"Hold it right there, Tolliver!"

But Tolliver had other ideas. Ducking to one side, he flicked up his rifle and snapped off a quick shot at Longarm. As he disappeared behind a boulder, Longarm clutched at his belly and crumpled to the ground, face down, his Colt still clutched in his outstretched hand...

"You ain't dead!" Tolliver cried. "You can't fool me."

TABOR EVANS

LONGARM

AND THE
DESERT DUCHESS

A JOVE BOOK

LONGARM AND THE DESERT DUCHESS

A Jove Book / published by arrangement with
the author

PRINTING HISTORY
Jove edition / August 1984

ISBN: 0-515-06269-3

Jove books are published by The Berkley Publishing Group,
200 Madison Avenue, New York, N.Y. 10016. The words
"A JOVE BOOK" and the "J" with sunburst are trademarks
belonging to Jove Publications, Inc.

LONGARM

AND THE DESERT DUCHESS

Chapter 1

The night was black as sin as Longarm stepped out onto the sidewalk in front of the Windsor Hotel. There had been a downpour earlier, but at the moment only a very light, intermittent rain was falling, hardly enough to bother about. The city's streets and sidewalks gleamed under the gas-lit street lamps.

Halting at the curb, Longarm flung away his cheroot and let the cool, damp breeze gently buffet his tall person. Though it was after midnight, there was still enough traffic for him to watch carefully before crossing the wide street. As soon as the traffic thinned, he strode swiftly across, then ducked down an alley, a shortcut he usually took to reach his rooming house on the other side of Cherry Creek.

As he strode along, he thought back on the poker

game he had just left. It had made him eighty-three dollars richer, but his three partners in the game had been somewhat unhappy at his departure, two of them especially. But from the moment they sat down at his table, Longarm had not liked them, and he had come to like them even less as the game progressed. For that reason he had not hesitated to pull out when it suited him. With grim satisfaction, Longarm recalled the frustration that had distorted both their faces when he stood up a few minutes ago and brushed his chips into his hat.

He left the alley and cut down a narrow street. He moved with a swift, catlike stride, a tall, looming presence that caused the few denizens of the night still abroad to duck hastily aside as he swept past them. He was alert enough to increase his pace considerably when a stallion standing in the traces of a beer truck voided a thick, steaming gout of urine that pounded heavily into the mash of manure and mud at its feet.

Above the sound of its splatter, Longarm thought he heard a cry from behind him. Someone had gotten caught, he realized. He glanced back. A shadowy form darted into a storefront doorway and became part of the night's shadows. Turning back around, Longarm increased his pace. He doubted there was only one. And if there were two, he would prefer to pick his own time and place.

By the time Longarm crossed the Colfax Avenue bridge and was crunching along the damp cinder path on the other side, he knew for sure there were two men following him. He also knew who they were—the two gents who'd been so unhappy at his early departure from the poker table, Milt Conant and Jake Tolliver. Longarm was reasonably sure they were not following him to tell him a bedtime story and tuck him in for the night. They

2

wanted something else—his scalp and, along with it, the money they had dropped at that poker table.

Sore losers, that was for sure.

A block before the rooming house, Longarm ducked into a narrow alley and loped swiftly around the building, cutting across a soggy backyard, coming out just as the two men tailing him peered cautiously into the alley down which he had just disappeared. Moving as silently as a cat, he came up behind the taller one, Tolliver, grabbed his shoulder, and spun him around. Startled, Tolliver only had time to cry out as Longarm punched him on the side of his lantern jaw. Tolliver reeled back against a cast-iron picket fence. His head sagging forward, he managed to stay upright as the back of his jacket caught on one of the spikes. The man was not unconscious, however, and this amazed Longarm. He had given the lanky son of a bitch his best shot.

Milt Conant spun to face him, then crouched. The small, blocky fellow had a thin leather sap in his right hand. It gleamed wetly in the light rain. Longarm thought he knew what was in it: ball bearings or silver coins, more than likely.

Conant rushed Longarm and swung the sap. Ducking back, Longarm felt the sap breeze past his face. The weight of it pulled Conant off balance. Having drawn his Colt, Longarm stepped in closer and brought its barrel down on Conant's right forearm. There was a sickening crunching sound. The sap dropped from Conant's hand. Holding onto his shattered arm, Conant went down on one knee, his face twisting in agony.

That left Tolliver. Longarm started to turn. The sound of Tolliver's jacket ripping free of the fence post filled the street as Tolliver lunged at Longarm. Longarm tried

3

to spin out of his path, but Tolliver caught him a numbing blow on the side of the head, then caught him again in the stomach, driving Longarm back. Longarm felt his legs go out from under him. He hit the sidewalk heavily. The back of his head cracked with numbing force against a fireplug.

The inside of his head exploded. He barely heard his Colt skitter away from him over the sidewalk. By the time his vision cleared, Tolliver was standing over him, a satanic grin on his long face, and Conant was back on his feet, his right arm hanging loosely, a large Remington revolver in his left hand.

"Get out of the way, Tolliver!" Conant snarled. "I'm going to kill the son of a bitch!"

Longarm rolled over and then managed to lift himself groggily onto his hands and knees. Chuckling, Tolliver moved away to give his partner a clear shot.

Still on his hands and knees, Longarm glanced up at Conant. "You pull that trigger," he said, "and it'll be murder. Over a lousy eighty-three dollars."

"You just broke my arm."

"What were you planning with that sap?"

"You can't weasel out of this, lawman. You got it coming!"

"Now hold it just a goddamn minute!" Longarm protested. "I got the money right here! Let me get it for you!"

As he reached back to his vest, Longarm heard Tolliver's harsh, gravelly voice. "That's it, you bastard. Give it here to me!"

"Make sure it's all there," said Conant, "then stand back."

Tolliver started toward Longarm, but Longarm had

4

already palmed the double-barrelled .44 derringer that rode in the left breast pocket of his vest. He fired up at Conant. The .44 slug caught the man full in the chest. He dropped his revolver and staggered backward, then collapsed to the sidewalk.

Longarm swung the derringer toward Tolliver, but he was already ducking down the alley. Scrambling to his feet, Longarm sent his remaining .44 slug after the fleeing figure, then searched the sidewalk and gutter for his Colt. By the time he found the weapon, however, it was too late to go after Tolliver. He walked over to inspect Conant.

He was bending over the lifeless form when he became aware of the heavy sweet smell of his own blood pouring from the open laceration in the back of his head. He tried to straighten up, but found that impossible.

He did not remember hitting the pavement.

Longarm could tell it was Marshal Billy Vail at his door from the two sharp knocks. Reaching for a fresh cheroot, he called out, "Come in, Billy!"

Vail pushed open the door and stepped inside the room. He looked relieved to find Longarm sitting up, a pillow bunched at his back. One bushy eyebrow cocked upward, the pink-cheeked, balding official tried to appear angry as he stopped at the foot of Longarm's bed. He was holding a folder in one hand.

"Sitting up, are you?" Vail demanded. "How long you goin' to maintain this fraud? You been out of action for more than a week now!"

Longarm smiled at the old fake and lit his cheroot. "To tell you the truth, Billy, I've been getting a mite anxious. You didn't get any line on that son of a bitch who put me here, did you?"

"Nothing more than I already told you. Tolliver's been in trouble of one sort and another ever since he hit Denver a year ago. But, like Wallace told you, nothing solid, just scrapes and occasional assaults. One thing you did accomplish, though."

"What's that?"

"He's cleared out of Denver."

Longarm shrugged and glanced at the folder in Billy's hand. "You got anything interesting in that for me?"

Vail drew up a chair and sat down beside Longarm's bed. "Before I say anything, the doc been here yet today?"

"Just left. The old fart told me I should stop smoking. Says it'll stunt my growth."

"Good idea, that. Have you considered it?"

"I figure it's too late for me, Billy. So tell me, what've you got there?"

"I hesitate to tell you, you being in such a delicate condition and all. This might finish what that knock on the head started."

"Try me."

"You do good on deserts, Longarm. I remember you telling me about your adventure on the Great Salt Lake Desert. You really had me spellbound."

"Cut it out, Billy. Let's hear it."

The old lawman got serious—or tried to—as he opened his folder. He ran a pudgy hand over his flaccid face as he scanned the report he was holding, then leaned back in the chair and looked at Longarm, his eyes alight with mischief. "Like I said, Longarm, you do very well on deserts, so try this one on for size. The U. S. marshal's office in San Bernardino needs your services."

6

"Go on." Longarm had stopped puffing on his cheroot.

"There's a duchess on the Mojave Desert and they want you to find out what the hell she's up to."

"A *what?*"

"You heard me. That knock on the head didn't affect your hearin' none. A duchess, that's what. She's got herself a castle or some such thing out there in the middle of the Mojave Desert."

"Well, let her stay there, then. What harm's she doing?"

"Just let me get a word in here edgewise. The fact is the San Bernardino office has already sent out two deputies to look into it, and both of them have disappeared."

"Disappeared?" Longarm felt a flicker of interest.

"Without a trace."

"Now, that is interesting—and downright unlawful. So what does the marshal in San Bernardino want from me?"

"Go in there. Exert some charm on this here duchess, sniff around some, and find out if there are any grounds for grand jury action. If there are, the office will go in there in force. But so far they've got no grounds."

"Just two missing deputies."

"That's it."

"And this here castle of hers is in the Mojave Desert?"

"Right smack dab in the middle. It's near the only water hole for miles. And she has her own army of retainers."

"Is this on the level?"

"You mean is she legitimate?"

"That's just what I mean."

Vail sighed and nodded his head. "Apparently. The king of Spain gave her mother a title and a land grant.

7

To get rid of her maybe. The land is worthless except for the water hole. The daughter's claim has been checked out by the State Department and seems legitimate."

"And she's calling herself a duchess, is she?"

"She has that right."

"My head is beginning to bother me again," Longarm said. "I feel a dizzy spell coming on."

"I could send Wallace," Vail offered.

"He'd get killed."

"I admit. He ain't had your experience with crazy dames or deserts. He just might end up being the third deputy to disappear."

Longarm groaned. "All right. When do you want me to start?"

"As soon as you can."

Longarm shrugged and stubbed out his cheroot, then flung back the covers. "Hold on and I'll go back to the office with you to pick up my expense vouchers and a railroad pass."

Smiling, Vail reached into the folder. "No need for that, Longarm. I brought both with me. Your train'll be pulling out in an hour. Should give you plenty of time."

Longarm sat back down on the bed and fixed the old lawman with a baleful eye. "Sometimes, Billy," he said, "I think you take me too much for granted."

Billy laughed. "No, I don't, Longarm. But I'd sure as hell rather see you out on assignment than flat on your back. That fireplug took a real bite out of your head, and that fool doctor just kept muttering as he wound that bandage around your head. He wouldn't tell us anything, 'cept that maybe we ought to scare up your next of kin. I don't mind telling you, you had us all nervous for a while."

Stepping into his trousers, Longarm frowned. He did not want the chief to know how gratified he had been by everyone's genuine concern. "Just drop them vouchers and the train pass on the bed and get out of here before you have me crying all over you. I got a train to catch. Remember?"

Grinning, Marshal Vail got to his feet and walked to the door.

"See the marshal, Ivar Thorrson, in San Bernardino for what you'll need," Vail said, opening the door. "And just make sure you don't join them other two deputies."

"Don't you worry none about me," Longarm told him, looking up. "There's no fireplugs on the Mojave Desert."

Marshal Vail laughed and pulled the door shut behind him.

Marshal Ivor Thorrson did not seem to mind the heat. A raw-boned, wiry man in his early fifties, he looked as dry and as tough as an old cornhusk. His once yellow hair reached to his shoulders, and his thick brows and drooping mustache had been bleached white by the sun. His sky-blue eyes snapped alertly as Longarm came to a halt in front of his desk.

"Sit down, Mr. Long," he said, indicating with a nod the wooden chair beside his desk. "Sorry I couldn't meet you at the station. How was your trip?"

"The train was slow and hot," Longarm replied, slumping into the chair.

"Usually is this time of year. And how's old Billy Vail these days?"

"Billy's doing just fine."

"Great lawman in his day. Could track as good as any Apache. Show them a few lessons, he could. As persistent as a summer cold and twice as deadly."

"He's put on a few pounds since then."

"Yeah. And I just get skinnier. Must be the heat. What'd he tell you about this duchess?"

"Not much. Not even her name."

"It's Marta Zapolya. Want me to spell that for you?"

"I'd appreciate it."

Thorrson spelled it for Longarm, then went on, "I've never laid eyes on her myself, and neither have any of my men, but I've heard stories. She keeps herself pretty well hidden, as I understand it—and seems able to get absolute loyalty from the gunslicks and other human refuse she has hired to act as her retainers."

"And aside from the fact that you've lost two deputies you sent out there to say hello, you know nothing else about her."

"That's it."

"Why do you care? Vail says her claim is legitimate enough."

"She's too damn rich, I'm thinking. Where the hell's she getting all this money to keep that place up? In other words, there's more to her than she's willing to let on. Some travelers have reported she lets them water their stock at her place and even puts them up overnight, free. But then other travelers, last seen heading her way, have never been seen again."

"You sure they were heading for her place?"

"Where the hell else could they have been heading? You seen the Mojave Desert, Long?"

"Nope."

"Well, let me tell you, it's a real one. You won't get across it without you visit her water hole."

10

"Go on."

"I don't like that army of hers. Like I told you, it's made up of prime gunslicks and assorted desperadoes. Besides, she's beginning to draw a crowd. Some tough hombres have been slipping into San Berdoo lately, asking the same questions about this crazy duchess as I'm asking you. She's trouble, Long, but I don't know what kind for sure, and I want to find that out before it reaches up and takes me by the neck."

"So you'd like me to go out there and have a chat with her."

"Hell, Long, it won't be that easy! I was hoping you'd think of something original."

"I was wondering when you'd ask." Longarm leaned back in the chair and thought a moment. "No sense in my going in there waving a badge. I'll have to find another reason. Would you say she's a mite touchy about her claim?"

"From what I hear she is. And it stands to reason she would be. One of them travelers who stayed at her place mentioned she got riled when he asked her if she really owned the castle and all the land around the water hole."

"That makes it easy, then. I'll tell her I'm a tax assessor. That'll give me an excuse to poke around some, check all the hidden places to see what the value of her place is. And that should make her welcome me with open arms."

"Now how in hell do you figure that?"

"Holders of land grants are expected to pay modest federal taxes on the land they occupy. Once I show up, it'll mean the government accepts her claim to this land

11

she's been squatting on. It might even make her feel she doesn't need that army of hired guns to keep her claim."

Ivar's eyes lit up. "Danged if I don't think that might work."

"Sure it'll work. She'll be happy to cooperate with me if she's on the level. If she ain't and detains me— or throws me to the wolves—we'll know she's up to no good. No one but an out-and-out crook—and a damn fool one, at that—would kill a man trying to prove her claim. Send in the army with some field guns and blast down them adobe walls, if she does."

"Sounds logical. And I promise if you don't get back in a week, I'll send in them field guns."

"Don't be so anxious. I'm hoping you won't need them. Now, can you get me the papers?"

"What papers?"

"The papers proving I'm a tax assessor."

"Hell, Long, I don't know nothin' about collecting taxes. I'm a lawman, not a tax collector."

"Who does?"

"Try the land office down the street."

Longarm got up. "As soon as I'm ready to pull out, I'll let you know. I'll need at least two burros for packing and Spanish mules to ride, at least two. I don't feel so gallant astride one of them long-eared critters, but I do feel a mite safer."

"I'll get them for you."

"I'll be back as soon as I can with the papers."

The land office was a two-story adobe building across from the livery stable. Longarm entered. There was a counter across the width of the room, with a low gate for access beyond it. A woman in a light blue dress, her

12

hair as black as a raven's wing, was busy at a desk behind the counter. As he came to a halt in front of the counter, she looked up. The woman was obviously Spanish. Her eyes were as dark as a moonless night and just as mysterious.

"What can I do for you, *señor?*"

"I need help." Longarm smiled.

The girl got to her feet and approached the counter. She was easily as tall as Longarm, and as supple as a sapling. She looked him over as quickly and as deftly as he was looking her over. Her smile was sudden and dazzling, indicating she approved.

"What kind of help, *señor?*"

"It's more or less confidential. I need to tell you somewhere else, where it's more private. Would you care to have dinner with me?"

"Señor, I do not know you."

"You will after we have dinner." Longarm smiled.

Despite herself, she smiled back.

Longarm took out his wallet and showed her his badge. "I'm a deputy U. S. marshal, ma'am," he told her. "The name is Long, Custis Long. This would be official business."

"And the dinner—it, too, would be official business?"

"Of course. I have an expense voucher."

"You will not need that." She turned and glanced at the wall clock over her desk. "I will be closing up in less than an hour. I live over this office." She smiled. "I will provide the dinner, Marshal. There's an open stairway at the rear of the office. I'll be expecting you."

A rancher entered at that moment, his face intent on the business he had come to transact. "Delores—" he began, addressing the girl. Longarm touched the brim of his hat to the girl and left.

He didn't even know her last name, he realized. But he didn't think he'd have too much trouble finding out what it was. As he started across the street to the livery stable to look over the mules he'd be using, he caught sight of a long, lanky fellow ducking into a saloon door a block down the street.

It startled him and he pulled up. Then he continued on across the street, shaking his head in disgust. For a minute there he had imagined the fellow was Jake Tolliver. He was jumping at shadows, he told himself as he entered the livery stable. That knock on the head had left him a mite skittish.

Chapter 2

Delores answered Longarm's knock promptly. Smiling brilliantly, she pulled the door open and stepped back to let him in. She was not wearing the same prim dress she had been wearing in the land office, he noticed at once. She had changed into a blouse and skirt more in keeping with her Spanish heritage. The skirt was high and colorful, the blouse snow-white, loose about the shoulders, and open at the neck, giving him an enticing view of the swell of her ample breasts.

Moving past her, he doffed his hat and glanced toward the small dining room. The table was already set with two candles, bright silverware, and gleaming china. The aroma of beefsteak and onions filled the small apartment. His stomach rolled a little in anticipation.

"Custis, will you make yourself comfortable, please?"

15

she said, taking his hat. "The dinner is not quite ready."

"Smells ready to me."

"Just a few moments. I wait for you before I put on the vegetables. You will have a drink?"

"You wouldn't happen to have any Maryland rye, would you?"

"Alas, no. But I have some very good whiskey."

"That'll do fine."

"With water?"

"Neat."

Longarm was ready for another drink when Delores called him softly. He got up from the easy chair where he had almost fallen asleep and saw her lighting the two candles. Covered dishes had been placed down on the table and a huge platter containing thick slabs of steak garnished with herbs, onions, and mushrooms dominated the table.

Delores turned to smile at him. "You will not do much better in San Berdoo, Custis."

"I don't doubt it, Delores."

He waited until she was ready to sit down, then moved behind her and lifted the chair in for her. Leaning over as he did so, he gazed for a moment into her dark cleft and was assailed by the intoxicating perfume of her body. The scent was not store-bought, but was the natural combination of her perspiration and the cooking odors that still clung to her. He found the combination more arousing than any Paris perfume.

They ate in decorous silence, Longarm perfectly willing to concentrate on the food, which he found more than delicious. It was spicy, but not outrageously so, flavorful and savory, the meat cooked to a tenderness

16

that made a knife seem unnecessary.

When they were finished and he pushed his plate from him, she produced a thick wedge of apple pie and dared him not to eat it. He did not argue with her, and a few moments later he was stretched out on the sofa in the living room. She had made the meal an assault on almost all his senses and he felt as satiated as an oriental potentate.

The sound of her washing the dishes lulled him. He dropped off and was awakened by the cool feel of her hand on his forehead. Opening his eyes, he smiled up at her. She had pulled a chair up beside the sofa and was sitting in it.

"That was a meal fit for a king," he told her.

"I am glad you liked it."

"You made that miserable trip from Denver worthwhile. I am flattered that you should go to such lengths to make a stove-up stranger feel welcome."

She smiled sadly, a sudden weariness washing over her face. "Do you have any idea what a dreary place this can be, Custis? For a woman like me, that is. Or how welcome the sight of a new face could be to a woman? I have needs like any other. But the men here, they have no romance, no charm, no manners. I will marry one of them some day. It will be my fate, I am sure. But they are not gentlemen, Custis. They are not like you."

"You'll make me blush if you don't hold off," Longarm replied with a grin. "I wasn't aware I possessed such famous qualities. Perhaps you are imagining it."

She leaned forward. "Let me ask you a question, Custis. You were not brought up in the West, were you?"

"No, I wasn't."

17

"You were brought up in the South. Is that not so?"

"Yes, it is, as a matter of fact. In West-by-God-Virginia."

"And there you learned manners. I could tell the moment your tall figure strode into the land office." She smiled. "When my father lived, he was wealthy enough to send me to St. Louis for my education. I am Spanish. Full-blooded," she added proudly. "But I know Americans well—too well. It has always been my experience that Southern men are gentlemen. They have a code of honor. They appreciate a woman."

He reached out and took her hand in his. "True enough," he said. "At least this here lawman does."

She withdrew her hand gently and leaned back in her chair. "Now, how can I help you, Custis?"

He shook what drowsiness remained from his senses and sat up. "I need papers that will enable me to pass myself off as a tax assessor. I imagine you have such forms. Marshal Thorrson said you might."

"You have come all the way from Denver to collect taxes?"

"No. I have come out here to check on that duchess living in that castle out there in the middle of the desert. I figure she'll welcome me a little more heartily if she thinks I'm only trying to verify her claim to that land grant."

"Ah, yes, I have heard of that one. And I have looked at the records, Custis. I can tell you now. Her claim is valid. The king of Spain granted her mother the land—for favors rendered." She smiled wryly. "And I am sure he must have known it was a desert."

"He was not a gentleman."

She shook her head. "No, he was not."

18

"Can you help me?"

"Of course."

"And could you give me some pointers in assessing. I mean, what to look for, how to sound—that sort of thing."

"As soon as you wish, Custis."

He leaned back. "How can I thank you?"

"I just fed you. You are no longer hungry. But I have a different kind of hunger, Custis. And it has not been satisfied—not for a long, long time."

Smiling, Longarm got to his feet and swept Delores up into his arms. She flung her arms around his neck and rested her head against his chest as he carried her into the bedroom.

"Set me down, Custis," she whispered, nibbling on his earlobe.

He did as he was told.

"Let me take your clothes off," she said. "I love to do that. It adds to the suspense, don't you think?"

"Well, maybe it does, at that, but you better let me give you a little helping hand."

Grinning, Longarm sat back on the bed and yanked both boots off. Then he stood up and shrugged out of his vest and started to unbutton his shirt.

"Now, that's enough help," Delores said, stepping closer and slapping his hand away. "I told you, I want to do it."

Longarm shrugged and gave her no more argument. Her hands were deft and light as she took his shirt off, then dropped to the waistband of his skin-tight brown tweed pants, unbuttoning the fly and peeling them down to his ankles. As he kicked his woolen socks away and stepped out of his trousers, Delores unbuttoned his tight cotton knit longjohns. The tips of her fingers lightly touched his swollen member. She appeared not to notice, but there was a smoky look in her eyes when she glanced up and leaned against him to peel off the top of his longjohns.

Then he was standing before her as naked as a jaybird, a very important part of his anatomy standing rigidly at attention. She took him by the upper arm and moved him gently closer to a commode standing in a corner. Dipping a sponge into the pan of water standing on it, she began sponging his genitals.

"Hey! What's that?"

"Whiskey and water. How does it feel?"

"Can't you tell?"

She laughed, the sound of it low, husky. "Yes," she said, "I think I can."

Working with a light but effective stroke, she soon had him on the verge of mayhem. He was about to grab her when she pushed him gently back to the bed until he was reclining on it face up. Then she rolled him over onto his stomach and, employing remarkably strong fingers, massaged the back of his neck, his back, and kept on past his buttocks to his thighs. Then she turned him so that he was once again looking up at her. He was as erect as a telegraph pole and so eager he was about to spring off the bed and take her.

She sensed his arousal. Laughing softly, she stepped back. In an instant, her skirt and blouse had become a silken mound at her feet as she stood before him, stark naked, her olive body burnished like silk.

"Well," she said, cocking her head, "aren't you ready yet?"

"You devil," he muttered cheerfully.

Jumping up, he caught her about the thighs and lifted her boldly up onto his erection. Opening herself, she slammed down onto him, then threw both legs around his waist and locked her ankles. Longarm groaned with pleasure as she settled her thighs against his hip bones and began to work him still deeper into her.

Abruptly, she leaned close to him. "Spin me!" she whispered fiercely. "Spin me, Longarm!"

Astonished, he nevertheless did as she directed, turning slowly at first, then faster and faster. All the while she gyrated wildly, her head flung back, her lustrous hair flying, moaning softly—and then not so softly. At last he lost his balance and went listing toward the bed. He almost went down, but she clung to him, laughing now, her eyes glittering, her lips drawn back in a fierce grimace. He managed to get her onto the bed first, then collapsed on top of her.

She cried out and began thrashing her head from side to side. He didn't know if it was in pain or delight, but when he saw her still straining under him, her neck taut, her eyes wide and unseeing, he resumed his own frantic thrusting. Deeper and deeper he probed, driving her into the bed, impaling her. It didn't take long, and when he climaxed, she followed in a matter of seconds.

Laughing softly, she clung to Longarm as he rolled off her.

"It has been so long!" Delores whispered. "You do not know, Longarm, how long I have waited for that! I could not let just anyone have me. You understand? I must be so discreet in this small place. I am Spanish, and if these Americans think I am like the *cantina* girls,

21

I can never marry. So I must wait, you see. Wait for someone like you. Big enough and strong enough to satisfy me."

"And then move on."

"Yes. It is so. You understand, don't you?"

"Sure. Just so you understand it, too."

"Do not worry," she said, running a finger down his nose and then past his lips to his chin. "I will not fall in love with you. I will not let myself do such a foolish thing. Not right away, I think. It will take maybe a day or so longer."

He laughed. "So I better get out of here tomorrow."

"Yes. Go after the duchess. See what you can do for her."

"Enough of such talk," Longarm growled, pulling Delores closer.

Delores's fingers had not stopped at his chin, and now they were proving to both of them what a man he was. With an impish laugh, she snuggled down quickly and Frenched him for a moment, returning Longarm to full efficiency.

Laughing, he pulled her over on top of him. With an exultant cry, she began riding his bucking torso like an Apache, her raven hair flinging out behind her. From that moment on, neither of them thought of the desert Duchess—only of each other's pleasure.

Longarm did not return to his hotel room that night.

A little before dawn, Delores shook Longarm awake and told him school was in session. She disappeared then and returned soon after with some legal-looking documents. As Longarm shook the cobwebs out of his head,

22

she lit a lantern, placed it on the kitchen table, and proceeded to give Longarm a pretty good idea of what he would have to ask the duchess when he began his inventory of her place and what he should look for.

As soon as that portion of his education was complete, he asked her what she knew of the duchess and her castle and found Delores to be full of useful information. The desert duchess, it seemed, had been intriguing the townsfolk—and Delores—for close to a year now. She had materialized on the Mojave Desert like Morgan le Fay, complete with castle and private force of armed retainers. It was a mystery that everyone in the town and thereabouts was anxious to solve. As a result, it was probably the single most important topic in every saloon and at every sewing circle.

Dawn was breaking when Delores announced that school was out. She got up from the table and prepared a hearty breakfast for them both. Thanking her afterward with a warm kiss, Longarm left her apartment and went straight up to his hotel room. He had only visited it long enough after checking in the day before to drop his gear on the bed.

A few feet from the door he pulled up.

As was his custom whenever he was on assignment, Longarm had left a toothpick between the door and the doorjamb, high enough to be off the ground but low enough not to be noticed by anyone approaching the door. Especially anyone approaching in the dark.

The toothpick had dropped from the doorjamb. It was resting on the carpet, a portion of it under the door. Someone had entered his room, and it was much too early in the morning to be the chambermaid.

Flattening himself against the wall, Longarm withdrew his Colt from his cross-draw rig, then moved close enough to the door to be able to listen for sounds coming from within. He thought he heard something. Stepping out into the hallway in front of the door, he raised his foot and kicked at it viciously, his boot coming down close by the doorknob. The flimsy lock gave and the door slammed open, striking the wall beside it sharply. Longarm ducked back for an instant. Then, crouching, he flung himself into the room, his revolver at the ready.

The room was empty, but the window on the other side of the bed was open. He vaulted the bed and stuck his head out in time to see a lanky figure scuttling from the back of the alley. There was a narrow porch roof about ten feet below his window. That sound he had heard had been Jake Tolliver dropping to the roof.

He wasn't seeing things, after all. And it wasn't his nerves. Jake Tolliver had followed him to San Bernardino and had been waiting in his room for him all through the night.

An hour after he had kicked open the door to his hotel room, Longarm was slumped in the chair by Thorrson's desk.

"And you're sure he was in there," Thorrson said.

"I'm sure."

Thorrson's snow-white brows lifted. "You're a lucky man, looks like. Two ways. Not to be in your room—and to be able to find a friendlier place to spend the night."

Longarm saw no reason to comment on that. It was

24

enough for Thorrson to know he had not slept in his hotel room.

"What's this here gent look like?" Thorrson asked.

Longarm gave the marshal a description of Jake Tolliver. The marshal took it down hastily on a tablet in front of him. "I'll get one of my deputies on this right away, Long. We don't want this jasper putting you out of action before you get to see the duchess."

"I thought you'd say that. Will you still be as anxious after I've seen her?"

Thorrson allowed himself a smile. "Sure I will, Long. But we'll have this fellow long before that. There ain't too many places he can hide in San Berdoo."

"If he's still in San Bernardino."

"Like I say, I'll put my best man on it."

"That makes me feel a whole hell of a lot better."

"Jesus, Long. We got you out here to see about the duchess. We got your mules and pack animals all ready to go. I suggest the best thing for you to do now would be to hightail it out of here before that fellow tries again."

"I was thinking the same thing," said Long, getting to his feet. "See you when I get back, Marshal."

Thorrson unfolded himself from his swivel chair and leaned over to shake Longarm's hand. Longarm took it. Thorrson's grip had the strength of a hickory stick.

A moment later Longarm was staring into the fierce sun at his four sorry-looking beasts of burden, two burros and two large Mexican mules. One of the mules flung him a glance that would have turned a holy man to stone, then flicked his long ears at him. Longarm was unable to take the warning, however, since this was the mule

25

he had saddled earlier in the livery stable.

Longarm checked the cinch one more time and mounted up. The mule's head dropped forward fatalistically. Longarm kicked the animal into motion and a moment later he was on his way out of San Berdoo heading for the Mojave Desert.

And the desert duchess.

Chapter 3

Delores Sandoz had given Longarm directions to the duchess's castle. Once he reached the fringes of the Mojave by the middle of the afternoon, he had little difficulty finding the wagon trace she had described to him. Pulling up, he peered out into the desert, noting how the trace disappeared completely in the shimmering haze that hung over its dead, flat surface.

Only a fool would attempt to move across that shimmering stovetop in daylight. Longarm decided to spend the time left before sunset filling up his water bags and canteens. Delores had told him of a water hole in among some rocks a little farther south. Shading his eyes, Longarm looked in that direction and saw a dim pile of granite blocks piled on the horizon.

He dug his heels into the mule's flanks and reached

the rocks less than an hour later. Dismounting, he climbed a tall rock and spotted the water hole somewhat north of his present position. It was surrounded by yucca scrub and burnt-over grass. Returning to his mount, Longarm mounted up and rode to the water hole.

He filled both water bags and his two canteens, keeping the mules and burros back so they would not muddy the water hole. Sturdy beasts, they were better than horses when it came to water and forage, and they waited patiently for him to get to them. Longarm was on his way back to his mule with his hat full of water when the first shot came from the rocks above him.

The bullet ricocheted off a granite block chin-high, splattering his face with tiny shards of rock. Slapping his hat back on and blinking through the sudden deluge, he dove for cover among some low rocks. Blinking up at the skyline, his Colt out, Longarm cursed himself for not having taken his rifle from its scabbard when he dismounted. He should have known Jake Tolliver would try again.

"Jake!" Longarm cried, swiftly removing his spurs. "This is crazy! Killing me won't bring Conant back to life!"

"Who gives a shit about him?" came the response from some rimrocks to Longarm's left. "All I want is satisfaction. And that's what I'll get when I kill you!"

As Tolliver was shouting his reply, Longarm ducked back out of sight, then circled around. Keeping his head down, he headed for the patch of high rocks from behind which Tolliver's voice had come. He ran swiftly, almost silently, his low-heeled cavalry stovepipes giving him excellent footing.

Cutting around a tall finger of rock, he came face to

face with Jake Tolliver. He had just finished scrambling down the rear face of the rocks he had been using for cover and was less than ten feet from Longarm, heading right for him. He was as surprised to see Longarm as Longarm was to see him.

Longarm flung up his Colt. "Hold it right there, Tolliver!"

But Tolliver had other ideas. Ducking to one side, he flicked up his rifle and snapped off a quick shot at Longarm. As he disappeared behind a boulder, Longarm clutched at his belly and crumpled to the ground, face down, his Colt still clutched in his outstretched hand. Breathing as shallowly as possible, Longarm played possum. His hat had spilled to the ground and now lay just in front of his head. Though it was effectively shielding most of his face, Longarm had an unobstructed view of the boulder behind which Tolliver was crouching.

"You ain't dead!" Tolliver cried. "You can't fool me."

He popped his head up from behind the boulder, sighted quickly, and snapped off a shot. The bullet struck the ground just in front of Longarm's hat. The small explosion of sand and rock knocked the hat slightly askew. Longarm did not move.

In the ensuing silence Longarm heard Tolliver jacking a fresh round into his Winchester's firing chamber. Longarm waited. Tolliver stepped out from behind the boulder. He looked carefully down at Longarm for a moment, then calmly raised his rifle. From the way he stood there, it was clear he was convinced by now that Longarm was unconscious. This shot was just to make damn sure.

Longarm lifted his double-action Colt and squeezed off three quick shots. The first two rounds punched black holes in Tolliver's chest, slamming him back against a boulder. The third caught him in the jaw. The lower portion of his face exploded. His teeth clattering against the rocks beside him, Tolliver slid lifelessly to the ground.

Longarm got to his feet and walked over to the dead man. Looking down, he felt a little sick. *What in hell possesses a man to go to such lengths?* he wondered. A card game in a distant hotel had started Tolliver on this fool errand. Tolliver had lost a little money. His pride had been hurt. So now he was sprawled on his back in the middle of nowhere with half his face blown away.

What was that about pride going before a fall?

Longarm glanced up at the sky. There were no buzzards yet, but there would be. Tolliver might yet serve a useful purpose. Leaving Tolliver's body, Longarm searched among the rocks and found Tolliver's mount, a sorrel. He pulled the saddle off the animal, dumped it, and slapped the sorrel smartly on the rump. The horse took off in the direction of San Bernardino. Longarm returned to his mules, finished watering them, mounted up, and rode out of the rocks, heading for the wagon trace.

The sun was low in the sky when he ventured out onto the Mojave. From the very first it looked grim and unfriendly. There were no sand dunes. Instead, Longarm found himself traveling over a flat, salt-crusted plain blazing still in the late afternoon sun. The vegetation was sparse and just as uninteresting, slate-gray greasewood for the most part, yucca scrub and spiny cactus. He saw a few water holes with the telltale salt weed growing on their fringes. He knew the salt weed would not hurt his stock, but the alkali water in the holes would. There were no skeletons around the water holes, but that proved nothing. Any cattle or wild creatures unlucky enough to drink the water would simply get sick as hell and stagger off some distance from the well, keel over, and die.

He had not gone far when he saw in the dying light of the setting sun a dry lake bed off to his right. For a moment it gleamed like water, but only for a moment. He knew it was only cement-hard, dun-colored clay. Miles and miles of nothing. Caliche, it was called, gravel crusted together by salts and other minerals. He kept going, following the wagon trace, grateful it was there, and just in time, it seemed, the red eye of the sun ducked below the horizon. Not long after, the chill of the desert night fell over him.

He stopped only once during the first night, and kept going well into the next morning. But as soon as the sun began to bother him, he found a low spot, unpacked his tarpaulin, and made himself and his animals a crude tentlike shelter, under which the five of them spent the worst part of the day, effectively shielded from the direct rays of the sun if not from its awful heat. Longarm managed to get a good bit of sleep, nevertheless, and early the second evening, he was well on his way again.

From what Delores had told him, he expected to reach the duchess's castle a little after dawn of the second day. Resting himself and his mount only once during the night, he pushed on, his slicker wrapped around him once again to protect himself from the cold desert night.

At daybreak, he saw nothing on the horizon to cheer him on, but he kept going anyway. He paid no attention to the lizards. It was the desert diamondbacks that concerned him and made him wary. The most likely time for Longarm or one of his animals to get hit by a snake, he knew, was just after sundown or at dawn. The rattlers came out to hunt as the desert cooled off, got lethargic once the desert night turned cold, and woke up as soon as the rays of the rising sun caught them.

He kept going well into the morning. By this time the sun's baleful eye was fixing him with an unsettling intensity, beginning to beat on his eyes like a fist. Longarm wondered if he wasn't going to find himself in trouble if he didn't reach this damned castle before long. He did not have enough water to spend another day under the tarpaulin. And if he kept going, he had only enough water for ten, maybe fifteen miles.

An hour later, like some enchantment out of a King Arthur legend, the duchess's turreted castle materialized on the desert horizon in front of him. The heat radiating up from the desert floor caused the castle to appear to tremble magically, and for a moment it looked as if a shimmering lake surrounded the castle's walls. That part of it was only a desert mirage. The rest, however, was real enough.

As Longarm well knew, desert distances were tricky. He rode for close to an hour before the castle took on any real solidity. At just about this time, he saw the riders approaching—ten of them. These would be the duchess's retainers. Hardcases, Thorrson had called them. Delores had heard they were worse than that—cutthroats and murderers culled from the San Francisco waterfront.

As they rode closer on sleek, well-fed horses, Longarm saw that each rider wore roughly the same costume, as befitted a duchess's armed retinue. They wore dark hats with the brims turned down; a white silk scarf knotted at the neck; dark leather buttonless vests; and black, snug-fitting trousers. The similarity in dress ended there, however, as each rider wore a different colored shirt, and each man carried his iron suited to his own individual taste.

Longarm reined in and waited for the riders to reach him. They fanned out as they approached, then surrounded him. The leader pulled up in front of Longarm and peered at him from under his hatbrim. He was a chunky fellow with bloodless lips and pale-blue, dead-looking eyes in a pocked face. A Bull Durham tag dangled from his vest pocket. He wore his gun tied down in an oiled, flapless holster. "Who're you, mister?"

Longarm smiled. "I might ask the same question."

"You might, but it wouldn't do you no good."

"Name's Long, Custis Long. I'm here to assess your mistress's taxes."

"Hell, man! You mean to tell me you're a tax collector?"

"No, I am a tax assessor. The tax collecting will come later. My job is to see what taxes your mistress is liable for."

"How the hell do I know you're who you say you are?"

"I have papers."

"You could've stolen them."

Longarm shrugged. "Yes, I suppose so, but I didn't."

"Hey, Ruel," a rider behind him said, "why don't we just keep his mules and burros and send him back the way he came?" As the rider made this suggestion, he nudged his horse up beside Ruel's.

"Shut up, Hansen," Ruel said to him. "I'll handle this."

But Hansen ignored Ruel and nudged his horse closer

33

to Longarm, a thin smile on his face. He was a blond, blue-eyed young man of twenty or so with brows so pale he seemed to have none. This gave his expression the deceptive wide-eyed innocence of a babe. But though he had the face of an angel, his smile sent a cold knife edge of apprehension down Longarm's back.

Longarm had met this type before. They were usually the fruit of widowed or single mothers and doting grandmothers who spoiled and petted and turned rancid the young boys in their care. Often, these young men—so sweet and wide-eyed as children—grew up to murder and rape and pillage, and always with a smile on their smooth faces. They had been taught from the cradle that they could do no wrong and what they coveted was theirs by right. Accordingly, no matter what crimes they committed, they felt no shame or guilt. They were the most unpredictable and dangerous of men.

Even as Longarm thought about this, Hansen took out his gun. Still smiling, he fired almost negligently at a point just over Longarm's hat. The round passed close enough for Longarm to hear it sear through the air. Longarm's mule shied nervously. Reaching down quickly, Longarm patted the mule's neck to soothe it.

"Damn it, Hansen!" Ruel cried. "I'm in charge here!" As Ruel spoke, he pushed down Hansen's Colt.

"So you are. So you are," Hansen allowed, turning around to smile maliciously at his boss. "But maybe you're goin' soft, Ruel. I just wanted to see the son of a bitch jump a little, that's all."

Longarm reached casually under his frock coat and drew his Colt from his cross-draw rig. As soon as the revolver cleared his coat's skirt he fired, catching Hansen's gun hand. The Colt went flying.

Then Longarm kicked his mule forward. With the barrel of his gun, he took one vicious swipe at Hansen and sent him flying backward off his horse. The man landed heavily on his back.

Then Longarm poked the muzzle of his .44 into Ruel's face.

From the riders all around Longarm came the sudden creak of saddle leather and the sound of gun sights scraping free. Longarm did not bother to look about him as he fixed Ruel with his cold eyes.

"Tell your men to drop their sixguns and unbuckle their gunbelts," he told Ruel, "or I'll blow a hole in your face."

"You're bluffin'."

"Try me and see."

Ruel took another look into the muzzle of Longarm's .44 and swallowed. Beads of perspiration stood out suddenly on his forehead.

"All right, men," he rasped. "You heard him. Do what he says!"

"Aw, hell, Ruel!" a rider behind Longarm cried. "We can blow this son of a bitch away before he squeezes the trigger!"

"Damn it! You heard me! Drop your gunbelts!"

Without further protest, the men dropped their weapons and let their gunbelts slip to the hard desert ground. Hansen had regained consciousness by this time and, out of the corner of his eye, Longarm saw him reaching out with his left hand in an effort to grab his sixgun. Longarm fired at Hansen's gun. The weapon skittered across the desert floor well out of Hansen's reach. Then he fired a second shot. A geyser of sand and gravel exploded under Hansen's chin. Clasping his shattered right hand in his left, Hansen sat up and glared at Longarm.

"I'll get you for this, you son of a bitch!" he roared.

"Sure you will. Get on your horse!"

Hansen grabbed his mount's reins with his left hand and hauled himself into his saddle.

Longarm turned to the other riders. "Leave your weapons out here and ride to the castle ahead of us," he told them. "Try anything, and I'll let Ruel have it first."

The riders pulled their mounts around and started back to the castle. As Longarm dug the barrel of his Colt into Ruel's back, the two men clapped spurs to their mounts and followed after Ruel's men.

The castle wall appeared to be at least twelve feet high and was constructed of solid adobe. It was strong enough to hold off a disorganized band, Longarm judged, but it would afford little real protection in the event it was invested by a large, determined force. But that, obviously, was not its function. The wall was built primarily for show. As such, Longarm found it most impressive.

Reining in, Ruel yelled up at a rifle-toting Mexican standing on the wall and told him to open the gates. The old man disappeared down a ladder. A moment later the two massive doors swung open and the men rode into the compound, Longarm and Ruel still at the rear.

Longarm glanced quickly around. Beyond the spacious courtyard loomed the castle he had glimpsed from afar. It was just as impressive close up. Three stories high, it boasted elaborate balconies, buttresses, and two turrets, one on each end of the building. From a tall pole on the highest turret streamed a single yellow banner. It would have snapped more bravely had there been any wind at all, but Longarm appreciated the touch nevertheless.

Alongside the castle were two large stables, a carriage house, and three bunkhouses. Every building, including the castle, was constructed of adobe and all of the roofs were of red tile. As he pulled his mule to a halt, Longarm heard the distant clang of an anvil. All about the busy courtyard men and women, most of them in Spanish dress, were moving about as they would in any small town, each intent on his or her own business.

"Dismiss your men, Ruel," Longarm snapped.

"You heard him," Ruel told the riders.

With more than one surly glance back at them, the nine men—including Hansen—rode toward the larger of the two bunkhouses.

"Keep going, Ruel," Longarm told him, "and don't make any sudden moves."

Once they reached the castle, Longarm saw that he did not have to worry about a moat or drawbridge. The two men pulled their mounts to a halt at the foot of the stairs leading to the entrance. One of the two double doors opened and a tall fellow dressed in butler's livery strode out onto the topmost step.

"Who is this man?" the butler asked Ruel.

"Some bastard I found on the desert. Says he's a tax assessor."

Longarm cracked Ruel on the side of the head. Ruel almost fell from his horse.

"It's *Mister* Bastard to you," Longarm told Ruel. "I don't like you getting familiar."

"Son of a bitch!" Ruel cried, rubbing his skull. "I'll get you for that."

"And if you don't, Hansen will."

"You can bet on it!"

Ignoring him, Longarm got down from his mule and mounted the castle's broad steps. Again he was impressed. The steps were cut from solid granite and seemed to have been fitted by an expert. It must have cost a pretty penny to haul these enormous slabs this far into the desert.

Longarm stopped in front of the butler. The fellow had a swarthy face, bright dark eyes, a black Vandyke beard, and gleaming hair slicked back with macassar oil. "Your business, sir?" the man asked. "I did not quite understand Mr. Ruel." The butler enunciated every syllable perfectly. Longarm detected a faint accent, but he could not place it.

"I am here on federal business," Longarm told him.

"I do not understand."

"The treasury, to be more exact. I am a tax assessor."

That seemed to register. The man understood about taxes and tax collectors, it seemed. He stiffened slightly. "And your name, sir?"

"Custis Long."

"Was the mistress expecting you?"

"Sure. I dropped by yesterday and left a calling card."

The butler frowned.

Longarm still held his weapon in his hand. He lifted it and pointed the barrel at the butler's midsection. "Just take me in to see the duchess," Longarm said wearily. "It's getting hot as the hinges of hell out here, and I want someone to look after my animals."

The butler's black eyes grew a little darker and smaller, but otherwise he kept his equanimity perfectly. "Of course. This way, Mr. Long."

38

He stepped back. Longarm walked into the castle past him and found himself in a large reception hall. A broad, winding staircase led to a spacious second-floor balcony that ringed the hall. Along the walls stood cast-iron free-standing candelabra. Longarm had no difficulty imagining them fitted out with tall candles, their soft glow filling the hall as dancers swung their partners across the floor, an orchestra playing against the far wall.

The butler led Longarm across the hall into a room lined with bookshelves—the library, Longarm assumed. About the room there were many leather armchairs and two large divans. The room was pleasantly cool.

"Just make yourself comfortable," the butler said. "The duchess or the governor will see you promptly."

"What about my stock? The mules and burros will need plenty of water and generous graining."

"I will see to them at once."

Longarm nodded, holstered his weapon, slumped into one of the armchairs, and took out a cheroot. The sound of the butler's sharp heels faded as he went back across the reception hall. Longarm lit his cheroot and looked around.

French doors led from the library to a sun-drenched inner courtyard. There was a lush flower garden in the courtyard's center, containing a profusion of desert flowers, shrubs, and cacti. In the middle of the garden Longarm glimpsed a fountain, the drowsy sound of its splattering water coming to him through the French windows. A flagstone walk bordered the garden and wrought-iron benches faced it.

Puffing on his cheroot, Longarm shook his head in sheer admiration. Nothing Billy Vail or Thorrson had told him had prepared him for this castle. He leaned back and crossed his legs. He was sitting in the lap of luxury. No doubt about it.

A moment later he sat bolt upright, listening.

The music came again. His ears had not been playing tricks on him. Someone somewhere in this castle was playing a powerful church organ. The swelling chords rang through the castle's walls, the mournful music rising and falling in a long, tremulous, dirgelike melody. How long he listened to it Longarm did not know, but when the music halted after a crashing chord, his cheroot was dead in his mouth.

Slowly the deep, shuddering reverberations died, to be replaced by an unnerving silence.

Chapter 4

A moment later, Longarm heard sharp footsteps crossing the hall. He got to his feet as a tall Spanish gentleman strode in, his hand outstretched, a smile on his face. His eyes were dark, his tanned face lean.

"I am José Duarte," he said, as he shook Longarm's hand warmly. "I am most happy to meet you, *Señor* Long."

"Thanks," said Longarm. "Will the duchess be joining us soon?"

José shrugged unhappily. "I am afraid not. The duchess is—how do you put it?—indisposed."

"Sorry to hear that."

"I have been assured it is nothing serious. She will be feeling better soon. In the meantime, allow me to be of service."

"Have my animals been taken care of yet?"

"I believe Janos has seen to that."

"Janos is the butler?"

"Yes."

"And who might you be? The duke?"

The man smiled. His teeth gleamed like pearls in his swarthy face. "I am the castellan, *señor,* the governor of the castle. It is what a foreman would be for one of your ranches."

"You mean you run this place for the duchess."

"Precisely, *Señor* Long. And you? Janos says you have come to collect taxes. Does that mean you have come all the way from the federal government in Washington?"

"I have come from San Bernardino, and I am not here to collect taxes, just to see what's taxable. I'm a tax assessor."

"Ah, I see. Janos is not familiar with such terms, I am afraid. In any event, I am sure everything is in order." He smiled. "But would you be kind enough to show me your credentials?"

Longarm took out the documents Delores had given him. She had put on enough stamps and ribbons to make them look quite official. Jose glanced perfunctorily at them, then handed the papers back to Longarm.

"So you will be staying with us, *señor*. It will take a while for you to inspect our oasis out here in the Mojave Desert. But I am sure you will enjoy your stay. We have other visitors as well. We have the only fresh water, you see, and many travelers stop by on their way. Some like it so well, they stay longer than they had anticipated. This makes the duchess very happy."

"And you?"

"I am happy when the duchess is happy. It does not

matter how much more work it makes for the rest of us."

"Including that band of outlaws who greeted me on my arrival?"

"My apologies, *señor*," he said, again smiling brilliantly. "That was all a terrible mistake. Let me take you to the men. I will explain your mission to them, and you will hear their apologies. I insist on it."

"If you don't mind, I'll keep my weapon handy."

"By all means." José led Longarm from the room. As they started down a long hallway, Duarte glanced sidelong at Longarm. "If you don't mind my saying it, *Señor* Long, from what I hear, you handle a gun very well for a tax assessor."

Longarm shrugged. "Have you any idea how some people regard taxes—and those sent to levy and collect them?"

José laughed. "I most assuredly have!"

"It doesn't seem to bother you, I notice."

"It is something the duchess will have to deal with, I am afraid. I am just her castellan. But I understand she will not be unhappy at the prospect of paying her taxes. After all, does this not mean her claim to this land has been accepted as genuine?"

"It does. This land is hers, or we wouldn't be taxing her for its use, and since this is a Spanish land grant, her taxes will be minimal."

"She will be most pleased to hear that, I am sure."

They walked a while in silence.

"Tell me," Longarm said abruptly, "did I hear someone in the castle playing an organ before you arrived?"

The man shrugged. "Yes, I believe you did. Our chapel has the finest organ this side of the Mississippi. It was shipped from Boston and freighted all the way from San

Francisco. A magnificent instrument."

"Who was that playing? The music sounded rather grim."

"Did it? I thought the music quite powerful myself. It was Bach's Toccata and Fugue, I believe."

They had reached a door by this time. José opened it for Longarm and they stepped out into the bright sunlight and headed across the compound toward the larger bunkhouse. It did not pass unnoticed by Longarm that José had deftly avoided telling him who had been playing the organ.

As they walked, they passed an old man wearing a huge sombrero. He was hurrying toward one of the barns, clutching a pitchfork in one gnarled old hand. The respect and fear in his eyes when he glanced up and saw José was startling in its intensity. Just before they reached the bunkhouse, two women with brightly colored Spanish skirts and long, gleaming black hair left the bunkhouse chattering gaily, baskets of laundry perched miraculously on their heads. The moment they saw José approaching with Longarm, however, their laughter ceased. Averting their eyes, they hurried swiftly, almost abjectly, past them.

José Duarte, the governor of this castle, ran a tight ship.

The interior of the bunkhouse was spacious and, due to the extra thickness of the adobe walls, comfortably cool. The men who inhabited these quarters were enjoying a level of luxury they could not easily duplicate elsewhere in the West. Colorful lanterns hung from the beams. Extra tables and chairs were placed conveniently about the room. The beds were not crowded together and they were roomy, their bedspreads bright and clean. There

44

were even curtains at the windows, and a small, wizened Indian woman was busy sweeping an already clean floor as they entered.

Except for the old woman, the large room was empty. But there was another room beyond this one, and through the thick adobe wall that separated them Longarm could hear the steady boom of male voices. José headed for the door. Pushing it open, he entered, Longarm on his heels. Glancing about him, Longarm found himself in a room as spacious as the first. Clouds of pipe and cigar smoke hung in the air and at small saloon tables scattered about the room men were drinking and playing cards.

All of them glanced up as José appeared in the doorway, and the boom of their voices halted on the instant. From a table in the middle of the room, Ruel got to his feet. He did not look at all happy to see Longarm standing so casually beside José.

"Ruel," José said, his voice cutting through the room like a lash, *"Señor* Long has made a long journey to this oasis to be of great service to our mistress, the duchess. With his help, her claim to this land will be verified. I am sure even you realize how important this is. I have brought *Señor* Long here now so you can apologize to him for your execrable behavior."

Ruel took a deep breath and looked directly at Longarm. Moistening suddenly dry lips, he said, "Guess I made a mistake, Long. Thought you might be trouble for the duchess."

"Is that an apology?" snapped José.

Ruel's face went white with panic. "Hell, José. It was Hansen started shootin'. You know what he gets like when he's riled!"

"Apologize! Hansen is your man. You hired him. If

you cannot control him, that is your responsibility!"

Ruel looked quickly at Longarm. "I'm . . . sorry, Mr. Long."

Longarm could see how much it was costing Ruel to say that. But he was under no illusion that it meant very much. Ruel would be more anxious now than before to get even with Longarm for causing him this public humiliation.

"Where's Hansen?" José demanded.

"He's with one of the girls. She's . . . fixin' his hand."

A whisper of laughter swept the room.

"Hansen!" José boomed.

A door opened and Hansen appeared in its doorway. He was wearing only his pants and his right hand was covered with a clean bandage. A girl in a slip was sitting upright on the small cot behind him. When she caught sight of José, she ducked out of sight.

"You lookin' for me, José?" Hansen asked, almost lightly.

"Yes. You owe Mr. Long here an apology!"

"Why, sure, José."

Hansen looked at Longarm and smiled. It was as sunny and lighthearted a smile as Longarm had seen in a long time. "I sure am sorry I shot at you, Mr. Long," Hansen said. "I was just funnin' is all. Sure didn't mean to get you all riled."

Longarm nodded curtly. Hansen's apology sent a shiver down his back. His words were so complete and lighthearted a deception. The man lied as easily as he drew breath.

José looked at Hansen. Tension was building in the room. In the silence that followed Hansen's apology, the sound of a woman's sudden, piercing laughter came from a room to Longarm's right. A thin fellow close to the door got swiftly to his feet and burst into the room. The laughter stopped instantly. Longarm heard a hurried, hushed conversation and a moment later came the girl's voice, frightened and apologetic. The thin fellow left the room, closed the door firmly behind him, and returned to his table.

The incident broke the tension. José looked slowly about the room, his eye fixing each man in turn. Then he cleared his throat. *"Señor* Long is our guest," he told them. "While he is here I will expect every single one of you to do all in your power to welcome him and make his stay with us a pleasant one. Is that clear?"

A sullen but prompt murmur of assent swept the room.

"Good," José snapped, his voice still having the effect of a lash. "If any of you fail in this, you will find yourself walking back the way you came. If you have any legs left to walk on, that is." José looked over at Hansen. "Did you hear me, Hansen?"

"Sure did, José," Hansen responded heartily. "You can count on me."

José spun then, nodded curtly to Longarm, and led the way back out of the room. As José closed the door behind him, he glanced at Longarm.

"You see? It was all a mistake. I am sure they will give you no more trouble."

Longarm nodded. He had seen men cowed, but José was a master at it. Raw power emanated from his person. But it was more than that. Duarte was a feared man in this castle because he enjoyed unlimited sway over its inhabitants. As the duchess's castellan, he owed allegiance to no one but her. And she was undisputed ruler of her desert realm.

As they approached another door, José paused. "My quarters are in here," he said, opening the door. "You are welcome to join me at any time for a drink, conversation—anything you might wish."

As he spoke, he ushered Longarm into a large, magnificently furnished room. There was a huge bed, an oaken, flat-topped desk, leather armchairs, and a divan. In a sizable alcove there was a liquor cabinet and floor-to-ceiling shelves containing what appeared to be an extensive library. In a rocking chair beside the cabinet, a young, dark-haired girl was busy sewing buttons on a man's jacket. She glanced up for a moment as José and Longarm entered, then went back to her sewing.

Longarm paused and looked around. Four large windows along one wall, thoroughly shaded from the desert sun by extensive eaves, added a cheery brightness to the room, while the thick adobe walls kept the temperature in the room quite comfortable. In front of the windows, long window boxes contained a profusion of plants and flowers. Their bright blossoms added a heavy, perfumed scent to the room.

"The duchess is very generous, as you can see," José said, indicating his quarters with a sweeping motion of his hand.

As he walked about the room with Longarm, he made no effort to introduce Longarm to the girl sewing his jacket, nor did the girl herself bother even to look up at Longarm. She might have been just one more piece of furniture.

"All this, of course, is taxable," said Longarm.

"Of course," José said, smiling.

"The duchess must have considerable resources."

José smiled. "Considerable. Have you seen enough?"

"For now, yes."

José ushered Longarm from the room. As he pulled his door shut, he said, "You have had a long, weary journey. Let me show you to your quarters. Your room should be ready by now."

They returned to the castle. José led Longarm up the stairs to the second floor and down a long corridor. Stopping before a large oak door, he knocked once, then pushed it open and stepped back.

A dark, squat Indian housekeeper turned as they entered. She was holding a feather duster. Her dark liquid eyes regarded José solemnly as she moved past him and out of the room. Longarm found himself in a room almost as luxurious as José's. The furniture was solid, heavy drapes kept out the sunlight, and the bed looked large enough to enable him to really stretch out.

"The second floor housekeeper's name is Teresa," José told Longarm. "She has a daughter." He smiled. "Taller, younger. I believe it is she who will attend to your needs. Rest up after your bath. Dinner will be at eight in the guests' dining hall. At that time you will meet the other guests." He smiled. "They will be anxious to hear all the news, I am sure. Tomorrow, *Señor* Long, I will be at your disposal."

He smiled, bowed curtly, then backed from the room, pulling the door shut behind him.

Before Longarm had a chance to slip off his coat, there was a light rap on his door and Teresa entered, a young girl behind her. This would be the Indian housekeeper's daughter. As José had told him, she was indeed taller and younger. No more than twenty, Longarm judged. Her gleaming black hair hung to her waist. They

49

were lugging a large, ornate bathtub. It was of gleaming white porcelain, the front of it shaped to resemble the neck and face of a swan. There was even a swan's tail at its rear.

They placed the tub down in the center of the room and hurried out. Longarm began to undress. A moment later the two women returned lugging buckets of steaming water. Two more trips followed, after which the girl returned alone. She was carrying one more steaming bucket, blankets, a bar of soap, and a brush. Longarm hurried to help her close the door.

"Thank you, *senor,*" she said, flashing him a smile.

He was dressed only in the lower portion of his longjohns by this time. She looked at him and frowned.

"Please, *señor*, the water will grow cold. You must hurry."

She hurried over to the two windows and drew the heavy drapes. Some sunlight filtered in, bathing the room in a warm glow. Longarm peeled himself out of his longjohns and stepped swiftly into the water. Too swiftly. His shins sizzled.

The girl laughed and, stepping closer, pushed him lightly. Longarm went down into the steaming tub, causing the water to lap almost over the sides of his white swan. He felt a little foolish, as if he should now be given a toy boat to play with.

"What is your name?" he asked the girl.

"Maria, *señor.*"

"Stop calling me *señor,*" he told her. "My friends call me Longarm.

"Yes? I will call you Longarm, then. Now put your head down."

"What?"

She did not wait to explain. She placed her hand on the back of his head and pushed his face down into the steaminq cauldron. She kept his head down for what seemed like an eternity, then let him up. Blowing like a beached whale, Longarm blinked his eyes frantically. He felt like a scalded cat. He was certain there was not a trace of skin left on his bones. He started to protest, but Maria was too busy to listen. She was soaping his head.

He forgot about protesting and gave himself over to the delight he felt as her fingers dug deliciously into his scalp. So vigorously did she work the suds into his hair, Longarm had to hang on to the sides of the tub. Soon, thick gobs of stinging suds were flowing down his forehead into his eyes.

Just in time, it seemed, Maria shoved his head forward into the water. When he tried to pull his head up, she only pushed him down more firmly. At last, when he thought he was never going to see the light of day again, she released him. He pulled his head out of the water, only to be greeted by a sudden, brutal cascade of steaming water, as Maria emptied over him the last bucket she had brought in.

"Stand up, Longarm," she told him.

He pushed his long frame up out of the water and stood unashamedly before her as she proceeded to soap the brush she had brought in earlier. He braced himself, but her energetic use of the brush almost catapulted him from the tub, nevertheless. He hung on grimly, and soon found delight in the way in which she scrubbed up over his shoulders, dug into the hollow of his back, then attacked the front of his chest. Nor did she neglect his long thighs and calves. Years of grime were scraped from his torso with a diligence that elated him. His entire body was glowing when she had finished.

"Sit back down in the tub," she said.

He nodded obediently and glanced down to grab hold of the tub's side. What he saw astounded and embarrassed rim. He was as erect as a telegraph pole. Swiftly, he dropped his long frame into the water, causing a minor tidal wave to lap over the sides of the tub. With no comment or apparent concern, Maria knelt down beside him and began rinsing the soap off his back and chest.

As she worked, her dark face and glowing eyes remained close to his. Her hand reached into the water and she began scrubbing his buttocks and stomach. She smiled suddenly at him, and he felt her hand brushing his erection. Impishly, she squeezed it. He reached out for her, but she moved deftly to one side and stood up.

"You may stand up now, Longarm," she told him.

Sheepishly, he did as she instructed. As soon as he was upright, she draped a huge towel over his long frame. He stepped out of the tub. She directed him gently toward the bed. When he reached it, he sat down facing her while she toweled him dry.

Pulling the towel away suddenly, she smiled at him. "Yes," she said. "It is true. You are a long one."

She was looking boldly down at him now, making no effort to hide her pleased astonishment at his masculinity. This time she did not duck aside when he reached for her. Catching her about the waist, he swung her onto the bed beside him and swiftly moved a hand up her skirt. To his delight he found nothing under it but her warm, silken thighs and between them a moist thatch. She flung her arms around his neck.

"Are you going to thank me for your bath, Longarm?"

"Yes," he told her, his voice husky. "I sure as hell am."

He closed his mouth over hers and rolled swiftly onto her. She moved eagerly under him, her eyes bright with anticipation, her tongue reaching deep into his mouth, fluttering with a wild abandon. He pushed up her dress and slid into her quickly, her warmth thrilling him. Then she closed her inner muscles tightly about him. He was astonished. It was as if she had clasped his erection in both her hands.

He began thrusting slowly, determined to thank her adequately for that marvelous bath. She opened her mouth still wider and lifted her thighs, grinding them upward with each downward thrust of his. Uttering tiny, animal-like cries, she began to fling her head back and forth. At once he slowed, pulled back, then plunged fully into her hot depths, holding her tightly and pressing in as deeply as he could go, impaling her. The urgency in his loins quieted, but his erection remained intact.

She clung to him, both arms about his neck. Her breathing eased somewhat, and she grew silent as the muscles deep within her closed still more tightly about him. He groaned at the sensation and heard her laugh softly, deeply. Unable to hold off any longer, he began to thrust again. Once more she began to cry out. He increased his tempo, driving deeper and deeper. She started trembling from head to foot. This time he knew he could not prolong it for her, and soon he was soaring himself, past the point of no return, bringing her with him to a final, dazed explosion. For an incredible moment, the two clung to each other fiercely, while the muscles within her continued to milk him, draining him of every last ounce.

That accomplished, she uttered a broken cry and collapsed under him. Weak as a kitten, he rolled off her and lay beside her, his arm over her waist.

She was as silent as death.

He propped himself up on his arms and shook her. Dazedly, she opened her eyes, then crinkled them in silent laughter.

"Are you all right?" he asked.

"I was just thinking of it again. I like very much to do that. It is like I can still feel you inside me."

"Must be nice."

"Do not think of me," she told him. "You must sleep now, and I think you will. Like a baby. There will be a fine dinner later, and you will meet the other guests."

"And will I meet the duchess then?"

Her face clouded suddenly. "I do not know. She is a strange one. But there is one other woman. I think she is very lonely for a man such as you. But you will not forget Maria, no?"

"I will not forget Maria." He grinned at her.

She left the bed and flung a blanket over his body, then leaned down and kissed him lightly on the cheek. Through a fog of sudden drowsiness, he reached out for her, but she laughed lightly and danced away. A moment later she left the room, to return not long after with her mother.

He was asleep before the two women had finished removing the water and the bathtub and did not hear them close the door softly behind them—or the shuddering organ that began to play soon thereafter.

Chapter 5

For Longarm, the dinner that night proved to be a gloomy, disappointing affair. Gloomy because of its location, disappointing because the duchess did not attend.

Longarm and the other guests sat at a long table in a cavernous banquet hall. The many candles placed about the room and table seemed to have little effect on the damp, inky blackness crowding in upon them. Despite this, the food—served by impassive Indian and Mexican servants—was excellent. The servants hovered close about the table, serving them with a deft, silent efficiency that was almost unnerving as the black chamber in which they dined. The butler Janos kept tabs on everything, giving only a wave or a glance to direct the servants.

At the head of the table sat José Duarte, dressed for the occasion in a silver-brocaded black waistcoat, white silk shirt, and string tie, his dark hair slicked back, his swarthy complexion glowing in the candlelight. To his right sat a Colonel Halsey Forsyth and his daughter, Jennifer. On his left sat John Wesley Jarvis and his mother, Esmeralda. Longarm sat next to Esmeralda and directly across from Jennifer.

Throughout the meal they spoke softly, their words at times lost in the yawning void above them. José did his best to keep the conversation light, and everyone was curious about Longarm—Jennifer Forsyth, especially. The colonel said little. He was a small man with keen gray eyes and a snow-white, meticulously barbered Vandyke beard. He was polite but said little in response to Longarm's casual attempt to get a conversation going.

Giving up finally, Longarm allowed Jennifer to move into the vacuum, which she did eagerly. Jennifer was taller than her father, with luxurious brown hair combed down to her shoulders. She wore a bright orange dress, open at the neck, and a magnificent jeweled cross rested on her bosom. Her hazel eyes glowed with excitement as she leaned over to speak to Longarm. It was clear she was bored silly with the castle's dull routine and saw in Longarm's arrival a welcome bit of excitement.

Esmeralda Jarvis, the guest sitting beside Longarm, was a cold, aloof woman with a broad slab of a face, pale and massive and unforgiving. She wore her gray hair in a bun on top of her head and had on a severe black dress that extended down to the insteps of her high-button shoes. Her son was in his early twenties. A short, small-boned child of a man, he had the pallid complexion and luminous eyes of a woman. Wearing a suit as somber and as severely tailored as his mother's dress, he seemed attached to her by invisible strings. His eyes flicked to her constantly for guidance. It was clear that he said and did little without first consulting his mother.

As the table was being cleared off, the wine was brought and poured. Getting to his feet and lifting his glass high, Duarte intoned solemnly, "Ladies and gentlemen, I propose a toast!"

The others dutifully got to their feet also and lifted their glasses.

"To Mr. Custis Long," Duarte said, his voice resonant in the oversized room, almost threatening. "May his sojourn with us be as prosperous for our mistress as for the federal government in Washington."

There was some nervous laughter at that, but they all drank up willingly, then sat down.

Longarm sipped his wine and was suitably impressed. The wine was an excellent vintage. "It is too bad," Longarm said to Duarte, "that the duchess is still indisposed. I am anxious to meet her."

"And she to meet you," Duarte responded. "I assure you. But she will be feeling better soon. Meanwhile, until such time, I shall be more than happy to escort you about the castle."

Duarte finished the wine in his glass, got to his feet, and bowed slightly to his guests. "And now," he said, "if you will excuse me, I wish you all a pleasant good night."

As Duarte strode from the room it served as a signal for everyone to finish their wine and do the same. Everyone promptly gulped down what remained in the glasses, scraped back their high-backed, ornate chairs, and stood up. Longarm exchanged pleasantries for a while with the other guests. Then, excusing himself, he left the room.

He was moving down a long corridor heading for the

57

stairway leading to the second floor when he heard light footsteps overtaking him. He turned to see Jennifer Forsyth coming up beside him, her face flushed with excitement.

"Are you going to retire so soon?" she asked.

"Do you have any better ideas?"

"There's a lovely balcony on the third floor. There's always a breeze up there, and the stars at this time of night are simply glorious."

He smiled at her. "Lead the way."

Halfway up the first flight of stairs, the sound of the organ came again, filling the stairwell with its mournful shuddering. Longarm stopped to listen. "I wish to hell I knew who was playing that thing," he said.

"You mean you don't know?"

Longarm looked down at Jennifer. "No, I don't."

"It's the duchess! She's an accomplished organist. She studied in Europe."

"Well, she certainly doesn't play like someone who is indisposed."

"She has moods. Dark moods. Maria told me."

"Moods? You mean she's..."

"Oh, I don't think she's mentally disturbed. Nothing like that. But... well, she's an artist, you see."

"No, I don't see."

"Temperament. She has an artist's temperament."

"That so?" Longarm was unimpressed by Jennifer's explanation. "Where's the chapel?" he asked.

"To the left off the main hall."

Longarm nodded. He was thinking seriously of going back down to introduce himself, but the organ stopped abruptly. The silence that followed was almost deafening.

Jennifer took his arm. "The night is really beautiful."

"All right, Jennifer. Let's go on up."

As soon as Longarm stepped out onto the balcony, he realized that Jennifer had not been exaggerating. The night was glorious. The stars were spectacular and there was a strong, cooling breeze that caught her long hair and sent it flying. Above him in the night Longarm could hear that banner he had noted earlier snapping in the wind.

They stood with their hands on the balcony railing looking about them at the sky and the world below. No one moved in the courtyard, and the desert beyond the high walls was a pale, moonlit sea stretching as far as the eye could see.

Longarm directed his gaze down to the courtyard. From the balcony he was able to obtain a marvelous bird's-eye view. The castle and grounds were quite extensive and seemed prosperous enough—a small adobe village, complete in itself, secreted away within the walls of the duchess's castle. Surely the duchess had to be enormously wealthy to allow for such extravagance. But for a woman with these resources, any place in the world could be made over to her liking. Why on earth, then, would she choose to build her duchy here on the Mojave Desert?

Jennifer moved closer to him. "You're really quite handsome for a tax collector," she said.

Longarm started to explain the difference between an assessor and a tax collector, but by this time he had become quite weary of the chore and decided not to bother. "And you're very pretty yourself," he told her, "to be hidden away in this castle. How long have you and your father been here?"

"Only a couple of days. We were on our way to California and stopped for water. At the same time we found out our wagon needed repairs. The duchess's people are repairing it for us. Aren't we lucky? Isn't this a wonderful place? So mysterious!"

"And they haven't asked you for a cent?"

"No, they haven't. All this hospitality, and not once have we been asked to pay for a thing."

"Remarkable," said Longarm.

"Yes."

"Have you met the duchess?"

"She greeted my father and me on our first day here, in the main hall. She is very beautiful."

"Did she play for you?"

Jennifer laughed. "No. At that time I had no idea she played anything. She was holding court."

He looked at her in some surprise.

"Yes," she said, grinning mischievously, "you heard right. She was holding court."

"Describe it to me."

"She was sitting in a handsome chair with a high back. Mr. Duarte stood on one side of her. He acted as a translator as the butler kept bringing people in—the people who work and live here. Some wanted a chance to go home to their families for visits and others just wanted different jobs around the place. One young married couple was not getting along, and I guess their bickering was disturbing everyone. There were complaints about that. The duchess listened to all of them and made her judgments."

"She played Solomon, you mean."

"Yes." She laughed lightly. "Fortunately, there was

no dispute about a baby. But I am sure she would have been able to handle it if there had been."

"She impressed you?"

"Oh, yes. It was quite exciting watching her. And then she left her chair and came down to welcome my father and me personally." Jennifer paused a moment as she recalled the scene in her mind. "Yes," she concluded, "she is a very beautiful woman."

"I am anxious to meet her."

Jennifer sighed. "If you do, I'm afraid I will not see much of you from then on."

"Never fear. This castle is not as spacious as all that. I am sure we will meet often."

She rested her head on his shoulder. "That's not what I meant."

"Jennifer . . . !"

Longarm spun. The girl's father was standing in the doorway to the balcony, his gray eyes snapping angrily.

"Father!" Jennifer cried. "You shouldn't be sneaking around like that!"

"Enough of your tongue, young lady. It is *you* who are sneaking around. I had no idea where you had gone. It is time for you to retire."

Jennifer looked helplessly up at Longarm. "Good night, Mr. Long. I do hope I see you again soon."

Then, flinging a hurt, angry look at her father, Jennifer brushed away tears and fled past the colonel to the stairs and vanished from sight. As soon as she was gone, the colonel turned to Longarm.

"As for you, sah, I do not regard your actions as those of a gentleman. No, sah, Ah do not!"

"Hell, Colonel," Longarm said mildly, "if I were you,

I'd just be grateful I had a daughter as pretty, obedient, and intelligent as Jennifer. And I'd trust her a whole lot more."

"Sah, it is not your place to question my behavior as a parent."

"Not your behavior, I guess—just your good sense."

The man drew himself up to his full five feet five. "I regard that as an insult, sah! I demand satisfaction!"

"You going to let me choose the weapons?"

"At your service, sah!"

"Good. Horse manure at five paces."

Without another word to the irate colonel, Longarm moved brusquely past him and down the stairs.

He was almost to his room when he heard the sombre quaking of the organ start up again. The very walls seemed to tremble. He pulled up, thought a minute, then turned back around. A moment later he found the door to the chapel and pushed it open.

Stepping inside, he pulled the door shut softly and turned. The organ's great golden pipes were perched high above the altar, the organ itself off to the right. Sitting at the organ, a candelabrum with four lighted candles standing beside her, was the duchess.

She was dressed all in black. It looked like an evening gown. Her hair, as black as midnight, flowed down her back clear to her waist. As she played, she swayed back and forth over the keys, the music filling the chapel with a great, surging ocean of sound. It was the same melody Duarte had identified earlier—something by a fellow named Bach, called Toccata and Fugue. Longarm had never heard such music before. It stirred him clear down to his boot heels.

He walked down the aisle until he reached the first

row of pews and slumped into one to wait for her to finish. She seemed to be working very hard, energetically yanking out stops and reaching with her feet to depress the pedals, her fingers leaping from one row of keys to another. Her energy never flagged, however, and the music that poured forth was like a sustained, shuddering lament.

At last she brought the piece to its climax, the music building upward with an inevitability that swept all before it. For a moment she held all the forces of the stunning climax together under her fingers, the chords sustained for an agonizing interval. Then it was over, the echoing cry of the music fading into the night.

The duchess slumped forward over the keyboard, her head down, her shoulders sagging.

Longarm got to his feet and cleared his voice. "That was very beautiful," he said.

She spun, uttering a tiny cry of surprise, her hand up to her mouth. "I did not know you were there!"

She jumped to her feet, and he could see that she was tall and imposing. She wore no jewelry except a single diamond-studded comb. Her eyes were dark, gleaming coals in the candlelight, her complexion flawless, her prominent cheekbones and the slight upward cant to her brows giving her face a slightly oriental cast.

"I am sorry for intruding, Duchess. The music drew me into the chapel."

She frowned. "You . . . you are Custis Long?"

"Yes."

"I have not been well, or I would have seen you sooner."

"You sounded pretty good just now."

"You don't understand. You must go. I do not wish

63

to see you now. If you do not leave, I will send for José. He will see that you do not disturb me."

"It is not necessary for you to send for him," Longarm said. "I can wait. As soon as you . . . feel better, I will be most happy to go over the castle with you. Again, my apologies for intruding."

She said nothing as Longarm turned and started back up the aisle. He was opening the door on his way out when she called his name. He turned.

"Thank you, Mr. Long. For being so . . . understanding. I assure you, we will meet again."

Longarm smiled. "I hope so."

He strode out.

The door to his room was slightly ajar. Halting, Longarm flattened himself against the wall and took out his derringer. He had not worn his gunbelt to dinner. Moving forward silently, he reached out and pushed the door gently. It swung slowly open. When it was wide enough, he stepped quickly inside his room and then crouched.

Longarm had cat's eyes. In a matter of seconds he could see into every corner of his room. He left his crouching position and made a swift inspection of its perimeter, then walked over to the dresser and lit the lamp sitting on it. As he placed the chimney back on, he glanced at his bed.

Maria was sleeping on it, a blanket thrown over her. Frowning, he strode to her side, intent on sending her back to her quarters. He did not need another bath. What he needed was sleep.

Looking down at her, he felt as if someone had just punched him in the pit of his stomach. Maria was lying on her back, her eyes opened wide in terror, her face frozen into a silent, eternal scream. Reaching down, he flung back the covers and saw the hilt of a knife protruding from between her breasts. The blow had been so powerful that a portion of the hilt had been driven beneath the skin.

He flung the blanket back over her, covering her face this time, and hurried from the room to find José Duarte—and to escape the horror of what he had found.

The next morning Longarm visited Duarte in the bunkhouse. In order for them to discuss matters privately, Duarte had sent his woman from his room. Duarte was sitting at his desk, Longarm in a wooden chair beside it.

"There's also the chance," Longarm was saying, "that whoever killed Maria entered my room to kill me."

Duarte's eyebrows went up slightly. "And found Maria in your bed?"

"Why not? In the darkness, he might have mistaken her for me."

"It would appear from the expression on her face that she saw the knife descending."

"Yes."

"She must have screamed. Would that not have told him it was not you sleeping in that bed?"

"By that time it would have been too late."

Duarte shrugged. "Tell me, *Señor* Long. What was Maria doing in your bed?"

Longarm shrugged. "Waiting for me, I suppose."

"For what purpose?"

"If you don't know, Duarte, it would be foolish of me to explain. But Maria's attraction for me is not what we are discussing now. It is Maria's murder. And, damn it, I want to find the son of a bitch who killed her!"

65

"I am sure you do. The duchess most assuredly does, as well. We are all anxious to find the murderer of this unfortunate girl. And of course you would be the most anxious of all, especially if, as you suggest, Maria's murderer had really been seeking to kill you."

"You must admit it makes sense, doesn't it?"

Duarte shrugged. "And whom do you suspect?"

"One of your boys. Ruel or Hansen for starters."

Duarte shook his head. "I am afraid neither man could have done it. Both men's whereabouts last night have already been accounted for."

"That so?"

"From the beginning of our dinner until well into this morning, Ruel and Hansen were in the company of two local girls. Somehow they managed to get into the wine cellar. Maria's mother said that Maria did not leave her room until nine o'clock. By that time both men were sodden with drink. It was Janos who told me they had broken into the wine cellar."

"You think drink would stop either one of them?"

Duarte smiled sardonically. "Apparently. Both girls complained that neither man could, shall we say, perform by then. I have seen them, *Señor* Long. They are even now almost too sick to stand." He smiled. "It was not a very good vintage they chose, I am afraid."

"They could have hired someone else. There's eight other men who would have done it gladly."

Duarte leaned forward onto his desk, his eyes studying Longarm closely. *"Señor* Long, what would be their motive?"

"They didn't like the way I handled them out there on the desert. Hurt their pride, maybe."

"You did indeed take care of them with some despatch. Those two were my toughest and meanest, dredged from the back alleys and gambling dens of San Francisco. A surly, murderous couple. Yet you handled them with almost casual ease. For a tax assessor, I would say you have already displayed somewhat deadly talents."

"I wasn't always a tax assessor."

"I can imagine."

"I'd like to see Ruel and Hansen."

Duarte shrugged. "As you wish."

Duarte got to his feet and went to the door. His sharp call brought someone running. Longarm heard him speaking rapidly in Spanish and caught most of it. Duarte returned to his desk, sat down, and started drumming with his fingers on the blotter. Longarm took out a cheroot and lit it, offering one to Duarte. The man shook his head.

There was a knock on Duarte's door. "Come in," Duarte called, his voice sharp.

Ruel and Hansen entered. One look at them and Longarm knew why Duarte was so convinced that neither of them had killed Maria. They were dreadfully sick, their eyes sunken, their faces drawn and pale despite their tans, giving them both a yellowish cast. They stood upright, but only with a tremendous effort of will.

Longarm got out of his chair and approached them. He studied them both closely, as he would vermin he had just found scurrying out from under a rock.

"Maria's dead," he told them. "Did you know that?"

Hansen tried to smile. "I'll bet she died happy. She always was eager to please."

Longarm punched the man. He went reeling back against the wall, struck it hard, and slid to the floor, unconscious. Ruel tried to swing on Longarm, but he

67

was so wild he lost his balance and sagged to his hands and knees. For a moment it looked as if he were going to be sick to his stomach.

Longarm stared down Ruel, then glanced over at Hansen. His mouth was open, his head lolling loosely to one side. Longarm looked back at Ruel.

"Get Hansen out of here."

Ruel muttered something and remained on his hands and knees.

"You heard him, Ruel!" snapped Duarte.

At once Ruel staggered to his feet, made it over to Hansen's side, then proceeded to drag the unconscious man from the room. Even as the two disappeared through the doorway, two very frightened girls entered.

"I thought you might want to speak to them as well," Duarte explained. "The short one is Rosita, her companion is Constance. They were with the men all last night. Go ahead, ask them whatever you want."

Longarm strode close to the girls. Clinging to each other, they took a step back. They appeared terrified of Longarm and seemed to be bracing themselves for a blow.

"I am not going to hurt you," Longarm told them. "Just tell me what you know. Were those two men with you last night?"

Both women nodded frantically.

"Did either of them ever leave you?"

"No, *señor!*" the women cried.

They were trembling, their eyes darting constantly to Duarte. So terrified were they that Longarm was certain they were not lying. He waved them out and returned to his chair by the desk.

"All right, then. Who?" he asked, slumping into it.

"Someone's out to kill me. Who? And why?"

Duarte raised his eyebrows and shrugged. "That, *señor*, is as much a mystery to me as it is to you. I suggest you take precautions for the rest of your stay here. And of course I will do all in my power to see that no harm comes to you." He got to his feet. "And now, would you care to inspect the grounds and begin your assessment? The sooner you finish your business here, the sooner will you be free to go on your way."

Longarm stubbed out his cheroot and followed Duarte from his room. As Duarte closed the door behind him, he glanced at Longarm.

"The duchess has been most disturbed by all this," he said coldly. "Your coming upon her so unexpectedly last night—and now this terrible murder. Maria was one of her favorite servants. She would like to see you when we complete this day's inspection. I do not need to remind you," he went on, his voice growing as cold as steel, "that you must be gentle with her. She is a delicate flower blooming on this desert. I would be most unhappy if your presence here upset her any further."

Longarm glanced at Duarte. The man was threatening him, of that there could be no doubt. And his threat, Longarm was certain, carried as much weight as did those of Ruel or Hansen. Perhaps more.

Longarm realized he sure as hell was going to find it difficult to sleep with both eyes closed in this place.

Chapter 6

Longarm did his best, but it was not easy for him to concentrate on assessing the value of the duchess's holdings—especially when he and Duarte left the storeroom an hour or so later and caught sight of Maria's funeral cortege returning to the castle grounds.

Stopping in his tracks, he watched the black-garbed mourners file in through the gate behind the mule-driven wagon that had borne Maria's casket to its final resting place. He found it almost impossible to reconcile the reality of Maria's death with the memory of her vibrant presence the day before. He could still feel the delicious way she dug the suds into his hair, the impudent force of her hand on the back of his neck as she plunged his face down into the boiling water, and later, the sweet imprint of her lips on his.

All morning Duarte had been eagerly showing off the extent of the duchess's wealth. Longarm had been dutifully impressed, especially when he noted the many blooded thoroughbreds in the stable and the fact that their expensive oats and hay were freighted in fresh every week. A moment before, in the small outbuilding containing the extensive pantry and cupboards supporting the kitchen staff, Duarte had pointed out unnecessarily that the duchess's plate was sterling, her glass Waterford.

Now Longarm was weary. The charade that he was interested in all this pointless extravagance was fraying his patience. By this time he was quite willing to believe that the duchess's wardrobe consisted almost exclusively of Paris gowns and that she probably took daily baths in the most expensive perfumes, freighted in by the gallon for that purpose.

Yet he still had no clue as to the source of all this wealth, nor why she had planted this showplace of luxury and elegance in the middle of the Mojave Desert. What in hell was really going on here? And, even more important, what had happened to those two deputies Ivar Thorrson had sent out to inquire about the duchess?

And who had murdered Maria?

The gate closed behind the returning mourners, and Duarte led Longarm around to the back of the castle and through a rear entrance into the kitchen serving the castle and the bunkhouse. Chatting amiably, Duarte pointed out the hanging sides of beef, the huge ice locker, the gleaming cookware. Longarm decided he had had enough and stopped. For a while Duarte continued on, oblivious to the fact that Longarm was no longer at his elbow. When Duarte discovered that fact, he turned around, visibly annoyed.

"I've had enough for today," Longarm told him.

Duarte walked back to Longarm. "What is it, *Señor* Long? Is all this too much for you?"

Longarm shrugged. "Guess so. I'm used to assessing much more modest spreads, I can tell you."

"Yes. In this godforsaken land, I imagine you must be."

"We can continue tomorrow."

"As you wish. But there is still a considerable amount yet to show you. We have only scratched the surface. And we have yet to tour the castle itself. I assure you, the library alone is worth a day's inspection. Additional volumes are being freighted in monthly."

"We'll get to it, I promise you. I've got plenty of time."

"Are you quite sure of that, *Señor* Long?"

Longarm knew at once what Duarte meant. There was still every reason to believe that whoever murdered Maria had been after Longarm instead. If this were so, every day Longarm remained at the castle increased the odds against him. Until, of course, the murderer was apprehended.

".You will have to let me worry about that, Duarte."

"Of course, *Señor* Long."

Duarte's smile was thin and cold. It held no comfort at all.

Longarm left the kitchen by the rear door and started around to the front of the castle. When he reached the courtyard, he heard distant shouts and two quick gunshots sounding from the desert beyond the walls. As he turned to watch, he saw the gatekeeper hurrying down his ladder to pull open the gate. A moment later, a rider leading a huge, canvas-covered freight wagon and four horses burst through the gate and into the compound.

Once safely inside, the rider turned his mount and rode back to see to the Mexican freighter driving the wagon. The old man appeared to be wounded, though not seriously. José Duarte rushed past Longarm toward the wagon. Ruel and Hansen and the rest of the men streamed out of their bunkhouse. Soon, from all parts of the castle grounds, others came running as well.

Keeping in the background, Longarm hurried over himself to see what all the excitement was about. The newcomer was a tall, lean fellow with wide shoulders, long, sandy hair, and a drooping mustache. He was wearing a gray duster and a black, wide-brimmed hat, with the brim turned down on all sides. He looked to be in his early forties. His eyes were an icy blue, his long, pale face hard. Despite the heat, not a single bead of perspiration moved down his face.

After he had seen to the driver of his wagon and made sure he was not hurt all that seriously, he called for someone to take charge of the wagon and horses. Then he turned to José.

"Damn it! Where were your men, Duarte?" he asked furiously. "If I hadn't noticed them bastards closing in on us last night, we never would have made it!"

"They were in here. I had no reason to send them out. How many men were after you?"

"Tarnation, Duarte! I didn't take time to count. Ten, maybe twenty. They were a motley, unshaven band of brigands—that's all I know for sure. They saw my wagon as perfect plunder. And if we don't stop them, they'll be back to find out what's behind these walls."

"I'll send the men out right now," Duarte told him.

"Then do it! They couldn't be too far. They just turned back when they came in sight of the castle. And tell your men I'm offering a fifty-dollar gold piece to the first man who brings back one of them, dead or alive."

"You hear that?" José asked, swinging around to face the men now crowding around.

"We heard," said Hansen, grinning. He looked beyond Duarte at the newcomer. "How much for two?"

"I'll double it," the man snapped.

"Done," said Hansen.

"Get on your horses," ordered Duarte. "All of you. And get going!"

The men hurried to the stables.

An old Mexican hurried up and climbed onto the wagon seat beside the wounded driver and drove the wagon off, the horses trailing it. The animals looked like still more thoroughbreds for the duchess's stables—and why in blazes she needed that kind of horseflesh, this far out in the middle of nowhere, was just one more mystery to Longarm.

Duarte and the newcomer started across the courtyard, heading for the castle. Longarm decided to find out who the fellow was. He strode boldly toward them, nodding briskly to Duarte and his companion.

The newcomer halted and glanced at Duarte for an introduction. Duarte quickly introduced Longarm, explaining what he was doing at the castle. The fellow's name was Dudley Jacobson and he was from San Francisco. As Jacobson shook Longarm's hand, he explained that, as Longarm had surmised, he had just delivered four thoroughbred horses and a wagonload of valuables for the duchess. He was her principal buyer in San Francisco.

"So you've come to see what the duchess is worth, have you?" Jacobson asked, his frosted eyebrows canting ironically.

Longarm nodded.

"Should keep you busy for a while, I'm thinking," the buyer said as the three of them started walking across the compound.

"I got the impression *Señor* Long is already wearying of his task," commented José.

"I would not doubt it," Jacobson said, glancing at Longarm. "Your eyes would grow as big as saucers if you could see what's in that wagon."

"I'm sure," Longarm said. "You mind telling me what happened out on that desert?"

The tall man shrugged. "Nothing for a tax assessor to bother about," he said. "A band of marauders, that's all. We've always had trouble since the duchess began building here. This was the largest and boldest bunch, however. They tried to sneak up on me last night, so I lit out."

"Looks like you traded some lead."

"We did," Jacobson said. "I think I stopped their leader at the outset. It disorganized them some and gave us the chance we needed to get some distance on them."

"Nice going."

"I can handle such riffraff, Mr. Long," Jacobson declared scornfully. "The pity of it is that Ruel's men were not out there to catch them as they approached the castle. We would have been rid of that gang for good had Ruel's men been on hand."

He turned to José. "I suggest you keep a patrol outside the walls from now on, night and day. It'll keep the men from getting flabby. The flies are beginning to buzz around

76

the honey, Duarte. We can't relax a minute."

José nodded quickly. It was clear to Longarm that Jacobson wielded considerable influence—as much as, if not more than, the duchess herself. A moment later Jacobson bid Longarm goodbye, then left him to accompany Duarte to the castellan's office in the large bunkhouse. Longarm watched them stride off for a moment, then continued on to the castle.

He was almost to his room when he saw Jennifer running down the hallway toward him. He waited for her.

"I must see you!" she cried.

"Here I am."

"No! Not out here! In your room."

"I don't think the colonel would like that, Jennifer."

"Please, Mr. Long!"

Longarm opened the door to his room and stepped aside as Jennifer hurried in past him. He entered after her, closed the door, then turned to face her.

"Now," he said, "what is this all about?"

Jennifer held out an envelope for him. "I found this on my dresser, Mr. Long. It's addressed to you."

He took it from her.

"I think it's from the duchess," she said in a hushed voice.

He opened it, read it quickly, and looked up at Jennifer. "You're right. It is from the duchess. She would like to meet me."

"Where?"

He smiled. "In your room."

"Why, what do you mean?"

He smiled. "That's what the note says, Jennifer. The duchess wants to meet me this afternoon around three in your room. Do you suppose you could persuade your father to leave the room at that time? Maybe both of you could take a walk."

"Oh, we could do better than that," she said. "Father is anxious to check on the progress of our wagon. It should certainly be ready by now, and he is getting impatient. I'll suggest we go to the carriage barn and see how it's coming."

"Reckon that should do it, then."

"You'll need my key."

"Leave it under the rug outside your door."

"But that's where everyone hides a key, isn't it?"

"I reckon. But put it there anyway, okay?"

She nodded. "Mr. Long . . . ?"

"Yes, Jennifer?"

"Isn't it just awful, what happened to poor Maria?"

"Yes, Jennifer, it is."

"Do you have any idea who could have killed her?"

"No, I don't. I thought I did last night and this morning, but I'm not so sure now."

"It gives me the shivers. I just want to get out of here. Imagine! Someone in this castle is a murderer!"

"Yes."

"Perhaps that's why the duchess wants to see you."

"That may be so."

"I'll go find Father," Jennifer said, moving past him to the door. As she pulled it open, she glanced back to Longarm. "I'll be glad to leave this castle, but I will miss you, Mr. Long."

"That's very kind of you, Jennifer."

"I suppose now that you'll be seeing the duchess you won't have any time for me."

"Not at all," he told her gently. "I will always have

time for my friends. And that includes you, doesn't it, Jennifer?"

She nodded happily and left.

Jennifer left the key where Longarm suggested. He let himself into Jennifer's room and checked it quickly, his derringer out and ready, but there were no surprises. The room was empty enough. He selected a comfortable upholstered chair by one window and sat down. As he waited, he took out the note Jennifer had delivered to him and read it again.

Dear Mr. Long,
I would appreciate it if you would meet me in Jennifer Forsyth's room at three this afternoon. Please do what you can to arrange it. I am sure Jennifer will cooperate.

Marta Zapolya

Longarm folded the note and placed it back in his pocket. He consulted his watch. It was already past three. At any moment now, he should hear a light tap on the door. He leaned back in the chair and took out a cheroot.

"I wish you wouldn't smoke."

Longarm almost dropped his match. Stepping out from behind the head of the canopied bed, the duchess strode into view. It was uncanny—as if she had materialized out of thin air. Jumping to his feet, Longarm hastily pocketed his cheroot.

She smiled when she saw the surprise on his face. Longarm was impressed. She had seemed beautiful enough in the chapel, but close up she was even more breathtaking. He could not help wondering how much she must resemble her mother, a fiery courtesan who had seduced the king of Spain.

She held out her hand to him and he took it. Her hand grasped his warmly. She still favored black, he saw, but the dress she wore now was not as severely modest as the one she had worn in the chapel. It granted Longarm a generous view of her ample bosom and of her flawless shoulders and neck, composed, it seemed, of a radiant, almost translucent ivory. As she looked into his eyes, her own dark eyes burned with a passionate fire. She had Spanish blood, of course, but there was something else mixed in there too—a strain Longarm could not place. But it did not matter. The mix was a good one.

"Shall I call you Marta?" he asked her.

"Yes. Please do."

"I am flattered you wanted to see me. And I'm sure amazed at the way you managed it."

She smiled. "I came through a hidden door."

"I figured something like that."

She sat back on the bed and faced him, her hands clasped in her lap. "Please sit down. There's no need to stand on ceremony here," she said, her tone revealing a touch of irony. "After all, I am only a duchess."

"And also a very fine organist," he said, sitting back down in his chair.

"I am glad you liked it."

"I had never heard such music before," Longarm admitted. "But it had a certain..." He shrugged, unable to find the right word.

"Power?" she finished for him. "Is that the word?"

He smiled quickly, nodding. "Yes, that's it. The music has power all right—the power to reach deep into you."

"Exactly. When I am feeling . . . under the weather, or lonely, that is when I play Bach. His music is a great comfort to me."

"Do you feel better now?"

She shrugged. "The mood has passed. And perhaps it was the music that carried me through."

"Fine. I'm glad you are feeling better," Longarm said.

"But now comes this frightening murder, Mr. Long. Poor Maria! I can still hardly believe it. José told me as much as he could. But I understand it was you who discovered her body—in your bed."

"Yes."

"Why was she there, Mr. Long? Why was she in your bed?"

"She was waiting for me, I suppose."

"You mean that you and Maria . . ."

He returned her gaze unflinchingly. "Yes," he replied, in answer to her unspoken question.

"But, Mr. Long, you hardly knew the girl."

"She was . . . very warm. A very attractive young lady."

"Do you usually find women so quickly?"

"This conversation is not really necessary, is it, Duchess?"

She sighed and looked away. "I suppose not," she admitted, looking back at him. "Your private affairs are your own business, of course. And that is not why I wanted to see you, anyway. Not entirely, that is."

"Why did you send me that note, Duchess?"

"Because I thought I detected something in your face when you visited the chapel."

"I don't understand."

"I cannot believe you are what you say you are—an ordinary tax assessor."

"But of course I am."

She looked at him for a long moment, her eyes probing deep into his, then she smiled. "All right, have it your way. You are a tax assessor. If you say you are a tax assessor, then that is what you are. It is just that when I saw you in the chapel, you simply did not strike me as one more government functionary. You stand too straight, too tall for that."

"Thank you, Marta."

She smiled. "It feels so good to hear my name."

"Your mother," Longarm said. "Where was she from?"

"You know her history, do you?"

"Yes."

"Then you mean before she met the king of Spain." He nodded.

"A tiny little country in eastern Europe, now a part of Hungary. It is called Transylvania. Janos, my butler, is from there, as well, He was a small boy when my mother brought him to Spain to serve the family."

"He is still doing so, I see."

"Yes, he is very loyal."

"As loyal as your castellan, Duarte?"

"Of course. More so. I would trust Janos with my life," the duchess replied.

"But not Duarte?"

"Not Duarte."

"You have much wealth, Marta."

She shrugged, as if this was of no real importance.

"So maybe you won't mind if I ask you a question," Longarm went on. "Why did you build this castle in the middle of the Mojave Desert? You could have built it anywhere in the world."

She shrugged and looked at him with brooding eyes.

"One place—one prison—is as good as another. It does not matter where I live, Mr. Long. Everywhere I go, my wealth creates walls about me. Here, at least, I am not being continually plagued by those who seek only my wealth."

"Well, you've found the right place. You couldn't have picked a more desolate spot."

She sighed. "I agree."

"And this is what you want, really?"

"No, of course not. When one gets what one wants, all one really gets is what one deserves."

Longarm laughed. It was a cynical but wise observation.

"Mr. Long, I am frightened," she said. "Someone behind these walls is a murderer. I had hoped you might be able to tell me more about Maria's death, and that you might even be the kind of person who could investigate this terrible crime. Do something about it, perhaps."

"You mean you think I am a lawman?"

"As I told you before, you stand too tall to be just another tax man."

"It takes all kinds to collect the government's taxes, Marta. Tall men, short men, fat men."

She got to her feet. "Yes, yes," she said wearily, heading around the bed for the hidden door. "We need not go through that again. Spare me the many numerous examples. I am sorry to have bothered you, Mr. Long. Make your assessment of my possessions. Measure my wealth. Then you may leave."

"I am sorry if I am not what you think—what you had hoped for, at any rate."

She smiled at him. "Forgive me. I should not have

asked you to be anything more than what you are. It was most unfair of me."

He had followed her to the wall. Without a pause, she reached out and pushed a portion of the wall closest to the headboard. The wall pivoted almost silently on a bearing or on a rock imbedded in the wall. There was a barely audible grating sound. Before Marta stepped into the passageway, she looked back at him. "This was what took the longest to build. I find these passages very convenient."

"Tell me, do these passageways run through all the walls?"

"Of course."

She vanished as she replied, and the wall swung back into place.

The light, barely audible sound of her footsteps faded rapidly. Longarm waited just a moment longer. Then, moving closer to the apparently solid wall, he tried to see the break that would indicate the doorway. After a few moments he detected a slight but noticeable line tracing from the ceiling to the floor. Unless the person studying the wall knew almost precisely where to look for it, however, the break in the wall was virtually invisible to the naked eye.

He touched the wall where Marta had. Nothing happened. He pressed harder and this time he felt something give. Increasing the pressure steadily without letting up, he watched the wall swing in smoothly, pivoting on the stone. He stepped into the passageway and pushed the door shut. It swung easily back into place—too easily. The sudden darkness was almost enough to convince Longarm he had gone blind.

He stood patiently until his eyes grew accustomed to

the dimness. He saw ahead of him a steep, crude stairway, a dim light filtering up from below. He moved down the stairs and found himself in a long corridor. Sunlight was streaming in through foot-long slits in the top of the wall. They were probably hidden from the outside by being placed well up under the eaves. Everywhere Longarm looked he saw evidence of sloppy, hasty workmanship. But it didn't matter. The passageways were intact and they afforded secret and swift access to almost every room in the castle.

As he walked, he followed the dim impression left by Marta's footprints. At last they vanished into what appeared to be a solid wall. He pressed against the wall firmly. It took a while to find the right spot. When he did, the wall swung open into Marta's room.

She was on the bed, naked, waiting for him.

"I was beginning to think you would not come after me," she said, as the wall swung shut behind him.

Chapter 7

"You see?" she said, laughing softly, seductively. "I was right. You are too tall to be just a tax man. Such a functionary would not have followed me. Do you insist on denying it, Mr. Long? Are you not a lawman?"

He looked down at her, his knees somewhat shaky at the prospect before him. "If I am a lawman—and I ain't sayin' you're right, Marta—then this is sure one hell of a way to find out."

"Then you will not admit it?"

"All I'm admittin' to is a desire to join you on that bed."

"Then do it."

He was all thumbs, but he managed to peel out of his clothes quickly enough, and was careful to keep his derringer hidden from her as he folded his pants around it and placed them down on the floor at the head of the bed.

"My," she said, "you are so neat."

"Shut up," he said hoarsely.

He was on the bed then, straddling her, his lips plastered over hers. If this was trouble, and she was it, he was determined to make the most of it. He just hoped to hell Duarte or some other henchman of hers didn't come barging through that wall at the wrong time.

She clung to him and swung her body up to meet his. With his knee, he pushed aside her thighs. Already her moist pubis had touched the tip of his erection.

"It's been such a long time, Mr. Long," she murmured feverishly. "So terribly, terribly long!"

Her fingers flew down his flanks, and with a swift, heated urgency that aroused him even more, she took hold of him in a hasty, frantic effort to guide him into her. He felt his erection, raw now with desire, probing at her moist entrance. He pulled back for just an instant in a deliberate ploy to drive her even wilder. It succeeded.

"You bastard!" she cried out. "What are you waiting for? I want you! Now!"

He went in, thrusting full and deep, grunting with the exertion. She moaned from deep within her and fastened her lips to his again, her tongue probing wildly as she brought her legs up and locked her ankles around his back. With each thrust she hugged him still tighter, her hips grinding, sucking him deeper into her.

Pulling back, careful not to come out entirely, he waited a moment, then thrust back in, deeper this time, hitting bottom. He felt her shudder under the impact. She opened her mouth to gasp, her head thrown back, her eyes shut tightly as he continued his long, deep plunges. Keeping it up steadily, driving fiercely into her each time, he felt himself moving inexorably toward his climax. Tiny, inarticulate cries broke from her throat. She began twisting her head from side to side. Still deeper he thrust, rocking her violently, slamming into her so swiftly now that he felt as if a switch deep within his groin had been turned on and he was now completely out of control.

Marta cried out, a high, keening shriek. Her eyes flew open. He felt her go rigid under him. Her inner muscles tightened convulsively. He bore in then with a sudden powerful thrust that nailed her to the bed. In that single instant, both of them came in a shuddering orgasm that left Longarm pulsing deep within her. Again and again he came in a series of uncontrollable spasms.

A blissful sense of relief engulfed him. He fell forward onto her, his shaft still enclosed in her soft, warm snugness, her legs still clasped tightly about his waist. She would not, it seemed, let him go.

"It has been too long for me," she told him, her voice husky with desire. "I will not let you roll over and go to sleep. Do you hear me, Mr. Long?"

He laughed softly, his face nestled in her luxurious hair. "I hear you."

"Good!"

She rolled over, still holding him with her legs. A moment later she was astride him, her head thrown back, the lines of her neck muscles taut and straining. Then she began to raise and lower herself, allowing the lips of her vagina to caress his erection. At first it had little effect. But she was patient. Slowly at first, but gradually, with maddening deliberation, she increased her pace.

Longarm felt the first faint ache of a new urgency growing within his loins. Soon, to his astonishment, he was growing larger and still larger. Moaning, she increased her tempo, driving deeper now with each thrust, impaling herself with a fierce, reckless abandon that startled Longarm.

He reached up to cup her breasts in his big, rough hands. She nodded her head frantically. Yes. That was what she wanted. Longarm could feel her erect nipples thrusting against the palms of his hands. Her movements became more violent now. Short, explosive sounds escaped from her. She rose and came down on his shaft with a violence that threatened to split her asunder—or injure him fearfully. He dropped his hands from her breasts and grabbed her hips in an effort to keep her from riding too high, to control her wild gyrations. This was sure as hell no time for her to come out.

"Faster!" she told him, with a sudden, fierce hoarseness. "Faster! And deeper! Damn you!"

She flung herself forward suddenly, her lips fastening to his. He opened his mouth and her tongue darted frantically in, flicking like the tongue of a snake. He lifted his buttocks while he continued to thrust. He was almost flinging her backward over his head.

He let go of her hips then and encircled her shoulders, holding his mouth hard against hers, their tongues entwined now in a lewd embrace of their own. Her hips were grinding down on him now with a control that was as amazing as it was effective, achieving a synchronization that both excited and astonished him. They were welded together in a fierce, passionate dance that had become sheer instinct. In a wild but perfectly controlled coupling, his hips rose to meet each one of her down-thrusts.

Abruptly there came the inevitable, headlong rush. Plunging upward, he felt himself exploding deep within her. She flung back her head and once more cried out in a high, keening wail as her inner muscles continued to suck his erection clean. Then she too was shuddering to a climax. It lasted for what seemed an interminable time until finally she collapsed, laughing delightedly, onto his massive chest.

Her face was gleaming with perspiration. She panted as she raised her face to look at him and then she was covering his face with soft, grateful kisses. She was in a transport of delight. And this pleased Longarm as much as it pleased her. When she slid off him finally, it was slowly, lingeringly.

"Had enough?"

"Never," she said. "Give me a few minutes."

He chuckled. "It'll take me longer than that, Marta. There ain't any sense in you going to the well again today. You'll only come up with an empty bucket."

She sat up and looked down at him, then reached over and traced her cool fingers lightly down his cheeks. She leaned over and kissed him on the shoulder, then rested her cheek on the tightly coiled hair of his chest.

"You must think me shameless," she said.

"And you must think I am two men."

She kissed him almost demurely on the lips and sighed. "Alas, you are not two men, are you? But you did your best, poor dear. Thank you, Mr. Long. Thank you so very much."

He laughed softly. "My first name is Custis."

"Is that what people call you?"

"My friends call me Longarm."

"Mmm! Is that so?" She laughed delightedly and let her fingers move swiftly down his long flanks. "You are well named, Longarm. Truly."

He chuckled and pulled her mischievous hand away.

"I must return to Jennifer's room. I still have her key. She and her father will have difficulty getting back into her room, and if she has to go for another key, it may lead to questions."

"I won't let you go back until you give me a direct answer to my question, Longarm. Are you a lawman?"

"Why is that so important? Aren't you satisfied that I am a tax assessor? Isn't it to your advantage that I am what I say I am—someone able to verify your claim?"

"I am not worried about my claim. There is no doubt I am who I say I am and that the king of Spain gave my mother this empty patch of desert. I am worried about other things."

"Like the death of Maria?"

"Her brutal murder, you mean."

"I don't think the murderer of Maria is after you. Remember, Maria was found dead in my bed. I still think Maria was killed because she was mistaken for me. If anyone should be worried, it's me, not you. I'm sure you are perfectly safe."

"What you say makes sense. But . . . it is not just the murder of Maria that makes me wish you were a lawman. I have other fears as well."

"What fears, Marta?"

"I cannot tell you. If I am not sure who you really are, how can I possibly trust you?"

"What you are saying is that you have no faith in José or his men."

"His bandits, you mean. No, I have no faith in them."

"So you are hoping for a miracle—that I am some kind of lawman who might be able to apprehend Maria's murderer and also with whom you might be able to share your other fears."

"Yes."

"Sorry, Duchess. I'm just a little ol' functionary from the land office. But maybe that newcomer who rode in just a little while ago will be able to find out who did it. He sure did act like a fellow who knew how to take charge. He had José and the rest of his men jumping."

She sat up. "What man are you talking about?"

"Dudley Jacobson."

"You mean he's here?"

"He just rode in a few hoofbeats ahead of a bunch of outlaws. He brought along four more thoroughbreds for that stable of yours and a wagonload of treasure for the desert duchess."

All business suddenly, she got to her feet. "You are right, Longarm. It is getting late. I think you should go now. Jacobson will be coming to see me, I am sure. And those horses! I really do want to see them."

Longarm got to his feet. "Just one thing. Call me Mr. Long in front of everyone else. Promise?"

Her eyes narrowed. "Of course," she said.

"That's the girl."

"Then you *aren't* just a tax man."

He looked at her for a long minute. "Well, now, you'll just have to figure that out for yourself."

She sat back down on the bed, watching him closely

93

while he dressed. As he was moving back out through the wall a moment later, she reached out and took his arm. She was still naked.

"If I need you, Longarm, will you come?"

He grinned back at her. "There's no doubt about that, is there?"

Then he stepped into the passageway, the wall swung back into place, and she vanished from his sight.

A moment later, as he was placing the key back under the carpet where Jennifer had left it, Longarm glimpsed young Jarvis ducking back out of sight at the far end of the hallway. He dropped the rug over the key and hurried down the hall. Rounding the corner, he saw Jarvis scurrying away as fast as he could go without running.

Longarm's long legs overtook Jarvis easily. He grabbed the fellow's shoulder and spun him around. "What are you doing down here, junior? Who you looking for?"

"Jennifer!" he spat, furious. "But not any more!"

At once Longarm understood. "You think I was just with her, is that it?"

"What else am I to think?"

Longarm sighed. Indeed, if Jarvis had seen him putting the key back, what else could he think but that Longarm and Jennifer had developed a somewhat special relationship?

"Well," he said lamely, "it won't do you much good to go skulking around the hallways. That ain't necessarily the best way to attract a woman, you know."

"I beg your pardon. I was doing just fine before you came along."

"Were you now?"

"Yes, I was," he blurted miserably. "And the same

94

with Maria. But you took her, too. I know you did. You are an animal, sir—a base, unprincipled animal!"

As he said this, he hurled himself forward, flailing his white, knobby knuckles at Longarm. But he was hopelessly ineffectual. Longarm simply stuck his left arm out and held him at a distance as the little man continued to swing hopelessly at nothing more substantial than the air surrounding him.

At that moment Esmeralda Jarvis made her appearance. She hove into sight, steaming around a corner, her huge block of a face crimson with embarrassment and rage as she bore down on the two of them.

"John!" she cried. "Stop that at once! I will not have you brawling in public with his man!"

Still swinging furiously at Longarm, Jarvis cried, "But he took Jennifer from me!"

"Nonsense! Jennifer was not yours to lose, you silly boy!" she cried, hauling him around. "Now you come with me and stop this at once."

All the fight drained out of young Jarvis. His shoulders sagged. With the back of his hand, he wiped his nose. In his rage, he had shed real tears.

As Esmeralda dragged her son off, she glanced back at Longarm. "And as for you, sir, I am sure you will roast in hell for your wicked, sinful ways."

"Possibly," Longarm drawled. "I've been worried about that myself for years."

There was a faint smile on his face as he turned and headed back to his own room. But not for long. Not when he began to consider what had just happened a little more closely.

Young Jarvis might be quite ineffectual in a hand-to-hand encounter with someone who overmatched him as much as Longarm. But Jarvis's anger had been genuine. In fact, it seemed to verge on something close to fury—a mad, ungovernable fury. And he had mentioned Maria, as well. She, too, he had proclaimed, had once been his. Which meant that, in young Jarvis's eyes, Longarm had taken two women from him.

Reaching his room, Longarm let himself in and locked the door behind him. Then he systematically probed the walls until he found the hidden doorway. He went down on one knee to inspect the carpeting near the wall. If it had been swung open and someone had entered his room, fine traces of adobe dust or faint footprints might still remain. He found nothing. But then he realized that one of the Indian housekeepers must already have cleaned his room that day, despite Maria's funeral.

He got back up onto his feet and propped a chair against the portion of the wall designed to swing into his room, effectively blocking it. After that, he jammed the back of another chair against the door. Only then did he sit down, take out a cheroot, and do some serious thinking about that furious little man, John Wesley Jarvis. Just how dangerous could such a fellow be? Longarm wondered. Could it have been Jarvis's knife, the hilt of which Longarm had seen protruding from poor Maria's chest?

At last, his thoughts wearying of the ceaseless, tail-chasing speculation, he stubbed out his cheroot and flung himself down onto his bed. Thrusting his sixgun under his pillow, he closed his right fist about its grips and allowed himself to drift off for a much-needed nap.

The desert duchess had sure as hell taken the starch out of him.

• • •

The soft but persistent knock on his door finally managed to penetrate Longarm's almost drugged sleep. He sat up and found himself looking blearily down at the Colt in his hand. Then the knock came again, this time with Jennifer's voice calling softly through the door after it.

Longarm placed the revolver back under his pillow, removed the chair from the door, and pulled it open.

Jennifer burst in.

"What's wrong?" he asked. "The end of the world— or has the sky fallen?"

"Mr. Long! Something is wrong! Terribly wrong!"

"What do you mean? What happened?"

"It's our wagon. They wouldn't let us see it."

Longarm frowned and scratched his head. "You want to go over that again for me?"

"They wouldn't let my father and me see the wagon because they haven't even begun to repair it."

"Why not? They've had it long enough, haven't they?"

"Almost a week!"

"Look, why don't you start at the beginning?"

"Father and I went down to see if our wagon was ready. But when we tried to get into the repair shed, they wouldn't let us. They said the wagon was almost ready, but that if we went in to watch the men work, it would only make them nervous."

"Who said this?"

"One of the wheelwrights. He was the one who assured us he would have the wagon repaired in just a few days."

"How do you know they haven't done any work on it if they wouldn't let you in to see it?"

She straightened up proudly. "While father was arguing with the wheelwright, I sneaked into the building.

I saw our wagon with my own eyes. It's exactly as it was on the day we drove it into the shed. Not a single thing has been done to it."

"Maybe I'd better go down there and take a look myself."

"Oh, I wish you would!" she said.

"You don't think your father would mind?"

"Oh, no! Absolutely not. He's just as upset as I am."

"Let's go, then."

One of the wheelwrights had been posted to look for Jennifer, in case she should return. As soon as she was spotted approaching the shed with Longarm, two burly workers, one a Mexican, the other Mojave Indian, placed themselves in front of the shed door. The Indian folded his arms and watched impassively as the Mexican shook his head sadly and smiled, both at the same time.

"I am sorry, *señorita*," he told Jennifer. "You cannot go in to see your wagon."

"Sure she can," Longarm said. "It's her wagon."

"I cannot allow it, *señor*."

"Why can't you?" demanded Jennifer, seething.

"*Señor* Duarte, he say you should not go in to the shed now, *señorita*. He tell me to send you to see him," the workman replied.

"Well, then, where is he? If he's the one behind this, I'll be more than anxious to give him a piece of my mind."

The Mexican smiled with sudden relief and pointed. Jennifer and Longarm turned. Duarte was hurrying across the compound toward them in the company of Dudley Jacobson.

Jennifer hurried at once to meet the two men with

Longarm tagging along. He was beginning to wonder why Jennifer needed him. She was doing just fine all by herself.

"Mr. Duarte," she said, pulling up before the man, "just what is going on here? Why can't I see our wagon?"

Duarte smiled, not very convincingly. "It is not ready yet."

"Of course it's not ready. No one has touched it!"

"The men have been very busy, Miss Forsyth."

"Is that so?"

"Yes. Very busy."

"Then why didn't anyone tell my father that no work was being done on our wagon?"

"We did not wish to disturb you."

"She's sure as hell disturbed now," Longarm commented.

Duarte smiled coldly at Longarm. "Yes, I can see that."

"May I make a suggestion?" said Dudley Jacobson.

"That depends," snapped Jennifer. "Who are you, anyway? I don't even know you."

"Oh, excuse me," said Duarte, quickly introducing Jacobson to Jennifer.

As soon as the formalities were completed, Jacobson bowed courteously to Jennifer. "Miss Forsyth, I am sure that if you will wait just one or two more days, your wagon will be ready to go. My freighter was wounded slightly, but soon he will be well enough to give the others a hand. He is a master with wheels. Just give us a little more time."

"Meanwhile," Duarte added hastily, "you are welcome to stay here and rest up at no charge whatsoever."

"Yes," Jacobson, smiling benignly. "What better ac-

99

commodations could you find at those prices, my dear?"

Jennifer took a deep breath and surveyed both men. It was plain to her—as it was to Longarm—that she could get nothing more from these two men. She would just have to take their word and hope for the best.

"Come on," she said, turning on her heels and stalking off.

Longarm did his best to keep up with her.

After a few minutes, she turned her head and glared up at him. "Do you see what I mean? We are prisoners here! I don't know why, but we are!"

"Isn't that a rather hasty judgment?"

"No, it isn't. But what I can't understand is why on earth these people would want to keep my father and me here."

"It does seem rather odd, doesn't it?"

Jennifer glanced quickly up at Longarm with the trace of a smile on her face. "Unless John Jarvis is behind it. He's pretty sweet on me, I'm afraid."

"Not any more, Jennifer," Longarm said.

"Why, whatever do you mean?"

Longarm described to her the altercation he had had with young Jarvis and his mother outside her door earlier that afternoon.

"John fought with you? Over me? What on earth could have gotten into him?"

Longarm told her what John had said about him and Jennifer. Her face flamed. "He had no right to assume what he did," she said. "How dare he?"

"It seems he was quite friendly with Maria, also."

She became playful again. "And did you really think she favored only you, Mr. Long?"

"I didn't give it any thought. But young Jarvis was

angry enough to kill back there. He's a little man, but he certainly impressed me with his capacity for trouble."

She pulled up quickly. "Mr. Long! You don't think he had anything to do with Maria's murder, do you?"

"I find it hard to believe, myself. But someone killed her."

"Not John," she said, shaking her head. "He's such a pipsqueak. Not John."

"If he is such a pipsqueak, Jennifer, why did you lead him on, as you must have?"

Again Jennifer stopped and studied Longarm's face carefully. "I suppose I have no choice now. I might as well tell you where I am going—and why. But not out here, Mr. Long. Someplace where we can talk in private."

"My room?"

"Yes." She smiled bleakly. "Since my honor has already been compromised."

On the way up to his room, Jennifer asked if he had enjoyed his meeting with the mysterious duchess. He told her he had found her charming. He then went on to remark that for some reason the duchess seemed to think he was a lawman, not someone from the tax department. He wondered aloud why she was so anxious to find out if he was a lawman.

They were inside his room by this time. As Longarm closed the door, Jennifer considered his question.

"Well," she said, "it's not so strange, really. You see yourself how odd things are in this place. Here are my father and I, virtual prisoners. And now there's this terrible murder. Something's wrong here, Mr. Long. I don't find it at all unusual that the duchess is looking for someone to help."

101

"You've never seen this Jacobson fellow before?"

"No, I haven't."

"Do you like him?" Longarm asked.

"No. He is too oily. And I am not his 'dear' either."

Longarm laughed. "No, you are not. Now, what is this big, dark secret you could not reveal to me downstairs in the courtyard?"

Jennifer flung herself into one of Longarm's easy chairs. "I am on my way to San Diego," she told him bluntly, "to my betrothed."

"Congratulations."

"They are not in order, Mr. Long."

"I don't understand."

"I have never met the young gentleman I am going to marry. My father has arranged the marriage. It will be a most fortunate alliance for him. It will give him the added capital he needs."

"For what?"

"He is about to purchase additional stock in a railroad that will serve the southern coast of California. I know little more than that, but he regards this opportunity as his big chance."

"And for that he is willing to sell his daughter to a stranger."

"It's not as bad as it sounds, Mr. Long. Father has known this man and his son for many years. I have the young man's picture and he has mine. We have written to each other for many months. I confess I find his letters charming—and if his picture is any judge, he is a most handsome man. It was not difficult for me to go along with Father in this."

"You are being very noble, if foolish."

102

"Foolish, mostly. I see that now. I have had time to think. I no longer want to go through with the marriage unless I am granted much more time to get to know the man. But the wedding date is set, and there seems no way to stop things."

"Sometimes events gain a momentum of their own."

"Yes. That is so. But I have devised a plan." She smiled sadly. "A wicked plan, I must admit. But perhaps I was not thinking as clearly as I might have."

"Go on, Jennifer."

"Paul—that's his name, Paul Martinez—is very sure of one thing, about what he wants in a woman, I mean." She hesitated. Longarm smiled encouragingly, and Jennifer plunged on. "It seems he insists that the woman he marries be a virgin."

"And are you a virgin, Jennifer?"

"Yes."

Longarm understood at once. He sat down in the chair by his window and smiled. "So you decided you would not be a virgin when you reached San Diego."

Her face flamed, but she did not look away as she nodded.

"And poor John Wesley Jarvis was your first hope."

"I'm afraid so," she said, looking with sudden boldness at Longarm. "Until I saw you, Mr. Long. Then I knew that when it happened, I wanted it to be with someone like you—someone who would know how to treat a woman."

It was Longarm's turn to blush. He laughed instead. "So that is why young Jarvis is so upset with me."

"Yes. I must admit, though, I had no idea he and Maria . . ."

103

"I don't figure it amounted to anything. Little boys dream big dreams. And I must admit, Maria could be quite provocative on occasion."

"Yes," Jennifer said mischievously, swiftly regaining her composure. "I knew of Maria—and the baths she could give. It was not a very well-kept secret around here." She smiled. "She gave my father a bath when he first arrived. It did him a world of good, I must admit. But I am quite sure John's mother would not have let Maria get that close to him."

Longarm smiled. "If anyone gave John a bath, it would be her."

"Yes. The poor boy. Esmeralda would not let anyone else near him, I'm certain of that."

"So am I."

Jennifer got up. Longarm did also. She looked up into his eyes, more boldly than at any time in the past. "I have been very honest with you, Mr. Long," she told him.

"Yes, you have."

"But I am sure I can count on your discretion."

"You can, Jennifer."

She smiled then. "I have been speaking to the duchess. I know why she wanted to meet you, and I think she is right. You could not be just someone who goes around computing the value of property. There is more—so much more—to you than that."

Longarm shrugged and strode ahead of her to the door. As he opened it for her, he smiled. "You are certainly welcome to your opinion, Jennifer."

As she passed him, she went suddenly up on tiptoe and kissed him full on the lips. It pleased him as much as it pleased her. He watched her go for a moment, then closed the door and turned back to his room.

His mind was racing.

If Jennifer was correct, and she and the other guests were being held virtual prisoners, the question was, what purpose was being served by keeping them prisoner? Was there some reason other than the whim of an eccentric duchess for building a castle here in the middle of the Mojave Desert?

And now that Longarm considered it more closely, why had Dudley Jacobson's arrival affected Marta the way it did? Jacobson had given orders as if he and no one else was in charge here, not the duchess, and certainly not José Duarte. Who the hell was he, anyway?

Could he possibly be the key to what was going on around here?

Chapter 8

Close to sundown the next day, a weary Longarm left the bunkhouse with Duarte. He was finally finished with his inventory of the duchess's wealth. The tax on what he had seen would undoubtedly be enough to add another wing to the White House.

Duarte had made sure that Longarm had not missed a thing, starting off the day with a complete inspection of the duchess's extensive wine cellar. No sooner was that completed than Longarm found himself embarked on an exasperatingly extensive inventory of the two blacksmith shops, following that up with a tour of the carpentry, furniture, and weaving shops. Most of the afternoon was taken up with an inspection of the Mexicans' small houses and apartments along the northern wall.

It was obvious that Duarte took a malicious delight in Longarm's weariness. And for his part, Longarm found that toting up someone else's worldly goods was about the dreariest occupation he had ever undertaken. He hoped to hell he would never have to suffer through such a chore again.

Longarm and Duarte were on their way back to the castle when Dudley Jacobson appeared, coming from one of the horse barns. He waved and hurried to meet them.

"Well, well," Jacobson said as he pulled up alongside Longarm. "Have you finished your assessment, Mr. Long?"

"I have."

"I suppose you have been eaten up with jealousy."

"I wouldn't exactly say that," Longarm drawled.

Jacobson peered shrewdly at Longarm. "I suppose not," he said. "It takes someone with a little more sophistication than the average Western functionary to appreciate what we have here."

Longarm decided he would not bother to comment on that. When a man talked like a fatuous ass it was always best not to try to curb him. He derived too much comfort from the activity. It was kind of like farting.

Encouraged by Longarm's silence, Jacobson swept his hand about him expansively and said, "Can't you see it, Long? This castle is nothing less than a fist shaken in the face of God Almighty. A thriving universe! Just imagine what we have here in the middle of the Mojave Desert."

"That's what I have been trying to do," drawled Longarm. "I'd say it's about as useful as a new breed of mosquito."

"Oh, never fear, Mr. Long. This castle and grounds

will be useful, quite useful. I did not go to all this trouble just to create another nest for rattlers and desert lizards."

"You? I thought this was the duchess's idea."

"Of course, of course," he amended hastily, "but who do you think it was who took her dream and made it a reality?"

"I'll bet it was you."

Jacobson laughed. "You are a cool one, Mr. Long. I guess it is just every man to his own tastes."

"That about sums it up, I reckon."

At that moment they heard shouting near the gate. Turning, they saw the gatekeeper hauling back on the gate. As soon as it was open, Ruel and his men rode through. Behind Ruel came a cow pony with the body of a man slung over its back. From the slack look of him, Longarm knew the pony was carrying a dead man. Ruel, it seemed, was about to claim his gold piece.

Ruel's crew did not slow until they got to within ten yards of Longarm and his two companions. The dust they raised caused Jacobson and Duarte to duck their heads irritably. Longarm heard Jacobson's curse. A weary but triumphant Ruel dismounted and strode up to them.

"I claim that hundred-dollar gold piece," he told Jacobson. "You said dead or alive, didn't you?"

"That I did," responded Jacobson. "But are you sure this is one of those brigands who attacked me?"

"He's one of them, all right. He was the leader. When we cut him down, the rest turned tail and lit out."

"You've driven them off, have you?"

"I'd say so. We caught them unexpected while they made camp. Some of them are walking now and quite a few are riding double. Not every one of them is going to get off this here desert alive."

Jacobson nodded emphatically. "Excellent. Good work. Come to Duarte's headquarters in an hour. Your gold piece will be waiting for you." He looked over at the other riders. "Is everyone back safely?"

"All except Hansen."

"What happened to him?"

Ruel shrugged. "Took a slug, I guess, when we first caught up with them."

Duarte spoke up. "I won't miss him."

Ruel fixed Duarte with a hard stare. "Maybe you think I will."

He turned, waved the rest of the men off their horses, and strode with them toward the bunkhouse. Stable boys and hostlers were already swarming around to take care of the horses. The corpse, Longarm noted, was accepted as casually as the lathered horses.

Jacobson was pleased. "Well, now," he said, his eyes gleaming, "that's just fine. Ruel's a tough man, and that's a fact. Him and those cutthroats of his have yet to be bested."

Duarte looked at Longarm. "Looks like it's safe for you to head back to San Bernardino now."

"Yes, reckon so. What about the others—the Forsyths and the Jarvises—will they be free to leave now also?"

"I don't know what you're implying," Duarte said blandly. "They can leave whenever it suits them. Of course, it would be much wiser for the colonel to wait until we repair his wagon. And young Jarvis and his battleship of a mother will be lucky to make it through another day in that coach they purchased. Their horses are little better than Central Park hacks."

"Then you've just been looking out for their best interests."

"That is correct, Mr. Long."

"And that's why you have been discouraging them from leaving."

"What other reason could we possibly have, Mr. Long?" Jacobson asked sharply.

"And as for you, Mr. Long," Duarte repeated, "you may leave any time you wish."

"Then I'll be leaving tonight," Longarm told Duarte. "I would appreciate it if your hostler could see to my two mules and the burros."

"All will be in readiness for your journey," Duarte assured him.

"But before you go, you really must join us for dinner," Jacobson said, smiling. "I insist."

"All right," Longarm told him. "I'll leave after."

"Fine! Fine! It will give you a warm glow—something to remember us by. And I am sure the duchess will want to join us at dinner so that she may say goodbye to you personally."

Longarm smiled. "I would like that, Mr. Jacobson."

Despite Jacobson's best intentions, the dinner was a gloomy affair. The death of Maria still hung over them like a curse. Marta presided at the head of the table, with Jacobson and Duarte on either side of her. But she exhibited little enthusiasm, though she dutifully managed to smile at all the right times and did her best to keep the conversation light and cheerful.

John and Esmeralda Jarvis had refused to come. The colonel kept his own dour counsel, and nothing seemed capable of arousing Jennifer. She seemed gloomily preoccupied from the very start.

When it came time at last for the dinner party to break

up, Marta was the one who proposed a toast to Longarm, wishing him a safe journey back to San Bernardino. As she did so, Marta exhibited the only genuine warmth she had shown all evening. A moment later, as everyone got up and filed from the room, Marta was escorted out with unseemly haste by Jacobson. Longarm was disappointed, since he had wanted to say goodbye personally.

He was about to head for his room when he found Jennifer tugging on his arm, imploring him to join her one more time on the balcony they had visited his first night there.

"You're sure your father won't storm up there a second time and drag you away?" he asked.

"I've already spoken to him," she said firmly.

Once they reached the balcony, Jennifer sighed deeply. "Are you really going?" she asked.

"My business here is finished."

"Is it? Really?"

It was uncanny how close Jennifer's question came to the truth of the matter. If he were to answer her directly, he would have to reply that, in truth, his business here was not finished.

He still had no clue at all as to why those two deputies had been murdered—and certainly he was no closer to tracking down the maniac who had killed Maria. And there was something else. He could not put his finger on it, but things were not quite right in this castle, despite the fact that it seemed to run so smoothly. Longarm had the feeling that this entire operation was being held together by a thread, and that at any moment it would snap.

Still, it had not done so yet.

"I guess I have to say my mission here is finished, Jennifer," Longarm admitted reluctantly. "I've assessed the duchess's wealth, and that's why I came."

"Are you telling me the truth, Mr. Long? Is that *really* why you came?"

He smiled at her. "Of course. And now I've good news for you. I spoke to Duarte and Jacobson. You and your father can leave as soon as your wagon is ready, and they assured me there will be no attempt to stop you."

"Thank you, Mr. Long," she said, her voice small and discouraged. "I am sure Father will be very glad to hear that."

"But you aren't."

She sighed. "I guess I simply must accept my fate. My father is counting on me so much."

"Cheer up, Jennifer. You may be in for a pleasant surprise. This young gentleman you have been writing to may turn out to be quite nice."

"He may. All the same, I have read and reread his letters, and I think he is a prig."

"If that's true, then you must loosen him up. I'm sure you will be able to do so."

"Really?"

"Yes."

Impulsively, she flung her arms about his neck and kissed him hard. Her young, pliant lips moved hungrily. He pushed her away gently.

"Mmm," she said, resting her head against his chest. "I'm being very bad, I know. I shouldn't have done that. But I'm glad I did, and I wish you didn't have to go."

He hugged her gently and said nothing. After a while, Jennifer pushed away from him, sighed, and looked up into his eyes dreamily. "Would you mind if I waited for you at the gate? I want to say goodbye as you ride out."

"I would not mind at all," he told her.

"And when you go, will you turn in your saddle and wave to me?"

He laughed softly. "Yes, Jennifer, if that is what you want. I just hope I don't fall off when I turn to wave!"

She giggled. "Oh, you won't, I'm sure. And when you wave, I'll wave back. It will be so romantic. And I'll always have that picture of you in my mind."

He laughed softly and escorted her from the balcony. Leaving her at the door to her room a moment later, he continued on down the hallway to his own room. Entering it, he found his already packed gear on the bed where he had left it before going down to the dinner. He consulted his watch. It was close to eight. He had better get moving. The more ground he covered during the night, the better off he would be.

He was reaching for his saddle roll and bag when he heard the unmistakable sound of stone grating on stone. Had Marta come to say goodbye personally? He spun about to see Esmeralda stepping through the wall into his room with a huge kitchen knife in her hand. Behind her came her son, holding a lighted candelabrum.

"You are evil!" the woman cried, advancing toward him.

"Now, hold it right there, ma'am. I ain't perfect, that's for sure. But that's no reason for you to get all riled."

"You make women evil, too!" Esmeralda continued, pointing the knife at Longarm as she continued to advance on him. The candlelight gleamed on the long blade.

Young Jarvis moved to one side of Longarm. "Mother is right," he said. "We are going to have to punish you."

"Ours is the vengeance of God!" Esmeralda cried.

That was when Longarm swung. Bringing his right

fist around with all the force he could muster, he caught Esmeralda flush on the jaw. She went hurtling back, her feet flying out from under her. Her head struck the wall with an ugly thud. She dropped the knife and began to slide down the wall.

With a furious cry, young Jarvis sprang upon Longarm. As he managed to ward off the infuriated young man, Longarm drew his derringer. But he was reluctant to use the gun on Jarvis and did not see the heavy iron candelabrum until it crashed down upon his head. Lights exploded deep inside his skull. His knees turned to suet as he toppled head first to the floor.

But he did not entirely lose consciousness as Esmeralda and Jarvis dragged him feet first into the passageway. She was still somewhat groggy from Longarm's punch, it appeared. Longarm heard Esmeralda snapping impatiently at her frail son, who was not very helpful at this juncture. Longarm had not the slightest idea where they were taking him. Most of the lines governing his limbs were still down, but as the wall swung to, he managed to reach out and shove a large piece of adobe into the opening, preventing the wall from shutting completely.

They were not gentle as they dragged him face down along the narrow stairway. After one mean crack on his forehead, he almost passed out completely. Then he was being dragged into Marta's apartment and dumped face up on her bed alongside the bound and naked duchess. Swiftly, Esmeralda and her son bound his ankles and wrists with strips of bedsheet. As he watched Esmeralda tie his bound ankles to a bedpost, he took some comfort from the purpling patch on the side of her jaw.

As he regained more control over his limbs, he was

able to turn his head and look at the duchess. A cruel gag had been shoved into her mouth. From the look in her eyes, he could tell she was terrified.

Esmeralda leaned close to Longarm. "This is your punishment for the sin of fornication!" she snapped.

As she spoke, her face was distorted with maniacal rage. Longarm had seen the same look on the faces of some women he had watched once crashing into a saloon with axes in their hands. The look on Esmeralda's face matched the expressions on their faces perfectly. She was experiencing the same orgy of righteousness.

"Punishment?" Longarm asked, frowning.

"Yes!"

"You old bat! You're as crazy as a loon!"

Young Jarvis took a step closer to the bed, his face flaming with rage. "Don't you dare talk to Mother like that!" he cried.

"Why not? She's a genuine, fourteen-carat madwoman! And a murderer, too, if I'm not mistaken!"

Young Jarvis's face went pale.

Longarm turned his head and looked coldly up at Esmeralda. "That's right, isn't it? Why, you damned old she-devil, you're going to kill us both! You're going to drive that knife up to the hilt in both of us! Ain't that right?"

"Yes!" she cried, her voice quavering with lust as she contemplated the action. "Yes!"

"Just like you did to Maria."

"Yes! Just like Maria!" she agreed.

"Mother!" young Jarvis cried. "You said *he* killed Maria!"

"Of course he did," Esmeralda said. "Don't you see? He made her evil. How could I possibly let her live? I

116

could not let an evil force seduce you!"

"But I loved her!"

"No! You are my little boy. I must protect you from evil—from women such as Maria."

"No, Mother!" young Jarvis cried. "You shouldn't've done it!"

"But she seduced you!"

"She just gave me a bath, that's all!" Jarvis protested.

"Hah!"

"I swear it, that was all! Just a bath!"

"But don't you see? That was only the beginning!"

"Oh, Mother! Not Maria!"

"I had to! She would have turned you from me. She would have corrupted you!"

All the while the two were arguing, Longarm was twisting his wrists in a desperate effort to break free of the frail cloth strips holding them. At last one of them gave slightly. Encouraged, he made one more supreme effort and this time broke free.

Seeing this, Esmeralda shrieked out a warning to her son and flung herself, knife raised, toward Longarm. As she plunged the knife down in a flashing arc, Longarm managed to reach up and grab her wrist.

With his ankles bound, Longarm could muster very little leverage. Esmeralda pulled back and almost broke free. Retaining his grip on her wrist, Longarm twisted. With a shriek, Esmeralda dropped the knife. It fell to the floor beside the bed. With a powerful heave, Longarm flung Esmeralda away from the bed. She stumbled back, struck a footstool, and slammed to the floor. Stunned, she remained on the floor, moaning slightly.

With his feet still bound to the bedpost, Longarm reached down for the knife, but found himself unable to reach it. Young Jarvis darted forward and snatched it up. As he scurried out of Longarm's reach with the knife, the wall beside the bed slid open and Jennifer stepped into the room.

One look around her and Jennifer was shocked into immobility. Eyes wide, she stared first at the naked duchess, then at Longarm. In her hand Longarm caught sight of the derringer he had dropped when Jarvis struck him down.

"Throw the gun, Jennifer!" Longarm cried. "Throw it to me!"

His shout roused the girl to action, and she threw the derringer. Snatching the weapon out of the air, Longarm aimed the muzzle at Jarvis.

"All right, Jarvis," Longarm told the young man. "Relax now and take it easy. The curtain's coming down on this whole crazy show. Cut my ankles free."

Jarvis sagged. He stared at the gun in Longarm's hand and licked suddenly dry lips. Perspiration stood out on his forehead.

"You heard me, Jarvis," Longarm repeated. "Get over here. Free my ankles."

Jarvis started to walk over to the bed.

"John!" his mother screamed. Her voice cut through the room like a razor. "Give me that knife!"

Jarvis kept coming.

"Stop, I tell you!"

Young Jarvis winced visibly. Nevertheless, he reached the foot of the bed and began cutting away the cloth strips binding Longarm's ankles. The knowledge that his mother had been the one who killed Maria seemed to have shattered his will. A fierce internal struggle was consuming him.

"What are you doing?" Esmeralda cried furiously as she heaved herself to her feet. "Don't you dare free that man!"

Even Longarm winced at the way her voice cut through the room. Jarvis pulled his knife back and began to tremble. By now he did not know which way to turn.

"John!" his mother warned, starting toward him, her voice chilling in its intensity. "Do as I say! THIS INSTANT!"

Jarvis swung around to face his mother.

"No, I won't!" he told her, his face suddenly livid with rage. "No, I won't! Not any more!"

He rushed at his mother, the knife held high.

"No!" Esmeralda cried, ducking back. "No, John! Oh, please, John! No!"

But Jarvis was not listening. Eyes gleaming madly, he began to stalk his mother. Moaning in terror, Esmeralda stumbled away from him until she was wedged into a corner. She flung her arms up to protect herself.

"Stop, Jarvis!" Longarm cried. "Stop or I'll fire!"

But young Jarvis was listening to different voices now. He slashed downward, the blade slicing into his mother's upraised arm. Esmeralda screamed out in pain and terror as blood pulsed from her wound.

Longarm fired.

The slug caught Jarvis in the back. He dropped the knife as the force of the slug flung him forward into his mother's arms. She clutched at him, trying to hold him up. But young Jarvis slipped from her grasp, already dead.

Screaming, Esmeralda watched her son collapse at her feet.

Chapter 9

Longarm did not leave the castle that night. The next morning John Wesley Jarvis was lowered into his final resting place alongside Maria. Esmeralda Jarvis remained in the castle during the ceremony, bound securely upright in a chair in a room in the castle's west wing. Even so, her screams echoed and reechoed throughout the place. The death of her son had toppled what little reason remained. She was now a raving lunatic.

Late in the afternoon, the duchess and Jennifer joined Longarm in the inner courtyard off the library. The gentle splashing of the fountain soothed them somewhat. Jennifer and Marta were sitting together on a bench while Longarm, restless, was pacing before them, his head swathed in bandages, a nasty laceration over his left eye.

This was the first time Jennifer had been able to tell

Longarm and Marta the complete story of how she had managed to show up in Marta's apartment when she had. She had just finished relating how, impatient at Longarm's delay in riding out, she had left the gate and gone to his room.

"I called out to you first, Mr. Long," Jennifer said, "then pushed your door open and saw the candelabrum on the floor alongside your little gun. I could see at once there had been a scuffle and knew something was terribly wrong. Then I noticed where something had been dragged toward the wall."

"That was my face," Longarm commented wryly.

"It was clear that whoever had attacked you had gone through the wall. So when I saw that long crack in the wall where the door was jammed open I knew at once there must be a secret passageway on the other side."

"Some secret," Marta commented sourly.

Longarm smiled at her. "Yeah. It got to be a real highway, didn't it? In the future, you might consider charging fees and conducting guided tours."

"Please!" Marta laughed. Then she turned to Jennifer. "Go on, Jennifer."

"Well, the rest was easy enough. I went back and picked up Mr. Long's little gun from the floor, and—"

"That's called a derringer," Longarm told her, smiling. "It's a mean little fellow. Packs quite a wallop."

Jennifer nodded. "Then I went back to the wall and pushed until the door in the wall swung open. The passageway was dark, but when my eyes got accustomed to it, I saw a dim light and followed it down some narrow stairs. The dragging marks came to another wall. I heard some scuffling on the other side of it and started pushing on the wall."

122

"And that's when you found yourself staring at all hell breaking loose," Longarm said.

"Yes. I was so surprised—and frightened!"

"I don't wonder," said Marta, shaking her head. "But thank you, Jennifer. Longarm and I both owe you our lives."

"Yes, Jennifer," Longarm acknowledged. "We wouldn't be in this garden today if it hadn't been for you."

"Do you really think Esmeralda and John would have killed you?"

"I don't doubt it for a minute," Longarm replied. "They were both drooling at the prospect. They were going to bring righteousness back to earth and destroy sin and fornication all in one master stroke."

"They were both insane," said Marta, shuddering.

"Esmeralda is, for sure," Longarm said. "I think for a moment there Jarvis was coming out of it. Then his mother went at him again and he snapped like a bowstring." Longarm shook his head. "I only wish I could have stopped him without using the derringer."

"I think it's better for him to be dead," Marta said coldly.

There was no response Longarm or Jennifer could make to that. They grew silent then, contemplating the horror of that moment in Marta's apartment. Only there was no longer any real silence left in the castle. Dimly, the could hear the faint screaming still coming at ragged intervals from the farthest reaches of the castle.

"Do you think she'll ever stop screaming?" Jennifer asked, her voice hushed.

"Sure. When her voice gives out," Longarm said.

"If it ever does," Marta said wearily. She looked

sharply at Longarm. "When did you realize it was Esmeralda who had killed Maria—and not John?"

"A portion of the blade's hilt had been driven into Maria's chest. That meant a very forceful blow. Young Jarvis was not capable of striking so hard."

Jennifer shuddered. "What a fearsome woman she is!"

"Are you leaving tonight?" Marta asked Longarm.

"Yes."

"Jennifer and I will miss you."

"I'll miss both of you—but not this place, I'm afraid. And not the wails of that demented woman."

Marta got to her feet. Jennifer did also. Silently, the three of them left the garden.

Both Jennifer and Marta were at the gate when Longarm rode out later that evening. There had been no farewell dinner this time, and Longarm had seen neither Duarte or Dudley Jacobson since the burial of John Jarvis that morning.

Longarm's stock had been well cared for. The extra grain had made his mule somewhat sassy, and he farted a bit as he moved along. The moon and stars rode into a clear night sky. There was no haze at all. The moon hung in the sky as clear and sharp as a new silver dollar. It was a quiet, beautiful desert night, yet on more than one occasion, Longarm got an itchy feeling between his shoulder blades. But no matter how often he pulled up and looked back, he saw no sign that he was being followed.

A little after midnight, the desert chill caused him to hold up and put on his slicker. As he was repacking his saddle roll, he noticed a glow on the horizon off to the west. He stood quiet for a moment, studying the glow until he realized what it was.

A greasewood fire. Someone was camping on the Mojave Desert miles off the wagon trace, and that could mean a party had wandered off the trace and become lost. If they didn't know the desert well enough they could be in real trouble. The flat expanse of nothingness could be confusing and deadly to anyone without visible landmarks to follow.

Then again, it could mean trouble of another kind: more outlaws. What was it Jacobson had said? The flies were beginning to buzz around the honey.

There was only one way to find out which it was. Mounting up, he headed toward the glow.

When he got close enough, he saw that the fire was coming from a wash. He dismounted and snaked his Winchester out of its scabbard. Crouching, he moved closer. He was flat on his belly when he peered finally down into the wash and saw the five men hunkered around the fire. Two or three others were busy gathering greasewood to feed it. The smell of coffee was on the wind, and occasionally a sharp bark of laughter reached Longarm.

From the moment he caught sight of them, Longarm realized they sure as hell were not lost.

So what were they doing out here?

There was only one way to find out. Moving carefully and keeping a constant vigil for desert rattlers, he edged closer to the ring of men around the fire. When he was close enough to catch individual words, he held up, kept his head down, and listened.

It wasn't long before he realized that he recognized

one voice: that of Rolf Hansen. Hansen was supposed to be dead. At least that was how Ruel had told it. Yet here he was, conversing amiably with the same desperadoes Ruel and his riders had supposedly sent packing.

Longarm frowned. No, he was wrong. Hansen was not conversving amiably. He was giving orders. From the sound of it, the man was in charge.

Unable to hear all that was being said, Longarm edged closer, using his rifle barrel to poke the ground ahead of him to warn him of any snakes. Caught out hunting when the temperature dropped, they would be quite sluggish by now. But Longarm was not anxious to do anything that would arouse them from their torpor.

Pulling up behind a greasewood bush, he was able to hear the men talking among themselves. They were waiting to move out and they seemed a bit jumpy. There was a lot of nervous laughter and some boasting.

"All right, all right," said Rolf Hansen, his smooth voice cutting sharply across the desert floor. "Just remember. I get to that bitch first." He glanced around at those hunkered around him. "You fellers can have her when I'm done—but I've seen the duchess up close, and I know she's goin' to be a good one. I figure her for a real wildcat."

"Aw, hell, Rolf," said the fellow across the fire from him. "Why don't we cut cards to see who goes first? I ain't never laid a duchess."

Hansen laughed. "And you ain't goin' to if you don't shut up. You heard me. I go first. You'll get a piece of her when I'm through."

"Shit! There won't be nothin' left."

"What else we got there?" said another, his voice

126

betraying his eagerness. "I ain't had a woman in a coon's age."

"Don't worry. You'll have your pick. The place has all the women you'd want," Hansen assured him. "But, like I told you, first things first. There's got to be gold there. And loot, plenty of it. We'll clean the damn place out, take our split, then light out."

"I been thinking on that," said another, "and I don't like that part of it much."

"Why not?" Hansen asked, his voice deceptively soft.

"Why do we have to share all that loot with Ruel and the others?"

Longarm saw Hansen reach back for his weapon. It was in his hand in an instant, tracing a swift arc as it came crashing against the unhappy outlaw's jaw. As the man went tumbling back out of sight, Hansen laughed softly, then dropped his weapon back into his holster.

"We share the loot, you stupid son of a bitch," he snapped, "because it will be Ruel and them other riders who're goin' to open the gates for us. What makes you think you could get within a mile of them walls if we didn't want you to? Wise up, you asshole!"

Longarm saw the fellow Hansen had struck rubbing his jaw unhappily as he sat back up. "Sure, Rolf," he said. "Sure. I was just askin'."

"Oh, sure you were." Hansen snorted derisively. "Sure you were, you silly bastard."

Longarm had heard enough—more than enough. Ruel had thrown in with the outlaws he had been sent out to get rid of, and Hansen was now running the show from outside. As soon as Ruel opened up the castle to Hansen and these outlaws, there would be enough pillaging to keep an army of Huns busy for a week. When it was all over, they would ride off with their loot. The only thing they would leave alive would be the buzzards—and they would be feeding.

Longarm began to inch backward.

"Hold it, Long," a quiet, deadly voice whispered from behind him. "Just lay there nice and still."

Cursing bitterly, Longarm froze. He recognized the voice at once. It was the same rider who earlier had assured Ruel he could blast Longarm out of his saddle.

"Hey, Hansen!" the fellow cried. "We got ourselves a visitor!"

"Who's there?" Hansen asked, jumping to his feet.

"It's Riley!"

"What the hell?" Hansen raced toward them, his sixgun out.

Riley bent down and took Longarm's rifle, then reached under him and slipped Longarm's Colt from its rig. As Hansen pounded up, he straightened, grinning at Hansen.

"What've you got here, Riley?"

"The tax man, Long. You remember him?"

Hansen looked down in pleased astonishment, then kicked Longarm brutally, lifting him over onto his back.

"Hot damn!" Hansen cried. "So it is!"

The others had run over by this time as well. Looking up at the ring of bearded, grinning faces peering down at him, Longarm felt as if he had fallen into the clutches of a wolf pack.

Hansen hunkered down and smiled easily at Longarm. "Well, well, Mr. Taxman. Ain't you a sight for sore eyes!"

"Ruel sent me after him," Riley explained. "And the poor sap was so damned eager to find out what you fellers was doing over here, he never once looked back. Ruel figured the son of a bitch might cause us trouble. So he sent me to take care of him if he did."

Hansen looked up at Riley and grinned. "Well, why in hell didn't you?"

"Hell, I thought you might like a piece of him. I know how you feel about the son of a bitch."

"Yeah," Hansen chuckled. "You're right. Looks like I owe you one. Planting a slug between his shoulder blades, like them other two nosy bastards, would be letting him off too easy."

Hansen stood back up and kicked Longarm again.

Before he could pull his foot back, Longarm grabbed it, then twisted violently, sending Hansen hurtling backward into a greasewood bush. Hansen struck heavily, then began to scream something about snakes. The others quickly scattered.

Hansen had landed in a rattlers' nest, Longarm realized. Lethargic though they were, Hansen's sudden crunch into their midst had them moving about unhappily. Longarm could hear their rattles sounding feebly.

He jumped to his feet, knocked Riley to one side, and snatched up his rifle. He heard someone breathing heavily behind him. Before he could turn, a gun barrel crashed down onto the back of his neck. He sagged, paralyzed, to the desert floor. The others came running and began to kick him, but the blows rained upon him painlessly as he sank into oblivion.

When Longarm revived, he found himself sitting with his back to the fire, his wrists bound tightly behind his back with rawhide, his ankles bound together as well. Hansen's men were all watching him from about ten feet away. Their eyes glittered in the firelight. Beside Long-arm stood Hansen. He was dropping a small greasewood branch into the fire.

"We're movin' out now, Long," he said. "We got ourselves a castle to loot, damned if we don't." He smiled in happy anticipation.

Longarm took a deep breath and tested the rawhide. The strips were tight and getting tighter.

"Look around you," Hansen said.

Longarm did. At first he did not know what Hansen wanted him to see, then he realized what it was. Like clumps of twigs, coiled and uncoiled snakes had been placed all around him. At first he had mistaken them for rocks or depressions in the wash. Now he knew better. The men had searched out the sleeping snakes, then dragged them or poked them closer while they were still too groggy to protest.

"It's cold right now," Hansen said. "They ain't very active. But they soon will be. Look there, between your legs."

Longarm did not want to look, but he forced himself. A small rattler had been placed inches from his right knee. He was coiled tightly and was not moving, but his serpentine head was pointed directly at Longarm's crotch. And the heat from the campfire behind him would revive him soon enough.

"Now look behind you."

Longarm decided not to.

"That's all right," said Hansen, chuckling. "I guess you know what's back there, too."

Longarm said nothing.

Hansen left him then, picking his way carefully across the moonlit wash. Longarm watched him go. Pausing for a moment, Hansen lit a greasewood branch and began touching off other patches of greasewood. The rest of his men did the same, and in a matter of seconds, Longarm was surrounded by a series of blazing campfires. A moment longer and they had become one single ring of fire, closing inexorably around him. Only then did Hansen and the others mount up.

"Them snakes'll be a mite nervous with them flames lickin' at them," Hansen called out. "I'd sure like to stay and watch, but this here gully has a million rattlers, we just found out—and I hate the bastards!"

He laughed, dug his spurs into his horse, and rode off.

Chapter 10

The hoofbeats of Hansen and his men faded into the silence of the desert. Longarm glanced swiftly around. Already the rattlers closest to the crackling greasewood were beginning to stir. The diamondback under his knee seemed to be moving slightly also. Apparently, the campfire blazing at Longarm's back was having its effect on the snake. Nevertheless, Longarm was grateful to Hansen for gloating about the rattler he had dropped between him and the fire. That critter should be fairly well aroused by now. Longarm would be careful not to move any closer to it.

Bracing himself on his heels and his bound wrists, Longarm lifted himself off the ground and thrust himself gently sideways, away from the rattler beneath his legs and the one at his back. He repeated the maneuver until he could see that both snakes were no longer within striking distance.

This brought him closer to the other diamondbacks circling the campfire, however. But so far it appeared that most of them were still dormant.

Twisting his head around, he saw nothing between him and the blazing campfire. He edged closer to it, then turned back around and extended his wrists out over the fire. A flame enclosed both wrists, prompting him to yank them back swiftly, groaning. A little more carefully the next time, he held them out over the fire, keeping them higher this time. He gritted his teeth as the flames singed his flesh. But he could smell the cooking rawhide, too, and that encouraged him. Closing his eyes and grinding his teeth against the pain, he lowered his rawhide-bound wrists ruthlessly into the fire. He felt the rawhide giving, kept them in the flames a moment longer, then flexed powerfully.

His hands flew apart. The raw, smoking skin was already peeling from them, and the pain was intense. But there was no time for him to think of that. A rattler had come alive within striking distance of his right leg, and Longarm's sudden movement had alerted it.

The sound of the snake's rattles filled the night as it lifted its head. Its tongue flicked wildly up at Longarm. The snake dropped its head slightly, preparatory to striking. Longarm palmed his derringer and fired, shearing off the rattler's head. The headless snake's rattle continued to vibrate, and looking about him, Longarm saw the other diamondbacks lifting their heads also. Another snake materialized on his left, close to his hip. Longarm aimed swiftly and fired, cutting this one in two.

As swiftly as he could manage it with his scorched

134

hands, Longarm reached into the fire for a flaming branch and burned through the rawhide binding his ankles. He jumped to his feet then and bolted toward the rapidly closing ring of fire.

By this time the heat had banished the night's chill and almost every snake had come awake. The wash was alive with them. They writhed in the light of the dancing flames like an oversized can of worms, the din of their rattles filling the night. Two struck at Longarm's flying feet. The first missed, the second buried its fangs in the heel of his right boot. Without slowing, Longarm struck down at the snake's head with the barrel of his derringer, knocking it free.

A moment later, his arm held up to protect his face, he broke through the flaming greasewood. Once through them, he did not slow down. Even on the other side of the flaming barrier, the desert floor appeared to be alive with the squirming reptiles. As he ran, he beat at his smoking clothes and did what he could to ignore the excruciating pain that pulsed up from his seared wrists.

He slowed down only when he reached the wagon trace. Pulling up then, he looked back at the glow on the horizon. In his mind's eye, he could still see the floor of the wash trembling with the frantic, rippling bodies of the rattlers attempting to escape that enclosing ring of fire. Rolf Hansen was a devil of a man, truly—an inspired architect of calculated brutality. The prospect of him loose in Marta Zapolya's castle was not a pleasant one.

He started walking back to the castle. It would be one hell of a long trek, but it was closer than San Bernardino. He had gone less than a mile when he saw something remarkable just ahead of him—his mules and burros ambling peacefully along, like him, heading back to the castle. When Longarm had not returned for them, they had remembered their last stable—a luxurious place with fresh bedding, plenty of water, and fresh grain—and had simply turned around and started back toward it.

When Longarm overtook them, he took the reins of the mule he had been riding and swung into the saddle. Then he clapped spurs to the mule and left the other stock behind, confident they would find the way back without any trouble. His only hope now was that there would be something left in the castle to make their return worth the bother.

Longarm's mule did not have the speed of a Cheyenne war horse, but it covered the ground steadily enough and at a pace that brought Longarm within sight of the castle walls at least two hours before dawn. The moon was down and the night was inky black. Longarm could not be sure, but it appeared to him that Ruel would wait until it got just a bit lighter before signaling to Hansen to enter the compound. If something went wrong, it would lessen the chance of them cutting each other to ribbons by mistake in the stygian desert night. If that surmise was correct, Longarm had probably an hour to alert Marta and those still loyal to her.

Longarm pulled the mule around and headed in a wide circle, not bothering to keep the castle wall in sight. Only when he was well behind the castle did he ride directly for the wall. Reaching it, he reined in the mule, then stood up on the saddle and grabbed for the top of the wall. He almost made it, but his weakened hands could not hold on, and he fell to the ground. He brushed himself off, pulled the mule closer to the wall, and climbed back up into the saddle. This time he stood on the cantle, crouched, and leaped. Both hands got a reasonably firm hold on the edge of the wall. A moment later, he managed to get one arm up onto it. The sand and gravel dug cruelly into his raw wrists, but he hung on grimly, and a moment later was able to haul himself up onto the wall.

Jumping down, he ran through the darkness to the rear of the castle. His interminable inspection of the castle and its grounds with Duarte had given Longarm an excellent acquaintance with the grounds and the castle itself. Going in through the rear door, he slipped past the kitchen staff, already up and making breakfast, moved up a back stairway, and a moment later knocked on the door to Jennifer's room.

There was a long wait. Longarm heard someone stirring and then the sound of a chimney being placed back on a lamp. A moment later Jennifer pulled the door open. She was dressed in bedroom slippers and a long white nightgown with plenty of lace at the throat and hem. She peered in astonishment at Longarm. "Why, Mr. Long!" she cried. "You're back!"

"May I come in?"

"Of course!"

She stepped back hastily. As soon as Longarm was inside and Jennifer had closed the door, he smiled apologetically and stuck out both hands.

"Could you do something about these burns, Jennifer? I need something to cover them, at least."

"Oh, my!" she cried. "They look terrible. Whatever happened?"

"It's a long story. Can you get bandages?"

"Of course! Just stay right here. I'll go down to the kitchen. I know just what to get for burns like that."

As she hurried over to her bed and slipped into a

wrap, he slumped into one of her chairs.

"Jennifer . . . ?" he said.

She paused at the door.

"Don't tell anyone I'm in the castle. And hurry. Make it as fast as you can."

Jennifer simply nodded and left.

A moment later there was a sharp knock on the door. Longarm had already reloaded his derringer. He took it out and leveled it at the door.

"Come in," he called softly.

Colonel Forsyth strode in. He occupied the room next door and must have heard Jennifer greeting Longarm and letting him into her room. The colonel had dressed hastily in a rumpled pair of white pants and jacket and a floppy Panama hat. He was carrying a cane the way one would a club. When he saw the derringer in Longarm's hand, he pulled up, his eyes blazing fiercely.

"Sah! What are you doin' in mah daughter's room!"

"Getting some help," Longarm replied, pocketing his derringer.

"May Ah inquire as to what you mean by that, sah?"

"I burned myself a while back. My wrists need to be bandaged." As Longarm spoke, he held up one wrist. "I mean no disrespect to Jennifer, Colonel. She is a fine and honorable young lady, and my presence in no way compromises her honor. I came to Jennifer because I knew she would be able to help me."

"Surely, sah, I am not one to deny the truth of what you say. Jennifer is certainly capable of treating such a fearful burn. She has many talents."

The colonel was only slightly mollified by Longarm's words. It was not easy for him to be civil to the man who had made so light of him earlier.

138

The colonel strode into the room, closed the door, and sat down on the edge of his daughter's bed. Resting his hands and his chin on the head of his cane, he peered warily at Longarm, his bright keen eyes alert.

"With all due respects, Mistah Long, would you care to enlighten me as to how you acquired those fearful burns?"

Longarm considered how much he should reveal to the colonel, but it did not take him long to come to a decision. If they were to hold off that pack waiting now in the desert and neutralize Ruel and his men at the same time, they would need the guns of every able-bodied man in the castle. And Colonel Forsyth was quite clearly a combative sort.

"Colonel, I stumbled on a band getting ready to storm the castle. They tied me up and left me to die beside a campfire. I used the fire to burn through the rawhide and rode to warn the duchess and the rest of you."

"Ah see. Very commendable, sah. Very. You are a brave man indeed." He straightened up, lifting his chin from the head of his cane. "If your story is to be believed."

"What proof do you require?"

"More than your word, sah. Why would you be up here in Jennifer's room when you should be reporting this dire news to Ruel and his men? Ah believe, sah, it is their job to make short work of such no-accounts."

Longarm smiled grimly. "That's the point, Colonel. Rolf Hansen, one of Ruel's lieutenants, is leading the outlaws. Ruel and his men have joined them."

"Sah, Ah find that hard to believe. You must give me more than your word, Ah am afraid."

Longarm reached for his wallet and flipped it open,

revealing his badge. The colonel took it, examined the badge in some surprise, then handed it back to Longarm. His face had gone white. "Then what you say is true!" he cried.

"Yes. Ruel's men are ready to move—ready right now to open the gates to Hansen and his men."

"The Trojan horse," he muttered in alarm.

"You might say that," Longarm agreed, nodding. "Only Ruel and his men didn't need any big hollow horse to get inside the gates. They've been in here all along."

At that moment Jennifer arrived with one of the old Mexican women who worked in the kitchen. The Mexican was carrying a steaming pan of hot water. Jennifer had a pair of scissors, bandages, and a jar of honey. She was not surprised to see her father there, and greeted him as she hurried into the room.

She pulled up before Longarm and went down on one knee beside his chair. "This is going to hurt, but trust me."

"I will," Longarm responded.

The two women set to work on Longarm's wrists. Jennifer was right. Washing off the wound and cutting away the blackened, dead strips of burned flesh was excruciatingly painful, but Longarm did not utter a sound as they worked. As soon as the burns were clean, Jennifer covered them with honey, then bandaged both wrists. In a surprisingly short time the pain eased. So expertly did Jennifer bandage his hands, in fact, that he found himself able to flex both of them. He could hold things with either hand—his derringer, especially.

"We don't have much time," Longarm told Jennifer as the Mexican woman hurried from the room. "Use that passageway beside your bed and bring the duchess in here. I'll go get Duarte and bring him back with me. While I'm gone, your father will explain."

Longarm glanced at the colonel. "By the way, Colonel, you do have a firearm, don't you?"

"Ah do, sah!"

"Get it. We'll need it."

"And perhaps Ah should alert Dudley Jacobson as well."

"That might be a good idea."

Longarm got up then and hurried from the room. The courtyard was already stirring to life. Men and women were moving in the shadows, setting about the day's work even before daylight. As Longarm neared the main bunkhouse, he caught sight of José Duarte striding from the horse barn. Halting, Longarm peered closely at Duarte through the cloaking darkness.

Duarte was fully armed.

Longarm ducked back into the shadows. A moment later Ruel joined Duarte in front of the bunkhouse. Like Duarte, he was wearing gunbelt and holster and was carrying a rifle. This could mean only one thing: José Duarte and Ruel were in this betrayal together.

Longarm had counted on Duarte to disarm Ruel and lock him and his crew in the bunkhouse until the danger was passed. But he saw now how foolishly optimistic such a plan had been from the very first. Ruel would never have dared such a mutiny without bringing Duarte into it with him.

As Duarte and Ruel turned and started for the bunkhouse, Longarm moved back around behind one of the smaller barns, then ducked through the darkness to the rear of the bunkhouse. The windows were lit. He peered in. Every man was up and dressed, and—like Duarte and Ruel—armed to the teeth.

Time was getting short. Longarm hurried to the front of the bunkhouse and peered around the corner. Duarte and Ruel had almost reached the bunkhouse door. Longarm stepped into view, leveling his derringer at them.

"Freeze," he told them.

Both men pulled up. Longarm was close to the wall, partially hidden by the roof's shadow. The two men could see he was armed, but they probably could not tell he was carrying only a derringer.

"Drop your gunbelts," Longarm told them, still speaking softly. "If you raise a fuss, I'll have to kill you."

"Where the hell did you come from?" muttered Ruel as he unbuckled his belt.

Longarm understood his surprise. "Next time send a better man," he told Ruel. "Riley wasn't up to it."

Both gunbelts thudded to the ground.

"Now step back!" he ordered.

As soon as they had, Longarm snatched up the two sixguns. He stuck one into his cross-draw rig and kept the other trained on both men. He dropped the derringer back into his vest pocket.

"Turn around," Longarm said.

"Damn you!" said Ruel. "You ain't goin' to shoot us!"

"Turn around, I said!"

Both men turned.

Longarm strode forward and brought his gun barrel down onto Ruel's skull. The man dropped like a sack of potatoes. Duarte braced himself for a similar blow. Instead, Longarm prodded him in the back with the muzzle of his gun.

"We're going inside," he told Duarte. "I'll keep out

of sight while you tell your men that the raid has been called off for now—and to put their weapons away."

"They won't believe me."

"It's your job to convince them. You do and you live. You don't, and you're a dead man, and half of them will be, too, when the dust clears."

"I don't care about them," Duarte said.

"Then think about yourself."

"Long! This is madness. Don't try to stop us! I'll deal you in! I'll see you get a full share. More than a full share!"

Longarm dug the barrel deeper into Duarte's back. "Get inside, I told you."

Duarte protested no longer. He opened the door and stepped into the bunkhouse. The men were all waiting in the larger room, the one containing the bar and the cribs for their whores. Longarm could hear an occasional short bark of laughter above the general mutter and the sound of clinking glasses.

"I'll stand by the door," Longarm told Duarte. "This gun is inches from your back. Stay in the doorway and convince them that the raid is off. Do it!"

Duarte approached the door. Longarm flattened himself against the wall beside him. Duarte pushed the door open and remained in the doorway. The sound of voices inside the other room ceased abruptly.

"When do we move out, Duarte?" someone yelled.

"We don't," the man replied. "The raid is off. There's been a change in plans."

"The hell you say!" came from another one. "Where's Ruel?"

"He's coming."

"Well, he better! This stinks. We been waiting long

143

enough. He told us as soon as Jacobson brought in that gold, we'd move."

"We will. But not now. Later."

"We want to hear that from Ruel," another growled.

"Damn you!" Duarte told them, his voice once again cracking like a whip. "You'll do as I say!"

There was a bit of grumbling then, but the back of the rebellion appeared to have been broken. José Duarte was, after all, the man in charge.

"Now go ahead and put those weapons away," Duarte snapped. "You won't be needing them for awhile yet."

There was sullen acquiesence to that. Longarm heard the men call for drinks. Before Duarte moved back and closed the door, there was a general rush for the bar.

Duarte looked at Longarm.

"Now what are you going to do?" he asked. "They'll be in here in a minute. When they see you with that gun..."

"They won't. Get into your room. I'll be right behind you."

A moment later Longarm had trussed Duarte securely, then gagged him, after which he shoved him under his bed. Climbing out the window, he ran around to the front of the bunkhouse, dragged the still unconscious Ruel into the shadows, and slapped him back to life.

"All right, Ruel," he told the man, his sixgun nudging Ruel's nose, "you're going to tell me how you planned to alert Hansen."

"I ain't tellin' you nothin'!" Ruel snarled.

Longarm slapped him hard.

"Go on. Beat the shit out of me. I'll get it all back,

144

Long. Hansen will be in here soon and there ain't nothin' you can do about it."

Longarm dragged Ruel to his feet. The only choice now was to put Ruel on the wall, a gun to his head. That would certainly discourage Hansen and his band. They would see there was no chance for an easy entry.

A deep Mexican voice came from behind Longarm.

"Hey, *señor!* What are you doing here with thees man?"

"Get him, Manuel!" Ruel cried, jumping back. "He's an outlaw!"

Before Longarm could protest, a heavy arm circled his neck from behind, crunching against his Adam's apple and yanking him cruelly back. Ruel snatched Longarm's gun from him and, with a grunt, brought it down onto Longarm's head. Longarm managed to duck just enough so that the barrel slammed down onto his shoulder instead. Feigning a more serious injury, Longarm slumped heavily in the Mexican's arms.

The Mexican stepped back and let Longarm fall. Without waiting to examine him, Ruel turned and raced toward the gate. In some confusion, the Mexican turned and watched him run off.

"You fool," Longarm told Manuel. "Ruel is opening the gate for the outlaws. I was trying to stop him. You will all be wiped out!"

The Mexican spun and looked down at Longarm. "Is this true, *señor?*"

"Damn it! I'm a U. S. deputy," Longarm said, pushing himself upright and flashing his badge at the Mexican. "Of course it's true!"

Glancing over at the wall, Longarm saw Ruel pulling

up under it just beside the gate. The Mexican lookout on the wall called down something to Ruel. It sounded like a question. Ruel fired up at the man. The Mexican toppled from the wall.

That was the signal. As Ruel headed for the gate, from outside the wall came the dim thunder of horses' hooves. Longarm realized that that gunshot must have already alerted Ruel's men. He spun on the big Mexican. "Do you have a gun, Manuel?"

The Mexican nodded.

"Get it! Find all the help you can! Ruel's men are inside the bunkhouse. Keep them from breaking out!"

The Mexican nodded, then turned and raced toward the nearest stable. Other Mexicans were streaming across the compound by now. Manuel called to them, and at once they hurried toward him.

Longarm ran toward the gate. As he did so, he drew the other Colt from his rig. He heard a shout from his left, turned, and saw the colonel, Marta, and Jacobson hurrying from the castle. Behind them came most of the castle staff, men and women both, including Janos, the butler. All of them except Marta were carrying weapons.

Longarm waved them toward the gate.

By this time, Ruel was tugging on the gate, pulling one door open. Longarm stopped, aimed carefully, and fired. The round did not strike Ruel, but it came close. He ducked low and returned the fire. Longarm dodged aside and continued to race toward him. Ruel fired again. The ground at Longarm's feet exploded. He zigged, then zagged. He was much closer now. Ruel's shots were whining past his head. Ruel was too anxious, firing too high. Meanwhile, the rising thunder of the oncoming horses outside the gate filled the night.

146

Firing from the hip, Longarm bolted straight for Ruel. Longarm's third shot caught him low. Ruel doubled up and sent a round into the ground at his feet. A second later, Longarm was at the gate. Slamming his shoulder against it, he rammed it shut, then swiftly ran the beam through. A second later the wall was struck from the other side. He heard shouts, an angry, frustrated fusillade of gunfire.

Longarm clambered up the ladder, flung himself flat on the wall, and did his best to return the fire. Meanwhile, on the other side of the gate, other ladders were hastily propped against the side of the wall as the colonel and Jacobson and a few armed Mexicans clambered up to add their firepower to Longarm's.

It was not long before their combined fire proved discouraging enough to send Hansen's riders galloping away from the gate, following the curve of the wall. In a moment they were out of sight, leaving one of their number face down on the desert floor, his blood staining the ground.

At that moment gunfire erupted behind Longarm. Turning, he saw a Mexican staggering to one knee as a rifleman within the bunkhouse raked the compound.

Ruel's men were breaking out!

Chapter 11

Climbing down from the wall, Longarm led the others across the compound to the bunkhouse. The four or five Mexicans firing into it did not seem to be having much effect. Not a window was broken yet.

Jacobson and Colonel Forsyth fell in beside Longarm. Longarm glanced at them angrily. "What the hell is the duchess doing out here? Ruel's men may get loose yet— and I'm not sure we've seen the last of Hansen and his men."

"I'll organize these Mexicans," Jacobson told him. "You see to Marta!"

Letting Jacobson and the colonel continue on toward the men firing into the bunkhouse, Longarm waited as Marta, her face flushed, a silly little pearl-handled pepperbox in her hand, overtook him. With her was Janos, the butler, sticking grimly by his mistress's side.

Longarm pulled them both to a halt. "I want you to get back into the castle," he told Marta. "It's too dangerous for you out here." He turned to Janos. "Stay with Marta. Guard her. Find a good spot to hole up. This thing ain't over yet."

The butler nodded grimly. There was no doubt he saw the wisdom of Longarm's words.

"What have you got for a weapon?" Longarm asked.

Janos showed him his revolver. It was an enormous Remington Frontier .44. A bulky, poorly balanced weapon, it would do well enough in close quarters. Longarm nodded to Janos, then looked at Marta. "Where's Jennifer?"

"In her room. Do you think the colonel would let her come down into this?"

"Keep an eye out for her, too, Janos," Longarm told the butler. "Now get on back into that castle, both of you!"

Janos took his mistress's arm and guided her swiftly back across the compound.

By this time Jacobson and the colonel had managed to drag from the barns and the carriage house what wagons they could find, overturn them, and create a breastworks, behind which they were now beginning to pour fire into the front of the bunkhouse. At the rear of the bunkhouse, Longarm glimpsed other men using adjacent buildings and outhouses for cover.

Keeping low, he ran over to Jacobson and dropped down beside him. Crouching behind one of the wagons, Jacobson was obviously enjoying himself. He had a rifle and knew how to use it as he poked its barrel between two wagon-wheel spokes and systematically shot out windows in the bunkhouse.

The return fire from the bunkhouse was deadly, however. Longarm heard one of the Mexicans cry out. He turned in time to see the man sag to the ground, clutching at his left shoulder. Ruel and Duarte had evidently picked choice gunslicks for their force. Meanwhile, the sky overhead was turning pale. It would be daylight soon, which would make it a lot easier for the bunkhouse's defenders and its attackers to see what they were shooting at.

"You think these men out here can keep those gunslicks from breaking out?" Longarm asked Jacobson.

"They're lousy shots, but I think they'll do," he replied.

"Sure, but it'll take all day to flush them at this rate. And I'm worried about Hansen and his men. They're outside the walls, but not for long. I got over the wall easy enough."

"What do you suggest?"

"We light a wagonload of hay and send it against the bunkhouse. That'll smoke 'em out."

"Good idea," Jacobson said. "I'll see to it."

"No. You keep the fire heavy enough to prevent a breakout. I'll get the colonel."

Jacobson nodded, turned back around, and began sending rounds into one of the corner windows. Longarm left him and moved along the ring of wagons until he found the colonel. The man was peppering the walls of the bunkhouse with shots from his nickel-plated Smith and Wesson. He did not seem to be having much luck.

"Colonel, I need you," said Longarm.

"At your service, sah," the man said.

Longarm quickly explained what he had in mind. With some alacrity, the colonel left his post and followed Longarm into the horse barn. A Mexican with a slight flesh wound helped them select a high-backed wagon that already was half buried in loose hay. The three of them put their shoulders to the rear of the wagon and pushed it out into the barn's massive doorway.

Waiting until the Mexican had cleared a path through the barrier of wagons, Longarm lit the hay with a match and waited a moment or two for the flames to spread. Then he nodded to the colonel. They put their shoulders to the wagon again and sent it down the slight slope toward the bunkhouse. After a moment or two, the flames caused Longarm and the colonel to fall back, but by that time the wagon had a momentum of its own.

Ducking behind one of the wagons, Longarm and the colonel watched the wagon strike the bunkhouse door. It seemed to explode when it hit. Embers shot into the air, some landing on the roof, others littering the ground in front of the building. On impact, the bunkhouse door had exploded inward and the blazing hay was now filling the interior with smoke. Flames flickered in the windows.

"Hold your fire!" Longarm cried as the first of Ruel's men began to climb out of one of the windows.

The man flung down his weapon and, with hands flung skyward, staggered toward the wagons. A moment later two others followed his example. A shout from the rear of the building announced the surrender of a fourth man. Longarm waited, but that was all that came out. The remaining three, not counting Duarte, remained inside the bunkhouse. As Longarm watched the interior of the adobe bunkhouse turn into a furious, roaring oven, he

152

hoped fervently that any man still inside was already dead.

Duarte, unable to call out and bound hand and foot, must surely have been trapped under his bed, which meant he had either suffocated or been burned alive. This realization gave Longarm little comfort. There were very few men for which he would have fashioned such a miserable fate.

Rolf Hansen was the problem now.

Longarm could not believe he had given up—not this easily. Leaving Jacobson to deal with the four men who had just stumbled from the bunkhouse, Longarm put the colonel in charge of a small force of armed defenders he posted at the gate. Then he gathered up the most battle-wise of the Mexicans and set out to patrol the wall.

A half-hour later, close to the spot where Longarm had himself managed to pull himself up onto the wall, Long-arm spotted the hoofprints of Hansen's riders where they had milled about the base of the wall. There was clear sign also that the horses had then turned and galloped straight off across the desert. They were gone, then. Hansen and his riders had seen the futility of an attempt to gain entry into the castle grounds.

Yet something about this victory dissatisfied Long-arm. For one thing, it was too damned easy.

A moment later his fears appeared to be confirmed when the big Mexican who had almost strangled him not long before found indisputable sign that Hansen and his men had succeeded in scaling the wall. About ten yards farther down the wall, the Mexican found the spot where they had dropped into the compound. The tracks led them to the rear of the castle. There they got hopelessly lost

153

in the heavy stream of traffic going to and from it.

Returning to the spot where Hansen and his riders appeared to gave ridden off, Longarm dropped to the desert and walked out to examine the tracks. He counted eight riders in all, and as they rode off, they were not sparing their mounts any. Longarm glanced up at the steel-blue sky. It had only been daylight for less than an hour and already the sun's stare was heavy and unrelenting.

The big Mexican reached down and helped Longarm back up onto the wall. Brushing himself off, Longarm turned and looked back out over the grim expanse of the Mojave Desert. Less than an hour ago, Hansen and his men had ridden into that blazing expanse of nothingness. Longarm shook his head. It had probably seemed like a good idea at the time.

A few moments later Longarm was standing beside Jacobson in front of the smouldering ruins of the bunkhouse. Jacobson had already seen to the removal of the three who had been caught inside. The roof had caved in. What remained of Duarte's room was off to the right. His bed had been partially consumed, and charred adobe bricks had collapsed down onto it.

"You think the poor son of a bitch might be under that?" Jacobson asked unhappily.

Longarm nodded grimly. "I had him bound pretty tightly and had stuffed a gag into his mouth. No one else knew he was in there. When the fighting began, he might have been able to spit out the gag, but no one would have heard him in all that racket."

"Jesus," said Jacobson. "That poor bastard."

Longarm nodded.

"I'll go in with you, Deputy," Jacobson said. "Help

you lift that bed off him."

"Thanks."

Longarm went first, picking his way carefully through the still-burning debris. The smoke bit cruelly into his eyes and the heat retained by the adobe was fierce. Heavy beads of sweat stood out on Longarm's forehead by the time they reached Duarte's bed. The two men each grabbed one end of the bedframe and heaved upward. The frame and mattress went flying.

There was nothing under it. No shrivelled body. Nothing.

Longarm bent close to the rug that had been protected by the collapsed mattress. There was a thin, even coating of cinders across its entire surface. Duarte had managed to pull himself out from under the bed before the fire started.

"So where is the son of a bitch?" Jacobson said.

"Gone, I'm thinking."

"Gone?"

"That's right. With Hansen and his men. I counted the tracks of eight riders. There should only have been seven. We killed one of their men outside the gate. That eighth one is Duarte. He must have met them behind the castle during the fighting after they scaled the wall."

"You mean he just happened on them like that?"

"Looks like it. All hell was breaking loose, and all he wanted was to save his hide. Looks like he convinced Hansen and his men to hightail it."

Jacobson took a deep breath and grinned through his sweat at Longarm. "Well, that suits me just fine. I'm glad to be rid of the son of a bitch. Now let's get the hell out of this inferno."

"Suits me," said Longarm.

• • •

Longarm still had some questions he wanted answered, and he asked Jacobson to join him in Marta's apartment as soon as he could manage it. Jacobson assured him he would be there in less than an hour. Longarm cleaned himself up and found Marta waiting nervously in her apartment with a grim-faced Janos sitting between her and the door, the Remington .44 looking as big as a cannon in his hand.

As soon as Longarm told her it was over, Marta jumped to her feet, opened her arms, and rushed toward him.

"Oh, Longarm!" she cried. "You've saved us!"

Instead of stepping into her arms, Longarm took both her hands in his and smiled. "Jacobson is joining us in a few minutes. I think I'd like to know what this castle—this damned fairy tale here in the middle of the desert—is really all about."

"Why, whatever do you mean?"

"Jacobson's gold. That's what I mean."

She went pale. "You know about that?"

"And so did every one of Ruel's men. That's why they were waiting so patiently for Jacobson to arrive before making their move."

There was a sharp knock on the door. "That'll be Jacobson," Longarm said, as the butler hurried to answer it.

But it wasn't. Instead, Teresa entered, her face distraught.

"Mistress!" she cried, sweeping in past Janos, "the woman who screams is gone!"

Marta jumped up. "Gone? What do you mean?"

"I left the castle when the shooting began. Just now

156

I come back. The door, it is open! That crazy woman, she is gone!"

Marta closed her eyes in exasperation at this new calamity. Then she got hold of herself and spoke sharply, decisively to Teresa. "Get everyone you can," she told the woman. "Scour the castle. Look everywhere. Get some men. And arm them. That woman is very dangerous!"

"Yes, mistress!"

As Teresa hurried from the room, Marta turned to Longarm. "Oh, my God! The thought of that terrible woman running loose—on top of everything else!"

"She won't get far."

"No, I suppose not. But just the thought of it! I won't sleep until she is caught."

At that moment, there was a quick knock on the door and Jacobson entered. They told him the latest and he shrugged fatalistically.

"It is all a curse on Marta and me for our transgressions," he suggested, winking at Marta. Then he slumped into one of her easy chairs.

Marta glanced at Janos. "Thank you, Janos. You can go now."

The butler bowed and left, the oversized Remington hanging from his right hand like a gleaming deformity.

As soon as the door closed behind him, Marta looked at Jacobson. "The cat is out of the bag, darling," she told him.

Jacobson frowned. "I don't understand."

"The gold. Longarm knows about it."

"Well, of course. If he hadn't rushed off, I would have shown it to him." He turned to face Longarm. "It was in that last wagonload I brought here from San Francisco—along with the four thoroughbred horses."

"It was that gold which set Ruel and his men—and Duarte, too—against you," Longarm told him. "That first band that attacked you in the desert probably knew nothing about it. They were just after you because you were heading for the castle. But when Ruel and his men overtook them, Ruel saw his chance. He killed their leader and put Hansen in charge of the remaining outlaws. That gave Ruel a force he knew could take the castle and all its inhabitants—as long as they had a chance to get past the gate with one swift maneuver."

"And that you foiled. You did brilliantly, Deputy."

"Thank you. Now, I would like you to tell me just what in hell you and the duchess are doing out here in this desert. I want to know and I want to know without any farting around about it. Pardon me, Duchess."

"Tell him, Dudley," the duchess said.

"I'd rather you did, Marta."

With a shrug, Marta turned to face Longarm. "Longarm, Dudley is my lawyer and my . . . lover. I guess that's the proper term, isn't it, Dudley? He found me with barely a penny to my name—just a worthless patch of desert, something that had been a family joke until now. But Dudley was privy to some information which he shared with me, and which he has generously allowed me to exploit."

"Most generously."

"Yes, Dudley," she said, flicking an appreciative glance at him. "I certainly have no complaints on that score."

"And just how," Longarm asked, "could you possibly exploit a piece of the Mojave Desert?"

"Simple. It has the only fresh water rights for miles

158

around. That, of course, is no secret. But what is a secret is that a railroad building a line up the California coast has decided to build a shortcut across the desert. Otherwise the railroad would not be able to link up with the transcontinental lines coming from the East."

Longarm nodded. He understood perfectly now. "And this place would be ideal for a tank stop."

"Precisely." Marta smiled. "And for it, we plan to ask a price commensurate with our investment here. Furthermore, we expect to get it."

"What makes you think you will?"

"The investors are already in too deep to pull back now, Longarm. They absolutely must have the water rights we've built this castle on. You see, when they floated the stock for this railroad, they had no idea the government did not own the entire desert. They had expected to get the land for very little."

"And of course," Jacobson broke in, "that meant there were a few men in Washington who expected to realize a sizable portion of stock in payment for their cooperation."

Marta laughed softly. "You can imagine how red their faces were when they found out this desert was not theirs to deliver. Not the most important part of it, that is."

"But they do now?"

"Yes. The cat—as they say—is out of the bag."

"That was why the colonel was sniffing around," Marta said, smiling slyly. "We told him he could go any time, but it was he who told the wheelwrights not to touch his wagon. He is one of the earliest investors in the railroad."

"And how did Duarte figure in all this?" Longarm asked.

"He knew nothing."

"Perhaps you should have let him in on the secret. He might not have been so willing to throw in with Ruel if he had known."

Marta shrugged. "Such a man would not be satisfied no matter what you gave him." She spoke with profound disgust. It was obvious she loathed the man who had served as her castellan.

As if her scornful words had drawn him, José Duarte appeared from behind the large canopied bed, a revolver gleaming dully in his hand, his eyes fixed on Marta with a reptilian fixity.

Jacobson gasped. Marta spun in her chair.

"José!" she cried, half-rising from her seat.

"Yes, José," he sneered. "José, the man who would not be satisfied, no matter what you gave him. And you gave him plenty, didn't you, you damned slut!"

Longarm started to reach under his coat.

"Go ahead, Long," Duarte snarled. "Go for your gun! Give me an excuse!"

Longarm let his hand relax on his knee and leaned back in his chair. "Be grateful you are alive, Duarte," he told the man. "And get out of this apartment and out of this place."

"Oh, I'll get out! Never fear. I got out from under that bed, didn't I? But I'll not go until I've taken care of this damned witch!"

"Duarte!" Marta cried. "Don't be a fool! Shut up!"

"You'd like that, wouldn't you? You don't want anyone to know what you really are!"

Duarte looked back at Longarm. "She promised me that gold, said it would all be mine, once I helped her kill Jacobson. Then she changed her mind and told me she would have me flogged if I told anyone about it."

160

He laughed shortly, bitterly, at the recollection. "That was your doing, Long. Soon as you arrived, she found other pleasures."

"Longarm!" Marta pleaded. "Don't believe him. He's lying! Lying!"

"Shut up, bitch," he told her.

Duarte looked back at Longarm. "Did she tell you how long it had been for her, how terribly, terribly long? Of all her lies, that was the biggest!"

With a piercing cry of rage and fury, Marta leaped out of her chair and flung herself on Duarte. Her long fingers frozen into claws, she raked him down one cheek, then began tearing at his face. Perhaps it was unintended, but as he stumbled backward under Marta's furious assault, his gun detonated.

Marta was flung back. She stopped herself by grabbing at one of the bedposts. A sob broke from her lips. With both hands, she grabbed at her stomach as blood spouted through her fingers. She collapsed onto her knees, then fell forward to the carpet, her head striking almost lightly. Except for the rapidly spreading stain of blood growing under her, she might have been sleeping peacefully.

Distraught, Duarte looked up at Longarm and Jacobson. He had done what he had come to do, yet it seemed to have destroyed him.

"Stay back!" he cried.

"Get out of here, Duarte," Jacobson told him. "Now!"

"I . . . she came at me! I didn't mean to fire!"

Longarm got to his feet and started for Duarte. "You heard him!" he told Duarte.

Duarte turned and flung himself back into the passageway. Longarm drew his gun, cut around the bed,

161

and managed to slip through the wall before it swung shut. The sudden dimness momentarily blinded him. Pulling up, he peered through narrowed eyes at the passageway ahead of him. He remembered there should be some light filtering in from narrow slits high on the wall.

He heard Duarte's stumbling feet as he fled, and went after him. He was gaining on Duarte when he heard an abrupt, horrified gasp just ahead of him. Then came a second cry, this one more like a muffled scream.

Longarm pulled up. His eyes were accustomed now to the dimness, and just ahead of him contorted shapes materialized out of the gloom. Duarte was struggling with a woman, her hair piled atop her head like a cone. The scuffle was fierce and prolonged. Longarm caught the dim flash of a knife as it plunged down. This time Duarte simply groaned. The heavy sound of his body crumpling to the floor filled the narrow passageway.

Esmeralda turned to face Longarm, her looming presence blotting out what little light filtered down from the top of the wall. Even in the semi-darkness, Longarm saw the mad glitter in her eyes.

"God has sent me!" she cried.

Longarm turned and fumbled back to Marta's room. Pushing open the door, he slipped through it, then slammed it shut. He dragged the bed over to block the door. He knew what he would do within the hour: he would get the butler to organize the help, and they would nail braces against every one of these damned secret doors.

Let Duarte's corpse rot in the walls, and when Esmeralda Jarvis got hungry enough, she would ask to come out—quietly.

He turned to look down at Marta. Jacobson, weeping,

was holding her head in his lap. It did not matter to Jacobson if Duarte's accusations were true. All he felt was her loss.

Longarm thought he understood. Without a word, he stepped swiftly past Marta's grieving lover and hurried from the apartment.

Chapter 12

Two hours later, Longarm was on his way to the stables to see if his remaining mule and the two burros had shown up yet. He wanted to leave as soon as night fell. Another day in this gaudy palace of madness and death would be too much for him. Everything in this place had been fashioned out of deceit and connivance. Even the colonel's presence here and Jennifer's upcoming marriage to that fine gentleman from San Diego was a part of it.

He entered the barn and, to his surprise, found both his mules and the two burros in fresh, clean stalls, crunching on grain, looking as sleek and fit as seals. They must have been discovered outside the walls by one of the hostlers and brought in. Longarm looked them over. It was a good sign. He would be on his way as soon as night fell. And this time he would not leave the wagon trace to check out any campfires on the horizon.

He was on his way from the barn when the colonel burst in. "Deputy Long!" he cried. "Have you seen Jennifer?"

"No. I haven't, Colonel. What's wrong?"

"My God, sah! She's gone! Cleared out. Not a sight of her!"

The man was close to hysteria. Longarm reached out and held him gently by the shoulders to calm him. "Just slow down, Colonel," he said. "Tell me what you know."

"I left her in her room. I gave her a derringer and made her swear not to let anyone in. When I went back after the fighting, she was not in her room. But the danger had passed, so I gave it no thought."

"When was the last time you saw her?"

"Before the fighting. Ah haven't seen her since! Ah thought surely when she heard about the duchess, she'd have shown up. But Ah have not seen her nowhere! Ah had that post at the gate to look aftah! Mah God, deputy, Ah have been so busy since all this started . . . !"

"The first thing to do is search the grounds," said Longarm. "Look everywhere. She may have sneaked down to watch the fighting and been wounded slightly."

"Oh, God!"

"Now, we don't know that for sure, Colonel. I was just thinking out loud. Go on back to the castle. Get that butler, Janos, to help you search it. I'll stay out here and go over the grounds thoroughly."

As the colonel hurried off, Longarm thought suddenly of that eighth rider with Hansen's men. He had assumed it was Duarte, but he had sure as hell guessed wrong on

166

that one. Now, with Jennifer missing, a sick apprehension started to grow in the pit of his stomach.

He forced himself not to think of it and went looking for that big Mexican, to begin a search of the grounds.

The search of the castle grounds revealed no sign of Jennifer. The search of the castle itself netted nothing until the colonel, beside himself, returned to Jennifer's room. In his first frantic search of it he had rushed about blindly. This time, as he sat brokenly at her vanity table, he found a note in plain sight, neatly folded, leaning against the mirror.

Longarm was brought to the room by Janos, a shadowy, broken Jacobson following behind. When they entered the room, the colonel was still sitting at the vanity. He turned his pallid face to them and wordlessly handed the note he had found to Longarm.

Longarm opened it quickly and read what it said. It was in Jennifer's neat hand.

Dear Father,

Rolf Hansen is forcing me to write this note to you. But he cannot read or write, so I'll just put down more than he tells me to. He wants you to tell Mr. Long that I will be safe as long as no one but Mr. Long comes after me. If he sees a posse, he will kill me.

He wants Mr. Long to come after him alone, but I don't think Mr. Long should do this. Mr. Hansen will kill me anyway when he gets tired of me, so there's no sense in endangering Mr. Long on my account.

Goodbye, Father. I love you very much. I hope

167

you will be able to swing the railroad deal in San Diego.

> Your loving daughter,
> Jennifer

Longarm read the note twice, then handed it back to the colonel.

"What does it say?" Jacobson asked.

"Hansen has Jennifer," Longarm told him. "He must have taken her when he scaled the wall. She was probably down in the yard watching the fighting when he came upon her. He says he won't hurt Jennifer as long as I'm the only one who comes after him. If he sees a posse, he'll kill Jennifer. It's me Hansen wants."

"What are you going to do?"

"I want Hansen."

"My God, Deputy, he'll kill you!"

Longarm looked at the colonel. "Colonel, get out of this place. Go on to San Diego. If I get Jennifer back, I'll bring her to you. What hotel will you be staying at?"

"There's only one," the colonel told him, his voice barely above a whisper.

"That's where I'll bring her, then."

"What if you..." The colonel could not finish his question.

"If Jennifer or I don't join you in two weeks, you can figure we aren't going to."

The colonel nodded, then bowed his face into his hands.

Longarm turned and strode from the room.

He was ready to ride out in less than an hour. He had his two burros loaded with two casks of water each. His

168

spare mule was carrying water bags. Longarm had flung over his shoulder a serape he had soaked thoroughly, and in addition, he had thrown over himself and his mule a heavy wool blanket saturated with water.

His eyes narrowed to slits, Longarm rode out through the gate, the heat recoiling from the flat surface of the desert like the wind from an open furnace door. It was early yet, not quite ten o'clock in the morning. Hansen had left around daybreak. At best, Hansen had a four-hour lead.

And Hansen and his men were riding horses, not mules, and there was little doubt in Longarm's mind that Hansen had not had the time nor the foresight to provision himself as Longarm had.

By noon the blanket had been burned so dry it was hot to the touch. The serape had long since been abandoned. Longarm wrapped the blanket around him in much the way he imagined the bedouins did. Soon, however, he was forced to discard the blistering wool blanket also. By four that afternoon, he had already changed mounts twice, but his mule was beginning to falter.

Ahead of him he saw buzzards. He kept going and a mile farther on saw them crouching and flapping over a horse and the prone figure of a man a few feet beyond it. Longarm rode slowly up to the dead horse and rider. The horse appeared to have just given out, but the rider had been shot just below the neck. He was still holding his revolver. The sun glancing off its barrel lanced cruelly into Longarm's eyes.

Longarm rode on past. The buzzards waddled back to their feast.

An hour or two before sunset, Hansen's tracks began to swing toward the wagon trace. A half-hour later, Long-

169

arm passed another dead horse, its flanks covered with dried lather, its dead eyes wild. Flies were nesting in its flared nostrils and, overhead, vultures were tilting more steeply as they spiraled down. Not too long after that, Longarm saw one of Hansen's men on his hands and knees.

The man turned at Longarm's approach and went for his gun.

"Don't!" called Longarm, swinging his rifle out of his scabbard.

But the outlaw was not thinking clearly. His bloodshot eyes wild, he began firing. Though his shots were well off the mark, Longarm realized a single lucky round could rupture one of his water casks. He pulled up.

"I'll give you some water! Stop shooting!" he said.

The outlaw staggered to his feet and began to run ahead of Longarm. He ran crookedly, drunkenly, then sprawled forward. As Longarm started up again and rode after him, the crazed outlaw started crawling on his hands and knees. Longarm kept a safe distance back and followed until the fellow collapsed forward into the sand.

Longarm reined in and watched the outlaw for a while. The low sun peered redly at them both, its glare still a punishment. After a few minutes Longarm dismounted and, with the barrel of his rifle trained on the outlaw's head, walked slowly toward him.

When he reached him, he saw a fly crawling on the back of the man's leathery neck. Slowly, carefully, Longarm placed the toe of his boot under his chest and rolled him over. The man flopped over and stared blindly up at him. There was sand in his mouth and nostrils. But he was no longer breathing, so it did not matter.

• • •

Night was a blessing. Longarm rested a little after sunset, emptied the second cask of water, then mounted a fresh mule and kept on. He was able to push his mules a little harder now, and the sturdy animals responded gallantly. He kept up this pace throughout the night, changing mounts frequently. Only when the sun climbed above the horizon once more did he pull up, seek out a gully free of snakes, and give himself and his mounts a rest.

Using the water sparingly, he watered them and himself, kept them as quiet as he could as the sun rose into the steel-blue sky. He protected them from the sun's blistering rays with a tarpaulin he had brought with him for this purpose. He propped it over them with branches of dead greasewood, and was careful to keep the roof of the tarpaulin high enough above them so that some air could pass through. Meanwhile, he continually wrapped the muzzle of each animal with wet towels.

After two hours, he packed the tarpaulin, watered the animals once more, then started up again. He was certain he had gained on Hansen enough during the night to allow that two-hour respite. What he was counting on now was the total exhaustion of Hansen's men and horses, since there was no sign that they had camped at all during the night.

At first Longarm wondered at Hansen's foolhardy pace until he realized that Hansen had no idea when Jennifer's note had been found. He could not have realized that it would have taken so long for the colonel to spot a note placed so prominently on Jennifer's vanity. Hansen was undoubtedly convinced that Longarm was just below the horizon and still coming on.

About noon, Longarm passed another dead horse. Less than an hour later, he caught sight of two men astride a

171

horse. They were about half a mile ahead of him and not moving very fast. The horse was apparently on its last legs. As Longarm pulled up to watch, one of the men slipped from the horse and began to lead it. There was a good chance the animal had gone blind. Longarm had seen it happen to steers driven too long without water, and he had heard of it happening to horses.

Longarm urged his mule on. If he could reach them in time, he might be able to save the horse. The two men were in such poor condition that not until Longarm was within a hundred yards of them did they spot him. The one still in the saddle slipped painfully off the horse. He appeared to have been wounded—by Hansen, possibly. The one leading the horse snatched a rifle out of its scabbard and levered a fresh cartridge into the firing chamber. The sound it made came clearly across the desert.

"I have water!" Longarm called to them as he pulled up. "Throw down your weapons."

Almost in unison, the two men started firing at Longarm. The shots went wild. Some of them landed twenty or thirty feet in front of him. They were not thinking clearly. But that made them almost as dangerous as a clear-headed Hansen.

Longarm waited a while longer, hoping they would come to their senses. When they continued to fire, reloading frantically every time they ran out of ammunition, he pulled his mule off the trace and decided to go around them. When he regained the wagon trace a half-hour later, he looked back and saw them clearly on the shimmering horizon, following doggedly after him.

But a few minutes later when he looked back, they were gone.

• • •

An hour later, Longarm pulled up, took out his binoculars, and focused them on a small group of riders on the horizon ahead of him. There were four of them, trembling in the waves of heat emanating from the desert floor. At times they disappeared entirely; at others they loomed eerily closer.

Longarm put away the glasses. Jennifer was one of the riders, and riding beside her was Hansen. The other two were trailing at a distance. What Hansen had done, Longarm surmised, was to keep changing to the strongest horse, shooting anyone who would not exchange horses with him.

By now, all four were probably desperate for water, and their mounts were undoubtedly suffering at least as much. They would be off the desert by nightfall, and Hansen would want to make for water immediately. He would not be able to wait until he reached San Bernardino. But an hour's ride south of where the trace left the desert there was a water hole in among the rocks. According to Delores, it was known to everyone in this county who used the wagon trace to cross the desert, and there was little doubt Hansen knew of it as well.

It was also where the bones of Jake Tolliver lay mouldering.

Longarm held up until the four riders had vanished over the horizon, then left the wagon trace and headed southwest, straight for the rocks. He stopped to water his mules and burros frequently. This close to the water hole he could afford to be generous. The mules almost kicked up their heels as they began to trot over the hard, briny surface of the desert. Could they possibly smell

173

the water hole this far out? Longarm wondered.

Longarm reached the rocks an hour or so before sunset and cut through them to the water hole. Dismounting swiftly, he plunged his head in, holding it under for a while, glorying in its icy grip. Afterward, he drank his fill, slowly at first so he wouldn't get sick. Then he watered his mules and the two burros. They were sensible beasts and would not normally overdrink. But to be on the safe side, he led them off into a small arroyo where he removed the casks from the burros and off-saddled the mules. Then, carrying his Winchester and binoculars, he climbed up into the rocks to wait.

There was only a faint crimson finger of light remaining in the sky when Longarm caught movement out beyond the rocks. He lifted his binoculars. Two people, both on foot, were approaching. One was Jennifer. Longarm could not be sure, but the other one looked like Riley. Their faces were barely discernible in the darkness that now hugged the ground. From the way they straggled along, it was clear neither of them was in very good shape. As Longarm watched, Jennifer stumbled, then fell. Riley kept on past her without looking back. In a moment, Jennifer managed to push herself up off the ground and follow after him.

Frowning, Longarm lowered his binoculars. Was it possible only Riley and Jennifer had made it this far? Where was Hansen and the other one? He lifted his glasses and raked the darkening horizon. Nothing. No one. Hansen could have tried to take one of their horses and been gunned down by Riley or the other one.

Longarm watched Riley and Jennifer approach the rocks. He made no move to leave his perch. Every once in a while, he brought his binoculars up and searched

174

the horizon. But it was too dark now to see any riders, even if there had been any out there. It was too pat, damn it! He felt cheated. Hansen wanted him—and he wanted Hansen.

Riley reached the water hole before Jennifer. Two more times Jennifer stumbled and fell headlong onto the cruel rocks. Longarm winced each time he saw her go down. Yet an instinctive wariness prevented him from revealing his presence to her or Riley. Not just yet. It was a stubbornness that surprised him, but he obeyed this instinct and remained hidden in the rocks above them.

Riley had thrown himself face down in front of the water hole and plunged his head down into the water. Every once in a while he would lift his head, shake his hair, then duck his head back down again. Jennifer reached the water hole finally. Longarm watched her, puzzled. Instead of plunging into the water as Longarm would have expected, she sat on the edge of the water hole, hugging her knees, rocking back and forth, but not drinking.

Pushing himself out of the water, Riley snarled something at her. From this height, Longarm could not hear a word. In response, Jennifer just ducked her head, hugged her knees, and continued to rock. Longarm could take it no longer. Something was terribly wrong with Jennifer. She was obviously frantic for water, yet was unable to drink. What had those devils done to her?

As silently as a great cat, Longarm dropped from ledge to ledge, found the trail he had used earlier, and followed it to the ground. This put him finally on a smooth patch of bedrock directly behind the water hole. His rifle on his hip, he strode swiftly toward Jennifer and Riley.

175

They heard him coming and turned their heads. In that instant, Longarm saw why Jennifer could not drink the water. A cruel gag had been shoved into her mouth, a thin strip of rawhide keeping it in place. But why? And then he knew.

It was to keep Jennifer from calling out a warning to him.

Instinctively, he flung himself to one side, just as a series of gunshots erupted behind him. He felt a slug burn through his right sleeve and another catch him in the heel of his boot. Turning around and crabbing to the right, he levered his Winchester rapidly and sent a devastating fusillade in among the rocks behind which Hansen and his companion were crouching.

Then he dove for cover behind a boulder and continued going until he reached a tall finger of rock jutting at a forty-five-degree angle out of the ground. He found a foothold and launched himself up the steep face of it. When he reached the top, he flung himself flat and peered over the edge, his revolver in his hand. Hansen was peering out from behind a boulder, looking straight ahead of him at the boulder behind which Longarm had just ducked.

Beside him, writhing silently on the ground, was the other outlaw.

"Up here, Hansen," Longarm said softly.

Hansen glanced up, firing at Longarm in the same motion. His bullet whined off the rock an inch under Longarm's chin. Longarm squeezed off two quick shots. Each round slammed into Hansen. The first one punched him down into a sitting position. The second one took away part of his face.

176

"Riley!" Longarm cried. "You want to live?"

"Yes!"

"Throw your gun down and step out!"

Riley flung his gun onto the ground, then stepped out from behind a rock, his hands in the air.

"Jennifer," Longarm called, "take his gun!"

She darted forward and snatched it up.

"Cover Riley until I get down there."

As soon as he was beside her, Longarm took Riley's gun from her, clubbed Riley to the ground, then swiftly rid Jennifer of the gag that bound her mouth. Without a word, she turned from him and ran to the water hole.

As she drank, Longarm walked over to inspect Hansen and his companion. Hansen was dead, the other one wounded fearfully and no longer conscious. Counting Jake Tolliver, this meant that three men—seeking only to even the score with Longarm—had found in this pile of rocks a common burial ground. Once again Longarm found himself wondering at the vanity of gunfighters, and the stupid, unproductive futility of their lives.

Returning to the stunned Riley, Longarm hauled him to his feet. "Hansen left the horses out there somewhere. Is that right?"

"Yes," Riley managed.

"What shape are they in?"

"Bad. Real bad."

"Go get them and bring them to the water hole. And if you're thinking of running out, just figure how far you'll be able to get on those horses in their present condition."

With a sullen nod, Riley moved off.

• • •

Jennifer was sitting up beside the water hole. She had ducked her entire head into the icy water and now her hair hung in ratty snarls about her shoulders. But she looked a lot better than she had a few minutes before.

"They saw you coming after them," she said, looking forlornly up at Longarm. "They caught the glint of your binoculars."

Longarm shook his head in disgust and hunkered down beside her. He hadn't thought of that. "And that was when they planned this surprise for me."

"Yes. They knew I'd shout a warning to you if I could, so they waited until dark. Then they gagged me."

She began to cry.

He reached out and took her gently into his arms. As he stroked her wet hair to soothe her, she wailed, "I'm such a mess! I must look awful, and I feel so dirty!"

He hugged her close until she brought her tears under some control. He handed her his handkerchief.

"There's a fine hotel in San Bernardino," he assured her, "and a general store. You'll look as fresh and pretty as a daisy when your father comes through on his way to San Diego. And that's a promise!"

She hugged him tightly. "But I don't want to go to San Diego, Longarm. Not right away. I want to stay with you in San Bernardino. Please?"

"What've you got in mind?" he asked, almost as if he didn't know.

"I told you once before. Have you forgotten?"

Longarm took a deep breath. "Well, now, why don't we just cross that bridge when we come to it?"

"Yes," she said, brightening. "That's a fine idea!"

• • •

Two months later, on his way across the lobby of the Windsor Hotel, Longarm heard a familiar voice call his name. He halted and spun about. Jennifer Forsyth was running across the lobby to greet him, her arms out.

"It *is* you, Longarm!" she cried. "How wonderful to see you again!"

He took her hands in his and squeezed. She looked wonderful, but better than that, she looked happy. "My," he said, "don't you look fine! What are you doing in Denver?"

"I'm with father—and my fiancé!"

"You must introduce me."

"And I shall! I'm dying for you to meet Paul!"

As she led him across the lobby to the parlor, he asked, "Is this the young man you told me about? The one who was so anxious to marry a virgin?"

She giggled. "Yes."

"Have you told him?"

"Of course!"

"You are a devil."

"Where you are concerned, Longarm, I will always be a devil. But you will see. He is very handsome and very nice and is coming East with us so we may become better acquainted before the ceremony."

"Whose idea was that?"

"Mine, of course."

"Of course."

Paul Martinez was indeed handsome, and almost as tall as Longarm. He was standing with the colonel looking over a train schedule. As Jennifer approached, the colonel and Martinez turned. The colonel's eyes lit up when he saw Longarm.

179

"Paul," said Jennifer, "I want you to meet the man who saved my life, U. S. Deputy Custis Long."

"I am pleased to meet you, Mr. Long," Paul said, reaching out and shaking Longarm's hand quite firmly. "I sure hope I can take care of Jennifer as well as you did."

"Well, you'd better," Longarm remarked. "But watch out. She needs a strong hand."

Both Paul and Jennifer laughed at that, and Jennifer moved close to Paul and put her arm through his. It was obvious she was already very pleased with him.

"Deputy," Colonel Forsyth said, "would you care to join me at the bar?"

"Delighted, Colonel."

Excusing themselves, they left Jennifer and Paul and found a quiet corner at the hotel bar. Longarm was about to order, but noticed that the colonel was hanging back.

"What would you like, Colonel?"

"Your choice is mine, Mistah Long."

"Would Maryland rye be to your liking?"

"Indeed. Indeed. An auspicious choice. I drink it with great regularity mahself."

When it came they sipped in solemn silence for a while, then the colonel indicated with a nod of his head a small table in a corner. They retired to it. Longarm leaned back and took out a cheroot, offering one to the colonel. He accepted it.

Once they had both lit up, the colonel cleared his throat. "Ah fear Ah have never had the oppo'tunity to thank you properly fo' all you have done for Jennifer and me, Deputy. Ah would like to take that oppo'tunity now. Ah am in your debt, sah, and Ah dutifully acknowledge it. If there is ever anything Ah can do for

180

you, you have but to ask."

"Thank you, Colonel, that's very decent of you. But, remember, I was just doing my job. There is one thing, though."

"What's that, sah? Name it!"

"Just take good care of Jennifer, and make sure that young man sidling up to her treats her decent."

"You can rest assured Ah will do that, sah. You can rest assured."

They smoked in silence awhile, sipping the Maryland rye.

"What about that railroad deal?" Longarm asked. "I trust it went through according to plan."

"Ah have sold all my stock in that enterprise, sah. Ah am proud to say Ah had second thoughts. My daughter means more to me than all the wealth in the world. If she and Paul find happiness together, it will have nothing to do whatever with my dreams of wealth and high finance."

"But is there still going to be a railroad across that desert?"

"With the duchess dead, there is nothing to stop the railroad. But Ah will not be a part of it. And neither will Dudley Jacobson. Ah thought you might have heard."

"I've been chasing a varmint up in the high country these past weeks."

"Dudley's castle burned down—right to the ground. That madwoman set the fire, Ah would most certainly bet. Poor Jacobson. He died in the fire. Those Mexicans who were living there fled, and there's nothing left now but rubble."

"And rattlers."

"Ah fear so, sah."

They finished their drink and their smoke, shook hands, and bid each other goodbye. The train the colonel had to catch would leave in less than an hour. Longarm said one last goodbye in the lobby to Jennifer and Paul Martinez, then watched them hail a cab and ride off to the station.

He went back to the bar for another glass of Maryland rye. As he sipped it, he thought of the desert duchess, and imagined he could still hear that shuddering organ of hers resounding through the halls and rooms—and, later, the screams of that other poor, demented creature.

It had all been a mad dream—fueled by greed and doomed from the start. It was some comfort that Jennifer and the colonel, at least, had managed to survive it. He decided he would have another glass of Maryland rye and drink to them both.

Watch for

LONGARM ON THE PAINTED DESERT

sixty-ninth novel in the bold
LONGARM series from Jove

coming in September!

6

continued...

Bitter Sweet
The poignant tale of high school sweethearts reunited...

"A journey of self-discovery and reawakening."
—*Booklist*

The Endearment
A woman's love is threatened by the secrets of her past...

"A tender, sensual story."
—Lisa Gregory, author of *Before the Dawn*

Morning Glory
Two misfit hearts find unexpected tenderness in a Southern town...

"A superb book...it leaves the reader breathless."
—*New York Daily News*

Spring Fancy
A bride-to-be falls in love—with another man...

"You will never forget the incredible beauty of LaVyrle's gifted pen."
—*Affaire de Coeur*

The Hellion
The sparks fly when a lady tries to tame a hellraiser...

"A truly special story...superb!"　　—*Chicago Sun-Times*

Vows
The unforgettable story of two willful lovers—and one special promise...

"LaVyrle Spencer is magic!"
—*Affaire de Coeur*

The Gamble
Taking a chance on love is the only way to win it...

"A grand new bestseller!" —*Good Housekeeping*

A Heart Speaks
Two of her favorite novels—*A Promise to Cherish* and *Forsaking All Others*—together in one volume.

Years
Across the Western plains, only the strongest survived...

"Splendid!" —*Publishers Weekly*

Separate Beds
First came the baby, then came marriage. And then came love...

"A superb story." —*Los Angeles Times*

Twice Loved
A woman's missing husband returns—after she's remarried...

"A beautiful love story...emotional."
—*Rocky Mountain News*

Hummingbird
The novel that launched LaVyrle Spencer's stunning career...

"Will leave you breathless." —*Affaire de Coeur*

LaVyrle Spencer

Hummingbird

JOVE BOOKS, NEW YORK

HUMMINGBIRD

A Jove Book / published by arrangement with
the author

PRINTING HISTORY
Jove edition / May 1983

The Putnam Berkley World Wide Web site address is
http://www.berkley.com/berkley

ISBN: 0-515-09160-X

A JOVE BOOK®
Jove Books are published by The Berkley Publishing Group,
200 Madison Avenue, New York, New York 10016.
JOVE and the "J" design
are trademarks belonging to Jove Publications, Inc.

PRINTED IN THE UNITED STATES OF AMERICA

45   44   43   42   41   40   39   38   37

With love to Mom and Pat

And thanks to Janis Ian,
whose poignant love song
"Jesse" inspired me
to write this story

Chapter 1

———

WHEN THE 9:50 pulled into Stuart's Junction, it always attracted a crowd, for the train was still a novelty which the whole town anticipated daily. Barefoot children squatted like quail in the sand reed and needlegrass just outside town till the loud, gaseous monstrosity flushed them up and raced them the last quarter-mile toward the gabled depot. Ernie Turner, the town drunk, came each day to meet it, too. Belching and weaving his way out of the saloon, he would settle on a bench by the depot porch and sleep it off till the afternoon train sent him back for his evening round. Down at the smithy, Spud Swedeen laid down his maul, let loose of his bellows, and came to stand in the gaping door with black arms crossed upon blacker apron. And when the ringing of Spud's iron ceased, all the ears of Stuart's Junction, Colorado, perked up. Then along the short expanse of Front Street shopkeepers stepped from their doorways onto the weather-bleached planks of the boardwalk.

That early June morning in 1879 was no different. When Spud stopped his clanging, the barber chair emptied, bank clerks left their cages, and scales in the assay office swung empty while everybody stepped outside to face northeast and watch for the arrival of the 9:50.

But the 9:50 didn't come.

Before long, fingers nervously toyed with watch fobs; timepieces were pulled out, opened, and snapped shut before dubious glances were exchanged. Murmurs of speculation were eventually replaced by restlessness as one by one the townsfolk returned to their shops to peer out occasionally through their windows and wonder at the train's delay.

Time crawled while every ear was cocked for the moan of that whistle, which didn't come and didn't come. An hour, and the stillness over Stuart's Junction became a hush of reverence, as if someone had died, but nobody knew who.

At 11:06 heads lifted, one by one. The first, then the second merchant stepped to his doorsill once again as the livening summer wind lifted the incoming steam whistle on its heated breath.

"That's her! But she's comin' in too fast!"

"If that's Tuck Holloway drivin' her, he's settin' to put 'er right through the depot! Stand back—she might jump the rails!"

The cowcatcher came on in a blur of speed while steam and dust wafted away behind it, and a red plaid arm flailed from the open window of the cab. It was Tuck Holloway, all right, whose words were lost in the slamming of iron and the hiss of steam as the engine overshot the depot by a hundred yards— still miraculously on both tracks. But Tuck's hoarse voice could not be heard above the babbling crowd who'd surged toward the depot. Then a single gunshot made every head turn and every jaw stop as Max Smith, the newly appointed station agent, stood with a pistol still smoking in his hand.

"Where's Doc Dougherty?" Tuck bellowed into the lull. "Better get him fast 'cause the train got held up about twenty miles north of here and we got two injured men aboard. One of 'em's bad shot, for sure."

"Who are they?" Max asked.

"Didn't stop to ask for names. Both of 'em's strangers to me. The one tried to rob my train and the other one saved it. Got hisself shot while he was doin' it, though. I need a couple men to tote 'em off."

Within minutes, two limp bodies were borne from the depths of the train, down its steps, into the waiting arms of bank clerk, hostler, assayer, and blacksmith.

"Someone get a wagon!"

Through the crowd came a buckboard, and onto it the motionless bodies were placed, while from around the saloon corner Doctor Cleveland Dougherty came panting and snorting, his black bag whacking his overweight calves as he ran. A moment later he knelt beside the first stranger, whose face was chalky and unnaturally pacified.

"He's alive," Doc pronounced. "Just barely." The second man was likewise checked. "Can't tell about this one. Get 'em to my place quick, and Spud, you make damn sure you miss every rock and pothole on the street between here and there!"

All who came to town that day lingered. The saloon did a roadhouse business. Down at the livery, Gem Perkins ran out of stalls. The floor beneath the cuspidors in the hotel lobby was well stained long before midafternoon, while underneath the beech trees in Doc's front yard townspeople sat with their eyes trained on his door, waiting now as they'd earlier waited for the arrival of the 9:50. Waiting to hear the fate of the two who'd ridden it in on their backs.

Miss Abigail McKenzie heaved a sigh that lifted her breasts beneath the pleated bodice of her proper Victorian blouse. She ran one small, efficient finger around the inside of the lace-edged choker collar to free it from her sticky skin. She made a quarter-turn to the left, blue eyes glancing askance into the mirror, and placed the back side of one hand beneath her jaw— just so—lifting the skin there to test it for tautness.

Yes, the skin was still firm, still young, she assured herself soberly.

Then she quickly slipped the oversized filigreed hatpin from the crown of her daisy-trimmed hat, placed the hat carefully upon her sternly backswept brown hair, rammed the pin home, and picked up her pristine white gloves from the seat of the huge umbrella stand—a thronelike affair with a mirror on its backrest and umbrellas and canes threaded through holes in its outsized arms.

She considered her gloves a moment, looked out front through the screen door at the shimmering heat ripples radiating skyward, laid the gloves down, hesitated, then resolutely picked them up again, dutifully drawing them over her slim hands. The heat is no excuse to go over town improperly dressed, she scolded herself.

She walked to the rear of her house, rechecking each shade

on each south window, assuring herself they were all drawn low against the harsh sun. She glanced in a full circle around her kitchen, but nothing needed straightening, putting away, or taking out. Her house was kept as fastidiously as was her clothing. Indeed, everything in Miss Abigail McKenzie's life was always as orderly and precise and correct as it could possibly be.

She sighed again, crossed the straight shot from kitchen to dining room to front parlor, and stepped onto the porch. But abruptly she reentered, checking the doorstop fussily, in the way of those who manufacture worry because their lives contain too little of the genuine article.

"No sense risking your lovely oval window," she said aloud to the door. That window was her pride and joy. Satisfied that the door was secure, out she went, closing the screen as gently as if it had feelings. She crossed the porch, walked down the path, and nodded hello to her well-tended roses beside the pickets.

She walked erectly, chin parallel to the earth, as a lady of propriety ought. Let it never be said that Miss Abigail stooped, slouched, or slogged when she walked over town. Oh, never! Her carriage was utterly proper at all times. Her sensible shoes scarcely peeked from beneath her skirts, for she never hurried—rushing was most undignified!

She had things on her mind, Miss Abigail did, which didn't rest lightly there. Her errand was not one she relished. But one would never guess from perusing her as she strode down Front Street that there could be the slightest thing amiss with Miss Abigail McKenzie, if indeed one ever could.

Coming along past the houses and yards, her eye was caught by the unusual scene up ahead. Doc Dougherty's lawn was crowded with people, while across the street the benches of the boardwalk were hidden behind solid skirts and men sat on its high ledge while children scuffled in the dirt and horses waited at the hitching rails.

One could always rely upon Miss Abigail to keep her nose out of other people's business. Seeing the crowd, she swung left, walked the short block over to Main, and finished her trek over town along its all but deserted length. Thus Miss Abigail avoided what was probably some sordid spectacle at Doc Dougherty's. That kind of thing attracted riffraff, and she was not about to be one of their number!

Miss Abigail thought it truly lamentable to have to do what she was about to do. Oh, not that there was anything wrong with Louis Culpepper's establishment. He ran a neat and orderly eatery—she'd give him that. But waiting tables was truly a last resort—oh, truly a last! It was not at all the kind of thing she'd choose to do, had she the choice. But Miss Abigail had no choice. It was either Louis Culpepper's place or starve. And Abigail McKenzie was too ornery to starve.

Sensible black squat heels aclicking, she entered beneath the sign hailing, THE CRITERION—FINE FOOD AND DRINKS, LOUIS CULPEPPER, PROP. As she carefully closed the door, she ran a hand over her blouse front, making sure it was tightly tucked into her skirtband, then, turning, she again sighed. But the place looked deserted. There was a faint odor of yesterday's cabbage adrift in the air, but nothing resembling the aroma of meats stewing for the supper clientele, who wouldn't be long in coming. Why, one would have thought Louis to be better organized than this!

"Hello?" she called, cocking her head, listening.

From somewhere in the rear came a tiny, tinny sound. She walked toward the kitchen to find the alley door open and a hot breeze buffeting the saucepans that hung above the wood range. The place *was* abandoned.

"Well, I declare!" Miss Abigail exclaimed to no one at all. Then, glancing in a circle, repeated, "Well, I *do* declare!"

It had taken her some weeks to finally decide she must speak to Louis. To find his restaurant empty was most disconcerting. Wiping an errant bead of perspiration from her forehead with a single finger of her pristine glove, Miss Abigail chafed at this unexpected turn of events. Inspecting the fingertip, she found it dampened by her own sweat and knew she could not put herself through this a second time. She must find Louis now, today!

Adjusting her already well placed hat, she again took to Main Street, then over one block to Front, on which both she and Doc lived, some two blocks apart. Rounding the corner, she found herself part of the throng that filled Doc Dougherty's yard and the surrounding area. Doc himself was standing under his beech trees, sleeves rolled up, speaking loudly so everyone could hear.

". . . lost a lot of blood and I had to operate to clean up the hole and shut it up. It's too early to tell if he'll make it yet. But you all know it's my duty to do whatever I can to keep him alive, no matter what he's done."

A distracted murmur passed among the townspeople while Miss Abigail glanced around hopefully, looking for Louis Culpepper. Spying a towheaded youth who lived next door to her, she whispered, "Good day, Robert."

"Howdy, Miss Abigail."

"Have you seen Mr. Culpepper, Robert?"

But the boy's neck was stretched and his ears tuned to Doc again as he grunted, "Un-uh."

"Who is Doctor Dougherty talking about?"

"Don't rightly know. Some strangers got themselves shot on the train."

Relieved that it was none of the town's own, Miss Abigail was nonetheless forced to give up her cause as fruitless until the crowd dispersed, so turned her attention to the doctor.

"The other one's not in as bad of a shape, but he'll be out of commission for a few days. Between the two of 'em, I'll have my hands full. You know Gertie's gone off to her cousin's wedding in Fairplay and I'm caught shorthanded here. There's plenty of you'll be hollering for me, and I just plain can't be in more than one place at a time. So if there's anybody that'd volunteer to give me a hand looking after these two, well, I'd be obliged."

From somewhere in the crowd a woman's voice spoke what many were thinking. "I'd like to know why we should feel obliged to take care of some outlaw tried his hardest to do us dirt! Robbing our train that way and shooting that innocent young man in there. Why, what if it'd been Tuck he shot?"

Doc raised his hands to quiet the swell of agreement.

"Now, hold on! I got two men in here, and granted, the one done wrong and the other done right, but they're both in need of help. Would you people have me tend the one that's hurt less and turn out the one that's nearly dead?"

Some of them had the grace to drop their eyes, but still they demurred.

Doc continued while he had 'em feeling guilty. "Well, a man can do just so much alone, and that's all he can do. I need help and I'm leaving it up to you to find it for me. The problem isn't just mine—it's all of ours. Now, we all wanted the Rocky Mountain Railroad to put their spur line through here, didn't we? And sure enough we got it! 'Course, we only banked on it hauling our quartz and copper and silver out of here and bringing our conveniences in from the East. But now that we get a little trouble hauled in too, we're not so all-fired anxious to stand up and pay the price, are we?

Still nobody volunteered.

What Doc said was undeniably true. The railroad was an asset from which they all benefited. Having a spur line run into a hidden mountain town like Stuart's Junction opened it up to both East and West, bringing the town commerce, transportation, and a stable future that it had lacked before the R.M.R. laid tracks up here.

The citizens chose to forget all that now, though, leaving Doc Dougherty to plead his case, and leaving Miss Abigail somehow inexplicably angry at their heartlessness.

"I could pay anyone that took on to help me—the same as I pay Gertie when she's here," Doc offered hopefully.

Miss Abigail glanced around. Her mouth puckered.

"Hell, Doc," someone hollered, "Gertie's the only nurse this town's ever saw or prob'ly ever will. You ain't gonna find nobody to take her place nohow."

"Well, maybe not anybody as qualified as Gertie, but anybody that's willing is qualified enough to suit me. Now what do you say?"

The sweat broke out upon Miss Abigail's upper lip. What she was considering was too sudden, too unprecedented, yet she had no time for rumination. And the smug attitudes surrounding her made her unutterably angry! The thought of tending two injured men in the privacy of her own home seemed far, far preferable to carrying stew and soup to the lot of them. Furthermore, she was almost as skilled as Gertie Burtson. Her pulse thrummed a little behind her proper, tight collar, but her chin was high as ever as she stepped forward, squelching her misgivings, putting those around her in their proper place.

"I believe, Doctor Dougherty, that I would qualify," Miss Abigail stated in her ladylike way. But since a lady does not shout, Doc didn't quite hear her. Nobody believed what they were seeing as Miss Abigail raised a meticulous white glove.

"Miss Abigail, is that you?" he called; somehow the crowd had silenced.

"Yes, Doctor Dougherty, it is. I should like very much to volunteer."

Before he could check his reaction, Doc Dougherty raised
his brows, ran a grizzled hand over his balding head, and
blurted out, "Well, I'll be damned!"

Excusing herself, Miss Abigail made her way to Doc's side.
She parted the crowd almost as Moses parted the Red Sea, still
with that level chin and that all-fired dignity she always
maintained. As she passed, men actually reached as if to doff
hats they weren't wearing.

"G'day, Miss Abigail."

"How do, Miss Abigail."

"Howdy, Miss Abigail."

The ladies greeted her with silent, smiling nods, most of
them awed by her cool, flowing presence as she glided toward
Doc in her customary, pure-bred way while they fanned
themselves and raised their arms to let the breeze at their wet
armpits. Moving through their midst, Miss Abigail somehow
managed to make them all feel gross and lardy and—worse—
small, for the help they'd stubbornly refused.

"Come inside, Miss Abigail," Doc said, then raised his
voice to the crowd. "You might as well go home now. I'll leave
word up at the station with Max if there's any change." Then,
solicitously taking Miss Abigail's elbow, he led her inside.

His widower's house was a mishmash of flotsam, collected
and never discarded. The big front room looked like a willful
child had messed it up in retaliation for being spanked, except
that the strewn articles obviously were an adult's. Doc
Dougherty removed a stack of journals and newspapers from
an armchair, kicked aside a pair of forlorn house slippers, and
said, "Sit down, Miss Abigail, sit down."

"Thank you," she replied, sitting in the cleared spot as if it
were the dais in a throneroom.

While she gave the impression that none of the debris around
her infiltrated her superb hauteur, Miss Abigail noticed all
right. Old Doc Dougherty meant well enough, but since his
Emma died the place had become slovenly. Doc kept absurd
hours, running to anyone who needed him at any hour of the
day or night, but leaving himself little time for such refine-
ments as housecleaning. Gertie Burtson was hired as his nurse,
not as his housekeeper. That was all too evident by the looks of
the room.

Doc Dougherty sat down on the arm of an old lumpy
horsehair sofa, spread his old lumpy knees, and covered them

with his old lumpy hands. As his rump came into contact with the overstuffed arm, Miss Abigail saw a puff of dust emanate from the horsehair and overcast the air around him. He studied the floor a minute before speaking.

"Miss Abigail, I appreciate your offer." He didn't know exactly how to say this. "But you know, Miss Abigail, I hardly thought you'd be the one to step forward and volunteer. This is probably a job somebody else is better suited for."

Irritation pricked her. Crisply, she asked, "Are you refusing my help, Doctor Dougherty?"

"I . . . I'd hate to say I'm refusing. I'm asking you to consider what you're getting into."

"I believe I have considered it. As a result, I've offered my services. If there is some inexplicable reason why I shan't do, then we are both wasting our time." When Miss Abigail was piqued, her voice became curt and she tended to get eloquently wordy. She rose, looking down her nose as she tugged her gloves more securely on her hands.

He moved quickly to press her back into her chair, his dust cloud swirling with him. She looked up at him from under her hat brim, inwardly gratified that he'd seen her pique. Fine time for him to get choosy!

"Hold on now, don't get yourself all in a huff."

"In a huff, Doctor Dougherty? I hardly would describe myself as being in a huff." She arched one brow and tipped her head.

Doc Dougherty stood above her, smiling, peering at her upturned face under its crisp bonnet of daisies. "No, Miss Abigail, I doubt you've ever been in a huff in your life. What I'm trying to make you see is that you might be if I agree to let you nurse those two."

"Pray tell why, Doctor?"

"Well, the truth is . . . because you're a . . . a maiden lady."

The phrase echoed cruelly through Miss Abigail McKenzie's thirty-three-year-old head, and within her fast-tripping, lonely heart.

"A maiden lady?" she repeated, mouth puckered a little tighter.

"Yes, Miss Abigail."

"And what possible bearing does my being a . . . a

maiden lady—as you so kindly put it—have upon my being capable of helping you?"

"You must understand that I hoped for a married woman to volunteer."

"Why?" she asked.

Doc Dougherty turned his back and walked away, searching for a delicate way to phrase it. He cleared his throat. "You'd be exposed to parts of these men that you'd probably rather not be and asked to perform duties that would be—to say the least—unpalatable to a lady of your—" But his words faltered. He found himself unwilling to embarrass her further.

Miss Abigail finished for him. "Tender sensibilities, Doctor?" Then with a little false laugh asked, "Were you about to expound upon my being a lady of tender sensibilities?"

"Yes, you might put it that way." He turned once again to face her.

"Are you forgetting, Doctor, about the years I cared for my father while he was ill?"

"No, Miss Abigail, I'm not. But he was your father, not some gunshot stranger."

"Posh, Mister Dougherty," she said, giving the impression she'd spit out the words when they'd come out with calculated control, along with the word *Mister* instead of *Doctor*. "Give me one good reason why I should not care for these two gentlemen."

He flung his hands out in frustration. "Gentlemen! How do you know they're gentlemen? And what if they're not? What'll you do when I'm fourteen miles out in the country and you're wishing I weren't? One of those *gentlemen* just tried to rob a train and I'm willing to treat him, but that doesn't mean I'll trust him. Suppose he tries to overpower you and escape?"

"A moment ago you advised me not to get into a huff. May I now advise you the same, Doctor? You've been shouting."

"I'm sorry, Miss Abigail. I guess I was. But it's my responsibility to make you see the risk involved."

"You've done your duty then, Doctor Dougherty. But since I see your plea for help did not raise a plethora of willing volunteers, I hardly see that you have a choice but to accept my offer."

Doc shook his head at the threadbare carpet, wondering what her father would have said. Abbie had always been the apple of the old man's eye.

Miss Abigail looked up at him, so prim and erect from her spot on the forlorn old armchair, her mind made up.

"I have a strong stomach, a hand full of common sense, and a nearly empty bank account, Doctor," she stated. "And you have two wounded men who need looking after. I suspect that neither of them is healthy enough right now to either harm me or escape from me, so shall we get on with it?"

She knew she had him with that reference to her bank account.

"You're sure one smooth talker, Miss Abigail, and I'm up a crick, I'll grant you that. But I can't pay you much, you know. Thirty dollars for the week is about it. It's as much as I pay Gertie."

"Thirty dollars will do nicely . . . oh, and one thing more," she added, easing to the edge of her chair.

"Yes?"

"What do you propose to do with them when your patients arrive tomorrow morning?"

Miss Abigail's eyes had not scanned the room; they didn't have to for Doc to know that his place wasn't exactly her idea of a suitable hospital. He had no delusions regarding the condition of his house. What could be seen from their present vantage point was a sorry mess at best. They both knew what she'd find if she were to peruse the upstairs or—worse—the kitchen. They both knew, too, that she had a penchant for cleanliness. And so when Doc finally finished eyeballing the room, he was totally aware of the place's shortcomings.

"I don't suppose we could put 'em upstairs?" he asked fruitlessly.

"I don't suppose that would be the most convenient place. I propose that we remove them to my house as soon as you think that would be possible. It would be infinitely easier for me to care for them were I to have my own kitchen at my disposal."

"You're right," Doc agreed, and abruptly Miss Abigail got to her feet.

"Now, may I see our patients?"

"Of course. One's on the surgery table and the other on the sofa in the waiting room, but they're both out cold for the time being. Tomorrow'll be time enough for you to take charge of them."

They walked through an archway into Doc Dougherty's waiting room, which was only slightly tidier than the parlor.

On a sagging sofa beneath a triple window a man lay unmoving. He wore a city suit, its vest and jacket unbuttoned. One of his feet, brown-stockinged, stuck out from a pant leg while the other sported a bandage covering the forefoot but leaving the heel bare where it rested on a pillow. His face, in repose, was pleasant. His hair was nondescript brown and fell away from his forehead in boyish waves. His ears were flat and his nails clean. And that was good enough for Miss Abigail.

"This is the man who robbed the train?" she asked.

"No. The other one robbed the train. This one—Melcher's his name—apparently interrupted the proceedings. The way Tuck tells it, Melcher here took a stray bullet from that one's gun." Doc thumbed over his shoulder in the direction of the surgery. "Must've been some kind of scuffle involving a bunch of passengers because by the time Tuck got the train stopped and got back there to see what was going on, everybody was telling the story a different way and these two were lying there bleeding. One of the shots took Melcher's big toe clean off his right foot."

"His big toe!" she exclaimed, pressing her fingers to her lips to hide the smile.

"Could've been worse if the shot had been higher. On the other hand, it could've been little or nothing if he'd had a sensible pair of boots on instead o' them flimsy city shoes he was wearing."

Miss Abigail looked to where Doc Dougherty pointed, and there on the floor sat a single stylish brown shoe of fine, soft leather.

"Had to cut the other one off him," Doc informed her. "Wasn't any good anyway, with the end shot off like it was."

Miss Abigail had to smile in spite of herself. First at Doc's keeping the single shoe, which was no good without its mate, and secondly at the absurdity of the town's first hero saving the day by getting his big toe shot off!

"Is something funny, Miss Abigail?" She sobered at once, chagrined at being caught in a state of levity at this unfortunate man's expense.

"No . . . no, forgive me, Doctor. Tell me, is the loss of a toe a serious injury? I mean, is his life in danger?"

"No, hardly. The toe came off real clean, and there was no lead shavings or powder left on him once the bullet went through that shoe. He was in awful shock and lost some blood, but I put him to sleep and stitched him up and he'll be good as new in no time. When he wakes up, that toe is gonna throb like a bitch in heat, though . . ." Doc suddenly seemed to realize to whom he was talking. "Oh . . . forgive me, Miss Abigail. I forgot myself."

Miss Abigail colored deeply, stammering, "I . . . oh, I shall certainly sympathize with poor Mr. Melcher."

"Yes . . . well . . ." Doctor Dougherty cleared his throat. "Mr. Melcher will undoubtedly find himself walking with a limp from now on, but that should be the worst of it. We'll keep the foot propped up, keep it bandaged for a couple of days, and I'll give you some salve for it. But mostly time and air will have to heal the stitches. You're right—Mr. Melcher will need good old-fashioned sympathy most of all."

"So much for the damage done here. And what about the other?" Miss Abigail asked, relieved that her composure was returning.

Turning toward the surgery door, the doctor walked a step or two toward it. "The other bullet, I fear, did far more damage. This scoundrel will undoubtedly rue the day he set foot on that R.M.R. train . . . if he lives long enough."

They came to the doorway and Miss Abigail preceded him into its cream-colored depths. Here at last was cleanliness, although she devoted not even the quickest glance to it. Her eyes were drawn to the rectangular table where a sheet shrouded an inert figure. The table faced the doorway, so all that was visible was the sole of a left foot—a very long left foot, thought Miss Abigail—and the rise of sheet covering an updrawn right knee and leg.

"This one is lucky to be alive. He lost plenty of blood from the gunshot and more when I had to clean the wound out. He'd have been better off if the bullet had stayed in him. As it was, it came out the other side and blew a hole in him twenty times bigger than the one it made going in. Left a pretty big mess on its way through, too."

"Will he die?" Miss Abigail whispered, staring at that long foot that made her insides jitter. She'd never seen a man's bare foot before, other than her father's.

"No need to whisper. He's dead to the world and he's going to stay that way for a while, or I miss my guess. But as to whether or not the poor son of a b— the poor fool will die, that I can't say yet. Looked to be healthy as a horse before this happened to him." Doc Dougherty had walked farther than Miss Abigail into the room and now stood beside the man on the surgery table. "Come and have a look at him."

Miss Abigail experienced a sudden stab of reluctance but ventured far enough to see bare shoulders with the sheet slicing them at armpit level. Above was a chest shadowed with dark, curled hair, broad, tanned shoulders, and the bottom of a dark-skinned face that sported an evil-looking moustache. She couldn't see any of the features above the moustache from this angle, only the nostrils, which were shaped like half hearts, and the lower lip, which suddenly twitched as she looked at it. His chin wore only a trace of the day's growth of whiskers, and she suddenly found herself thinking that for a train robber he certainly kept himself up, if the clean foot and the recent shave were any indication.

The sheet covered him from biceps to ankle, giving no indication of where he was injured or how seriously. From here he looked as if he might have stretched out for a nap, one knee slung up haphazardly as he serenely dozed.

"He was shot in the groin," Doc said, and Miss Abigail suddenly blanched and felt her stomach go weightless.

"In . . . in the—" she stammered, then halted.

"Not quite . . . but very close. Do you still want the job?"

She didn't know. Frantically she thought of everyone in town hearing the reason she had changed her mind. She stood there considering a man coming to such an end. Whether she still wanted to care for him or not, she felt somehow sorry for the unconscious fellow.

"A train robber might expect to come to a bad end, yet nobody should come to this."

"No, Miss Abigail. It's not a pretty sight, but it could've been worse. A few inches difference and he could've lost . . . well, he could have been dead."

Miss Abigail blushed again but nevertheless looked resolutely at Doc Dougherty. Nobody else had come forward but herself. Even a hapless train robber deserved human consideration.

"I quite understand, Doctor, what the man's dilemma might have been, but don't you agree that even a robber deserves our sympathies, in his present state?"

"My sympathies he's got, Miss Abigail, and plenty of them.

He'll get every bit of care I can give him, but I got to warn you, I'm no miracle worker. If he lives it'll be just that—a dad-blamed miracle."

"What am I to do for him, Doctor?" she asked, suddenly deciding that a man this age—he looked to be thirty-five or so—was much too young to die.

"You're sure about this? Very sure?"

"Just tell me what to do." The look in her eyes, just like years ago when she'd taken on the care of her father, told Doc Dougherty she meant business.

"You'll keep the knee raised, keep the thigh up, so the air can get at the underside as well as the top. I managed to staunch the flow of blood, but if it starts up again, you'll have to apply alum to try to stop it. Keep the wound clean—I'll tell you what to disinfect it with. Watch for any putrefaction and if you see any, come runnin' like a cat with her tail on fire the minute you see any sign of it. We'll have to try to keep his fever down. For the pain there's not much we can do. Keep him still. Try to get him to eat. Do you think you can handle that, Miss Abigail?"

"Everything but setting my tail on fire," she replied dryly, surprising Doc with her wit. He smiled.

"Good. You go home now and get a good night's rest because it'll probably be your last for a while. I'm expecting a run on the place in the morning and I'd like to have these two out of here before it starts. I 'spect everyone with so much as an ingrown hair will be in here hoping for a glimpse of either a genuine robber or a genuine hero."

"Ah well, I expect I'm the lucky one then, to have seen them both at close range." A brief smile tugged at the corner of Miss Abigail's mouth.

"I 'spect you are at that. How can I thank you?"

"I'll see you in the morning. Everything shall be in order for their arrival."

"I'm sure it will be, Miss Abigail. Knowing you, I'm sure it will be."

She turned to leave, but at the door turned back.

"What . . . what is his name, the robber's?"

"We don't know. Men in his profession don't carry calling cards like Mr. Melcher did."

"Oh . . . oh, of course not," she replied, then hesitated a moment longer to add, "but it would be a shame if he should die and we should not know whom to inform. He must have someone somewhere.''

Doc Dougherty had scarcely had time to think of that yet.

"Only a woman with a heart would think of that at a time like this.''

"Nonsense," Miss Abigail said briskly, then turned to leave.

But of course he was right, for her heart was doing monkeyshines as she walked home, remembering a bare long foot; a dark, furred chest; and the prospect of caring for a wound near the man's—

But Miss Abigail McKenzie not only avoided speaking such a word. She could not even think it!

Chapter 2

———◆———

THE SUN WAS hotter than ever the following day as Doc approached the loiterers on the sagging veranda of Mitch Field's feedstore. They congregated there to drape on the feed sacks, spit and chew, and never give poor Mitch so much as a lick of business.

"All right, which of you lazy no-goods is gonna give me a hand," Doc challenged.

They even laughed lazily, then squinted at the sun, gauging the discomfort of exerting themselves against the chance of getting a gander at them two up at Doc's house. Old Bones Binley scratched his grizzled jaw with the dull edge of a whittling knife and drawled, "Reckon you can count me in, Doc."

It was Doc's turn to laugh. Bones had a yen for Miss Abigail and the whole town knew it. Bones looked just like his name, but along with some help from Mitch and Seth Carter, the transfer of patients was handled without mishap.

Miss Abigail was waiting at her front door and directed Doc and Mitch to place David Melcher in the southeast bedroom upstairs and the other man in the downstairs bedroom, since it was probably inadvisable to carry him up the steps.

The train robber was too long for the mattress, and his feet

17

hung beyond the footrail, so the sheet covered him only up to the waist. Bones and Seth watched Miss Abigail's face as she came around the doorway and saw that bare, hairy chest lying there, but she barely gave it a glance before turning to the pair and dismissing them coolly and unquestionably. "Thank you, gentlemen. I'm sure you have pressing business down at the feedstore."

"Why, uh, yes . . . yes we do, Mizz Abigail." Bones grinned while Seth elbowed him in the ribs to get him moving.

Outside, Seth said, "It might be ninety-nine degrees everywhere else, but a body could freeze to death anywhere within fifteen feet o' Miss Abigail McKenzie."

"Ain't she somethin', though?" Bones gulped, his Adam's apple protruding.

"Whole town knows she can twist you around her finger, but that sugary voice of hers don't fool me none. Underneath that sugar is mostly vinegar!"

"You really think so, Seth?"

"Why, sheee-oot, I know so. Why, lookit how she just excused us, like we was clutterin' up her bedroom or somethin'."

"Yeah, but she took in that there train robber, didn't she?"

"Did it for the money, the way I heard tell. It's prob'ly the only way she could get a man in her bed. And that one that's in it now will be sorry he didn't die when he comes to and finds hisself bein' nursed by the likes of her."

There were those in town, like Seth, who considered Miss Abigail just a touch above herself. Granted, she was always soft-spoken, but she had that way, just the same, of elevating herself and acting lofty.

When Doc had settled the patients and told her to send Rob Nelson if she needed anything, he promised to check in again that evening, then left with Mitch in tow.

She thought Mr. Melcher was asleep when she crept to the door of his room, for his arm lay over his forehead and his eyes were closed. Though his beard had grown overnight, he had a very nice mouth. It reminded her of Grandfather McKenzie's mouth, which had always smiled readily. Mr. Melcher looked to be perhaps in his late twenties—it was hard to tell with his eyes closed. Glancing around, she spied his suitcase under the Phyfe library table near the window and tiptoed across to open it and find his nightshirt. When she turned, she found that Mr. Melcher had been watching her.

"Ah, you're awake," she said gaily, disconcerted at being caught searching through his personal belongings.

"Yes. You must be Miss McKenzie. Doc Dougherty said you'd volunteered. It was very good of you."

"Not really. I live alone and have the time that Doctor Dougherty doesn't." She looked at his foot then, asking, "How does it feel this morning?"

"It's throbbing some," he answered honestly, and she immediately colored and fussed with the nightshirt.

"Yes, well . . . we'll see if we can't relieve it somewhat. But first I believe we'd best get you out of your suit. It looks as if it could stand a flour bath." The brown wool worsted was indeed wrinkled but Miss Abigail had grave misgivings about how to gracefully get him out of it.

"A flour bath?"

"Yes, a dredging in clean flour to absorb the soil and freshen it. I'll take care of it for you."

Although he moved his arm off his forehead and smiled, he was smitten with discomfort at the thought of undressing before a lady.

"Are you able to sit up, Mr. Melcher?"

"I don't know. I think so." He raised his head but grunted, so she crossed the room quickly and touched his lapel, saying, "Save your energy for now. I shall be right back." She returned shortly, bearing pitcher and bowl, towel and wash-cloth, and a bar of soap balanced across a glass of bubbling water. When she had set things down, she stood beside him, saying, "Now, let's get your jacket off."

The whole thing was done so slickly that David Melcher later wondered how she'd accomplished it. She managed to remove his jacket, vest, and shirt and wash his upper half with a minimum of embarrassment to either of them. She held the bowl while he rinsed his mouth with the soda water, then she helped him don his nightshirt before removing his trousers from beneath it. All the while she chatted, putting them both at ease. She said she would rub flour into his suit jacket and let it sit for a few hours, and by the time she hung it on the line and beat the flour from it with her rug-beater, it would be as fresh as a daisy. He'd never heard of such a thing! Furthermore, he wasn't used to a woman fussing over him this way. Her voice flowed sweetly while she attended him, easing him through what would otherwise have been a sticky situation had she been less talkative or less efficient.

"It seems you have become something of a local hero, Mr. Melcher," she noted, giving him only the beginnings of a smile.

"I don't feel much like a hero. I feel like a fool, ending up stretched out here with a toe shot off."

"The townspeople have a great interest in our new railroad and wouldn't like to see it jeopardized in any way. You've saved it from its first serious mishap. That's nothing to feel foolish about. It is also something which the town won't forget soon, Mr. Melcher."

"My name is David." But when he would have caught her eye she averted hers.

"Well, I'm pleased to meet you, though I regret the circumstances, on your behalf. From where do you hail, Mr. Melcher?"

When she used his surname he felt put in his place and colored slightly. "I'm from back East." He watched her precise movements and suddenly asked, "Are you a nurse, Miss Abigail?"

"No, sir, I'm not."

"Well, you should be. You're very efficient and gentle."

At last she beamed. "Why, thank you, Mr. Melcher. I take that as one of the nicest things you could say, under the circumstances. Are you hungry?"

"Yes, I don't remember when I ate last."

"You've been through an ordeal, I'm sure, that you'll be long in forgetting. Perhaps the right food will make your stay here seem shorter and your bad memories disappear the faster."

Her speech was as refined as her manners, he thought, watching her move about the room gathering his discarded clothing, stacking the toilet articles to carry away. He felt secure and cared for as she saw to his needs, and he wondered if this was how it felt to be a husband.

"I'll see to your suit after I prepare your breakfast. Oh! I forgot to comb your hair." She had stopped halfway out the door.

"I can do that myself."

"Have you a comb?"

"Not that I can reach."

"Then take the one from my apron pocket."

She came back and raised her laden arms so he could get at the comb. His hesitation before reaching to take it told her things about him that a thousand words could not tell. David Melcher, she could see, was a gentleman. Everything about him pleased her, and she later found herself inexplicably buoyant and humming while she worked in the kitchen preparing his meal. Perhaps she even felt the slightest bit wifely as she delivered the tray of bacon, eggs, and coffee, and wished she could stay and visit. But she had yet another patient needing her attention.

At the bedroom doorway downstairs, she hesitated, gazing at the stranger on her bed. Just the fact that he was a criminal was disquieting, though he remained unconscious, unable to harm her in any way. His beard was coal black, as were his moustache and hair, but his skin, since last night, had taken on the color of tallow. Coming fully into the room, she studied him more closely. There was a sheen of sweat on his bare chest and arms, and she reached out tentatively to touch him, finding his body radiating an unhealthy inner heat.

Quickly she fetched a bowl of vinegar water and sponged his face, neck, arms, and chest, as far as his waist, where the sheet stopped, then left the cool compresses on his brow in an effort to bring down his fever. She knew she must check his wound, but at the thought her palms went damp. She held her breath and gingerly lifted a corner of the sheet. Flames shot through her body at the sight of his nakedness. Her years of caring for an incontinent father had done nothing to prepare her for this! With a shaky hand she lay the sheet at an angle across his stomach, his genitals, and left leg, then fetched two firm bolsters to boost up his right knee. She snipped away the gauze bindings, but the bandages stuck to his skin, so next she mixed vinegar water with saltpeter and applied the dripping compresses to loosen the cotton from his wounds. The shot had hit him very high on the inner thigh, which had been firm before the bullet did its dirty work. But now, when the bangage fell free, she saw that the wound had begun bleeding again. One look and she knew she had her work cut out if he wasn't to bleed to death.

Back in the kitchen she spooned alum into an iron frying pan, shaking it over the hot range until it smoked and

darkened. She sprinkled the burnt alum liberally onto a fresh
piece of gauze, but when she hurried back to the bedroom with
the poultice, she stood horrified, gaping at the blood of this
nameless train robber as it welled in the bullet hole then ran the
short distance into the shallow valley of his groin, where
coarse hair caught and held it.

How long she stood staring at the raw wound and the
collecting blood she did not know. But suddenly it was as if
someone had shot her instead of him. Her body jerked as if
from the recoil, and once again she was frantically bathing,
staunching, praying. In the hours which followed, she fought
against time as a mortal enemy. Realizing that he must soon
eat . . . or die . . . she beat a piece of steak with a mallet
and put it into salt water to steep into beef tea. But he kept
bleeding and she began to doubt that he'd live to drink
it. Remembering her Grandmother McKenzie saying they'd
packed arrow wounds with dried ergot, she next made a
poultice of the powdery rye fungus and applied it. Feeling the
man's dark, wide brow, she realized it had not cooled, so she
swabbed him with alcohol. But when she stopped sponging, he
immediately grew hot again. The fever, she realized, must be
fought from within rather than without. She scoured her mind
and found yet another possibility.

Wild gingerroot tea!

But when she brought the ginger tea back to him, he lay as
still as death, and the first spoonful dribbled from his lips,
rolled past his ear, and stained the pillowcase a weak brown.
She tried again to force another spoonful into his mouth,
succeeding only in making him cough.

"Drink it! Drink it!" she willed the unconscious man almost
in an angry whisper. But it was no use; he'd choke if she forced
the tea into his mouth this way.

She pressed her knuckles to her teeth, despairing, near tears.
Suddenly she had an inspiration and ran through her house like
a demented being, flew out the back door, and found Rob
Nelson playing in his backyard next door.

"Robert!" she bellowed, and Rob jumped to stand at
attention. Never in his life had he seen Miss Abigail look so
bedeviled or raise her voice that way.

"Yes, ma'am?" he gulped, wide-eyed.

Miss Abigail grabbed him by the shoulders so tight she like
to break his bones. "Robert, run fast up to the livery stable and

ask Mr. Perkins for a handful of straw. Clean straw, do you understand? And run like your tail's on fire!" Then she gave Rob a push that nearly put him on his nose.

"Yes, ma'am," the amazed boy called, scuttling away as fast as his legs would carry him.

It seemed to Miss Abigail that hours passed while she paced feverishly, waiting. When Rob returned, she grabbed the straw without so much as a thank you, ran into her house, and slammed the screen in the boy's face.

Leaning over the robber's dark face, she tipped up his chin and forced two fingers into his mouth. His tongue was ominously hot and dry. But the straw was too flimsy, she could see after several unsuccessful attempts to get it down his throat. Harried, she scoured her mind, wasting precious minutes until she found an answer. Cattails! She plucked one from a dried bouquet in the parlor, reamed the pith from its center with a knitting needle, and—hardening her resolve—lifted the dark chin again, pried open his mouth with her fingers, and rammed the cattail down his throat, half gagging herself at what she was doing to him.

But it worked! It was a small success, but it made her hopeful: the ginger tea went down smoothly. With not a thought for delicacy, Miss Abigail filled her mouth again and again, and shot the tea into him, but as she was removing the straw from his mouth, some reflex in him decided to work and he swallowed, clamping down unknowingly upon her two fingers. She yelped and straightened up in a pained, arching snap, pulling her fingers free to find the skin broken between the first and second knuckles of both. Immediately she stuck them in her mouth and sucked, only to find a trace of his saliva on them. An outlaw! she thought, and yanked a clean handkerchief from within her sleeve, fastidiously wiping her tongue and fingers dry. But staring at his unconscious face, she felt her own flood with heat and her heart thrum from something she did not understand.

Realizing it was near noon, she left the man to prepare David Melcher's tray. When she brought it to his doorway, Melcher's jaw dropped.

"Miss Abigail! What's happened to you?"

She looked down to find flecks of blood strewn across her breasts from beating the steak, maybe even some from the body of the man downstairs. Raising a hand to her hair, she found it scattered like wind-whipped grass. As her arm went up, a large wet ring of sweat came into view beneath the underarm of the trim blue blouse which had looked so impeccable this morning. Too, there were those two bloody tooth marks on her fingers, but those she hid in the folds of her skirt.

Gracious! she thought, I hadn't realized! I simply hadn't realized!

"Miss Abigail, are you all right?"

"I'm quite all right, really, Mr. Melcher. I've been trying to save a man's life, and believe me, at this point I think I'd be grateful to see him with enough strength to try to harm me."

Melcher's face went hard. "He's still alive, then?"

"Just barely."

It was all David Melcher could do to refrain from snapping, "Too bad!"

Miss Abigail sensed his disapproval, but saw how he made an effort to submerge his anger, which was altogether justifiable, considering the man downstairs had done Mr. Melcher out of a big toe. "Just don't overdo it. I don't think you're used to such hard work. I shouldn't want you becoming ill over the care of a common thief."

An undeniable warmth came at his words, and she replied, "Don't worry about me, Mr. Melcher. I am here to worry about you."

Which is just what she did when he'd finished eating. She brought his shaving gear and held the mirror for him while he performed the ritual. She studied him surreptitiously, the gentle mouth and straight nose, strong chin with no cleft, no dimples. But it was his eyes she liked best. They were pale brown and very boyish, especially when he smiled. He looked up and she dropped her eyes. But when he tended his chore again, swiveling his head this way and that, his jaw jutting forward and the cords of his neck standing out, it made the pulse beat low in her stomach. Without warning came the memory of the robber's sharper features, thicker neck and longer, darker face. Forbidding countenance, she thought, compared to the inviting face of David Melcher.

"The robber wears a moustache," she observed.

All the gentleness left David Melcher's face. "Typical!" he snapped.

"Is it?"

"It certainly is! The most infamous outlaws in history wore them!"

She lowered the mirror, rose, and twisted her hands together, sorry to have angered him.

"I can see that you don't like to speak of him, so why don't you just forget he's down there and think about getting yourself better? Doctor Dougherty said I should change the bandage on your foot and apply some ointment if it gives you pain."

"It's feeling better all the time. Don't bother."

Rebuffed, she turned quickly to leave, sorry to have riled him by talking about the robber, especially after Mr. Melcher had been so complimentary over the fried steak and potatoes and the fresh linen napkin on the tray. She could see there was going to be friction in this house if the criminal managed to live. Yet she'd taken on the job of nursing him, and she was bound to give it her best.

Returning to the downstairs bedroom, she found he'd moved his right hand—it now lay across his stomach. She studied its long, lean fingers, curled slightly, the shading of hair upon its narrows, and saw what appeared to be a smear of dirt on it. Edging closer, she looked again. What she had taken for dirt was actually a black and blue mark in the distinct shape of a boot heel. Carefully picking up the injured hand by the wrist, she laid it back down at his side. But when it touched the sheet, he rolled slightly, protectively cradling it in his good left hand as if it pained him. Instinctively she pressed him onto his back, her hands seeming ridiculously minuscule upon his powerful chest. But he fell back as before, subdued and still again.

It was hard to tell if the hand was broken, but just in case, she padded a small piece of wood, fit it into his palm, and bound it, winding gauze strips up and around his hairy wrist, crossing them over the thumb until any broken bones could not easily be shifted. She noticed as she worked that his hands were clean, the nails well tended, the palms callused.

Checking his forehead again, she found it somewhat cooled but still hotter than it should be. Thinking back wearily to yesterday when she'd set out for town and a job at Culpepper's, she thought how little she'd suspected she'd end up with a job like this instead. Perhaps Culpepper's would have been preferable after all, she thought tiredly, slogging back to the kitchen for cotton and alcohol again. She looked around in dismay at the room: pieces of torn rags and gauze everywhere;

used wet lumps of cotton in bowls; vinegar cruet, salt bowl, herb bags, scissors, dirty dishes everywhere; blood splatters on the wall and the highboy, and the stench of burnt alum hanging sickeningly over everything.

Turning on her heel, she uncharacteristically disregarded it all and returned to her bedroom.

Dear God! He'd turned over . . . and onto his right leg!

Pushing and grunting, struggling with his limp weight, she managed to get him onto his back again, then fell across his stomach, panting. But she knew even before she looked what she'd find: the wound was bleeding profusely again.

So, sighing heavily, almost stumbling now, she fought the entire battle once more: cleansing the wound, burning the alum, staunching the blood, applying ergot, and praying to see the flow stop. He seemed to be rousing more often as the afternoon wore on. Each time he moved a limb, she poured her strength on him, holding him flat if need be, willing him to lie still, badgering him aloud, sweating with the effort, but wiping the sweat from his fevered body rather than from her own. Toward evening when he still hadn't gained consciousness, she gave up hoping for him to awaken fully enough to drink the beef tea and force-fed him again.

Sometime later she was standing staring trancelike at his exposed white hip, counting the minutes since the bleeding had stopped, when Doc Dougherty's knock brought her from her reverie. "Come in." But she barely had the strength left to call out.

Doc had had a tough day himself, but he took one look at her and demanded, "Miss Abigail, what in tarnation did you do to yourself?" She looked ghastly! Her eyes were red-rimmed and for a moment he thought she might start crying.

"I never knew before how hard it is to save a life," she said hoarsely. Doc led her by the arm into her disastrous kitchen. She laughed a little madly as he forced her into a chair. "And now I know why your house looks the way it does, too."

Rather than feel insulted, he snorted laughingly. She'd been initiated then, he thought, as we all must be at first.

"You need a good dose of coffee, Miss Abigail, and a bigger dose of sleep."

"The coffee I'll accept, but the sleep must wait until after he revives and I know he'll make it."

Doc poured her a cup of coffee and left her to check the

patients, but as he walked from the kitchen he saw Miss Abigail's back wilt against her chair and knew he was lucky it was she who'd offered to help. Yet, entering the room where the robber lay, he wondered again if she wasn't too delicate to handle wounds like this. At first he'd considered only her sense of propriety, but seeing her so whipped, he wondered if the physical strain wasn't too much for her.

But one look at her handiwork and he marveled at her ingenuity and tenacity. What he found when he checked the wound genuinely surprised him. The man doesn't know how lucky he is that he ended up where he did, Doc thought. The wound looked good, the fever was low, no bleeding, no gangrene. She'd done as much as Doc himself could have.

Upstairs, he said, "Mr. Melcher, I think you're in good hands with Miss Abigail dancing attendance on you. However, I thought I'd lend my meager medical assistance just the same."

"Ah, Doctor Dougherty, I'm happy to see you." Melcher looked fit as a fiddle.

"Foot giving you much pain?"

"No more than I can handle. It throbs now and then, but the salve you gave Miss Abigail helps immensely."

"Laudanum salve, my man. Laudanum salve applied by Miss Abigail—a very effective combination, don't you agree?"

Melcher smiled. "She is wonderful, isn't she? I want to thank you for . . . well, I'm very happy I'm here in her house."

"I didn't have much to do with it, Melcher. She volunteered! And even though she's being paid, I think she puts out more than the money will compensate her for. The two of you are a real handful for her."

At the reminder of the other patient, Melcher's face soured. "Tell me . . . how is he?"

"He's alive and not bleeding, and both facts seem to be more than believable. I don't know what Miss Abigail did for him, but whatever it was, it worked." Then, noting the expression on Melcher's face, Doc thumped the man's good leg. "Cheer up, my man! You won't need to be here under the same roof with the scoundrel too much longer. This toe is looking up. Shouldn't hold you up here for long at all."

"Thank you," Melcher offered, but his face remained untouched by warmth as he said it.

"My advice to you is to forget he's down there if it bothers you so much," Doc said, preparing to leave.

"How can I forget it when Miss Abigail has to be down there too . . . and caring for him!"

Ah, so that's the way the wind blows, thought Doc. "Sounds like Miss Abigail has made quite an impression on you."

"I dare say she has," admitted Melcher.

Doc laughed shortly, then said, "Don't worry about Miss Abigail. She can take care of herself. I'll be around again soon. Meanwhile, move that foot and use it as much as you want, as long as you feel comfortable doing it. It's doing well." But Doc was smiling at this unexpected turn of events as he headed downstairs.

The coffee had revived Miss Abigail somewhat.

"Got a cup for me?" Doc asked, returning to the kitchen. "Naw, don't get up. Cups in here? I'll pour my own." As he did, he continued visiting. "Miss Abigail, I'm sorry I doubted you yesterday, I can see what kind of fool I was to do so. You've not only done a proper job of nursing those two . . . it seems you've made a devotee of Mr. Melcher."

"A devotee?" She looked up, startled, over her cup.

Doc Dougherty leaned back against the edge of her sideboard as he sipped, his eyes alight.

Flustered, she looked into her cup. "Nonsense, Doctor, he's simply grateful for a clean bed and hot food."

"As you say, Miss Abigail . . . as you say." But still Doc's eyes were mischievous. Then abruptly he changed the subject. "Word came in by telegraph that the railroad wants us to keep that stranger here till they can send someone up here to question him."

"Ah, if he lives to talk." Once again he could see the weariness in her, could hear the dread in her voice.

"He'll live. I examined the wounds and they look real good, Miss Abigail, real good. What in blazes have you got on those poultices?"

"Powdered ergot. It healed the wounds from Indian arrows. I figured it might heal his."

"Why didn't you call me when he got bad?"

Her eyes looked incredulous. "I didn't think of it, I guess."

He chuckled and shook his head. "You planning to run me a

little competition in the healing business, are you?'' he asked, eyes twinkling.

"No, Doctor. It's far too hard on a maiden lady. When these men are fit, I shall give up my life in medicine, and gladly.''

"Well, don't give it up yet, Miss Abigail, please. You're doing one damn fine job for me.''

Too tired to even object to his language, she only answered, "Why, thank you, Doctor." And he could have sworn she beamed, there in her evening kitchen amidst the mess and the smell that was so unlike her usual tidiness. He knew she'd be okay then; she had qualities in her that most women didn't. Also, she was experiencing the first fledgling joy afforded to those who beat the odds against death.

On his way to the door, Doc turned. "Oh, I forgot to mention, the railroad said they'll foot the bill for as long as it takes to get these two healthy. I think they mean to pacify Melcher and keep him from kicking up a fuss about getting shot while on board one of the R.M.R. trains. As for the other one . . . he must be wanted for more than just one holdup for them to be that interested. I don't mean to scare you, just wanted you to rest easy about the money. Are you afraid, being here alone with him?''

She almost laughed. "No, I'm not afraid. I've never been afraid of anything in my life. Not even when I thought I was running out of money. Things have a way of working out. Yesterday I was facing penury and tonight here I am with a railroad supporting me. Isn't that handy?''

He patted her arm and chuckled. "That's more like it, Miss Abigail. Now see that you get some sleep so you can stay this way.''

As he opened the screen door, she stopped him momentarily, asking, "Doctor, did the telegram say what that man's name is? It seems strange always referring to him as 'that man' or 'that . . . robber.' ''

"No, it didn't. Just said they want him kept here and no question about it. They want to get their hands on him pretty bad.''

"How can they possibly know if he's wanted for other charges when they haven't seen him?''

"We sent out a description. Somebody along the line must have recognized him by it.''

"But suppose the man does die? It wouldn't seem proper for a man to die where not a soul even knew his name."

"It's happened before," Doc stated truthfully.

Her shoulders squared, and a look of pure resolve came over her face. "Yes, but it shan't this time. I will make it my goal, a sort of talisman if you like, to see that he revives sufficiently to state his name. If he can do that, perhaps he can recuperate fully. As you see, Doctor, I intend to be a tenacious healer." She gave Doc a wry grin. "Now hurry along. I have a kitchen to see to and a supper to prepare." Doc was chuckling as she whisked him away. It took more than weariness to defeat Abigail McKenzie!

She hadn't time to worry about her own appearance while she prepared David Melcher's supper tray, yet her heart was light as she pondered Doc's words. A devotee. David Melcher was her devotee. A delicious sense of expectation rippled through Miss Abigail at the thought. She took extra care with his meal and paused to tuck a few stray wisps of hair into place before stepping into his room. He was lying quietly, facing the window with its view of the apricot sky. As she paused in the doorway, he sensed her there and turned with a smile. Her heart flitted gaily, filling her with some new sense of herself.

"I've brought your supper," she said softly.

"Please sit with me while I eat it and keep me company," he invited. She wanted to . . . oh, how she wanted to, but it simply wasn't proper.

"I'm afraid I have things to do downstairs," was her excuse. His face registered disappointment. But he was afraid to be too insistent; she'd done so much already. The room grew silent, and from outside came the wistful cry of a mourning dove. Miss Abigail set the tray on his lap, then offered brightly, "But I've brought you something to read if you'd care to, after you've finished your supper." From her pocket she pulled a book of sonnets.

"Ah, sonnets! Do you enjoy sonnets too? I might have guessed you would."

At his smile of approval she grew flustered and raised her eyes to the cotton candy clouds beyond the window. Again came the call of the mourning dove, singing its question, "Who? Who? Who?" It suddenly seemed to Miss Abigail that the question was being asked of her. It was a question she'd asked herself more times than she cared to remember. Who would there ever be to brighten her life? To give her reason for living?

Lost in reverie, Miss Abigail said rather dreamily, "I find the evening a particularly appropriate time of day for sonnets—rather the softest time of day, don't you think?"

"I couldn't agree more," came his gentle reply. "It seems we have something in common."

"Yes, we do." She became suddenly aware of how she looked, and touched her lower lip with the tips of her fingers. She still wore her stained, sweaty dress that she'd worn all day, and her hair was terribly untidy. Yet even as she fled the room, she realized he'd smiled sweetly and spoken almost tenderly. Was it true, what Doc had said? Abigail McKenzie, you're so tired you're getting fanciful!

But tired or not, her day was not over.

Dusk had fallen and in the gloom of her downstairs bedroom its occupant looked darker than ever. She found herself comparing him to Mr. Melcher. The whiskers on his chin had nearly doubled in length, and she decided that tomorrow she would shave him. She had never liked dark-whiskered men anyway. And moustaches! Well, if dark chin whiskers were sinister, black moustaches were positively forbidding! This one—she stepped closer—bordered his upper lip like thick, drooping bat's wings. She shuddered as she studied it and crossed her arms protectively. Vile! she thought. Why would any man want to wear a bristly, unattractive thing like that on his very face?

But suddenly Miss Abigail's grip on her upper arms loosened. She had a dim recollection of—but no, it couldn't have been, could it? She frowned, remembering the feel of that moustache when she'd fed him, and in her memory it was not bristly, but soft.

Surely I'm mistaken, she thought, shaking herself a little. How could it be soft when it looks so prickly? Yet she was suddenly sure it had been. She glanced warily behind her, but of course nobody was there. It was simply silly to have looked! But she checked again, stealthily, before reaching out a tentative finger to touch the thick black hair beneath the robber's nose. It came as a near shock to find it almost silky! She felt his warm breath on her finger, and quickly, guiltily, recrossed her arms. The softness was disconcerting. Suddenly feeling sheepish, she spoke aloud. "Moustache or not, thief or not, I'm going to make you tell me your name, do you understand? You are not going to die on me, sir, because I simply shan't allow it! We shall take it one step at a time, and the first shall be getting your name out of you. It's best if you understand at the onset that I am not accustomed to being crossed up!"

He didn't move a muscle.

"Oh, just look at you, you're a mess. I'd better comb your hair for you. There's little else I can do right now."

She got her own comb from the dresser and ran it through his thick hair, experiencing a queer thrill at the thought that he was a robber of trains yet she was seeing to his intimate needs. "I can't say I've ever combed the hair of an outlaw before," she told him. "The only reason I'm doing so now is that, just in case you can hear me, you'll know you're not allowed to just . . . just lie there without fighting. This hair is dirty, and if you want it washed, you shall simply have to come around."

Suddenly his arm jerked and a small sound came from him. He tossed his head to one side and would have rolled over, but she prevented it by holding him down with restraining hands. "You've got to lie flat. I insist! Doctor Dougherty says you must!" He seemed to acquiesce then. She felt his forehead and found it cool. But just in case, she brought a sewing rocker from the living room—an armless, tiny thing offering little comfort—and sat down for only a moment, only until she was sure he wouldn't thrash around anymore and hurt himself.

In no time at all her head lolled and her thoughts grew dim as she faded into a dream world where the stranger awakened and smiled at her from behind his soft black moustache. His wide chest moved near and she pressed it with her hands. She avoided his tempting lips, arguing that he was a thief, but he only laughed deep in his throat and agreed that he was, and wanted to steal something from her now. But I don't know your name, she sighed like the night wind. He smiled and teased, Ah, but you know more of me than my name. And she saw again his naked body—soft, curled, intimate—and felt again the wondrous shame of sensuousness. And upon the tiny sewing rocker her sleeping body jerked.

His flailing limbs awakened her and she jumped up and flattened him, using her own body to keep him on his back and still. The strange, forbidden dream was strong in her as she felt the flesh of this man beneath her own. She should not think such thoughts, or touch him so.

Yet she stayed beside him, guarding him through the night. Time and again he tossed, and she ordered, "Stay on your back . . . keep that knee up . . . tell me your name . . ." until she could fight him no longer. In the deep of night she fumbled into the dark kitchen, found a roll of gauze, and tied his left ankle to the brass footboard, his left wrist to the headboard. Blurred by sleep, she again sat on the armless rocker. But sometime during the night she arose insensibly, clambered over the footboard, and fell asleep near the end of the bed with her lips near his hip.

Chapter 3

———

SLOWLY . . . HAZILY . . . HE became aware of a great, steady heat on his face. And he could tell by its constancy that it was sun.

Mistily . . . lazily . . . he became aware of a soft, lush heat against his side. And he could tell by its curves that it was woman.

Progressively . . . painfully . . . he became aware of raw, gnawing heat in his flesh. But this he could not identify, knew only that it pained in a way nothing ever had before. His eyeballs rolled behind closed lids, refusing yet to give up their private dark, hemming him in with the three heats that melded to scorch his very fiber. He wondered, if he opened his eyes, would he rouse from this dream? Or was it real? Was he alive? Was he in hell? His eyes grated open but he stared up at a ceiling, not the roof of a tent. His body ached in many places. Sweet Jesus, he thought, and his eyes faded closed to leave him wondering where he was and who lay down there near the foot of his bed. He tried to swallow but couldn't, lifted drugged lids again and gritted his teeth till his jaw popped, then raised his head with a painful effort.

A female satyr of some kind was braced on its elbows, gaping at him with wide eyes.

He had only one conscious thought: I must be slipping. This one's a hag and she had to tie me up to get me to stay.

Then he slipped once more into blackness. But he took with him the image of the ugly hag, her hair strewn like vile straw around a face that seemed to have fallen into collapsing folds from her eyes downward. In his insensibility he dreamed she harped at him, commanding him to do feats of which he was incapable. She insisted that he speak, roll over, don't roll over, answer her, be still. Sometimes he dreamed her voice had turned to honey, but then it intruded, thorny-like again, until he finally escaped her altogether and slept dreamlessly.

Miss Abigail despaired when his head fell back and he was lost in oblivion before she could wrest his name from him. All she knew that she hadn't known before was that his near-black eyes held a faint touch of hazel. She'd expected they'd be jet, hueless, as foreboding as the rest of him. But the hazel flecks saved them from all that.

Groaning, she pulled herself off the bed.

Never in her life had Miss Abigail looked into a morning mirror and seen a sight like that which confronted her today. The night had taken its toll, seemingly having shrunken the skin above her eyes and stretched that below. Plum-colored shadings accentuated her too-wide, distraught eyes while elongated lines parenthesized her lips. Tangled, devastated hair set it all off with cruel truthfulness.

She studied her reflection and felt very old indeed.

The thought of David Melcher brought her out of her maunderings.

She bathed in the kitchen and brushed her hair, coiling it neatly at the base of her neck, then donned a soft, cream-colored blouse much like that she'd worn yesterday and a brown broadcloth skirt. On an impulse she applied the tiniest bit of attar of roses to her wrists.

"Miss Abigail, don't you look lovely this morning!" David Melcher exclaimed appreciatively when she stepped to his doorway with a breakfast tray.

"And aren't you chipper, Mr. Melcher!"

Again he invited her to stay while he ate, and this time she accepted, though propriety demanded she stay only briefly. But he praised her cooking, the coddled eggs, toast, and apple butter, teasing, "Why, Miss Abigail, I'll be plain spoiled by the time you throw me out of here."

His appreciation ruffled her ego in a gentle, stirring way, like a low breeze can lift the fine hair at the back of one's neck and create delicious shivers.

"I would not, as you say, throw you out of here, Mr. Melcher. You are free to stay as long as you need."

"That, Miss Abigail, is truly a dangerous offer. I may take you at your word and never leave." His eyes held just the right amount of mischief to make the comment thoroughly proper. Yet that tickle stirred the back of her neck again. But she'd stayed as long as it was prudent.

"I'd like to visit longer, but I do have work I should like to complete while the morning coolness prevails."

"Why, Miss Abigail, you made that sound just like a sonnet. You have such an eloquent way of speaking." Then he cleared his throat and added, in a more formal manner, "I'd like to read through the sonnets again today, if you don't mind."

"Not at all. Perhaps you'd enjoy some others I have also."

"Yes . . . yes, I'm sure I would."

As she rose from her chair and ran her hands down her sleeves to free them of any nonexistent wrinkles, he thought of how delicate the high collar and long sleeves made her look and of how she smelled like roses and of what a perfect little lady she was.

She fed the robber warm broth through the cattail again. Now, nearing him, her pulse did strange, forbidden things, and as if to get even with him, she scolded the unconscious man, "When will you make up your mind to awaken and tell me your name and take some decent nourishment? You're being an awful lot of trouble, you know, lying there like a great hibernating grizzly! You've put me to the task of feeding you as I did yesterday. I know it seems a vicious method, but it's the only way I can think of . . . and believe me, sir, it's no more palatable to me than it is to you, especially with that moustache."

The feeding finished, she brought out the shaving gear and intrepidly set out to clean him up, not at all sure how well she'd do. She lay thick towels beneath his jaw, lathered him up, and set to work with the blade, all the while puzzling over that moustache.

Should she or shouldn't she?

It truly was a dirty, ominous-looking feature. And maybe if

David Melcher hadn't pointed out how typical the moustache was of outlaws, and maybe if it hadn't been so alarmingly soft, and maybe if her heart hadn't betrayed her when she touched it, she wouldn't have shaved it off.

But in the end she did.

When it was half gone she had a pang of guilt. But it was too late now. After she had finished, she stood back to evaluate the face without the moustache and found, to her chagrin, that she'd spoiled it completely! The moustache belonged on him just as surely as did his thick black eyebrows and his swarthy coloring. Suppose when he awoke he thought the same thing? The thought did little to calm her misgivings, and the next task did even less. It was time to give him a bath.

She set about doing so, a section at a time, first lightly soaping an arm, then rinsing it and wiping it dry. His armpit was a bed of straight, thick black hair—unnerving. So she concentrated on his shoulder and tried not to look at it. The far arm presented a problem, for the bed was pushed up into a corner of the room. She tried pulling the bed out to get at him from that side, but he was too heavy and it wouldn't budge. She ended up climbing once again onto the bed with him to facilitate matters.

His upper half was done . . .

She gulped, then remembered he was, after all, unconscious.

Slipping the oilcloth beneath his right leg, she washed it carefully, avoiding the damaged thigh. His foot was long, and it evoked a queer exhilaration as she washed the sole, then between the toes, which were shaded with hair between the knuckles. She admitted now that what Doctor Dougherty said was true: it was infinitely more disconcerting tending the intimate needs of a stranger than those of a father. The sheet still shrouded his private parts. She managed to keep them covered while doing his other leg. *That part* of him she did not wash.

But she had seen it once, and couldn't get the picture from her mind.

As the day progressed, his eyes moved more often, though they remained closed. Now and then she saw muscles flex, and he tossed repeatedly, so she kept him safely tied to the bedrails.

* * *

While Miss Abigail freshened up David's room that morning, she learned he was a shoe salesman out of Philadelphia. Then he surprised her by announcing, "When I get back, I'll be sure to send you a pair of our best."

She placed one small hand on the high collar of her blouse, fingers spreading delicately over her neck as if to hide a pulsebeat there.

"Oh, Mr. Melcher . . . it wouldn't do at all, I'm afraid, much as I'd love a fine pair of city-made shoes."

"Wouldn't do? But why?"

Miss Abigail dropped her eyes. "A lady simply does not accept such a personal gift from a gentleman unless he's . . ."

"Unless he's what, Miss Abigail?" he asked softly.

She felt herself color and stared at her hem. "Why, Mr. Melcher, it simply wouldn't be proper." She looked up to find his brown eyes on her. "But I thank you anyway," she added wistfully.

She thought the issue was settled, but at noon Mr. Melcher announced he felt good enough to come downstairs to eat his dinner, but apologized for having nothing to put on his feet.

"I believe I can find a pair of Father's slippers here somewhere."

She brought them and knelt before him.

Such a feeling welled up inside David Melcher, watching her. She was genteel, soft-spoken, refined, and each favor she did for him made David Melcher revere her more. He got up shakily, hopping on one foot to catch his balance, and she whisked an arm around his waist while his came about her shoulder.

"The floor is slippery, so hold the banister," she warned.

They started down, one step at a time, and each time he leaned on her, his face came close to her temple. Again she smelled of roses.

Her free hand was on his shirtfront and she felt his chest muscles flex each time he braced on the banister.

"What color would you like, Miss Abigail?" he asked, between jumps.

"Color?" They stopped and she looked up into his face, only inches from hers.

"What color shoes shall I pick for you?" They took one more step.

"Don't be silly, Mr. Melcher." Again they'd stopped, but now she was afraid to raise her eyes to his.

"How about a pale dun-colored kid leather?" He lightly squeezed her shoulder, sending her heart battering around wildly. "They'd look grand with what you're wearing now. Imagine the leather with this soft lace." He touched the lace of her cuff.

"Come . . . take another step, Mr. Melcher."

"I'd be honored if you'd accept the shoes."

She kept her eyes averted, her hand still upon his chest.

"I'd have no place to wear them."

"That I cannot believe. A fine-looking woman like you."

"No . . . I'd have no place. Please . . . our dinner is ready." She nudged him, but he resisted, and beneath her hand she felt his heart drumming as rapidly as her own.

"Don't be surprised if a pair of shoes arrives one day for you. Then you'll know I've been thinking of you." His voice was scarcely above a whisper as he murmured, "Miss Abigail . . ."

At last she looked up to find a multitude of feelings expressed in his eyes. Then his arm tightened upon her shoulder, he squeezed the soft sleeve, the arm beneath. She saw him swallow, and the breath caught in her throat as his pale brown eyes held hers. As his soft lips touched her she again felt the commotion beneath the palm on his chest. His gentle kiss was as light as a sigh upon her lips before he drew back and looked into her liquid gaze. Her heart thrilled, her knees weakened, and for a moment she feared she might tumble headlong down the stairs, so dizzy was she. But then she dropped her lashes demurely, and they continued on their halting, heart-bound way to the kitchen.

It had been years since David Melcher had lived in a house with a kitchen like this. The tabletop was covered with a starched yellow gingham to match the window curtains that lifted in a whispering wind. Dishes and silver had been precisely laid, and a clean linen napkin lay folded atop his plate. His eyes followed Abigail McKenzie as she brought simple, fragrant foods—three puffed, golden biscuits were dropped on his plate, then she returned with a blue-speckled kettle and spooned thick chunks of chicken and gravy over the top.

"How long has it been since you were home, Mr. Melcher?"

"You might say I have no home. When I go back to Philadelphia, I take a room at the Elysian Club. Believe me, it's nothing at all like this."

"Then you . . . you have no family?"

"None." Their eyes met, then parted. Birds chittered from somewhere in the shade-dappled yard, and the heady scent of nasturtiums drifted in. He thought he never wanted to leave, and wondered if she might be feeling the nesting urge as strongly as he.

The black-haired, clean-shaven man became aware of the smells around him this time much as he'd become aware of the heat once before. With his eyes still closed, he caught the scent of something sweet, like flowers. There was, too, the starchy, agreeable smell of laundry soap in fresh linens. Now and then came the tantalizing aroma of chicken cooking. He opened his eyes and his lashes brushed against some fancy, knotted stitchery on a pillow slip. So . . . this wasn't a dream. The sweet smell came from a bouquet of orange things over there on a low table near a bay window. The window seat had yellow-flowered cushions that matched the curtains.

He shut his eyes, trying to recall whose bedroom it was. Obviously a woman's, for there were more yellow flowers over the papered walls and a dressing table with hinged mirrors.

He had not moved—nothing more than the opening and closing of his eyelids. His left hand was tingling, it prickled as if no blood ran through it. When he flexed the fingers they closed around a cylinder of metal, and he realized with a shock that he was tied onto a bed.

So that hag was no nightmare! Who else could have tied him up? He was no stranger to caution. Stealthily he tested the bindings to see if he could break them. But they were tight on both hand and foot.

He lifted his lids to a brown skirt, smack in front of him, standing beside the bed. He assessed it warily, wondering if he should use his right hand to knock her off her feet with one surprise punch in the gut. He let his eyelids droop shut again, pretending to go back under so he could get a look at her face through a veil of near-closed lashes.

But he couldn't tell much. She had both hands clasped over her face, forming a steeple above her nose as if she was in joy, distress, or praying. From what he could tell, he'd never laid

eyes on her before. There wasn't much to her, and from the
stark hairdo she wore he knew she was no saloon girl. Her long
sleeves and high collar were no dance hall getup either. At last,
surmising he was safe from her, he opened his eyes fully.

Immediately she withdrew her hands and leaned close to lay
one—ah, so cool—along his cheek.

She didn't smell like a saloon girl either.

"Your name . . . tell me your name," she said with a note
of intense appeal.

He wondered why the hell she wouldn't know his name if
she was supposed to, so he didn't say a thing.

"Please," she implored again. "Please, just tell me your
name."

But suddenly he writhed, twisted at his bindings, and looked
frantically around the room in search of something.

"My camera!" he tried to croak, but his voice was a
pathetic, grating thing, and pain assailed him everywhere. At
his wild thrashing, she became big-eyed and jumped back a
step, her eyes riveted on his lips as he mouthed again, "My
camera." The attempt to utter his first words shot a searing
pain through his throat. He tried again, but all that came of it
was a thick rasp. But she read his lips and that was all she
needed to make her suddenly vibrant.

"Cameron," she whispered in disbelief.

He wanted to correct her but couldn't.

"Mike Cameron," she said louder, as if the words were
some kind of miracle. "Cameron . . . just imagine that!"
Then she beamed and clasped her hands joyfully before her,
saying, "Thank God, Mr. Cameron. I knew you could do it!"

Was she zany or what? She resembled the witch he'd
imagined in the bed beside him, only she was neat and clean
and easy on the eye. Still, she acted as if she didn't exactly
have all her marbles, and he thought maybe he *should* have
punched her one broadside when he'd had the chance, to bring
her out of a spell.

She whirled now, facing the bay window, and from behind it
looked like she was wiping her eyes. But why the hell would
she be crying over him?

When she faced him again, he tried to say, "My name's not
Cameron," but once more the pain shot through his throat, and
the sound was unrecognizable.

"Don't try to speak, Mr. Cameron. You've had some foreign

objects in your mouth and throat, that's why it hurts so badly. Please lie still."

He attempted to sit up, but she came immediately and pressed those cool hands of hers on his chest to stay him. "Please, Mr. Cameron," she pleaded, "please don't. You're in no condition to move yet. If you promise you won't try to get up, I will remove these gauze bindings." She peered into his stark eyes that were lined with dark suspicion of her.

He had a damn good look at her then, and she looked about as strong as a ten-year-old boy, but her eyes told him she'd give it her best shot at subduing him if need be. So far, every time he'd moved, some muscle pained him like a blue bitch. He felt disinclined to tussle with even such a hummingbird as her. He scowled, gave her the merest nod, then there was a snipping sound above his head and again at his foot and she came away holding the gauze strips, freeing him to move limbs that somehow now refused to do his bidding. "Dear me, Mr. Cameron, you can see what a weakened condition you're in." She lowered his dead arm and began rubbing it deftly, massaging the muscles. "Give the blood a chance to get back. . . . It'll be all right in a minute. You mustn't move, though, please. I have to leave you alone for a bit while I prepare you some food. You've been unconscious for two days."

But suddenly the blood came racing back like a spring cataract, pounding through his arm, shooting needles of hot ice everywhere. He gasped and arched. But gasping hurt his throat and arching hurt everything else. He tried to swear but that hurt worse, so with a drooping of eyelids he subsided, fighting the giddy sensation that his skin was trying to explode. She clasped the inert hand under her armpit while he lay there listening to the deft sound of her beating the blood back into his prickling limb; it sounded like she was making a meat patty for his dinner. He felt nothing of her and a moment later opened his eyes to find his hand again on the sheet at his side, the woman gone from the room.

His right knee was raised. When he flexed its muscles a film of sweat erupted from his forehead and armpits. What the hell! he thought. He looked down his bare torso. A white patch decorated his right thigh. Automatically lifting his right hand to explore the bandage, a new pain gripped him, this time centered in the hand. It felt as if some giant paw were doling out a grisly handshake. He used his left hand instead, exploring damp, clinging cloths that guarded some secret near his groin. It told him nothing. Feeling around, he found a sheet drawn across his left leg, covering his privates, and folded back across his navel. To wake up naked in a woman's bed didn't surprise him at all, but to wake up in one belonging to a woman like this sure as hell did!

His eyes wandered while he listened to clinking, domestic sounds from around the doorway, and he wondered how long it had been since he'd been in a place like this. The room looked like some old maid's flower garden—flowers everywhere! He had no doubt it was her room, that like a hummingbird she'd fit into it. He saw a pair of portraits beside the bouquet, in a hinged, oval frame, and an open book on the bay window seat, with the tail end of a crocheted bookmark trailing from its pages. There was a small rocker with a needlepoint cushion, and a basket of sewing things on the floor beside it. A chifforobe stood against one wall, the dressing table against another.

Through the doorway he saw a green velvet settee in what must be her parlor. A little table beside it, and an oil lamp with globes of opaque white glass painted with roses. God, more flowers! he thought. A corner of a lace-curtained window with fringed, tassled shades. The parlor of a goody twoshoes, he thought, and wondered, as his eyes slid shut, how the hell he had gotten here.

"Here we are, Mr. Cameron." His eyes flew open; he jumped and winced. "I've prepared a light broth and some tea. It's not much, but we'll have to cater to your throat rather than your appetite for a short while." She held a carved wooden tray, white triangles of linen falling over its edges.

Lordy, he thought, would you look at that! Probably handstitched those edges herself. Bracing the tray against her midriff, she cleared a space on the bedside table. He was surprised to see the tray pull her blouse against a pair of healthy, resilient breasts—she dressed like a woman who didn't want the world to suspect she had any! But if there was one thing he knew how to find, it was a pair of healthy breasts. His eyes followed while she crossed to the chifforobe and found a pillow. When she came to mound it up beneath his head, he again caught the drift of that starchy, fresh smell, both from her and the pillow, and he thought of many nights sleeping on the floor of a wet canvas tent with a musty blanket over him as the only comfort. As she cupped the back of his head and lifted it, ripples of pain undulated from muscles far down his body. Automatically his eyes sank shut and he sucked in a sharp breath. When his pain had subsided, her voice came again.

"I've brought something to freshen your mouth. It's just soda water." A cloth pressed his jowl and a glass touched his lips, then he pulled the salty solution into his mouth. "Hold it a minute and let it bubble around. The effervescence is very refreshing." He was too weak to argue, but watched her covertly as she brought the bowl for him to spit into. When dribbles wet his chin, she immediately applied a warm, damp cloth, then proceeded to wash his entire face as if he were a schoolboy. He tried to jerk aside, but it hurt, so he submitted. Next she placed a napkin under his chin and dipped the spoon, cupping her hand beneath it on its way to his mouth.

She wondered why he scowled so, and talked because his near-black eyes were frightening. "You're a lucky man, Mr. Cameron. You were critically shot and nearly bled to death. Luckily Doctor Dougherty . . ."

She rambled on but he heard little beyond the statement that he'd been shot. He tried to lift his right hand, remembered how it hurt, used his left instead to stop the spoon. But he bumped her hand and the soup spilled on his chin, running down his neck. Goddamnit! he thought, and tried to say it—unsuccessfully—while she dabbed, wiped, and sponged fussily.

"Behave yourself, Mr. Cameron. See the mess you've made here!"

She knew perfectly well that any man who'd just found out he'd been shot would want to know who did it! Did he have to ask, with this inflamed throat of his! She dabbed away at the stupid soup, and this time when he grabbed, he got her by the wrist, catching the washcloth, too, under his grip, bringing her startled eyes wide.

"Who shot me?" he tried, but the pain assaulted his throat from every angle, so he mouthed the words broadly, *oooo . . . shawt . . . mee?* She stared at him as if struck dumb, knotted her fist, and twisted it beneath his fingers until he felt the birdlike bones straining to be free.

"It wasn't I, Mr. Cameron," she snapped, "so you've no need to accost me!" His grip loosened and she wrenched free, amazed at how strong he was in his anger. "I fear I untied you too hastily," she said down her nose, rubbing her fingers over the redness where the stiff lace had scratched her wrist.

He could tell from her face that she wasn't used to being manhandled. He really hadn't meant to scare her, but he wanted some answers. She'd had plenty of time to fill him in while flitting around getting that pillow and washing his face. He reached for her wrist again but she flinched away. But he only touched it to make her look at his lips. Who shot me? he mouthed once more.

She stiffened her face and snapped, "I don't know!" then jammed the spoon into his mouth, clacking it against his teeth.

The spoon kept coming faster and faster, barely giving him time to swallow between each thrust. The bitch is going to drown me, damn her! he cursed silently. This time he grabbed the spoon in midair and sent chicken broth spraying all over the front of her spotless blouse. She recoiled, sucked in her belly, and closed her eyes as if beseeching the gods for patience. Her nostrils flared as she glared hatred at him. He jerked his chin at the soup bowl, glowering furiously until she picked it up and held it near his chin. He'd discovered while eating the broth that he was nearly starved. But with his left hand he was clumsy, so after a few inept attempts, he flung the spoon aside, grabbed the bowl, and slurped directly from it, taking perverse pleasure in shocking her.

A barbarian! she thought. I have been fighting to save the life of a barbarian! Like some slobbering beast, he went on till the bowl was empty. But as her thumb curled over it, he jerked it back, mouthing, "Who shot me?" She jerked the bowl stubbornly again, but with a painful lunge he yanked it from her, flung it across the room, where it shattered against the base of the window seat. He pierced her with eyes which knew no end of rage. His face went livid as he was forced to use the voice that cut his throat to ribbons.

"Goddamn you, bitch! Was it you!" he croaked.

Oh, the pain! The pain! He clutched his throat as she jumped back, squeezing both hands before her while two spots of color appeared in her cheeks. Never in her life had anyone spoken to Miss Abigail McKenzie in such a manner. To think she had nursed this . . . this baboon and struggled to get him to awaken, to speak, only to be cursed at, called a bitch, and accused of being the one who shot him! She drew her mouth into a disdainful pucker, but before she could say anything more, the alarmed voice of David Melcher rang through the house.

"Miss Abigail! Miss Abigail! Are you all right down there?"

"Who's that!" the rasping voice demanded.

It gave her immense pleasure to answer him at last. "That, sir, is the man who shot you!"

Before her answer could sink in, the voice came again. "Did that animal try to harm you?"

She scurried out, presumably to the bottom of the steps. "I'm fine, Mr. Melcher, now go back to bed. I just had an accident with a soup bowl."

Melcher? Who the hell was this Melcher to call him an animal? And why did she lie about the soup bowl?

She came back in and knelt to pick up the broken pieces. He longed to hurl questions at her, to jump up and shake her, make her fill in the blanks, but he hurt everywhere now from throwing the damn bowl. All he could do was glare at her while she came to stand beside the bed with a supercilious attitude.

"Cursing, Mr. Cameron, is a crutch for the dim-witted. Furthermore, I am not a bitch, but if I were, perhaps I *would* shoot you to put you out of your own self-inflicted misery and to be rid of you. I, unlike you, am civilized, thus I shall only stand back and hope that you will choke to death!" She punctuated this statement by dropping the broken china on the tray with a clatter. But before she left, she plagued him further by dropping one last morsel, just enough to rouse a thousand unaskable questions.

"You were shot, Mr. Cameron, while attempting to hold up a train . . ." She arched a brow, then added, "As if you didn't know." And with that she was gone.

Chapter 4

———————————

HE CLENCHED HIS good fist. Oh, she was some smug bitch! What train? I'm no goddamn train robber! And who is this Melcher anyway? Obviously not her husband. Her protector? Ha! She needs protecting like a tarantula needs protecting.

Miss Abigail stood in her kitchen quaking like an aspen, looking at the broken fragments of china, wondering why she hadn't heeded Doctor Dougherty's warning. Never in her life had she been spoken to this way! She would have him out of here—out!—before this day ended, that much she promised herself. Pressing a hand to her throbbing forehead, she considered running down to Doctor Dougherty's and pleading illness, but if she did that he would certainly remove Mr. Melcher, too. Then she remembered how desperately she needed the money and steeled herself for a long day ahead.

In the bedroom, he longed to raise his voice and bellow like a bull moose until somebody told him what the hell was going on around here. He lay instead sweating profusely, having writhed far more than he should have. His leg, hip, and lower stomach had turned to fire. Resting the back of a hand across his eyes, he gritted his teeth at the pain. That was how she found him.

"It has been two days since . . ."

He jumped and another pain grabbed him. Damn her! Did she have to pussyfoot around like that all the time?

Very collectedly now, she began again, with exaggerated control. "I thought you might have to relieve yourself." But she looked at the knob on the headboard while she said it.

Eyeing her mistrustfully, he knew she had him over a barrel. He did have to relieve himself, but he knew he wasn't going anywhere to do it. So just what did she have in mind?

With a voice like ice, she issued orders. "Don't try to speak or strain your leg in any way. I shall help you roll onto your side first." And coming to the side of the bed, she removed the bolsters from under his knee, lowered it with surprising gentleness, then snapped the ends of the under sheet loose from their moorings and rolled him with it until he faced the wall, still covered by the top sheet. She laid a flat porcelain pan next to him and without another word left the room, closing the door with not so much as a click of the latch.

What kind of woman was she anyway? She sashayed in here carrying that bedpan as if she had no idea that he was the one who'd only minutes before shattered her china soup bowl and called her a bitch. Most women would have refused any further services on spite alone . . . but not her. Why should that aggravate him too? Maybe because she looked frail enough to cow with a savage glare. Maybe because he'd tried it and it didn't work.

She came to collect the bedpan with the same silent poker face as before. They needn't have spoken anyway to tell each other they'd met their matches.

She had the perfect revenge for his insufferable attitude this morning: she left him alone. Miss Abigail knew perfectly well he was lying there with a hundred unasked questions eating him up. Well, good! Let them eat him up! It's no more than he deserves.

In the flowery bedroom that's exactly what was happening. Bitch! he thought time and again, unable to shout, to ask anything he wanted now worse than ever to know. He seethed for the remainder of the day, caught like some damn fool bumblebee in a glass jar, in that insufferable yellow flower garden she'd trapped him in. Once he even heard her humming out there in what seemed to be the kitchen, and it made him all the madder. She was out there humming while he couldn't make so much as a squeak without paying dearly.

Much later he heard her go upstairs, then the two of them come down to supper. Snatches of their conversation drifted through the quiet house, and he heard enough to know they were feeling pretty cozy with each other.

"Oh, Miss Abigail, nasturtiums on the table!"

"Ah, how pleasant it is to find a man who can actually identify a nasturtium."

"How pleasant it is to find a woman who still grows them." The eavesdropper in the bedroom rolled his eyes.

"Perhaps tomorrow you'll feel well enough to sit in the backyard while I do some weeding."

"I'd love that, Miss Abigail, I truly would."

"Then you shall do it, Mr. Melcher," she promised before inquiring, "Do you like fresh lemonade?"

"I wish you'd call me David. Yes, I love lemonade."

"We'll have some, tomorrow . . . in the garden?"

"I'll look forward to it."

She helped him back to bed. The man downstairs heard them go up and a silence that followed and thought to himself, no it couldn't be. But indeed it could be, and David Melcher kissed Miss Abigail adoringly, then watched her go all peach-colored and fluttery.

She came back downstairs from her pleasant interlude to face the horrifying prospect of feeding that black brute again. She'd like to let him starve to death. Furthermore, she was afraid to go near him, and more afraid that it might show. She prepared milk toast for him, and entered the bedroom armed with it, ready to fling it on him and scald him should he make a grab for her again.

"I've brought you milk toast," she informed him. He thought he looked like it had soured in her mouth.

"Bah!" was all he could get out to let her know just what he thought of milk toast. "I'm starving!" he mouthed.

"I wish you were," she said, all honey-voiced, and rammed a napkin under his chin. "Hold still and eat."

The hot milk nearly gagged him, the lumps of slimy bread slithered down his throat, disgustingly. Even so, every swallow was torture. He wondered just what had been in his mouth to make it hurt this way, but it appeared she was still in a snit and wasn't going to tell him anything.

They eyed each other menacingly. He, waiting for the chance to ask questions, she, ready to spring to safety at the first sign of brutality. She could hardly stand the sight of him and thought the only good thing about feeding him was that he couldn't speak. And since he looked in no way ready to carry on a dignified conversation, she left him to stew. She put her kitchen back in order and found herself exhausted. Alas, all of her night things were in her bedroom and the last thing she wanted was to go in there again. So she dreamed up an excuse: a gargle.

Before entering, she tiptoed to the doorway, peeped in, gathering her courage. He faced the window, jaw muscles tensing repeatedly. Ah, so he is still angry, she thought. His beard had grown again, darkening his entire face. Studying the lip, which she had willfully denuded, she trembled to think about what would happen when he discovered his moustache gone. She willed it to please . . . please, hurry up and grow back!

She tread soundlessly across the threshold, her insides ascatter with apprehension.

"Are you ready to act civil?" she asked. His head snapped around and his good fist clenched. Then he grimaced in pain.

Damn that pussyfooting! he thought. "Are you trying to kill me with neglect?" he whispered stridently and pressed a hand to his abdomen, "or just let that slimy milk toast do the job for you?"

The thought of David Melcher's warm compliments made her voice all the more frigid as she replied, "I attempted to teach you a lesson, but apparently I failed." She turned to leave.

"No . . . wait!" he grated hoarsely.

"Wait, Mr. Cameron? For what? To be insulted and cursed at and to have my possessions shattered as repayment for bringing you food?"

"You call that slop food? I'm half starved and you bring me broth and milk toast, then hustle your fanny out of here without so much as a fare-thee-well! I've been laying here waiting for some answers for who the hell knows how long, so just keep your bones where they are, missus!"

Appalled by his rude outburst, she attempted to level him with a little cool, sarcastic superiority.

"My! What an extensive vocabulary you harbor, Mr. Cameron. Slop . . . fanny . . . bones . . . spoken like a true scholar." She threw him a disparaging look, then stiffened her spine and tried to give the impression she was taking command, although she felt far less cocksure than she sounded.

"If you want answers to any questions, quit your cursing, *sir*, treat me with respect, and stop issuing orders! I shall issue orders if any are to be issued, is that understood? You have fallen under my care and—despicable as you are—I am committed to giving it to you. But I do not—repeat, *do not*—have to accept your grossness or your abuse. Now, shall I leave or will you comply?"

He jerked his chin once, gave her a withering look, and whispered something that sounded like, "Sheece!" Then in a guttering voice he obliged, "Enter, Goody Twoshoes, and I'll try to hold my temper."

"You had better do more than try, *sir*." She could say sir in the most cutting way he's ever heard, considering that sweet little voice she had.

"Yes, *ma'am*," he countered, giving her a dose of her own hot tongue.

"Very well. I've made a gargle to ease your throat. If you use it, I'm sure it will offer some relief by morning." But she hesitated, just beyond his reach, as if still unsure of him. He considered winking at her just to see her jump, but nodded instead, agreeing to lay off the rough stuff.

She came nearer. "Here, just gargle, don't swallow." She helped him sip sideways. He pulled half the contents into his mouth, but it flew out again in a flume.

"What kind of piss is this!"

"*Missster* Cameron!" she hissed, pulling her blouse from her skin.

He really hadn't meant to spray her that time. After all, he wanted his questions answered, even if he had to toe the line to get his way.

"Sorry," he whispered insincerely.

It seemed to appease her momentarily, for she shoved the cup in his direction and he grimaced, gulped, and gargled while she took vast pleasure in informing him, "It's an old remedy of my grandmother's—vinegar, salt, and red pepper."

This time he hit the bowl, but he couldn't help gagging.

"Rinse!" she ordered imperiously, handing him a glass. He eyed it suspiciously, finally taking it. But it was only water this time.

"What the hell happened to my throat?" he guttered.

"As I said, it had some foreign objects in it while you were unconscious. It should feel better by tomorrow. I'd appreciate it if you would keep your crudities to yourself."

"It's not enough I get shot . . . I have to get choked, too. That would make any man cuss. And what's the matter with this hand?"

"Your gun hand?" she inquired sweetly, intimating a gross guilt upon him with that single arched eyebrow of hers.

He scowled, causing forbidding creases to line his forehead.

"I assume somebody trounced on it in the scuffle, since it has the perfect imprint of a boot heel on its back."

"It hurts like hell."

"Yes, it should, from the looks of it. But then you brought it all on yourself by robbing that train."

"I didn't rob any goddamn train!" he whispered fiercely. Across the room, where she'd been taking things out of a dresser, her back stiffened like a ramrod. It was obvious to Miss Abigail that cursing flowed from his lips more readily than blood from his wound. She would be hard put trying to keep a civil tongue in his head. But there were other barbs with which to admonish him.

"Then why is Mr. Melcher lying upstairs at this very moment, wounded by you, and why has he sworn out a legal complaint against you for the damage you've done?"

"Who is this Melcher anyway?"

"The man you shot . . . and who shot you."

"What!"

"The two of you were carried off the train here at Stuart's Junction, and there was a car full of witnesses to prove you attempted to rob the R.M.R. passengers and he attempted to stop you. In the tussle, the two of you shot each other."

He couldn't believe it, but apparently she did, and a few others in this town, too, by the sound of it. At least he knew where he was now.

"So, I'm in Stuart's Junction."

"Yes."

"And I'm the villain?"

"Of course," she agreed with that uppity look.

"And this Melcher's the town hero, I presume."

This she declined to answer.

"And why did you get the honor of caring for us . . . *Miss* Abigail, is it?"

She disregarded his sarcastic tone to answer, "I volunteered. The R.M.R. is paying me and I need the money."

"The *R.M.R.* is paying *you*?"

"That's right."

"Hasn't this town got a doctor?"

"Yes, Doctor Dougherty. And you'll probably see him again tomorrow. He didn't come by today, so I expect he was called out to the country. You may save the rest of your questions for him. I am extremely fatigued. Good night, Mr. Cameron." She sallied out with her head up like a giraffe, cutting off the rest of his queries, and he got mad all over again. He'd seen some cold-hearted women in his day, but this one beat them all. And stiff! She was so stiff he figured she'd go lean herself in the corner out there someplace and go to sleep for the night. Good night, Mr. Cameron, my eye! My name's not Cameron, but you didn't give me a chance to say so. Just come strutting in here throwing orders around like some pinched-up shrew who takes pleasure from paining a man just because he is one. Oh, I've seen your kind before—bound up so tight with corset stays that you've got permanent indigestion.

Still, from what he'd heard of the conversation between her and this Melcher, he wondered if Melcher had miraculously made some of her juices flow. Then, glancing down at his own bare hip, he wondered what the old shrew's reaction had been to him sprawled out naked in her bed. If it wouldn't have hurt so bad, he would've laughed. No, he decided, she's as cold as frog's blood, that one. He fell to plotting how he might get even with her for shutting him off like this.

In the darkness, a light rustling sounded. He supposed she was changing clothes out in the parlor. He half expected to hear an explosion when those corset stays came undone.

There were spare bedrooms upstairs, of course. But somehow Miss Abigail thought it would be less than appropriate for her to go up there to sleep, now that she and David Melcher were getting along so well. It would be far better for her to stay down here on the parlor settee. True, the formidable Mr. Cameron was just around the other side of the wall, but their antagonism made this arrangement acceptable. After all, by now she had ceased caring whether he lived or died.

* * *

She awakened and shivered and stretched her neck taut, aware that something had roused her. It was deep night—no bird sounds came through the windows, only a chill damp, coming in on the dew-laden air.

"Miss Abigail . . ."

She heard her name whispered hoarsely and knew it was he calling her, and unconsciously she checked the buttons up the neck of her nightie.

"Miss Abigail?" he whispered again, and this time she didn't hesitate, not even long enough to light a lamp. She walked surely through the dark, familiar house to the side of the bed.

"Miss Abigail?" he rasped weakly.

"Yes, I'm here, Mr. Cameron."

"It's . . . it's worse. Can you help me?"

"I shall have a look." Something told her he was not feigning, and she lit the lamp quickly to find his eyes closed, the covering sheet kicked completely off him. She flickered it in place and bent to remove the bindings and poultice.

"Oh, dear God," she breathed when the odor assaulted her nostrils. "Dear God, no." The edge of the bullet hole had turned a dirty gray, and the stench of putrefaction all but knocked her from her feet. "I must get Doctor Dougherty," she cried in a choked voice, then hurried out.

Barefoot she ran, the always proper, always fastidious Miss Abigail McKenzie, heedless of the dew that wet the hem of her nightie, made her feet slip on the sharp gravel. Hair flying wildly, she took the length of Front Street to Doc's house. But she knew even as she mauled his front door that he wasn't home. He hadn't come to see the men tonight, which meant he could be sleeping in some forlorn barn with a sick horse or delivering a baby in a country home any number of miles away. Running back home, she alternately cursed herself and prayed, scanning her mind for answers to questions she'd never asked Doc Dougherty, never believing she'd have to know. Never should she have allowed anger to overcome common sense. But that's just what she'd done today. That man had made her so irate that she couldn't bear the thought of checking those poultices to see if they needed repacking. Oh, why hadn't she done it, even in spite of her anger? Her mother had always said, "Anger serves no purpose but its own," and now she knew exactly what that meant.

She leaped the front porch steps, night skirts lifted above the knees, and panted to a halt at the foot of her bed. He lay upon it with eyes closed, breath too shallow and sweet to be healthy. Forgotten now was her anger at him, her fear of him. All she knew was that she must do all she could to save his life. She dropped to her knees to scramble through a cedar chest at the foot of the bed, searching for a much-used book that had crossed the prairies in a conestoga wagon years before with her grandparents. It contained cures for humans and animals alike, and she desperately hoped it held answers for her now.

He moved restlessly as her frantic fingers scanned the pages. "Where's the doc?" he whispered hoarsely. She flew to his side.

"Shh . . ." she soothed. Eyes dark, hair ascatter, she flopped the pages, reading snatches aloud before finally finding the remedy. Then she lurched toward the door, cast the book aside, muttering, "Charcoal and yeast, charcoal and yeast," like a litany.

He drifted for a long time in a kind of peaceful reverie from which he was curiously removed yet somehow aware of his surroundings. He heard the stove lids clang, heard her exclaim, "Ouch!" and he smiled, wondering what she'd done to hurt herself, such a careful woman like her. Some glassy, tinkly sounds, fabric ripping, water being poured. She seemed to float in, arms and hands laden. But he was smacked from his blissful nether state when she began cleaning his wound.

"I'm sorry, Mr. Cameron, but I've got to do this."

He reached down to combat her hands.

"Please don't fight me," she pleaded. "Please. I don't have time to tie you again." He groaned, deep and long and raspy, and she gritted her teeth and bit on her inner cheek. He clasped the sheet with his one good hand while the other tapped listlessly against the mattress. She removed the useless, dead flesh, swallowing the gorge in the back of her throat, wiping at her forehead with the back of a hand.

Tears formed in her eyes, leaked down the corners while she bathed the wounds with disinfectant, then whispered, "I'm almost done, Mr. Cameron." She felt his hand grope at her chest and thought stupidly how he was using his battered hand and that he shouldn't be. Still, she let him grab a weak handful of the front of her nightgown and pull her up close to his mouth.

"My name's not Cameron. It's Jesse," he croaked.

"Jesse what?" she whispered.

But he drifted into oblivion then, his grip falling slack, his lips grown still, close beneath hers.

It became a personal thing then, refusing to let him die. She mixed warm, damp yeast with the remnants of charcoal, forming the mixture she hoped would keep him alive, all the while feeling for the second time that obdurate will to prevent the death of another human being. What he was and how he had treated her became insignificant against the fact that he was flesh and blood. Stubbornly she vowed that he would live.

If the night before had been difficult, the remainder of this one was a horror.

The book said to keep the poultices warm, so she made two, running to the kitchen to reheat them. The fire flagged and she slogged outside for more wood. Still the poultices cooled too fast, so she topped them with mustard plasters, the only thing she knew that would retain heat. But they needed frequent changing, so rather than bind them, she propped the bottom one and held the top one lightly in place with her hand. He often jerked spasmodically or tossed wildly, and when his moans brought her flying back from the kitchen, she wet his lips with a damp cloth, squeezing a drizzle of water into his mouth, massaging his throat, trying to make him swallow. Sometimes she said his name, the new name—Jesse—encouraging him to fight with her.

"Come on, Jesse," she whispered fiercely. "Come on, help me!"

She knew not if he heard her.

"Don't die on me now, Jesse, not now that we've come this far." He tossed, wild with delirium, and she fought him, throwing what she thought was the last of her strength on him to keep him flat. He muttered insensibly.

She argued with intense urgency, "Fight with me, Jesse. I know what a fighter you are. Fight with me now!"

But she herself could fight just so long. She fought long after she knew what she was saying or who she was or who he was or where they were.

When unconsciousness overtook her she never knew it.

Chapter 5

MR. MELCHER WAS truly on top of the world the next morning. His toe gave him nearly no pain at all, so he decided to surprise Miss Abigail by going down to breakfast unaided. The house was abnormally quiet as he limped downstairs. From the bottom step he eyed the bedroom doorway leading off the parlor. He was repelled by the thought of that felon sleeping under the same roof as himself and Miss Abigail, but he had an urge to sneak a small peak at the man nevertheless. It would be something to tell the boys back at the Elysian Club just what that robber looked like after he'd laid him low.

But he hadn't expected the shocking sight that greeted him when he stuck his carefully groomed head around the door-frame!

There was the wounded robber all right, but the man had absolutely not a stitch of clothing on, save his bandages. He lay stark naked and hairy, one leg draped over a pair of bolsters, the other sprawled lasciviously sideways, riding the curve of a woman's stomach. She occupied the lower half of the bed, her gown scrunched up to mid-thigh, feet dangling, along with his, between the footrails. Her face was nearly at his hip, but buried beneath a mop of plical-looking hair in which the man's fingers were twined. But most lurid of all: the harlot had one arm stretched out across the brute's hairy thighs, her palm precariously near the man's genitals!

From the looks of her, none of this was surprising. The slut was a mess. The soles of her feet were filthy, her gown the same, smirched with ocher and gray stains; the lace cuffs were grimy. Her hands looked no better than the rest of her, fingernails encrusted, knuckles long in need of scrubbing, those of her left hand wrapped in a piece of dirty gauze, as if she'd been in a saloon brawl.

How the man had managed to get the woman in here was a mystery, but Miss Abigail would be shocked to her very core to witness such a spectacle!

At that moment the man twitched restlessly and mumbled something incoherent. The woman came out of her deep sleep just enough to sigh, grope toward the bandage, and mumble, "Be still, Jesse." Then her hand fell away limply across his knee as she slumbrously snuggled against his long, bare leg, turning her face.

"Is that you, Abbie?" he mumbled, eyes still closed.

"Yes, Jesse, it's me, now go back to sleep."

He sighed, then a gentle snore sounded as his hand relaxed in her hair. And soon her rhythmic breathing joined his while a horrified David Melcher crept soundlessly back to his room.

The scene remained fixed in his memory during the awful days that followed, during the bittersweet afternoons in Miss Abigail's garden, when he longed to ask her for explanations but feared there were no good ones. His jealousy grew, for she spent most of her time with the outlaw, who recovered at a snail's pace. There were times when David paused, passing the room, and looked inside, nursing his hatred for the man who had not only maimed him but stolen the greatest joy from his life. David's limp seemed permanent now, and it undermined his self-esteem, making him believe no woman could possibly find him attractive. He watched the care with which Miss Abigail attended the man, though he was drugged now with laudanum for his own good, and each minute she spent in that downstairs bedroom was a minute of which David felt robbed of her attention.

Miss Abigail puzzled over his withdrawal. She longed for him to kiss her again, to buoy her tired spirits at the end of an arduous day, but he didn't. David's toe seemed completely healed and she dreaded the thought that he might leave without ever again pressing his suit. When she tried to please him with small favors, he thanked her considerately, but his old compliments were part of the past.

After Doc finally gave the orders to drop the laudanum, Jesse awoke one sunny morning, weak, but hungry as a bear, and amazed to find himself still alive. He flexed his muscles, found them stiff and sore from disuse, but those grinding pains had faded. He heard voices from the kitchen and remembered the man who'd put him here, wondered how many days he'd lain unconscious.

He heard not so much as a footstep, yet somehow knew she was standing there in the doorway. He turned from his study of the trees outside the window to find her watching him with all traces of her former antagonism gone.

She looked as crisp as a spring leaf in a skirt of forest green and a white lawn blouse, her brown hair knotted in its careful coil at the base of her neck, her skin fresh and peachy. And he saw for the first time how a smile could transform her face.

"So you've made it," she said quietly.

He studied her for a moment. "So I have." Softly, he added, "Come over here."

She paused uncertainly, then drifted slowly to the side of the bed.

"You been busy?" He smiled up at her crookedly.

"A little," came her mellow reply.

He flopped an arm out, gathered her in by her forest green skirts, and boldly caressed her buttocks, saying, "I guess I owe you." It was nothing Jesse hadn't done to a hundred women a hundred times, but it was just Miss Abigail's luck he chose that precise moment to do it to her, for the sound of their voices had brought David Melcher to the doorway.

The blood flooded his face before he remarked dryly, "Well, well . . ."

Miss Abigail froze, horrified, helpless. It had happened so fast. She squirmed, but Jesse only held tight and drawled with a lopsided grin, "Mr. Melcher, our avenging hero, I presume?"

"Have you no decency!" David hissed.

Undaunted, Jesse only turned his grin up at Abbie as she struggled to break his hold. "None whatever, have I, Abbie?"

"Abbie, is it?" returned the outraged David while she at last managed to struggle out of Jesse's hold, her eyes on the man in the doorway.

"This . . . this is not what it seems," she implored David.

"Yes it is," Jesse teased, enjoying Melcher's discomfort intensely, but Miss Abigail whirled on Jesse, all her venom returned in full force.

"Shut up!" she spit, little hands clenched into angry balls.

David gave the pair a scathing look. "This is the second time I've found you with him in wh . . . what I'd term a c . . . compromising position," he accused.

"The second time! What are you talking about? Why, I've never—"

"I *saw* you, Miss Abigail, curled up beside him with your hand on—" But he pursed his mouth suddenly, unable to go on.

"You're a liar!" Miss Abigail exclaimed, her hands now on her hips.

"Now, Abbie," put in Jesse, "there were those couple nights—" She whirled on him, sparks seeming to fly from her eyes.

"I'll thank you to shut your despicable mouth, Mr. . . . whatever your name is!"

"You called him Jesse in your sleep," David declared.

"In my—" She didn't understand. Jesse just smiled, enjoying it all.

"I thought you were such a lady. What a fool I was," Melcher disdained.

"I have never done any of what you've intimated. Never!"

"Oh? Then where had you been that night if not out romping in the grass? Your gown, your feet, your hands . . ."

She remembered them all too clearly, the knuckles bound because she'd burned herself on a live coal as she dug for charcoal, her feet and gown soiled by running to Doc's house.

"He was unconscious, and gangrene had set in. I went to fetch Doctor Dougherty."

"Oh? I don't seem to remember the doctor coming that night."

"Well, he didn't . . . I mean, he wasn't home, so I had to treat Jesse—Mr. Cameron, I mean, as best I could."

"You seem to have treated him to more than a mustard poultice," David accused.

"But I—"

"Save your explanations for someone who'll buy them, *Miss* McKenzie."

She was as pale as a sheet by this time and clutching her hands together to stop their trembling.

"I think you had better go, Mr. Melcher," she said quietly. A muscle worked in his jaw as he looked at her standing so still and erect beside the smirking man.

"Yes, I think I had," he agreed, quietly now too, and turned from the room. He went upstairs to gather his things together with a heavy heart. When he returned downstairs she stood clear across the parlor, the pain in her heart well hidden as she faced him.

"I have no shoes," he said forlornly.

"You may wear Father's slippers and have someone return them when they come for your valise." Her hands were clutched as their eyes locked, then parted.

"Miss Abigail, I . . ." He swallowed. "Perhaps I was hasty."

"Yes, perhaps you were," she said in clipped tones, too hurt to soften.

He limped to the screen door and each step crushed a petal of some fragile flower which had blossomed within her since he'd come here. He pushed the door open, and her hand instinctively reached toward him. "You . . ." He turned and she retracted the guilty hand. "You may take one of Father's canes. There's no need to return it."

He took one from the umbrella stand, looked balefully across at her, and said, "I'm ever so sorry." She longed to cross the room, draw an arm through his, and say, "It's all a big mistake. Stay and we'll set it straight. Stay and we'll have lemonade in the garden. I too am sorry." But pride kept her aloof. He turned and limped away.

She watched him until he turned a corner and was lost to her. He was a gentle man and a gentleman, and both attributes had lifted Miss Abigail's waning spinster hopes, but those hopes were firmly dashed now. There would be no lemonade in the garden, no soft, kid city shoes arriving to tell her he was thinking of her. There would be only her quiet afternoons of weeding and her twilights spent with the sonnets. What have I done to deserve this? she thought painfully. I've done nothing but save an outlaw's life.

As if on cue, his voice came, clear and resonant. "Abbie?"

Impossible to believe how a single word could make one so angry.

"There's no one here by that name!" she exploded, swiping at an errant tear.

"Abbie, come on," he wheedled, louder this time.

She wished she could ram a fork down his throat and incapacitate it again! She ignored him and went to do her morning chores in the kitchen.

"Abbie!" he called after several minutes, his voice growing stronger and more impatient. But she went on with her tasks, drawing extreme pleasure now from disregarding him. Hate lodged in her throat like a fishbone.

"Goddamnit, Abbie! Get in here!"

She cringed at the profanity but vowed it would never put her at a disadvantage again. Two could play this wily game, and she wasn't above trying to get even for what he'd done. She calmly ignored his calls until finally, in a voice filled with rage, he bellowed.

"Miss Abigail, if you don't get in here this minute, I'm going to piss all over your lily white bed!"

Appalled, blushing, but believing every word he said, she grabbed the bedpan and ran. "You just try it!" she shouted, and flung the bedpan from the doorway. It came down on his good knee with a resounding *twin-n-n-g,* but she was gone before the reverberations ended. In her wake she heard him hiss something about a vicious asp.

Horrified and shaking, she knew she'd made it worse, for she'd have to go back in there and collect the thing and—oh! he'd been so angry again! Maybe she shouldn't have flung it at him, but he deserved it, and worse. He'd have deserved it had it been full! She pressed her hands to her cheeks. What am I thinking? He's turning me into the same sort of uncouth barbarian he is. I must get control of myself, pull myself together. I'll get rid of him as soon as I can, but until I do, I'll level my temper, like Mother always warned me I must, and somehow squelch this urge for revenge. She was in careful control by the time she reentered his room and spoke with cold disdain.

"I suggest, sir, that for the duration of your convalescence we draw a truce. I should like to see you well and on your way again, but I simply cannot brook your hostility."

"My hostility! I deserve a fit of hostility! First I got shot by that . . . that *fool* for something I didn't do, then tortured by a woman who whacks me in the teeth with her spoon, refuses to tell me where I am or why, calls me by somebody else's name, ties me to the bedpost, and holds out on me when I need a bedpan! Lady, you talk about hostility, I've got plenty, and more where that came from!"

His shouting shattered her nerves, but she carefully hid it, purring, "I see you've regained full use of your vocal chords."

Her high and mighty attitude made him bellow all the louder. "You're goddamn right I have!" Her eyes actually twitched.

"I do not allow profanity in this house," she gritted.

"Like hell you say!" he roared.

"How brave you are when you shout like a madman." And finally he started to simmer down. Using her finest diction, her quietest tones, and her explicit vocabulary, she laid down the law while she had him feeling sheepish. "At the onset, sir, you must understand that I shall not accept your calling me by such familiar and disparaging terms as Abigail, Abbie or . . . or *lady*. You shall call me Miss Abigail, and I will call you by your surname if you will kindly give it to me."

"Like hell I will."

How easily he could rout the importance of etiquette and make her feel the one in error.

"What's the matter with calling me Jesse?" he asked now. "It's my name. You were so anxious for me to tell you what it was when you thought I might not make it."

"Yes, for your tombstone," she said smugly.

Unexpectedly, he smirked. "Now I'll never tell you the rest of it." She turned away quickly, fearing she might smile.

"Please, can't we quit this bantering and resolve our dispute?"

"Damn right we can. Just call me Jesse, *Miss* Abigail." Once he'd said it, she wished he hadn't—not that way! He was the most irritating man she'd ever met.

"Very well, if you won't tell me your last name, I'll continue to call you Mr. Cameron. I've grown used to it, in any case. However, if you persist in using crudities as you did earlier, we won't get along at all. I'd appreciate it if you'd temper your tongue."

"My tongue doesn't take to tempering too readily. Most of the places I go it doesn't have to."

"That has become very obvious already. However, I think

neither of us likes being cast together this way, but seeing that we are, shall we make the best of it?''

Again he considered her words, analyzing her highfalutin way of speaking and that cocky eyebrow that constantly prickled his desire to irritate her.

"Are you going to poison me with any more of your potions you concoct for naughty gunslingers?'' he queried mischievously.

"You have proven this morning, without a doubt, that you don't need it," she replied, her ears still ringing from his tirade.

"In that case, I accept your truce, Miss Abigail." And with that, the tension seemed to ease somewhat.

She went to the bay window and opened it to the morning air. "This room smells foul. It and you need a thorough airing and cleaning. You have grown as rank as your bedclothes,'' she finished, her back to him as she flung the curtains up over their rods.

"Tut-tut, Miss Abigail, now who's goading?"

That "tut-tut" sounded preposterous coming from a man like him. She wasn't sure if she could handle his newfound sense of humor.

"I only meant to say I thought you might appreciate a bath, sir. If you would rather lie in your own effluvia, I will thankfully let you.'' By now he knew that she cut loose with her high-class words whenever she got flustered. It was fun seeing her color up that way, so he went on teasing.

"Are you proposing to give me a bath while I lay naked in this bed?" He gasped in mock chagrin and pulled the sheet up like some timid virgin.

Turning, she had all she could do to keep from laughing at him in that ridiculous pose. She cast him a look of pure challenge and stated in no uncertain terms, "I did it before . . . I can do it again."

His thick black eyebrows shot up in surprise. "You did it before!" He pushed the sheet back down, just below his navel. "Well, then . . ." He drawled, relaxing back with his good hand cradling his head.

When she spun from the room he lay there smiling, wondering if she'd really give him a *thorough* cleaning. His smile grew broader. Hell, I'm willing if you are, Abbie, he thought, and lay in the best fit of humor he'd enjoyed since falling into this flower bed of hers.

When she returned, he watched her roll up her sleeves, thinking, ah, the lady bares her wrists to me at last. He knew he had her pegged right. She was virtuous to the point of fanaticism, and he couldn't figure out how she was going to handle this situation and come out as innocent as she went in. He enjoyed himself immensely, potent buck that he was, lying back waiting for her discomfort to begin.

She had very delicate hands that looked incapable of managing the job. But some minutes later she had an oilcloth under him so fast, he didn't remember raising up to have it slid into place. He submitted complacently, raising his chin, turning his head, lifting his arm upon command. He had to hand it to her, she really knew how to give a man a decent bed bath. It felt damn good. He couldn't believe it when she climbed up next to him to get at his left side. But she did it, by Jove! She did it! And raised a new grudging respect in him.

"Now that we've drawn a truce, maybe you'll tell me why you started calling me Cameron," he said while she lathered away.

"I thought you were awake and sensible that first time you spoke. I asked you your name and you said 'Mike Cameron.' I heard it, or rather saw it, distinctly."

He remembered back and suddenly laughed. "I didn't say Mike Cameron, I said 'my camera,' but at the time it felt like somebody was drying their green rawhide around my neck, so it might not have come out too clear." He looked around. "By the way, where is it?"

"Where is what?" She kept on ascrubbing, kneeling there beside him.

"My camera."

"Camera?" She glanced up dubiously. "You've actually lost a camera and you think *I* know where it is?"

He raised a sardonic eyebrow. "Well, don't you?"

She'd been washing his side. The cloth in her hand rested nearly on his hip now, the sheet still covering him from there down. She looked at him and said dryly, "Believe me, Mr. Cameron, I have not come upon a camera on you . . . anyplace." It was out before she could control it, and Miss Abigail was immediately chagrined at what she'd said. Her startled eyes found his, then veered away as she set to work with renewed intensity.

"Why, Miss Abigail, shame on you," he drawled, grinning at the rising color in her cheeks. But he was sincerely worried about his equipment. "A camera and plates take up one hell of a lot of space. What could have happened to them?" he asked. "And my grip was with my photographic gear. Where is it?"

"I'm sure I don't know what you're talking about. You were brought to me just as you are, sir, and nobody said anything about any camera or plates. Do you think I'm hiding them from you? Put your arm up, please."

Up went his arm while she scrubbed the length of it, including his armpit.

"Well, they've got to be someplace. Didn't anybody get them off the train?" She started rinsing the soap off the arm.

"The only things they carried off that train were you, Mr. Melcher, and his valise. I'm sure nobody expected a thief to be carrying a camera." The little upward tilt of her eyebrow told him just how preposterous she thought his little fable. "Tell me, sir, what an outlaw does with a camera." She looked him square in the eye, wondering what lie he'd concoct.

He couldn't resist. "Take pictures of his dead victims for his scrapbook." His evil grin met her appalled look.

"That, Mr. Cameron, isn't even remotely funny!" she snapped, suddenly scrubbing too hard.

"Ouch! Take it easy! I'm a convalescent, you know."

"Please don't remind me," she said sourly.

His tone became conversational. "You wouldn't believe me anyway, about my camera, so I won't bother to tell you. You'd rather think I was merrily robbing trains, then you can feel justified in . . ." his voice raised a few decibals as he yanked away ". . . . tanning my hide instead of just scrubbing it! Ouch, I said! Don't you know what ouch means, woman?" He nursed his knuckles. But he could almost hear the bones snap in her neck, she stiffened up so fast.

"Don't call me woman, I said!"

She snatched his hand back and began drying it roughly.

"Why? Aren't you?" Her hands fell still, for he had taken hold of her hand, towel and all, and was holding it prisoner in his long, dark fingers. Panic knifed through her at the flutter of her heart. She looked up at his dark eyes, probing with an intensity that alarmed her.

"Not to you," she answered starchily, and pulled her hand free, then quickly clambered off the bed.

Something indefinable had changed between them in that instant when he grasped her hand. They were now quiet while she proceeded with the washing of his right leg. She soaped the length of it, working gingerly at the area near the wound. Once he arched his chest high and dug his head back into the pillow with a swift sucking breath of pain.

"It's healing, no matter what it might feel like."

But she was still upset about his earlier comments. She was briskly working her way toward his foot with fresh lather when he looked down his chest at her and asked quietly, "Are you to old Melcher?"

Her head snapped up. "What?"

"A woman. Are you a woman to old Melcher?"

But his timing was ill chosen. She had him by the bad leg and was none too gentle about slamming it back down, suds and all. He gritted his teeth and gasped, but she stood there with an outraged expression on her face, hands jammed on the hips of her wet-spotted apron, eyes glaring.

"Haven't you done enough damage where Mr. Melcher is concerned without pushing my nose in it? He's a gentleman . . . but then you wouldn't know anything about gentlemen, would you? Does it satisfy your ego to know you've managed to lose him for me, too?"

His leg hurt like hell now and a white line appeared around his lips, but she had little sympathy. How much more could she take from him?

"If he's such a gentleman, why did you throw him out?" Jesse retorted.

Her mouth puckered and she flung the cloth into the bowl, sending water splattering onto his face, the floor, and pillow. He recoiled, hollering after her retreating figure, "Hey, where are you going? You haven't finished yet!"

"You have one good hand, sir. Use it!" And her skirts disappeared around the door. He looked down at his soapy foot.

"But what'll I do with the soap?"

"Why don't you try washing your mouth out with it, which your mother should have done years ago!"

The soap was beginning to itch. "Don't you leave this soap on me!"

"Feel lucky I've conceded to wash as much of you as I have!"

He drove his good fist into the mattress and shouted at the top of his lungs, "Get back here, you viper!"

But she didn't return, and the soap stayed until the itching became unbearable and he was forced to lean painfully to remove most of it, then dry his foot and calf with the sheets.

As Miss Abigail left the house, she whacked the screen door shut harder than she'd ever done in her life. She pounded down the back steps like a Hessian soldier, thinking, *I have to get out of the same house with that monster!* Nobody she'd ever known had managed to anger her like he had. Standing in the shade of the linden tree, gazing at the garden, she longed for a return of tranquility to her life. But not even the peaceful, nodding heads of her flax flowers could calm her today. She wondered how she would ever endure that odious man until he was well enough to walk out of here on his own. He was the crudest creature she'd ever encountered. She almost had to laugh now at the memory of Doc worrying about her "tender sensibilities." If only he knew how those sensibilities had been outraged by the man she'd freely allowed into her house.

Miss Abigail's mother and father had been people with faultless manners. Cursing and raging had been foreign to her life. She had always been taught to hide anger because it was not a genteel emotion. But Mr. Cameron had managed to elicit more than just her anger. She was smitten by guilt at all she'd done—withheld a bedpan from an invalid, then thrown it at him, then abused his leg, causing him intentional pain, and slamming out of the house like a petulant child. Why, she'd even made one unforgivable ribald comment! The memory of it scalded her cheeks even now.

But the one who had precipitated it all would not allow her escape, not even out here in her garden. His voice riveted through the still summer air, abrading her once more.

"Miss Abigail, what's the railroad paying you for, half a job? Where's my breakfast?" he needled.

Oh, the gall of that man to make demands on her! She wanted nothing so badly as to starve him out of here. Loathsome creature! But she was caught in a trap of her own making. All she could do was gather her ladyhood around her like a mantle while she returned to the kitchen to prepare his meal.

* * *

When she came in with the tray, the first thing he noticed was that there was no linen napkin lining it like before.

"What? Don't I get flowers like old Melcher did?"

"How did you know . . ." she said before she could think. He laughed.

"Sounds carry in your house. Is that a real blush I see on the woman's cheek? My, my, I wonder if old Melcher knew he had what it takes to put it there. He certainly didn't look as if he did." The way he said "old Melcher" made her want to smack him!

"Remember our truce, *sir?*" she said stiffly.

"I only wondered why I don't get equal consideration around here," he complained in mock dismay.

"You wanted food, sir. I've brought you food. Do you wish to lie there and blather all morning or to eat it?"

"That depends on what you've chosen to poison me with this time."

It didn't help her temper any to recall all the warm, appreciative comments Mr. Melcher had made about her cooking. She brought a pillow to boost up that black devil's head, wishing she could use it instead to smother him. The thought must have been reflected in her face, for he eyed her warily as she spread a cloth on his chest and picked up the spoon. The glimmer in his eye warned her she'd better look out for those precious, sparkling teeth of his!

"Would you rather do it yourself?" she asked brittlely.

"No, it doesn't work when I have to lie so flat. Besides, I know how you enjoy doing it for me, *Miss* Abigail." A slow grin began at the corner of his mouth. "What is this stuff?"

"This . . . *stuff* . . . is beef broth."

"Are you determined to starve me?" he asked in that horrible, teasing tone she found more offensive than his belligerent one.

"At dinner time tonight you may have something heavier, but for now, it's only broth and a coddled egg."

"Terrific." He grimaced.

"You may consider it terrific when you taste what will follow your breakfast."

"And what's that?"

"I'll prepare a decoction of balm of Gilead, and while you may find it quite bitter, rest assured it's very fortifying for one of your debility." He considered this while she poked a few more spoons of broth into him, carefully avoiding his teeth.

"Do you ever talk like other people, Miss Abigail?" he asked then.

Immediately she knew he was trying to rile her again. "Is there something wrong with the way I speak?"

"There's nothing wrong with it. That's what's wrong with it. Don't you ever talk plain, like—'I mixed up some medicine and it'll make you stronger'?"

She could not help remembering how David Melcher had likened her speech to a sonnet. A light flush came to her face at this newest unfair criticism. She had always prided herself on her literacy and began to turn away to cover the hurt at being criticized for it now. But he grabbed her wrist.

"Hey, Miss Abigail, why don't you just bend a little sometime?" he asked, and for once the teasing seemed absent from his voice.

"You've seen me as . . . as . . . *bent* as you ever shall, Mr. Cameron. You have managed to anger me, make me lose my patience, shout like a fishwife, and more. I assure you it is not my way at all. I am a civilized person and my manner of speech reflects it, I hope. You have goaded me in countless ways, but I find no reason for this newest assault. Do you intend to wring that spoon from my wrist again?"

"No . . . no, I don't," he answered quietly, but neither did he release it. Instead, he held it loosely, very narrow and fine within the circle of his wide, dark fingers while his hazel-flecked eyes looked from her hand to her eyes and back again. He shook it gently; the hand flopped, telling him that she was not about to try to resist his superior strength. "But you're more believable when you're angry and impatient and shouting. Why don't you get that way more often? I won't mind."

Surprised, she slipped easily from his grasp.

"Eat your eggs." He opened his mouth and she put a spoonful in.

"These things are slimy."

"Yes, aren't they?" she agreed, as if overjoyed. "But they'll build your strength, and the faster you get strong, the sooner I shall be rid of you, so I intend to take excellent care of you from now on. When you've finished your breakfast, I shall walk over town to Mr. Field's feedstore to buy flax seed for a poultice. Flax seed will heal that wound as fast as anything can, but never too fast to suit me."

"How about something for this sore hand, too? Must be something broken in there because it hurts like hell." She gave him a sharp look. "Well, it does. Don't get me wrong, Miss Abigail. I positively glow at your doting, but with two good hands I might have one free for you to hold."

"Save your ill-advised wit for someone who'll appreciate it."

Jesse was beginning to appreciate her more and more. She had a caustic tongue, which he liked, and whether she knew it or not, she didn't have such a bad sense of humor. If he could just get her to bend that ramrod back and those ramrod ideals just a little she might be almost human, he thought. Breakfast really hadn't been so bad after all.

"Oh," he said. "One more thing before you leave. How about a shave?"

She looked like she'd just swallowed a junebug.

"There's no . . . no hurry, is there?" She acted suddenly fidgety. "I mean, it's been growing ever since you've been unconscious. What will a few more hours matter?" He rubbed his chin and she held her breath, feeling suddenly nauseous. But she was given a temporary reprieve, for his hand stopped its investigation before getting to his upper lip. Suddenly she seemed eager to leave the house. "I'll make you the decoction of balm of Gilead, then go up to the feedstore, and you can . . . well, you can rest while I'm gone . . . and . . ."

"Go . . . go, if you want." He motioned her toward the door, puzzled by her sudden nervousness, which was so unlike her. When she returned a minute later with the balm of Gilead, he opened wide and gulped it down. It was vile.

"Bluhhh . . ." he grunted, closing his eyes, shivering once, sticking out his tongue. Normally his grimace of displeasure would have been all it took to make Miss Abigail happy, but she was too worried about his missing moustache to gloat.

She worried about it all the way over town.

The bay window faced south, with east and west facets. He saw her as she passed along the road, straight and proper, and he couldn't believe she'd donned a hat and gloves on a hot June day like this. She was something, Miss Abigail was. The woman had starch in everything from her bloomers to her backbone, and it was amusing trying to make it crackle. She passed out of his limited range of vision and he thought of other things.

He wondered if they'd found his camera and gear down in Rockwell, at the end of the line. If it had stayed on the train, the crew in Rockwell more than likely had it by now and had let Jim Hudson know it had arrived without Jesse. Jim would get word to him sooner or later.

A knock on the door disturbed Jesse from his thoughts. "Come in!" he called. The man who came was stubby, short of hair and of breath, but long on smiles. He raised his bag by way of introduction.

"Cleveland Dougherty's the name, better known as just plain Doc around here. How you doing, boy? You look more alive than I ever thought to see you again."

Jesse liked him instantly. "That woman's too stubborn to let me die."

Doc howled in laughter, already sensing that the man had sized up Miss Abigail quite accurately. "Abigail? Aw, Abigail's all right. You were damn lucky she took you in. Nobody else in town would, you know."

"So I gathered."

"You were in some shape when we got you off that train. All that's left of your stuff is this shirt and boots. We had to cut the pants off you, o' course. And I guess this belongs to you, too." Doc lifted a pistol, weighing it in his hand while he peered over lowered brows at the man on the bed. " 'Course it's empty," Doc said pointedly. Then, as if that subject were totally cut and dried, Doc tossed the gun onto the bed.

"I guess you can put my boots and shirt under the bed," Jesse said. "That way we won't clutter up Miss Abigail's house."

"Sounds like you already know her ways, eh? Where is she anyway?"

"She went '*over town*' to the feedstore." He managed to say it just like she would have.

"I see you've had the full lash of Miss Abigail's tongue," Doc said, chuckling again. "What in thunderation is she doing there?"

"She said she was going to get flax seed for a poultice."

"That sounds like Miss Abigail all right. Got more cures up

her sleeve than a chicken's got lice. Let's see here what she's done to you." He lifted the sheet and found the wound looking surprisingly healthy. "I'd have sworn the best you'd come out of this was losing the leg to gangrene, the way it looked. But she made up a mixture of charcoal and yeast that purified it and kept working the matter to the surface. It seems to have saved your life, boy, or the very least your leg."

"But I hear you did surgery first. I guess I owe you for taking me on when they dragged me off that train. They said I was robbing it and that might've made some men hesitate to patch me up."

"Some men, maybe. Even some men around here. But we're not all that way. Ah . . . what the hell's your name anyway?" Jesse liked the man's down-to-earth language and the fact that he seemed not to care whether it was a train robber or someone else whom he saved.

"Just call me Jesse."

"Well, Jesse, I figure a man's got a right to medical treatment first and a trial second."

"A trial?"

"Well, there's talk around. 'Course, there's bound to be, the way you came in."

"Raised an uproar, did I?"

"Uproar isn't the word for it. Whole damn town congregated on my lawn to raise objections to me taking you on as a patient. Riled me up something fierce, let me tell you! Still, it's natural folks were a mite jumpy about having you under their roofs, considering the circumstances. You can hardly blame them in some ways."

"Still, Miss Abigail braved it?"

"She sure did. Marched right down there in the middle of that crowd, cool as a cucumber salad, and told the whole damn town she was willing to take you in—the pair of you yet! Left everybody feeling a little sheepish, being what she is and all."

"And what's that, Doc?"

"You mean you don't know?"

"Well, I've got a pretty fair idea, but I'd like to hear your version."

"I can tell you, but it's nothing you don't know after spending any time with her at all. I'm sure you've divined she's no floozy. Miss Abigail is more or less the town yardstick." Doc scratched his head thoughtfully, puzzling out a way to describe how everybody felt about her. "I mean, if you want to see just what a proper lady ought to be, you measure her against Miss Abigail, 'cause she's the damnedest most proper lady this town's ever seen. You want to know what a devoted daughter should act like, you measure her up against Miss Abigail, after the way she saw to her old man in his last years. There's a few women in this town could take a lesson from her on keeping their noses out of other folks' business, too. Oh, she's exactly what she appears, make no mistake about that— every inch a lady. I guess that's why the townspeople were pretty surprised that she'd take in a gunslinger like she did." The word might have rankled, but Doc had a way of saying it, offhand, as if it didn't matter to him.

"Has she ever been married?" Jesse asked.

"Miss Abigail? No . . ." Then, recalling back, Doc added, "Now wait a minute. She almost did once. A rounder he was, never could see the two of them together. But, as I recall, he courted her right up until the time her father got bad. Seems he wasn't willing to take on a bedridden old man along with his bride, so he left her high and dry. You know, over the years a person forgets those things. She was different then, of course. But it's hard to think of Miss Abigail as anything but a maiden lady. Guess that's why we were all so surprised when she took you in." Doc looked up. "How's she bearing up?"

"Staunch as a midwife."

"That'd be typical of her too. She's that way, you know. When she takes on a responsibility she's prepared to see it through, come hell or high water. She gave up the better part of her youth seeing after her father, and by the time he died, we all kind of took for granted that she'd become the town's resident old maid. Some folks thought she got a little uppity, but then you can't blame her. Hell, who wouldn't, being so young when all your neighbors labeled you a spinster? Ah well, in any case, we'd all appreciate it if you gave her her due respect."

"You've got my word on it. Oh, and Doc, could you check this hand of mine?"

Doc pronounced the hand only bruised, then summed up his findings. "Well, you're healing fast, thanks to her, but don't push it. Take 'er slow and easy. Try sitting up tomorrow, but no more than that. I'd say, by the looks of you, you'll be managing a slow shuffle by the end of the week anyway. Just don't overdo it."

Jesse smiled and nodded, liking the man more than ever as Doc prepared to leave.

"Doc?"

"Yup?"

"What's up with that Melcher fellow?"

"Wondered when you'd ask about him." Doc could see the first hard lines in Jesse's face since he'd walked in the room. "Seems he's leaving town today. Went to the depot and bought himself a ticket for Denver on the afternoon train. Did you know you shot his toe off?"

"I heard."

"He probably will limp for the rest of his life. Plenty of grounds for a lawsuit, huh?"

"You'll pardon me if I'm not overcome by guilt," Jesse said with a bitter edge to his voice. "Look what he nearly did to me!"

"Around here that's not going to count for much, I don't think. You see, you're the villain—he's the hero."

Strange, but even at those frank words, Jesse felt no criticism from Doc. As the two eyed each other, it was with mutual silent approval.

"Tell Miss Abigail I'll try to be around if she needs me again, but I don't think she will."

"Thanks, Doc."

Doc stopped in the doorway, turned one last time, saying, "Thank Miss Abigail. She's the one that kept you alive." Then he was gone.

Jesse lay thinking of all Doc had told him, trying to imagine a young and vibrant Miss Abigail courted by an ardent suitor, but the picture wouldn't gel. The image of her taking care of a sickly father seemed far more believable. He wondered just how old she was, guessing her to be thirty or thereabouts. But her bearing and actions made her seem far older, stodgy, and fusty. To picture her with a husband and children seemed ludicrous. She would seem miscast in that role, with a child's sticky fingers pulling at her spotless apron or admiring a mud pie brought for her approval. Neither could he imagine her moaning in ecstasy beneath a man.

But like the change of cards in a stereoscope came the picture of Miss Abigail as she'd been that night fighting for his life, hair and gown and skin a mess, leaning over him, pleading, urging him to fight with her. How intense she'd been then, all fire and dedication, so different from the primness which she usually exuded. The two just didn't go together. But according to Doc Dougherty, he owed his life to her. He felt a prickle of discomfort, thinking about how she'd been jilted by that other man so many years ago just because she'd accepted the responsibility of caring for a sick man, and now the same thing had happened again and it was his fault. Guilt was a new thing to Jesse. Still, he decided he owed her something and would temper his tongue because she'd lost her boyfriend on his account.

But I'll surely miss teasing her, he thought. Yup, I'll surely miss it.

Chapter 6

ALL THE WAY home Miss Abigail knew she couldn't avoid shaving him any longer. He was bound to find out sooner or later that she'd shorn him, if he hadn't already! She'd intended to get the ordeal over with at the same time as his bath, but he'd riled her so that she simply couldn't face it. Oh, if only it were all over. He was simply going to explode when he found that moustache gone, and now that she knew how volatile he was, the thought made her quaver.

"I'm home," she announced from the bedroom doorway, surprising him, as usual. How a woman could move through a house without making a sound that way beat him.

"Aha."

With a half sigh of relief that he still hadn't made the discovery, she came into the room, pulling the white gloves from her hands on her way to the mirror. He was surprised to find himself glad she was back.

"And have you brought your flax seed?" he asked, eyeing her in semiprofile as she raised her arms above her head and removed the ornate, filigreed hatpin. He noticed again that she had generous breasts. Her usual starch-fronted blouses concealed the fact, but from this angle, and with her arms raised that way, they jutted forward, giving themselves away.

"Indeed I have," she said, turning now. "And some fresh lemons for a cool drink."

He bit back a cute remark about Melcher and asked instead, "Did you bring a beer for me?"

She soured up. "Your days of ebriosity are recessed temporarily. Lemonade will have to do while you're here." He understood her now, the way his teasing made her pluck some pretentious word from her ample store of them and use it to bring him down. Ebriosity! But again his newfound agreeability stopped him from teasing, and he agreed pleasantly, "Actually, lemonade will do quite nicely, Miss Abigail."

She stood there in the center of the room, ill at ease for some reason she couldn't define, and the shifting breeze from the open window caught her skirt, billowing it out before her. She took her hat and used it to flatten the skirt down again, the gesture very youthful and enchanting, making him wonder again what she'd been like as a young girl.

"I . . . I'll shave you now, if you like." Her eyes avoided his, and she fussed distractedly with the daisies on her hat. He rubbed his jaw while her heart jumped into her throat.

"I probably look like a grizzly bear," he ventured, smiling.

"Yes," she agreed rather weakly, thinking, and you'll probably act like one in a minute, too. "I'll go heat water and gather the necessary things."

She left the room to stoke up the fire, then found clean cloths and her father's old cup and brush. She was reaching for the basin when his voice roared from the other room.

"Miss Abigail, get your ass in here and fast!" She straightened up as if the toe of his boot had given her a little impetus, then closed her eyes to count to ten, but before she finished, he was yelling again. "Miss Abigail . . . *now*!"

He had completely forgotten his promise to be nice to her. She came in holding the washbasin like a shield before her.

"Yes, Mr. Cameron?" she almost whispered.

"Don't you 'yes Mr. Cameron' me!" he roared. "Where the hell is my moustache?"

"It's gone," she squeaked.

"I've just now discovered the fact. And who is responsible?"

"Responsible? I don't see why you put it that—"

"I'll put it any way I damn well please, you interfering—"

He was so angry he didn't trust himself to call her a name, not knowing what might come out. "Who in the hell gave you permission to shave me?"

"I didn't need permission. I am being paid to see after you."

"You call this seeing after me!" His black, piercing eyes held no softening hazel flecks now. "I suppose you figured as long as you were changing everything around here—sheets, bedpans, bandages—you might as well keep right on changing. Well, you changed just one thing too many, do you hear me, woman! Just one thing too many!"

Though she quailed before his wrath, she was unwilling to be spoken to this way. "You're shouting at me and I don't like it. Please lower your voice." But her very control seemed only to raise his temperature and his volume.

"Oh God," he implored the ceiling, "save me from this female!" Then he glared at her. "What did you do, decide the big bad train robber needed his fingers slapped, is that it? I suppose you picked this way to do it. Or did you shave it off just for spite because it's masculine? Oh, I've got you pegged, *Miss* Abigail. I've seen your kind before. Anything male is a threat to you, isn't it? Anything that smacks of virility dries you up till you squeak when you walk. Well, you've picked the wrong man to wreak your puritanical vengeance on, do you hear me, woman? You'll pay for this and dearly!"

Miss Abigail stood red-faced, horrified that he'd struck so near the truth.

"I am paying for this, just standing still for your abuse and your name calling, which I do not deserve."

"You want to talk about deserving? Did I deserve this?" He made a disgusted gesture near his wounded leg. "Or this?" He next pointed to his upper lip. She was again struck by the fact that he looked very naked and unnatural without the facial hair.

"I may have acted hastily," she began, still trembling but willing to compromise now with a sort of apology, if only to silence him. He let out a derisive snort and lay there glaring at the ceiling. "If it makes you feel any better," she said, "I'm sorry I did it."

"Believe it or not, it doesn't make me feel a damn bit better." Then he went on in an injured tone, "Just why the hell did you do it? Was it bothering you?"

"It looked dirty and gave you the appearance of a typical outlaw." Then her voice brightened noticeably. "Why, don't you know that some of the most famous outlaws in history had moustaches?"

"Oh?" He raised his head a little to peer at her. "And how many of us have you met?"

"You're the only one," she answered lamely.

"I'm the only one."

"Yes," she said very meekly.

"And you shaved me so I wouldn't look like the others, huh?"

Miss Abigail, who always had such control, came very close to blubbering. "Actually n . . . no. Well, not . . . I mean, it is very much trouble when . . . well, when you're eating. I mean . . . well, it tickled."

His head came up off the pillow. "It what!"

"Nothing!" she snapped. "Nothing!"

"It tickled?"

Mortified by her traitorous tongue, she was forced to expound. "Yes, when I was feeding you." That brought his head up even further.

"Would you care to explain that, Miss Abigail?" But she had turned so red he could almost smell the starch scorching in her collar as she spun from the room. While she gathered his shaving things, he lay considering. A crazy notion took hold of him, and being very much a ladies' man, it swelled his considerable ego and cooled his anger somewhat. But common sense told him it couldn't be true—not of the ramrod-spined Miss Abigail! Still, the notion gained credence when she returned, for she was skittish as a cat at howling time, fussing around with that shaving stuff, avoiding his eyes, and obviously very uncomfortable.

She felt his eyes following her with a feral glint, but steeled herself and approached, poured some hot water into the cup, and worked up a lather. But when she made a move toward his face, his black eyes snapped warningly.

"I'll do it myself," he protested, and grabbed the soapy brush from her hand. "Just hold the mirror," he ordered. But once he got an eyeful of his naked face in it, he grew disgusted again. "Damnit, Abbie, you might as well have changed the shape of my nose. A moustache is part of a man he doesn't feel the same without." He managed to sound quite wounded now. Looking into the mirror, he shook his head woefully at his own reflection, then started lathering as if to cover up what he saw.

As the black whiskers became covered with white he looked less fearsome, so she admitted, "I knew that as soon as I did it. I'm sorry." She sounded genuinely contrite, so he stopped brushing the soap on his jaws and turned to study her. She kept her eyes on the mirror but said, "I . . . I found that I'd liked you far better with it." Fearing she'd again said the wrong thing and given him ammunition, she ventured a peek at him. But his scowl was gone and, surprisingly, so was much of the anger from his voice.

"It'll grow back."

Something told her that the worst was over, that he was trying, really trying to control himself for her.

Pleased, she offered, "Yes, your beard grows exceedingly fast." They assessed each other for a few seconds, and in that time he realized she'd studied him in his sleep long enough or hard enough to mark the speed with which his beard grew.

"How observant you are, Miss Abigail," he said quietly. And damn if she didn't blush. "Here, you can take over." He handed her the brush. "I'm not too coordinated with my left hand."

"Are you sure you trust me?" Her one fine eyebrow was hoisted higher than the other, but still he smiled.

"No, should I?"

"Mr. Melcher did," she lied, not knowing why she should want this man to think she had shaved David Melcher.

"He didn't look like he had enough man in him to grow a beard. Are you sure there was hair on his face when you started?"

"Hold still or I may cut your nose off yet." She poised the blade above his cheek. "And, unlike your moustache, it shan't grow back."

"Just stay away from my upper lip," he warned, then pulled his mouth muscles to tighten them and could feel the blade as she scraped around none too proficiently. He reached up to stop her so he could talk without getting cut.

"Shape it down around here—"

"I remember the shape well enough, sir," she interrupted, "and you have me by the wrist again." An interminable moment charged past while his brown fingers circled her little wrist.

"So I do," he grinned. "I shall take the razor from you and slit it if you take off one more hair than I think you should." He released her and shut his eyes while she finished. She was getting better at it as she went along. So, he thought, she remembers the shape well enough, does she? For some reason that vastly pleased him.

"Miss Abigail?" She turned from rinsing the razor to find his black eyes filled with wicked amusement as they smiled from his freshly shaved face. "I shall spend time thinking of a way to get even with you for the loss of my moustache."

"I'm sure you shall, sir. Meanwhile, we'll drink lemonade together as if we were the best of friends, shan't we?"

When she brought the lemonade, he had a difficult time drinking from the glass.

"Here, try this," she said, handing him something that looked like a willow twig.

"What's this?"

"A piece of cattail which I reamed out with a knitting needle. You may drink your lemonade through it." He tried it and it worked.

"How ingenious of you. Why didn't you bring it for the broth this morning? Were you so anxious to spoon-feed me?"

"I simply did not think of it."

"Ah," he said knowingly, his expression saying only a fool would believe that.

"I have things to do," she said abruptly, deciding not to stay and drink her lemonade after all, not if he was going to tease again.

"Aren't you having any lemonade? Bring it in here and let's talk a minute."

"I grow weary of your talk. I almost wish your voice hadn't come back."

"How cruel of you to deny me the use of my voice when it's one of the few parts of me that's working right." Before she could decide if he meant the remark to be suggestive, he encouraged, "Don't go. I just want to talk awhile."

She hesitated, then perched on the sewing rocker, wondering why she stayed in the room with him. She sipped daintily while he pulled thirstily at the fresh drink through the piece of cattail, then growled, "Ahhhh, that's almost as good as beer."

"I wouldn't know." No, he supposed she wouldn't.

"Doc Dougherty was here while you were gone."

"And how did he find your condition?"

"Much better than expected." She lifted her glass but not

her eyes. "He told me I ought to thank you for saving my life."

"And are you?" she challenged.

"I'm not sure yet," he answered. "Just what all did you have to do to save it? I'm curious."

"Not much. A poultice here and a compress there."

"Why so modest, Miss Abigail? I know it took more than a pat on the head to bring me around. I have a natural curiosity about what you did to keep my carcass from rotting."

Unconsciously, Miss Abigail studied her two bitten fingers, rubbing her thumb over the small scabs which had formed, unaware that his eyes followed hers.

"There was very little for me to do. You were strong and healthy and the bullet couldn't do you in, that's all."

"Doc and I are both wondering as to how you fed me. I heard you say I ate—more than once today you referred to it. How can an unconscious man eat?"

"Very well, I'll tell you. I force-fed you, using that piece of cattail you're drinking through. I had to insert it into your throat. That's why it hurt so severely when you first awakened." Again he noted her preoccupation with the marks between her knuckles and began putting two and two together.

"Are you saying you spooned medicine and food through this little hole?" She was growing very uncomfortable under this line of questioning, then suddenly realized his eyes were on the knuckles she'd been nursing and hid them in her skirt.

"I did not spoon it. I blew it," she admitted impatiently.

"With your mouth, Miss Abigail?" he asked in surprise.

"With my mouth, Mr. Cameron." But she would not meet his eyes.

"Well I'll be damned."

"Yes, you probably already are, but please refrain from saying so in my presence."

"Is that how you got tickled by my moustache? By this little bitty short straw here? It sure seems to me like it could have been cut a little longer."

Feeling her face heat up, she shot out of the rocker but he was too quick. He grabbed and got her by the back of her hand. He looked at her exposed fingers, then up at her face, with a mischievous smile creasing one side of his mouth.

"And these . . ." he said, studying the fingers, "what are these?"

"Turn my hand loose, sir!"

"As soon as I'm satisfied about what took place here while I was not coherent. Could these be my tooth marks?"

"Yes!"

He held the hand in a viselike grip while she struggled to pull it free. "What were your fingers doing in my mouth?"

"Holding it open and forcing your tongue down while I inserted the straw into your throat."

"And you call that *nothing much*?"

She glared at him silently, red to the ears now.

"To feed a common thief, mouth to mouth, to put your fingers into his mouth and suffer him to bite them until he broke the skin, and to take broth into your own mouth and blow it into his? That is much more than *nothing much*. That is dedication, Miss Abigail. That is stalwart, admirable dedication, isn't it? It seems I do owe you my gratitude."

"You owe me nothing . . . Let my—"

"I owe you my gratitude. How shall I express it?"

"Just let my hand go and that will be quite enough."

"Ah no, Miss Abigail. Surely that won't do. After all, you've been forced into some unorthodox—not to mention intimate—methods of caring for me. I would be ungrateful to let your generosity pass without notice." With his thumb he gently stroked the tooth marks on her fingers. Their sparring eyes met while a queer thrill grabbed her stomach and she strained to pull free of his grasp. "Since I have no more ticklish moustache to offend you with, allow me . . . by way of apology for this . . ." Then in slow motion he pulled her fingers to his lips and kissed the small scars. He felt the change when she stopped fighting and let him take the fingers to his mouth. Then he turned the hand over, kissed the palm with a light, lingering touch, and lightly ran his tongue out to wet her skin. She jerked then and grabbed the stricken hand with her other.

"I must have been out of my mind to bring you into my house!" she spit.

"I only meant to apologize for biting you. Don't worry, it won't happen again."

"And is this . . . this form of apology your way of getting even for my having shaved your moustache?"

"Oh, that. No, never, Miss Abigail. When I choose the time and the method of getting even, you'll well know it."

His implication was plain, and all Miss Abigail could do was scuttle out, escaping those casually smiling lips and eyes which were so much more of a threat in his newfound good humor than they'd ever been in his anger.

She kept as far away from that bedroom door as she possibly could for the remainder of the day, telling herself that each time she remembered his kiss and her stomach trembled, it was from anger.

At noon she was forced to go to him with his dinner. She made the thickest stew she could manage and unceremoniously plopped the bowl on his chest.

He'd been dozing and awoke with a start. All he had time to say was, "Boy, the service is really going downhill around this place." But she was gone again. She didn't care how he managed or failed to manage eating that stew. Furthermore, she hoped it was thick enough to tear his gut out!

"Got any more of that stew out there?" he hollered a few minutes later.

She should have guessed that a goat like him would eat everything in the house and never be bothered by it at all! She slapped more stew into his bowl and again plopped it wordlessly onto his chest while he lay there grinning as if he knew something she didn't.

In the afternoon she went up to clean Mr. Melcher's room, only to find the book of sonnets lying like a love letter from a lost beau. In a lifetime of much loneliness, she remembered how for those few treasured days he had been a harbinger of something better to come. But he was gone from her life as suddenly as he'd entered it.

A timid knock on the downstairs door brought Miss Abigail from her brown study. Coming down the steps she recognized the fabric of David Melcher's suit sleeve, which was all she could see of him. It brought a flutter to her heart as, crossing the parlor, she paused, put a hand to her breathless lips, then smoothed her blouse front, her waistband, then touched a hand to the coil of hair at the nape of her neck. She didn't realize that from the bedroom Jesse saw it all.

She moved beyond his range of vision, but every word was audible, and even from the bedroom he could detect her breathlessness.

"Why, Mr. Melcher, it's you."

"Yes . . . ahem . . . I came to return your father's slippers."

"Yes . . . yes, of course. Thank you." The screen door spring went twinnng, and a long silence followed.

"I'm afraid I've been a lot of trouble to you."

"No, no, you've been no trouble at all."

Melcher seemed to be having some trouble with his throat. He cleared it several times, followed by a second lengthy silence. When they spoke again, it was simultaneously.

"Miss Abigail, I may have jumped to . . ."

"Mr. Melcher, this morning was . . ."

Silence again while the man in the bedroom cocked his ear.

"You were within your rights to get angry with me this morning."

"No, Mr. Melcher. I don't know what came over me."

"You had good cause, though. I never should have said those things."

"Well, it really doesn't matter, does it, since you're leaving Stuart's Junction on the train within an hour?"

"I want you to know what it meant to me, this time I've spent in your lovely house while you cared for me. You did far more than was expected of you."

"Nonsense, Mr. Melcher . . ." Conscious now of the man in the bedroom, she realized he could hear every word, but there was nowhere else she could take David Melcher. The front porch was too public, the kitchen too private.

"No, it's not, Miss Abigail. Why, your . . . your nasturtiums and the sonnets and your tasteful way of doing things . . . I mean, I'm not used to such treatment. And all that delicious food and your fine care—"

"All in the line of duty."

"Was it?" he asked. "I'd hoped . . ." But this he didn't finish, and Miss Abigail toyed with the lace edging of her high, stiff collar.

"Hopes can be very hurtful things, Mr. Melcher," she said quietly.

"Yes . . . well . . ."

"I see you have purchased yourself a pair of new shoes."

"Yes. Not quite as fine as those I sell, but . . ." Once again his words trailed away.

"Feel welcome to keep Father's cane. I have no use for it since he's gone."

"Are you sure?"

She suddenly wanted very badly for him to take it, for him to carry away some small thing from her house which would always remind him of her.

"I shan't miss it, but you might, if you had to go without it."

"Yes . . . well . . . thank you again, Miss Abigail."

It grew silent again and Jesse pictured the two of them, both probably gaping at the old man's cane. The spring on the screen door sang again.

"If I ever get back through here, I'll return the cane to you."

"You needn't bother."

"Ah . . . I see," he said, rather forlornly.

"I didn't mean . . ." But her words, too, trailed away.

"I will always think of this place when I smell the scent of nasturtiums."

She swallowed, her heart threatening to explode, her eyes to flood.

"Goodbye, Miss Abigail," he said, backing away slowly.

"Goodbye, Mr. Melcher."

It grew so quiet then that Jesse could hear each and every one of Melcher's irregular steps shuffling off down the road. He saw the limping figure through the east facet of the bay window, below the half-drawn shade, and thought, damn fool should've used his head on that train and he wouldn't be limping now. It was the first time Jesse was able to think of Melcher without getting frustrated and angry at his own incapacity. He heard the footsteps of Miss Abigail go back upstairs long, long after Melcher limped away. She must have watched him out of sight, Jesse thought. He couldn't help recalling all that Doc had told him about the other man who'd walked out on her once before, couldn't help comparing now to then. And he could not stop the irritating twitch of conscience that prickled him.

From an upstairs window Miss Abigail watched the puffs of smoke as the afternoon train pulled in. Its whistle swooned through the stillness as she held the lace curtains aside. She pictured Mr. Melcher limping aboard the train. Her heart called to him not to forget her. A puffy cloud lifted above the roof of the depot and the steam whistle cried mournfully once more, bearing David Melcher out of her life. Her eyes stung as she turned to put fresh sheets on his bed.

She fully expected to be teased again after everything the man in her house had overheard. She came to his doorway to find him sound asleep. It gave her a moment of perverse pleasure to disturb him.

"I found some wild weeds that will help your hand," she said loudly, businesslike.

He roused at her words, clenched his good hand, and gave one of those shivering, all-over stretches. It was slow, masculine, and she averted her eyes, remembering how he'd earlier said that anything masculine threatened her. He growled lazily, deep in his throat, twisting and yawing. At last he opened his eyes and drawled, "Howdy, Miss Abigail. Have you been there long?"

"I just . . ." But she had. She'd been watching those muscles twisting and turning.

"Studying my beard grow again?"

"You flatter yourself, sir. I'd as soon watch grass grow."

He smiled, again slowly and lazily.

"I came to put a fomentation on that bruised hand. The sooner it heals, the sooner I'll be excused from wringing out your shaving cloths."

He laughed. He seemed for once to be in a halfway human mood. "Spoken like a true adversary, Miss Abigail. Come on in. I can use the company now that I've been so rudely awakened anyway. I expect you can too, now that Melcher is gone."

"Leave Mr. Melcher out of this, if you please," she said acidly. "Do you want the compress on your hand or not?"

"By all means. After all, it's my gun hand, isn't it?" He extended it toward her and she came to unwrap the old gauze strips and pad. As she unwound the pieces, he added, "And my loving hand, too." She automatically halted all movement, realized her mistake, continued unwrapping while he went on. "Hard for a right-handed man to make love with only one good hand and that his left."

She could already feel the color creeping up behind her choker collar.

"How indelicate of you to say so."

The hand was free now and he flexed it only a little, at the same time moving it toward her face. She jerked back.

"And how indelicate of you to flinch, Miss Abigail, as if I

had designs on you. After all, a hand like this is in no shape for loving or shooting, either one. When it is, you'll know it."

Rattled now, she turned her back on him, and her voice was almost pleading. "What do I have to do to keep you from teasing me this way? I am unused to it, thus I have no defense against it. I'm sure the women you've known in the past were quick with rebuttal, but I am simply tongue-tied, time and again, and deeply embarrassed. I realize this is precisely the outcome you hope to achieve with me, so it must pleasure you endlessly to hear me finally admit it. But I lay my soul bare to you and admit that these taunts are disconcerting. I ask you to make my job easier by treating me fairly and honorably."

"Do you want me to beseech you to put fresh nasturtiums in my room?"

When she spoke her voice was exceedingly quiet, almost defeated. "I want absolutely nothing from you except to be treated like a lady, as I was by Mr. Melcher. But then you obviously disdain Mr. Melcher. His qualities of kindness and consideration are foreign to you, I know, but you only make yourself more offensive by making fun of him."

"Old Melcher got to you, did he?"

With an effort she kept her voice calm. "Mr. Melcher knows how to treat a lady, how to make her feel valued and appreciated, how to eke a bit of the sublime out of the everyday tedium. These things may seem soft and weak to you, but it is because you have never learned the strengths to be found in the beautiful and gentle things of this life. Strength to you is only . . . only . . . anger and cursing and goading and making others do what you want by the force of these things. I pity you, Mr. Cameron, for you've somehow been denied the knowledge that such well-worn attributes as politeness, respect, patience, forbearance, even gratitude, have a peculiar strengthening quality all their own."

"And you've practiced these virtues all your life?"

"I've tried." He saw her shoulder blades draw erect proudly as she admitted it.

"And what good did it do you? Here you are, polite and bitter, and left with me and deserted by Melcher."

Still with her back to him, she cried, "You have no right, Mr. Cameron! No right at all! *You* are the reason he is lost to me, you and your teasing tongue. I'm sure you feel supremely self-satisfied that he is gone and that with him went my last

chance for . . . for . . ." But at last Miss Abigail broke
down, lowered her face into her hands and sobbed, her small
shoulders shaking as Jesse had never thought to see them. The
last woman he'd caused to cry had been his mother, the last
time he'd left New Orleans to come back out West again.
Seeing Miss Abigail cry now was equally as disturbing. It
made him feel exactly as she had many times said he was:
callous and coarse. And this feeling was something new and
disturbing. He wanted suddenly to make up for the hurt he'd
caused, but before he could say more, she gulped, "Excuse
me, sir," and fled the room.

It struck him that even in her discomposure she clung to her
impeccable manners as tightly as possible.

Miss Abigail was aghast at her own actions. Never in her life
had she cried before a man. Strength came from many sources,
but crying, she believed, was not one of them. Still, it was
peculiar how purged she felt when she finished. All the
bitterness and waste of her life, all the given years, all the
unexperienced joys, all the foregone pleasures which she had
never before begrudged her father or Richard . . . ah Richard . . . it was a blissful relief to even think his name
again . . . welled now in a great, crushing hurt which she
allowed herself to explore. All the pent-up frustrations which a
lady never shows felt like a blessed release after years in
prison.

She stood in her shaded backyard and cried at last for the
loss of Richard, of her father, of David Melcher, of children
and warmth and companionship. And for the first time ever she
rued those years she had sacrificed to her father.

And her breakdown before Jesse made her something which
she had never seemed to him before: vulnerable.

And his having caused it made him something she could
hardly have suspected him capable of being: contrite.

And so it was that in the late afternoon, when she came to
him next, there was a first hint of harmony between them. She
came with the same self-assured dignity as before her outburst,
as if it had never taken place. The only residual of her tears was
a faint puffiness beneath her eyelids. Her face held neither
challenge nor rebuke as she stood in the doorway, saying, "It
seems I've neglected your hand again."

"My fault," he said simply. He seemed agreeable, no hint of teasing showed in his face.

"I'll take care of it now?" she asked more than stated.

"Come in," he replied. "What have you got this time?"

"The trappings for a fomentation. May I put it on?" What she was really asking was if she could come in without being tortured again by his tongue. He nodded, fully understanding. She entered, took his bruised hand, and began working over it. A grudging admiration once again overtook him. Time and again she came to him, no matter what he did or what he said. There seemed no end to her tenacity in the face of duty.

"How is it feeling?" she asked, studying the hand.

"Not good."

"Do you think any bones are broken?"

"Doc says no, but it hurts every time I move it."

"It would be surprising if none were broken," she said. The bruise was by now a ghastly yellowish-green. She picked up a small, filled cloth bag from a steaming cup.

"What's that?" he asked suspiciously.

"Be still." Holding it gingerly between two fingers, she blew on it.

"Are you punishing me with that thing?" But she only squeezed it against the side of the cup and laid it on the colorful bruise. It didn't quite burn him, but was mighty uncomfortable. "I guess I deserve it," he ventured while she only concentrated on wrapping the hand. "What have you put in that?"

"Something that will take away the aching, heal the bruise."

"Well, is it a secret or what?"

"No, it's no secret. It's just a weed."

"A weed? What weed?"

"A weed called arsesmart."

"Arsesmart! Are you serious?" It was all he could do to keep from making choice remarks about that, but he resolutely refrained.

Meanwhile Miss Abigail thought, Is there nothing we can say to each other that hasn't some ulterior meaning? He was, of course, wearing a grin, which she ignored. To cover her discomfort, she lectured.

"My grandmother taught my mother, and she taught me the value of arsesmart. It can dissolve congealed blood, which is why I'm using it on your hand. My grandmother used it for everything. She even used it on a small mole she had on her chin right here." At last Miss Abigail looked into Jesse's eyes, touching her own chin. Lamely, she finished, "But as far as I can recall, that mole never disappeared. She never . . ." Her words trailed off as she looked into Jesse's dark face, still painfully aware of the tears he had seen her shed earlier, wondering if he would mention them. But he said nothing and now looked deep in thought.

She gathered up the roll of gauze. "I believe that by morning you'll find those muscles noticeably relieved." Her eyes slid to his hand. Now, she thought, now he will taunt me. But instead he only held out the hand, shook his head as if scolding himself.

"Well, that puts one pistol hand out of commission. But it feels much better."

It was not a thank you, but it was close, and Miss Abigail thought about it all the while she fixed his supper tray. An apology was too much to hope for—he had probably never apologized for anything in his life. Still, her outburst of tears had mollified him somewhat, and to let him know she would not be faulted for a genteel life style, she picked a small nosegay of nasturtiums and put them in a delicate cut glass ewer on his tray, which was again spread with a spotless linen liner.

When he saw the neat tray and fresh flowers, he quirked an eyebrow questioningly but took it all as a peace offering and decided he'd accept.

"Is it these things that smell so sweet?" He flicked a petal.

"It is."

"Nasturtiums, I presume?"

"They are."

They eyed one another like two bighorns deciding whether to butt or back off.

"With this hand I won't be able to handle a knife." And with those words her olive branch was accepted.

"I'll handle the knife," she offered. Then added, "I hope you like liver, Mr. Cameron. It was simply too warm a day to keep the range stoked for long. Liver and onions was the fastest thing I could think of."

At her words he felt a curious swelling at the base of his tongue, warning him not to open his mouth for any liver. But there she sat on the sewing rocker beside his bed, cutting the meat, extending it to his mouth, some sort of unspoken, rocky truce at last between them. So he took it, chewed slowly, and swallowed, willing himself not to gag, not to displease her again as he seemed to do so easily. But oh! how he despised liver!

She kept it coming and coming and finally he had to think of something. "What's in the cup?" he asked.

"Coffee."

"Where's your straw?"

"Right here." She produced it from under the linen napkin on the tray.

"I'll have a drink of that." He was in too much of a hurry and burned his mouth, opened it wide, exclaiming, "Waugh!"

"Oops," she said innocently. "I guess I should have warned you it might be too hot."

But by this time he was too concerned about finishing that liver to ride her about scalding him with coffee. She wanted peace and she would have it, by God! He steeled himself for more liver and never uttered a word, but ate dutifully until the plate was empty.

Meanwhile she rambled on, talking about the many home cures and remedies she'd learned from her mother and grandmother, telling him about the book where she'd found the yeast and charcoal remedy that had saved his life.

And all the while his stomach rebelled.

At last she said, "By morning your hand could be so much improved that you might be slicing your own liver . . . I mean, slicing the liver by yourself."

But he was lying with closed eyes, curiously impassive. Please, no, he was thinking. Anything but liver. Unaware of his roiling stomach, she left with the tray, gratified for the first time at how docile and obedient he had been.

Halfway through the dishes she heard him weakly call, "Miss Abigail?" She cocked an ear, smiled, pleased that he at last was calling her Miss Abigail without his usual annoying tone, yet wondering at the same time what trick he might be up to now.

"Miss Abigail . . . bring me a bucket, please—quick!"

Was that *please* she heard? Then suddenly she realized he'd asked for a bucket. His silence during supper, his closed eyes

right afterward, his uncharacteristic passivity . . . oh no!
"I'm coming!" she bellowed at the top of her lungs.

The bucket had no more than hit the floor beside the bed
when he groaned, struggling to roll over toward it. She
whipped the bolsters from under his leg, reached across, and
grabbed him—sheet and all—by the buttocks and rolled him to
the edge of the bed just in time. He upchucked every bit of her
fried liver, onions, coffee, green beans, and even the cherry
cobbler. He lay sweating, face down over the edge of the bed,
his eyes closed.

At last he took a fortifying gulp of air, then said to the floor,
"Has it occurred to you, Miss Abigail, that perhaps we're fated
to aggravate each other without even trying?"

"Here, roll over," she ordered. "You must not lie on your
wounded leg that way." She helped him onto his back again
and saw his chalky complexion beneath the black, black
whiskers. "Perhaps I'd better check your wound again."

He flung an arm across his forehead and eyes. "It's got
nothing to do with my wound. I just detest liver, that's all."

"What?" she gasped. "And still you ate it all anyway?"

"Well, I tried," he managed with a rueful laugh. "I tried,
but it didn't work. I was bound and determined not to
antagonize you again, especially when I saw how you'd done
up that tray. But it seems I can't keep peace even when I try."
He flopped his arm weakly away from his eyes to find Miss
Abigail McKenzie in a state of suspended humor, her wide
smile hidden behind both hands, and he couldn't help his own
sheepish grin from spreading across his face. And then Miss
Abigail did the most amazing thing! She collapsed onto the
rocker, sending it rolling backward while she laughed and
laughed, clutching her waist and letting her merriment fill the
room. It was the last thing in the world Jesse had expected her
to do. Forward she came, then back again, forgetting herself
for once, lifting her feet as a child pumps on a swing, a flash of
petticoat lace accompanying her libation. And, oh, how
enchanting she looked limp and laughing that way.

"I'm sorry I can't join you," he said, "but it hurts to laugh
right after you've just heaved your guts out." But his smile
was there just the same while he continued thinking how
surprisingly beguiling she looked with her guard down.

"Oh, Mr. Cameron," she sighed at last, "perhaps you're
right and we are fated, you and I. Even when you try to do my

cooking justice it backfires." She laughed once more, gaily.

"Backfires? For once you've chosen the perfect word," he said, chuckling in spite of his sore stomach muscles. "Oh God, don't make me laugh . . . please." He hugged himself.

"You deserve it after the way you have just insulted my cooking."

"Who insulted whom? You're the one who poked that liver down me without bothering to ask if I liked it or not. It was more than an insult to have to eat it. Believe me, lady, it was a lethal weapon."

By now she was so amused that she forgot to take offense at either his profanity or the way he'd laughingly called her *lady*. She only lolled back in the rocker while he enjoyed just watching her.

"One by one I'm discovering the chinks in your armor," she said, coasting to a stop, with her head tilted back lazily. "And one of them is liver." She was relaxed as he'd never seen her before, hands lying palms-up in her lap. The golden evening sun came through the west window, lighting her hair, her chin, her high collar, the tips of her earlobes and eyelashes, turning them all to gilt.

He wondered again how old she was, for she looked suddenly young, leaning back on the chair that way, and he experienced again a momentary flash of regret for what he'd said earlier about how she'd been deserted by Melcher. He wanted the air cleared of that, thought that maybe now when she was relaxed and affable they might talk about it and exorcise the lingering bad feelings it had caused.

"How old are you?" he asked.

"Too old for it to be any business of yours."

"Too old to let a good prospect like Melcher get away?"

"You're despicable," she said, but without much fight, still easy in that chair. She rolled her head toward him, met his eyes, and a faint smile limned her lips.

"Maybe," he admitted, smiling too. "And you're worried."

"What am I worried about?"

"About getting old and having no man. But there are more where Melcher came from."

"Not in Stuart's Junction there aren't," she said resignedly.

"So . . . I fixed it good between you and Melcher and he was the last prospect around, huh?"

She didn't reply, but then she didn't need to. He studied her appreciatively as she looked into the sun's rays through slitted eyes, as if playing some game with them.

"Should I apologize for that, Miss Abigail?"

She quit playing with the sunbeams and rolled her head his way, quiet for the moment, considering. "If you must ask, it counts for naught," she said softly.

"Does it?" Then after a moment, "Anyway, it would be a bit of a letdown to have apologies between us now, wouldn't it? After all, we started out fighting like alley cats. You'd miss it if I suddenly became meek."

"And it would pain you to apologize, wouldn't it?" she countered.

"Pain me? Why, you do me an injustice, Miss Abigail. I'm as capable of apologies as anyone." But still he didn't say he was sorry.

"I apologized about your moustache, didn't I?"

"Out of fear, I think."

She rolled her head away, back toward the light that poured through the window, and shrugged her shoulders. "An apology is a move denoting strength—not strength of body, which I'm sure you've always had, but strength of character such as Mr. Melcher has."

His mellow mood was suddenly soured by her words. He was getting sick and tired of being compared unfavorably to that man. His ego was definitely singed. He didn't like being found lacking, even by such a sexless woman as her, and certainly not when put up against a milktoast like Melcher. If it took an apology to sate the woman's eternal appetite for mitigation, well she'd have it, by God!

"I'm sorry, Miss Abigail. Does that make you feel better?"

She didn't even turn his way, just sat intent upon that sunlight. But she heard the defensiveness in his voice, making the apology less than sincere.

"No, not really. It's supposed to make *you* feel better. Did it?"

He felt the blood leap to his face, scourged by her refusal to gracefully accept his apology after it had taken much soul-searching to bring it out. Never in his life had he lowered himself to apologize to any woman, and now that he had, look what had come of it. Suddenly angered, he laughed once, harshly and short.

"Tell you what'd make me feel better—if you'd just get out of here and take your liver and all your rosy pictures of Melcher with you!"

Turning, she found his face suffused with irritability. Her amused eyes remained upon his hard ones. She could see that he thought she should have blithely accepted his apology; it did not occur to him that it had been given for all the wrong reasons, making it totally without contrition. The color was back in his face again, and the bite of his words suddenly sowed a seed of suspicion within Miss Abigail. Why, he's jealous of David Melcher! Unbelievable as it was, it had to be true. What other reason could there possibly be for him to react as he had? He glared at her while she, wearing a secret cozening smile, rose and sweetly wished him good night.

It was her smug attitude and that sugary good night that drove him to call after her, "I now owe you two! One for the moustache and one for the liver!"

When she had gone upstairs for the night, he lay awake a long time, puzzling over how she could manage to anger him this way. What was it about Abigail McKenzie that got under his skin? He reviewed all the obvious irritations she'd caused—the moustache and the bedpan and such—but none of these was really the crux of his anger. It stemmed from the way she'd managed to make him feel guilty about scaring Melcher off. Why, he'd had women from New Orleans to the Great Divide, any one of whom would make Abigail McKenzie look like a sorry scarecrow, and here she was, mooning over that pantywaist Melcher, flinching from so much as a finger twitched her way by himself. And when she had finally wheedled an apology out of him, what had she done? Thrown it back in his face, that's what! For a while there tonight, while she sat in that rocker laughing, he wondered if she could be human, with impulses like other women had. Well, he thought, we'll soon find out if that female has impulses or not. If she wants to moon around making me feel guilty about Melcher, always reminding me what a gentleman he is and what a despicable cad I am, even when I'm trying to apologize, I'll give her something to back it up, by God! And maybe next time she forces an apology from me—if that day ever comes—she'll show some of that impeccable breeding she's always throwing in my face and accept it like the lady she claims to be!

Chapter 7

————

HE HEARD HER creeping softly down the stairs before dawn had fully blossomed in the sky. She flashed past the area he could view from his bed, and he heard the front door open. After a stretch of silence he heard her humming ever so faintly. Off in the unseen distance a rooster crowed. He imagined her standing there at the east door, looking out at the dawn, listening to it. She passed his door on catfeet.

"Taking in the dawn, Miss Abigail?" he asked. And her head popped back around the doorsill. She still had her nightie on, so hid behind the wall.

"Why, Mr. Cameron, you're awake, and you're sitting up!"

"Doc Dougherty said I could."

"And how does it feel?"

"Like I ought to be out there with you watching the sun come up. I'm used to watching it rise over the roughlands, but I haven't seen it for a while. What's it like today?"

She gazed toward the front door, still shielding herself behind the doorframe, but he could see the mere tip of her nose. "It is a myriad of pinks today—striated feathers of color, from deepest murrey to palest primrose, with the spaces between each color as deep and clear as the thoughts of sages."

He laughed, not unpleasantly, and said, "Well put, Miss Abigail. But all I understood was pink."

She felt foolish for having been carried away by the beauty of the dawn, but he would, of course, not be the kind to apprecite it in the same way she did.

"I . . . I need some things for today. May I come in and get them?"

"It's your room. Why the sudden request for permission?"

"I . . . I forgot my robe last night. Would you please look away while I come in?"

From around the doorway came the healthiest laugh she'd ever heard.

"Unless I miss my guess, Miss Abigail, you're swathed in white cotton down to your wrists, up to your ears, and down again to your heels. Am I right?"

"Mr. Cameron!"

"Yes ma'am," he drawled, "yes ma'am, you can come in. You're safe from me." Naturally he sat there leaning against the head of the bed, watching her boldly as she gathered up fresh clothing for the day. She saw his smile from the corner of her eye, and once he had the audacity to ask, "What's that?" She tucked the undergarment out of sight, assuring herself that she would not again forget to get her things out of here while he was sleeping.

"The leg feels fine today," he said conversationally, "and so does the hand. The only thing that hurts is my stomach after the liver you flushed it out with last night. I'm so hungry I could eat a horse and chase the rider!"

She almost laughed out loud. Sometimes it happened so easily that she couldn't control herself, for usually she did not want to be amused by him. But now she replied, "If I see any coming this way, I'll be sure to warn them off. I somehow don't doubt that you'd do it!"

"Feisty this morning, Miss Abigail?"

"I might ask you the same thing, Mr. Cameron," she rejoined, making for the door with her cumulate riggings.

"Abbie?" The shortened name brought her up short.

"*Miss* Abigail," she corrected, raising her chin and turning toward him.

And it was then that she saw the gun.

It was black, oiled, sleek, and he held it loosely in his left hand. She had not the slightest doubt that he could use it accurately at this range, left-handed or not.

All he said was "Abbie" again, reiterating much more than the name. There followed a vast silence while he let the significance of the gun and the shortened name sink in. Then he said in a casual, mellow voice, "You know, I am feeling a bit feisty this morning after all." A sinister half smile played upon his generous lips, beneath the shadowed skin to which she'd once taken a blade.

She stared at that lip, then back at the gun as he hefted it in his hand carelessly, making her clutch the articles of clothing tightly against her chest.

"Wh . . . where did you get that . . . that thing?" she asked in a quivering voice, her eyes riveted to it.

"I'm a train robber, am I not? How can I rob trains without a gun?"

"B . . . but where did you get it?"

"Never mind that now." But there was little else she could mind. Her eyes were like moons while he took perverse pleasure in the fearful way she gawked at it.

"Abbie?" he repeated. She didn't move, just gaped at the gun while he used the end of it to point at the floor at her feet.

"Drop the duds," he ordered, almost mildly.

"Th . . . the duds?" she choked.

"The ones in your arms." It took some time before the words seemed to get through to her. When they did, she released the clothes in slow motion, letting sleeves, stockings, underwear trail regrettably down to the floor at her bare feet.

"Come here," he ordered quietly. She swallowed but didn't budge. "I said come here," he repeated, lifting the pistol now to point it directly at her, and she began slowly inching around the foot of the bed.

"What did I do?" she managed to squeak.

"Nothing . . . yet." His left eyebrow arched provocatively. "But the day is young."

"Why are you doing this?"

"I'm going to teach you a couple of lessons today." Her eyes, like a cornered rabbit's, didn't even blink. "Do you know what I'm going to teach you?" he asked, and her head moved dumbly on her neck. "Number one . . ." he went on, "I'm going to teach you never to shave the moustache off an unsuspecting outlaw. I said come here and I meant it." She moved nearer but still not near enough for him to reach from where he sat leaning leisurely against the brass headboard. He swung the pistol slowly her way.

"Here," he ordered, pointing with it to the floor directly beside him.

"Wh . . . why are you threatening me?"

"Have I made any threats?"

"The gun is a threat, Mr. Cameron!"

"*Jesse!*" he spit suddenly, and she jumped. "Call me Jesse!"

"Jesse," she repeated meekly.

"That's better." Once again his voice went quiet, almost silky. "Lesson number two, Abbie, is what happens when you wheedle an apology out of a man then use it to slap him in the face with."

"I did not wheed—"

"You wheedled, Abbie, you wheedled," he wheedled. "You got me to the point where I was actually sorry I'd made old Melcher run off like a scared chipmunk. Did you know you got me to that point, Abbie?"

She shook her head, staring blindly.

"And when I apologized, what did you say?"

"I don't remember."

"I mean to make you remember, Abbie, so you'll never do it again."

"I won't," she promised, "just put your gun away."

"I will . . . after I've taught you your lesson. What you said was that my apology should make *me* feel good, only it didn't . . . because you wouldn't let it. But I aim to feel good—real good, real soon."

She clutched her arms tightly over her breasts, gripping the sleeves of her batiste nightgown.

"Put your arms down, Abbie." She stared into his black, amused eyes, unable to make her muscles move.

"What?" she gulped.

"You heard me." At last she did as ordered, but again in slow motion. "Since I scared Melcher away and you declined to accept my apology for it, I figured the least I could do is make up for what you missed, huh?"

Here it comes, she thought in panic, and her eyes slid closed while she quaked all over.

"But I'm stuck in this bed, so you'll have to come to me,

Abbie . . . come on." He made a beckoning motion with the tip of the gun. When she stood directly beside and above him, he pointed the pistol at her, not even looking up as he did so. "You were so all-fired breathless with Melcher, there were times when I heard you heart pitty-patting clear in here. But if old Melcher had any spine, he'd have hung around at least for a little billing and cooing. You know what I mean? Since the big, bad train robber chased him off, the least he can do now is stand in for old Melcher, right?" When she only stood quaking, saying nothing, his silky voice continued. "I know you get the picture, Abbie, so kiss me. I'm waiting."

"No . . . no. I won't," she answered, wondering where she got the air to speak—her chest felt crushed by fear. He moved the pistol then and even through her nightie she could feel the cold metal barrel against her hip. He still didn't even look up, just nudged her hip with the gun. She slowly leaned over and, with eyes wide open, touched his lips quickly with hers.

"You call that a kiss?" he scoffed when she jumped away again. "That felt like some dry, old lizard whipped her tail across my lips. Try it again, like you would if I were Melcher."

"Why are you doing this—" she began, but he cut her off.

"Again, Abbie! And shut your eyes this time. Only a lizard keeps her eyes open while she's kissing."

She lowered her face to his, seeing his black, amused eyes close before her as she dropped her eyelids and kissed him again. The new growth of moustache was like the stem of a wild rose bush.

"Getting better," he said when she again leaped away. "Now give me some tongue."

"Dear God . . ." she moaned, mortified.

"He's not going to help you now, Abbie, so get down here and do as I say."

"Please . . ." she whispered.

"Please, Jesse!" he corrected.

"Please, Jesse . . . I've never . . . I haven't . . ."

"Quit stalling and get to it," he ordered. "And sit down here. I'm getting dizzy watching you bounce up and down."

With her insides trembling, she sat down gingerly on the edge of the bed, hating every black whisker that shadowed his skin, every hair that surrounded his hatefully handsome face.

"What is it you want of me? Please get it over with," she begged.

"I want a responsive, wet female kiss out of you. Haven't you ever kissed a man before, Abbie? I have nothing but time while you practice. What are you afraid of?" When her eyes refused to lower to the gun at her side, he chuckled. "Let's get back to the lesson at hand. You were going to give me some tongue. It's called french kissing and everybody does it that way, probably even lizards." He lounged there insolently, and when she sat stiffly he had to put the gun to her again, this time beneath her right jaw. "Wet!" was all he said, then cocked the gun, making her jump at the metallic click.

She closed her eyes and resigned herself. He didn't quite close his, saw hers pinched tightly shut beneath woven eyebrows, saw her brows twitch as the tip of her tongue touched his upper lip and his tongue came out to meet it. Against her lips he said, "Relax, Abbie," and he lowered the gun and put an arm around her shoulders, pulling her against his bare chest, turning his mouth sideways on hers. "Put your arms around me," he said as he felt her elbows digging against him in resistance. "Come on, Abbie, unless you want to be here all day." And one of her arms crept up around his neck, the other around his bare side. She felt the gun, still in the hand which he used to press the back of her head, forcing their mouths so tightly together. His lips opened farther; the inside of his mouth was hot. He pushed his tongue into the secret crevices of her mouth, withdrew it again, then lightly bit her tongue making her fearfully push against his chest. But he somehow wrestled her arms away, pulling her against him, squashing her breasts flat against his skin, combating her every move while his mouth retained its hold on hers. He broke away then, sliding his lips down, taking her lower lip gently between his teeth. "Jesse!" he ordered in a fierce whisper, ". . . say it."

"Jesse," she whimpered before his mouth slid onto hers again, warm and wet and melting some of her resistance.

"Jesse . . . again," he demanded, feeling her thundering heartbeat through the thin batiste nightgown upon his chest.

"Jesse," she whispered while he rubbed the back of her neck with his fingers and the butt of the gun: warm and cold together. Then he silenced the word again, kissing her with that same intercourse of tongues as before, compounding fear and delight, sensuality and shame, refusal and acceptance all within her confused body.

"Ab . . ." he whispered then, "Ab . . ." Her lips were free to correct him but the thought never entered her head, for some strange languor had befallen her. Then, using his hands and mouth, he pushed her abruptly away, stunning her by asking, "Did it tickle that time?"

She could not look at him. Her head hung down and she felt suddenly filthy, violated in some way she could not comprehend. Not by him but by herself, because she'd stopped fighting him sometime while his tongue moved within her mouth, because she'd begun liking the wet, warm touch of it, the feel of his broad, muscled shoulders beneath her hand, her racing heart upon his chest.

"Today's lesson is over," he said dismissingly, the satisfied smile once again about his eyes. "I told you, when I set out to get even you'd know it."

"And I told you that force is not strength. Gentleness is strength."

"Force is damn effective, though, isn't it, Abbie?"

Once free of him, off the bed, her courage returned. "I want you out of here, do you hear? Immediately!"

"Don't forget who holds the gun, Abbie. Besides, I can't walk yet. What reason will you give all your inquisitive neighbors when they ask why you threw a helpless man out of your house? Will you tell them it was because he taught you how to kiss properly?"

"They won't ask. None of them was willing to take you in in the first place. They won't find fault with me for putting you out now."

"I've been meaning to talk to you about that, Abbie. Doc Dougherty said you were the only one who stood up and spoke for me out of this whole town. I've been meaning to thank you for that."

His words brought her blood to the boiling point. Oh, the nerve of the conceited fool to sit there thanking her after what he'd just done! "Your thanks are not essential, nor are they wanted anymore. The railroad is paying me to keep you until they can get their hands on you. It's all the thanks I need!"

He reared back and laughed. "Have you thought of why they want me, Abbie?" he asked, with a knowing look in his eyes.

"What a question from a *train robber*!" She longed to smack the disgusting smirk from his face. "I shall go to the depot today and wire whomever it is that wants you next to come and get you! The railroad can have you, wound, moustache, and all!"

"You'll miss the money you could make off me during my recuperation."

"I will miss nothing of you, you filthy, conceited goat!" she all but shrieked.

"Enough!" he suddenly roared. "Get out of here and get yourself dressed and make me some breakfast before I decide to get even with you for feeding me that liver last night. How long can a man live without decent food?"

She stomped to the pile of clothing at the foot of his bed, flailing the air with each piece before hooking it in the crook of an arm and stamping her way out. Her lips were pursed so tightly that her teeth were dry from sucking wind. When she was gone, Jesse's head arched back and his body bounced with great gasps of silent laughter. Then he dug his dirty shirt out from under the sheet near his feet, wrapped the empty gun in it, and put it back under the mattress.

She had absolutely no intention of cooking him one morsel of food. She made a fire, bathed, dressed, and all the while he periodically bellyached for his breakfast.

"What the hell's taking you so long out there?"

"I'm starving, woman!"

"Where's my food?"

She kept her eye on the clock, anxious for it to reach a proper hour so she could go over town and send the wire. But in the midst of her extreme pleasure in starving the goat in the other room, he informed her, "I don't smell anything cooking out there. I have this gun trained at the wall where I think you are. Should I try for a lucky shot?"

His answer was the loud, tinny whack of a kettle as she smacked it onto the range. She'd fill him up to shut him up, but she'd be blinkered if she'd feed him anything remotely delectable! Cornmeal was the fastest, cheapest, least appetizing thing she could think of. He kept up the needling while she cooked.

"What are you doing now, butchering the hog for bacon? . . . I smell something cooking. What is it? . . . If you're thinking of wasting time bringing me the pitcher and bowl, forget it, unless they're filled with food. A man could starve here and go unnoticed while he's doing it!"

On and on he yammered until by the time she took his tray in she was livid.

"Ah, I see you heard me at last," he said, with a stupid grin on his face. She looked for the gun but it was nowhere in sight.

"The people clear over town heard, I'm sure."

"Good! Maybe somebody will take pity on me and bring me some hardtack and jerky to store under my mattress. It would sure beat the cooking around here—not to mention the service. You didn't bring me any more of your slimy eggs, did you?"

"You are insufferable! Despicable!" she spit venomously.

He only smiled broader than before. "You too, Miss Abigail, you too." He sounded downright jovial. "Now stand back and let me at this Epicurean delight of the week. Ahhh, cornmeal. Takes a skilled hand to make cornmeal."

The only thing she could think of at the moment was, "Even animals wash before they eat."

"Oh yeah? Name me one," he said through a mouthful of cornmeal. She looked aside in distaste.

"A racoon."

"Coons wash their food, not their faces. Besides, they can afford the time. Nobody makes them throw up then leaves them to starve all night."

It was beyond her why she spoke to him at all. But just once she'd like to get the best of him. But there was no dealing with a swine. Irritated, she flounced out. In a ridiculously short time he called for more cornmeal mush.

"I could use another bowl of that Epicurean cornmeal," he informed her loudly. She took the kettle right in there and plopped a now-cold gob of the stuff in his bowl. It had, in the ensuing time, acquired the look and texture of dried adobe.

"When you get rid of me, why don't you get a job slinging hash?" He grinned devilishly. "You've got a real knack for it." He chopped the cornmeal brick into smaller pellets that sat like islands sticking out of the lake of cream he poured over them. As she turned on her heel, he was smiling crookedly and digging in again.

Why in the world did I ever think that taking care of him would be preferable to "slinging hash" at Louis Culpepper's,

she wondered. *I would work for Louis now . . . and gladly
. . . if only I could!*

By the time he'd filled that empty leg of his he'd cleaned up
enough cornmeal to stuff a flock of geese. All he said by way
of appreciation was, "We could use you in camp, Abbie." It
crossed her mind that any woman foolish enough to be found in
a bandit's camp would undoubtedly find herself used, all right!

Next he raised his voice and shouted, "What does a man
have to do to get a pot of hot water around here? I need to wash
up and shave. Do you hear me, Abbie?"

She had no source of comparison by which to measure the
man's capacity for being overbearing and rude, but surely he
must set the world's record, she thought. She delivered the
water and as stinging an insult as she could manage. "Wash
yourself . . . if you've ever learned how!"

He only laughed and observed, "Witty little chit this
morning, aren't you?"

He made a real sideshow out of his washing. Even from the
kitchen she knew every single thing he was doing. He sang out
loud, splashed, exclaimed how good this felt, and that felt. It
was disgusting. She had no idea how he was coping with one
hand, but she didn't care. Several times she became angrier
because he almost made her smile. Finally he called, "I'm as
fresh as a blinkin' nasturtium. Come and smell!"

Even in the kitchen she blushed. Never in her life had she
been so worked up. He had to threaten her with the gun again
to get her to bring the shaving gear. When she carried it in, she
cast her eyes down her nose at an angle suggesting that perhaps
she was trying to outstare a fly on its end. "Shall we proceed?"
she asked acidly. Half expecting him to be buck naked, she was
at least relieved to see he'd covered himself with the sheet.

"We?"

She stood with strained patience, awaiting his newest
objection, wishing she could take the blade and scrape every
hair off his entire head.

Maybe the look in her eye told him to beware, for he finally
said, "Keep away from my beard, woman. You made me wash
up by myself—just why so anxious to help me shave? As if I
didn't know. I've got one and a half good hands and I can sit up
now. I'll manage without your help." Then, as she turned to
leave, he added, ". . . Delila."

Her back stiffened, and he began his shave. He was damned

if he was going to let her near his moustache again after what he'd done to her this morning. He smiled, remembering it. But shaving turned out to be more difficult than he'd planned, being only slightly better than one-handed. The mirror was one of hers. Damn female gizmo! he thought. He tried to hold the long handle between his knees while he pulled at one cheek, used the other hand to work the blade, but the useless thing slipped down or turned sideways, refusing to stay where he wanted it. He finally gave up in frustration and called, "Miss Abigail, I can't manage the mirror. Come and hold it for me."

She only began singing as if she hadn't heard a word he said. But his voice was deep and strong again, and there was no way it could be missed. "Did somebody step on a cat's tail out there? Seems I have to shout to be heard above the caterwauling! Come and hold the mirror!"

"You have one and a half good hands and can sit up again. Hold it yourself!" She listened, heard him sigh disgustedly. Then—lo and behold!—out came the magic word.

"Please?" That brought an enormous smile to Miss Abigail's lips.

"I'm sorry, did you say something, Mr. Cameron?" she called, the smile growing wider.

"I said please, and you know damn well I did, so quit basking in self-righteousness and get in here."

"I'm coming," she sang. She was fast learning what exquisite joy it could be to be snide. From the doorway she said pleasantly, "How can I refuse a man with such sterling manners?" She eyed his foamy face, which spoke for itself. "What would you have me do?" His eyes, like chunks of coal in a snowman, were stark and snapping.

"Just hold the damn mirror, Your Highness!"

Taking it, she noted, "You're obviously in more than one kind of a lather. If you'd like, I'll shave it for you. My hand is undoubtedly steadier anyway—see the way you're shaking?" He ignored her and peered at himself sideways in the mirror, scraping a cheek, circumscribing a black, thick sideburn, outlining one side of his precious moustache.

She raised a little finger. "Ah, be careful of the moustache," she warned, watching the lather come away black-speckled while his scowl was revealed beneath it.

"Just hold the thing still so I can see." He drew his top lip down, curling it against his teeth, shaping the moustache. "It's damn hard to follow . . . a shape . . . that isn't there anymore."

"I think you should have etched it a bit more deeply along this side," she advised, lowering her brows as if seriously studying the fault.

"Damnit, Abigail, shut up! You were easier to put up with before you found your sense of humor. You moved the mirror again!"

"Oops, sorry." She settled back and watched him finish. It was surprisingly enjoyable. Amazing, she thought, how fast the man's beard grows. When he finished his shave, the moustache stood out blackly again. Funny thing, she thought, but the fool actually looks better with it.

"Intriguing?" he asked. She jumped, abashed at being caught regarding him that way. "You can feel it any time you want. The pleasure will be mine."

"I'd as soon feel the whiskers of a billy goat!" she snapped.

"You're excused," he laughed, as she headed for the door. On second thought, added, "But just be good."

It seemed to take forever until it was late enough to go over town while she wondered just what "be good" meant. Would he try to stop her with that gun again? She tiptoed to the back door, knowing she could not cross the open bedroom doorway without being seen. But the spring gave her away, and his voice told her he knew exactly what she was up to.

"While you're gone, see if they have any meat in this town besides liver, will you? Nobody's going to come for me tomorrow. It's Sunday."

She gave into some deep, deep need and slammed the screen door until it whacked against the frame and bounced halfway open again before settling shut. Naturally he laughed.

Chapter 8

"I can't send no such wire on your say-so," Max insisted.

"Why ever not?" Miss Abigail bristled.

"Got to be the sheriff does 'at," Max said importantly. "You go over and see Sam about it, then he'll send the wire. He knows who's the right person to send it to anyways. I don't."

Stymied, Miss Abigail stood, stiff-backed and upset, at a loss now. She didn't want to traipse all over town letting the entire citizenry know she was anxious to have that man out of her house. What rankled was that he was partially right. She was afraid that if she ran all over saying "I want him out," people would wonder why. And then what would she say? That he'd drawn a gun on her and made her kiss him? No power on earth could make her confess such a thing. Could she say he drew a gun on her to make her fix him his breakfast? Hardly. After all, she was being paid by the railroad to do those things for him. How would it look if she admitted she'd tried to starve him out of her house? What if she said he'd forced her at gunpoint to help him shave? The implications became worse all the time. Oh, why did that fool Maxwell Smith have to get all uppity with her? One quiet telegram is all it would have taken. Against her better judgment she went to Sheriff Samuel Harris next.

"Sorry, Miss Abigail," Sheriff Harris said. "Got to have a release from Doc Dougherty first. It's the law. Any prisoner under a doctor's care has got to be released officially by the doc before he can be transferred from one jail to the next—oh, begging your pardon ma'am, that's not to say your house is a jail. You know what I mean, Miss Abigail."

"Yes, of course, Mr. Harris," she condescended. "I shall speak to Doctor Dougherty then."

But Doc Dougherty wasn't home, so she went back to Main Street again, headed for the butcher shop, thoroughly disgusted now.

"Howdy, Miss Abigail," Bill Tilden greeted, coming out of his barbershop.

"Good day, Mr. Tilden."

"Hot, ain't it?" he observed, glancing at her unhatted hair. She nodded briskly, moving on. "Going over to Culpepper's for dinner," he called after her conversationally just as Frank Adney hung up his sign next door that said OUT TO LUNCH.

"How do, Miss Abigail," he greeted.

"Mr. Adney," she acknowledged.

"Some scorcher, huh?

"Indeed." She headed on up the boardwalk thinking how limited the range of conversation was in Stuart's Junction. Behind her, Bill Tilden asked Frank Adney, "You ever seen Miss Abigail uptown without her hat and gloves before?"

"Come to think of it, I ain't."

"Well, wonders never cease!" they turned to watch Miss Abigail as she entered the door of Porter's Meat Market, shaking their heads in disbelief.

"Howdy, Miss Abigail," Gabe Porter said.

"Good day, Mr. Porter."

"Heard tell you took in that train robber up to your house."

"Indeed?"

Gabe stood with his ham-sized arms crossed over his mammoth, aproned stomach, the flies buzzing around the blood stains there, one occasionally landing on the fly paper that hung coiled from the ceiling. "Shucks, everybody knows about it. He ain't giving you no trouble, now, is he?"

"No, he's not, Mr. Porter."

"Heard 'at other city dude cleared out on the train yesterday, huh?"

"Yes, he did."

"Ain't it a little risky, you bein' up there all alone with 'at other one?"

"Do I look as if I'm in jeopardy, Mr. Porter?"

"No, no indeed you don't, Miss Abigail. Folks is just wonderin' is all."

"Well, folks may cease their wondering, Mr. Porter. The gravest danger I'm in is that of being eaten out of house and home."

Then Gabe jumped, realizing she was waiting to buy some meat. "Ah . . . right! And what'll it be today?"

"How are your pork chops today? Are they fresh and lean?"

"Oh both, ma'am. Fresh cut today and kept on ice for as long as I can keep it from melting."

"Very well, Mr. Porter. I shall have three of them."

"Yup, coming right up!"

"On second thought, perhaps I shall need, four—no, five."

"Five? These ain't gonna keep till tomorrow, Miss Abigail, even down the well."

"I nevertheless shall take five, and a length of smoked sausage, oh, say—this long." She held up her palms six inches apart, then lengthened the span to ten or so and said, "No, this long."

"What in Hades you feedin' up there, Miss Abigail, a gorilla?"

It was all she could do to keep from replying, "Exactly!" Instead she thrust poor Gabe into total dismay by requesting, "I should like one pig's bladder added to my order."

"One . . . pig's bladder, Miss Abigail?" Gabe asked, bug-eyed.

"You just butchered, did you not? Where are the entrails?"

"Oh, I got 'em. I mean, they ain't been buried yet, but what—"

"Just wrap up one bladder, if you please," she ordered imperiously, and he finally gave up and did as she requested. When she was gone Gabe muttered to the flies,". . . a pig's bladder . . . now what in the hell is she gonna do with that?"

When Miss Abigail reached her house again there were fresh buggy tracks in the fine, dry dust out front, and she realized she'd missed Doctor Dougherty again. What dismal luck to have missed him when she needed his help to get that man out of here.

In her customary way, she stopped to peak at her reflection in the mirror of the umbrella stand. There was no hat to remove, so she smoothed her hair, her sleeves, her waistband, then quickly tested the tautness of the skin beneath her chin with the back of her hand.

"Is it firm?" a deep voice asked, and she whirled and jumped a foot off the floor, pressing a hand to her heart.

"What are you doing up?" He was standing just this side of the kitchen archway, leaning on crutches, his dark chest, calves, and feet sticking out of a sheet he had wound around himself.

"I asked first," he said.

"What?" All she could think of was, what if that sheet dropped off!

"Is it firm? It should be, the way you point that saucy little chin at the ceiling all the time." As if to verify it, up went her chin.

"If you are up, you are strong enough to get out of here. How heartening!"

"Doc brought me the crutches and I needed to go out back after he left, so I decided to give it a go. But I'm not as strong as I thought."

"You traipsed clear across the backyard dressed in that sheet?" she gasped. "What if someone saw you?"

"What if they did?"

"I have a reputation to uphold, sir!"

"Don't flatter yourself, Miss Abigail," he smirked. She stood there with the blood cascading into her face, until even her ears felt hot. "You know, I'm getting a bit lightheaded," he said.

"Lightheaded? Don't you dare pass out wrapped in that sheet! Get back into bed, do you hear? I should never be able to budge you if you collapsed on the floor!"

He stumped his way across the far end of the parlor and all went well until he came to a hooked rug that lay in the bedroom doorway. One crutch caught in it and he began to waver. She hurried across, grabbed him around his middle to keep him from tipping over, and when he was steadied, went down on one knee to remove the rug. But the crutch was still planted on it, holding it down. "I can't pick it up. Can you move the crutch?" she asked, looking up the long length of him. It was a long, long way indeed to the top of that length, and she warned, "Mr. Cameron, if you tip over on top of me I'll never forgive you."

"There'd be nothing left to forgive with. You'd be one . . . squashed . . . hummingbird." He swayed against the doorjamb as one crutch crashed to the floor.

"Quickly, get to bed," she ordered, taking his arm over her shoulders. He was as tall as a barn door and nearly as broad at the shoulders, but they made it to the bed all right and sat down on the edge side by side. She quickly unwound his arm from her shoulder and rose.

"I'll thank you to use some common sense from now on. First of all, if you intend to parade around, you shall do so in pajamas and a robe. Secondly, you shall tend to necessities and not stand around yammering while you make a hazard of your big self in my house. If a . . . a gorilla like you ever fell, how would I ever get you up?"

In spite of his haziness, he asked, "Did you send your telegram, Miss Abigail?"

"Yes!" she lied, "and they cannot come too soon to get you off my hands."

"If you want to get rid of me, you'd better start feeding me better. I'm as weak as a mosquito. Did you buy some decent meat?"

"Yes! I bought something perfectly suited to you!"

He awakened from a dream that there was rain spattering on the canvas of his tent, but it was the pork chops splattering away on top of Miss Abigail's kitchen range. He stretched, feeling the skin of his right leg tight but healing and hurting less all the time. Something smelled so good his stomach lurched over, his mouth salivated, and a rumble sounded somewhere deep inside of him. By the time she brought the tray in he was ravenous.

"Mmm . . . it smells like pork chops. Is it some real meat at last?" He brightened as she set the tray on his lap. She had even considerately covered the plate with an upturned bowl to keep it hot.

"Yes, real meat," she confirmed, all smiles.

"Could it be you have a heart after all?"

"Decide for yourself," she replied saucily as the bowl came up in her hands, revealing the raw pig's bladder. She simply had to stay long enough to see the expression on his face. It was a black, shaking visage of anger while a spate of filth poured from him. At some time while he cursed, he asked what the hell it was on the plate.

"Real meat. Isn't that what you wanted?" she asked innocently, enjoying every minute of this. "As a matter of fact, it is pork. A pig's bladder . . . simply perfect for a goat like you."

He glared at her venomously and roared, "I smell pork chops, Abbie! Don't tell me I don't! Now do I get some or do I walk uptown in my sheet and tell them that the hussy Abigail McKenzie refuses to feed me as she's being paid to?"

She was in a fine fury, little fists clenched into tight balls, eyes bright with vindication as she stamped her foot.

"It is *my* turn to teach *you* a lesson, *sir*! I have pork chops, potatoes, gravy, vegetables, everything to sate your fool appetite and get you strong and out of here. All I want from you in return is some decent treatment. You give me that filthy gun!"

"Bring me my pork chops!" he shouted, glowering at her.

"Give me the gun!"

"Like hell I will!"

"Then you shan't have pork chops!" But the gun appeared so quickly she'd have sworn it was there in his hand all the time. It shut her up like a sprung trap.

"Give . . . me . . . my . . . pork . . . chops," he growled.

She stammered, "Keep th . . . that filthy thing out of m . . . my sight!"

"I'll put it away when you bring me the pork chops you're being paid to give me!"

"Please!" she bellowed now.

"PLEASE!" he bellowed back.

Then silence crashed around them, and for one self-conscious moment they both felt foolish, glaring at each other that way.

He got his pork chops all right. And by that time, Miss Abigail was in a state! She admitted that it was a blame good thing tomorrow was Sunday. She was definitely in need of divine guidance after all the transgressions she'd been committing lately. Anger, spite, vengeance, lying, even promiscuity. Yes, she even admitted that what had happened during that kiss had been undeniably promiscuous—well, it had ended that way, anyway. But if she was guilty of all this, think of what he had to ask forgiveness for—not that he ever would. Besides his own, he'd caused every single one of her sins!

The pig's bladder had mysteriously disappeared. She didn't know where it had gone and didn't ask. Being the goat that he is, she thought, he probably ate the thing and enjoyed every bite!

"I've brought you some bed clothes of my father's. Put them on and leave them on. I'm sick and tired of looking at your hairy legs and chest."

"So you say." He puffed out the chest in question and rubbed its furred surface as if it were spun gold. She ignored his conceit, moving away, but then she spied the bladder soaking in the water bowl. She reached two fingers in to pick up the smelly thing and take it away, but he ordered, "Leave it where it is."

"What!"

"I said leave it where is it."

"But it stinks!" She made a face at the offensive innard which had left a residue of scum on the surface of the water.

"Leave it!" he repeated, "and leave the pajamas and get out."

She dropped the gut back in its swampy water and left, thankfully.

It was Saturday afternoon and she spent it cleaning the house for Sunday, as she'd done all her life. When she had cleaned everything else, she came near the door to his room, calling first, "Are you decent now, Mr. Cameron?"

"Does a snake have armpits?" came the reply.

She grabbed her cheeks to keep from laughing. How could that infernal man make her laugh so easily when she was thoroughly disgusted with him?

"I'm covered, if that's what you're asking, but I'll never be decent, hopefully."

She took one look at him and had to work diligently to prevent her face from smiling again. He looked utterly ridiculous. The pajama legs stopped halfway down his hairy calves.

"Well, what are you smirking at?" he grumbled.

"Nothing."

"The hell you say. Keep it up and I'll take these idiotic things off. I feel like a damn coolie in them anyway . . . or at

least I would if they were long enough. Your old man must've
been a midget!"

"They'll just have to do. I have none that are longer." But in
spite of herself she stood there smiling openly now at the hairy
calves and feet sticking out of the drawers.

"All right! Get to your cleaning if that's what you came in
here for because if you stand there smirking one minute longer
I'll take these damn things off!"

"You have the vilest tongue of any man I've ever known.
I'm tempted to fix it with the cattail again."

"Just get on with the cleaning and quit hassling me."

Their constant bickering had come to have a pattern. When
they were angry their tongues cut sharp and deep with words
they seldom meant. And when it went too far they reverted to
sarcasm or teasing, scrimmaging verbally in a way which even
Miss Abigail had come to enjoy. Cleaning the room, she felt
his eyes on her all the while. He moved to the window seat
while she changed his sheets and dustmopped under the bed.
Kneeling, she saw his boots pushed deeply beneath it, and the
lump of what must be his shirt with the gun wrapped in it,
between the mattress and the open wire spring. The only way it
could have gotten there was if Doc Dougherty had brought it to
him, but she couldn't believe the man's idiocy to do such a
thing. She didn't mention the gun again, but made as if she
hadn't seen it there, then went on to her featherdusting, and
finally to clean the tabletop where the pitcher and bowl sat.

"May I ask what you propose to keep this filthy thing for?"
She looked distastefully at the bladder.

"Never mind," was all he'd say. "Just leave it."

Supper passed uneventfully, except that he let her know he
hated those bloody-looking beets.

The bladder still lay in the bowl. And a plan was forming in
Miss Abigail's head.

Evening came and Jesse grew bored and listless. It was
funny how he'd grown used to her coming and going. The
minute it grew quiet and he was left alone, he almost wished
she'd come in, even if only to argue. Like a child who's fought
with a playmate, he found he preferred her aggravation to her
absence. He heard her making a lot of watery noises and got up
with the crutches and came to find her leaning over the back
step, washing her hair. He opened the screen door and tapped it
against her head twice, softly, just enough to vex her. "This is a

hell of a place to wash your hair. You're directly in the path between bedroom and outhouse.''

"Get that screen door off my head!" she exclaimed from under her sopping hair. 'I'll wash my hair anywhere I like. It just so happens I do it here because it makes less mess to clean up than in the kitchen.''

He stood looking down at her, kneeling on the earth with her head over the basin. The hollow at the nape of her neck held some soap suds, and he found it hard to take his eyes off it. He opened the screen door enough to get out, causing her to sidestep on her knees. She felt vulnerable, knowing he stood above her, watching her.

The way he stood, right foot hanging conveniently before him, it was easy to reach out and put his big toe right there in that little hollow that held the shampoo captive at the back of her neck.

"Getting rid of all the nasty *effluvia* so you're all polished and shined for church tomorrow?" he teased, using the pretentious word she'd once used on him. She swatted blindly at the foot, but he'd swung on down the yard, wearing only those short pajama pants, calling back, "Whose redemption are you going to pray for, Miss Abigail, yours or mine?"

And from the yard next door Rob Nelson heard and saw it all and ran into his house, hollering, "Maw! Maw! Guess what I just seen!"

She was gone, pan and all, when he came back to the house. He felt weak again and went straight to his bed, making up his mind that he must continue to work up his strength by staying up longer each time with the crutches. He sank down on the edge of the bed and ran a hand through his hair. It itched. In spite of his teasing, that shampoo had looked mighty inviting.

"Miss Abigail?" he called, but the house was quiet. "Can you hear me?"

No answer.

"Don't I get a shampoo?"

There still was no answer but he heard a floorboard creak above him.

"Hey, I could use one myself, you know." He didn't really expect an answer, neither was she about to give one. To himself, he said, "She keeps typical old maid's hours. Closeted in her bedroom before eight o'clock on a Saturday night." He was bored to death and wished she'd come down and keep him company. If she could just hold that sharp tongue of hers, he'd try to do the same, just for somebody to talk to for a while. The sounds of light revelry drifted from the direction of town, and he longed for a beer and a little company, maybe even a woman on his knee.

Miss Abigail was drying her hair at an open upstairs window, fluffing it with a thick towel, wondering when she would find her first gray hair. He called something again, but she ignored him, thinking of how he'd touched the back of her neck with his toe, secretly smiling. He could be so exasperating and so funny at the same time. She thought of what she'd wear for church in the morning; this time she'd gathered all her things from his room. She thought of the gun beneath his bed. She thought of his kiss, but pushed the thought aside because it did funny things to her stomach. The air was so still you could hear every sound from the saloon, but then it was nearly July and the summer heat did that. How many Saturday nights had she washed her hair and combed it dry, gone to bed early, and wished to be doing something else? Something with a man. Now she was thrown together with a man who might have been company had he not turned out to be the height of loathsomeness. How much longer would she be stuck with him? She heard him call, saying he wanted a shampoo too. Nonsense! He couldn't stand up long enough to have his hair washed. How many days had it been since he'd had his hair washed? Nine? Ten? She remembered how she'd promised when he was unconscious that she'd wash it for him. She was stuck with him until the railroad took him off her hands. At least if he was clean he would be that much less offensive, she told herself, not wanting to admit that she was lonely, that even his company was preferable to none.

When she stepped into his room and saw what he held, she asked in disgust, "Whatever are you doing with that vile thing?"

The pig bladder was scraped clean, blown up, and tied with yarn from her sewing basket. He clenched it in his right hand, squeezing repeatedly, then relaxing time and again. The action was as suggestive as the licking of lips, and he smiled as he drawled, "Exercising my *gun* hand."

Mortified, her eyes could not seem to leave the dark, supple fingers as they squeezed, squeezed, squeezed. Her lips fell open and her stomach went light and fluttery. Should she turn and escape? And let him have the satisfaction of humiliating her once again? Though her cheeks blazed, she ordered, "Put that horrible thing away if you want me to help you with your hair."

He gave it several more slow, suggestive squeezes before tossing it aside negligently, with that same knowing smile on his lips. Well, well, he thought, the queen descendeth! And in her nightie and wrapper, no less!

"You're too weak to stand or lean over long enough to shampoo your hair with water, so I'll give you the next best thing, an oatmeal shampoo. It's not as fragrant, but it works."

"No offense, Abbie, but do you know what you're doing?"

"Precisely, but you'll have to lie down."

"Oatmeal?" he asked skeptically, making no move to lie down yet.

"Exactly," she said crisply. "Do you want the dry treatment or none at all?" Too late she realized what she'd said. The smile was already sneaking around the outer edges of his eyes, and by the time it made it to his lips she was the color of cinnamon.

He stretched out full length and drawled, "By all means, give it to me dry."

Flustered beyond belief, she fussed with her bowl of dry oatmeal, a towel, and three clothespins while he eyed them inquisitively. "The towel goes *under* your head," she said testily, as if he were truly a dolt.

"Oh yes, how stupid of me." He grinned, lifting his head while she arranged the towel under it. Then, to his amazement, she dumped half of the bowl of oatmeal on his hair and started working it in as if it were soap and water.

"Serves double duty, huh?" he quipped. "Tomorrow you can cook it for my breakfast instead of cornmeal." She was caught unaware and let out a huff of laughter while he peeked up at her prankishly. Finally he shut his eyes and let himself enjoy the feeling of her hands in his hair—a Saturday night feeling remembered from childhood. He believed he could nearly smell the fresh shoe blacking on all the shoes of his sisters and brothers, lined up at the bottom of the stairs awaiting Sunday morning. How long since he'd been in a house where Saturday was set aside for those get-ready things?

"Up!" she ordered, interrupting his reverie. "I must shake this. Hold still till I come back." She took the towel gingerly by its four corners and went away with the soiled oatmeal. She repeated the process once again, only this time when she had the clean oatmeal in his hair, she bound the towel up turban-style and secured it with the clothespins. "The oatmeal will absorb the oils. We'll leave it on for a while," she said, and went to the bowl to wash her own hands. But the water was still there from the pig bladder. With a grimace she took it away to dump.

When she returned, he was exercising his hand with that *thing* again, but he invited, "Stay while I soak."

She glanced at the flexing hand, back up at him skeptically.

"What can I do bound up like a sheik with the fleas?" he asked, rolling his eyes upward. Unconsciously she tightened the ends of her tie belt that held the wrapper. Finally, he tossed the thing aside and said cajolingly, "Hey, it's Saturday night, Abbie, the social hour . . . remember? I've been in this bed for almost two weeks now and, truthfully, I'm getting a little stir crazy. All I want is a little talk."

She sighed and perched on the trunk at the foot of the bed. "If you're growing restless you must be healing."

"I'm not used to sitting still for so long."

"What are you used to?" She wasn't really sure if she wanted any sordid details about his robber's life, yet the prospect of hearing about it was strangely alluring. He, meanwhile, was wondering whether she'd believe him if he told her the truth.

"I'm not used to a place like this, that's for sure, or spending time with a woman like you. I travel around a lot."

"Yes, I supposed you did, in your occupation. Doesn't it grow tiresome?"

"Sometimes, but I have to do it, so I do."

She looked him dead in the eye—Miss Goody Twoshoes giving her reformer's pitch. "Nobody has to live that kind of life. Why don't you give it up and find a wholesome occupation?"

"Believe it or not, being a photographer isn't far from wholesome."

"Oh, come now, you can't think I believed your story about the camera you left on the train?"

"No, a woman like you wouldn't believe it, I guess."

"What is it that you claim you photograph?" she asked, making it clear that this was all too farfetched.

"The building of the railroads," he said, with that half smile on his face. "The grandeur of history in the making," he emoted, raising his arms dramatically. "The spanning of our land by twin iron rails, capturing it forever for our posterity to share." But then he dropped his arms and his dramatizing and fell thoughtful, introspective. "You know, it'll never happen again just like it's happening now. It's been something to see, Abbie." He sighed, entwined his fingers behind his head, and studied the ceiling. And for a moment she almost believed him, he sounded so sincere.

"I'm sure you would like me to believe you, Mr. Cameron."

"Would it hurt you to call me Jesse? It would make it more pleasant while we talk this way."

"I thought I'd made you understand that I live by rules of propriety."

"There's nobody here but you and me. I won't tell," he teased mischievously.

"No, you won't, because I shan't call you Jesse . . . ever. Now quit changing the subject and tell me about your occupation. Try to convince me that you are not a robber of trains."

He laughed, then said, "All right. I work for the railroad, photographing every phase of its construction, just like I said. I have free passage as long as I work for them, and I travel to the railhead—wherever that may be—to take most of my photographs. I live in camps and on trains most of the time. There's not much more to tell."

"Except why, if you have a decent job, you chose to steal from the very hand that feeds you."

"That was a mistake, Abbie."

"Miss Abigail," she corrected.

"Very well, Miss Abigail, then. Have you ever seen a railroad camp?"

"Hardly."

"No, you wouldn't have. Well, it's no Abigail McKenzie's house, I'll tell you that. It's wild out in the middle of nowhere, and the men who work there are not exactly parlor fare."

"Like you?" she couldn't resist saying. Again he laughed lightly, letting her think what she would.

"I'm a veritable goldmine of manners compared to the navvies who build the railroads. Their life is rough, their language is rougher, and anybody who crosses anybody else can expect a bullet between the eyes. There's no law where they live, none at all. They settle their disputes with guns and fists and sometimes even with hammers—anything that's convenient. There not only is no law at the end of a railroad line, there's no town. No houses, stores, churches, depots—in other words, no shelter of any kind. A man who lives in the wilds like that won't survive long without a gun. There are bobcats in the mountains, wolves on the prairies, and everything that grows teeth in between. Naturally they all go to water, which is usually where bridges and trestles go up. About this time of day the animals always come to drink."

"What's your point, Mr. Cameron?"

"My point is that I carry a gun like every other smart fellow who expects to tame the West and live to see it. I'm not denying I had a gun on me on that train. I am denying I used it to pull a holdup."

"You're forgetting you were caught red-handed."

"Doing what? I had just taken it out, thinking I'd clean it, but before I got it unloaded, some nervous old biddy was screaming, and I found myself on the floor, shot, and the next thing I knew I woke up here in your house. That's all I know."

"A likely story. You would make a fine actor, Mr. Cameron."

"I don't need to be a fine actor—I'm a fine photographer. When I get my plates back, you'll see."

"You seem very confident about that."

"I am, wait and see."

"Oh, I shall wait, but I doubt that there will be anything to see."

"You're a hard woman to convince."

"I'm a woman who recognizes the truth when it's staring her in the face."

"But that's what I do as a photographer. Recognize the truth and record it permanently in pictures."

"The truth?"

He considered for a moment, then cocked his head to the side as if studying her. "Well, take last night for instance. You'd have made a very fetching subject last night when you sat in that rocker there, laughing. The light fell on you at precisely the right angle to take all of the affected hardness away from your face and lend it a natural quality it was meant to reflect. Call it unpretentiousness, if you will. In that brief moment, if I'd had my camera I might have captured you as you really are, not as you pretend to be. I might have exposed you as a charlatan."

Faintly smarting at his words, denial sprang instantly to her lips. "I am no charlatan." Rather than argue, he studied her with cocked head, as if he could see into her depths and knew exactly what he was talking about. "If there is any charlatan here it is you. You have proven it by your own words. Any photographer knows that a subject could not be photographed rocking in a rocking chair. Even I know that subjects must be stiff, sometimes even braced into place in order to take successful photographs."

"You've missed my point completely, but on purpose, I think. However, if that's how you want it, it's all right with me. Let me only say that if you want stiff, braced-looking results, they're easy to obtain. My photographs lack such artifice. It's why I do what I do for the railroad. They want their history photographed as it happens, not as some fools see fit to pose and posture the real thing. It can be the same with people. Someday I'll take your picture and it will prove to you what I meant. It will show you what the real Abbie is like."

It was easy to tell from her expression that she had censured out of his words all she chose to disbelieve. "The real me is inutterably weary," she said, rising from the trunk. "But not weary enough to fall for such a story as yours. I still believe you're a finer actor than either train robber or photographer."

"Have it your way, Miss Abigail," he said. "Charlatans usually do."

"You should know," she replied, but his eyes caught and held hers, making her wonder just what he'd meant by all he'd said. At last she glanced at his turbaned head and said, "I believe we can remove the oatmeal now." She went to the dressing table to get her brush.

"I can brush it myself," he offered, but she waved away his hand, removed the clothespins, stretched out the towel, and began brushing.

"You'd have it all over everything and oatmeal attracts mice," she said. "They are not as opposed to eating it secondhand as you are."

He closed his eyes and rolled his head this way and that when she told him to. What a Saturday night, he thought, getting oatmeal brushed out of my hair by a woman who

dislikes me and mice. "I can't reach the back. Could you sit up
and lean over the edge of the bed?" He sat up, hunched
forward, elbows to knees, and she spread the towel carefully
on the floor between his feet. He watched the oatmeal dust
drifting down as she brushed from the nape of his neck forward
in deft strokes. There were times when she could be quite
appealing, like last night in the rocker, and now, doing a
common thing like brushing his hair. It was seldom, though,
that she did anything in a common way. She preferred, for
some reason, to pose herself, taut, rigid, as inflexible as the
everlasting restrictions she put upon her behavior. It was
beyond him why he should try to make her see herself
truthfully. If she was happy with the artifice, let her be, he
thought. Still, it was hard for him to understand why anyone
would set such a mold for themselves.

The brushing made goose pimples shiver up his arms. It was
deliciously relaxing. In his drowsy thoughts he wondered
about Abigail McKenzie, thought of other things he might say
to her, but then he realized the brushing had stopped; she had
gone as silently as she'd come, leaving the brush lying bristles-
down on the back of his neck.

Chapter 9

───────◆───────

SHE HAD LEFT him relaxed and drowsy and lay now listening to the muffled sounds below. She heard the bedsprings twang beneath his weight, then the muted chiming of the brass headboard as he pulled against it. She visualized him turning on his side, sighing and falling asleep while she waited patiently. She fought drowsiness, listening to the occasional sounds from town petering out until all was as still as eternity. A dog barked, once, far away and lonely, but it made her flinch awake and sit up straighter, resisting slumber.

After an interminably long time she arose, quickly and lightly, creating only one little twank that was then gone. Again she waited, patient as a cat on the stalk, and when she moved, it was to the accompaniment of sheer soundlessness. She took the stairs barefoot, in a swift, gliding descent, knowing she risked less sound going that way than if she hesitated on each step. But once at the bottom, she waited again. She could hear his breathing in the stillness—long, rhythmic, somnolent. And she moved again, stopping not at the bedroom door, or the foot of his bed or to peer down to make sure he was sleeping; any of these hesitations, especially the last, might key some instinctual reaction and arouse him. Instead, surefooted and silent, she glided to the side of the bed and lay down on the floor half under it.

He breathed on as before while her breath came in short, scared spurts.

The shirt-wrapped gun was close to the outer edge of the mattress, where he could get at it without having to reach too far underneath. She touched it, exploring the fabric of the shirt, the hard lump inside, the ridges of the cartridge chamber, the sharp, crooked hammer, the butt, the barrel. She shivered. If she were to try to pull it through the rectangular spaces between the wires of the spring, it would undoubtedly get caught, for the gun was bigger than the holes. Instead, she studied the shape as a blind person might: using her fingertips, determining that it was so near the edge that no more than the slightest upward pressure on the mattress would free the gun so she could slip it out sideways.

The problem was raising the mattress an inch or so.

She would simply have to wait until he decided to roll over. Maybe when the springs squeaked she could yank the gun out quickly and he'd never know the difference. The floor grew as hard as an anvil. She grew chilled and needed badly to fidget, and still he slept on peacefully. She heard the dog again, far off, and the answering call of a wolf even farther, and in spite of the hard floor, began to get sleepy. To keep awake she reached out a hand and it touched something cold and fleshy. She recoiled in fear, then realized it was only the pig bladder. The memory of his long, strong fingers squeezing it came back to haunt her, and she pinched her eyes shut to blot out the picture. But just then Jesse snuffled, sighed, and shifted onto his side, causing the bedsprings to creak. At that exact moment, she pushed with one hand through the open spaces of the bedspring while with her other she pulled the shirt free, gun and all. It landed in the small of her chest, thudding heavily, and she checked the impulse to gasp at the weight of it.

She lay absolutely motionless, repulsed by the thing weighing her down. But she had the ominous weapon at last! Slowly she unwrapped it. The shirt lay upon her stomach and breasts and she could smell the smell of him in it. She shuddered. Then she slowly rolled the shirt into a tight ball, making sure not so much as a button clicked on the floor. While she waited with the cold steel upon her chest, she imagined what kind of a person it took to draw it, raise it, and aim it at another human being. She saw herself at the other end of it as she'd been this morning, and once again told herself it would take an animal to do such a thing.

He was breathing evenly again. She held her breath, shivering at the thought of getting caught. But the hardest part was done—the rest was easy. Be patient, be patient, she admonished herself. He was snoring lightly now. With the gun in one hand and his shirt in the other she sat up, alert, poised to spring should he move, almost startled to see how near she'd actually been to his head all this time. He faced the wall so she raised herself further, soundlessly as ever, and the moment her soles touched the floor she hit for safety.

She had taken less than one full step when an arm lashed out, caught her, and flipped her over backward, somersaulting her across a lumpy hipbone till her toes cracked high against the wall. As she slithered down into a heap, a horrible weight settled upon her chest. In the next moment she was sure she was dying, for he'd knocked the wind out of her. The small of her back where it had bumped across him felt like there were two boulders beneath it and she reached to knead the pain, but just that fast he pinned the arm beneath him and pinioned the other one against the mattress over her head, the gun still tight in her grasp.

"All right, lady, you want to sneak around under my bed, this is what you get!" he snarled. "Give me the goddamn gun! Now!" He pushed her wrist into the mattress, trying to wrest the pistol from her fingers. But it was useless. They were clenched in a death-grip, locked in mid-motion when he'd flattened the breath from her. The pain in her chest grew to a choking, hammering, crushing insistence while she struggled for air that refused her. He pummeled her wrist against the bed, leaning on her, adding stress to her lungs until she felt her eyes would pop from their sockets.

"Give me the gun, you asinine woman! Did you think I was fool enough to let you get away with it?" Still no breath came and her fear swelled and swelled and she panicked, unable to tell him what was wrong. And just when she knew more certainly than ever that she was starting to die, a rattling issued from her throat and her hand went lax, loosing the gun. He heard the hissing and gasping as she fought for breath. Then suddenly her knees pulled up fetally.

He jumped off her chest, exclaiming, "Christ, Abbie!" She

curled up like an armadillo, half crying, half gasping, and rolled from side to side, grasping her knees. He tried to make her straighten out so the air could get in, but she only curled tighter.

Finally he flung her onto her belly like a rag doll, the gun flying to the wall, then clunking to the floor in the corner behind the bed. With her forehead now screwing itself into the mattress, she clutched her stomach, writhing, her hind side hoisted up by nature trying to renew her life force. Jesse got her by the hips, his giant hands holding her up, trying to help her breathe again.

"I didn't mean to knock the wind out of you." Still her breath came hoarse and rasping. She could feel her posterior shimmed up against something warm. "Abbie, are you okay?" But his thumb pressed a spot that had been brusied by his hipbone. Heaving, gasping, crying all at once, she tried to break free.

"Put me . . ." But her voice wasn't working yet and he held her in that ignominious position against his pajama-clad body.

"Don't try to talk yet," he ordered, "let your breath come back first."

Then finally it came. Blessed, pure, giant puffs of air, flowing into her lungs and fortifying her. "Put . . . me . . . down," she managed while her fists still gripped the sheet and she flailed one foot dissolutely. He released her at last and she slumped flat. She felt her weight roll as he moved to kneel beside her.

"Hurt?" he asked, and she felt his hand rubbing the small of her back while she lay there limp, panting, waiting for her near-bursting heart to ease.

"Get . . . your . . . filthy . . . hands . . . off . . . me," she sputtered into the mattress between gasps of air.

"It's your own fault," he said, ignoring her order, still rubbing, warmer now and in longer sweeps. "Just what were you trying to do, shoot me?"

"Nothing would pleasure me more," she puffed.

"That goes to show what you know," he said, and purposely ran his long, lean fingers—one swipe—down her spine where its hollow widened, then narrowed. She jumped like a jackrabbit in a desperate leap toward the corner of the bed, lunging for the gun. But her head hit the corner wall with a resounding crack! The bedsprings twanged and he grabbed her by the calves and dragged her backward, her fingers never touching the pistol, her nightgown shinnying up in a roll beneath her. She reached for it desperately, but just then he flew and landed full-length on top of her, reaching easily with one long arm to retrieve the gun from the floor. His chest pushed her face into the bed, then the weight was gone, settled farther down as he straddled her like a cowboy on a bronc, holding her arms pinned to her sides by his knees.

But now he was panting too, gritting his teeth while he pressed a hand to his throbbing wound. He rocked a time or two, suddenly angry because of the pain.

"All right, Miss High-And-Mighty, so you want to play guns, do you? Okay, I'll play." Through the ringing in her head she heard his ragged breathing. Then he swung off her hips and she heard the gun click by her ear. "Roll over," he ordered.

She struggled with the nightgown, but as she tugged, the gun barrel skewered it to the center of her back, holding it where it was.

"Roll over," he repeated, tight and hard now, and nudged her a little harder with the barrel. She rolled fearfully away from him, shivering near the wall. "Why is it that every time I wake up you seem to be in my bed?" he accused.

She clutched her head, which was aching uncontrollably now, closed her eyes while his unctuous voice flowed. "Is this why you took me into your house, Abbie? So you could weasel your way into a gunslinger's bed? Why didn't you just say so instead of pretending to be the gracious nurse? Nurse . . . ha! Do you know what all you've done to me under the guise of nursing? Let me recount every one so you'll know what I'm about to get even with here. First you shaved off my moustache for no apparent reason at all. You made me lie in need until I thought my bladder would burst. Then you threw the bedpan at me. Then you pushed branches down my throat until it was practically useless to me, then claimed afterward that it was for my own good you had to starve me. Next, you proceeded to calmly poison me with liver until I puked like a buzzard. Then, you presented me with a raw pig's bladder while I groaned for a square meal. And now—last but not least—you try to shoot me!"

"I did not try to shoot you!"

"You, Miss Abigail, were caught red-handed. Are those familiar words? Do you remember hearing them recently?"

"You shot Mr. Melcher and he has a toe gone to prove it. I shot nobody. I was only after the gun."

"You shot nobody because I was faster than you. What's the matter, your head hurt now?"

"I hit it on the wall."

"As you also said to me once, it's your own fault. You brought it on yourself when you came sneaking in here. You pulled your pussyfooting act just once too often."

"I saved your life, you ingrate!" she spit, and was going to call his bluff, thinking he wouldn't really harm her. But her shoulders got no more than a hand's width off the mattress before she found herself pushed flat again, his knuckles prying into the bones of her chest.

"Ingrate?" he chuckled wickedly. "Yes, perhaps I have been an ingrate. Perhaps I haven't shown the proper gratitude for all you've done for me. Maybe I'd better do it now . . . in kind. Pay you back for all you've done to me, is that what you want?"

"N . . . no, I didn't mean it."

"But of course you meant it. Let's just call it payment for services rendered."

"Don't . . ." She crossed her arms protectively over her chest.

"Let's see how you like having your mouth invaded, Abbie." He moved so swiftly she had no chance to fight. The next moment one of her arms was imprisoned between the mattress and his body, the other wrist pressed against a rail of the brass headboard while he held it there with a powerful hand. His mouth swooped down but she rolled her face aside and he missed. He tried again but she rolled the other way.

"So you still want to play games, huh?" She struggled while he yanked her arm down. But he rolled her easily to her side, forcing the arm up behind her back before her own weight and his rendered it useless. His newly freed hand came to the back of her neck, long fingers trailing up through her freshly washed hair, controlling her as he lowered his mouth to hers again and ran his tongue across her bared teeth. She gasped and bucked, but pain shot into her arm so she fell still, realizing she was no match for his strength. He lightened his hold on her lips, teasing now with his tongue, running it to the corners of her mouth, torturing her with its sleek, wet insinuation. Unable to combat him, her only recourse was to lay limp and submissive, determined to show neither fight nor fear.

He sensed what she was doing and slid his lips down to the hollow beneath her jaw, whispered near her ear, "I'm going to pay you back for every single thing you did to me, Abbie." Then he nuzzled his way back to the corner of her mouth, his full lips closing upon it leisurely while she resolutely kept her jaws clamped shut. He chuckled low in his throat and she felt him smile against her lips. "How do you like it, Abbie?" Her heart danced to her throat and her eyelids trembled as she held them tightly shut. He moved to catch the side of one nostril as a stallion nips a mare, leaving her skin damp as he moved on, bending lower. He took her small pointed chin in his mouth, sucking gently, sending shafts of heat darting through her body. And far down the bed she felt him grow harder and harder against the back of her captured hand. Wanting to die, yet feeling more alive than ever before in her life, Abbie absorbed the feeling of it all. Held prisoner, she suddenly felt as if she soared free.

His hand slid away from her hair and he ran only the outer edges of its little finger down the valley between her breasts, to her waist. Then, hooking each button with that single finger, he flicked them open on his leisurely way back up. "Hey," he whispered against her neck, "did you think you were going to get away with my shirt tonight? You steal mine . . . I steal yours." Then slowly he pushed aside the bodice of her gown, opening first the left side, then the right, still using only that little finger, but sailing its back side against the surface of her breasts, over each smooth mound to each erect nipple, skimming them like warm wind and creating uninvited goose bumps upon her skin.

"You know what you do to me, Abbie? You rub me in a hundred wrong ways. Let me show you the one right way." His palm cupped her bare breast and her eyes flew open. She saw his dark moustache so close to her face, felt his breath on her mouth, his hot hardness against the back of her hand. And all the while he kneaded her breast with its unforgivable taut nipple, he caressed her ribs and stomach with his forearm. Her eyelids slid closed, the breath which he'd earlier knocked from her caught now in her helpless throat.

"How about a bed bath, Abbie? I owe you one." Her senses

fled to one central spot as he fondled one breast while leaning to circle the other with his warm, wet tongue, slowly and painstakingly bathing it, from rigid crest to softest perimeter. She felt the forbidden lick of grain upon smoothness, made sleek by moisture. His teeth, open, gently sliced, their edges unhurting, knowing. Between tongue and upper teeth he took the ruby crown of her breast, lightly, lightly, stroking, tugging until her shoulder strained off the mattress. He lowered his mouth to the soft cay where breast met rib and there washed her with warmth before continuing downward while her body reached its dewpoint. He dipped his tongue into the cupule of her navel as a bee dips into the chalice of a flower for honey. His warm tongue disappeared, then he kissed her lightly a little lower, raised his face to ask, "Should I do a thorough job or leave you half-finished like you did me?"

"Please . . ." she begged in a ragged whisper.

"Please what? Please finish or please stop?"

"Please stop." Tears seemed to have gathered in her eyes, her throat, and between her legs.

"Not yet. Not till I bring some life to these limbs like you did to mine. Remember, Abbie? Remember how you massaged the life back into me and made my blood beat again after you tied me up?" She could no longer tell if this was torture or treat. It seemed her heart beat in every pore of her body as once again, in that slow, slow motion, he did what he wanted with her, sliding his arms along the lengths of her own, catching one up high above her head, sealing the other beneath them. He stretched his length out upon her, holding her now from behind while her wrist was clamped against brass which chimed a muted knell each time he pulled, grinding his tumescent body against her aroused one. Her lips fell open as her traitorous body responded. Her breath beat fast and warm upon his face. She'd made no sound, yet he heard her whimper all the same. Whimper for all the fear mingled with this new sensual turbulence so suddenly awakened in her, the pulsing void that seemed to cry for fulfillment.

Suddenly he stilled, looking down into her shadowed face with its closed, trembling eyes, its open, trembling lips. He touched the crest of her cheek softly. "How old are you, Abbie? You lied to me, didn't you? You said you're old because it's a shield you hide behind, afraid of what life is all about. But what do you fear now, living with this or without this?"

A sob caught in her throat. "I am thirty-three and I hate you," she whispered. "I shall hate you till my dying day." Her fear of him was gone, replaced by fear of a new and different kind: a fear of herself. A fear of the muscle and blood that had responded too plainly to all he'd said and done.

How long had her hands been free? They rested inanimately, curled in limp abandon, commanded now only by the air, for he was smoothing the hair back from her brow—too gently, too gently. He had claimed his victory over her, true, but somehow it left him hollow and beaten himself. As she lay beneath him, disheveled and defeated, he suddenly wished he had the old Abbie back, all starch and spitfire.

"Hey, what started this anyway?" She heard the change in his voice and it did nothing to calm the riotous vibrations of her flesh. She swallowed the tears in her throat, but her voice was thick, the back of her wrist falling across her eyes.

"If I remember correctly, somebody brought a train robber into my house and he wore a moustache."

"Abbie . . ." he said tentatively, as if there were so much more unsaid. But she pushed him off her and struggled to the edge of the bed, leaving him sorry he'd done as much as he had, sorrier still that he hadn't done more. But as she slid across the rumpled sheets her hand touched cold steel, abandoned in their struggle which had ceased to be a struggle. Her fingers closed over it as she moved off silently in the dark.

Chapter 10

—————

It was a fine Sunday, bright and fresh, the sky as blue as a robin's egg. But all through services Miss Abigail found it difficult to pay attention. Even while praying to be forgiven for the responses she'd been unable to control last night, she felt her skin ripple sweetly in remembrance. Standing to join in a hymn, her lips parted to form the words, but the memory of his tongue between them scorched her with shame and a tingling, forbidden want. Putting a hand to the nape of her neck to smooth her hair, the memory of his hand there made her hang her head in shame. But as she did she looked down the lace-covered bodice of her proper, high-necked dress only to know that within it her nipples were puckered up like gumdrops. And within her pristine soul Abigail McKenzie knew that she was truly damned now, yet all through no real fault of her own. She had lived a demure life, one in which—granted—little temptation of last night's sort had been put in her way. But she had not deserved to be treated so ruthlessly.

While Miss Abigail contemplated all this she occasionally caught herself eyeing the back of Doc Dougherty's bald head, wishing she could take the butt of that gun and rap some sense into it!

When the service was over she lost track of how many times

she was asked how everything was going up at her house, how many times she was forced to lie and answer, "Fine, fine." She was asked everything from how the outlaw's wounds were healing to what in the world she wanted with that pig bladder! To the latter she again replied with the half lie that the train robber used it to strengthen his bruised hand—true enough, but hardly the reason she'd bought it. When she finally got Doc Dougherty off to one side, she was upset not only with him but with everyone who'd asked her what was none of their business.

Doc was his usual congenial self as he greeted, "How-do, Miss Abigail."

"Doctor, I must talk to you."

"Something wrong with our patient? What's his name again? Jesse, isn't it? Has he been up getting some exercise?"

"Yes he has, but—"

"Fine! Fine! That limb will stiffen up like an uncured pelt if he doesn't move it. Feed him good and see that he gets up and around, maybe even out of the house."

"Out of the house! Why the man has no clothes. He went to the outhouse yesterday wrapped in nothing more than a sheet!"

Doc laughed, his belly hefting jovially. "Never thought about that when I brought his stuff back the other day. Guess we'll have to buy him some clothes, eh? The railroad'll pay for—"

Impatiently, she interrupted, "Doctor, whatever were you thinking to return his gun to him? He . . . he threatened me with it, after all I've done for him."

Doc scowled worriedly. "Threatened you?"

"Shh!" She looked quickly around, then lied again. "It was nothing too serious. He just wanted some fried pork chops for his dinner."

Suddenly Doc suspected just what sort of rivalry might have sprung up between two such willful people, and a telltale sparkle lit his eyes as he inquired, "And did he get them?"

She colored, fussed about pulling her glove on tighter, and stammered, "Why . . . I . . . he . . . yes, he did."

Doc reached into a breast pocket, found a cigar, bit off the end, and gazed off across the distance reflectively. Then he spit the cigar end into the dirt and smiled. "Pretty crafty of him, considering the gun had no bullets."

Miss Abigail felt like somebody had just opened her chemise and poured ice water inside.

"Bullets?" she snapped, her jaw so tight she could have bitten one in half just then.

"Bullets, Miss Abigail. You didn't think I'd turn his gun over to him with a cylinder full of bullets, did you?"

"I . . . I . . ." But she realized how very stupid she must appear to Doc Dougherty, admitting that she'd been duped by a felon with an empty pistol. "I had not thought the gun might be empty. I . . . I . . . should have known."

"Of course you should have. But I'm sorry he pulled it on you anyway. Sounds like you've had your trials with him. Is everything else all right?"

Miss Abigail could not, would not admit to a living soul how extremely unright everything was. She could never again face a person in this town if people found out what she had suffered at the hands of that scoundrel up at her house. She prided herself on control, good breeding, fine manners, and the town respected her for those things. She would not give them any reason to raise eyebrows at her now. Not at this late date!

"I assure you that everything is all right, Doctor Dougherty. The man has harmed me in no way whatsoever. But he is a loutish brute, crude-mannered and vain, and I have grown thoroughly sick of having him in my house. The sooner he gets out, the better. I should like it if you would sign a release immediately so that Sheriff Harris may wire the railroad authorities to come and get him."

"Sure enough! I'll do it first thing in the morning. He should be well enough to travel soon."

"Just how long do you think it will be before they come and get him?"

Doc scratched his chin. "That's hard to say, but it shouldn't be too long, and I'll be up every day. You can count on that, Miss Abigail. As soon as I see he's able to travel, we'll have him out of there and off your hands for you. Anything else I can do for you?"

"Yes. You may purchase some britches for him. If he is to be traipsing around on those crutches I insist he dress properly."

"Sure thing. I'll have 'em up there first thing."

"The earlier the better," she suggested, none too placatingly. Then with that little upward nudge of chin she wished him good day and turned toward home, angrier than she ever remembered being in her life. To think that she'd been duped, gulled, toyed with in such a manner by that . . . that *dog* she'd taken in off the streets when nobody else in town would so much as throw their table scraps to him! He had victimized her not once, but *twice* . . . and with an empty gun yet! The thought had her positively sizzling by the time she reached the house.

Jesse heard the loud Clack! Clack! Clack! of her heels on the steps as she went noisily upstairs. A moment later she came down again, marching loudly, regularly, as if some band accompanied her parade. The uncharacteristic noise surprised him; before church she'd been pussyfooting again. She flashed past his door, went to the kitchen, and opened the pantry door. He heard her pouring something, then here she came again, still marching. Around the bedroom doorway she swished. Up to the bed she hiked, and before he could say a word, wound up, hauled off, and smacked him across the face so hard that his cheek reverberated off the headboard. The brass sang out like she'd slammed it with a ball peen hammer. While he was still stunned senseless, she crossed calmly to the water pitcher, dumped a cupful of something into it, then held his pistol over it, using thumb and forefinger only.

"Never again will you threaten me with this distasteful object you once called a gun," she said, all eloquent and self-righteous, before releasing the gun with a plop! into the water. "Neither *with* nor *without* bullets!" Still too surprised to move, he heard burbles from within the pitcher as water gurgled its way into the barrel. When it finally struck him what she'd done, he leaped from the bed and hobbled to the pitcher. He was about to plunge his hand in after the gun when she coolly advised, "I wouldn't try dunking for it unless you want your hand dissolved, too, by the lye." She had retreated a safe distance.

He hopped around, swinging awkwardly to face her, but jostling the table in the process. "You daughter of a snake! Get that gun out of there or I'll dump the whole thing on the floor, I swear!"

"My tabletop!" she exclaimed, as the lye water puddled on the varnish. She lurched a few steps toward it, but stopped uncertainly.

"Get it out!" he roared. They glowered at each other, his

jaws grinding, her mouth pinched and quivering. Like feral animals they poised, wary, tensile, cautious. In a scarcely controlled fit, from between clenched teeth he spoke, punctuating his words with grand, empty gaps: "Get . . . it . . . out!"

And she knew she'd better get it out.

With a toss of shoulders and thrusting out of ribs, she carried the pitcher away, out the back screen door. He heard it slam, then the slosh as she emptied the whole mess into the yard. She came running back with a rag to wipe off her precious tabletop. While she dabbed at it, Jesse collapsed into the rocker, burying his face in his hands, muttering disgustedly, "What did you do a goddamn thing like that for?"

In a voice oozing sarcasm, she began, "Your foray into the prolix is truly impressive—"

"Just don't start in on me with your three-dollar words," he barked, "because we both know that every damn time you do it, it's because you're running scared! I'll say anything I want, any way I want to!"

"So will I! You may have thought you bested me last night, but Miss Abigail McKenzie shall not be bested, do you hear!" She scrubbed at the tabletop with violent motions. "I take you into my house—You! A common train robber!—and keep your rotting hulk alive, and for what! To be criticized for my cooking, my language, my manners, even the flowers I grow in my garden! To be pawed and degraded in repayment for my care!"

"Care?" He laughed harshly. "You never cared about anything in your entire, dismal life! Your blood is as cold as a frog's. And just like a frog, you live on your lonely lily pad, jumping in and hiding whenever anything resembling life comes anywhere near you! So you found out the gun wasn't loaded, huh? And that's why you marched in here and smacked me clear into next week, then dropped my gun into lye? Is it?"

"Yes!" she screeched, whirling on him, tears seeping to her eyes now.

"Like hell it is *Miss* Abigail McKenzie! The reason you did it is because you knew that gun wasn't even pointed at you anymore when you turned to jelly beneath me, isn't it? Because what you felt last night had absolutely nothing to do with a gun. You've lived your whole life in this godforsaken old maid's house, scared to death to show any emotion whatever, until I came along. Me! A common train robber! A man your warped sense of decency has told you to beware of since the first minute I was hauled in here. Only you can't admit to yourself that you're human, that you could be lit up by the likes of me, that you could lie there on that bed and find that bare skin can be something less than sordid, in spite of who it's touching, in spite of what you've forced yourself to believe all these years. You've also learned that a little fight now and then can be pretty invigorating, not to mention downright sexually stimulating. Only it's not supposed to be, is it? Since I've been here you've experienced every emotion that's been forbidden to you your entire life. And the truth is, you blame me because you like them all and you don't think you're supposed to."

"Lies!" she argued. "You lie to defend yourself when you know that what you did last night was low and cruel and immoral!"

"Low? Cruel? Immoral?" Again he laughed harshly. "Why, if you had any sense, Abbie, you'd be thanking me for showing you last night that there's hope for you after all. The way you've been pussyfooting your life away with your clean white gloves and your fastidiously clean thoughts, I'm surprised you didn't ask the congregation to stone you as a martyr this morning. Admit it, Abbie. You're sore because you enjoyed rolling around on that bed with me last night!"

"Stop it! Stop it!" she shrieked. Then she whirled and threw the lye-soaked rag at him. It landed across his lower face, a sodden end cloying like a rat's tail around his jaw and neck. Instantly his skin began to burn and his eyes grew wide. He clawed at the rag wildly as she realized, horrified, what she'd done. The next moment she was reacting as her life had programmed her to react, grabbing a dry towel from the washstand, lunging to wrap his face. Their hands worked together frantically to dry his skin before any damage was done. He saw her eyes widen with fear, telling him she knew she'd gone one step too far.

"You . . ." she choked out, scrubbing at his skin harder than she had at the tabletop. "You laugh at all I do for you and de . . . deride me for everything that is your fault. Never once since you've been here have you ap . . . appreciated a single thing I've done for you. Instead, you criticize and berate and slander. Well, if I'm so cold-blooded and straight-laced and undesirable, why did you start what you did on that bed last night? Why?" Stricken, on the verge of breaking down, she met his eyes nevertheless. "Do you think that I don't know the reason you turned me loose? Do you think I'm so naive that I couldn't tell you ended up in self-defeat by liking it yourself?" Her hands had fallen still on the towel, which trailed away behind his shoulders. It covered his mouth, but his moustache appeared blacker than ever, contrasted against its whiteness. They faced each other now in silent standoff. His black eyes bored into hers, which dropped to his bronze chest. Her hands fluttered from the towel as her eyes had from his relentless, knowing gaze. She suddenly wished she could reclaim her words. In slowest motion his swarthy fingers pulled the towel free from his mouth. His words, when at last they came, were the most fearsome yet, for they were spoken in a hushed, confused voice.

"And what if I did, Abbie? What if I did?"

Stricken anew, she felt her nerves gathering into wary knots, the skin at the back of her neck prickle, while confusion sluiced through her. He was a player of games, a law breaker, her enemy. He could not be trusted. Still she looked up at his disconcerting train robber's eyes and they skewered her to the spot as no gun ever could. He neither smiled nor frowned, but looked at her with an expression of intense sincerity.

"I did not ask for it," she managed in a choked whisper.

"Neither did I," he said low.

Quickly she turned from him, asking, "Is your skin burned?" But his strong hand came out to stay her in a firm grip just above her elbow.

"Did you really want to burn me?" he asked, studying the taut cords of her neck as she arched sharply away from him and swallowed.

"I . . . no . . . I don't know what I wanted." Her voice was timorous and uncertain. "I don't know how to survive around you. You make me so angry when I don't want to be. I want . . ." But she sighed to a halt, unable to finish. All she wanted was peace, not this hammering heart, this threatening desire for a person like him.

"You make me angry too," he said most gently, squeezing the flesh beneath his sinewed fingers.

He watched the profile of her right breast lift as she drew in a great, shuddering breath. He saw her eyelashes drift down upon her pinkened cheek.

"Let my arm go," she begged shakily. "I don't want to be touched by you."

"I think you're too late, Abbie," he said. "I think you already are." He shook her arm gently. "Hey, look at me."

When she wouldn't, he gripped her narrow shoulders and forced her to face him. She studied the floor at his feet while his hands burned a trail down her limp arms to her elbows and on to her wrists. He took her hands loosely in his while she fought the compulsion to raise her gaze to those dark, dark eyes.

"It's Sunday, Abbie. Should we just be friends for one day and see how it works?"

"I'd . . ." She swallowed. Her heart clamored in her throat and she braved raising her eyes as far as his chin. He had shaved while she was gone, and he smelled of soap. His moustache was thick and black, but she would not raise her eyes farther. Suddenly he sighed and dropped back down into the rocker again, still holding her hands, doing something soft and wonderful to the backs of them, rubbing them slowly with his thumbs, from cuff to knuckle, while she stood in confusion, telling herself to pull her hands free from his, yet absorbing the very niceness of the touch, so different from how he'd ever touched her before. This was gentle, tender in a way she would have sworn this man could never be. She stared at their joined hands and knew fully what he was doing, but she let him go about it.

Slowly he turned a palm to his mouth, and his eyes closed as warm lips and soft moustache grew lost in it. Her fingers lay curled beneath his chin and she stood like a statue feeling the touch of a magic wand, suddenly imbued with life-giving current while his kiss lingered in her cupped hand. Then his hand stole up to her waist and he tugged her toward his lap.

"No, don't—not again," she begged even as he eased her down expertly.

"Why not?" he whispered as strong hands closed over her shoulders and turned her inexorably toward his chest.

"Because we hate each—" He stopped her words with his open lips while his hands went aroving up and down her back. His moustache was soft now, almost as soft as before she'd shaved it, and his warm tongue came seeking, thrilling, inviting with supple sensuousness before she broke away, claiming, "This is crazy, we must not—" But his long palms spanned her cheeks and he had his way with her again. He pulled her mouth to his, then found her arms and placed them behind his neck, holding them in place until he felt her acquiesce and curl them around his head.

And she thought, I am crazy, and let him go on kissing her until his hands were on her back again, running up and down, up and down. Then at her waist, pressing firmly at her sides, down low, just above her belt line.

He whispered things into her mouth. "Don't fight it, Abbie . . . for once, don't fight it," and the words were blurred from his tongue moving against hers as he spoke. His hands moved lower, to her hips, swiveling them around until she half lay, half sat on his lap. He stiffened his body in the very small chair, lifting and shifting her until she no longer controlled where she was or how she rested upon him. With chest and waist arched away from the chair, Jesse manipulated her until she lay upon him. He was one smooth, hard plane of flesh upon which she settled while both of his arms circled her waist, holding her very still, allowing her to know the feel of him through flounced petticoats.

And he was long . . . and hard . . . and somehow very good.

Sense intruded and she broke away, resisting. "No . . . you are a thief. You are my enemy."

"You are your own enemy, Abbie," he whispered. Then she felt his hands cup her beneath her arms while he raised her whole body, sliding it effortlessly upward until her breasts were over his face and he held her that way, breathing through the starched front of her proper dress, blowing hot life into her who fought against wanting it.

"Oh, please . . . please, put me down." She was almost in tears now, pain and pleasure intermingling in her breasts, her heart, her hands upon his hard shoulders . . . and the part of her that now rested against his chest.

"Abbie, let me," he said into her breasts, "let me."

"No, oh, no, please," she begged, her lips brushing against his soft hair as she spoke into it.

"Let me make a woman of you, Ab."

"No, don't," she gasped. "I . . . I won't touch your gun or your moustache again. I promise. I'll feed you anything you want, only let me go, please."

"You don't want me to," he said, letting her slide back

down the length of him until her lips were at his again. But the
towel had worked its way between their mouths somehow.

"Take the towel away, Abbie," he entreated, his arms firm
and solid about her waist.

"No, Jesse, no," she breathed tremulously.

And hearing her utter his name, Jesse knew that she wanted
him, too. He raised his chin, nudging the towel down with it,
nuzzling her neck. "Let's be friends," he said against her high,
stiff collar.

"Never," she denied as his lips eased back to hers. He
pushed the rocker back and lay further horizontally, his hips
plying hers, rocking a little bit, a little bit, each movement of
the chair driving his hard body against hers. He knew it was
truly beyond her to say yes to him, that the only way he'd ever
have her would be nothing short of rape, for even if she gave
in, she'd be doing so against her will. He had to hear her say
yes or turn her loose. But he understood, too, that that one
word—yes—was impossible for her to utter. When he released
her, she'd be shamed even by what she'd done so far. But
release her he must, and so, to make it easier on her, he
quipped, "Say yes quick, Abbie, because my leg hurts like a
bitch."

At his teasing she jumped back, too peeved for shame. "Oh,
you! You are egotistical and insufferable!" To her dismay, he
laughed, holding her down just a moment longer.

"But let's still be friends, for today anyway. I'm sick of the
fighting too."

She struggled up from his lap, adjusting her clothing. "If
you promise not to do anything like this again."

"Well, could I maybe just think about it?" His dark
moustache curled above a teasing smile while Abby scarcely
knew where to let her eyes light, she was so flustered. She
headed for the kitchen and he followed on his crutches.

"Mind if I sit out here awhile?" he asked. "I'm getting
pretty sick of that bedroom."

She wouldn't look at him, but allowed, "Do whatever you
like as long as you stay out of my way."

He sat down nonchalantly beside the table, leaning the
crutches on the floor beneath his legs. "I won't be any bother,"
he promised. However, it bothered her already, the way he sat
there with his legs sprawled and those walking sticks resting
against his crotch. It took a supreme effort to keep her eyes

from straying to it, and she had no doubt he knew exactly what he was doing to her. But before he could fluster her further, Doc Dougherty's voice came from the front door.

"Hello in there. Can I come in?" And in he came, for the way Miss Abigail's house was designed he could see down the straight shot from front to back that they were both in the kitchen. "W-e-e-ll," he drawled at the sight of Jesse, "you're looking fit as a fiddle, sitting up on that kitchen chair. How do you feel?"

"Stronger every day, thanks to Miss Abigail," Jesse answered, pleased, as usual, to see the doc.

"So she told me at church earlier. Oh, Miss Abigail, I got those britches you asked me to get. Avery opened his store special. We figured pants for a real necessity, so he obliged. If they don't fit, it'll be too bad, because Avery already locked up again."

Miss Abigail gave the denims a scant glance, then continued with her dinner preparations again as Doc and Jesse retired to the bedroom to have a look at his leg. She could hear their muffled voices before Doc came back to repeat his order of earlier. "He's long past any danger and he can do whatever he feels strong enough to do—inside, outside, doesn't matter. A little fresh air and sunshine might do him good. Now that he's got decent clothes, it wouldn't hurt to take a ride in the country or sit in that garden of yours."

"I doubt that he'd enjoy either of those things."

"I already suggested it and he seemed real anxious to get out. Might not do you any harm either. Well, I better be off now. You need anything else, just holler."

She showed him to the front door, but halfway there Jesse came out of the bedroom, dressed now in blue denims and a pale blue cotton shirt, which hung open.

"Thanks for stopping, Doc, and for the clothes," he said, and went along to the front door as if the house were his own.

"It was Miss Abigail's idea," Doc informed him.

"Then maybe I should thank Miss Abigail," Jesse said, casting a brief grin her way. But Doc was away, out the door, down the porch steps, calling as he went, "See you tomorrow, you two!" The way he said it, lumping the two of them together that way, left a curious warm feeling almost like security in Abbie, standing there beside Jesse at the front door after having ushered Doc out together.

Unexpectedly, Jesse's voice beside her was polite and sincere as he said, "It feels good to have some clothes on that fit me again. Thanks, Abbie." It took her aback because she had grown so used to his teasing and criticism, she hardly knew how to handle politeness from him. She was acutely aware of the fact that while Doc was here Jesse had politely called her Miss Abigail, but as soon as he left, he reverted to the familiar Abbie again. She could feel him looking down at her, caught sight of that bare, black-haired chest, those long naked feet, and wondered what to say to him. But he turned then, lifted a crutch, and gestured politely for her to move ahead of him back to the kitchen. She felt his eyes branding her back as he thumped along behind her.

She returned to her cooking and he to his chair, but the room remained strained with silence until Jesse commented, "Doc gave me hell for pulling that gun on you."

She could not conceal her surprise. Out of the clear blue sky he said a thing like that. Then he added, "I was surprised you admitted it to him."

Sheepishly, she said, "I only told him you made demands regarding pork chops, nothing more."

"Ah," he returned, "is that all?"

She was disconcerted by his sitting behind her, probably staring at every move she made. At last she ventured a peek over her shoulder. The crutches were resting against the same distracting spot as before as he leaned an elbow on the table, scowling, running a forefinger repeatedly over his moustache as if deep in thought.

She turned her back on him before inquiring innocently, "Did he say anything else?"

Silence for a long moment, then, "He wanted to know why my chin and neck were red. I told him I'd been eating fresh strawberries from your garden and they make me break out. You'd better have some strawberries in that garden of yours . . ." From behind, he saw her hands fall idle.

Abbie could feel the coloring working its way up her neck. "You . . . you mean . . . you didn't tell him about the lye in the rag?"

"No." He watched her shoulders slump slighty in relief.

To the top of the range, she said, "Yes, I do have strawberries in my garden."

Behind her, he sat watching as she started whipping

something with a spoon. The motion stirred her skirts until they swayed about her narrow hips. Suddenly she stood very still, and said quietly, "Thank you."

A strange feeling gripped him. She had never spoken so nicely to him before. He cleared his throat and it sounded like thunder in the quiet room. "Have you got anything to put on it, though, Abbie? It's starting to sting pretty bad."

She whirled quickly, and he caught an unguarded look of concern on her face as she crossed the room to him. Her hand reached tentatively for his chin, withdrew, and their eyes met, each wondering why the other had softened the truth when Doc Dougherty had asked his questions.

"Buttermilk should help it." Her eyes dropped to the crutches.

"Have you got any?" he asked.

"Yes, outside in the well. I'll get it."

He watched her walk down the yard and draw the bucket up and bring a fruit jar back into the house. All the while the frown stayed on his face. "I'll get some gauze to apply it with," she said when she returned. Bringing it, she stood hesitantly, somehow afraid to touch him now.

He reached out a hand, palm-up, saying, "I can do it myself. You're busy." When she was back at the stove he surprised her once more by asking, "Are your hands okay?"

"My hands?"

"From the lye. Are they okay, or do you need some buttermilk too?"

"Oh, they're all right. I barely got them damp."

When she collected the buttermilk and wet gauze to begin setting the table for their dinner, she stopped in the pantry door, looked across the room at him. "Do you like buttermilk?" she asked.

"Yes, I do."

"Do you want some with your dinner?"

"Sounds good."

She disappeared, returned with a glass of frothy white, and handed it to him. His fingers looked tawnier than ever against the milk.

"Thank you," he said to her for the second time that day.

At last she joined him at the table, extended a platter his way, asking politely, "Chicken?"

"Help yourself first," he suggested. And pretty soon—

unbelievably—their plates were filled and they were eating dinner across from each other without so much as one cross word between them.

"We used to have chicken every single Sunday when I was little," he recalled.

"Who is we?"

"We," he repeated. "My mom and dad and Rafe and June and Clare and Tommy Joe. My family."

"And where was that?"

"New Orleans."

Somehow the picture of him in a circle of brothers and sisters and parents seemed ludicrous. He was—she reminded herself—a consummate liar.

"You don't believe me, do you?" He smiled and took a bite of chicken.

"I don't know."

"Even train robbers have mothers and fathers. Some of us even have siblings." He was back to his customary teasing again, but somehow she didn't mind this time. The word *siblings* was a surprise, too, the kind he now and then tossed out unexpectedly. It was her kind of word, not his.

"And how many *siblings* did you have?"

"I had . . . *have* . . . four. Two brothers and two sisters."

"Indeed?" She raised an eyebrow dubiously.

He raised his buttermilked chin a little and laughed enjoyably. "I can hear the skepticism in your voice and I know why. Sorry if I don't fit your notion of where I should or shouldn't have come from, but I have two parents, still living in New Orleans, in a real house, still eating real chicken on Sundays— only Creole-style—and I have two older brothers and two younger sisters and last night when you washed my hair it reminded me of Saturday nights back there at home. We all washed our hair on Saturday nights, and Mom polished our shoes for Sunday."

She was unabashedly staring at him now. The truth was, she wanted to be convinced that it was all true. Could it possibly be? She reminded herself again that he was an accused felon, that the last thing she should do was believe him.

"Surprised?" he asked, smiling at her amazed expression. But she wasn't ready to believe it yet.

"If you had such a nice home, why did you leave it?"

"Oh, I didn't leave it permanently. I go back regularly and visit. I left my family because I was young and had my fortune to seek, and a good and loyal friend who wanted to seek his along with me. But I miss them sometimes."

"And so you left New Orleans together?"

"We did."

"And did you find your fortunes?"

"We did. On the railroads—together."

"Ahhh, the railroads again," she crooned knowingly.

"What can I say?" He threw his hands out guiltily. "I was caught red-handed."

His blithe, devil-may-care attitude puzzled her, but she smiled at his affability, wondering if it was all true about New Orleans and his family.

"And what about you?" He had finished eating and leaned back relaxedly in his chair, one elbow slung on the table. "Any brothers or sisters?"

She immediately gazed out the screen door, faraway things in her expression as she answered, "None."

"I gathered as much from Doc. I left my family when I was twenty. He said you stayed with yours."

"Yes." She picked away a nonexistent thread from her skirt.

"Not by choice?"

She looked up sharply. It would not do to admit such a thing, no matter what the truth. A good daughter simply would not begrudge a father anything, would she? Jesse was absently toying with his moustache again, resting his forefinger beneath his nose as he continued. "Doc told me once that you gave up your youth to care for an ailing father. I find that commendable." She glanced to his eyes to see if he was teasing again, but they were serious. "How long ago was that?"

She swallowed, weighing the risks of telling him things she never talked about. Finally she admitted, "Thirteen years."

"When you were twenty?"

"Yes." Her eyes dropped to her lap again.

"What a waste," he commented quietly, making the skin at the back of her neck prickle. She didn't know what to reply or where to look or what to do with her hands. "It's not everyone who'd do a thing like that, Abbie. Do you regret it now?"

The fact that she did not deny her regret was the closest she had ever come to admitting it.

"When did he die?" Jesse went on.

"A year ago."

"Twelve years you gave him?" Only silence answered him while she demurely looked at her hands. "Twelve years, and all that time you learned how to do all the things you do so well, all the things it takes to make a house run smoothly, and a family . . . yet you never had one. Why?"

She was startled and embarrassed by his question. She'd thought they had come to a silent agreement not to intentionally hurt each other anymore. But some shred of pride kept her eyes from tearing as she replied, "I believe that's obvious, isn't it?"

"You mean you had little choice in the matter?"

She swallowed, and her face became mottled. I should have known better than to confide in him, she thought, her heart near bursting with bitter pain.

"Until Melcher came along and I took the choice away from you by scaring him away."

She could not tolerate his barbs anymore. She flew from her chair to run, but he stopped her with a hand on her arm. "I see now I was wrong," he said quietly, making her eyes fly to his. It was the last thing she had expected him to say. It wilted her resolve to hate him, yet she was now afraid of what would take hate's place should she relinquish it.

"Do we have to talk about this?" she asked the tan hand upon her sleeve.

"I'm trying to apologize, Abbie," he said. "I haven't done it many times in my life." She looked up, startled, to find utter sincerity in his eyes, and her heart set up a flurry of wingbeats at the somber look he wore.

Knowing that once she said it she would be on even more precarious footing, she said anyway, "Apology accepted." His dark fingers squeezed her arm once, then slid away. But it felt as if he had branded her with that touch while he spoke the words she had never thought to hear from him.

Chapter 11

———

MISS ABIGAIL KEPT her gardens just as fastidiously as she kept everything else, Jesse thought as he lounged against a tree, hands laced on his stomach, watching her. There was a predominance of blues, but being a man, he could not identify bachelor buttons, canterbury bells, or forget-me-nots, though he did know a morning glory. He squinted as Abbie flitted to explore them where they climbed a white trellis against the wall of the house. He almost expected her to dip and sip from one, he had thought of her as a hummingbird for so long. Lazy and sated, he watched her move from flower to flower. She leaned to pull an errant weed and he smiled privately as her derriere pointed his way. The backs of her calves came into view beneath her skirt. He closed one eye, leaving the other open as if taking a bead on her. When she seemed about to turn around, he pretended to be asleep. Then, in a moment, he carefully peered out at her again. Once more he assessed her slim ankles, realizing that she was a damn fine-looking woman. Let that tight knot of hair down, unbutton a couple buttons, teach her it's all right to laugh, and she'd make some man sit up and take notice. Realizing what he was thinking, he shut his eyes completely and thought, *That hummingbird's not for you, Jess.* But then why had they goaded and fought with each other like they had? It had all the earmarks of a mating ritual and he knew it. Didn't the stallion bite the mare before mounting her? And the she-cat—how she screamed and growled and spit at the tom before he jumped her. Even the gentle rabbits became vicious beforehand, the doe using her powerful back legs to box and kick the buck as if repulsed by him.

He studied Abigail McKenzie through scarcely opened eyelids. She picked some yellow thing and raised it to her nose. She had a cute little turned up nose.

He considered the hummingbird. Even its disposition turned pugnacious at mating time, both male and female becoming quarrelsome and snappish in their own avian way. He'd seen hummingbirds countless times in the woods, feeding from honey trees sweet with blossoms. Each male marked his feeding territory, defending it against all comers who sought to sip the nectar of his chosen flowers. He fought off all invaders until one special female arrived to tempt him. Together they would flit through the air flirting, toward and away from the prized flowers. Then, at the last, the female stilled her wings and hesitated just long enough for the male to mate with her, thus paying for the taste of his flowers before sipping quickly and caroming away too fast for the eye to follow.

He recalled how Abbie had withheld food from him, trying to starve him out of her house. He remembered all the teasing, the fighting, the baiting they'd each done.

She straightened and wiped her forehead with the back of a hand, her breast thrown into sharp relief against the mass of blue flowers behind her.

Damnit, Jess, get your carcass healed and out of here! he thought, and sat up quickly.

"What do you say we go for that ride?" he asked, needing some distraction.

She turned. "I thought you were asleep."

"I've slept so much in the last couple of weeks I don't care if I never do again." He wore a faint scowl as he looked away at the mountains.

"How is your skin?" she asked.

"Sour, I think. This buttermilk was soothing but I think it'd better come off before the neighbors start complaining." An amused smile lifted her lips and she wiped the back of her forehead again.

"I'll get some water." Soon she returned with a basin of cold water, a cloth, and a bar of soap, placing them on the ground near him.

"Pew! You do stink!" she exclaimed, backing away.

"If you think it smells bad from over there, you should smell it from over here." Again she laughed, then sat down a proper distance away, tucking both feet to one side beneath her skirts, watching him draw the basin between his legs and lean over to bathe his face. He lathered his hands instead of the cloth, raised his chin, running the soap back around his jaw and neck. He rinsed, opened his eyes, and caught her watching him, and she quickly glanced off across the flats to where the mountains rose, blue-hued and hazy, even in the high daytime sun.

"It'd be nice to take a buggy ride out there," he said.

"But I don't own a buggy or a horse," she explained.

"Hasn't this town got a livery stable?"

"Yes. Mr. Perkins runs it, but I don't think it's a good idea."

"But Doc said it's okay. I've been up a lot. I was up all the while you were gone. I even washed my hair with soap and water, didn't you notice?"

Oh, she'd noticed all right. She could still remember the smell of it while he breathed into her breasts on the rocker this morning.

"Being up is different than riding along in a bumpy buggy." But she looked wistfully at the road, lifting smoothly out of the valley into the foothills that gently inclined toward the ridges above the town.

"Are you afraid to go for a ride with me?"

Startled because he'd guessed the truth, she was forced to lie. "Why . . . why no. No, why should I be?"

"I'm a wanted man."

"You're an injured man, and in spite of what Doc Dougherty says, I refuse to believe it could do you any good to go riding on a hard buggy seat."

"When's the last time you saw my wound, Abbie? Doc's been the one looking at it and he says buggy riding's okay."

"It's not a good idea," she repeated lamely, picking a blade of grass.

"It's not me you don't think should go off in a buggy, it's you. Admit it."

"Me!"

He squinted up at the mountains, while her eyes strayed to

the black hairs on the tops of his bare toes. "I mean," he
drawled, biting on a piece of grass now himself, "it would
probably look pretty queer, Miss Abigail McKenzie renting a
rig to take her train robber off to who knows where on a
Sunday afternoon."

"You are not *my* train robber, Mr. Cameron, and I'd
appreciate it if you'd not refer to yourself as such."

"Oh, pardon," he said with a lopsided smile, "then the
town's train robber." He could see her weakening—damnit,
but she was getting to look more appealing by the minute—and
he wondered if he should stay put.

"Why are you after me like this again? You promised you
would behave."

"I'm behaving, aren't I? All I want to do is get out of here
for awhile. Furthermore, I promised Doc I wouldn't harm you
or try to escape. It's Sunday, everybody in town's relaxing and
doing exactly as they please, and here you sit, gazing at the
mountains from your hot backyard while we could be up where
it's cooler, riding along and enjoying the day."

"I'm enjoying it right here—at least I was until you started
with this preposterous idea." But she tucked a slim forefinger
into the high, tight band of her collar and worked it back and
forth.

He wondered if ever in her life she'd taken a buggy ride with
a man. Maybe with that one thirteen years ago, she had. He
found himself again trying to picture how she'd looked and
acted when being courted.

"I wouldn't bite you, Abbie. What do you say?"

Her blue eyes seemed to appeal to him not to convince her
this way, yet as her finger slid out of her collar her lips parted
expectantly and she glanced once more at the mountains. Her
cheeks took on a delicate pink color of her own primroses.
Then she dropped her eyes to her lap as she spoke. "You would
have to button up your shirt and put your boots on."

All was silent but for the chirp of a katydid. She raised her
eyes to his and he thought, what the hell are you up to, Jess?
He suddenly felt like some damn fool bumblebee sitting in her
garden while she poised a glass jar above him, ready to slam it
down and clap the cover on. But, against his better judgment,
he smiled and said, "Agreed."

* * *

"Why, howdy, Miss Abigail," Gem Perkins said, answering her knock, trying hard not to show his surprise. Never before had she come to his door, but here she was, decked out flawlessly in white hat and gloves.

"Good afternoon, Mr. Perkins. I should like to rent a horse and buggy with a well-sprung seat. One that will jostle as little as possible."

"A buggy, Miss Abigail?" Gem asked, as if she'd requested instead a saddled gila monster.

"Do you or do you not rent buggies, Mr. Perkins?" she asked dryly.

"Why, o' course I do, you know that, Miss Abigail. I just never knew you to take one out before."

"And I wouldn't be now, except that Dr. Dougherty wants that invalid up at my place to grow accustomed to riding again so that he may be packed off on the train as soon as possible. However, we shall need an upholstered seat with lithe springs."

"Why, sure thing, Miss Abigail, upholstered seat and what was that other again?" He led the way to the livery, still surprised at her showing up here this way.

"Springy springs, Mr. Perkins," she stated again, wondering how long it would take for the news to spread to every resident of town what she was doing.

Jesse chuckled, watching her drive the rig up the street. He could see she didn't know the first thing about handling a horse. The mare threw her head and nickered in objection to the cut of the bit in Abbie's too-cautious hands. She pulled up in front of the pickets and he watched her carefully dismount, then swish up the walk. No, he decided, she'd never done anything like this before in her life.

By the time she entered the parlor, he was waiting on her graceful settee. Miss Abigail resisted the urge to laugh at how ridiculous he looked there—the only discrepancy in her otherwise tidy room. No, she thought, he'll never make *parlor fare*.

"The leg's a little stiff," he said, "and so is the new denim. Could you help me with my boots?" She looked down at his bare toes, chagrined to feel a peculiar thrill at the sight of them, then quickly she knelt and held first his socks, then his boots. They were fine boots, she noticed for the first time, well oiled

and made of heavy, expensive cowhide. She wondered if he'd
robbed a train to pay for them and was again surprised that the
thought did nothing to deter her from wanting to ride out with
him.

When the boots were on she rose, carefully avoiding looking
at his dark-skinned chest behind the gaping garment. "You
promised you'd button up your shirt," she reminded him.

He looked down at himself. "Oh, yeah." Then he struggled
to stand clumsily on one foot, buttoned the shirt, then turned
his back to her and unceremoniously unbuttoned his fly and
began stuffing his shirttails in. Her cheeks flared red yet she
stood and watched the play of his shoulder muscles while he
made the necessary adjustments. Finally realizing what she
was doing, she spun from the room and went to wait for him on
the porch.

He stumped his way out on his crutches and moved to the
side of the buggy. The denims were indeed very stiff. It
immediately became apparent that he'd have trouble boarding.
There was only a single, small footrest high on the buggy, and
after three attempts to lift his foot to it, she ordered, "Wait on
the steps and I'll pull up near them."

He withdrew to the porch steps to watch her inexpertly drive
the rig around the end of the picket fence.

"You're pulling too sharp!" he warned. "Ease off!" He held
his breath for fear she'd overturn the thing before the mission
even got under way. But the rig arrived safely at the porch and
he poised on his crutches on the second step.

"Can you make it?" she asked, measuring the distance
visually.

He grinned, quipping, "If I don't, just ship my bones back
to New Orleans." Then he swung both feet toward the floor of
the rig, dangling momentarily by his armpits on the crutches.
But the rest of his body didn't come along with his feet, and he
teetered precariously, on the verge of going over backward.

"No!" Miss Abigail exclaimed, reacting automatically,
reaching to grab the only thing she could see to grab: the
waistband of his new denims. It did the trick, all right, but she
yanked a little too hard and he came plummeting like a felled
tree, nearly wiping her clean out the other side of the buggy.
The next moment she found herself squashed beneath him, one
hand splayed on his hard chest, the other still delving into his
waistband. Suddenly realizing where that hand was buried, she

jerked it out. But not before his suggestive smile made her face flame. She pushed him away and fussily adjusted her hat, whisked at her skirt, and refused to look at him. But his smirk remained in her peripheral vision. He was up to his cute tricks again, naturally! Red to the ears and trying to pretend she wasn't, she stiffened her back while he took the reins, clicked, whistled, and the mare set off while Abbie sat like a lump of her own cornmeal being taken for a ride.

"Are you all right?" he asked. But she could hear that smirk still coloring his words.

"I'm perfectly fine!" she snapped.

"Then what are you snapping at me for?"

"You know perfectly well why I'm snapping at you!"

"What did I do now?" All innocence and light.

"You know perfectly well what you did! You and your shifty, suggestive eyes!"

He smiled sideways at her starchy, affronted pose. "Well, I wasn't going to mention it, but as long as you did, what's a man supposed to do when a woman's got her hand in his pants?"

"My hand was not in your pants!" she spit, really puckered now.

He laughed boldly. "Oh, a thousand pardons, Miss Abigail. I guess I was mistaken. It must have been some other woman's hand in my pants just now." He looked around as if searching for the culprit. He chuckled low in his throat once, assessing her mirthfully. She wasn't taking his teasing too well today. He liked it best when she gave him tit for tat. He grinned, casting sideward glances at her stern face, and relaxed back and started whistling some little ditty softly between his teeth, deciding he'd be nice for a while and see if he couldn't sweeten her up some.

They headed north on a double track that paralleled the railroad tracks toward the foothills. It was scorching, and Miss Abigail was grateful for even the sliver of shade afforded by her narrow hatbrim. The leg space was inadequate for his long limbs, so his knees sprawled sideways, brushing against her skirts, though she kept her feet primly together and her hands in her lap. She inched away as far as possible, but they hit a bump and his knee lolled over and thumped against her and his smiling eyes leisurely roved her way. When she sat stiff and silent, he finally glanced off at the scenery without saying a word.

As they neared the foothills the undergrowth thickened and Jesse raised an arm, silently pointing. She followed his finger to where a cottontail hit for cover, and without knowing it, she smiled. Her eyes stayed riveted to the spot until they reached and passed it, and Jesse furtively watched her search for more animal life. A hawk appeared, circling above him, and she lifted her face to follow it. The greenery hedged closer to the road, and she seemed enchanted by a flock of lark buntings flitting in and out, feeding upon piñon nuts. The rails swung right while the wagon track bore left, and once again they broke into an open space where spikes of blue lupines created a moving sea all about them, as if part of the sky had fallen into the peaceful mountainside. Her lips formed a silent "Ohhh," and he smiled appreciatively. Silently they swayed along, climbing higher and higher until the terrain became rockier, with outcroppings here and there holding a strangling yew. They passed a cluster of bright orange painted cups, and again her eyes strayed behind to linger on the flowers as long as possible.

He turned his slow gaze upon her. "Where does this go?"

She perched like a little chipping sparrow, on the edge of her seat, alert and taking everything in. "To Eagle Butte, then along the Cascade Creek to Great Pine Rock and over the ridge to Hicksville."

Again they fell silent, he smiling and she taking in everything, while the mare trotted along. Once Jesse wiped his forehead on his shirtsleeve. They entered a patch of quaking aspen and the trembling, dappled shade the trees created. Here and there was a fragrant evergreen—juniper or spruce—vying for sky as the branches formed a tunnel overhead. Soon they came to a flat, shapeless gray rock precipice.

"Is this Eagle Butte?"

She looked around in a full circle. "I think so. It's been a long time since I was up here."

He stopped the horse and they sat with the sun pelting them mercilessly as they gazed beyond the enormity of Eagle Butte to a similar ridge that rose across a chasm along which they'd been riding for some distance. Over there the firs were in deep shadow—a rich, lush haven of coolness, while on this side the afternoon sun still blazed. Studying the scene opposite, Jesse absently unbuttoned two buttons of his shirt and ran a hand inside. Mingling with the scent of pine was that of ripe grass and the pleasantly fecund scent of the sweating horse.

"If you continue on, we should soon reach Cascade Creek and it should be much cooler there."

He clucked to the mare and they moved on. When they reached Cascade Creek it was, indeed, cool and inviting, brattling its way shallowly down a rocky bed between shady willows and alders.

The horse plodded to the water, dipped her head, and drank, then stood blinking slowly. Both of the riders watched the animal for several long, silent minutes.

At last Jesse asked, "Would you like to get down for a while?"

She knew it would be best to keep this outing strictly to riding, but she cast a wishful glance at the water. Instead of waiting for an answer, Jesse flicked the reins and turned the horse, nudging her toward a low-hanging branch on a gnarled pine tree. He stood, grabbed the sturdy branch, and swung easily to the ground. He retrieved his crutches from the buggy while she concealed her surprise at his lithe agility—for someone as big as he was, he moved like a puma. He reached up a brown hand to help her down, and she glanced, startled, at it, quite unprepared for this civility.

"Don't bump your head," he said, indicating the branch above her.

His palm waited, callused and hard, becoming more of an issue the longer she delayed placing her own in it. But she recalled that she was wearing her white gloves, and at last placed one in his firm grip as he helped her jump to the ground. She moved ahead of him toward the inviting water, but she had those gloves on, and he was on crutches so neither of them touched it. Instead they watched it bubble away at their feet. After some time he pulled his shirttails completely free of his pants again and unbuttoned the shirt the rest of the way. She stood stiff and formal, yet. Jesse glanced around, and spied a comfortable-looking spot where the water had scooped away the bank to form a rude, but natural chair. He hobbled over, threw his crutches down, then settled himself with a sigh. The creek burbled. The birds spoke. The woods were redolent with pine spice and leaf mold. Jesse crossed his arms behind his head and leaned back, watching the woman who stood on the creek bank.

Her back was as straight as a ramrod: she never allowed herself to relax those infernal gentilities of hers. Now she stood as stiffly as the boles of the pine trees, although he knew she was hot, too, for she'd raised a white glove to touch her forehead, then again to brush at the nape of her neck. What was she thinking as she looked at the creek? What did she want to do that her silly manners would not allow? He wondered if she'd even sit down, if she'd touch the water, if she'd condescend to talk to him.

"The water looks nice and cool," he commented finally, watching her carefully to see what she'd do. When she neither replied nor moved, he added, "Tell me if it is. I can't reach."

Her hands remained as motionless as a watched clock for a long, long time. Finally she drew her gloves off. He could tell by the hesitant way she leaned to touch the water that she wished he weren't watching her. Even a simple, sensual gesture like that caused her second thoughts. For a moment he pitied her. The hem of her dress slipped a little bit and she hurriedly clutched it up, away from the surface of the stream.

And he thought, let it fall, Abbie, let it fall, then wallow in behind it and see how great it feels. But he knew, of course, that she never would.

"Bring me some," he called anyway, just to see what she'd do.

She turned a brief, quizzical glance over her shoulder. "But I have nothing to carry it in."

"So carry it in your hands."

Abruptly she stood up. "There is a ridiculous suggestion if I ever heard one."

"Not to a thirsty man."

"Don't be foolish, you can't drink from my hands."

"Why not?" he asked casually.

He could hear her thinking, as clearly as if she'd spoken the words aloud, "It is just not done!"

"If I could drink from your mouth while I was unconscious, why can't I drink from your hands now?"

Her shoulder blades snapped closer together and she said, still facing away from him, "You take very great pleasure in persecuting me, don't you?"

"All I want is some water," he said reasonably, still with his head hanging backward in the cradle of his two hands. Then he sighed, looked upstream, and muttered, "Aw, what the hell, just forget it then," and laid his head back on the creekbank and closed his eyes.

He looked very harmless that way when she ventured to peek at him. Funny, but she really did not like being on the bad side of him, yet she never quite knew what he was up to. She glanced at his moustache—it was almost as thick as when she first saw him—then to the water, then back at him again. She looked around for something she could shape into a cone or vessel, but there was nothing. Never in her life had she done such a thing, but the thought of doing it caused an earthy sensation in the pit of her stomach. The water had felt deliciously cool. Even the horse had needed a long drink. And Jesse was obviously very hot. He'd unbuttoned that shirt again, and she remembered how he'd run his hand inside it earlier. She looked at him dozing peacefully. She looked at the water.

Jesse's eyes flew open as two large splats of water hit his bare chest. He jumped but then grinned: she was standing over him with cupped hands.

"Open up," she ordered.

Well I'll be damned, he thought, and opened his mouth like a communicant. She lowered her palms, created a split in their seam, but the water trailed away, down inside her cuffs, some hitting his chest and chin, but none reaching his lips. She half expected him to jump up and smack her hands aside, remembering the time she'd clacked the spoon against his teeth, but he surprised her by rubbing a hand over his dark chest, spreading the water wide.

"Ah, that's cool," he said appreciatively, then his eyes twinkled. "But I'd like a little in my mouth, too."

"Oh, I got my cuffs wet," she complained, pulling at them. But they stuck to her wrists and would not even slide on her skin.

"As long as they're already wet, may as well try again."

This time it worked better, for he reached to cup the backs of her hands and pour the water into his mouth from her fingertips as if they were the lip of a pitcher.

It was a decidedly sensuous thing, watching him drink from her fingertips. It made queer quivers start way down low in her stomach. After he swallowed, droplets were left upon his moustache. Fascinated, she watched his tongue run along its edge and lap them up. She realized suddenly that she'd been staring. Immediately her eyes flitted to some distant bush.

"Why don't you have some?"

She touched her throat just below her jaw. "N . . . No, I don't want any."

He knew it was not true, but understood—she'd already gone too far.

"Come on, sit down awhile. It's nice and cool here and really quite comfortable."

She glanced around as if someone might catch her at it if she dared. Reaching some sort of compromise with herself, she said, "I'll sit here," and perched on a rock near his feet.

"You've never been up here before?" he asked, studying her back as she faced the creek.

"When I was a girl, I was."

"Who brought you?"

"My father. He came to cut wood and I helped him load it."

"If I lived around here I'd come up here all the time. It's too flat and hot down in the valley to suit me." He laced his hands behind his head and looked up into the trees. "When my brothers and I were small, we spent hours and hours by the Gulf, catching sand crabs, playing in the surf, shell hunting. I miss the ocean."

"I've never seen the ocean," she said plaintively.

"It's no prettier than this, just pretty in a different way. Do you want to?"

"Want to?" She glanced back at him.

"See the ocean?"

"I don't know. Richard was—" But she stopped dead and quickly faced the creek.

"Richard? Who is Richard?"

"Nothing . . . nobody . . . I don't even know why I brought him up."

"He must be *somebody*, or you wouldn't have."

"Oh . . ." She circled her knees with her hands. "He was just someone I knew once who always said he wanted to live by the ocean."

"Did he make it?"

"I don't know."

"You lost touch with him?"

She sighed and shrugged. "What does it matter? It was a long time ago."

"How long ago?"

But she didn't answer. She was afraid to confide in him. Yet he urged her to speak of things which no other person had ever cared enough to ask about.

"Thirteen years ago?" he prompted. Still she didn't reply, and he thought long and hard before finally admitting, "I know about Richard, Abbie."

He heard her breath catch in her throat before she turned startled eyes to him. "How could you know about Richard?"

"Doc Dougherty told me."

Her nostrils distended and her lips tightened. "Doctor Dougherty talks too much for his own good."

"And you talk too little for yours."

She hugged herself and turned away. "I keep my private affairs to myself. That is exactly how it should be."

"Is it? Then why did you bring up Richard?"

"I don't know. His name slipped out inadvertently. I've never talked about him since he left and I assure you I am not about to start now."

"Why? Is he taboo, just like everything else?"

"You talk like a fool."

"No, I suspect somebody did that long before I came along, or you wouldn't be so tied up in knots over letting go a little bit."

"I don't even know why I listen to you—a completely impulsive person like you. You have no notion of restraint or self-control of any kind. You . . . you charge through life as if to give it a shock so it will remember you've been there. That may work well for you, but I assure you it is not my way. I live by strict standards."

"Has it occurred to you, Abbie, that maybe you set your standards too high, or that somebody else may have done it for you?"

"That is impossible for any living person to do."

"Then tell me why you're sitting out here five miles from civilization yet you wouldn't take your hat off if it grew tentacles or even unbutton the cuffs that are probably chafing you raw right now. But worst of all you won't talk about something that caused you pain, because some fool said a lady shouldn't? Nor does she show regret or anger, is that right? A lady just doesn't spill her guts. She sits instead with them all tied in neat, prim knots. Of course talking would make you human, and maybe you prefer to think you're above being human." He knew he was making her angry, but knew too that was the only time she truly opened up.

"I was taught, sir, that it is both ill-mannered and—yes—unladylike to wail out one's dissatisfactions with life. It simply is not done."

"Who said so, your mother?"

"Yes, if you must know!"

"Humph!" He could just about picture her mother. "The best thing in the world for you would be to come right out and say, 'I loved a man named Richard once but he jilted me and it makes me mad as hell.'"

Her fists knotted and she spun to face him, eyes dangerously glistening. "You have no right!"

"No, but you do, Abbie, don't you see?" He sat straighter, intense now.

"All I see is that I should never have come up here with you today. You have succeeded again in making me so angry that I should like to . . . to slap your hateful face!"

"It'd be the second time today you slapped my face for making you feel something. Is it that frightful to you to feel? If slapping me would make you feel good, why don't you come over here and do it? How mad do I have to make you before you'll break out? Why can't you just cuss or laugh or cry when something inside Abbie says she should?"

"What is it you want of me!"

"Just to teach you that what comes natural shouldn't be forbidden."

"Oh, certainly! Slapping, crying . . . and . . . and that . . . that little scene on the rocker this morning! Why, if you had your way you would turn me into a wanton!" Tears brimmed at the rims of her eyes.

"Those things aren't wanton, but you can't see it because of all the silly rules your mother made you live by."

"You leave my mother out of this! Ever since you came to my house you've been contrary and fault-finding. I will not let you attack my mother when your own could have taught you a few manners!"

"Listen to yourself, Abbie. Why is it you can call me names and get angry with me when the ones you really blame are your mother and father and Richard for what they did to you?"

"I said leave them out of this! What they were to me is none of your business!" Her eyes blazed as she jumped to her feet.

"Why so belligerent, Abbie? Because I hit on the truth? Because it's them you blame when you think you're not supposed to? Doc Dougherty didn't have to tell me much to fit the pieces together. Correct me if I'm wrong. Your mother taught you that a good daughter honors her father and mother, even if it means sacrificing her own joy. She taught you that virtue is natural and carnality isn't, when actually it's the other way around."

"How dare you sit there and pour acerbations on innocent people who wanted only the best for me?"

"They had no idea of what was best for you—all except Richard, I suspect, and he was smart enough to know he couldn't fight your dead mother's code of ethics, so he got out!"

"Oh! And you know what's best for me, I suppose!"

He assessed her dispassionately. "Maybe."

She assessed him passionately. "And maybe you'll sprout wings and fly away from the law when they come to get you!" She waggled a finger in the direction of town.

Comprehension dawned in his eyes. "Ah, now we're getting down to the truth here, aren't we?" He reached for his crutches without taking his menacing eyes from her. "It baffles you how some common, no-good train robber like me could possibly hit on the truth about you, doesn't it?"

"Exactly!" she spit, facing him, fists clenched angrily at her sides. "A common, no-good train robber!"

"Well, let this common, no-good train robber tell you a few things about yourself, Miss Abigail McKenzie, that you've been denying ever since you laid eyes on me." He struggled to his feet, advancing upon her. "It is precisely *because* I'm an outlaw that you have, on several occasions, ventured forth from your righteous ways and lost control. With me you did things you never dared do before—you sneaked a peek at life. And do you know why you tried it? Because afterward you could wipe your conscience clean and blame me for goading you into it. After all, I'm the bad one anyway, right?"

"You talk in circles!" she scoffed, quaking now because he'd hit upon the truth and that truth was too awful for her to admit.

"Are you denying that it's because I'm a . . . a criminal

that you dared to bend your holy bylaws around me a little?" They were nose to nose now.

"I don't know what you're talking about," she said prissily, and turned away, crossing her arms tightly across her breasts.

He reached out to grab her upper arm and try to make her turn to face him. "Oh, pull your head out of the sand, Miss Abigail Ostrich, and admit it!" She yanked herself free of his grip, but he moved in close behind her, pursuing her with his relentless accusations. "You slammed doors and threw bed-pans and kissed me and hollered at me and even got yourself a little sexually excited, and you found out it all felt pretty damn fun at times. But you could blame all those forbidden things on me, right? Because I'm the nasty one here, not you. But what would happen to all your grand illusions if I turned out to be something other than the brigand you think I am?" Again he got her by the arm. "Come on, talk to me. Tell me all your well-guarded secret guilts! You can tell me—what the hell, I'll be gone soon enough and take them all with me!"

At last she spun on him, whacking his hand off her arm. "I have no secret guilts!" she shouted angrily.

His eyes bored into hers as he shouted back, with ferocity equal to hers, "Now *that's* what I've been trying to make you see all this time!"

Silence fell like a hundred-year oak. Their eyes locked. She struggled to understand what it was he was saying, and when the truth came to her at last, she was stricken by her own comprehension, and she turned away.

"Don't keep turning away from me, Abbie," he said, making his way to her on the clumsy crutches, touching her arm more gently now, trying to make her face him willingly, which she stubbornly refused to do. "Do I have to say it for you, Abbie?" he asked softly.

Tears began gathering in her throat.

"I . . . I don't know what it is you want me to . . . to say."

In the quietest tones he had ever used with her, Jesse spoke. "Why not start by admitting that Richard was a randy youth, that something happened between you and him that made him leave." Jesse paused a long moment, then added even softer, while with his thumb he stroked the arm he still held, "That it had nothing to do with your father."

"No, no . . . it's not true!" She covered her face with her palms. "Why do you goad me like this?"

"Because I think Richard was exactly like me and it's got you scared to death."

She whirled then and hit him once with her pathetic little fist in the center of his bare chest. It send him hobbling backward, but he didn't quite fall. "Wasn't he?" Jesse persisted.

She looked into his relentless eyes like a demented woodland nymph, shaken, tears now streaming down her cheeks. "Leave me alone!" she begged miserably.

"Admit it, Abbie," he said softly.

"Damn you!" she cried, sobbing now, and raised a hand to strike him again. He did not cringe or back away as the blow, and another and another rained upon his shoulders and chest. "Damn you . . . R . . . Richard!" she choked, but Jesse stood sturdy as she hit the side of his neck and her nails scraped two red welts upon it.

He did not fight her, did not block her swing, only said very gently, "I'm not Richard, Abbie. I'm Jesse."

"I know . . . I kn . . . I know," she sobbed into her hands, ashamed now of having sunk to such depths.

He reached out and encircled her shaking shoulders, gathering her near, pulling her forehead against his hard chest. Her tears scalded his bare skin and brought some wholly new and disturbing stinging behind his eyes. A crutch dropped to the ground, but he steadied himself and let it fall. Her hat had gone askew and he reached to pull the pin from it.

Her hands flew up and she choked, "Wh . . . what are y . . . you doing?"

"Just something you wouldn't do for yourself—taking your hat off. Nothing more, okay?" He stuck the filigreed pin through the straw, tossed it behind him onto the creek bank, then pulled her again into his arms, circling her neck with one large hand, rubbing a thumb across the hair pulled so prudishly taut behind her ear.

She cried against him with her elbows folded tightly between them, comforted more than she'd thought possible by the feel of his forearm spanning her narrow shoulders and his palm stroking her sleeve. He touched her soft earlobe. He laid his cheek against her hair, and she felt a queer sense of security, staying within his arms that way.

Abbie, Abbie, he thought, *my little hummingbird, what are you doing to me?*

He smelled different than her father—better. He felt different than David—harder. She reminded herself who he was, what he was, but for the moment it didn't matter. He was here, and warm, and real, and the beat of his heart was firm and sure beneath her cheek upon his chest. And she needed so terribly badly to talk about everything at last.

When her crying eased, he leaned back, taking her face in both hands, wiping at the wetness beneath her eyes with his thumbs.

"Come on, Abbie, let's sit down and talk. Don't you see you've got to talk about it?"

She nodded limply, then he drew her by the hand toward the creek bank, and she followed docilely, exhausted now from her fit of tears.

A blackbird sang in the willows. The creek rushed past with its whispered accompaniment as Abbie began to speak. Jesse did not touch her again, but let her talk it all out, drawing from her the truths which he'd guessed days ago. He pieced together the picture of a pathetic, retiring husband and the single child, both of whom the mother had wronged with her narrow version of love. A rigid woman of stern discipline who taught her daughter that duty was more important than the urgings of her own body. And Richard, the man who made Abbie aware of those urgings, but could not free her from the stringent laws laid down by her mother. And Abbie, hiding all these years behind the delusion that Richard had deserted her because of the invalid father.

But Jesse now saw the imprisoned Abbie escape, as the bullfrogs set up their late-day chorus. He watched the woman on the creek bank change into a mellow, human entity, with fears, misgivings, frailties, and regrets. And it was this transformed Abbie of whom Jesse knew he'd best be careful.

Things were infinitely different between them by the time they started back to town. The myths were shattered. The truth now rode like a passenger on the seat, intimately, between them. There was a disturbing ease, born of a deeper understanding, and far more threatening than the animosities which had earlier riddled their relationship.

For she had learned he could be kind.

And he had learned she could be human.

They rode in silence, aware of each brush of elbow and knee. White moths of evening came out and the song of the cicada ceased. The shadows of the trees grew to long-stretching tendrils then disappeared in the cease of sun. The leaves whispered their last hushed vespers. The mare quickened her step toward home, her voice the only one heard as she nickered to the growing twilight. Abbie's sleeve brushed Jesse's shoulder and he leaned forward, away from it, staring straight ahead, elbows to knees and the reins limp in his hands. He had helped her break down many barriers today, but she was still bound by propriety. She was not at all his kind of woman. Yet he looked back over his shoulder and caught her watching him, her eyes quite the color of the evening sky, her piquant little face showing signs of confusion, but her hands again in white gloves, glowing almost purple now as dusk came on.

Her eyes strayed, then came back to meet his, and she knew the swift, intimidating yearning of the woman who feels herself drawn to the wrong man. The wheels hushed along, the riders rocked in unison, their eyes locked. At last her troubled gaze drifted aside, as did his. She thought of a gun in his hand on that train and her eyes slid shut, not wanting to picture it yet unable to keep the image at bay. She opened her eyes again and studied his broad shoulders with blue cotton pulled taut against rippling muscle, black hair curling down over his collar, thick sideburns curving low on a crisp jaw, sleeves rolled to elbows upon arms limned with dark hair, the limp wrist, those long fingers. She remembered them upon her, then looked away, distracted.

God help me, she thought, I want him.

Town approached. Jesse shifted the reins to one hand and, without saying a word, considerately buttoned up his shirt. In the gathering dusk she felt herself blush. He leaned back, their shoulders touched again, then her familiar white picket fence was beside them and he pulled up before the porch steps.

He handed her the reins. They were warm from his hands.

He spoke gently. "Don't turn her so sharp this time. I don't want you tipping over."

Something too good happened within her at his quiet admonition.

He stood in the twilight watching her again cut too sharply

around the pickets, holding his breath, releasing it only when she'd straightened the rig and was heading up the street. Then he clumped to the swing at the north end of the porch to wait for her. He braced his crutches in the corner and swung idly, surveying the porch, which was so typical of her. It was tidy, freshly painted, surrounded by a spooled rail that quit only where the wide steps gave onto the yard. At the opposite end was a pair of white wicker chairs with a matching table between them holding a sprawling fern. He thought of her while he swung, accompanied by the soft, jerking squeak of the ropes.

She rounded a corner down the street and he watched her come on, small and straight, and felt the strength of his healing muscles and knew he'd damn well better leave this place soon.

She started slightly when she saw him there in the shadows, one arm stretched carelessly along the back of the double seat. She wondered how it would feel to simply settle down in the lea of that arm and lean her head back against him and swing away companiably until full darkness fell and he should say, "It's time for bed now, Abbie."

But he was Jesse the ominous train robber, so she stood uncertainly at the top of the steps. Only, he did not look very ominous swinging away idly there. The ropes spoke a creaky complaint about his weight, and for a moment she remembered the awesomeness of it upon her. She dropped her eyes guiltily.

"Are you hungry?" she asked, unable to think of anything else to say.

"A little," he replied. He realized only too clearly what it was he was hungry for.

"Would cold chicken and bread be all right?"

"Sure. Why don't we eat it out here?"

"I don't think—" She cast a glance at the house next door, then seemed to change her mind. "All right. I'll get it." She left him swinging there, and when she returned with the tray she sensed her hesitation to approach him.

"Put it on the floor at our feet and come sit with me," he invited. "It's getting dark—nobody will see us." But her eyes skittered to the elbow slung along the back of the swing, and only when he lowered it did she set the tray down and perch beside him.

They nibbled silently, caught up by awareness, lashed into silence by the new tension which had sprung up between them.

They ate little. She told herself to take the tray back inside, but sat instead as if her legs had wills of their own.

He crossed his near ankle over his knee, dropped a dark hand over the boot to hold it there while each stroke of the swing now whispered his knee across Abbie's skirts. Her eyes were drawn to the sturdy thigh tight-wrapped in straining denim. She clenched her hand in the folds of her skirts to keep it from reaching out and resting upon that firm muscle which flexed repeatedly with each nudge of his heel upon the floor. She could almost feel how warm and hard that thigh would be, how sensual it would feel to run her palm along its long, inner side, to know the intimate shift of muscle as it moved with the swing. But she only stared at it while her unwieldy imagination did strange things to the low reaches of her stomach. A tightness tugged there, and queer trembles afflicted her most intimate parts. She sat there coveting that masculine thigh and becoming enamored with the mere touch of her own clothing against her skin.

He draped his wrist lazily over the back of the swing, never touching her, yet making her heart career when she realized how close it hung to her shoulder.

"Well, I guess it's bedtime," he said quietly at last. Her pulses pounded and the blood beat its way up her cheeks. But he only removed his hand from the back of the swing and craned around for his crutches in the corner, then rose and positioned them, politely waiting for her to precede him.

He managed the screen door, and when she passed before him into the parlor, asked behind her, "Do you want the inside door closed?"

She was afraid to look back at him, so continued toward the kitchen, answering, "No. It's a warm night, just hook the screen."

Jesse felt a sense of home, coming in with her this way, putting things in order for the night, and knew more than ever that it was time to move on. He shuffled through the dark in the direction of the kitchen.

"Where are the matches?" he asked.

Her voice came from someplace near the pantry door. "In the matchbox on the wall to the left of the stove."

He groped, found, struck a wooden tip and held it high. Abbie sprang into light, hovering in the pantryway with the tray pressed against her waist, and her eyes big and luminous in the lamplight. He put the chimney back on the lamp and looked across at her, tempted . . . oh so tempted.

For a minute neither knew what to say.

"I'll . . . I'll just set these dirty dishes in the pantry."

"Oh . . . oh, sure," he shrugged, looked around as if he'd lost something. "Guess I'll go out back then before bed." Resolutely, Jesse headed for the door, knowing he was doing the right thing. But as he was negotiating the dark steps he found her behind him holding the lantern aloft to illuminate his way. He swung around and looked up at her.

Unsmiling, she studied his face glowing red-gold below her, his hair blending with the backdrop of the night. The lantern caught the measureless depths of his eyes, like those of a cat impaled by a ray of direct light.

"Thanks, Abbie," he said quietly, ". . . good night." Then his arms flexed upon the crutches and he was gone, downyard, swallowed by the dark.

She put the pantry in order for the night, and still he hadn't come in. She went to the back screen and peered out. The moon had risen and she made out his shape by its pale white light, sitting in the backyard under the linden tree. His face was in lacy night shadow, but she made out his boots and the way one knee was raised with an arm slung over it.

"Jesse?" she called softly.

"Aha."

"Are you all right?"

"I'm fine. Go to bed, Abbie."

When she did, she lay a long time listening, but never did hear him come back inside.

Chapter 12

———————

THE FOLLOWING MORNING a grinning Bones Binley stood on Miss Abigail's front porch, looking like a jack-o'-lantern atop a knobby fence post, with his over-large head, gap-teeth, and protruding Adam's apple.

"Mornin', Mizz Abigail. Fine mornin'. Fine mornin'. This package . . . ah . . . come for you at the depot on yesterday's train, Mizz Abigail, but there wasn't nobody around to bring it on up, so Max he ast me to this mornin'."

"Thank you, Mr. Binley," she answered, opening the screen only enough to slip the package through, disappointing old Bones, who'd have given a half plug of tobacco to see just what was inside that box and the other half to see what that train robber was doing inside her house. But when Bones continued to grin at her through the screen, she added, "It was very obliging of you to deliver it to me, Mr. Binley."

She was the only person ever called him Mister that way.

"Sure thing, Mizz Abigail," Bones said almost reverently, nodding and shifting enormous feet while she wondered if she'd have to swat him off her porch with the screen door, like some pesky fly.

Once when they were younger Bones had bought Miss Abigail's basket at a Fourth of July picnic, and he'd never

forgotten the taste of her sour cream cake and fried chicken, or
her ladylike ways and the time she had him up to do a little
repair work on the shingles and how she'd asked him in
afterward for cake and coffee. But he could see now that he
was no more going to get inside her house than any train robber
was going to get inside her pants, which was after all what the
whole town was buzzing about.

"How's that there robber feller doing?" he asked, lifting his
battered hat and scratching his forehead.

"I'm not qualified to give a medical opinion on his state of
health, Mr. Binley. If you want that information to pass around
with your snuff down at the feedstore, I suggest you ask Doctor
Dougherty."

Bones had just then worked up a good hock and was about to
let 'er fly when Miss Abigail warned from her front door, "Do
not leave your residue on my property, if you please, Mr.
Binley!"

Well, by damn! thought old Bones, if she was talking about
spit, why in tarnal didn't she just come right out and say spit?
Maybe folks was right when they said she got a little uppity at
times. But anyways, Bones waited till he got to the road before
he laid a good gob. He wasn't gonna go messin' with her—
nossir!—not old Bones. And unless he missed his guess,
wasn't no man ever gonna mess with her, train robber or not!

The package was unmarked, except for a Denver postmark
and her name and Stuart's Junction, Colorado. She did not
recognize the handwriting. It was angular, tall, and made her
heart race. In her entire life she might have gotten maybe three
packages. There was one a long time ago that had brought the
small picture frame she'd sent for, to hold her mother's and
father's tintypes. Then there was the time she'd sent away for
the bedpan when her father could no longer execute the walk to
the backyard. This package now was Miss Abigail's third, and
she wanted to savor its mystery as long as possible.

She shook it and it clunked like dried muffins in a pie safe.
She saw Bones disappear down the street and on an impulse
took the box back outside to the porch swing. She savored it
for a long while before finally carefully removing the outside
wrapper, keeping the paper in one piece to save away and
treasure later. She shook the box again and even sniffed at it.
But all it smelled like was the pages of an old book, papery and
dry. She set it on her knees and ran a bemused hand over the lid

and swung idly upon the swing, drawing out the delicious wonderment while curiosity welled beautifully in her throat. She took some moments to cherish the anticipatory feeling and file it away for future memory. Finally she lifted the lid and her breath caught in her throat. Nestled within, like two pieces of a jigsaw puzzle, was a pair of the most beautiful shoes she had ever seen. There was a folded note, but she reached for neither note nor shoes immediately, sat instead with her hand over her opened lips, remembering David Melcher's face as she had last seen it, stricken with regret.

At last she lifted the note in one hand and a single shoe in the other.

Oh my! she thought. Red! They are red! Whatever shall I do with a pair of red shoes?

But she examined the exquisite leather, soft as a gentian petal, so soft that she wondered how such supple stuff could possibly support a person's weight. They were buskin styled, with delicate lacets running from ankle to top and sporting heels shaped like the waists of fairies, concave and chic. Touching the chamois-soft texture, she knew without needing to be told that they were indeed made of kidskin, the finest money could buy. David, she thought, oh, David, thank you. And she pressed a shoe to her cheek, suddenly missing him and wishing he were here. She would have liked to put the shoes on while she read his note, but she could never put these scarlet shoes on where they might be seen. Oh, perhaps sometime in the privacy of her bedroom. But for now she laid the shoe back in the box beside its mate and read his note:

My Dear Miss Abigail,

I take the liberty—no, the honor—of sending the finest and newest pair of shoes from the shipment awaiting me when I arrived in Denver. It will please me to imagine them on your dainty feet as you snip nasturtiums and take them into your gracious home. I think of you in that setting and even now rue my rashness in speaking to you as I did. If you can find it in your heart to forgive me, know that I would have willed things to take a different course than they've taken.

Yours in humility and gratitude,
David Melcher

She'd thought thirteen years ago that she'd realized what a broken heart felt like, when she was spurned by the man she'd grown to love through all her growing years. But it felt now as if this sense of a thing lost before it was ever gained was sorrier than anything she'd suffered back then. Her heart stung at the thought that David Melcher pined for her—impossible as it seemed, herself being the age she was. Such a refined man, who was just what she'd been looking for for so many years, ever since Richard ran away. And now she had no way to reach him, to say, "Come back . . . I forgive you . . . let us begin from here." The shoebox told her nothing. It held no company name, no color or style markings. There was no clue as to whom he worked for. All she knew was that he'd mentioned Philadelphia and that this package had been posted in Denver. But they were big cities, Denver and Philadelphia, cities in which there were undoubtedly many shoe manufacturers, many hawkers. It would be impossible to find a man who did not even possess a permanent address. But at the thought of his lack of a residence, the words *Elysian Club* came back to her.

The Elysian Club! Phildelphia!

That was where he stayed when he went back there. With a leaping heart she knew she would write a thank you to him in care of the Elysian Club, Philadelphia, and just hope he would somehow receive it on one of his return trips, and maybe—just maybe—he would come back to Stuart's Junction some day and look her up.

"Abbie? What're you doing out there?" A tousled Jesse, fresh up, stood barefoot, bare-chested in the front door.

Excitement animated her voice as she bubbled, "Oh, Mr. Cameron, look at what has just arrived for me." She had eyes for nothing but the shoes, which he could not see yet. She brought the package into the front parlor, crossed, and laid it on the dining room table at the far end, the wrapping paper address-side-up so there could be no mistaking the shoes were meant for her.

Jesse hobbled over to see what it was. "Where did you order those from?" he asked, surprised when he saw the scarlet shoes, for they didn't seem at all the kind of thing she'd choose.

"I didn't order them. They are a gift from David Melcher."

Suddenly Jesse needed a second look, and after taking it,

decided he disliked the shoes wholeheartedly. "*David* Melcher? My, my, aren't we becoming informal all of a sudden? And shoes yet! How shocking, Miss Abigail."

"I find it rather endearing myself," she said, fingering the leather, her mind scarcely on what she was doing. "Not the kind of gift that just any man would choose."

Jesse could sense her excitement as she let her fingers flutter over the red leather, butterflylike, touching the laces, the tongue, the toes, almost reverently.

"You can wear 'em over town every time you need a pig's bladder from the butcher shop," he said testily, "or whenever you need to send a wire asking somebody to get rid of a gunslinger for you."

She was too happy to heed his attempt to snub the gift.

"Oh my, I fear I cannot wear them anyplace at all. They simply aren't—well, they're much too fine and elegant for Stuart's Junction."

A black scowl drew his eyebrows down. She was damn near fondling the red leather now, and her face wore a beatific expression while she raved on about the exquisite workmanship and the quality of the leather. He'd never seen her glow so before, or bubble this way. Her eyes were as blue and bright as her morning glories, and her lips were parted in a rare, pliant smile. Watching it, he wanted to smack those damn red shoes from her hands.

But suddenly Jesse realized that Abbie's hair was less than tidy and she was wearing an old, shapeless dark floral shirt with sleeves rolled up to her elbows and a dishtowel tied triangularly around her belly. She looked as ordinary as a scullery maid, and the effect was devastating. He found himself studying the knot of the dishtowel which rode the shallows of her spine.

"Oh, my heavens!" she said gaily, "you slept so late and here I stand gaping at these things while you're probably fit to starve." She plopped the cover back over the shoes and looked up to catch the dark frown on his face.

For a moment it seemed to Abbie that he'd grown taller overnight, but she suddenly realized why.

"Why, you're walking without crutches!" she exclaimed gladly. Then she thought, gracious, but he is tall! And immediately afterward, gracious, but he is only half-dressed! He was shirtless and barefoot, as usual, wearing nothing but the new dungarees. "Now, Doctor Dougherty said you must take it a little at a time," she scolded, to cover her flustration at the sight of his bare skin.

Her concern assuaged some of the nettlesome annoyance he'd felt over the shoes, and his anger faded.

"I'm starved. What time is it?" He rubbed his hard, flat belly, pleased to see her eyes skitter away.

"Approaching noon. You slept very late." She turned toward the kitchen and he followed.

"Did you miss me?" He gave the shoebox a last scathing look and eyed that knotted dishtowel as it lifted perkily, bustlelike, with each step she took. She had one of the trimmest backsides he'd ever seen.

"I hardly had time. I was busy doing the washing."

"Oh, so that's why you're dressed like a scullery maid. I don't mind saying it's a pleasant change."

Suddenly she became self-conscious and began unrolling one of her shirtsleeves, flicking the folds down to cover her exposed arms, and he wondered if she'd have left them rolled up were he David Melcher. The thought irritated him further.

"Dirty jobs do not magically get done," she said, all businessy again, efficiently buttoning up her cuffs, then reaching behind to untie her dishtowel. He was sorry to see it go as she set about preparing their noon dinner. There was no evidence of her having washed clothes in the kitchen, but outside he found lines strung now, holding bedding, dish-towels, and some skirts and blouses. Limping his way to the privy, he caught sight, too, of pantalets and chemises trimmed with eyelet, hidden as inconspicuously as possible behind the larger, more mundane pieces of laundry. The corset he'd imagined her in, giving her chronic gastric and emotional indigestion, was nowhere in evidence.

However, when he got back to the house he figured the reason it was not on the line was because it must be busily binding her up in knots! Her waspish temperament had inexplicably returned. She started in on him the minute he walked in the door.

"I've asked you not to go about undressed that way, *sir*!" she stated tartly, obviously in a snit over a damn fool thing like that.

"Undressed!" He looked down at himself. "I'm not undressed!"

"Where is your shirt!"

"It's in the bedroom, for God's sake!"

"Mister Cameron, would you set aside your own offensive vernacular until you are once again in the sort of company that will appreciate it?"

"All right, all right, what bit you all of a sudden?"

"Nothing *bit* me, I just—" But she turned away without finishing.

"A minute ago you were all sloe-eyed over old Melcher's shoes and now—"

"I was *not* sloe-eyed!" She spun, eyes snapping, hands on hips.

"Huh!" he snorted, gripping the edge of the highboy behind him, tapping out a vexed rhythm with his fingertips. "He lit you up like a ball of swamp gas with those . . . those pieces of frippery!" He flung a disparaging hand toward the dining room.

Her eyebrows shot up. "Yesterday you were telling me to throw caution to the wind and feel things. Today you disparage me for a simple show of appreciation."

They stared at each other for a few crackling seconds before Jesse said the most absurd thing.

"But they're red!"

"They're what?" she asked, baffled.

"I said, they're red!" he roared. "The goddamn shoes are red!"

"Well, so what?"

"So . . . so they're red, that's all." He started pacing around in the corner by the pantry door, feeling silly. "What the hell kind of woman wears red shoes?" he squawked, forgetting that he'd just been admiring the way that dishtowel made her look like precisely the kind of woman who might wear red shoes.

"Did I say I wanted to wear them?"

"You didn't have to say it. The look on your face said it for you."

She pointed out the back door. "While I am trying to preserve some decorum around here, you limp out to the outhouse, naked as a savage, then have the audacity to scold me for thinking I should like to wear red shoes!"

"Let's get the issue straight here, *Miss* Abigail. You're not mad about me going out in the open without a shirt and shoes.

You're mad because I caught you looking sloe-eyed over those insufferable shoes!"

"And you're not mad because the shoes are red, you're mad because they're from David Melcher!"

"David Melcher!" he squawked disbelievingly, almost in her ear as she thundered past him into the pantry. "Don't make me laugh!" He followed right behind her, nose first, like a bloodhound. "If you think I'm jealous of a pantywaist like that—" But just then she swung around and stepped on his bare toe. "Ouch!" he yelped, while she didn't even slow down or say excuse me.

"You wouldn't get stepped on if you'd dress properly." She clapped some dishes on the table.

"The hell you say! You did that on purpose!"

"Maybe I did." She sounded pleased.

He nursed his toe against his calf. "Over nothing. I didn't do a damn thing this time!"

But she whirled on him, pointing an outraged finger at the backyard. "Nothing, you say? How dare you, sir, walk across my yard dressed like *that* and gape at my underthings in front of the whole town!"

His eyebrows shot up and a slow smile crept across his countenance, lifting one corner of his moustache before it lit up his mischievous eyes and he started laughing deep in his throat, then louder and louder until at last he collapsed onto a chair.

"Oh you . . . you . . . just . . . just shut up!" she spluttered. "Do you want the whole town to hear you?" She clapped herself down on the chair opposite and created a gross breach of etiquette for Miss Abigail McKenzie, serving herself without waiting for him. She whacked the serving spoon against her plate, splatting potatoes onto it while he sat there snickering. Finally she shoved a bowl in his direction and grunted, "Eat!"

He loaded his plate in between maddening chuckles while she felt like kicking his bad leg under the table. Finally he braced an elbow on the corner of the table, leaned near, and whispered very loudly, "Is it better if I whisper? This way the neighbors won't hear me." Even staring at her plate she could see that insufferable moustache right by her cheek. "Hey, Abbie, you know what I was looking for out there? Corsets. I wanted to see just how much rigging I'd have to get through before I hit skin."

She dropped her fork and knife with a clatter and left her chair as if ejected from it, but he made a grab and caught her by the back of her skirt.

"Let me go!" She yanked at the skirt, but he hauled away and pulled her back between his spraddled thighs while her arms flailed ineffectually.

"How many layers are under there, Abbie?" he teased, trying to get an arm around her waist and pull her down to his lap. She yanked and slapped and tried to free her skirt but he hauled it in like lanyard, all the while chortling deep in his throat.

"Get away!" she barked while he got her up against his lap like a schooner against a piling. She battled frantically, then luffed around till she could push against his shoulder, still trying to control her skirt with the other hand.

His smile was wicked, his hands deadly, as he breathed hard in her ear, "Don't you wear petticoats, Abbie? Come on, let's see." They were a dervish of arms and hands and elbows and petticoats and knees by this time. He gained and she struggled. He captured and she flapped. He fended off a misaimed slap, feinting back expertly while she rapidly lost ground.

"You maniac!" she bellowed, clawing his fingers loose from her wrist.

"Come on, Ab, quit teasin'." He got her wrist again, tighter than before.

"Me! Let me go!" she squawked. But somehow he had her turned around facing him. He pulled her up against his crotch, her thigh against his vitals while she fell upon his stone-hard chest. But once more she yanked loose, spun in a half turn till his hands got her by the hips and took her into port again.

"God, can you scrap for such a hummingbird," he puffed. And as if to prove it she almost got away. But his powerful arm caught her waist and she felt her backside hauled unceremoniously against his lap. "Ugh!" he grunted when she hit his sore leg, but his grip held at her waist.

"Good!" she spit, "I hope I hurt you! Get your hand down! Leave my buttons alone!"

He had her from behind, cinched the arm tight around her little middle, grappling for the buttons at her throat with his other hand. He managed to get one undone while she struggled to snatch his hand away and contend with the other that snaked up her midriff to her breast.

"Come on, Abbie, I won't hurt you." Her struggle only seemed to amuse him further while the skirmish at her blouse front went on.

"I'll hurt you any way I can!" she vowed—a mosquito threatening a rhinocerous. "I warn you!" She struggled valiantly, breathless now, but he kept her pinned so tightly she couldn't get far enough away to do any damage.

"God, how I like you in this old faded shirt," he panted, and somehow managed to spirit a second button free while she tried to seize both of his hands and gain her freedom at the same time.

"You filthy louse . . . I hope they . . . hang you!" she grunted.

"If I hang . . ." he grunted back, "at least give me . . . one last . . . sweet memory to take al . . . along." He had one breast now and she twisted around violently while he ducked to avoid a flying elbow.

"Atta girl, Abbie, turn around here where I can get at you." His black moustache came swooping for her mouth, but she clutched a hank of hair at his temple and pulled with all her might.

"Ouch!" he yelped, and she yanked harder until suddenly, unexpectedly, he released her. Sprawled as she was, she went down at a full slide, landing on her knees with her mouth just above his navel. But her elbow caught him precisely in the spot where he'd been shot, and he gasped and stiffened back, arms outflung, as if she'd just crucified him to that chair. His throaty groan told her the battle was over.

She scrambled up out of his thighs, fastening her two neck buttons while his eyes remained closed, the lids flinching. His lips had fallen open, his tongue tip came out to ride the lower edges of his even, upper teeth, then he sucked in a long, pained breath and looked up at the ceiling, with his head still hanging backward. Limply he touched the hair at his temple, massaging it gingerly while she watched, quivering and wary. His arm flopped back down and he finally grunted, pulling himself up by degrees until he was L-shaped again. The silence in the room was rife as he leaned an elbow on either side of his plate and stared down at it as if some piece of food there had moved. She eased to her chair, sat with her hands in her lap, then listlessly picked up a knife that was stuck at a precarious angle into a mound of mashed potatoes. She cleaned it off against the edge of her plate and laid it down very carefully and still neither of them said anything. She tried a bite, but it seemed to stick in her throat. He raised his head and stared past her down the length of the house, out the front door. There was no use pretending to eat, so she carefully wiped her mouth, folded her napkin, laid it down precisely, as if awaiting her penance.

He knew now why he'd done it. It really came as no surprise to him to find that he was jealous, just that he should be so over a woman like her. Yet, never had he been able to make her smile, laugh, or twinkle as that pair of shoes from Melcher had done.

Her chair scraped back into the silence at the same moment he finally decided to speak.

"Abbie, I think—"

"What?" She halted, half up, plate in hand.

He stared out the far front door, not trusting himself to look at her. "I think I'd better get out of here before we do hurt each other."

She stared at the plate in her hand, suddenly very sorry she'd hurt him.

"Yes," she said meekly. "I think you had better."

"Would you get my crutches from the bedroom please?" he asked, very politely.

"Of course," she agreed, equally as polite, and went to get them. She wanted to say she was sorry, but thought he should say it first. He had started it. Silently, she handed him the sticks.

"Thank you," he said, again too politely, pulling himself to his feet, then stumping off toward his room, gingerly favoring the right leg again. There followed a long, deep sigh as he lowered himself to the bedsprings.

Abbie stared out the back door for the longest time, seeing nothing. Finally, she sighed and put the room in order, then crept off to her upstairs room to discard the floral blouse.

But she slumped to the edge of the bed disconsolately, burying her face in her hands. Oh, she was so confused by everything. Nothing seemed simple like it had before the two men had entered her life. She could no longer deny her attraction for Jesse. At times he could be so warm and sympathetic. Like yesterday, when she'd told him things she'd never told another living soul and had begun to trust him, only to have him do what he'd just done. Why couldn't he be like

David? David—so much more like her. David—a gentleman whose values ran parallel to hers. David—who had kissed her so sweetly on the stairs but would never have tried anything like Jesse had just pulled on that chair downstairs. But thinking of it, she felt that odd, forbidden exhilaration that would not be quelled. Why was she unable to resist the dark, foreboding charms that drew her into Jesse's web time and time again?

She tried to imagine her father ever carrying on with her mother in that fashion but simply could not. Why, her mother would have left home. Yet Abbie wondered now why her father and mother never touched or kissed. She had always assumed that their polite way was the way all well-bred married couples acted.

Abbie pressed her hands to her heated face, remembering her mother saying that all men were beasts. She remembered Richard tackling her in the livery stable one time and how she'd slapped him. She remembered Jesse grappling with her on that chair, and that night in the bed with his tongue all over her breasts and belly. She shivered, there in the heat of the upstairs bedroom, assuring herself that what she'd felt that night and today was fear and nothing more. For anything else would be sinful.

She pulled herself up sharply, changed into proper clothing, and made up her mind she must offer him some apology for hurting him and would go down and make lemonade, which would suffice if she could not bring herself to utter the words.

Chapter 13

SHE WAS JUST about ready to pour the lemonade when there was a knock at the front door. There, on the porch, stood a swarthy, well-dressed man of perhaps forty-five years. Everything from his cordoban shoes to his Stetson hat was impeccably crisp, clean, and correct. He doffed his hat with a flawlessly groomed hand and bowed slightly, adjusting a package he held beneath an arm.

"Good day. Miss Abigail McKenzie?"

"Yes."

"I was told in town that you have a Mr. DuFrayne here."

"DuFrayne?" she repeated, confused.

"Jesse DuFrayne," he clarified.

She was momentarily taken aback by the name. Jesse *DuFrayne*? Jesse DuFrayne. It rhymed with train and had a rhythmic, beat-of-the-rails motion to it. Of its own accord, the name repeated itself in her mind, as if steel drivers churned out the message:

> Jesse DuFrayne
> Rode in on a train . . .
> Jesse DuFrayne
> Rode in on a train . . .

Still, somehow she thought the name could not belong to the Jesse she knew. To lend him a genuine surname would be to afford him unwarranted validity.

"Is he here, Miss McKenzie?"

Abruptly she twitched from her musings.

"Oh, I'm sorry, Mr—?"

"Hudson. James Hudson, of the Rocky Mountain Railroad. We have, Miss McKenzie, as you've probably already guessed, a vested interest in Jesse DuFrayne."

So, she thought, Mr. Jesse DuFrayne is no train robber, is he not? This was the moment she had waited for; vengeance was hers. But it somehow lost its savor.

"Come in, Mr. Hudson, please do come in," she said, opening the screen and gesturing him inside. "I believe the man you're looking for is here. He refused to tell—"

But at that moment his voice came from the bedroom. "Hey, Doc, is that you out there? Come on in here."

A smile suddenly covered Mr. Hudson's face, and he made a move toward the voice, then halted—properly if impatiently—asking, "May I?"

She nodded and pointed to the bedroom door. "He's in there."

James Hudson did not conceal the fact that he was in an overjoyed hurry to hit that bedroom doorway. Six or seven long strides across the living room and their voices were booming.

"Jesse, Gol-damnit, how did you end up here?"

"Jim! Am I glad to see you!"

Abbie tiptoed timidly to the door. Jesse'd been shaving, but even through the suds she could tell that he had absolutely no fear of Jim Hudson, was instead elated to see him. To her amazement the two bear-hugged and affably pounded each other's backs.

"Goddamn if you aren't a sight for sore eyes!" DuFrayne exclaimed, pulling back.

"Look at yourself! I could say the same thing. Word came along the line that you'd been shot. What happened? Somebody take your moustache off with a stray bullet? It looks kind of ragged."

DuFrayne's laughter, genuine, spontaneous, filled the room while he glanced in the mirror he held. "I wish that was all a stray bullet had bothered."

"Yeah? What else got hit?"

"My right leg, but it's doing fine, thanks to Miss Abigail here. They hauled me off the R.M.R. coach and plunked me down here and she's been stuck with me ever since."

"Miss McKenzie, how can we thank you?" Jim Hudson asked, but as if to answer his own question lifted the package he'd brought and came to her, extending it. It was wrapped, but even so the shape of a bottle was evident. "This isn't much, but please accept it with my heartfelt thanks."

She stood in startled confusion, reached for his proffered gift with the hands of an automaton, quite stunned by what all this seemed to mean, but Hudson immediately turned back to DuFrayne.

"What happened, Jesse? We were worried as hell. You turned up missing and the boys down at Rockwell found your gear on the train, and no Jesse! Then somebody from the depot in Stuart's Junction wired down a description of an alleged robber they pulled off a train up here and it sounded like you: coal black moustache and tall as a barn door. I said to myself, if that's not Jess I'll eat my fifteen-dollar Stetson."

Jesse laughed again from behind the lather and sank back onto the bed where he'd been when Hudson came in. "Well, you can wear your fifteen-dollar Stetson out of here because I'm all right." He cast a cautious glance at Abbie. "Leg's been acting up a little this afternoon so I thought I'd sit down while I shave is all."

"So . . . what happened? Are you going to keep me in suspense all day?"

"No, not all day, but just a little longer. This shaving soap is drying up and starting to itch. Mind if I finish this first?"

"No, no, go ahead."

"Come on in, Abbie. No need to hover in the door. Jim, this is Abbie. She's done a damn fine job of keeping my carcass from rotting for nearly three weeks now. If it hadn't been for her, I'd be crow bait by this time. Miss Abigail McKenzie, meet Jim Hudson."

"Mr. Hudson and I met at the door. Won't you have a seat, Mr. Hudson?" she invited, pulling the rocker forward. "I'll leave you two alone."

"Wait a minute, will you, Abbie?" Jesse had again taken up razor and hand mirror but was having trouble executing everything at once, needing both hands for the straightedge. "Hold this damn thing, so I can finish." The request was made so amiably that she forgot to take offense and came to do his bidding.

Watching the two of them, Jim Hudson thought this little domestic scene quite unlike his friend Jesse and wondered what had taken place around here during the last few weeks.

"Jess, what in the heck happened to your moustache? Looks like you took the blade to it," he observed. "I never thought I'd live to see the day."

Jesse's and Abbie's eyes met briefly over the mirror before he replied, "Neither did I. I just decided I'd see what I looked like plain-faced. I guess you can tell what I thought of myself. One day without it and I was growing it back as fast as possible. Abbie agrees I look best with a moustache too."

She felt her face flush and was grateful that her back was to Jim Hudson. Jesse swabbed off his face, then his eyes merrily met hers again while she knew a profound confusion at the very different way he always treated her before others, always respectful, hiding any trace of her transgressions, blaming only himself. What manner of man is this, she wondered, while his eyes danced away again.

Shaving done, Jesse stayed on the bed while the men continued talking.

"What's wrong with your hand, Jess?"

"It got jimmied up somehow on that train."

"Come on, I've waited long enough. Tell me what happened here."

"There's nothing much to tell. It was a damn fool mistake is all. I was headed up to Rockwell, as you know . . ." While Jesse told his account of the incident on the train, Abbie leaned over the bed to collect his shaving equipage. As she did, he absently laid a hand on her waist, then gave it a light pat as she straightened and moved away. Jim Hudson noted the touch with interest. The heedless gesture was as intimate as a caress might have been, for while he did it, Jess kept right on talking, and Jim was certain he was oblivious of the fact that he'd touched the woman at all. Hudson did a good job of concealing his surprise. Miss McKenzie wasn't Jess's type at all. It hadn't taken more than thirty seconds at her front door for Hudson to recognize that fact. He watched her leave the room, puzzled by what he'd just witnessed.

While Jesse was unconscious of what he'd done, Abbie was not. The spot on her spine where his palm had rested seemed afire. In her entire life no man had ever laid a hand upon Abigail McKenzie in so casual a fashion. It was totally different from the many ways in which Jesse DuFrayne had touched her before: sometimes teasing, sometimes daring, sometimes angry, but always for a reason. No, this touch was different. It was the kind she'd wondered about between her parents, the kind she'd never seen between them, and it raised her bloodbeat by its very offhandedness.

All the while she prepared more lemonade in the kitchen, the thought rang through her mind—Jesse DuFrayne has just touched the small of my back before his friend . . .

In the bedroom, Jim Hudson said, "Now listen, Jess, we'll have all of this straightened out in no time. You know there's no beef with the railroad." He laughed, shook his head good-naturedly, and continued. "Why, hell, we know you weren't robbing any train. But this Melcher fellow is raising a stink. He's up in arms and out to sue us for everything he can get, because of his permanent disability."

"Just what do you think he'll get?"

"We'll find out tomorrow. I've got a meeting set up right here in town for noon and we'll settle it then if we can. Melcher will be coming in, but I'll be there to represent the railroad, so you don't need to come unless you want to, of course, and only if you're feeling up to it. Melcher will have his lawyer present, I'm sure. It'll be best to settle this thing with as little publicity as possible, don't you agree?"

"I agree, Jim, but it still riles me to think what that little shrimp can get by pointing an accusing finger at the railroad and walk away two days later while I lie here with a hole as big as a goose egg blown in me."

"And that's the main thing you should be concerned with. Let me handle the legal stuff. Hell, everybody's more worried about you than about what Melcher plans to ask for as a payoff. He'll probably turn out to be more bluff than threat anyway. But how about you? Just how is that leg healing?"

"Oh, it's stiff as hell, so's the hand, but I couldn't have been luckier if the shot had blown me straight into the arms of Doc Dougherty—he's the local medic. Abbie's got remedies up her sleeve that Doc Dougherty never dreamed of. He fixed me up that first day, but it was Abbie who kept me alive afterward."

"Which reminds me," Hudson put in, "did she get our

message saying we'd compensate her for putting up you and Melcher?"

"She got it . . . and Jim?" He lowered his voice, even though they'd been talking in low tones already. "See that she gets plenty. I've been a regular son of a bitch to her."

In the kitchen Miss Abigail heard a burst of laughter, though she didn't hear what prompted it.

"I take it you're impressed with the lady?" Jim Hudson asked quietly, with one eyebrow raised.

"Have you ever seen a lady that didn't impress me, Jim?"

"Hell, I don't think I've ever seen you with a *lady* before, Jess." There was good humor written all over both of their faces.

"I admit she's something of an oddity for me, but all in all I'm not having a half bad time of it here, other than the fact that she considers me a robber of trains, a defiler of women, a teller of lies, and the blackest of blackguards. And she's doing her damnedest to reform me. I put up with it because I like her cooking—watery broth, slimy eggs, and lethal liver." Jesse laughed, remembering it all.

"Sounds like she's just what you've always avoided, Jess— a straight woman. Maybe she's just what you need."

"What I need, James-Smart-Boy-Hudson, is a train out of here, and the sooner the better. I'll be at that meeting tomorrow whether Doc turns me loose or not. I thought you were Doc when you came in. He's supposed to give me my walking papers, so to speak. I'm already pretty handy on those crutches, though."

"Well, don't rush it, Jess. I'll have to look up this man Dougherty, too, while I'm in town. I expect you ran up a bill with him too, huh?"

"I'm still running it, but I knew you'd come along after me and pick up the bill."

Hudson laughed. "Say, the boys up in Rockwell want to know what to do with your gear."

"Is it okay, Jim?"

"Intact, I assure you. Everything. They stored it all in the line shack up there."

"In the line shack! Hell, those galoots will have every one of my plates shattered. I want them out of there. Are you going up that way?"

"No, I'm headed back to Denver again after the meeting

tomorrow. You know we're listening to every mayor of every mining town in this state beg for a spur line to get their ore out. We can't build 'em fast enough, so hurry and get well."

"I'll trust your judgment on that, Jim. Just let me know what's up because I'm already tired of this leisure life. As soon as Doc even relaxes his grizzled old eyebrows my way, I'll be up and gone from here back to the railhead. I just want to make damn sure my gear is safe in the meantime."

"I could have Stoker bring it down on the supply train," Hudson suggested with a knowing grin.

"God, no! Save me from Stoker!" They both laughed. "He does all right with steel and wood, but I'd just as soon have my gear rolled down the side of the mountain as brought down in Stoker's engine. Just leave it there for the time being. Maybe I'll think of something. I might even make it out of here with you tomorrow. Who knows?"

"Well, rest up, boy. I have this Doc Dougherty to see yet, and as long as I'm up here, I may as well see if the depot agent has any complaints on this new spur. I guess I'd better be going, Jess. One way or another, I'll see you before I leave town."

As Hudson prepared to take his leave, Miss Abigail appeared in the doorway with a tray. "May I offer you a glass of lemonade before you leave, Mr. Hudson?"

"I think we've been enough trouble to you already, Miss McKenzie. I'm the one who must offer you something before I leave. How much do I owe you for your care of the two men?"

Regardless of how many times she had reminded Jesse that she'd taken him in only for the money, when offered payment now she became disconcerted.

Jesse could read her discomfiture over Jim's question, saw her reluctance to put a dollar value on what she'd done. Like many other subjects, money was an indelicate subject for a lady to discuss. "Give the lady a fair price, Jim."

"Just what do you think your hide is worth, DuFrayne?"

The two of them exchanged a look of amused conspiracy before Jess answered, "I don't know what my hide is worth, but a glass of Abbie's lemonade is worth a thousand bucks any day."

"In that case, I'll have to try a glass before I leave," Jim Hudson said, smiling now at Abbie.

"I shall pour one for you then," Abbie offered, uncomfortable before their obvious teasing.

"Where will you take it, Mr. Hudson?" she asked.

"How about on your front porch, Miss McKenzie? Will you join me?"

Why did she glance at Jesse first before answering, as if she needed his permission to sit on the porch with another man?

"Go ahead, Abbie, you deserve a rest," he said, noting the pink in her cheeks. "Jim, you big galoot, thanks a hulluva lot for coming."

Hudson approached the bed and the two shook hands again, Hudson squeezing the back of Jess's as he said, "Get your bones out of here and back on those tracks, do you hear? And don't give the lady any fuss while you're doing it. That's an order!"

"Get the hell out of here before that lemonade evaporates in this heat." Then as the two left the room, he called after them, "See that you use your best manners out on the front porch, Jim. Miss Abigail is a lady of utmost propriety."

The north end of Miss Abigail's porch was in cool shadow now in midafternoon. Hudson saw the slatted wooden swing there but gestured Abbie instead to the opposite end, where the wicker chairs were. His manners showed in everything he did, she thought, even in his choosing separate chairs in the beating sun rather than the more intimate double swing in the inviting shade. He remained on his feet until she was seated. She noted how he pulled his sharply creased trousers up at the knees as he took the opposite chair.

"I take it Jesse has been less than a model patient," he opened.

"He was gravely wounded, Mr. Hudson, hardly expected to live. It would be difficult for anyone to be a model patient under those circumstances." Once said, she didn't know why she had defended Jesse that way, just as he had her.

"I think you're tiptoeing around the mulberry bush, Miss McKenzie, but I know Jess better than that. You've earned every penny you get. I fear he's not one who takes to coddling and being cooped up too gracefully. In his own element he's a damn fine man, the best there is."

"Just what is his element, Mr. Hudson?"

"The railroad, of course."

"So he does work for the railroad?"

"Yes, and a damn fine job he does."

Hearing it, Abbie's senses whirled. So it was true after all. With an effort she kept her hand from fluttering to her throat.

"Your loyalty does him credit, Mr. Hudson, since you yourself seem to be a respectable sort." Taking in his flawless elegance, his politeness, his obvious admiration of Jesse DuFrayne, she felt overcome by the swift shift of her patient's status.

"Men earn respect in different ways, Miss McKenzie. If I'm respected, it's for different reasons than he is. Take my word for it, Jess DuFrayne is a gem in the rough, and there's not a man on the R.M.R. line that'll say different."

"Just what has he done to earn that respect?" She wondered if he could see the glass trembling in her hand.

"I hear rebuttal in your tone, Miss McKenzie, and I'm thinking he's given you little reason to see good in him. I'd do him an injustice to list his merits. You'll only believe them if you discover them yourself. If you ever get a chance to see his photographs, study them well. You'll see more than sepia images . . . you'll see where his heart lies."

Funny, she had never thought of Jesse as having a heart before.

"Yes, I shall, Mr. Hudson, if I ever see them." He *is* a photographer, she was thinking as wings seemed to beat about her temples, he really is!

"Jess was right," Jim Hudson said, placing his empty glass on the wicker table between them. "This lemonade is worth a thousand dollars a glass on a day like today."

"I'm glad you enjoyed it."

"If there's anything you need while he's here, you have only to say the word and it's yours."

"How very gracious of you, sir."

"I'm sure if our graces were held up for comparison, mine should be found sadly lacking beside yours. Good day, Miss McKenzie. Take care of him for me." Jim Hudson looked at the front door as he said it.

That curiously heartfelt remark put the final touch of confusion upon Miss Abigail's already confounded emotions. She had thought Jim Hudson had come to her door to mete out justice, but instead he had vindicated the man she had repeatedly called "robber." Watching Hudson's trouser legs as he walked off down the dusty road, she was shaken anew by the revelations regarding Jesse Cameron-DuFrayne.

Once again, the ironic rhyme came to her out of nowhere:

> Jesse DuFrayne
> Rode in on a train . . .

She could not stand out here on the porch indefinitely. She had to go in and face him. But what could she say? She seemed to be having great difficulty breathing and could feel the blood welled up to her hairline, her pulse clicking off the passing seconds as memories came hurtling back, memories of the countless times she'd taunted him because he was a train robber. She tried to compose herself but found that she was feeling inexplicably feminine, and somehow very vulnerable. How he must have laughed to himself all these days, she thought. And what is he thinking now?

She opened the door silently, stepped before the umbrella stand to check her reflection, but her hand paused before it reached her hair. There on the seat lay a rectangular piece of paper. Something seemed to warn her, for her hand hesitated, then finally picked it up.

There followed an audible gasp.

It was a check boasting the payer's name across the top in block letters: ROCKY MOUNTAIN RAILROAD, DENVER, COLORADO. It was made out to Abigail McKenzie in the amount of one thousand dollars!

Her stomach began to tremble and the paper quivered in her fingers. She looked up at the bedroom doorway, suddenly more afraid than ever to face him again.

One thousand dollars! Why, it would take her two years or more of waiting tables at Louis Culpepper's to earn such a sum. Just what was this Jesse DuFrayne that the railroad would put out money like this for his safekeeping? Utterly befuddled, she gaped at the check, knowing she'd earned not even a quarter of this amount. She remembered the knowing looks exchanged by Jesse and Jim Hudson and the words, "A glass of Abbie's lemonade is worth a thousand bucks any day." More confused than ever, she swallowed back the lump in her throat.

"Abbie, is Jim gone?" he called.

"Yes, he is, Mr.——" But what should she call him now? She could still not connect him with his new name, or with his old.

Everything had suddenly changed. She looked at herself in the mirror, saw her flushed face, the paper in her hand, the confusion in her eyes, and stood rooted, not knowing, suddenly, how to act before the man on the other side of the wall. He had a real name and a very respectable job and a very impressive friend, plus a whole railroad full of cohorts who apparently respected him immensely. But all that seemed secondary to the fact that his being shot had had enough impact to cause the railroad to pay her grandly for his care.

How should she act?

She had called him Mr. Cameron, train robber for so long that it was perplexing to suddenly have to change her opinion, which—she admitted now—had been largely based upon the supposition that he was guilty as accused. But then, how many times had he himself implied he was an outlaw? Why, just yesterday he'd said he wouldn't be around long enough for it to matter what she told him about herself and . . . and Richard. She understood now that he'd been toying with her, implying that it was justice which would come to take him, when he'd known all along it was Jim Hudson.

With a sinking feeling, she recalled all those other things— the fighting and kissing and pulling the gun on each other and the terrible ways they'd goaded and hazed. Was he right about all that? Had she lost her sense of decency thinking he, the train robber, was the indecent one responsible?

Only he was no robber.

But she suddenly came to her senses, realizing she could treat him no differently than she had before James Hudson's visit. He was not instantly exonerated of all he'd put her through! But she held a thousand dollars in her unsteady hand, and deny it though she might, it *did* exonerate him in some way.

Her heart thumped crazily as she approached his room and found Jesse sitting on the floral cushions of the window seat, looking so black and brown against all those yellows and greens, so masculinely out of place in his dungarees and unbuttoned shirt. He was watching Jim Hudson walk back uptown and didn't know she stood there observing him. She swallowed thickly, for he looked too handsome and excusable and she wanted him to look neither. He dropped the curtain, absently scratched his bare chest, and her eyes followed the lean fingers that tracked across his skin. At last she cleared her throat.

He looked up, surprised. "Oh, I probably shouldn't sit here, huh?" He moved as if to rise.

"No, you're fine. It's cool there between the windows, stay where you are."

He settled back down. "Well, come on in. Maybe you're not afraid to now." But all traces of teasing were gone from his voice and eyes, and she suddenly wished they would return and ease this dread fascination she felt for him.

"I . . . I still am," she admitted. But neither of them smiled. "I want to say 'Why didn't you tell me,' only—silly as it seems—you did."

He was gracious enough not to rub it in, and now all she wished was that he would. It would be far preferable to this strained seriousness. All he said was, "I could use a glass of lemonade too, Abbie. Would you mind getting me one, please?"

"How can I mind? After all, it *is* paid for now." She felt his eyes upon her, and her hands shook as she poured the drink. Who are you? her mind cried out. And why? She was totally disturbed by the change she sensed in him since Jim Hudson left. He accepted the glass, thanked her, took a swallow, and leaned forward, bracing his elbows on his knees, staring at her in silence.

"Before I say anything else," she began nervously, "I want to make it explicitly clear that I did not hurt you intentionally in the kitchen before, and . . . and the reason I say so now has nothing whatever to do with whether or not you hold up trains for a living."

"That's nice to know. And of course I believe you. You're a most honorable person, Abbie." His eyes seemed to delve into her very depths.

"And how about yourself?"

"Sit down, Abbie, for God's sake . . . there in your little rocker, where I can talk to you." She hesitated, then sat, but hardly relaxed. "Every damn thing I ever told you about myself is true. I never lied to you."

"Jim Hudson is the friend of whom you spoke? The one who left New Orleans with you when you were twenty?"

He nodded, then stared out the window, disturbed anew by this woman and wishing he were not.

"He's very personable," she admitted, looking down into her glass, then added in the quietest of tones, "and very rich."

He turned his hazel-flecked eyes on her again but said nothing.

"I simply cannot accept a thousand dollars. It's far too much."

"Jim doesn't seem to think so." Her eyes met his directly.

"I don't think Jim alone decided."

"No?" His expression was noncommittal. He raised the glass to his lips as if it really didn't matter to him. She caught herself watching his full mouth upon the rim of the glass, his dark, dark moustache, which he brushed with a forefinger after he drank.

"Who are you?" she asked when she could stand it no longer.

"Jesse DuFrayne at your service, ma'am," he returned, raising the glass as if toasting her in introduction.

"That's not what I meant and you know it."

"I know." He now made a deep study of the lemonade. "But I don't want you to have to reestablish your commitment to me in any way, which may happen if I suddenly become a real person to you."

She drew a deep, ragged breath. "You are a real person to me and you know it, so I may as well have it all."

He continued studying the glass intently, swirling it so the liquid eddied into a whirlpool, leaving transparent bits of lemon meat on its sides. "I don't want to be a real person to you. Let me put it that way then." His disturbing eyes challenged as he at last raised them and looked directly into hers. "But nevertheless, you already know what I am. I'm a photographer, just like I said."

"Hired by James Hudson?"

He took a long pull while looking over the rim of the glass, then dropped his eyes as he swallowed, and said, "Yup."

"Why should the railroad protect you if all you are is a picture taker?"

"I guess they must like my stuff."

"Yes, they certainly must. I'll be anxious to see it, if I'm allowed. Your photos must be something really extraordinary."

"Not at all. They're graphic, but the only thing about them that might be considered extraordinary is the fact that they depict railroad life as it really is."

"That's not what you said the other night."

He smiled for the first time, a little crookedly. "Oh well . . . that's the one time I may have lied just a little. But you can judge for yourself if you ever see them."

"And will I?" she dared, her heart in her throat.

"It's hard to say. Jim and I are going to tie up some loose ends around here tomorrow." He braced a dark arm upon the window frame and studied the road beyond it. "Then I'll be leaving town."

No, not yet! her thoughts cried silently. Already she felt an emptiness, realizing this was unwarranted after all the times she'd wished him gone. Sober eyes still on the road, he added, "If I ever get the chance to drop back in and show you my photographs, I'll be sure to do it."

Sadly she knew she never would. "Are you sure you're well enough to travel?"

He flicked a glance her way. "Well, you want me out of here, don't you?"

"Yes, I do," she lied, then finished truthfully, "but not hurting."

His eyes moved to her face and their expression grew momentarily soft. "Don't worry your head over me, Abbie. You've done all the worrying about me that you'll have to."

"But you've paid me too highly for it," she claimed. He noted her stiff posture on the rocker, the hands clutched around her glass as if still scared to death of him. He supposed she suspected the real truth about him, but leaving would be easier if he never verified it.

"It was the railroad who paid you, not Jim or me," he said convincingly.

"I know. It was just a figure of speech. I only meant it was too much."

"How much would you say my life is worth?" he asked, just to see what she'd say, knowing now how much it mattered that she value him in some way.

Her eyes skimmed the room in a semicircle, ended up studying the glass in his hand. "More than a glass of lemonade . . ." But at last her composure slipped. "Oh, I don't know," she sighed and slumped, resting her forehead on a hand, studying her lap.

"How much would you say it was all worth—all the things you had to do to save my life? I never really did find out for sure everything you did. Some of it I knew that night when I had you—" His eyes went to the bed, then he abruptly looked out the window again. Damn, but the woman did things to his head! Staring out unseeingly at the summer afternoon he said gruffly, "Abbie, I'm damn sorry about it all."

Her head snapped up to study his profile. She saw him swallow, his Adam's apple rising, settling back down. He seemed intrigued by that yard out there, which was fine, for her face was burning and her own mouth and eyes seemed suddenly filled with salt.

"I . . . I'm sorry too, Mr. D . . . DuFrayne," she got out.

Palm braced against the window frame, he turned his head to look across his biceps, resting his lips there against his own skin while studying her. Then he said one last, quiet time, from behind that tan arm, "Jesse . . . the name is Jesse." He wanted somehow to hear her say it, just once, now that she knew he was no criminal.

She lifted her eyes to his face, searching for a trace of humor, finding none this time, finding only that quiet intensity which threatened to undo her. The name hung in the air between them, and she wanted to echo it, but had she done so they'd both have been lost, and in that poignant moment they knew it. Her eyes traveled the length of that muscular arm, lingering at the point where his lips must be. His moustache glanced darkly back at her from behind the arm. It took a perceptive eye by now to tell that it had ever been shaved: Mr. Hudson knew this man very well to discern it. So, must he now know equally as well all those inner qualities he'd hinted at? Abbie wondered.

Minutes ago, studying Jesse from the doorway, it had been obvious that he followed his friend's progress down the street as if anxious to follow him out of here, back to the brawling, tough railroad life the two had shared for many years. She had absolutely no business wishing he didn't have to go quite yet.

The silence grew long and strained, but at last he dropped his arm from the window frame and glanced around the room, surveying it fully as if for the final time. "I want to thank you for the use of your room, Abbie. It's pretty. A real lady's room. I imagine you'll be glad to get back into it again."

"I haven't been uncomfortable upstairs," she said inanely.

"It must be a lot hotter up there these nights than down here.

Sorry I put you out." Then he looked at the small double oval picture frame. He reached to pick it up. "Are these your parents?"

"Yes," she answered, following the frame with her eyes, watching a tan finger curve and tap it thoughtfully.

"You don't look much like her. More like him."

"People always said I looked like him and acted like her." It was out before she realized what she'd said. The room grew quiet. Jesse cleared his throat, studied the picture, bounced it on his palm a time or two, then it hung forgotten in his fingers as he leaned forward and spoke to the floor between his feet, his tone as near emotional as she'd ever heard it.

"Abbie, forget what I said about your mother. What the hell—I mean . . . I didn't even know her."

She stared at the tintype and the familiar hand which held it. A lump lodged in her throat and tears formed on her lids. "Yes . . . yes you did. You knew her better than I did, I think."

He raised his startled eyes while his elbows came off his knees in slow motion and his muscles seemed to strain toward her even though he never left the edge of the window seat. For a heart-stopping moment she thought he would. She saw the battle going on in him while he sat poised in indecision. He uttered then the familiar name he'd spoken so often to tease her, but it came out now with gruff emotion.

"Abbie?"

The way he said it made her want to impress the word into a solid lump to carry in a locket maybe, or to press between the pages of a sonnet book. She should correct him, but those days when she'd chided him seemed part of a misty forever ago, for light years seemed to have passed during this conversation. Here, now, with her name fresh on his lips, with his dark troubled eyes seeming to ask her questions best left unanswered, with his black moustache unbroken by smile, she silently begged him not to look as if he too hurt.

"Abbie?" he said again, soft as before: too beautifully threatening. And she shivered once, then broke the spell which should not have been cast in the first place.

"I have at least two more meals to feed you, Mr. DuFrayne, and not a thing in the house resembling meat. I'd best walk over town before the butcher shop closes. What would you like?"

His eyes pored over her face, then slowly, thankfully, the old hint of humor returned to his lips. "Since when have you bothered to ask?"

"Since the buttermilk," she answered, knowing the exact moment.

He laughed lightly, enjoying her immensely, as he so often could. She was a pretty little thing, he had to admit as he scanned her crisp, high collar and swept-back hair. She, in turn, enjoyed his swarthy handsomeness and the imposing breadth of partially exposed muscle before her.

"Ah yes, the buttermilk," he remembered, shaking his head in amusement. They both realized the buttermilk had been a turning point.

"And for your supper?" she asked.

He allowed his warm smile to linger upon her bewitching eyes. His glance, of its own accord, lowered to her breasts, then raised again.

"I'll let you choose," he said, very unlike the Jesse she'd grown used to.

"Very well," she returned, very like the Miss Abigail he'd grown used to.

When she rose, her knees felt curiously watery, as if she'd run a long way. Yet she ran again, though her steps were slow and measured as ever. She ran from the smile in Jesse's eyes . . . to the umbrella stand, to arm herself with a daisy-trimmed hat and a pair of gloves that bore smudges of dirt from leather reins and a creek bank.

Chapter 14

THE TOWN WAS buzzing with the news. Miss Abigail knew it. She sensed eyes peering at her from behind every window of the boardwalk. But she carried herself proudly, flouncing into the meat market as if unaware of all the curious stares following her.

"Why, Mizz Abigail," Gabe Porter plunged right in. "What do you think about that man up to your house turning out not to be a train robber atall? Isn't that something? Whole town's talking about this railroad feller that come in today to pay off your patient's debts. Seems we had him all wrong. Seems he works for the railroad after all. What do you think of that!"

"It's of little interest to me, Mr. Porter. What he is has no bearing on how he is. He is not fully healed and shall be under my care for one more day before he's ready to leave Stuart's Junction."

"You mean you're gonna keep him up there even though he ain't got to stay if he don't want to now?"

Miss Abigail's eyes snapped fire enough to precook the meats hanging on the hooks of the huge tooled iron rack on Gabe's wall. "What exactly are you implying, Mr. Porter? That I was safe with him as long as he was a felon but that I'm not now that he's a photographer?"

That didn't make much sense, even to Gabe Porter. "Why, I didn't mean nothin' by it, Miss Abigail. Just lookin' out for a maiden lady's welfare is all." Gabe Porter couldn't have cut her any deeper had he chopped her a good one with his greasy meat cleaver, but Miss Abigail's face showed no trace of the stark ache his words struck in her heart.

"You may best look after my welfare by cutting two especially thick beef steaks, Mr. Porter," she ordered. "Meat is what builds one up when one has been weakened. We owe that man some good red meat after the blood he lost because of this unfortunate incident, wouldn't you agree?"

Gabe did as ordered, all the while remembering how Bones Binley had said that Gem Perkins had said that Miss Abigail had been out in a trap with that photographer, riding in the hills, and right after young Rob Nelson had seen the man prancing around Miss Abigail's backyard dressed in nothing but pajama pants, mind you. And from the sound of it, he had took to having presents shipped in to her by railroad express from Denver. It had to be from him. Hell, she didn't know nobody else from Denver!

But if Gabe Porter was white-faced at all that, he had the jolt of his life still coming. For on his way home Gabe heard that on her way home Miss Abigail had stopped over to the bank and deposited a check for no less than one thousand dollars, and it drawn against the Rocky Mountain Railroad Company, which, everyone in town knew by that time, the man up at her house took "pitchers" for.

Coming around the corner between the buildings, Miss Abigail was disconcerted to see Jesse waiting for her on the porch swing again. She controlled the urge to glance up and down the street and see if anyone else had seen him there. Ah, at least he has his shirt on, she thought, and coming nearer saw that it was buttoned nearly to the point of decency. But when she mounted the steps she saw that his feet were bare and one of his legs half slung across the swing seat, causing it to go all crooked when he set it on the move.

"Hi," he greeted. "What did you decide on?"

Sheepishly remembering the bugging eyes of Blair Simmons as she slid the check under his cage at the bank only minutes ago, she answered, "I kept it."

Confused, he asked, "What?"

"I kept it," she repeated. "I deposited it at the bank. Thank you."

He laughed and shook his head. "No, that's not what I meant. I meant what did you decide on for supper." The thousand dollars didn't seem to faze him at all. He scarcely seemed to give it a second thought, as if he really thought it was her due, and that was the end of that.

"Steak," she answered, pleased now at how he played down that thousand.

"Goddamn, but that sounds good!" he exclaimed, slapping his stomach, rubbing it, rumpling his shirt and stretching all at once.

All of a sudden she found it impossible to grow peeved with him for his coarse language, and harder yet to keep from smiling. "You are incorrigible, sir. I think that if you stayed around here any longer I might be in danger of failing to note your crassness."

"If I stayed here any longer, you'd either have to convert me or run me out on a rail—probably right beside you, though. I am what I am, Miss Abigail, and steak sounds goddamn good right now."

"If you said it in any other way, I'm not sure I would believe you any more, Mr. Came—Mr. DuFrayne." Her smile was broad now, and charmed him fully.

It was infinitely easier exchanging light badinage with him again. This, she knew, would get them safely through the evening ahead. But just then he swung his foot to the floor, leaned his dark, square palms on the edge of the seat, and with the now familiar grin all over one side of his face, said quietly, "Go fry the steak, woman."

And after all they'd been through, it was the last thing in the world that should have made her blush.

The sun fell behind the mountains while the steak was frying, and the front porch was cool and lavender-shadowed. Jesse DuFrayne sat there listening to the sounds of children playing "Run Sheep Run," drifting in on the wings of twilight. From the shrill babble he could hear occasional childish arguments: "No he didn't! . . . Yes, he did. . . . He din't neither! . . ." Then a swell of argument again before the squabble was apparently settled and the sheep ran again in a peaceful fold. The smell of meat drifted out to him, augmented by an iron clank every now and then and an occasional tinkle of glassware. He got up lazily and limped inside and there she was, coming out of the pantry with a heap of plates and glasses and cups balanced against her midriff. They pulled her blouse tight against her breasts and he admired the sight, then raised his eyes to find she'd caught him at it. He grinned and shrugged.

"Can I help?" he asked.

Oh, he was just full of surprises tonight, she thought. But she handed him the stack of dishes anyway. When he turned toward the kitchen table she surprised him.

"No, not there. Put them in the dining room. That table is never used anymore. I thought we might tonight."

His moustache teased. "Is it going to be a little going-away party then?"

"Rather."

"Whatever you say, Abbie." He moved off toward the dining room.

"Just a minute, I'll get the linen."

"Oh? It's a linen occasion too?"

She came with a spotless, stiff cloth and asked, "Can you pick up those candlesticks too?"

"Sure." He got the pair off the table, along with his other burden, and held everything while she snapped the cloth out in the air. He watched it billow and balloon and fall precisely where she wanted it to.

"Why, that's the damnedest thing I've ever seen!"

"What is?" she asked, leaning over to smooth the already perfect surface of the cloth.

"Well if I tried that, the thing would probably go in the opposite direction and carry me off with it." He cocked his head and hung on to his stack of dishes and watched her little butt as she leaned over the table edge that way, ironing wrinkles with her hands. He snapped back up straight when she turned around.

"Do you want to finish this or stand holding those things all night?"

"I want to see you do that once more," he said.

"What?"

"Flip that thing up and get it to land exactly centered like that. I'll make you a bet that you can't do it again."

"You're insane. And you're going to smash the rest of my dishes if you don't set them down."

"What do you wanna bet?"

"Now you want me to take up gambling on top of everything else?"

"Come on, Abbie, what will you put up? One throw of the cloth."

"I've put up with you, that's enough!" She smiled engagingly.

"How about one photographic portrait against one good home-cooked meal?" he suggested, thinking it would bring him back to Stuart's Junction again with a plausible excuse for coming.

What in the sam scratch got into Abigail McKenzie she couldn't say, but the next thing she knew, she was taking that tablecloth back off the table, flapping it high again while he watched. Of course, the cloth landed crooked this time . . . and the next . . . and the next . . . and by then they were both laughing like loons when it really wasn't *that* hilarious!

The dishes clinked against Jesse's chest as he mirthfully teased, "See, I told you you'd never be able to do it again with one toss. I win."

"But I did it the first time, so it doesn't matter. It was hardly fair after all the air currents were stirred up. Anyway, what am I doing here flapping a tablecloth like a fool?"

"Damned if I know, Abbie," he quipped, and finally set his stack down.

And for the first time in her life she thought, damned if I know either.

"I'd better turn those steaks," she said, and went back to the kitchen.

He followed in a moment with the flat-bottomed glasses she'd given him. "Hey, if this is a party, shouldn't we use champagne glasses and drink the champagne Jim brought?"

"Champagne?"

"I opened the bag while you were gone, and good old Jim brought you champagne. Just in time for my going away party. What do you say we pop it open?"

"I'm afraid I don't drink spirits, and I don't think you—" But things were different now. He was respectable. "You may have champagne if you wish."

"Where are the glasses?"

"Those are all I have."

"Okay, what's the difference?" And he went off to put them back on the table.

He opened the bottle out in the backyard, using a knife blade, and she was sure that the whole blasted town could hear that cork pop—not that too many of them would recognize the sound.

"All set?" he asked, coming back in. She took off her apron, preceded him into the dining room carrying the beef steaks and vegetables on a wide, ivory-colored platter. But all that was there for light were the candles.

"Bring the lantern, too," she said over her shoulder, "it's growing dark." He grabbed if off the kitchen table and came behind her, swinging none too jauntily on his impaired leg, oil sloshing in one container, champagne in the other.

"The matches . . ." she said.

"Coming up."

It struck her that by now he knew where many things were kept in her house and that she liked having him know. She suffered a sudden, wistful pride, watching while he fetched the matches as if he were lord of the manor come to light its fires.

"Sit down, Abbie, I'll do the honors. I'm in charge of the table anyway tonight." He lit not only the lantern but the two candles also, casting the room into blushing rosiness around them. His hand captivated her with its long fingers curled around the match, the dark hairs sweeping down from his forearm and wrist as he blew out the match. The table was twice the size of that in the kitchen, but he had set their two places cozily at right angles. "You'll have to forgive me, Abbie, I'm not dressed for the occasion," he said, checking his buttons as he sat down.

She smiled. "Mr. DuFrayne, for you that *is* dressed."

He patted his ribs and laughed. "I guess you're right."

On his plate she put steak and round, browned potatoes and old gold carrots, and he eyed them all while she served, then began eating with obvious relish, groaning, "God, I'm hungry. Dinner wasn't—" But they weren't going to bring up dinner. He shrugged and went on eating.

"Dinner was interrupted," she finished for him, raising an eyebrow. She'd never in her life seen anyone who enjoyed eating quite like he. Surprisingly, he did it quietly, using the proper moves, using the knife for cutting only, not for stabbing with and eating from. He used his linen napkin instead of his sleeve, relaxed back in his chair when he drank. Abbie could not help comparing this pleasant, polite man to the scoundrel who'd criticized her during those first meals she'd served him. Why couldn't he have been this smiling and amenable right from the first?

"I'll miss this good food when it's not available anymore," he said, as if reading her mind and reinforcing her newly formed opinions of him.

"Like most things, once beyond reach, my cooking will seem better than it truly was."

"Oh, I doubt that, Abbie. Once we stopped fighting at mealtime, I really enjoyed your food."

"I didn't know that before. I thought there was nothing you enjoyed so much as a good . . . or should I say a *bad* fight."

"You're partially right. I do enjoy a good fight. I find it invigorating, good for the emotional system. A good fight purges and leaves you clean to start over again." He peered up impishly at her, adding, "Kind of like liver."

She laughed and had to snatch the napkin to her lips quickly to keep the food from flying out. Ah, she would miss his wit after all. When she could swallow and speak once more, she did so with a bedeviling smile for him.

"But does your emotional system need purging quite so often, Mr. DuFrayne?"

He laughed openly, leaning back in his chair in pure enjoyment. He loved her this way, at her witty best, and took his turn at thinking he would miss this lively banter they'd grown so skilled at tossing back and forth. "Your wry wit is showing, Abbie, but I've come to love it. It has spiced up the days as much as the little fights we had now and then." Behind his glass his eyes looked all black, the night light not bright enough for her to make out those hazel flecks she knew so well by now.

"*Little* fights?" she returned. "*Now and then?*"

He stabbed a chunk of meat, eyeing her amusedly across the table. "I guess you got more than your share of my bad temper . . ." Here he brandished his fork almost under her nose. "But you deserved it, you know, woman."

She leveled him with a look of mock severity and pushed the fork aside with a tiny forefinger. "Quit pointing your meat at me, Jesse."

Too late she realized what she'd said. His expression turned to a suggestive smirk while her face grew scorching. Amused, he watched the blood rise from her chin to her hairline. He hadn't the decency to say something diverting, which would have been the chivalrous thing to do. But when had Jesse ever been chivalrous? He only sat back and used her ill-advised remark to his advantage, his teeth sparkling in a broad smile while she patted the napkin again to her lips and dropped her eyes to her plate, stammering for something to say. "I . . . I . . . did not deserve to . . . to have my best china thrown across my c . . . clean bedroom, and . . . and soup and glass all over everything."

He drew circles on his plate with the chunk of meat which had started all this, finally deciding to let her off the hook. He popped the meat into his mouth, studied the ceiling thoughtfully, and mused, "Now why the hell did I do that again, do you remember?"

This time his ridiculous innocent act caught her unaware. She laughed without warning and spit out a chunk of meat. It sailed clear across the way and landed on her clean linen tablecloth while she clasped her mouth with both palms and laughed until her shoulders shook.

He picked up the errant meat, laughing now too, and scolded, "Why, Miss Abigail McKenzie, you put this right back where it belongs!" Then he held it over her nose. Not quite believing it was herself acting so giddy, she obliged, finding it very hard to open one's mouth when one is laughing so hard.

She listened to a humorous recap of all the indignities he'd suffered at her hands, ending with his accusation that she'd tried to drown him with soup.

"So you grabbed the bowl and slurped like a hog at a trough," she finished.

"Aw, there's a new one—a hog at a trough. I'm a regular menagerie all rolled into one. Do you realize, Miss McKenzie, that you have called me by the names of more animals than Noah had on his ark?"

"I have?" She sounded surprised.

"You have."

"I have not!" But as she smirked, he started naming them.

"Goat, swine, baboon, hog . . . even louse. He held knife

and fork very correctly, feigning a sterling table etiquette. "Now I ask you, Abbie, do I have the manners of a goat?"

"What about the liver?"

"Oh, that. Well, that night, as many others, just when I was ready to make peace with you, you brought that lethal liver. It's true, Ab, every time I made up my mind to be nice to you, you came charging in with some new scheme to make me miserable and mad at you." He wiped his mouth, hiding a smile behind the napkin while she realized how enjoyable it was to laugh at all of it now with him.

"But you know what, Abbie?" he asked, reaching for the champagne bottle. "You were a worthy adversary. I don't know how we put up with each other all this time, but I think we both deserved everything we got." He filled both of their glasses and said, "I propose a toast." He handed her a glass and looked steadily into her pansy-colored eyes. "To Abigail McKenzie, the woman who saved my life and nearly killed me, all at the same time."

His glass touched hers, and the dark knuckle of his second finger grazed her fairer one. She looked away. "I don't drink," she reiterated as the room grew hushed.

"Oh, no, of course you don't. You only try to kill wayward gunslingers." He still held his glass aloft, waiting for her. She felt silly denying him the right to end this all gracefully, which he'd been managing nicely all through their pleasant supper so far. And so she touched his glass and took a small, wicked sip and found it did not hurt her at all, only made her want to sneeze. So she took another, and did sneeze. And they laughed together and he drained his glass and refilled it, and hers.

"You must return a toast of your own," he insisted, leaning back nonchalantly in his chair, "it's the only acceptable way."

Her eyes, meeting his, were violet in the soft light, registering deep thought. He wondered if she was remembering . . . as he was . . . the good times they'd shared since he'd been here. He wished that he could see what images went through her mind, for she looked thoroughly adorable tonight.

Abbie sat with her elbow resting on the table, the unfamiliar champagne bubbling before her eyes.

"Very well," she agreed at last, then sat a moment longer peering at him through the pale gold liquid, puzzling over how to say it. At last she lowered her glass enough to see his face above it and intoned quietly, "To Jesse DuFrayne, who actually admires my morals all the while he tries to sully them."

But this time after their glasses touched it was he who did not drink from his. Instead his brow furrowed and he scowled slightly.

"What did you say?"

"I said, 'To Jesse DuFrayne who—"

"I know what you said, Abbie, I want to know why you said it."

Do you, Jesse, she thought. Do you? Or do you understand perfectly, just as I do, that you could have forced yourself on me any one of countless times, yet you always backed off. Must I tell you why? Do you understand so little of yourself? Abbie drew a deep breath and met his eyes.

"Because it's true. Perhaps because I have noted that when others are around you refer to me respectfully as Miss Abigail, no matter what you might call me when we're alone together. Maybe too because you—Oh, never mind." She didn't think she could go through with it and tell him what he couldn't see for himself.

"No, I want to know what you were going to say." He leaned forward now, bracing his forearms against the edge of the table, rolling the glass between his palms, the frown lingering about his eyes.

She considered a moment, sipped a little, then looked away from his mouth: he was chewing somehow on the fringe of his moustache, and she thought it might be a danger sign. "The truth as I see it would sound blatantly conceited were I to say it. I don't want you to leave here thinking of me in that light."

"You of all people are the farthest thing from conceited I've ever met. Self-righteous maybe, but not conceited."

"I'm not sure whether I should say thank you or spit in your eye."

"Neither. Just explain what you meant about me and your morals."

She sipped again for false courage, her eyes picking up some of the champagne bubbles and refracting the lamplight off them. "Very well," she agreed at last, looking into her glass to find it surprisingly empty. He refilled it as she began. "I think that you find me . . . let us say, not totally unattractive. I also, however, think that my feminine gender in itself would serve that purpose for you, because you just plain *like women*.

But that's beside the point. I only mentioned it to point out that I do not say this in a vain way. I think you are attracted to me by the very thing that you seek to change in me. Unless I miss my guess, I am the first woman you've encountered in a good long time who possesses any of the qualities that the old beatitudes praise. And all the time you berate me for my inability to bend, you are hoping I will not do so. In other words, Mr. DuFrayne, I think that for perhaps the first time in your life you have found something besides flesh to admire in a woman, but you've never learned how to handle admiration of that sort, so you resort to breaking down my morals in order to feel at ease in your relationship with me."

He sat there with his shoulders lounging at a slant against the back of his chair, but the scowl on his lips belied the lax attitude of his body. He had an elbow propped on the arm of his chair and ran an index finger repeatedly along the lower fringe of his moustache.

"Perhaps you're right, Abbie." He took a sip, measuring her over the glass. "And if you are, why do you blush like a schoolgirl? Your beatific nature is all intact—everything right where it was when I first found you." Lazily he leaned and reached out that bronze finger that had been stroking his moustache, touched her lightly beneath the chin, and made her look up at him. But she stiffened, drawing her eyes away again, turning her chin aside to avoid the finger that seemed too, too warm and exciting. When she would not look up again he ran the callused finger lightly along her delicate jawbone. That at last made her eyes fly to his.

"Don't!" She jerked back, but something strange happened inside her head. For a moment things looked like they had fuzzy edges.

His eyes traveled over her open lips, noted her quick breath, the distended nostrils, then lazily eased back to the blue threatened depths of her wide eyes.

"All right," he agreed softly, "and this time I won't even ask why."

Panicked by the sudden change in him, she lurched up from her chair, but a tornado seemed to be whirling inside her. She fell forward, hands pressed flat on the tabletop on either side of her plate. Her head reverberated. Her neck felt limp, and a lock of damp hair hung down across her collar.

"You've duped me again, have you, Mr. DuFrayne? This

time with your innocent toasts." Her head hung down
disgracefully but she couldn't seem to raise it, not even to look
daggers at him for doing this to her.

"No I haven't. If so, I didn't mean to. Why, you hardly had
enough wine to inebriate a hummingbird." He picked up the
bottle and tipped it, looking at the lantern light through it. It
was still half full.

"Well, this hum . . . hummingbird is in . . . inebriated
just the same," she said to the slanting tabletop, her head
sinking lower between her shoulder blades all the time.

He smiled down at the part in her hair, thinking how appalled
she'd be in the morning and how they weren't going to get out
of this without another fight after all. Abbie drunk, imagine
that, he thought, unable to keep from smiling at her.

"It must be the altitude," he said now. "Up this high it
doesn't take much, especially if you've never drunk before."
He came to put an arm around her and lead her toward the back
door. "Come on, Abbie, let's get you some fresh air." She
stumbled. "Be careful, Abbie, the steps are here." He took
one floppy hand and put it around his waist and it grabbed a
handful of shirt obediently. "Come on, Ab, let's walk, or
you'll find your bed spinning when you lie down."

"I'm sure you kn . . . know all about . . . sp . . .
spinning b . . . beds," she mumbled, then pulled herself up
and slapped lamely at his helping hands. "I'm fine. I'm fine,"
she repeated drunkenly, thinking she was regaining a little
decorum. But she started humming next and knew perfectly
well that she wouldn't be humming if she were truly fine.

"Shhh!" he whispered, forcing her to walk.

She flung a palm up. "But I'm a . . . a hummingbird, am
I not?" She actually giggled, then swayed around and fell
against him, tapping him on the chest. "Am I not a hummingbird, Jesse? Hmm? Hmmm?" Her forefinger drilled teasingly
into his chin, and he lifted it aside.

"Yes, you are. Now shut up and keep walking and breathe
deeply, all right?"

She tried to take careful steps, but the ground seemed so far
away from her soles, and so evasive and tipsy. They walked
and walked, all around the backyard. And once more she
giggled. And more than once stumbled so he'd grab her more
tightly around the waist to set her aright. "Keep walking," he
insisted again and again. "Damnit, Abbie, I did *not* do this to

you on purpose. I never in my life saw anybody get tight on a thimbleful of champagne. Do you believe me?"

"Who cares if *I* believe *you*. Do *you* believe *me*?"

"Keep walking."

"I said *do you believe me!*" she suddenly demanded, her words ringing out through the still air. "Do you believe what I said in there about you and me!" She got belligerent and tried to yank away, but he steadied her close against his hip and she submitted to his strong, forceful arm.

"Don't raise your voice, Abbie. The neighbors might still be up."

"Ha!" she all but bellowed. "Carve that one on marble! *You* worried about what *my* neighbors might think!" She lurched and grabbed his shirtfront in both fists, shaking it, tugging till it pulled against his neck.

"Shh! You're drunk."

"I'm as sober as a judge now. Why won't you answer me?"

Was she drunk or sober when she reared back and began trumpeting in the most unladylike way, "Jesse DuFrayne loves Abbie Mc—" and he plastered his mouth over hers to shut her up? Her arms came around his neck and he lifted her clean up off the ground, her breasts flattened mercilessly against his rigid chest. But once his mouth covered hers, he forgot he was only trying to shut her up. He took her mouth wholly, and there was nothing dry about it. She had both of her arms folded behind his strong neck, her toes dangling half a foot off the earth, and they stood that way in the silver moonlight, kissing and kissing, and forgetting they had vowed to be enemies, all tongue and tooth and lip and a soft, thick moustache. Her mouth was hot and sweet and tasted of champagne. The smell of roses came from the fabric of her starched blouse and she made a small groaning whimper deep in her throat, her breath coming warm against his cheek. And in no time at all his body grew uncomfortably hard, so he set her down on her feet none too gently, pulled her arms away from his neck, and ordered fiercely, "Get the hell up to bed, Abbie. Do you hear me!"

She stood there drooping, conquered.

"Can you walk by yourself?" His warm hand still gripped her elbow.

"I told you I'm not drunk," she muttered to the earth at her feet.

"Then prove it and get inside where you belong."

"I, Mr. DuFrayne, am as sober as a veritable judge!" she
boasted, still to the night earth, for she could not raise her
head. He carefully released her elbow, and she swayed a little
but remained upright.

"Don't judge me for this, Abbie, just get the hell out of
here!"

"Well, you don't have to sound so mad about it," she said
childishly, and knew somewhere in her bleary head just how
drunk she really was to be talking that way, almost whining.
Ashamed now of what she'd done, she turned and weaved her
way to the house, gulping deep draughts of the stringent night
air. On her way past the dining room table she gulped a whole
cup of cold coffee. And by the time she made her way upstairs
it was herself she was judging, not him. Champagne was no
excuse, none at all. The pure, unadulterated truth was that
she'd been wanting him to kiss her all night. Worse, she'd been
wanting to kiss him back. Worse yet, she didn't think that was
all she wanted anymore.

Upstairs, she flopped backward onto the bed, arms as limp
as the excuses she tried to think up. Heavens, that man can
kiss! One finger wound around a tendril of hair until she'd
curled it all the way to her scalp. She closed her eyes and
groaned, then hugged her belly and curled up, suddenly
tragically sure her mother had been dead wrong. Here she was,
Abigail McKenzie, spinster, thirty-three and heading upward,
never to know just what it was that her mother had so warned
her against. Certainly it couldn't be kissing. It had been
nothing short of a swift, sweet miracle, the way that kiss had
felt. It had been so long ago with Richard that it was
impossible to recall if it had been this good. And certainly
David's kiss had not started such a volcanic throbbing in her.
But always before she had held back, afraid of what her mother
had said. But when you loosen your reserve and put everything
into it, kissing was a different matter entirely. It started such
strange and pleasant rippling sensations shimmying downward
through one's body.

Lying in the darkness above Jesse, she again pictured his
body. Ah, she knew it so well. She knew the shape and hue and
texture of each part of it, the valleys of his shoulder blades
where strong muscles welled up to leave inviting hollows. His
dark arms, long, strong, etched with veins at the inner bend of
elbow. His legs and feet, how often she'd seen them, washed

them. She knew his hands, large, square, with equal capacity for teasing and gentling. His eyes seemed to seek her out in the darkness, from beneath brows whose outline she traced on her stomach now from memory. Those eyes crinkled at the corners in the instant before his soft, soft moustache lifted with a lazy smile. She knew the spot where the skin grew smooth, down low where the hair of his broad chest narrowed and dove in a thinner line, narrowing, narrowing along his hard belly to his groin.

She rolled onto her stomach because her breasts hurt. She clamped her arms against the swelling sides of those breasts and squeezed her thighs together, locking her ankles, holding them tightly, tightly, trying to forget the image of the naked Jesse. But forgetfulness refused her. She opened her mouth, waiting for the heat of his imaginary kiss. But she touched only the pillow, not warm, soft lips. She rolled to her side clutching a knob of nightgown between her legs, feeling what was happening there, this awful aching need to be filled.

Was this then how it was? How it ought to be? What her mother had known? What her mother had never known? It was fullness and emptiness, acceptance and denial, hot and cold, shiver and sweat, yes and no. It was the coming apart of scruples, ethics, codes, standards, and virtues and not caring in the slightest, because your body spoke louder than your conscience.

Jesse had been right all along, and her mother had been wrong. How could such compulsion be wrong? Senses Abbie had never realized she possessed were now expanded to their fullest. Her body throbbed and beat and begged. How right . . . how utterly right . . . it would be to simply go to him and say, "Show me, for I want to see. Give me, for I deserve. Let me, for I feel the right."

The question no longer was could she do that and live with it afterward. The question now was could she not do that and watch her one chance walk out the door tomorrow to leave her ignorant and unfulfilled.

Chapter 15

THE MOON WAS rich cream, high, melting down through the wide bay window, running all over him as he lay, sprawled carelessly, naked on the bed. His head and chin were screwed around at an odd angle, as if trying to see the headboard backward. She had listened to his restless movements for what seemed like hours, working up the courage to creep downstairs. But now he slept, she could tell by his measured breath and the one dark foot that dangled off the end of the bed where he had never fit and never would. She came trembling to the bedroom doorway, afraid to enter, afraid not to. What if he turned her away?

Little tight fists pressed against chin and teeth, she eased closer. Her chest felt as if it were in a vise. How should she awaken him? What should she say? Should she touch him? Maybe say, "Mr. DuFrayne, wake up and make love to me"? How absurd that she didn't even know what to call him anymore. Suddenly she felt awkward and sexless and knew for sure he'd tell her to get back upstairs and she would die of humiliation.

Yet she whispered his name anyway. Or did she whimper it? "J . . . Jesse?"

It might have been the brush of curtain upon sill, so tentative was the sound.

"Jesse?" she asked again of his moon-clad body.

He straightened his head around on the pillow drowsily. Although she couldn't make out his eyes, she saw the moon's reflection on the bolder lines of his face. His moustache made a darker, beckoning shadow. His chin lowered and he looked across his chest and saw her, and pulled a hank of sheet over to cover himself.

"Abbie? What is it?" he asked sleepily, disoriented, braced up on his elbows now.

"J . . . Jesse?" She quavered, suddenly not knowing what else to say. This was awful. This was so awful. It was worse than any of the insults she'd suffered at his hands, yet she stood as she was, her two hands, fisted tight, bound together against her chin.

But he knew. He knew by the tremulous way she spoke his name at last. He sat up, taking more of the sheet across his lap, dropping a single leg over the edge of the bed for equilibrium.

"What are you doing down here?"

"Don't ask . . . please," she pleaded.

The silent night surrounded them and time seemed to cease its coursing until out of the creamy night quiet came his voice, low and knowing.

"I don't need to ask, do I?"

She gulped, shook her head no, unable to speak.

He didn't know what to do; he knew what he must do.

"Go back upstairs, Abbie. For God's sake, go. You don't know what you're doing. I shouldn't have let you have that champagne."

"I'm not drunk, Jesse. I . . . I'm not. And I do not want to go back upstairs."

"You don't need this in your life."

"What life?" she asked chokily, and his heart was clutched with remorse for having made her question the blandness that had always been enough before.

"The life you've always prided yourself on, the one I don't want to ruin for you."

"There have been so many times I thought I knew what would ruin my life. My mother always warned me that men like Richard would ruin it. Then she died and he ran away and I wondered how to exist from one day to the next with all that nothingness. Then a man named David Melcher came into my house and made me hope again, but—"

"Abbie, I tried to apologize for that. I know I shouldn't have done that to you. I'm sorry."

"No, you shouldn't have, but you did, and he's gone and shall never be back. And I need . . . I . . ." She stood as still as a mannequin, the moonlight limning her in ivory, her hands pressed to her throbbing throat.

"Abbie, don't say it. You were right at the supper table tonight. I do value all your old-fashioned morals or I'd have taken you long ago. I don't want to be the one to make them come crashing down now, so just go back upstairs and tomorrow I'll be gone."

"Don't you think I *know* that!" she cried desperately. "You are the one who made me realize the truth about Richard and me. You are the one who accused me of stagnating, so who better shall I ask? Don't change on me now, Jesse, not now that I've come this far. You . . . you are my last chance, Jesse. I want what every other woman has known long before she's thirty-three."

He jumped off the bed, twisting the sheet around him, holding it low against one hip. "Goddamnit, that's not fair! I will not be the one to aid in your undoing!" He tugged the sheet viciously but it was anchored beneath the mattress, tethering him before her. "I lay there thinking about you for hours after I went to bed and I found you were a hundred percent right about my motives. I don't know what it is about you that mixes me up so, but one minute I want to bend you and the next I'm cussing because you're so godalmighty moral that if you bend, I'm the one who breaks. But you know that and you're using it against me!"

She was. She knew it. But she swallowed her pride and spoke in a strained whisper. "You're sending me away then?"

Oh, God, he thought. God, Abbie, don't do this to me when I'm trying to be noble for the first time in my life! "Abbie, I couldn't live with myself afterward. You're not some . . . some two-bit whore following the railroad camps."

"If I were, could I stay?" Her plaintive plea made him ache with want.

Why the hell did I push her so far, he berated himself, wondering how to get them both out of this without lasting hurt to either. This was the moment when her morals and her mother's morals faced off. How ironic that he should now be the spokesman for the mother he had criticized.

"Abbie," he reasoned, "it's because you're not that you can't. Do you understand the difference?" Had she no idea what she did to him, standing there hugging herself, swathed in moonlight and trembles? "You'll hate me afterward, just like you hate Richard. Because I'm going, Abbie. I'm going and you know it."

"The difference is that I know it beforehand."

Sweat broke out across his chest and he tightened the twist of sheet at his hip until it dug into his skin. "But you know what I am, Abbie."

She raised her chin proudly, though her body quaked. "Yes, you are Jesse DuFrayne, photographer, seer of life as it really is. But you are the one running from reality now, not I."

"You're damn right I'm running." His labored breath sounded like he actually had been. "But the reason is you. Tomorrow you'd look at this differently and you'd hate me."

"And would you mind?" she braved, her chin lifting defensively.

"You're damn right I'd mind, or I wouldn't be standing here arguing, wrapped in these sheets like some timid schoolboy!"

"But you know that if you send me back upstairs, I shall hate you anyway."

The moonlight scintillated off their outlined bodies as they strained to see each other's faces. He thought he could smell roses clear across the room. Her shoulders were so small, and she looked all vulnerable and scared with her arms folded up the center of her chest that way. But her hair was loose, lit by moonglow, like a nimbus about her shadowed face.

"Abbie . . ." His voice sounded tortured. "I'm not for you. I've had too damn many quick women." But his conviction somehow faded into appeal and he took a halting step toward her. She too took one tremulous step, then another, until he could make out the quick rise and fall of her breathing.

"All the better that it be you, Jesse, my one and only time— you who know so well." Her words were soft, breathy, and raised the hair along his arms. They were so close that Jesse's shadow blocked the moonlight from her upraised face. Tension tugged at their hovering, unsure bodies. The whisper of curtains in the night breeze was now the only sound in the room. Jesse's nostrils flared while he clutched the sheet tighter,

tighter. He thought of tomorrow and knew she had no idea that David Melcher would be back in town. All he had to do was tell her so and she would turn back upstairs obediently. But the thought of leaving her to Melcher flooded him with livid jealousy. He could take her now, but how she'd hate him afterward, when she found out he'd known all along of Melcher's return.

She knew absolutely nothing about what he could do to her, he was sure. There she stood, imploring him for that of which she was ignorant—his tiny little hummingbird Abbie, who'd fought for his life and defied death right here in this very room. And in return she asked just one thing of him now . . . and he wanted to give it to her so badly that it physically hurt. She was a scant four feet in front of him now. All he had to do was take one step more. Standing there, fighting desire, smelling the aura of roses drifting from her, Jesse floundered, became lost in her. "Abbie," he uttered, the name strained, deep in his throat, "you're so damn small." And the sheet, like a puddle of rippling milk, moved with him as he leaned to whisper in her ear, "Don't hate me, Abbie, promise you won't hate me." His gruff words moved the hair behind her ear and trapped her heart in her throat. A sinewy hand reached through the moonlight to close itself about her upper arm.

Her lips fell open. She raised her face and her nose touched his firm shoulder. His skin smelled of night warmth and sleep and held a faint trace of dampness, not wholly unpleasant. She raised a hesitant hand to brush it with her fingertips. He was so hard, so warm, and she so unsure. He poised, his breath beating upon her ear, and she wondered what he would have her do. She knew so little, only that to kiss as they'd kissed in the yard had turned her body to sweet, shaking jelly. So she raised her lips and asked near his, "Would you kiss me first, like you did in the yard, Jesse?"

His grip on her arm grew painful. "Oh, God, Abbie," he groaned, and let the sheet spill from him as he scooped her up in powerful arms and held her against the heart that hammered wildly in his breast. He buried his face in her hair, knowing he should not do this, but was unable to deny himself any longer.

She rubbed her temple against his lips, eager for the touch of them on her own. Then slowly, timidly, her face turned up, seeking that remembered rapture.

"Abbie, this is wrong," he reiterated one last, useless time.

"Just once, like in the yard," she whispered. "Oh, Jess, please . . . I liked it so much."

Sanity fled. Her childlike plea threw his heart cracking against his ribs. He lowered open lips to her warm, waiting ones. As she met his kiss her arms went twining around his neck, fingers delving the mysteries of thick, black hair at the back of his head. His tongue, once dry with fever, was now wet with fervor, dipping against hers, slipping to explore her mouth greedily. She responded timidly at first, but imitating his actions, her pleasure grew and her tongue became bolder within his mouth. He released her suddenly and her knees and legs went sliding down along his until her feet touched the floor. He cinched powerful arms about her ribs, lifting her untutored body up and in against him. His mouth slanted demandingly across hers and his tongue delved deeper, plying, playing, melting her insides like sugar candy until she felt it drizzle, sweet and warm, far down from the depths of her.

For Abbie it was the wonder of the first kiss magnified a hundred times as her body pressed willingly against his. He made a faint growling sound in his throat, then threaded his long fingers back through the hair at her temples, cradling her head in his palms while he scattered little kisses everywhere. He seemed to be eating her up by nibbles, making her feel delicious as he took a piece of her chin, then her lip, her nose, her eyebrow, ear, neck, settling back upon her mouth again, biting her tongue lightly as if finding it the tastiest. She forgot everything but the slow, sweet yearning inside her body. She let it control her, leaving her with the wonder of this man whom she had so long feared, but whom she wanted now with a desire that shut out all thoughts of wrong. She forgot that his was a practiced kiss, knew only that it was the prelude to all she was so eager to learn from him, of him. He buried his face in her neck, his breath summer warm on her skin.

"Abbie, I have to know, so I don't hurt you," he said in a hoarse, stranger's voice, "did you and Richard ever do this?"

Her hands fell still upon his neck.

"No . . . no!" she answered in a startled whisper, straining away suddenly. "I told you—" She would have turned aside, abashed, but he took her jaw in both of his warm hands, tipping her face up as if it were a chalice from which he would sip, forcing her to look at him.

"Abbie, it doesn't matter," he said low, brushing his thumbs lightly, lightly upon the crests of her cheeks. "I don't want to hurt you is all. I had to ask."

"I . . . I don't understand," she said tremulously, her eyes wide on his, lips fallen open in dismay.

She swallowed hard; he felt it beneath the heels of his hands, and thought, Lord, she's so small, I'll kill her. Yet he brushed her cheek with his lips and hushed, "Shhh . . . it's all right," and lifted her face to meet his kiss again, making them both forget all but the turbulent senses aroused now beyond recall. With his tongue in her mouth, he picked her up again and carried her to the edge of the bed, where he sat with her upon his lap. Silently he vowed to go slow with her, to make it good, right, memorable if he could. He lifted her bashful arms and looped them around his neck. She was ever aware that he was naked, that his skin burned warmly through her wrapper and gown. His lips slid to the warm cay of her collarbone, and he murmured, "You smell like roses . . . so good." She twisted her head sensuously, rubbing a jaw against his temple. He touched her neck with his tongue, and she shuddered with some new, vital want. "Can I take your wrapper off, Abbie?" he asked, trailing brief kisses to a soft spot on the underside of her chin.

"Is that how it's done?" she asked rather dreamily.

"Only if you want."

"I want," she confessed simply, sending his senses thrumming. So he found the twist of belt at her waist and tugged it free and brushed the garment away until it lay tumbling across his bare knees.

He kissed her once more, then said into her mouth, "Abbie, I'm shaking as if it's my first time."

"That's good," she whispered.

Yes, he thought, it's good.

Then she added, "So am I," and he heard the smile in her words. He smiled too, against her cheek, then bit the tip of her ear.

"Remember when we were sitting on the swing? I really wanted to do this then, but I was afraid to put my arm around you all of a sudden."

"You've never been afraid, I don't think. Not of this." But still it pleased her that he said so. His hand slid to her ribs, rubbing sideways, abrading her skin softly through the thin cloth of her nightgown.

"I'm afraid now, Ab, afraid this might melt away beneath my hand."

She held her breath, her skin tingling with anticipation until at last his palm filled itself with her breast, warm and peaked and generous. The pressure of his other hand grew insistent at the back of her neck until she obeyed its command and turned her mouth again to his. But this time his kiss was no heavier than the touch of a moth's wing, more a kiss of breath than of lips. But it made shivers ride outward from every pore of her body. His caresses were loving, gentle, as he took a nipple, hard and expectant, between his thumb and the edge of his palm, squeezing it gently until she sighed against his lips. His hands roamed her shoulders and the nightgown fell down about her hips, letting first the warm fingers of night air ripple over her bare skin . . . then the warm fingers of Jesse DuFrayne. When his hand at last cupped her bare breast, she laid her forehead against his chin, lost in the magic of his touch. He brushed the erect nipple with the backs of his fingers while her wrists went limp, hanging across his shoulders. Drifting in sensation, she unconsciously pulled back to free a space so he could explore further. Finding her other breast as aroused as the first, he made a satisfied sound in his throat. "Ahhh, they're so hard," he said thickly.

She murmured some wordless reply, adrift in pleasure, wanting this to go on forever. She seemed to be floating above herself, looking down at a strange, lucky woman being pleasured by her man. She'd never imagined people talking when they did things like this, yet his soothing tones freed her from the bonds of restraint, and the lover she watched from above answered her consort, "Sometimes all I have to do is think of you and they get that way. Once it even happened in church."

He chuckled softly against her neck, but it was all he could do to keep from tumbling her backward and delving into her, deep and hard and now. He felt like he would burst from his skin! He wanted to taste her, smell her, hear her whimper, feel her flesh surround his. But he restrained himself, knowing it best to make it last long and good for both of them. He plied her with more kisses, running a hand up her back, then low along her spine. His fingers slid to her waist and pulled her bare hip up hard against the erect evidence of his desire, giving her time to learn the newness of a man, teaching her the difference between himself and her. He eased a hand onto her stomach, the other to the base of her spine, and sat as if praying, with her between his folded hands. Then his large palm swallowed up her breast as he took her with him, back, back, onto the softness of rumpled sheets. She fell atop his hard chest, but he rolled her onto her back, dipping his head down to kiss her shoulder, her collarbone, then the warm swell of skin below it. She felt his soft moustache, pictured it vividly as his hot, wet tongue trailed nearer and nearer a nipple until at last he was upon it, receiving the cockled tip beneath his stroking tongue, making her gasp, arch her ribs, and reach blindly for his hair. He tugged and sucked, sending billows of feeling flowing outward, downward from where he taught her skin to crave the moistness of his loving. He left one nipple wet, and she shivered as he moved to the other, her palm now guiding his jaw. With his ardent kiss upon her breast, all of her long-unused senses came to life, sluicing downward in a grand, liquid rush. Her nipples ached sweetly for more, but he stretched out beside her then, bending an arm beneath his ear, tickling her chest with a single playful fingertip. Goose bumps erupted all over her body, then she laughed girlishly and rolled a little bit, pushing the teasing finger away.

"I want to touch you all over," he said. But, curiously, he had removed his touch from her altogether, making her long greedily for its return. They stared into each other's eyes for a long, intense minute, neither of them speaking or moving. She sent him a tacit invitation to come back and try again, unable to say it in words. His hand lay down along his hip. He lifted it slowly and saw her eyelids flinch and widen as he touched her stomach lightly with the tip of an index finger, drawing tendrils and grapevines around her navel, up her ribs, around her nipples, up to her throat. Then, still with that single fingertip, he surveyed the line along which the fine hairs of her body met, joined, and pointed like nature's arrows, to the place which wept for want of him. He pressed her stomach, letting his fingertips trail into Spanish moss, lingering there while she lay with the breath caught in her pleasured throat. But as his fingers moved lower she recoiled, instinctively protecting herself against intrusion.

Realizing what she'd done, she felt awkward and stupid, covering herself that way, but she was suddenly, inexplicably afraid. Surely he would get disgusted now and think her utterly childish and realize he'd been wasting his time with her.

But instead, he whispered near her ear, "It's all right, Abbie, it's all right." He looped an arm loosely about her waist and kissed her again, exploring her back, shoulders, and the firm rises at the base of her spine. He lifted his head, looking down into her face. "Abbie, have you changed your mind?" he whispered, husky and strained. Her wide, uncertain eyes looked up at him, but she could not speak. Sensing her last-minute fear, he soothed her with whispered words, running the backs of his knuckles down her shoulder and around the outer perimeter of a breast. "Your skin, Ab, I never felt such skin. It's like warm custard pudding . . . smooth . . . and soft . . . and sweet." And as if to prove it, he leaned to take a taste, just inside her elbow where the soft pulse throbbed. He took the velvety skin gently between his teeth, tugging at it tenderly, then buried his face in the hollow of her abdomen. Her spine went taut, so he eased up to whisper into her mouth, "Don't be afraid, Abbie."

Then gently, insistently, his hand flowed downward, warm, slow, but sure. She squeezed her eyes shut, took a deep breath and held it tightly, envisioning the exact length and strength of his fingers before they sought, found, and entered.

She was sweetly swollen and wholly aroused, all sleek, wet satin. He braced up on an elbow, the better to see her. He moved his finger, watching her face all the while—the eyelids that trembled, the lips that fell open, the cheeks that grew hollow. She arched and gasped at what was happening within her. He plied her with the certain knowledge that she was ripe with the need for this. He teased her knowingly until, in abandon, she flung an arm over her head, eyes hidden now behind her elbow, her breath fast, hot and urgent.

He smiled, watching her go all sensuous and stretching. Then his touch slipped away.

She opened her startled eyes to his smiling face above her. "Jesse . . ." she choked, dying of need.

"Shhh . . . we have all night." He circled her with a strong arm and turned them onto their sides, pulling her up tightly against his hot length. His knee slid silkily between her legs, rode up high against the place his hand had abandoned. With the sole of his foot he caressed the back of her calf and the softness behind her knee. Even in the vague light he could see the look of longing in her eyes. He kissed her just enough to keep the fever high, then pressed her shoulder blades back against the sheets again. With agonizing slowness he slid his hand along her belly, her ribs, her breast, her armpit, then on up, up, up the length of her loose-flung arm, finally closing over her palm, carrying it down between their two bodies. He felt her tense as she sensed where he was taking that hand.

"No . . ." she uttered before she could stop herself. Her fingers strained against his grip, leaving him doubtful of how to proceed with her. At last he laid her hand upon his ribs, leaving the choice up to her. But to tip the scales in his favor he used ardent words and a timeless language of body to tempt her.

"Touch me, Abbie," he encouraged, "touch me like I just touched you." His voice was a racked whisper, his kisses trailed fire paths across her face, his knees and hips spoke intimate promises against her. The hand remained on his ribs, trembling there, warm and slightly damp. "That's how it's done, Ab, we touch each other first. Did you like it when I touched you?" He heard her swallow convulsively. "It was good, wasn't it? Men like it just as much as women do."

A fearful timidity swelled her throat but the hand would not move. Do it! Do it! she told herself, her heart leaping and lunging within her breast. But nothing had prepared her for this. She had thought to lie passively and let him do what he would with her. The thought of fondling him made her palm burn to know him, but she was afraid once she reached, touched, her mother's spirit would somehow know what she was doing.

"Just a touch, then you'll know." He reached to titillate her again, hinting at bestowing the fire that had driven her wanton before, and she found herself thrusting up in welcome. But his teasing fingers left again, and she understood frustration as she never had before. She swallowed and made her hand move. He fell dead still, waiting. But when at last her fingertips came into contact with his tumescence they retracted into a quick clinch: he was so unexpectedly hot!

He lost all sense of caution then and moved swiftly, capturing her wrist between their bellies. "Just take it, Ab, just touch," he begged in a strident whisper. Fear lodged in her throat. The back of her hand now rested against that soft-hard heat, but timidity crushed her will to do what he asked. She pinched her eyes shut as he relentlessly forced her fingers to close around his engorged flesh and showed her how he would have her please him. A racked sound fell into the night and her eyes flashed open to find him raised on an elbow, his head flung back, mouth open almost as if in the throes of pain. He groaned raggedly and she jerked her hand away guiltily.

"Jesse, what is it! Did I hurt you?"

He swooped over her in a rough, swift enveloping turn, clutching her hand back where it had been.

"Lord . . . no, no, you didn't hurt me. You can do anything you want. . . . Do it . . . please." His lips smothered hers, almost violently, his tongue and hips thrusting rhythmically while his hand slid over her stomach in a frantic search now.

Her senses were torn between the sinuous ebb and flow within her grasp and the warm hand sliding up her thigh, the faint feather strokes with which he again quickened her, his knowing fingertips never faltering. Femininity had lain fallow within her for thirty-three years, planted by nature, nourished by time, until it took now but a kiss-breadth to make it erupt and flower.

She was dimly aware that he roughly jerked her hand off his flesh, but her eyes could no more open than could her body control the volcanic climax which he brought to it so effortlessly. And all the while he chanted murmurously, leaning on an elbow above her, kissing her eyes, stroking her flesh. "Let it come, Ab . . . let yourself fly . . . fly, Abbie . . . fly with me . . ."

His name escaped her throat as spasms of heat pulsated from deep in her stomach downward, downward, and her hips reached high, yearning. When the final seizure gripped her, she was unprepared for its force. She had never, never guessed . . . aaah, the power of it, the rapture . . . Jesse, she thought, ah, Jess, it's so good. . . . Jess, you were right. . . . Mother, why did you warn me against this?

Her nails cut into his arm. A rasping cry of ecstasy was wrenched from her throat and even as she shuddered his body covered hers. He spoke her name as the silken hair of his chest pressed upon her bare breasts, absorbing the faint sheen of moisture there. His tumescent body searched, probed, and found its home. He flanked her narrow shoulders with his hands, bracing away.

"Abbie, it's going to hurt, love, but just once, I promise."

Hot flesh entered her; her own resisted. She started to struggle, pushing against his chest. "Relax, Abbie, relax and it'll be better. Don't fight me, Abbie." But her fists pummeled him, so he captured them and pinned them to the mattress. "I want to make it good for you," he intoned as his weight pressed heavily and he plunged. She gasped and a cry of appeal tore from her throat, but he smothered it with his kiss, then spoke her name in loving apology.

From the ecstasy of a moment ago she was seared by pain. Her shoulders strained up off the mattress, but he held her helpless, moving within her. Delicate membrane tore and sent stabbing anguish through her recently pleasured limbs. She struggled uselessly, for her every resistance was controlled by his awesome strength and size. His breath scraped harshly with each thrust until at last she gave up, throwing her face aside, waiting passively for the torment to end.

As Jesse moved, each stroke brought shards of glassy pain to him, too. The long-unused muscles of his leg flamed as if a hot poker had been thrust into his wound. He gritted his teeth, his hands clinching her wrists like talons, thinking of how small she was, causing himself more misery by shimming his weight high to keep from hurting her. He fought pain in an effort to derive the most from his pleasure, but the faster he moved, the more it hurt. Sweat broke out on his brow as pain slowly but surely got the upper hand. His head sagged down, and his efforts at release grew grim. His arms shook mightily and a deep groan escaped him when finally he collapsed upon her, burning jets of white-hot fire searing his loins. He sighed, but it was not a replete sound, it was filled rather with relief.

He fell half off her, one leg still sprawled across her thighs, and she knew even in the depth of her naiveté that something was wrong. It had not been good for him as it had been earlier for her. He groaned into the pillow beside her ear and rolled himself away, limb by limb. But she could hear him gritting his teeth, and could feel his tensile muscles still shaking. She reviewed it all and knew exactly whose fault it was. His sudden withdrawal could only have been caused by her lack of prowess. Unsure of what she'd done wrong, she knew beyond doubt it was something, for it came back to her how he'd roughly jerked her hand off his body. He lay now with the back of a wrist over his eyes, obviously greatly relieved that it was over. Chagrined, she rolled away, cursing herself for being a stupid virgin of thirty-three, unable to perform even the simplest act to his satisfaction.

"Where are you going?"

"Upstairs." She began to sit up, but a long arm pinned her flat.

"What's the matter?"

"Let me go." She could already feel tears gathering in her throat.

"Not until you tell me what's wrong."

Her eyelids stung. She bit the inside of her lip, disappointment, anger, and guilt settling in with a sudden, deflating whump.

"Thank you, Mr. DuFrayne, for a heartfelt performance," she said stingingly.

"For *what*!" His neck crimped up, his fingers bit into her arm.

"What else shall I call such a sham?"

"What's wrong, Abbie, didn't I do it to suit you?" he asked sarcastically.

"Oh, you suited me fine. I fear I'm the one who did not suit."

He instantly softened. "Hey, it's your first time. It takes time to learn, all right?"

She pried his fingers from her arm and rolled away from him, thoroughly ashamed now of all the moaning and groaning she'd done when he had, in his turn, acted as if he couldn't wait to be done with her. He'd rolled off and out of her as fast as he could, then just lay there like a big, silent lump, saying nothing. All right then! If he had nothing to say, neither did she! She stared at the moonlit window, battling tears, remembering how he hadn't wanted to make love to her in the first place, how she'd practically had to beg him. Mortified, she lurched up as if to leave, but he got her by the shoulders and toppled her back down.

"Oh, no you don't! You're not running out of this bed and leaving this unsettled, because I'm not about to let you! You're going to stay right here until I find out what's got you prickled up, then you're going to give me a chance to put it right!"

"I am not prickled up!"

"Like hell you aren't! Can't we even do *this* without a fight! Not even this!" She bit her lip to keep from bawling out loud.

He went on, "I thought we did rather well, myself, considering it was our first time together. So what's your gripe?"

"Let me up. You're all done with me anyway." Martyrdom felt blessedly sweet. But one hard arm pressed her shoulders relentlessly, allowing no escape.

"I'm *what*!" he barked, growing angrier by the minute at her sudden, unexplained peevishness. "Don't you use that tone of voice on me, as if I'd slung you here against your will and raped you!"

"I didn't mean it that way. I only meant that it was obvious I was nothing."

"Abbie, don't say that." His voice lost its harshness. "This shouldn't happen between a man and a woman and leave them as nothing. It should always leave them as more."

"But I was nothing. You said so."

"I never said any such thing!"

"You said it takes s . . . some time t . . . to learn." The tears were growing plumper on her lids.

"Well, damnit, it does! But that's nothing against you."

"Don't you dare lie there over me, swearing right into my face, Jesse DuFrayne!"

"I'll lie here and do any damn thing I please, Miss Abigail McKenzie! You've got the story all wrong anyway. Look at you! Why, you're half the size of me. Just what do you think would happen if I laid into you with all I've got?" She turned her face aside. He grabbed her cheeks and made her look him in the eyes. "Abbie, I didn't want to hurt you so I held back . . . and there's not as much in it, is all, when a man does that. And yes, you're inexperienced, and no, you don't know all the moves, but I didn't care. By the time we got to the end I knew exactly how painful it was for you—the first time is always like that for a woman. I just wanted to end it quick for you."

"I am not made of china like the soup bowl you shattered once in this room!" she pouted.

"I don't think I know exactly what you're bitching about! Just what is it!"

Her chin trembled and a tear spilled. She looked at the moonlight streaming across the windowseat. "I . . . I don't kn . . . know either. You just . . . you acted like you were glad it was ov . . . over, that's all."

He sighed, tired and disgusted now. "Abbie, my leg hurt

like hell and I was worried about hurting you any more and
. . . and . . . *oh, goddamnit!*" he exclaimed, pounding a
fist into the mattress and flopping onto his back to stare at the
ceiling.

She knew he was done with her for sure then, so sat up. But
he touched her arm, gently though. "Stay a minute," he
placated. "Will you stay?" There was a new note of sincerity
in his voice as he dropped his hand from her arm. She pushed
her hair back and wiped her eyes, so sorry now that she'd ever
started this. "Don't go, Abbie, not like this," he pleaded,
raising up on an elbow.

"I'm just getting the sheet." She found it on the floor and
wiped her eyes with it before lying down and flinging it over
her. It fell across him too, and they lay there like a pair of
scarecrows under the sheet and the silence and the misunder-
standing. Finally he rolled onto his side facing her and folded
an elbow beneath his ear, studying her stiff profile against the
square of milk-white window. His voice came again, soft and
disarming. "Abbie, do you think it's always so easy for a man?
Well, it's not. A man is expected to lead the way and a woman
relies on him to do the right thing. But being the leader doesn't
make him either infallible or fearless." She stared at the
ceiling, the sheet clinched tightly beneath her armpits as tears
dripped down into her ears. He ran an absent finger back and
forth along the taut edge of the sheet while he went on quietly.
"I took a virgin tonight. Do you know what goes through a
man's mind when he does that? Do you think I didn't fear
you'd push me away or think I went too fast or too hard or too
far? Do you think I didn't know how you recoiled from
touching me, Abbie? What was I supposed to do then? Stop,
for God's sake?" Back and forth, back and forth went his
finger, lightly whisking her skin and the edge of the sheet. "I
promised to make it good for you, as good as I could, but the
first time is never too good for a woman. Abbie, can you
believe that I was afraid after that? Every step of the way I had
doubts just like you, just like all lovers do the first time. The
farther I went, the more afraid I was that you'd get up and run
out of here in the middle of it all. Abbie, look at me."

She did, because he sounded very hurt and sincere.

"Abbie, what did I do wrong?" he asked softly. His hand
had stopped toying with the sheet and lay unmoving between

her breasts, his elbow resting lightly along the shallows of her ribcage.

"Nothing . . . nothing. It was m . . . me. I was terribly noisy, and afraid to do what I knew you wanted me to do, and I blamed you because it hurt at the end, and . . . and . . . oh, everything." Chagrined, she turned her face against his biceps. Tears were coming fast now. "It . . . it's just easier to get m . . . mad at you than it is t . . . to get mad at mys . . . self."

"Shhh, Abbie," he hushed, "you were fine."

"N . . . no, I was not f . . . fine. I was sc . . . scared and childish, but I d . . . didn't expect—"

A big hand found her cheek, its thumb brushed near a lower eyelid. "I know, Ab, I know. It's all new to you. Don't cry, though, and don't think you didn't give me pleasure, because you did."

She was horrified that she could not stem the flow of tears. His thumb grew sleek upon the hot puddle in the hollow beneath her eye. Her chest felt like it was near bursting from holding the sobs back.

"Th . . . then why were you in such a hurry to have it over with? I even h . . . heard you gritting your t . . . teeth."

"I told you why I hurried. My leg hurt and I thought I'd crush you. Besides, my own performance was none too great at the end either." He lifted his head off its cradling arm to look down into her face and find her eyes tightly jammed shut. In all his life he'd never faced a situation such as this after lovemaking. He too felt inept and wanting, dissatisfied in spite of what had passed. But at the same time he felt singularly protective toward this woman: the first he'd ever encountered who was as much concerned with fulfilling his needs as her own. He leaned to kiss the river of salt that streamed from her eyes, and she suddenly choked and clutched his neck, sobbing pitifully, her arms tenaciously trapping him too close for him to watch her misery. Her chest heaved with wrenching sobs that shook his own and made his stomach cinch tight with the need to comfort her and make things right.

"Abbie, Abbie, don't cry," he whispered throatily against her hair. "We'll try it again and it'll be better." But he understood what she really cried about. He understood how far she'd come from propriety to this. So he held her tenderly, cooing soft endearments as he smoothed the hair up from the nape of her neck and back from her temples, wondering miserably how things could have gone so wrong.

"Oh, Jess, I w . . . wanted my memories of this n . . . night to be good. I didn't w . . . want us to f . . . fight tonight. I wanted us to pl . . . please each other."

"Shhh, Abbie, there are lots of ways." He dried her cheeks with the tail of a sheet. "Lots of ways and lots of time."

"Then show me, Jess, show me," she pleaded, desperate now to see that this night not end in desolation. His hand stopped moving. He kissed her forehead. She heard him swallow.

"I can't right now. A man needs time in between, Abbie, and my leg needs a rest too. But in a while . . . all right?"

But she didn't believe him. She was sure now that he was only placating her because she'd done such a miserable job the first time. He rolled to his back again, swallowing the sigh which formed as he fully rested his leg. She lay very still, staring at the ceiling, going over it all in her memory, recategorizing Jesse DuFrayne once again according to what this night had taught her about him. No longer could she consider him a defiler of women, but a tender, considerate lover instead. Not fearless, as she'd thought, but human, with misgivings not unlike her own. He'd always seemed so bold and doubtless in his teasing. What a revelation to think that there lurked trepidation behind his bravado. Yet even in his disappointment he eased her with kind, sweet words and assuaged her feelings of inadequacy by taking the blame upon himself.

But how could she face him come morning? How could she awaken here and look into his dark eyes when neither would be able to deny that their lovemaking had been disastrous? As she had once before in this room, she lay falsely still, waiting for sleep to overtake him so she could slip away. But a large, heavy hand sought and found her hair, smoothed it, then drew her to his side and pulled her up against his chest. He rested his chin upon the top of her head and her eyelashes fluttered shut as she sighed and stayed, unwilling to deny herself the comfort of being cradled that way. After some minutes his hand moved lazily against her hair. His brawny chest had a silken texture beneath her cheek. She told herself she must get up and go— what would she say to him in the morning? But like a bridling in its nesting place, she felt secure. His hand grew weighted upon her skull, then fell still. His other hand, which lay flung across her hip, twitched once spasmodically. His breathing became heavy and buffeted the top of her hair. A lethargy unlike any she'd known before came to lower her lids and sap her limbs. She knew she was falling asleep in the arms of Jesse DuFrayne. She knew he'd been a gentle and considerate lover. She knew she must awaken tomorrow to the fact that he was leaving. But it all ceased to matter.

And they slept, unaware.

The Colorado Rockies spread protective arms about the lovers. The moon pulled the earth around, climbed the clouds, and slid down the other side, to the west. The dawn peepings of birds stirred upon the pinkening air. A sleeping man rolled over and settled his face against a fair, warm arm. A sleeping woman pulled her pillow into the deep curve of her shoulder, bent a bare knee toward her nose. The man snored lightly and shifted onto his stomach, and a lock of hair caught in his moustache, fluttering as he breathed, tickling him distractingly. The edge of a long, dark hand scratched the nose, tried to brush the nuisance away. But his breath fluttered it again, still caught, still tickling. He snuffled, roused, felt something warm covering his fingers, and opened his eyes groggily to see what it was.

Abbie.

He grinned at the sight of a single rose-tipped breast half covering the back of his hand. Her other breast was buried beneath her someplace, for she too was half on her belly, one knee drawn up high, presenting a beautifully turned hip, but hiding her feminine secrets. He smiled crookedly. She likes to hog the bed, he thought. The smile dissolved as he remembered how she'd cried last night. He carefully extracted his hand, rolled onto his side, and braced his jaw on a palm. His eyes leisurely traveled the length of her, several times. Tiny toes, delicate ankles, shapely calves. He remembered glimpsing them before, but never as freely as this. Her hip was as round as the swell of a sea wave, and her waist as sharp as the trough created by tides. The deep crevice carved an enticing angle, buttressed by the knee she'd cast upward toward her chest. Myriad memories flitted through his mind. Abbie, you saved my life. Abbie, I made you cry. Abbie, I must leave soon. He looked at the window where pink-gray light crept over the sill and knew an emptiness unlike any he'd ever faced

upon leaving a woman's bed. No, last night's pleasures, for
him, had been minimal at best, yet his body sprang to life now
at the sight of her. He leaned to drop a light kiss upon her ribs,
then on that pale hip. He placed a much more lingering one in
the trough of her waist. A small hand came down and swatted
unconsciously at him. Then she flopped over, facing away
from him, with her top leg pulled up high as before.

His heart went crazy and moisture erupted on his brow. She
was small and exquisite and—yes, it was still true—innocent,
for she knew nothing of the ways in which he yet desired her.
He released a pent-up breath and eased down low on the bed,
touched his tongue to the soft place behind her knee, closed his
eyes and breathed against her skin, knowing he was taking
unfair advantage while she slept, yet he was aroused so
ardently that his body felt it would burst its bounds. He tasted
salt and roses and maybe a little of himself. He followed the
contour of her leg, his hair brushing against her thigh, recalling
how very familiar she had long ago become with his own body.

What he did seemed inevitable; the weeks of intimacy they
had shared made it almost preordained. He kissed her
everywhere but the one spot he wanted most to taste, waiting
for her to awaken that he might kiss it, too. He learned the
ridges of her vertebrae, the firmness of her hip, the resilience
of her thighs, buttocks, calves. He memorized even her half-
flattened breast. She awakened when he lightly bit the arch of
her updrawn foot, and with a start she looked back over her
shoulder at the man behind her. Vague, predawn light caught in
his black, aroused eyes as he braced up and searched her face
for permission. Above his open lips his moustache was a dark,
trembling shadow. Her eyes were drawn to it, sensing that it
had just explored her skin. Her startled eyes again fled to his,
and she read in that gaze a kind of ardent agony which she'd
not suspected a man could harbor. It brought her heart and
blood alive with a leap of sensuality and expectation.

"J . . . Jesse?" she stammered croakily. Slowly she eased
her leg down, realizing how immodest her pose had been and
that he'd undoubtedly been awake for some time. "Y . . .
you woke me up."

"I meant to, love," he whispered, holding her captive by
only the strong, sensuous tether of his gaze. She rolled
backward slightly, twisting at the waist, bracing up on an
elbow now and watching his eyes drop to the peak of her other

breast, which curved into view, then return to her face. She felt his warm palm travel from the small of her back, around one buttock, along the back side of her calf, gently tucking her knee back up as it had been before. And all the while his eyes never left hers.

"It's my turn to know your body like you've known mine all these weeks, Abbie." She became aware of all the places where her body was wet, where his tongue had trailed as she slept, where her skin now cooled as it dried. Naiveté vanished as she read his eyes and understood his intention. Involuntarily she shivered, then slowly hid her breast behind her upper arm, not quite knowing how to hide the rest of her. Mesmerized by the hunger in his gaze, she watched in fascination as he dipped his head again to her white hip, his eyes sliding closed while a sound of deep passion rumbled from his throat. He braced up on one hand, twisted now at the waist, and with a warm, caressing palm, pushed her back down onto her stomach. Her cheek grew lost in a pillow and her heart thrust wildly against the mattress as his warm lips brushed up and down her back and he began uttering her name against her skin. "Abbie . . . Abbie . . . Abbie . . ." Over and over, roaming her body with his soft moustache and his softer mouth until everything inside her grew yearning and outreaching. He turned her gently onto her back, moving her limbs where he would have them, trailing wetness and love words as his kisses tracked across her flesh. His gravelly voice whispered that the second time was better, begged her to be still, to let him. "Don't fight me, Abbie, I'll show you . . . Abbie, you're so tiny . . . God, you're beautiful . . . Shhhh, don't hide from me . . . there's more. . . . Trust me, Ab." When she reached instinctively to cover herself, he nudged her hand aside with his nose. Then his teeth gently closed upon the side of her thumb and he carried it to the hollow of her hip.

"Jesse . . ." she rasped once, beseeching him for she knew not what.

"Nothing's going to hurt this time, Abbie, I promise."

No, she thought, people don't do this! But people did, she learned, for his mouth possessed her everywhere, sent her spinning into mindless wonder while she lost all will to resist. He sailed her high and writhing until heat exploded like a skyrocket inside her, sending sparks sizzling from the core of her stomach to the tips of her toes and fingers in a gigantic burning burst of sensation. She opened her eyes to the sight of him gazing in undisguised need up her stomach, into her dazed, glazed eyes. She groaned and rolled a shoulder languorously away from the mattress, then let it sag back again. She pulled her senses up from their debilitated depths and opened her eyes, realizing that he needed fulfillment equally as much as she had a moment ago. So she raised her drugged arms in welcome.

He lunged up, rasping instructions in her ear, encompassing her with powerful brown arms that lifted her, turned her, and set her on top of his stomach, then brought her down until her breasts were crushed against the mat of hair on his chest. Words became unnecessary, for her body and his hands told her what to do. Innocence, timidity, naiveté all fled as she started to move, watching his pleasured face as his eyes slid closed and his head arched back against the jumbled pillows. As his lips fell open and his breath scraped harshly, she saw in his face the plenary abandon which he'd earlier brought to her. Her heart soared. Her eyes stung. This, this, this, is how it should be for both man and woman, she realized. The one giving to the other, the one taking from the other, with as much joy derived from the giving as from the taking. She faltered and his eyelids flickered opened momentarily, then closed again and his temple turned sharply against the pillow as she regained the rhythm. Unbelievably, when he reached his climax he cried out—was it her name or some mindless profanity or both? It mattered not, for it made her smile, made her feel skilled and agile, and bursting with joy.

She collapsed onto his broad chest, her forehead nestling beneath his jaw. One of his hands fell tiredly onto her shoulder, rubbed it in a light, caressing circle of satisfaction before flopping weakly onto the pillow again. Then, surprisingly, beneath her ear, a slow, quiet, wonderful chuckle began. It rumbled there like sweet thunder until, puzzled, she raised her head to study him. But his eyes remained closed while his chest rose and fell beneath her own, with silent laughter. And suddenly she understood why he laughed—it was a laugh of elemental satisfaction. A smile blossomed upon her lips, and a slow glow began deep down in her belly, in answering gladness. He slung his tired arms about her, hugged her tightly, and smiled against her hair as he rolled them both from side to side several times.

"Ahh, Abbie, you're good," came his lover's hosannah, "you're so damn good."

Nothing he might have said could have pleased Abbie more at that moment. She smiled against his chest. Then his hands flopped back, palms-up, on either side of his head. She sat up, peered at him, but his eyes remained peacefully closed, and while she watched in astonishment, he fell asleep, with her sitting yet astride him—stunned, naked, and new.

Chapter 16

———◆———

WITH HER FIRST rising movement, Abbie knew she'd overdone it. She was thirty-three years old and some of the muscles she'd stretched last night hadn't been stretched for years. Suppressing a groan, she rolled to the edge of the bed.

"Good morning, Miss Abigail," drawled a pleasant, raspy voice behind her. But she couldn't endure the thought of facing him, knowing that in a few short hours he would simply be walking out of her life. Two strong brown hands circled her white hips, and he kissed her down low, almost where she sat, laying behind her, strewn all over the bed hazardly, like the tumbled sheets.

"Where you going?" he inquired lazily, giving her a fond squeeze.

She sucked in her breath and her back went rigid. "Don't do that, it hurts!"

His hands slipped away and he watched her get up slowly with one hand bracing the small of her back. Two or three steps told them both that her back wasn't the only thing that hurt. But she eased her way to the pile of discarded clothing on the floor, bent over painfully to pick up her wrapper.

Ooooo, did he enjoy that!

He'd planned on a little morning morsel of her but could see that was definitely off. She straightened up just fine, but wasn't moving any too spryly. She shuffled out wiltedly while he felt like the first rose of summer—no doubt about it! He flexed, yawned, scratched his chest, and popped up happily to slip into his pants.

Abbie stood looking at the greasy, ivory-colored platter, the bones and hardened fat with dry, curling edges. She surveyed the coffee cups with brown rings and residue in their bottoms, the plain everyday glasses with now-flat champagne lying lifeless in their depths, the spot on the linen where the laughing piece of steak had hit when it flew from her mouth. Miserably she remembered their gay laughter while she'd tried in vain to settle the tablecloth perfectly all those times. She studied it all and it sickened her, standing in the middle of the room, gripping both ends of her tie-belt as if considering pulling, pulling, pulling, until it cut her in half. She told herself she would *not* think of last night as sordid! *She could not*! But eyeing the mess on the table, she wondered sadly which she wanted to wash up first, the dishes or herself.

Behind her, Jesse crossed his brown arms and leaned a shoulder against the doorframe. He could read her as accurately as if the old beatitudes were suddenly running ticker-tape fashion across the back of her sensible, sexless wrapper.

He wondered what to do or say. If he made a joke, it would fall flat. If he tried to take her in his arms, he was sure she'd push him away. If he conferred upon her the right to place the blame on him, it would only make matters worse. Still, he could not let her stand there interminably, being her own censor.

He came up behind her, placed both hands on her shoulders, and decided to simply say the truth. "In the morning sometimes a person needs reassurance, sometimes both people need reassurance." Her neck was very stiff and he slowly rubbed his long thumbs along its taut cords. He felt her swallow and went on soothingly, "It always seems different in the morning, so the best thing to do is wait until later in the day to decide just how you feel about it. In the meantime, it's customary to at least acknowledge one's partner. That is usually done in a very charming and old-fashioned way—like this."

Abbie felt herself being turned by her shoulders. She knew her hair and face were a fright, that this whole situation was frightful. But he made all that seem petty by lowering her hands when she sought to hide her hair and eyes, by kissing her ever so lightly while softly kneading her neck. She wanted to respond, but was afraid and guilty, thus Jesse had to settle for no reassurance at all, nothing more than the closing of her eyelids. Yet he understood that self-retribution already had her in its clutches, so he kissed her tenderly again, touching her fleetingly on each corner of her mouth.

His kiss was a new surprise, a unique, nice sensation which threatened her only with gentleness. But in the middle of it, with his warm lips wishing her the first lover's good morning of her life, she remembered that before the day wore out he'd be gone. Stricken, she controlled the urge to cling to him. She bit her lip as he rested his chin on top of her head. His hands rubbed her lower spine in heartrending consideration while he murmured, "The soreness will go away in no time."

And her thoughts cried, Oh, but so will you, Jesse, so will you!

She was shaken by his sensitivity, his depth of understanding. Both last night and this morning he had been tenderhearted in his treatment of her, and she now wished this weren't true. It made his imminent departure too abrupt and harsh to quite accept. Were he to turn again to his former ways, teasing, needling, or irritating her in some fashion, it would suit her far better, for she told herself rigidly that she would not—*would not!*—beg him to stay.

He patted her then, back there low, and said, "Why don't you take a nice hot bath and don't worry about breakfast? We ate late last night anyway."

She turned stiffly from his embrace, his consideration ripping some new wound in her with each passing moment. But still it went on, for when she was laying the fire and he saw her wince as she lifted a heavy chunk of wood, he came to take it from her, saying, "Here, let me do that. You go gather up your clothes or those dishes or something while I get a fire going and bring in some water."

As she turned away, burdened by his sweetness, he stopped her, calling quietly, "Abbie?"

She craned around, meeting his eyes directly for the first time across the morning expanse of kitchen. He looked as engagingly natural as ever: nothing on but his jeans, standing there barefoot, with that hunk of wood in his long brown fingers, his hair tousled and dark, his moustache and eyes as unsettlingly attractive as ever.

"What?" she got out.

"You haven't said anything to me yet this morning except 'Don't do that, it hurts.' "

She thought, damn you, Jesse, don't do this to me! I don't deserve it—not all this!

Why did he have to stand there looking so damn handsome and considerate and warm and likeable only now when he was on the very brink of leaving?

"I'm all right," she said evenly, disguising her turmoil. "Don't worry about last night. I can live with it."

"That's better," he said, putting the chunk of wood down, brushing bark bits off his palms. "Abbie, I have to ask you for a favor."

"Yes?"

"Are the stores open in town yet?"

"Yes."

"Well, all my stuff went on the train with my photographic gear. It was all packed together. I want to go buy a set of clothes, but I don't have any money. I never thought to ask Jim for some. If you could lend me some out of that thousand, I'll see that you get it back."

"Don't be silly. You do not need to pay it back. The money was for anything you need, and if you need clothes, of course you may have as much as you wish."

"I thought I'd just wash my face quick and run a comb through my hair and go on up to buy what I need, then come back here and get cleaned up and changed before I leave. Is that all right with you?"

"You're leaving on the morning train, then?"

"No. I'm meeting some people at noon to discuss . . . some business, then I'll take the three-twenty out this afternoon."

"Meeting some people?" she asked, puzzled, but he looked away, busying himself at his firebuilding.

"Yeah, Jim set up a meeting here and told me about it yesterday. He said I don't have to be there, but I want to since it's . . . well, it's railroad business and I'm involved in it."

She couldn't help but wonder what kind of meeting a railroad photographer would be attending in a town as remote and insignificant as Stuart's Junction, but decided it was none of her business whatsoever. She was acting like a presuming lover on the basis of a one-night consortion. He had no obligation to explain his business dealings to her at all.

"Of course," she agreed, watching him poke at the fire. He looked so natural, bare-chested and barefoot that way. It was hard to imagine him in a full set of clothes. She'd never thought to see the day he'd actually buy and wear them, railroad meeting or not. It struck her that he must be inordinately eager to leave, for he had memorized the exact time of the train whistles.

Some minutes later she was sitting at the secretary in the parlor when he came out of the bedroom, shirt buttoned, all tucked in neat and proper, boots on, hair combed.

"I hope it's all right if I used your brush, Abbie, since I don't have one of my own."

She didn't know whether to laugh or cry at that remark after what the two of them had shared last night. She handed him a bank draft she'd written out, saying, "Yes, of course it's all right. Here. I hope this will do. I haven't much cash in the house."

He reached out slowly, his eyes never leaving her downcast face while he scissored the check between two lean fingers.

"I'll be back soon." He hesitated, wishing she'd look at him, but finally swung away, seeing she would not.

As he went out, limping slightly, she called, "It's Holmes's Dry Goods Store, on the left side of the street about half a block down."

Her eyes devoured his broad back. But suddenly he stopped, braced a palm against the porch column, and studied his boots. Then he slapped the column, muttered, "Damn," and pivoted.

The screen door squeaked like her love-sprung bones, and her heart careened while she wished desperately that he'd just go, get out fast. But he came instead to stand dejectedly beside the desk, his weight slung on one hip, a thumb hanging from the waist of his denims. He slumped one shoulder, leaning his half of the way, but she refused to look up from the pigeonholes of the desk. The thumb left the waistband and came to her chin, but she jerked aside, snapping, "Don't!" He hesitated a moment longer, then leaned the rest of the way, and dropped a kiss on her nose.

"I'll be back." His voice sounded a little shaky, and her chin quivered. He straightened, touched her lips with the back of a forefinger, then left the house as fast as he should have the first time. The screen door slammed and she leaned both elbows onto the desktop, then dropped her face into her hands. She sat that way a long time, miserable, knowing she would get far more miserable before she managed to get over him. Yet get over him she must.

At last she rose, bathed, and went upstairs to dress for the day. She donned a black skirt and a pastel blue organdy blouse. She closed the loops over the many buttons of the deep cuffs, then stretched her neck high and smoothed the tight lace up her throat until it nearly grazed her ears. All the evidence of last night's tryst had been erased, but as she studied her reflection in the oval dresser mirror, she looked ten years older than she had yesterday morning. Behind her, reflected in the glass, she saw the red shoes. She raised her own castigating eyes once more, wondering if after last night those red shoes might fit. She turned, picked one up, studied it, closed her eyes, judging herself. Finally she sat down on the bed and drew a red shoe on.

From downstairs she heard the screen door slam, then Jesse, call, "Abbie? I'm back. Hey, where are you?"

"I'm upstairs," she called, casting a baleful look at the shoe.

He came to the foot of the steps and called up, "Is it all right if I take a bath?"

"Yes. There's hot water left in the reservoir, and clean linens in the bureau drawer across from the pantry."

"I know where you keep them." His footsteps moved away.

She closed her eyes against the onslaught of welcome she felt at his returning, calling up the stairs in that familiar way.

Oh, God, God, she didn't want him to go, not so soon.

The red shoe still dangled from her toe, and she leaned to lace it up. She stuck her foot out, rotated the ankle this way and that, admiring the look and feel of David Melcher's gift.

And somehow Miss Abigail felt reassured, so she put on the second shoe.

She examined them again and the red color seemed to fade into a less offensive, less improper shade. She stood up, balanced on the comfortable shoes, and found they had a heavenly fit. They made her feel petite and feminine. It was the first brief wisp of vanity Abigail McKenzie had allowed herself in her entire life. By the time she'd paced off four trial steps, the shoes had lost all garishness and were actually now quite appealing. It did not concern her that this was true only because she wanted it to be. Pacing back and forth across the bedroom floor, hearing the baby french heels click on the floorboards, there was nothing within Miss Abigail's conscience to suggest that the reason she was going to wear these shoes downstairs was to show Jesse DuFrayne that even though he was about to walk out of her life forever, he could just bear in mind that he wasn't the only fish in the sea.

"Where the hell do you keep the razor anyway?" Jesse called from downstairs, sounding like his old self again. "Abbie? I've got to hurry."

"Just a moment, I'm coming," she answered, hustling down the steps, the red shoes forgotten. She produced the razor from its kitchen hiding place and turned to find Jesse standing behind her in a pair of greenish-blue stovepipe pants—that's all. Her eyes traveled from his waist to his long toes, then back to his face as he reached for the razor.

"Could you fetch me the strop too, Abbie?" he asked, seemingly unaware of anything that might be happening inside of her.

And something was definitely happening.

Here was a bittersweet pang of a new kind. Here was her house filled with the sight and sound and smell of a man's toilette, something she'd long thought it would never again see. Oh, he had shaved and bathed and dressed here before, but now he did it in preparation to desert her. Now she was intimate with the muscle beneath the trouser, the ridges beneath the razor, the texture beneath the comb, the warmth beneath the smell. Now she wanted to call back time, forbid him to beautify his body for any cause other than her. But she had no right.

So she tried to keep from watching his bare shoulders curl toward the mirror, his head angle away, his eyes strain askance as he shaved near an ear. She tried not to dote upon the scent of shaving soap drifting through her old maid's kitchen. She tried to keep her eyes from coveting the rich fabric of the new pants he was wearing. She tried to ignore the whistle of the 9:50 from Denver when it keened through the house, the same train that had brought him here initially. She pretended that there would be no afternoon train to take him away.

"I left the change on the secretary in the parlor," he said, drying his face, leaning to comb his moustache. She'd never seen him do that before. She tore her greedy eyes away and moved into the parlor to sit before the secretary in an effort to appear busy, rummaging through some papers officiously. But all the time her heart grew heavier. He went into the bedroom and from around the doorway came the rustle of clothing, clunk of boot, chink of buckle, soft whistle through teeth, all punctuated by proclamations of silence during which her imagination took fire with images too familiar and forbidden.

And then out he came.

He stepped through the bedroom doorway and it was all she could do to keep from gasping and letting her jaw drop slack. He might have been a stranger, some striking dandy come to call as he paused, smoothing his vest almost self-consciously with a queer look on his face. His bronze skin beneath the slash of moustache was foiled against a high, stiff wing collar of pristine white, its corners turned back to create a 'V' at his Adam's apple. A four-in-hand tie was meticulously knotted and boasted a scarf pin against its bedeviling silken stripes. The rolled collar of a double-breasted waistcoat peeped from beneath impeccable lapels of a faultless cutaway jacket shorter and more contouring than the frock coats she saw in church on Sundays. The sight of him was breath-stopping, especially in this town, where miners trudged in dirt-grimed britches held by weary suspenders over grayed union suits. Jesse's entire suit was made of that startling color that reminded Abbie of the head of a drake mallard.

She suddenly knew a stab of jealousy so great that she dropped her eyes to keep him from reading them, jealousy for a cause which could make him dress like a peacock only as he left her, when all this time she could scarcely get him to don boots or shirt.

She spoke to her desktop. "You found all these . . . *habiliments* in Stuart's Junction?"

He'd thought she'd be pleased to see him dressed civilly at last, but the three-dollar word was definitely irritated and fault-finding.

"You seem surprised, but you shouldn't be." He moved gracefully to the side of the secretary, touched its writing surface lightly with three fingertips. "The railroads bring in everything they have in the East these days. The Yankees no longer have a monopoly on the up-to-date."

"Hmph," she snorted, "I should think you'd have chosen a less obtrusive color at least."

"What's the matter with this? It's called verdigris, I'm told, and it's all the rage in the East and Europe."

"Verdigris indeed?" she disdained, cocking an eyebrow at the fingers that haunted her, no matter how she tried to ignore them. "Peacock would have been more apropos."

"Peacock?" At last he withdrew his hand to tug his new lapels. "Why, this is no more peacock than . . . than the shoes old Melcher sent you."

Reflexively, she tucked her feet behind the gambriole legs of the desk chair while silently admitting the verdigris was not a bit offensive. It was deep, masculine, and utterly proper. But none of that mattered, for it wasn't really the color which riled her, and by now they both knew it.

"Perhaps it is not the suit that is peacock but only its wearer," she said stringently, and could sense Jesse bristling now.

"Why don't you make up your mind what you want out of me, Miss Abigail?" he asked hotly, referring of course to the clothing, but making her color at the memory of last night's request. Her mouth grew pinched.

"It must be a vital assignation you are going to, to bring about such a transformation when I could scarcely get a shirt on you for love or money!" Their eyes at last met in a clash of wills, but her dubious, ill-chosen phrase became poignant with unintended meaning.

"Not for love or money?" he repeated, slowly, precisely. She realized she had employed both in the last ten hours.

"Do not dare take those words figuratively, sir!" she snapped. "Just go! Be off to your *tête-à-tête*—whatever it is—in your *verdigris* suit. But don't forget to take your everyday britches along. You never can tell when you'll get these shot off for you!"

They glared at each other while Jesse wondered how to get out of here gracefully without further recriminations on either side. At last he placed his hands on his hips, his stance wilted, and he shook his head at the floor. "Abbie," he asked entreateningly, "for God's sake, can't we at least say goodbye without all this again?"

"Why? It makes it far more familiar to see you leave with anger in your eyes."

He realized that this was true, that wrapped in the security blanket of anger she needn't make appeals or excuses. He squatted beside her chair as she stared unblinkingly into the pigeonholed depths of the desktop.

"Abbie," he said quietly, taking one of her small, clenched hands, which refused to open, "I don't want to leave you in anger. I want to see you smiling and I want to be smiling myself."

"If you'll pardon me, I don't seem to have a lot to smile about this morning."

He sighed, stared at her hem, and absently rubbed his fingers over her tightly knotted fist that he had placed on his upraised knee.

Damn! Damn! she thought, why does he have to smell so good and be so nice? Why now?

"I knew you'd be bitter this morning," he went on. "I tried to warn you but you wouldn't listen. Abbie, I don't have time to stay here and help you straighten out your conscience. Just believe me. What happened happened, and you have nothing to be ashamed of. Tell me you won't go on feeling guilty."

But she would not say any such thing, or loosen her fist, or even look at him. Had she done any of those things she would end up in his arms again, and already she was bound for a long stint in hell, she was sure. Jesse realized it was getting late, that he must soon leave. "Abbie, there's one thing that's . . . . Listen, Abbie, what we did might not be over yet, you know. If anything happens, I mean if you should be pregnant, will you let me know?"

It had never, never entered her mind. Not before, during, or after making love with him, but his considering the possibility gave her the final, unforgivable cut, for she knew he would never come back and marry her if it did turn out that way.

He was saying, "You can reach me any time by wiring the central R.M.R. office in Denver," when she slowly pivoted toward him and slipped two scarlet kidskin toes from beneath her skirt, right next to that verdigris knee on the floor. He saw the red toes peep slowly from beneath her skirt, like two insolent, protruding tongues, and jumped to his feet, fists clenched at his sides, two small horizontal creases now behind the knee of the very pant leg which he had bent to her with the kindest of intentions.

"Goddammit, Abbie, what do you expect of me! he

shouted. "I told you last night I was going, and I am! Don't think I don't know why you're wearing those . . . those strumpet's shoes! But it's not going to work. You're not going to beat me over the head with the kidskin fact that you are now a scarlet woman, because it takes more than one night in bed with a man to make you one! You wanted what you got and so did I, so don't make me the fall guy. Grow up, Abbie. Grow up and realize that we're both a little right and both a little wrong and that you do not have the corner on guilt in this world!"

She kept her eyes trained on his knee and innocently intoned, "My, my, what a shame, Mr. DuFrayne, to have crimped your faultless peacock pant leg that way."

"All right, Abbie, have it your way, but don't make a fool of yourself by parading down Main Street in those goddamn red shoes!"

At that moment a querulous voice spoke from the front door. "Miss . . . Miss Abigail, are you all right?" David Melcher peered in, suffering the unsettling feeling of *déjà vu,* for it seemed he'd lived through this scene once before.

Miss Abigail shot to her feet, gaping. You could easily have stuffed both red shoes into the cavern of her mouth just then before she gathered her scattered wits enough to stammer, "M . . . Mr. Melcher . . . how . . . how long have you b . . . been standing there?" Frantically she heard the echo of Jesse's comments about scarlet women and pregnancy.

"I only just got here this minute. How long has *he* been here?"

But Jesse DuFrayne would not be talked past as if he were some cigar store Indian. His tone was icy and challenging as he faced the door. "I've been here since before you left, Melcher, so what of it!"

David pierced him with a look of pure hate. "I'll speak with you across a bargaining table at high noon and not a minute before. I am here to see Miss Abigail. I assumed you would have relieved her of your presence long before this, especially since you are obviously well enough to be arranging arbitration discussion these days."

DuFrayne angrily jerked a cuff into place, confirming flatly, "As you say, at noon then." He spun toward the bedroom to get his few things, leaving Abbie to seethe with shock yet unable to show it.

He knew! He knew! All the time he knew! He knew since

Jim Hudson came that David would be returning to Stuart's Junction. He knew because the meeting today was between the two of them, apparently to settle the liability over the shootings on the train. The pompous, conceited bag of arrogance knew that he was not her last chance, yet he stole her virginity anyway, knowing she'd never have given it had she known of Melcher's imminent return. Neither did it take much perception to guess that a man like David Melcher would never accept a soiled bride. Miss Abigail wanted to fly at Jesse DuFrayne and pummel him to a pulp, scream out her rage at how she'd been taken advantage of when he could simply have told her the truth and David might have been hers!

Melcher saw the anger blotch her face, but could not guess at what the foul-mouthed DuFrayne had said this time to place it there. Miss Abigail seemed to gather her equilibrium again, for she turned and invited sweetly, "Please come in, Mr. Melcher," and even opened the screen for him.

"Thank you." He came in bearing her father's cane, but just then Jesse shouldered his way around the bedroom doorway, gripping his wadded-up britches and gun in one hand as he clomped through the parlor.

"Your man has arrived in town then?" Melcher inquired expressionlessly.

"He got here yesterday," DuFrayne answered, the quivers of anger scarcely held in check. "And yours?"

"He's waiting at the depot as the wire stated he should."

DuFrayne nodded once sharply, feeling Abbie's eyes boring into the back of his head in cold, suppressed wrath. He turned, relaxed his jaw long enough to say stiffly, "Goodbye, Miss Abigail."

She was suddenly revisited by all the hate she'd felt for Jesse DuFrayne that other morning when his insinuations had lost David to her. Now it scarcely mattered that it was DuFrayne going and Melcher staying, for the mild-mannered man was again lost to her as surely as if Jesse DuFrayne had raised his gun, pointed, and shot David Melcher square between the eyes.

Jesse read before him the face of woman spurned, and his insides twisted with guilt.

"The same to you . . . *Mister* Dufrayne!"

His eyes bored into hers for a moment before he turned on his heel, banked past David Melcher, and hit for the door. In his wake, Abbie's nostrils were filled with the distressing scent of his shaving soap.

"Well, at least he's learned to address you in terms of respect," David noted stiffly.

Watching Jesse limp away down the street, she murmured, "Yes . . . yes, he has," though she longed to shriek a last *dementi* at the sarcasm now reflected by the term.

David cleared his throat. "I . . . I've returned your fa . . . father's cane, Miss Abigail." When she did not respond, he repeated, "Miss Abigail?"

She turned absently, forcing her mind away from Jesse DuFrayne. "I'm happy you did, Mr. Melcher, I really am. Not because I wanted it back, but because it gives me a chance to see you again."

He colored slightly, rather surprised by her directness, so different than the last time he'd spoken to her. He thought that he detected a brittle edge to her voice that he didn't remember from before either.

"Yes, well . . . I . . . I had to return to Stuart's Junction to attend a meeting at which we will attempt to ascertain who was to blame for the entire fiasco aboard the train."

"Yes, I only heard of the meeting this morning. How *is* your foot?"

He looked down at it, then back up. "The discomfort is gone. The limp is not."

At last the old solicitude returned to her voice. "Ah, I am so sorry. Perhaps in time it too will disappear." But she recalled how Doc said he would walk with a limp for the rest of his life.

"I see you . . . ahum . . . got the gift I sent," he stammered.

Now it was Miss Abigail's turn to glance at her feet. Gracious! she thought, I would have to have these things on just when he arrived!

"They're even lovelier on your feet than off," Melcher said, completely unaware of the shoe's unacceptability, and she hadn't the heart to crush his pride.

"They're a perfect fit," she said, truthfully enough, raising her skirt a few inches and flexing her toes within the supple kidskin. "I wanted to thank you but I had no address where I might reach you." Looking up then, she saw that David Melcher was embarrassed by how much of her ankle she'd revealed. Quickly she dropped her skirts. How rapidly one forgot propriety before a true gentleman after even a brief sojourn with a rounder like Jesse.

"You must forgive my rude manners, Mr. Melcher. Please sit down," she insisted, indicating the settee and taking a side chair. "I've had a somewhat trying morning and I'm afraid I've allowed my manners to lapse because of it. Please . . . please sit. Enough about me. What about you? Will you be on your way again selling shoes as soon as this meeting today is concluded?"

"I'd hoped . . . that is to say . . . I had considered spending . . . ah well, a couple of days right . . . right here in Stuart's Junction. I've taken a room at the ah, hotel, and deposited my gear there. I have the largest shipment of shoes ever—it was waiting for me in Denver. I thought I would see about finding some new markets for them right here and in the towns close around."

"Well in that case, perhaps you'll be free this evening to pay a call on me and tell me the outcome of today's meeting. I am most interested, of course, since both you and—" she found it difficult to say his name now "—Mr. DuFrayne were both under my care."

"Yes," David said a little breathlessly. "I . . . I'd like that ev . . . ever so much. Of course I realize you'll be anxious for the . . . the news."

"The whole town will be, Mr. Melcher. Nothing quite like this has ever happened in Stuart's Junction before and I'm sure tongues have been wagging fit to kill. When the meeting commences, the townspeople will be even more curious, I'm sure."

He fiddled with his vest buttons nervously before finally asking, with countless clearings of his throat, "Miss . . . Miss Abigail, did . . . agh . . . did you, or rather . . . has your . . . agh . . . has your repu—that is to say, have the townspeople . . . agh, said anything . . ."

She finally took pity on his overstrained sense of delicacy. "No, Mr. Melcher. My reputation has not suffered because of either you or Mr. DuFrayne being here at my house. I believe it's fair to say the people of this town know me better than that."

"Oh, of course," he quickly put in, "I didn't mean—"

"Please," she extended one delicate hand toward him, "let's not speak in parables. It brings only misunderstandings. Let us agree to start over as the best of friends and forget anything which has passed."

Again her directness befuddled him, but he reached out and took the proferred fingertips in his own for a fraction of a second while his raddled face told her again how very, very different this man was from Jesse DuFrayne.

"Until this evening then," she said softly.

"Yes . . . agh . . . until this evening."

He cleared his throat for perhaps the fiftieth time since entering her house, and suddenly it irritated Miss Abigail profoundly.

The inquisitive citizens of Stuart's Junction knew something was up when Max kicked Ernie off his customary bench on the depot porch long before the 3:20 was due, declaring the station was closed for official railroad business until further notice.

All up and down the boardwalk the news spread that that Melcher fellow with the shot off toe had checked in up at Albert's Hotel, along with some dandy in a yellow-checkered suit. They knew, too, that some fancy-dressed railroad bigwig had been in town since yesterday. And it was no secret that the one from up't Miss Abigail's house came uptown this morning and bought that fancy suit they'd all been starin' at in the window of Holmes's Dry Goods Store. When they saw him limp down the street wearing it, speculation grew heavy.

"Well, if he ain't no train robber, what do you reckon he is, and what do you reckon's goin' on up to the depot?"

But all they could get out of Max was that a representative of the R.M.R. had called a meeting here.

Max dusted the runged oak chairs and gathered them around a makeshift conference table made of a couple of raw planks balanced on two nail kegs, since the station was too new to boast a real table yet. Word had it the men were gussied up fit to kill. Max picked a sliver off a raw-edged plank, anxious to please. Yessir, he thought, looks like this is real important, whatever it is. So he rounded up a pitcher and four glasses, and filled it with water from the giant holding tank looming above the tracks outside where the steam engines drank their fill.

The four of them converged on the depot at the same time, the quartet looking altogether like a rainbow trout. There was James Hudson, in a wine-colored business suit. He shook

Max's hand. "Nice clean depot you keep here, Smith."
Instantly he gained Max's sympathy. Jesse DuFrayne appeared
in the teal blue suit which even Max had been eyeballing at
Holmes's Dry Goods. When Hudson introduced Maxwell
Smith, he said, "Smith is our station agent here in Stuart's
Junction."

DuFrayne, extending his hand, noted congenially, "Mr.
Smith, the man who refused to deport me without a release
from Doc Dougherty? I want to thank you for that, sir."

Though Max said, "Aw, think nuthin' of it," he was
enormously pleased and proud.

Hudson seemed to take the lead in all the introductions and
Max kept his ears open, learning that the man in the yellow-
checkered suit was Peter Crowley, Melcher's lawyer. By the
time Hudson suggested, "Gentlemen, shall we all be seated?"
Max was relieved. All this commotion and color during the
hand shaking was getting him dizzy. He'd never seen such a
bunch of dandies in his life!

James Hudson took a seat at the makeshift table as if it were
polished mahogany. There was an air of leadership about him
that stood out among the four. "Now, Crowley," he began, "I
suggest we forego accusations and stick to the straight facts
regarding the circumstances surrounding the shootings. Both
Mr. Melcher and Mr. DuFrayne have obviously undergone
some incapacitation due to the incident on the train."

"Mr. Melcher has come here to discuss liability," Crowley
replied. Melcher nodded. DuFrayane sat like a statue, glowering at him while verdigris arms remained folded tightly across
his chest. Hudson and Crowley went on.

"Do you mean liability on both sides or just one?" Hudson
asked.

"By that I take you to mean that DuFrayne sees Mr. Melcher
as liable in some way?"

"Well, isn't he?"

"He doesn't think so."

"He is the one who precipitated the scuffle in which Mr.
DuFrayne was shot."

"He did not precipitate it. He came in in the middle of it."

"Causing DuFrayne to receive a nearly fatal gunshot."

"From which your client has obviously recovered, according to reports I have here from one . . ." Crowley
examined a sheaf of papers before him ". . . Dr. Cleveland

Dougherty, who states that DuFrayne will, in all likelihood, recover full use of the leg, while Mr. Melcher will undoubtedly walk with a limp for the remainder of his life."

"For which Mr. Melcher presumably feels he is entitled to a settlement of some sort?"

"Indeed." Crowley leaned back in his chair.

"To the tune of what?" Hudson asked, steepling his fingertips.

"Mr. Melcher was riding aboard an R.M.R. coach when he was shot. Should not the owners of the railway be liable?"

More sharply this time, Hudson asked, "To the tune of what, I asked, Mr. Crowley?"

"Shall we say ten thousand dollars?"

Then all hell broke loose. DuFrayne leaped to his feet like a springing panther, glaring at Melcher with feral eyes. "Shall we *not* say ten thousand, you scheming little parasite!" he shouted.

"Parasite!" the shaken Melcher braved in his angriest tone while Hudson and Crowley tried to settle the pair down. "Just who is the parasite here, I ask!"

"Well, it sure as hell isn't me!" DuFrayne stormed. "You're the one looking for a handout, thinking that the railroad can afford it. After all, railroads are rich, aren't they? Why not milk this one for as much as you can get?"

"Any railroad can well afford that amount, it's true."

"Why, you little—"

"Jess, settle down!" Hudson got him by an arm and pushed him back toward his chair.

"Gentlemen, control yourselves," Crowley interjected.

"DuFrayne obviously doesn't know the meaning of the word. He never has!" Melcher claimed irately.

Crowley took his client in hand. "Mr. Melcher, we're here to discuss liability."

"And so we shall. He is liable, all right, for far more than a physical wound to me. What about the wounds he caused Miss Abigail?"

A fine white line appeared around the entire circumferance of DuFrayne's lips, but hidden on the upper one by his moustache, which outlined his formidable scowl. Rage bubbled in him, spawned by Melcher's accusation, but swelled by his own secret guilt over Abbie. Having Melcher unwittingly remind him of it only increased his hatred of the man.

"You leave Miss Abigail out of this!" DuFrayne barked.

"Yes, you'd like that, I'm sure. You were insufferable to her and would probably like not to be reminded of just exactly how insufferable!"

Confused, James Hudson spoke. "Miss Abigail? Do you mean Miss Abigail McKenzie? I cannot see what possible bearing she could have on any of this."

"Nor I," agreed Crowley. "Mr. Melcher, please—"

"No amount of money can atone for his treatment of her," Melcher said.

"Miss Abigail has already been recompensed for her help," Hudson assured him. "Mr. DuFrayne saw to that."

"Oh, yes, I've seen just how DuFrayne pays her back for everything she does. He forces her—"

Again DuFrayne flew to his feet. "You leave Abbie out of this, you little pipsqueak, or so help me—"

"Damnit, Jess, sit down!" Hudson at last lost patience. But in his anger, Jesse had used the familiar first name of the woman. Max noted it with great interest. When things cooled down a little, Hudson placed ten fingertips on the pine plank and spoke carefully. "It seems you two are picking bones that have nothing to do with the issue at hand. Now, you have asked Mr. Crowley and myself here as your arbiters. Will you allow us to arbitrate or shall we leave the two of you to haggle by yourselves?" A pause, then, "Mr. Crowley, suppose that Mr. DuFrayne agrees to a settlement on Mr. Melcher, what consideration would he receive in return?"

"I'm afraid you confuse me, sir. I didn't think it was DuFrayne's decision. I thought that you spoke for the railroad in this matter."

Hudson cleared the tabletop of his fingers, glanced at Jesse.

"Jess?" he asked quietly. All eyes in the room trained on DuFrayne.

"No."

"It's time, Jess. Do you want to pay out ten thousand for nothing?"

But DuFrayne clamped his lips tightly and brooded while the two arbiters went on discussing. Jesse's dark face was unreadable, although Melcher pierced him with hating eyes. Fraught by guilt over the night before, and by anger that Melcher should be squeezing for every penny he could get, Jesse was plagued by an idea that would not desist. Suppose they settled enough money on the vulture to set him up for life? Suppose they made the damn fool so rich that he could settle down in one place and sell shoes till hell froze over? Suppose they fixed him up comfy and cozy right here where all he'd need next was a woman to settle with? As distasteful as it was, it would at least salve Jesse DuFrayne's conscience over last night. If he could arrange it, Abbie would end up with everything she'd ever need or want—that sheep-faced shoe peddler, the means to set up a substantial business, and enough money to keep the two of them in red kidskin for the rest of their lackluster lives! DuFrayne again pictured Abbie's face as she'd come to him last night, saying, "David Melcher is gone and he shall never return. You're my last chance, Jesse." Glimmers of what had followed painted Jesse's mind. She was a woman with too much fire to be wasted on the likes of Melcher, but she was probably right in assuming that Stuart's Junction offered no better alternatives. Better she should have Melcher to shower a few sparks on than burn for nobody at all. He came out of his ruminations and picked up the thread of argument still going on.

". . . hardly think the sentence of life as a partial cripple would be considered nothing if this were taken to court, do you? You must consider the fact also that Mr. Melcher thought he was *defending* the railroad against what he considered an armed thief." Crowley's tone sounded slightly smug, and at last Hudson lost patience.

"Mr. Crowley," he rebutted testily, "I want to get something straight for the record. I'm tired of DuFrayne's name being bandied about as a train robber when it's the most preposterous accusation in the world! Now I ask you, why would any man want to rob his own train?"

"Jim!" barked DuFrayne, but his friend paid him little mind.

"Yes, you heard me correctly. You see, gentlemen, Jesse DuFrayne is a major shareholder of stock in the R.M.R. In other words, he owns the railroad—which he is accused of robbing."

In his corner, Max sat like a katydid with stilled wings. Crowley looked like he was trying to spit up a goose egg caught in his throat. Melcher looked like he was trying to swallow one. DuFrayne sat like a stone, facing the window, staring at the blue sky beyond, where a tip of the water tank showed. Hudson waited for the spell to take full effect. Melcher was the first to speak.

"If you think that this changes what you owe Miss Abigail, it doesn't. Your being a big railroad owner in no way excuses your actions toward her. You may be innocent of robbing that train, but where she is concerned, you are guilty of the most grossly unforgivable breaches of con—"

"Pay him!" Jesse snapped with agate hardness, attempting to shut the man up, for by now Jesse had become aware of the station agent, gawking like a hawk from his corner. The man had ears, and it didn't take much straining to hear everything being said in the room.

"Now wait a minute, Jess—"

"I said pay him, Jim, and I mean it," barked DuFrayne. Melcher couldn't believe his ears. Only a moment ago he'd have sworn all chance for monetary gain was nil, realizing how thoroughly he'd misjudged DuFrayne's intentions aboard that train. Still, he could not hold his tongue.

"Conscience money is just as sp—"

"And you shut up, little man, if you want so much as a penny out of me!" Jesse spit, jumping to his feet, pointing a finger. "Jim, just do as I say."

"Now wait a minute, Jess, the railroad is partly mine. I want some satisfaction out of this before we just hand him what he wants."

Suddenly DuFrayne lurched around. The scrape of chair legs made Melcher twitch back from the table. "I want to talk to you outside, Jim." DuFrayne was oblivious to the curious stares from across the street. He stood steely, furious, on the depot porch, his thumbs hooked into his waistcoat pockets, eyes narrowed vacantly at the gold pans hanging on display before a store across the way.

"Jess, I had to tell them about your ownership," Hudson reasoned.

"That's all right, Jim, it was bound to come out sooner or later. I just didn't want Abbie to find out about it before I left town, that's all."

"There's something going on here that I don't understand and maybe it's none of my business, but I just want you to think of what you're doing before you make any rash decisions about handing over what that leech wants."

"I've been considering it and my mind is made up."

"You're sure?"

"With several stipulations, and with the understanding that the money paid to Melcher is from my profits only, not yours."

They spoke quietly for several minutes, then reentered the station and took their places at the makeshift table.

"Mr. Crowley," Hudson addressed the man rather than his client, "if the railroad agrees to imburse Mr. Melcher ten thousand for damages, we will in turn demand that certain stipulations be fulfilled by him. First, Melcher will issue a statement to the local newspaper to the effect the railroad was in no way liable for this incident due to the fact that Mr. DuFrayne was carrying a gun, but only to the extent that your client was aboard one of our coaches when he was shot. The statement must in no way denigrate Mr. DuFrayne's name or that of Miss Abigail McKenzie but shall instead make it explicitly clear that Mr. DuFrayne was indeed not robbing the train, but that Mr. Melcher misjudged DuFrayne's intentions at the time. He may indicate that he acted for what he thought was the good of the passengers if he wishes, but that is the only defense he must give for his actions.

"Our second stipulation is that Mr. Melcher invest no less than two-thirds of this settlement money in a business or livelihood based in Stuart's Junction. He may choose whatever type of venture he wishes, but it must be in this town and it cannot be sold within the next five years.

"The third stipulation is that Mr. Melcher, personally, never again ride aboard an R.M.R. train. He may, of course, use the railroad to further his business venture by transporting goods, but he himself shall never again set foot on one of our coaches.

"We shall want these terms validated in writing and notarized, and of course there shall be an inclusion stating that if any of these terms are not fulfilled Mr. Melcher shall be liable to repay the R.M.R. the full amount of ten thousand dollars upon demand."

Crowley raised a silent, inquiring eyebrow at Melcher, who still floundered in the backwash of shock. Not only was DuFrayne vindicated of attempted robbery, he was rich enough and powerful enough to put the final nod to a settlement of ten thousand dollars of what, in retrospect, was his own capital anyway! The fact made Melcher's face flame and his hands shake. He clearly did not understand the man's reasons for stipulating that the money be reinvested in Stuart's Junction, but he was certainly not about to inquire. It was appalling enough to be subjected to the man's self-satisfied supremacy without being subjected to his reasoning, which might be as galling as the fact that he was issuing ultimatums in the first place.

"I will agree," Melcher stated flatly, "but with one condition of my own."

"And that?" Hudson asked.

"That DuFrayne pr . . . privately apologize to Miss Mc . . . McKenzie."

"You go too far, Melcher!" DuFrayne warned stormily, his face now livid. "Any animosity between Miss McKenzie and myself has no bearing on this bargaining session and, furthermore, is none of your business!"

"You made it my business, sir, one morning when you took gross liberties in her bedroom right before my eyes!"

"Enough!" roared DuFrayne, while Max nearly swallowed his tongue. The big man took to his feet, bumping the table and nearly upsetting it, sending the water pitcher careening precariously, glasses teetering. One circled and finally tipped, sending a splash of water over the table edge onto Melcher's lap while DuFrayne, with feet aspraddle, glared venomously, clenching his fists. "Our differences are settled, Abbie's and mine, so say no more of her, do you hear? You can take your ten thousand in blood money or toe money or whatever you choose to call it and live in splendor the rest of your days, or you can watch me walk out of here with the control of it still in my pocket and never see me again! Now which will it be?"

Melcher glared at the black moustache, envisioning again that bold, bare body that had taunted both him and Miss Abigail, wishing fervently that the bullet had struck DuFrayne's anatomy about four inches to the left of where it had! But were he to voice his thought, he stood to lose ten thousand dollars of this devil's own lucre. Neither did he doubt that DuFrayne meant it when he said one more word and David would see his back but not his money. And so David bit his tongue, daring not to insist again on the apology he so badly wanted for Miss Abigail. His Adam's apple bulged where his pride was stuck in his throat. But he only nodded woodenly.

"Very well. I'll give the newspapers only the answers you want, but don't you ever come back to Stuart's Junction again, DuFrayne. You have no reason to." They both knew he alluded to Abigail McKenzie, but DuFrayne carefully thrust one last riposte at Melcher.

"You're forgetting, Melcher, that I own property here, some of which you are standing upon at this very minute. Don't dictate to me where I can and cannot go . . . in business interests, of course," he finished sarcastically, with one eyebrow quirked.

Hudson interjected, "There seems little more to be said here," attempting to dull the animosity between the two and draw an end to the proceeding before they came to blows. "Mr. Crowley, if you will remain, we can draw up the agreement, have it verified before I leave town, and we will see about getting a bank draft to Mr. Melcher within three days at whatever destination he signifies. You understand that Mr. DuFrayne will have to free that amount personally from his accounts in Denver."

"Yes, I understand. If that is agreeable to Mr. Melcher, that is agreeable to me."

Melcher stood stiffly.

When things broke up, Hudson and DuFrayne stepped outside into the arid midday heat, which didn't help Jesse's temper any.

"What the hell's wrong with you anyway, Jess?" Hudson took his friend's elbow as if to cool his temper. "I've never seen you quite this defensive and belligerent over a woman before."

"Woman, hell! I just signed over ten thousand of my hard-earned bucks to that pipsqueak in there! How the hell would you feel?"

"Now hold on, Jess. You're the one who said give it to him, and I gathered at the time it was as much to shut him up as for any other reason. Just what did go on up there at Miss McKenzie's house anyway?"

Jesse's eyes moved to the gable of Abbie's house, visible beyond the false-fronted saddlery and harness shop. His stare was mechanical, his lips taut as he replied, "You have an inquisitive mind, Jim, and I have a temper. And that's why you do the business and I do the field work. Let's just keep it that way, only reserve your inquisitions for the likes of Melcher there, old buddy, huh?"

"All right . . . as you like it. But if you're after preserving Miss McKenzie's reputation, how about that station agent with his cocked ear and bulging eyes? I don't know what that remark meant, about your taking liberties in the bedroom of the lady in question, but it could come to have all kinds of unexpected ramifications once it rolls off the tongue of our station agent. Shall I go inside and bribe him or will you?"

"Goddamnit, Jim, didn't I take enough abuse from Melcher with you adding to it?"

But Hudson understood his friend's frustration, thus his scolding was taken with a grain of salt. But there was something eating Jess that he wasn't letting on about. Hudson couldn't help but wonder exactly what it was.

"Just trying to be practical," Hudson added.

"Well, you go on inside and be practical any way you see fit. I've already lost enough . . . *practicality* for one day."

They made arrangements to meet back at the hotel just before train time, then Hudson went back into the depot while DuFrayne made for the local saloon, to be stared at by everybody in the place except Ernie Turner, who was sound asleep with his head in a puddle of sweat from his beer glass.

Chapter 17

———————

FROM THE SECOND-STORY window in his hotel room on Main Street, David Melcher watched Hudson and DuFrayne board the 3:20. He had done as promised, had given the newspaper only the information agreed upon, yet it vexed Melcher mercilessly to have had to gild DuFrayne in any way whatsoever. It would vex him even more to accidentally run into DuFrayne at Miss Abigail's house again, thus he waited until DuFrayne was safely aboard the train and it had ground its way out of town.

Then and only then did David Melcher allow his victory to overwhelm him, to make him smile at its limitless possibilities. The thought of owning ten thousand dollars elated him, and he hummed as he changed clothes and brushed his hair, thinking of the sudden rosy future ahead of him. By the time he arrived at Miss Abigail's doorstep, he was beaming like the headlamp of an R.M.R. engine.

"Why, Mr. Melcher, you're early!" she said when she saw him there. But she was relieved to have his company, for the past five hours had been the longest of her life. Not only had her imagination run rife with scenes from the meeting at the depot, she had had to allow it to run its course with visions of Jesse boarding the 3:20, which she could not see from her place, and riding out of Stuart's Junction in that stunning suit, with his likable friend, James Hudson, the two of them never to return again. When the steam whistle raised its billow of white above the rooftops and sighed its departing scream, she had crossed her arms tightly across her chest and thought, Good. He is getting out of my life forever. But when the last clack of wheels had died away into summer silence, she had felt suddenly bereft and lonely.

Having David Melcher arrive, with his cheerful expression, was exactly what she needed to chase away lingering thoughts of Jesse DuFrayne. Standing now on her porch step, David wore an almost cherubic look, his pink cheeks blossoming into a little boy smile, almost as if he wanted to flatten his nose against the screen in delight. She knew immediately that the decision at the depot must have gone in his favor.

"And what has brought such a look of jubilation to your face?" Miss Abigail asked.

For once he forgot himself and asked, "Can I come in?" He had the door open before she could give him permission or open it for him. "Yes, I'm early, and yes, I'm jubilant, and can you guess why, Miss Abigail?"

She could not help but smile with him. "Well, I guess the meeting's results met with your approval, but—my goodness, Mr. Melcher—you're almost dancing. Do sit down."

He perched on the edge of the settee, then popped back up like a jack-in-the-box.

"Miss Abigail, I hope you're still wearing those red shoes, because I want to take you out for supper to celebrate."

"To celebrate? . . . Out to supper? . . . Why . . . why, Mr. Melcher!" She'd never been taken out to supper in her life.

He forgot himself even further and clasped both of her hands in his and, looking down into her amazed face, said, "Why, our victory of course. The railroad has agreed to settle ten thousand dollars on me for damages."

For a moment she couldn't speak, she was so stunned. Her jaw dropped down so far that her high collar bit into her neck. "Ten . . . thousand . . . dollars?" she repeated incredulously, then dropped off her feet into a side chair.

"Exactly!" He beamed at her a moment longer, then seemed to remember himself and dropped her hands to take his seat over on the settee again.

"My, how admirably generous," she said lamely, picturing James Hudson again, and the check for the thousand dollars he'd left on the seat of the umbrella stand.

David Melcher knew he should tell her now about DuFrayne being part-owner of the railroad, but he did not want anything putting a damper on their evening together.

"Do say you'll allow me to take you out this evening to celebrate with me. I consider it our victory, yours and mine together. It seems only right that we should commemorate it with an evening on the town."

"But it's your compensation, not mine."

"Miss Abigail, I don't care to cast shadows over the bright joy of the moment, but considering the circumstances under which we met, I feel—shall we say—rather liable to you for the indignities you suffered at the hands of that vile man DuFrayne. I have felt helpless to make up in any way for all that. Now, coming out the winner in this dispute seems like we've somehow brought him to bay at last. Not only for what he did to me, but what he did to you, too."

She studied the man perched on the edge of her settee. He spoke with such earnestness, wanting to be her champion, that she was suddenly swept by guilt that he should still consider her a flawless lady, worthy of his chivalry. She felt, too, an utter hopelessness, because she could not undo what she and Jesse DuFrayne had done together. How she wished that it had never happened, that she could honestly deserve David Melcher's advocation and admiration. She touched a hand to her high collar and looked away.

"Oh, Mr. Melcher, I'm truly touched, but I think it would be best for me not to celebrate your victory. Let me just congratulate you and keep the shoes as your thank you."

Disappointment covered his face. "You won't even let me buy you dinner?"

But their relationship had no future now. She got up from the side chair and walked over to the secretary and pretended that a cluster of papers there needed straightening. With her back to him, she answered, "I simply think it's best if you don't."

David Melcher swallowed, flushed, then stammered, "Is . . . is it that you c . . . cannot forgive me for what I ac . . . accused you of, that awf . . . f . . . ful morning when I left here?"

"Oh, no!" She swung to face him, an imploring look upon

her face. "That's all forgotten, please believe me, Dav—Mr.
Melcher."

But he'd heard her slip. He stood up, gathered his courage,
and approached her. Flustered, she turned toward the desk
again.

"Then pr . . . pr . . . prove it," he got out finally.

She turned to look over her shoulder at him, one hand still
trailing on the desktop.

"Prove it?" she repeated.

"C . . . come to dinner with m . . . me and pr . . .
prove that everything up t . . . till now is f . . . f
. . . forgotten."

Again she touched the lace at her throat, a winsome
expression softening her features. Oh, how she wanted to go to
dinner with a fine gentleman like him, for the first time in her
life. She wanted the gaiety and carelessness that her youth had
never tasted, the charm and companionship of a man at her
elbow. She wanted to share the mutual interests which she
knew the two of them were capable of sharing.

He still waited for her answer, the invitation alight in his
brown eyes.

Recriminations jangled through her mind. If only it were
yesterday. If only I had not done what I did with Jesse. If
only . . . if only. Anger touched her, too. Damn you, Jesse,
why didn't you tell me he was coming back?

She knew she must refuse, but in the end David's invitation
was too tempting. What will it hurt if I spend one evening with
him—just one? He, too, is here today and gone tomorrow, so
what harm can come of a single evening in his company?

"Dinner sounds nice," she understated, already feeling
guilty for accepting.

"Then you'll come?" He again looked jubilant.

"I'll come."

"And you'll wear the red shoes?"

Oh, dear! she thought, feeling herself flush. But there was
no graceful way to get out of it now, for he was totally unaware
of the shoes' flamboyance. But then, as if in answer to her
discomfort, came Jesse's belittling voice, as she remembered
him warning, "Just don't make a fool of yourself by parading
down Main Street in those goddamn red shoes!" And so,
diffidently, she left them on, praying all the way that none of
the townspeople noticed them on her feet. But she'd have

given that thousand-dollar bank deposit if Jesse DuFrayne himself could have seen her wearing them uptown to have dinner with David Melcher, her gloved hand in the crook of his arm as they walked along the boardwalk.

Not a soul in town could find fault with their demeanor.

By the next morning everyone in Stuart's Junction knew exactly how polite David Melcher had been and just how proper and prim Miss Abigail had been. They also knew what the couple had ordered and exactly how long they'd stayed and how many times they'd smiled at each other. But they had it straight from Louis Culpepper's mouth how Miss Abigail showed up wearing *red* shoes, of all things. Red! They must've been a gift from Melcher, 'cause it seemed he was a shoe peddler out of the East somewhere.

Imagine that! they all said, Miss Abigail taking up with a shoe peddler, and an easterner no less. And doing it decked out like December twenty-fifth in red shoes the man had given her after sleeping in her house!

"What a memorable evening," Miss Abigail said as they walked idly back to her house after supper. It was the slowest she had ever walked home from town. "How can I thank you?"

He limped along beside her. With each step he took, she could feel the hitch of his stride pull lightly at the hand with which she held his elbow.

"By not refusing me the next time I ask you."

She controlled the urge to turn her startled eyes up at him. "The next time? Why, aren't you leaving Stuart's Junction soon?"

"No, I'm not. As I said earlier, I have a large stock of shoes to sell and I intend to approach some local merchants in hopes that they'll act as outlets for us. Also, the railroad will be sending my settlement money to Stuart's Junction, so I'll have to wait here till it arrives."

Again she controlled the urge to ask how many days it would take.

He refrained from telling her that he was being forced to invest the major portion of the settlement money right here, for it made him look like DuFrayne's puppet, and the fact that David was galled him. David wanted her to believe that the decision to stay and settle here had been his own, which it probably would have been if it had been left up to him.

"How . . . how many days do you think it will take?" she finally asked.

"Three days maybe."

Three days, she thought. Oh, glorious three days! What harm can come of enjoying his company for three days? They're all I'll have, and then he'll be gone for good.

"In that case, I shall not refuse you anything while you're here," she said, and felt him tighten his elbow around her gloved hand and pull it against his ribs.

"Miss Abigail, you won't be sorry," he promised.

But deep inside Miss Abigail already was, for tonight had been so wonderful. And because her heart had jumped when he pulled her hand against his ribs.

"Tell me what grand things you intend to do with that money once it comes," she said, to distract her thoughts.

"I hadn't thought about it much. It's enough for now just to feel the sense of freedom it brings. I've never been wanting, but I've never had security such as this either."

They were nearly at her house, their steps slower than ever.

"It's strange, isn't it," she asked, "that much the same sort of thing has happened to me because of all this? Did I tell you that the railroad paid me a thousand dollars for my care of you and . . . and Mr. DuFrayne?" It was dreadfully hard to say his name now, and when she did, she felt David's arm tense, but she went on. "It brings me a sense of security too. Temporary, of course, but security nevertheless."

David Melcher certainly did not begrudge her the thousand dollars, only the fact that DuFrayne was the one who'd paid her off and was rich enough to do it so easily.

But he submerged his irritation and asked, "How did that come about?"

"Mr. Hudson came here and left a bank draft for me. He seems to be in a position of authority on the railroad. Is he the owner?"

David swallowed, still reluctant to tell her that DuFrayne was the other owner. "Yes," he answered tightly. "You deserved every penny he paid you, I'm sure."

They reached her porch then, and she asked, "Would you care to sit for a while? Your foot is probably tired."

"No . . . I mean yes . . . I mean, my f . . . foot is f . . . fine, but I'd like to sit awhile anyway."

She glanced at the pair of wicker chairs but led the way to the swing instead, justifying her choice by reiterating silently how little time they had together.

When she had seated herself, David asked politely before sitting, "May I?"

She pulled her skirt aside and made room while he settled quite stiffly and formally beside her, making sure that his coat sleeve did not touch her. There were restless night sounds all around them—insects, the saloon piano, leaves astir in the faint breeze.

He cleared his throat.

She sighed.

"Is something wrong?" he asked.

"Wrong? No . . . no, everything is . . . is wonderful." And indeed it should have been. He had his money, she had hers, he'd taken her to dinner, she was at last rid of Jesse DuFrayne.

He cleared his throat. "You seem . . . dif . . . different some . . . sometimes."

She hadn't realized it showed. She would have to be more careful.

"It's just that I'm not used to everything turning out so well. It all happened so fast. And I'm sure you've guessed that I don't get dinner invitations just every night. I was still thinking about how enjoyable it was."

"It—" He cleared his throat once more. "It was for me, too. I thought of it all the t . . . time after I left St . . . Stuart's Junction, about how I w . . . wanted to come back and take you to dinner." Here he cleared his throat yet again. "And now here we are."

Yes, like two pokers, she thought, surprising herelf, wishing that he would put his arm along the back of the swing like Jesse had done. But he was no Jesse, and she had no business wishing David would act even remotely like him! Still she grew more disappointed as the minutes passed and David sat sticklike beside her. His attitude seemed suddenly puerile. She wondered if she could soften him up somewhat.

"This was where I was when I opened the package with the shoes."

"Right here? On the swing?"

"Yes. Mr. Binley brought them up from the station. Remember Mr. Binley—the one who helped carry you to my house that first morning?"

"Would he be the tall, skinny one they called Bones?"

"The same. He seemed fascinated by the fact that I'd received a package. I'm sure he was hoping I'd open it before him."

"But you didn't?"

"Gracious no. I sat down and took the package here on the swing after he was gone and opened it all alone."

"And what did you . . . ahem!"—that was his throat again—"think?"

"Why, I was amazed, Mr. Melcher, simply amazed. I don't think another woman in this town owns a pair of red shoes." That was the truth!

"Well they will before long, because I have others in my stock. Red is the coming thing, you know."

She simply hadn't the heart to tell him her true feelings about the shoes. He would just have to find out for himself when his stock of reds didn't sell. Out here in the West, the staid, hard-working woman wanted sturdy browns and blacks, but he, like so many people in sales, was convinced that what he sold was the best, and could not see any fault with it.

"Would you have preferred another color?" he asked now.

She lied. "Oh, no! Of course not! I love these!" When had she become so glib at lying?

He once more cleared his throat. He placed his hands over his kneecaps and stared straight ahead. "Miss Abigail, when I approached your door today, I distinctly heard you and DuFrayne arguing about the shoes."

"We were," she admitted candidly.

"Why?" he asked, surprising himself at his own temerity. But where his products were concerned, he had backbone.

"He disliked them."

"Good!" he exclaimed, suddenly feeling very self-satisfied. It was perhaps the most romantic thing he had said that night, but she was too busy worrying about what else he'd overheard this morning to note David's pleased expression.

Her heart thudded as she worked up her courage and asked, "What else did you hear?"

"Nothing. Only his remark about the shoes."

She concealed a sigh but was greatly relieved.

David looked at her entreatingly and said, "He's gone now and we can both forget him."

"Yes," she agreed. But there was a sick feeling in the pit of her stomach and she could not meet David's eyes, knowing that for as long as she lived she would never forget Jesse DuFrayne. She attempted to lighten the atmosphere by suggesting, "Let's talk of more pleasant things. Tell me what it's like in the East."

"Have you never been there?"

"No. I've never been farther than Denver, and I was there only twice, both times as a child."

"The East . . ." He stopped momentarily and ruminated. "Well, the East has absolutely everything one could want to buy. Factories everywhere producing everything, especially since the war is over. The newest innovations and the grandest inventions. Did you know that a man named Lyman Blake in Massachusetts invented a machine for sewing soles onto shoes?"

"No, no I didn't, but I guess I must thank him for his glorious invention." Miss Abigail realized she was bored to death by this conversation.

"The East has all the up-and-coming modern advancements, including women's suffragettes voicing their absurd ideas and encouraging such outlandish activities as the game of tennis for females. Not everything in the East is proper," he finished, making it clear what he thought of women playing tennis.

"I've heard of Mrs. Stanton's Suffrage Association, of course, but what is tennis?"

"Nothing at all for you, Miss Abigail, I assure you," he said distastefully. "Why, it's the most . . . the most unladylike romp that France ever invented! Women actually running and . . . and sweating and swatting at balls with these gut-string rackets."

"It sounds like the Indian game of lacrosse."

"One might expect such behavior out of an uncivilized savage, but the women of the East should know better than to wear shortened hems and shortened sleeves and carry on like . . . well, it's disgraceful! They have lost their sense of decency. Some of them even drink spirits! I much prefer you women out West, who still conform to the old social graces, and for my money I want to see it left that way. Leave the upstart ideas out East where they belong."

He had scarcely stammered at all during that long diatribe.

She realized he was very incensed about the subject. Miss Abigail sat on the porch swing, rocking quietly, and suddenly found herself comparing David Melcher's opinions to those of Jesse DuFrayne on the many occasions he'd encouraged her to set aside her prim and proper ways. She remembered that day up in the hills when he'd taken her hat off for her and teased her about not unbuttoning her wet cuffs. She pictured his dark hand pouring champagne and recalled the loose, easy feeling as it ran through her blood. And then there was that untidy scrap they'd had on that kitchen chair and somehow in the middle of it he'd said he liked her in that old faded shirt . . ."

". . . . don't you agree, Miss Abigail?"

She came out of her reverie to realize David had been expounding upon the virtues of a western woman while she'd been wool-gathering about Jesse, comparing him—and unfavorably yet!—to David.

"Oh, yes," she sat up straight. "I quite agree, I'm sure." But she wasn't even sure what she was agreeing with. Would Jesse's memory always distract her so?

Apparently she had agreed that one o'clock would be a good time for them to meet tomorrow, for he was rising from the swing and making his way across the porch while she followed.

He went down one step, turned, cleared his throat volubly, came back up the same step, fumbled for her hand, and kissed it quickly, then retreated down the step hurriedly.

"Good night, Miss Abigail."

"Thank you for dinner, Mr. Melcher."

For some reason, watching him disappear up the street, she found herself wishing he had not cleared his throat that way or fumbled as he reached for her hand or even kissed *it!* She wished that he might have kissed her mouth instead, and that when he had, she'd have found it preferable to the kisses of Jesse DuFrayne.

Inside, the house was beastly quiet.

She wandered in without even lighting a lamp, listless and dissatisfied. She raised the back of the kissed hand to her lips, trying to draw some feeling from the memory. David Melcher approved of her wholeheartedly, she was sure. She willed that to be enough for now, but the memory of Jesse DuFrayne contraposed every action and mannerism that David had displayed tonight. Why should it be that even though he was gone Jesse had the power to impose himself on her this way? And at the most inopportune times possible? Instead of reveling in David's seeming attraction for her, her joy was blighted by her endless contrasting of the two men in which Jesse invariably came out the winner. With these couple of days so precious, while David remained, she wanted to find him perfect, flawless, incontestable. But Jesse wouldn't let her. Jesse dominated in every way.

Even here in her house, from which he was gone, she found herself listening for his breathing, his yawning, the squeak of the bedsprings as he turned. Perhaps by taking over her old room she could exorcise him. But wandering into it she was smitten by a sense of emptiness for her "gunslinger." The bed was dark and vacant. The pall of silence grew awesome. She dropped down onto the edge of the bed, feeling his absence keenly, knowing a bleakness more complete and sad than that which she had felt at the death of her father.

Twisting at the waist, she suddenly punched one small fist into the pillow he'd occupied so lately, demanding angrily, "Get out of my house, Jesse DuFrayne!"

Only he was out.

She punched the pillow again, her delicate fist creating a thick, muffled sound of loneliness. He's gone, she despaired. He's gone. How could she have grown so used to him that his absence assaulted her by its mere vacuity? She wanted her life back the way it had been before he'd come into it. She wanted to take a man like David Melcher into that old life and forge a relationship of genteel, sensible normalcy, instead she sank both hands into the soft feathers of Jesse's pillow, taking great fistfuls of his absence, her head slung low between her sagging shoulders as she braced there in the gloom.

"Damn you, Jesse!" she shouted at the dark ceiling. "Damn you for ever coming here!"

Then she fell lonely upon his bed, rolling onto her side and hugging his pillow to her stomach while she cried.

Chapter 18

———————

AWAKENING THE FOLLOWING morning, Abbie forgot she was in the house alone. She stretched and rolled over, wondering what to fix Jesse for breakfast. Realizing her mistake, she sat up abruptly and looked around. She was back in her own bedroom—alone.

She flopped back down, studied the ceiling, closed her eyes and admonished herself to be sensible. Life must go on. She could and she would get over Jesse DuFrayne. But she opened her eyes and felt empty. The day had nothing to inspire her to get out of bed.

She spent it trying to scrub every last vestige of Jesse from her bedroom. She washed the smell of him from her sheets, polished his fingerprints from the brass headboard, and fluffed his imprint from the cushions of the window seat. But even so, she could not reclaim the room as her own. He remained present in its memory, possessing each article he'd touched, lingering in each place he'd rested, an unwanted reminder of what he'd been to her.

When her cleaning was done, she had an hour to spare before David would arrive. But the *Junction County Courier* arrived before he did. She heard it thwack upon the porch floor and retrieved it, grateful for any diversion that would keep her mind off Jesse.

Idly, she went back inside, pausing before the umbrella stand and using the folded up newspaper to check the tautness of her chin. But even that longtime, private habit now reminded her of Jesse, standing half-naked in the doorway, teasing, "Is it firm?" Abruptly she turned away from the mirror and snapped the newspaper open, seeking to scatter his memory.

Lotta Crabtree was appearing at the famed Teller Opera House in Central City and would be followed by the great Madjeska.

Another railroad baron had chosen to build his mansion in the vastly popular Colorado Springs, playground of the rich, who flocked there to soak away their ailments in the famous mineral springs.

Some accused train robber . . .

Miss Abigail's eyes widened and her tongue seemed to grow thick in her throat.

ACCUSED TRAIN ROBBER PROVES TO BE OWNER OF RAILROAD

At a meeting Tuesday afternoon in the Stuart's Junction Depot, arbiters debated . . .

It was all there, including the truth about Jesse DuFrayne, which she should have guessed long ago. Standing in the middle of her proper Victorian parlor, Miss Abigail placed the back of a lacy wrist to her throat. Jesse owns the railroad! The man I called train robber *owns* the railroad! And so he has the last laugh after all. But then, didn't he always?

With a mixture of horror and dismay she recalled the awful things she had done to him—the owner of a railroad!

And suddenly she was laughing, raising her delicate chin high, covering her forehead with a palm. The daft, sad sound cracked pitifully into the silence. And when at last it faded away, she was left staring at the article like a glassy-eyed statue, while its significance sank in, while she absorbed what she should have guessed that day Jim Hudson had come. Maybe she had guessed but simply hadn't wanted to admit it could be true. What she read again pounded home the facts in black and white. The article described the meeting right down to the clothing the four men had worn. It described James Hudson as the business agent-co-owner of the railroad, while Jesse DuFrayne was called the hidden partner who oversaw his enterprise from behind the hood of a photographic camera. The meeting itself was described as a "sometimes placid discussion of terms, sparked at times by fiery clashes of animosity between DuFrayne and Melcher over the seemingly alien subject of one Miss Abigail McKenzie, a longtime resident of Stuart's Junction, who had nursed both DuFrayne and Melcher during their convalescence."

As she finished, she stood mortified! By this time she was in a state of anger that would have delighted Jesse DuFrayne.

David Melcher, however, who happened to the door at that precise moment was dismayed when he stepped inside and she gave him a flat slap across his chest with the folded newspaper.

"Mi . . . Miss Abigail, what's wr . . . wrong?" he stammered.

"What's wrong?" she repeated, barely controlling the volume of her voice. "Read this and then ask me what's wrong! I am a respectable woman who must live in this town after you and Mr. DuFrayne have long left it. I do not care to have my name spewed from the lips of every gossipmonger in Stuart's Junction after the two of you saw to it that I made the front page of the newspaper in the most intriguing way possible!"

Perplexed, he glanced at the article, back at her, then silently started reading, finding more in the paper than he had told the newspaper editor.

"Whatever possessed you to argue about me in a meeting with the press present?"

"There was n . . . no press . . . pre . . . present. It was strictly pr . . . private. I . . . he . . . DuFrayne even made me pr . . . promise that no word would l . . . leak out about you."

That surprised her. "Then how did it?" she demanded.

"I . . . I don't know."

"Just what brought my name into a discussion of liability settlements?"

He'd only meant the best for her yesterday and quavered now at the thought that he'd messed everything up so badly.

"I thought he sh . . . should apologize to you for . . . for all he put you through."

She turned her back on him and plucked at her blouse front. "Had it occurred to you that perhaps he might already have done so?"

"Miss Abigail! Are you defending him against me, when it is I who set out to d . . . defend you against him?"

"I am defending no one. I am simply chagrined at finding myself the object of two men's animosity and having it appear in newsprint. I—What will it look like to the people of this town? And why didn't you tell me last night that he is part owner of the railroad?"

He considered her question a moment, then asked, "Does that change your opinion of him now?"

Realizing that if it did she was nothing but a hypocrite, she turned to show David she was sincere.

"No, it doesn't. I simply think you would have told me that the money was coming from him, that's all."

"It's only right that he should pay me. He's the one who shot me."

"But he was *not* robbing that train when he did it. There lies the difference."

"You *are* defending him!" David Melcher accused.

"I am not! I'm defending myself!" Her voice had risen until she was shouting like a fishwife, and when she realized it she suddenly put her fingertips over her lips. She found she'd been haranguing him in the same way she'd done countless times with Jesse. Angry now at Jesse too, she'd attacked David as if he were both of them. To her horror, she found herself anticipating the exhilaration of the fight, welcoming the kind of verbiage Jesse had taught her to enjoy with him.

But David was no Jesse DuFrayne. In fact, David was stunned by her almost baiting attitude and unladylike shouting. His face grew mottled, and he stared at her as if he'd never seen her before. Indeed he hadn't—not like this. In a calm voice, he said, "We are having a fight."

His words brought her to her senses. Chagrined at what she had just caught herself doing, she felt suddenly small and completely in the wrong. She sat down properly on the edge of the settee, looking at the hands she'd clasped tighty in her lap.

"I'm sorry," she said contritely.

He sat down beside her, pleasantly surprised by her change back to the Miss Abigail he knew.

"So am I."

"No, it was my fault. I don't know what came over me to speak to you in such tones. I . . ." But she stumbled to a halt, for it was a lie. She was not sorry, and she did know what had come over her. The ways of Jesse DuFrayne had come over her, for it was as he'd said, fighting was like an emetic. It felt good. It purged.

David spoke softly beside her. "Maybe we wouldn't fight if we didn't . . ." He was going to say "care for each other," but stopped himself in time. It was too soon to say a thing like that, so he finished, ". . . didn't talk about . . . him."

The tension remained between them, each displeased with the other as they sat silently.

After a moment David said, "You know I would not do or say anything to jeopardize your reputation. Why, it would be as good as ruining my own now, don't you see?"

She looked up at him, perched beside her on the settee.

"No, of course you don't see," he continued. "I haven't told you yet. I was going to tell you when I c . . . came to the door, but you were there with that . . . that newspaper and didn't give me a chance."

"Tell me what?"

He smiled boyishly, the soft, brown eyes locked with hers. "That I am going to stay in Stuart's Junction and open a shoe store right here with the money I have coming from the railroad."

Her heart hit the roof of her mouth. Remorse and fear welled in her throat, then drifted through her veins. His words sieved their way downward and dropped hollowly at last into the womb she had begged Jesse DuFrayne to unseal. She'd been so sure no other man would come along in her lifetime to do it. It was all too, too ironic to think that not only had Jesse done her bidding on the very eve of David's return, but had then given David the fistful of money that would enable him to establish himself right here under her nose and court her, when that was now out of the question. What was she supposed to do? Abet the situation when she knew that under no circumstances must she encourage David Melcher now? Furthermore, it was becoming increasingly obvious that he intended to actively court her.

She had been hazed by Jesse DuFrayne for the final, most

humiliating time of all: he had given David the means for marriage while robbing her of the same.

David Melcher watched myriad expressions drift across Miss Abigail's face. At first she looked surprised, then happy, then perplexed, quizzical, stunned, and lastly, he could have sworn that she looked guilty. At what he had no idea. But after watching that parade of emotions, he certainly did not expect her final reaction, which was the placing of her tiny fingers upon her lips as she whispered, "Oh no!"

He was stricken with disappointment at her words. "I thought you'd be happy, Miss Abigail."

"Oh, I am, I am," she said quickly, touching his sleeve. "Oh, how wonderful for you. I know that you're not a man who likes wandering ways." But she did not look at all happy.

"No, I don't. I've wanted to settle in one spot for the longest time. It's just that I never had the means and I never found the right spot." Timidly he took one of her hands. "Now I think I've found both. Will you come with me this afternoon? You could be such a big help. I must arrange to find a place to rent or find some land to put up a place on. There's a corner at the far end of Main Street that I like. You know who to see and where to find people I'd need to talk to, and of course you could introduce me to those I might need to look up. Oh, Miss Abigail," he implored, "come with me. We'll look them all in the eye and make them take back any gossip the paper might have started."

Sensibly, she withdrew her hand and dropped her eyes. "I'm afraid you don't know the people of this town too well. If we show up arranging business agreements together after what was printed in the paper, they'll take nothing back. I'm afraid we would start more gossip than we'll stop."

"I hadn't thought of that, and of course you're right."

She had quite decided to end any budding relationship with him here and now. It would be the best way. But he looked so depressed at her refusal to help him that she felt mean denying him her help. It was true that she could expedite matters for him, for he was a stranger here.

"On the other hand," she procrastinated, "if we were to face the town and show them we are associating solely on a business basis, we might just put the gossip to rout, mightn't we?"

He looked up hopefully, his face suddenly youthfully attractive, like that first day he'd been carried into her house.

"Then you'll come? You'll help me today?"

She controlled the urge to sigh. Whatever was she doing?

"Yes, I'll come. But only as an ambassador, you must understand."

"Oh, of course, of course," he agreed.

David Melcher was a man who left good impressions in his wake. While he and Miss Abigail made business contacts that day, his soft-spoken, likable approach made people realize he was no "slick talker" from the East, as they considered most peddlers to be. Indeed, there were those who said that were it not for Miss Abigail's effrontery Melcher would have gotten nowhere, for he was unpushy and retiring. She, however, opened the way for him in the businesslike manner she always used on the townspeople. If any of them objected to her briskness, they didn't say so. As usual, they treated her—and thus him—with deference. Perhaps it was because they'd grown used to granting her wide berth, perhaps because she had not had an easy life and they all knew it, or perhaps because they were just plain nosy about her relationship to the two men who'd had words over her. For whatever reason, while she and David traversed the town that day they seemed to gain the town's approval and along with it many invitations to attend the following day's Fourth of July celebrations. Indeed, some businessmen seemed more intent upon making sure the two appeared at the morrow's festivities than they were about selling land, leasing property, or discussing lumber prices.

But behind them speculation was rife. That settlement money raised questions they all wished they had answers for. It's no wonder they all said, "Now don't forget to join the fun over in Hake's Meadow tomorrow," or "You're coming, aren't you, Miss Abigail?" or "You're both coming, aren't you?"

Someone else put it more bluntly: "There's to be a basket social and a greased pig contest and log rolling and sack races and what not. Good way for you to get acquainted with all the folks you'll be calling customers afore long, Melcher."

Someone else bid them goodbye by saying, "Bring her over and help us all celebrate. Wagons'll be loading up in front of Avery's store at a quarter to ten or so."

They were also bribed. "It's the only time of the summer you'll find ice cream in Stuart's Junction. You wouldn't want to miss that now, would you?"

But what *they* all really didn't want to miss was a chance to observe Miss Abigail with that new beau she'd apparently taken up with the minute the old one left town. Of course they all knew Melcher was going to be filthy rich on the other guy's money yet. Now who'd've dreamed Miss Abigail would ever become a pants-chaser, and furthermore that she'd make sure those pants had full pockets? 'Course, they all said, it was a fact she was almost clean out of money since her pa died. You couldn't hardly blame the woman. There was that thousand the railroad had paid her, but how long would that last? She was probably just investing in her future, hooking up with Melcher this way. Not a soul in town but couldn't wait to see if the two of them'd show up tomorrow and if she'd seem sweet on him. Nobody could really tell from her businessy attitude today. But tomorrow would be another story!

When he saw her home it was with a mutual feeling of satisfaction. They'd accomplished much in one day. They'd checked out some rental property, found out Nels Nordquist owned the vacant lot next to his saddlery and leather shop, spoken to him about a selling price, checked on the deed at the land office, arranged for blueprints to be drawn up for a simple, single-story frame building with storage at the rear, sales area at the center, and display windows at the fore, and found out whom to see about lumber prices and delivery.

Back at her house now, she led the way to the wicker chairs on the porch.

"I can't thank you enough," he said.

"Nonsense, you were right. I do know everyone in this town and it would have been foolish for you to try to make the necessary contacts alone."

"But you were marvelous. People just seem to . . . to bend to your will."

Before the advent of Jesse DuFrayne in her life she would not have dreamed of replying as she did now. "I tend to cow people and make them afraid of me." She knew it was a graceless, unfeminine admission, and she could see it made David uncomfortable. But she herself felt oddly free after admitting it.

"Nonsense," David said, "a lady like you? Why, you're not . . . pushy."

But she suddenly knew she was and that he did not want to admit it. Pushiness was unfeminine. Ladies should be shyly retiring. But Jesse had taught her much about self-delusion, and she was getting better and better at ridding herself of it.

"It's not nonsense. I'm afraid it's true. However, today it served our purpose, so I shan't complain." Yet it hurt her a little that people opened doors for her because she cowed them while they'd opened doors for David because they instantly liked him.

"There's still so much to be done besides making building decisions. I'll have to take inventory of my stock and put in an order for a much larger number of shoes than I've ever been able to carry with me on the road. And there's the furnishings to order and the awning and the window glass. I'll have to drive out to see about a winter wood supply somewhere—And, oh! I'll need to order a stove from the East and—"

He stopped abruptly, breathlessly, realizing he'd been running on.

But she suddenly looked at him differently and found herself laughing, enjoying his enthusiasm.

"I guess I got carried away by my plans," he admitted sheepishly.

"Yes, you did," she said agreeably, "but you have every right. It's such a big step you're taking. It will take a lot of planning and enthusiasm."

His face suddenly looked worried. "Oh, I didn't mean that I expected you to be running along beside me each step of the way. I wouldn't expect that of you. You've done more than your share today."

But they went on making plans for the store, its furnishing, accoutrements and prospects. He was very animated, but forced himself to sit still and contain his excitement.

Time and again she compared him to Jesse. Jesse with his boundless ego and limited crassness. Never would he sit there like he'd gotten himself caned into that chair seat the way David did. He'd be pacing up and down, probably bellowing, "Goddamnit, Abbie, I know this business can go, and you're going to help it!" Abigail McKenzie! she scolded herself, stop making these unjustifiable comparisons and pay attention to what David is saying!

"It seems we've g . . . gotten ourselves almost . . .
ah . . . expected at the fes . . . festivites tomorrow," he
stammered. "Do you mind?"

She tried not to be annoyed by his lack of assertiveness, but
guilty for having compared him to Jesse all afternoon, she
made up for it by answering, "It's almost a matter of good
business by now, isn't it? No, I don't mind. I attend the
festivities annually anyway. Everybody in town does."

"I . . . ahem . . . we could . . . ah . . . go out together then," he stammered.

It was not at all the way Miss Abigail would like to have
been invited. She was reminded that Jesse had once called
David a milktoast, then kicked herself mentally for being
unfair to him.

"Well . . . if . . . if you'd rather not."

"Oh, I didn't mean— Of course I'll go out with you."

He stood to leave, and she found herself actually quite glad
he was going.

"Where is Hake's Meadow?" he asked.

"It's out northeast of town where Rum Creek broadens. As
you heard earlier, several wagons leave from Avery Holmes's
Dry Goods Store and anyone who wants may ride out from
there."

"At qu . . . quarter to ten?"

"Yes."

"Then I'll come. . . . Should I . . . well, come for you
a little before then?"

"I'll be ready," she replied, growing irritated by his
stammering.

"I'd better be leaving now . . ." His voice had a way of
trailing off uncertainly at the end of phrases, which was
beginning to make her nerves jangle. It seemed that only the
subject of business could wring a positive, assured note from
him. Personal subjects made him stutter and stammer. At the
steps he did it again.

"I . . . I . . . could I . . ."

But he seemed unable to finish, and only looked down at her
with spaniel eyes. She was suddenly very sure that he wanted
to kiss her but didn't dare. Even though she had no business
thinking it, she wondered, Why doesn't he just grab me and do
it? She need not add, like Jesse would. By now she was
comparing every action, every inflection, every mannerism of

the two men. And unbelievably, in each instance she'd found David lacking. It stunned her to realize, while she watched him walk away, that though David's manners were impeccable, she now preferred Jesse's boorishness.

Chapter 19

MISS ABIGAIL DID not approve of everything that went on out at Hake's Meadow on the Fourth of July, but she was always in attendance nevertheless. She had a feeling for patriotism, and this was a patriotic holiday, though somehow it always seemed to turn into one sprawling, noisy beer-soaked melee. Each year it started with the mayor's inept speech while children held flags, but before long the politicians lost ground to beer and the ribaldry that inevitably followed. For the beer flowed as freely as did the baked beans tended by the D.A.R. members, who cooked them in an open fifty-gallon drum. It was, too, a perennial joke that had those D.A.R.s stirred up a few drums of their infamous beans back in 1776 and fed them to the British, they might have cut the war short by seven years. And when those beans merged with beer . . . well, rumor had it that Royal Gorge was no natural wonder; it was ripped out one Fourth of July when the picnic was held down there instead of at Hake's Meadow.

There were battles of every sort imaginable—some scheduled, some not. Rum Creek slid coolly out of the mountains and slithered to a halt above a beaver dam, creating Hake's Pond, where loggers from up mountain whupped the hell out of every aspiring log roller and tree skinner from Stuart's

Junction, who later returned the favor at horsehoes and chasing a greased pig.

Then, too, there was the kissing, which grew more uninhibited as the day wore on and people just seemed to do it whenever and with whomever they could manage. Of course, the darker it got, the easier it was to manage.

The whole affair started at ten A.M. and officially ended with the ten P.M. fireworks display, unofficially when the last roaring drunk was hauled home by his wife, still singing loudly and probably more amorous than he'd been since last Fourth of July.

Miss Abigail had brought a basket for the basket social—her way of joining wholeheartedly in the festivities. She deposited it with all the others under a huge oak tree where the bidding was always done. She wore her daisy-trimmed hat, as usual, and a dove gray dress with matching overjacket of simple lines, which fairly clung to her skin by eleven o'clock. David Melcher, in a brown day suit, white shirt, and string tie, grew equally as hot as the sun rose toward its apex.

The two of them were sitting in the shade sipping sarsaparilla.

"Don't you drink beer?" she asked.

"I never developed a taste for it, I guess."

"Beer, as you've probably already guessed, is the drink of the day here, though I've never been able to understand why these men don't stop at their quota. On the Fourth of July they just don't seem to. Look! Look at Mr. Diggens. He's the one in the blue shirt who is challenging that logger twice his size. Is it the beer that makes him believe he can actually beat that logger at arm wrestling?"

They watched the mismatched contestants across the way as the pair knelt on either side of a stump, and of course the smaller Mr. Diggens lost, though he came up laughing and gamely warned the huge, strapping logger, "A few more beers and I beat you good!"

"Is that so!" the logger bellowed. "Well, let's get 'em into you then!" And before Diggens could protest, the logger lifted him bodily as if he were a bride being carried across a threshhold and carried him to the beer kegs, ballyhooing, "Feed my friend here some beer, Ivan. I want to see him beat me!"

A shout of laughter went up from the crowd and the logger

took off his shirt, tied it by its sleeves around his waist, and stood like Paul Bunyan himself, drinking beer beside the dwarfed Diggens, as if waiting for him to suddenly sprout up and grow bigger.

Looking on, Miss Abigail and David joined in the laughter.

"As you can see, these little duels enhance the real contest which will all take place this afternoon," Miss Abigail explained.

David's eyes scanned the area. "I've never been much at physical things," he admitted unabashedly.

"Neither has Diggens, I'm afraid."

Then, as their eyes met, they both burst into laughter again.

"I think the speech makers are losing their audience," he noted some time later. Most of the listeners had drifted away from the pondside as soon as the mayor had finished his windy oratory.

"They'd rather listen to the nonsense at the beer kegs."

Another bit of revelry had started up there. Now the hairy-chested logger who'd tied his shirt around his waist was curtseying with that same shirt to Diggens before the two embraced and began a ridiculous impromptu dance while a fiddle scraped in the background. As they spun, beer flew out of their mugs, splattering two young women, who jumped back and shrieked joyously, only to be profusely apologized to by the men. The girls giggled as the logger again made his ridiculous curtsey to them.

"Something just seems to come over people out here on the Fourth of July," Miss Abigail said, unbuttoning her overjacket, which was becoming unbearable in the heat.

"It's a beautiful spot. It makes me happy all over again that I decided to stay in Stuart's Junction. These people . . . they were all so nice to me yesterday. I can't help but feel like I'm welcome here."

"Why shouldn't you be? Don't you think they know that your new business is going to be an asset to this town?"

"Do you think so? Do you really think it will succeed?"

He was very transparent. At times he displayed an almost childish need of her support and encouragement.

"Can you think of a thing more necessary than shoes? Why, just look at all those feet out there." She turned to survey the picnic grounds. A bunch of little boys scuffled under a nearby tree, playing some sort of rugby game they had improvised, kicking at a stuffed bag with curled-toed boots; a mother passed by, leading a little girl who was wailing over a stubbed, bare toe; the mother herself wore down-at-the-heel oxfords, long in need of replacing. "Look at the beating all those shoes are taking. Chances are that later every one of these people will come directly to your store to buy new ones."

He beamed at the thought, spinning visions of the future, but at that moment they were approached by a giant of a man wearing the familiar logger's uniform of loose-slung britches, black suspenders, and a red plaid shirt.

"Hey there, Melcher, you're the man I'm looking for!" A huge, hairy, friendly paw was extended. "Michael Morneau's the name. I hear you'll be needing some timber for a building you aim to put up. I'm the man's got just what you need. I brung you a beer so we can talk about it friendly like."

David Melcher found himself pulled to his feet and a beer slapped into his hand.

To Miss Abigail, the amiable logger said, "Hope you don't mind, lady, if we mix a little business with pleasure. I'll bring him right back." A big arm circled David's shoulders and herded him away. "Come on over here, Melcher. Got some people I want you to meet."

Miss Abigail saw how David was rather bulldozed into drinking that beer. It was more than a drink—it was the symbol of goodwill among those men who swilled together in great camaraderie. Even from this distance she could tell when they talked business, from the forgotten way the mugs hung in their hands. But when some point was agreed upon, up in the air went the beers before everyone, including David, drank.

She watched his brown shoulders buffeted along among the mixture of shirts: red plaids, white businesses, even some yellowed union suits, and into each new group came fresh beer. Once he caught her eye across the expanse of meadow and made a gesture of helpless apology for abandoning her, but she shrugged and smiled and swished her hand to tell him not to worry. She was fine. She sat contentedly watching all the commotion around her. David was concluding more business arrangements and gathering more goodwill among the beer swillers than he could garner in a fortnight of selling quality shoes or beating the boardwalks downtown.

So Miss Abigail wandered off to watch the children's sack races.

Rob Nelson came running past but shied to a halt when he saw her.

"Howdy, Miss Abigail."

"Hello, Robert. Are you entering the sack race?"

"Sure am."

"Well, good luck to you then."

There was something different about Miss Abigail today. She didn't look like she just ate a pickle.

"Thank y', ma'am," the boy said, spinning away only to screech to a halt and return, squinting up at her, scratching his head, something obviously on his mind.

"What is it, Robert?"

"Well, y' know them there straws I brung you that time for that train robber?" He watched for danger signs, but she looked kind of young and pretty and her mouth kind of fell open and she touched her blouse where her heart was.

"Yes?"

"Did they work?"

"Why, yes they did, Robert, and I want to thank you very much for getting them."

"What'd you do with 'em?"

To Rob's surprise, Miss Abigail smiled and leaned down conspiratorially. "I blew soup into him," she whispered near his ear. She straightened then. "Now run along to your race."

But Rob didn't move. Just stood there slack-mouthed, in wonder. "*You* blew soup into a *train robber*, Miss Abigail?" he asked incredulously.

"He wasn't a train robber after all."

"Oh," Robert said shortly, then looked thoughtful before stuffing his hands into his pants pockets and saying, "You know, he really didn't look much like a train robber in those pajama pants."

Now it was Miss Abigail's turn to go slack-jawed. Horrified, she spun Rob about by the shoulders, controlling the urge to paddle his little backside. "Robert Nelson, don't you dare repeat that to a single living soul, do you hear? Now git!"

And the impetuous child ran off toward the sack race, trailing a burlap bag as he ran.

But when he was gone she crossed an arm upon her waist, rested her elbow upon it, and lightly covered her smiling mouth. Her shoulders shook mirthfully as she recaptured the

picture of Jesse stumping around in pajama pants much too
short for him.

"Is something funny, Miss Abigail?"

"Oh, Doctor Dougherty, hello. I was just enjoying the
children's sack races."

"I've been meaning to get up to your place and thank you
for all you did. You sure helped me out of a pickle."

"I was only too happy to help."

"Did that man behave himself and put that gun away? I sure
didn't mean to put you in any ticklish spots by returning it to
him."

"Oh, it's all over and done with now, water under the
bridge." But she refused to meet his eyes, squinted into the sun
instead to watch the races now in full swing.

"Yup!" he agreed, following her eyes to the jumping,
writhing boys, some now sprawled out on their stomachs,
struggling to regain their feet. "I heard you got paid real
well."

Her eyes snapped to him. Only the doc would have the
temerity to come right out with a thing like that. "Everybody
in this town hears everything," she said.

"Yup," he agreed, "and what they don't hear, they damn
well guess at."

"I hear Gertie got back from Fairplay," she said quickly,
changing the subject.

"Yeah, she's got my office running slicker'n a greased pig
again. And I heard you were all over town yesterday
introducing that Melcher around and blazing trails for him to
open up a new business."

"That's right. This town owes him that much, I think."

"Why so?"

It was an odd question. She gave him a puzzled look. But
Doc had drawn a penknife from his pocket and was calmly
cleaning his nails as he went on. "Seems to me we owe Jesse
something if we owe anybody. Folks around here were mighty
nasty about even letting him off his own train in our midst. If it
weren't for you he could've rotted right there on it, for all they
cared. And all the time it's his railroad that's brought new
prosperity to Stuart's Junction. Just goes to show how wrong
about a person you can be."

Doc didn't so much as glance at Miss Abigail, just snapped
his penknife shut, tucked it away in a baggy pocket, and

glanced out toward the sack races, where a lad lay humped up on the ground clutching his stomach. "Well," Doc murmured, as if ruminating to himself, "guess I'd better go see if I can get the scare out of him and the wind back in." And he shambled off to the rescue, leaving Miss Abigail to wonder just how much he guessed about her relationship with Jesse.

As she watched Doc moving toward the boy, she remembered the night she'd had the wind knocked out of her, and of the things which had followed, and she thought about Doc's words, "Just goes to show how wrong about a person you can be."

"Miss Abigail, I've been looking all over for you," David said, making her jump. She gasped and put a hand to her heart. "I'm sorry, I didn't mean to scare you."

"Oh, I was just daydreaming, that's all."

"Come. They're going to auction off the baskets now. You've been standing here in the sun too long. Your face is all red."

But it was memories of Jesse which had heightened her color, and she was grateful that David could not read her mind. He took her by the arm to where the crowd had gathered under the huge, sprawling oak for the pairing off and picnicking. He continued to hold her elbow as the auctioning began, and she could smell the yeastiness about him from the beer he'd drunk. Now and then he'd weave a bit unsteadily, but he was apparently sober enough to recognize the napkin that matched her kitchen curtains peeking out from under the lid of her picnic basket. When it came up for bids, he raised a looping arm and called out, "Seventy-five cents!"

"Way to go!" Someone slapped him on the back and he barely retained his stance. Then some unseen voice hollered, "That's Miss Abigail's basket, Melcher. Bid 'em up!"

Laughter, good-natured and teasing, went up, and her cheeks grew pinker.

"A dollar!" came the second bid.

"A dollar ten!" called David.

"Hell, that ain't no way to pay back a lady that saved your life! A dollar twenty!"

David rocked back on his heels, grinning quite drunkenly.

From the crowd someone hollered, "Melcher, you ain't too drunk to see Miss Abigail's colors flying from under that there basket lid, are you?"

"A dollar and a quarter!" Melcher thought he shouted, only he hiccuped in the middle and it came out, "A dollar and a quor-horter!" raising a whoop of laughter.

The auctioneer bawled, "Anybody got more'n a dollar and a *quor-horter* for this here basket?" Laughter billowed and so did Miss Abigail's blush.

"Sold!"

The gavel smacked down, and from all around rose catcalls, whistles, and hoots. David just grinned.

"Give 'er hell, David!" someone encouraged as David made his unsteady way forward to get the basket. As he passed Michael Morneau, a hand steered David and steadied him while the lumberman laughed, "We got all that business taken care of. Time for a little fun now, eh, Melcher?"

Miss Abigail thought David would never make it to that basket and back again, but soon he returned, offering an arm, leading her proudly. She was as red as a raspberry by now, moving through the crowd, being watched by the entire town while he plunked the basket down in the shade of a nearby tree. Finally the bidding resumed and drew people's attention away from them for the time being.

She knelt and opened the lid of the basket and began taking food out while he dropped to his knees, bracing his hands onto his thighs.

"Miss Abigail, I have to beg your forgi-hiveness," he hiccuped. "I said I-hime no beer drinker, but the bo-hoys took me in hand. I thought it'd be good business to mingle with the boys a li-hittle."

She was embarrassed by the entire scene, but still there was something unblamable about his tipsy state. She remembered all too well how easily she herself had gotten that way on a "thimbleful of champagne." She suddenly couldn't find it in her heart to be angry with him.

He sat with head hung low, hands still grasping thighs—a disconsolate drunk having a staring contest with the ground between his knees. Now and then he would quietly hiccup behind closed lips. She went about calmly laying out their food.

"I'm really sorry. I shouldn't have left you alone like tha-hat."

"Here. If you eat a little something, those hiccups will stop."

He looked at the piece of fried chicken she extended as if trying to identify what it was.

"Here," she repeated, gesturing with the drumstick as if to wake him up. "I'm not angry."

He looked up dumbly. "You're naw-hot?"

"No, but I will be if you don't take this thing and begin eating so people will stop staring at us."

"Oh . . . oh, sure." he said, taking the drumstick very carefully, as if it were porcelain. He bit into it, looked around, then stupidly waved the piece of meat toward a clump of gawking people as if signaling, "Hey there . . . how's it goin'?"

"You know, I really don't like beer," he mumbled to the chicken.

"Yes, so you told me. And as I told you, something just seems to come over people out here on the Fourth of July."

"But I shouldn't have drunk so much."

"Something good seems to have come of it though, hasn't it? I believe you've had your initiation today and now you truly are an accepted member of the community."

"Do you really think so?" He looked up, surprised.

"When you sat down here do you remember what you said? You said something about *the boys* insisting you have another beer."

"Did I say that?"

"Yes you did, just as if you were one of them."

He raised his eyebrows foolishly and grinned. "Well now, maybe I am, maybe I am." Then after a long pause, "Wouldn't that be somethin'?"

"I have a feeling that at first some of the men around here took you for the usual high and mighty easterner . . . and a peddler to boot. That combination doesn't always meet with the approval of Stuart's Junction's businessmen. I wouldn't be surprised if they actually set you up to see if you'd pass their rites."

"Do you think so?" He continued to ask dumb, rhetorical questions but she could not help smiling because he was obviously abashed at his state . . . and it was funny in its own way.

"Oh, I'm only guessing. Don't be alarmed. If they did set you up, it'll be for this once only, and my guess is you already passed muster."

"Do you think so?" he asked again, in the exact dumb tone he'd used all the other times.

"Well, you got some business handled in between beers, didn't you? Or wasn't that what all those raised glasses were all about?"

"Come to think of it, I did." He looked astounded.

"Well then, where's the loss?"

Even in his drunkenness he was touched by her magnanimity. "You're being awfully understanding, Miss Abigail, considering how embarrassed you must have been during the bidding."

"Would you like to know a secret?" she asked.

"A secret?"

"Mm-hmm." She tilted her head sideways, a mischievous look in her eye. "Today was nothing compared to the year that Mr. Binley bought my picnic basket."

"Bones Binley?" he asked, amazed. His mouth hung open, displaying a bite of chicken.

"Yes . . . one and the same."

"Bones Binley bought your basket?" The chicken fell out and she hid her laughter behind her hand and came up smiling.

"Aha. It sounds like a tongue twister, doesn't it?" There was no artful coyness in her admission whatsoever. It simply seemed easier for her to erase his discomfiture and have a pleasant day than to hold him responsible for the teasing of the townspeople and the fact that they'd coerced him into getting drunk.

"Bones Binley with the tobacco and the brown teeth at the feedstore all day long spitting?"

It *was* funny, although she'd never seen it as funny before. She rocked forward on her knees, smiling, chuckling as she remembered. "It's funny, isn't it? But it wasn't then. He . . . he bought my basket and nobody teased him at all. It was horrible, just horrible, walking through the crowd with him. And he's looked at me with cow eyes ever since."

"Musta been your fried chicken that did it." He was sobering up a little bit by now, but was still elevated enough to laugh at his joke. Then he sucked at his greasy fingers and they happened to be both laughing when another contingent came past with a basket of their own. Frank Adney waved to David as he passed, calling, "Sounds like she's not too mad after all, eh, David?" Then he tipped the brim of his hat up briefly at her. "No hard feelings, Miss Abigail?"

"None at all, Mr. Adney." She smiled back. Frank was surprised to see what a pretty woman Miss Abigail actually was with that smile on her face and laughing the way she was. He mentioned so to his wife, and she agreed as they moved away.

Miss Abigail, watching the Adneys move on, felt suddenly more a part of the town than ever before. David, watching her, felt expansive and wonderful. In two short days he'd melded into both the social and business environment of Stuart's Junction with an almost magical smoothness, and it was all due to her support.

"Miss Abigail?"

"Yes?" She looked up.

"I love this chicken, and the deviled eggs too." What he really thought he loved was her.

Suddenly she realized that all of this was simply too, too enjoyable and that she should not be encouraging him with smiles and laughter this way.

"You've lost your suit jacket somewhere," she observed.

Looking down at his chest he acted surprised to find it clad only in shirt and tie. "It's out there somewhere." He waved the chicken at the world at large. "It'll be around when I need it. It's too hot anyway for all that. Don't you want to take your jacket off?"

Informality breeding familiarity, she knew she shouldn't. But it was ghastly hot, and she'd been schooled by Jesse to rid herself of her too-rigid proprieties. She tried not to think of how pleased he'd be if he could see the change in her today. "It is awfully hot," she said, beginning to shrug the garment off.

David quickly used his napkin and walked on his knees, coming to help her out of it.

"Yes, that's much better," she said, laying it across the top of the picnic basket, swiping a hand upward from the nape of her neck to tuck up absolutely nothing; her hair was perfectly in place.

He had finished eating but still felt very mellow from the beer and stretched out on the grass, relaxed. He wondered how it would feel to lay his head in her lap. Instead, he said, "Tomorrow I'm supposed to go up to the logging camp and put in an order with Morneau for some lumber at the mill. But I don't know where it is for sure."

"It's about halfway up that ridge over there," she said, pointing and squinting, conscious of his eyes on her.

He liked the way the shade dappled her forehead when she raised her head to look at the ridge.

"Would you . . ." he began, but stopped. Should he simply invite her out for a ride or tell her he needed her help to find the place? She seemed to shy away from anything personal, but as long as he kept things on a business basis, she was more amenable. "Could you come along and show me where to find it?"

She wanted to say yes, but said instead, "Tomorrow I must do the ironing."

"Oh," he replied flatly. He lay there considering her while she began to pack up the remnants of their meal. Finally he said, "If it didn't take you all day maybe you could make it in the afternoon?"

She was pleased about one thing regarding the beer: since he'd been under its influence he'd stopped stammering. It almost made her break down and say yes, but again she realized she had no right to involve herself with him, not anymore.

"No. I simply can't make it at all," she said crisply, continuing to fuss with the picnic basket.

Rebuffed, he immediately sat up. Her abrupt changes of mood confused him. A minute ago she'd been very amiable, but suddenly she became cold and terse, refusing to look at him.

"I said before that I didn't expect you to follow me hand and foot through this entire opening up of the business, and now here I am, asking you again, the first thing. I shouldn't have asked."

Once again she felt irritated by the way David extended his invitation. Even though she knew better than to encourage him, she wished he would not always dream up an excuse to be with him. Female vanity, she chided herself, remembering the way Jesse had goaded and teased her into taking her for a ride. She put Jesse firmly from her mind, wishing he'd stay away.

As if to make up for his transgression, David asked, "Do you want some ice cream?"

But she was preoccupied, irritated with herself for leading

David on, and at David for not being manly enough to lead her on. It was all very confusing.

"Do you?"

She came out of her maunderings to find him standing beside her. She blinked once, hypnotically. "What?"

"I asked, do you want some ice cream," he repeated. "It's ready." He was handsome and polite and unassuming, and she stared up his body for a moment, confused by the sharp comings and goings of feelings she experienced for him.

"Yes, please," she said, sorry that she'd snapped at him.

The smile was gone from his face as he turned and limped away, only to remind her again of Jesse limping away from her down the street the last time she saw him.

David was thoroughly confused by Miss Abigail since he'd come back to Stuart's Junction. Her quicksilver mood changes were totally different from the steady, sweet woman she had been before. There were times when he swore she liked him—more than liked him—and other times that cold light would come into her gaze, making him sure that she cared nothing at all for him.

But he was reminded again of what she could mean to him when he was served ahead of the children who'd been waiting their turns around the ice cream churn. The whole town seemed to treat him solicitously! Even the fat woman who scooped out ice cream and served him out of turn.

"You tell Mizz Abigail I picked them peaches myself last fall. Tell her Fanny Hastings says she brought a real swell feller here when she brung you," the ingratiating woman said, her dimples disappearing into her plump cheeks.

He thanked the woman and picked his way back to Miss Abigail, wondering what mood she would be in now.

He stood above her, smitten all over again with her cool, calm ladylike demeanor, studying her breasts beneath the high-necked blouse.

"Fanny Hastings says to tell you she picked the peaches for the ice cream herself."

Abbie looked up and reached for his peace offering, knowing by the look in his face that he thought he'd done something wrong, something to upset her, when it was she who continuously upset herself these days. And because he truly had done nothing wrong, and because Jesse DuFrayne refused to free her from the grip of memory, and because there was such a whipped-pup look in David's eyes as he offered her the streaming ice cream, she said, "Mr. Melcher, I believe I'll have time to show you the way to the mill tomorrow after all."

His face was immediately transformed into cherubic radiance. She realized when he smiled so quickly, so joyfully, how little it took for her to make him happy. Gratitude and admiration shone from his eyes at each little bit of attention she showed him.

This man, she realized, could be manipulated by nothing more than a smile. It should have been a heady thought, but it left her inexplicably unexcited. Still, she made up her mind she would be nice to him for the rest of the day, because he did not deserve to suffer the consequences of her constant thoughts of Jessy DuFrayne.

"Let's go watch the tree skinners choose up sides," she suggested, reaching a hand up to him. Like a grateful puppy, he helped her to her feet, his expression one of devotion.

David Melcher's initiation had only begun with the morning draught session and the subsequent bidding on the picnic baskets. Being the subject of much conjecture, he was greeted profusely wherever he and Miss Abigail went. Each greeting was enhanced in cordiality by the offer of a mug of beer, and just like that morning, David found his hand filled with a sweating glass through the entire afternoon, through no wish of his own. It was understood that Miss Abigail would not drink beer, but the mere fact that she accompanied David while he did seemed to make Miss Abigail more human in the eyes of the citizens of Stuart's Junction. At times she was actually seen smiling and laughing, and the townswomen took note of this, poking their elbows into one another's ribs, winking. And hour by hour, David became increasingly inebriated, and more thoroughly accepted.

Before the end of the day, Miss Abigail too felt herself accepted in a way she'd never been before. The women included her in their plans for the next meeting of the Ladies of Diligence Sewing Circle, gave her an apron and a spatula when the pie eating contest took place, kept her in their cheering circle when David participated with their men, and took her by the elbow as they moved to the more rowdy contests. David participated in everything—the sack jousting, pole climbing, Indian wrestling, and even the tobacco spitting contest. And he was a miserable failure at everything he tried. But only if success was measured by the official contest results, for in goodwill he was the greatest achiever of the day. The fact that he tried all the contests, in spite of his lost toe, in spite of his limp, in spite of the fact that he was assured of a loss even before he started, endeared him to the men. And the fact that he had wrought such a change in Miss Abigail endeared both of them to the women.

David was finally forced to desist at the final event of the day, the log rolling contest. It took the nimblest of feet and a perfection of balance to even enter the event—obviously he lacked both. He had been slapped on the back and hugged by more than one of the log rollers, though, as they slogged out of the pond, defeated, dripping, laughing. Thus, by the time he at last returned to Miss Abigail he was as wet as if he'd participated himself. He was roaring drunk too, stained with tobacco and pie, reeking to high heaven of beer—an unequivocal mess. In this deplorable state he was carried to Miss Abigail's side, to where she was working with the women who were putting away pie tins, picking up forks and glasses, and distributing picnic baskets to their rightful owners.

"Miss Abigail," roared Michael Morneau, "this man is the best goddamn sport that ever got a toe shot off!"

The women noticed how she didn't so much as bat an eyelash at the word *goddamn*. Instead she turned to find the disheveled David actually borne to her on the shoulders of the well oiled men who were to be his cohorts for as long as he chose to live in this town. They were all laughing, staggering, singing, swaggering, arms around each other so that if one of them leaned to the left, the lot of them leaned. Swaying back to the right, the lot of them swayed.

"Town's got a helluva wunnerful newcomer here, ain't that right, Jim?"

Whomever Jim was, he roared even louder than his companions and drunkenly doubled the motion. "Damn right, and we got Miss Abigail here to thank for bringin' him in! Ain't that right, boys?"

More amiable cussing and approval followed, and Miss Abigail looked up to where David swayed on their shoulders.

"See? We brung him back to you, Miss Abigail." But the inebriated speaker seemed unable to locate David all of a sudden and looked around searchingly. "Didn't we?" he asked, raising another hullabaloo. "Where the hell'd we put 'im?"

"I'm up here!" called a grinning David from his perch on the men's shoulders.

The one who'd been searching looked up. "There you are! Well, how the hell'd you git up there?"

"Why, you dummy, we was bringin' him back to Miss Abigail, remember?" another voice slurred while somebody stumbled and the gleeful band swayed, *en masse*, in the other direction.

"Well, put 'im down then, 'cause here she is!"

She could see it happening even before it actually did. One minute David was up there smiling like a besotted wall-eyed pike, the next minute the shoulders separated almost as if choreographed—half in one direction, half in another. Like the Red Sea they parted, dropping David Melcher, still smiling and waving, down the chasm. Miss Abigail saw him coming and gasped, then lurched futilely to save him. He fell, octopus-like, a tangle of jellied arms and legs, but just as he plummeted, she gained the cleft in the human sea and David's disappearing shoulder caught her on the side of the neck and down she went with him! She landed flat on top of him, arms and legs splayed in the most unladylike fashion imaginable.

As soon as the crowd realized what had happened, solicitous hands reached toward the pair of casualties piled up in their midst. The men "ooh-ed." The women clucked. But David, with that pikey grin still all over his face, opened his eyes to find Miss Abigail McKenzie's face smack in front of him—and Lord! if she wasn't lying on top of him! Her hair was falling sideways out of its knot, her breasts were smashed against his damp, beery shirtfront, her blue eyes were startled, and her cheeks were a darling pink. He didn't care how she got there, or when. This was just too good a chance to miss.

He threw two very loose-jointed arms around her and kissed her so long and hard he thought he'd throw up for lack of wind and dizziness and the bump his head had just suffered.

Miss Abigail felt his arms tighten and saw his lopsided grin become even more lopsided, and she knew beyond a doubt what he was going to do, but she could not scramble off of him in time to prevent it. She felt her hair go sliding to hang over their two cheeks as he kissed her with the smell of tobacco juice and beer and sweat and cherry pies all around them.

And suddenly she was aware that a great, pulsing roar of applause had burst out. Even the ladies were clapping and cheering. Men whistled through their teeth and kids came scrambling among long legs and petticoats to see what was going on within the circle.

"Atta boy, David, give it to 'er!" somebody yelled.

Miss Abigail pushed and rolled and finally broke free, tumbled to the dirt, and sat beside him. She was positively scorching! But what made the final difference, what everyone could not quite believe they were seeing, was the way she burst out laughing, trying to hide her blushing cheeks behind a small, uncharacteristically grimy hand. Sitting there in the dirt, she reached both hands toward the hovering men and said, "Well, are you going to stand there applauding all day or is somebody going to help me up?"

Everyone was laughing with her as they tugged her to her feet, followed by David. The ladies fussily dusted off her skirts and scolded their foolish husbands. But secretly they were all well pleased. Miss Abigail, it seemed, wasn't the stick-in-the-mud she'd seemed all these years, and David—why, he was perfect for her. Every citizen of the town congratulated himself on what a tidy bit of matchmaking had been accomplished here today. From that moment on David Melcher and Abigail McKenzie were accepted not individually, but as a pair.

She felt it happening all day long, the curious tide of that acceptance. It was a new feeling to her, one that had been denied to Abigail McKenzie all her single life. The subtle change that had started that morning had grown more palpable as the day wore on. If she were to try to define it she could not, in her vast store of words, find just the right ones to describe the exclusion of the single person from the immutable charmed circle of those who live life two by two. Only in retrospect did she feel it fully. Not until the end of this day during which she had felt so much included did she realize how much she had been excluded until now.

Basking in the glow of the feeling she found herself again beside David Melcher, seated on the ground beneath the deep blue night sky of Hake's Meadow. Legs stretched out before them, faces raised, they watched the intermittent bursts of fireworks that illuminated both them and the sky.

From the corner of her eye she could see that David was watching her.

"I ought not to have . . . have kissed you that way," he stammered, sobering for the second time that day, admiring her chin, nose, and cheeks as explosions came and went. She kept her face raised, but said nothing. "I . . . I didn't exactly know . . . what I was doing."

"Didn't you?" she asked.

He looked up as a skyrocket exploded. "I mean, I had too much beer."

"Like everyone else."

He took heart. "You're not . . . you're not angry?"

"No."

The two of them leaned back, elbows stiff, palms on the grass behind them. He edged one hand sideways until his fingers touched hers, and when the next firefall burst, he saw that she was smiling up at the sky.

David's fingers were warm, his eyes upon her admiring. She was filled with a sense of well-being from the day they'd shared and wondered, when they reached the doorstep would he kiss her?

On the ride back to town aboard the crowded wagon, David held her hand as they sat side by side on a bundle of hay, their hands concealed beneath the folds of her skirt. Their hands grew very damp and once he released hers and wiped his palm on his pant leg, then found her fingers again beneath the skirt of dove gray. She thought of Jesse, of his straightforward moves so unlike David's unsure ones. Guiltily, then, as David's hand returned to hers she squeezed it.

He walked her home when the buckboard unloaded, but there were others walking their way so he kept his distance. At her door, with hammering heart, he took her hand once again in his damp one.

"I . . . ." he began, but stopped, as usual.

She wished he would simply say what he was thinking, without these false starts. He's not Jesse, she reminded herself, give him time.

"Thank you," he said in the end, and dropped her hand, stepping back as the Nelsons came home next door.

"I didn't do anything deserving thanks," she said quietly, disappointed that he'd dropped her hand.

"Yes you did."

"What?"

"Well . . ." He seemed to search his mind a moment. "How about the picnic?" He spied the basket on the porch floor.

She said nothing.

"You . . . you did more, Miss Abigail, you know you did. You m . . . made . . . m . . . me accepted in Stuart's Junction today."

The night was quiet, contentment seemed to spread around Abbie like a comfortable warm wind. "No, you made me accepted."

"I . . . I . . . what?"

She looked down at her hands and joined them together. "I've lived here all my life and have never felt as much a part of this town as I do right now. You did that for me today, Mr. Melcher."

He suddenly took both of her hands again. "Why, that's what I feel like. Like . . . like I've found my home at last."

"You have," she assured him, "one where you are liked by everyone."

"Everyone?" he swallowed as he asked.

"Yes, everyone."

He stood squeezing her hands a long time and she heard him swallow again. His hands were much smaller than Jesse's. She tried not to compare them. Kiss me, she thought. Kiss me and chase him from my mind.

But he could not gather the courage, sober as he was now. And he knew he was in a sorry state, smelling of beer and tobacco, clothing soiled and damp.

"You'll show me the way to the mill tomorrow?" he asked.

"Certainly. The sooner the building goes up, the sooner you'll be open for business."

"Yes."

He let her hands go, disappointing her immensely, for she knew by the way he did it that he'd rather have continued holding them.

Jesse would have held them.

Damn you, Jesse, leave us alone.

"I had a marvelous day," she urged, finding an almost compulsive need within her to be kissed by this man, although perhaps not solely for the right reasons.

But David only said, "So did I," then wished her good night and turned to go.

Her heart fell. She was doomed to another night of thoughts of Jesse after all. Wearily, she went to the swing and sat there in the dark, listening to the sound of David's irregular footsteps retreating up the gravel street. Soon he moved beyond earshot and the sound of his steps was replaced by the gentle creaking of ropes as she nudged the swing. A cricket answered the ropes. She stared hypnotically up the dark street, saw not dark street but dark moustache instead.

David . . . Jesse . . . David . . . Jesse . . .

David, why didn't you kiss me?

Jesse, why did you?

David, would I have let you?

Jesse, why did I let you?

David, what if you knew about Jesse?

Jesse, if it weren't for you there'd be nothing for David to know. Why didn't you force me to leave your room that night as any gentleman should have? Why did I force my way in as a lady should not have? All it has brought me is pain. No, that's not true, it brought me David, who is all the gentle, refined and likable things I ever wanted in my life. Why must I compare him to you, Jesse DuFrayne? Why should he have to measure up to you, who did everything wrong from start to finish? David, David, I'm sorry . . . believe me. How could I know that you would come back? What would it do to you, with your gentle nature, if you learned the truth about me? Why do I find fault with you for being hesitant and polite and being a gentleman? Jesse was fast and rude and nothing gentlemanly whatsoever and I hated it . . .

Ah, but not at the last . . . not at the last, her disloyal body claimed.

She crossed an arm over her stomach, rested an elbow on it, and cradled her forehead tiredly, trying to forget.

The swing ropes squeaked rhythmically, and memory descended mercilessly. A bare chest showing behind the open buttons of a shirt, an arm slung along the back of a swing, a smile that began slowly at the corner of a moustache, hands upon her skin, lips and tongue upon her skin.

At the instant tears gathered in the corners of her eyes, she realized that her breasts were puckered up like tight little rosebuds.

Get out of my life, Jesse DuFrayne! Do you hear me! Get off my swing and out of my bed so I may go to it in peace again.

Chapter 20

THE TOWNSPEOPLE GREW accustomed to seeing Miss Abigail and David together in the days that followed. The two of them spent long hours making the many decisions necessary for establishing a new business from the ground up. The day after the picnic, when they showed up at Silver Pine Mill, Miss Abigail was right beside David as the arrangements for the sale of lumber were handled. Demonstrating her keen business acumen, she secured his lumber at a better price than he'd have gotten on his own by insisting that they be shown the less desirable knotted pine, which brought the price down. These, she wisely noted, were good enough for building storage shelves at the rear of the building.

The plate glass for the windows, which would be shipped by train from Ohio, would have been one of their most expensive commodities had they purchased plates of the large size he envisioned. She suggested instead that they order numerous small panes that could be shipped at a far smaller price due to the fact that they were far less liable to break in transit. Thus the plan for a flat, cold, indifferent storefront was scrapped in favor of a warm, inviting Cape Cod bow window, the first Main Street was to boast. In the words of Miss Abigail, why not let women ogle the shoes from three directions instead of just one? Perhaps they could sell three times as many that way.

While the store's first studs began rising she marched one day down to the feedstore and presented Bones Binley with a proposition he found impossible to refuse: she would furnish him and his cronies with a picnic basket each day for seven days if during that time they could whittle a set of twenty-eight matched spools of which a railing would be made for the back of the display window. The railing, rather than a wall, would allow the window display items to be seen from inside the store while at the same time creating a warm, inviting atmosphere when viewed from outside.

When it was announced at services one Sunday that pews had finally been ordered for the church, she suggested to David that they see about purchasing the old wooden benches at a fraction of what new chairs would have cost. This done, she next raided Avery Holmes's back room and came up with a dusty bolt of sturdy rep that had been lying there untouched for years simply because it was bright scarlet. She considered scarlet the perfect color to lend the shoe store the interior warmth she was striving for. She talked Avery into selling her the entire bolt at a ridiculously low price and left him feeling only too glad that he'd unloaded it at last. Afterward, she talked the ladies of the sewing circle into experimenting with upholstering, which none of them had ever tried before. They padded and covered the old church benches with the red rep, all the while thanking Miss Abigail for giving them a chance to try their hand at this new craft.

The bolt of rep seemed to have no end. When the benches were completed, there were still yards and yards left. Abbie fashioned simple, flat curtain panels with which to frame the bow window, to be tied back, giving the whole display a stagelike affect. Still she hadn't run out of the red fabric, so the remainder of the bolt she began tearing into strips whenever she found time, to be used later in braided rugs for in front of the door and before the iron stove at the rear of the store.

As August neared and the building took shape, Abbie and David worked together on the massive order that needed placing with the factory in Philadelphia for the first stocking of the shelves. The heat remained intense, the air seeming always to carry its low haze of dust motes. One such late afternoon the two of them were in the coolest spot they could find: on the grass out under the linden tree in Abbie's backyard, with ledgers, lists, and catalogues spread all about them.

"But you have to think about winter coming!" Abbie was insisting. "Be practical, David. If you were to place an order from your company only, for nothing but high-fashion shoes, you'll lose out on the far greater share of your potential business."

"I've always sold fine, up-to-date shoes," he argued. "People can buy boots in a dry goods store—so let them."

"But why lose their business?"

"Because I don't think I'll need it. I'll have all the business I need selling the more fashionable styles I've always handled."

"Maybe in the East you would, and maybe traveling in a circuit like you did in the past, because what you carried was a novelty and those who saw them thought they'd lose the chance to buy such shoes once you moved on. But out here, in one place, you'll need to suit all needs. Work boots would be your best seller of all."

"But how will work boots look in that lovely little Cape Cod window you talked me into?"

"Horrible!"

He blinked at her questioningly. "Well?"

Immediately she was planning: she was always filled with fresh ideas. "Well . . . we'll put them in the back of the store, in a spot more suited to them. We'll display them where the men will feel more comfortable looking at them. That's it!" she exclaimed, the idea suddenly gelling. "We'll make a spot exclusively for the men! Men are so funny that way, they like to have a spot of their own. We'll get a few captain's chairs like the ones out in front of Mitch's feedstore and we'll circle them around the stove and . . . and . . . let's see . . ." She pondered again, placing a finger against her teeth. "We'll make it homey and masculine both at once—a red rug in the middle of the circle of chairs, and maybe we can display the boots in a masculine way that's attractive and takes a little of the dullness away."

"I don't know," David said doubtfully.

She became impatient with him and jumped up, spilling ledgers and scattering notes and papers. "Oh, David, be sensible!"

"I am being sensible. This town already has an outlet for work boots and everyday shoes. I specialize in fashionable

shoes and they are what I know how to sell. It's the ladies I
want to appeal to. When they see what is in the front window, I
want them to run straight home and exclaim to their husbands,
'Guess what I saw today!' "

Abbie stood very still now, hands on her hips, challenging
him. "And what exactly will they describe?"

"Well, the window display, of course, filled with the kind of
shoes that appeal to their vanity or maybe their husband's
vanities. Heavenly shoes the likes of which they've never seen
in their lives, straight from the East."

Whether or not it was wise, she asked, "Red shoes?"

"What?" He blinked up at her.

"Red shoes, I said. Will they be describing red shoes?"

"Why . . . why, yes, some of them. Red shoes just like
yours."

But they both knew she'd never worn those red shoes since
that one and only night when he'd taken her out to dinner.

"You . . . you like the red shoes, d . . . don't you,
Abigail?"

She came near him and squatted down, her skirt forming a
billowy mushroom about her as she reached to lay an arm upon
his sleeve. "Please understand, David. I like them because
they are from you, but I . . ."

When she hesitated, he insisted, "Go on."

She looked into his face, then away, then nervously stood up
and turned her back on him. "Do you know what . . . what
Mr. DuFrayne said when he saw them?"

David instantly bristled at the mention of DuFrayne. "What
does DuFrayne have to do with it?"

"He was here the day they arrived, as you know."
Resolutely she turned to face David before adding, "He called
them strumpet's shoes." David's face burned and his lips
pursed.

"Why do you bring him up? What does it matter what he
thinks?"

Her tone became imploring. "Because I want your business
to succeed. I want you to realize that here in Stuart's Junction
people don't wear red shoes, but they wear a lot of work boots
and sensible utility shoes. If you are going to succeed, it is
imperative that you understand. In the East, where bright
colors are all the rage, it is perfectly acceptable to sell them and
to wear them. It's different here. You look at those colors from

the salesman's point of view. People here, particularly women, are far more conservative. No matter how much they might even secretly admire them, most of these women would not dream of purchasing them. That is the only reason I repeated Mr. DuFrayne's comment, because it symbolizes the views of the town.''

"Abigail." His mouth was pinched, his jaw rigid. He had completely forgotten the reason for her soliloquy. Only one thing now possessed his thoughts. "Are you saying he called you a strumpet?"

Without thinking, she replied, "Oh, no, he was just jealous, that's all."

David jumped to his feet, snapping, "What?"

She tried to make light of it, realizing her mistake. "We're getting off the subject. We were speaking of the most sensible shoes for you to order."

"*You* were speaking of the most sensible shoes for me to order. *I* was speaking of why DuFrayne should have cause to feel jealous. Was there something between you two after all?" David Melcher became strangely self-assured and glib-tongued whenever DuFrayne's name came up. He possessed a firm authority which was missing at other times.

"No!" she exclaimed—too fast—then, calming herself, repeated more quietly, "No . . . there was nothing between us. He was hateful and inconsiderate and insulting whenever he got the chance to be." But she knew that wasn't entirely true, and she could not meet David's eyes.

"Then why should he care one way or another if I sent you a pair of strumpet's shoes? After that scene on the bed the morning I left, I should think he'd be the type to applaud red shoes, if what you say is true and they really are considered inappropriate.''

Unwittingly, David had hit on one of those inconsistencies about Jesse DuFrayne that rankled her still, all these weeks after he had left. It was disconcerting to have it put into words by someone else when it was in her thoughts so often, seemingly inexpressible.

"I cannot answer for him," she said, "and I don't think it's your place to upbraid me. After all, you and I are nothing more than—" But she suddenly came up short, chagrined at herself. She dropped her eyes and fidgeted with the button on her cuff. She really did not know what she and David were to each other.

He had been the epitome of politeness in the weeks they'd been working together on plans for the store. The only change—and it was natural—was that they'd begun using each other's first names. He'd made no further attempt to kiss her or even hold her hand. In no other way did he indicate that he was wooing her. She supposed that he thought he'd offended her by getting drunk and kissing her that way before the entire populace of Stuart's Junction on the Fourth of July and was making amends by his extreme politeness since then.

Again with that aura of authority, he said unequivocally, "I don't want that man's name mentioned between us again, Abigail."

Her eyes came up sharply to meet his. By what right did he give her orders? They were not betrothed.

Suddenly David softened. The wind lifted the brown hair from his forehead, and the expression about his eyes grew wistful. He stood with his weight on his good leg—he often did that, perhaps because his other foot gave him discomfort—and it lent him a relaxed look, especially when he had the thumb and forefinger of one hand hidden inside his vest pocket, where he carried his watch.

"Abigail, what were you going to say just then? That you and I are no more than what? You didn't finish."

But how could she finish? It had been a slip of the tongue. He should be the one to finish, to understand what it was she had meant. She had grown so used to being with him, and she enjoyed him most of the time. Now and then she thought of her lost virginity and the fact that she should cease encouraging David, but as time went on she thought of it less and less. Still, he never made any advances toward her or even acted as if he thought about doing so. They shared a platonic relationship at most. And so Abbie thought up a likely answer for him.

"I was going to say business partners, but I guess we're not even that. The business is yours." She could not quite meet his eyes.

"I feel like it's half yours too. You've done as much or m . . . more than I." He began to stammer as soon as the subject broached anything personal. While speaking of the store his enthusiasm kept his voice steady. But now, perilously close to clarifying his relationship with Abigail, he grew timorous again.

"I've done no more than any friend would do," she said humbly, hoping he would deny it.

"No, Abigail, you've done much more. I don't know how I could have done it all without you. You . . . your judgments are m . . . much better than mine."

She waited with her heart in her throat, wondering if he'd go on to more personal things, but she could sense his shyness—for some men it is not easy to be the man in a situation like this. The silence lengthened between them and became uncomfortable and she could see he'd lost his nerve.

"We still haven't agreed on the ordering of the stock," she said, and the moment of discomfort passed.

"Something tells me I should trust your judgment again on this."

"There is room at the rear of the store for boots. I am also very sure that we'll sell more of them if we do it the way I've envisioned it. Come to the store and we'll look around and I'll show you just where we could put the boot section and how we'll plan it."

"Now?"

"Why not?"

"But it's Sunday."

"So it is, and there'll be no noisy hammering and banging and we should be able to talk in peace and study the possibilities."

He smiled, conceding. "You're right. Let's go."

She no longer wore her hat and gloves when the weather was too hot for them. They walked uptown in the late-day sun, nodding hello to an occasional neighbor who now called an amiable greeting to both of them. "Afternoon, David, Miss Abigail. How you doin'?" There were times when Miss Abigail already felt married to him.

The skeleton of the building was up. It had walls and part of a roof, but inside the studs showed. The framework of the bow window lay in wait of panes, and there was no front door yet. The interior walls were to be of tin wainscot above the shelves—the stacks of wainscot lay amid sawhorses and planks.

Abigail picked her way among pails of nails, stacks of shelving, the carved posts Bones and the boys had already completed. "See here?" At the rear of the building she pointed to a spot where a hole had been left for the chimney pipe.

"Now here's where the stove will be. Suppose we cut some giant rounds of oak and leave them, bark and all, just as they come from the woods. We'll put them here near the stove and set the rugged work boots on the wood to add just the right touch of masculinity. A basket of nuts here, the ring of sturdy chairs around the stove, or leaning up against the wall behind it, almost as if reserved for each man. Why, they'll love it! Men love it near a stove. Women get enough of stoves working in their kitchens, so we'll put their shoes up front where it's cool, in the display window surrounded by the spooled railing. And while it might be true that no woman around here might like the color red on her shoes, they will find it cheerful and gay when it is brightening up the store as a background for displays. Imagine it at Christmas with the fire snapping and a hot pot of coffee back here on the stove for the men. We could invite them to leave their mugs right here, hanging on the wall on pegs. We'll sell boots all right, and plenty of them. At the same time the ladies will be up front oohing and aahing over your fancy shoes, and gossiping, away from their husbands."

Abigail didn't know it, but carried away as she was by her plans for the store, her face had taken on the same lovely look that Jesse had discovered upon it the day the red shoes came. Neither did she realize she had said "*we'll* sell boots all right." Her face was animated, bright-eyed and radiant. And just as Jesse DuFrayne had been moved by it weeks ago, David Melcher was moved by it now. The hem of Abigail's skirt had stirred up sawdust in the air, and the sun, glinting down through the chimney hole and half-finished roof, caught it in hovering cantles as she gestured, moved, turned, and spoke. She raised a hand to point at where the coffee pot would be, bubbling away on a winter stove . . . and David forgot the summer heat, imagined her here then, helping the ladies select shoes, bringing her enthusiasm along with her good business sense. He imagined helping the husbands while he told their ladies, "My wife will help you up front."

And suddenly he knew it could not possibly be any other way.

She swung around and he surprised her hand by capturing it in mid-air. For a moment the words stuck in his timid throat. The sawdust drifted around them like summer snow, settling here and there on their shoulders. It was silent and wood-scented and private. And he loved her very much.

"Abigail . . ." he said, then swallowed.

"Yes, David?"

"Abigail, may I . . . k . . . kiss you?" He had made so many blunders with her already that he thought it best to ask first.

She wished he had not asked. Jesse would not have asked. Afraid David might have read the unwanted thought, she lowered her lashes. Instead, he took it for her demure refusal and dropped her hand.

"I'm sorry . . ." he began.

Her eyes flew back up. "How can you be sorry?" she asked quickly. "You haven't done anything." It was unreasonable for her to feel piqued when all he meant to do was be polite, but enough was enough!

"I . . . do . . . don't . . . " he stammered, but her reply had confused him so, he didn't know what to do.

"Yes, you may kiss me, David."

But by now the situation had lost the grace that a spontaneous kiss would have lent. In spite of this, he took both of her hands and leaned toward her. There was a short piece of planking between their feet, but rather than move around it or step over it to take her in his arms, he leaned over the barrier and, with closed eyes, gently placed his lips over hers.

He had fine, soft, warm, shapely lips. And she thought, what a shame he does not know how to use them.

He laid them over hers for a wasting flight of seconds while Abigail felt absolutely nothing. The talk about how they should display the shoes had excited her more than his kiss. He straightened then and remained perfectly silent, as silent as his kiss had been. She gazed down at the sawdust beneath their feet, at the plank which separated them, thinking it might as well have been between their torsos as well as there on the floor for all the contact there'd been during that kiss. A kiss of the lips only, she determined, was a decidedly unsatisfying thing. So she raised her lips to David's again and dared to put her hand behind his neck for a brief moment. But the kiss was brief, and immediately afterward David said the appropriate thing.

"Shall we go?"

She wanted to say, "No, let's try that again without the plank between us. Let's try that again with a little tongue." But he finally came around the plank and took her elbow, leading her toward the nonexistent door. She could tell, though, that the kiss had flustered him, for he talked nervously all the way home, about how she was right and he'd immediately put in an order for boots so they would arrive in time for the planned October opening, about how there might even be snow by then and he'd better get his wood stacked in the back, and how they would plan a special announcement in the paper, even though everyone in town knew the store would open and when.

He refused to stay for supper, which he'd done quite often recently—indeed, suppers together had become the rule rather than the exception—but collected his materials and left, insisting that he'd better get started putting the order on paper.

That night she tried to analyze her feelings toward David Melcher, to sort out her reasons for encouraging him as she had today. By now she was sure that she was not pregnant, so the biggest potential obstacle to their relationship had been removed. Oddly enough, the overwhelming guilt she had once felt no longer riddled her. She had performed an immoral act, but she did not think she had to pay for it for the rest of her life. She did deserve some happiness, and if David Melcher offered it to her, she no longer believed she'd be deceiving him to take him up on it.

No, her problem with David was no longer a problem of morality, it was one of sexuality. She simply was not stimulated by him. She tried not to think of Jesse . . . oh, she really, really tried. But it did not work. Being kissed as she had been by David, it was impossible not to contrast his kisses with that of the practiced, the fiery, the tempting Jesse. Vivid memories came flooding back until they swept everything from her mind except her intimate knowledge of him. She knew every part of his body as well as she did her own, and it no longer seemed shameful to admit it. She thought of each part of it, wondering if the importance of sexual attraction would wane in time if she married David. Ah, but David had not asked her. Ah, but David would. It would take a little more time, but she was sure he would. And when he did, what would she say? No—I won't marry you because you don't make my blood run high like Jesse? Or yes—because in every other way we are compatible. She thought, as she lay awake into the wee hours, that if she could entice David into displaying more ardor, she might at least have a larger basis of comparison between him and Jesse DuFrayne.

* * *

The following evening David accepted her invitation to supper. It was a pleasant meal, shared at her kitchen table in the familiar way they had so often shared such meals. Over coffee, David was hugely complimentary, as he always was.

"What a delicious meal. Everything you make is always delicious. It warms more than a man's stomach."

If she was going to contrast the two men, then let her do it truthfully, and garner for herself an honest choice about them. She let the voice of Jesse echo back, with its infernal teasing, which at the time had so galled her but which now only tempted. "And what are you planning to poison me with this time, Abbie?" She was unaware of the lingering smile the memory brought to her lips.

"Did I say something funny?" David asked, noting it.

"What?" She brought herself back to the present—regretfully.

"You were laughing just then. What were you thinking?"

"I wasn't laughing."

"Well, your shoulders were moving as if you were laughing inside."

She shook her head. "It was nothing. I'm just glad you enjoyed your supper."

Her answer appeased him. He pushed his chair back from the table, suggesting, "I thought maybe we'd read some of your sonnets after supper. That's all it would take to make the evening perfect."

Why all of a sudden did sonnets sound as dry as his kisses had been?

"You always say the nicest things," she said to atone for the errant thought. I really must be more fair to him, she promised herself, for it was not he who had changed. It was she.

They read sonnets, he sitting on the settee and she sitting on a stiff side chair. The lamps were lit, they had nothing to do but enjoy the verses together. But he sensed an impatience, almost a relief, in her when they finally put the book aside. He puzzled once again at the change he sometimes sensed in her, a restlessness that continued to intrude upon the tranquility he loved and sought.

He kissed her good night. A chaste kiss, David thought. A dry kiss, Abbie thought.

Several days later they sat on the swing in the early evening.

September was upon them, the hint of winter not far behind it.

"Something has been . . . bo . . . bothering you, has . . . hasn't it?"

"Bothering me?" But her tone was sharp. She was working on the strips for the rugs, and her hands tore and rolled the rags almost frantically.

"I can tell that I displease you, but I d . . . don't know what it is that br . . . brings it on."

"Don't be silly, David," she said reprovingly. "You don't displease me at all. Quite the contrary."

She ripped a long strip of the cloth, her eyes never leaving it, and the harsh sound scraped on his nerves. He wished that she would stop the rag work while they talked.

"There's no need for you to . . . t . . . try to be kind by disguising it. I would only like t . . . to know what it is that bothers you."

"Nothing, I said!" Her hands were a blur, winding the strips up into a ball. How could she say that everyone in town was expecting the two of them to get married and that she'd give anything if only he would ask her, yet feared more each day that he would? Just how could she explain such a confusion of thoughts to him when she couldn't straighten it out for herself.

Quietly he reached out to lay a hand over hers, which were furiously rolling those rag strips into a tight, tight ball.

"Whatever it is that you call nothing is a very large lump of something. Much larger than I thought. You're winding those rags like you wish they were choking somebody. Is it me?"

She dropped the rag ball into her lap and her forehead onto the heel of her hand, but said not one word.

He sat staring down at the tattered red threads that lay all over her lap like a web. "It started that d . . . day I asked if I could k . . . k . . . kiss you. I could tell you were disgusted w . . . with me. Is that it, Abigail? Are you angry b . . . because I k . . . kissed you?"

She tapped her fingers against her forehead and looked at her lap, not knowing what to say. She didn't know if she wanted him to pursue this subject or not. How could she tell after those two lackluster kisses?

"Oh, David . . ." She sighed heavily and looked away, across the yard.

"What is it? What have I done?" he asked pleadingly.

"You haven't done anything," she said, now wishing

fervently that he would so she could know once and for all what she felt for him.

"Abigail, when I first came here I sensed a . . . a rapport between us. I thought you felt it too. I thought how we were the same k . . . kind of people, but . . . well, since I've been back you seem d . . . different."

It was time she admitted the truth.

"I am," she said tiredly.

"How?" he braved.

The tiredness left her and she jumped to her feet, snapping in irritation, "I don't like sonnets anymore." The rag ball rolled onto the porch floor, untwining, but she paid it not the scantest attention. She crossed her arms over her ribs and left him to contemplate her erect shoulder blades.

He sat staring at them, thoroughly befuddled. In a moment she entered the parlor, slamming the screen door shut behind her. He remained on the swing for some time, wondering just what she wanted out of him, wondering what sonnets had to do with anything. Finally he sighed, rose, and limped to the door. He opened it quietly and entered to find her standing before the monstrous throne-shaped umbrella stand, gazing at her reflection in the mirror. As he watched she did a most curious thing. She raised a hand and pressed the backs of her fingers upward against the skin on her jaw, studying the movement in the glass.

"What are you doing?" he asked.

She did not answer immediately, but continued pressing her chin. At last she dropped the hand as if she were very weary, then turned to him with a sad expression on her face, and answered almost dolefully, "Wishing you might kiss me again."

His lips opened slightly and she could almost see his thoughts drift across his transparent face: he'd been worried for so long that he'd gone too far, kissing her in the store that day. He was relieved yet timid, perhaps a tiny bit shocked that she should ask him. But at last he moved toward her, and she read one last look in his face—awe that she should really, really want him.

This time there was no plank between them, but when he kissed her he still held her undemandingly, fragilely. It was like before, only worse, because now, without hindrance, he could have pulled her flush against him, but he didn't. He held her instead in a wan imitation of an embrace, afraid to believe his lips were on hers at last, and with her full consent.

Suddenly she needed to know about David Melcher, about herself. She lifted her arms and they swirled onto his shoulders as she raised up on tiptoe and offered her lips to him with feigned passion. She pressed her breasts against his vested chest, but rather than accepting her invitation he sucked in his breath, taking himself away from the touch of her, afraid the contact was too intimate yet.

"Abigail, I've thought about this for so long," he said, looking into her eyes. "I thought about you and the house and the store and everything, and it just seemed too good to be true to think that you might feel the same about me as I do about you."

"How do you feel, David?" she asked, trying to force the words from him.

He released her fully, properly, stepping back and holding her only by her upper arms. "I want to marry you and live here in this house and work in the store with you by my side."

She had the sinking feeling that he desired all three equally. She had the even more sinking feeling that she did, too.

"I love you," he said then, and added, "I guess I should have said that first."

What could she say to that? Yes, you should have? Tell me again and kiss me and pull me against you and touch my body here and here and inspire me to love you also? Touch my skin, touch my hair, touch my heart and make it race and touch my breast and make my blood pound and touch me beneath my skirt and show me you're as good at it as another man was before you?

But the cool fact was, none of these things happened. He did not kiss her passionately or pull her against him or touch her hair or heart or breast or any other part of her as Jesse had done. Instead, he drew back, gave her shoulders a loving squeeze, contolling all his body's urges with a will that she suddenly detested. He waited for her reply. She moved to him and kissed him, allowing her lips to grow lax, to be opened by his tongue should he choose. But his soft lips remained together, guarded by discretion.

But discretion was the last thing she yearned for. She longed to be reduced—no, heightened—by the ecstasy she knew could sluice through her body should he wield it in just the right way.

But standing in David's hands she thought, He's not Jesse. He'll never be Jesse.

But might that not cease to matter? Here he was, offering her safe keeping for life. One did not decline an offer of marriage simply because of the way a man kissed or didn't kiss. She ought to be flattered by his courtliness, not be insulted by it. But Jesse had managed to change her sense of values somewhere along the line.

"There's time enough for you to decide," David was saying. "You don't have to answer me tonight. After all, I know this is a bit sudden."

She had the awful urge to laugh aloud. She had known him over three months and her blouse buttons had never touched his vest, yet he thought his chaste kiss and this invitation sudden.

What would he think if he knew that in three weeks she'd touched every part of Jesse DuFrayne's body and had pleaded with him to take her to the limits?

"Are you sure you want to marry me?" Abigail asked David, knowing it was not him but herself she should be asking.

"I've been quite sure since the day you threw me out after I accused—" But there he stopped, not wanting to bring DuFrayne's name into it, not realizing it had been in it all the time. "Can you forgive me for what I accused you of? I was very foolish and very jealous myself that morning. I know now that you're not at all that kind of woman. You're pure and fine and good . . . and that's why I love you."

If ever there was a point of no return, it was now. Now, when his words could easily be denied if they were going to be. But deny them she did not. She kept her silence, knowing that even it was a lie.

David gave her shoulders one last squeeze. "Besides," he said in a light attempt at gaiety, "what would my store be without you?"

But again she wondered if he did not value her more because she could help in his store, and because he could live in her house, than he did because she could be his wife.

"David, I'm very proud to have been asked. I'd like to think about it, though, at least overnight."

He nodded understandingly, then pulled her toward him by her shoulders and kissed her on the forehead before leaving. He left her standing next to the umbrella stand. For a long moment she stared disconsolately at nothing. Finally she turned her head and confronted her reflection, admitting once and for all how old she was getting. She sighed deeply, rubbed the small of her back, and went out onto the porch to collect the rag ball and rewind it mechanically as she wandered aimlessly into her bedroom. She stood beside the window seat winding, winding, remembering Jesse sitting here that afternoon after Jim Hudson left. She dropped the ball into the sewing basket on the floor, remembering how Jesse had taken a hank of yarn from it to tie up that pig bladder with which he had so mercilessly teased her. She pictured his long-fingered hands, dark of skin, gentle of touch, flexing on that inflated bladder, flexing upon her own breast. She thought of David, afraid to pull her against him as he kissed her on the eve of his marriage proposal to her.

She sighed, dropped down onto the window seat, leaned her elbows to her knees, cupped her face in both hands, and cried.

Fortunately, during that night good common sense took over and made Abigail realize that David Melcher was a decent, honest man who would treat her decently, honestly for the rest of her life. She, too, could offer the same, from here on out. Whether it was scheming or not to consider it, she admitted that David, in his naiveté, would probably not know whether or not she was a virgin anyway. If she were mistaken about that, she would tell him it was Richard, those many years ago. If her marriage had to begin with that one, last lie, it was a necessary lie—necessary to prevent David's being hurt any further. And since there was no chance of her ever falling into promiscuity again, her decision was made.

David kissed her tenderly, if dryly, when she told him that she was accepting his proposal. Standing in his light embrace, she felt a sense of relief that the decision was made. This time he did hug her to his chest, but his eyes were scanning her front parlor.

"Abigail, we're going to be so happy here," he said near her temple. A deep sense of peace overcame him here in her house.

"You'll have roots at last," she returned.

"Yes, thanks to you."

And to Jesse DuFrayne, she thought, but she said, "And the citizens of Stuart's Junction."

"I think they were half expecting us to get married."

"I know they were, especially after the Fourth of July."

He released her, smiling his very youngish smile. "When shall we announce it?"

She looked thoughtful for a moment, then quirked an eyebrow. "How about in Thursday's paper? Mr. Riley started all this when he linked my name with yours in June. Shall we give him the opportunity to print the ensuing chapter?"

The announcement in Thursday's paper read:

> Miss Abigail McKenzie and Mr. David Melcher happily announce their intentions to be married on October 20, 1879, in Christ Church, Stuart's Junction. Miss McKenzie, a lifetime resident of this town, is the daughter of the late Andrew and Martha McKenzie. Mr. Melcher, formerly of Philadelphia, Pennsylvania, has traveled for several years in this area as a circuit salesman for the Hi-Style Shoe Company of that city. Upon marriage to Miss McKenzie, Melcher will open for business in the Melcher Shoe Salon, the edifice currently under construction at the south end of Main Street directly adjacent to Perkins' Livery Stable. The business is slated to open its doors immediately upon the couple's return from a two-week honeymoon in Colorado Springs.

The first frosts came. The quaking aspens blanketed the hills with brilliant splashes of amber. Mornings, even the cart ruts were beautiful, trimmed in rime, glistening in the touch of new light. Sunsets turned the color of melons and became jaggedly streaked with purple, presaging the cold breath of winter soon to follow. The mourning doves left; the nuthatches stayed. Weather eyes were cast at the mountains as the first leaves tumbled like golden gems to the earth.

A flood of good wishes poured into Miss Abigail's house and David's store, which was fast nearing completion. Neighbors and townsfolk could not resist stopping at one place or the other when passing by. Their good wishes reaffirmed to Abigail that she had done the right thing in accepting David's proposal.

It was easy and natural now to be with David, and daily they reaffirmed the fact that they were very much alike in ideals, likes, dislikes, goals. He was a totally adoring suitor, ever ready with a compliment, a smile, a look which told her he approved of her in every way. His kisses became more ardent, which pleased her, but his immense respect for her kept improper advances at bay. He stammered less and less as they became more familiar with each other. This newfound ease pleased her immeasurably.

Often as not, David and Abigail could be found at the shoe store, stacking a winter supply of wood at the rear, staining the lovely spooled rail, building shelves, hanging red draperies in the bow window, carrying in the huge oak rounds, or unpacking a partial shipment of stock, which had finally arrived. They worked together constantly, becoming a fixture of the small town's society even before their wedding took place. Those who stopped by to say hello or to ask if they needed a hand with anything went their way again thinking they'd never seen a pair more suited to each other; it really was a match made in heaven. Some chuckled, patting themselves on the back, thinking, well, if not in heaven, then at Hake's Meadow.

Abigail was a mistress of efficiency as the wedding day neared. Besides helping David make preparations for the opening of the store, there were countless personal details demanding her attention. She had decided to wear her mother's wedding gown of ivory silk, but it needed alterations. The lace veil was in excellent condition. However, some of the seed pearls had come loose from the headpiece and needed replacing, thus it had been' sent to a jeweler in Denver for renovation. David had ordered a special pair of white satin pumps for her and she anxiously awaited both headpiece and shoes. Once the entire bridal ensemble was in her possession, she would pose for a photograph—her bridal gift to David. She contracted a Denver photographer, Damon Smith, to come out to do the portrait. They'd planned to have a wedding reception at the house, and Abbie began baking cookies and *petits fours*, freezing them now that frosts had come to stay. The garden was cleaned out until spring. The little iron stove was installed in the store, and the coffee pot there was already a fixture. She was often happy to have it, for between the store and the house, her duties kept her juggling her precious time and attention between wedding and grand opening preparations.

The store was turning out beautifully. There, it seemed, was where Abigail and David shared their closest intimacies. Times when they found themselves alone, stocking shelves in the storeroom, he would steal kisses, making her impatient for their wedding day to arrive . . . and, more importantly, their honeymoon. There were times when she knew he was on the brink of breaking down his own self-imposed restrictions, but either he would back away or they would be interrupted, for people came in and out of the store as if it were already open for business.

The interior was as bright, warm, and cheerful as she'd imagined it, with its red curtains, braided rugs, and upholstered benches. The circle of comfortable chairs wreathed the fireplace where a cheering blaze beckoned. The smell of fresh wood and bark permeated the air, combined with coffee, leather, and the clean smell of shoe wax. People loved it and there were always friends gathered around the stove. There was not a doubt in the world that the business would thrive, or the marriage either.

Chapter 21

IT WAS ONE of those dark, steely late afternoons when the thought of supper in a toasty kitchen made footsteps hurry homeward. The murky clouds played games with the top of the mountain, gathering, scattering—wind-whipped shreds scudding in a darksome sky, making all mortals feel lowly indeed.

The bell and the pearl headpiece had arrived from Denver. Bones Binley had walked the packages up from the depot after the late train pulled through. Pleased, Abigail now donned her new green coat, wrapped a matching scarf about her head, and flung its tails back over her shoulders. Smiling, she left the house with the small brass bell tucked warmly in her white fur muff.

Snow flecks stung her forehead and the wind sent the scarf tails slapping about her cheeks. She shivered. David would already have the lanterns lit at the store. The stove would be warm, and she pictured David standing with one foot braced on its fender, a cup of coffee in his hand. Oh, he would be pleased that she'd thought of the bell. She skipped once and hurried on.

Coming around the corner of the saloon, she stepped up onto the boardwalk and the wind shifted, hitting her full in the face, driving icy needles of snow against her skin. She glanced down the street at the welcome orange lanternlight spilling from the bow window. A man was standing looking in through the small panes, a big man in a heavy sheepskin jacket with its collar turned up and his hands plunged deep into its pockets. He stood motionless, bareheaded, with his back to her, while for some inexplicable reason her footsteps slowed. Then he hung his head low, stared at his boots a moment before turning toward the livery stable next door and disappearing inside. He was very tall, very broad. From behind he'd reminded her of Jesse, except that he had no limp. Once more she hurried, keeping her eyes on the door of the livery stable, but no one came out as she advanced toward the door of the store, above which hung a fresh, new sign, swinging wildly in the wind.

MELCHER'S SHOE SALON, it said, DAVID AND ABIGAIL MELCHER, PROPS.

It was lusciously warm in the store. As usual, there was a circle of men around the stove, David among them, sipping coffee.

He came forward immediately to greet her. "Hello, Abigail. You should have stayed at the house. There's weather brewing out there."

She radiated toward the stove, removing her coat, scarf, and muff, tossing them onto a red-padded bench along the way.

"I had to come to tell you the good news. My headpiece came back from Denver this afternoon, all repaired at last."

"Good!" David exclaimed, then winking at his cronies around the stove, added, "Now maybe I won't have to listen to her fretting about that photograph anymore." The men chuckled and sipped.

"And look what else came." She held up the tinkling, brass bell. "It's for your door—a good luck charm. Every new store must have a bell to announce its first customer."

David smiled in genuine delight and set his coffee cup down, coming to squeeze and chafe her upper arms affectionately. "It's just the right touch. Thank you, Abigail." The smile on his face made her feel treasured and precious. "Here," he said, "let me hang it."

"Oh, no," she said pertly, lifting the bell out of his reach, "it's my gift. I shall do the hanging."

David laughed, turning back to the men. "Never saw such a nuisance of a woman—always wants her own way."

"Well, David, you just gotta learn to step on 'er a little bit when she gets outta line." Then the men all laughed in easy camaraderie. They could do that now, laugh at Miss Abigail this way—she had changed so much since David Melcher came around.

She got a hammer and tacks from the back room and hauled one of the chairs up near the front door. The bell tinkled as she climbed up, reaching toward the sill above the door to find the perfect spot for the bracket. But even on the chair she couldn't quite reach, so she put one foot up on the spooled railing beside her and stepped onto it.

That was how Jesse DuFrayne saw her when he came out of the livery stable and stopped again before the shop with the sign reading, . . . DAVID AND ABIGAIL MELCHER . . .

She had two tacks in her mouth and was holding the brass bracket against the doorframe, hammer poised, when she saw a man's legs stop outside the Cape Cod window. With her arms raised that way she could not see his face, but she saw cowboy boots, dark-clad legs spraddled wide against the wind, and the bottom half of a thick, old sheepskin jacket. Something made her duck down to peer beneath her sleeve at the face above those wide-braced legs.

Her eyes widened and one of the nails fell from her lips. An agonizing, wonderful, horrible terror filled her heart.

Jesse! My God, no . . . Jesse.

He was gazing up at her with that big sheepskin collar turned high around his jaw while the wind caught at his thick black hair, whipping it like the dark clouds above the mountain. The lantern glow coming through the window illuminated his face and kindled his dark, intense eyes that were raised in an unsmiling study of her. It lit, too, his forehead, cheeks, and chin, making them stand out starkly against the stormy darkness behind him. His moustache was as black as a crow's wing, and as she stared, hammer forgotten in hand, he smiled just a little and lifted one bare hand from his pocket in silent hello. But still she seemed unable to move, to do anything more than gape as if struck dumb, filled with pounding emotions, all at odds with each other.

Then one of the men behind her asked how she was doing up there, and she came back to life, turning to look over her shoulder at the stove and mutter something. When she looked outside again, Jesse had stepped back beyond the circle of window light, but she could still see his boots and knew he stood there watching her with those jet black eyes and his old familiar half grin.

She scuttled down to search for the tack on the floor, but couldn't find it, so clambered back up again and started hammering the one she had, ever conscious now of the angle from which he studied her, the way her breasts thrust out against her dress front and jiggled with each fall of the hammer.

The other tack winked at her from inside the spooled railing and she climbed down to retrieve it, unable to keep her eyes from seeking the waiting figure beyond the window. For a moment she stood framed by red curtains, like a dumbstruck mannequin on display, quite unable to move her limbs or draw her eyes away from the dim figure who watched from the street, frowning as the wind tried to blow him over.

Jesse, go away, she pleaded silently, terrified of his pull on her.

Somehow her limbs found their ability to move, and she climbed up on the railing again and pounded in the second nail, her heart cracking against her ribs in rhythm with the hammer.

David came from the rear of the store then, admiring her handiwork.

"Should we hang the bell together?" he asked.

"Yes, let's," she choked, hoping he would not note the hysteria in her voice. "That way it will bring good luck to both of us." She could see now that Jesse's legs were gone and wondered if David had spied them out there.

When the bell was on the bracket, David brought her coat and helped her into it. "You'd better get back home before the weather gets worse."

"You're coming up for supper, aren't you?" she asked, trying to keep the desperation from reverberating in her tone.

"What do you think?" he answered, then pulled her scarf protectively around her neck and turned her by the shoulders toward the door before he opened it for her and smiled her away.

The bell tinkled.

Two steps outside she turned, imploring, "Hurry home, David."

"I will."

She lowered her head to hold the scarf more tightly around her neck, but the wind lifted its fringed end and threw it back at her face. She scanned the dark street ahead.

He was gone!

The snow was fine and stinging and had glazed the streets with dangerous ice, which left no tracks for her to either follow or avoid. The wind slashed at her back, buffeting her along the slick boardwalks while her skirts luffed like a mainsail in a gale. She looked into each lighted store as she passed but he was in none of them. Turning at the saloon corner, the wind eddied into a whirlpool and twisted her skirts about her with renewed mastery. She ducked her head, hanging on to her scarf to keep it on her head, pulling her chin down low into her coat collar.

"Hello, Abbie."

Her head snapped up as if the trap door of a gallows had opened beneath her feet. His voice came out of the wild darkness, so near that she realized she'd nearly bumped into him rounding the corner. He stood with feet spread wide, hands in pockets, the swirling wind lifting his white, misty breath up and away.

"Jesse," she got out, "I thought it was you." She had come to a stop and could not help staring.

"It was."

The way they stood, the wind pelted his back but riveted the icy snow into her face, stinging it. She had forgotten how big he was, strapping wide and so tall that she had to look up sharply to see his face.

"What are you doing here?" she asked, but her teeth had begun to chatter, the cold having little to do with it.

"I heard there's going to be a wedding in town," he said, as conversationally as if they were still in her summer garden on a mellow, floral afternoon. Without asking, he withdrew a bare hand from his pocket and turned her by an elbow so that her back was to the wind, his face into it. He moved her nearer the clapboard wall, stood close before her, and jammed his hand back into his pocket again.

"How did you know I was getting married?"

"I figured it before I left, so I kept my eye on the papers."

"Then why didn't you just stay away and leave us in peace?"

His smileless face looked as ominous as the roiling clouds that had brought on the early dark. He scowled, black brows curling together as he ignored her question and asked one of his own.

"Are you pregnant?"

He couldn't have stunned her more had he kicked her in the side of the head with his slant-heeled cowboy boot.

"Why, you insufferable—" But the wind stole the rest of her lashing epithet, muffling her voice as the scarf flapped at her lips.

"Are you pregnant!" he repeated, hard, demanding, standing like a barrier before her. She moved as if to lurch around him, but he blocked her way simply by taking a step sideways, with his hands still buried in his pockets, keeping her between his bulk and the saloon wall.

"Let me past," she said coldly, glaring up at him.

"Like hell I will, woman! I asked you a question and I deserve an answer."

"You deserve nothing and that is precisely what you shall get!"

In an injured tone he went on, "Damnit, Abbie, I left him enough money to set the two of you up in high style for life. All I want in return is to know if the baby is mine."

Rage swooped over her. How dare he sashay into town and imply such a thing—that she had allowed David to make love to her to disguise the mistake she'd made with him, Jesse. At that moment she hated him. She wound up and swung, forgetting that the muff was on her hand. It caught him on the side of the face, doing no damage whatsoever with the soft white rabbit's fur, the pathetic attempt at violence made all the more pitiful by its ineffectuality.

With his hands in his pockets he couldn't block her swing in time, but shrugged and feinted to one side and the muff glanced off his cheek and rolled away onto the icy street behind him.

She made a move toward it, but he caught her by the shoulders, swinging her in a half circle to face him.

"Listen to me, you! I came back here to get the truth out of you and—by God!—I'll have it!"

She skewered him with her eyes and moved again as if to pick up the muff. But he pushed her back against the wall, his eyes warning her not to move, then he knelt and retrieved the muff, but when he handed it to her she had forgotten all about it.

"You despicable goat!" she cried, tears now freezing paths down her cheeks. "If you think I'm going to stand here in the middle of a blizzard and be insulted by you again, you are sadly mistaken!''

"All it takes is a simple yes or no," he argued, holding her in place while the wind threatened to rip them both off their feet. "Are you pregnant, damnit!"

Again she tried to jerk away, but his fingers closed over her coat sleeves like talons. "Are you?" he demanded, giving her a little shake.

"No!" she shouted into his face, stamping her foot and at last spinning free, running away from him. But the ground was glare ice now and a little foot flew sideways, and the next thing she knew she was sprawled at his feet. Immediately he went down on one knee and reached for her elbow, still holding the white muff in his massive, dark hand.

"Abbie, I'm sorry," he said, but she shook his hand off, sat up and whisked at her skirts, fighting back tears of mortification. "Damnit, Abbie, we can't talk here," he said, reaching as if to aid her once more, but she slapped his hand away.

"We cannot talk anywhere!" she exploded, still sitting on the street, glaring up at him. "We never could! All we could ever do was *fight*, and here you are, back for more. Well, what's the matter, Mr. DuFrayne, couldn't you find any other woman to force yourself on?"

All traces of temper left his voice as he looked into her angry eyes, kneeling there on one knee, engulfed in that dreadfully masculine sheepskin jacket, and said simply, "I haven't been looking for one."

God help me, she thought, and gathered her outrage about her like armor, struggling to her feet while he held her elbow solicitously and offered her the muff, which she yanked out of his hand. As she swung away and stalked up the street again, everything in her stomach threatened to erupt.

He watched her retreating back a moment, then called out to her, "Abbie, are you happy?"

Don't! Don't! Don't! she wanted to scream at him. Not again! Instead, she whirled into the banshee wind and yelled, "What do you care! Leave me alone. Do you hear! I've been screaming it to an empty house for three months now, but at last I can scream it to you in person. *Get out of my life, Jesse DuFrayne*!"

Then she spun again toward home, running as best she could on the precarious ice.

For some minutes after she rounded Doc's corner and
disappeared, Jesse stared at the empty street, then he stamped
the gathering snow off his boots and turned back toward the
corner saloon. Inside, he ordered a drink, sat brooding until it
arrived, then downed it in a single gulp, his mind made up.
He'd damn well go back up to her place and get some answers
out of that woman!

The roses were gone now from beside her white pickets,
which looked forlorn in the wintry gale. Walking up the path he
studied the porch. The wicker furniture was gone now. The
swing hung disconsolately, shivering in the wind as if a ghost
had just risen from it—maybe two. He took the steps and
peered through the long oval window of her front door. He
could see her rump and the back of her skirts at the far end of
the house. It looked like she was bending over, putting wood
into the kitchen range.

Hitching his collar up, he rapped on the door, watching her
hurry toward him down the length of the house. He stepped
back into the shadows.

As she opened the door, she began, "Supper's not ready yet,
David, but it—" The words died upon her lips as Jesse stepped
into the light. She lurched to slam the door, but his long fingers
curled around the edge of it and a boot wedged it open at the
floor.

"Abbie, can we talk a minute?"

Her cheeks made up for the missing roses outside.

"You get off my front porch! Do you hear me, *sir*. That is all
I need right now, for you to be seen here." She darted a look
beyond him, but the yard and street were empty.

"It won't take a minute, and shouldn't an old friend be
allowed to wish the bride well?"

"Go away before David comes and sees you here. He is
coming for supper any minute."

"Then I can congratulate the groom too."

Her eyes quickly assessed the hand and boot holding the
door open; there was no possible way she could force him to
leave.

"Neither David nor I wish anything from you except that
you be gone from our lives." The cold air swirled into the
house causing the flames to flicker in the lanterns. Jesse's hand
was nearly frozen to that door.

"Very well. I'll leave now, but I'll be seeing you again, *Miss Abigail*. I still owe you one photograph and that twenty-three dollars I borrowed from you."

Then, before she could harp once more about wanting absolutely nothing from him, he released the door, bounded down the porch steps, hit the path at a run, and jogged off toward town, kicking up snow behind him.

His limp was completely gone.

When David arrived for supper, Abigail's greeting was far warmer than usual. She took his arm and squeezed his hand, saying, "Oh, David, I'm so glad you're here."

"Where else would I be three days before my wedding?" he asked, smiling.

But she squeezed his arm harder, then helped him out of his coat. "David, you're so good for me," she said, holding his coat in both arms against her body, hoping, hoping, that it was true.

"Why, Abigail, what is it?" he asked, noting the glitter of tears in her eyes, moving to take her in his arms.

"Oh, I don't know," she said chokily. "I guess it's all the plans and jitters and getting everything done in time. I've been so worried about the headpiece not arriving in time for the photograph, and now this storm is starting and what if the photographer can't make it in from Denver?" She backed away, swiped at a single tear which had spilled over, and said to the floor between them, "I guess I'm just having what I've heard most brides have sooner or later—an attack of last-minute nerves."

"You've done too much, that's all," he sympathized. "What with the store and the preparations for the reception and getting all your clothes ready for the ceremony and our trip. It isn't *all* necessary, you know. I've told you that before."

"I know you did," she said plaintively, feeling foolish now at her display of jangling nerves, "but a woman has only one wedding in her lifetime and she wants it perfect, with all the amenities."

He circled her shoulders with an arm and herded her toward the kitchen. "But most women have mothers and sisters and aunts to help carry the load. You're doing too much. Just make sure you don't overdo it, Abigail. I want you well and happy on Saturday."

His concern made her feel somewhat better, but it was extremely difficult to forget that somewhere out there Jesse DuFrayne was spending the night, and should David encounter him between now and Saturday and stir up old animosities, there was no telling what might happen. The results could be unpleasant, to say the least, disastrous, to say the most. For she wouldn't put anything past Jesse.

All through supper she found her thoughts returning time and again to one plaguing question: would Jesse stoop so low that he'd tell David about what they'd done together?

An instinct for preservation made her broach the subject of Richard. David was relaxed and lethargic, sitting back on the settee with his hands laced over his full stomach, feet outstretched and crossed at the ankle.

"David?"

"Yes, Abigail?" He had never taken to using any shortened form of her name like Jesse had. It had always disappointed her just a little.

"Did I ever tell you I was engaged once?" She knew perfectly well she'd never told him before. He suddenly sat up and took interest. "It was long ago—when I was twenty."

She could tell by the stunned look on his face that there were a hundred questions he wanted to ask, but he just sat there waiting for her to go one.

"His name was Richard and he grew up here in Stuart's Junction. We . . . we used to play hopscotch together. I'm actually surprised that nobody has mentioned his name to you because people around here have long memories."

"No, nobody has," he said, red around the collar.

"I just thought that you should know, David, before we got married. We've never spoken much about our pasts. We've had such a mutual interest in our future, with the store to plan and everything, that it has rather superseded other topics, hasn't it?"

"Perhaps it has—you're right. But if you don't want to tell me about Richard you don't have to. It doesn't matter, Abigail."

"I want to," she said gazing at him directly, "so that perhaps you'll understand my sudden jitters." Then she looked at her lap again as she went on. "There had never been anyone except Richard, and we more or less grew up suspecting that one day we'd marry. My mother died when I was nineteen, and within a short time Richard and I became engaged. I was very young and naive and believed in such things as destiny then." She paused, creating the effect of the passage of time in her narrative. Then she sighed. "Richard apparently believed differently, though, for when my father fell ill and became a total invalid within a year of my mother's death, it seems Richard found me less desirable as a future wife. I guess you might say he considered my father excess baggage. At any rate, my . . . my fiancé disappeared scarcely a week before the wedding. His family moved too, shortly afterward, and I have never seen them or him since."

David's face wore a caring expression. He reached for her hand. "I'm sorry, Abigail. I truly am."

She looked up at his gentle, unassuming face, knowing at that instant just what a good, moral man he was and knowing also that she was very lucky to have found someone like him so late in her life.

"I understand your jitters now," he said into her eyes, "but I would never leave you like he did. Surely you know that."

"Yes, I do," she assured him. But she felt small and guilty, for she knew he was too good to read into her story the possibility that she and Richard had been intimate. "David," she said, really meaning what she was about to say, "I do so want everything to be perfect in our lives together, that's all."

"It will be," he promised. But he promised it holding nothing more than her hand, and she could not help thinking that this was the kind of thing which two people in love should be sharing wrapped up tightly in each other's arms. "I'm glad you told me, Abigail. I could see that something had you upset tonight, and now that the story is out, consider it forgotten."

At last he kissed her, and she clung to him with a sudden desperation very much unlike her. Taking his lips away, he said, "I think it's best if I go now, Abigail."

But she clung harder, willing him to stay a little longer, to keep the threat of Jesse DuFrayne at bay. "Do you have to go so soon?"

He put her firmly away from him. "You can use a good night's rest, you said so yourself a while ago. I'll see you tomorrow evening, like we agreed."

He kissed her at the door before leaving, but he had put on his overcoat first, so all of the warm contact of hugging was lost in the bulk of woolen coat and muslin skirt.

Chapter 22

———————

IMMEDIATELY AFTER DAVID left, Abbie dressed for bed and retired, wanting to get the lanterns blown out as quickly as possible. The wind buffeted the house, rattling shingles, tapping barren branches against eaves, promising a full night of its wrath. The storm sounds only multiplied her trepidation. Resolutely she closed her eyes and recounted the needs David effectively fulfilled in her life: security, companionship, admiration, love. She spent time analyzing each. He was paving the way to the most secure life she had ever known. Companionship was unquestionable—they had recognized it between themselves from the first. And when it came to admiration— out of all the people she'd known in her entire life none had been more complimentary, appreciative, or admiring. And love—

Her thoughts were hammered to an abrupt halt by the loudest beating her back door had ever suffered. Nobody ever came to her back door. She knew before her feet hit the icy floor who it would be and realized she'd been lying there riddling herself with thoughts of David to keep them off of Jesse DuFrayne.

For a moment she considered letting him bang away until he gave up, but then he shouted at the top of his lungs, and even above the howling storm, she was afraid someone next door would hear.

She found her wrapper and hurried to the back door, listening, her toes curled against the drafty floorboards. He banged and hollered again so she lit a lantern but left the wick low, almost guttering, still afraid of anyone seeing him through the windows.

"Abbie, open up!"

She did, but only partway, refusing to step back and let him in.

He was standing in the wind and snow, hair, eyebrows, and moustache laced with the stuff, determination boring into her from eyes as black as the night.

"I told you to keep away from me. Do you realize what time of the night it is?"

"I don't give a damn."

"No, you never did."

"Are you going to let me in or not? Nobody saw me, but they sure as hell will hear me beat the door down if you slam it in my face again." The wind invaded the house while she clutched her wrapper together over her breastbone. Her feet were freezing and the wrapper did little to protect her against the shudders that overtook her.

Suddenly he ordered, "Get in there before you freeze to death along with me," and in he came, filling the kitchen with ten pounds of sheepskin jacket, three inches of wet moustache, and nearly two hundred pounds of stubbornness.

She lit into him before he even got the door shut. "How dare you come barging in here as if you owned the place! Get out!"

He just gave a large, exaggerated shiver, rubbed his palms together, and exclaimed, "God, but it's cold out there!" completely ignoring her order, shrugging out of his jacket without so much as a by-your-leave. "We're going to need some wood on that fire to keep us from freezing solid." He jerked a chair from the kitchen table, clapped it down right in front of the stove, hung his jacket on the back of it, then opened a stove lid and reached for a log from the woodbox—all this time he hardly looked at her.

"This is my house and you are not welcome in it. Put that wood back in my woodbox!"

Again he paid no heed but stuffed the wood into the stove, replaced the lid, then turned and bent over at the waist, brushing snow curds from his hair. He spied her bare toes peeking from beneath the hem of her wrapper, pointed at them, and said, "You'd better get something on those tootsies, tootsie, because this is going to take a while."

By this time she was livid. "This will take no time at all because you are leaving. And don't call me tootsie!"

"I'm not leaving," he said matter-of-factly.

She knew he meant it. What was she supposed to do with a bull-headed fool like him? She clenched her fists and grunted in exasperation while he took anoher chair and clapped it down beside the first, then stood back with a thumb hooked in his waistband.

"We've got some talking to do, Abbie."

The frost was melting from his moustache now and a drop fell from it as he stood patiently waiting for her to give in and sit down. His nose was red from the cold, hair glistening and tousled from its recent whisking. He looked more like a gunslinger than ever in those boots and denims, dark shirt and rough leather vest. His skin was swarthy, the perfect foil for his black hair, moustache, and swooping sideburns. He might have ridden in from the range just now after rounding up cattle in the blizzard or outrunning a posse. His appearance was totally masculine, from the clothing to the ruddy cheeks, the wind-reddened nose to the untidy hair. Her eyes fell to his hip—no gun.

"You don't have to be afraid of me, Abbie," he assured her, following the direction of her eyes. Then he drew a handkerchief from his hip pocket and blew his nose, all the while studying her above the hankie, his eyes refusing to let her go.

How could her feelings betray her like this? How could she stand here thinking that even the way he blew his nose was attractive? Yet it was. Oh, Lord, Lord, it was because Jesse DuFrayne was undeniably all man. Angry with herself for these thoughts, she lashed out at him.

"Why did you come here again? You know that if David finds out, he'll be terribly angry, but I suppose you're planning on that. You haven't done enough to me, have you?"

He bent forward at the waist, reaching behind to stuff the hankie away in his pocket, and said calmly, "Come on, Abbie, sit down. I'm half-frozen from standing out there waiting for him to leave." Then he sat down himself and held his palms toward the heat.

"You've been standing out in the street watching my house? How dare you!"

He continued leaning toward the stove, not even bothering to turn around as he said, "You're forgetting that I'm financing this setup. I figure that gives me plenty of rights around here."

"Rights!" She came one angry step closer behind him. "You come in here spouting rights to me in my own house and put wood in my stove and . . . and sit on my chair and say you have rights? What about my rights!"

He slowly brought his elbows off his knees, straightened his shoulders almost one muscle at a time, sighed deeply, then got up from the chair with exaggerated patience, and swaggered across the room to her with deliberate, slow clunking boot-steps. His eyes told her he'd put up with no more of her defiance. And he took her upper arm in one hand, the back of her neck in the other, then steered her toward the pair of chairs. This time when he ordered, "Sit down," she did.

But stiffly, on the very edge of the chair, her arms crossed tightly over her chest while she poised like a ramrod. "If David finds out about this and I lose him I'll . . . I'll . . . ." But she spluttered to a stop, unable to find harsh enough words, he infuriated her so.

Jesse just stretched his long legs out and leaned back, relaxed, fingers laced over his stomach. "So are you happy with him then?" he asked, studying her stiff profile.

"When you left here that was the last thing on your mind!"

"Don't make assumptions, Abbie. When I left here things were in a jumble and I don't like leaving things in a jumble, so I came back. When I didn't hear from you but I read that you were getting married, I had to know for sure if you might be in a family way."

She pierced him with a malevolent look. "Oh, that's big of you—really big!" she spit. "I suppose I should get all fluttery at your tardy concern."

"I hadn't thought you might, not after the iceberg treatment I got on my way out of here that morning." He grinned crookedly, and out of nowhere there came to Abbie the memory of Jesse in that stunning verdigris suit, bending to her on one knee.

"Well, you deserved it," she said petulantly, but with a little less venom.

"Yes, I guess I did," he admitted good-naturedly, an amiable expression about his eyes.

Behind them the low-burning lantern guttered, sending their shadows dancing on the wall behind the stove. Before them the fire grew, licking against the isinglass window in the cast-iron door of the stove. Outside the wind keened, and for a moment they looked at each other, thinking back.

Then Jesse asked softly, "You're not, are you, Abbie?"

"Not what?"

"Pregnant."

Beleaguered once again by those conflicting emotions that this infernal man could always rouse in her, she turned to stare at the isinglass window. She was so confused. All he had to do was walk in here and start being nice and it started all over again. She pulled her feet up off the drafty floor, hooked her heels over the edge of the chairseat, and hugged her knees up tight, laying her forehead on her arms.

"Oh, Jesse, how could you?" she asked, the words coming muffled into the cacoon of her lap. "Out there in the street you practically accused me of . . . of consorting with David to confuse the issue of . . . of this nonexistent paternity."

"I didn't mean it to sound that way, Abbie." He touched her elbow, but she jerked it away, still keeping her head buried in her arms.

"Don't touch me, Jesse." Now she looked up, accusingly, "Not after that."

"All right . . . all right." He put his hands up as if a gun were pointed at him, then slowly lowered them as he saw the fierce, hurt expression on her face.

"Just why did you have to come back here? Didn't you do enough the first time without coming back to haunt me?"

Their eyes locked, held for a moment, while he asked softly, "Do I haunt you, Abbie?"

She looked away. "No, not in the way you mean."

He looked down at her bare toes curling over the edge of the chair, then sprawled back lazily, studying her while he slung a wrist over the back of her chair. "Well, you haunt me," he admitted. "I guess that's why I came back, to settle all the misunderstandings between us that still haunt me." Without removing his wrist from the chair back, he took a lock of her hair between index and middle fingers, rubbing the silky skein back and forth a couple of times. At the fluttering touch she worked her shoulder muscles in an irritated gesture and pulled her head forward to free the hair.

"I thought we understood each other fully that last day," she said, hugging her knees tighter.

"Not hardly."

Memories of that last day came hurtling back as they sat side by side, warming by the stove, warming to each other again, anger dissipating with the cold. Something unwanted seemed to seep into their pores along with the radiating warmth from the stove. After some time her voice came again, small and injured.

"Why didn't you tell me you knew David was coming back before we . . ." But she was afraid to finish. He was too near to put that into words.

He considered her for a long moment before asking quietly, "Why didn't you go back upstairs when I told you to?"

But neither of them had the answers to these questions that echoed through the windswept night. Abbie lowered her forehead onto her crossed arms again and silently shook her head. She heard Jesse move, sitting forward on the edge of his chair, leaning his elbows on his knees again.

"Is there any coffee in that pot?"

She got up, lifted the blue-speckled pot, found it full, then placed both palms around it. He watched from under lowered brows, reminded of those hands upon him, feeling for fever. She disappeared into the dark pantry.

There, alone, she pressed her hands to her open mouth as if it might help her control this urge to cry when she got back out there where he could see her.

His eyes followed her as she came back out with cups, filled them, then turned to find he had removed his boots and braced his feet up on the fender of the range to warm them. Wordlessly she handed him his cup, their eyes locked while he lowered his feet so she could step past to her chair.

Side by side they sipped, not talking, both of them staring introspectively at the little patch of fire visible through the stove window. He rested his feet once more against the fender while she wound her toes around each other. There was something about sitting barefoot together before a snapping fire that was disconcertingly calming. Animosity ebbed away, leaving them almost at peace with each other.

"Did you think that I knew Melcher was coming back to stay?" he asked without turning to look at her.

"Well, didn't you?" she asked his toes. She remembered what his feet looked like bare and was conscious of how bare her own were right now.

"I know that's what you've been thinking all these months, but it's not true. I knew he was coming for the meeting the next day, but I had no idea he'd end up staying."

She turned to study his profile, following the line of his forehead, nose, moustache, and lips that were lit to a burning, glowing yellow-red. He lifted his cup, took a swallow, and she watched his Adam's apple lift and settle back down. He was, she admitted, a decidedly handsome man.

Almost tiredly she said, "Don't lie to me anymore, Jesse. At least don't lie."

He lifted his eyes to hers, to the firelight dancing away on her smileless face. "I never lied to you. When did I lie?"

"Silence can be a lie."

He knew she was right. He had deceived her by his silence many times, not only about Melcher coming back, but about owning the railroad and being the one who paid her for his keep. She took a drink of coffee, then held the cup carefully in both palms, looking down into it.

"You knew what hopes I'd pinned on him, Jesse, you knew it all the time. How could you not tell me?" She looked perhaps seventeen, and broken-hearted and all golden-skinned in the blush of the dancing firelight. It was all he could do to keep both of his hands around his cup.

"Because if I'd told you he was coming back I couldn't have had you that night, isn't that right?"

Startled, she found his eyes. She didn't know what to say. All this time she had thought . . .

"B . . . but Jesse," she said, eyes gone wide, "it was I who came to you that night. it was I doing the asking."

"No it wasn't." He scanned her face, those wide eyes which looked black in the shadowy kitchen, then forced himself to look away. "Not from the first day it wasn't. It was me, always me, right up to the very end, trying to break you down until I finally succeeded. But you know something, Abbie?" He pulled his stocking feet off the fender, leaned elbows to knees and spoke into the depths of his coffee cup. "When it was over, I didn't like myself for what I'd done."

At that moment the lantern on the table behind them guttered, spluttered, and went out. Shaken, she studied the back of his neck, the hair that grew thick and curling about his ear. "I don't understand you at all."

He glanced back over his shoulder. "I want you to be happy, Abbie. Is that so hard to understand?"

"I just . . . it doesn't . . . well, it doesn't fit the Jesse I know, that's all."

He eyed her over his shoulder for a moment longer, then turned his eyes to the fire again and took a drink of coffee. "What fits me then? The image of a train robber? You're having trouble untangling me from that image. That's part of the reason I came back here. Because I cared what you thought of me afterward, and that's never happened to me before with a woman. You're different. The way we started out was different. We started so . . ." But he stopped, going back to the beginning in his thoughts, enjoying some memories, sorry about some others, but unable to encapsulate his feelings into words.

"How did we start?" she encouraged, wondering what he'd been about to say.

"Oh, all the fighting and baiting and getting even. When I woke up the first time in this house and found out how I got here, you know how mad I was, and you were convenient so I took it out on you. But I just didn't want you to go on thinking that I was still getting even that last night when we made love. That had nothing to do with getting even."

She realized there had been countless times since when she'd thought exactly that. It was part of what haunted her. He looked back over his shoulder, but she was afraid to meet the disturbing eyes of this new, sincere Jesse.

"Is that what you thought, Abbie? That I made love to you so I could hand Melcher the money with one hand and a soiled bride with the other and watch him squirm while he decided what to do with them?" He still sat a little forward of her, coffee cup slung on a single finger, empty, forgotten, looking back, waiting for the answer she was afraid to give. "Did you?" he quietly insisted.

And at last her eyes could not resist. They trembled to find his as she managed to choke out, "I . . . d . . . didn't want to."

Her words were greeted by a long silence before Jesse sat

back in his chair, crossing an ankle over a knee so his stockinged foot brushed her gown, almost touching her knee. One dark hand fell over his anklebone, the other dangled the cup over his upraised knee.

"Abbie, I'm going to tell you the truth, whether you believe it or not. It *was* conscience money I gave Melcher, but not because I'd shot him. It wasn't him I was paying off, it was you, because I felt guilty about the night before. But I swear to you, the idea came to me in the middle of that arbitration meeting. I figured if I gave him that much money he *could* settle here and probably *would*. Oh, I admit I forced his hand a little bit, but I didn't do it to put you on the spot, Abbie. Not at all. I thought if I could fix it so you could have him and a nice cozy marriage and a nice cozy business and a secure financial future, I'd have you off my conscience."

She looked at the side of his face. He was watching the coffee cup as he tapped it on his knee.

"And am I?"

The cup fell still. He looked into her eyes.

"No."

She picked at a thread on her lap. "Are you always so generous with your mistresses?" she asked, seeking to break this spell of madness that was weaving itself about them like some silken, seductive web.

He surprised her by simply answering, "No."

She realized she'd been expecting him to deny the others, and that it suddenly hurt when he didn't. What did it matter that there had been others? Yet she could not look him in the eye for fear he'd understand more about her feelings for him than was prudent at the moment.

"Wouldn't it have been much easier to just turn me away when I came to you?"

His foot came off his knee and hit the floor and he was on his feet, suddenly absorbed in refilling his cup. With his back to her, he answered, "Hardly." Then he took a long pull of coffee while, stunned, she stared at the thick hair on the back of his neck. He stood there for a long time before finally asking, "Did you know you were the first woman who ever said no to me, Abbie?"

Again he had managed to surprise her; what he said made no sense.

"But I—"

He turned to face her suddenly, interrupting. "Don't blame yourself, Abbie, not one more time. It was me who did the asking, no matter who came to whose room, and you know it. But you were different from the rest."

"I should think that in bed one woman is no different from the rest."

His hand shot out, grabbed her by the chin, and lifted her face roughly. He looked for a moment like he might strike her. "You cut it out, Abbie! You know damn well you were different and that it was more than your just being a virgin. It was all we'd been through together that made you different. That and the fact that you'd saved my life."

Suddenly, at his angry touch, at the intensity in his eyes, she felt her own sting with tears. She twisted her chin out of his grip, her eyes never leaving his as at last she unburdened herself.

"Do you know how low I thought you were for using what I didn't know against me? For not telling me David was coming back? For not telling me you owned the railroad? For not telling me it was your money that was . . . was paying me off like . . . like some whore?"

"Abbie—"

"No, let me finish. I've been angry at how you sashayed out of here and thought a little tumble in the hay didn't matter to a woman like me, who—"

"I never thought—" He sat down, putting one hand on the back of her chair again.

"Be quiet!" she ordered. "I want you to know what hell you put me through, Jesse DuFrayne, because you did . . . you did. You made me feel unworthy of David's love, like I had no right to marry him even if he asked. You cannot imagine what that did to me, Jesse. I don't want you to leave here with a clear conscience. I want it to hurt you like it did me, because even after you were gone all I had to do was walk through this house to be reminded of what I'd done with you, or to walk into David's store to be reminded that you'd paid for it all. Even there you seemed to be laughing at me from the very walls you'd financed. I waned to strike back at you, but there was no way, and I'd begun to think I couldn't be free of you."

"Do you want to be?"

"I want it more than anything in the world," she said in utter sincerity.

"Meaning you're not?" He looked up at her hair, down at her trembling lips.

"No, I'm not. Maybe I'll never be, and that's why I'm glad I'm on your conscience. Because all it would have taken was one single statement of fact that night and none of this guilt would have been necessary. Now I face a wedding night of . . ." She looked down at her lap. ". . . . of questionable outcome, to say the least. And you say *you* want a clear conscience?"

"Abbie," he pleaded, moving nearer, turning to face her, with his hand still on the back of her chair. "I told you, I didn't know he'd stay—"

But she cut him off. "You realize, don't you, that I still stand to lose it all. Now, when I am on the very brink of everything I ever hoped for—a husband who thinks the sun rises and sets on me, a business that will mean security for as long as we live." She looked up at him squarely. He was very close, leaning toward her. "Why, I've even acquired an acceptance from this community that I never had before I knew David. As his wife I will at last fit in, where before I was nothing more than 'that . . . that *maiden lady* up the street.'"

It grew quiet, all but for the wind and the fire. He studied her, sitting there in her nightgown and wrapper, looking down at her lap. And he suddenly knew that to stay here was to hurt her further.

"What do you want me to say?" he asked miserably. "That I'm sorry?" His fingers touched the back of her hair again, but she did not flinch away this time. "I am. You know it. I'm sorry, Abbie." She looked up and found his face filled with sincerity, all hint of smile or teasing erased.

"I've gone through hell because of you, Jesse. Maybe sorry isn't enough. I knew from the first day David told me he was going to settle in Stuart's Junction that he was settling here because of me. I knew he had me on a pedestal, but I couldn't tell him differently. He would never, never understand why I did what I did with you. But do you know what my deception is doing to me, inside?"

It was clear to Jesse what it was doing to her. He could see the pain in her face and wished he had not been the cause of it. He moved back a little bit.

"What will you say on your wedding night if he suspects?"

Her eyes moved to the isinglass door. "That it was Richard."

"You've told him about Richard?" he asked, surprised.

"Not all that I've told you, but enough."

"Will he believe you?"

She smiled, somewhat ruefully. "He's not like you, Jesse. He hasn't had every woman who came along the pike."

Repeatedly he lifted the hair from the back of her neck, letting it drop back down. Very quietly he said to her ear, "There've been no women along my pike since I left here."

Shivers tingled up her spine and down her arms. But he was what he was. "I'm going to marry David, Jesse. He's very good for me."

"So was I once."

"Not in that way."

"In lots of ways. We could always talk, and laugh and—"

"And fight?"

His hand stopped toying with her hair for a second. "Yes, and fight," he admitted unabashedly, with a smile in his voice.

"Even after you left I was still fighting you. When I read the truth in that newspaper the day after the meeting I smoldered for days."

He grinned. "You were always good at smoldering," he said, low in his throat.

"Remove your arm from the back of my chair, Mr. DuFrayne, or I shall smolder all over again."

"The name's Jesse," he said, leaving the arm where it was.

"Oh, spare me from all that again. The next thing I know you'll be claiming you're a train robber with a bullet in your hip."

He laughed and squeezed the back of her neck, then gave it a gentle shake and rubbed her earlobe with his thumb. "Let's see you smolder a little bit, huh, Abbie? For old times' sake?" His hand left her neck and he got her by a little piece of hair and yanked it lightly.

But she calmly faced him, repeating, "I'm going to marry David Melcher and until I do you're going to get out of my house and out of my life."

He finally faced the stove again, stretched out with his hands on his stomach, slung down low with the nape of his neck hooked on the chair back.

"Did you really have to scream that to the empty rooms when I was gone?"

"Oh, don't let your ego swell up so," she said testily. "I hated you every time I did it."

He rolled his face her way.

"You never hated me."

"Yes I did."

"You hate me now?"

But instead of answering, she stretched out on her chair too, putting her feet up on the fender beside his.

"Tell me now that you hate me," he challenged, moving his foot to cover the top of hers.

"I will if you don't get your foot off mine and leave here this very minute." He got her foot now between both of his, rubbed it sensuously.

"Make me."

She looked at him to find the old teasing smile back on his lips, certain at that moment that if she could make him believe her, she would at last be free of him. She lounged there on her chair, just as indolently as he, and said without a qualm, "You are still convinced that forcefulness is strength, aren't you? I can't make you go and you know it. But I can repeat what I said long ago, that David Melcher has all the beautiful and gentle strengths which I admire in a man, and I'm going to marry him for them."

Jesse perused her silently for a moment, then reached out and took her hand. Her heart did crazy things, but she watched his thumb stroke hers and kept outward appearances unruffled.

"You know, I think you really mean it."

"I do," she said, letting him have his way with her hand to prove that she was no longer affected by him.

"Is he good to you?" Jesse asked, and she suddenly wanted to lace her fingers with his and pull that hand against her stomach. This was the hardest of all—it always was—when Jesse became concerned and caring and let it show in his voice and his touch.

"Always . . . and in all ways," she answered softly.

The wind moaned about something that hurt.

"And is he good *for* you?"

The snow tittered its secrets against the house.

"Abbie?" he persisted when she didn't answer.

"They're one and the same."

"No they're not."

"Then perhaps the question is, am I good for him."

"That goes without saying," came Jesse's gentle words.

To their joined hands she said, "Don't be kind. It's when you've been kind that we've traditionally made fools of ourselves."

That broke the spell and he released her hand with a light laugh, saying, "Tell me all about your plans. I really want to hear them."

Funny, she thought, but here she was two days away from her wedding and she'd never had a friend with whom to discuss it. How ironic that it should be Jesse who drew her out. But he was right about one thing—they could always talk, and by now she was feeling very comfortable with him. And for some reason she was telling him everything. All about the wedding plans, the reception plans, and about how hard she and David had worked setting up the store. She told him they were going to Colorado Springs on their honeymoon.

He quirked a cute sideways smile at her and teased, "Oh, so I'm paying for a honeymoon too?" But then he told her that the store was nicely done. He could see her hand in it.

And she told how her mother's seed-pearl headpiece had worried her by not arriving until today for the photograph tomorrow. He asked who she'd hired to take it and told her he knew Damon Smith. Smith did good work and she'd be pleased. Then she made him laugh by asking him if he really was a photographer then, and when he smiled at her and said, "You mean you still don't believe me," they ended up laughing together.

They were getting very lazy and woozy-tired by now, and the conversation was becoming a little punchy and lethargic. She told him he looked more like an outlaw than a photographer in those clothes of his, and he asked if she preferred him in that verdigris suit and she admitted no, these clothes suited him better. From time to time during this lazy exchange, he'd cast that damnably sleepy grin her way before they'd both stare at the isinglass window again, all natural and relaxed and getting sleepier and looser by the minute. The hour ceased to matter as they talked on into the stormy night.

He told her about how he and Jim had started out surveying on a railroad crew and had gone from there to blasting tunnels, building trestles, and even laying tracks before they'd finally started laying down rails of their own, beginning with one little spur line, because by that time they could see the money was not in laying down rails but in owning them. She'd see, he said, when she got to Colorado Springs where all the railroad barons built their mansions.

"You too?" she asked indolently.

"No," he laughed, he didn't go for that stuff. Besides, his railroad wasn't really that big. But he talked more about how photography had started as a diversion for him, then how he'd come to love it.

By this time he was slung low upon his chair, feet crossed on the fender, contented, half-asleep. Still he asked, "And you believe me now?"

"Yes, I guess I do."

It had taken a long time to hear her say that, a long time and a lot of misunderstandings.

The howling night sounds came and went as they sat, listening in companionable silence now.

"It's very late," Abbie finally said. "I think you should be going or my photograph will be of one very wrinkled looking bride tomorrow."

He chuckled, hands rising and falling on his stomach, remembering. "Just like the first time I ever saw you. God, you were a mess, Abbie."

"You certainly have a way with words." But they were both too lazy to care anymore. They rolled their heads to look at each other.

"Don't let me fool you, though, Abbie," he said quietly.

He'd never change, she realized. He'd always be the same teasing Jesse. But he was not for her.

"I'm glad we talked," he said, sitting up at last, stretching, then yawning widely.

She followed suit, stiff and tired. "So am I. But Jesse?"

"Mmm?" he said, blinking slow at her, his hands hanging limp between his knees.

"Could you sneak back into your room without being seen, or will I have to think up quick excuses for David again?"

"Only a fool would be up this late. I'd be sneaking for nothing."

"You will try not to be seen, though, won't you?"

"Yes, Abbie." And for once he didn't tease.

He tensed every muscle in his body then, grasping the back

of one hand, stretching them both out before him while he perched on the very edge of his chair in one of those quivering, shivering, all-over stretches that involves legs, stomach, neck, arms, even head. She'd seen him do it a hundred times before.

Memories.

Then he doubled up and began slowly pulling his boots on. Watching, she recalled once when she'd helped him do that.

He stood. He stretched again. He tucked his shirttails in and she got to her feet, standing uncertainly beside him.

He hooked a thumb in his belt and stood there looking at her.

"I guess I'm not invited to the wedding, huh?"

She stilled the wild thrumming of her heart and smiled. "Mr. DuFrayne, you are incorrigible."

Without taking his eyes off her, he reached for his jacket from the back of the chair and shrugged it on. She stood watching every movement, hugging her arms.

The jacket was on. But instead of buttoning it up, he used the front panels to hang his hands on, then just stood there that way, making no move toward the door.

"Well . . ." he said, relative to nothing. She smiled shakily, then shrugged.

"Well . . ." she repeated stupidly.

Then their eyes met. Neither of them smiled.

"Do I get to kiss the bride before I go?" he asked, but there was a husky note of emotion in his voice.

"No!" she exclaimed too quickly, and backed a step away from him, but tripped on the chair rung behind her. He reached for her elbow to keep her from falling, then pulled her slowly, slowly, inexorably into the deep, fuzzy pile of his jacket front. His eyes slid shut while he cupped the back of her head to keep her there against him.

Abbie, he thought, my little hummingbird.

And like the heart of the hummingbird, which beats faster than all others in creation, the heart of Abigail McKenzie felt as if it would beat its way out of her body.

Standing against Jesse felt nothing whatever like standing against David earlier. Jesse's coat was more bulky but through all these thick, thick layers of sheepskin she could feel the thrum of his heart.

"Be happy, Abbie," he said against her hair, and kissed it.

She squeezed her eyes shut tight while a button impressed itself into the soft skin of her cheek.

"I will," she said against the sheepskin and his hammering heart. The big hand moved in her hair, petting it, smoothing it down against her neck, tightening almost painfully as he held her tightly against him for one last second.

Then he stepped back, his hands trailing down her arms until he captured her hands. With a last searching look into her startled eyes, he took her palms to his cheeks and placed them there for a moment, her thumbs resting at the outer corners of his black moustache. His eyelids slid closed and trembled for just a moment. Then he opened them again and said so softly she scarcely heard, " 'Bye, Ab."

Her hands wanted suddenly to linger upon his dark, warm face, to stroke his moustache, touch his eyes, and move from there down his well remembered body. But he squeezed them painfully, and she swallowed and said into his eyes. " 'Bye, Jess."

Then he backed away and stood looking at her all the while he slowly buttoned up his jacket and turned the collar up around his ears.

He turned. The door opened and the snow swirled in about her feet.

And in the silence after the door closed, slicing off a quick chunk of cold, she whispered to the emptiness, " 'Bye, Jess."

Chapter 23

———◆———

WHEN ABBIE AWAKENED the following morning and saw her haggard face in the mirror, she was relieved that David wouldn't have a chance to see her this way. They had agreed she would not go down to the store at all today, so she wouldn't see him until seven this evening, when he came by to walk her over to church for their wedding rehearsal.

Assessing herself in the mirror, she found her face a disaster and her nerves ruined. Both needed immediate help.

The best she could do for her face was to give it the astringent benefits of a freshly sliced lemon. The results were an infinite improvement over the perdition which had shown in every pore when she first woke up. She managed to dim the telltale puffiness and shadows beneath her eyes by using handfuls of snow to soothe and invigorate them. After a bath and hair wash, she began to feel even more human. The visible devastation was repaired.

But what about the invisible?

It certainly didn't help her quivering stomach at all to think about Jesse, but she couldn't help it. She paused in putting the finishing touches to her hair. How different Jesse had seemed last night.

Forget him, Abigail McKenzie!

She forced herself to think of David, of the store, the photograph, the practice tonight, the ceremony tomorrow, the reception. The honeymoon. For a moment her thoughts strayed back to Jesse, but she brought them up short.

Go through the list of things that need doing for the reception! Get out the lace tablecloth, lay out the plates, forks, cups. Frost the tea cakes, slice the breads and set them aside. Press Mama's gown. Worry about the snow.

She glanced out the window but the blizzard had blown itself out toward dawn. Still, snow in the mountains often meant delayed trains, since not all lines had adequate snow sheds so trains were forced to wait while crews cleared the tracks after a blizzard like they'd had last night. Suppose the train was late or never came at all. The photograph was no life and death matter, she told herself one minute. Then the next, watched the clock, listening for the whistle, railing, oh, why did it have to snow!

Jesse—with snow melting off his hair, his moustache . . .

Forget him! Think of David. Get your clothing ready to carry to the hotel.

The 9:50 whistle! At last! That meant Damon Smith had arrived and would be setting up his photographic equipment at the hotel.

Did it mean, too, that Jesse was boarding the train to leave town?

Oh yes, yes, please be gone, Jesse.

Would David find out Jesse had been in town, even for such a short time? Did anyone see Jesse returning to the hotel at three o'clock in the morning?

Don't think about it! Pack the pearl headpiece and veil in tissue, cover the wedding dress on its hanger, get shoes ready to take. Your face looks fine, Abbie, quit looking in the mirror! Your dress is beautiful, everything will turn out fine if you simply forget Jesse DuFrayne.

With fifteen minutes to spare, Miss Abigail McKenzie stood before her umbrella stand beside the front door with its lovely oval window. She glanced outside at the windless, dazzling day, dressed as it was in white, in honor of her wedding. On the seat of the umbrella stand were her garments, stacked all neatly. On top of the stack was a pair of delicate white satin slippers of tapering heel and pointed toe—her wedding gift from David.

In the mirror determined eyes stared back at her, chastising Abbie for her foolish, tremulous misgivings. She watched herself draw arms into a new jade green coat with capelet and hood, purchased for her honeymoon trip. She forced herself to refrain from thinking it was Jesse's money that had bought it. She drew her hands into her muff. He'd bought it, too.

Lifting her eyes, she thought, pick up your wedding garments, Abigail McKenzie, and carry them over town and get this photograph taken and get yourself married to David Melcher and quit being a simpering schoolgirl. She thought of how long it had been since she'd checked the tautness of her chin. She need not do that anymore; she was not old. Yet neither was she young. She was in between, and it was a blessed relief not to have to worry about it anymore. David accepted middle age with total unconcern, which made her do the same. She need not fear life passing her by again. From now on there'd be David.

Edwin Young was behind his front desk when Miss Abigail came into the hotel lobby, lightly stamping snow from her feet as she closed the door behind her.

"Here, let me help you with those things, Miss Abigail," he offered, coming across the lobby.

"Thank you, Edwin, but I've got them in hand."

"These're your wedding things, I suspect."

"They certainly are."

"Too bad the weather had to turn nasty right before your wedding."

"I really don't mind the snow," she said. "I had the thought this morning that it makes the entire mountain look as if it dressed up for David's and my wedding."

Miss Abigail sure has changed, Edwin thought, since David Melcher came to town. She was just as nice and common and friendly as could be. A person felt comfortable around her now. Edwin even dared to touch her chin lightly.

"You just keep that smile on your face, Miss Abigail, and— if you'll pardon my saying so—your photograph will be pretty as a picture."

They laughed and Edwin noted how Miss Abigail had lost her loftiness which used to make him think she considered herself a cut above the others in this town.

"I take it Damon Smith has arrived on the morning train as expected?"

"Oh, he sure did, Miss Abigail. Drug in enough gear to photograph the entire population of Colorado, the way it looked."

"I worried about the snow blocking the tracks. I was relieved to hear the whistle."

"Nope. He's here, all right, and if you'll follow me I'll be happy to show you to his room and help you carry these things."

"You don't need to do that, but thank you anyway. As long as I have everything in hand I'll just go up if you'll tell me what room he's in."

"He's in number eight. You sure I can't help you?"

But she was halfway up the stairs by that time.

The long, narrow upstairs hall dissected the building down the middle, with four rooms on either side. Number eight was the last one on the left, where a long window lit the hall, sun glancing in off brilliant snow, giving life to the faded moss roses on the carpet.

Juggling the garments in one arm and holding the ivory dress folded over the other, she knocked on the door with its centered brass numeral eight. She had never been in a hotel room in her life and was rather discomfited at being here now. She intended to make sure the door remained open during the session.

Footsteps came across the floor on the other side of the door and she wondered what Damon Smith would be like. David had met him and thought highly of his work. The doorknob turned and the door was opened by Jesse DuFrayne.

She gaped at him as if she'd gone snowblind. She blinked exaggeratedly, but, no, it was Jesse all right, gesturing with a sweep of hand for her to enter.

"I must have the wrong room," she said, standing rooted to the spot, the eight on the open door seeming to wink at her.

"No, it's the right one," he said, unperturbed.

"But it's supposed to be Damon Smith's room."

"It is."

"Then where is he?"

"In my room, right there." He pointed to the closed door of number seven. "I persuaded him to trade rooms with me for a while."

"You persuaded him?"

"Yes, rather. A favor between fellow photographers, you might say."

"I don't believe you. What have you done to him?" She turned toward number seven, half expecting Jesse to try to stop her. But he leaned against the doorframe, arms folded, and said—oh so casually, "I paid him off. He won't be taking your photograph. I will."

Angry already, she flung at him, "You are just as pompous as always!"

He grinned charmingly. "Just paying my debts is all. I got that free dinner, but I still owe you one portrait, just like we wagered. I'll take it for you today."

"You will not!" And Abigail rapped soundly at the door of number seven. While she waited for an answer, behind her Jesse said, "I told him you and I are old friends, that you'd even saved my life once and by a lucky coincidence I'm here in town to do you a favor in return."

Just as she raised her knuckles to rap again, the door was opened by a blond, blinking man who was buttoning his vest and suppressing a yawn. It was apparent he'd been sleeping. He ran a hand through his tousled hair, grinned in a friendly manner, and glanced from one to the other. "What's up, Jesse? Is this Miss McKenzie?"

"Yes, this is Miss McKenzie!" snapped Miss McKenzie herself.

"Is something wrong?" he asked, surprised.

"Are you Damon Smith?"

"Yes . . . sorry, I should have intro—"

"And were you commissioned to take a wedding portrait of me?"

"Why, yes, but Jesse explained how he just happened to be in town at the right time to do it instead, and since the two of you are such close friends I have no objection to stepping aside. As long as he paid me for my trouble, there are no hard feelings. No need to apologize, Miss McKenzie."

"I am not knocking on your door to apologize, Mr. Smith. I am knocking to get my photograph taken as we agreed!"

Smith scowled. "Hey, Jesse, what the hell is this anyway?"

"A lovers' quarrel," Jesse answered easily, in a stage whisper. "If you'll just bow out, we'll get it settled. See, she's marrying this guy on the rebound." Jesse continued lounging against the doorframe.

Smith grunted while Abbie, outraged, swung first to one man, then to the other, claiming to deaf ears, "He's lying! I hired you to do my picture, not him. Now will you do it or not?"

"Listen, I didn't even set up my equipment, and besides, I don't want anything to do with whatever bones you two are picking. Just leave me out of it. Jesse already paid me twice what you would have, so why should I go through the trouble of setting up my gear? If you want your picture taken, let him do it. He's all set up for it anyway."

And before her astonished eyes, Damon Smith withdrew, mumbling about how in the hell he'd got into the middle of this in the first place, and slammed the door.

Immediately Abbie whirled on Jesse, incensed. "How dare you—" But he came away from that door, propelled her toward number eight, looking back over his shoulder down the hall with a conspiratorial grin.

"Shh," he teased. "If you want to pull your fishwife act, wait until the door is closed or the whole town will know about it."

She balked, outraged, jerking her elbow out of his grasp and taking root.

Rather than force her, he again made a gallant, sweeping gesture, saying politely, "Step into my parlor . . ."

Venomously, she added, ". . . said the spider to the fly!"

"Touché!" he saluted, smiling at her clever riposte. "But all I want to do is take your photograph, and you really don't have much choice in the matter now, do you?"

"I have the choice of having no photograph taken at all."

"Do you?" he asked, quirking one eyebrow.

"Haven't I?"

"Not if you want Melcher to remain blissfully ignorant of your midnight *tête-à-tête* last night with a caller who crept out of your house at three in the morning. Then, too, there's that clerk downstairs who knows perfectly well that you're up here at this very minute, having Damon take your photograph. Just how are you going to explain away your time spent with him if you can't produce a picture?"

She glared at the closed door of number seven and knew the spider had trapped her even before she entered his parlor. She could see that he did indeed have a hooded camera set up on a tripod, but it was little consolation. She thoroughly mistrusted him.

"Having created such a sensation the first time you entered this town," she reasoned, "you're certain not to have been missed this second time. The clerk knows you are up here too. One way or another David is bound to learn that you've been in town."

"But I have a perfectly legitimate business holding in this town, which he probably also knows I came to check on. So far nobody knows that you and I were together last night, or today for that matter, except Smith and he's been taken care of."

The man totally frustrated her. How could he change from the understanding warm person of last night to this conniving sneak?

"Ohhh! You and your railroad and your money! You think you can buy your way into or out of anything, don't you—that you can manipulate people's lives with the flash of your money."

"What good is my money if I don't use it to make me happy?" he asked innocently, once more indicating the open door.

She was licked and she knew it. She entered huffily while he began closing the door.

"Leave it open, if you please," she snapped, thinking, what can he do with the door wide open?

"Whatever you say," he agreed amiably, leaving the door as it happened to be, nearly closed, but unlatched. He advanced toward her, reaching politely for the things she held. She was now so leery of him that when he would have taken the garments, she refused to relinquish them.

Glancing at her hand clutching the ivory satin, he warned, "You'll wrinkle your wedding dress before you pose. What will David say?"

He took the garments and placed them on the bed, then came back to her. "Let me help you with your coat," he said, standing behind her while she unbuttoned it and let him remove it. "Nice coat," he noted as she shrugged it off. "Is it new?" She didn't have to see his face to recognize the knowing gleam in his eye. The coat was obviously part of her trousseau: it was obvious whose money had paid for it.

He laid it on the bed along with the other things, then turned to face her. They said nothing for a moment, and Abbie began to feel uneasy. What was she supposed to do, change clothes now?

"Isn't this where you're supposed to ask me if I'd like to see your etchings?" she asked sarcastically.

He surprised her by exclaiming, "Good idea!" with a single clap of his hands. "They're right over here."

Impossible as it was to believe, he meant it, for he squatted down by three large black cases and began unbuckling the straps on one of them. She knew immediately that these must be his photographs he'd mentioned so often.

"I was being facetious," she said, more mellowly.

"I know. Come and have a look anyway. I've wanted you to see these for a long time and maybe once you do you'll feel better about posing for me."

"You said you don't do portraits."

"I don't," he said, glancing up, sitting on his haunches with his hands resting on his thighs, "just yours."

He opened the first case and began removing layers of velvet padding from around the many heavy glass photographic plates, then the plates themselves.

"Come on, Abbie, don't be so skeptical and stubborn. I'll show you what it takes to build a railroad."

She was curious to see what kind of photographs he took, but still hesitated uncertainly. She'd been disarmed by him many times before.

"C'mon." He reached a hand up as if to pull her down beside him where he sat now, encircled by glass squares. He looked very appealing and even a little proud as he waited for her to join him. She ignored the hand but picked her way to the clear spot on the floor beside him and knelt in a puff of skirts, her eyes moving immediately to the photographs. The first one she saw was not of a train but of a square-sailed windjammer.

"I think this vessel would have a little trouble negotiating the rails," she observed.

He laughed and picked up the photograph, dusted it with his sleeve, and smiled down at it. "She's the *Nantucket*, and she made it around the Cape, from Philadelphia to San Francisco in just one hundred twelve days in eighteen sixty-three. The *Nantucket* brought the first two engines."

"Railroad engines?" she asked, surprised and interested in spite of herself. He gave her a brief smile, but his interest was mainly for the photographs.

"Everything came by ship then and everything rounded the Horn—engines, rails, spikes, fishplates, frogs—everything but wood for the ties and trestles."

Fishplates? Frogs? He sounded like he knew what he was talking about. Furthermore, while he talked, a delight shone from his eyes like none she'd ever seen there before. Next, he pointed to a picture of a locomotive riding aboard a lithe, graceful river schooner whose stern wheel churned the waters of the Sacramento levee.

"The railroads had to rely on the river steamers," he explained. "Did you know that the levee was built especially to transport supplies for the railroad, only to lose its own lifeblood to the railroads after doing so?"

He studied the picture, and she could not help being touched by the sadness that came into his eyes. He might have forgotten she was in the room, so absorbed was he. He reached to dust the picture with his fingers and she saw things about him she had never seen before.

Without taking his eyes from the picture, he reminisced, "I rode on a riverboat several times when I was a boy. New Orleans will never be the same without them." In his voice, in his touch of fingertips to glass plate, were both passion and compassion, and they moved Abbie deeply.

Next came pictures of trestles, their diamond girders snaking away into the hearts of mountains or the abysses of canyons.

"Sometimes the cinders set them on fire," he ruminated, frowning as if unable to forget a bad memory.

Next was a picture showing hundreds of antlike coolies pushing minute wooden barrows toward those endlessly stretching trestles, ballasting them by hand against the threat of fire. Jesse explained each photo, often smiling, sometimes frowning, but always, always with a concentrated emotion which struck Abbie deeper and deeper.

"That's Chen," he said of a wrinkled, sweating Chinese man.

She looked at the ugly, leathery looking face, then up at Jesse, who smiled down at some good memory.

"Was Chen's skin really yellow like I've heard?" she asked, mystified.

Jesse laughed softly and said, almost as if to himself, "No, more like the color of the earth he carried in his barrow, never complaining, always smiling." Again he dusted the picture with his sleeve. "I wonder where old Chen is now."

There were tunnels that stretched into black nothingness, their domed tops cavernous and foreboding. Even they made Abbie shiver. There were tent towns Jesse had once described to her, pictured in sun, in mud, at dinnertime, at fight time, even at dancing time—men dancing with men at the end of a dirty day. At these Jesse laughed, as if he remembered those good times vividly and had shared them. There were faces seamed with silt, backs bent bare over hammers, pot-bellied dignitaries in faultless silk suits with gold watch chains stretched across their bellies, contrasted against the sweat-streaked stomachs of soiled, tired navvies. There were two well-groomed hands clasped above the golden spike. There was a single stiff, gnarled hand sticking out of a mountain of rubble at which men frantically clawed.

"That was Will Fenton," Jesse said quietly. "He was a good old boy."

But this picture he did not dust. He just stared at it while Abbie watched pain drift across his face, and swallowed at a thick lump in her throat. She had the compulsion to reach out and lay a hand on his arm, soothe the tight, sad expression from his brow. Jesse, she thought, what else is inside you that I've never guessed? She looked at his long fingers resting along his thighs and again at Will Fenton's hand in the photograph.

What Abbie saw round her was a gallery of contrasts, a conscientious account of what it had cost to connect America's two shores with iron rails, of what some had paid while others profited, a pictorial statement from a man who'd done some of each—some paying and some profiting—and who knew the value of both.

James Hudson had been right.

"Well, do I pass muster?" Jesse asked, breaking into her reverie.

"Impressively," she answered, quite humbled by what lay around her, no longer sorry he'd tricked her into this room.

"Then why don't you get on all that wedding finery while I put these away?"

He bent to his task as if forgetting that she was there, and she glanced at the clothing still lying on the bed, then at the hinged screen in the far corner of the room and hoped she was doing the right thing as she went to collect her garments.

Behind the screen, she told herself that although she was very impressed by his photographs, she was not imbecile enough not to realize she'd just been soft-soaped by Jesse.

Step into my parlor, said the spider to the fly . . .

But all the while she was getting into her wedding gown, she kept remembering those photographs and the expression on Jesse's face. She hurried, telling herself to be wary of him, whether he'd won her respect as a photographer or not. He was still the wily Jesse DuFrayne.

He was clattering around out there, putting away his plates, whistling, then it sounded like he was shoving a piece of furniture about. When she stepped from behind the screen, his back was to her. He was kneeling down, taking something from the floor beside his camera. While she watched, he put it beneath the rockers of a chair he'd set before the camera. She caught his eyes while he knelt beside the rocking chair, but he continued that nonchalant whistling, obviously enjoying his trade.

"I need to see in your mirror," she said, noting that he'd rolled his shirtsleeves up as if he meant to do business.

"Fine," he said, rising and stepping aside so she could get between him and his camera to the dresser. He watched out of the corner of his eye while she smoothed back her hair and tightened the hairpins holding the severe french knot pulled back. In the mirror she watched him pull a pedestal table and fern over beside the rocking chair, obviously as a backdrop. Surely he wasn't planning to photograph her sitting in a rocking chair! What about her headpiece and the trailing veil? But she didn't question him yet, just lifted the seed-pearl circle. But when she was about to place it on her head, he ordered, "No, don't put that on!"

"But it's my bridal veil. I want it in the picture."

"It will be. Bring it here," he said, gesturing her toward the rocker.

"Surely you don't intend to have me sitting in a rocking chair in my wedding picture. I'm not *that* old, Jesse."

He laughed, a full-throated, wonderful laugh. He'd never known another woman with her great sense of humor. He stood loose, relaxed, hands on hips, letting his eyes take in the sight of Abbie in her mother's wedding dress. "I'm glad I've taught you that fact anyway, but yes, you're sitting in the rocker."

"Jesse . . ." she started to argue.

"I think I know a little more about this than you, so get over here." When she didn't move, he said, "Trust me."

She thought, look what happened last time I trusted you, but she did as he asked and neared the chair. He had propped it back at a sharp angle, shimming a block of wood beneath the rockers, and she suddenly realized what he was up to.

"This is supposed to be a picture of a bride, not a boudoir," she noted caustically.

"Don't be so suspicious, Ab, I know what I'm doing. David will love it when he sees it."

That made her more suspicious than ever.

"I want you to take my picture standing up."

"I'll be standing up. Don't worry."

"Don't be ridiculous, you know what I mean."

"Yes, of course I do. Just some facetiae of my own. But either we do this my way or David wonders why there's no picture to show for all your time up here today."

He reached out a palm, stood waiting to hand her into the chair. Stymied, she had to do as he wanted. With grave misgivings she let him take her hand and help her into the tilted rocker. His hand was hard and warm and somehow very secure-feeling as he squeezed hers, lending some balance while she lowered herself into the propped-back chair. This rocker was larger than her little sewing one, and had arms and a high back decorated with turned finials on each side of the curved backrest. The way he had the thing listing at such a severe angle, once she fell back into it she was quite helpless to get back out again. She felt positively adrift with her feet dangling free, and tried to hold her head away from the back of the chair.

Jesse took the veil from her hand and moved around behind her to lay it on the bed. He stepped to the back of the chair and looked down at her hair. Laying a hand on her forehead, he pulled her head back against the carved oak which caught her just above the nape of the neck.

"Like this," he said, "relaxed and natural."

At the touch of his hand, her heartbeat became pronounced within the high, tight collar of Mechlin lace. As her french knot touched the back of the chair, she found herself looking at Jesse upside down. They stared at each other for a moment and she wondered frantically what he was going to do to her.

In a velvety voice he began speaking as he slowly moved

around the chair, never taking his eyes off hers. "What we have here is the bride not before the ceremony, but after—the way every groom wants to remember his bride. When her hair is a little less than perfect and she doesn't know it."

He seemed to be moving in slow motion, reaching toward a pocket, producing a small comb while her eyes never left his, but she saw the comb coming toward her temple, where it bit lightly, loosing some strands from their moorings while she failed, for once, to protest. She knew she should put her hands up to stop him from this madness, but he seemed to have hypnotized her with those dark, probing eyes and that low, crooning voice.

"There is a look a man likes about his bride," came that voice again. "Call it tousled maybe . . . less than perfect after all the cheeks that have pressed hers that day and all the arms that have hugged her, all the losers that have danced with her and touched her temple with theirs." He leaned toward her slowly, reaching a dark hand again to hook a wisp of hair in front of the opposite ear, not smiling, but studying, studying. She knew her french knot was being annihilated, but sat entranced while he freed the fine strand, then moved around the rocking chair while she followed him with her eyes.

"He likes tendrils that cling here and there and stick to her damp skin."

No, Jesse, no, she thought, yet sat mesmerized while he wet the tip of his own finger with his tongue, touched it to the crest of her cheek, then stuck the curl onto it. She saw and felt it all as if only an observer at a distance—the tip of his tongue, his long finger, the wet, cold spot of his saliva on her cheek. She tried not to think of how many places on her body he had touched with his tongue, but his finger went to his mouth again and he did the same on her other cheek, then backed away a little, approving, "Oh, much better, Abbie. David will love this."

She gripped the arms of the chair and stared up at him, her errant pulse skipping to every part of her he had touched and many he had not.

"Oh, but you're so tense. No bride should clutch the arms of her chair as if she's scared to death." His hair came very close to her face as he took both of her hands from the arms of the chair and ordered in that same dreamlike voice, "Loosen up," then shook them lightly until her wrists acquiesced and grew limp. "Just like in your bedroom that night when you first laughed," he reminded her. "Remember?" She let him do what he would with those lacebound wrists. He turned one over and laid it palm-up on her thigh. "That's right," he murmured, then ran one of his fingertips from its wrist to the end of her middle finger, flicking it, finding it relaxed. Shivers ran across her belly. He rose and disappeared momentarily, and her wide eyes only waited for the return of his dark face before her.

"Now the veil . . ." He brought it, a cloud of white in his swarthy, masculine hands, "the symbol of purity, about to be discarded." Her heart leaped wildly as his arm came toward her, but he only hung the headpiece on a spooled finial beside her temple and brought the lace train over one arm to lay in a flowing heap cascading from her lap. "Palm-up, okay, Ab?" The texture of netting crossed her palm as he placed it there, as if she had just tiredly removed it from her head. Then he lifted her other arm and draped its wrist like a willow branch over the chair arm. He knelt on one knee before her.

"It's the end of the day, right? Far too late for tight shoes and stiff collars." And before she realized what was happening, he had swept David's satin gift from her feet, his palm sliding over her sole in a sensuous fleeting touch. She gazed, awestruck, into silence as he rose and moved behind her again, hypnotizing her with his dark eyes above the slash of moustache which curved in the direction of a smile as she once again viewed it upside down. She knew he was reaching for the buttons at her throat but was powerless to stop him. His fingers slowly freed the first one, relieving some of the pressure where her heartbeat threatened to shut off her breath. He freed a second button, then a third—tiny buttons, close together, held by delicate loops that took time, time, time before he had finally exposed the hollow of her throat. She stared up into his black eyes. His hands slid from her throat to the finials of the chair and tipped it farther back, holding it as he looked down into her tortured eyes and asked throatily, "What man would not like to remember his bride this way?"

His eyes, even upside down, burned like firebrands, scorching her cheeks, making her want to cover her face with the inverted palm that lay instead lax upon her lap. Had she wanted to get up and run from him she could not. She had no recourse now but to submit to his narcotic voice and eyes.

Looking down at her, Jesse could see a tricky sunshaft emphasize the heartbeat in the hollow of her throat behind the filigreed lace which lay open and inviting. He released the chair slowly until it rested against its shim again, then equally as slowly moved to its side, never taking his eyes from Abbie's face, trailing one hand on the finial very close to her cheek.

"Wet your lips, Abbie," he said softly. "They should be wet when the picture is snapped." But he made no move toward the camera, neither did she wet her lips.

"Wet them," he urged, "as if David has just now kissed them and said . . . I love you, Abbie." Jesse stared down at her soft, parted lips, his eyes roved up to hers, then back down to her mouth again, waiting. The tip of her tongue crept out and slipped across her lips, leaving them glistening, opened yet as the breath came labored between them.

He leaned down, placing one hand on each arm of the chair, his face only inches from hers, his voice like warm honey. "Your eyes are opened too wide, Abbie. When a man tells his wife he loves her, don't her eyelids flutter closed?" She fought for breath, staring at his handsome, handsome face, so near that when he spoke, she felt the words against her skin. "Let's try it once more and see," he whispered, still leaning above her.

"I love you, Abbie." And her eyelids lost their moorings.

"I love you, Abbie," she heard again . . . and they were at half mast.

"I love you, Abbie." And they closed against his cheek as his mouth came hungering. She no longer wanted to get up from the chair, for his open lips claimed hers and his long hands cinched her shoulders, thumbs reaching to stroke the spot where he'd seen her heart fluttering in her throat. He knelt on one knee at the side of the rocker while he kissed her back against it, his tongue dancing and stroking upon hers while everything in her reached and yearned for more.

But suddenly she felt panic rise within, tightening her lungs, her throat, her scalp. "No, I'm being married tomorrow," she choked, turning her head aside from his kiss which taunted her to forget.

"Exactly—tomorrow," he murmured softly into her neck.

Her eyes slid closed, and she turned sharply away from him in a vain attempt to combat the feelings he unleashed in her. "Let me up from this chair," she pleaded, close to tears.

"Not until I get a proper kiss from the bride," he said, kissing the underside of her jaw. "Ab, you're not his wife yet, but when you are, I won't be here to kiss the bride. Just one day early, that's all . . ."

When she still refused to turn toward him, he said, "Why not, Ab? Let's make you look like a kissed woman for David's photograph. That's how a woman looks on her wedding night, isn't it?" Then a strong hand spanned her chin and turned her mouth to his. But when he swooped to kiss her again, she began struggling against him, using arms, hands, and elbows. But he captured her arms effortlessly and lifted them around his neck, holding them there forcibly until he felt her struggling begin to quell.

Those arms had been denied for so long. Now at last they curled around the dark hair at the back of his neck while she arched up and opened the lips she had wet at his command, for David.

Jesse's mouth twisted hungrily across hers, then suddenly jerked away as he knocked the block of wood from beneath the rocker with a thrust of his knee. The chair came reeling forward and he was there to meet her as she came with it. Their mouths met almost desperately and he pulled Abbie from the chair onto her knees before him. He wrapped a powerful arm about her waist, forcing her against his hard, bulging loins, which moved in slow, sensuous circles against her satin wedding dress. His hands moved down to hold her tightly against him while their tongues spoke messages of want into each other's mouths and their lips spoke like messages against flesh that arched and pressed until both ached sweetly.

Tearing his lips from hers, he uttered against her temple, "You can't marry him, Ab. Say you can't." But before she could make a sound his impatient mouth sought hers once more, delving into its warmth and wetness with his seeking tongue. "Say it," he demanded in a voice gruff with passion as he lowered his lips to her jaw, then down, down to the open neck of her wedding dress. But she was adrift in splendor, could think of nothing but the pleasured sound which his touch brought from her throat. She leaned her face into his hair, kissing the top of his head while her hands caressed his face. His mouth moved beneath her palms, opening wide as he tasted her skin and buttons sprayed like sundrops around them, glancing off his face as he lowered it to the newly cloven garment where her breasts waited for his lips.

She recaptured enough sanity to murmur, "Jess . . . my wedding dress . . ."

Into her breasts he answered, "I'll buy you a new one." Then his head came up and his palms slid within the torn garment, touching a taut nipple, flattening it, then stroking it to an erect, pink peak.

"But it's my mother's," she said senselessly.

"Good," he grunted, running both of his palms upward past her breasts, onto her shoulders, then peeling the garment away with an outward thrust of wrists. He forced it down in back until it lay tight just above her elbows, imprisoning them within the long, lace sleeves but freeing her breasts to his hands, his tongue, his teeth, while her throat arched backward in abandon. He tugged at a nipple, groaned deep in his throat, then released it to rub the soft hair of his moustache back and forth across it as he admitted, "God, Abbie, I couldn't get you out of my mind."

"Please, Jess, we've got to stop."

But he didn't, only moved to her other breast.

"Did you think about me too?" he asked in a choked voice.

She tried halfheartedly to pull his head away from her breasts, but he continued kissing and suckling while her arms remained pinioned by the garment, useless.

"I tried not to. Oh, Jess, I tried."

"I did too . . ."

"Stop, Jess . . ."

"I love it when you call me Jess that way. What do you call him when he does this to you?" He knelt up straight again and held the back of her head in his two wide hands, searching her eyes before pulling her to him to kiss her with an almost savage anguish. Breaking away, he touched her very deliberately in her most sensitive spots—breast, belly, down her ivory skirts that remained between his hand and the warm, weeping female flesh within. "Can David make you quiver like this, want like this? Can he make your breasts get hard and your body go dewy like I can?"

And he knew from the tortured look upon her face what the answer was before she touched his face and kissed his chin, moving close.

"No . . . not like you, Jess, never like you . . ."

And she knew if she lived with David a thousand years the answer would remain the same.

Chapter 24

———————

THE BELL TINKLED and David looked up to find Bones Binley shambling toward him between the red benches. Now that the cold weather was here, Bones had taken to loitering in the store, which was far more comfortable than Mitch's veranda, and where the coffee was hot. Then, too, it gave him a chance to eye Mizz Abigail now and again.

She wasn't here today . . . but Bones knew that before he came in.

"Howdy, Bones," David greeted the gangly stalk, experiencing the peculiar momentary twinge of ego he always felt in Bones's presence ever since he'd heard Bones had eyes for his woman. As Abbie's "chosen one," David often patronized Bones just the smallest bit. As the "non-chosen," Bones sensed this and bridled inwardly. He couldn't figure out what Mizz Abigail saw in Melcher anyway.

"What say, David?" Bones returned.

"Thanks for taking Abigail's packages up from the depot yesterday. She was really happy to see them. She'd been waiting for the headpiece for days and was worried it might not get here in time."

Bones nodded at the floor. "Yup."

"She said to thank you again when I saw you."

"Yup."

"She's up at the hotel having her picture taken."

"Yup."

David laughed. "I don't know why I bother telling you anything. There's not a thing happens in this town you don't know about before it does."

Bones again laughed at the floor—a soundless shake of shoulders.

"Yup, that's a fact. Now y' take like yesterday, with that blizzard brewin', I musta been the only one out when the two-twenty come in and that DuFrayne feller gits off carryin' all that pitcher-takin' gear and checks in up at Edwin's." Bones found his twist of tobacco and bit off a good-size chew.

David went white as the new snow.

"D . . . D . . . DuFrayne?"

"Yup."

"Y . . . you . . . m . . . must be mistaken, Bones. That wasn't D . . . DuFrayne, it was D . . . Damon Smith with the picture-taking gear."

"Him? He the blond one? Short? About so-high? Naw, he din't come in till the nine-fifty this morning. No, that other one, he come in on the late train yesterday and checks in at Edwin's just like I said. Far as I know he's still right there." Bones lifted the lid off the pot-bellied stove, took deadly aim, and let fly with a brown streak of tobacco juice that sizzled into the lull that had suddenly fallen. Then he wiped the side of his mouth with the edge of his hand, keeping the corner of his eye on David.

"I . . . I see it's time for me to go m . . . meet Abigail, Bones. I t . . . told her I w . . . would, after she was d . . . done with the ph . . . photograph. If you'll excuse me . . ."

"Sure thing, sure thing," returned the pleased Bones as David hurried to the back room for his coat.

Three and a half minutes later, David entered the hotel lobby.

"Well, David, my man, how's business?"

"All s . . . set to go, right af . . . after the w . . . wedding."

Edwin chuckled amiably, noting David's nervousness. He gave David a conspiratorial grin. "Last twenty-four hours before a wedding are the toughest, eh, David?"

David swallowed.

"Don't you worry now, with that store and that wife, you're gonna be as happy as a hog in slop."

Normally David would have laughed heartily with Edwin, but he only asked now, with a worried look upon his face, "Is she here, Ed?"

"Sure is." Ed thumbed toward the ceiling. "Been up there an hour already. Should have a dandy photograph by this time."

"I . . . I n . . . need to talk to her a m . . . minute."

"Sure thing, go right on up. Smith's in number eight, end o' the hall on your left."

"Thanks, Ed. I'll find it."

Upstairs the sunlight streamed through sheer lace on the long, narrow window at the end of the hall as David strode silently upon the long runner strewn with faded moss roses. His toe had begun to hurt, and his heart felt swollen, as if it were choking him. An hour? She had been here an hour? Did it take an hour to have a photograph made? But it *was* Damon Smith she was with, It was! Yes, it surely must take at least an hour for the posing and the developing, which was done on the spot.

As he approached number eight, he saw that the door was closed but not latched.

A murmur of voices came from inside—a man's, husky and low, a woman's, strained and throaty. David felt suddenly weak and placed his palm against the wall for support. The voices were muffled, and David strained to hear.

"Stop, Jess . . ."

Oh, God, that was Abigail's voice. David's eyes slid closed. He willed his feet to move, to take him away, but it felt as if those moss roses had suddenly sent up tendrils to hold his ankles to the carpet. Tortured, he listened to the husky words that followed.

"I love it when you call me Jess that way. What do you call him when he does this to you?"

David's mind filled with terrible moving pictures as a long, long silence followed and sweat broke out on his brow. Move! he told himself. Get out! But before he could, DuFrayne's voice, fierce, passionate, asked, "Can David make you quiver like this, want like this? Can he make your breasts get hard and your body go dewy like I can?"

And Abigail's shaken reply, "No . . . not like you, Jess, never like you . . ."

David hesitated a moment longer, nausea and fear plummeting through him while from within the room came the sounds of lovers who forget themselves, and the temptation became too great.

Stepping to the door, he pushed it open, then gulped down the gorge that threatened to erupt from his throat.

Abigail knelt on the floor, eyes closed, head slung back as hair tumbled in wanton disarray down her bared back. The bodice of her wedding gown was lowered, pinning her elbows to her sides, baring her breasts to Jesse DuFrayne, who knelt on one knee before her, his mouth upon her skin. Abigail's bridal veil was crushed beneath their knees, its headpiece lay in a misshapen gnarl under the rocking chair behind her. Pearl buttons lay ascatter amid hairpins, a comb, the satin shoes he'd given Abigail as a wedding gift. Sickened yet unable to tear his eyes away, David watched as the woman he was supposed to marry tomorrow reached blindly to cup the jaw of the dark man before her, guiding his mouth from one breast to the other as a soft moan escaped her lips.

The shamed blood came surging to David's face as he bleated out a single word. "Abigail!"

She jerked back. "David! Oh, my God!"

"Well, you certainly had me fooled!"

The blood drained from her face, but as quickly as she pulled back, Jesse instinctively pulled her against his chest, shielding her bare breasts from intruding eyes, cupping the back of her head protectively, even his raised knee tightening against her hip as he settled her safely against the lee of his loins.

"You'd better watch what you say, Melcher, because this time it will be me who answers, not her," Jesse warned, his voice resounding mightily against Abigail's ear which lay against his chest.

"You . . . you scum!" David hissed. "I was right all along. You're two of a kind!"

"It seems we are, which makes me wonder why in the living hell she'd want to marry you."

"She won't be! You can have her!"

"Sold!" barked Jesse, piercing Melcher with an ominous

glare while he reached blindly to pull the shoulders of Abigail's dress back up.

"An apt word, I'd say, considering the money she's already taken from you, you son of a bitch!"

Abigail felt Jesse's muscles tense as he put her away from him and made as if to rise.

"Stop it! Stop it, both of you!" Abbie cried, clutching her dress front and struggling to her feet, followed by Jesse, who kept a shoulder between her and the door. The torn garment, their compromising pose, and what David had overheard made denial impossible. She felt as if she were freefalling through endless space into the horrifying noplace of *déjà vu*. She lurched around to move toward David, but he backed away in distaste.

"David, I'm sorry . . . I'm sorry, David, please forgive me. I didn't intend for this to happen." She reached a supplicating hand toward him even as the other continued to hold her bodice together. But apologies and excuses were so pitifully inadequate they only added to her shame.

"You lying harlot," he ground out venomously, all signs of stammering somehow surprisingly gone from his voice. "Did you think I wouldn't find out? Just one more time before you married me, is that it? Just one more time with this son of a bitch you'd rather have than me? Well, fine—keep him!"

Today was the first time she'd ever heard David swear. She reached to clutch his sleeve, horrified at what he'd witnessed, at herself for having fallen so low.

"David, please . . ."

But he jerked free, as if her touch were poison.

"Don't touch me. Don't you ever touch me again," he said in cold, hard hate. Then he tugged his coat squarely onto his shoulders, turned on his good foot, and limped away without a backward glance.

Standing there staring at the empty doorway the enormity of her offense washed over her. Tears formed in her eyes and her hands came to cover her open mouth, from which no sound issued for a long time. She felt sickened by herself and her eyes slid shut as she started quaking uncontrollably.

"He'll never marry me now. Oh God, the whole town will know within an hour. What am I going to do?" She covered her temples with her fingertips and rubbed them, then clutched her arms tightly and rocked back and forth as if nearing hysteria.

Jesse stood several feet behind her, did not approach or try to
touch her as he said quietly, "It's simple. . . . Marry me."

"What!" She spun to face him, staring for a moment as if
he'd gone mad. But she was the one suddenly laughing,
crying, shaking all at once in a queer fit tinged by frenzy. "Oh,
wouldn't that be jolly. Marry you and we could spend the rest
of our lives screaming and biting and scratching and trying to
get the better of each other. Oh . . ." She laughed again
hysterically, "Oh, that's very funny, Mr. DuFrayne," she
ended, tears streaming down her face.

But Jesse was not laughing. He was stone serious, his face
an unmoving mask as he said intensely, "Yes, sometimes it is
very funny, Miss McKenzie—funny and exhilarating and
wonderful, because that's our way of courting each other. I
found I missed it so much when I was away from you that I had
to come back here to see if you were as good as I
remembered."

"You purposely came back to cause trouble between David
and me, don't deny it."

"I'm not denying it. But I changed my mind last night while
we talked. What happened here today was not planned. It just
happened."

"But you . . . you tricked me into this room, into . . .
into sitting in that rocking chair and . . . and . . ."

"But you wanted it just as bad as I did."

The truth was still too frightening for her to face, and she
was, as always, confounded by his changeability. She could
not help wondering what his motives were today. She swung
around him and swooped toward the screen in the corner,
accusing, "It's all a big game to you, manipulating people so
th—"

"This is not a game, Abbie," he argued, following her right
around the screen, talking to her shoulder as she turned her
back on him. "I'm asking you to marry me."

She unbuttoned her cuffs as if they were made of itchweed.
"Oh, wouldn't we be the laughingstock of Stuart's Junction—
Miss Abigail and her train robber!" She turned to him, yanking
at the sleeves, affecting the sugary tone of a gossip. "Oh, you
remember, don't you? The couple who were caught in the act
the day before her impending marriage to another man?" She
yanked the bodice down, fuming. He moved up close behind
her.

"That in itself should tell you that we're right for each other. You know damn well you enjoy it more with me than with him or you never would have let me get as far as I did today."

She whirled on him, holding some garment over her breasts. "How dare you insinuate that I did anything with David! We did nothing—absolutely nothing! We were as pure as the driven snow and this town knew it!"

They stood nose to nose, each of them glaring.

"Who gives a damn about what this town thinks? What has this town ever done for you besides label you a spinster when you were only twenty years old?"

"Get out of here when I'm changing my clothes!" she shouted, and presented her back to step out of the wedding dress, bending forward and giving him a rear view of white pantalets more ruffled than any he'd seen on her clothesline. His eyes traveled down her skin, down the shadowed hollow that receded into the white cotton waistband.

"When I get out of here, it will be with you on my arm, wearing that expensive green coat I paid for, telling this town to kiss off as we board my train!"

She yanked a camisole over her head and he watched the fine hair at the back of her neck as she looked down and tied the string at her waist.

"You're still not done flaunting your money, are you?" She threw a brief, disparaging look over her shoulder. "Well, you've come up against the one thing you can't buy!" She pulled a petticoat and skirt on and buttoned them at her waist.

"Buy you!" he shouted, "I don't want to buy you. I want you free! You have to give yourself to me freely if we get married, because you want to."

"You planned this seduction today, don't tell me you didn't." She pulled a blouse off the top of the screen and slipped her arms into it.

He reached out and got her from behind by both breasts, pulling her back against his hardness. She purposely remained aloof, acting as if his touch went thoroughly unnoticed except when she had to push his hands aside to close the buttons of her blouse.

"So we're even then, aren't we, Ab?" he asked, pressing the side of his mouth against the hair behind her ear. "Didn't you plan my seduction once? Only you succeeded where I haven't . . . so far." As he nuzzled her rose-scented neck, he

fervently began caressing her breasts, at last awakening the
fight in her. She fought his hands, but he only held her tighter,
slipping his palm inside her partially opened blouse, leaning to
kiss the nape of her neck, sliding his other hand down her
stomach, then lower. They grappled together, elbows flying,
sending the screen crashing to the floor.

"You have the most unscrupulous courting methods I've
ever seen!" she bawled, pulling at his wrists, but just then he
got one powerful arm cinched around her stomach, his other
hand once more finding its way to her breast and forcing her
back against his tumescent body.

"Feel that. Tell me you don't want it. Tell me I don't know
what's best for you."

For a moment she wilted and his grip slackened, giving her
enough advantage to break free and spin to face him.

"How can you know what's best for me when I don't even
know myself?"

Her eyes flicked to the door David had left open.

"Then I think it's time I showed you again," he threatened
with honey in his voice, taking a step nearer.

Her heart was hammering wildly now, confused by the
mixture of emotions Jesse could always stir up in her. They
eyed each other like a pair of cats at howling time, beginning
slowly, slowly to circle until she gained the side of the room
closest to the hall. Suddenly she turned and hit for the door, but
he had it slammed so fast the wind dried her eyeballs. She
backed away, big-eyed, panting, feeling the throb of her pulse
in every wary nerve of her body.

He leaned back casually, holding the doorknob behind his
back. One foot was flat on the floor, the other crossed in front
of it with only the toe of his boot on the floor. He wasn't even
breathing heavily. He lounged there as if he had all the time in
the world, the ghost of a grin crawling up one side of his mouth
while those hazel-flecked eyes assessed her with a tinge of
knowing mirth. His voice was soft, cajoling, seductive.

"You know we're doing it again, don't you? The old
courting dance we both love so much. This is the way we
always start out, Abbie—me pursuing, you fighting me off.
But this is no fight and you know it, because in the end we both
win." He brought his shoulders away from the door in slow
motion. "So come here you little hell-cat," he ended with a

hoarse whisper, "because I'll only stalk you so long before I pounce."

She loved it, she'd missed it, she wanted it, this hammering of the senses that exhilarated like nothing else she'd ever experienced as she waited, waited, knowing what he'd do. Her breasts were heaving and her eyes sparkled, but like a true hellcat she spit one more time. "Come here! Do this! Do that! Marry me! And then what? Go through this for the rest of our lives!"

His grin grew bolder. "You're goddamn right," he said, low.

"Oh, you . . . you . . ."

But he was done waiting.

"Damn . . ." he muttered, and sprang! He grabbed her wrists and swung her adeptly until her back slammed flat against the closed door. His hands grasped her beneath the armpits and she felt her feet leave the floor as he lifted her bodily, holding her plastered against the mahogany panel, kissing her. His wide palms bracketed the sides of her breasts while his lips, too, held her prisoner, controlling hers, sending spasms of desire rippling through her body, directed each to its own nerve by his mastering tongue. Emotions stormed her senses while Jesse stormed her body, breathing now like a hurricane while he besieged her with deep kisses, his tongue fierce and probing, impaling her against the door.

At last he freed her mouth, gazing with dark, tempestuous eyes into hers.

"Damnit, Abbie, I love you. It was me saying I love you before, for myself, not for David."

She seemed unable to speak, and they both suddenly realized he still had her up against that door. He let her slide slowly down, a last hairpin dropping unnoticed from her hair. When her toes touched the floor, he continued holding her lightly by both breasts, searching her eyes for some sign of entente.

"What do you say, Abbie?"

Her eyes, kindled yet confused, sparkled within the shock of loosened hair framing her face.

"How can I marry a man I'm afraid of half the time, who just flung me against a door?"

A pained expression crossed his face and he dropped his hands from her breasts to her ribs, touching her gently, caringly.

"Oh, God, did I hurt you, Abbie? I didn't mean to hurt you." He kissed one of her eyelids, then the other, then backed away to look into her blue eyes, his voice as close to tortured as she'd ever heard it. "Are you really afraid of me, Abbie? You don't ever have to be afraid of me. All I want to do is make you happy, make you laugh, maybe moan . . . but not from hurt. From this . . ."

He closed her eyes once again with his lips, then trailed them down her nose to her cheek, along her delicate jaw to her chin, then finally up to her lips, which had fallen open by the time he reached them. His hands went to the shoulders of her unbuttoned blouse, squeezing until she thought her bones would crack. But his mouth upon hers was a direct contrast to the pressure of his hands—soft, gentle, convincing, while his warm tongue skimmed lightly, lightly over her lips, then over her teeth before he moved to her ear and said into it. "Admit it, Abbie, it's what you want too. Be honest with me and with yourself."

"How can I be honest when you've got a hold on me this way? Jesse, I can't think."

He cautiously dropped his hands, but only to her ribs, riding them lightly as if afraid she might escape him yet. And there they lay, warm, large, spanning her torso, one of his thumbs reaching up to brush the underside of her breast while he searched her face.

"Abbie, you said you had to shout to the empty rooms when I was gone, trying to be free of me. Doesn't that tell you something?"

Her eyes pleaded but he did not relinquish his hold on her. Instead, the warmth from his palms seeped through the layer of cotton over her skin, his hands now inside the blouse, on her ribs, that long thumb still arousing her to shivery sensuality as it slid slowly back and forth.

"I'm so mixed up," she said in a trembling voice, eyes sliding closed, head resting back wearily against the door.

"You have a right to be. I'm exactly the opposite of what you've been told all your life was right for you. But I am right, Ab, I am."

She rolled her head from side to side, swallowing. "I don't know . . . I don't know."

"Yes, you do, Abbie. You know what kind of life we'd have. We're good together at everything we do. Talking, arguing, making love, making sense . . . and nonsense. What are you afraid of, Abbie, that you'll get hurt again? Or of what this town will say? Or what David will say?"

She opened her eyes but looked over his shoulder at the lacy window curtain and the snow beyond.

"I've hurt David so badly." Her nostrils flared and her eyes slid shut.

"Maybe you had to, for your own salvation."

"No, nobody deserves to be hurt like that."

"Did you, thirteen years ago?"

She looked into his eyes again.

"I refuse to appease my conscience by saying two wrongs make a right."

"Then let me share part of the blame for hurting him. Hell, I'll even march up the street and apologize to him if that's what it takes to win you. Is that what you want me to do, Abbie?"

Tears suddenly stung her nose, for the loss of David, for this man's devotion. She somehow believed Jesse meant it and would actually face David and apologize. After all, Jesse was a man who'd go to any lengths to get what he wanted. It struck her just how badly he wanted her. Still, she leaned against that door and let him go on convincing her, for it was heavenly standing there with his dark face so close to hers as he leaned both forearms now on either side of her head.

"There's a whole country out there, Abbie. You can pick any city you want to live in. I'll take you anyplace. You want to live like the wife of a railroad baron in some mansion in Colorado Springs, all right. It's yours. You name the place and we'll go. How about starting in New Orleans? I'll take you to see the ocean, Abbie, and to meet my family. You've always wanted to see the ocean, you told me so. You even tried to bring a little of it here by designing that Cape Cod window in that shoe store, but I'll take you to Cape Cod to see the real thing if you want." His eyes were filled with sincerity as he went on. "Abbie, I don't want to buy you, but I would if I had to. I'm rich, Abbie, so what's wrong with that? What's wrong with me wanting to spend my money making you happy? I owe you my life, Abbie, let me give it to you . . ."

This, this, this, she thought, was what she had always dreamed of, the Jesse she'd always dreamed of, whispering love words in her ear, making her blood pound and her senses soar. Her eyes drifted open and found his, dark, intense, promising her the world. She floated in the warm security of the knowledge of his love for her, quite unable to speak at the moment.

Is this me, she thought, Abigail McKenzie? Is this really happening? This startlingly handsome man, with his elbows leanings beside my ears, convincing me with utter sincerity in his every word that he loves me? Her heart felt ready to explode.

He leaned to nuzzle her neck, to nip her earlobe, then touch the inside of it with the tip of his damp tongue.

"That's what I want, Ab, but what about what you want right now?"

She felt his breath—warm, fast—beating upon her ear, then his voice came again, strangled and strange, making things melt within her body. "Don't discount it as unimportant. If I slipped my hand beneath your skirt and touched your body, I know what I'd find. Don't deny that it's important, Ab. I've felt it there before because you wanted me, and I know it's there again."

And deep inside Abbie felt a welcome liquid rush of femininity, accompanied by the sensual swelling of that part of her which no man except Jesse had ever touched.

Her eyes slid closed. Her chest tightened. Her breath came jerky. Even the hair at the back of her neck felt like it had nerves, each of them aroused, ready for response.

Across the fullest part of her stomach, she felt him press his aroused body, lightly, lightly brushing from left to right, right to left, making circles on her while his palms remained pressed flat against the door above her head. Her own palms tingled, eager to be released and to touch him, yet she kept them pressed flat against the door behind her hips, drawing out this sensual mating dance to its fullest, wanting it to build slowly, slowly, slowly in tempo and heat while he rubbed against her, his shirt buttons now lightly grazing the tips of her nipples, which were drawn up tight like tiny, hard bells beneath the flimsy cotton camisole.

She trembled with sensation. Jesse, Jesse, she thought, you are so good at this . . . so good . . .

He looked down to find a faint smile upon her lips, her eyes still closed, her breasts now straining as far forward as she could manage and still keep her shoulder blades against the door. He smiled slowly, understanding her well, letting his elbows slide several inches lower, bringing his midsection away from hers, then flicking his tongue out to touch the very corner of her eye.

She's had so little love, he thought, I will drown her in it for the rest of her life.

No word was said. Her hands came from behind her to blindly find his hips and pull them back against her, bringing his heat and hardness where she wanted them, making him smile against her hair and slip one arm between her shoulder blades and the door, down to her waist. His other hand grasped the doorknob for leverage as he ground himself against her, a hand clapped tight now upon the seat of her petticoats, quite unable to feel much more through all those layers.

Her hips began to move with his, while her palms remained just below his belt as if she must know fully his every motion—she must, she must, she had waited so long. She opened her eyes as if drugged, pleading silently until his mouth came down to find hers open, waiting, yearning. And together their tongues dove deep while their flesh pressed so tightly together that pulses seemed inseparable.

She writhed between him and the door and he moved his mouth to her ear, whispering hoarsely, "Abbie, I'm going to take you to that bed and make love to you like you never imagined you'd be made love to again."

He felt her shudder and understood what was happening inside her. His own body was straining against the confines of clothing. Still, he leaned low and lightly bit one of her nipples—as if in passing—through the cloth and all, making her twist and suck her breath in sharply and open her eyes.

He slipped an arm around her shoulder, the other beneath her knees, and lifted her effortlessly from her feet, her arms twining up and about his broad shoulders, fingers twining into the hair at the back of his neck while he turned slowly, slowly toward the bed.

"And I'm going to keep it up . . . and keep it up . . . and keep it up . . . until you admit that you love me and say you'll marry me," he said throatily.

They stared into each other's eyes as he strode toward the bed, the muscles of his chest hard and warm against her breast.

She heard the springs sing out as he knelt with one knee and leaned to lay her down. With a hand on either side of her head, he hung above her, and said into her eyes, "And I don't intend to be hindered by the petticoats you chose to wear for any wedding to another man—whether I paid for them or not." Then without watching what he was doing, he found the buttons at her waist and she felt them come free. Tingles shafted through her and she smiled, a glitter of eagerness now playing up at him from behind fringed lashes.

"But, Jesse, you paid so dearly to arrange that wedding," she said softly, seductively.

"Well, I'm unarranging it," he said gruffly, and he stripped the petticoats away down her calves, then grabbed her hand and pulled her to a sitting position.

"And neither will I contend with Victorian collars that signify nothing."

With agonizing slowness he removed her blouse. She obediently complied, but when his dark head dipped near hers as he slid the garment away she informed him, "Whether I marry you or not, I will dress as I see fit—like a lady."

"Fine," he returned as the blouse came off. "You do that. In our parlor when you have the ladies of the other railroad barons to tea." He tossed the blouse over his shoulder. "In our bedroom you leave them hanging in the chiffonier along with your camisole and these." He inserted a single finger into the waistband of her pantaloons, tugging.

She fell back languidly, arms flung loosely above her head, and lay there in wait, loving him more with each passing word.

"You paid for these too. I suppose that gives you the right to do what you will with them."

He knelt beside her and without taking his eyes from her face, removed his vest and shirt, flinging them over his shoulder to join her petticoat and skirt on the floor.

"Exactly. Just like I paid for that green coat you were going to wear on your honeymoon. And if you weren't proud of the fact that I'm rich you wouldn't keep pointing it out time and again." And off came his belt.

"I would have been content to run a simple shoe store," she purred, reaching out to brush the backs of her fingers against the part of him she'd first seen when he was dying upon her bed, making his eyes burn bright before her fingers trailed away from his trousers.

Then slowly, tantalizingly, he freed the buttons up the front of his pants, while his voice poured over her like liquid silk.

"When I'm done here, I'm going to shoot down that

goddamn sign that's got your name on it with his." The ardor in his tone made the word *goddamn* almost an endearment. Then his pants, too, were gone.

"Signifying nothing," she murmured with a slow smile.

"Like hell," he said gruffly, reaching to untie the string at the waist of her camisole, then sliding a hand inside, up, up, over her ribs as he sat on the bed and stretched his long, dark limbs toward Abbie.

Her nostrils widened and her breath came jagged.

"You don't think it's significant that I'm taking back what I once gave away so foolishly?" he asked possessively, pushing the camisole up by increments, leaning his dark head to kiss the hollow between her ribs, then that beneath her left breast.

Eyes closing, she whispered, "This whole town probably knows what we're doing right now," caring not the least, loving it anyway.

He moved his tongue to the hollow beneath her other breast, chuckling deep in his throat, his lips nuzzling against her skin.

"And they'll probably run home and do a little of it themselves, just at the thought."

"Not everyone's like you, Jess," she said, smiling behind closed lids, wishing he would hurry up.

But he moved like a seductive snail, unbuttoning the waist of her pantaloons and slipping them only to her hips, exposing their hollows provocatively.

"No, but you are, and that's all that counts." Again his mouth found her hollows, these just inside her hipbones, while she stirred sinuously. And after some moments the last garment moved slowly, slowly downward while he kissed a path in its wake and she lay with a wrist across her forehead, all resistance gone, her lips parted as his tongue danced upon her.

"I remember this best," he whispered hoarsely before delving into her, following as she arched, stroking until she moaned and fell back, shuddering beneath him.

"I did too . . . I did too," came her strangled voice.

He knew her well, he loved her well, he drew his head back just at her breaking point, moving up her body to thread his fingers back through her hair and lay his hot, hard length upon her, not in her.

"Say it, Abbie," he begged, kissing her beneath the jaw as her head arched back. "Say it now while I come into you."

She opened her eyes and found his filled with love as they probed hers. His elbows quivered beside her as he braced away, waiting to hear the words.

She reached between them and found him, guided him home, her eyes never leaving his as he came into her, moving strong and sure to the rhythm of her repeated words, "I love you, Jesse . . . love you . . . love you . . . love you . . ." over and over again in accompaniment to his long, slow strokes. He saw tears well and slip from the corners of her eyes as her lips formed and reformed the words, faster and faster, until her lips fell open. And shortly, he followed the way she had gone, through that plunging ride of ecstasy.

The room grew quiet, the afternoon light reflecting in off the snow as her hand lay on the damp nape of his neck. She toyed with his hair absently. Then, closing her eyes tightly, she suddenly grasped him to her, holding him, possessing him, lying perfectly still for that moment, recording it in her memory to carry with her into the length of their days together.

"Jesse . . . oh, Jesse."

Lost in love, he rocked her, rolling wordlessly from side to side, and finally falling still beside her, looking into her serene face.

"The train is coming," he said softly.

She smiled and touched his lower lip, then trailed a fingertip from the center of his moustache to its outer tip. "Even the train schedule accommodates you, doesn't it?"

"And what about Miss Abigail McKenzie?" he asked, holding his breath.

She gazed into his beloved eyes. "She too," she said softly, "she too."

His eyes slid shut and he sighed, content.

But she made them open again when she asked, "But what shall she do with her houseful of wedding cakes and sandwiches?"

"Leave them to the mice. They'll like them better than oatmeal."

"Leave them?" she asked, puzzled.

He braced up on one elbow, all trace of smile gone from his face as he gazed at her intently.

"I'm asking you to get up off this bed and put on your clothes and walk to the train depot with me, holding my arm, never looking back. Everything starts with now."

"Leave my house, my possessions, everything—just like that?"

"Just like that."

"But the whole town is probably out there waiting for us to come out of this hotel. If we go straight to the depot, they'll know."

"Yes, they will. Won't we create a sensation walking out right under their noses, boarding the executive coach—Miss Abigail and her train robber?"

She eyed him, considering it.

"Why, Jesse, you want to shock them, don't you?"

"I think we already have, so why not finish it off with aplomb?"

She couldn't help laughing. At least she tried to, but he hugged her again, pressing his chest across hers, and he was very, very heavy. All that came out was a soundless bouncing, which made him relieve her of some of his weight, but not quite all—not until she said yes.

"We are so very different, Jesse," she said, serious again, touching him upon his temples. "In spite of what we have in common, we are still opposites. I could not change for you."

"I don't want you to. Do you want me to?" For a moment he was afraid of what she might answer. Instead she said nothing, so he sat up on the edge of the bed, turning his back on her.

But she knew him well enough by now to recognize the tensing of his jaw muscle for what it was. She sat up behind him and ran a hand over one of his shoulders, then kissed his back.

"No," she said quietly against his skin, "just as you are, Jess. I love you just as you are."

He turned to her with a smile aslant his lips, the bedeviling moustache inviting as he reached out a single hand, palm-up.

"Then let's go."

She placed her hand in his and let him tug her off the bed, almost catapulting into his arms, laughing.

He hugged her naked body long against his, running his hand down her spine while her bare toes dangled above the floor.

"Back off, woman," he warned with a chuckle, "or we're going to miss that three-twenty to Denver."

Then he let her slip down and slapped her lightly on her naked rump.

* * *

They dressed, their eyes on each other instead of what they were doing. But when she began gathering up the torn wedding gown and the buttons and satin shoes, he ordered gently, "Leave them."

"But—"

"Leave them."

She looked down at the dress. The touch of its satin beneath her fingers reminded her again of David, and she knew what she must do. "Jesse, I can leave everything else, but I must . . ." She looked up entreatingly. "I must not leave David—not this way." Jesse did not move a muscle or smile. "Not hurting him as I have. May I just go back to the store and try to make him understand I never meant to hurt him?"

Jesse's eyes were dark, inscrutable, as he knelt before her, buckling the straps on one of his photograph cases.

"Yes. If it'll mean not having him between us for the rest of our lives, yes." They were the hardest words Jesse DuFrayne had ever spoken.

A few moments later he held the new green coat as she slipped her arms into it. Then they turned at the door to survey the room for a moment—the overturned screen still lying on its side, wedding gown in a heap, torn and wrinkled, its buttons strewn around the room along with her crushed veil and the discarded satin pumps.

Hoping he'd understand, she went back in and retrieved the shoes, tucking them into her coat as they left the hotel and stepped into the cold, sparkling sunlit afternoon.

He held her arm as they walked along the boardwalks to the shoe store at the end of the street, and he stood outside stoically, his hands buried in his pockets, waiting, while she went inside to return the white satin pumps to David Melcher. It seemed to take forever, though it was a matter of only several minutes.

The bell tinkled and Jesse looked up, searching her face as she came back out and took his arm to walk back toward the depot.

There was an odd, sick feeling in the pit of his stomach. He looked down at her gravely.

She smiled up at him. "I love you, Jesse."

And he breathed again.

They walked the length of Main Street, feeling eyes upon

them every step of the way. At the station the train waited, chugging and puffing impatiently, its breath white upon the cold Colorado air.

On the side of the second to the last car glittered an ornate crest bearing an R.M.R. insignia done in gold leaf, intertwined with a design of dogwood petals.

Puzzled, Abbie looked at it, then up at Jesse, but before she could ask, he scooped her up in his arms and mounted the steps of the executive coach.

But suddenly he stopped, turned, looked thoughtfully out at the deserted street, deposited her on her feet again, and said, "Just a minute. Don't go away." Then he swung down the steps again.

And cool as you please, Jesse DuFrayne drew a gun, took a bead on the sign down the street that bore the names of David and Abigail Melcher, and popped off two shots that brought every person out of the shops from one end of Main Street to the other to see what in tarnation was going on.

But all they saw was that sign lying in the snow down there in front of the shoe store and the back of Jesse DuFrayne disappearing up the steps into the train.

Inside, he again scooped Abbie into his arms, closing her surprised lips with his own.

"There's no place like home," he said when he had kissed her thoroughly, kicking the door shut behind them.

"Home?" she repeated, glancing around at the lush emerald green velvet interior of the car. "What is this?"

She strained to see around his head. As she turned this way and that he nuzzled her neck, for she was still in his arms and he had no intention of putting her down just yet.

"This, my darling Ab, is your honeymoon suite, especially ordered for the occasion."

What Abbie saw was no common steerage. She had never seen such luxury in her life—a massive bed covered in green velvet, an intimate dinner table set for two, a magnum of champagne in a loving cup, an ornate copper tub off to one side near an ornate pot-bellied stove, where a fire crackled, deep chairs, thick rugs.

"Jesse DuFrayne, you conniving devil! How did you get this coach to Stuart's Junction at the exact time we needed it? And quit kissing my neck as if you don't hear a word of what I'm accusing you of." But in spite of her scolding, she was giggling.

"It'll be a cold day in hell before I quit kissing your neck, Miss Abigail McKenzie, just because you order me to."

"But this *is* an executive coach. You ordered this car to be here. You *did* plan my seduction right down to the last minute!"

"Shut your precious mouth," he said, shutting it for her as the train started moving, and he strode to the oversized bed at the far end of the car, the kiss actually becoming quite slippery and misguided as the coach rocked and gained speed.

They laughed into each other's mouths, then he tossed her onto the bed, stood back, and asked, "What's first? A bath, dinner, champagne . . . or me?"

"How much time do we have?" she asked, already undoing her coat buttons.

"We can go all the way to New Orleans without coming up for air," he replied, that roguish grin tempting her while his eyes danced wickedly.

Taking her coat off she eyed the copper tub, the magnum of champagne, the table set for two, the window beside it where the world raced past. And the man . . . unbuttoning his cuffs.

"Well then, how about all four at once?" Abigail McKenzie suggested.

His eyebrows flew up, and his hands fell still momentarily before starting down the buttons on his chest.

"Well, goddamn . . ." muttered Jesse DuFrayne deliciously, his moustache coming at her in the most tantalizingly menacing way.

That CAMDEN SUMMER

LAVYRLE SPENCER

The heart has a mind of its own . . .

G. P. PUTNAM'S SONS
A MEMBER OF THE PUTNAM BERKLEY GROUP, INC.

Do it Now. George Merriam, one of the founders of Merriam-Webster, kept that motto posted above his rolltop desk. It was this slogan that motivated George and his younger brother, Charles, as they carried forward the work of Noah Webster, the United States' first great lexicographer, after his death in 1843. George and Charles Merriam recognized the significance of Webster's great dictionary and worked to continue his tradition of excellence. Their efforts made "Merriam-Webster" the most important name in American dictionaries.

Today, Merriam-Webster maintains an ongoing commitment to innovation and scholarship. Our dictionaries and other reference products are prepared by a distinguished staff of scholars who rely on a file of more than 14,500,000 citations documenting actual word usage to ensure that every Merriam-Webster publication meets the highest standards of quality and reliability. Other publishers may use the name *Webster*, but only Merriam-Webster products are backed by 150 years of accumulated knowledge and experience. The name *Merriam-Webster* is your assurance that you are purchasing the most authoritative, accurate, and well-designed language reference products in the world.

Not just Webster. Merriam Webster.

®

Merriam-Webster's
Medical
Dictionary

MERRIAM-WEBSTER, INCORPORATED
Springfield, Massachusetts, U.S.A.

A GENUINE MERRIAM-WEBSTER

The name *Webster* alone is no guarantee of excellence. It is used by a number of publishers and may serve mainly to mislead an unwary buyer.

Merriam-Webster™ is the name you should look for when you consider the purchase of dictionaries or other fine reference books. It carries the reputation of a company that has been publishing since 1831 and is your assurance of quality and authority.

Contents

Preface

MERRIAM-WEBSTER'S MEDICAL DICTIONARY is a concise guide to the essential language of medicine. It is an abridged version of *Merriam-Webster's Medical Desk Dictionary*, and it shares many of the features of its parent volume. These are features that are standard for most desk dictionaries of the English language but are often missing from medical dictionaries. For example, users of this book will find how to pronounce *CABG, NSAID*, and *RU 486;* how to spell and pronounce the plurals of *arthritis, chlamydia*, and *uterus;* where to divide *arteriosclerosis* and *thrombolytic* at the end of a line; and the part-of-speech labels of *spermicide, spermicidal*, and *spermicidally*.

The 35,000 vocabulary entries include the most frequently used words of human and veterinary medicine. The reader will find entries not only for human diseases such as *AIDS, Lyme disease*, and *chronic fatigue syndrome* but also for those of domestic animals such as *heartworm* of dogs, *panleukopenia* of cats, and *foot-and-mouth disease* of cattle. In addition this dictionary includes the scientific and medically related words that are essential to understanding the definitions of the core vocabulary. Every word used in a definition in this book appears as a boldface vocabulary entry either in this dictionary or in its companion general paperback, *The Merriam-Webster Dictionary*.

This dictionary is designed to serve as an interface between the language of doctor and the language of patient, between sports medicine and the sports page, between the technical New Latin names of plants and animals and their common names, and between the old and the new in medical terminology. The user of this dictionary will find, for example, that the *abs, delts, glutes, lats*, and *pecs* of the physical fitness enthusiast are the *abdominal muscles, deltoidei, glutei, latissimi dorsi*, and *pectorales* of the anatomist. Both medicine and science sometimes give the impression that the latest technical terminology has no antecedents. There may be no clue on the medical page of the reader's daily newspaper that the bacteria referred to as *Gardnerella* and *Helicobacter* were formerly classified as *Haemophilus* and *Campylobacter*. Medical writers may neglect to mention that the *auditory tube* and *uterine tubes* of formal anatomy are still widely known as the *eustachian tube* and *fallopian tubes*. All of these words are entered and defined in this dictionary with mention of synonymous or former terminology when appropriate.

Entries known to be trademarks or service marks are so labeled and are treated in accordance with a formula approved by the United States Trademark Association. No entry in this dictionary, however, should be regarded as affecting the validity of any trademark or service mark.

When a trademark or service mark for a drug is entered in this dictionary, it is also mentioned in a cross-reference following the definition of its generic equivalent, so that, for example, from either of the entries for *diazepam* or *Valium, fluoxetine* or *Prozac, finasteride* or *Proscar*, the reader can determine which is a generic name and which a proprietary name for the same drug.

This dictionary contains material from its parent work supplemented by new material from the research files in the Merriam-Webster editorial offices which now include more than 14,500,000 citations (examples of English words used in context). Of these, a ten-year sample of approximately 1,300,000 citations containing about 20,000,000 words of text is available on-line for search and retrieval. The editors frequently consulted these sources in abridging the parent work as well as in evaluating new words for entry.

The language of medicine is vast, and as a result, infrequently used medical terms must be excluded from a book of this size. However, many of the excluded terms are compound words and this book compensates in large part for their omission by generous coverage of the prefixes, suffixes, and combining forms that are used in creating medical vocabulary. The entries for these forms can often be used to determine the meaning of words that are not common enough to warrant entry in this dictionary. For example, from the combining form *hemo-* and the noun *transfusion*, it can be determined that *hemotransfusion* means a blood transfusion.

Another important feature of this book is that words occurring only as part of compound terms are entered at their own place in alphabetical sequence with a cross-reference to the compound terms themselves. Thus, *herpetiformis* has a cross-reference to *dermatitis herpetiformis*, and *longus* is followed by a list of eleven compound terms of which it is part. These lists may help the reader unfamiliar with medical terminology to find the place of definition of compound terms.

The biographical information following words derived from the names of persons has been limited to the person's name, birth and death dates, nationality, and occupation or status. Such information is entered only for historical figures, not for fictional or mythical characters.

It is the intent of the editors that this dictionary serve the purposes of all those who seek information about medical English as it is currently spoken and written, whether in the context of a clinical setting, in correctly rendering spoken and written text, or from the perspective of lexicography as an art and science.

Merriam-Webster's Medical Dictionary is the result of a collective effort by the staff of Merriam-Webster Incorporated. The editor was assisted by Joan I. Narmontas, Assistant Editor, in preparing the basic text. Stephen J. Perrault, Senior Editor, copyedited the entire manuscript and identified areas where technical material needed to be clarified. Brian M. Sietsema, Ph.D., Associate Editor, prepared the pronunciations. The cross-referencing was done by Maria A. Sansalone, Assistant Editor, and Donna L. Rickerby, Assistant Editor, with the help of Adrienne M. Scholz. Robert D. Copeland, Senior Editor, adapted typesetting tapes for use on the personal computers in the editorial offices and wrote computer programs to facilitate specific cross-reference tasks. Other specialized editorial assistance was provided by Michael G. Belanger, Paul F. Cappellano, Jennifer N. Cislo, Jill J. Cooney, Peter D. Haraty, Amy K. Harris, Brett P. Palmer, James L. Rader, and Katherine C. Sietsema. Joan I. Narmontas supervised proofreading by Deanna Chiasson, Jennifer N. Cislo, Jill J. Cooney, Michael G. Guzzi, Amy K. Harris, Thomas F. Pitoniak, Ph.D., James L. Rader, Donna L. Rickerby, and Maria A. Sansalone. Ruth W. Gaines, Senior General Clerk, kept track of the copy as it moved about the editorial office and was assisted in the final stages by Carol A. Fugiel. Madeline L. Novak, Senior Editor, coordinated production. John M. Morse, Executive Editor, made numerous suggestions for improving the book and gave encouragement and moral support throughout.

Roger W. Pease, Jr., Ph.D.
Editor

Explanatory Notes

Entries

Main Entries

A boldface letter or a combination of such letters, including punctuation marks and diacritics where needed, that is set flush with the left-hand margin of each column of type is a main entry or entry word. The main entry may consist of letters set solid, of letters joined by a hyphen, or of letters separated by one or more spaces:

> al·ler·gy . . . *n*
>
> ¹an·ti–in·flam·ma·to·ry . . . *adj*
>
> **blood vessel** *n*
>
> **non–A, non–B hepatitis** . . . *n*

The material in lightface type that follows each main entry explains and justifies its inclusion in the dictionary.

Variation in the styling of compound words in English is frequent and widespread. It is often completely acceptable to choose freely among open, hyphenated, and closed alternatives. To save space for other information, this dictionary usually limits itself to a single styling for a compound. When a compound is widely used and one styling predominates, that styling is shown. When a compound is uncommon or when the evidence indicates that two or three stylings are approximately equal in frequency, the styling shown is based on the analogy of parallel compounds.

Order of Main Entries

The main entries follow one another in alphabetical order letter by letter without regard to intervening spaces or hyphens: *elastic stocking* follows *elasticity* and *right-handed* follows *right hand*. Words that often begin with the abbreviation *St.* in common usage have the abbreviation spelled out: *Saint Anthony's fire, Saint Vitus' dance*.

Full words come before parts of words made up of the same letters. Parts of words with no hyphen in front but followed by a hyphen come before parts of words preceded by a hyphen. Solid words come first and are followed by hyphenated compounds and then by open compounds. Lowercase entries come before entries that begin with a capital letter:

> ²**path** *abbr*
>
> **path-** . . . *comb form*
>
> **-path** . . . *n comb form*
>
> **workup** . . . *n*
>
> **work up** . . . *vb*
>
> **tri·chi·na** . . . *n*
>
> **Trichina** . . . *n*

Entries containing an Arabic numeral within or at the end of the word are alphabetized as if the number were spelled out: *glucose phosphate* comes after *glucose-1-phosphate* and before *glucose-6-phosphate* while *LD50* is between *LD* and *LDH*. Some chemical terms are preceded by one or more Arabic numerals or by a chemical prefix abbreviated to a Roman or Greek letter or by a combination of the two usually set off by a hyphen. In general the numerical or abbreviated prefix is ignored in determining the word's alphabetical place: *N-allylnormorphine* is entered in the letter *a*, *5-hydroxytryptamine* in the letter *h*, and *β₂-microglobulin* in the letter *m*. However, if the prefix is spelled out, it is used in alphabetizing the word: *beta globulin* is entered in the letter *b*, and *levo-dihydroxyphenylalanine* in the letter *l*. In a few cases, entries have been made at more than one place to assist the reader in finding the place of definition, especially when the prefix has variants: *gamma-aminobutyric acid*, defined in the letter *g*, is often written with a Greek letter as *γ-aminobutyric acid*, and an entry has been made in the letter *a* to direct the reader to the place of definition.

If the names of two chemical substances differ only in their prefixes, the terms are alphabetized first by the main part of the word and then in relation to each other according to the prefix: *L-PAM* immediately precedes *2-PAM* in the letter *p*.

Guide Words

A pair of guide words is printed at the top of each page. The entries that fall alphabetically between the guide words are found on that page.

It is important to remember that alphabetical order rather than position of an entry on the page determines the selection of guide words. The first guide word is the alphabetically first entry on the page. The second guide word is usually the alphabetically last entry on the page:

acyanotic • adductor pollicis

The entry need not be a main entry. Another boldface word — a variant, an inflected form, or a defined or undefined run-on — may be selected as a guide word. For this reason the last main entry on a page is not always the last entry alphabetically.

All guide words must themselves be in alphabetical order from page to page throughout the dictionary; thus, the alphabetically last entry on a page is not used if it follows alphabetically the first guide word on the next page.

Homographs

When main entries are spelled alike, they are distinguished by superscript numerals preceding each word:

¹ano·rex·ic . . . *adj*   ¹se·rum . . . *n*

²anorexic *n*   ²serum *adj*

Although homographs are spelled alike, they may differ in pronunciation, derivation, or functional classification (as part of speech). The order of homographs is historical: the one first used in English is entered first with the exception that abbreviations and symbols are listed last in a series of homographs. Abbreviations appear before symbols when both are present.

End-of-Line Division

The centered dots within entry words indicate division points at which a hyphen may be put at the end of a line of print or writing. Centered dots are not shown after a single initial letter or before a single terminal letter because printers seldom cut off a single letter:

abort . . . *vb*

body . . . *n*

Nor are they shown at second and succeeding homographs unless these differ among themselves in division or pronunciation:

¹mu·tant . . . *adj*   ¹pre·cip·i·tate . . . *vb*

²mutant . . . *n*   ²pre·cip·i·tate . . . *n*

There are acceptable alternative end-of-line divisions just as there are acceptable variant spellings and pronunciations. No more than one division is, however, shown for an entry in this dictionary.

Many words have two or more common pronunciation variants, and the same end-of-line division is not always appropriate for each of them. The division *ho·me·op·a·thy*, for example, best fits the variant \hō-mē-'ä-pə-thē\ whereas the division *hom·e·op·a·thy* best fits the variant \hä-mē-'ä-pə-thē\. In instances like this, the division falling farther to the left is used, regardless of the order of the pronunciations:

ho‑me‑op‑a‑thy \ˌhō‑mē‑ˈä‑pə‑thē, ˌhä‑\

A double hyphen at the end of a line in this dictionary stands for a hyphen that belongs at that point in a hyphenated word and that is retained when the word is written as a unit on one line.

Variants

When a main entry is followed by the word *or* and another spelling, the two spellings are equal variants.

¹neu‑tro‑phil . . . *or* neu‑tro‑phil‑ic

If two variants joined by *or* are out of alphabetical order, they remain equal variants. The one printed first is, however, slightly more common than the second:

phys‑i‑o‑log‑i‑cal . . . *or* phys‑i‑o‑log‑ic

When another spelling is joined to the main entry by the word *also*, the spelling after *also* is a secondary variant and occurs less frequently than the first:

lip‑id *also* lip‑ide

If there are two secondary variants, the second is joined to the first by *or*. Once the word *also* is used to signal a secondary variant, all following variants are joined by *or*:

taen‑ *or* taeni‑ *also* ten‑ *or* teni‑

A variant whose own alphabetical place is at some distance from the main entry is entered at its own place with a cross-reference to the main entry. Such variants at consecutive or nearly consecutive entries are listed together.

tendonitis *var of* TENDINITIS

anchylose, anchylosis *var of* ANKYLOSE, ANKYLOSIS

Variants having a usage label (as *Brit* or *chiefly Brit*) appear only at their own alphabetical places:

-aemia *also* -haemia *chiefly Brit var of* -EMIA
anae‑mia *chiefly Brit var of* ANEMIA
haem‑ *or* haemo‑ *chiefly Brit var of* HEM-
hae‑mo‑glo‑bin *chiefly Brit var of* HEMOGLOBIN

When long lists of such variants would be generated by entering all those at consecutive entries, only one or a few are given. The rest can be deduced by analogy with those which are entered. For example, the chiefly British variant *haemoglobinaemia* is formed analogously with *haemoglobin* and *anaemia* (it might also be recognized from the combining forms *-aemia* and *haem-* or *haemo-*).

Run-on Entries

A main entry may be followed by one or more derivatives or by a homograph with a different functional label. These are run-on entries. Each is introduced by a boldface dash and each has a functional label. They are not defined, however, since their meanings can readily be derived from the meaning of the root word:

> **healthy** . . . *adj* . . . **— health·i·ly** . . . *adv* **— health·i·ness** . . . *n*
>
> **drift** . . . *n* . . . **— drift** *vb*

A main entry may be followed by one or more phrases containing the entry word. These are also run-on entries. Each is introduced by a boldface dash but there is no functional label. They are, however, defined since their meanings are more than the sum of the meanings of their elements:

> **²couch** *n* . . . **— on the couch :** . . .
>
> **risk** . . . *n* . . . **— at risk :** . . .

A run-on entry is an independent entry with respect to function and status. Labels at the main entry do not apply unless they are repeated.

Pronunciation

The matter between a pair of reversed virgules \ \ following the entry word indicates the pronunciation. The symbols used are listed in the chart printed on the page facing the first page of the dictionary proper and on the inside of the back cover.

Syllables

A hyphen is used in the pronunciation to show syllabic division. These hyphens sometimes coincide with the centered dots in the entry word that indicate end-of-line division; sometimes they do not:

> **ab·scess** \ˈab-ˌses\
>
> **met·ric** \ˈme-trik\

Stress

A high-set mark \\'\\ indicates primary (strongest) stress or accent; a low-set mark \\ˌ\\ indicates secondary (medium) stress or accent:

ear·ache \\'ir-ˌāk\\

The stress mark stands at the beginning of the syllable that receives the stress.

Variant Pronunciations

The presence of variant pronunciations indicates that not all educated speakers pronounce words the same way. A second-place variant is not to be regarded as less acceptable than the pronunciation that is given first. It may, in fact, be used by as many educated speakers as the first variant, but the requirements of the printed page are such that one must precede the other:

oral \\'ȯr-əl, 'är-\\

um·bi·li·cus \\ˌəm-bə-'lī-kəs, ˌəm-'bi-li-\\

Parentheses in Pronunciations

Low-set stress marks enclosed in parentheses indicate that the following syllable may be pronounced with secondary stress or with no stress:

de·sen·si·tize \\(ˌ)dē-'sen-sə-ˌtīz\\

RNA \\ˌär-(ˌ)en-'ā\\

Partial and Absent Pronunciations

When a main entry has less than a full pronunciation, the missing part is to be supplied from a pronunciation in a preceding entry or within the same pair of reversed virgules:

psy·cho·sur·gery \\-'sər-jə-rē\\

vit·i·li·go \\ˌvi-tə-'lī-gō, -'lē-\\

The pronunciation of the first two syllables of *psychosurgery* is found at the main entry *psychosurgeon:*

psy·cho·sur·geon \\ˌsī-kō-'sər-jən\\

The hyphens before and after \-ˈlē-\ in the pronunciation of *vitiligo* indicate that both the first and the last parts of the pronunciation are to be taken from the immediately preceding pronunciation.

When a variation of stress is involved, a partial pronunciation may be terminated at the stress mark which stands at the beginning of a syllable not shown:

li·gate \ˈlī-ˌgāt, lī-ˈ\

In general, no pronunciation is indicated for open compounds consisting of two or more English words that have own-place entry:

lateral collateral ligament *n*

A pronunciation is shown, however, for any unentered element of an open compound:

Meiss·ner's corpuscle \ˈmīs-nərz-\

Only the first entry in a sequence of numbered homographs is given a pronunciation if their pronunciations are the same:

¹**sig·moid** \ˈsig-ˌmȯid\ *adj*
²**sigmoid** *n*

The pronunciation of unpronounced derivatives run on at a main entry is a combination of the pronunciation at the main entry and the pronunciation of the suffix or final element.

Abbreviations, Acronyms, and Symbols

Pronunciations are not usually shown for entries with the functional labels *abbr* or *symbol* since they are usually spoken by saying the individual letters in sequence or by giving the expansion. The pronunciation is given only if there is an unusual and unexpected way of saying the abbreviation or symbol:

ICU *abbr* intensive care unit
Al *symbol* aluminum
CABG \ˈka-bij\ *abbr* coronary artery bypass graft

Acronyms (as *DNA* and *NSAID*) and compounds (as *ACE inhibitor*) consisting of an acronym and a word element which have one of the traditional parts of speech labels (usually *n*, *adj*, *adv*, or *vb* in this book) are given a pronunciation even when the word is spoken by pronouncing the letters in sequence:

DNA \ˌdē-(ˌ)en-ˈā\ *n*

ACE inhibitor \ˈās-, ˌā-(ˌ)sē-ˈē-\ *n*

NSAID \ˈen-ˌsed, -ˌsād\ *n*

Functional Labels

An italic label indicating a part of speech or some other functional classification follows the pronunciation or, if no pronunciation is given, the main entry. Of the eight traditional parts of speech, five appear in this dictionary as follows:

healthy. . . *adj*   per . . . *prep*

psy·cho·log·i·cal·ly . . . *adv*   pre·scribe . . . *vb*

hos·pi·tal . . . *n*

Other italic labels used to indicate functional classifications that are not traditional parts of speech include:

tid *abbr*   -lyt·ic . . . *adj suffix*

pleur- *or* pleuro- *comb form*   -i·a·sis . . . *n suffix*

-poi·e·sis . . . *n comb form*   Rolf·ing . . . *service mark*

-poi·et·ic . . . *adj comb form*   Ca *symbol*

dys- *prefix*   Val·ium . . . *trademark*

Functional labels are sometimes combined:

sap·phic . . . *adj or n*

cold turkey *n* : . . . — cold turkey *adv or adj or vb*

Inflected Forms

The inflected forms recorded in this dictionary include the plurals of nouns; the past tense, the past participle when it differs from the past tense, and the present participle of verbs; and the comparative and superlative forms of adjectives and adverbs. When these inflected forms are created in a manner considered regular in English (as by adding -*s* or -*es* to nouns, -*ed* and -*ing* to verbs, and -*er* and -*est* to adjectives and adverbs) and when it seems that there is nothing about the formation to give the dictionary user doubts, the inflected form is not shown in order to save space for information more likely to be sought.

If the inflected form is created in an irregular way or if the dictionary user is likely to have doubts about it (even if it is formed regularly), the inflected form is shown in boldface either in full or, especially when the word has three or more syllables, cut back to a convenient and easily recognizable point.

The inflected forms of nouns, verbs, adjectives, and adverbs are shown in this dictionary when suffixation brings about a change in final *y* to *i*, when the word ends in *-ey*, when there are variant inflected forms, and when the dictionary user might have doubts about the spelling of the inflected form:

> **scaly** . . . *adj* **scal·i·er; -est**
>
> ²**atrophy** . . . *vb* **-phied; -phy·ing**
>
> **kid·ney** . . . *n, pl* **kid·neys**
>
> **sar·co·ma** . . . *n, pl* **-mas** *also* **-ma·ta**
>
> ¹**burn** . . . *vb* **burned** . . . *or* **burnt** . . . **burn·ing**
>
> **sta·tus** . . . *n, pl* **sta·tus·es**

A plural is also shown for a noun when it ends in a consonant plus *o* or in a double *oo*, and when its plural is identical with the singular. Many nouns in medical English have highly irregular plurals modeled after their language of origin. Sometimes more than one element of a compound term is pluralized:

> **ego** . . . *n, pl* **egos**
>
> **HMO** . . . *n, pl* **HMOs**
>
> **tattoo** *n, pl* **tattoos**
>
> ¹**pu·bes** . . . *n, pl* **pubes**
>
> **en·ceph·a·li·tis** . . . *n, pl* **-lit·i·des**
>
> **cor pul·mo·na·le** . . . *n, pl* **cor·dia pul·mo·na·lia**

Nouns that are plural in form and that are regularly used with a plural verb are labeled *n pl:*

> **in·nards** . . . *n pl*

If nouns that are plural in form are regularly used with a singular verb, they are labeled *n* or if they are used with either a singular or plural verb, they are labeled *n sing or pl:*

> **rick·ets** . . . *n*
>
> **blind stag·gers** . . . *n sing or pl*

The inflected forms of verbs, adjectives, and adverbs are also shown whenever suffixation brings about a doubling of a final consonant, elision of a final *e*, or a radical change in the base word itself. The principal parts of a verb are shown when a final *-c* changes to *-ck* in suffixation:

re•fer . . . *vb* re•ferred; re•fer•ring

hot . . . *adj* hot•ter; hot•test

op•er•ate . . . *vb* -at•ed; -at•ing

sane . . . *adj* san•er; san•est

¹break . . . *vb* broke . . . bro•ken . . . break•ing

¹ill . . . *adj* worse . . . worst

²physic *vb* phys•icked; phys•ick•ing

Inflected forms are not shown at undefined run-ons.

Capitalization

Most entries in this dictionary begin with a lowercase letter, indicating that the word is not ordinarily capitalized. A few entries have an italic label *often cap*, indicating that the word is as likely to begin with a capital letter as not and is equally acceptable either way. Some entries begin with an uppercase letter, which indicates that the word is usually capitalized.

pan•cre•as . . . *n*

braille . . . *n, often cap*

Gol•gi . . . *adj*

The capitalization of entries that are open or hyphenated compounds is similarly indicated by the form of the entry or by an italic label:

heart attack *n*

¹neo–Freud•ian . . . *adj, often cap N*

Agent Orange . . . *n*

Many acronyms are written entirely or partly in capitals, and this fact is shown by the form of the entry or by an italic label:

DNA . . . *n*

cgs *adj, often cap C&G&S*

A word that is capitalized in some senses and lowercase in others shows variations from the form of the main entry by the use of italic labels at the appropriate senses:

strep•to•coc•cus . . . *n* 1 *cap*

pill . . . *n* . . . 2 *often cap*

Attributive Nouns

The italicized label *often attrib* placed after the functional label *n* indicates that the noun is often used as an adjective equivalent in attributive position before another noun:

> **blood** . . . *n, often attrib*
>
> **hos·pi·tal** . . . *n, often attrib*

Examples of the attributive use of these nouns are *blood clot* and *hospital ward*.

While any noun may occasionally be used in attribution, the label *often attrib* is limited to those having broad attributive use. This label is not used when an adjective homograph (as *serum*) is entered. And it is not used at open compounds that are used in attribution with an inserted hyphen.

Etymology

Etymologies showing the origin of particular words are given in this dictionary only for some abbreviations and for all eponyms.

If any entry for an abbreviation is followed by the expansion from which it is derived, no etymology is given. However, if the abbreviation is derived from a phrase in a foreign language or in English that is not mentioned elsewhere in the entry, that phrase and its language of origin (if other than English) are given in square brackets following the functional label:

> **IFN** *abbr* interferon
>
> **bid** *abbr* [Latin *bis in die*] twice a day

Words derived from the names of persons are called eponyms. Eponymous entries in this dictionary that are derived from the names of one or more real persons are followed by the last name, personal name, birth and death dates where known, nationality, and occupation or status of the person (or persons) from whose name the term is derived:

> **pas·teu·rel·la** . . . *n* . . .
>
> **Pas·teur** . . . , Louis (1822–1895), French chemist and bacteriologist.

Doubtful dates are followed by a question mark, and approximate dates are preceded by *ca* (circa). In some instances only the years of principal activity are given, preceded by the abbreviation *fl* (flourished):

> **sap·phic** . . . *adj or n*
>
> **Sap·pho** . . . (*fl ca* 610 BC–*ca* 580 BC), Greek lyric poet.

If a series of main entries is derived from the name of one person, the data usually follow the first entry. The dictionary user who turns, for example, to *pasteurellosis, pasteurization,* or *Pasteur treatment* and seeks biographical information is expected to glance back to the first entry in the sequence, *pasteurella.*

If an eponymous entry is defined by a synonymous cross-reference to the entry where the biographical data appear, no other cross-reference is made. However, if the definition of an eponymous entry contains no clue as to the location of the data, the name of the individual is given following the entry and a directional cross-reference is made to the appropriate entry:

> **gland of Bartholin** *n* : BARTHOLIN'S GLAND
>
> **gland of Bow·man** . . . *n* : any of the tubular and often
>   branched glands occurring beneath the olfactory epi-
>   thelium of the nose . . .
>   W. Bowman — see BOWMAN'S CAPSULE

The data for C. T. Bartholin can be found at *Bartholin's gland* and that for William Bowman at *Bowman's capsule.*

Usage

Usage Labels

Status labels are used in this dictionary to signal that a word or a sense of a word is restricted in usage.

A word or sense limited in use to a specific region of the English-speaking world has an appropriate label. The adverb *chiefly* precedes a label when the word has some currency outside the specified region, and a double label is used to indicate currency in each of two specific regions:

> **red bug** . . . *n, Southern & Midland*
>
> **ap·pen·di·cec·to·my** . . . *n* . . . *Brit*
>
> **fru·se·mide** . . . *n, chiefly Brit*

The stylistic label *slang* is used with words or senses that are especially appropriate in contexts of extreme informality, that usually have a currency not limited to a particular region or area of interest, and that are composed typically of shortened forms or extravagant or facetious figures of speech. Words with the label *slang* are entered if they have been or in the opinion of the editors are likely to be encountered in communicating with patients especially in emergencies. A few words from the huge informal argot of medicine are entered with the label *med slang* because they have appeared in general context or have been the subject of discussion in medical journals:

> ben•ny . . . *n* . . . *slang*
>
> go•mer . . . *n, med slang*

Subject orientation is generally given in the definition; however, a guide phrase is sometimes used to indicate a specific application of a word or sense:

> ¹drug . . . *n* 1 . . . **b** *according to the Food, Drug, and Cosmetic Act*
>
> erupt . . . *vb* 1 *of a tooth*

Illustrations of Usage

Definitions are sometimes followed by verbal illustrations that show a typical use of the word in context. These illustrations are enclosed in angle brackets, and the word being illustrated is usually replaced by a lightface swung dash. The swung dash stands for the boldface entry word, and it may be followed by an italicized suffix:

> ab•er•rant . . . *adj* . . . 2 . . . ⟨∼ salivary tissue⟩
>
> treat . . . *vb* . . . ⟨∼*ed* their diseases⟩ ⟨∼*s* a patient⟩

The swung dash is not used when the form of the boldface entry word is changed in suffixation, and it is not used for open compounds:

> ab•nor•mal•i•ty . . . *n* . . . 2 . . . ⟨brain-wave *abnormalities*⟩
>
> work up . . . *vb* . . . ⟨*work up* a patient⟩

Usage Notes

Definitions are sometimes followed by usage notes that give supplementary information about such matters as idiom, syntax, semantic relationship, and status. For trademarks and service marks, a usage note is used in place of a definition. A usage note is introduced by a lightface dash:

> pill . . . *n* . . . 2 . . . : . . . — usu. used with *the*
>
> bug . . . *n* 1 a : . . . — not used technically
>
> hs *abbr* . . . — used esp. in writing prescriptions
>
> pec . . . *n* . . . — usu. used in pl.
>
> Val•ium . . . *trademark* — used for a preparation of diazepam

Sometimes a usage note calls attention to one or more terms that mean the same thing as the main entry:

> lep•ro•sy . . . *n* . . . : a chronic disease caused by infection with an acid-fast bacillus of the genus *Mycobacterium* (*M. leprae*) . . . — called also *Hansen's disease, lepra*

The called-also terms are shown in italic type. If the called-also term falls alphabetically at some distance from the principal entry, the called-also term is entered in alphabetical sequence with the sole definition being a synonymous cross-reference to the entry where it appears in the usage note:

> **Hansen's disease** *n* : LEPROSY
>
> **lep·ra** . . . *n* : LEPROSY

Two or more usage notes are separated by a semicolon.

> **can·tha·ris** . . . *n* . . . **2 cantharides** . . . : a preparation of dried beetles . . . — used with a sing. or pl. verb: called also *Spanish fly*

Sense Division

A boldface colon is used in this dictionary to introduce a definition:

> **pul·mo·nary** . . . *adj* : relating to, functioning like, associated with, or carried on by the lungs

It is also used to separate two or more definitions of a single sense:

> **quack** . . . *n* : a pretender to medical skill : an ignorant or dishonest practitioner

Boldface Arabic numerals separate the senses of a word that has more than one sense:

> **nerve** . . . *n* **1** : any of the filamentous bands of nervous tissue that connect parts of the nervous system with other organs . . . **2** *pl* : a state or condition of nervous agitation or irritability **3** : the sensitive pulp of a tooth

Boldface lowercase letters separate the subsenses of a word:

> **¹dose** . . . *n* **1 a** : the measured quantity of a therapeutic agent to be taken at one time **b** : the quantity of radiation administered or absorbed **2** : a gonorrheal infection

Lightface numerals in parentheses indicate a further division of subsenses:

> **ra·di·a·tion** . . . *n* . . . **2 a** : . . . **b** (1) : the process of emitting radiant energy . . . (2) : the combined processes of emission, transmission, and absorption of radiant energy

A lightface colon following a definition and immediately preceding two or more subsenses indicates that the subsenses are subsumed by the preceding definition:

> **mac·u·la** . . . *n* . . . **2** : an anatomical structure having the form of a spot differentiated from surrounding tissue: as **a** : MACULA ACUSTICA **b** : MACULA LUTEA

extensor ret·i·nac·u·lum . . . *n* **1** : either of two fibrous bands of fascia crossing the front of the ankle: **a** : a lower band . . . **b** : an upper band . . .

The word *as* may or may not follow the lightface colon. Its presence (as at *macula*) indicates that the following subsenses are typical or significant examples. Its absence (as at *extensor retinaculum*) indicates that the subsenses which follow are exhaustive.

Sometimes a particular semantic relationship between senses is suggested by the use of one of four italic sense dividers: *esp, specif, also*, or *broadly*. The sense divider *esp* (for *especially*) is used to introduce the most common meaning subsumed in the more general preceding definition. The sense divider *specif* (for *specifically*) is used to introduce a common but highly restricted meaning subsumed in the more general preceding definition. The sense divider *also* is used to introduce a meaning that is closely related to but may be considered less important than the preceding sense. The sense divider *broadly* is used to introduce an extended or wider meaning of the preceding definition.

The order of senses within an entry is historical: the sense known to have been first used in English is entered first. This is not to be taken to mean, however, that each sense of a multisense word developed from the immediately preceding sense. It is altogether possible that sense 1 of a word has given rise to sense 2 and sense 2 to sense 3, but frequently sense 2 and sense 3 may have arisen independently of one another from sense 1.

Information coming between the entry word and the first definition of a multisense word applies to all senses and subsenses. Information applicable only to some senses or subsenses is given between the appropriate boldface numeral or letter and the symbolic colon.

bur . . . *n* **1** *usu* **burr**

chla·myd·ia . . . *n* **1** *cap* . . . **2** *pl* **-iae** *also* **-ias**

Names of Plants & Animals

The entries in this dictionary that define the names of plants and animals include common or vernacular names (as *mosquito* and *poison ivy*) and names of genera (as *Ctenocephalides* and *Rhus*) from the formal, codified, New Latin vocabulary of biological systematics. The vocabulary of biological nomenclature has been developed and used in accordance with international codes for the purpose of identifying and indicating the relationships of plants and animals. Organisms are classified into a hierarchy of groups — taxa — with each kind of organism having one — and only one — correct name and belonging to one — and only one — taxon at each level of classification in the hierarchy.

The fundamental taxon is the genus, which includes a group of closely related species of organisms and of which the name is a capitalized singular noun:

Cteno-ce-phal-i-des . . . *n* : a genus of fleas (family Pulicidae) including
the dog flea (*C. canis*) and cat flea (*C. felis*)

rhus . . . *n* 1 *cap* : a genus of shrubs and trees of the cashew family
(Anacardiaceae) that . . . include some (as poison ivy, poison oak,
and poison sumac) producing irritating oils that cause dermatitis

Names of taxa higher than the genus (as family, order, class, and phylum) are not given main-entry status in this dictionary but may be
used in parentheses within definitions (as the family names *Pulicidae*
and *Anacardiaceae* at *Ctenocephalides* and *Rhus*, above).

The unique name of each kind of organism or species — the binomial or species name — consists of a singular capitalized genus name
combined with an uncapitalized specific epithet. The name for a variety or subspecies — the trinomial, variety name, or subspecies name
— adds a similar varietal or subspecific epithet. The head louse
(*Pediculus humanus capitis*) is a subspecies of the species (*Pediculus
humanus*) to which the body louse belongs.

If the name of a genus from biological nomenclature is used outside
of parentheses as part of a definition, it appears in this dictionary as
a vocabulary entry at its own place. If such a name is used inside parentheses in a definition, it may or may not appear as an entry. No
binomial, specific, subspecific, or varietal name appears as a vocabulary entry (although common names derived from such names may
be entered). In contrast, every common or vernacular name which is
used in a definition whether inside or outside of parentheses is entered
in this dictionary or in its companion volume, The Merriam-Webster
Dictionary.

Many common names are derived directly from the names of taxa
and especially genera with little or no modification. The genus name
(as *Chlamydia* or *Giardia*) is capitalized and italicized but never takes
a plural. In contrast the common name (as chlamydia or giardia) is not
usually capitalized or italicized but does take a plural (as chlamydiae
or giardias). In many cases both the systematic taxonomic name and
the common name derived from it are entered in this dictionary.

chla-myd-ia . . . *n* 1 *cap* : a genus of coccoid to spherical gram-
negative intracellular bacteria (family Chlamydiaceae) . . . 2 *pl*
-iae *also* **-ias a** : a bacterium of the genus *Chlamydia*

giar-dia . . . *n* 1 *cap* : a genus of flagellate protozoans inhabiting
the intestines of various mammals and including one (*G. lamblia*)
that is associated with diarrhea in humans 2 : any flagellate of
the genus *Giardia*

The entries defining the names of plants and animals are usually
oriented to a taxon higher in the systematic hierarchy by a systematic
name of higher rank (as *Chlamydiaceae* at *Chlamydia*), by a common
name (as *mosquito* at *Anopheles* or *carrot family* at *hemlock*), or by
a technical adjective (as *digenetic* at *fluke* or *dipteran* at *mosquito*) so
that the systematic name of a higher, more inclusive taxon can usually
be found by consulting another entry if it is not explicitly mentioned
at the entry itself.

A genus name may be abbreviated to its initial letter when it is used
as part of a binomial or trinomial name in the definition of the genus

itself or when it is listed more than once in senses not separated by a boldface number.

A capitalized entry for a systematic taxonomic name of the form **X** *n, syn of* Y means that *X* has the same taxonomic rank and meaning as *Y* but that it is technically inferior to and less valid than *Y*. In a few cases a widely used synonym may be added after the currently recognized systematic name in some definitions:

> **Piro‑plas‑ma** . . . *n, syn of* BABESIA
>
> **plague** . . . *n* . . . 2 : a virulent contagious febrile disease that is caused by a bacterium of the genus *Yersinia* (*Y. pestis* syn. *Pasteurella pestis*)

Cross-Reference

Four different kinds of cross-references are used in this dictionary: directional, synonymous, cognate, and inflectional. In each instance the cross-reference is readily recognized by the lightface small capitals in which it is printed.

A cross-reference usually following a lightface dash and beginning with *see* or *compare* is a directional cross-reference. It directs the dictionary user to look elsewhere for further information. A *compare* cross-reference is regularly appended to a definition; a *see* cross-reference may stand alone:

> **can‑cer** . . . *n* 1 . . . — compare CARCINOMA, SARCOMA; NEOPLASM, TUMOR
>
> **iron** . . . *n* 1 . . . — symbol *Fe; see* ELEMENT table
>
> **mammary artery** — SEE INTERNAL THORACIC ARTERY

A *see* cross-reference may be used to indicate the place of definition of an entry containing one or more Arabic numerals or abbreviated chemical prefixes that might cause doubt. Examples of chemical names are given above at "Order of Main Entries." The entry below follows the entry for the abbreviation *GP:*

> **G₁ phase, G₂ phase** — see entries alphabetized as G ONE PHASE, G TWO PHASE

A *see* cross-reference may follow a main entry that consists of a single word which does not stand alone but appears only in a compound term or terms; the *see* cross-reference at such entries indicates the compound term or terms in which the single word appears:

> **herpetiformis** — see DERMATITIS HERPETIFORMIS
>
> **dorsi** — see ILIOCOSTALIS DORSI, LATISSIMUS DORSI, LONGISSIMUS DORSI

A *see* cross-reference may appear after the definition of the name of a generic drug to refer the reader to a trademark used for a preparation of the drug:

di·az·e·pam . . . *n* . . . — see VALIUM

A cross-reference immediately following a boldface colon is a synonymous cross-reference. It may stand alone as the only definitional matter, it may follow an analytical definition, or it may be one of two synonymous cross-references separated by a comma:

serum hepatitis *n* : HEPATITIS b

liv·id . . . *adj* : discolored by bruising : BLACK-AND-BLUE

af·fec·tion . . . *n* . . . 2 . . . b : DISEASE. MALADY

A synonymous cross-reference indicates that a definition at the entry cross-referred to can be substituted as a definition for the entry or the sense or subsense in which the cross-reference appears.

A cross-reference following an italic *var of* is a cognate cross-reference:

pro·cary·ote *var of* PROKARYOTE

manoeuvre *Brit var of* MANEUVER

A cross-reference following an italic label that identifies an entry as an inflected form is an inflectional cross-reference. Inflectional cross-references appear only when the inflected form falls alphabetically at some distance from the main entry.

corpora *pl of* CORPUS

broke *past of* BREAK

When guidance seems needed as to which one of several homographs or which sense of a multisense word is being referred to, a superscript numeral may precede the cross-reference or a sense number may follow it or both:

ossa *pl of* ¹OS

lateral cuneiform bone *n* : CUNEIFORM BONE 1c

Combining Forms, Prefixes & Suffixes

An entry that begins or ends with a hyphen is a word element that forms part of an English compound:

pharmaco- *comb form* . . . ⟨*pharmaco*logy⟩

dys- *prefix* . . . ⟨*dys*plasia⟩

-i·a·sis *n suffix, pl* **-i·a·ses** . . . ⟨ancylostom*iasis*⟩

Combining forms, prefixes, and suffixes are entered in this dictionary for two reasons: to make understandable the meaning of many undefined run-ons and to make recognizable the meaningful elements of words that are not entered in the dictionary.

Abbreviations & Symbols

Abbreviations and symbols for chemical elements are included as main entries in the vocabulary:

> **RQ** *abbr* respiratory quotient
>
> **Al** *symbol* aluminum

Abbreviations are entered without periods and have been normalized to one form of capitalization. In practice, however, there is considerable variation, and stylings other than those given in this dictionary are often acceptable.

The more common abbreviations and the symbols of chemical elements also appear after the definition at the entries for the terms they represent:

> **respiratory quotient** *n* : . . . abbr. *RQ*

Symbols that are not capable of being alphabetized are included in a separate section in the back of this book headed "Signs and Symbols."

Abbreviations Used in This Work

abbr	abbreviation	*n pl*	noun plural
adj	adjective	*occas*	occasionally
adv	adverb	*orig*	originally
attrib	attributive	*part*	participle
b	born	*pl*	plural
B.C.	before Christ	*pres*	present
Brit	British	*prob*	probably
C	Celsius	*sing*	singular
ca	circa	*So*	South
Canad	Canadian	*SoAfr*	South African
cap	capitalized	*specif*	specifically
comb	combining	*spp*	species (*pl*)
d	died	*syn*	synonym
esp	especially	*U.S.*	United States
F	Fahrenheit	*usu*	usually
fl	flourished	*var*	variant
n	noun	*vb*	verb
No	North		

PRONUNCIATION SYMBOLS

ə .... abut, collect, suppose

ˈə, ˌə humdrum

ᵊ .... (in ᵊl, ᵊn) battle, cotton; (in lᵊ, mᵊ, rᵊ) French table, prisme, titre

ər ... operation, further

a .... map, patch

ā .... day, fate

ä .... bother, cot, father

ȧ .... a sound between \a\ and \ä\, as in an Eastern New England pronunciation of aunt, ask

au̇ ... now, out

b .... baby, rib

ch ... chin, catch

d .... did, adder

e .... set, red

ē .... beat, easy

f .... fifty, cuff

g .... go, big

h .... hat, ahead

hw ... whale

i .... tip, banish

ī .... site, buy

j .... job, edge

k .... kin, cook

k̲ .... German Bach, Scots loch

l .... lily, cool

m .... murmur, dim

n .... nine, own

ⁿ .... indicates that a preceding vowel is pronounced through both nose and mouth, as in French bon \bōⁿ\

ŋ .... sing, singer, finger, ink

ō .... bone, hollow

ȯ .... saw

œ .... French bœuf, German Hölle

œ̄ .... French feu, German Höhle

ȯi ... toy

p .... pepper, lip

r .... rarity

s .... source, less

sh ... shy, mission

t .... tie, attack

th ... thin, ether

t̲h̲ ... then, either

ü .... boot, few \ˈfyü\

u̇ .... put, pure \ˈpyu̇r\

ue ... German füllen

œ̄ ... French rue, German fühlen

v .... vivid, give

w ... we, away

y .... yard, cue \ˈkyü\

ʸ .... indicates that a preceding \l\, \n\, or \w\ is modified by having the tongue approximate the position for \y\, as in French digne \dēnʸ\

z .... zone, raise

zh ... vision, pleasure

\ .... slant line used in pairs to mark the beginning and end of a transcription: \ˈpen\

ˈ .... mark at the beginning of a syllable that has primary (strongest) stress: \ˈshə-fəl-ˌbȯrd\

ˌ .... mark at the beginning of a syllable that has secondary (next-strongest) stress: \ˈshə-fəl-ˌbȯrd\

- .... mark of a syllable division in pronunciations (the mark of end-of-line division in boldface entries is a centered dot ·)

() ... indicate that what is symbolized between sometimes occurs and sometimes does not occur in the pronunciation of the word: bakery \ˈbā-k(ə-)rē\ = \ˈbā-kə-rē, ˈbā-krē\

A

A *abbr* 1 adenine 2 ampere

Å *symbol* angstrom unit

a- *or* **an-** *prefix* : not : without ⟨asexual⟩ — *a-* before consonants other than *h* and sometimes even before *h*, *an-* before vowels and usu. before *h* ⟨achromatic⟩ ⟨anhydrous⟩

āā *also* **aa** *abbr* [Latin *ana*] of each — used at the end of a list of two or more substances in a prescription to indicate that equal quantities of each are to be taken

AA *abbr* Alcoholics Anonymous

ab \'ab\ *n* : an abdominal muscle — usu. used in pl.

ab- *prefix* : from : away : off ⟨aboral⟩

abac·te·ri·al \ˌā-(ˌ)bak-'tir-ē-əl\ *adj* : not caused by or characterized by the presence of bacteria ⟨∼ prostatitis⟩

A band *n* : one of the cross striations in striated muscle that contains myosin filaments and appears dark under the light microscope and light in polarized light

aba·sia \ə-'bā-zhə, -zhē-ə\ *n* : inability to walk caused by a defect in muscular coordination — compare ASTASIA

Ab·be-Est·lan·der operation \'a-bē-'āst-ˌlän-dər-, -'est-ˌlan-\ *n* : the grafting of a flap of tissue from one lip of the oral cavity to the other lip to correct a defect using a pedicle with an arterial supply

  Abbe, Robert (1851–1928), American surgeon.

  Estlander, Jakob August (1831–1881), Finnish surgeon.

abdom *abbr* abdomen; abdominal

ab·do·men \'ab-də-mən, (ˌ)ab-'dō-\ *n* 1 **a** : the part of the body between the thorax and the pelvis — called also *belly* **b** : the cavity of this part of the trunk lined by the peritoneum, enclosed by the body walls, the diaphragm, and the pelvic floor, and containing the visceral organs (as the stomach, intestines, and liver) **c** : the portion of this cavity between the diaphragm and the brim of the pelvis — compare PELVIC CAVITY 2 : the posterior often elongated region of the body behind the thorax in arthropods — **ab·dom·i·nal** \ab-'dä-mən-əl\ *adj* — **ab·dom·i·nal·ly** *adv*

abdomin- *or* **abdomino-** *comb form* 1 : abdomen ⟨*abdomino*plasty⟩ 2 : abdominal and ⟨*abdomino*perineal⟩

abdominal aorta *n* : the portion of the aorta between the diaphragm and the bifurcation into the right and left common iliac arteries

abdominal cavity *n* : ABDOMEN 1b

abdominal reflex *n* : contraction of the muscles of the abdominal wall in response to stimulation of the overlying skin

abdominal region *n* : any of the nine areas into which the abdomen is divided by four imaginary planes of which two are vertical passing through the middle of the inguinal ligament on each side and two are horizontal passing respectively through the junction of the ninth rib and costal cartilage and through the top of the iliac crest — see EPIGASTRIC 2b, HYPOCHONDRIAC 2b, HYPOGASTRIC 1, ILIAC 2, LUMBAR 2, UMBILICAL 2

abdominis — see OBLIQUUS EXTERNUS ABDOMINIS, OBLIQUUS INTERNUS ABDOMINIS, RECTUS ABDOMINIS, TRANSVERSUS ABDOMINIS

ab·dom·i·no·pel·vic \(ˌ)ab-ˌdä-mə-nō-'pel-vik\ *adj* : relating to or being the abdominal and pelvic cavities of the body

ab·dom·i·no·per·i·ne·al \-ˌper-ə-'nē-əl\ *adj* : relating to the abdominal and perineal regions

abdominoperineal resection *n* : resection of a part of the lower bowel together with adjacent lymph nodes through abdominal and perineal incisions

ab·dom·i·no·plas·ty \ab-'dä-mə-nō-ˌplas-tē\ *n, pl* **-ties** : cosmetic surgery of the abdomen (as for removing wrinkles and tightening the skin over the stomach)

ab·du·cens nerve \ab-'dü-ˌsenz-, -'dyü-\ *n* : either of the 6th pair of cranial nerves which are motor nerves, arise beneath the floor of the fourth ventricle, and supply the lateral rectus muscle of each eye — called also *abducens, sixth cranial nerve*

ab·du·cent nerve \-sənt-\ *n* : ABDUCENS NERVE

ab·duct \ab-'dəkt *also* 'ab-ˌ\ *vb* : to draw or spread away (as a limb or the fingers) from a position near or parallel to the median axis of the body or from the axis of a limb — **ab·duc·tion** \ab-'dək-shən\ *n*

ab·duc·tor \ab-'dək-tər\ *n, pl* **ab·duc·to·res** \ˌab-ˌdək-'tōr-(ˌ)ēz\ *or* **abductors** : a muscle that draws a part away from the median line of the body or from the axis of an extremity

abductor di·gi·ti min·i·mi \-'di-jə-(ˌ)tē-'mi-nə-(ˌ)mē\ *n* 1 : a muscle of the hand that abducts the little finger and flexes the phalanx nearest the hand 2 : a muscle of the foot that abducts the little toe

abductor hal·lu·cis \-'hal-yə-səs; -'ha-lə-səs, -kəs\ *n* : a muscle of the foot that abducts the big toe

abductor pol·li·cis brev·is \-'pä-lə-səs-'bre-vəs, -lə-kəs-\ *n* : a thin flat muscle of the hand that abducts the thumb at right angles to the plane of the palm

abductor pollicis lon·gus \-'lȯṅ-gəs\ *n* : a muscle of the forearm that abducts the thumb and wrist

ab·er·rant \a-'ber-ənt; 'a-bə-rənt, -ˌber-ənt\ *adj* 1 : straying from the right or normal way (~ behavior) 2 : deviating from the usual or natural type : ATYPICAL (~ salivary tissue)

ab·er·ra·tion \ˌa-bə-'rā-shən\ *n* 1 : failure of a mirror, refracting surface, or lens to produce exact point-to-point correspondence between an object and its image 2 : unsoundness or disorder of the mind 3 : an aberrant organ or individual — **ab·er·ra·tion·al** \-sh(ə-)nəl\ *adj*

abey·ance \ə-'bā-əns\ *n* : temporary inactivity or suspension (as of function or a symptom)

ab·i·ence \'a-bē-əns\ *n* : a tendency to withdraw from a stimulus object or situation — compare ADIENCE — **abi·ent** \-ənt\ *adj*

abi·ot·ro·phy \ˌā-(ˌ)bī-'ä-trə-fē\ *n*, *pl* **-phies** : degeneration or loss of function or vitality in an organism or in cells or tissues not due to any apparent injury

ab·late \a-'blāt\ *vb* **ab·lat·ed; ab·lat·ing** : to remove esp. by cutting

ab·la·tion \a-'blā-shən\ *n* : the process of ablating; *esp* : surgical removal

ab·la·tio pla·cen·tae \a-'blā-shē-ō-plə-'sen-(ˌ)tē\ *n* : ABRUPTIO PLACENTAE

¹ab·nor·mal \(ˌ)ab-'nȯr-məl\ *adj* : deviating from the normal or average; *esp* : departing from the usual or accepted standards of social behavior — **ab·nor·mal·ly** *adv*

²abnormal *n* : an abnormal person

ab·nor·mal·i·ty \ˌab-nȯr-'ma-lə-tē\ *n*, *pl* **-ties** 1 : the quality or state of being abnormal 2 : something abnormal (brain-wave *abnormalities*)

abnormal psychology *n* : a branch of psychology concerned with mental and emotional disorders (as neuroses and psychoses) and with certain incompletely understood normal phenomena (as dreams)

ABO blood group \ˌā-(ˌ)bē-'ō-\ *n* : one of the four blood groups A, B, AB, or O comprising the ABO system

ab·o·ma·sum \ˌa-bō-'mā-səm\ *n*, *pl* **-sa** \-sə\ : the fourth compartment of the ruminant stomach that follows the omasum and has a true digestive function — compare RUMEN, RETICULUM — **ab·oma·sal** \-səl\ *adj*

ab·oral \(ˌ)a-'bȯr-əl, -'bȯr-\ *adj* : situated opposite to or away from the mouth

abort \ə-'bȯrt\ *vb* 1 : to cause or undergo abortion 2 : to stop in the early stages (~ a disease) — **abort·er** *n*

¹abor·ti·fa·cient \ə-ˌbȯr-tə-'fā-shənt\ *adj* : inducing abortion

²abortifacient *n* : an agent (as a drug) that induces abortion

abor·tion \ə-'bȯr-shən\ *n* 1 : the termination of a pregnancy after, accompa-

nied by, resulting in, or closely followed by the death of the embryo or fetus: **a** : spontaneous expulsion of a human fetus during the first 12 weeks of gestation — compare MISCARRIAGE **b** : induced expulsion of a human fetus **c** : expulsion of a fetus by a domestic animal often due to infection at any time before completion of pregnancy — see CONTAGIOUS ABORTION 2 : arrest of development of an organ so that it remains imperfect or is absorbed 3 : the arrest of a disease in its earliest stage

abor·tion·ist \-sh(ə-)nist\ *n* : one who induces abortion

abor·tive \ə-'bȯr-tiv\ *adj* 1 : imperfectly formed or developed : RUDIMENTARY 2 **a** : ABORTIFACIENT **b** : cutting short (~ treatment of pneumonia) **c** : failing to develop completely or typically

abor·tus \ə-'bȯr-təs\ *n* : an aborted fetus; *specif* : a human fetus less than 12 weeks old or weighing at birth less than 17 ounces

ABO system \ˌā-(ˌ)bē-'ō-\ *n* : the basic system of antigens of human blood behaving in heredity as an allelic set to produce any of the ABO blood groups

aboulia *var of* ABULIA

abrade \ə-'brād\ *vb* **abrad·ed; abrad·ing** : to irritate or roughen by rubbing : CHAFE

abra·sion \ə-'brā-zhən\ *n* 1 : wearing, grinding, or rubbing away by friction 2 **a** : the rubbing or scraping of the surface layer of cells or tissue from an area of the skin or mucous membrane; *also* : a place so abraded **b** : the mechanical wearing away of the tooth surfaces by chewing

¹abra·sive \ə-'brā-siv, -ziv\ *adj* : tending to abrade — **abra·sive·ness** *n*

²abrasive *n* : a substance used for abrading, smoothing, or polishing

ab·re·ac·tion \ˌa-brē-'ak-shən\ *n* : the expression and emotional discharge of unconscious material (as a repressed idea or emotion) by verbalization esp. in the presence of a therapist — compare CATHARSIS 2 — **ab·re·act** \-'akt\ *vb* — **ab·re·ac·tive** \-'ak-tiv\ *adj*

ab·rup·tio pla·cen·tae \ə-'brəp-shē-ō-plə-'sen-(ˌ)tē, -tē-ō-\ *n* : premature detachment of the placenta from the wall of the uterus — called also *ablatio placentae*

abs \'abz\ *pl of* AB

ab·scess \'ab-ˌses\ *n*, *pl* **ab·scess·es** \'ab-sə-ˌsēz, -(ˌ)se-səz\ : a localized collection of pus surrounded by inflamed tissue — **ab·scessed** \-ˌsest\ *adj*

ab·scis·sion \ab-'si-zhən\ *n* : the act or process of cutting off : ABLATION

ab·sco·pal \ab-'skō-pəl\ *adj* : relating to or being an effect on a nonirradiated part of the body that results from radiation of another part

ab·sence \'ab-səns\ n : a transient loss or impairment of consciousness beginning and ending abruptly, unremembered afterward, and seen chiefly in mild types of epilepsy

ab·so·lute \ab-sə-'lüt\ adj : pure or relatively free from mixture

absolute alcohol n : ethyl alcohol that contains no more than one percent by weight of water — called also *dehydrated alcohol*

absolute humidity n : the amount of water vapor present in a unit volume of air — compare RELATIVE HUMIDITY

absolute refractory period n : the period immediately following the firing of a nerve fiber when it cannot be stimulated no matter how great a stimulus is applied — called also *absolute refractory phase*; compare RELATIVE REFRACTORY PERIOD

absolute temperature n : temperature measured on a scale based on absolute zero

absolute zero n : a theoretical temperature characterized by complete absence of heat and exactly equal to $-273.15°C$ or $-459.67°F$

ab·sorb \əb-'sȯrb, -'zȯrb\ vb 1 : to take up esp. by capillary, osmotic, solvent, or chemical action 2 : to transform (radiant energy) into a different form usu. with a resulting rise in temperature — **ab·sorb·able** \əb-'sȯr-bə-bəl, -'zȯr-\ adj — **ab·sorb·er** n

ab·sor·bent also **ab·sor·bant** \-bənt\ adj : able to absorb — **ab·sor·ben·cy** \-bən-sē\ n — **absorbent** also **absorbant** n

absorbent cotton n : cotton made absorbent by chemically freeing it from its fatty matter

ab·sorp·tion \əb-'sȯrp-shən, -'zȯrp-\ n : the process of absorbing or of being absorbed — compare ADSORPTION — **ab·sorp·tive** \-tiv\ adj

ab·stain \ab-'stān\ vb : to refrain deliberately and often with an effort of self-denial from an action or practice — **ab·stain·er** n

ab·sti·nence \'ab-stə-nəns\ n 1 : voluntary forbearance esp. from indulgence of an appetite or craving or from eating some foods 2 : habitual abstaining from intoxicating beverages — **ab·sti·nent** \-nənt\ adj

ab·stract \'ab-ˌstrakt\ n : a pharmaceutical preparation made by mixing a powdered solid extract of a vegetable substance with lactose in such proportions that one part of the final product represents two parts of the original drug from which the extract was made — **ab·stract** \'ab-ˌstrakt, ab-'\ vb

abu·lia \ā-'bü-lē-ə, ə-, -'byü-\ n : abnormal lack of ability to act or to make decisions characteristic of certain psychotic and neurotic conditions — **abu·lic** \-lik\ adj

¹**abuse** \ə-'byüs\ n 1 : improper or excessive use or treatment ⟨drug ∼⟩ — see SUBSTANCE ABUSE 2 : physical maltreatment: as **a** : the act of violating sexually : RAPE **b** *under some statutes* : rape or indecent assault not amounting to rape

²**abuse** \ə-'byüz\ vb **abused; abus·ing** 1 : to put to a wrong or improper use ⟨∼ drugs⟩ 2 : to treat so as to injure or damage ⟨∼ a child⟩ 3 **a** : MASTURBATE **b** : to subject to abuse and esp. to rape or indecent assault — **abus·able** \-'byü-zə-bəl\ adj — **abus·er** n

abut·ment \ə-'bət-mənt\ n : a tooth to which a prosthetic appliance (as a denture) is attached for support

ac abbr 1 acute 2 [Latin *ante cibum*] before meals — used in writing prescriptions

Ac symbol actinium

aca·cia \ə-'kā-shə\ n : GUM ARABIC

acal·cu·lia \ˌā-ˌkal-'kyü-lē-ə\ n : lack or loss of the ability to perform simple arithmetic tasks

acanth- or **acantho-** comb form : spine : prickle : projection ⟨acanthoma⟩ ⟨acanthocyte⟩

acan·tho·ceph·a·lan \ə-ˌkan-thə-'se-fə-lən\ n : any of a group of elongated parasitic intestinal worms with a hooked proboscis that as adults lack a digestive tract and absorb food through the body wall and that are usu. considered a separate phylum (Acanthocephala) related to the flatworms — **acanthocephalan** adj

acan·tho·cyte \ə-'kan-thə-ˌsīt\ n : an abnormal red blood cell characterized by variously shaped protoplasmic projections

ac·an·tho·ma \ˌa-(ˌ)kan-'thō-mə, ˌā-\ n, pl **-mas** \-məz\ or **-ma·ta** \-mə-tə\ : a neoplasm originating in the skin and developing through excessive growth of skin cells esp. of the stratum spinosum

ac·an·tho·sis \-'thō-səs\ n, pl **-tho·ses** \-ˌsēz\ : a benign overgrowth of the stratum spinosum of the skin — **ac·an·thot·ic** \-'thä-tik\ adj

acanthosis ni·gri·cans \-'ni-grə-ˌkanz, -'nī-\ n : a skin disease characterized by gray-black warty patches usu. situated in the axilla or groin or on elbows or knees and sometimes associated with cancer of abdominal viscera

acap·nia \ə-'kap-nē-ə, (ˌ)ā-\ n : a condition of carbon dioxide deficiency in blood and tissues

acar- or **acari-** or **acaro-** comb form : mite ⟨acariasis⟩ ⟨acaricide⟩

ac·a·ri·a·sis \ˌa-kə-'rī-ə-səs\ n, pl **-a·ses** \-ˌsēz\ : infestation with or disease caused by mites

acar·i·cide \ə-'kar-ə-ˌsīd\ n : a pesticide that kills mites and ticks — **acar·i·cid·al** \-ˌkar-ə-'sīd-əl\ adj

ac·a·rid \'a-kə-rəd\ n : any of an order (Acarina) of arachnids comprising the mites and ticks of which many are parasites of plants, animals, or humans; *esp* : any of a family (Acaridae) of mites that feed on organic substances and are sometimes responsible for dermatitis in persons exposed to repeated contacts with infested products — compare GROCER'S ITCH — **acarid** *adj*

ac·a·rine \'ak-ə-ˌrīn, -ˌrēn, -rən\ *adj* : of, relating to, or caused by mites or ticks (~ dermatitis) — **acarine** *n*

ac·a·rus \'a-kə-rəs\ *n*, *pl* **-ri** \-ˌrī, -ˌrē\ : MITE; *esp* : one of a formerly extensive genus (*Acarus*)

ac·cel·er·ate \ik-'se-lə-ˌrāt, ak-\ *vb* **-at·ed; -at·ing** : to speed up; *also* : to undergo or cause to undergo acceleration

ac·cel·er·a·tion \ik-ˌse-lə-'rā-shən, ak-\ *n* 1 : the act or process of accelerating : the state of being accelerated 2 : change of velocity; *also* : the rate of this change 3 : advancement in mental growth or achievement beyond the average for one's age

acceleration of gravity *n* : the acceleration of a body in free fall under the influence of the earth's gravity that has a standard value of 980.665 centimeters per second per second — abbr. *g*

ac·cel·er·a·tor \ik-'se-lə-ˌrā-tər, ak-\ *n* : a muscle or nerve that speeds the performance of an action (a cardiac ~)

accelerator globulin *n* : FACTOR V

accelerator nerve *n* : a nerve whose impulses increase the rate of the heart

ac·cel·er·om·e·ter \ik-ˌse-lə-'rä-mə-tər, ak-\ *n* : an instrument for measuring acceleration or for detecting and measuring vibrations

ac·cep·tor \ik-'sep-tər, ak-\ *n* : a compound, atom, or elementary particle capable of receiving another entity (as an atom, radical, or elementary particle) to form a compound — compare DONOR 2

ac·ces·so·ry \ik-'se-sə-rē, ak-, -'ses-rē\ *adj* 1 : aiding, contributing, or associated in a secondary way: as **a** : being or functioning as a vitamin **b** : associated in position or function with something (as an organ or lesion) usu. of more importance 2 : SUPERNUMERARY (~ spleens)

accessory hemiazygos vein *n* : a vein that drains the upper left side of the thoracic wall, descends along the left side of the spinal column, and empties into the azygos or hemiazygos veins near the middle of the thorax

accessory nerve *n* : either of a pair of motor nerves that are the 11th cranial nerves, arise from the medulla and the upper part of the spinal cord, and supply chiefly the pharynx and muscles of the upper chest, back, and shoulders — called also *accessory*, *spinal accessory nerve*

accessory olivary nucleus *n* : any of several small masses or layers of gray matter that are situated adjacent to the inferior olive and of which there are typically two on each side

accessory pancreatic duct *n* : a duct of the pancreas that branches from the chief pancreatic duct and opens into the duodenum above it — called also *duct of Santorini*

ac·ci·dent \'ak-sə-dənt, -ˌdent\ *n* 1 : an unfortunate event resulting from carelessness, unawareness, ignorance, or a combination of causes 2 : an unexpected and medically important bodily event esp. when injurious (a cerebral vascular ~) 3 : an unexpected happening causing loss or injury which is not due to any fault or misconduct on the part of the person injured but for which legal relief may be sought — **ac·ci·den·tal** \ˌak-sə-'dent-ᵊl\ *adj* — **ac·ci·den·tal·ly** \-'dent-lē, -ᵊl-ē\ *also* **ac·ci·dent·ly** \-'dent-lē\ *adv*

accident-prone *adj* 1 : having a greater than average number of accidents 2 : having personality traits that predispose to accidents

ac·cli·mate \'a-klə-ˌmāt; ə-'klī-mət, -ˌmāt\ *vb* **-mat·ed; -mat·ing** : ACCLIMATIZE

ac·cli·ma·tion \ˌa-klə-'mā-shən, -ˌklī-\ *n* : acclimatization esp. by physiological adjustment of an organism to environmental change

ac·cli·ma·tize \ə-'klī-mə-ˌtīz\ *vb* **-tized; -tiz·ing** : to adapt to a new temperature, altitude, climate, environment, or situation — **ac·cli·ma·ti·za·tion** \ə-ˌklī-mə-tə-'zā-shən\ *n*

ac·com·mo·date \ə-'kä-mə-ˌdāt\ *vb* **-dat·ed; -dat·ing** : to adapt oneself; *also* : to undergo visual accommodation — **ac·com·mo·da·tive** \-ˌdā-tiv\ *adj*

ac·com·mo·da·tion \ə-ˌkä-mə-'dā-shən\ *n* : an adaptation or adjustment esp. of a bodily part (as an organ): as **a** : the automatic adjustment of the eye for seeing at different distances effected chiefly by changes in the convexity of the crystalline lens **b** : the range over which such adjustment is possible

ac·couche·ment \ˌa-ˌküsh-'mäⁿ, ə-'küsh-ˌ\ *n* : the time or act of giving birth

ac·cou·cheur \ˌa-kü-'shər\ *n* : one that assists at a birth; *esp* : OBSTETRICIAN

ac·cou·cheuse \ˌa-kü-'shərz, -'shüz\ *n* : MIDWIFE

ac·cre·tio cor·dis \ə-'krē-shē-ō-'kòr-dəs\ *n* : adhesive pericarditis in which there are adhesions extending from the pericardium to the mediastinum, pleurae, diaphragm, and chest wall

ac·cre·tion \ə-'krē-shən\ *n* : the process of growth or enlargement; *esp* : increase by external addition or accumulation — compare APPOSITION 1

ac·cre·tion·ary \-shə-ˌner-ē\ *adj*

accumbens — see NUCLEUS ACCUMBENS

Ac·cu·tane \'a-kyù-ıtān\ *trademark* — used for a preparation of isotretinoin

Ace\'ās\ *trademark* — used for a bandage with elastic properties

ACE inhibitor \'ās-, ıā-(ı)sē-'ē-\ *n* : any of a group of antihypertensive drugs (as captopril) that relax arteries and promote renal excretion of salt and water by inhibiting the activity of angiotensin converting enzyme

acel·lu·lar \(ı)ā-'sel-yə-lər\ *adj* 1 : containing no cells (~ vaccines) 2 : not divided into cells : consisting of a single complex cell — used esp. of protozoa and ciliates

acen·tric \(ı)ā-'sen-trik\ *adj* : lacking a centromere (~ chromosomes)

acetabular notch \-'näch\ *n* : a notch in the rim of the acetabulum through which blood vessels and nerves pass

ac·e·tab·u·lo·plas·ty \ıa-sə-'tab-yə-(ı)lō-ıplas-tē\ *n, pl* **-ties** : a plastic operation on the acetabulum intended to restore its normal state

ac·e·tab·u·lum \-'ta-byə-ləm\ *n, pl* **-lums** *or* **-la** \-lə\ : the cup-shaped socket in the hipbone — **ac·e·tab·u·lar** \-lər\ *adj*

ac·et·al·de·hyde \ıa-sə-'tal-də-ıhīd\ *n* : a colorless volatile water-soluble liquid aldehyde C_2H_4O used chiefly in organic synthesis that can cause irritation to mucous membranes

acet·amin·o·phen \ə-ısē-tə-'mi-nə-fən, -ıset-, -'mē-, ıa-sə-tə-\ *n* : a crystalline compound $C_8H_9NO_2$ used in medicine instead of aspirin to relieve pain and fever — called also *paracetamol*; see TYLENOL

ac·et·an·i·lide *or* **ac·et·an·i·lid** \ıa-sə-'tan-ᵊl-ıid, -əd\ *n* : a white crystalline compound C_8H_9NO used esp. to relieve pain or fever

ac·e·tate \'a-sə-ıtāt\ *n* : a salt or ester of acetic acid

ac·et·azol·amide \ıa-sə-tə-'zō-lə-ımīd, -'zā-, -məd\ *n* : a diuretic drug $C_4H_6N_4O_3S_2$ used esp. in the treatment of edema associated with congestive heart failure and of glaucoma

ace·tic acid \ə-'sē-tik-\ *n* : a colorless pungent acid $C_2H_4O_2$ that is the chief acid of vinegar and is used occas. in medicine as an astringent and styptic

ace·to·ace·tate \ıa-sə-tō-'a-sə-ıtāt, ə-ısē-tō-\ *n* : a salt or ester of acetoacetic acid

ace·to·ace·tic acid \ıa-sə-(ı)tō-ə-ısē-tik-, ə-ısē-tō-\ *n* : an unstable acid $C_4H_6O_3$ that is one of the ketone bodies found in abnormal amounts in the blood and urine in certain conditions of impaired metabolism (as in starvation and diabetes mellitus) — called also *diacetic acid*

ace·to·hex·amide \ıa-sə-tō-'hek-sə-ıməd, ə-ısē-tō-, -ımīd\ *n* : a sulfonylurea drug $C_{15}H_{20}N_2O_4S$ used in the oral treatment of some of the milder forms of diabetes in adults to lower the level of glucose in the blood

ace·to·me·roc·tol \ıa-sə-(ı)tō-mə-'räk-ıtōl, ə-ısē-tō-, -ıtōl\ *n* : a white crystalline mercury derivative $C_{16}H_{24}HgO_3$ of phenol used in solution as a topical antiseptic

ace·ton·ae·mia *chiefly Brit var of* ACETONEMIA

ace·tone \'a-sə-ıtōn\ *n* : a volatile fragrant flammable liquid ketone C_3H_6O found in abnormal quantities in diabetic urine

acetone body *n* : KETONE BODY

ace·ton·emia \ıa-sə-tō-'nē-mē-ə\ *n* : KETOSIS 2; *also* : KETONEMIA 1

ace·ton·uria \ıa-sə-tō-'nùr-ē-ə, -'nyùr-\ *n* : KETONURIA

ace·to·phe·net·i·din \ıa-sə-(ı)tō-fə-'net-əd-ən, ə-ısē-tō-\ *n* : PHENACETIN

ace·tyl \ə-'sēt-ᵊl, 'a-sət-; 'a-sə-ıtēl\ *n* : the radical CH_3CO of acetic acid

acet·y·lase \ə-'set-ᵊl-ıās\ *n* : any of a class of enzymes that accelerate the synthesis of esters of acetic acid

acet·y·late \ə-'set-ᵊl-ıāt\ *vb* **-lat·ed; -lat·ing** : to introduce the acetyl radical into (a compound) — **acet·y·la·tion** \-ıset-ᵊl-'ā-shən\ *n*

ace·tyl·cho·line \ə-ıset-ᵊl-'kō-ılēn, -ısēt-; ıa-sə-ıtēl-\ *n* : a neurotransmitter $C_7H_{17}NO_3$ released at autonomic synapses and neuromuscular junctions, active in the transmission of nerve impulse, and formed enzymatically in the tissues from choline

ace·tyl·cho·lin·ester·ase \-ıkō-lə-'nes-tə-ırās, -ırāz\ *n* : an enzyme that occurs esp. in some nerve endings and in the blood and promotes the hydrolysis of acetylcholine

acetyl CoA \-ıkō-'ā\ *n* : ACETYL COENZYME A

acetyl coenzyme A *n* : a compound $C_{25}H_{38}N_7O_{17}P_3S$ formed as an intermediate in metabolism and active as a coenzyme in biological acetylations

ace·tyl·cys·te·ine \ə-ısēt-ᵊl-'sis-tə-ıēn, -ıset-; ıa-sə-ıtēl-, ıa-sət-ᵊl-\ *n* : a mucolytic agent $C_5H_9NO_3S$ used esp. to reduce the viscosity of abnormally viscid respiratory tract secretions — see MUCOMYST

ace·tyl·phen·yl·hy·dra·zine \-ıfen-ᵊl-'hī-drə-ızēn, -ıfēn-\ *n* : a white crystalline compound $C_8H_{10}ON_2$ used in the symptomatic treatment of polycythemia

ace·tyl·sal·i·cy·late \ə-ısēt-ᵊl-sə-'li-sə-ılāt\ *n* : a salt or ester of acetylsalicylic acid

ace·tyl·sal·i·cyl·ic acid \ə-ısēt-ᵊl-ısa-lə-'si-lik-\ *n* : ASPIRIN 1

AcG *abbr* [accelerator globulin] factor V

ACh *abbr* acetylcholine

acha·la·sia \ıā-kə-'lā-zhē-ə, -zhə\ *n* : failure of a ring of muscle (as a

sphincter) to relax — compare CAR-
DIOSPASM

¹ache \\'āk\\ *vb* **ached; ach·ing** : to suffer
a usu. dull persistent pain

²ache *n* 1 : a usu. dull persistent pain 2
: a condition marked by aching

achieve·ment age \\ə-'chēv-mənt-\\ *n*
: the level of an individual's educa-
tional achievement as measured by a
standardized test and expressed as
the age for which the test score would
be the average score — compare
CHRONOLOGICAL AGE

achievement test *n* : a standardized test
for measuring the skill or knowledge
attained by an individual in one or
more fields of work or study

Achil·les reflex \\ə-'ki-lēz-\\ *n* : ANKLE
JERK

Achilles tendon *n* : the strong tendon
joining the muscles in the calf of the
leg to the bone of the heel — called
also *tendon of Achilles*

achlor·hyd·ria \\ā-klōr-'hī-drē-ə\\ *n*
: absence of hydrochloric acid from
the gastric juice — compare HYPER-
CHLORHYDRIA, HYPOCHLORHYDRIA —
achlor·hy·dric \\-'hī-drik, -'hī-\\ *adj*

acho·lia \\(,)ā-'kō-lē-ə, -'kä-\\ *n* : defi-
ciency or absence of bile

achol·ic \\(,)ā-'kä-lik\\ *adj* : exhibiting
deficiency of bile ⟨~ stools⟩

achol·uria \\ā-kō-'lùr-ē-ə, -kä-, -lyùr-\\
n : absence of bile pigment from the
urine — **achol·uric** \\-'lùr-ik, -'lyùr-\\
adj

achon·dro·pla·sia \\ā-kän-drə-'plā-
zhē-ə, -zhə\\ *n* : a genetic disorder disturbing normal growth of cartilage,
resulting in a form of dwarfism
characterized by a usu. normal torso
and shortened limbs, and usu. inherited as an autosomal dominant —
compare ATELIOSIS — **achon·dro·plas-
tic** \\-'plas-tik\\ *adj*

achromat- *or* **achromato-** *comb form*
: uncolored except for shades of
black, gray, and white ⟨*achromatop-
sia*⟩

ach·ro·mat·ic \\a-krə-'ma-tik\\ *adj* 1
: not readily colored by the usual
staining agents 2 : possessing or involving no hue : being or involving
only black, gray, or white ⟨~ visual
sensations⟩ — **ach·ro·mat·i·cal·ly** \\-ti-
k(ə-)lē\\ *adv* — **ach·ro·mat·ism** \\(,)ā-
'krō-mə-ˌti-zəm, a-\\ *n*

achro·ma·top·sia \\ā-krō-mə-'täp-sē-ə\\
n : a visual defect marked by total
color blindness in which the colors of
the spectrum are seen as tones of
white-gray-black

achro·mia \\(,)ā-'krō-mē-ə\\ *n* : absence
of normal pigmentation esp. in red
blood cells and skin

achy \\'ā-kē\\ *adj* **ach·i·er; ach·i·est** : afflicted with aches — **ach·i·ness** *n*

achy·lia \\(,)ā-'kī-lē-ə\\ *n* : ACHYLIA GAS-
TRICA — **achy·lous** \\(,)ā-'kī-ləs\\ *adj*

achylia gas·tri·ca \\-'gas-tri-kə\\ *n* 1 : par-

tial or complete absence of gastric
juice 2 : ACHLORHYDRIA

¹ac·id \\'a-səd\\ *adj* 1 : sour, sharp, or biting to the taste 2 **a** : of, relating to, or
being an acid; *also* : having the reactions or characteristics of an acid **b** *of
salts and esters* : derived by partial
exchange of replaceable hydrogen ⟨~
sodium carbonate NaHCO₃⟩ **c**
: marked by or resulting from an abnormally high concentration of acid
⟨~ indigestion⟩ — not used technically

²acid *n* 1 : a sour substance; *specif* : any
of various typically water-soluble and
sour compounds that in solution are
capable of reacting with a base to
form a salt, redden litmus, and have a
pH less than 7, that are hydrogen-
containing molecules or ions able to
give up a proton to a base, or that are
substances able to accept a pair of
electrons from a base 2 : LSD

ac·i·dae·mia *chiefly Brit var of* ACIDE-
MIA

acid–base balance \\'a-səd-'bās-\\ *n* : the
state of equilibrium between proton
donors and proton acceptors in the
buffering system of the blood that is
maintained at approximately pH 7.35
to 7.45 under normal conditions in arterial blood

ac·i·de·mia \\ˌa-sə-'dē-mē-ə\\ *n* : a condition in which the hydrogen-ion concentration in the blood is increased

acid–fast \\'a-səd-ˌfast\\ *adj* : not easily
decolorized by acids (as when
stained) — used esp. of bacteria and
tissues

acid·ic \\ə-'si-dik, a-\\ *adj* 1 : acid-forming 2 : ACID

acid·i·fy \\ə-'si-də-ˌfī\\ *vb* **-fied; -fy·ing** 1 : to
make acid 2 : to convert into an acid
— **acid·i·fi·ca·tion** \\ə-ˌsi-də-fə-'kā-
shən, a-\\ *n* — **acid·i·fi·er** \\ə-'si-də-ˌfī-
ər, a-\\ *n*

acid·i·ty \\ə-'si-də-tē, a-\\ *n, pl* **-ties** 1
: the quality, state, or degree of being
sour or chemically acid 2 : the quality
or state of being excessively or abnormally acid : HYPERACIDITY

acid maltase deficiency *n* : POMPE'S DIS-
EASE

acid·o·gen·ic \\ˌa-ˌsi-də-'je-nik, ˌa-sə-
dō-\\ *adj* : acid-forming

¹acid·o·phil \\ə-'si-də-ˌfil, a-\\ *also* **acid-
o·phile** \\-ˌfil\\ *adj* : ACIDOPHILIC l

²acidophil *also* **acidophile** *n* : a substance, tissue, or organism that stains
readily with acid stains

acid·o·phil·ic \\ə-ˌsi-də-'fi-lik\\ *adj* 1 : staining
readily with acid stains 2 : preferring
or thriving in a relatively acid environment ⟨~ bacteria⟩

ac·i·doph·i·lus milk \\ˌa-sə-ˌdä-fə-ləs-\\ *n*
: milk fermented by any of several
bacteria and used therapeutically to
change the intestinal flora

ac·i·do·sis \\ˌa-sə-'dō-səs\\ *n, pl* **-do·ses**
\\-ˌsēz\\ : a condition of decreased alkalinity of the blood and tissues

marked by sickly sweet breath. headache. nausea and vomiting. and visual disturbances and usu. a result of excessive acid production — compare ALKALOSIS, KETOSIS 1 — **ac·i·dot·ic** \-'dä-tik\ *adj*

acid phosphatase *n* : a phosphatase (as the phosphomonoesterase from the prostate gland) active in acid medium

acid·u·late \ə-'si-jə-ˌlāt\ *vb* **-lat·ed; -lat·ing** : to make acid or slightly acid — **acid·u·la·tion** \-ˌsi-jə-'lā-shən\ *n*

ac·id·uria \ˌa-sə-'dur-ē-ə. -ˈdyur-\ *n* : the condition of having acid in the urine esp. in abnormal amounts — see AMINOACIDURIA

ac·id·uric \ˌa-sə-'dur-ik. -'dyur-\ *adj* : tolerating a highly acid environment; *also* : ACIDOPHILIC 2

ac·i·nar \'a-sə-nər, -ˌnär\ *adj* : of. relating to. or comprising an acinus

acin·ic \ə-'si-nik\ *adj* : ACINAR (∼ and follicular carcinoma)

ac·i·nous \'a-sə-nəs, ə-'sī-nəs\ *adj* : consisting of or containing acini

aci·nus \'a-sə-nəs, ə-'sī-\ *n, pl* **aci·ni** \-ˌnī\ : any of the small sacs terminating the ducts of some exocrine glands and lined with secretory cells

ackee *var of* AKEE

ac·ne \'ak-nē\ *n* : a disorder of the skin caused by inflammation of the skin glands and hair follicles; *specif* : a form found chiefly in adolescents and marked by pimples esp. on the face — **ac·ned** \-nēd\ *adj*

ac·ne·form \'ak-nē-ˌfȯrm\ *or* **ac·nei·form** \'ak-nē-ə-ˌfȯrm. ak-'nē-\ *adj* : resembling acne (an ∼ eruption)

ac·ne·gen·ic \ˌak-ni-'je-nik\ *adj* : producing or increasing the severity of acne (the ∼ effect of some hormones)

ac·ne ro·sa·cea \ˌak-nē-rō-'zā-shē-ə. -shə\ *n, pl* **ac·nae ro·sa·ce·ae** \ˌak-nē-rō-'zā-shē-ˌē\ : acne involving the skin of the nose. forehead. and cheeks that is common in middle age and characterized by congestion. flushing. telangiectasia. and marked nodular swelling of tissues esp. of the nose — called also *rosacea*

acne ur·ti·ca·ta \-ˌər-tə-'kā-tə\ *n* : an acneform eruption of the skin characterized by itching papular wheals

acne vul·gar·is \-ˌvəl-'gar-əs\ *n, pl* **ac·nae vul·gar·es** \-ˌgar-ˌēz\ : a chronic acne involving mainly the face. chest. and shoulders that is common in adolescent humans and various domestic animals and characterized by the intermittent formation of discrete papular or pustular lesions often resulting in considerable scarring

ACNM *abbr* American College of Nurse-Midwives

acous·tic \ə-'kü-stik\ *or* **acous·ti·cal** \-sti-kəl\ *adj* : of or relating to the sense or organs of hearing. to sound. or to the science of sounds — **acous·ti·cal·ly** \-k(ə-)lē\ *adv*

acoustic meatus *n* : AUDITORY CANAL

acoustic nerve *n* : AUDITORY NERVE

acoustic tubercle *n* : a pear-shaped prominence on the inferior cerebellar peduncle including the dorsal nucleus of the cochlear nerve

ac·quired \ə-'kwīrd\ *adj* **1** : arising in response to the action of the environment on the organism (as in the use or disuse of an organ) — compare GENIC. HEREDITARY **2** : developed after birth — compare CONGENITAL, FAMILIAL. HEREDITARY

acquired immune deficiency syndrome *n* : AIDS

acquired immunity *n* : immunity that develops after exposure to a suitable agent (as by an attack of a disease or by injection of antigens) — compare ACTIVE IMMUNITY, NATURAL IMMUNITY. PASSIVE IMMUNITY

acquired immunodeficiency syndrome *n* : AIDS

acr- *or* **acro-** *comb form* **1** : top : peak : summit (*acrocephaly*) **2** : height (*acrophobia*) **3** : extremity of the body (*acrocyanosis*)

ac·rid \'a-krəd\ *adj* : irritatingly sharp and harsh or unpleasantly pungent in taste or odor — **ac·rid·ly** *adv*

ac·ri·dine \'a-krə-ˌdēn\ *n* : a colorless crystalline compound $C_{13}H_9N$ occurring in coal tar and important as the parent compound of dyes and pharmaceuticals

ac·ri·fla·vine \ˌa-krə-'flā-ˌvēn. -vən\ *n* : a yellow acridine dye $C_{14}H_{14}N_3Cl$ obtained by methylation of proflavine as red crystals or usu. in admixture with proflavine as a deep orange powder and used often in the form of its reddish brown hydrochloride as an antiseptic esp. for wounds

ac·ro·cen·tric \ˌa-krō-'sen-trik\ *adj* : having the centromere situated so that one chromosomal arm is much shorter than the other — compare METACENTRIC. TELOCENTRIC — **acrocentric** *n*

ac·ro·ceph·a·lo·syn·dac·ty·ly \-ˌse-fə-(ˌ)lō-sin-ˌdak-tə-lē\ *n, pl* **-lies** : a congenital syndrome characterized by a peaked head and webbed or fused fingers and toes

ac·ro·ceph·a·ly \ˌa-krə-'se-fə-lē\ *n, pl* **-lies** *also* **-lias** : OXYCEPHALY

ac·ro·chor·don \ˌa-krə-'kȯr-ˌdän\ *n* : SKIN TAG

ac·ro·cy·a·no·sis \ˌa-krō-ˌsī-ə-'nō-səs\ *n, pl* **-no·ses** \-ˌsēz\ : a disorder of the arterioles of the exposed parts of the hands and feet involving abnormal contraction of the arteriolar walls intensified by exposure to cold and resulting in bluish mottled skin. chilling. and sweating of the affected parts — **ac·ro·cy·a·not·ic** \-'nä-tik\ *adj*

ac·ro·der·ma·ti·tis \ˌa-krō-ˌdər-mə-'tī-təs\ *n* : inflammation of the skin of the extremities

acrodermatitis chron·i·ca atroph·i·cans

\-ˌkrä-ni-kə-ə-ˈträ-fī-ˌkanz\ *n* : a skin condition of the extremities related to Lyme disease and characterized by erythematous and edematous lesions which tend to become atrophic giving the skin the appearance of wrinkled tissue paper

acrodermatitis en·tero·path·i·ca \-ˌen-tə-rō-ˈpa-thi-kə\ *n* : a severe human skin and gastrointestinal disease inherited as a recessive autosomal trait that is characterized by the symptoms of zinc deficiency and clears up when zinc is added to the diet

ac·ro·dyn·ia \ˌa-krō-ˈdi-nē-ə\ *n* : a disease of infants and young children that is an allergic reaction to mercury, is characterized by dusky pink discoloration of hands and feet with local swelling and intense itching, and is accompanied by insomnia, irritability, and sensitivity to light — called also *erythredema*, *pink disease*, *Swift's disease* — **ac·ro·dyn·ic** \-ˈdi-nik\ *adj*

¹**ac·ro·meg·al·ic** \ˌa-krō-mə-ˈga-lik\ *adj* : exhibiting acromegaly

²**acromegalic** *n* : one affected with acromegaly

ac·ro·meg·a·ly \ˌa-krō-ˈme-gə-lē\ *n, pl* **-lies** : chronic hyperpituitarism that is characterized by a gradual and permanent enlargement of the flat bones (as the lower jaw) and of the hands and feet, abdominal organs, nose, lips, and tongue and that develops after ossification is complete — compare GIGANTISM

acro·mi·al \-ˈkrō-mē-əl\ *adj* : of, relating to, or situated near the acromion

acromial process *n* : ACROMION

ac·ro·mi·cria \ˌa-krō-ˈmi-krē-ə, -ˈmī-\ *n* : abnormal smallness of the extremities

acromio- *comb form* : acromial and (*acromio*clavicular)

acro·mio·cla·vic·u·lar \ə-ˌkrō-mē-(ˌ)ō-klə-ˈvi-kyə-lər\ *adj* : relating to, being, or affecting the joint connecting the acromion and the clavicle

acro·mi·on \ə-ˈkrō-mē-ən, -ˌän\ *n* : the outer end of the spine of the scapula that protects the glenoid cavity, forms the outer angle of the shoulder, and articulates with the clavicle — called also *acromial process, acromion process*

acro·mi·on·ec·to·my \ə-ˌkrō-mē-ˌän-ˈek-tə-mē, -mē-ə-ˈnek-\ *n, pl* **-mies** : partial or total surgical excision of the acromion

acro·pa·chy \ˈa-krō-ˌpa-kē, ə-ˈkrä-pə-kē\ *n, pl* **-pa·chies** : OSTEOARTHROPATHY

ac·ro·par·es·the·sia \ˌa-krō-ˌpar-əs-ˈthē-zhē-ə, -zhə\ *n* : a condition of burning, tingling, or pricking sensations or numbness in the extremities present on awaking and of unknown cause or produced by compression of nerves during sleep

acrop·a·thy \ə-ˈkrä-pə-thē\ *n, pl* **-thies** : a disease affecting the extremities

ac·ro·phobe \ˈa-krə-ˌfōb\ *n* : a person affected with acrophobia

ac·ro·pho·bia \ˌa-krə-ˈfō-bē-ə\ *n* : abnormal or pathological fear of being at a great height

ac·ro·sclero·der·ma \ˌa-krō-ˌskler-ə-ˈdar-mə\ *n* : scleroderma affecting the extremities, face, and chest

ac·ro·scle·ro·sis \ˌa-krō-sklə-ˈrō-səs\ *n, pl* **-ro·ses** \-ˌsēz\ : ACROSCLERODERMA

ac·ro·some \ˈa-krə-ˌsōm\ *n* : an anterior prolongation of a spermatozoon that releases egg-penetrating enzymes — **ac·ro·so·mal** \ˌa-krə-ˈsō-məl\ *adj*

ac·ry·late \ˈak-rə-ˌlāt\ *n* : a salt or ester of acrylic acid

¹**acryl·ic** \ə-ˈkri-lik\ *adj* : of or relating to acrylic acid or its derivatives

²**acrylic** *n* : ACRYLIC RESIN

acrylic acid *n* : an unsaturated liquid acid $C_3H_4O_2$ that is obtained by synthesis and that polymerizes readily

acrylic resin *n* : a glassy acrylic thermoplastic used for cast and molded parts (as of medical prostheses and dental appliances) or as coatings and adhesives

ACSW *abbr* Academy of Certified Social Workers

ACTH \ˌā-ˌsē-(ˌ)tē-ˈāch\ *n* : a protein hormone of the anterior lobe of the pituitary gland that stimulates the adrenal cortex — called also *adrenocorticotropic hormone*

ac·tin \ˈak-tən\ *n* : a cellular protein found esp. in microfilaments (as those comprising myofibrils) and active in muscular contraction, cellular movement, and maintenance of cell shape — see F-ACTIN, G-ACTIN

actin- or **actini-** or **actino-** *comb form* : of, utilizing, or caused by actinic radiation (as X rays) (*actino*therapy)

ac·tin·ic \ak-ˈti-nik\ *adj* : of, relating to, resulting from, or exhibiting chemical changes produced by radiant energy esp. in the visible and ultraviolet parts of the spectrum (∼ keratosis) (∼ injury)

ac·tin·i·um \ak-ˈti-nē-əm\ *n* : a radioactive trivalent metallic element — symbol *Ac*; see ELEMENT table

ac·ti·no·bac·il·lo·sis \ˌak-tə-(ˌ)nō-ˌba-sə-ˈlō-səs, ak-ˌti-nō-\ *n, pl* **-lo·ses** \-ˌsēz\ : a disease that affects domestic animals and sometimes humans, resembles actinomycosis, and is caused by a bacterium of the genus *Actinobacillus* (*A. lignieresi*) — see WOODEN TONGUE

ac·ti·no·ba·cil·lus \-bə-ˈsi-ləs\ *n* 1 *cap* : a genus of aerobic gram-negative parasitic bacteria (family Pasteurellaceae) forming filaments resembling streptobacilli — see ACTINOBACILLOSIS 2 *pl* **-li** \-ˌlī\ : a bacterium of the genus *Actinobacillus*

ac·ti·no·my·ces \ˌak-tə-(ˌ)nō-ˈmī-ˌsēz, ak-ˌti-nō-\ *n* 1 *cap* : a genus of filamentous or rod-shaped gram-positive bacteria (family Actinomycetaceae) that includes usu. commensal and sometimes pathogenic forms inhabiting mucosal surfaces esp. of the oral cavity — compare ACTINOMYCOSIS 2 *pl* **actinomyces** : a bacterium of the genus *Actinomyces*

ac·ti·no·my·cete \-'mī-₁sēt, -mī-'sēt\ *n* : any of an order (Actinomycetales) of filamentous or rod-shaped bacteria (as the actinomyces or streptomyces)

ac·ti·no·my·cin \-'mīs-³n\ *n* : any of various red or yellow-red mostly toxic polypeptide antibiotics isolated from soil bacteria (esp. *Streptomyces antibioticus*)

actinomycin D *n* : DACTINOMYCIN

ac·ti·no·my·co·sis \₁ak-tə-nō-₁mī-'kō-səs\ *n, pl* **-co·ses** \-₁sēz\ : infection with or disease caused by actinomycetes

ac·ti·no·spec·ta·cin \₁ak-tə-(₁)nō-'spek-tə-sən, ak-₁ti-nō-\ *n* : SPECTINOMYCIN

ac·ti·no·ther·a·py \-'ther-ə-pē\ *n, pl* **-pies** : application for therapeutic purposes of the chemically active rays of the spectrum (as ultraviolet light or X rays)

ac·tion \'ak-shən\ *n* 1 : the process of exerting a force or bringing about an effect that results from the inherent capacity of an agent 2 : a function or the performance of a function of the body (as defecation) or of one of its parts (heart ∼) 3 : an act of will 4 *pl* : BEHAVIOR (aggressive ∼*s*)

action potential *n* : a momentary change in electrical potential (as between the inside of a nerve cell and the extracellular medium) that occurs when a cell or tissue has been activated by a stimulus — compare RESTING POTENTIAL

ac·ti·vat·ed charcoal *n* : a highly absorptive, fine, black, odorless, and tasteless powdered charcoal used in medicine esp. as an antidote in many forms of poisoning and as an antiflatulent

ac·ti·va·tor \'ak-tə-₁vā-tər\ *n* 1 : a substance (as a chloride ion) that increases the activity of an enzyme — compare COENZYME 2 : a substance given off by developing tissue that stimulates differentiation of adjacent tissue; *also* : a structure giving off such a stimulant

ac·tive \'ak-tiv\ *adj* 1 : capable of acting or reacting esp. in some specific way (an ∼ enzyme) 2 : tending to progress or to cause degeneration (∼ tuberculosis) 3 : exhibiting optical activity 4 : requiring the expenditure of energy — **ac·tive·ly** *adv*

active immunity *n* : usu. long-lasting immunity that is acquired through production of antibodies within the organism in response to the presence of antigens — compare ACQUIRED IMMUNITY, NATURAL IMMUNITY, PASSIVE IMMUNITY

active site *n* : a region esp. of a biologically active protein (as an enzyme or an antibody) where catalytic activity takes place and whose shape permits the binding only of a specific reactant molecule

active transport *n* : movement of a chemical substance by the expenditure of energy through a gradient (as across a cell membrane) in concentration or electrical potential and opposite to the direction of normal diffusion

ac·tiv·i·ty \ak-'ti-və-tē\ *n, pl* **-ties** 1 : natural or normal function (digestive ∼) 2 : the characteristic of acting chemically or of promoting a chemical reaction (the ∼ of a catalyst)

ac·to·my·o·sin \₁ak-tə-'mī-ə-sən\ *n* : a viscous contractile complex of actin and myosin concerned together with ATP in muscular contraction

act out *vb* : to express (as an impulse or a fantasy) directly in overt behavior without modification to comply with social norms

acu- *comb form* : performed with a needle (*acu*puncture)

acu·ity \ə-'kyü-ə-tē\ *n, pl* **-ities** : keenness of sense perception (∼ of hearing) — see VISUAL ACUITY

acuminata — see CONDYLOMA ACUMINATUM, VERRUCA ACUMINATA

acuminatum — see CONDYLOMA ACUMINATUM

acu·pres·sure \'a-kyü-₁pre-shər\ *n* : SHIATSU — **acu·pres·sur·ist** \-₁pre-shə-rist\ *n*

acu·punc·ture \-₁pəŋk-chər\ *n* : an orig. Chinese practice of puncturing the body (as with needles) at specific points to cure disease or relieve pain (as in surgery) — **acu·punc·tur·ist** \-chə-rist\ *n*

-acusis *n comb form* : hearing (diplac*usis*) (hyperac*usis*)

acustica — see MACULA ACUSTICA

acusticus — see MEATUS ACUSTICUS EXTERNUS, MEATUS ACUSTICUS INTERNUS

acuta — see PITYRIASIS LICHENOIDES ET VARIOLIFORMIS ACUTA

acute \ə-'kyüt\ *adj* 1 : sensing or perceiving accurately, clearly, effectively, or sensitively (∼ vision) 2 a : characterized by sharpness or severity (∼ pain) (∼ infection) b : having a sudden onset, sharp rise, and short course (∼ disease) — compare CHRONIC — **acute·ly** *adv* — **acute·ness** *n*

acute abdomen *n* : an acute internal abdominal condition requiring immediate operation

acute care *n* : short-term medical care in a hospital or emergency room esp. for serious acute disease or trauma

acute febrile neutrophilic dermatosis *n* : SWEET'S SYNDROME

acy·a·not·ic \ā-ˌsī-ə-ˈnä-tik\ *adj* : characterized by the absence of cyanosis (~ patients) (~ heart disease)

acy·clo·vir \ā-ˈsī-klō-ˌvir\ *n* : a cyclic nucleoside $C_8H_{11}N_5O_3$ used esp. to treat the symptoms of the genital form of herpes simplex — see ZOVIRAX

ac·yl \ˈa-səl, -ˌsēl; ˈā-səl\ *n* : a radical derived usu. from an organic acid by removal of the hydroxyl from all acid groups

ADA *abbr* 1 adenosine deaminase 2 American Dietetic Association

adac·tyl·ia \ˌā-ˌdak-ˈti-lē-ə\ *n* : congenital lack of fingers or toes

ad·a·man·ti·no·ma \ˌa-də-ˌmant-ᵊn-ˈō-mə\ *n*, *pl* **-mas** *also* **-ma·ta** \-mə-tə\ : AMELOBLASTOMA

Ad·am's ap·ple \ˈa-dəmz-ˈa-pəl\ *n* : the projection in the front of the neck that is formed by the thyroid cartilage and is particularly prominent in males

ad·am·site \ˈa-dəm-ˌzīt\ *n* : a yellow crystalline arsenical $C_{12}H_9AsClN$ used as a respiratory irritant in some forms of tear gas

Adams, Roger (1889–1971), American chemist.

Adams–Stokes syndrome *n* : STOKES-ADAMS SYNDROME

R. Adams — see STOKES-ADAMS SYNDROME

J. Stokes — see CHEYNE-STOKES RESPIRATION

adapt \ə-ˈdapt\ *vb* : to make or become fit often by modification

ad·ap·ta·tion \ˌa-ˌdap-ˈtā-shən\ *n* 1 : the act or process of adapting : the state of being adapted 2 : adjustment to environmental conditions — **adap·tive** \ə-ˈdap-tiv\ *adj*

ad·der \ˈa-dər\ *n* 1 : the common venomous European viper of the genus *Vipera* (*V. berus*); broadly : a terrestrial viper (family Viperidae) 2 : any of several No. American snakes that are harmless but are popularly believed to be venomous

¹ad·dict \ə-ˈdikt\ *vb* : to cause (a person) to become physiologically dependent upon a substance

²ad·dict \ˈa-(ˌ)dikt\ *n* : one who is addicted to a substance

ad·dic·tion \ə-ˈdik-shən\ *n* : compulsive need for and use of a habit-forming substance (as heroin, nicotine, or alcohol) characterized by tolerance and by well-defined physiological symptoms upon withdrawal; broadly : persistent compulsive use of a substance known by the user to be physically, psychologically, or socially harmful — compare HABITUATION, SUBSTANCE ABUSE — **ad·dic·tive** \-ˈdik-tiv\ *adj*

Ad·dis count \ˈa-dis-ˌkau̇nt\ *n* : a technique for the quantitative determination of cells, casts, and protein in a 12-hour urine sample used in the diagnosis and treatment of kidney disease

Addis, Thomas (1881–1949), American physician.

Ad·di·so·ni·an \ˌa-də-ˈsō-nē-ən, -nyən\ *adj* : of, relating to, or affected with Addison's disease (~ crisis)

Addison, Thomas (1793–1860), English physician.

addisonian anemia *n, often cap 1st A* : PERNICIOUS ANEMIA

Addison's disease *n* : a destructive disease marked by deficient adrenocortical secretion and characterized by extreme weakness, loss of weight, low blood pressure, gastrointestinal disturbances, and brownish pigmentation of the skin and mucous membranes

¹ad·di·tive \ˈa-də-tiv\ *adj* : characterized by, being, or producing effects (as drug responses or gene products) that when the causative factors act together are the sum of their individual effects — **ad·di·tive·ly** *adv* — **ad·di·tiv·i·ty** \ˌa-də-ˈti-və-tē\ *n*

²additive *n* : a substance added to another in relatively small amounts to impart or improve desirable properties or suppress undesirable properties (food ~s)

ad·duct \ə-ˈdəkt, a-\ *vb* : to draw (as a limb) toward or past the median axis of the body; *also* : to bring together (similar parts) (~ the fingers) — **ad·duc·tion** \ə-ˈdək-shən, a-\ *n*

ad·duc·tor \-ˈdək-tər\ *n* 1 : any of three powerful triangular muscles that contribute to the adduction of the human thigh: **a** : one arising from the superior or ramus of the pubis and inserted into the middle third of the linea aspera — called also *adductor longus* **b** : one arising from the inferior ramus of the pubis and inserted into the iliopectineal line and the upper part of the linea aspera — called also *adductor brevis* **c** : one arising from the inferior ramus of the pubis and the ischium and inserted behind the first two into the linea aspera — called also *adductor magnus* 2 : any of several muscles other than the adductors of the thigh that draw a part toward the median line of the body or toward the axis of an extremity

adductor brev·is \-ˈbre-vəs\ *n* : ADDUCTOR 1b

adductor hal·lu·cis \-ˈhal-yə-sis; -ˈha-lə-səs, -kəs\ *n* : a muscle of the foot that adducts and flexes the big toe and helps to support the arch of the foot — called also *adductor hallucis muscle*

adductor lon·gus \-ˈlȯŋ-gəs\ *n* : ADDUCTOR 1a

adductor mag·nus \-ˈmag-nəs\ *n* : ADDUCTOR 1c

adductor pol·li·cis \-ˈpä-lə-səs, -kəs\ *n* : a muscle of the hand with two heads that adducts the thumb by bringing it toward the palm — called also *adductor pollicis muscle*

adductor tubercle *n* : a tubercle on the proximal part of the medial epicondyle of the femur that is the site of insertion of the adductor magnus

aden- *or* **adeno-** *comb form* : gland : glandular (*adenitis*) (*adeno*carcinoma)

ad•e•nine \'ad-ʰn-ˌēn\ *n* : a purine base $C_5H_5N_5$ that codes hereditary information in the genetic code in DNA and RNA — compare CYTOSINE, GUANINE, THYMINE, URACIL

adenine arabinoside *n* : VIDARABINE

ad•e•ni•tis \ˌad-ʰn-ʰī-təs\ *n* : inflammation of a gland; *esp* : LYMPHADENITIS

ad•e•no•ac•an•tho•ma \ˌad-ʰn-(ˌ)ō-ˌa-ˌkan-ʰthō-mə\ *n, pl* **-mas** *or* **-ma•ta** \-mə-tə\ : an adenocarcinoma with epithelial cells differentiated and proliferated into squamous cells

ad•e•no•car•ci•no•ma \-ˌkärs-ʰn-ʰō-mə\ *n, pl* **-mas** *or* **-ma•ta** \-mə-tə\ : a malignant tumor originating in glandular epithelium — **ad•e•no•car•ci•no•ma•tous** \-mə-təs\ *adj*

ad•e•no•fi•bro•ma \-ˌfī-ʰbrō-mə\ *n, pl* **-mas** *or* **-ma•ta** \-mə-tə\ : a benign tumor of glandular and fibrous tissue

ad•e•no•hy•poph•y•sis \-hī-ʰpä-fə-səs\ *n, pl* **-y•ses** \-ˌsēz\ : the anterior part of the pituitary gland that is derived from the embryonic pharynx and is primarily glandular in nature — called also *anterior lobe*; compare NEUROHYPOPHYSIS — **ad•e•no•hy•poph•y•se•al** \-(ˌ)hī-ˌpä-fə-ʰsē-əl\ *or* **ad•e•no•hy•po•phys•i•al** \-hī-pə-ʰfi-zē-əl\ *adj*

¹ad•e•noid \'ad-ʰn-ˌȯid, ʰad-ˌnȯid\ *adj* **1** : of, like, or relating to glands or glandular tissue; *esp* : like or belonging to lymphoid tissue **2** : of or relating to the adenoids **3 a** : of, relating to, or affected with abnormally enlarged adenoids **b** : characteristic of one affected with abnormally enlarged adenoids (~ facies)

²adenoid *n* **1** : an abnormally enlarged mass of lymphoid tissue at the back of the pharynx characteristically obstructing the nasal and ear passages and inducing mouth breathing, a nasal voice, postnasal discharge, and dullness of facial expression — usu. used in pl. **2** : PHARYNGEAL TONSIL

ad•e•noi•dal \ˌad-ʰn-ʰȯid-ʰl\ *adj* : exhibiting the characteristics (as snoring, mouth breathing, and a nasal voice) of one affected with abnormally enlarged adenoids : ADENOID — not usu. used technically

ad•e•noid•ec•to•my \ˌad-ʰn-ˌȯi-ʰdek-tə-mē\ *n, pl* **-mies** : surgical removal of the adenoids

ad•e•noid•itis \ˌad-ʰn-ˌȯi-ʰdī-təs\ *n* : inflammation of the adenoids

ad•e•no•ma \ˌad-ʰn-ʰō-mə\ *n, pl* **-mas** *also* **-ma•ta** \-mə-tə\ : a benign tumor of a glandular structure or of glandular origin — **ad•e•no•ma•tous** \-mə-təs\ *adj*

ad•e•no•ma•toid \ˌad-ʰn-ʰō-mə-ˌtȯid\ *adj* : relating to or resembling an adenoma

ad•e•no•ma•to•sis \ˌad-ʰn-ˌō-mə-ʰtō-səs\ *n, pl* **-to•ses** \-ˌsēz\ : a condition marked by multiple growths consisting of glandular tissue

ad•e•no•my•o•ma \ˌad-ʰn-(ˌ)ō-ˌmī-ʰō-mə\ *n, pl* **-mas** *or* **-ma•ta** \-mə-tə\ : a benign tumor composed of muscular and glandular elements

ad•e•no•my•o•sis \-ˌmī-ʰō-səs\ *n, pl* **-o•ses** \-ˌsēz\ : endometriosis esp. when the endometrial tissue invades the myometrium

ad•e•nop•a•thy \ˌad-ʰn-ʰä-pə-thē\ *n, pl* **-thies** : any disease or enlargement involving glandular tissue; *esp* : one involving lymph nodes

aden•o•sine \ə-ʰde-nə-ˌsēn, -sən\ *n* : a nucleoside $C_{10}H_{13}N_5O_4$ that is a constituent of RNA yielding adenine and ribose on hydrolysis

adenosine deaminase *n* : an enzyme which catalyzes the conversion of AMP, ADP, and ATP to inosine, whose deficiency causes a severe immunodeficiency disease by inhibiting DNA replication in lymphocytes, and whose marked increase is associated with a mild chronic hemolytic anemia — abbr. *ADA*

adenosine diphosphate *n* : ADP

adenosine mo•no•phos•phate \-ˌmä-nə-ʰfäs-ˌfāt, -ˌmō-\ *n* : AMP

adenosine phosphate *n* : any of three phosphates of adenosine: **a** : AMP **b** : ADP **c** : ATP

adenosine 3′,5′–monophosphate \-ʰthrē-ʰfīv-\ *n* : CYCLIC AMP

adenosine tri•phos•pha•tase \-trī-ʰfäs-fə-ˌtās, -ˌtāz\ *n* : ATPASE

adenosine tri•phos•phate \-trī-ʰfäs-ˌfāt\ *n* : ATP

ad•e•no•sis \ˌad-ʰn-ʰō-səs\ *n, pl* **-no•ses** \-ˌsēz\ : a disease of glandular tissue; *esp* : one involving abnormal proliferation or occurrence of glandular tissue (vaginal ~)

ad•e•not•o•my \ˌad-ʰn-ʰä-tə-mē\ *n, pl* **-mies** : the operation of dissecting, incising, or removing a gland and esp. the adenoids

ad•e•no•vi•rus \ˌad-ʰn-ō-ʰvī-rəs\ *n* : any of a group of DNA-containing viruses shaped like a 20-sided polyhedron and orig. identified in human adenoid tissue, causing respiratory diseases (as catarrh), and including some capable of inducing malignant tumors in experimental animals — **ad•e•no•vi•ral** \-rəl\ *adj*

ad•e•nyl•ic acid \ˌad-ʰn-ʰi-lik-\ *n* : AMP

ADH *abbr* antidiuretic hormone

ADHD *abbr* attention-deficit hyperactivity disorder

ad•here \ad-ʰhir\ *vb* **ad•hered; ad•her•ing 1** : to hold fast or stick by or as if by gluing, suction, grasping, or fusing **2** : to become joined (as in pathological adhesion) — **ad·her·ence** \-'hir-ᵊns\ n

ad·he·sion \ad-'hē-zhən\ n 1 : the action or state of adhering; *specif* : a sticking together of substances 2 a : the abnormal union of surfaces normally separated by the formation of new fibrous tissue resulting from an inflammatory process; *also* : the newly formed uniting tissue (pleural ~s) b : the union of wound edges esp. by first intention

¹**ad·he·sive** \-'hē-siv, -ziv\ adj 1 a : relating to or having the ability to stick things together b : prepared for adhering 2 : characterized by adhesions — **ad·he·sive·ly** adv

²**adhesive** n 1 : a substance that bonds two materials together by adhering to the surface of each 2 : ADHESIVE TAPE

adhesive pericarditis n : pericarditis in which adhesions form between the two layers of pericardium — see AC-CRETIO CORDIS

adhesive tape n : tape coated on one side with an adhesive mixture; *esp* : one used for covering wounds

adi·a·do·ko·ki·ne·sis or **adi·a·do·cho·ki·ne·sis** \a-dē-ₐ-dₐ-ₖō-kₐ-'nē-sₐs, ₐ-dī-ₐ-ₗdō-(ₗ)kō-, -kī-'nē-\ n, pl **-ne·ses** \-ₗsēz\ : inability to make movements exhibiting a rapid change of motion (as in quickly rotating the wrist one way and then the other) due to cerebellar dysfunction — compare DYSDIADOCHOKINESIA

ad·i·ence \'a-dē-əns\ n : a tendency to approach or accept a stimulus object or situation — compare ABIENCE — **ad·i·ent** \-ənt\ adj

Ad·ie's syndrome \'a-dēz-\ or **Ad·ie syndrome** \-dē-\ n : a neurologic syndrome that affects esp. women between 20 and 40 and is characterized by an abnormally dilated pupil, absent or diminished light reflexes of the eye, abnormal accommodation, and lack of ankle-jerk and knee-jerk reflexes

Adie \'ā-dē\, **William John (1886–1935),** British neurologist.

adip- or **adipo-** comb form : fat : fatty tissue (*adipo*cyte)

ad·i·phen·ine \ₐ-di-'fe-ₙnēn\ n : an antispasmodic drug $C_{20}H_{25}NO_2$ administered in the form of the hydrochloride — see TRASENTINE

ad·i·po·cere \'a-də-pə-ₗsir\ n : a waxy or unctuous brownish substance consisting chiefly of fatty acids and calcium soaps produced by chemical changes affecting dead body fat and muscle long buried or immersed in moisture

ad·i·po·cyte \'a-də-pə-ₗsīt\ n : FAT CELL

ad·i·pose \'a-də-ₗpōs\ adj : of or relating to fat; *broadly* : FAT

adipose tissue n : connective tissue in which fat is stored and which has the cells distended by droplets of fat

ad·i·pos·i·ty \ₐ-də-'pä-sə-tē\ n, pl **-ties** : the quality or state of being fat : OBESITY

adi·po·so·gen·i·tal dystrophy \ₐ-də-dₒ-dō-sō-'je-nət-ᵊl-\ n : FRÖHLICH'S SYNDROME

adiposus — see PANNICULUS ADIPOSUS

adip·sia \ā-'dip-sē-ə, ə-\ n : loss of thirst; *also* : abnormal and esp. prolonged abstinence from the intake of fluids

ad·i·tus \'a-də-təs\ n, pl **aditus** or **ad·i·tus·es** : a passage or opening for entrance

ad·junct \'a-ₗjəŋkt\ n : ADJUVANT b

ad·junc·tive \ə-'jəŋk-tiv, a-\ adj : involving the medical use of an adjunct (~ therapy) — **ad·junc·tive·ly** adv

ad·just \ə-'jəst\ vb 1 : to bring about orientation or adaptation of (oneself) 2 : to achieve mental and behavioral balance between one's own needs and the demands of others — **ad·just·ment** \-mənt\ n

ad·just·ed adj : having achieved an often specified and usu. harmonious relationship with the environment or with other individuals

¹**ad·ju·vant** \'a-jə-vənt\ adj 1 : serving to aid or contribute 2 : assisting in the prevention, amelioration, or cure of disease (~ chemotherapy following surgery)

²**adjuvant** n : one that helps or facilitates: as a : an ingredient (as in a prescription) that facilitates or modifies the action of the principal ingredient b : something (as a drug or method) that enhances the effectiveness of a medical treatment c : a substance enhancing the immune response to an antigen

ADL abbr activities of daily living

Ad·le·ri·an \ad-'lir-ē-ən, äd-\ adj : of, relating to, or being a theory and technique of psychotherapy emphasizing the importance of feelings of inferiority, a will to power, and overcompensation in neurotic processes

Ad·ler \'äd-lər\, **Alfred (1870–1937),** Austrian psychiatrist.

ad lib \ₗ)ad-'lib\ adv : without restraint or imposed limit : as much or as often as is wanted — often used in writing prescriptions

ad li·bi·tum \ₗ)ad-'li-bə-təm\ adv : AD LIB (rats fed *ad libitum*)

ad·min·is·ter \ad-'mi-nə-stər\ vb **ad·min·is·tered; ad·min·is·ter·ing** : to give remedially (as medicine) — **ad·min·is·tra·tion** \ad-ₗmi-nə-'strā-shən\ n

ad·nexa \ad-'nek-sə\ n pl : conjoined, subordinate, or associated anatomic parts (the uterine ~ include the ovaries and fallopian tubes) — **ad·nex·al** \-səl\ adj

ad·nex·i·tis \ₗad-ₗnek-'sī-təs\ n : inflammation of adnexa (as of the uterus)

ad·o·les·cence \ₗad-ᵊl-'es-ᵊns\ n 1 : the state or process of growing up 2 : the period of life from puberty to maturity terminating legally at the age of majority

ad·o·les·cent \-ᵊnt\ *n* : one in the state of adolescence — **adolescent** *adj* — **ad·o·les·cent·ly** *adv*

ADP \ā-(ˌ)dē-ˈpē\ *n* : an ester of adenosine that is reversibly converted to ATP for the storing of energy by the addition of a high-energy phosphate group — called also *adenosine diphosphate, adenosine phosphate*

adren- *or* **adreno-** *comb form* **1 a** : adrenal glands (*adrenocortical*) **b** : adrenal and (*adrenogenital*) **2** : adrenaline (*adrenergic*)

¹ad·re·nal \ə-ˈdrēn-ᵊl\ *adj* : of, relating to, or derived from the adrenal glands or their secretion — **ad·re·nal·ly** *adv*

²adrenal *n* : ADRENAL GLAND

ad·re·nal·ec·to·my \ə-ˌdrēn-ᵊl-ˈek-tə-mē\ *n, pl* **-mies** : surgical removal of one or both adrenal glands

adrenal gland *n* : either of a pair of complex endocrine organs near the anterior medial border of the kidney consisting of a mesodermal cortex that produces glucocorticoid, mineralocorticoid, and androgenic hormones and an ectodermal medulla that produces epinephrine and norepinephrine — called also *adrenal, suprarenal gland*

Adren·a·lin \ə-ˈdren-ᵊl-ən\ *trademark* — used for a preparation of levorotatory epinephrine

adren·a·line \ə-ˈdren-ᵊl-ən\ *n* : EPINEPHRINE

ad·ren·er·gic \ˌa-drə-ˈnər-jik\ *adj* **1** : liberating or activated by adrenaline or a substance like adrenaline — compare CHOLINERGIC 1, NORADRENERGIC **2** : resembling adrenaline esp. in physiological action — **ad·ren·er·gi·cal·ly** \-ji-k(ə-)lē\ *adv*

adreno- — see ADREN-

ad·re·no·cor·ti·cal \ə-ˌdrē-nō-ˈkȯr-ti-kəl\ *adj* : of, relating to, or derived from the cortex of the adrenal glands

ad·re·no·cor·ti·coid \-ˌkȯid\ *n* : a hormone secreted by the adrenal cortex — **adrenocorticoid** *adj*

ad·re·no·cor·ti·co·ste·roid \-ˈstir-ˌȯid, -ˈster-\ *n* : a steroid (as cortisone or hydrocortisone) obtained from, resembling, or having physiological effects like those of the adrenal cortex

ad·re·no·cor·ti·co·tro·pic \-ˈtrō-pik, -ˈträ-\ *also* **ad·re·no·cor·ti·co·tro·phic** \-ˈtrō-fik, -ˈträ-\ *adj* : acting on or stimulating the adrenal cortex

adrenocorticotropic hormone *n* : ACTH

ad·re·no·cor·ti·co·tro·pin \-ˈtrō-pən\ *also* **ad·re·no·cor·ti·co·tro·phin** \-fən\ *n* : ACTH

adre·no·gen·i·tal syndrome \ə-ˌdrē-nō-ˈje-nət-ᵊl-, -ˌdre-\ *n* : CUSHING'S SYNDROME

adre·no·leu·ko·dys·tro·phy \-ˌlü-kō-ˈdis-trə-fē\ *n, pl* **-phies** : SCHILDER'S DISEASE

adre·no·lyt·ic \ə-ˌdrēn-ᵊl-ˈi-tik, -ˌdren-\

adj : blocking the release or action of adrenaline at nerve endings

adre·no·med·ul·lary \ə-ˌdrē-nō-ˈmed-ᵊl-ˌer-ē, -ˌdre-, -ˈme-jə-ˌler-; -mə-ˈdə-lə-ˌrē\ *adj* : relating to or derived from the medulla of the adrenal glands (~ extracts)

adre·no·re·cep·tor \ə-ˌdrē-nō-ri-ˈsep-tər, -ˌdre-\ *n* : an adrenergic receptor

adre·no·ste·rone \ə-ˌdrē-nō-stə-ˈrōn, -ˌdre-; ˌa-drə-ˈnäs-tə-\ *n* : a crystalline steroid $C_{19}N_{24}O_3$ obtained from the adrenal cortex and having androgenic activity

Adria·my·cin \ˌā-drē-ə-ˈmīs-ᵊn, ˌa-\ *trademark* — used for a preparation of the hydrochloride of doxorubicin

ad·sorb \ad-ˈsȯrb, -ˈzȯrb\ *vb* : to take up and hold by adsorption — **ad·sorb·able** \-ˈsȯr-bə-bəl, -ˈzȯr-\ *adj*

ad·sor·bent \-bənt\ *adj* : having the capacity or tendency to adsorb — **adsorbent** *n*

ad·sorp·tion \ad-ˈsȯrp-shən, -ˈzȯrp-\ *n* : the adhesion in an extremely thin layer of molecules (as of gases) to the surfaces of solid bodies or liquids with which they are in contact — compare ABSORPTION — **ad·sorp·tive** \-ˈsȯrp-tiv, -ˈzȯrp-\ *adj*

adult \ə-ˈdəlt, ˈa-ˌdəlt\ *n* **1** : one that has arrived at full development or maturity esp. in size, strength, or intellectual capacity **2** : a human male or female after a specific age (as 21) — **adult** *adj*

adul·ter·ate \ə-ˈdəl-tə-ˌrāt\ *vb* **-at·ed; -at·ing** : to corrupt, debase, or make impure by the addition of a foreign or inferior substance — **adul·ter·ant** \-rənt\ *n or adj* — **adul·ter·a·tion** \-ˈrā-shən\ *n*

adult·hood \ə-ˈdəlt-ˌhúd\ *n* : the state or time of being an adult

adult–on·set diabetes *n* : NON-INSULIN=DEPENDENT DIABETES MELLITUS

adult respiratory distress syndrome *n* : respiratory failure in adults or children that results from diffuse injury to the endothelium of the lung (as in sepsis, chest trauma, massive blood transfusion, aspiration of the gastric contents, or diffuse pneumonia) and is characterized by pulmonary edema with an abnormally high amount of protein in the edematous fluid, and by respiratory distress, and hypoxemia — abbr. *ARDS*

ad·vance·ment \ad-ˈvans-mənt\ *n* : detachment of a muscle or tendon from its insertion and reattachment (as in the surgical correction of strabismus) at a more advanced point from its insertion (flexor tendon ~)

advancement flap *n* : a flap of tissue stretched and sutured in place to cover a defect at a nearby position

ad·ven·ti·tia \ˌad-vən-ˈti-shə, -ven-\ *n* : the outer layer that makes up a tubular organ or structure and esp. a blood vessel, is composed of collagenous and elastic fibers, and is not covered with peritoneum — called also *tunica adventitia* — **ad·ven·ti·tial** \-shəl\ *adj*

ad·ven·ti·tious \-shəs\ *adj* : arising sporadically or in other than the usual location (an ~ part in embryonic development)

ady·na·mia \ˌā-dī-ˈna-mē-ə, ˌa-də-, -ˈnā-\ *n* : asthenia caused by disease

ady·nam·ic \ˌā-(ˌ)dī-ˈna-mik, ˌa-də-\ *adj* : characterized by or causing a loss of strength or function (~ ileus)

ae·des \ā-ˈē-(ˌ)dēz\ *n* 1 *cap* : a large cosmopolitan genus of mosquitoes that includes vectors of some diseases (as yellow fever and dengue) 2 *pl* **aedes** : any mosquito of the genus *Aedes* — **ae·dine** \-ˌdīn, -ˌdēn\ *adj*

ae·goph·o·ny *chiefly Brit var of* EGOPHONY

ae·lu·ro·phobe, ae·lu·ro·pho·bia *var of* AILUROPHOBE, AILUROPHOBIA

-aemia *also* **-haemia** *chiefly Brit var of* -EMIA

aer- *or* **aero-** *comb form* 1 : air : atmosphere (*aerate*) (*aerobic*) 2 : gas (*aerosol*) 3 : aviation (*aeromedicine*)

aer·ate \ˈar-ˌāt, ˈa-ər-\ *vb* **aer·at·ed; aer·at·ing** 1 : to supply (the blood) with oxygen by respiration 2 : to supply or impregnate (as a liquid) with air 3 : to combine or charge with a gas (as carbon dioxide) — **aer·a·tion** \ar-ˈā-shən, ˌa-ər-\ *n*

aer·obe \ˈar-ˌōb, ˈa-ər-\ *n* : an organism (as a bacterium) that lives only in the presence of oxygen

aer·o·bic \ar-ˈō-bik, ˌa-ər-\ *adj* 1 : living, active, or occurring only in the presence of oxygen (~ respiration) 2 : of, relating to, or induced by aerobes 3 : involving or utilizing aerobics (~ exercises) — **aer·o·bi·cal·ly** \-bi-k(ə-)lē\ *adv*

aer·o·bics \-biks\ *n pl* 1 : a system of physical conditioning involving exercises (as running, walking, swimming, or calisthenics) strenuously performed so as to cause marked temporary increase in respiration and heart rate — used with a sing. or pl. verb 2 : aerobic exercises

aero·bi·ol·o·gy \ar-ō-bī-ˈä-lə-jē\ *n, pl* **-gies** : the science dealing with the occurrence, transportation, and effects of airborne materials or microorganisms (as viruses or pollen)

aer·odon·tal·gia \ar-ō-dän-ˈtal-jē-ə, -jə\ *n* : toothache resulting from atmospheric decompression

aero·em·bo·lism \-ˈem-bə-ˌli-zə,n\ *n* : decompression sickness caused by rapid ascent to high altitudes and resulting exposure to rapidly lowered air pressure — called also *air bends*

aero·med·i·cine \ar-ō-ˈme-də-sən\ *n* : a branch of medicine that deals with the diseases and disturbances arising from flying and the associated physiological and psychological problems

— **aero·med·i·cal** \-ˈme-di-kəl\ *adj*

aer·o·oti·tis \ar-ə-wō-ˈti-təs\ *n* : AEROOTITIS MEDIA

aero·otitis me·dia \-ˈmē-dē-ə\ *n* : the traumatic inflammation of the middle ear resulting from differences between atmospheric pressure and pressure in the middle ear

aero·pha·gia \ar-ō-ˈfā-jē-ə, -jə\ *also* **aer·oph·a·gy** \ar-ˈä-fə-jē, ˌa-ər-\ *n, pl* **-gias** *also* **-gies** : the swallowing of air esp. in hysteria

aero·pho·bia \ar-ō-ˈfō-bē-ə\ *n* : abnormal or excessive fear of drafts or of fresh air — **aero·pho·bic** \-bik\ *adj*

aero·sol \ˈar-ə-ˌsäl, -ˌsȯl\ *n* 1 : a suspension of fine solid or liquid particles in gas (smoke and mist are ~s) 2 : a substance (as a medicine) dispensed from a pressurized container as an aerosol; *also* : the container for this

aero·sol·i·za·tion \ar-ə-ˌsä-lə-ˈzā-shən, -ˌsȯl-\ *n* : dispersal (as of a medicine) in the form of an aerosol — **aero·sol·ize** \ˈar-ə-ˌsä-ˌlīz, -ˌsȯl-\ *vb* — **aero·sol·iz·er** *n*

aero·space medicine \ˈar-ō-ˌspās-\ *n* : a medical specialty concerned with the health and medical problems of flight personnel both in the earth's atmosphere and in space

aer·oti·tis \ar-ō-ˈtī-təs\ *n* : AEROOTITIS MEDIA

Aes·cu·la·pi·an staff \ˌes-kyə-ˈlā-pē-ən-\ *n* : STAFF OF AESCULAPIUS

aetio- *chiefly Brit var of* ETIO-

ae·ti·o·log·ic, ae·ti·ol·o·gy, ae·ti·o·patho·gen·e·sis *chiefly Brit var of* ETIOLOGIC, ETIOLOGY, ETIOPATHOGENESIS

afe·brile \(ˌ)ā-ˈfe-ˌbril *also* -ˈfē-\ *adj* : free from fever : not marked by fever

¹**af·fect** \ˈa-ˌfekt\ *n* : the conscious subjective aspect of an emotion considered apart from bodily changes

²**af·fect** \ə-ˈfekt, a-\ *vb* : to produce an effect upon; *esp* : to produce a material influence upon or alteration in

af·fec·tion \ə-ˈfek-shən\ *n* 1 : the action of affecting : the state of being affected 2 **a** : a bodily condition **b** : DISEASE, MALADY (a pulmonary ~)

af·fec·tive \a-ˈfek-tiv\ *adj* : relating to, arising from, or influencing feelings or emotions : EMOTIONAL (~ disorders) — **af·fec·tive·ly** *adv* — **af·fec·tiv·i·ty** \a-ˌfek-ˈti-və-tē\ *n*

¹**af·fer·ent** \ˈa-fə-rənt, -ˌfer-ənt\ *adj* : bearing or conducting inward; *specif* : conveying impulses toward a nerve center (as the brain or spinal cord) — compare EFFERENT — **af·fer·ent·ly** *adv*

²**afferent** *n* : an afferent anatomical part (as a nerve)

af·fin·i·ty \ə-ˈfin-ət-ē\ *n, pl* **-ties** : an attractive force between substances or particles that causes them to enter into and remain in chemical combination

afi·brin·o·gen·emia \ā-(ˌ)fī-ˌbri-nə-jə-ˈnē-mē-ə\ *n* : an abnormality of blood clotting caused by usu. congenital absence of fibrinogen in the blood

af·la·tox·in \ˌa-flə-ˈtäk-sən\ *n* : any of several carcinogenic mycotoxins that are produced esp. in stored agricultural crops (as peanuts) by molds (as *Aspergillus flavus*)

AFP *abbr* alpha-fetoprotein

Af·ri·can·ized bee \ˈa-fri-kə-ˌnīzd-\ *n* : a honeybee that originated in Brazil as an accidental hybrid between an aggressive African subspecies (*Apis mellifera scutellata*) and previously established European honeybees and has spread to Mexico and the southernmost U.S. by breeding with local bees producing populations retaining most of the African bee's traits — called also *Africanized honeybee, killer bee*

African sleeping sickness *n* : SLEEPING SICKNESS 1

African trypanosomiasis *n* : any of several trypanosomiases caused by African trypanosomes; *esp* : SLEEPING SICKNESS 1

af·ter·birth \ˈaf-tər-ˌbərth\ *n* : the placenta and fetal membranes that are expelled after delivery — called also *secundines*

af·ter·care \-ˌkar\ *n* : the care, treatment, help, or supervision given to persons discharged from an institution (as a hospital or prison)

af·ter·ef·fect \ˈaf-tər-i-ˌfekt\ *n* 1 : an effect that follows its cause after an interval 2 : a secondary result esp. in the action of a drug coming on after the subsidence of the first effect

af·ter·im·age \-ˌi-mij\ *n* : a usu. visual sensation occurring after stimulation by its external cause has ceased — called also *aftersensation, aftervision*

af·ter·load \ˈaf-tər-ˌlōd\ *n* : the force against which a ventricle contracts that is contributed to by the vascular resistance esp. of the arteries and by the physical characteristics (as mass and viscosity) of the blood

af·ter·pain \-ˌpān\ *n* : pain that follows its cause only after a distinct interval (the ~ of a tooth extraction)

af·ter·taste \-ˌtāst\ *n* : persistence of a sensation (as of flavor or an emotion) after the stimulating agent or experience has gone

af·to·sa \af-ˈtō-sə, -zə\ *n* : FOOT-AND-MOUTH DISEASE

Ag *symbol* [Latin *argentum*] silver

aga·lac·tia \ˌā-gə-ˈlak-shē-ə, -shə, -tē-ə\ *n* : the failure of the secretion of milk from any cause other than the normal ending of the lactation period — **aga·lac·tic** \-ˈlak-tik\ *adj*

agam·ma·glob·u·lin·emia \(ˌ)ā-ˌga-mə-ˌglä-byə-lə-ˈnē-mē-ə\ *n* : a pathological condition in which the body forms few or no gamma globulins or anti-

bodies — compare DYSGAMMAGLOBU-LINEMIA

agan·gli·on·ic \(ˌ)ā-ˌgaŋ-glē-ˈä-nik\ *adj* : lacking ganglia

agar \ˈä-gər\ *n* 1 : a gelatinous colloidal extractive of a red alga (as of the genera *Gelidium, Gracilaria,* and *Eucheuma*) used esp. in culture media or as a gelling and stabilizing agent in foods 2 : a culture medium containing agar

agar–agar \ˌä-gər-ˈä-gər\ *n* : AGAR

aga·rose \ˈa-gə-ˌrōs, ˈä-, -ˌrōz\ *n* : a polysaccharide obtained from agar that is used esp. as a supporting medium in gel electrophoresis

¹age \ˈäj\ *n* 1 a : the part of life from birth to a given time (a child 10 years of ~) b : the time or part of life at which some particular event, qualification, or capacity arises, occurs, or is lost (of reproductive ~) — see MIDDLE AGE c : an advanced stage of life 2 : an individual's development measured in terms of the years requisite for like development of an average individual — see BINET AGE, MENTAL AGE

²age *vb* **aged; ag·ing** *or* **age·ing** : to grow old or cause to grow old

agen·e·sis \(ˌ)ā-ˈje-nə-səs\ *n, pl* **-e·ses** \-ˌsēz\ : lack or failure of development (as of a body part)

agent \ˈā-jənt\ *n* 1 : something that produces or is capable of producing an effect 2 : a chemically, physically, or biologically active principle — see OXIDIZING AGENT, REDUCING AGENT

Agent Orange \-ˈȯr-inj\ *n* : an herbicide widely used as a defoliant in the Vietnam War that is composed of 2,4-D and 2,4,5-T and contains dioxin as a contaminant

ageu·sia \ə-ˈgyü-zē-ə, (ˌ)ā-, -ˈjü-, -sē-\ *n* : the absence or impairment of the sense of taste — **ageu·sic** \-zik, -sik\ *adj*

ag·glu·ti·na·bil·i·ty \ə-ˌglüt-ᵊn-ə-ˈbi-lə-tē\ *n, pl* **-ties** : capacity to be agglutinated — **ag·glu·ti·na·ble** \-ˈglüt-ᵊn-ə-bəl\ *adj*

¹ag·glu·ti·nate \ə-ˈglüt-ᵊn-ˌāt\ *vb* **-nat·ed; -nat·ing** : to undergo or cause to undergo agglutination

²ag·glu·ti·nate \-ᵊn-ət, -ᵊn-ˌāt\ *n* : a clump of agglutinated material (as blood cells or bacteria)

ag·glu·ti·na·tion \ə-ˌglüt-ᵊn-ˈā-shən\ *n* : a reaction in which particles (as red blood cells or bacteria) suspended in a liquid collect into clumps and which occurs esp. as a serological response to a specific antibody — **ag·glu·ti·na·tive** \ə-ˈglüt-ᵊn-ˌā-tiv, -ə-tiv\ *adj*

agglutination test *n* : any of several tests based on the ability of a specific serum to cause agglutination of a suitable system and used in the diagnosis of infections, the identification of microorganisms, and in blood typing — compare WIDAL TEST

ag·glu·ti·nin \ə-ˈglüt-ᵊn-ən\ *n* : a substance (as an antibody) producing agglutination

ag·glu·ti·no·gen \ə-ˈglüt-ᵊn-ə-jən\ *n* : an antigen whose presence results in the formation of an agglutinin — **ag·glu·ti·no·gen·ic** \-glüt-ᵊn-ə-ˈje-nik\ *adj*

ag·gre·gate \ˈa-gri-gät\ *vb* -**gat·ed**; -**gat·ing** : to collect or gather into a mass or whole — **ag·gre·gate** \-gət\ *adj or n*

ag·gres·sion \ə-ˈgre-shən\ *n* : hostile, injurious, or destructive behavior or outlook esp. when caused by frustration

ag·gres·sive \ə-ˈgre-siv\ *adj* 1 : tending toward or exhibiting aggression (∼ behavior) 2 : more severe, intensive, or comprehensive than usual esp. in dosage or extent (∼ chemotherapy) — **ag·gres·sive·ly** *adv* — **ag·gres·sive·ness** *n* — **ag·gres·siv·i·ty** \ˌa-gre-ˈsi-və-tē\ *n*

agitans — see PARALYSIS AGITANS

agly·cone \a-ˈglī-ˌkōn\ *also* **agly·con** \-ˌkän\ *n* : an organic compound (as a phenol or alcohol) combined with the sugar portion of a glycoside

ag·na·thia \ag-ˈnā-thē-ə, ˌ)āg-, -ˈnā-thē-\ *n* : the congenital complete or partial absence of one or both jaws

ag·no·gen·ic \ag-nō-ˈje-nik\ *adj* : of unknown cause (∼ metaplasia)

ag·no·sia \ag-ˈnō-zhə, -shə\ *n* : loss or diminution of the ability to recognize familiar objects or stimuli usu. as a result of brain damage

-agogue *n comb form* : substance that promotes the secretion or expulsion of (cholagogue) (emmenagogue)

ag·o·nal \ˈa-gən-ᵊl\ *adj* : of, relating to, or associated with agony and esp. the death agony — **ag·o·nal·ly** *adv*

ag·o·nist \ˈa-gə-nist\ *n* 1 : a muscle that on contracting is automatically checked and controlled by the opposing simultaneous contraction of another muscle — called also *agonist muscle*, *prime mover*; compare ANTAGONIST a, SYNERGIST 2 : a chemical substance (as a drug) capable of combining with a receptor on a cell and initiating a reaction or activity (binding of adrenergic ∼s) — compare ANTAGONIST b

ag·o·ny \ˈa-gə-nē\ *n, pl* -**nies** 1 : intense pain of mind or body 2 : the struggle that precedes death

ag·o·ra·pho·bia \ˌa-gə-rə-ˈfō-bē-ə\ *n* : abnormal fear of being helpless in a situation from which escape may be difficult or embarrassing that is characterized initially often by panic or anticipatory anxiety and finally by avoidance of open or public places

¹**ag·o·ra·pho·bic** \-ˈfō-bik\ *adj* : of, relating to, or affected with agoraphobia

²**agoraphobic** *or* **ag·o·ra·phobe** \ˈa-gə-rə-ˌfōb\ *also* **ag·o·ra·pho·bi·ac** \ˌa-gə-rə-ˈfō-bē-ˌak\ *n* : a person affected with agoraphobia

-agra *n comb form* : seizure of pain (pellagra) (podagra)

agram·ma·tism \(ˌ)ā-ˈgra-mə-ˌti-zəm\ *n* : the pathological inability to use words in grammatical sequence

agran·u·lo·cyte \(ˌ)ā-ˈgran-yə-lō-ˌsīt\ *n* : a leukocyte without cytoplasmic granules — compare GRANULOCYTE

agran·u·lo·cyt·ic angina \ā-ˌgran-yə-lō-ˈsi-tik-\ *n* : AGRANULOCYTOSIS

agran·u·lo·cy·to·sis \ā-ˌgran-yə-lō-ˌsī-ˈtō-səs\ *n, pl* -**to·ses** \-ˌsēz\ : an acute febrile condition marked by severe depression of the granulocyte-producing bone marrow and by prostration, chills, swollen neck, and sore throat sometimes with local ulceration and believed to be basically a response to the side effects of certain drugs of the coal-tar series (as aminopyrine) — called also *agranulocytic angina*, *granulocytopenia*

agraph·ia \(ˌ)ā-ˈgra-fē-ə\ *n* : the pathological loss of the ability to write — **agraph·ic** \-fik\ *adj*

ague \ˈā-(ˌ)gyü\ *n* 1 : a fever (as malaria) marked by paroxysms of chills, fever, and sweating that recur at regular intervals 2 : a fit of shivering : CHILL

AHF *abbr* 1 antihemophilic factor 2 [antihemophilic factor] factor VIII

AHG *abbr* antihemophilic globulin

AI *abbr* artificial insemination

aid \ˈād\ *n* 1 : the act of helping or treating; *also* : the help or treatment given 2 : an assisting person or group (a laboratory ∼) — compare AIDE 3 : something by which assistance is given : an assisting device; *esp* : HEARING AID

AID *abbr* artificial insemination by donor

aide \ˈād\ *n* : a person who acts as an assistant (volunteer ∼s) (psychiatric ∼s) — see NURSE'S AIDE

AIDS \ˈādz\ *n* : a disease of the human immune system that is caused by infection with HIV, that is characterized cytologically esp. by reduction in the numbers of CD4-bearing helper T cells to 20 percent or less of normal, that in modern industrialized nations occurs esp. in homosexual and bisexual men and in intravenous users of illicit drugs, that is commonly transmitted in blood and bodily secretions (as semen), and that renders the subject highly vulnerable to life-threatening conditions (as Pneumocystis carinii pneumonia) and to some that become life-threatening (as Kaposi's sarcoma) — called also *acquired immune deficiency syndrome*, *acquired immunodeficiency syndrome*

AIDS–related complex *n* : a group of symptoms (as fever, weight loss, and lymphadenopathy) that is associated with the presence of antibodies to HIV and is followed by the development of AIDS in a certain proportion of cases — abbr. *ARC*

AIDS virus *n* : HIV

AIH *abbr* artificial insemination by husband

ail \ʼāl\ *vb* 1 : to affect with an unnamed disease or physical or emotional pain or discomfort — used only of unspecified causes 2 : to be or become affected with pain or discomfort

ail·ment \ʼāl-mənt\ *n* : a bodily disorder or chronic disease

ai·lu·ro·phobe \ī-ʼlur-ə-ˌfōb, ā-\ *n* : a person who hates or fears cats

ai·lu·ro·pho·bia \-ʼfō-bē-ə\ *n* : abnormal fear of cats

air \ʼar\ *n* : a mixture of invisible odorless tasteless sound-transmitting gases that is composed by volume chiefly of 78 percent nitrogen, 21 percent oxygen, 0.9 percent argon, 0.03 percent carbon dioxide, varying amounts of water vapor, and minute amounts of rare gases (as helium), that surrounds the earth with half its mass within four miles of the earth's surface, that has a pressure at sea level of about 14.7 pounds per square inch, and that has a density of 1.293 grams per liter at 0°C and 760 mm. pressure

air bends *n pl* : AEROEMBOLISM

air·borne \ʼar-ˌbōrn\ *adj* : carried or transported by the air (∼ allergens) (∼ bacteria)

air embolism *n* : obstruction of the circulation by air that has gained entrance to veins usu. through wounds — compare AEROEMBOLISM

air hunger *n* : deep labored breathing at an increased or decreased rate

air sac *n* : ALVEOLUS b

air·sick \ʼar-ˌsik\ *adj* : affected with motion sickness associated with flying — **air·sick·ness** *n*

air·way \-ˌwā\ *n* : a passageway for air into or out of the lungs; *specif* : a device passed into the trachea by way of the mouth or nose or through an incision to maintain a clear respiratory passageway (as during anesthesia or convulsions)

aka·thi·sia \ˌā-ka-ʼthi-zhē-ə, -zhə, ˌa-, -ʼthē-\ *n* : a condition characterized by uncontrollable motor restlessness

ak·ee \ʼa-kē, a-ʼkē\ *n* : the fruit of an African tree (*Blighia sapida* of the family Sapindaceae) that has edible flesh when ripe but is poisonous when immature or overripe; *also* : the tree

aki·ne·sia \ˌā-kī-ʼnē-zhē-ə, -zhə\ *n* : loss or impairment of voluntary activity (as of a muscle) — **aki·net·ic** \ˌā-kə-ʼne-tik, -kī-\ *adj*

Al *symbol* aluminum

ala \ʼā-lə\ *n, pl* **alae** \-ˌlē\ : a wing or a winglike anatomic process or part; *esp* : ALA NASI

alaeque — see LEVATOR LABII SUPERIORIS ALAEQUE NASI

ala na·si \-ʼnā-ˌsī, -ˌzī\ *n, pl* **alae na·si** \-ˌsī, -ˌzī\ : the expanded outer wall of cartilage on each side of the nose

al·a·nine \ʼa-lə-ˌnēn\ *n* : a simple nonessential crystalline amino acid $C_3H_7NO_2$ formed esp. by the hydrolysis of proteins

alar cartilage \ʼā-lər-\ *n* : one of the pair of lower lateral cartilages of the nose

alar ligament *n* : either of a pair of strong rounded fibrous cords of which one arises on each side of the cranial part of the odontoid process, passes obliquely and laterally upward, and inserts on the medial side of a condyle of the occipital bone — called also *check ligament*

alarm reaction *n* : the initial reaction of an organism (as increased hormonal activity) to stress

alas·trim \ʼa-lə-ˌstrim, ˌa-lə-ʼ; ə-ʼlastrəm\ *n* : VARIOLA MINOR

alba — see LINEA ALBA, MATERIA ALBA, PHLEGMASIA ALBA DOLENS

Al·bers–Schön·berg disease \ʼal-bərz-ˈsharn-ˌbərg-, -ˈshōn-\ *n* : OSTEOPETROSIS

Albers–Schönberg, Heinrich Ernst (1865–1921), German roentgenologist.

albicans, albicantia — see CORPUS ALBICANS

albicantes — see LINEAE ALBICANTES

al·bi·nism \ʼal-bə-ˌni-zəm, al-ʼbī-\ *n* : the condition of an albino — **al·bi·nis·tic** \ˌal-bə-ʼnis-tik\ *adj*

al·bi·no \al-ʼbī-(ˌ)nō\ *n, pl* **-nos** : an organism exhibiting deficient pigmentation; *esp* : a human being who is congenitally deficient in pigment and usu. has a milky or translucent skin, white or colorless hair, and eyes with pink or blue iris and deep-red pupil — **al·bin·ic** \-ʼbi-nik\ *adj*

al·bi·not·ic \ˌal-bə-ʼnä-tik\ *adj* 1 : of, relating to, or affected with albinism 2 : tending toward albinism

albuginea — see TUNICA ALBUGINEA

al·bu·men \al-ʼbyü-mən; ʼal-ˌbyü-, -byə-\ *n* 1 : the white of an egg 2 : ALBUMIN

al·bu·min \al-ʼbyü-mən; ʼal-ˌbyü-, -byə-\ *n* : any of numerous simple heat-coagulable water-soluble proteins that occur in blood plasma or serum, muscle, the whites of eggs, milk, and other animal substances and in many plant tissues and fluid

¹**al·bu·min·oid** \-mə-ˌnȯid\ *adj* : resembling albumin

²**albuminoid** *n* 1 : PROTEIN 1 2 : SCLEROPROTEIN

al·bu·min·uria \al-ˌbyü-mə-ʼnur-ē-ə, -ʼnyur-\ *n* : the presence of albumin in the urine that is usu. a symptom of disease of the kidneys but sometimes a response to other diseases or physiological disturbances of benign nature — **al·bu·min·uric** \-'nür-ik, -'nyùr-\ *adj*

al·cap·ton·uria *var of* ALKAPTONURIA

al·co·hol \'al-kə-,hòl\ *n* 1 a : ethanol esp. when considered as the intoxicating agent in fermented and distilled liquors b : drink (as whiskey or beer) containing ethanol c : a mixture of ethanol and water that is usu. 95 percent ethanol 2 : any of various compounds that are analogous to ethanol in constitution and that are hydroxyl derivatives of hydrocarbons

¹al·co·hol·ic \,al-kə-'hò-lik, -'hä-\ *adj* 1 a : of, relating to, or caused by alcohol ⟨~ hepatitis⟩ b : containing alcohol 2 : affected with alcoholism — **al·co·hol·i·cal·ly** \-li-k(ə-)lē\ *adv*

²alcoholic *n* : one affected with alcoholism

al·co·hol·ism \'al-kə-,hò-,li-zəm, -kə-hə-\ *n* 1 : continued excessive or compulsive use of alcoholic drinks 2 a : poisoning by alcohol b : a chronic, progressive, potentially fatal, psychological and nutritional disorder associated with excessive and usu. compulsive drinking of ethanol and characterized by frequent intoxication leading to dependence on or addiction to the substance, impairment of the ability to work and socialize, destructive behaviors (as drunken driving), tissue damage (as cirrhosis of the liver), and severe withdrawal symptoms upon detoxification

al·de·hyde \'al-də-,hīd\ *n* : ACETALDEHYDE; *broadly* : any of various highly reactive compounds typified by acetaldehyde and characterized by the group CHO — **al·de·hy·dic** \,al-də-'hī-dik\ *adj*

al·do·hex·ose \,al-dō-'hek-,sōs, -,sōz\ *n* : a hexose (as glucose or mannose) of an aldehyde nature

al·dose \'al-,dōs, -,dōz\ *n* : a sugar containing one aldehyde group per molecule

al·do·ste·rone \al-'däs-tə-,rōn; ,al-dō-'stir-,ōn, -stə-'rōn\ *n* : a steroid hormone $C_{21}H_{28}O_5$ of the adrenal cortex that functions in the regulation of the salt and water balance of the body

al·do·ste·ron·ism \al-'däs-tə-,rō-,ni-zəm, ,al-dō-stə-'rō-\ *n* : a condition that is characterized by excessive secretion of aldosterone and typically by loss of body potassium, muscular weakness, and elevated blood pressure — called also *hyperaldosteronism*

al·drin \'òl-drən, 'al-\ *n* : an exceedingly poisonous insecticide $C_{12}H_8Cl_6$

K. Alder — see DIELDRIN

aleu·ke·mia \,ā-lü-'kē-mē-ə\ *n* : leukemia in which the circulating leukocytes are normal or decreased in number; *esp* : ALEUKEMIC LEUKEMIA

aleu·ke·mic \-'kē-mik\ *adj* : not marked by increase in circulating white blood cells

aleukemic leukemia *n* : leukemia resulting from changes in the leukocyte-forming tissues and characterized by a normal or decreased number of leukocytes in the circulating blood — called also *aleukemic myelosis*

alex·ia \ə-'lek-sē-ə\ *n* : aphasia characterized by loss of ability to read — **alex·ic** \-'lek-sik\ *adj*

alex·in \ə-'lek-sən\ *n* : COMPLEMENT 2 — **al·ex·in·ic** \,a-,lek-'si-nik\ *adj*

ALG *abbr* antilymphocyte globulin; antilymphocytic globulin

alg- *or* **algo-** *comb form* : pain ⟨algolagnia⟩

al·ga \'al-gə\ *n*, *pl* **al·gae** \'al-(,)jē\ *also* **algas** : a plant or plantlike organism (as a seaweed) of any of several phyla, divisions, or classes of chiefly aquatic usu. chlorophyll-containing nonvascular organisms including green, yellow-green, brown, and red forms — see BROWN ALGA, RED ALGA — **al·gal** \-gəl\ *adj*

al·ge·sia \al-'jē-zē-ə, -'jē-zhə\ *n* : sensitivity to pain — **al·ge·sic** \-'jē-zik, -sik\ *adj*

-al·gia \'al-jə, -jē-ə\ *n comb form* : pain ⟨neuralgia⟩

al·gi·cide *or* **al·gae·cide** \'al-jə-,sīd\ *n* : an agent used to kill algae — **al·gi·cid·al** \,al-jə-'sīd-ºl\ *adj*

al·gin \'al-jən\ *n* : any of various colloidal substances (as an alginate or alginic acid) derived from marine brown algae and used esp. as emulsifiers or thickeners

al·gi·nate \'al-jə-,nāt\ *n* : a salt of alginic acid

al·gin·ic acid \(,)al-'ji-nik-\ *n* : an insoluble colloidal acid $(C_6H_8O_6)_n$ that is used in making dental preparations and in preparing pharmaceuticals

algo- — see ALG-

al·go·gen·ic \,al-gō-'je-nik\ *adj* : producing pain

al·go·lag·nia \,al-gō-'lag-nē-ə\ *n* : a perversion (as masochism or sadism) in which pleasure and esp. sexual gratification is obtained by inflicting or suffering pain — **al·go·lag·nic** \-nik\ *adj*

al·gor mor·tis \'al-,gòr-'mòr-təs\ *n* : the gradual cooling of the body following death

ali- *comb form* : wing or winglike part ⟨alisphenoid⟩

alien·ate \'ā-lē-ə-,nāt, 'āl-yə-\ *vb* -at·ed; -at·ing : to make unfriendly, hostile, or indifferent where attachment formerly existed

alien·a·tion \,ā-lē-ə-'nā-shən, ,āl-yə-\ *n* 1 : a withdrawing or separation of a person or a person's affections from an object or position of former attachment 2 : a state of abnormal function; *esp* : mental derangement : INSANITY

alien·ist \'ā-lē-ə-nist, 'āl-yə-\ *n* : PSYCHIATRIST

al·i·men·ta·ry \ˌa-lə-ˈmen-tə-rē, ˈmen-trē\ *adj* : of, concerned with, or relating to nourishment or to the function of nutrition : NUTRITIVE

alimentary canal *n* : the tubular passage that extends from mouth to anus, functions in digestion and absorption of food and elimination of residual waste, and includes the mouth, pharynx, esophagus, stomach, small intestine, and large intestine

alimentary system *n* : the organ system devoted to the ingestion, digestion, and assimilation of food and the discharge of residual wastes and consisting of the alimentary canal and those glands or parts of complex glands that secrete digestive enzymes

al·i·men·ta·tion \ˌa-lə-mən-ˈtā-shən, -ˌmen-\ *n* : the act or process of affording nutriment or nourishment

al·i·phat·ic \ˌa-lə-ˈfa-tik\ *adj* : of, relating to, or being an organic compound having an open-chain structure (as an alkane)

¹**al·i·quot** \ˈa-lə-ˌkwät\ *adj* : being an equal fractional part (as of a solution) — **aliquot** *n*

²**aliquot** *vb* : to divide (as a solution) into equal parts

al·i·sphe·noid \ˌa-ləs-ˈfē-ˌnoid, ˌa-\ *adj* : belonging or relating to or forming the wings of the sphenoid or the pair of bones that fuse with other sphenoidal elements to form the greater wings of the sphenoid in the adult

²**alisphenoid** *n* : an alisphenoid bone; *esp* : GREATER WING

alive \ə-ˈliv\ *adj* : having life : not dead or inanimate

al·ka·lae·mia *chiefly Brit var of* ALKALEMIA

al·ka·le·mia \ˌal-kə-ˈlē-mē-ə\ *n* : a condition in which the hydrogen ion concentration in the blood is decreased

al·ka·li \ˈal-kə-ˌlī\ *n, pl* **-lies** *or* **-lis** : a substance having marked basic properties — compare BASE

alkali disease *n* : SELENOSIS

al·ka·line \ˈal-kə-lən, -ˌlīn\ *adj* : of, relating to, containing, or having the properties of an alkali or alkali metal : BASIC; *esp, of a solution* : having a pH of more than 7 — **al·ka·lin·i·ty** \ˌal-kə-ˈli-nə-tē\ *n*

alkaline phosphatase *n* : any of the phosphatases optimally active in alkaline medium and occurring in esp. high concentrations in bone, the liver, the kidneys, and the placenta

al·ka·lin·ize \ˈal-kə-lə-ˌnīz\ *vb* **-ized; -iz·ing** : to make alkaline — **al·ka·lin·i·za·tion** \ˌal-kə-ˌli-nə-ˈzā-shən, -lə-\ *n*

al·ka·lize \ˈal-kə-ˌlīz\ *vb* **-lized; -liz·ing** : ALKALINIZE — **al·ka·li·za·tion** \ˌal-kə-lə-ˈzā-shən\ *n*

alkali reserve *n* : the concentration of one or more basic ions or substances in a fluid medium that buffer its pH by neutralizing acid; *esp* : the concentration of bicarbonate in the blood

al·ka·liz·er \ˈal-kə-ˌlī-zər\ *n* : an alkalinizing agent

al·ka·loid \ˈal-kə-ˌloid\ *n* : any of numerous usu. colorless, complex, and bitter organic bases (as morphine or codeine) containing nitrogen and usu. oxygen that occur esp. in seed plants — **al·ka·loi·dal** \ˌal-kə-ˈloid-ᵊl\ *adj*

al·ka·lo·sis \ˌal-kə-ˈlō-səs\ *n, pl* **-lo·ses** \-ˌsēz\ : an abnormal condition of increased alkalinity of the blood and tissues — compare ACIDOSIS — **al·ka·lot·ic** \ˌal-kə-ˈlä-tik\ *adj*

al·kane \ˈal-ˌkān\ *n* : any of a series of aliphatic hydrocarbons C_nH_{2n+2} (as methane) in which each carbon is bonded to four other atoms — called also *paraffin*

al·kap·ton·uria \(ˌ)al-ˌkap-tə-ˈnur-ē-ə, -ˈnyur-\ *n* : a rare recessive metabolic anomaly marked by inability to complete the degradation of tyrosine and phenylalanine resulting in the presence of homogentisic acid in the urine — **al·kap·ton·uric** \-ˈnur-ik, -ˈnyur-\ *n or adj*

al·kene \ˈal-ˌkēn\ *n* : any of numerous unsaturated hydrocarbons having one double bond; *specif* : any of a series of open-chain hydrocarbons C_nH_{2n} (as ethylene)

¹**al·kyl** \ˈal-kəl\ *adj* : having an organic group with a chemical valence of one and esp. one C_nH_{2n+1} (as methyl) derived from an alkane (as methane)

²**alkyl** *n* : a compound of one or more alkyl groups with a metal

al·kyl·ate \ˈal-kə-ˌlāt\ *vb* **-at·ed; -at·ing** : to introduce one or more alkyl groups into (a compound) — **al·kyl·a·tion** \ˌal-kə-ˈlā-shən\ *n*

alkylating agent *n* : a substance that causes replacement of hydrogen by an alkyl group esp. in a biologically important molecule; *specif* : one with mutagenic activity that inhibits cell division and growth and is used to treat some cancers

ALL *abbr* acute lymphoblastic leukemia

all- *or* **allo-** *comb form* 1 : other : different : atypical ⟨*allergy*⟩ ⟨*allopathy*⟩ 2 *allo-* : isomeric form or variety of (a specified chemical compound) ⟨*allopurinol*⟩

al·lan·to·ic \ˌa-lən-ˈtō-ik, -ˌlan-\ *adj* : relating to, contained in, or characterized by an allantois

al·lan·to·in \ə-ˈlan-tə-wən\ *n* : a crystalline oxidation product $C_4H_6N_4O_3$ of uric acid used to promote healing of local wounds and infections

al·lan·to·is \ə-ˈlan-tə-wəs\ *n, pl* **al·lan·to·ides** \ˌa-lən-ˈtō-ə-ˌdēz, -ˌlan-\ : a vascular fetal membrane that is formed as a pouch from the hindgut and that in placental mammals is intimately associated with the chorion in formation of the placenta

al·lele \ə-ˈlēl\ *n* 1 : any of the alternative forms of a gene that may occur at a given locus 2 : either of a pair of alternative Mendelian characters (as ability versus inability to taste the chemical phenylthiocarbamide) — **al·le·lic** \-'lē-lik. -'le-\ *adj* — **al·lel·ism** \-'lē-ₗli-zəm. -'le-\ *n*

allelo- *comb form* : a native (*allelomorph*)

al·le·lo·morph \ə-'lē-lə-ₗmȯrf. -'le-\ *n* : ALLELE — **al·le·lo·mor·phic** \-ₗlē-lə-'mȯr-fik. -ₗle-\ *adj* — **al·le·lo·mor·phism** \ə-'lē-lə-ₗmȯr-ₗfi-zəm. -'lē-\ *n*

al·ler·gen \'a-lər-jən\ *n* : a substance that induces allergy

al·ler·gen·ic \ₗa-lər-'je-nik\ *adj* : having the capacity to induce allergy (~ plants) — **al·ler·ge·nic·i·ty** \-jə-'ni-sə-tē\ *n*

al·ler·gic \ə-'lər-jik\ *adj* 1 : of, relating to, or characterized by allergy (an ~ reaction) 2 : affected with allergy : subject to an allergic reaction

allergic encephalomyelitis *n* : encephalomyelitis produced by an allergic response following the introduction of an antigenic substance into the body

al·ler·gist \-jist\ *n* : a specialist in allergy

al·ler·gol·o·gy \ₗa-lər-'jä-lə-jē\ *n, pl* **-gies** : a branch of medicine concerned with allergy

al·ler·gy \'a-lər-jē\ *n, pl* **-gies** 1 : altered bodily reactivity (as hypersensitivity) to an antigen in response to a first exposure 2 : exaggerated or pathological reaction (as by sneezing, respiratory embarrassment, itching, or skin rashes) to substances, situations, or physical states that are without comparable effect on the average individual 3 : medical practice concerned with allergies

al·le·thrin \'a-lə-thrən\ *n* : a light yellow oily synthetic insecticide $C_{19}H_{26}O_3$ used esp. in household aerosols

al·le·vi·ate \ə-'lē-vē-ₗāt\ *vb* **-at·ed; -at·ing** : to make (as symptoms) less severe or more bearable — **al·le·vi·a·tion** \-ₗlē-vē-'ā-shən\ *n*

al·le·vi·a·tive \ə-'lē-vē-ₗā-tiv\ *adj* : tending to alleviate : PALLIATIVE (a medicine that is ~ but not curative)

al·li·cin \'a-lə-sən\ *n* : a liquid compound $C_6H_{10}OS_2$ with a garlic odor and antibacterial properties

allo- — see ALL-

al·lo·an·ti·body \ₗa-lō-'an-ti-ₗbä-dē\ *n, pl* **-bod·ies** : an antibody produced following introduction of an alloantigen into the system of an individual of a species lacking that particular antigen — called also *isoantibody*

al·lo·an·ti·gen \ₗa-lō-'an-tə-jən\ *n* : a genetically determined antigen present in some but not all individuals of a species (as those of a particular blood group) and capable of inducing the production of an alloantibody by individuals which lack it — called also

isoantigen — **al·lo·an·ti·gen·ic** \-ₗan-tə-'je-nik\ *adj*

al·lo·bar·bi·tal \ₗa-lə-'bär-bə-ₗtȯl\ *n* : a white crystalline barbiturate $C_{10}H_{12}$-N_2O_3 used as a sedative and hypnotic

al·lo·bar·bi·tone \-ₗtōn\ *n, chiefly Brit* : ALLOBARBITAL

al·lo·cor·tex \-'kȯr-ₗteks\ *n* : ARCHIPALLIUM

Al·lo·der·ma·nys·sus \-ₗdər-mə-'ni-səs\ *n* : a genus of bloodsucking mites parasitic on rodents including one (*A. sanguineus*) implicated as a vector of rickettsialpox in humans

al·lo·gene·ic \ₗa-lō-jə-'nē-ik\ *also* **al·lo·gen·ic** \-'je-nik\ *adj* : involving, derived from, or being individuals of the same species that are sufficiently unlike genetically to interact antigenically (~ skin grafts) — compare SYNGENEIC, XENOGENEIC

al·lo·graft \'a-lə-ₗgraft\ *n* : a homograft between allogeneic individuals — **allograft** *vb*

al·lo·iso·leu·cine \ₗa-lō-ₗī-sə-'lü-ₗsēn\ *n* : either of two stereoisomers of isoleucine of which one is present in bodily fluids of individuals affected with maple syrup urine disease

al·lo·path \'a-lə-ₗpath\ *n* : one who practices allopathy

al·lop·a·thy \ə-'lä-pə-thē. a-\ *n, pl* **-thies** 1 : a system of medical practice that aims to combat disease by use of remedies producing effects different from those produced by the special disease treated 2 : a system of medical practice making use of all measures that have proved of value in treatment of disease — compare HOMEOPATHY — **al·lo·path·ic** \ₗa-lə-'pa-thik\ *adj* — **al·lo·path·i·cal·ly** \-thi-k(ə-)lē\ *adv*

al·lo·pu·ri·nol \ₗa-lō-'pyur-ə-ₗnȯl. -ₗnōl\ *n* : a drug $C_5H_4N_4O$ used to promote excretion of uric acid esp. in the treatment of gout

all-or-none *adj* : marked either by complete operation or effect or by none at all (~ response of a nerve cell)

all-or-none law *n* : a principle in physiology: in any single nerve or muscle fiber the response to a stimulus above threshold level is maximal and independent of the intensity of the stimulus

all-or-noth·ing *adj* : ALL-OR-NONE

al·lo·ster·ic \ₗa-lō-'ster-ik. -'stir-\ *adj* : of, relating to, or being a change in the shape and activity of a protein (as an enzyme) that results from combination with another substance at a point other than the chemically active site — **al·lo·ster·i·cal·ly** \-i-k(ə-)lē\ *adv*

al·lo·trans·plant \ₗa-lō-trans-'plant\ *vb* : to transplant between genetically different individuals — **al·lo·trans·plant** \-'trans-ₗ\ *n* — **al·lo·trans·plan·ta·tion** \-ₗtrans-ₗplan-'tā-shən\ *n*

al·lo·type \'a-lə-ₗtīp\ *n* : an alloantigen

that is part of a plasma protein (as an antibody) — compare IDIOTYPE, ISOTYPE — **al·lo·typ·ic** \,a-lə-'ti-pik\ *adj* — **al·lo·typ·i·cal·ly** \-pi-k(ə-)lē\ *adv* — **al·lo·ty·py** \'a-lə-,tī-pē\ *n*

al·lox·an \ə-'läk-sən\ *n* : a crystalline compound $C_4H_2N_2O_4$ causing diabetes mellitus when injected into experimental animals — called also *mesoxalylurea*

al·loy \'a-,loí, ə-'loí\ *n* : a substance composed of two or more metals or of a metal and a nonmetal intimately united usu. by being fused together and dissolving in each other when molten; *also* : the state of union of the components — **al·loy** \ə-'loí, 'a-,loí\ *vb*

al·lo·zyme \'a-lə-,zīm\ *n* : any of the variants of an enzyme that are determined by alleles at a single genetic locus — **al·lo·zy·mic** \,a-lə-'zī-mik\ *adj*

al·lyl \'a-ləl\ *n* : an unsaturated radical C_3H_5 compounds of which are found in the oils of garlic and mustard — **al·lyl·ic** \ə-'li-lik, a-\ *adj*

allyl iso·thio·cy·a·nate \-,ī-sō-,thī-ə-'sī-ə-,nāt, -nət\ *n* : a colorless pungent irritating liquid ester C_4H_5NS that is the chief constituent of mustard oil used in medicine and is used as a medical counterirritant

N-**al·lyl·nor·mor·phine** \en-,al-əl-,nòr-'mòr-,fēn\ *n* : NALORPHINE

al·oe \'a-(,)lō\ *n* 1 *cap* : a large genus of succulent chiefly southern African plants of the lily family (Liliaceae) 2 : a plant of the genus *Aloe* 3 : the dried juice of the leaves of various aloes used esp. formerly as a purgative and tonic — usu. used in pl. with a sing. verb

aloe vera \-'ver-ə, -'vir-\ *n* : an aloe (*Aloe barbadensis*) whose leaves furnish an emollient extract used esp. in cosmetics and skin creams; *also* : such a preparation

al·o·in \'a-lə-wən\ *n* : a bitter yellow crystalline cathartic obtained from the aloe and containing one or more glycosides

al·o·pe·cia \,a-lə-'pē-shē-ə, -shə\ *n* : loss of hair, wool, or feathers : BALDNESS — **al·o·pe·cic** \-'pē-sik\ *adj*

alopecia ar·e·a·ta \-,ar-ē-'ā-tə, -'ä-\ *n* : sudden loss of hair in circumscribed patches with little or no inflammation

¹**al·pha** \'al-fə\ *n* 1 : the 1st letter of the Greek alphabet — symbol A or α 2 : ALPHA RAY

²**alpha** *or* α- *adj* 1 : of or relating to one of two or more closely related chemical substances (the *alpha* chain of hemoglobin) — used somewhat arbitrarily to specify ordinal relationship or a particular physical form 2 : closest in position in the structure of an organic molecule to a particular group or atom; *also* : of, relating to, or having a structure characterized by such a position (α-substitution)

al·pha-ad·ren·er·gic \'al-fə-,a-drə-'nər-jik\ *adj* : of, relating to, or being an alpha-receptor (~ blocking action)

al·pha-ad·re·no·cep·tor \-ə-'drē-nō-,sep-tər\ *also* **al·pha-ad·re·no·re·cep·tor** \-ri-,sep-tər\ *n* : ALPHA-RECEPTOR

al·pha-ami·no acid *or* α-**ami·no acid** \ə-?-'mē-nō-\ *n* : any of the more than 20 amino acids that have an amino group in the alpha position with most having the general formula RCH-$(NH_2)COOH$, that are synthesized in plant and animal tissues, that are considered the building blocks of proteins from which they can be obtained by hydrolysis, and that play an important role in metabolism, growth, maintenance, and repair of tissue

alpha cell *n* : an acidophilic glandular cell (as of the pancreas or the adenohypophysis) — compare BETA CELL

al·pha-fe·to·pro·tein *or* α-**fetoprotein** *n* : a fetal blood protein present abnormally in adults with some forms of cancer (as of the liver) and normally in the amniotic fluid of pregnant women with very low levels tending to be associated with Down's syndrome in the fetus and very high levels with neural tube defects (as spina bifida) in which the tube remains open

alpha globulin *n* : any of several globulins of plasma or serum that have at alkaline pH the greatest electrophoretic mobility next to albumin — compare BETA GLOBULIN, GAMMA GLOBULIN

al·pha-he·lix *or* α-**he·lix** \,al-fə-'hē-liks\ *n* : the coiled structural arrangement of many proteins consisting of a single chain of amino acids stabilized by hydrogen bonds — compare DOUBLE HELIX — **al·pha-he·li·cal** \-'he-li-kəl, -'hē-\ *adj*

al·pha-ke·to·glu·tar·ic acid \-,kē-tō-glü-'tar-ik-\ *n* : the alpha keto isomer of glutaric acid : the alpha keto isomer of ketoglutaric acid formed in various metabolic processes (as the Krebs cycle)

alpha-lipoprotein *or* α-**lipoprotein** *n* : HDL

al·pha-1-an·ti·tryp·sin \-,wən-,an-ti-'trip-sən, -,tī-\ *n* : a trypsin-inhibiting serum protein whose deficiency has been implicated as a factor in emphysema

alpha particle *n* : a positively charged nuclear particle identical with the nucleus of a helium atom that consists of two protons and two neutrons and is ejected at high speed in certain radioactive transformations

alpha ray *n* 1 : an alpha particle moving at high speed (as in radioactive emission) 2 : a stream of alpha particles — called also *alpha radiation*

al·pha-re·cep·tor \'al-fə-ri-,sep-tər\ *n* : any of a group of receptors postulated to exist on nerve cell membranes of the sympathetic nervous system to explain the specificity of certain adrenergic agents in affecting only some sympathetic activities (as vasoconstriction, relaxation of intestinal muscle, and contraction of most smooth muscle) — compare BETA-RECEPTOR

al·pha–to·coph·er·ol \al-fə-tō-'kä-fə-ˌrȯl, -ˌrōl\ n : a tocopherol $C_{29}H_{50}O_2$ with high vitamin E potency — called also *vitamin E*

alpha wave n : an electrical rhythm of the brain with a frequency of 8 to 13 cycles per second that is often associated with a state of wakeful relaxation — called also *alpha rhythm*

al·praz·o·lam \al-'praz-ə-ˌlam\ n : a benzodiazepine tranquilizer $C_{17}H_{13}ClN_4$ used esp. in the treatment of mild to moderate anxiety — see XANAX

al·pren·o·lol \al-'pre-nə-ˌlȯl, -ˌlōl\ n : a beta-adrenergic blocking agent $C_{15}H_{23}NO_2$ that has been used as the hydrochloride in the treatment of cardiac arrhythmias

ALS abbr 1 amyotrophic lateral sclerosis 2 antilymphocyte serum; antilymphocytic serum

al·ser·ox·y·lon \al-sə-'räk-sə-ˌlän\ n : a complex extract from a rauwolfia (*Rauwolfia serpentina*) that has a physiological action resembling but milder than that of reserpine

al·ter \'ȯl-tər\ vb **al·tered; al·ter·ing** : CASTRATE, SPAY

al·ter·ative \'ȯl-tə-ˌrā-tiv, -rə-\ n : a drug used empirically to alter favorably the course of an ailment

altered state of consciousness n : any of various states of awareness that deviate from and are usu. clearly demarcated from ordinary waking consciousness

alternans — see PULSUS ALTERNANS

al·ter·nate host \'ȯl-tər-nət-\ n : INTERMEDIATE HOST 1

alternating personality n : MULTIPLE PERSONALITY

alternation of generations n : the occurrence of two or more forms differently produced in the life cycle of a plant or animal usu. involving the regular alternation of a sexual with an asexual generation

altitude sickness n : the effects (as nosebleed or nausea) of oxygen deficiency in the blood and tissues developed in rarefied air at high altitudes

al·um \'a-ləm\ n : a potassium aluminum sulfate $KAl(SO_4)_2 \cdot 12H_2O$ or an ammonium aluminum sulfate $NH_4Al(SO_4)_2 \cdot 12H_2O$ used esp. as an emetic and as an astringent and styptic

alu·mi·na \ə-'lü-mə-nə\ n : an oxide of aluminum Al_2O_3 that occurs native as corundum and in hydrated forms and is used in antacids — called also *aluminum oxide*

al·u·min·i·um \al-yü-'mi-nē-əm\ n, chiefly Brit : ALUMINUM

alu·mi·num \ə-'lü-mə-nəm\ n, often attrib : a bluish silver-white malleable ductile light trivalent metallic element — symbol *Al*; see ELEMENT table

aluminum chloride n : a deliquescent compound $AlCl_3$ or Al_2Cl_6 that is used as a topical astringent and antiseptic on the skin, in some deodorants to control sweating, and in the anhydrous form as a catalyst

aluminum hydroxide n : any of several white gelatinous or crystalline hydrates $Al_2O_3 \cdot nH_2O$ of alumina; *esp* : one $Al_2O_3 \cdot 3H_2O$ or $Al(OH)_3$ used in medicine as an antacid

aluminum oxide n : ALUMINA

aluminum sulfate n : a colorless salt $Al_2(SO_4)_3$ that is a powerful astringent and is used as a local antiperspirant and in water purification

Al·u·pent \'a-lü-ˌpent\ trademark — used for a preparation of the sulfate of metaproterenol

alvei pl of ALVEUS

alveol- or **alveolo-** comb form : alveolus (alveolectomy)

al·ve·o·lar \al-'vē-ə-lər\ adj : of, relating to, resembling, or having alveoli; *esp* : of, relating to, or constituting the part of the jaws where the teeth arise, the air-containing cells of the lungs, or glands with secretory cells about a central space

alveolar arch n : the arch of the upper or lower jaw formed by the alveolar processes

alveolar artery n : any of several arteries supplying the teeth; *esp* : POSTERIOR SUPERIOR ALVEOLAR ARTERY — compare INFERIOR ALVEOLAR ARTERY

alveolar canals n pl : the canals in the jawbones for the passage of the dental nerves and associated vessels

alveolar ducts n pl : the somewhat enlarged terminal sections of the bronchioles that branch into the terminal alveoli

alveolar process n : the bony ridge or raised thickened border on each side of the upper or lower jaw that contains the sockets of the teeth — called also *alveolar ridge*

al·ve·o·lec·to·my \al-ˌvē-ə-'lek-tə-mē, ˌal-vē-\ n, pl **-mies** : surgical excision of a portion of an alveolar process usu. as an aid in fitting dentures

al·ve·o·li·tis \al-ˌvē-ə-'lī-təs, ˌal-vē-\ n : inflammation of one or more alveoli esp. of the lung

al·ve·o·lo·plas·ty \al-'vē-ə-(ˌ)lō-ˌplas-tē\ or **al·ve·o·plas·ty** \'al-vē-ō-\ n, pl **-ties** : surgical shaping of the dental alveoli and alveolar processes esp. after extraction of several teeth or in preparation for dentures

al·ve·o·lus \al-'vē-ə-ləs\ n, pl **-li** \-ˌlī, -(ˌ)lē\ : a small cavity or pit: as **a** : a socket for a tooth **b** : an air cell of the lungs **c** : an acinus of a compound gland d : any of the pits in the wall of the stomach into which the glands open

al·ve·us \'al-vē-əs\ *n, pl* **al·vei** \-vē-ᵢī, -ᵢē\ : a thin layer of medullary nerve fibers on the ventricular surface of the hippocampus

Alz·hei·mer's disease \'älts-ᵢhī-mərz-, 'alts-\ *n* : a degenerative disease of the central nervous system characterized esp. by premature senile mental deterioration — called also *Alzheimer's;* see NEUROFIBRILLARY TANGLE; compare PRESENILE DEMENTIA

Alzheimer, Alois (1864–1915), German neurologist.

Am *symbol* americium

AMA *abbr* 1 against medical advice 2 American Medical Association

am·a·crine cell \'a-mə-ᵢkrīn-, (ᵢ)ā-'ma-ᵢkrīn-\ *n* : a unipolar nerve cell found in the retina, in the olfactory bulb, and in close connection with the Purkinje cells of the cerebellum

amal·gam \ə-'mal-gəm\ *n* : an alloy of mercury with another metal that is solid or liquid at room temperature according to the proportion of mercury present and is used esp. in making tooth cements

am·a·ni·ta \ᵢa-mə-'nī-tə, -'nē-\ *n* 1 *cap* : a genus of widely distributed whitespored basidiomycetous fungi that includes some deadly poisonous forms (as the death cap) 2 : a fungus of the genus *Amanita*

am·a·ni·tin \-'nit-ᵊn, -'nēt-\ *n* : a highly toxic cyclic peptide produced by the death cap (*Amanita phalloides*) that selectively inhibits mammalian RNA polymerase

aman·ta·dine \ə-'man-tə-ᵢdēn\ *n* : a drug used esp. as the hydrochloride C₁₀H₁₇N·HCl to prevent infection (as by an influenza virus) by interfering with virus penetration into host cells and in the treatment of Parkinson's disease — see SYMMETREL

Am·a·ran·thus \ᵢa-mə-'ran-thəs\ *n* : a large genus of coarse herbs (family Amaranthaceae including some which produce pollen that is an important hay fever allergen

amas·tia \(ᵢ)ā-'mas-tē-ə\ *n* : the absence or underdevelopment of the mammary glands

am·au·ro·sis \ᵢa-mȯ-'rō-səs\ *n, pl* **-ro·ses** \-ᵢsēz\ : partial or complete loss of sight occurring esp. without an externally perceptible change in the eye — **am·au·rot·ic** \-'rä-tik\ *adj*

amaurosis fu·gax \-'fü-ᵢgaks, -'fyü-\ *n* : temporary partial or complete loss of sight esp. from the effects of excessive acceleration (as in flight)

amaurotic idiocy *n* : any of several recessive genetic conditions characterized by the accumulation of lipid-containing cells in the viscera and nervous system, mental retardation,

and impaired vision or blindness; *esp* : TAY-SACHS DISEASE

ambi- *prefix* : both ⟨*ambivalence*⟩ ⟨*ambisexuality*⟩

am·bi·dex·ter·i·ty \ᵢam-bi-(ᵢ)dek-'ster-ə-tē\ *n, pl* **-ties** : the quality or state of being ambidextrous

am·bi·dex·trous \ᵢam-bi-'dek-strəs\ *adj* : using both hands with equal ease — **am·bi·dex·trous·ly** *adv*

am·bi·ent \'am-bē-ənt\ *adj* : surrounding on all sides (∼ air pollution)

am·bi·sex·u·al \ᵢam-bi-'sek-shə-wəl\ *adj* : BISEXUAL — **àmbisexual** *n* — **am·bi·sex·u·al·i·ty** \-ᵢsek-shə-'wa-lə-tē\ *n*

ambiguus — see NUCLEUS AMBIGUUS

am·biv·a·lence \am-'bi-və-ləns\ *also* **am·biv·a·len·cy** \-lən-sē\ *n, pl* **-ces** *also* **-cies** : simultaneous and contradictory attitudes or feelings (as attraction and repulsion) toward an object, person, or action — **am·biv·a·lent** \-lənt\ *adj* — **am·biv·a·lent·ly** *adv*

am·bi·ver·sion \ᵢam-bi-'vər-zhən, -shən\ *n* : the personality configuration of an ambivert — **am·bi·ver·sive** \-'vər-siv, -ziv\ *adj*

am·bi·vert \'am-bi-ᵢvərt\ *n* : a person having characteristics of both extrovert and introvert

ambly- *or* **amblyo-** *comb form* : connected with amblyopia ⟨*amblyoscope*⟩

Am·bly·om·ma \ᵢam-blē-'ä-mə\ *n* : a genus of ixodid ticks including the lone star tick (*A. americanum*) of the southern U.S. and the African bont tick (*A. hebraeum*)

am·bly·ope \'am-blē-ᵢōp\ *n* : an individual affected with amblyopia

am·bly·opia \ᵢam-blē-'ō-pē-ə\ *n* : dimness of sight esp. in one eye without apparent change in the eye structures — called also *lazy eye, lazy-eye blindness* — **am·bly·opic** \-'ō-pik, -'ä-\ *adj*

am·bly·o·scope \'am-blē-ə-ᵢskōp\ *n* : an instrument for training amblyopic eyes to function properly

Am·bro·sia \am-'brō-zhə, -zhē-ə\ *n* : a genus of mostly American composite herbs that includes the ragweeds

am·bu·lance \'am-byə-ləns\ *n* : a vehicle equipped for transporting the injured or sick

am·bu·lant \'am-byə-lənt\ *adj* : walking or in a walking position; *specif* : AMBULATORY (an ∼ patient)

am·bu·late \-ᵢlāt\ *vb* **-lat·ed; -lat·ing** : to move from place to place — **am·bu·la·tion** \ᵢam-byə-'lā-shən\ *n*

am·bu·la·to·ry \'am-byə-lə-ᵢtȯr-ē\ *adj* 1 : of, relating to, or adapted to walking 2 a : able to walk about and not bedridden ⟨an ∼ patient⟩ b : performed on or involving an ambulatory patient or an outpatient ⟨an ∼ electrocardiogram⟩ ⟨∼ medical care⟩ — **am·bu·la·to·ri·ly** \ᵢam-byə-lə-'tȯr-ə-lē\ *adv*

ame·ba \ə-'mē-bə\ *n, pl* **-bas** *or* **-bae** \-(ᵢ)bē\ : a protozoan of the genus

Amoeba; broadly : an ameboid protozoan (as a naked rhizopod) — **ame·bic** \-bik\ *adj*

am·e·bi·a·sis \₁a-mi-'bī-ə-səs\ *n, pl* -a·ses \-₁sēz\ : infection with or disease caused by amebas

amebic abscess *n* : a specific purulent invasive lesion commonly of the liver caused by parasitic amebas (esp. *Entamoeba histolytica*)

amebic dysentery *n* : acute human intestinal amebiasis caused by a common ameba of the genus *Entamoeba* (*E. histolytica*) and marked by dysentery, griping, and erosion of the intestinal wall

ame·bi·cide \ə-'mē-bə-₁sīd\ *n* : a substance used to kill or capable of killing amebas and esp. parasitic amebas — **ame·bi·cid·al** \ə-₁mē-bə-'sīd-ᵊl\ *adj*

ame·bo·cyte \ə-'mē-bə-₁sīt\ *n* : a cell (as a phagocyte) having ameboid form or movements

ame·boid \-₁bȯid\ *adj* : resembling an ameba specif. in moving or changing shape by means of protoplasmic flow

amel·a·not·ic \ā-₁mē-lə-'nä-tik\ *adj* : containing little or no melanin (~ melanocytes)

ame·lia \ə-'mē-lē-ə, (₁)ā-\ *n* : congenital absence of one or more limbs

am·e·lo·blast \'a-mə-lō-₁blast\ *n* : any of a group of columnar cells that produce and deposit enamel on the surface of a developing tooth — **am·e·lo·blas·tic** \₁a-mə-lō-'blas-tik\ *adj*

am·e·lo·blas·to·ma \₁a-mə-lō-blas-'tō-mə\ *n, pl* -mas *or* -ma·ta \-mə-tə\ : a tumor of the jaw derived from remnants of the embryonic rudiment of tooth enamel — called also *adamantinoma*

am·e·lo·den·tin·al \-'den-₁tēn-ᵊl, -den-'tēn-\ *adj* : of or relating to enamel and dentin

am·e·lo·gen·e·sis \-'je-nə-səs\ *n, pl* -e·ses \-₁sēz\ : the process of forming tooth enamel

amelogenesis im·per·fec·ta \-₁im-(₁)pər-'fek-tə\ *n* : faulty development of tooth enamel that is genetically determined

amen·or·rhea \₁ā-₁me-nə-'rē-ə, ₁ā-\ *n* : abnormal absence or suppression of menstruation — **amen·or·rhe·ic** \-'rē-ik\ *adj*

amen·tia \(₁)ā-'men-chē-ə, -chə, (₁)ā-\ *n* : MENTAL RETARDATION; *specif* : a condition of lack of development of intellectual capacity — compare DEMENTIA

American cockroach *n* : a free-flying cockroach (*Periplaneta americana*) that is a common domestic pest infesting ships or buildings in the northern hemisphere

American dog tick *n* : a common No. American ixodid tick of the genus *Dermacentor* (*D. variabilis*) esp. of dogs and humans that is an important vector of Rocky Mountain spotted fe-

ver and tularemia — called also *dog tick*

am·er·i·ci·um \₁a-mə-'ri-shē-əm, -sē-\ *n* : a radioactive metallic element produced by bombardment of plutonium with high-energy neutrons — symbol *Am*; see ELEMENT table

Ames test \'āmz-\ *n* : a test for identifying potential carcinogens by studying the frequency with which they cause histidine-producing genetic mutants in bacterial colonies of the genus *Salmonella* (*S. typhimurium*) initially lacking the ability to synthesize histidine

Ames, Bruce Nathan (*b* 1928), American biochemist.

ameth·o·caine \ə-'me-thə-₁kān\ *n* : TETRACAINE

am·e·thop·ter·in \₁a-mə-'thäp-tə-rən\ *n* : METHOTREXATE

am·e·tro·pia \₁a-mə-'trō-pē-ə\ *n* : an abnormal refractive eye condition (as myopia, hyperopia, or astigmatism) in which images fail to focus upon the retina — **am·e·tro·pic** \-'trō-pik, -'trä-\ *adj*

AMI *abbr* acute myocardial infarction

am·ide \'am-₁īd, -əd\ *n* : a compound resulting from replacement of an atom of hydrogen in ammonia by an element or radical or of one or more atoms of hydrogen in ammonia by acid radicals having a chemical valence of one

am·i·done \'a-mə-₁dōn\ *n* : METHADONE

amil·o·ride \ə-'mil-ə-₁rīd\ *n* : a diuretic $C_6H_8ClN_7O$ that promotes sodium excretion and potassium retention

amine \ə-'mēn, 'a-₁mēn\ *n* : any of a class of organic compounds derived from ammonia by replacement of hydrogen by one or more alkyl groups

ami·no \ə-'mē-(₁)nō\ *adj* : relating to, being, or containing the amine group NH_2 or a substituted group NHR or NR_2 united to a radical other than an acid radical — often used in combination

amino acid *n* : an amphoteric organic acid containing the amino group NH_2; *esp* : ALPHA-AMINO ACID

ami·no·ac·i·de·mia \ə-₁mē-nō-₁a-sə-'dē-mē-ə\ *n* : a condition in which the concentration of amino acids in the blood is abnormally increased

ami·no·ac·id·uria \-₁a-sə-'dùr-ē-ə, -'dyùr-\ *n* : a condition in which one or more amino acids are excreted in excessive amounts

ami·no·ben·zo·ic acid \ə-₁mē-nō-ben-'zō-ik-\ *n* : any of three crystalline derivatives $C_7H_7NO_2$ of benzoic acid; *esp* : PARA-AMINOBENZOIC ACID

γ-aminobutyric acid *var of* GAMMA-AMINOBUTYRIC ACID

ami·no·glu·teth·i·mide \-glü-'te-thə-₁mīd\ *n* : a glutethimide derivative $C_{13}H_{16}N_2O_2$ used esp. as an anticonvulsant

ami·no·gly·co·side \-'glī-kə-₁sīd\ *n* : any

of a group of antibiotics (as strepto-mycin and neomycin) that inhibit bacterial protein synthesis and are active esp. against gram-negative bacteria

ami·no·pep·ti·dase \ə-₁mē-nō-ˈpep-tə-₁dās, -₁dāz\ *n* : an enzyme (as one found in the duodenum) that hydro-lyzes peptides

am·i·noph·yl·line \₁a-mə-ˈnä-fə-lən\ *n* : a theophylline derivative $C_{16}H_{24}$-$N_{10}O_4$ used esp. to stimulate the heart in congestive heart failure and to dilate the air passages in respira-tory disorders — called also *theophyl-line ethylenediamine*

β–ami·no·pro·pio·ni·trile \₁bä-tə-ə-₁mē-nō-₁prō-pē-ō-ˈnī-trəl, -₁trīl\ *n* : a po-tent lathyrogen $C_3H_6N_2$

am·i·nop·ter·in \₁a-mə-ˈnäp-tə-rən\ *n* : a derivative of glutamic acid C_{19}-$H_{20}N_8O_5$ used esp. as a rodenticide

ami·no·py·rine \ə-₁mē-nō-ˈpīr-₁ēn\ *n* : a white crystalline compound $C_{13}H_{17}$-N_3O formerly used to relieve pain and fever but now largely abandoned for this purpose because of the occur-rence of fatal agranulocytosis as a side effect in some users

ami·no·sal·i·cyl·ic acid \ə-₁mē-nō-₁sa-lə-ˈsi-lik-\ *n* : any of four isomeric deriv-atives $C_7H_8O_3N$ of salicylic acid that have a single amino group; *esp* : PARA-AMINOSALICYLIC ACID

ami·no·thi·a·zole \ə-₁mē-nō-ˈthī-ə-₁zōl\ *n* : a light yellow crystalline heterocy-clic amine $C_3H_4N_2S$ that has been used as a thyroid inhibitor in the treatment of hyperthyroidism

ami·no·trans·fer·ase   \-ˈtrans-fə-₁rās, -₁rāz\ *n* : TRANSAMINASE

am·i·trip·ty·line \₁a-mə-ˈtrip-tə-₁lēn\ *n* : a tricyclic antidepressant drug $C_{20}H_{23}N$ administered as the hydro-chloride salt

am·mo·nia \ə-ˈmō-nyə\ *n* **1** : a pungent colorless gaseous alkaline compound of nitrogen and hydrogen NH_3 that is very soluble in water and can easily be condensed to a liquid by cold and pressure **2** : AMMONIA WATER

am·mo·ni·a·cal \₁a-mə-ˈnī-ə-kəl\ *also* **am·mo·ni·ac** \ə-ˈmō-nē-₁ak\ *adj* : of, relating to, containing, or having the properties of ammonia

ammonia water *n* : a water solution of ammonia — called also *spirit of hartshorn*

am·mo·ni·um \ə-ˈmō-nē-əm\ *n* : an ion NH_4^+ derived from ammonia by combination with a hydrogen ion

ammonium carbonate *n* : a carbonate of ammonium; *specif* : the commer-cial mixture of the bicarbonate and carbamate used esp. in smelling salts

ammonium chloride *n* : a white crystal-line volatile salt NH_4Cl that is used in dry cells and as an expectorant — called also *sal ammoniac*

ammonium nitrate *n* : a colorless crys-talline salt $N_2H_4NO_3$ used in veteri-nary medicine as an expectorant and urinary acidifier

ammonium sulfate *n* : a colorless crys-talline salt $(NH_4)_2SO_4$ used in medi-cine as a local analgesic

am·ne·sia \am-ˈnē-zhə\ *n* **1** : loss of memory sometimes including the memory of personal identity due to brain injury, shock, fatigue, repres-sion, or illness or sometimes induced by anesthesia **2** : a gap in one's mem-ory

am·ne·si·ac \am-ˈnē-zhē-₁ak, -zē-\ *also* **am·ne·sic** \-zik, -sik\ *n* : a person af-fected with amnesia

am·ne·sic \am-ˈnē-zik, -sik\ *also* **am·ne·si·ac** \-zhē-₁ak, -zē-\ *adj* : of or re-lating to amnesia : affected with or caused by amnesia (an ~ patient)

am·nes·tic \am-ˈnes-tik\ *adj* : AMNESI-AC; *also* : causing amnesia (~ agents)

amnii — see LIQUOR AMNII

amnio- *comb form* : amnion (*amnio-centesis*)

am·nio·cen·te·sis \₁am-nē-ō-(₁)sen-ˈtē-səs\ *n, pl* **-te·ses** \-₁sēz\ : the surgical insertion of a hollow needle through the abdominal wall and into the uter-us of a pregnant female to obtain am-niotic fluid esp. to examine the fetal chromosomes for an abnormality and for the determination of sex

am·ni·og·ra·phy \₁am-nē-ˈä-grə-fē\ *n, pl* **-phies** : radiographic visualization of the outlines of the uterine cavity, pla-centa, and fetus after injection of a ra-diopaque substance into the amnion

am·ni·on \ˈam-nē-₁än, -ən\ *n, pl* **amni-ons** *or* **am·nia** \-nē-ə\ : a thin mem-brane forming a closed sac about the embryos of reptiles, birds, and mam-mals and containing a serous fluid in which the embryo is immersed

am·nio·scope \ˈam-nē-ə-₁skōp\ *n* : an endoscope for observation of the am-nion and its contents

am·ni·os·co·py \₁am-nē-ˈäs-kə-pē\ *n, pl* **-pies** : visual observation of the amni-on and its contents by means of an endoscope

am·ni·ote \ˈam-nē-₁ōt\ *n* : any of a group (Amniota) of vertebrates that undergo embryonic development within an amnion and include the birds, reptiles, and mammals — **amniote** *adj*

am·ni·ot·ic \₁am-nē-ˈä-tik\ *adj* **1** : of or relating to the amnion **2** : character-ized by the development of an amni-on

amniotic band *n* : a band of fibrous tis-sue extending between the embryo and amnion and often associated with faulty development of the fetus

amniotic cavity *n* : the fluid-filled space between the amnion and the fetus

amniotic fluid *n* : the serous fluid in which the embryo is suspended with-in the amnion

amniotic sac *n* : AMNION

am·ni·ot·o·my \₁am-nē-ˈä-tə-mē\ *n, pl*

-mies : intentional rupture of the fetal membranes to induce or facilitate labor

amo·bar·bi·tal \\,a-mō-'bär-bə-,tȯl\ *n* : a barbiturate $C_{11}H_{18}N_2O_3$ used as a hypnotic and sedative; *also* : its sodium salt — called also *amylobarbitone;* see AMYTAL, TUINAL

amo·di·a·quine \\,a-mə-'dī-ə-,kwin, -,kwēn\ *or* **amo·di·a·quin** \-,kwin\ *n* : a compound $C_{20}H_{22}ClN_3O$ derived from quinoline and used in the form of its dihydrochloride as an antimalarial

amoe·ba *chiefly Brit var of* AMEBA

Amoe·ba \ə-'mē-bə\ *n* : a large genus of naked rhizopod protozoans that have lobed and never anastomosing pseudopodia and are widely distributed in fresh and salt water and moist terrestrial environments

amoe·bi·a·sis, amoe·bi·cide, amoe·bocyte, amoe·boid *chiefly Brit var of* AMEBIASIS, AMEBICIDE, AMEBOCYTE, AMEBOID

Amoe·bo·tae·nia \ə-,mē-(,)bō-'tē-nē-ə\ *n* : a genus of tapeworms (family Dilepididae) parasitic in the intestines of poultry

amor·phous \ə-'mȯr-fəs\ *adj* 1 : having no apparent shape or organization 2 : having no real or apparent crystalline form

amox·a·pine \ə-'mäk-sə-,pēn\ *n* : an antidepressant drug $C_{17}H_{16}ClN_3O$

amox·i·cil·lin \ə-,mäk-si-'si-lən\ *n* : a semisynthetic penicillin $C_{16}H_{19}N_3$-O_5S derived from ampicillin — see LAROTID

amox·y·cil·lin \ə-,mäk-sē-'si-lən\ *Brit var of* AMOXICILLIN

AMP \,ā-(,)em-'pē\ *n* : a mononucleotide of adenine $C_{10}H_{12}N_5O_3H_2PO_4$ that was orig. isolated from mammalian muscle and is reversibly convertible to ADP and ATP in metabolic reactions — called also *adenosine monophosphate, adenosine phosphate;* compare CYCLIC AMP

am·pere \'am-,pir, -,per\ *n* : a unit of electric current equivalent to a steady current produced by one volt applied across a resistance of one ohm

am·phet·amine \am-'fe-tə-,mēn, -mən\ *n* : a racemic sympathomimetic amine $C_9H_{13}N$ or one of its derivatives (as dextroamphetamine or methamphetamine) frequently abused as a stimulant of the central nervous system but used clinically esp. as the sulfate or hydrochloride salt to treat hyperactive children and the symptoms of narcolepsy and as a short-term appetite suppressant in dieting — compare BENZEDRINE

amphi- *or* **amph-** *prefix* : on both sides : of both kinds : both (*amphi*mixis)

am·phi·ar·thro·sis \,am-fē-(,)är-'thrō-səs\ *n, pl* **-thro·ses** \-,sēz\ : a slightly movable articulation (as a symphysis)

am·phi·bol·ic \,am-fə-'bä-lik\ *adj* : having an uncertain or irregular outcome — used of stages in fevers or the critical period of disease when prognosis is uncertain

am·phi·mix·is \,am-fə-'mik-səs\ *n, pl* **-mix·es** \-,sēz\ : the union of gametes in sexual reproduction

am·phi·path·ic \,am-fə-'pa-thik\ *adj* : AMPHIPHILIC — **am·phi·path** \'am-fə-,path\ *n*

am·phi·phil·ic \,am-fə-'fi-lik\ *adj* : of, relating to, consisting of, or being one or more molecules (as of a glycolipid or sphingolipid in a biological membrane) having a polar water-soluble terminal group attached to a water-insoluble hydrocarbon chain — **amphi·phile** \'am-fə-,fīl\ *n*

am·phi·stome \'am-fi-,stōm\ *n* : any of a suborder (Amphistoma) of digenetic trematodes — compare GASTRODISCOIDES — **amphistome** *adj*

am·phor·ic \am-'for-ik\ *adj* : resembling the sound made by blowing across the mouth of an empty bottle (~ breathing) (~ sounds)

am·pho·ter·ic \,am-fə-'ter-ik\ *adj* : partly one and partly the other; *specif* : capable of reacting chemically either as an acid or as a base — **am·pho·ter·ism** \-'ter-ı-zəm\ *n*

am·pho·ter·i·cin B \,am-fə-'ter-ə-sən\ *n* : an antifungal antibiotic obtained from a soil actinomycete (*Streptomyces nodosus*) and used esp. to treat systemic fungal infections

am·pi·cil·lin \,am-pə-'si-lən\ *n* : a penicillin $C_{16}H_{19}N_3O_4S$ that is effective against gram-negative and gram-positive bacteria and is used to treat various infections of the urinary, respiratory, and intestinal tracts — see PENBRITIN

am·pli·fi·ca·tion \,am-plə-fə-'kā-shən\ *n* 1 : an act, example, or product of amplifying 2 : a usu. massive replication esp. of a gene or DNA sequence (as in a polymerase chain reaction)

am·pli·fy \'am-plə-,fī\ *vb* **-fied; -fying** 1 : to make larger or greater (as in amount or intensity) 2 : to cause (a gene or DNA sequence) to undergo amplification

am·pule *or* **am·poule** *also* **am·pul** \'am-,pyül, -,pül\ *n* 1 : a hermetically sealed small bulbous glass vessel that is used to hold a solution for esp. hypodermic injection 2 : a vial resembling an ampule

am·pul·la \am-'pu̇-lə, 'am-,pyü-lə\ *n, pl* **-lae** \-,lē\ : a saccular anatomic swelling or pouch; as **a** : the dilatation containing a patch of sensory epithelium at one end of each semicircular canal of the ear **b** : one of the dilatations of the milk-carrying tubules of the mammary glands that serve as reservoirs for milk **c** (1) : the middle portion of the fallopian tube (2) : the distal dilatation of a vas deferens near the opening of the duct leading from the seminal vesicle **d** : a terminal dilatation of the rectum just before it joins the anal canal

ampulla of Va·ter \-ˈfä-tər\ *n* : a trumpet-mouthed dilatation of the duodenal wall at the opening of the fused pancreatic and common bile ducts — called also *papilla of Vater* **Vater, Abraham (1684–1751),** German anatomist.

am·pul·la·ry \am-ˈpu̇-lə-rē\ *also* **am·pul·lar** \-ˈpu̇-lər\ *adj* : resembling or relating to an ampulla

am·pu·tate \ˈam-pyə-ˌtāt\ *vb* **-tat·ed; -tat·ing** : to cut (as a limb) from the body — **am·pu·ta·tion** \ˌam-pyə-ˈtā-shən\ *n*

amputation neuroma *n* : NEUROMA 2

am·pu·tee \ˌam-pyə-ˈtē\ *n* : one that has had a limb amputated

amygdal- *or* **amygdalo-** *comb form* **1** : almond (*amygdalin*) **2** : amygdala (*amygdalectomy*) (*amygdalotomy*)

amyg·da·la \ə-ˈmig-də-lə\ *n, pl* **-lae** \-ˌlē, -ˌlī\ : the one of the four basal ganglia in each cerebral hemisphere that is part of the limbic system and consists of an almond-shaped mass of gray matter in the roof of the lateral ventricle — called also *amygdaloid body, amygdaloid nucleus*

amyg·da·lec·to·my \ə-ˌmig-də-ˈlek-tə-mē\ *n, pl* **-mies** : surgical removal of the amygdala — **amyg·da·lec·to·mized** \-tə-ˌmizd\ *adj*

amyg·da·lin \ə-ˈmig-də-lən\ *n* : a white crystalline cyanogenetic glucoside $C_{20}H_{27}NO_{11}$ found esp. in the seeds of the apricot (*Prunus armeniaca*), peach (*Prunus persica*), and bitter almond

amyg·da·loid \-ˌloid\ *adj* **1** : almond-shaped **2** : of, relating to, or affecting an amygdala (~ lesions)

amygdaloid body *n* : AMYGDALA

amygdaloid nucleus *n* : AMYGDALA

amyg·da·lot·o·my \ə-ˌmig-də-ˈlät-ə-mē\ *n, pl* **-mies** : destruction of part of the amygdala of the brain (as for the control of epilepsy) esp. by surgical incision

amyl- *or* **amylo-** *comb form* : starch (*amylase*)

am·y·lase \ˈa-mə-ˌlās, -ˌlāz\ *n* : any of a group of enzymes (as amylopsin) that catalyze the hydrolysis of starch and glycogen or their intermediate hydrolysis products

am·yl nitrite \ˈa-məl-\ *n* : a pale yellow pungent flammable liquid ester $C_5H_{11}NO_2$ that is used chiefly in medicine as a vasodilator esp. in angina pectoris and illicitly as an aphrodisiac — called also *isoamyl nitrite;* compare POPPER

am·y·lo·bar·bi·tone \ˌa-mə-lō-ˈbär-bə-ˌtōn\ *n, Brit* : AMOBARBITAL

¹**am·y·loid** \ˈa-mə-ˌloid\ *adj* : resembling or containing starch

²**amyloid** *n* : a waxy translucent substance consisting of protein in combination with polysaccharides that is deposited in some animal organs and tissue under abnormal conditions (as in Alzheimer's disease)

am·y·loid·osis \ˌa-mə-ˌloi-ˈdō-səs\ *n, pl* **-oses** \-ˌsēz\ : a disorder characterized by the deposition of amyloid in organs or tissues of the animal body — see PARAMYLOIDOSIS

am·y·lop·sin \ˌa-mə-ˈläp-sən\ *n* : the amylase of the pancreatic juice

am·y·lum \ˈa-mə-ləm\ *n* : STARCH

amyo·to·nia \ˌā-ˌmī-ə-ˈtō-nē-ə\ *n* : deficiency of muscle tone

amyotonia con·gen·i·ta \-kən-ˈje-nə-tə\ *n* : a congenital disease of infants characterized by flaccidity of the skeletal muscles

amyo·tro·phia \ˌā-ˌmī-ə-ˈtrō-fē-ə\ *or* **amy·ot·ro·phy** \-ˌmī-ˈä-trə-fē\ *n, pl* **-phias** *or* **-phies** : atrophy of a muscle — **amyo·tro·phic** \-ˌmī-ə-ˈträ-fik, -ˈtrō-\ *adj*

amyotrophic lateral sclerosis *n* : a rare fatal progressive degenerative disease that affects pyramidal motor neurons, usu. begins in middle age, and is characterized esp. by increasing and spreading muscular weakness — called also *Lou Gehrig's disease;* abbr. ALS

Am·y·tal \ˈa-mə-ˌtȯl\ *trademark* — used for a preparation of amobarbital

an- — see A-

ana \ˈä-nə\ *adv* : of each an equal quantity — used in prescriptions

ana- *or* **an-** *prefix* : up : upward (*anabolism*)

ANA *abbr* American Nurses Association

anabolic steroid *n* : any of a group of usu. synthetic hormones that increase constructive metabolism and are sometimes abused by athletes in training to increase temporarily the size of their muscles

anab·o·lism \ə-ˈna-bə-ˌli-zəm\ *n* : the constructive part of metabolism concerned esp. with macromolecular synthesis — compare CATABOLISM — **an·a·bol·ic** \ˌa-nə-ˈbä-lik\ *adj*

an·ac·id·i·ty \ˌa-nə-ˈsi-də-tē\ *n, pl* **-ties** : ACHLORHYDRIA

an·a·clit·ic \ˌa-nə-ˈkli-tik\ *adj* : of, relating to, or characterized by the direction of love toward an object (as the mother) that satisfies nonsexual needs (as hunger)

anaclitic depression *n* : impaired development of an infant resulting from separation from its mother

ana·cro·tism \ə-ˈna-krə-ˌti-zəm\ *n* : an abnormality of the blood circulation characterized by a secondary notch in the ascending part of a sphygmographic tracing of the pulse — **an·a·crot·ic** \ˌa-nə-ˈkrä-tik\ *adj*

anae·mia *chiefly Brit var of* ANEMIA

an·aer·obe \ˈa-nə-ˌrōb, (ˌ)a-ˈnar-ˌōb\ *n* : an anaerobic organism

an·aer·o·bic \ˌa-nə-ˈrō-bik, ˌa-ˌnar-ˈō-\ *adj* **1 a** : living, active, or occurring in the absence of free oxygen ⟨∼ respiration⟩ **b** : of, relating to, or being active in which the body incurs an oxygen debt ⟨∼ exercise⟩ **2** : relating to or induced by anaerobes — **an·aer·o·bi·cal·ly** \-bi-k(ə-)lē\ *adv*

an·aes·the·sia, an·aes·the·si·ol·o·gist, an·aes·the·si·ol·o·gy, an·aes·the·tic, an·aes·the·tist, an·aes·the·tize *chiefly Brit var of* ANESTHESIA, ANESTHESIOLOGIST, ANESTHESIOLOGY, ANESTHETIC, ANESTHETIST, ANESTHETIZE

an·a·gen \ˈa-nə-ˌjen\ *n* : the active phase of the hair growth cycle preceding telogen

anal \ˈān-ᵊl\ *adj* **1** : of, relating to, or situated near the anus **2 a** : of, relating to, or characterized by the stage of psychosexual development in psychoanalytic theory during which the child is concerned esp. with its feces **b** : of, relating to, or characterized by personality traits (as parsimony, meticulousness, and ill humor) considered typical of fixation at the anal stage of development — compare GENITAL 3, ORAL 2, PHALLIC 2 — **anal·ly** *adv*

anal *abbr* **1** analysis **2** analytic **3** analyze

anal canal *n* : the terminal section of the rectum

¹an·a·lep·tic \ˌa-nə-ˈlep-tik\ *adj* : of, relating to, or acting as an analeptic

²analeptic *n* : a restorative agent: *esp* : a drug that acts as a stimulant on the central nervous system

anal eroticism *n* : the experiencing of pleasurable sensations or sexual excitement associated with or symbolic of stimulation of the anus — called also *anal erotism* — **anal erotic** *adj*

an·al·ge·sia \ˌan-ᵊl-ˈjēzhə, -zhē-ə, -zē-\ *n* : insensibility to pain without loss of consciousness

¹an·al·ge·sic \-ˈjē-zik, -sik\ *adj* : relating to, characterized by, or producing analgesia

²analgesic *n* : an agent for producing analgesia

an·al·get·ic \-ˈje-tik\ *n or adj* : ANALGESIC

anal·i·ty \ā-ˈna-lə-tē\ *n, pl* **-ties** : an anal psychological state, stage, or quality

anal·o·gous \ə-ˈna-lə-gəs\ *adj* : having similar function but a different structure and origin ⟨∼ organs⟩

an·a·logue *or* **an·a·log** \ˈan-ᵊl-ˌȯg, -ˌäg\ *n* **1** : an organ similar in function to an organ of another animal or plant but different in structure and origin **2** *usu* **analog** : a chemical compound that is structurally similar to another but differs slightly in composition (as in the replacement of one atom by an atom of a different element or in the presence of a particular functional group)

anal·o·gy \ə-ˈna-lə-jē\ *n, pl* **-gies** : functional similarity between anatomical

parts without similarity of structure and origin — compare HOMOLOGY 1

anal–re·ten·tive \ˈān-ᵊl-ri-ˈten-tiv\ *adj* : characterized by personality traits (as frugality and obstinacy) held to be psychological sequelae of toilet training — compare ANAL 2b — **anal retentive** *n* — **anal retentiveness** *n*

anal sadism *n* : the cluster of personality traits (as aggressiveness, negativism, destructiveness, and outwardly directed rage) typical of the anal stage of development — **anal–sa·dis·tic** \ˌān-ᵊl-sə-ˈdis-tik\ *adj*

anal sphincter *n* : either of two sphincters controlling the closing of the anus: **a** : an outer sphincter of striated muscle surrounding the anus immediately beneath the skin — called also *external anal sphincter, sphincter ani externus* **b** : an inner sphincter formed by thickening of the circular smooth muscle of the rectum — called also *internal anal sphincter, sphincter ani internus*

anal verge \-ˈvərj\ *n* : the distal margin of the anal canal comprising the muscular rim of the anus

anal·y·sand \ə-ˈna-lə-ˌsand\ *n* : one who is undergoing psychoanalysis

anal·y·sis \ə-ˈna-lə-səs\ *n, pl* **-y·ses** \-ˌsēz\ **1** : separation of a whole into its component parts **2 a** : the identification or separation of ingredients of a substance **b** : a statement of the constituents of a mixture **3** : PSYCHOANALYSIS

an·a·lyst \ˈan-ᵊl-ist\ *n* : PSYCHOANALYST

an·a·lyt·ic \ˌan-ᵊl-ˈi-tik\ *or* **an·a·lyt·i·cal** \-ti-kəl\ *adj* **1** : of or relating to analysis; *esp* : separating something into component parts or constituent elements **2** : PSYCHOANALYTIC — **an·a·lyt·i·cal·ly** \-ti-k(ə-)lē\ *adv*

analytic psychology *n* : a modification of psychoanalysis due to C. G. Jung that adds to the concept of the personal unconscious a racial or collective unconscious and advocates that psychotherapy be conducted in terms of the patient's present-day conflicts and maladjustments

an·a·lyze \ˈan-ᵊl-ˌīz\ *vb* **-lyzed; -lyz·ing 1** : to study or determine the nature and relationship of the parts of by analysis; *esp* : to examine by chemical analysis **2** : PSYCHOANALYZE

an·am·ne·sis \ˌa-nam-ˈnē-səs\ *n, pl* **-ne·ses** \-ˌsēz\ **1** : a recalling to mind **2** : a preliminary case history of a medical or psychiatric patient — **an·am·nes·tic** \-ˈnes-tik\ *adj*

ana·phase \ˈa-nə-ˌfāz\ *n* : the stage of mitosis and meiosis in which the chromosomes move toward the poles of the spindle — **ana·pha·sic** \ˌa-nə-ˈfā-zik\ *adj*

an·aph·ro·dis·i·ac \-ˈdē-zē-ˌak, -ˈdi-\ *adj* : of, relating to, or causing absence or impairment of sexual desire — **anaphrodisiac** *n*

ana·phy·lac·tic \ˌa-nə-fə-ˈlak-tik\ *adj* : of, relating to, affected by, or causing anaphylaxis or anaphylactic shock — **ana·phy·lac·ti·cal·ly** \-ti-k(ə-)lē\ *adv*

anaphylactic shock *n* : an often severe and sometimes fatal systemic reaction in a susceptible individual upon a second exposure to a specific antigen (as wasp venom or penicillin) after previous sensitization that is characterized esp. by respiratory symptoms, fainting, itching, and hives

ana·phy·lac·toid \ˌa-nə-fə-ˈlak-ˌtoid\ *adj* : resembling anaphylaxis or anaphylactic shock

ana·phy·lax·is \ˌa-nə-fə-ˈlak-səs\ *n, pl* **-lax·es** \-ˌsēz\ 1 : hypersensitivity (as to foreign proteins or drugs) resulting from sensitization following prior contact with the causative agent 2 : ANAPHYLACTIC SHOCK

an·a·pla·sia \ˌa-nə-ˈplā-zhē-ə, -zē-\ *n* : reversion of cells to a more primitive or undifferentiated form

an·a·plas·ma \ˌa-nə-ˈplaz-mə\ *n* 1 *cap* : a genus of bacteria (family Anaplasmataceae) that are found in the red blood cells of ruminants, are transmitted by biting arthropods, and cause anaplasmosis 2 *pl* **-ma·ta** \-mə-tə\ *or* **-mas** : any bacterium of the genus *Anaplasma*

an·a·plas·mo·sis \-ˌplaz-ˈmō-səs\ *n, pl* **-mo·ses** \-ˌsēz\ : a tick-borne disease of cattle, sheep, and deer caused by a bacterium of the genus *Anaplasma* (*A. marginale*) and characterized esp. by anemia and by jaundice

an·a·plas·tic \ˌa-nə-ˈplas-tik\ *adj* : characterized by, composed of, or being cells which have reverted to a relatively undifferentiated state

an·a·plas·tol·o·gy \-ˌplas-ˈtä-lə-jē\ *n, pl* **-gies** : a branch of medical technology concerned with the preparation and fitting of prosthetic devices (as artificial eyes and surgical implants) to individual specifications and with the study of the materials from which they are fabricated — **an·a·plas·tol·o·gist** \-jist\ *n*

an·ar·thria \a-ˈnär-thrē-ə\ *n* : inability to articulate remembered words as a result of a brain lesion — compare APHASIA

an·a·sar·ca \ˌa-nə-ˈsär-kə\ *n* : generalized edema with accumulation of serum in the connective tissue

an·a·stal·sis \ˌa-nə-ˈstȯl-səs, -ˈstäl-, -ˈstal-\ *n, pl* **-stal·ses** \-ˌsēz\ : ANTIPERISTALSIS

anas·to·mose \ə-ˈnas-tə-ˌmōz, -ˌmōs\ *vb* **-mosed; -mos·ing** : to connect, join, or communicate by anastomosis

anas·to·mo·sis \ə-ˌnas-tə-ˈmō-səs, ˌa-nəs-\ *n, pl* **-mo·ses** \-ˌsēz\ 1 a : a communication between or coalescence of blood vessels b : the surgical union of parts and esp. hollow tubular parts 2 : a product of anastomosis; *esp* : a

network (as of channels or branches) produced by anastomosis — **anas·to·mot·ic** \-ˈmä-tik\ *adj*

anat *abbr* anatomic; anatomical; anatomy

an·a·tom·ic \ˌa-nə-ˈtä-mik\ *or* **an·a·tom·i·cal** \-mi-kəl\ *adj* 1 : of or relating to anatomy 2 : STRUCTURAL 1 (an ∼ obstruction) — **an·a·tom·i·cal·ly** \-mi-k(ə-)lē\ *adv*

Anatomica — see BASLE NOMINA ANATOMICA, NOMINA ANATOMICA

anatomical dead space *n* : the dead space in that portion of the respiratory system which is external to the alveoli and includes the air-conveying ducts from the nostrils to the terminal bronchioles — compare PHYSIOLOGICAL DEAD SPACE

anatomical position *n* : the normal position of the human body when active

anat·o·mist \ə-ˈna-tə-mist\ *n* : a student of anatomy; *esp* : one skilled in dissection

anat·o·my \ə-ˈna-tə-mē\ *n, pl* **-mies** 1 : a branch of morphology that deals with the structure of organisms — compare PHYSIOLOGY 1 2 : a treatise on anatomic science or art 3 : the art of separating the parts of an organism in order to ascertain their position, relations, structure, and function : DISSECTION 4 : structural makeup esp. of an organism or any of its parts

ana·tox·in \ˌa-nə-ˈtäk-sən\ *n* : TOXOID

anchyl- *or* **anchylo-** — see ANKYL-

an·chy·lose, an·chy·lo·sis *var of* ANKYLOSE, ANKYLOSIS

an·cil·lary \ˈan-sə-ˌler-ē\ *adj* : being auxiliary or supplementary

an·co·ne·us \aŋ-ˈkō-nē-əs\ *n, pl* **-nei** \-nē-ˌī\ : a small triangular extensor muscle that is superficially situated behind and below the elbow joint and that extends the forearm — called also *anconeus muscle*

An·cy·los·to·ma \ˌaŋ-ki-ˈläs-tə-mə, ˌan-sə-\ *n* : a genus of hookworms (family Ancylostomatidae) that are intestinal parasites of mammals including humans — compare NECATOR

an·cy·los·tome \aŋ-ˈki-lə-ˌstōm, -ˈsi-\ *n* : any of the genus *Ancylostoma* of hookworms

an·cy·lo·sto·mi·a·sis \ˌaŋ-ki-lō-stə-ˈmī-ə-səs, ˌan-sə-\ *n, pl* **-a·ses** \-ˌsēz\ : infestation with or disease caused by hookworms; *esp* : a lethargic anemic state due to blood loss through the feeding of hookworms in the small intestine — called also *hookworm disease*

andr- *or* **andro-** *comb form* 1 : male ⟨*androgen*⟩ 2 : male and ⟨*androgynous*⟩

an·dro·gen \ˈan-drə-jən\ *n* : a male sex hormone (as testosterone) — **an·dro·gen·ic** \ˌan-drə-ˈje-nik\ *adj*

an·drog·e·nize \an-ˈdrä-jə-ˌnīz\ *vb* **-nized; -niz·ing** : to treat or influence with male sex hormone esp. in excessive amounts

an·drog·y·nous \an-ˈdrä-jə-nəs\ *adj* : having the characteristics or nature of both male and female — **an·drog·y·ny** \-nē\ *n*

an·droid \ˈan-ˌdrȯid\ *adj, of the pelvis* : having the angular form and narrow outlet typical of the human male — compare ANTHROPOID, GYNECOID, PLATYPELLOID

an·drom·e·do·tox·in \an-ˌdrä-mə-dō-ˈtäk-sən\ *n* : a toxic compound $C_{31}H_{50}O_{10}$ found in various plants of the heath family (Ericaceae)

an·dro·stene·di·one \ˌan-drə-ˈstēn-ˈdī-ˌōn, -ˈstēn-dē-ˌōn\ *n* : a steroid sex hormone that is secreted by the testis, ovary, and adrenal cortex and acts more strongly in the production of male characteristics than testosterone

an·dros·ter·one \an-ˈdräs-tə-ˌrōn\ *n* : an androgenic hormone that is a hydroxy ketone $C_{19}H_{30}O_2$ found in human urine

Anec·tine \ə-ˈnek-tən\ *trademark* — used for a preparation of succinylcholine

an·elec·trot·o·nus \ˌan-əl-ˌek-ˈträt-ᵊn-əs\ *n* : the decreased irritability of a nerve in the region of a positive electrode or anode on the passage of a current of electricity through it

ane·mia \ə-ˈnē-mē-ə\ *n* 1 : a condition in which the blood is deficient in red blood cells, in hemoglobin, or in total volume — see APLASTIC ANEMIA, HYPERCHROMIC ANEMIA, HYPOCHROMIC ANEMIA, MEGALOBLASTIC ANEMIA, MICROCYTIC ANEMIA, PERNICIOUS ANEMIA, SICKLE-CELL ANEMIA 2 : ISCHEMIA — **ane·mic** \ə-ˈnē-mik\ *adj* — **ane·mi·cal·ly** \-mi-k(ə-)lē\ *adv*

an·en·ceph·a·lus \ˌan-(ˌ)en-ˈse-fə-ləs\ *n, pl* -li \-ˌlī\ : ANENCEPHALY

an·en·ceph·a·ly \ˌan-(ˌ)en-ˈse-fə-lē\ *n, pl* -lies : congenital absence of all or a major part of the brain — **an·en·ce·phal·ic** \-ˌen-sə-ˈfa-lik\ *adj or n*

aneph·ric \(ˌ)ā-ˈne-frik, (ˌ)ā-\ *adj* : being without functioning kidneys

an·er·gy \ˈa-(ˌ)nər-jē\ *n, pl* -gies : a condition in which the body fails to react to an injected allergen or antigen (as tuberculin) — **an·er·gic** \-jik\ *adj*

an·es·the·sia \ˌa-nəs-ˈthē-zhə\ *n* 1 : loss of sensation esp. to touch usu. resulting from a lesion in the nervous system or from some other abnormality 2 : loss of sensation and usu. of consciousness without loss of vital functions artificially produced by the administration of one or more agents that block the passage of pain impulses along nerve pathways to the brain

Anes·the·sin \ə-ˈnes-thə-sən\ *trademark* — used for a preparation of benzocaine

an·es·the·si·ol·o·gist \ˌa-nəs-ˌthē-zē-ˈä-lə-jist\ *n* : ANESTHETIST; *specif* : a physician specializing in anesthesiology

an·es·the·si·ol·o·gy \-jē\ *n, pl* -gies : a branch of medical science dealing with anesthesia and anesthetics

¹**an·es·thet·ic** \ˌa-nəs-ˈthe-tik\ *adj* 1 : capable of producing anesthesia (~ agents) 2 : of, relating to, or caused by anesthesia (~ effect) (~ symptoms) — **an·es·thet·i·cal·ly** \-ti-k(ə-)lē\ *adv*

²**anesthetic** *n* : a substance that produces anesthesia

anes·the·tist \ə-ˈnes-thə-tist\ *n* : one who administers anesthetics — compare ANESTHESIOLOGIST

anes·the·tize \-ˌtīz\ *vb* -tized; -tiz·ing : to subject to anesthesia — **anes·the·ti·za·tion** \ə-ˌnes-thə-tə-ˈzā-shən\ *n*

an·es·trous \(ˌ)a-ˈnes-trəs\ *adj* 1 : not exhibiting estrus 2 : of or relating to anestrus

an·es·trus \-trəs\ *n* : the period of sexual quiescence between two periods of sexual activity in cyclically breeding mammals — compare ESTRUS

an·eu·ploid \ˈan-yü-ˌplȯid\ *adj* : having or being a chromosome number that is not an exact multiple of the usu. haploid number — **aneuploid** *n* — **an·eu·ploi·dy** \-ˌplȯi-dē\ *n*

an·eu·rine \ˈan-yə-ˌrēn, (ˌ)a-ˈnyur-ˌēn\ *n* : THIAMINE

an·eu·rysm *also* **an·eu·rism** \ˈan-yə-ˌri-zəm\ *n* : an abnormal blood-filled dilatation of a blood vessel and esp. an artery resulting from disease of the vessel wall — **an·eu·rys·mal** *also* **an·eu·ris·mal** \ˌan-yə-ˈriz-məl\ *adj* — **an·eu·rys·mal·ly** *adv*

angel dust *n* : PHENCYCLIDINE

An·gel·man syndrome \ˈaŋ-jəl-mən-\ *also* **An·gel·man's syndrome** \-mənz-\ *n* : a genetic disorder characterized by severe mental retardation, hyperactivity, seizures, hypotonia, jerky movements, lack of speech, and frequent smiling and laughter

Angelman, Harry (*fl* 1965), British physician.

angi- *or* **angio-** *comb form* 1 : blood or lymph vessel (*angioma*) (*angiogenesis*) 2 : blood vessels and (*angiocardiography*)

-angia *pl of* -ANGIUM

an·gi·i·tis \ˌan-jē-ˈī-təs\ *n, pl* -it·i·des \-ˈi-tə-ˌdēz\ : inflammation of a blood or lymph vessel or duct

an·gi·na \an-ˈjī-nə, ˈan-jə-\ *n* : a disease marked by spasmodic attacks of intense suffocative pain: as a : a severe inflammatory or ulcerated condition of the mouth or throat (diphtheritic ~) — see LUDWIG'S ANGINA, VINCENT'S ANGINA b : ANGINA PECTORIS — **an·gi·nal** \an-ˈjīn-ᵊl, ˈan-jən-\ *adj*

angina pec·to·ris \-ˈpek-tə-rəs\ *n* : a disease marked by brief paroxysmal attacks of chest pain precipitated by deficient oxygenation of the heart muscles — see UNSTABLE ANGINA:

compare CORONARY INSUFFICIENCY, HEART FAILURE, MYOCARDIAL INFARCTION

an·gi·nose \ˈan-jə-ˌnōs, an-ˈjī-\ *or* **an·gi·nous** \(ˌ)an-ˈjī-nəs, ˈan-jə-\ *adj* : relating to angina or angina pectoris

an·gio·car·dio·gram \ˌan-jē-ō-ˈkär-dē-ə-ˌgram\ *n* : a roentgenogram of the heart and its blood vessels prepared by angiocardiography

an·gio·car·di·og·ra·phy \-ˌkär-dē-ˈä-grə-fē\ *n, pl* **-phies** : the roentgenographic visualization of the heart and its blood vessels after injection of a radiopaque substance — **an·gio·car·dio·graph·ic** \-dē-ə-ˈgra-fik\ *adj*

an·gio·ede·ma \ˌan-jē-ō-i-ˈdē-mə\ *n, pl* **-mas** *or* **-ma·ta** \-mə-tə\ : an allergic skin disease characterized by patches of circumscribed swelling involving the skin and its subcutaneous layers, the mucous membranes, and sometimes the viscera — called also *angioneurotic edema, giant urticaria, Quincke's disease, Quincke's edema*

an·gio·gen·e·sis \-ˈje-nə-səs\ *n, pl* **-e·ses** \-ˌsēz\ : the formation and differentiation of blood vessels

an·gio·gram \ˈan-jē-ə-ˌgram\ *n* : a roentgenogram made by angiography

an·gi·og·ra·phy \ˌan-jē-ˈä-grə-fē\ *n, pl* **-phies** : the roentgenographic visualization of the blood vessels after injection of a radiopaque substance — **an·gio·graph·ic** \ˌan-jē-ə-ˈgra-fik\ *adj* — **an·gio·graph·i·cal·ly** \-fi-k(ə-)lē\ *adv*

an·gio·ker·a·to·ma \ˌan-jē-ō-ˌker-ə-ˈtō-mə\ *n, pl* **-mas** *or* **-ma·ta** \-mə-tə\ : a skin disease characterized by small warty elevations or telangiectasias and epidermal thickening

an·gi·ol·o·gy \ˌan-jē-ˈä-lə-jē\ *n, pl* **-gies** : the study of blood vessels and lymphatics

an·gi·o·ma \ˌan-jē-ˈō-mə\ *n, pl* **-mas** *or* **-ma·ta** \-mə-tə\ : a tumor (as a hemangioma) composed chiefly of blood vessels or lymphatic vessels — **an·gi·o·ma·tous** \-mə-təs\ *adj*

an·gio·ma·to·sis \ˌan-jē-(ˌ)ō-mə-ˈtō-səs\ *n, pl* **-to·ses** \-ˌsēz\ : a condition characterized by the formation of multiple angiomas

an·gio·neu·rot·ic edema \-nú-ˌrä-tik, -nyü-\ *n* : ANGIOEDEMA

an·gi·op·a·thy \ˌan-jē-ˈä-pə-thē\ *n, pl* **-thies** : a disease of the blood or lymph vessels

an·gio·plas·ty \ˈan-jē-ə-ˌplas-tē\ *n, pl* **-ties** : surgical repair of a blood vessel; *esp* : BALLOON ANGIOPLASTY

an·gio·sar·co·ma \ˌan-jē-ō-sär-ˈkō-mə\ *n, pl* **-mas** *or* **-ma·ta** \-mə-tə\ : a rare malignant tumor affecting esp. the liver

an·gio·spasm \ˈan-jē-ō-ˌspa-zəm\ *n* : spasmodic contraction of the blood vessels with increase in blood pressure — **an·gio·spas·tic** \ˌan-jē-ō-ˈspas-tik\ *adj*

an·gio·ten·sin \ˌan-jē-ō-ˈten-sən\ *n* 1

: either of two forms of a kinin of which one has marked physiological activity: *esp* : ANGIOTENSIN II 2 : a synthetic amide derivative of angiotensin II used to treat some forms of hypotension

an·gio·ten·sin·ase \ˌan-jē-ō-ˈten-sə-ˌnās, -ˌnāz\ *n* : any of several enzymes in the blood that hydrolyze angiotensin — called also *hypertensinase*

angiotensin converting enzyme *n* : a proteolytic enzyme that converts angiotensin I to angiotensin II — see ACE INHIBITOR

an·gio·ten·sin·o·gen \-ten-ˈsi-nə-jən\ *n* : a serum globulin formed by the liver that is cleaved by renin to produce angiotensin I — called also *hypertensinogen*

angiotensin I \-ˈwən\ *n* : the physiologically inactive form of angiotensin that is composed of 10 amino-acid residues and is a precursor of angiotensin II

angiotensin II \-ˈtü\ *n* : a protein with vasoconstrictive activity that is composed of eight amino-acid residues and is the physiologically active form of angiotensin

an·gio·to·nin \-ˈtō-nən\ *n* : ANGIOTENSIN

-angium *n comb form, pl* **-angia** : vessel : receptacle ⟨mes*angium*⟩

an·gle \ˈaŋ-gəl\ *n* 1 : a corner whether constituting a projecting part or a partially enclosed space 2 : the figure formed by two lines extending from the same point

an·gle·ber·ry \ˈaŋ-gəl-ˌber-ē\ *n, pl* **-ries** : a papilloma or warty growth of the skin or mucous membranes of cattle and sometimes horses often occurring in great numbers

angle of the jaw *n* : GONIAL ANGLE

angle of the mandible *n* : GONIAL ANGLE

ang·strom \ˈaŋ-strəm\ *n* : a unit of length equal to one ten-billionth of a meter — used esp. for wavelengths of light

Ångström, Anders Jonas (1814–1874), Swedish astronomer and physicist.

angstrom unit *n* : ANGSTROM

an·gu·lar \ˈaŋ-gyə-lər\ *adj* 1 a : having an angle or angles b : forming an angle or corner : sharp-cornered 2 : relating to or situated near an anatomical angle: *specif* : relating to or situated near the inner angle of the eye — **an·gu·lar·i·ty** \ˌaŋ-gyü-ˈlar-ə-tē\ *n* — **an·gu·lar·ly** *adv*

angular artery *n* : the terminal part of the facial artery that passes up alongside the nose to the inner angle of the orbit

angular gyrus *n* : the cerebral gyrus of the posterior part of the external surface of the parietal lobe that arches over the posterior end of the sulcus between the superior and middle gyri of the temporal lobe — called also *angular convolution*

angularis — see INCISURA ANGULARIS

angular vein *n* : a vein that comprises the first part of the facial vein and runs obliquely down at the side of the upper part of the nose

an·gu·la·tion \aŋ-gyə-ˈlā-shən\ *n* : an angular position, formation or shape; *esp* : an abnormal bend or curve in an organ — **an·gu·late** \ˈaŋ-gyə-ˌlāt\ *vb*

anguli — see LEVATOR ANGULI ORIS

an·gu·lus \ˈaŋ-gyə-ləs\ *n, pl* **an·gu·li** \-ˌlī, -ˌlē\ : an anatomical angle; *also* : an angular part or relationship

an·he·do·nia \ˌan-hē-ˈdō-nē-ə\ *n* : a psychological condition characterized by inability to experience pleasure in normally pleasurable acts — compare ANALGESIA — **an·he·don·ic** \-ˈdä-nik\ *adj*

an·hi·dro·sis \ˌan-hi-ˈdrō-səs, -hī-\ *n, pl* **-dro·ses** \-ˌsēz\ : abnormal deficiency or absence of sweating

¹**an·hi·drot·ic** \-ˈdrä-tik\ *adj* : tending to check sweating

²**anhidrotic** *n* : an anhidrotic agent

anhydr- *or* **anhydro-** *comb form* : lacking water (*anhydremia*)

an·hy·drase \an-ˈhī-ˌdrās, -ˌdrāz\ *n* : an enzyme (as carbonic anhydrase) promoting a specific dehydration reaction and the reverse hydration reaction

an·hy·dre·mia \ˌan-(ˌ)hī-ˈdrē-mē-ə\ *n* : an abnormal reduction of water in the blood

an·hy·dride \(ˌ)an-ˈhī-ˌdrīd\ *n* : a compound derived from another (as an acid) by removal of the elements of water

an·hy·dro·hy·droxy·pro·ges·ter·one \an-ˌhī-drō-ˌhī-ˌdräk-sē-prō-ˈjes-tə-ˌrōn\ *n* : ETHISTERONE

an·hy·dro·sis, an·hy·drot·ic *var of* AN-HIDROSIS, ANHIDROTIC

an·hy·drous \(ˌ)an-ˈhī-drəs\ *adj* : free from water and esp. water that is chemically combined in a crystalline substance (~ ammonia)

ani — see LEVATOR ANI, PRURITUS ANI

an·ic·ter·ic \ˌa-(ˌ)nik-ˈter-ik\ *adj* : not accompanied or characterized by jaundice (~ hepatitis)

an·i·line \ˈan-ᵊl-ən\ *n* : an oily liquid poisonous amine C₆H₅NH₂ used chiefly in organic synthesis (as of dyes and pharmaceuticals) — **aniline** *adj*

ani·lin·gus \ˌā-ni-ˈliŋ-gəs\ *or* **ani·linc·tus** \-ˈliŋk-təs\ *n* : erotic stimulation achieved by contact between mouth and anus

an·i·ma \ˈa-nə-mə\ *n* : an individual's true inner self that in the analytic psychology of C. G. Jung reflects archetypal ideals of conduct; *also* : an inner feminine part of the male personality — compare ANIMUS, PERSONA

animal heat *n* : heat produced in the body of a living animal by functional chemical and physical activities — called also *body heat*

animal model *n* : an animal sufficiently like humans in its anatomy, physiology, or response to a pathogen to be used in medical research in order to obtain results that can be extrapolated to human medicine

animal starch *n* : GLYCOGEN

an·i·mate \ˈa-nə-mət\ *adj* 1 : possessing or characterized by life 2 : of or relating to animal life as opposed to plant life

an·i·mus \ˈa-nə-məs\ *n* : an inner masculine part of the female personality in the analytic psychology of C. G. Jung — compare ANIMA

an·ion \ˈa-ˌnī-ən\ *n* : the ion in an electrolyzed solution that migrates to the anode; *broadly* : a negatively charged ion — **an·ion·ic** \ˌa-(ˌ)nī-ˈä-nik\ *adj* — **an·ion·i·cal·ly** \-ni-k(ə-)lē\ *adv*

an·irid·ia \ˌa-ˌnī-ˈri-dē-ə\ *n* : congenital or traumatically induced absence or defect of the iris

anis- *or* **aniso-** *comb form* : unequal (*aniseikonia*) (*anisocytosis*)

an·is·ei·ko·nia \ˌa-ˌnī-ˌsī-ˈkō-nē-ə\ *n* : a defect of binocular vision in which the two retinal images of an object differ in size — **an·is·ei·kon·ic** \-ˈkä-nik\ *adj*

an·iso·co·ria \ˌa-ˌnī-sō-ˈkōr-ē-ə\ *n* : inequality in the size of the pupils of the eyes

an·iso·cy·to·sis \-ˌsī-ˈtō-səs\ *n, pl* **-to·ses** \-ˌsēz\ : variation in size of cells and esp. of the red blood cells (as in pernicious anemia) — **an·iso·cy·tot·ic** \-ˈtä-tik\ *adj*

an·iso·me·tro·pia \ˌa-ˌnī-sə-mə-ˈtrō-pē-ə\ *n* : unequal refractive power in the two eyes — **an·iso·me·tro·pic** \-ˈträ-pik, -ˈtrō-\ *adj*

an·kle \ˈaŋ-kəl\ *n* 1 : the joint between the foot and the leg that constitutes in humans a ginglymus joint between the tibia and fibula above and the talus below — called also *ankle joint* 2 : the region of the ankle joint

an·kle·bone \-ˌbōn\ *n* : TALUS 1

ankle jerk *n* : a reflex downward movement of the foot produced by a spasmodic contraction of the muscles of the calf in response to sudden extension of the leg or the striking of the Achilles tendon above the heel — called also *Achilles reflex*

ankle joint *n* : ANKLE 1

ankyl- *or* **ankylo-** *also* **anchyl-** *or* **anchylo-** *comb form* : stiffness : immobility (*ankylosis*)

an·ky·lose \ˈaŋ-ki-ˌlōs, -ˌlōz\ *vb* **-losed; -los·ing** 1 : to unite or stiffen by ankylosis 2 : to undergo ankylosis

ankylosing spondylitis *n* : rheumatoid arthritis of the spine — called also *Marie-Strümpell disease, rheumatoid spondylitis*

an·ky·lo·sis \ˌaṅ-ki-ˈlō-səs\ *n, pl* **-lo·ses** \ˌsēz\ : stiffness or fixation of a joint by disease or surgery — **an·ky·lot·ic** \-ˈlä-tik\ *adj*

an·kylo·stome, an·ky·lo·sto·mi·a·sis *var of* ANCYLOSTOME, ANCYLOSTOMIASIS

an·la·ge \ˈän-ˌlä-gə\ *n, pl* **-gen** \-gən\ *also* **-ges** \-əz\ : the foundation of a subsequent development; *esp* : PRIMORDIUM

an·neal \ə-ˈnēl\ *vb* 1 : to heat and then cool (nucleic acid) in order to separate strands and induce combination at lower temperatures esp. with complementary strands of a different species 2 : to be capable of combining with complementary nucleic acid by a process of heating and cooling

an·ne·lid \ˈan-ᵊl-əd\ *n* : any of a phylum (Annelida) of usu. elongated segmented invertebrates (as earthworms and leeches) — **annelid** *adj*

annexa *var of* ADNEXA

an·nu·lar \ˈan-yə-lər\ *adj* : of, relating to, or forming a ring

annulare — see GRANULOMA ANNULARE

annular ligament *n* : a ringlike ligament or band of fibrous tissue encircling a part: as **a** : a strong band of fibers surrounding the head of the radius and retaining it in the radial notch of the ulna **b** : a ring attaching the base of the stapes to the oval window

an·nu·lus \ˈan-yə-ləs\ *n, pl* **-li** \-ˌlī\ *also* **-lus·es** : a ringlike part, structure, or marking; *esp* : any of various ringlike anatomical parts (as the inguinal ring)

annulus fi·bro·sus \-fī-ˈbrō-səs, -fi-\ *n* : a ring of fibrous or fibrocartilaginous tissue (as of an intervertebral disk)

¹**ano-** *prefix* : upward ⟨*anoopsia*⟩

²**ano-** *comb form* 1 : anus ⟨*anoscope*⟩ 2 : anus and ⟨*anorectal*⟩

ano·ci·as·so·ci·a·tion \ə-ˌnō-sē-ə-ˌsō-sē-ˈā-shən, a-, -ˌsō-shē-\ *n* : a method of preventing shock and exhaustion incident to surgical operations by preventing communication between the area of operation and the nervous system esp. by means of a local anesthetic or sharp dissection

an·odon·tia \ˌa-nō-ˈdän-chə, -chē-ə\ *n* : an esp. congenital absence of teeth

¹**an·o·dyne** \ˈa-nə-ˌdīn\ *adj* : serving to ease pain

²**anodyne** *n* : a drug that allays pain

ano·gen·i·tal \ˌā-nō-ˈje-nə-tᵊl\ *adj* : of, relating to, or involving the genital organs and the anus ⟨an ~ infection⟩

anom·a·lo·scope \ə-ˈnä-mə-lə-ˌskōp\ *n* : an optical device designed to test color vision

anom·a·lous \ə-ˈnä-mə-ləs\ *adj* : deviating from normal; *specif* : having abnormal vision with respect to a particular color but not color-blind

anom·a·ly \ə-ˈnä-mə-lē\ *n, pl* **-lies** : a deviation from normal esp. of a bodily part

ano·mia \ə-ˈnä-mē-ə, -ˈnō-\ *n* : ANOMIC APHASIA

ano·mic \ə-ˈnä-mik, ā-, -ˈnō-\ *adj* : relating to or characterized by anomie

anomic aphasia *n* : loss of the power to use or understand words denoting objects

an·o·mie *also* **an·o·my** \ˈa-nə-mē\ *n* : personal unrest, alienation, and anxiety that comes from a lack of purpose or ideals

an·onych·ia \ˌa-nə-ˈni-kē-ə\ *n* : congenital absence of the nails

ano·op·sia \ˌa-nō-ˈäp-sē-ə\ *n* : upward strabismus

anoph·e·les \ə-ˈnä-fə-ˌlēz\ *n* 1 *cap* : a genus of mosquitoes that includes all mosquitoes that transmit malaria to humans 2 : any mosquito of the genus *Anopheles* — **anopheles** *adj* — **an·oph·e·line** \-ˌlīn\ *adj or n*

an·oph·thal·mia \ˌa-näf-ˈthal-mē-ə, -äp-\ *n* : congenital absence of the eyes — **an·oph·thal·mic** \-ˈthal-mik\ *adj*

an·oph·thal·mos \-ˈthal-məs\ *n* 1 : ANOPHTHALMIA 2 : an individual born without eyes

an·opia \ə-ˈnō-pē-ə, a-\ *n* : a defect of vision; *esp* : HEMIANOPIA

ano·plas·ty \ˈā-nə-ˌplas-tē, ˈa-\ *n, pl* **-ties** : a plastic operation on the anus (as for stricture)

An·o·plo·ceph·a·la \ˌa-nə-(ˌ)plō-ˈse-fə-lə\ *n* : a genus of taenioid tapeworms including some parasites of horses

an·op·sia \ə-ˈnäp-sē-ə, a-, -ˈnōp-\ *var of* ANOOPSIA

an·or·chid·ism \ə-ˈnór-ki-ˌdi-zəm, a-\ *n* : congenital absence of one or both testes

ano·rec·tal \ˌā-nō-ˈrekt-ᵊl, ˌa-nə-\ *adj* : of, relating to, or involving both the anus and rectum ⟨~ surgery⟩

¹**an·o·rec·tic** \ˌa-nə-ˈrek-tik\ *also* **an·o·ret·ic** \-ˈre-tik\ *adj* 1 **a** : lacking appetite **b** : ANOREXIC 2 2 : causing loss of appetite ⟨~ drugs⟩

²**anorectic** *also* **anoretic** *n* 1 : an anorectic agent 2 : ANOREXIC

an·orex·ia \ˌa-nə-ˈrek-sē-ə, -ˈrek-shə\ *n* 1 : loss of appetite esp. when prolonged 2 : ANOREXIA NERVOSA

anorexia ner·vo·sa \-(ˌ)nər-ˈvō-sə, -zə\ *n* : a serious eating disorder primarily of young women in their teens and early twenties that is characterized esp. by a pathological fear of weight gain leading to faulty eating patterns, malnutrition, and usu. excessive weight loss

¹**an·o·rex·i·ant** \ˌa-nə-ˈrek-sē-ənt, -ˈrek-shənt\ *n* : a drug that suppresses appetite

²**anorexiant** *adj* : ANORECTIC 2

¹**ano·rex·ic** \-ˈrek-sik\ *adj* 1 : ANORECTIC 1a, 2 2 : affected with anorexia nervosa

²**anorexic** *n* : a person affected with anorexia nervosa

ano·rex·i·gen·ic \-ˌrek-sə-ˈje-nik\ *adj*
: ANORECTIC 2

an·or·gas·mia \ˌa-nȯr-ˈgaz-mē-ə\ *n*
: sexual dysfunction characterized by
failure to achieve orgasm — **an·or·gas·mic** \-mik\ *adj*

ano·scope \ˈā-nə-ˌskōp\ *n* : an instrument for facilitating visual examination of the anal canal

ano·sco·py \ā-ˈnäs-kə-pē, ə-\ *n, pl* -**pies**
: visual examination of the anal canal
with an anoscope — **ano·scop·ic** \ˌā-nə-ˈskä-pik\ *adj*

an·os·mia \a-ˈnäz-mē-ə\ *n* : loss or impairment of the sense of smell — **an·os·mic** \-mik\ *adj*

ano·vag·i·nal \ˌā-nō-ˈva-jən-əl\ *adj*
: connecting the anal canal and the
vagina (a congenital ~ fistula)

an·ovu·la·tion \ˌa-ˌnä-vyə-ˈlā-shən,
-ˌnō-\ *n* : failure or absence of ovulation

an·ovu·la·to·ry \(ˌ)a-ˈnä-vyə-lə-ˌtȯr-ē,
-ˈnō\ *adj* 1 : not involving or associated with ovulation (~ bleeding) 2
: suppressing ovulation (~ drugs)

an·ox·emia \ˌa-ˌnäk-ˈsē-mē-ə\ *n* : a
condition of subnormal oxygenation
of the arterial blood — **an·ox·emic** \-mik\ *adj*

an·ox·ia \ə-ˈnäk-sē-ə, a-\ *n* : hypoxia
esp. of such severity as to result in
permanent damage — **an·ox·ic** \-sik\ *adj*

ANS *abbr* autonomic nervous system

an·sa \ˈan-sə\ *n, pl* **an·sae** \-ˌsē\ : a
loop-shaped anatomical structure

ansa cer·vi·ca·lis \-ˌsər-və-ˈka-ləs,
-ˈkā-\ *n* : a nerve loop from the upper
cervical nerves that accompanies the
hypoglossal nerve and innervates the
infrahyoid muscles

ansa hy·po·glos·si \-ˌhī-pə-ˈglä-ˌsī,
-ˌglō-, -(ˌ)sē\ *n* : ANSA CERVICALIS

ansa sub·cla·via \-ˌsəb-ˈklā-vē-ə\ *n* : a
nerve loop of sympathetic fibers
passing around the subclavian artery

anserinus — see PES ANSERINUS

ant- — see ANTI-

Ant·a·buse \ˈan-tə-ˌbyüs\ *trademark* —
used for a preparation of disulfiram

¹ant·ac·id \(ˌ)ant-ˈa-səd\ *also* **an·ti·ac·id** \ˌan-tē-ˈa-səd, -ˌtī-\ *adj* : tending to
counteract acidity

²antacid *also* **antiacid** *n* : an agent (as an
alkali or absorbent) that counteracts
or neutralizes acidity

an·tag·o·nism \an-ˈta-gə-ˌni-zəm\ *n*
: opposition in physiological action: **a**
: contrariety in the effect of contraction of muscles **b** : interaction of two
or more substances such that the action of any one of them on living cells
or tissues is lessened — compare SYN-
ERGISM — **an·tag·o·nize** \an-ˈta-gə-ˌnīz\ *vb*

an·tag·o·nist \-nist\ *n* : an agent that
acts in physiological opposition: as **a**
: a muscle that contracts with and
limits the action of an agonist with
which it is paired — called also *an-*
tagonistic muscle; compare AGONIST
1. SYNERGIST 2 **b** : a chemical substance that opposes the action on the
nervous system of a drug or a substance occurring naturally in the
body by combining with and blocking
its nervous receptor — compare AGO-
NIST 2

an·tag·o·nis·tic \(ˌ)an-ˌta-gə-ˈnis-tik\
adj 1 : characterized by or resulting
from antagonism 2 : relating to or being muscles that are antagonists —
an·tag·o·nis·ti·cal·ly \-ti-k(ə-)lē\ *adv*

ante- *prefix* 1 : anterior : forward (*an-
tehyophysis*) 2 **a** : prior to : earlier
than (*antepartum*) **b** : in front of (*antebrachium*)

an·te·bra·chi·um \ˌan-ti-ˈbrā-kē-əm\ *n,
pl* -**chia** \-kē-ə\ : the part of the arm or
forelimb between the brachium and
the carpus : FOREARM

an·te·cu·bi·tal \ˌan-ti-ˈkyü-bət-ᵊl\ *adj*
: of or relating to the inner or front
surface of the forearm

antecubital fossa *n* : a triangular cavity
of the elbow joint that contains a tendon of the biceps, the median nerve,
and the brachial artery

an·te·flex·ion \ˌan-ti-ˈflek-shən\ *n* : a
displacement forward of an organ (as
the uterus) so that its axis is bent
upon itself

an·te·grade \ˈan-ti-ˌgrād\ *adj* : occurring or performed in the usual direction of conduction or flow

an·te·hy·poph·y·sis \-hī-ˈpä-fə-səs\ *n, pl*
-**y·ses** \-ˌsēz\ : the anterior lobe of the
pituitary gland

an·te·mor·tem \-ˈmȯr-təm\ *adj* : preceding death

an·te·na·tal \-ˈnāt-ᵊl\ *adj* : PRENATAL (~
diagnosis of birth defects) — **an·te·na·tal·ly** *adv*

an·te·par·tum \-ˈpär-təm\ *adj* : relating
to the period before parturition : before childbirth (~ infection) (~ care)

an·te·ri·or \an-ˈtir-ē-ər\ *adj* 1 : relating
to or situated near or toward the head
or toward the part in headless animals most nearly corresponding to
the head 2 : situated toward the front
of the body : VENTRAL — used in human anatomy because of the upright
posture of humans — **an·te·ri·or·ly**
adv

anterior cerebral artery *n* : CEREBRAL
ARTERY a

anterior chamber *n* : a space in the eye
bounded in front by the cornea and in
back by the iris and middle part of the
lens — compare POSTERIOR CHAMBER

anterior column *n* : VENTRAL HORN

anterior commissure *n* : a band of nerve
fibers crossing from one side of the
brain to the other just anterior to the
third ventricle

anterior communicating artery *n* : COM-
MUNICATING ARTERY a

anterior corticospinal tract *n* : VEN-
TRAL CORTICOSPINAL TRACT

anterior cruciate ligament *n* : CRUCIATE LIGAMENT a(1)

anterior facial vein *n* : FACIAL VEIN

anterior fontanel *or* **anterior fontanelle** *n* : the fontanel occurring at the meeting point of the coronal and sagittal sutures

anterior funiculus *n* : a longitudinal division on each side of the spinal cord comprising white matter between the anterior median fissure and the ventral root — called also *ventral funiculus;* compare LATERAL FUNICULUS, POSTERIOR FUNICULUS

anterior gray column *n* : VENTRAL HORN

anterior horn *n* **1** : VENTRAL HORN **2** : the cornu of the lateral ventricle of each cerebral hemisphere that curves outward and forward into the frontal lobe — compare INFERIOR HORN, POSTERIOR HORN 2

anterior humeral circumflex artery *n* : an artery that branches from the axillary artery in the shoulder, curves around the front of the humerus, and is distributed esp. to the shoulder joint, head of the humerus, biceps brachii, and deltoid muscle — compare POSTERIOR HUMERAL CIRCUMFLEX ARTERY

anterior inferior cerebellar artery *n* : an artery that arises from the basilar artery and divides into branches distributed to the anterior parts of the inferior surface of the cerebellum

anterior inferior iliac spine *n* : a projection on the anterior margin of the ilium that is situated below the anterior superior iliac spine and is separated from it by a notch — called also *anterior inferior spine*

anterior intercostal artery *n* : INTERCOSTAL ARTERY a

anterior jugular vein *n* : JUGULAR VEIN c

anterior lingual gland *n* : either of two mucus-secreting glands of the tip of the tongue

anterior lobe *n* : ADENOHYPOPHYSIS

anterior median fissure *n* : a groove along the anterior midline of the spinal cord that incompletely divides it into symmetrical halves — called also *ventral median fissure*

anterior nasal spine *n* : the nasal spine that is formed by the union of processes of the two premaxillae

anterior pillar of the fauces *n* : PALATOGLOSSAL ARCH

anterior root *n* : VENTRAL ROOT

anterior sacrococcygeal muscle *n* : SACROCOCCYGEUS VENTRALIS

anterior spinal artery *n* : SPINAL ARTERY a

anterior spinothalamic tract *n* : SPINOTHALAMIC TRACT a

anterior superior iliac spine *n* : a projection at the anterior end of the iliac crest — called also *anterior superior spine*

anterior synechia *n* : SYNECHIA a

anterior temporal artery *n* : TEMPORAL ARTERY 3a

anterior tibial artery *n* : TIBIAL ARTERY b

anterior tibial nerve *n* : DEEP PERONEAL NERVE

anterior tibial vein *n* : TIBIAL VEIN b

anterior triangle *n* : a triangular region that is a landmark in the neck and has its apex at the sternum pointing downward — compare POSTERIOR TRIANGLE

anterior ulnar recurrent artery *n* : ULNAR RECURRENT ARTERY a

antero- *comb form* : anterior and : extending from front to ⟨*antero*lateral⟩ ⟨*antero*posterior⟩

an·tero·grade \'an-tə-(ˌ)rō-ˌgrād\ *adj* **1** : effective for a period immediately following a shock or seizure; *specif* : effective for and in effect during the period from the time of seizure to the present ⟨∼ amnesia⟩ **2** : occurring along nerve cell processes away from the cell body ⟨∼ axonal transport⟩ — compare RETROGRADE 3

an·tero·in·fe·ri·or \ˌan-tə-(ˌ)rō-in-'fir-ē-ər\ *adj* : located in front and below ⟨the ∼ aspect of the femur⟩ — **an·tero·in·fe·ri·or·ly** *adv*

an·tero·lat·er·al \-'la-tə-rəl, -trəl\ *adj* : situated or occurring in front and to the side — **an·tero·lat·er·al·ly** *adv*

an·tero·me·di·al \-'mē-dē-əl\ *adj* : located in front and toward the middle

an·tero·pos·te·ri·or \-pō-'stir-ē-ər, -pä-\ *adj* : concerned with or extending along a direction or axis from front to back or from anterior to posterior — **an·tero·pos·te·ri·or·ly** *adv*

an·tero·su·pe·ri·or \-sù-'pir-ē-ər\ *adj* : located in front and above — **an·tero·su·pe·ri·or·ly** *adv*

an·te·ver·sion \ˌan-ti-'vər-zhən, -shən\ *n* : a condition of being anteverted — used esp. of the uterus

an·te·vert \'an-ti-ˌvərt, ˌan-ti-'\ *vb* : to displace (a body organ) so that the whole axis is directed farther forward than normal

anth- — see ANTI-

anthelix *var of* ANTIHELIX

¹**an·thel·min·tic** \ˌant-ˌhel-'min-tik, ˌan-ˌthel-\ *also* **an·thel·min·thic** \-'min-thik\ *adj* : expelling or destroying parasitic worms (as tapeworms) esp. of the intestine

²**anthelmintic** *also* **anthelminthic** *n* : an anthelmintic drug

-anthem *or* **-anthema** *n comb form, pl* **-anthems** *or* **-anthemata** : eruption : rash ⟨en*anthem*⟩ ⟨ex*anthema*⟩

anthrac- *or* **anthraco-** *comb form* : carbon : coal ⟨*anthraco*sis⟩ ⟨*anthraco*silicosis⟩

an·thra·co·sil·i·co·sis \ˌan-thrə-(ˌ)kō-ˌsi-lə-'kō-səs\ *n, pl* **-co·ses** \-ˌsēz\ : massive fibrosis of the lungs resulting from inhalation of carbon and quartz dusts and marked by shortness of breath

an·thra·co·sis \ˌan-thrə-ˈkō-səs\ *n, pl* **-co·ses** \-ˌsēz\ : a benign deposition of coal dust within the lungs from inhalation of sooty air — compare ANTHRACOSILICOSIS — **an·thra·cot·ic** \-ˈkä-tik\ *adj*

an·thra·cy·cline \ˌan-thrə-ˈsī-ˌklēn\ *n* : any of a class of antineoplastic drugs (as doxorubicin) derived from an actionmycete of the genus *Streptomyces* (esp. *S. peucetius*)

an·thra·lin \ˈan-thrə-lən\ *n* : a yellowish brown crystalline compound $C_{14}H_{10}O_3$ used in the treatment of skin diseases (as psoriasis) — called also *dithranol*

an·thra·sil·i·co·sis \ˌan-thrə-ˌsi-lə-ˈkō-səs\ *var of* ANTHRACOSILICOSIS

an·thrax \ˈan-ˌthraks\ *n, pl* **-thra·ces** \-thrə-ˌsēz\ : an infectious disease of warm-blooded animals (as cattle and sheep) caused by a spore-forming bacterium (*Bacillus anthracis*), transmissible to humans esp. by the handling of infected products (as wool), and characterized by external ulcerating nodules or by lesions in the lungs

anthrop- *or* **anthropo-** *comb form* : human being (*anthropophilic*)

an·thro·poid \ˈan-thrə-ˌpȯid\ *adj, of the pelvis* : having a relatively great anteroposterior dimension — compare ANDROID, GYNECOID, PLATYPELLOID

an·thro·pom·e·try \ˌan-thrə-ˈpä-mə-trē\ *n, pl* **-tries** : the study of human body measurements esp. on a comparative basis — **an·thro·po·met·ric** \-pə-ˈmetrik\ *adj*

an·thro·po·phil·ic \ˌan-thrə-(ˌ)pō-ˈfi-lik\ *also* **an·thro·poph·i·lous** \-ˈpä-fə-ləs\ *adj* : attracted to humans esp. as a source of food (~ mosquitoes)

anti- *or* **ant-** *or* **anth-** *prefix* 1 : opposing in effect or activity : inhibiting (*antacid*) (*anthelmintic*) (*antihistamine*) 2 : serving to prevent, cure, or alleviate (*antianxiety*)

an·ti·abor·tion \ˌan-tē-ə-ˈbȯr-shən, -ˌtī-\ *adj* : opposed to abortion — **an·ti·abor·tion·ist** \-shə-nist\ *n*

antiacid *var of* ANTACID

an·ti·ac·ne \-ˈak-nē\ *adj* : alleviating the symptoms of acne (an ~ ointment)

an·ti·AIDS \-ˈādz\ *adj* : used to treat or delay the development of AIDS (the ~ drug AZT)

¹an·ti·al·ler·gic \-ə-ˈlər-jik\ *also* **an·ti·al·ler·gen·ic** \-ˌa-lər-ˈje-nik\ *adj* : tending to relieve or control allergic symptoms

²antiallergic *also* **antiallergenic** *n* : an antiallergic agent

an·ti·an·a·phy·lax·is \ˌa-nə-fə-ˈlak-səs\ *n, pl* **-lax·es** \-ˌsēz\ : the state of desensitization to an antigen

an·ti·an·dro·gen \ˌan-ˈan-drə-jən\ *n* : a substance that tends to inhibit the production, activity, or effects of a male sex hormone — **an·ti·an·dro·gen·ic** \-ˌan-drə-ˈje-nik\ *adj*

an·ti·ane·mic \-ə-ˈnē-mik\ *adj* : effective in or relating to the prevention or correction of anemia

an·ti·an·gi·nal \-an-ˈjin-°l, -ˈan-jən-°l\ *adj* : used or tending to prevent or relieve angina pectoris (~ drugs)

an·ti·an·ti·body \ˌan-tē-ˈan-ti-ˌbä-dē, ˌan-ˌtī-\ *n, pl* **-bod·ies** : an antibody with specific immunologic activity against another antibody

an·ti·anx·i·ety \-(ˌ)aŋ-ˈzī-ə-tē\ *adj* : tending to prevent or relieve anxiety

¹an·ti·ar·rhyth·mic \-(ˌ)ā-ˈrith-mik\ *adj* : counteracting or preventing cardiac arrhythmia (an ~ agent)

²antiarrhythmic *n* : an antiarrhythmic agent

¹an·ti·ar·thrit·ic \-är-ˈthri-tik\ *or* **an·ti·ar·thri·tis** \-ˈthrī-təs\ *adj* : tending to relieve or prevent arthritic symptoms

²antiarthritic *n* : an antiarthritic agent

an·ti·asth·ma \-ˈaz-mə\ *adj* : used to relieve the symptoms of asthma (~ drugs)

¹an·ti·bac·te·ri·al \ˌan-ti-bak-ˈtir-ē-əl, ˌan-ˌtī-\ *adj* : directed or effective against bacteria

²antibacterial *n* : an antibacterial agent

an·ti·bi·o·sis \ˌan-ti-bī-ˈō-səs, ˌan-ˌtī-; ˌan-ti-bē-\ *n, pl* **-o·ses** \-ˌsēz\ : antagonistic association between organisms to the detriment of one of them or between one organism and a metabolic product of another

¹an·ti·bi·ot·ic \-bī-ˈä-tik, -bē-\ *adj* 1 : tending to prevent, inhibit, or destroy life 2 : of or relating to antibiotics or to antibiosis — **an·ti·bi·ot·i·cal·ly** \-ti-k(ə-)lē\ *adv*

²antibiotic *n* : a substance produced by or a semisynthetic substance derived from a microorganism and able in dilute solution to inhibit or kill another microorganism

an·ti·body \ˈan-ti-ˌbä-dē\ *n, pl* **-bod·ies** : any of a large number of proteins of high molecular weight that are produced normally by specialized B cells after stimulation by an antigen and act specifically against the antigen in an immune response, that are produced abnormally by some cancer cells, and that typically consist of four subunits including two heavy chains and two light chains — called also *immunoglobulin*

an·ti·bra·chi·um *var of* ANTEBRACHIUM

an·ti·can·cer \ˌan-ti-ˈkan-sər, ˌan-ˌtī-\ *adj* : used against or tending to arrest cancer (~ drugs) (~ activity)

an·ti·car·cin·o·gen \-kär-ˈsi-nə-jən, -ˈkärs-°n-ə-ˌjen\ *n* : an anticarcinogenic agent

an·ti·car·cin·o·gen·ic \-ˌkärs-°n-ō-ˈje-nik\ *adj* : tending to inhibit or prevent the activity of a carcinogen or the development of carcinoma

an·ti·car·ies \ˌan-ti-ˈkar-ēz, ˌan-ˌtī-\ *adj* : tending to inhibit the formation of caries

¹**an·ti·cho·lin·er·gic** \-ˌkō-lə-ˈnər-jik\ *adj* : opposing or blocking the physiological action of acetylcholine

²**anticholinergic** *n* : a substance having an anticholinergic action

an·ti·cho·lin·es·ter·ase \-ˈnes-tə-ˌrās, -ˌrāz\ *n* : any substance (as neostigmine) that inhibits a cholinesterase by combination with it

an·tic·i·pa·tion \(ˌ)an-ˌti-sə-ˈpā-shən\ *n* **1** : occurrence (as of a symptom) before the normal or expected time **2** : mental attitude that influences a later response — **an·tic·i·pate** \an-ˈti-sə-ˌpāt\ *vb*

an·ti·clot·ting \ˌan-ti-ˈklä-tiŋ, ˌan-ˌtī-\ *adj* : inhibiting the clotting of blood (~ factors)

¹**an·ti·co·ag·u·lant** \-kō-ˈa-gyə-lənt\ *adj* : of, relating to, or utilizing anticoagulants (~ therapy)

²**anticoagulant** *n* : a substance (as a drug) that hinders coagulation and esp. coagulation of the blood

an·ti·co·ag·u·la·tion \-kō-ˌa-gyə-ˈlā-shən\ *n* : the process of hindering the clotting of blood esp. by treatment with an anticoagulant — **an·ti·co·ag·u·late** \-kō-ˈa-gyə-ˌlāt\ *vb* — **an·ti·co·ag·u·la·to·ry** \-ˌə-tōr-ē\ *adj*

an·ti·co·ag·u·la·tive \-ˈa-gyə-ˌlā-tiv\ *adj* : ANTICOAGULANT (~ activity)

an·ti·co·ag·u·lin \-gyə-lən\ *n* : a substance (as one in snake venom) that retards clotting of vertebrate blood

an·ti·co·don \ˌan-ti-ˈkō-ˌdän\ *n* : a triplet of nucleotide bases in transfer RNA that identifies the amino acid carried and binds to a complementary codon in messenger RNA during protein synthesis at a ribosome

an·ti·com·ple·ment \-ˈkäm-plə-mənt\ *n* : a substance that interferes with the activity of complement — **an·ti·com·ple·men·ta·ry** \-ˌkäm-plə-ˈmen-tə-rē, -men-trē\ *adj*

¹**an·ti·con·vul·sant** \-kən-ˈvəl-sənt\ *also* **an·ti·con·vul·sive** \-siv\ *n* : an anticonvulsant drug

²**anticonvulsant** *also* **anticonvulsive** *adj* : used or tending to control or prevent convulsions (as in epilepsy)

anticus — see SCALENUS ANTICUS, SCALENUS ANTICUS SYNDROME, TIBIALIS ANTICUS

an·ti·dan·druff \-ˈdan-drəf\ *adj* : tending to remove or prevent dandruff (an ~ shampoo)

¹**an·ti·de·pres·sant** \-di-ˈpres-ᵊnt\ *also* **an·ti·de·pres·sive** \-ˈpre-siv\ *adj* : used or tending to relieve or prevent psychic depression

²**antidepressant** *also* **antidepressive** *n* : an antidepressant drug — called *also* *energizer*, *psychic energizer*; compare TRICYCLIC ANTIDEPRESSANT

¹**an·ti·di·a·bet·ic** \-ˌdī-ə-ˈbe-tik\ *n* : an antidiabetic drug

²**antidiabetic** *adj* : tending to relieve diabetes (~ drugs)

¹**an·ti·di·ar·rhe·al** \-ˌdī-ə-ˈrē-əl\ *adj* : tending to prevent or relieve diarrhea

²**antidiarrheal** *n* : an antidiarrheal agent

an·ti·di·ure·sis \-ˌdī-yù-ˈrē-səs\ *n*, *pl* **-ure·ses** \-ˌsēz\ : reduction in or suppression of the excretion of urine

¹**an·ti·di·uret·ic** \-ˈre-tik\ *adj* : tending to oppose or check excretion of urine

²**antidiuretic** *n* : an antidiuretic substance

antidiuretic hormone *n* : VASOPRESSIN

an·ti·dote \ˈan-ti-ˌdōt\ *n* : a remedy that counteracts the effects of poison — **an·ti·dot·al** \an-ti-ˈdōt-ᵊl\ *adj* — **an·ti·dot·al·ly** *adv*

an·ti·dro·mic \ˌan-ti-ˈdrä-mik, -ˈdrō-\ *adj* : proceeding or conducting in a direction opposite to the usual one — used esp. of a nerve impulse or fiber (~ action potentials) — **an·ti·dro·mi·cal·ly** \-mi-k(ə-)lē\ *adv*

¹**an·ti·dys·en·ter·ic** \ˌan-ti-ˌdis-ᵊn-ˈter-ik, ˌan-ˌtī-\ *adj* : tending to relieve or prevent dysentery

²**antidysenteric** *n* : an antidysenteric agent

¹**an·ti·emet·ic** \-ə-ˈme-tik\ *adj* : used or tending to prevent or check vomiting (~ drugs)

²**antiemetic** *n* : an antiemetic agent

¹**an·ti·ep·i·lep·tic** \-ˌe-pə-ˈlep-tik\ *adj* : tending to suppress or prevent epilepsy (~ treatment)

²**antiepileptic** *n* : an antiepileptic drug

an·ti·es·tro·gen \-ˈes-trə-jən\ *n* : a substance that inhibits the physiological action of an estrogen — **an·ti·es·tro·gen·ic** \-ˌes-trə-ˈje-nik\ *adj*

an·ti·fer·til·i·ty \-(ˌ)fər-ˈti-lə-tē\ *adj* : having the capacity or tending to reduce or destroy fertility : CONTRACEPTIVE (~ agents)

an·ti·fi·bril·la·to·ry \-ˈfi-brə-lə-ˌtōr-ē, -ˈfī-\ *adj* : tending to suppress or prevent cardiac fibrillation

an·ti·fi·bri·no·ly·sin \-ˌfi-brən-ᵊl-ˈīs-ᵊn\ *n* : an antibody that acts specifically against fibrinolysins of hemolytic streptococci and that is used chiefly in some diagnostic tests — called *also* *antistreptokinase* — **an·ti·fi·bri·no·ly·sis** \-ˈli-səs\ *n* — **an·ti·fi·bri·no·lyt·ic** \-ˈi-tik\ *adj*

¹**an·ti·flat·u·lent** \-ˈfla-chə-lənt\ *adj* : preventing or relieving flatulence

²**antiflatulent** *n* : an antiflatulent agent

an·ti·flu \-ˈflü\ *adj* : used to prevent infection by the myxovirus causing influenza (an ~ drug)

¹**an·ti·fun·gal** \ˌan-ti-ˈfəŋ-gəl, ˌan-ˌtī-\ *adj* : destroying fungi; *also* : inhibiting the growth of fungi

²**antifungal** *n* : an antifungal agent

an·ti·gen \ˈan-ti-jən\ *n* : a usu. protein or carbohydrate substance (as a toxin or enzyme) capable of stimulating an immune response — **an·ti·gen·ic** \ˌan-ti-ˈje-nik\ *adj* — **an·ti·gen·i·cal·ly** \-ni-k(ə-)lē\ *adv*

an·ti·gen·emia \ˌan-ti-jə-ˈnē-mē-ə\ *n* : the condition of having an antigen in the blood

antigenic determinant *n* : EPITOPE

an·ti·gen·ic·i·ty \-ˈni-sə-tē\ *n, pl* -ties : the capacity to act as an antigen

an·ti·glob·u·lin \ˌan-ti-ˈglä-byə-lən, ˌan-ˌtī-\ *n* : an antibody that combines with and precipitates globulin

an·ti·go·nad·o·trop·ic \-ˌgō-ˌna-də-ˈträ-pik\ *adj* : tending to inhibit the physiological activity of gonadotropic hormones

an·ti·go·nad·o·tro·pin \-ˈtrō-pən\ *n* : an antigonadotropic substance

an·ti·he·lix \-ˈhē-liks\ *n, pl* -li·ces \-ˈhe-lə-ˌsēz, -ˈhē-\ *or* -lix·es \-ˈhē-lik-səz\ : the curved elevation of cartilage within or in front of the helix

an·ti·he·mo·phil·ic factor \-ˌhē-mə-ˈfi-lik-\ *n* : FACTOR VIII — called also *antihemophilic globulin*

an·ti·hem·or·rhag·ic \-ˌhe-mə-ˈra-jik\ *adj* : tending to prevent or arrest hemorrhage

an·ti·her·pes \-ˈhər-(ˌ)pēz\ *adj* : acting against a herpesvirus or the symptoms caused by infection with it (the ~ drug acyclovir)

an·ti·hi·drot·ic \-hi-ˈdrä-tik, -hī-\ *adj* : tending to reduce or prevent sweat secretion

¹**an·ti·his·ta·mine** \-ˈhis-tə-ˌmēn, -mən\ *adj* : tending to block or counteract the physiological action of histamine

²**antihistamine** *n* : any of various compounds that oppose the actions of histamine and are used esp. for treating allergic reactions (as hay fever), cold symptoms, and motion sickness

an·ti·his·ta·min·ic \-his-tə-ˈmi-nik\ *adj or n* : ANTIHISTAMINE

an·ti·hu·man \-ˈhyü-mən, -ˈyü-\ *adj* : reacting strongly with human antigens (~ antibodies)

an·ti·hy·per·lip·id·emic \-ˌhī-pər-ˌli-pə-ˈdē-mik\ *adj* : acting to prevent or counteract the accumulation of lipids in the blood (an ~ drug)

¹**an·ti·hy·per·ten·sive** \-ˌhī-pər-ˈten-siv\ *also* **an·ti·hy·per·ten·sion** \-ˈhī-pər-ˈten-chən\ *adj* : used for or effective against high blood pressure (~ drugs)

²**antihypertensive** *n* : an antihypertensive agent (as a drug)

an·ti·id·io·type \ˌan-tī-ˈi-dē-ə-ˌtīp\ *n* : an antibody that treats another antibody as an antigen and suppresses its immunoreactivity — **an·ti·id·io·typ·ic** \-ˌi-dē-ə-ˈti-pik\ *adj*

¹**an·ti·im·mu·no·glob·u·lin** \ˌan-tē-i-myə-nō-ˈglä-byə-lən, ˌan-ˌtī-, -ˌi-ˌmyü-nō-\ *adj* : acting against specific antibodies (~ antibodies) (~ sera)

²**anti-immunoglobulin** *n* : an anti-immunoglobulin substance

¹**an·ti·in·fec·tive** \-in-ˈfek-tiv\ *adj* : used against or tending to counteract or prevent infection (~ agents)

²**anti-infective** *n* : an anti-infective agent

¹**an·ti·in·flam·ma·to·ry** \-in-ˈfla-mə-ˌtōr-ē\ *adj* : counteracting inflammation

²**anti-inflammatory** *n, pl* -ries : an anti-inflammatory agent (as a drug)

¹**an·ti·in·su·lin** \-ˈin-sə-lən\ *adj* : tending to counteract the physiological action of insulin

²**anti-insulin** *n* : an anti-insulin substance

an·ti·ke·to·gen·ic \-ˈje-nik\ *adj* : tending to prevent or counteract ketosis

an·ti·leu·ke·mic \-lü-ˈkē-mik\ *also* **an·ti·leu·ke·mia** \-mē-ə\ *adj* : counteracting the effects of leukemia

an·ti·lu·et·ic \-lü-ˈe-tik\ *n* : ANTISYPHILITIC

an·ti·lym·pho·cyte globulin \-ˈlim-fə-ˌsīt-\ *n* : serum globulin containing antibodies against lymphocytes that is used similarly to antilymphocyte serum

antilymphocyte serum *n* : a serum containing antibodies against lymphocytes that is used for suppressing graft rejection

an·ti·lym·pho·cyt·ic globulin \-ˌlim-fə-ˈsi-tik-\ *n* : ANTILYMPHOCYTE GLOBULIN

antilymphocytic serum *n* : ANTILYMPHOCYTE SERUM

¹**an·ti·ma·lar·i·al** \-mə-ˈler-ē-əl\ *or* **an·ti·ma·lar·ia** \-ə\ *adj* : serving to prevent, check, or cure malaria

²**antimalarial** *n* : an antimalarial drug

an·ti·me·tab·o·lite \-mə-ˈta-bə-ˌlīt\ *n* : a substance (as a sulfa drug) that replaces or inhibits the utilization of a metabolite

¹**an·ti·mi·cro·bi·al** \-mī-ˈkrō-bē-əl\ *also* **an·ti·mi·cro·bic** \-ˈkrō-bik\ *adj* : destroying or inhibiting the growth of microorganisms (~ drugs)

²**antimicrobial** *also* **antimicrobic** *n* : an antimicrobial substance

¹**an·ti·mi·tot·ic** \-mi-ˈtä-tik\ *adj* : inhibiting or disrupting mitosis (~ agents) (~ activity)

²**antimitotic** *n* : an antimitotic substance

an·ti·mo·ny \ˈan-tə-ˌmō-nē\ *n, pl* -nies : a metalloid element that is commonly silvery white, crystalline, and brittle and is used in medicine as a constituent of various antiprotozoal agents (as tartar emetic) — symbol *Sb*; see ELEMENT TABLE

antimonyltartrate — see POTASSIUM ANTIMONYLTARTRATE

antimony potassium tartrate *n* : TARTAR EMETIC

an·ti·mus·ca·rin·ic \-ˌməs-kə-ˈri-nik\ *adj* : inhibiting muscarinic physiological effects (an ~ agent)

an·ti·mu·ta·gen·ic \-ˌmyü-tə-ˈje-nik\ *adj* : reducing the rate of mutation (~ substances)

an·ti·my·cin A \ˌan-ti-ˌmīs-ᵊn-ˈā\ *n* : a crystalline antibiotic $C_{28}H_{40}N_2O_9$ used esp. as a fungicide, insecticide, and miticide — called also *antimycin*

an·ti·my·cot·ic \,an-ti-mī-ˈkä-tik, ,an-,tī-\ *adj or n* : ANTIFUNGAL

an·ti·nau·sea \-ˈnȯ-zē-ə, -sē-; -ˈnȯ-zhə, -shə\ *also* **an·ti·nau·se·ant** \-ˈnȯ-zē-ənt, -zhē-, -sē-, -shē-\ *adj* : preventing or counteracting nausea (~ drugs)

an·ti·nau·se·ant \-ˈnȯ-zē-ənt, -zhē-, -sē-, -shē-\ *n* : an antinausea agent

¹**an·ti·neo·plas·tic** \-ˌnē-ə-ˈplas-tik\ *adj* : inhibiting or preventing the growth and spread of neoplasms or malignant cells (~ drugs)

²**antineoplastic** *n* : an antineoplastic agent

an·ti·neu·rit·ic \-nu̇-ˈri-tik, -nyu̇-\ *adj* : preventing or relieving neuritis

an·ti·no·ci·cep·tive \,an-ti-nō-si-ˈsep-tiv, ,an-ˌtī-\ *adj* : ANALGESIC

an·ti·nu·cle·ar \-ˈnü-klē-ər, -ˈnyü-\ *adj* : tending to react with cell nuclei or their components (as DNA)

an·ti·ox·i·dant \-ˈäk-sə-dənt\ *n* : a substance (as beta-carotene or alpha‑tocopherol) that inhibits oxidation or reactions promoted by oxygen or peroxides — **antioxidant** *adj*

an·ti·par·a·sit·ic \-ˌpar-ə-ˈsi-tik\ *adj* : acting against parasites

an·ti·par·kin·so·nian \-ˌpär-kən-ˈsō-nē-ən, -nyən\ *also* **an·ti·par·kin·son** \-ˈpär-kən-sən\ *adj* : tending to relieve parkinsonism (~ drugs)

¹**an·ti·pe·ri·od·ic** \-ˌpir-ē-ˈä-dik\ *adj* : preventing periodic returns of disease

²**antiperiodic** *n* : an antiperiodic agent

an·ti·peri·stal·sis \-ˌper-ə-ˈstȯl-səs, -ˈstäl-, -ˈstal-\ *n, pl* **-stal·ses** \-ˌsēz\ : reversed peristalsis

an·ti·peri·stal·tic \-tik\ *adj* **1** : opposed to or checking peristaltic motion **2** : relating to antiperistalsis

an·ti·per·spi·rant \-ˈpər-spə-rənt\ *n* : a preparation used to check perspiration

an·ti·phlo·gis·tic \-flə-ˈjis-tik\ *adj or n* : ANTI-INFLAMMATORY

an·ti·plas·min \-ˈplaz-mən\ *n* : a substance (as an antifibrinolysin) that inhibits the action of plasmin

an·ti·plate·let \-ˈplāt-lət\ *adj* : acting against or destroying blood platelets

an·ti·pneu·mo·coc·cal \-ˌnü-mə-ˈkä-kəl, -ˌnyü-\ *or* **an·ti·pneu·mo·coc·cic** \-ˈkäk-(ˌ)sik\ *or* **an·ti·pneu·mo·coc·cus** \-ˈkä-kəs\ *adj* : destroying or inhibiting pneumococci

an·ti·pro·lif·er·a·tive \-prə-ˈli-fə-ˌrā-tiv\ *adj* : used or tending to inhibit cell growth (~ effects on tumor cells)

an·ti·pro·te·ase \-ˈprō-tē-ˌās, -ˌāz\ *n* : a substance that inhibits the enzymatic activity of a protease

an·ti·pro·throm·bin \-(ˌ)prō-ˈthräm-bən\ *n* : a substance that interferes with the conversion of prothrombin to thrombin — compare ANTITHROMBIN, HEPARIN

¹**an·ti·pro·to·zo·al** \-ˌprō-tə-ˈzō-əl\ *adj* : tending to destroy or inhibit the growth of protozoa

²**antiprotozoal** *n* : an antiprotozoal agent

¹**an·ti·pru·rit·ic** \-prü-ˈri-tik\ *adj* : tending to check or relieve itching

²**antipruritic** *n* : an antipruritic agent

an·ti·pseu·do·mo·nal \-ˌsü-də-ˈmōn-əl, -sü-ˈdä-mən-əl\ *adj* : tending to destroy bacteria of the genus *Pseudomonas* (~ activity)

an·ti·psy·chot·ic \-sī-ˈkä-tik\ *n or adj* : NEUROLEPTIC

an·ti·py·re·sis \-ˌpī-ˈrē-səs, -ˌpī-\ *n, pl* **-re·ses** \-ˌsēz\ : treatment of fever by use of antipyretics

¹**an·ti·py·ret·ic** \-pī-ˈre-tik\ *n* : an antipyretic agent — called also *febrifuge*

²**antipyretic** *adj* : preventing, removing, or allaying fever

an·ti·py·rine \-ˈpīr-ˌēn\ *also* **an·ti·py·rin** \-ən\ *n* : an analgesic and antipyretic $C_{11}H_{12}N_2O$ formerly widely used but now largely replaced in oral use by less toxic drugs (as aspirin) — called also *phenazone*

¹**an·ti·ra·chit·ic** \-rə-ˈki-tik\ *adj* : used or tending to prevent the development of rickets (an ~ vitamin)

²**antirachitic** *n* : an antirachitic agent

an·ti·re·jec·tion \-ri-ˈjek-shən\ *adj* : used or tending to prevent organ transplant rejection (~ drugs)

an·ti·ret·ro·vi·ral \-ˈre-trō-ˌvi-rəl\ *adj* : acting, used, or effective against retroviruses (~ drugs) (~ therapy)

¹**an·ti·rheu·mat·ic** \-ru̇-ˈma-tik\ *adj* : alleviating or preventing rheumatism

²**antirheumatic** *n* : an antirheumatic agent

an·ti·schis·to·so·mal \-ˌshis-tə-ˈsō-məl\ *adj* : tending to destroy or inhibit the development and reproduction of schistosomes

an·ti·schizo·phren·ic \-ˌskit-sə-ˈfre-nik\ *adj* : tending to relieve or suppress the symptoms of schizophrenia

¹**an·ti·scor·bu·tic** \-skȯr-ˈbyü-tik\ *adj* : counteracting scurvy (the ~ vitamin is vitamin C)

²**antiscorbutic** *n* : a remedy for scurvy

an·ti·se·cre·to·ry \-ˈsē-krə-ˌtȯr-ē\ *adj* : tending to inhibit secretion

an·ti·sei·zure \-ˈsē-zhər\ *adj* : preventing or counteracting seizures (~ drugs)

an·ti·sense ¹**an-ˌtī-ˌsens**, **an-ti-** *adj* : having a complementary sequence to a segment of genetic material (as mRNA) and serving to inhibit gene function (~ nucleotides) — compare MISSENSE, NONSENSE

an·ti·sep·sis \ˌan-tə-ˈsep-səs\ *n, pl* **-sep·ses** \-ˌsēz\ : the inhibiting of the growth and multiplication of microorganisms by antiseptic means

¹**an·ti·sep·tic** \ˌan-tə-ˈsep-tik\ *adj* **1 a** : opposing sepsis, putrefaction, or decay; *esp* : preventing or arresting the growth of microorganisms (as on living tissue) **b** : acting or protecting like an antiseptic **2** : relating to or characterized by the use of antiseptics **3** : free of living microorganisms : scru-

pulously clean : ASEPTIC — **an·ti·sep·ti·cal·ly** \-ti-k(ə-)lē\ *adv*

²**antiseptic** *n* : a substance that checks the growth or action of microorganisms esp. in or on living tissue; *also* : GERMICIDE

an·ti·se·rum \ˈan-ti-ˌsir-əm, ˈan-ˌtī-, -ˌser-\ *n* : a serum containing antibodies — called also *immune serum*

an·ti·so·cial \ˈsō-shəl\ *adj* : hostile or harmful to organized society: as a : being or marked by behavior deviating sharply from the social norm b : PSYCHOPATHIC (~ personality disorder)

¹**an·ti·spas·mod·ic** \-spaz-ˈmä-dik\ *n* : an antispasmodic agent

²**antispasmodic** *adj* : capable of preventing or relieving spasms or convulsions

an·ti·sperm \-ˈspərm\ *adj* : destroying or inactivating sperm (~ pills)

an·ti·strep·to·coc·cal \-ˌstrep-tə-ˈkä-kəl\ *or* **an·ti·strep·to·coc·cic** \-ˈkä-kik, -ˈkäk-sik\ *adj* : tending to destroy or inhibit the growth and reproduction of streptococci (~ antibodies)

an·ti·strep·to·ki·nase \-ˌstrep-tō-ˈkī-ˌnās, -ˌnāz\ *n* : ANTIFIBRINOLYSIN

an·ti·strep·to·ly·sin \-ˌstrep-tə-ˈlīs-ᵊn\ *n* : an antibody against a streptolysin produced by an individual injected with a streptolysin-forming streptococcus

¹**an·ti·syph·i·lit·ic** \-ˌsi-fə-ˈli-tik\ *adj* : effective against syphilis (~ treatment)

²**antisyphilitic** *n* : an antisyphilitic agent

an·ti·throm·bin \-ˈthräm-bən\ *n* : any of a group of substances in blood that inhibit blood clotting by inactivating thrombin — compare ANTIPROTHROMBIN, HEPARIN

an·ti·throm·bo·plas·tin \-ˌthräm-bə-ˈplas-tən\ *n* : an anticoagulant substance that counteracts the effects of thromboplastin

an·ti·throm·bot·ic \-thräm-ˈbä-tik\ *adj* : used against or tending to prevent thrombosis (~ agents) (~ therapy)

an·ti·thy·roid \-ˈthī-ˌroid\ *adj* : able to counteract excessive thyroid activity (~ drugs)

an·ti·tox·ic \-ˈtäk-sik\ *adj* 1 : counteracting toxins 2 : being or containing antitoxins (~ serum)

an·ti·tox·in \ˌan-ti-ˈtäk-sən\ *n* : an antibody that is capable of neutralizing the specific toxin (as a specific causative agent of disease) that stimulated its production in the body and is produced in animals for medical purposes by injection of a toxin or toxoid with the resulting serum being used to counteract the toxin in other individuals; *also* : an antiserum containing antitoxins

an·ti·trag·i·cus \ˌan-ti-ˈtra-jə-kəs\ *n, pl -i·ci* \-jə-ˌsī, -ˌsē\ : a small muscle arising from the outer part of the antitragus and inserted into the antihelix

an·ti·tra·gus \-ˈtrā-gəs\ *n, pl -gi* \-ˌjī, -ˌgī\ : a prominence on the lower posterior portion of the concha of the external ear opposite the tragus

an·ti·try·pano·som·al \-tri-ˌpa-nə-ˈsō-məl\ *or* **an·ti·try·pano·some** \-tri-ˈpa-nə-ˌsōm\ *adj* : TRYPANOCIDAL

an·ti·tryp·sin \ˈan-ti-ˈtrip-sən, ˌan-ˌtī-\ *n* : a substance that inhibits the action of trypsin — see ALPHA-1-ANTITRYPSIN — **an·ti·tryp·tic** \-ˈtrip-tik\ *adj*

an·ti·tu·ber·cu·lous \ˌan-ti-tü-ˈbər-kyə-ləs, ˌan-ˌtī-, -tyü-\ *or* **an·ti·tu·ber·cu·lo·sis** \-bər-kyə-ˈlō-səs\ *also* **an·ti·tu·ber·cu·lar** \-ˈbər-kyə-lər\ *adj* : used for or effective against tuberculosis

an·ti·tu·mor \ˈan-ti-ˈtü-mər, ˈan-ˌtī-, -tyü\ *also* **an·ti·tu·mor·al** \-mə-rəl\ *adj* : ANTICANCER (~ agents)

¹**an·ti·tus·sive** \ˌan-ti-ˈtə-siv, -ˌtī-\ *adj* : tending or having the power to act as a cough suppressant (~ action)

²**antitussive** *n* : a cough suppressant

an·ti·ty·phoid \-ˈtī-ˌfoid, -ˌtī-ˈfoid\ *adj* : tending to prevent or cure typhoid

an·ti·ul·cer \-ˈəl-sər\ *adj* : tending to prevent or heal ulcers (~ drugs)

an·ti·ven·in \-ˈve-nən\ *n* : an antitoxin to a venom; *also* : an antiserum containing such an antitoxin

An·ti·vert \ˈan-ti-ˌvərt, -ˌtī-\ *trademark* — used for a preparation of the hydrochloride of meclizine

an·ti·vi·ral \ˌan-ti-ˈvī-rəl, ˌan-ˌtī-\ *also* **an·ti·vi·rus** \-ˈvī-rəs\ *adj* : acting, effective, or directed against viruses (~ drugs)

an·ti·vi·ta·min \ˈan-ti-ˌvī-tə-mən, ˈan-ˌtī-\ *n* : a substance that makes a vitamin metabolically ineffective

antr- *or* **antro-** *comb form* : antrum (*antrostomy*)

an·tral \ˈan-trəl\ *adj* : of or relating to an antrum

an·trec·to·my \an-ˈtrek-tə-mē\ *n, pl -mies* : excision of an antrum (as of the stomach or mastoid)

an·tros·to·my \an-ˈträs-tə-mē\ *n, pl -mies* : the operation of opening an antrum (as for drainage); *also* : the opening made in such an operation

an·trot·o·my \-ˈträ-tə-mē\ *n, pl -mies* : incision of an antrum; *also* : ANTROSTOMY

an·trum \ˈan-trəm\ *n, pl* **an·tra** \-trə\ : the cavity of a hollow organ or a sinus (the ~ of the Graafian follicle)

antrum of High·more \-ˈhī-ˌmōr\ *n* : MAXILLARY SINUS

Highmore, Nathaniel (1613–1685), British surgeon.

anu·cle·ate \(ˌ)ā-ˈnü-klē-ət, -ˈnyü-\ *also* **anu·cle·at·ed** \-klē-ˌā-təd\ *adj* : lacking a cell nucleus

an·u·lus fibrosus *var of* ANNULUS FIBROSUS

an·uria \ə-ˈnu̇r-ē-ə, a-, -ˈnyu̇r-\ *n* : absence of or defective urine excretion — **an·uric** \-ˈnu̇r-ik, -ˈnyu̇r-\ *adj*

anus \ˈā-nəs\ *n, pl* **anus·es** *or* **ani** \ˈā-

(ˌ)nī\ : the posterior opening of the alimentary canal

an·vil \ˈan-vəl\ n : INCUS

anx·i·e·ty \aŋ-ˈzī-ə-tē\ n, pl **-eties 1 a** : a painful or apprehensive uneasiness of mind usu. over an impending or anticipated ill **b** : a cause of anxiety **2** : an abnormal and overwhelming sense of apprehension and fear often marked by physiological signs (as sweating, tension, and increased pulse), by doubt concerning the reality and nature of the threat, and by self-doubt about one's capacity to cope with it

anxiety neurosis n : a psychoneurotic disorder characterized by anxiety unattached to any obvious source and often accompanied by physiological manifestations of fear (as sweating, cardiac disturbances, diarrhea, or vertigo) — called also *anxiety reaction, anxiety state*

¹anx·io·lyt·ic \ˌaŋ-zē-ō-ˈli-tik, ˌaŋ-sē-\ n : a drug that relieves anxiety

²anxiolytic adj : relieving anxiety

anx·ious \ˈaŋk-shəs\ adj **1** : characterized by extreme uneasiness of mind or brooding fear about some contingency **2** : characterized by, resulting from, or causing anxiety

AOB abbr alcohol on breath

aort- or **aorto-** comb form **1** : aorta ⟨*aorti*tis⟩ **2** : aortic and ⟨*aorto*coronary⟩

aor·ta \ā-ˈȯr-tə\ n, pl **-tas** or **-tae** \-ˈtē\ : the large arterial trunk that carries blood from the heart to be distributed by branch arteries through the body

aor·tic \ā-ˈȯr-tik\ also **aor·tal** \-ˈȯrt-əl\ adj : of, relating to, or affecting an aorta (an ~ aneurysm)

aortic arch n : ARCH OF THE AORTA

aortic hiatus n : an opening in the diaphragm through which the aorta passes

aortic incompetence n : AORTIC REGURGITATION

aortic insufficiency n : AORTIC REGURGITATION

aor·ti·co·pul·mo·nary \ā-ˌȯr-tə-kō-ˈpȯl-mə-ˌner-ē, -ˈpəl-\ adj : relating to or joining the aorta and the pulmonary artery

aor·ti·co·re·nal \-ˈrēn-əl\ adj : relating to or situated near the aorta and the kidney

aortic regurgitation n : leakage of blood from the aorta back into the left ventricle during diastole because of failure of an aortic valve to close properly — called also *aortic incompetence, aortic insufficiency, Corrigan's disease*

aortic sinus n : SINUS OF VALSALVA

aortic stenosis n : a condition usu. the result of disease in which the aorta and esp. its orifice is abnormally narrow

aortic valve n : the semilunar valve separating the aorta from the left ventricle that prevents blood from flowing back into the left ventricle

aor·ti·tis \ˌā-ȯr-ˈtī-təs\ n : inflammation of the aorta

aor·to·cor·o·nary \ˌā-ˌȯr-tō-ˈkȯr-ə-ˌner-ē, -ˈkär-\ adj : of, relating to, or joining the aorta and the coronary arteries (~ bypass surgery)

aor·to·fem·o·ral \-ˈfe-mə-rəl\ adj : of, relating to, or joining the abdominal aorta and the femoral arteries (~ bypass graft)

aor·to·gram \ā-ˈȯr-tə-ˌgram\ n : an X-ray picture of the aorta made by arteriography

aor·tog·ra·phy \ˌā-ȯr-ˈtä-grə-fē\ n, pl **-phies** : arteriography of the aorta — **aor·to·graph·ic** \(ˌ)ā-ˌȯr-tə-ˈgra-fik\ adj

aor·to·il·i·ac \ˌā-ˌȯr-tō-ˈi-lē-ˌak\ adj : of, relating to, or joining the abdominal aorta and the iliac arteries

aor·to·pul·mo·nary window \ˌā-ˌȯr-tō-ˈpȯl-mə-ˌner-ē, -ˈpəl-\ n : a congenital circulatory defect in which there is direct communication between the aorta and the pulmonary artery — called also *aortopulmonary fenestration*

aor·to·sub·cla·vi·an \-ˌsəb-ˈklā-vē-ən\ adj : relating to or joining the aorta and the subclavian arteries

AOTA abbr American Occupational Therapy Association

ap- — see APO-

apar·a·lyt·ic \ˌā-ˌpar-ə-ˈli-tik\ adj : not characterized by paralysis

ap·a·thet·ic \ˌa-pə-ˈthe-tik\ adj : having or showing little or no feeling or emotion — **ap·a·thet·i·cal·ly** \-ti-k(ə-)lē\ adv

ap·a·thy \ˈa-pə-thē\ n, pl **-thies** : lack of feeling or emotion

ap·a·tite \ˈa-pə-ˌtīt\ n : any of a group of calcium phosphate minerals comprising the chief constituent of bones and teeth; specif : calcium phosphate fluoride $Ca_5F(PO_4)_3$

APC abbr aspirin, phenacetin, and caffeine

¹aper·i·ent \ə-ˈpir-ē-ənt\ adj : gently causing the bowels to move : LAXATIVE

²aperient n : an aperient agent

ape·ri·od·ic \ˌā-ˌpir-ē-ˈä-dik\ adj : of irregular occurrence

aperi·stal·sis \ˌā-ˌper-ə-ˈstȯl-səs, -ˈstäl-, -ˈstal-\ n, pl **-stal·ses** \-ˌsēz\ : absence of peristalsis

apex \ˈā-ˌpeks\ n, pl **apex·es** or **api·ces** \ˈā-pə-ˌsēz\ : a narrowed or pointed end of an anatomical structure: as **a** : the narrow somewhat conical upper part of a lung extending into the root **b** : the lower pointed end of the heart situated in humans opposite the space between the cartilages of the fifth and sixth ribs on the left side **c** : the extremity of the root of a tooth

apex·car·di·og·ra·phy \ˌā-ˌpeks-ˌkär-dē-ˈä-grə-fē\ n, pl **-phies** : a procedure for measuring the beat in the apex region of the heart by recording movements in the nearby wall of the chest

Ap·gar score \\'ap-₁gär-\ *n* : an index used to evaluate the condition of a newborn infant based on a rating of 0, 1, or 2 for each of the five characteristics of color, heart rate, response to stimulation of the sole of the foot, muscle tone, and respiration with 10 being a perfect score

Apgar, Virginia (1909–1974), American physician.

aph- — see APO-

apha·gia \ə-'fā-jə, a-, -jē-ə\ *n* : loss of the ability to swallow

apha·kia \ə-'fā-kē-ə, a-\ *n* : absence of the crystalline lens of the eye; *also* : the resulting anomalous state of refraction

[1]**apha·kic** \ə-'fā-kik, a-\ *adj* : of, relating to, or affected with aphakia

[2]**aphakic** *n* : an individual who has had the lens of an eye removed

apha·sia \ə-'fā-zhə, -zhē-ə\ *n* : loss or impairment of the power to use or comprehend words usu. resulting from brain damage — compare ANARTHRIA; see MOTOR APHASIA

[1]**apha·sic** \ə-'fā-zik\ *adj* : of, relating to, or affected with aphasia

[2]**aphasic** *or* **apha·si·ac** \ə-'fā-zē-₁ak, -zhē-\ *n* : an individual affected with aphasia

apha·si·ol·o·gy \ə-₁fā-zē-'ä-lə-jē, -zhē-\ *n*, *pl* **-gies** : the study of aphasia — **apha·si·ol·o·gist** \-jist\ *n*

aphe·re·sis \ə-fə-'rē-səs\ *n*, *pl* **-re·ses** \-₁sēz\ : PHERESIS

apho·nia \(₁)ā-'fō-nē-ə\ *n* : loss of voice and of all but whispered speech — **apho·nic** \-'fä-nik, -'fō-\ *adj*

aphos·pho·ro·sis \ā-₁fäs-fə-'rō-səs\ *n*, *pl* **-ro·ses** \-₁sēz\ : a deficiency disease esp. of domestic cattle caused by inadequate intake of dietary phosphorus

[1]**aph·ro·di·si·ac** \₁a-frə-'dē-zē-₁ak, -'di-\ *also* **aph·ro·di·si·a·cal** \₁a-frə-də-'zī-ə-kəl, -'si-\ *adj* : exciting sexual desire

[2]**aphrodisiac** *n* : an aphrodisiac agent

aph·tha \'af-thə\ *n*, *pl* **aph·thae** \-₁thē\ : a speck, flake, or blister on the mucous membranes (as of the mouth, gastrointestinal tract, or lips) — **aph·thous** \-thəs\ *adj*

aph·thoid \'af-₁thóid\ *adj* : having the characteristics of aphthae; *specif* : resembling thrush

aphthous fever *n* : FOOT-AND-MOUTH DISEASE

aphthous stomatitis *n* : a very common disorder of the oral mucosa that is characterized by the formation of canker sores on movable mucous membranes and that has a multiple etiology but is not caused by the virus causing herpes simplex

apic- *or* **apici-** *or* **apico-** *comb form* : apex : tip esp. of an organ (*apicectomy*)

api·cal \'ā-pi-kəl, 'a-\ *adj* : of, relating to, or situated at an apex — **api·cal·ly** \-k(ə-)lē\ *adv*

apical foramen *n* : the opening of the pulp canal in the root of a tooth

apic·ec·to·my \₁ā-pə-'sek-tə-mē\ *n*, *pl* **-mies** : surgical removal of an anatomical apex (as of the root of a tooth)

apices *pl of* APEX

api·co·ec·to·my \₁ā-pi-(₁)kō-'ek-tə-mē, ₁a-\ *n*, *pl* **-mies** : excision of the root tip of a tooth

apla·sia \(₁)ā-'plā-zhə, -zhē-ə, ə-\ *n* : incomplete or faulty development of an organ or part — **aplas·tic** \-'plas-tik\ *adj*

aplastic anemia *n* : anemia that is characterized by defective function of the blood-forming organs (as the bone marrow) and is caused by toxic agents (as chemicals or X rays) or is idiopathic in origin — called also *hypoplastic anemia*

ap·nea \'ap-nē-ə, ap-'nē-\ *n* 1 : transient cessation of respiration 2 : ASPHYXIA — **ap·ne·ic** \ap-'nē-ik\ *adj*

ap·neu·sis \ap-'nü-səs, -'nyü-\ *n*, *pl* **ap·neu·ses** \-₁sēz\ : sustained tonic contraction of the respiratory muscles resulting in prolonged inspiration — **ap·neus·tic** \-'nü-stik, -'nyü-\ *adj*

ap·noea \ap-'nē-ə, 'ap-nē-\ *chiefly Brit var of* APNEA

apo- *or* **ap-** *or* **aph-** *prefix* : formed from : related to (*apo*morphine)

apo·crine \'a-pə-krən, -₁krīn, -₁krēn\ *adj* : producing a fluid secretion by pinching off one end of the secreting cells which then reform and repeat the process; *also* : produced by an apocrine gland — compare ECCRINE, HOLOCRINE, MEROCRINE

apo·en·zyme \₁a-pō-'en-₁zīm\ *n* : a protein that forms an active enzyme system by combination with a coenzyme and determines the specificity of this system for a substrate

apo·fer·ri·tin \₁a-pə-'fer-ət-ən\ *n* : a colorless crystalline protein capable of storing iron in bodily cells esp. of the liver

apo·li·po·pro·tein \₁a-pə-₁lī-pō-'prō-₁tēn, -₁li-\ *n* : a protein that combines with a lipid to form a lipoprotein

apo·mor·phine \₁a-pə-'mȯr-₁fēn\ *n* : a crystalline morphine derivative $C_{17}H_{17}NO_2$ that is a dopamine agonist and is administered as the hydrochloride for its powerful emetic action

apo·neu·ro·sis \₁a-pə-nü-'rō-səs, -nyü-\ *n*, *pl* **-ro·ses** \-₁sēz\ : any of the broad flat sheets of dense fibrous collagenous connective tissue that cover, invest, and form the terminations and attachments of various muscles — **apo·neu·rot·ic** \-'rä-tik\ *adj*

aponeurotica — see GALEA APONEUROTICA

apoph·y·sis \ə-'pä-fə-səs\ *n*, *pl* **-y·ses** \-₁sēz\ : an expanded or projecting part esp. of an organism — **apoph·y·se·al** \-ˌpä-fə-ˈsē-əl\ *adj*

ap·o·plec·tic \ˌa-pə-ˈplek-tik\ *adj* **1** : of, relating to, or causing stroke **2** : affected with, inclined to, or showing symptoms of stroke — **ap·o·plec·ti·cal·ly** \-ti-k(ə-)lē\ *adv*

ap·o·plexy \ˈa-pə-ˌplek-sē\ *n, pl* **-plex·ies 1** : STROKE **2** : copious hemorrhage into a cavity or into the substance of an organ ⟨abdominal ~⟩ ⟨adrenal ~⟩

apo·pro·tein \ˌa-pə-ˈprō-ˌtēn\ *n* : a protein that combines with a prosthetic group to form a conjugated protein

apothecaries' measure *n* : a system of liquid units of measure used in compounding medical prescriptions that include the gallon, pint, fluid ounce, fluid dram, and minim

apothecaries' weight *n* : a system of weights used chiefly by pharmacists in compounding medical prescriptions that include the pound of 12 ounces, the dram of 60 grains, and the scruple

apoth·e·cary \ə-ˈpä-thə-ˌker-ē\ *n, pl* **-car·ies 1** : a person who prepares and sells drugs or compounds for medicinal purposes : DRUGGIST, PHARMACIST **2** : PHARMACY 2a

ap·pa·ra·tus \ˌa-pə-ˈra-təs, -ˈrā-\ *n, pl* **-tus·es** *or* **-tus** : a group of anatomical or cytological parts functioning together — see GOLGI APPARATUS

append- *or* **appendo-** *or* **appendic-** *or* **appendico-** *comb form* : vermiform appendix ⟨*append*ectomy⟩ ⟨*appendi*citis⟩

ap·pend·age \ə-ˈpen-dij\ *n* : a subordinate or derivative body part; *esp* : a limb or analogous part

ap·pen·dec·to·my \ˌa-pən-ˈdek-tə-mē\ *n, pl* **-mies** : surgical removal of the vermiform appendix

ap·pen·di·ceal \ə-ˌpen-də-ˈsē-əl\ *also* **ap·pen·di·cal** \ə-ˈpen-di-kəl\ *adj* : of, relating to, or involving the vermiform appendix ⟨~ inflammation⟩

ap·pen·di·cec·to·my \ə-ˌpen-də-ˈsek-tə-mē\ *n, pl* **-mies** *Brit* : APPENDECTOMY

ap·pen·di·ces epi·plo·i·cae \ə-ˈpen-də-ˌsēz-ˌe-pi-ˈploi-ˌsē\ *n pl* : small peritoneal pouches filled with fat that are situated along the large intestine

ap·pen·di·ci·tis \ə-ˌpen-də-ˈsī-təs\ *n* : inflammation of the vermiform appendix

ap·pen·dic·u·lar \ˌa-pən-ˈdi-kyə-lər\ *adj* : of or relating to an appendage: **a** : of or relating to a limb or limbs ⟨the ~ skeleton⟩ **b** : APPENDICEAL

ap·pen·dix \ə-ˈpen-diks\ *n, pl* **-dix·es** *or* **-di·ces** \-də-ˌsēz\ : a bodily outgrowth or process; *specif* : VERMIFORM APPENDIX

ap·per·ceive \ˌa-pər-ˈsēv\ *vb* **-ceived; -ceiv·ing** : to have apperception of

ap·per·cep·tion \ˌa-pər-ˈsep-shən\ *n* : mental perception; *esp* : the process of understanding something perceived in terms of previous experience — compare ASSIMILATION 3 —

ap·per·cep·tive \-ˈsep-tiv\ *adj*

ap·pe·stat \ˈa-pə-ˌstat\ *n* : the neural center in the brain that regulates appetite and is thought to be in the hypothalamus

ap·pe·tite \ˈa-pə-ˌtīt\ *n* : any of the instinctive desires necessary to keep up organic life; *esp* : the desire to eat — **ap·pe·ti·tive** \-ˌtī-tiv\ *adj*

ap·pla·na·tion \ˌa-plə-ˈnā-shən\ *n* : abnormal flattening of a convex surface (as of the cornea of the eye)

applanation tonometer *n* : an ophthalmologic instrument used to determine pressure within the eye by measuring the force necessary to flatten an area of the cornea with a small disk

ap·pli·ance \ə-ˈplī-əns\ *n* : an instrument or device designed for a particular use ⟨prosthetic ~s⟩

ap·pli·ca·tion \ˌa-plə-ˈkā-shən\ *n* **1** : an act of applying **2** : a medicated or protective layer or material

ap·pli·ca·tor \ˈa-plə-ˌkā-tər\ *n* : one that applies; *specif* : a device for applying a substance (as medicine)

ap·ply \ə-ˈplī\ *vb* **ap·plied; ap·ply·ing** : to lay or spread on

ap·po·si·tion \ˌa-pə-ˈzi-shən\ *n* **1** : the placing of things in juxtaposition or proximity; *specif* : deposition of successive layers upon those already present (as in cell walls) — compare ACCRETION **2** : the state of being in juxtaposition or proximity (as in the drawing together of cut edges of tissue in healing) — **ap·pose** \a-ˈpōz\ *vb* — **ap·po·si·tion·al** \ˌa-pə-ˈzi-shə-nəl\ *adj*

ap·proach \ə-ˈprōch\ *n* : the surgical procedure by which access is gained to a bodily part

approach–approach conflict *n* : psychological conflict that results when a choice must be made between two desirable alternatives — compare APPROACH-AVOIDANCE CONFLICT, AVOIDANCE-AVOIDANCE CONFLICT

approach–avoidance conflict *n* : psychological conflict that results when a goal is both desirable and undesirable — compare APPROACH-APPROACH CONFLICT, AVOIDANCE-AVOIDANCE CONFLICT

ap·prox·i·mate \ə-ˈpräk-sə-ˌmāt\ *vb* **-mat·ed; -mat·ing** : to bring together ⟨~ cut edges of tissue⟩

aprax·ia \ˌā-ˈprak-sē-ə\ *n* : loss or impairment of the ability to execute complex coordinated movements without impairment of the muscles or senses — **aprac·tic** \-ˈprak-tik\ *or* **aprax·ic** \-ˈprak-sik\ *adj*

apro·ti·nin \ā-ˈprō-tə-nin\ *n* : a polypeptide used for its proteinase-inhibiting properties esp. in the treatment of pancreatitis — see TRASYLOL

aptha *var of* APHTHA

ap·ti·tude \ˈap-tə-ˌtüd, -ˌtyüd\ *n* : a natural or acquired capacity or ability; *esp* : a tendency, capacity, or inclination to learn or understand

aptitude test *n* : a standardized test designed to predict an individual's ability to learn certain skills — compare INTELLIGENCE TEST

apy·rex·ia \ā-ₐpī-ˈrek-sē-ə, ₐa-pə-ˈrek-\ *n* : absence or intermission of fever

aqua \ˈa-kwə, ˈā-\ *n, pl* **aquae** \ˈa-(ₐ)kwē, ˈä-ₐkwī\ *or* **aquas** : WATER; *esp* : an aqueous solution

aq·ue·duct \ˈa-kwə-ₐdəkt\ *n* : a canal or passage in a part or organ

aqueduct of Syl·vi·us \-ˈsil-vē-əs\ *n* : a channel connecting the third and fourth ventricles of the brain — called also *cerebral aqueduct*
  Du·bois \dū-ˈbwä, dü-, dyü-\, **Jacques** (Latin, **Jacobus Sylvius**) (1478–1555), French anatomist.

¹**aque·ous** \ˈā-kwē-əs, ˈa-\ *adj* **1 a** : of, relating to, or resembling water (an ~ vapor) **b** : made from, with, or by water (an ~ solution) **2** : of or relating to the aqueous humor

²**aqueous** *n* : AQUEOUS HUMOR

aqueous flare *n* : FLARE 3

aqueous humor *n* : a transparent fluid occupying the space between the crystalline lens and the cornea of the eye

Ar *symbol* argon

ara-A \ₐär-ə-ˈā\ *n* : VIDARABINE

arab·i·nose \ə-ˈra-bə-ₐnōs, -ₐnōz\ *n* : a white crystalline aldose sugar $C_5H_{10}O_5$ occurring esp. in vegetable gums

ara·bi·no·side \ₐar-ə-ˈbi-nə-ₐsīd, ə-ˈra-bə-nō-ₐsīd\ *n* : a glycoside that yields arabinose on hydrolysis

ara·chi·don·ic acid \ₐar-ə-kə-ˈdä-nik-\ *n* : a liquid unsaturated fatty acid $C_{20}H_{32}O_2$ that occurs in most animal fats, is a precursor of prostaglandins, and is considered essential in animal nutrition

arachn- *or* **arachno-** *comb form* : spider ⟨*arachnodactyly*⟩

arach·nid \ə-ˈrak-nəd\ *n* : any of a large class of arthropods (Arachnida) comprising mostly air-breathing invertebrates, including the spiders and scorpions, mites, and ticks, and having a segmented body divided into two regions of which the anterior bears four pairs of legs but no antennae — **arach·nid** *adj*

arach·nid·ism \-nə-ₐdi-zəm\ *n* : poisoning caused by the bite or sting of an arachnid (as a spider, tick, or scorpion); *esp* : a syndrome marked by extreme pain and muscular rigidity due to the bite of a black widow spider

arach·no·dac·ty·ly \ə-ₐrak-nō-ˈdak-tə-lē\ *n, pl* **-lies** : a hereditary condition characterized esp. by excessive length of the fingers and toes

arach·noid \ə-ˈrak-ₐnȯid\ *n* : a thin membrane of the brain and spinal cord that lies between the dura mater and the pia mater — **arachnoid** *also* **arach·noi·dal** \ə-ₐrak-ˈnȯid-əl\ *adj*

arachnoid granulation *n* : any of the small whitish processes that are enlarged villi of the arachnoid membrane of the brain which protrude into the superior sagittal sinus and into depressions in the neighboring bone — called also *arachnoid villus, pacchionian body*

arach·noid·itis \ə-ₐrak-ₐnȯi-ˈdī-təs\ *n* : inflammation of the arachnoid membrane

ar·bor \ˈär-bər\ *n* : a branching anatomical structure resembling a tree

ar·bo·ri·za·tion \ₐär-bə-rə-ˈzā-shən\ *n* : a treelike figure or arrangement of branching parts; *esp* : a treelike part or process (as a dendrite) of a nerve cell

ar·bo·rize \ˈär-bə-ₐrīz\ *vb* **-rized; -riz·ing** : to branch freely and repeatedly

ar·bo·vi·rus \ˈär-bə-ˈvī-rəs\ *n* : any of a group of RNA viruses (as the causative agents of encephalitis, yellow fever, and dengue) transmitted by arthropods

ARC *abbr* **1** AIDS-related complex **2** American Red Cross

ar·cade \är-ˈkād\ *n* **1** : an anatomical structure comprising a series of arches **2** : DENTAL ARCH

arch \ˈärch\ *n* **1** : an anatomical structure that resembles an arch in form or function: as **a** : either of two vaulted portions of the bony structure of the foot that impart elasticity to it **b** : ARCH OF THE AORTA **2** : a fingerprint in which all the ridges run from side to side and make no backward turn

arch- *or* **archi-** *prefix* : primitive : original : primary ⟨*archenteron*⟩

arch·en·ter·on \är-ˈken-tə-ₐrän, -rən\ *n, pl* **-tera** \-tə-rə\ : the cavity of the gastrula of an embryo forming a primitive gut

ar·che·type \ˈär-ki-ₐtīp\ *n* : an inherited idea or mode of thought in the psychology of C. G. Jung that is derived from the experience of the race and is present in the unconscious of the individual — **ar·che·typ·al** \ₐär-ki-ˈtī-pəl\ *adj*

ar·chi·pal·li·um \ₐär-ki-ˈpa-lē-əm\ *n* : the olfactory part of the cerebral cortex comprising the hippocampus and the part of the hippocampal gyrus — compare NEOPALLIUM

ar·chi·tec·ton·ics \-tek-ˈtä-niks\ *n sing or pl* : the structural arrangement or makeup of an anatomical part or system — **ar·chi·tec·ton·ic** \-nik\ *adj*

ar·chi·tec·ture \ˈär-kə-ₐtek-chər\ *n* : the basic structural form esp. of a bodily part or of a large molecule — **ar·chi·tec·tur·al** \ₐär-kə-ˈtek-chə-rəl, -ˈtek-shrəl\ *adj* — **ar·chi·tec·tur·al·ly** *adv*

arch of the aorta *n* : the curved transverse part of the aorta that connects the ascending aorta with the descending aorta — called also *aortic arch*

ar·cu·ate \'är-kyə-wət, -ˌwāt\ adj : curved like a bow

arcuate artery n : any of the branches of the interlobar arteries of the kidney that form arches over the base of the pyramids

arcuate ligament — see LATERAL ARCUATE LIGAMENT, MEDIAL ARCUATE LIGAMENT, MEDIAN ARCUATE LIGAMENT

arcuate nucleus n : any of several cellular masses in the thalamus, hypothalamus, or medulla oblongata

arcuate popliteal ligament n : a triangular ligamentous band in the posterior part of the knee that passes medially downward from the lateral condyle of the femur to the area between the condyles of the tibia and to the head of the fibula — compare OBLIQUE POPLITEAL LIGAMENT

arcuate vein n : any of the veins of the kidney that accompany the arcuate arteries, drain blood from the interlobular veins, and empty into the interlobar veins

ar·cus \'är-kəs\ n, pl **arcus** : an anatomical arch

arcus se·nil·is \-sə-'ni-ləs\ n. : a whitish ring-shaped or bow-shaped deposit in the cornea that frequently occurs in old age

ARDS abbr adult respiratory distress syndrome

ar·ea \'ar-ē-ə\ n : a part of the cerebral cortex having a particular function — see ASSOCIATION AREA, MOTOR AREA, SENSORY AREA

area po·stre·ma \-pōs-'trē-mə, -päs-\ n : a tongue-shaped structure in the caudal region of the fourth ventricle of the brain

areata — see ALOPECIA AREATA

arec·o·line \ə-'re-kə-ˌlēn\ n : a toxic parasympathomimetic alkaloid $C_8H_{13}NO_2$ that is used as a veterinary anthelmintic and occurs naturally in betel nuts

are·flex·ia \ˌā-ri-'flek-sē-ə\ n : absence of reflexes — **are·flex·ic** \-'flek-sik\ adj

ar·ena·vi·rus \ˌar-ə-nə-'vī-rəs\ n : any of a group of viruses containing a single strand of RNA, having a grainy appearance due to the presence of ribosomes in the virion, and including the Machupo virus and the causative agents of lymphocytic choriomeningitis and Lassa fever

are·o·la \ə-'rē-ə-lə\ n, pl **-lae** \-ˌlē\ or **-las 1** : the colored ring around the nipple or around a vesicle or pustule **2** : the portion of the iris that borders the pupil of the eye

are·o·lar \-lər\ adj **1** : of, relating to, or like an areola **2** : of, relating to, or consisting of areolar tissue

areolar tissue n : fibrous connective tissue having the fibers loosely arranged in a net or meshwork

Ar·gas \'är-gəs, -ˌgas\ n : a genus of ticks (family Argasidae) including the fowl ticks (as A. persicus)

argent- or **argenti-** or **argento-** comb form : silver (argentophil)

ar·gen·taf·fin cell \är-'jen-tə-fən-\ or **ar·gen·taf·fine cell** \-fon-, -ˌfēn-\ n : one of the specialized epithelial cells of the gastrointestinal tract that stain readily with silver salts

ar·gen·to·phil \är-'jen-tə-ˌfil\ or **ar·gen·to·phile** \-ˌfil\ or **ar·gen·to·phil·ic** \-ˌjen-tə-'fi-lik\ adj : having an affinity for silver — used of certain cells, structures, or tissues

ar·gi·nine \'är-jə-ˌnēn\ n : a crystalline basic amino acid $C_6H_{14}N_4O_2$ derived from guanidine

ar·gon \'är-ˌgän\ n : a colorless odorless inert gaseous element — symbol Ar; see ELEMENT table

Ar·gyll Rob·ert·son pupil \'är-gil-'rä-bərt-sən-, är-'gil-\ n : a pupil characteristic of neurosyphilis that fails to react to light but still reacts in accommodation to distance

Robertson, Douglas Argyll (1837–1909), British ophthalmologist.

argyr- or **argyro-** comb form : silver (argyria)

ar·gyr·ia \är-'jir-ē-ə\ n : permanent dark discoloration of skin caused by overuse of medicinal silver preparations

Ar·gy·rol \'är-jə-ˌról, -ˌról\ trademark — used for a silver-protein compound whose aqueous solution is used as a local antiseptic esp. for mucous membranes

ar·gy·ro·phil \'är-jə-(ˌ)rō-ˌfil, -rə-\ or **ar·gy·ro·phile** \-ˌfil\ or **ar·gy·ro·phil·ic** \ˌär-jə-(ˌ)rō-'fi-lik, -rə-\ adj : ARGENTOPHIL (~ cytoplasmic inclusions)

ari·bo·fla·vin·osis \ˌā-ˌrī-bə-ˌflā-və-'nō-səs\ n, pl **-oses** \-ˌsēz\ : a deficiency disease due to inadequate intake of riboflavin and characterized by sores on the mouth

arith·mo·ma·nia \ə-ˌrith-mō-'mā-nē-ə, -nyə\ n : a morbid compulsion to count objects

-ar·i·um \'ar-ē-əm\ n suffix, pl **-ariums** or **-aria** \-ē-ə\ : thing or place belonging to or connected with (sanitarium)

arm \'ärm\ n **1** : a human upper limb; esp : the part between the shoulder and the wrist **2 a** : the forelimb of a vertebrate other than a human being **b** : a limb of an invertebrate animal **c** : any of the usu. two parts of a chromosome lateral to the centromere — **armed** \'ärmd\ adj

ar·ma·men·tar·i·um \ˌär-mə-ˌmen-'ter-ē-əm, -mən-\ n, pl **-tar·ia** \-ē-ə\ : the equipment and methods used esp. in medicine

arm·pit \'ärm-ˌpit\ n : the hollow beneath the junction of the arm and shoulder : AXILLA

aro·ma·ther·a·py \ə-ˌrō-mə-'ther-ə-pē\ n, pl **-pies** : massage of the body and esp. of the face with a preparation of fragrant essential oils extracted from herbs, flowers, and fruits — **aro·ma·ther·a·pist** \-pist\ *n*

aromatic ammonia spirit *n* : a solution of ammonia and ammonium carbonate in alcohol and distilled water used as a stimulant, carminative, and antacid — called also *aromatic spirit of ammonia*

arous·al \ə-ˈraú-zəl\ *n* : the act of arousing : state of being aroused (sexual ~); *specif* : responsiveness to stimuli

arouse \ə-ˈraúz\ *vb* **aroused; arousing** : to rouse or stimulate to action or to physiological readiness for activity

ar·rec·tor pi·li muscle \ə-ˈrek-tər-ˈpi-ˌlī-, -ˈpi-lē-\ *n* : one of the small fan-shaped smooth muscles associated with the base of each hair that contract when the body surface is chilled and erect the hairs, compress an oil gland above each muscle, and produce the appearance of goose bumps

¹**ar·rest** \ə-ˈrest\ *vb* : to bring to a standstill or state of inactivity

²**arrest** *n* : the condition of being stopped — see CARDIAC ARREST

ar·rhe·no·blas·to·ma \ˌar-ə-ˌnō-ˌbla-ˈstō-mə, ə-ˌrē-ˌnō-\ *n*, *pl* **-mas** *also* **-ma·ta** \-mə-tə\ : a sometimes malignant tumor of the ovary that by the secretion of male hormone induces development of secondary male characteristics — compare GYNANDRO-BLASTOMA

ar·rhyth·mia \ā-ˈrith-mē-ə\ *n* : an alteration in rhythm of the heartbeat either in time or force

ar·rhyth·mic \-mik\ *adj* : lacking rhythm or regularity

ar·row·root \ˈar-ō-ˌrüt, -ˌrút\ *n* : an easily digested starch obtained from the rootstock of a tropical American plant (esp. *Maranta arundinacea* of the family Marantaceae)

ARRT *abbr* **1** American registered respiratory therapist **2** American Registry of Radiologic Technologists

ars- *comb form* : arsenic (*arsine*) (*ars*phenamine)

arse·nate \ˈär-sə-nət, -ˌnāt\ *n* : a salt or ester of an arsenic acid

¹**ar·se·nic** \-nik\ *n* **1** : a solid poisonous element that is commonly metallic steel-gray, crystalline, and brittle — symbol *As*; see ELEMENT table **2** : ARSENIC TRIOXIDE

²**ar·sen·ic** \är-ˈse-nik\ *adj* : of, relating to, or containing arsenic esp. with a valence of five

arsenic acid \är-ˈse-nik-\ *n* : any of three arsenic-containing acids that are analogous to the phosphoric acids

¹**ar·sen·i·cal** \är-ˈse-ni-kəl\ *adj* : of, relating to, containing, or caused by arsenic (~ poisoning)

²**arsenical** *n* : a compound or preparation containing arsenic

ar·se·nic trioxide \ˈär-sə-nik-\ *n* : a poisonous trioxide As_2O_3 or As_4O_6 of arsenic that was formerly used in medicine and dentistry and is now used esp. as an insecticide and weed killer — called also *arsenic*

ar·sine \är-ˈsēn, ˈär-ˌ\ *n* : a colorless flammable extremely poisonous gas AsH_3 with an odor like garlic

ars·phen·a·mine \ärs-ˈfe-nə-ˌmēn, -mən\ *n* : a toxic powder $C_{12}Cl_2$-$H_{14}As_2N_2O_2 \cdot 2H_2O$ formerly used in the treatment esp. of syphilis and yaws — called also *salvarsan*, *six-o-six*

ART *abbr* accredited record technician

ar·te·fact *chiefly Brit var of* ARTIFACT

ar·te·ria \är-ˈtir-ē-ə\ *n*, *pl* **-ri·ae** \-ē-ˌē\ : ARTERY

arteri- *or* **arterio-** *comb form* **1** : artery (*arteriography*) **2** : arterial and (*arteriovenous*)

ar·te·ri·al \är-ˈtir-ē-əl\ *adj* **1** : of or relating to an artery **2** : relating to or being the bright red blood present in most arteries that has been oxygenated in lungs or gills — compare VENOUS **3** — **ar·te·ri·al·ly** *adv*

ar·te·rio·gram \är-ˈtir-ē-ə-ˌgram\ *n* : a roentgenogram of an artery made by arteriography

ar·te·ri·og·ra·phy \är-ˌtir-ē-ˈä-grə-fē\ *n*, *pl* **-phies** : the roentgenographic visualization of an artery after injection of a radiopaque substance — **ar·te·rio·graph·ic** \-ē-ə-ˈgra-fik\ *adj* — **ar·te·rio·graph·i·cal·ly** \-fi-k(ə-)lē\ *adv*

ar·te·ri·ola \är-ˌtir-ē-ˈō-lə\ *n*, *pl* **-lae** \-ˌlē\ : ARTERIOLE

ar·te·ri·ole \är-ˈtir-ē-ˌōl\ *n* : any of the small terminal twigs of an artery that ends in capillaries — **ar·te·ri·o·lar** \-ˌtir-ē-ˈō-ˌlär, -lər\ *adj*

ar·te·ri·o·li·tis \är-ˌtir-ē-ō-ˈlī-təs\ *n* : inflammation of the arterioles

ar·te·rio·lu·mi·nal \är-ˌtir-ē-ō-ˈlü-mən-ᵊl\ *adj* : relating to or being the small vessels that branch from the arterioles of the heart and empty directly into its lumen

ar·te·ri·op·a·thy \är-ˌtir-ē-ˈä-pə-thē\ *n*, *pl* **-thies** : a disease of the arteries

ar·te·ri·or·rha·phy \är-ˌtir-ē-ˈōr-ə-fē\ *n*, *pl* **-phies** : a surgical operation of suturing an artery

ar·te·rio·scle·ro·sis \är-ˌtir-ē-ō-sklə-ˈrō-səs\ *n*, *pl* **-ro·ses** \-ˌsēz\ : a chronic disease characterized by abnormal thickening and hardening of the arterial walls with resulting loss of elasticity

arteriosclerosis ob·lit·er·ans \-ə-ˈbli-tə-ˌranz\ *n* : chronic arteriosclerosis marked by occlusion of arteries and esp. those supplying the extremities

¹**ar·te·rio·scle·rot·ic** \-ˈrä-tik\ *adj* : of, relating to, or affected with arteriosclerosis

²**arteriosclerotic** *n* : an arteriosclerotic individual

arteriosi — see CONUS ARTERIOSUS

ar·te·rio·si·nu·soi·dal \är-ˌtir-ē-ō-ˌsi-nyə-ˈsóid-ᵊl, -nə-\ *adj* : relating to or being the vessels that connect the arterioles and sinusoids of the heart

ar·te·rio·spasm \är-ˈtir-ē-ō-ˌspa-zəm\ n : spasm of an artery — **ar·te·rio·spas·tic** \-ˌtir-ē-ō-ˈspas-tik\ adj

arteriosum — see LIGAMENTUM ARTERIOSUM

arteriosus — see CONUS ARTERIOSUS, DUCTUS ARTERIOSUS, PATENT DUCTUS ARTERIOSUS

ar·te·ri·ot·o·my \är-ˌtir-ē-ˈä-tə-mē\ n, pl -mies : the surgical incision of an artery

ar·te·rio·ve·nous \ˌär-ˌtir-ē-ō-ˈvē-nəs\ adj : of, relating to, or connecting the arteries and veins (∼ anastomoses)

ar·ter·i·tis \ˌär-tə-ˈrī-təs\ n : arterial inflammation — see GIANT CELL ARTERITIS — **ar·ter·it·ic** \-ˈri-tik\ adj

ar·tery \ˈär-tə-rē\ n, pl -ter·ies : any of the tubular branching muscular- and elastic-walled vessels that carry blood from the heart through the body

arthr- or **arthro-** comb form : joint ⟨arthralgia⟩ ⟨arthropathy⟩

ar·thral·gia \är-ˈthral-jə, -jē-ə\ n : pain in one or more joints — **ar·thral·gic** \-jik\ adj

ar·threc·to·my \är-ˈthrek-tə-mē\ n, pl -mies : surgical excision of a joint

¹ar·thrit·ic \är-ˈthri-tik\ adj : of, relating to, or affected with arthritis — **ar·thrit·i·cal·ly** \-ti-k(ə-)lē\ adv

²arthritic n : a person affected with arthritis

ar·thri·tis \är-ˈthrī-təs\ n, pl -thrit·i·des \-ˈthri-tə-ˌdēz\ : inflammation of joints due to infectious, metabolic, or constitutional causes; also : a specific arthritic condition (the gonococcal and pneumococcal arthritides)

arthritis de·for·mans \-dē-ˈfor-ˌmanz\ n : a chronic arthritis marked by deformation of affected joints

ar·thro·cen·te·sis \ˌär-(ˌ)thrō-sen-ˈtē-səs\ n, pl -te·ses \-ˌsēz\ : surgical puncture of a joint

ar·throd·e·sis \är-ˈthrä-də-səs\ n, pl -e·ses \-ˌsēz\ : the surgical immobilization of a joint so that the bones grow solidly together : artificial ankylosis

ar·thro·dia \är-ˈthrō-dē-ə\ n, pl -di·ae \-dē-ˌē\ : GLIDING JOINT

ar·thro·dys·pla·sia \ˌär-(ˌ)thrō-dis-ˈplā-zhə, zhē-ə, -zē-ə\ n : abnormal development of a joint

ar·thro·gram \ˈär-thrō-ˌgram\ n : a roentgenogram of a joint made by arthrography

ar·throg·ra·phy \är-ˈthrä-grə-fē\ n, pl -phies : the roentgenographic visualization of a joint after the injection of a radiopaque substance — **ar·thro·graph·ic** \ˌär-thrə-ˈgra-fik\ adj

ar·thro·gry·po·sis \ˌär-(ˌ)thrō-gri-ˈpō-səs\ n : permanent flexure of a joint

arthrogryposis mul·ti·plex con·gen·i·ta \ˈməl-tə-ˌpleks-kən-ˈje-nə-tə\ n : a congenital syndrome characterized by deformed joints with limited

movement, atrophy of muscles, and contractures

ar·throl·o·gy \är-ˈthrä-lə-jē\ n, pl -gies : a science concerned with the study of joints

ar·throp·a·thy \är-ˈthrä-pə-thē\ n, pl -thies : a disease of a joint

ar·thro·plas·ty \ˈär-thrə-ˌplas-tē\ n, pl -ties : plastic surgery of a joint : the operative formation or restoration of a joint

ar·thro·pod \ˈär-thrə-ˌpäd\ n : any of a phylum (Arthropoda) of invertebrate animals (as insects, arachnids, and crustaceans) having a segmented body and jointed appendages, usu. a shell of chitin molted at intervals, and an anterior brain dorsal to the alimentary canal and connected with a ventral chain of ganglia — **arthropod** adj — **ar·throp·o·dan** \är-ˈthrä-pəd-ᵊn\ adj

ar·thro·scope \ˈär-thrə-ˌskōp\ n : a surgical instrument for the visual examination of the interior of a joint (as the knee)

ar·thros·co·py \är-ˈthrä-skə-pē\ n, pl -pies : examination of a joint with an arthroscope; also : joint surgery using an arthroscope — **ar·thro·scop·ic** \ˌär-thrə-ˈskä-pik\ adj

ar·thro·sis \är-ˈthrō-səs\ n, pl -thro·ses \-ˌsēz\ 1 : an articulation or line of juncture between bones 2 : a degenerative disease of a joint

ar·throt·o·my \är-ˈthrä-tə-mē\ n, pl -mies : incision into a joint

Ar·thus reaction \ˈär-thəs-, är-ˈtūes-\ n : a reaction that follows injection of an antigen into an animal in which hypersensitivity has been previously established and that involves infiltrations, edema, sterile abscesses, and in severe cases gangrene — called also Arthus phenomenon

Arthus, Nicolas Maurice (1862-1945), French bacteriologist and physiologist.

ar·tic·u·lar \är-ˈti-kyə-lər\ adj : of or relating to a joint

articular capsule n : a ligamentous sac that surrounds the articular cavity of a freely movable joint, is attached to the bones, completely encloses the joint, and is composed of an outer fibrous membrane and an inner synovial membrane — called also joint capsule

articular cartilage n : cartilage that covers the articular surfaces of bones

articular disc n : a cartilage interposed between two articular surfaces and partially or completely separating the joint cavity into two compartments

articular process n : either of two processes on each side of a vertebra that articulate with adjoining vertebrae: a : one on each side of the neural arch that projects upward and articulates with an inferior articular process of the next more cranial vertebra —

called also *superior articular process* **b** : one on each side of the neural arch that projects downward and articulates with a superior articular process of the next more caudal vertebra — called also *inferior articular process*

ar·tic·u·late \är-ˈti-kyə-ˌlāt\ *vb* **-lat·ed; -lat·ing** 1 : to unite or be united by means of a joint (bones that ~ with each other) 2 : to arrange (artificial teeth) on an articulator

ar·tic·u·la·tion \är-ˌti-kyə-ˈlā-shən\ *n* 1 : the action or manner in which the parts come together at a joint 2 **a** : a joint between bones or cartilages in the vertebrate skeleton that is immovable when the bones are directly united, slightly movable when they are united by an intervening substance, or more or less freely movable when the articular surfaces are covered with smooth cartilage and surrounded by an articular capsule — see AMPHIARTHROSIS, DIARTHROSIS, SYNARTHROSIS **b** : a movable joint between rigid parts of any animal (as between the segments of an insect appendage) 3 **a** (1) : the act of properly arranging artificial teeth (2) : an arrangement of artificial teeth **b** : OCCLUSION 2a

ar·tic·u·la·tor \är-ˈti-kyə-ˌlā-tər\ *n* : an apparatus used in dentistry for obtaining correct articulation of artificial teeth

ar·tic·u·la·to·ry \är-ˈti-kyə-lə-ˌtōr-ē\ *adj* : of or relating to articulation

ar·ti·fact \ˈär-tə-ˌfakt\ *n* 1 : a product of artificial character due to usu. extraneous (as human) agency; *specif* : a product or formation in a microscopic preparation of a fixed tissue or cell that is caused by manipulation or reagents and is not indicative of actual structural relationships 2 : an electrocardiographic and electroencephalographic wave that arises from sources other than the heart or brain — **ar·ti·fac·tu·al** \ˌär-tə-ˈfak-chə-wəl, -shə-wəl\ *adj*

ar·ti·fi·cial \ˌär-tə-ˈfi-shəl\ *adj* : humanly contrived often on a natural model ⟨an ~ limb⟩ ⟨an ~ eye⟩ — **ar·ti·fi·cial·ly** *adv*

artificial insemination *n* : introduction of semen into the uterus or oviduct by other than natural means

artificial kidney *n* : an apparatus designed to do the work of the kidney during temporary stoppage of kidney function — called also *hemodialyzer*

artificial respiration *n* : the process of restoring or initiating breathing by forcing air into and out of the lungs to establish the rhythm of inspiration and expiration — see MOUTH-TO-MOUTH

ary·ep·i·glot·tic \ˌar-ē-ˌep-ə-ˈglä-tik\ *adj* : relating to or linking the arytenoid cartilage and the epiglottis ⟨~ folds⟩

¹**ary·te·noid** \ˌar-ə-ˈtē-ˌnȯid, ə-ˈrit-ᵊn-ˌȯid\ *adj* 1 : relating to or being either of two small cartilages to which the vocal cords are attached and which are situated at the upper back part of the larynx 2 : relating to or being either of a pair of small muscles or an unpaired muscle of the larynx

²**arytenoid** *n* : an arytenoid cartilage or muscle

ary·te·noi·dec·to·my \ˌar-ə-ˌtē-ˌnȯi-ˈdek-tə-mē, ə-ˌrit-ᵊn-ˌȯi-\ *n, pl* **-mies** : surgical excision of an arytenoid cartilage

ary·te·noi·do·pexy \ˌar-ə-tə-ˈnȯi-də-ˌpek-sē, ə-ˌrit-ᵊn-ˈȯid-\ *n, pl* **-pex·ies** : surgical fixation of arytenoid muscles or cartilages

As *symbol* arsenic

AS *abbr* 1 aortic stenosis 2 arteriosclerosis

ASA *abbr* [*acetylsalicylic acid*] aspirin

asa·fet·i·da *or* **asa·foet·i·da** \ˌa-sə-ˈfi-tə-də, -ˈfe-tə-də\ *n* : the fetid gum resin of various Asian plants (genus *Ferula*) of the carrot family (Umbelliferae) that was formerly used in medicine as an antispasmodic and in folk medicine as a general prophylactic against disease

as·bes·tos \as-ˈbes-təs, az-\ *n* : any of several minerals that readily separate into long flexible fibers, that have been implicated as causes of certain cancers, and that have been used esp. formerly as fireproof insulating materials

as·bes·to·sis \ˌas-ˌbes-ˈtō-səs, ˌaz-\ *n, pl* **-to·ses** \-ˌsēz\ : a pneumoconiosis due to asbestos particles

as·ca·ri·a·sis \ˌas-kə-ˈrī-ə-səs\ *n, pl* **-a·ses** \-ˌsēz\ : infestation with or disease caused by ascarids

as·car·i·cid·al \ə-ˌskar-ə-ˈsīd-ᵊl\ *adj* : capable of destroying ascarids

as·car·i·cide \ə-ˈskar-ə-ˌsīd\ *n* : an agent destructive of ascarids

as·ca·rid \ˈas-kə-rəd\ *n* : any of a family (Ascaridae) of nematode worms that are usu. parasitic in the intestines of vertebrates — see ASCARIDIA, ASCARIS — **ascarid** *adj*

As·ca·rid·ia \ˌas-kə-ˈri-dē-ə\ *n* : a genus of ascarid nematode worms that include an important intestinal parasite (*A. galli*) of some domestic fowl

as·ca·rid·i·a·sis \ə-ˌskar-ə-ˈdī-ə-səs\ *n, pl* **-a·ses** : ASCARIASIS

as·car·i·do·sis \ə-ˌskar-ə-ˈdō-səs\ *n, pl* **-do·ses** \-ˌsēz\ : ASCARIASIS

as·ca·ris \ˈas-kə-rəs\ *n* 1 *cap* : a genus of ascarid nematode worms that resemble earthworms in size and superficial appearance and include one (*A. lumbricoides*) parasitic in the human intestine 2 *pl* **as·car·i·des** \ə-ˈskar-ə-ˌdēz\ : ASCARID

As·ca·rops \ˈas-kə-ˌräps\ *n* : a genus of nematode worms (family Spiruridae) including a common reddish stomach worm (*A. strongylina*) of wild and domestic swine

as·cend \ə-'send\ *vb* : to move upward: as a : to conduct nerve impulses toward or to the brain b : to affect the extremities and esp. the lower limbs first and then the central nervous system

ascending aorta *n* : the part of the aorta from its origin to the beginning of the arch

ascending colon *n* : the part of the large intestine that extends from the cecum to the bend on the right side below the liver — compare DESCENDING COLON, TRANSVERSE COLON

ascending lumbar vein *n* : a longitudinal vein on each side that connects the lumbar veins and is frequently the origin of the azygos vein on the right side and of the hemiazygos vein on the left

ascending palatine artery *n* : PALATINE ARTERY 1a

Asch·heim–Zon·dek test \'äsh-,hīm-'zän-dik-, -'tsän-\ *n* : a test formerly used esp. to determine human pregnancy in its early stages on the basis of the effect of a subcutaneous injection of the patient's urine on the ovaries of an immature female mouse

Asch·heim \'äsh-,hīm\, Selmor Samuel (1878–1965), and Zon·dek \'tsón-,dek\, Bernhard (1891–1966), German obstetrician-gynecologists.

Asch·off body \'ä-,shof-\ *n* : one of the tiny lumps in heart muscle typical of rheumatic heart disease; *also* : one of the similar but larger lumps found under the skin esp. in rheumatic fever or polyarthritis — called also *Aschoff nodule*

Aschoff, Karl Albert Ludwig (1866–1942), German pathologist.

as·ci·tes \ə-'sī-tēz\ *n, pl* ascites : accumulation of serous fluid in the spaces between tissues and organs in the cavity of the abdomen — as·cit·ic \-'si-tik\ *adj*

as·co·my·cete \,as-kō-'mī-,sēt, -,mī-'sēt\ *n* : any of a class (Ascomycetes) or subdivision (Ascomycotina) of fungi (as yeasts or molds) with spores formed in asci — as·co·my·ce·tous \-,mī-'sē-təs\ *adj*

ascor·bate \ə-'skor-,bāt, -bət\ *n* : a salt of ascorbic acid

ascor·bic acid \ə-'skor-bik-\ *n* : VITAMIN C

ASCP *abbr* American Society of Clinical Pathologists

as·cus \'as-kəs\ *n, pl* as·ci \'as-,kī, -,kē; 'a-,sī\ : the oval or tubular spore case of an ascomycete

ASCVD *abbr* arteriosclerotic cardiovascular disease

-ase *n suffix* : enzyme ⟨protease⟩ ⟨urease⟩

asep·sis \(,)ā-'sep-səs, ə-\ *n, pl* asep·ses \-,sēz\ 1 : the condition of being aseptic 2 : the methods of producing or maintaining an aseptic condition

asep·tic \-'sep-tik\ *adj* 1 : preventing infection ⟨~ techniques⟩ 2 : free or freed from pathogenic microorganisms ⟨an ~ operating room⟩ — asep·ti·cal·ly \-ti-k(ə-)lē\ *adv*

asex·u·al \(,)ā-'sek-shə-wəl\ *adj* 1 : lacking sex or functional sexual organs 2 : produced without sexual action or differentiation ⟨~ spores⟩ — asex·u·al·ly *adv*

asexual generation *n* : a generation that reproduces only by asexual processes — used of organisms exhibiting alternation of generations

asexual reproduction *n* : reproduction (as spore formation, fission, or budding) without union of individuals or germ cells

ASHD *abbr* arteriosclerotic heart disease

Asian influenza *n* : influenza caused by a mutant strain of the influenza virus isolated during the 1957 epidemic in Asia — called also *Asian flu*

Asi·at·ic cholera \,ā-zhē-'a-tik-, -zē-\ *n* : cholera of Asian origin that is produced by virulent strains of the causative bacterium (*Vibrio cholerae*)

aso·cial \(,)ā-'sō-shəl\ *adj* : not social: as a : rejecting or lacking the capacity for social interaction b : ANTISOCIAL

as·par·ag·i·nase \,as-pə-'ra-jə-,nās, -,nāz\ *n* : an enzyme that hydrolyzes asparagine to aspartic acid and ammonia

L-asparaginase — see entry alphabetized as L-ASPARAGINASE

as·par·a·gine \ə-'spar-ə-,jēn\ *n* : a white crystalline amino acid $C_4H_8N_2O_3$ that is an amide of aspartic acid

as·par·tame \'as-pər-,tām, ə-'spär-\ *n* : a crystalline protein $C_{14}H_{18}N_2O_5$ that is derived from the amino acids phenylalanine and aspartic acid and is used as a low-calorie sweetener — see NUTRASWEET

as·par·tate \-,tāt\ *n* : a salt or ester of aspartic acid

as·par·tic acid \ə-'spär-tik-\ *n* : a crystalline amino acid $C_4H_7NO_4$ that is obtained from many proteins by hydrolysis

as·par·tyl \ə-'spär-təl, a-, -,tēl\ *n* : the bivalent radical $-OCCH_2CH(NH_2)-CO-$ of aspartic acid

as·pect \'as-,pekt\ *n* : the part of an object (as an organ) in a particular position

aspera — see LINEA ASPERA

as·per·gil·lin \,as-pər-'ji-lən\ *n* : an antibacterial substance isolated from two molds of the genus *Aspergillus* (*A. flavus* and *A. fumigatus*)

as·per·gil·lo·sis \,as-pər-(,)ji-'lō-səs, -'lo-ses \-,sēz\ : infection with or disease caused (as in poultry) by molds of the genus *Aspergillus*

as·per·gil·lus \-'ji-ləs\ *n* 1 *cap* : a genus of ascomycetous fungi that include many common molds 2 *pl* -gil·li \-'ji-

ꞏlī, -(ꞏ)lē\ : any fungus of the genus *Aspergillus*

asꞏperꞏmia \-\ꞏspər-mē-ə\ *n* : inability to produce or ejaculate semen — compare AZOOSPERMIA — **asperꞏmic** \-mik\ *adj*

asꞏphyxꞏia \as-ꞏfik-sē-ə, əs-\ *n* : a lack of oxygen or excess of carbon dioxide in the body that is usu. caused by interruption of breathing and that causes unconsciousness — **asꞏphyxꞏiꞏal** \-sē-əl\ *adj*

asꞏphyxꞏiꞏant \-sē-ənt\ *n* : an agent (as a gas) capable of causing asphyxia

asꞏphyxꞏiꞏate \-sē-ꞏāt\ *vb* **-atꞏed; -atꞏing** 1 : to cause asphyxia in; *also* : to kill or make unconscious by inadequate oxygen, presence of noxious agents, or other obstruction to normal breathing 2 : to become asphyxiated — **asꞏphyxꞏiꞏaꞏtion** \-ꞏfik-sē-ꞏā-shən\ *n* — **asꞏphyxꞏiꞏaꞏtor** \-ꞏfik-sē-ꞏā-tər\ *n*

¹**asꞏpiꞏrate** \ꞏas-pə-ꞏrāt\ *vb* **-ratꞏed; -ratꞏing** 1 : to draw by suction 2 : to remove (as blood) by aspiration 3 : to take into the lungs by aspiration

²**asꞏpiꞏrate** \-rət\ *n* : material removed by aspiration

asꞏpiꞏraꞏtion \ꞏas-pə-ꞏrā-shən\ *n* 1 : the act of breathing and esp. of breathing in 2 : the withdrawal of fluid or friable tissue from the body 3 : the taking of foreign matter into the lungs with the respiratory current — **asꞏpiꞏraꞏtionꞏal** \-sh(ə-)nəl\ *adj*

asꞏpiꞏraꞏtor \ꞏas-pə-ꞏrā-tər\ *n* : an apparatus for producing suction or moving or collecting materials by suction: *esp* : a hollow tubular instrument connected with a partial vacuum and used to remove fluid or tissue or foreign bodies from the body

asꞏpiꞏrin \ꞏas-prən, -pə-rən\ *n, pl* aspirin *or* aspirins 1 : a white crystalline derivative $C_9H_8O_4$ of salicylic acid used for relief of pain and fever 2 : a tablet of aspirin

asꞏsay \ꞏa-ꞏsā, a-ꞏsā\ *n* 1 : examination and determination as to characteristics (as weight, measure, or quality) 2 : analysis (as of a drug) to determine the presence, absence, or quantity of one or more components — compare BIOASSAY 3 : a substance to be assayed; *also* : the tabulated result of assaying — **asꞏsay** \a-ꞏsā, ꞏa-ꞏsā\ *vb*

asꞏsimꞏiꞏlaꞏble \ə-ꞏsi-mə-lə-bəl\ *adj* : capable of being assimilated

¹**asꞏsimꞏiꞏlate** \ə-ꞏsi-mə-ꞏlāt\ *vb* **-latꞏed; -latꞏing** 1 : to take in and appropriate as nourishment : absorb into the system 2 : to become absorbed or incorporated into the system

²**asꞏsimꞏiꞏlate** \-lət, -ꞏlāt\ *n* : something that is assimilated

asꞏsimꞏiꞏlaꞏtion \ə-ꞏsi-mə-ꞏlā-shən\ *n* 1 a : an act, process, or instance of assimilating b : the state of being assimilated 2 : the incorporation or conversion of nutrients into protoplasm

that in animals follows digestion and absorption 3 : the process of receiving new facts or of responding to new situations in conformity with what is already available to consciousness — compare APPERCEPTION

asꞏsoꞏciꞏaꞏtion \ə-ꞏsō-sē-ꞏā-shən, -shē-\ *n* 1 : something linked in memory or imagination with a thing or person 2 : the process of forming mental connections or bonds between sensations, ideas, or memories 3 : the aggregation of chemical species to form (as with hydrogen bonds) loosely bound chemical complexes — compare POLYMERIZATION — **asꞏsoꞏciꞏaꞏtionꞏal** \-sh(ə-)nəl\ *adj*

association area *n* : an area of the cerebral cortex considered to function in linking and coordinating the sensory and motor areas

association fiber *n* : a nerve fiber connecting different parts of the brain; *esp* : any of the fibers connecting different areas within the cortex of each cerebral hemisphere — compare PROJECTION FIBER

asꞏsoꞏciaꞏtive \ə-ꞏsō-shē-ꞏā-tiv, -sē-; -shə-tiv\ *adj* 1 : of or relating to association esp. of ideas or images 2 a : dependent on or characterized by association (an ~ reaction) b : acquired by a process of learning (an ~ reflex)

associative learning *n* : a learning process in which discrete ideas and percepts which are experienced together become linked to one another — compare PAIRED-ASSOCIATE LEARNING

associative neuron *n* : a neuron that conveys nerve impulses from one neuron to another — compare MOTONEURON, SENSORY NEURON

asꞏsortꞏment \ə-ꞏsort-mənt\ — see INDEPENDENT ASSORTMENT

asꞏtaꞏsia \ə-ꞏstā-zhə, -zhē-ə\ *n* : muscular incoordination in standing — compare ABASIA — **asꞏtatꞏic** \ə-ꞏsta-tik\ *adj*

asꞏtaꞏtine \ꞏas-tə-ꞏtēn\ *n* : a radioactive halogen element discovered by bombarding bismuth with helium nuclei and also formed by radioactive decay — symbol *At;* see ELEMENT table

asꞏter \ꞏas-tər\ *n* : a system of microtubules arranged radially about a centriole at either end of the mitotic or meiotic spindle

asterꞏeꞏogꞏnoꞏsis \(ꞏ)ā-ꞏster-ē-äg-ꞏnō-səs, -ꞏstir-\ *n, pl* **-noꞏses** \-ꞏsēz\ : loss of the ability to recognize the shapes of objects by handling them

asꞏteꞏrixꞏis \ꞏas-tə-ꞏrik-sis\ *n* : a motor disorder characterized by jerking movements (as of the outstretched hands) and associated with various encephalopathies due esp. to faulty metabolism

asthen- *or* **astheno-** *comb form* : weak ⟨*asthen*opia⟩

as·the·nia \as-'thē-nē-ə\ *n* : lack or loss of strength : DEBILITY

as·then·ic \as-'the-nik\ *adj* **1** : of, relating to, or exhibiting asthenia : DEBILITATED **2** : characterized by slender build and slight muscular development : ECTOMORPHIC

as·the·no·pia \ˌas-thə-'nō-pē-ə\ *n* : weakness or rapid fatigue of the eyes often accompanied by pain and headache — **as·the·no·pic** \-'nä-pik, -'nō-\ *adj*

asth·ma \'az-mə\ *n* : a condition often of allergic origin that is marked by continuous or paroxysmal labored breathing accompanied by wheezing, by a sense of constriction in the chest, and often by attacks of coughing or gasping

¹asth·mat·ic \az-'ma-tik\ *adj* : of, relating to, or affected with asthma (an ∼ attack) — **asth·mat·i·cal·ly** \-ti-k(ə-)lē\ *adv*

²asthmatic *n* : a person affected with asthma

asthmaticus — see STATUS ASTHMATICUS

asth·mo·gen·ic \ˌaz-mə-'je-nik\ *adj* : causing asthmatic attacks

¹as·tig·mat·ic \ˌas-tig-'ma-tik\ *adj* : affected with, relating to, or correcting astigmatism

²astigmatic *n* : a person affected with astigmatism

astig·ma·tism \ə-'stig-mə-ˌti-zəm\ *n* **1** : a defect of an optical system (as a lens) causing rays from a point to fail to meet in a focal point resulting in a blurred and imperfect image **2** : a defect of vision due to astigmatism of the refractive system of the eye and esp. to corneal irregularity — compare EMMETROPIA, MYOPIA

as tol *abbr* as tolerated

astr- or **astro-** *comb form* **1** : star (*astrocyte*) **2** : astrocyte (*astro*blastoma) (*astro*glia)

astragal- or **astragalo-** *comb form* : astragalus (*astragal*ectomy)

astrag·a·lec·to·my \ə-ˌstra-gə-'lek-tə-mē\ *n, pl* -mies : surgical removal of the astragalus

as·trag·a·lus \ə-'stra-gə-ləs\ *n, pl* -li \-ˌlī, -ˌlē\ : one of the proximal bones of the tarsus of the higher vertebrates — see TALUS 1

astral ray *n* : one of the thin fibrils that make up the mitotic or meiotic aster

¹as·trin·gent \ə-'strin-jənt\ *adj* : having the property of drawing together the soft organic tissues (∼ cosmetic lotions): **a** : tending to shrink mucous membranes or raw or exposed tissues : checking discharge (as of serum or mucus) : STYPTIC **b** : tending to pucker the tissues of the mouth — **as·trin·gen·cy** \-jən-sē\ *n*

²astringent *n* : an astringent agent or substance

as·tro·blas·to·ma \ˌas-trō-(ˌ)blas-'tō-mə\ *n, pl* -mas or -ma·ta \-mə-tə\ : an

astrocytoma of moderate malignancy

as·tro·cyte \'as-trə-ˌsīt\ *n* : a star-shaped cell; *esp* : any comparatively large much-branched neuroglial cell — **as·tro·cyt·ic** \ˌas-trə-'si-tik\ *adj*

as·tro·cy·to·ma \ˌas-trə-sī-'tō-mə\ *n, pl* -mas or -ma·ta \-mə-tə\ : a nerve-tissue tumor composed of astrocytes

as·tro·glia \ə-'strä-glē-ə, ˌas-trə-'glī-ə\ *n* : neuroglia tissue composed of astrocytes — **as·tro·gli·al** \-əl\ *adj*

asy·lum \ə-'sī-ləm\ *n* : an institution for the relief or care of the destitute or sick and esp. the insane

asym·bo·lia \ˌā-(ˌ)sim-'bō-lē-ə\ *n* : loss of the power to understand previously familiar symbols and signs

asym·met·ri·cal \ˌā-sə-'me-tri-kəl\ or **asym·met·ric** \-trik\ *adj* **1** : not symmetrical **2** : characterized by bonding to different atoms or groups — **asym·met·ri·cal·ly** \-tri-k(ə-)lē\ *adv*

asym·me·try \(ˌ)ā-'si-mə-trē\ *n, pl* -tries **1** : lack or absence of symmetry: as **a** : lack of proportion between the parts of a thing; *esp* : want of bilateral symmetry (∼ in the development of the two sides of the brain) **b** : lack of coordination of two parts acting in connection with one another (∼ of convergence of the eyes) **2** : lack of symmetry in spatial arrangement of atoms and groups in a molecule

asymp·tom·at·ic \ˌā-ˌsimp-tə-'ma-tik\ *adj* : presenting no symptoms of disease — **asymp·tom·at·i·cal·ly** \-ti-k(ə-)lē\ *adv*

asyn·ap·sis \ˌā-sə-'nap-səs\ *n, pl* -ap·ses \-ˌsēz\ : failure of pairing of homologous chromosomes in meiosis

asyn·clit·ism \(ˌ)ā-'sin-klə-ˌti-zəm, -'sin-\ *n* : presentation of the fetal head during childbirth with the axis oriented obliquely to the axial planes of the pelvis

asy·ner·gia \ˌā-sə-'nər-jē-ə, -jə\ or **asyn·er·gy** \(ˌ)ā-'si-nər-jē\ *n, pl* -gias or -gies : lack of coordination (as of muscles) — **asy·ner·gic** \ˌā-sə-'nər-jik\ *adj*

asys·to·le \(ˌ)ā-'sis-tə-(ˌ)lē\ *n* : a condition of weakening or cessation of systole — **asys·tol·ic** \ˌā-sis-'tä-lik\ *adj*

At *symbol* astatine

Ata·brine \'a-tə-brən\ *trademark* — used for a preparation of quinacrine

¹at·a·rac·tic \ˌa-tə-'rak-tik\ or **at·a·rax·ic** \-'rak-sik\ *adj* : tending to tranquilize (∼ drugs)

²ataractic or **ataraxic** *n* : TRANQUILIZER

at·a·rax·ia \ˌa-tə-'rak-sē-ə\ or **at·a·raxy** \'a-tə-ˌrak-sē\ *n, pl* -rax·ias or -rax·ies : calmness untroubled by mental or emotional disquiet

at·a·vism \'a-tə-ˌvi-zəm\ *n* : recurrence in an organism of a trait or character typical of an ancestral form and usu. due to genetic recombination **2** : an individual or character manifesting atavism : THROWBACK — **at·a·vis·tic** \ˌa-tə-'vis-tik\ *adj*

atax·ia \ə-'tak-sē-ə, (ˌ)ā-\ *n* : an inability to coordinate voluntary muscular movements that is symptomatic of some nervous disorders — **atax·ic** \-sik\ *adj*

atel- *or* **atelo-** *comb form* : defective ⟨*atelectasis*⟩

at·el·ec·ta·sis \₁at-ᵊl-ᵊek-tə-səs\ *n, pl* **-ta·ses** \-₁sēz\ : collapse of the expanded lung; *also* : defective expansion of the pulmonary alveoli at birth — **at·el·ec·tat·ic** \-ek-ᵊta-tik\ *adj*

ate·li·o·sis \ə-₁te-lē-ᵊō-səs, -₁tē-\ *n, pl* **-o·ses** \-₁sēz\ : incomplete development; *esp* : dwarfism associated with anterior pituitary deficiencies and marked by essentially normal intelligence and proportions — compare ACHONDROPLASIA

¹**ate·li·ot·ic** \-ᵊä-tik\ *adj* : of, relating to, or affected with ateliosis

²**ateliotic** *n* : a person affected with ateliosis

aten·o·lol \ə-ᵊte-nə-₁lòl, -₁lōl\ *n* : a beta-blocker $C_{14}H_{22}N_2O_3$ used in the treatment of hypertension

athero- *comb form* : atheroma ⟨*atherogenic*⟩

ath·er·o·gen·e·sis \₁a-thə-rō-ᵊje-nə-səs\ *n, pl* **-e·ses** \-₁sēz\ : the process of developing atheroma

ath·er·o·gen·ic \-ᵊje-nik\ *adj* : relating to or producing degenerative changes in arterial walls ⟨∼ diet⟩ — **ath·er·o·ge·nic·i·ty** \-jə-ᵊni-sə-tē\ *n*

ath·er·o·ma \₁a-thə-ᵊrō-mə\ *n, pl* **-mas** *also* **-ma·ta** \-mə-tə\ 1 : fatty degeneration of the inner coat of the arteries 2 : an abnormal fatty deposit in an artery — **ath·er·o·ma·tous** \-ᵊrō-mə-təs\ *adj*

ath·er·o·ma·to·sis \₁a-thə-rō-mə-ᵊtō-səs\ *n, pl* **-to·ses** \-₁sēz\ : a disease characterized by atheromatous degeneration of the arteries

ath·er·o·scle·ro·sis \₁a-thə-rō-sklə-ᵊrō-səs\ *n, pl* **-ro·ses** \-₁sēz\ : an arteriosclerosis characterized by atheromatous deposits in and fibrosis of the inner layer of the arteries — **ath·er·o·scle·rot·ic** \-ᵊrä-tik\ *adj* — **ath·er·o·scle·rot·i·cal·ly** \-i-k(ə-)lē\ *adv*

¹**ath·e·toid** \ᵊa-thə-₁tòid\ *adj* : exhibiting or characteristic of athetosis

²**athetoid** *n* : an athetoid individual

ath·e·to·sis \₁a-thə-ᵊtō-səs\ *n, pl* **-to·ses** \-₁sēz\ : a nervous disorder that is marked by continual slow movements esp. of the extremities and is usu. due to a brain lesion

athlete's foot *n* : ringworm of the feet — called also *tinea pedis*

ath·let·ic \ath-ᵊle-tik\ *adj* : characterized by heavy frame, large chest, and powerful muscular development : MESOMORPHIC

athletic supporter *n* : a supporter for the genitals worn by men participating in sports or strenuous activities — called also *jockstrap*; see CUP 1

ath·ro·cyte \ᵊa-thrə-₁sīt\ *n* : a cell capable of athrocytosis — **ath·ro·cyt·ic** \₁a-thrə-ᵊsi-tik\ *adj*

ath·ro·cy·to·sis \₁a-thrə-sī-ᵊtō-səs\ *n, pl* **-to·ses** \-₁sēz\ : the capacity of some cells (as of the proximal convoluted tubule of the kidney) to pick up foreign material and store it in granular form in the cytoplasm

athy·mic \(₁)ā-ᵊthī-mik\ *adj* : lacking a thymus

At·i·van \ᵊat-i-₁van\ *trademark* — used for a preparation of lorazepam

atlant- *or* **atlanto-** *comb form* 1 : atlas ⟨*atlant*al⟩ 2 : atlantal and ⟨*atlanto*occipital⟩

at·lan·tal \-ᵊlant-ᵊl\ *adj* 1 : of or relating to the atlas 2 : ANTERIOR 1, CEPHALIC

at·lan·to·ax·i·al \ət-₁lan-tō-ᵊak-sē-əl, at-\ *adj* : relating to or being anatomical structures that connect the atlas and the axis

at·lan·to·oc·cip·i·tal \-äk-ᵊsi-pət-ᵊl\ *adj* : relating to or being structures (as a joint or ligament) joining the atlas and the occipital bone

at·las \ᵊat-ləs\ *n* : the first vertebra of the neck

at·mo·sphere \ᵊat-mə-₁sfir\ *n* 1 : the whole mass of air surrounding the earth 2 : the air of a locality 3 : a unit of pressure equal to the pressure of the air at sea level or approximately 14.7 pounds per square inch (101,000 newtons per square meter) — **at·mo·spher·ic** \₁at-mə-ᵊsfir-ik, -ᵊsfer-\ *adj*

atmospheric pressure *n* : the pressure exerted in every direction at any given point by the weight of the atmosphere

at·om \ᵊa-təm\ *n* : the smallest particle of an element that can exist either alone or in combination — **atom·ic** \ə-ᵊtä-mik\ *adj*

atomic cocktail *n* : a radioactive substance (as iodide of sodium) dissolved in water and administered orally to patients with cancer

atomic energy *n* : energy that can be liberated by changes in the nucleus of an atom (as by fission of a heavy nucleus or fusion of light nuclei into heavier ones with accompanying loss of mass)

atomic number *n* : the number of protons in the nucleus of an element — see ELEMENT table

atomic weight *n* : the average relative mass of one atom of an element usu. with carbon of atomic weight 12 being taken as the standard — see ELEMENT table

at·om·ize \ᵊa-tə-₁mīz\ *vb* **-ized; -iz·ing** : to convert to minute particles or to a fine spray — **at·om·iza·tion** \₁a-tə-mə-ᵊzā-shən\ *n*

at·om·iz·er \ᵊa-tə-₁mī-zər\ *n* : an instrument for atomizing usu. a perfume, disinfectant, or medicament

aton·ic \(₁)ā-ᵊtä-nik, (₁)a-\ *adj* : characterized by atony

at·o·ny \ᵊat-ᵊn-ē\ *or* **ato·nia** \(₁)ā-ᵊtō-nē-**

ə\ *n, pl* **-nies** *or* **-ni·as** : lack of physiological tone esp. of a contractile organ

at·o·py \'a-tə-pē\ *n, pl* **-pies** : a probably hereditary allergy characterized by symptoms (as asthma, hay fever, or hives) produced upon exposure to the exciting antigen without inoculation — **ato·pic** \(ₐ)ā-'tä-pik, -'tō-\ *adj*

ATP \ₐā-(ₐ)tē-'pē\ *n* : a phosphorylated nucleoside $C_{10}H_{16}N_5O_{13}P_3$ of adenine that when reversibly converted esp. to ADP releases energy in the cell for many metabolic reactions (as protein synthesis) — called also *adenosine triphosphate*

ATPase \ₐā-(ₐ)tē-'pē-ₐās, -ₐāz\ *n* : an enzyme that hydrolyzes ATP; *esp* : one that hydrolyzes ATP to ADP and inorganic phosphate — called also *adenosine triphosphatase*

atre·sia \ə-'trē-zhə\ *n* 1 : absence or closure of a natural passage of the body (~ of the small intestine) 2 : absence or disappearance of an anatomical part (as an ovarian follicle) by degeneration — **atret·ic** \ə-'tre-tik\ *adj*

atri- *or* **atrio-** *comb form* 1 : atrium ⟨*atrial*⟩ 2 : atrial and ⟨*atrioventricular*⟩

atria *pl of* ATRIUM

atri·al \'ā-trē-əl\ *adj* : of, relating to, or affecting an atrium (~ disorder)

atrial fibrillation *n* : very rapid uncoordinated contractions of the atria of the heart resulting in a lack of synchronism between heartbeat and pulse beat — called also *auricular fibrillation*

atrial flutter *n* : an irregularity of the heartbeat in which the contractions of the atrium exceed in number those of the ventricle — called also *auricular flutter*

atrial natriuretic factor *n* : a peptide hormone secreted by the cardiac atria that stimulates natriuresis and diuresis and helps regulate blood pressure

atrial septum *n* : INTERATRIAL SEPTUM

atrich·ia \ā-'tri-kē-ə, ə-\ *n* : congenital or acquired baldness : ALOPECIA

atrio·ven·tric·u·lar \ₐā-trē-(ₐ)ō-ₐven-'tri-kyə-lər\ *adj* 1 : of, relating to, or situated between an atrium and ventricle 2 : of, involving, or being the atrioventricular node

atrioventricular bundle *n* : BUNDLE OF HIS

atrioventricular canal *n* : the canal joining the atrium and ventricle in the tubular embryonic heart

atrioventricular node *n* : a small mass of tissue that is situated in the wall of the right atrium adjacent to the septum between the atria and passes impulses received from the sinoatrial node to the ventricles by way of the bundle of His

atrioventricular valve *n* : a valve between an atrium and ventricle of the

heart: **a** : BICUSPID VALVE **b** : TRICUSPID VALVE

atri·um \'ā-trē-əm\ *n, pl* **atria** \-trē-ə\ *also* **atri·ums** : an anatomical cavity or passage; *esp* : a chamber of the heart that receives blood from the veins and forces it into a ventricle or ventricles

At·ro·pa \'a-trə-pə\ *n* : a genus of Eurasian and African herbs (as belladonna) of the nightshade family (Solanaceae) that are a source of medicinal alkaloids (as atropine and scopolamine)

atro·phic \(ₐ)ā-'trō-fik, ə-, -'trä-\ *adj* : relating to or characterized by atrophy (an ~ jaw)

atrophicans — see ACRODERMATITIS CHRONICA ATROPHICANS

atrophic rhinitis *n* 1 : a disease of swine that is characterized by purulent inflammation of the nasal mucosa, atrophy of the nasal conchae, and abnormal swelling of the face 2 : OZENA

atrophicus — see LICHEN SCLEROSUS ET ATROPHICUS

atrophic vaginitis *n* : inflammation of the vagina with thinning of the epithelial lining that occurs following menopause

¹**at·ro·phy** \'a-trə-fē\ *n, pl* **-phies** : decrease in size or wasting away of a body part or tissue; *also* : arrested development or loss of a part or organ incidental to the normal development or life of an animal or plant — **atro·phic** \(ₐ)ā-'trō-fik\ *adj*

²**atrophy** \'a-trə-fē, -ₐfī\ *vb* **-phied; -phy·ing** : to undergo or cause to undergo atrophy

at·ro·pine \'a-trə-ₐpēn\ *n* : a racemic mixture of hyoscyamine obtained from belladonna and related plants (family Solanaceae) and used esp. in the form of its sulfate for its anticholinergic effects (as relief of smooth muscle spasms or dilation of the pupil of the eye)

at·ro·pin·ism \-ₐpē-ₐni-zəm\ *n* : poisoning by atropine

at·ro·pin·iza·tion \ₐa-trə-ₐpē-nə-'zā-shən\ *n* : the physiological condition of being under the influence of atropine — **at·ro·pin·ize** \'a-trə-pə-ₐnīz\ *vb*

at·ro·scine \'a-trə-ₐsēn, -sən\ *n* : racemic scopolamine

at·tach·ment \ə-'tach-mənt\ *n* : the physical connection by which one thing is attached to another — **at·tach** \ə-'tach\ *vb*

¹**at·tack** \ə-'tak\ *vb* : to begin to affect or to act on injuriously

²**attack** *n* : a fit of sickness; *esp* : an active episode of a chronic or recurrent disease

at·tend \ə-'tend\ *vb* : to visit or stay with professionally as a physician or nurse

¹**at·tend·ing** \ə-'ten-diŋ\ *adj* : serving as a physician or surgeon on the staff of a hospital, regularly visiting and

treating patients, and often supervising students, fellows, and the house staff

²**attending** *n* : an attending physician or surgeon

at·ten·tion \ə-'ten-chən\ *n* 1 : the act or state of attending : the application of the mind to any object of sense or thought 2 **a** : an organismic condition of selective awareness or perceptual receptivity **b** : the process of focusing consciousness to produce greater vividness and clarity of certain of its contents relative to others — **at·ten·tion·al** \-'ten-chə-nəl\ *adj*

attention deficit disorder *n* : a syndrome of learning and behavioral problems that is not caused by any serious underlying physical or mental disorder and is characterized esp. by difficulty in sustaining attention, by impulsive behavior (as in speaking out of turn), and usu. by excessive activity — called also *minimal brain dysfunction*

attention–deficit hyperactivity disorder *n* : ATTENTION DEFICIT DISORDER

at·ten·u·ate \ə-'ten-yə-ˌwāt\ *vb* **-at·ed; -at·ing** : to reduce the severity of (a disease) or virulence or vitality of (a pathogenic agent) (a procedure to ∼ severe diabetes) ⟨*attenuated* bacilli⟩

at·ten·u·a·tion \ə-ˌten-yə-'wā-shən\ *n* : a decrease in the pathogenicity or vitality of a microorganism or in the severity of a disease

at·tic \'a-tik\ *n* : the small upper space of the middle ear — called also *epitympanic recess*

at·ti·co·to·my \ˌa-tə-'kä-tə-mē\ *n, pl* **-mies** : surgical incision of the tympanic attic

at·ti·tude \'a-tə-ˌtüd, -ˌtyüd\ *n* 1 : the arrangement of the parts of the body : POSTURE 2 **a** : a mental position with regard to a fact or state **b** : a feeling or emotion toward a fact or state 3 : an organismic state of readiness to respond in a characteristic way to a stimulus (as an object, concept, or situation)

at·ti·tu·di·nal \ˌa-tə-'tüd-ᵊn-əl, -'tyüd-\ *adj* : relating to, based on, or expressive of personal attitudes or feelings

at·tri·tion \ə-'tri-shən\ *n* : the act of rubbing together; *also* : the act of wearing or grinding down by friction (∼ of teeth)

atyp·ia \(ˌ)ā-'ti-pē-ə\ *n* : ATYPISM

atyp·i·cal \(ˌ)ā-'ti-pi-kəl\ *adj* : not typical : not like the usual or normal type — **atyp·i·cal·ly** \-pi-k(ə-)lē\ *adv*

atypical pneumonia *n* : PRIMARY ATYPICAL PNEUMONIA

atyp·ism \(ˌ)ā-'ti-ˌpi-zəm\ *n* : the condition of being uncharacteristic or lacking uniformity

Au *symbol* [L *aurum*] gold

au·di·ble \'o-də-bəl\ *adj* : heard or capable of being heard — **au·di·bil·i·ty** \ˌo-də-'bi-lə-tē\ *n* — **au·di·bly** \'o-də-blē\ *adv*

¹**au·dile** \'o-ˌdīl\ *n* : a person whose mental imagery is auditory rather than visual or motor — compare TACTILE, VISUALIZER

²**audile** *adj* 1 : of or relating to hearing : AUDITORY 2 : of, relating to, or being an audile

audio- *comb form* 1 : hearing ⟨*audiol*ogy⟩ 2 : sound ⟨*audio*genic⟩

au·dio·gen·ic \ˌo-dē-ō-'je-nik\ *adj* : produced by frequencies corresponding to sound waves — used esp. of epileptoid responses (∼ seizures)

au·dio·gram \'o-dē-ō-ˌgram\ *n* : a graphic representation of the relation of vibration frequency and the minimum sound intensity for hearing

au·di·ol·o·gist \ˌo-dē-'ä-lə-jist\ *n* : a specialist in audiology

au·di·ol·o·gy \ˌo-dē-'ä-lə-jē\ *n, pl* **-gies** : a branch of science dealing with hearing; *specif* : therapy of individuals having impaired hearing — **au·di·o·log·i·cal** \-dē-ə-'lä-ji-kəl\ *also* **au·di·o·log·ic** \-dē-ə-'lä-jik\ *adj*

au·di·om·e·ter \ˌo-dē-'ä-mə-tər\ *n* : an instrument used in measuring the acuity of hearing

au·di·om·e·try \ˌo-dē-'ä-mə-trē\ *n, pl* **-tries** : the testing and measurement of hearing acuity for variations in sound intensity and pitch and for tonal purity — **au·dio·met·ric** \-ō-'me-trik\ *adj* — **au·di·om·e·trist** \-'ä-mə-trist\ *n*

au·di·to·ry \'o-də-ˌtōr-ē\ *adj* 1 : of or relating to hearing 2 : attained, experienced, or produced through or as if through hearing (∼ images) (∼ hallucinations) 3 : marked by great susceptibility to impressions and reactions produced by acoustic stimuli

auditory area *n* : a sensory area in the temporal cortex associated with the organ of hearing — called also *auditory center, auditory cortex*

auditory canal *n* : either of two passages of the ear — called also *acoustic meatus, auditory meatus;* compare EXTERNAL AUDITORY MEATUS, INTERNAL AUDITORY MEATUS

auditory cortex *n* : AUDITORY AREA

auditory nerve *n* : either of the 8th pair of cranial nerves connecting the inner ear with the brain, transmitting impulses concerned with hearing and balance, and composed of the cochlear nerve and the vestibular nerve — called also *acoustic nerve, auditory, eighth cranial nerve, vestibulocochlear nerve*

auditory tube *n* : EUSTACHIAN TUBE

Auer·bach's plexus \'aủ-ər-ˌbäks-, -ˌbäks-\ *n* : MYENTERIC PLEXUS

Auer·bach \'aủ-ər-ˌbäk, -ˌbäk\, **Leopold (1828–1897)**, German anatomist.

aug·ment \og-'ment, 'og-ˌment\ *vb* : to increase in size, amount, degree, or severity — **aug·men·ta·tion** \ˌȯg-mən-ˈtā-shən, -ˌmen-\ n

aur- or **auri-** comb form : ear ⟨aural⟩

au·ra \ˈȯr-ə\ n, pl **auras** also **au·rae** \-ē\ : a subjective sensation (as of voices or colored lights) experienced before an attack of some disorders (as epilepsy or migraine)

au·ral \ˈȯr-əl\ adj : of or relating to the ear or to the sense of hearing — **au·ral·ly** adv

Au·reo·my·cin \ˌȯr-ē-ō-ˈmī-sən\ trademark — used for a preparation of the hydrochloride of chlortetracycline

au·ri·cle \ˈȯr-i-kəl\ n 1 a : PINNA b : an atrium of the heart 2 : an angular or ear-shaped anatomical lobe or process

au·ric·u·la \ȯ-ˈri-kyu̇-lə\ n, pl **-lae** \-ˌlē\ : AURICLE; esp : AURICULAR APPENDAGE

au·ric·u·lar \ȯ-ˈri̇-kyu̇-lər\ adj 1 : of, relating to, or using the ear or the sense of hearing 2 : understood or recognized by the sense of hearing 3 : of or relating to an auricle or auricular appendage ⟨∼ fibrillation⟩

auricular appendage n : an ear-shaped pouch projecting from each atrium of the heart — called also auricular appendix

auricular artery — see POSTERIOR AURICULAR ARTERY

auricular fibrillation n : ATRIAL FIBRILLATION

auricular flutter n : ATRIAL FLUTTER

au·ric·u·lar·is \ȯ-ˌri-kyu̇-ˈlar-əs, -ˈlär-\ n, pl **-lar·es** \-ˌēz\ : any of three muscles attached to the cartilage of the external ear that assist in moving the scalp and in some individuals the external ear itself and that consist of one that is anterior, one superior, and one posterior in position — called also respectively auricularis anterior, auricularis superior, and auricularis posterior

auricular tubercle of Darwin n : DARWIN'S TUBERCLE

auricular vein — see POSTERIOR AURICULAR VEIN

auriculo- comb form : of or belonging to an auricle of the heart and ⟨auriculoventricular⟩

au·ric·u·lo·tem·po·ral nerve \ȯ-ˌri-kyu̇-(ˌ)lō-ˈtem-pə-rəl-\ n : the branch of the mandibular nerve that supplies sensory fibers to the skin of the external ear and temporal region and autonomic fibers from the otic ganglion to the parotid gland

au·ric·u·lo·ven·tric·u·lar \-ven-ˈtri-kyu̇-lər-, -vən-\ adj : ATRIOVENTRICULAR

au·ro·thio·glu·cose \ˌȯr-ō-ˌthī-ō-ˈglü-ˌkōs, -ˌkōz\ n : GOLD THIOGLUCOSE

aus·cul·ta·tion \ˌȯ-skəl-ˈtā-shən\ n : the act of listening to sounds arising within organs (as the lungs or heart) as an aid to diagnosis and treatment — **aus·cul·tate** \ˈȯ-skəl-ˌtāt\ vb — **aus·cul·ta·to·ry** \ȯ-ˈskəl-tə-ˌtȯr-ē\ adj

Aus·tra·lia antigen \ȯ-ˈstrāl-yə-\ also **Aus·tra·lian antigen** \-yən-\ n : HEPATITIS B SURFACE ANTIGEN

aut- or **auto-** comb form : self : same one ⟨autism⟩: a : of, by, affecting, from, or for the same individual ⟨autograft⟩ ⟨autotransfusion⟩ ⟨autovaccination⟩ b : arising or produced within the individual and acting or directed toward or against the individual or the individual's own body, tissues, or molecules ⟨autoimmunity⟩ ⟨autosuggestion⟩ ⟨autoerotism⟩

au·ta·coid \ˈȯ-tə-ˌkȯid\ n : a physiologically active substance (as serotonin, bradykinin, or angiotensin) produced by and acting within the body

au·tism \ˈȯ-ˌti-zəm\ n 1 : absorption in self-centered subjective mental activity (as daydreams, fantasies, delusions, and hallucinations) esp. when accompanied by marked withdrawal from reality 2 : a mental disorder originating in infancy that is characterized by self-absorption, inability to interact socially, repetitive behavior, and language dysfunction (as echolalia)

¹**au·tis·tic** \ȯ-ˈtis-tik\ adj : of, relating to, or marked by autism ⟨∼ behavior⟩ ⟨∼ children⟩

²**autistic** n : a person affected with autism

au·to·ag·glu·ti·na·tion \ˌȯ-tō-ə-ˌglüt-ᵊn-ˈā-shən\ n : agglutination of red blood cells by cold agglutinins in an individual's own serum usu. at lower than body temperature

au·to·ag·glu·ti·nin \-ə-ˈglüt-ᵊn-ən\ n : an antibody that agglutinates the red blood cells of the individual producing it — compare COLD AGGLUTININ

Au·to·an·a·lyz·er \ˌȯ-tō-ˈan-ᵊl-ˌī-zər\ trademark — used for an instrument designed for automatic chemical analysis (as of blood glucose level)

au·to·an·ti·body \ˌȯ-(ˌ)tō-ˈan-ti-ˌbä-dē\ n, pl **-bod·ies** : an antibody active against a tissue constituent of the individual producing it

au·to·an·ti·gen \ˌȯ-tō-ˈan-ti-jen\ n : an antigen that is a normal bodily constituent and against which the immune system produces autoantibodies

au·toch·tho·nous \(ˌ)ȯ-ˈtäk-thə-nəs\ adj 1 a : indigenous or endemic to a region ⟨∼ malaria⟩ b : contracted in the area where reported 2 : originated in that part of the body where found — used chiefly of pathological conditions — **au·toch·tho·nous·ly** adv

au·to·clav·able \ˈȯ-tə-ˌklā-və-bəl\ adj : able to withstand the action of an autoclave — **au·to·clav·abil·i·ty** \ˌȯ-tə-ˌklā-və-ˈbi-lə-tē\ n

au·to·clave \ˈȯ-tō-ˌklāv\ n : an apparatus (as for sterilizing) using superheated steam under pressure — **autoclave** vb

au·to·er·o·tism \ˌȯ-tō-ˈer-ə-ˌti-zəm\ or

au·to·erot·i·cism \-i-'rä-tə-₋si-zəm\ n 1 : sexual gratification obtained solely through stimulation by oneself of one's own body 2 : sexual feeling arising without known external stimulation — **au·to·erot·ic** \-i-'rä-tik\ adj — **au·to·erot·i·cal·ly** \-ti-k(ə-)lē\ adv

au·to·gen·ic \₋ȯ-tə-'je-nik\ adj 1 : AUTOGENOUS 2 : of or relating to any of several relaxation techniques that actively involve the patient (as by meditation or biofeedback) in attempts to control physiological variables (as blood pressure)

au·tog·e·nous \ȯ-'tä-jə-nəs\ adj 1 : produced independently of external influence or aid : ENDOGENOUS 2 : originating or derived from sources within the same individual (an ~ graft) (~ vaccine)

au·to·graft \'ȯ-tō-₋graft\ n : a tissue or organ that is transplanted from one part to another part of the same body — **autograft** vb

au·to·he·mo·ly·sin \₋ȯ-tō-₋hē-mə-'līs-ᵊn\ n : a hemolysin that acts on the red blood cells of the individual in whose blood it is found

au·to·he·mo·ly·sis \-hi-'mä-lə-səs, -₋hē-mə-'li-səs\ n, pl -ly·ses \-₋sēz\ : hemolysis of red blood cells by factors in the serum of the person from whom the blood is taken

au·to·he·mo·ther·a·py \-₋hē-mō-'ther-ə-pē\ n, pl -pies : treatment of disease by modification (as by irradiation) of the patient's own blood or by its introduction (as by intramuscular injection) outside the bloodstream

au·to·hyp·no·sis \₋ȯ-tō-hip-'nō-səs\ n, pl -no·ses \-₋sēz\ : self-induced and usu. automatic hypnosis — **au·to·hyp·not·ic** \-'nä-tik\ adj

au·to·im·mune \-i-'myün\ adj : of, relating to, or caused by antibodies or T cells that attack molecules, cells, or tissues of the organism producing them (~ diseases)

au·to·im·mu·ni·ty \₋ȯ-tō-i-'myü-nə-tē\ n, pl -ties : a condition in which the body produces an immune response against its own tissue constituents — **au·to·im·mu·ni·za·tion** \-₋i-myə-nə-'zā-shən also i-₋myü-nə-\ n — **au·to·im·mu·nize** \-'i-myə-₋nīz\ vb

au·to·in·fec·tion \in-'fek-shən\ n : reinfection with larvae produced by parasitic worms already in the body — compare HYPERINFECTION

au·to·in·oc·u·la·tion \-i-₋nä-kyə-'lā-shən\ n 1 : inoculation with vaccine prepared from material from one's own body 2 : spread of infection from one part to other parts of the same body — **au·to·in·oc·u·la·ble** \₋ȯ-tō-i-'nä-kyə-lə-bəl\ adj

au·to·ki·ne·sis \₋ȯ-tō-kə-'nē-səs, -kī-\ n, pl -ne·ses \-₋sēz\ : spontaneous or voluntary movement

au·tol·o·gous \ȯ-'tä-lə-gəs\ adj 1 : derived from the same individual (~

grafts) — compare HETEROLOGOUS 1, HOMOLOGOUS 2 2 : involving one individual as both donor and recipient (as of blood) (~ transfusion)

au·tol·y·sate \ȯ-'tä-lə-₋sāt, -₋zāt\ also **au·tol·y·zate** \-₋zāt\ n : a product of autolysis

au·tol·y·sin \-lə-sən\ n : a substance that produces autolysis

au·tol·y·sis \-lə-səs\ n, pl -y·ses \-lə-₋sēz\ : breakdown of all or part of a cell or tissue by self-produced enzymes — **au·to·lyt·ic** \₋ȯt-ᵊl-'i-tik\ adj — **au·to·lyze** \'ȯt-ᵊl-₋īz\ vb

au·tom·a·tism \ȯ-'tä-mə-₋ti-zəm\ n 1 : an automatic action; esp : any action performed without the doer's intention or awareness 2 : the power or fact of moving or functioning without conscious control either independently of external stimulation (as in the beating of the heart) or more or less directly under the influence of external stimuli (as in the dilating or contracting of the pupil of the eye)

au·to·nom·ic \₋ȯ-tə-'nä-mik\ adj 1 a : acting or occurring involuntarily (~ reflexes) b : relating to, affecting, or controlled by the autonomic nervous system (~ ganglia) 2 : having an effect upon tissue supplied by the autonomic nervous system (~ drugs) — **au·to·nom·i·cal·ly** \-mi-k(ə-)lē\ adv

autonomic nervous system n : a part of the vertebrate nervous system that innervates smooth and cardiac muscle and glandular tissues and governs involuntary actions (as secretion, vasoconstriction, or peristalsis) and that consists of the sympathetic nervous system and the parasympathetic nervous system — compare CENTRAL NERVOUS SYSTEM, PERIPHERAL NERVOUS SYSTEM

au·ton·o·my \ȯ-'tä-nə-mē\ n, pl -mies 1 : the quality or state of being independent, free, and self-directing 2 : independence from the organism as a whole in the capacity of a part for growth, reactivity, or responsiveness — **au·ton·o·mous** \-məs\ adj — **au·ton·o·mous·ly** adv

au·to·pro·throm·bin \₋ȯ-tō-prō-'thräm-bən\ n : any of several blood factors formed in the conversion of prothrombin to thrombin: as a : FACTOR VII — called also autoprothrombin I b : FACTOR IX — called also autoprothrombin II

¹**au·top·sy** \'ȯ-₋täp-sē, -təp-\ n, pl -sies : an examination of the body after death usu. with such dissection as will expose the vital organs for determining the cause of death or the character and extent of changes produced by disease — called also necropsy, postmortem, postmortem examination

²**autopsy** vb -sied; -sy·ing : to perform an autopsy on

au·to·ra·dio·gram \ȯ-tō-ˈrā-dē-ə-ˌgram\ *n* : AUTORADIOGRAPH

au·to·ra·dio·graph \-ˌgraf\ *n* : an image produced on a photographic film or plate by the radiations from a radioactive substance in an object which is in close contact with the emulsion — called also *radioautogram, radioautograph* — **autoradiograph** *vb* — **au·to·ra·dio·graph·ic** \-ˌrä-dē-ə-ˈgra-fik\ *adj* — **au·to·ra·dio·graph·y** \-ˌrä-dē-ˈä-grə-fē\ *n*

au·to·reg·u·la·tion \ˌȯ-tō-ˌre-gyə-ˈlā-shən\ *n* : the maintenance of relative constancy of a physiological process by a bodily part or system under varying conditions; *esp* : the maintenance of a constant supply of blood to an organ in spite of varying arterial pressure — **au·to·reg·u·late** \-ˈre-gyə-ˌlāt\ *vb* — **au·to·reg·u·la·to·ry** \-ˈre-gyə-lə-ˌtȯr-ē\ *adj*

au·to·sen·si·ti·za·tion \ˌȯ-tō-ˌsen-sə-tə-ˈzā-shən\ *n* : AUTOIMMUNIZATION

au·to·some \ˈȯ-tə-ˌsōm\ *n* : a chromosome other than a sex chromosome — **au·to·som·al** \ˌȯ-tə-ˈsō-məl\ *adj* — **au·to·som·al·ly** *adv*

au·to·sug·ges·tion \-səg-ˈjes-chən, -jesh-\ *n* : an influencing of one's own attitudes, behavior, or physical condition by mental processes other than conscious thought : SELF-HYPNOSIS — **au·to·sug·gest** \-səg-ˈjest\ *vb*

au·to·ther·a·py \ˈȯ-tō-ˌther-ə-pē\ *n, pl* **-pies** : SELF-TREATMENT

au·to·top·ag·no·sia \ˌȯ-tō-ˌtä-pig-ˈnō-zhə\ *n* : loss of the power to recognize or orient a bodily part due to a brain lesion

autotoxicus — see HORROR AUTOTOXICUS

au·to·trans·fu·sion \-trans-ˈfyü-zhən\ *n* : return of autologous blood to the patient's own circulatory system — **au·to·trans·fuse** \-trans-ˈfyüz\ *vb*

au·to·trans·plant \-ˈtrans-ˌplant\ *n* : AUTOGRAFT — **au·to·trans·plant** \-trans-ˈ\ *vb* — **au·to·trans·plan·ta·tion** \-ˌtrans-ˌplan-ˈtā-shən\ *n*

au·to·troph \ˈȯ-tə-ˌtrȯf, -ˌträf\ *n* : autotrophic organism

au·to·tro·phic \ˌȯ-tə-ˈtrō-fik\ *adj* **1** : needing only carbon dioxide or carbonates as a source of carbon and a simple inorganic nitrogen compound for metabolic synthesis **2** : not requiring a specified exogenous factor for normal metabolism — **au·to·tro·phi·cal·ly** \-fi-k(ə-)lē\ *adv* — **au·to·tro·phy** \ˈȯ-tə-ˌtrō-fē, ȯ-ˈtä-trə-fē\ *n*

au·to·vac·ci·na·tion \ˌȯ-tō-ˌvak-sə-ˈnā-shən\ *n* : vaccination of an individual by material from the individual's own body or with a vaccine prepared from such material

au·tumn cro·cus \ˌȯ-təm-ˈkrō-kəs\ *n* : an autumn-blooming herb (*Colchicum autumnale*) of the lily family (Liliaceae) that is the source of medicinal colchicum

aux·il·ia·ry \ȯg-ˈzil-yə-rē, -ˈzi-lə-rē, -ˈzil-rē\ *adj* : serving to supplement or assist (~ springs in a dental appliance)

²auxiliary *n* **1** : one who assists or serves another person esp. in dentistry **2** : an organization that assists (as by donations or volunteer services) the work esp. of a hospital

auxo·troph \ˈȯk-sə-ˌtrȯf, -ˌträf\ *n* : an auxotrophic strain or individual

auxo·tro·phic \ˌȯk-sə-ˈtrō-fik\ *adj* : requiring a specific growth substance beyond the minimum required for normal metabolism and reproduction of the parental or wild-type strain (~ mutants of bacteria) — **aux·ot·ro·phy** \ȯk-ˈsä-trə-fē\ *n*

AV *abbr* **1** arteriovenous **2** atrioventricular

avas·cu·lar \(ˌ)ā-ˈvas-kyə-lər\ *adj* : having few or no blood vessels (~ necrosis) — **avas·cu·lar·i·ty** \-ˌvas-kyə-ˈlar-ə-tē\ *n*

Aven·tyl \ˈa-vən-ˌtil\ *trademark* — used for a preparation of nortriptyline

aver·sion \ə-ˈvər-zhən, -shən\ *n* **1** : a feeling of repugnance toward something with a desire to avoid or turn from it **2** : a tendency to extinguish a behavior or to avoid a thing or situation and esp. a usu. pleasurable one because it is or has been associated with a noxious stimulus

aversion therapy *n* : therapy intended to change habits or antisocial behavior by inducing a dislike for them through association with a noxious stimulus

aver·sive \ə-ˈvər-siv, -ziv\ *adj* : tending to avoid or causing avoidance of a noxious or punishing stimulus (behavior modification by ~ conditioning) — **aver·sive·ly** *adv* — **aver·sive·ness** *n*

avi·an influenza \ˈā-vē-ən-\ *n* : any of several highly variable diseases of domestic and wild birds that are caused by orthomyxoviruses and characterized usu. by respiratory symptoms but sometimes by gastrointestinal, integumentary, and urogenital symptoms — called also *fowl plague*

avian tuberculosis *n* : tuberculosis of birds usu. caused by a bacterium of the genus *Mycobacterium* (*M. avium*); *also* : infection of mammals (as swine) by the same bacterium

avi·din \ˈa-və-din\ *n* : a protein found in egg white that inactivates biotin by combining with it

avir·u·lent \(ˌ)ā-ˈvir-ə-lənt, -ˈvir-yə-\ *adj* : not virulent (an ~ tubercle bacillus) — compare NONPATHOGENIC

avis — see CALCAR AVIS

avi·ta·min·osis \ˌā-ˌvī-tə-mə-ˈnō-səs\ *n, pl* **-oses** \-ˌsēz\ : disease (as pellagra) resulting from a deficiency of one or more vitamins — called also *hypovi-*

taminosis — avi·ta·min·ot·ic \-mə-ˈnä-tik\ adj

A–V node or AV node \ā-ˈvē-\ n : ATRIOVENTRICULAR NODE

avoid·ance \ə-ˈvȯid-ᵊns\ n, often attrib : the act or practice of keeping away from or withdrawing from something undesirable; esp : an anticipatory response undertaken to avoid a noxious stimulus

avoidance–avoidance conflict n : psychological conflict that results when a choice must be made between two undesirable alternatives — compare APPROACH-APPROACH CONFLICT, APPROACH-AVOIDANCE CONFLICT

avoid·ant \ə-ˈvȯid-ᵊnt\ adj : characterized by turning away or by withdrawal or defensive behavior (an ~ personality)

av·oir·du·pois \ˌa-vər-də-ˈpȯiz, -ˈpwä\ adj : expressed in avoirdupois weight (~ units) (5 ounces ~)

avoirdupois pound n : POUND b

avoirdupois weight n : a system of weights based on a pound of 16 ounces and an ounce of 437.5 grains (28.350 grams) and in general use in the U.S. except for precious metals, gems, and drugs

avul·sion \ə-ˈvəl-shən\ n : a tearing away of a body part accidentally or surgically — avulse \ə-ˈvəls\ vb

ax- or axo- comb form : axon (axodendritic)

axe·nic \(ˌ)ā-ˈze-nik, -ˈzē-\ adj : free from other living organisms (an ~ culture of bacteria) — axe·ni·cal·ly \-ni-k(ə-)lē\ adv

ax·i·al \ˈak-sē-əl\ adj 1 : of, relating to, or having the characteristics of an axis 2 : situated around, in the direction of, on, or along an axis

axial skeleton n : the skeleton of the trunk and head

ax·il·la \ag-ˈzi-lə, ak-ˈsi-\ n, pl -lae \-(ˌ)lē, -ˌlī\ or -las : the cavity beneath the junction of the arm or anterior appendage and shoulder or pectoral girdle containing the axillary artery and vein, a part of the brachial plexus of nerves, many lymph nodes, and fat and areolar tissue; esp : ARMPIT

ax·il·lary \ˈak-sə-ˌler-ē\ adj : of, relating to, or located near the axilla (~ lymph nodes)

axillary artery n : the part of the main artery of the arm that lies in the axilla and that is continuous with the subclavian artery above and the brachial artery below

axillary nerve n : a large nerve arising from the posterior cord of the brachial plexus and supplying the deltoid and teres minor muscles and the skin of the shoulder

axillary node n : any of the lymph nodes of the axilla

axillary vein n : the large vein passing through the axilla continuous with the basilic vein below and the subclavian vein above

ax·is \ˈak-səs\ n, pl ax·es \-ˌsēz\ 1 a : a straight line about which a body or a geometric figure rotates or may be thought of as rotating b : a straight line with respect to which a body, organ, or figure is symmetrical 2 a : the second vertebra of the neck of the higher vertebrates that is prolonged anteriorly within the foramen of the first vertebra and united with the odontoid process which serves as a pivot for the atlas and head to turn upon — called also epistropheus b : any of various central, fundamental, or axial parts (the cerebrospinal ~) (the skeletal ~) c : AXILLA

axis cylinder n : AXON; esp : the axon of a myelinated neuron

axo- — see AX-

axo·ax·o·nal \ˌak-sō-ˈak-sən-ᵊl, -akˈsän-, -ˈsōn-\ or axo·ax·on·ic \-ak-ˈsä-nik\ adj : relating to or being a synapse between an axon of one neuron and an axon of another

axo·den·drit·ic \ˌak-sō-den-ˈdri-tik\ adj : relating to or being a nerve synapse between an axon of one neuron and a dendrite of another

axo·lem·ma \ˈak-sə-ˌle-mə\ n : the plasma membrane of an axon

ax·on \ˈak-ˌsän\ also ax·one \-ˌsōn\ n : a usu. long and single nerve-cell process that usu. conducts impulses away from the cell body — ax·o·nal \ˈak-sən-ᵊl; ak-ˈsän-, -ˈsōn-\ adj

axon·ot·me·sis \ˌak-sə-nət-ˈmē-səs\ n, pl -me·ses \-ˌsēz\ : axonal nerve damage that does not completely sever the surrounding endoneurial sheath so that regeneration can take place

axo·plasm \ˈak-sə-ˌpla-zəm\ n : the protoplasm of an axon — axo·plas·mic \ˌak-sə-ˈplaz-mik\ adj

axo·so·mat·ic \ˌak-sō-sō-ˈma-tik\ adj : relating to or being a nerve synapse between the cell body of one neuron and an axon of another

Ayer·za's disease \ə-ˈyər-zəz-\ n : a complex of symptoms marked esp. by cyanosis, dyspnea, polycythemia, and sclerosis of the pulmonary artery

Ayerza, Abel (1861–1918), Argentinean physician.

az- or azo- comb form : containing (azotemia)

aza·thi·o·prine \ˌa-zə-ˈthī-ə-ˌprēn\ n : a purine antimetabolite $C_9H_7N_7O_2S$ that is used esp. as an immunosuppressant — see IMURAN

az·i·do·thy·mi·dine \ˌa-zi-dō-ˈthī-mə-ˌdēn\ n : an antiviral drug $C_{10}H_{13}$-N_5O_4 that inhibits replication of some retroviruses (as HIV) and is used to treat AIDS — called also AZT, zidovudine; see RETROVIR

azo \ˈā-(ˌ)zō, ˈa-\ adj : relating to or containing the bivalent group N=N united at both ends to carbon

azo dye *n* : any of numerous dyes containing azo groups

azo·osper·mia \ ˌā-ˌzō-ə-ˈspər-mē-ə, ˌa-zō-\ *n* : absence of spermatozoa from the seminal fluid — compare ASPERMIA — **azo·osper·mic** \-ˈspər-mik\ *adj*

azo·sul·fa·mide \ ˌa-zō-ˈsəl-fə-ˌmīd\ *n* : a dark red crystalline azo compound $C_{18}H_{14}N_4Na_2O_{10}S_3$ of the sulfa class having antibacterial effect similar to that of sulfanilamide — called also *prontosil*

azo·te·mia \ ˌa-zō-ˈtē-mē-ə\ *n* : an excess of nitrogenous bodies in the blood as a result of kidney insufficiency — compare UREMIA — **azo·te·mic** \-ˈtē-mik\ *adj*

azo·tu·ria \ ˌa-zō-ˈtùr-ē-ə, -ˈtyùr-\ *n* : an abnormal condition of horses characterized by an excess of urea or other nitrogenous substances in the urine and by muscle damage esp. to the hindquarters

AZT \ ˌā-(ˌ)zē-ˈtē\ *n* : AZIDOTHYMIDINE

azygo- *comb form* : azygos ⟨*azygogra*phy⟩

azy·gog·ra·phy \ ˌa-zī-ˈgä-grə-fē\ *n, pl* **-phies** : roentgenographic visualization of the azygos system of veins after injection of a radiopaque medium

¹azy·gos \ ˌā-ˈzī-gəs\ *n* : an azygos anatomical part

²azy·gos *also* **azy·gous** \(ˌ)ā-ˈzī-gəs\ *adj* : not being one of a pair (the ∼ muscle of the uvula)

azygos vein *n* : any of a system of three veins which drain the thoracic wall and much of the abdominal wall and which form a collateral circulation when either the inferior or superior vena cava is obstructed; *esp* : a vein that receives blood from the right half of the thoracic and abdominal walls, ascends along the right side of the vertebral column, and empties into the superior vena cava — compare ACCESSORY HEMIAZYGOS VEIN, HEMIAZYGOS VEIN

B

b *abbr* bicuspid
B *symbol* boron
Ba *symbol* barium

ba·be·sia \ bə-ˈbē-zhə, -zhē-ə\ *n* 1 *cap* : a genus of sporozoans (family Babesiidae) parasitic in mammalian red blood cells (as in Texas fever) and transmitted by the bite of a tick 2 : any sporozoan of the genus *Babesia* or sometimes the family (Babesiidae) to which it belongs — called also *piroplasm*

Babès, Victor (1854–1926), Romanian bacteriologist.

babe·si·a·sis \ ˌba-bə-ˈsī-ə-səs\ *n, pl* **-ases** \-ˌsēz\ : BABESIOSIS

ba·be·si·o·sis \ ˌba-bə-ˈsī-ə-səs, ˌbā-bə-, bə-ˌbē-zē-ˈō-səs\ *n, pl* **-oses** \-ˌsēz\ : infection with or disease caused by babesias — called also *babesiasis*

Ba·bin·ski reflex \ bə-ˈbin-skē\ *also* **Babin·ski's reflex** \-skēz-\ *n* : a reflex movement in which when the sole is tickled the great toe turns upward instead of downward and which is normal in infancy but indicates damage to the central nervous system (as in the pyramidal tracts) when occurring later in life — called also *Babinski sign, Babinski's sign;* compare PLANTAR REFLEX

Babinski, Joseph–François–Felix (1857–1932), French neurologist.

ba·by \ ˈbā-bē\ *n, pl* **babies** : an extremely young child or animal; *esp* : INFANT — see BLUE BABY

baby talk *n* 1 : the imperfect speech or modified forms used by small children learning to talk 2 : the consciously imperfect or altered speech often used by adults in speaking to small children

baby tooth *n* : MILK TOOTH

bacill- *or* **bacilli-** *or* **bacillo-** *comb form* : bacillus ⟨*bacillo*sis⟩

ba·cil·la·ry \ ˈba-sə-ˌler-ē, bə-ˈsi-lə-rē\ *also* **ba·cil·lar** \ bə-ˈsi-lər, ˈba-sə-lər\ *adj* 1 : shaped like a rod; *also* : consisting of small rods 2 : of, relating to, or caused by bacilli (∼ meningitis)

bac·il·le·mia \ ˌba-sə-ˈlē-mē-ə\ *n* : BACTEREMIA

bac·il·lo·sis \ ˌba-sə-ˈlō-səs\ *n, pl* **-loses** \-ˌsēz\ : infection with bacilli

bac·il·lu·ria \ ˌba-sə-ˈlur-ē-ə, -ˈlyur-\ *n* : the passage of bacilli with the urine — **bac·il·lu·ric** \-ik\ *adj*

ba·cil·lus \ bə-ˈsi-ləs\ *n, pl* **-li** \-ˌlī *also* -lē\ 1 *a cap* : a genus of aerobic rod-shaped gram-positive bacteria (family Bacillaceae) that include many saprophytes and some parasites (as *B. anthracis* of anthrax) b : any bacterium of the genus *Bacillus; broadly* : a straight rod-shaped bacterium 2 : BACTERIUM; *esp* : a disease-producing bacterium

bacillus Cal·mette–Gué·rin \-ˌkal-ˈmet-(ˌ)gā-ˈraⁿ, -ˈraⁿ\ *n* : an attenuated strain of tubercle bacillus developed by repeated culture on a medium containing bile and used in preparation of tuberculosis vaccines — compare BCG VACCINE

Calmette, Albert Léon Charles (1863–1933), French bacteriologist, and Guérin, Camille (1872–1961), French veterinarian.

bac·i·tra·cin \ ˌba-sə-ˈtrās-ᵊn\ *n* : a toxic polypeptide antibiotic isolated from a bacillus (*Bacillus subtilis*) and usu. used topically esp. against gram-positive bacteria

Tra·cy \'trā-sē\, **Margaret,** American hospital patient.

back \'bak\ *n* **1 a :** the rear part of the human body esp. from the neck to the end of the spine **b :** the corresponding part of a lower animal (as a quadruped) **c :** SPINAL COLUMN **2 :** the part of the upper surface of the tongue behind the front and lying opposite the soft palate when the tongue is at rest

back·ache \'bak-∎āk\ *n* **:** a pain in the lower back

back·bone \-∎bōn\ *n* **:** SPINAL COLUMN, SPINE

¹back·cross \'bak-∎krós\ *vb* **:** to cross (a first-generation hybrid) with one of the parental types

²backcross *n* **:** a mating that involves backcrossing; *also* **:** an individual produced by backcrossing

back·ing \'ba-kiŋ\ *n* **:** the metal portion of a dental crown, bridge, or similar structure to which a porcelain or plastic tooth facing is attached

back·rest \'bak-∎rest\ *n* **:** a rest for the back

back·side \-'sīd\ *n* **:** BUTTOCKS — often used in pl.

bac·lo·fen \'ba-klō-∎fen\ *n* **:** a gamma-aminobutyric acid analogue $C_{10}H_{12}ClNO_2$ used as a relaxant of skeletal muscle esp. in treating spasticity (as in multiple sclerosis)

bact *abbr* **1** bacterial; bacterial **2** bacteriological; bacteriology **3** bacterium

bac·ter·emia \∎bak-tə-'rē-mē-ə\ *n* **:** the usu. transient presence of bacteria in the blood — **bac·ter·emic** \-mik\ *adj*

bacteri- *or* **bacterio-** *comb form* **:** bacteria **:** bacterial (*bacteri*olysis)

¹bacteria *pl of* BACTERIUM

²bacteria *n* **:** BACTERIUM — not usu. used technically

bac·te·ri·al \bak-'tir-ē-əl\ *adj* **:** of, relating to, or caused by bacteria (a ~ chromosome) (~ infection) — **bac·te·ri·al·ly** *adv*

bac·te·ri·cid·al \bak-∎tir-ə-'sīd-əl\ *also* **bac·te·ri·o·cid·al** \-∎tir-ē-ə-'sīd-\ *adj* **:** destroying bacteria — **bac·te·ri·cid·al·ly** *adv* — **bac·te·ri·cide** \-'tir-ə-∎sīd\ *n*

bac·te·ri·cid·in \∎bak-∎tir-ə-'sīd-ᵊn\ *or* **bac·te·ri·o·cid·in** \-∎tir-ē-ə-'sīd-\ *n* **:** a bactericidal antibody

bac·ter·in \'bak-tə-rən\ *n* **:** a suspension of killed or attenuated bacteria for use as a vaccine

bac·te·ri·o·cin \bak-'tir-ē-ə-sən\ *n* **:** an antibiotic (as colicin) produced by bacteria

bac·te·ri·ol·o·gist \(∎)bak-∎tir-ē-'ä-lə-jist\ *n* **:** a specialist in bacteriology

bac·te·ri·ol·o·gy \(∎)bak-∎tir-ē-'ä-lə-jē\ *n, pl* **-gies 1 :** a science that deals with bacteria and their relations to medicine, industry, and agriculture **2 :** bacterial life and phenomena — **bac-**

te·ri·o·log·ic \bak-∎tir-ē-ə-'lä-jik\ *or* **bac·te·ri·o·log·i·cal** \-ji-kəl\ *adj* — **bac·te·ri·o·log·i·cal·ly** \-ji-k(ə)lē\ *adv*

bac·te·ri·o·ly·sin \bak-∎tir-ē-ə-'lis-ᵊn\ *n* **:** an antibody that acts to destroy a bacterium

bac·te·ri·ol·y·sis \(∎)bak-∎tir-ē-'ä-lə-səs\ *n, pl* **-y·ses** \-∎sēz\ **:** destruction or dissolution of bacterial cells — **bac·te·ri·o·lyt·ic** \bak-∎tir-ē-ə-'li-tik\ *adj*

bac·te·ri·o·phage \bak-'tir-ē-ə-∎fāj, -∎fäzh\ *n* **:** a virus that infects bacteria — called also *phage*

bacteriophage lambda *n* **:** PHAGE LAMBDA

bac·te·ri·o·sta·sis \bak-∎tir-ē-ō-'stā-səs\ *n, pl* **-sta·ses** \-∎sēz\ **:** inhibition of the growth of bacteria without destruction

bac·te·ri·o·stat \-'tir-ē-ō-∎stat\ *also* **bac·te·ri·o·stat·ic** \-∎tir-ē-ō-'sta-tik\ *n* **:** an agent that causes bacteriostasis

bac·te·ri·o·stat·ic \-∎tir-ē-ō-'sta-tik\ *adj* **:** causing bacteriostasis (a ~ agent) — **bac·te·ri·o·stat·i·cal·ly** \-ti-k(ə)lē\ *adv*

bac·te·ri·um \bak-'tir-ē-əm\ *n, pl* **-ria** \-ē-ə\ **:** any of a group (as Kingdom Procaryotae or Kingdom Monera) of prokaryotic unicellular round, spiral, or rod-shaped single-celled microorganisms that are often aggregated into colonies or motile by means of flagella, that live in soil, water, organic matter, or the bodies of plants and animals, and that are autotrophic, saprophytic, or parasitic in nutrition and important because of their biochemical effects and pathogenicity

bac·te·ri·uria \bak-∎tir-ē-'ur-ē-ə, -'yùr-\ *n* **:** the presence of bacteria in the urine — **bac·te·ri·uric** \-ik\ *adj*

bac·te·roi·des \-'rói-(∎)dēz\ *n* **1** *cap* **:** a genus of gram-negative anaerobic bacteria (family Bacteroidaceae) that have rounded ends and occur usu. in the normal intestinal flora **2** *pl* **-roides :** a bacterium of the genus *Bacteroides* or of a closely related genus

Bac·trim \'bak-trim\ *trademark* — used for a preparation of sulfamethoxazole and trimethoprim

bag \'bag\ *n* **:** a pouched or pendulous bodily part or organ

ba·gasse \bə-'gas\ *n* **:** plant residue (as of sugarcane or grapes) left after a product (as juice) has been extracted

bag·as·so·sis \∎ba-gə-'sō-səs\ *n, pl* **-so·ses** \-∎sēz\ **:** an industrial disease characterized by cough, difficult breathing, chills, fever, and prolonged weakness and caused by the inhalation of the dust of bagasse — called also *bagasse disease*

bag of waters *n* **:** the double-walled fluid-filled sac that encloses and protects the fetus in the mother's womb and that breaks releasing its fluid during the birth process

Bain·bridge reflex \'bān-(∎)brij-\ *n* **:** a homeostatic reflex mechanism that causes acceleration of heartbeat following the stimulation of local muscle spindles when blood pressure in the venae cavae and right atrium is increased

Bainbridge, Francis Arthur (1874–1921), British physiologist.

Ba·ker's cyst \'bā-kərz-\ *n* : a swelling behind the knee that is composed of a membrane-lined sac filled with synovial fluid and is associated with certain joint disorders (as arthritis)

Baker, William Morrant (1839–1896), British surgeon.

bak·er's itch \-bā-kərz-\ *n* : GROCER'S ITCH

bak·ing soda \'bā-kiŋ-\ *n* : SODIUM BICARBONATE

BAL \-bē-(-)ā-'el\ *n* : DIMERCAPROL

balan- *or* **balano-** *comb form* : glans penis (balanitis) (balanoposthitis)

bal·ance \'ba-ləns\ *n* 1 : an instrument for weighing 2 : mental and emotional steadiness 3 : the relation in physiology between the intake of a particular nutrient and its excretion — see NITROGEN BALANCE, WATER BALANCE

bal·anced \-lənst\ *adj* 1 : having the physiologically active elements mutually counteracting (a ~ solution) 2 *of a diet or ration* : furnishing all needed nutrients in the amount, form, and proportions needed to support healthy growth and productivity

bal·a·ni·tis \ba-lə-'nī-təs\ *n* : inflammation of the glans penis

bal·a·no·pos·thi·tis \ba-lə-(-)nō-päs-'thī-təs\ *n* : inflammation of the glans penis and of the prepuce

bal·an·ti·di·a·sis \ba-lən-tə-'dī-ə-səs, bə-lan-\ *also* **bal·an·tid·i·o·sis** \balən-ti-dē-'ō-səs\ *n, pl* -a·ses *also* -o·ses \-sēz\ : infection with or disease caused by protozoans of the genus *Balantidium*

bal·an·tid·i·um \ba-lən-'ti-dē-əm\ *n* 1 *cap* : a genus of large parasitic ciliate protozoans (order Heterotricha) including one (*B. coli*) that infests the intestines of some mammals and esp. swine and may cause a chronic ulcerative dysentery in humans 2 *pl* -ia \-dē-ə\ : a protozoan of the genus *Balantidium* — **bal·an·tid·i·al** \-dē-əl\ *adj*

bald \'bȯld\ *adj* : lacking all or a significant part of the hair on the head or sometimes on other parts of the body — **bald** *vb*

bald·ness *n* : the state of being bald — see MALE-PATTERN BALDNESS

Bal·kan frame \'bȯl-kən-\ *n* : a frame employed in the treatment of fractured bones of the leg or arm that provides overhead weights and pulleys for suspension, traction, and continuous extension of the splinted fractured limb

ball \'bȯl\ *n* 1 : a roundish protuberant part of the body; as a : the rounded eminence by which the base of the thumb is continuous with the palm of

the hand b : the rounded broad part of the sole of the human foot between toes and arch and on which the main weight of the body first rests in normal walking 2 : EYEBALL 3 : TESTIS — usu. considered vulgar

ball–and–socket joint *n* : an articulation (as the hip joint) in which the rounded head of one bone fits into a cuplike cavity of the other and admits movement in any direction — called also *enarthrosis*

bal·lism \'ba-ıli-zəm\ *or* **bal·lis·mus** \bə-'liz-məs\ *n, pl* -isms *or* -is·mus·es : the abnormal swinging jerking movements sometimes seen in chorea

bal·lis·to·car·dio·gram \bə-ılis-tō-'kär-dē-ə-ıgram\ *n* : the record made by a ballistocardiograph

bal·lis·to·car·dio·graph \-ıgraf\ *n* : a device for measuring the amount of blood passing through the heart in a specified time by recording the recoil movements of the body that result from contraction of the heart muscle in ejecting blood from the ventricles — **bal·lis·to·car·dio·graph·ic** \-ıkär-dē-ə-'gra-fik\ *adj* — **bal·lis·to·car·di·og·ra·phy** \-ē-'ä-grə-fē\ *n*

¹**bal·loon** \bə-'lün\ *n* : a nonporous bag of tough light material that can be inflated (as in a bodily cavity) with air or gas

²**balloon** *vb* : to inflate, swell, or puff out like a balloon

balloon angioplasty *n* : dilatation of an atherosclerotically obstructed artery by the passage of a balloon catheter through the vessel to the area of disease where inflation of the catheter compresses the plaque against the vessel wall

balloon catheter *n* : a catheter that has two lumens and an inflatable tip which can be expanded by the passage of gas, water, or a radiopaque medium through one of the lumens and that is used esp. to measure blood pressure in a blood vessel or to expand a partly closed or obstructed bodily passage or tube (as a coronary artery) — see PERCUTANEOUS TRANSLUMINAL ANGIOPLASTY, SWAN-GANZ CATHETER

bal·lotte·ment \bə-'lät-mənt\ *n* : a sharp upward pushing against the uterine wall with a finger inserted into the vagina for diagnosing pregnancy by feeling the return impact of the displaced fetus; *also* : a similar procedure for detecting a floating kidney

balm \'bäm, 'bälm, 'bäm\ *n* 1 : an aromatic preparation (as a healing ointment) 2 : a soothing restorative agency

balne- *or* **balneo-** *comb form* : bath : bathing (balneotherapy)

bal·ne·ol·o·gy \bal-nē-'ä-lə-jē\ *n, pl* -gies : the science of the therapeutic use of baths

bal·neo·ther·a·py \bal-nē-ō-'ther-ə-pē\

n, pl **-pies** : the treatment of disease by baths

bal·sam \'bȯl-səm\ *n* **1** : any of several resinous substances used esp. in medicine **2** : BALM 2 — **bal·sam·ic** \bȯl-'sa-mik\ *adj*

balsam of Pe·ru \-pə-'rü\ *n* : a leguminous balsam from a tropical American tree (*Myroxylon pereirae*) used esp. as an irritant and to promote wound healing — called also *Peru balsam, Peruvian balsam*

balsam of To·lu \-tə-'lü\ *n* : a balsam from a tropical American leguminous tree (*Myroxylon balsamum*) used esp. as an expectorant and as a flavoring for cough syrups — called also *tolu, tolu balsam*

bam·boo spine \(ˌ)bam-'bü-\ *n* : a spinal column in the advanced stage of ankylosing spondylitis esp. as observed in an X ray with ossified layers at the margins of the vertebrae giving the whole an appearance of a stick of bamboo

Ban·croft·i·an filariasis \'ban-ˌkrȯf-tē-ən-, 'baṅ-\ *or* **Ban·croft's filariasis** \-ˌkrȯfts-\ *n* : filariasis caused by a slender white filaria of the genus *Wuchereria* (*W. bancrofti*) that is transmitted in larval form by mosquitoes, lives in lymph vessels and lymphoid tissues, and often causes elephantiasis by blocking lymphatic drainage

Ban·croft \'ban-ˌkrȯft, 'baṅ-\, **Jo·seph** (1836–1894), British physician.

band \'band\ *n* **1** : a thin flat encircling strip esp. for binding: as **a** : a strip of cloth used to protect a newborn baby's navel — called also *bellyband* **b** : a thin flat strip of metal that encircles a tooth (orthodontic ∼s) **2** : a strip separated by some characteristic color or texture or considered apart from what is adjacent: as **a** : a line or streak of differentiated cells **b** : one of the alternating dark and light segments of skeletal muscle fibers **c** : a strip of abnormal tissue either congenital or acquired; *esp* : a strip of connective tissue that causes obstruction of the bowel

¹ban·dage \'ban-dij\ *n* : a strip of fabric used to cover a wound, hold a dressing in place, immobilize an injured part, or apply pressure — see CAPELINE, ESMARCH BANDAGE, PRESSURE BANDAGE, SPICA, VELPEAU BANDAGE

²bandage *vb* **ban·daged; ban·dag·ing** : to bind, dress, or cover with a bandage (∼ a wound) (∼ a sprained ankle)

Band-Aid \'ban-ˌdād\ *trademark* — used for a small adhesive strip with a gauze pad for covering minor wounds

band form *n* : a young neutrophil in the stage of development following a metamyelocyte and having an elongated nucleus that has not yet become lobed as in a mature neutrophil — called also *band cell, stab cell*

band keratopathy *n* : calcium deposition in Bowman's membrane and the stroma of the cornea that appears as an opaque gray streak and occurs in hypercalcemia and various chronic inflammatory conditions of the eye

bane·ber·ry \'bān-ˌber-ē, -bə-rē, -brē\ *n, pl* **-ber·ries** : the acid poisonous berry of any plant of a genus (*Actaea*) of the buttercup family (Ranunculaceae); *also* : one of these plants

bang \'baṅ\ *var of* BHANG

Bang's disease \'baṅz-\ *n* : BRUCELLOSIS; *specif* : contagious abortion of cattle caused by a bacterium of the genus *Brucella* (*B. abortus*) — called also *Bang's*

Bang \'baṅ\, **Bernhard Lauritz Frederik** (1848–1932), Danish veterinarian.

bank \'baṅk\ *n* : a depot for the collection and storage of a biological product of human origin for medical use (bone ∼) — see BLOOD BANK

Ban·thine \'ban-ˌthin\ *trademark* — used for a preparation of methantheline

Ban·ti's disease \'ban-tēz-\ *n* : a disorder characterized by congestion and great enlargement of the spleen usu. accompanied by anemia, leukopenia, and cirrhosis of the liver — called also *Banti's syndrome*

Ban·ti \'ban-tē\, **Guido** (1852–1925), Italian physician.

¹bar \'bär\ *n, often attrib* **1** : a piece of metal that connects parts of a removable partial denture **2** : a straight stripe, band, or line much longer than it is wide **3** : the space in front of the molar teeth of a horse in which the bit is placed

²bar *vb* **barred; bar·ring** : to cut free and ligate (a vein in a horse's leg) above and below the site of a projected operative procedure

³bar *n* : a unit of pressure equal to one million dynes per square centimeter

bar- *or* **baro-** *comb form* : weight : pressure (*bariatrics*) (*barotrauma*)

Bá·rá·ny chair \bə-'rän-(y)ē-ˌcha(ə)r, -ˌche(ə)r\ *n* : a chair for testing the effects of circular motion esp. on airplane pilots

Bá·rá·ny \'bä-ˌrän\, **Robert** (1876–1936), Austrian otologist.

barb \'bärb\ *n, slang* : BARBITURATE

barbae — see SYCOSIS BARBAE

bar·ber's itch \ˌbär-bərz-\ *n* : ringworm of the face and neck

bar·bi·tal \'bär-bə-ˌtȯl\ *n* : a white crystalline addictive hypnotic $C_8H_{12}N_2O_3$ often administered in the form of its soluble sodium salt — see MEDINAL, VERONAL

bar·bi·tone \'bär-bə-ˌtōn\ *n, Brit* : BARBITAL

bar·bi·tu·rate \bär-'bi-chə-rət\ *n* **1** : a salt or ester of barbituric acid **2** : any of various derivatives of barbituric acid used esp. as sedatives, hypnotics, and antispasmodics

bar·bi·tu·ric acid \ˌbär-bə-ˈtür-ik, -ˈtyür-\ n : a synthetic crystalline acid $C_4H_4N_2O_3$ that is a derivative of pyrimidine; *also* : any of its acid derivatives of which some are used as hypnotics

bar·bi·tur·ism \bär-ˈbi-chə-ˌri-zəm, ˈbär-bi-\ n : a condition characterized by deleterious effects on the mind or body by excess use of barbiturates

barefoot doctor n : an auxiliary medical worker trained to provide health care in rural areas of China

bar·ia·tri·cian \bar-ē-ə-ˈtri-shən\ n : a specialist in bariatrics

bar·iat·rics \ˌbar-ē-ˈa-triks\ n : a branch of medicine that deals with the treatment of obesity — **bar·iat·ric** \-trik\ adj

bar·i·to·sis \ˌbar-ə-ˈtō-səs\ n, pl **-to·ses** \-ˌsēz\ : pneumoconiosis caused by inhalation of dust composed of barium or its compounds

bar·i·um \ˈbar-ē-əm\ n : a silver-white malleable toxic bivalent metallic element — symbol Ba; see ELEMENT table

barium chloride n : a water-soluble toxic salt $BaCl_2 \cdot 2H_2O$ used as a reagent in analysis and as a cardiac stimulant

barium enema n : a suspension of barium sulfate injected into the lower bowel to render it radiopaque, usu. followed by injection of air to inflate the bowel and increase definition, and used in the roentgenographic diagnosis of intestinal lesions

barium meal n : a solution of barium sulfate that is swallowed by a patient to facilitate fluoroscopic or roentgenographic diagnosis

barium sulfate n : a colorless crystalline insoluble salt $BaSO_4$ used medically chiefly as a radiopaque substance

Bar·low's disease \ˈbär-ˌlōz-\ n : INFANTILE SCURVY

    Barlow, Sir Thomas (1845–1945), British physician.

baro- — see BAR-

baro·re·cep·tor \ˌbar-ō-ri-ˈsep-tər\ also **baro·cep·tor** \-ō-ˈsep-\ n : a neural receptor (as of the carotid sinus) sensitive to changes in pressure

baro·trau·ma \-ˈtrau̇-mə, -ˈtrȯ-\ n, pl **-ma·ta** \-mə-tə\ : injury of a part or organ as a result of changes in barometric pressure; *specif* : AERO-OTITIS MEDIA

Barr body \ˈbär-\ n : material of the inactivated X chromosome present in each somatic cell of most female mammals that is used as a test of genetic femaleness (as in a fetus or an athlete) — called also *sex chromatin*

    Barr, Murray Llewellyn (b 1908), Canadian anatomist.

bar·rel chest \ˈbar-əl-\ n : the enlarged chest with a rounded cross section and fixed horizontal position of the ribs that occurs in chronic pulmonary emphysema

bar·ren \ˈbar-ən\ adj : incapable of producing offspring — used esp. of females or matings — **bar·ren·ness** \-ən-nəs\ n

bar·ri·er \ˈbar-ē-ər\ n : a material object or set of objects that separates, demarcates, or serves as a barricade — see BLOOD-BRAIN BARRIER, PLACENTAL BARRIER

bar·tho·lin·itis \bär-ˌtō-lə-ˈnī-təs\ n, pl **-lin·ites** \-ˌtēz\ : inflammation of the Bartholin's glands

Bar·tho·lin's gland \ˈbärt-ᵊl-ənz-, ˈbär-thə-lənz-\ n : either of two oval racemose glands lying one to each side of the lower part of the vagina and secreting a lubricating mucus — called also *gland of Bartholin, greater vestibular gland*; compare COWPER'S GLAND

    Bar·tho·lin \bär-ˈtü-lin\, **Caspar Thomèson** (1655–1738), Danish anatomist.

bar·ton·el·la \ˌbärt-ᵊn-ˈe-lə\ n 1 cap : a genus of gram-negative bacteria (family Bartonellaceae) that include the causative agent (B. bacilliformis) of bartonellosis 2 : any bacterium of the genus *Bartonella*

    Bar·ton \ˈbär-ˌtōn\, **Alberto L.** (b 1874), Peruvian physician.

bar·ton·el·lo·sis \ˌbärt-ᵊn-e-ˈlō-səs\ n, pl **-lo·ses** \-ˌsēz\ : a disease that occurs in So. America, is characterized by severe anemia and high fever followed by an eruption like warts on the skin, and is caused by a bacterium of the genus *Bartonella* (B. bacilliformis) that invades the red blood cells and is transmitted by sand flies (genus *Phlebotomus*) — called also *Carrión's disease*

ba·sal \ˈbā-səl, -zəl\ adj 1 : relating to, situated at, or forming the base 2 : of, relating to, or essential for maintaining the fundamental vital activities of an organism (as respiration, heartbeat, or excretion) ⟨~ diet⟩ 3 : serving as or serving to induce an initial comatose or unconscious state that forms a basis for further anesthetization ⟨~ narcosis⟩ ⟨~ anesthetic⟩ — **ba·sal·ly** adv

basal cell n : one of the innermost cells of the deeper epidermis of the skin

basal–cell carcinoma n : a skin cancer derived from and preserving the form of the basal cells of the skin

basal ganglion n : any of four deeply placed masses of gray matter within each cerebral hemisphere comprising the caudate nucleus, the lentiform nucleus, the amygdala, and the claustrum — usu. used in pl.; called also *basal nucleus*

basale, basalia — see STRATUM BASALE
basalis — see DECIDUA BASALIS

basal lamina *n* : the part of the gray matter of the embryonic neural tube from which the motor nerve roots arise

basal metabolic rate *n* : the rate at which heat is given off by an organism at complete rest

basal metabolism *n* : the turnover of energy in a fasting and resting organism using energy solely to maintain vital cellular activity, respiration, and circulation as measured by the basal metabolic rate

basal plate *n* : an underlying structure: as a : the ventral portion of the neural tube b : the part of the decidua of a placental mammal that is intimately fused with the placenta

base \'bās\ *n*, *pl* **bas•es** \'bā-səz\ 1 : that portion of a bodily organ or part by which it is attached to another more central structure of the organism (the ~ of the thumb) 2 a : the usu. inactive ingredient of a preparation serving as the vehicle for the active medicinal preparation b : the chief active ingredient of a preparation — called also *basis* 3 a : any of various typically water-soluble and bitter tasting compounds that in solution have a pH greater than 7, are capable of reacting with an acid to form a salt, and are molecules or ions able to take up a proton from an acid or are substances able to give up a pair of electrons to an acid — compare ALKALI b : any of the five purine or pyrimidine bases of DNA and RNA that include cytosine, guanine, adenine, thymine, and uracil — **based** \'bāst\ *adj*

Ba•se•dow's disease \'bä-zə-ıdō\ *n* : GRAVES' DISEASE

Basedow \'bä-zə-ıdō\, **Karl Adolph von** (1799–1854), German physician.

base•line \'bās-ılīn\ *n* : a set of critical observations or data used for comparison or a control

base•ment membrane \'bā-smənt-\ *n* : a thin membranous layer of connective tissue that separates a layer of epithelial cells from the underlying lamina propria

base pair *n* : one of the pairs of chemical bases composed of a purine on one strand of DNA joined by hydrogen bonds to a pyrimidine on the other that hold together the two complementary strands much like the rungs of a ladder and include adenine linked to thymine or sometimes to uracil and guanine linked to cytosine

base•plate \'bās-ıplāt\ *n* 1 : the portion of an artificial denture in contact with the jaw 2 : the sheet of plastic material used in the making of trial denture plates

basi- *also* **baso-** *comb form* 1 : of or belonging to the base or lower part of (*basi*cranial) 2 : chemical base (*baso*philic)

ba•sic \'bā-sik, -zik\ *adj* 1 : of, relating to, or forming the base or essence 2 a : of, relating to, containing, or having the character of a base b : having an alkaline reaction

ba•si•cra•ni•al \ıbā-si-'krā-nē-əl\ *adj* : of or relating to the base of the skull

ba•sid•io•my•cete \bə-ısid-ē-ō-'mī-ısēt\ *n* : any of a large class (Basidiomycetes) or subdivision (Basidiomycotina) of higher fungi that include rusts (order Uredinales), smuts (order Ustilaginales), and numerous edible forms (as many mushrooms) — **ba•sid•io•my•ce•tous** \-mī-'sē-təs\ *adj*

bas•i•lar \'ba-zə-lər, -sə- *also* 'bā-\ *adj* : of, relating to, or situated at the base

basilar artery *n* : an unpaired artery that is formed by the union of the two vertebral arteries, runs forward within the skull just under the pons, divides into the two posterior cerebral arteries, and supplies the pons, cerebellum, posterior part of the cerebrum, and the internal ear

basilar membrane *n* : a membrane that extends from the margin of the bony shelf of the cochlea to the outer wall and that supports the organ of Corti

basilar process *n* : an anterior median projection of the occipital bone in front of the foramen magnum articulating in front with the body of the sphenoid by the basilar suture

basilic vein *n* : a vein of the upper arm lying along the inner border of the biceps muscle, draining the whole limb, and opening into the axillary vein

¹ba•si•oc•cip•i•tal \ıbā-sē-äk-'sip-ət-əl\ *adj* : relating to or being a bone in the base of the cranium immediately in front of the foramen magnum that is represented in humans by the basilar process of the occipital bone

²basioccipital *n* : the basioccipital bone

ba•si•on \'bā-sē-ıän, -zē-\ *n* : the midpoint of the anterior margin of the foramen magnum

ba•sis \'bā-səs\ *n*, *pl* **ba•ses** \-ısēz\ 1 : any of various anatomical parts that function as a foundation 2 : BASE 2b

ba•si•sphe•noid \ıbā-səs-'fē-ınȯid\ *also* **ba•si•sphe•noi•dal** \-səs-fi-'nȯid-əl\ *adj* : relating to or being the part of the base of the cranium that lies between the basioccipital and the presphenoid bones and that usu. ossifies separately and becomes a part of the sphenoid bone only in the adult — **basisphenoid** *n*

basket cell *n* : any of the cells in the molecular layer of the cerebellum whose axons pass inward and end in a basketlike network around the Purkinje cells

Basle Nom•i•na An•a•tom•i•ca \'bä-zəl-'nä-mə-nə-ıa-nə-'tä-mi-kə\ *n* : the anatomical nomenclature adopted at the 1895 meeting of the German Anatomical Society at Basel, Switzerland, and superseded by the Nomina Anatomica adopted at the Sixth International Congress of Anatomists in 1955 — abbr. *BNA*

baso- — see BASI-

ba·so·phil \'bā-sə-ˌfĭl, -zə-\ *or* **ba·so·phile** \-ˌfīl\ *n* : a basophilic substance or structure; *esp* : a white blood cell with basophilic granules that is similar in function to a mast cell

ba·so·phil·ia \ˌbā-sə-'fĭl-ē-ə, -zə-\ *n* 1 : tendency to stain with basic dyes 2 : an abnormal condition in which some tissue element has increased basophilia

ba·so·phil·ic \-'fĭl-ĭk\ *also* **ba·so·phil** \'bā-sə-ˌfĭl, -zə-\ *or* **ba·so·phile** \-ˌfīl\ *adj* : staining readily with or being a basic stain

bath \'bath, 'bàth\ *n, pl* **baths** \'bathz, 'baths, 'bàthz, 'bàths\ 1 : a washing or soaking (as in water) of all or part of the body — see MUD BATH, SITZ BATH 2 : water used for bathing 3 : a place resorted to esp. for medical treatment by bathing : SPA — usu. used in pl.

bathe \'bāth\ *vb* **bathed; bath·ing** 1 : to wash in a liquid (as water) 2 : to apply water or a liquid medicament to

Bath·i·nette \ˌba-thə-'net, ˌbà-\ *trademark* — used for a portable bathtub for babies

ba·tracho·tox·in \bə-ˌtra-kə-'tăk-sən, ˌba-trə-kō-\ *n* : a very powerful steroid venom $C_{31}H_{42}N_2O_6$ extracted from the skin of a So. American frog (*Phyllobates aurotaenia*)

battered child syndrome *n* : the complex of physical injuries (as fractures, hematomas, and contusions) that results from gross abuse (as by a parent) of a young child

bat·tery \'ba-tə-rē\ *n, pl* **-ter·ies** : a group or series of tests; *esp* : a group of intelligence or personality tests given to a subject as an aid in psychological analysis

battle fatigue *n* : COMBAT FATIGUE — **bat·tle–fa·tigued** *adj*

Bau·hin's valve \'bō-ˌanz-, bō-'aⁿz-\ *n* : ILEOCECAL VALVE

Bauhin, Gaspard *or* Caspar (1560–1624), Swiss anatomist and botanist.

B cell *n* : any of the lymphocytes that have antibody molecules on the surface and comprise the antibody-secreting plasma cells when mature — called also *B lymphocyte*; compare T CELL

BCG *abbr* bacillus Calmette-Guérin

BCG vaccine \ˌbē-(ˌ)sē-'jē-\ *n* : a vaccine prepared from a living attenuated strain of tubercle bacilli and used to vaccinate human beings against tuberculosis

A. L. C. Calmette and C. Guérin — see BACILLUS CALMETTE-GUÉRIN

BCNU \ˌbē-(ˌ)sē-(ˌ)en-'yü\ *n* : a nitrosourea $C_5H_9Cl_2N_3O_2$ used as an antineoplastic drug — called also *carmustine*

B complex *n* : VITAMIN B COMPLEX

b.d. *abbr* [Latin *bis die*] twice a day — used in writing prescriptions

Bdel·lo·nys·sus \ˌde-lə-'nĭ-səs\ *n* : a genus of mites (family Dermanyssidae) that are parasitic on vertebrates and include the rat mite (*B. bacoti*) and serious pests (as *B. bursa* and *B. sylviarum*) of domestic fowl

Be *symbol* beryllium

bead·ing \'bē-dĭŋ\ *n* : the beadlike nodules occurring in rickets at the junction of the ribs with their cartilages — called also *rachitic rosary*

bear down *vb* : to contract the abdominal muscles and the diaphragm during childbirth

¹**beat** \'bēt\ *vb* **beat; beat·en** \'bēt-ᵊn\ *or* **beat; beat·ing** : PULSATE, THROB

²**beat** *n* : a single stroke or pulsation (as of the heart) (ectopic ∼s) — see EXTRASYSTOLE

bec·lo·meth·a·sone \ˌbe-klə-'me-thə-ˌzōn, -ˌsōn\ *n* : a steroid anti-inflammatory drug administered in the form of its dipropionate $C_{28}H_{37}$-ClO_7 as an inhalant in the treatment of asthma

Bec·que·rel ray \be-'krel-, ˌbe-kə-'rel-\ *n* : a ray emitted by a radioactive substance — used before adoption of the terms *alpha ray, beta ray, gamma ray*

Becquerel, Antoine–Henri (1852–1908), French physicist.

bed \'bed\ *n* 1 a : a piece of furniture on or in which one may lie and sleep — see HOSPITAL BED b : the equipment and services needed to care for one hospitalized patient 2 : a layer of specialized or altered tissue esp. when separating dissimilar structures — see NAIL BED, VASCULAR BED

bed·bug \'bed-ˌbəg\ *n* : a wingless bloodsucking bug (*Cimex lectularius*) sometimes infesting houses and esp. beds and feeding on human blood — called also *chinch*

bed·pan \'bed-ˌpan\ *n* : a shallow vessel used by a bedridden person for urination or defecation

bed rest *n* : confinement of a sick person to bed

bed·rid·den \'bed-ˌrid-ᵊn\ *or* **bed·rid** \-ˌrid\ *adj* : confined to bed (as by illness)

¹**bed·side** \'bed-ˌsīd\ *n* : a place beside a bed esp. of a bedridden person

²**bedside** *adj* 1 : of, relating to, or conducted at the bedside of a bedridden patient (a ∼ diagnosis) 2 : suitable for a bedridden person

bedside manner *n* : the manner that a physician assumes toward patients

bed·so·nia \bed-'sō-nē-ə\ *n, pl* **-ni·ae** \-nē-ˌē, -ˌī\ : CHLAMYDIA 2a

Bedson, \'bed-sᵊn\, Sir Samuel Phillips (1886–1969), English bacteriologist.

bed·sore \'bed-ˌsōr\ *n* : an ulceration of tissue deprived of adequate blood supply by prolonged pressure —

called also *decubitus, decubitus ulcer;* compare PRESSURE POINT

bed-wet-ting \-₁we-tiŋ\ *n* : enuresis esp. when occurring in bed during sleep — **bed-wet-ter** \-₁we-tər\ *n*

bee \'bē\ *n* : HONEYBEE; *broadly* : any of numerous hymenopterous insects (superfamily Apoidea) that differ from the related wasps esp. in the heavier hairier body and in having sucking as well as chewing mouthparts — see AFRICANIZED BEE

beef measles *n sing or pl* : the infestation of beef muscle by cysticerci of the beef tapeworm which make oval white vesicles giving a measly appearance to beef

beef tapeworm *n* : a tapeworm of the genus *Taenia* (*T. saginata*) that infests the human intestine as an adult, has a cysticercus larva that develops in cattle, and is contracted through ingestion of the larva in raw or rare beef

bees-wax \'bēz-₁waks\ *n* 1 : WAX 1 2 : YELLOW WAX

be-hav-ior \bi-'hā-vyər\ *n* 1 : the manner of conducting oneself 2 a : anything that an organism does involving action and response to stimulation b : the response of an individual, group, or species to its environment — **be-hav-ior-al** \-vyə-rəl\ *adj* — **be-hav-ior-al-ly** *adv*

behavioral science *n* : a science (as psychology, sociology, or anthropology) that deals with human action and seeks to generalize about human behavior in society — **behavioral scientist** *n*

be-hav-ior-ism \bi-'hā-vyə-₁ri-zəm\ *n* : a school of psychology that takes the objective evidence of behavior (as measured responses to stimuli) as the only concern of its research and the only basis of its theory without reference to conscious experience — **be-hav-ior-ist** \-rist\ *n or adj* — **be-hav-ior-is-tic** \-₁hā-vyə-'ris-tik\ *adj*

behavior therapist *n* : a specialist in behavior therapy

behavior therapy *n* : psychotherapy that emphasizes the application of the principles of learning to substitute desirable responses and behavior patterns for undesirable ones — called also *behavior modification;* compare COGNITIVE THERAPY

be-hav-iour, be-hav-iour-ism *chiefly Brit var of* BEHAVIOR, BEHAVIORISM

Beh-çet's syndrome \bə-'chets-\ *n* : a group of symptoms of unknown etiology that occur esp. in young men and include esp. ulcerative lesions of the mouth and genitalia and inflammation of the eye (as uveitis and iridocyclitis) — called also *Behcet's disease*

Behçet, Hulusi (1889–1948), Turkish dermatologist.

bej-el \'be-jəl\ *n* : a disease that is chiefly endemic in children in northern Africa and Asia Minor, is marked by bone and skin lesions, and is caused by a spirochete of the genus *Treponema* very similar to the causative agent of syphilis

bel \'bel\ *n* : ten decibels

Bell \'bel\, Alexander Graham (1847–1922), American inventor.

¹belch \'belch\ *vb* : to expel gas from the stomach suddenly : ERUCT

²belch *n* : an act or instance of belching : ERUCTATION

bel-la-don-na \₁be-lə-'dä-nə\ *n* 1 : an Old World poisonous plant of the genus *Atropa* (*A. belladonna*) having purple or green flowers, glossy black berries, and a root and leaves that yield atropine — called also *deadly nightshade* 2 : a medicinal extract (as atropine) from the belladonna plant

Bell-Ma-gen-die law \'bel-₁mä-zhạn-'dē-\ *n* : BELL'S LAW

Bell, Sir Charles (1774–1842), British anatomist.

Magendie, François (1783–1855), French physiologist.

bel-lows \'be-(₁)lōz\ *n sing or pl* : LUNGS

Bell's law \'belz-\ *n* : a statement in physiology: the roots of the spinal nerves coming from the ventral portion of the spinal cord are motor in function and those coming from the dorsal portion are sensory — called also *Bell-Magendie law*

Bell's palsy *n* : paralysis of the facial nerve producing distortion on one side of the face

bel-ly \'be-lē\ *n, pl* **bellies** 1 a : ABDOMEN 1a b : the undersurface of an animal's body c : the stomach and its adjuncts 2 : the enlarged fleshy body of a muscle

bel-ly-ache \'be-lē-₁āk\ *n* : pain in the abdomen and esp. in the bowels : COLIC

bel-ly-band \-₁band\ *n* : a band around or across the belly; *esp* : BAND 1a

belly button *n* : the human navel

be-me-gride \'be-mə-₁grīd, 'bē-\ *n* : an analeptic drug $C_{18}H_{13}NO_2$ used esp. to counteract the effects of barbiturates — see MEGIMIDE

Ben-a-dryl \'be-nə-₁dril\ *trademark* — used for a preparation of the hydrochloride of diphenhydramine

Bence-Jones protein \'bens-'jōnz-\ *n* : a polypeptide composed of one or two antibody light chains that is found esp. in the urine of persons affected with multiple myeloma

Bence-Jones, Henry (1814–1873), British physician.

Ben-der Gestalt test \₁ben-dər-\ *n* : a test in which the subject copies geometric figures and which is used esp. to assess organic brain damage and degree of nervous system maturation

Bender, Lauretta (*b* 1897), American psychiatrist.

bends \'bendz\ *n sing or pl* : the painful

manifestations (as joint pain) of decompression sickness; *also* : DECOMPRESSION SICKNESS — usu. used with preceding *the* (a case of the ∼)

Ben·e·dict's solution \'be-nə-ˌdikts-\ *n* : a blue solution that contains sodium carbonate, sodium citrate, and copper sulfate $CuSO_4$ and is used to test for reducing sugars in Benedict's test

Ben·e·dict \'be-nə-ˌdikt\, **Stanley Rossiter (1884–1936),** American chemist.

Benedict's test *n* : a test for the presence of a reducing sugar (as in urine) by heating the solution to be tested with Benedict's solution which yields a red, yellow, or orange precipitate upon warming with a reducing sugar (as glucose or maltose)

be·nign \bi-'nīn\ *adj* 1 : of a mild type or character that does not threaten health or life (∼ malaria) (a ∼ tumor) — compare MALIGNANT 1 2 : having a good prognosis : responding favorably to treatment (a ∼ psychosis) — **be·nig·ni·ty** \bi-'nig-nə-tē\ *n*

ben·ny \'be-nē\ *n, pl* **bennies** *slang* : a tablet of amphetamine taken as a stimulant

ben·ton·ite \'bent-ᵊn-ˌīt\ *n* : an absorptive and colloidal clay used in pharmacy esp. to stabilize suspensions

benz- *or* **benzo-** *comb form* 1 : related to benzene or benzoic acid (*benzoate*) 2 : containing a benzene ring fused on one side to one side of another ring (*benzimidazole*)

benz·al·ko·ni·um chloride \ˌben-zal-'kō-nē-əm-\ *n* : a white or yellowish white mixture of chloride salts used as an antiseptic and germicide — see ZEPHIRAN

ben·za·thine penicillin G \'ben-zə-ˌthēn-, -thən-\ *n* : a long-acting relatively insoluble salt of penicillin G

Ben·ze·drine \'ben-zə-ˌdrēn\ *trademark* — used for a preparation of the sulfate of amphetamine

ben·zene \'ben-ˌzēn, ben-'\ *n* : a colorless volatile flammable toxic liquid aromatic hydrocarbon C_6H_6 used in organic chemistry, as a solvent, and as a motor fuel

benzene hexa·chlor·ide \-ˌhek-sə-'klōr-ˌīd\ *n* : a compound $C_6H_6Cl_6$ occurring in several stereoisomeric forms : BHC; *esp* : GAMMA BENZENE HEXACHLORIDE — see LINDANE

benzene ring *n* : a ring of six carbon atoms linked by alternate single and double bonds in a plane symmetrical hexagon that occurs in benzene and related compounds

ben·zes·trol \ben-'zes-ˌtrȯl, -ˌtrōl\ *n* : a crystalline estrogenic compound $C_{20}H_{26}O_2$

ben·zi·dine \'ben-zə-ˌdēn\ *n* : a crystalline base $C_{12}H_{12}N_2$ used esp. in making dyes and in a test for blood

benzidine test *n* : a test for blood (as in feces) based on its production of a blue color in a solution containing benzidine

benzilate — see QUINUCLIDINYL BENZILATE

benz·imid·azole \ˌben-zi-mə-'da-ˌzōl, ˌben-zə-'mi-də-ˌzōl\ *n* : a crystalline base $C_7H_6N_2$ used esp. to inhibit the growth of various viruses, parasitic worms, and fungi; *also* : one of its derivatives

benzo- — see BENZ-

ben·zo·[a]·py·rene \ˌben-zō-ˌā-'pīr-ˌēn, -zō-ˌal-fə-, -ˌpī-'rēn\ *also* **3,4-benzpyrene** \-benz-'pīr-ˌēn, -ˌbenz-pī-'rēn\ *n* : the yellow crystalline highly carcinogenic isomer of the benzopyrene mixture that is formed esp. in the burning of cigarettes, coal, and gasoline

ben·zo·ate \'ben-zə-ˌwāt\ *n* : a salt or ester of benzoic acid

ben·zo·caine \'ben-zə-ˌkān\ *n* : a crystalline ester $C_9H_{11}NO_2$ used as a local anesthetic — called also *ethyl aminobenzoate*

ben·zo·di·az·e·pine \ˌben-zō-dī-'a-zə-ˌpēn\ *n* : any of a group of aromatic lipophilic amines (as diazepam and chlordiazepoxide) used esp. as tranquilizers

ben·zo·ic acid \ben-ˌzō-ik-\ *n* : a white crystalline acid $C_6H_6O_2$ used as a preservative of foods and in medicine

ben·zo·in \'ben-zə-wən, -ˌwēn; -ˌzóin\ *n* 1 : a yellowish balsamic resin from trees (genus *Styrax* of the family styracaceae) of southeastern Asia used esp. as an expectorant and topically to relieve skin irritations 2 : a white crystalline hydroxy ketone $C_{14}H_{12}O_2$

ben·zo·mor·phan \ˌben-zō-'mȯr-ˌfan\ *n* : any of a group of synthetic compounds whose best-known members are analgesics (as phenazocine or pentazocine)

ben·zo·phe·none \ˌben-zō-fi-'nōn, -'fē-ˌnōn\ *n* : a colorless crystalline ketone $C_{13}H_{10}O$ used in sunscreens

ben·zo·py·rene \ben-zō-'pīr-ˌēn, -ˌpī-'rēn\ *or* **benz·py·rene** \benz-'pīr-ˌēn, ˌbenz-pī-'rēn\ *n* : a mixture of two isomeric hydrocarbons $C_{20}H_{12}$ of which one is highly carcinogenic — see BENZO[A]PYRENE

ben·zo·yl \'ben-ˌzȯil, 'ben-zə-ˌwil\ *n* : the radical C_6H_5CO of benzoic acid

benzoyl peroxide *n* : a white crystalline flammable compound $C_{14}H_{10}O_4$ used in medicine esp. in the treatment of acne

benz·pyr·in·i·um bromide \ˌbenz-pə-'ri-nē-əm-\ *n* : a cholinergic drug $C_{15}H_{17}BrN_2O_2$ that has actions and uses similar to those of neostigmine and has been used esp. to relieve postoperative urinary retention — called also *benzpyrinium*

benz·tro·pine \benz-'trō-ˌpēn, -pən\ *n* : a parasympatholytic drug used in the form of one of its salts $C_{21}H_{25}NO\cdot$

CH_4O_3S esp. in the treatment of Parkinson's disease

ben·zyl \'ben-ˌzēl, -zəl\ n : the radical $C_6H_5CH_2$ having a chemical valence of one

benzyl benzoate n : a colorless oily ester $C_{14}H_{12}O_2$ used esp. as a scabicide

ben·zyl-pen·i·cil·lin \ˌben-zēl-(ˌ)pe-nə-'si-lən, -zəl-\ n : PENICILLIN G

beri·beri \ˌber-ē-'ber-ē\ n : a deficiency disease marked by inflammatory or degenerative changes of the nerves, digestive system, and heart and caused by a lack of or inability to assimilate thiamine

berke·li·um \'bər-klē-əm\ n : a radioactive metallic element — symbol Bk; see ELEMENT table

ber·lock dermatitis \'bər-ˌläk-\ n : a brownish discoloration of the skin that develops on exposure to sunlight after the use of perfume containing certain essential oils

Ber·tin's column \ber-'taⁿz-\ n : RENAL COLUMN

Ber·tin \ber-taⁿ\, Exupère Joseph (1712–1781), French anatomist.

be·ryl·li·o·sis \bə-ˌri-lē-'ō-səs\ also **beryl·lo·sis** \ˌber-ə-'lō-\ n, pl -li·o·ses \-ˌsēz\ or -lo·ses \-ˌsēz\ : poisoning resulting from exposure to fumes and dusts of beryllium compounds or alloys and occurring chiefly as an acute pneumonitis or as a granulomatosis involving esp. the lungs

be·ryl·li·um \bə-'ri-lē-əm\ n : a steelgray light strong brittle toxic bivalent metallic element — symbol Be; see ELEMENT table

bes·ti·al·i·ty \ˌbes-chē-'a-lə-tē, ˌbēs-\ n, pl -ties : sexual relations between a human being and a lower animal

¹be·ta \'bā-tə\ n 1 : the second letter of the Greek alphabet — B or β 2 : BETA PARTICLE 3 : BETA WAVE

²beta or **β-** adj 1 : of or relating to one of two or more closely related chemical substances ⟨the beta chain of hemoglobin⟩ — used somewhat arbitrarily to specify ordinal relationship or a particular physical form 2 : second in position in the structure of an organic molecule from a particular group or atom; also : of, relating to, or having a structure characterized by such a position (β–substitution) 3 : producing a zone of decolorization when grown on blood media — used of some hemolytic streptococci or of the hemolysis they cause

be·ta–ad·ren·er·gic \-ˌa-drə-'nər-jik\ adj : of, relating to, or being a beta-receptor ⟨~ blocking action⟩

be·ta–adrenergic receptor n : BETA-RECEPTOR

be·ta–ad·re·no·cep·tor \-ə-'drē-nə-ˌsep-tər\ also **be·ta–ad·re·no·re·cep·tor** \-ˌri-ˌsep-tər\ n : BETA-RECEPTOR

be·ta–block·er \-'blä-kər\ n : any of a class of heart drugs (as propranolol)

that combine with and block the activity of a beta-receptor

be·ta–block·ing \-'blä-kiŋ\ adj : blocking or relating to the blocking of beta-receptor activity ⟨~ drugs⟩

be·ta–car·o·tene or **β-carotene** \-'kar-ə-ˌtēn\ n : an isomer of carotene that is found in dark green and dark yellow vegetables and fruits

beta cell n : any of various secretory cells distinguished by their basophilic staining characters: as a : a pituitary basophil b : an insulin-secreting cell of the islets of Langerhans — compare ALPHA CELL

Be·ta·dine \'bā-tə-ˌdīn\ trademark — used for a preparation of povidone-iodine

be·ta–en·dor·phin or **β-endorphin** \ˌbā-tə-en-'dór-fən\ n : an endorphin of the pituitary gland with much greater analgesic potency than morphine — see BETA-LIPOPROTEIN

beta globulin n : any of several globulins of plasma or serum that have at alkaline pH electrophoretic mobilities intermediate between those of the alpha globulins and gamma globulins

beta hemolysis n : a sharply defined clear colorless zone of hemolysis surrounding colonies of certain streptococci on blood agar plates — **be·ta–he·mo·lyt·ic** \ˌbā-tə-ˌhē-mə-'li-tik\ adj

be·ta–lac·tam or **β-lactam** \ˌbā-tə-'lak-ˌtam\ n : any of a large class of antibiotics (as the penicillins and cephalosporins) with a lactam ring

be·ta–lac·ta·mase or **β-lactamase** \-'lak-tə-ˌmās, -ˌmāz\ n : PENICILLINASE

beta–lipoprotein or **β-lipoprotein** n : LDL

be·ta–li·po·tro·pin \ˌbā-tə-ˌli-pə-'trō-pən, -ˌlī-\ n : a lipotropin of the anterior pituitary that contains beta-endorphin as the terminal sequence of 31 amino acids in its polypeptide chain

be·ta·meth·a·sone \ˌbā-tə-'me-thə-ˌzōn, -ˌsōn\ n : a potent glucocorticoid $C_{22}H_{29}FO_5$ that is isomeric with dexamethasone and has potent anti-inflammatory activity

beta particle n : an electron or positron ejected from the nucleus of an atom during radioactive decay; also : a high-speed electron or positron

beta ray n 1 : BETA PARTICLE 2 : a stream of beta particles

be·ta–re·cep·tor \ˌbā-tə-ri-'sep-tər\ n : any of a group of receptors postulated to exist on nerve cell membranes of the sympathetic nervous system to explain the specificity of certain adrenergic agents in affecting only some sympathetic activities (as vasodilation, increase in muscular contraction and beat of the heart, and relaxation of smooth muscle in the bronchi and intestine) — called also beta-adren-

ergic receptor, beta-adrenoceptor; compare ALPHA-RECEPTOR

beta–thalassemia or **β-thalassemia** *n* : thalassemia in which the hemoglobin chain designated beta is affected and which comprises Cooley's anemia in the homozygous condition and thalassemia minor in the heterozygous condition

beta wave *n* : an electrical rhythm of the brain with a frequency of 13 to 30 cycles per second that is associated with normal conscious waking experience — called also *beta, beta rhythm*

betel nut *n* : the astringent seed of an Asian palm (*Areca catechu*) that is a source of arecoline

be·tha·ne·chol \bə-ˈthā-nə-ˌkȯl, -ˈtha-, -ˌkȯl\ *n* : a parasympathomimetic agent administered in the form of its chloride $C_7H_{17}ClN_2O_2$ and used esp. to treat gastric and urinary retention — see URECHOLINE

be·tween·brain \bi-ˈtwēn-ˌbrān\ *n* : DIENCEPHALON

Betz cell \ˈbets-\ *n* : a very large pyramidal nerve cell of the motor area of the cerebral cortex

Betz, Vladimir Aleksandrovich (1834–1894), Russian anatomist.

be·zoar \ˈbē-ˌzȯr\ *n* : any of various calculi found in the gastrointestinal organs esp. of ruminants — called also *bezoar stone*

BFP *abbr* biologic false-positive

BHA \ˌbē-(ˌ)āch-ˈā\ *n* : a phenolic antioxidant $C_{11}H_{16}O_2$ used esp. to preserve fats and oils in food — called also *butylated hydroxyanisole*

bhang \ˈbäŋ, ˈbȯŋ, ˈbaŋ\ *n* **1 a** : HEMP **1 b** : the leaves and flowering tops of uncultivated hemp : CANNABIS — compare MARIJUANA **2** : an intoxicant product obtained from bhang — compare HASHISH

BHC \ˌbē-(ˌ)āch-ˈsē\ *n* **1** : BENZENE HEXACHLORIDE **2** : LINDANE

BHT \ˌbē-(ˌ)āch-ˈtē\ *n* : a phenolic antioxidant $C_{15}H_{24}O$ used esp. to preserve fats and oils in food, cosmetics, and pharmaceuticals — called also *butylated hydroxytoluene*

Bi *symbol* bismuth

¹bi- *prefix* **1 a** : two (*bi*lateral) **b** : into two parts (*bi*furcate) **2** : twice : doubly : on both sides (*bi*convex) **3** : between, involving, or affecting two (specified) symmetrical parts (*bi*labial) **4 a** : containing one (specified) constituent in double the proportion of the other constituent or in double the ordinary proportion (*bi*carbonate) **b** : DI- (*bi*phenyl)

²bi- or **bio-** *comb form* : life : living organisms or tissue (*bio*chemistry)

bib·li·o·ther·a·py \ˌbi-blē-ō-ˈther-ə-pē\ *n, pl* **-pies** : the use of selected reading materials as therapeutic adjuvants in medicine and in psychiatry; *also* : guidance in the solution of personal

problems through directed reading — **bib·li·o·ther·a·peu·tic** \-ˌther-ə-ˈpyüt-ik\ *adj* — **bib·li·o·ther·a·pist** \-ˈther-ə-pist\ *n*

bi·carb \ˈbi-ˌkärb, bi-ˈ\ *n* : SODIUM BICARBONATE

bi·car·bon·ate \(ˌ)bi-ˈkär-bə-ˌnāt, -nət\ *n* : an acid carbonate

bicarbonate of soda *n* : SODIUM BICARBONATE

bi·ceps \ˈbi-ˌseps\ *n, pl* **biceps** *also* **bi·cepses** : a muscle having two heads: as **a** : the large flexor muscle of the front of the upper arm **b** : the large flexor muscle of the back of the upper leg

biceps bra·chii \-ˈbrā-kē-ˌē, -ˌī\ *n* : BICEPS a

biceps fe·mo·ris \-ˈfē-mə-rəs, -ˈfe-\ *n* : BICEPS b

biceps flex·or cu·bi·ti \-ˈflek-ˌsȯr-ˈkyü-bə-ˌtī, -tē\ *n* : BICEPS a

bi·chlo·ride of mercury \(ˌ)bī-ˈklȯr-ˌīd-\ *n* : MERCURIC CHLORIDE

bi·cip·i·tal \(ˌ)bī-ˈsi-pət-ᵊl\ *adj* **1** of muscles : having two heads or origins **2** : of or relating to a biceps muscle

bicipital aponeurosis *n* : an aponeurosis given off from the tendon of the biceps of the arm and continuous with the deep fascia of the forearm

bicipital groove *n* : a furrow on the upper part of the humerus occupied by the long head of the biceps — called also *intertubercular groove*

bicipital tuberosity *n* : the rough eminence which is on the anterior inner aspect of the neck of the radius and into which the tendon of the biceps is inserted

bi·con·cave \(ˌ)bī-(ˌ)kän-ˈkāv, (ˌ)bī-ˈkän-ˌ\ *adj* : concave on both sides — **bi·con·cav·i·ty** \ˌbī-(ˌ)kän-ˈka-və-tē\ *n*

bi·con·vex \(ˌ)bī-ˈkän-ˌ, ˌbī-kən-ˈ\ *adj* : convex on both sides — **bi·con·vex·i·ty** \ˌbī-kən-ˈvek-sə-tē, -(ˌ)kän-ˈ\ *n*

bi·cor·nu·ate \(ˌ)bī-ˈkȯrn-yə-ˌwāt, -wət\ *also* **bi·cor·nate** \-ˈkȯr-ˌnāt, -nət\ *adj* : having two horns or horn-shaped processes (a ~ uterus)

bi·cu·cul·line \bī-ˈkü-kyə-ˌlēn, -lən\ *n* : a convulsant alkaloid $C_{20}H_{17}NO_6$ obtained from plants (family Fumariaceae) and having the capacity to antagonize the action of gamma-aminobutyric acid in the central nervous system

¹bi·cus·pid \(ˌ)bī-ˈkəs-pəd\ *adj* : having or ending in two points (~ teeth)

²bicuspid *n* : either of the two double-pointed teeth that in humans are situated between the canines and the molars on each side of each jaw : PREMOLAR

bicuspid valve *n* : a valve in the heart consisting of two triangular flaps which allow only unidirectional flow from the left atrium to the ventricle — called also *left atrioventricular valve, mitral valve*

bi·cy·clic \(ˌ)bī-ˈsī-klik, -ˈsi-\ *adj* : containing two usu. fused rings in the structure of a molecule

bid *abbr* [Latin *bis in die*] twice a day — used in writing prescriptions

bi·det \bi-ˈdā\ *n* : a bathroom fixture used esp. for bathing the external genitals and the posterior parts of the body

bi·di·rec·tion·al \ˌbī-də-ˈrek-sh(ə-)nəl, -dī-\ *adj* : involving, moving, or taking place in two usu. opposite directions (~ flow of materials in axons) — **bi·di·rec·tion·al·ly** *adv*

bi·fid \ˈbī-ˌfid, -fəd\ *adj* : divided into two equal lobes or parts by a median cleft (repair of a ~ digit)

bifida — see SPINA BIFIDA, SPINA BIFIDA OCCULTA

¹bi·fo·cal \(ˌ)bī-ˈfō-kəl\ *adj* 1 : having two focal lengths 2 : having one part that corrects for near vision and another for distant vision (a ~ eyeglass lens)

²bifocal *n* 1 : a bifocal glass or lens 2 *pl* : eyeglasses with bifocal lenses

bi·func·tion·al \ˌbī-ˈfəŋk-sh(ə-)nəl\ *adj* : having two functions (~ neurons)

bi·fur·cate \ˈbī-(ˌ)fər-ˌkāt, bī-ˈfər-\ *vb* -cat·ed; -cat·ing : to divide into two branches or parts — **bi·fur·cate** \(ˌ)bī-ˈfər-kət, -ˌkāt; ˈbī-(ˌ)fər-ˌkāt\ *or* **bi·fur·cat·ed** \-ˌkā-təd\ *adj* — **bi·fur·ca·tion** \ˌbī-(ˌ)fər-ˈkā-shən\ *n*

bi·gem·i·ny \bī-ˈje-mə-nē\ *n, pl* **-nies** : the state of having a pulse characterized by two beats close together with a pause following each pair of beats — **bi·gem·i·nal** \-nəl\ *adj*

big·head \ˈbig-ˌhed\ *n* : any of several diseases of animals: as **a** : equine osteoporosis **b** : an acute photosensitization of sheep and goats that follows the ingestion of various plants — compare FAGOPYRISM

big toe *n* : the innermost and largest digit of the foot — called also *great toe*

bi·gua·nide \(ˌ)bī-ˈgwä-ˌnīd, -nəd\ *n* : any of a group of hypoglycemia-inducing drugs (as phenformin) used esp. in the treatment of diabetes — see PALUDRINE

bi·la·bi·al \(ˌ)bī-ˈlā-bē-əl\ *adj* : of or relating to both lips

bi·lat·er·al \(ˌ)bī-ˈla-tə-rəl, -ˈla-trəl\ *adj* 1 : of, relating to, or affecting the right and left sides of the body or the right and left members of paired organs (~ nephrectomy) 2 : having bilateral symmetry — **bi·lat·er·al·i·ty** \(ˌ)bī-ˌla-tə-ˈra-lə-tē\ *n* — **bi·lat·er·al·ly** *adv*

bilateral symmetry *n* : symmetry in which similar anatomical parts are arranged on opposite sides of a median axis so that one and only one plane can divide the individual into essentially identical halves

bi·lay·er \ˈbī-ˌlā-ər\ *n* : a film or membrane with two molecular layers — **bilayer** *adj*

bile \ˈbīl\ *n* : a yellow or greenish viscid alkaline fluid secreted by the liver and passed into the duodenum where it aids esp. in the emulsification and absorption of fats

bile acid *n* : any of several steroid acids (as cholic acid) that occur in bile usu. in the form of sodium salts conjugated with glycine or taurine

bile duct *n* : a duct by which bile passes from the liver or gallbladder to the duodenum

bile fluke *n* : CHINESE LIVER FLUKE

bile pigment *n* : any of several coloring matters (as bilirubin or biliverdin) in bile

bile salt *n* 1 : a salt of bile acid 2 **bile salts** *pl* : a dry mixture of the salts of the gall of the ox used as a liver stimulant and as a laxative

bil·har·zia \bil-ˈhär-zē-ə, -ˈhärt-sē-\ *n* 1 : SCHISTOSOME 2 : SCHISTOSOMIASIS — **bil·har·zi·al** \-zē-əl, -sē-\ *adj*

Bil·harz \ˈbil-ˌhärts\, **Theodor Maximilian** (1825–1862), German anatomist and helminthologist.

bil·har·zi·a·sis \ˌbil-ˌhär-ˈzī-ə-səs, -ˌhärt-ˈsī-\ *n, pl* **-a·ses** \-ˌsēz\ : SCHISTOSOMIASIS

bili- *comb form* 1 : bile (*biliary*) 2 : derived from bile (*bilirubin*)

bil·i·ary \ˈbi-lē-ˌer-ē\ *adj* 1 : of, relating to, or conveying the bile 2 : affecting the bile-conveying structures

biliary cirrhosis *n* : cirrhosis of the liver due to inflammation or obstruction of the bile ducts resulting in the accumulation of bile in and functional impairment of the liver

biliary dyskinesia *n* : pain or discomfort in the epigastric region resulting from spasm esp. of the sphincter of Oddi following cholecystectomy

biliary fever *n* : piroplasmosis esp. of dogs and horses

biliary tree *n* : the bile ducts and gallbladder

bil·ious \ˈbil-yəs\ *adj* 1 : of or relating to bile 2 : marked by or affected with disordered liver function and esp. excessive secretion of bile — **bil·ious·ness** *n*

bil·i·ru·bin \ˌbi-li-ˈrü-bən, ˈbi-li-ˌ\ *n* : a reddish yellow pigment $C_{33}H_{36}N_4O_6$ that occurs esp. in bile and blood and causes jaundice if accumulated in excess

bil·i·ru·bi·nae·mia \ˌbi-li-ˌrü-bə-ˈnē-mē-ə\ *chiefly Brit var of* BILIRUBINEMIA

bil·i·ru·bi·ne·mia \-ˈnē-mē-ə\ *n* : HYPERBILIRUBINEMIA

bil·i·ru·bi·nu·ria \-ˈnür-ē-ə, -ˈnyür-\ *n* : excretion of bilirubin in the urine

bil·i·ver·din \ˌbi-li-ˈvərd-ən, ˈbi-li-ˌ\ *n* : a green pigment $C_{33}H_{34}N_4O_6$ that occurs in bile and is an intermediate in the degradation of hemoglobin heme groups to bilirubin

bi·lobed \(ˌ)bī-ˈlōbd\ *adj* : divided into two lobes (a ~ organ)

Bil·tri·cide \\'bil-trə-ₐsīd\ *trademark* — used for a preparation of praziquantel

bi·man·u·al \(ₐ)bī-'man-yə-wəl\ *adj* : done with or requiring the use of both hands (~ pelvic examination)

bin- *comb form* : two : two by two : two at a time (*bin*aural)

bi·na·ry \'bī-nə-rē\ *adj* 1 : compounded or consisting of or marked by two things or parts 2 : composed of two chemical elements, an element and a radical that acts as an element, or two such radicals

binary fission *n* : reproduction of a cell by division into two approximately equal parts

bin·au·ral \(ₐ)bī-'nór-əl, (ₐ)bi-\ *adj* : of, relating to, or involving two or both ears — **bin·au·ral·ly** \-ē\ *adv*

bind \'bīnd\ *vb* **bound** \'baund\; **binding** 1 : to wrap up (an injury) with a cloth : BANDAGE 2 : to take up and hold usu. by chemical forces : combine with (cellulose ~s water) 3 : to combine or be taken up esp. by chemical action (an antibody *bound* to a specific antigen) 4 : to make costive : CONSTIPATE

bind·er \'bīn-dər\ *n* 1 : a broad bandage applied (as about the chest) for support 2 : a substance (as glucose or acacia) used in pharmacy to hold together the ingredients of a compressed tablet

Bi·net age \bē-'nā-, bi-\ *n* : mental age as determined by the Binet-Simon scale

    Bi·net \bē-nā\, **Alfred (1857–1911),** French psychologist, and **Si·mon** \sē-mōⁿ\, **Théodore (1873–1961),** French physician.

Bi·net–Si·mon scale \bi-'nā-sē-'mōⁿ-\ *n* : an intelligence test consisting orig. of tasks graded from the level of the average 3-year-old to that of the average 12-year-old but later extended in range — called also *Binet-Simon test, Binet test;* see STANFORD-BINET TEST

binge \'binj\ *vb* **binged; binge·ing** or **bing·ing** : to eat compulsively or greedily esp. as a symptom of bulimia — **bing·er** \'bin-jər\ *n*

bin·oc·u·lar \bī-'nä-kyə-lər, bə-\ *adj* : of, relating to, using, or adapted to the use of both eyes (a ~ infection) (~ vision) — **bin·oc·u·lar·ly** *adv*

bi·no·mi·al \bī-'nō-mē-əl\ *n* : a biological species name consisting of two terms — **binomial** *adj*

binomial nomenclature *n* : a system of nomenclature in which each species of animal or plant receives a name of two terms of which the first identifies the genus to which it belongs and the second the species itself

bin·ovu·lar \(ₐ)bi-'nä-vyə-lər, -'nō-\ *adj* : BIOVULAR (~ twins)

bi·nu·cle·ate \(ₐ)bī-'nü-klē-ət, -'nyü-\ *also* **bi·nu·cle·at·ed** \-klē-ₐā-təd\ *adj* : having two nuclei (~ lymphocytes)

bio- — see BI-

bio·ac·cu·mu·la·tion \ₐbī-(ₐ)ō-ə-ₐkyü-myə-'lā-shən\ *n* : the accumulation of a substance (as a pesticide) in a living organism

bio·ac·tive \ₐbī-ō-'ak-tiv\ *adj* : having an effect on a living organism (~ pharmaceuticals and pesticides) — **bio·ac·tiv·i·ty** \-ak-'ti-və-tē\ *n*

bio·as·say \ₐbī-(ₐ)ō-'a-ₐsā, -a-'sā\ *n* : determination of the relative strength of a substance (as a drug) by comparing its effect on a test organism with that of a standard preparation — **bio·as·say** \-a-'sā, -'a-ₐsā\ *vb*

bio·avail·abil·i·ty \ₐbī-(ₐ)ō-ə-ₐvā-lə-'bi-lə-tē\ *n, pl* **-ties** : the degree and rate at which a substance (as a drug) is absorbed into a living system or is made available at the site of physiological activity — **bio·avail·able** \-'vā-lə-bəl\ *adj*

bio·cat·a·lyst \ₐbī-ō-'kat-əl-əst\ *n* : ENZYME

bio·chem·i·cal \ₐbī-ō-'ke-mi-kəl\ *adj* 1 : of or relating to biochemistry 2 : characterized by, produced by, or involving chemical reactions in living organisms (~ derangements) — **biochemical** *n* — **bio·chem·i·cal·ly** \-k(ə-)lē\ *adv*

bio·chem·is·try \ₐbī-ō-'ke-mə-strē\ *n, pl* **-tries** 1 : chemistry that deals with the chemical compounds and processes occurring in organisms 2 : the chemical characteristics and reactions of a particular living system or biological substance — **bio·chem·ist** \-'ke-mist\ *n*

bio·cide \'bī-ə-ₐsīd\ *n* : a substance (as DDT) that is destructive to many different organisms — **bio·cid·al** \ₐbī-ə-'sīd-əl\ *adj*

bio·com·pat·i·bil·i·ty \ₐbī-ō-kəm-ₐpa-tə-'bi-lə-tē\ *n, pl* **-ties** : the condition of being compatible with living tissue or a living system by not being toxic or injurious and not causing immunological rejection — **bio·com·pat·i·ble** \-kəm-'pa-tə-bəl\ *adj*

bio·de·grad·able \ₐbī-(ₐ)ō-di-'grā-də-bəl\ *adj* : capable of being broken down esp. into innocuous products by the action of living things (as microorganisms) — **bio·de·grad·abil·i·ty** \-ₐgrā-də-'bi-lə-tē\ *n* — **bio·de·gra·da·tion** \-ₐde-grə-'dā-shən\ *n* — **bio·de·grade** \-di-'grād\ *vb*

bio·elec·tri·cal \-i-'lek-tri-kəl\ *also* **bio·elec·tric** \-trik\ *adj* : of or relating to electric phenomena in living organisms (human cortical ~ activity) — **bio·elec·tric·i·ty** \-ₐlek-'tri-sə-tē\ *n*

bio·elec·tron·ics \-i-(ₐ)lek-'trä-niks\ *n* 1 : a branch of the life sciences that deals with electronic control of physiological function 2 : a branch of science that deals with the role of electron transfer in biological processes

bio·en·er·get·ics \-ₐe-nər-'je-tiks\ *n* : a

system of therapy that combines breathing and body exercises, psychological therapy, and the free expression of impulses and emotions and that is held to increase well-being by releasing blocked physical and psychic energy — **bio·en·er·get·ic** \-tik\ adj

bio·en·gi·neer·ing \-ₐen-jə-ˈnir-iŋ\ n : biological or medical application of engineering principles or engineering equipment; broadly : BIOTECHNOLOGY — **bio·en·gi·neer** \-ˈnir\ n or vb

bio·equiv·a·lence \-i-ˈkwi-və-ləns\ n : the property that two drugs or dosage forms have when they have the same bioavailability and produce the same effect at the site of physiological activity — **bio·equiv·a·lent** \-lənt\ adj

bio·equiv·a·len·cy \-lən-sē\ n, pl -cies : BIOEQUIVALENCE

bio·eth·i·cist \-ˈe-thə-sist\ n : an expert in bioethics

bio·eth·ics \-ˈe-thiks\ n : the discipline dealing with the ethical implications of biological research and applications esp. in medicine — **bio·eth·ic** \-thik\ n — **bio·ethical** \-thi-kəl\ adj

bio·feed·back \-ˈfēd-ₐbak\ n : the technique of making unconscious or involuntary bodily processes (as heartbeat or brain waves) perceptible to the senses (as by the use of an oscilloscope) in order to manipulate them by conscious mental control

bio·fla·vo·noid \-ˈflā-və-ₐnȯid\ n : biologically active flavonoid

bio·gen·ic \-ˈje-nik\ adj : produced by living organisms (~ amines)

bio·haz·ard \ˈbī-ō-ₐha-zərd\ n : a biological agent or condition (as an infectious organism or insecure laboratory procedures) that constitutes a hazard to humans or the environment; also : a hazard posed by such an agent or condition — **bio·haz·ard·ous** \ₐbī-ō-ˈha-zər-dəs\ adj

biol abbr biologic; biological; biologist; biology

bio·log·ic \ₐbī-ə-ˈlä-jik\ or **bio·log·i·cal** \-ji-kəl\ n : a biological product (as a globulin, serum, vaccine, antitoxin, or antigen) used in the prevention or treatment of disease

biological also **biologic** adj 1 : of or relating to biology or to life and living processes 2 : used in or produced by applied biology 3 : related by direct genetic relationship rather than by adoption or marriage (~ parents) — **bi·o·log·i·cal·ly** \-ji-k(ə-)lē\ adv

biological clock n : an inherent timing mechanism that is inferred to exist in some living systems (as a cell) in order to explain various cyclical behaviors and physiological processes

biological control n : reduction in numbers or elimination of pest organisms by interference with their ecology

biological half–life or **biologic half–life** n

: the time that a living body requires to eliminate one half the quantity of an administered substance (as a radioisotope) through its normal channels of elimination

biological warfare n : warfare involving the use of living organisms (as disease germs) or their toxic products as weapons; also : warfare involving the use of herbicides

biologic false–positive n : a positive serological reaction for syphilis given by blood of a person who does not have syphilis

bi·ol·o·gist \bī-ˈä-lə-jist\ n : a specialist in biology

bi·ol·o·gy \bī-ˈä-lə-jē\ n, pl -gies 1 : a branch of science that deals with living organisms and vital processes 2 : the laws and phenomena relating to an organism or group

bio·ma·te·ri·al \ₐbī-ō-mə-ˈtir-ē-əl\ n : material used for or suitable for use in prostheses that come in direct contact with living tissues

bio·me·chan·ics \ₐbī-ō-mi-ˈka-niks\ n sing or pl : the mechanical bases of biological, esp. muscular, activity; also : the study of the principles and relations involved — **bio·me·chan·i·cal** \-ni-kəl\ adj

bio·med·i·cal \-ˈme-di-kəl\ adj 1 : of or relating to biomedicine (~ studies) 2 : of, relating to, or involving biological, medical, and physical science — **bio·med·i·cal·ly** \-k(ə-)lē\ adv

biomedical engineering n : BIOENGINEERING

bio·med·i·cine \-ˈme-də-sən\ n : medicine based on the application of the principles of the natural sciences and esp. biology and biochemistry

bio·met·rics \-ˈme-triks\ n sing or pl : BIOMETRY

bi·om·e·try \bī-ˈä-mə-trē\ n, pl -tries : the statistical analysis of biological observations and phenomena — **bio·met·ric** \ₐbī-ō-ˈme-trik\ or **bio·met·ri·cal** \-tri-kəl\ adj — **bio·me·tri·cian** \-me-ˈtri-shən\ n

bio·mi·cro·scope \ₐbī-ō-ˈmī-krə-ₐskōp\ n : a binocular microscope used for examination of the anterior part of the eye

bio·mi·cros·co·py \-mī-ˈkräs-kə-pē\ n, pl -pies : the microscopic examination and study of living cells and tissues; specif : examination of the living eye with the biomicroscope

bio·mol·e·cule \ₐbī-ō-ˈmä-li-ₐkyül\ n : an organic molecule and esp. a macromolecule (as a protein or nucleic acid) in living organisms — **bio·mo·lec·u·lar** \-mə-ˈle-kyə-lər\ adj

bi·on·ic \bī-ˈä-nik\ adj 1 : of or relating to bionics 2 : having natural biological capability or performance enhanced by or as if by electronic or electrically actuated mechanical devices

bi·on·ics \bī-ˈä-niks\ n sing or pl : a science concerned with the application of data about the functioning of biological systems to the solution of engineering problems

bio·phar·ma·ceu·tics \'bī-ō-‖fär-mə-'sü-tiks\ *n* : the study of the relationships between the physical and chemical properties, dosage, and form of administration of a drug and its activity in the living body — **bio·phar·ma·ceu·ti·cal** \-ti-kəl\ *adj*

bio·phys·i·cist \-'fi-zə-sist\ *n* : a specialist in biophysics

bio·phys·ics \‖bī-ō-'fi-ziks\ *n* : a branch of knowledge concerned with the application of physical principles and methods to biological problems — **bio·phys·i·cal** \-zi-kəl\ *adj*

bio·poly·mer \‖bī-ō-'pä-lə-mər\ *n* : a polymeric substance (as a protein or polysaccharide) formed in a biological system

bi·op·sy \'bī-‖äp-sē\ *n, pl* **-sies** : the removal and examination of tissue, cells, or fluids from the living body — **biopsy** *vb*

bio·psy·chol·o·gy \‖bī-ō-sī-'kä-lə-jē\ *n, pl* **-gies** : psychology as related to biology or as a part of the vital processes — **bio·psy·chol·o·gist** \-jist\ *n*

bio·re·ac·tor \-rē-'ak-tər\ *n* : a device or apparatus in which living organisms and esp. bacteria synthesize useful substances (as interferon) or break down harmful ones (as in sewage)

bio·rhythm \'bī-ō-‖ri-thəm\ *n* : an innately determined rhythmic biological process or function (as sleep behavior); *also* : an innate rhythmic determiner of such a process or function — **bio·rhyth·mic** \‖bī-ō-'rith-mik\ *adj*

bio·sci·ence \'bī-ō-‖sī-əns\ *n* : BIOLOGY; *also* : LIFE SCIENCE — **bio·sci·en·tist** \‖bī-ō-'sī-ən-tist\ *n*

bio·sen·sor \'bī-ō-‖sen-‖sòr, -sər\ *n* : a device that is sensitive to a physical or chemical stimulus (as heat or an ion) and transmits information about a life process

-bi·o·sis \(‖)bī-'ō-səs, bē-\ *n comb form, pl* **-bi·o·ses** \-‖sēz\ : mode of life ⟨parabiosis⟩ ⟨symbiosis⟩

bio·sta·tis·tics \‖bī-ō-stə-'tis-tiks\ *n* : statistical processes and methods applied to the analysis of biological phenomena — **bio·stat·is·ti·cian** \-‖sta-tə-'sti-shən\ *n*

bio·syn·the·sis \‖bī-ō-'sin-thə-səs\ *n, pl* **-the·ses** : production of a chemical compound by a living organism — **bio·syn·the·size** \-'sin-thə-‖sīz\ *vb* — **bio·syn·thet·ic** \-sin-'the-tik\ *adj* — **bio·syn·thet·i·cal·ly** \-ti-k(ə-)lē\ *adv*

bio·tech·ni·cal \-'tek-ni-kəl\ *adj* : of or relating to biotechnology

bio·tech·nol·o·gy \‖bī-ō-tek-'nä-lə-jē\ *n, pl* **-gies** 1 : applied biological science (as bioengineering or recombinant DNA technology) 2 : ERGONOMICS —

bio·tech·no·log·i·cal \-‖tek-nə-'lä-ji-kəl\ *adj*

bio·te·lem·e·try \-tə-‖le-mə-trē\ *n, pl* **-tries** : remote detection and measurement of a human or animal condition, activity, or function (as heartbeat or body temperature) — **bio·tel·e·met·ric** \-‖te-lə-'me-trik\ *adj*

bi·ot·ic \bī-'ä-tik\ *adj* : of or relating to life; *esp* : caused or produced by living beings

-bi·ot·ic \bī-'ä-tik\ *adj comb form* 1 : relating to life ⟨anti*biotic*⟩ 2 : having a (specified) mode of life ⟨necro*biotic*⟩

bi·o·tin \'bī-ə-tən\ *n* : a colorless crystalline growth vitamin $C_{10}H_{16}N_2O_3S$ of the vitamin B complex found esp. in yeast, liver, and egg yolk — called also *vitamin H*

bio·trans·for·ma·tion \'bī-ō-‖trans-fər-'mā-shən, -‖fȯr-\ *n* : the transformation of chemical compounds within a living system

bi·ovu·lar \(‖)bī-'ä-vyə-lər, -'ō-\ *adj, of fraternal twins* : derived from two ova

bi·pa·ri·etal \‖bī-pə-'rī-ət-əl\ *adj* : of or relating to the parietal bones; *specif* : being a measurement between the most distant opposite points of the two parietal bones

bi·ped \'bī-‖ped\ *n* : a two-footed animal — **biped** *or* **bi·ped·al** \(‖)bī-'ped-əl\ *adj*

bi·pen·nate \(‖)bī-'pe-‖nāt\ *adj* : BIPENNIFORM

bi·pen·ni·form \-'pe-ni-‖fȯrm\ *adj* : resembling a feather barbed on both sides — used of muscles

bi·per·i·den \bī-'per-ə-dən\ *n* : a white crystalline muscle relaxant $C_{21}H_{29}$NO used esp. to reduce the symptoms (as tremors, akinesia, and muscle rigidity) associated with Parkinson's disease

bi·phe·nyl \(‖)bī-'fen-əl, -'fēn-\ *n* : a white crystalline hydrocarbon C_6H_5-C_6H_5

bi·po·lar \(‖)bī-'pō-lər\ *adj* 1 : having or involving the use of two poles ⟨~ encephalograph leads⟩ 2 *of a neuron* : having an efferent and an afferent process 3 : characterized by the alternation of manic and depressive states (a ~ affective disorder)

bird louse *n* : BITING LOUSE

bi·re·frin·gence \‖bī-ri-'frin-jəns\ *n* : the refraction of light in two slightly different directions to form two rays — **bi·re·frin·gent** \-jənt\ *adj*

birth \'bərth\ *n, often attrib* 1 : the emergence of a new individual from the body of its parent 2 : the act or process of bringing forth young from the womb — **birth** *vb*

birth canal *n* : the channel formed by the cervix, vagina, and vulva through which the fetus is expelled during birth

birth certificate *n* : a copy of an official

record of a person's date and place of birth and parentage

birth control n : control of the number of children born esp. by preventing or lessening the frequency of conception : CONTRACEPTION

birth defect n : a physical or biochemical defect (as cleft palate, phenylketonuria, or Down's syndrome) that is present at birth and may be inherited or environmentally induced

birthing center n : a facility usu. staffed by nurse-midwives that provides a less institutionalized setting than a hospital for women who wish to deliver by natural childbirth

birthing room n : a comfortably furnished hospital room where both labor and delivery take place and in which the baby usu. remains during the hospital stay

birth·mark \'bərth-ˌmärk\ n : an unusual mark or blemish on the skin at birth : NEVUS — **birthmark** vb

birth pang n : one of the regularly recurrent pains that are characteristic of childbirth — usu. used in pl.

birth·rate \'bərth-ˌrāt\ n : the ratio between births and individuals in a specified population and time often expressed as number of live births per hundred or per thousand population per year — called also *natality*

birth trauma n : the physical injury or emotional shock sustained by an infant in the process of birth

bis·a·co·dyl \ˌbi-sə-'kō-(ˌ)dil\ n : a white crystalline laxative $C_{22}H_{19}NO_4$ administered orally or as a suppository

¹bi·sex·u·al \(ˌ)bī-'sek-shə-wəl\ adj 1 a : possessing characters of both sexes : HERMAPHRODITIC b : sexually oriented toward both sexes ⟨a ∼ person who engages in both heterosexual and homosexual practices⟩ 2 : of, relating to, or involving two sexes — **bi·sex·u·al·i·ty** \ˌbī-ˌsek-shə-'wa-lə-tē\ n — **bi·sex·u·al·ly** adv

²bisexual n : a bisexual individual

bis·hy·droxy·cou·ma·rin \ˌbis-(ˌ)hī-ˌdrak-sē-'kü-mə-rən\ n : DICUMAROL

bis·muth \'biz-məth\ n : a brittle grayish white chiefly trivalent metallic element — symbol *Bi*; see ELEMENT table

bismuth sub·car·bon·ate \-ˌsəb-'kär-bə-ˌnāt, -nət\ n : a white or pale yellowish white powder used chiefly in treating gastrointestinal disorders, topically as a protective in lotions and ointments, and in cosmetics

bismuth sub·ni·trate \-ˌsəb-'nī-ˌtrāt\ n : a white powder $Bi_5O(OH)_9(NO_3)_4$ that is used in medicine similarly to bismuth subcarbonate

bis·tou·ry \'bis-tə-rē\ n, pl **-ries** : a small slender straight or curved surgical knife that is sharp-pointed or probe-pointed

¹bite \'bīt\ vb **bit** \'bit\; **bit·ten** \'bit-ᵊn\

also **bit**; **bit·ing** 1 : to seize esp. with teeth or jaws so as to enter, grip, or wound 2 : to wound, pierce, or sting esp. with a fang or a proboscis

²bite n 1 : the act or manner of biting: *esp* : OCCLUSION 2a 2 : a wound made by biting

bite block n : a device used in dentistry for recording the spatial relation of the jaws esp. in respect to the occlusion of the teeth

bi·tem·po·ral \(ˌ)bī-'tem-pə-rəl\ adj : relating to, involving, or joining the two temporal bones or the areas that they occupy

bite plane n : a removable dental appliance used to cover the occlusal surfaces of the teeth so that they cannot be brought into contact

bite plate n : a dental appliance used in orthodontics and prosthodontics that is usu. made of plastic and wire and is worn in the palate or sometimes on the lower jaw

bite·wing \'bīt-ˌwiŋ\ n : dental X-ray film designed to show the crowns of the upper and lower teeth simultaneously

biting fly n : a dipteran fly (as a mosquito, midge, or horsefly) having mouthparts adapted for piercing and biting

biting louse n : any of numerous wingless insects (order Mallophaga) parasitic esp. on birds — called also *bird louse*

biting midge n : any of a large family (Ceratopogonidae) of tiny dipteran flies of which some are vectors of filarial worms

Bi·tot's spots \bē-'tōz-\ n : shiny pearly spots of triangular shape occurring on the conjunctiva in severe vitamin A deficiency esp. in children

Bi·tot \bē-'tō\, **Pierre A.** (1822–1888), French physician.

bit·ter \'bit-ər\ adj : being or inducing the one of the four basic taste sensations that is peculiarly acrid, astringent, or disagreeable — compare SALT, SOUR, SWEET — **bit·ter·ness** n

bitter almond n : an almond with a bitter taste that contains amygdalin; *also* : a tree (*Prunus dulcis amara*) of the rose family (Rosaceae) producing bitter almonds

bi·uret \ˌbī-yə-'ret\ n : a white crystalline compound $N_3H_5C_2O_2$ formed by heating urea

biuret reaction n : a reaction that is shown by biuret, proteins, and most peptides on treatment in alkaline solution with copper sulfate and that results in a violet color

biuret test n : a test esp. for proteins using the biuret reaction

¹bi·va·lent \(ˌ)bī-'vā-lᵊnt\ adj : associated in pairs in synapsis

²bivalent n : a pair of synaptic chromosomes

bi·valve \'bī-ˌvalv\ vb **bi·valved**; **bi-**

valv•ing : to split (a cast) along one or two sides (as to renew surgical dressings or to restore circulation)

Bk *symbol* berkelium

BK *abbr* below knee

black-and-blue \‚blak-ᵊn-ˈblü\ *adj* : darkly discolored from blood effused by bruising

black damp *n* : a nonexplosive mine gas that is a mixture containing carbon dioxide and is incapable of supporting life or flame — compare FIREDAMP

black death *n, often cap B&D* 1 : PLAGUE 2 2 : a severe epidemic of plague and esp. bubonic plague that occurred in Asia and Europe in the 14th century

black disease *n* : a fatal toxemia of sheep associated with simultaneous infection by liver flukes (*Fasciola hepatica*) and an anaerobic toxin-producing clostridium (*Clostridium novyi*) and characterized by liver necrosis and subcutaneous hemorrhage — compare BLACKLEG, BRAXY, LIVER ROT, MALIGNANT EDEMA

black eye *n* : a discoloration of the skin around the eye from bruising

black-fly \ˈblak-‚flī\ *n, pl* **-flies** : any of a family (Simuliidae) and esp. genus *Simulium* of bloodsucking dipteran flies

black hairy tongue *n* : BLACKTONGUE 1

black-head \ˈblak-‚hed\ *n* 1 : a small plug of sebum blocking the duct of a sebaceous gland esp. on the face — compare MILIUM 2 : a destructive disease of turkeys and related birds caused by a protozoan of the genus *Histomonas* (*H. meleagridis*) that invades the intestinal ceca and liver — called also *enterohepatitis, histomoniasis, infectious enterohepatitis*

black henbane *n* : HENBANE

black-leg \ˈblak-‚leg\ *n* : a usu. fatal toxemia esp. of young cattle caused by toxins produced by an anaerobic soil bacterium of the genus *Clostridium* (*C. chauvoei*) — compare BLACK DISEASE, MALIGNANT EDEMA

black lung *n* : pneumoconiosis caused by habitual inhalation of coal dust — called also *black lung disease*

black-out \ˈblak-‚aut\ *n* : a transient dulling or loss of vision, consciousness, or memory (as from temporary impairment of cerebral circulation, retinal anoxia, a traumatic emotional blow, or an alcoholic binge) — compare GRAYOUT, REDOUT — **black out** *vb*

black quarter *n* : BLACKLEG

black rat *n* : a rat of the genus *Rattus* (*R. rattus*) that infests houses and has been the chief vector of bubonic plague

black-tongue \ˈblak-‚tᵊng\ *n* 1 : a dark furry or hairy discoloration of the tongue that is due to hyperplasia of the filiform papillae with an over-growth of microorganisms and is often associated with prolonged use of antibiotics — called also *black hairy tongue* 2 : a disease of dogs that is caused by a deficient diet and that is identical with pellagra in humans

black-wa•ter \ˈblak-‚wo-tər, -‚wä-\ *n* : any of several diseases (as blackwater fever or Texas fever) characterized by dark-colored urine

blackwater fever *n* : a rare febrile complication of repeated malarial attacks that is marked by destruction of blood cells with hemoglobinuria and extensive kidney damage

black widow *n* : a venomous New World spider of the genus *Latrodectus* (*L. mactans*) the female of which is black with an hourglass-shaped red mark on the abdominal underside

blad•der \ˈbla-dər\ *n* 1 : a membranous sac in animals that serves as the receptacle of a liquid or contains gas; *esp* : URINARY BLADDER 2 : a vesicle or pouch forming part of an animal body (the ~ of a tapeworm larva)

bladder worm *n* : CYSTICERCUS

blade \ˈblād\ *n* 1 : a broad flat body part (as the shoulder blade) 2 : the flat portion of the tongue immediately behind the tip; *also* : this portion together with the tip 3 : a flat working and esp. cutting part of an implement (as a scalpel)

blain \ˈblān\ *n* : an inflammatory swelling or sore

Bla•lock-Taus•sig operation \ˈblā-‚läk-ˈtaú-sig-\ *n* : surgical correction of the tetralogy of Fallot — called also *blue= baby operation*

Blalock, Alfred (1899–1964), and Taussig, Helen B. (1898–1986), American physicians.

blast \ˈblast\ *n* : an immature or imperfectly developed cell (leukemic ~s) — **blas•tic** \ˈblas-tik\ *also* blast *adj*

blast- *or* **blasto-** *comb form* : bud : budding : germ (*blasto*disc) (*blastula*)

-blast \ˈblast\ *n comb form* : formative unit esp. of living matter : germ : cell layer (epi*blast*)

blast cell *n* : a blood cell precursor that is in the earliest stage of development in which it is recognizably committed to development along a particular cell lineage

blas•te•ma \bla-ˈstē-mə\ *n, pl* **-mas** *or* **-ma•ta** \-mə-tə\ : a mass of living substance capable of growth and differentiation

-blas•tic \ˈblas-tik\ *adj comb form* : sprouting or germinating (in a specified way) (hemocyto*blastic*) : having (such or so many) sprouts, buds, or germ layers (meso*blastic*)

blas•to•coel *or* **blas•to•coele** \ˈblas-tə-‚sēl\ *n* : the cavity of a blastula — **blas•to•coe•lic** \‚blas-tə-ˈsē-lik\ *adj*

blas•to•cyst \ˈblas-tə-‚sist\ *n* : the modified blastula of a placental mammal

blas•to•derm \-‚dərm\ *n* : a blastodisc

after completion of cleavage and formation of the blastocoel

blas·to·derm·ic vesicle \blas-tə-'dər-mik-\ *n* : BLASTOCYST

blas·to·disc *or* **blas·to·disk** \'blas-tə-ˌdisk\ *n* : the embryo-forming portion of an egg with discoidal cleavage usu. appearing as a small disc on the upper surface of the yolk mass

blas·to·gen·e·sis \ˌblas-tə-'je-nə-səs\ *n, pl* **-e·ses** \-ˌsēz\ : the transformation of lymphocytes into larger cells capable of undergoing mitosis — **blas·to·gen·ic** \-'je-nik\ *adj*

blas·to·mere \'blas-tə-ˌmir\ *n* : a cell produced during cleavage of a fertilized egg — called also *cleavage cell*

Blas·to·my·ces \ˌblas-tə-'mī-ˌsēz\ *n, in some classifications* : a genus of yeastlike fungi to which the causative agents of blastomycosis are sometimes assigned

blas·to·my·cin \-'mīs-ᵊn\ *n* : a preparation of growth products of the causative agent of North American blastomycosis that is used esp. to test for this disease

blas·to·my·co·sis \-ˌmī-'kō-səs\ *n, pl* **-co·ses** \-ˌsēz\ : either of two infectious diseases caused by yeastlike fungi — see BLASTOMYCES; NORTH AMERICAN BLASTOMYCOSIS, SOUTH AMERICAN BLASTOMYCOSIS — **blas·to·my·cot·ic** \-'kä-tik\ *adj*

blas·to·pore \'blas-tə-ˌpō(ə)r, -ˌpȯ(ə)r\ *n* : the opening of the archenteron

blas·tu·la \'blas-chə-lə\ *n, pl* **-las** *or* **-lae** \-ˌlē\ : an early metazoan embryo typically having the form of a hollow fluid-filled rounded cavity bounded by a single layer of cells — compare GASTRULA, MORULA — **blas·tu·lar** \-lər\ *adj* — **blas·tu·la·tion** \ˌblas-chə-'lā-shən\ *n*

Blat·ta \'bla-tə\ *n* : a genus (family Blattidae) of cockroaches including the common oriental cockroach (*B. orientalis*) that infests buildings in America and most other parts of the world

Blat·tel·la \blə-'te-lə\ *n* : a genus of cockroaches including the abundant small domestic German cockroach (*B. germanica*)

bleb \'bleb\ *n* : a small blister — compare BULLA 2

bleed \'blēd\ *vb* **bled** \'bled\; **bleed·ing 1** : to emit or lose blood **2** : to escape by oozing or flowing (as from a wound); *also* : to remove or draw blood from

bleed·er \'blē-dər\ *n* **1** : one that draws blood; *esp* : a person who draws blood for medical reasons : BLOOD-LETTER **2** : one that gives up blood : a : HEMOPHILIAC b : a large blood vessel divided during surgery

bleed·ing *n* : an act, instance, or result of being bled or the process by which something is bled: as **a** : the escape of blood from vessels : HEMORRHAGE b

: the operation of bleeding a person medically : PHLEBOTOMY

bleeding time *n* : a period of time of usu. about two and a half minutes during which a small wound (as a pinprick) continues to bleed

blem·ish \'ble-mish\ *n* : a mark of physical deformity or injury; *esp* : any small mark on the skin (as a pimple or birthmark)

blen·nor·rha·gia \ˌble-nə-'rä-jē-ə, -jə\ *n* **1** : BLENNORRHEA **2** : GONORRHEA

blennorrhagica — see KERATOSIS BLENNORRHAGICA

blennorrhagicum — see KERATODERMA BLENNORRHAGICUM

blen·nor·rhea \ˌble-nə-'rē-ə\ *n* : an excessive secretion and discharge of mucus — **blen·nor·rheal** \-'rē-əl\ *adj*

blen·nor·rhoea *chiefly Brit var of* BLENNORRHEA

bleo·my·cin \ˌblē-ə-'mīs-ᵊn\ *n* : a mixture of glycoprotein antibiotics derived from a streptomyces (*Streptomyces verticillus*) and used in the form of the sulfates as an antineoplastic agent

blephar- *or* **blepharo-** *comb form* : eyelid (*blepharo*spasm)

bleph·a·ri·tis \ˌble-fə-'rī-təs\ *n, pl* **-rit·i·des** \-'ri-tə-ˌdēz\ : inflammation esp. of the margins of the eyelids

bleph·a·ro·con·junc·ti·vi·tis \ˌble-fə-(ˌ)rō-kən-ˌjəŋk-tə-'vī-təs\ *n* : inflammation of the eyelid and conjunctiva

bleph·a·ro·plas·ty \'ble-fə-rō-ˌplas-tē\ *n, pl* **-ties** : plastic surgery on an eyelid esp. to remove fatty or excess tissue

bleph·a·rop·to·sis \ˌble-fə-rəp-'tō-səs\ *n, pl* **-to·ses** \-ˌsēz\ : a drooping or abnormal relaxation of the upper eyelid

bleph·a·ro·spasm \'ble-fə-rō-ˌspa-zəm, -rə-\ *n* : spasmodic winking from involuntary contraction of the orbicularis oculi muscle of the eyelids

bleph·a·rot·o·my \ˌble-fə-'rä-tə-mē\ *n, pl* **-mies** : surgical incision of an eyelid

blind \'blīnd\ *adj* **1 a** : lacking or deficient in sight; *esp* : having less than ¹/₁₀ of normal vision in the more efficient eye when refractive defects are fully corrected by lenses **b** : of or relating to sightless persons (~ care) **2** : made or done without sight of certain objects or knowledge of certain facts by the participants that could serve for guidance (a ~ test) — see DOUBLE-BLIND, SINGLE-BLIND **3** : having but one opening or outlet (the cecum is a ~ pouch) — **blind** *vb* — **blind·ly** *adv* — **blind·ness** *n*

blind gut *n* : the cecum of the large intestine

blind spot *n* : the point in the retina where the optic nerve enters that is not sensitive to light — called also *optic disk*

blind stag·gers \-'sta-gərz\ *n sing or pl* : a severe form of selenosis characterized esp. by impairment of vision and an unsteady gait; *also* : a similar condition not caused by selenium poisoning

blink \\'bliŋk\ *vb* 1 : to close and open the eye involuntarily 2 : to remove (as tears) from the eye by blinking — **blink** *n*

blis·ter \\'blis-tər\ *n* 1 : an elevation of the epidermis containing watery liquid 2 : an agent that causes blistering — **blister** *vb* — **blis·tery** \-tə-rē\ *adj*

¹**bloat** \\'blōt\ *vb* : to make or become turgid: a : to produce edema in b : to cause or result in accumulation of gas in the digestive tract of

²**bloat** *n* : a flatulent digestive disturbance of domestic animals and esp. cattle marked by abdominal bloating

¹**block** \\'bläk\ *n*, *often attrib* 1 : interruption of normal physiological function of a tissue or organ; *esp* : HEART BLOCK 2 a : BLOCK ANESTHESIA b : NERVE BLOCK 1 3 : interruption of a train of thought by competing thoughts or psychological suppression

²**block** *vb* 1 : to prevent normal functioning of (a bodily element); *also* : to experience or exhibit psychological blocking or blockage 2 : to obstruct the effect of

block·ade \blä-'kād\ *n* : interruption of normal physiological function (as transmission of nerve impulses) of a tissue or organ — **blockade** *vb*

block·age \\'blä-kij\ *n* 1 : the action of blocking or the state of being blocked 2 : internal resistance to understanding a communicated idea, to learning new material, or to adopting a new mode of response because of existing habitual ways of thinking, perceiving, and acting — compare BLOCKING

block anesthesia *n* : local anesthesia (as by injection) produced by interruption of the flow of impulses along a nerve trunk — compare REGIONAL ANESTHESIA

block·er \\'blä-kər\ *n* : one that blocks — see BETA-BLOCKER, CALCIUM CHANNEL BLOCKER

block·ing \\'blä-kiŋ\ *n* : interruption of a trend of associative thought by the arousal of an opposing trend or through the welling up into consciousness of a complex of unpleasant ideas — compare BLOCKAGE 2

blocking antibody *n* : an antibody that combines with an antigen without visible reaction but prevents another antibody from later combining with or producing its usual effect on that antigen

blood \\'bləd\ *n*, *often attrib* 1 : the fluid that circulates in the heart, arteries, capillaries, and veins of a vertebrate animal carrying nourishment and oxygen to and bringing away waste products from all parts of the body 2 : a fluid of an invertebrate comparable to blood

blood bank *n* : a place for storage of or an institution storing blood or plasma; *also* : blood so stored

blood banking *n* : the activity of administering or working in a blood bank

blood–brain barrier *n* : a barrier created by the modification of brain capillaries (as by reduction in fenestration and formation of tight cell-to-cell contacts) that prevents many substances from leaving the blood and crossing the capillary walls into the brain tissues

blood cell *n* : a cell normally present in blood — see RED BLOOD CELL, WHITE BLOOD CELL

blood count *n* : the determination of the blood cells in a definite volume of blood; *also* : the number of cells so determined — see COMPLETE BLOOD COUNT, DIFFERENTIAL BLOOD COUNT

blood doping *n* : a technique for temporarily improving athletic performance in which oxygen-carrying red blood cells from blood previously withdrawn from an athlete are injected back just before an event — called also *blood packing*

blood fluke *n* : SCHISTOSOME

blood group *n* : one of the classes (as A, B, AB, or O) into which individual vertebrates and esp. human beings or their blood can be separated on the basis of the presence or absence of specific antigens in the blood — called also *blood type*

blood grouping *n* : BLOOD TYPING

blood island *n* : any of the reddish areas in the extraembryonic mesoblast of developing vertebrate eggs where blood cells and vessels are forming — called also *blood islet*

blood·less \\'bləd-ləs\ *adj* : free from or lacking blood (a ~ surgical field)

blood·let·ter \\'bləd-₁le-tər\ *n* : a practitioner of phlebotomy

blood·let·ting \-₁le-tiŋ\ *n* : PHLEBOTOMY

blood·mo·bile \-mō-₁bēl\ *n* : a motor vehicle staffed and equipped for collecting blood from donors

blood platelet *n* : one of the minute protoplasmic disks of vertebrate blood that assist in blood clotting — called also *platelet*, *thrombocyte*

blood poisoning *n* : SEPTICEMIA

blood pressure *n* : pressure exerted by the blood upon the walls of the blood vessels and esp. arteries, usu. measured on the radial artery by means of a sphygmomanometer, and expressed in millimeters of mercury either as a fraction having as numerator the maximum pressure that follows systole of the left ventricle of the heart and as denominator the minimum pressure that accompanies cardiac diastole or as a whole number representing the first value only ⟨a *blood pressure* of 120/80⟩ ⟨a *blood pressure* of 120⟩ — abbr. *BP*

blood serum *n* : SERUM a (1)

blood·shot \'bləd-ˌshät\ *adj, of an eye* : inflamed to redness

blood·stain \-ˌstān\ *n* : a discoloration caused by blood — **blood-stained** \-ˌstānd\ *adj*

blood·stream \-ˌstrēm\ *n* : the flowing blood in a circulatory system

blood·suck·er \-ˌsə-kər\ *n* : an animal that sucks blood; *esp* : LEECH — **blood·suck·ing** \-kiŋ\ *adj*

blood sugar *n* : the glucose in the blood; *also* : its concentration (as in milligrams per 100 milliliters)

blood test *n* : a test of the blood; *esp* : a serological test for syphilis

blood type *n* : BLOOD GROUP

blood typ·ing \-ˌtī-piŋ\ *n* : the action or process of determining an individual's blood group

blood vessel *n* : any of the vessels through which blood circulates in the body

blood·worm \'bləd-ˌwərm\ *n* : any of several nematode worms of the genus *Strongylus* that are parasitic in the large intestine of horses — called also *palisade worm, red worm*

bloody \'blə-dē\ *adj* **blood·i·er; -est 1 a** : containing or made up of blood **b** : of or contained in the blood **2 a** : smeared or stained with blood **b** : dripping blood : BLEEDING (a ~ nose)

blot \'blät\ *n* : a sheet usu. of a cellulose derivative that contains spots of immobilized macromolecules (as of DNA, RNA, or protein) or their fragments and that is used to identify specific components of the spots by applying a suitable molecular probe (as a complementary nucleic acid or a radioactively labeled antibody) — see NORTHERN BLOT, SOUTHERN BLOT, WESTERN BLOT — **blot** *vb*

blotch \'bläch\ *n* : a blemished patch on the skin (a face covered with ~es) — **blotch** *vb* — **blotchy** \'blä-chē\ *adj*

blow·fish \'blō-ˌfish\ *n* : PUFFER

blow·fly \-ˌflī\ *n, pl* **-flies** : any of a family (Calliphoridae) of dipteran flies (as a bluebottle or screwworm)

blue baby *n* : an infant with a bluish tint usu. from a congenital heart defect marked by mingling of venous and arterial blood

blue–baby operation *n* : BLALOCK-TAUSSIG OPERATION

blue bag *n* : gangrenous mastitis of sheep

blue·bot·tle \'blü-ˌbät-ᵊl\ *n* : any of several blowflies (genus *Calliphora*) that have the abdomen or the whole body iridescent blue in color and that make a loud buzzing noise in flight

blue comb *n* : a severe avian disease esp. of domestic fowl caused by a coronavirus

blue heaven *n, slang* : amobarbital or its sodium derivative in a blue tablet or capsule

blue nevus *n* : a small blue or bluish black spot on the skin that is sharply circumscribed, rounded, and flat or slightly raised and is usu. benign but often mistaken for a melanoma

blue-tongue \'blü-ˌtəŋ\ *n* : a virus disease esp. of sheep marked by hyperemia, cyanosis, and by swelling and sloughing of the epithelium esp. about the mouth and tongue and caused by an orbivirus

blunt dissection *n* : surgical separation of tissue layers by means of an instrument without a cutting edge or by the fingers

blunt trauma *n* : an injury caused by a blunt object

B lym·pho·cyte \'bē-ˈlim-fə-ˌsīt\ *n* : B CELL

BM *abbr* **1** Bachelor of Medicine **2** bowel movement

BMR *abbr* basal metabolic rate

BNA *abbr* Basle Nomina Anatomica

BO *abbr* body odor

board \'bōrd\ *n* **1** : a group of persons having supervisory, managerial, investigative, or advisory powers (medical licensing ~s) (a ~ of health) **2** : an examination given by an examining board — often used in pl.

board–certified *adj* : being a physician who has graduated from medical school, completed residency, trained under supervision in a specialty, and passed a qualifying exam given by a medical specialty board

Bo·dan·sky unit \bə-ˈdan-skē-, -ˈdän-\ *n* : a unit that is used as a measure of phosphatase concentration (as in the blood) esp. in the diagnosis of various pathological conditions and that has a normal value for the blood averaging about 7 for children and about 4 for adults

Bodansky, Aaron (1887–1960), American biochemist.

bod·i·ly \'bäd-ᵊl-ē\ *adj* : of or relating to the body (~ organs)

body \'bä-dē\ *n, pl* **bod·ies 1 a (1)** : the material part or nature of a human being **(2)** : the dead organism : CORPSE **b** : a human being **2 a** : the main part of a plant or animal body esp. as distinguished from limbs and head : TRUNK **b** : the main part of an organ (as the uterus) **3** : a kind or form of matter : a material substance — see KETONE BODY

body bag *n* : a large zippered usu. rubber bag in which a human corpse is placed esp. for transportation

body–build \-ˌbild\ *n* : the distinctive physical makeup of a human being

body cavity *n* : a cavity within an animal body; *specif* : COELOM

body heat *n* : ANIMAL HEAT

body image *n* : a subjective picture of one's own physical appearance established both by self-observation and by noting the reactions of others

body louse *n* : a louse feeding primarily on the body; *esp* : a sucking louse of the genus *Pediculus* (*P. humanus humanus*) feeding on the human body and living in clothing — called also *cootie*

body odor *n* : an unpleasant odor from a perspiring or unclean person

body stalk *n* : the mesodermal cord that contains the umbilical vessels and that connects a fetus with its chorion

Boeck's sarcoid \'beks-\ *n* : SARCOIDO-SIS

   Boeck \'bek\, **Caesar Peter Moeller** (1845–1917), Norwegian dermatologist.

Bohr effect \'bōər-\ *n* : the decrease in oxygen affinity of a respiratory pigment (as hemoglobin) in response to decreased blood pH resulting from increased carbon dioxide concentration

   Bohr, Christian (1855–1911), Danish physiologist.

boil \'bȯil\ *n* : a localized swelling and inflammation of the skin resulting from bacterial infection in a skin gland, having a hard central core, and forming pus — called also *furuncle*

boiling point *n* : the temperature at which a liquid boils

bo·lus \'bō-ləs\ *n* : a rounded mass: as **a** : a large pill **b** : a soft mass of chewed food

bombé — see IRIS BOMBÉ

bom·be·sin \'bäm-bə-sin\ *n* : a polypeptide that is found in the brain and gastrointestinal tract and has been shown experimentally to cause the secretion of various substances (as gastrin and cholecystokinin) and to inhibit intestinal motility

bond \'bänd\ *n* : an attractive force that holds together atoms, ions, or groups of atoms in a molecule or crystal — usu. represented in formulas by a line or dot — **bond** *vb*

bond·ing *n* **1** : the formation of a close personal relationship (as between a mother and child) esp. through frequent or constant association — see MALE BONDING **2** : a dental technique in which a material and esp. plastic or porcelain is attached to a tooth surface to correct minor defects (as chipped or discolored teeth) esp. for cosmetic purposes

bone \'bōn\ *n, often attrib* **1** : one of the hard parts of the skeleton of a vertebrate (the ∼s of the arm) **2** : the hard largely calcareous connective tissue of which the adult skeleton of most vertebrates is chiefly composed (cancellous ∼) (compact ∼) — compare CARTILAGE **1**

bone marrow *n* : MARROW

bont tick \'bänt-\ *n* : a southern African tick of the genus *Amblyomma* (*A. hebraeum*) that attacks livestock, birds, and sometimes humans and transmits heartwater of sheep, goats, and cattle: *broadly* : any African tick of the genus *Amblyomma*

bony *also* **bon·ey** \'bō-nē\ *adj* **bon·i-**er; -est : consisting of or resembling bone (∼ prominences of the skull)

bony labyrinth *n* : the cavity in the petrous portion of the temporal bone that contains the membranous labyrinth of the inner ear — called also *osseous labyrinth*

Bo·oph·i·lus \bō-'ä-fə-ləs\ *n* : a genus of ticks some of which are pests esp. of cattle and vectors of disease — see CATTLE TICK

boost·er \'bü-stər\ *n* : a substance that increases the effectiveness of a medicament; *esp* : BOOSTER SHOT

booster shot *n* : a supplementary dose of an immunizing agent — called also *booster, booster dose*

bo·rac·ic acid \bə-'ra-sik-\ *n* : BORIC ACID

bo·rate \'bȯr-ˌāt\ *n* : a salt or ester of a boric acid

bor·bo·ryg·mus \ˌbȯr-bə-'rig-məs\ *n, pl* **-mi** \-ˌmī\ : a rumbling sound made by the movement of gas in the intestine — **bor·bo·ryg·mic** \-mik\ *adj*

bor·der·line \'bȯr-dər-ˌlīn\ *adj* **1** : being in an intermediate position or state : not fully classifiable as one thing or its opposite: *esp* : not quite up to what is usual, standard, or expected (∼ intelligence) **2** : exhibiting typical but not altogether conclusive symptoms **3** : characterized by psychological instability in several areas (as interpersonal relations, behavior, mood, and identity) often with impaired social and vocational functioning but with brief or no psychotic episodes (a ∼ personality disorder)

Bor·de·tel·la \ˌbȯr-də-'te-lə\ *n* : a genus of bacteria comprising minute and very short gram-negative strictly aerobic coccuslike bacilli and including the causative agent (*B. pertussis*) of whooping cough

   J.-J.-B.-V. Bordet — see BORDET=GENGOU BACILLUS

Bor·det-Gen·gou bacillus \bȯr-'dā-zhän-'gü-\ *n* : a small ovoid bacillus of the genus *Bordetella* (*B. pertussis*) that is the causative agent of whooping cough

   Bordet, Jules–Jean–Baptiste–Vincent (1870–1961), Belgian bacteriologist, and **Gengou, Octave** (1875–1957), French bacteriologist.

bo·ric acid \'bȯr-ik-\ *n* : a white crystalline acid H_3BO_3 used esp. as a weak antiseptic — called also *boracic acid*

Born·holm disease \'bȯrn-ˌhōlm-\ *n* : EPIDEMIC PLEURODYNIA

bo·ron \'bȯr-ˌän\ *n* : a trivalent metalloid element found in nature only in combination — symbol *B*; see ELEMENT table

bor·re·lia \bə-'re-lē-ə, -'rē-\ *n* **1** *cap* : a genus of small spirochetes (family Spirochaetaceae) that are parasites of humans and warm-blooded animals and include the causative agents of septicemia in chickens (*B. recur-*

rentis), relapsing fever in Africa (*B. duttoni*), and Lyme disease in the U.S. (*B. burgdorferi*) 2 : a spirochete of the genus *Borrelia*

bos•se•lat•ed \'bä-sə-ˌlā-təd, 'bö-\ *adj* : marked or covered with protuberances (a ~ tumor)

bot *also* **bott** \'bät\ *n* : the larva of a botfly; *esp* : one infesting the horse

bo•tan•i•cal \bə-'ta-ni-kəl\ *n* : a vegetable drug esp. in the crude state

bot•fly \'bät-ˌflī\ *n, pl* **-flies** : any of various stout dipteran flies (family Oestridae) with larvae parasitic in cavities or tissues of various mammals including humans

botry- *or* **botryo-** *comb form* 1 : bunch of grapes (*botryoid*) 2 : botryoid (*botryomycosis*)

bot•ry•oid \'bä-trē-ˌöid\ *adj* : having the form of a bunch of grapes (~ sarcoma)

botryoides — *see* SARCOMA BOTRYOIDES

bot•ry•o•my•co•sis \ˌbä-trē-(ˌ)ö-ˌmī-'kö-səs\ *n, pl* **-co•ses** \-ˌsēz\ : a bacterial infection of domestic animals and humans marked by the formation of usu. superficial vascular granulomatous masses, associated esp. with wounds, and sometimes followed by metastatic visceral tumors — **bot•ry•o•my•cot•ic** \-'kä-tik\ *adj*

bot•tle \'bät-ᵊl\ *n, often attrib* 1 : a container typically of glass or plastic having a comparatively narrow neck or mouth and usu. no handle 2 : liquid food usu. consisting of milk and supplements that is fed from a bottle (as to an infant) in place of mother's milk

bottle baby *n* : a baby fed chiefly or wholly on the bottle as contrasted with a baby that is chiefly or wholly breast-fed

bot•tle–feed \'bät-ᵊl-ˌfēd\ *vb* **-fed; -feeding** : to feed (an infant) from a bottle rather than by breast-feeding

bottle jaw *n* : a pendulous edematous condition of the tissues under the lower jaw in cattle and sheep resulting from infestation with bloodsucking gastrointestinal parasites (as of the genus *Haemonchus*)

bot•u•lin \'bä-chə-lən\ *n* : a neurotoxin formed by botulinum and causing botulism

bot•u•li•num \ˌbä-chə-'lī-nəm\ *also* **bot•u•li•nus** \-nəs\ *n* : a spore-forming bacterium of the genus *Clostridium* (*C. botulinum*) that secretes botulin — **bo•tu•li•nal** \-'lī-nᵊl\ *adj*

bot•u•lism \'bä-chə-ˌli-zəm\ *n* : acute food poisoning caused by a toxic product produced in food by a bacterium of the genus *Clostridium* (*C. botulinum*) and characterized by muscle weakness and paralysis, disturbances of vision, swallowing, and speech, and a high mortality rate — *compare* BOTULIN

bou•gie \'bü-ˌzhē, -ˌjē\ *n* 1 : a tapering cylindrical instrument for introduction into a tubular passage of the body 2 : SUPPOSITORY

bou•gie•nage *or* **bou•gi•nage** \ˌbü-zhē-'näzh\ *n* : the dilation of a tubular cavity (as a constricted esophagus) with a bougie

-boulia — *see* -BULIA

bound \'baund\ *adj* 1 : made costive : CONSTIPATED 2 : held in chemical or physical combination

bou•ton \bü-'tō̃\ *n* : a terminal club-shaped enlargement of a nerve fiber at a synapse with another neuron

bou•ton•neuse fever \ˌbü-tȯ-'nüz-, -'nœz-\ *n* : a disease of the Mediterranean area that is characterized by headache, pain in muscles and joints, and an eruption over the body and is caused by a tick-borne rickettsia (*Rickettsia conorii*) — called also *fièvre boutonneuse, Marseilles fever;* see TICK TYPHUS

Bo•vic•o•la \bō-'vi-kə-lə\ *n* : a genus of biting lice (order Mallophaga) including several that infest the hair of domestic mammals

bo•vine \'bō-ˌvīn, -ˌvēn\ *n* : an ox (genus *Bos*) or a closely related animal — **bovine** *adj*

bovine mastitis *n* : inflammation of the udder of a cow resulting from injury or more commonly from bacterial infection

bovinum — *see* COR BOVINUM

bow \'bō\ *n* : a frame for the lenses of eyeglasses; *also* : the curved sidepiece of the frame passing over the ear

bow•el \'baül\ *n* : INTESTINE, GUT; *also* : one of the divisions of the intestines — usu. used in pl. except in medical use (move your ~s) (surgery of the involved ~)

bowel worm *n* : a common strongylid nematode worm of the genus *Chabertia* (*C. ovina*) infesting the colon of sheep and feeding on blood and tissue

Bow•en's disease \'bō-ənz-\ *n* : a precancerous lesion of the skin or mucous membranes characterized by small solid elevations covered by thickened horny tissue

Bow•en \'bō-ən\, **John Templeton** (1857–1941), American dermatologist.

bow•leg \'bō-ˌleg\ *n* : a leg bowed outward at or below the knee — called also *genu varum*

bow•legged \'bō-ˌle-gəd, -ˌlegd\ *adj* : having bowlegs

Bow•man's capsule \'bō-mənz-\ *n* : a thin membranous double-walled capsule surrounding the glomerulus of a vertebrate nephron — called also *capsule of Bowman, glomerular capsule*

Bow•man \'bō-mən\, **Sir William** (1816–1892), British ophthalmologist, anatomist, and physiologist.

Bowman's gland *n* : GLAND OF BOWMAN

Bowman's membrane *n* : the thin outer layer of the substantia propria of the cornea immediately underlying the epithelium

box·ing \'bäk-siŋ\ *n* : construction of the base of a dental cast by building up the walls of an impression while preserving important landmarks

bp *abbr* base pair

BP *abbr* blood pressure

Br *symbol* bromine

¹**brace** \'brās\ *n, pl* **brac·es** 1 : an appliance that gives support to movable parts (as a joint), to weak muscles (as in paralysis), or to strained ligaments (as of the lower back) 2 *pl* : dental appliances used to exert pressure to straighten misaligned teeth

²**brace** *vb* **braced; brac·ing** : to furnish or support with a brace

brachi- *or* **brachio-** *comb form* 1 : arm ⟨*brachi*oradialis⟩ 2 : brachial and ⟨*brachio*cephalic artery⟩

bra·chi·al \'brā-kē-əl\ *adj* : of or relating to the arm

brachial artery *n* : the chief artery of the upper arm that is a direct continuation of the axillary artery and divides into the radial and ulnar arteries just below the elbow — see DEEP BRACHIAL ARTERY

bra·chi·alis \ˌbrā-kē-ˈa-ləs, -ˈä-, -ˈä-\ *n* : a flexor that lies in front of the lower part of the humerus whence it arises and is inserted into the ulna

brachial plexus *n* : a complex network of nerves that is formed chiefly by the lower four cervical nerves and the first thoracic nerve and supplies nerves to the chest, shoulder, and arm

brachial vein *n* : one of a pair of veins accompanying the brachial artery and uniting with each other and with the basilic vein to form the axillary vein

brachii — see BICEPS BRACHII, TRICEPS BRACHII

bra·chio·ce·phal·ic \ˌbrā-kē-(ˌ)ō-sə-ˈfa-lik\ *n* : a short artery that arises from the arch of the aorta and divides into the carotid and subclavian arteries of the right side — called also *innominate artery*

brachiocephalicus — see TRUNCUS BRACHIOCEPHALICUS

brachiocephalic vein *n* : either of two large veins that occur one on each side of the neck, receive blood from the head and neck, are formed by the union of the internal jugular and the subclavian veins, and unite to form the superior vena cava — called also *innominate vein*

bra·chio·ra·di·alis \ˌbrā-kē-ō-ˌrā-dē-ˈa-ləs, -ˈä-, -ˈä-\ *n, pl* **-ales** \-ˌlēz\ : a flexor of the radial side of the forearm arising from the lateral supracondylar ridge of the humerus and inserted into the styloid process of the radius

bra·chi·um \'brā-kē-əm\ *n, pl* **-chia**

\-kē-ə\ : the upper segment of the arm extending from the shoulder to the elbow

brachium con·junc·ti·vum \-ˌkän-(ˌ)jəŋk-ˈtī-vəm\ *n* : CEREBELLAR PEDUNCLE a

brachium pon·tis \-ˈpän-təs\ *n* : CEREBELLAR PEDUNCLE b

brachy- *comb form* : short ⟨*brachy*cephalic⟩ ⟨*brachy*dactylous⟩

brachy·ce·phal·ic \ˌbra-ki-sə-ˈfa-lik\ *adj* : short-headed or broad-headed with a cephalic index of over 80 — **brachy·ceph·a·ly** \-ˈse-fə-lē\ *n*

brachy·dac·ty·lous \ˌbra-ki-ˈdak-tə-ləs\ *adj* : having abnormally short digits — **brachy·dac·ty·ly** \-lē\ *n*

brachy·ther·a·py \-ˈther-ə-pē\ *n, pl* **-pies** : radiotherapy in which the source of radiation is close to the area being treated

Brad·ford frame \'brad-fərd-\ *n* : a frame used to support a patient with disease or fractures of the spine, hip, or pelvis

Bradford, Edward Hickling (1848–1926), American orthopedist.

brad·sot \'brad-sət\ *n* : BRAXY

brady- *comb form* : slow ⟨*brady*cardia⟩

bra·dy·car·dia \ˌbrā-di-ˈkär-dē-ə *also* ˌbra-\ *n* : relatively slow heart action whether physiological or pathological — compare TACHYCARDIA

bra·dy·ki·ne·sia \-kī-ˈnē-zhē-ə, -zhə, -zē-ə\ *n* : extreme slowness of movements and reflexes (as in catatonic schizophrenia)

bra·dy·ki·nin \-ˈkī-nən\ *n* : a kinin that is formed locally in injured tissue, acts in vasodilation of small arterioles, is considered to play a part in inflammatory processes, and is composed of a chain of nine amino-acid residues

bra·dy·pnea \ˌbrā-dəp-ˈnē-ə, ˌbra-\ *n* : abnormally slow breathing

bra·dy·pnoea *chiefly Brit var of* BRADYPNEA

braille \'brāl\ *n, often cap* : a system of writing for the blind that uses characters made up of raised dots — **braille** *vb*

Braille \'brī, ˈbrāl\, Louis (1809–1852), French inventor and teacher.

brain \'brān\ *n* : the portion of the vertebrate central nervous system that constitutes the organ of thought and neural coordination, includes all the higher nervous centers receiving stimuli from the sense organs and interpreting and correlating them to formulate the motor impulses, is made up of neurons and supporting and nutritive structures, is enclosed within the skull, and is continuous with the spinal cord through the foramen magnum

brain·case \-ˌkās\ *n* : the part of the skull that encloses the brain — see CRANIUM

brain death *n* : final cessation of activity in the central nervous system esp. as indicated by a flat electroencephalogram for a predetermined length of time — **brain-dead** *adj*

brain stem *n* : the part of the brain composed of the midbrain, pons, and medulla oblongata and connecting the spinal cord with the forebrain and cerebrum

brain vesicle *n* : any of the divisions into which the developing embryonic brain of vertebrates is marked off by incomplete transverse constrictions

brain-wash-ing \'brān-ˌwȯ-shiṇ, -ˌwä-\ *n* : a forcible indoctrination to induce someone to give up basic political, social, or religious beliefs and attitudes and to accept contrasting regimented ideas — **brain-wash** *vb*

brain wave *n* 1 : rhythmic fluctuations of voltage between parts of the brain resulting in the flow of an electric current 2 : a current produced by brain waves — compare ALPHA WAVE, BETA WAVE

bran \'bran\ *n* : the edible broken seed coats of cereal grain separated from the flour or meal by sifting

branch \'branch\ *n* : something that extends from or enters into a main body or source (a ～ of an artery) — **branch** *vb*

bran-chi-al \'bran-kē-əl\ *adj* : of or relating to the parts of the body derived from the embryonic branchial arches and clefts

branchial arch *n* : one of a series of bony or cartilaginous arches that develop in the walls of the mouth cavity and pharynx of a vertebrate embryo and correspond to the gill arches of fishes and amphibians — called also *pharyngeal arch, visceral arch*

branchial cleft *n* : one of the open or potentially open clefts that occur on each side of the neck region of a vertebrate embryo between the branchial arches and correspond to the gill slits of fishes and amphibians — called also *pharyngeal cleft*

brash \'brash\ *n* : WATER BRASH

Brax-ton-Hicks contractions \'brak-stən-ˈhiks-\ *n pl* : relatively painless nonrhythmic contractions of the uterus that occur during pregnancy with increasing frequency over time but are not associated with labor

Hicks, John Braxton (1823–1897), British gynecologist.

braxy \'brak-sē\ *n, pl* **brax-ies** : a malignant edema of sheep that involves gastrointestinal invasion by a bacterium of the genus *Clostridium* (*C. septicum*) — compare BLACK DISEASE

¹**break** \'brāk\ *vb* **broke** \'brōk\; **bro-ken** \'brō-kən\; **break-ing** 1 a : to snap into pieces : FRACTURE (～ a bone) b : to fracture the bone of (a bodily part) (the bone *broke* her arm) c : DISLOCATE (～*ing* his neck) 2 a : to cause an open wound in : RUPTURE (～ the

skin) b : to rupture the surface of and permit flowing out or effusing (～ an artery) 3 : to fail in health or strength — often used with *down* 4 : to suffer complete or marked loss of resistance, composure, resolution, morale, or command of a situation — often used with *down*

²**break** *n* 1 : an act or action of breaking : FRACTURE 2 : a condition produced by breaking (gave him something to relieve the pain of the ～ in his leg)

break-bone fever \'brāk-ˌbōn-\ *n* : DENGUE

¹**break-down** \'brāk-ˌdau̇n\ *n* 1 : a failure to function 2 : a physical, mental, or nervous collapse 3 : the process of decomposing (～ of food during digestion) — **break down** *vb*

²**breakdown** *adj* : obtained or resulting from disintegration or decomposition of a substance (a ～ product of hemoglobin)

break out *vb* 1 : to become affected with a skin eruption 2 *of a disease* : to manifest itself by skin eruptions 3 : to become covered with (*break out* in a sweat)

break-through bleeding \ˌbrāk-ˌthrü-\ *n* : prolonged bleeding due to irregular sloughing of the endometrium in the menstrual cycle in women on contraceptive hormones

breast \'brest\ *n* 1 : either of the pair of mammary glands extending from the front of the chest in pubescent and adult females; *also* : either of the analogous but rudimentary organs of the male chest esp. when enlarged 2 : the fore or ventral part of the body between the neck and the abdomen

breast-bone \'brest-ˌbōn\ *n* : STERNUM

breast-feed \'brest-ˌfēd\ *vb* : to feed (an infant) from a mother's breast rather than from a bottle

breath \'breth\ *n* 1 a : the faculty of breathing b : an act or instance of breathing or inhaling (fought to his last ～) 2 a : air inhaled and exhaled in breathing (bad ～) b : something (as moisture on a cold surface) produced by breath or breathing — **out of breath** : breathing very rapidly

Breath-a-ly-zer \'bre-thə-ˌlī-zər\ *trademark* — used for a device that is used to determine the alcohol content of a breath sample

breathe \'brēth\ *vb* **breathed; breath-ing** 1 : to draw air into and expel it from the lungs : RESPIRE; *broadly* : to take in oxygen and give out carbon dioxide through natural processes 2 : to inhale and exhale freely

breath-er \'brē-thər\ *n* : one that breathes usu. in a specified way — see MOUTH BREATHER

breath-less \'breth-ləs\ *adj* 1 : panting or gasping for breath 2 : suffering from dyspnea

breech \'brēch\ *n* 1 : the hind end of the body : BUTTOCKS 2 : BREECH PRESEN-

TATION; *also* : a fetus that is presented breech first

breech delivery *n* : delivery of a fetus by breech presentation

breech presentation *n* : presentation of the fetus in which the breech is the first part to appear at the uterine cervix

breg·ma \'breg-mə\ *n, pl* -ma·ta \-mə-tə\ : the point of junction of the coronal and sagittal sutures of the skull — **breg·mat·ic** \breg-'ma-tik\ *adj*

bre·tyl·i·um \brə-'ti-lē-əm\ *n* : an antiarrhythmic drug administered in the form of its tosylate $C_{18}H_{24}BrNO_3S$ in the treatment of ventricular fibrillation and tachycardia and formerly used as an antihypertensive

brevis — see ABDUCTOR POLLICIS BREVIS, ADDUCTOR BREVIS, EXTENSOR CARPI RADIALIS BREVIS, EXTENSOR DIGITORUM BREVIS, EXTENSOR HALLUCIS BREVIS, EXTENSOR POLLICIS BREVIS, FLEXOR DIGITI MINIMI BREVIS, FLEXOR DIGITORUM BREVIS, FLEXOR HALLUCIS BREVIS, FLEXOR POLLICIS BREVIS, PALMARIS BREVIS, PERONEUS BREVIS

brewer's yeast *n* : the dried pulverized cells of a yeast of the genus *Saccharomyces* (*S. cerevisiae*) used as a source of B-complex vitamins

bridge \'brij\ *n* **1 a** : the upper bony part of the nose **b** : the curved part of a pair of glasses that rests upon this part of the nose **2 a** : PONS **b** : a strand of protoplasm extending between two cells **c** : a partial denture held in place by anchorage to adjacent teeth

bridge·work \-ˌwərk\ *n* : dental bridges; *also* : prosthodontics concerned with their construction

bright·ness \'brīt-nəs\ *n* : the one of the three psychological dimensions of color perception by which visual stimuli are ordered continuously from light to dark and which is correlated with light intensity — compare HUE, SATURATION

Bright's disease \'brīts-\ *n* : any of several kidney diseases marked esp. by albumin in the urine

    Bright \'brīt\, **Richard** (1789–1858), British internist and pathologist.

Brill's disease \'brilz-\ *n* : an acute infectious disease milder than epidemic typhus but caused by the same rickettsia

    Brill \'bril\, **Nathan Edwin** (1860–1925), American physician.

bring up *vb* : VOMIT

British an·ti·lew·is·ite \-ˌan-tē-'lü-ə-ˌsīt, -ˌan-ˌti-\ *n* : DIMERCAPROL

    W. L. Lewis — see LEWISITE

brit·tle \'brit-ᵊl\ *adj* : affected with or being a form of insulin-dependent diabetes mellitus characterized by large and unpredictable fluctuations in blood glucose level (∼ diabetes)

broach \'brōch\ *n* : a fine tapered flexible instrument used in dentistry in removing the dental pulp and in dressing a root canal

broad bean *n* : the large flat edible seed of an Old World upright vetch (*Vicia faba*); *also* : the plant itself — see FAVISM

broad ligament *n* : either of the two lateral ligaments of the uterus composed of a double sheet of peritoneum and bearing the ovary supended from the dorsal surface

broad-spectrum *adj* : effective against a wide range of organisms (as insects or bacteria) — compare NARROW-SPECTRUM

Bro·ca's aphasia \'brō-ˌkəz-\ *n* : MOTOR APHASIA

    Bro·ca \brō-'kä\, **Pierre–Paul** (1824–1880), French surgeon and anthropologist.

Broca's area *n* : a brain center associated with the motor control of speech and usu. located in the left but sometimes in the right inferior frontal gyrus — called also *Broca's convolution, Broca's gyrus, convolution of Broca*

Brod·mann area \'bräd-mən-\ *or* **Brodmann's area** \-mənz-\ *n* : one of the several structurally distinguishable and presumably functionally distinct regions into which the cortex of each cerebral hemisphere can be divided

    Brod·mann \'brōt-ˌmän, 'bräd-mən\, **Korbinian** (1868–1918), German neurologist.

broke *past of* BREAK

bro·ken \'brō-kən\ *adj* : having undergone or been subjected to fracture

broken wind *n* : HEAVES 1 — **bro·ken–wind·ed** \-'wind-əd\ *adj*

brom- *or* **bromo-** *comb form* **1** : bromine (*bromide*) **2** *now usu* **bromo-** : containing bromine in place of hydrogen — in names of organic compounds (*bromo*uracil)

bro·me·lain *also* **bro·me·lin** \'brō-mə-lən\ *n* : a protease obtained from the juice of the pineapple (*Ananas comosus* of the family Bromeliaceae)

bro·mide \'brō-ˌmīd\ *n* **1** : a binary compound of bromine with another element or a radical including some (as potassium bromide) used as sedatives **2** : a dose of bromide taken usu. as a sedative

brom·hi·dro·sis \ˌbrō-mə-'drō-səs *also* ˌbrōm-hə-\ *also* **bro·mi·dro·sis** \ˌbrō-mə-\ *n, pl* **-dro·ses** \-ˌsēz\ : foul-smelling sweat

bro·mine \'brō-ˌmēn\ *n* : a nonmetallic element that is normally a red corrosive toxic liquid — symbol *Br*; see ELEMENT table

bro·mism \'brō-ˌmi-zəm\ *n* : an abnormal state due to excessive or prolonged use of bromides

bro·mo \'brō-(ˌ)mō\ *n, pl* **bromos** : a proprietary effervescent mixture used as a headache remedy, sedative, and alkalinizing agent; *also* : a dose of such a mixture

bro·mo·crip·tine \ˌbrō-mō-ˈkrip-ˌtēn\ *n* : a polypeptide alkaloid $C_{32}H_{40}$-BrN_5O_5 that is a derivative of ergot and mimics the activity of dopamine in selectively inhibiting prolactin secretion

bro·mo·de·oxy·ur·i·dine \ˌbrō-mō-ˌdē-ˌäk-sē-ˈyur-ə-ˌdēn, -dən\ *or* 5-**bro·mo·de·oxy·ur·i·dine** \ˈfīv-\ *n* : a mutagenic analog $C_9H_{11}O_5NBr$ of thymidine that induces chromosomal breakage esp. in heterochromatic regions — *abbr. BUdR*

bro·mo·der·ma \ˈbrō-mə-ˌdər-mə\ *n* : a skin eruption caused in susceptible persons by the use of bromides

bro·mo·ura·cil \ˌbrō-mō-ˈyur-ə-ˌsil, -səl\ *n* : a mutagenic uracil derivative $C_4H_3N_2O_2Br$ that is an analog of thymine and pairs readily with adenine and sometimes with guanine

Brom·sul·pha·lein \ˌbrōm-(ˌ)səl-ˈfa-lē-ən, -ˈfā\ *trademark* — used for a dye derived from phenolphthalein that is used in the form of its disodium salt in a liver function test

bronch- *or* **broncho-** *comb form* : bronchial tube : bronchial (*bronchitis*)

bronchi *pl of* BRONCHUS

bronchi- *or* **bronchio-** *comb form* : bronchial tubes (*bronchiectasis*)

bron·chi·al \ˈbräŋ-kē-əl\ *adj* : of or relating to the bronchi or their ramifications in the lungs — **bron·chi·al·ly** *adv*

bronchial artery *n* : any branch of the descending aorta or first intercostal artery that accompanies the bronchi

bronchial asthma *n* : asthma resulting from spasmodic contraction of bronchial muscles

bronchial pneumonia *n* : BRONCHO-PNEUMONIA

bronchial tree *n* : the bronchi together with their branches

bronchial tube *n* : a primary bronchus; *also* : any of its branches

bronchial vein *n* : any vein accompanying the bronchi and their branches and emptying into the azygos and superior intercostal veins

bron·chi·ec·ta·sis \ˌbräŋ-kē-ˈek-tə-səs\ *also* **bron·chi·ec·ta·sia** \-ek-ˈtā-zhə, -zhē-ə\ *n, pl* **-ta·ses** \-ˈsēz\ *also* **-ta·sias** \-zhəz, -zhē-əz\ : a chronic inflammatory or degenerative condition of one or more bronchi or bronchioles marked by dilatation and loss of elasticity of the walls — **bron·chi·ec·tat·ic** \-ek-ˈta-tik\ *adj*

bron·chio·gen·ic \ˌbräŋ-kē-ō-ˈje-nik\ *adj* : BRONCHOGENIC

bron·chi·ole \ˈbräŋ-kē-ˌōl\ *n* : a minute thin-walled branch of a bronchus — **bron·chi·o·lar** \ˌbräŋ-kē-ˈō-lər\ *adj*

bron·chi·ol·itis \ˌbräŋ-kē-ō-ˈlī-təs\ *n* : inflammation of the bronchioles

bron·chi·o·lus \ˈbräŋ-kī-ə-ləs\ *n, pl* **-o·li** \-ˌlī\ : BRONCHIOLE

bron·chi·tis \brän-ˈkī-təs, bräŋ-\ *n*

: acute or chronic inflammation of the bronchial tubes; *also* : a disease marked by this — **bron·chit·ic** \-ˈki-tik\ *adj*

broncho- — see BRONCH-

bron·cho·al·ve·o·lar \ˌbräŋ-kō-al-ˈvē-ə-lər\ *adj* : of, relating to, or involving the bronchioles and alveoli of the lungs (∼ lavage as a diagnostic technique)

bron·cho·con·stric·tion \-kən-ˈstrik-shən\ *n* : constriction of the bronchial air passages — **bron·cho·con·stric·tor** \-ˈstrik-tər\ *adj*

bron·cho·di·la·ta·tion \-ˌdi-lə-ˈtā-shən, -ˌdī-\ *n* : BRONCHODILATION

bron·cho·di·la·tion \-dī-ˈlā-shən\ *n* : expansion of the bronchial air passages

¹bron·cho·di·la·tor \-dī-ˈlā-tər, -ˈdī-ˌlā-\ *also* **bron·cho·di·la·to·ry** \-dī-ˈlā-tə-rē\ *adj* : relating to or causing expansion of the bronchial air passages (∼ activity) (∼ drugs)

²bronchodilator *n* : a drug that relaxes bronchial muscle resulting in expansion of the bronchial air passages

bron·cho·gen·ic \ˌbräŋ-kə-ˈje-nik\ *adj* : of, relating to, or arising in or by way of the air passages of the lungs (∼ carcinoma)

bron·cho·gram \ˈbräŋ-kə-ˌgram, -kō-\ *n* : a roentgenogram of the bronchial tree after injection of a radiopaque substance

bron·chog·ra·phy \brän-ˈkä-grə-fē, bräŋ-\ *n, pl* **-phies** : the roentgenographic visualization of the bronchi and their branches after injection of a radiopaque substance — **bron·cho·graph·ic** \ˌbräŋ-kə-ˈgra-fik\ *adj*

bron·choph·o·ny \brän-ˈkä-fə-nē\ *n, pl* **-nies** : the sound of the voice heard through the stethoscope over a healthy bronchus and over other portions of the chest in cases of consolidation of the lung tissue — compare PECTORILOQUY

bron·cho·plas·ty \ˈbräŋ-kə-ˌplas-tē\ *n, pl* **-ties** : surgical repair of a bronchial defect

bron·cho·pleu·ral \ˌbräŋ-kō-ˈplür-əl\ *adj* : joining a bronchus and the pleural cavity (a ∼ fistula)

bron·cho·pneu·mo·nia \ˌbräŋ-(ˌ)kō-nu̇-ˈmō-nyə, -nyü-\ *n* : pneumonia involving many relatively small areas of lung tissue — called also *bronchial pneumonia* — **bron·cho·pneu·mon·ic** \-ˈmä-nik\ *adj*

bron·cho·pul·mo·nary \ˌbräŋ-kō-ˈpul-mə-ˌner-ē, -ˈpəl-\ *adj* : of, relating to, or affecting the bronchi and the lungs

bron·cho·scope \ˈbräŋ-kə-ˌskōp\ *n* : a tubular illuminated instrument used for inspecting or passing instruments into the bronchi — **bron·cho·scop·ic** \ˌbräŋ-kə-ˈskä-pik\ *adj* — **bron·chos·co·pist** \brän-ˈkäs-kə-pist\ *n* — **bron·chos·co·py** \brän-ˈkäs-kə-pē\ *n*

bron·cho·spasm \ˈbräŋ-kə-ˌspa-zəm\ *n* : constriction of the air passages of the lung (as in asthma) by spasmodic contraction of the bronchial muscles — **bron·cho·spas·tic** \ˌbrän-kə-ˈspas-tik\ adj

bron·cho·spi·rom·e·try \ˌbrän-kō-spī-ˈrä-mə-trē\ n, pl **-tries** : independent measurement of the vital capacity of each lung by means of a spirometer in direct continuity with one of the primary bronchi — **bron·cho·spi·rom·e·ter** \-ˈrä-mə-tər\ n

bron·cho·ste·no·sis \ˌbrän-kō-stə-ˈnō-səs\ n, pl **-no·ses** \-ˌsēz\ : stenosis of a bronchus

bron·chus \ˈbrän-kəs\ n, pl **bron·chi** \ˈbräŋ-ˌkī, -ˌkē\ : either of the two primary divisions of the trachea that lead respectively into the right and the left lung; broadly : BRONCHIAL TUBE

broth \ˈbroth\ n, pl **broths** \ˈbroths, ˈbrothz\ 1 : liquid in which meat or sometimes vegetable food has been cooked 2 : a fluid culture medium

brow \ˈbrau̇\ n 1 : EYEBROW 2 : either of the lateral prominences of the forehead 3 : FOREHEAD

brown alga n : any of a major taxonomic group (Phaeophyta) of variable mostly marine algae with chlorophyll masked by brown pigment — see ALGIN

brown dog tick n : a widely distributed reddish brown tick of the genus Rhipicephalus (R. sanguineus) that occurs esp. on dogs and that transmits canine babesiosis

brown fat n : a mammalian heat-producing tissue occurring esp. in human newborn infants — called also brown adipose fat

brown lung disease n : BYSSINOSIS

brown rat n : a common domestic rat of the genus Rattus (R. norvegicus) that has been introduced worldwide — called also Norway rat

brown recluse spider n : a venomous spider of the genus Loxosceles (L. reclusa) introduced into the southern U.S. that produces a dangerous cytotoxin — called also brown recluse

brown snake n : any of several Australian venomous elapid snakes (genus Demansia); esp : a widely distributed brownish or blackish snake (D. textilis)

brow·ridge \ˈbrau̇-ˌrij\ n : SUPERCILIARY RIDGE

BRP abbr bathroom privileges

bru·cel·la \brü-ˈse-lə\ n 1 cap : a genus of nonmotile capsulated bacteria (family Brucellaceae) that cause disease in humans and domestic animals 2 pl **-cel·lae** \-ˈse-(ˌ)lē\ or **-cel·las** : any bacterium of the genus Brucella

Bruce \ˈbrüs\, Sir David (1855–1931), British bacteriologist.

bru·cel·lo·sis \ˌbrü-sə-ˈlō-səs\ n, pl **-lo·ses** \-ˌsēz\ : a disease caused by bacteria of the genus Brucella: **a** : a dis-

ease of humans caused by any of four organisms (Brucella melitensis of goats, B. suis of hogs, B. abortus of cattle, and B. canis of dogs), characterized by weakness, extreme exhaustion on slight effort, night sweats, chills, remittent fever, and generalized aches and pains, and acquired through direct contact with infected animals or animal products or from the consumption of milk, dairy products, or meat from infected animals — called also Malta fever, undulant fever **b** : CONTAGIOUS ABORTION

bru·cine \ˈbrü-ˌsēn\ n : a poisonous alkaloid $C_{23}H_{26}N_2O_4$ found with strychnine esp. in nux vomica

Bruce \ˈbrüs\, James (1730–1794), British explorer.

Brud·zin·ski sign \brü-ˈjin-skē-, brüd-ˈzin-\ or **Brud·zin·ski's sign** \-skēz-\ n : any of several symptoms of meningeal irritation occurring esp. in meningitis: as **a** : flexion of the lower limbs induced by passive flexion of the head on the chest **b** : flexion of one lower limb following passive flexion of the other

Brudzinski, Josef (1874–1917), Polish physician.

¹**bruise** \ˈbrüz\ vb **bruised; bruis·ing** 1 : to inflict a bruise on : CONTUSE 2 : WOUND, INJURE; esp : to inflict psychological hurt on 3 : to become bruised

²**bruise** n 1 : an injury transmitted through unbroken skin to underlying tissue causing rupture of small blood vessels and escape of blood into the tissue with resulting discoloration : CONTUSION 2 : an injury or hurt (as to the feelings or the pride)

bruit \ˈbrü-ē\ n : any of several generally abnormal sounds heard on auscultation

Brun·ner's gland \ˈbrü-nərz-\ n : any of the compound racemose glands in the submucous layer of the duodenum that secrete alkaline mucus and a potent proteolytic enzyme — called also gland of Brunner

Brun·ner \ˈbrü-nər\, Johann Conrad (1653–1727), Swiss anatomist.

brush border n : a stria of microvilli on the plasma membrane of an epithelial cell (as in a kidney tubule) that is specialized for absorption

brux·ism \ˈbrək-ˌsi-zəm\ n : the habit of unconsciously gritting or grinding the teeth esp. in situations of stress or during sleep

BS abbr 1 bowel sounds 2 breath sounds

BSN abbr bachelor of science in nursing

BST abbr blood serological test

bu·bo \ˈbü-(ˌ)bō, ˈbyü-\ n, pl **buboes** : an inflammatory swelling of a lymph node esp. in the groin — **bu·bon·ic** \bü-ˈbä-nik, byü-\ adj

bubonic plague *n* : plague caused by a bacterium of the genus *Yersinia* (*Y. pestis* syn. *Pasteurella pestis*) and characterized esp. by the formation of buboes — compare PNEUMONIC PLAGUE

buc·cal \\'bə-kəl\\ *adj* 1 : of, relating to, near, involving, or supplying a cheek (the ∼ surface of a tooth) 2 : of, relating to, involving, or lying in the mouth — **buc·cal·ly** *adv*

buccal gland *n* : any of the small racemose mucous glands in the mucous membrane lining the cheeks

buc·ci·na·tor \\'bək-sə-ˌnā-tər\\ *n* : a thin broad muscle forming the wall of the cheek and serving to compress the cheek against the teeth — called also *buccinator muscle*

bucco- *comb form* : buccal and (*buccolingual*)

buc·co·lin·gual \\ˌbə-kō-'liŋ-gwəl, -gyə-wəl\\ *adj* 1 : relating to or affecting the cheek and the tongue 2 : of or relating to the buccal and lingual aspects of a tooth (the ∼ width of a molar) — **buc·co·lin·gual·ly** *adv*

buc·co·pha·ryn·geal \\-ˌfar-ən-'jē-əl, -fə-'rin-jəl, -jē-əl\\ *adj* : relating to or near the cheek and the pharynx

buck·thorn \\'bək-ˌthȯrn\\ *n* : any of a genus (*Rhamnus* of the family Rhamnaceae) of shrubs and trees some of which yield purgative principles in their bark or sap

buck·tooth \\-'tüth\\ *n* : a large projecting front tooth — **buck-toothed** \\-ˌtütht\\ *adj*

¹**bud** \\'bəd\\ *n* 1 **a** : an asexual reproductive structure **b** : a primordium having potentialities for growth and development into a definitive structure (an embryonic limb ∼) 2 : an anatomical structure (as a tactile corpuscle) resembling a bud

²**bud** *vb* **bud·ded; bud·ding** : to reproduce asexually esp. by the pinching off of a small part of the parent

BUdR *abbr* bromodeoxyuridine

Buer·ger's disease \\'bər-gərz-, 'bùr-\\ *n* : THROMBOANGIITIS OBLITERANS

Buer·ger \\'bər-gər, 'bùr-\\, **Leo** (1879–1943), American pathologist.

¹**buff·er** \\'bə-fər\\ *n* : a substance or mixture of substances (as bicarbonates) that in solution tends to stabilize the hydrogen-ion concentration by neutralizing within limits both acids and bases

²**buffer** *vb* : to treat (as a solution or its acidity) with a buffer; *also* : to prepare (aspirin) with an antacid

buffy coat \\'bə-fē-\\ *n* : the superficial layer of yellowish or buff coagulated plasma from which the red corpuscles have settled out in slowly coagulated blood

bu·fo·ten·ine \\ˌbyü-fə-'te-ˌnēn, -nən\\ *or* **bu·fo·ten·in** \\-nən\\ *n* : a toxic hallucinogenic alkaloid $C_{12}H_{16}N_2O$ that is obtained esp. from poisonous secretions of toads (order Anura and esp. family Bufonidae) and from some mushrooms and has hypertensive and vasoconstrictor activity

bug \\'bəg\\ *n* 1 **a** : an insect or other creeping or crawling invertebrate animal (as a spider) — not used technically **b** : any of various insects commonly considered esp. obnoxious: as (1) : BEDBUG (2) : COCKROACH (3) : HEAD LOUSE **c** : any of an order (Hemiptera and esp. its suborder Heteroptera) of insects that have sucking mouthparts and forewings thickened at the base and that lack a pupal stage between the immature stages and the adult — called also *true bug* 2 **a** : a disease-producing microorganism and esp. a germ **b** : a disease caused by such microorganisms; *esp* : any of various respiratory conditions (as influenza or grippe) of virus origin

bulb \\'bəlb\\ *n* 1 : a protuberance resembling a plant bulb: as **a** : a rounded dilatation or expansion of something cylindrical (the ∼ of a thermometer); *esp* : a rounded or pear-shaped enlargement on a small base (the ∼ of an eyedropper) 2 : a rounded part: as **a** : a rounded enlargement of one end of a part — see BULB OF THE PENIS, BULB OF THE VESTIBULE, END BULB, OLFACTORY BULB **b** : MEDULLA OBLONGATA; *broadly* : the hindbrain exclusive of the cerebellum

bulb- *or* **bulbo-** *comb form* 1 : bulb (*bulbar*) 2 : bulbar and (*bulbospinal*) (*bulbourethral gland*)

bul·bar \\'bəl-bər, -ˌbär\\ *adj* : of or relating to a bulb; *specif* : involving the medulla oblongata

bulbar paralysis *n* : destruction of nerve centers of the medulla oblongata and paralysis of the parts innervated from the medulla with interruption of their functions (as swallowing or speech)

bulbi — see PHTHISIS BULBI

bul·bo·cav·er·no·sus \\ˌbəl-(ˌ)bō-ˌkavər-'nō-səs\\ *n, pl* **-no·si** \\-ˌsī\\ : a muscle that in the male surrounds and compresses the bulb of the penis and the bulbar portion of the urethra and in the female serves to compress the vagina — see SPHINCTER VAGINAE

bulb of the penis *n* : the proximal expanded part of the corpus cavernosum of the male urethra

bulb of the vestibule *n* : a structure in the female vulva that is homologous to the bulb of the penis and the adjoining corpus spongiosum in the male and that consists of an elongated mass of erectile tissue on each side of the vaginal opening united anteriorly to the contralateral mass by a narrow median band passing along the lower surface of the clitoris

bul·bo·spi·nal \\ˌbəl-bō-'spin-əl\\ *adj* : of,

relating to. or connecting the medulla oblongata and the spinal cord

bul·bo·spon·gi·o·sus muscle \ˌbəl-(ˌ)bō-ˌspən-jē-ˈō-səs-\ *n* : BULBOCAVERNOSUS

bul·bo·ure·thral gland \-yü-ˈrē-thrəl-\ *n* : COWPER'S GLAND

bul·bous \ˈbəl-bəs\ *adj* : resembling a bulb esp. in roundness or the gross enlargement of a part

bul·bus \ˈbəl-bəs\ *n, pl* **bul·bi** \-ˌbī, -ˌbē\ : a bulb-shaped anatomical part

-bulia *also* **-boulia** *n comb form* : condition of having (such) will (*abulia*)

-bulic *adj comb form* : of, relating to, or characterized by a (specified) state of will (*abulic*)

bu·lim·a·rex·ia \ˌbü-ˌli-mə-ˈrek-sē-ə, byü-, -ˌlē-\ *n* : BULIMIA 2 — **bu·lim·a·rex·ic** \-sik\ *n or adj*

bu·lim·ia \bü-ˈli-mē-ə, byü-, -ˈlē-\ *n* 1 : an abnormal and constant craving for food 2 : a serious eating disorder that occurs chiefly in females. is characterized by compulsive overeating usu. followed by self-induced vomiting or laxative or diuretic abuse, and is often accompanied by guilt and depression

bulimia ner·vo·sa \-(ˌ)nər-ˈvō-sə, -zə\ *n* : BULIMIA 2

¹**bu·lim·ic** \-mik\ *adj* : of, relating to, or affected with bulimia

²**bulimic** *n* : a person affected with bulimia

bulk \ˈbəlk\ *n* : material (as indigestible fibrous residues of food) that forms a mass in the intestine; *esp* : FIBER 2

bul·la \ˈbu̇-lə\ *n, pl* **bul·lae** \ˈbu̇-ˌlē, -ˌlī\ 1 : a hollow thin-walled rounded bony prominence 2 : a large vesicle or blister — compare BLEB

bull-nose \ˈbu̇l-ˌnōz\ *n* : a necrobacillosis arising in facial wounds of swine

bul·lous \ˈbu̇-ləs\ *adj* : resembling or characterized by bullae : VESICULAR (~ lesions)

bullous pemphigoid *n* : a chronic skin disease affecting esp. elderly persons that is characterized by the formation of numerous hard blisters over a widespread area

BUN \ˌbē-(ˌ)yü-ˈen\ *n* : the concentration of nitrogen in the form of urea in the blood

bun·dle \ˈbənd-ᵊl\ *n* : a small band of mostly parallel fibers (as of nerve or muscle) : FASCICULUS. TRACT

bundle branch *n* : either of the parts of the bundle of His passing respectively to the right and left ventricles

bundle branch block *n* : heart block due to a lesion in one of the bundle branches

bundle of His \-ˈhis\ *n* : a slender bundle of modified cardiac muscle that passes from the atrioventricular node in the right atrium to the right and left ventricles by way of the septum and that maintains the normal sequence of the heartbeat — called also *atrioventricular bundle, His bundle*

His, Wilhelm (1863–1934), German physician.

bun·ga·ro·tox·in \ˈbəŋ-gə-rō-ˌtäk-sən\ *n* : a potent neurotoxin obtained from the venom of an Asian elapid snake (genus *Bungarus*)

bun·ion \ˈbən-yən\ *n* : an inflamed swelling of the small sac on the first joint of the big toe — compare HALLUX VALGUS

bun·io·nec·to·my \ˌbən-yə-ˈnek-tə-mē\ *n, pl* **-mies** : surgical excision of a bunion

Bu·nos·to·mum \byü-ˈnäs-tə-məm\ *n* : a genus of nematode worms including the hookworms of sheep and cattle

buph·thal·mos \ˈbüf-ˌthal-məs, byüf-, ˌbəf-, -ˌmäs\ *also* **buph·thal·mia** \-mē-ə\ *n, pl* **-mos·es** *also* **-mias** : marked enlargement of the eye that is usu. congenital and attended by symptoms of glaucoma

bu·piv·a·caine \byü-ˈpi-və-ˌkān\ *n* : a local anesthetic $C_{18}H_{28}N_2O$ that is like lidocaine in its action but is longer acting

bur \ˈbər\ *n* 1 *usu* **burr** : a small surgical cutting tool (as for making an opening in bone) 2 : a bit used on a dental drill

bur·den \ˈbər-dən\ *n* : the amount of a deleterious parasite. growth. or substance present in the body (worm ~) (cancer ~) — called also *load*

Bur·kitt's lymphoma \ˈbər-kəts-\ *also* **Burkitt lymphoma** \-kət-\ *n* : a malignant lymphoma that occurs esp. in children of central Africa and is associated with Epstein-Barr virus

Burkitt, Denis Parsons (1911–1993), British surgeon.

Burkitt's tumor *also* **Burkitt tumor** *n* : BURKITT'S LYMPHOMA

¹**burn** \ˈbərn\ *vb* **burned** \ˈbərnd. ˈbərnt\ *or* **burnt** \ˈbərnt\; **burn·ing** 1 : to produce or undergo discomfort or pain (iodine ~s so); *also* : to injure or damage by exposure to fire. heat. or radiation (~ed his hand) 2 : to receive sunburn

²**burn** *n* 1 : bodily injury resulting from exposure to heat, caustics. electricity. or some radiations. marked by varying degrees of skin destruction and hyperemia often with the formation of watery blisters and in severe cases by charring of the tissues. and classified according to the extent and degree of the injury — see FIRST-DEGREE BURN, SECOND-DEGREE BURN, THIRD-DEGREE BURN 2 : an abrasion having the appearance of a burn (friction ~s) 3 : a burning sensation (the ~ of iodine applied to a cut)

¹**burn·ing** \ˈbər-niŋ\ *adj* 1 : affecting with or as if with heat (a ~ fever) 2 : resembling that produced by a burn

²**burning** *n* : a sensation of being on fire or excessively heated (gastric ~)

burnout • BZ

burn·out \\'bərn-,aút\ *n* **1 a** : exhaustion of physical or emotional strength usu. as a result of prolonged stress or frustration **b** : a person affected with burnout **2** : a person showing the effects of drug abuse

Bu·row's solution \\'bü-(,)rōz-\ *n* : a solution of the acetate of aluminum used as an antiseptic and astringent

Bu·row \\'bü-(,)rō\, **Karl August von** (1809–1874), German military surgeon and anatomist.

¹burp \\'bərp\ *n* : BELCH

²burp *vb* **1** : BELCH **2** : to help (a baby) expel gas from the stomach esp. by patting or rubbing the back

burr *var of* BUR

bur·row \\'bər-(,)ō\ *n* : a passage or gallery formed in or under the skin by the wandering of a parasite (as the mite of scabies or a foreign hookworm) — **burrow** *vb*

bur·sa \\'bər-sə\ *n, pl* **bur·sas** \-səz\ *or* **bur·sae** \-,sē, -,sī\ : a bodily pouch or sac: as **a** : a small serous sac between a tendon and a bone **b** : BURSA OF FABRICIUS — **bur·sal** \-səl\ *adj*

bursa of Fa·bri·cius \-fə-'brī-shəs, -shē-əs\ *n* : a blind glandular sac that opens into the cloaca of birds and functions in B cell production

Fabricius, Johann Christian (1745–1808), Danish entomologist.

bur·si·tis \(,)bər-'sī-təs\ *n* : inflammation of a bursa esp. of the shoulder or elbow

bush·mas·ter \\'bush-,mas-tər\ *n* : a tropical American pit viper (*Lachesis mutus*)

Bu·Spar \\'byü-,spär\ *trademark* — used for a preparation of the hydrochloride of buspirone

bu·spi·rone \byü-'spī-,rōn\ *n* : a mild antianxiety tranquilizer $C_{21}H_{31}N_5O_2$ that is used in the form of its hydrochloride and does not induce significant tolerance or psychological dependence — see BUSPAR

bu·sul·fan \byü-'səl-fən\ *n* : an antineoplastic agent $C_6H_{14}O_6S_2$ used in the treatment of chronic myelogenous leukemia — see MYLERAN

bu·ta·bar·bi·tal \,byü-tə-'bär-bə-,tal\ *n* : a synthetic barbiturate used esp. in the form of its sodium salt $C_{10}H_{15}N_2NaO_3$ as a sedative and hypnotic

bu·ta·caine \\'byü-tə-,kān\ *n* : a local anesthetic that is an ester of para-aminobenzoic acid and is applied in the form of its sulfate $(C_{18}H_{30}N_2O_2)_2 \cdot H_2SO_4$ to mucous membranes

Bu·ta·zol·i·din \,byü-tə-'zä-lə-dən\ *trademark* — used for a preparation of phenylbutazone

bute \\'byüt\ *n* : PHENYLBUTAZONE

butoxide — see PIPERONYL BUTOXIDE

¹but·ter·fly \\'bət-ər-,flī\ *n, pl* **-flies 1** *pl* : a feeling of hollowness or queasiness caused esp. by emotional or nervous tension or anxious anticipation **2** : a bandage with wing-shaped extensions

²butterfly *adj* : being, relating to, or affecting the area of the face including both cheeks connected by a band across the nose (the typical ∼ lesion of lupus erythematosus)

but·tock \\'bət-ək\ *n* **1** : the back of a hip that forms one of the fleshy parts on which a person sits **2** *pl* : the seat of the body; *also* : the corresponding part of a quadruped : RUMP

but·ton \\'bət-ᵊn\ *n* : something that resembles a small knob or disk: as **a** : the terminal segment of a rattlesnake's rattle **b** : COTYLEDON 1

bu·tyl·at·ed hy·droxy·an·i·sole \\'byüt-ᵊl-,ā-təd-,hī-,dräk-sē-'a-nə-,sōl\ *n* : BHA

butylated hy·droxy·tol·u·ene \-(,)hī-,dräk-sē-'täl-yə-,wēn\ *n* : BHT

bu·tyl nitrite \\'byüt-ᵊl-\ *n* : ISOBUTYL NITRITE

bu·ty·rate \\'byü-tə-,rāt\ *n* : a salt or ester of butyric acid

bu·tyr·ic acid \byü-'tir-ik-\ *n* : either of two isomeric fatty acids $C_4H_8O_2$: *esp* : a normal acid of unpleasant odor found in rancid butter and in perspiration

bu·ty·ro·phe·none \,byü-tə-rō-fə-'nōn\ *n* : any of a class of neuroleptic drugs (as haloperidol) used esp. in the treatment of schizophrenia

Bx [by analogy with *Rx*] *abbr* biopsy

by·pass \\'bī-,pas\ *n* : a surgically established shunt; *also* : a surgical procedure for the establishment of a shunt (have a coronary ∼) — **bypass** *vb*

bys·si·no·sis \,bi-sə-'nō-səs\ *n, pl* **-no·ses** \-,sēz\ : an occupational respiratory disease asssociated with inhalation of cotton, flax, or hemp dust and characterized initially by chest tightness, shortness of breath, and cough, and eventually by irreversible lung disease — called also *brown lung, brown lung disease*

BZ \,bē-'zē\ *n* : a gas $C_{21}H_{23}NO_3$ that when breathed produces incapacitating physical and mental effects — called also *quinuclidinyl benzilate*

C

c *abbr* 1 canine 2 centimeter 3 curie 4 or **c̄** [Latin *cum*] with — used in writing prescriptions

¹C *abbr* 1 Celsius 2 centigrade 3 cervical — used esp. with a number from 1 to 7 to indicate a vertebra or segment of the spinal cord 4 cocaine 5 [Latin *congius*] gallon 6 cytosine

²C *symbol* carbon

Ca *symbol* calcium

CA *abbr* chronological age

CABG \'ka-bü\ *abbr* coronary artery bypass graft

cacao butter *var of* COCOA BUTTER

ca·chec·tic \kə-'kek-tik, ka-\ *adj* : relating to or affected by cachexia

ca·chet \ka-'shā\ *n* : a medicinal preparation for swallowing consisting of a case usu. of rice-flour paste containing an unpleasant-tasting medicine

ca·chex·ia \kə-'kek-sē-ə, ka-\ *n* : general physical wasting and malnutrition usu. associated with chronic disease

cac·o·dyl·ic acid \ka-kə-'di-lik-\ *n* : a toxic crystalline compound of arsenic $C_2H_7AsO_2$ used esp. as an herbicide

ca·cos·mia \kə-'käs-mē-ə, ka-,-'käz-\ *n* : a hallucination of a disagreeable odor

CAD *abbr* coronary artery disease

ca·dav·er \kə-'da-vər\ *n* : a dead body; *specif* : one intended for dissection — **ca·dav·er·ic** \-və-rik\ *adj*

ca·dav·er·ous \kə-'da-və-rəs\ *adj* 1 : of or relating to a corpse 2 *of a complexion* : being pallid or livid like a corpse

cade oil *n* : JUNIPER TAR

cad·mi·um \'kad-mē-əm\ *n* : a bluish white malleable ductile toxic bivalent metallic element — symbol Cd; see ELEMENT table

cadmium sulfide *n* : a yellow-brown poisonous salt CdS used esp. in the treatment of seborrheic dermatitis of the scalp

ca·du·ceus \kə-'dü-sē-əs, -'dyü-, -shəs\ *n, pl* -cei \-sē-ī\ : a medical insignia bearing a representation of a staff with two entwined snakes and two wings at the top — compare STAFF OF AESCULAPIUS

caec- or **caeci-** or **caeco-** *chiefly Brit var of* CEC-

cae·sar·ean *also* **cae·sar·ian** *var of* CESAREAN

cae·si·um *chiefly Brit var of* CESIUM

ca·fé au lait spot \ka-'fā-ō-'lā-\ *n* : any of the medium brown spots usu. on the trunk, pelvis, and creases of the elbow and knees that are often numerous in neurofibromatosis — usu. used in pl.

caf·feine \ka-'fēn, 'ka-\ *n* : a bitter alkaloid $C_8H_{10}N_4O_2$ found esp. in coffee and tea and used medicinally as a stimulant and diuretic — **caf·fein·ic** \ka-'fē-nik\ *adj*

caf·fein·ism \-,ni-zəm\ *n* : a morbid condition caused by caffeine (as from excessive consumption of coffee)

-caine *n comb form* : synthetic alkaloid anesthetic ⟨pro*caine*⟩ ⟨lido*caine*⟩

cais·son disease \'kā-sän-, 'käs-³n-\ *n* : DECOMPRESSION SICKNESS

caj·e·put·ol *or* **caj·u·put·ol** \'ka-jə-pə-,tol, -,tōl\ *n* : EUCALYPTOL

caked breast \'kākt-\ *n* : a localized hardening in one or more segments of a lactating breast caused by accumulation of blood in dilated veins and milk in obstructed ducts

cal *abbr* small calorie

Cal *abbr* large calorie

Cal·a·bar swelling \'ka-lə-,bär-\ *n* : a transient subcutaneous swelling marking the migratory course through the tissues of the adult filarial eye worm of the genus *Loa* (*L. loa*) — compare LOAIASIS

cal·a·mine \'ka-lə-,mīn, -mən\ *n* : a mixture of zinc oxide or zinc carbonate with a small amount of ferric oxide that is used in lotions, liniments, and ointments

cal·ca·ne·al \kal-'kā-nē-əl\ *adj* 1 : relating to the heel 2 : relating to the calcaneus

calcaneal tendon *n* : ACHILLES TENDON

calcaneo- *comb form* : calcaneal and ⟨*calcaneo*cuboid⟩

cal·ca·neo·cu·boid \(,)kal-,kā-nē-ō-'kyü-,bȯid\ *adj* : of or relating to the calcaneus and the cuboid bone

cal·ca·ne·um \kal-'kā-nē-əm\ *n, pl* -nea \-nē-ə\ : CALCANEUS

cal·ca·ne·us \-nē-əs\ *n, pl* -nei \-nē-ī\ : a tarsal bone that in humans is the large bone of the heel — called also *heel bone, os calcis*

cal·car \'kal-,kär\ *n, pl* **cal·car·ia** \kal-'kar-ē-ə\ : a spurred anatomical prominence

calcar avis \-'ā-vəs, -'ä-\ *n, pl* **calcaria avi·um** \-vē-əm\ : a curved ridge on the medial wall of the posterior horn of each lateral ventricle of the brain opposite the calcarine sulcus

cal·car·e·ous \kal-'kar-ē-əs\ *adj* : resembling, consisting of, or containing calcium carbonate; *also* : containing calcium

cal·ca·rine sulcus \'kal-kə-,rīn-\ *n* : a sulcus in the mesial surface of the occipital lobe of the cerebrum — called also *calcarine fissure*

cal·cif·er·ol \kal-'si-fə-,rȯl, -,rōl\ *n* : an alcohol $C_{28}H_{43}OH$ usu. prepared by irradiation of ergosterol and used as a dietary supplement in nutrition and medicinally esp. in the control of rickets — called also *ergocalciferol, viosterol, vitamin D, vitamin D₂*; see DRISDOL

cal·cif·ic \kal-'si-fik\ *adj* : involving or

caused by calcification (~ lesions)

cal·ci·fi·ca·tion \\kal-sə-fə-'kā-shən\ n 1 : impregnation with calcareous matter: as **a** : deposition of calcium salts within the matrix of cartilage often as the preliminary step in the formation of bone — compare OSSIFICATION 1a b : abnormal deposition of calcium salts within tissue 2 : a calcified structure or part — **cal·ci·fy** \'kal-sə-ˌfī\ vb

cal·ci·no·sis \\kal-sə-'nō-səs\ n, pl -no·ses \-ˌsēz\ : the abnormal deposition of calcium salts in a part or tissue of the body

calcis — see OS CALCIS

cal·ci·to·nin \\kal-sə-'tō-nən\ n : a polypeptide hormone esp. from the thyroid gland that tends to lower the level of calcium in the blood plasma — called also *thyrocalcitonin*

cal·ci·um \'kal-sē-əm\ n, often attrib : a silver-white bivalent metal that is an essential constituent of most plants and animals — symbol *Ca;* see ELEMENT table

calcium blocker n : CALCIUM CHANNEL BLOCKER

calcium carbonate n : a calcium salt $CaCO_3$ that is found in limestone, chalk, and bones and that is used in dentifrices and in pharmaceuticals as an antacid and to supplement bodily calcium stores

calcium channel blocker n : any of a class of drugs (as verapamil) that prevent or slow the influx of calcium ions into smooth muscle cells esp. of the heart and that are used to treat some forms of angina pectoris and some cardiac arrhythmias — called also *calcium blocker*

calcium chloride n : a salt $CaCl_2$ used in medicine as a source of calcium and as a diuretic

calcium gluconate n : a white crystalline or granular powdery salt $C_{12}H_{22}CaO_{14}$ used to supplement bodily calcium stores

calcium hydroxide n : a strong alkali $Ca(OH)_2$ — see SODA LIME

calcium lactate n : a white almost tasteless crystalline salt $C_6H_{10}CaO_6 \cdot 5H_2O$ used chiefly in medicine as a source of calcium and in foods (as in baking powder)

calcium levulinate n : a white powdery salt $C_{10}H_{14}CaO_6 \cdot H_2O$ used in medicine as a source of calcium

calcium oxalate n : a crystalline salt $CaC_2O_4 \cdot H_2O$ that is noted for its insolubility and is sometimes excreted in urine or retained in the form of urinary calculi

calcium pantothenate n : a white powdery salt $C_{18}H_{32}CaN_2O_{10}$ made synthetically and used as a source of pantothenic acid

calcium phosphate n 1 : a phosphate of calcium $CaHPO_4$ used in pharmaceutical preparations and animal feeds 2 : a naturally occurring phosphate of calcium $Ca_5(F,Cl,OH,½CO_3)(PO_4)_3$ that contains other elements or radicals and is the chief constituent of bones and teeth

calcium propionate n : a mold-inhibiting salt $(CH_3CH_2COO)_2Ca$ used chiefly as a food preservative

calcium stearate n : a white powder consisting essentially of calcium salts of stearic acid and palmitic acid and used as a conditioning agent in food and pharmaceuticals

calcium sulfate n : a white calcium salt $CaSO_4$ used esp. as a diluent in tablets and in hydrated form as plaster of paris

cal·co·sphe·rite \\kal-kō-'sfir-ˌīt\ n : a granular or laminated deposit of calcium salts in the body

cal·cu·lo·sis \\kal-kyə-'lō-səs\ n, pl -lo·ses \-ˌsēz\ : the formation of or the condition of having a calculus or calculi

cal·cu·lous \'kal-kyə-ləs\ adj : caused or characterized by a calculus or calculi

cal·cu·lus \-ləs\ n, pl -li \-ˌlī, -ˌlē\ also -lus·es 1 : a concretion usu. of mineral salts around organic material found esp. in hollow organs or ducts 2 : a concretion on teeth : TARTAR

Cald·well–Luc operation \'kōld-ˌwel-'lük-, 'käld-, -ˈlÜek-\ n : a surgical procedure used esp. for clearing a blocked or infected maxillary sinus that involves entering the sinus through the mouth by way of an incision into the canine fossa above a canine tooth, cleaning the sinus, and creating a new and enlarged opening for drainage through the nose

Caldwell, George Walter (1866–1946), American surgeon.
Luc \lÜek\, Henri (1855–1925), French laryngologist.

calf \'kaf, 'käf\ n, pl calves \'kavz, 'kävz\ : the fleshy back part of the leg below the knee

calf bone n : FIBULA

calf diphtheria n : an infectious disease of the mouth and pharynx of calves and young cattle associated with the presence of large numbers of a bacterium of the genus *Fusobacterium* (*F. necrophorum*) and commonly passing into pneumonia or generalized septicemia if untreated

cal·i·ber \'ka-lə-bər\ n : the diameter of a round body; *esp* : the internal diameter of a hollow cylinder

cal·i·bre chiefly Brit var of CALIBER

ca·li·ce·al var of CALYCEAL

cal·i·for·ni·um \\ka-lə-'för-nē-əm\ n : an artificially prepared radioactive element — symbol *Cf;* see ELEMENT table

cal·i·per splint \'ka-lə-pər-\ n : a support for the leg consisting of two metal rods extending between a foot plate and a padded thigh band and worn so that the weight is borne mainly by the hipbone — called also *caliper*

cal·is·then·ics \ˌka-ləs-ᵊthe-niks\ *n sing or pl* **1** : systematic rhythmic bodily exercises performed usu. without apparatus **2** *usu sing* : the art or practice of calisthenics — **cal·is·then·ic** \-nik\ *adj*

ca·lix *n, pl* **ca·li·ces** *var of* CALYX

cal·li·per splint *chiefly Brit var of* CALIPER SPLINT

cal·is·then·ics *Brit var of* CALISTHENICS

cal·lo·sal \ka-ᵊlō-səl\ *adj* : of, relating to, or adjoining the corpus callosum

cal·los·i·ty \ka-ᵊlä-sə-tē\ *n, pl* **-ties** : the quality or state of being callous; *esp* : marked or abnormal hardness and thickness (as of the skin)

callosum — see CORPUS CALLOSUM

cal·lous \ᵊka-ləs\ *adj* **1** : being hardened and thickened **2** : having calluses

cal·loused *or* **cal·lused** \ᵊka-ləst\ *adj* : CALLOUS 2 (~ hands)

cal·lus \ᵊka-ləs\ *n* **1** : a thickening of or a hard thickened area on skin **2** : a mass of exudate and connective tissue that forms around a break in a bone and is converted into bone in the healing of the break

calm·ant \ᵊkä-mənt, ᵊkälm-\ *n* : SEDATIVE

calm·ative \ᵊkä-mə-tiv, ᵊkäl-mə-\ *n or adj* : SEDATIVE

cal·mod·u·lin \kal-ᵊmä-jə-lən\ *n* : a calcium-binding protein that regulates cellular metabolic processes (as muscle-fiber contraction) by modifying the activity of specific calcium–sensitive enzymes

cal·o·mel \ᵊka-lə-məl, -ˌmel\ *n* : a white tasteless compound Hg_2Cl_2 used esp. as a fungicide and insecticide and occas. in medicine as a purgative — called also *mercurous chloride*

cal·or \ᵊka-ˌlȯr\ *n* : bodily heat that is a sign of inflammation

calori- *comb form* : heat (*calorigenic*) (*calorimeter*)

ca·lor·ic \kə-ᵊlȯr-ik, -ᵊlär-; ᵊka-lə-rik\ *adj* **1** : of or relating to heat **2** : of or relating to calories — **ca·lor·i·cal·ly** \kə-ᵊlȯr-i-k(ə-)lē, -ᵊlär-\ *adv*

cal·o·rie *also* **cal·o·ry** \ᵊka-lə-rē\ *n, pl* **-ries 1 a** : the amount of heat required at a pressure of one atmosphere to raise the temperature of one gram of water one degree centigrade — called also *gram calorie, small calorie;* abbr. **cal b** : the amount of heat required to raise the temperature of one kilogram of water one degree centigrade : 1000 gram calories — called also *kilocalorie, kilogram calorie, large calorie;* abbr. **Cal 2 a** : a unit equivalent to the large calorie expressing heat-producing or energy–producing value in food when oxidized in the body **b** : an amount of food having an energy-producing value of one large calorie

cal·o·rif·ic \ˌka-lə-ᵊri-fik\ *adj* **1** : CALOR-

IC 2 : of or relating to the production of heat

ca·lor·i·gen·ic \kə-ˌlȯr-ə-ᵊje-nik, -ˌlär-; ˌka-lə-rə-\ *adj* : generating heat or energy (~foodstuffs)

cal·o·rim·e·ter \ˌka-lə-ᵊri-mə-tər\ *n* : any of several apparatuses for measuring quantities of absorbed or evolved heat or for determining specific heats — **ca·lo·ri·met·ric** \ˌka-lə-rə-ᵊme-trik; kə-ˌlȯr-ə-, -ˌlär-\ *adj* — **ca·lo·ri·met·ri·cal·ly** \-tri-k(ə-)lē\ *adv* — **cal·o·rim·e·try** \ˌka-lə-ᵊri-mə-trē\ *n*

cal·va \ᵊkal-və\ *n, pl* **calvas** *or* **cal·vae** \-ˌvē, -ˌvī\ : the upper part of the human cranium — compare CALVARIUM

cal·var·ia \kal-ᵊvar-ē-ə\ *n, pl* **-i·ae** \-ē-ˌē, -ē-ˌī\ : CALVARIUM

cal·var·i·um \-ē-əm\ *n, pl* **-ia** \-ē-ə\ : an incomplete skull; *esp* : the portion of a skull including the braincase and excluding the lower jaw or lower jaw and facial portion — **cal·var·i·al** \-ē-əl\ *adj*

calves *pl of* CALF

cal·vi·ties \kal-ᵊvi-shē-ˌēz, -(ˌ)shēz\ *n, pl* **calvities** : the condition of being bald : BALDNESS

calx \ᵊkalks\ *n, pl* **cal·ces** \ᵊkal-ˌsēz\ : HEEL

ca·ly·ce·al \ˌka-lə-ᵊsē-əl, ˌkā-\ *adj* : of or relating to a calyx

calyces *pl of* CALYX

Ca·lym·ma·to·bac·te·ri·um \kə-ˌli-mə-tō-bak-ᵊtir-ē-əm\ *n* : a genus of pleomorphic nonmotile rod bacteria (family Brucellaceae) including only the causative agent (*C. granulomatis*) of granuloma inguinale — see DONOVAN BODY

ca·lyx \ᵊkā-liks, ᵊka-\ *n, pl* **ca·lyx·es** *or* **ca·ly·ces** \ᵊkā-lə-ˌsēz, ᵊka-\ : a cuplike division of the renal pelvis surrounding one or more renal papillae

cam·i·sole \ᵊka-mə-ˌsōl\ *n* : a long-sleeved straitjacket

cAMP *abbr* cyclic AMP

cam·phor \ᵊkam-fər\ *n* : a tough gummy volatile aromatic crystalline compound $C_{10}H_{16}O$ that is obtained esp. from the wood and bark of a large evergreen tree (*Cinnamomum camphora*) of the laurel family (Lauraceae) and is used esp. as a liniment and mild topical analgesic and as an insect repellent

cam·phor·at·ed \ᵊkam-fə-ˌrā-təd\ *adj* : impregnated or treated with camphor

cam·phor·ic acid \kam-ᵊfȯr-ik-, -ᵊfär-\ *n* : the dextrorotatory form of a white crystalline acid $C_{10}H_{16}O_2$ that is used in pharmaceuticals

cam·pim·e·ter \kam-ᵊpi-mə-tər\ *n* : instrument for testing indirect or peripheral visual perception of form and color — **cam·pim·e·try** \-trē\ *n*

camp·to·cor·mia \ˌkam-tə-ᵊkȯr-mē-ə\ *n* : an hysterical condition marked by forward bending of the trunk and sometimes accompanied by lumbar pain

camp·to·dac·ty·ly \,kam-tə-'dak-tə-lē\ n, pl **-lies** : permanent flexion of one or more finger joints

camp·to·the·cin \,kamp-tə-'thē-sən\ n : an alkaloid $C_{20}H_{16}N_2O_4$ from the wood of a Chinese tree (*Camptotheca acuminata* of the family Nyssaceae) that has shown some antileukemic and antitumor activity

cam·py·lo·bac·ter \'kam-pə-lō-,bak-tər\ n 1 cap : a genus of slender spirally curved rod bacteria (family Spirillaceae) that include some forms pathogenic for domestic animals or humans — see HELICOBACTER 2 : any bacterium of the genus *Campylobacter*

ca·nal \kə-'nal\ n : a tubular anatomical passage or channel : DUCT — see ALIMENTARY CANAL, HAVERSIAN CANAL, INGUINAL CANAL

can·a·lic·u·lus \,kan-əl-'i-kyə-ləs\ n, pl **-li** \-,lī, -,lē\ : a minute canal in a bodily structure — **can·a·lic·u·lar** \-lər\ adj

ca·na·lis \kə-'na-ləs, -'nä-\ n, pl **ca·na·les** \-'na-(,)lēz, -'nä-(,)lās\ : CANAL

ca·na·li·za·tion \,kan-əl-ə-'zā-shən\ n 1 : surgical formation of holes or canals for drainage without tubes 2 : natural formation of new channels in tissue (as formation of new blood vessels through a blood clot) 3 : establishment of new pathways in the central nervous system by repeated passage of nerve impulses

can·a·lize \'kan-əl-,īz\ vb **-lized; -lizing** 1 : to drain (a wound) by forming channels without the use of tubes 2 : to develop new channels (as new capillaries in a blood clot)

canal of Schlemm \-'shlem\ n : a circular canal lying in the substance of the sclerocorneal junction of the eye and draining the aqueous humor from the anterior chamber into the veins draining the eyeball — called also *Schlemm's canal, sinus venosus sclerae*

  Schlemm, Friedrich S. (1795–1858), German anatomist.

can·cel·lous \kan-'sel-əs, 'kan-sə-\ adj : having a porous structure made up of intersecting plates and bars that form small cavities or cells (~bone) — compare COMPACT

can·cer \'kan-sər\ n 1 : a malignant tumor of potentially unlimited growth that expands locally by invasion and systemically by metastasis — compare CARCINOMA, SARCOMA; NEOPLASM, TUMOR 2 : an abnormal state marked by a cancer — **can·cer·ous** \-sə-rəs\ adj

can·cer·i·ci·dal or **can·cer·o·ci·dal** \,kan-sə-rə-'sīd-əl\ adj : destructive of cancer cells

can·cer·i·za·tion \-'zā-shən\ n : transformation into cancer or from a normal to a cancerous state

can·cer·o·gen·ic \-'je-nik, -rō-\ or **can·cer·i·gen·ic** \-rə-\ adj : CARCINOGENIC

can·cer·ol·o·gist \-'rä-lə-jist\ n : a cancer specialist

can·cer·ol·o·gy \-lə-jē\ n, pl **-gies** : the study of cancer

can·cer·pho·bia \,kan-sər-'fō-bē-ə\ or **can·cer·o·pho·bia** \-sər-ō-'fō-\ n : an abnormal dread of cancer

can·crum oris \,kaŋ-krəm-'ōr-əs, -'är-\ n, pl **can·cra oris** \-krə-\ : noma of the oral tissues — called also *gangrenous stomatitis*

can·de·la \kan-'dē-lə, -'de-\ n : CANDLE 2

can·di·ci·din \,kan-də-'sīd-ən\ n : an antibiotic obtained from a streptomyces (*Streptomyces griseus*) and active against some fungi of the genus *Candida*

can·di·da \'kan-də-də\ n 1 cap : a genus of parasitic imperfect fungi (order Moniliales) that resemble yeasts, occur esp. in the mouth, vagina, and intestinal tract, are usu. benign but can become pathogenic, and include the causative agent (*C. albicans*) of thrush 2 : any fungus of the genus *Candida* — **can·di·dal** \-dəd-əl\ adj

can·di·di·a·sis \,kan-də-'dī-ə-səs\ n, pl **-a·ses** \-,sēz\ : infection with or disease caused by a fungus of the genus *Candida* — called also *monilia, moniliasis*

can·dle \'kand-əl\ n 1 : a medicated candle or lozenge used for fumigation 2 : a unit of luminous intensity — called also *candela, new candle*

candy striper n : a volunteer nurse's aide

ca·nic·o·la fever \kə-'ni-kə-lə-\ n : an acute disease of humans and dogs characterized by gastroenteritis and mild jaundice and caused by a spirochete of the genus *Leptospira* (*L. canicola*)

¹ca·nine \'kā-,nīn\ n 1 : a conical pointed tooth; esp : one situated between the lateral incisor and the first premolar 2 : a canine mammal : DOG

²canine adj : of or relating to dogs or to the family (Canidae) to which they belong

canine fossa n : a depression external to and somewhat above the prominence on the surface of the superior maxillary bone caused by the socket of the canine tooth

ca·ni·nus \kā-'nī-nəs, kə-\ n, pl **ca·ni·ni** \-'nī-,nī\ : LEVATOR ANGULI ORIS

ca·ni·ties \kə-'ni-shē-,ēz\ n : grayness or whiteness of the hair

can·ker \'kaŋ-kər\ n 1 a : an erosive or spreading sore b : CANKER SORE 2 a : a chronic inflammation of the ear in dogs, cats, or rabbits; esp : a localized form of mange b : a chronic and progressive inflammation of the hooves of horses resulting in softening and destruction of the horny layers — **can·kered** \ˈkər̄d\ *adj*

canker sore *n* : a painful shallow ulceration of the oral mucous membranes that has a grayish-white base surrounded by a reddish inflamed area and is characteristic of aphthous stomatitis — compare COLD SORE

can·na·bi·noid \ˈka-nə-bə-ˌnȯid, kəˈna-\ *n* : any of various chemical constituents (as THC) of cannabis or marijuana

can·na·bis \ˈka-nə-bəs\ *n* **1** *a cap* : a genus of annual herbs (family Moraceae) that have leaves with three to seven elongate leaflets and pistillate flowers in spikes along the leafy erect stems and that include the hemp (*C. sativa*) **b** : HEMP 1 **2** : any of the preparations (as marijuana or hashish) or chemicals (as THC) that are derived from the hemp and are psychoactive

cannabis in·di·ca \-ˈin-di-kə\ *n, pl* **can·na·bes in·di·cae** \ˈka-nə-ˌbēz-ˈin-də-ˌsē, -bās-ˈin-di-ˌkī\ : cannabis of a variety obtained in India

can·na·bism \ˈka-nə-ˌbi-zəm\ *n* **1** : habituation to the use of cannabis **2** : chronic poisoning from excessive smoking or chewing of cannabis

can·ni·bal \ˈka-nə-bəl\ *n* : one that eats the flesh of its own kind — **cannibal** *adj*

can·ni·bal·ism \-bə-ˌli-zəm\ *n* **1** : the usu. ritualistic eating of human flesh by a human being **2** : the eating of the flesh or the eggs of any animal by its own kind

can·non \ˈka-nən\ *n* : the part of the leg in which the cannon bone is found

cannon bone *n* : a bone in hoofed mammals that supports the leg from the hock joint to the fetlock

can·nu·la *also* **can·u·la** \ˈkan-yə-lə\ *n, pl* **-las** *or* **-lae** \-ˌlē, -ˌlī\ : a small tube for insertion into a body cavity, duct, or vessel

can·nu·late \-ˌlāt\ *vb* **-lat·ed; -lat·ing** : to insert a cannula into — **can·nu·la·tion** \ˌkan-yə-ˈlā-shən\ *n*

can·nu·lize \ˈkan-yə-ˌlīz\ *vb* **-lized; -liz·ing** : CANNULATE — **can·nu·li·za·tion** \ˌkan-yə-lə-ˈzā-shən\ *n*

ca·no·la \kə-ˈnō-lə\ *n* **1** : a rape plant (*Brassica napus*) of the mustard family of an improved variety with seeds that are low in erucic acid and are the source of canola oil **2** : CANOLA OIL

canola oil *n* : an edible vegetable oil obtained from the seeds of canola that is high in monounsaturated fatty acids

can·thar·i·din \kan-ˈthar-əd-ᵊn\ *n* : a bitter crystalline compound $C_{10}H_{12}O_4$ that is the active blister-producing ingredient of cantharides

can·thar·is \ˈkan-thə-rəs\ *n, pl* **can·thar·i·des** \kan-ˈthar-ə-ˌdēz\ **1** : SPANISH FLY 1 **2** *cantharides* : a preparation of dried beetles and esp. Spanish flies that contains cantharidin and is used in medicine as a blister-pro-

ducing agent and formerly as an aphrodisiac — used with a *sing.* or *pl.* verb; called also *Spanish fly*

can·tha·xan·thin \ˌkan-thə-ˈzan-ˌthin\ *n* : a carotenoid $C_{40}H_{52}O_2$ used esp. as a color additive in food

can·thus \ˈkan-thəs\ *n, pl* **can·thi** \ˈkan-ˌthī, -ˌthē\ : either of the angles formed by the meeting of the upper and lower eyelids

¹cap \ˈkap\ *n, often attrib* **1** : something that serves as a cover or protection esp. for a tip, knob, or end (as of a tooth) **2** : PATELLA, KNEECAP **3** *Brit* : CERVICAL CAP

²cap *vb* **capped; cap·ping 1** : to invest (a student nurse) with a cap as an indication of completion of a probationary period of study **2** : to cover (a diseased or exposed part of a tooth) with a protective substance

³cap *abbr* capsule

ca·pac·i·ta·tion \kə-ˌpa-sə-ˈtā-shən\ *n* : the change undergone by sperm in the female reproductive tract that enables them to penetrate and fertilize an egg — **ca·pac·i·tate** \-ˌtāt\ *vb*

ca·pac·i·ty \kə-ˈpa-sə-tē, -ˈpas-tē\ *n, pl* **-ties 1** : a measure of content : VOLUME — see VITAL CAPACITY **2** : legal qualification, competency, power, or fitness

cap·e·line \ˈka-pə-ˌlēn, -lən\ *n* : a cup-shaped bandage for the head, the shoulder, or the stump of an amputated limb

cap·il·lar·ia \ˌka-pə-ˈlar-ē-ə\ *n* **1** *cap* : a genus of slender white nematode worms (family Trichuridae) that include serious pathogens of the alimentary tract of fowls and some tissue and organ parasites of mammals including one (*C. hepatica*) which is common in rodents and occas. invades the human liver sometimes with fatal results **2** : a nematode worm of the genus *Capillaria* — **cap·il·lar·id** \-ˈlar-əd, kə-ˈpi-lə-rəd\ *n*

cap·il·la·ri·a·sis \kə-ˌpi-lə-ˈrī-ə-səs\ *also* **cap·il·lar·i·o·sis** \ˌka-pə-ˌler-ē-ˈō-səs\ *n, pl* **-a·ses** \-ˈrī-ə-ˌsēz\ *also* **-o·ses** \-ˈō-ˌsēz\ : infestation with or disease caused by nematode worms of the genus *Capillaria*

cap·il·laro·scope \ˌka-pə-ˈlar-ə-ˌskōp\ *n* : a microscope that permits visual examination of the living capillaries in nail beds, skin, and conjunctiva — **cap·il·la·ros·co·py** \ˌka-pə-lə-ˈräs-kə-pē\ *n*

¹cap·il·lary \ˈka-pə-ˌler-ē\ *adj* **1 a** : resembling a hair esp. in slender elongated form **b** : having a very small bore (a ~ tube) **2** : of or relating to capillaries

²capillary *n, pl* **-lar·ies** : a capillary tube; *esp* : any of the smallest blood vessels connecting arterioles with venules and forming networks throughout the body

capillary bed *n* : the whole system of

capillaries of a body, part, or organ

capita *pl of* CAPUT

¹cap·i·tate \ˈka-pə-ˌtāt\ *adj* : abruptly enlarged and globe-shaped

²capitate *n* : the largest bone of the wrist that is situated between the hamate and the trapezoid in the distal row of carpal bones and that articulates with the third metacarpal

cap·i·ta·tum \ˌka-pə-ˈtā-təm, -ˈtä-\ *n, pl* **cap·i·ta·ta** \-tə\ : CAPITATE

cap·i·tel·lum \ˌka-pə-ˈte-ləm\ *n, pl* **-tel·la** \-lə\ : a knoblike protuberance esp. at the end of a bone (as the humerus)

capitis — see LONGISSIMUS CAPITIS, LONGUS CAPITIS, OBLIQUUS CAPITIS INFERIOR, OBLIQUUS CAPITIS SUPERIOR, PEDICULOSIS CAPITIS, RECTUS CAPITIS POSTERIOR MAJOR, RECTUS CAPITIS POSTERIOR MINOR, SEMISPINALIS CAPITIS, SPINALIS CAPITIS, SPLENIUS CAPITIS, TINEA CAPITIS

ca·pit·u·lum \kə-ˈpi-chə-ləm\ *n, pl* **-la** \-lə\ : a rounded protuberance of an anatomical part — **ca·pit·u·lar** \-lər, -ˌlär\ *adj*

Cap·lets \ˈka-pləts\ *trademark* — used for capsule-shaped medicinal tablets

-capnia *n comb form* : carbon dioxide in the blood (hyper*capnia*) (hypo*capnia*)

Cap·o·ten \ˈka-pō-ˌten\ *trademark* — used for a preparation of captopril

cap·re·o·my·cin \ˌka-prē-ō-ˈmīs-ᵊn\ *n* : an antibiotic obtained from a bacterium of the genus *Streptomyces* (*S. capreolus*) that is used to treat tuberculosis

ca·pro·ic acid \kə-ˈprō-ik-\ *n* : a liquid fatty acid $C_6H_{12}O_2$ that is found as a glycerol ester in fats and oils and is used in pharmaceuticals and flavors

cap·ry·late \ˈka-prə-ˌlāt\ *n* : a salt or ester of caprylic acid — see SODIUM CAPRYLATE

ca·pryl·ic acid \kə-ˈpri-lik-\ *n* : a fatty acid $C_8H_{16}O_2$ of rancid odor occurring in fats and oils

cap·sa·i·cin \kap-ˈsā-ə-sən\ *n* : a colorless irritant substance $C_{18}H_{27}NO_3$ obtained from various capsicums

cap·si·cum \ˈkap-si-kəm\ *n* **1** : any of a genus (*Capsicum*) of tropical plants of the nightshade family (Solanaceae) that are widely cultivated for their many-seeded usu. fleshy-walled berries **2** : the dried ripe fruit of some capsicums (as *C. frutescens*) used as a gastric and intestinal stimulant

cap·sid \ˈkap-səd\ *n* : the outer protein shell of a virus particle

cap·so·mer \ˈkap-sə-mər\ *or* **cap·so·mere** \ˈkap-sə-ˌmir\ *n* : one of the subunits making up a viral capsid

capsul- *or* **capsuli-** *or* **capsulo-** *comb form* : capsule (*capsul*itis) (*capsule*ctomy)

cap·su·la \ˈkap-sə-lə\ *n, pl* **cap·su·lae** \-ˌlē, -ˌlī\ : CAPSULE

cap·su·lar \ˈkap-sə-lər\ *adj* : of, relating to, affecting, or resembling a capsule

capsularis — see DECIDUA CAPSULARIS

cap·su·lat·ed \-lā-təd\ *also* **cap·su·late** \-ˌlāt, -lət\ *adj* : enclosed in a capsule

cap·su·la·tion \ˌkap-sə-ˈlā-shən\ *n* : enclosure in a capsule

cap·sule \ˈkap-səl, -(ˌ)sül\ *n* **1 a** : a membrane or saclike structure enclosing a part or organ (the ~ of the kidney) **b** : either of two layers or laminae of white matter in the cerebrum: (1) : a layer that consists largely of fibers passing to and from the cerebral cortex and that lies internal to the lentiform nucleus — called also *internal capsule* (2) : one that lies between the lentiform nucleus and the claustrum — called also *external capsule* **2** : a shell usu. of gelatin for packaging something (as a drug or vitamins); *also* : a usu. medicinal or nutritional preparation for oral use consisting of the shell and its contents **3** : a viscous or gelatinous often polysaccharide envelope surrounding certain microscopic organisms (as the pneumococcus)

cap·su·lec·to·my \ˌkap-sə-ˈlek-tə-mē\ *n, pl* **-mies** : excision of a capsule (as of a joint, kidney, or lens)

capsule of Bow·man \ˈbō-mən\ *n* : BOWMAN'S CAPSULE

capsule of Te·non \-tə-ˈnōⁿ\ *n* : TENON'S CAPSULE

cap·su·li·tis \ˌkap-sə-ˈlī-təs\ *n* : inflammation of a capsule (as that of the crystalline lens)

cap·su·lor·rha·phy \ˌkap-sə-ˈlòr-ə-fē\ *n, pl* **-phies** : suture of a cut or wounded capsule (as of the knee joint)

cap·su·lot·o·my \-ˈlä-tə-mē\ *n, pl* **-mies** : incision of a capsule esp. of the crystalline lens (as in a cataract operation)

cap·to·pril \ˈkap-tə-ˌpril\ *n* : an antihypertensive drug $C_9H_{15}NO_3S$ that is an ACE inhibitor — see CAPOTEN

ca·put \ˈkä-ˌpút, -pət\ *n, pl* **ca·pi·ta** \ˈkä-pə-ˌtä, ˈka-pə-tə\ **1** : a knoblike protuberance (as of a bone or muscle) **2** : CAPUT SUCCEDANEUM

caput suc·ce·da·ne·um \-ˌsək-sə-ˈdā-nē-əm\ *n, pl* **capita suc·ce·da·nea** \-ə\ : a swelling formed upon the presenting part of the fetus during labor

ca·ra·te \kə-ˈrä-tē\ *n* : PINTA

car·a·way oil \ˈkar-ə-ˌwā-\ *n* : an essential oil obtained from the seeds of caraway (*Carum carvi*) of the carrot family (Umbelliferae) and used in pharmaceuticals and as a flavoring agent

car·ba·chol \ˈkär-bə-ˌkól, -ˌkōl\ *n* : a synthetic parasympathomimetic drug $C_6H_{15}ClN_2O_2$ that is used in veterinary medicine and topically in glaucoma

car·ba·mate \ˈkär-bə-ˌmāt, kär-ˈba-ˌmāt\ *n* : a salt or ester of carbamic acid — see URETHANE

car·ba·maz·e·pine \ˌkär-bə-ˈma-zə-ˌpēn\ *n* : a tricyclic anticonvulsant and analgesic $C_{15}H_{12}N_2O$ used in the treatment of trigeminal neuralgia and epilepsy — see TEGRETOL

car·bam·ic acid \(,)kär-'ba-mik-\ *n* : an acid CH_3NO_2 known in the form of salts and esters

carb·ami·no·he·mo·glo·bin \kär-bə-mē-(,)nō-'hē-mə-,glō-bən\ *n* : CARBHEMOGLOBIN

car·bar·sone \kär-'bär-,sōn\ *n* : a white powder $C_7H_9N_2O_4As$ used esp. in treating intestinal amebiasis

car·ba·zole \'kär-bə-,zōl\ *n* : a crystalline slightly basic cyclic compound $C_{12}H_9N$ used in testing for carbohydrates (as sugars)

car·ben·i·cil·lin \kär-,be-nə-'si-lən\ *n* : a broad-spectrum semisynthetic penicillin that is used esp. against gram-negative bacteria (as pseudomonas)

carb·he·mo·glo·bin \(,)kärb-'hē-mə-,glō-bən\ *n* : a compound of hemoglobin with carbon dioxide

car·bo·hy·drase \,kär-bō-'hī-,drās, -bə-, -,drāz\ *n* : any of a group of enzymes (as amylase) that promote hydrolysis or synthesis of a carbohydrate (as a disaccharide)

car·bo·hy·drate \-'drāt, -,drāt\ *n* : any of various neutral compounds of carbon, hydrogen, and oxygen (as sugars, starches, and celluloses) most of which are formed by green plants and which constitute a major class of animal foods

car·bol·fuch·sin paint \'kär-(,)bäl-'fyük-sən, -(,)bôl-\ *n* : a solution containing boric acid, phenol, resorcinol, and fuchsin in acetone, alcohol, and water that is applied externally in the treatment of fungal infections of the skin — called also *Castellani's paint*

car·bol·ic \kär-'bä-lik\ *n* : PHENOL 1

carbolic acid *n* : PHENOL 1

car·bo·my·cin \,kär-bə-'mīs-ᵊn\ *n* : a colorless crystalline basic macrolide antibiotic $C_{42}H_{67}NO_{16}$ produced by a bacterium of the genus *Streptomyces* (*S. halstedii*) and active esp. in inhibiting the growth of gram-positive bacteria — see MAGNAMYCIN

car·bon \'kär-bən\ *n*, *often attrib* : a nonmetallic element found native (as in diamonds and graphite) or as a constituent of coal, petroleum, asphalt, limestone, and organic compounds or obtained artificially (as in activated charcoal) — symbol *C*; see ELEMENT table

car·bon·ate \'kär-bə-,nāt, -nət\ *n* : a salt or ester of carbonic acid

carbon dioxide *n* : a heavy colorless gas CO_2 that does not support combustion, dissolves in water to form carbonic acid and is formed esp. in animal respiration and in the decay or combustion of animal and vegetable matter

carbon 14 *n* : a heavy radioactive isotope of carbon of mass number 14 used esp. in tracer studies

car·bon·ic acid \kär-'bä-nik-\ *n* : a weak acid H_2CO_3 known only in solution that reacts with bases to form carbonates

carbonic anhydrase *n* : a zinc-containing enzyme that occurs in living tissues (as red blood cells) and aids carbon-dioxide transport from the tissues and its release from the blood in the lungs by catalyzing the reversible hydration of carbon dioxide to carbonic acid

carbon monoxide *n* : a colorless odorless very toxic gas CO that is formed as a product of the incomplete combustion of carbon

carbon tetrachloride *n* : a colorless nonflammable toxic carcinogenic liquid CCl_4 that has an odor resembling that of chloroform and is used as a solvent and a refrigerant

car·boxy·he·mo·glo·bin \(,)kär-,bäk-sē-'hē-mə-,glō-bən\ *n* : a very stable combination of hemoglobin and carbon monoxide formed in the blood when carbon monoxide is inhaled with resulting loss of ability of the blood to combine with oxygen

car·boxyl \kär-'bäk-səl\ *n* : a univalent group —COOH typical of organic acids — called also *carboxyl group* — **car·box·yl·ic** \,kär-(,)bäk-'si-lik\ *adj*

car·box·yl·ase \kär-'bäk-sə-,lās, -,lāz\ *n* : an enzyme that catalyzes decarboxylation or carboxylation

car·box·yl·ate \-,lāt, -lət\ *n* : a salt or ester of a carboxylic acid — **car·box·yl·ate** \-,lāt\ *vb* — **car·box·yl·ation** \(,)kär-,bäk-sə-'lā-shen\ *n*

carboxylic acid *n* : an organic acid (as an acetic acid) containing one or more carboxyl groups

car·boxy·meth·yl·cel·lu·lose \(,)kär-,bäk-sē-,me-thəl-'sel-yə-,lōs, -,lōz\ *n* : a derivative of cellulose that in the form of its sodium salt is used as a bulk laxative in medicine

car·boxy·pep·ti·dase \'pep-tə-,dās, -,dāz\ *n* : an enzyme that hydrolyzes peptides and esp. polypeptides by splitting off sequentially the amino acids at the end of the peptide chain which contain free carboxyl groups

car·bun·cle \'kär-,bəŋ-kəl\ *n* : a painful local purulent inflammation of the skin and deeper tissues with multiple openings for the discharge of pus and usu. necrosis and sloughing of dead tissue — **car·bun·cu·lar** \kär-'bəŋ-kyə-lər\ *adj*

car·bun·cu·lo·sis \,kär-,bəŋ-kyə-'lō-səs\ *n*, *pl* **-lo·ses** \-,sēz\ : a condition marked by the formation of many carbuncles simultaneously or in rapid succession

carcin- *or* **carcino-** *comb form* : tumor : cancer ⟨*carcinogenic*⟩

car·ci·no·em·bry·on·ic antigen \,kärs-ᵊn-ō-,em-brē-'ä-nik-\ *n* : a glycoprotein present in fetal gut tissues during the first two trimesters of pregnancy and in peripheral blood of patients with cancer of the digestive system — abbr. *CEA*

car·cin·o·gen \kär-ˈsi-nə-jən, ˈkärs-ᵊn-ə-ˌjen\ *n* : a substance or agent causing cancer

car·ci·no·gen·e·sis \ˌkärs-ᵊn-ō-ˈje-nə-səs\ *n, pl* **-e·ses** \-ˌsēz\ : the production of cancer

car·ci·no·gen·ic \ˌkärs-ᵊn-ō-ˈje-nik\ *adj* : producing or tending to produce cancer — **car·ci·no·gen·i·cal·ly** \-ni-k(ə-)lē\ *adv* — **car·ci·no·ge·nic·i·ty** \-jə-ˈni-sə-tē\ *n*

car·ci·noid \ˈkärs-ᵊn-ˌöid\ *n* : a benign or malignant tumor arising esp. from the mucosa of the gastrointestinal tract (as in the stomach or appendix)

carcinoid syndrome *n* : a syndrome that is caused by vasoactive substances secreted by carcinoid tumors and is characterized by flushing, cyanosis, abdominal cramps, diarrhea, and valvular heart disease

car·ci·no·ma \ˌkärs-ᵊn-ō-ˈō-mə\ *n, pl* **-mas** *or* **-ma·ta** \-mə-tə\ : a malignant tumor of epithelial origin — compare CANCER 1, SARCOMA — **car·ci·no·ma·tous** \-mə-təs\ *adj*

carcinoma in situ *n* : carcinoma in the stage of development when the cancer cells are still within their site of origin (as the mouth or uterine cervix)

car·ci·no·ma·to·sis \-ˌō-mə-ˈtō-səs\ *n, pl* **-to·ses** \-ˌsēz\ : a condition in which multiple carcinomas develop simultaneously usu. after dissemination from a primary source

car·ci·no·sar·co·ma \ˈkärs-ᵊn-ō-(ˌ)sär-ˈkō-mə\ *n, pl* **-mas** *or* **-ma·ta** \-mə-tə\ : a malignant tumor combining elements of carcinoma and sarcoma

cardi- *or* **cardio-** *comb form* : heart : cardiac : cardiac and (*cardiogram*) (*cardiovascular*)

car·dia \ˈkär-dē-ə\ *n, pl* **car·di·ae** \-ˌē\ *or* **cardias 1** : the opening of the esophagus into the stomach **2** : the part of the stomach adjoining the cardia

¹-car·dia \ˈkär-dē-ə\ *n comb form* : heart action or location (of a specified type) (dextro*cardia*) (tachy*cardia*)

²-cardia *pl of* -CARDIUM

¹car·di·ac \ˈkär-dē-ˌak\ *adj* **1 a** : of, relating to, situated near, or acting on the heart **b** : of or relating to the cardia of the stomach **2** : of, relating to, or affected with heart disease

²cardiac *n* : a person with heart disease

cardiac arrest *n* : temporary or permanent cessation of the heartbeat

cardiac asthma *n* : asthma due to heart disease (as heart failure) that occurs in paroxysms usu. at night and is characterized by difficult wheezing respiration, pallor, and anxiety — called also *paroxysmal dyspnea*

cardiac cycle *n* : the complete sequence of events in the heart from the beginning of one beat to the beginning of the following beat : a complete heartbeat including systole and diastole

cardiac failure *n* : HEART FAILURE

cardiac gland *n* : any of the branched tubular mucus-secreting glands of the cardia of the stomach; *also* : one of the similar glands of the esophagus

cardiac muscle *n* : the principal muscle tissue of the vertebrate heart made up of striated fibers that appear to be separated from each other under the electron microscope but that function in long-term rhythmic contraction as if in protoplasmic continuity — compare SMOOTH MUSCLE, STRIATED MUSCLE

cardiac nerve *n* : any of the three nerves connecting the cervical ganglia of the sympathetic nervous system with the cardiac plexus

cardiac neurosis *n* : NEUROCIRCULATORY ASTHENIA

cardiac output *n* : the volume of blood ejected from the left side of the heart in one minute — called also *minute volume*

cardiac plexus *n* : a nerve plexus of the autonomic nervous system supplying the heart and neighboring structures and situated near the heart and the arch and ascending part of the aorta

cardiac reserve *n* : the difference between the rate at which a heart pumps blood at a particular time and its maximum capacity for pumping blood

cardiac sphincter *n* : the somewhat thickened muscular ring surrounding the opening between the esophagus and the stomach

cardiac tamponade *n* : mechanical compression of the heart by large amounts of fluid or blood within the pericardial space that limits the normal range of motion and function of the heart

cardiac vein *n* : any of the veins returning the blood from the tissues of the heart that open into the right atrium either directly or through the coronary sinus

car·di·al·gia \ˌkär-dē-ˈal-jə, -jē-ə\ *n* **1** : HEARTBURN **2** : pain in the heart

car·di·ec·to·my \ˌkär-dē-ˈek-tə-mē\ *n, pl* **-mies** : excision of the cardiac portion of the stomach

cardinal vein *n* : any of four longitudinal veins of the vertebrate embryo running anteriorly and posteriorly along each side of the spinal column with the pair on each side meeting at and discharging blood to the heart through a large venous sinus — called also *cardinal sinus, Cuvierian vein*

cardio- — see CARDI-

car·dio·ac·cel·er·a·tor \ˌkär-dē-(ˌ)ō-ik-ˈse-lə-ˌrā-tər, -ak-\ *adj* : speeding up the action of the heart — **car·dio·ac·cel·er·a·tion** \-ˌse-lə-ˈrā-shən\ n

car·dio·ac·tive \-ˈak-tiv\ adj : having an influence on the heart (~ drugs)

car·dio·cir·cu·la·to·ry \ˈsər-kyə-lə-ˌtôr-ē\ adj : of or relating to the heart and circulatory system (temporary ~ assist)

car·dio·dy·nam·ics \-dī-ˈna-miks\ n sing or pl : the dynamics of the heart's action in pumping blood — **car·dio·dy·nam·ic** \-mik\ adj

car·dio·gen·ic \ˈ-je-nik\ adj : originating in the heart : caused by a cardiac condition (~ shock)

car·dio·gram \ˈkär-dē-ə-ˌgram\ n : the curve or tracing made by a cardiograph

car·dio·graph \ˌ-graf\ n : an instrument that registers graphically movements of the heart — **car·dio·graph·ic** \ˌkär-dē-ə-ˈgra-fik\ adj — **car·di·og·ra·phy** \ˌkär-dē-ˈä-grə-fē\ n

car·dio·in·hib·i·to·ry \ˌkär-dē-(ˌ)ō-in-ˈhi-bə-ˌtôr-ē\ adj : interfering with or slowing the normal sequence of events in the cardiac cycle (the ~ center of the medulla)

car·dio·lip·in \ˌkär-dē-ō-ˈli-pən\ n : a phospholipid used in combination with lecithin and cholesterol as an antigen in diagnostic blood tests for syphilis

car·di·ol·o·gy \ˌkär-dē-ˈä-lə-jē\ n, pl -gies : the study of the heart and its action and diseases — **car·di·o·log·i·cal** \-ə-ˈlä-ji-kəl\ adj — **car·di·ol·o·gist** \-ˈä-lə-jist\ n

car·dio·meg·a·ly \ˌkär-dē-ō-ˈme-gə-lē\ n, pl -lies : enlargement of the heart

car·dio·my·op·a·thy \ˈkär-dē-ō-(ˌ)mī-ˈä-pə-thē\ n, pl -thies : a typically chronic disorder of heart muscle that may involve hypertrophy and obstructive damage to the heart

car·di·op·a·thy \ˌkär-dē-ˈä-pə-thē\ n, pl -thies : any disease of the heart

car·dio·plas·ty \ˈkär-dē-ō-ˌplas-tē\ n, pl -ties : a plastic operation performed on the gastric cardiac sphincter

car·dio·ple·gia \ˌkär-dē-ō-ˈplē-jə, -jē-ə\ n : temporary cardiac arrest induced (as by drugs) during heart surgery — **car·dio·ple·gic** \-jik\ adj

car·dio·pul·mo·nary \ˌkär-dē-ō-ˈpùl-mə-ˌner-ē, -ˈpəl-\ adj : of or relating to the heart and lungs (a ~ bypass)

cardiopulmonary resuscitation n : a procedure designed to restore normal breathing after cardiac arrest that includes the clearance of air passages to the lungs, the mouth-to-mouth method of artificial respiration, and heart massage by the exertion of pressure on the chest — abbr. **CPR**

car·dio·re·nal \-ˈrēn-ᵊl\ adj : of or relating to the heart and the kidneys (~ disorders)

car·dio·re·spi·ra·to·ry \ˌkär-dē-ō-ˈres-pə-rə-ˌtôr-ē, -ˌri-ˈspī-rə-\ adj : of or relating to the heart and the respiratory system : CARDIOPULMONARY (~ ailments) (~ responses)

car·dio·scle·ro·sis \ˌkär-dē-(ˌ)ō-sklə-ˈrō-səs\ n, pl -ro·ses \-ˌsēz\ : induration of the heart caused by formation of fibrous tissue in the cardiac muscle

car·dio·spasm \ˈkär-dē-ō-ˌspa-zəm\ n : failure of the cardiac sphincter to relax during swallowing with resultant esophageal obstruction — compare ACHALASIA

car·dio·ta·chom·e·ter \ˌkär-dē-(ˌ)ō-ta-ˈkä-mə-tər\ n : a device for prolonged graphic recording of the heartbeat

car·dio·tho·ra·cic \-thə-ˈra-sik\ adj : relating to, involving, or specializing in the heart and chest (~ surgeon) (~ surgery)

car·di·ot·o·my \ˌkär-dē-ˈä-tə-mē\ n, pl -mies 1 : surgical incision of the heart 2 : surgical incision of the stomach cardia

¹**car·dio·ton·ic** \ˌkär-dē-ō-ˈtä-nik\ adj : tending to increase the tonus of heart muscle (~ steroids)

²**cardiotonic** n : a cardiotonic substance

car·dio·tox·ic \ˈ-ˈtäk-sik\ adj : having a toxic effect on the heart — **car·dio·tox·ic·i·ty** \-ˌtäk-ˈsi-sə-tē\ n

¹**car·dio·vas·cu·lar** \-ˈvas-kyə-lər\ adj : of, relating to, or involving the heart and blood vessels (~ disease)

²**cardiovascular** n : a substance (as a drug) that affects the heart or blood vessels

car·dio·ver·sion \-ˈvər-zhən, -shən\ n : application of an electric shock in order to restore normal heartbeat

car·dio·ver·ter \ˈkär-dē-ō-ˌvər-tər\ n : a device for the administration of an electric shock in cardioversion

car·di·tis \kär-ˈdī-təs\ n, pl **car·dit·i·des** \-ˈdi-tə-ˌdēz\ : inflammation of the heart muscle : MYOCARDITIS

-car·di·um \ˈkär-dē-əm\ n comb form, pl **-car·dia** \-ē-ə\ : heart (epicardium)

care \ˈker, ˈkar\ n : responsibility for or attention to health, well-being, and safety — see HEALTH CARE, INTENSIVE CARE, PRIMARY CARE, TERTIARY CARE — **care** vb

care·giv·er \-ˌgi-vər\ n : a person who provides direct care (as for children or the chronically ill) esp : one who has primary responsibility for a child — **care·giv·ing** \-ˌgi-viŋ\ n

car·ies \ˈkar-ēz, ˈker-\ n, pl **caries** : a progressive destruction of bone or tooth; esp : tooth decay

ca·ri·na \kə-ˈrī-nə, -ˈrē-\ n, pl **carinas** or **ca·ri·nae** \ˈrī-ˌnē, -ˈrē-ˌnī\ : any of various keel-shaped anatomical structures, ridges, or processes

carinii — see PNEUMOCYSTIS CARINII PNEUMONIA

cario- comb form : caries (cariogenic) (cariostatic)

car·io·gen·ic \ˌkar-ē-ō-ˈje-nik\ adj : producing or promoting the development of tooth decay (~ foods)

car·io·stat·ic \-ˈsta-tik\ adj : tending to

inhibit the formation of dental caries (the ∼ action of fluorides)

car·i·ous \'kar-ē-əs, 'ker-\ *adj* : affected with caries ⟨∼ teeth⟩

car·i·so·pro·dol \kə-₁rī-sə-'prō-₁dȯl, -zə-, -₁dȯl\ *n* : a drug $C_{12}H_{24}N_2O_4$ related to meprobamate that is used to relax muscle and relieve pain

¹car·min·a·tive \kär-'mi-nə-tiv, 'kär-mə-₁nā-\ *adj* : expelling or causing the expulsion of gas from the alimentary canal so as to relieve colic or griping

²carminative *n* : a carminative agent

car·mus·tine \'kär-mə-₁stēn\ *n* : BCNU

car·ni·tine \'kär-nə-₁tēn\ *n* : a quaternary ammonium compound $C_7H_{15}NO_3$ present esp. in vertebrate muscle and involved in the transfer of fatty acids across mitochondrial membranes

car·o·ten·ae·mia *chiefly Brit var of* CAROTENEMIA

car·o·tene \'kar-ə-₁tēn\ *n* : any of several orange or red hydrocarbon pigments (as $C_{40}H_{56}$) that occur in plants and plant-eating animals and are convertible to vitamin A — see BETA-CAROTENE

car·o·ten·emia \₁kar-ə-tə-'nē-mē-ə\ *n* : the presence in the circulating blood of carotene which may cause a yellowing of the skin resembling jaundice

ca·rot·enoid \kə-'rät-ᵊn-₁ȯid\ *n* : any of various usu. yellow to red pigments (as carotenes) found widely in plants and animals — **carotenoid** *adj*

caroticum — see GLOMUS CAROTICUM

ca·rot·id \kə-'rä-təd\ *adj* : of, situated near, or involving a carotid artery

carotid artery *n* : either of the two main arteries that supply blood to the head of which the left in humans arises from the arch of the aorta and the right by bifurcation of the brachiocephalic artery — called also *carotid*; see COMMON CAROTID ARTERY, EXTERNAL CAROTID ARTERY, INTERNAL CAROTID ARTERY

carotid body *n* : a small body of vascular tissue that adjoins the carotid sinus, functions as a chemoreceptor sensitive to change in the oxygen content of blood, and mediates reflex changes in respiratory activity — called also *carotid gland, glomus caroticum*

carotid canal *n* : the canal by which the internal carotid artery enters the skull — called also *carotid foramen*

carotid plexus *n* : a network of nerves of the sympathetic nervous system surrounding the internal carotid artery

carotid sinus *n* : a small but richly innervated arterial enlargement that is located near the point in the neck where the common carotid artery divides into the internal and the external carotid arteries and that functions in the regulation of heart rate and blood pressure

carp- or **carpo-** *comb form* 1 : carpus ⟨*carpectomy*⟩ 2 : carpal and ⟨*carpo-metacarpal*⟩

¹car·pal \'kär-pəl\ *adj* : relating to the carpus

²carpal *n* : a carpal element : CARPALE

car·pa·le \kär-'pa-(₁)lē, -'pä-, -'pä-\ *n*, *pl* **-lia** \-lē-ə\ : a carpal bone; *esp* : one of the distal series articulating with the metacarpals

carpal tunnel *n* : a passage between the flexor retinaculum of the hand and the carpal bones that is sometimes a site of compression of the median nerve

carpal tunnel syndrome *n* : a condition caused by compression of the median nerve in the carpal tunnel and characterized esp. by weakness, pain, and disturbances of sensation in the hand

car·pec·to·my \kär-'pek-tə-mē\ *n*, *pl* **-mies** : excision of a carpal bone

carpi — see EXTENSOR CARPI RADIALIS BREVIS, EXTENSOR CARPI RADIALIS LONGUS, EXTENSOR CARPI ULNARIS, FLEXOR CARPI RADIALIS, FLEXOR CARPI ULNARIS

carpo- — see CARP-

car·po·meta·car·pal \₁kär-pō-'me-tə-₁kär-pəl\ *adj* : relating to, situated between, or joining a carpus and metacarpus ⟨a ∼ joint⟩

car·po·ped·al spasm \₁kär-pə-'ped-ᵊl-, -'pēd-\ *n* : a spasmodic contraction of the muscles of the hands and feet or esp. of the wrists and ankles in disorders such as alkalosis and tetany

car·pus \'kär-pəs\ *n*, *pl* **car·pi** \-₁pī, -₁pē\ 1 : WRIST 2 : the group of bones supporting the wrist comprising in humans a proximal row which contains the scaphoid, lunate, triquetrum, and pisiform that articulate with the radius and a distal row which contains the trapezium, trapezoid, capitate, and hamate that articulate with the metacarpals

car·ri·er \'kar-ē-ər\ *n* 1 a : a person, animal, or plant that harbors and disseminates the specific agent (as a microorganism) causing an infectious disease from which it has recovered or to which it is immune ⟨a ∼ of typhoid fever⟩ — compare RESERVOIR 2, VECTOR 1 b : an individual possessing a specified gene and capable of transmitting it to offspring but not of showing its typical expression; *esp* : one that is heterozygous for a recessive factor 2 : a vehicle serving esp. as a diluent (as for a drug)

Car·ri·ón's disease \₁kar-ē-'ȯnz-\ *n* : BARTONELLOSIS

Carrión, Daniel A. (1850–1885), Peruvian medical student.

car·sick \'kär-₁sik\ *adj* : affected with motion sickness esp. in an automobile — **car sickness** *n*

car·ti·lage \'kärt-ºl-ij, 'kärt-lij\ *n* **1** : a usu. translucent somewhat elastic tissue that composes most of the skeleton of vertebrate embryos and except for a small number of structures (as some joints, respiratory passages, and the external ear) is replaced by bone during ossification in the higher vertebrates **2** : a part or structure composed of cartilage

car·ti·lag·i·nous \ˌkärt-ºl-'a-jə-nəs\ *adj* : composed of, relating to, or resembling cartilage

car·un·cle \'kar-əŋ-kəl, kə-'rəŋ-\ *n* : a small fleshy growth; *specif* : a reddish growth situated at the urethral meatus in women causing pain and bleeding — see LACRIMAL CARUNCLE

ca·run·cu·la \kə-'rəŋ-kyə-lə\ *n, pl* **-lae** \-ˌlē, -ˌlī\ : CARUNCLE

cary- *or* **caryo-** — see KARY

cas·cade \(ˌ)kas-'kād\ *n* : a molecular, biochemical, or physiological process occurring in a succession of stages each of which is closely related to or depends on the output of the previous stage (a ~ of enzymic reactions) (the ~ of events comprising the immune response)

cas·cara sa·gra·da \kas-'kar-ə-sə-'grä-də, -ˌkär-; 'kas-kə-rə-\ *n* : the dried bark of a buckthorn (*Rhamnus purshiana*) of the Pacific coast of the U.S. that is used as a mild laxative — called also cascara

case \'kās\ *n* **1** : the circumstances and situation of a particular person or group **2 a** : an instance of disease or injury (10 ~s of pneumonia) **b** : PATIENT 1

ca·se·ation \ˌkā-sē-'ā-shən\ *n* : necrosis with conversion of damaged tissue into a soft cheesy substance — **ca·se·ate** \'kā-sē-ˌāt\ *vb*

case·book \'kās-ˌbük\ *n* : a book containing medical records of illustrative cases that is used for reference and instruction

case history *n* : a record of an individual's personal or family history and environment for use in analysis or instructive illustration

ca·sein \kā-'sēn, 'kā-sē-ən\ *n* : any of several phosphoproteins of milk

case load *n* : the number of cases handled in a particular period (as by a clinic)

caseosa — see VERNIX CASEOSA

ca·se·ous \'kā-sē-əs\ *adj* : marked by caseation

caseous lymphadenitis *n* : a chronic infectious disease of sheep and goats characterized by caseation of the lymph glands and occas. of parts of the lungs, liver, spleen, and kidneys that is caused by a bacterium of the genus *Corynebacterium* (*C. pseudotuberculosis*) — called also pseudotuberculosis

case·work \'kās-ˌwərk\ *n* : social work involving direct consideration of the problems, needs, and adjustments of the individual case (as a person or family in need of psychiatric aid) — **case·work·er** \-ˌwər-kər\ *n*

cas·sette *also* **ca·sette** \kə-'set, ka-\ *n* : a lightproof magazine for holding the intensifying screens and film in X-ray photography

cassia oil *n* : CINNAMON OIL

cast \'kast\ *n* **1** : a slight strabismus **2** : a rigid dressing of gauze impregnated with plaster of paris for immobilizing a diseased or broken part **3** : a mass of plastic matter formed in cavities of diseased organs (as the kidneys) and discharged from the body

Cas·tel·la·ni's paint \ˌkas-tə-'lä-nēz-\ *n* : CARBOLFUCHSIN PAINT

Cas·tel·la·ni \ˌkas-tə-'lä-nē, Aldo (1878–1971), Italian physician.**

cas·tor bean \'kas-tər-\ *n* : the very poisonous seed of the castor-oil plant; *also* : CASTOR-OIL PLANT

castor oil *n* : a pale viscous fatty oil from castor beans used esp. as a cathartic

castor-oil plant *n* : a tropical Old World herb (*Ricinus communis*) of the spurge family (Euphorbiaceae) widely grown as an ornamental or for its oil-rich castor beans that are a source of castor oil

¹cas·trate \'kas-ˌtrāt\ *vb* **cas·trat·ed; cas·trat·ing 1 a** : to deprive of the testes : GELD **b** : to deprive of the ovaries : SPAY **2** : to render impotent or deprive of vitality esp. by psychological means — **cas·trat·er** *or* **cas·tra·tor** \-'trā-tər\ *n* — **cas·tra·tion** \kas-'trā-shən\ *n*

²castrate *n* : a castrated individual

castration complex *n* : a child's fear or delusion of genital injury at the hands of the parent of the same sex as punishment for unconscious guilt over oedipal strivings; *broadly* : the often unconscious fear or feeling of bodily injury or loss of power at the hands of authority

ca·su·al·ty \'ka-zhəl-tē, 'ka-zhə-wəl-\ *n, pl* **-ties 1** : a serious or fatal accident **2** : a military person lost through death, wounds, injury, sickness, internment, or capture or through being missing in action **3 a** : injury or death from accident **b** : one injured or killed (as by accident)

ca·su·is·tic \ˌka-zhə-'wis-tik\ *adj* : of or based on the study of actual cases or case histories

cat \'kat\ *n, often attrib* **1** : a carnivorous mammal (*Felis catus*) long domesticated and kept as a pet or for catching rats and mice **2** : any of a family (Felidae) of mammals including the domestic cat, lion (*Panthera leo*), tiger (*Panthera tigris*), leopard (*Panthera pardus*), cougar (*Felis concolor*), and their relatives

CAT *abbr* computed axial tomography; computerized axial tomography

cata- or **cat-** or **cath-** prefix : down (cat-amnesis) (cataplexy)

ca·tab·o·lism \kə-'ta-bə-ˌli-zəm\ n : destructive metabolism involving the release of energy and resulting in the breakdown of complex materials within the organism — compare ANABOLISM — **cat·a·bol·ic** \ˌka-tə-'bä-lik\ adj — **cat·a·bol·i·cal·ly** \-li-k(ə-)lē\ adv

ca·tab·o·lite \-ˌlīt\ n : a product of catabolism

ca·tab·o·lize \-ˌlīz\ vb -lized; -liz·ing : to subject to or undergo catabolism

cat·a·lase \'kat-əl-ˌās, -ˌāz\ n : an enzyme that consists of a protein complex with hematin groups and catalyzes the decomposition of hydrogen peroxide into water and oxygen

cat·a·lep·sy \'kat-əl-ˌep-sē\ n, pl -sies : a condition of suspended animation and loss of voluntary motion associated with hysteria and schizophrenia in humans and with organic nervous disease in animals and characterized by a trancelike state of consciousness and a posture in which the limbs hold any position they are placed in — compare WAXY FLEXIBILITY

¹**cat·a·lep·tic** \ˌkat-əl-'ep-tik\ adj : of, having the characteristics of, or affected with catalepsy (a ~ state)

²**cataleptic** n : one affected with catalepsy

ca·tal·y·sis \kə-'ta-lə-səs\ n, pl -y·ses \-ˌsēz\ : a change and esp. increase in the rate of a chemical reaction brought about by a substance (catalyst \'kat-əl-ˌist\ that is itself unchanged at the end of the reaction — **cat·a·lyt·ic** \ˌkat-əl-'i-tik\ adj — **cat·a·lyt·i·cal·ly** \-ti-k(ə-)lē\ adv

cat·a·lyze \'kat-əl-ˌīz\ vb -lyzed; -lyz·ing : to bring about the catalysis of (a chemical reaction) — **cat·a·lyz·er** n

cata·me·nia \ˌka-tə-'mē-nē-ə\ n pl : MENSES — **cata·me·ni·al** \-nē-əl\ adj

cat·am·ne·sis \ˌkat-ˌam-'nē-səs\ n, pl -ne·ses \-ˌsēz\ : the follow-up medical history of a patient — **cat·am·nes·tic** \-'nes-tik\ adj

cat·a·plasm \'kat-ə-ˌpla-zəm\ n : POULTICE

cat·a·plexy \'ka-tə-ˌplek-sē\ n, pl -plex·ies \-ˌsēz\ : sudden loss of muscle power with retention of clear consciousness following a strong emotional stimulus (as fright, anger, or shock)

cat·a·ract \'ka-tə-ˌrakt\ n : a clouding of the lens of the eye or its surrounding transparent membrane that obstructs the passage of light

cat·a·ract·ous \ˌka-tə-ˌrak-təs\ adj : of, relating to, or affected with an eye cataract

ca·tarrh \kə-'tär\ n : inflammation of a mucous membrane in humans or animals; esp : one chronically affecting the human nose and air passages — **ca·tarrh·al** \-əl\ adj

catarrhal fever n : MALIGNANT CATARRHAL FEVER

cata·to·nia \ˌka-tə-'tō-nē-ə\ n : catatonic schizophrenia

¹**cata·ton·ic** \ˌka-tə-'tä-nik\ adj : of, relating to, being, or affected with schizophrenia characterized esp. by a marked psychomotor disturbance that may involve stupor or mutism, negativism, rigidity, purposeless excitement, and inappropriate or bizarre posturing — **cata·ton·i·cal·ly** \-ni-k(ə-)lē\ adv

²**catatonic** n : a catatonic person

catch·ment area \'kach-mənt-\ n : the geographical area served by an institution

cat cry syndrome n : CRI DU CHAT SYNDROME

cat distemper n : PANLEUKOPENIA

cat·e·chol·amine \ˌka-tə-'kō-lə-ˌmēn, -'kō-\ n : any of various substances (as epinephrine, norepinephrine, and dopamine) that function as hormones or neurotransmitters or both

cat·e·chol·amin·er·gic \-ˌkō-lə-mē-'nər-jik\ adj : involving, liberating, or mediated by catecholamine (~ transmission in the nervous system)

cat fever n : PANLEUKOPENIA

cat flea n : a common often pestiferous flea of the genus Ctenocephalides (C. felis) that breeds chiefly on cats, dogs, and rats

cat·gut \'kat-ˌgət\ n : a tough cord made usu. from sheep intestines and used esp. for sutures in closing wounds

cath abbr 1 cathartic 2 catheter

cath- — see CATA-

ca·thar·sis \kə-'thär-səs\ n, pl ca·thar·ses \-ˌsēz\ 1 : PURGATION 2 : elimination of a complex by bringing it to consciousness and affording it expression

¹**ca·thar·tic** \kə-'thär-tik\ adj : of, relating to, or producing catharsis

²**cathartic** n : a cathartic medicine : PURGATIVE

ca·thect \kə-'thekt, ka-\ vb : to invest with mental or emotional energy

ca·thec·tic \kə-'thek-tik, ka-\ adj : of, relating to, or invested with mental or emotional energy

cath·e·ter \'ka-thə-tər, 'kath-tər\ n : a tubular medical device for insertion into canals, vessels, passageways, or body cavities usu. to permit injection or withdrawal of fluids or to keep a passage open

cath·e·ter·i·za·tion \ˌka-thə-tə-rə-'zā-shən, ˌkath-tə-rə-\ n : the use of or insertion of a catheter (as in or into the bladder, trachea, or heart) — **cath·e·ter·ize** \'ka-thə-tə-ˌrīz, 'kath-tə-\ vb

cath·e·ter·ized adj : obtained by catheterization (~ urine specimens)

ca·thex·is \kə-'thek-səs, ka-\ n, pl ca·thex·es \-ˌsēz, -səs\ 1 : investment of mental or emotional energy in a person, object, or idea 2 : libidinal energy that is either invested or being invested

cath·ode–ray oscilloscope \'ka-ˌthōd-\ n : OSCILLOSCOPE

cathode–ray tube n : a vacuum tube in which a beam of electrons is projected on a fluorescent screen to produce a luminous spot

cat·ion \'kat-ˌī-ən, ˌka-(ˌ)tī-ən\ n : the ion in an electrolyte that migrates to the cathode; also : a positively charged ion — **cat·ion·ic** \ˌkat-(ˌ)ī-'ä-nik, ˌka-(ˌ)tī-\ adj — **cat·ion·i·cal·ly** adv

cat louse n : a biting louse (Felicola subrostratus of the family Trichodectidae) common on cats esp. in warm regions

CAT scan \'kat-\ n : a sectional view of the body constructed by computed tomography — **CAT scanning** n

CAT scanner n : a medical instrument consisting of integrated X-ray and computing equipment and used for computed tomography

cat scratch disease n : an illness that is characterized by chills, slight fever, and swelling of the lymph glands and is caused by a gram-negative bacillus (Afipia felis) transmitted esp. by a cat scratch — called also cat scratch fever

cat tapeworm n : a common tapeworm of the genus Taenia (T. taeniaeformis) of cats who ingest cysticercus-infected livers of various rodents

cattle grub n : either of two warble flies of the genus Hypoderma esp. in the larval stage: **a** : COMMON CATTLE GRUB **b** : NORTHERN CATTLE GRUB

cattle louse n : a louse infesting cattle — see LONG-NOSED CATTLE LOUSE, SHORT-NOSED CATTLE LOUSE

cattle tick n : either of two ixodid ticks of the genus Boophilus (B. annulatus and B. microplus) that infest cattle and transmit the protozoan which causes Texas fever

cau·dad \'kô-ˌdad\ adv : toward the tail or posterior end

cau·da equi·na \ˌkaù-də-ē-'kwē-nə, ˌkô-də-, -'kwī-\ n, pl **caudae equi·nae** \ˌkaù-ˌdī-ē-'kwē-nē, -ˌnī, ˌkô-ˌdē-ē-'kwī-ˌnē\ : the roots of the upper sacral nerves that extend beyond the termination of the spinal cord at the first lumbar vertebra in the form of a bundle of filaments within the spinal canal resembling a horse's tail

cau·dal \'kôd-ᵊl\ adj 1 : of, relating to, or being a tail 2 : situated in or directed toward the hind part of the body — **cau·dal·ly** adv

caudal anesthesia n : loss of pain sensation below the umbilicus produced by injection of an anesthetic into the caudal portion of the spinal canal — called also caudal analgesia

cau·date lobe \'kô-ˌdāt-\ n : a lobe of the liver bounded on the right by the inferior vena cava, on the left by the fissure of the ductus venosus, and

connected with the right lobe by a narrow prolongation

caudate nucleus n : the one of the four basal ganglia in each cerebral hemisphere that comprises a mass of gray matter in the corpus striatum, forms part of the floor of the lateral ventricle, and is separated from the lentiform nucleus by the internal capsule — called also caudate

caul \'kôl\ n 1 : GREATER OMENTUM 2 : the inner embryonic membrane of higher vertebrates esp. when covering the head at birth

cauliflower ear n : an ear deformed from injury and excessive growth of reparative tissue

cau·sal·gia \kô-'zal-jə, -'sal-, -jē-ə\ n : a constant usu. burning pain resulting from injury to a peripheral nerve — **cau·sal·gic** \-jik\ adj

¹**caus·tic** \'kô-stik\ adj : capable of destroying or eating away organic tissue and esp. animal tissue by chemical action

²**caustic** n : a caustic agent; esp : a substance or means that can burn, corrode, or destroy animal or other organic tissue by chemical action : ESCHAROTIC

cau·ter·ize \'kô-tə-ˌrīz\ vb -ized; -iz·ing : to sear with a cautery or caustic — **cau·ter·i·za·tion** \ˌkô-tə-rə-'zā-shən\ n

cau·tery \'kô-tə-rē\ n, pl -ter·ies 1 : the act or effect of cauterizing : CAUTERIZATION 2 : an agent (as a hot iron or caustic) used to burn, sear, or destroy tissue

¹**ca·va** \'kä-və, 'kā-\ n, pl **ca·vae** \'kä-ˌvē, -ˌvī; 'kā-ˌvē\ : VENA CAVA — **ca·val** \-vəl\ adj

²**cava** pl of CAVUM

cavernosum, cavernosa — see CORPUS CAVERNOSUM

cav·ern·ous \'ka-vər-nəs\ adj 1 : having caverns or cavities 2 of tissue : composed largely of vascular sinuses and capable of dilating with blood to bring about the erection of a body part

cavernous sinus n : either of a pair of large venous sinuses situated in a groove at the side of the body of the sphenoid bone in the cranial cavity and opening behind into the petrosal sinuses

cav·i·tary \'ka-və-ˌter-ē\ adj : of, relating to, or characterized by bodily cavitation (~ tuberculosis) (~ lesions)

cav·i·ta·tion \ˌka-və-'tā-shən\ n 1 : the process of cavitating; esp : the formation of cavities in an organ or tissue esp. in disease 2 : a cavity formed by cavitation — **cav·i·tate** \'ka-və-ˌtāt\ vb

cav·i·ty \'ka-və-tē\ n, pl -ties 1 : an unfilled space within a mass — see PELVIC CAVITY 2 : an area of decay in a tooth : CARIES

ca·vum \'kä-vəm, 'kä-\ *n, pl* **ca·va** \-və\ : an anatomical recess or hollow

cavus — see PES CAVUS

Cb *symbol* columbium

CB *abbr* [Latin *Chirurgiae Baccalaureus*] bachelor of surgery

CBC *abbr* complete blood count

CBW *abbr* chemical and biological warfare

cc *abbr* cubic centimeter

CC *abbr* 1 chief complaint 2 current complaint

CCK *abbr* cholecystokinin

CCU *abbr* 1 cardiac care unit 2 coronary care unit 3 critical care unit

Cd *symbol* cadmium

CD *abbr* cluster of differentiation — used with an integer to denote any of numerous antigenic proteins on the surface of thymocytes and esp. T cells; see CD4

CDC *abbr* Centers for Disease Control

CD4 \¡sē-(¡)dē-'fȯr\ *n* : a large glycoprotein esp. on the surface of helper T cells that is the receptor for HIV; *also* : a cell and esp. a helper T cell bearing the CD4 receptor

cDNA \¡sē-(¡)dē-(¡)en-'ā\ *n* : DNA that is complementary to a given messenger RNA and that serves as a template for production of the messenger RNA in the presence of a reverse transcriptase — called also *complementary DNA*

Ce *symbol* cerium

CEA *abbr* carcinoembryonic antigen

cec- or **ceci-** or **ceco-** *comb form* : cecum (*cecitis*) (*cecostomy*)

ce·cal \'sē-kəl\ *adj* : of or like a cecum — **ce·cal·ly** *adv*

ce·ci·tis \sē-'sī-təs\ *n* : inflammation of the cecum

ce·co·pexy \'sē-kə-¡pek-sē\ *n, pl* **-pex·ies** : a surgical operation to fix the cecum to the abdominal wall

ce·cos·to·my \sē-'käs-tə-mē\ *n, pl* **-mies** : the surgical formation of an opening into the cecum to serve as an artificial anus

ce·cum \'sē-kəm\ *n, pl* **ce·ca** \-kə\ : the blind pouch at the beginning of the large intestine into which the ileum opens from one side and which is continuous with the colon

¹-cele *n comb form* : tumor : hernia (cystocele)

²-cele — see -COELE

celi- or **celio-** *comb form* : belly : abdomen (*celioscopy*) (*celiotomy*)

¹ce·li·ac \'sē-lē-¡ak\ *adj* 1 : of or relating to the abdominal cavity 2 : belonging to or prescribed for celiac disease (the ~ syndrome) (a ~ diet)

²celiac *n* : a celiac part (as a nerve)

celiac artery *n* : a short thick artery arising from the aorta just below the diaphragm and dividing almost immediately into the gastric, hepatic, and splenic arteries — called also *celiac axis, truncus celiacus*

celiac disease *n* : a chronic nutritional disorder esp. in young children that is characterized by defective digestion and utilization of fats and often by abdominal distension, diarrhea, and fatty stools — called also *nontropical sprue*

celiac ganglion *n* : either of a pair of collateral sympathetic ganglia that are the largest of the autonomic nervous system and lie one on each side of the celiac artery near the adrenal gland on the same side

celiac plexus *n* : a nerve plexus that is situated in the abdomen behind the stomach and in front of the aorta and the crura of the diaphragm, surrounds the celiac artery and the root of the superior mesenteric artery, contains several ganglia of which the most important are the celiac ganglia, and distributes nerve fibers to all the abdominal viscera — called also *solar plexus*

celiacus — see TRUNCUS CELIACUS

ce·li·os·co·py \¡sē-lē-'äs-kə-pē\ *n, pl* **-pies** : examination of the abdominal cavity by surgical insertion of an endoscope through the abdominal wall

ce·li·ot·o·my \¡sē-lē-'ä-tə-mē\ *n, pl* **-mies** : surgical incision of the abdomen

cell \'sel\ *n* : a small usu. microscopic mass of protoplasm bounded externally by a semipermeable membrane, usu. including one or more nuclei and various nonliving products, capable alone or interacting with other cells of performing all the fundamental functions of life, and forming the smallest structural unit of living matter capable of functioning independently

cell body *n* : the nucleus-containing central part of a neuron exclusive of its axons and dendrites that is the major structural element of the gray matter of the brain and spinal cord, the ganglia, and the retina — called also *soma*

cell count *n* : a count of cells esp. of the blood or other body fluid in a standard volume (as a cubic millimeter)

cell cycle *n* : the complete series of events from one cell division to the next — see G₁ PHASE, G₂ PHASE, M PHASE, S PHASE

cell division *n* : the process by which cells multiply involving both nuclear and cytoplasmic division — compare MEIOSIS, MITOSIS

celled \'seld\ *adj* : having (such or so many) cells — used in combination (single-*celled* organisms)

cell line *n* : a cell culture selected for uniformity from a cell population derived from a usu. homogeneous tissue source (as an organ) (a *cell line* derived from a malignant tumor)

cell—me·di·at·ed \'sel-¡mē-dē-¡ā-təd\ *adj* : relating to or being the part of immunity or the immune response that is mediated primarily by T cells and esp. cytotoxic T cells rather than by antibodies secreted by B cells (~ immunity) — compare HUMORAL 2

cell membrane *n* **1** : PLASMA MEMBRANE **2** : CELL WALL

cell of Ley·dig \-'lī-dig\ *n* : LEYDIG CELL

cell plate *n* : a disk formed in a dividing plant cell that eventually forms the middle lamella of the wall between the daughter cells

cell sap *n* **1** : the liquid contents of a plant cell vacuole **2** : CYTOSOL

cell theory *n* : a theory in biology that includes one or both of the statements that the cell is the fundamental structural and functional unit of living matter and that the organism is composed of autonomous cells with its properties being the sum of those of its cells

cel·lu·lar \'sel-yə-lər\ *adj* **1** : of, relating to, or consisting of cells **2** : CELL-MEDIATED — **cel·lu·lar·i·ty** \ˌsel-yə-'lar-ə-tē\ *n*

cel·lu·lite \'sel-yə-ˌlīt, -ˌlēt\ *n* : lumpy fat found in the thighs, hips, and buttocks of some women

cel·lu·li·tis \ˌsel-yə-'lī-təs\ *n* : diffuse and esp. subcutaneous inflammation of connective tissue

cel·lu·lose \'sel-yə-ˌlōs, -ˌlōz\ *n* : a polysaccharide ($C_6H_{10}O_5$), of glucose units that constitutes the chief part of the cell walls of plants — **cel·lu·los·ic** \ˌsel-yə-'lō-sik, -zik\ *adj*

cellulose acetate phthal·ate \-'ta-ˌlāt\ *n* : a derivative of cellulose used as a coating for enteric tablets

cell wall *n* : the usu. rigid nonliving permeable wall that surrounds the plasma membrane and encloses and supports the cells of most plants, bacteria, fungi, and algae

Cel·sius \'sel-sē-əs, -shəs\ *adj* : relating to or having a scale for measuring temperature on which the interval between the triple point and the boiling point of water is divided into 99.99 degrees with 0.01° being the triple point and 100.00° the boiling point — abbr. *C;* compare CENTIGRADE

Celsius, Anders (1701–1744), Swedish astronomer.

ce·ment \si-'ment\ *n* **1** : CEMENTUM **2** : a plastic composition used esp. of zinc or silica for filling dental cavities

ce·men·ta·tion \ˌsē-ˌmen-'tā-shən\ *n* : the act or process of attaching (as a dental restoration to a natural tooth) by means of cement

ce·ment·i·cle \si-'men-ti-kəl\ *n* : a calcified body formed in the periodontal membrane of a tooth

ce·men·to·enam·el \si-ˌmen-tō-i-'na-məl\ *adj* : of, relating to, or joining the cementum and enamel of a tooth (the ~ junction)

ce·men·to·ma \ˌsē-ˌmen-'tō-mə\ *n*, *pl* **-mas** *or* **-ma·ta** \-mə-tə\ : a tumor resembling cementum in structure

ce·men·tum \si-'men-təm\ *n* : a specialized external bony layer covering the dentin of the part of a tooth normally within the gum — called also *cement;* compare DENTIN, ENAMEL

cen·sor \'sen-sər\ *n* : a hypothetical psychic agency that represses unacceptable notions before they reach consciousness — **cen·so·ri·al** \sen-'sōr-ē-əl\ *adj*

cen·sor·ship \'sen-sər-ˌship\ *n* : exclusion from consciousness by the psychic censor

cen·ter \'sen-tər\ *n* : a group of nerve cells having a common function (respiratory ~) — called also *nerve center*

cen·te·sis \sen-'tē-səs\ *n*, *pl* **cen·te·ses** \-ˌsēz\ : surgical puncture (as of a tumor or membrane) — usu. used in compounds (para*centesis*)

cen·ti·grade \'sen-tə-ˌgrād, 'sän-\ *adj* : relating to, conforming to, or having a thermometer scale on which the interval between the freezing and boiling points of water is divided into 100 degrees with 0° representing the freezing point and 100° the boiling point (10° ~) — abbr. *C;* compare CELSIUS

cen·ti·gram \-ˌgram\ *n* : a unit of mass and weight equal to $\frac{1}{100}$ gram

cen·ti·li·ter \-ˌlē-tər\ *n* : a unit of liquid capacity equal to $\frac{1}{100}$ liter

cen·ti·me·ter \-ˌmē-tər\ *n* : a unit of length equal to $\frac{1}{100}$ meter

centimeter–gram–second *adj* : CGS

cen·ti·pede \'sen-tə-ˌpēd\ *n* : any of a class (Chilopoda) of long flattened many-segmented predaceous arthropods with each segment bearing one pair of legs of which the foremost pair is modified into poison fangs

centra *pl of* CENTRUM

cen·tral \'sen-trəl\ *adj* **1** : of or concerning the centrum of a vertebra **2** : of, relating to, or comprising the brain and spinal cord; *also* : originating within the central nervous system — **cen·tral·ly** *adv*

central artery *n* : a branch of the ophthalmic artery or the lacrimal artery that enters the substance of the optic nerve and supplies the retina

central artery of the retina *n* : a branch of the ophthalmic artery that passes to the retina in the middle of the optic nerve and branches to form the arterioles of the retina — called also *central retinal artery*

central canal *n* : a minute canal running through the gray matter of the whole length of the spinal cord and continuous anteriorly with the ventricles of the brain

central deafness *n* : hearing loss or impairment resulting from defects in the central nervous system (as in the auditory area) rather than in the ear itself or the auditory nerve — compare CONDUCTION DEAFNESS, NERVE DEAFNESS

centralis — see FOVEA CENTRALIS

central lobe n : INSULA

central nervous system n : the part of the nervous system which in vertebrates consists of the brain and spinal cord, to which sensory impulses are transmitted and from which motor impulses pass out, and which supervises and coordinates the activity of the entire nervous system — compare AUTONOMIC NERVOUS SYSTEM, PERIPHERAL NERVOUS SYSTEM

central pontine myelinolysis n : disintegration of the myelin sheaths in the pons that is associated with malnutrition and esp. with alcoholism

central retinal artery n : CENTRAL ARTERY OF THE RETINA

central retinal vein n : CENTRAL VEIN OF THE RETINA

central sulcus n : the sulcus separating the frontal lobe of the cerebral cortex from the parietal lobe — called also *fissure of Rolando*

central tendon n : a 3-lobed aponeurosis located near the central portion of the diaphragm caudal to the pericardium and composed of intersecting planes of collagenous fibers

central vein n : any of the veins in the lobules of the liver that occur one in each lobule running from the apex to the base, receive blood from the sinusoids, and empty into the sublobular veins — called also *intralobular vein*

central vein of the retina n : a vein that is formed by union of the veins draining the retina, passes with the central artery of the retina in the optic nerve, and empties into the superior ophthalmic vein — called also *central retinal vein*

central venous pressure n : the venous pressure of the right atrium of the heart obtained by inserting a catheter into the median cubital vein and advancing it to right atrium through the superior vena cava — abbr. CVP

centre *chiefly Brit var of* CENTER

cen·tric \'sen-trik\ adj 1 : of or relating to a nerve center 2 of dental occlusion : involving spatial relationships such that all teeth of both jaws meet in a normal manner and forces exerted by the lower on the upper jaw are perfectly distributed in the dental arch

cen·trif·u·gal \sen-'tri-fyə-gəl, -fi-\ adj : passing outward (as from a nerve center to a muscle or gland) : EFFERENT — **cen·trif·u·gal·ly** adv

cen·trif·u·ga·tion \ˌsen-trə-fyü-'gā-shən\ n : the process of centrifuging

¹cen·tri·fuge \'sen-trə-ˌfyüj\ n : a machine using centrifugal force for separating substances of different densities, for removing moisture, or for simulating gravitational effects

²centrifuge vb **-fuged; -fug·ing** : to subject to centrifugal action esp. in a centrifuge

cen·tri·lob·u·lar \ˌsen-trə-'lä-byə-lər\ adj : relating to or affecting the center of a lobule ⟨~ necrosis in the liver⟩; also : affecting the central parts of the lobules containing clusters of branching functional and anatomical units of the lung ⟨~ emphysema⟩

cen·tri·ole \'sen-trē-ˌōl\ n : one of a pair of cellular organelles that occur esp. in animals, are adjacent to the nucleus, function in the formation of the spindle apparatus during cell division, and consist of a cylinder with nine microtubules arranged peripherally in a circle

cen·trip·e·tal \sen-'tri-pət-əl\ adj : passing inward (as from a sense organ to the brain or spinal cord) : AFFERENT — **cen·trip·e·tal·ly** adv

cen·tro·mere \'sen-trə-ˌmir\ n : the point or region on a chromosome to which the spindle attaches during mitosis and meiosis — called also *kinetochore* — **cen·tro·mer·ic** \ˌsen-trə-'mer-ik, -'mir-\ adj

cen·tro·some \'sen-trə-ˌsōm\ n : the centriole-containing region of clear cytoplasm adjacent to the cell nucleus

cen·trum \'sen-trəm\ n, pl **centrums** or **cen·tra** \-trə\ 1 : the center esp. of an anatomical part 2 : the body of a vertebra ventral to the neural arch

Cen·tru·roi·des \ˌsen-trə-'rói-(ˌ)dēz\ n : a genus of scorpions containing the only U.S. forms dangerous to humans

cephal- or **cephalo-** comb form 1 : head ⟨cephalalgia⟩ ⟨cephalometry⟩ 2 : cephalic and ⟨cephalopelvic⟩

ceph·a·lad \'se-fə-ˌlad\ adv : toward the head or anterior end of the body

ceph·a·lal·gia \ˌse-fə-'lal-jə, -jē-ə\ n : HEADACHE

ceph·a·lex·in \ˌse-fə-'lek-sən\ n : a semisynthetic cephalosporin $C_{16}H_{17}$-N_3O_4S with a spectrum of antibiotic activity similar to the penicillins

ce·phal·gia \se-'fal-jə, -jē-ə\ n : HEADACHE

ceph·al·he·ma·to·ma \ˌse-fəl-ˌhē-mə-'tō-mə\ n, pl **-mas** or **-ma·ta** \-mə-tə\ : a blood-filled tumor or swelling beneath the pericardium that occurs frequently in newborn infants as a result of injury (as by forceps) during birth

-cephali pl of -CEPHALUS

ce·phal·ic \sə-'fa-lik\ adj 1 : of or relating to the head 2 : directed toward or situated on or in or near the head — **ce·phal·i·cal·ly** \-li-k(ə-)lē\ adv

cephalic flexure n : the middle of the three anterior flexures of an embryo in which the front part of the brain bends downward in an angle of 90 degrees

cephalic index n : the ratio multiplied by 100 of the maximum breadth of the head to its maximum length — compare CRANIAL INDEX

cephalic vein n : any of various superficial veins of the arm : specif : a large vein of the upper arm lying along the outer edge of the biceps muscle and emptying into the axillary vein

ceph·a·lin \'ke-fə-lən, 'se-\ n : PHOSPHATIDYLETHANOLAMINE

cephalo- — see CEPHAL-

ceph·a·lo·cau·dal \,se-fə-lō-'kȯd-əl\ adj : proceeding or occurring in the long axis of the body esp. in the direction from head to tail — **ceph·a·lo·cau·dal·ly** adv

ceph·a·lom·e·ter \,se-fə-'lä-mə-tər\ n : an instrument for measuring the head

ceph·a·lom·e·try \,se-fə-'lä-mə-trē\ n, pl **-tries** : the science of measuring the head in living individuals — **ceph·a·lo·met·ric** \-lō-'me-trik\ adj

ceph·a·lo·pel·vic disproportion \,se-fə-lō-'pel-vik-\ n : a condition in which a maternal pelvis is small in relation to the size of the fetal head

ceph·a·lor·i·dine \,se-fə-'lȯr-ə-,dēn, -'lär-\ n : a semisynthetic broad-spectrum antibiotic $C_{19}H_{17}N_3O_4S_2$ derived from cephalosporin

ceph·a·lo·spo·rin \,se-fə-lə-'spȯr-ən\ n : any of several antibiotics produced by an imperfect fungus (genus *Cephalosporium*)

ceph·a·lo·thin \'se-fə-lə-(,)thin\ n : a semisynthetic broad-spectrum antibiotic $C_{16}H_{15}N_2NaO_6S_2$ that is an analog of a cephalosporin and is effective against penicillin-resistant staphylococci

ceph·a·lo·tho·ra·cop·a·gus \,se-fə-lō-,thȯr-ə-'kä-pə-gəs\ n, pl **-agi** \-,gī, -,gē\ : teratological twin fetuses joined at the head, neck, and thorax

-cephalus n comb form, pl **-cephali** : cephalic abnormality (of a specified type) (hydro*cephalus*) (micro*cephalus*)

cer·amide \'sir-ə-,mīd\ n : any of a group of amides formed by linking a fatty acid to sphingosine and found widely but in small amounts in plant and animal tissue

cer·amide·tri·hexo·si·dase \,sir-ə-,mīd-,trī-,hek-sə-'sī-,dās, -,dāz\ n : an enzyme that breaks down ceramidetrihexoside and is deficient in individuals affected with Fabry's disease

cer·amide·tri·hexo·side \-(,)trī-'hek-sə-,sīd\ n : a lipid that accumulates in body tissues of individuals affected with Fabry's disease

ce·rate \'sir-,āt\ n : an unctuous preparation for external use consisting of wax or resin mixed with oil, lard, and medicinal ingredients

cer·a·to·hy·al \,ser-ə-(,)tō-'hī-əl\ or **cer·a·to·hy·oid** \-'hī-,ȯid\ n : the smaller inner projection of the two lateral projections on each side of the human hyoid bone — called also *lesser cornu*; compare THYROHYAL

cer·car·ia \(,)sər-'kar-ē-ə, -'ker-\ n, pl **-iae** \-ē-,ē\ : a usu. tadpole-shaped larval trematode worm that develops in a molluscan host from a redia — **cer·car·i·al** \-əl\ adj

cer·clage \ser-'kläzh, (,)sər-\ n : any of several procedures for increasing tissue resistance in a functionally incompetent uterine cervix that usu. involve reinforcement with an inert substance esp. in the form of sutures near the internal opening

ce·rea flex·i·bil·i·tas \,sir-ē-ə-,flek-sə-'bi-lə-,tas, -,täs\ n : the capacity (as in catalepsy) to maintain the limbs or other bodily parts in whatever position they have been placed

cerebell- or **cerebelli-** or **cerebello-** comb form : cerebellum (*cerebell*itis)

cerebella pl of CEREBELLUM

cerebellar artery n : any of several branches of the basilar and vertebral arteries that supply the cerebellum

cerebellaris — see PEDUNCULUS CEREBELLARIS INFERIOR, PEDUNCULUS CEREBELLARIS MEDIUS, PEDUNCULUS CEREBELLARIS SUPERIOR

cerebellar peduncle n : any of three large bands of nerve fibers that join each hemisphere of the cerebellum with the parts of the brain below and in front: a : one connecting the cerebellum with the midbrain — called also *brachium conjunctivum*, *pedunculus cerebellaris superior*, *superior cerebellar peduncle* b : one connecting the cerebellum with the pons — called also *brachium pontis*, *middle cerebellar peduncle*, *middle peduncle*, *pedunculus cerebellaris medius* c : one that connects the cerebellum with the medulla oblongata and the spinal cord — called also *inferior cerebellar peduncle*, *pedunculus cerebellaris inferior*, *restiform body*

cerebelli — see FALX CEREBELLI, TENTORIUM CEREBELLI

cer·e·bel·li·tis \,ser-ə-bə-'lī-təs, -be-\ n : inflammation of the cerebellum

cer·e·bel·lo·pon·tine angle \,ser-ə-,be-lō-,pän-,tēn-, -,tīn-\ n : a region of the brain at the junction of the pons and cerebellum that is a frequent site of tumor formation

cer·e·bel·lum \,ser-ə-'be-ləm\ n, pl **-bellums** or **-bel·la** \-lə\ : a large dorsally projecting part of the brain concerned esp. with the coordination of muscles and the maintenance of bodily equilibrium, situated between the brain stem and the back of the cerebrum and formed in humans of two lateral lobes and a median lobe — **cer·e·bel·lar** \-lər\ adj

cerebr- or **cerebro-** comb form 1 : brain : cerebrum (*cerebr*ation) 2 : cerebral and (*cerebro*spinal)

cerebra pl of CEREBRUM

ce·re·bral \sə-'rē-brəl, 'ser-ə-\ adj 1 : of or relating to the brain or the intellect 2 : of, relating to, or being the cerebrum

cerebral accident n : an occurrence of sudden damage (as by hemorrhage) to the cerebral vascular system — compare STROKE

cerebral aqueduct n : AQUEDUCT OF SYLVIUS

cerebral artery n : any of the arteries supplying the cerebral cortex: a : an artery that arises from the internal carotid artery, forms the anterior portion of the circle of Willis where it is linked to the artery on the opposite side by the anterior communicating artery, and passes on to supply the medial surfaces of the cerebrum — called also *anterior cerebral artery* b : an artery that arises from the internal carotid artery, passes along the lateral fissure, and supplies the lateral surfaces of the cerebral cortex — called also *middle cerebral artery* c : an artery that arises by the terminal forking of the basilar artery where it forms the posterior portion of the circle of Willis and passes on to supply the lower surfaces of the temporal and occipital lobes — called also *posterior cerebral artery*

cerebral cortex n : the surface layer of gray matter of the cerebrum that functions chiefly in coordination of sensory and motor information — called also *pallium*

cerebral dominance n : dominance in development and functioning of one of the cerebral hemispheres

cerebral hemisphere n : either of the two hollow convoluted lateral halves of the cerebrum

cerebral hemorrhage n : the bleeding into the tissue of the brain and esp. of the cerebrum from a ruptured blood vessel

cerebral palsy n : a disability resulting from damage to the brain before, during, or shortly after birth and outwardly manifested by muscular incoordination and speech disturbances — compare SPASTIC PARALYSIS — **cerebral palsied** adj

cerebral peduncle n : either of two large bundles of nerve fibers passing from the pons forward and outward to form the main connection between the cerebral hemispheres and the spinal cord

cerebral vein n : any of various veins that drain the surface and inner tissues of the cerebral hemispheres — see GALEN'S VEIN, GREAT CEREBRAL VEIN

cer·e·brate \'ser-ə-ˌbrāt\ vb -brat·ed; -brat·ing : to use the mind — **cer·e·bra·tion** \ˌser-ə-'brā-shən\ n

cerebri — see CRURA CEREBRI, FALX CEREBRI, HYPOPHYSIS CEREBRI, PSEUDOTUMOR CEREBRI

cerebro- — see CEREBR-

ce·re·bro·side \sə-'rē-brə-ˌsīd, 'ser-ə-\ n : any of various lipids composed of ceramide and a monosaccharide and found esp. in the myelin sheath of nerves

ce·re·bro·spi·nal \sə-ˌrē-brō-'spīn-əl, ˌser-ə-\ adj : of or relating to the brain and spinal cord or to these together with the cranial and spinal nerves that innervate voluntary muscles

cerebrospinal fluid n : a liquid that is comparable to serum but contains less dissolved material, that is secreted from the blood into the lateral ventricles of the brain, and that serves chiefly to maintain uniform pressure within the brain and spinal cord — called also *spinal fluid*

cerebrospinal meningitis n : inflammation of the meninges of both brain and spinal cord; specif : an infectious epidemic and often fatal meningitis caused by the meningococcus

ce·re·bro·vas·cu·lar \sə-ˌrē-brō-'vas-kyə-lər, ˌser-ə-\ adj : of or involving the cerebrum and the blood vessels supplying it (~ disease)

ce·re·brum \sə-'rē-brəm, 'ser-ə-\ n, pl -brums or -bra \-brə\ : the expanded anterior portion of the brain that overlies the rest of the brain, consists of cerebral hemispheres and connecting structures, and is considered to be the seat of conscious mental processes : TELENCEPHALON

ce·re·sin \'ser-ə-sən\ n : a white or yellow hard brittle wax used as a substitute for beeswax

ce·ri·um \'sir-ē-əm\ n : a malleable ductile metallic element — symbol Ce; see ELEMENT table

ce·roid \'sir-ˌoid\ n : a yellow to brown pigment found esp. in the liver in cirrhosis

cert abbr certificate: certification: certified: certify

cer·ti·fy \'sər-tə-ˌfī\ vb -fied; -fy·ing 1 : to attest officially to the insanity of 2 : to designate as having met the requirements to practice medicine or a particular medical specialty — **cer·ti·fi·able** \ˌsər-tə-'fī-ə-bəl\ adj — **cer·ti·fi·ably** \-blē\ adv — **cer·ti·fi·ca·tion** \-fə-'kā-shən\ n

cerulea — see PHLEGMASIA CERULEA DOLENS

ceruleus, cerulei — see LOCUS COERULEUS

ce·ru·lo·plas·min \sə-ˌrü-lō-'plaz-mən\ n : a blue alpha globulin active in the biological storage and transport of copper

ce·ru·men \sə-'rü-mən\ n : EARWAX

ce·ru·mi·nous gland \sə-'rü-mə-nəs-\ n : one of the modified sweat glands of the ear that produce earwax

cervic- or **cervici-** or **cervico-** comb form 1 : neck : cervix of an organ (cervicitis) 2 : cervical and (cervicothoracic) (cervicovaginal)

cer·vi·cal \'sər-vi-kəl\ adj : of or relating to a neck or cervix (~ cancer)

cervical canal n : the passage through the cervix uteri

cervical cap n : a usu. rubber or plastic contraceptive device in the form of a thimble-shaped molded cap that fits snugly over the uterine cervix and blocks sperm from entering the uterus — called also *Dutch cap*

cervical flexure *n* : a ventral bend in the neural tube of the embryo marking the point of transition from brain to spinal cord

cervical ganglion *n* : any of three sympathetic ganglia on each side of the neck

cervicalis — see ANSA CERVICALIS

cervical nerve *n* : one of the spinal nerves of the cervical region of which there are eight on each side in most mammals including humans

cervical plexus *n* : a plexus formed by the anterior divisions of the four upper cervical nerves

cervical plug *n* : a mass of tenacious secretion by glands of the uterine cervix present during pregnancy and tending to close the uterine orifice

cervical rib *n* : a supernumerary rib sometimes found in the neck above the usual first rib

cervical vertebra *n* : any of the seven vertebrae of the neck

cer·vi·cec·to·my \ˌsər-və-ˈsek-tə-mē\ *n*, *pl* **-mies** : surgical excision of the uterine cervix — called also *trachelectomy*

cervici- *or* **cervico-** — see CERVIC-

cervicis — see ILIOCOSTALIS CERVICIS, LONGISSIMUS CERVICIS, SEMISPINALIS CERVICIS, SPINALIS CERVICIS, SPLENIUS CERVICIS, TRANSVERSALIS CERVICIS

cer·vi·ci·tis \ˌsər-və-ˈsi-təs\ *n* : inflammation of the uterine cervix

cer·vi·co·fa·cial nerve \ˌsər-və-(ˌ)kō-ˈfā-shəl-\ *n* : a branch of the facial nerve supplying the lower part of the face and upper part of the neck

cer·vi·co·tho·rac·ic \ˌsər-vi-(ˌ)kō-thə-ˈra-sik, -thō-\ *adj* : of or relating to the neck and thorax ⟨~ sympathectomy⟩

cer·vi·co·vag·i·nal \-ˈva-jən-ᵊl\ *adj* : of or relating to the uterine cervix and the vagina ⟨~ flora⟩ ⟨~ carcinoma⟩

cer·vix \ˈsər-viks\ *n*, *pl* **cer·vi·ces** \-və-ˌsēz, ˌsər-ˈvī-(ˌ)sēz\ *or* **cervixes** 1 : NECK 1a; *esp* : the back part of the neck 2 : a constricted portion of an organ or part: as a : the narrow lower or outer end of the uterus b : the constricted cementoenamel junction on a tooth

cervix uteri \-ˈyü-tə-ˌrī\ *n* : CERVIX 2a

¹**ce·sar·e·an** *also* **ce·sar·i·an** \si-ˈzar-ē-ən\ *adj* : of, relating to, or being a cesarean section ⟨~ birth⟩

²**cesarean** *also* **cesarian** *n* : CESAREAN SECTION

Cae·sar \ˈsē-zər\, **Gaius Julius** (100–44 B.C.), Roman general and statesman.

cesarean section *n* : surgical incision of the walls of the abdomen and uterus for delivery of offspring

ce·si·um \ˈsē-zē-əm\ *n* : a silver-white

soft ductile element — symbol *Cs*; see ELEMENT table

ces·tode \ˈses-ˌtōd\ *n* : TAPEWORM — **cestode** *adj*

cet·ri·mide \ˈse-trə-ˌmīd\ *n* : a mixture of bromides of ammonium used esp. as a detergent and antiseptic

ce·tyl alcohol \ˈsēt-ᵊl-\ *n* : a waxy crystalline alcohol $C_{16}H_{34}O$ used in pharmaceutical and cosmetic preparations

ce·tyl·py·ri·din·i·um chloride \ˌsēt-ᵊl-ˌpi-rə-ˈdi-nē-əm-\ *n* : a white powder consisting of a quaternary ammonium salt $C_{21}H_{38}ClN \cdot H_2O$ and used as a detergent and antiseptic

Cf *symbol* californium

CF *abbr* cystic fibrosis

CG *abbr* chorionic gonadotropin

cgs *adj*, *often cap C&G&S* : of, relating to, or being a system of units based on the centimeter as the unit of length, the gram as the unit of mass, and the second as the unit of time ⟨~ system⟩ ⟨~ units⟩

Cha·ber·tia \shə-ˈber-tē-ə, -ˈbər-\ *n* : a genus of strongylid nematode worms including one (*C. ovina*) that infests the colon esp. of sheep and causes a bloody diarrhea

Cha·bert \shä-ˈber\, **Philibert** (1737–1814), French veterinarian.

chafe \ˈchāf\ *n* : injury caused by friction — **chafe** *vb*

Cha·gas' disease \ˈshä-gəs-, -gə-səz-\ *n* : a tropical American disease that is caused by a flagellate of the genus *Trypanosoma* (*T. cruzi*) and is marked by prolonged high fever, edema, and enlargement of the spleen, liver, and lymph nodes

Chagas, Carlos Ribeiro Justiniano (1879–1934), Brazilian physician.

cha·go·ma \shə-ˈgō-mə\ *n*, *pl* **-mas** *or* **-ma·ta** \-tə\ : a swelling resembling a tumor that appears at the site of infection in Chagas' disease

κ-chain \ˈka-pə-\ *var of* KAPPA CHAIN

chain reflex *n* : a series of responses each serving as a stimulus that evokes the next response

chair·side \ˈchar-ˌsīd\ *adj* : relating to, performed in the vicinity of, or assisting in the work done on a patient in a dentist's chair ⟨a dental ~ assistant⟩ ⟨a good ~ manner⟩

chair time *n* : the time that a dental patient spends in the dentist's chair

cha·la·sia \kə-ˈlā-zhə, ka-\ *n* : the relaxation of a ring of muscle (as the cardiac sphincter of the esophagus) surrounding a bodily opening

cha·la·zi·on \kə-ˈlā-zē-ən, -ˌän\ *n*, *pl* **-zia** \-zē-ə, -zē-ə\ : a small circumscribed tumor of the eyelid formed by retention of secretions of the meibomian gland and sometimes accompanied by inflammation

chal·i·co·sis \ˌka-li-ˈkō-səs\ *n*, *pl* **-co·ses** \-ˌsēz\ : a pulmonary affection occurring among stone cutters that is caused by inhalation of stone dust

chalk \'chȯk\ n : a soft white, gray, or buff limestone sometimes used medicinally as a source of calcium carbonate — see PRECIPITATED CHALK, PREPARED CHALK — **chalky** \'chȯ-kē\ adj

chal·lenge \'cha-lənj\ n : the process of provoking or testing physiological activity by exposure to a specific substance; esp : a test of immunity by exposure to an antigen after immunization against it — **challenge** vb

cha·lone \'kā-ˌlōn, 'ka-\ n : an endogenous secretion that is held to inhibit mitosis in a specific tissue

cham·ber \'chām-bər\ n : an enclosed space within the body of an animal — see ANTERIOR CHAMBER, POSTERIOR CHAMBER

chamber pot n : a bedroom vessel for urination and defecation

chan·cre \'shaŋ-kər\ n : a primary sore or ulcer at the site of entry of a pathogen (as in tularemia); esp : the initial lesion of syphilis

chan·croid \'shaŋ-ˌkrȯid\ n : a venereal disease caused by a hemophilic bacterium of the genus Haemophilus (H. ducreyi) and characterized by chancres that unlike those of syphilis lack firm indurated margins — called also soft chancre; see DUCREY'S BACILLUS

change of life n : CLIMACTERIC

chan·nel \'chan-ᵊl\ n 1 : a usu. tubular enclosed passage 2 : a passage created in a selectively permeable membrane by a conformational change in membrane proteins

chap \'chap\ n : a crack in or a sore roughening of the skin caused by exposure to wind or cold — **chap** vb

Chap Stick \'chap-ˌstik\ trademark — used for a lip balm in stick form

char·ac·ter \'kar-ik-tər\ n 1 : one of the attributes or features that make up and distinguish the individual 2 : the detectable expression of the action of a gene or group of genes 3 : the complex of mental and ethical traits marking and often individualizing a person, group, or nation

¹**char·ac·ter·is·tic** \ˌkar-ik-tə-'ris-tik\ adj : serving to reveal and distinguish the individual character — **char·ac·ter·is·ti·cal·ly** \-ti-k(ə-)lē\ adv

²**characteristic** n : a distinguishing trait, quality, or property

cha·ras \'chär-əs\ n : HASHISH

char·coal \'chär-ˌkōl\ n : a dark or black porous carbon prepared from vegetable or animal substances — see ACTIVATED CHARCOAL

Char·cot–Ley·den crystals \ˌshär-kō-'lī-dᵊn-\ n pl : minute colorless crystals that occur in various pathological discharges and esp. in the sputum following an asthmatic attack and that are thought to be formed by the disintegration of eosinophils

Char·cot \shär-'kō\, **Jean–Martin (1825–1893),** French neurologist.

Leyden, Ernst Viktor von (1832–1910), German physician.

Char·cot–Ma·rie–Tooth disease \(ˌ)shär-'kō-mə-'rē-'tüth-\ n : PERONEAL MUSCULAR ATROPHY

P. Marie — see MARIE-STRÜMPELL DISEASE

Tooth, Howard Henry (1856–1925), British physician.

Char·cot's joint \(ˌ)shär-'kōz-\ or **Char·cot joint** \-'kō-\ n : a destructive condition affecting one or more joints, occurring in diseases of the spinal cord, and ultimately resulting in a flail joint — called also Charcot's disease

charge \'chärj\ n 1 : a plaster or ointment used on a domestic animal 2 : CATHEXIS 2

charge nurse n : a nurse who is in charge of a health-care unit (as a hospital ward, emergency room, or nursing home)

char·la·tan \'shär-lə-tən\ n : QUACK

char·ley horse \'chär-lē-ˌhȯrs\ n : a muscular pain, cramping, or stiffness esp. of the quadriceps that results from a strain or bruise

chart \'chärt\ n : a record of medical information for a patient

Chas·tek paralysis \'chas-ˌtek-\ n : a fatal paralytic vitamin deficiency of foxes and minks that are bred in captivity and fed raw fish and that is caused by enzymatic inactivation of thiamine by thiaminase present in the fish

Chastek, John Simeon (1886–1954), American breeder of fur-bearing animals.

CHD abbr coronary heart disease

check·bite \'chek-ˌbīt\ n 1 a : an act of biting into a sheet of material (as wax) to record the relation between the opposing surfaces of upper and lower teeth b : the record obtained 2 : the material for checkbites

check ligament n 1 : ALAR LIGAMENT 2 : either of two expansions of the sheaths of rectus muscles of the eye each of which prob. restrains the activity of the muscle with which it is associated

check·up \'chek-ˌəp\ n : EXAMINATION; esp : a general physical examination

Che·diak–Hi·ga·shi syndrome \shäd-'yäk-hē-'gä-shē\ n : a genetic disorder inherited as an autosomal recessive and characterized by partial albinism, abnormal granules in the white blood cells, and marked susceptibility to bacterial infections

Che·diak \shäd-'yäk\, **Moises (fl 1952),** French physician.

Hi·ga·shi \hē-'gä-shē\, **Ototaka (fl 1954),** Japanese physician.

cheek \'chēk\ n 1 : the fleshy side of the

face below the eye and above and to the side of the mouth: *broadly* : the lateral aspect of the head **2** : BUTTOCK 1

cheek·bone \'chēk-ˌbōn\ *n* : the prominence below the eye that is formed by the zygomatic bone; *also* : ZYGOMATIC BONE

cheek tooth *n* : any of the molar or premolar teeth

cheese skipper *n* : a dipteran fly (*Piophila casei*) whose larva lives in cheese and cured meats and is a cause of intestinal myiasis

cheesy \'chē-zē\ *adj* **chees·i·er; -est** : resembling cheese in consistency ⟨∼ lesions⟩ ⟨a ∼ discharge⟩

cheil- *or* **cheilo-** *also* **chil-** *or* **chilo-** *comb form* : lip ⟨*cheil*itis⟩ ⟨*cheilo*plasty⟩

cheil·i·tis \kī-'lī-təs\ *n* : inflammation of the lip

cheil·o·plas·ty \'kī-lō-ˌplas-tē\ *n*, *pl* **-ties** : plastic surgery to repair lip defects

cheil·os·chi·sis \kī-'läs-kə-səs\ *n*, *pl* **-chi·ses** \-ˌsēz\ : CLEFT LIP

chei·lo·sis \kī-'lō-səs\ *n*, *pl* **-lo·ses** \-ˌsēz\ : an abnormal condition of the lips characterized by scaling of the surface and by the formation of fissures in the corners of the mouth

cheir- *or* **cheiro-** — see CHIR-

chei·ro·pom·pho·lyx \ˌkī-rō-'päm-fə-ˌliks\ *n* : a skin disease characterized by itching vesicles or blebs occurring in groups on the hands or feet

che·late \'kē-ˌlāt\ *n* : a compound having a ring structure that usu. contains a metal ion held by coordinate bonds — **chelate** *adj or vb* — **che·la·tion** \kē-'lā-shən\ *n*

che·lat·ing agent \'kē-ˌlā-tiŋ-\ *n* : any of various compounds that combine with metals to form chelates and that include some used medically in the treatment of metal poisoning (as by lead)

che·la·tion therapy \kē-'lā-shən-\ *n* : the use of a chelating agent to bind with a metal in the body to form a chelate so that the metal loses its toxic effect or physiological activity

che·la·tor \'kē-ˌlā-tər\ *n* : CHELATING AGENT

chem *abbr* chemical; chemist; chemistry

chem- *or* **chemo-** *also* **chemi-** *comb form* : chemical : chemistry ⟨*chemo*therapy⟩

¹**chem·i·cal** \'ke-mi-kəl\ *adj* **1** : of, relating to, used in, or produced by chemistry **2** : acting or operated or produced by chemicals — **chem·i·cal·ly** \-mi-k(ə-)lē\ *adv*

²**chemical** *n* : a substance obtained by a chemical process or used for producing a chemical effect

chemical peel *n* : PEEL

chemical warfare *n* : warfare using incendiary mixtures, smokes, or irritant, burning, poisonous, or asphyxiating gases

chem·ist \'ke-məst\ *n* **1** : one trained in chemistry **2** *Brit* : PHARMACIST

chem·is·try \'ke-mə-strē\ *n*, *pl* **-tries 1** : a science that deals with the composition, structure, and properties of substances and of the transformations that they undergo **2 a** : the composition and chemical properties of a substance ⟨the ∼ of hemoglobin⟩ **b** : chemical processes and phenomena (as of an organism) ⟨blood ∼⟩

chemist's shop *n*, *Brit* : a place where medicines are sold

chemo \'kē-ˌmō\ *n* : CHEMOTHERAPY

chemo- — see CHEM-

che·mo·dec·to·ma \ˌkē-mō-'dek-tə-mə, ˌke-\ *n*, *pl* **-mas** *or* **-ma·ta** \-mə-tə\ : a tumor that affects tissue (as of the carotid body) populated with chemoreceptors

che·mo·nu·cle·ol·y·sis \-ˌnü-klē-'ä-lə-səs, -ˌnyü-\ *n*, *pl* **-y·ses** \-ˌsēz\ : treatment of a slipped disk by the injection of chymopapain to dissolve the displaced nucleus pulposus

che·mo·pal·li·dec·to·my \-ˌpa-lə-'dek-tə-mē\ *n*, *pl* **-mies** : destruction of the globus pallidus by the injection of a chemical agent (as ethyl alcohol) esp. for the relief of parkinsonian tremors

che·mo·pro·phy·lax·is \-ˌprō-fə-'lak-səs, -ˌprä-\ *n*, *pl* **-lax·es** \-ˌsēz\ : the prevention of infectious disease by the use of chemical agents — **che·mo·pro·phy·lac·tic** \-'lak-tik\ *adj*

che·mo·re·cep·tion \-ri-'sep-shən\ *n* : the physiological reception of chemical stimuli — **che·mo·re·cep·tive** \-'tiv\ *adj*

che·mo·re·cep·tor \-ri-'sep-tər\ *n* : a sense organ (as a taste bud) responding to chemical stimuli

che·mo·re·flex \ˌkē-mō-'rē-ˌfleks *also* ˌke-\ *n* : a physiological reflex initiated by a chemical stimulus or in a chemoreceptor — **chemoreflex** *adj*

che·mo·re·sis·tance \-ri-'zis-təns\ *n* : the quality or state of being resistant to a chemical (as a drug) — **che·mo·re·sis·tant** \-tənt\ *adj*

che·mo·sen·si·tive \-'sen-sə-tiv\ *adj* : susceptible to the action of a (particular) chemical — used esp. of strains of bacteria — **che·mo·sen·si·tiv·i·ty** \-ˌsen-sə-'ti-və-tē\ *n*

che·mo·sis \kə-'mō-səs\ *n*, *pl* **-mo·ses** \-ˌsēz\ : swelling of the conjunctival tissue around the cornea

che·mo·sur·gery \ˌkē-mō-'sər-jə-rē\ *n*, *pl* **-ger·ies** : removal by chemical means of diseased or unwanted tissue — **che·mo·sur·gi·cal** \-'sər-ji-kəl\ *adj*

che·mo·tac·tic \-'tak-tik\ *adj* : involving, inducing, or exhibiting chemotaxis — **che·mo·tac·ti·cal·ly** \-ti-k(ə-)lē\ *adv*

che·mo·tax·is \-'tak-səs\ *n*, *pl* **-tax·es** \-ˌsēz\ : orientation or movement of an organism or cell in relation to chemical agents

¹**che·mo·ther·a·peu·tic** \-ˌther-ə-'pyü-tik\

adj : of, relating to, or used in chemotherapy — **che·mo·ther·a·peu·ti·cal·ly** \-ti-k(ə-)lē\ *adv*

²**chemotherapeutic** *n* : an agent used in chemotherapy

che·mo·ther·a·py \-'ther-ə-pē\ *n, pl* **-pies** : the use of chemical agents in the treatment or control of disease or mental illness — **che·mo·ther·a·pist** \-pist\ *n*

che·mot·ic \ki-'mä-tik\ *adj* : marked by or belonging to chemosis

che·mot·ro·pism \ki-'mä-trə-,pi-zəm, ke-\ *n* : orientation of cells or organisms in relation to chemical stimuli

che·no·de·ox·y·cho·lic acid \,kē-(,)nō-,dē-,äk-si-'kō-lik-, -'kä-\ *n* : a bile acid $C_{24}H_{40}O_4$

cher·ub·ism \'cher-ù-,bi-zəm\ *n* : a hereditary condition characterized by swelling of the jawbones and esp. in young children by a characteristic facies marked by protuberant cheeks and upturned eyes

chest \'chest\ *n* **1** : a cupboard used esp. for storing medicines or first-aid supplies — called also *medicine cabinet, medicine chest* **2** : the part of the body enclosed by the ribs and sternum

chest·nut \'ches-(,)nət\ *n* : a callosity on the inner side of the leg of the horse

chesty \'ches-tē\ *adj* : of, relating to, or affected with disease of the chest — not used technically

Cheyne–Stokes respiration \'chān-'stōks-\ *n* : cyclic breathing marked by a gradual increase in the rapidity of respiration followed by a gradual decrease and total cessation for from 5 to 50 seconds and found esp. in advanced kidney and heart disease, asthma, and increased intracranial pressure — called also *Cheyne-Stokes breathing*

Cheyne \'chān, 'chā-nē\, **John** (1777–1836), British physician.

Stokes \'stōks\, **William** (1804–1878), British physician.

CHF *abbr* congestive heart failure

Chi·ari–From·mel syndrome \kē-'är-ē-'frō-məl-, -'frä-\ *n* : a condition usu. occurring postpartum and characterized by amenorrhea, galactorrhea, obesity, and atrophy of the uterus and ovaries

Chiari, Johann Baptist (1817–1854), German surgeon.

Frommel, Richard Julius Ernst (1854–1912), German gynecologist.

chi·asm \'kī-,a-zəm, 'kē-\ *n* : CHIASMA 1

chi·as·ma \kī-'az-mə, kē-\ *n, pl* **-ma·ta** \-mə-tə\ **1** : an anatomical intersection or decussation — see OPTIC CHIASMA **2** : a cross-shaped configuration of paired chromatids visible in the diplotene of meiotic prophase and considered the cytological equivalent of genetic crossing-over — **chi·as·mat·ic** \,kī-əz-'ma-tik, ,kē-\ *adj*

chiasmatic groove *n* : a narrow transverse groove that lies near the front of the superior surface of the body of the sphenoid bone, is continuous with the optic foramen, and houses the optic chiasma

chicken mite *n* : a small mite of the genus *Dermanyssus* (*D. gallinae*) that infests poultry esp. in warm regions

chicken pox *n* : an acute contagious disease esp. of children marked by low-grade fever and formation of vesicles and caused by a herpes virus — called also *varicella;* compare SHINGLES

chief cell *n* **1** : one of the cells that line the lumen of the fundic glands of the stomach; *esp* : a small cell with granular cytoplasm that secretes pepsin — compare PARIETAL CELL **2** : one of the secretory cells of the parathyroid glands

chig·ger \'chi-gər, 'ji-\ *n* **1** : CHIGOE 1 2 : a 6-legged mite larva (family Trombiculidae) that sucks the blood and causes intense irritation

chi·goe \'chi-(,)gō, 'chē-\ *n* **1** : a tropical flea belonging to the genus *Tunga* (*T. penetrans*) of which the fertile female causes great discomfort by burrowing under the skin — called also *chigger, sand flea* **2** : CHIGGER 2

chil- *or* **chilo-** — see CHEIL-

chil·blain \'chil-,blān\ *n* : an inflammatory swelling or sore caused by exposure (as of the feet or hands) to cold — called also *pernio*

child \'chīld\ *n, pl* **chil·dren** \'chil-drən, -dərn\ **1** : an unborn or recently born person **2** : a young person esp. between infancy and youth — **with child** : PREGNANT

child·bear·ing \'chīld-,bar-iŋ\ *n* : the act of bringing forth children : PARTURITION — **childbearing** *adj*

child·bed \-,bed\ *n* : the condition of a woman in childbirth

childbed fever *n* : PUERPERAL FEVER

child·birth \-,bərth\ *n* : PARTURITION

child guidance *n* : the clinical study and treatment of the personality and behavior problems of esp. maladjusted and delinquent children by a staff of specialists usu. comprising a physician or psychiatrist, a clinical psychologist, and a psychiatric social worker

child·hood \'chīld-,hùd\ *n* : the state or period of being a child

child psychiatry *n* : psychiatry applied to the treatment of children

child psychology *n* : the study of the psychological characteristics of infants and children and the application of general psychological principles to infancy and childhood

¹**chill** \'chil\ *n* **1** : a sensation of cold accompanied by shivering **2** : a disagreeable sensation of coldness

²**chill** *vb* **1 a** : to make or become cold b : to shiver or quake with or as if with

cold 2 : to become affected with a chill

chill factor *n* : WINDCHILL

chi·me·ra *or* **chi·mae·ra** \kī-'mir-ə, kə-\ *n* : an individual, organ, or part consisting of tissues of diverse genetic constitution — **chi·me·ric** \-'mir-ik, -'mer-\ *adj* — **chi·me·rism** \-'mir-ˌi-zəm, kə-; 'kī-mə-ˌri-\ *n*

chin \'chin\ *n* : the lower portion of the face lying below the lower lip and including the prominence of the lower jaw — called also *mentum* — **chin·less** \-ləs\ *adj*

chin·bone \'chin-ˌbōn\ *n* : JAW 1b; *esp* : the median anterior part of the bone of the lower jaw

chinch \'chinch\ *n* : BEDBUG

Chinese liver fluke *n* : a common and destructive Asian liver fluke of the genus *Clonorchis* (*C. sinensis*) that invades the human liver causing clonorchiasis

Chinese restaurant syndrome *n* : a group of symptoms (as numbness of the neck, arms, and back with headache, dizziness, and palpitations) that is held to affect susceptible persons eating food and esp. Chinese food heavily seasoned with monosodium glutamate

chip-blow·er \'chip-ˌblō-ər\ *n* : a dental instrument typically consisting of a rubber bulb with a long metal tube that is used to blow drilling debris from a cavity being prepared for filling

chir- *or* **chiro-** *also* **cheir-** *or* **cheiro-** *comb form* : hand ⟨*chiro*practic⟩

chi·rop·o·dy \kə-'rä-pə-dē, shə-, kī-\ *n, pl* **-dies** : PODIATRY — **chi·ro·po·di·al** \ˌkī-rə-'pō-dē-əl\ *adj* — **chi·rop·o·dist** \kə-'rä-pə-dist, shə-, kī-\ *n*

chi·ro·prac·tic \'kī-rə-ˌprak-tik\ *n* : a system of therapy which holds that disease results from a lack of normal nerve function and which employs manipulation and specific adjustment of body structures (as the spinal column) — **chi·ro·prac·tor** \-tər\ *n*

chi·rur·gi·cal \kī-'rər-ji-kəl\ *adj, archaic* : of or relating to surgery : SURGICAL

chis·el \'chi-zəl\ *n* : a metal tool with a cutting edge at the end of a blade; *esp* : one used in dentistry (as for shaping enamel)

chi·tin \'kīt-ən\ *n* : a horny polysaccharide that forms part of the hard outer integument esp. of insects, arachnids, and crustaceans — **chi·tin·ous** \'kīt-ən-əs\ *adj*

chla·myd·ia \klə-'mi-dē-ə\ *n* **1** *cap* : a genus of coccoid to spherical gram-negative intracellular bacteria (family Chlamydiaceae) including one (*C. trachomatis*) that causes or is associated with various diseases of the eye and genitourinary tract including trachoma, lymphogranuloma venereum,

cervicitis, and some forms of nongonococcal urethritis **2** *pl* **-iae** *also* **-ias a** : a bacterium of the genus *Chlamydia* **b** : an infection or disease caused by chlamydiae — **chla·myd·i·al** \-əl\ *adj*

chlo·as·ma \klō-'az-mə\ *n, pl* **-ma·ta** \-mə-tə\ : irregular brownish or blackish spots esp. on the face that occur sometimes in pregnancy and in disorders of or functional changes in the uterus and ovaries — see LIVER SPOTS

chlor- *or* **chloro-** *comb form* **1** : green ⟨*chlor*ine⟩ ⟨*chlor*osis⟩ **2** : chlorine : containing or caused by chlorine ⟨*chlor*acne⟩ ⟨*chlor*dane⟩

chloracetophenone *var of* CHLOROACETOPHENONE

chlor·ac·ne \(ˌ)klȯr-'ak-nē\ *n* : a skin eruption resembling acne and resulting from exposure to chlorine or its compounds

chlo·ral \'klȯr-əl\ *n* : CHLORAL HYDRATE

chloral hydrate *n* : a bitter white crystalline drug $C_2H_3Cl_3O_2$ used as a hypnotic and sedative

chlo·ral·ose \'klȯr-ə-ˌlōs, -ˌlōz\ *n* : a bitter crystalline compound $C_8H_{11}Cl_3$-O_6 used esp. to anesthetize animals — **chlo·ral·osed** \-ˌlōst, -ˌlōzd\ *adj*

chlor·am·bu·cil \klȯr-'am-byə-ˌsil\ *n* : an anticancer drug $C_{14}H_{19}Cl_2NO_2$ used esp. to treat leukemias, multiple myeloma, some lymphomas, and Hodgkin's disease

chlo·ra·mine \'klȯr-ə-ˌmēn\ *n* : any of various organic compounds containing nitrogen and chlorine; *esp* : CHLORAMINE-T

chloramine–T \-'tē\ *n* : a white or faintly yellow crystalline compound C_7-$H_7ClNNaO_2S·3H_2O$ used as an antiseptic (as in treating wounds)

chlor·am·phen·i·col \klȯr-ˌam-'fe-ni-kȯl, -ˌkōl\ *n* : a broad-spectrum antibiotic $C_{11}H_{12}Cl_2N_2O_5$ isolated from cultures of a soil actinomycete of the genus *Streptomyces* (*S. venezuelae*) or prepared synthetically — see CHLOROMYCETIN

chlor·bu·tol \'klȯr-byə-ˌtȯl\ *n, chiefly Brit* : CHLOROBUTANOL

chlor·cy·cli·zine \klȯr-'sī-klə-ˌzēn\ *n* : a cyclic antihistamine $C_{18}H_{21}ClN_2$ administered as the hydrochloride

chlor·dane \'klȯr-ˌdān\ *n* : a highly chlorinated viscous volatile liquid insecticide $C_{10}H_6Cl_8$

chlor·di·az·epox·ide \ˌklȯr-dī-ˌa-zə-'pak-ˌsīd\ *n* : a benzodiazepine $C_{16}H_{14}ClN_3O$ structurally and pharmacologically related to diazepam that is used in the form of its hydrochloride esp. as a tranquilizer and to treat the withdrawal symptoms of alcoholism — see LIBRIUM

chlor·hex·i·dine \klȯr-'hek-sə-ˌdīn, -ˌdēn\ *n* : a biguanide derivative $C_{22}H_{30}Cl_2N_{10}$ used as a local antiseptic esp. in the form of its hydrochloride or acetate

chlo·ride \\'klōr-ˌīd\ *n* : a compound of chlorine with another element or radical; *esp* : a salt or ester of hydrochloric acid

chloride shift *n* : the passage of chloride ions from the plasma into the red blood cells when carbon dioxide enters the plasma from the tissues and their return to the plasma when the carbon dioxide is discharged in the lungs that is a major factor both in maintenance of blood pH and in transport of carbon dioxide

chlo·ri·nate \\'klōr-ə-ˌnāt\ *vb* **-nat·ed; -nat·ing** : to treat or cause to combine with chlorine or a chlorine compound — **chlo·ri·na·tion** \ˌklōr-ə-'nā-shən\ *n*

chlo·rine \\'klōr-ˌēn, -ən\ *n* : a halogen element that is isolated as a heavy greenish yellow gas of pungent odor and is used esp. as a bleach, oxidizing agent, and disinfectant in water purification — symbol *Cl*; see ELEMENT table

chlor·mer·o·drin \klōr-'mer-ə-drən\ *n* : a mercurial diuretic $C_5H_{11}ClHgN_2O_2$ used in the treatment of some forms of edema, ascites, and nephritis

chloro- — see CHLOR-

chlo·ro·ace·to·phe·none \ˌklōr-ō-ˌa-sə-(ˌ)tō-fə-'nōn, -ə-'sē-\ *n* : a chlorine-containing compound C_8H_7ClO used esp. as a tear gas

chlo·ro·az·o·din \ˌklōr-ō-'a-zəd-ᵊn\ *n* : a yellow crystalline compound $C_2H_4Cl_2$-N_6 used in solution as a surgical antiseptic

chlo·ro·bu·ta·nol \-'byüt-ᵊn-ˌol, -ōl\ *n* : a white crystalline alcohol C_4H_7-Cl_3O with an odor and taste like camphor that is used as a local anesthetic, sedative, and preservative (as for hypodermic solutions)

chlo·ro·cre·sol \-'krē-ˌsol, -ˌsōl\ *n* : a chlorine derivative C_7H_7ClO of cresol used as an antiseptic and preservative

¹**chlo·ro·form** \\'klōr-ə-ˌform\ *n* : a colorless volatile heavy toxic liquid $CHCl_3$ with an ether odor that is used esp. as a solvent or as a veterinary anesthetic — called also *trichloromethane*

²**chloroform** *vb* : to treat with chloroform esp. so as to produce anesthesia or death

chlo·ro·gua·nide \ˌklōr-ō-'gwä-ˌnīd, -nəd\ *n* : an antimalarial drug C_{11}-$H_{16}N_5Cl$ administered as the bitter crystalline hydrochloride — called also *proguanil*

chlo·ro·leu·ke·mia \-lü-'kē-mē-ə\ *n* : CHLOROMA 1

chlo·ro·ma \klə-'rō-mə\ *n, pl* **-mas** or **-ma·ta** \-mə-tə\ **1** : leukemia originating in the bone marrow and marked by the formation of growths of myeloid tissue resembling tumors beneath the periosteum of flat bones (as the skull, ribs, or pelvis) **2** : one of the tumorous growths characteristic of chloroma

Chlo·ro·my·ce·tin \ˌklōr-ō-mī-'sēt-ᵊn\ *trademark* — used for chloramphenicol

chlo·ro·phyll \\'klōr-ə-ˌfil, -fəl\ *n* **1** : the green photosynthetic coloring matter of plants **2** : a waxy green chlorophyll-containing substance extracted from green plants and used as a coloring agent or deodorant

chlo·ro·pic·rin \ˌklōr-ə-'pik-rən\ *n* : a heavy colorless liquid CCl_3NO_2 that causes tears and vomiting and is used esp. as a soil fumigant

chlo·ro·pro·caine \ˌklōr-ō-'prō-ˌkān\ *n* : a local anesthetic $C_{13}H_{19}ClN_2O_2$ — see NESACAINE

chlo·ro·quine \\'klōr-ə-ˌkwēn\ *n* : an antimalarial drug $C_{18}H_{26}ClN_3$ administered as the bitter crystalline diphosphate

chlo·ro·sis \klə-'rō-səs\ *n, pl* **-ro·ses** \-ˌsēz\ : an iron-deficiency anemia esp. of adolescent girls that may impart a greenish tint to the skin — called also *greensickness* — **chlo·rot·ic** \-'rä-tik\ *adj*

chlo·ro·thi·a·zide \ˌklōr-ə-'thī-ə-ˌzīd, -zəd\ *n* : a thiazide diuretic C_7H_6-$ClN_3O_4S_2$ used esp. in the treatment of edema and hypertension — see DIURIL

chlo·ro·tri·an·i·sene \-ˌtrī-'a-nə-ˌsēn\ *n* : a synthetic estrogen $C_{23}H_{21}ClO_3$ used to treat menopausal symptoms

chlor·phen·e·sin carbamate \(ˌ)klōr-'fe-nə-sin-\ *n* : a drug $C_{10}H_{12}ClNO_4$ used to relax skeletal muscle — see MAOLATE

chlor·prom·a·zine \klōr-'prä-mə-ˌzēn\ *n* : a phenothiazine $C_{17}H_{19}ClN_2S$ used as a tranquilizer esp. in the form of its hydrochloride to suppress the more flagrant symptoms of psychotic disorders (as in schizophrenia) — see LARGACTIL, THORAZINE

chlor·prop·amide \-'prä-pə-ˌmīd, -'prō-\ *n* : a sulfonylurea drug $C_{10}H_{13}$-ClN_2O_3S used orally to reduce blood sugar in the treatment of mild diabetes

chlor·tet·ra·cy·cline \ˌklōr-ˌte-trə-'sī-ˌklēn\ *n* : a yellow crystalline broad-spectrum antibiotic $C_{22}H_{23}ClN_2O_8$ produced by a soil actinomycete of the genus *Streptomyces* (*S. aureofaciens*) and sometimes used in animal feeds to stimulate growth — see AUREOMYCIN

chlor·thal·i·done \klōr-'tha-lə-ˌdōn\ *n* : a diuretic sulfonamide $C_{14}H_{11}Cl$-N_2O_4S used esp. in the treatment of edema and hypertension — see HYGROTON

cho·a·nae \\'kō-ə-ˌnē\ *n pl* : the pair of posterior apertures of the nasal cavity that open into the nasopharynx —

called also *posterior nares* — **cho·a·nal** \-nəl\ *adj*

Cho·a·no·tae·nia \ˌkō-ə-(ˌ)nō-ˈtē-nē-ə\ *n* : a genus of tapeworms including one (*C. infundibulum*) which is an intestinal parasite of birds

¹**choke** \ˈchōk\ *vb* **choked; chok·ing 1** : to keep from breathing in a normal way by compressing or obstructing the windpipe or by poisoning or adulterating available air **2** : to have the windpipe blocked entirely or partly

²**choke** *n* **1** : the act of choking **2 chokes** *pl* : decompression sickness when marked by suffocation — used with *the*

choked disk *n* : PAPILLEDEMA

chol- *or* **chole** *or* **cholo-** *comb form* : bile : gall (*cholate*) (*cholelith*) (*cholorrhea*)

cho·lae·mia *chiefly Brit var of* CHOLEMIA

cho·la·gogue \ˈkä-lə-ˌgäg, ˈkō-\ *n* : an agent that promotes an increased flow of bile — **cho·la·gog·ic** \ˌkä-lə-ˈgä-jik, ˌkō-\ *adj*

chol·an·gio·gram \kə-ˈlan-jē-ə-ˌgram, kō-\ *n* : a roentgenogram of the bile ducts made after the ingestion or injection of a radiopaque substance

chol·an·gi·og·ra·phy \kə-ˌlan-jē-ˈä-grə-fē, (ˌ)kō-\ *n, pl* **-phies** : radiographic visualization of the bile ducts after ingestion or injection of a radiopaque substance — **chol·an·gio·graph·ic** \-jē-ə-ˈgra-fik\ *adj*

chol·an·gi·o·li·tis \-ə-ˈlī-təs, (ˌ)kō-\ *n, pl* **-lit·i·des** \-ˈli-tə-ˌdēz\ : inflammation of bile capillaries — **chol·an·gi·o·lit·ic** \-ˈli-tik\ *adj*

chol·an·gi·tis \ˌkō-ˌlan-ˈjī-təs\ *n, pl* **-git·i·des** \-ˈji-tə-ˌdēz\ : inflammation of one or more bile ducts

cho·late \ˈkō-ˌlāt\ *n* : a salt or ester of cholic acid

chole- — *see* CHOL-

cho·le·cal·cif·er·ol \ˌkō-lə-(ˌ)kal-ˈsi-fə-ˌrȯl, -ˌrōl\ *n* : a sterol $C_{27}H_{43}OH$ that is a natural form of vitamin D found esp. in fish, egg yolks, and fish-liver oils and is formed in the skin on exposure to sunlight or ultraviolet rays — called also *vitamin D, vitamin D₃*

cho·le·cys·tec·to·my \ˌkō-lə-(ˌ)sis-ˈtek-tə-mē\ *n, pl* **-mies** : surgical excision of the gallbladder — **cho·le·cys·tec·to·mized** \-ˈmīzd\ *adj*

cho·le·cys·ti·tis \-(ˌ)sis-ˈtī-təs\ *n, pl* **-tit·i·des** \-ˈti-tə-ˌdēz\ : inflammation of the gallbladder

cho·le·cys·to·en·ter·os·to·my \-sis-tō-ˌen-tə-ˈräs-tə-mē\ *n, pl* **-mies** : surgical union of and creation of a passage between the gallbladder and the intestine

cho·le·cys·to·gram \-ˈsis-tə-ˌgram\ *n* : a roentgenogram of the gallbladder made after ingestion or injection of a radiopaque substance

cho·le·cys·tog·ra·phy \-(ˌ)sis-ˈtä-grə-fē\ *n, pl* **-phies** : the roentgenographic visualization of the gallbladder after ingestion or injection of a radiopaque substance — **cho·le·cys·to·graph·ic** \-ˌsis-tə-ˈgra-fik\ *adj*

cho·le·cys·to·ki·net·ic \-ˌsis-tə-kə-ˈne-tik, -ˌkī-\ *adj* : tending to cause the gallbladder to contract and discharge bile

cho·le·cys·to·ki·nin \-ˌsis-tə-ˈkī-nən\ *n* : a hormone secreted esp. by the duodenal mucosa that regulates the emptying of the gallbladder and secretion of enzymes by the pancreas and that has been found in the brain — called also *cholecystokinin-pancreozymin, pancreozymin*

cho·le·cys·tor·rha·phy \-(ˌ)sis-ˈtȯr-ə-fē\ *n, pl* **-phies** : repair of the gallbladder by suturing

cho·le·cys·tos·to·my \-(ˌ)sis-ˈtäs-tə-mē\ *n, pl* **-mies** : surgical incision of the gallbladder usu. to effect drainage

cho·le·cys·tot·o·my \-ˈtä-tə-mē\ *n, pl* **-mies** : surgical incision of the gallbladder esp. for exploration or to remove a gallstone

cho·led·o·chal \ˈkō-lə-ˌdä-kəl, kə-ˈle-də-kəl\ *adj* : relating to, being, or occurring in the common bile duct

cho·led·o·chi·tis \kə-ˌle-də-ˈkī-təs, ˌkō-lə-\ *n* : inflammation of the common bile duct

cho·led·o·cho·je·ju·nos·to·my \kə-ˌle-də-(ˌ)kō-ji-(ˌ)jü-ˈnäs-tə-mē\ *n, pl* **-mies** : surgical creation of a passage uniting the common bile duct and the jejunum

cho·led·o·cho·li·thi·a·sis \-li-ˈthī-ə-səs\ *n, pl* **-a·ses** \-ˌsēz\ : a condition marked by presence of calculi in the gallbladder and common bile duct

cho·led·o·cho·li·thot·o·my \-li-ˈthä-tə-mē\ *n, pl* **-mies** : surgical incision of the common bile duct for removal of a gallstone

cho·led·o·chor·ra·phy \kə-ˌle-də-ˈkōr-ə-fē\ *n, pl* **-ra·phies** : surgical union of the separated ends of the common bile duct by suturing

cho·led·o·chos·to·my \-ˈkäs-tə-mē\ *n, pl* **-mies** : surgical incision of the common bile duct usu. to effect drainage

cho·led·o·chot·o·my \-ˈkä-tə-mē\ *n, pl* **-mies** : surgical incision of the common bile duct

cho·led·o·chus \kə-ˈle-də-kəs\ *n, pl* **-o·chi** \-ˌkī, -ˌkē\ : COMMON BILE DUCT

cho·le·glo·bin \ˈkō-lə-ˌglō-bən, ˈkä-\ *n* : a green pigment that occurs in bile and is formed by breakdown of hemoglobin

cho·le·lith \ˈkō-li-ˌlith, ˈkä-\ *n* : GALLSTONE

cho·le·li·thi·a·sis \ˌkō-li-li-ˈthī-ə-səs\ *n, pl* **-a·ses** \-ˌsēz\ : production of gallstones : *also* : the resulting abnormal condition

cho·le·mia \kō-ˈlē-mē-ə\ *n* : the presence of excess bile in the blood usu. indicative of liver disease — **cho·le·mic** \-mik\ *adj*

cho·le·poi·e·sis \ˌkō-lə-ˌpȯi-ˈē-səs, ˌkä-\ *n, pl* **-e·ses** \-ˌsēz\ : production of bile — compare CHOLERESIS — **cho·le·poi·et·ic** \-ˈe-tik\ *adj*

chol·era \ˈkä-lə-rə\ *n* : any of several diseases of humans and of domestic animals usu. marked by severe gastrointestinal symptoms: as **a** : an acute diarrheal disease caused by an enterotoxin produced by a comma-shaped gram-negative bacillus of the genus *Vibrio* (*V. cholerae* syn. *V. comma*) when it is present in large numbers in the proximal part of the human small intestine — see ASIATIC CHOLERA **b** : FOWL CHOLERA **c** : HOG CHOLERA — **chol·e·ra·ic** \ˌkä-lə-ˈrā-ik\ *adj*

cholera mor·bus \-ˈmȯr-bəs\ *n* : a gastrointestinal disturbance characterized by griping, diarrhea, and sometimes vomiting — not used technically

cho·le·re·sis \ˌkō-lə-ˈrē-səs, ˌkä-\ *n, pl* **-re·ses** \-ˌsēz\ : the flow of bile from the liver esp. when increased above a previous or normal level — compare CHOLAGOGUE, CHOLEPOIESIS, HYDRO-CHOLERESIS

¹**cho·le·ret·ic** \ˌkō-lə-ˈre-tik, ˌkä-\ *adj* : promoting bile secretion by the liver (~ action of bile salts)

²**choleretic** *n* : a choleretic agent

cho·le·sta·sis \ˌkō-lə-ˈstā-səs, ˌkä-\ *n, pl* **-sta·ses** \-ˈstā-ˌsēz\ : a checking or failure of bile flow — **cho·le·stat·ic** \-ˈsta-tik\ *adj*

cho·le·ste·a·to·ma \kə-ˌles-tē-ə-ˈtō-mə, ˌkō-lə-ˌstē-, ˌkä-lə-\ *n, pl* **-tomas or -to·ma·ta** \-mə-tə\ **1** : an epidermoid cyst usu. in the brain appearing as a compact shiny flaky mass **2** : a tumor usu. growing in a confined space (as the middle ear) and frequently constituting a sequel to chronic otitis media — **cho·le·ste·a·to·ma·tous** \-mə-təs\ *adj*

cho·les·ter·ol \kə-ˈles-tə-ˌrōl, -ˌról\ *n* : a steroid alcohol $C_{27}H_{45}OH$ present in animal cells and body fluids that regulates membrane fluidity, functions as a precursor molecule in various metabolic pathways, and as a constituent of LDL may cause arteriosclerosis — **cho·les·ter·ic** \kə-ˈles-tə-rik; ˌkō-lə-ˈster-ik, ˌkä-\ *adj*

cho·les·ter·ol·ae·mia *also* **cho·les·ter·rae·mia** *chiefly Brit var of* CHOLESTEROLEMIA

cho·les·ter·ol·emia \kə-ˌles-tə-rə-ˈlē-mē-ə\ *also* **cho·les·ter·emia** \-ˈrē-mē-ə\ *n* : the presence of cholesterol in the blood

cho·les·ter·ol·osis \kə-ˌles-tə-rə-ˈlō-səs\ *or* **cho·les·ter·o·sis** \kə-ˌles-tə-ˈrō-səs\ *n, pl* **-oses** \-ˌsēz\ : abnormal deposition of cholesterol (as in blood vessels)

cho·le·styr·amine \kō-ˈles-tir-ə-ˌmēn\ *n* : a strongly basic synthetic resin used to lower cholesterol levels in hypercholesterolemic patients

cho·lic acid \ˈkō-lik-\ *n* : a crystalline bile acid $C_{24}H_{40}O_5$

cho·line \ˈkō-ˌlēn\ *n* : a base $C_5H_{15}NO_2$ that occurs as a component of phospholipids esp. in animals, is a precursor of acetylcholine, and is essential to liver function

cho·lin·er·gic \ˌkō-lə-ˈnər-jik\ *adj* **1** *of autonomic nerve fibers* : liberating, activated by, or involving acetylcholine — compare ADRENERGIC 1, NORADRENERGIC 2 : resembling acetylcholine esp. in physiologic action — **cho·lin·er·gi·cal·ly** \-ji-k(ə-)lē\ *adv*

cho·lin·es·ter·ase \ˌkō-lə-ˈnes-tə-ˌrās, -ˌrāz\ *n* **1** : ACETYLCHOLINESTERASE 2 : an enzyme that hydrolyzes choline esters and that is found esp. in blood plasma — called also *pseudocholinesterase*

¹**cho·li·no·lyt·ic** \ˌkō-lə-nō-ˈli-tik\ *adj* : interfering with the action of acetylcholine or cholinergic agents

²**cholinolytic** *n* : a cholinolytic substance

cho·li·no·mi·met·ic \ˌkō-lə-nō-mə-ˈme-tik, ˌkä-, -mī-\ *adj* : resembling acetylcholine or simulating its physiologic action

²**cholinomimetic** *n* : a cholinomimetic substance

cholo- — see CHOL-

cho·lor·rhea \ˌkä-lə-ˈrē-ə, ˌkō-\ *n* : excessive secretion of bile

cho·lor·rhoea *chiefly Brit var of* CHOLORRHEA

chol·uria \kō-ˈlūr-ē-ə, kōl-ˈyūr-\ *n* : presence of bile in urine

chondr- *or* **chondri-** *or* **chondro-** *comb form* : cartilage (*chondral*) (*chondro-dysplasia*)

chon·dral \ˈkän-drəl\ *adj* : of or relating to cartilage

chon·dri·tis \kän-ˈdrī-təs\ *n* : inflammation of cartilage

chon·dro·blast \ˈkän-drə-ˌblast, -drō-\ *n* : a cell that produces cartilage — **chon·dro·blas·tic** \ˌkän-drə-ˈblas·tik, -drō-\ *adj*

chon·dro·clast \ˈkän-drə-ˌklast, -drō-\ *n* : a cell that absorbs cartilage — compare OSTEOCLAST 1

chon·dro·cos·tal \ˌkän-drə-ˈkäst-əl, -drō-\ *adj* : of or relating to the costal cartilages and the ribs

chon·dro·cyte \ˈkän-drə-ˌsīt, -drō-\ *n* : a cartilage cell

chon·dro·dys·pla·sia \ˌkän-drə-dis-ˈplā-zhə, -drō-, -zhē-ə\ *n* : a hereditary skeletal disorder characterized by the formation of exostoses at the epiphyses and resulting in arrested development and deformity — called also *dyschondroplasia*

chon·dro·dys·tro·phia \-dis-ˈtrō-fē-ə\ *n* : ACHONDROPLASIA

chon·dro·dys·tro·phy \-ˈdis-trə-fē\ *n, pl* **-phies** : ACHONDROPLASIA — **chon·dro·dys·tro·phic** \-dis-ˈtrō-fik\ *adj*

chon·dro·gen·e·sis \-ˈje-nə-səs\ *n, pl* **-e·ses** \-ˌsēz\ : the development of cartilage — **chon·dro·gen·ic** \-ˈje-nik\ *adj*

chon·droid \'kän-₁dròid\ *adj* : resembling cartilage

chon·droi·tin \kän-'dròit-ᵊn. -'dró͞t-ᵊn\ *n* : any of several glycosaminoglycans occurring in sulfated form in various tissues (as cartilage and tendons)

chon·drol·o·gy \kän-'drä-lə-jē\ *n, pl* **-gies** : a branch of anatomy concerned with cartilage

chon·dro·ma \kän-'drō-mə\ *n, pl* **-mas** \-məz\ *also* **-ma·ta** \-mə-tə\ : a benign tumor containing the structural elements of cartilage — compare CHONDROSARCOMA — **chon·dro·ma·tous** \('\)kän-'drä-mə-təs, -'drō-\ *adj*

chon·dro·ma·la·cia \₁kän-drō-mə-'lā-shə, -shē-ə\ *n* : abnormal softness of cartilage

chon·dro·os·teo·dys·tro·phy \-₁äs-tē-ō-'dis-trə-fē\₁*n, pl* **-phies** : any of several mucopolysaccharidoses (as Hurler's syndrome) characterized esp. by disorders of bone and cartilage

chon·dro·phyte \'kän-drō-₁fit\ *n* : an outgrowth or spur of cartilage

chon·dro·sar·co·ma \₁kän-drō-sär-'kō-mə\ *n, pl* **-mas** *or* **-ma·ta** \-mə-tə\ : a sarcoma containing cartilage cells

chon·dro·ster·nal \₁kän-drō-'stərn-ᵊl\ *adj* : of or relating to the costal cartilages and sternum

Cho·part's joint \(₁)shō-'pärz-\ *n* : the tarsal joint that comprises the talonavicular and calcaneocuboid articulations

 Cho·part \shō-pár\, **François** (1743-1795), French surgeon.

chor·da ten·din·ea \'kòr-də-₁ten-'di-nē-ə\ *n, pl* **chor·dae ten·din·e·ae** \-nē-₁ē\ : any of the delicate tendinous cords that are attached to the edges of the atrioventricular valves of the heart and to the papillary muscles and serve to prevent the valves from being pushed into the atrium during the ventricular contraction

chor·da tym·pa·ni \-'tim-pə-₁nī\ *n* : a branch of the facial nerve that traverses the middle ear cavity and the infratemporal fossa and supplies autonomic fibers to the sublingual and submandibular glands and sensory fibers to the anterior part of the tongue

chor·dee \'kòr-₁dē, -₁dā, ₁kòr-'\ *n* : painful erection of the penis often with a downward curvature that may be present in a congenital condition (as hypospadias) or accompany gonorrhea

chor·do·ma \kòr-'dō-mə\ *n, pl* **-mas** *or* **-ma·ta** \-mə-tə\ : a malignant tumor that is derived from remnants of the embryonic notochord and occurs along the spine

chor·dot·o·my *var of* CORDOTOMY

cho·rea \kə-'rē-ə\ *n* : any of various nervous disorders of infectious or organic origin marked by spasmodic movements of the limbs and facial muscles and by incoordination —

called also *Saint Vitus' dance*; see HUNTINGTON'S DISEASE, SYDENHAM'S CHOREA — **cho·re·at·ic** \₁kòr-ē-'a-tik\ *adj* — **cho·re·ic** \kə-'rē-ik\ *adj*

cho·re·i·form \kə-'rē-ə-₁fòrm\ *adj* : resembling chorea (∼ convulsions)

cho·reo·ath·e·to·sis \-₁a-thə-'tō-səs\ *n, pl* **-to·ses** \-₁sēz\ : a nervous disturbance marked by the involuntary movements characteristic of chorea and athetosis

cho·rio·al·lan·to·is \₁kòr-ē-ō-ə-'lan-tə-wəs\ *n, pl* **-to·ides** \-ō-₁a-lən-'tō-ə-₁dēz, -₁lan-\ : a vascular fetal membrane composed of the fused chorion and adjacent wall of the allantois — called also *chorioallantoic membrane* — **cho·rio·al·lan·to·ic** \-₁a-lən-'tō-ik\ *adj*

cho·rio·am·ni·o·ni·tis \-₁am-nē-ō-'nī-təs\ *n* : inflammation of the fetal membranes

cho·rio·cap·il·lar·is \-₁ka-pə-'lar-əs\ *n* : the inner of the two vascular layers of the choroid of the eye that is composed largely of capillaries

cho·rio·car·ci·no·ma \₁kärs-ᵊn-'ō-mə\ *n, pl* **-mas** *or* **-ma·ta** \-mə-tə\ : a malignant tumor developing in the uterus from the trophoblast and rarely in the testes from a neoplasm

cho·rio·epi·the·li·o·ma \-₁e-pə-₁thē-lē-'ō-mə\ *n, pl* **-mas** *or* **-ma·ta** \-mə-tə\ : CHORIOCARCINOMA

cho·ri·oid·i·tis \₁kòr-ē-₁òi-'dī-təs\ *var of* CHOROIDITIS

cho·ri·o·ma \₁kòr-ē-'ō-mə\ *n, pl* **-mas** *or* **-ma·ta** \-mə-tə\ : a tumor formed of chorionic tissue

cho·rio·men·in·gi·tis \₁kòr-ē-(₁)ō-₁me-nən-'jī-təs\ *n, pl* **-git·i·des** \-'ji-tə-₁dēz\ : cerebral meningitis; *specif* : LYMPHOCYTIC CHORIOMENINGITIS

cho·ri·on \'kòr-ē-₁än\ *n* : the highly vascular outer embryonic membrane that is associated with the allantois in the formation of the placenta

cho·rio·epi·the·li·o·ma \₁kòr-ē-₁ä-₁ne-pə-₁thē-lē-'ō-mə\ *n, pl* **-mas** *or* **-o-ma·ta** \-mə-tə\ : CHORIOCARCINOMA

chorion fron·do·sum \-₁frän-'dō-səm\ *n* : the part of the chorion that has persistent villi and that with the decidua basalis forms the placenta — see CHORIONIC VILLUS SAMPLING

cho·ri·on·ic \₁kòr-ē-'ä-nik\ *adj* **1** : of, relating to, or being part of the chorion (∼ villi) **2** : secreted or produced by chorionic or a related tissue (as in the placenta or a choriocarcinoma) (human ∼ gonadotropin)

chorionic villus sampling *also* **chorionic villi sampling** *n* : biopsy of the chorion frondosum through the abdominal wall or by way of the vagina and uterine cervix at nine to 12 weeks of gestation to obtain fetal cells for the prenatal diagnosis of genetic disorder — abbr. *CVS*

Cho·ri·op·tes \₁kòr-ē-'äp-₁tēz\ *n* : a genus of small parasitic mites infesting domestic animals — **cho·ri·op·tic** \-'äp-tik\ adj

chorioptic mange n : mange caused by mites of the genus *Chorioptes* that usu. attack only the surface of the skin — compare DEMODECTIC MANGE, SARCOPTIC MANGE

cho·rio·ret·i·nal \ˌkōr-ē-ō-'ret-ᵊn-əl\ adj : of, relating to, or affecting the choroid and the retina of the eye (~ burns) (~ lesions)

cho·rio·ret·i·ni·tis \-ˌret-ᵊn-'ī-təs\ n, pl **-nit·i·des** \-'i-tə-ˌdēz\ : inflammation of the retina and choroid of the eye

cho·roid \'kōr-ˌoid\ n : a vascular membrane containing star branched pigment cells that lies between the retina and the sclera of the eye — called also *choroid coat* — **choroid** or **cho·roi·dal** \kə-'roid-ᵊl\ adj

choroidea — see TELA CHOROIDEA

cho·roi·de·re·mia \ˌkōr-ˌoi-də-'rē-mē-ə\ n : progressive degeneration of the choroid

cho·roid·itis \ˌkōr-ˌoi-'dī-təs\ n : inflammation of the choroid of the eye

cho·roi·do·iri·tis \kə-ˌroid-dō-ī-'rī-təs\ : inflammation of the choroid and the iris of the eye

cho·roi·dop·a·thy \ˌkōr-ˌoi-'dä-pə-thē\ n, pl **-thies** : a diseased condition affecting the choroid of the eye

cho·roi·do·ret·i·ni·tis \kə-ˌroi-dō-ˌret-ᵊn-'ī-təs\ var of CHORIORETINITIS

choroid plexus n : a highly vascular portion of the pia mater that projects into the ventricles of the brain and is thought to secrete the cerebrospinal fluid

Christ·mas disease \'kris-məs-\ n : a hereditary sex-linked hemorrhagic disease involving absence of a coagulation factor in the blood and failure of the clotting mechanism — called also *hemophilia B*; compare HEMOPHILIA

Christmas, Stephen, British child patient.

Christmas factor n : FACTOR IX

chrom·aes·the·sia *chiefly Brit var of* CHROMESTHESIA

chro·maf·fin \'krō-mə-fən\ adj : staining deeply with chromium salts

chro·maf·fi·no·ma \ˌkrō-mə-fə-'nō-mə, krō-ˌma-\ n, pl **-mas** or **-ma·ta** \-mə-tə\ : a tumor containing chromaffin cells; esp : PHEOCHROMOCYTOMA

chro·ma·phil \'krō-mə-ˌfil\ adj : CHROMAFFIN (~ tissue)

chromat- or **chromato-** *comb form* 1 : color (*chromatid*) 2 : chromatin (*chromatolysis*)

chro·mat·ic \krō-'ma-tik\ adj 1 : of, relating to, or characterized by color or color phenomena or sensations (~ stimuli) 2 : capable of being colored by staining agents (~ substances)

chromatic vision n 1 : normal color vision in which the colors of the spectrum are distinguished and evaluated 2 : CHROMATOPSIA

chro·ma·tid \'krō-mə-təd\ n : one of the usu. paired and parallel strands of a duplicated chromosome joined by a single centromere — see CHROMONEMA

chro·ma·tin \'krō-mə-tən\ n : a complex of a nucleic acid with basic proteins (as histone) in eukaryotic cells that is usu. dispersed in the interphase nucleus and condensed into chromosomes in mitosis and meiosis — **chro·ma·tin·ic** \ˌkrō-mə-'tin-ik\ adj

chro·ma·tism \'krō-mə-ˌti-zəm\ n : CHROMESTHESIA

chromato- — see CHROMAT-

chro·ma·to·gram \krō-'ma-tə-ˌgram, krə-\ n : the pattern formed on the adsorbent medium by the layers of components separated by chromatography

chro·ma·to·graph \krō-'ma-tə-ˌgraf, krə-\ n : an instrument for producing chromatograms — **chromatograph** vb

chro·ma·tog·ra·phy \ˌkrō-mə-'tä-grə-fē\ n, pl **-phies** : a process in which a chemical mixture carried by a liquid or gas is separated into components as a result of differential distribution of the solutes as they flow around or over a stationary liquid or solid phase — **chro·mato·graph·ic** \krō-ˌma-tə-'gra-fik, krə-\ adj — **chro·mato·graph·i·cal·ly** \-fi-k(ə-)lē\ adv

chro·ma·tol·y·sis \ˌkrō-mə-'tä-lə-səs\ n, pl **-y·ses** \-ˌsēz\ : the dissolution and breaking up of chromophil material (as chromatin) of a cell — **chro·mato·lyt·ic** \krō-ˌmat-ᵊl-'i-tik, krə-\ adj

chro·ma·to·phore \krō-'ma-tə-ˌfōr, krə-\ n : a pigment-bearing cell esp. in the skin

chro·ma·top·sia \ˌkrō-mə-'täp-sē-ə\ n : a disturbance of vision which is sometimes caused by drugs and in which colorless objects appear colored

chro·ma·to·sis \ˌkrō-mə-'tō-səs\ n, pl **-to·ses** \-ˌsēz\ : PIGMENTATION; specif : deposit of pigment in a normally unpigmented area or excessive pigmentation in a normally pigmented site

chrom·es·the·sia \ˌkrō-mes-'thē-zhə, -zhē-ə\ n : synesthesia in which color is perceived in response to stimuli (as words or numbers) that contain no element of color — called also *chromatism*

chrom·hi·dro·sis \ˌkrōm-hī-'drō-səs\ var of CHROMIDROSIS

chro·mid·i·al substance \krō-'mi-dē-əl-\ n : NISSL SUBSTANCE

chro·mi·dro·sis \ˌkrō-mə-'drō-səs\ n, pl **-dro·ses** \-ˌsēz\ : secretion of colored sweat

chro·mi·um \'krō-mē-əm\ n : a blue-white metallic element found naturally only in combination — symbol *Cr*; see ELEMENT table

chro·mo·blas·to·my·co·sis \ˌkrō-mə-ˌblas-tə-ˌmī-'kō-səs\ n, pl **-co·ses** \-ˌsēz\ : a skin disease that is caused by any of several pigmented fungi (esp. genera *Phialophora*, *Cladosporium*, and *Fonsecaea*) and is marked by the formation of warty colored nodules usu. on the legs — called also *chromomycosis*

¹chro·mo·mere \'krō-mə-₁mir\ *n* : the highly refractile portion of a thrombocyte or blood platelet — compare HYALOMERE

²chromomere *n* : one of the small bead-shaped and heavily staining concentrations of chromatin that are linearly arranged along the chromosome — chro·mo·mer·ic \₁krō-mə-'mer·ik. -'mir-\ *adj*

chro·mo·my·co·sis \₁krō-mə-₁mī-'kō-səs\ *n, pl* -co·ses \-₁sēz\ : CHROMOBLASTOMYCOSIS

chro·mo·ne·ma \₁krō-mə-'nē-mə\ *n, pl* -ne·ma·ta \-'nē-mə-tə\ : the coiled filamentous core of a chromatid — chro·mo·ne·mat·ic \-ni-'ma·tik\ *adj*

chro·mo·phil \'krō-mə-₁fil\ *adj* : staining readily with dyes

¹chro·mo·phobe \'krō-mə-₁fōb\ *adj* : not readily absorbing stains : difficult to stain (~ tumors)

²chromophobe *n* : a chromophobe cell esp. of the pituitary gland

chro·mo·pro·tein \₁kro-mə-'prō-₁tēn\ *n* : any of various proteins (as hemoglobins, carotenoids, or flavoproteins) having a pigment as a prosthetic group

chro·mo·some \'krō-mə-₁sōm. -₁zōm\ *n* : one of the linear or sometimes circular basophilic bodies of viruses, prokaryotic organisms. and the cell nucleus of eukaryotic organisms that contain most or all of the genes of the individual — chro·mo·som·al \₁krō-mə-'sō-məl. -'zō-\ *adj* — chro·mo·som·al·ly *adv*

chromosome complement *n* : the entire group of chromosomes in a nucleus

chromosome number *n* : the usu. constant number of chromosomes characteristic of a particular kind of animal or plant

chron·ax·ie *or* chron·axy \'krō-₁nak-sē. 'krä-\ *n, pl* -ax·ies : the minimum time required for excitation of a structure (as a nerve cell) by a constant electric current of twice the threshold voltage

¹chron·ic \'krä-nik\ *also* chron·i·cal \-ni-kəl\ *adj* 1 a : marked by long duration. by frequent recurrence over a long time, and often by slowly progressing seriousness : not acute (~ indigestion) b : suffering from a disease or ailment of long duration or frequent recurrence (~ arthritic) 2 : having a slow progressive course of indefinite duration — used esp. of degenerative invasive diseases. some infections. psychoses, inflammations, and the carrier state (~ heart disease) (~ arthritis) — compare ACUTE 2b — chron·i·cal·ly \-ni-k(ə-)lē\ *adv* — chro·nic·i·ty \krä-'ni-sə-tē. krō-\ *n*

²chronic *n* : one that suffers from a chronic disease

chronica — see ACRODERMATITIS CHRONICA ATROPHICANS

chronic alcoholism *n* : ALCOHOLISM 2b

chronic fatigue syndrome *n* : a group of symptoms of unknown cause including fatigue, cognitive dysfunction. and sometimes fever and lymphadenopathy that affect esp. young adults between the ages of 20 and 40 — called also *yuppie flu*

chronicum — see ERYTHEMA CHRONICUM MIGRANS

chronicus — see LICHEN SIMPLEX CHRONICUS

chro·no·bi·ol·o·gy \₁krä-nə-bī-'ä-lə-jē. ₁krō-\ *n, pl* -gies : the study of biological rhythms — chro·no·bi·o·log·ic \-₁bī-ə-'lä-jik\ *or* chro·no·bi·o·log·i·cal \-ji-kəl\ *adj* — chro·no·bi·ol·o·gist \-bī-'ä-lə-jist\ *n*

chro·no·log·i·cal age \₁krän-əl-'ä-ji-kəl. ₁krōn-\ *n* : the age of a person as measured from birth to a given date — compare ACHIEVEMENT AGE

chro·no·ther·a·py \₁krä-nə-'ther-ə-pē. ₁krō-\ *n, pl* -pies : treatment of a sleep disorder (as insomnia) by changing sleeping and waking times in an attempt to reset the patient's biological clock

chro·no·trop·ic \-'trä-pik\ *adj* : influencing the rate esp. of the heartbeat

chro·not·ro·pism \krə-'nä-trə-₁pi-zəm\ *n* : interference with the rate of the heartbeat

chrys·a·ro·bin \₁kri-sə-'rō-bən\ *n* : a powder derived from the wood of a tropical tree (*Andira araroba*) of the legume family (Leguminosae) that is used to treat skin diseases

chry·si·a·sis \krə-'sī-ə-səs\ *n, pl* -a·ses \-₁sēz\ : an ash-gray or mauve pigmentation of the skin due to deposition of gold in the tissues

Chrys·ops \'kri-₁säps\ *n* : a genus of small horseflies (family Tabanidae) of which the American deerflies in certain areas transmit tularemia while the African mango flies are vectors of the eye worm (*Loa loa*)

chryso·ther·a·py \₁kri-sə-'ther-ə-pē\ *n, pl* -pies : treatment (as of arthritis) by injection of gold salts

Chvos·tek's sign \'vós-₁teks-. 'kvós-\ *or* Chvos·tek sign \-₁tek-\ *n* : a twitch of the facial muscles following gentle tapping over the facial nerve in front of the ear that indicates hyperirritability of the facial nerve

  Chvostek, Franz (1835–1884), Austrian surgeon.

chyl- *or* chyli- *or* chylo- *comb form* : chyle (*chyluria*) (*chylothorax*)

chyle \'kīl\ *n* : lymph that is milky from emulsified fats. is characteristically present in the lacteals. and is most apparent during intestinal absorption of fats

chyli — see CISTERNA CHYLI

-chylia *n comb form* : condition of having (such) chyle ⟨*achylia*⟩

chy·lo·mi·cron \ˌkī-lō-ˈmī-ˌkrän\ *n* : a microscopic lipid particle common in the blood during fat digestion and assimilation

chy·lo·mi·cro·nae·mia *chiefly Brit var of* CHYLOMICRONEMIA

chy·lo·mi·cro·ne·mia \-ˌmī-krə-ˈnē-mē-ə\ *n* : an excessive number of chylomicrons in the blood (postprandial ∼)

chy·lo·tho·rax \-ˈthōr-ˌaks\ *n, pl* **-rax·es** *or* **-ra·ces** \-ˈthōr-ə-ˌsēz\ : an effusion of chyle or chylous fluid into the thoracic cavity

chy·lous \ˈkī-ləs\ *adj* : consisting of or like chyle ⟨∼ ascites⟩

chy·lu·ria \kī-ˈlür-ē-ə, kīl-ˈyür-\ *n* : the presence of chyle in the urine as a result of organic disease (as of the kidney) or of mechanical lymphatic esp. parasitic obstruction

chyme \ˈkīm\ *n* : the semifluid mass of partly digested food expelled by the stomach into the duodenum — **chymous** \ˈkī-məs\ *adj*

chy·mo·pa·pa·in \ˌkī-mō-pə-ˈpā-ən, -ˈpī-ən\ *n* : a proteolytic enzyme from the latex of the papaya that is used in meat tenderizer and has been used medically in chemonucleolysis

chy·mo·tryp·sin \ˌkī-mō-ˈtrip-sən\ *n* : a protease that hydrolyzes peptide bonds and is formed in the intestine from chymotrypsinogen — **chy·mo·tryp·tic** \-ˈtrip-tik\ *adj*

chy·mo·tryp·sin·o·gen \-ˌtrip-ˈsi-nə-jən\ *n* : a zymogen that is secreted by the pancreas and is converted by trypsin to chymotrypsin

ci·ca·trix \ˈsi-kə-ˌtriks, sə-ˈkā-triks\ *n, pl* **ci·ca·tri·ces** \ˌsi-kə-ˈtrī-(ˌ)sēz, sə-ˈkā-trə-ˌsēz\ : a scar resulting from formation and contraction of fibrous tissue in a flesh wound — **ci·ca·tri·cial** \ˌsi-kə-ˈtri-shəl\ *adj*

ci·ca·tri·zant \ˌsi-kə-ˈtriz-ənt\ *adj* : promoting the healing of a wound or the formation of a cicatrix

ci·ca·tri·za·tion \ˌsi-kə-trə-ˈzā-shən\ *n* : scar formation at the site of a healing wound — **ci·ca·trize** \ˈsi-kə-ˌtriz\ *vb*

CICU *abbr* coronary intensive care unit

cic·u·tox·in \ˌsi-kyə-ˈtäk-sən, ˈsi-kyə-ˌ\ *n* : an amorphous poisonous principle $C_{19}H_{26}O_3$ in water hemlock, spotted cowbane, and related plants (genus *Cicuta*)

cigarette drain *n* : a cigarette-shaped gauze wick enclosed in rubber dam tissue or rubber tubing for draining wounds — called also *Penrose drain*

ci·gua·te·ra \ˌsē-gwə-ˈter-ə, ˌsi-\ *n* : poisoning caused by the ingestion of various normally edible tropical fish in whose flesh a toxic substance has accumulated

ci·gua·tox·in \ˈsē-gwə-ˌtäk-sən, ˈsi-\ : a potent lipid neurotoxin associated

with ciguatera that has been found widely in normally edible fish

cil·ia *pl of* CILIUM

ciliaris — see ORBICULARIS CILIARIS, ZONULA CILIARIS

cil·i·ary \ˈsi-lē-ˌer-ē\ *adj* 1 : of or relating to cilia 2 : of, relating to, or being the annular suspension of the lens of the eye

ciliary artery *n* : any of several arteries that arise from the ophthalmic artery or its branches and supply various parts of the eye — see LONG POSTERIOR CILIARY ARTERY, SHORT POSTERIOR CILIARY ARTERY

ciliary body *n* : an annular structure on the inner surface of the anterior wall of the eyeball composed largely of the ciliary muscle and bearing the ciliary processes

ciliary ganglion *n* : a small autonomic ganglion on the nasociliary branch of the ophthalmic nerve receiving preganglionic fibers from the oculomotor nerve and sending postganglionic fibers to the ciliary muscle and to the sphincter pupillae

ciliary muscle *n* : a circular band of smooth muscle fibers situated in the ciliary body and serving as the chief agent in accommodation when it contracts by drawing the ciliary processes centripetally and relaxing the suspensory ligament of the lens so that the lens is permitted to become more convex

ciliary nerve — see LONG CILIARY NERVE, SHORT CILIARY NERVE

ciliary process *n* : any of the vascular folds on the inner surface of the ciliary body that give attachment to the suspensory ligament of the lens

ciliary ring *n* : ORBICULUS CILIARIS

cil·i·ate \ˈsi-lē-ət, -ˌāt\ *n* : any of a phylum or subphylum (Ciliophora) of ciliate protozoans

cil·i·at·ed \ˈsi-lē-ˌā-təd\ *or* **ciliate** *adj* : provided with cilia ⟨*ciliated* epithelium⟩ ⟨the *ciliate* protozoans⟩

cil·io·ret·i·nal \ˌsi-lē-ō-ˈret-ᵊn-əl\ *adj* : of, relating to, or supplying the part of the eye including the ciliary body and the retina

cil·i·um \ˈsi-lē-əm\ *n, pl* **-ia** \-ə\ 1 : EYELASH 2 : a minute short hairlike process often forming part of a fringe: *esp* : one of a cell that in free unicellular organisms produces locomotion or in higher forms a current of fluid

ci·met·i·dine \si-ˈme-tə-ˌdēn\ *n* : a histamine analog $C_{10}H_{16}N_6S$ used in the treatment of duodenal ulcers and pathological hypersecretory disorders — see TAGAMET

ci·mex \ˈsī-ˌmeks\ *n* 1 *pl* **ci·mi·ces** \ˈsī-mə-ˌsēz, ˈsi-\ : BEDBUG 2 *cap* : a genus of bloodsucking bugs (family Cimicidae) that includes the common bedbug

cin- *or* **cino-** — see KIN-

cin·cho·caine \'siŋ-kə-ˌkân, 'sin-\ n, *chiefly Brit* : DIBUCAINE

cin·cho·na \siŋ-'kō-nə, sin-'chō-\ n : the dried bark of any of several trees (genus *Cinchona* of the family Rubiaceae and esp. *C. ledgeriana* and *C. succirubra*) containing alkaloids (as quinine) used esp. formerly as a specific in malaria, an antipyretic in other fevers, and a tonic and stomachic — called also *cinchona bark*

Chin·chón \chin-'chōn\, **Countess of** (Doña Francisca Henriquez de Ribera), Peruvian noblewoman.

cin·cho·nism \'siŋ-kə-ˌni-zəm, 'sin-chə-\ n : a disorder due to excessive or prolonged use of cinchona or its alkaloids and marked by temporary deafness, ringing in the ears, headache, dizziness, and rash

cine·an·gio·car·di·og·ra·phy \ˌsi-nē-ˌan-jē-ō-ˌkär-dē-'ä-grə-fē\ n, *pl* **-phies** : motion-picture photography of a fluoroscopic screen recording passage of a contrasting medium through the chambers of the heart and large blood vessels — **cine·an·gio·car·dio·graph·ic** \-ˌkär-dē-ə-'gra-fik\ adj

cine·an·gi·og·ra·phy \-ˌan-jē-'ä-grə-fē\ n, *pl* **-phies** : motion-picture photography of a fluorescent screen recording passage of a contrasting medium through the blood vessels — **cine·an·gio·graph·ic** \-jē-ə-'gra-fik\ adj

cine·flu·o·rog·ra·phy \-ˌflùr-'ä-grə-fē\ n, *pl* **-phies** : the process of making motion pictures of images of objects by means of X rays with the aid of a fluorescent screen (as for revealing the motions of organs in the body) — compare CINERADIOGRAPHY — **cine·flu·o·ro·graph·ic** \-ˌflùr-ə-'gra-fik\ adj

cin·e·ole \'si-nē-ˌōl\ n : EUCALYPTOL

cine·plas·ty \'si-nə-ˌplas-tē\ n, *pl* **-ties** 1 : surgical fitting of a lever to a muscle in an amputation stump to facilitate the operation of an artificial hand 2 : surgical isolation of a loop of muscle of chest or arm, covering it with skin, and attaching to it a prosthetic device to be operated by contraction of the muscle in the loop — **cin·e·plas·tic** \ˌsi-nē-'plas-tik\ adj

cine·ra·di·og·ra·phy \ˌsi-nē-ˌrā-dē-'ä-grə-fē\ n, *pl* **-phies** : the process of making radiographs of moving objects (as the heart or joints) in sufficiently rapid sequence so that the radiographs or copies made from them may be projected as motion pictures — compare CINEFLUOROGRAPHY — **cine·ra·dio·graph·ic** \-ˌrä-dē-ō-'gra-fik\ adj

ci·ne·rea \sə-'nir-ē-ə\ n : the gray matter of nerve tissue

cinereum — see TUBER CINEREUM

cine·roent·gen·og·ra·phy \ˌsi-nē-ˌrent-gən-'ä-grə-fē\ n, *pl* **-phies** : CINERADIOGRAPHY

cin·gu·late gyrus \'siŋ-gyə-lət-, -ˌlāt-\ n : a medial gyrus of each cerebral hemisphere that partly surrounds the corpus callosum

cin·gu·lot·o·my \ˌsiŋ-gyə-'lä-tə-mē\ n, *pl* **-mies** : surgical destruction of all or part (as the cingulum) of the cingulate gyrus

cin·gu·lum \'siŋ-gyə-ləm\ n, *pl* **cin·gu·la** \-lə\ 1 : a ridge about the base of the crown of a tooth 2 : a tract of association fibers lying within the cingulate gyrus and connecting the callosal and hippocampal convolutions of the brain

cin·na·mon \'si-nə-mən\ n, *often attrib* 1 : any of several Asian trees (genus *Cinnamomum*) of the laurel family (Lauraceae) 2 : an aromatic spice prepared from the dried inner bark of a cinnamon (esp. *C. zeylanicum*); *also* : the bark

cino— see KIN-

cinnamon oil n : a yellowish or brownish essential oil obtained from the leaves and young twigs of a cinnamon tree (*Cinnamomum cassia*) and used chiefly as a flavoring — called also *cassia oil*

cir·ca·di·an \ˌsər-'ka-dē-ən, -'kä-; ˌsər-kə-'dī-ən, -'dē-\ adj : being, having, characterized by, or occurring in approximately 24-hour periods or cycles (as of biological activity or function) (~ rhythms in behavior)

cir·ci·nate \'sərs-ᵊn-ˌāt\ adj, *of lesions* : having a sharply circumscribed and somewhat circular margin

circle of Wil·lis \-'wi-ləs\ n : a complete ring of arteries at the base of the brain that is formed by the cerebral and communicating arteries and is a site of aneurysms

Willis, Thomas (1621–1675), British physician.

circling disease n : listeriosis of sheep or cattle

cir·cu·lar \'sər-kyə-lər\ adj : MANIC-DEPRESSIVE; *esp* : BIPOLAR 3

circulares — see PLICAE CIRCULARES

circular sinus n : a circular venous channel around the pituitary gland formed by the cavernous and intercavernous sinuses

cir·cu·late \'sər-kyə-ˌlāt\ vb **-lat·ed; -lat·ing** : to flow or be propelled naturally through a closed system of channels (as blood vessels)

cir·cu·la·tion \ˌsər-kyə-'lā-shən\ n : the movement of blood through the vessels of the body that is induced by the pumping action of the heart and serves to distribute nutrients and oxygen to and remove waste products from all parts of the body — see PULMONARY CIRCULATION, SYSTEMIC CIRCULATION

cir·cu·la·to·ry \'sər-kyə-lə-ˌtōr-ē\ adj : of or relating to circulation or the circulatory system (~ failure)

circulatory system n : the system of blood, blood vessels, lymphatics, and heart concerned with the circulation of the blood and lymph

cir·cu·lus \'sər-kyə-ləs\ n, pl -li \-ˌlī\ : an anatomical circle or ring esp. of veins or arteries

cir·cum·cise \'sər-kəm-ˌsīz\ vb -cised; -cis·ing : to cut off the prepuce of (a male) or the clitoris of (a female) — cir·cum·cis·er n

cir·cum·ci·sion \ˌsər-kəm-'si-zhən\ n 1 : the act of circumcising; esp : the cutting off of the prepuce of males that is practiced as a religious rite by Jews and Muslims and as a sanitary measure in modern surgery 2 : the condition of being circumcised

cir·cum·cor·ne·al injection \ˌsir-kəm-'kȯr-nē-əl-\ n : enlargement of the ciliary and conjunctival blood vessels near the margin of the cornea with reduction in size peripherally

cir·cum·duc·tion \ˌsər-kəm-'dək-shən\ n : movement of a limb or extremity so that the distal end describes a circle while the proximal end remains fixed — cir·cum·duct \-'dəkt\ vb

cir·cum·flex \'sər-kəm-ˌfleks\ adj, of nerves and blood vessels : bending around

circumflex artery n : any of several paired curving arteries: as a : either of two arteries that branch from the deep femoral artery or from the femoral artery itself: (1) : LATERAL FEMORAL CIRCUMFLEX ARTERY (2) : MEDIAL FEMORAL CIRCUMFLEX ARTERY b : either of two branches of the axillary artery that wind around the neck of the humerus: (1) : ANTERIOR HUMERAL CIRCUMFLEX ARTERY (2) : POSTERIOR HUMERAL CIRCUMFLEX ARTERY c : CIRCUMFLEX ILIAC ARTERY d : a branch of the subscapular artery supplying the muscles of the shoulder

circumflex iliac artery n : either of two arteries arching anteriorly near the inguinal ligament: a : an artery lying internal to the iliac crest and arising from the external iliac artery b : a more superficially located artery that is a branch of the femoral artery

circumflex nerve n : AXILLARY NERVE

cir·cum·oral \ˌsər-kəm-'ōr-əl, -'ȯr-\ adj : surrounding the mouth (~ pallor)

cir·cum·scribed \'sər-kəm-ˌskrībd\ adj : confined to a limited area (a ~ neurosis) (~ loss of hair)

cir·cum·stan·ti·al·i·ty \ˌsər-kəm-ˌstan-chē-'a-lə-tē\ n, pl -ties : a conversational pattern (as in some manic states) exhibiting excessive attention to irrelevant and digressive details

cir·cum·val·late \ˌsər-kəm-'va-ˌlāt, -lət\ adj : enclosed by a ridge of tissue

circumvallate papilla n : any of approximately 12 large papillae near the back of the tongue each of which is surrounded with a marginal sulcus and supplied with taste buds responsive esp. to bitter flavors — called also vallate papilla

cir·rho·sis \sə-'rō-səs\ n, pl -rho·ses \-ˌsēz\ : widespread disruption of normal liver structure by fibrosis and the formation of regenerative nodules that is caused by any of various chronic progressive conditions affecting the liver (as long-term alcohol abuse or hepatitis) — see BILIARY CIRRHOSIS

¹cir·rhot·ic \sə-'rä-tik\ adj : of, relating to, caused by, or affected with cirrhosis (~ degeneration) (a ~ liver)

²cirrhotic n : an individual affected with cirrhosis

cirs- or cirso- comb form : swollen vein : varix (cirsoid)

cir·soid \'sər-ˌsȯid\ adj : resembling a dilated tortuous vein (a ~ aneurysm of the scalp)

cis·plat·in \'sis-ˌplat-ᵊn\ n : a platinum-containing antineoplastic drug PtN₂-H₆Cl₂ used esp. as a palliative therapy in testicular and ovarian tumors and in advanced bladder cancer — see PLATINOL

cis–platinum \-'plat-ᵊn-əm\ n : CISPLATIN

cis·ter·na \sis-'tər-nə\ n, pl -nae \-ˌnē\ : a fluid-containing sac or cavity in an organism : as a : CISTERNA MAGNA b : CISTERNA CHYLI

cisterna chy·li \-'kī-ˌlī\ n, pl cisternae chyli : a dilated lymph channel usu. opposite the 1st and 2d lumbar vertebrae and marking the beginning of the thoracic duct

cis·ter·nal \(ˌ)sis-'tərn-ᵊl\ adj : of or relating to a cisterna and esp. the cisterna magna (~ puncture) — cis·ter·nal·ly adv

cisterna mag·na \-'mag-nə\ n, pl cisternae mag·nae \-ˌnē\ : a large subarachnoid space between the caudal part of the cerebellum and the medulla oblongata

cis·ter·nog·ra·phy \ˌsis-(ˌ)tər-'nä-grə-fē\ n, pl -phies : roentgenographic visualization of the subarachnoid spaces containing cerebrospinal fluid following injection of an opaque contrast medium

cis·tron \'sis-ˌträn\ n : a segment of DNA that is equivalent to a gene and that specifies a single functional unit (as a protein or enzyme) — cis·tron·ic \sis-'trä-nik\ adj

cit·rate \'si-ˌtrāt\ n : a salt or ester of citric acid

cit·rat·ed \'si-ˌtrā-təd\ adj : treated with a citrate esp. of sodium or potassium to prevent coagulation (~ blood)

cit·ric acid \'si-trik-\ n : a sour organic acid $C_6H_8O_7$ occurring in cellular metabolism, obtained esp. from lemon and lime juices or by fermentation of sugars, and used as a flavoring

citric acid cycle n : KREBS CYCLE

ci·tri·nin \si-'trī-nən\ n : a toxic antibiotic $C_{13}H_{14}O_5$ that is produced esp. by two molds of the genus Penicillium

(*P. citrinum*) and the genus *Aspergillus* (*A. niveus*) and is effective against some gram-positive bacteria

ci·trov·o·rum factor \sə-ˈträ-və-rəm-\ *n* : a metabolically active form of folic acid that has been used in cancer therapy to protect normal cells against methotrexate — called also *folinic acid, leucovorin*

cit·rul·line \ˈsi-trə-ˌlēn; si-ˈtrə-ˌlēn, -lən\ *n* : a crystalline amino acid $C_6H_{13}N_3O_3$ formed esp. as an intermediate in the conversion of ornithine to arginine in the living system

cit·rul·lin·ae·mia *chiefly Brit var of* CITRULLINEMIA

cit·rul·lin·emia \ˌsi-trə-lə-ˈnē-mē-ə, si-ˌtrə-lə-ˈnē-\ *n* : an inherited disorder of amino acid metabolism accompanied by excess amounts of citrulline in the blood, urine, and cerebrospinal fluid and ammonia intoxication

cit·rus \ˈsi-trəs\ *n, often attrib* : any plant or fruit of a genus (*Citrus*) of the rue family (Rutacexae) of often thorny trees and shrubs that are grown in warm regions and include the oranges (esp. *C. sinensis*), lemon (*C. limon*), lime (*C. aurantifolia*), and related plants

CK *abbr* creatine kinase

cl *abbr* centiliter

Cl *symbol* chlorine

CLA *abbr* certified laboratory assistant

clair·voy·ance \klar-ˈvȯi-əns, kler-\ *n* : the power or faculty of discerning objects or matters not present to the senses — clair·voy·ant \-ənt\ *adj*

clam·my \ˈkla-mē\ *adj* clam·mi·er; -est : being moist and sticky (~ hands) (~ sweating)

clamp \ˈklamp\ *n* : any of various instruments or appliances having parts brought together for holding or compressing something; *esp* : an instrument used to hold, compress, or crush vessels and hollow organs and to aid in surgical excision of parts — clamp *vb*

clang association *n* : word association (as in a psychological test) based on sound rather than meaning

clap \ˈklap\ *n* : GONORRHEA — often used with *the*

clasp \ˈklasp\ *n* : a device designed to encircle a tooth to hold a denture in place

class \ˈklas\ *n* : a major category in biological taxonomy ranking above the order and below the phylum

clas·sic \ˈkla-sik\ *or* clas·si·cal \-si-kəl\ *adj* : standard or recognized esp. because of great frequency or consistency or occurrence (the ~ symptoms of a disease)

classical conditioning *n* : conditioning in which the conditioned stimulus (as the sound of a bell) is paired with and precedes the unconditioned stimulus (as the sight of food) until the conditioned stimulus alone is sufficient to elicit the response (as salivation in a dog) — compare OPERANT CONDITIONING

clau·di·ca·tion \ˌklȯ-də-ˈkā-shən\ *n* 1 : the quality or state of being lame 2 : INTERMITTENT CLAUDICATION

claus·tro·phobe \ˈklȯ-strə-ˌfōb\ *n* : one affected with claustrophobia

claus·tro·pho·bia \ˌklȯ-strə-ˈfō-bē-ə\ *n* : abnormal dread of being in closed or narrow spaces

¹claus·tro·pho·bic \ˌklȯ-strə-ˈfō-bik\ *adj* 1 : suffering from or inclined to claustrophobia 2 : inducing or suggesting claustrophobia — claus·tro·pho·bi·cal·ly \-bi-k(ə-)lē\ *adv*

²claustrophobic *n* : CLAUSTROPHOBE

claus·trum \ˈklȯ-strəm, ˈklaù-\ *n, pl* claus·tra \-strə\ : the one of the four basal ganglia in each cerebral hemisphere that consists of a thin lamina of gray matter between the lentiform nucleus and the insula

clav·i·cle \ˈkla-vi-kəl\ *n* : a bone of the pectoral girdle that links the scapula and sternum, is situated just above the first rib on either side of the neck, and has the form of a narrow elongated S — called also *collarbone* — cla·vic·u·lar \kla-ˈvi-kyə-lər, klə-\ *adj*

clavicular notch *n* : a notch on each side of the upper part of the manubrium that is the site of articulation with a clavicle

cla·vic·u·lec·to·my \kla-ˌvi-kyə-ˈlek-tə-mē, klə-\ *n, pl* -mies : surgical removal of all or part of a clavicle

cla·vus \ˈklā-vəs, ˈklä-\ *n, pl* cla·vi \ˈklā-ˌvi, ˈklä-ˌvē\ : CORN

claw foot *n* : a deformity of the foot characterized by an exaggerated curvature of the longitudinal arch

claw hand *n* : a deformity of the hand characterized by extreme extension of the wrist and the first phalanges and extreme flexion of the other phalanges

claw toe *n* : HAMMERTOE

¹clean \ˈklēn\ *adj* 1 a : free from dirt or pollution b : free from disease or infectious agents 2 : free from drug addiction

²clean *vb* 1 : to brush (the teeth) with a cleanser (as a dentifrice) 2 : to perform dental prophylaxis on (the teeth)

¹clear \ˈklir\ *adj* 1 *of the skin or complexion* : good in texture and color and without blemish or discoloration 2 : free from abnormal sounds on auscultation

²clear *vb* : to rid (the throat) of phlegm or of something that makes the voice indistinct or husky

clear·ance \ˈklir-əns\ *n* : the volume of blood or plasma that could be freed of a specified constituent in a specified time (usu. one minute) by excretion of the constituent into the urine through the kidneys — called also *renal clearance*

cleav·age \'klē-vij\ n 1 : the series of synchronized mitotic cell divisions of the fertilized egg that results in the formation of the blastomeres and changes the single-celled zygote into a multicellular embryo; *also* : one of these cell divisions 2 : the splitting of a molecule into simpler molecules — **cleave** \'klēv\ vb

cleavage cell n : BLASTOMERE

cleft \'kleft\ n 1 : a usu. abnormal fissure or opening esp. when resulting from failure of parts to fuse during embryonic development 2 : a usu. V-shaped indented formation : a hollow between ridges or protuberances 3 : SYNAPTIC CLEFT

cleft lip n : a birth defect characterized by one or more clefts in the upper lip resulting from failure of the embryonic parts of the lip to unite — called also *cheiloschisis, harelip*

cleft palate n : congenital fissure of the roof of the mouth produced by failure of the two maxillae to unite during embryonic development and often associated with cleft lip

cleid- or **cleido-** comb form : clavicular : clavicular and ⟨cleidocranial⟩

clei·do·cra·ni·al dysostosis \‚klī-dō-‚krā-nē-əl-\ n : a rare condition inherited as an autosomal dominant and characterized esp. by partial or complete absence of the clavicles, defective ossification of the skull, and faulty occlusion due to missing, misplaced, or supernumerary teeth

cle·oid \'klē-‚oid\ n : a dental excavator with a claw-shaped working point

click \'klik\ n : a short sharp sound heard in auscultation and associated with various abnormalities of the heart

cli·mac·ter·ic \klī-'mak-tə-rik, ‚klī-‚mak-'ter-ik\ n 1 : MENOPAUSE 2 : a period in the life of a male corresponding to female menopause and usu. occurring with less well-defined physiological and psychological changes — **climacteric** adj

cli·mac·te·ri·um \‚klī-‚mak-'tir-ē-əm\ n, pl **-ria** \-ē-ə\ : the bodily and psychic involutional changes accompanying the transition from middle life to old age; *specif* : menopause and the bodily and mental changes that accompany it

cli·mac·tic \klī-'mak-tik\ adj : of, relating to, or constituting a climax

cli·ma·to·ther·a·py \‚klī-mə-tō-'ther-ə-pē\ n, pl **-pies** : treatment of disease by means of residence in a suitable climate

cli·max \'klī-‚maks\ n 1 : the highest or most intense point 2 : ORGASM 3 : MENOPAUSE

clin abbr clinical

clin·da·my·cin \‚klin-də-'mī-sən\ n : an antibiotic $C_{18}H_{33}ClN_2O_5S$ derived from and used similarly to lincomycin

clin·ic \'kli-nik\ n 1 a : a session or class

of medical instruction in a hospital held at the bedside of patients serving as case studies b : a group of selected patients presented with discussion before doctors for purposes of instruction 2 a : an institution connected with a hospital or medical school where diagnosis and treatment are made available to outpatients b : a form of group practice in which several physicians work in cooperative association

clin·i·cal \'kli-ni-kəl\ adj : of, relating to, or conducted in or as if in a clinic: as a : involving or depending on direct observation of the living patient ⟨~ diagnosis⟩ b : observable or diagnosable by clinical inspection ⟨~ tuberculosis⟩ c : based on clinical observation ⟨~ treatment⟩ d : applying objective or standardized methods (as interviews and personality tests) to the description, evaluation, and modification of human behavior ⟨~ psychology⟩ — **clin·i·cal·ly** \-k(ə-)lē\ adv

clinical crown n : the part of a tooth that projects above the gums

clinical thermometer n : a thermometer for measuring body temperature that has a constriction in the tube where the column of liquid breaks when the temperature drops from its maximum and that continues to indicate the maximum temperature by the part of the column above the constriction until reset by shaking — called also *fever thermometer*

cli·ni·cian \kli-'ni-shən\ n : one qualified in the clinical practice of medicine, psychiatry, or psychology

clinico- comb form : clinical : clinical and ⟨clinicopathologic⟩

clin·i·co·path·o·log·ic \'kli-ni-(‚)kō-‚pa-thə-'lä-jik\ or **clin·i·co·path·o·log·i·cal** \-'lä-ji-kəl\ adj : relating to or concerned both with the signs and symptoms directly observable by the physician and with the results of laboratory examination ⟨a ~ study of the patient⟩ — **clin·i·co·path·o·log·i·cal·ly** \-ji-k(ə-)lē\ adv

cli·no·dac·ty·ly \‚klī-nō-'dak-tə-lē\ n, pl **-ty·lies** : a deformity of the hand marked by deviation or deflection of the fingers

cli·noid process \'klī-‚nòid-\ n : any of several processes of the sphenoid bone

clip \'klip\ n : a device used to arrest bleeding from vessels or tissues during operations

clitorid- or **clitorido-** comb form : clitoris ⟨clitoridectomy⟩

clit·o·ri·dec·to·my \‚kli-tə-rə-'dek-tə-mē\ also **clit·o·rec·to·my** \-'rek-tə-mē\ n, pl **-mies** : excision of all or part of the clitoris

clitoridis — see PREPUTIUM CLITORIDIS

cli·to·ris \'kli-tə-rəs, kli-'tòr-əs\ n, pl **cli·to·ri·des** \kli-'tòr-ə-‚dēz\ : a small erectile organ at the anterior or ventral part of the vulva homologous to the penis — **cli·to·ral** \'klī-tə-rəl\ also **cli·tor·ic** \klī-'tȯr-ik, -'tär-\ adj

cli·vus \'klī-vəs\ n, pl **cli·vi** \-ˌvī\ : the smooth sloping surface on the upper posterior part of the body of the sphenoid bone supporting the pons and the basilar artery

CLL abbr chronic lymphocytic leukemia

clo·aca \klō-'ā-kə\ n, pl **-acae** \-ˌkē, -ˌsē\ 1 : the terminal part of the embryonic hindgut of a mammal before it divides into rectum, bladder, and genital precursors 2 : a passage in a bone leading to a cavity containing a sequestrum — **clo·acal** \-kəl\ adj

cloacal membrane n : a plate of fused embryonic ectoderm and endoderm closing the fetal anus

clo·a·ci·tis \klō-ə-'sī-təs\ n : a chronic inflammatory process of the cloaca of the domestic chicken that is of undetermined cause but is apparently transmitted by copulation — called also *vent gleet*

clock \'kläk\ n : BIOLOGICAL CLOCK

clo·fi·brate \klō-'fī-ˌbrāt, -'fi-\ n : a synthetic drug $C_{12}H_{15}ClO_3$ used esp. to lower abnormally high concentrations of fats and cholesterol in the blood

clo·mi·phene \'klä-mə-ˌfēn, 'klō-\ n : a synthetic drug $C_{26}H_{28}ClNO$ used in the form of its citrate to induce ovulation

clo·mip·ra·mine \klō-'mi-prə-ˌmēn\ n : a tricyclic antidepressant $C_{19}H_{23}-ClN_2$ used in the form of its hydrochloride to treat obsessive-compulsive disorder

clo·naz·e·pam \(ˌ)klō-'na-zə-ˌpam\ n : a benzodiazepine $C_{15}H_{10}ClN_3O_3$ used as an anticonvulsant in the treatment of epilepsy

clone \'klōn\ n 1 : the aggregate of the asexually produced progeny of an individual 2 : an individual grown from a single somatic cell of its parent and genetically identical to it — **clon·al** \'klōn-əl\ adj — **clon·al·ly** adv — **clone** vb

clon·ic \'klä-nik\ adj : exhibiting, relating to, or involving clonus (~ contraction) (~ spasm) — **clo·nic·i·ty** \klō-'ni-sə-tē, klä-\ n

clo·ni·dine \'klä-nə-ˌdēn, 'klō-, -ˌdīn\ n : an antihypertensive drug $C_9H_9-Cl_2N_3$ used esp. to treat essential hypertension, to prevent migraine headache, and to diminish opiate withdrawal symptoms

clo·nor·chi·a·sis \ˌklō-nȯr-'kī-ə-səs\ n, pl **-a·ses** \-ˌsēz\ : infestation with or disease caused by the Chinese liver fluke (*Clonorchis sinensis*) that invades bile ducts of the liver after ingestion in uncooked fish and when present in numbers causes severe systemic reactions including edema, liver enlargement, and diarrhea

Clo·nor·chis \klō-'nȯr-kəs\ n : a genus of trematode worms (family Opisthorchiidae) that includes the Chinese liver fluke (*C. sinensis*)

clo·nus \'klō-nəs\ n : a series of alternating contractions and partial relaxations of a muscle that in some nervous diseases occurs in the form of convulsive spasms — compare TONUS 2

closed \'klōzd\ adj 1 : covered by unbroken skin (~ fracture) 2 : not discharging pathogenic organisms to the outside (a case of ~ tuberculosis) — compare OPEN 1c

closed–angle glaucoma n : glaucoma in which the drainage channel for the aqueous humor composed of the attachment at the edge of the iris and the junction of the sclera and cornea is blocked by the iris — called also *narrow-angle glaucoma;* compare OPEN-ANGLE GLAUCOMA

closed reduction n : the reduction of a displaced part (as a fractured bone) by manipulation without incision — compare OPEN REDUCTION

clos·trid·i·um \kläs-'tri-dē-əm\ n 1 cap : a genus of saprophytic anaerobic bacteria (family Bacillaceae) that are commonly found in soil and in the intestinal tracts of humans and animals and that include important pathogens — see BLACKLEG, BOTULISM, GAS GANGRENE, TETANUS BACILLUS; compare LIMBERNECK 2 pl **clos·trid·ia** \-dē-ə\ a : any bacterium of the genus *Clostridium* b : a spindle-shaped or ovoid bacterial cell; esp : one swollen at the center by an endospore — **clos·trid·i·al** \-dē-əl\ adj

clo·sure \'klō-zhər\ n 1 a : an act of closing up or condition of being closed up b : a drawing together of edges or parts to form a united integument (wound ~ by suture) 2 : the perception of incomplete figures or situations as though complete by ignoring the missing parts or by compensating for them by projection based on past experience

¹**clot** \'klät\ n : a coagulated mass produced by clotting of blood

²**clot** vb **clot·ted; clot·ting** : to undergo a sequence of reactions that results in conversion of fluid blood into a coagulum and that involves shedding of blood, release of thromboplastin, inactivation of heparin, conversion of prothrombin to thrombin, interaction of thrombin with fibrinogen to form an insoluble fibrin network, and contraction of the network to squeeze out excess fluid : COAGULATE

clot-bust·er \'klät-ˌbəs-tər\ n : a drug (as streptokinase or tissue plasminogen activator) used to dissolve blood clots — **clot-bust·ing** \-tiŋ\ adj

clot retraction n : the process by which

a blood clot becomes smaller and draws the edges of a broken blood vessel together and which involves the shortening of fibrin threads and the squeezing out of excess serum

clo·tri·ma·zole \klō-'trī-mə-ˌzōl, -ˌzól\ *n* : an antifungal agent $C_{22}H_{17}ClN_2$ used to treat candida infections, tinea, and ringworm — see LOTRIMIN

clotting factor *n* : any of several plasma components (as fibrinogen, prothrombin, and thromboplastin) that are involved in the clotting of blood — see TRANSGLUTAMINASE; compare FACTOR V, FACTOR VII, FACTOR VIII, FACTOR IX, FACTOR X, FACTOR XII, FACTOR XIII

clove \'klōv\ *n* : the fragrant dried aromatic flower bud of a tropical tree (*Syzygium aromaticum*) of the myrtle family (Myrtaceae) that yields a colorless to pale yellow essential oil (**clove oil**) which is a source of eugenol, has a powerful germicidal action, and is used topically to relieve toothache

cloverleaf skull *n* : a birth defect in which some or all of the usu. separate bones of the skull have grown together resulting in a 3-lobed skull with associated deformities of the features and skeleton

clox·a·cil·lin \ˌkläk-sə-'si-lən\ *n* : a semisynthetic oral penicillin $C_{19}H_{17}$ ClN_3NaO_5S effective esp. against staphylococci which secrete penicillinase — see TEGOPEN

clo·za·pine \'klō-zə-ˌpēn\ *n* : an antipsychotic drug $C_{18}H_{19}ClN_4$ with serious side effects that is used in the management of severe schizophrenia — see CLOZARIL

Clo·za·ril \'klō-zə-ril\ *trademark* — used for a preparation of clozapine

clubbed \'kləbd\ *adj* **1** : having a bulbous enlargement of the tip with convex overhanging nail ⟨a ~ finger⟩ **2** : affected with clubfoot — **club·bing** \'klə-biŋ\ *n*

club·foot \'kləb-ˌfút\ *n, pl* **club·feet** \-ˌfēt\ **1** : any of numerous congenital deformities of the foot in which it is twisted out of position or shape — called also *talipes*; compare TALIPES EQUINOVARUS, TALIPES EQUINUS, TALIPES VALGUS, TALIPES VARUS **2** : a foot affected with clubfoot — **club·foot·ed** \-ˌfú-təd\ *adj*

club·hand \-ˌhand\ *n* **1** : a congenital deformity in which the hand is short and distorted **2** : a hand affected with clubhand

clump \'kləmp\ *n* : a clustered mass of particles (as bacteria or blood cells) — compare AGGLUTINATION — **clump** *vb*

cluster headache *n* : a headache that is characterized by severe unilateral pain in the eye or temple, affects primarily men, and tends to recur in a series of attacks

clut·ter·ing \'klə-tə-riŋ\ *n* : a speech defect in which phonetic units are dropped, condensed, or otherwise distorted as a result of overly rapid agitated utterance

Clut·ton's joints \'klət-ᵊnz-\ *n pl* : symmetrical hydrarthrosis esp. of the knees or elbows that occurs in congenital syphilis

Clut·ton \'klət-ᵊn\, **Henry Hugh** (1850–1909), British surgeon.

cly·sis \'klī-səs\ *n, pl* **cly·ses** \-ˌsēz\ : the introduction of large amounts of fluid into the body usu. by parenteral injection to replace that lost (as from hemorrhage or in dysentery or burns), to provide nutrients, or to maintain blood pressure — see HYPODERMOCLYSIS, PROCTOCLYSIS

clys·ter \'klis-tər\ *n* : ENEMA

cm *abbr* centimeter

Cm *symbol* curium

CMA *abbr* certified medical assistant

CMHC *abbr* Community Mental Health Center

CMV *abbr* cytomegalovirus

cne·mi·al \'nē-mē-əl\ *adj* : relating to the shin or shinbone

cne·mis \'nē-məs\ *n, pl* **cnem·i·des** \'ne-mə-ˌdēz\ : SHIN, TIBIA

cni·dar·i·an \nī-'dar-ē-ən\ *n* : COELENTERATE — **cnidarian** *adj*

CNM *abbr* certified nurse-midwife

CNS *abbr* central nervous system

Co *symbol* cobalt

c/o *abbr* complains of

co·ag·u·lant \kō-'a-gyə-lənt\ *n* : something that produces coagulation

co·ag·u·lase \kō-'a-gyə-ˌlās, -ˌlāz\ *n* : any of several enzymes that cause coagulation (as of blood)

¹co·ag·u·late \kō-'a-gyə-ˌlāt\ *vb* **-lat·ed; -lat·ing** : to become or cause to become viscous or thickened into a coherent mass : CLOT — **co·ag·u·la·bil·i·ty** \kō-ˌa-gyə-lə-'bi-lə-tē\ *n* — **co·ag·u·la·ble** \-'a-gyə-lə-bəl\ *adj*

²co·ag·u·late \-lət, -ˌlāt\ *n* : COAGULUM

co·ag·u·la·tion \kō-ˌa-gyə-'lā-shən\ *n* **1 a** : the process of becoming viscous, jellylike, or solid; *esp* : the change from a liquid to a thickened curdlike state not by evaporation but by chemical reaction **b** : the process by which such change of state takes place consisting of the alteration of a soluble substance (as protein) into an insoluble form or of the flocculation or separation of colloidal or suspended matter **2** : a substance or body formed by coagulation : COAGULUM

coagulation time *n* : the time required by shed blood to clot that is a measure of the normality of the blood

co·ag·u·lop·a·thy \kō-ˌa-gyə-'lä-pə-thē\ *n, pl* **-thies** : a disease affecting blood coagulation

co·ag·u·lum \kō-'a-gyə-ləm\ *n, pl* **-u·la** \-lə\ *or* **-u·lums** : a coagulated mass or substance : CLOT

coal tar *n* : tar obtained by distillation

of bituminous coal and used in the treatment of some skin diseases by direct local application to the skin

co·apt \kō-'apt\ *vb* : to close or fasten together : cause to adhere — **co·ap·ta·tion** \(,)kō-,ap-'tā-shən\ *n*

co·arct \kō-'ärkt\ *vb* : to cause (the aorta) to become narrow or (the heart) to constrict

co·arc·ta·tion \(,)kō-,ärk-'tā-shən\ *n* : a stricture or narrowing esp. of a canal or vessel (as the aorta)

coarse \'kōrs\ *adj* **1** : visible to the naked eye or by means of a compound microscope **2** *of a tremor* : of wide excursion **3** : harsh, raucous, or rough in tone — used of some sounds heard in auscultation in pathological states of the chest (∼ rales)

coat \'kōt\ *n* **1** : the external growth on an animal **2** : a layer of one substance covering or lining another; *esp* : one covering or lining an organ (the ∼ of the eyeball)

coat·ed \'kō-təd\ *adj, of the tongue* : covered with a yellowish white deposit of desquamated cells, bacteria, and debris usu. as an accompaniment of digestive disorder

Coats's disease \'kōts, 'kōt-səz-\ *n* : a chronic inflammatory disease of the eye that is characterized by white or yellow areas around the optic disk due to edematous accumulation under the retina and that leads to destruction of the macula and to blindness

    Coats \'kōts\, **George (1876–1915)**, British ophthalmologist.

co·bal·a·min \kō-'ba-lə-mən\ *n* : VITAMIN B₁₂

co·balt \'kō-,bȯlt\ *n* : a tough lustrous silver-white magnetic metallic element — symbol *Co*; see ELEMENT table

cobalt 60 *n* : a heavy radioactive isotope of cobalt having the mass number 60 and used as a source of gamma rays esp. in place of radium (as in the treatment of cancer and in radiography) — called also *radio-cobalt*

co·bra \'kō-brə\ *n* **1** : any of several very venomous Asian and African elapid snakes (genera *Naja* and *Ophiophagus*) **2** : RINGHALS **3** : MAMBA

co·ca \'kō-kə\ *n* **1** : any of several So. American shrubs (genus *Erythroxylon* of the family Erythroxylaceae); *esp* : one (*E. coca*) that is the primary source of cocaine **2** : dried leaves of a coca (esp. *E. coca*) containing alkaloids including cocaine

co·caine \kō-'kān, 'kō-,\ *n* : a bitter crystalline alkaloid C₁₇H₂₁NO₄ obtained from coca leaves that is used medically esp. in the form of its hydrochloride as a topical anesthetic and illicitly for its euphoric effects and that may result in a compulsive psychological need

co·cain·ize \kō-'kā-,nīz\ *vb* **-ized; -iz·ing** : to treat or anesthetize with cocaine — **co·cain·i·za·tion** \-,kā-nə-'zā-shən\ *n*

co·car·cin·o·gen \kō-kär-'si-nə-jən, kō-'kärs-ᵊn-ə-,jen\ *n* : an agent that aggravates the carcinogenic effects of another substance — **co·car·cin·o·gen·ic** \kō-,kärs-ᵊn-ō-'je-nik\ *adj*

coc·cal \'kä-kəl\ *adj* : of or relating to a coccus

cocci *pl of* COCCUS

coc·cid·ia \käk-'si-dē-ə\ *n pl* : a sporozoans of an order (Coccidia) parasitic in the digestive epithelium of vertebrates and higher invertebrates and including several forms of economic importance — compare CRYPTOSPORIDIUM, EIMERIA, ISOSPORA — **coc·cid·ian** \-dē-ən\ *adj or n*

Coc·cid·i·oi·des \käk-,si-dē-'ȯi-,dēz\ *n* : a genus of imperfect fungi including one (*C. immitis*) causing coccidioidomycosis

coc·cid·i·oi·din \-'ȯid-ᵊn, -'ȯi-,din\ *n* : an antigen prepared from a fungus of the genus *Coccidioides* (*C. immitis*) and used to detect skin sensitivity to and, by inference, infection with this organism

coc·cid·i·oi·do·my·co·sis \-,ȯi-dō-(,)mī-'kō-səs\, *n, pl* **-co·ses** \-,sēz\ : a disease of humans and domestic animals caused by a fungus of the genus *Coccidioides* (*C. immitis*) and marked esp. by fever and localized pulmonary symptoms — called also *San Joaquin fever, San Joaquin valley fever, valley fever*

coc·cid·io·my·co·sis \(,)käk-,si-dē-ō-(,)mī-'kō-səs\ *n, pl* **-co·ses** \-,sēz\ : COCCIDIOIDOMYCOSIS

coc·cid·i·o·sis \(,)käk-,si-dē-'ō-səs\ *n, pl* **-o·ses** \-,sēz\ : infestation with or disease caused by coccidia

coc·cid·io·stat \(,)käk-'si-dē-ō-,stat\ *n* : a chemical agent added to animal feed (as for poultry) that serves to retard the life cycle or reduce the population of a pathogenic coccidium to the point that disease is minimized and the host develops immunity

coc·co·ba·cil·lus \,käk-(,)kō-bə-'si-ləs\ *n, pl* **-li** \-,lī, -,lē\ : a very short bacillus esp. of the genus *Pasteurella* — **coc·co·ba·cil·la·ry** *adj* \-'ba-sə-,ler-ē, -bə-'si-lə-rē\

coc·coid \'kä-,kȯid\ *adj* : of, related to, or resembling a coccus — **coccoid** *n*

coc·cus \'kä-kəs\ *n, pl* **coc·ci** \'kä-,kī, -,kē; 'käk-,sī, -,sē\ : a spherical bacterium

coccyg- *or* **coccygo-** *comb form* : coccyx (*coccygectomy*)

coc·cy·ge·al \käk-'si-jəl, -jē-əl\ *adj* : of, relating to, or affecting the coccyx

coccygeal body *n* : GLOMUS COCCYGEUM

coccygeal gland *n* : GLOMUS COCCYGEUM

coccygeal nerve *n* : either of the 31st or lowest pair of spinal nerves

coc·cy·gec·to·my \ˌkäk-sə-ˈjek-tə-mē\ n, pl **-mies** : the surgical removal of the coccyx

coccygeum — see GLOMUS COCCYGEUM

coc·cyg·e·us \käk-ˈsi-jē-əs\ n, pl **coc·cyg·ei** \-jē-ˌī\ : a muscle arising from the ischium and sacrospinous ligament and inserted into the coccyx and sacrum — called also *coccygeus muscle, ischiococcygeus*

coc·cy·go·dyn·ia \ˌkäk-sə-(ˌ)gō-ˈdi-nē-ə\ n : pain in the coccyx and adjacent regions

coc·cyx \ˈkäk-siks\ n, pl **coc·cy·ges** \-sə-ˌjēz\ also **coc·cyx·es** \-sik-səz\ : a small bone that articulates with the sacrum and that usu. consists of four fused vertebrae which form the terminus of the spinal column

coch·lea \ˈkō-klē-ə, ˈkä-\ n, pl **co·chle·as** or **co·chle·ae** \-ˌē, -ˌī\ : a division of the bony labyrinth of the inner ear coiled into the form of a snail shell and consisting of a spiral canal in the petrous part of the temporal bone in which lies a smaller membranous spiral passage that communicates with the saccule at the base of the spiral, ends blindly near its apex, and contains the organ of Corti — **coch·le·ar** \-ər\ adj

cochlear canal n : SCALA MEDIA

cochlear duct n : SCALA MEDIA

cochlear nerve n : a branch of the auditory nerve that arises in the spiral ganglion of the cochlea and conducts sensory stimuli from the organ of hearing to the brain — called also *cochlear, cochlear branch, cochlear division*

cochlear nucleus n : the nucleus of the cochlear nerve situated in the caudal part of the pons and consisting of dorsal and ventral parts which are continuous and lie on the dorsal and lateral aspects of the inferior cerebellar peduncle

co·chleo·ves·tib·u·lar \ˌkō-klē-(ˌ)ō-ve-ˈsti-byə-lər, ˌkä-\ adj : relating to or affecting the cochlea and vestibule of the ear

Coch·lio·my·ia \ˌkä-klē-ə-ˈmī-ə\ n : a genus of No. American blowflies that includes the screwworms (C. hominivorax and C. macellaria)

cock·roach \ˈkäk-ˌrōch\ n : any of an order or suborder (Blattodea) of chiefly nocturnal insects including some that are domestic pests — see BLATTA, BLATTELLA

cock·tail \ˈkäk-ˌtāl\ n : a solution of agents taken or used together esp. for medical treatment or diagnosis

cocoa butter n : a pale vegetable fat obtained from cacao beans that is used in the manufacture of chocolate candy, in cosmetics as an emollient, and in pharmacy for making suppositories — called also *theobroma oil*

co·con·scious \(ˌ)kō-ˈkän-chəs\ n : mental processes outside the main stream of consciousness but sometimes available to it — **coconscious** adj

co·con·scious·ness n : COCONSCIOUS

¹**code** \ˈkōd\ n : GENETIC CODE

²**code** vb **cod·ed; cod·ing** : to specify the genetic code ⟨a gene that ∼s for a protein⟩

co·deine \ˈkō-ˌdēn, ˈkō-dē-ən\ n : a morphine derivative $C_{18}H_{21}NO_3 \cdot H_2O$ that is found in opium, is weaker in action than morphine, and is used esp. in cough remedies

co·de·pen·dence \ˌkō-di-ˈpen-dəns\ n : CODEPENDENCY

co·de·pen·den·cy \-dən-sē\ n, pl **-cies** : a psychological condition or a relationship in which a person is controlled or manipulated by another who is affected with a pathological condition (as an addiction to alcohol or heroin)

¹**co·de·pen·dent** \-dənt\ n : a codependent person

²**codependent** adj : participating in or exhibiting codependency

co·dex \ˈkō-ˌdeks\ n, pl **co·di·ces** \ˈkō-də-ˌsēz, ˈkä-\ : an official or standard collection of drug formulas and descriptions (the British Pharmaceutical Codex)

cod-liver oil n : a pale yellow fatty oil obtained from the liver of the cod (Gadus morrhua of the family Gadidae) and related fishes and used in medicine chiefly as a source of vitamins A and D in conditions (as rickets) due to abnormal calcium and phosphorus metabolism

co·dom·i·nant \(ˌ)kō-ˈdä-mə-nənt\ adj : being fully expressed in the heterozygous condition — **codominant** n

co·don \ˈkō-ˌdän\ n : a specific sequence of three consecutive nucleotides that is part of the genetic code and that specifies a particular amino acid in a protein or starts or stops protein synthesis — called also *triplet*

co·ef·fi·cient \ˌkō-ə-ˈfi-shənt\ n : a number that serves as a measure of some property (as of a substance) or characteristic (as of a device or process)

-coele or **-coel** also **-cele** n comb form : cavity : chamber : ventricle (blastocoel)

coe·len·ter·ate \si-ˈlen-tə-ˌrāt, -rət\ n : any of a phylum (Cnidaria syn. Coelenterata) of invertebrate animals with radial symmetry including some forms (as the jellyfishes) with tentacles studded with stinging cells — called also *cnidarian* — **coelenterate** adj

coeli- or **coelio-** chiefly Brit var of CELI-

coe·li·ac, coe·li·os·co·py, coe·li·ot·o·my chiefly Brit var of CELIAC, CELIOSCOPY, CELIOTOMY

coe·lom \ˈsē-ləm\ n, pl **coeloms** or **coe·lo·ma·ta** \si-ˈlō-mə-tə\ : the usu. epithelium-lined body cavity of metazoans above the lower worms that forms a large space when well developed between the alimentary viscera and the body walls — **coe·lo·mate** \'sē-lə-ˌmāt\ *adj or n* — **coe·lo·mic** \si-'lä-mik, -'lō-\ *adj*

coe·nu·ro·sis \ˌsēn-yə-'rō-səs, ˌsen-\ *or* **coe·nu·ri·a·sis** \-'rī-ə-səs\ *n, pl* **-oses** \-ˌsēz\ *or* **-ases** \ˌsēz\ : infestation with or disease caused by coenuri (as gid of sheep)

coe·nu·rus \sə-'nür-əs, sē-. -'nyur-\ *n, pl* **-nu·ri** \-'nür-ˌī. -'nyur-\ : a complex tapeworm larva growing interstitially in vertebrate tissues and consisting of a large fluid-filled sac from the inner wall of which numerous scolices develop — see GID, MULTICEPS

co·en·zyme \(ˌ)kō-'en-ˌzīm\ *n* : a thermostable nonprotein compound that forms the active portion of an enzyme system after combination with an apoenzyme — compare ACTIVATOR 1 — **co·en·zy·mat·ic** \-en-zə-'ma·tik, -(ˌ)zī-\ *adj* — **co·en·zy·mat·i·cal·ly** \-ti-k(ə-)lē\ *adv*

coenzyme A *n* : a coenzyme $C_{21}H_{36}$-$N_7O_{16}P_3S$ that occurs in all living cells and is essential to the metabolism of carbohydrates, fats, and some amino acids

coenzyme Q *n* : UBIQUINONE

coeruleus, coerulei — see LOCUS COE-RULEUS

co·fac·tor \'kō-ˌfak-tər\ *n* : a substance that acts with another substance to bring about certain effects; *esp* : CO-ENZYME

co·ge·ner *var of* CONGENER

Coggins test \'kä-gənz-\ *n* : a serological immunodiffusion test for the diagnosis of equine infectious anemia esp. in horses by the presence of antibodies to the causative virus — called also *Coggins* — **Coggins test** *vb*
  Coggins, Leroy (1932–), American veterinary virologist.

cog·ni·tion \käg-'ni-shən\ *n* 1 : cognitive mental processes 2 : a conscious intellectual act (conflict between ~ s)

cog·ni·tive \'käg-nə-tiv\ *adj* : of, relating to, or being conscious intellectual activity (as thinking, reasoning, remembering, imagining, or learning words) — **cog·ni·tive·ly** *adv*

cognitive dissonance *n* : psychological conflict resulting from simultaneously held incongruous beliefs and attitudes

cognitive therapy *n* : psychotherapy esp. for depression that emphasizes the substitution of desirable patterns of thinking for undesirable ones — compare BEHAVIOR THERAPY, CHEMO-THERAPY

co·he·sion \kō-'hē-zhən\ *n* 1 : the act or process of sticking together tightly 2 : the molecular attraction by which the particles of a body are united throughout the mass — **co·he·sive** \kō-'hē-siv, -ziv\ *adj* — **co·he·sive·ly** *adv* — **co·he·sive·ness** *n*

coin lesion *n* : a round well-circum-scribed nodule in a lung that is seen in an X-ray photograph as a shadow the size and shape of a coin

coital exanthema *n* : a highly contagious disease of horses that is caused by a herpesvirus transmitted chiefly by copulation

co·ition \kō-'i-shən\ *n* : COITUS — **co·ition·al** \-'ish-nəl, -'i-shən-ᵊl\ *adj*

co·itus \'kō-ə-təs, kō-'ē-; 'kȯi-təs\ *n* : physical union of male and female genitalia accompanied by rhythmic movements leading to the ejaculation of semen from the penis into the female reproductive tract; *also* : INTER-COURSE — compare ORGASM — **co·ital** \-ət-ᵊl, -'ēt-\ *adj* — **co·ital·ly** \-ᵊl-ē\ *adv*

coitus in·ter·rup·tus \-ˌin-tə-'rəp-təs\ *n* : coitus in which the penis is withdrawn prior to ejaculation to prevent the deposit of sperm in the vagina

coitus res·er·va·tus \-ˌre-zər-'vä-təs\ *n* : prolonged coitus in which ejaculation of sperm is deliberately withheld

col- *or* **coli-** *or* **colo-** *comb form* 1 : colon (*colitis*) (*colostomy*) 2 : colon bacillus (*coli*form)

cola *pl of* COLON

col·chi·cine \'käl-chə-ˌsēn. 'käl-kə-\ *n* : a poisonous alkaloid $C_{22}H_{25}NO_6$ that inhibits mitosis, is extracted from the corms or seeds of the autumn crocus, and is used in the treatment of gout and acute attacks of gouty arthritis

col·chi·cum \-kəm\ *n* : the dried corm or dried ripe seeds of the autumn crocus containing the alkaloid colchicine

¹**cold** \'kōld\ *adj* 1 **a** : having or being a temperature that is noticeably lower than body temperature and esp. that is uncomfortable for humans **b** : having a relatively low temperature or one that is lower than normal or expected **c** : receptive to the sensation of coldness : stimulated by cold 2 : marked by the loss of normal body heat (~ hands) 3 : DEAD 4 : exhibiting little or no radioactivity when subjected to radionuclide scanning — **cold·ness** *n*

²**cold** *n* 1 : bodily sensation produced by loss or lack of heat 2 : a bodily disorder popularly associated with chilling: **a** *in humans* : COMMON COLD **b** *in domestic animals* : CORYZA

COLD *abbr* chronic obstructive lung disease

cold agglutinin *n* : any of several agglutinins sometimes present in the blood (as that of many patients with primary atypical pneumonia) that at low temperatures combine compatible as well as incompatible erythrocytes, including the patient's own — compare AUTOAGGLUTININ

cold–blood·ed \'kōld-'blə-dəd\ *adj* : having a body temperature not internally regulated but approximating that of the environment : POIKILO-THERMIC — **cold–blood·ed·ness** *n*

cold cream *n* : a soothing and cleansing cosmetic basically consisting of a perfumed emulsion of a bland vegetable oil or heavy mineral oil

cold pack *n* : a sheet or blanket wrung out of cold water, wrapped around the patient's body, and covered with dry blankets — compare HOT PACK

cold sore *n* : a group of blisters appearing about or within the mouth and caused by a herpes simplex virus — called also *fever blister*; compare CANKER SORE

cold sweat *n* : perspiration accompanied by feelings of chill or cold and usu. induced by or accompanied by dread, fear, or shock

cold turkey *n* : abrupt complete cessation of the use of an addictive drug; *also* : the symptoms experienced by one undergoing withdrawal from a drug — **cold turkey** *adv or adj or vb*

col·ec·to·my \kä-ᵇlek-tə-mē, kō-\ *n, pl* **-mies** : excision of a portion or all of the colon

co·les·ti·pol \kə-ᵇles-tə-ˌpȯl\ *n* : a strongly basic resin with an affinity for bile acids that is used in the form of its hydrochloride to treat hypercholesterolemia and disorders associated with the accumulation of bile acids

co·li \ᵇkō-ˌlī\ *adj* : of or relating to bacteria normally inhabiting the intestine or colon and esp. to species of the genus *Escherichia* (as *E. coli*) — **coli** *n*

coli— see COL-

co·li·ba·cil·lo·sis \ˌkō-lə-ˌba-sə-ᵇlō-səs\ *n, pl* **-lo·ses** \-ˌsēz\ : infection with or disease caused by colon bacilli (esp. *Escherichia coli*)

¹**col·ic** \ᵇkä-lik\ *n* : a paroxysm of acute abdominal pain localized in a hollow organ and often caused by spasm, obstruction, or twisting

²**colic** *adj* : of or relating to colic : COLICKY ⟨∼ crying⟩

³**co·lic** \ᵇkō-lik, ᵇkä-\ *adj* : of or relating to the colon

colic artery *n* : any of three arteries that branch from the mesenteric arteries and supply the large intestine

co·li·cin \ᵇkō-lə-sən\ *also* **co·li·cine** \-ˌsēn\ *n* : any of various antibacterial proteins that are produced by strains of intestinal bacteria (as *Escherichia coli*) and that often act to inhibit macromolecular synthesis in related strains

col·icky \ᵇkä-li-kē\ *adj* 1 : relating to or associated with colic ⟨∼ pain⟩ 2 : suffering from colic ⟨∼ babies⟩

co·li·form \ᵇkō-lə-ˌfȯrm, ᵇkä-\ *adj* : relating to, resembling, or being colon bacilli — **coliform** *n*

co·li·phage \ᵇkō-lə-ˌfāj, -ˌfäzh\ *n* : a bacteriophage active against colon bacilli

co·lis·tin \kə-ᵇlis-tən, kō-\ *n* : a polymyxin produced by a bacterium of the genus *Bacillus* (*B. polymyxa* var. *colistinus*)

co·li·tis \kō-ᵇlī-təs, kə-\ *n* : inflammation of the colon — see ULCERATIVE COLITIS

colla *pl of* COLLUM

col·la·gen \ᵇkä-lə-jən\ *n* : an insoluble fibrous protein of vertebrates that is the chief constituent of the fibrils of connective tissue (as in skin and tendons) and of the organic substance of bones and yields gelatin and glue on prolonged heating with water — **col·lag·e·nous** \kə-ᵇla-jə-nəs\ *adj*

col·la·ge·nase \kə-ᵇla-jə-ˌnās, ᵇkä-lə-, -ˌnāz\ *n* : any of a group of proteolytic enzymes that decompose collagen and gelatin

collagen disease *n* : CONNECTIVE TISSUE DISEASE

col·la·gen·o·lyt·ic \ˌkä-lə-jə-nə-ᵇli-tik, -je-\ *adj* : relating to or having the capacity to break down collagen

col·la·ge·no·sis \ˌkä-lə-jə-ᵇnō-səs\ *n, pl* **-no·ses** \-ˌsēz\ : CONNECTIVE TISSUE DISEASE

collagen vascular disease *n* : CONNECTIVE TISSUE DISEASE

¹**col·lapse** \kə-ᵇlaps\ *vb* **col·lapsed**; **col·laps·ing** 1 : to fall or shrink together abruptly and completely : fall into a jumbled or flattened mass through the force of external pressure ⟨a blood vessel that *collapsed*⟩ 2 : to break down in vital energy, stamina, or self-control through exhaustion or disease; *esp* : to fall helpless or unconscious — **col·laps·ibil·i·ty** \-ˌlap-sə-ᵇbi-lə-tē\ *n* — **col·laps·ible** \-ᵇlap-sə-bəl\ *adj*

²**collapse** *n* 1 : a breakdown in vital energy, strength, or stamina : complete sudden enervation 2 : a state of extreme prostration and physical depression resulting from circulatory failure, great loss of body fluids, or heart disease and occurring terminally in diseases such as cholera, typhoid fever, and pneumonia 3 : an airless state of a lung of spontaneous origin or induced surgically — see ATELECTASIS 4 : an abnormal falling together of the walls of an organ ⟨∼ of blood vessels⟩

col·lar \ᵇkä-lər\ *n* : a band (as of cotton) worn around the neck for therapeutic purposes (as support or retention of body heat)

col·lar·bone \ᵇkä-lər-ˌbōn\ *n* : CLAVICLE

¹**col·lat·er·al** \kə-ᵇla-tə-rəl, -trəl\ *adj* 1 : relating to or being branches of a bodily part ⟨∼ sprouting of nerves⟩ 2 : relating to or being part of the collateral circulation

²**collateral** *n* 1 : a branch esp. of a blood vessel, nerve, or the axon of a nerve cell 2 : a bodily part that is lateral in position

collateral circulation *n* : circulation of blood established through enlargement of minor vessels and anastomosis of vessels with those of adjacent parts when a major vein or artery is functionally impaired (as by obstruction); *also* : the modified vessels through which such circulation occurs

col•lat•er•al ligament *n* : any of various ligaments on one or the other side of a hinge joint (as the knee, elbow, or the joints between the phalanges of the toes and fingers): as **a** : LATERAL COLLATERAL LIGAMENT **b** : MEDIAL COLLATERAL LIGAMENT

collateral sulcus *n* : a sulcus of the tentorial surface of the cerebrum lying below and external to the calcarine sulcus and causing an elevation on the floor of the lateral ventricle between the hippocampi — called also *collateral fissure*

collecting tubule *n* : a nonsecretory tubule that receives urine from several nephrons and discharges it into the pelvis of the kidney — called also *collecting duct*

collective unconscious *n* : the genetically determined part of the unconscious that esp. in the psychoanalytic theory of C. G. Jung occurs in all the members of a people or race

Col•les' fracture \ˈkä-ləs-, -ˌlēz-\ *n* : a fracture of the lower end of the radius with backward displacement of the lower fragment and radial deviation of the hand at the wrist that produces a characteristic deformity — compare SMITH FRACTURE

    Col•les \ˈkä-ləs\, **Abraham (1773–1843),** British surgeon.

col•lic•u•lus \kə-ˈli-kyə-ləs\ *n, pl* **-li** \-ˌlī, -ˌlē\ : an anatomical prominence; *esp* : any of the four prominences constituting the corpora quadrigemina — see INFERIOR COLLICULUS, SUPERIOR COLLICULUS

col•li•ma•tor \ˈkä-lə-ˌmā-tər\ *n* : a device for obtaining a beam of radiation (as X rays) of limited cross section

col•li•qua•tion \ˌkä-lə-ˈkwā-zhən, -shən\ *n* : the breakdown and liquefaction of tissue — **col•li•qua•tive** \ˈkä-li-ˌkwā-tiv, kə-ˈli-kwə-\ *adj*

col•lo•di•on \kə-ˈlō-dē-ən\ *n* : a viscous solution of pyroxylin used as a coating for wounds

col•loid \ˈkä-ˌlȯid\ *n* **1** : a gelatinous or mucinous substance found in tissues in disease or normally (as in the thyroid) **2 a** : a substance that consists of particles dispersed throughout another substance which are too small for resolution with an ordinary light microscope but are incapable of passing through a semipermeable membrane **b** : a mixture (as smoke) consisting of a colloid together with the medium in which it is dispersed — **col•loi•dal** \kə-ˈlȯid-əl, kä-\ *adj* — **col•loi•dal•ly** *adv*

col•lum \ˈkä-ləm\ *n, pl* **col•la** \-lə\ : an

anatomical neck or neckline part or process

col•lu•to•ri•um \ˌkä-lə-ˈtȯr-ē-əm\ *n, pl* **-to•ria** \-ē-ə\ : MOUTHWASH

col•lyr•i•um \kə-ˈlir-ē-əm\ *n, pl* **-ia** \-ē-ə\ *or* **-i•ums** : an eye lotion : EYEWASH

colo- — see COL-

col•o•bo•ma \ˌkä-lə-ˈbō-mə\ *n, pl* **-ma•ta** \-mə-tə\ : a fissure of the eye usu. of congenital origin

co•lon \ˈkō-lən\ *n, pl* **colons** *or* **co•la** \-lə\ : the part of the large intestine that extends from the cecum to the rectum

colon bacillus *n* : any of several bacilli esp. of the genus *Escherichia* that are normally commensal in vertebrate intestines; *esp* : one (*E. coli*) used extensively in genetic research

¹co•lon•ic \kō-ˈlä-nik, kə-\ *adj* : of or relating to the colon

²colonic *n* : irrigation of the colon : ENEMA — see HIGH COLONIC

col•o•nize \ˈkä-lə-ˌnīz\ *vb* **-nized; -nizing** : to establish a colony in or on — **col•o•ni•za•tion** \ˌkä-lə-nə-ˈzā-shən\ *n*

co•lon•o•scope \kō-ˈlä-nə-ˌskōp\ *n* : a flexible tube containing a fiberscope for visual inspection of the colon and apparatus for taking tissue samples

co•lo•nos•co•py \ˌkō-lə-ˈnäs-kə-pē, ˌkä-\ *n, pl* **-pies** : endoscopic examination of the colon — **co•lon•o•scop•ic** \kō-ˌlä-nə-ˈskä-pik\ *adj*

col•o•ny \ˈkä-lə-nē\ *n, pl* **-nies** : a circumscribed mass of microorganisms usu. growing in or on a solid medium

colony–stimulating factor *n* : any of several glycoproteins that promote the differentiation of stem cells esp. into blood granulocytes and macrophages and that stimulate their proliferation into colonies in culture

co•lo•proc•tos•to•my \ˌkō-lə-ˌpräk-ˈtäs-tə-mē, ˌkä-\ *n, pl* **-mies** : surgical formation of an artificial passage between the colon and the rectum

col•or \ˈkə-lər\ *n, often attrib* **1 a** : a phenomenon of light (as red, brown, pink, or gray) or visual perception that enables one to differentiate otherwise identical objects **b** : the aspect of objects and light sources that may be described in terms of hue, lightness, and saturation for objects and hue, brightness, and saturation for light sources **c** : a hue as contrasted with black, white, or gray **2** : complexion tint; *esp* : the tint characteristic of good health

Colorado tick fever *n* : a mild disease of the western U.S. and western Canada that is characterized by the absence of a rash, intermittent fever, malaise, headaches, and myalgia and is caused by an orbivirus transmitted by the Rocky Mountain wood tick

col•or–blind \-ˌblīnd\ *adj* : affected with partial or total inability to distinguish one or more chromatic colors — **color blindness** *n*

co•lo•rec•tal \ˌkō-lə-ˈrekt-əl, ˌkä-\ *adj*

: relating to or affecting the colon and the rectum (~ cancer) (~ surgery)

col·or·im·e·ter \ˌkə-lə-ˈri-mə-tər\ n : any of various instruments used to objectively determine the color of a solution — **col·or·i·met·ric** \ˌkə-lə-rə-ˈme-trik\ adj — **col·or·i·met·ri·cal·ly** \-tri-k(ə-)lē\ adv — **col·or·im·e·try** \ˌkə-lə-ˈri-mə-trē\ n

color index n : a figure that represents the ratio of the amount of hemoglobin to the number of red cells in a given volume of blood and that is a measure of the normality of the hemoglobin content of the individual cells

color vision n : perception of and ability to distinguish colors

co·los·to·mize \kə-ˈläs-tə-ˌmīz\ vb -mized; -miz·ing : to perform a colostomy on

co·los·to·my \kə-ˈläs-tə-mē\ n, pl -mies : surgical formation of an artificial anus by connecting the colon to an opening in the abdominal wall

colostomy bag n : a container kept constantly in position to receive feces discharged through a colostomy

co·los·trum \kə-ˈläs-trəm\ n : milk secreted for a few days after parturition and characterized by high protein and antibody content — **co·los·tral** \-trəl\ adj

col·our chiefly Brit var of COLOR

colp- or **colpo-** comb form : vagina (colpitis) (colposcope)

col·pec·to·my \käl-ˈpek-tə-mē\ n, pl -mies : partial or complete surgical excision of the vagina — called also vaginectomy

col·pi·tis \käl-ˈpī-təs\ n : VAGINITIS

col·po·cen·te·sis \ˌkäl-(ˌ)pō-sen-ˈtē-səs\ n, pl -te·ses \-ˌsēz\ : surgical puncture of the vagina

col·po·clei·sis \ˌkäl-pō-ˈklī-səs\ n, pl -clei·ses \-ˌsēz\ : the suturing of posterior and anterior walls of the vagina to prevent uterine prolapse

col·po·per·i·ne·or·rha·phy \ˌkäl-pō-ˌper-ə-(ˌ)nē-ˈòr-ə-fē\ n, pl -phies : the suturing of an injury to the vagina and the perineum

col·po·pexy \ˈkäl-pə-ˌpek-sē\ n, pl -pex·ies : fixation of the vagina by suturing it to the adjacent abdominal wall

col·por·rha·phy \käl-ˈpòr-ə-fē\ n, pl -phies : surgical repair of the vaginal wall

-colpos n comb form : vaginal disorder (of a specified type) (hydrometrocolpos)

col·po·scope \ˈkäl-pə-ˌskōp\ n : an instrument designed to facilitate visual inspection of the vagina — **col·po·scop·ic** \ˌkäl-pə-ˈskä-pik\ adj — **col·po·scop·i·cal·ly** \-pi-k(ə-)lē\ adv — **col·pos·co·py** \käl-ˈpäs-kə-pē\ n

col·pot·o·my \käl-ˈpä-tə-mē\ n, pl -mies : surgical incision of the vagina

co·lum·bi·um \kə-ˈləm-bē-əm\ n : NIOBIUM

col·u·mel·la \ˌkä-lə-ˈme-lə, ˌkäl-yə-\ n, pl -mel·lae \-ˈme-(ˌ)lē, -ˈlī\ : any of various anatomical parts likened to a column: **a** : the bony central axis of the cochlea **b** : the lower part of the nasal septum — **col·u·mel·lar** \-lər\ adj

col·umn \ˈkä-ləm\ n : a longitudinal subdivision of the spinal cord that resembles a column or pillar: as **a** : any of the principal longitudinal subdivisions of gray matter or white matter in each lateral half of the spinal cord — see DORSAL HORN, GRAY COLUMN, LATERAL COLUMN 1, VENTRAL HORN; compare FUNICULUS a **b** : any of a number of smaller bundles of spinal nerve fibers : FASCICULUS

co·lum·nar \kə-ˈləm-nər\ adj : of, relating to, being, or composed of tall narrow somewhat cylindrical epithelial cells

column chromatography n : chromatography in which the substances to be separated are introduced onto the top of a column packed with an adsorbent (as silica gel or alumina), pass through the column at different rates that depend on the affinity of each substance for the adsorbent and for the solvent or solvent mixture, and are usu. collected in solution as they pass from the column at different times — compare PAPER CHROMATOGRAPHY, THIN-LAYER CHROMATOGRAPHY

column of Ber·tin \-ber-ˈtaⁿ\ n : RENAL COLUMN

E. J. Bertin — see BERTIN'S COLUMN

column of Bur·dach \-ˈbər-dək, -ˈbùr-, -däk\ n : FASCICULUS CUNEATUS

Bur·dach \ˈbùr-däk\, **Karl Friedrich** (1776–1847), German anatomist.

co·ma \ˈkō-mə\ n : a state of profound unconsciousness caused by disease, injury, or poison

co·ma·tose \ˈkō-mə-ˌtōs, ˈkä-\ adj : of, resembling, or affected with coma (a ~ patient) (a ~ condition)

combat fatigue n : a traumatic psychoneurotic reaction or an acute psychotic reaction occurring under conditions (as wartime combat) that cause intense stress — called also battle fatigue; compare POST-TRAUMATIC STRESS DISORDER

com·e·do \ˈkä-mə-ˌdō\ n, pl com·e·do·nes \ˌkä-mə-ˈdō-(ˌ)nēz\ : BLACKHEAD 1

com·e·do·car·ci·no·ma \ˌkä-mə-ˌdō-ˌkärs-ᵊn-ˈō-mə\ n, pl -mas or -ma·ta \-mə-tə\ : a breast cancer that arises in the larger ducts and is characterized by slow growth, late metastasis, and the accumulation of solid plugs of atypical and degenerating cells in the ducts

come to vb : to recover consciousness

comitans — see VENA COMITANS

com·men·sal·ism \kə-ˈmen-sə-ˌli-zəm\ n : a relation between two kinds of organisms in which one obtains food or other benefits from the other without damaging or benefiting it — **com·men·sal** \-səl\ *adj or n* — **com·men·sal·ly** *adv*

com·mi·nut·ed \ˈkä-mə-ˌnü-təd, -ˈnyü-\ *adj* : being a fracture in which the bone is splintered or crushed into numerous pieces

com·mis·su·ra \ˌkä-mə-ˈshür-ə\ *n*, *pl* **-rae** \-ˈshür-ē\ : COMMISSURE

com·mis·sure \ˈkä-mə-ˌshür\ *n* 1 : a point or line of union or junction between two anatomical parts (as the lips at their angles or adjacent heart valves) 2 : a connecting band of nerve tissue in the brain or spinal cord — see ANTERIOR COMMISSURE, GRAY COMMISSURE, HABENULAR COMMISSURE, HIPPOCAMPAL COMMISSURE, POSTERIOR COMMISSURE; compare CORPUS CALLOSUM, MASSA INTERMEDIA — **com·mis·su·ral** \ˌkä-mə-ˈshür-əl\ *adj*

com·mis·sur·ot·o·my \ˌkä-mə-ˌshür-ˈä-tə-mē, -shə-ˈrä-\ *n*, *pl* **-mies** : the operation of cutting through a band of muscle or nerve fibers; *specif* : separation of the flaps of a bicuspid valve to relieve mitral stenosis : VALVULOTOMY

com·mit \kə-ˈmit\ *vb* **com·mit·ted**; **com·mit·ting** : to place in a prison or mental institution — **com·mit·ment** \kə-ˈmit-mənt\ *n* — **com·mit·ta·ble** \-ˈmi-tə-bəl\ *adj*

com·mon \ˈkä-mən\ *adj* : formed of or dividing into two or more branches (the ~ facial vein) (~ iliac vessels)

common bile duct *n* : the duct formed by the union of the hepatic and cystic ducts and opening into the duodenum

common carotid artery *n* : the part of either carotid artery between its point of origin and its division into the internal and external carotid arteries — called also *common carotid*

common cattle grub *n* : a cattle grub of the genus *Hypoderma* (*H. lineatum*) which is found throughout the U.S. and whose larva is particularly destructive to cattle

common cold *n* : an acute contagious disease of the upper respiratory tract caused by a virus and characterized by inflammation of the mucous membranes of the nose, throat, eyes, and eustachian tubes with a watery and purulent discharge

common iliac artery *n* : ILIAC ARTERY 1

common iliac vein *n* : ILIAC VEIN a

common interosseous artery *n* : a short thick artery that arises from the ulnar artery near the proximal end of the radius and that divides into anterior and posterior branches which pass down the forearm toward the wrist

common peroneal nerve *n* : the smaller of the branches into which the sciatic nerve divides passing outward and downward from the popliteal space and to the neck of the fibula where it divides into the deep peroneal nerve

and the superficial peroneal nerve — called also *lateral popliteal nerve*, *peroneal nerve*

com·mu·ni·ca·ble \kə-ˈmyü-ni-kə-bəl\ *adj* : capable of being transmitted from person to person, animal to animal, animal to human, or human to animal : TRANSMISSIBLE — **com·mu·ni·ca·bil·i·ty** \-ˌmyü-ni-kə-ˈbi-lə-tē\ *n*

communicable disease *n* : an infectious disease transmissible (as from person to person) by direct contact with an affected individual or the individual's discharges or by indirect means (as by a vector) — compare CONTAGIOUS DISEASE

communicans — see RAMUS COMMUNICANS, WHITE RAMUS COMMUNICANS

communicantes — see RAMUS COMMUNICANS

communicating artery *n* : any of three arteries in the brain that form parts of the circle of Willis: a : one connecting the anterior cerebral arteries — called also *anterior communicating artery* b : either of two arteries that occur one on each side of the circle of Willis and connect an internal carotid artery with a posterior cerebral artery — called also *posterior communicating artery*

com·mu·ni·ca·tion \kə-ˌmyü-nə-ˈkā-shən\ *n* 1 : the act or process of transmitting information (as about ideas, attitudes, emotions, or objective behavior) (nonverbal interpersonal ~) 2 : information communicated 3 : a connection between bodily parts (an artificial ~ between the esophagus and the stomach)

communis — see EXTENSOR DIGITORUM COMMUNIS

com·pact \kəm-ˈpakt, käm-ˈ, ˈkäm-ˌ\ *adj* : having a dense structure without small cavities or cells (~ bone) — compare CANCELLOUS

compacta — see PARS COMPACTA

compactum — see STRATUM COMPACTUM

com·par·a·tive \kəm-ˈpar-ə-tiv\ *adj* : characterized by the systematic comparison of phenomena and esp. of likenesses and dissimilarities (~ anatomy)

com·pat·i·ble \kəm-ˈpa-tə-bəl\ *adj* 1 : capable of existing together in a satisfactory relationship (as marriage) 2 : capable of being used in transfusion or grafting without immunological reaction (as agglutination or tissue rejection) 3 *of medications* : capable of being administered jointly without interacting to produce deleterious effects or impairing their respective actions — **com·pat·i·bil·i·ty** \-ˌpa-tə-ˈbi-lə-tē\ *n*

Com·pa·zine \ˈkäm-pə-ˌzēn\ *trademark* — used for a preparation of prochlorperazine

com·pen·sate \ˈkäm-pən-ˌsāt, -ˌpen-\ *vb* **-sat·ed**; **-sat·ing** 1 : to subject to or remedy by physiological compensation 2 : to undergo or engage in psychic or physiological compensation

com·pen·sat·ed *adj* : buffered so that there is no change in the pH of the blood ⟨∼ acidosis⟩ — compare UNCOMPENSATED

com·pen·sa·tion \ˌkäm-pən-ˈsā-shən, -ˌpen-\ *n* 1 : correction of an organic defect by excessive development or by increased functioning of another organ or unimpaired parts of the same organ ⟨cardiac ∼⟩ — see DECOMPENSATION 2 : a psychological mechanism by which feelings of inferiority, frustration, or failure in one field are counterbalanced by achievement in another

com·pen·sa·to·ry \kəm-ˈpen-sə-ˌtōr-ē\ *adj* : making up for a loss; *esp* : serving as psychic or physiological compensation

com·pe·tence \ˈkäm-pə-təns\ *n* : the quality or state of being functionally adequate ⟨drugs that improve the ∼ of a failing heart⟩

com·pe·ten·cy \-tən-sē\ *n, pl* -cies : COMPETENCE

com·pe·tent \ˈkäm-pə-tənt\ *adj* : having the capacity to function or develop in a particular way

com·pet·i·tive \kəm-ˈpe-tə-tiv\ *adj* : depending for effectiveness on the relative concentration of two or more substances ⟨∼ inhibition of an enzyme⟩ ⟨∼ protein binding⟩

com·plain \kəm-ˈplān\ *vb* : to speak of one's illness or symptoms ⟨the patient visited the office ∼*ing* of jaundice⟩

com·plaint \kəm-ˈplānt\ *n* : a bodily ailment or disease

com·ple·ment \ˈkäm-plə-mənt\ *n* 1 : a group or set ⟨as of chromosomes⟩ that is typical of the complete organism or one of its parts — see CHROMOSOME COMPLEMENT 2 : the thermolabile group of proteins in normal blood serum and plasma that in combination with antibodies causes the destruction esp. of particulate antigens

com·ple·men·tar·i·ty \ˌkäm-plə-(ˌ)men-ˈtar-ə-tē, -mən-\ *n, pl* -ties : correspondence in reverse of part of one molecule to part of another: as **a** : the arrangement of chemical groups and electric charges that enables a combining group of an antibody to combine with a specific determinant group of an antigen or hapten **b** : the correspondence between strands or nucleotides of DNA or sometimes RNA that permits their precise pairing

com·ple·men·ta·ry \ˌkäm-plə-ˈmen-tə-rē, -trē\ *adj* : characterized by molecular complementarity; *esp* : characterized by the capacity for precise pairing of purine and pyrimidine bases between strands of DNA and sometimes RNA such that the structure of one strand determines the oth-er — **com·ple·men·ta·ri·ly** \-ˈmen-trə-lē, -(ˌ)men-ˈter-ə-lē, -ˈmen-tə-rə-lē\ *adv* — **com·ple·men·ta·ri·ness** \-ˈmen-tə-rē-nəs, -ˈmen-ˌtrē-\ *n*

complementary DNA *n* : CDNA

complement fixation *n* : the process of binding serum complement to the product formed by the union of an antibody and the antigen for which it is specific that occurs when complement is added to a mixture ⟨in proper proportion⟩ of such an antibody and antigen

complement-fixation test *n* : a diagnostic test for the presence of a particular antibody in the serum of a patient that involves inactivation of the complement in the serum, addition of measured amounts of the antigen for which the antibody is specific and of foreign complement, and detection of the presence or absence of complement fixation by the addition of a suitable indicator system — see WASSERMAN TEST

com·plete \kəm-ˈplēt\ *adj* 1 *of insect metamorphosis* : having a pupal stage intercalated between the motile immature stages and the adult — compare INCOMPLETE 1 2 *of a bone fracture* : characterized by a break passing entirely across the bone — compare INCOMPLETE 2

complete blood count *n* : a blood count that includes separate counts for red and white blood cells — called also *complete blood cell count*; compare DIFFERENTIAL BLOOD COUNT

¹**com·plex** \käm-ˈpleks, kəm-ˈ, ˈkäm-ˌ\ *adj* : formed by the union of simpler chemical substances ⟨∼ proteins⟩

²**com·plex** \ˈkäm-ˌpleks\ *n* 1 : a group of repressed memories, desires, and ideas that exert a dominant influence on the personality and behavior ⟨a guilt ∼⟩ — see CASTRATION COMPLEX, ELECTRA COMPLEX, INFERIORITY COMPLEX, OEDIPUS COMPLEX, PERSECUTION COMPLEX, SUPERIORITY COMPLEX 2 : a group of chromosomes arranged or behaving in a particular way — see GENE COMPLEX 3 : a complex chemical substance ⟨molecular ∼es⟩ 4 : the sum of the factors ⟨as symptoms and lesions⟩ characterizing a disease ⟨primary tuberculous ∼⟩

³**com·plex** \käm-ˈpleks, kəm-ˈ, ˈkäm-ˌ\ *vb* : to form or cause to form into a complex ⟨RNA ∼ed with protein⟩

com·plex·ion \kəm-ˈplek-shən\ *n* : the hue or appearance of the skin and esp. of the face ⟨a dark ∼⟩ — **com·plex·ioned** \-shənd\ *adj*

com·plex·us \kəm-ˈplek-səs, käm-\ *n* : SEMISPINALIS CAPITIS — called also *complexus muscle*

com·pli·ance \kəm-ˈplī-əns\ *n* 1 : the ability or process of yielding to changes in pressure without disruption of structure or function ⟨a study of pulmonary ∼⟩ 2 : the process of complying with a regimen of treatment

com·pli·cate \ˈkäm-plə-ˌkāt\ vb **-cat·ed; -cat·ing** : to cause to be more complex or severe (a virus disease *complicated* by bacterial infection)

com·pli·cat·ed adj, *of a bone fracture* : characterized by injury to nearby parts

com·pli·ca·tion \ˌkäm-plə-ˈkā-shən\ n : a secondary disease or condition that develops in the course of a primary disease or condition and arises either as a result of it or from independent causes

com·pos men·tis \ˌkäm-pəs-ˈmen-təs\ adj : of sound mind, memory, and understanding

¹**com·pound** \käm-ˈpaủnd, kəm-ˈ, ˈkäm-ˌ\ vb : to form by combining parts (~ a medicine)

²**com·pound** \ˈkäm-ˌpaủnd, käm-ˈ, kəm-ˈ\ adj : composed of or resulting from union of separate elements, ingredients, or parts (a ~ substance) (~ glands)

³**com·pound** \ˈkäm-ˌpaủnd\ n : something formed by a union of elements or parts; *specif* : a distinct substance formed by chemical union of two or more ingredients in definite proportion by weight

compound benzoin tincture n : FRIAR'S BALSAM

compound fracture n : a bone fracture resulting in an open wound through which bone fragments usu. protrude — compare SIMPLE FRACTURE

compound microscope n : a microscope consisting of an objective and an eyepiece mounted in a telescoping tube

¹**com·press** \kəm-ˈpres\ vb : to press or squeeze together

²**com·press** \ˈkäm-ˌpres\ n 1 : a covering consisting usu. of a folded cloth that is applied and held firmly by the aid of a bandage over a wound dressing to prevent oozing 2 : a folded wet or dry cloth applied firmly to a part (as to allay inflammation)

compressed-air illness n : DECOMPRESSION SICKNESS

com·pres·sion \kəm-ˈpre-shən\ n : the act, process, or result of compressing esp. when involving a compressing force on a bodily part (~ of an artery by forceps)

compression fracture n : fracture (as of a vertebra) caused by compression of one bone against another

com·pro·mise \ˈkäm-prə-ˌmīz\ vb **-mised; -mis·ing** : to cause the impairment of (a *compromised* immune system) (a seriously *compromised* patient)

com·pul·sion \kəm-ˈpəl-shən\ n : an irresistible impulse to perform an irrational act — compare OBSESSION, PHOBIA

¹**com·pul·sive** \-siv\ adj : of, relating to, caused by, or suggestive of psycho-

logical compulsion or obsession (repetitive and ~ behavior) (a ~ gambler) — **com·pul·sive·ly** adv — **com·pul·sive·ness** n — **com·pul·siv·i·ty** \ˌkäm-ˌpəl-ˈsi-və-tē, käm-\ n

²**compulsive** n : one who is subject to a psychological compulsion

com·put·ed axial tomography \kəm-ˈpyü-təd-\ n : COMPUTED TOMOGRAPHY — abbr. CAT

computed tomography n : radiography in which a three-dimensional image of a body structure is constructed by computer from a series of plane cross-sectional images made along an axis — abbr. CT

com·pu·ter·ized axial tomography \kəm-ˈpyü-tə-ˌrīzd-\ n : COMPUTED TOMOGRAPHY — abbr. CAT

computerized tomography n : COMPUTED TOMOGRAPHY — abbr. CT

co·na·tion \kō-ˈnā-shən\ n : an inclination (as an instinct, a drive, a wish, or a craving) to act purposefully : IMPULSE 2 — **co·na·tive** \ˈkō-nə-tiv, -ˌnā-; ˈkä-\ adj

conc abbr concentrated; concentration

con·ca·nav·a·lin \ˌkän-kə-ˈna-və-lən\ n : either of two crystalline globulins occurring esp. in the seeds of a tropical American leguminous plant (*Canavalia ensiformis*): esp : one that is a potent hemagglutinin

con·ceive \kən-ˈsēv\ vb **con·ceived; con·ceiv·ing** : to become pregnant

con·cen·trate \ˈkän-sən-ˌtrāt, -ˌsen-\ vb **-trat·ed; -trat·ing 1 a** : to bring or direct toward a common center or objective **b** : to accumulate (a toxic substance) in bodily tissues (fish ~ mercury) **2** : to make less dilute **3** : to fix one's powers, efforts, or attention on one thing

con·cen·tra·tion \ˌkän-sən-ˈtrā-shən, -ˌsen-\ n 1 : the act or action of concentrating: as **a** : a directing of the attention or of the mental faculties toward a single object **b** : an increasing of strength (as of a solute) by partial or total removal of diluents **2** : a crude active principle of a vegetable esp. for pharmaceutical use in the form of a powder or resin **3** : the relative content of a component (as dissolved or dispersed material) of a solution, mixture, or dispersion that may be expressed in percentage by weight or by volume, in parts per million, or in grams per liter

con·cep·tion \kən-ˈsep-shən\ n 1 a : the process of becoming pregnant involving fertilization or implantation or both **b** : EMBRYO, FETUS **2 a** : the capacity, function, or process of forming or understanding ideas or abstractions or their symbols **b** : a general idea

con·cep·tive \kən-ˈsep-tiv\ adj : capable of or relating to conceiving

con·cep·tus \kən-ˈsep-təs\ n : a fertilized egg, embryo, or fetus

conch \'känk, 'känch, 'kóŋk\ n, pl conchs \'käŋks, 'kóŋks\ or conch·es \'kän-chəz\ : CONCHA 1

con·cha \'käŋ-kə, 'kóŋ-\ n, pl con·chae \-ıkē, -ıkī\ 1 : the largest and deepest concavity of the external ear 2 : NASAL CONCHA — con·chal \-kəl\ adj

con·cor·dant \kən-'körd-ᵊnt\ adj, of twins : similar with respect to one or more particular characters — compare DISCORDANT — con·cor·dance \-ᵊn(t)s\ n

con·cre·ment \'käŋ-krə-mənt, 'kän-\ n : CONCRETION

con·cre·tion \kän-'krē-shən, kən-\ n : a hard usu. inorganic mass (as a bezoar or tophus) formed in a living body

con·cuss \kən-'kəs\ vb : to affect with concussion

con·cus·sion \kən-'kə-shən\ n 1 : a hard blow or collision 2 : a condition resulting from the effects of a hard blow; esp : a jarring injury of the brain resulting in disturbance of cerebral function — con·cus·sive \-'kə-siv\ adj

con·den·sa·tion \ıkän-ıden-'sā-shən, -dən-\ n 1 : the act or process of condensing: as a : a chemical reaction involving union between molecules often with elimination of a simple molecule (as water) b : a reduction to a denser form (as from steam to water) 2 : representation of several apparently discrete ideas by a single symbol esp. in dreams 3 : an abnormal hardening of an organ or tissue (connective tissue ∼s)

con·dense \kən-'dens\ vb con·densed; con·dens·ing : to make denser or more compact; esp : to subject to or undergo condensation

¹con·di·tion \kən-'di-shən\ n 1 : something essential to the appearance or occurrence of something else; esp : an environmental requirement 2 a : a usu. defective state of health (a serious heart ∼) b : a state of physical fitness

²condition vb con·di·tioned; con·di·tion·ing : to cause to undergo a change so that an act or response previously associated with one stimulus becomes associated with another — con·di·tion·able \kən-'di-sh(ə-)nə-bəl\ adj

con·di·tion·al \kən-'dish-nəl, -'di-shən-ᵊl\ adj 1 : CONDITIONED (∼ reflex) 2 : eliciting a conditional response (a ∼ stimulus) — con·di·tion·al·ly \-'dish-nə-lē, -'di-shən-ᵊl-ē\ adv

con·di·tioned adj : determined or established by conditioning

con·dom \'kän-dəm\ n 1 : a sheath commonly of rubber worn over the penis (as to prevent conception or venereal infection during coitus) — called also sheath 2 : a device inserted into the vagina that is similar to a condom

con·duct \kən-'dəkt, 'kän-ıdəkt\ vb 1 : to act as a medium for conveying 2 : to have the quality of transmitting something — con·duc·tance \kən-'dək-təns\ n

con·duc·tion \kən-'dək-shən\ n 1 : transmission through or by means of something (as a conductor) 2 : the transmission of excitation through living tissue and esp. nervous tissue

conduction deafness n : hearing loss or impairment resulting from interference with the transmission of sound waves to the organ of Corti — called also conductive deafness, transmission deafness; compare CENTRAL DEAFNESS, NERVE DEAFNESS

con·duc·tive \-'dək-tiv\ adj 1 : having the power to conduct 2 : caused by failure in the mechanisms for sound transmission in the external or middle ear (∼ hearing loss) — con·duc·tiv·i·ty \ıkän-ıdək-'ti-və-tē, kən-\ n

con·duc·tor \kən-'dək-tər\ n 1 : a substance or body capable of transmitting electricity, heat, or sound 2 : a bodily part (as a nerve fiber) that transmits excitation

condyl- or condylo- comb form : joint : condyle (condylectomy) (condyloid joint)

con·dy·lar·thro·sis \ıkän-də-lär-'thrō-səs\ n, pl -thro·ses \-ısēz\ : articulation by means of a condyle

con·dyle \'kän-ıdīl, 'känd-ᵊl\ n : an articular prominence of a bone — used chiefly of such as occur in pairs resembling a pair of knuckles (as those of the occipital bone for articulation with the atlas, those at the distal end of the humerus and femur, and those of the lower jaw); see LATERAL CONDYLE, MEDIAL CONDYLE — con·dy·lar \'kän-də-lər\ adj — con·dy·loid \'kän-də-ılóid\ adj

con·dyl·ec·to·my \ıkän-dī-'lek-tə-mē, ıkänd-ᵊl-'ek-\ n, pl -mies : surgical removal of a condyle

con·dy·loid joint \'kän-də-ılóid-\ n : an articulation in which an ovoid head is received into an elliptical cavity permitting all movements except axial rotation

condyloid process n : the rounded process by which the ramus of the mandible articulates with the temporal bone

con·dy·lo·ma \ıkän-də-'lō-mə\ n, pl -ma·ta \-mə-tə\ also -mas : CONDYLOMA ACUMINATUM — con·dy·lo·ma·tous \-mə-təs\ adj

condyloma acu·mi·na·tum \-ə-ıkyü-mə-'nä-təm\ n, pl condylomata acu·mi·na·ta \-'nä-tə\ : a warty growth on the skin or adjoining mucous membrane usu. near the anus and genital organs — called also genital wart, venereal wart

condyloma la·tum \-'lä-təm\ n, pl condylomata la·ta \-tə\ : a highly infectious flattened often hypertrophic papule of secondary syphilis that forms in moist areas of skin and at mucocutaneous junctions

cone \'kōn\ *n* **1** : any of the conical photosensitive receptor cells of the retina that function in color vision — compare ROD 1 **2** : any of a family (Conidae) of numerous somewhat conical tropical gastropod mollusks that include a few highly poisonous forms **3** : a cusp of a tooth esp. in the upper jaw

cone-nose \'kōn-,nōz\ *n* : any of various large bloodsucking bugs esp. of the genus *Triatoma* including some capable of inflicting painful bites — called also *kissing bug*

con-fab-u-la-tion \kən-,fa-byə-'lā-shən, ,kän-\ *n* : a filling in of gaps in memory by unconstrained fabrication — **con-fab-u-late** \kən-'fa-byə-,lāt\ *vb*

con-fec-tion \kən-'fek-shən\ *n* : a medicinal preparation usu. made with sugar, syrup, or honey — called also *electuary*

con-fine \kən-'fīn\ *vb* **con-fined; con-fin-ing** : to keep from leaving accustomed quarters (as one's room or bed) under pressure of infirmity, childbirth, or detention

con-fined \kən-'fīnd\ *adj* : undergoing childbirth

con-fine-ment \kən-'fīn-mənt\ *n* : an act of confining : the state of being confined; *esp* : LYING-IN

con-flict \'kän-,flikt\ *n* : mental struggle resulting from incompatible or opposing needs, drives, wishes, or external or internal demands — **con-flict-ful** \-,flikt-fəl\ *adj* — **con-flic-tu-al** \kän-'flik-chə-wəl, kən-\ *adj*

con-flict-ed \kən-'flik-təd\ *adj* : having or expressing emotional conflict 〈~ about one's sexual identity〉

con-flu-ence of sinuses \'kän-,flü-ənts-, kən-'flü-\ *n* : the junction of several of the sinuses of the dura mater in the internal occipital region — called also *confluence of the sinuses*

con-flu-ent \'kän-,flü-ənt, kən-'\ *adj* **1** : flowing or coming together; *also* : run together 〈~ pustules〉 **2** : characterized by confluent lesions 〈~ smallpox〉 — compare DISCRETE

coni *pl of* CONUS

con-for-ma-tion \,kän-(,)för-'mā-shən, -fər-\ *n* : any of the spatial arrangements of a molecule that can be obtained by rotation of the atoms about a single bond — **con-for-ma-tion-al** \-shnəl, -shən-əl\ *adj* — **con-for-ma-tion-al-ly** *adv*

con-form-er \kən-'för-mər\ *n* : a mold (as of plastic) used to prevent collapse or closing of a cavity, vessel, or opening during surgical repair

con-fu-sion \kən-'fyü-zhən\ *n* : disturbance of consciousness characterized by inability to engage in orderly thought or by lack of power to distinguish, choose, or act decisively — **con-fused** \-'fyüzd\ *adj* — **con-fu-sion-al** \-zhnəl, -zhən-əl\ *adj*

con-geal \kən-'jēl\ *vb* **1** : to change from

a fluid to a solid state by or as if by cold **2** : to make viscid or curdled : COAGULATE

con-ge-ner \'kän-jə-nər, kən-'jē-\ *n* **1** : a member of the same taxonomic genus as another plant or animal **2** : a chemical substance related to another 〈tetracycline and its ~s〉 — **con-ge-ner-ic** \,kän-jə-'ner-ik\ *adj*

congenita — see AMYOTONIA CONGENITA, ARTHROGRYPOSIS MULTIPLEX CONGENITA, MYOTONIA CONGENITA, OSTEOGENESIS IMPERFECTA CONGENITA

con-gen-i-tal \kän-'je-nət-əl\ *adj* **1** : existing at or dating from birth 〈~ deafness〉 **2** : acquired during development in the uterus and not through heredity 〈~ syphilis〉 — compare ACQUIRED 2, FAMILIAL, HEREDITARY — **con-gen-i-tal-ly** *adv*

congenital megacolon *n* : HIRSCHSPRUNG'S DISEASE

con-gest-ed \kən-'jes-təd\ *adj* : containing an excessive accumulation of blood : HYPEREMIC 〈~ mucous membranes〉

con-ges-tion \kən-'jes-chən, -'jesh-\ *n* : an excessive accumulation esp. of blood in the blood vessels of an organ or part whether natural or artificially induced (as for therapeutic purposes) — **con-ges-tive** \-'jes-tiv\ *adj*

congestive heart failure *n* : heart failure in which the heart is unable to maintain adequate circulation of blood in the tissues of the body or to pump out the venous blood returned to it by the venous circulation

con-glu-ti-nate \kən-'glüt-ən-,āt, kän-\ *vb* **-nat-ed; -nat-ing** : to unite or become united by or as if by a glutinous substance (blood platelets ~ in blood clotting) — **con-glu-ti-na-tion** \-,glüt-ən-'ā-shən\ *n*

Congo red \'käŋ-(,)gō-\ *n* : an azo dye $C_{32}H_{22}N_6Na_2O_6S_2$ used in a number of diagnostic tests and esp. for the detection of amyloidosis since the injected dye tends to be retained by abnormal amyloid deposits

con-gress \'käŋ-grəs, -rəs\ *n* : COITUS

con-iza-tion \,kō-nə-'zā-shən, ,kä-\ *n* : the electrosurgical excision of a cone of tissue from a diseased uterine cervix

con-ju-ga-ta \,kän-jə-'gā-tə\ *n, pl* **-ga-tae** \-'gā-,tē\ : CONJUGATE DIAMETER

¹con-ju-gate \'kän-ji-gət, -jə-,gāt\ *adj* **1** : functioning or operating simultaneously as if joined **2** *of an acid or base* : related by the difference of a proton — **con-ju-gate-ly** *adv*

²con-ju-gate \-jə-,gāt\ *vb* **-gat-ed; -gat-ing 1** : to unite (as with the elimination of water) so that the product is easily broken down (as by hydrolysis) into the original compounds **2** : to pair and fuse in conjugation **3** : to pair in synapsis

³con-ju-gate \-ji-gət, -jə-,gāt\ *n* : a chemical compound formed by the union of two compounds or united with another compound — **con·ju·gat·ed** \'kän-jə-ˌgā-təd\ *adj*

conjugate diameter *n* : the anteroposterior diameter of the human pelvis measured from the sacral promontory to the pubic symphysis — called also *conjugata, true conjugate*

conjugated protein *n* : a compound of a protein with a nonprotein (hemoglobin is a *conjugated protein* of heme and globin)

con·ju·ga·tion \ˌkän-jə-'gā-shən\ *n* 1 : the act of conjugating : the state of being conjugated 2 a : temporary cytoplasmic union with exchange of nuclear material that is the usual sexual process in ciliated protozoans b : the one-way transfer of DNA between bacteria in cellular contact — **con·ju·ga·tion·al** \-shnəl, -shən-əl\ *adj*

con·junc·ti·va \ˌkän-ˌjəŋk-'tī-və, kən-\ *n, pl* **-vas** *or* **-vae** \-(ˌ)vē\ : the mucous membrane that lines the inner surface of the eyelids and is continued over the forepart of the eyeball — **con·junc·ti·val** \-vəl\ *adj*

con·junc·ti·vi·tis \kən-ˌjəŋk-ti-'vī-təs\ *n* : inflammation of the conjunctiva

con·junc·ti·vo·plas·ty \kən-'jəŋk-ti-(ˌ)vō-ˌplas-tē\ *n, pl* **-ties** : plastic repair of a defect in the conjunctiva

con·junc·ti·vo·rhi·nos·to·my \kən-ˌjəŋk-ti-(ˌ)vō-ˌrī-'näs-tə-mē\ *n, pl* **-mies** : surgical creation of a passage through the conjunctiva to the nasal cavity

conjunctivum — see BRACHIUM CONJUNCTIVUM

connective tissue *n* : a tissue of mesodermal origin rich in intercellular substance or interlacing processes with little tendency for the cells to come together in sheets or masses; *specif* : connective tissue of stellate or spindle-shaped cells with interlacing processes that pervades, supports, and binds together other tissues and forms ligaments, tendons, and aponeuroses

connective tissue disease *n* : any of various diseases or abnormal states (as rheumatoid arthritis, systemic lupus erythematosus, polyarteritis nodosa, rheumatic fever, and dermatomyositis) characterized by inflammatory or degenerative changes in connective tissue — called also *collagen disease, collagenolysis, collagen vascular disease*

con·nec·tor \kə-'nek-tər\ *n* : a part of a partial denture which joins its components

conniventes — see VALVULAE CONNIVENTES

Conn's syndrome \'känz-\ *n* : PRIMARY ALDOSTERONISM

Conn, Jerome W. (*b* 1907), American physician.

con·san·guine \kän-'saŋ-gwən, kən-\ *adj* : CONSANGUINEOUS

con·san·guin·e·ous \ˌkän-ˌsan-'gwi-nē-əs, -ˌsaŋ-\ *adj* : of the same blood or origin; *specif* : relating to or involving persons (as first cousins) that are relatively closely related (~ marriages) — **con·san·guin·i·ty** \-nə-tē\ *n*

con·science \'kän-chəns\ *n* : the part of the superego in psychoanalysis that transmits commands and admonitions to the ego

¹**con·scious** \'kän-chəs\ *adj* 1 : capable of or marked by thought, will, design, or perception : relating to, being, or being part of consciousness (the ~ mind) 2 : having mental faculties undulled by sleep, faintness, or stupor — **con·scious·ly** *adv*

²**conscious** *n* : CONSCIOUSNESS 3

con·scious·ness \-nəs\ *n* 1 : the totality in psychology of sensations, perceptions, ideas, attitudes, and feelings of which an individual or a group is aware at any given time or within a given time span 2 : waking life (as that to which one returns after sleep, trance, or fever) in which one's normal mental powers are present 3 : the upper part of mental life of which the person is aware as contrasted with unconscious processes

con·sen·su·al \kän-'sen-chə-wəl\ *adj* 1 : existing or made by mutual consent (~ sexual behavior) 2 : relating to or being the constrictive pupillary response of an eye that is covered when the other eye is exposed to light — **con·sen·su·al·ly** *adv*

con·ser·va·tive \kən-'sər-və-tiv\ *adj* : designed to preserve parts or restore function (~ surgery) — compare RADICAL — **con·ser·va·tive·ly** *adv*

con·serve \kən-'sərv\ *vb* **con·served; con·serv·ing** : to maintain (a quantity) constant during a process of chemical, physical, or evolutionary change

con·sol·i·da·tion \kən-ˌsä-lə-'dā-shən\ *n* : the process by which an infected lung passes from an aerated collapsible condition to one of airless solid consistency through the accumulation of exudate in the alveoli and adjoining ducts; *also* : tissue that has undergone consolidation

con·spe·cif·ic \ˌkän-spi-'si-fik\ *adj* : of the same species — **conspecific** *n*

constant region *n* : the part of the polypeptide chain of a light or heavy chain of an antibody that ends in a free carboxyl group —COOH and that is relatively constant in its sequence of amino-acid residues from one antibody to another — called also *constant domain*; compare VARIABLE REGION

con·stel·la·tion \ˌkän-stə-'lā-shən\ *n* : a set of ideas, conditions, symptoms, or traits that fall into or appear to fall into a pattern

con·sti·pa·tion \ˌkän-stə-ˈpā-shən\ n : abnormally delayed or infrequent passage of usu. dry hardened feces — **con·sti·pate** \ˈkän-stə-ˌpāt\ vb — **con·sti·pat·ed** \-ˌpā-təd\ adj

con·sti·tu·tion \ˌkän-stə-ˈtü-shən, -ˈtyü-\ n : the physical makeup of the individual comprising inherited qualities modified by environment — **con·sti·tu·tion·al** \-shnəl, -shən-ᵊl\ adj

con·sti·tu·tion·al \-shnəl, -shən-ᵊl\ n : a walk taken for one's health

con·strict \kən-ˈstrikt\ vb 1 : to make narrow or draw together 2 : to subject (as a body part) to compression 〈∼ a nerve〉 — **con·stric·tion** \-ˈstrik-shən\ n — **con·stric·tive** \-ˈstrik-tiv\ adj

con·stric·tor \-ˈstrik-tər\ n : a muscle that contracts a cavity or orifice or compresses an organ — see INFERIOR CONSTRICTOR, MIDDLE CONSTRICTOR, SUPERIOR CONSTRICTOR

constrictor pha·ryn·gis inferior \-fə-ˈrin-jəs-\ n : INFERIOR CONSTRICTOR

constrictor pharyngis me·di·us \-ˈmē-dē-əs\ n : MIDDLE CONSTRICTOR

constrictor pharyngis superior n : SUPERIOR CONSTRICTOR

con·struct \ˈkän-ˌstrəkt\ n : something constructed esp. by mental synthesis 〈form a ∼ of a physical object〉

con·sult \kən-ˈsəlt\ vb : to ask the advice or opinion of 〈∼ a doctor〉

con·sul·tant \kən-ˈsəlt-ᵊnt\ n : a physician asked by esp. a specialist called in for professional advice or services usu. at the request of another physician — called also *consulting physician*

con·sul·ta·tion \ˌkän-səl-ˈtā-shən\ n : a deliberation between physicians on a case or its treatment — **con·sul·ta·tive** \kən-ˈsəl-tə-tiv, ˈkän-səl-ˌtā-tiv\ adj

con·sum·ma·to·ry \kən-ˈsə-mə-ˌtōr-ē\ adj : of, relating to, or being a response or act (as eating or copulating) that terminates a period of usu. goal-directed behavior

con·sump·tion \kən-ˈsəmp-shən\ n 1 : a progressive wasting away of the body esp. from pulmonary tuberculosis 2 : TUBERCULOSIS

¹con·sump·tive \-ˈsəmp-tiv\ adj : of, relating to, or affected with consumption 〈a ∼ cough〉

²consumptive n : a person affected with consumption

¹con·tact \ˈkän-ˌtakt\ n 1 : union or junction of body surfaces 〈sexual ∼〉 2 : direct experience through the senses 3 : CONTACT LENS

²contact adj : caused or transmitted by direct or indirect contact (as with an allergen or a contagious disease)

contact lens n : a thin lens designed to fit over the cornea and usu. worn to correct defects in vision

con·ta·gion \kən-ˈtā-jən\ n 1 : the transmission of a disease by direct or indirect contact 2 : CONTAGIOUS DISEASE 3 : a disease-producing agent (as a virus)

contagiosa — see IMPETIGO CONTAGIOSA, MOLLUSCUM CONTAGIOSUM

contagiosum — see MOLLUSCUM CONTAGIOSUM

con·ta·gious \-jəs\ adj 1 : communicable by contact — compare INFECTIOUS 2 2 : bearing contagion 3 : used for contagious diseases 〈a ∼ ward〉 — **con·ta·gious·ly** adv — **con·ta·gious·ness** n

contagious abortion n 1 : brucellosis in domestic animals characterized by abortion; *esp* : a disease affecting esp. cattle that is caused by a brucella (*Brucella abortus*), that is contracted by ingestion, by copulation, or possibly by wound infection, and that is characterized by proliferation of the causative organism in the fetal membranes inducing abortion 2 : any of several contagious or infectious diseases of domestic animals marked by abortion (as vibrionic abortion of sheep) — called also *infectious abortion*

contagious disease n : an infectious disease communicable by contact with one suffering from it, with a bodily discharge of such a patient, or with an object touched by such a patient or by bodily discharges — compare COMMUNICABLE DISEASE

con·ta·gium \kən-ˈtā-jəm, -jē-əm\ n, pl -gia \-jə, -jē-ə\ : a virus or living organism capable of causing a communicable disease

con·tam·i·nant \kən-ˈta-mə-nənt\ n : something that contaminates

con·tam·i·nate \kən-ˈta-mə-ˌnāt\ vb -nat·ed; -nat·ing 1 : to soil, stain, or infect by contact or association 〈bacteria *contaminated* the wound〉 2 : to make inferior or impure by admixture 〈air *contaminated* by sulfur dioxide〉 — **con·tam·i·na·tion** \kən-ˌta-mə-ˈnā-shən\ n

con·tent \ˈkän-ˌtent\ n : the subject matter or symbolic significance of something — see LATENT CONTENT, MANIFEST CONTENT

con·ti·nence \ˈkänt-ᵊn-əns\ n 1 : self-restraint in refraining from sexual intercourse 2 : the ability to retain a bodily discharge voluntarily 〈fecal ∼〉 — **con·ti·nent** \-ənt\ adj — **con·ti·nent·ly** adv

continuous positive airway pressure n : a technique of assisting breathing by maintaining the air pressure in the lungs and air passages constant and above atmospheric pressure throughout the breathing cycle — abbr. *CPAP*

con·tra·cep·tion \ˌkän-trə-ˈsep-shən\ n : deliberate prevention of conception or impregnation — **con·tra·cep·tive** \-ˈsep-tiv\ adj or n

con·tract \kən-ˈtrakt, ˈkän-ˌtrakt\ vb 1 : to become affected with 〈∼ pneumonia〉 2 : to draw together so as to become diminished in size; *also* : to shorten and broaden (muscle ~s in tetanus)

con·trac·tile \kən-'trakt-əl, -'trak-,tīl\ *adj* : having or concerned with the power or property of contracting

con·trac·til·i·ty \,kän-,trak-'til-ə-tē\ *n, pl* **-ties** : the capability or quality of shrinking or contracting : *esp* : the power of muscle fibers of shortening into a more compact form

con·trac·tion \kən-'trak-shən\ *n* **1** : the action or process of contracting : the state of being contracted **2** : the shortening and thickening of a functioning muscle or muscle fiber

con·trac·tor \'kän-,trak-tər, kən-'\ *n* : something (as a muscle) that contracts or shortens

con·trac·ture \kən-'trak-chər\ *n* : a permanent shortening (as of muscle or scar tissue) producing deformity or distortion — see DUPUYTREN'S CONTRACTURE

con·tra·in·di·ca·tion \,kän-trə-,in-də-'kā-shən\ *n* : something (as a symptom or condition) that makes a particular treatment or procedure inadvisable — **con·tra·in·di·cate** \-'in-də-,kāt\ *vb*

con·tra·lat·er·al \-'la-tə-rəl, -'la-trəl\ *adj* : occurring on or acting in conjunction with a part on the opposite side of the body — compare IPSILATERAL

contrast bath *n* : a therapeutic immersion of a part of the body (as an extremity) alternately in hot and cold water

contrast medium *n* : a material comparatively opaque to X rays that is injected into a hollow organ to provide contrast with the surrounding tissue and make possible radiographic and fluoroscopic examination

con·tre·coup \'kōn-trə-,kü, 'kän-\ *n* : injury occurring on one side of an organ (as the brain) when it recoils against a hard surface (as of the skull) following a blow on the opposite side

¹con·trol \kən-'trōl\ *vb* **con·trolled; con·trol·ling 1 a** : to check, test, or verify by evidence or experiments **b** : to incorporate suitable controls in (a *controlled* experiment) **2** : to reduce the incidence or severity of esp. to innocuous levels (~ outbreaks of cholera)

²control *n* **1** : an act or instance of controlling something (~ of acute intermittent porphyria) **2** : one that is used in controlling something: as **a** : an experiment in which the subjects are treated as in a parallel experiment except for omission of the procedure or agent under test and which is used as a standard of comparison in judging experimental effects — called also *control experiment* **b** : one (as an organism) that is part of a control

con·trolled \kən-'trōld\ *adj* : regulated by law with regard to possession and use (~ drugs)

controlled hypotension *n* : low blood pressure induced and maintained to reduce blood loss or to provide a bloodless field during surgery

con·tu·sion \kən-'tü-zhən, -'tyü-\ *n* : injury to tissue usu. without laceration : BRUISE 1 — **con·tuse** \-'tüz, -tyüz\ *vb*

co·nus \'kō-nəs\ *n, pl* **co·ni** \-,nī, -(,)nē\ : CONUS ARTERIOSUS

co·nus ar·te·ri·o·sus \'kō-nəs-är-,tir-ē-'ō-səs\ *n, pl* **co·ni ar·te·ri·o·si** \-,nī-är-,tir-ē-'ō-,sī, -(,)nē-\ : a conical prolongation of the right ventricle from which the pulmonary arteries emerge — called also *conus*

conus med·ul·lar·is \-,med-əl-'er-əs, -,me-jə-'ler-\ *n* : a tapering lower part of the spinal cord at the level of the first lumbar segment

con·va·les·cence \,kän-və-'les-³ns\ *n* **1** : gradual recovery of health and strength after disease **2** : the time between the subsidence of a disease and complete restoration to health — **con·va·lesce** \,kän-və-'les\ *vb*

¹con·va·les·cent \,kän-və-'les-³nt\ *adj* **1** : recovering from sickness or debility : partially restored to health or strength **2** : of, for, or relating to convalescence or convalescents (a ~ ward)

²convalescent *n* : one recovering from sickness

convalescent home *n* : an institution for the care of convalescing patients

con·ver·gence \kən-'vər-jəns\ *n* **1** : movement of the two eyes so coordinated that the images of a single point fall on corresponding points of the two retinas **2** : overlapping synaptic innervation of a single cell by more than one nerve fiber — compare DIVERGENCE 2 — **con·verge** \-'vərj\ *vb* — **con·ver·gent** \-'vər-jənt\ *adj*

con·ver·sion \kən-'vər-zhən, -shən\ *n* : the transformation of an unconscious mental conflict into a symbolically equivalent bodily symptom

conversion reaction *n* : a psychoneurosis in which bodily symptoms (as paralysis of the limbs) appear without physical basis — called also *conversion hysteria*

con·vo·lut·ed \'kän-və-,lü-təd\ *adj* : folded in curved or tortuous windings; *specif* : having convolutions

convoluted tubule *n* **1** : PROXIMAL CONVOLUTED TUBULE **2** : DISTAL CONVOLUTED TUBULE

con·vo·lu·tion \,kän-və-'lü-shən\ *n* : any of the irregular ridges on the surface of the brain and esp. of the cerebrum — called also *gyrus*; compare SULCUS

convolution of Broca *n* : BROCA'S AREA

¹con·vul·sant \kən-'vəl-sənt\ *adj* : causing convulsions : CONVULSIVE

²convulsant *n* : an agent and esp. a drug that produces convulsions

con·vulse \kən-'vəls\ *vb* **con·vulsed; con·vuls·ing 1** : to shake or agitate violently: *esp* : to shake or cause to shake with or as if with irregular spasms **2** : to become affected with convulsions

con·vul·sion \kən-ʹvəl-shən\ *n* : an abnormal violent and involuntary contraction or series of contractions of the muscles — often used in pl. (a patient suffering from ∼*s*) — **con·vul·sive** \-siv\ *adj* — **con·vul·sive·ly** *adv*

convulsive therapy *n* : SHOCK THERAPY

Coo·ley's anemia \ʹkü-lēz-\ *n* : a severe thalassemic anemia that is associated with the presence of microcytes, enlargement of the liver and spleen, increase in the erythroid bone marrow, and jaundice and that occurs esp. in children of Mediterranean parents — called also *thalassemia major*

   Coo·ley \ʹkü-lē\, **Thomas Benton (1871–1945),** American pediatrician.

Coo·mas·sie blue \kü-ʹma-sē-, -ʹmä-\ *n* : a bright blue acid dye used as a biological stain esp. for proteins in gel electrophoresis

Coombs test \ʹkümz-\ *n* : an agglutination test used to detect proteins and esp. antibodies on the surface of red blood cells

   Coombs, Robert Royston Amos (*b* 1921), British immunologist.

Coo·pe·ria \kü-ʹpir-ē-ə\ *n* : a genus of small reddish brown nematode worms (family Trichostrongylidae) including several species infesting the small intestine of sheep, goats, and cattle

   Curtice, Cooper (1856–1939), American veterinarian.

coordinate bond *n* : a covalent bond that consists of a pair of electrons supplied by only one of the two atoms it joins

co·or·di·na·tion \(ˌ)kō-ˌȯrd-ᵊn-ʹā-shən\ *n* **1** : the act or action of bringing into a common action, movement, or condition **2** : the harmonious functioning of parts (as muscle and nerves) for most effective results — **co·or·di·nate** \kō-ʹȯrd-ᵊn-ˌāt\ *vb* — **co·or·di·nat·ed** \-ˌā-təd\ *adj*

coo·tie \ʹkü-tē\ *n* : BODY LOUSE

co·pay·ment \(ˌ)kō-ʹpā-mənt\ *n* : a relatively small fixed fee required by a health insurer (as an HMO) to be paid by the patient at the time of each office visit, outpatient service, or filling of a prescription

COPD *abbr* chronic obstructive pulmonary disease

cope \ʹkōp\ *vb* **coped; cop·ing** : to deal with and attempt to overcome problems and difficulties — usu. used with *with* (teachers *coping* with violence in schools)

COPE *abbr* chronic obstructive pulmonary emphysema

cop·per \ʹkä-pər\ *n, often attrib* : a common reddish metallic element that is ductile and malleable — symbol *Cu*; see ELEMENT table

cop·per·head \ʹkä-pər-ˌhed\ *n* : a pit viper (*Agkistrodon contortrix*) widely distributed in upland areas of the eastern U.S. that attains a length of three feet or 0.9 meter, is coppery brown above with dark transverse blotches that render it inconspicuous among fallen leaves, and is usu. regarded as much less dangerous than a rattlesnake of comparable size

copper sulfate *n* : a sulfate of copper: *esp* : the sulfate of copper that is most familiar in its blue hydrous crystalline form $CuSO_4 \cdot 5H_2O$, is used as an algicide and fungicide, and has been used medicinally in solution as an emetic but is not now recommended for such use because of its potential toxicity

copr- *or* **copro-** *comb form* **1** : dung : feces (*copro*phagy) **2** : obscenity (*copro*lalia)

cop·ro·an·ti·body \ˌkä-prō-ʹan-ti-ˌbä-dē\ *n, pl* **-bod·ies** : an antibody whose presence in the intestinal tract can be demonstrated by examination of an extract of the feces

cop·ro·la·lia \ˌkä-prə-ʹlā-lē-ə\ *n* **1** : obsessive or uncontrollable use of obscene language **2** : the use of obscene (as scatological) language as sexual gratification — **cop·ro·la·lic** \-ʹla-lik\ *adj*

cop·ro·pha·gia \ˌkä-prə-ʹfā-jə, -jē-ə\ *n* : COPROPHAGY

co·proph·a·gy \kə-ʹprä-fə-jē\ *n, pl* **-gies** : the eating of excrement that is normal behavior among many esp. young animals but in humans is a symptom of some forms of insanity — **co·proph·a·gous** \-gəs\ *adj*

cop·ro·phil·ia \ˌkä-prə-ʹfi-lē-ə\ *n* : marked interest in excrement; *esp* : the use of feces or filth for sexual excitement — **cop·ro·phil·i·ac** \-ˌak\ *n*

cop·ro·por·phy·rin \ˌkä-prə-ʹpȯr-fə-rən\ *n* : any of four isomeric porphyrins $C_{36}H_{38}N_4O_8$ of which types I and III are found in feces and urine esp. in certain pathological conditions

cop·u·late \ʹkä-pyə-ˌlāt\ *vb* **-lat·ed; -lat·ing** : to engage in sexual intercourse — **cop·u·la·tion** \ˌkä-pyə-ʹlā-shən\ *n* — **cop·u·la·to·ry** \ʹkä-pyə-lə-ˌtōr-ē\ *adj*

coraco- *comb form* : coracoid and (*coraco*humeral)

cor·a·co·acro·mi·al \ˌkȯr-ə-(ˌ)kō-ə-ʹkrō-mē-əl\ *adj* : relating to or connecting the acromion and the coracoid process

cor·a·co·bra·chi·a·lis \ˌkȯr-ə-(ˌ)kō-ˌbrā-kē-ʹā-ləs\ *n, pl* **-a·les** \-ˌlēz\ : a muscle extending between the coracoid process and the middle of the medial surface of the humerus — called also *coracobrachialis muscle*

cor·a·co·cla·vic·u·lar ligament \-klə-ˌvi-kyə-lər-, -klä-\ *n* : a ligament that joins the clavicle and the coracoid process of the scapula

cor·a·co·hu·mer·al \-ʹhyü-mə-rəl\ *adj*

: relating to or connecting the coracoid process and the humerus

¹cor·a·coid \ˈkȯr-ə-ˌkȯid, ˈkär-\ *adj* : of, relating to, or being a process of the scapula in most mammals or a well-developed cartilage bone of many lower vertebrates that extends from the scapula to or toward the sternum

²coracoid *n* : a coracoid bone or process

coracoid process *n* : a process of the scapula in most mammals representing the remnant of the coracoid bone of lower vertebrates that has become fused with the scapula and in humans is situated on its superior border and serves for the attachment of various muscles

coral snake \ˈkȯr-əl-, ˈkär-\ *n* : any of several venomous chiefly tropical New World elapid snakes of the genus *Micrurus* that are brilliantly banded in red, black, and yellow or white and include two (*M. fulvius* and *M. euryxanthus*) ranging northward into the southern U.S.

cor bo·vi·num \ˈkȯr-bō-ˈvī-nəm\ *n* : a greatly enlarged heart

cord \ˈkȯrd\ *n* : a slender flexible anatomical structure (as a nerve) — see SPERMATIC CORD, SPINAL CORD, UMBILICAL CORD, VOCAL CORD 1

cord blood *n* : blood from the umbilical cord of a fetus or newborn

cor·dec·to·my \kȯr-ˈdek-tə-mē\ *n, pl* **-mies** : surgical removal of one or more vocal cords

cordia pulmonalia *pl of* COR PULMONALE

cordis — see ACCRETIO CORDIS, VENAE CORDIS MINIMAE

cor·dot·o·my \kȯr-ˈdä-tə-mē\ *n, pl* **-mies** : surgical division of a tract of the spinal cord for relief of severe intractable pain

core \ˈkȯr\ *n* : the central part of a body, mass, or part

co·re·pres·sor \kō-ri-ˈpres-ər\ *n* : a substance that activates or inactivates a particular genetic repressor by combining with it

core temperature *n* : the temperature deep within a living body (as in the viscera)

Co·ri cycle \ˈkȯr-ē-\ *n* : the cycle in carbohydrate metabolism consisting of the conversion of glycogen to lactic acid in muscle, diffusion of the lactic acid into the bloodstream which carries it to the liver where it is converted into glycogen, and the breakdown of liver glycogen to glucose which is transported to muscle by the bloodstream and reconverted into glycogen

Cori, Carl Ferdinand (1896–1984) **and Gerty Theresa** (1896–1957), American biochemists.

co·ri·um \ˈkȯr-ē-əm\ *n, pl* **co·ria** \-ē-ə\ : DERMIS

corn \ˈkȯrn\ *n* : a local hardening and thickening of epidermis (as on a toe)

corne- *or* **corneo-** *comb form* : cornea : corneal and ⟨*corneo*scleral⟩

cor·nea \ˈkȯr-nē-ə\ *n* : the transparent part of the coat of the eyeball that covers the iris and pupil and admits light to the interior — **cor·ne·al** \-əl\ *adj*

cor·neo·scler·al \ˌkȯr-nē-ə-ˈskler-əl\ *adj* : of, relating to, or affecting both the cornea and the sclera (the ~ junction)

cor·ner \ˈkȯ(r)-nər\ *n* : CORNER TOOTH

corner tooth *n* : one of the third or outer pair of incisor teeth of each jaw of a horse — compare DIVIDER, NIPPER

cor·ne·um \ˈkȯr-nē-əm\ *n, pl* **cornea** \-nē-ə\ : STRATUM CORNEUM

cor·nic·u·late cartilage \kȯr-ˈni-kyə-lət-\ *n* : either of two small nodules of yellow elastic cartilage articulating with the apex of the arytenoid

cor·ni·fi·ca·tion \ˌkȯr-nə-fə-ˈkā-shən\ *n* 1 : conversion into horn or a horny substance or tissue 2 : the conversion of the vaginal epithelium from the columnar to the squamous type — **cor·ni·fy** \ˈkȯr-nə-fī\ *vb*

corn oil *n* : a yellow fatty oil obtained from the germ of Indian corn kernels that is used in medicine as a solvent and as a vehicle for injections

cor·nu \ˈkȯr-(ˌ)nü, -(ˌ)nyü\ *n, pl* **cornua** \-nü-ə, -nyü-\ : a horn-shaped anatomical structure (as either of the lateral divisions of a bicornuate uterus or one of the lateral processes of the hyoid bone) — **cor·nu·al** \-nü-əl, -nyü-\ *adj*

co·ro·na \kə-ˈrō-nə\ *n* : the upper portion of a bodily part

co·ro·nal \ˈkȯr-ən-əl, ˈkär-; kə-ˈrōn-\ *adj* 1 : of, relating to, or being a corona 2 : lying in the direction of the coronal suture 3 : of or relating to the frontal plane that passes through the long axis of the body

coronal suture *n* : a suture extending across the skull between the parietal and frontal bones — called also *frontoparietal suture*

co·ro·na ra·di·a·ta \kə-ˈrō-nə-ˌrā-dē-ˈä-tə, -ˈä-\ *n, pl* **co·ro·nae ra·di·a·tae** \-(ˌ)nē-ˌrā-dē-ˈā-(ˌ)tē, -ˈä-\ 1 : the zone of small follicular cells immediately surrounding the ovum in the graafian follicle and accompanying the ovum on its discharge from the follicle 2 : a large mass of myelinated nerve fibers radiating from the internal capsule to the cerebral cortex

¹cor·o·nary \ˈkȯr-ə-ˌner-ē, ˈkär-\ *adj* 1 : of, relating to, affecting, or being the coronary arteries or veins of the heart (~ bypass) (~ sclerosis); *broadly* : of or relating to the heart 2 : of, relating to, or affected with coronary heart disease (~ care unit)

²coronary *n, pl* **-nar·ies** 1 a : CORONARY ARTERY b : CORONARY VEIN 2 : CORONARY THROMBOSIS; *broadly* : HEART ATTACK

coronary artery *n* : either of two arteries that arise one from the left and one from the right side of the aorta immediately above the semilunar valves and supply the tissues of the heart itself

coronary band *n* : a thickened band of extremely vascular tissue that lies at the upper border of the wall of the hoof of the horse and related animals and that plays an important part in the secretion of the horny walls — called also *coronary cushion*

coronary failure *n* : heart failure in which the heart muscle is deprived of the blood necessary to meet its functional needs as a result of narrowing or blocking of one or more of the coronary arteries — compare CONGESTIVE HEART FAILURE

coronary heart disease *n* : a condition (as sclerosis or thrombosis) that reduces the blood flow through the coronary arteries to the heart muscle — called also *coronary artery disease, coronary disease*

coronary insufficiency *n* : cardiac insufficiency of relatively mild degree — compare ANGINA PECTORIS, HEART FAILURE 1, MYOCARDIAL INFARCTION

coronary ligament *n* 1 : the folds of peritoneum connecting the posterior surface of the liver and the diaphragm 2 : a part of the articular capsule of the knee connecting each semilunar cartilage with the margin of the head of the tibia

coronary occlusion *n* : the partial or complete blocking (as by a thrombus or by sclerosis) of a coronary artery

coronary plexus *n* : one of two nerve plexuses that are extensions of the cardiac plexus along the coronary arteries

coronary sinus *n* : a venous channel that is derived from the sinus venosus, is continuous with the largest of the cardiac veins, receives most of the blood from the walls of the heart, and empties into the right atrium

coronary thrombosis *n* : the blocking of a coronary artery of the heart by a thrombus

coronary vein *n* 1 a : any of several veins that drain the tissues of the heart and empty into the coronary sinus b : CARDIAC VEIN — not used technically 2 : a vein draining the lesser curvature of the stomach and emptying into the portal vein

co·ro·na·vi·rus \kə-ˈrō-nə-ˌvī-rəs\ *n* : any of a group of viruses that resemble myxoviruses and include some causing respiratory symptoms in humans

cor·o·ner \ˈkȯr-ə-nər, ˈkär-\ *n* : a public officer whose principal duty is to inquire by an inquest into the cause of any death which there is reason to suppose is not due to natural causes

cor·o·net \ˌkȯr-ə-ˈnet, ˌkär-\ *n* : the lower part of a horse's pastern where the horn terminates in skin

cor·o·noid·ec·to·my \ˌkȯr-ə-ˌnȯi-ˈdek-tə-mē\ *n, pl* **-mies** : surgical removal of the mandibular coronoid process

coronoid fossa *n* : a depression of the humerus into which the coronoid process fits when the arm is flexed — compare OLECRANON FOSSA

coronoid process *n* 1 : the anterior process of the superior border of the ramus of the mandible 2 : a flared process of the lower anterior part of the upper articular surface of the ulna fitting into the coronoid fossa when the arm is flexed

corpora *pl of* CORPUS

cor·po·ral \ˈkȯr-pə-rəl, -prəl\ *adj* : of, relating to, or affecting the body (~ punishment)

cor·po·ra quad·ri·gem·i·na \ˌkȯr-pə-rə-ˌkwä-drə-ˈje-mə-nə, ˌkȯr-prə-\ *n pl* : two pairs of colliculi on the dorsal surface of the midbrain composed of white matter externally and gray matter within, the superior pair containing correlation centers for optic reflexes and the inferior pair containing correlation centers for auditory reflexes

cor·po·re·al \kȯr-ˈpȯr-ē-əl\ *adj* : having, consisting of, or relating to a physical material body

corporis — see PEDICULOSIS CORPORIS, TINEA CORPORIS

corpse \ˈkȯrps\ *n* : a dead body esp. of a human being

corps·man \ˈkȯr-mən, ˈkȯrz-\ *n, pl* **corps·men** \-mən\ : an enlisted man trained to give first aid and minor medical treatment

cor pul·mo·na·le \ˌkȯr-ˌpu̇l-mə-ˈnä-lē, -ˌpəl-, -ˈna-\ *n, pl* **cor·dia pul·mo·na·lia** \ˈkȯr-dē-ə-ˌpu̇l-mə-ˈnä-lē-ə, -ˌpəl-, -ˈna-\ : disease of the heart characterized by hypertrophy and dilatation of the right ventricle and secondary to disease of the lungs or their blood vessels

cor·pus \ˈkȯr-pəs\ *n, pl* **cor·po·ra** \-pə-rə, -prə\ 1 : the human or animal body esp. when dead 2 : the main part or body of a bodily structure or organ

corpus al·bi·cans \-ˈal-bə-ˌkanz\ *n, pl* **corpora al·bi·can·tia** \-ˌal-bə-ˈkan-chē-ə\ 1 : MAMMILLARY BODY 2 : the white fibrous scar that remains in the ovary after resorption of the corpus luteum and replaces a discharged graafian follicle

corpus cal·lo·sum \-ka-ˈlō-səm\ *n, pl* **corpora cal·lo·sa** \-sə\ : the great band of commissural fibers uniting the cerebral hemispheres

corpus ca·ver·no·sum \-ˌka-vər-ˈnō-səm\ *n, pl* **corpora ca·ver·no·sa** \-sə\ : a mass of erectile tissue with large interspaces capable of being distended with blood; *esp* : one of those that form the bulk of the body of the penis or of the clitoris

cor·pus·cle \'kȯr-(ˌ)pə-səl\ n 1 : a living cell; esp : one (as a red or white blood cell or a cell in cartilage or bone) not aggregated into continuous tissues 2 : any of various small circumscribed multicellular bodies — usu. used with a qualifying term (Malpighian ~s) — **cor·pus·cu·lar** \kȯr-'pəs-kyə-lər\ adj

corpuscle of Krause n : KRAUSE'S CORPUSCLE

corpus hem·or·rhag·i·cum \-ˌhe-mə-'ra-ji-kəm\ n : a ruptured graafian follicle containing a blood clot that is absorbed as the cells lining the follicle form the corpus luteum

corpus lu·te·um \-'lü-tē-əm, -lü-'tē-əm\ n, pl **corpora lu·tea** \-ə\ : a yellowish mass of progesterone-secreting endocrine tissue that consists of pale secretory cells derived from granulosa cells, that forms immediately after ovulation from the ruptured graafian follicle in the mammalian ovary, and that regresses rather quickly if the ovum is not fertilized but persists throughout the ensuing pregnancy if it is fertilized

corpus spon·gi·o·sum \-ˌspən-jē-'ō-səm, -ˌspän-\ n : the median longitudinal column of erectile tissue of the penis that contains the urethra and is ventral to the two corpora cavernosa

corpus stri·a·tum \-ˌstrī-'ā-təm\ n, pl **corpora stri·a·ta** \-'ā-tə\ : either of a pair of masses of nerve tissue which lie beneath and external to the anterior cornua of the lateral ventricles of the brain and form part of their floor and each of which contains a caudate nucleus and a lentiform nucleus separated by sheets of white matter to give the mass a striated appearance in section

corpus uteri \-'yü-tə-ˌrī\ n : the main body of the uterus above the constriction behind the cervix and below the openings of the fallopian tubes

¹cor·rec·tive \kə-'rek-tiv\ adj : intended to correct (~ lenses) (~ surgery) — **cor·rec·tive·ly** adv

²corrective n : a medication that removes undesirable or unpleasant side effects of other medication

corresponding points n pl : points on the retinas of the two eyes which when simultaneously stimulated normally produce a single visual impression

Cor·ri·gan's disease \'kȯr-i-gənz-\ n : AORTIC REGURGITATION

Cor·ri·gan \'kȯr-i-gən\, **Sir Dominic John** (1802–1880), British pathologist.

Corrigan's pulse or **Corrigan pulse** n : a pulse characterized by a sharp rise to full expansion followed by immediate collapse that is seen in aortic insufficiency — called also water-hammer pulse

cor·rode \kə-'rōd\ vb **cor·rod·ed; cor·rod·ing** : to eat or be eaten away gradually (as by chemcial action) — **cor·ro·sion** \kə-'rō-zhən\ n

¹cor·ro·sive \-'rō-siv, -ziv\ adj : tending or having the power to corrode (~ acids) — **cor·ro·sive·ness** n

²corrosive n : a substance that corrodes : CAUSTIC

corrosive sublimate n : MERCURIC CHLORIDE

cor·ru·ga·tor \'kȯr-ə-ˌgā-tər\ n : a muscle that contracts the skin into wrinkles; esp : one that draws the eyebrows together and wrinkles the brow in frowning

cor·tex \'kȯr-ˌteks\ n, pl **cor·ti·ces** \'kȯr-tə-ˌsēz\ or **cor·tex·es** : the outer or superficial part of an organ or body structure (as the kidney, adrenal gland, or a hair); esp : the outer layer of gray matter of the cerebrum and cerebellum

cor·ti·cal \'kȯr-ti-kəl\ adj 1 : of, relating to, or consisting of cortex (~ tissue) 2 : involving or resulting from the action or operation of the cerebral cortex — **cor·ti·cal·ly** adv

cortico- comb form 1 : cortex (cortico-tropin) 2 : cortical and (corticospinal)

cor·ti·co·ad·re·nal \ˌkȯr-ti-kō-ə-'drēn-əl\ adj : of or relating to the cortex of the adrenal gland (~ hormones) (~ insufficiency)

cor·ti·co·bul·bar \-'bəl-bər, -ˌbär\ adj : relating to or connecting the cerebral cortex and the medulla oblongata

cor·ti·coid \'kȯr-ti-ˌkȯid\ n : CORTICOSTEROID — **corticoid** adj

cor·ti·co·pon·tine \ˌkȯr-ti-kō-'pän-ˌtīn\ adj : relating to or connecting the cerebral cortex and the pons

cor·ti·co·pon·to·cer·e·bel·lar \-ˌpän-tō-ˌser-ə-'be-lər\ adj : of, relating to, or being a tract of nerve fibers or a path for nervous impulses that passes from the cerebral cortex through the internal capsule to the pons to the white matter and cortex of the cerebellum

cor·ti·co·spi·nal \-'spīn-əl\ adj : of or relating to the cerebral cortex and spinal cord or to the corticospinal tract

corticospinal tract n : any of four columns of motor fibers of which two run on each side of the spinal cord and which are continuations of the pyramids of the medulla oblongata: a : LATERAL CORTICOSPINAL TRACT b : VENTRAL CORTICOSPINAL TRACT

cor·ti·co·ste·roid \ˌkȯr-ti-kō-'stir-ˌȯid, -'ster-\ n : any of various adrenal-cortex steroids (as corticosterone, cortisone, and aldosterone) used medically esp. as anti-inflammatory agents

cor·ti·co·ste·rone \ˌkȯr-tə-'käs-tə-ˌrōn, -kō-stə-ˈ; ˌkȯr-ti-kō-ˈstir-ˌōn, -ˈster-\ n : a colorless crystalline corticosteroid $C_{21}H_{30}O_4$ of the adrenal cortex that is important in protein and carbohydrate metabolism

cor·ti·co·tro·pic \ˌkȯr-ti-kō-ˈtrō-pik\ *also* **cor·ti·co·tro·phic** \-fik\ *adj* : influencing or stimulating the adrenal cortex

cor·ti·co·tro·pin \-ˈtrō-pən\ *also* **cor·ti·co·tro·phin** \-fən\ *n* : ACTH; *also* : a preparation of ACTH that is used esp. in the treatment of rheumatoid arthritis and rheumatic fever

corticotropin–releasing factor *or* **corticotrophin–releasing factor** *n* : a substance secreted by the median eminence of the hypothalamus that regulates the release of ACTH by the anterior lobe of the pituitary gland

cor·tin \ˈkȯrt-ᵊn\ *n* : the active principle of the adrenal cortex now known to consist of several hormones

cor·ti·sol \ˈkȯrt-ə-ˌsȯl, -ˌzȯl, -ˌsōl, -ˌzōl\ *n* : HYDROCORTISONE

cor·ti·sone \-ˌsōn, -ˌzōn\ *n* : a glucocorticoid $C_{21}H_{28}O_5$ of the adrenal cortex used esp. in the treatment of rheumatoid arthritis — compare *11*-DEHYDROCORTICOSTERONE

cor·y·ne·bac·te·ri·um \kȯr-ə-(ˌ)nē-bak-ˈtir-ē-əm\ *n* **1** *cap* : a large genus (family Corynebacteriaceae) of usu. gram-positive nonmotile bacteria that occur as irregular or branching rods and include a number of important parasites — see DIPHTHERIA *2 pl* **-ria** \-ē-ə\ : any bacterium of the genus *Corynebacterium*

co·ry·ne·form \kə-ˈri-nə-ˌfȯrm\ *adj* : being or resembling bacteria of the genus *Corynebacterium*

co·ry·za \kə-ˈrī-zə\ *n* : an acute inflammatory contagious disease involving the upper respiratory tract: **a** : COMMON COLD **b** : any of several diseases of domestic animals characterized by inflammation of and discharge from the mucous membranes of the upper respiratory tract, sinuses, and eyes; *esp* : INFECTIOUS CORYZA — **co·ry·zal** \-zəl\ *adj*

¹cos·met·ic \käz-ˈme-tik\ *n* : a cosmetic preparation for external use

²cosmetic *adj* **1** : of, relating to, or making for beauty esp. of the complexion (~ salves) **2** : correcting defects esp. of the face (~ surgery) — **cos·met·i·cal·ly** *adv*

cos·mid \ˈkäz-məd\ *n* : a plasmid whose original genome has been altered so that a large segment of DNA can be inserted for cloning purposes

cost- *or* **costi-** *or* **costo-** *comb form* : rib (costal and (costochondral)

cos·ta \ˈkäs-tə\ *n, pl* **cos·tae** \-(ˌ)tē, -ˌtī\ : RIB

cos·tal \ˈkäst-ᵊl\ *adj* : of, relating to, involving, or situated near a rib

costal breathing *n* : inspiration and expiration produced chiefly by movements of the ribs

costal cartilage *n* : any of the cartilages that connect the distal ends of the ribs with the sternum and by their elastic-ity permit movement of the chest in respiration

costarum — see LEVATORES COSTARUM

cos·tive \ˈkäs-tiv, ˈkȯs-\ *adj* **1** : affected with constipation **2** : causing constipation — **cos·tive·ness** *n*

cos·to·cer·vi·cal trunk \ˌkäs-tə-ˈsər-və-kəl-, -tō-\ *n* : a branch of the subclavian artery that divides to supply the first or first two intercostal spaces and the deep structures of the neck — see INTERCOSTAL ARTERY b

cos·to·chon·dral \-ˈkän-drəl\ *adj* : relating to or joining a rib and costal cartilage (a ~ junction)

cos·to·chon·dri·tis \-kän-ˈdrī-təs\ *n* : TIETZE'S SYNDROME

cos·to·di·a·phrag·mat·ic \ˌkäs-tə-ˌdī-ə-frə-ˈma-tik, ˌkäs-tō-, -frag-, -ˈfrag-\ *adj* : relating to or involving the ribs and diaphragm

cos·to·phren·ic \ˌkäs-tə-ˈfre-nik, -tō-\ *adj* : of or relating to the ribs and the diaphragm

cos·to·trans·verse \ˌkäs-tə-trans-ˈvərs, -tō-, -tranz-, -ˈtrans-, -ˈtranz-\ *adj* : relating to or connecting a rib and the transverse process of a vertebra (a ~ joint)

cos·to·trans·ver·sec·to·my \-ˌtrans-(ˌ)vər-ˈsek-tə-mē, -ˌtranz-\ *n, pl* **-mies** : surgical excision of part of a rib and the transverse process of the adjoining vertebra

cos·to·ver·te·bral \-(ˌ)vər-ˈtē-brəl, -ˈvər-tə-\ *adj* : of or relating to a rib and its adjoining vertebra (~ pain)

¹cot \ˈkät\ *n* : a protective cover for a finger — called also *fingerstall*

²cot *n* : a wheeled stretcher for hospital, mortuary, or ambulance service

COTA *abbr* certified occupational therapy assistant

cot death *n, chiefly Brit* : SUDDEN INFANT DEATH SYNDROME

co·throm·bo·plas·tin \(ˌ)kō-ˌthräm-bō-ˈplas-tən\ *n* : FACTOR VII

co·tri·mox·a·zole \ˌkō-ˌtrī-ˈmäk-sə-ˌzōl\ *n* : a bactericidal combination of trimethoprim and sulfamethoxazole in the ratio of one to five used esp. for chronic urinary tract infections

cot·ton·mouth \ˈkät-ᵊn-ˌmauth\ *n* : WATER MOCCASIN

cottonmouth moccasin *n* : WATER MOCCASIN

cotton–wool *n, Brit* : ABSORBENT COTTON

cot·y·le·don \ˌkät-ᵊl-ˈēd-ᵊn\ *n* : a lobule of a mammalian placenta — **cot·y·le·don·ary** \-ˈēd-ᵊn-ˌer-ē\ *adj*

¹couch \ˈkauch\ *vb* : to treat (a cataract or a person having a cataract) by displacing the lens of the eye into the vitreous humor

²couch *n* : an article of furniture used (as by a patient undergoing psychoanalysis) for sitting or reclining — **on the couch** : receiving psychiatric treatment

¹cough \ˈkȯf\ *vb* **1** : to expel air from the

lungs suddenly with an explosive noise usu. in a series of efforts **2** : to expel by coughing — often used with *up* ⟨~ up mucus⟩

²**cough** *n* **1** : an ailment manifesting itself by frequent coughing ⟨he has a bad ~⟩ **2** : an explosive expulsion of air from the lungs acting as a protective mechanism to clear the air passages or as a symptom of pulmonary disturbance

cough drop *n* : a lozenge used to relieve coughing

cough syrup *n* : any of various sweet usu. medicated liquids used to relieve coughing

cou·lomb \'kü-₁läm, -₁lōm, kü-'\ *n* : the practical mks unit of electric charge equal to the quantity of electricity transferred by a current of one ampere in one second

Coulomb, Charles–Augustin de (1736–1806), French physicist.

Cou·ma·din \'kü-mə-dən\ *trademark* — used for a preparation of warfarin

cou·ma·phos \'kü-mə-₁fäs\ *n* : an organophosphorus systemic insecticide $C_{14}H_{16}ClO_5PS$ administered esp. to cattle and poultry as a feed additive

cou·ma·rin \'kü-mə-rən\ *n* : a toxic white crystalline lactone $C_9H_6O_2$ found in plants or made synthetically and used as the parent compound in various anticoagulant agents (as warfarin)

coun·sel·ing \'kaún-s(ə-)liŋ\ *n* : professional guidance of the individual by utilizing psychological methods

coun·sel·or *or* **coun·sel·lor** \'kaún-s(ə-)lər\ *n* : a person engaged in counseling

¹**count** \'kaúnt\ *vb* : to indicate or name by units or groups so as to find the total number of units involved

²**count** *n* : the total number of individual things in a given unit or sample (as of blood) obtained by counting all or a subsample of them

¹**coun·ter** \'kaún-tər\ *n* : a level surface over which transactions are conducted or food is served or on which goods are displayed or work is conducted — **over the counter** : without a prescription ⟨drugs available *over the counter*⟩

²**counter** *n* : a device for indicating a number or amount — see GEIGER COUNTER

coun·ter·act \₁kaún-tər-'akt\ *vb* : to make ineffective or restrain or neutralize the usu. ill effects of by an opposite force — **coun·ter·ac·tion** \-'ak-shən\ *n*

coun·ter·con·di·tion·ing \-kən-'di-shə-niŋ\ *n* : conditioning in order to replace an undesirable response (as fear) to a stimulus (as an engagement in public speaking) by a favorable one

coun·ter·cur·rent \₁kaún-tər-'kər-ənt, -'kə-rənt\ *adj* **1** : flowing in an opposite direction **2** : involving flow of ma-

terials in opposite directions ⟨~ dialysis⟩

coun·ter·elec·tro·pho·re·sis \-i-₁lek-trə-fə-'rē-səs\ *n, pl* **-re·ses** \-₁sēz\ : an electrophoretic method of testing blood esp. for hepatitis antigens

coun·ter·im·mu·no·elec·tro·pho·re·sis \-₁im-yə-nō-i-₁lek-trō-fə-'rē-səs\ *n, pl* **-re·ses** : COUNTERELECTROPHORESIS

coun·ter·ir·ri·tant \-'ir-ə-tənt\ *n* : an agent applied locally to produce superficial inflammation with the object of reducing inflammation in deeper adjacent structures — **counterirritant** *adj*

coun·ter·ir·ri·ta·tion \-₁tā-shən\ *n* : the reaction produced by treatment with a counterirritant; *also* : the treatment itself

coun·ter·pho·bic \-₁fō-bik\ *adj* : relating to or characterized by a preference for or the seeking out of a situation that is feared ⟨~ reaction patterns⟩

coun·ter·pul·sa·tion \-₁pəl-₁sä-shən\ *n* : a technique for reducing the work load on the heart by lowering systemic blood pressure just before or during expulsion of blood from the ventricle and by raising blood pressure during diastole — see INTRAAORTIC BALLOON COUNTERPULSATION

coun·ter·shock \-₁shäk\ *n* : therapeutic electric shock applied to a heart for the purpose of altering a disturbed rhythm

coun·ter·stain \-₁stān\ *n* : a stain used to color parts of a microscopy specimen not affected by another stain; *esp* : a cytoplasmic stain used to contrast with or enhance a nuclear stain — **counterstain** *vb*

coun·ter·trac·tion \'kaún-tər-₁trak-shən\ *n* : a traction opposed to another traction used in reducing fractures

coun·ter·trans·fer·ence \₁kaún-tər-trans-'fər-əns, -'trans-(₁)\ *n* **1** : psychological transference esp. by a psychotherapist during the course of treatment; *esp* : the psychotherapist's reactions to the patient's transference **2** : the complex of feelings of a psychotherapist toward the patient

cou·pling \'kə-pliŋ, -pə-liŋ\ *n* : the joining of or the part of the body that joins the hindquarters to the forequarters of a quadruped

course \'kōrs\ *n* : an ordered process or succession; *esp* : a series of doses or medications administered over a designated period

court plaster \'kōrt-\ *n* : an adhesive plaster esp. of silk coated with isinglass and glycerin

cou·vade \kü-'väd\ *n* : a custom in some cultures in which when a child is born the father takes to bed as if bearing the child and submits himself to fasting, purification, or taboos

Cou·ve·laire uterus \₁kü-və-'ler-\ *n* : a pregnant uterus in which the placenta has detached prematurely with extravasation of blood into the uterine musculature

Cou·ve·laire, Alexandre (1873–1948), French obstetrician.

co·va·lent bond \(͵)kō-ˈvā-lənt-\ *n* : a chemical bond that is not ionic and is formed by one or more shared pairs of electrons

cover glass *n* : a piece of very thin glass used to cover material on a glass microscope slide

cov·er·slip \ˈkə-vər-͵slip\ *n* : COVER GLASS

Cow·dria \ˈkaů-drē-ə\ *n* : a genus of small pleomorphic intracellular rickettsial bacteria known chiefly from ticks but including the causative organism (*C. ruminantium*) of heartwater of ruminants

Cow·dry \ˈkaů-drē\ **, Edmund Vincent (1888–1975),** American anatomist.

cow·hage *also* **cow·age** \ˈkaů-ij\ *n* : a tropical leguminous woody vine (*Mucuna pruriens*) with crooked pods covered with barbed hairs that cause severe itching; *also* : these hairs formerly used as a vermifuge

Cow·per's gland \ˈkaů-pərz-, ˈkü-, ˈkü-\ *n* : either of two small glands of which one lies on each side of the male urethra below the prostate gland and discharges a secretion into the semen — called also *bulbourethral gland*; compare BARTHOLIN'S GLAND

Cow·per \ˈkaů-pər, ˈkü-, ˈkü-\ **, William (1666–1709),** British anatomist.

cow·pox \ˈkaů-͵päks\ *n* : a mild eruptive disease of the cow that is caused by a poxvirus and when communicated to humans protects against smallpox — called also *variola vaccinia*

cox- *or* **coxo-** *comb form* : hip : thigh : of the hip and (*coxo*femoral)

coxa \ˈkäk-sə\ *n, pl* **cox·ae** \-͵sē, -͵sī\ : HIP JOINT, HIP

coxa vara \ˈkäk-sə-ˈvar-ə\ *n* : a deformed hip joint in which the neck of the femur is bent downward

Cox·i·el·la \͵käk-sē-ˈe-lə\ *n* : a genus of small pleomorphic rickettsial bacteria occurring intercellularly in ticks and intracellularly in the cytoplasm of vertebrates and including the causative organism (*C. burnetii*) of Q fever

Cox \ˈkäks\ **, Herald Rea (b 1907),** American bacteriologist.

coxo·fem·o·ral \͵käk-sō-ˈfe-mə-rəl\ *adj* : of or relating to the hip and thigh

cox·sack·ie·vi·rus \(͵)käk-͵sa-kē-ˈvī-rəs\ *n* : any of several enteroviruses associated with human diseases (as meningitis) — see EPIDEMIC PLEURODYNIA

CP *abbr* cerebral palsy

CPAP *abbr* continuous positive airway pressure

CPB *abbr* competitive protein binding

C-pep·tide \ˈsē-ˈpep-͵tīd\ *n* : a protein fragment 35 amino-acid residues long produced by enzymatic cleavage of

proinsulin in the formation of insulin

CPK *abbr* creatine phosphokinase

CPR *abbr* cardiopulmonary resuscitation

Cr *symbol* chromium

CR *abbr* conditioned response

crab louse *n, pl* **crab lice** : a sucking louse of the genus *Phthirius* (*P. pubis*) infesting the pubic region of the human body

crabs \ˈkrabz\ *n pl* : infestation with crab lice

crack \ˈkrak\ *n, often attrib* : potent highly purified cocaine in the free-based form of small chips used illicitly usu. for smoking

cra·dle \ˈkrād-ᵊl\ *n* : a frame to keep the bedding from contact with an injured part of the body

cradle cap *n* : a seborrheic condition in infants that usu. affects the scalp and is characterized by greasy gray or dark brown adherent scaly crusts

¹**cramp** \ˈkramp\ *n* 1 : a painful involuntary spasmodic contraction of a muscle (a ~ in the leg) 2 : a temporary paralysis of muscles from overuse — see WRITER'S CRAMP 3 a : sharp abdominal pain — usu. used in pl. b : persistent and often intense though dull lower abdominal pain associated with dysmenorrhea — usu. used in pl.

²**cramp** *vb* : to affect with or be affected with a cramp or cramps

crani- *or* **cranio-** *comb form* 1 : cranium (*cranio*synostosis) 2 : cranial and (*cranio*sacral)

-crania *n comb form* : condition of the skull or head (hemi*crania*)

cra·ni·ad \ˈkrā-nē-͵ad\ *adv* : toward the head or anterior end

cra·ni·al \ˈkrā-nē-əl\ *adj* 1 : of or relating to the skull or cranium 2 : CEPHALIC — **cra·ni·al·ly** *adv*

cranial arteritis *n* : GIANT CELL ARTERITIS

cranial fossa *n* : any of the three large depressions in the posterior, middle, and anterior aspects of the floor of the cranial cavity

cranial index *n* : the ratio multiplied by 100 of the maximum breadth of the bare skull to its maximum length from front to back — compare CEPHALIC INDEX

cranial nerve *n* : any of the 12 paired nerves that arise from the lower surface of the brain with one of each pair on each side and pass through openings in the skull to the periphery of the body — see ABDUCENS NERVE, ACCESSORY NERVE, AUDITORY NERVE, FACIAL NERVE, GLOSSOPHARYNGEAL NERVE, HYPOGLOSSAL NERVE, OCULOMOTOR NERVE, OLFACTORY NERVE, OPTIC NERVE, TRIGEMINAL NERVE, TROCHLEAR NERVE, VAGUS NERVE

cra·ni·ec·to·my \͵krā-nē-ˈek-tə-mē\ *n, pl* **-mies** : the surgical removal of a portion of the skull

cra·nio·ce·re·bral \͵krā-nē-ō-sə-ˈrē-brəl. -'ser-ə-\ *adj* : involving both cranium and brain (~ injury)

cra·nio·fa·cial \·krā-nē-ō-'fā-shəl\ *adj* : of, relating to, or involving both the cranium and the face

cra·ni·ol·o·gy \·krā-nē-'ä-lə-jē\ *n, pl* -gies : a science dealing with variations in size, shape, and proportions of skulls among human races

cra·ni·om·e·try \-'ä-mə-trē\ *n, pl* -tries : a science dealing with cranial measurement

cra·ni·op·a·gus \·krā-nē-'ä-pə-gəs\ *n, pl* -agi \-pə-,jē, -,jī\ : a pair of twins joined at the heads

cra·nio·pha·ryn·geal \·krā-nē-ō-,far-ən-'jē-əl, -fə-'rin-jəl, -jē-əl\ *adj* : relating to or connecting the cavity of the skull and the pharynx

cra·nio·pha·ryn·gi·o·ma \-,far-ən-jē-'ō-mə, -fə-,rin-jē-'ō-mə\ *n, pl* -mas *or* -ma·ta \-mə-tə\ : a tumor of the brain near the pituitary gland that develops esp. in children or young adults from epithelium derived from the embryonic craniopharyngeal canal and that is often associated with increased intracranial pressure

cra·nio·plas·ty \'krā-nē-(,)ō-,plas-tē\ *n, pl* -ties : the surgical correction of skull defects

cra·nio·ra·chis·chi·sis \,krā-nē-(,)ō-rə-'kis-kə-səs\ *n, pl* -chi·ses \-,sēz\ : a congenital fissure of the skull and spine

cra·nio·sa·cral \,krā-nē-ō-'sa-krəl, -'sā-\ *adj* 1 : of or relating to the cranium and the sacrum 2 : PARASYMPATHETIC

cra·ni·os·chi·sis \,krā-nē-'äs-kə-səs\ *n, pl* -chi·ses \-,sēz\ : a congenital fissure of the skull

cra·nio·ste·no·sis \,krā-nē-(,)ō-stə-'nō-səs\ *n, pl* -no·ses \-,sēz\ : malformation of the skull caused by premature closure of the cranial sutures

cra·nio·syn·os·to·sis \-,si-,näs-'tō-səs\ *n, pl* -to·ses \-,sēz\ *or* -to·sis·es : premature fusion of the sutures of the skull

cra·nio·ta·bes \,krā-nē-ə-'tā-(,)bēz\ *n, pl* **craniotabes** : a thinning and softening of the infantile skull in spots usu. due to rickets or syphilis

cra·ni·ot·o·my \,krā-nē-'ä-tə-mē\ *n, pl* -mies 1 : the operation of cutting or crushing the fetal head to effect delivery 2 : surgical opening of the skull

cra·ni·um \'krā-nē-əm\ *n, pl* -ni·ums *or* -nia \-nē-ə\ : SKULL; *specif* : BRAINCASE

crank \'kraŋk\ *n* : CRYSTAL 2

cra·ter \'krā-tər\ *n* : an eroded lesion of a wall or surface (ulcer ~s)

cra·ter·i·za·tion \,krā-tər-ə-'zā-shən\ *n* : surgical excision of a crater-shaped piece of bone

craz·ing \'krāz-iŋ\ *n* : the formation of minute cracks (as in acrylic resin teeth) usu. attributed to shrinkage or to moisture

cra·zy \'krā-zē\ *adj* **craz·i·er; -est** : MAD 1, INSANE — **cra·zi·ly** \-zə-lē\ *adv* — **cra·zi·ness** \-zē-nəs\ *n*

crazy bone *n* : FUNNY BONE

CRD *abbr* chronic respiratory disease

C-re·ac·tive protein \'sē-rē-'ak-tiv-\ *n* : a protein present in blood serum in various abnormal states (as inflammation)

cream \'krēm\ *n* 1 : the yellowish part of milk containing from 18 to about 40 percent butterfat 2 : something having the consistency of cream: *esp* : a usu. emulsified medicinal or cosmetic preparation — **creamy** \'krē-mē\ *adj*

crease \'krēs\ *n* : a line or mark made by or as if by folding a pliable substance (as the skin) — **crease** *vb*

cre·atine \'krē-ə-,tēn, -ət-ən\ *n* : a nitrogenous substance $C_4H_9N_3O_2$ found esp. in vertebrate muscles either free or as phosphocreatine

creatine kinase *n* : an enzyme of vertebrate skeletal and myocardial muscle that catalyzes the transfer of a high-energy phosphate group from phosphocreatine to ADP with the formation of ATP and creatine

creatine phosphate *n* : PHOSPHOCREATINE

creatine phosphokinase *n* : CREATINE KINASE

cre·at·i·nine \krē-'at-ə-,nēn, -ən-ən\ *n* : a white crystalline strongly basic compound $C_4H_7N_3O$ formed from creatine and found esp. in muscle, blood, and urine

cre·a·tin·uria \,krē-ə-tə-'nur-ē-ə, -'nyur-\ *n* : the presence of creatine in urine; *esp* : an increased or abnormal amount in the urine

creeping eruption *n* : a human skin disorder that is characterized by a red line of eruption which fades at one end as it progresses at the other and that is usu. caused by insect or worm larvae and esp. those of the dog hookworm burrowing in the deeper layers of the skin — called also *larval migrans, larva migrans*

creeps \'krēps\ *n pl* : a deficiency disease esp. of sheep and cattle associated with an abnormal dietary calcium-phosphorus ratio

cre·mas·ter \krē-'mas-tər, krə-\ *n* : a thin muscle consisting of loops of fibers derived from the internal oblique muscle and descending upon the spermatic cord to surround and suspend the testicle — called also *cremaster muscle* — **cre·mas·ter·ic** \,krē-mə-'ster-ik\ *adj*

crème \'krem, 'krēm\ *n, pl* **crèmes** \'krem, 'kremz, 'krēmz\ : CREAM 2

cre·nat·ed \'krē-,nā-təd\ *also* **cre·nate** \-,nāt\ *adj* : having the margin or surface cut into rounded scallops (~ red blood cells)

cre·na·tion \kri-'nā-shən\ *n* : shrinkage of red blood cells resulting in crenated margins

cre·o·sote \'krē-ə-ˌsōt\ n 1 : an oily liquid mixture of phenolic compounds obtained by the distillation of wood tar and used esp. as a disinfectant and as an expectorant in chronic bronchitis 2 : a brownish oily liquid consisting chiefly of aromatic hydrocarbons obtained by distillation of coal tar and used esp. as a wood preservative

crep·i·tant rale \'krep-ə-tənt-\ n : a peculiar crackling sound audible with inspiration in pneumonia and other lung diseases

crep·i·ta·tion \ˌkre-pə-'tā-shən\ n : a grating or crackling sound or sensation (as that produced by the fractured ends of a bone moving against each other) (∼ in the arthritic knee)

crep·i·tus \'kre-pə-təs\ n, pl **crepitus** : CREPITATION

crescent of Gian·nuz·zi or **crescent of Gia·nuz·zi** \-jə-'nüt-sē\ n : DEMILUNE

G. Giannuzzi — see DEMILUNE OF GIANNUZZI

cre·sol \'krē-ˌsȯl, -ˌsōl\ n : any of three poisonous colorless crystalline or liquid isomeric phenols C_7H_8O that are used as disinfectants, in making phenolic resins, and in organic synthesis — see METACRESOL

crest \'krest\ n : a ridge esp. on a bone (the ∼ of the tibia) — see OCCIPITAL CREST

cre·tin \'krēt-ᵊn\ n : one affected with cretinism — **cre·tin·ous** \-ᵊn-əs\ adj

cre·tin·ism \-ᵊn-ˌi-zəm\ n : a usu. congenital abnormal condition marked by physical stunting and mental deficiency and caused by severe thyroid deficiency

Creutz·feldt–Ja·kob disease also **Creutz·feld–Ja·cob disease** \'kroits-ˌfelt-'yä-(ˌ)kōb-, -(ˌ)kȯp-\ n : a rare progressive fatal encephalopathy caused by a slow virus and marked by development of porous brain tissue, premature dementia in middle age, and gradual loss of muscular coordination — called also *Jakob-Creutzfeldt disease*

    Creutzfeldt, Hans Gerhard (1885–1964) and **Jakob, Alfons Maria (1884–1931), German psychiatrists.**

crev·ice \'kre-vəs\ n : a narrow fissure or cleft — see GINGIVAL CREVICE

cre·vic·u·lar \krə-'vi-kyə-lər\ adj : of, relating to, or involving a crevice and esp. the gingival crevice (gingival ∼ fluid)

crib·bing \'kri-biŋ\ n : a vice of horses characterized by gnawing (as at a manger) while slobbering and salivating

crib biting n : CRIBBING

crib death n : SUDDEN INFANT DEATH SYNDROME

crib·ri·form plate \'kri-brə-ˌfȯrm-\ n 1 : the horizontal plate of the ethmoid bone perforated with numerous foramina for the passage of the olfactory nerve filaments from the nasal cavity — called also *lamina cribrosa* 2 : LAMINA DURA

cribrosa — see LAMINA CRIBROSA

crick \'krik\ n : a painful spasmodic condition of muscles (as of the neck or back) — **crick** vb

crico- comb form 1 : cricoid cartilage and (cricothyroid) 2 : of the cricoid cartilage and (cricopharyngeal)

cri·co·ar·y·te·noid \ˌkrī-kō-ˌar-ə-'tē-ˌnȯid, -kō-ə-'rit-ᵊn-ˌȯid\ n 1 : a muscle of the larynx that arises from the upper margin of the arch of the cricoid cartilage, inserts into the front of the process of the arytenoid cartilage, and helps to narrow the opening of the vocal cords — called also *lateral cricoarytenoid* 2 : a muscle of the larynx that arises from the posterior surface of the lamina of the cricoid cartilage, inserts into the posterior of the process of the arytenoid cartilage, and widens the opening of the vocal cords — called also *posterior cricoarytenoid*

cri·coid cartilage \'krī-ˌkȯid-\ n : a cartilage of the larynx which articulates with the lower cornua of the thyroid cartilage and with which the arytenoid cartilages articulate — called also **cricoid**

cri·co·pha·ryn·ge·al \ˌkrī-kō-ˌfar-ən-'jē-əl, -fə-'rin-jəl, -jē-əl\ adj : of or relating to the cricoid cartilage and the pharynx

¹**cri·co·thy·roid** \-'thī-ˌrȯid\ adj : relating to or connecting the cricoid cartilage and the thyroid cartilage

²**cricothyroid** n : a triangular muscle of the larynx that is attached to the cricoid and thyroid cartilages and is the principal tensor of the vocal cords — called also *cricothyroid muscle*

cri·co·thy·roi·de·us \ˌkrī-kō-thi-'rȯi-dē-əs\ n, pl **-dei** \-dē-ˌī\ : CRICOTHYROID

cri du chat syndrome \ˌkrē-dü-'shä-, -də-\ n : an inherited condition characterized by a mewing cry, mental retardation, physical anomalies, and the absence of part of a chromosome — called also *cat cry syndrome*

¹**crip·ple** \'kri-pəl\ n : a lame or partly disabled individual — sometimes taken to be offensive

²**cripple** vb **crip·pled; crip·pling** \-p(ə-)liŋ\ : to deprive of the use of a limb and esp. a leg (crippled by arthritis)

crip·pler \-p(ə-)lər\ n : a disease that results in crippling

cri·sis \'krī-səs\ n, pl **cri·ses** \-ˌsēz\ 1 : the turning point for better or worse in an acute disease or fever; esp : a sudden turn for the better (as sudden abatement in severity of symptoms or abrupt drop in temperature) — compare LYSIS 2 : a paroxysmal attack of pain, distress, or disordered function (tabetic ∼) (cardiac ∼) 3 : an emotionally significant event or radical change of status in a person's life 4 : a psychological or social condition characterized by unusual instability caused by excessive stress and either endangering or felt to endanger the continuity of an individual or group; *esp* : such a social condition requiring the transformation of cultural patterns and values

crisis center *n* : a facility run usu. by nonprofessionals who counsel those who telephone for help in a personal crisis

cris·ta \'kris-tə\ *n, pl* **cris·tae** \-₋tē₋ -₋tī\ 1 : one of the areas of specialized sensory epithelium in the ampullae of the semicircular canals of the ear serving as end organs for the labyrinthine sense 2 : an elevation of the surface of a bone for the attachment of a muscle or tendon 3 : any of the inwardly projecting folds of the inner membrane of a mitochondrion

crista gal·li \-'gal-ē, -'go-\ *n* : an upright process on the anterior portion of the cribriform plate to which the anterior part of the falx cerebri is attached

crit·i·cal \'kri-ti-kəl\ *adj* 1 : relating to, indicating, or being the stage of a disease at which an abrupt change for better or worse may be anticipated with reasonable certainty (the ∼ phase of a fever) 2 : being or relating to an illness or condition involving danger of death (∼ care) (a ∼ head injury) — **crit·i·cal·ly** \-k(ə-)lē\ *adv*

CRNA *abbr* certified registered nurse anesthetist

crock \'kräk\ *n* : a complaining medical patient whose illness is largely imaginary or psychosomatic

Crohn's disease \'krōnz-\ *n* : ileitis that typically involves the distal portion of the ileum, often spreads to the colon, and is characterized by diarrhea, cramping, and loss of appetite and weight with local abscesses and scarring — called also *regional enteritis, regional ileitis*

Crohn \'krōn\, **Burrill Bernard** (1884–1983), American physician.

cro·mo·gly·cate \₋krō-mō-'gli-₋kāt\ — see CROMOLYN SODIUM

cro·mo·lyn sodium \'krō-mə-lən-\ *n* : a drug $C_{23}H_{14}Na_2O_{11}$ that inhibits the release of histamine from mast cells and is used usu. as an inhalant to prevent the onset of bronchial asthma attacks — called also *cromolyn, disodium cromoglycate, sodium cromoglycate*

¹**cross** \'krós\ *n* 1 : an act of crossing dissimilar individuals 2 : a crossbred individual or kind

²**cross** *vb* : to interbreed or cause (an animal or plant) to interbreed with one of a different kind : HYBRIDIZE

³**cross** *adj* : CROSSBRED, HYBRID

cross·bred \'krós-'bred\ *adj* : produced by crossbreeding : HYBRID — **cross·bred** \-'bred\ *n*

¹**cross·breed** \'krós-₋brēd, -'brēd\ *vb* -**bred** \-₋bred, -'bred\; -**breed·ing** : HYBRIDIZE, CROSS; *esp* : to cross (two varieties or breeds) within the same species

²**cross·breed** \-₋brēd\ *n* : HYBRID

cross·bridge \'krós-₋brij\ *n* : the globular head of a myosin molecule that projects from a myosin filament in muscle and in the sliding filament hypothesis of muscle contraction is held to attach temporarily to an adjacent actin filament and draw it into the A band of a sarcomere between the myosin filaments

crossed \'króst\ *adj* : forming a decussation (a ∼ tract of nerve fibers)

cross-eye \'krós-₋ī\ *n* 1 : squint in which the eye turns inward toward the nose — called also *esotropia*; compare WALLEYE 2a 2 **cross-eyes** \-'īz\ *pl* : eyes affected with cross-eye — **cross-eyed** \-'īd\ *adj*

cross·ing-over \₋krós-siŋ-'ō-vər\ *n* : an interchange of genes or segments between homologous chromosomes

cross·match·ing \'krós-'ma-chiŋ\ *or* **cross·match** \-'mach\ *n* : the testing of the compatibility of the bloods of a transfusion donor and a recipient by mixing the serum of each with the red cells of the other to determine the absence of agglutination reactions — **crossmatch** *vb*

¹**cross·over** \'krós-₋ō-vər\ *n* 1 : an instance or product of genetic crossing-over 2 : a crossover interchange in an experiment

²**crossover** *adj* : involving or using interchange of the control group and the experimental group during the course of an experiment

cross-re·ac·tion \₋krós-rē-'ak-shən\ *n* : reaction of one antigen with antibodies developed against another antigen — **cross-re·act** \-'akt\ *vb* — **cross-re·ac·tive** \-rē-'ak-tiv\ *adj* — **cross-re·ac·tiv·i·ty** \-(₋)rē-₋ak-'ti-və-tē\ *n*

cross section *n* : a cutting or piece of something cut off at right angles to an axis; *also* : a representation of such a cutting — **cross-sec·tion·al** \'krós-'sek-shə-nəl\ *adj*

cross-tol·er·ance \'krós-'tä-lə-rəns\ *n* : tolerance or resistance to a drug that develops through continued use of another drug with similar pharmacological action

cro·ta·lar·ia \₋krō-tə-'lar-ē-ə, ₋krä-\ *n* 1 *cap* : a large genus of usu. tropical and subtropical plants (family Leguminosae) with yellow flowers and inflated pods including some containing toxic alkaloids esp. in the seeds that are poisonous to farm animals and humans 2 : any plant of the genus *Crotalaria* — called also *rattlebox*

Cro·ta·lus \'krót-əl-əs, 'krät-\ *n* : a genus of American pit vipers including many of the rattlesnakes

crotch \'kräch\ *n* : an angle formed by

the parting of two legs, branches, or members

-crotic *adj comb form* : having (such) a heartbeat or pulse (di*crotic*)

-crotism *n comb form* : condition of having (such) a heartbeat or pulse (di*crotism*)

Cro-ton bug \'krōt-ᵊn-\ *n* : GERMAN COCKROACH

cro-ton oil \'krōt-ᵊn-\ *n* : a viscid acrid fixed oil from an Asian plant (*Croton tiglium* of the family Euphorbiaceae) that was formerly used as a drastic cathartic but is now used esp. in pharmacological experiments as an irritant

croup \'krüp\ *n* : a spasmodic laryngitis esp. of infants marked by episodes of difficult breathing, stridor, and a hoarse grating cough — **croup-ous** \'krü-pəs\ *adj* — **croupy** \-pē\ *adj*

¹crown \'kraün\ *n* **1** : the topmost part of the skull or head **2** : the part of a tooth external to the gum or an artificial substitute for this

²crown *vb* **1** : to put an artificial crown on (a tooth) **2** *in childbirth* : to appear at the vaginal opening — used of the first part (as the crown of the head) of the infant to appear (an anesthetic was given when the head ~ed)

crow's–foot \'krōz-ˌfüt\ *n, pl* **crow's– feet** \-ˌfēt\ : a wrinkle extending from the outer corner of the eye — usu. used in pl.

CRT \ˌsē-(ˌ)är-'tē\ *n, pl* **CRTs** *or* **CRT's** : CATHODE-RAY TUBE; *also* : a display device incorporating a cathode-ray tube

CRTT *abbr* certified respiratory therapy technician

cru-ci-ate \'krü-shē-ˌāt\ *adj* : shaped like a cross

cruciate ligament *n* : any of several more or less cross-shaped ligaments: as **a** : either of two ligaments in the knee joint which cross each other from femur to tibia: (1) : an anterior one that limits extension and rotation — called also *anterior cruciate ligament* (2) : a posterior one that prevents dislocation of the femur in a forward direction — called also *posterior cruciate ligament* **b** : a complex ligament made up of the transverse ligament of the atlas and vertical fibrocartilage extending from the odontoid process to the border of the foramen magnum

crude protein *n* : the approximate amount of protein in foods that is calculated from the determined nitrogen content by multiplying by a factor (as 6.25 for many foods and 5.7 for wheat) derived from the average percentage of nitrogen in the food proteins and that may contain an appreciable error if the nitrogen is derived from nonprotein material or from a protein of unusual composition

crura *pl of* CRUS

cru-ra ce-re-bri \ˌkrür-ə-'ser-ə-ˌbrī, -ᵊker-ə-ˌbrē\ *n pl* : CRUS 2c

crura for-ni-cis \-ᵊfȯr-nə-ˌsis, -ə-ˌkis\ *n pl* : CRUS 2e

cru-ral \'krür-əl\ *adj* : of or relating to the thigh or leg; *specif* : FEMORAL

cruris — see TINEA CRURIS

crus \'krüs, 'krəs\ *n, pl* **cru-ra** \'krür-ə\ **1** : the part of the hind limb between the femur or thigh and the ankle or tarsus : SHANK **2** : any of various anatomical parts likened to a leg or to a pair of legs: as **a** : either of the diverging proximal ends of the corpora cavernosa **b** : the tendinous attachments of the diaphragm to the bodies of the lumbar vertebrae forming the sides of the aortic opening — often used in pl. **c** *pl* : the peduncles of the cerebrum — called also *crura cerebri* **d** *pl* : the peduncles of the cerebellum **e** *pl* : the posterior pillars of the fornix — called also *crura fornicis* **f** (1) : a long bony process of the incus that articulates with the stapes; *also* : a shorter one projecting from the body of the incus perpendicular to this (2) : either of the two bony processes forming the sides of the arch of the stapes

crush syndrome *n* : the physical responses to severe crushing injury of muscle tissue involving esp. shock and partial or complete renal failure; *also* : the renal failure associated with such responses

crust \'krəst\ *n* **1** : SCAB **2** **2** : an encrusting deposit of serum, cellular debris, and bacteria present over or about lesions in some skin diseases (as impetigo or eczema) — **crust** *vb*

crutch \'krəch\ *n* **1** : a support typically fitting under the armpit for use as an aid in walking **2** : the crotch esp. of an animal

cry- *or* **cryo-** *comb form* : cold : freezing (*cryo*surgery)

cryo-bi-ol-o-gy \ˌkrī-ō-bī-'ä-lə-jē\ *n, pl* **-gies** : the study of the effects of extremely low temperature on biological systems (as cells or organisms) — **cryo-bi-o-log-i-cal** \-ˌbī-ə-'lä-ji-kəl\ *adj* — **cryo-bi-ol-o-gist** \ˌkrī-ō-bī-'ä-lə-jist\ *n*

cryo-cau-tery \-'kȯ-tə-rē\ *n, pl* **-ter-ies** : destruction of tissue by use of extreme cold

cryo-ex-trac-tion \-ik-'strak-shən\ *n* : extraction of a cataract through use of a cryoprobe whose refrigerated tip adheres to and freezes tissue of the lens permitting its removal

cryo-ex-trac-tor \-ik-'strak-tər, -'ek-\ *n* : a cryoprobe used for removal of cataracts

cryo-fi-brin-o-gen \-fī-'bri-nə-jən\ *n* : fibrinogen that precipitates upon cooling to 4° C (39° F) and redissolves at 37° C (98.6° F)

cryo-gen-ic \ˌkrī-ə-'je-nik\ *adj* **1 a** : of or relating to the production of very low temperatures **b** : being or relating to very low temperatures **2** : requiring or involving the use of a cryogenic temperature (∼ surgery) — **cryo-gen-i-cal-ly** \-ni-k(ə-)lē\ *adv*

cryo-gen-ics \-niks\ *n* : a branch of physics that deals with the production and effects of very low temperatures

cryo-glob-u-lin \₁krī-ō-ˈglä-byə-lən\ *n* : any of several proteins similar to gamma globulins (as in molecular weight) that precipitate usu. in the cold from blood serum esp. in pathological conditions (as multiple myeloma)

cryo-glob-u-lin-emia \-₁glä-byə-lə-ˈnē-mē-ə\ *n* : the condition of having abnormal quantities of cryoglobulins in the blood

cry-on-ics \krī-ˈä-niks\ *n* : the practice of freezing the body of a person who has died from a disease in hopes of restoring life at some future time when a cure for the disease has been developed — **cry-on-ic** \-nik\ *adj*

cryo-pexy \ˈkrī-ə-₁pek-sē\ *n, pl* **-pex-ies** : cryosurgery for fixation of the retina in retinal detachment or for repair of a retinal tear or hole

cryo-pre-cip-i-tate \₁krī-ō-prə-ˈsi-pə-tət, -₁tāt\ *n* : a precipitate that is formed by cooling a solution — **cryo-pre-cip-i-ta-tion** \-₁si-pə-ˈtā-shən\ *n*

cryo-pres-er-va-tion \-₁pre-zər-ˈvā-shən\ *n* : preservation (as of sperm or eggs) by subjection to extremely low temperatures — **cryo-pre-serve** \-pri-ˈzərv\ *vb*

cryo-probe \ˈkrī-ə-₁prōb\ *n* : a blunt chilled instrument used to freeze tissues in cryosurgery

cryo-pro-tec-tive \₁krī-ō-prə-ˈtek-tiv\ *adj* : serving to protect against the deleterious effects of subjection to freezing temperatures (a ∼ agent) — **cryo-pro-tec-tant** \-tənt\ *n or adj*

cryo-stat \ˈkrī-ə-₁stat\ *n* : an apparatus for maintaining a constant low temperature esp. below 0°C or 32°F (as by means of liquid helium); *esp* : one containing a microtome for obtaining sections of frozen tissue — **cryo-stat-ic** \₁krī-ə-ˈsta-tik\ *adj*

cryo-sur-gery \₁krī-ō-ˈsərj-rē, -ˈsər-jə-rē\ *n, pl* **-ger-ies** : surgery in which the tissue to be treated or operated on is frozen (as by liquid nitrogen) — **cryo-sur-geon** \-ˈsər-jən\ *n* — **cryo-sur-gi-cal** \-ˈsər-ji-kəl\ *adj*

cryo-ther-a-py \-ˈther-ə-pē\ *n, pl* **-pies** : the therapeutic use of cold

crypt \ˈkript\ *n* **1** : an anatomical pit or depression **2** : a simple tubular gland (as a crypt of Lieberkühn)

crypt- *or* **crypto-** *comb form* : hidden : covered (*cryptogenic*)

crypt-ec-to-my \krip-ˈtek-tə-mē\ *n, pl* **-mies** : surgical removal or destruction of a crypt

cryp-tic \ˈkrip-tik\ *adj* : not recognized (a ∼ infection)

cryp-ti-tis \krip-ˈtī-təs\ *n* : inflammation of a crypt (as an anal crypt)

cryp-to-coc-co-sis \₁krip-tə-(₁)kä-ˈkō-səs\ *n, pl* **-co-ses** \-(₁)sēz\ : an infectious disease that is caused by a fungus of the genus *Cryptococcus* (*C. neoformans*) and is characterized by the production of nodular lesions or abscesses in the lungs, subcutaneous tissues, joints, and esp. the brain and meninges — called also *torulosis*

cryp-to-coc-cus \-ˈkä-kəs\ *n* **1** *cap* : a genus of imperfect fungi (family Cryptococcaceae) that resemble yeasts and include a number of saprophytes and a few serious pathogens **2** *pl* **-coc-ci** \-ˈkäk-₁sī, -₁sē; -ˈkä-₁kī, -₁kē\ : any fungus of the genus *Cryptococcus* — **cryp-to-coc-cal** \-ˈkä-kəl\ *adj*

crypt of Lie-ber-kühn \-ˈlē-bər-₁kün, -₁kyün, -₁kün-\ *n* : any of the tubular glands of the intestinal mucous membrane — called also *intestinal gland*

Lieberkühn, Johannes Nathanael (1711–1756), German anatomist.

crypt of Mor-ga-gni \-mȯr-ˈgän-yē\ *n* : any of the pouched cavities of the rectal mucosa immediately above the anorectal junction, intervening between vertical folds of the rectal mucosa

Morgagni, Giovanni Battista (1682–1771), Italian anatomist and pathologist.

cryp-to-ge-net-ic \₁krip-tō-jə-ˈne-tik\ *adj* : CRYPTOGENIC

cryp-to-gen-ic \₁krip-tə-ˈje-nik\ *adj* : of obscure or unknown origin (∼ epilepsy)

crypt-or-chid \krip-ˈtȯr-kəd\ *n* : one affected with cryptorchidism — compare MONORCHID — **cryptorchid** *adj*

crypt-or-chi-dism \-kə-₁di-zəm\ *n* *also* **crypt-or-chism** \-₁ki-zəm\ : a condition in which one or both testes fail to descend normally — compare MONORCHIDISM

cryp-to-spo-rid-i-o-sis \₁krip-tō-spȯr-₁i-dē-ˈō-səs\ *n, pl* **-o-ses** \-₁sēz\ : a disease caused by cryptosporidia

cryp-to-spo-rid-i-um \₁krip-tō-spȯr-ˈi-dē-əm\ *n* **1** *cap* : a genus of coccidian protozoans parasitic in the gut of many vertebrates including humans and sometimes causing diarrhea esp. in individuals who are immunocompromised (as in AIDS) **2** *pl* **-rid-ia** \-dē-ə\ : any protozoan of the genus *Cryptosporidium*

cryp-to-xan-thin \₁krip-tə-ˈzan-thən\ *n* : a red crystalline carotenoid alcohol $C_{40}H_{55}OH$ that occurs in many plants, in blood serum, and in some animal products (as butter and egg yolk) and that is a precursor of vitamin A

cryp-to-zo-ite \-ˈzō-₁īt\ *n* : a malaria parasite that develops in tissue cells and gives rise to the forms that invade

blood cells — compare METACRYPTO-
ZOITE

crys·tal \'krist-ªl\ *n* **1** : a body that is formed by the solidification of a chemical element, a compound, or a mixture and has a regularly repeating internal arrangement of its atoms and often external plane faces **2** : powdered methamphetamine — **crystal** *adj* — **crys·tal·line** \'kris-tə-lən, -ªlin, -ªlēn\ *adj*

crys·tal·lin \'kris-tə-lən\ *n* : either of two globulins in the crystalline lens

crystallina — see MILIARIA CRYSTALLINA

crystalline lens *n* : the lens of the eye

crys·tal·lize *also* **crys·tal·ize** \'kris-tə-ªlīz\ *vb* **-lized** *also* **-ized**; **-liz·ing** *also* **-iz·ing** : to cause to form crystals or assume crystalline form — **crys·tal·liz·able** \-ªkris-tə-ªlī-zə-bəl\ *adj* — **crys·tal·li·za·tion** \ªkris-tə-lə-ªzā-shən\ *n*

crys·tal·lu·ria \ªkris-tə-ªlùr-ē-ə, -təl-ªyùr-\ *n* : the presence of crystals in the urine indicating renal irritation

cs *abbr* conditioned stimulus

Cs *symbol* cesium

CS \ªsē-ªes\ *n* : a potent lacrimatory and nausea-producing gas $C_{10}H_5ClN_2$ used in riot control and chemical warfare

C-sec·tion \'sē-ªsek-shən\ *n* : CESAREAN

CSF \ªsē-(ª)es-ªef\ *n* : COLONY-STIMULATING FACTOR

CSF *abbr* cerebrospinal fluid

CT *abbr* computed tomography; computerized tomography

Cteno·ce·phal·i·des \ªte-nō-sə-ªfa-lə-ªdēz\ *n* : a genus of fleas (family Pulicidae) including the dog flea (*C. canis*) and cat flea (*C. felis*)

CT scan \'sē-ªtē-\ *n* : CAT SCAN — **CT scanning** *n*

CT scanner *n* : CAT SCANNER

C–type \'sē-ªtīp\ *adj* : TYPE C

Cu *symbol* copper

¹cu·bi·tal \'kyü-bət-ªl\ *adj* : of or relating to a cubitus

²cubital *n* : CUBITUS

cubiti — see BICEPS FLEXOR CUBITI

cu·bi·tus \'kyü-bə-təs\ *n, pl* **cu·bi·ti** \-ªtī\ **1** : FOREARM, ANTEBRACHIUM **2** : ULNA

cubitus valgus *n* : a condition of the arm in which the forearm deviates away from the midline of the body when extended

cubitus varus *n* : a condition of the arm in which the forearm deviates toward the midline of the body when extended

¹cu·boid \'kyü-ªbóid\ *adj* **1** : relating to or being the cuboid (the ~ bone) **2** : shaped approximately like a cube

²cuboid *n* : the outermost bone* in the distal row of tarsal bones of the foot that supports the fourth and fifth metatarsals

cu·boi·dal \kyü-ªbóid-ªl\ *adj* **1** : CUBOID

2 2 : composed of nearly cubical elements (~ epithelium)

cud \'kəd\ *n* : food brought up into the mouth by a ruminating animal from its first stomach to be chewed again

cue \'kyü\ *n* : a minor stimulus acting as an indication of the nature of the perceived object or situation

cuff \'kəf\ *n* **1** : an inflatable band that is wrapped around an extremity to control the flow of blood through the part when recording blood pressure with a sphygmomanometer **2** : an anatomical structure shaped like a cuff; *esp* : ROTATOR CUFF

cui·rass \kwi-ªras, kyü-\ *n* **1** : a plaster cast for the trunk and neck **2** : a respirator that covers the chest or the chest and abdomen and provides artificial respiration by means of an electric pump

cul-de-sac \ªkəl-di-ªsak, ªkúl-\ *n, pl* **culs-de-sac** *same or* ªkəlz-, ªkúlz-\ *also* **cul-de-sacs** \-ªsaks\ **1** : a blind diverticulum or pouch; *also* : the closed end of such a pouch **2** : POUCH OF DOUGLAS

cul-de-sac of Douglas *n* : POUCH OF DOUGLAS

culdo- *comb form* : pouch of Douglas (*culdoscopy*)

cul·do·cen·te·sis \ªkəl-dō-ªsen-ªtē-səs, ªkúl-\ *n, pl* **-te·ses** \-ªsēz\ : removal of material from the pouch of Douglas by means of puncture of the vaginal wall

cul·dos·co·py \kəl-ªdäs-kə-pē, ªkúl-\ *n, pl* **-pies** : a technique for endoscopic visualization and minor operative procedures on the female pelvic organs in which the instrument is introduced through a puncture in the wall of the pouch of Douglas — **cul·do·scop·ic** \ªkəl-də-ªskä-pik, ªkúl-\ *adj*

cul·dot·o·my \kəl-ªdä-tə-mē, ªkúl-\ *n, pl* **-mies** : surgical incision of the pouch of Douglas

cu·lex \'kyü-ªleks\ *n* **1** *cap* : a large cosmopolitan genus of mosquitoes (family Culicidae) that includes the common house mosquito (*C. pipiens*) of Europe and No. America, a widespread tropical mosquito (*C. quinquefasciatus* syn. *C. fatigans*) which transmits some filarial worms parasitic in humans, and other mosquitoes which have been implicated as vectors of virus encephalitides and possibly of other diseases — compare ANOPHELES **2** : a mosquito of the genus *Culex* — **cu·li·cine** \'kyü-lə-ªsīn\ *adj or n*

cu·li·cide \'kyü-lə-ªsīd\ *n* : an insecticide that destroys mosquitoes

Cu·li·coi·des \ªkyü-lə-ªkói-ªdēz\ *n* : a genus of bloodsucking midges (family Ceratopogonidae) of which some are intermediate hosts of filarial parasites

cul·men \'kəl-mən\ *n* : a lobe of the cerebellum lying in the superior vermis just in front of the primary fissure

cul·ti·vate \'kəl-tə-₁vāt\ vb -vat·ed; -vat·ing : CULTURE 1

cul·ti·va·tion \₁kəl-tə-'vā-shən\ n : CULTURE 2

¹**cul·ture** \'kəl-chər\ n 1 a : the integrated pattern of human behavior that includes thought, speech, action, and artifacts and depends upon the human capacity for learning and transmitting knowledge to succeeding generations b : the customary beliefs, social forms, and material traits of a racial, religious, or social group 2 a : the act or process of growing living material (as bacteria or viruses) in prepared nutrient media b : a product of cultivation in nutrient media — **cul·tur·al** \'kəl-chə-rəl\ adj — **cul·tur·al·ly** adv

²**culture** vb **cul·tured; cul·tur·ing** 1 : to grow (as microorganisms or tissues) in a prepared medium 2 : to start a culture from; also : to make a culture of (~ milk)

culture shock n : a sense of confusion and uncertainty sometimes with feelings of anxiety that may affect people exposed to an alien culture or environment without adequate preparation

cu·mu·la·tive \'kyü-myə-lə-tiv, -₁lā-\ adj : increasing in effect by successive doses (as of a drug or poison) — **cu·mu·la·tive·ly** adv

cu·mu·lus \'kyü-myə-ləs\ n, pl **cu·mu·li** \-₁lī, -₁lē\ : the projecting mass of granulosa cells that bears the developing ovum in a graafian follicle — called also discus proligerus

cumulus ooph·o·rus \-ō-'ä-fə-rəs\ n : CUMULUS

cu·ne·ate fasciculus \'kyü-nē-₁āt-, -ət-,\ n, pl **cuneate fasciculi** : FASCICULUS CUNEATUS

cuneate nucleus n : NUCLEUS CUNEATUS

cuneatus — see FASCICULUS CUNEATUS, NUCLEUS CUNEATUS

¹**cu·ne·i·form** \kyü-'nē-ə-₁fórm, 'kyü-; 'kyü-nə-\ adj 1 : of, relating to, or being a cuneiform bone or cartilage 2 of a human skull : wedge-shaped as viewed from above

²**cuneiform** n : a cuneiform bone or cartilage

cuneiform bone n 1 : any of three small bones of the tarsus situated between the navicular and the first three metatarsals a : one on the medial side of the foot that is just proximal to the first metatarsal bone and is the largest of the three bones — called also medial cuneiform, medial cuneiform bone b : one that is situated between the other two bones proximal to the second metatarsal bone and is the smallest of the three bones — called also intermediate cuneiform, intermediate cuneiform bone c : one that is situated proximal to the third metatarsal bone and that lies between the intermediate cuneiform bone and the

cuboid — called also lateral cuneiform bone 2 : TRIQUETRAL BONE

cuneiform cartilage n : either of a pair of rods of yellow elastic cartilage of which each lies on one side of the larynx in an aryepiglottic fold just below the arytenoid cartilage

cu·ne·us \'kyü-nē-əs\ n, pl **cu·nei** \-nē-₁ī\ : a convolution of the mesial surface of the occipital lobe of the brain above the calcarine sulcus that forms a part of the visual area

cun·ni·lin·gus \₁kə-ni-'liŋ-gəs\ also **cun·ni·linc·tus** \-'liŋk-təs\ n : oral stimulation of the vulva or clitoris

¹**cup** \'kəp\ n 1 : an athletic supporter reinforced for providing extra protection to the wearer in certain strenuous sports (as boxing, hockey, football) 2 : a cap of metal shaped like the femoral head and used in plastic reconstruction of the hip joint

²**cup** vb **cupped; cup·ping** 1 : to treat by cupping 2 : to undergo or perform cupping

cup·ping n : a technique formerly employed for drawing blood to the surface of the body by application of a glass vessel from which air had been evacuated by heat to form a partial vacuum

cu·pu·la \'kyü-pyü-lə, -pü-\ n, pl **cu·pu·lae** \-₁lē\ 1 : the bony apex of the cochlea 2 : the peak of the pleural sac covering the apex of the lung

cur·able \'kyür-ə-bəl\ adj : capable of being cured

cu·ra·re also **cu·ra·ri** \kyü-'rär-ē, kü-\ n : a dried aqueous extract esp. of a vine (as Strychnos toxifera of the family Loganiaceae or Chondodendron tomentosum of the family Menispermaceae) used in arrow poisons by So. American Indians and in medicine to produce muscular relaxation

cu·ra·ri·form \kyü-'rär-ə-₁fórm, kü-\ adj : producing or characterized by the muscular relaxation typical of curare (~ drugs)

cu·ra·rize \-'rär-₁īz\ vb **-rized; -riz·ing** : to treat with curare — **cu·ra·ri·za·tion** \-₁rär-ə-'zā-shən\ n

cu·ra·tive \'kyür-ə-tiv\ adj : relating to or used in the cure of diseases — **curative** n — **cu·ra·tive·ly** adv

curb \'kərb\ n : a swelling on the back of the hind leg of a horse just behind the lowest part of the hock joint that is due to strain or rupture of the ligament and generally causes lameness

¹**cure** \'kyür\ n 1 : recovery from a disease (his ~ was complete); also : remission of signs or symptoms of a disease esp. during a prolonged period of observation (clinical ~) — compare ARREST, REMISSION 2 : a drug, treatment, regimen, or other agency that cures a disease 3 : a course or period of treatment; esp : one designed to interrupt an addic-

tion or compulsive habit or to improve general health **4** : SPA

²**cure** *vb* **cured; cur·ing 1 a** : to make or become healthy, sound, or normal again ⟨*curing* his patients rapidly by new procedures⟩ **b** : to bring about recovery from ⟨antibiotics ∼ many formerly intractable infections⟩ **2** : to take a cure (as in a sanatorium or at a spa) — **cur·er** *n*

cu·ret·tage \ˌkyùr-ə-ˈtäzh\ *n* : a surgical scraping or cleaning by means of a curette

¹**cu·rette** *also* **cu·ret** \kyù-ˈret\ *n* : a surgical instrument that has a scoop, loop, or ring at its tip and is used in performing curettage

²**curette** *also* **curet** *vb* **cu·rett·ed; cu·rett·ing** : to perform curettage on — **cu·rette·ment** \-ˈret-mənt\ *n*

cu·rie \ˈkyùr-(ˌ)ē, kyù-ˈrē\ *n* **1** : a unit quantity of any radioactive nuclide in which 3.7×10^{10} disintegrations occur per second **2** : a unit of radioactivity equal to 3.7×10^{10} disintegrations per second

Curie, Pierre (1859–1906), and **Marie Sklodowska** (1867–1934), French chemists and physicists.

cu·ri·um \ˈkyùr-ē-əm\ *n* : a metallic radioactive trivalent element artificially produced — symbol *Cm;* see ELEMENT table

Cur·ling's ulcer \ˈkər-liŋz-\ *n* : acute gastroduodenal ulceration following severe skin burns

Cur·ling \ˈkər-liŋ\, **Thomas Blizard** (1811–1888), British surgeon.

cur·rent \ˈkər-ənt\ *n* : a flow of electric charge; *also* : the rate of such flow

cur·va·ture \ˈkər-və-ˌchùr, -chər, -ˌtyùr\ *n* **1** : an abnormal curving (as of the spine) — see KYPHOSIS, SCOLIOSIS **2** : a curved surface of an organ (as the stomach) — see GREATER CURVATURE, LESSER CURVATURE

cush·ing·oid \ˈkù-shiŋ-ˌoid\ *adj, often cap* : resembling Cushing's disease esp. in facies or habitus

Cush·ing's disease \ˈkù-shiŋz-\ *n* : Cushing's syndrome esp. when caused by excessive production of ACTH by the pituitary gland

Cush·ing, Harvey Williams (1869–1939), American neurosurgeon.

Cushing's syndrome *n* : an abnormal bodily condition characterized by obesity and muscular weakness due to excess corticosteroids and esp. hydrocortisone from adrenal or pituitary hyperfunction — called also *adrenogenital syndrome*

cush·ion \ˈkù-shən\ *n* **1** : a bodily part resembling a pad **2** : a medical procedure or drug that eases discomfort without necessarily affecting the basic condition of the patient

cusp \ˈkəsp\ *n* **1** : a point on the grinding surface of a tooth **2** : a fold or flap of a cardiac valve

cus·pid \ˈkəs-pəd\ *n* : a canine tooth

cus·pi·date \ˈkəs-pə-ˌdāt\ *adj* : having a cusp : terminating in a point ⟨∼ molars⟩

cus·to·di·al \ˌkəs-ˈtō-dē-əl\ *adj* : marked by or given to watching and protecting rather than seeking to cure ⟨∼ care⟩

¹**cut** \ˈkət\ *vb* **cut; cut·ting 1 a** : to penetrate with or as if with an edged instrument **b** : to cut or operate on in surgery: as (1) : to subject (a domestic animal) to castration (2) : to perform lithotomy on **c** : to experience the emergence of (a tooth) through the gum **2** : to function as or in the manner of an edged tool ⟨a knife that ∼s well⟩ **3** : to subject to trimming or paring ⟨∼ one's nails⟩

²**cut** *n* **1 a** : an opening made with an edged instrument **b** : a wound made by something sharp **2** : a stroke or blow with the edge of a sharp implement (as a knife)

cu·ta·ne·ous \kyù-ˈtā-nē-əs\ *adj* : of, relating to, or affecting the skin ⟨a ∼ infection⟩ — **cu·ta·ne·ous·ly** *adv*

cut·down \ˈkət-ˌdaùn\ *n* : incision of a superficial blood vessel (as a vein) to facilitate insertion of a catheter (as for administration of fluids)

Cu·te·re·bra \ˌkyù-tə-ˈrē-brə, kyù-ˈter-ə-brə\ *n* : a genus of large usu. dark-colored botflies (family Cuterebridae) with larvae that form tumors under the skin of rodents, cats, and other small mammals

cu·ti·cle \ˈkyù-ti-kəl\ *n* **1 a** : the outermost layer of integument composed of epidermis **b** : the outermost membranous layer of a hair consisting of cornified epithelial cells **2** : dead or horny epidermis (as that surrounding the base and sides of a fingernail or toenail) — **cu·tic·u·lar** \kyù-ˈti-kyə-lər\ *adj*

cu·ti·re·ac·tion \ˌkyù-ti-rē-ˈak-shən, ˈkyù-ti-rē-\ *n* : a local inflammatory reaction of the skin that occurs in certain infectious diseases following the application to or injection into the skin of a preparation of organisms producing the disease

cu·tis \ˈkyù-təs\ *n, pl* **cu·tes** \-ˌtēz\ *or* **cu·tis·es** : DERMIS

cu·vette \kyù-ˈvet\ *n* : a small often transparent laboratory vessel (as a tube)

Cu·vie·ri·an vein \ˌ(ˌ)kyù-ˈvir-ē-ən-, ˌkyù-vē-ˈir-\ *n* : CARDINAL VEIN

Cu·vier \ˈkü-vē-ˌā, ˈkyù-; klē-ˈvyā\, **Georges** (*orig.* Jean-Léopold-Nicolas-Frédéric) (†1769–1832), French naturalist.

CVA *abbr* cerebrovascular accident

CVP *abbr* central venous pressure

CVS *abbr* chorionic villus sampling

cyan- *or* **cyano-** *comb form* **1** : blue ⟨*cyanosis*⟩ **2** : cyanide ⟨*cyanogenetic*⟩

cy·a·nide \ˈsī-ə-ˌnīd, -nəd\ *n* : any of several compounds (as potassium cyanide) that contain the radical CN having a chemical valence of one, re-act with and inactivate respiratory enzymes, and are rapidly lethal pro-ducing drowsiness, tachycardia, coma, and finally death

cy·a·no·ac·ry·late \ˌsī-ə-nō-ˈa-krə-ˌlāt, sī-ˌa-nō-\ *n* : any of several liquid ac-rylate monomers used as adhesives in medicine on living tissue to close wounds in surgery

cy·a·no·co·bal·a·min \-kō-ˈba-lə-mən\ *also* **cy·a·no·co·bal·a·mine** \-ˌmēn\ *n* : VITAMIN B₁₂

cy·a·no·ge·net·ic \ˌsī-ə-nō-jə-ˈne-tik, sī-ˌa-nō-\ *or* **cy·a·no·gen·ic** \-ˈje-nik\ *adj* : capable of producing cyanide (as hydrogen cyanide) (a ~ plant that is dangerous to livestock) — **cy·a·no·gen·e·sis** \-ˈje-nə-səs\ *n*

cy·a·no·met·he·mo·glo·bin \ˌsī-ə-nō-(ˌ)met-ˈhē-mə-ˌglō-bən\ *or* **cy·an·met·he·mo·glo·bin** \ˌsī-ˌan-(ˌ)met-, sī-ˌan-\ *n* : a bright red crystalline compound formed by the action of hydrogen cy-anide on methemoglobin in the cold or on oxyhemoglobin at body temper-ature

cy·a·nosed \ˈsī-ə-ˌnōst, -ˌnōzd\ *adj* : af-fected with cyanosis

cy·a·no·sis \ˌsī-ə-ˈnō-səs\ *n, pl* **-no·ses** \-ˌsēz\ : a bluish or purplish discolor-ation (as of skin) due to deficient ox-ygenation of the blood — **cy·a·not·ic** \-ˈnä-tik\ *adj*

cycl- *or* **cyclo-** *comb form* : ciliary body (of the eye) (cyclitis) (cyclodialysis)

cy·cla·mate \ˈsī-klə-ˌmāt, -mət\ *n* : an artificially prepared salt of sodium or calcium used esp. formerly as a sweetener but now largely discontin-ued because of the possibly harmful effects of its metabolic breakdown product cyclohexylamine

cy·clan·de·late \ˌsī-ˈkland-əl-ˌāt\ *n* : an antispasmodic drug $C_{17}H_{24}O_3$ used esp. as a vasodilator in the treatment of diseased arteries

cy·claz·o·cine \ˌsī-ˈkla-zə-ˌsēn, -sən\ *n* : an analgesic drug $C_{18}H_{25}NO$ that in-hibits the effect of morphine and re-lated addictive drugs and is used in the treatment of drug addiction

¹**cy·cle** \ˈsī-kəl\ *n* : a recurring series of events: as a (1) : a series of stages through which an organism tends to pass once in a fixed order; *also* : a se-ries of stages through which a popu-lation of organisms tends to pass more or less together — see LIFE CY-CLE (2) : a series of physiological, biochemical, or psychological stages that recur in the same individual — see CARDIAC CYCLE, MENSTRUAL CY-CLE; KREBS CYCLE b : one complete performance of a vibration, electric oscillation, current alternation, or other periodic process — **cy·clic** \ˈsī-klik, ˈsī-\ *or* **cy·cli·cal** \ˈsī-kli-kəl, ˈsī-\ *adj* — **cy·cli·cal·ly** *also* **cy·clic·ly** *adv*

²**cycle** *vb* **cycled; cycling** : to undergo estrous cycle

cy·clec·to·my \sī-ˈklek-tə-mē, si-\ *n, pl* **-mies** : surgical removal of part of the ciliary muscle or body

cyclic adenosine monophosphate *n* : CY-CLIC AMP

cyclic AMP *n* : a cyclic mononucleotide of adenosine that is formed from ATP and is responsible for the intracellular mediation of hormonal effects on var-ious cellular processes — *abbr. CAMP*

cyclic GMP \-ˌjē-(ˌ)em-ˈpē\ *n* : a cyclic mononucleotide of guanosine that acts similarly to cyclic AMP as a sec-ondary messenger in response to hor-mones

cyclic guanosine monophosphate *n* : CY-CLIC GMP

cy·clic·i·ty \sī-ˈkli-sə-tē, si-\ *n, pl* **-ties** : the quality or state of being cyclic (estrous ~)

cy·cli·tis \sə-ˈklī-təs, sī-\ *n* : inflamma-tion of the ciliary body

cy·cli·zine \ˈsī-klə-ˌzēn\ *n* : an anti-emetic drug $C_{18}H_{22}N_2$ used esp. in the form of its hydrochloride in the treatment of motion sickness — see MAREZINE

cyclo- — see CYCL-

cy·clo·di·al·y·sis \ˌsī-klō-dī-ˈa-lə-səs\ *n, pl* **-y·ses** \-ˌsēz\ : surgical detachment of the ciliary body from the sclera to reduce tension in the eyeball in some cases of glaucoma

cy·clo·dia·ther·my \-ˈdī-ə-ˌthər-mē\ *n, pl* **-mies** : partial or complete destruc-tion of the ciliary body by diathermy to relieve some conditions (as glauco-ma) characterized by increased ten-sion within the eyeball

Cy·clo·gyl \ˈsī-klō-ˌgil\ *trademark* — used for a preparation of the hydro-chloride of cyclopentolate

cy·clo·hex·ane \ˌsī-klō-ˈhek-ˌsān\ *n* : a pungent saturated hydrocarbon C_6H_{12} found in petroleum or made syn-thetically

cy·clo·hex·yl·a·mine \-hek-ˈsi-lə-ˌmēn\ *n* : a colorless liquid amine $C_6H_{11}N$-H_2 of cyclohexane that is believed to be harmful as a metabolic breakdown product of cyclamate

¹**cy·cloid** \ˈsī-ˌklȯid\ *n* : a cycloid indi-vidual

²**cycloid** *adj* : relating to or being a per-sonality characterized by alternating high and low moods — compare CY-CLOTHYMIC

cy·clo·oxy·gen·ase \ˌsī-klō-ˈäk-si-jə-ˌnās, -äk-ˈsi-jə-, -ˌnāz\ *n* : an enzyme that catalyzes the conversion of ara-chidonic acid into prostaglandins of which some are associated with ar-thritic inflammation and that is held to be inactivated by aspirin giving temporary partial relief of arthritic symptoms

cy·clo·pen·to·late \ˌsī-klō-ˈpen-tə-ˌlāt, ˌsi-\ *n* : an anticholinergic drug used esp. in the form of its hydrochloride

$C_{17}H_{25}NO_3 \cdot HCl$ to dilate the pupil of the eye for ophthalmologic examination — see CYCLOGYL

cy·clo·phos·pha·mide \-ⁱfäs-fə-₊mīd\ n : an immunosuppressive and antineoplastic drug $C_7H_{15}Cl_2N_2O_2P$ used in the treatment of lymphomas and some leukemias — see CYTOXAN

cy·clo·pia \sīⁱklō-pē-ə\ n : a developmental anomaly characterized by the presence of a single median eye

cy·clo·ple·gia \ₛsī-klōⁱplē-jə, ₊si-, -jē-ə\ n : paralysis of the ciliary muscle of the eye

¹cy·clo·ple·gic \-ⁱplē-jik\ adj : producing, involving, or characterized by cycloplegia ⟨~ agents⟩ ⟨~ refraction⟩

²cycloplegic n : a cycloplegic agent

cy·clo·pro·pane \-ⁱprō-₊pān\ n : a flammable gaseous saturated cyclic hydrocarbon C_3H_6 sometimes used as a general anesthetic

cy·clops \ⁱsī-₊kläps\ n, pl **cy·clo·pes** \sī-ⁱklō-(₊)pēz\ : an individual or fetus abnormal in having a single eye or the usual two orbits fused

cy·clo·ser·ine \ₛsī-klō-ⁱser-₊ēn, ₊si-\ : an amino antibiotic $C_3H_6N_2O_2$ produced by an actinomycete of the genus Streptomyces (S. orchidaceus) and used esp. in the treatment of tuberculosis

cy·clo·spor·in \ₛsī-klō-ⁱspȯr-ᵊn\ n : any of a group of polypeptides obtained as metabolites from various imperfect fungi (as Tolypocladium inflatum Gams syn. Trichoderma polysporum); esp : CYCLOSPORINE

cyclosporin A n : CYCLOSPORINE

cy·clo·spor·ine \ₛsī-klə-ⁱspȯr-ən, -₊ēn\ n : a cyclosporin $C_{62}H_{111}N_{11}O_{12}$ used as an immunosuppressive drug esp. to prevent rejection of transplanted organs

cy·clo·thyme \ⁱsī-klə-₊thīm\ n : a cyclothymic individual

cy·clo·thy·mia \ₛsī-klə-ⁱthī-mē-ə\ n : a cyclothymic affective disorder

¹cy·clo·thy·mic \-ⁱthī-mik\ adj : relating to or being an affective disorder characterized by the alternation of depressed moods with elevated, expansive, or irritable moods without psychotic features (as hallucinations or delusions) — compare CYCLOID

²cyclothymic n : a cyclothymic individual

cy·clo·tome \ⁱsī-klə-₊tōm\ n : a knife used in cyclotomy

cy·clot·o·my \sī-ⁱklä-tə-mē\ n, pl **-mies** : incision or division of the ciliary body

cy·clo·tro·pia \ₛsī-klə-ⁱtrō-pē-ə\ n : squint in which the eye rolls outward or inward around its front-to-back axis

cy·e·sis \sī-ⁱē-səs\ n, pl **cy·e·ses** \-₊sēz\ : PREGNANCY

cyl·in·droid \ⁱsi-lən-₊drȯid, sə-ⁱlin-\ n : a spurious or mucous urinary cast

that resembles a hyaline cast but has one tapered, stringy, twisted end

cyl·in·dro·ma \ₛsi-lən-ⁱdrō-mə\ n, pl **-mas** or **-ma·ta** \mə-tə\ : a tumor characterized by cylindrical masses consisting of epithelial cells and hyalinized stroma: **a** : a malignant tumor esp. of the respiratory tract or salivary glands **b** : a benign tumor of the skin and esp. the scalp

cyl·in·dru·ria \ₛsi-lən-ⁱdrür-ē-ə\ n : the presence of casts in the urine

cy·no·mol·gus monkey \ₛsī-nə-ⁱmäl-gəs-\ n : a macaque (Macaca fascicularis syn. M. cynomolgus) of southeastern Asia, Borneo, and the Philippines that is often used in medical research

cy·no·pho·bia \-ⁱfō-bē-ə\ n : a morbid fear of dogs

cy·pro·hep·ta·dine \ₛsī-prō-ⁱhep-tə-₊dēn\ n : a drug $C_{21}H_{21}N$ that acts antagonistically to histamine and serotonin and is used esp. in the treatment of asthma

cy·prot·er·one \sī-ⁱprä-tə-₊rōn\ n : a synthetic steroid $C_{22}H_{27}ClO_3$ used in the form of its acetate to inhibit androgenic secretions (as testosterone)

cyst \ⁱsist\ n **1** : a closed sac having a distinct membrane and developing abnormally in a body cavity or structure **2** : a body resembling a cyst: as **a** : a capsule formed about a minute organism going into a resting or spore stage; also : this capsule with its contents **b** : a resistant cover about a parasite produced by the parasite or the host — compare HYDATID 2a

cyst- or **cysti-** or **cysto-** comb form **1** : bladder ⟨cystitis⟩ ⟨cystoplasty⟩ **2** : cyst ⟨cystogastrostomy⟩

-cyst \₊sist\ n comb form : bladder : sac ⟨blastocyst⟩

cyst·ad·e·no·ma \ₛsis-₊tad-ᵊn-ⁱō-mə\ n, pl **-mas** or **-ma·ta** \mə-tə\ : an adenoma marked by a cystic structure — **cyst·ad·e·no·ma·tous** \-mə-təs\ adj

cys·te·amine \sis-ⁱtē-ə-mən\ n : a cysteine derivative C_2H_7NS that has been used experimentally in the prevention of radiation sickness (as in cancer patients)

cys·tec·to·my \sis-ⁱtek-tə-mē\ n, pl **-mies 1** : the surgical excision of a cyst (ovarian ~) **2** : the removal of all or a portion of the urinary bladder

cys·teine \ⁱsis-tə-₊ēn\ n : a sulfur-containing amino acid $C_3H_7NO_2S$ occurring in many proteins and glutathione and readily oxidizable to cystine

cysti- — see CYST-

cys·tic \ⁱsis-tik\ adj **1** : relating to, composed of, or containing cysts ⟨a ~ tumor⟩ **2** : of or relating to the urinary bladder or the gallbladder **3** : enclosed in a cyst ⟨a ~ worm larva⟩

cystica — see OSTEITIS FIBROSA CYSTICA. OSTEITIS FIBROSA CYSTICA GENERALISTA

cystic duct *n* : the duct from the gall-bladder that unites with the hepatic duct to form the common bile duct

cys·ti·cer·coid \ˌsis-tə-ˈsər-ˌkȯid\ *n* : a tapeworm larva having an invaginated scolex and solid hind part

cys·ti·cer·co·sis \-(ˌ)sər-ˈkō-səs\ *n, pl* **-co·ses** \-ˌsēz\ : infestation with or disease caused by cysticerci

cys·ti·cer·cus \-ˈsər-kəs\ *n, pl* **-cer·ci** \-ˈsər-ˌsī, -ˌkī\ : a tapeworm larva that consists of a fluid-filled sac containing an invaginated scolex, is situated in the tissues of an intermediate host, and is capable of developing into an adult tapeworm when eaten by a suitable definitive host — called also *bladder worm, measle* — **cys·ti·cer·cal** \-ˈsər-kəl\ *adj*

cystic fibrosis *n* : a common hereditary disease esp. in Caucasian populations that appears usu. in early childhood, involves functional disorder of the exocrine glands, and is marked esp. by faulty digestion due to a deficiency of pancreatic enzymes, by difficulty in breathing due to mucus accumulation in airways, and by excessive loss of salt in the sweat — called also *fibrocystic disease of the pancreas, mucoviscidosis*

cys·tine \ˈsis-ˌtēn\ *n* : a crystalline amino acid $C_6H_{12}N_2O_4S_2$ that is widespread in proteins (as keratins) and is a major metabolic sulfur source

cys·ti·no·sis \ˌsis-tə-ˈnō-səs\ *n, pl* **-no·ses** \-ˌsēz\ : a recessive autosomally inherited disease characterized esp. by cystinuria and deposits of cystine throughout the body — **cys·ti·not·ic** \-ˈnä-tik\ *adj*

cys·tin·uria \ˌsis-tə-ˈnür-ē-ə, -ˈnyur-\ *n* : a metabolic defect characterized by excretion of excessive amounts of cystine in the urine and sometimes by the formation of stones in the urinary tract and inherited as an autosomal recessive trait — **cys·tin·uric** \-ˈnür-ik, -ˈnyur-\ *adj*

cys·ti·tis \sis-ˈtī-təs\ *n, pl* **cys·tit·i·des** \-ˈti-tə-ˌdēz\ : inflammation of the urinary bladder — **cys·tit·ic** \(ˈ)sis-ˈti-tik\ *adj*

cysto- — see CYST-

cys·to·cele \ˈsis-tə-ˌsēl\ *n* : hernia of a bladder and esp. the urinary bladder : vesical hernia

cys·to·gas·tros·to·my \ˌsis-tō-(ˌ)gas-ˈträs-tə-mē\ *n, pl* **-mies** : creation of a surgical opening between the stomach and a nearby cyst for drainage

cys·to·gram \ˈsis-tə-ˌgram\ *n* : a roentgenogram made by cystography

cys·tog·ra·phy \sis-ˈtä-grə-fē\ *n, pl* **-phies** : X-ray photography of the urinary bladder after injection of a contrast medium — **cys·to·graph·ic** \-tə-ˈgra-fik\ *adj*

cys·toid \ˈsis-ˌtȯid\ *adj* : resembling a bladder

cys·to·lith \ˈsis-tə-ˌlith\ *n* : a urinary calculus

cys·to·li·thi·a·sis \ˌsis-tō-li-ˈthī-ə-səs\ *n, pl* **-a·ses** \-ˌsēz\ : the presence of calculi in the urinary bladder

cys·to·li·thot·o·my \-li-ˈthä-tə-mē\ *n, pl* **-mies** : surgical removal of a calculus from the urinary bladder

cys·tom·e·ter \sis-ˈtä-mə-tər\ *n* : an instrument designed to measure pressure within the urinary bladder in relation to its capacity — **cys·to·met·ric** \ˌsis-tə-ˈme-trik\ *adj* — **cys·tom·e·try** \sis-ˈtä-mə-trē\ *n*

cys·to·met·ro·gram \ˌsis-tə-ˈme-trə-ˌgram, -ˈmē-\ *n* : a graphic recording of a cystometric measurement

cys·to·me·trog·ra·phy \-mə-ˈträ-grə-fē\ *n, pl* **-phies** : the process of making a cystometrogram

cys·to·plas·ty \ˈsis-tə-ˌplas-tē\ *n, pl* **-ties** : a plastic operation upon the urinary bladder

cys·to·py·eli·tis \ˌsis-tə-ˌpī-ə-ˈlī-təs\ *n* : inflammation of the urinary bladder and of the pelvis of one or both kidneys

cys·tor·rha·phy \sis-ˈtȯr-ə-fē\ *n, pl* **-phies** : suture of a wound, injury, or rupture in the urinary bladder

cys·to·sar·co·ma phyl·lodes \ˌsis-tō-sär-ˈkō-mə-fi-ˈlōdz\ *n* : a slow-growing tumor of the breast that resembles a fibroadenoma

cys·to·scope \ˈsis-tə-ˌskōp\ *n* : a medical instrument for the visual examination of the urinary bladder and the passage of instruments under visual control — **cys·to·scop·ic** \ˌsis-tə-ˈskä-pik\ *adj* — **cys·tos·co·pist** \sis-ˈtäs-kə-pist\ *n*

cys·tos·co·py \sis-ˈtäs-kə-pē\ *n, pl* **-pies** : the use of a cystoscope to examine the bladder

cys·tos·to·my \sis-ˈtäs-tə-mē\ *n, pl* **-mies** : formation of an opening into the urinary bladder by surgical incision

cys·tot·o·my \sis-ˈtä-tə-mē\ *n, pl* **-mies** : surgical incision of the urinary bladder

cys·to·ure·ter·itis \ˌsis-tō-ˌyür-ə-tə-ˈrī-təs\ *n* : combined inflammation of the urinary bladder and ureters

cys·to·ure·thro·cele \ˌsis-tō-yü-ˈrē-thrə-ˌsēl\ *n* : herniation of the neck of the female bladder and associated urethra into the vagina

cys·to·ure·thro·gram \-yü-ˈrē-thrə-ˌgram\ *n* : an X-ray photograph of the urinary bladder and urethra made after injection of these organs with a contrast medium — **cys·to·ure·throg·ra·phy** \-ˌyür-i-ˈthrä-grə-fē\ *n*

cys·to·ure·thro·scope \ˌsis-tō-yü-ˈrē-thrə-ˌskōp\ *n* : an instrument used for the examination of the posterior urethra and bladder — **cys·to·ure·thros·co·py** \-ˌyür-i-ˈthräs-kə-pē\ *n*

cyt- or **cyto-** *comb form* **1** : cell ⟨*cytology*⟩ **2** : cytoplasm ⟨*cytokinesis*⟩

cyt·ar·a·bine \sĭ-'tar-ə-ˌbēn\ n : CYTOSINE ARABINOSIDE

-cyte \ˌsīt\ n comb form : cell ⟨leukocyte⟩

cy·to·ar·chi·tec·ton·ics \ˌsī-tō-ˌär-kə-(ˌ)tek-'tä-niks\ n sing or pl : CYTOARCHITECTURE — **cy·to·ar·chi·tec·ton·ic** \-nik\ adj

cy·to·ar·chi·tec·ture \ˌsī-tō-'är-kə-ˌtek-chər\ n : the cellular makeup of a bodily tissue or structure — **cy·to·ar·chi·tec·tur·al** \-ˌär-kə-'tek-chə-rəl\ adj — **cy·to·ar·chi·tec·tur·al·ly** adv

cy·to·chem·is·try \-'ke-mə-strē\ n, pl -tries 1 : microscopic biochemistry 2 : the chemistry of cells — **cy·to·chem·i·cal** \-'ke-mi-kəl\ adj — **cy·to·chem·i·cal·ly** \-mi-k(ə-)lē\ adv — **cy·to·chem·ist** \-'ke-mist\ n

cy·to·chrome \'sī-tə-ˌkrōm\ n : any of several intracellular hemoprotein respiratory pigments that are enzymes functioning in electron transport as carriers of electrons

cytochrome c n, often italicized 3d c : the most abundant and stable of the cytochromes

cytochrome oxidase n : an iron-porphyrin enzyme important in cell respiration because of its ability to catalyze the oxidation of reduced cytochrome c in the presence of oxygen

cy·to·cid·al \ˌsī-tə-'sīd-ᵊl\ adj : killing or tending to kill individual cells ⟨~ RNA-containing viruses⟩

cy·to·di·ag·no·sis \ˌsī-tō-ˌdī-ig-'nō-səs, -əg-\ n, pl -no·ses \-ˌsēz\ : diagnosis based upon the examination of cells found in the tissues or fluids of the body — **cy·to·di·ag·nos·tic** \-'näs-tik\ adj

cy·to·dif·fer·en·ti·a·tion \ˌsī-tō-ˌdi-fə-ˌren-chē-'ā-shən\ n : the development of specialized cells (as muscle, blood, or nerve cells) from undifferentiated precursors

cy·to·ge·net·ics \-jə-'ne-tiks\ n sing or pl : a branch of biology that deals with the study of heredity and variation by the methods of both cytology and genetics — **cy·to·ge·net·ic** \-jə-'ne-tik\ or **cy·to·ge·net·i·cal** \-ti-kəl\ adj — **cy·to·ge·net·i·cal·ly** \-ti-k(ə-)lē\ adv — **cy·to·ge·net·i·cist** \-'ne-tə-sist\ n

cy·toid body \'sī-ˌtoid-\ n : one of the white globular masses resembling cells that are found in the retina in some abnormal conditions

cy·to·kine \'sī-tə-ˌkīn\ n : any of a class of immunoregulatory substances (as lymphokines) that are secreted by cells of the immune system

cy·to·ki·ne·sis \ˌsī-tō-kə-'nē-səs, -kī-\ n, pl -ne·ses \-ˌsēz\ 1 : the cytoplasmic changes accompanying mitosis 2 : cleavage of the cytoplasm into daughter cells following nuclear division — compare KARYOKINESIS — **cy·to·ki·net·ic** \-'ne-tik\ adj

cytol abbr cytological; cytology

cy·tol·o·gy \sī-'tä-lə-jē\ n, pl -gies 1 : a branch of biology dealing with the structure, function, multiplication, pathology, and life history of cells 2 : the cytological aspects of a process or structure — **cy·to·log·i·cal** \ˌsīt-ᵊl-'ä-ji-kəl\ or **cy·to·log·ic** \-'ä-jik\ adj — **cy·to·log·i·cal·ly** \-ji-k(ə-)lē\ adv — **cy·tol·o·gist** \sī-'tä-lə-jist\ n

cy·to·ly·sin \ˌsīt-ᵊl-'īs-ᵊn\ n : a substance (as an antibody that lyses bacteria) producing cytolysis

cy·tol·y·sis \sī-'tä-lə-səs\ n, pl -y·ses \-ˌsēz\ : the usu. pathologic dissolution or disintegration of cells — **cy·to·lyt·ic** \ˌsīt-ᵊl-'i-tik\ adj

cy·to·me·gal·ic \ˌsī-tō-mi-'ga-lik\ adj : characterized by or causing the formation of enlarged cells

cytomegalic inclusion disease n : a severe disease esp. of newborns that is caused by a cytomegalovirus and usu. affects the salivary glands, brain, kidneys, liver, and lungs — called also inclusion disease

cy·to·meg·a·lo·vi·rus \ˌsī-tə-ˌme-gə-lō-'vī-rəs\ n : any of several herpesviruses that cause cellular enlargement and formation of eosinophilic inclusion bodies esp. in the nucleus and include some acting as opportunistic infectious agents in immunosuppressed conditions (as AIDS)

cy·tom·e·ter \sī-'tä-mə-tər\ n : an apparatus for counting and measuring cells

cy·tom·e·try \sī-'tä-mə-trē\ n, pl -tries : a technical specialty concerned with the counting of cells and esp. blood cells — **cy·to·met·ric** \ˌsī-tə-'me-trik\ adj

cy·to·mor·phol·o·gy \ˌsī-tə-mór-'fä-lə-jē\ n, pl -gies : the morphology of cells — **cy·to·mor·pho·log·i·cal** \-ˌmór-fə-'lä-ji-kəl\ adj

cy·to·path·ic \ˌsī-tə-'pa-thik\ adj : of, relating to, characterized by, or producing pathological changes in cells

cy·to·patho·gen·ic \-ˌpa-thə-'je-nik\ adj : pathologic for or destructive to cells — **cy·to·patho·ge·nic·i·ty** \-jə-'ni-sə-tē\ n

cy·to·pa·thol·o·gy \-pə-'thä-lə-jē, -pa-\ n, pl -gies : a branch of pathology that deals with manifestations of disease at the cellular level — **cy·to·patho·log·ic** \-ˌpa-thə-'lä-jik\ also **cy·to·patho·log·i·cal** \-ji-kəl\ adj — **cy·to·pa·thol·o·gist** \-pə-'thä-lə-jist, -pa-\ n

cy·to·pe·nia \-'pē-nē-ə\ n : a deficiency of cellular elements of the blood; esp : deficiency of a specific element (as granulocytes in granulocytopenia) — **cy·to·pe·nic** \-'pē-nik\ adj

cy·to·phil·ic \ˌsī-tə-'fi-lik\ adj : having an affinity for cells

cy·to·pho·tom·e·ter \ˌsī-tō-fō-'tä-mə-tər\ n : a photometer for use in cytophotometry

cy·to·pho·tom·e·try \-(ˌ)fō-'tä-mə-trē\ n, pl -tries : photometry applied to the study of the cell or its constituents — **cy·to·pho·to·met·ric** \-ˌfō-tə-ˈme-trik\ adj — **cy·to·pho·to·met·ri·cal·ly** \-tri-k(ə-)lē\ adv

cy·to·phys·i·ol·o·gy \-ˌfi-zē-ˈä-lə-jē\ n, pl **-gies** : the physiology of cells — **cy·to·phys·i·o·log·i·cal** \-zē-ə-ˈlä-ji-kəl\ adj

cy·to·pi·pette \ˈsī-tō-pī-ˈpet\ n : a pipette with a bulb that contains a fluid which is released into the vagina and then sucked back with a sample of cells for a vaginal smear

cy·to·plasm \ˈsī-tə-ˌpla-zəm\ n : the organized complex of inorganic and organic substances external to the nuclear membrane of a cell and including the cytosol and membrane-bound organelles (as mitochondria) — **cy·to·plas·mic** \ˌsī-tə-ˈplaz-mik\ adj — **cy·to·plas·mi·cal·ly** \-mi-k(ə-)lē\ adv

cy·to·sine \ˈsī-tə-ˌsēn\ n : a pyrimidine base $C_4H_5N_3O$ that codes genetic information in the polynucleotide chain of DNA or RNA — compare ADENINE, GUANINE, THYMINE, URACIL

cytosine arabinoside n : a cytotoxic antineoplastic agent $C_9H_{13}N_3O_5$ that is a synthetic isomer of the naturally occurring nucleoside of cytosine and arabinose and is used esp. in the treatment of acute myelogenous leukemia in adults

cy·to·skel·e·ton \ˌsī-tō-ˈske-lət-ᵊn\ n : the network of protein filaments and microtubules in the cytoplasm that controls cell shape, maintains intracellular organization, and is involved in cell movement — **cy·to·skel·e·tal** \-ᵊl\ adj

cy·to·sol \ˈsī-tə-ˌsäl, -ˌsol\ n : the fluid portion of the cytoplasm exclusive of organelles and membranes — called also *hyaloplasm*, *ground substance* — **cy·to·sol·ic** \ˌsī-tə-ˈsä-lik, -ˈso-\ adj

cy·to·stat·ic \ˌsī-tə-ˈsta-tik\ adj : tending to retard cellular activity and multiplication (~ treatment of tumors) — **cy·to·stat·i·cal·ly** \-ti-k(ə-)lē\ adv

²**cytostatic** n : a cytostatic agent

cy·to·tech·ni·cian \-ˌsī-tə-(ˌ)tek-ˈni-shən\ n : CYTOTECHNOLOGIST

cy·to·tech·nol·o·gist \-ˈnä-lə-jist\ n : a medical technician trained in cytotechnology

cy·to·tech·nol·o·gy \-ˈnä-lə-jē\ n, pl **-gies** : a specialty in medical technology concerned with the identification of cells and cellular abnormalities (as in cancer)

cy·to·tox·ic \ˌsī-tə-ˈtäk-sik\ adj : toxic to cells (~ lymphocytes) (~ drugs) — **cy·to·tox·ic·i·ty** \-(ˌ)täk-ˈsi-sə-tē\ n

cy·to·tox·in \-ˈtäk-sən\ n : a substance (as a toxin or antibody) having a toxic effect on cells

cy·to·tro·pho·blast \ˌsī-tə-ˈtrō-fə-ˌblast\ n : the inner cellular layer of the trophoblast of an embryonic placenta-forming mammal that gives rise to the plasmodial syncytiotrophoblast covering the placental villi — **cy·to·tro·pho·blas·tic** \-ˌtrō-fə-ˈblas-tik\ adj

Cy·tox·an \sī-ˈtäk-sən\ trademark — used for a preparation of cyclophosphamide

D

d abbr **1** died **2** diopter **3** disease

d- \ˈdē, ˈdē\ prefix **1** : dextrorotatory — usu. printed in italic ⟨d-tartaric acid⟩ **2** : having a similar configuration at a selected carbon atom to the configuration of dextrorotatory glyceraldehyde — usu. printed as a small capital ⟨D-fructose⟩

2,4–D — see entry alphabetized as TWO,FOUR-D in the letter t

da·car·ba·zine \dä-ˈkär-bə-ˌzēn\ n : an antineoplastic agent $C_6H_{10}N_6O$ used to treat esp. metastatic malignant melanoma, tumors of adult soft tissue, and Hodgkin's disease

dacry- or **dacryo-** comb form : lacrimal ⟨dacryocystitis⟩

dac·ry·o·ad·e·nec·to·my \ˌda-krē-(ˌ)ō-ˌad-ᵊn-ˈek-tə-mē\ n, pl **-mies** : excision of a lacrimal gland

dac·ry·o·cyst \ˈda-krē-ə-ˌsist\ n : LACRIMAL SAC

dac·ry·o·cys·tec·to·my \ˌda-krē-(ˌ)ō-sis-ˈtek-tə-mē\ n, pl **-mies** : excision of a lacrimal sac

dac·ry·o·cys·ti·tis \-sis-ˈtī-təs\ n : inflammation of the lacrimal sac

dac·ry·o·cys·tog·ra·phy \-sis-ˈtä-grə-fē\ n, pl **-phies** : radiographic visualization of the lacrimal sacs and associated structures after injection of a contrast medium

dac·ry·o·cys·to·rhi·nos·to·my \-ˌsis-tə-ˌrī-ˈnäs-tə-mē\ n, pl **-mies** : surgical creation of a passage for drainage between the lacrimal sac and the nasal cavity

dac·ry·o·cys·tos·to·my \-sis-ˈtäs-tə-mē\ n, pl **-mies** : an operation on a lacrimal sac to form a new opening (as for drainage)

dac·ry·o·cys·tot·o·my \-sis-ˈtä-tə-mē\ n, pl **-mies** : incision (as for drainage) of a lacrimal sac

dac·ry·o·lith \ˈda-krē-ə-ˌlith\ n : a concretion formed in a lacrimal passage

dac·ry·o·ste·no·sis \ˌda-krē-(ˌ)ō-sti-ˈnō-səs\ n, pl **-oses** \-ˌsēz\ : a narrowing of the lacrimal duct

dac·ti·no·my·cin \ˌdak-tə-nō-ˈmīs-ᵊn\ n : a toxic antineoplastic drug $C_{62}H_{86}N_{12}O_{16}$ of the actinomycin group — called also *actinomycin D*

dactyl- or **dactylo-** comb form : finger : toe : digit ⟨dactylology⟩

-dactylia *n comb form* : -DACTYLY ⟨adactylia⟩

-dactylism *n comb form* : -DACTYLY ⟨oligodactylism⟩

dac·ty·lol·o·gy \ˌdak-tə-ˈlä-lə-jē\ *n, pl* -gies : the art of communicating ideas by signs made with the fingers

-dactylous *adj comb form* : having (such or so many) fingers or toes ⟨brachydactylous⟩

-dactyly *n comb form* : condition of having (such or so many) fingers or toes ⟨polydactyly⟩ ⟨syndactyly⟩

dag·ga \ˈda-gə, ˈdä-\ *n, chiefly SoAfr* : MARIJUANA

DAH *abbr* disordered action of the heart

Dal·mane \ˈdal-ˌmān\ *trademark* — used for a preparation of flurazepam hydrochloride

Dal·ton·ism \ˈdȯlt-ᵊn-ˌi-zəm\ *n* : red-green blindness occurring as a recessive sex-linked genetic trait; *broadly* : any form of color blindness

Dalton, John (1766–1844), British chemist and physicist.

¹dam \ˈdam\ *n* : a female parent — used esp. of a domestic animal

²dam *n* : RUBBER DAM — see DENTAL DAM

³dam *abbr* dekameter

damp \ˈdamp\ *n* : a noxious or stifling gas or vapor; *esp* : one occuring in coal mines — usu. used in pl.; see BLACK DAMP, FIREDAMP

da·na·zol \ˈdä-nə-ˌzȯl, ˈda-, -ˌzōl\ *n* : a synthetic androgenic derivative $C_{22}H_{27}NO_2$ of ethisterone that suppresses hormone secretion by the adenohypophysis and is used esp. in the treatment of endometriosis

D&C *abbr* dilation and curettage

D&E *abbr* dilation and evacuation

dan·der \ˈdan-dər\ *n* : DANDRUFF; *specif* : minute scales from hair, feathers, or skin that may act as allergens

dan·druff \ˈdan-drəf\ *n* : a scurf that forms on the skin esp. of the scalp and comes off in small white or grayish scales — dan·druffy \-drə-fē\ *adj*

dan·dy fever \ˈdan-dē-\ *n* : DENGUE

Dane particle \ˈdān-\ *n* : a spherical particle found in the serum in hepatitis B that is the virion of the causative virus

Dane, David Maurice Surrey (*b* 1923), British pathologist.

Da·nysz phenomenon \ˈdä-nish-\ *n* : the exhibition of residual toxicity by a mixture of toxin and antitoxin in which the toxin has been added in several increments to an amount of antitoxin sufficient to completely neutralize it if it had been added as a single increment — called also *Danysz effect*

Danysz, Jean (1860–1928), Polish-French pathologist.

dap·pen dish \ˈda-pən-\ *n* : a small heavy 10-sided piece of glass each end of which is ground into a small cup for mixing dental medicaments or fillings — called also *dappen glass*

dap·sone \ˈdap-ˌsȯn, -ˌzȯn\ *n* : an antimicrobial agent $C_{12}H_{12}N_2O_2S$ used esp. against leprosy and sometimes against malaria — called also *diaminodiphenyl sulfone*

Da·rier's disease \dar-ˈyāz-\ *n* : a genetically determined skin condition characterized by patches of keratotic papules — called also *keratosis follicularis*

Da·rier \dár-ˈyā\, **Jean Ferdinand** (1856–1938), French dermatologist.

dark adaptation *n* : the phenomena including dilation of the pupil, increase in retinal sensitivity, shift of the region of maximum luminosity toward the blue, and regeneration of rhodopsin by which the eye adapts to conditions of reduced illumination — compare LIGHT ADAPTATION — **dark–adapted** *adj*

dark field *n* : the dark area that serves as the background for objects viewed in an ultramicroscope — **dark–field** *adj*

dark–field microscope *n* : ULTRAMICROSCOPE — **dark–field microscopy** *n*

dar·tos \ˈdär-ˌtäs, -təs\ *n* : a thin layer of vascular contractile tissue that contains smooth muscle fibers but no fat and is situated beneath the skin of the scrotum or beneath that of the labia majora

Dar·von \ˈdär-ˌvän\ *trademark* — used for a preparation of the hydrochloride of propoxyphene

Dar·win·ism \ˈdär-wə-ˌni-zəm\ *n* : a theory of the origin and perpetuation of new species of animals and plants that offspring of a given organism vary, that natural selection favors the survival of some of these variations over others, that new species have arisen and may continue to arise by these processes, and that widely divergent groups of plants and animals have arisen from the same ancestors; *broadly* : a theory of biological evolution — **Dar·win·ist** \-nist\ *n or adj*

Dar·win \ˈdär-wən\, **Charles Robert** (1809–1882), British naturalist.

Darwin's tubercle *n* : the slight projection occas. present on the edge of the external human ear and assumed by some scientists to represent the pointed part of the ear of quadrupeds — called also *auricular tubercle of Darwin*

da·ta \ˈdā-tə, ˈda-, ˈdä-\ *n sing or pl* : factual information (as measurements or statistics) used as a basis for reasoning, discussion, or calculation ⟨comprehensive ~ on the incidence of sexually transmitted diseases⟩

da·tu·ra \də-ˈtür-ə, -ˈtyür-\ *n 1 cap* : a genus of widely distributed strong-scented herbs, shrubs, or trees (family Solanaceae) related to the potato and tomato and including some used as sources of medicinal alkaloids (as stramonium from jimsonweed) or in folk rites or illicitly for their poisonous, narcotic, or hallucinogenic properties 2 : any plant or flower of the genus *Datura*

dau *abbr* daughter

¹daugh·ter \'do-tər\ *n* 1 a : a human female having the relation of child to a parent b : a female offspring of an animal 2 : an atomic species that is the immediate product of the radioactive decay of a given element (radon, the ~ of radium)

²daughter *adj* 1 : having the characteristics or relationship of a daughter 2 : belonging to the first generation of offspring, organelles, or molecules produced by reproduction, division, or replication (~ cell) (~ chromosomes) (~ DNA molecules)

dau·no·my·cin \ˌdȯ-nə-¹mīs-ᵊn, ˌdaȯ-\ : DAUNORUBICIN

dau·no·ru·bi·cin \-¹rü-bə-sən\ *n* : an antibiotic nitrogenous glycoside used in the form of its hydrochloride $C_{27}H_{29}NO_{10}\cdot HCl$ esp. in the treatment of some leukemias

day·dream \'dā-ˌdrēm\ *n* : a visionary creation of the imagination experienced while awake; *esp* : a gratifying reverie usu. of wish fulfillment — **daydream** *vb* — **day·dream·er** *n*

day·mare \'dā-ˌmar\ *n* : a nightmarish fantasy experienced while awake

day nursery *n* : a public center for the care and training of young children

DBCP \ˌdē-(ˌ)bē-ˌsē-¹pē\ *n* : an agricultural pesticide $C_3H_5Br_2Cl$ that is a suspected carcinogen and cause of sterility in human males

DBP *abbr* diastolic blood pressure

DC *abbr* doctor of chiropractic

DD *abbr* developmentally disabled

DDC *or* **ddC** \ˌdē-(ˌ)dē-¹sē\ *n* : an antiviral drug $C_{10}H_{33}N_3O_3$ used to reduce virus growth and reproduction in AIDS and HIV infection — called also *dideoxycytidine, zalcitabine*

DDD \-¹dē\ *n* : an insecticide $C_{14}H_{10}Cl_4$ closely related chemically and similar in properties to DDT

DDE \-¹ē\ *n* : a persistent organochlorine $C_{15}H_8Cl_4$ that is produced by the metabolic breakdown of DDT

DDI *or* **ddI** \-¹ī\ *n* : an antiviral drug $C_{10}H_{12}N_4O_3$ used to reduce virus growth and reproduction in AIDS and HIV infection — called also *didanosine, dideoxyinosine;* see VIDEX

DDS *abbr* doctor of dental surgery

DDT \ˌdēd-(ˌ)ē-¹tē\ *n* : a colorless odorless water-insoluble crystalline insecticide $C_{14}H_9Cl_5$ that tends to accumulate in ecosystems and has toxic effects on many vertebrates

DDVP \ˌdē-(ˌ)dē-(ˌ)vē-¹pē\ *n* : DICHLORVOS

¹dead \'ded\ *adj* 1 : deprived of life

: having died 2 : lacking power to move, feel, or respond : NUMB

²dead *n, pl* **dead** : one that is dead — usu. used collectively

dead·ly \'ded-lē\ *adj* **dead·li·er; -est** : likely to cause or capable of causing death (a ~ disease) (a ~ poison) — **dead·li·ness** \-nəs\ *n*

deadly nightshade *n* : BELLADONNA 1

dead space *n* 1 : space in the respiratory system in which air does not undergo significant gaseous exchange — see ANATOMICAL DEAD SPACE, PHYSIOLOGICAL DEAD SPACE 2 : a space (as that in the chest following excision of a lung) left in the body as the result of a surgical procedure

deaf \'def\ *adj* : lacking or deficient in the sense of hearing — **deaf·ness** *n*

deaf-aid \'def-ˌād\ *n, chiefly Brit* : HEARING AID

deaf·en \'de-fən\ *vb* **deaf·ened; deaf·en·ing** 1 : to make deaf 2 : to cause deafness or stun one with noise — **deaf·en·ing·ly** \-f(ə-)niŋ-lē\ *adv*

de·af·fer·en·ta·tion \ˌdē-ˌa-fə-ˌren-¹tā-shən\ *n* : the freeing of a motor nerve from sensory components by severing the dorsal root central to the dorsal ganglion

¹deaf-mute \'def-¹myüt\ *adj* : lacking the sense of hearing and the ability to speak — **deaf-mute·ness** *n* — **deaf-mut·ism** \-¹myü-ˌti-zəm\ *n*

²deaf-mute *n* : a person who is deaf-mute

de·am·i·nase \(ˌ)dē-¹a-mə-ˌnās, -ˌnāz\ *also* **des·am·i·nase** \(ˌ)des-\ *n* : an enzyme that hydrolyzes amino compounds (as amino acids) with removal of the amino group

de·am·i·nate \-ˌnāt\ *vb* **-nat·ed; -nat·ing** : to remove the amino group from (a compound) — **de·am·i·na·tion** \(ˌ)dē-ˌa-mə-¹nā-shən\ *n*

death \'deth\ *n* 1 : the irreversible cessation of all vital functions esp. as indicated by permanent stoppage of the heart, respiration, and brain activity : the end of life — see BRAIN DEATH 2 : the cause or occasion of loss of life (drinking was the ~ of him) 3 : the state of being dead (in ~ as in life)

death·bed \'deth-ˌbed\ *n* 1 : the bed in which a person dies 2 : the last hours of life — **on one's deathbed** : near the point of death

death cap *n* : a very poisonous mushroom of the genus *Amanita* (*A. phalloides*) of deciduous woods of No. America and Europe that varies in color from pure white to olive or yellow and has a prominent cup at the base of the stem — called also *death cup;* see THIOCTIC ACID

death instinct *n* : an innate and unconscious tendency toward self-destruction postulated in psychoanalytic theory to explain aggressive and destructive behavior not satisfactorily explained by the pleasure principle — called also *Thanatos*; compare EROS

death rate *n* : the ratio of deaths to number of individuals in a population usu. expressed as number of deaths per hundred or per thousand population for a given time

death rattle *n* : a rattling or gurgling sound produced by air passing through mucus in the lungs and air passages of a dying person

death wish *n* : the conscious or unconscious desire for the death of another or of oneself

de·bil·i·tate \di-'bi-lə-ˌtāt\ *vb* **-tat·ed; -tat·ing** : to impair the strength of (a body *debilitated* by disease) — **de·bil·i·ta·tion** \-ˌbi-lə-'tā-shən\ *n*

de·bil·i·ty \di-'bi-lə-tē\ *n, pl* **-ties** : the quality or state of being weak, feeble, or infirm; *esp* : physical weakness

de·bride·ment \di-'brēd-mənt, dā-, -ˌmänt, -ˌmäⁿ\ *n* : the surgical removal of lacerated, devitalized, or contaminated tissue — **de·bride** \də-'brēd, dā-\ *vb*

de·bris \də-'brē, dā-', 'dā-ˌ\ *n, pl* **debris** : organic waste from dead or damaged tissue

de·bris·o·quin \di-'bri-sō-ˌkwin\ *or* **de·bris·o·quine** \-ˌkwīn\ *n* : an antihypertensive drug $C_{10}H_{13}N_3$ used esp. in the form of the sulfate

dec *abbr* deceased

Deca·dron \'de-kə-ˌdrän\ *trademark* — used for a preparation of dexamethasone

de·cal·ci·fi·ca·tion \(ˌ)dē-ˌkal-sə-fə-'kā-shən\ *n* : the removal or loss of calcium or calcium compounds (as from bones) — **de·cal·ci·fy** \-'kal-sə-ˌfī\ *vb*

deca·me·tho·ni·um \ˌde-kə-mə-'thō-nē-əm\ *n* : a synthetic ion used in the form of either its bromide or iodide salts ($C_{16}H_{38}Br_2N_2$ or $C_{16}H_{38}I_2N_2$) as a skeletal muscle relaxant; *also* : either of these salts

¹de·cap·i·tate \di-'ka-pə-ˌtāt\ *vb* **-tat·ed; -tat·ing** : to cut off the head of — **de·cap·i·ta·tion** \-ˌka-pə-'tā-shən\ *n*

²de·cap·i·tate \-ˌtāt, -tət\ *adj* : relating to or being a decapitated experimental animal

de·cap·su·late \(ˌ)dē-'kap-sə-ˌlāt\ *vb* **-lat·ed; -lat·ing** : to remove the capsule from (~ a kidney) — **de·cap·su·la·tion** \-ˌkap-sə-'lā-shən\ *n*

de·car·box·yl·ase \ˌdē-kär-'bäk-sə-ˌlās, -ˌlāz\ *n* : any of a group of enzymes that accelerate decarboxylation esp. of amino acids

de·car·box·yl·ate \-sə-ˌlāt\ *vb* **-at·ed; -at·ing** : to remove carboxyl from — **de·car·box·yl·ation** \-ˌbäk-sə-'lā-shən\ *n*

de·cay \di-'kā\ *n* **1 a** : ROT 1; *specif* : aerobic decomposition of proteins chiefly by bacteria **b** : the product of decay **2 a** : spontaneous decrease in the number of radioactive atoms in

radioactive material **b** : spontaneous disintegration (as of an atom or a nuclear particle) — **decay** *vb*

decay constant *n* : the constant ratio of the number of radioactive atoms disintegrating in any specified short unit interval of time to the total number of atoms of the same kind still intact at the beginning of that interval

de·cer·e·brate \(ˌ)dē-'ser-ə-brət, -ˌbrāt; ˌdē-sə-'rē-brət\ *also* **de·cer·e·brat·ed** \-'ser-ə-ˌbrā-təd\ *adj* : having the cerebrum removed or made inactive; *also* : characteristic of the resulting condition (~ rigidity) — **de·cer·e·bra·tion** \-ˌser-ə-'brā-shən\ *n*

deci·bel \'de-sə-ˌbel, -bəl\ *n* : a unit for expressing the relative intensity of sounds on a scale from zero for the average least perceptible sound to about 130 for the average pain level

de·cid·ua \di-'si-jə-wə\ *n, pl* **-uae** \-ˌwē\ **1** : the part of the mucous membrane lining the uterus that in higher placental mammals undergoes special modifications in preparation for and during pregnancy and is cast off at parturition, being made up in the human of a part lining the uterus, a part enveloping the embryo, and a part participating with the chorion in the formation of the placenta — see DECIDUA BASALIS, DECIDUA CAPSULARIS, DECIDUA PARIETALIS **2** : the mucous membrane of the uterus cast off in the ordinary process of menstruation — **de·cid·u·al** \-wəl\ *adj*

decidua ba·sa·lis \-bə-'sā-ləs\ *n* : the part of the endometrium in the pregnant human female that participates with the chorion in the formation of the placenta

decidua cap·su·lar·is \-ˌkap-sə-'lar-əs\ *n* : the part of the decidua in the pregnant human female that envelops the embryo

decidua pa·ri·etal·is \-pə-ˌrī-ə-'ta-ləs\ *n* : the part of the decidua in the pregnant human female lining the uterus

decidua pla·cen·tal·is \-ˌplā-sən-'ta-ləs, -sen-\ *n* : DECIDUA BASALIS

de·cid·u·ate \di-'si-jə-wət\ *adj* : having the fetal and maternal tissues firmly interlocked so that a layer of maternal tissue is torn away at parturition and forms a part of the afterbirth

decidua ve·ra \-'vir-ə, -'ver-\ *n* : DECIDUA PARIETALIS

de·cid·u·oma \di-ˌsi-jə-'wō-mə\ *n, pl* **-mas** *or* **-ma·ta** \-mə-tə\ **1** : a mass of tissue formed in the uterus following pregnancy that contains remnants of chorionic or decidual tissue **2** : decidual tissue induced in the uterus (as by trauma) in the absence of pregnancy

de·cid·u·ous \di-'si-jə-wəs\ *adj* **1** : falling off or shed at a certain stage in the life cycle **2** : having deciduous parts (a ~ dentition)

deciduous tooth *n* : MILK TOOTH

deci·gram \'de-sə-ˌgram\ *n* : a metric

unit of mass and weight equal to ¹⁄₁₀ gram

deci·li·ter \'de-sə-ˌlē-tər\ *n* : a metric unit of capacity equal to ¹⁄₁₀ liter

deci·me·ter \'de-sə-ˌmē-tər\ *n* : a metric unit of length equal to ¹⁄₁₀ meter

de·cline \di-'klīn, 'dē-ˌklīn\ *n* 1 : a gradual physical or mental sinking and wasting away 2 : the period during which the end of life is approaching 3 : a wasting disease: *esp* : pulmonary tuberculosis — **de·cline** \di-'klīn\ *vb*

de·clive \di-'klīv\ *n* : a part of the monticulus of the cerebellum that is dorsal to the culmen

de·clot \(ˌ)dē-'klät\ *vb* **de·clot·ted; de·clot·ting** : to remove blood clots from

de·coc·tion \di-'käk-shən\ *n* 1 : the act or process of boiling usu. in water so as to extract the flavor or active principle — compare INFUSION 2a 2 : an extract or liquid preparation obtained by decoction esp. of a medicinal plant — **de·coct** \-'käkt\ *vb*

de·col·or·ize \(ˌ)dē-'kə-lə-ˌrīz\ *vb* -**or·ized; -or·iz·ing** : to remove color from — **de·col·or·iza·tion** \-ˌkə-lə-rə-'zā-shən\ *n*

de·com·pen·sa·tion \(ˌ)dē-ˌkäm-pən-'sā-shən, -pen-\ *n* : loss of physiological compensation or psychological balance: *esp* : inability of the heart to maintain adequate circulation — **de·com·pen·sate** \-'käm-pən-ˌsāt, -pen-\ *vb* — **de·com·pen·sa·to·ry** \ˌdē-kəm-'pen-sə-ˌtōr-ē\ *adj*

de·com·pose \ˌdē-kəm-'pōz\ *vb* -**posed; -pos·ing** 1 : to separate into constituent parts or elements or into simpler compounds 2 : to undergo chemical breakdown : DECAY, ROT — **de·com·pos·able** \-'pō-zə-bəl\ *adj* — **de·com·po·si·tion** \(ˌ)dē-ˌkäm-pə-'zi-shən\ *n*

de·com·pres·sion \ˌdē-kəm-'pre-shən\ *n* 1 a : the decrease of ambient air pressure experienced in an air lock on return to atmospheric pressure after a period of breathing compressed air (as in a diving apparatus or caisson) or experienced in ascent to a great altitude without a pressure suit or pressurized cabin b : the decrease of water pressure experienced by a diver when ascending rapidly 2 : an operation or technique used to relieve pressure upon an organ (as in fractures of the skull or spine) or within a hollow organ (as in intestinal obstruction) — **de·com·press** \-'pres\ *vb*

decompression chamber *n* 1 : a chamber in which excessive pressure can be reduced gradually to atmospheric pressure 2 : a chamber in which an individual can be gradually subjected to decreased atmospheric pressure (as in simulating conditions at high altitudes)

decompression sickness *n* : a sometimes fatal disorder that is marked by neuralgic pains and paralysis, distress in breathing, and often collapse and that is caused by the release of gas bubbles (as of nitrogen) in tissue upon too rapid decrease in air pressure after a stay in a compressed atmosphere — called also *bends, caisson disease*; see AEROEMBOLISM

de·com·pres·sive \ˌdē-kəm-'pre-siv\ *adj* : tending to relieve or reduce pressure ⟨a ~ operation in obstruction of the large bowel⟩

de·con·di·tion \ˌdē-kən-'di-shən\ *vb* 1 : to cause to lose physical fitness 2 : to cause extinction of (a conditioned response)

de·con·di·tion·ing \-'di-shə-niŋ\ *n* : a decrease in the responsiveness of heart muscle that sometimes occurs after long periods of weightlessness and may be marked by decrease in blood volume and pooling of the blood in the legs upon return to normal conditions

¹**de·con·ges·tant** \ˌdē-kən-'jes-tənt\ *n* : an agent that relieves congestion (as of mucous membranes)

²**decongestant** *adj* : relieving or tending to relieve congestion

de·con·ges·tion \-'jes-chən\ *n* : the process of relieving congestion — **de·con·ges·tive** \-'jes-tiv\ *adj*

de·con·tam·i·nate \ˌdē-kən-'ta-mə-ˌnāt\ *vb* -**nat·ed; -nat·ing** : to rid of contamination (as radioactive material) — **de·con·tam·i·na·tion** \-ˌta-mə-'nā-shən\ *n*

¹**de·cor·ti·cate** \(ˌ)dē-'kȯr-tə-ˌkāt\ *vb* -**cat·ed; -cat·ing** : to remove all or part of the cortex from (as the brain)

²**de·cor·ti·cate** \-kät, -kət\ *adj* : lacking a cortex and esp. the cerebral cortex

de·cor·ti·ca·tion \-ˌkȯr-ti-'kā-shən\ *n* : the surgical removal of the cortex of an organ, an enveloping membrane, or a constrictive fibrinous covering (the ~ of a lung)

de·cu·bi·tal \di-'kyü-bət-ᵊl\ *adj* 1 : relating to or resulting from lying down ⟨a ~ sore⟩ 2 : relating to or resembling a decubitus

de·cu·bi·tus \-bə-təs\ *n, pl* -**bi·ti** \-ˌtī, -ˌtē\ 1 : a position assumed in lying down (the dorsal ~) 2 a : ULCER b : BEDSORE 3 : prolonged lying down (as in bed)

decubitus ulcer *n* : BEDSORE

de·cus·sa·tion \ˌdē-(ˌ)kə-'sā-shən\ *n* 1 : the action of intersecting or crossing (as of nerve fibers) esp. in the form of an X — see DECUSSATION OF PYRAMIDS 2 a : a band of nerve fibers that connects unlike centers on opposite sides of the nervous system b : a crossed tract of nerve fibers passing between centers on opposite sides of the central nervous system : COMMISSURE — **de·cus·sate** \'de-kə-ˌsāt, di-'kə-ˌsāt\ *vb*

decussation of pyramids *n* : the crossing of the fibers of the corticospinal tracts from one side of the central nervous system to the other near the junction of the medulla and the spinal cord

de·dif·fer·en·ti·a·tion \(,)dē-,di-fə-,ren-chē-'ā-shən\ n : reversion of specialized structures (as cells) to a more generalized or primitive condition of ten as a preliminary to major change — de·dif·fer·en·ti·ate \-'ren-chē-,āt\ vb

deep \'dēp\ adj 1 a : extending well inward from an outer surface (a ~ gash) b (1) : not located superficially within the body or one of its parts (~ veins) (2) : resulting from or involving stimulation of deep structures (~ pain) (~ reflexes) 2 : being below the level of the conscious (~ neuroses) — deep·ly adv

deep brachial artery n : the largest branch of the brachial artery in the upper part of the arm

deep external pudendal artery n : EXTERNAL PUDENDAL ARTERY b

deep facial vein n : a tributary of the facial vein draining part of the pterygoid plexus and nearby structures

deep fascia n : a firm fascia that ensheathes and binds together muscles and other internal structures — compare SUPERFICIAL FASCIA

deep femoral artery n : the large deep branch of the femoral artery formed where it divides about two inches (five centimeters) below the inguinal ligament

deep inguinal ring n : the internal opening of the inguinal canal — called also internal inguinal ring; compare SUPERFICIAL INGUINAL RING, INGUINAL RING

deep palmar arch n : PALMAR ARCH a

deep peroneal nerve n : a nerve that arises as a branch of the common peroneal nerve and that innervates or gives off branches innervating the muscles of the anterior part of the leg, the extensor digitorum brevis of the foot, and the skin between the big toe and the second toe — compare SUPERFICIAL PERONEAL NERVE

deep petrosal nerve n : a sympathetic nerve that originates in the carotid plexus, passes through the cartilage of the Eustachian tube, joins with the greater petrosal nerve to form the Vidian nerve, and as part of this nerve is distributed to the mucous membranes of the nasal cavity and palate

deep temporal artery n : TEMPORAL ARTERY 1

deep temporal nerve n : either of two motor branches of the mandibular nerve on each side of the body that are distributed to the temporalis

deep temporal vein n : TEMPORAL VEIN b

deer·fly \'dir-,flī\ n : any of numerous small horseflies esp. of the genus

Chrysops that include important vectors of tularemia

deer tick n : a tick of the genus Ixodes (I. dammini) that transmits the bacterium causing Lyme disease

def·e·cate \'de-fi-,kāt\ vb -cat·ed; -cat·ing 1 : to discharge from the anus 2 : to discharge feces from the bowels — def·e·ca·tion \de-fi-'kā-shən\ n

de·fect \'dē-,fekt, di-'\ n : a lack or deficiency of something necessary for adequacy in form or function

¹de·fec·tive \di-'fek-tiv\ adj : falling below the norm in structure or in mental or physical function (~ eyesight) — de·fec·tive·ness \-nəs\ n

²defective n : one that is subnormal physically or mentally

de·fem·i·nize \(,)dē-'fe-mə-,nīz\ vb -nized; -niz·ing : to divest of feminine qualities or physical characteristics : MASCULINIZE — de·fem·i·ni·za·tion \-fe-mə-nə-'zā-shən\ n

de·fense \di-'fens\ n : a means or method of protecting the physical or functional integrity of body or mind (a ~ against anxiety)

defense mechanism n : an often unconscious mental process (as repression, projection, or sublimation) that makes possible compromise solutions to personal problems

de·fen·sive \di-'fen-siv, 'dē-\ adj 1 : serving to defend or protect (as the ego) 2 : devoted to resisting or preventing aggression or attack (~ behavior) — de·fen·sive·ly adv — de·fen·sive·ness n

deferens — see DUCTUS DEFERENS, VAS DEFERENS

deferentes — see DUCTUS DEFERENS

deferentia — see VAS DEFERENS

de·fer·ves·cence \,dē-(,)fər-'ves-əns, ,de-fər-\ n : the subsidence of a fever

de·fi·bril·la·tion \(,)dē-,fi-brə-'lā-shən, -,fī-\ n : restoration of the rhythm of a fibrillating heart — de·fi·bril·late \(')dē-'fi-brə-,lāt, -'fī-\ vb

de·fi·bril·la·tor \-'fi-brə-,lā-tər, -'fī-\ n : an electronic device used to defibrillate a heart by applying an electric shock to it

de·fi·brin·ate \-'fi-brə-,nāt, -'fī-\ vb -at·ed; -at·ing : to remove fibrin from (blood) — de·fi·brin·ation \-,fi-brə-'nā-shən, -,fī-\ n

de·fi·cien·cy \di-'fi-shən-sē\ n, pl -cies 1 : a shortage of substances (as vitamins) necessary to health 2 : DELETION

deficiency anemia n : NUTRITIONAL ANEMIA

deficiency disease n : a disease (as scurvy) caused by a lack of essential dietary elements and esp. a vitamin or mineral

¹de·fi·cient \di-'fi-shənt\ adj 1 : lacking in some necessary quality or element (a ~ diet) 2 : not up to a normal standard or complement (~ strength)

²deficient n : one that is deficient

de·fi·cit \'de-fə-sət\ *n* : a deficiency of a substance; *also* : a lack or impairment of a functional capacity (cognitive ~s)

de·fin·i·tive \di-'fi-nə-tiv\ *adj* : fully differentiated or developed (a ~ organ)

definitive host *n* : the host in which the sexual reproduction of a parasite takes place — compare INTERMEDIATE HOST 1

de·flo·ra·tion \de-flə-'rā-shən, dē-\ *n* : rupture of the hymen — **de·flo·rate** \'de-flə-rāt, dē-\ *vb*

de·flu·vi·um \dē-'flü-vē-əm\ *n* : the pathological loss of a part (as hair or nails)

de·fo·cus \(,)dē-'fō-kəs\ *vb* **de·fo·cused; de·fo·cus·ing** : to cause to be out of focus (~ed his eye) (a ~ed image)

deformans — see ARTHRITIS DEFORMANS, DYSTONIA MUSCULORUM DEFORMANS, OSTEITIS DEFORMANS

de·formed \di-'formd, dē-\ *adj* : misshapen esp. in body or limbs

de·for·mi·ty \di-'for-mə-tē\ *n, pl* **-ties 1** : the state of being deformed **2** : a physical blemish or distortion

deg *abbr* degree

de·gen·er·a·cy \di-'je-nə-rə-sē\ *n, pl* **-cies 1** : sexual perversion **2** : the coding of an amino acid by more than one codon of the genetic code

¹de·gen·er·ate \-rət\ *adj* **1 a** : having declined (as in nature, character, structure, or function) from an ancestral or former state; *esp* : having deteriorated progressively (as in the process of evolution) esp. through loss of structure and function **b** : having sunk to a lower and usu. corrupt and vicious state **2** : having more than one codon representing an amino acid; *also* : being such a codon

²degenerate *n* : one that is degenerate

de·gen·er·a·tion \di-je-nə-'rā-shən, dē-\ *n* **1** : progressive deterioration of physical characters from a level representing the norm of earlier generations or forms : regression of the morphology of a group or kind of organism toward a simpler less highly organized state (parasitism leads to ~) **2** : deterioration of a tissue or an organ in which its vitality is diminished or its structure impaired; *esp* : deterioration in which specialized cells are replaced by less specialized cells (as in fibrosis or in malignancies) or in which cells are functionally impaired (as by deposition of abnormal matter in the tissue) — **de·gen·er·ate** \-'je-nə-rāt\ *vb* — **de·gen·er·a·tive** \di-'je-nə-rā-tiv, -rə-\ *adj*

degenerative arthritis *n* : OSTEOARTHRITIS

degenerative disease *n* : a disease (as arteriosclerosis, diabetes mellitus, or osteoarthritis) characterized by progressive degenerative changes in tissue

degenerative joint disease *n* : OSTEOARTHRITIS

de·germ \(,)dē-'jərm\ *vb* : to remove germs from (as the skin) — **de·germ·ation** \-jər-'mā-shən\ *n*

de·glu·ti·tion \dē-,glü-'ti-shən, ,de-\ *n* : the act, power, or process of swallowing

deg·ra·da·tion \,de-grə-'dā-shən\ *n* : change of a chemical compound to a less complex compound — **deg·ra·da·tive** \'de-grə-,dā-tiv\ *adj*

de·grade \di-'grād\ *vb* **1** : to reduce the complexity of (a chemical compound) by splitting off one or more groups or larger components : DECOMPOSE **2** : to undergo chemical degradation — **de·grad·able** \-'grā-də-bəl\ *adj*

de·gran·u·la·tion \(,)dē-,gran-yə-'lā-shən\ *n* : the process of losing granules (~ of leukocytes) — **de·gran·u·late** \-'gran-yə-,lāt\ *vb*

de·gree \di-'grē\ *n* **1** : a measure of damage to tissue caused by injury or disease — see FIRST-DEGREE BURN, SECOND-DEGREE BURN, THIRD-DEGREE BURN **2** : one of the divisions or intervals marked on a scale of a measuring instrument; *specif* : any of various units for measuring temperature

de·his·cence \di-'his-°ns\ *n* : the parting of the sutured lips of a surgical wound — **de·hisce** \-'his\ *vb*

de·hu·mid·i·fy \,dē-hyü-'mi-də-,fī, ,dē-yü-\ *vb* **-fied; -fy·ing** : to remove moisture from (as air) — **de·hu·mid·i·fi·ca·tion** \-,mi-də-fə-'kā-shən\ *n* — **de·hu·mid·i·fi·er** \-'mi-də-,fī-ər\ *n*

de·hy·drate \(,)dē-'hī-,drāt\ *vb* **-drated; -drat·ing 1** : to remove bound water or hydrogen and oxygen from (a chemical compound) in the proportion in which they form water **2** : to remove water from (as foods) **3** : to lose water or body fluids — **de·hy·dra·tor** \-,drā-tər\ *n*

dehydrated alcohol *n* : ABSOLUTE ALCOHOL

de·hy·dra·tion \,dē-hī-'drā-shən\ *n* : the process of dehydrating; *esp* : an abnormal depletion of body fluids

de·hy·dro·ascor·bic acid \(,)dē-,hī-drō-ə-'skor-bik-\ *n* : a crystalline oxidation product $C_6H_6O_6$ of vitamin C

de·hy·dro·cho·late \(,)dē-'hī-drō-'kō-,lāt\ *n* : a salt of dehydrocholic acid

7-de·hy·dro·cho·les·ter·ol \'se-vən-(,)dē-,hī-drō-kə-'les-tə-,rol, -,rōl\ *n* : a crystalline steroid alcohol $C_{27}H_{43}$-OH that occurs (as in the skin) chiefly in higher animals and humans and that yields vitamin D_3 on irradiation with ultraviolet light

de·hy·dro·cho·lic acid \(,)dē-,hī-drə-'kō-lik-\ *n* : a colorless crystalline acid $C_{23}H_{33}O_3COOH$ used often in the form of its sodium salt esp. as a laxative and choleretic

11-de·hy·dro·cor·ti·co·ste·rone \i-'le-vən-(,)dē-,hī-drō-,kor-tə-'käs-tə-,rōn, -,kō-stə-'rōn, ,kō-'stir-,ōn\ *n* : a steroid $C_{21}H_{28}O_4$ extracted from the adrenal cortex and also made synthetically — compare CORTISONE

de·hy·dro·epi·an·dros·ter·one \(₁)dē-₁hī-drō-₁e-pē-an-ᵈdräs-tə-₁rōn\ n : an androgenic ketosteroid $C_{19}H_{28}O_2$ found in human urine and the adrenal cortex that is thought to be an intermediate in the biosynthesis of testosterone

de·hy·dro·ge·nase \₁dē-(₁)hī-ᵈdrä-jə-₁nās, -ᵈhī-drə-jə-, -₁nāz\ n : an enzyme that accelerates the removal of hydrogen from metabolites and their transfer to other substances

de·hy·dro·ge·nate \(₁)dē-(₁)hī-ᵈdrä-jə-₁nāt, -ᵈhī-drə-jə-\ vb -nat·ed; -nat·ing : to remove hydrogen from — de·hy·dro·ge·na·tion \(₁)dē-(₁)hī-drä-jə-ᵈnā-shən, -₁hī-drə-jə-\ n

de·hy·dro·ge·nize \(₁)dē-ᵈhī-drə-jə-₁nīz\ vb -ized; -iz·ing : DEHYDROGENATE

de·in·sti·tu·tion·al·iza·tion \₁dē-in-stə-₁tü-shə-nə-lə-ᵈzā-shən, -₁tyü-\ n : the release of institutionalized individuals (as mental patients) from institutional care to care in the community — de·in·sti·tu·tion·al·ize \-ᵈtü-shə-nə-₁līz, -ᵈtyü-\ vb

de·ion·ize \(₁)dē-ᵈī-ə-₁nīz\ vb -ized; -iz·ing : to remove ions from (∼ water) — de·ion·iza·tion \-₁ī-ə-nə-ᵈzā-shən\ n — de·ion·iz·er \-ᵈī-ə-₁nī-zər\ n

Dei·ters' nucleus \ᵈdī-tərz-\ n : LATERAL VESTIBULAR NUCLEUS

dé·jà vu \₁dā-₁zhä-ᵈvü\ n : PARAMNESIA b

delayed–stress disorder n : POST-TRAUMATIC STRESS DISORDER

delayed–stress syndrome n : POST-TRAUMATIC STRESS DISORDER

de·lead \(₁)dē-ᵈlēd\ vb : to remove lead from (∼ a chemical)

del·e·te·ri·ous \₁de-lə-ᵈtir-ē-əs\ adj : harmful often in a subtle or an unexpected way (∼ genes)

de·le·tion \di-ᵈlē-shən\ n 1 : the absence of a section of genetic material from a chromosome 2 : the mutational process that results in a deletion

de·lin·quen·cy \di-ᵈliŋ-kwən-sē, -ᵈlin-\ n, pl -cies : conduct that is out of accord with accepted behavior or the law; esp : JUVENILE DELINQUENCY

¹de·lin·quent \-kwənt\ n : a transgressor against duty or the law esp. in a degree not constituting crime; specif : one whose behavior has been labeled juvenile delinquency

²delinquent adj 1 : offending by neglect or violation of duty or of law 2 : of, relating to, or characteristic of delinquents : marked by delinquency — de·lin·quent·ly adv

de·lir·i·um \di-ᵈlir-ē-əm\ n : a mental disturbance characterized by confusion, disordered speech, and hallucinations — de·lir·i·ous \-ē-əs\ adj — de·lir·i·ous·ly adv

delirium tremens \-ᵈtrē-mənz, -ᵈtre-\ n : a violent delirium with tremors that

is induced by excessive and prolonged use of alcoholic liquors — called also d.t.'s \ᵈdē-ᵈtēz\

de·liv·er \di-ᵈli-vər\ vb de·liv·ered; de·liv·er·ing 1 a : to assist (a parturient female) in giving birth (she was ∼ed of a fine boy) b : to aid in the birth of (∼ a child with forceps) 2 : to give birth to (she ∼ed a pair of healthy twins)

de·liv·ery \di-ᵈli-və-rē\ n, pl -er·ies 1 : the act of giving birth : the expulsion or extraction of a fetus and its membranes : PARTURITION 2 : the procedure of delivering the fetus and placenta by manual, instrumental, or surgical means

delivery room n : a hospital room esp. equipped for the delivery of pregnant women

de·louse \(₁)dē-ᵈlaus, -ᵈlauz\ vb de·loused; de·lous·ing : to remove lice from

del·phin·i·um \del-ᵈfin-ē-əm\ n 1 cap : a large genus of the buttercup family (Ranunculaceae) comprising chiefly perennial branching herbs with divided leaves and showy flowers and including several esp. of the western U.S. that are toxic to grazing animals and esp. cattle 2 : any plant of the genus Delphinium

delt \ᵈdelt\ n : DELTOID — usu. used in pl.

¹del·ta \ᵈdel-tə\ n 1 : the fourth letter of the Greek alphabet — symbol Δ or δ 2 : DELTA WAVE

²delta or δ- adj : of or relating to one of four or more closely related chemical substances (the delta chain of hemoglobin) — used somewhat arbitrarily to specify ordinal relationship or a particular physical form

delta wave n : a high amplitude electrical rhythm of the brain with a frequency of less than 6 cycles per second that occurs esp. in deep sleep, in infancy, and in many diseased conditions of the brain — called also delta, delta rhythm

¹del·toid \ᵈdel-₁toid\ n : a large triangular muscle that covers the shoulder joint, serves to raise the arm laterally, arises from the upper anterior part of the clavicle and from the acromion and spine of the scapula, and is inserted into the outer side of the middle of the shaft of the humerus — called also deltoid muscle; see DELTOID TUBEROSITY

²deltoid adj : relating to, associated with, or supplying the deltoid

del·toi·de·us \del-ᵈtoi-dē-əs\ n, pl -dei \-dē-₁ī\ : DELTOID

deltoid ligament n : a strong radiating ligament of the inner aspect of the ankle that binds the base of the tibia to the bones of the foot

deltoid tuberosity n : a rough triangular bump on the outer side of the middle of the humerus that is the site of insertion of the deltoid

delts \'delts\ *pl of* DELT

de·lude \di-'lüd\ *vb* **de·lud·ed; de·lud·ing** : to mislead the mind or judgment of

de·lu·sion \di-'lü-zhən\ *n* **1 a** : the act of deluding : the state of being deluded **b** : an abnormal mental state characterized by the occurrence of psychotic delusions **2** : a false belief regarding the self or persons or objects outside the self that persists despite the facts and occurs in some psychotic states — **de·lu·sion·al** \di-'lü-zhən-ᵊl\ *adj*

delusion of reference *n* : IDEA OF REFERENCE

de·mas·cu·lin·ize \(₁)dē-'mas-kyə-lə-₁nīz, di-\ *vb* **-ized; -iz·ing** : to remove the masculine character or qualities of — **de·mas·cu·lin·iza·tion** \-₁mas-kyə-lə-nə-'zā-shən, -₁ni-\ *n*

dem·e·car·i·um \₁de-mi-'kar-ē-əm, -'ker-\ *n* : a long-acting cholinesterase-inhibiting ammonium compound that is used as the bromide $C_{32}H_{52}Br_2N_4O_4$ in an ophthalmic solution esp. in the treatment of glaucoma and esotropia

de·ment·ed \di-'men-təd\ *adj* : MAD, INSANE — **de·ment·ed·ly** *adv* — **de·ment·ed·ness** *n*

de·men·tia \di-'men-chə\ *n* : a condition of deteriorated mentality that is characterized by marked decline from the individual's former intellectual level and often by emotional apathy — compare AMENTIA — **de·men·tial** \-chəl\ *adj*

dementia par·a·lyt·i·ca \-₁par-ə-'li-ti-kə\ *n, pl* **de·men·ti·ae par·a·lyt·i·cae** \-'men-chē-₁ē-₁par-ə-'li-ti-₁sē\ : GENERAL PARESIS

dementia prae·cox \-'prē-₁käks\ *n* : SCHIZOPHRENIA

de·ment·ing \di-'men-tiŋ\ *adj* : causing or characterized by dementia (a ~ illness)

Dem·er·ol \'de-mə-₁rol, -₁rōl\ *trademark* — used for meperidine

demi·lune \'de-mē-₁lün\ *n* : one of the small crescentic groups of granular deeply staining zymogen-secreting cells lying between the clearer mucus-producing cells and the basement membrane in the alveoli of mixed salivary glands — called also *crescent of Giannuzzi*

demilune of Gian·nuz·zi *also* **demilune of Gia·nuz·zi** \-jä-'nüt-sē\ *n* : DEMILUNE

Giannuzzi, Giuseppe (1839–1876), Italian anatomist.

de·min·er·al·iza·tion \(₁)dē-₁mi-nə-rə-lə-'zā-shən\ *n* **1** : loss of minerals (as salts of calcium) from the body esp. in disease **2** : the process of removing mineral matter or salts (as from water) — **de·min·er·al·ize** \-'mi-nə-rə-₁līz\ *vb*

dem·o·dec·tic mange \₁de-mə-'dek-tik-\

n : mange caused by mites of the genus *Demodex* that burrow in the hair follicles esp. of dogs — compare CHORIOPTIC MANGE, SARCOPTIC MANGE

de·mo·dex \'de-mə-₁deks, 'dē-\ *n* **1** *cap* : a genus (family Demodicidae) of minute mites that live in the hair follicles esp. about the face of humans and various furred mammals and in the latter often cause demodectic mange **2** : any mite of the genus *Demodex* : FOLLICLE MITE

de·mog·ra·phy \di-'mä-grə-fē\ *n, pl* **-phies** : the statistical study of human populations esp. with reference to size and density, distribution, and vital statistics — **de·mog·ra·pher** \-fər\ *n* — **de·mo·graph·ic** \₁de-mə-'gra-fik, ₁dē-\ *adj* — **de·mo·graph·i·cal·ly** \-fi-k(ə-)lē\ *adv*

¹**de·mul·cent** \di-'məl-sᵊnt\ *adj* : tending to sooth or soften (~ expectorants)

²**demulcent** *n* : a usu. mucilaginous or oily substance that can soothe or protect an abraded mucous membrane

de·my·elin·at·ing \(₁)dē-'mī-ə-lə-₁nā-tiŋ\ *adj* : causing or characterized by the loss or destruction of myelin

de·my·eli·na·tion \-₁mī-ə-lə-'nā-shən\ *n* : the state resulting from the loss or destruction of myelin; *also* : the process of such loss or destruction

de·my·elin·iza·tion \-lə-nə-'zā-shən\ *n* : DEMYELINATION

de·na·tur·ant \(₁)dē-'nā-chər-ənt\ *n* : a denaturing agent

de·na·ture \-'nā-chər\ *vb* **de·na·tured; de·na·tur·ing** : to deprive or become deprived of natural qualities: as **a** : to make (alcohol) unfit for drinking (as by adding an obnoxious substance) without impairing usefulness for other purposes **b** : to modify the molecular structure of (as a protein or DNA) esp. by heat, acid, alkali, or ultraviolet radiation so as to destroy or diminish some of the original properties and esp. the specific biological activity — **de·na·tur·ation** \-₁nā-chə-'rā-shən\ *n*

den·drite \'den-₁drīt\ *n* : any of the usu. branching protoplasmic processes that conduct impulses toward the body of a nerve cell — **den·drit·ic** \den-'dri-tik\ *adj*

den·dro·den·drit·ic \₁den-drō-₁den-'dri-tik\ *adj* : relating to or being a nerve synapse between a dendrite of one cell and a dendrite of another

de·ner·vate \'dē-(₁)nər-₁vāt\ *vb* **-vat·ed; -vat·ing** : to deprive of a nerve supply (as by cutting a nerve) — **de·ner·va·tion** \₁dē-(₁)nər-'vā-shən\ *n*

den·gue \'deŋ-gē, -₁gā\ *n* : an acute infectious disease caused by an arbovirus, transmitted by aedes mosquitoes, and characterized by headache, severe joint pain, and a rash — called also *breakbone fever, dengue fever*

de·ni·al \di-'nī-əl\ *n* : a psychological defense mechanism in which confrontation with a personal problem or with reality is avoided by denying the existence of the problem or reality

den·i·da·tion \ˌde-nə-ˈdā-shən\ *n* : the sloughing of the endometrium of the uterus esp. during menstruation

de·ni·trog·e·nate \ˌ)dē-ˈnī-ˈträ-jə-ˌnāt\ *vb* **-nat·ed; -nat·ing** : to reduce the stored nitrogen in the body of by forced breathing of pure oxygen for a period of time esp. as a measure designed to prevent development of decompression sickness — **de·ni·trog·e·na·tion** \-ˌträ-jə-ˈnā-shən\ *n*

dens \ˈdenz\ *n, pl* **den·tes** \ˈden-ˌtēz\ : ODONTOID PROCESS

densa — see MACULA DENSA

den·si·tom·e·ter \ˌden-sə-ˈtä-mə-tər\ *n* : an instrument for determining optical or photographic density — **den·si·to·met·ric** \ˌden-sə-tə-ˈme-trik\ *adj* — **den·si·tom·e·try** \ˌden-sə-ˈtä-mə-trē\ *n*

den·si·ty \ˈden-sə-tē\ *n, pl* **-ties** 1 : the quantity per unit volume, unit area, or unit length: as **a** : the mass of a substance per unit volume **b** : the distribution of a quantity (as mass, electricity, or energy) per unit usu. of space **c** : the average number of individuals or units per space unit 2 : the degree of opacity of a translucent medium

dent- or **denti-** or **dento-** *comb form* 1 : tooth : teeth ⟨*dental*⟩ 2 : dental and ⟨*dentofacial*⟩

den·tal \ˈdent-ᵊl\ *adj* 1 : relating to, specializing in, or used in dentistry 2 : relating to or used on the teeth ⟨∼ paste⟩ — **den·tal·ly** *adv*

dental arch *n* : the curve of the row of teeth in each jaw — called also *arcade*

dental dam *n* : a rubber dam used in dentistry

dental floss *n* : a thread used to clean between the teeth

dental formula *n* : an abridged expression for the number and kind of teeth of mammals in which the kind of teeth are represented by *i* (incisor), *c* (canine), *pm* (premolar) or *b* (bicuspid), and *m* (molar) and the number in each jaw is written like a fraction with the figures above the horizontal line showing the number in the upper jaw and those below the number in the lower jaw and with a dash separating the figures representing the teeth on each side of the jaw (the *dental formula* of a human adult is

$$i \ \frac{2\text{-}2}{2\text{-}2}, \ c \ \frac{1\text{-}1}{1\text{-}1}, \ b \ \text{or} \ pm \ \frac{2\text{-}2}{2\text{-}2},$$

$$m \ \frac{3\text{-}3}{3\text{-}3} = 32)$$

dental hygienist *n* : one who assists a dentist esp. in cleaning teeth

dental lamina *n* : a linear zone of epithelial cells of the covering of each embryonic jaw that gives rise to the enamel organs of the teeth — called also *dental ridge*

dental nerve *n* — see INFERIOR ALVEOLAR NERVE

dental papilla *n* : the mass of mesenchyme that gives rise to the dentin and the pulp of the tooth

dental plate *n* : DENTURE 2

dental pulp *n* : the highly vascular sensitive tissue occupying the central cavity of a tooth

dental surgeon *n* : DENTIST; *esp* : one engaging in oral surgery

dental technician *n* : a technician who makes dental appliances

den·tate \ˈden-ˌtāt\ *adj* : having teeth or pointed conical projections (the ∼ border of the retina)

dentate gyrus *n* : a narrow strip of cortex associated with the hippocampal sulcus that continues forward to the uncus

dentate nucleus *n* : a large laminar nucleus of gray matter forming an incomplete capsule within the white matter of each cerebellar hemisphere

dentes *pl of* DENS

denti- — see DENT-

den·ti·cle \ˈden-ti-kəl\ *n* : PULP STONE

den·tic·u·late ligament \den-ˈti-kyə-lət-\ *n* : a band of fibrous pia mater extending along the spinal cord on each side between the dorsal and ventral roots

den·ti·frice \ˈden-tə-frəs\ *n* : a powder, paste, or liquid for cleaning the teeth

den·tig·er·ous cyst \den-ˈti-jə-rəs-\ *n* : an epithelial cyst containing fluid and one or more imperfect teeth

den·tin \ˈdent-ᵊn\ *or* **den·tine** \ˈden-ˌtēn, den-ˈtēn\ *n* : a calcareous material similar to bone but harder and denser that composes the principal mass of a tooth and is formed by the odontoblasts — compare CEMENTUM, ENAMEL — **den·tin·al** \ˈdent-ᵊn-əl; ˈden-ˌtēn-ᵊl, den-ˈ\ *adj*

dentinal tubule *n* : one of the minute parallel tubules of the dentin of a tooth that communicate with the dental pulp

den·tino·enam·el \den-ˌtē-nō-i-ˈna-məl\ *n* : relating to or connecting the dentin and enamel of a tooth (the ∼ junction)

den·tino·gen·e·sis \den-ˌtē-nə-ˈje-nə-səs\ *n, pl* **-e·ses** \-ˌsēz\ : the formation of dentin

den·tist \ˈden-tist\ *n* : one who is skilled in and licensed to practice the prevention, diagnosis, and treatment of diseases, injuries, and malformations of the teeth, jaws, and mouth and who makes and inserts false teeth — **den·tist·ry** \ˈden-tə-strē\ *n*

den·ti·tion \den-ˈti-shən\ *n* 1 : the development and cutting of teeth 2 : the character of a set of teeth esp. with regard to their number, kind, and arrangement **3** : TEETH

dento- — see DENT-

den·to·al·ve·o·lar \ˌden-tō-al-ˈvē-ə-lər\ *adj* : of, relating to, or involving the teeth and their sockets (~ structures)

den·to·fa·cial \ˌden-tə-ˈfā-shəl\ *adj* : of or relating to the dentition and face

den·to·gin·gi·val \ˌden-tō-ˈjin-jə-vəl\ *adj* : of, relating to, or connecting the teeth and the gums (the ~ junction)

den·tu·lous \ˈden-chə-ləs\ *adj* : having teeth

den·ture \ˈden-chər\ *n* **1** : a set of teeth **2** : an artificial replacement for one or more teeth; *esp* : a set of false teeth

den·tur·ist \-chə-rist\ *n* : a dental technician who makes, fits, and repairs dentures directly for the public

de·nu·da·tion \ˌdē-nü-ˈdā-shən, ˌde-, -nyü-\ *n* : the act or process of removing surface layers (as of skin) or an outer covering (as of myelin); *also* : the condition that results from this — **de·nude** \di-ˈnüd, -ˈnyüd\ *vb*

¹de·odor·ant \dē-ˈō-də-rənt\ *adj* : destroying or masking offensive odors

²deodorant *n* : any of various preparations or solutions (as a soap or disinfectant) that destroy or mask unpleasant odors; *esp* : a cosmetic that neutralizes perspiration odors

de·odor·ize \dē-ˈō-də-ˌrīz\ *vb* **-ized; -iz·ing** : to eliminate or prevent the offensive odor of — **de·odor·iza·tion** \-ˌō-də-rə-ˈzā-shən\ *n* — **de·odor·iz·er** *n*

de·oxy \ˌdē-ˈäk-sē\ *also* **des·oxy** \ˌdez-\ *adj* : containing less oxygen per molecule than the compound from which it is derived (~ sugars) — usu. used in combination (*deoxy*ribonucleic acid) (*desoxy*corticosterone)

de·oxy·cho·late \ˌdē-ˌäk-sē-ˈkō-ˌlāt\ *n* : a salt or ester of deoxycholic acid

de·oxy·cho·lic acid \-ˈkō-lik-\ *n* : a crystalline acid $C_{24}H_{40}O_4$ found esp. in bile

de·oxy·cor·ti·co·ste·rone *var of* DESOXYCORTICOSTERONE

de·oxy·cor·tone *chiefly Brit var of* DESOXYCORTONE

de·oxy·gen·ate \ˌdē-ˈäk-si-jə-ˌnāt, ˌdē-äk-ˈsi-jə-\ *vb* **-at·ed; -at·ing** : to remove oxygen from — **de·oxy·gen·ation** \-ˌäk-si-jə-ˈnā-shən, ˌdē-äk-ˌsi-jə-\ *n*

de·oxy·gen·at·ed *adj* : having the hemoglobin in the reduced state

de·oxy·ri·bo·nu·cle·ase \ˌdē-ˌäk-si-ˌrī-bō-ˈnü-klē-ˌās, -ˈnyü-, -ˌāz\ *n* : an enzyme that hydrolyzes DNA to nucleotides — called also *DNase*

de·oxy·ri·bo·nu·cle·ic acid \ˌdē-ˌäk-si-ˌrī-bō-nü-ˈklē-ik-, -nyü-, -ˈklā-\ *n* : DNA

de·oxy·ri·bo·nu·cle·o·tide \-ˈnü-klē-ə-ˌtīd, -ˈnyü-\ *n* : a nucleotide that contains deoxyribose and is a constituent of DNA

de·oxy·ri·bose \ˌdē-ˌäk-si-ˈrī-bōs,

-ˌbōz\ *n* : a pentose sugar $C_5H_{10}O_4$ that is a structural element of DNA

de·pen·dence \di-ˈpen-dəns\ *n* **1** : the quality or state of being dependent upon or unduly subject to the influence of another **2 a** : drug addiction **b** : HABITUATION 2b

de·pen·den·cy \-dən-sē\ *n, pl* **-cies** : DEPENDENCE

de·pen·dent \di-ˈpen-dənt\ *adj* **1** : unable to exist, sustain oneself, or act appropriately or normally without the assistance or direction of another **2** : affected with a drug dependence — **de·pen·dent·ly** *adv*

de·per·son·al·iza·tion \ˌdē-ˌpər-sə-nə-lə-ˈzā-shən\ *n* : the act or process of causing or the state resulting from loss of the sense of personal identity; *esp* : a psychopathological syndrome characterized by loss of identity and feelings of unreality or strangeness about one's own behavior — **de·per·son·al·ize** \ˈdē-ˈpər-sə-nə-ˌlīz\ *vb*

de·phos·phor·y·la·tion \ˌdē-ˌfäs-ˌfōr-ə-ˈlā-shən\ *n* : the process of removing phosphate groups from an organic compound (as ATP) by hydrolysis; *also* : the resulting state — **de·phos·phor·y·late** \-ˈfäs-ˈfor-ə-ˌlāt\ *vb*

de·pig·men·ta·tion \ˌdē-ˌpig-mən-ˈtā-shən, -ˌmen-\ *n* : loss of normal pigmentation

dep·i·la·tion \ˌde-pə-ˈlā-shən\ *n* : the removal of hair, wool, or bristles by chemical or mechanical methods — **dep·i·late** \ˈde-pə-ˌlāt\ *vb*

¹de·pil·a·to·ry \di-ˈpi-lə-ˌtōr-ē\ *adj* : having the power to remove hair

²depilatory *n* : a cosmetic for the temporary removal of undesired hair

de·plete \di-ˈplēt\ *vb* **de·plet·ed; de·plet·ing** : to empty of a principal substance (tissues *depleted* of vitamins)

de·ple·tion \di-ˈplē-shən\ *n* : the act or process of depleting or the state of being depleted: as **a** : the reduction or loss of blood, body fluids, chemical constituents, or stored materials from the body (as by hemorrhage or malnutrition) **b** : a debilitated state caused by excessive loss of body fluids or other constituents

de·po·lar·iza·tion \ˌdē-ˌpō-lə-rə-ˈzā-shən\ *n* : loss of polarization; *esp* : loss of the difference in charge between the inside and outside of the plasma membrane of a muscle or nerve cell due to a change in permeability and migration of sodium ions to the interior — **de·po·lar·ize** \ˈpō-lə-ˌrīz\ *vb*

Depo–Pro·vera \ˈde-pō-prō-ˈver-ə\ *trademark* — used for an aqueous suspension of medroxyprogesterone acetate

de·pos·it \də-ˈpä-zət\ *n* : something laid down; *esp* : matter deposited by a natural process — **deposit** *vb*

¹de·pot \ˈde-(ˌ)pō, ˈdē-\ *n* : a bodily location where a substance is stored usu. for later utilization

²**de·pot** *adj* : being in storage 〈~ fat〉; *also* : acting over a prolonged period 〈~ insulin〉

de·press \di-ˈpres\ *vb* **1** : to diminish the activity, strength, or yield of **2** : to lower in spirit or mood

¹**de·pres·sant** \-ᵊnt\ *adj* : tending to depress; *esp* : lowering or tending to lower functional or vital activity 〈a drug with a ~ effect on heart rate〉

²**depressant** *n* : one that depresses; *specif* : an agent that reduces bodily functional activity or an instinctive desire (as appetite)

de·pressed \di-ˈprest\ *adj* **1** : low in spirits; *specif* : affected by psychological depression 〈a severely ~ patient〉 **2** : having the central part lower than the margin

depressed fracture *n* : a fracture esp. of the skull in which the fragment is depressed below the normal surface

de·pres·sion \di-ˈpre-shən\ *n* **1** : a displacement downward or inward 〈~ of the jaw〉 **2** : an act of depressing or a state of being depressed: as a (1) : a state of feeling sad (2) : a psychoneurotic or psychotic disorder marked esp. by sadness, inactivity, difficulty with thinking and concentration, a significant increase or decrease in appetite and time spent sleeping, feelings of dejection and hopelessness, and sometimes suicidal thoughts or an attempt to commit suicide **3** : a reduction in functional activity, amount, quality, or force 〈~ of autonomic function〉

¹**de·pres·sive** \di-ˈpre-siv\ *adj* **1** : tending to depress **2** : of, relating to, marked by, or affected by psychological depression

²**depressive** *n* : one who is affected with or prone to psychological depression

de·pres·sor \di-ˈpre-sər\ *n* : one that depresses: as **a** : a muscle that draws down a part — compare LEVATOR **b** : a device for pressing a part down or aside — see TONGUE DEPRESSOR **c** : a nerve or nerve fiber that decreases the activity or the tone of the organ or part it innervates

depressor sep·ti \-ˈsep-ˌtī\ *n* : a small muscle of each side of the upper lip that is inserted into the nasal septum and wing of the nose on each side and constricts the nasal opening by drawing the wing downward

de·pri·va·tion \ˌde-prə-ˈvā-shən, ˌdē-ˌprī-\ *n* : the act or process of removing or the condition resulting from removal of something normally present and usu. essential for mental or physical well-being 〈emotional ~ in childhood〉 〈sensory ~〉 — **de·prive** \di-ˈprīv\ *vb*

de·pro·tein·ate \(ˌ)dē-ˈprō-ˌtē-ˌnāt, -ˈprō-tē-ə-ˌnāt\ *vb* **-at·ed; -at·ing** : DE-

PROTEINIZE — **de·pro·tein·ation** \(ˌ)dē-ˌprō-tē-ˈnā-shən, -ˌprō-tē-ə-\ *n*

de·pro·tein·i·za·tion \(ˌ)dē-ˌprō-ˌtē-nə-ˈzā-shən, -ˌprō-tē-ə-nə-\ *n* : the process of removing protein

de·pro·tein·ize \(ˌ)dē-ˈprō-ˌtē-ˌnīz, -ˈprō-tē-ə-ˌnīz\ *vb* **-ized; -iz·ing** : to subject to deproteinization

depth \ˈdepth\ *n, pl* **depths 1** : the distance between upper and lower or between dorsal and ventral points of a body **2** : the quality of a state of consciousness, a bodily state, or a physiological function of being intense or complete 〈the ~ of anesthesia〉

depth perception *n* : the ability to judge the distance of objects and the spatial relationship of objects at different distances

depth psychology *n* : PSYCHOANALYSIS; *also* : psychology concerned esp. with the unconscious mind

de-Quer·vain's disease \də-(ˌ)kər-ˈvaⁿz-\ *n* : inflammation of tendons and their sheaths at the styloid process of the radius that often causes pain in the thumb side of the wrist

    Quer·vain \ker-ˈvaⁿ\, **Fritz de** (1868–1940), Swiss physician.

de·range·ment \di-ˈrānj-mənt\ *n* **1** : a disturbance of normal bodily functioning or operation **2** : INSANITY — **de·range** \di-ˈrānj\ *vb*

de·re·al·iza·tion \(ˌ)dē-ˌrē-ə-lə-ˈzā-shən\ *n* : a feeling of altered reality that occurs often in schizophrenia and in some drug reactions

de·re·press \ˌdē-ri-ˈpres\ *vb* : to activate (a gene or enzyme) by releasing from a blocked state — **de·re·pres·sion** \-ˈpre-shən\ *n*

¹**de·riv·a·tive** \di-ˈri-və-tiv\ *adj* **1** : formed by derivation **2** : made up of or marked by derived elements

²**derivative** *n* **1** : something that is obtained from, grows out of, or results from an earlier or more fundamental state or condition **2 a** : a chemical substance related structurally to another substance and theoretically derivable from it **b** : a substance that can be made from another substance in one or more steps

de·rive \di-ˈrīv\ *vb* **de·rived; de·riv·ing** : to take, receive, or obtain. esp. from a specified source; *specif* : to obtain (a chemical substance) actually or theoretically from a parent substance — **der·i·va·tion** \ˌder-ə-ˈvā-shən\ *n*

derm- *or* **derma-** *or* **dermo-** *comb form* : skin 〈*dermal*〉 〈*dermopathy*〉

-derm \ˌdərm\ *n comb form* : skin : covering 〈ecto*derm*〉

-der·ma \ˈdər-mə\ *n comb form, pl* **-dermas** *or* **-der·ma·ta** \-mə-tə\ : skin or skin ailment of a (specified) type 〈sclero*derma*〉

derm·abra·sion \ˌdər-mə-ˈbrā-zhən\ *n* : surgical removal of skin blemishes or imperfections (as scars or tattoos) by abrasion

Der·ma·cen·tor \'dər-mə-ˌsen-tər\ n : a large widely distributed genus of ornate ixodid ticks including several vectors of important diseases (as Rocky Mountain spotted fever)

der·mal \'dər-məl\ adj 1 : of or relating to skin and esp. to the dermis : CUTANEOUS 2 : EPIDERMAL

Der·ma·nys·sus \ˌdər-mə-'ni-səs\ n : a genus (family Dermanyssidae) of blood-sucking mites that are parasitic on birds — see CHICKEN MITE

dermat- or **dermato-** comb form : skin ⟨dermatitis⟩ ⟨dermatology⟩

der·ma·ti·tis \ˌdər-mə-'tī-təs\ n, pl -ti·tis·es or -tit·i·des \-'ti-tə-ˌdēz\ : inflammation of the skin — **der·ma·tit·ic** \-'ti-tik\ adj

dermatitis her·pe·ti·for·mis \-ˌhər-pə-tə-'för-məs\ n : chronic dermatitis characterized by eruption of itching papules, vesicles, and lesions resembling hives typically in clusters

Der·ma·to·bia \ˌdər-mə-'tō-bē-ə\ n : a genus of botflies including one (D. hominis) whose larvae live under the skin of domestic mammals and sometimes of humans in tropical America

der·ma·to·fi·bro·ma \ˌdər-mə-tō-fī-'brō-mə\ n, pl -mas also -ma·ta \-mə-tə\ : a benign chiefly fibroblastic nodule of the skin found esp. on the extremities of adults

der·ma·to·fi·bro·sar·co·ma \-ˌfī-brō-sär-'kō-mə\ n, pl -mas or -ma·ta \-mə-tə\ : a fibrosarcoma affecting the skin

dermatofibrosarcoma pro·tu·ber·ans \ˌprō-'tü-bə-ranz, -'tyü-\ n : a dermal fibroblastic neoplasm composed of firm nodular masses that usu. do not metastasize

der·ma·to·glyph·ics \ˌdər-mə-tə-'gli-fiks\ n 1 : skin patterns; esp : patterns of the specialized skin of the inferior surfaces of the hands and feet 2 : the science of the study of skin patterns — **der·ma·to·glyph·ic** \-fik\ adj

der·ma·to·graph·ia \-'gra-fē-ə\ n : DERMOGRAPHISM

der·ma·to·graph·ism \-'gra-ˌfi-zəm\ n : DERMOGRAPHISM

der·ma·to·log·ic \ˌdər-mət-ᵊl-'ä-jik\ or **der·ma·to·log·i·cal** \-ji-kəl\ adj : of or relating to dermatology

der·ma·to·log·i·cal \-ji-kəl\ n : a medicinal agent for application to the skin

der·ma·tol·o·gy \ˌdər-mə-'tä-lə-jē\ n, pl -gies : a branch of science dealing with the skin, its structure, functions, and diseases — **der·ma·tol·o·gist** \-mə-'tä-lə-jist\ n

der·ma·tome \'dər-mə-ˌtōm\ n 1 : an instrument for cutting skin for use in grafting 2 : the lateral wall of a somite from which the dermis is produced — **der·ma·to·mal** \ˌdər-mə-'tō-məl\ or **der·ma·to·mic** \-mik\ adj

der·ma·to·my·co·sis \ˌdər-mə-tō-ˌmī-'kō-səs, ˌ)dər-ˌma-\ n, pl -co·ses \-ˌsēz\ : a disease (as ringworm) of

the skin caused by infection with a fungus

der·ma·to·my·o·si·tis \-ˌmī-ə-'sī-təs\, n, pl -si·tis·es or -sit·i·des \-'si-tə-ˌdēz\ : a chronic inflammation of the skin, subcutaneous tissue, and skeletal muscles of unknown cause

der·ma·to·pa·thol·o·gy \-pə-'thä-lə-jē, -pa-\ n, pl -gies : pathology of the skin — **der·ma·to·pa·thol·o·gist** \-jist\ n

der·ma·to·phyte \(ˌ)dər-'ma-tə-ˌfīt, 'dər-mə-tə-\ n : a fungus parasitic upon the skin or skin derivatives (as hair or nails) — compare DERMATOMYCOSIS

der·ma·to·phy·tid \(ˌ)dər-ˌma-tə-'fī-təd, ˌdər-mə-\ n : a skin eruption associated with a fungus infection: esp : one considered to be due to allergic reaction

der·ma·to·phy·to·sis \-ˌfī-'tō-səs\ n, pl -to·ses \-ˌsēz\ : a disease (as athlete's foot) of the skin or skin derivatives that is caused by a dermatophyte

der·ma·to·plas·ty \(ˌ)dər-'ma-tə-ˌplas-tē, 'dər-mə-\ n, pl -ties : plastic surgery of the skin

der·ma·to·sis \ˌdər-mə-'tō-səs\ n, pl -to·ses \-ˌsēz\ : a disease of the skin

-der·ma·tous \'dər-mə-təs\ adj comb form : having a (specified) type of skin ⟨sclerodermatous⟩

-der·mia \'dər-mē-ə\ n comb form : skin or skin ailment of a (specified) type ⟨keratodermia⟩

der·mis \'dər-məs\ n : the sensitive vascular inner mesodermic layer of the skin — called also corium, cutis

-der·mis \'dər-məs\ n comb form : layer of skin or tissue ⟨epidermis⟩

dermo- — see DERM-

der·mo·graph·ia \ˌdər-mə-'gra-fē-ə\ n : DERMOGRAPHISM

der·mog·ra·phism \(ˌ)dər-'mä-grə-ˌfi-zəm\ n : a condition in which pressure or friction on the skin gives rise to a transient raised usu. reddish mark so that a word traced on the skin becomes visible — called also dermatographia, dermatographism

der·moid \'dər-ˌmoid\ also **der·moi·dal** \(ˌ)dər-'moid-ᵊl\ adj 1 : made up of cutaneous elements and esp. ectodermal derivatives ⟨a ~ tumor⟩ 2 : resembling skin

dermoid cyst n : a cystic tumor often of the ovary that contains skin and skin derivatives (as hair or teeth) — called also dermoid

der·mo·ne·crot·ic \ˌdər-mō-ni-'krä-tik\ adj : relating to or causing necrosis of the skin ⟨a ~ toxin⟩ ⟨~ effects⟩

der·mop·a·thy \(ˌ)dər-'mä-pə-thē\ n, pl -thies : a disease of the skin

DES \ˌdē-(ˌ)ē-'es\ n : DIETHYLSTILBESTROL

des·am·i·nase \dē-'za-mə-ˌnās, -ˌnāz\ var of DEAMINASE

des·ce·met·o·cele \ˌde-sə-'me-tə-ˌsēl\ n : protrusion of Descemet's membrane through the cornea

Des·ce·met's membrane \de-sə-'māz-, ˌdes-'māz-\ n : a transparent highly elastic apparently structureless membrane that covers the inner surface of the cornea and is lined with endothelium — called also *membrane of Descemet, posterior elastic lamina*
Des·ce·met \des-'mā\, **Jean** (1732–1810), French physician.

descending adj 1 : moving or directed downward 2 : being a nerve, nerve fiber, or nerve tract that carries nerve impulses in a direction away from the central nervous system : EFFERENT, MOTOR

descending aorta n : the part of the aorta from the arch to its bifurcation into the two common iliac arteries that passes downward in the thoracic and abdominal cavities

descending colon n : the part of the large intestine on the left side that extends from the bend below the spleen to the sigmoid flexure — compare ASCENDING COLON, TRANSVERSE COLON

de·scen·sus \di-'sen-səs\ n : the process of descending or prolapsing

de·sen·si·tize \(ˌ)dē-'sen-sə-ˌtīz\ vb **-tized; -tiz·ing** 1 : to make (a sensitized or hypersensitive individual) insensitive or nonreactive to a sensitizing agent 2 : to extinguish an emotional response (as of fear, anxiety, or guilt) to stimuli which formerly induced it : make emotionally insensitive — **de·sen·si·ti·za·tion** \-ˌsen-sə-tə-'zā-shən\ n

de·sen·si·tiz·er \-'sen-sə-ˌtī-zər\ n : a desensitizing agent; esp : a drug that reduces sensitivity to pain

de·sex \(ˌ)dē-'seks\ vb : CASTRATE, SPAY

¹**des·ic·cant** \'de-si-kənt\ adj : tending to dry or desiccate

²**desiccant** n : a drying agent (as calcium chloride)

des·ic·cate \'de-si-ˌkāt\ vb **-cat·ed; -cat·ing** : to dry up or cause to dry up : deprive or exhaust of moisture; esp : to dry thoroughly

des·ic·ca·tion \ˌde-si-'kā-shən\ n : the act or process of desiccating or the state of being or becoming desiccated; esp : a complete or nearly complete deprivation of moisture or of water not chemically combined : DEHYDRATION

designer drug n : a synthetic version of a controlled substance (as heroin) that is produced with a slightly altered molecular structure to avoid classification as an illicit drug

de·si·pra·mine \ˌde-zə-'pra-mən, də-'zi-prə-ˌmēn\ n : a tricyclic antidepressant $C_{18}H_{22}N_2$ administered as the hydrochloride esp. in the treatment of endogenous depressions (as a manic-depressive psychosis) — see PERTOFRANE

-de·sis \də-səs\ n comb form, pl **-de-**

ses \-ˌsēz\ : binding or fixation (arthro*desis*)

desm- or **desmo-** comb form : connective tissue (*desmo*plasia)

des·meth·yl·imip·ra·mine \ˌdes-ˌmethəl-im-'i-prə-ˌmēn\ n : DESIPRAMINE

des·moid \'dez-ˌmȯid\ n : a dense benign connective-tissue tumor

des·mo·pla·sia \ˌdez-mə-'plā-zhə, -zhē-ə\ n : formation of fibrous connective tissue by proliferation of fibroblasts

des·mo·plas·tic \-'plas-tik\ adj : characterized by the formation of fibrous tissue (~ fibromas)

des·mo·some \'dez-mə-ˌsōm\ n : a specialized local thickening of the cell membrane of an epithelial cell that serves to anchor contiguous cells together — **des·mo·som·al** \-ˌsō-məl\ adj

des·oxy \de-'zäk-sē\ var of DEOXY

des·oxy·ri·bo·nu·cle·ic acid var of DEOXYRIBONUCLEIC ACID

des·oxy·cor·ti·co·ste·rone \(ˌ)dez-ˌäk-si-ˌkȯr-ti-'käs-tə-ˌrōn, -ˌkō-stə-'rōn\ n : a steroid hormone $C_{21}H_{30}O_3$ of the adrenal cortex

des·oxy·cor·tone \(ˌ)dez-ˌäk-si-'kȯr-ˌtōn\ n : DESOXYCORTICOSTERONE

des·qua·mate \'des-kwə-ˌmāt\ vb **-mat·ed; -mat·ing** : to peel off in the form of scales : scale off (*desquamated* epithelial cells) — **des·qua·ma·tion** \ˌdes-kwə-'mā-shən\ n — **des·qua·ma·tive** \'des-kwə-ˌmā-tiv, di-'skwa-mə-\ adj

destroying angel n : DEATH CAP; also : a mushroom of the genus *Amanita* (*A. verna*) closely related to the death cap

detached retina n : RETINAL DETACHMENT

detachment of the retina n : RETINAL DETACHMENT

detail man n : a representative of a drug manufacturer who introduces new drugs esp. to physicians and pharmacists

¹**de·ter·gent** \di-'tər-jənt\ adj : having a cleansing action

²**detergent** n : a cleansing agent (as a soap)

de·te·ri·o·rate \di-'tir-ē-ə-ˌrāt\ vb **-rat·ed; -rat·ing** : to become impaired in quality, functioning, or condition : DEGENERATE — **de·te·ri·o·ra·tion** \di-ˌtir-ē-ə-'rā-shən\ n

de·ter·mi·nant \di-'tər-mə-nənt\ n 1 : GENE 2 : EPITOPE

de·ter·mi·nate \di-'tər-mə-nət\ adj : relating to, being, or undergoing determinate cleavage

determinate cleavage n : cleavage of an egg in which each division irreversibly separates portions of the zygote with specific potencies for further development — compare INDETERMINATE CLEAVAGE

de·ter·min·er \-'tər-mə-nər\ n : GENE

de·tick \(ˌ)dē-'tik\ vb : to remove ticks from (~ dogs)

¹**de·tox** \(ˌ)dē-'täks\ vb : DETOXIFY 2

²**de·tox** \'dē-ˌtäks\ n, often attrib : de-

de·tox·i·cant \(ˌ)dē-ˈtäk-si-kənt\ *n* : a detoxicating agent

de·tox·i·cate \-ˈtäk-sə-ˌkāt\ *vb* **-cat·ed; -cat·ing** : DETOXIFY — **de·tox·i·ca·tion** \-ˌtäk-sə-ˈkā-shən\ *n*

de·tox·i·fy \-ˈtäk-sə-ˌfī\ *vb* **-fied; -fy·ing** **1 a** : to remove a poison or toxin or the effect of such from **b** : to render (a harmful substance) harmless **2** : to free (as a drug user or an alcoholic) from an intoxicating or an addictive substance in the body or from dependence on or addiction to such a substance — **de·tox·i·fi·ca·tion** \-ˌtäk-sə-fə-ˈkā-shən\ *n*

de·tru·sor \di-ˈtrü-zər, -sər\ *n* : the outer largely longitudinally arranged musculature of the bladder wall — called also *detrusor muscle*

detrusor uri·nae \-yə-ˈrī-(ˌ)nē\ *n* : the external longitudinal musculature of the urinary bladder

de·tu·mes·cence \ˌdē-tü-ˈmes-ᵊns, -tyü-\ *n* : subsidence or diminution of swelling or erection — **de·tu·mes·cent** \-ᵊnt\ *adj*

deu·ter·anom·a·lous \ˌdü-tə-rə-ˈnä-mə-ləs, ˌdyü-\ *adj* : exhibiting partial loss of green color vision so that an increased intensity of this color is required in a mixture of red and green to match a given yellow

deu·ter·anom·a·ly \-mə-lē\ *n, pl* **-lies** : the condition of being deuteranomalous — compare PROTANOMALY, TRICHROMATISM

deu·ter·an·ope \ˈdü-tə-rə-ˌnōp, ˈdyü-\ *n* : an individual affected with deuteranopia

deu·ter·an·opia \ˌdü-tə-rə-ˈnō-pē-ə, ˌdyü-\ *n* : color blindness marked by confusion of purplish red and green — **deu·ter·an·opic** \-ˈnō-pik, -ˈnä-\ *adj*

deux see FOLIE À DEUX

de·vas·cu·lar·iza·tion \(ˌ)dē-ˌvas-kyə-lə-rə-ˈzā-shən\ *n* : loss of the blood supply to a bodily part due to destruction or obstruction of blood vessels — **de·vas·cu·lar·ized** \ˈvas-kyə-lə-ˌrīzd\ *adj*

de·vel·op \di-ˈve-ləp\ *vb* **1 a** : to expand by a process of growth **b** : to go through a process of natural growth, differentiation, or evolution by successive stages **2** : to have (something) unfold or differentiate within one — used esp. of diseases and abnormalities (~ed tuberculosis) **3** : to acquire secondary sex characters

de·vel·op·ment \di-ˈve-ləp-mənt\ *n* **1** : the action or process of developing: as **a** : the process of growth and differentiation by which the potentialities of a zygote, spore, or embryo are realized **b** : the gradual advance through evolutionary stages : EVOLUTION **2** : the state of being developed — **de·vel·op·men·tal** \-ˌve-ləp-ˈment-ᵊl\ *adj* — **de·vel·op·men·tal·ly** *adv*

developmentally disabled *adj* : having a physical or mental handicap (as mental retardation) that impedes or prevents normal development — abbr. *DD*

developmental quotient *n* : a number expressing the development of a child determined by dividing the age of the group into which test scores place the child by the child's chronological age and multiplying by 100

de·vi·ance \ˈdē-vē-əns\ *n* : deviant quality, state, or behavior

¹de·vi·ant \-ənt\ *adj* **1** : deviating esp. from some accepted norm **2** : characterized by deviation (as from a standard of conduct) (~ children)

²deviant *n* : something that deviates from a norm; *esp* : a person who differs markedly (as in intelligence, social adjustment, or sexual behavior) from what is considered normal for a group

¹de·vi·ate \ˈdē-vē-ət, -vē-ˌāt\ *adj* : characterized by or given to significant departure from the behavioral norms of a particular society

²deviate *n* : one that deviates from a norm; *esp* : a person who differs markedly from a group norm

de·vi·a·tion \ˌdē-vē-ˈā-shən\ *n* : an act or instance of diverging (as in growth or behavior) from an established way or in a new direction

de·vi·tal·iza·tion \(ˌ)dē-ˌvīt-ᵊl-ə-ˈzā-shən\ *n* : destruction and usu. removal of the pulp from a tooth — **de·vi·tal·ize** \-ˈvīt-ᵊl-ˌīz\ *vb*

dew·claw \ˈdü-ˌklò, ˈdyü-\ *n* : a vestigial digit not reaching to the ground on the foot of a mammal; *also* : a claw or hoof terminating such a digit — **dew·clawed** \-ˌklòd\ *adj*

dew·lap \-ˌlap\ *n* : loose skin hanging under the neck esp. of a bovine animal — **dew·lapped** \-ˌlapt\ *adj*

de·worm \(ˌ)dē-ˈwərm\ *vb* : to rid (as a dog) of worms : WORM

de·worm·er \-ˈwər-mər\ *n* : WORMER 1

dex \ˈdeks\ *n* : the sulfate of dextroamphetamine

dexa·meth·a·sone \ˌdek-sə-ˈme-thə-ˌsōn, -zōn\ *n* : a synthetic glucocorticoid $C_{22}H_{29}FO_5$ used esp. as an anti-inflammatory and antiallergic agent — see DECADRON

Dex·e·drine \ˈdek-sə-ˌdrēn, -drən\ *trademark* — used for a preparation of the sulfate of dextroamphetamine

dex·ies \ˈdek-sēz\ *n pl* : tablets or capsules of the sulfate of dextroamphetamine

dextr- *or* **dextro-** *comb form* **1** : right : on or toward the right (*dextro*cardia) **2** *usu* **dextro-** : dextrorotatory (*dex*troamphetamine)

¹dex·tral \ˈdek-strəl\ *adj* : of or relating to the right; *esp* : RIGHT-HANDED — **dex·tral·ly** *adv*

²**dextral** *n* : a person exhibiting dominance of the right hand and eye

dex·tral·i·ty \dek-ˈstra-lə-tē\ *n, pl* **-ties** : the quality or state of having the right side or some parts (as the hand or eye) different from and usu. more efficient than the left or corresponding parts; *also* : RIGHT-HANDEDNESS

dex·tran \ˈdek-ˌstran, -strən\ *n* : any of numerous glucose biopolymers ($C_6H_{10}O_5$)$_n$ of variable molecular weight that are produced esp. by the fermentation of sucrose by bacteria (genus *Leuconostoc*), are found in dental plaque, and are used esp. to increase the volume of blood plasma

dex·tran·ase \-strə-ˌnās, -ˌnāz\ *n* : a hydrolase that prevents tooth decay by breaking down dextran and eliminating plaque

dex·trin \ˈdek-strən\ *n* : any of various soluble gummy polysaccharides ($C_6H_{10}O_5$)$_n$ obtained from starch by the action of heat, acids, or enzymes

dex·tro \ˈdek-(ˌ)strō\ *adj* : DEXTRORO-TATORY

dex·tro·am·phet·amine \ˌdek-(ˌ)strō-am-ˈfe-tə-ˌmēn, -mən\ *n* : a drug consisting of dextrorotatory amphetamine that is usu. administered as the sulfate ($C_9H_{13}N$)$_2$·H_2SO_4, is a strong stimulant of the central nervous system, is a common drug of abuse, and is used medicinally esp. in the treatment of narcolepsy and attention deficit disorder — see DEXEDRINE

dex·tro·car·dia \ˌdek-strō-ˈkär-dē-ə\ *n* : an abnormal condition in which the heart is situated on the right side and the great blood vessels of the right and left sides are reversed — **dex·tro·car·di·al** \-dē-əl\ *adj*

dex·tro·pro·poxy·phene \ˌdek-strə-prō-ˈpäk-sə-ˌfēn\ *n* : PROPOXYPHENE

dex·tro·ro·ta·to·ry \-ˈrō-tə-ˌtōr-ē\ *also* **dex·tro·ro·ta·ry** \-ˈrō-tə-rē\ *adj* : turning clockwise or toward the right; *esp* : rotating the plane of polarization of light toward the right (~ crystals) — compare LEVOROTATORY

dex·trose \ˈdek-ˌstrōs, -ˌstrōz\ *n* : dextrorotatory glucose — called also *grape sugar*

DFP \ˌdē-(ˌ)ef-ˈpē\ *n* : ISOFLUROPHATE

DHPG \ˌdē-(ˌ)āch-(ˌ)pē-ˈjē\ *n* : GANCI-CLOVIR

di- *comb form* **1** : twice : twofold : double (*diphasic*) (*dizygotic*) **2** : containing two atoms, radicals, or groups (*dioxide*)

di·a·be·tes \ˌdī-ə-ˈbē-tēz, -təs\ *n, pl* **diabetes** : any of various abnormal conditions characterized by the secretion and excretion of excessive amounts of urine; *esp* : DIABETES MELLITUS

diabetes in·sip·i·dus \-in-ˈsi-pə-dəs\ *n* : a disorder of the pituitary gland characterized by intense thirst and by the excretion of large amounts of urine

diabetes mel·li·tus \-ˈme-lə-təs\ *n* : a variable disorder of carbohydrate metabolism caused by a combination of hereditary and environmental factors and usu. characterized by inadequate secretion or utilization of insulin, by excessive urine production, by excessive amounts of sugar in the blood and urine, and by thirst, hunger, and loss of weight — see INSULIN-DEPENDENT DIABETES MELLITUS, NON-INSULIN-DEPENDENT DIABETES MELLITUS

¹**di·a·bet·ic** \ˌdī-ə-ˈbe-tik\ *adj* **1** : of or relating to diabetes or diabetics **2** : affected with diabetes **3** : occurring in or caused by diabetes (~ coma) **4** : suitable for diabetics (~ food)

²**diabetic** *n* : a person affected with diabetes

diabeticorum — see NECROBIOSIS LIPOIDICA DIABETICORUM

di·a·be·to·gen·ic \ˌdī-ə-ˌbē-tə-ˈje-nik\ *adj* : producing diabetes (~ drugs) (a ~ diet)

di·a·be·tol·o·gist \ˌdī-ə-bə-ˈtä-lə-jist\ *n* : a specialist in diabetes

di·ace·tic acid \ˌdī-ə-ˌsēt-ik-\ *n* : ACETO-ACETIC ACID

di·ace·tyl·mor·phine \ˌdī-ə-ˌsēt-əl-ˈmor-ˌfēn, dī-ˌa-sət-əl-\ *n* : HEROIN

di·ag·nose \ˈdī-ig-ˌnōs, -ˌnōz, ˌdī-ig-ˈ-, -əg-\ *vb* **-nosed; -nos·ing 1** : to recognize (as a disease) by signs and symptoms **2** : to diagnose a disease or condition in (*diagnosed* the patient) — **di·ag·nos·able** *also* **di·ag·nose·able** \ˌdī-ig-ˈnō-sə-bəl, -əg-, -zə-\ *adj*

di·ag·no·sis \ˌdī-ig-ˈnō-səs, -əg-\ *n, pl* **-no·ses** \-ˌsēz\ **1** : the art or act of identifying a disease from its signs and symptoms **2** : the decision reached by diagnosis

diagnosis related group *n* : DRG

¹**di·ag·nos·tic** \-ˈnäs-tik\ *also* **di·ag·nos·ti·cal** \-ti-kəl\ *adj* **1** : of, relating to, or used in diagnosis **2** : using the methods of or yielding a diagnosis — **di·ag·nos·ti·cal·ly** \-ti-k(ə-)lē\ *adv*

²**diagnostic** *n* : the art or practice of diagnosis — often used in pl.

di·ag·nos·ti·cian \-(ˌ)näs-ˈti-shən\ *n* : a specialist in medical diagnostics

dia·ki·ne·sis \ˌdī-ə-kə-ˈnē-səs, -(ˌ)kī-\ *n, pl* **-ne·ses** \-ˌsēz\ : the final stage of the meiotic prophase marked by contraction of each chromosome pair — **dia·ki·net·ic** \-ˈne-tik\ *adj*

di·al·y·sance \di-ˈa-lə-səns\ *n* : blood volume in milliliters per unit time cleared of a substance by dialysis (as by an artificial kidney)

di·al·y·sate \dī-ˈa-lə-ˌzāt, -ˌsāt\ *also* **di·al·y·zate** \-ˌzāt\ *n* **1** : the material that passes through the membrane in dialysis **2** : the liquid into which material passes by way of the membrane in dialysis

di·al·y·sis \dī-ˈa-lə-səs\ *n, pl* **-y·ses** \-ˌsēz\ **1** : the separation of substances in solution by means of their unequal diffusion through semipermeable membranes; *esp* : such a separation of colloids from soluble substances 2 : HEMODIALYSIS — **di·a·lyt·ic** \ˌdī-ə-ˈli-tik\ *adj*

di·a·lyze \ˈdī-ə-ˌlīz\ *vb* **-lyzed; -lyz·ing** 1 : to subject to or undergo dialysis 2 : to separate or obtain by dialysis — **di·a·lyz·abil·i·ty** \-ˌlī-zə-ˈbi-lə-tē\ *n* — **di·a·lyz·able** \-ˈlī-zə-bəl\ *adj*

di·a·lyz·er \-ˌlī-zər\ *n* : an apparatus in which dialysis is carried out consisting essentially of one or more containers for liquids separated into compartments by membranes

di·am·e·ter \dī-ˈa-mə-tər\ *n* 1 : a unit of magnification of a magnifying device equal to the number of times the linear dimensions of the object are increased (a microscope magnifying 60 ~*s*) 2 : one of the maximal breadths of a part of the body (the transverse ~ of the inlet of the pelvis)

di·ami·no·di·phe·nyl sul·fone \ˌdī-ə-ˌmē-(ˌ)nō-ˌdī-ˈfen-ᵊl-ˈsəl-ˌfōn, -ˈfēn-\ *n* : DAPSONE

di·a·mond·back rattlesnake \ˈdī-mənd-ˌbak-, ˈdī-ə-\ *n* : either of two large and deadly rattlesnakes of the genus *Crotalus* (*C. adamanteus* of the southeastern U.S. and *C. atrox* of the south central and southwestern U.S. and Mexico) — called also *diamondback, diamondback rattler*

dia·mor·phine \ˈdī-ə-ˈmor-ˌfēn\ *n* : HEROIN

di·a·pe·de·sis \ˌdī-ə-pə-ˈdē-səs\ *n, pl* **-de·ses** \-ˌsēz\ : the passage of blood cells through capillary walls into the tissues — **di·a·pe·det·ic** \-ˈde-tik\ *adj*

¹**di·a·per** \ˈdī-pər, ˈdī-ə-\ *n* : a basic garment esp. for infants consisting of a folded cloth or other absorbent material drawn up between the legs and fastened about the waist

²**diaper** *vb* **di·a·pered; di·a·per·ing** : to put on or change the diaper of (an infant)

diaper rash *n* : skin irritation of the diaper-covered area and usu. the buttocks of an infant esp. from exposure to feces and urinary ammonia

di·a·pho·re·sis \ˌdī-ə-fə-ˈrē-səs, (ˌ)dī-ˌa-fə-\ *n, pl* **-re·ses** \-ˌsēz\ : PERSPIRATION; *esp* : profuse perspiration artificially induced

¹**di·a·pho·ret·ic** \-ˈre-tik\ *adj* : having the power to increase sweating

²**diaphoretic** *n* : an agent capable of inducing sweating

di·a·phragm \ˈdī-ə-ˌfram\ *n* 1 : a body partition of muscle and connective tissue; *specif* : the partition separating the chest and abdominal cavities in mammals — compare PELVIC DIAPHRAGM, UROGENITAL DIAPHRAGM 2 : a device that limits the aperture of a lens or optical system 3 : a molded cap usu. of thin rubber fitted over the uterine cervix to act as a mechanical contraceptive barrier

di·a·phrag·ma sel·lae \ˌdī-ə-ˈfrag-mə-

ˈse-ˌlī, -ˌlē\ *n, pl* : a small horizontal fold of the dura mater that roofs over the sella turcica and is pierced by a small opening for the infundibulum

di·a·phrag·mat·ic \ˌdī-ə-frə-ˈma-tik, -ˌfrag-\ *adj* : of, involving, or resembling a diaphragm (~ hernia)

di·aph·y·se·al \dī-ˌa-fə-ˈsē-əl, -ˌzē-\ *or* **di·a·phys·i·al** \ˌdī-ə-ˈfi-zē-əl\ *adj* : of, relating to, or involving a diaphysis

di·a·phy·sec·to·my \ˌdī-ə-fə-ˈzek-tə-mē, -ˈsek-\ *n, pl* **-mies** : surgical excision of all or part of a diaphysis (as of the femur)

di·aph·y·sis \dī-ˈa-fə-səs\ *n, pl* **-y·ses** \-ˌsēz\ : the shaft of a long bone

di·ar·rhea \ˌdī-ə-ˈrē-ə\ *n* : abnormally frequent intestinal evacuations with more or less fluid stools

di·ar·rhe·al \-ˈrē-əl\ *adj* : DIARRHEIC

di·ar·rhe·ic \-ˈrē-ik\ *adj* : of or relating to diarrhea

di·ar·rhet·ic \-ˈre-tik\ *adj* : DIARRHEIC

di·ar·rhoea, di·ar·rhoe·al, di·ar·rhoe·ic, di·ar·rhoet·ic *chiefly Brit var of* DIARRHEA, DIARRHEAL, DIARRHEIC, DIARRHETIC

di·ar·thro·sis \ˌdī-är-ˈthrō-səs\ *n, pl* **-thro·ses** \-ˌsēz\ 1 : articulation that permits free movement 2 : a freely movable joint — called also *synovial joint* — **di·ar·thro·di·al** \ˌdī- är-ˈthrō-dē-əl\ *adj*

di·a·stase \ˈdī-ə-ˌstās, -ˌstāz\ *n* 1 : AMYLASE: *esp* : a mixture of amylases from malt 2 : ENZYME

di·as·ta·sis \dī-ˈas-tə-səs\ *n, pl* **-ta·ses** \-ˌsēz\ 1 : an abnormal separation of parts normally joined together 2 : the rest phase of cardiac diastole occurring between filling of the ventricle and the start of atrial contraction

di·a·stat·ic \ˌdī-ə-ˈsta-tik\ *adj* : relating to or having the properties of diastase; *esp* : converting starch into sugar

di·a·ste·ma \ˌdī-ə-ˈstē-mə\ *n, pl* **-ma·ta** \-mə-tə\ : a space between teeth in a jaw

di·a·ste·ma·to·my·e·lia \ˌdī-ə-ˌstē-mə-tō-mī-ˈē-lē-ə, -ˌste-\ *n* : congenital division of all or part of the spinal cord

di·as·to·le \dī-ˈas-tə-(ˌ)lē\ *n* : the passive rhythmical expansion or dilation of the cavities of the heart during which they fill with blood — compare SYSTOLE — **di·a·stol·ic** \ˌdī-ə-ˈstä-lik\ *adj*

diastolic pressure *n* : the lowest arterial blood pressure of a cardiac cycle occurring during diastole of the heart — compare SYSTOLIC PRESSURE

di·a·stroph·ic dwarfism \ˌdī-ə-ˈsträ-fik\ *n* : an inherited dysplasia affecting bones and joints and characterized esp. by clubfoot, deformities of the digits of the hand, malformed pinnae, and cleft palate

dia·ther·my \ˈdī-ə-ˌthər-mē\ *n, pl* **-mies** : the generation of heat in tissue by electric currents for medical or surgical purposes — see ELECTROCOAG-ULATION — **dia·ther·mic** \dī-ə-ˈthər-mik\ *adj*

di·ath·e·sis \dī-ˈa-thə-səs\ *n, pl* **-e·ses** \-ˌsēz\ : a constitutional predisposition toward a particular state or condition and esp. one that is abnormal or diseased

dia·tri·zo·ate \ˌdī-ə-ˌtrī-ˈzō-ˌāt\ *n* : either of two salts of the acid $C_{11}H_9$-$I_3N_2O_4$ administered in solution as a radiopaque medium for various forms of radiographic diagnosis — see HY-PAQUE

di·az·e·pam \dī-ˈa-zə-ˌpam\ *n* : a synthetic tranquilizer $C_{16}H_{13}ClN_2O$ used esp. to relieve anxiety and tension and as a muscle relaxant — see VAL-IUM

Di·az·i·non \dī-ˈa-zə-ˌnän\ *trademark* — used for an organophosphate insecticide $C_{12}H_{21}N_2O_3PS$ that is a cholinesterase inhibitor dangerous to humans if ingested

di·az·ox·ide \ˌdī-ˌa-ˈzäk-ˌsīd\ *n* : an antihypertensive drug $C_8H_7ClN_2O_2S$ that has a structure similar to chlorothiazide but no diuretic activity

di·benz·an·thra·cene or **1,2:5,6-di·benz·an·thra·cene** \(ˌ)wən-ˌtü-ˌfīv-ˌsiks-)dī-ˌben-ˈzan-thrə-ˌsēn\ *n* : a carcinogenic cyclic hydrocarbon $C_{22}H_{14}$ found in trace amounts in coal tar

di·ben·zo·fu·ran \ˈdī-ˌben-zō-ˈfyu̇-ˌran, -fyə-ˈran\ *n* : a highly toxic chemical compound $C_{12}H_8O$ that is used in chemical synthesis and as an insecticide and is a hazardous pollutant in its chlorinated form

di·bu·caine \ˈdī-ˌbyü-ˌkān, ˈdī-ˌ\ *n* : a local anesthetic $C_{20}H_{29}N_3O_2$ used for temporary relief of pain and itching esp. from burns, sunburn, insect bites, or hemorrhoids — called also *cinchocaine*; see NUPERCAINE

dibucaine number *n* : a number expressing the percentage by which cholinesterase activity in a serum sample is inhibited by dibucaine

di·cen·tric \(ˌ)dī-ˈsen-trik\ *adj* : having two centromeres (a ~ chromosome) — **dicentric** *n*

dich- *or* **dicho-** *comb form* : apart : separate (*dichotic*)

di·chlo·ra·mine-T \ˌdī-ˌklōr-ə-ˌmēn-ˈtē\ *n* : a yellow crystalline compound $C_7H_7Cl_2NO_2S$ used esp. formerly as an antiseptic — compare CHLORA-MINE-T

p–di·chlo·ro·ben·zene *var of* PARADI-CHLOROBENZENE

2,4-di·chlo·ro·phen·oxy·ace·tic acid *also* **di·chlo·ro·phen·oxy·ace·tic acid** \(ˌtü-ˌfōr-)dī-ˌklōr-ō-(ˌ)phe-ˌnäk-sē-ə-ˈsē-tik-\ *n* : 2,4-D

di·chlor·vos \(ˌ)dī-ˈklȯr-ˌväs, -vəs\ *n* : an organophosphorus insecticide and anthelmintic $C_4H_7Cl_2O_4P$ used esp. in veterinary medicine — called also *DDVP*

dich·ot·ic \(ˌ)dī-ˈkō-tik\ *adj* : relating to

or involving the presentation of a stimulus to one ear that differs in some respect (as pitch, loudness, frequency, or energy) from a stimulus presented to the other ear (~ listening) — **dich·oti·cal·ly** \-ti-k(ə-)lē\ *adv*

di·chot·o·my \dī-ˈkä-tə-mē\ *n, pl* **-mies** : a division or forking into branches; *esp* : repeated bifurcation — **di·chot·o·mous** \(ˌ)dī-ˈkä-tə-məs\ *adj*

di·chro·mat \ˈkä-krō-ˌmat, (ˌ)dī-ˈ\ *n* : one affected with dichromatism

di·chro·ma·tism \dī-ˈkrō-mə-ˌti-zəm\ *n* : partial color blindness in which only two colors are perceptible — **di·chro·mat·ic** \ˌdī-krō-ˈma-tik\ *adj*

Dick test \ˈdik-\ *n* : a test to determine susceptibility or immunity to scarlet fever by an injection of scarlet fever toxin

di·clox·a·cil·lin \(ˌ)dī-ˌkläk-sə-ˈsi-lən\ *n* : a semisynthetic penicillin used in the form of its sodium salt $C_{19}H_{16}Cl_2N_3$-$NaO_5S·H_2O$ esp. against penicillinase-producing staphylococci

di·cou·ma·rin \(ˌ)dī-ˈkü-mə-rən\ *n* : DI-CUMAROL

Di·cro·coe·li·um \ˌdī-krə-ˈsē-lē-əm\ *n* : a widely distributed genus (family Dicrocoeliidae) that includes small digenetic trematodes infesting the livers of ruminants or occas. other mammals including humans — see LANCET FLUKE

di·crot·ic \(ˌ)dī-ˈkrä-tik\ *adj* **1** *of the pulse* : having a double beat (as in certain febrile states in which the heart is overactive and the arterial walls are lacking in tone) — compare MONOCROTIC **2** : being or relating to the second part of the arterial pulse occurring during diastole of the heart or of an arterial pressure recording made during the same period — **di·cro·tism** \ˈdī-krə-ˌti-zəm\ *n*

dicrotic notch *n* : a secondary upstroke in the descending part of a pulse tracing corresponding to the transient increase in aortic pressure upon closure of the aortic valve

Dic·ty·o·cau·lus \ˌdik-tē-ə-ˈkȯ-ləs\ *n* : a genus (family Metastrongylidae) of small slender lungworms infesting mammals (as ruminants) and often causing severe bronchial symptoms or even pneumonia in young animals

dic·ty·o·some \ˈdik-tē-ə-ˌsōm\ *n* : any of the membranous or vesicular structures making up the Golgi apparatus

di·cu·ma·rol *also* **di·cou·ma·rol** \dī-ˈkü-mə-ˌrȯl, -ˈkyü-, -ˌrȯl\ *n* : a crystalline compound $C_{19}H_{12}O_6$ used to delay clotting of blood esp. in preventing and treating thromboembolic disease

di·cy·clo·mine \(ˌ)dī-ˈsī-klə-ˌmēn, -ˈsi-\ *n* : an anticholinergic drug used in the form of its hydrochloride salt C_{19}-$H_{35}NO_2·HCl$ for its antispasmodic effect on smooth muscle in gastrointestinal functional disorders

di·dan·o·sine \dī-ˈda-nə-ˌsēn\ *n* : DDI

di·de·oxy·cy·ti·dine \ˌdī-(ˌ)dē-ˌäk-sē-ˈsi-tə-ˌdēn, -ˈsī-\ *n* : DDC

di·de·oxy·ino·sine \-ˈi-nə-ˌsēn, -ˈī-, -sən\ *n* : DDI

die \ˈdī\ *vb* **died; dy·ing** \ˈdī-iŋ\ 1 : to suffer total and irreversible loss of the bodily attributes and functions that constitute life 2 : to suffer or face the pains of death

diel·drin \ˈdēl-drən\ *n* : a white crystalline persistent chlorinated hydrocarbon insecticide $C_{12}H_8Cl_6O$

Diels \ˈdēls\, Otto Paul Hermann (1876–1954), and Al·der \ˈól-dər\, Kurt (1902–1958), German chemists.

di·en·ceph·a·lon \ˌdī-ən-ˈse-fə-ˌlän, -ˌdī-(ˌ)en-, -lən\ *n* : the posterior subdivision of the forebrain — called also *betweenbrain* — **di·en·ce·phal·ic** \-sə-ˈfa-lik\ *adj*

die·ner \ˈdē-nər\ *n* : a laboratory helper esp. in a medical school

di·en·es·trol \ˌdī-ə-ˈnes-ˌtról, -ˌtról\ *n* : a white crystalline estrogenic compound $C_{18}H_{18}O_2$ structurally related to diethylstilbestrol and used topically to treat atrophic vaginitis and kraurosis vulvae

di·en·oes·trol \ˌdī-ə-ˈnēs-ˌtról, -ˌtról\ *chiefly Brit var of* DIENESTROL

Di·ent·amoe·ba \ˌdī-ˌen-tə-ˈmē-bə\ *n* : a genus of amebic protozoans parasitic in the intestines of humans and monkeys that include one (*D. fragilis*) known to cause abdominal pain, anorexia, and loose stools in humans

di·es·trus \(ˌ)dī-ˈes-trəs\ *n* : a period of sexual quiescence that intervenes between two periods of estrus — **di·es·trous** \-trəs\ *adj*

¹**di·et** \ˈdī-ət\ *n* 1 : food and drink regularly provided or consumed 2 : habitual nourishment 3 : the kind and amount of food prescribed for a person or animal for a special reason

²**diet** *vb* : to eat or cause to eat less or according to a prescribed rule

³**diet** *adj* : reduced in calories ⟨a ∼ soft drink⟩

¹**di·etary** \ˈdī-ə-ˌter-ē\ *n, pl* **di·etar·ies** : the kinds and amounts of food available to or eaten by an individual, group, or population

²**dietary** *adj* : of or relating to a diet or to the rules of a diet ⟨∼ habits⟩ — **di·etari·ly** \ˌdī-ə-ˈter-ə-lē\ *adv*

dietary fiber *n* : FIBER 2

di·et·er \ˈdī-ə-tər\ *n* : one that diets; *esp* : a person that consumes a reduced allowance of food in order to lose weight

di·etet·ic \ˌdī-ə-ˈte-tik\ *adj* 1 : of or relating to diet 2 : adapted (as by the elimination of salt or sugar) for use in special diets — **di·etet·i·cal·ly** \-ti-k(ə-)lē\ *adv*

di·etet·ics \-ˈte-tiks\ *n sing or pl* : the

science or art of applying the principles of nutrition to feeding

diethylamide — see LYSERGIC ACID DIETHYLAMIDE

di·eth·yl·car·bam·azine \ˌdī-ˌe-thəl-kär-ˈba-mə-ˌzēn, -zən\ *n* : an anthelmintic derived from piperazine and administered in the form of its crystalline citrate $C_{10}H_{21}N_3O \cdot C_6H_8O_7$ esp. to control filariasis in humans and large roundworms in dogs and cats

di·eth·yl ether \(ˌ)dī-ˈe-thəl-\ *n* : ETHER 1

di·eth·yl·pro·pi·on \(ˌ)dī-ˌe-thəl-ˈprō-pē-ˌän\ *n* : a sympathomimetic amine related structurally to amphetamine and used esp. in the form of its hydrochloride $C_{13}H_{19}NO \cdot HCl$ as an appetite suppressant to promote weight loss — see TENUATE

di·eth·yl·stil·bes·trol \-stil-ˈbes-ˌtról, -ˌtról\ *n* : a colorless crystalline synthetic compound $C_{18}H_{20}O_2$ used as a potent estrogen but contraindicated in pregnancy for its tendency to cause cancer or birth defects in offspring — called also *DES, stilbestrol*

di·eth·yl·stil·boes·trol \-ˈbes-ˌtról, -ˌtról\ *chiefly Brit var of* DIETHYLSTILBESTROL

di·eti·tian *or* **di·eti·cian** \ˌdī-ə-ˈti-shən\ *n* : a specialist in dietetics

Dietl's crisis \ˈdēt-lz-\ *n* : an attack of violent pain in the kidney region accompanied by chills, nausea, vomiting, and collapse that is caused by the formation of kinks in the ureter and is usu. associated with a floating kidney

Dietl \ˈdēt-ˈl\, Josef (1804–1878), Polish physician.

differential blood count *n* : a blood count which includes separate counts for each kind of white blood cell — compare COMPLETE BLOOD COUNT

differential diagnosis *n* : the distinguishing of a disease or condition from others presenting similar symptoms

dif·fer·en·ti·ate \ˌdi-fə-ˈren-chē-ˌāt\ *vb* **-at·ed; -at·ing** 1 : to constitute a difference that distinguishes 2 a : to cause differentiation of in the course of development b : to undergo differentiation 3 : to sense, recognize, or give expression to a difference (as in stimuli) 4 : to cause differentiation in (a specimen for microscopic examination) by staining

dif·fer·en·ti·a·tion \-ˌren-chē-ˈā-shən\ *n* 1 a : the act or process of differentiating b : the enhancement of microscopically visible differences between tissue or cell parts by partial selective decolorization or removal of excess stain 2 a : modification of different parts of the body for performance of particular functions; *also* : specialization of parts or organs in the course of evolution b : the sum of the developmental processes whereby apparently unspecialized cells, tissues, and structures attain their adult form and function

dif·flu·ent \'dif-(,)flü-ənt\ *adj* : soft like mush (a ~ spleen)

dif·fu·sate \di-'fyü-,zāt\ *n* : DIALYSATE

¹**dif·fuse** \di-'fyüs\ *adj* : not concentrated or localized (~ sclerosis)

²**dif·fuse** \di-'fyüz\ *vb* **dif·fused; dif·fus·ing 1** : to subject to or undergo diffusion **2** : to break up and distribute (incident light) by reflection (as from a rough surface) — **dif·fus·ible** \di-'fyü-zə-bəl\ *adj* — **dif·fus·ibil·i·ty** \-,fyü-zə-'bi-lə-tē\ *n*

dif·fu·sion \di-'fyü-zhən\ *n* **1** : the process whereby particles of liquids, gases, or solids intermingle as the result of their spontaneous movement caused by thermal agitation and in dissolved substances move from a region of higher to one of lower concentration **2 a** : reflection of light by a rough reflecting surface **b** : transmission of light through a translucent material — **dif·fu·sion·al** \-'fyü-zhə-nəl\ *adj*

di·flu·ni·sal \(,)dī-'flü-nə-,sal\ *n* : a nonsteroidal anti-inflammatory drug $C_{13}H_8F_2O_3$ related to aspirin that is used to relieve mild to moderately severe pain — see DOLOBID

di·gas·tric muscle \(,)dī-'gas-trik-\ *n* : either of a pair of muscles having two bellies separated by a tendon that extend from the anterior inferior margin of the mandible to the temporal bone and serve to open the jaw — called also *digastric*

di·gas·tri·cus \-tri-kəs\ *n* : DIGASTRIC MUSCLE

di·ge·net·ic \,dī-jə-'ne-tik\ *adj* : of or relating to a subclass (Digenea) of trematode worms in which sexual reproduction as an internal parasite of a vertebrate alternates with asexual reproduction in a mollusk and which include a number of parasites (as the Chinese liver fluke) of humans

¹**di·gest** \'dī-,jest\ *n* : a product of digestion

²**di·gest** \dī-'jest, də-\ *vb* **1** : to convert (food) into absorbable form **2 a** : to soften, decompose, or break down by heat and moisture or chemicals **b** : to extract soluble ingredients from by warming with a liquid — **di·gest·er** \-'jes-tər\ *n*

di·gest·ant \-'jes-tənt\ *n* : a substance that digests or aids in digestion — compare DIGESTIVE 1

di·gest·ibil·i·ty \-,jes-tə-'bi-lə-tē\ *n*, *pl* **-ties 1** : the fitness of something for digestion **2** : the percentage of a foodstuff taken into the digestive tract that is absorbed into the body

di·gest·ible \-'jes-tə-bəl\ *adj* : capable of being digested

di·ges·tion \-'jes-chən\ *n* : the action, process, or power of digesting; *esp* : the process of making food absorb-

able by dissolving it and breaking it down into simpler chemical compounds that occurs in the living body chiefly through the action of enzymes secreted into the alimentary canal

¹**di·ges·tive** \-'jes-tiv\ *n* **1** : something that aids digestion esp. of food — compare DIGESTANT 2 : a substance which promotes suppuration

²**digestive** *adj* **1** : relating to or functioning in digestion (the ~ system) **2** : having the power to cause or promote digestion (~ enzymes)

digestive gland *n* : a gland secreting digestive enzymes

dig·i·la·nid \,dij-ə-'la-nəd\ *or* **dig·i·lan·ide** \-,nīd, -nəd\ *n* : LANATOSIDE

digilanid A *or* **digilanide A** *n* : LANATOSIDE A

digilanid B *or* **digilanide B** *n* : LANATOSIDE B

digilanid C *or* **digilanide C** *n* : LANATOSIDE C

dig·it \'di-jət\ *n* : any of the divisions (as a finger or toe) in which the limbs of amphibians and all higher vertebrates terminate and which in humans are five in number on each limb

dig·i·tal \'di-jət-³l\ *adj* **1** : of, relating to, or supplying one or more fingers or toes (a ~ branch of an artery) **2** : done with a finger (a ~ examination) — **dig·i·tal·ly** *adv*

dig·i·tal·in \,di-jə-'ta-lən, -'tā-\ *n* **1** : a white crystalline steroid glycoside $C_{36}H_{56}O_{14}$ obtained from seeds esp. of the common foxglove **2** : a mixture of the glycosides of digitalis leaves or seeds

dig·i·tal·is \-ləs\ *n* **1 a** *cap* : a genus of Eurasian herbs (family Scrophulariaceae) that have alternate leaves and stalks of snowy bell-shaped flowers and comprise the foxgloves **b** : FOXGLOVE **2** : the dried leaf of the common European foxglove (*D. purpurea*) containing the active principles digitoxin and gitoxin, serving as a powerful cardiac stimulant and a diuretic, and used in standardized powdered form esp. in the treatment of congestive heart failure

dig·i·ta·li·za·tion \,di-jət-³l-ə-'zā-shən\ *n* : the administration of digitalis (as in heart disease) until the desired physiological adjustment is attained; *also* : the bodily state so produced — **dig·i·ta·lize** \'di-jət-³l-,īz\ *vb*

digital nerve *n* **1** : any of several branches of the median nerve and the ulnar nerve supplying the fingers and thumb **2** : any of several branches of the medial plantar nerve supplying the toes

digiti — see ABDUCTOR DIGITI MINIMI, EXTENSOR DIGITI MINIMI, EXTENSOR DIGITI QUINTI PROPRIUS, FLEXOR DIGITI MINIMI BREVIS, OPPONENS DIGITI MINIMI

digitorum — see EXTENSOR DIGITORUM BREVIS, EXTENSOR DIGITORUM COM-

digitoxin • dimer 178

MUNIS, EXTENSOR DIGITORUM LONGUS, FLEXOR DIGITORUM BREVIS, FLEXOR DIGITORUM LONGUS, FLEXOR DIGITORUM PROFUNDUS, FLEXOR DIGITORUM SUPERFICIALIS

dig·i·tox·in \ˌdi-jə-ˈtäk-sən\ n : a poisonous glycoside $C_{41}H_{64}O_{13}$ that is the most active constituent of digitalis; also : a mixture of digitalis glycosides consisting chiefly of digitoxin

di·glyc·er·ide \ˌdī-ˈgli-sə-ˌrīd\ n : an ester of glycerol that contains two ester groups and involves one or two acids

di·gox·in \dī-ˈjäk-sən, -ˈgäk-\ n : a poisonous cardiotonic glycoside $C_{41}H_{64}O_{14}$ obtained from the leaves of a foxglove (Digitalis lanata) and used similarly to digitalis — see LANOXIN

di·hy·dro·chlo·ride \ˌdī-hī-drə-ˈklōr-ˌīd\ n : a chemical compound with two molecules of hydrochloric acid (quinine ~ $C_{20}H_{24}N_2O_2 \cdot 2HCl$)

di·hy·dro·co·de·inone \-ˌkō-ˈdē-ə-ˌnōn\ n : a habit-forming codeine derivative $C_{18}H_{21}NO_3$ used as an analgesic and cough sedative — called also hydrocodone; see HYCODAN

di·hy·dro·er·got·a·mine \-hī-drō-ˌər-ˈgä-tə-ˌmēn\ n : a hydrogenated derivative $C_{33}H_{37}N_5O_5$ of ergotamine that is used in the treatment of migraine

di·hy·dro·mor·phi·none \-ˈmòr-fə-ˌnōn\ n : HYDROMORPHONE

di·hy·dro·strep·to·my·cin \-ˌstrep-tə-ˈmīs-ᵊn\ n : a toxic antibiotic $C_{21}H_{41}N_7O_{12}$ formerly used but abandoned because of its tendency to impair hearing

di·hy·dro·tachy·ste·rol \-ˌta-ki-ˈster-ˌòl, -ˈstir-, -ˌōl\ n : an alcohol $C_{28}H_{45}OH$ used in the treatment of hypocalcemia

di·hy·dro·tes·tos·ter·one \-te-ˈstäs-tə-ˌrōn\ n : a derivative $C_{19}H_{30}O_2$ of testosterone with similar androgenic activity

di·hy·dro·the·elin \-ˈthē-ə-lən\ n : ESTRADIOL

di·hy·droxy·ac·e·tone \ˌdī-hī-ˌdräk-sē-ˈa-sə-ˌtōn\ n : a glyceraldehyde isomer $C_3H_6O_3$ that is used esp. to stain the skin to simulate a tan

1,25-di·hy·droxy·cho·le·cal·cif·er·ol \-ˌwən-ˌtwen-tē-ˌfīv-ˌchō-lē-ˌdräk-sē-kō-lə-(ˌ)kal-ˈsi-fə-ˌròl, -ˌrōl\ n : a physiologically active metabolic derivative $C_{27}H_{44}O_3$ of vitamin D that is synthesized in the kidney

di·hy·droxy·phe·nyl·al·a·nine \ˌdī-hī-ˌdräk-sē-ˌfen-ᵊl-ˈa-lə-ˌnēn, -ˌfēn-\ n 1 or 3,4-dihydroxyphenylalanine \ˌthrē-ˈfòr-\ : DOPA 2 or L-3,4-dihydroxyphenylalanine \el-\ or L-dihydroxyphenylalanine : L-DOPA

di·io·do·hy·droxy·quin \ˌdī-ˌī-ə-dō-hī-ˈdräk-si-kwən\ n : IODOQUINOL

di·io·do·hy·droxy·quin·o·line \-hī-ˈdräk-si-ˈkwin-ᵊl-ˌēn\ n : IODOQUINOL

di·io·do·ty·ro·sine \-ˈtī-rə-ˌsēn\ n : a compound $C_9H_9I_2NO_3$ of tyrosine and iodine that is produced in the thyroid gland from monoiodotyrosine and that combines with monoiodotyrosine to form triiodothyronine

di·iso·pro·pyl flu·o·ro·phos·phate \ˌdī-ˌī-sə-ˈprō-pəl-ˌflùr-ō-ˈfäs-ˌfāt\ n : ISOFLURPHATE

di·lac·er·a·tion \(ˌ)dī-ˌla-sə-ˈrā-shən\ n : injury (as partial fracture) to a developing tooth that results in a curve in the long axis as development continues — **di·lac·er·at·ed** \(ˌ)dī-ˈla-sə-ˌrā-təd\ adj

Di·lan·tin \dī-ˈlant-ᵊn, də-\ trademark — used for a preparation of phenytoin

di·la·ta·tion \ˌdi-lə-ˈtā-shən, ˌdī-\ n 1 : the condition of being stretched beyond normal dimensions esp. as a result of overwork or disease or of abnormal relaxation 2 : DILATION 2

di·la·ta·tor \ˈdi-lə-ˌtā-tər, ˈdī-\ n : DILATOR b

di·late \dī-ˈlāt, ˈdī-\ vb **di·lat·ed; di·lat·ing** 1 : to enlarge, stretch, or cause to expand 2 : to become expanded or swollen

di·la·tion \dī-ˈlā-shən\ n 1 : the state of being dilated : DILATATION 2 : the action of stretching or enlarging an organ or part of the body

di·la·tor \(ˌ)dī-ˈlā-tər, də-\ n : one that dilates: as a : an instrument for expanding a tube, duct, or cavity (a urethral ~) b : a muscle that dilates a part c : a drug (as a vasodilator) causing dilation

Di·lau·did \(ˌ)dī-ˈlò-did\ trademark — used for a preparation of hydromorphone

dil·do \ˈdil-(ˌ)dō\ n, pl **dildos** : an object serving as a penis substitute for vaginal insertion

di·lti·a·zem \dil-ˈtī-ə-(ˌ)zem\ n : a calcium channel blocker $C_{22}H_{26}N_2O_4S$ used esp. in the form of its hydrochloride as a coronary vasodilator

¹dil·u·ent \ˈdil-yə-wənt\ n : a diluting agent (as the vehicle in a medicinal preparation)

²diluent adj : making thinner or less concentrated by admixture : DILUTING

¹di·lute \dī-ˈlüt, də-\ vb **di·lut·ed; di·lut·ing** : to make thinner or more liquid by admixture — **di·lut·or** also **di·lut·er** \-ˈlü-tər\ n

²dilute adj : of relatively low strength or concentration

di·lu·tion \dī-ˈlü-shən, də-\ n 1 : the action of diluting : the state of being diluted 2 : something (as a solution) that is diluted

di·men·hy·dri·nate \ˌdī-ˌmen-ˈhī-drə-ˌnāt\ n : a crystalline antihistaminic compound $C_{24}H_{28}ClN_5O_3$ used esp. to prevent nausea (as in motion sickness)

di·mer \ˈdī-mər\ n : a compound formed by the union of two radicals or two molecules of a simpler compound; *specif* : a polymer formed from two molecules of a monomer — **di·mer·ic** \(ˌ)dī-ˈmer-ik\ *adj*

di·mer·cap·rol \dī-(ˌ)mər-ˈka-ˌprȯl, -ˌprōl\ *n* : a colorless viscous oily compound $C_3H_8OS_2$ with an offensive odor used in treating arsenic, mercury, and gold poisoning — called also *BAL, British anti-lewisite*

di·meth·yl·ni·tros·amine \(ˌ)dī-ˌme-thəl-(ˌ)nī-ˈtrō-sə-ˌmēn\ *n* : a carcinogenic nitrosamine $C_2H_6N_2O$ that occurs esp. in tobacco smoke — called also *nitrosodimethylamine*

dimethyl sul·fox·ide \-səl-ˈfäk-ˌsīd\ *n* : an anti-inflammatory agent $(CH_3)_2SO$ used in the treatment of interstitial cystitis — called also *DMSO*

di·meth·yl·tryp·ta·mine \-ˈtrip-tə-ˌmēn\ *n* : a hallucinogenic drug $C_{12}H_{16}N_2$ that is chemically similar to but shorter acting than psilocybin — called also *DMT*

dim·ple \ˈdim-pəl\ *n* : a slight natural indentation or hollow in the surface of some part of the human body (as on a cheek or the chin) — **dimple** *vb*

dinitrate — see ISOSORBIDE DINITRATE

di·ni·tro·phe·nol \dī-ˌnī-trō-ˈfē-ˌnȯl, -fi-\ *n* : any of six isomeric compounds $C_6H_4N_2O_5$ some of whose derivatives are pesticides; *esp* : a highly toxic compound formerly used in weight control

di·no·fla·gel·late \ˌdī-nō-ˈfla-jə-lət, -ˌlāt, -flə-ˈje-lət\ *n* : any of an order (Dinoflagellata) of chiefly marine planktonic plantlike unicellular flagellates of which some cause red tide

Di·oc·to·phy·me \(ˌ)dī-ˌäk-tə-ˈfī-(ˌ)mē\ *n* : a genus (family Dioctophymidae) of nematode worms including a single species (*D. renale*) which is a destructive parasite of the kidney of dogs, minks, and sometimes humans

Di·o·drast \ˈdī-ə-ˌdrast\ *trademark* — used for a sterile solution of iodopyracet for injection

di·oes·trus *chiefly Brit var of* DIESTRUS

di·op·ter \dī-ˈäp-tər, ˈdī-ˌäp-\ *n* : a unit of measurement of the refractive power of a lens equal to the reciprocal of the focal length in meters

di·op·tric \(ˌ)dī-ˈäp-trik\ *adj* **1** : producing or serving in refraction of a beam of light : REFRACTIVE; *specif* : assisting vision by refracting and focusing light **2** : produced by means of refraction

di·ox·ide \(ˌ)dī-ˈäk-ˌsīd\ *n* : an oxide (as carbon dioxide) containing two atoms of oxygen in a molecule

di·ox·in \dī-ˈäk-sən\ *n* : any of several heterocyclic hydrocarbons that occur esp. as persistent toxic impurities in herbicides; *esp* : TCDD — see AGENT ORANGE

di·oxy·ben·zone \(ˌ)dī-ˌäk-sē-ˈben-ˌzōn, -ben-ˈ\ *n* : a sunscreen $C_{14}H_{12}O_4$ that absorbs throughout the ultraviolet spectrum

dip \ˈdip\ *n* : a liquid preparation of an insecticide or parasiticide which is applied to animals by immersing them in it — see SHEEP-DIP — **dip** *vb*

di·pep·ti·dase \dī-ˈpep-tə-ˌdās, -ˌdāz\ *n* : any of various enzymes that hydrolyze dipeptides but not polypeptides

di·pep·tide \(ˌ)dī-ˈpep-ˌtīd\ *n* : a peptide that yields two molecules of amino acid on hydrolysis

di·pha·sic \(ˌ)dī-ˈfā-zik\ *adj* : having two phases: as **a** : exhibiting a stage of stimulation followed by a stage of depression or vice versa (the ∼ action of certain drugs) **b** : relating to or being a record of a nerve impulse that is negative and positive — compare MONOPHASIC 1, POLYPHASIC 1

di·phen·hy·dra·mine \ˌdī-ˌfen-ˈhī-drə-ˌmēn\ *n* : an antihistamine $C_{17}H_{21}NO$ used esp. in the form of its hydrochloride to treat allergy symptoms and motion sickness

di·phen·oxy·late \ˌdī-ˌfen-ˈäk-sə-ˌlāt\ *n* : an antidiarrheal agent chemically related to meperidine and used in the form of its hydrochloride $C_{30}H_{32}N_2O_2·HCl$ — see LOMOTIL

di·phe·nyl·hy·dan·to·in \(ˌ)dī-ˌfen-ᵊl-hī-ˈdan-tə-wən, -ˌfen-ˌ\ *n* : PHENYTOIN

di·phos·phate \(ˌ)dī-ˈfäs-ˌfāt\ *n* : a phosphate containing two phosphate groups

2,3-di·phos·pho·glyc·er·ate *also* **di·phos·pho·glyc·er·ate** \(ˌ)tü-ˌthrē-)dī-ˌfäs-fō-ˈgli-sə-ˌrāt\ *n* : a phosphate that occurs in human erythrocytes and facilitates release of oxygen by decreasing the oxygen affinity of hemoglobin

di·phos·pho·pyr·i·dine nucleotide \-ˌpir-ə-ˌdēn-\ *n* : NAD

diph·the·ria \dif-ˈthir-ē-ə, dip-\ *n* : an acute febrile contagious disease marked by the formation of a false membrane esp. in the throat and caused by a bacterium of the genus *Corynebacterium* (*C. diphtheriae*) which produces a toxin causing inflammation of the heart and nervous system — **diph·the·ri·al** \-ē-əl\ *adj*

diph·the·rit·ic \ˌdif-thə-ˈri-tik, ˌdip-\ *adj* : relating to, produced in, or affected with diphtheria; *also* : resembling diphtheria esp. in the formation of a false membrane (∼ dysentery)

¹diph·the·roid \ˈdif-thə-ˌrȯid\ *adj* : resembling diphtheria

²diphtheroid *n* : a bacterium (esp. genus *Corynebacterium*) that resembles the bacterium of diphtheria but does not produce diphtheria toxin

di·phyl·lo·both·ri·a·sis \ˌdī-ˌfi-lō-bä-ˈthrī-ə-səs\ *n, pl* **-a·ses** \-ˌsēz\ : infestation with or disease caused by the fish tapeworm (*Diphyllobothrium latum*)

Di·phyl·lo·both·ri·um \-ˈbä-thrē-əm\ *n* : a large genus of tapeworms (family Diphyllobothriidae) that includes the common fish tapeworm (*D. latum*)

dipl- or **diplo-** comb form : double : twofold ⟨diplococcus⟩ ⟨diplopia⟩

dip·la·cu·sis \ˌdi-plə-ˈkyü-səs\ n, pl **-cu·ses** \-ˌsēz\ : the hearing of a single tone as if it were two tones of different pitch

di·ple·gia \dī-ˈplē-jə, -jē-ə\ n : paralysis of corresponding parts (as the legs) on both sides of the body

dip·lo·coc·cus \ˌdi-plō-ˈkä-kəs\ n, pl **-coc·ci** \-ˈkä-ˌkī, -ˌkē; ˈkäk-ˌsī, -ˌsē\ : any of various encapsulated bacteria (as the pneumococcus) that usu. occur in pairs and that were formerly grouped in a single taxon (genus Diplococcus) but are now all assigned to other genera — **di·plo·coc·cal** \-kəl\ adj

dip·loe \ˈdi-plə-ˌwē\ n : cancellous bony tissue between the external and internal layers of the skull — **di·plo·ic** \də-ˈplō-ik, -dī-\ adj

diploic vein n : any of several veins situated in channels in the diploe

¹dip·loid \ˈdi-ˌplȯid\ adj : having the basic chromosome number doubled — **dip·loi·dy** \-ˌplȯi-dē\ n

²diploid n : a single cell, individual, or generation characterized by the diploid chromosome number

dip·lo·mate \ˈdi-plə-ˌmāt\ n : a physician qualified to practice in a medical specialty by advanced training and experience in the specialty followed by passing an intensive examination by a national board of senior specialists

dip·lo·pia \di-ˈplō-pē-ə\ n : a disorder of vision in which two images of a single object are seen because of unequal action of the eye muscles — called also double vision — **dip·lo·pic** \-ˈplō-pik, -ˈplä-\ adj

dip·lo·tene \ˈdi-plə-ˌtēn\ n : a stage of meiotic prophase which follows the pachytene and during which the paired homologous chromosomes begin to separate and chiasmata become visible — **diplotene** adj

di·pole \ˈdi-ˌpōl\ n 1 : a pair of equal and opposite electric charges or magnetic poles of opposite sign separated by a small distance 2 : a body or system (as a molecule) having such charges — **di·po·lar** \-ˌpō-lər, -ˈpō-\ adj

di·pro·pi·o·nate \(ˌ)dī-ˈprō-pē-ə-ˌnāt\ n : an ester containing two propionate groups

dip·so·ma·nia \ˌdip-sə-ˈmā-nē-ə, -nyə\ n : an uncontrollable craving for alcoholic liquors — **dip·so·ma·ni·ac** \-nē-ˌak\ n — **dip·so·ma·ni·a·cal** \ˌdip-sō-mə-ˈnī-ə-kəl\ adj

dip·stick \ˈdip-ˌstik\ n : a chemically sensitive strip of cellulose used to identify the constituents (as glucose) of urine by immersion

dip·ter·an \ˈdip-tə-rən\ adj : of, relating to, or being a fly (sense 2a) — **dipteran** n — **dip·ter·ous** \-rəs\ adj

Di·py·lid·i·um \ˌdī-pī-ˈli-dē-əm, -pə-\ n : a genus of taenioid tapeworms including the common dog tapeworm (D. caninum)

di·pyr·i·dam·ole \(ˌ)dī-ˌpir-ə-ˈda-ˌmōl, -ˌmōl\ n : a drug $C_{24}H_{40}N_8O_4$ used as a coronary vasodilator — see PERSANTINE

di·rec·tive \də-ˈrek-tiv, dī-\ adj : of or relating to psychotherapy in which the therapist introduces information, content, or attitudes not previously expressed by the client

di·rec·tor \də-ˈrek-tər, dī-\ n : an instrument grooved to guide and limit the motion of a surgical knife

direct pyramidal tract n : VENTRAL CORTICOSPINAL TRACT

Di·ro·fi·lar·ia \ˌdī-(ˌ)rō-fə-ˈlar-ē-ə\ n : a genus of filarial worms (family Dipetalonematidae) that includes the heartworm (D. immitis) — **di·ro·fi·lar·i·al** \-ē-əl\ adj

di·ro·fil·a·ri·a·sis \-ˌfi-lə-ˈrī-ə-səs\ n, pl **-a·ses** \-ˌsēz\ : infestation with filarial worms of the genus Dirofilaria and esp. with the heartworm (D. immitis)

dirty \ˈdər-tē\ adj **dirt·i·er; -est** : contaminated with infecting organisms

dis·abil·i·ty \ˌdi-sə-ˈbi-lə-tē\ n, pl **-ties** 1 : the condition of being disabled 2 : inability to pursue an occupation because of physical or mental impairment

dis·able \di-ˈsā-bəl, -ˈzā-\ vb **dis·abled; dis·abling** : to deprive of a mental or physical capacity

dis·abled adj : incapacitated by illness, injury, or wounds; broadly : physically or mentally impaired

dis·able·ment \-mənt\ n : the act of becoming disabled to the extent that full wages cannot be earned; also : the state of being so disabled

di·sac·cha·ri·dase \(ˌ)dī-ˈsa-kə-rə-ˌdās, -ˌdāz\ n : an enzyme (as maltase) that hydrolyzes disaccharides

di·sac·cha·ride \(ˌ)dī-ˈsa-kə-ˌrīd\ n : any of a class of sugars (as sucrose) that on hydrolysis yields two monosaccharide molecules

dis·ar·tic·u·la·tion \ˌdi-sär-ˌti-kyə-ˈlā-shən\ n : separation or amputation of a body part at a joint ⟨~ of the shoulder⟩ — **dis·ar·tic·u·late** \-ˈti-kyə-ˌlāt\ vb

disc var of DISK

disc- or **disci-** or **disco-** comb form : disk ⟨disciform⟩

¹dis·charge \dis-ˈchärj, ˈdis-ˌ\ vb **discharged; dis·charg·ing** 1 : to release from confinement, custody, or care ⟨~ a patient from the hospital⟩ 2 a : to give outlet to or emit ⟨a boil discharging pus⟩ b : to release or give expression to

²dis·charge \ˈdis-ˌchärj, dis-ˈ\ n 1 : the act of relieving of something ⟨~ of a repressed impulse⟩ 2 : release from confinement, custody, or care 3

: something that is emitted or evacuated (a purulent ~)

disci *pl of* DISCUS

dis·ci·form \'di-sə-ˌförm\ *adj* : round or oval in shape

dis·cis·sion \də-'si-shən, -zhən\ *n* : an incision (as in treating cataract) of the capsule of the lens of the eye

dis·clos·ing \dis-'klō-ziŋ\ *adj* : being or using an agent (as a tablet or liquid) that contains a usu. red dye that adheres to and stains dental plaque

disc·o·gram, dis·cog·ra·phy *var of* DISKOGRAM, DISKOGRAPHY

¹**dis·coid** \'dis-ˌköid\ *adj* **1** : resembling a disk : being flat and circular **2** : characterized by macules (~ lupus erythematosus)

²**discoid** *n* : an instrument with a disk-shaped blade used in dentistry for carving

dis·coi·dal \dis-'köid-ᵊl\ *adj* : of, resembling, or producing a disk; *esp* : having the villi restricted to one or more disklike areas

dis·cop·a·thy \dis-'kä-pə-thē\ *n*, *pl* **-thies** : any disease affecting an intervertebral disk

dis·cor·dant \dis-'körd-ᵊnt\ *adj*, *of twins* : dissimilar with respect to one or more particular characters — compare CONCORDANT — **dis·cor·dance** \-ᵊns\ *n*

dis·crete \dis-'krēt, 'dis-ˌ\ *adj* : characterized by distinct unconnected lesions (~ smallpox) — compare CONFLUENT 2

dis·crim·i·nate \dis-'kri-mə-ˌnāt\ *vb* **-nat·ed; -nat·ing** : to respond selectively to (a stimulus)

dis·crim·i·na·tion \dis-ˌkri-mə-'nā-shən\ *n* : the process by which two stimuli differing in some aspect are responded to differently

dis·cus \'dis-kəs\ *n*, *pl* **disci** \-ˌkī, -kē\ : any of various rounded and flattened anatomical structures

discus pro·lig·er·us \-prō-'li-jə-rəs\ *n* : CUMULUS

dis·ease \di-'zēz\ *n* : an impairment of the normal state of the living body or one of its parts that interrupts or modifies the performance of the vital functions and is a response to environmental factors (as malnutrition), to specific infective agents (as viruses), to inherent defects of the organism (as genetic anomalies), or to combinations of these factors : SICKNESS, ILLNESS — **dis·eased** \-'zēzd\ *adj*

dis·equi·lib·ri·um \(ˌ)di-ˌē-sē-kwə-'li-brē-əm, -ˌse-\ *n*, *pl* **-ri·ums** *or* **-ria** : loss or lack of equilibrium

dis·func·tion *var of* DYSFUNCTION

dis·har·mo·ny \(ˌ)dis-'här-mə-nē\ *n*, *pl* **-nies** : lack of harmony — see OCCLUSAL DISHARMONY

dis·in·fect \ˌdis-ᵊn-'fekt\ *vb* : to free from infection esp. by destroying harmful microorganisms — **dis·in·fec·tion** \-'fek-shən\ *n*

¹**dis·in·fec·tant** \-'fek-tənt\ *n* : an agent that frees from infection; *esp* : a chemical that destroys vegetative forms of harmful microorganisms but not ordinarily bacterial spores

²**disinfectant** *adj* : serving or tending to disinfect : suitable for use in disinfecting

dis·in·fest \ˌdis-ᵊn-'fest\ *vb* : to rid of small animal pests (as insects or rodents) — **dis·in·fes·ta·tion** \(ˌ)dis-ˌin-ˌfes-'tā-shən\ *n*

dis·in·fes·tant \ˌdis-ᵊn-'fes-tənt\ *n* : a disinfesting agent

dis·in·hi·bi·tion \(ˌ)di-ˌsin-hə-'bi-shən, -ˌsi-nə-\ *n* : loss or reduction of an inhibition (as by the action of interfering stimuli or events) (~ of a reflex)

dis·in·hib·i·to·ry \-in-'hi-bə-ˌtör-ē\ *adj* : tending to overcome psychological inhibition (~ drugs)

dis·in·ter \ˌdis-in-'tər\ *vb* : to take out of the grave or tomb — **dis·in·ter·ment** \-mənt\ *n*

dis·junc·tion \dis-'jəŋk-shən\ *n* : the separation of chromosomes or chromatids during anaphase of mitosis or meiosis

disk \'disk\ *n* : any of various rounded or flattened anatomical structures: as **a** : a mammalian blood cell **b** : BLIND SPOT **c** : INTERVERTEBRAL DISK — see SLIPPED DISK

disk·ec·to·my \dis-'kek-tə-mē\ *n*, *pl* **-mies** : surgical removal of an intervertebral disk

disk·o·gram \'dis-kə-ˌgram\ *n* : a roentgenogram of an intervertebral disk made after injection of a radiopaque substance

dis·kog·ra·phy \dis-'kä-grə-fē\ *n*, *pl* **-phies** : the process of making a diskogram

dis·lo·cate \'dis-lō-ˌkāt, -lə-; ˌdis-'lō-ˌkāt\ *vb* **-cat·ed; -cat·ing** : to put (a body part) out of order by displacing a bone from its normal connections with another bone; *also* : to displace (a bone) from normal connections with another bone

dis·lo·ca·tion \ˌdis-(ˌ)lō-'kā-shən, -lə-\ *n* : displacement of one or more bones at a joint : LUXATION

dismutase — see SUPEROXIDE DISMUTASE

di·so·di·um \(ˌ)dī-'sō-dē-əm\ *adj* : containing two atoms of sodium in a molecule

disodium cromoglycate *n* : CROMOLYN SODIUM

disodium ed·e·tate \-'e-də-ˌtāt\ *n* : a hydrated disodium salt $C_{10}H_{14}N_2Na_2O_8 \cdot 2H_2O$ of EDTA that has an affinity for calcium and is used to treat hypercalcemia and pathological calcification

di·so·pyr·a·mide \ˌdī-(ˌ)sō-'pir-ə-ˌmīd\ *n* : a cardiac depressant $C_{21}H_{29}N_3O$

used in the treatment of ventricular arrhythmias

¹dis·or·der \(ˌ)di-ˈsȯr-dər, -ˈzȯr-\ *vb* **dis·or·dered**; **dis·or·der·ing** : to disturb the regular or normal functions of

²disorder *n* : an abnormal physical or mental condition : AILMENT

dis·or·dered *adj* 1 : not functioning in a normal orderly healthy way (~ bodily functions) 2 : mentally unbalanced (a ~ patient)

dis·or·ga·ni·za·tion \(ˌ)di-ˌsȯr-gə-nə-ˈzā-shən\ *n* : psychopathological inconsistency in personality, mental functions, or overt behavior — **dis·or·ga·nize** \(ˌ)di-ˈsȯr-gə-ˌnīz\ *vb*

dis·ori·ent \(ˌ)di-ˈsȯr-ē-ˌent\ *vb* : to produce a state of disorientation in : DISORIENTATE

dis·ori·en·ta·tion \(ˌ)di-ˌsȯr-ē-ən-ˈtā-shən, -ˌen-\ *n* : a usu. transient state of confusion esp. as to time, place, or identity often as a result of disease or drugs — **dis·ori·en·tate** \-ˈsȯr-ē-ən-ˌtāt, -ˌen-\ *vb*

dis·par·i·ty \dis-ˈspar-ə-tē\ *n, pl* **-ties** : the state of being different or dissimilar (as in the sensory information received) — see RETINAL DISPARITY

dis·pen·sa·ry \di-ˈspen-sə-rē\ *n, pl* **-ries** : a place where medicine or medical or dental treatment is dispensed

dis·pen·sa·to·ry \di-ˈspen-sə-ˌtȯr-ē\ *n, pl* **-ries** 1 : a book or medicinal formulary containing a systematic description of the drugs and preparations used in medicine — compare PHARMACOPOEIA 2 : DISPENSARY

dis·pense \dis-ˈpens\ *vb* **dis·pensed**; **dis·pens·ing** 1 : to put up (a prescription or medicine) 2 : to prepare and distribute (medication) — **dis·pen·sa·tion** \ˌdis-pən-ˈsā-shən, -pen-\ *n*

dispensing optician *n, Brit* : a person qualified and licensed to fit and supply eyeglasses

dispersion medium *n* : the liquid, gaseous, or solid phase in a two-phase system in which the particles of the other phase are distributed

dis·place·ment \di-ˈsplā-smənt\ *n* 1 : the act or process of removing something from its usual or proper place or the state resulting from this : DISLOCATION (the ~ of a knee joint) 2 : the quantity in which or the degree to which something is displaced 3 a : the direction of an emotion or impulse away from its original object (as an idea or person) to something more acceptable b : SUBLIMATION c : the substitution of another form of behavior for what is usual or expected esp. when the usual response is nonadaptive — **dis·place** \-ˈsplās\ *vb*

dis·pro·por·tion \ˌdis-prə-ˈpȯr-shən\ *n* : absence of symmetry or the proper dimensional relationship — see CEPHALOPELVIC DISPROPORTION

dis·rup·tive \dis-ˈrəp-tiv\ *adj* : characterized by psychologically disorgan-

ized behavior (a confused, incoherent, and ~ patient in the manic phase)

dissecans — see OSTEOCHONDRITIS DISSECANS

dis·sect \di-ˈsekt, dī-; ˈdī-ˌ\ *vb* 1 : to cut so as to separate into pieces or to expose the several parts of (as an animal or a cadaver) for scientific examination; *specif* : to separate or follow along natural lines of cleavage (as through connective tissue) 2 : to make a medical dissection — **dis·sec·tor** \-ˈsek-tər, -ˌsek-\ *n*

dis·sec·tion \di-ˈsek-shən, dī-; ˈdī-ˌ\ *n* 1 : the act or process of dissecting or separating: as **a** : the surgical removal along natural lines of cleavage of tissues which are or might become diseased **b** : the digital separation of tissues (as in heart-valve operations) — compare FINGER FRACTURE 2 **a** : something (as a part or the whole of an animal) that has been dissected **b** : an anatomical specimen prepared in this way

dis·sem·i·nat·ed \di-ˈse-mə-ˌnā-təd\ *adj* : widely dispersed in a tissue, organ, or the entire body (~ gonococcal disease) — **dis·sem·i·na·tion** \-ˌse-mə-ˈnā-shən\ *n*

dis·so·ci·a·tion \(ˌ)di-ˌsō-sē-ˈā-shən, -shē-\ *n* 1 : the process by which a chemical combination breaks up into simpler constituents 2 : the separation of whole segments of the personality (as in multiple personality) or of discrete mental processes (as in the schizophrenias) from the mainstream of consciousness or of behavior — **dis·so·ci·ate** \-ˈsō-sē-ˌāt, -shē-\ *vb* — **dis·so·cia·tive** \(ˌ)di-ˈsō-shē-ˌā-tiv, -sē-, -shə-tiv\ *adj*

dis·so·lu·tion \ˌdi-sə-ˈlü-shən\ *n* : the act or process of dissolving

dis·solve \di-ˈzälv, -ˈzȯlv\ *vb* **dis·solved**; **dis·solv·ing** 1 : to pass or cause to pass into solution 2 : to cause to melt or liquefy 3 : to become fluid — **dis·solv·er** *n*

dis·so·nance \ˈdi-sə-nəns\ *n* : inconsistency between the beliefs one holds or between one's actions and one's beliefs — see COGNITIVE DISSONANCE

dist- — see DISTO-

dis·tal \ˈdist-əl\ *adj* 1 : situated away from the point of attachment or origin or a central point: as **a** : located away from the center of the body (the ~ end of a bone) — compare PROXIMAL 1a **b** : located away from the mesial plane of the body — compare MESIAL 2 **c** : of, relating to, or being the surface of a tooth that is next to the following tooth counting from the middle of the front of the upper or lower jaw or that faces the back of the mouth in the case of the last tooth on each side — compare MESIAL 3, PROXIMAL 1b 2 : physical or social rather than sensory — compare PROXIMAL 2 — **dis·tal·ly** adv

distal convoluted tubule n : the convoluted portion of the nephron lying between the loop of Henle and the nonsecretory part of the nephron and concerned esp. with the concentration of urine — called also *convoluted tubule, distal tubule*

distalis see PARS DISTALIS

distal radioulnar joint n : a pivot joint between the lower end of the ulna and the ulnar notch on the lower end of the radius that permits rotation of the distal end of the radius around the longitudinal axis of the ulna — called also *inferior radioulnar joint*

dis·tem·per \dis-ˈtem-pər\ n : a disordered or abnormal bodily state esp. of quadruped mammals: as a : a highly contagious virus disease esp. of dogs that is marked by fever, leukopenia, and respiratory, gastrointestinal, and neurological symptoms and that is caused by a paramyxovirus b : STRANGLES c : PANLEUKOPENIA

dis·tend \di-ˈstend\ vb : to enlarge or stretch out (as from internal pressure) — **dis·ten·si·ble** \-ˈsten-sə-bəl\ adj : capable of being distended, extended, or dilated — **dis·ten·si·bil·i·ty** \-ˌsten-sə-ˈbi-lə-tē\ n

dis·ten·sion or **dis·ten·tion** \di-ˈsten-chən\ n : the act of distending or the state of being distended esp. unduly or abnormally

disto- also **dist-** or **disti-** comb form : distal (distobuccal)

dis·to·buc·cal \ˌdis-tō-ˈbə-kəl\ adj : relating to or located on the distal and buccal surfaces of a molar or premolar — **dis·to·buc·cal·ly** adv

dis·to·lin·gual \-ˈliŋ-gwel, -gyə-wəl\ adj : relating to or situated on the distal and lingual surfaces of a tooth

dis·to·ma·to·sis \ˌdī-ˌstō-mə-ˈtō-səs\ n, pl -to·ses \-ˌsēz\ : infestation with or disease (as liver rot) caused by digenetic trematode worms

dis·to·mi·a·sis \ˌdī-stō-ˈmī-ə-səs\ n, pl -a·ses \-ˌsēz\ : DISTOMATOSIS

dis·tor·tion \di-ˈstòr-shən\ n 1 : the censorship of unacceptable unconscious impulses so that they are unrecognizable to the ego in the manifest content of a dream 2 : a lack of correspondence of size or intensity in an image resulting from defects in an optical system

dis·tract·i·bil·i·ty \di-ˌstrak-tə-ˈbi-lə-tē\ n, pl -ties : a condition in which the attention of the mind is easily distracted by small and irrelevant stimuli — **dis·tract·ible** \-ˈstrak-tə-bəl\ adj

dis·trac·tion \di-ˈstrak-shən\ n 1 a : diversion of the attention b : mental derangement 2 : excesssive separation (as from improper traction) of fracture fragments — **dis·tract** \di-ˈstrakt\ vb

dis·tress \di-ˈstres\ n : pain or suffering

affecting the body, a bodily part, or the mind (gastric ~) (respiratory ~)

dis·tri·bu·tion \ˌdis-trə-ˈbyü-shən\ n : the pattern of branching and termination of a ramifying anatomical structure (as a nerve or artery)

district nurse n, Brit : a qualified nurse who is employed by a local authority to visit and treat patients in their own homes — compare VISITING NURSE

dis·turbed \di-ˈstərbd\ adj : showing symptoms of emotional illness (~ children) — **dis·tur·bance** \-ˈstər-bəns\ n

di·sul·fi·ram \di-ˈsəl-fə-ˌram\ n : a compound $C_{10}H_{20}N_2S_4$ that causes a severe physiological reaction to alcohol and is used esp. in the treatment of alcoholism — called also *tetraethylthiuram disulfide*; see ANTABUSE

di·sul·phi·ram chiefly Brit var of DISULFIRAM

di·thra·nol \ˈdī-thrə-ˌnöl, ˈdi-, -ˌnöl\ n, chiefly Brit : ANTHRALIN

di·ure·sis \ˌdī-yə-ˈrē-səs\ n, pl **di·ure·ses** \-ˌsēz\ : an increased excretion of urine

¹**di·uret·ic** \ˌdī-yə-ˈre-tik\ adj : tending to increase the flow of urine — **di·uret·i·cal·ly** \-i-k(ə-)lē\ adv

²**diuretic** n : an agent that increases the flow of urine

Di·ur·il \ˈdī-yür-il\ trademark — used for a preparation of chlorothiazide

di·ur·nal \dī-ˈərn-əl\ adj 1 : having a daily cycle (~ rhythms) 2 : of, relating to, or occurring in the daytime (~ activity) — **di·ur·nal·ly** adv

di·ver·gence \də-ˈvər-jəns, dī-\ n 1 : a drawing apart 2 : dissemination of the effect of activity of a single nerve cell through multiple synaptic connections — compare CONVERGENCE 2 — **di·verge** \-ˈvərj\ vb — **di·ver·gent** \-ˈvər-jənt\ adj

di·ver·tic·u·lar \ˌdī-vər-ˈti-kyə-lər\ adj : consisting of or resembling a diverticulum

di·ver·tic·u·lec·to·my \ˌdī-vər-ˌti-kyə-ˈlek-tə-mē\ n, pl -mies : the surgical removal of a diverticulum

di·ver·tic·u·li·tis \-ˈlī-təs\ n : inflammation of a diverticulum — called also *diverticular disease*

di·ver·tic·u·lop·exy \-ˈlä-pək-sē\ n, pl -ex·ies : surgical obliteration or fixation of a diverticulum

di·ver·tic·u·lo·sis \-ˈlō-səs\ n, pl -lo·ses \-ˌsēz\ : an intestinal disorder characterized by the presence of many diverticula

di·ver·tic·u·lum \ˌdī-vər-ˈti-kyə-ləm\ n, pl -la \-lə\ 1 : an abnormal pouch or sac opening from a hollow organ (as the intestine or bladder) 2 : a blind tube or sac branching off from a cavity or canal of the body

di·vide \də-ˈvīd\ vb **di·vid·ed; di·vid·ing** 1 : to separate into two or more parts (~ a nerve surgically) 2 : to undergo replication, multiplication, fission, or separation into parts (actively *dividing* cells)

di·vid·er \də-'vī-dər\ *n* : the second incisor tooth of a horse situated between the center and corner incisors on each side — compare NIPPER

di·vi·sion \də-'vi-zhən\ *n* 1 : the act or process of dividing : the state of being divided — see CELL DIVISION 2 : a group of organisms forming part of a larger group; *specif* : a primary category of the plant kingdom that is equivalent to a phylum — **di·vi·sion·al** \-'vi-zhə-nəl\ *adj*

di·zy·got·ic \ˌdī-zī-'gä-tik\ *adj, of twins* : FRATERNAL

di·zy·gous \(ˌ)dī-'zī-gəs\ *var of* DIZYGOTIC

diz·zi·ness \'di-zē-nəs\ *n* : the condition of being dizzy; *esp* : a sensation of unsteadiness accompanied by a feeling of movement within the head — compare VERTIGO 1

diz·zy \'di-zē\ *adj* **diz·zi·er; -est** 1 : having a whirling sensation in the head with a tendency to fall 2 : mentally confused — **diz·zi·ly** \'di-zə-lē\ *adv*

DJD *abbr* degenerative joint disease

DM *abbr* diabetes mellitus

DMD *abbr* [Latin *dentariae medicinae doctor*] doctor of dental medicine

DMF *abbr* decayed, missing, and filled teeth

DMSO \ˌdē-(ˌ)em-(ˌ)es-'ō\ *n* : DIMETHYL SULFOXIDE

DMT \ˌdē-(ˌ)em-'tē\ *n* : DIMETHYLTRYPTAMINE

DNA \ˌdē-(ˌ)en-'ā\ *n* : any of various nucleic acids that are usu. the molecular basis of heredity, are localized esp. in cell nuclei, and are constructed of a double helix held together by hydrogen bonds between purine and pyrimidine bases which project inward from two chains containing alternate links of deoxyribose and phosphate — called also *deoxyribonucleic acid*; see RECOMBINANT DNA

DNA fingerprinting *n* : a method of identification (as for forensic purposes) by determining the sequence of base pairs in the DNA esp. of a person — **DNA fingerprint** *n*

DNA polymerase *n* : any of several polymerases that promote replication or repair of DNA usu. using single-stranded DNA as a template

DN·ase \(ˌ)dē-'en-ˌās, -ˌāz\ *also* **DNAase** \(ˌ)dē-en-'ā-ˌās, -ˌāz\ *n* : DEOXYRIBONUCLEASE

DNR *abbr* do not resuscitate

DO *abbr* doctor of osteopathy

DOA *abbr* dead on arrival

DOB *abbr* date of birth

do·bu·ta·mine \dō-'byü-tə-ˌmēn\ *n* : a strongly inotropic catecholamine used in the form of its hydrochloride $C_{18}H_{23}NO_3 \cdot HCl$ esp. to increase cardiac output and lower wedge pressure in heart failure and after cardiopulmonary bypass surgery

doc \'däk\ *n* : DOCTOR — used chiefly as a familiar term of address

¹doc·tor \'däk-tər\ *n* 1 a : a person who has earned one of the highest academic degrees (as a PhD) conferred by a university b : a person awarded an honorary doctorate by a college or university 2 : one skilled or specializing in healing arts; *esp* : a physician, surgeon, dentist, or veterinarian licensed to practice his or her profession

²doctor *vb* **doc·tored; doc·tor·ing** 1 a : to give medical treatment to b : to practice medicine 2 : CASTRATE, SPAY

doc·u·sate \'dä-kyü-ˌsāt\ *n* : any of several laxative salts and esp. the sodium salt $C_{20}H_{37}NaO_7S$ used to soften stools

dog \'dog\ *n, often attrib* : a highly variable carnivorous domesticated mammal (*Canis familiaris*); *broadly* : any member of the family (Canidae) to which the dog belongs

dog flea *n* : a flea of the genus *Ctenocephalides* (*C. canis*) that feeds chiefly on dogs and cats

dog tapeworm *n* : a tapeworm of the genus *Dipylidium* (*D. caninum*) occurring in dogs and cats and sometimes in humans

dog tick *n* : AMERICAN DOG TICK

dolens — see PHLEGMASIA ALBA DOLENS, PHLEGMASIA CERULEA DOLENS

dolicho- *comb form* : long (*dolichocephalic*)

dol·i·cho·ce·phal·ic \ˌdä-li-kō-sə-'fa-lik\ *adj* : having a relatively long head with a cephalic index of less than 75 — **dol·i·cho·ceph·a·ly** \-'se-fə-lē\ *n*

Do·lo·bid \'dō-lə-ˌbid\ *trademark* — used for a preparation of diflunisal

do·lor \'dō-lər, 'dä-\ *n* 1 *obs* : physical pain — used in old medicine as one of five cardinal symptoms of inflammation 2 : mental suffering or anguish

DOM \ˌdē-(ˌ)ō-'em\ *n* : STP

dome \'dōm\ *n* : a rounded-arch element in the wave tracing in an electroencephalogram

do·mi·cil·i·ary \ˌdä-mə-'si-lē-ˌer-ē, ˌdō-\ *adj* 1 : provided or attended in the home rather than in an institution (~ midwifery) 2 : providing, constituting, or provided by an institution for chronically ill or permanently disabled persons requiring minimal medical attention (~ care)

dom·i·nance \'dä-mə-nəns\ *n* : the fact or state of being dominant: as a : the property of one of a pair of alleles or traits that suppresses expression of the other in the heterozygous condition b : functional asymmetry between a pair of bodily structures (as the right and left hands)

¹dom·i·nant \-nənt\ *adj* 1 : exerting forcefulness or having dominance in a social hierarchy 2 : being the one of a pair of bodily structures that is the more effective or predominant in action (the ~ eye) **3** : of, relating to, or exerting genetic dominance — **dom-i-nant-ly** adv

²**dominant** n **1** : a dominant genetic character or factor **2** : a dominant individual in a social hierarchy

do-nee \dō-ˈnē\ n : a recipient of biological material (as blood or a graft)

Don Juan-ism \ˈdän-ˈhwä-ˌni-zəm, -ˈwä-\ n, pl **Don Juanisms** : male sexual promiscuity that is motivated by impotence or feelings of inferiority or unconscious homosexual impulses

do-nor \ˈdō-nər, -ˌnȯr\ n **1** : one used as a source of biological material (as blood or an organ) **2** : a compound capable of giving up a part (as an atom) for combination with an acceptor

Don-o-van body \ˈdä-nə-vən-, ˈdə-\ n : an encapsulated gram-negative bacterium of the genus *Calymmatobacterium* (*C. granulomatis*) that is the causative agent of granuloma inguinale and is characterized by one or two opposite polar chromatin masses — compare LEISHMAN-DONOVAN BODY

C. Donovan — see LEISHMAN-DONOVAN BODY

do-pa \ˈdō-pə, -(ˌ)pä\ n : an amino acid $C_9H_{11}NO_4$ that in the levorotatory form is found in the broad bean and is used in the treatment of Parkinson's disease

L-dopa — see entry alphabetized in the letter *l*

do-pa-mine \ˈdō-pə-ˌmēn\ n : a monoamine $C_8H_{11}NO_2$ that is a decarboxylated form of dopa and occurs esp. as a neurotransmitter in the brain and as an intermediate in the biosynthesis of epinephrine — see INTROPIN

do-pa-mi-ner-gic \ˌdō-pə-ˌmē-ˈnər-jik\ adj : relating to, participating in, or activated by the neurotransmitter activity of dopamine or related substances ⟨~ activity⟩ ⟨~ neurons⟩

dope \ˈdōp\ n **1** : a preparation of an illicit, habit-forming, or narcotic drug (as opium, heroin, or marijuana) **2** : a preparation given to a racehorse to help or hinder its performance — **dope** vb

Dopp-ler \ˈdä-plər\ adj : of, relating to, or utilizing a shift in frequency in accordance with the Doppler effect

Doppler, Christian Johann (1803-1853), Austrian physicist and mathematician.

Doppler effect n : a change in the frequency with which waves (as sound or light) from a given source reach an observer when the source and the observer are in rapid motion with respect to each other so that the frequency increases or decreases according to the speed at which the distance is decreasing or increasing

dors- — see DORSO-

dorsa pl of DORSUM

¹**dor-sal** \ˈdȯr-səl\ adj **1** : being or located near, on, or toward the upper surface of an animal (as a quadruped) opposite the lower or ventral surface **2** : being or located near, on, or toward the back or posterior part of the human body — **dor-sal-ly** \-sə-lē\ adv

²**dorsal** n : a dorsally located part; esp : a thoracic vertebra

dorsal column n : DORSAL HORN

dorsal horn n : a longitudinal subdivision of gray matter in the dorsal part of each lateral half of the spinal cord that receives terminals from some afferent fibers of the dorsal roots of the spinal nerves — called also *dorsal column, posterior column, posterior gray column, posterior horn*; compare LATERAL COLUMN 1, VENTRAL HORN

dorsal interosseus n **1** : any of four small muscles of the hand that act to draw the fingers away from the long axis of the middle finger, flex the fingers at the metacarpophalangeal joints, and extend their distal two phalanges **2** : any of four small muscles of the foot that act to draw the toes away from the long axis of the second toe, flex their proximal phalanges, and extend the distal phalanges

dorsalis — see INTEROSSEUS DORSALIS, SACROCOCCYGEUS DORSALIS, TABES DORSALIS

dorsalis pe-dis \dȯr-ˈsa-ləs-ˈpe-dəs, -ˈsä-, -ˈsä-, -ˈpē-\ n : an artery of the upper surface of the foot that is a direct continuation of the anterior tibial artery — called also *dorsalis pedis artery*

dorsal lip n : the margin of the fold of blastula wall that delineates the dorsal limit of the blastopore

dorsal mesogastrium n : MESOGASTRIUM 2

dorsal root n : the one of the two roots of a spinal nerve that passes posteriorly to the spinal cord separating the posterior and lateral funiculi and that consists of sensory fibers — called also *posterior root*; compare VENTRAL ROOT

dorsal root ganglion n : SPINAL GANGLION

dorsal spinocerebellar tract n : SPINOCEREBELLAR TRACT a

dorsi — see ILIOCOSTALIS DORSI, LATISSIMUS DORSI, LONGISSIMUS DORSI

dor-si-flex-ion \ˌdȯr-sə-ˈflek-shən\ n : flexion in a dorsal direction; esp : flexion of the foot in an upward direction — compare PLANTAR FLEXION — **dor-si-flex** \ˈdȯr-sə-ˌfleks\ vb

dor-si-flex-or \ˈdȯr-sə-ˌflek-sər\ n : a muscle causing flexion in a dorsal direction

dorso- or **dorsi-** also **dors-** comb form **1** : dorsal ⟨*dorsi*flexion⟩ **2** : dorsal and ⟨*dorso*lateral⟩

dor-so-lat-er-al \ˌdȯr-sō-ˈla-tə-rəl, -ˈla-trəl\ adj : of, relating to, or involving both the back and the sides (lesions of the ~ hypothalamus) — **dor·so·lat·er·al·ly** *adv*

dorsolateral tract *n* : a slender column of white matter between the dorsal gray column and the periphery of the spinal cord — called also *tract of Lissauer*

dor·so·me·di·al \-'mē-dē-əl\ *adj* : located toward the back and near the midline

dor·so·ven·tral \-'ven-trəl\ *adj* : relating to, involving, or extending along the axis joining the dorsal and ventral sides — **dor·so·ven·tral·ly** *adv*

dor·sum \'dȯr-səm\ *n, pl* **dor·sa** \-sə\ 1 : the upper surface of an appendage or part 2 : BACK; *esp* : the entire dorsal surface of an animal

dos·age \'dō-sij\ *n* 1 a : the addition of an ingredient or the application of an agent in a measured dose b : the presence and relative representation or strength of a factor or agent (as a gene) 2 a : DOSE 1 b (1) : the giving of a dose (2) : regulation or determination of doses

¹**dose** \'dōs\ *n* 1 a : the measured quantity of a therapeutic agent to be taken at one time b : the quantity of radiation administered or absorbed 2 : a gonorrheal infection

²**dose** *vb* **dosed; dos·ing** 1 : to divide (as a medicine) into doses 2 : to give a dose to; *esp* : to give medicine to 3 : to take medicine 4 : to treat with an application or agent

do·sim·e·ter \dō-'si-mə-tər\ *n* : a device for measuring doses of radiations (as X rays) — **do·si·met·ric** \dō-sə-'me-trik\ *adj* — **do·sim·e·try** \dō-'si-mə-trē\ *n*

double bind *n* : a psychological predicament in which a person receives from a single source conflicting messages that allow no appropriate response to be made

dou·ble–blind \də-bəl-'blīnd\ *adj* : of, relating to, or being an experimental procedure in which neither the subjects nor the experimenters know the identity of the individuals in the test and control groups during the actual course of the experiments — compare SINGLE-BLIND

double bond *n* : a chemical bond consisting of two covalent bonds between two atoms in a molecule — compare TRIPLE BOND; see UNSATURATED b

double chin *n* : a fleshy or fatty fold under the chin — **dou·ble–chinned** \-'chind\ *adj*

double helix *n* : the structural arrangement of DNA in space that consists of paired polynucleotide strands stabilized by chemical bonds between the chains linking purine and pyrimidine bases — compare ALPHA-HELIX, WATSON-CRICK MODEL — **dou·ble–he·li·cal** \-'he-li-kəl, -'hē-\ *adj*

dou·ble–joint·ed \də-bəl-'jȯin-təd\ *adj* : having a joint that permits an exceptional degree of freedom of motion of the parts joined

double pneumonia *n* : pneumonia affecting both lungs

double vision *n* : DIPLOPIA

douche \'düsh\ *n* 1 a : a jet or current esp. of water directed against a part or into a cavity of the body b : an act of cleansing with a douche 2 : a device for giving douches — **douche** *vb*

Doug·las bag \'də-gləs-\ *n* : an inflatable bag used to collect expired air for the determination of oxygen consumption and basal metabolic rate

    Douglas, Claude Gordon (1882–1963), British physiologist.

Douglas's cul–de–sac \-'də-glə-səz-\ *n* : POUCH OF DOUGLAS

Douglas's pouch *n* : POUCH OF DOUGLAS

douloureux — see TIC DOULOUREUX

dow·a·ger's hump \'daü-i-jərz-\ *n* : an abnormal outward curvature of the upper back with round shoulders and stooped posture caused esp. by bone loss and anterior compression of the vertebrae in osteoporosis

down·er \'daü-nər\ *n* : a depressant drug; *esp* : BARBITURATE

Down's syndrome \'daünz-\ *or* **Down syndrome** \'daün-\ *n* : a congenital condition characterized by moderate to severe mental retardation, slanting eyes, a broad short skull, broad hands with short fingers, and by trisomy of the human chromosome numbered 21 — called also *Down's, trisomy 21*

    Down \'daün, John Langdon Haydon (1828–1896), British physician.

down·stream \'daün-'strēm\ *adv or adj* : in the same direction along a molecule of DNA or RNA as that in which transcription and translation take place and toward the end having a hydroxyl group attached to the position labeled 3' in the terminal nucleotide — compare UPSTREAM

dox·e·pin \'däk-sə-pin, -pən\ *n* : a tricyclic antidepressant administered as the hydrochloride salt $C_9H_{21}NO\cdot HCl$ — see SINEQUAN

doxo·ru·bi·cin \däk-sə-'rü-bə-sən\ *n* : an anthracycline antibiotic with broad antitumor activity that is obtained from a bacterium of the genus *Streptomyces* (*S. peucetius*) and is administered in the form of its hydrochloride $C_{27}H_{29}NO_{11}\cdot HCl$ — see ADRIAMYCIN

doxy·cy·cline \däk-sə-'sī-klēn\ *n* : a broad-spectrum tetracycline antibiotic $C_{22}H_{24}N_2O_8$ with potent antibacterial activity that is often taken orally by travelers as a prophylactic against diarrhea — see VIBRAMYCIN

dox·yl·amine \däk-'si-lə-mēn, -mən\ *n* : an antihistamine usu. used in the form of its succinate $C_{17}H_{22}N_2O\cdot C_4H_6O_4$

DP *abbr* doctor of podiatry

DPH *abbr* **1** department of public health **2** doctor of public health

DPM *abbr* doctor of podiatric medicine

DPT *abbr* diphtheria-pertussis-tetanus (vaccines)

dr *abbr* dram

Dr *abbr* doctor

drac·on·ti·a·sis \ˌdra-kän-ˈtī-ə-səs\ *n, pl* **-a·ses** \-ˌsēz\ : DRACUNCULIASIS

dra·cun·cu·li·a·sis \ˌdra-ˌkən-kyə-ˈlī-ə-səs\ *n, pl* **-a·ses** \-ˌsēz\ : infestation with or disease caused by the guinea worm

dra·cun·cu·lo·sis \-ˈlō-səs\ *n, pl* **-lo·ses** \-ˌsēz\ : DRACUNCULIASIS

Dra·cun·cu·lus \drə-ˈkən-kyə-ləs\ *n* : a genus (family Dracunculidae) of greatly elongated nematode worms including the guinea worm

draft \ˈdraft, ˈdráft\ *n* **1** : a portion (as of medicine) poured out or mixed for drinking : DOSE **2** : a current of air in a closed-in space — **drafty** \ˈdraf-tē, ˈdráf-\ *adj*

¹**drain** \ˈdrān\ *vb* **1** : to draw off (liquid) gradually or completely (~ pus from an abscess) **2** : to carry away or give passage to a bodily fluid or a discharge from (~ an abscess)

²**drain** *n* : a tube or cylinder usu. of absorbent material for drainage of a wound — see CIGARETTE DRAIN

drain·age \ˈdrā-nij\ *n* : the act or process of drawing off fluids from a cavity or wound by means of suction or gravity

Draize test \ˈdrāz-\ *n* : a test that is used as a criterion for harmfulness of chemicals to the human eye and that involves dropping the test substance into one eye of rabbits without anesthesia with the other eye used as a control — called also *Draize eye test*

   Draize, John H. (*b* 1900), American pharmacologist.

dram \ˈdram\ *n* **1** : either of two units of weight: **a** : an avoirdupois unit equal to 1.772 grams or 27.344 grains **b** : a unit of apothecaries' weight equal to 3.888 grams or 60 grains **2** : FLUID DRAM

Dram·amine \ˈdra-mə-ˌmēn\ *trademark* — used for dimenhydrinate

drape *n* : a sterile covering used in an operating room — usu. used in pl. — **drape** *vb*

dras·tic \ˈdras-tik\ *adj* : acting rapidly or violently — used chiefly of purgatives — **dras·ti·cal·ly** \-ti-k(ə-)lē\ *adv*

draught *chiefly Brit var of* DRAFT

draw \ˈdró\ *vb* **drew** \ˈdrü\; **drawn** \ˈdrón\; **draw·ing 1** : INHALE **2 a** : to localize in or cause to move toward a surface — used in the phrase *draw to a head* (using a poultice to ~ inflammation to a head) **b** : to cause local congestion : induce blood or other body fluid to localize at a particular point

draw·sheet \ˈdró-ˌshēt\ *n* : a narrow sheet used chiefly in hospitals and stretched across the bed lengthwise often over a rubber sheet underneath the patient's trunk

dream \ˈdrēm\ *n, often attrib* : a series of thoughts, images, or emotions occurring during sleep and esp. during REM sleep — compare DAYDREAM — **dream** *vb*

¹**drench** \ˈdrench\ *n* : a poisonous or medicinal drink; *specif* : a large dose of medicine mixed with liquid and put down the throat of an animal

²**drench** *vb* : to administer a drench to (an animal)

dress \ˈdres\ *vb* : to apply dressings or medicaments to

dress·ing *n* : a covering (as of ointment or gauze) applied to a lesion

DRG \ˌdē-(ˌ)är-ˈjē\ *n* : any of about 500 payment categories that are used to classify patients and esp. Medicare patients for the purpose of reimbursing hospitals for each case in a given category with a fixed fee regardless of the actual costs incurred and that are based esp. on the principal diagnosis, surgical procedure used, age of patient, and expected length of stay in the hospital — called also *diagnosis related group*

drier *comparative of* DRY

driest *superlative of* DRY

drift \ˈdrift\ *n* **1** : movement of a tooth in the dental arch **2** : GENETIC DRIFT — **drift** *vb*

drill *n* : an instrument with an edged or pointed end for making holes in hard substances (as teeth) by revolving — **drill** *vb*

Drink·er respirator \ˈdriŋ-kər-\ *n* : IRON LUNG

   Drinker, Philip (1894–1972), American can industrial hygienist.

drip \ˈdrip\ *n* **1 a** : a falling in drops **b** : liquid that falls, overflows, or is extruded in drops **2** : a device for the administration of a fluid at a slow rate esp. into a vein; *also* : a material so administered (a glucose ~) — **drip** *vb*

Dris·dol \ˈdris-ˌdól, -ˌdōl\ *trademark* — used for a preparation of calciferol

drive \ˈdrīv\ *n* : an urgent, basic, or instinctual need : a motivating physiological condition of the organism (a sexual ~)

drool \ˈdrül\ *vb* **1** : to secrete saliva in anticipation of food **2** : to let saliva or some other substance flow from the mouth — **drool** *n*

¹**drop** \ˈdräp\ *n* **1 a** : the quantity of fluid that falls in one spherical mass **b** : **drops** *pl* : a dose of medicine measured by drops; *specif* : a solution for dilating the pupil of the eye **2** : the smallest practical unit of liquid measure that varies in size according to the specific gravity and viscosity of the liquid and to the conditions under which it is formed — compare MINIM

²**drop** *vb* **dropped; drop·ping 1** : to fall in

drops 2 *of an animal* : to give birth to (lambs *dropped* in June) 3 : to take (a drug) orally ⟨~ acid⟩

drop-let \'dräp-lət\ *n* : a tiny drop (as of a liquid)

droplet infection *n* : infection transmitted by airborne droplets of sputum containing infectious organisms

drop-per \'drä-pər\ *n* : a short glass tube fitted with a rubber bulb and used to measure liquids by drops — called also *eyedropper, medicine dropper* — **drop-per-ful** \-ˌfu̇l\ *n*

drop-si-cal \'dräp-si-kəl\ *adj* : relating to or affected with edema

drop-sy \'dräp-sē\ *n, pl* **drop-sies** : EDEMA

drown \'drau̇n\ *vb* **drowned** \'drau̇nd\; **drown-ing** \'drau̇-niŋ\ 1 : to suffocate in water or some other liquid 2 : to suffocate because of excess of body fluid that interferes with the passage of oxygen from the lungs to the body tissues (as in pulmonary edema)

DrPH *abbr* doctor of public health

¹**drug** \'drəg\ *n* 1 a : a substance used as a medication or in the preparation of medication b *according to the Food, Drug, and Cosmetic Act* (1) : a substance recognized in an official pharmacopoeia or formulary (2) : a substance intended for use in the diagnosis, cure, mitigation, treatment, or prevention of disease (3) : a substance other than food intended to affect the structure or function of the body (4) : a substance intended for use as a component of a medicine but not a device or a component, part, or accessory of a device 2 : something and often an illicit substance that causes addiction, habituation, or a marked change in consciousness

²**drug** *vb* **drugged; drug-ging** 1 : to affect with a drug; *esp* : to stupefy by a narcotic drug 2 : to administer a drug to 3 : to take drugs for narcotic effect

drug-gist \'drə-gist\ *n* : one who sells or dispenses drugs and medicines: as a : PHARMACIST b : one who owns or manages a drugstore

drug-mak-er \'drəg-ˌmā-kər\ *n* : one that manufactures pharmaceuticals

drug-store \-ˌstȯr\ *n* : a retail store where medicines and miscellaneous articles (as food, cosmetics, and film) are sold — called also *pharmacy*

drum \'drəm\ *n* : TYMPANIC MEMBRANE

drum-head \-ˌhed\ *n* : TYMPANIC MEMBRANE

drum-stick \-ˌstik\ *n* : a small projection from the cell nucleus that occurs in a small percentage of the polymorphonuclear leukocytes in the normal human female

druse \'drüz, 'drüz\ *n, pl* **dru-sen** \'drü-zən\ : one of the small hyaline usu. laminated bodies sometimes appearing behind the retina of the eye

dry \'drī\ *adj* **dri-er** \'drī-ər\; **dri-est** \-əst\ 1 : marked by the absence or scantiness of secretions, effusions, or other forms of moisture 2 *of a cough* : not accompanied by the raising of mucus or phlegm

dry gangrene *n* : gangrene that develops in the presence of arterial obstruction, is sharply localized, and is characterized by dryness of the dead tissue which is distinguishable from adjacent tissue by a line of inflammation

dry mouth *n* : XEROSTOMIA

dry out *vb* : to undergo an extended period of withdrawal from alcohol or drug use esp. at a special clinic : DETOXIFY

dry socket *n* : a tooth socket in which after tooth extraction a blood clot fails to form or disintegrates without undergoing organization; *also* : a condition that is marked by the occurrence of such a socket or sockets and that is usu. accompanied by neuralgic pain but without suppuration

DSC *abbr* doctor of surgical chiropody

DT *abbr* delirium tremens

DTP *abbr* diphtheria, tetanus, pertussis (vaccines)

d.t.'s \ˌdē-'tēz\ *n pl, often cap D&T* : DELIRIUM TREMENS

Du-chenne \dü-'shen, də-\ *also* **Du-chenne's** \-'shenz\ *adj* : relating to or being a severe form of muscular dystrophy of males that affects the muscles of the pelvic and shoulder girdles and the pectoral muscles first and is inherited as a sex-linked recessive trait ⟨muscular dystrophy of the ~ type⟩

Du-chenne \dü-'shen\, **Guillaume–Benjamin–Amand (1806–1875),** French neurologist.

Du-crey's bacillus \dü-'krāz-\ *n* : a gram-negative bacillus of the genus *Haemophilus* (*H. ducreyi*) that is the causative agent of chancroid

Du-crey \dü-'krā\, **Augusto (1860–1940),** Italian dermatologist.

duct \'dəkt\ *n* : a bodily tube or vessel esp. when carrying the secretion of a gland

duc-tal \'dək-tᵊl\ *adj* : of or belonging to a duct : made up of ducts ⟨the biliary ~ system⟩

duc-tion \'dək-shən\ *n* : a turning or rotating movement of the eye

duct-less \'dəkt-ləs\ *adj* : being without a duct

ductless gland *n* : ENDOCRINE GLAND

duct of Bel-li-ni \-be-'lē-nē\ *n* : any of the large excretory ducts of the uriniferous tubules of the kidney that open on the free surface of the papillae

Bellini, Lorenzo (1643–1704), Italian anatomist and physiologist.

duct of Gart-ner \-'gärt-nər\ *n* : GARTNER'S DUCT

duct of Ri-vi-nus \-rə-'vē-nəs\ *n* : any of several small inconstant efferent ducts of the sublingual gland

Rivinus, Augustus Quirinus (1652–

1723), German anatomist and botanist.

duct of San·to·ri·ni \-ˌsan-tə-ˈrē-nē, -ˌsän-\ *n* : ACCESSORY PANCREATIC DUCT

Santorini, Giovanni Domenico (1681–1737), Italian anatomist.

duct of Wir·sung \-ˈvir-(ˌ)zùŋ, -zəŋ\ *n* : PANCREATIC DUCT a — compare ACCESSORY PANCREATIC DUCT

Wirsung, Johann Georg (1600–1643), German anatomist.

duct·ule \ˈdək-(ˌ)tyül\ *n* : a small duct

duc·tu·li ef·fe·ren·tes \ˈdək-tyü-ˌlī-ˌef-ə-ˈren-(ˌ)tēz, -tù-, -(ˌ)lē-\ *n pl* : a group of ducts that convey sperm from the testis to the epididymis

duc·tu·lus \ˈdək-tyù-ləs, -tù-\ *n, pl* **-li** \-ˌlī, -(ˌ)lē\ : DUCTULE

duc·tus \ˈdək-təs\ *n, pl* **ductus** : DUCT

ductus ar·te·ri·o·sus \-är-ˌtir-ē-ˈō-səs\ *n* : a short broad vessel in the fetus that connects the pulmonary artery with the aorta and conducts most of the blood directly from the right ventricle to the aorta bypassing the lungs

ductus de·fer·ens \-ˈde-fə-ˌrenz, -rənz\ *n, pl* **ductus de·fer·en·tes** \-ˌde-fə-ˈren-tēz\ : VAS DEFERENS

ductus re·uni·ens \-rē-ˈyü-nē-ˌenz, -ˈü-\ *n* : a passage in the ear that connects the cochlea and the saccule

ductus ve·no·sus \-vi-ˈnō-səs\ *n* : a vein passing through the liver and connecting the left umbilical vein with the inferior vena cava of the fetus, losing its circulatory function after birth, and persisting as the ligamentum venosum of the liver

Duf·fy \ˈdə-fē\ *adj* : relating to, characteristic of, or being a system of blood groups determined by the presence or absence of any of several antigens in red blood cells (~ blood typing)

Duffy, Richard (1906–1956), British hemophiliac.

Dührs·sen's incisions \ˈdüer-sənz-\ *n pl* : a set of three incisions in the cervix of the uterus to facilitate delivery if dilation is inadequate

Dührs·sen \ˈdüer-sən\, **Alfred (1862–1933),** German obstetrician-gynecologist.

dull \ˈdəl\ *adj* **1** : mentally slow or stupid **2** : slow in perception or sensibility **3** : lacking sharpness or edge or point (a ~ scalpel) **4** : lacking in force, intensity, or acuteness (a ~ pain) — **dull** *vb* — **dull·ness** *or* **dul·ness** \ˈdəl-nəs\ *n* — **dul·ly** *adv*

dumb \ˈdəm\ *adj* : lacking the power of speech

dumb rabies *n* : PARALYTIC RABIES

dum-dum fever \ˈdəm-ˌdəm-\ *n* : KALA-AZAR

dum·my \ˈdə-mē\ *n, pl* **dummies** : PLACEBO

dump·ing syndrome \ˈdəm-piŋ-\ *n* : a condition characterized by weakness, dizziness, flushing and warmth, nausea, and palpitation immediately or shortly after eating and produced by abnormally rapid emptying of the stomach in persons who have had part of the stomach removed or in hypersensitive or neurotic individuals

duoden- *or* **duodeno-** *comb form* **1** : duodenum (*duoden*itis) **2** : duodenal and (*duodeno*jejunal)

du·o·de·nal ulcer \ˌdü-ə-ˈdēn-əl-, ˌdyü-; dù-ˈäd-ən-əl-, dyù-\ *n* : a peptic ulcer situated in the duodenum

du·o·de·ni·tis \ˌdù-ˌäd-ən-ˈī-təs, dyù-\ *n* : inflammation of the duodenum

du·o·de·no·cho·led·o·chot·o·my \ˌdù-ˌäd-ən-ō-kə-ˌle-də-ˈkä-tə-mē, dyù-\ *n, pl* **-mies** : choledochotomy performed by approach through the duodenum by incision

du·o·de·nog·ra·phy \ˌdù-ˌäd-ən-ˈä-grə-fē, dyù-\ *n, pl* **-phies** : radiographic visualization of the duodenum with a contrast medium

du·o·de·no·je·ju·nal \ˌdù-ˌäd-ən-ō-ji-ˈjün-əl, dyù-\ *adj* : of, relating to, or joining the duodenum and the jejunum

du·o·de·no·je·ju·nos·to·my \-ji-jü-ˈnäs-tə-mē\ *n, pl* **-mies** : a surgical operation that joins part of the duodenum and the jejunum with creation of an artificial opening between them

du·o·de·not·o·my \ˌdù-ˌäd-ən-ˈä-tə-mē, dyù-\ *n, pl* **-mies** : incision of the duodenum

du·o·de·num \ˌdü-ə-ˈdē-nəm, ˌdyü-; dù-ˈäd-ən-əm, dyù-\ *n, pl* **-de·na** \-ˈdē-nə, -ən-ə\ *or* **-de·nums** : the first, shortest, and widest part of the small intestine that in humans is about 10 inches (25 centimeters) long and that extends from the pylorus to the undersurface of the liver where it descends for a variable distance and receives the bile and pancreatic ducts and then bends to the left and finally upward to join the jejunum near the second lumbar vertebra — **du·o·de·nal** \-ˈdēn-əl, -ən-əl\ *adj*

¹du·plex \ˈdü-ˌpleks, ˈdyü-\ *adj* : having complementary polynucleotide strands of DNA or of DNA and RNA

²duplex *n* : a duplex molecule of DNA or of DNA and RNA

du·pli·cate \ˈdü-pli-ˌkāt, ˈdyü-\ *vb* **-cat·ed; -cat·ing** : to become duplicate : REPLICATE ⟨DNA in chromosomes ~ s⟩

du·pli·ca·tion \ˌdü-pli-ˈkā-shən, ˌdyü-\ *n* **1** : the act or process of duplicating : the quality or state of being duplicated **2** : a part of a chromosome in which the genetic material is repeated; *also* : the process of forming a duplication

Du·puy·tren's contracture \də-ˌpwē-ˈtraⁿz-, -ˌpwē-trenz-\ *n* : a condition marked by fibrosis with shortening and thickening of the palmar aponeurosis resulting in flexion contracture of the fingers into the palm of the hand

Du·puy·tren \də-pwē-²tram\, Guillaume (1777–1835), French surgeon.

dura — see LAMINA DURA

du·ral \²dur-əl, ²dyur-\ *adj* : of or relating to the dura mater

dural sinus *n* : SINUS OF THE DURA MATER

du·ra ma·ter \²dur-ə-²mā-tər, ²dyur-, -₁mä-\ *n* : the tough fibrous membrane lined with endothelium on the inner surface that envelops the brain and spinal cord external to the arachnoid and pia mater, that in the cranium closely lines the bone, does not dip down between the convolutions, and contains numerous blood vessels and venous sinuses, and that in the spinal cord is separated from the bone by a considerable space and contains no venous sinuses — called also **dura**

dust cell *n* : a pulmonary histiocyte that takes up and eliminates foreign particles introduced into the lung alveoli with inspired air

dust·ing powder \²dəs-tiŋ-\ *n* : a powder used on the skin or on wounds esp. for allaying irritation or absorbing moisture

Dutch cap *n* : CERVICAL CAP

DVM *abbr* doctor of veterinary medicine

¹**dwarf** \²dworf\ *n, pl* **dwarfs** \²dworfs\ *also* **dwarves** \²dworvz\ *often attrib* 1 : a person of unusually small stature; *esp* : one whose bodily proportions are abnormal 2 : an animal much below normal size

²**dwarf** *vb* : to restrict the growth of

dwarf·ism \²dwor-₁fi-zəm\ *n* : the condition of stunted growth

Dx *abbr* diagnosis

Dy *symbol* dysprosium

dy·ad \²dī-₁ad, -əd\ *n* : a meiotic chromosome after separation of the two homologous members of a tetrad — **dy·ad·ic** \dī-²a-dik\ *adj*

dy·dro·ges·ter·one \dī-drō-²jes-tə-₁rōn\ *n* : a synthetic progestational agent $C_{21}H_{28}O_2$ — called also *isopregnenone*

dying *pres part of* DIE

-dynamia *n comb form* : strength : condition of having (such) strength ⟨adynamia⟩

dy·nam·ic \dī-²na-mik\ *also* **dy·nam·i·cal** \-mi-kəl\ *adj* 1 a : of or relating to physical force or energy b : of or relating to dynamics 2 : FUNCTIONAL 1b ⟨a ~ disease⟩ 3 a : marked by continuous usu. productive activity or change b : marked by energy ⟨a ~ personality⟩ — **dy·nam·i·cal·ly** \-mi-k(ə-)lē\ *adv*

dy·nam·ics \dī-²na-miks\ *n sing or pl* 1 : a branch of mechanics that deals with forces and their relation primarily to the motion but sometimes also to the equilibrium of bodies 2 : PSYCHODYNAMICS 3 : the pattern of change or growth of an object or phe-

nomenon ⟨personality ~⟩ ⟨population ~⟩

dy·na·mom·e·ter \₁dī-nə-²mä-mə-tər\ *n* : an instrument for measuring the force of muscular contraction esp. of the hand

dyne \²dīn\ *n* : the unit of force in the cgs system equal to the force that would give a free mass of one gram an acceleration of one centimeter per second per second

dy·nein \²dī-₁nēn, -₁nē-ən\ *n* : an ATPase that is associated esp. with microtubules involved in the ciliary and flagellar movement of cells

dy·nor·phin \dī-²nor-fən\ *n* : any of a group of potent opioid peptides found in the mammalian central nervous system that have a strong affinity for opiate receptors

dy·phyl·line \dī-²fi-₁lēn\ *n* : a theophylline derivative $C_{10}H_{14}N_4O_4$ used as a diuretic and for its bronchodilator and peripheral vasodilator effects — see NEOTHYLLINE

dys- *prefix* 1 : abnormal ⟨dysplasia⟩ 2 : difficult ⟨dyspnea⟩ 3 : impaired ⟨dysfunction⟩

dys·aes·the·sia *chiefly Brit var of* DYSESTHESIA

dys·ar·thria \dis-²är-thrē-ə\ *n* : difficulty in articulating words due to disease of the central nervous system — compare DYSPHASIA — **dys·ar·thric** \-thrik\ *adj*

dys·ar·thro·sis \dis-₁är-²thrō-səs\ *n, pl* **-thro·ses** \-₁sēz\ 1 : a condition of reduced joint motion due to deformity, dislocation, or disease 2 : DYSARTHRIA

dys·au·to·no·mia \dis-₁o-tə-²nō-mē-ə\ *n* : a familial disorder of the nervous system characterized esp. by multiple sensory deficiency (as of taste and pain) and by excessive sweating and salivation — **dys·au·to·nom·ic** \-²nä-mik\ *adj*

dys·ba·rism \²dis-bə-₁ri-zəm\ *n* : the complex of symptoms (as bends or headache) that accompanies exposure to excessively low or rapidly changing environmental air pressure

dys·cal·cu·lia \dis-₁kal-²kyü-lē-ə\ *n* : impairment of mathematical ability due to an organic condition of the brain

dys·che·zia \dis-²kē-zē-ə, -²ke-, -zhə, -zhē-ə\ *n* : constipation associated with a defective reflex for defecation — **dys·che·zic** \-²kē-zik, -²ke-\ *adj*

dys·chon·dro·pla·sia \dis-₁kän-drō-²plā-zhə, -zhē-ə\ *n* : CHONDRODYSPLASIA

dys·cra·sia \dis-²krā-zhə, -zhē-ə\ *n* : an abnormal condition of the body; *esp* : an imbalance of components of the blood

dys·di·ad·o·cho·ki·ne·sia *or* **dys·di·ad·o·ko·ki·ne·sia** \₁dis-₁dī-₁a-də-₁kō-ki-²nē-zhə, -zhē-ə\ *n* : impairment of the ability to make movements exhibiting a rapid change of motion that is caused by cerebellar dysfunction — compare ADIADOKOKINESIS

dys·en·ter·ic \ˌdis-ᵊn-ˈter-ik\ *adj* : of or relating to dysentery

dys·en·tery \ˈdis-ᵊn-ˌter-ē\ *n, pl* **-ter·ies** 1 : a disease characterized by severe diarrhea with passage of mucus and blood and usu. caused by infection 2 : DIARRHEA

dys·es·the·sia \ˌdi-ses-ˈthē-zhə, -zhē-ə\ *n* : impairment of sensitivity esp. to touch — **dys·es·thet·ic** \-ˈthe-tik\ *adj*

dys·func·tion \(ˈ)dis-ˈfəŋk-shən\ *n* : impaired or abnormal functioning (as of an organ of the body) — **dys·func·tion·al** \-shnəl, -shən-ᵊl\ *adj* — **dys·func·tion·ing** \-shə-niŋ\ *n*

dys·gam·ma·glob·u·li·ne·mia \ˌdis-ˌgamə-ˌglä-byə-lə-ˈnē-mē-ə\ *n* : a disorder involving abnormality in structure or frequency of gamma globulins — compare AGAMMAGLOBULINEMIA

dys·gen·e·sis \(ˌ)dis-ˈje-nə-səs\ *n, pl* **-e·ses** \-ˌsēz\ : defective development esp. of the gonads (as in Klinefelter's syndrome or Turner's syndrome)

dys·ger·mi·no·ma \dis-ˌjər-mə-ˈnō-mə\ *n, pl* **-mas** *or* **-ma·ta** \-mə-tə\ : a malignant tumor of the ovary arising from undifferentiated germinal epithelium

dys·geu·sia \(ˌ)dis-ˈgü-zē-ə, -ˈgyü-, -zhə, -zhē-ə\ *n* : dysfunction of the sense of taste

dys·graph·ia \(ˌ)dis-ˈgra-fē-ə\ *n* : impairment of the ability to write caused by brain damage

dys·hi·dro·sis \dis-ˌhī-ˈdrō-səs, -hə-\ *n, pl* **-dro·ses** \-ˌsēz\ : POMPHOLYX 2

dys·kary·o·sis \dis-kar-ē-ˈō-səs\ *n, pl* **-o·ses** \-ˌsēz\ *or* **-o·sis·es** : abnormality esp. of exfoliated cells (as from the uterine cervix) that affects the nucleus but not the cytoplasm

dys·ker·a·to·sis \ˌdis-ˌker-ə-ˈtō-səs\ *n, pl* **-to·ses** \-ˌsēz\ : faulty development of the epidermis with abnormal keratinization — **dys·ker·a·tot·ic** \-ˈtä-tik\ *adj*

dys·ki·ne·sia \ˌdis-kə-ˈnē-zhə, -kī-, -zhē-ə\ *n* : impairment of voluntary movements resulting in fragmented or jerky motions (as in Parkinson's disease) — see TARDIVE DYSKINESIA — **dys·ki·net·ic** \-ˈne-tik\ *adj*

dys·lec·tic \dis-ˈlek-tik\ *adj or n* : DYSLEXIC

dys·lex·ia \dis-ˈlek-sē-ə\ *n* : a disturbance of the ability to read; *broadly* : disturbance of the ability to use language

¹**dys·lex·ic** \-ˈlek-sik\ *adj* : affected with dyslexia

²**dyslexic** *n* : a dyslexic person

dys·men·or·rhea \(ˌ)dis-ˌme-nə-ˈrē-ə\ *n* : painful menstruation — **dys·men·or·rhe·ic** \-ˈrē-ik\ *adj*

dys·met·ria \dis-ˈme-trē-ə\ *n* : impaired ability to estimate distance in muscular action

dys·mor·phia \-ˈmȯr-fē-ə\ *n* : DYSMORPHISM — **dys·mor·phic** \-fik\ *adj*

dys·mor·phism \-ˈmȯr-ˌfi-zəm\ *n* : an anatomical malformation

dys·os·mia \di-ˈsäz-mē-ə, -ˈsäs-\ *n* : dysfunction of the sense of smell

dys·os·to·sis \ˌdi-ˌsäs-ˈtō-səs\ *n, pl* **-to·ses** \-ˌsēz\ : defective formation of bone — **dys·os·tot·ic** \-ˈtä-tik\ *adj*

dys·pa·reu·nia \ˌdis-pə-ˈrü-nē-ə, -nyə\ *n* : difficult or painful sexual intercourse

dys·pep·sia \dis-ˈpep-shə, -sē-ə\ *n* : INDIGESTION

¹**dys·pep·tic** \-ˈpep-tik\ *adj* : relating to or having dyspepsia

²**dyspeptic** *n* : a person having dyspepsia

dys·pha·gia \dis-ˈfā-jə, -jē-ə\ *n* : difficulty in swallowing — **dys·phag·ic** \-ˈfa-jik\ *adj*

dys·pha·sia \dis-ˈfā-zhə, -zhē-ə\ *n* : loss of or deficiency in the power to use or understand language as a result of injury to or disease of the brain — compare DYSARTHRIA

¹**dys·pha·sic** \-ˈfā-zik\ *adj* : relating to or affected with dysphasia

²**dysphasic** *n* : a dysphasic person

dys·pho·nia \dis-ˈfō-nē-ə\ *n* : defective use of the voice

dys·pho·ria \dis-ˈfȯr-ē-ə\ *n* : a state of feeling unwell or unhappy — compare EUPHORIA — **dys·phor·ic** \-ˈfȯr-ik, -ˈfär-\ *adj*

dys·pla·sia \dis-ˈplā-zhə, -zhē-ə\ *n* : abnormal growth or development (as of organs or cells); *broadly* : abnormal anatomic structure due to such growth — **dys·plas·tic** \-ˈplas-tik\ *adj*

dys·pnea \ˈdis-nē-ə, ˈdisp-\ *n* : difficult or labored respiration — compare EUPNEA — **dys·pne·ic** \-nē-ik\ *adj*

dys·pnoea *chiefly Brit var of* DYSPNEA

dys·prax·ia \dis-ˈprak-sē-ə, -ˈprak-shə, -shē-ə\ *n* : impairment of the ability to perform coordinated movements

dys·pro·si·um \dis-ˈprō-zē-əm, -zhəm, -zhē-əm\ *n* : an element that forms highly magnetic compounds — symbol *Dy*; see ELEMENT table

dys·pro·tein·ae·mia *chiefly Brit var of* DYSPROTEINEMIA

dys·pro·tein·emia \ˌdis-ˌprōt-ᵊn-ˈē-mē-ə, -ˌprō-ˌtē-ˈnē-, -ˌprō-ˌtē-ə-ˈnē-\ *n* : any abnormality of the protein content of the blood — **dys·pro·tein·emic** \-mik\ *adj*

dys·reg·u·la·tion \ˌdis-ˌre-gyə-ˈlā-shən\ *n* : impairment of regulatory mechanisms (as those governing concentration of a substance in the blood or the function of an organ)

dys·rhyth·mia \dis-ˈrith-mē-ə\ *n* 1 : an abnormal rhythm; *esp* : a disordered rhythm exhibited in a record of electrical activity of the brain or heart 2 : JET LAG — **dys·rhyth·mic** \-mik\ *adj*

dys·syn·er·gia \dis-sə-ˈnər-jə, -jē-ə\ *n* : DYSKINESIA — **dys·syn·er·gic** \-ˈnər-jik\ *adj*

dys·thy·mia \dis-ˈthī-mē-ə\ *n* : an affective disorder characterized by chronic mildly depressed or irritable mood often accompanied by other symptoms (as eating and sleeping disturbances, fatigue, and poor self-esteem) — **dys·thy·mic** \-ˈmik\ adj

dys·to·cia \dis-ˈtō-shə, -shē-ə\ or **dys·to·kia** \-ˈtō-kē-ə\ n : slow or difficult labor or delivery

dys·to·nia \dis-ˈtō-nē-ə\ n : a state of disordered tonicity of tissues (as of muscle) — **dys·ton·ic** \-ˈtä-nik\ adj

dystonia mus·cu·lo·rum de·for·mans \-ˌməs-kyə-ˈlȯr-əm-di-ˈfȯr-ˌmanz\ n : a rare inherited neurological disorder characterized by progressive muscular spasticity causing severe involuntary contortions esp. of the trunk and limbs — called also *torsion dystonia*

dys·tro·phic \dis-ˈtrō-fik\ adj 1 : relating to or caused by faulty nutrition 2 : relating to or affected with a dystrophy

dystrophica — see MYOTONIA DYSTROPHICA

dys·tro·phy \ˈdis-trə-fē\ n, pl **-phies** 1 : a condition produced by faulty nutrition 2 : any myogenic atrophy: esp : MUSCULAR DYSTROPHY

dys·uria \dis-ˈyu̇r-ē-ə\ n : difficult or painful discharge of urine — **dys·uric** \-ˈyu̇r-ik\ adj

E

e- prefix : missing : absent ⟨edentulous⟩

ear \ˈir\ n 1 : the vertebrate organ of hearing and equilibrium consisting in the typical mammal of a sound-collecting outer ear separated by the tympanic membrane from a sound-transmitting middle ear that in turn is separated from a sensory inner ear by membranous fenestrae 2 a : the external ear of humans and most mammals b : a human earlobe — **eared** \ˈird\ adj

ear·ache \ˈir-ˌāk\ n : an ache or pain in the ear — called also *otalgia*

ear·drum \-ˌdrəm\ n : TYMPANIC MEMBRANE

ear·lobe \ˈir-ˌlōb\ n : the pendent part of the ear esp. of humans

ear mange n : canker of the ear esp. in cats and dogs that is caused by mites; esp : OTODECTIC MANGE

ear mite n : any of various mites attacking the ears of mammals

ear pick n : a device for removing wax or foreign bodies from the ear

ear·piece \ˈir-ˌpēs\ n 1 : a part of an instrument (as a stethoscope or hearing aid) that is applied to the ear 2 : one of the two sidepieces that support eyeglasses by passing over or behind the ears

ear·plug \-ˌpləg\ n : a device of pliable material for insertion into the outer opening of the ear (as to keep out water or deaden sound)

ear tick n : any of several ticks infesting the ears of mammals; esp : SPINOSE EAR TICK

ear·wax \ˈir-ˌwaks\ n : the yellow waxy secretion from the glands of the external ear — called also *cerumen*

east coast fever n : an acute highly fatal febrile disease of cattle esp. of eastern and southern Africa that is caused by a protozoan of the genus *Theileria* (*T. parva*) transmitted by ticks esp. of the genera *Rhipicephalus* and *Hyalomma*

eastern equine encephalomyelitis n : EQUINE ENCEPHALOMYELITIS a

eating disorder n : any of several psychological disorders (as anorexia nervosa or bulimia) characterized by gross disturbances of eating behavior

Ea·ton agent \ˈēt-ᵊn-\ n : a microorganism of the genus *Mycoplasma* (*M. pneumoniae*) that is the causative agent of primary atypical pneumonia

Eaton, Monroe Davis (b 1904), American microbiologist.

eb·ur·nat·ed \ˈe-bər-ˌnā-təd, ˈē-\ adj : hard and dense like ivory ⟨~ cartilage⟩ ⟨~ bone⟩ — **eb·ur·na·tion** \ˌe-bər-ˈnā-shən, ˌē-\ n

EBV abbr Epstein-Barr virus

EB virus \ˌē-ˈbē-\ n : EPSTEIN-BARR VIRUS

ec- prefix : out of : outside of : outside ⟨eccrine⟩

eccentric hypertrophy n : hypertrophy of the wall of a hollow organ and esp. the heart with dilatation of its cavity

ec·chon·dro·ma \ˌe-kən-ˈdrō-mə\ n, pl **-ma·ta** \-mə-tə\ or **-mas** : a cartilaginous tumor projecting from bone or cartilage

ec·chy·mo·sis \ˌe-kə-ˈmō-səs\ n, pl **-mo·ses** \-ˌsēz\ : the escape of blood into the tissues from ruptured blood vessels marked by a livid black-and-blue or purple spot or area; also : the discoloration so caused — compare PETECHIA — **ec·chy·mosed** \ˈe-kə-ˌmōzd, -ˌmōst\ adj — **ec·chy·mot·ic** \-ˈmä-tik\ adj

ec·crine \ˈe-krən, -ˌkrīn, -ˌkrēn\ adj : of, relating to, having, or being eccrine glands — compare APOCRINE, HOLOCRINE, MEROCRINE

eccrine gland n : any of the rather small sweat glands that produce a fluid secretion without removing cytoplasm from the secreting cells and that are restricted to the human skin — called also *eccrine sweat gland*

ECG abbr electrocardiogram

Echid·noph·a·ga \ˌek-(ˌ)id-ˈnä-fə-gə\ n

: a genus of fleas (family Pulicidae) including the sticktight flea (*E. gallinacea*

echi·no·coc·co·sis \i-ˌkī-nə-kä-ˈkō-səs\ *n, pl* **-co·ses** \-ˌsēz\ : infestation with or disease caused by a small tapeworm of the genus *Echinococcus* (*E. granulosus*): *esp* : HYDATID DISEASE

echi·no·coc·cus \-nə-ˈkä-kəs\ *n* 1 *cap* : a genus of taeniid tapeworms that alternate a minute adult living as a harmless commensal in the intestine of dogs and other carnivores with a hydatid larva invading tissues esp. of the liver of cattle, sheep, swine, and humans, and acting as a serious often fatal pathogen 2 *pl* **-coc·ci** \ˈkä-ˌkī, -ˌkē; -ˈkäk-ˌsī, -ˌsē\ : any tapeworm of the genus *Echinococcus*; *also* : HYDATID

echo·car·dio·gram \ˌe-kō-ˈkär-dē-ə-ˌgram\ *n* : a visual record made by echocardiography

echo·car·di·og·ra·phy \-kär-dē-ˈä-grə-fē\ *n, pl* **-phies** : the use of ultrasound to examine and measure structure and functioning of the heart and to diagnose abnormalities and disease — **echo·car·dio·graph·er** *n* \-grə-fər\ — **echo·car·dio·graph·ic** \-dē-ə-ˈgra-fik\ *adj*

echo·en·ceph·a·lo·gram \ˌe-kō-in-ˈse-fə-lə-ˌgram\ *n* : a visual record obtained by echoencephalography

echo·en·ceph·a·log·ra·phy \-in-ˌse-fə-ˈlä-grə-fē\ *n, pl* **-phies** : the use of ultrasound to examine and measure internal structures (as the ventricles) of the skull and to diagnose abnormalities and disease — **echo·en·ceph·a·lo·graph·ic** \-fə-lə-ˈgra-fik\ *adj*

echo·gram \ˈe-kō-ˌgram\ *n* : the record made by echography — called also *ultrasonogram*

echo·graph \-ˌgraf\ *n* : an instrument used for echography

echog·ra·phy \i-ˈkä-grə-fē\ *n, pl* **-phies** : ULTRASOUND 2 — **echo·graph·ic** \ˌe-kō-ˈgra-fik\ *adj* — **echo·graph·i·cal·ly** \-fi-k(ə-)lē\ *adv*

echo·la·lia \ˌe-kō-ˈlä-lē-ə\ *n* : the often pathological repetition of what is said by other people as if echoing them — **echo·lal·ic** \-ˈla-lik\ *adj*

echo·prax·ia \ˌe-kō-ˈprak-sē-ə\ *n* : pathological repetition of the actions of other people as if echoing them

echo·thi·o·phate iodide \-ˈthī-ə-ˌfāt-\ *n* : a long-acting anticholinesterase $C_9H_{21}INO_3PS$ used esp. to reduce intraocular pressure in the treatment of glaucoma — called also *echothiophate*

echo·vi·rus \ˈe-kō-ˌvī-rəs\ *n* : any of a group of picornaviruses that are found in the gastrointestinal tract, that cause cytopathic changes in cells in tissue culture, and that are sometimes associated with respiratory ailments and meningitis

ec·lamp·sia \i-ˈklamp-sē-ə, e-\ *n* : a convulsive state : an attack of convulsions: as **a** : toxemia of pregnancy esp. when severe and marked by convulsions and coma — compare PREECLAMPSIA b : a condition comparable to milk fever of cows occurring in domestic animals (as dogs and cats) — **ec·lamp·tic** \-tik\ *adj*

¹**eclec·tic** \e-ˈklek-tik, i-\ *adj* 1 : selecting what appears to be best in various doctrines or methods 2 : of. relating to. or practicing eclecticism — **eclec·ti·cal·ly** \-ti-k(ə-)lē\ *adv*

²**eclectic** *n* : one who uses an eclectic method or approach

eclec·ti·cism \-ˈklek-tə-ˌsi-zəm\ *n* 1 : a theory or practice (as of medicine or psychotherapy) that combines doctrines or methods (as therapeutic procedures) from diverse sources 2 : a system of medicine once popular in the U.S. that depended on plant remedies

ecol·o·gy \i-ˈkä-lə-jē, e-\ *n, pl* **-gies** 1 : a branch of science concerned with the interrelationship of organisms and their environments 2 : the totality or pattern of relations between organisms and their environment 3 : HUMAN ECOLOGY — **eco·log·i·cal** \ˌe-kə-ˈlä-ji-kəl, ˌē-\ *also* **eco·log·ic** \-jik\ *adj* — **eco·log·i·cal·ly** \-ji-k(ə-)lē\ *adv* — **ecol·o·gist** \i-ˈkä-lə-jist, e-\ *n*

eco·sys·tem \ˈē-kō-ˌsis-təm, ˈe-\ *n* : the complex of a community and its environment functioning as an ecological unit in nature

écra·seur \ˌā-krä-ˈzər, ˌē-\ *n* : a surgical instrument used to encircle and sever a projecting mass of tissue

ec·sta·sy \ˈek-stə-sē\ *n, pl* **-sies** 1 : a trance state in which intense absorption is accompanied by loss of sense perception and voluntary control 2 : a synthetic amphetamine analog $C_{11}H_{15}NO_2$ used illicitly for its mood-enhancing and hallucinogenic properties — called also *MDMA* — **ec·stat·ic** \ek-ˈsta-tik\ *adj*

ECT *abbr* electroconvulsive therapy

ec·ta·sia \ek-ˈtā-zhē-ə, -zhə\ *n* : the expansion of a hollow or tubular organ — **ec·tat·ic** \ek-ˈta-tik\ *adj*

ec·ta·sis \ˈek-tə-səs\ *n, pl* **-ta·ses** \-ˌsēz\ : ECTASIA

ec·thy·ma \ek-ˈthī-mə\ *n* 1 : a cutaneous eruption marked by large flat pustules that have a hardened base surrounded by inflammation and occur esp. on the lower legs 2 : sore mouth of sheep — **ec·thy·ma·tous** \ek-ˈthī-mə-təs, -ˈthī-\ *adj*

ecto- *also* **ect-** *comb form* : outside : external (*ecto*derm) — compare END- 1, EXO-

ec·to·cyst \ˈek-tə-ˌsist\ *n* : the external layer of a hydatid cyst

ec·to·derm \-ˌdərm\ *n* 1 : the outermost of the three primary germ layers of an embryo 2 : a tissue (as neural tissue) derived from ectoderm — **ec·to·der·mal** \ek-tə-'dər-məl\ adj

ec·to·en·zyme \ek-tō-'en-₁zīm\ n : an enzyme acting outside the cell

ec·to·mor·phic \ek-tə-'mȯr-fik\ adj 1 : of or relating to the component in W. H. Sheldon's classification of body types that measures the body's degree of thinness, angularity, and fragility — compare ENDOMORPHIC 1, MESOMORPHIC 2 2 : having a light body build — **ec·to·morph** \'ek-tə-₁mȯrf\ n — **ec·to·mor·phy** \'ek-tə-₁mȯr-fē\ n

-ec·to·my \'ek-tə-mē\ n comb form, pl **-ec·to·mies** : surgical removal (appendectomy)

ec·to·par·a·site \ek-tō-'par-ə-₁sīt\ n : a parasite that lives on the exterior of its host — compare ENDOPARASITE — **ec·to·par·a·sit·ic** \-₁par-ə-'si-tik\ adj

ec·to·pia \ek-'tō-pē-ə\ n : an abnormal congenital or acquired position of an organ or part (~ of the heart)

ec·top·ic \ek-'tä-pik\ adj 1 : occurring in an abnormal position (an ~ kidney) 2 : originating in an area of the heart other than the sinoatrial node (~ beats); also : initiating ectopic heartbeats — **ec·top·i·cal·ly** \-pi-k(ə-)lē\ adv

ectopic pregnancy n : gestation elsewhere than in the uterus (as in a fallopian tube or in the peritoneal cavity) — called also ectopic gestation, extrauterine pregnancy

ec·to·pla·cen·ta \ek-tō-plə-'sen-tə\ n : TROPHOBLAST — **ec·to·pla·cen·tal** \-'sent-ᵊl\ adj

ec·to·plasm \'ek-tə-₁pla-zəm\ n : the outer relatively rigid granule-free layer of the cytoplasm — compare ENDOPLASM

ec·to·py \'ek-tə-pē\ n, pl **-pies** : ECTOPIA

ectro- comb form : congenitally absent — usu. indicating absence of a particular limb or part (ectrodactyly)

ec·tro·dac·tyl·ia \ek-trō-dak-'ti-lē-ə\ n : ECTRODACTYLY

ec·tro·dac·tyl·ism \-'dak-tə-₁li-zəm\ n : ECTRODACTYLY

ec·tro·dac·ty·ly \-'dak-tə-lē\ n, pl **-lies** : congenital complete or partial absence of one or more digits

ec·tro·me·lia \ek-trō-'mē-lē-ə\ n 1 : congenital absence or imperfection of one or more limbs 2 : MOUSEPOX

ec·tro·pi·on \ek-'trō-pē-₁än, -ən\ n : an abnormal turning out of a part (as an eyelid)

ec·ze·ma \ig-'zē-mə, 'eg-zə-mə, 'ek-sə-\ n : an inflammatory condition of the skin characterized by redness, itching, and oozing vesicular lesions which become scaly, crusted, or hardened — **ec·zem·a·tous** \ig-'ze-mə-təs\ adj

ec·ze·ma·toid \ig-'ze-mə-₁tȯid, -'ze-\ adj : resembling eczema

ED abbr effective dose

EDB abbr ethylene dibromide

ede·ma \i-'dē-mə\ n : an abnormal excess accumulation of serous fluid in connective tissue or in a serous cavity — called also dropsy — **edem·a·tous** \-'de-mə-təs\ adj

eden·tu·lous \(₁)ē-'den-chə-ləs\ adj : TOOTHLESS (an ~ upper jaw)

edetate — see DISODIUM EDETATE

Ed·ing·er–West·phal nucleus \₁e-diŋ-ər-'west-₁fäl-, -₁fȯl-\ n : the lateral portion of the group of nerve cells lying ventral to the aqueduct of Sylvius which give rise to autonomic fibers of the oculomotor nerve

Ed·ing·er \'e-diŋ-ər\, **Ludwig** (1855–1918), German neurologist.

West·phal \'west-₁fäl, -₁fȯl\, **Carl Friedrich Otto** (1833–1890), German neurologist.

EDR abbr electrodermal response

ed·ro·pho·ni·um \₁e-drə-'fō-nē-əm\ n : an anticholinesterase $C_{10}H_{16}ClNO$ used esp. to stimulate skeletal muscle and in the diagnosis of myasthenia gravis — called also edrophonium chloride; see TENSILON

EDTA \₁ē-(₁)dē-(₁)tē-'ā\ n : a white crystalline acid $C_{10}H_{16}N_2O_8$ used in medicine as an anticoagulant and in the treatment of lead poisoning — called also ethylenediaminetetraacetic acid

ed·u·ca·ble \'e-jə-kə-bəl\ adj : affected with mild mental retardation and capable of developing academic, social, and occupational skills within the capabilities of one with a mental age between 9 and 12 years — compare TRAINABLE

EEE abbr eastern equine encephalomyelitis

EEG abbr electroencephalogram; electroencephalograph

EENT abbr eye, ear, nose, and throat

ef·face·ment \i-'fās-mənt, e-\ n : obliteration of the uterine cervix by shortening and softening during labor so that only the external orifice remains — **ef·face** \-'fās\ vb

ef·fect \i-'fekt\ n : something that is produced by an agent or cause

ef·fec·tive \i-'fek-tiv\ adj : producing a decided, decisive, claimed, or desired effect — **ef·fec·tive·ness** n

ef·fec·tor \i-'fek-tər, -₁tȯr\ n 1 : a bodily organ (as a gland or muscle) that becomes active in response to stimulation 2 : a substance (as an inducer or corepressor) that controls protein synthesis by combining allosterically with a genetic repressor

¹ef·fer·ent \'e-fə-rənt, 'e-₁fer-ənt, 'ē-₁fer-\ adj : conducting outward from a part or organ; specif : conveying nervous impulses to an effector (~ neurons) — compare AFFERENT

²efferent n : an efferent part (as a blood vessel or nerve fiber)

efferentes — see DUCTULI EFFERENTES

efferentia — see VASA EFFERENTIA

ef·fleu·rage \₁e-flə-'räzh, -(₁)flü-\ n : a

light stroking movement used in massage

effort syndrome *n* : NEUROCIRCULATORY ASTHENIA

ef·fuse \i-ᵇfyüs, e-\ *adj* : spread out flat without definite form

ef·fu·sion \i-ᵇfyü-zhən, e-\ *n* **1** : the escape of a fluid from anatomical vessels by rupture or exudation **2** : the fluid that escapes by extravasation — see PLEURAL EFFUSION

eges·tion \i-ᵇjes-chən\ *n* : the act or process of discharging undigested or waste material from a cell or organism; *specif* : DEFECATION — **egest** \i-ᵇjest\ *vb*

EGF *abbr* epidermal growth factor

egg \ᵇeg, ᵇāg\ *n* **1** : the hard-shelled reproductive body produced by a bird and esp. by the common domestic chicken (*Gallus gallus*) **2** : an animal reproductive body consisting of an ovum together with its nutritive and protective envelopes and having the capacity to develop into a new individual capable of independent existence **3** : OVUM

egg cell *n* : OVUM

ego \ᵇē-(ₐ)gō\ *n, pl* **egos 1** : the self esp. as contrasted with another self or the world **2** : the one of the three divisions of the psyche in psychoanalytic theory that serves as the organized conscious mediator between the person and reality esp. by functioning both in the perception of and adaptation to reality — compare ᵇID, SUPEREGO

¹ego·cen·tric \ₐē-gō-ᵇsen-trik\ *adj* **1** : limited in outlook or concern to one's own activities or needs **2** : being self-centered or selfish — **ego·cen·tri·cal·ly** \-tri-k(ə-)lē\ *adv* — **ego·cen·tric·i·ty** \ₐē-gō-(ₐ)sen-ᵇtris-ət-ē, -sən-\ *n* — **ego·cen·trism** \-ᵇsen-ₐtri-zəm\ *n*

²egocentric *n* : an egocentric person

ego-defense *n* : DEFENSE MECHANISM

ego-dys·ton·ic \-dis-ᵇtä-nik\ *adj* : incompatible with or unacceptable to the ego — compare EGO-SYNTONIC

ego ideal *n* : the positive standards, ideals, and ambitions that according to psychoanalytic theory are assimilated from the superego

ego-involvement *n* : an involvement of one's self-esteem in the performance of a task or in an object — **ego-involve** *vb*

ego·ism \ᵇē-gə-ₐwi-zəm \ *n* **1 a** : a doctrine that individual self-interest is the actual motive of all conscious action **b** : a doctrine that individual self-interest is the valid end of all actions **2** : excessive concern for oneself without exaggerated feelings of self-importance — compare EGOTISM — **ego·ist** \-wist\ *n* — **ego·is·tic** \ₐē-gə-ᵇwis-tik \ *also* **ego·is·ti·cal** \-ti-kəl\ *adj* — **ego·is·ti·cal·ly** \-ti-k(ə-)lē\ *adv*

ego·ma·nia \ₐē-gō-ᵇmä-nē-ə, -nyə\ *n* : the quality or state of being ex-

tremely egocentric — **ego·ma·ni·ac** \-nē-ₐak\ *n* — **ego·ma·ni·a·cal** \-mə-ᵇnī-ə-kəl\ *adj* — **ego·ma·ni·a·cal·ly** \-k(ə-)lē\ *adv*

egoph·o·ny \ē-ᵇgä-fə-nē\ *n, pl* **-nies** : a modification of the voice resembling bleating heard on auscultation of the chest in some diseases (as in pleurisy with effusion)

ego-syn·ton·ic \ₐē-gō-sin-ᵇtä-nik\ *adj* : compatible with or acceptable to the ego — compare EGO-DYSTONIC

ego·tism \ᵇē-gə-ₐti-zəm\ *n* : an exaggerated sense of self-importance — compare EGOISM **2** — **ego·tist** \-tist\ *n* — **ego·tis·tic** \ₐē-gə-ᵇtis-tik\ *or* **ego·tis·ti·cal** \-ᵇtis-ti-kəl\ *adj* — **ego·tis·ti·cal·ly** \-ᵇtis-ti-k(ə-)lē\ *adv*

Eh·lers–Dan·los syndrome \ᵇā-lərz-ᵇdan-(ₐ)läs-\ *n* : a rare inherited disorder of connective tissue characterized by extremely flexible joints and elastic skin

Ehlers \ᵇā-(ₐ)lerz\. **Edvard L.** (1863–1937), Danish dermatologist.

Dan·los \dä°-ᵇlō\. **Henri-Alexandre** (1844–1912), French dermatologist.

Ehr·lich·ia \er-ᵇli-kē-a\ *n* : a genus of gram-negative nonmotile rickettsial bacteria that are intracellular parasites infecting the cytoplasm of reticuloendothelial cells and circulating leukocytes but not erythrocytes

Ehr·lich \ᵇār-₁lik\. **Paul** (1854–1915), German chemist and bacteriologist.

ehrlichiosis *n* : infection with or a disease caused by rickettsial bacteria of the genus *Ehrlichia*

ei·co·sa·noid \ī-ᵇkō-sə-ₐnòid\ *n* : any of a class of compounds (as the prostaglandins, leukotrienes, and thromboxanes) derived from polyunsaturated fatty acids and involved in cellular activity

ei·det·ic \ī-ᵇde-tik\ *adj* : marked by or involving extraordinarily accurate and vivid recall esp. of visual images — **ei·det·i·cal·ly** \-ti-k(ə-)lē\ *adv*

eighth cranial nerve *n* : AUDITORY NERVE

eighth nerve *n* : AUDITORY NERVE

ei·ko·nom·e·ter \ₐī-kə-ᵇnä-mə-tər\ *n* : a device to detect aniseikonia or to test stereoscopic vision

Ei·me·ria \ī-ᵇmir-ē-ə\ *n* : a genus of coccidian protozoans that invade the visceral epithelia and esp. the intestinal wall of many vertebrates and include serious pathogens

Ei·mer \ᵇī-mər\. **Theodor Gustav Heinrich** (1843–1898), German zoologist.

ein·stei·ni·um \īn-ᵇstī-nē-əm\ *n* : a radioactive element produced artificially — symbol *Es*; see ELEMENT table

Einstein \ᵇīn-₁stīn, -₁shtīn\. **Albert** (1879–1955), German physicist.

ejac·u·late \i-ᵇja-kyə-ₐlāt\ *vb* **-lat·ed; -lat·ing** : to eject from a living body; *specif* : to eject (semen) in orgasm — **ejac·u·la·tor** \-ₐlā-tər\ *n*

²ejac·u·late \-lət\ n : the semen released by one ejaculation

ejac·u·la·tion \i-₁ja-kyə-ˈlā-shən\ n : the act or process of ejaculating; specif : the sudden or spontaneous discharging of a fluid (as semen in orgasm) from a duct — see PREMATURE EJACULATION

ejac·u·la·tio prae·cox \-ˈlā-shē-ō-ˈprē-₁käks\ n : PREMATURE EJACULATION

ejac·u·la·to·ry \i-ˈja-kyə-lə-₁tȯr-ē\ adj : associated with or concerned in physiological ejaculation (∼ vessels)

ejaculatory duct n : either of the paired ducts in the human male that are formed by the junction of the duct from the seminal vesicle with the vas deferens, pass through the prostate, and open into or close to the prostatic utricle

ejection fraction n : the ratio of the volume of blood the heart empties during systole to the volume of blood in the heart at the end of diastole expressed as a percentage normally between 56 and 78 percent

ejec·tor \i-ˈjek-tər\ n : something that ejects — see SALIVA EJECTOR

EKG \₁ē-(₁)kā-ˈjē\ n 1 : ELECTROCARDIOGRAM 2 : ELECTROCARDIOGRAPH

elab·o·rate \i-ˈla-bə-₁rāt\ vb -rat·ed; -rat·ing of a living organism : to build up (complex organic compounds) from simple ingredients — elab·o·ra·tion \i-₁la-bə-ˈrā-shən\ n

ela·pid \ˈe-lə-pəd\ n : any of a family (Elapidae) of venomous snakes with grooved fangs that include the cobras and mambas, the coral snakes of the New World, and the majority of Australian snakes — elapid adj

elast- or elasto- comb form : elasticity (elastosis)

elas·tase \i-ˈlas-₁tās, -₁tāz\ n : an enzyme esp. of pancreatic juice that digests elastin

¹elas·tic \i-ˈlas-tik\ adj : capable of being easily stretched or expanded and resuming former shape — elas·ti·cal·ly \-ti-k(ə-)lē\ adv

²elastic n 1 a : easily stretched rubber usu. prepared in cords, strings, or bands b : a band of elastic used esp. in orthodontics; also : one placed around a tooth at the gum line in effecting its nonsurgical removal 2 a : an elastic fabric usu. made of yarns containing rubber b : something made from this fabric

elastic cartilage n : a yellowish flexible cartilage having the matrix infiltrated in all directions by a network of elastic fibers and occurring chiefly in the external ear, eustachian tube, and some cartilages of the larynx and epiglottis

elastic fiber n : a thick very elastic smooth yellowish anastomosing fiber of connective tissue that contains elastin

elas·tic·i·ty \i-₁las-ˈti-sə-tē, ₁ē-\ n, pl

-ties : the quality or state of being elastic

elastic stocking n : a stocking woven or knitted with an elastic material and used (as in the treatment of varicose veins) to provide support for the leg

elastic tissue n : tissue consisting chiefly of elastic fibers that is found esp. in some ligaments and tendons

elasticum — see PSEUDOXANTHOMA ELASTICUM

elas·tin \i-ˈlas-tən\ n : a protein that is similar to collagen and is the chief constituent of elastic fibers

elas·to·sis \i-₁las-ˈtō-səs\ n, pl -to·ses \-₁sēz\ : a condition marked by loss of elasticity of the skin in elderly people due to degeneration of connective tissue

El·a·vil \ˈe-lə-₁vil\ trademark — used for a preparation of amitriptyline

el·bow \ˈel-₁bō\ n : the joint between the human forearm and the upper arm that supports the outer curve of the arm when bent — called also elbow joint

elec·tive \i-ˈlek-tiv\ adj : beneficial to the patient but not essential for survival (an ∼ appendectomy)

Elec·tra complex \i-ˈlek-trə-\ n : the Oedipus complex when it occurs in a female

electrical potential or electric potential n : the potential energy measured in volts of a unit of positive charge in an electric field

electric eel n : a large eel-shaped bony fish (Electrophorus electricus of the family Electrophoridae) of the Orinoco and Amazon basins that is capable of giving a severe shock with electricity generated by a special tract of tissue

electric ray n : any of various round-bodied short-tailed rays (family Torpedinidae) of warm seas that have a pair of specialized tracts of tissue in which electricity is generated

electric shock n 1 : SHOCK 3 2 : ELECTROSHOCK THERAPY

electric shock therapy n : ELECTROSHOCK THERAPY

electric shock treatment n : ELECTROSHOCK THERAPY

elec·tro·car·dio·gram \-ˈkär-dē-ə-₁gram\ n : the tracing made by an electrocardiograph

elec·tro·car·dio·graph \-₁graf\ n : an instrument for recording the changes of electrical potential occurring during the heartbeat used esp. in diagnosing abnormalities of heart action — elec·tro·car·dio·graph·ic \-₁kär-dē-ə-ˈgra-fik\ adj — elec·tro·car·dio·graph·i·cal·ly \-fi-k(ə-)lē\ adv — elec·tro·car·di·og·ra·phy \-dē-ˈä-grə-fē\ n

elec·tro·cau·tery \-ˈkȯ-tə-rē\ n, pl -ter·ies 1 : a cautery operated by an electric current 2 : the cauterization of tissue by means of an electrocautery

elec·tro·co·ag·u·la·tion \-kō-₁a-gyə-ˈlāshan\ *n* : the surgical coagulation of tissue by diathermy — **elec·tro·co·ag·u·late** \-kō-ˈa-gyə-ˌlāt\ *vb*

elec·tro·con·vul·sive \i-ˌlek-trō-kən-ˈvəl-siv\ *adj* : of, relating to, or involving convulsive response to electroshock

electroconvulsive therapy *n* : ELECTRO-SHOCK THERAPY

elec·tro·cor·ti·cal \-ˈkȯr-ti-kəl\ *adj* : of, relating to, or being the electrical activity occurring in the cerebral cortex

elec·tro·cor·ti·co·gram \-ˈkȯr-ti-kə-ˌgram\ *n* : an electroencephalogram made with the electrodes in direct contact with the brain

elec·tro·cor·ti·cog·ra·phy \-ˌkȯr-ti-ˈkä-grə-fē\ *n, pl* **-phies** : the process of recording electrical activity in the brain by placing electrodes in direct contact with the cerebral cortex — **elec·tro·cor·ti·co·graph·ic** \-kə-ˈgra-fik\ *adj* — **elec·tro·cor·ti·co·graph·i·cal·ly** \-fi-k(ə-)lē\ *adv*

elec·tro·c·u·lo·gram \i-ˌlek-ˈträ-kyə-lə-ˌgram\ *n* : a recording of the moving eye

elec·tro·cute \i-ˈlek-trə-ˌkyüt\ *vb* **-cut·ed; -cut·ing** 1 : to execute (a criminal) by electricity 2 : to kill by electric shock — **elec·tro·cu·tion** \i-ˌlek-trə-ˈkyü-shən\ *n*

elec·trode \i-ˈlek-ˌtrōd\ *n* : a conductor used to establish electrical contact with a nonmetallic part of a circuit

elec·tro·der·mal \i-ˌlek-trō-ˈdər-məl\ *adj* : of or relating to electrical activity in or electrical properties of the skin

elec·tro·des·ic·ca·tion \-ˌde-si-ˈkā-shən\ *n* : the drying of tissue by a high-frequency electric current applied with a needle-shaped electrode — called also *fulguration* — **elec·tro·des·ic·cate** \-ˈde-si-ˌkāt\ *vb*

elec·tro·di·ag·no·sis \-ˌdī-ig-ˈnō-səs\ *n, pl* **-no·ses** \-ˌsēz\ : diagnosis based on electrodiagnostic tests or procedures

elec·tro·di·ag·nos·tic \-ˌdī-ig-ˈnäs-tik\ *adj* : involving or obtained by the recording of responses to electrical stimulation or of spontaneous electrical activity (as in electromyography) for purposes of diagnosing a pathological condition (~ studies) — **elec·tro·di·ag·nos·ti·cal·ly** \-ti-k(ə-)lē\ *adv*

elec·tro·di·al·y·sis \i-ˌlek-trō-dī-ˈa-lə-səs\ *n, pl* **-y·ses** \-ˌsēz\ : dialysis accelerated by an electromotive force applied to electrodes adjacent to the membranes — **elec·tro·di·a·lyt·ic** \-ˌdī-ə-ˈli-tik\ *adj* — **elec·tro·di·a·lyze** \-ˈdī-ə-ˌlīz\ *vb* — **elec·tro·di·a·lyz·er** *n*

elec·tro·en·ceph·a·lo·gram \-in-ˈse-fə-lə-ˌgram\ *n* : the tracing of brain waves made by an electroencephalograph

elec·tro·en·ceph·a·lo·graph \-ˌgraf\ *n* : an apparatus for detecting and recording brain waves — called also *encephalograph* — **elec·tro·en·ceph·a·lo·graph·ic** \-ˌse-fə-lə-ˈgra-fik\ *adj* —

elec·tro·en·ceph·a·lo·graph·i·cal·ly \-fi-k(ə-)lē\ *adv* — **elec·tro·en·ceph·a·log·ra·phy** \-ˈlä-grə-fē\ *n*

elec·tro·en·ceph·a·log·ra·pher \-in-ˌse-fə-ˈlä-grə-fər\ *n* : a person who specializes in electroencephalography

elec·tro·gen·ic \-ˈje-nik\ *adj* : of or relating to the production of electrical activity in living tissue — **elec·tro·gen·e·sis** \i-ˌlek-trə-ˈje-nə-səs\ *n*

elec·tro·gram \i-ˈlek-trə-ˌgram\ *n* : a tracing of the electrical potentials of a tissue (as the brain or heart) made by means of electrodes placed directly in the tissue instead of on the surface of the body

elec·tro·graph·ic \i-ˌlek-trə-ˈgra-fik\ *adj* : relating to, involving, or produced by the use of electrodes implanted directly in living tissue (~ stimulation of the brain) — **elec·tro·graph·i·cal·ly** \-fi-k(ə-)lē\ *adv*

elec·tro·ky·mo·graph \-ˈkī-mə-ˌgraf\ *n* : an instrument for recording graphically the motion of the heart as seen in silhouette on a fluoroscopic screen — **elec·tro·ky·mog·ra·phy** \-kī-ˈmä-grə-fē\ *n*

elec·trol·o·gist \i-ˌlek-ˈträ-lə-jist\ *n* : a person who removes hair, warts, moles, and birthmarks by means of an electric current applied to the body with a needle-shaped electrode

elec·trol·y·sis \i-ˌlek-ˈträ-lə-səs\ *n, pl* **-y·ses** \-ˌsēz\ 1 a : the producing of chemical changes by passage of an electric current through an electrolyte b : subjection to this action 2 : the destruction of hair roots with an electric current

elec·tro·lyte \i-ˈlek-trə-ˌlīt\ *n* 1 : a nonmetallic electric conductor in which current is carried by the movement of ions 2 : a substance (as an acid or salt) that when dissolved in a suitable solvent (as water) or when fused becomes an ionic conductor

elec·tro·lyt·ic \i-ˌlek-trə-ˈli-tik\ *adj* : of or relating to electrolysis or an electrolyte; *also* : involving or produced by electrolysis — **elec·tro·lyt·i·cal·ly** \-ti-k(ə-)lē\ *adv*

elec·tro·mag·net·ic \-mag-ˈne-tik\ *adj* : of, relating to, or produced by electromagnetism

electromagnetic field *n* : a field (as around a working computer or a transmitting high voltage power line) that is made up of associated electric and magnetic components, that results from the motion of an electric charge, and that possesses a definite amount of electromagnetic energy (the purported effects of *electromagnetic fields* on human health)

electromagnetic radiation *n* : a series of electromagnetic waves

electromagnetic spectrum *n* : the entire range of wavelengths or frequencies of electromagnetic radiation extending from gamma rays to the longest radio waves and including visible light

electromagnetic wave *n* : one of the waves that are propagated by simultaneous periodic variations of electric and magnetic field intensity and that include radio waves, infrared, visible light, ultraviolet, X rays, and gamma rays

elec·tro·mag·ne·tism \i-ˌlek-trō-ˈmag-nə-ˌti-zəm\ *n* 1 : magnetism developed by a current of electricity 2 : physics dealing with the relations between electricity and magnetism

elec·tro·mo·tive force \i-ˌlek-trō-ˈmō-tiv-, -trə-\ *n* : something that moves or tends to move electricity : the amount of energy derived from an electrical source per unit quantity of electricity passing through the source (as a cell or generator)

elec·tro·myo·gram \i-ˌlek-trō-ˈmī-ə-ˌgram\ *n* : a tracing made with an electromyograph

elec·tro·myo·graph \-ˌgraf\ *n* : an instrument that converts the electrical activity associated with functioning skeletal muscle into a visual record or into sound and has been used to diagnose neuromuscular disorders and in biofeedback training — **elec·tro·myo·graph·ic** \-ˌmī-ə-ˈgra-fik\ *adj* — **elec·tro·myo·graph·i·cal·ly** \-fi-k(ə-)lē\ *adv* — **elec·tro·my·og·ra·phy** \-mī-ˈä-grə-fē\ *n*

elec·tron \i-ˈlek-ˌträn\ *n* : an elementary particle consisting of a charge of negative electricity equal to about 1.602×10^{-19} coulomb and having a mass when at rest of about 9.109534×10^{-28} gram or about $1/1836$ that of a proton

elec·tro·nar·co·sis \i-ˌlek-trō-när-ˈkō-səs\ *n*, *pl* **-co·ses** \-ˌsēz\ : unconsciousness induced by passing a weak electric current through the brain

elec·tron·ic \i-ˌlek-ˈträ-nik\ *adj* : of or relating to electrons or electronics — **elec·tron·i·cal·ly** \-ni-k(ə-)lē\ *adv*

elec·tron·ics \i-ˌlek-ˈträ-niks\ *n* 1 : the physics of electrons and electronic devices 2 : electronic devices or equipment

electron micrograph *n* : a micrograph made with an electron microscope

electron microscope *n* : an electron-optical instrument in which a beam of electrons is used to produce an enlarged image of a minute object on a fluorescent screen or photographic plate — **electron microscopist** *n* — **electron microscopy** *n*

electron transport *n* : the sequential transfer of electrons esp. by cytochromes in cellular respiration from an oxidizable substrate to molecular oxygen by a series of oxidation-reduction reactions

elec·tro·nys·tag·mog·ra·phy \i-ˌlek-trō-ˌnis-ˌtag-ˈmä-grə-fē\ *n*, *pl* **-phies** : the use of electrooculography to study

nystagmus — **elec·tro·nys·tag·mo·graph·ic** \-(ˌ)nis-ˌtag-mə-ˈgra-fik\ *adj*

elec·tro·oc·u·lo·gram \-ˈä-kyə-lə-ˌgram\ *n* : a record of the standing voltage between the front and back of the eye that is correlated with eyeball movement (as in REM sleep) and obtained by electrodes suitably placed on the skin near the eye

elec·tro·oc·u·log·ra·phy \-ˌä-kyə-ˈlä-grə-fē\ *n*, *pl* **-phies** : the preparation and study of electrooculograms — **elec·tro·oc·u·lo·graph·ic** \-lə-ˈgra-fik\ *adj*

elec·tro·phe·ro·gram \i-ˈtrə-ˈfir-ə-ˌgram, -ˈfer-\ *n* : ELECTROPHORETOGRAM

elec·tro·pho·re·sis \-trə-fə-ˈrē-səs\ *n*, *pl* **-re·ses** \-ˈsēz\ : the movement of suspended particles through a fluid or gel under the action of an electromotive force applied to electrodes in contact with the suspension — **elec·tro·pho·rese** \-ˈrēs, -ˈrēz\ *vb* — **elec·tro·pho·ret·ic** \-ˈre-tik\ *adj* — **elec·tro·pho·ret·i·cal·ly** \-ti-k(ə-)lē\ *adv*

elec·tro·pho·reto·gram \-fə-ˈre-tə-ˌgram\ *n* : a record that consists of the separated components of a mixture (as of proteins) produced by electrophoresis in a supporting medium

elec·tro·phren·ic \i-ˌlek-trə-ˈfre-nik\ *adj* : relating to or induced by electrical stimulation of the phrenic nerve (~ respiration) (~ respirator)

elec·tro·phys·i·ol·o·gy \i-ˌlek-trō-ˌfi-zē-ˈä-lə-jē\ *n*, *pl* **-gies** 1 : physiology that is concerned with the electrical aspects of physiological phenomena 2 : electrical phenomena associated with a physiological process (as the function of a body or bodily part) — **elec·tro·phys·i·o·log·i·cal** \-ə-ˈlä-ji-kəl\ *also* **elec·tro·phys·i·o·log·ic** \-jik\ *adj* — **elec·tro·phys·i·o·log·i·cal·ly** \-ji-k(ə-)lē\ *adv* — **elec·tro·phys·i·ol·o·gist** \-ˈä-lə-jist\ *n*

elec·tro·re·sec·tion \-rē-ˈsek-shən\ *n* : resection by electrosurgical means

elec·tro·ret·i·no·gram \-ˈret-ᵊn-ə-ˌgram\ *n* : a graphic record of electrical activity of the retina

elec·tro·ret·i·no·graph \-ˌgraf\ *n* : an instrument for recording electrical activity in the retina — **elec·tro·ret·i·no·graph·ic** \-ˌret-ᵊn-ə-ˈgra-fik\ *adj* — **elec·tro·ret·i·nog·ra·phy** \-ᵊn-ˈä-grə-fē\ *n*

elec·tro·shock \i-ˈlek-trō-ˌshäk\ *n* 1 : SHOCK 3 2 : ELECTROSHOCK THERAPY

electroshock therapy *n* : the treatment of mental disorder and esp. depression by the induction of unconsciousness and convulsions through the use of an electric current now usu. on an anesthetized patient — called also *electric shock, electric shock therapy, electric shock treatment, electroconvulsive therapy*

elec·tro·sleep \-ˌslēp\ *n* : profound relaxation or a state of unconsciousness induced by the passage of a very low voltage electric current through the brain

elec·tro·stat·ic \i-ˌlek-trə-ˈsta-tik\ *adj* : of or relating to stationary electric charges or to the study of the forces of attraction and repulsion acting between such charges

elec·tro·stim·u·la·tion \i-ˌlek-trō-ˌstim-yə-ˈlā-shən\ *n* : electroshock administered in nonconvulsive doses

elec·tro·sur·gery \-ˈsər-jə-rē\ *n, pl* -ger·ies : surgery by means of diathermy — **elec·tro·sur·gi·cal** \-ji-kəl\ *adj*

elec·tro·ther·a·py \-ˈther-ə-pē\ *n, pl* -pies : treatment of disease by means of electricity (as in diathermy)

elec·tro·tome \i-ˈlek-trə-ˌtōm\ *n* : an electric cutting instrument used in electrosurgery

elec·tro·ton·ic \i-ˌlek-trə-ˈtä-nik\ *adj* 1 : of, induced by, relating to, or constituting electrotonus (the ~ condition of a nerve) 2 : of, relating to, or being the spread of electrical activity through living tissue or cells in the absence of repeated action potentials — **elec·tro·ton·i·cal·ly** \-ni-k(ə-)lē\ *adv*

elec·trot·o·nus \i-ˌlek-ˈträt-ᵊn-əs\ *n* : the altered sensitivity of a nerve when a constant current of electricity passes through any part of it

elec·tu·ary \i-ˈlek-chə-ˌwer-ē\ *n, pl* -ar·ies : CONFECTION; *esp* : a medicated paste prepared with a sweet (as honey) and used in veterinary practice

el·e·doi·sin \e-lə-ˈdois-ᵊn\ *n* : a small protein $C_{54}H_{85}N_{13}O_{15}S$ from the salivary glands of several octopuses (genus *Eledone*) that is a powerful vasodilator and hypotensive agent

el·e·ment \ˈe-lə-mənt\ *n* 1 : any of more than 100 fundamental substances that consist of atoms of only one kind and that singly or in combination constitute all matter 2 : one of the basic constituent units (as a cell or fiber) of a tissue

CHEMICAL ELEMENTS

ELEMENT	SYMBOL	ATOMIC NUMBER	ATOMIC WEIGHT (C = 12)
actinium	Ac	89	227.0278
aluminum	Al	13	26.98154
americium	Am	95	
antimony	Sb	51	121.75
argon	Ar	18	39.948
arsenic	As	33	74.9216
astatine	At	85	
barium	Ba	56	137.33
berkelium	Bk	97	
beryllium	Be	4	9.01218
bismuth	Bi	83	208.9804
boron	B	5	10.81
bromine	Br	35	79.904
cadmium	Cd	48	112.41
calcium	Ca	20	40.08
californium	Cf	98	

ELEMENT	SYMBOL	ATOMIC NUMBER	ATOMIC WEIGHT (C = 12)
carbon	C	6	12.011
cerium	Ce	58	140.12
cesium	Cs	55	132.9054
chlorine	Cl	17	35.453
chromium	Cr	24	51.996
cobalt	Co	27	58.9332
copper	Cu	29	63.546
curium	Cm	96	
dysprosium	Dy	66	162.50
einsteinium	Es	99	
erbium	Er	68	167.26
europium	Eu	63	151.96
fermium	Fm	100	
fluorine	F	9	18.998403
francium	Fr	87	
gadolinium	Gd	64	157.25
gallium	Ga	31	69.72
germanium	Ge	32	72.59
gold	Au	79	196.9665
hafnium	Hf	72	178.49
helium	He	2	4.00260
holmium	Ho	67	164.9304
hydrogen	H	1	1.0079
indium	In	49	114.82
iodine	I	53	126.9045
iridium	Ir	77	192.22
iron	Fe	26	55.847
krypton	Kr	36	83.80
lanthanum	La	57	138.9055
lawrencium	Lr	103	
lead	Pb	82	207.2
lithium	Li	3	6.941
lutetium	Lu	71	174.967
magnesium	Mg	12	24.305
manganese	Mn	25	54.9380
mendelevium	Md	101	
mercury	Hg	80	200.59
molybdenum	Mo	42	95.94
neodymium	Nd	60	144.24
neon	Ne	10	20.179
neptunium	Np	93	237.0482
nickel	Ni	28	58.69
niobium	Nb	41	92.9064
nitrogen	N	7	14.0067
nobelium	No	102	
osmium	Os	76	190.2
oxygen	O	8	15.9994
palladium	Pd	46	106.42
phosphorus	P	15	30.97376
platinum	Pt	78	195.08
plutonium	Pu	94	
polonium	Po	84	
potassium	K	19	39.0983
praseodymium	Pr	59	140.9077
promethium	Pm	61	
protactinium	Pa	91	231.0359
radium	Ra	88	226.0254
radon	Rn	86	
rhenium	Re	75	186.207
rhodium	Rh	45	102.9055
rubidium	Rb	37	85.4678
ruthenium	Ru	44	101.07
samarium	Sm	62	150.36
scandium	Sc	21	44.9559
selenium	Se	34	78.96
silicon	Si	14	28.0855
silver	Ag	47	107.868

ELEMENT	SYMBOL	ATOMIC NUMBER	ATOMIC WEIGHT (C = 12)
sodium	Na	11	22.98977
strontium	Sr	38	87.62
sulfur	S	16	32.06
tantalum	Ta	73	180.9479
technetium	Tc	43	
tellurium	Te	52	127.60
terbium	Tb	65	158.9254
thallium	Tl	81	204.383
thorium	Th	90	232.0381
thulium	Tm	69	168.9342
tin	Sn	50	118.69
titanium	Ti	22	47.88
tungsten	W	74	183.85
unnilhexium	Unh	106	
unnilpentium	Unp	105	
unnilquadium	Unq	104	
uranium	U	92	238.0289
vanadium	V	23	50.9415
xenon	Xe	54	131.29
ytterbium	Yb	70	173.04
yttrium	Y	39	88.9059
zinc	Zn	30	65.38
zirconium	Zr	40	91.22

el·e·men·tal \ₑe-lə-'ment-ᵊl\ *adj* : of, relating to, or being an element; *specif* : existing as an uncombined chemical element

elementary body *n* : an infectious particle of any of several microorganisms; *esp* : a chlamydial cell of an extracellular infectious form that attaches to receptors on the membrane of the host cell and is taken up by endocytosis — compare RETICULATE BODY

elementary particle *n* : any of the subatomic units of matter and energy (as the electron, neutrino, proton, or photon) that do not appear to be made up of other smaller particles

el·e·phan·ti·a·sis \ₑe-lə-fən-'tī-ə-səs, -ₑfan-\ *n, pl* **-a·ses** \-ₑsēz\ : enlargement and thickening of tissues; *specif* : the enormous enlargement of a limb or the scrotum caused by obstruction of lymphatics by filarial worms of the genus *Wuchereria* (*W. bancrofti*) or a related genus (*Brugia malayi*)

el·e·vat·ed \'e-lə-ₑvā-təd\ *adj* : increased esp. abnormally (an ~ pulse rate)

el·e·va·tion \ₑe-lə-'vā-shən\ *n* 1 : a swelling esp. on the skin 2 : a usu. abnormal increase (as in degree or amount) (an ~ of temperature)

el·e·va·tor \'e-lə-ₑvā-tər\ *n* 1 : a dental instrument that is used for removing teeth or the roots of teeth which cannot be gripped with a forceps 2 : a surgical instrument for raising a depressed part (as a bone) or for separating contiguous parts

eleventh cranial nerve *n* : ACCESSORY NERVE

elim·i·nate \i-'li-mə-ₑnāt\ *vb* **-nat·ed;**

-**nat·ing** : to expel (as waste) from the living body

elim·i·na·tion \i-ₑli-mə-'nā-shən\ *n* 1 : the act of discharging or excreting waste products or foreign substances from the body 2 **eliminations** *pl* : bodily discharges including urine, feces, and vomit

ELISA \ē-'lī-sə, -zə\ *n* : ENZYME-LINKED IMMUNOSORBENT ASSAY

elix·ir \i-'lik-sər\ *n* : a sweetened liquid usu. containing alcohol that is used in medication either for its medicinal ingredients or as a flavoring

Eliz·a·be·than collar \i-ₑli-zə-'bē-thən-\ *n* : a broad circle of stiff cardboard or other material placed about the neck of a cat or dog to prevent it from licking or biting an injured part

el·lip·to·cyte \i-'lip-tə-ₑsīt\ *n* : an elliptical red blood cell

el·lip·to·cy·to·sis \i-ₑlip-tə-ₑsī-'tō-səs\ *n, pl* **-to·ses** \-ₑsēz\ : a human hereditary trait manifested by the presence in the blood of red blood cells which are oval in shape with rounded ends — compare SICKLE-CELL TRAIT

el·u·ant *or* **el·u·ent** \'el-yə-wənt\ *n* : a solvent used in eluting

el·u·ate \'el-yə-wət, -ₑwāt\ *n* : the washings obtained by eluting

elute \ē-'lüt\ *vb* **elut·ed; elut·ing** : to wash out or extract; *specif* : to remove (adsorbed material) from an adsorbent by means of a solvent — **elu·tion** \-'lü-shən\ *n*

ema·ci·ate \i-'mā-shē-ₑāt\ *vb* **-at·ed; -at·ing** 1 : to cause to lose flesh so as to become very thin 2 : to waste away physically — **ema·ci·a·tion** \-ₑmā-shē-'ā-shən, -sē-\ *n*

emas·cu·late \i-'mas-kyə-ₑlāt\ *vb* **-lat·ed; -lat·ing** : to deprive of virility or procreative power : CASTRATE — **emas·cu·la·tion** \-ₑmas-kyə-'lā-shən\ *n*

emas·cu·la·tor \i-'mas-kyə-ₑlā-tər\ *n* : an instrument often with a broad surface and a cutting edge used in castrating livestock

em·balm \im-'bäm, -'bälm\ *vb* : to treat (a dead body) so as to protect from decay — **em·balm·er** *n*

em·bar·rass \im-'bar-əs\ *vb* : to impair the activity of (a bodily function) or the function of (a bodily part)

em·bar·rass·ment \im-'bar-əs-mənt\ *n* : difficulty in functioning as a result of a disease (cardiac ~) (respiratory ~)

em·bed \im-'bed\ *vb* **em·bed·ded; em·bed·ding** : to prepare (a microscopy specimen) for sectioning by infiltrating with and enclosing in a supporting substance — **em·bed·ment** \-'bed-mənt\ *n*

embol- *comb form* : embolus (*embol*ectomy)

em·bo·lec·to·my \ₑem-bə-'lek-tə-mē\ *n, pl* **-mies** : surgical removal of an embolus

em·bol·ic \em-'bä-lik, im-\ *adj* : of or relating to an embolus or embolism

em·bo·lism \'em-bə-ˌli-zəm\ n 1 : the sudden obstruction of a blood vessel by an embolus 2 : EMBOLUS

em·bo·li·za·tion \ˌem-bə-lə-'zā-shən\ n : the process by which or state in which a blood vessel or organ is obstructed by the lodgment of a material mass (as an embolus) ⟨pulmonary ∼⟩ ⟨∼ of a thrombus⟩; also : an operation in which pellets are introduced into the circulatory system in order to induce embolization in specific abnormal blood vessels

em·bo·lize \'em-bə-ˌliz\ vb **-lized; -liz·ing** 1 of an embolus : to lodge in and obstruct (as a blood vessel or organ) 2 : to break up into emboli or become an embolus

em·bo·lus \'em-bə-ləs\ n, pl **-li** \-ˌli\ : an abnormal particle (as an air bubble) circulating in the blood — compare THROMBUS

em·bra·sure \im-'brā-zhər\ n : the sloped valley between adjacent teeth

em·bro·ca·tion \ˌem-brə-'kā-shən\ n : LINIMENT

embry- or **embryo-** comb form : embryo ⟨embryoma⟩ ⟨embryogenesis⟩

em·bryo \'em-brē-ˌō\ n, pl **em·bry·os** : an animal in the early stages of growth and differentiation that are characterized by cleavage, the laying down of fundamental tissues, and the formation of primitive organs and organ systems; esp : the developing human individual from the time of implantation to the end of the eighth week after conception — compare FETUS

em·bryo·gen·e·sis \ˌem-brē-ō-'je-nə-səs\ n, pl **-e·ses** \-ˌsēz\ : the formation and development of the embryo — **em·bryo·ge·net·ic** \-jə-'ne-tik\ adj

em·bry·og·e·ny \ˌem-brē-'ä-jə-nē\ n, pl **-nies** : EMBRYOGENESIS — **em·bryo·gen·ic** \-brē-ō-'je-nik\ adj

em·bry·ol·o·gist \ˌem-brē-'ä-lə-jist\ n : a specialist in embryology

em·bry·ol·o·gy \-jē\ n, pl **-gies** 1 : a branch of biology dealing with embryos and their development 2 : the features and phenomena exhibited in the formation and development of an embryo — **em·bry·o·log·i·cal** \-brē-ə-'lä-ji-kəl\ also **em·bry·o·log·ic** \-jik\ adj — **em·bry·o·log·i·cal·ly** \-ji-k(ə-)lē\ adv

em·bry·o·ma \ˌem-brē-'ō-mə\ n, pl **-mas** or **-ma·ta** \-mə-tə\ : a tumor derived from embryonic structures : TERATOMA

embryon- or **embryoni-** comb form : embryo ⟨embryonic⟩

em·bry·o·nal \em-'brī-ən-ᵊl\ adj : EMBRYONIC 1

embryonal carcinoma n : a highly malignant cancer of the testis

em·bry·o·nate \'em-brē-ə-ˌnāt\ vb **-nat·ed; -nat·ing** of an egg or zygote : to produce or differentiate into an embryo

em·bry·o·nat·ed adj : having an embryo

em·bry·on·ic \ˌem-brē-'ä-nik\ adj 1 : of or relating to an embryo 2 : being in an early stage of development : INCIPIENT, RUDIMENTARY — **em·bry·on·i·cal·ly** \-ni-k(ə-)lē\ adv

embryonic disk or **embryonic disc** n 1 a : BLASTODISC b : BLASTODERM 2 : the part of the inner cell mass of a blastocyst from which the embryo of a placental mammal develops

embryonic membrane n : a structure (as the amnion) that derives from the fertilized ovum but does not form a part of the embryo

em·bry·op·a·thy \ˌem-brē-'ä-pə-thē\ n, pl **-thies** : a developmental abnormality of an embryo or fetus esp. when caused by a disease (as German measles or mumps) in the mother

em·bry·o·tox·i·c·i·ty \ˌem-brē-ō-ˌtäk-'si-sə-tē\ n, pl **-ties** : the state of being toxic to embryos — **em·bry·o·tox·ic** \-'täk-sik\ adj

embryo transfer n : a procedure used esp. in animal breeding in which an embryo from a superovulated female is removed and reimplanted in the uterus of another female — called also embryo transplant

emer·gence \i-'mər-jəns\ n : a recovering of consciousness (as from anesthesia)

emer·gen·cy \i-'mər-jən-sē\ n, pl **-cies** : an unforeseen combination of circumstances or the resulting state that calls for immediate action: as a : a sudden bodily alteration (as a ruptured appendix) such as is likely to require immediate medical attention b : a usu. distressing event or condition that can often be anticipated or prepared for but seldom exactly foreseen

emergency medical technician n : EMT

emergency room n : a hospital room or area staffed and equipped for the reception and treatment of persons with conditions (as illness or trauma) requiring immediate medical care

emer·gent \i-'mər-jənt\ adj : calling for prompt or urgent action

eme·sis \'e-mə-səs, i-'mē-\ n, pl **eme·ses** \-ˌsēz\ : VOMITING

¹**emet·ic** \i-'me-tik\ n : an agent that induces vomiting

²**emetic** adj : having the capacity to induce vomiting

em·e·tine \'e-mə-ˌtēn\ n : an amorphous alkaloid $C_{29}H_{40}N_2O_4$ extracted from ipecac root and used as an emetic and expectorant

EMF abbr 1 electromotive force 2 electromagnetic field

EMG abbr electromyogram; electromyograph; electromyography

-emia \'ē-mē-ə\ or **-hemia** \'hē-\ n comb form 1 : condition of having (such) blood ⟨leukemia⟩ ⟨septicemia⟩ 2 : condition of having (a specified thing) in the blood ⟨cholemia⟩ ⟨uremia⟩

em·i·nence \'e-mə-nəns\ n : a protuberance or projection on a bodily part and esp. a bone

emissary vein n : any of the veins that pass through apertures in the skull and connect the venous sinuses of the dura mater with veins external to the skull

emis·sion \ē-ˈmi-shən\ n 1 : a discharge of fluid from a living body; esp : EJACULATE — see NOCTURNAL EMISSION 2 : substances and esp. pollutants discharged into the air (as by a smokestack or an automobile gasoline engine)

em·men·a·gogue \ə-ˈme-nə-ˌgäg, e-\ n : an agent that promotes the menstrual discharge

em·me·tro·pia \ˌe-mə-ˈtrō-pē-ə\ n : the normal refractive condition of the eye in which with accommodation relaxed parallel rays of light are all brought accurately to a focus upon the retina — compare ASTIGMATISM, MYOPIA — **em·me·trop·ic** \-ˈträ-pik, -ˈtrō-\ adj

¹**emol·lient** \i-ˈmäl-yənt\ adj : making soft or supple; also : soothing esp. to the skin or mucous membrane

²**emollient** n : an emollient agent (an ~ for the hands)

emo·tion \i-ˈmō-shən\ n : a psychic and physical reaction (as anger or fear) subjectively experienced as strong feeling and physiologically involving changes that prepare the body for immediate vigorous action — **emo·tion·al** \-shə-nəl\ adj — **emo·tion·al·i·ty** \-ˌmō-shə-ˈna-lə-tē\ n — **emo·tion·al·ly** adv

em·pa·thy \ˈem-pə-thē\ n, pl -thies : the action of understanding, being aware of, being sensitive to, and vicariously experiencing the feelings, thoughts, and experience of another of either the past or present without having the feelings, thoughts, and experience fully communicated in an objectively explicit manner; also : the capacity for empathy — **em·path·ic** \em-ˈpa-thik, im-\ adj — **em·path·i·cal·ly** adv — **em·pa·thize** \ˈem-pə-ˌthīz\ vb

em·phy·se·ma \ˌem-fə-ˈzē-mə, -ˈsē-\ n : a condition characterized by air-filled expansions like blisters in interstitial or subcutaneous tissues; specif : a local or generalized condition of the lung marked by distension, progressive loss of elasticity, and eventual rupture of the alveoli and accompanied by labored breathing, a husky cough, and frequently by impairment of heart action — **em·phy·se·ma·tous** \-ˈze-mə-təs, -ˈse-, -ˈzē-, -ˈsē-\ adj — **em·phy·se·mic** \-ˈzē-mik, -ˈsē-\ adj

em·pir·ic \im-ˈpir-ik, em-\ n : EMPIRICIST

em·pir·i·cal \-i-kəl\ or **em·pir·ic** \ik-\ adj 1 : originating in or based on observation or experiment 2 : capable of being confirmed, verified, or disproved by observation or experiment (~ statements or laws) — **em·pir·i·cal·ly** \-i-k(ə-)lē\ adv

empirical formula n : a chemical formula showing the simplest ratio of elements in a compound rather than the total number of atoms in the molecule (CH_2O is the empirical formula for glucose)

em·pir·i·cism \im-ˈpir-ə-ˌsi-zəm, em-\ n 1 a : a former school of medical practice founded on experience without the aid of science or theory b : QUACKERY 2 : the practice of relying on observation and experiment esp. in the natural sciences

em·pir·i·cist \-sist\ n : one that advocates or practices empiricism

em·py·ema \ˌem-ˌpī-ˈē-mə\ n, pl -ema·ta \-mə-tə\ or -emas : the presence of pus in a bodily cavity (as the pleural cavity) — called also pyothorax — **em·py·emic** \-mik\ adj

EMT \ˌē-(ˌ)em-ˈtē\ n : a specially trained medical technician licensed to provide basic emergency services (as cardiopulmonary resuscitation) before and during transportation to a hospital — called also emergency medical technician; compare PARAMEDIC 2

emul·si·fi·er \i-ˈməl-sə-ˌfī-ər\ n : one that emulsifies; esp : a surface-active agent (as a soap) promoting the formation and stabilization of an emulsion

emul·si·fy \-ˌfī\ vb **-fied; -fy·ing** : to disperse (as an oil) in an emulsion — **emul·si·fi·ca·tion** \-ˌməl-sə-fə-ˈkā-shən\ n

emul·sion \i-ˈməl-shən\ n 1 a : a system (as fat in milk) consisting of a liquid dispersed with or without an emulsifier in an immiscible liquid usu. in droplets of larger than colloidal size b : the state of such a system 2 : SUSPENSION 2

enal·a·pril \e-ˈna-lə-ˌpril\ n : an antihypertensive drug $C_{20}H_{28}N_2O_5$ that is an ACE inhibitor administered orally in the form of its maleate — see VASOTEC

enal·a·pril·at \e-ˈna-lə-ˌpril-ˌat\ n : the metabolically active form $C_{18}H_{24}N_2O_5 \cdot 2H_2O$ of enalapril administered intravenously

enam·el \in-ˈa-məl\ n : the hard calcareous substance that forms a thin layer partly covering the teeth and consists of minute prisms secreted by ameloblasts, arranged at right angles to the surface, and bound together by a cement substance — compare CEMENTUM, DENTIN

enamel organ n : an ectodermal ingrowth from the dental lamina that forms a cap with two walls separated by a reticulum of stellate cells, encloses the anterior part of the developing dental papilla and the cells of the inner enamel layer adjacent to the

papilla, and differentiates into columnar ameloblasts which lay down the
enamel rods of the tooth

enamel rod n : one of the elongated
prismatic bodies making up the enamel of a tooth — called also *enamel
prism*

enanthate — see TESTOSTERONE ENAN-
THATE

en·an·them \i-ˈnan-thəm\ *or* **en·an·the-
ma** \in-ˌan-ˈthē-mə\ n, pl **-thems** *or*
-the·ma·ta \-mə-tə\ : an eruption on a
mucous surface

en·an·tio·mer \i-ˈnan-tē-ə-mər\ n : either of a pair of chemical compounds
whose molecular structures have a
mirror-image relationship to each
other — **en·an·tio·mer·ic** \-ˌnan-tē-ə-
ˈmer-ik\ adj — **en·an·tio·mer·i·cal·ly**
\-i-k(ə-)lē\ adv

en·an·tio·morph \i-ˈnan-tē-ə-ˌmórf\ n
: ENANTIOMER

en·ar·thro·sis \ˌe-när-ˈthrō-səs\ n, pl
-thro·ses \-ˌsēz\ : BALL-AND-SOCKET
JOINT

en·cap·su·late \in-ˈkap-sə-ˌlāt\ vb **-lat-
ed; -lat·ing** : to encase or become en-
cased in or as if in a capsule — **en·
cap·su·la·tion** \-ˌkap-sə-ˈlā-shən\ n

en·cap·su·lat·ed adj : surrounded by a
gelatinous or membranous envelope

en·ceinte \äⁿ-ˈsant\ adj : PREGNANT

encephal- *or* **encephalo-** comb form 1
: brain (*encephalitis*) (*encephalocele*)
2 : of, relating to, or affecting the
brain and (*encephalo*myelitis)

-encephalus pl of -ENCEPHALUS

en·ceph·a·li·tis \in-ˌse-fə-ˈlī-təs\ n, pl
-lit·i·des \-ˈli-tə-ˌdēz\ : inflammation
of the brain — **en·ceph·a·lit·ic** \-ˈli-tik\
adj

encephalitis le·thar·gi·ca \-li-ˈthär-ji-kə,
-le-\ n : epidemic virus encephalitis in
which somnolence is marked

en·ceph·a·lit·o·gen \in-ˌse-fə-ˈli-tə-jən,
-ˌjen\ n : an encephalitogenic agent
(as a virus)

en·ceph·a·lit·o·gen·ic \in-ˌse-fə-ˌli-tə-
ˈje-nik\ adj : tending to cause encephalitis (an ∼ strain of a virus)

en·ceph·a·lo·cele \in-ˈse-fə-lō-ˌsēl\ n
: hernia of the brain that is either congenital or due to trauma

en·ceph·a·lo·gram \in-ˈse-fə-lō-ˌgram\ n
: an X-ray picture of the brain made
by encephalography

en·ceph·a·lo·graph \-ˌgraf\ n 1 : EN-
CEPHALOGRAM 2 : ELECTROENCEPHA-
LOGRAPH

en·ceph·a·log·ra·phy \in-ˌse-fə-ˈlä-grə-
fē\ n, pl **-phies** : roentgenography of
the brain after the cerebrospinal fluid
has been replaced by a gas (as air) —
en·ceph·a·lo·graph·ic \-lə-ˈgra-fik\ adj
— **en·ceph·a·lo·graph·i·cal·ly** \-fi-k(ə)-
lē\ adv

en·ceph·a·lo·ma·la·cia \in-ˌse-fə-lō-mə-
ˈlā-shē-ə, -shə\ n : softening of the
brain due to degenerative changes in
nervous tissue

en·ceph·a·lo·my·eli·tis \in-ˌse-fə-lō-ˌmī-

ə-ˈlī-təs\ n, pl **-elit·i·des** \-ə-ˈli-tə-ˌdēz\
: concurrent inflammation of the
brain and spinal cord; specif : EQUINE
ENCEPHALOMYELITIS — **en·ceph·a·lo-
my·elit·ic** \-ə-ˈli-tik\ adj

en·ceph·a·lo·my·elop·a·thy \-ˌmī-ə-ˈlä-
pə-thē\ n, pl **-thies** : any disease that
affects the brain and spinal cord

en·ceph·a·lo·myo·car·di·tis \-ˌmī-ə-kär-
ˈdī-təs\ n : an acute febrile virus disease characterized by degeneration
and inflammation of skeletal and cardiac muscle and lesions of the central
nervous system

en·ceph·a·lop·a·thy \in-ˌse-fə-ˈlä-pə-
thē\ n, pl **-thies** : a disease of the
brain; esp : one involving alterations
of brain structure — **en·ceph·a·lo-
path·ic** \-ˈlə-pa-thik\ adj

-en·ceph·a·lus \in-ˈse-fə-ləs\ n comb
form, pl **-en·ceph·a·li** \-ˌlī, -ˌlē\ 1 : fetus having (such) a brain (*iniencephal-
alus*) 2 : condition of having (such) a
brain (hydr*encephalus*)

-en·ceph·a·ly \in-ˈse-fə-lē\ n comb
form, pl **-en·ceph·a·lies** \in-ˈse-fə-lēz\
: condition of having (such) a brain
(micr*encephaly*)

en·chon·dral \(ˌ)en-ˈkän-drəl, (ˌ)eŋ-\
adj : ENDOCHONDRAL

en·chon·dro·ma \ˌen-ˌkän-ˈdrō-mə,
ˌeŋ-\ n, pl **-mas** *or* **-ma·ta** \-mə-tə\ : a
tumor consisting of cartilaginous tissue; esp : one arising where cartilage
does not normally exist

en·code \in-ˈkōd, en-\ vb : to specify
the genetic code for

en·co·pre·sis \ˌen-skä-ˈprē-səs, -kə-\ n,
pl **-re·ses** \-ˌsēz\ : involuntary defecation of psychic origin

encounter group n : a usu. unstructured
group that seeks to develop the capacity of the individual to express
feelings and to form emotional ties by
unrestrained confrontation of individuals — compare T-GROUP

en·crus·ta·tion \in-ˌkrəs-ˈtā-shən,
ˌen-\ var of INCRUSTATION

en·cyst \in-ˈsist, en-\ vb : to enclose in
or become enclosed in a cyst (protozoans ∼*ing* in order to resist desicca-
tion) — **en·cyst·ment** n

end- *or* **endo-** comb form 1 : within : inside (*end*aural) (*endo*skeleton) —
compare ECT-, EXO- 1 2 : taking in (*en·
do*cytosis)

end·ar·ter·ec·to·my \ˌen-ˌdär-tə-ˈrek-
tə-mē\ n, pl **-mies** : surgical removal
of the inner layer of an artery when
thickened and atheromatous or occluded (as by intimal plaques)

end·ar·te·ri·tis \ˌen-ˌdär-tə-ˈrī-təs\ n
: inflammation of the intima of one or
more arteries

endarteritis oblit·er·ans \-ə-ˈbli-tə-
ˌranz, -rənz\ n : endarteritis in which
the intimal tissue plugs the lumen of
an affected artery — called also *obliterating endarteritis*

end artery n : a terminal artery (as a

coronary artery) supplying all or most of the blood to a body part

end·au·ral \(ˌ)en-'dȯr-əl\ *adj* : performed or applied within the ear (~ surgery)

end·brain \'end-ˌbrān\ *n* : TELENCEPHALON

end brush *n* : END PLATE

end bud *n* : TAIL BUD

end bulb *n* : a bulbous termination of a sensory nerve fiber (as in the skin) — compare KRAUSE'S CORPUSCLE

end·di·a·stol·ic \ˌen-ˌdī-ə-'stä-lik\ *adj* : relating to or occurring in the moment immediately preceding contraction of the heart (~ pressure)

¹**en·dem·ic** \en-'de-mik, in-\ *adj* : restricted or peculiar to a locality or region (~ diseases) — compare EPIDEMIC 1, SPORADIC — **en·dem·i·cal·ly** \-mi-k(ə)lē\ *adv*

²**endemic** *n* 1 : an endemic disease or an instance of its occurrence 2 : an endemic organism

en·de·mic·i·ty \ˌen-ˌde-'mi-sə-tē, -də-\ *n, pl* **-ties** : the quality or state of being endemic

endemic typhus *n* : MURINE TYPHUS

en·de·mism \'en-də-ˌmi-zəm\ *n* : ENDEMICITY

end foot *n, pl* **end feet** : BOUTON

endo- — see END-

en·do·ab·dom·i·nal \ˌen-dō-ab-'dä-mən-əl\ *adj* : relating to or occurring in the interior of the abdomen

en·do·an·eu·rys·mor·rha·phy \ˌen-dō-ˌan-yə-ˌriz-'mȯr-ə-fē\ *n, pl* **-phies** : a surgical treatment of aneurysm that involves opening its sac and collapsing, folding, and suturing its walls

en·do·bron·chi·al \ˌen-dō-'brän-kē-əl\ *adj* : located within a bronchus (~ tuberculosis) — **en·do·bron·chi·al·ly** *adv*

en·do·car·di·al \-'kär-dē-əl\ *adj* 1 : situated within the heart 2 : of or relating to the endocardium (~ biopsy)

endocardial fibroelastosis *n* : a condition usu. associated with congestive heart failure and enlargement of the heart that is characterized by conversion of the endocardium to fibroelastic tissue

en·do·car·di·tis \-ˌkär-'dī-təs\ *n* : inflammation of the lining of the heart and its valves

en·do·car·di·um \-'kär-dē-əm\ *n, pl* **-dia** \-dē-ə\ : a thin serous membrane lining the cavities of the heart

en·do·cer·vi·cal \ˌen-dō-'sər-vi-kəl\ *adj* : of, relating to, or affecting the endocervix

en·do·cer·vi·ci·tis \-ˌsər-və-'sī-təs\ *n* : inflammation of the lining of the uterine cervix

en·do·cer·vix \-'sər-viks\ *n, pl* **-vi·ces** \-və-ˌsēz\ : the epithelial and glandular lining of the uterine cervix

en·do·chon·dral \ˌen-də-'kän-drəl\ *adj* : relating to, formed by, or being ossification that takes place from centers arising in cartilage and involves deposition of lime salts in the carti-

lage matrix followed by secondary absorption and replacement by true bony tissue

¹**en·do·crine** \'en-də-krən, -ˌkrīn, -ˌkrēn\ *adj* 1 : secreting internally; *specif* : producing secretions that are distributed in the body by way of the bloodstream (an ~ system) 2 : of, relating to, affecting, or resembling an endocrine gland or secretion

²**endocrine** *n* 1 : HORMONE 2 : ENDOCRINE GLAND

endocrine gland *n* : a gland (as the thyroid or the pituitary) that produces an endocrine secretion — called also *ductless gland, gland of internal secretion*

endocrine system *n* : the glands and parts of glands that produce endocrine secretions, help to integrate and control bodily metabolic activity, and include esp. the pituitary, thyroid, parathyroids, adrenals, islets of Langerhans, ovaries, and testes

en·do·cri·no·log·ic \ˌen-də-ˌkrin-əl-'ä-jik, -ˌkrīn-, -ˌkrēn-\ *or* **en·do·cri·no·log·i·cal** \-ji-kəl\ *adj* : involving or relating to the endocrine glands or secretions or to endocrinology

en·do·cri·nol·o·gy \ˌen-də-kri-'nä-lə-jē, -ˌkrī-\ *n, pl* **-gies** : a science dealing with the endocrine glands — **en·do·cri·nol·o·gist** \-jist\ *n*

en·do·cri·nop·a·thy \-krə-'nä-pə-thē, -ˌkrī-, -ˌkrē-\ *n, pl* **-thies** : a disease marked by dysfunction of an endocrine gland — **en·do·crin·o·path·ic** \-ˌkri-nə-'pa-thik, -ˌkrī-, -ˌkrē-\ *adj*

en·do·cyt·ic \-'si-tik\ *adj* : of or relating to endocytosis : ENDOCYTOTIC (~ vesicles)

en·do·cy·to·sis \-sī-'tō-səs\ *n, pl* **-to·ses** \-ˌsēz\ : incorporation of substances into a cell by phagocytosis or pinocytosis — **en·do·cy·tose** \-'sī-ˌtōs, -ˌtōz\ *vb* — **en·do·cy·tot·ic** \-sī-'tä-tik\ *adj*

en·do·derm \'en-də-ˌdərm\ *n* : the innermost of the germ layers of an embryo that is the source of the epithelium of the digestive tract and its derivatives; *also* : a tissue that is derived from this germ layer — **en·do·der·mal** \ˌen-də-'dər-məl\ *adj*

end·odon·tia \ˌen-də-'dän-chē-ə, -chə\ *n* : ENDODONTICS

end·odon·tics \-'dän-tiks\ *n* : a branch of dentistry concerned with diseases of the pulp — **end·odon·tic** \-tik\ *adj* — **end·odon·ti·cal·ly** \-ti-k(ə-)lē\ *adv*

end·odon·tist \-tist\ *n* : a specialist in endodontics

en·do·en·zyme \ˌen-dō-'en-ˌzīm\ *n* : an enzyme that functions inside the cell — compare EXOENZYME

en·dog·e·nous \en-'dä-jə-nəs\ *also* **en·do·gen·ic** \ˌen-də-'je-nik\ *adj* 1 : caused by factors within the body or mind or arising from internal structural or functional causes (~ malnutrition) (~ psychic depression) 2 : relating to or produced by metabolic synthesis in the body ⟨ ∼ opioids⟩ — compare EXOGENOUS — **en·dog·e·nous·ly** adv

en·do·lymph \'en-də-ˌlimf\ n : the watery fluid in the membranous labyrinth of the ear — **en·do·lym·phat·ic** \ˌen-də-lim-'fa-tik\ adj

en·do·me·ninx \ˌen-də-'mē-niks, -'me-\ n, pl **-nin·ges** \-mə-'nin-(ˌ)jēz\ : the layer of embryonic mesoderm from which the arachnoid coat and pia mater of the brain develop

en·do·me·tri·al \ˌen-də-'mē-trē-əl\ adj : of, belonging to, or consisting of endometrium

en·do·me·tri·o·ma \-ˌmē-trē-'ō-mə\ n, pl **-mas** or **-ma·ta** \-mə-tə\ **1** : a tumor containing endometrial tissue **2** : ENDOMETRIOSIS — used chiefly of isolated foci of endometrium outside the uterus

en·do·me·tri·o·sis \ˌen-dō-ˌmē-trē-'ō-səs\ n, pl **-oses** \-ˌsēz\ : the presence and growth of functioning endometrial tissue in places other than the uterus that often results in severe pain and infertility — see ADENOMYOSIS

en·do·me·tri·tis \-mə-'trī-təs\ n : inflammation of the endometrium

en·do·me·tri·um \-'mē-trē-əm\ n, pl **-tria** \-trē-ə\ : the mucous membrane lining the uterus

en·do·morph \'en-də-ˌmȯrf\ n : an endomorphic individual

en·do·mor·phic \ˌen-də-'mȯr-fik\ adj **1** : of or relating to the component in W. H. Sheldon's classification of body types that measures the degree to which the digestive viscera are massive and the body build rounded and soft — compare ECTOMORPHIC 1, MESOMORPHIC 2 **2** : having a heavy rounded body build often with a marked tendency to become fat — **en·do·mor·phy** \'en-də-ˌmȯr-fē\ n

en·do·myo·car·di·al \ˌen-dō-ˌmī-ə-'kär-dē-əl\ adj : of, relating to, or affecting the endocardium and the myocardium ⟨∼ fibrosis⟩ ⟨∼ biopsy⟩ — **en·do·myo·car·di·um** \-dē-əm\ n

en·do·my·si·um \ˌen-də-'mi-zē-əm, -zhē-əm, -zhəm\ n, pl **-sia** \-zē-ə, -zhē-ə, -zhə\ : the delicate connective tissue surrounding the individual muscular fibers — compare EPIMYSIUM

en·do·neu·ri·um \ˌen-dō-'nur-ē-əm, -'nyur-\ n, pl **-ria** \-ē-ə\ : the delicate connective tissue network holding together the individual fibers of a nerve trunk — **en·do·neu·ri·al** \-ē-əl\ adj

en·do·nu·cle·ase \-'nü-klē-ˌās, -'nyü-, -ˌāz\ n : an enzyme that breaks down a nucleotide chain into two or more shorter chains by breaking it at points not adjacent to the ends — see RESTRICTION ENZYME; compare EXONUCLEASE

en·do·nu·cleo·lyt·ic \-ˌnü-klē-ō-'li-tik, -ˌnyü-\ adj : breaking a nucleotide chain into two parts at an internal point ⟨∼ nicks⟩

en·do·par·a·site \-'par-ə-ˌsīt\ n : a parasite that lives in the internal organs or tissues of its host — compare ECTOPARASITE — **en·do·par·a·sit·ic** \-ˌpar-ə-'si-tik\ adj — **en·do·par·a·sit·ism** \-ˌsi-ˌti-zəm, -sə-\ n

en·do·pep·ti·dase \-'pep-tə-ˌdās, -ˌdāz\ n : any of a group of enzymes that hydrolyze peptide bonds within the long chains of protein molecules : PROTEASE — compare EXOPEPTIDASE

en·do·per·ox·ide \-pə-'räk-ˌsīd\ n : any of various biosynthetic intermediates in the formation of prostaglandins

en·do·phle·bi·tis \ˌen-dō-fli-'bī-təs\ n, pl **-bi·tis·es** or **-bit·i·des** \-'bi-tə-ˌdēz\ : inflammation of the intima of a vein

en·doph·thal·mi·tis \ˌen-ˌdäf-thal-'mī-təs\ n : inflammation that affects the interior of the eyeball

en·do·phyt·ic \ˌen-dō-'fi-tik\ adj : tending to grow inward into tissues in fingerlike projections from a superficial site of origin — used of tumors; compare EXOPHYTIC

en·do·plasm \'en-də-ˌpla-zəm\ n : the inner relatively fluid part of the cytoplasm — compare ECTOPLASM — **en·do·plas·mic** \ˌen-də-'plaz-mik\ adj

endoplasmic reticulum n : a system of mutually connected vesicular and lamellar cytoplasmic membranes that functions esp. in the transport of materials within the cell and that is studded with ribosomes in some places

en·do·pros·the·sis \ˌen-dō-präs-'thē-səs\ n, pl **-the·ses** \-ˌsēz\ : an artificial device to replace a missing bodily part that is placed inside the body

end organ n : a structure forming the peripheral end of a path of nerve conduction and consisting of an effector or a receptor with its associated nerve terminations

en·dor·phin \en-'dȯr-fən\ n : any of a group of proteins with potent analgesic properties that occur naturally in the brain — see BETA-ENDORPHIN; compare ENKEPHALIN

β-endorphin var of BETA-ENDORPHIN

en·do·scope \'en-də-ˌskōp\ n : an instrument for visualizing the interior of a hollow organ (as the rectum or urethra) — **en·dos·co·py** \en-'däs-kə-pē\ n

en·do·scop·ic \ˌen-də-'skä-pik\ adj : of, relating to, or performed by means of an endoscope or endoscopy — **en·do·scop·i·cal·ly** \-pi-k(ə-)lē\ adv

en·dos·co·pist \en-'däs-kə-pist\ n : a person trained in the use of the endoscope

en·do·skel·e·ton \ˌen-dō-'skel-ət-ᵊn\ n : an internal skeleton or supporting framework in an animal — **en·do·skel·e·tal** \-ət-ᵊl\ adj

en·do·spore \-ˌspȯr\ n : an asexual spore developed within the cell esp. in bacteria

end·os·te·al \en-ˈdäs-tē-əl\ *adj* **1** : of or relating to the endosteum **2** : located within bone or cartilage — **end·os·te·al·ly** *adv*

end·os·te·um \en-ˈdäs-tē-əm\ *n, pl* **-tea** \-ə\ : the layer of vascular connective tissue lining the medullary cavities of bone

endotheli- *or* **endothelio-** *comb form* : endothelium (*endothelioma*)

en·do·the·li·al \ˌen-dō-ˈthē-lē-əl\ *adj* : of, relating to, or produced from endothelium

en·do·the·li·o·ma \-ˌthē-lē-ē-ō-mə\ *n, pl* **-omas** *or* **-o·ma·ta** \-ˈmə-tə\ : a tumor developing from endothelial tissue

en·do·the·li·um \ˌen-də-ˈthē-lē-əm\ *n, pl* **-lia** \-ə\ : an epithelium of mesoblastic origin composed of a single layer of thin flattened cells that lines internal body cavities (as the serous cavities or the interior of the heart)

en·do·tox·emia \ˌen-dō-tӓk-ˈsē-mē-ə\ *n* : the presence of endotoxins in the blood

en·do·tox·in \ˌen-dō-ˈtäk-sən\ *n* : a toxin of internal origin; *specif* : a poisonous substance present in bacteria but separable from the cell body only on its disintegration — compare EXOTOXIN — **en·do·tox·ic** \-sik\ *adj*

en·do·tra·che·al \-ˈtrā-kē-əl\ *adj* **1** : placed within the trachea (an ~ tube) **2** : applied or effected through the trachea

end plate *n* : a complex terminal arborization of a motor nerve fiber — called also *end brush*

en·e·ma \ˈe-nə-mə\ *n, pl* **enemas** *also* **ene·ma·ta** \ˌe-nə-ˈmä-tə, ˈe-nə-mə-tə\ : the injection of liquid into the intestine by way of the anus (as for cleansing); *also* : the liquid so injected

en·er·get·ic \ˌe-nər-ˈje-tik\ *adj* : of or relating to energy

en·er·get·ics \-tiks\ *n* **1** : a branch of physics that deals primarily with energy and its transformations **2** : the total energy relations and transformations of a physical, chemical, or biological system (~ of muscular contraction)

en·er·giz·er \ˈe-nər-ˌjī-zər\ *n* : ANTIDEPRESSANT

en·er·gy \ˈe-nər-jē\ *n, pl* **-gies** **1** : the force driving and sustaining mental activity **2** : the capacity for doing work

en·er·vate \ˈe-nər-ˌvāt\ *vb* **-vat·ed; -vat·ing** : to lessen the vitality or strength of — **en·er·va·tion** \ˌe-nər-ˈvā-shən\ *n*

en·flur·ane \en-ˈflu̇r-ˌān\ *n* : a liquid inhalational general anesthetic $C_3H_2ClF_5O$ prepared from methanol

en·gage·ment \in-ˈgāj-mənt\ *n* : the phase of parturition in which the fetal head passes into the cavity of the true pelvis

en·gi·neer \ˌen-jə-ˈnir\ *vb* : to modify or produce by genetic engineering

English system \ˈiŋ-glish-, ˈiŋ-lish-\ *n* : the foot-pound-second system of units

en·gorge \in-ˈgȯrj\ *vb* **en·gorged; en·gorg·ing** **1** : to fill with blood to the point of congestion (the gastric mucosa was greatly *engorged*) **2** : to suck blood to the limit of body capacity (a tick *engorging* on its host) — **en·gorge·ment** *n*

en·graft \in-ˈgraft\ *vb* : GRAFT — **en·graft·ment** *n*

en·gram *also* **en·gramme** \ˈen-ˌgram\ *n* : a hypothetical change in neural tissue postulated in order to account for persistence of memory — called also *memory trace*

en·hanc·er \in-ˈhan-sər, en-\ *n* : a nucleotide sequence that increases the rate of genetic transcription by increasing the activity of the nearest promoter on the same DNA molecule

en·keph·a·lin \in-ˈke-fə-lən, -(ˌ)lin\ *n* : either of two pentapeptides with opiate and analgesic activity that occur naturally in the brain and have a marked affinity for opiate receptors: **a** : LEUCINE-ENKEPHALIN **b** : METHIONINE-ENKEPHALIN — compare ENDORPHIN

en·keph·a·lin·er·gic \-ˌke-fə-lə-ˈnər-jik\ *adj* : liberating or activated by enkephalins (~ neurons)

eno·lase \ˈē-nə-ˌlās, -ˌlāz\ *n* : an enzyme that is found esp. in muscle and is important in the metabolism of carbohydrates

en·oph·thal·mos \ˌe-ˌnäf-ˈthal-məs, -ˌnäp-, -ˌmäs\ *also* **en·oph·thal·mus** \-məs\ *n* : a sinking of the eyeball into the orbital cavity

en·os·to·sis \ˌe-ˌnäs-ˈtō-səs\ *n, pl* **-to·ses** \-ˌsēz\ : a bony tumor arising within a bone

Eno·vid \e-ˈnō-vid\ *trademark* — used for an oral contraceptive containing norethynodrel and mestranol

en·sheathe \in-ˈshēth\ *vb* : to cover with or as if with a sheath

ensiform cartilage *n* : XIPHOID PROCESS

ensiform process *n* : XIPHOID PROCESS

ENT *abbr* ear, nose, and throat

ent- *or* **ento-** *comb form* : inner : within (*entoptic*) (*entoderm*)

ent·amoe·ba \ˌent-ə-ˈmē-bə\ *n, pl* **-bas** *or* **-bae** \-(ˌ)bē\ : any ameba of the genus *Entamoeba* — **ent·amoe·bic** \-bik\ *adj*

ent·am·e·bi·a·sis \ˌen-ˌta-mi-ˈbī-ə-səs\ *n, pl* **-a·ses** \-ˌsēz\ : infection with or disease caused by a protozoan of the genus *Entamoeba* : AMEBIASIS

ent·amoe·ba *chiefly Brit var of* ENTAMEBA

Ent·amoe·ba \ˌen-tə-ˈmē-bə, ˈen-tə-\ *n* : a genus of ameboid protozoans (order Amoebida) that are parasitic in the alimentary canal and esp. in the intestines and that include the causative agent (*E. histolytica*) of amebic dysentery

enter- *or* **entero-** *comb form* **1** : intestine (*enteritis*) **2** : intestinal and (*enterohepatic*)

en·ter·al \\'en-tə-rəl\\ *adj* : ENTERIC — **en·ter·al·ly** *adv*

en·ter·ec·to·my \\,en-tə-'rek-tə-mē\\ *n, pl* **-mies** : the surgical removal of a portion of the intestine

en·ter·ic \\en-'ter-ik, in-\\ *adj* **1** : of or relating to the intestines; *broadly* : ALIMENTARY **2** : of, relating to, or being a medicinal preparation treated to pass through the stomach unaltered and disintegrate in the intestines

enteric fever *n* : TYPHOID FEVER; *also* : PARATYPHOID

entericus — see SUCCUS ENTERICUS

en·ter·itis \\,en-tə-'rī-təs\\ *n, pl* **en·ter·it·i·des** \\-'ri-tə-,dēz\\ *or* **en·ter·i·tis·es 1** : inflammation of the intestines and esp. of the human ileum **2** : a disease of domestic animals (as panleukopenia of cats) marked by enteritis and diarrhea

En·tero·bac·ter \\'en-tə-rō-,bak-tər\\ *n* : a genus of enterobacteria that are widely distributed in nature (as in feces, soil, water, and the contents of human and animal intestines) and include some that may be pathogenic

en·tero·bac·te·ri·um \\,en-tə-rō-bak-'tir-ē-əm\\ *n, pl* **-ria** \\-ē-ə\\ : any of a family (Enterobacteriaceae) of gram-negative rod-shaped bacteria (as a salmonella or colon bacillus) that ferment glucose and include some serious animal pathogens — **en·tero·bac·te·ri·al** \\-ē-əl\\ *adj*

en·tero·bi·a·sis \\-'bī-ə-səs\\ *n, pl* **-a·ses** \\-,sēz\\ : infestation with or disease caused by pinworms of the genus *Enterobius* that occurs esp. in children

En·tero·bi·us \\,en-tə-'rō-bē-əs\\ *n* : a genus of small nematode worms (family Oxyuridae) that includes the common pinworm (*E. vermicularis*) of the human intestine

en·tero·cele \\'en-tə-rō-,sēl\\ *n* : a hernia containing a portion of the intestines

en·tero·chro·maf·fin \\,en-tə-rō-'krō-mə-fən\\ *adj* : of, relating to, or being epithelial cells of the intestinal mucosa that stain esp. with chromium salts and usu. contain serotonin

en·tero·coc·cus \\,en-tə-rō-'kä-kəs\\ *n, pl* **-coc·ci** \\-'käk-,sī, -,sē; -'kä-,kī, -,kē\\ : STREPTOCOCCUS **2**; *esp* : a streptococcus (as *Streptococcus faecalis*) normally present in the intestine — **en·tero·coc·cal** \\-'kä-kəl\\ *adj*

en·tero·co·li·tis \\,en-tə-rō-kə-'lī-təs\\ *n* : enteritis affecting both the large and small intestine

en·tero·en·ter·os·to·my \\-,en-tə-'räs-tə-mē\\ *n, pl* **-mies** : surgical anastomosis of two parts of the intestine with creation of an opening between them

en·tero·gas·tric reflex \\-,gas-trik-\\ *n* : reflex inhibition of the emptying of the stomach's contents through the pylorus that occurs when the duodenum is stimulated by the presence of irri-

tants, is overloaded, or is obstructed

en·tero·gas·trone \\-'gas-,trōn\\ *n* : a hormone that is held to be produced by the duodenal mucosa and to inhibit gastric motility and secretion — compare UROGASTRONE

en·tero·he·pat·ic \\-hi-'pa-tik\\ *adj* : of or involving the intestine and the liver (~ circulation of bile salts)

en·tero·hep·a·ti·tis \\-,he-pə-'tī-təs\\ *n* : BLACKHEAD **2**

en·tero·ki·nase \\-'kī-,nās, -,nāz\\ *n* : an enzyme that activates trypsinogen by converting it to trypsin

en·tero·lith \\'en-tə-rō-,lith\\ *n* : an intestinal calculus

enteropathica — see ACRODERMATITIS ENTEROPATHICA

en·tero·patho·gen·ic \\,en-tə-rō-,pa-thə-'je-nik\\ *adj* : tending to produce disease in the intestinal tract (~ bacteria) — **en·tero·patho·gen** \\-'pa-thə-jen\\ *n*

en·ter·op·a·thy \\,en-tə-'rä-pə-thē\\ *n, pl* **-thies** : a disease of the intestinal tract

en·ter·os·to·my \\,en-tə-'räs-tə-mē\\ *n, pl* **-mies** : a surgical formation of an opening into the intestine through the abdominal wall — **en·ter·os·to·mal** \\-tə-məl\\ *adj*

en·ter·ot·o·my \\,en-tə-'rä-tə-mē\\ *n, pl* **-mies** : incision into the intestines

en·tero·tox·emia \\,en-tə-rō-,täk-'sē-mē-ə\\ *n* : a disease (as pulpy kidney disease of lambs) attributed to absorption of a toxin from the intestine — called also *overeating disease*

en·tero·toxi·gen·ic \\-,täk-sə-'je-nik\\ *adj* : producing enterotoxin

en·tero·tox·in \\-'täk-sən\\ *n* : a toxin that is produced by microorganisms (as some staphylococci) and causes gastrointestinal symptoms

en·tero·vi·rus \\-'vī-rəs\\ *n* : any of a group of picornaviruses (as the poliomyelitis virus) that typically occur in the gastrointestinal tract but may be involved in respiratory ailments, meningitis, and neurological disorders — **en·tero·vi·ral** \\-rəl\\ *adj*

ento- — see ENT-

en·to·derm \\'en-tə-,dərm\\ *n* : ENDODERM

en·to·mo·pho·bia \\,en-tə-mō-'fō-bē-ə\\ *n* : fear of insects

ent·op·tic \\(,)en-'täp-tik\\ *adj* : lying or originating within the eyeball — used esp. of visual sensations due to the shadows of retinal blood vessels or of opaque particles in the vitreous humor falling upon the retina

en·tro·pi·on \\en-'trō-pē-,än, -ən\\ *n* : the inversion or turning inward of the border of the eyelid against the eyeball

¹enu·cle·ate \\(,)ē-'nü-klē-,āt, -'nyü-\\ *vb* **-at·ed; -at·ing 1** : to deprive of a nucleus **2** : to remove without cutting into (~ a tumor) (~ the eyeball) — **enu·cle·ation** \\(,)ē-,nü-klē-'ā-shən, ,nyü-\\

n — enu·cle·a·tor \(ͺ)ē-ˈnü-klē-ͺā-tər, -ˈnyü-\ *n*

²enu·cle·ate \-klē-ͺət, -ͺāt\ *adj* : lacking a nucleus (~ cells)

en·ure·sis \ͺen-yů-ˈrē-səs\ *n*, *pl* -ure·ses \-ͺsēz\ : an involuntary discharge of urine : incontinence of urine — en·uret·ic \-ˈre-tik\ *adj or n*

en·ve·lope \ˈen-və-ͺlōp, ˈän-\ *n* : a natural enclosing covering (as a membrane or integument)

en·ven·om·ation \in-ͺve-nə-ˈmā-shən\ *n* : an act or instance of impregnating with a venom (as of a snake or spider); *also* : ENVENOMIZATION

en·ven·om·iza·tion \-mə-ˈzā-shən\ *n* : a poisoning caused by a bite or sting

en·vi·ron·ment \in-ˈvī-rən-mənt, -ˈvī-ərn-\ *n* 1 : the complex of physical, chemical, and biotic factors (as climate, soil, and living things) that act upon an organism or an ecological community and ultimately determine its form and survival 2 : the aggregate of social and cultural conditions that influence the life of an individual or community — en·vi·ron·men·tal \-ͺvī-rən-ˈment-ᵊl, -ͺvī-ərn-\ *adj* — en·vi·ron·men·tal·ly *adv*

¹en·zo·ot·ic \ͺen-zə-ˈwä-tik\ *adj*, *of animal diseases* : peculiar to or constantly present in a locality — en·zo·ot·i·cal·ly \-ti-k(ə-)lē\ *adv*

²enzootic *n* : an enzootic disease

en·zy·mat·ic \ͺen-zə-ˈma-tik\ *also* en·zy·mic \en-ˈzī-mik\ *adj* : of, relating to, or produced by an enzyme — en·zy·mat·i·cal·ly \-ti-k(ə-)lē\ *also* en·zy·mi·cal·ly \en-ˈzī-mi-k(ə-)lē\ *adv*

en·zyme \ˈen-ͺzīm\ *n* : any of numerous complex proteins that are produced by living cells and catalyze specific biochemical reactions at body temperatures

enzyme–linked immunosorbent assay *n* : a quantitative in vitro test for an antibody or antigen in which the test material is adsorbed on a surface and exposed to a complex of an enzyme linked to an antibody specific for the suspected antibody or antigen being tested for with a positive result indicated by a treatment yielding a color in proportion to the amount of antigen or antibody in the test material — called also *ELISA*

en·zy·mol·o·gy \ͺen-ͺzī-ˈmä-lə-jē, -zə-\ *n*, *pl* -gies : a branch of biochemistry dealing with enzymes, their nature, activity, and significance — en·zy·mo·log·i·cal \-mə-ˈlä-ji-kəl\ *adj* — en·zy·mol·o·gist \ͺen-ͺzī-ˈmä-lə-jist\ *n*

EOG *abbr* electrooculogram

eon·ism \ˈē-ə-ͺni-zəm\ *n* : TRANSVESTISM

Éon de Beau·mont \ā-ōⁿ-də-bō-mōⁿ\, **Charles (1728–1810),** French chevalier and adventurer.

eo·sin \ˈē-ə-sən\ *also* eo·sine \-sən, -ͺsēn\ *n* : a red fluorescent dye $C_{20}H_8Br_4O_5$; *also* : its red to brown sodium or potassium salt used esp. as a biological stain for cytoplasmic structures

eo·sin·o·pe·nia \ͺē-ə-ͺsi-nə-ˈpē-nē-ə, -nyə\ *n* : an abnormal decrease in the number of eosinophils in the blood — eo·sin·o·pe·nic \-ˈpē-nik\ *adj*

¹eo·sin·o·phil \ˈē-ə-ˈsi-nə-ͺfil\ *also* eo·sin·o·phile \-ͺfil\ *adj* : EOSINOPHILIC 1

²eosinophil *also* eosinophile *n* : a leukocyte or other granulocyte with cytoplasmic inclusions readily stained by eosin

eo·sin·o·phil·ia \-ͺsi-nə-ˈfi-lē-ə\ *n* : abnormal increase in the number of eosinophils in the blood that is characteristic of allergic states and various parasitic infections

eo·sin·o·phil·ic \-ͺsi-nə-ˈfi-lik\ *adj* 1 : staining readily with eosin 2 : of, relating to, or characterized by eosinophilia

eosinophilic granuloma *n* : a disease of adolescents and young adults marked by the formation of granulomas in bone and the presence in them of histiocytes and eosinophilic cells with secondary deposition of cholesterol

ep- — see EPI-

ep·ar·te·ri·al \ͺe-pär-ˈtir-ē-əl\ *adj* : situated above an artery; *specif* : of or relating to the first branch of the right bronchus

ependym- *or* ependymo- *comb form* : ependyma (*ependymitis*)

ep·en·dy·ma \e-ˈpen-də-mə\ *n* : an epithelial membrane lining the ventricles of the brain and the canal of the spinal cord — ep·en·dy·mal \(ͺ)e-ˈpen-də-məl\ *adj*

ep·en·dy·mi·tis \ͺe-ͺpen-də-ˈmī-təs\ *n*, *pl* -mit·i·des \-mi-tə-ͺdēz\ : inflammation of the ependyma

ep·en·dy·mo·ma \(ͺ)e-ͺpen-də-ˈmō-mə\ *n*, *pl* -mas *also* -ma·ta \-mə-tə\ : a glioma arising in or near the ependyma

ep·eryth·ro·zo·on \e-pə-ͺrith-rə-ˈzō-ͺän\ *n* 1 *cap* : a genus of bacteria (family Anaplasmataceae) comprising blood parasites of vertebrates 2 *pl* -zoa \-ˈzō-ə\ : a bacterium of the genus *Eperythrozoon*

ep·eryth·ro·zo·on·o·sis \-ͺzō-ə-ˈnō-səs\ *n*, *pl* -oses \-ͺsēz\ : infection with or disease caused by bacteria of the genus *Eperythrozoon* that is esp. severe in young pigs

ephed·rine \i-ˈfe-drən\ *n* : a crystalline alkaloid $C_{10}H_{15}NO$ extracted from a Chinese shrub (*Ephedra sinica* of the family Gnetaceae) or synthesized that has the physiological action of epinephrine and is used in the form of a salt for relief of hay fever, asthma, and nasal congestion

ephe·lis \i-ˈfē-ləs\ *n*, *pl* -li·des \-ˈfē-lə-ͺdēz, -ˈfe-\ : FRECKLE

ephem·er·al \i-ˈfe-mə-rəl\ *adj* : lasting a very short time

epi- *or* ep- *prefix* : upon (*epicranial*)

besides ⟨*epi*phenomenon⟩ : attached to ⟨*epi*didymis⟩ : outer ⟨*epi*blast⟩

epi·an·dros·ter·one \₁e-pē-₁an-ˈdräs-tə-₁rōn\ *n* : an androsterone derivative $C_{19}H_{30}O_2$ that occurs in normal human urine

epi·blast \ˈe-pə-₁blast\ *n* : the outer layer of the blastoderm : ECTODERM — **epi·blas·tic** \₁e-pə-ˈblas-tik\ *adj*

epi·can·thic fold \₁e-pə-ˈkan-thik-\ *n* : a prolongation of a fold of the skin of the upper eyelid over the inner angle or both angles of the eye

epi·can·thus \-ˈkan-thəs\ *n* : EPICAN-THIC FOLD

epi·car·di·um \₁e-pi-ˈkär-dē-əm\ *n, pl* -**dia** \-ə\ : the visceral part of the pericardium that closely envelops the heart — called also *visceral pericardium;* compare PARIETAL PERICARDIUM — **epi·car·di·al** \-dē-əl\ *adj*

epi·con·dyle \₁e-pi-ˈkän-₁dīl, -dəl\ *n* : any of several prominences on the distal part of a long bone serving for the attachment of muscles and ligaments: **a** : one on the outer aspect of the distal part of the humerus or proximal to the lateral condyle of the femur — called also *lateral epicondyle* **b** : a larger and more prominent one on the inner aspect of the distal part of the humerus or proximal to the medial condyle of the femur — called also *medial epicondyle;* see EPITROCHLEA — **epi·con·dy·lar** \-də-lər\ *adj*

epi·con·dy·li·tis \-₁kän-dī-ˈlī-təs, -də-\ *n* : inflammation of an epicondyle or of adjacent tissues — compare TENNIS ELBOW

epi·cra·ni·al \-ˈkrā-nē-əl\ *adj* : situated on the cranium

epicranial aponeurosis *n* : GALEA APONEUROTICA

epi·cra·ni·um \-ˈkrā-nē-əm\ *n, pl* -**nia** \-nē-ə\ : the structures covering the vertebrate cranium

epi·cra·ni·us \₁e-pə-ˈkrā-nē-əs\ *n, pl* -**cra·nii** \-nē-₁ī\ : OCCIPITOFRONTALIS

epi·crit·ic \-ˈkri-tik\ *adj* : of, relating to, being, or mediating cutaneous sensory reception that is marked by accurate discrimination between small degrees of sensation — compare PROTOPATHIC

¹**epi·dem·ic** \₁e-pə-ˈde-mik\ *also* **ep·i·dem·i·cal** \-mi-kəl\ *adj* **1** : affecting or tending to affect an atypically large number of individuals within a population, community, or region at the same time ⟨typhoid was ∼⟩ — compare ENDEMIC, SPORADIC **2** : of, relating to, or constituting an epidemic — **ep·i·dem·i·cal·ly** \-mi-k(ə-)lē\ *adv*

²**epidemic** *n* : an outbreak of epidemic disease

epidemic hemorrhagic fever *n* : KOREAN HEMORRHAGIC FEVER

ep·i·de·mic·i·ty \₁e-pə-₁de-ˈmi-sə-tē, -də-\ *n, pl* -**ties** : the quality or state of being epidemic; *specif* : the relative

ability to spread from one host to others (∼ of typhoid bacteria)

epidemic keratoconjunctivitis *n* : an infectious often epidemic disease that is caused by an adenovirus and is marked by pain, by redness and swelling of the conjunctiva, by edema of the tissues around the eye, and by tenderness of the adjacent lymph nodes

epidemic parotitis *n* : MUMPS

epidemic pleurodynia *n* : an acute virus infection that is typically caused by a coxsackievirus and is characterized by sudden onset with fever, headache, and acute diaphragmatic pain

epidemic typhus *n* : TYPHUS a

ep·i·de·mi·ol·o·gist \₁e-pə-₁dē-mē-ˈä-lə-jist, -₁de-\ *n* : a specialist in epidemiology

ep·i·de·mi·ol·o·gy \-jē\ *n, pl* -**gies 1** : a branch of medical science that deals with the incidence, distribution, and control of disease in a population **2** : the sum of the factors controlling the presence or absence of a disease or pathogen — **ep·i·de·mi·o·log·i·cal** \-ə-ˈläj-i-kəl\ *also* **ep·i·de·mi·o·log·ic** \-jik\ *adj* — **ep·i·de·mi·o·log·i·cal·ly** \-ji-k(ə-)lē\ *adv*

epiderm- *or* **epidermo-** *comb form* : epidermis ⟨*epiderm*itis⟩ ⟨*epidermo*lysis⟩

ep·i·derm \ˈe-pə-₁dərm\ *n* : EPIDERMIS

epi·der·mal \₁e-pə-ˈdər-məl\ *adj* : of, relating to, or arising from the epidermis

epidermal growth factor *n* : a polypeptide hormone that stimulates cell proliferation esp. of epithelial cells by binding to receptor proteins on the cell surface — abbr. *EGF*

epidermal necrolysis *n* : TOXIC EPIDERMAL NECROLYSIS

epi·der·mic \₁e-pə-ˈdər-mik\ *adj* : EPIDERMAL

epi·der·mis \-məs\ *n* : the outer epithelial layer of the external integument of the animal body that is derived from the embryonic epiblast; *specif* : the outer nonsensitive and nonvascular layer of the skin that overlies the dermis

epi·der·mi·tis \-(₁)dər-ˈmī-təs\ *n, pl* -**tis·es** *or* -**mit·i·des** \-ˈmi-tə-₁dēz\ : inflammation of the epidermis

epidermo- — see EPIDERM-

epi·der·moid \-ˈdər-₁mȯid\ *adj* : resembling epidermis or epidermal cells : made up of elements like those of epidermis (∼ cancer of the lung)

epidermoid cyst *n* : a cystic tumor containing epidermal or similar tissue — called also *epidermoid;* see CHOLESTEATOMA

epi·der·mol·y·sis \₁e-pə-(₁)dər-ˈmä-lə-səs\ *n, pl* -**y·ses** \-₁sēz\ : a state of detachment or loosening of the epidermis

Ep·i·der·moph·y·ton \-(₁)dər-ˈmä-fə-₁tän\ *n* : a genus of fungi that comprises dermatophytes causing disease (as athlete's foot and tinea cruris), that now usu. includes a single species (*E. floccosums* syn. *E. inguinale* and *E. cruris*), and that is sometimes considered a synonym of *Trichophyton*

epi·i·der·moph·y·to·sis \-₁mä-fə-'tō-səs\ *n, pl* **-to·ses** \-₁sēz\ : a disease (as athlete's foot) of the skin or nails caused by a dermatophyte

epididym- *or* **epididymo-** *comb form* **1** : epididymis (*epididym*ectomy) **2** : epididymis and (*epididymo*orchitis)

epi·did·y·mec·to·my \-₁di-də-'mek-tə-mē\ *n, pl* **-mies** : excision of the epididymis

epi·did·y·mis \-'di-də-məs\ *n, pl* **-mi·des** \-mə-₁dēz\ : a system of ductules that emerges posteriorly from the testis, holds sperm during maturation, and forms a tangled mass before uniting into a single coiled duct which comprises the highly convoluted body and tail of the system and is continuous with the vas deferens — see VASA EFFERENTIA — **epi·did·y·mal** \-məl\ *adj*

epi·did·y·mi·tis \-₁di-də-'mī-təs\ *n* : inflammation of the epididymis

epi·did·y·mo–or·chi·tis \-₁di-də-₁mō-ȯr-'kī-təs\ *n* : combined inflammation of the epididymis and testis

epi·did·y·mo·vas·os·to·my \-va-'säs-tə-mē\ *n, pl* **-mies** : surgical severing of the vas deferens with anastomosis of the distal part to the epididymis esp. to circumvent an obstruction

¹**epi·du·ral** \₁ep-i-'dúr-əl, -'dyúr-\ *adj* : situated upon or administered outside the dura mater — **epi·du·ral·ly** *adv*

²**epidural** *n* : EPIDURAL ANESTHESIA

epidural anesthesia *n* : anesthesia produced by injection of a local anesthetic into the peridural space of the spinal cord beneath the ligamentum flavum — called also *peridural anesthesia*

epi·gas·tric \₁ep-ə-'gas-trik\ *adj* **1** : lying upon or over the stomach **2 a** : of or relating to the anterior walls of the abdomen (∼ *veins*) **b** : of or relating to the abdominal region lying between the hypochondriac regions and above the umbilical region

epigastric artery *n* : any of the three arteries supplying the anterior walls of the abdomen

epi·gas·tri·um \₁ep-ə-'gas-trē-əm\ *n, pl* **-tria** \-trē-ə\ : the epigastric region

epi·glot·tic \₁ep-ə-'glä-tik\ *or* **epi·glot·tal** \-'glät-ᵊl\ *adj* : of, relating to, or produced with the aid of the epiglottis

epi·glot·ti·dec·to·my \-₁glä-tə-'dek-tə-mē\ *n, pl* **-mies** : excision of all or part of the epiglottis

epi·glot·tis \-'glä-təs\ *n* : a thin lamella of yellow elastic cartilage that ordinarily projects upward behind the tongue and just in front of the glottis and that with the arytenoid cartilages

serves to cover the glottis during the act of swallowing

epi·glot·ti·tis \-₁glä-'tī-təs\ *n* : inflammation of the epiglottis

epi·la·tion \₁ep-ə-'lā-shən\ *n* : the loss or removal of hair

epi·lep·sy \'ep-ə-₁lep-sē\ *n, pl* **-sies** : any of various disorders marked by disturbed electrical rhythms of the central nervous system and typically manifested by convulsive attacks usu. with clouding of consciousness — called also *falling sickness*; see GRAND MAL, PETIT MAL; JACKSONIAN EPILEPSY

epilept- *or* **epilepti-** *or* **epilepto-** *comb form* : epilepsy (*epilept*oid) (*epilepti*form) (*epilepto*genic)

epi·lep·tic \₁ep-ə-'lep-tik\ *adj* : relating to, affected with, or having the characteristics of epilepsy — **epileptic** *n* — **epi·lep·ti·cal·ly** \-ti-k(ə-)lē\ *adv*

epilepticus — see STATUS EPILEPTICUS

epi·lep·ti·form \-'lep-tə-₁fȯrm\ *adj* : resembling that of epilepsy (an ∼ convulsion)

epi·lep·to·gen·ic \-₁lep-tə-'je-nik\ *adj* : inducing or tending to induce epilepsy (an ∼ *drug*)

epi·lep·toid \-'lep-₁tȯid\ *adj* **1** : EPILEPTIFORM **2** : exhibiting symptoms resembling those of epilepsy

epi·loia \₁ep-ə-'lȯi-ə\ *n* : a deleterious dominant genetic trait marked by mental deficiency and multiple tumor formation of the skin and brain and maintained in human populations by a high mutation rate — called also *tuberous sclerosis*

epi·my·si·um \₁ep-ə-'mizh-ē-əm, -zē-\ *n, pl* **-sia** \-zhē-ə, -zē-ə\ : the external connective-tissue sheath of a muscle — compare ENDOMYSIUM

epi·neph·rine *also* **epi·neph·rin** \₁ep-ə-'ne-frən\ *n* : a crystalline feebly basic sympathomimetic hormone $C_9H_{13}N-O_3$ that is the principal blood-pressure-raising hormone secreted by the adrenal medulla, is prepared from adrenal extracts or made synthetically, and is used medicinally esp. as a heart stimulant, as a vasoconstrictor in controlling hemorrhages of the skin and in prolonging the effects of local anesthetics, and as a muscle relaxant in bronchial asthma — called also *adrenaline*

¹**epi·neu·ral** \₁ep-ə-'nùr-əl, -'nyùr-\ *adj* : arising from the neural arch of a vertebra

²**epineural** *n* : a spine or process arising from the neural arch of a vertebra

epi·neu·ri·um \₁ep-ə-'nùr-ē-əm, -'nyùr-\ *n* : the external connective-tissue sheath of a nerve trunk

epi·phe·nom·e·non \₁ep-i-fə-'nä-mə-₁nän, -nən\ *n* : an accidental or accessory event or process occurring in the course of a disease but not necessarily related to that disease

epiph·o·ra \i-'pi-fə-rə\ *n* : a watering of

the eyes due to excessive secretion of tears or to obstruction of the lacrimal passages

epiph·y·se·al \i-ˌpi-fə-ˈsē-əl\ also **epi·phys·i·al** \ˌe-pə-ˈfi-zē-əl\ adj : of or relating to an epiphysis

epiphyseal line n : the line marking the site of the epiphyseal plate

epiphyseal plate n : the cartilage that contains an epiphysis, unites it with the shaft, and is the site of longitudinal growth of the bone — called also epiphyseal cartilage

epiph·y·si·od·e·sis \i-ˌpi-fə-sē-ˈä-də-səs, ˌe-pə-ˌfi-zē-\ n, pl **-e·ses** \-ˌsēz\ : the surgical reattachment of a separated epiphysis to the shaft of its bone

epiph·y·sis \i-ˈpi-fə-səs\ n, pl **-y·ses** \-ˌsēz\ 1 : a part or process of a bone that ossifies separately and later becomes ankylosed to the main part of the bone; esp : an end of a long bone — compare DIAPHYSIS 2 : PINEAL GLAND

epiph·y·si·tis \i-ˌpi-fə-ˈsī-təs\ n : inflammation of an epiphysis

epi·plo·ec·to·my \ˌe-pə-plō-ˈek-tə-mē\ n, pl **-mies** : OMENTECTOMY

epi·plo·ic \ˌe-pə-ˈplō-ik\ adj : of or associated with an omentum : OMENTAL

epiploicae — see APPENDICES EPIPLOICAE

epiploic foramen n : the only opening between the omental bursa and the general peritoneal sac — called also foramen of Winslow

epi·plo·on \ˌe-pə-ˈplō-ˌän\ n, pl **-ploa** \-ˈplō-ə\ : OMENTUM; specif : GREATER OMENTUM

epi·pter·ic \ˌep-ip-ˈter-ik\ adj : relating to or being a small Wormian bone sometimes present in the human skull between the parietal and the greater wing of the sphenoid

epi·sclera \ˌe-pə-ˈskler-ə\ n : the layer of connective tissue between the conjunctiva and the sclera of the eye

epi·scler·al \-ˈskler-əl\ adj 1 : situated upon the scleral coat of the eye 2 : of or relating to the episclera

epi·scle·ri·tis \-sklə-ˈrī-təs\ n : inflammation of the superficial layers of the sclera

episio- comb form 1 : vulva ⟨episiotomy⟩ 2 : vulva and ⟨episioperineorrhaphy⟩

epi·sio·per·i·ne·or·rha·phy \i-ˌpi-zē-ō-ˌper-ə-nē-ˈor-ə-fē, -ˌpē-\ n, pl **-phies** : surgical repair of the vulva and perineum by suturing

epi·si·or·rha·phy \-zē-ˈor-ə-fē\ n, pl **-phies** : surgical repair of injury to the vulva by suturing

epi·si·ot·o·my \i-ˌpi-zē-ˈä-tə-mē, -ˌpē-\ n, pl **-mies** : surgical enlargement of the vulval orifice for obstetrical purposes during parturition

ep·i·sode \ˈe-pə-ˌsōd, -ˌzōd\ n : an event that is distinctive and separate although part of a larger series; esp : an occurrence of a usu. recurrent

pathological abnormal condition — **ep·i·sod·ic** \ˌe-pə-ˈsä-dik, -ˈzä-\ adj — **ep·i·sod·i·cal·ly** \-di-k(ə-)lē\ adv

ep·some \ˈe-pə-ˌsōm, -ˌzōm\ n : a genetic determinant (as the DNA of some bacteriophages) that can replicate either autonomously in bacterial cytoplasm or as an integral part of their chromosomes — compare PLASMID — **epi·som·al** \ˌe-pə-ˈsō-məl, -ˈzō-\ adj — **epi·som·al·ly** \-mə-lē\ adv

epi·spa·di·as \ˌe-pə-ˈspā-dē-əs\ n : a congenital defect in which the urethra opens upon the upper surface of the penis

epis·ta·sis \i-ˈpis-tə-səs\ n, pl **-ta·ses** \-ˌsēz\ 1 a : suppression of a secretion or discharge b : a scum on the surface of urine 2 : suppression of the effect of a gene by a nonallelic gene — **epi·stat·ic** \ˌe-pə-ˈsta-tik\ adj

epi·stax·is \ˌe-pə-ˈstak-səs\ n, pl **-stax·es** \-ˌsēz\ : NOSEBLEED

epi·stro·phe·us \ˌe-pə-ˈstrō-fē-əs\ n : AXIS 2a

epi·thal·a·mus \ˌe-pə-ˈtha-lə-məs\ n, pl **-mi** \-ˌmī\ : a dorsal segment of the diencephalon containing the habenula and the pineal gland

epithel- comb form : epithelium ⟨epithelize⟩

epitheli- or **epithelio-** comb form : epithelium ⟨epithelioma⟩

ep·i·the·li·al \ˌe-pə-ˈthē-lē-əl\ adj : of or relating to epithelium ⟨~ cells⟩

ep·i·the·li·oid \-ˈthē-lē-ˌoid\ adj : resembling epithelium

ep·i·the·li·o·ma \-ˌthē-lē-ˈō-mə\ n, pl **-mas** or **-ma·ta** \-mə-tə\ : a tumor derived from epithelial tissue

ep·i·the·li·um \ˌe-pə-ˈthē-lē-əm\ n, pl **-lia** \-lē-ə\ : a membranous cellular tissue that covers a free surface or lines a tube or cavity of an animal body and serves esp. to enclose and protect the other parts of the body, to produce secretions and excretions, and to function in assimilation

ep·i·the·li·za·tion \ˌe-pə-ˌthē-lə-ˈzā-shən\ or **ep·i·the·lial·i·za·tion** \-ˌthē-lē-ə-lə-\ n : the process of becoming covered with or converted to epithelium — **ep·i·the·lize** \ˌe-pə-ˈthē-ˌlīz\ or **ep·i·the·li·al·ize** \-ˈthē-lē-ə-ˌlīz\ vb

ep·i·thet \ˈe-pə-ˌthet, -thət\ n : the part of a scientific name identifying the species, variety, or other subunit within in a genus — see SPECIFIC EPITHET

epi·tope \ˈe-pə-ˌtōp\ n : a molecular region on the surface of an antigen capable of eliciting an immune response and of combining with the specific antibody produced by such a response — called also determinant, antigenic determinant

epi·troch·lea \ˌe-pi-ˈträ-klē-ə\ n : the medial epicondyle at the distal end of the humerus — **epi·troch·le·ar** \-klē-ər\ adj

epi·tym·pan·ic \-tim-ˈpa-nik\ adj : situated above the tympanic membrane

epitympanic recess *n* : ATTIC

epi·tym·pa·num \-ˈtim-pə-nəm\ *n* : the upper portion of the middle ear — compare HYPOTYMPANUM

epi·zo·ot·ic \ɪe-pə-zō-ˈwä-tik\ *n* : an outbreak of disease affecting many animals of one kind at the same time; *also* : the disease itself — **epizootic** *adj*

epizootic lymphangitis *n* : a chronic contagious inflammation that affects chiefly the superficial lymphatics and lymph nodes of horses, mules, and donkeys and is caused by a fungus of the genus *Histoplasma* (*H. farciminosum*)

epi·zo·oti·ol·o·gy \ɪe-pə-zō-ɪwä-tē-ˈä-lə-jē\ *also* **epi·zo·otol·o·gy** \-ɪzō-ə-ˈtä-lə-jē\ *n, pl* **-gies** 1 : a science that deals with the character, ecology, and causes of outbreaks of animal diseases 2 : the sum of the factors controlling the occurrence of a disease or pathogen of animals — **epi·zo·oti·o·log·i·cal** \-ɪzō-ɪwō-tē-ə-ˈlä-ji-kəl, -ɪwä-\ *also* **epi·zo·oti·o·log·ic** \-jik\ *adj*

ep·o·nych·i·um \ɪe-pə-ˈni-kē-əm\ *n* : the quick of a nail

ep·onym \ˈe-pə-ɪnim\ *n* 1 : the person for whom something (as a disease) is or is believed to be named 2 : a name (as of a drug or a disease) based on or derived from the name of a person — **epon·y·mous** \i-ˈpä-nə-məs. e-\ *adj*

ep·oph·o·ron \ɪe-pō-ˈä-fə-ɪrän\ *n* : a rudimentary organ homologous with the male epididymis that lies in the broad ligament of the uterus — called also *organ of Rosenmüller, parovarium*

Ep·som salt \ˈep-səm-\ *n* : EPSOM SALTS

Epsom salts *n* : a bitter colorless or white crystalline salt $MgSO_4 \cdot 7H_2O$ that is a hydrated magnesium sulfate with cathartic properties

Ep·stein–Barr virus \ˈep-ɪstīn-ˈbär-\ *n* : a herpesvirus that causes infectious mononucleosis and is associated with Burkitt's lymphoma and nasopharyngeal carcinoma — called also *EB virus*

  Epstein, Michael Anthony (*b* 1921) and Barr, Y. M. (*fl* 1964), British virologists.

epu·lis \ə-ˈpyü-ləs\ *n, pl* **epu·li·des** \-lə-ɪdēz\ : a tumor or tumorous growth of the gum

equa·tion·al \i-ˈkwā-zhə-nəl\ *adj* : dividing into two equal parts — used esp. of the mitotic cell division usu. following reduction in meiosis — **equa·tion·al·ly** *adv*

equa·tor \i-ˈkwā-tər, ˈē-ɪ\ *n* 1 : a circle dividing the surface of a body into two usu. equal and symmetrical parts esp. at the place of greatest width (the ~ of the lens of the eye) 2 : EQUATORIAL PLANE — **equa·to·ri·al** \ɪē-kwə-ˈtōr-ē-əl, ɪe-\ *adj*

equatorial plane *n* : the plane perpendicular to the spindle of a dividing cell and midway between the poles

equatorial plate *n* 1 : METAPHASE PLATE 2 : EQUATORIAL PLANE

equi·an·al·ge·sic \ɪē-kwi-ɪan-əl-ˈjē-zik, ɪe-, -sik\ *adj* : producing the same degree of analgesia

equi·len·in \ɪe-kwə-ˈle-nən, ə-ˈkwi-lə-nən\ *n* : a weakly estrogenic steroid hormone $C_{18}H_{18}O_2$ obtained from the urine of pregnant mares

equi·lib·ri·um \ɪē-kwə-ˈli-brē-əm, ɪe-\ *n, pl* **-ri·ums** *or* **-ria** \-brē-ə\ 1 : a state of balance between opposing forces or actions that is either static (as in a body acted on by forces whose resultant is zero) or dynamic (as in a reversible chemical reaction when the velocities in both directions are equal) 2 : a state of intellectual or emotional balance

equina — see CAUDA EQUINA

equine \ˈē-ɪkwīn, ˈe-\ *n* : any of a family (Equidae) of hoofed mammals that include the horses, asses and zebras; *esp* : HORSE — **equine** *adj*

equine babesiosis *n* : a babesiosis that affects horses and related equines. is caused by two protozoans of the genus *Babesia* (*B. caballi* and *B. equi*), and is characterized esp. by fever, anemia, weakness, icterus, and sometimes hemoglobinuria and edema just below the skin around the head — called also *equine piroplasmosis*

equine encephalitis *n* : EQUINE ENCEPHALOMYELITIS

equine encephalomyelitis *n* : any of three encephalomyelitides that attack chiefly equines and humans and are caused by three related strains of arbovirus: a : one that occurs esp. in the eastern U.S. — called also *eastern equine encephalomyelitis* b : one that occurs esp. in the western U.S. — called also *western equine encephalomyelitis* c : one that occurs esp. from northern S. America to Mexico — called also *Venezuelan equine encephalitis, Venezuelan equine encephalomyelitis*

equine infectious anemia *n* : a serious sometimes fatal disease of horses that is caused by a lentivirus and is marked by intermittent fever, depression, weakness, edema and anemia — called also *swamp fever*

equine piroplasmosis *n* : EQUINE BABESIOSIS

equinovarus — see TALIPES EQUINOVARUS

equinus — see TALIPES EQUINUS

equi·po·tent \ɪē-kwə-ˈpōt-ənt, ɪe-\ *adj* : having equal effects or capacities (~ doses of different drugs)

Er *symbol* erbium

ER *abbr* emergency room

er·bi·um \ˈər-bē-əm\ *n* : a metallic element that occurs with yttrium — symbol *Er*; see ELEMENT table

Erb's palsy *erbz-. *erps-\ *n* : paralysis affecting the muscles of the upper arm and shoulder that is caused by an injury during birth to the upper part of the brachial plexus

erect \i *rekt\ *adj* 1 : standing up or out from the body (~ hairs) 2 : being in a state of physiological erection

erec•tile \i-*rekt-ʾl. -*rek-.tīl\ *adj* : capable of being raised to an erect position; *esp* : CAVERNOUS 2 — **erec•til•i•ty** \-.rek-*ti-lə-tē\ *n*

erec•tion \i-*rek-shən\ *n* 1 : the state marked by firm turgid form and erect position of a previously flaccid bodily part containing cavernous tissue when that tissue becomes dilated with blood 2 : an occurrence of erection in the penis or clitoris

erec•tor \i-*rek-tər\ *n* : a muscle that raises or keeps a part erect

erector spi•nae \-*spī-.nē\ *n* : SACROSPINALIS

erep•sin \i-*rep-sən\ *n* : a proteolytic fraction obtained esp. from the intestinal juice

ere•thism *er-ə-.thi-zəm\ *n* : abnormal irritability or responsiveness to stimulation

erg *ərg\ *n* : a cgs unit of work equal to the work done by a force of one dyne acting through a distance of one centimeter

ERG *abbr* electroretinogram

erg- or ergo- *comb form* : work (*ergometer*)

-er•gic *ər-jik\ *adj comb form* 1 : allergic (hyper*ergic*) 2 : exhibiting or stimulating activity esp. of (such) a neurotransmitter substance (adren*ergic*) (dopamin*ergic*)

ergo- *comb form* : ergot (*ergosterol*)

er•go•cal•cif•er•ol \.ər-(.)gō-kal-*si-fə-.rōl. -.rōl\ *n* : CALCIFEROL

er•go•loid mesylates *er-gə-.lòid-\ *n pl* : a combination of equal amounts of three ergot alkaloids used with varying success in the treatment of cognitive decline and dementia esp. in elderly patients — see HYDERGINE

er•gom•e•ter \(.)ər-*gä-mə-tər\ *n* : an apparatus for measuring the work performed (as by a person exercising); *also* : an exercise machine equipped with an ergometer — **er•go•met•ric** \.ər-gə-*me-trik\ *adj*

er•go•met•rine \.ər-gə-*me-.trēn, -trən\ *n* : ERGONOVINE

er•go•nom•ics \.ər-gə-*nä-miks\ *n sing or pl* : an applied science concerned with the characteristics of people that need to be considered in designing and arranging things that they use in order that those things may be used most easily, effectively, and safely — called also *human engineering, human factors engineering* — **er•go•nom•ic** \-mik\ *adj* — **er•go•nom•i•cal•ly** \-mi-k(ə-)lē\ *adv* — **er•gon•o•mist** \(.)ər-*gä-nə-mist\ *n*

er•go•no•vine \.ər-gə-*nō-.vēn, -vən\ *n*

: an alkaloid $C_{19}H_{23}N_3O_2$ that is derived from ergot and is used esp. in the form of its maleate to prevent or treat postpartum bleeding

er•gos•ter•ol \(.)ər-*gäs-tə-.ròl. -.ròl\ *n* : a crystalline steroid alcohol $C_{28}H_{44}O$ that occurs esp. in yeast, molds, and ergot and is converted by ultraviolet irradiation ultimately into vitamin D_2

er•got *ər-gət. -.gät\ *n* 1 : the black or dark purple sclerotium of fungi of an ascomycetous genus (*Claviceps*); *also* : any fungus of this genus 2 a : the dried sclerotial bodies of an ergot fungus grown on rye and containing several alkaloids (as ergonovine. ergotamine) b : any of such alkaloids used medicinally for their contractile effect on smooth muscle (as of the uterus) — see ERGOTISM

er•got•a•mine \(.)ər-*gä-tə-.mēn\ *n* : an alkaloid $C_{33}H_{35}N_5O_5$ that is derived from ergot and is used chiefly in the form of its tartrate esp. in treating migraine

er•got•ism *ər-gə-.ti-zəm\ *n* : a toxic condition produced by eating grain, grain products (as rye bread). or grasses infected with ergot fungus or by chronic excessive use of an ergot drug

er•got•ized \-.tīzd\ *adj* : infected with ergot (~ grain); *also* : poisoned by ergot (~ cattle)

erigens, erigentes — see NERVUS ERIGENS

er•i•o•dic•ty•on \.er-ē-ə-*dik-tē-.än\ *n* : the dried leaves of yerba santa used as a flavoring in medicine esp. to disguise the taste of quinine

erode \i-*rōd\ *vb* **erod•ed; erod•ing** 1 : to eat into or away by slow destruction of substance (acids that ~ the teeth) (bone *eroded* by cancer) 2 : to remove with an abrasive

erog•e•nous \i-*rä-jə-nəs\ *adj* 1 : producing sexual excitement or libidinal gratification when stimulated : sexually sensitive 2 : of, relating to, or arousing sexual feelings — **er•o•ge•ne•ity** \.er-ə-jə-*nē-ə-tē\ *n*

Eros *er-.äs. *ir-\ *n* : the sum of life-preserving instincts that are manifested as impulses to gratify basic needs (as sex), as sublimated impulses motivated by the same needs. and as impulses to protect and preserve the body and mind — compare DEATH INSTINCT

ero•sion \i-*rō-zhən\ *n* **1 a** : the superficial destruction of a surface area of tissue (as mucous membrane) by inflammation, ulceration, or trauma (~ of the uterine cervix) **b** : progressive loss of the hard substance of a tooth 2 : an instance or product of erosion — **ero•sive** \i-*rō-siv. -ziv\ *adj*

erot•ic \i-*rä-tik\ *also* **erot•i•cal** \i-*rä-ti-kəl\ *adj* 1 : of, devoted to, or tending to arouse sexual love or desire 2

: strongly marked or affected by sexual desire — **erot·i·cal·ly** \-ti-k(ə-)lē\ adv

erot·i·ca \i-ˈrä-ti-kə\ n sing or pl : literary or artistic works having an erotic theme or quality

erot·i·cism \i-ˈrä-tə-ˌsi-zəm\ n 1 : a state of sexual arousal or anticipation 2 : insistent sexual impulse or desire

erot·i·cize \-ˌsīz\ vb -cized; -ciz·ing : to make erotic — **erot·i·ci·za·tion** \i-ˌrä-tə-sə-ˈzā-shən\ n

ero·tism \ˈer-ə-ˌti-zəm\ n : EROTICISM

ero·tize \ˈer-ə-ˌtīz\ vb -tized; -tiz·ing : to invest with erotic significance or sexual feeling — **ero·ti·za·tion** \ˌer-ə-tə-ˈzā-shən\ n

eroto- comb form : sexual desire (erotomania)

ero·to·gen·ic \i-ˌrō-tə-ˈje-nik, -ˌrä-\ adj : EROGENOUS

ero·to·ma·nia \-ˈmā-nē-ə\ n : excessive sexual desire esp. as a symptom of mental disorder

ero·to·ma·ni·ac \-ˈmā-nē-ˌak\ n : one affected with erotomania

ero·to·pho·bia \-ˈfō-bē-ə\ n : a morbid aversion to sexual love or desire

eru·cic acid \i-ˈrü-sik-\ n : a crystalline fatty acid $C_{22}H_{42}O_2$ found in the form of glycerides esp. in an oil obtained from the seeds of the rape plant (*Brassica napus* of the mustard family)

eruct \i-ˈrəkt\ vb : BELCH

eruc·ta·tion \i-ˌrək-ˈtā-shən, -ˌē-\ n : an act or instance of belching

erupt \i-ˈrəpt\ vb 1 of a tooth : to emerge through the gum 2 : to break out (as with a skin eruption) — **erup·tive** \-ˈrəp-tiv\ adj

erup·tion \i-ˈrəp-shən\ n 1 : an act, process, or instance of erupting; specif : the breaking out of an exanthem or enanthem on the skin or mucous membrane (as in measles) 2 : something produced by an act or process of erupting; as a : the condition of the skin or mucous membrane caused by erupting b : one of the lesions (as a pustule) constituting this condition

er·y·sip·e·las \ˌer-ə-ˈsi-pə-ləs, ˌir-\ n 1 : an acute febrile disease that is associated with intense often vesicular and edematous local inflammation of the skin and subcutaneous tissues and that is caused by a hemolytic streptococcus 2 : SWINE ERYSIPELAS — used esp. when the disease affects other hosts than swine

er·y·sip·e·loid \ˌer-ə-ˈsi-pə-ˌlóid, ˌir-\ n : a localized nonfebrile dermatitis resembling erysipelas, caused by the parasite of the genus *Erysipelothrix* (*E. rhusiopathiae*) that causes swine erysipelas, and occurring esp. about the hands of persons exposed to this organism (as by handling contaminated flesh) — **erysipeloid** adj

er·y·sip·e·lo·thrix \ˌer-ə-ˈsi-pə-lō-ˌthriks\ n 1 cap : a genus of gram-

positive, rod-shaped bacteria (family Corynebacteriaceae) that are usu. considered to comprise a single form (*E. rhusiopathiae*) which is the causative agent of swine erysipelas, an arthritis of lambs, and erysipeloid of humans 2 : a bacterium of the genus *Erysipelothrix*

er·y·the·ma \ˌer-ə-ˈthē-mə\ n : abnormal redness of the skin due to capillary congestion (as in inflammation) — **er·y·the·mal** \-məl\ adj

erythema chron·i·cum mi·grans \-ˈkrä-nə-kəm-ˈmi-grənz\ n : a spreading annular erythematous skin lesion that is an early symptom of Lyme disease and that develops at the site of the bite of a tick (as the deer tick) infected with the causative spirochete

erythema in·fec·ti·o·sum \-ˌin-ˌfek-shē-ˈō-səm\ n : an acute eruptive disease esp. of children that is caused by a parvovirus and is first manifested by a blotchy maculopapular rash on the cheeks which gradually spreads to the extremities and that is usu. accompanied by fever and malaise — called also *fifth disease*

erythema mul·ti·for·me \-ˌməl-tə-ˈfȯr-mē\ n : a skin disease characterized by papular or vesicular lesions and reddening or discoloration of the skin often in concentric zones about the lesions

erythema no·do·sum \-nō-ˈdō-səm\ n : a skin condition characterized by small tender reddened nodules under the skin (as over the shin bones) often accompanied by fever and transitory arthritic pains

erythematosus — see LUPUS ERYTHE-MATOSUS, LUPUS ERYTHEMATOSUS CELL, PEMPHIGUS ERYTHEMATOSUS, SYSTEMIC LUPUS ERYTHEMATOSUS

er·y·them·a·tous \ˌer-ə-ˈthe-mə-təs, -ˈthē-\ adj : relating to or marked by erythema

er·y·thor·bate \ˌer-ə-ˈthȯr-ˌbāt\ n : a salt of erythorbic acid that is used in foods as an antioxidant

erythorbic acid n : a stereoisomer of vitamin C

erythr- or **erythro-** comb form 1 : red (*erythrocyte*) 2 : erythrocyte (*erythroid*)

er·y·thrae·mia chiefly Brit var of ERY-THREMIA

er·y·thras·ma \ˌer-ə-ˈthraz-mə\ n : a chronic contagious dermatitis that affects warm moist areas of the body (as the axilla and groin) and is caused by a bacterium of the genus *Corynebacterium* (*C. minutissimum*)

eryth·re·de·ma \i-ˌri-thrə-ˈdē-mə\ n : ACRODYNIA

er·y·thre·mia \ˌer-ə-ˈthrē-mē-ə\ n : POLY-CYTHEMIA VERA

er·y·thrism \ˈer-ə-ˌthri-zəm\ n : a condition marked by exceptional prevalence of red pigmentation (as in skin or hair) — **er·y·thris·tic** \ˌer-ə-ˈthris-

tik\ *also* **er·y·thris·mal** \-ᵊthriz-məl\
adj

eryth·ri·tyl tet·ra·ni·trate \i-ᵊri-thrə-ᵊtil-
ᵢte-trə-ᵊni-ᵢtrāt\ *n* : a vasodilator
$C_4H_{10}N_4O_{12}$ used to prevent angina
pectoris — called also *erythritol tetranitrate*

erythro- — see ERYTHR-

eryth·ro·blast \i-ᵊri-thrə-ᵢblast\ *n* : a
polychromatic nucleated cell of red
marrow that synthesizes hemoglobin
and that is an intermediate in the initial stage of red blood cell formation;
broadly : a cell ancestral to red blood
cells — compare NORMOBLAST —
eryth·ro·blas·tic \-ᵢri-thrə-ᵊblas-tik\
adj

eryth·ro·blas·to·pe·nia \i-ᵢri-thrə-ᵢblas-
tə-ᵊpē-nē-ə\ *n* : a deficiency in bone-
marrow erythroblasts

eryth·ro·blas·to·sis \-ᵢblas-ᵊtō-səs\ *n, pl*
-to·ses \-ᵢsēz\ : abnormal presence of
erythroblasts in the circulating blood;
esp : ERYTHROBLASTOSIS FETALIS

erythroblastosis fe·ta·lis \-fi-ᵊta-ləs\ *n*
: a hemolytic disease of the fetus and
newborn that is characterized by an
increase in circulating erythroblasts
and by jaundice and that occurs when
the system of an Rh-negative mother
produces antibodies to an antigen in
the blood of an Rh-positive fetus —
called also *hemolytic disease of the
newborn, Rh disease*

eryth·ro·blas·tot·ic \i-ᵢri-thrə-ᵊblas-ᵊtä-
tik\ *adj* : of, relating to, or affected by
erythroblastosis (an ~ infant)

eryth·ro·cyte \i-ᵊri-thrə-ᵢsīt\ *n* : RED
BLOOD CELL — **eryth·ro·cyt·ic** \-ᵢri-
thrə-ᵊsi-tik\ *adj*

eryth·ro·cy·to·pe·nia \i-ᵢri-thrə-ᵢsī-tə-
ᵊpē-nē-ə\ *n* : red-blood-cell deficiency

eryth·ro·cy·tor·rhex·is \-ᵊrek-səs\ *n, pl*
-rhex·es \-ᵊrek-ᵢsēz\ : rupture of a red
blood cell

eryth·ro·cy·to·sis \i-ᵢri-thrə-ᵢsī-ᵊtō-səs\
n, pl -to·ses \-ᵊtō-ᵢsēz\ : an increase in
the number of circulating red blood
cells resulting from a known stimulus
(as hypoxia) — compare POLYCYTHE-
MIA VERA

eryth·ro·der·ma \-ᵊdər-mə\ *n, pl* -mas
\-məz\ *or* -ma·ta \-mə-tə\ : ERYTHEMA

eryth·ro·der·mia \-ᵊdər-mē-ə\ *n* : ERY-
THEMA

eryth·ro·gen·ic \-ᵊje-nik\ *adj* 1 : producing red blood cells : ERYTHROPOIETIC
2 : inducing reddening of the skin

ery·throid \i-ᵊri-ᵢthroid, ᵊer-ə-\ *adj* : relating to erythrocytes or their precursors

eryth·ro·leu·ke·mia \i-ᵢri-thrə-lü-ᵊkē-
mē-ə\ *n* : a malignant disorder that is
marked by proliferation of erythro-
blastic and myeloblastic tissue and in
later stages by leukemia — **eryth·ro·
leu·ke·mic** \-mik\ *adj*

eryth·ro·mel·al·gia \-mə-ᵊlal-jə\ *n* : a
state of excessive dilation of the superficial blood vessels usu. of the feet
accompanied by hyperemia, in-

creased skin temperature, and burning pain

eryth·ro·my·cin \i-ᵢri-thrə-ᵊmīs-ᵊn\ *n*
: a broad-spectrum antibiotic C_{37}-
$H_{67}NO_{13}$ produced by a bacterium of
the genus *Streptomyces* (*S. ery-
threus*), resembling penicillin in antibacterial activity, and effective also
against amebae, treponemata, and
pinworms — see ILOSONE, ILOTYCIN

eryth·ro·phago·cy·to·sis \i-ᵢri-thrə-ᵢfa-
gə-sə-ᵊtō-səs, -ᵢsī-\ *n, pl* -to·ses \-ᵊtō-
ᵢsēz\ : consumption of red blood cells
by histiocytes and sometimes other
phagocytes

eryth·ro·pla·sia \-ᵊplā-zhə, -zhē-ə\ *n* : a
reddened patch with a velvety sur-
face on the oral or genital mucosa
that is considered to be a precancerous lesion

eryth·ro·poi·e·sis \i-ᵢri-thrō-pói-ᵊē-səs\
n, pl -e·ses \-ᵢsēz\ : the production of
red blood cells (as from the bone marrow) — **eryth·ro·poi·et·ic** \-ᵊe-tik\ *adj*

erythropoietic protoporphyria *n* : a rare
porphyria usu. appearing in young
children and marked by excessive
protoporphyrin in erythrocytes,
blood plasma, and feces and by skin
lesions resulting from photosensitivity

eryth·ro·poi·e·tin \-ᵊpói-ət-ᵊn\ *n* : a hormonal substance that is formed esp.
in the kidney and stimulates red
blood cell formation

eryth·ro·sine \i-ᵊri-thrə-sən, -ᵢsēn\ *also*
eryth·ro·sin \-sən\ *n* : a brick-red powdered xanthene dye $C_{20}H_6I_4Na_2O_5$
that is used as a biological stain and
in dentistry as an agent to disclose
plaque on teeth — called also *eryth-
rosine sodium*

Es *symbol* einsteinium

ESB *abbr* electrical stimulation of the
brain

¹**es·cape** \i-ᵊskāp\ *n* 1 : evasion of something undesirable (~ from pain and
suffering) 2 : distraction or relief from
routine or reality; *esp* : mental distraction or relief by flight into ideal-
izing fantasy or fiction — **escape** *vb* —
escape *adj*

escape mechanism *n* : a mode of behavior or thinking adopted to evade unpleasant facts or responsibilities
: DEFENSE MECHANISM

es·cap·ism \i-ᵊskā-ᵢpi-zəm\ *n* : habitual
diversion of the mind to purely imag-
inative activity or entertainment as
an escape from reality or routine —
es·cap·ist \-pist\ *adj or n*

es·char \ᵊes-ᵢkär\ *n* : a scab formed
esp. after a burn

¹**es·cha·rot·ic** \ᵢes-kə-ᵊrä-tik\ *adj* : producing an eschar

²**escharotic** *n* : an escharotic agent (as a
drug)

Esch·e·rich·ia \ᵢe-shə-ᵊri-kē-ə\ *n* : a genus of aerobic gram-negative rod-
shaped bacteria (family Enterobacteriaceae) that include occas. patho-

genic forms (as some strains of *E. coli*) normally present in the human intestine and other forms which typically occur in soil and water

Esch·e·rich \\'e-shə-ˌrik\\, **Theodor** (1857–1911), German pediatrician.

es·cutch·eon \i-'skə-chən\ *n* : the configuration of adult pubic hair

es·er·ine \\'e-sə-ˌrēn\\ *n* : PHYSOSTIGMINE

Es·march bandage \\'es-ˌmärk, 'ez-\ *or* **Es·march's bandage** \-ˌmärks-\ *n* : a tight rubber bandage for driving the blood out of a limb

Esmarch, Johannes Friedrich August von (1823–1908), German surgeon.

eso- *prefix* : inner (*esotropia*)

esophag- *or* **esophago-** *comb form* **1** : esophagus (*esophagectomy*) (*esophagoplasty*) **2** : esophagus and (*esophagogastrectomy*)

esoph·a·ge·al \i-ˌsä-fə-'jē-əl\ *adj* : of or relating to the esophagus

esophageal artery *n* : any of several arteries that arise from the front of the aorta, anastomose along the esophagus, and terminate by anastomosis with adjacent arteries

esophageal gland *n* : one of the racemose glands in the walls of the esophagus that in humans are small and serve principally to lubricate the food but in some birds secrete a milky fluid on which the young are fed

esophageal hiatus *n* : the aperture in the diaphragm that gives passage to the esophagus — see HIATAL HERNIA

esophageal plexus *n* : a nerve plexus formed by the branches of the vagus nerve which surround and supply the esophagus

esophageal speech *n* : a method of speaking which is used by individuals whose larynx has been removed and in which phonation is achieved by expelling swallowed air from the esophagus

esoph·a·gec·to·my \i-ˌsä-fə-'jek-tə-mē\ *n*, *pl* -**mies** : excision of part of the esophagus

esophagi *pl of* ESOPHAGUS

esoph·a·gi·tis \i-ˌsä-fə-'ji-təs, -'gī-, (ˌ)ē-\ *n* : inflammation of the esophagus

esophago- — see ESOPHAG-

esoph·a·go·gas·trec·to·my \i-ˌsä-fə-gō-ˌgas-'trek-tə-mē\ *n*, *pl* -**mies** : excision of part of the esophagus (esp. the lower third) and the stomach

esoph·a·go·gas·tric \-'gas-trik\ *adj* : of, relating to, involving, or affecting the esophagus and the stomach (∼ ulcers)

esoph·a·go·gas·tros·co·py \-ˌgas-'träs-kə-pē\ *n*, *pl* -**pies** : examination of the interior of the esophagus and stomach by means of an endoscope

esoph·a·go·gas·tros·to·my \-ˌgas-'träs-tə-mē\ *n*, *pl* -**mies** : the surgical formation of an artificial communication between the esophagus and the stomach

esoph·a·go·je·ju·nos·to·my \-ˌje-jə-'näs-tə-mē\ *n*, *pl* -**mies** : the surgical formation of an artificial communication between the esophagus and the jejunum

esoph·a·go·my·ot·o·my \-ˌmī-'ä-tə-mē\ *n*, *pl* -**mies** : incision through the musculature of the esophagus and esp. the distal part (as for the relief of esophageal achalasia)

esoph·a·go·plas·ty \i-'sä-fə-gə-ˌplas-tē\ *n*, *pl* -**ties** : plastic repair or reconstruction of the esophagus

esoph·a·go·scope \-ˌskōp\ *n* : an instrument for inspecting the interior of the esophagus

esoph·a·gos·co·py \i-ˌsä-fə-'gäs-kə-pē\ *n*, *pl* -**pies** : examination of the esophagus by means of an esophagoscope — **esoph·a·go·scop·ic** \i-ˌsä-fə-gə-'skä-pik\ *adj*

esoph·a·go·sto·mi·a·sis *var of* OESOPHAGOSTOMIASIS

esoph·a·gos·to·my \i-ˌsä-fə-'gäs-tə-mē\ *n*, *pl* -**mies** : surgical creation of an artificial opening into the esophagus

esoph·a·got·o·my \-'gä-tə-mē\ *n*, *pl* -**mies** : incision of the esophagus (as for the removal of an obstruction or the relief of esophageal achalasia)

esoph·a·gus \i-'sä-fə-gəs\ *n*, *pl* -**gi** \-ˌgī, -ˌjī\ : a muscular tube that in humans is about nine inches (23 centimeters) long and passes from the pharynx down the neck between the trachea and the spinal column and behind the left bronchus where it pierces the diaphragm slightly to the left of the middle line and joins the cardiac end of the stomach

es·o·pho·ria \ˌe-sə-'fōr-ē-ə, *sometimes* ˌē-\ *n* : squint in which the eyes tend to turn inward toward the nose

es·o·tro·pia \ˌe-sə-'trō-pē-ə, ˌē-\ *n* : CROSS-EYE 1 — **es·o·trop·ic** \-'trä-pik\ *adj*

ESP \ˌē-(ˌ)es-'pē\ *n* : EXTRASENSORY PERCEPTION

es·pun·dia \is-'pün-dē-ə, -'pün-\ *n* : leishmaniasis of the mouth, pharynx, and nose that is prevalent in Central and So. America

ESR *abbr* erythrocyte sedimentation rate

es·sen·tial \i-'sen-chəl\ *adj* : having no obvious or known cause : IDIOPATHIC (∼ disease)

essential amino acid *n* : any of various alpha-amino acids that are required for normal health and growth, are either not manufactured in the body or manufactured in insufficient quantities, are usu. supplied by dietary protein, and in humans include isoleucine, leucine, lysine, methionine, phenylalanine, threonine, tryptophan, and valine

essential hypertension *n* : abnormally high systolic and diastolic blood pressure occurring in the absence of any evident cause and resulting typically in marked hypertrophic and degenerative changes in small arteries, hypertrophy of the heart, and often more or less severe kidney damage — called also *primary hypertension*; see MALIGNANT HYPERTENSION

essential oil *n* : any of a large class of volatile oils of vegetable origin that give plants their characteristic odors and are used esp. in perfumes, flavorings, and pharmaceutical preparations — called also *volatile oil*; compare FATTY OIL, FIXED OIL

EST *abbr* electroshock therapy

es·ter \'es-tər\ *n* : any of a class of often fragrant compounds that can be represented by the formula RCOOR' and that are usu. formed by the reaction between an acid and an alcohol usu. with elimination of water

es·ter·ase \'es-tə-ˌrās, -ˌrāz\ *n* : an enzyme that accelerates the hydrolysis or synthesis of esters

es·ter·i·fy \'es-ter-ə-ˌfī\ *vb* -**fied**; -**fy·ing** : to convert into an ester — **es·ter·i·fi·ca·tion** \e-ˌster-ə-fə-'kā-shən\ *n*

estr- *or* **estro-** *comb form* : estrus (*estrogen*)

es·tra·di·ol \ˌes-trə-'dī-ˌōl, -ˌol\ *n* : an estrogenic hormone that is a phenolic steroid alcohol $C_{18}H_{24}O_2$ usu. made synthetically and that is often used combined as an ester esp. in treating menopausal symptoms — called also *dihydrotheelin*

es·tral cycle \'es-trəl-\ *n* : ESTROUS CYCLE

es·trin \'es-trən\ *n* : an estrogenic hormone; *esp* : ESTRONE

es·tri·ol \'es-ˌtrī-ˌōl, e-'strī-, -ˌol\ *n* : a crystalline estrogenic hormone $C_{18}H_{24}O_3$ usu. obtained from the urine of pregnant women

estro- — see ESTR-

es·tro·gen \'es-trə-jən\ *n* : a substance (as a sex hormone) tending to promote estrus and stimulate the development of female secondary sex characteristics

es·tro·gen·ic \ˌes-trə-'je-nik\ *adj* 1 : promoting estrus 2 : of, relating to, caused by, or being an estrogen — **es·tro·gen·i·cal·ly** \-ni-k(ə-)lē\ *adv* — **es·tro·gen·ic·i·ty** \-jə-'ni-sə-tē\ *n*

es·trone \'es-ˌtrōn\ *n* : an estrogenic hormone that is a ketone $C_{18}H_{22}O_2$, is usu. obtained from the urine of pregnant women, and is used similarly to estradiol — see THEELIN

es·trous \'es-trəs\ *adj* 1 : of, relating to, or characteristic of estrus 2 : being in heat

estrous cycle *n* : the correlated phenomena of the endocrine and generative systems of a female mammal from the beginning of one period of estrus to the beginning of the next — called also *estral cycle, estrus cycle*

es·tru·al \'es-trə-wəl\ *adj* : ESTROUS

es·trus \'es-trəs\ *n* : a regularly recurrent state of sexual excitability during which the female of most mammals will accept the male and is capable of conceiving : HEAT; *also* : a single occurrence of this state

eth·a·cryn·ic acid \ˌe-thə-'kri-nik-\ *n* : a potent synthetic diuretic $C_{13}H_{12}Cl_2$-O_4 used esp. in the treatment of edema

eth·am·bu·tol \e-'tham-byü-ˌtȯl, -ˌtōl\ *n* : a synthetic drug $C_{10}H_{24}N_2O_2$ used esp. in the treatment of tuberculosis — see MYAMBUTOL

etha·mi·van \e-'tha-mə-ˌvan, ˌe-thə-'mī-vən\ *n* : an analeptic drug and central nervous stimulant $C_{12}H_{17}NO_3$ used as a respiratory stimulant for intoxication with central nervous depressants (as barbiturates) and for chronic lung diseases

eth·a·nol \'e-thə-ˌnȯl, -ˌnōl\ *n* : a colorless volatile flammable liquid C_2H_5-OH that is the intoxicating agent in liquors and is also used as a solvent — called also *ethyl alcohol, grain alcohol*; see ALCOHOL 1

eth·chlor·vy·nol \ˌeth-'klȯr-və-ˌnȯl, -ˌnōl\ *n* : a pungent liquid alcohol C_7H_9ClO derived from methanol and used esp. as a mild hypnotic — see PLACIDYL

eth·ene \'e-ˌthēn\ *n* : ETHYLENE

ether \'ē-thər\ *n* 1 : a light volatile flammable liquid $C_4H_{10}O$ used esp. formely as an anesthetic — called also *diethyl ether, ethyl ether* 2 : any of various organic compounds characterized by an oxygen atom attached to two carbon atoms

ether·ize \'ē-thə-ˌrīz\ *vb* -**ized**; -**iz·ing** : to treat or anesthetize with ether

¹eth·i·cal \'e-thi-kəl\ *also* **eth·ic** \-thik\ *adj* 1 : conforming to accepted professional standards of conduct 2 *of a drug* : restricted to sale only on a doctor's prescription — **eth·i·cal·ly** \-thi-k(ə-)lē\ *adv*

²ethical *n* : an ethical drug

eth·ics \'e-thiks\ *n sing or pl* : the principles of conduct governing an individual or a group (medical ~)

ethid·i·um bromide \e-'thi-dē-əm-\ *n* : a biological dye used to block nucleic acid synthesis (as in mitochondria) and to destroy trypanosomes

ethi·nyl *var of* ETHYNYL — used esp. in pharmacology

eth·i·nyl estra·di·ol \ˌe-thə-ni-ˌles-trə-'dī-ˌol, -ˌōl\ *n* : a very potent synthetic estrogen $C_{20}H_{24}O_2$ used orally

eth·i·on·amide \ˌe-thē-'ä-nə-ˌmīd\ *n* : a compound $C_8H_{10}N_2S$ used against mycobacteria (as in tuberculosis and leprosy)

ethi·o·nine \e-'thī-ə-ˌnēn\ *n* : an amino acid $C_6H_{13}NO_2S$ that is biologically antagonistic to methionine

eth·is·ter·one \i-'this-tə-ˌrōn\ *n* : a synthetic female sex hormone $C_{21}H_{28}O_2$ administered in cases of deficiency of progesterone — called also *anhydrohydroxyprogesterone*

ethmo- *comb form* : ethmoid and ⟨*ethmo*maxillary⟩

¹**eth·moid** \'eth-₁mȯid\ *or* **eth·moi·dal** \eth-'mȯid-ᵊl\ *adj* : of, relating to, adjoining, or being one or more bones of the walls and septum of the nasal cavity

²**ethmoid** *n* : ETHMOID BONE

ethmoidal air cells *n pl* : the cavities in the lateral masses of the ethmoid bone that are partly completed by adjoining bones and communicate with the nasal cavity

ethmoid bone *n* : a light spongy cubical bone forming much of the walls of the nasal cavity and part of those of the orbits

eth·moid·ec·to·my \₁eth-₁mȯi-'dek-tə-mē\ *n, pl* **-mies** : excision of all or some of the ethmoidal air cells or part of the ethmoid bone

eth·moid·itis \-'dī-təs\ *n* : inflammation of the ethmoid bone or its sinuses

ethmoid sinus *also* **ethmoidal sinus** *n* : either of two sinuses each of which is situated in a lateral part of the ethmoid bone alongside the nose and consists of ethmoidal air cells

eth·mo·max·il·lary \₁eth-(₁)mō-'mak-sə-₁ler-ē\ *adj* : of or relating to the ethmoid and maxillary bones

etho·sux·i·mide \₁e-(₁)thō-'sək-sə-₁mīd. -₁məd\ *n* : an antidepressant drug $C_7H_{11}NO_2$ used to treat epilepsy

eth·o·to·in \₁e-thə-'tō-ən\ *n* : an anticonvulsant drug $C_{11}H_{12}N_2O_2$ used in the treatment of epilepsy — see PEGANONE

eth·yl alcohol \'e-thəl-\ *n* : ETHANOL

ethyl aminobenzoate *n* : BENZOCAINE

ethyl bromide *n* : a volatile liquid compound C_2H_5Br used as an inhalation anesthetic

ethyl carbamate *n* : URETHANE

ethyl chloride *n* : a colorless pungent flammable gaseous or volatile liquid C_2H_5Cl used esp. as a local surface anesthetic

eth·yl·ene \'e-thə-₁lēn\ *n* : a colorless flammable gaseous unsaturated hydrocarbon C_2H_4 used in medicine as a general inhalation anesthetic and occurring in plants where it functions esp. as a natural growth regulator that promotes the ripening of fruit — called also *ethene*

ethylene bromide *n* : ETHYLENE DIBROMIDE

ethylene di·amine \-'dī-ə-₁mēn. -dī-'a-mən\ *n* : a colorless volatile liquid base $C_2H_8N_2$ used in medicine to stabilize aminophylline when used in injections

eth·yl·ene·di·amine·tetra·ace·tate \₁e-thə-₁lēn-₁dī-ə-₁mēn-₁te-trə-'a-sə-₁tāt. -dī-'a-mən-\ *n* : a salt of EDTA

eth·yl·ene·di·amine·tetra·ace·tic acid \-ə-'sē-tik-\ *n* : EDTA

ethylene dibromide *n* : a colorless toxic liquid compound $C_2H_4Br_2$ that has been shown by experiments with lab-oratory animals to be strongly carcinogenic and that was used formerly in the U.S. as an agricultural pesticide — abbr. *EDB*; called also *ethylene bromide*

ethylene glycol *n* : a thick liquid alcohol $C_2H_6O_2$ used esp. as an antifreeze

ethylene oxide *n* : a colorless flammable toxic gaseous or liquid compound C_2H_4O used in fumigation and sterilization (as of medical instruments)

eth·yl·es·tren·ol \₁e-thəl-'es-trə-₁nȯl. -₁nōl\ *n* : an anabolic steroid $C_{20}H_{32}O$ having androgenic activity — see MAXIBOLIN

eth·yl·mor·phine \₁e-thəl-'mȯr-₁fēn\ *n* : a synthetic toxic alkaloid $C_{19}H_{23}$-NO_3 used esp. in the form of its hydrochloride similarly to morphine and codeine

ethy·nyl \e-'thīn-ᵊl. 'e-thə-₁nil\ *n* : a monovalent unsaturated group $HC≡C–$

ethy·nyl·es·tra·di·ol *var of* ETHINYL ESTRADIOL

etio- *comb form* : cause ⟨*etio*logic⟩ ⟨*etio*pathogenesis⟩

etio·chol·an·ol·one \₁e-tē-ō-₁kō-'la-nə-₁lōn. ₁e-\ *n* : a testosterone metabolite $C_{19}H_{30}O_2$ that occurs in urine

eti·o·log·ic \₁e-tē-ə-'lä-jik\ *or* **eti·o·log·i·cal** \-ji-kəl\ *adj* 1 : of, relating to, or based on etiology ⟨~ investigations⟩ 2 : causing or contributing to the cause of a disease or condition — **eti·o·log·i·cal·ly** \-ji-k(ə-)lē\ *adv*

eti·ol·o·gy \₁e-tē-'ä-lə-jē\ *n, pl* **-gies** 1 : all of the causes of a disease or abnormal condition 2 : a branch of medical science dealing with the causes and origin of diseases

etio·patho·gen·e·sis \₁e-tē-ō-₁pa-thə-'je-nə-səs. ₁e-\ *n, pl* **-e·ses** \-₁sēz\ : the cause and development of a disease or abnormal condition

etor·phine \e-'tȯr-₁fēn. i-\ *n* : a synthetic narcotic drug $C_{25}H_{33}NO_4$ related to morphine but with more potent analgesic properties

eu- *comb form* 1 : good : normal ⟨*eu*thyroid⟩ 2 : true ⟨*eu*globulin⟩

Eu *symbol* europium

eu·ca·lyp·tol *also* **eu·ca·lyp·tole** \₁yü-kə-'lip-₁tȯl. -₁tōl\ *n* : a liquid $C_{10}H_{18}O$ with an odor of camphor that is contained in many essential oils (as of eucalyptus) and is used esp. as an expectorant — called also *cajeputol*, *cineole*

eu·ca·lyp·tus oil \₁yü-kə-'lip-təs-\ *n* : any of various essential oils obtained from the leaves of an Australian tree (genus *Eucalyptus* and esp. *E. globulus*) of the myrtle family (Myrtaceae) and used in pharmaceutical preparations (as antiseptics or cough drops)

eu·cary·ote *var of* EUKARYOTE

euc·at·ro·pine \yü-'ka-trə-₁pēn\ *n* : a synthetic alkaloid used in the form of its white crystalline hydrochloride $C_{17}H_{25}NO_3 \cdot HCl$ as a mydriatic

eu·chro·ma·tin \(ˌ)yü-ˈkrō-mə-tən\ *n* : the genetically active portion of chromatin that is largely composed of genes — **eu·chro·mat·ic** \ˌyü-krō-ˈma-tik\ *adj*

eu·gen·ics \yü-ˈje-niks\ *n* : a science that deals with the improvement (as by control of human mating) of hereditary qualities of a race or breed — **eu·gen·ic** \-nik\ *adj* — **eu·gen·i·cist** \-nə-sist\ *n* — **eu·gen·i·cal·ly** *adv*

eu·ge·nol \ˈyü-jə-ˌnȯl, -ˌnōl\ *n* : an aromatic liquid phenol $C_{10}H_{12}O_2$ found esp. in clove oil and used in dentistry as an analgesic

eu·glob·u·lin \yü-ˈglä-byə-lən\ *n* : a simple protein that does not dissolve in pure water

eu·gly·ce·mia \ˌyü-ˌglī-ˈsē-mē-ə\ *n* : a normal level of sugar in the blood

eu·kary·ote \(ˌ)yü-ˈkar-ē-ˌōt, -ē-ət\ *n* : an organism composed of one or more cells containing visibly evident nuclei and organelles — compare PROKARYOTE — **eu·kary·ot·ic** *also* **eu·cary·ot·ic** \-ˌkar-ē-ˈä-tik\ *adj*

eu·nuch \ˈyü-nək, -nik\ *n* : a man or boy deprived of the testes or external genitals — **eu·nuch·ism** \-nə-ˌki-zəm, -ni-\ *n*

¹eu·nuch·oid \ˈyü-nə-ˌkȯid\ *adj* : of, relating to, or characterized by eunuchoidism : resembling a eunuch

²eunuchoid *n* : a sexually deficient individual; *esp* : one lacking in sexual differentiation and tending toward the intersex state

eu·nuch·oid·ism \ˈyü-nə-ˌkȯi-ˌdi-zəm\ *n* : a state suggestive of that of a eunuch in being marked by deficiency of sexual development, by persistence of prepubertal characteristics, and often by the presence of characteristics typical of the opposite sex

eu·pep·sia \yü-ˈpep-shə, -sē-ə\ *n* : good digestion — **eu·pep·tic** \ˈpep-tik\ *adj*

eu·phen·ics \yü-ˈfe-niks\ *n* : a science that deals with the biological improvement of human beings after birth — **eu·phen·ic** \-nik\ *adj*

eu·pho·ria \yü-ˈfōr-ē-ə\ *n* : a feeling of well-being or elation; *esp* : one that is groundless, disproportionate to its cause, or inappropriate to one's life situation — compare DYSPHORIA — **eu·phor·ic** \-ˈfōr-ik, -ˈfär-\ *adj* — **eu·phor·i·cal·ly** \-i-k(ə-)lē\ *adv*

¹eu·pho·ri·ant \yü-ˈfōr-ē-ənt\ *n* : a drug that tends to induce euphoria

²euphoriant *adj* : tending to induce euphoria ⟨a ~ drug⟩

eu·phor·i·gen·ic \yü-ˌfōr-ə-ˈje-nik\ *adj* : tending to cause euphoria

eup·nea \yüp-ˈnē-ə\ *n* : normal respiration — compare DYSPNEA — **eup·ne·ic** \-ˈnē-ik\ *adj*

eup·noea *chiefly Brit var of* EUPNEA

eu·ro·pi·um \yü-ˈrō-pē-əm\ *n* : a biva-

lent and trivalent metallic element — symbol *Eu*; see ELEMENT table

-eus \ē-əs\ *n comb form, pl* **-ei** \ē-ī\ *also* **-eus·es** \ē-ə-səz\ : muscle that constitutes, has the form of, or joins a (specified) part, thing, or structure (glut*eus*) (rhomboid*eus*) (iliococcyg*eus*)

eu·sta·chian tube \yü-ˈstā-shən-, -shē-ən-, -kē-ən-\ *n, often cap E* : a bony and cartilaginous tube connecting the middle ear with the nasopharynx and equalizing air pressure on both sides of the tympanic membrane — called also *auditory tube, pharyngotympanic tube*

Eu·sta·chio \āü-ˈstäk-yō\, **Bartolomeo** (*ca* 1520–1574), Italian anatomist.

eu·tha·na·sia \ˌyü-thə-ˈnā-zhə, -zhē-ə\ *n* : the act or practice of killing hopelessly sick or injured individuals (as persons or domestic animals) in a relatively painless way for reasons of mercy; *also* : the act or practice of allowing a hopelessly sick or injured patient to die by taking less than complete medical measures to prolong life — called also *mercy killing*

eu·than·a·tize \yü-ˈtha-nə-ˌtīz\ *also* **eu·tha·nize** \ˈyü-thə-ˌnīz\ *vb* **-tized** *also* **-nized; -tiz·ing** *also* **-niz·ing** : to subject to euthanasia

eu·then·ics \yü-ˈthe-niks\ *n sing or pl* : a science that deals with development of human well-being by improvement of living conditions — **eu·the·nist** \yü-ˈthe-nist, ˈyü-thə-\ *n*

eu·thy·roid \(ˌ)yü-ˈthī-ˌrȯid\ *adj* : characterized by normal thyroid function — **eu·thy·roid·ism** \-ˌrȯi-ˌdi-zəm\ *n*

¹evac·u·ant \i-ˈva-kyə-wənt\ *n* : an evacuant agent

²evacuant *adj* : EMETIC, DIURETIC, PURGATIVE, CATHARTIC

evac·u·ate \i-ˈva-kyə-ˌwāt\ *vb* **-at·ed; -at·ing** 1 : to remove the contents of ⟨~ an abscess⟩ 2 : to discharge (as urine or feces) from the body as waste : VOID — **evac·u·a·tive** \-ˌwā-tiv\ *adj*

evac·u·a·tion \i-ˌva-kyə-ˈwā-shən\ *n* 1 : the act or process of evacuating 2 : something evacuated or discharged

evag·i·na·tion \i-ˌva-jə-ˈnā-shən\ *n* 1 : a process of turning outward or inside out (~ of a cell membrane) 2 : a part or structure that is produced by evagination — called also *outpocketing, outpouching* — **evag·i·nate** \i-ˈva-jə-ˌnāt\ *vb*

ev·a·nes·cent \ˌe-və-ˈnes-ᵊnt\ *adj* : tending to disappear quickly : of relatively short duration ⟨an ~ rash⟩

Ev·ans blue \ˈe-vənz-\ *n* : a dye $C_{34}H_{24}N_6Na_4O_{14}S_4$ that on injection into the blood stream combines with serum albumin and is used to determine blood volume colorimetrically

Evans, Herbert McLean (1882–

1971), American anatomist and physiologist.

even·tra·tion \ē-ᵢven-ᵗtrā-shən\ n : protrusion of abdominal organs through the abdominal wall

ever·sion \i-ᵗvər-zhən, -shən\ n 1 : the act of turning inside out : the state of being turned inside out (~ of the eyelid) 2 : the condition (as of the foot) of being turned or rotated outward — compare INVERSION 1b

evert \i-ᵗvərt\ vb : to turn outward (~ the foot); also : to turn inside out

evis·cer·ate \i-ᵗvis-sə-ᵢrāt\ vb -at·ed; -at·ing 1 a : to remove the viscera of b : to remove an organ from (a patient) or the contents of (an organ) 2 : to protrude through a surgical incision or suffer protrusion of a part through an incision — evis·cer·a·tion \i-ᵢvis-sə-ᵗrā-shən\ n

evo·ca·tion \ᵢē-vō-ᵗkā-shən, ᵢe-\ n : INDUCTION 2b

evo·ca·tor \ᵗē-vō-ᵢkā-tər, ᵗe-\ n : the specific chemical constituent responsible for the physiological effects of an organizer

evoked potential \ē-ᵗvōkt-\ n : an electrical response esp. in the cerebral cortex as recorded following stimulation of a peripheral sense receptor

evo·lu·tion \ᵢe-və-ᵗlü-shən, ᵢē-\ n 1 : a process of change in a certain direction 2 a : the historical development of a biological group (as a race or species) : PHYLOGENY b : a theory that the various types of animals and plants have their origin in other preexisting types and that the distinguishable differences are due to modifications in successive generations — **evo·lu·tion·ar·i·ly** \-shə-ᵢner-ə-lē\ adv — **evo·lu·tion·ary** \-shə-ᵢner-ē\ adj — **evo·lu·tion·ist** \-shə-nist\ n

evolve \i-ᵗvälv, -ᵗvȯlv\ vb evolved; evolv·ing : to produce or develop by natural evolutionary processes

evul·sion \i-ᵗvəl-shən\ n : the act of extracting forcibly : EXTRACTION (~ of a tooth) — **evulse** \i-ᵗvəls\ vb

ewe-neck \ᵗyü-ᵗnek\ n : a thin neck with a concave arch occurring as a defect in dogs and horses — **ewe-necked** \-ᵗnekt\ adj

Ew·ing's sarcoma \ᵗyü-iŋz-\ n : a tumor that invades the shaft of a long bone and that tends to recur but rarely metastasizes — called also Ewing's tumor

Ewing, James (1866–1943), American pathologist.

ex- — see EXO-

ex·ac·er·bate \ig-ᵗza-sər-ᵢbāt\ vb -bat·ed; -bat·ing : to cause (a disease or its symptoms) to become more severe — **ex·ac·er·ba·tion** \-ᵢza-sər-ᵗbā-shən\ n

ex·al·ta·tion \ᵢeg-ᵢzȯl-ᵗtā-shən, ᵢek-ᵢsȯl-\ n 1 : marked or excessive intensification of a mental state or of the activity of a bodily part or function 2 : an abnormal sense of personal well-

being, power, or importance : a delusional euphoria

ex·am \ig-ᵗzam\ n : EXAMINATION

ex·am·i·na·tion \ig-ᵢza-mə-ᵗnā-shən\ n : the act or process of inspecting or testing for evidence of disease or abnormality — see PHYSICAL EXAMINATION — **ex·am·ine** \ig-ᵗza-mən\ vb

ex·am·in·ee \ig-ᵢza-mə-ᵗnē\ n : a person who is examined

ex·am·in·er \ig-ᵗza-mə-nər\ n : one that examines — see MEDICAL EXAMINER

ex·an·them \eg-ᵗzan-thəm, ᵗek-ᵢsan-them\ also **ex·an·the·ma** \eg-ᵗzan-ᵗthē-mə\ n, pl -thems also -them·a·ta \ᵢeg-ᵢzan-ᵗthe-mə-tə\ or -themas : an eruptive disease (as measles) or its symptomatic eruption — **ex·an·them·a·tous** \ᵢeg-ᵢzan-ᵗthe-mə-təs\ or **ex·an·the·mat·ic** \ᵢeg-ᵢzan-ᵗthe-ᵢma-tik\ adj

ex·ca·va·tion \ᵢek-skə-ᵗvā-shən\ n 1 : the action or process of forming or undergoing formation of a cavity or hole 2 : a cavity formed by or as if by cutting, digging, or scooping — **ex·ca·vate** vb \ᵗek-skə-ᵢvāt\

ex·ca·va·tor \ᵗek-skə-ᵢvā-tər\ n : an instrument used to open bodily cavities (as in the teeth) or remove material from them

excavatum — see PECTUS EXCAVATUM

ex·ce·men·to·sis \ᵢeks-si-mən-ᵗtō-səs\ n, pl -to·ses \-ᵢsēz\ or -to·sis·es : abnormal outgrowth of the cementum of the root of a tooth

ex·change transfusion \iks-ᵗchānj-\ n : simultaneous withdrawal of the recipient's blood and transfusion with the donor's blood esp. in the treatment of erythroblastosis

ex·ci·mer laser \ᵗek-si-mər-\ n : a laser that uses a compound of a halogen and a noble gas to generate radiation usu. in the ultraviolet region of the spectrum

ex·cip·i·ent \ik-ᵗsi-pē-ənt\ n : a usu. inert substance (as gum arabic or starch) that forms a vehicle (as for a drug)

ex·ci·sion \ik-ᵗsi-zhən\ n : surgical removal or resection (as of a diseased part) — **ex·cise** \-ᵗsīz\ vb — **ex·ci·sion·al** \-ᵗsi-zhə-nəl\ adj

ex·cit·able \ik-ᵗsī-tə-bəl\ adj, of living tissue or an organism : capable of being activated by and reacting to stimuli : exhibiting irritability — **ex·cit·abil·i·ty** \-ᵢsī-tə-ᵗbi-lə-tē\ n

ex·ci·tant \ik-ᵗsīt-ᵊnt, ᵗek-sə-tənt\ n : an agent that arouses or augments physiological activity (as of the nervous system) — **excitant** adj

ex·ci·ta·tion \ᵢek-ᵢsī-ᵗtā-shən, -sə-\ n : EXCITEMENT: as a : the disturbed or altered condition resulting from arousal of activity (as by neural or electrical stimulation) in an individual organ or tissue b : the arousing of such activity

ex·cit·a·to·ry \ik-ᵗsī-tə-ᵢtōr-ē\ adj 1 : tending to induce excitation (as of a

neuron 2 : exhibiting, resulting from, related to, or produced by excitement or excitation

ex·cite \ik-ˈsīt\ *vb* **ex·cit·ed; ex·cit·ing** : to increase the activity of (as a living organism) — **STIMULATE**

ex·cite·ment \-ˈsīt-mənt\ *n* **1** : the act of exciting **2** : the state of being excited: as **a** : aroused, augmented, or abnormal activity of an organism or functioning of an organ or part **b** : extreme motor hyperactivity (as in catatonic schizophrenia)

ex·co·ri·a·tion \(ˌ)ek-ˌskōr-ē-ˈā-shən\ *n* **1** : the act of abrading or wearing of the skin **2** : a raw irritated lesion (as of the skin or a mucosal surface) — **ex·co·ri·ate** \ek-ˈskōr-ē-ˌāt\ *vb*

ex·cre·ment \ˈek-skrə-mənt\ *n* : waste matter discharged from the body; *esp* : waste (as feces) discharged from the alimentary canal — **ex·cre·men·tal** \ˌek-skrə-ˈment-ᵊl\ *adj*

ex·cres·cence \ik-ˈskres-ᵊns\ *n* : an outgrowth or enlargement: as **a** : a natural and normal appendage or development **b** : an abnormal outgrowth — **ex·cres·cent** \ik-ˈskres-ᵊnt\ *adj*

ex·cre·ta \ik-ˈskrē-tə\ *n pl* : waste matter eliminated or separated from an organism — compare EXCRETION 2 — **ex·cre·tal** \-ˈskrē-təl\ *adj*

ex·crete \ik-ˈskrēt\ *vb* **ex·cret·ed; ex·cret·ing** : to separate and eliminate or discharge (waste) from the blood or tissues or from the active protoplasm

ex·cret·er \-ˈskrē-tər\ *n* : one that excretes something and esp. an atypical bodily product (as a pathogenic microorganism)

ex·cre·tion \ik-ˈskrē-shən\ *n* **1** : the act or process of excreting **2 a** : something eliminated by the process of excretion that is composed chiefly of urine or sweat in mammals including humans and of comparable materials in other animals, characteristically includes products of protein degradation (as urea or uric acid), usu. differs from ordinary bodily secretions by lacking any further utility to the organism that produces it, and is distinguished from waste materials (as feces) that have merely passed into or through the alimentary canal without being incorporated into the body proper **b** : a waste product (as urine, feces, or vomitus) eliminated from an animal body : EXCREMENT — not used technically

ex·cre·to·ry \ˈek-skrə-ˌtōr-ē\ *adj* : of, relating to, or functioning in excretion (~ ducts)

ex·cur·sion \ik-ˈskər-zhən\ *n* **1** : a movement outward and back or from a mean position or axis **2** : one complete movement of expansion and contraction of the lungs and their membranes (as in breathing)

ex·cyst \eks-ˈsist\ *vb* : to emerge from a cyst — **ex·cys·ta·tion** \ˌeks-ˌsis-ˈtā-shən\ *n* — **ex·cyst·ment** \eks-ˈsist-mənt\ *n*

ex·en·ter·a·tion \ig-ˌzen-tə-ˈrā-shən\ *n* : surgical removal of the contents of a bodily cavity (as the orbit, pelvis, or a sinus) — **ex·en·ter·ate** \ig-ˈzen-tə-ˌrāt\ *vb*

ex·er·cise \ˈek-sər-ˌsīz\ *n* **1** : regular or repeated use of a faculty or bodily organ **2** : bodily exertion for the sake of developing and maintaining physical fitness — **exercise** *vb*

ex·er·cis·er \ˈek-sər-ˌsī-zər\ *n* **1** : one that exercises **2** : an apparatus for use in physical exercise

ex·er·e·sis \ig-ˈzer-ə-səs\ *n, pl* **-e·ses** \-ˌsēz\ : surgical removal of a part or organ (as a nerve)

ex·fla·gel·la·tion \(ˌ)eks-ˌfla-jə-ˈlā-shən\ *n* : the formation of microgametes in sporozoans (as the malaria parasite) by extrusion of nuclear material into peripheral processes resembling flagella — **ex·fla·gel·late** \-ˈfla-jə-ˌlāt\ *vb*

ex·fo·li·ate \(ˌ)eks-ˈfō-lē-ˌāt\ *vb* **-at·ed; -at·ing** **1** : to cast or come off in scales or laminae **2** : to remove the surface of in scales or laminae **3** : to shed (teeth) by exfoliation

ex·fo·li·a·tion \(ˌ)eks-ˌfō-lē-ˈā-shən\ *n* : the action or process of exfoliating: as **a** : the peeling of the horny layer of the skin **b** : the shedding of surface components **c** : the shedding of a superficial layer of bone or of a tooth or part of a tooth — **ex·fo·li·a·tive** \eks-ˈfō-lē-ˌā-tiv\ *adj*

exfoliative cytology *n* : the study of cells shed from body surfaces esp. for determining the presence or absence of a cancerous condition

ex·ha·la·tion \ˌeks-hə-ˈlā-shən, ˌeks-ə-ˈ\ *n* **1** : the action of forcing air out of the lungs **2** : something (as the breath) that is exhaled or given off — **ex·hale** \eks-ˈhāl, ek-ˈsāl\ *vb*

ex·haust \ig-ˈzȯst\ *vb* **1 a** : to draw off or let out completely **b** : to empty by drawing off the contents: *specif* : to create a vacuum in **2 a** : to use up : consume completely **b** : to tire extremely or completely (~ed by overwork) **3** : to extract completely with a solvent

ex·haus·tion \ig-ˈzȯs-chən\ *n* **1** : the act or process of exhausting: the state of being exhausted **2** : neurosis following overstrain or overexertion esp. in military combat

ex·hib·it \ig-ˈzi-bət\ *vb* : to administer for medical purposes

ex·hi·bi·tion·ism \ˌek-sə-ˈbi-shə-ˌni-zəm\ *n* **1 a** : a perversion marked by a tendency to indecent exposure **b** : an act of such exposure **2** : the act or practice of behaving so as to attract attention to oneself — **ex·hi·bi·tion-**

ist \-nist\ *n* — **ex·hi·bi·tion·is·tic** \-bish-ə-⁵nis-tik\ *also* **exhibitionist** *adj* — **ex·hi·bi·tion·is·ti·cal·ly** \-ti-k(ə-)lē\ *adv*

ex·hume \ig-⁵züm, igz-⁵yüm; iks-⁵hyüm, -⁵yüm\ *vb* **ex·humed; ex·hum·ing** : DISINTER — **ex·hu·ma·tion** \eks-hyü-⁵mā-shən, eks-yü-; egz-yü-, eg-zü-\ *n*

ex·i·tus \⁵ek-sə-təs\ *n, pl* **exitus** : DEATH; *esp* : fatal termination of a disease

exo- *or* **ex- comb form** : outside : outer ⟨*exoenzyme*⟩ — compare ECT-, END- 1

exo·crine \⁵ek-sə-krən, -krin, -⁵krēn\ *adj* : producing, being, or relating to a secretion that is released outside its source

exocrine gland *n* : a gland (as a salivary gland) that releases a secretion external to or at the surface of an organ by means of a canal or duct — called also *gland of external excretion*

exo·cri·nol·o·gy \ek-sə-kri-⁵nä-lə-jē, -krī-, -krē-\ *n, pl* **-gies** : the study of external secretions (as pheromones) that serve an integrative function

exo·cy·to·sis \ek-sō-sī-⁵tō-səs\ *n, pl* **-to·ses** \-sēz\ : the release of cellular substances (as secretory products) contained in cell vesicles by fusion of the vesicular membrane with the plasma membrane and subsequent release of the contents to the exterior of the cell — **exo·cy·tot·ic** \-⁵tä-tik\ *adj*

ex·odon·tia \ek-sə-⁵dän-chə, -chē-ə\ *n* : a branch of dentistry that deals with the extraction of teeth — **ex·odon·tist** \-⁵dän-tist\ *n*

exo·en·zyme \ek-sō-⁵en-ₐzīm\ *n* : an extracellular enzyme

exo·eryth·ro·cyt·ic \ek-sō-i-ₐri-thrə-⁵si-tik\ *adj* : occurring outside the red blood cells — used of stages of malaria parasites

ex·og·e·nous \ek-⁵sä-jə-nəs\ *also* **ex·o·gen·ic** \ek-sō-⁵je-nik\ *adj* 1 : growing from or on the outside 2 : caused by factors (as food or a traumatic factor) or an agent (as a disease-producing organism) from outside the organism or system ⟨∼ obesity⟩ ⟨∼ psychic depression⟩ 3 : introduced from or produced outside the organism or system; *specif* : not synthesized within the organism or system — compare ENDOGENOUS — **ex·og·e·nous·ly** *adv*

ex·on \⁵ek-ₐsän\ *n* : a polynucleotide sequence in a nucleic acid that codes information for protein synthesis and that is copied and spliced together with other such sequences to form messenger RNA — compare INTRON — **ex·on·ic** \ek-⁵sä-nik\ *adj*

exo·nu·cle·ase \ek-sō-⁵nü-klē-ₐās, -⁵nyü-, -ₐāz\ *n* : an enzyme that breaks down a nucleic acid by removing nucleotides one by one from the end of a chain — compare ENDONU-CLEASE

exo·nu·cleo·lyt·ic \ek-sō-ₐnü-klē-ə-⁵li-

tik, -ₐnyü-\ *adj* : breaking a nucleotide chain into two parts at a point adjacent to one of its ends

exo·pep·ti·dase \-⁵pep-tə-ₐdās, -ₐdāz\ *n* : any of a group of enzymes that hydrolyze peptide bonds formed by the terminal amino acids of peptide chains : PEPTIDASE — compare ENDO-PEPTIDASE

exo·pho·ria \ek-sə-⁵fōr-ē-ə\ *n* : latent strabismus in which the visual axes tend outward toward the temple — compare HETEROPHORIA

ex·oph·thal·mia \ek-ₐsäf-⁵thal-mē-ə\ *n* : EXOPHTHALMOS

ex·oph·thal·mic goiter \ek-säf-⁵thal-mik-\ *n* : GRAVES' DISEASE

ex·oph·thal·mos *also* **ex·oph·thal·mus** \ek-säf-⁵thal-məs, -səf-\ *n* : abnormal protrusion of the eyeball — **exophthalmic** *adj*

exo·phyt·ic \ek-sō-⁵fi-tik\ *adj* : tending to grow outward beyond the surface epithelium from which it originates — used of tumors; compare ENDOPHYT-IC

ex·os·tec·to·my \ek-(ₐ)säs-⁵tek-tə-mē\ *n, pl* **-mies** : excision of an exostosis

ex·os·to·sis \ek-(ₐ)säs-⁵tō-səs\ *n, pl* **-to·ses** \-ₐsēz\ : a spur or bony outgrowth from a bone or the root of a tooth — **ex·os·tot·ic** \-⁵tä-tik\ *adj*

exo·tox·in \ek-sō-⁵täk-sən\ *n* : a soluble poisonous substance produced during growth of a microorganism and released into the surrounding medium (tetanus ∼) — compare ENDO-TOXIN

exo·tro·pia \ek-sə-⁵trō-pē-ə\ *n* : WALL-EYE 2a

ex·pan·der \ik-⁵span-dər\ *n* : any of several colloidal substances (as dextran) of high molecular weight used as a blood or plasma substitute for increasing the blood volume — called also *extender*

ex·pect \ik-⁵spekt\ *vb* : to be pregnant : await the birth of one's child — used in progressive tenses (she's ∼*ing* next month)

ex·pec·tan·cy \-⁵spek-tən-sē\ *n, pl* **-cies** : the expected amount (as of the number of years of life) based on statistical probability — see LIFE EXPEC-TANCY

ex·pec·tant \-⁵spek-tənt\ *adj* : expecting the birth of a child

ex·pec·to·rant \ik-⁵spek-tə-rənt\ *n* : an agent that promotes the discharge or expulsion of mucus from the respiratory tract; *broadly* : ANTITUSSIVE — **expectorant** *adj*

ex·pec·to·rate \-ₐrāt\ *vb* **-rat·ed; -rat·ing** 1 : to eject matter from the throat or lungs by coughing or hawking and spitting 2 : SPIT

ex·pec·to·ra·tion \ik-ₐspek-tə-⁵rā-shən\ *n* 1 : the act or an instance of expectorating 2 : expectorated matter

ex·per·i·ment \ik-⁵sper-ə-mənt, -⁵spir-\ *n* 1 : a procedure carried out under controlled conditions in order to discover an unknown effect or law, to test or establish a hypothesis, or to illustrate a known law **2** : the process of testing — **experiment** *vb* — **ex·per·i·men·ta·tion** \ik-ˌsper-ə-mən-ˈtā-shən, -ˌspir-, -ˌmen-\ *n* — **ex·per·i·ment·er** \-ˈsper-ə-ˌmen-tər, -ˈspir-\ *n*

ex·per·i·men·tal \ik-ˌsper-ə-ˈment-ᵊl, -ˌspir-\ *adj* **1** : of, relating to, or based on experience or experiment **2** : founded on or derived from experiment **3** *of a disease* : intentionally produced esp. in laboratory animals for the purpose of study ⟨~ diabetes⟩ — **ex·per·i·men·tal·ly** *adv*

ex·pi·ra·tion \ˌek-spə-ˈrā-shən\ *n* **1 a** : the act or process of releasing air from the lungs through the nose or mouth **b** : the escape of carbon dioxide from the body protoplasm (as through the blood and lungs or by diffusion) **2** : something produced by breathing out

ex·pi·ra·to·ry \ik-ˈspī-rə-ˌtōr-ē, ek-\; ˈek-spə-rə-\ *adj* : of, relating to, or employed in the expiration of air from the lungs ⟨~ muscles⟩

expiratory reserve volume *n* : the additional amount of air that can be expired from the lungs by determined effort after normal expiration — compare INSPIRATORY RESERVE VOLUME

ex·pire \ik-ˈspīr, ek-\ *vb* **ex·pired; ex·pir·ing 1** : to breathe one's last breath : DIE 2 a : to breathe out from or as if from the lungs **b** : to emit the breath

ex·plant \ˈek-ˌsplant\ *n* : living tissue removed from an organism and placed in a medium for tissue culture — **ex·plant** \(ˌ)ek-ˈsplant\ *vb* — **ex·plan·ta·tion** \ˌek-ˌsplan-ˈtā-shən\ *n*

ex·plor·a·to·ry \ik-ˈsplōr-ə-ˌtōr-ē\ *adj* : of, relating to, or being exploration ⟨~ surgery⟩

ex·plore \ik-ˈsplōr\ *vb* **ex·plored; ex·plor·ing** : to examine minutely (as by surgery) esp. for diagnostic purposes — **ex·plo·ra·tion** \ˌek-splə-ˈrā-shən\ *n*

ex·plor·er \ik-ˈsplōr-ər\ *n* : an instrument for exploring cavities esp. in teeth : PROBE 1

ex·pose \ik-ˈspōz\ *vb* **ex·posed; ex·pos·ing 1** : to make liable to or accessible to something (as a disease or environmental conditions) that may have a detrimental effect ⟨children *exposed* to diphtheria⟩ **2** : to lay open to view: **as a** : to conduct (oneself) as an exhibitionist **b** : to reveal (a bodily part) esp. by dissection

ex·po·sure \ik-ˈspō-zhər\ *n* **1** : the act or an instance of exposing — see INDECENT EXPOSURE **2** : the condition of being exposed to severe weather conditions

ex·press \ik-ˈspres, ek-\ *vb* **1** : to make known or exhibit by an expression **2** : to cause (a gene) to manifest its effects in the phenotype

ex·pres·sion \ik-ˈspre-shən\ *n* **1 a** : something that manifests, represents, reflects, embodies, or symbolizes something else ⟨the first clinical ~ of a disease⟩ **b** : the detectable effect of a gene; *also* : EXPRESSIVITY 2 : facial aspect or vocal intonation as indicative of feeling

ex·pres·siv·i·ty \ˌek-ˌspre-ˈsi-və-tē\ *n*, *pl* **-ties** : the relative capacity of a gene to affect the phenotype of the organism of which it is a part — compare PENETRANCE

ex·pul·sive \ik-ˈspəl-siv\ *adj* : serving to expel ⟨~ efforts during labor⟩

ex·san·gui·na·tion \(ˌ)eks-ˌsaŋ-gwə-ˈnā-shən\ *n* : the action or process of draining or losing blood — **ex·san·gui·nate** \eks-ˈsaŋ-gwə-ˌnāt\ *vb*

ex·sic·co·sis \ˌek-si-ˈkō-səs\ *n*, *pl* **-co·ses** \-ˌsēz\ : insufficient intake of fluids; *also* : the resulting condition of bodily dehydration

ex·stro·phy \ˈek-strə-fē\ *n*, *pl* **-phies** : eversion of a part or organ; *specif* : a congenital malformation of the bladder in which the normally internal mucosa of the organ lies exposed on the abdominal wall

ex·tend \ik-ˈstend\ *vb* : to straighten out (as an arm or leg)

extended family *n* : a family that includes in one household near relatives in addition to a nuclear family

ex·tend·er \ik-ˈsten-dər\ *n* **1** : a substance added to a product esp. in the capacity of a diluent, adulterant, or modifier **2** : EXPANDER

ex·ten·si·bil·i·ty \ik-ˌsten-sə-ˈbi-lə-tē\ *n*, *pl* **-ties** : the capability of being stretched ⟨~ of muscle⟩ — **ex·ten·si·ble** \ik-ˈsten-sə-bəl\ *adj*

ex·ten·sion \ik-ˈsten-chən\ *n* **1** : the stretching of a fractured or dislocated limb so as to restore it to its natural position **2** : an unbending movement around a joint in a limb (as the knee or elbow) that increases the angle between the bones of the limb at the joint — compare FLEXION 1

ex·ten·sor \ik-ˈsten-sər, -ˌsȯr\ *n* : a muscle serving to extend a bodily part (as a limb) — called also *extensor muscle*; compare FLEXOR

extensor car·pi ra·di·al·is brev·is \-ˈkär-ˌpī-ˌrā-dē-ˈā-ləs-ˈbre-vəs, -ˈkär-ˌpē-\ *n* : a short muscle on the radial side of the back of the forearm that extends and may abduct the hand

extensor carpi radialis lon·gus \-ˈlȯŋ-gəs\ *n* : a long muscle on the radial side of the back of the forearm that extends and abducts the hand

extensor carpi ul·na·ris \-ˌəl-ˈnar-əs\ *n* : a muscle on the ulnar side of the back of the forearm that extends and adducts the hand

extensor dig·i·ti min·i·mi \-ˈdi-jə-ˌtī-ˈmi-nə-ˌmī, -ˈdi-jə-ˌtē-ˈmi-nə-ˌmē\ *n* : a slender muscle on the medial side of the extensor digitorum communis that extends the little finger

extensor digiti quin·ti pro·pri·us \-ˈkwin-ˌtī-ˈprō-prē-əs, -ˈkwin-ˌtē-\ *n* : EXTENSOR DIGITI MINIMI

extensor dig·i·to·rum brev·is \-ˌdi-jə-ˈtōr-əm-ˈbre-vəs\ *n* : a muscle on the dorsum of the foot that extends the toes

extensor digitorum com·mu·nis \-kə-ˈmyü-nəs, -ˈkä-myə-\ *n* : a muscle on the back of the forearm that extends the fingers and wrist

extensor digitorum lon·gus \-ˈlȯṅ-gəs\ *n* : a pennate muscle on the lateral part of the front of the leg that extends the four small toes and dorsally flexes and pronates the foot

extensor hal·lu·cis brev·is \-ˈha-lü-səs-ˈbre-vəs, -lyü-, -ˈha-lə-kəs-\ *n* : the part of the extensor digitorum brevis that extends the big toe

extensor hallucis lon·gus \-ˈlȯṅ-gəs\ *n* : a long thin muscle situated on the shin that extends the big toe and dorsiflexes and supinates the foot

extensor in·di·cis \-ˈin-də-səs, -də-kəs\ *n* : a thin muscle that arises from the ulna in the more distal part of the forearm and extends the index finger

extensor indicis pro·pri·us \-ˈprō-prē-əs\ *n* : EXTENSOR INDICIS

extensor pol·li·cis brev·is \-ˈpä-lə-səs-ˈbre-vəs, -lə-kəs-\ *n* : a muscle that arises from the dorsal surface of the radius, extends the first phalanx of the thumb, and adducts the hand

extensor pollicis lon·gus \-ˈlȯṅ-gəs\ *n* : a muscle that arises dorsolaterally from the middle part of the ulna, extends the second phalanx of the thumb, and abducts the hand

extensor ret·i·nac·u·lum \-ˌret-ᵊn-ˈa-kyə-ləm\ *n* **1** : either of two fibrous bands of fascia crossing the front of the ankle: **a** : a lower band that is attached laterally to the superior aspect of the calcaneus and passes medially to divide in the shape of a Y and that passes over or both over and under the tendons of the extensor muscles at the ankle — called also *inferior extensor retinaculum* **b** : an upper band passing over and binding down the tendons of the tibialis anterior, extensor hallucis longus, extensor digitorum longus, and peroneus tertius just above the ankle joint — called also *superior extensor retinaculum, transverse crural ligament* **2** : a fibrous band of fascia crossing the back of the wrist and binding down the tendons of the extensor muscles

ex·te·ri·or·ize \ek-ˈstir-ē-ə-ˌrīz\ *vb* **-ized; -iz·ing 1** : EXTERNALIZE **2** : to bring out of the body (as for surgery) ⟨the section of perforated colon was *exteriorized*⟩ — **ex·te·ri·or·iza·tion** \-ˌstir-ē-ə-rə-ˈzā-shən\ *n*

ex·tern \ˈek-ˌstərn\ *n* : a nonresident doctor or medical student at a hospital — **ex·tern·ship** \-ˌship\ *n*

externa — see MUSCULARIS EXTERNA, OTITIS EXTERNA, THECA EXTERNA

ex·ter·nal \ek-ˈstərn-ᵊl\ *adj* **1** : capable of being perceived outwardly : BODILY ⟨~ signs of a disease⟩ **2 a** : situated at, on, or near the outside ⟨an ~ muscle⟩ **b** : directed toward the outside : having an outside object ⟨~ perception⟩ **c** : used by applying to the outside ⟨an ~ lotion⟩ **3 a** (1) : situated near or toward the surface of the body; *also* : situated away from the mesial plane ⟨the ~ condyle of the humerus⟩ (2) : arising or acting from outside : having an outside origin ⟨~ stimuli⟩ **b** : of, relating to, or consisting of something outside the mind : having existence independent of the mind ⟨~ reality⟩ — **ex·ter·nal·ly** *adv*

external anal sphincter *n* : ANAL SPHINCTER a

external auditory meatus *n* : the passage leading from the opening of the external ear to the eardrum — called also *external acoustic meatus, external auditory canal, meatus acusticus externus*

external capsule *n* : CAPSULE 1b(2)

external carotid artery *n* : the outer branch of the carotid artery that supplies the face, tongue, and external parts of the head — called also *external carotid*

external ear *n* : the parts of the ear that are external to the eardrum; *also* : PINNA

external iliac artery *n* : ILIAC ARTERY 2

external iliac node *n* : any of the lymph nodes grouped around the external iliac artery and the external iliac vein — compare INTERNAL ILIAC NODE

external iliac vein *n* : ILIAC VEIN b

external inguinal ring *n* : SUPERFICIAL INGUINAL RING

external intercostal muscle *n* : INTERCOSTAL MUSCLE a — called also *external intercostal*

ex·ter·nal·ize \ek-ˈstern-ᵊl-ˌīz\ *vb* **-ized; -iz·ing 1 a** : to transform from a mental image into an apparently real object (as in hallucinations) : attribute (a mental image) to external causation b : to invent an explanation for by attributing to causes outside the self : RATIONALIZE, PROJECT **2** : to direct outward socially ⟨*externalized* anger⟩ — **ex·ter·nal·iza·tion** \-ˌstern-ᵊl-ə-ˈzā-shən\ *n*

external jugular vein *n* : JUGULAR VEIN b — called also *external jugular*

external malleolus *n* : MALLEOLUS a

external maxillary artery *n* : FACIAL ARTERY

external oblique *n* : OBLIQUE a (1)

external occipital crest *n* : OCCIPITAL CREST a

external occipital protuberance *n* : OCCIPITAL PROTUBERANCE a

225 external pterygoid muscle • extrapyramidal

external pterygoid muscle *n* : PTERYGOID MUSCLE a

external pudendal artery *n* : either of two branches of the femoral artery: **a** : one that is distributed to the skin of the lower abdomen, to the penis and scrotum in the male, and to one of the labia majora in the female — called also *superficial external pudendal artery* **b** : one that follows a deeper course, that is distributed to the medial aspect of the thigh, to the skin of the scrotum and perineum in the male, and to one of the labia majora in the female — called also *deep external pudendal artery*

external respiration *n* : exchange of gases between the external environment and the lungs or between the alveoli of the lungs and the blood — compare INTERNAL RESPIRATION

ex·terne *var of* EXTERN

externus — see MEATUS ACUSTICUS EXTERNUS, OBLIQUUS EXTERNUS ABDOMINIS, OBTURATOR EXTERNUS, SPHINCTER ANI EXTERNUS

ex·tero·cep·tive \ˌek-stə-rō-ˈsep-tiv\ *adj* : activated by, relating to, or being stimuli received by an organism from outside

ex·tero·cep·tor \-ˈsep-tər\ *n* : a sense receptor (as of touch, temperature, smell, vision, or hearing) excited by exteroceptive stimuli — compare INTEROCEPTOR

ex·tinc·tion \ik-ˈstiŋk-shən\ *n* : the process of eliminating or reducing a conditioned response by not reinforcing it

ex·tin·guish \ik-ˈstiŋ-gwish\ *vb* : to cause extinction of (a conditioned response)

ex·tir·pa·tion \ˌek-stər-ˈpā-shən\ *n* : complete excision or surgical destruction of a body part — **ex·tir·pate** \ˈek-stər-ˌpāt\ *vb*

extra- *prefix* : outside : beyond ⟨*extra*uterine⟩

ex·tra·cap·su·lar \ˌek-strə-ˈkap-sə-lər, -syü-lər\ *adj* **1** : situated outside a capsule **2** *of a cataract operation* : involving removal of the front part of the lens — compare INTRACAPSULAR 2

ex·tra·cel·lu·lar \-ˈsel-yə-lər\ *adj* : situated or occurring outside a cell or the cells of the body ⟨∼ digestion⟩ ⟨∼ enzymes⟩ — **ex·tra·cel·lu·lar·ly** *adv*

ex·tra·chro·mo·som·al \-ˌkrō-mə-ˈsō-məl, -ˌzō-\ *adj* : situated or controlled by factors outside the chromosome ⟨∼ inheritance⟩ ⟨∼ DNA⟩

ex·tra·cor·po·re·al \-kȯr-ˈpōr-ē-əl\ *adj* : occurring or based outside the living body ⟨heart surgery employing ∼ circulation⟩ — **ex·tra·cor·po·re·al·ly** *adv*

ex·tra·cra·ni·al \-ˈkrā-nē-əl\ *adj* : situated or occurring outside the cranium

¹ex·tract \ik-ˈstrakt\ *vb* **1** : to pull or take out forcibly ⟨∼ed a wisdom tooth⟩ **2** : to separate the medicinally-

active components of a plant or animal tissue by the use of solvents —

ex·trac·tion \-ˈstrak-shən\ *n*

²ex·tract \ˈek-ˌstrakt\ *n* : something prepared by extracting; *esp* : a medicinally-active pharmaceutical solution

¹ex·trac·tive \ik-ˈstrak-tiv, ˈek-ˌ\ *adj* : of, relating to, or involving the process of extracting

²extractive *n* : EXTRACT

ex·tra·du·ral \ˌek-strə-ˈdʉr-əl, -dyʉr-\ *adj* : situated or occurring outside the dura mater but within the skull ⟨an ∼ hemorrhage⟩

ex·tra·em·bry·on·ic \-ˌem-brē-ˈä-nik\ *adj* : situated outside the embryo proper; *esp* : developed from the zygote but not part of the embryo ⟨∼ membranes⟩

extraembryonic coelom *n* : the space between the chorion and amnion which in early stages is continuous with the coelom of the embryo proper

ex·tra·fu·sal \ˌek-strə-ˈfyü-zəl\ *adj* : situated outside a striated muscle spindle ⟨∼ muscle fibers⟩ — compare INTRAFUSAL

ex·tra·gen·i·tal \-ˈje-nə-təl\ *adj* : situated or originating outside the genital region or organs

ex·tra·he·pat·ic \-hi-ˈpa-tik\ *adj* : situated or originating outside the liver

ex·tra·in·tes·ti·nal \-in-ˈtes-tə-nəl\ *adj* : situated or occurring outside the intestines ⟨∼ infections⟩

ex·tra·mac·u·lar \-ˈma-kyə-lər\ *adj* : relating to or being the part of the retina other than the macula lutea

ex·tra·med·ul·lary \-ˈmed-əl-ˌer-ē, -ˈme-jə-ˌler-ē, -mə-ˈdəl-ə-rē\ *adj* **1** : situated or occurring outside the spinal cord or the medulla oblongata **2** : located or taking place outside the bone marrow

ex·tra·mi·to·chon·dri·al \-ˌmī-tə-ˈkän-drē-əl\ *adj* : situated or occurring in the cell outside the mitochondria

ex·tra·nu·cle·ar \-ˈnü-klē-ər, -ˈnyü-\ *adj* : situated in or affecting the parts of a cell external to the nucleus : CYTOPLASMIC

ex·tra·oc·u·lar muscle \-ˈä-kyə-lər-\ *n* : any of six small voluntary muscles that pass between the eyeball and the orbit and control the movement of the eyeball in relation to the orbit

ex·tra·oral \-ˈȯr-əl, -ˈär-\ *adj* : situated or occurring outside the mouth ⟨an ∼ abscess⟩

ex·tra·peri·to·ne·al \-ˌper-ət-ᵊn-ˈē-əl\ *adj* : located or taking place outside the peritoneal cavity

ex·tra·pi·tu·itary \-pə-ˈtü-ə-ˌter-ē, -ˈtyü-\ *adj* : situated or arising outside the pituitary gland

ex·tra·pla·cen·tal \-plə-ˈsent-ᵊl\ *adj* : being outside of or independent of the placenta

ex·tra·py·ra·mi·dal \-pə-ˈra-məd-ᵊl, -ˌpir-ə-ˈmid-ᵊl\ *adj* : situated outside of and esp. involving descending nerve tracts other than the pyramidal tracts ⟨∼ brain lesions⟩

ex·tra·re·nal \-ˈrēn-ᵊl\ *adj* : situated or occurring outside the kidneys

ex·tra·ret·i·nal \-ˈre-tə-nəl\ *adj* : situated or occurring outside the retina ⟨∼ photoreception⟩

ex·tra·sen·so·ry \ek-strə-ˈsen-sə-rē\ *adj* : residing beyond or outside the ordinary senses

extrasensory perception *n* : perception (as in telepathy, clairvoyance, and precognition) that involves awareness of information about events external to the self not gained through the senses and not deducible from previous experience — called also *ESP*

ex·tra·sys·to·le \-ˈsis-tə-(,)lē\ *n* : a prematurely occurring beat of one of the chambers of the heart that leads to momentary arrhythmia but leaves the fundamental rhythm unchanged — called also *premature beat* — **ex·tra·sys·tol·ic** \-,sis-ˈtä-lik\ *adj*

ex·tra·uter·ine \-ˈyü-tə-rən, -,rīn\ *adj* : situated or occurring outside the uterus

extrauterine pregnancy *n* : ECTOPIC PREGNANCY

ex·trav·a·sate \ik-ˈstra-və-,sāt, -,zāt\ *vb* **-sat·ed; -sat·ing** : to force out, cause to escape, or pass by infiltration or effusion from a proper vessel or channel (as a blood vessel) into surrounding tissue

ex·trav·a·sa·tion \ik-,stra-və-ˈzā-shən, -ˈsā-\ *n* 1 : the action of extravasating 2 a : an extravasated fluid (as blood) ⟨∼s from the nose and mouth⟩ b : a deposit formed by extravasation

ex·tra·vas·cu·lar \ek-strə-ˈvas-kyə-lər\ *adj* : not occurring or contained in body vessels — **ex·tra·vas·cu·lar·ly** *adv*

ex·tra·ven·tric·u·lar \-ven-ˈtri-kyə-lər, -vən-\ *adj* : located or taking place outside a ventricle ⟨∼ lesions⟩

ex·tra·ver·sion, ex·tra·vert *var of* EXTROVERSION, EXTROVERT

ex·trem·i·ty \ik-ˈstre-mə-tē\ *n, pl* **-ties** 1 : the farthest or most remote part, section, or point 2 : a limb of the body; *esp* : a hand or foot

ex·trin·sic \ek-ˈstrin-zik, -sik\ *adj* 1 : originating or due to causes or factors from or on the outside of a body, organ, or part 2 : originating outside a part and acting on the part as a whole — used esp. of certain muscles; compare INTRINSIC 2 — **ex·trin·si·cal·ly** \-zi-k(ə-)lē, -si-\ *adv*

extrinsic factor *n* : VITAMIN B₁₂

extro- *prefix* : outside : outward ⟨*extro*vert⟩ — compare INTRO-

ex·tro·ver·sion \ek-strə-ˈvər-zhən, -shən\ *n* : the act, state, or habit of being predominantly concerned with and obtaining gratification from what is outside the self — compare INTROVERSION

ex·tro·vert \ˈek-strə-,vərt\ *n* : one whose personality is characterized by extroversion; *broadly* : a gregarious and unreserved person — compare INTROVERT — **extrovert** *adj* — **ex·tro·vert·ed** \-,vər-təd\ *adj*

ex·trude \ik-ˈstrüd\ *vb* **ex·trud·ed; ex·trud·ing** : to force, press, or push out; *also* : to become extruded ⟨blood *extruding* through arteries⟩ — **ex·tru·sion** \ik-ˈstrü-zhən\ *n*

ex·tu·ba·tion \,ek-,stü-ˈbā-shən, -,styü-\ *n* : the removal of a tube esp. from the larynx after intubation — **ex·tu·bate** \ek-ˈstü-,bāt, -ˈstyü-, ˈek-,stü-, -,styü-\ *vb*

ex·u·date \ˈek-sù-,dāt, -syu-, -shù-\ *n* : exuded matter; *esp* : the material composed of serum, fibrin, and white blood cells that escapes from blood vessels into a superficial lesion or area of inflammation

ex·u·da·tion \,ek-sù-ˈdā-shən, -syu-, -shù-\ *n* 1 : the process of exuding 2 : EXUDATE — **ex·u·da·tive** \ig-ˈzü-də-tiv; ˈek-sù-,dā-tiv, -syu-, -shù-\ *adj*

ex·ude \ig-ˈzüd\ *vb* **ex·ud·ed; ex·ud·ing** 1 : to ooze or cause to ooze out 2 : to undergo diffusion

eye \ˈī\ *n* 1 : a nearly spherical hollow organ that is lined with a sensitive retina, is lodged in a bony orbit in the skull, is the vertebrate organ of sight, and is normally paired 2 : all the visible structures within and surrounding the orbit and including eyelids, eyelashes, and eyebrows 3 : the faculty of seeing with eyes

eye·ball \ˈī-,bol\ *n* : the more or less globular capsule of the vertebrate eye formed by the sclera and cornea together with their contained structures

eye bank *n* : a storage place for human corneas from the newly dead for transplanting to the eyes of those blind through corneal defects

eye·brow \ˈī-,braù\ *n* : the ridge over the eye or hair growing on it — called also *brow*

eye chart *n* : a chart that is read at a fixed distance for purposes of testing sight; *esp* : one with rows of letters or objects of decreasing size

eye·cup \ˈī-,kəp\ *n* 1 : a small oval cup with a rim curved to fit the orbit of the eye used for applying liquid remedies to the eyes 2 : OPTIC CUP

eyed \ˈīd\ *adj* : having an eye or eyes esp. of a specified kind or number — often used in combination ⟨a blue-*eyed* patient⟩

eyed·ness \ˈīd-nəs\ *n* : preference for the use of one eye instead of the other

eye doctor *n* : a specialist (as an optometrist or ophthalmologist) in the examination, treatment, or care of the eyes

eye·drop·per \ˈī-,drä-pər\ *n* : DROPPER

eye·drops \ˈī-,dräps\ *n pl* : a medicated solution for the eyes that is applied in drops — **eye·drop** \-,dräp\ *adj*

eye-glass \'ī-ˌglas\ *n* **1 a** : a lens worn to aid vision; *specif* : MONOCLE **b** *pl* : GLASSES, SPECTACLES **2** : EYECUP 1

eye gnat *n* : any of several small dipteran flies (genus *Hippelates* of the family Chloropidae and esp. *H. pusio*) including some that are held to be vectors of pinkeye and yaws — called also *eye fly*

eye-ground \'ī-ˌgraund\ *n* : the fundus of the eye; *esp* : the retina as viewed through an ophthalmoscope

eye-lash \'ī-ˌlash\ *n* **1** : the fringe of hair edging the eyelid — usu. used in pl. **2** : a single hair of the eyelashes

eye-lid \'ī-ˌlid\ *n* : either of the movable lids of skin and muscle that can be closed over the eyeball — called also *palpebra*

eye-sight \'ī-ˌsīt\ *n* : SIGHT 2

eye socket *n* : ORBIT

eye-strain \'ī-ˌstrān\ *n* : weariness or a strained state of the eye

eye-tooth \'ī-ˌtüth\ *n*, *pl* **eye-teeth** \-ˌtēth\ : a canine tooth of the upper jaw

eye-wash \'ī-ˌwȯsh, -ˌwȧsh\ *n* : an eye lotion

eye-wear \'ī-ˌwar, -ˌwer\ *n* : corrective or protective devices (as glasses or contact lenses) for the eyes

eye worm *n* **1** : either of two slender nematode worms of the genus *Oxyspirura* (*O. mansoni* and *O. petrowi*) living beneath the nictitating membrane of the eyes of birds and esp. chickens **2** : any member of the nematode genus *Thelazia* living in the tear duct and beneath the eyelid of dogs, cats, sheep, humans, and other mammals and sometimes causing blindness **3** : an African filarial worm of the genus *Loa* (*L. loa*) that migrates through the eyeball and subcutaneous tissues of humans — compare CALABAR SWELLING

F

f *symbol* focal length

¹F *abbr* Fahrenheit

²F *symbol* **1** filial generation — usu. used with a subscript F_1 for the first, F_2 for the second, etc. **2** fluorine

fab-ri-ca-tion \ˌfa-bri-ˈkā-shən\ *n* : CONFABULATION

Fa-bry's disease \'fä-brēz-\ *n* : a sex-linked inherited disorder of lipid catabolism characterized esp. by renal dysfunction, a rash in the inguinal, scrotal, and umbilical regions, and corneal defects

Fabry, Johannes (1860–1930), German dermatologist.

FACC *abbr* Fellow of the American College of Cardiology

FACD *abbr* Fellow of the American College of Dentists

face \'fās\ *n, often attrib* : the front part of the head including the chin, mouth, nose, cheeks, eyes, and usu. the forehead

face-bow \'fās-ˌbō\ *n* : a device used in dentistry to determine the positional relationships of the maxillae to the temporomandibular joints of a patient

face fly *n* : a European fly of the genus *Musca* (*M. autumnalis*) that is similar to the house fly, is widely established in No. America, and causes distress in livestock by clustering about the face

face-lift \'fās-ˌlift\ *n* : a plastic surgical operation for removal of facial defects (as wrinkles) typical of aging — called also *rhytidectomy* — **face-lift** *vb*

face-lifting \-ˌlif-tiŋ\ *n* : FACE-LIFT

fac-et \'fa-sət\ *n* : a smooth flat or nearly flat circumscribed anatomical surface (the articular ~ of a bone) — **fac-et-ed** *or* **fac-et-ted** \'fa-sə-təd\ *adj*

fac-et-ec-to-my \ˌfa-sə-ˈtek-tə-mē\ *n, pl* **-mies** : excision of a facet esp. of a vertebra

¹fa-cial \'fā-shəl\ *adj* **1** : of, relating to, or affecting the face ⟨~ neuralgia⟩ **2** : concerned with or used in improving the appearance of the face **3** : relating to or being the buccal and labial surface of a tooth — **fa-cial-ly** \-shə-lē\ *adv*

²facial *n* : a treatment to improve the appearance of the face

facial artery *n* : an artery that arises from the external carotid artery and gives off branches supplying the neck and face — called also *external maxillary artery;* compare MAXILLARY ARTERY

facial bone *n* : any of the 14 bones of the facial region of the human skull that do not take part in forming the braincase

facial canal *n* : a passage in the petrous part of the temporal bone that transmits various branches of the facial nerve

facial colliculus *n* : a medial eminence on the floor of the fourth ventricle of the brain produced by the nucleus of the abducens nerve and the flexure of the facial nerve around it

facial nerve *n* : either of the seventh pair of cranial nerves that supply motor fibers esp. to the muscles of the face and jaw and sensory and parasympathetic fibers to the tongue, palate, and fauces — called also *seventh cranial nerve, seventh nerve*

facial vein *n* : a vein that arises as the angular vein, drains the superficial structures of the face, and empties into the internal jugular vein — called also *anterior facial vein;* see DEEP FACIAL VEIN, POSTERIOR FACIAL VEIN

-fa·cient \'fā-shənt\ *adj comb form* : making : causing ⟨aborti*facient*⟩ ⟨rube*facient*⟩

fa·cies \'fā-ıshēz, -shē-ıēz\ *n, pl* **facies** 1 : an appearance and expression of the face characteristic of a particular condition esp. when abnormal ⟨adenoid ~⟩ 2 : an anatomical surface

fa·cil·i·ta·tion \fə-ısi-lə-'tā-shən\ *n* 1 : the lowering of the threshold for reflex conduction along a particular neural pathway 2 : the increasing of the ease or intensity of a response by repeated stimulation — **fa·cil·i·tate** \-'si-lə-ıtāt\ *vb* — **fa·cil·i·ta·to·ry** \-'si-lə-tə-ıtōr-ē\ *adj*

fac·ing \'fā-siŋ\ *n* : a front of porcelain or plastic used in dental crowns and bridgework to face the metal replacement and simulate the natural tooth

facio- *comb form* : facial and ⟨*facio*scapulohumeral⟩

fa·cio·scap·u·lo·hu·mer·al \ıfā-shē-ō-ıska-pyə-lō-'hyü-mə-rəl\ *adj* : relating to or affecting the muscles of the face, scapula, and arm

FACOG *abbr* Fellow of the American College of Obstetricians and Gynecologists

FACP *abbr* Fellow of the American College of Physicians

FACR *abbr* Fellow of the American College of Radiology

FACS *abbr* Fellow of the American College of Surgeons

F-ac·tin \'ef-ıak-tən\ *n* : a fibrous actin polymerized in the form of a double helix that is produced in the presence of some salts (as divalent calcium) and ATP — compare G-ACTIN

fac·ti·tious \fak-'ti-shəs\ *adj* : not produced by natural means

fac·tor \'fak-tər\ *n* 1 a : something that actively contributes to the production of a result b : a substance that functions in or promotes the function of a particular physiological process or bodily system 2 : GENE — **fac·to·ri·al** \fak-'tōr-ē-əl\ *adj*

factor VIII \-'āt\ *n* : a glycoprotein of blood plasma that is essential for blood clotting and is absent or inactive in hemophilia — called also *antihemophilic factor, thromboplastinogen*

factor XI \-i-'le-vən\ *n* : PLASMA THROMBOPLASTIN ANTECEDENT

factor V \-'fiv\ *n* : a globulin occurring in inactive form in blood plasma that in its active form is one of the factors accelerating the formation of thrombin from prothrombin in the clotting of blood — called also *accelerator globulin, labile factor, proaccelerin*

factor IX \-'nīn\ *n* : a clotting factor whose absence is associated with Christmas disease — called also *autoprothrombin II, Christmas factor*

factor VII \-'se-vən\ *n* : a clotting fac-

tor in normal blood that is formed in the kidney under the influence of vitamin K and may be deficient due to a hereditary disorder or to a vitamin K deficiency — called also *autoprothrombin I, cothromboplastin, proconvertin, stable factor*

factor X \-'ten\ *n* : a clotting factor that is converted to a proteolytic enzyme which converts prothrombin to thrombin in a reaction dependent on calcium ions and other clotting factors — called also *Stuart-Prower factor*

factor XIII \-ıthərt-'tēn\ *n* : a substance that aids in clotting blood by causing monomeric fibrin to polymerize and become stable and insoluble — called also *fibrinase;* see TRANSGLUTAMINASE

factor XII \-'twelv\ *n* : a clotting factor that facilitates blood coagulation in vivo and initiates coagulation on a firm surface (as glass) in vitro but whose deficiency tends not to promote hemorrhage — called also *Hageman factor*

facts of life *n pl* : the fundamental physiological processes and behavior involved in sex and reproduction

fac·ul·ta·tive \'fa-kəl-ıtā-tiv\ *adj* 1 : taking place under some conditions but not under others ⟨~ parasitism⟩ 2 : exhibiting an indicated lifestyle under some environmental conditions but not under others ⟨~ anaerobes⟩ — **fac·ul·ta·tive·ly** *adv*

FAD \ef-(ı)ā-'dē\ *n* : FLAVIN ADENINE DINUCLEOTIDE

Each boldface word in the list below is a chiefly British variant of the word to its right in small capitals.

faecal	FECAL
faecalith	FECALITH
faecaloid	FECALOID
faeces	FECES

fag·o·py·rism \ıfa-gō-'pī-ıri-zəm\ *n* : a photosensitization esp. of swine and sheep that is due to eating large quantities of buckwheat (esp. *Fagopyrum esculentum* of the family Polygonaceae) and that appears principally on the nonpigmented parts of the skin as an intense redness and swelling with severe itching and the formation of vesicles and later sores and scabs — compare BIGHEAD b, HYPERICISM

Fahr·en·heit \'far-ən-ıhīt\ *adj* : relating or conforming to a thermometric scale on which under standard atmospheric pressure the boiling point of water is at 212 degrees above the zero of the scale and the freezing point is at 32 degrees above zero — *abbr.* F

fahrenheit, Daniel Gabriel (1686–1736), German physicist.

fail \'fāl\ *vb* 1 : to weaken or lose strength 2 : to stop functioning ⟨the patient's heart ~ed⟩

fail·ure \'fāl-yər\ *n* : a state of inability

to perform a vital function (acute renal ~) ⟨respiratory ~⟩ — see HEART FAILURE

¹faint \'fānt\ adj : weak, dizzy, and likely to faint — **faint·ness** \-nəs\ n

²faint vb : to lose consciousness because of a temporary decrease in the blood supply to the brain

³faint n : the physiological action of fainting; also : the resulting condition : SYNCOPE

faith healing n : a method of treating diseases by prayer and exercise of faith in God — **faith healer** n

falces pl of FALX

falciform ligament n : an anteroposterior fold of peritoneum attached to the under surface of the diaphragm and sheath of the rectus muscle and along a line on the anterior and upper surfaces of the liver extending back from the notch on the anterior margin

fal·cip·a·rum malaria \fal-'si-pə-rəm-, fŏl-\ n : severe malaria caused by a parasite of the genus *Plasmodium* (*P. falciparum*) and marked by recurrence of paroxysms usu. in less than 48 hours — called also *malignant malaria, malignant tertian malaria;* compare VIVAX MALARIA

fallen arch n : FLATFOOT

falling sickness n : EPILEPSY

fal·lo·pian tube \fə-'lō-pē-ən-\ n, often cap F : either of the pair of tubes that carry the eggs from the ovary to the uterus — called also *uterine tube*

Fal·lop·pio \fäl-'lȯp-yō\ *or* **Fal·lop·pia** \-'lȯp-yä\, **Gabriele** (*Latin* Gabriel **Fal·lo·pi·us** \fə-'lō-pē-əs\) (1523–1562), Italian anatomist.

Fallot's tetralogy \,fa-'lōz-\ n : TETRALOGY OF FALLOT

fall·out \'fȯ-,laút\ n 1 : the often radioactive particles stirred up by or resulting from a nuclear explosion and descending through the atmosphere; *also* : other polluting particles (as volcanic ash) descending likewise 2 : descent (as of fallout) through the atmosphere

false \'fȯls\ adj **fals·er; fals·est** 1 : not corresponding to truth or reality ⟨a test for syphilis which gave ~ results⟩ 2 : artificially made ⟨a set of ~ teeth⟩

false joint n : PSEUDARTHROSIS

false labor n : pains resembling those of normal labor but occuring at irregular intervals and without dilation of the cervix

false membrane n : a fibrinous deposit with enmeshed necrotic cells formed esp. in croup and diphtheria — called also *pseudomembrane*

false mo·rel \-mȯ-'rel\ n : any fungus of the genus *Gyromitra*

false–negative adj : relating to or being an individual or a test result that is erroneously classified in a negative category (as of diagnosis) because of imperfect testing methods or procedures — compare FALSE-POSITIVE — **false negative** n

false pelvis n : the upper broader portion of the pelvic cavity — called also *false pelvic cavity;* compare TRUE PELVIS

false–positive adj : relating to or being an individual or a test result that is erroneously classified in a positive category (as of diagnosis) because of imperfect testing methods or procedures — compare FALSE-NEGATIVE — **false positive** n

false pregnancy n : PSEUDOCYESIS, PSEUDOPREGNANCY

false rib n : a rib whose cartilages unite indirectly or not at all with the sternum — compare FLOATING RIB

false vocal cords n pl : the upper pair of vocal cords that are not directly concerned with speech production — called also *superior vocal cords, ventricular folds, vestibular folds*

falx \'falks, 'fȯlks\ n, pl **fal·ces** \'fal-,sēz, 'fȯl-\ : a sickle-shaped part or structure: as a : FALX CEREBRI b : FALX CEREBELLI

falx ce·re·bel·li \-,ser-ə-'be-,lī\ n : the smaller of the two folds of dura mater separating the hemispheres of the brain that lies between the lateral lobes of the cerebellum

falx cer·e·bri \-'ser-ə-,brī\ n : the larger of the two folds of dura mater separating the hemispheres of the brain that lies between the cerebral hemispheres and contains the sagittal sinuses

FAMA abbr Fellow of the American Medical Association

fa·mil·ial \fə-'mil-yəl\ adj : tending to occur in more members of a family than expected by chance alone ⟨a ~ disorder⟩ — compare ACQUIRED 2, CONGENITAL 2, HEREDITARY

fam·i·ly \'fam-lē, 'fa-mə-\ n, pl **-lies** 1 : the basic unit in society having as its nucleus two or more adults living together and cooperating in the care and rearing of their own or adopted children 2 : a group of related plants or animals forming a category ranking above a genus and below an order and usu. comprising several to many genera — **family** adj

family doctor n 1 : a doctor regularly consulted by a family 2 : a doctor specializing in family practice

family physician n : FAMILY DOCTOR

family planning n : planning intended to determine the number and spacing of one's children through effective methods of birth control

family practice n : a medical practice or specialty which provides continuing general medical care for the individual and family — called also *family medicine*

family practitioner n : FAMILY DOCTOR

Fan·co·ni's anemia \fän-'kō-nēz-, fan-\ n : a rare disease inherited as an autosomal recessive trait that is characterized by progressive hypoplastic pancytopenia, skeletal anomalies (as short stature), and a predisposition to cancer and esp. leukemia

Fanconi, Guido (*b* 1892), Swiss pediatrician.

Fanconi syndrome *n* : a disorder of reabsorption in the proximal convoluted tubules of the kidney marked esp. by the presence of glucose, amino acids, and phosphates in the urine

fang \'faŋ\ *n* **1** : a long sharp tooth: as **a** : one by which an animal's prey is seized and held or torn **b** : one of the long hollow or grooved and often erectile teeth of a venomous snake **2** : the root of a tooth or one of the processes or prongs into which a root divides — **fanged** \'faŋd\ *adj*

fan·go \'faŋ-(ˌ)gō, 'fäŋ-\ *n* : mud and esp. a clay mud from hot springs at Battaglio, Italy, that is used in the form of hot external applications in the therapeutic treatment of certain medical conditions (as rheumatism)

fan·ta·size \'fan-tə-ˌsīz\ *vb* **-sized; -sizing 1** : to indulge in fantasy **2** : to portray in the mind by fantasy

¹fan·ta·sy \'fan-tə-sē, -zē\ *n, pl* **-sies** : the power or process of creating esp. unrealistic or improbable mental images in response to psychological need; *also* : a mental image or a series of mental images (as a daydream) so created (sexual *fantasies*)

²fantasy *vb* **-sied; -sy·ing** : FANTASIZE

FAPA *abbr* Fellow of the American Psychological Association

fa·rad·ic \fə-'ra-dik, far-'a-\ *also* **far·a·da·ic** \far-ə-'dā-ik\ *adj* : of or relating to an asymmetric alternating current of electricity (∼ muscle stimulation)

Far·a·day \'far-ə-ˌdā\, **Michael** (1791-1867), British physicist and chemist.

far·a·dism \'far-ə-ˌdi-zəm\ *n* : the application of a faradic current of electricity (as for therapeutic purposes)

far·cy \'fär-sē\ *n, pl* **far·cies** : GLANDERS; *esp* : cutaneous glanders

farmer's lung *n* : an acute pulmonary disorder that is characterized by sudden onset, fever, cough, expectoration, and breathlessness and that results from the inhalation of dust from moldy hay or straw

far point *n* : the point farthest from the eye at which an object is accurately focused on the retina when the accommodation is completely relaxed — compare NEAR POINT

far·sight·ed \'fär-ˌsī-təd\ *adj* **1** : seeing or able to see to a great distance **2** : affected with hyperopia — **far·sight·ed·ly** *adv*

far·sight·ed·ness *n* **1** : the quality or state of being farsighted **2** : HYPEROPIA

FAS *abbr* fetal alcohol syndrome

fasc *abbr* fasciculus

fas·cia \'fa-shə, 'fā-, -shē-ə\ *n, pl* **-ci·ae** \-shē-ˌē\ *or* **-cias** : a sheet of connective tissue (as an aponeurosis) covering or binding together body structures; *also* : tissue occurring in such a sheet — see DEEP FASCIA, SUPERFICIAL FASCIA — **fas·cial** \-shəl, -shē-\ *adj*

fasciae — see TENSOR FASCIAE LATAE

fascia la·ta \-'lä-tə, -'lā-\ *n, pl* **fasciae latae** \-'lä-tē, -'lā-\ : the deep fascia that forms a complete sheath for the thigh

fas·ci·cle \'fa-si-kəl\ *n* : a small bundle; *esp* : FASCICULUS

fasciculata — see ZONA FASCICULATA

fas·cic·u·la·tion \fə-ˌsi-kyə-'lā-shən, fa-\ *n* : muscular twitching involving the simultaneous contraction of contiguous groups of muscle fibers

fas·cic·u·lus \fə-'si-kyə-ləs, fa-\ *n, pl* **-li** \-ˌlī\ : a slender bundle of fibers: **a** : a bundle of skeletal muscle cells bound together by fasciae and forming one of the constituent elements of a muscle **b** : a bundle of nerve fibers that follow the same course but do not necessarily have like functional connections **c** : TRACT 2

fasciculus cu·ne·a·tus \-ˌkyü-nē-'ā-təs\ *n* : either of a pair of nerve tracts of the posterior funiculus of the spinal cord that are situated on opposite sides of the posterior median septum lateral to the fasciculus gracilis and that carry nerve fibers from the upper part of the body — called also *column of Burdach*

fasciculus grac·i·lis \-'gra-sə-ləs\ *n* : either of a pair of nerve tracts of the posterior funiculus of the spinal cord that carry nerve fibers from the lower part of the body — called also *gracile fasciculus*

fas·ci·ec·to·my \ˌfa-shē-'ek-tə-mē, -sē-\ *n, pl* **-mies** : surgical excision of strips of fascia

fas·ci·itis \ˌfa-shē-'ī-təs, -sē-\ *n* : inflammation of a fascia

Fas·ci·o·la \fə-'sē-ə-lə, -'sī-\ *n* : a genus of digenetic trematode worms (family Fasciolidae) including common liver flukes of various mammals

fa·sci·o·li·a·sis \fə-ˌsē-ə-'lī-ə-səs, -ˌsī-\ *n, pl* **-a·ses** \-ˌsēz\ : infestation with or disease caused by liver flukes of the genus *Fasciola*

fas·ci·o·li·cide \fə-'sē-ə-lə-ˌsīd, fa-\ *n* : an agent that destroys liver flukes of the genus *Fasciola*

Fas·ci·o·loi·des \fə-ˌsē-ə-'loi-(ˌ)dēz, -ˌsī-\ *n* : a genus of trematode worms (family Fasciolidae) including the giant liver flukes of ruminant mammals

fas·ci·o·lop·si·a·sis \ˌlãp-'sī-ə-səs\ *n, pl* **-a·ses** \-ˌsēz\ : infestation with or disease caused by a large intestinal fluke of the genus *Fasciolopsis* (*F. buski*)

Fas·ci·o·lop·sis \-'läp-səs\ *n* : a genus of trematode worms (family Fasciolidae) that includes an important intestinal parasite (*F. buski*) of humans, swine, dogs, and rabbits in much of eastern Asia

fas·ci·ot·o·my \ˌfa-shē-ˈä-tə-mē\ *n*, *pl* **-mies** : surgical incision of a fascia

fas·ci·tis \fa-ˈshī-təs. -ˈsī-\ *var of* FASCIITIS

¹fast \ˈfast\ *adj* : resistant to change (as from destructive action) — used chiefly of organisms and in combination with the agent resisted (acid-*fast* bacteria)

²fast *vb* **1 a** : to abstain from food **b** : to eat sparingly or abstain from some foods **2** : to deny food to (the patient was ~ed before treatment)

³fast *n* **1** : the practice of fasting **2** : a time of fasting

fastigial nucleus \fa-ˈsti-jē-əl-\ *n* : a nucleus lying near the midline in the roof of the fourth ventricle of the brain

fas·tig·i·um \fa-ˈsti-jē-əm\ *n* : the period at which the symptoms of a disease (as a febrile disease) are most pronounced

fast–twitch \ˈfast-ˌtwich\ *adj* : of. relating to, or being muscle fiber that contracts quickly esp. during brief high-intensity physical activity requiring strength — compare SLOW-TWITCH

¹fat \ˈfat\ *adj* **fat·ter; fat·test** : fleshy with superfluous flabby tissue that is not muscle : OBESE — **fat·ness** *n*

²fat *n* **1** : animal tissue consisting chiefly of cells distended with greasy or oily matter — compare BROWN FAT **2 a** : oily or greasy matter making up the bulk of adipose tissue **b** : any of numerous compounds of carbon, hydrogen, and oxygen that are glycerides of fatty acids, are the chief constituents of plant and animal fat, are a major class of energy-rich food, and are soluble in organic solvents but not in water **c** : a solid or semisolid fat as distinguished from an oil **3** : the condition of fatness : OBESITY

fa·tal \ˈfāt-ᵊl\ *adj* : causing death — **fa·tal·ly** *adv*

fa·tal·i·ty \fā-ˈta-lə-tē, fə-\ *n*, *pl* **-ties 1** : the quality or state of causing death or destruction : DEADLINESS **2 a** : death resulting from a disaster **b** : one who suffers such a death

fat cell *n* : a fat-containing cell of adipose tissue — called also *adipocyte*

fat de·pot \-ˈde-(ˌ)pō, -ˈdē-\ *n* : ADIPOSE TISSUE

fat farm *n* : a health spa that specializes in weight reduction

father figure *n* : one often of particular power or influence who serves as an emotional substitute for a father

father image *n* : an idealization of one's father often projected onto someone to whom one looks for guidance and protection

fa·ti·ga·bil·i·ty *also* **fa·ti·gua·bil·i·ty** \fə-ˌtē-gə-ˈbi-lə-tē, ˌfa-ti-\ *n*, *pl* **-ties** : susceptibility to fatigue

fa·tigue \fə-ˈtēg\ *n* **1** : weariness or exhaustion from labor, exertion, or stress **2** : the temporary loss of power to respond induced in a sensory receptor or motor end organ by continued stimulation — **fatigue** *vb*

fat pad *n* : a flattened mass of fatty tissue

fat·ty \ˈfa-tē\ *adj* **fat·ti·er; -est 1 a** : unduly stout **b** : marked by an abnormal deposit of fat (a ~ liver) (~ cirrhosis) **2** : derived from or chemically related to fat — **fat·ti·ness** *n*

fatty acid *n* **1** : any of numerous saturated acids $C_nH_{2n+1}COOH$ containing a single carboxyl group and including many that occur naturally usu. in the form of esters in fats, waxes, and essential oils **2** : any of the saturated or unsaturated acids (as palmitic acid) with a single carboxyl group and usu. an even number of carbon atoms that occur naturally in the form of glycerides in fats and fatty oils

fatty degeneration *n* : a process of tissue degeneration marked by the deposition of fat globules in the cells — called also *steatosis*

fatty infiltration *n* : infiltration of the tissue of an organ with excess amounts of fat

fatty oil *n* : a fat that is liquid at ordinary temperatures — called also *fixed oil;* compare ESSENTIAL OIL. OIL 1

fau·ces \ˈfȯ-ˌsēz\ *n sing or pl* : the narrow passage from the mouth to the pharynx situated between the soft palate and the base of the tongue — called also *isthmus of the fauces* — **fau·cial** \ˈfȯ-shəl\ *adj*

fau·na \ˈfȯn-ə. ˈfän-\ *n*, *pl* **faunas** *also* **fau·nae** \-ˌē. -ˌī\ : animal life; *esp* : the animals characteristic of a region, period, or special environment — compare FLORA — **fau·nal** \-ᵊl\ *adj* — **fau·nal·ly** \-ᵊl-ē\ *adv*

fava bean \ˈfä-və-\ *n* : BROAD BEAN

fa·vism \ˈfä-ˌvi-zəm, ˈfä-\ *n* : a hereditary allergic condition esp. of males of Mediterranean descent that causes a severe reaction to the broad bean or its pollen which is characterized by hemolytic anemia, fever, and jaundice

fa·vus \ˈfā-vəs\ *n* : a contagious skin disease of humans and many domestic animals and fowls that is caused by a fungus (as *Trichophyton schoenleinii*) — **fa·vic** \-vik\ *adj*

FDA *abbr* Food and Drug Administration

Fe *symbol* iron

febri- *comb form* : fever (*febrifuge*)

feb·ri·fuge \ˈfe-brə-ˌfyüj\ *n or adj* : ANTIPYRETIC

fe·brile \ˈfe-ˌbril, ˈfē-\ *adj* : FEVERISH

fe·cal \ˈfē-kəl\ *adj* : of, relating to, or constituting feces — **fe·cal·ly** *adv*

fe·ca·lith \ˈfē-kə-ˌlith\ *n* : a concretion

of dry compact feces formed in the intestine or vermiform appendix

fe·cal·oid \'fē-kə-₁lȯid\ *adj* : resembling dung

fe·ces \'fē-(₁)sēz\ *n pl* : bodily waste discharged through the anus : EXCREMENT

Fech·ner's law \'fek-nərz-, 'fek-\ *n* : WEBER-FECHNER LAW

fec·u·lent \'fe-kyə-lənt\ *adj* : foul with impurities : FECAL

fe·cund \'fe-kənd, 'fē-\ *adj* **1** : characterized by having produced many offspring **2** : capable of producing : not sterile or barren — **fe·cun·di·ty** \fi-'kən-də-tē, fe-\ *n*

fe·cun·date \'fe-kən-₁dāt, 'fē-\ *vb* **-dat·ed; -dat·ing** : IMPREGNATE — **fe·cun·da·tion** \fe-kən-'dā-shən, ₁fē-\ *n*

fee·ble-mind·ed \₁fē-bəl-'mīn-dəd\ *adj* : mentally deficient — **fee·ble-mind·ed·ness** *n*

feed·back \'fēd-₁bak\ *n* **1** : the partial reversion of the effects of a process to its source or to a preceding stage **2** : the return to a point of origin of evaluative or corrective information about an action or process; *also* : the information so transmitted

feedback inhibition *n* : inhibition of an enzyme controlling an early stage of a series of biochemical reactions by the end product when it reaches a critical concentration

fee–for–service *n* : separate payment to a health-care provider for each medical service rendered to a patient

feel·ing \'fē-liŋ\ *n* **1** : the one of the basic physical senses of which the skin contains the chief end organs and of which the sensations of touch and temperature are characteristic : TOUCH; *also* : a sensation experienced through this sense **2** : an emotional state or reaction (guilt ~s) **3** : the overall quality of one's awareness as measured along a pleasantness-unpleasantness continuum — compare AFFECT, EMOTION

fee splitting *n* : payment by a medical specialist (as a surgeon) of a part of the specialist's fee to the physician who made the referral — **fee splitter** *n*

feet *pl of* FOOT

Feh·ling's solution \'fā-liŋz-\ *or* **Fehling solution** \-liŋ-\ *n* : a blue solution of Rochelle salt and copper sulfate used as an oxidizing agent in a test for sugars and aldehydes in which the precipitation of a red oxide of copper indicates a positive result

Fehling, Hermann von (1812–1885), German chemist.

fe·line \'fē-₁līn\ *adj* : of, relating to, or affecting cats or the cat family (Felidae) — **feline** *n*

feline distemper *n* : PANLEUKOPENIA

feline enteritis *n* : PANLEUKOPENIA

feline infectious anemia *n* : a widespread contagious disease of cats characterized by weakness, lethargy, loss of appetite, and hemolytic anemia and caused by a bacterial parasite of red blood cells belonging to the genus *Haemobartonella* (*H. felis*)

feline infectious peritonitis *n* : an almost invariably fatal infectious disease of cats caused by one or more coronaviruses and characterized by fever, weight and appetite loss, and ascites with a thick yellow fluid

feline leukemia *n* : a disease of cats caused by the feline leukemia virus, characterized by leukemia and lymphoma, and often resulting in death

feline leukemia virus *n* : a retrovirus that is widespread in cat populations, is prob. transmitted by direct contact, and in cats is associated with or causes malignant lymphoma, feline leukemia, anemia, glomerulonephritis, and immunosuppression

feline panleukopenia *n* : PANLEUKOPENIA

feline pneumonitis *n* : an infectious disease of the eyes and upper respiratory tract of cats that is caused by a bacterium of the genus *Chlamydia* (*C. psittaci*) and is characterized esp. by conjunctivitis and rhinitis

fel·late \'fe-₁lāt, fə-'lāt\ *vb* **fel·lat·ed; fel·lat·ing** : to perform fellatio on someone — **fel·la·tor** \-₁lā-tər, -'lā-\ *n*

fel·la·tio \fə-'lā-shē-₁ō, fe-, -'lā-tē-\ *also* **fel·la·tion** \-'lā-shən\ *n, pl* **-tios** *also* **-tions** : oral stimulation of the penis

fel·la·tor \'fe-₁lā-tər, fə-'lā-\ *n* : one and esp. a man who performs fellatio

fel·la·trice \'fe-lə-₁trēs\ *n* : FELLATRIX

fel·la·trix \'fe-'lā-triks\ *n, pl* **-trix·es** *or* **-tri·ces** \-trə-₁sēz, ₁fe-lə-'trī-(₁)sēz\ : a woman who performs fellatio

fel·on \'fe-lən\ *n* : WHITLOW

Fel·ty's syndrome \'fel-tēz-\ *n* : a condition characterized esp. by rheumatoid arthritis, neutropenia, and splenomegaly

Felty, Augustus Roi (1895–1964), American physician.

FeLV *abbr* feline leukemia virus

fe·male \'fē-₁māl\ *n* : an individual that bears young or produces eggs as distinguished from one that produces sperm; *esp* : a woman or girl as distinguished from a man or boy — **female** *adj* — **fe·male·ness** *n*

female hormone *n* : a sex hormone (as an estrogen) primarily produced and functioning in the female

fem·i·nize \'fe-mə-₁nīz\ *vb* **-nized; -niz·ing** : to cause (a male or castrate) to take on feminine characters (as by implantation of ovaries or administration of estrogenic substances) — **fem·i·ni·za·tion** \₁fe-mə-nə-'zā-shən\ *n*

femora *pl of* FEMUR

fem·o·ral \'fe-mə-rəl\ *adj* : of or relating to the femur or thigh

femoral artery *n* : the chief artery of the thigh that lies in the anterior part of the thigh — see DEEP FEMORAL ARTERY

femoral canal n : the space that is situated between the femoral vein and the inner wall of the femoral sheath

femoral nerve n : the largest branch of the lumbar plexus that supplies extensor muscles of the thigh and skin areas on the front of the thigh and medial surface of the leg and foot and that sends articular branches to the hip and knee joints

femoral ring n : the oval upper opening of the femoral canal often the seat of a hernia

femoral sheath n : the fascial sheath investing the femoral vessels

femoral triangle n : an area in the upper anterior part of the thigh bounded by the inguinal ligament, the sartorius, and the adductor longus — called also *femoral trigone*, *Scarpa's triangle*

femoral vein n : the chief vein of the thigh that is a continuation of the popliteal vein and continues above Poupart's ligament as the external iliac vein

femoris — see BICEPS FEMORIS, PROFUNDA FEMORIS, PROFUNDA FEMORIS ARTERY, QUADRATUS FEMORIS, QUADRICEPS FEMORIS, RECTUS FEMORIS

femoro- comb form : femoral and ⟨*femoropopliteal*⟩

fem·o·ro·pop·li·te·al \ˌfe-mə-rō-ˌpä-plə-ᵗtē-əl, -pä-ᵖpli-tē-əl\ adj : of, relating to, or connecting the femoral and popliteal arteries (a ~ bypass)

fe·mur \ᵗfē-mər\ n, pl **fe·murs** or **fem·o·ra** \ᵗfē-mə-rə\ : the proximal bone of the hind or lower limb that is the longest and largest bone in the human body, extends from the hip to the knee, articulates above with the acetabulum, and articulates with the tibia below by a pair of condyles — called also *thighbone*

fe·nes·tra \fə-ᵗnes-trə\ n, pl **-trae** \-ˌtrē, -ˌtrī\ 1 : a small anatomical opening (as in a bone): as a : OVAL WINDOW b : ROUND WINDOW 2 a : an opening like a window cut in bone b : a window cut in a surgical instrument (as an endoscope) — **fe·nes·tral** \-trəl\ adj

fenestra coch·le·ae \-ᵗkä-klē-ē, -ᵗkō-klē-ī\ n : ROUND WINDOW

fenestra oval·is \-ō-ᵗvä-ləs\ n : OVAL WINDOW

fenestra ro·tun·da \-rō-ᵗtən-də\ n : ROUND WINDOW

fen·es·trat·ed \ᵗfe-nə-ˌstrā-təd\ adj : having one or more openings or pores (~ blood capillaries)

fen·es·tra·tion \ˌfe-nə-ᵗstrā-shən\ n 1 a : a natural or surgically created opening in a surface b : the presence of such openings 2 : the operation of cutting an opening in the bony labyrinth between the inner ear and tympanum to replace natural fenestrae that are not functional

fenestra ves·ti·bu·li \-ˌves-ᵗti-byə-ˌlī\ n : OVAL WINDOW

fen·flur·amine \ˌfen-ᵗflúr-ə-ˌmēn\ n : an amphetamine derivative $C_{12}H_{16}F_3N$ used esp. as the hydrochloride salt to suppress appetite in the treatment of obesity

fen·o·pro·fen \ˌfe-nə-ᵗprō-fən\ n : an anti-inflammatory analgesic $C_{15}H_{14}O_3$ used esp. in the treatment of arthritis

fen·ta·nyl \ᵗfent-ᵊn-ˌil\ n : a narcotic analgesic $C_{22}H_{28}N_2O$ with pharmacological action similar to morphine that is administered esp. as the citrate

fer·ment \ᵗfər-ˌment, (ˌ)fər-ᵗ\ n : ENZYME; also : FERMENTATION

fer·men·ta·tion \ˌfər-mən-ᵗtā-shən, -ˌmen-\ n : an enzymatically controlled anaerobic breakdown of an energy-rich compound (as a carbohydrate to carbon dioxide and alcohol); broadly : an enzymatically controlled transformation of an organic compound — **fer·ment** \(ˌ)fər-ᵗment\ vb — **fer·men·ta·tive** \(ˌ)fər-ᵗmen-tə-tiv\ adj

fer·mi·um \ᵗfer-mē-əm, ᵗfər-\ n : a radioactive metallic element artificially produced — symbol Fm; see ELEMENT table

fer·ric \ᵗfer-ik\ adj 1 : of, relating to, or containing iron 2 : being or containing iron usu. with a valence of three

ferric chloride n : a salt $FeCl_3$ that is used in medicine in a water solution or tincture usu. as an astringent or styptic

ferric oxide n : the red or black oxide of iron Fe_2O_3

ferric py·ro·phos·phate \-ˌpī-rō-ᵗfäs-ˌfāt\ n : a green or yellowish green salt, approximately $Fe_4(P_2O_7)_3$·$9H_2O$, used as a source of iron esp. when dietary intake is inadequate

fer·ri·he·mo·glo·bin \ˌfer-ˌi-ᵗhē-mə-ˌglō-bən, ˌfer-i-\ n : METHEMOGLOBIN

fer·ri·tin \ᵗfer-ət-ᵊn\ n : a crystalline iron-containing protein that functions in the storage of iron and is found esp. in the liver and spleen

fer·rous \ᵗfer-əs\ adj 1 : of, relating to, or containing iron 2 : being or containing iron with a valence of two

ferrous fumarate n : a reddish orange to red-brown powder $C_4H_2FeO_4$ used orally in the treatment of iron-deficiency anemia

ferrous gluconate n : a yellowish gray or pale greenish yellow powder or granules $C_{12}H_{22}FeO_{14}$ used as a hematinic in the treatment of iron-deficiency anemia

ferrous sulfate n : an astringent iron salt obtained usu. in pale green crystalline form $FeSO_4$·$7H_2O$ and used in medicine chiefly for treating iron-deficiency anemia

fer·tile \ᵗfərt-ᵊl, ᵗfər-ˌtīl\ adj 1 : capable of growing or developing ⟨~ egg⟩ 2 : developing spores or spore-bearing organs **3 a** : capable of breeding or reproducing **b** *of an estrous cycle* : marked by the production of one or more viable eggs

fer·til·i·ty \(ˌ)fər-ˈti-lə-tē\ *n, pl* **-ties 1** : the quality or state of being fertile **2** : the birthrate of a population — compare MORTALITY 2b

fer·til·i·za·tion \ˌfərt-ᵊl-ə-ˈzā-shən\ *n* : an act or process of making fertile; *specif* : the process of union of two gametes whereby the somatic chromosome number is restored and the development of a new individual is initiated — **fer·til·ize** \ˈfərt-ᵊl-ˌīz\ *vb*

fertilization membrane *n* : a resistant membranous layer in eggs of many animals that forms following fertilization by the thickening and separation of the vitelline membrane from the cell surface and that prevents multiple fertilization

fes·cue foot \ˈfes-(ˌ)kyü-\ *n* : a disease of the feet of cattle resembling ergotism that is associated with feeding on fescue grass (genus *Festuca* and esp. *F. elatior* var. *arundinacea*)

¹**fes·ter** \ˈfes-tər\ *n* : a suppurating sore : PUSTULE

²**fester** *vb* **fes·tered; fes·ter·ing** : to generate pus

fes·ti·nat·ing \ˈfes-tə-ˌnā-tiŋ\ *adj* : being a walking gait (as in Parkinson's disease) characterized by involuntary acceleration — **fes·ti·na·tion** \ˌfes-tə-ˈnā-shən\ *n*

fe·tal \ˈfēt-ᵊl\ *adj* : of, relating to, or being a fetus

fetal alcohol syndrome *n* : a highly variable group of birth defects including mental retardation, deficient growth, and defects of the skull, face, and brain that tend to occur in the infants of women who consume large amounts of alcohol during pregnancy — abbr. *FAS*

fetal hemoglobin *n* : a hemoglobin variant that predominates in the blood of a newborn and persists in increased proportions in some forms of anemia (as thalassemia) — called also *hemoglobin F*

fe·ta·lis \fi-ˈta-ləs\ — see ERYTHROBLASTOSIS FETALIS, HYDROPS FETALIS

fetal position *n* : a position (as of a sleeping person) in which the body lies curled up on one side with the arms and legs drawn up toward the chest and the head bowed forward and which is assumed in some forms of psychic regression

feti— see FETO-

fe·ti·cide \ˈfē-tə-ˌsīd\ *n* : the action or process of causing the death of a fetus

fe·tish *also* **fe·tich** \ˈfe-tish, ˈfē-\ *n* : an object or bodily part whose real or fantasized presence is psychologically necessary for sexual gratification and that is an object of fixation to the extent that it may interfere with complete sexual expression

fe·tish·ism *also* **fe·tich·ism** \-ˌti-ˌshi-zəm\ *n* : the pathological displacement of erotic interest and satisfaction to a fetish — **fe·tish·ist** \-shist\ *n* — **fe·tish·is·tic** \ˌfe-ti-ˈshis-tik *also* ˌfē-\ *adj* — **fe·tish·is·ti·cal·ly** \-ti-k(ə-)lē\ *adv*

fet·lock \ˈfet-ˌläk\ *n* **1 a** : a projection bearing a tuft of hair on the back of the leg above the hoof of a horse or similar animal **b** : the tuft of hair itself **2** : the joint of the limb at the fetlock

feto- *or* **feti-** *comb form* : fetus ⟨*feticide*⟩ ⟨*fetology*⟩

fe·tol·o·gist \fē-ˈtä-lə-jist\ *n* : a specialist in fetology

fe·tol·o·gy \fē-ˈtä-lə-jē\ *n, pl* **-gies** : a branch of medical science concerned with the study and treatment of the fetus in the uterus

fe·to·pro·tein \ˌfē-tō-ˈprō-ˌtēn, -tē-ən\ *n* : any of several fetal antigens present in the adult in some abnormal conditions; *esp* : ALPHA-FETOPROTEIN

fe·tor he·pat·i·cus \ˈfē-tər-hi-ˈpa-ti-kəs, -ˌtor\ *n* : a characteristically disagreeable odor to the breath that is a sign of liver failure

fe·to·scope \ˈfē-tə-ˌskōp\ *n* : a fiber-optic tube used to perform fetoscopy

fe·tos·co·py \fē-ˈtäs-kə-pē\ *n, pl* **-pies** : examination of the pregnant uterus by means of a fiber-optic tube

fe·to·tox·ic \ˌfē-tə-ˈtäk-sik\ *adj* : toxic to fetuses — **fe·to·tox·ic·i·ty** \-ˌtäk-ˈsi-sə-tē\ *n*

fe·tus \ˈfē-təs\ *n, pl* **fe·tus·es** : an unborn or unhatched vertebrate esp. after attaining the basic structural plan of its kind; *specif* : a developing human from usu. three months after conception to birth — compare EMBRYO

Feul·gen reaction \ˈfoil-gən\ *n* : the development of a purple color by DNA in a microscopic preparation stained with a modified Schiff's reagent

Feulgen, Robert Joachim (1884–1955), German biochemist.

¹**fe·ver** \ˈfē-vər\ *n* **1** : a rise of body temperature above the normal **2** : an abnormal bodily state characterized by increased production of heat, accelerated heart action and pulse, and systemic debility with weakness, loss of appetite, and thirst **3** : any of various diseases of which fever is a prominent symptom — see YELLOW FEVER, TYPHOID FEVER — **fe·ver·ish** \-və-rish\ *adj*

²**fever** *vb* **fe·vered; fe·ver·ing** : to affect with or be in a fever

fever blister *n* : COLD SORE

fever therapy *n* : a treatment of disease by fever induced by various artificial means

fever thermometer *n* : CLINICAL THERMOMETER

FFA *abbr* free fatty acids

fi·ber *or* **fi·bre** \ˈfi-bər\ *n* **1 a** : a strand of nerve tissue : AXON, DENDRITE **b** : one of the filaments composing most of the intercellular matrix of connective tissue c : one of the elongated contractile cells of muscle tissue 2 : indigestible material in food that stimulates the intestine to peristalsis — called also **bulk, dietary fiber, roughage**

fiber of Mül·ler \-ˈmyü-lər, -ˈmə-\ n : any of the neuroglia fibers that extend through the entire thickness of the retina — called also **Müller cell, sustentacular fiber of Müller**

H. Müller — see MÜLLER CELL

fiber optics n pl 1 : thin transparent fibers of glass or plastic that transmit light throughout their length by internal reflections; also : a bundle of such fibers used in an instrument (as for viewing body cavities) 2 : the technique of the use of fiber optics — used with a sing. verb — **fi·ber·op·tic** adj

fi·ber·scope \ˈfi-bər-ˌskōp\ n : a flexible instrument utilizing fiber optics for examination of inaccessible areas (as the stomach)

fiber tract n : TRACT 2

fibr- or **fibro-** comb form 1 : fiber : fibrous tissue (fibrogenesis) 2 : fibrous and (fibroelastic)

fi·bril \ˈfī-brəl, ˈfi-\ n : a small filament or fiber: as a : one of the fine threads into which a striated muscle fiber can be longitudinally split b : NEUROFIBRIL

fi·bril·la \fī-ˈbri-lə, fi-; ˈfib-rə-lə, ˈfī-\ n, pl **fi·bril·lae** \-ˌlē\ : FIBRIL

fi·bril·lar \ˈfī-brə-lər, ˈfi-; fī-ˈbri-, fi-\ adj 1 : of or like fibrils or fibers (a ~ network) 2 : of or exhibiting fibrillation

fi·bril·lary \ˈfī-brə-ˌler-ē, ˈfi-; fī-ˈbri-lə-rē, fi-\ adj 1 : of or relating to fibrils or fibers (~ overgrowth) 2 : of, relating to, or marked by fibrillation (~ chorea)

fi·bril·la·tion \ˌfi-brə-ˈlā-shən, ˌfī-\ n 1 : an act or process of forming fibers or fibrils 2 a : a muscular twitching involving individual muscle fibers acting without coordination b : very rapid irregular contractions of the muscle fibers of the heart resulting in a lack of synchronism between heartbeat and pulse — **fi·bril·late** \ˈfi-brə-ˌlāt, ˈfī-\ vb

fi·bril·lo·gen·e·sis \ˌfi-brə-lō-ˈje-nə-səs, ˌfī-\ n, pl **-e·ses** \-ˌsēz\ : the development of fibrils

fi·brin \ˈfī-brən\ n : a white insoluble fibrous protein formed from fibrinogen by the action of thrombin esp. in the clotting of blood

fi·brin·ase \-brə-ˌnās, -ˌnāz\ n : FACTOR XIII

fi·brin·o·gen \fī-ˈbri-nə-jən\ n : a plasma protein that is produced in the liver and is converted into fibrin during blood clot formation

fi·brin·o·gen·o·pe·nia \(ˌ)fī-ˌbri-nə-ˌje-nə-ˈpē-nē-ə, -nyə\ n : a deficiency of fibrin or fibrinogen or both in the blood

fi·bri·noid \ˈfi-brə-ˌnȯid, ˈfī-\ n, often attrib : a homogeneous material that resembles fibrin and is formed in the walls of blood vessels and in connective tissue in some pathological conditions and normally in the placenta

fi·bri·no·ly·sin \ˌfi-brən-ᵊl-ˈīs-ᵊn\ n : any of several proteolytic enzymes that promote the dissolution of blood clots; esp : PLASMIN

fi·bri·no·ly·sis \ˈfī-səs, -brə-ˈnä-lə-səs\ n, pl **-ly·ses** \-ˌsēz\ : the usu. enzymatic breakdown of fibrin — **fi·bri·no·lyt·ic** \-brən-ᵊl-ˈi-tik\ adj

fi·bri·no·pe·nia \ˌfī-brə-nō-ˈpē-nē-ə, -nyə\ n : FIBRINOGENOPENIA

fi·bri·no·pep·tide \-ˈpep-ˌtīd\ n : any of the polypeptides that are cleaved from fibrinogen by thrombin during blood clot formation

fi·bri·no·pu·ru·lent \-ˈpyu̇r-yə-lənt, -ˌpyu̇r-\ adj : containing, characterized by, or exuding fibrin and pus (as in certain inflammations)

fi·bri·nous \ˈfi-brə-nəs, ˈfī-\ adj : marked by the presence of fibrin

fibro- — see FIBR-

fi·bro·ad·e·no·ma \ˌfī-(ˌ)brō-ˌad-ᵊn-ˈō-mə\ n, pl **-mas** or **-ma·ta** \-mə-tə\ : adenoma with a large amount of fibrous tissue

fi·bro·blast \ˈfī-brə-ˌblast, ˈfi-\ n : a connective-tissue cell of mesenchymal origin that secretes proteins and esp. molecular collagen from which the extracellular fibrillar matrix of connective tissue forms — **fi·bro·blas·tic** \ˌfī-brə-ˈblas-tik, ˌfi-\ adj

fi·bro·car·ti·lage \ˈfī-(ˌ)brō-ˈkärt-ᵊl-ij\ n : cartilage in which the matrix except immediately about the cells is largely composed of fibers like those of ordinary connective tissue; also : a structure or part composed of such cartilage — **fi·bro·car·ti·lag·i·nous** \-ˌkärt-ᵊl-ˈa-jə-nəs\ adj

fi·bro·cys·tic \ˌfī-brə-ˈsis-tik, ˌfi-\ adj : characterized by the presence or development of fibrous tissue and cysts

fibrocystic disease of the pancreas n : CYSTIC FIBROSIS

fi·bro·cyte \ˈfī-brə-ˌsīt, ˈfi-\ n : FIBROBLAST; specif : a spindle-shaped cell of fibrous tissue

fi·bro·elas·tic \ˌfī-(ˌ)brō-i-ˈlas-tik\ adj : consisting of both fibrous and elastic elements (~ tissue)

fi·bro·elas·to·sis \-ˌlas-ˈtō-səs\ n, pl **-to·ses** \-ˌsēz\ : a condition of the body or one of its organs characterized by proliferation of fibroelastic tissue — see ENDOCARDIAL FIBROELASTOSIS

fi·bro·gen·e·sis \ˌfī-brə-ˈje-nə-səs, n, pl **-e·ses** \-ˌsēz\ : the development or proliferation of fibers or fibrous tissue

fi·bro·gen·ic \-ˈje-nik\ adj : promoting the development of fibers (a ~ agent)

fi·broid \ˈfī-ˌbrȯid, ˈfi-\ adj : resembling, forming, or consisting of fibrous tissue

²fibroid *n* : a benign tumor that consists of fibrous and muscular tissue and occurs esp. in the uterine wall

fi·bro·ma \fī-ˈbrō-mə\ *n, pl* **-mas** *also* **-ma·ta** \-tə\ : a benign tumor consisting mainly of fibrous tissue — **fi·bro·ma·tous** \-təs\ *adj*

fi·bro·ma·toid \fī-ˈbrō-mə-ˌtȯid\ *adj* : resembling a fibroma

fi·bro·ma·to·sis \(ˌ)fī-ˌbrō-mə-ˈtō-səs\ *n, pl* **-to·ses** \-ˌsēz\ : a condition marked by the presence of or a tendency to develop multiple fibromas

fi·bro·my·al·gia \-ˌmī-ˈal-jə, -jē-ə\ *n* : any of a group of nonarticular rheumatic disorders characterized by pain, tenderness, and stiffness of muscles and associated connective tissue structures — called also *fibromyositis*

fi·bro·my·o·ma \-ˌmī-ˈō-mə\ *n, pl* **-mas** *also* **-ma·ta** \-mə-tə\ : a mixed tumor containing both fibrous and muscle tissue — **fi·bro·my·o·ma·tous** \-mə-təs\ *adj*

fi·bro·my·o·si·tis \-ˌmī-ə-ˈsī-təs\ *n* : FIBROMYALGIA

fi·bro·myx·o·ma \-mik-ˈsō-mə\ *n, pl* **-mas** *or* **-ma·ta** \-mə-tə\ : a myxoma containing fibrous tissue

fi·bro·nec·tin \ˌfī-brə-ˈnek-tən\ *n* : any of a group of glycoproteins of cell surfaces, blood plasma, and connective tissue that promote cellular adhesion and migration

fi·bro·pla·sia \ˌfī-brə-ˈplā-zhə, -zhē-ə\ *n* : the process of forming fibrous tissue — **fi·bro·plas·tic** \-ˈplas-tik\ *adj*

fibrosa — see OSTEITIS FIBROSA, OSTEITIS FIBROSA CYSTICA, OSTEITIS FIBROSA CYSTICA GENERALISATA, OSTEODYSTROPHIA FIBROSA

fi·bro·sar·co·ma \-sär-ˈkō-mə\ *n, pl* **-mas** *or* **-ma·ta** \-mə-tə\ : a sarcoma of relatively low malignancy consisting chiefly of spindle-shaped cells that tend to form collagenous fibrils

fi·brose \ˈfī-ˌbrōs\ *vb* **-brosed; -brosing** : to form fibrous tissue ⟨a *fibrosed* wound⟩

fi·bro·se·rous \ˌfī-brō-ˈsir-əs\ *adj* : composed of a serous membrane supported by a firm layer of fibrous tissue

fi·bro·sis \fī-ˈbrō-səs\ *n, pl* **-bro·ses** \-ˌsēz\ : a condition marked by increase of interstitial fibrous tissue : fibrous degeneration — **fi·brot·ic** \-ˈbrä-tik\ *adj*

fi·bro·si·tis \ˌfī-brə-ˈsī-təs\ *n* : a muscular condition that is commonly accompanied by the formation of painful subcutaneous nodules — **fi·bro·sit·ic** \-ˈsi-tik\ *adj*

fibrosus — see ANNULUS FIBROSUS

fi·brous \ˈfī-brəs\ *adj* **1** : containing, consisting of, or resembling fibers **2** : characterized by fibrosis

fibrous ankylosis *n* : ankylosis due to the growth of fibrous tissue

fib·u·la \ˈfī-byə-lə\ *n, pl* **-lae** \-lē, -ˌlī\ *or* **-las** : the outer or postaxial and usu. the smaller of the two bones of the hind or lower limb below the knee that is the slenderest bone of the human body in proportion to its length and articulates above with the external tuberosity of the tibia and below with the talus — called also *calf bone* — **fib·u·lar** \-lər\ *adj*

fibular collateral ligament *n* : LATERAL COLLATERAL LIGAMENT

Fick principle \ˈfik-\ *n* : a generalization in physiology which states that blood flow is proportional to the difference in concentration of a substance (as oxygen) in the blood as it enters and leaves an organ and which is used to determine cardiac output — called also *Fick method*

Fick, Adolf Eugen (1829–1901), German physiologist.

FICS *abbr* Fellow of the International College of Surgeons

field \ˈfēld\ *n* **1** : a complex of forces that serve as causative agents in human behavior **2** : a region of embryonic tissue potentially capable of a particular type of differentiation **3 a** : an area that is perceived or under observation **b** : the site of a surgical operation

field hospital *n* : a military organization of medical personnel with equipment for establishing a temporary hospital in the field

field of vision *n* : VISUAL FIELD

fièvre bou·ton·neuse \ˈfyev-rə-ˌbü-tȯ-ˈnœz\ *n* : BOUTONNEUSE FEVER

fifth cranial nerve *n* : TRIGEMINAL NERVE

fifth disease *n* : ERYTHEMA INFECTIOSUM

fifth nerve *n* : TRIGEMINAL NERVE

figure–ground \ˈfi-gyər-ˈgraund\ *adj* : relating to or being the relationships between the parts of a perceptual field which is perceived as divided into a part consisting of figures having form and standing out from the part comprising the background and being relatively formless

fil·a·ment \ˈfi-lə-mənt\ *n* : a single thread or a thin flexible threadlike object, process, or appendage; *esp* : an elongated thin series of cells attached one to another (as of some bacteria) — **fil·a·men·tous** \ˌfi-lə-ˈmen-təs\ *adj*

fi·lar·ia \fə-ˈlar-ē-ə\ *n, pl* **fi·lar·i·ae** \-ē-ˌē, -ˌī\ : any of numerous slender filamentous nematodes that as adults are parasites in the blood or tissues and as larvae usu. develop in biting insects and that for the most part were once included in one genus (*Filaria*) but are now divided among various genera (as *Wuchereria* and *Onchocerca*) — **fi·lar·i·al** \-ē-əl\ *adj* — **fi·lar·i·id** \-ē-əd\ *adj or n*

fil·a·ri·a·sis \ˌfi-lə-ˈrī-ə-səs\ *n, pl* **-a-**

ses \-ˌsēz\ : infestation with or disease caused by filariae

fi·lar·i·cide \fə-ˈlar-ə-ˌsīd\ n : an agent that is destructive to filariae — **fi·lar·i·cid·al** \-ˌlar-ə-ˈsīd-ᵊl\ adj

fi·lar·i·form \-ə-ˌfȯrm\ adj, of a larval nematode : resembling a filaria esp. in having a slender elongated form and in possessing a delicate capillary esophagus

fili- or **filo-** comb form : thread (fili-form)

fil·i·al generation \ˈfi-lē-əl-, ˈfil-yəl-\ n : a generation in a breeding experiment that is successive to a parental generation — symbol F_1 for the first, F_2 for the second, etc.

fi·li·form \ˈfi-lə-ˌfȯrm, ˈfī-\ n : an extremely slender bougie

filiform papilla n : any of numerous minute pointed papillae on the tongue

fil·i·pin \ˈfi-lə-pin\ n : an antifungal antibiotic $C_{35}H_{58}O_{11}$ produced by a bacterium of the genus *Streptomyces* (*S. filipinensis*)

fill \ˈfil\ vb **1** : to repair the cavities of (teeth) **2** : to supply as directed (∼ a prescription)

fil·let \ˈfi-lət\ n : a band of anatomical fibers; specif : LEMNISCUS

fill·ing \ˈfi-liŋ\ n **1** : material (as gold or amalgam) used to fill a cavity in a tooth **2** : simple sporadic lymphangitis of the leg of a horse commonly due to overfeeding and insufficient exercise

film \ˈfilm\ n **1 a** : a thin skin or membranous covering **b** : an abnormal growth on or in the eye **2** : an exceedingly thin layer : LAMINA

film badge n : a small pack of sensitive photographic film worn as a badge for indicating exposure to radiation

filo- — see FILI-

fil·ter \ˈfil-tər\ n **1** : a porous article or mass (as of paper) through which a gas or liquid is passed to separate out matter in suspension **2** : an apparatus containing a filter medium — **filter** vb

fil·ter·able \ˈfil-tə-rə-bəl\ also **fil·tra·ble** \-trə-bəl\ adj : capable of being filtered or of passing through a filter — **fil·ter·abil·i·ty** \ˌfil-tə-rə-ˈbi-lə-tē\ n

filterable virus n : any of the infectious agents that pass through a fine filter (as of unglazed porcelain) with the filtrate and remain virulent and that include the viruses as presently understood and various other groups (as the mycoplasmas and rickettsias) which were orig. considered viruses before their cellular nature was established

filter paper n : porous paper used esp. for filtering

fil·trate \ˈfil-ˌtrāt\ n : fluid that has passed through a filter

fil·tra·tion \fil-ˈtrā-shən\ n **1** : the process of filtering **2** : the process of passing through or as if through a filter; also : DIFFUSION

fi·lum ter·mi·na·le \ˈfī-ləm-ˌtər-mə-ˈnā-(ˌ)lē, ˈfē-ləm-ˌter-mə-ˈnä-ˌlā\ n, pl **fi·la ter·mi·na·lia** \ˈfī-lə-ˌtər-mə-ˈnā-lē-ə, ˈfē-lə-ˌter-mə-ˈnä-lē-ə\ : the slender threadlike prolongation of the spinal cord below the origin of the lumbar nerves : the last portion of the pia mater

fim·bria \ˈfim-brē-ə\ n, pl **-bri·ae** \-brē-ˌē, -ˌī\ **1** : a bordering fringe esp. at the entrance of the fallopian tubes **2** : a band of nerve fibers bordering the hippocampus and joining the fornix — **fim·bri·al** \-brē-əl\ adj

fimbriata — see PLICA FIMBRIATA

fim·bri·at·ed \ˈfim-brē-ˌā-təd\ also **fimbri·ate** \-ˌāt\ adj : having the edge or extremity fringed or bordered by slender processes

fi·nas·te·ride \fə-ˈnas-tə-ˌrīd\ n : an antineoplastic drug $C_{23}H_{36}N_2O_2$ used esp. to shrink an enlarged prostate gland by inhibiting an enzyme catalyzing conversion of testosterone to dihydrotestosterone — see PROSCAR

fin·ger \ˈfiŋ-gər\ n : any of the five terminating members of the hand : a digit of the forelimb; esp : one other than the thumb — **fin·gered** \ˈfiŋ-gərd\ adj

finger fracture n : valvulotomy of the mitral commissures performed by a finger thrust through the valve

fin·ger·nail \ˈfiŋ-gər-ˌnāl\ n : the nail of a finger

fin·ger·print \-ˌprint\ n **1** : an ink impression of the lines on the fingertip taken for purpose of identification **2** : chromatographic, electrophoretic, or spectrographic evidence of the presence or identity of a substance — compare DNA FINGERPRINTING — **fingerprint** vb — **fin·ger·print·ing** n

fin·ger·stall \-ˌstȯl\ n : COT

fin·ger·tip \-ˌtip\ n : the tip of a finger

fire \ˈfīr\ vb fired; fir·ing : to transmit or cause to transmit a nerve impulse

fire ant n : any ant of the genus *Solenopsis*; esp : IMPORTED FIRE ANT

fire·damp \-ˌdamp\ n : a combustible mine gas that consists chiefly of methane; also : the explosive mixture of this gas with air — compare BLACK DAMP

first aid n : emergency care or treatment given to an ill or injured person before regular medical aid can be obtained

first cranial nerve n : OLFACTORY NERVE

first–degree burn n : a mild burn characterized by heat, pain, and reddening of the burned surface but not exhibiting blistering or charring of tissues

first intention n : the healing of an incised wound by the direct union of skin edges without granulations — compare SECOND INTENTION

first polar body n : POLAR BODY a

fish–liv·er oil \ˈfish-ˌli-vər-\ n : a fatty oil from the livers of various fishes (as cod, halibut, or sharks) used chiefly as a source of vitamin A — compare COD-LIVER OIL

fish tapeworm *n* : a large tapeworm of the genus *Diphyllobothrium* (*D. latum*) that as an adult infests the human intestine and goes through its intermediate stages in freshwater fishes from which it is transmitted to humans when raw fish is eaten

fis·sion \'fi-shən, -zhən\ *n* 1 : a method of reproduction in which a living cell or body divides into two or more parts each of which grows into a whole new individual 2 : the splitting of an atomic nucleus resulting in the release of large amounts of energy — called also *nuclear fission* — **fis·sion·able** \'fi-shə-nə-bəl, -zhə-\ *adj*

fis·sure \'fi-shər\ *n* 1 : a natural cleft between body parts or in the substance of an organ: as **a** : any of several clefts separating the lobes of the liver **b** : any of various clefts between bones or parts of bones in the skull **c** : any of the deep clefts of the brain; *esp* : one of those located at points of elevation in the walls of the ventricles — compare SULCUS **d** : ANTERIOR MEDIAN FISSURE; *also* : POSTERIOR MEDIAN SEPTUM 2 : a break or slit in tissue usu. at the junction of skin and mucous membrane (~ of the lip) 3 : a linear developmental imperfection in the enamel of a tooth — **fis·sured** \'fi-shərd\ *adj*

fissure of Ro·lan·do \-rō-'lan-(ˌ)dō, -'lä-\ *n* : CENTRAL SULCUS
Rolando, Luigi (1773–1831), Italian anatomist and physiologist.

fissure of Syl·vi·us \-'sil-vē-əs\ *n* : a deep fissure of the lateral aspect of each cerebral hemisphere that divides the temporal from the parietal and frontal lobes — called also *lateral fissure, lateral sulcus, Sylvian fissure*
Du·bois \dē-'bwä\ *or* **De Le Boë** \də-lä-'bō-ā\, **François** *or* **Franz** (*Latin* **Franciscus Sylvius**) **1614–1672),** Dutch anatomist, physician, and chemist.

fis·tu·la \'fis-chə-lə, -tyù-lə\ *n*, *pl* **-las** *or* **-lae** \-ˌlē, -ˌlī\ : an abnormal passage leading from an abscess or hollow organ to the body surface or from one hollow organ to another and permitting passage of fluids or secretions — **fis·tu·lat·ed** \-ˌlā-təd\ *adj*

fis·tu·lec·to·my \ˌfis-chə-'lek-tə-mē, -tyū-\ *n*, *pl* **-mies** : surgical excision of a fistula

fis·tu·li·za·tion \-lə-'zā-shən, -ˌlī-\ *n* 1 : the condition of having a fistula 2 : surgical production of an artificial channel

fis·tu·lous \-ləs\ *adj* : of, relating to, or having the form or nature of a fistula

fistulous withers *n sing or pl* : a deep-seated chronic inflammation of the withers of the horse that discharges seropurulent or bloody fluid through

one or more openings and is prob. associated with infection by bacteria of the genus *Brucella* (esp. *B. abortus*)

¹**fit** \'fit\ *n* 1 : a sudden violent attack of a disease (as epilepsy) esp. when marked by convulsions or unconsciousness : PAROXYSM 2 : a sudden but transient attack of a physical disturbance

²**fit** *adj* **fit·ter; fit·test** : sound physically and mentally : HEALTHY — **fit·ness** *n*

¹**fix** \'fiks\ *vb* 1 **a** : to make firm, stable, or stationary **b** (1) : to change into a stable compound or available form (bacteria that ~ nitrogen) (2) : to kill, harden, and preserve for microscopic study 2 : SPAY, CASTRATE

²**fix** *n* : a shot of a narcotic

fix·at·ed \'fik-ˌsā-təd\ *adj* : arrested in development or adjustment; *esp* : arrested at a pregenital level of psychosexual development

fix·a·tion \fik-'sā-shən\ *n* 1 **a** : the act or an instance of focusing the eyes upon an object **b** (1) : a persistent concentration of libidinal energies upon objects characteristic of psychosexual stages of development preceding the genital stage (2) : an obsessive or unhealthy preoccupation or attachment 2 : the immobilization of the parts of a fractured bone esp. by the use of various metal attachments — **fix·ate** \'fik-ˌsāt\ *vb*

fixation point *n* : the point in the visual field that is fixated by the two eyes in normal vision and for each eye is the point that directly stimulates the fovea of the retina

fix·a·tive \'fik-sə-tiv\ *n* : a substance used to fix living tissue

fix·a·tor \'fik-ˌsā-tər\ *n* : a muscle that stabilizes or fixes a part of the body to which a muscle in the process of moving another part is attached

fixed idea *n* : IDÉE FIXE

fixed oil *n* : a nonvolatile oil; *esp* : FATTY OIL — compare ESSENTIAL OIL

fl *abbr* fluid

flac·cid \'fla-səd, 'flak-\ *adj* : not firm or stiff; *also* : lacking normal or youthful firmness (~ muscles) — **flac·cid·i·ty** \fla-'si-də-tē, flak-\ *n*

flaccid paralysis *n* : paralysis in which muscle tone is lacking in the affected muscles and in which tendon reflexes are decreased or absent

fla·gel·lant \'fla-jə-lənt, flə-'je-lənt\ *n* : a person who responds sexually to being beaten by or to beating another person — **flagellant** *adj* — **fla·gel·lant·ism** \-lən-ˌti-zəm\ *n*

fla·gel·lar \flə-'je-lər, 'fla-jə-\ *adj* : of or relating to a flagellum

¹**fla·gel·late** \'fla-jə-lət, -ˌlāt; flə-'je-lət\ *adj* 1 **a** *or* **flag·el·lat·ed** \'fla-jə-ˌlā-təd\ : having flagella **b** : shaped like a flagellum 2 : of, relating to, or caused by flagellates

²**flagellate** *n* : a flagellate protozoan or alga

¹flag·el·la·tion \ˌfla-jə-ˈlā-shən\ *n* : the practice of a flagellant

²flagellation *n* : the formation or arrangement of flagella

fla·gel·lum \flə-ˈje-ləm\ *n, pl* **-la** \-lə\ *also* **-lums** : a long tapering process that projects singly or in groups from a cell and is the primary organ of motion of many microorganisms

flail \ˈflāl\ *adj* : exhibiting abnormal mobility and loss of response to normal controls — used of body parts (as joints) damaged by paralysis, accident, or surgery ⟨~ foot⟩

flame photometer *n* : a spectrophotometer in which a spray of metallic salts in solution is vaporized in a very hot flame and subjected to quantitative analysis by measuring the intensities of the spectral lines of the metals present — **flame photometric** *adj* — **flame photometry** *n*

flammeus — see NEVUS FLAMMEUS

flank \ˈflaŋk\ *n* : the fleshy part of the side between the ribs and the hip; *broadly* : the side of a quadruped

flap \ˈflap\ *n* : a piece of tissue partly severed from its place of origin for use in surgical grafting

¹flare \ˈflar\ *vb* **flared; flar·ing** : to break out or intensify rapidly : become suddenly worse or more painful — often used with *up*

²flare *n* **1** : a sudden outburst or worsening of a disease — see FLARE-UP **2** : an area of skin flush resulting from and spreading out from a local center of vascular dilation and hyperemia (urticaria ~) **3** : the presence of floating particles in the fluid of the anterior chamber of the eye — called also *aqueous flare*

flare-up \-ˌəp\ *n* : a sudden increase in the symptoms of a latent or subsiding disease (a ~ of malaria)

flash \ˈflash\ *n* : RUSH **1** — see HOT FLASH

flat \ˈflat\ *adj* **flat·ter; flat·test 1** : being or characterized by a horizontal line or tracing without peaks or depressions **2** : characterized by general impoverishment in the presence of emotion-evoking stimuli — **flat·ness** *n*

flat bone *n* : any of various bones (as of the skull, the jaw, the pelvis, or the rib cage) not rounded in cross section

flat·foot \-ˌfu̇t\ *n, pl* **flat·feet** \-ˌfēt\ **1** : a condition in which the arch of the instep is flattened so that the entire sole rests upon the ground **2** : a foot affected with flatfoot — **flat·foot·ed** \-ˌfu̇-təd\ *adj*

flat plate *n* : a radiograph esp. of the abdomen taken with the subject lying flat

flat·u·lence \ˈfla-chə-ləns\ *n* : the quality or state of being flatulent

flat·u·lent \-lənt\ *adj* **1** : marked by or affected with gases generated in the intestine or stomach **2** : likely to

cause digestive flatulence — **flat·u·lent·ly** *adv*

fla·tus \ˈflā-təs\ *n* : gas generated in the stomach or bowels

flat·worm \ˈflat-ˌwərm\ *n* : PLATYHELMINTH; *esp* : TURBELLARIAN

fla·vin \ˈflā-vən\ *n* : any of a class of yellow water-soluble nitrogenous pigments derived from isoalloxazine and occurring in the form of nucleotides as coenzymes of flavoproteins; *esp* : RIBOFLAVIN

flavin adenine di·nu·cle·o·tide \-ˌdī-ˈnü-klē-ō-ˌtīd, -ˈnyü-\ *n* : a coenzyme $C_{27}H_{33}N_9O_{15}P_2$ of some flavoproteins — called also *FAD*

flavin mononucleotide *n* : FMN

fla·vi·vi·rus \ˈflā-vi-ˌvī-rəs\ *n* : any of a group of arboviruses that contain a single strand of RNA, are transmitted by ticks and mosquitoes, and include the causative agents of dengue, Japanese B encephalitis, and yellow fever

fla·vo·noid \ˈflā-və-ˌnȯid, ˈfla-\ *n* : any of a group of compounds that includes many common pigments — **flavonoid** *adj*

fla·vo·pro·tein \ˌflā-vo-ˈprō-ˌtēn, ˌfla-, -ˈprō-tē-ən\ *n* : a dehydrogenase that contains a flavin and often a metal and plays a major role in biological oxidations

flavum — see LIGAMENTUM FLAVUM

flax·seed \ˈflaks-ˌsēd\ *n* : the seed of flax that is used medicinally as a demulcent and emollient

flea \ˈflē\ *n* : any of an order (Siphonaptera) comprising small wingless bloodsucking insects that have a hard laterally compressed body and legs adapted to leaping and that feed on warm-blooded animals

flea·bite \-ˌbīt\ *n* : the bite of a flea; *also* : the red spot caused by such a bite — **flea·bit·ten** \-ˌbit-ᵊn\ *adj*

flea collar *n* : a collar for animals that contains insecticide for killing fleas

flea·wort \-ˌwȯrt, -ˌwȯrt\ *n* : any of three Old World plantains of the genus *Plantago* (esp. *P. psyllium*) that are the source of psyllium seed — called also *psyllium*

flec·tion *var of* FLEXION

flesh \ˈflesh\ *n* : the soft parts of the body; *esp* : the parts composed chiefly of skeletal muscle as distinguished from visceral structures, bone, and integuments — see GOOSE BUMPS, PROUD FLESH — **fleshed** \ˈflesht\ *adj* — **fleshy** \ˈfle-shē\ *adj*

flesh fly *n* : any of a family (Sarcophagidae) of dipteran flies some of which cause myiasis

flesh wound *n* : an injury involving penetration of the body musculature without damage to bones or internal organs

Fletch·er·ism \ˈfle-chər-ˌi-zəm\ *n* : the practice of eating in small amounts and only when hungry and of chewing one's food thoroughly — **fletch-er·ize** \-ˌīz\ *vb*

Fletcher, Horace (1849–1919), American dietitian.

flex \ˈfleks\ *vb* **1** : to bend esp. repeatedly **2 a** : to move muscles so as to cause flexion of (a joint) **b** : to move or tense (a muscle) by contraction

flexibilitas — see CEREA FLEXIBILITAS

flex·i·ble \ˈflek-sə-bəl\ *adj* : capable of being flexed : capable of being turned, bowed, or twisted without breaking — **flex·i·bil·i·ty** \ˌflek-sə-ˈbi-lə-tē\ *n*

flex·ion \ˈflek-shən\ *n* **1** : a bending movement around a joint in a limb (as the knee or elbow) that decreases the angle between the bones of the limb at the joint — compare EXTENSION 2 **2** : a forward raising of the arm or leg by a movement at the shoulder or hip joint

flex·or \ˈflek-sər, -ˌsȯr\ *n* : a muscle serving to bend a body part (as a limb) — called also *flexor muscle*

flexor car·pi ra·di·al·is \-ˈkär-ˌpī-ˌrā-dē-ˈā-ləs, -ˈkär-ˌpē-\ *n* : a superficial muscle of the palmar side of the forearm that flexes the hand and assists in abducting it

flexor carpi ul·nar·is \-ˌəl-ˈnar-əs\ *n* : a superficial muscle of the ulnar side of the forearm that flexes the hand and assists in adducting it

flexor dig·i·ti min·i·mi brev·is \-ˈdi-jə-ˌtī-ˈmi-nə-ˌmī-ˈbre-vəs, -ˈdi-jə-ˌtē-ˈmi-nə-ˌmē-\ *n* **1** : a muscle of the ulnar side of the palm of the hand that flexes the little finger **2** : a muscle of the sole of the foot that flexes the first proximal phalanx of the little toe

flexor dig·i·to·rum brevis \-ˌdi-jə-ˈtȯr-əm-\ *n* : a muscle of the middle part of the sole of the foot that flexes the second phalanx of each of the four small toes

flexor digitorum lon·gus \-ˈlȯŋ-gəs\ *n* : a muscle of the tibial side of the leg that flexes the terminal phalanx of each of the four small toes

flexor digitorum pro·fund·us \-prō-ˈfən-dəs\ *n* : a deep muscle of the ulnar side of the forearm that flexes esp. the terminal phalanges of the four fingers

flexor digitorum su·per·fi·cial·is \-ˌsü-pər-ˌfi-shē-ˈā-ləs\ *n* : a superficial muscle of the palmar side of the forearm that flexes esp. the second phalanges of the four fingers

flexor hal·lu·cis brev·is \-ˈha-lü-səs-ˈbre-vəs, -lyü-, -ˌha-lə-kəs-\ *n* : a short muscle of the sole of the foot that flexes the proximal phalanx of the big toe

flexor hallucis longus *n* : a long deep muscle of the fibular side of the leg that flexes esp. the second phalanx of the big toe

flexor muscle *n* : FLEXOR

flexor pol·li·cis brevis \-ˈpä-lə-səs-, -kəs-\ *n* : a short muscle of the palm that flexes and adducts the thumb

flexor pollicis longus *n* : a muscle of the radial side of the forearm that flexes esp. the second phalanx of the thumb

flexor ret·in·ac·u·lum \-ˌret-ᵊn-ˈa-kyə-ləm\ *n* **1** : a fibrous band of fascia on the medial side of the ankle that extends downward from the medial malleolus of the tibia to the calcaneus and that covers over the bony grooves containing the tendons of the flexor muscles, the posterior tibial artery and vein, and the tibial nerve as they pass into the sole of the foot **2** : a fibrous band of fascia on the palm side of the wrist and base of the hand that forms the roof of the carpal tunnel and covers the tendons of the flexor muscles and the median nerve as they pass into the hand — called also *transverse carpal ligament*

flex·ure \ˈflek-shər\ *n* **1** : the quality or state of being flexed : FLEXION **2** : an anatomical turn, bend, or fold; *esp* : one of three sharp bends of the anterior part of the primary axis of the vertebrate embryo that serve to establish the relationship of the parts of the developing brain — see CEPHALIC FLEXURE, HEPATIC FLEXURE, PONTINE FLEXURE; SPLENIC FLEXURE — **flex·ur·al** \-shər-əl\ *adj*

flick·er \ˈfli-kər\ *n* : the wavering or fluttering visual sensation produced by intermittent light when the interval between flashes is not small enough to produce complete fusion of the individual impressions

flicker fusion *n* : FUSION b(2)

flight of ideas *n* : a rapid shifting of ideas that is expressed as a disconnected rambling and occurs esp. in the manic phase of manic-depressive psychosis

flight surgeon *n* : a medical officer (as in the U.S. Air Force) qualified by additional training for specialization in the psychological and medical problems associated with flying

float·er \ˈflō-tər\ *n* : a bit of optical debris (as a dead cell) in the vitreous humor or lens that may be perceived as a spot before the eye — usu. used in pl.; compare MUSCAE VOLITANTES

float·ing \ˈflōt-iŋ\ *adj* : located out of the normal position or abnormally movable (a ~ kidney)

floating rib *n* : any rib in the last two pairs of ribs that have no attachment to the sternum — compare FALSE RIB

floc·cu·lar \ˈflä-kyə-lər\ *adj* : of or relating to a flocculus

floc·cu·late \ˈflä-kyə-ˌlāt\ *vb* **-lat·ed; -lat·ing** : to aggregate or cause to aggregate into a flocculent mass — **floc·cu·la·tion** \ˌflä-kyə-ˈlā-shən\ *n*

floc·cu·la·tion test \ˌflä-kyə-ˈlā-shən-\ *n* : any of various serological tests (as the Mazzini test for syphilis) in which a positive result depends on the combination of an antigen and antibody to produce a flocculent precipitate

floc·cu·lent \-kyə-lənt\ *adj* : made up of loosely aggregated particles (a ∼ precipitate)

floc·cu·lo·nod·u·lar lobe \ˌflä-kyə-(ˌ)lō-ˈnä-jə-lər-\ *n* : the posterior lobe of the cerebellum that consists of the nodulus and paired lateral flocculi and is concerned with equilibrium

floc·cu·lus \-ləs\ *n, pl* **-li** \-ˌlī, -ˌlē\ : a small irregular lobe on the undersurface of each hemisphere of the cerebellum that is linked with the corresponding side of the nodulus by a peduncle

floor \ˈflȯr\ *n* : the lower inside surface of a hollow anatomical structure (the ∼ of the pelvis)

flo·ra \ˈflȯr-ə\ *n, pl* **floras** *also* **flo·rae** \ˈflȯr-ˌē, -ˌī\ : plant life; *esp* : the plant life characteristic of a region, period, or special environment (the bacterial ∼ of the human intestine) — compare FAUNA a — **flo·ral** \ˈflȯr-əl\ *adj*

flor·id \ˈflȯr-əd, ˈflär-\ *adj* : fully developed : manifesting a complete and typical clinical syndrome (∼ schizophrenia) (∼ adolescent acne) — **flor·id·ly** *adv*

¹**floss** \ˈfläs, ˈflȯs\ *n* : DENTAL FLOSS

²**floss** *vb* : to use dental floss on (one's teeth)

¹**flow** \ˈflō\ *vb* **1** : to move with a continual change of place among the constituent particles **2** : MENSTRUATE

²**flow** *n* **1** : the quantity that flows in a certain time **2** : MENSTRUATION

flow cy·tom·e·try \-sī-ˈtä-mə-trē\ *n* : a technique for identifying and sorting cells and their components (as DNA) by staining with a fluorescent dye and detecting the fluorescence usu. by laser beam illumination

flowers of zinc *n pl* : zinc oxide esp. as obtained as a light white powder by burning zinc for use in pharmaceutical and cosmetic preparations — called also *pompholyx*

flow·me·ter \ˈflō-ˌmē-tər\ *n* : an instrument for measuring the velocity of flow of a fluid (as blood) in a tube or pipe

fl oz *abbr* fluid ounce

flu \ˈflü\ *n* **1** : INFLUENZA **2** : any of several virus or bacterial diseases marked esp. by respiratory symptoms — see INTESTINAL FLU

fluc·tu·ant \ˈflək-chə-wənt\ *adj* : movable and compressible — used of abnormal body structures (as some abscesses or tumors)

fluc·tu·a·tion \ˌflək-chə-ˈwā-shən\ *n* : the wavelike motion of a fluid collected in a natural or artificial cavity of the body observed by palpation or percussion

flu·cy·to·sine \ˌflü-ˈsī-tə-sēn\ *n* : a white crystalline drug $C_4H_4FN_3O$ used to treat fungal infections esp. by mem-

bers of the genera *Candida* and *Cryptococcus* (esp. *Cryptococcus neoformans*)

flu·dro·cor·ti·sone \ˌflü-drō-ˈkȯr-tə-ˌsōn, -ˌzōn\ *n* : a potent mineralocorticoid drug $C_{23}H_{31}FO_6$ with some glucocorticoid activity that is administered esp. as the acetate

fluid *n* : a substance (as a liquid or gas) tending to flow or conform to the outline of its container; *specif* : one in the body of an animal or plant — see CEREBROSPINAL FLUID, SEMINAL FLUID — **fluid** *adj*

fluid dram *or* **flu·i·dram** \ˌflü-ə-ˈdram\ *n* : either of two units of liquid capacity: **a** : a U.S. unit equal to ⅛ U.S. fluid ounce or 0.226 cubic inch or 3.697 milliliters **b** : a British unit equal to ⅛ British fluid ounce or 0.2167 cubic inch or 3.5516 milliliters

flu·id·ex·tract \ˌflü-əd-ˈek-ˌstrakt\ *n* : an alcohol preparation of a vegetable drug containing the active constituents of one gram of the dry drug in each milliliter

fluid ounce *n* **1** : a U.S. unit of liquid capacity equal to ¹⁄₁₆ pint or 1.805 cubic inches or 29.573 milliliters **2** : a British unit of liquid capacity equal to ¹⁄₂₀ pint or 1.7339 cubic inches or 28.412 milliliters

fluke \ˈflük\ *n* : a flattened digenetic trematode worm; *broadly* : TREMATODE — see LIVER FLUKE

flu·o·cin·o·lone ace·to·nide \ˌflü-ə-ˈsin-ᵊl-ˌōn-ˌa-sə-ˈtō-ˌnīd\ *n* : a glucocorticoid steroid $C_{24}H_{30}F_2O_6$ used esp. as an anti-inflammatory agent in the treatment of skin diseases.

fluor- *or* **fluoro-** *comb form* **1** : fluorine (fluorosis) *also* **fluori-** : fluorescence (fluoroscope)

flu·o·res·ce·in \ˌflü-ə-ˈre-sē-ən, ˌflȯr-\ *n* : a dye $C_{20}H_{12}O_5$ with a bright yellow-green fluorescence in alkaline solution that is used as the sodium salt as an aid in diagnosis (as of brain tumors)

flu·o·res·cence \-ˈes-ᵊns\ *n* : emission of or the property of emitting electromagnetic radiation usu. as visible light resulting from and occurring only during the absorption of radiation from some other source; *also* : the radiation emitted — **flu·o·resce** \-ˈes\ *vb* — **flu·o·res·cent** \-ˈes-ᵊnt\ *adj*

fluorescence microscope *n* : ULTRAVIOLET MICROSCOPE

flu·o·ri·date \ˈflu̇r-ə-ˌdāt, ˈflȯr-\ *vb* **-dat·ed; -dat·ing** : to add a fluoride to (as drinking water) to reduce tooth decay — **flu·o·ri·da·tion** \ˌflu̇r-ə-ˈdā-shən, ˌflȯr-\ *n*

flu·o·ride \ˈflu̇r-ˌīd\ *n* **1** : a compound of fluorine usu. with a more electrically positive element or radical **2** : the monovalent anion of fluorine — **fluoride** *adj*

flu·o·rine \ˈflu̇r-ˌēn, ˈflȯr-, -ən\ *n* : a nonmetallic halogen element having a chemical valence of one that is normally a pale yellowish flammable irritating toxic gas — symbol F; see ELEMENT table

flu·o·rom·e·ter \\flü-ər-'ä-mə-tər\ or **flu·o·rim·e·ter** \-'i-mə-tər\ n : an instrument for measuring fluorescence and related phenomena (as intensity of radiation) — **flu·o·ro·met·ric** or **flu·o·ri·met·ric** \\flü-ər-ə-'me-trik, -flȯr-\ adj — **flu·o·rom·e·try** \-'ä-mə-trē\ or **flu·o·rim·e·try** \-'i-mə-trē\ n

flu·o·ro·pho·tom·e·ter \\flü-ər-ō-fō-'tä-mə-tər, -flȯr-ō-\ n : FLUOROMETER — **flu·o·ro·pho·to·met·ric** \-ˌfō-tə-'me-trik\ adj — **flu·o·ro·pho·tom·e·try** \-ˌfō-'tä-mə-trē\ n

flu·o·ro·scope \\'flur-ə-ˌskōp, 'flȯr-\ n : an instrument used in medical diagnosis for observing the internal structure of the body by means of X rays — **fluoroscope** vb — **flu·o·ro·scop·ic** \\flur-ə-'skä-pik, -flȯr-\ adj — **flu·o·ro·scop·i·cal·ly** \-pi-k(ə-)lē\ adv — **flu·o·ros·co·pist** \-'äs-kə-pist\ n — **flu·o·ros·co·py** \-pē\ n

flu·o·ro·sis \\flü-ər-'ō-səs, -flȯr-\ n : an abnormal condition (as mottled enamel of human teeth) caused by fluorine or its compounds

flu·o·ro·ura·cil \\flü-ər-ō-'yur-ə-ˌsil, -ˌsəl\ or **5-flu·o·ro·ura·cil** \'fīv-\ n : a fluorine-containing pyrimidine base $C_4H_3FN_2O_2$ used to treat some kinds of cancer

flu·ox·e·tine \\flü-'äk-sə-ˌtēn\ n : an antidepressant drug $C_{17}H_{18}F_3NO$ that enhances serotonin activity

flu·phen·azine \\flü-'fe-nə-ˌzēn\ n : a phenothiazine tranquilizer $C_{22}H_{26}$-F_3N_3OS used esp. combined as a salt or ester — see PROLIXIN

flur·az·e·pam \\flur-'a-zə-ˌpam\ n : a benzodiazepine closely related structurally to diazepam that is used as a hypnotic in the form of its hydrochloride $C_{21}H_{23}ClFN_3O·2HCl$ — see DALMANE

flur·o·thyl \\'flur-ə-thil\ n : a clear colorless volatile liquid convulsant C_4H_4-F_6O that has been used in place of electroshock therapy in the treatment of mental illness — see INDOKLON

¹flush \\'fləsh\ n : a transitory sensation of extreme heat (as in response to some physiological states)

²flush vb 1 : to blush or become suddenly suffused with color due to vasodilation 2 : to cleanse or wash out with or as if with a rush of liquid

flut·ter \\'flə-tər\ n : an abnormal rapid spasmodic and usu. rhythmic motion or contraction of a body part (a serious ventricular ~) — **flutter** vb

flux \\'fləks\ n 1 : a flowing of fluid from the body; esp : an excessive abnormal discharge from the bowels 2 : the matter discharged in a flux

fly \\'flī\ n, pl **flies** 1 : any of a large order (Diptera) of usu. winged insects (as the housefly or a mosquito) that

have the anterior wings functional and the posterior wings modified to function as sensory flight stabilizers and that have a segmented larva often without a head, eyes, or legs 2 : a large stout-bodied fly (as a horsefly)

fly agar·ic \\'a-gə-rik, -ə-'gar-ik\ n : a poisonous mushroom of the genus *Amanita* (*A. muscaria*) that has a usu. bright red cap and that with the related death cap is responsible for most cases of severe mushroom poisoning — called also *fly amanita, fly mushroom*

¹fly·blow \\'flī-ˌblō\ vb **-blew; -blown** : to deposit eggs or young larvae of a flesh fly or blowfly in

²flyblow n : FLY-STRIKE

fly-blown \-ˌblōn\ adj 1 : infested with fly maggots 2 : covered with fly-specks

fly-strike \-ˌstrīk\ n : infestation with fly maggots — **fly-struck** \-ˌstrək\ adj

Fm symbol fermium

FMN \\ˌef-(ˌ)em-'en\ n : a yellow crystalline phosphoric ester $C_{17}H_{21}N_4$-O_9P of riboflavin that is a coenzyme of several flavoprotein enzymes — called also *flavin mononucleotide, riboflavin phosphate*

foam \\'fōm\ n : a light frothy mass of fine bubbles formed in or on the surface of a liquid (a contraceptive ~) — **foam** vb

foam cell n : a swollen vacuolate reticuloendothelial cell filled with lipid inclusions and characteristic of some conditions of disturbed lipid metabolism

focal infection n : a persistent bacterial infection of some organ or region; esp : one causing symptoms elsewhere in the body

focal length n : the distance of a focus from the surface of a lens or concave mirror — symbol f

focal point n : FOCUS 1

fo·cus \\'fō-kəs\ n, pl **fo·ci** \\'fō-ˌsī, -ˌkī\ also **fo·cus·es** 1 : a point at which rays (as of light) converge or from which they diverge or appear to diverge usu. giving rise to an image after reflection by a mirror or refraction by a lens or optical system 2 : a localized area of disease or the chief site of a generalized disease or infection — **focus** vb

foe·ti·cide chiefly Brit var of FETICIDE

foeto- or **foeti-** chiefly Brit var of FETO-

foe·tol·o·gy, foe·tus chiefly Brit var of FETOLOGY, FETUS

fog \\'fäg, 'fȯg\ vb **fogged; fog·ging** : to blur (a field of vision) with lenses that prevent a sharp focus in order to relax accommodation before testing vision

foil \\'fȯil\ n : very thin sheet metal (as of gold or platinum) used esp. in filling teeth

fo·la·cin \\'fō-lə-sən\ n : FOLIC ACID

fo·late \\'fō-ˌlāt\ n : FOLIC ACID; also : a salt or ester of folic acid

fold \'fōld\ *n* : a margin apparently formed by the doubling upon itself of a flat anatomical structure (as a membrane)

Fo·ley catheter \'fō-lē-\ *n* : a catheter with an inflatable balloon tip for retention in the bladder

Foley, Frederic Eugene Basil (1891–1966), American urologist.

fo·lic acid \'fō-lik-\ *n* : a crystalline vitamin $C_{19}H_{19}N_7O_6$ of the B complex that is used esp. in the treatment of nutritional anemias — called also *folacin, folate, pteroylglutamic acid, vitamin B_c, vitamin M*

folie à deux \fō-'lē-(ˌ)ä-'dœ, -'dər\ *n, pl* **folies à deux** *same or* fō-'lēz-\ : the presence of the same or similar delusional ideas in two persons closely associated with one another

fo·lin·ic acid \fō-'li-nik-\ *n* : CITROVORUM FACTOR

fo·li·um \'fō-lē-əm\ *n, pl* **fo·lia** \-lē-ə\ : one of the lamellae of the cerebellar cortex

folk medicine *n* : traditional medicine as practiced esp. by people isolated from modern medical services and usu. involving the use of plant-derived remedies on an empirical basis

fol·li·cle \'fä-li-kəl\ *n* **1** : a small anatomical cavity or deep narrow-mouthed depression; *esp* : a small simple or slightly branched gland : CRYPT **2** : a small lymph node **3** : a vesicle in the mammalian ovary that contains a developing egg surrounded by a covering of cells : OVARIAN FOLLICLE; *esp* : GRAAFIAN FOLLICLE — **fol·lic·u·lar** \fə-'li-kyə-lər, fä-\ *adj*

follicle mite *n* : any of several minute mites of the genus *Demodex* that are parasitic in the hair follicles

follicle–stimulating hormone *n* : a hormone from an anterior lobe of the pituitary gland that stimulates the growth of the ovum-containing follicles in the ovary and that activates sperm-forming cells

follicularis — see KERATOSIS FOLLICULARIS

folliculi — see LIQUOR FOLLICULI, THECA FOLLICULI

fol·lic·u·lin \fə-'li-kyə-lən, fä-\ *n* : ESTROGEN; *esp* : ESTRONE

fol·lic·u·li·tis \fə-ˌli-kyə-'lī-təs\ *n* : inflammation of one or more follicles esp. of the hair

fol·li·tro·pin \fä-lə-'trō-pən\ *n* : FOLLICLE-STIMULATING HORMONE

follow–up \'fä-lō-ˌəp\ *n* : maintenance of contact with or reexamination of a patient at usu. prescribed intervals following diagnosis or treatment; *also* : a patient with whom such contact is maintained — **follow–up** *adj* — **follow up** *vb*

fo·men·ta·tion \ˌfō-mən-'tā-shən, -ˌmen-\ *n* **1** : the application of hot moist substances to the body to ease

pain **2** : the material applied in fomentation : POULTICE

fomi·tes \'fä-mə-ˌtēz, 'fō-\ *n pl* : inanimate objects (as clothing, dishes, toys, or books) that may be contaminated with infectious organisms and serve in their transmission

fon·ta·nel *or* **fon·ta·nelle** \ˌfänt-ᵊn-'el\ *n* : any of the spaces closed by membranous structures between the uncompleted angles of the parietal bones and the neighboring bones of a fetal or young skull

food \'füd\ *n, often attrib* **1** : material consisting essentially of protein, carbohydrate, and fat used in the body of an organism to sustain growth, repair, and vital processes and to furnish energy; *also* : such food together with supplementary substances (as minerals, vitamins, and condiments) **2** : nutriment in solid form

food poisoning *n* **1** : either of two acute gastrointestinal disorders caused by bacteria or their toxic products: **a** : a rapidly developing intoxication marked by nausea, vomiting, prostration, and often severe diarrhea and caused by the presence in food of toxic products produced by bacteria (as some staphylococci) **b** : a less rapidly developing infection esp. with salmonellas that has generally similar symptoms and that results from multiplication of bacteria ingested with contaminated food **2** : a gastrointestinal disturbance occurring after consumption of food that is contaminated with chemical residues or food (as some fungi) that is inherently unsuitable for human consumption

food·stuff \'füd-ˌstəf\ *n* : a substance with food value; *esp* : a specific nutrient (as a fat or protein)

foot \'fut\ *n, pl* **feet** \'fēt\ *also* **foot 1** : the terminal part of the vertebrate leg upon which an individual stands **2** : a unit equal to ⅓ yard and comprising 12 inches or 30.48 centimeters — *pl foot* used between a number and a noun (a 10-*foot* pole); *pl feet or foot* used between a number and an adjective (6 *feet* tall)

foot–and–mouth disease *n* : an acute contagious febrile disease esp. of cloven-hoofed animals that is caused by a picornavirus related to the rhinoviruses and that is marked by ulcerating vesicles in the mouth, about the hoofs, and on the udder and teats — called also *aftosa, aphthous fever, foot-and-mouth, hoof-and-mouth disease*; compare HAND-FOOT-AND-MOUTH DISEASE

foot·bath \'fut-ˌbath\ *n* : a bath for cleansing, warming, or disinfecting the feet

foot drop *n* : an extended position of the foot caused by paralysis of the flexor muscles of the leg

foot·ed \'fu-təd\ *adj* : having a foot or

feet esp. of a specified kind or number — often used in combination (a 4-*footed* animal)

foot-plate \'fut-,plāt\ *n* : the flat oval base of the stapes

foot-pound \-'paund\ *n, pl* **foot-pounds** : a unit of work equal to the work done by a force of one pound acting through a distance of one foot in the direction of the force

foot-pound-second \-,fut-,paund-'se-kənd\ *adj* : being or relating to a system of units based upon the foot as the unit of length, the pound as the unit of weight or mass, and the second as the unit of time — abbr. *fps*

foot-print \'fut-,print\ *n* : an impression of the foot on a surface

foot rot *n* : a necrobacillosis of tissues of the foot esp. of sheep and cattle that is marked by sloughing, ulceration, suppuration, and sometimes loss of the hoof

fo-ra-men \fə-'rā-mən\ *n, pl* **fo-ram-i-na** \-'ra-mə-nə\ *or* **fo-ra-mens** \-'rā-mənz\ : a small opening, perforation, or orifice : FENESTRA 1 — **fo-ram-i-nal** \fə-'ra-mən-ᵊl\ *adj*

foramen ce-cum \-'sē-kəm\ *n* : a shallow depression in the posterior dorsal midline of the tongue that is the remnant of the more cranial part of the embryonic duct from which the thyroid gland developed

foramen lac-er-um \-'la-sər-əm\ *n* : an irregular aperture on the lower surface of the skull bounded by parts of the temporal, sphenoid, and occipital bones that gives passage to the internal carotid artery

foramen mag-num \-'mag-nəm\ *n* : the opening in the skull through which the spinal cord passes to become the medulla oblongata

foramen of Lusch-ka \-'lush-kə\ *n* : either of two openings each of which is situated on one side of the fourth ventricle of the brain and communicates with the subarachnoid space

 Luschka, Hubert von (1820–1875), German anatomist.

foramen of Ma-gen-die \-mə-,zhän-'dē\ *n* : a passage through the midline of the roof of the fourth ventricle of the brain that gives passage to the cerebrospinal fluid from the ventricles to the subarachnoid space

 F. Magendie — see BELL-MAGENDIE LAW

foramen of Mon-ro \-mən-'rō\ *n* : INTERVENTRICULAR FORAMEN

 Monro, Alexander (Secundus) (1733–1817), British anatomist.

foramen of Wins-low \-'winz-,lō\ *n* : EPIPLOIC FORAMEN

 Winslow, Jacob (or Jacques–Bénigne) (1669–1760), Danish anatomist.

foramen ova-le \-ō-'va-(,)lē, -'vā-, -'vä-\ *n* 1 : an opening in the septum between the two atria of the heart that is normally present only in the fe-

tus 2 : an oval opening in the greater wing of the sphenoid for passage of the mandibular nerve

foramen ro-tun-dum \-rō-'tən-dəm\ *n* : a circular aperture in the anterior and medial part of the greater wing of the sphenoid that gives passage to the maxillary nerve

foramen spin-o-sum \-spi-'nō-səm\ *n* : an aperture in the great wing of the sphenoid that gives passage to the middle meningeal artery

foramina *pl of* FORAMEN

for-ceps \'fôr-səps, -,seps\ *n, pl* **forceps** : an instrument for grasping, holding firmly, or exerting traction upon objects esp. for delicate operations

For-dyce's disease \'fôr-,dī-səz-\ *also* **For-dyce disease** \'fôr-,dīs-\ *n* : a common anomaly of the oral mucosa in which misplaced sebaceous glands form yellowish white nodules on the lips or the lining of the mouth

 Fordyce, John Addison (1858–1925), American dermatologist.

fore- *comb form* 1 : situated at the front : in front (*fore*leg) 2 : front part of (something specified) (*fore*arm)

fore-arm \'fōr-,ärm\ *n* : the part of the arm between the elbow and the wrist

fore-brain \-,brān\ *n* : the anterior of the three primary divisions of the developing vertebrate brain or the corresponding part of the adult brain that includes esp. the cerebral hemispheres, the thalamus, and the hypothalamus and that esp. in higher vertebrates is the main control center for sensory and associative information processing, visceral functions, and voluntary motor functions — called also *prosencephalon*; see DIENCEPHALON, TELENCEPHALON

forebrain bundle — see MEDIAL FOREBRAIN BUNDLE

fore-fin-ger \'fōr-,fiŋ-gər\ *n* : the finger next to the thumb — called also *index finger*

fore-foot \-,fut\ *n* 1 : one of the anterior feet esp. of a quadruped 2 : the front part of the human foot

fore-gut \-,gət\ *n* : the anterior part of the alimentary canal of a vertebrate embryo that develops into the pharynx, esophagus, stomach, and extreme anterior part of the intestine

fore-head \'fōr-əd, 'fär-; 'fōr-,hed\ *n* : the part of the face above the eyes — called also *brow*

for-eign \'fôr-ən, 'fär-\ *adj* : occurring in an abnormal situation in the living body and often introduced from outside

fore-leg \'fôr-,leg\ *n* : a front leg

fore-limb \-,lim\ *n* : a limb (as an arm, wing, fin, or leg) that is situated anteriorly

fo-ren-sic \fə-'ren-sik, -zik\ *adj* : relating to or dealing with the application of scientific knowledge to legal problems (~ pathologist) (~ experts)

forensic medicine n : a science that deals with the relation and application of medical facts to legal problems — called also *legal medicine*

forensic psychiatry n : the application of psychiatry in courts of law (as for the determination of criminal responsibility or liability to commitment for insanity) — **forensic psychiatrist** n

fore·play \'fōr-ˌplā\ n : erotic stimulation preceding sexual intercourse

fore·skin \-ˌskin\ n : a fold of skin that covers the glans of the penis — called also *prepuce*

-form \ˌform\ adj comb form : in the form or shape of : resembling (chore*iform*) (epilepti*form*)

form·al·de·hyde \fȯr-'mal-də-ˌhīd, fər-\ n : a colorless pungent irritating gas CH_2O used as a disinfectant and preservative

for·ma·lin \'fȯr-mə-lən, -ˌlēn\ n : a clear aqueous solution of formaldehyde containing a small amount of methanol

formed element n : one of the red blood cells, white blood cells, or blood platelets as contrasted with the fluid portion of the blood

forme fruste \ˌform-'früest, -'früst\ n, pl **formes frustes** \same or -'früsts\ : an atypical and usu. abortive manifestation of a disease

for·mic acid \'fȯr-mik-\ n : a colorless pungent fuming vesicant liquid acid CH_2O_2 found esp. in ants and in many plants

for·mi·ca·tion \ˌfȯr-mə-'kā-shən\ n : an abnormal sensation resembling that made by insects creeping in or on the skin

for·mu·la \'fȯr-myə-lə\ n, pl **-las** or **-lae** \-ˌlē, -ˌlī\ 1 a : a recipe or prescription giving method and proportions of ingredients for the preparation of some material (as a medicine) b : a milk mixture or substitute for feeding an infant typically consisting of prescribed proportions and forms of cow's milk, water, and sugar; *also* : a batch of this made up at one time to meet an infant's future requirements (as during a 24-hour period) 2 : a symbolic expression showing the composition or constitution of a chemical substance and consisting of symbols for the elements present and subscripts to indicate the relative or total number of atoms present in a molecule (the ∼s for water and ethyl alcohol are H_2O and C_2H_5OH respectively)

for·mu·lary \'fȯr-myə-ˌler-ē\ n, pl **-lar·ies** : a book containing a list of medicinal subtances and formulas

for·ni·ca·tion \ˌfȯr-nə-'kā-shən\ n : consensual sexual intercourse between two persons not married to each other — **for·ni·cate** \'fȯr-nə-ˌkāt\ vb — **for·ni·ca·tor** \-ˌkā-tər\ n — **for·ni·ca·trix** \-'kā-triks\ n, pl **-tri·ces**

\-kə-'trī-ˌsēz\ : a woman who engages in fornication

fornices — see CRURA FORNICIS

for·nix \'fȯr-niks\ n, pl **for·ni·ces** \-nə-ˌsēz\ : an anatomical arch or fold: as **a** : the vault of the cranium **b** : the part of the conjunctiva overlying the cornea **c** : a body of nerve fibers lying beneath the corpus callosum and serving to integrate the hippocampus with other parts of the brain **d** : the vaulted upper part of the vagina surrounding the uterine cervix **e** : the fundus of the stomach **f** : the vault of the pharynx

fos·sa \'fä-sə\ n, pl **fos·sae** \-ˌsē, -ˌsī\ : an anatomical pit, groove, or depression (the temporal ∼ of the skull)

fossa na·vic·u·lar·is \-nə-ˌvi-kyə-'lar-əs\ n : a depression between the posterior margin of the vaginal opening and the fourchette

fossa ova·lis \-ō-'va-ləs, -'vā-, -'vä-\ n 1 : a depression in the septum between the right and left atria that marks the position of the foramen ovale in the fetus 2 : SAPHENOUS OPENING

Fos·sar·ia \fä-'sar-ē-ə, fȯ-\ n : a genus of small freshwater snails (family Lymnaeidae) including intermediate hosts of liver flukes — compare GALBA, LYMNAEA

¹foun·der \'faün-dər\ vb **foun·dered**; **foun·der·ing** 1 : to become disabled; *esp* : to go lame 2 : to disable (an animal) esp. by inducing laminitis through excessive feeding

²founder n : LAMINITIS

four·chette or **four·chet** \fur-'shet\ n : a small fold of membrane connecting the labia minora in the posterior part of the vulva

fourth cranial nerve n : TROCHLEAR NERVE

fourth ventricle n : a somewhat rhomboidal ventricle of the posterior part of the brain that connects at the front with the third ventricle through the aqueduct of Sylvius and at the back with the central canal of the spinal cord

fo·vea \'fō-vē-ə\ n, pl **fo·ve·ae** \-vē-ˌē, -ˌī\ 1 : a small fossa 2 : a small area of the retina without rods that affords acute vision — **fo·ve·al** \-əl\ adj

fovea cen·tra·lis \-sen-'tra-ləs, -'trä-, -'trā-\ n : FOVEA 2

fo·ve·o·la \fō-'vē-ə-lə\ n, pl **-lae** \-ˌlē, -ˌlī\ or **-las** : a small pit; *specif* : one of the pits in the embryonic gastric mucosa from which the gastric glands develop — **fo·ve·o·lar** \-lər\ adj

fowl cholera n : an acute contagious septicemic disease of birds that is marked by fever, weakness, diarrhea, and petechial hemorrhages in the mucous membranes and is caused by a bacterium of the genus *Pasteurella* (*P. multocida*)

fowl mite n : CHICKEN MITE — see NORTHERN FOWL MITE

fowl pest *n* : NEWCASTLE DISEASE

fowl plague *n* : AVIAN INFLUENZA

fowl pox *n* : either of two forms of a virus disease esp. of chickens and turkeys that is characterized by head lesions: **a** : a cutaneous form marked by pustules, warty growths, and scabs esp. on skin that lacks feathers **b** : a more serious form occurring as cheesy lesions of the mucous membranes of the mouth, throat, and eyes

fowl tick *n* : any of several ticks of the genus *Argas* (as *A. persicus*) that attack fowl in the warmer parts of the world causing anemia and transmitting various diseases (as spirochetosis)

fowl typhoid *n* : an infectious disease of poultry characterized by diarrhea, anemia, and prostration and caused by a bacterium of the genus *Salmonella* (*S. gallinarum*)

fox·glove \'fäks-ˌgləv\ *n* : any plant of the genus *Digitalis*; *esp* : a common European biennial or perennial (*D. purpurea*) cultivated for its stalks of showy dotted white or purple tubular flowers and as a source of digitalis

fps *abbr* foot-pound-second

Fr *symbol* francium

FR *abbr* flocculation reaction

frac·tion \'frak-shən\ *n* : one of several portions (as of a distillate) separable by fractionation

frac·tion·al \-shə-nəl\ *adj* : of, relating to, or involving a process for fractionating components of a mixture

frac·tion·ate \-shə-ˌnāt\ *vb* -at·ed; -at·ing : to separate (as a mixture) into different portions (as by distillation or precipitation) — **frac·tion·a·tion** \-ˈnā-shən\ *n*

frac·ture \'frak-chər, -shər\ *n* 1 : the act or process of breaking or the state of being broken: *specif* : the breaking of hard tissue (as bone) — see POTT'S FRACTURE 2 : the rupture (as by tearing) of soft tissue (kidney ~) — **fracture** *vb*

fragile X syndrome \-ˈeks-\ *n* : an inherited disorder that is associated with an abnormal X chromosome, that is characterized esp. by moderate to severe mental retardation, by large ears, chin, and forehead, and by enlarged testes in males, and that often has limited or no effect in heterozygous females

fra·gil·i·tas os·si·um \frə-ˈji-lə-təs-ˈä-sē-əm\ *n* : OSTEOGENESIS IMPERFECTA

fram·be·sia \fram-ˈbē-zhə, -zhē-ə\ *n* : YAWS

frame \'frām\ *n* 1 : the physical make-up of an animal and esp. a human body : PHYSIQUE 2 **a** : a part of a pair of glasses that holds one of the lenses **b** *pl* : that part of a pair of glasses other than the lenses

frame·shift \-ˌshift\ *adj* : relating to, being, or causing a mutation in which a number of nucleotides not divisible by three is inserted or deleted so that some triplet codons are read incorrectly during genetic translation — **frameshift** *n*

fran·ci·um \'fran-sē-əm\ *n* : a radioactive element discovered as a disintegration product of actinium and obtained artificially by the bombardment of thorium with protons — symbol *Fr*; see ELEMENT table

frank \'fraŋk\ *adj* : clinically evident (~ pus) (~ gout)

Frank·fort horizontal plane \'fraŋk-fərt-\ *n* : a plane used in craniometry that is determined by the highest point on the upper margin of the opening of each external auditory meatus and the low point on the lower margin of the left orbit and that is used to orient a human skull or head usu. so that the plane is horizontal — called also *Frankfort horizontal*, *Frankfort plane*

Frank–Star·ling law \'fraŋk-ˈstär-liŋ-\ *n* : STARLING'S LAW OF THE HEART

Frank, Otto (1865–1944), German physiologist.

Starling, Ernest Henry (1866–1927), British physiologist.

Frank–Starling law of the heart *n* : STARLING'S LAW OF THE HEART

fra·ter·nal \frə-ˈtərn-əl\ *adj* : derived from two ova : DIZYGOTIC (~ twins)

FRCP *abbr* Fellow of the Royal College of Physicians

FRCS *abbr* Fellow of the Royal College of Surgeons

freck·le \'fre-kəl\ *n* : one of the small brownish spots in the skin that are usu. due to precipitation of pigment and that increase in number and intensity on exposure to sunlight — called also *ephelis*; compare LENTIGO — **freckle** *vb* — **freck·led** \-kəld\ *adj*

¹free \'frē\ *adj* **fre·er; fre·est** 1 **a** (1) : not united with, attached to, combined with, or mixed with something else (a ~ surface of a bodily part) (2) : having the bare axon exposed in tissue (a ~ nerve ending) **b** : not chemically combined (~ oxygen) 2 : having all living connections severed before removal to another site (a ~ graft)

free association *n* 1 **a** : the expression (as by speaking or writing) of the content of consciousness without censorship as an aid in gaining access to unconscious processes esp. in psychoanalysis **b** : the reporting of the first thought that comes to mind in response to a given stimulus (as a word) 2 : an idea or image elicited by free association 3 : a method using free association — **free-as·so·ci·ate** \ˈfrē-ə-ˈsō-shē-ˌāt, -sē-\ *vb*

¹free·base \'frē-ˌbās\ *vb* -based; -bas·ing : to prepare or use (cocaine) as freebase — **free·bas·er** \-ˌbā-sər\ *n*

²freebase *n* : cocaine freed from impurities by treatment (as with ether) and heated to produce vapors for inhalation or smoked as crack

free fall *n* : the condition of unrestrained motion in a gravitational field; *also* : such motion

free-float-ing \'frē-'flō-tiŋ\ *adj* : felt as an emotion without apparent cause ⟨~ anxiety⟩

free-liv-ing \-'li-viŋ\ *adj* 1 : not fixed to the substrate but capable of motility ⟨a ~ protozoan⟩ 2 : being metabolically independent : neither parasitic nor symbiotic

free-mar-tin \'frē-,märt-ʰn\ *n* : a sexually imperfect usu. sterile female calf born as a twin with a male

free radical *n* : an esp. reactive atom or group of atoms that has one or more unpaired electrons

free-swimming *adj* : able to swim about : not attached ⟨a ~ larva of a trematode⟩

freeze \'frēz\ *vb* **froze** \'frōz\; **fro-zen** \'frōz-ʰn\; **freez-ing** 1 : to harden or cause to harden into a solid (as ice) by loss of heat 2 : to chill or become chilled with cold 3 : to anesthetize (a part) by cold

freeze-dry \'frēz-'drī\ *vb* **freeze-dried**; **freeze-dry-ing** : to dry and preserve (as food, vaccines, or tissue) in a frozen state under high vacuum — **freeze-dried** *adj*

freeze-etch-ing \-'e-chiŋ\ *n* : preparation of a specimen (as of tissue) for electron microscopic examination by freezing, fracturing along natural structural lines, and preparing a replica (as by simultaneous vapor deposition of carbon and platinum) — **freeze-etch** \-'ech\ *adj* — **freeze-etched** \-,echt\ *adj*

freeze fracture *also* **freeze-fracturing** *n* : FREEZE-ETCHING — **freeze-fracture** *vb*

freezing point *n* : the temperature at which a liquid solidifies

Frei test \'frī-\ *n* : a serological test for the identification of lymphogranuloma venereum — called also *Frei skin test*

    Frei, Wilhelm Siegmund (1885–1943), German dermatologist.

frem-i-tus \'fre-mə-təs\ *n* : a sensation felt by a hand placed on a part of the body (as the chest) that vibrates during speech

fren-ec-to-my \frə-'nek-tə-mē\ *n, pl* **-mies** : excision of a frenulum

fren-u-lum \'fren-yə-ləm\ *n, pl* **-la** \-lə\ : a connecting fold of membrane serving to support or restrain a part (as the tongue)

fre-num \'frē-nəm\ *n, pl* **frenums** *or* **frena** \-nə\ : FRENULUM

freq *abbr* frequency

fre-quen-cy \'frē-kwən-sē\ *n, pl* **-cies** 1 : the number of individuals in a single class when objects are classified according to variations in a set of one or more specified attributes 2 : the number of repetitions of a periodic process in a unit of time

Freud-ian \'froi-dē-ən\ *adj* : of, relating to, or according with the psychoanalytic theories or practices of Freud — **Freudian** *n* — **Freud-ian-ism** \-ə-,ni-zəm\ *n*

    Freud \'froid\, **Sigmund** (1856–1939), Austrian neurologist and psychiatrist.

Freudian slip *n* : a slip of the tongue that is motivated by and reveals some unconscious aspect of the mind

Freund's adjuvant \'froindz-\ *n* : any of several oil and water emulsions that contain antigens and are used to stimulate antibody production in experimental animals

    Freund \'froind\, **Jules Thomas** (1890–1960), American immunologist.

fri-a-ble \'frī-ə-bəl\ *adj* : easily crumbled or pulverized ⟨~ carcinomatous tissue⟩ — **fri-a-bil-i-ty** \,frī-ə-'bi-lə-tē\ *n*

friar's balsam *n* : an alcoholic solution containing essentially benzoin, storax, balsam of Tolu, and aloes used chiefly as a local application (as for small fissures) and after addition to hot water as an inhalant (as in laryngitis) — called also *compound benzoin tincture*

Fried-man test \'frēd-mən-\ *also* **Fried-man's test** *n* : a modification of the Aschheim-Zondek test for pregnancy using rabbits as test animals

    Friedman, Maurice Harold (1903–1991), American physiologist.

Fried-reich's ataxia \'frēd-riks-, 'frēt-riks-\ *n* : a recessive hereditary degenerative disease affecting the spinal column, cerebellum, and medulla, marked by muscular incoordination and twitching, and usu. becoming manifest in the adult

    Friedreich \'frēt-rīk\, **Nikolaus** (1825–1882), German neurologist.

frig-id \'fri-jəd\ *adj* 1 : abnormally averse to sexual intercourse — used esp. of women 2 *of a female* : unable to achieve orgasm during sexual intercourse — **fri-gid-i-ty** \fri-'ji-də-tē\ *n*

fringed tapeworm *n* : a tapeworm of the genus *Thysanosoma* (*T. actinioides*) found in the intestine and bile ducts of ruminants esp. in the western U.S.

frog \'frog, 'fräg\ *n* 1 : the triangular elastic horny pad in the middle of the sole of the foot of a horse 2 : a condition in the throat that produces hoarseness ⟨had a ~ in his throat⟩

Fröh-lich's syndrome *or* **Froeh-lich's syndrome** \'frā-liks-, 'frœ-liks-\ *also* **Fröhlich syndrome** *n* : ADIPOSOGENITAL DYSTROPHY

    Fröhlich \'frœ-lik\, **Alfred** (1871–1953), Austrian pharmacologist and neurologist.

frondosum — see CHORION FRONDOSUM

fron-tal \'frənt-ʰl\ *adj* 1 : of, relating to,

or adjacent to the forehead or the frontal bone 2 : of, relating to, or situated at the front or anteriorly 3 : parallel to the main axis of the body and at right angles to the sagittal plane (a ∼ plane) — **fron·tal·ly** adv

frontal bone n : a bone that forms the forehead and roofs over most of the orbits and nasal cavity and that at birth consists of two halves separated by a suture

frontal eminence n : the prominence of the human frontal bone above each superciliary ridge

frontal gyrus n : any of the convolutions of the outer surface of the frontal lobe of the brain — called also *frontal convolution*

fron·ta·lis \frən-ˈtā-ləs\ n : the muscle of the forehead that forms part of the occipitofrontalis — called also *frontalis muscle*

frontal lobe n : the anterior division of each cerebral hemisphere having its lower part in the anterior fossa of the skull and bordered behind by the central sulcus

frontal lobotomy n : PREFRONTAL LOBOTOMY

frontal nerve n : a branch of the ophthalmic nerve supplying the forehead, scalp, and adjoining parts

frontal process n 1 : a long plate that is part of the maxillary bone and contributes to the formation of the lateral part of the nose and of the nasal cavity — called also *nasal process* 2 : a process of the zygomatic bone articulating superiorly with the frontal bone, forming part of the orbit anteriorly, and articulating with the sphenoid bone posteriorly

frontal sinus n : either of two air spaces lined with mucous membrane each of which lies within the frontal bone above one of the orbits

fronto- comb form : frontal bone and (frontoparietal)

fron·to·oc·cip·i·tal \frən-tō-äk-ˈsip-ət-ᵊl, -frän-\ adj : of or relating to the forehead and occiput

fron·to·pa·ri·etal \-pə-ˈrī-ət-ᵊl\ adj : of, relating to, or involving both frontal and parietal bones of the skull

frontoparietal suture n : CORONAL SUTURE

fron·to·tem·po·ral \-ˈtem-pə-rəl\ adj : of or relating to the frontal and the temporal bones

frost·bite \ˈfrost-ˌbīt\ n : the freezing or the local effect of a partial freezing of some part of the body — **frostbite** vb

frot·tage \frō-ˈtäzh\ n : masturbation by rubbing against another person

frot·teur \fro-ˈtər\ n : one who engages in frottage

froze past of FREEZE

frozen past part of FREEZE

frozen shoulder n : a shoulder affected by severe pain and stiffening

fruc·to·kin·ase \frək-tō-ˈkī-ˌnās, -ˈki-,

-ˌnāz, ˌfrük-\ n : a kinase that catalyzes the transfer of phosphate groups to fructose

fruc·tose \ˈfrək-ˌtōs, ˈfrük-, ˈfrük-, -ˌtōz\ n 1 : a sugar $C_6H_{12}O_6$ known in three forms that are optically different with respect to polarized light 2 : the very sweet soluble levorotatory D-form of fructose that occurs esp. in fruit juices and honey — called also *levulose*

fruc·tos·uria \frək-tə-ˈsür-ē-ə\ n : the presence of fructose in the urine

fruit·ar·i·an \frü-ˈter-ē-ən\ n : one who lives chiefly on fruit

fruiting body n : a plant organ specialized for producing spores; esp : SPOROPHORE

fruit sugar n : FRUCTOSE 2

fru·se·mide \ˈfrü-sə-ˌmīd\ n, chiefly Brit : FUROSEMIDE

frus·trat·ed adj : filled with a sense of frustration : feeling deep insecurity, discouragement, or dissatisfaction

frus·tra·tion \(ˌ)frəs-ˈtrā-shən\ n 1 : a deep chronic sense or state of insecurity and dissatisfaction arising from unresolved problems or unfulfilled needs 2 : something that frustrates — **frus·trate** \ˈfrəs-ˌtrāt\ vb

FSH abbr follicle-stimulating hormone

ft abbr feet; foot

fuch·sin or **fuch·sine** \ˈfyük-sən, -ˌsēn\ n : a dye that yields a brilliant bluish red and is used in carbolfuchsin paint, in Schiff's reagent, and as a biological stain

fu·cose \ˈfyü-ˌkōs, -ˌkōz\ n : an aldose sugar that occurs in bound form in the dextrorotatory D-form in various glycosides and in the levorotatory L-form in some brown algae and in mammalian polysaccharides typical of some blood groups

fu·co·si·dase \fyü-ˈkō-sə-ˌdās, -ˌdāz\ n : an enzyme existing in stereoisomeric alpha and beta forms that catalyzes the metabolism of fucose

fu·co·si·do·sis \-ˌkō-sə-ˈdō-səs\ n, pl -do·ses \-ˌsēz\ : a disorder of metabolism inherited as a recessive trait and characterized by progressive neurological degeneration, deficiency of the alpha stereoisomer of fucosidase, and accumulation of fucose-containing carbohydrates

fugax — see AMAUROSIS FUGAX, PROCTALGIA FUGAX

-fuge \ˌfyüj\ n comb form : one that drives away (febrifuge) (vermifuge)

fu·gi·tive \ˈfyü-jə-tiv\ adj : tending to be inconstant or transient

fu·gu \ˈfyü-(ˌ)gü, ˈfü-\ n : any of various very poisonous puffers that contain tetrodotoxin and that are used as food in Japan after the toxin-containing organs are removed

fugue \ˈfyüg\ n : a disturbed state of consciousness in which the one affected seems to perform acts in full awareness but upon recovery cannot recollect them

ful·gu·ra·tion \ˌful-gə-ˈrā-shən, ˌfəl-, -gyə-, -jə-\ n : ELECTRODESICCATION — **ful·gu·rate** \ˈful-gə-ˌrāt, ˈfəl-, -gyə-, -jə-\ vb

full-mouthed \ˈful-ˈmau̇thd, -ˈmau̇tht\ adj : having a full complement of teeth — used esp. of sheep and cattle

ful·mi·nant \ˈful-mə-nənt, ˈfəl-\ adj : FULMINATING

ful·mi·nat·ing \-ˌnā-tiŋ\ adj : coming on suddenly with great severity ⟨∼ infection⟩ — **ful·mi·na·tion** \ˌful-mə-ˈnā-shən, ˌfəl-\ n

fu·ma·rate \ˈfyü-mə-ˌrāt\ n : a salt or ester of fumaric acid

fu·mar·ic acid \fyü-ˈmar-ik-\ n : a crystalline acid C₄H₄O₄ formed from succinic acid as an intermediate in the Krebs cycle

fu·mi·gant \ˈfyü-mi-gənt\ n : a substance used in fumigating

fu·mi·gate \ˈfyü-mə-ˌgāt\ vb -gat·ed; -gat·ing : to apply smoke, vapor, or gas to esp. for the purpose of disinfecting or of destroying pests — **fu·mi·ga·tion** \ˌfyü-mə-ˈgā-shən\ n — **fu·mi·ga·tor** \ˈfyü-mə-ˌgā-tər\ n

func·tion \ˈfəŋk-shən\ n : any of a group of related actions contributing to a larger action; esp : the normal and specific contribution of a bodily part to the economy of a living organism — **function** vb — **func·tion·less** \-ləs\ adj

func·tion·al \ˈfəŋk-shə-nəl\ adj 1 a : of, connected with, or being a function — compare STRUCTURAL 1 b : affecting physiological or psychological functions but not organic structure ⟨∼ heart disease⟩ ⟨a ∼ psychosis⟩ — compare ORGANIC 1b 2 : performing or able to perform a regular function — **func·tion·al·ly** adv

fun·dal \ˈfənd-ᵊl\ adj : FUNDIC

fun·da·ment \ˈfən-də-mənt\ n 1 : BUTTOCKS 2 : ANUS

fun·dic \ˈfən-dik\ adj : of or relating to a fundus

fundic gland n : one of the tubular glands of the fundus of the stomach secreting pepsin and mucus — compare CHIEF CELL 1

fun·do·pli·ca·tion \ˌfən-dō-pli-ˈkā-shən\ n : surgical plication of the fundus of the stomach around the lower end of the esophagus as a treatment for the reflux of stomach contents into the esophagus

fun·dus \ˈfən-dəs\ n, pl **fun·di** \-ˌdī, -ˌdē\ : the bottom of or part opposite the aperture of the internal surface of a hollow organ: as a : the greater curvature of the stomach b : the lower back part of the bladder c : the large upper end of the uterus d : the part of the eye opposite the pupil

fun·du·scop·ic also **fun·do·scop·ic** \ˌfən-də-ˈskä-pik\ adj : of, relating to, or by means of ophthalmoscopic examina-

tion of the fundus of the eye — **fun·dus·co·py** \ˌfən-ˈdəs-kə-pē\ also **fun·dos·co·py** \-ˈdäs-\ n

fun·gae·mia Brit var of FUNGEMIA

fun·gal \ˈfəŋ-gəl\ adj 1 : of, relating to, or having the characteristics of fungi 2 : caused by a fungus ⟨∼ infections⟩

fun·gate \ˈfəŋ-ˌgāt\ vb -gat·ed; -gat·ing : to assume a fungal form or grow rapidly like a fungus ⟨a fungating lesion⟩ — **fun·ga·tion** \ˌfəŋ-ˈgā-shən\ n

fun·ge·mia \fən-ˈgē-mē-ə\ n : the presence of fungi in the blood

fungi pl of FUNGUS

fungi- comb form : fungus ⟨fungicide⟩

fun·gi·cid·al \ˌfən-jə-ˈsīd-ᵊl, ˌfəŋ-gə-\ adj : destroying fungi; broadly : inhibiting the growth of fungi — **fun·gi·cid·al·ly** adv

fun·gi·cide \ˈfən-jə-ˌsīd, ˈfəŋ-gə-\ n : an agent that destroys fungi or inhibits their growth

fun·gi·form \ˈfən-jə-ˌfȯrm, ˈfəŋ-gə-\ adj : shaped like a mushroom

fungiform papilla n : any of numerous papillae on the upper surface of the tongue that are flat-topped and noticeably red from the richly vascular stroma and usu. contain taste buds

fun·gi·stat \ˈfən-jə-ˌstat, ˈfəŋ-gə-\ n : a fungistatic agent

fun·gi·stat·ic \ˌfən-jə-ˈsta-tik, ˌfəŋ-gə-\ adj : capable of inhibiting the growth and reproduction of fungi without destroying them ⟨a ∼ agent⟩ — **fun·gi·stat·i·cal·ly** \-ti-k(ə-)lē\ adv

Fun·gi·zone \ˈfən-jə-ˌzōn\ trademark — used for a preparation of amphotericin B

fun·goid \ˈfən-ˌgȯid\ adj : resembling, characteristic of, caused by, or being a fungus ⟨a ∼ ulcer⟩ ⟨a ∼ growth⟩

fungoides — see MYCOSIS FUNGOIDES

fun·gous \ˈfəŋ-gəs\ adj : FUNGAL

fun·gus \ˈfəŋ-gəs\ n, pl **fun·gi** \ˈfən-ˌjī, ˈfəŋ-ˌgī\ also **fun·gus·es** \ˈfəŋ-gə-səz\ often attrib 1 : any of a major group (Fungi) of saprophytic and parasitic spore-producing organisms that lack chlorophyll, are usu. classified as plants, and include molds, rusts, mildews, smuts, mushrooms, and yeasts 2 : infection with a fungus

fu·nic·u·li·tis \fyü-ˌni-kyə-ˈlī-təs, fə-\ n : inflammation of the spermatic cord

fu·nic·u·lus \fyü-ˈni-kyə-ləs, fə-\ n, pl **-li** \-ˌlī, -ˌlē\ : any of various bodily structures more or less like a cord in form: as a : one of the longitudinal subdivisions of white matter in each lateral half of the spinal cord — see ANTERIOR FUNICULUS, LATERAL FUNICULUS, POSTERIOR FUNICULUS; compare COLUMN a b : SPERMATIC CORD

funnel chest n : a depression of the anterior wall of the chest produced by a sinking in of the sternum — called also funnel breast, pectus excavatum

funny bone n : the place at the back of

the elbow where the ulnar nerve rests against a prominence of the humerus — called also **crazy bone**

FUO *abbr* fever of undetermined origin

fur \\'fər\\ *n* : a coat of epithelial debris on the tongue

fu·ra·zol·i·done \\,fyur-ə-'zä-lə-,dōn\\ *n* : an antimicrobial drug $C_8H_7N_3O_5$ used against bacteria and some protozoa esp. in infections of the gastrointestinal tract

furious rabies *n* : rabies characterized by spasm of the muscles of throat and diaphragm, choking, salivation, extreme excitement, and evidence of fear often manifested by indiscriminate snapping at objects — compare PARALYTIC RABIES

fu·ro·se·mide \\fyü-'rō-sə-,mīd\\ *n* : a powerful diuretic $C_{12}H_{11}ClN_2O_5S$ used esp. to treat edema — called also *frusemide, fursemide;* see LASIX

furred \\'fərd\\ *adj* : having a coating consisting chiefly of mucus and dead epithelial cells (a ~ tongue)

fur·row \\'fər-(,)ō\\ *n* 1 : a marked narrow depression or groove 2 : a deep wrinkle

fur·se·mide \\'fər-sə-,mīd\\ *n* : FUROSEMIDE

fu·run·cle \\'fyur-,əŋ-kəl\\ *n* : BOIL — **fu·run·cu·lar** \\fyu-'rəŋ-kyə-lər\\ *adj* — **fu·run·cu·lous** \\-ləs\\ *adj*

fu·run·cu·lo·sis \\fyü-,rəŋ-kyə-'lō-səs\\ *n, pl* -**lo·ses** \\-,sēz\\ 1 : the condition of having or tending to develop multiple furuncles 2 : a highly infectious disease of various salmon and trout (genera *Salmo* and *Oncorhynchus*) and their relatives that is caused by a bacterium (*Aeromonas salmonicida* of the family Vibrionaceae)

fuse \\'fyüz\\ *vb* **fused; fus·ing** : to undergo or cause to undergo fusion

fusi- *comb form* : spindle (*fusi*form)

fu·si·form \\'fyü-zə-,fȯrm\\ *adj* : tapering toward each end (a ~ aneurysm)

fu·sion \\'fyü-zhən\\ *n, often attrib* : a union by or as if by melting together: as **a** : a merging of diverse elements into a unified whole: *specif* : the blending of retinal images in binocular vision **b** (1) : a blend of sensations, perceptions, ideas, or attitudes such that the component elements can seldom be identified by introspective analysis (2) : the perception of light from a source that is intermittent above a critical frequency as if the source were continuous — called also *flicker fusion;* compare FLICKER **c** : the surgical immobilization of a joint — see SPINAL FUSION

fu·so·bac·te·ri·um \\,fyü-zō-bak-'tir-ē-əm\\ *n* 1 *cap* : a genus of gramnegative anaerobic strictly parasitic rod-shaped bacteria (family Bacteroidaceae) that include some pathogens occurring esp. in purulent or gangrenous infections 2 *pl* -**ria** \\-ē-ə\\ : any bacterium of the genus *Fusobacterium*

fu·so·spi·ro·chet·al \\-,spī-rə-'kēt-əl\\ *adj* : of, relating to, or caused by fusobacteria and spirochetes

G

¹g \\'jē\\ *n, pl* **g's** *or* **gs** \\'jēz\\ : a unit of force equal to the force exerted by gravity on a body at rest and used to indicate the force to which a body is subjected when accelerated

²g *abbr* 1 gram 2 gravity; acceleration of gravity

G *abbr* guanine

Ga *symbol* gallium

GABA *abbr* gamma-aminobutyric acid

G-ac·tin \\'jē-,ak-tən\\ *n* : a globular monomeric form of actin produced in solutions of low ionic concentration — compare F-ACTIN

gad·fly \\'gad-,flī\\ *n, pl* -**flies** : any of various flies (as a horsefly or botfly) that bite or annoy livestock

gad·o·lin·i·um \\,gad-əl-'i-nē-əm\\ *n* : a magnetic metallic element — symbol *Gd;* see ELEMENT table

gag reflex *n* : reflex contraction of the muscles of the throat caused esp. by stimulation (as by touch) of the pharynx

gal *abbr* gallon

galact- *or* **galacto-** *comb form* 1 : milk (*galact*orrhea) 2 : galactose (*galacto*kinase)

ga·lac·to·cele \\gə-'lak-tə-,sēl\\ *n* : a cystic tumor containing milk or a milky fluid; *esp* : such a tumor of a mammary gland

ga·lac·to·ki·nase \\gə-,lak-tō-'kī-,nās, -'ki-, -,nāz\\ *n* : a kinase that catalyzes the transfer of phosphate groups to galactose

ga·lac·tor·rhea \\gə-,lak-tə-'rē-ə\\ *n* : a spontaneous flow of milk from the nipple

ga·lac·tor·rhoea *chiefly Brit var of* GALACTORRHEA

ga·lac·tos·ae·mia *chiefly Brit var of* GALACTOSEMIA

ga·lac·tos·amine \\gə-,lak-'tō-sə-,mēn, -zə-\\ *n* : an amino derivative $C_6H_{13}O_5N$ of galactose that occurs in cartilage

ga·lac·tose \\gə-'lak-,tōs, -,tōz\\ *n* : a sugar $C_6H_{12}O_6$ that is less soluble and less sweet than glucose and is known in dextrorotatory, levorotatory, and racemic forms

ga·lac·tos·emia \\gə-,lak-tə-'sē-mē-ə\\ *n* : an inherited metabolic disorder in which galactose accumulates in the blood due to deficiency of an enzyme catalyzing its conversion to glucose — **ga·lac·tos·emic** \-mik\ *adj*

ga·lac·to·si·dase \gə-ˈlak-ˈtō-sə-ˌdās, -zə-ˌdāz\ *n* : an enzyme (as lactase) that hydrolyzes a galactoside

ga·lac·to·side \-ˈlak-tə-ˌsīd\ *n* : a glycoside that yields galactose on hydrolysis

ga·lac·tos·uria \gə-ˌlak-(ˌ)tō-ˈsùr-ē-ə, -ˈsyùr-\ *n* : an excretion of urine containing galactose

Gal·ba \ˈgal-bə, ˈgòl-\ *n* : a genus of freshwater snails (family Lymnaeidae) that include hosts of a liver fluke of the genus *Fasciola* (*F. hepatica*) and that are sometimes considered indistinguishable from the genus *Lymnaea* — compare FOSSARIA

ga·lea \ˈgā-lē-a, ˈga-\ *n* : GALEA APONEUROTICA

galea apo·neu·ro·ti·ca \-ˌa-pō-nù-ˈrä-ti-kə, -nyù-\ *n* : the aponeurosis underlying the scalp and linking the frontalis and occipitalis muscles — called also *epicranial aponeurosis*

ga·len·i·cal \gə-ˈle-ni-kəl\ *n* : a standard medicinal preparation (as an extract or tincture) containing usu. one or more active constituents of a plant — **ga·len·ic** \-nik\ *also* **galenical** *adj*

Ga·len \ˈgā-lən\. (ca 129–ca 199), Greek physician.

Ga·len·ist \ˈgā-lə-nist\ *n* : a follower or disciple of the ancient physician Galen — **Ga·len·ism** \-ˌni-zəm\ *n*

Galen's vein *n* 1 : either of a pair of cerebral veins in the roof of the third ventricle that drain the interior of the brain 2 : GREAT CEREBRAL VEIN

¹**gall** \ˈgòl\ *n* : BILE; *esp* : bile obtained from an animal and used in the arts or medicine

²**gall** *n* : a skin sore caused by chronic irritation

³**gall** *vb* : to fret and wear away by friction : CHAFE

gal·la·mine tri·eth·io·dide \ˈga-lə-ˌmēn-ˌtri-e-ˈthī-ə-ˌdīd\ *n* : an iodide salt $C_{30}H_{60}I_3N_3O_3$ that is used to produce muscle relaxation esp. during anesthesia — called also *gallamine*

gal·late \ˈga-ˌlāt, ˈgò-\ *n* : a salt or ester of gallic acid — see PROPYL GALLATE

gall·blad·der \ˈgòl-ˌbla-dər\ *n* : a membranous muscular sac in which bile from the liver is stored

galli — see CRISTA GALLI

gal·lic acid \ˈga-lik-, ˈgò-\ *n* : a white crystalline acid $C_7H_6O_5$ found widely in plants or combined in tannins

gal·li·um \ˈga-lē-əm\ *n* : a rare bluish white metallic element — symbol *Ga*; see ELEMENT table

gal·lon \ˈga-lən\ *n* 1 : a U.S. unit of liquid capacity equal to four quarts or 231 cubic inches or 3.785 liters 2 : a British unit of liquid and dry capacity equal to four quarts or 277.42 cubic inches or 4.544 liters — called also *imperial gallon*

gal·lop \ˈga-ləp\ *n* : GALLOP RHYTHM

galloping *adj, of a disease* : progressing rapidly toward a fatal conclusion

gallop rhythm *n* : an abnormal heart rhythm marked by the occurrence of three distinct sounds in each heartbeat like the sound of a galloping horse — called also *gallop*

gall sickness *n* : ANAPLASMOSIS

gall·stone \ˈgòl-ˌstōn\ *n* : a calculus formed in the gallbladder or biliary passages — called also *cholelith*

gal·van·ic \gal-ˈva-nik\ *adj* : of, relating to, involving, or producing galvanism (~ stimulation of flaccid muscles) — **gal·van·i·cal·ly** \-ni-k(ə)-lē\ *adv*

Gal·va·ni \gäl-ˈvä-nē\. **Luigi** (1737–1798), Italian physician and physicist.

galvanic skin response *n* : a change in the electrical resistance of the skin in response to a change in emotional state — abbr. *GSR*

gal·va·nism \ˈgal-və-ˌni-zəm\ *n* : the therapeutic use of direct electric current

gal·va·nom·e·ter \ˌgal-və-ˈnä-mə-tər\ *n* : an instrument for detecting or measuring a small electric current

gamet- *or* **gameto-** *comb form* : gamete ⟨*gamet*ic⟩ ⟨*gameto*genesis⟩

gam·ete \ˈga-ˌmēt, gə-ˈmēt\ *n* : a mature male or female germ cell usu. possessing a haploid chromosome set and capable of initiating formation of a new diploid individual by fusion with a gamete of the opposite sex — called also *sex cell* — **ga·met·ic** \gə-ˈme-tik\ *adj* — **ga·met·i·cal·ly** \-ti-k(ə-)lē\ *adv*

ga·me·to·cide \gə-ˈmē-tə-ˌsīd\ *n* : an agent that destroys the gametocytes of a malaria parasite

ga·me·to·cyte \-ˌsīt\ *n* : a cell (as of a protozoan causing malaria) that divides to produce gametes

gam·e·to·gen·e·sis \ˌga-mə-tə-ˈje-nə-səs, gə-ˌmē-tə-\ *n, pl* **-e·ses** \-ˌsēz\ : the production of gametes — **gam·e·tog·e·nous** \ˌga-mə-ˈtä-jə-nəs\ *adj*

-gam·ic \ˈgam-ik\ *adj comb form* : -GAMOUS ⟨monogamic⟩

¹**gam·ma** \ˈga-mə\ *n* 1 : the 3d letter of the Greek alphabet — symbol Γ or γ 2 : GAMMA RAY

²**gamma** *or* γ- *adj* 1 : of or relating to one of three or more closely related chemical substances (the *gamma* chain of hemoglobin) — used somewhat arbitrarily to specify ordinal relationship or a particular physical form 2 : of *streptococci* : producing no hemolysis on blood agar plates

gam·ma–ami·no·bu·tyr·ic acid *also* γ-ami·no·bu·tyr·ic acid \ˌga-mə-ə-ˌmē-(ˌ)nō-byü-ˈtir-ik-, ˌga-mə-ˌa-mə-(ˌ)nō-\ *n* : an amino acid $C_4H_9NO_2$ that is a neurotransmitter in the central nervous system — abbr. *GABA*

gamma benzene hexa·chlo·ride \-ˌhek-sə-ˈklōr-ˌīd\ *n* : the gamma isomer of benzene hexachloride that comprises the insecticide lindane and is used in medicine esp. as a scabicide and pediculicide in a one-percent cream, lotion, or shampoo — called also *gamma BHC*

gamma camera *n* : a camera that detects the gamma-ray photons produced by radionuclide decay and is used esp. in medical diagnostic scanning to create a visible record of a radioactive substance injected into the body

gamma globulin *n* **1 a** : a protein fraction of blood rich in antibodies **b** : a sterile solution of gamma globulin from pooled human blood administered esp. for passive immunity against measles, German measles, hepatitis A, or poliomyelitis **2** : any of numerous globulins of blood plasma or serum that have less electrophoretic mobility at alkaline pH than serum albumins, alpha globulins, or beta globulins and that include most antibodies

gamma ray *n* **1** : a photon emitted spontaneously by a radioactive substance; *also* : a high-energy photon — usu. used in pl. **2** : a continuous stream of gamma rays — called also *gamma radiation*

gam·mop·a·thy \ga-'mä-pə-thē\ *n*, *pl* **-thies** : a disorder characterized by a disturbance in the body's synthesis of antibodies

-g·a·mous \gə-məs\ *adj comb form* **1** : characterized by having or practicing (such) a marriage or (such or so many) marriages (monog*amous*) **2** : having (such) gametes or reproductive organs or (such) a mode of fertilization (heterog*amous*)

-g·a·my \gə-mē\ *n comb form* **1** : marriage (monog*amy*) **2** : possession of (such) gametes or reproductive organs or (such) a mode of fertilization (heterog*amy*)

gan·ci·clo·vir \gan-'sī-klə-(₀)vir\ *n* : an antiviral drug $C_9H_{13}N_5O_4$ related to acyclovir and used esp. in the treatment of cytomegalovirus retinitis in immunocompromised patients — called also *DHPG*

gangli- *or* **ganglio-** *comb form* : ganglion (gang*lioma*) (gang*lioneuroma*)

gan·gli·al \'gaŋ-glē-əl\ *adj* : of, relating to, or resembling a ganglion

gan·gli·at·ed cord \'gaŋ-glē-ॱā-təd-\ *n* : either of the two main trunks of the sympathetic nervous system of which one lies on each side of the spinal column

gan·gli·o·ma \ॱgaŋ-glē-'ō-mə\ *n*, *pl* **-mas** *or* **-ma·ta** \-mə-tə\ : a tumor of a ganglion

gan·gli·on \'gaŋ-glē-ən\ *n*, *pl* **-glia** \-glē-ə\ *also* **-gli·ons** **1** : a small cystic tumor (as on the back of the wrist) containing viscid fluid and connected either with a joint membrane or tendon sheath **2** : a mass of nerve tissue

containing nerve cells: **a** : an aggregation of such cells forming an enlargement upon a nerve or upon two or more nerves at their point of junction or separation **b** : a mass of gray matter within the brain or spinal cord : NUCLEUS 2 — see BASAL GANGLION

gan·gli·on·at·ed \-ə-ॱnā-təd\ *adj* : furnished with ganglia

ganglion cell *n* : a nerve cell having its body outside the central nervous system

gan·gli·on·ec·to·my \ॱgaŋ-glē-ə-'nek-tə-mē\ *n*, *pl* **-mies** : surgical removal of a nerve ganglion

gan·glio·neu·ro·ma \-(₀)ō-nú-'rō-mə, -nyú-\ *n*, *pl* **-ro·mas** *or* **-ro·ma·ta** \-mə-tə\ : a neuroma derived from ganglion cells

gan·gli·on·ic \ॱgaŋ-glē-'ä-nik\ *adj* : of, relating to, or affecting ganglia or ganglion cells

ganglionic blocking agent *n* : a drug used to produce blockade at a ganglion

gan·gli·on·itis \ॱgaŋ-glē-ə-'nī-təs\ *n* : inflammation of a ganglion

gan·glio·side \'gaŋ-glē-ə-ॱsīd\ *n* : any of a group of glycolipids that are found esp. in the plasma membrane of cells of the gray matter and have sialic acid, hexoses, and hexosamines in the carbohydrate part and ceramide as the lipid

gan·glio·si·do·sis \ॱgaŋ-glē-ॱō-sī-'dō-səs\ *n*, *pl* **-do·ses** \-ॱsēz\ : any of several inherited metabolic diseases (as Tay-Sachs disease) characterized by an enzyme deficiency which causes accumulation of gangliosides in the tissues

gan·go·sa \gaŋ-'gō-sə\ *n* : a destructive ulcerative condition believed to be a manifestation of yaws that usu. originates about the soft palate, nasal structures, and outward to the face — compare GOUNDOU

gan·grene \'gaŋ-ॱgrēn, gaŋ-'\ *n* : local death of soft tissues due to loss of blood supply — **gangrene** *vb* — **gan·gre·nous** \'gaŋ-grə-nəs\ *adj*

gangrenous stomatitis *n* : CANCRUM ORIS

gan·ja \'gän-jə, 'gan-\ *n* : a potent preparation of marijuana used esp. for smoking; *broadly* : MARIJUANA

Gan·ser syndrome \'gän-zər-\ *or* **Ganser's syndrome** *n* : a pattern of psychopathological behavior characterized by the giving of approximate answers (as 2×2 = about 5)

Ganser, Sigbert Joseph Maria (1853–1931), German psychiatrist.

gapes \'gāps\ *n* : a disease of birds and esp. young birds in which gapeworms invade and irritate the trachea

gape·worm \'gāp-ॱwərm\ *n* : a nematode worm of the genus *Syngamus* (*S. trachea*) that causes gapes of birds

gap junction *n* : an area of contact between adjacent cells characterized by modification of the cell membranes for intercellular communication or transfer of low molecular-weight substances — **gap-junc·tion·al** \'gap-ˌjəŋk-shə-nəl\ *adj*

Gard·ner·el·la \ˌgärd-nə-'re-lə\ *n* : a genus of bacteria of uncertain taxonomic affinities that includes one (*G. vaginalis* syn. *Haemophilus vaginalis*) often present in the flora of the healthy vagina and present in greatly increased numbers in nonspecific vaginitis

Gard·ner, \'gärd-nər\ **Herman L.** (*fl* 1955–80), American physician.

gar·get \'gär-gət\ *n* : mastitis of domestic animals; *esp* : chronic bovine mastitis

¹**gar·gle** \'gär-gəl\ *vb* **gar·gled; gar·gling** : to hold (a liquid) in the mouth or throat and agitate with air from the lungs; *also* : to cleanse or disinfect (the oral cavity) in this manner

²**gargle** *n* : a liquid used in gargling

gar·goyl·ism \'gär-ˌgoi-ˌli-zəm\ *n* : MUCOPOLYSACCHARIDOSIS; *esp* : HURLER'S SYNDROME

Gärt·ner's bacillus \'gert-nərz-\ *n* : a motile bacterium of the genus *Salmonella* (*S. enteritidis*) that causes enteritis

Gärtner, August Anton Hieronymus (1848–1934), German hygienist and bacteriologist.

Gart·ner's duct \'gärt-nərz-, 'gert-\ *n* : the remains in the female mammal of a part of the Wolffian duct of the embryo — called also *duct of Gartner*
Gart·ner \'gert-nər\. **Hermann Treschow** (1785–1827), Danish surgeon and anatomist.

gas \'gas\ *n, pl* **gas·es** *also* **gas·ses** **1** : a fluid (as air) that has neither independent shape nor volume but tends to expand indefinitely **2** : a gaseous product of digestion; *also* : discomfort from this **3** : a gas or gaseous mixture used to produce anesthesia **4** : a substance that can be used to produce a poisonous, asphyxiating, or irritant atmosphere

gas chromatograph *n* : an instrument used to separate a sample into components in gas chromatography

gas chromatography *n* : chromatography in which the sample mixture is vaporized and injected into a stream of carrier gas (as helium) moving through a column containing a stationary phase composed of a liquid or a particulate solid and is separated into its component compounds according to the affinity of the components for the stationary phase — **gas chromatographic** *adj*

gas·eous \'ga-sē-əs, 'ga-shəs\ *adj* : having the form of or being gas; *also* : of or relating to gases

gas gangrene *n* : progressive gangrene marked by impregnation of the dead and dying tissue with gas and caused by one or more toxin-producing bacteria of the genus *Clostridium*

gash \'gash\ *n* : a deep long cut esp. in flesh — **gash** *vb*

gas–liquid chromatography *n* : gas chromatography in which the stationary phase is a liquid — **gas–liquid chromatographic** *adj*

gas·se·ri·an ganglion \ga-'sir-ē-ən-\ *n, often cap 1st G* : TRIGEMINAL GANGLION

Gas·ser \'gä-sər\. **Johann Laurentius** (1723–1765), Austrian anatomist.

Gas·ter·oph·i·lus \ˌgas-tə-'rä-fə-ləs\ *n* : a genus of botflies including several (esp. *G. intestinalis* in the U.S.) that infest horses and rarely humans

gastr- *or* **gastro-** *also* **gastri-** *comb form* **1** : stomach 〈*gastritis*〉 **2** : gastric and 〈*gastro*intestinal〉

gas·tral \'gas-trəl\ *adj* : of or relating to the stomach or digestive tract

gas·tral·gia \ga-'stral-jə\ *n* : pain in the stomach or epigastrium esp. of a neuralgic type — **gas·tral·gic** \-jik\ *adj*

gas·trec·to·my \ga-'strek-tə-mē\ *n, pl* **-mies** : surgical removal of all or part of the stomach

gas·tric \'gas-trik\ *adj* : of or relating to the stomach

gastrica — see ACHYLIA GASTRICA

gastric artery *n* **1** : a branch of the celiac artery that passes to the cardiac end of the stomach and along the lesser curvature — called also *left gastric artery*; see RIGHT GASTRIC ARTERY **2** : any of several branches of the splenic artery distributed to the greater curvature of the stomach

gastric gland *n* : any of various glands in the walls of the stomach that secrete gastric juice

gastric juice *n* : a thin watery acid digestive fluid secreted by the glands in the mucous membrane of the stomach and containing 0.2 to 0.4 percent free hydrochloric acid and several enzymes (as pepsin)

gastric pit *n* : any of the numerous depressions in the mucous membrane lining the stomach into which the gastric glands discharge their secretions

gastric ulcer *n* : a peptic ulcer situated in the stomach

gas·trin \'gas-trən\ *n* : any of various polypeptide hormones that are secreted by the gastric mucosa and induce secretion of gastric juice

gas·tri·no·ma \ˌgas-trə-'nō-mə\ *n, pl* **-mas** *or* **-ma·ta** \-mə-tə\ : a neoplasm that often involves blood vessels, usu. occurs in the pancreas or the wall of the duodenum, and produces excessive amounts of gastrin — see ZOLLINGER-ELLISON SYNDROME

gas·tri·tis \ga-'strī-təs\ *n* : inflammation esp. of the mucous membrane of the stomach

gastro- — see GASTR-

gas·troc·ne·mi·us \ˌgas-(ˌ)träk-'nē-mē-əs, -trək-\ *n*, *pl* -mii \-ˌmē-ˌī\ : the largest and most superficial muscle of the calf of the leg that arises by two heads from the condyles of the femur and has its tendon of insertion incorporated as part of the Achilles tendon — called also *gastrocnemius muscle*

gas·tro·co·lic \ˌgas-trō-ˈkä-lik, -ˈkō-\ *adj* : of, relating to, or uniting the stomach and colon (a ∼ fistula)

gastrocolic reflex *n* : the occurrence of peristalsis following the entrance of food into the empty stomach

Gas·tro·dis·coi·des \ˌgas-trō-dis-ˈkoi-(ˌ)dēz\ *n* : a genus of amphistome trematode worms including a common intestinal parasite (*G. hominis*) of humans and swine in southeastern Asia

gas·tro·du·o·de·nal \ˌgas-trō-ˌdü-ə-ˈdēn-əl, -ˌdyü-; -dü-ˈäd-ən-əl, -dyü-\ *adj* : of, relating to, or involving both the stomach and the duodenum

gastroduodenal artery *n* : an artery that arises from the hepatic artery and divides to form the right gastroepiploic artery and a branch supplying the duodenum and pancreas

gas·tro·du·o·de·nos·to·my \-ˌdü-ə-(ˌ)dē-ˈnäs-tə-mē, -ˌdyü-; -dü-ˌäd-ᵊn-ˈäs-tə-mē, -dyü-\ *n*, *pl* -mies : surgical formation of a passage between the stomach and the duodenum

gas·tro·en·ter·i·tis \-ˌen-tə-ˈrī-təs\ *n*, *pl* -en·ter·it·i·des \-ˈri-tə-ˌdēz\ : inflammation of the lining membrane of the stomach and the intestines

gas·tro·en·ter·ol·o·gist \-ˌen-tə-ˈrä-lə-jist\ *n* : a specialist in gastroenterology

gas·tro·en·ter·ol·o·gy \-ˌen-tə-ˈrä-lə-jē\ *n*, *pl* -gies : a branch of medicine concerned with the structure, functions, diseases, and pathology of the stomach and intestines — **gas·tro·en·ter·o·log·i·cal** \-ˌen-tə-rə-ˈlä-ji-kəl\ *or* **gas·tro·en·ter·o·log·ic** \-ˈlä-jik\ *adj*

gas·tro·en·ter·op·a·thy \-ˌen-tə-ˈrä-pə-thē\ *n*, *pl* -thies : a disease of the stomach and intestines

gas·tro·en·ter·os·to·my \-ˈräs-tə-mē\ *n*, *pl* -mies : the surgical formation of a passage between the stomach and small intestine

gas·tro·ep·i·plo·ic artery \-ˌe-pə-ˈplō-ik\ *n* : either of two arteries forming an anastomosis along the greater curvature of the stomach: **a** : one that is larger, arises as one of the two terminal branches of the gastroduodenal artery, and passes from right to left — called also *right gastroepiploic artery* **b** : one that is smaller, arises as a branch of the splenic artery, and passes from left to right — called also *left gastroepiploic artery*

gas·tro·esoph·a·ge·al \ˌgas-trō-i-ˌsä-fə-ˈjē-əl\ *adj* : of, relating to, or involving the stomach and esophagus (∼ reflux)

gas·tro·in·tes·ti·nal \-in-ˈtes-tən-əl\ *adj* : of, relating to, or affecting both stomach and intestine

gastrointestinal tract *n* : the stomach and intestine as a functional unit

gas·tro·je·ju·nal \-ji-ˈjün-əl\ *adj* : of, relating to, or involving both stomach and jejunum (∼ lesions)

gas·tro·je·ju·nos·to·my \-ji-(ˌ)jü-ˈnäs-tə-mē\ *n*, *pl* -mies : the surgical formation of a passage between the stomach and jejunum : GASTROENTEROSTOMY

gas·tro·lith \ˈga-strə-ˌlith\ *n* : a gastric calculus

gas·trop·a·thy \ga-ˈsträ-pə-thē\ *n*, *pl* -thies : a disease of the stomach

gas·tro·pexy \ˈgas-trə-ˌpek-sē\ *n*, *pl* -pex·ies : a surgical operation in which the stomach is sutured to the abdominal wall

gas·tro·pod \ˈgas-trə-ˌpäd\ *n* : any of a large class (Gastropoda) of mollusks (as snails and cones) usu. with a one-piece shell or none and a distinct head bearing sensory organs — **gastropod** *adj*

gas·tros·chi·sis \ga-ˈsträs-kə-səs\ *n*, *pl* -chi·ses \-ˌsēz\ : congenital fissure of the ventral abdominal wall

gas·tro·scope \ˈgas-trə-ˌskōp\ *n* : an instrument for viewing the interior of the stomach — **gas·tro·scop·ic** \ˌgas-trə-ˈskä-pik\ *adj* — **gas·tros·co·pist** \ga-ˈsträs-kə-pist\ *n* — **gas·tros·co·py** \-pē\ *n*

gas·tro·splen·ic ligament \ˌgas-trō-ˈsple-nik-\ *n* : a mesenteric fold passing from the greater curvature of the stomach to the spleen

gas·tros·to·my \ga-ˈsträs-tə-mē\ *n*, *pl* -mies **1** : the surgical formation of an opening through the abdominal wall into the stomach **2** : the opening made by gastrostomy

gas·trot·o·my \ga-ˈsträ-tə-mē\ *n*, *pl* -mies : surgical incision into the stomach

gas·tru·la \ˈgas-trə-lə\ *n*, *pl* -las *or* -lae \-ˌlē, -ˌlī\ : an early embryo that develops from the blastula and in mammals is formed by the differentiation of the upper layer of the blastodisc into the ectoderm and the lower layer into the endoderm and by the inward migration of cells through the primitive streak to form the mesoderm — compare BLASTULA, MORULA — **gas·tru·lar** \-lər\ *adj*

gas·tru·la·tion \ˌgas-trə-ˈlā-shən\ *n* : the process of becoming or of forming a gastrula — **gas·tru·late** \ˈgas-trə-ˌlāt\ *vb*

Gatch bed \ˈgach-\ *n* : HOSPITAL BED
Gatch, Willis Dew (1878–1954), American surgeon.

gath·er \ˈga-thər\ *vb* **gath·ered; gath·er·ing** : to swell and fill with pus (the boil is ∼ing)

gathering *n* : a suppurating swelling : ABSCESS

Gau·cher's disease \ˌgō-ˈshäz-\ *n* : a

rare hereditary disorder of lipid metabolism that is caused by an enzyme deficiency of glucocerebrosidase. that is characterized by enormous enlargement of the spleen. pigmentation of the skin. and bone lesions. and that is marked by the presence of large amounts of glucocerebroside in the cells of the reticuloendothelial system

Gaucher, Philippe Charles Ernest (1854–1918). French physician.

gaul·the·ria \gȯl-ᵇthir-ē-ə\ n 1 cap : a genus of evergreen shrubs of the heath family (Ericaceae) that includes the wintergreen (*G. procumbens*) which is a source of methyl salicylate 2 : a plant of the genus *Gaultheria*

Gaultier \gō-ᵇtyā\, **Jean François** (1708–1756), Canadian physician and botanist.

gaultheria oil n : OIL OF WINTERGREEN

gauze \ᵇgȯz\ n : a loosely woven cotton surgical dressing

ga·vage \gə-ᵇväzh, gä-\ n : introduction of material into the stomach by a tube

gave *past of* GIVE

¹GB \ᵇjē-ᵇbē\ n : SARIN

²GB *abbr* gallbladder

GC *abbr* 1 gas chromatograph; gas chromatography 2 gonococcus

G–CSF *abbr* granulocyte colony-stimulating factor

Gd *symbol* gadolinium

Ge *symbol* germanium

GE *abbr* gastroenterology

Gei·ger counter \ᵇgī-gər-\ n : an instrument for detecting the presence and intensity of radiations (as cosmic rays or particles from a radioactive substance) by means of the ionizing effect on an enclosed gas which results in a pulse that is amplified and fed to a device giving a visible or audible indication

Geiger, Hans (Johannes) Wilhelm (1882–1945), and **Müller** \ᵇmue-lər\, **Walther** (*fl* 1928), German physicists.

Geiger–Mül·ler counter \-ᵇmyü-lər-\ n : GEIGER COUNTER

¹gel \ᵇjel\ n : a colloid in a more solid form than a sol

²gel vb **gelled; gel·ling** : to change into or take on the form of a gel — **gel·able** \ᵇje-lə-bəl\ adj

gel·ate \ᵇje-ᵇlāt\ vb **gel·at·ed; gel·at·ing** : GEL

gel·a·tin *also* **gel·a·tine** \ᵇje-lə-tən\ n 1 : glutinous material obtained from animal tissues by boiling; *esp* : a colloidal protein used as a food and in medicine 2 a : any of various substances (as agar) resembling gelatin b : an edible jelly made with gelatin — **ge·lat·i·nous** \jə-ᵇlat-ᵊn-əs\ adj

gelatinosa — see SUBSTANTIA GELATINOSA

gel·ation \je-ᵇlā-shən\ n : the formation of a gel from a sol

geld \ᵇgeld\ vb : CASTRATE; *also* : SPAY

geld·ing \ᵇgel-diŋ\ n : a castrated animal; *specif* : a castrated male horse

gel electrophoresis n : electrophoresis in which molecules (as proteins and nucleic acids) migrate through a gel and esp. a polyacrylamide gel and separate into bands according to size

gel filtration n : chromatography in which the material to be fractionated separates primarily according to molecular size as it moves into a column of a gel and is washed with a solvent so that the fractions appear successively at the end of the column — called also *gel chromatography*

ge·mel·lus \jə-ᵇme-ləs\ n, pl **ge·mel·li** \-ᵇlī\ *also* **ge·mel·lus·es** : either of two small muscles of the hip that insert into the tendon of the obturator internus: a : a superior one originating chiefly from the outer surface of the ischial spine — called also *gemellus superior* b : an inferior one originating chiefly from the ischial tuberosity — called also *gemellus inferior*

gem·fi·bro·zil \jem-ᵇfi-brə-(ᵢ)zil, -ᵇfi-\ n : a drug $C_{15}H_{22}O_3$ that reduces the level of triglycerides in the blood and is used to treat hyperlipoproteinemia

gem·i·na·tion \ᵢje-mə-ᵇnā-shən\ n : a doubling. duplication. or repetition; *esp* : a formation of two teeth from a single tooth germ

gen- *or* **geno-** *comb form* : gene ⟨*gen*ome⟩

-gen \jən, ᵢjen\ *also* **-gene** \ᵢjēn\ n *comb form* 1 : producer ⟨aller*gen*⟩ ⟨carcino*gen*⟩ 2 : one that is (so) produced ⟨phos*gen*e⟩

gen·der \ᵇjen-dər\ n 1 : SEX 1 2 : the behavioral. cultural. or psychological traits typically associated with one sex

gender identity n : the totality of physical and behavioral traits that are designated by a culture as masculine or feminine

gene \ᵇjēn\ n : a specific sequence of nucleotides in DNA or RNA that is located in the germ plasm usu. on a chromosome and that is the functional unit of inheritance controlling the transmission and expression of one or more traits by specifying the structure of a particular polypeptide and esp. a protein or controlling the function of other genetic material — called also *determinant, determiner, factor*

gene amplification n : replication and esp. massive replication (as in the polymerase chain reaction) of the genetic material in part of a genome

gene complex n : a group of genes of an individual or of a potentially interbreeding group that constitute an interacting functional unit

gene flow n : the passage and establishment of genes typical of one breeding population into the gene pool of another by hybridization and back-crossing

gene frequency n : the ratio of the number of a specified allele in a population to the total of all alleles at its genetic locus

gene mutation n : POINT MUTATION

gene pool n : the collection of genes of all the individuals in an interbreeding population

genera pl of GENUS

gen·er·al \'je-nə-rəl, 'jen-rəl\ adj 1 : not confined by specialization or careful limitation (a ~ surgeon) 2 : involving or affecting practically the entire organism : not local (~ nervousness)

general anesthesia n : anesthesia affecting the entire body and accompanied by loss of consciousness

general anesthetic n : an anesthetic used to produce general anesthesia

general hospital n : a hospital in which patients with many different types of ailments are given care

gen·er·al·ist \'jen-rə-list, 'je-nə-rə-\ n : one whose skills or interests extend to several different medical fields; esp : GENERAL PRACTITIONER

generalista — see OSTEITIS FIBROSA CYSTICA GENERALISTA

gen·er·al·iza·tion \jen-rə-lə-'zā-shən, je-nə-rə-\ n 1 : the action or process of generalizing 2 : the process whereby a response is made to a stimulus similar to but not identical with a reference stimulus

gen·er·al·ize \'jen-rə-līz, 'je-nə-rə-\ vb -ized; -iz·ing : to spread or extend throughout the body

general paresis n : insanity caused by syphilitic alteration of the brain that leads to dementia and paralysis — called also *dementia paralytica, general paralysis of the insane*

general practitioner n : a physician or veterinarian whose practice is not limited to a specialty

gen·er·a·tion \je-nə-'rā-shən\ n 1 : a body of living beings constituting a single step in the line of descent from an ancestor 2 : the average span of time between the birth of parents and that of their offspring 3 : the action or process of producing offspring : PROCREATION

gen·er·a·tive \'je-nə-rə-tiv, -,rā-\ adj : having the power or function of propagating or reproducing (~ organs)

gen·er·a·tiv·i·ty \je-nə-rə-'ti-və-tē\ n : a concern for people besides self and family that usu. develops during middle age; esp : a need to nurture and guide younger people and contribute to the next generation — used in the psychology of Erik Erikson

¹**ge·ner·ic** \jə-'ner-ik\ adj 1 : not protected by trademark registration : NONPROPRIETARY 2 : relating to or having the rank of a biological genus — **ge·ner·i·cal·ly** \-i-k(ə-)lē\ adv

²**generic** n : a generic drug — usu. used in pl.

gene–splic·ing \'jēn-,splī-siŋ\ n : any of various techniques by which recombinant DNA is produced and made to function in an organism

gene therapy n : the insertion of normal or genetically altered genes into cells usu. to replace defective genes esp. in the treatment of genetic disorders

ge·net·ic \jə-'ne-tik\ also **ge·net·i·cal** \-ti-kəl\ adj 1 : of, relating to, or involving genetics 2 : GENIC — **ge·net·i·cal·ly** \-ti-k(ə-)lē\ adv

-ge·net·ic \jə-'ne-tik\ adj comb form : -GENIC (osteogenetic)

genetic code n : the biochemical basis of heredity consisting of codons in DNA and RNA that determine the specific amino acid sequence in proteins and that appear to be uniform for all known forms of life — **genetic coding** n

genetic counseling n : medical education of affected individuals and the general public concerning inherited disorders that includes discussion of the probability of producing offspring with a disorder, diagnostic tests, and available treatment

genetic drift n : random changes in gene frequency esp. in small populations when leading to preservation or extinction of particular genes

genetic engineering n : the directed alteration of genetic material by intervention in genetic processes; esp : GENE-SPLICING — **genetically engineered** adj — **genetic engineer** n

genetic map n : MAP

genetic marker n : a usu. dominant gene or trait that serves esp. to identify genes or traits linked with it — called also *marker*

ge·net·ics \jə-'ne-tiks\ n 1 a : a branch of biology that deals with the heredity and variation of organisms b : a treatise or textbook on genetics 2 : the genetic makeup and phenomena of an organism, type, group, or condition — **ge·net·i·cist** \jə-'ne-tə-sist\ n

ge·ni·al \ji-'nī-əl\ adj : of or relating to the chin

genial tubercle n : MENTAL TUBERCLE

gen·ic \'jē-nik, 'je-\ adj : of, relating to, or being a gene — **gen·i·cal·ly** \-nik(ə-)lē\ adv

-gen·ic \'je-nik, 'jē-\ adj comb form 1 : producing : forming (carcinogenic) 2 : produced by : formed from (nephrogenic)

ge·nic·u·lar artery \jə-'ni-kyə-lər-\ n : any of several branches of the femoral and popliteal arteries that supply the region of the knee — called also *genicular*

ge·nic·u·late \-lət, -,lāt\ adj 1 : bent abruptly at an angle like a bent knee 2 : relating to, comprising, or belonging to a geniculate body or geniculate ganglion (~ cells) (~ neurons)

geniculate body n : either of two prominences of the diencephalon that comprise the metathalamus: **a** : LATERAL GENICULATE BODY **b** : MEDIAL GENICULATE BODY

geniculate ganglion n : a small reddish ganglion consisting of sensory and sympathetic nerve cells located at the sharp backward bend of the facial nerve

ge·nic·u·lo·cal·ca·rine \jə-ˌni-kyə-(ˌ)lō-ˈkal-kə-ˌrīn\ adj : relating to or comprising the optic radiation from the lateral geniculate body and the pulvinar to the occipital lobe (~ tracts)

genio- comb form : chin and ⟨genioglossus⟩

ge·nio·glos·sus \ˌjē-nē-ō-ˈglä-səs, -ˈglō-\ n, pl **-glos·si** \-ˌsī\ : a fan-shaped muscle that arises from the superior mental spine, inserts on the hyoid bone and into the tongue, and serves to advance and retract and also to depress the tongue

ge·nio·hyo·glos·sus \-ˌhī-ō-ˈglä-səs, -ˈglō-\ n, pl **-glos·si** \-ˌsī\ : GENIOGLOSSUS

ge·nio·hy·oid \-ˈhī-ˌoid\ adj : of or relating to the chin and hyoid bone

ge·nio·hy·oid·eus \-ˌhī-ˈoi-dē-əs\ n, pl **-oid·ei** \-dē-ˌī\ : GENIOHYOID MUSCLE

geniohyoid muscle n : a slender muscle that arises from the inferior mental spine, is inserted on the hyoid bone and acts to raise the hyoid bone and draw it forward and to retract and depress the lower jaw — called also geniohyoid

gen·i·tal \ˈje-nə-t³l\ adj **1** : GENERATIVE **2** : of, relating to, or being a sexual organ **3** : of, relating to, or characterized by the stage of psychosexual development in psychoanalytic theory during which oral and anal impulses are subordinated to adaptive interpersonal mechanisms — compare ANAL 2a, ORAL 2a, PHALLIC 2 — **gen·i·tal·ly** adv

genital herpes n : HERPES GENITALIS

genital herpes simplex n : HERPES GENITALIS

gen·i·ta·lia \ˌje-nə-ˈtāl-yə\ n pl : the organs of the reproductive system; esp : the external genital organs — see HERPES GENITALIS

gen·i·tal·i·ty \-ˈta-lə-tē\ n, pl **-ties** : possession of full genital sensitivity and capacity to develop orgasmic potency in relation to a sexual partner of the opposite sex

genital ridge n : a ridge of embryonic mesoblast developing from the mesonephros and giving rise to the gonad on either side of the body

gen·i·tals \ˈje-nə-t³lz\ n pl : GENITALIA

genital tubercle n : a conical protuberance on the belly wall of an embryo that develops into the penis in the male and the clitoris in the female

genital wart n : CONDYLOMA ACUMINATUM

genito- comb form : genital and ⟨genitourinary⟩

gen·i·to·cru·ral nerve \jə-nə-(ˌ)tō-ˈkrúr-əl-\ n : GENITOFEMORAL NERVE

gen·i·to·fem·o·ral nerve \-ˈfe-mə-rəl-\ n : a nerve that arises from the first and second lumbar nerves and is distributed by way of branches to the skin of the scrotum, labia majora, and the upper anterior aspect of the thigh

gen·i·to·uri·nary \-ˈyúr-ə-ˌner-ē\ adj : UROGENITAL

genitourinary system n : GENITOURINARY TRACT

genitourinary tract n : the system of organs comprising those concerned with the production and excretion of urine and those concerned with reproduction — called also genitourinary system, urogenital system, urogenital tract

geno- — see GEN-

ge·nome \ˈjē-ˌnōm\ n : one haploid set of chromosomes with the genes they contain — **ge·no·mic** \ji-ˈnō-mik, -ˈnä-\ adj

¹ge·no·type \ˈjē-nə-ˌtīp, ˈje-\ n : all or part of the genetic constitution of an individual or group — compare PHENOTYPE — **ge·no·typ·ic** \ˌjē-nə-ˈti-pik, ˌje-\ also **ge·no·typ·i·cal** \-pi-kəl\ adj — **ge·no·typ·i·cal·ly** \-pi-k(ə-)lē\ adv

²genotype vb **-typed; -typ·ing** : to determine the genotype of

-g·e·nous \jə-nəs\ adj comb form **1** : producing : yielding ⟨erogenous⟩ **2** : produced by : arising or originating in ⟨neurogenous⟩ ⟨endogenous⟩

gen·ta·mi·cin \ˌjen-tə-ˈmīs-³n\ n : a broad-spectrum antibiotic mixture that is derived from an actinomycete of the genus Micromonospora (M. purpurea and M. echinospora) and is used extensively in the form of the sulfate in treating infections esp. of the urinary tract

gen·tian violet \ˈjen-chən-\ n, often cap G&V : a greenish mixture that contains not less than 96% of the derivative of pararosaniline containing six methyl groups in each molecule and is used esp. as a bactericide, fungicide, and anthelmintic

gen·tis·ic acid \jen-ˈti-sik-, -zik\ n : a crystalline acid $C_7H_6O_4$ used medicinally as an analgesic and diaphoretic

ge·nu \ˈjē-ˌnü, ˈjen-yü\ n, pl **gen·ua** \ˈjen-yə-wə\ : an abrupt flexure; esp : the bend in the anterior part of the corpus callosum — compare GENU VALGUM, GENU VARUM

ge·nus \ˈjē-nəs, ˈje-\ n, pl **gen·era** \ˈje-nə-rə\ : a category of biological classification ranking between the family and the species, comprising structurally or phylogenetically related species or an isolated species exhibiting unusual differentiation, and being designated by a capitalized singular noun that is Latin or has a Latin form

genu val·gum \-ˈval-gəm\ n : KNOCK-KNEE

genu va·rum \-ˈvar-əm\ n : BOWLEG

-ge·ny \jə-nē\ n comb form : generation : production (embryogeny) (lysogeny)

geo·med·i·cine \jē-ō-ˈme-də-sən\ n : a branch of medicine that deals with geographic factors in disease

ge·o·pha·gia \ˈfā-jē-ə-, -jə\ n : GEOPHAGY

ge·oph·a·gy \jē-ˈä-fə-jē\ n, pl -gies : a practice of eating earthy substances (as clay) among primitive or economically depressed peoples to augment a scanty or mineral-deficient diet — compare PICA

ge·ot·ri·cho·sis \jē-ˌä-trə-ˈkō-səs\ n : infection of the bronchi or lungs and sometimes the mouth and intestines by a fungus of the genus Geotrichum (G. candidum)

Ge·ot·ri·chum \jē-ˈä-tri-kəm\ n : a genus of fungi (family Moniliaceae) including one (G. candidum) that causes human geotrichosis

ge·ri·at·ric \ˌjer-ē-ˈa-trik, ˌjir-\ n 1 ge·ri·at·rics \-triks\ : a branch of medicine that deals with the problems and diseases of old age and aging people — used with a sing. verb; compare GERONTOLOGY 2 : an aged person — geriatric adj

ge·ri·a·tri·cian \ˌjer-ē-ə-ˈtri-shən, ˌjir-\ n : a specialist in geriatrics

ge·ri·a·trist \ˌjer-ē-ˈa-trist, ˌjir-; jə-ˈrī-ə-\ n : GERIATRICIAN

germ \ˈjərm\ n 1 : a small mass of living substance capable of developing into an organism or one of its parts 2 : MICROORGANISM: esp : a microorganism causing disease

Ger·man cockroach \ˈjər-mən-\ n : a small active winged cockroach of the genus Blattella (B. germanica) prob. of African origin but now common in many urban buildings in the U.S. — called also Croton bug

ger·ma·nin \jər-ˈmä-nən\ n : SURAMIN

ger·ma·ni·um \(ˌ)jər-ˈmä-nē-əm\ n : a grayish white hard brittle element — symbol Ge; see ELEMENT table

German measles n sing or pl : an acute contagious virus disease that is milder than typical measles but is damaging to the fetus when occurring early in pregnancy — called also rubella

germ cell n : an egg or sperm cell or one of their antecedent cells

germ-free \ˈjərm-ˌfrē\ adj : free of microorganisms : AXENIC

ger·mi·cid·al \ˌjər-mə-ˈsid-ᵊl\ adj : of or relating to a germicide; also : destroying germs

ger·mi·cide \ˈjər-mə-ˌsīd\ n : an agent that destroys germs

ger·mi·nal \ˈjər-mə-nəl\ adj : of, relating to, or having the characteristics of a germ cell or early embryo

germinal cell n : an embryonic cell of the early vertebrate nervous system that is the source of neuroblasts and neuroglial cells

germinal center n : the lightly staining central proliferative area of a lymphoid follicle

germinal disk n 1 : BLASTODISC 2 : the part of the blastoderm that forms the embryo proper of an amniote vertebrate

germinal epithelium n : the epithelial covering of the genital ridges and of the gonads derived from them

germinal vesicle n : the enlarged nucleus of the egg before completion of meiosis

ger·mi·na·tive layer \ˈjər-mə-ˌnā-tiv-, -nə-\ n : the innermost layer of the epidermis from which new tissue is constantly formed

germinativum — see STRATUM GERMINATIVUM

germ layer n : any of the three primary layers of cells differentiated in most embryos during and immediately following gastrulation

germ plasm n 1 : germ cells and their precursors serving as the bearers of heredity and being fundamentally independent of other cells 2 : the hereditary material of the germ cells : GENES

germ-proof \ˈjərm-ˌprüf\ adj : impervious to the penetration or action of germs

germ theory n : a theory in medicine: infections, contagious diseases, and various other conditions (as suppurative lesions) result from the action of microorganisms

geront- or geronto- comb form : aged one : old age (gerontology)

ger·on·tol·o·gist \ˌjer-ən-ˈtä-lə-jist\ n : a specialist in gerontology

ger·on·tol·o·gy \-jē\ n, pl -gies : the comprehensive study of aging and the problems of the aged — compare GERIATRIC 1 — ge·ron·to·log·i·cal \jə-ˌränt-ᵊl-ˈä-ji-kəl\ also ge·ron·to·log·ic \-jik\ adj

Gerst·mann's syndrome \ˈgerst-mänz-, ˈgərst-mənz-\ n : cerebral dysfunction characterized esp. by finger agnosia, disorientation with respect to right and left, agraphia, and acalculia and caused by a lesion in the dominant cerebral hemisphere

Gerstmann, Josef (1887–1969), Austrian neurologist and psychiatrist.

Gerst·mann–Sträus·sler–Schein·ker syndrome \ˈgerst-män-ˈshtrȯis-lər-ˈshiŋ-kər-\ n : GERSTMANN'S SYNDROME — called also Gerstmann-Sträussler-Scheinker disease

ge·stalt \gə-ˈstält, -ˈshtält, -ˈstȯlt, -ˈshtȯlt\ n, pl ge·stalt·en \-ᵊn\ or ge·stalts : a structure, arrangement, or pattern of physical, biological, or psychological phenomena so integrated as to constitute a functional unit with properties not derivable by summation of its parts

ge·stalt·ist \gə-'stäl-tist, -'shtäl-, -'stòl-, -'shtòl-\ *n, often cap* : a specialist in Gestalt psychology

Gestalt psychology *n* : the study of perception and behavior from the standpoint of an individual's response to gestalten with stress on the uniformity of psychological and physiological events and rejection of analysis into discrete events of stimulus, percept, and response — **Gestalt psychologist** *n*

ges·ta·tion \je-'stā-shən\ *n* 1 : the carrying of young in the uterus from conception to delivery : PREGNANCY 2 : GESTATION PERIOD — **ges·tate** \'jes-ıtāt\ *vb* — **ges·ta·tion·al** \-shə-nəl\ *adj*

gestation period *n* : the length of time during which gestation takes place — called also *gestation*

ges·to·sis \je-'stō-səs\ *n, pl* **-to·ses** \-ısēz\ : any disorder of pregnancy; *esp* : TOXEMIA OF PREGNANCY

-geu·sia \'gü-zē-ə, 'jü-, -sē-ə, -zhə\ *n comb form* : a (specified) condition of the sense of taste (ag*eusia*) (dysg*eusia*)

GG *abbr* gamma globulin

GH *abbr* growth hormone

ghost \'gōst\ *n* : a structure (as a cell or tissue) that does not stain normally because of degenerative changes; *specif* : a red blood cell that has lost its hemoglobin

GI *abbr* gastrointestinal

giant cell *n* : a large multinucleate often phagocytic cell (as those characteristic of tubercular lesions or various sarcomas)

giant cell arteritis *n* : arterial inflammation that often involves the temporal arteries and may lead to blindness when the ophthalmic artery and its branches are affected, is characterized by the formation of giant cells, and may be accompanied by fever, malaise, fatigue, anorexia, weight loss, and arthralgia — called also *temporal arteritis*

giant–cell tumor *n* : an osteolytic tumor affecting the metaphyses and epiphyses of long bones that is usually benign but sometimes malignant — called also *osteoclastoma*

gi·ant·ism \'jī-ən-ıti-zəm\ *n* : GIGANTISM

giant kidney worm *n* : a blood-red nematode worm of the genus *Dioctophyme* (*D. renale*) that sometimes exceeds a yard in length and invades mammalian kidneys esp. of the dog and occas. of humans

giant urticaria *n* : ANGIOEDEMA

giant water bug *n* : any of a family (Belostomatidae and esp. genus *Lethocerus*) of very large predatory bugs capable of inflicting a painful bite

giar·dia \jē-'är-dē-ə, 'jär-\ *n* 1 *cap* : a genus of flagellate protozoans inhabiting the intestines of various mammals and including one (*G. lamblia*) that is associated with diarrhea in humans 2 : any flagellate of the genus *Giardia*

Giard \zhē-'är\, **Alfred Mathieu** (1846–1908), French biologist.

giar·di·a·sis \(ı)jē-ıär-'dī-ə-səs, ıjē-ər-, (ı)jär-\ *n, pl* **-a·ses** \-ısēz\ : infestation with or disease caused by a flagellate protozoan of the genus *Giardia* (esp. *G. lamblia*) that is often characterized by diarrhea — called also *lambliasis*

gid \'gid\ *n* : a disease esp. of sheep that is caused by the presence in the brain of the coenurus of a tapeworm of the genus *Multiceps* (*M. multiceps*) — called also *sturdy*

Giem·sa stain \gē-'em-zə-\ *also* **Giemsa's stain** *n* : a stain consisting of a mixture of eosin and a blue dye and used chiefly in differential staining of blood films — called also *Giemsa*

Giemsa, Gustav (1867–1948), German chemist and pharmacist.

gi·gan·tism \jī-'gan-ıti-zəm, jə-; 'jī-gən-\ *n* : development to abnormally large size from excessive growth of the long bones accompanied by muscular weakness and sexual impotence and usu. caused by hyperpituitarism before normal ossification is complete — called also *macrosomia*; compare ACROMEGALY

Gi·la monster \'hē-lə-\ *n* : a large orange and black venomous lizard of the genus *Heloderma* (*H. suspectum*) of the southwestern U.S.; *also* : the beaded lizard (*H. horridum*) of Mexico

Gil·bert's disease \zhil-'berz-\ *n* : a metabolic disorder prob. inherited as an autosomal dominant with variable penetrance and characterized by elevated levels of serum bilirubin caused esp. by defective uptake of bilirubin by the liver

Gilbert, Augustin–Nicholas (1858–1927), French physician.

Gil·christ's disease \'gil-ıkrists-\ *n* : NORTH AMERICAN BLASTOMYCOSIS

Gilchrist, Thomas Caspar (1862–1927), American dermatologist.

¹**gill** \'jil\ *n* : either of two units of capacity: **a** : a British unit equal to ¼ imperial pint or 8.669 cubic inches **b** : a U.S. liquid unit equal to ¼ U.S. liquid pint or 7.218 cubic inches

²**gill** \'gil\ *n* 1 : an organ (as of a fish) for obtaining oxygen from water 2 : one of the radiating plates forming the undersurface of the cap of a mushroom — **gilled** \'gild\ *adj*

gill arch *n* : one of the bony or cartilaginous arches placed one behind the other on each side of the pharynx and supporting the gills of fishes and amphibians; *also* : BRANCHIAL ARCH

gill cleft *n* : GILL SLIT

Gilles de la Tou·rette syndrome \'zhēl-də-lä-tü-'ret\ *also* **Gilles de la Tourette's syndrome** *n* : TOURETTE'S SYNDROME

gill slit *n* : one of the openings or clefts between the gill arches in vertebrates that breathe by gills through which water taken in at the mouth passes to the exterior and bathes the gills; *also* : BRANCHIAL CLEFT

gingiv- *or* **gingivo-** *comb form* 1 : gum : gums (*gingivitis*) 2 : gums and (*gingivostomatitis*)

gin·gi·va \ˌjin-jə-və, jin-ˈjī-\ *n, pl* **-vae** \-ˌvē, -ˌvī\ : ¹GUM — **gin·gi·val** \ˈjin-jə-vəl\ *adj*

gingival crevice *n* : a narrow space between the free margin of the gingival epithelium and the adjacent enamel of a tooth — called also *gingival trough*

gingival papilla *n* : INTERDENTAL PAPILLA

gingival trough *n* : GINGIVAL CREVICE

gin·gi·vec·to·my \ˌjin-jə-ˈvek-tə-mē\ *n, pl* **-mies** : the excision of a portion of the gingiva

gin·gi·vi·tis \ˌjin-jə-ˈvī-təs\ *n* : inflammation of the gums

gin·gi·vo·plas·ty \ˈjin-jə-və-ˌplas-tē\ *n, pl* **-ties** : a surgical procedure that involves reshaping the gums for aesthetic or functional purposes

gin·gi·vo·sto·ma·ti·tis \ˌjin-jə-vō-ˌstō-mə-ˈtī-təs\ *n, pl* **-tit·i·des** \-ˈti-tə-ˌdēz\ *or* **-ti·tis·es** : inflammation of the gums and of the mouth

gin·gly·mus \ˈjin-glə-məs, ˈgin-\ *n, pl* **gin·gly·mi** \-ˌmī, -ˌmē\ : a hinge joint (as between the humerus and ulna) allowing motion in one plane only

gin·seng \ˈjin-ˌseŋ, -ˌsiŋ\ *n* : the aromatic root of a Chinese perennial herb (*Panax schinseng* of the family Araliaceae, the ginseng family) valued esp. locally as a medicine; *also* : the plant

gir·dle \ˈgərd-ᵊl\ *n* : either of two more or less complete bony rings at the anterior and posterior ends of the vertebrate trunk supporting the arms and legs respectively: a : PECTORAL GIRDLE b : PELVIC GIRDLE

gi·tal·in \ˈji-tə-lən; jə-ˈtā-lən, -ˈta-\ *n* 1 : a crystalline glycoside $C_{35}H_{56}O_{12}$ obtained from digitalis 2 : an amorphous water-soluble mixture of glycosides of digitalis used similarly to digitalis

gi·tox·in \jə-ˈtäk-sən\ *n* : a poisonous crystalline steroid glycoside $C_{41}H_{64}O_{14}$ that is obtained from digitalis and from lanatoside B by hydrolysis

give \ˈgiv\ *vb* **gave** \ˈgāv\; **giv·en** \ˈgiv-ən\; **giv·ing** 1 : to administer as a medicine 2 : to cause a person to catch by contagion, infection, or exposure

giz·zard \ˈgi-zərd\ *n* : the muscular usu. horny-lined enlargement of the alimentary canal of a bird used for churning and grinding food

gla·bel·la \glə-ˈbe-lə\ *n, pl* **-bel·lae** \-ˈbe-(ˌ)lē, -ˌlī\ : the smooth prominence between the eyebrows — **gla·bel·lar** \-ˈbe-lər\ *adj*

gla·brous \ˈglā-brəs\ *adj* : having or being a smooth hairless surface (~ skin)

glacial acetic acid *n* : acetic acid containing usu. less than 1 percent of water

glad·i·o·lus \ˌgla-dē-ˈō-ləs\ *n, pl* **-li** \-(ˌ)lē, -ˌlī\ : the large middle portion of the sternum lying between the upper manubrium and the lower xiphoid process — called also *mesosternum*

glairy \ˈglar-ē\ *adj* **glair·i·er; -est** : having a slimy viscid consistency suggestive of an egg white

gland \ˈgland\ *n* 1 : a cell, group of cells, or organ of endothelial origin that selectively removes materials from the blood, concentrates or alters them, and secretes them for further use in the body or for elimination from the body 2 : any of various animal structures (as a lymph node) suggestive of glands though not secretory in function — **gland·less** *adj*

glan·dered \ˈglan-dərd\ *adj* : affected with glanders

glan·ders \-dərz\ *n sing or pl* : a contagious and destructive disease esp. of horses caused by a bacterium of the genus *Pseudomonas* (*P. mallei*) and characterized by caseating nodular lesions esp. of the respiratory mucosae and lungs

glandes *pl of* GLANS

gland of Bartholin *n* : BARTHOLIN'S GLAND

gland of Bow·man \-ˈbō-mən\ *n* : any of the tubular and often branched glands occurring beneath the olfactory epithelium of the nose — called also *Bowman's gland, olfactory gland*
W. **Bowman** — see BOWMAN'S CAPSULE

gland of Brunner *n* : BRUNNER'S GLAND

gland of external secretion *n* : EXOCRINE GLAND

gland of internal secretion *n* : ENDOCRINE GLAND

gland of Lit·tré \-lē-ˈtrā\ *n* : any of the urethral glands of the male
Littré, Alexis (1658–1726), French surgeon and anatomist.

gland of Moll \-ˈmōl, -ˈmȯl, -ˈmäl\ *n* : any of the small glands near the free margin of each eyelid regarded as modified sweat glands
Moll \ˈmȯl\, **Jacob Antonius** (1832–1914), Dutch ophthalmologist.

gland of Ty·son \-ˈtīs-ᵊn\ *n* : any of the small glands at the base of the glans penis that secrete smegma — called also *preputial gland*
Tyson, Edward (1650–1708), British anatomist.

glan·du·lar \ˈglan-jə-lər\ *adj* 1 : of, relating to, or involving glands, gland cells, or their products 2 : having the characteristics or function of a gland (~ tissue)

glandular fever *n* : INFECTIOUS MONONUCLEOSIS

glan·du·lous \'glan-jə-ləs\ *adj* : GLANDULAR

glans \'glanz\ *n, pl* **glan·des** \'glan-ˌdēz\ 1 : a conical vascular body forming the extremity of the penis 2 : a conical vascular body that forms the extremity of the clitoris and is similar to the glans penis

glans cli·tor·i·dis \-klə-'tȯr-ə-(ˌ)dis\ : GLANS 2

glans penis *n* : GLANS 1

Gla·se·ri·an fissure \glə-'zir-ē-ən-\ *n* : PETROTYMPANIC FISSURE

    Gla·ser \'glä-zər\, **Johann Heinrich (1629–1675),** Swiss anatomist and surgeon.

glass·es \'gla-səz\ *n pl* : a device used to correct defects of vision or to protect the eyes that consists typically of a pair of glass or plastic lenses and the frame by which they are held in place — called also *eyeglasses*

glass eye *n* 1 : an artificial eye made of glass 2 : an eye having a pale, whitish, or colorless iris — **glass-eyed** \-'īd\ *adj*

Glau·ber's salt \'glau̇-bərz-\ *also* **Glauber salt** \-bər-\ *n* : a colorless crystalline sodium sulfate $Na_2SO_4 \cdot 10H_2O$ used as a cathartic — sometimes used in pl.

    Glauber, Johann Rudolf (1604–1670), German physician and chemist.

glau·co·ma \glau̇-'kō-mə, glȯ-\ *n* : a disease of the eye marked by increased pressure within the eyeball that can result in damage to the optic disk and gradual loss of vision — **glau·coma·tous** \-'kō-mə-təs, -'kä-\ *adj*

GLC *abbr* gas-liquid chromatography

gleet \'glēt\ *n* : a chronic inflammation (as gonorrhea) of a bodily orifice usu. accompanied by an abnormal discharge; *also* : the discharge itself

gle·no·hu·mer·al \ˌgle-(ˌ)nō-'hyü-mə-rəl, ˌglē-\ *adj* : of, relating to, or connecting the glenoid cavity and the humerus

glen·oid \'gle-ˌnȯid, 'glē-\ *adj* 1 : having the form of a smooth shallow depression — used chiefly of skeletal articulatory sockets 2 : of or relating to the glenoid cavity or glenoid fossa

glenoid cavity *n* : the shallow cavity of the upper part of the scapula by which the humerus articulates with the pectoral girdle

glenoid fossa *n* : the depression in each lateral wall of the skull with which the mandible articulates — called also *mandibular fossa*

glenoid labrum *or* **glen·oid·al labrum** \gli-'nȯid-ᵊl-\ *n* : a fibrocartilaginous ligament forming the margin of the glenoid cavity of the shoulder joint that serves to broaden and deepen the cavity and gives attachment to the long head of the biceps brachii — called also *labrum*

gli- *or* **glio-** *comb form* 1 : gliomatous (*glioblastoma*) 2 : neuroglial (*glioma*)

glia \'glē-ə, 'glī-ə\ *n* : NEUROGLIA — **gli·al** \-əl\ *adj*

-glia \glē-ə\ *n comb form* : neuroglia made up of a (specified) kind or size of element (microglia) (oligodendroglia)

gli·a·din \'glī-ə-dən\ *n* : PROLAMIN; *esp* : one obtained by alcoholic extraction of gluten from wheat and rye

gliding joint *n* : a diarthrosis in which the articular surfaces glide upon each other without axial motion — called also *arthrodia, plane joint*

glio·blas·to·ma \ˌglī-(ˌ)ō-bla-'stō-mə\ *n, pl* **-mas** *or* **-ma·ta** \-mə-tə\ : a malignant tumor of the central nervous system and usu. of a cerebral hemisphere — called also *spongioblastoma*

glioblastoma mul·ti·for·me \-ˌməl-tə-'for-mē\ *n* : GLIOBLASTOMA

Glio·cla·di·um \ˌglī-ō-'klä-dē-əm\ *n* : a genus of molds resembling those of the genus *Penicillium* — see GLIOTOXIN

gli·o·ma \glī-'ō-mə, glē-\ *n, pl* **-mas** *or* **-ma·ta** \-mə-tə\ : a tumor arising from neuroglia — **gli·o·ma·tous** \-mə-təs\ *adj*

gli·o·ma·to·sis \glī-ˌō-mə-'tō-səs\ *n, pl* **-to·ses** \-ˌsēz\ : a glioma with diffuse proliferation of glial cells or with multiple foci

gli·o·sis \glī-'ō-səs\ *n, pl* **gli·o·ses** \-ˌsēz\ : excessive development of neuroglia esp. interstitially — **gli·ot·ic** \-'ä-tik\ *adj*

gli·o·tox·in \ˌglī-ō-'täk-sən\ *n* : a toxic antibiotic $C_{13}H_{14}N_2O_4S_2$ that is produced by various fungi esp. of the genus *Gliocladium*

Glisson's capsule \'glis-ᵊnz-\ *n* : an investment of loose connective tissue entering the liver with the portal vessels and sheathing the larger vessels in their course through the organ

    Glisson, Francis (1597–1677), British physician and anatomist.

globe \'glōb\ *n* : EYEBALL

globe·fish \'glōb-ˌfish\ *n* : PUFFER

glo·bin \'glō-bən\ *n* : a colorless protein obtained by removal of heme from a conjugated protein and esp. hemoglobin

glo·bo·side \'glō-bə-ˌsīd\ *n* : a complex glycolipid that occurs in the red blood cells, serum, liver, and spleen of humans and accumulates in tissues in one of the variants of Tay-Sachs disease

glob·u·lar \'glä-byə-lər\ *adj* 1 a : having the shape of a globe or globule b : having a compact folded molecular structure ⟨∼ proteins⟩ 2 : having or consisting of globules — **glob·u·lar·ly** \-lē\ *adv*

glob·ule \'glä-(ˌ)byül\ *n* : a small globular body or mass (as a drop of water, fat, or sweat)

glob·u·lin \\'glä-byə-lən\\ *n* : any of a class of simple proteins (as myosin) that occur widely in plant and animal tissues — see ALPHA GLOBULIN, BETA GLOBULIN, GAMMA GLOBULIN

glo·bus hys·ter·i·cus \\'glō-bəs-his-'ter-i-kəs\\ *n* : a choking sensation commonly experienced in hysteria

globus pal·li·dus \\-'pa-lə-dəs\\ *n* : the median portion of the lentiform nucleus — called also *pallidum*

glom·an·gi·o·ma \\,glō-man-jē-'ō-ma\\ *n, pl* **-mas** *or* **-ma·ta** \\-mə-tə\\ : GLOMUS TUMOR

glo·mec·to·my \\glō-'mek-tə-mē\\ *n, pl* **-mies** : excision of a glomus (as the carotid body)

glomerul- *or* **glomerulo-** *comb form* : glomerulus of the kidney ⟨*glomerulitis*⟩ ⟨*glomerulonephritis*⟩

glo·mer·u·lar \\glə-'mer-yə-lər, -ə-lər\\ *adj* : of, relating to, or produced by a glomerulus ⟨∼ nephritis⟩

glomerular capsule *n* : BOWMAN'S CAPSULE

glo·mer·u·li·tis \\glə-,mer-yə-'lī-təs, glō-, -ə-'lī-\\ *n* : inflammation of the glomeruli of the kidney

glo·mer·u·lo·ne·phri·tis \\-,mer-yə-lō-ni-'frī-təs, -ə-lō-\\ *n, pl* **-phrit·i·des** \\-'fri-tə-,dēz\\ : nephritis marked by inflammation of the capillaries of the renal glomeruli

glo·mer·u·lo·sa \\glə-,mer-yə-'lō-sə, -'lō-, -zə\\ *n, pl* **-sae** \\-,sē, -,sī, -,zē, -,zī\\ : ZONA GLOMERULOSA

glo·mer·u·lo·scle·ro·sis \\-,lō-sklə-'rō-səs\\ *n, pl* **-ro·ses** \\-,sēz\\ : nephrosclerosis involving the renal glomeruli

glo·mer·u·lus \\glə-'mer-yə-ləs, -ə-ləs\\ *n, pl* **-li** \\-,lī, -,lē\\ : a small convoluted or intertwined mass: as **a** : a tuft of capillaries at the point of origin of each nephron that passes a protein-free filtrate to the surrounding Bowman's capsule **b** : a dense entanglement of nerve fibers situated in the olfactory bulb and containing the primary synapses of the olfactory pathway

glo·mus \\'glō-məs\\ *n, pl* **glom·era** \\'glä-mə-rə\\ *also* **glo·mi** \\'glō-,mī, -,mē\\ : a small arteriovenous anastomosis together with its supporting structures: as **a** : a vascular tuft that suggests a renal glomerulus and that develops from the embryonic aorta in relation to the pronephros **b** : CAROTID BODY **c** : a tuft of the choroid plexus protruding into each lateral ventricle of the brain

glomus ca·rot·i·cum \\-kə-'rä-ti-kəm\\ *n* : CAROTID BODY

glomus coc·cy·ge·um \\-käk-'si-jē-əm\\ *n* : a small mass of vascular tissue situated near the tip of the coccyx — called also *coccygeal body, coccygeal gland*

glomus jug·u·la·re \\-,jə-gyə-'lar-ē\\ *n* : a mass of chemoreceptors in the adventitia of the dilation in the internal jug-ular vein where it arises from the transverse sinus in the jugular foramen

glomus tumor *n* : a painful benign tumor that develops by hypertrophy of a glomus — called also *glomangioma*

gloss- *or* **glosso-** *comb form* **1** : tongue ⟨*glossitis*⟩ ⟨*glossopathy*⟩ **2** : language ⟨*glossolalia*⟩

glos·sal \\'glä-səl, 'glō-\\ *adj* : of or relating to the tongue

-glos·sia \\'glä-sē-ə, 'glō-\\ *n comb form* : condition of having (such) a tongue ⟨*microglossia*⟩

Glos·si·na \\glä-'sī-nə, glō-, -'sē-\\ *n 1 cap* : an African genus of dipteran flies with a long slender sharp proboscis that includes the tsetse flies — compare SLEEPING SICKNESS **2** : any dipteran fly of the genus *Glossina* : TSETSE FLY

glos·si·tis \\-'sī-təs\\ *n* : inflammation of the tongue

glosso- — see GLOSS-

gloss·odyn·ia \\,glä-sō-'di-nē-ə, ,glō-\\ *n* : pain localized in the tongue

glos·so·la·lia \\,glä-sə-'lā-lē-ə, ,glō-\\ *n* : profuse and often emotionally charged speech that mimics coherent speech but is usu. unintelligible to the listener and that is uttered in some states of religious ecstasy and in some schizophrenic states

glos·so·pal·a·tine arch \\,glä-sō-'pa-lə-,tīn-, ,glō-\\ *n* : PALATOGLOSSAL ARCH

glossopalatine nerve *n* : NERVUS INTERMEDIUS

glos·so·pal·a·ti·nus \\-,pa-lə-'tī-nəs\\ *n, pl* **-ni** \\-,nī, -,nē\\ : PALATOGLOSSUS

glos·sop·a·thy \\glä-'sä-pə-thē\\ *n, pl* **-thies** : a disease of the tongue

glos·so·pha·ryn·geal \\,glä-sō-fə-'rin-jē-əl, ,glō-, -jəl; -,far-ən-'jē-əl\\ *adj* **1** : of or relating to both tongue and pharynx **2** : of, relating to, or affecting the glossopharyngeal nerve ⟨∼ lesions⟩

glossopharyngeal nerve *n* : either of the 9th pair of cranial nerves that are mixed nerves and supply chiefly the pharynx, posterior tongue, and parotid gland with motor and sensory fibers — called also *glossopharyngeal, ninth cranial nerve*

glottidis — see RIMA GLOTTIDIS

glot·tis \\'glä-təs\\ *n, pl* **glot·tis·es** *or* **glot·ti·des** \\-tə-,dēz\\ : the space between one of the true vocal cords and the arytenoid cartilage on one side of the larynx and those on the other side; *also* : the structures that surround this space — compare EPIGLOTTIS

gluc- *or* **gluco-** *comb form* : glucose ⟨*glucokinase*⟩ ⟨*gluconeogenesis*⟩

glu·ca·gon \\'glü-kə-,gän\\ *n* : a protein hormone that is produced esp. by the pancreatic islets of Langerhans and that promotes an increase in the sugar content of the blood by increasing the rate of breakdown of glycogen in the liver — called also *hyperglycemic factor*

glu·can \\'glü-ˌkan, -kən\ *n* : a polysaccharide (as glycogen) that is a polymer of glucose

glu·co·ce·re·bro·si·dase \ˌglü-kō-ˌser-ə-'brō-sə-ˌdās, -ˌdāz\ *n* : an enzyme that catalyzes the hydrolysis of the glucose part of a glucocerebroside and is deficient in patients affected with Gaucher's disease

glu·co·ce·re·bro·side \-'ser-ə-brə-ˌsīd, -sə-'rē-\ *n* : a lipid composed of a ceramide and glucose that accumulates in the tissues of patients affected with Gaucher's disease

glu·co·cor·ti·coid \-'kȯr-ti-ˌkȯid\ *n* : any of a group of corticosteroids (as hydrocortisone or dexamethasone) that are involved esp. in carbohydrate, protein, and fat metabolism, that tend to increase liver glycogen and blood sugar by increasing gluconeogenesis, that are anti-inflammatory and immunosuppressive, and that are used widely in medicine (as in the alleviation of the symptoms of rheumatoid arthritis) — compare MINERALOCORTICOID

glu·co·ki·nase \-'kī-ˌnās, -ˌnāz\ *n* : a hexokinase found esp. in the liver that catalyzes the phosphorylation of glucose

glu·co·nate \'glü-kə-ˌnāt\ *n* : a salt or ester of a crystalline acid $C_6H_{12}O_7$ — see CALCIUM GLUCONATE, FERROUS GLUCONATE

glu·co·neo·gen·e·sis \ˌglü-kə-ˌnē-ə-'je-nə-səs\ *n, pl* **-e·ses** \-ˌsēz\ : formation of glucose esp. by the liver and kidney from substances (as fats and proteins) other than carbohydrates — **glu·co·neo·gen·ic** \-'je-nik\ *adj*

glu·cos·amine \glü-'kō-sə-ˌmēn, -zə-\ *n* : an amino derivative $C_6H_{13}NO_5$ of glucose that occurs esp. as a constituent of polysaccharides in animal supporting structures and some plant cell walls

glu·cose \'glü-ˌkōs, -ˌkōz\ *n* : a sugar $C_6H_{12}O_6$ known in dextrorotatory, levorotatory, and racemic forms; *esp* : the sweet soluble dextrorotatory form that occurs widely in nature and is the usual form in which carbohydrate is assimilated by animals

glucose–1–phosphate *n* : an ester $C_6H_{13}O_9P$ that reacts in the presence of a phosphorylase with aldoses and ketoses to yield disaccharides or with itself in liver and muscle to yield glycogen and phosphoric acid

glucose phosphate *n* : a phosphate ester of glucose: as **a** : GLUCOSE-1-PHOSPHATE **b** : GLUCOSE-6-PHOSPHATE

glucose–6–phosphate *n* : an ester $C_6H_{13}O_9P$ that is formed from glucose and ATP in the presence of a glucokinase and that is an essential early stage in glucose metabolism

glucose–6–phosphate dehydrogenase *n* : an enzyme found esp. in red blood cells that dehydrogenates glucose-6-

phosphate in a glucose degradation pathway alternative to the Krebs cycle

glucose–6–phosphate dehydrogenase deficiency *n* : a hereditary metabolic disorder affecting red blood cells that is controlled by a variable gene on the X chromosome, that is characterized by a deficiency of glucose-6-phosphate dehydrogenase conferring marked susceptibility to hemolytic anemia which may be chronic, episodic, or induced by certain foods (as broad beans) or drugs (as primaquine), and that occurs esp. in individuals of Mediterranean or African descent

glucose tolerance test *n* : a test of the body's powers of metabolizing glucose that involves the administration of a measured dose of glucose to the fasting stomach and the determination of glucose levels in the blood and urine at measured intervals thereafter

glu·cos·uria \ˌglü-kō-'shuṙ-ē-ə, -'syuṙ-\ *n* : GLYCOSURIA

gluc·uron·ic acid \ˌglü-kyə-'rä-nik-\ : a compound $C_6H_{10}O_7$ that occurs esp. as a constituent of glycosaminoglycans and combined as a glucuronide

gluc·uron·i·dase \-'rä-nə-ˌdās, -ˌdāz\ *n* : an enzyme that hydrolyzes a glucuronide

gluc·uron·ide \glü-'kyuṙ-ə-ˌnīd\ *n* : any of various derivatives of glucuronic acid that are formed esp. as combinations with often toxic aromatic hydroxyl compounds (as phenols) and are excreted in the urine

glue–sniffing *n* : the deliberate inhalation of volatile organic solvents from plastic glues that may result in symptoms ranging from mild euphoria to disorientation and coma

glu·ta·mate \'glü-tə-ˌmāt\ *n* : a salt or ester of glutamic acid; *esp* : one that is an excitatory neurotransmitter in the central nervous system : MONOSODIUM GLUTAMATE

glutamate dehydrogenase *n* : an enzyme present esp. in liver mitochondria and cytosol that catalyzes the oxidation of glutamate to ammonia and α-ketoglutaric acid

glu·tam·ic acid \(ˌ)glü-'ta-mik-\ *n* : a crystalline amino acid $C_5H_9NO_4$ widely distributed in plant and animal proteins

glutamic–ox·a·lo·ace·tic transaminase \-ˌak-sə-lō-ə-'sē-tik-\ *also* **glutamic-ox·al·ace·tic transaminase** \-ˌak-sə-lə-'sē-tik-\ *n* : an enzyme that promotes transfer of an amino group from glutamic acid to oxaloacetic acid and that when present in abnormally high levels in the blood is a diagnostic indication of myocardial infarction or liver disease

glutamic pyruvic transaminase *n* : an enzyme that promotes transfer of an amino group from glutamic acid to pyruvic acid and that when present in abnormally high levels in the blood is a diagnostic indication of liver disease

glu·ta·mine \'glü-tə-ˌmēn\ n : a crystalline amino acid $C_5H_{10}N_2O_3$ that is found both free and in proteins in plants and animals and that yields glutamic acid and ammonia on hydrolysis

glu·tar·al·de·hyde \ˌglü-tə-'ral-də-ˌhīd\ n : a compound $C_5H_8O_2$ used esp. as a disinfectant and in fixing biological tissues

glu·tar·ic acid \glü-ˌtar-ik-\ n : a crystalline acid $C_5H_8O_4$ used esp. in organic synthesis

glu·ta·thi·one \ˌglü-tə-'thī-ˌōn\ n : a peptide $C_{10}H_{17}N_3O_6S$ that contains one amino-acid residue each of glutamic acid, cysteine, and glycine, that occurs widely in plant and animal tissues, and that plays an important role in biological oxidation-reduction processes and as a coenzyme

glute \'glüt\ n : GLUTEUS — usu. used in pl.

glu·te·al \'glü-tē-əl, glü-'tē-\ adj : of or relating to the buttocks or the gluteus muscles

gluteal artery n : either of two branches of the internal iliac artery that supply the gluteal region: **a** : the largest branch of the internal iliac artery that sends branches esp. to the gluteal muscles — called also superior gluteal artery **b** : a branch that is distributed esp. to the buttocks and the backs of the thighs — called also inferior gluteal artery

gluteal nerve n : either of two nerves arising from the sacral plexus and supplying the gluteal muscles and adjacent parts: **a** : one arising from the posterior part of the fourth and fifth lumbar nerves and from the first sacral nerve and distributed to the gluteus muscles and to the tensor fasciae latae — called also superior gluteal nerve **b** : one arising from the posterior part of the fifth lumbar nerve and from the first and second sacral nerves and distributed to the gluteus maximus — called also inferior gluteal nerve

gluteal tuberosity n : the lateral ridge of the linea aspera of the femur that gives attachment to the gluteus maximus

glu·ten \'glüt-ᵊn\ n : a gluey protein substance that causes dough to be sticky

glutes pl of GLUTE

glu·teth·i·mide \glü-'te-thə-ˌmīd, -məd\ n : a sedative-hypnotic drug $C_{13}H_{15}NO_2$ that induces sleep with less depression of respiration than occurs with comparable doses of barbiturates

glu·te·us \'glü-tē-əs, glü-'tē-\ n, pl glu-

tei \'glü-tē-ˌī, -tē-ˌē; glü-'tē-ˌī\ : any of three large muscles of the buttocks: **a** : GLUTEUS MAXIMUS **b** : GLUTEUS MEDIUS **c** : GLUTEUS MINIMUS

gluteus max·i·mus \-'mak-sə-məs\ n, pl **glutei max·i·mi** \-sə-ˌmī\ : the outermost of the three muscles in each buttock that acts to extend and laterally rotate the thigh

gluteus me·di·us \-'mē-dē-us\ n, pl **glutei me·dii** \-dē-ˌī\ : the middle of the three muscles in each buttock that acts to abduct and medially rotate the thigh

gluteus min·i·mus \-'mi-nə-məs\ n, pl **glutei min·i·mi** \-ˌmī\ : the innermost of the three muscles in each buttock that acts similarly to the gluteus medius

glyc- or **glyco-** comb form : carbohydrate and esp. sugar ⟨glycolysis⟩ ⟨glycoprotein⟩

gly·cae·mia chiefly Brit var of GLYCEMIA

gly·can \'glī-ˌkan\ n : POLYSACCHARIDE

gly·ce·mia \glī-'sē-mē-ə\ n : the presence of glucose in the blood — **gly·ce·mic** \-'sē-mik\ adj

glycer- or **glycero-** comb form 1 : glycerol ⟨glyceryl⟩ 2 : related to glycerol or glyceric acid ⟨glyceraldehyde⟩

glyc·er·al·de·hyde \ˌgli-sə-'ral-də-ˌhīd\ n : a sweet crystalline compound $C_3H_6O_3$ that is formed as an intermediate in carbohydrate metabolism

gly·cer·ic acid \gli-'ser-ik-\ n : a syrupy acid $C_3H_6O_4$ obtainable by oxidation of glycerol or glyceraldehyde

glyc·er·ide \'gli-sə-ˌrīd\ n : an ester of glycerol esp. with fatty acids

glyc·er·in or **glyc·er·ine** \'gli-sə-rən\ n : GLYCEROL

glycero- — see GLYCER-

glyc·er·ol \'gli-sə-ˌrȯl, -ˌrōl\ n : a sweet syrupy hygroscopic alcohol $C_3H_8O_3$ containing three hydroxy groups per molecule, usu. obtained by the saponification of fats, and used as a moistening agent, emollient, and lubricant, and as an emulsifying agent — called also glycerin

glyc·er·yl \'gli-sə-rəl\ n : a radical derived from glycerol by removal of hydroxide; esp : a trivalent radical CH_2CHCH_2

glyceryl guai·a·col·ate \-'gwī-ə-ˌkȯ-ˌlāt, -'gī-, -kə-\ n : GUAIFENESIN

gly·cine \'glī-ˌsēn, 'glīs-ᵊn\ n : a sweet crystalline amino acid $C_2H_5NO_2$ obtained esp. by hydrolysis of proteins and used esp. as an antacid

gly·cin·uria \ˌglīs-ᵊn-'ūr-ē-ə, -'yùr-\ n : a kidney disorder characterized by the presence of excessive amounts of glycine in the urine

glyco- — see GLYC-

gly·co·bi·ar·sol \ˌglī-kō-(ˌ)bī-'är-ˌsȯl, -ˌsōl\ n : an antiprotozoal drug $C_8H_9AsBiNO_6$ used esp. in the treatment of intestinal amebiasis — see MILIBIS

gly·co·chol·ic acid \glī-kō-ˈkä-lik-, -ˈkō-\ n : a crystalline acid $C_{26}H_{43}NO_6$ that occurs in bile

gly·co·con·ju·gate \glī-kō-ˈkän-ji-gət, -ˌgāt\ n : any of a group of compounds (as the glycolipids and glycoproteins) consisting of sugars linked to proteins or lipids

gly·co·gen \ˈglī-kə-jən\ n : a white amorphous tasteless polysaccharide $(C_6H_{10}O_5)x$ that constitutes the principal form in which carbohydrate is stored in animal tissues and esp. in muscle and liver tissue — called also *animal starch*

gly·cog·e·nase \glī-ˈkä-jə-ˌnās, -ˌnāz\ n : an enzyme that catalyzes the hydrolysis of glycogen

gly·co·gen·e·sis \glī-kə-ˈje-nə-səs\ n, pl -e·ses \-ˌsēz\ : the formation and storage of glycogen — compare GLYCOGENOLYSIS

gly·co·gen·ic \-ˈje-nik\ adj : of, relating to, or involving glycogen or glycogenesis

gly·co·gen·ol·y·sis \glī-kə-jə-ˈnä-lə-səs\ n, pl -y·ses \-ˌsēz\ : the breakdown of glycogen esp. to glucose in the body — compare GLYCOGENESIS — **gly·co·gen·o·lyt·ic** \-jən-ᵊl-ˈi-tik, -ˌjen-\ adj

gly·co·ge·no·sis \glī-kə-jə-ˈnō-səs\ n, pl -no·ses \-ˌsēz\ : GLYCOGEN STORAGE DISEASE

glycogen storage disease n : any of several metabolic disorders (as McArdle's disease or Pompe's disease) that are characterized esp. by abnormal deposits of glycogen in tissue, are caused by enzyme deficiencies in glycogen metabolism, and are usu. inherited as an autosomal recessive trait

gly·co·lip·id \glī-kō-ˈli-pəd\ n : a lipid (as a ganglioside or a cerebroside) that contains a carbohydrate radical

gly·col·y·sis \glī-ˈkä-lə-səs\ n, pl -y·ses \-ˌsēz\ : the enzymatic breakdown of a carbohydrate (as glucose) by way of phosphate derivatives with the production of pyruvic or lactic acid and energy stored in high-energy phosphate bonds of ATP — **gly·co·lyt·ic** \glī-kə-ˈli-tik\ adj — **gly·co·lyt·i·cal·ly** adv

gly·co·pep·tide \glī-kō-ˈpep-ˌtīd\ n : GLYCOPROTEIN

gly·co·pro·tein \-ˈprō-ˌtēn, -ˈprō-tē-ən\ n : a conjugated protein in which the nonprotein group is a carbohydrate — compare MUCOPROTEIN

gly·co·pyr·ro·late \-ˈpī-rə-ˌlāt\ n : a synthetic anticholinergic drug $C_{19}H_{28}BrNO_3$ used in the treatment of gastrointestinal disorders (as peptic ulcer) esp. when associated with hyperacidity, hypermotility, or spasm — see ROBINUL

gly·co·sa·mi·no·gly·can \glī-kō-sə-ˌmē-nō-ˈglī-ˌkan, -kō-ˌsa-mə-nō-\ n : any of various polysaccharides derived from an amino hexose that are constituents of mucoproteins, glycoproteins, and blood-group substances — called also *mucopolysaccharide*

gly·co·side \ˈglī-kə-ˌsīd\ n : any of numerous sugar derivatives that contain a nonsugar group attached through an oxygen or nitrogen bond and that on hydrolysis yield a sugar (as glucose) — **gly·co·sid·ic** \glī-kə-ˈsi-dik\ adj — **gly·co·sid·i·cal·ly** adv

gly·co·sphin·go·lip·id \glī-kō-ˌsfiŋ-gō-ˈli-pəd\ n : any of various lipids (as a cerebroside or a ganglioside) which are derivatives of ceramides and some of which accumulate in disorders of lipid metabolism (as Tay-Sachs disease)

gly·cos·uria \glī-kō-ˈshür-ē-ə, -ˈsyür-\ n : the presence in the urine of abnormal amounts of sugar — called also *glucosuria* — **gly·cos·uric** \-ˈshür-ik, -ˈsyür-\ adj

gly·cyr·rhi·za \glī-sə-ˈrī-zə\ n : the dried root of a licorice (*Glycyrrhiza glabra* of the legume family, Leguminosae) that is a source of extracts used to mask unpleasant flavors (as in drugs) or to give a pleasant taste (as to confections) — called also *licorice, licorice root*

gm abbr gram

GM and S abbr General Medicine and Surgery

GM–CSF abbr granulocyte-macrophage colony-stimulating factor

GN abbr graduate nurse

gnat \ˈnat\ n : any of various small usu. biting dipteran flies (as a midge or blackfly)

gna·thi·on \ˈnā-thē-ˌän, ˈna-\ n : the midpoint of the lower border of the human mandible

gna·thos·to·mi·a·sis \nə-ˌthäs-tə-ˈmī-ə-səs\ n, pl -a·ses \-ˌsēz\ : infestation with or disease caused by nematode worms (genus *Gnathostoma*) commonly acquired by eating raw fish

-gna·thous \g-nə-thəs\ adj comb form : having (such) a jaw (prognathous)

-gno·sia \g-ˈnō-zhə\ n comb form : -GNOSIS (agnosia) (prosopagnosia)

-gno·sis \g-ˈnō-səs\ n comb form, pl -g·no·ses \-ˌsēz\ : knowledge : cognition : recognition (stereognosis)

-gnos·tic \g-ˈnäs-tik\ adj comb form : characterized by or relating to (such) knowledge (pharmacognostic)

-gno·sy \g-nə-sē\ n comb form, pl -g·no·sies : -GNOSIS (pharmacognosy)

GnRH abbr gonadotropin-releasing hormone

goal–directed adj : aimed toward a goal or toward completion of a task ⟨~ behavior⟩

goblet cell n : a mucus-secreting epithelial cell (as of columnar epithelium) that is distended with secretion or its precursors at the free end

goi·ter \ˈgȯi-tər\ n : an enlargement of the thyroid gland that is commonly visible as a swelling of the anterior part of the neck, that often results from insufficient intake of iodine and then is usu. accompanied by hypothyroidism, and that in other cases is associated with hyperthyroidism usu. together with toxic symptoms and exophthalmos — called also *struma* — **goi·trous** \'goi-trəs\ *also* **goi·ter·ous** \'goi-tə-rəs\ *adj*

goi·tre *chiefly Brit var of* GOITER

goi·tro·gen \'goi-trə-jən\ *n* : a substance (as thiourea or thiouracil) that induces goiter formation

goi·tro·gen·ic \ˌgoi-tə-'je-nik\ *also* **goi·ter·o·gen·ic** \ˌgoi-tə-rō-'je-nik\ *adj* : producing or tending to produce goiter (a ~ agent) — **goi·tro·gen·ic·i·ty** \ˌgoi-trə-jə-'ni-sə-tē\ *n*

gold \'gōld\ *n, often attrib* : a malleable ductile yellow metallic element used in the form of its salts (as gold sodium thiomalate) esp. in the treatment of rheumatoid arthritis — symbol *Au*; see ELEMENT table

gold sodium thio·ma·late \-ˌthī-ō-'ma-ˌlāt, -'mā-\ *n* : a gold salt $C_4H_3Au-Na_2O_4S \cdot H_2O$ used in the treatment of rheumatoid arthritis — called also *gold thiomalate*; see MYOCHRYSINE

gold sodium thiosulfate *n* : a soluble gold compound $Na_3Au(S_2O_3)_2 \cdot 2H_2O$ administered by intravenous injection in the treatment of rheumatoid arthritis and lupus erythematosus

gold thio·glu·cose \-ˌthī-ō-'glü-ˌkōs\ *n* : an organic compound of gold $C_6H_{11}AuO_5S$ injected intramuscularly in the treatment of active rheumatoid arthritis and nondisseminated lupus erythematosus — called also *aurothioglucose*

Gol·gi \'gōl-(ˌ)jē\ *adj* : of or relating to the Golgi apparatus, Golgi bodies, or the Golgi method of staining nerve tissue

Golgi, Camillo (1843 *or* 1844–1926), Italian histologist and pathologist.

Golgi apparatus *n* : a cytoplasmic organelle that consists of a stack of smooth membranous saccules and associated vesicles and that is active in the modification and transport of proteins — called also *Golgi complex*

Golgi body *n* : GOLGI APPARATUS; *also* : DICTYOSOME

Golgi cell *n* : a neuron with short dendrites and with either a long axon or an axon that breaks into processes soon after leaving the cell body

Golgi complex *n* : GOLGI APPARATUS

Golgi tendon organ *n* : a spindle-shaped sensory end organ within a tendon that provides information about muscle tension — called also *neurotendinous spindle*

go·mer \'gō-mər\ *n, med slang* : a chronic problem patient who does not respond to treatment — usu. used disparagingly

gom·pho·sis \gäm-'fō-səs\ *n* : an im-

movable articulation in which a hard part is received into a bone cavity (as the teeth into the jaws)

go·nad \'gō-ˌnad\ *n* : a gamete-producing reproductive gland (as an ovary or testis) — **go·nad·al** \gō-'nad-əl\ *adj*

go·nad·o·troph \gō-'na-də-ˌtrōf\ *n* : a cell of the adenohypophysis that secretes a gonadotropic hormone (as luteinizing hormone)

go·nad·o·trop·ic \gō-ˌna-də-'trä-pik\ *also* **go·nad·o·troph·ic** \-'trō-fik, -'trä-\ *adj* : acting on or stimulating the gonads

go·nad·o·tro·pin \-'trō-pən\ *also* **go·nad·o·tro·phin** \-fən\ *n* : a gonadotropic hormone (as follicle-stimulating hormone)

gonadotropin–releasing hormone *n* : a hormone produced by the hypothalamus that stimulates the adenohypophysis to release gonadotropins (as luteinizing hormone and follicle-stimulating hormone) — called also *luteinizing hormone-releasing hormone*

G₁ phase \ˌjē-'wən-\ *n* : the period in the cell cycle from the end of cell division to the beginning of DNA replication — compare G₂ PHASE, M PHASE, S PHASE

goni- *or* **gonio-** *comb form* : corner : angle ⟨*goniometer*⟩

gonial angle *n* : the angle formed by the junction of the posterior and lower borders of the human lower jaw — called also *angle of the jaw, angle of the mandible*

go·ni·om·e·ter \ˌgō-nē-'ä-mə-tər\ *n* : an instrument for measuring angles (as of a joint or the skull) — **go·nio·met·ric** \-nē-ə-'me-trik\ *adj* — **go·ni·om·e·try** \-nē-'ä-mə-trē\ *n*

go·nio·punc·ture \'gō-nē-ə-ˌpəŋk-chər\ *n* : a surgical operation for congenital glaucoma that involves making a puncture into the sclera with a knife at the site of discharge of aqueous fluid at the periphery of the anterior chamber of the eye

go·nio·scope \-ˌskōp\ *n* : an instrument consisting of a contact lens to be fitted over the cornea and an optical system with which the interior of the eye can be viewed — **go·ni·os·co·py** \ˌgō-nē-'äs-kə-pē\ *n*

go·ni·ot·o·my \ˌgō-nē-'ä-tə-mē\ *n, pl* **-mies** : surgical relief of glaucoma used in some congenital types and achieved by opening the canal of Schlemm

go·ni·tis \gō-'nī-təs\ *n* : inflammation of the knee

gono·coc·cae·mia *chiefly Brit var of* GONOCOCCEMIA

gono·coc·ce·mia \ˌgä-nə-ˌkäk-'sē-mē-ə\ *n* : the presence of gonococci in the blood — **gono·coc·ce·mic** \-'sē-mik\ *adj*

gono·coc·cus \ˌgä-nə-'kä-kəs\ *n, pl* **-coc-**

ci \-ˈkäk-ˌsī, -ˌsē: -ˈkä-ˌkī, -ˌkē\ : a pus-producing bacterium of the genus *Neisseria* (*N. gonorrhoeae*) that causes gonorrhea — **gono·coc·cal** \-ˈkä-kəl\ *adj*

gon·or·rhea \ˌgä-nə-ˈrē-ə\ *n* : a contagious inflammation of the genital mucous membrane caused by the gonococcus — called also *clap* — **gon·or·rhe·al** \-ˈrē-əl\ *adj*

gon·or·rhoea *chiefly Brit var of* GONORRHEA

-g·o·ny \gə-nē\ *n comb form*, *pl* **-g·o·nies** : manner of generation or of reproduction (schizo*gony*)

go·ny·au·lax \ˌgō-nē-ˈô-ˌlaks\ *n* 1 *cap* : a large genus of phosphorescent marine dinoflagellates that when unusually abundant cause red tide 2 : any dinoflagellate of the genus *Gonyaulax*

Good·pas·ture's syndrome \ˈgud-ˌpas-chərz-\ *also* **Good·pas·ture syndrome** \-chər-\ *n* : a hypersensitivity disorder of unknown cause that is characterized by the presence of circulating antibodies in the blood which react with antigens in the basement membrane of the kidney's glomeruli and with antigens in the lungs producing combined glomerulonephritis and pulmonary hemorrhages

  Goodpasture, Ernest William (1886–1960), American pathologist.

goose bumps *n pl* : a roughness of the skin produced by erection of its papillae esp. from cold, fear, or a sudden feeling of excitement — called also *goose pimples*

goose·flesh \-ˌflesh\ *n* : GOOSE BUMPS

gork \ˈgork\ *n, med slang* : a terminal patient whose brain is nonfunctional and the rest of whose body can be kept functioning only by the extensive use of mechanical devices and nutrient solutions — usu. used disparagingly — **gorked** \ˈgorkt\ *adj, med slang*

goun·dou \ˈgün-(ˌ)dü\ *n* : a tumorous swelling of the nose often considered a late lesion of yaws — compare GANGOSA

gout \ˈgaut\ *n* : a metabolic disease marked by a painful inflammation of the joints, deposits of urates in and around the joints, and usu. an excessive amount of uric acid in the blood — **gouty** \ˈgau-tē\ *adj*

GP *abbr* general practitioner

G₁ phase, G₂ phase — see entries alphabetized as G ONE PHASE, G TWO PHASE

G protein \ˈjē-\ *n* : any of a group of proteins in cell membranes that upon activation by a hormone initiate a series of molecular events inside the cell

gr *abbr* 1 grain 2 gram 3 gravity

graaf·ian follicle \ˈgrä-fē-ən-, ˈgra-\ *n, often cap G* : a liquid-filled cavity in a mammalian ovary containing a ma-

ture egg before ovulation — called also *vesicular ovarian follicle*

  Graaf \də-ˈgräf\, Reinier de (1641–1673), Dutch physician and anatomist.

grac·ile fasciculus \ˈgra-səl-, -ˌsīl-\ *n, pl* **gracile fasciculi** : FASCICULUS GRACILIS

grac·i·lis \ˈgra-sə-ləs\ *n* : the most superficial muscle of the inside of the thigh that acts to adduct the thigh and to flex the leg at the knee and assist in rotating it medially

graduate nurse *n* : a person who has completed the regular course of study and practical hospital training in nursing school — called also *trained nurse*; abbr. GN

¹graft \ˈgraft\ *vb* : to implant (living tissue) surgically

²graft *n* 1 : the act of grafting 2 : something grafted; *specif* : living tissue used in grafting

graft-versus-host *adj* : relating to or being the bodily condition that results when cells from a tissue or organ transplant mount an immunological attack against the cells or tissues of the host (~ disease)

grain \ˈgrān\ *n* : a unit of avoirdupois, Troy, and apothecaries' weight equal to 0.0648 gram or 0.002286 avoirdupois ounce or 0.002083 Troy ounce — abbr. gr

grain alcohol *n* : ETHANOL

grain itch *n* : an itching rash caused by the bite of a mite of the genus *Pyemotes* (*P. ventricosus*) that occurs chiefly on grain, straw, or straw products — compare GROCER'S ITCH

gram \ˈgram\ *n* : a metric unit of mass and weight equal to ¹⁄₁₀₀₀ kilogram and nearly equal to one cubic centimeter of water at its maximum density — abbr. g

-gram \ˌgram\ *n comb form* : drawing : writing : record (cardio*gram*)

gram calorie *n* : CALORIE 1a

gram·i·ci·din \ˌgra-mə-ˈsid-ᵊn\ *n* : an antibacterial mixture produced by a soil bacterium of the genus *Bacillus* (*B. brevis*) and used topically against gram-positive bacteria in local infections esp. of the eye

gramme *chiefly Brit var of* GRAM

gram-negative *adj* : not holding the purple dye when stained by Gram's stain — used chiefly of bacteria

gram-positive *adj* : holding the purple dye when stained by Gram's stain — used chiefly of bacteria

Gram's solution \ˈgramz-\ *n* : a watery solution of iodine and the iodide of potassium used in staining bacteria by Gram's stain

  Gram \ˈgräm\, Hans Christian Joachim (1853–1938), Danish physician.

Gram's stain *or* **Gram stain** \ˈgram-\ *n* 1 : a method for the differential staining of bacteria by treatment with Gram's solution after staining with a triphenylmethane dye — called also *Gram's method* **2** : the chemicals used in Gram's stain

gram–variable *adj* : staining irregularly or inconsistently by Gram's stain

gran·di·ose \'gran-dē-ós, ˌgran-dē-'\ *adj* : characterized by affectation of grandeur or splendor or by absurd exaggeration (~ delusions) — **gran·di·os·i·ty** \ˌgran-dē-'äs-ət-ē\ *n*

grand mal \'grän-ˌmäl, 'grän-, 'grand-, -'mal\ *n* : epilepsy due to an inborn usu. inherited dysrhythmia of the electrical pulsations of the brain as demonstrated by an electroencephalogram and characterized by attacks of violent convulsions, coma, constitutional disturbances, and usu. amnesia — compare PETIT MAL

grand rounds *n* : rounds involving the formal presentation by an expert of a clinical issue sometimes in the presence of selected patients

granul- *or* **granuli-** *or* **granulo-** *comb form* : granule ⟨*granulo*cyte⟩

gran·u·lar \'gran-yə-lər\ *adj* **1** : consisting of or appearing to consist of granules : having a grainy texture **2** : having or marked by granulations (~ tissue) — **gran·u·lar·i·ty** \ˌgran-yə-'lar-ət-ē\ *n*

granular conjunctivitis *n* : TRACHOMA

granular leukocyte *n* : a blood granulocyte; *esp* : a polymorphonuclear leukocyte

gran·u·late \'gran-yə-ˌlāt\ *vb* **-lat·ed; -lat·ing 1** : to form or crystallize (as sugar) into grains or granules **2** : to form granulations ⟨a *granulating* wound⟩

gran·u·la·tion \ˌgran-yə-'lā-shən\ *n* **1** : the act or process of granulating : the condition of being granulated **2 a** : one of the small elevations of a granulated surface: (1) : a minute mass of tissue projecting from the surface of an organ (as on the eyelids in trachoma) (2) : one of the minute red granules made up of loops of newly formed capillaries that form on a raw surface (as of a wound) and that with fibroblasts are the active agents in the process of healing — see GRANULATION TISSUE **b** : the act or process of forming such elevations or granules

granulation tissue *n* : tissue made up of granulations that temporarily replaces lost tissue in a wound

gran·ule \'gran-(ˌ)yül\ *n* : a little grain or small particle; *esp* : one of a number of particles forming a larger unit

granule cell *n* : one of the small neurons of the cortex of the cerebellum and cerebrum

granuli- — see GRANUL-

granulo- — see GRANUL-

gran·u·lo·cyte \'gran-yə-lō-ˌsīt\ *n* : a polymorphonuclear white blood cell with granule-containing cytoplasm — compare AGRANULOCYTE — **gran·u·lo·cyt·ic** \ˌgran-yə-lō-'si-tik\ *adj*

granulocytic leukemia *n* : MYELOGENOUS LEUKEMIA

gran·u·lo·cy·to·pe·nia \ˌgran-yə-lō-ˌsī-tə-'pē-nē-ə\ *n* : deficiency of blood granulocytes; *esp* : AGRANULOCYTOSIS — **gran·u·lo·cy·to·pe·nic** \-'pē-nik\ *adj*

gran·u·lo·cy·to·poi·e·sis \-ˌsī-tə-pói-'ē-səs\ *n, pl* **-e·ses** \-ˌsēz\ : GRANULOPOIESIS

gran·u·lo·cy·to·sis \ˌgran-yə-lō-ˌsī-'tō-səs\ *n, pl* **-to·ses** \-ˌsēz\ : an increase in the number of blood granulocytes — compare LYMPHOCYTOSIS, MONOCYTOSIS

gran·u·lo·ma \ˌgran-yə-'lō-mə\ *n, pl* **-mas** *or* **-ma·ta** \-mə-tə\ : a mass or nodule of chronically inflamed tissue with granulations that is usu. associated with an infective process

granuloma an·nu·la·re \-ˌa-nyü-'lar-ē\ *n* : a benign chronic rash of unknown cause characterized by one or more flat spreading ringlike spots with lighter centers esp. on the feet, legs, hands, or fingers

granuloma in·gui·na·le \-ˌiŋ-gwə-'na-lē, -'nä-, -'nä-\ *n* : a sexually transmitted disease characterized by ulceration and formation of granulations on the genitalia and in the groin area and caused by a bacterium of the genus *Calymmatobacterium* (*C. granulomatis* syn. *Donovania granulomatis*) which is usu. recovered from lesions as Donovan bodies

gran·u·lo·ma·to·sis \ˌgran-yə-ˌlō-mə-'tō-səs\ *n, pl* **-to·ses** \-ˌsēz\ : a chronic condition marked by the formation of numerous granulomas

gran·u·lo·ma·tous \-'lō-mə-təs\ *adj* : of, relating to, or characterized by granuloma

gran·u·lo·poi·e·sis \-(ˌ)lō-ˌpói-'ē-səs\ *n, pl* **-e·ses** \-ˌsēz\ : the formation of blood granulocytes typically in the bone marrow — **gran·u·lo·poi·et·ic** \-ˌpói-'e-tik\ *adj*

gran·u·lo·sa cell \ˌgran-yə-'lō-sə-, -zə-\ *n* : one of the estrogen-secreting cells of the epithelial lining of a graafian follicle or its follicular precursor

granulosum — see STRATUM GRANULOSUM

grapes \'grāps\ *n sing or pl* **1** : a cluster of raw red nodules of granulation tissue in the hollow of the fetlock of horses that is characteristic of advanced or chronic grease heel **2** : tuberculous disease of the pleura in cattle — called also *grape disease*

grape sugar \'grāp-\ *n* : DEXTROSE

-graph \ˌgraf\ *n comb form* **1** : something written ⟨mono*graph*⟩ **2** : instrument for making or transmitting records ⟨electrocardio*graph*⟩

-graph·ia \'gra-fē-ə\ *n comb form* : writing characteristic of a (specified) usu. psychological abnormality ⟨dys*graphia*⟩ ⟨dermo*graphia*⟩

grapho- *comb form* : writing ⟨*graphol-ogy*⟩

gra·phol·o·gy \gra-'fä-lə-jē\ *n, pl* **-gies** : the study of handwriting esp. for the purpose of character analysis — **graph·o·log·i·cal** \gra-fə-'lä-ji-kəl\ *adj* — **gra·phol·o·gist** \gra-'fä-lə-jist\ *n*

grapho·ma·nia \gra-fō-'mā-nē-ə, -nyə\ *n* : a morbid and compulsive desire for writing — **grapho·ma·ni·ac** \-nē-ak\ *n*

grapho·spasm \'gra-fə-spa-zəm\ *n* : WRITER'S CRAMP

gras — see TULLE GRAS

GRAS *abbr* generally recognized as safe

grass \'gras\ *n* : MARIJUANA

grass sickness *n* : a frequently fatal disease of grazing horses of unknown cause that affects gastrointestinal functioning by causing difficulty in swallowing, interruption of peristalsis, and fecal impaction — called also *grass disease*

grass staggers *n* : GRASS TETANY

grass tetany *n* : a disease of cattle and esp. milk cows marked by tetanic staggering, convulsions, coma, and frequently death and caused by reduction of blood calcium and magnesium when overeating on lush pasture — called also *hypomagnesia*; compare MILK FEVER 2, STAGGERS 1

grav *abbr* gravida

grave \'grāv\ *adj* : very serious : dangerous to life — used of an illness or its prospects ⟨a ~ prognosis⟩

grav·el \'gra-vəl\ *n* 1 : a deposit of small calculous concretions in the kidneys and urinary bladder 2 : the condition that results from the presence of deposits of gravel

Graves' disease \'grāvz-\ *n* : a common form of hyperthyroidism characterized by goiter and often a slight protrusion of the eyeballs — called also *Basedow's disease, exophthalmic goiter*

    Graves, Robert James (1796–1853), British physician.

grav·id \'gra-vəd\ *adj* : PREGNANT

grav·i·da \'gra-və-də\ *n, pl* **-i·das** *or* **-i·dae** \-dē\ : a pregnant woman — often used in combination with a number or figure to indicate the number of pregnancies a woman has had ⟨a 4-*gravida*⟩; compare PARA — **gra·vid·ic** \gra-'vi-dik\ *adj*

gra·vid·i·ty \gra-'vi-də-tē\ *n, pl* **-ties** : PREGNANCY, PARITY

gra·vi·or — see ICHTHYOSIS HYSTRIX GRAVIOR

gra·vis — see ICTERUS GRAVIS, ICTERUS GRAVIS NEONATORUM, MYASTHENIA GRAVIS

grav·i·ta·tion \gra-və-'tā-shən\ *n* : a natural force of attraction that tends to draw bodies together and that occurs because of the mass of the bodies — **grav·i·ta·tion·al** \-shə-nəl\ *adj* — **grav·i·ta·tion·al·ly** *adv*

gravitational field *n* : the space around an object having mass in which the object's gravitational influence can be detected

grav·i·ty \'gra-və-tē\ *n, pl* **-ties** : the gravitational attraction of the mass of a celestial object (as earth) for bodies close to it; *also* : GRAVITATION

gray \'grā\ *n* : the mks unit of absorbed dose of ionizing radiation equal to an energy of one joule per kilogram of irradiated material — abbr. *Gy*

    Gray, Louis Harold (1905–1965), British radiobiologist.

gray column *n* : any of the longitudinal columns of gray matter in each lateral half of the spinal cord — compare COLUMN a

gray commissure *n* : a transverse band of gray matter in the spinal cord appearing in sections as the transverse bar of the H-shaped mass of gray matter

gray matter *n* : neural tissue esp. of the brain and spinal cord that contains cell bodies as well as nerve fibers, has a brownish gray color, and forms most of the cortex and nuclei of the brain, the columns of the spinal cord, and the bodies of ganglia — called also *gray substance*

gray·out \'grā-aut\ *n* : a transient dimming or haziness of vision resulting from temporary impairment of cerebral circulation — compare BLACKOUT, REDOUT — **gray out** *vb*

gray ramus *n* : RAMUS COMMUNICANS b

gray substance *n* : GRAY MATTER

gray syndrome *n* : a potentially fatal toxic reaction to chloramphenicol esp. in premature infants that is characterized by abdominal distension, cyanosis, vasomotor collapse, and irregular respiration

grease heel *n* : a chronic inflammation of the skin of the fetlocks and pasterns of horses marked by an excess of oily secretion, ulcerations, and in severe cases general swelling of the legs, nodular excrescences, and a foul-smelling discharge and usu. affecting horses with thick coarse legs kept or worked under unsanitary conditions — called also *greasy heel*; see GRAPES 1

great cerebral vein *n* : a broad unpaired vein formed by the junction of Galen's veins and uniting with the inferior sagittal sinus to form the straight sinus

great·er cornu \'grāt-ər-\ *n* : THYROHYAL

greater curvature *n* : the boundary of the stomach that forms a long usu. convex curve on the left from the opening for the esophagus to the opening into the duodenum — compare LESSER CURVATURE

greater multangular *n* : TRAPEZIUM — called also *greater multangular bone*

greater occipital nerve *n* : OCCIPITAL NERVE a

greater omentum *n* : a part of the peritoneum attached to the greater curvature of the stomach and to the colon and hanging down over the small intestine — called also *caul;* compare LESSER OMENTUM

greater palatine artery *n* : PALATINE ARTERY 1b

greater palatine foramen *n* : a foramen in each posterior side of the palate giving passage to the greater palatine artery and to a palatine nerve

greater petrosal nerve *n* : a mixed nerve that contains mostly sensory and some parasympathetic fibers, arises in the geniculate ganglion, joins with the deep petrosal nerve at the entrance of the pterygoid canal to form the Vidian nerve, and as part of this nerve sends sensory fibers to the soft palate with some to the eustachian tube and sends parasympathetic fibers forming the motor root of the pterygopalatine ganglion — called also *greater superficial petrosal nerve*

greater sciatic foramen *n* : SCIATIC FORAMEN a

greater sciatic notch *n* : SCIATIC NOTCH a

greater splanchnic nerve *n* : SPLANCHNIC NERVE a

greater superficial petrosal nerve *n* : GREATER PETROSAL NERVE

greater trochanter *also* **great trochanter** *n* : TROCHANTER a

greater tubercle *n* : a prominence on the upper lateral part of the end of the humerus that serves as the insertion for the supraspinatus, infraspinatus, and teres minor — compare LESSER TUBERCLE

greater vestibular gland *n* : BARTHOLIN'S GLAND

greater wing *also* **great wing** *n* : a broad curved winglike expanse on each side of the sphenoid bone — called also *alisphenoid;* compare LESSER WING

great ragweed *n* : RAGWEED b

great saphenous vein *n* : SAPHENOUS VEIN a

great toe *n* : BIG TOE

great white shark *n* : a large shark (*Carcharodon carcharias* of the family Lamnidae) that is bluish when young but becomes whitish with age and is noted for aggressively attacking humans — called also *white shark*

green \'grēn\ *adj* **1** *of a wound* : being recently incurred and unhealed **2** *of hemolytic streptococci* : tending to produce green pigment when cultured on blood media

green monkey *n* : a long-tailed African monkey (*Cercopithecus aethiops*) with greenish-appearing hair that is often used in medical research

green monkey disease *n* : a febrile infectious often fatal virus disease char-

acterized esp. by encephalitis, hepatitis, and renal involvement and orig. transmitted to humans from green monkeys — called also *Marburg disease;* see MARBURG VIRUS

green-sick-ness \'grēn-₊sik-nəs\ *n* : CHLOROSIS — **green-sick** *adj*

green soap *n* : a soft soap made from vegetable oils and used esp. in the treatment of skin diseases

green-stick fracture \'grēn-₊stik-\ *n* : a bone fracture in a young individual in which the bone is partly broken and partly bent

grew *past of* GROW

grey-out *chiefly Brit var of* GRAYOUT

¹**gripe** \'grīp\ *vb* **griped; grip-ing** : to cause or experience pinching and spasmodic pain in the bowels of

²**gripe** *n* : a pinching spasmodic intestinal pain — usu. used in pl.

grippe \'grip\ *n* : an acute febrile contagious virus disease; *esp* : INFLUENZA 1a — **grippy** \'gri-pē\ *adj*

gris-eo-ful-vin \₊gri-zē-ō-'fül-vən,₋sē-,₋'fal-\ *n* : a fungistatic antibiotic $C_{17}H_{17}ClO_6$ used systemically in treating superficial infections by fungi esp. of the genera *Epidermophyton, Microsporum,* and *Trichophyton*

grocer's itch *n* : an itching dermatitis that results from prolonged contact with some mites (esp. family Acaridae), their products, or materials (as feeds) infested with them — called also *baker's itch;* compare GRAIN ITCH

groin \'groin\ *n* : the fold or depression marking the juncture of the lower abdomen and the inner part of the thigh; *also* : the region of this line

groove \'grüv\ *n* : a long narrow depression occurring naturally on the surface of an anatomical part

gross \'grōs\ *adj* **1** : glaringly or flagrantly obvious **2** : visible without the aid of a microscope : MACROSCOPIC (~ lesions) — compare OCCULT

gross anatomist *n* : a specialist in gross anatomy

gross anatomy *n* : a branch of anatomy that deals with the macroscopic structure of tissues and organs — compare HISTOLOGY

ground itch *n* : an itching inflammation of the skin marking the point of entrance into the body of larval hookworms

ground substance *n* : a more or less homogeneous matrix that forms the background in which the specific differentiated elements of a system are suspended: **a** : the intercellular substance of tissues **b** : CYTOSOL

group dynamics *n sing or pl* : the interacting forces within a small human group; *also* : the sociological study of these forces

group practice *n* : medicine practiced by a group of associated physicians or dentists (as specialists in different fields) working as partners or as partners and employees

group psychotherapy *n* : GROUP THERAPY

group therapy *n* : therapy in the presence of a therapist in which several patients discuss and share their personal problems — **group therapist** *n*

grow \'grō\ *vb* **grew** \'grü\; **grown** \'grōn\; **grow·ing** 1 a : to spring up and develop to maturity b : to be able to grow in some place or situation c : to assume some relation through or as if through a process of natural growth ⟨the cut edges of the wound *grew* together⟩ 2 : to increase in size by addition of material by assimilation into the living organism or by accretion in a nonbiological process (as crystallization)

growing pains *n pl* : pains occurring in the legs of growing children having no demonstrable relation to growth

growth \'grōth\ *n* 1 a (1) : a stage in the process of growing (2) : full growth b : the process of growing 2 a : something that grows or has grown b : an abnormal proliferation of tissue (as a tumor)

growth factor *n* : a substance (as a vitamin B_{12} or an interleukin) that promotes growth and esp. cellular growth

growth hormone *n* : a polypeptide hormone that is secreted by the anterior lobe of the pituitary gland and regulates growth — called also *somatotropic hormone, somatotropin*

growth plate *n* : the region in a long bone between the epiphysis and diaphysis where growth in length occurs — called also *physis*

g's or **gs** *pl of* G

G6PD *abbr* glucose-6-phosphate dehydrogenase

GSR *abbr* galvanic skin response

G suit *n* : a suit designed to counteract the physiological effects of acceleration on an aviator or astronaut

GSW *abbr* gunshot wound

GTP \ˌjē-(ˌ)tē-'pē\ *n* : an energy-rich nucleotide analogous to ATP that is composed of guanine linked to ribose and three phosphate groups and is necessary for peptide-bond formation during protein synthesis — called also *guanosine triphosphate*

G_2 phase \ˌjē-'tü-\ *n* : the period in the cell cycle from the completion of DNA replication to the beginning of cell division — compare G_1 PHASE, M PHASE, S PHASE

GU *abbr* genitourinary

guai·ac \'gwī-ˌak\ *n* : GUAIACUM

guai·a·col \'gwī-ə-ˌkȯl, -ˌkōl\ *n* : a liquid or solid $C_7H_8O_2$ with an aromatic odor used chiefly as an expectorant and as a local anesthetic

guaiac test *n* : a test for blood in urine or feces using a reagent containing guaiacum that yields a blue color

when blood is present — see HEMOCCULT

guai·a·cum \'gwī-ə-kəm\ *n* : a resin with a faint balsamic odor obtained as tears or masses from the trunk of either of two trees (*Guaiacum officinale* and *G. sanctum* of the family Zygophyllaceae) and used in various tests (as the guaiac test)

guai·fen·e·sin \gwī-'fe-nə-sən\ *n* : the glyceryl ether of guaiacol $C_{10}H_{14}O_4$ that is used esp. as an expectorant — called also *glyceryl guaiacolate*

gua·neth·i·dine \gwä-'ne-thə-ˌdēn\ *n* : a drug $C_{10}H_{22}N_4$ used esp. as the sulfate in treating severe high blood pressure

gua·ni·dine \'gwä-nə-ˌdēn\ *n* : a base CH_5N_3 derived from guanine and used as a parasympathetic stimulant in medicine esp. as the hydrochloride salt

gua·nine \'gwä-ˌnēn\ *n* : a purine base $C_5H_5N_5O$ that codes genetic information in the polynucleotide chain of DNA or RNA — compare ADENINE, CYTOSINE, THYMINE, URACIL

gua·no·sine \'gwä-nə-ˌsēn\ *n* : a nucleoside $C_{10}H_{13}N_5O_5$ composed of guanine and ribose

guanosine 3′, 5′-monophosphate *n* : CYCLIC GMP

guanosine triphosphate *n* : GTP

gua·nyl·ate cy·clase \'gwän-ᵊl-ˌāt-'sī-ˌklās, -ˌklāz\ *n* : an enzyme that catalyzes the formation of cyclic GMP from GTP

guard·ing \'gär-diŋ\ *n* : involuntary reaction to protect an area of pain (as by spasm of muscle on palpation of the abdomen over a painful lesion)

gu·ber·nac·u·lum \ˌgü-bər-'na-kyü-ləm\ *n, pl* **-la** \-lə\ : a fibrous cord that connects the fetal testis with the bottom of the scrotum and by failing to elongate in proportion to the rest of the fetus causes the descent of the testis

guide \'gīd\ *n* : a grooved director for a surgical probe or knife

Guil·lain–Bar·ré syndrome \ˌgē-'lan-ˌbä-'rā-, ˌgē-'yaⁿ-\ *n* : a polyneuritis of unknown cause characterized esp. by muscle weakness and paralysis — called also *Landry's paralysis*

Guillain \gē-'yaⁿ\, **Georges Charles (1876–1961),** and **Barré** \bä-'rā\, **Jean Alexander (b 1880),** French neurologists.

guil·lo·tine \'gi-lə-ˌtēn, 'gē-ə-\ *n* : a surgical instrument that consists of a ring and handle with a knife blade which slides down the handle and across the ring and that is used for cutting out a protruding structure (as a tonsil) capable of being placed in the ring

Guil·lo·tin \gē-yȯ-'taⁿ, **Joseph–Ignace (1738–1814),** French surgeon.

guillotine amputation *n* : an emergency surgical amputation (as of a leg) in which the skin is incised around the part being amputated and is allowed to retract, successive layers of muscle are then divided around the part, and finally the bone is divided

guilt \'gilt\ *n* : feelings of culpability esp. for imagined offenses or from a sense of inadequacy : morbid self-reproach often manifest in marked preoccupation with the moral correctness of one's behavior

guin·ea worm \'gi-nē-\ *n* : a slender nematode worm of the genus *Dracunculus* (*D. medinensis*) attaining a length of several feet, being parasitic as an adult in the subcutaneous tissues of mammals including humans in tropical regions, and having a larva that develops in small freshwater crustaceans (as of the genus *Cyclops* of the order Copepoda) and when ingested with drinking water passes through the intestinal wall and tissues to lodge beneath the skin of a mammalian host where it matures — called also *Medina worm*

gul·let \'gə-lət\ *n* : ESOPHAGUS; *broadly* : THROAT

gum \'gəm\ *n* : the tissue that surrounds the necks of teeth and covers the alveolar parts of the jaws; *broadly* : the alveolar portion of a jaw with its enveloping soft tissues

gum ar·a·bic \-'ar-ə-bik\ *n* : a water-soluble gum obtained from several leguminous plants (genus *Acacia* and esp. *A. senegal* and *A. arabica*) and used esp. in pharmacy to suspend insoluble substances in water, to prepare emulsions, and to make pills and lozenges — called also *acacia, gum acacia*

gum·boil \'gəm-ˌbȯil\ *n* : an abscess in the gum

gum karaya *n* : KARAYA GUM

gum·line \'gəm-ˌlīn\ *n* : the line separating the gum from the exposed part of the tooth

gum·ma \'gə-mə\ *n, pl* **gummas** *also* **gum·ma·ta** \-mə-tə\ : a tumor of gummy or rubbery consistency that is characteristic of the tertiary stage of syphilis — **gum·ma·tous** \-mə-təs\ *adj*

gum tragacanth *n* : TRAGACANTH

gur·ney \'gər-nē\ *n, pl* **gurneys** : a wheeled cot or stretcher

gus·ta·tion \ˌgəs-'tā-shən\ *n* : the act or sensation of tasting

gus·ta·to·ry \'gəs-tə-ˌtōr-ē\ *adj* : relating to, affecting, associated with, or being the sense of taste

gut \'gət\ *n* **1 a** : the alimentary canal or part of it (as the intestine or stomach) **b** : ABDOMEN 1a, BELLY — usu. used in pl.; not often in formal use **2** : CATGUT

Guth·rie test \'gə-thrē-\ *n* : a test for phenylketonuria in which the plasma phenylalanine of an affected individual reverses the inhibition of a strain of bacteria of the genus *Bacillus* (*B. subtilis*) needing it for growth

Guthrie, Robert (*b* 1916), American microbiologist.

gut·ta-per·cha \ˌgə-tə-'pər-chə\ *n* : a tough plastic substance from the latex of several Malaysian trees (genera *Payena* and *Palaquium*) of the sapodilla family (Sapotaceae) that is used in dentistry in temporary fillings

gut·tate \'gə-ˌstāt\ *adj* : having small usu. colored spots or drops

gut·ter \'gə-tər\ *n* : a depressed furrow between body parts (as on the surface between a pair of adjacent ribs)

Gutzeit test \'güt-ˌsīt-\ *n* : a test for arsenic used esp. in toxicology

Gutzeit, Ernst Wilhelm Heinrich (1845–1888), German chemist.

GVH *abbr* graft-versus-host

Gy *abbr* gray

Gym·no·din·i·um \ˌjim-nə-'di-nē-əm\ *n* : a large genus of marine and freshwater dinoflagellates (family Gymnodiniidae) that includes a few forms which cause red tide

gyn *abbr* gynecologic; gynecologist; gynecology

gynaec- *or* **gynaeco-** *chiefly Brit var of* GYNEC-

gy·nae·coid, gy·nae·col·o·gy *chiefly Brit var of* GYNECOID, GYNECOLOGY

gyn·an·dro·blas·to·ma \(ˌ)gī-ˌnan-drə-blā-'stō-mə, (ˌ)ji-, ˌjī-\ *n, pl* **-mas** *or* **-ma·ta** \-mə-tə\ : a rare tumor of the ovary with both masculinizing and feminizing effects — compare ARRHENOBLASTOMA

gynec- *or* **gyneco-** *comb form* : woman (gynecoid) (gynecology)

gy·ne·cog·ra·phy \ˌgī-nə-'kä-grə-fē, ˌji-\ *n, pl* **-phies** : roentgenographic visualization of the female reproductive tract

gy·ne·coid \'gī-ni-ˌkȯid, 'ji-\ *adj, of the pelvis* : having the rounded form typical of the human female — compare ANDROID, ANTHROPOID, PLATYPELLOID

gy·ne·col·o·gist \ˌgī-nə-'kä-lə-jist, ˌji-, ˌjī-\ *n* : a specialist in gynecology

gy·ne·col·o·gy \ˌgī-nə-'kä-lə-jē, ˌji-, ˌjī-\ *n, pl* **-gies** : a branch of medicine that deals with the diseases and routine physical care of the reproductive system of women — **gy·ne·co·log·ic** \-ni-kə-'lä-jik\ *or* **gy·ne·co·log·i·cal** \-ji-kəl\ *adj*

gy·ne·co·mas·tia \ˌgī-nə-kō-'mas-tē-ə, 'ji-, 'ji-\ *n* : excessive development of the breast in the male

gyp·py tummy \ˌji-pē-\ *n* : diarrhea contracted esp. by travelers

gy·rase \'ji-ˌrās, -ˌrāz\ *n* : an enzyme that catalyzes the breaking and rejoining of bonds linking adjacent nucleotides in DNA to generate supercoiled DNA helices

gy·rate \'ji-ˌrāt\ *adj* : winding or coiled around : CONVOLUTED

gyrate atrophy *n* : progressive degeneration of the choroid and pigment epithelium of the retina that is inherited as an autosomal recessive trait and is characterized esp. by myopia, constriction of the visual field, night blindness, and cataracts

gy·ra·tion \jī-ˈrā-shən\ *n* : the pattern of convolutions of the brain

Gy·ro·mi·tra \jī-rō-ˈmī-trə, ˌjir-ə-\ *n* : a genus of ascomycetous fungi (family Helvellaceae) that include the false morels and typically contain toxins causing illness or death

gy·rus \ˈjī-rəs\ *n, pl* **gy·ri** \-ˌrī\ : a convoluted ridge between anatomical grooves; *esp* : CONVOLUTION

H

h *abbr* **1** height **2** [Latin *hora*] hour — used in writing prescriptions; see QH

¹H *abbr* heroin

²H *symbol* hydrogen

ha·ben·u·la \hə-ˈben-yə-lə\ *n, pl* **-lae** \-ˌlī, -ˌlē\ **1** : TRIGONUM HABENULAE **2** : either of two nuclei of which one lies on each side of the pineal gland under the corresponding trigonum habenulae, is composed of two groups of nerve cells, and forms a correlation center for olfactory stimuli — called also *habenular nucleus* — **ha·ben·u·lar** \-lər\ *adj*

habenular commissure *n* : a band of nerve fibers situated in front of the pineal gland that connects the habenular nucleus on one side with that on the other

hab·it \ˈha-bət\ *n* **1** : a behavior pattern acquired by frequent repetition or physiological exposure that shows itself in regularity or increased facility of performance **2** : an acquired mode of behavior that has become nearly or completely involuntary **3** : ADDICTION

hab·i·tat \ˈha-bə-ˌtat\ *n* : the place or environment where a plant or animal naturally occurs

habit-forming *adj* : inducing the formation of an addiction

ha·bit·u·al \hə-ˈbi-chə-wəl\ *adj* **1** : having the nature of a habit : being in accordance with habit **2** : doing, practicing, or acting in some manner by force of habit — **ha·bit·u·al·ly** *adv*

habitual abortion *n* : spontaneous abortion occurring in three or more successive pregnancies

ha·bit·u·a·tion \-ˌbi-chə-ˈwā-shən\ *n* **1** : the act or process of making habitual or accustomed **2 a** : tolerance to the effects of a drug acquired through continued use **b** : psychological dependence on a drug after a period of use — compare ADDICTION **3** : a form of nonassociative learning characterized by a decrease in responsiveness upon repeated exposure to a stimulus — compare SENSITIZATION **3** — **ha·bit·u·ate** \-ˈbi-chə-ˌwāt\ *vb*

hab·i·tus \ˈha-bə-təs\ *n, pl* **habitus** \-təs, -ˌtüs\ : HABIT; *specif* : body-build and constitution esp. as related to predisposition to disease (ulcer ∼)

Hab·ro·ne·ma \ˌha-brō-ˈnē-mə\ *n* : a genus of parasitic nematode worms (family Spiruridae) that live as adults in the stomach of the horse or the proventriculus of various birds — see HABRONEMIASIS, SUMMER SORES

hab·ro·ne·mi·a·sis \ˌha-brə-nē-ˈmī-ə-səs\ *n, pl* **-a·ses** \-ˌsēz\ : infestation with or disease caused by roundworms of the genus *Habronema*

hack \ˈhak\ *n* : a short dry cough — **hack** *vb*

haem- *or* **haemo-** *chiefly Brit var of* HEM-

haema- *chiefly Brit var of* HEMA-

hae·ma·cy·tom·e·ter, hae·mal, haem·an·gi·o·ma *chiefly Brit var of* HEMACYTOMETER, HEMAL, HEMANGIOMA

Hae·ma·phy·sa·lis \ˌhē-mə-ˈfi-sə-ləs, ˌhe-\ *n* : a cosmopolitan genus of small ixodid ticks including some that are disease carriers — see KYASANUR FOREST DISEASE

haemat- *or* **haemato-** *chiefly Brit var of* HEMAT-

hae·ma·tem·e·sis, hae·ma·tog·e·nous *chiefly Brit var of* HEMATEMESIS, HEMATOGENOUS

haematobium — see SCHISTOSOMIASIS HAEMATOBIUM

Hae·ma·to·pi·nus \-tə-ˈpī-nəs\ *n* : a genus of sucking lice including the hog louse (*H. suis*) and short-nosed cattle louse (*H. eurysternus*)

-haemia \ˈhē-mē-ə\ — see -EMIA

hae·mo·bar·ton·el·la \ˌhē-mō-ˌbär-tə-ˈne-lə, ˌhe-\ *n* **1** *cap* : a genus of bacteria (family Anaplasmataceae) that are blood parasites in various mammals **2** *pl* **-lae** \-ˌlē, -ˌlī\ : a bacterium of the genus *Haemobartonella*

hae·mo·bar·ton·el·lo·sis \-tə-nə-ˈlō-səs\ *n, pl* **-lo·ses** \-ˌsēz\ : an infection or disease caused by bacteria of the genus *Haemobartonella*

hae·mo·glo·bin *chiefly Brit var of* HEMOGLOBIN

Hae·mon·chus \ˌhē-ˈmäŋ-kəs\ *n* : a genus of nematode worms (family Trichostrongylidae) including a parasite (*H. contortus*) of the abomasum of ruminants (as sheep) and occurring rarely in humans

hae·mo·phil·ia *chiefly Brit var of* HEMOPHILIA

hae·moph·i·lus \hē-ˈmä-fə-ləs\ *n* **1** *cap* : a genus of nonmotile gram-negative facultatively anaerobic rod bacteria (family Pasteurellaceae) that include several important pathogens (as *H. influenzae* associated with human respiratory infections, conjunctivitis, and meningitis and *H. ducreyi* of chancroid) 2 *pl* -li \-•lī, -•lē\ : any bacterium of the genus *Haemophilus*

Hae·mo·pro·te·us \•hē-mō-•prō-tē-əs, •he-mə-\ *n* : a genus of protozoan parasites (family Haemoproteidae) occurring in the blood of some birds

haem·or·rhage, haem·or·rhoid *chiefly Brit var of* HEMORRHAGE, HEMORRHOID

haf·ni·um \•haf-nē-əm\ *n* : a metallic element that readily absorbs neutrons — symbol *Hf*; see ELEMENT table

Hag·e·man factor \•ha-gə-mən-, •hāg-mən-\ *n* : FACTOR XII

Hageman (fl 1963), hospital patient.

hair \•har\ *n, often attrib* 1 : a slender threadlike outgrowth of the epidermis of an animal: *esp* : one of the usu. pigmented filaments that form the characteristic coat of a mammal 2 : the hairy covering of an animal or a body part: *esp* : the coating of hairs on a human head — **hairlike** *adj*

hair ball *n* : a compact mass of hair formed in the stomach esp. of a shedding animal (as a cat) that cleanses its coat by licking — called also *trichobezoar*

hair bulb *n* : the bulbous expansion at the base of a hair from which the hair shaft develops

hair cell *n* : a cell with hairlike processes; *esp* : one of the sensory cells in the auditory epithelium of the organ of Corti

haired \•hard\ *adj* : having hair esp. of a specified kind — usu. used in combination (red-*haired*)

hair follicle *n* : the tubular epithelial sheath that surrounds the lower part of the hair shaft and encloses at the bottom a vascular papilla supplying the growing basal part of the hair with nourishment

hair·line \•har-•lin\ *n* : the outline of scalp hair esp. on the forehead

hairline fracture *n* : a fracture that appears as a narrow crack along the surface of a bone

hair root *n* : ROOT 2

hair shaft *n* : the part of a hair projecting beyond the skin

hair·worm \•har-•wərm\ *n* : any nematode worm of the genus *Capillaria*

hairy cell leukemia \•har-ē-\ *n* : a lymphocytic leukemia usu. of B cell origin and characterized by malignant cells with a ciliated appearance that replace bone marrow and infiltrate the spleen causing splenomegaly

hal·a·zone \•ha-lə-•zōn\ *n* : a white crystalline powdery acid $C_7H_5Cl_2NO_4S$ used as a disinfectant for drinking water

Hal·dol \•hal-•dȯl, -•dōl\ *trademark* — used for a preparation of haloperidol

half-life \•haf-•līf\ *n* 1 : the time required for half of the atoms of a radioactive substance to become disintegrated 2 : the time required for half the amount of a substance (as a drug or radioactive tracer) in or introduced into a living system or ecosystem to be eliminated or disintegrated by natural processes

half-moon \-•mün\ *n* : LUNULA a

half-value layer *n* : the thickness of an absorbing substance necessary to reduce by one half the initial intensity of the radiation passing through it

halfway house *n* : a center for formerly institutionalized individuals (as mental patients or drug addicts) that is designed to facilitate their readjustment to private life

halibut-liver oil *n* : a yellowish to brownish fatty oil from the liver of the halibut used chiefly as a source of vitamin A

hal·i·to·sis \•ha-lə-•tō-səs\ *n, pl* -to·ses \-•sēz\ : a condition of having fetid breath

hal·lu·ci·na·tion \hə-•lüs-ᵊn-•ā-shən\ *n* 1 : a perception of something (as a visual image or a sound) with no external cause usu. arising from a disorder of the nervous system (as in delirium tremens) or in response to drugs (as LSD) 2 : the object of an hallucinatory perception — compare DELUSION, ILLUSION — **hal·lu·ci·nate** \-•lüs-ᵊn-•āt\ *vb* — **hal·lu·ci·na·tor** \-•lüs-ᵊn-•ā-tər\ *n* — **hal·lu·ci·na·to·ry** \-•lüs-ᵊn-ə-•tȯr-ē\ *adj*

hal·lu·ci·no·gen \hə-•lüs-ᵊn-ə-jən\ *n* : a substance and esp. a drug that induces hallucinations

¹**hal·lu·ci·no·gen·ic** \hə-•lüs-ᵊn-ə-•je-nik\ *adj* : causing hallucinations — **hal·lu·ci·no·gen·i·cal·ly** \-ni-k(ə-)lē\ *adv*

²**hallucinogenic** *n* : HALLUCINOGEN

hal·lu·ci·no·sis \hə-•lüs-ᵊn-•ō-səs\ *n, pl* -no·ses \-•sēz\ : a pathological mental state characterized by hallucinations

hallucis — see ABDUCTOR HALLUCIS, ADDUCTOR HALLUCIS, EXTENSOR HALLUCIS BREVIS, EXTENSOR HALLUCIS LONGUS, FLEXOR HALLUCIS BREVIS, FLEXOR HALLUCIS LONGUS

hal·lux \•ha-ləks\ *n, pl* **hal·lu·ces** \•ha-lə-•sēz, •hal-yə-\ : the innermost digit of the foot : BIG TOE

hallux rig·id·us \-•ri-jə-dəs\ *n* : restricted mobility of the big toe due to stiffness of the metatarsophalangeal joint esp. when due to arthritic changes in the joint

hallux val·gus \-•val-gəs\ *n* : an abnormal deviation of the big toe away from the midline of the body or toward the other toes of the foot that is associated esp. with the wearing of ill-fitting shoes — compare BUNION

ha·lo \•hā-(•)lō\ *n, pl* **halos** *or* **haloes** 1 : a circle of light appearing to surround a luminous body; *esp* : one seen as the result of the presence of glaucoma 2 : a differentiated zone surrounding a central object (the ~ around a boil) 3 : the aura of glory, veneration, or sentiment surrounding an idealized person or thing

halo effect n : generalization from the perception of one outstanding personality trait to an overly favorable evaluation of the whole personality

halo·gen \ˈha-lə-jən\ n : any of the five elements fluorine, chlorine, bromine, iodine, and astatine that exist in the free state normally with two atoms per molecule

hal·o·ge·ton \ˌha-lə-ˈjē-ˌtän\ n : a coarse annual herb (*Halogeton glomeratus*) of the goosefoot family (Chenopodiaceae) that in western American ranges is dangerous to sheep and cattle because of its high oxalate content

halo·per·i·dol \ˌha-lō-ˈper-ə-ˌdȯl, -ˌdōl\ n : a depressant $C_{21}H_{23}ClFNO_2$ of the central nervous system used esp. as an antipsychotic drug — see HALDOL

halo·thane \ˈha-lə-ˌthän\ n : a nonexplosive inhalational anesthetic $C_2H_BrClF_3$

Hal·sted radical mastectomy \ˈhalˌsted-\ n : RADICAL MASTECTOMY

hal·zoun \ˈhal-ˈzün, ˈhal-zün\ n : infestation of the larynx and pharynx esp. by tongue worms (genus *Linguatula* and esp. *L. serrata*) consumed in raw liver

ham \ˈham\ n 1 : the part of the leg behind the knee : the hollow of the knee : POPLITEAL SPACE 2 : a buttock with its associated thigh or with the posterior part of a thigh — usu. used in pl.

hama·dry·ad \ˌha-mə-ˈdrī-əd, -ˌad\ n : KING COBRA

ham·ar·to·ma \ˌha-ˌmär-ˈtō-mə\ n, pl -mas or -ma·ta \-mə-tə\ : a mass resembling a tumor that represents anomalous development of tissue natural to a part or organ rather than a true tumor

ha·mate \ˈhā-ˌmāt, ˈha-mət\ n : a bone on the little-finger side of the second row of the carpus — called also *unciform, unciform bone*

ham·mer \ˈha-mər\ n : MALLEUS

ham·mer·toe \ˈha-mər-ˌtō\ n : a deformed claw-shaped toe and esp. the second that results from permanent angular flexion between one or both phalangeal joints — called also *claw toe*

¹**ham·string** \ˈham-ˌstriŋ\ n 1 a : either of two groups of tendons bounding the upper part of the popliteal space at the back of the knee and forming the tendons of insertion of some muscles of the back of the thigh b : HAMSTRING MUSCLE 2 : a large tendon above and behind the hock of a quadruped

²**hamstring** vb **-strung** \-ˌstrəŋ\; **-stringing** \-ˌstriŋ-iŋ\ : to cripple by cutting the leg tendons

hamstring muscle n : any of three muscles at the back of the thigh that function to flex and rotate the leg and extend the thigh: a : SEMIMEMBRANOSUS b : SEMITENDINOSUS c : BICEPS b

ham·u·lus \ˈha-myə-ləs\ n, pl -u·li \-ˌlī, -ˌlē\ : a hook or hooked process

hand \ˈhand\ n, often attrib : the terminal part of the vertebrate forelimb when modified (as in humans) as a grasping organ

hand·ed \ˈhan-dəd\ adj 1 : having a hand or hands esp. of a specified kind or number — usu. used in combination (a large-*handed* man) 2 : using a specified hand or number of hands — used in combination (right-*handed*)

hand·ed·ness \-nəs\ n : a tendency to use one hand rather than the other

hand–foot–and–mouth disease n : a usu. mild contagious disease esp. of young children that is caused by a picornavirus of the coxsackievirus group and is characterized by vesicular lesions in the mouth, on the hands and feet, and sometimes in the diaper-covered area — compare FOOT-AND-MOUTH DISEASE

hand·i·cap \ˈhan-di-ˌkap, -dē-\ n : a disadvantage that makes achievement unusually difficult; esp : a physical disability

hand·i·capped \-ˌkapt\ adj : having a physical or mental disability that substantially limits activity esp. in relation to employment or education

hand·piece \ˈhand-ˌpēs\ n : the handheld part of an electrically powered dental apparatus that holds the revolving instruments (as a bur)

Hand–Schül·ler–Chris·tian disease \ˈhand-ˈshü-lər-ˈkris-chən-\ n : an inflammatory histiocytosis associated with disturbances in cholesterol metabolism that occurs chiefly in young children and is marked by cystic defects of the skull, exophthalmos, and diabetes insipidus — called also *Schüller-Christian disease*

Hand, Alfred (1868–1949), American physician.

Schüller \ˈshue-ler\, Artur (1874–1958), Austrian neurologist.

Christian, Henry Asbury (1876–1951), American physician.

hang·nail \ˈhaŋ-ˌnāl\ n : a bit of skin hanging loose at the side or root of a fingernail

hang·over \-ˌō-vər\ n 1 : disagreeable physical effects following heavy consumption of alcohol 2 : disagreeable aftereffects from the use of drugs

hang-up \-ˌəp\ n : a source of mental or emotional difficulty

Han·sen's bacillus \ˈhan-sənz-\ n : a bacterium of the genus *Mycobacterium* (*M. leprae*) that causes leprosy

Han·sen \ˈhän-sen\, Gerhard Henrik Armauer (1841–1912), Norwegian physician.

Hansen's disease n : LEPROSY

han·ta·vi·rus \ˈhan-tə-ˌvī-rəs\ n : any of a group of closely related arboviruses that cause hemorrhagic fever accompanied by leakage of plasma and red blood cells through the endothelium of blood vessels and by necrosis of the kidney

H antigen \\'āch-\ *n* : any of various antigens associated with the flagella of motile bacteria and used in serological identification of various bacteria — compare O ANTIGEN

hap·a·lo·nych·ia \\,ha-pə-lō-'ni-kē-ə\ *n* : abnormal softness of the fingernails or toenails

hap·loid \\'ha-,plȯid\ *adj* : having the gametic number of chromosomes or half the number characteristic of somatic cells : MONOPLOID — **haploid** *n* — **hap·loi·dy** \\-,plȯi-dē\ *n*

hap·lo·scope \\'ha-plə-,skōp\ *n* : a simple stereoscope that is used in the study of depth perception

hap·lo·type \\-,tīp\ *n* : a set of genes that determine different antigens but are closely enough linked to be inherited as a unit; *also* : the antigenic phenotype determined by a haplotype

hapt- *or* **hapto-** *comb form* : contact : touch : combination ⟨hapten⟩ ⟨haptic⟩ ⟨haptoglobin⟩

hap·ten \\'hap-,ten\ *n* : a small separable part of an antigen that reacts specif. with an antibody but is incapable of stimulating antibody production except in combination with an associated protein molecule — **hap·ten·ic** \\hap-'te-nik\ *adj*

hap·tic \\'hap-tik\ *adj* 1 : relating to or based on the sense of touch 2 : characterized by a predilection for the sense of touch

hap·tics \\-tiks\ *n* : a science concerned with the sense of touch

hap·to·glo·bin \\'hap-tə-,glō-bən\ *n* : any of a family of glycoproteins that are serum alpha globulins and can combine with free hemoglobin in the plasma

hard \\'härd\ *adj* 1 : not easily penetrated : not easily yielding to pressure 2 : of or relating to radiation of relatively high penetrating power (~ X rays) 3 : being at once addictive and gravely detrimental to health (such ~ drugs as heroin) 4 : resistant to biodegradation (~ pesticides like DDT) — **hard·ness** *n*

hard·en·ing \\'härd-ᵊn-iŋ\ *n* : SCLEROSIS 1 (~ of the arteries)

hard·of·hearing *adj* : of or relating to a defective but functional sense of hearing

hard pad *n* : a serious and frequently fatal virus disease of dogs now considered to be a form of distemper — called also *hard pad disease*

hard palate *n* : the bony anterior part of the palate forming the roof of the mouth

hardware disease *n* : traumatic damage to the viscera of cattle due to ingestion of a foreign body (as a nail or barbed wire)

Har·dy-Wein·berg law \\'här-dē-'win-,bərg-\ *n* : a fundamental principle of population genetics that is approximately true for small populations and holds with increasing exactness for larger and larger populations: population gene frequencies and population genotype frequencies remain constant from generation to generation if mating is random and if mutation, selection, immigration, and emigration do not occur — called also *Hardy-Weinberg principle*

Hardy, Godfrey Harold (1877–1947), British mathematician.

Wein·berg \\'vīn-berk\\, **Wilhelm** (1862–1937), German physician and geneticist.

hare·lip \\'har-,lip\ *n* : CLEFT LIP — **hare·lipped** \\-lipt\ *adj*

har·ma·line \\'här-mə-'lēn\ *n* : a hallucinogenic alkaloid $C_{13}H_{14}N_2O$ found in several plants (*Peganum harmala* of the family Zygophyllaceae and *Banisteriopsis* spp. of the family Malpighiaceae) and used in medicine as a stimulant of the central nervous system

har·mine \\'här-'mēn\ *n* : a hallucinogenic alkaloid $C_{13}H_{12}N_2O$ similar to harmaline

Hart·nup disease \\'härt-,nəp-\ *n* : an inherited metabolic disease that is caused by abnormalities of the renal tubules and is characterized esp. by aminoaciduria involving only monoamines having a single carboxyl group, a dry red scaly rash, and episodic muscular incoordination due to the effects of the disease on the cerebellum

Hartnup (*fl* 1950s), British family.

harts·horn \\'härts-,hȯrn\ *n* : a preparation of ammonia used as smelling salts

hash \\'hash\ *n* : HASHISH

Ha·shi·mo·to's disease \\,hä-shē-'mō-(,)tōz-\ *n* : chronic thyroiditis characterized by goiter, thyroid fibrosis, infiltration of thyroid tissue by lymphoid tissue, and the production of autoantibodies that attack the thyroid — called also *Hashimoto's struma, Hashimoto's thyroiditis, struma lymphomatosa*

Hashimoto, Hakaru (1881–1934), Japanese surgeon.

hash·ish \\'ha-,shēsh, ha-'shēsh\ *n* : the concentrated resin from the flowering tops of the female hemp plant (*Cannabis sativa*) that is smoked, chewed, or drunk for its intoxicating effect — called also *charas*; compare BHANG, MARIJUANA

Has·sall's corpuscle \\'ha-səlz-\ *n* : one of the small bodies of the medulla of the thymus having granular cells at the center surrounded by concentric layers of modified epithelial cells — called also *thymic corpuscle*

Hassall, Arthur Hill (1817–1894), British physician and chemist.

hatch·et \'ha-chət\ n : a dental excavator

haus·tra·tion \hȯ-'strā-shən\ n 1 : the property or state of having haustra 2 : HAUSTRUM

haus·trum \'hȯ-strəm\ n, pl **haus·tra** \-strə\ : one of the pouches or sacculations into which the large intestine is divided — **haus·tral** \-strəl\ adj

ha·ver·sian canal \hə-'vər-zhən\ n, often cap H : any of the small canals through which the blood vessels ramify in bone

Ha·vers \'hā-vərz, 'ha-\, Clopton (1655?–1702), British osteologist.

haversian system n, often cap H : a haversian canal with the laminae of bone that surround it — called also osteon

haw \'hȯ\ n : NICTITATING MEMBRANE; esp : an inflamed nictitating membrane of a domesticated mammal

hawk \'hȯk\ vb : to make a harsh coughing sound in or as if in clearing the throat; also : to raise by hawking 〈~ up phlegm〉 — **hawk** n

hay fever n : an acute allergic rhinitis and conjunctivitis that is sometimes accompanied by asthmatic symptoms; specif : POLLINOSIS

Hb abbr hemoglobin

H band \'āch-\ n : a relatively pale band in the middle of the A band of striated muscle

HBsAg abbr hepatitis B surface antigen

HBV abbr hepatitis B virus

HCG abbr human chorionic gonadotropin

HCT abbr hematocrit

HDL \ach-(,)dē-'el\ n : a lipoprotein of blood plasma that is composed of a high proportion of protein with little triglyceride and cholesterol and that is associated with decreased probability of developing atherosclerosis — called also alpha-lipoprotein, high-density lipoprotein; compare LDL, VLDL

He symbol helium

head \'hed\ n 1 : the division of the human body that contains the brain, the eyes, the ears, the nose, and the mouth; also : the corresponding anterior division of the body of all vertebrates, most arthropods, and many other animals 2 : HEADACHE 3 : a projection or extremity esp. of an anatomical part: as a : the rounded proximal end of a long bone (as the humerus) b : the end of a muscle nearest the origin 4 : the part of a boil, pimple, or abscess at which it is likely to break — **head** adj

head·ache \'he-,dāk\ n : pain in the head — called also cephalalgia — **head·achy** \-,dā-kē\ adj

head cold n : a common cold centered in the nasal passages and adjacent mucous tissues

head louse n : one of a variety of louse of the genus Pediculus (P. humanus capitis) that lives on the human scalp

head nurse n : CHARGE NURSE; esp : one with overall responsibility for the supervision of the administrative and clinical aspects of nursing care

head-shrink·er \'hed-,shriŋ-kər\ n : SHRINK

heal \'hēl\ vb 1 : to make or become sound or whole esp. in bodily condition 2 : to cure of disease or affliction — **heal·er** \'hē-lər\ n

¹heal·ing \'hē-liŋ\ n 1 : the act or process of curing or of restoring to health 2 : the process of getting well

²healing adj : tending to heal or cure : CURATIVE 〈a ~ art〉

health \'helth\ n, often attrib 1 : the condition of an organism or one of its parts in which it performs its vital functions normally or properly : the state of being sound in body or mind : esp : freedom from physical disease and pain — compare DISEASE 2 : the condition of an organism with respect to the performance of its vital functions esp. as evaluated subjectively 〈how is your ~ today〉

health care n : the maintenance and restoration of health by the treatment and prevention of disease esp. by trained and licensed professionals — **health–care** adj

health department n : a division of a local or larger government responsible for the oversight and care of matters relating to public health

health·ful \'helth-fəl\ adj : beneficial to health of body or mind — **health·ful·ly** adv — **health·ful·ness** n

health insurance n : insurance against loss through illness of the insured; esp : insurance providing compensation for medical expenses

health maintenance organization n : HMO

health spa n : a commercial establishment (as a resort) providing facilities devoted to health and fitness

health visitor n, Brit : a trained person who is usu. a qualified nurse and is employed by a local British authority to visit people (as nursing mothers) in their homes and advise them on health matters

healthy \'hel-thē\ adj **health·i·er; -est** 1 : enjoying health and vigor of body, mind, or spirit 2 : revealing a state of health 3 : conducive to health — **health·i·ly** \-thə-lē\ adv — **health·i·ness** \-thē-nəs\ n

hear \'hir\ vb **heard** \'hərd\; **hear·ing** : to perceive or have the capacity to perceive sound

hearing n : one of the senses that is concerned with the perception of sound, is mediated through the organ of Corti, is normally sensitive in humans to sound vibrations between 16 and 27,000 cycles per second but most receptive to those between 2000 and 5000 cycles per second, is conducted centrally by the cochlear branch of the auditory nerve, and is coordinated esp. in the medial geniculate body

hearing aid *n* : an electronic device usu. worn by a person for amplifying sound before it reaches the receptor organs

hearing dog *n* : a dog trained to alert its deaf or hearing-impaired owner to sounds (as of a doorbell, alarm, or telephone) — called also *hearing ear dog*

heart \'härt\ *n* : a hollow muscular organ of vertebrate animals that by its rhythmic contraction acts as a pump maintaining the circulation of the blood and that in the human adult is about five inches (13 centimeters) long and three and one half inches (9 centimeters) broad, is of conical form, is enclosed in a serous pericardium, and consists as in other mammals and in birds of four chambers divided into an upper pair of rather thin-walled atria which receive blood from the veins and a lower pair of thick-walled ventricles into which the blood is forced and which in turn pump it into the arteries

heart attack *n* : an acute episode of heart disease (as myocardial infarction) due to insufficient blood supply to the heart muscle itself esp. when caused by a coronary thrombosis or a coronary occlusion

heart·beat \'härt-ˌbēt\ *n* : one complete pulsation of the heart

heart block *n* : incoordination of the heartbeat in which the atria and ventricles beat independently due to defective transmission through the bundle of His and which is marked by decreased cardiac output often with cerebral ischemia

heart·burn \-ˌbərn\ *n* : a burning discomfort behind the lower part of the sternum usu. related to spasm of the lower end of the esophagus or of the upper part of the stomach — called also *cardialgia, pyrosis*; compare WATER BRASH

heart disease *n* : an abnormal organic condition of the heart or of the heart and circulation

heart failure *n* 1 : a condition in which the heart is unable to pump blood at an adequate rate or in adequate volume — compare ANGINA PECTORIS, CONGESTIVE HEART FAILURE, CORONARY FAILURE 2 : cessation of heartbeat : DEATH

heart–lung machine *n* : a mechanical pump that maintains circulation during heart surgery by shunting blood away from the heart, oxygenating it, and returning it to the body

heart murmur *n* : MURMUR

heart rate *n* : a measure of cardiac activity usu. expressed as number of beats per minute

heart·wa·ter \'härt-ˌwȯ-tər, -ˌwä-\ *n* : a serious febrile disease of sheep, goats, and cattle in southern Africa that is caused by a bacterium of the genus *Cowdria* (*C. ruminantium*) transmitted by a bont tick — called also *heartwater disease, heartwater fever*

heart·worm \-ˌwərm\ *n* : a filarial worm of the genus *Dirofilaria* (*D. immitis*) that is a parasite esp. in the right heart of dogs and is transmitted by mosquitoes; *also* : infestation with or disease caused by the heartworm

heat \'hēt\ *n* 1 a : a feverish state of the body : pathological excessive bodily temperature (as from inflammation) b : a warm flushed condition of the body (as after exercise) 2 : sexual excitement esp. in a female mammal; *specif* : ESTRUS

heat cramps *n pl* : a condition that is marked by sudden development of cramps in skeletal muscles and that results from prolonged work in high temperatures accompanied by profuse perspiration with loss of sodium chloride from the body

heat exchanger *n* : a device (as in an apparatus for extracorporeal blood circulation) for transferring heat from one fluid to another without allowing them to mix

heat exhaustion *n* : a condition marked by weakness, nausea, dizziness, and profuse sweating that results from physical exertion in a hot environment — called also *heat prostration*; compare HEATSTROKE

heat prostration *n* : HEAT EXHAUSTION

heat rash *n* : PRICKLY HEAT

heat·stroke \'hēt-ˌstrōk\ *n* : a condition marked esp. by cessation of sweating, extremely high body temperature, and collapse that results from prolonged exposure to high temperature — compare HEAT EXHAUSTION

heave \'hēv\ *vb* **heaved; heav·ing** : VOMIT, RETCH

heaves \'hēvz\ *n sing or pl* 1 : chronic emphysema of the horse affecting the alveolae of the lungs — called also *broken wind* 2 : a spell of retching or vomiting

heavy chain *n* : either of the two larger of the four polypeptide chains comprising antibodies — compare LIGHT CHAIN

he·be·phre·nia \ˌhē-bə-ˈfrē-nē-ə, -ˈfre-\ *n* : a disorganized form of schizophrenia characterized esp. by incoherence, delusions which if present lack an underlying theme, and affect that is flat, inappropriate, or silly — **he·be·phre·nic** \-ˈfre-nik, -ˈfrē-\ *adj or n*

Heb·er·den's node \'he-bər-dənz-\ *n* : any of the bony knots at joint margins (as at the terminal joints of the fingers) commonly associated with osteoarthritis

Heberden, William (1710–1801), British physician.

hec·tic \'hek-tik\ *adj* 1 : of, relating to, or being a fluctuating but persistent fever (as in tuberculosis) 2 : having a hectic fever

heel \'hēl\ *n* 1 : the back of the human foot below the ankle and behind the arch 2 : the part of the palm of the hand nearest the wrist

heel bone *n* : CALCANEUS

heel fly *n* : CATTLE GRUB; *esp* : one in the adult stage

Heer·fordt's syndrome \'hār-,fórts-\ *n* : UVEOPAROTID FEVER

Heerfordt, Christian Frederik (*b* 1871), Danish ophthalmologist.

height \'hīt\ *n* : the distance from the bottom to the top of something standing upright; *esp* : the distance from the lowest to the highest point of an animal body esp. of a human being in a natural standing position or from the lowest point to an arbitrarily chosen upper point

Heim·lich maneuver \'hīm-lik-\ *n* : the manual application of sudden upward pressure on the upper abdomen of a choking victim to force a foreign object from the windpipe

Heimlich, Henry Jay (*b* 1920), American surgeon.

Heinz body \'hīnts-, 'hinz-\ *n* : a cellular inclusion in a red blood cell that consists of damaged aggregated hemoglobin and is associated with some forms of hemolytic anemia

Heinz \'hīnts\, **Robert** (1865–1924), German physician.

hela cell \'hē-lə-\ *n, often cap H & 1st L* : a cell of a continuously cultured strain isolated from a human uterine cervical carcinoma in 1951 and used in biomedical research esp. to culture viruses

Lacks \'laks\, **Henrietta** (*fl* 1951), American hospital patient.

helio- *or* **heli-** *comb form* : sun ⟨*heliotherapy*⟩

helic- *or* **helico-** *comb form* : helix : spiral ⟨*helical*⟩ ⟨*helicotrema*⟩

he·li·cal \'he-li-kəl, 'hē-\ *adj* : of, relating to, or having the form of a helix; *broadly* : SPIRAL 1a — **he·li·cal·ly** *adv*

hel·i·cine artery \'he-lə-,sēn-, 'hē-lə-,sīn-\ *n* : any of various convoluted and dilated arterial vessels that empty directly into the cavernous spaces of erectile tissue and function in its erection

hel·i·co·bac·ter \'he-li-kō-,bak-tər\ *n* 1 *cap* : a genus of bacteria formerly placed in the genus *Campylobacter* and including one (*H. pylori*) associated with gastritis and implicated in gastric and duodenal ulcers and gastric cancer 2 : any bacterium of the genus *Helicobacter*

hel·i·co·trema \,he-lə-kō-'trē-mə\ *n*

: the minute opening by which the scala tympani and scala vestibuli communicate at the top of the cochlea of the ear

he·lio·ther·a·py \,hē-lē-ō-'ther-ə-pē\ *n, pl* **-pies** : the use of sunlight or of an artificial source of ultraviolet, visible, or infrared radiation for therapeutic purposes

he·li·um \'hē-lē-əm\ *n* : a light nonflammable gaseous element — symbol *He*; see ELEMENT table

he·lix \'hē-liks\ *n, pl* **he·li·ces** \'he-lə-,sēz, 'hē-\ *also* **he·lix·es** \'hē-lik-səz\ 1 : the inward curved rim of the external ear 2 : a curve traced on a cylinder by the rotation of a point crossing its right sections at a constant oblique angle; *broadly* : SPIRAL 2 — see ALPHA-HELIX, DOUBLE HELIX

hel·le·bore \'he-lə-,bōr\ *n* 1 : any of a genus (*Helleborus*) of poisonous herbs of the buttercup family (Ranunculaceae) that have showy flowers with sepals like petals; *also* : the dried rhizome or an extract or powder of this formerly used in medicine 2 a : a poisonous herb of the genus *Veratrum* b : the dried rhizome of either of two hellebores (*Veratrum viride* of America and *V. album* of Europe) or a powder or extract of this containing alkaloids used as a cardiac and respiratory depressant and as an insecticide — called also *veratrum*

hel·minth \'hel-,minth\ *n* : a parasitic worm (as a tapeworm, liver fluke, ascarid, or leech); *esp* : an intestinal worm — **hel·min·thic** \hel-'min-thik\ *adj*

helminth- *or* **helmintho-** *comb form* : helminth ⟨*helminth*iasis⟩ ⟨*helminth*ology⟩

hel·min·thi·a·sis \,hel-mən-'thī-ə-səs\ *n, pl* **-a·ses** \-,sēz\ : infestation with or disease caused by parasitic worms

hel·min·thol·o·gy \-'thä-lə-jē\ *n, pl* **-gies** : a branch of zoology concerned with helminths; *esp* : the study of parasitic worms — **hel·min·thol·o·gist** \-'thä-lə-jist\ *n*

Helo·der·ma \,hē-lō-'dər-mə, ,he-\ *n* : a genus of lizards (family Helodermatidae) including the Gila monsters

helper T cell *n* : a T cell that participates in an immune response by recognizing a foreign antigen and secreting lymphokines to activate T cell and B cell proliferation, that usu. carries CD4 molecular markers on its cell surface, and that is reduced to 20 percent or less of normal numbers in AIDS — called also *helper cell, helper lymphocyte, helper T lymphocyte*

hem- *or* **hemo-** *comb form* : blood ⟨*he*mal⟩ ⟨*hem*angioma⟩ ⟨*hem*ophilia⟩

hema- *comb form* : HEM- ⟨*hema*cytometer⟩

he·ma·cy·tom·e·ter \,hē-mə-sī-'tä-mə-tər\ *n* : an instrument for counting blood cells — called also *hemocytometer*

hem·ad·sorp·tion \hē-(₁)mad-ˈsórp-shən, -ˈzórp-\ n : adherence of red blood cells to the surface of something (as a virus or cell) — **hem·ad·sorb·ing** \-ˈsòr-biŋ, -ˈzòr-\ *adj*

hem·ag·glu·ti·na·tion \ˌhē-mə-ˌglüt-ᵊn-ˈā-shən\ n : agglutination of red blood cells — **hem·ag·glu·ti·nate** \-ˈglüt-ᵊn-ˌāt\ *vb*

hem·ag·glu·ti·nin \ˌhē-mə-ˈglüt-ᵊn-ən\ n : an agglutinin (as an antibody or viral capsid protein) that causes hemagglutination — compare LEUKOAGGLUTININ

he·mal \ˈhē-məl\ *adj* 1 : of or relating to the blood or blood vessels 2 : relating to or situated on the side of the spinal cord where the heart and chief blood vessels are placed — compare NEURAL 2

he·man·gio·en·do·the·li·o·ma \ˌhē-ˌman-jē-ō-ˌen-dō-ˌthē-lē-ˈō-mə\ n, *pl* -**mas** *or* -**ma·ta** \-mə-tə\ : an often malignant tumor originating by proliferation of capillary endothelium

hem·an·gi·o·ma \ˌhē-ˌman-jē-ˈō-mə\ n, *pl* -**mas** *or* -**ma·ta** \-mə-tə\ : a usu. benign tumor made up of blood vessels that typically occurs as a purplish or reddish slightly elevated area of skin

he·man·gi·o·ma·to·sis \-ˌjē-ō-mə-ˈtō-səs\ n, *pl* -**to·ses** \-ˌsēz\ : a condition in which hemangiomas are present in several parts of the body

hem·an·gio·peri·cy·to·ma \-ˌjē-ō-ˌper-ə-ˌsī-ˈtō-mə\ n, *pl* -**mas** *or* -**ma·ta** \-mə-tə\ : a vascular tumor composed of spindle cells that are held to be derived from pericytes

he·man·gio·sar·co·ma \-ˌjē-ō-sär-ˈkō-mə\ n, *pl* -**mas** *or* -**ma·ta** \-mə-tə\ : a malignant hemangioma

he·mar·thro·sis \ˌhē-mär-ˈthrō-səs, ˌhe-\ n, *pl* -**thro·ses** \-ˌsēz\ : hemorrhage into a joint

hemat- *or* **hemato-** *comb form* : HEM- ⟨*hemat*emesis⟩ ⟨*hemato*genous⟩

he·ma·tem·e·sis \ˌhē-mə-ˈte-mə-səs, ˌhē-mə-tə-ˈmē-səs\ n, *pl* -**e·ses** \-ˌsēz\ : the vomiting of blood

he·ma·tin \ˈhē-mə-tən\ n 1 : a brownish black or bluish black derivative C₃₄H₃₃N₄O₅Fe of oxidized heme containing iron with a valence of three; *also* : any of several similar compounds 2 : HEME

he·ma·tin·ic \ˌhē-mə-ˈti-nik\ n : an agent that tends to stimulate blood cell formation or to increase the hemoglobin in the blood — **hematinic** *adj*

he·ma·to·cele \ˈhē-mə-tə-ˌsēl, hi-ˈma-tə-\ n : a blood-filled cavity of the body; *also* : the effusion of blood into a body cavity (as the scrotum)

he·ma·to·che·zia \ˌhē-mə-tə-ˈkē-zē-ə, ˌhē-; hi-ˌma-tə-\ n : the passage of blood in the feces — compare MELENA

he·ma·to·col·pos \ˌhē-mə-tō-ˈkäl-pəs, ˌhē-, -ˈpäs; hi-ˌma-tə-\ n : an accumulation of blood within the vagina

he·mat·o·crit \hi-ˈma-tə-krət, -ˌkrit\ n 1 : an instrument for determining usu. by centrifugation the relative amounts of plasma and corpuscles in blood 2 : the ratio of the volume of packed red blood cells to the volume of whole blood as determined by a hematocrit

he·ma·to·gen·ic \ˌhē-mə-tə-ˈje-nik\ *adj* : HEMATOGENOUS 2

he·ma·tog·e·nous \ˌhē-mə-ˈtä-jə-nəs\ *adj* 1 : producing blood 2 : involving, spread by, or arising in the blood — **he·ma·tog·e·nous·ly** *adv*

he·ma·to·log·ic \ˌhē-mət-ᵊl-ˈä-jik\ *also* **he·ma·to·log·i·cal** \-ji-kəl\ *adj* : of or relating to blood or to hematology

he·ma·tol·o·gy \ˌhē-mə-ˈtä-lə-jē\ n, *pl* -**gies** : a medical science that deals with the blood and blood-forming organs — **he·ma·tol·o·gist** \-jist\ n

he·ma·to·ma \ˌhē-mə-ˈtō-mə\ n, *pl* -**mas** *or* -**ma·ta** \-mə-tə\ : a mass of usu. clotted blood that forms in a tissue, organ, or body space as a result of a broken blood vessel

he·ma·to·me·tra \ˌhē-mə-tə-ˈmē-trə, ˌhe-\ n : an accumulation of blood or menstrual fluid in the uterus

he·ma·to·my·e·lia \hi-ˌma-tə-ˌmī-ˈē-lē-ə, ˌhē-mə-tō-\ n : a hemorrhage into the spinal cord

he·ma·to·pa·thol·o·gy \hi-ˌma-tə-pə-ˈthä-lə-jē, ˌhē-mə-tō-\ n, *pl* -**gies** : the medical science concerned with diseases of the blood and related tissues — **he·ma·to·pa·thol·o·gist** \-jist\ n

he·ma·toph·a·gous \ˌhē-mə-ˈtä-fə-gəs\ *adj* : feeding on blood ⟨∼ insects⟩

he·ma·to·poi·e·sis \hi-ˌma-tə-pói-ˈē-səs, ˌhē-mə-tə-\ n, *pl* -**e·ses** \-ˌsēz\ : the formation of blood or of blood cells in the living body — called also *hemopoiesis* — **he·ma·to·poi·et·ic** \-ˈe-tik\ *adj*

he·ma·to·por·phy·rin \ˌhē-mə-tə-ˈpór-fə-rən, ˌhe-\ n : any of several isomeric porphyrins C₃₄H₃₈O₆N₄ that are hydrated derivatives of protoporphyrins: *esp* : the deep red crystalline pigment obtained by treating hematin or heme with acid

he·ma·to·sal·pinx \ˌhē-mə-tə-ˈsal-(ˌ)piŋks, ˌhe-, hi-ˌma-tə-\ n, *pl* -**sal·pin·ges** \-sal-ˈpin-(ˌ)jēz\ : accumulation of blood in a fallopian tube

he·ma·tox·y·lin \ˌhē-mə-ˈtäk-sə-lən\ n : a crystalline phenolic compound C₁₆H₁₄O₆ used chiefly as a biological stain

he·ma·tu·ria \ˌhē-mə-ˈtùr-ē-ə, -ˈtyùr-\ n : the presence of blood or blood cells in the urine

heme \ˈhēm\ n : the deep red iron-containing prosthetic group C₃₄H₃₂N₄O₄Fe of hemoglobin and myoglobin

hem·er·a·lo·pia \ˌhe-mə-rə-ˈlō-pē-ə\ n 1

: a defect of vision characterized by a reduced visual capacity in bright lights **2** : NIGHT BLINDNESS — not considered good medical usage in this sense

hemi- *prefix* : half ⟨*hemi*block⟩ ⟨*hemi*pelvectomy⟩

-he·mia \ˈhē-mē-ə\ — see -EMIA

hemi·an·es·the·sia \-ˌan-əs-ˈthē-zhə\ *n* : loss of sensation in either lateral half of the body

hemi·an·o·pia \-ə-ˈnō-pē-ə\ *or* **hemi·an·op·sia** \-ˈnäp-sē-ə\ *n* : blindness in one half of the visual field of one or both eyes — called also *hemiopia* — **hemi·an·op·tic** \-ə-ˈnäp-tik\ *adj*

hemi·at·ro·phy \-ˈa-trə-fē\ *n*, *pl* **-phies** : atrophy that affects one half of an organ or part or one side of the whole body — compare HEMIHYPERTROPHY

hemi·a·zy·gos vein \-(ˌ)ā-ˈzī-gəs-, -ˈa-zə-gəs-\ *n* : a vein that receives blood from the lower half of the left thoracic wall and the left abdominal wall, ascends along the left side of the spinal column, and empties into the azygos vein near the middle of the thorax

hemi·bal·lis·mus \ˌhe-mi-ba-ˈliz-məs\ *also* **hemi·bal·lism** \-ˈba-li-zəm\ *n* : violent uncontrollable movements of one lateral half of the body usu. due to a lesion in the subthalamic nucleus of the contralateral side of the body

hemi·block \ˈhe-mi-ˌbläk\ *n* : inhibition or failure of conduction of the muscular excitatory impulse in either of the two divisions of the left branch of the bundle of His

he·mic \ˈhē-mik\ *adj* : of, relating to, or produced by the blood or the circulation of the blood

hemi·cho·lin·ium \-kō-ˈli-nē-əm\ *n* : any of several blockers of the parasympathetic nervous system that interfere with the synthesis of acetylcholine

hemi·cho·rea \ˌhe-mi-kə-ˈrē-ə\ *n* : chorea affecting only one lateral half of the body

hemi·col·ec·to·my \-kə-ˈlek-tə-mē, -kō-\ *n*, *pl* **-mies** : surgical excision of part of the colon

hemi·cra·nia \-ˈkrā-nē-ə\ *n* : pain in one side of the head — **hemi·cra·ni·al** \-nē-əl\ *adj*

hemi·des·mo·some \-ˈdez-mə-ˌsōm\ *n* : a specialization of the plasma membrane of an epithelial cell that serves to connect the basal surface of the cell to the basement membrane

hemi·di·a·phragm \-ˈdī-ə-ˌfram\ *n* : one of the two lateral halves of the diaphragm separating the chest and abdominal cavities

hemi·fa·cial \-ˈfā-shəl\ *adj* : involving or affecting one lateral half of the face

hemi·field \ˈhe-mi-ˌfēld\ *n* : one of two halves of a sensory field (as of vision)

hemi·gas·trec·to·my \ˌhe-mi-ˌga-ˈstrek-tə-mē\ *n*, *pl* **-mies** : surgical removal of one half of the stomach

hemi·glos·sec·to·my \-ˌglä-ˈsek-tə-mē,

-ˌglō-\ *n*, *pl* **-mies** : surgical excision of one lateral half of the tongue

hemi·hy·per·tro·phy \-hī-ˈpər-trə-fē\ *n*, *pl* **-phies** : hypertrophy of one half of an organ or part or of one side of the whole body (facial ∼) — compare HEMIATROPHY

hemi·lam·i·nec·to·my \-ˌla-mə-ˈnek-tə-mē\ *n*, *pl* **-mies** : laminectomy involving the removal of vertebral laminae on only one side

hemi·me·lia \-ˈmē-lē-ə\ *n* : a congenital abnormality (as total or partial absence) affecting only the distal half of a limb

he·min \ˈhē-mən\ *n* : a red-brown to blue-black crystalline salt $C_{34}H_{32}N_4O_4FeCl$ that inhibits the biosynthesis of porphyrin and is used to ameliorate the symptoms of some forms of porphyria

hemi·o·pia \ˌhe-mē-ˈō-pē-ə\ *or* **hemi·op·sia** \-ˈäp-sē-ə\ *n* : HEMIANOPIA

hemi·pa·re·sis \ˌhe-mi-pə-ˈrē-səs, -ˈpar-ə-\ *n*, *pl* **-reses** \-ˌsēz\ : muscular weakness or partial paralysis restricted to one side of the body — **hemi·pa·ret·ic** \-pə-ˈre-tik\ *adj*

hemi·pel·vec·to·my \-pel-ˈvek-tə-mē\ *n*, *pl* **-mies** : amputation of one leg together with removal of the half of the pelvis on the same side of the body

hemi·ple·gia \ˌhe-mi-ˈplē-jə, -jē-ə\ *n* : total or partial paralysis of one side of the body that results from disease of or injury to the motor centers of the brain

¹**hemi·ple·gic** \-ˈplē-jik\ *adj* : relating to or marked by hemiplegia

²**hemiplegic** *n* : a hemiplegic individual

hemi·ret·i·na \ˌhe-mi-ˈret-ᵊn-ə\ *n*, *pl* **-i·nas** *or* **-i·nae** \-ᵊn-ˌē, -ˌī\ : one half of the retina of one eye

hemi·sect \ˈhe-mi-ˌsekt\ *vb* : to divide along the mesial plane

hemi·sphere \-ˌsfir\ *n* : half of a spherical structure or organ: as **a** : CEREBRAL HEMISPHERE **b** : either of the two lobes of the cerebellum of which one projects laterally and posteriorly from each side of the vermis

hemi·spher·ec·to·my \-ˌsfi-ˈrek-tə-mē\ *n*, *pl* **-mies** : surgical removal of a cerebral hemisphere

hemi·spher·ic \ˌhe-mi-ˈsfir-ik, -ˈsfer-\ *adj* : of, relating to, or affecting a hemisphere (as a cerebral hemisphere)

hemi·tho·rax \-ˈthōr-ˌaks\ *n*, *pl* **-tho·rax·es** *or* **-tho·ra·ces** \-ˈthōr-ə-ˌsēz\ : a lateral half of the thorax

hemi·thy·roid·ec·to·my \-ˌthī-ˌröi-ˈdek-tə-mē\ *n*, *pl* **-mies** : surgical removal of one lobe of the thyroid gland

hemi·zy·gote \-ˈzī-ˌgōt\ *n* : one that is hemizygous

hemi·zy·gous \-ˈzī-gəs\ *adj* : having or characterized by one or more genes (as in a genetic deficiency or in an X chromosome paired with a Y chromosome) that have no allelic counter-parts

hem·lock \'hem-,läk\ *n* 1 : any of several poisonous herbs (as a poison hemlock) of the carrot family (Umbelliferae) having finely cut leaves and small white flowers 2 : a drug or lethal drink prepared from the poison hemlock

hemo- — see HEM-

he·mo·ag·glu·ti·nin *var of* HEMAGGLUTININ

he·mo·bar·to·nel·lo·sis *var of* HAEMOBARTONELLOSIS

he·mo·bil·ia \,hē-mə-'bi-lē-ə\ *n* : bleeding into the bile ducts and gallbladder

he·mo·blas·to·sis \,hē-mə-,blas-'tō-səs\ *n, pl* -to·ses \-,sēz\ : abnormal proliferation of the blood-forming tissues

he·mo·cult \'hē-mə-,kəlt\ *adj* : relating to or being a modified guaiac test for occult blood

he·mo·cho·ri·al \,hē-mə-'kōr-ē-əl\ *adj, of a placenta* : having the fetal epithelium bathed in maternal blood

he·mo·chro·ma·to·sis \,hē-mə-,krō-mə-'tō-səs\ *n, pl* -to·ses \-,sēz\ : a metabolic disorder esp. of males that is characterized by deposition of iron-containing pigments in the tissues and frequently by diabetes and weakness — compare HEMOSIDEROSIS — **he·mo·chro·ma·tot·ic** \-'tä-tik\ *adj*

he·mo·co·ag·u·la·tion \,hē-mō-kō-,a-gyə-'lā-shən\ *n* : coagulation of blood

he·mo·con·cen·tra·tion \,hē-mō-,kän-sən-'trā-shən\ *n* : increased concentration of cells and solids in the blood usu. resulting from loss of fluid to the tissues — compare HEMODILUTION

he·mo·cul·ture \'hē-mə-,kəl-chər\ *n* : a culture made from blood to detect the presence of pathogenic microorganisms

he·mo·cy·to·blast \,hē-mə-'sī-tə-,blast\ *n* : a stem cell for blood-cellular elements; *esp* : one considered competent to produce all types of blood cell — **he·mo·cy·to·blas·tic** \-,sī-tə-'blas-tik\ *adj*

he·mo·cy·tom·e·ter \-sī-'tä-mə-tər\ *n* : HEMACYTOMETER

he·mo·di·al·y·sis \,hē-mō-dī-'a-lə-səs\ *n, pl* -y·ses \-,sēz\ : the process of removing blood from an artery (as of a kidney patient), purifying it by dialysis, adding vital substances, and returning it to a vein

he·mo·di·a·lyz·er \-'dī-ə-,lī-zər\ *n* : ARTIFICIAL KIDNEY

he·mo·di·lu·tion \-dī-'lü-shən, -də-\ *n* : decreased concentration (as after hemorrhage) of cells and solids in the blood resulting from gain of fluid from the tissues — compare HEMOCONCENTRATION — **he·mo·di·lute** \-'lüt\ *vb*

he·mo·dy·nam·ic \-dī-'na-mik, -də-\ *adj* 1 : of, relating to, or involving hemodynamics 2 : relating to or functioning in the mechanics of blood circulation — **he·mo·dy·nam·i·cal·ly** *adv*

he·mo·dy·nam·ics \-miks\ *n sing or pl* 1 : a branch of physiology that deals with the circulation of the blood 2 a : the forces or mechanisms involved in circulation b : hemodynamic effect (as of a drug)

he·mo·glo·bin \'hē-mə-,glō-bən\ *n* : an iron-containing respiratory pigment of red blood cells that functions primarily in the transport of oxygen from the lungs to the tissues of the body, that consists of a globin of four subunits each of which is linked to a heme molecule, that combines loosely and reversibly with oxygen in the lungs or gills to form oxyhemoglobin and with carbon dioxide in the tissues to form carbhemoglobin, and that in humans is present normally in blood to the extent of 14 to 16 grams in 100 milliliters — compare CARBOXYHEMOGLOBIN, METHEMOGLOBIN — **he·mo·glo·bin·ic** \,hē-mə-glō-'bi-nik\ *adj* — **he·mo·glo·bi·nous** \-'glō-bə-nəs\ *adj*

hemoglobin A *n* : the hemoglobin in the red blood cells of normal human adults

hemoglobin C *n* : an abnormal hemoglobin that differs from hemoglobin A in having a lysine residue substituted for the glutamic-acid residue at position 6 in two of the four polypeptide chains making up the hemoglobin molecule

hemoglobin C disease *n* : an inherited hemolytic anemia that occurs esp. in blacks and is characterized esp. by splenomegaly and the presence of target cells and hemoglobin C in the blood

he·mo·glo·bin·emia \-,glō-bə-'nē-mē-ə\ *n* : the presence of free hemoglobin in the blood plasma resulting from the solution of hemoglobin out of the red blood cells or from their disintegration

hemoglobin F *n* : FETAL HEMOGLOBIN

he·mo·glo·bin·om·e·ter \-,glō-bə-'nä-mə-tər\ *n* : an instrument for the colorimetric determination of hemoglobin in blood — **he·mo·glo·bin·om·e·try** \-'nä-mə-trē\ *n*

he·mo·glo·bin·op·a·thy \,hē-mə-,glō-bə-'nä-pə-thē\ *n, pl* -thies : a blood disorder (as sickle-cell anemia) caused by a genetically determined change in the molecular structure of hemoglobin

hemoglobin S *n* : an abnormal hemoglobin occurring in the red blood cells in sickle-cell anemia and sickle-cell trait and differing from hemoglobin A in having a valine residue substituted for the glutamic-acid residue in position 6 of two of the four polypeptide chains making up the hemoglobin molecule

he·mo·glo·bin·uria \,hē-mə-,glō-bə-'nur-ē-ə, -'nyur-\ *n* : the presence of free hemoglobin in the urine — he·mo·glo·bin·uric \-'nür-ik, -'nyür-\ adj

he·mo·gram \'hē-mə-ˌgram\ n : a systematic report of the findings from a blood examination

he·mol·y·sate or he·mol·y·zate \hi-'mä-lə-ˌzāt, -ˌsāt\ n : a product of hemolysis

he·mol·y·sin \hi-'mä-lə-sᵊn, hi-'mä-lə-sən\ n : a substance that causes the dissolution of red blood cells — called also hemotoxin

he·mol·y·sis \hi-'mä-lə-səs, ˌhē-mə-'li-səs\ n, pl -y·ses \-ˌsēz\ : lysis of red blood cells with liberation of hemoglobin — see BETA HEMOLYSIS — he·mo·lyt·ic \ˌhē-mə-'li-tik\ adj

hemolytic anemia n : anemia caused by excessive destruction (as in infection or sickle-cell anemia) of red blood cells

hemolytic disease of the newborn n : ERYTHROBLASTOSIS FETALIS

hemolytic jaundice n : a condition characterized by excessive destruction of red blood cells accompanied by jaundice — compare HEREDITARY SPHEROCYTOSIS

he·mo·lyze \'hē-mə-ˌlīz\ vb -lyzed; -lyz·ing : to cause or undergo hemolysis of

he·mo·par·a·site \ˌhē-mō-'par-ə-ˌsīt\ n : an animal parasite (as a filarial worm) living in the blood of a vertebrate — he·mo·par·a·sit·ic \-ˌpar-ə-'si·tik\ adj

he·mop·a·thy \hē-'mä-pə-thē\ n, pl -thies : a pathological state (as anemia or agranulocytosis) of the blood or blood-forming tissues

he·mo·per·fu·sion \ˌhē-mō-pər-'fyü-zhən\ n : blood cleansing by adsorption on an extracorporeal medium (as activated charcoal) of impurities of larger molecular size than are removed by dialysis

he·mo·peri·car·di·um \-ˌper-ə-'kär-dē-əm\ n, pl -dia \-dē-ə\ : blood in the pericardial cavity

he·mo·peri·to·ne·um \-ˌper-ət-ᵊn-'ē-əm\ n : blood in the peritoneal cavity

he·mo·pex·in \-'pek-sən\ n : a glycoprotein that binds heme preventing its excretion in urine and that is part of the beta-globulin fraction of human serum

¹he·mo·phile \'hē-mə-ˌfīl\ adj 1 : HEMOPHILIAC 2 : HEMOPHILIC 2

²hemophile n 1 : HEMOPHILIAC 2 : a hemophilic organism (as a bacterium)

he·mo·phil·ia \ˌhē-mə-'fil-ē-ə\ n : a sex-linked hereditary blood defect that occurs almost exclusively in males and is characterized by delayed clotting of the blood and consequent difficulty in controlling hemorrhage even after minor injuries

hemophilia A n : hemophilia caused by the absence of factor VIII from the blood

hemophilia B n : CHRISTMAS DISEASE

¹he·mo·phil·i·ac \-'fi-lē-ˌak\ adj : of, resembling, or affected with hemophilia

²hemophiliac n : one affected with hemophilia — called also bleeder

¹he·mo·phil·ic \-'fi-lik\ adj 1 : HEMOPHILIAC 2 : tending to thrive in blood ⟨~ bacteria⟩

²hemophilic n : HEMOPHILIAC

He·moph·i·lus \hē-'mä-fə-ləs\ n, syn of HAEMOPHILUS

he·mo·pneu·mo·tho·rax \ˌhē-mə-ˌnü-mə-'thȯr-ˌaks, -myü-\ n, pl -rax·es or -ra·ces \-'thȯr-ə-ˌsēz\ : the accumulation of blood and air in the pleural cavity

he·mo·poi·e·sis \ˌhē-mə-pȯi-'ē-səs\ n, pl -e·ses \-ˌsēz\ : HEMATOPOIESIS — he·mo·poi·et·ic \-'e-tik\ adj

he·mo·pro·tein \-'prō-ˌtēn\ n : a conjugated protein (as hemoglobin or cytochrome) whose prosthetic group is a porphyrin combined with iron

he·mop·ty·sis \hi-'mäp-tə-səs\ n, pl -ty·ses \-ˌsēz\ : expectoration of blood from some part of the respiratory tract

he·mor·rhe·ol·o·gy \ˌhē-mə-rē-'ä-lə-jē\ n, pl -gies : the science of the physical properties of blood flow in the circulatory system

hem·or·rhage \'hem-rij, 'hem-ə-\ n : a copious discharge of blood from the blood vessels — hemorrhage vb — hem·or·rhag·ic \ˌhe-mə-'ra-jik\ adj

hemorrhagica — see PURPURA HEMORRHAGICA

hemorrhagic diathesis n : an abnormal tendency to spontaneous often severe bleeding — compare HEMOPHILIA, PURPURA HEMORRHAGICA

hemorrhagic fever n : any of a diverse group of virus diseases (as Korean hemorrhagic fever) usu. transmitted by arthropods or rodents and characterized by a sudden onset, fever, aching, bleeding in the internal organs (as of the gastrointestinal tract), petechiae, and shock — see HANTAVIRUS

hemorrhagic septicemia n : any of several pasteurelloses of domestic animals that are caused by a bacterium of the genus Pasteurella (P. multocida)

hemorrhagic shock n : shock resulting from reduction of the volume of blood in the body due to hemorrhage

hemorrhagicum — see CORPUS HEMORRHAGICUM

hem·or·rhoid \'hem-ˌrȯid, 'he-mə-\ n : a mass of dilated veins in swollen tissue at the margin of the anus or nearby within the rectum — usu. used in pl.; called also piles

¹hem·or·rhoid·al \ˌhem-'rȯid-ᵊl, ˌhe-mə-\ adj 1 : of, relating to, or involving hemorrhoids 2 : RECTAL

²hemorrhoidal n : a hemorrhoidal part (as an artery or vein)

hemorrhoidal artery n : RECTAL ARTERY

hemorrhoidal vein n : RECTAL VEIN

hem·or·rhoid·ec·to·my \ˌhe-mə-ˌrȯi-ˈdek-tə-mē\ *n, pl* **-mies** : surgical removal of a hemorrhoid

he·mo·sid·er·in \ˌhē-mō-ˈsi-də-rən\ *n* : a yellowish brown granular pigment formed by breakdown of hemoglobin, found in phagocytes and in tissues esp. in disturbances of iron metabolism (as in hemochromatosis, hemosiderosis, or some anemias) — compare FERRITIN

he·mo·sid·er·o·sis \-ˌsi-də-ˈrō-səs\ *n, pl* **-o·ses** \-ˌsēz\ : excessive deposition of hemosiderin in bodily tissues as a result of the breakdown of red blood cells — compare HEMOCHROMATOSIS

he·mo·sta·sis \ˌhē-mə-ˈstā-səs\ *n, pl* **-sta·ses** \-ˌsēz\ **1** : stoppage or sluggishness of blood flow **2** : the arrest of bleeding (as by a hemostatic agent)

he·mo·stat \ˈhē-mə-ˌstat\ *n* **1** : HEMOSTATIC 2 : an instrument and esp. forceps for compressing a bleeding vessel

¹he·mo·stat·ic \ˌhē-mə-ˈsta-tik\ *n* : an agent that checks bleeding; *esp* : one that shortens the clotting time of blood

²hemostatic *adj* **1** : of or caused by hemostasis **2** : serving to check bleeding

he·mo·ther·a·py \-ˈther-ə-pē\ *n, pl* **-pies** : treatment involving the administration of fresh blood, a blood fraction, or a blood preparation

he·mo·tho·rax \ˌhē-mə-ˈthȯr-ˌaks\ *n, pl* **-tho·rax·es** *or* **-tho·ra·ces** \ˈ-thȯr-ə-ˌsēz\ : blood in the pleural cavity

he·mo·tox·ic \-ˈtäk-sik\ *adj* : destructive to red blood corpuscles

he·mo·tox·in \-ˈtäk-sən\ *n* : HEMOLYSIN

he·mo·zo·in \ˌhē-mə-ˈzō-ən\ *n* : an iron-containing pigment which accumulates as cytoplasmic granules in malaria parasites and is a breakdown product of hemoglobin

hemp \ˈhemp\ *n* **1** : a tall widely cultivated Asian herb of the genus *Cannabis* (*C. sativa*) with a strong woody fiber used esp. for cordage **2** : the fiber of hemp **3** : a psychoactive drug (as marijuana or hashish) from hemp

hen·bane \ˈhen-ˌbān\ *n* : a poisonous fetid Old World herb of the genus *Hyoscyamus* (*H. niger*) that contains the alkaloids hyoscyamine and scopolamine and is the source of hyoscyamus — called also *black henbane*

Hen·le's layer \ˈhen-lēz-\ *n* : a single layer of cuboidal epithelium forming the outer boundary of the inner stratum of a hair follicle — compare HUXLEY'S LAYER

Hen·le \ˈhen-lə\, **Friedrich Gustav Jacob** (1809–1885), German anatomist and histologist.

Henle's loop *n* : LOOP OF HENLE

Henoch–Schönlein *adj* : SCHÖNLEIN-HENOCH (~ purpura)

He·noch's purpura \ˈhe-nȯks-\ *n* : Schönlein-Henoch purpura that is characterized esp. by gastrointestinal bleeding and pain — compare SCHÖNLEIN'S DISEASE

E. H. Henoch — see SCHÖNLEIN-HENOCH

hep·a·ran sulfate \ˈhe-pə-ˌran-\ *n* : a sulfated glycosaminoglycan that accumulates in bodily tissues in abnormal amounts in some mucopolysaccharidoses — called also *heparitin sulfate*

hep·a·rin \ˈhe-pə-rən\ *n* : a glycosaminoglycan sulfuric acid ester that occurs esp. in the liver and lungs, that prolongs the clotting time of blood by preventing the formation of fibrin, and that is administered parenterally as the sodium salt in vascular surgery and in the treatment of postoperative thrombosis and embolism — see LIQUAEMIN

hep·a·rin·ize \ˈhe-pə-rə-ˌnīz\ *vb* **-ized; -iz·ing** : to treat with heparin — **hep·a·rin·iza·tion** \-rə-nə-ˈzā-shən\ *n*

hep·a·rin·oid \-ˌnȯid\ *n* : any of various sulfated polysaccharides that have anticoagulant activity resembling that of heparin — **heparinoid** *adj*

hep·a·ri·tin sulfate \ˈhe-pə-ˌrī-tin-\ *n* : HEPARAN SULFATE

hepat- *or* **hepato-** *comb form* **1** : liver (*hepat*itis) (*hepato*toxic) **2** : hepatic and (*hepato*biliary)

hep·a·tec·to·my \ˌhe-pə-ˈtek-tə-mē\ *n, pl* **-mies** : excision of the liver or of part of the liver — **hep·a·tec·to·mized** \-tə-ˌmīzd\ *adj*

he·pat·ic \hi-ˈpa-tik\ *adj* : of, relating to, affecting, or associated with the liver

hepatic artery *n* : the branch of the celiac artery that supplies the liver with arterial blood

hepatic cell *n* : HEPATOCYTE

hepatic coma *n* : a coma that is induced by severe liver disease

hepatic duct *n* : a duct conveying the bile away from the liver and uniting with the cystic duct to form the common bile duct

hepatic flexure *n* : the right-angle bend in the colon on the right side of the body near the liver that marks the junction of the ascending colon and the transverse colon — called also *right colic flexure*

hep·at·i·cos·to·my \hi-ˌpa-ti-ˈkäs-tə-mē\ *n, pl* **-mies** : an operation to provide an artificial opening into the hepatic duct

hep·at·i·cot·o·my \-ˈkä-tə-mē\ *n, pl* **-mies** : surgical incision of the hepatic duct

hepatic portal system *n* : a group of veins that carry blood from the capillaries of the stomach, intestine, spleen, and pancreas to the sinusoids of the liver

hepatic portal vein *n* : a portal vein carrying blood from the digestive organs and spleen to the liver

hepaticus — see FETOR HEPATICUS

hepatic vein *n* : any of the veins that carry the blood received from the hepatic artery and from the hepatic portal vein away from the liver and that in humans are usu. three in number and open into the inferior vena cava

hepatis — see PORTA HEPATIS

hep·a·ti·tis \ˌhe-pə-ˈtī-təs\ *n, pl* **-tit·i·des** \-ˈti-tə-ˌdēz\ **1** : inflammation of the liver **2** : a disease or condition (as hepatitis A or hepatitis B) marked by inflammation of the liver — **hep·a·tit·ic** \-ˈti-tik\ *adj*

hepatitis A *n* : an acute usu. benign hepatitis caused by an RNA-containing virus that does not persist in the blood serum and is transmitted esp. in food and water contaminated with infected fecal matter — called also *infectious hepatitis*

hepatitis B *n* : a sometimes fatal hepatitis caused by a double-stranded DNA virus that tends to persist in the blood serum and is transmitted esp. by contact with infected blood (as by transfusion) or blood products — called also *serum hepatitis*

hepatitis B surface antigen *n* : an antigen that resembles a virus and is found in the sera esp. of patients with hepatitis B — called also *Australia antigen; HBsAg*

hepatitis C *n* : hepatitis that is caused by a single-stranded RNA-containing virus usu. transmitted by parenteral means (as injection of an illicit drug, blood transfusion, or exposure to blood or blood products) and that accounts for most cases of non-A, non-B hepatitis

hep·a·ti·za·tion \ˌhe-pə-tə-ˈzā-shən\ *n* : conversion of tissue (as of the lungs in pneumonia) into a substance which resembles liver tissue — **hep·a·tized** \ˈhe-pə-ˌtīzd\ *adj*

hepato- — see HEPAT-

he·pa·to·bil·i·ary \ˌhe-pə-tō-ˈbi-lē-ˌer-ē, hi-ˌpa-tə-\ *adj* : of, relating to, situated in or near, produced in, or affecting the liver and bile, bile ducts, and gallbladder (∼ disease)

he·pa·to·car·cin·o·gen \-kär-ˈsi-nə-jən, -ˌkärs-ᵊn-ə-jen\ *n* : a substance or agent causing cancer of the liver — **he·pa·to·car·cin·o·gen·ic** \-ˈje-nik\ *adj* — **he·pa·to·car·cin·o·ge·nic·i·ty** \-jə-ˈni-sə-tē\ *n*

he·pa·to·car·cin·o·gen·e·sis \-ˌkärs-ᵊn-ō-ˈjc-nə-səs\ *n, pl* **-e·ses** \-ˌsēz\ : the production of cancer of the liver

he·pa·to·car·ci·no·ma \-ˌkärs-ᵊn-ˈō-mə\ *n, pl* **-mas** *or* **-ma·ta** \-mə-tə\ : carcinoma of the liver

he·pa·to·cel·lu·lar \ˌhep-ət-ō-ˈsel-yə-lər, hi-ˌpat-ə-ˈsel-\ *adj* : of or involving hepatocytes (∼ carcinomas)

he·pa·to·cyte \hi-ˈpa-tə-ˌsīt, ˈhe-pə-tə-\ *n* : any of the polygonal epithelial parenchymatous cells of the liver that se-

crete bile — called also *hepatic cell, liver cell*

he·pa·to·gen·ic \ˌhe-pə-tō-ˈje-nik, -ˌpa-tə-\ *or* **he·pa·tog·e·nous** \ˌhe-pə-ˈtä-jə-nəs\ *adj* : produced or originating in the liver

he·pa·to·len·tic·u·lar degeneration \hi-ˌpa-tə-len-ˌti-kyə-lər-, ˌhe-pə-tō-\ *n* : WILSON'S DISEASE

hep·a·tol·o·gy \ˌhe-pə-ˈtä-lə-jē\ *n, pl* **-gies** : a branch of medicine concerned with the liver — **hep·a·tol·o·gist** \-jist\ *n*

hep·a·to·ma \ˌhe-pə-ˈtō-mə\ *n, pl* **-mas** *or* **-ma·ta** \-mə-tə\ : a usu. malignant tumor of the liver — **hep·a·to·ma·tous** \-mə-təs\ *adj*

hep·a·to·meg·a·ly \ˌhe-pə-tō-ˈme-gə-lē, hi-ˌpa-tə-ˈme-\ *n, pl* **-lies** : enlargement of the liver — **hep·a·to·meg·a·lic** \-ˈme-gə-lik\ *adj*

he·pa·to·pan·cre·at·ic \hi-ˌpa-tə-ˌpaŋ-krē-ˈa-tik, ˌhe-pə-tō-, -ˌpan-\ *adj* : of or relating to the liver and the pancreas

hep·a·top·a·thy \ˌhe-pə-ˈtä-pə-thē\ *n, pl* **-thies** : an abnormal or diseased state of the liver

hep·a·to·por·tal \ˌhe-pə-tō-ˈpȯrt-ᵊl, hi-ˌpa-tə-\ *adj* : of or relating to the hepatic portal system

he·pa·to·re·nal \-ˈrē-nəl\ *adj* : of, relating to, or affecting the liver and the kidneys (fatal ∼ dysfunction)

hepatorenal syndrome *n* : functional kidney failure associated with cirrhosis of the liver and characterized typically by jaundice, ascites, hypoalbuminemia, hypoprothrombinemia, and encephalopathy

hep·a·tor·rha·phy \ˌhe-pə-ˈtȯr-ə-fē\ *n, pl* **-phies** : suture of a wound or injury to the liver

he·pa·to·sis \ˌhe-pə-ˈtō-səs\ *n, pl* **-to·ses** \-ˌsēz\ : any noninflammatory functional disorder of the liver

he·pa·to·splen·ic \ˌhe-pə-tō-ˈsple-nik, hi-ˌpa-tə-\ *adj* : of or affecting the liver and spleen (∼ schistosomiasis)

he·pa·to·spleno·meg·a·ly \-ˌsple-nō-ˈme-gə-lē\ *n, pl* **-lies** : coincident enlargement of the liver and spleen

hep·a·tot·o·my \ˌhe-pə-ˈtä-tə-mē\ *n, pl* **-mies** : surgical incision of the liver

he·pa·to·tox·ic \ˌhe-pə-tō-ˈtäk-sik, hi-ˌpa-tə-ˈtäk-\ *adj* : relating to or causing injury to the liver — **he·pa·to·tox·ic·i·ty** \-täk-ˈsi-sə-tē\ *n*

he·pa·to·tox·in \-ˈtäk-sən\ *n* : a substance toxic to the liver

hep·ta·chlor \ˈhep-tə-ˌklȯr\ *n* : a persistent chlorinated hydrocarbon pesticide $C_{10}H_5Cl_7$ that causes liver disease in animals and is a suspected human carcinogen

herb \ˈərb, ˈhərb\ *n, often attrib* **1** : a seed plant that lacks woody tissue and dies to the ground at the end of a growing season **2** : a plant or plant part valued for medicinal or savory qualities

¹herb·al \'ər-bəl, 'hər-\ n : a book about plants esp. with reference to their medical properties

²herbal adj : of, relating to, or made of herbs

herb·al·ist \'ər-bə-list, 'hər-\ n 1 : one who practices healing by the use of herbs 2 : one who collects or grows herbs

herb doctor n : HERBALIST 1

herd immunity n : a reduction in the probability of infection that is held to apply to susceptible members of a population in which a significant proportion of the individuals are immune because the chance of coming in contact with an infected individual is less

he·red·i·tary \hə-'re-də-ˌter-ē\ adj 1 : genetically transmitted or transmittable from parent to offspring — compare ACQUIRED 2, CONGENITAL 2, FAMILIAL 2 : of or relating to inheritance or heredity — he·red·i·tar·i·ly \-ˌre-də-'ter-ə-lē\ adv

hereditary hemorrhagic telangiectasia n : a hereditary abnormality that is characterized by multiple telangiectasias and by bleeding into the tissues and mucous membranes because of abnormal fragility of the capillaries — called also Rendu-Osler-Weber disease

hereditary spherocytosis n : a disorder of red blood cells that is inherited as a dominant trait and is characterized by anemia, small thick fragile spherocytes which are extremely susceptible to hemolysis, enlargement of the spleen, reticulocytosis, and mild jaundice

he·red·i·ty \hə-'re-də-tē\ n, pl -ties 1 : the sum of the qualities and potentialities genetically derived from one's ancestors 2 : the transmission of traits from ancestor to descendant through the molecular mechanism lying primarily in the DNA or RNA of the genes — compare MEIOSIS

heredo- comb form : hereditary (heredofamilial)

her·e·do·fa·mil·ial \ˌher-ə-dō-fə-'mil-yəl\ adj : tending to occur in more than one member of a family and suspected of having a genetic basis (a ~ disease)

Her·ing-Breu·er reflex \'her-iŋ-'broi-ər-\ n : any of several reflexes that control inflation and deflation of the lungs; esp : reflex inhibition of inspiration triggered by pulmonary muscle spindles upon expansion of the lungs and mediated by the vagus nerve

Hering, Karl Ewald Konstantin (1834–1918), German physiologist and psychologist.

Breuer, Josef (1842–1925), Austrian physician and physiologist.

her·i·ta·bil·i·ty \ˌher-ə-tə-'bi-lə-tē\ n, pl -ties 1 : the quality or state of being heritable 2 : the proportion of ob-

served variation in a particular trait (as intelligence) that can be attributed to inherited genetic factors in contrast to environmental ones

her·i·ta·ble \'her-ə-tə-bəl\ adj : HEREDITARY

her·maph·ro·dite \(ˌ)hər-'ma-frə-ˌdīt\ n 1 : an abnormal individual having both male and female reproductive organs 2 : a plant or animal that normally has both male and female reproductive organs : BISEXUAL — hermaphrodite adj — her·maph·ro·dit·ic \-ˌma-frə-'di-tik\ adj — her·maph·ro·dit·ism \-'ma-frə-ˌdi-ˌti-zəm\ n

her·met·ic \(ˌ)hər-'me-tik\ adj : being airtight or impervious to air — her·met·i·cal·ly \-ti-k(ə-)lē\ adv

her·nia \'hər-nē-ə\ n, pl -ni·as or -ni·ae \-nē-ˌē, -nē-ˌī\ : a protrusion of an organ or part through connective tissue or through a wall of the cavity in which it is normally enclosed — called also rupture — her·ni·al \-nē-əl\ adj

hernial sac n : a protruding pouch of peritoneum that contains a herniated organ or tissue

her·ni·ate \'hər-nē-ˌāt\ vb -at·ed; -at·ing : to protrude through an abnormal body opening : RUPTURE

her·ni·a·tion \ˌhər-nē-'ā-shən\ n 1 : the act or process of herniating 2 : HERNIA

hernio- comb form : hernia (herniorrhaphy) (herniotomy)

her·nio·plas·ty \'hər-nē-ə-ˌplas-tē\ n, pl -ties : HERNIORRHAPHY

her·ni·or·rha·phy \ˌhər-nē-'or-ə-fē\ n, pl -phies : an operation for hernia that involves opening the coverings, returning the contents to their normal place, obliterating the hernial sac, and closing the opening with strong sutures

her·ni·ot·o·my \-'ä-tə-mē\ n, pl -mies : the operation of cutting through a band of tissue that constricts a strangulated hernia

he·ro·ic \hi-'rō-ik\ adj 1 : of a kind that is likely to be undertaken only to save life (~ surgery) 2 : having a pronounced effect — used chiefly of medicaments or dosage (~ doses) (a ~ drug)

her·o·in \'her-ə-wən\ n : a strongly physiologically addictive narcotic $C_{21}H_{23}NO_5$ that is made by acetylation of but is more potent than morphine and that is prohibited for medical use in the U.S. but is used illicitly for its euphoric effects — called also diacetylmorphine, diamorphine

her·o·in·ism \-wə-ˌni-zəm\ n : addiction to heroin

her·pan·gi·na \ˌhər-ˌpan-'jī-nə, ˌhər-'pan-jə-nə\ n : a contagious disease of children characterized by fever, headache, and a vesicular eruption in the throat and caused by a coxsackievirus

her·pes \'hǝr-(ˌ)pēz\ *n* : any of several inflammatory diseases of the skin caused by a herpesvirus and characterized by clusters of vesicles : *esp* : HERPES SIMPLEX

herpes gen·i·tal·is \ˌhǝr-(ˌ)pēz-ˌje-nǝ-'ta-lǝs\ *n* : herpes simplex of the type affecting the genitals — called also *genital herpes, genital herpes simplex*

herpes keratitis *n* : keratitis caused by any of the herpesviruses that produce herpes simplex or shingles

herpes la·bi·al·is \-ˌlā-bē-'a-lǝs\ *n* : herpes simplex affecting the lips and nose

herpes sim·plex \-'sim-ˌpleks\ *n* : either of two diseases caused by a herpesvirus and marked in one case by groups of watery blisters on the skin or mucous membranes (as of the mouth and lips) above the waist and in the other by such blisters on the genitals

her·pes·vi·rus \-'vī-rǝs\ *n* : any of a group of DNA-containing viruses (as cytomegalovirus, Epstein-Barr virus, or varicella zoster) that replicate in the nuclei of cells and include the causative agents of a number of diseases (as herpes simplex, chicken pox, and shingles) characterized esp. by blisters or vesicles on the skin and mucous membranes and often by recurrence sometimes after a long period of latency

herpes zos·ter \-'zäs-tǝr\ *n* : SHINGLES

herpet- *or* **herpeto-** *comb form* : herpes 〈*herpet*iform〉

her·pet·ic \(ˌ)hǝr-'pe-tik\ *adj* : of, relating to, or resembling herpes

her·pet·i·form \-'pe-tǝ-fȯrm\ *adj* : resembling herpes

herpetiformis — see DERMATITIS HERPETIFORMIS

Herx·heim·er reaction \'hǝrks-ˌhī-mǝr-\ *n* : JARISCH-HERXHEIMER REACTION

Heschl's gyrus \'he-shǝlz-\ *n* : a convolution of the temporal lobe that is the cortical center for hearing and runs obliquely outward and forward from the posterior part of the lateral sulcus

Heschl, Richard Ladislaus (1824–1881), Austrian anatomist.

het·a·cil·lin \ˌhe-tǝ-'sil-ǝn\ *n* : a semisynthetic oral penicillin $C_{19}H_{23}N_3$-O_4S that is converted to ampicillin in the body

heter- *or* **hetero-** *comb form* : other than usual : other : different 〈*hetero*graft〉

Het·er·a·kis \-'ra-kǝs\ *n* : a genus (family Heterakidae) of nematode worms including one (*H. gallinae*) that infests esp. chickens and turkeys and serves as an intermediate host and transmitter of the protozoan causing blackhead

het·ero \'he-tǝ-ˌrō\ *n, pl* **-er·os** : HETEROSEXUAL

het·ero·an·ti·body \ˌhe-tǝ-rō-'an-ti-ˌbä-

dē\ *n, pl* **-dies** : an antibody specific for a heterologous antigen

het·ero·an·ti·gen \-'an-ti-jǝn, -ˌjen\ *n* : an antibody produced by an individual of one species that is capable of stimulating an immune response in an individual of another species

het·ero·chro·ma·tin \-'krō-mǝ-tǝn\ *n* : densely staining chromatin that appears as nodules in or along chromosomes and contains relatively few genes — **het·ero·chro·mat·ic** \-ˌkrǝ-ma-tik\ *adj*

het·ero·chro·mia \ˌhe-tǝ-rō-'krō-mē-ǝ\ *n* : a difference in coloration in two anatomical structures or two parts of the same structure which are normally alike in color 〈~ of the iris〉

heterochromia ir·i·dis \-'ir-i-dǝs\ *n* : a difference in color between the irises of the two eyes or between parts of one iris

het·ero·cy·clic \ˌhe-tǝ-rō-'sī-klik, -'si-\ *adj* : relating to, characterized by, or being a ring composed of atoms of more than one kind

het·ero·du·plex \ˌhe-tǝ-rō-'dü-ˌpleks, -'dyü-\ *n* : a nucleic-acid molecule composed of two chains with each derived from a different parent molecule — **heteroduplex** *adj*

het·ero·gam·ete \ˌhe-tǝ-rō-'ga-ˌmēt, -gǝ-'mēt\ *n* : either of a pair of gametes that differ in form, size, or behavior and occur typically as large nonmotile female gametes and small motile sperm

het·ero·ga·met·ic \-gǝ-'me-tik, -'mē-\ *adj* : forming two kinds of gametes of which one determines offspring of one sex and the other determines offspring of the opposite sex — **het·ero·gam·e·ty** \-'ga-mǝ-tē\ *n*

het·er·og·a·my \ˌhe-tǝ-'rä-gǝ-mē\ *n, pl* **-mies** 1 : sexual reproduction involving fusion of unlike gametes 2 : the condition of reproducing by heterogamy — **het·er·og·a·mous** \-mǝs\ *adj*

het·ero·ge·neous \ˌhe-tǝ-rǝ-'jē-nē-ǝs\ *adj* : not uniform in structure or composition — **het·ero·ge·ne·i·ty** \ˌhe-tǝ-rō-jǝ-'nē-ǝ-tē\ *n*

het·ero·gen·ic \ˌhe-tǝr-ǝ-'je-nik\ *adj* : derived from or involving individuals of a different species 〈~ antigens〉 〈~ transplantation〉

het·er·og·e·nous \ˌhe-tǝ-'rä-jǝ-nǝs\ *adj* 1 : originating in an outside source; *esp* : derived from another species 〈~ bone graft〉 2 : HETEROGENEOUS

het·ero·graft \'he-tǝ-rō-ˌgraft\ *n* : XENOGRAFT

het·er·ol·o·gous \ˌhe-tǝ-'rä-lǝ-gǝs\ *adj* 1 : derived from a different species 〈~ DNAs〉 〈~ transplants〉 — compare AUTOLOGOUS, HOMOLOGOUS 2 2 : characterized by cross-reactivity 〈a ~ vaccine〉 — **het·er·ol·o·gous·ly** *adv*

¹het·ero·phile \'he-tǝ-rǝ-ˌfīl\ *or* **het·er·o·phil** \-ˌfil\ *adj* : relating to or being any of a group of antigens in organisms of different species that induce the formation of antibodies which will cross-react with the other antigens of the group; *also* : being or relating to any of the antibodies produced and capable of cross-reacting in this way

²**heterophile** *or* **heterophil** *n* : NEUTROPHIL — used esp. in veterinary medicine

het·ero·pho·ria \he-tə-rō-ʰfōr-ē-ə\ *n* : latent strabismus in which one eye tends to deviate either medially or laterally — compare EXOPHORIA

het·ero·plas·tic \he-tə-rə-ʰplas-tik\ *adj* : HETEROLOGOUS — **het·ero·plas·ti·cal·ly** *adv*

het·ero·plas·ty \ʰhe-tə-rə-ʰplas-tē\ *n, pl* **-ties** : the operation of making a xenograft

¹**het·ero·sex·u·al** \he-tə-rō-ʰsek-shə-wəl\ *adj* **1 a** : of, relating to, or characterized by a tendency to direct sexual desire toward individuals of the opposite sex — compare HOMOSEXUAL **1 b** : of, relating to, or involving sexual intercourse between individuals of the opposite sex — compare HOMOSEXUAL **2 2** : of or relating to different sexes — **het·ero·sex·u·al·i·ty** \-ʸsek-shə-ʰwa-lə-tē\ *n* — **het·ero·sex·u·al·ly** *adv*

²**heterosexual** *n* : a heterosexual individual

het·ero·top·ic \he-tə-rə-ʰtä-pik\ *adj* **1** : occurring in an abnormal place (~ bone formation) **2** : grafted or transplanted into an abnormal position (~ liver transplantation) — **het·ero·to·pia** \-ʰtō-pē-ə\ *also* **het·er·ot·o·py** \ʰhe-ʰrä-tə-pē\ *n* — **het·ero·top·i·cal·ly** *adv*

het·ero·trans·plant \he-tə-rō-ʰtrans-ʸplant\ *n* : XENOGRAFT — **het·ero·trans·plan·ta·tion** \-ʸtrans-ʸplan-ʰtā-shən\ *n*

het·ero·tro·pia \-ʰtrō-pē-ə\ *n* : STRABISMUS

het·ero·typ·ic \he-tə-rō-ʰti-pik\ *adj* : different in kind, arrangement, or form (~ aggregations of cells)

het·ero·zy·go·sis \he-tə-rō-(ʸ)zī-ʰgō-səs\ *n, pl* **-go·ses** \-ʸsēz\ : HETEROZYGOSITY

het·ero·zy·gos·i·ty \-(ʸ)zī-ʰgä-sə-tē\ *n, pl* **-ties** : the state of being heterozygous

het·ero·zy·gote \-ʰzī-ʸgōt\ *n* : a heterozygous individual — **het·ero·zy·got·ic** \-(ʸ)zī-ʰgä-tik\ *adj*

het·ero·zy·gous \-ʰzī-gəs\ *adj* : having the two genes at corresponding loci on homologous chromosomes different for one or more loci — compare HOMOZYGOUS

HEW *abbr* Department of Health, Education, and Welfare

hexachloride — see BENZENE HEXACHLORIDE, GAMMA BENZENE HEXACHLORIDE

hexa·chlo·ro·eth·ane \hek-sə-ʸklōr-ō-ʰeth-ʸān\ *or* **hexa·chlor·eth·ane** \-ʸklōr-ʰeth-ʸān\ *n* : a toxic compound C_2Cl_6 used in the control of liver flukes in veterinary medicine

hexa·chlo·ro·phane \-ʰklōr-ə-ʸfān\ *n, Brit* : HEXACHLOROPHENE

hexa·chlo·ro·phene \-ʰklōr-ə-ʸfēn\ *n* : a powdered phenolic bacteria-inhibiting agent $C_{13}Cl_6H_6O_2$

hexa·dac·ty·ly \-ʰdak-tə-lē\ *n, pl* **-lies** : the condition of having six fingers or toes on a hand or foot

hexa·flu·o·re·ni·um \-ʸflü-ər-ʰē-nē-əm\ *n* : a cholinesterase inhibitor used as the bromide $C_{36}H_{12}Br_2N_2$ in surgery to extend the skeletal-muscle relaxing activity of succinylcholine

hexa·me·tho·ni·um \hek-sə-mə-ʰthō-nē-əm\ *n* : either of two compounds $C_{12}H_{30}Br_2N_2$ or $C_{12}H_{30}Cl_2N_2$ used as ganglionic blocking agents in the treatment of hypertension — see METHIUM

hexa·meth·y·lene·tet·ra·mine \-ʸme-thə-ʸlēn-ʰte-trə-ʸmēn\ *n* : METHENAMINE

hex·amine \ʰhek-sə-ʸmēn\ *n* : METHENAMINE

hexanitrate — see MANNITOL HEXANITRATE

hex·es·trol \ʰhek-sə-ʸströl, -ʸströl\ *n* : a synthetic derivative $C_{18}H_{22}O_2$ of diethylstilbestrol

hexo·bar·bi·tal \hek-sə-ʰbär-bə-ʸtöl\ *n* : a barbiturate $C_{12}H_{16}N_2O_3$ used as a sedative and hypnotic and in the form of its soluble sodium salt as an intravenous anesthetic of short duration

hexo·bar·bi·tone \-ʰbär-bə-ʸtōn\ *n, chiefly Brit* : HEXOBARBITAL

hexo·cy·cli·um meth·yl·sul·fate \-ʰsī-klē-əm-ʸme-thəl-ʰsəl-ʸfāt\ *n* : a white crystalline anticholinergic agent $C_{21}H_{36}N_2O_5S$ that tends to suppress gastric secretion and has been used in the treatment of peptic ulcers — see TRAL

hex·oes·trol \ʰhek-sē-ʸströl, -ʸströl\ *n, chiefly Brit var of* HEXESTROL

hexo·ki·nase \hek-sə-ʰkī-ʸnās, -ʸnāz\ *n* : any of a group of enzymes that accelerate the phosphorylation of hexoses (as in the formation of glucose-6-phosphate from glucose and ATP) in carbohydrate metabolism

hex·os·a·mine \hek-ʰsä-sə-ʸmēn\ *n* : an amine derived from a hexose by replacement of hydroxyl by the amino group

hex·os·a·min·i·dase \hek-ʸsä-sə-ʰmi-nə-ʸdās, -ʸdāz\ *n* : either of two hydrolytic enzymes that catalyze the splitting off of a hexose from a ganglioside and are deficient in some metabolic diseases: **a** : HEXOSAMINIDASE A **b** : HEXOSAMINIDASE B

hexosaminidase A *n* : the more thermolabile hexosaminidase that is deficient in both typical Tay-Sachs disease and Sandhoff's disease

hexosaminidase B *n* : the more thermostable hexosaminidase that is deficient in Sandhoff's disease but present in elevated quantities in typical Tay-Sachs disease

hex·ose \'hek-₁sōs, -₁sōz\ *n* : any monosaccharide (as glucose) containing six carbon atoms in the molecule

hex·yl·res·or·cin·ol \₁hek-səl-rə-'zȯrs-³n-₁ȯl, -₁ōl\ *n* : a crystalline phenol $C_{12}H_{18}O_2$ used as an antiseptic (as in a throat lozenge) and as an anthelmintic against ascarids (esp. *Ascaris lumbricoides*), hookworms, and whipworms (esp. *Trichuris trichiura*)

Hf *symbol* hafnium

Hg *symbol* [New Latin *hydrargyrum*] mercury

Hgb *abbr* hemoglobin

HGH *abbr* human growth hormone

HHS *abbr* Department of Health and Human Services

HI *abbr* hemagglutination inhibition

hi·a·tal \hī-'āt-³l\ *adj* : of, relating to, or involving a hiatus

hiatal hernia *n* : a hernia in which an anatomical part (as the stomach) protrudes through the esophageal hiatus of the diaphragm — called also *hiatus hernia*

hi·a·tus \hī-'ā-təs\ *n* : a gap or passage through an anatomical part or organ; *esp* : a gap through which another part or organ passes

hiatus semi·lu·nar·is \-₁se-mi-lü-'nar-əs\ *n* : a curved fissure in the nasal passages into which the frontal and maxillary sinuses open

Hib *abbr* — used to denote a bacterium of the genus *Haemophilus* (*H. influenzae*) belonging to serotype B (~ vaccine)

hi·ber·no·ma \₁hī-bər-'nō-mə\ *n, pl* **-mas** *or* **-ma·ta** \-mə-tə\ : a rare benign tumor that contains fat cells

hic·cup *also* **hic·cough** \'hi-(₁)kəp\ *n* 1 : a spasmodic inhalation with closure of the glottis accompanied by a peculiar sound 2 : an attack of hiccuping — usu. used in pl. but with a sing. or pl. verb — **hiccup** *vb*

hick·ey \'hi-kē\ *n, pl* **hickeys** : a temporary red mark produced esp. in lovemaking by biting and sucking the skin

hide·bound \'hīd-₁baúnd\ *adj* 1 : having a dry skin lacking in pliancy and adhering closely to the underlying flesh — used of domestic animals 2 : having scleroderma — used of human beings

hidr- *or* **hidro-** *comb form* : sweat glands (*hidradenitis*)

hi·drad·e·ni·tis \hi-₁drad-³n-'ī-təs, ₁hī-\ *n* : inflammation of a sweat gland

hidradenitis sup·pu·ra·ti·va \-₁sə-pyùr-ə-'tī-və\ *n* : a chronic suppurative inflammatory disease of the apocrine sweat glands

hi·drad·e·no·ma \hī-₁drad-³n-'ō-mə\ *n, pl* **-mas** *or* **-ma·ta** \-mə-tə\ : any benign tumor derived from epithelial cells of sweat glands

hi·dro·sis \hi-'drō-səs, hī-\ *n, pl* **-dro-**

ses \-₁sēz\ : excretion of sweat : PERSPIRATION

hi·drot·ic \hi-'drät-ik, hī-\ *adj* : causing perspiration : DIAPHORETIC, SUDORIFIC

¹high \'hī\ *adj* 1 : having a complex organization : greatly differentiated or developed phylogenetically — usu. used in the comparative degree of advanced types of plants and animals (the ~er apes) — compare LOW 2 a : exhibiting elation or euphoric excitement (a ~ patient) b : being intoxicated; *also* : excited or stupefied by or as if by a drug (as marijuana or heroin)

²high *n* : an excited, euphoric, or stupefied state; *esp* : one produced by or as if by a drug (as heroin)

high blood pressure *n* : HYPERTENSION

high colonic *n* : an enema injected deeply into the colon

high–density lipoprotein *n* : HDL

high forceps *n* : a rare procedure for delivery of an infant by the use of forceps before engagement has occurred — compare LOW FORCEPS, MIDFORCEPS

high–grade \'hī-'grād\ *adj* : being near the upper or most favorable extreme of a specified range — compare LOW-GRADE

high–performance liquid chromatography *n* : a form of chromatography in which the mobile phase is a liquid under pressure and the stationary phase is in the form of small particles so that the rate of flow is increased to shorten the separation time — abbr. *HPLC*

high–power *adj* : of, relating to, being, or made with a lens that magnifies an image a relatively large number of times and esp. about 40 times

high–strung \'hī-'strəŋ\ *adj* : having an extremely nervous or sensitive temperament

hi·lar \'hī-lər\ *adj* : of, relating to, affecting, or located near a hilum

hill·ock \'hi-lək\ *n* : any small anatomical prominence or elevation

hi·lum \'hī-ləm\ *n, pl* **hi·la** \-lə\ : a notch in or opening from a bodily part esp. when it is where the blood vessels, nerves, or ducts leave and enter: as **a** : the indented part of a kidney **b** : the depression in the medial surface of a lung that forms the opening through which the bronchus, blood vessels, and nerves pass **c** : a shallow depression in one side of a lymph node through which blood vessels pass and efferent lymphatic vessels emerge

hi·lus \-ləs\ *n, pl* **hi·li** \-₁lī\ : HILUM

hind·brain \'hīnd-₁brān\ *n* : the posterior division of the three primary divisions of the developing vertebrate brain or the corresponding part of the adult brain that includes the cerebellum, pons, and medulla oblongata and that controls the autonomic functions and equilibrium — called also *rhombencephalon*; see METENCEPH-ALON, MYELENCEPHALON

hind-foot \-ˌfu̇t\ *n* **1** *usu* hind foot : one of the posterior feet of a quadruped **2** : the posterior part of the embryonic foot that contains the calcaneus, talus, navicular, and cuboid bones

hind-gut \-ˌgət\ *n* : the posterior part of the embryonic alimentary canal

hind leg *n* : the posterior leg of a quadruped

hind limb *n* : a posterior limb esp. of a quadruped

hinge joint \ˈhinj-\ *n* : a joint between bones (as at the elbow or knee) that permits motion in only one plane; *esp* : GINGLYMUS

hip \ˈhip\ *n* **1** : the laterally projecting region of each side of the lower or posterior part of the mammalian trunk formed by the lateral parts of the pelvis and upper part of the femur together with the fleshy parts covering them **2** : HIP JOINT

hip-bone \-ˌbōn\ *n* : the large flaring bone that makes a lateral half of the pelvis in mammals and is composed of the ilium, ischium, and pubis which are consolidated into one bone in the adult — called also *innominate bone, os coxae, pelvic bone*

hip joint *n* : the ball-and-socket joint comprising the articulation between the femur and the hipbone

hipped \ˈhipt\ *adj* : having hips esp. of a specified kind — often used in combination (broad-*hipped*)

hip-po-cam-pal \ˌhi-pə-ˈkam-pəl\ *adj* : of or relating to the hippocampus

hippocampal commissure *n* : a triangular band of nerve fibers joining the two crura of the fornix of the rhinencephalon anteriorly before they fuse to form the body of the fornix — called also *psalterium*

hippocampal gyrus *n* : a convolution of the cerebral cortex that borders the hippocampus and contains elements of both archipallium and neopallium — called also *hippocampal convolution*

hippocampal sulcus *n* : a fissure of the mesial surface of each cerebral hemisphere extending from behind the posterior end of the corpus callosum forward and downward to the hippocampal gyrus — called also *hippocampal fissure*

hip-po-cam-pus \ˌhi-pə-ˈkam-pəs\ *n, pl* -pi \-ˌpī, -ˌpē\ : a curved elongated ridge that is an important part of the limbic system, extends over the floor of the descending horn of each lateral ventricle of the brain, and consists of gray matter covered on the ventricular surface with white matter

Hip-po-crat-ic \ˌhi-pə-ˈkra-tik\ *adj* : of or relating to Hippocrates or to the school of medicine that took his name

Hip-poc-ra-tes \hi-ˈpä-krə-ˌtēz\ (*ca*

460 BC–*ca* 370 BC), Greek physician.

Hippocratic facies *n* : the face as it appears near death and in some debilitating conditions marked by sunken eyes and temples, pinched nose, and tense hard skin

Hippocratic oath *n* : an oath that embodies a code of medical ethics and is usu. taken by those about to begin medical practice

hip pointer *n* : a deep bruise to the iliac crest or to the attachments of the muscles attached to it that occurs esp. in contact sports (as football)

hip-pu-ran \ˈhi-pyu̇-ˌran\ *n* : a white crystalline iodine-containing powder $C_9H_7INNaO_3 \cdot 2H_2O$ used as a radiopaque agent in urography of the kidney — called also *iodohippurate sodium, sodium iodohippurate*

hip-pus \ˈhi-pəs\ *n* : a spasmodic variation in the size of the pupil of the eye caused by a tremor of the iris

Hirsch-sprung's disease \ˈhirsh-ˌpru̇ŋz-\ *n* : megacolon that is caused by congenital absence of ganglion cells in the muscular wall of the distal part of the colon with resulting loss of peristaltic function in this part and dilatation of the colon proximal to the aganglionic part — called also *congenital megacolon*

Hirschsprung, Harold (1830–1916), Danish pediatrician.

hir-sute \ˈhər-ˌsüt, ˈhir-, ˌhər-ˈ, hir-ˈ\ *adj* : very hairy — **hir-sute-ness** *n*

hir-sut-ism \ˈhər-sə-ˌti-zəm, ˈhir-\ *n* : excessive growth of hair of normal or abnormal distribution : HYPERTRICHOSIS

hi-ru-din \hir-ˈüd-ᵊn, ˈhir-yu̇-dən\ *n* : an anticoagulant extracted from the buccal glands of a leech

Hi-ru-do \hi-ˈrü-(ˌ)dō\ *n* : a genus of leeches (family Hirudinidae) that includes the common medicinal leech (*H. medicinalis*)

His bundle \ˈhis-\ *n* : BUNDLE OF HIS

hist- *or* **histo-** *comb form* : tissue (*histamine*) (*histo*compatibility)

His-ta-log \ˈhis-tə-ˌlȯg\ *trademark* — used for a preparation of an isomer of histamine which is a gastric stimulant and is used to test gastric secretion

his-ta-mine \ˈhis-tə-ˌmēn, -mən\ *n* : a compound $C_5H_9N_3$ esp. of mammalian tissues that causes dilatation of capillaries, contraction of smooth muscle, and stimulation of gastric acid secretion, that is released during allergic reactions, and that is formed by decarboxylation of histidine — **his-ta-min-ic** \ˌhis-tə-ˈmi-nik\ *adj*

his-ta-min-er-gic \ˌhis-tə-mə-ˈnər-jik\ *adj* : liberating or activated by histamine (~ receptors)

his-ta-mi-no-lyt-ic \ˌhis-tə-ˌmi-nə-ˈli-tik, hi-ˌsta-mə-nə-\ *adj* : breaking down or tending to break down histamine

histi- or **histio-** comb form : tissue ⟨histiocyte⟩

his·ti·di·nae·mia chiefly Brit var of HISTIDINEMIA

his·ti·dine \'his-tə-ˌdēn\ n : a crystalline essential amino acid $C_6H_9N_3O_2$ formed by the hydrolysis of most proteins

his·ti·di·ne·mia \ˌhis-tə-də-'nē-mē-ə\ n : a recessive autosomal metabolic defect that results in an excess amount of histidine in the blood and urine due to an enzyme deficiency and is characterized by speech defects and mild mental retardation

his·ti·din·uria \-ˈnur-ē-ə, -ˈnyur-\ n : the presence of an excessive amount of histidine in the urine (as in pregnancy)

his·tio·cyte \'his-tē-ə-ˌsīt\ n : MACROPHAGE — **his·tio·cyt·ic** \ˌhis-tē-ə-'si-tik\ adj

his·tio·cy·to·ma \ˌhis-tē-ō-sī-'tō-mə\ n, pl **-mas** also **-ma·ta** \-mə-tə\ : a tumor that consists predominantly of macrophages

his·tio·cy·to·sis \-'tō-səs\ n, pl **-to·ses** \-ˌsēz\ : abnormal multiplication of macrophages; broadly : a condition characterized by such multiplication

histo- — see HIST-

his·to·chem·is·try \-'ke-mə-strē\ n, pl **-tries** : a science that combines the techniques of biochemistry and histology in the study of the chemical constitution of cells and tissues — **his·to·chem·i·cal** \-'ke-mə-kəl\ adj — **his·to·chem·i·cal·ly** adv

his·to·com·pat·i·bil·i·ty \ˌhis-(ˌ)tō-kəm-ˌpa-tə-'bi-lə-tē\ n, pl **-ties** often attrib : a state of mutual tolerance between tissues that allows them to be grafted effectively — see MAJOR HISTOCOMPATIBILITY COMPLEX — **his·to·com·pat·i·ble** \-kəm-'pa-tə-bəl\ adj

histocompatibility antigen n : any of the antigenic glycoproteins on the surface membranes of cells that enable the body's immune system to recognize a cell as native or foreign and that are determined by the major histocompatibility complex

his·to·flu·o·res·cence \-ˌflor-'es-ᵊns, -ˌflur-\ n : fluorescence by a tissue upon radiation after introduction of a fluorescent substance into the body and its uptake by the tissue — **his·to·flu·o·res·cent** \-'es-ᵊnt\ adj

his·to·gen·e·sis \ˌhis-tə-'je-nə-səs\ n, pl **-e·ses** \-ˌsēz\ : the formation and differentiation of tissues — **his·to·ge·net·ic** \-jə-'ne-tik\ adj — **his·to·ge·net·i·cal·ly** adv

his·toid \'his-ˌtoid\ adj 1 : resembling the normal tissues ⟨~ tumors⟩ 2 : developed from or consisting of but one tissue

his·to·in·com·pat·i·bil·i·ty \ˌhis-(ˌ)tō-ˌin-kəm-ˌpa-tə-'bi-lə-tē\ n, pl **-ties** : a state of mutual intolerance between tissues (as of a fetus and its mother or

a graft and its host) that normally leads to reaction against or rejection of one by the other — **his·to·in·com·pat·i·ble** \-kəm-'pa-tə-bəl\ adj

his·tol·o·gy \hi-'stä-lə-jē\ n, pl **-gies** 1 : a branch of anatomy that deals with the minute structure of animal and plant tissues as discernible with the microscope 2 : a treatise on histology 3 : tissue structure or organization — **his·to·log·i·cal** \ˌhis-tə-'lä-ji-kəl\ or **his·to·log·ic** \-'lä-jik\ adj — **his·to·log·i·cal·ly** adv — **his·tol·o·gist** \hi-'stä-lə-jist\ n

His·to·mo·nas \ˌhis-tə-'mō-nəs\ n : a genus of flagellate protozoans (family Mastigamoebidae) that are parasites in the liver and intestinal mucosa esp. of poultry and are usu. considered to include a single species (H. meleagridis) that causes blackhead

his·to·mo·ni·a·sis \ˌhis-tə-mə-'nī-ə-səs\ n, pl **-a·ses** \-ˌsēz\ : infection with or disease caused by protozoans of the genus Histomonas : BLACKHEAD 2

his·tone \'his-ˌtōn\ n : any of various simple water-soluble proteins that are rich in the basic amino acids lysine and arginine and are complexed with DNA in nucleosomes

his·to·patho·gen·e·sis \ˌhis-tə-ˌpa-thə-'je-nə-səs\ n, pl **-e·ses** \-ˌsēz\ : the origin and development of diseased tissue

his·to·pa·thol·o·gist \ˌhis-tō-pə-'thä-lə-jist, -pa-\ n : a pathologist who specializes in the detection of the effects of disease on body tissues; esp : one who identifies neoplasms by their histological characteristics

his·to·pa·thol·o·gy \ˌhis-tō-pə-'thä-lə-jē, -pa-\ n, pl **-gies** 1 : a branch of pathology concerned with the tissue changes characteristic of disease 2 : the tissue changes that affect a part or accompany a disease — **his·to·path·o·log·ic** \-ˌpa-thə-'lä-jik\ or **his·to·path·o·log·i·cal** \-ji-kəl\ adj — **his·to·path·o·log·i·cal·ly** adv

his·to·plas·ma \ˌhis-tə-'plaz-mə\ n 1 cap : a genus of fungi (family Coccidioidaceae) that includes one (H. capsulatum) causing histoplasmosis and another (H. farciminosum) causing epizootic lymphangitis 2 : any fungus of the genus Histoplasma

his·to·plas·min \-'plaz-mən\ n : a sterile filtrate of a culture of a fungus of the genus Histoplasma (H. capsulatum) used in a cutaneous test for histoplasmosis

his·to·plas·mo·sis \-ˌplaz-'mō-səs\ n, pl **-mo·ses** \-ˌsēz\ : a respiratory disease with symptoms like those of influenza that is endemic in the Mississippi and Ohio river valleys of the U.S., is caused by a fungus of the genus Histoplasma (H. capsulatum), and is marked by benign involvement of lymph nodes of the trachea and bronchi usu. without symptoms or by severe progressive generalized involvement of the lymph nodes and the reticuloendothelial system with fever, anemia, leukopenia and often with local lesions (as of the skin, mouth, or throat)

his·to·ry \'his-tə-rē\ n, pl **-ries** : an account of a patient's family and personal background and past and present health

his·to·tox·ic \,his-tə-'täk-sik\ adj : toxic to tissues (~ agents)

histotoxic anoxia n : anoxia caused by poisoning of the tissues (as by alcohol) that impairs their ability to utilize oxygen

histotoxic hypoxia n : a deficiency of oxygen reaching the bodily tissues due to impairment of cellular respiration esp. by a toxic agent (as cyanide or alcohol)

HIV \,āch-(,)ī-'vē\ n : any of a group of retroviruses and esp. HIV-I that infect and destroy helper T cells of the immune system causing the marked reduction in their numbers that is diagnostic of AIDS — called also *AIDS virus, human immunodeficiency virus*

hive \'hīv\ n : an urticarial wheal

hives \'hīvz\ n sing or pl : an allergic disorder marked by raised edematous patches of skin or mucous membrane and usu. by intense itching and caused by contact with a specific precipitating factor (as a food, drug, or inhalant) either externally or internally — called also *urticaria*

HIV-1 \,āch-(,)ī-(,)vē-'wən\ n : a retrovirus that is the most common HIV — called also *HTLV-III, LAV*

HLA also **HL-A** \,āch-(,)el-'ā\ n [human leukocyte antigen] 1 : the major histocompatibility complex in humans 2 : a genetic locus, gene, or antigen of the major histocompatibility complex in humans — often used in attribution (HLA antigens) (HLA typing); often used with one or more letters to designate a locus or with letters and a number to designate an allele at the locus or the antigen corresponding to the locus and allele (HLA-B27 antigen)

HMD abbr hyaline membrane disease

HMO \,āch-(,)em-'ō\ n, pl **HMOs** : an organization that provides comprehensive health care to voluntarily enrolled individuals and families in a particular geographic area by member physicians with limited referral to outside specialists and that is financed by fixed periodic payments determined in advance — called also *health maintenance organization*

Ho symbol holmium

hoarse \'hōrs\ adj **hoars·er; hoars·est** 1 : rough or harsh in sound (a ~ voice) 2 : having a hoarse voice — **hoarse·ly** adv — **hoarse·ness** n

hob·nail liver \'häb-,nāl-\ or **hob·nailed**

liver \'häb-,nāld-\ n 1 : the liver as it appears in one form of cirrhosis in which it is shrunken and hard and covered with small projecting nodules 2 : the cirrhosis associated with hobnail liver : LAENNEC'S CIRRHOSIS

hock \'häk\ n : the joint or region of the joint that unites the tarsal bones in the hind limb of a quadruped (as the horse) and that corresponds to the human ankle but is elevated and bends backward

hock disease n : PEROSIS

Hodg·kin's disease \'häj-kənz-\ n : a neoplastic disease that is characterized by progressive enlargement of lymph nodes, spleen, and liver and by progressive anemia

Hodgkin, Thomas (1798–1866), British physician.

Hodgkin's paragranuloma n : PARAGRANULOMA 2

hog cholera n : a highly infectious often fatal disease of swine caused by a togavirus and characterized by fever, loss of appetite, weakness, erythematous lesions esp. in light-skinned animals, and severe leukopenia — called also *swine fever*

hog louse n : a large sucking louse of the genus Haematopinus (H. suis) that is parasitic on the hog

hol- or **holo-** comb form 1 : complete : total (holoenzyme) 2 : completely : totally (holoendemic)

hold·fast \'hōld-,fast\ n : an organ by which a parasitic animal (as a tapeworm) attaches itself to its host

ho·lism \'hō-,li-zəm\ n 1 : a theory that the universe and esp. living nature is correctly seen in terms of interacting wholes (as of living organisms) that are more than the mere sum of elementary particles 2 : a holistic study or method of treatment

ho·lis·tic \hō-'lis-tik\ adj 1 : of or relating to holism 2 : relating to or concerned with wholes or with complete systems rather than with the analysis of, treatment of, or dissection into parts (~ medicine attempts to treat both the mind and the body) — **ho·lis·ti·cal·ly** adv

Hol·land·er test \'hä-lən-dər-\ n : a test for function of the vagus nerve (as after vagotomy for peptic ulcer) in which insulin is administered to induce hypoglycemia and gastric acidity tends to increase if innervation by the vagus nerve remains and decrease if severance is complete

Hollander, Franklin (1899–1966), American physiologist.

hol·low \'hä-(,)lō\ n : a depressed part of a surface or a concavity (the ~ at the back of the knee)

hollow organ n : a visceral organ that is a hollow tube or pouch (as the stomach or intestine) or that includes a cavity (as of the heart or bladder) which serves a vital function

hol·mi·um \\'hōl-mē-əm\ *n* : a metallic element that occurs with yttrium and forms highly magnetic compounds — symbol *Ho*; see ELEMENT table

ho·lo·blas·tic \\hō-lə-'blas-tik, ˌhä-\ *adj* : characterized by cleavage planes that divide the whole egg into distinct and separate though coherent blastomeres (∼ eggs) — compare MERO-BLASTIC

ho·lo·crine \\'hō-lə-krən, 'hä-, -ˌkrīn, -ˌkrēn\ *adj* : producing or being a secretion resulting from lysis of secretory cells (∼ gland) — compare APO-CRINE, ECCRINE, MEROCRINE

ho·lo·en·dem·ic \\hō-lō-en-'de-mik\ *adj* : affecting all or characterized by the infection of essentially all the inhabitants of a particular area

ho·lo·en·zyme \\hō-lō-'en-ˌzīm\ *n* : a catalytically active enzyme consisting of an apoenzyme combined with its cofactor

ho·lo·sys·tol·ic \\hō-lō-sis-'tä-lik\ *adj* : relating to an entire systole (a ∼ murmur)

Hol·ter monitor \\'hōl-tər-\ *n* : a portable device that makes a continuous record of electrical activity of the heart and that can be worn by an ambulatory patient during the course of daily activities for the purpose of detecting fleeting episodes of abnormal heart rhythms — **Holter monitoring** *n*

hom- — see HOMO-

Ho·mans' sign \\'hō-mənz-\ *n* : pain in the calf of the leg upon dorsiflexion of the foot with the leg extended that is diagnostic of thrombosis in the deep veins of the area

    Homans, John (1877–1954), American surgeon.

hom·at·ro·pine \\hō-'ma-trə-ˌpēn\ *n* : a poisonous drug $C_{16}H_{21}NO_3$ used esp. in the form of its hydrobromide for dilating the pupil of the eye — see MESOPIN

home- *or* **homeo-** *also* **homoi-** *or* **homoio-** *comb form* : like : similar (*homeo*stasis) (*homoio*thermy)

ho·meo·box \\'hō-mē-ō-ˌbäks\ *n* : a short usu. highly conserved DNA sequence in various genes (as many homeotic genes) that codes for a peptide which may be a DNA-binding protein

ho·meo·path \\'hō-mē-ə-ˌpath\ *n* : a practitioner or adherent of homeopathy

ho·me·op·a·thy \\hō-mē-'ä-pə-thē, ˌhä-\ *n, pl* **-thies** : a system of medical practice that treats a disease esp. by the administration of minute doses of a remedy that would in healthy persons produce symptoms similar to those of the disease — compare ALLOPATHY 2 — **ho·meo·path·ic** \\hō-mē-ə-'pa-thik\ *adj* — **ho·meo·path·i·cal·ly** *adv*

ho·meo·sta·sis \\hō-mē-ō-'stā-səs\ *n* : the maintenance of relatively stable internal physiological conditions (as body temperature or the pH of blood)

under fluctuating environmental conditions — **ho·meo·stat·ic** \-'sta-tik\ *adj* — **ho·meo·stat·i·cal·ly** *adj*

ho·meo·ther·my \\'hō-mē-ə-ˌthər-mē\ *n, pl* **-mies** : the condition of being warm-blooded : WARM-BLOODEDNESS — **ho·meo·therm** \-ˌthərm\ *n* — **ho·meo·ther·mic** \ˌhō-mē-ō-'thər-mik\ *adj*

ho·me·ot·ic \\hō-mē-'ä-tik\ *adj* : relating to, caused by, or being a gene producing a usu. major shift in structural development (∼ mutation)

home remedy *n* : a simply prepared medication or tonic often of unproven effectiveness administered without prescription or professional supervision — compare FOLK MEDICINE

ho·mi·cid·al \\hä-mə-'sīd-əl, ˌhō-\ *adj* : of, relating to, or tending toward homicide — **ho·mi·cid·al·ly** *adv*

ho·mi·cide \\'hä-mə-ˌsīd, 'hō-\ *n* : a killing of one human being by another

hom·i·nid \\'hä-mə-nəd, -ˌnid\ *n* : any of a family (Hominidae) of bipedal primate mammals comprising recent humans together with extinct ancestral and related forms — **hominid** *adj*

ho·mo \\'hō-(ˌ)mō\ *n* **1** *cap* : a genus of primate mammals (family Hominidae) that includes modern humans (*H. sapiens*) and several extinct related species (as *H. erectus*) **2** *pl* **homos** : any primate mammal of the genus *Homo*

homo- *or* **hom-** *comb form* **1** : one and the same : similar : alike (*homo*zygous) **2** : derived from the same species (*homo*graft) **3** : homosexual (*homo*phobia)

ho·mo·cys·te·ine \\hō-mō-'sis-tə-ˌēn, -ˌhä-\ *n* : an amino acid $C_4H_9NO_2S$ that is produced in animal metabolism by removal of a methyl group from methionine and forms a complex with serine that breaks up to produce cysteine and homoserine

ho·mo·cys·tine \-'sis-ˌtēn\ *n* : an amino acid $C_8H_{16}N_2O_4S_2$ formed by oxidation of homocysteine and excreted in the urine in homocystinuria

ho·mo·cys·tin·uria \-ˌsis-ti-'nür-ē-ə, -'nyür-\ *n* : a metabolic disorder inherited as a recessive autosomal trait, caused by deficiency of an enzyme important in the metabolism of homocystine with resulting accumulation of homocystine in the body and its excretion in the urine, and characterized typically by mental retardation, dislocation of the crystalline lenses, and cardiovascular and skeletal involvement — **ho·mo·cys·tin·uric** \-'nür-ik, -'nyür-\ *n*

ho·mo·cy·to·tro·pic \-ˌsī-tə-'trō-pik\ *adj* : of, relating to, or being any antibody that attaches to cells of the species in which it originates but not to cells of other species

homoe- *or* **homoeo-** chiefly Brit var of HOME-

ho·moe·o·path, **ho·moe·op·a·thy,** **ho·moe·o·sta·sis,** **ho·moe·o·ther·my,** **ho·moe·ot·ic** *chiefly Brit var of* HOMEO- PATH, HOMEOPATHY, HOMEOSTASIS, HO- MEOTHERMY, HOMEOTIC

ho·mo·erot·ic \ˌhō-mō-i-'rä-tik\ *adj* : HOMOSEXUAL — **ho·mo·erot·i·cism** \-i-'rä-tə-ˌsi-zəm\ *also* **ho·mo·erot·ism** \-'er-ə-ˌti-zəm\ *n*

ho·mo·ga·met·ic \-gə-'me-tik, -'mē-\ *adj* : forming gametes which all have the same type of sex chromosome

ho·moge·nate \hō-'mä-jə-ˌnāt, hə-\ *n* : a product of homogenizing

ho·mo·ge·neous \ˌhō-mə-'jē-nē-əs, -nyəs\ *adj* : of uniform structure or composition throughout — **ho·mo·ge·ne·ity** \ˌhō-mə-jə-'nē-ə-tē, -'hā-, -'nā-\ *adj* — **ho·mo·ge·neous·ly** *adv* — **ho·mo·ge·neous·ness** *n*

ho·mo·ge·nize \hō-'mä-jə-ˌnīz, hə-\ *vb* **-nized; -niz·ing 1** : to reduce to small particles of uniform size and distrib- ute evenly usu. in a liquid **2** : to re- duce the particles of so that they are uniformly small and evenly distribut- ed; *specif* : to break up the fat glob- ules (of milk) into very fine particles — **ho·mo·ge·ni·za·tion** \hō-ˌmä-jə-nə- 'zā-shən, hə-\ *n* — **ho·mo·ge·niz·er** \-'mä-jə-ˌnī-zər\ *n*

ho·mo·ge·nous \-nəs\ *adj* **1** : HOMOPLAS- TIC (∼ bone grafts) **2** : HOMOGENEOUS

ho·mo·gen·tis·ic acid \ˌhō-mō-ˌjen-'ti- zik, ˌhä-\ *n* : a crystalline acid $C_8H_8O_4$ formed as an intermediate in the metabolism of phenylalanine and ty- rosine and found esp. in the urine of those affected with alkaptonuria

ho·mo·graft \'hō-mə-ˌgraft, 'hä-\ *n* : a graft of tissue from a donor of the same species as the recipient — called also *homotransplant;* compare XENOGRAFT — **homograft** *vb*

homoi- *or* **homoio-** — see HOME-

ho·moio·ther·my *var of* HOMEOTHERMY

ho·mo·lat·er·al \ˌhō-mō-'la-tər-əl, ˌhä-\ *adj* : IPSILATERAL

ho·mo·log *var of* HOMOLOGUE

ho·mol·o·gous \hō-'mä-lə-gəs, hə-\ *adj* **1 a** : having the same relative position, value, or structure **b** : having the same or allelic genes with genetic loci usu. arranged in the same order (∼ chromosomes) **2** : derived from or involving organisms of the same spe- cies (∼ tissue graft) — compare AU- TOLOGOUS, HETEROLOGOUS **1 3** : re- lating to or being immunity or a se- rum produced by or containing a spe- cific antibody corresponding to a specific antigen — **ho·mol·o·gous·ly** *adv*

ho·mo·logue \'hō-mə-ˌlòg, 'hä-, -ˌläg\ *n* : something (as a chromosome) that is homologous

ho·mol·o·gy \hō-'mä-lə-jē, hə-\ *n, pl* **-gies 1** : likeness in structure between parts of different organisms due to evolutionary differentiation from the same or a corresponding part of a re-

mote ancestor — compare ANALOGY **2** : correspondence in structure be- tween different parts of the same in- dividual **3** : similarity of nucleotide or amino-acid sequence in nucleic acids, peptides, or proteins

hom·on·y·mous \hō-'mä-nə-məs\ *adj* **1** : affecting the same part of the visual field of each eye (right ∼ hemiano- pia) **2** : relating to or being diplopia in which the image that is seen by the right eye is to the right of the image that is seen by the left eye

¹ho·mo·phile \'hō-mə-ˌfil\ *adj* : of, relat- ing to, or concerned with homosexu- als or homosexuality (∼ lifestyles); *also* : being homosexual

²homophile *n* : HOMOSEXUAL

ho·mo·pho·bia \ˌhō-mə-'fō-bē-ə\ *n* : ir- rational fear of, aversion to, or dis- crimination against homosexuality or homosexuals — **ho·mo·phobe** \'hō- mə-ˌfōb\ *n* — **ho·mo·pho·bic** \ˌhō-mə- 'fō-bik\ *adj*

ho·mo·plas·tic \ˌhō-mə-'plas-tik, ˌhä-\ *adj* : of, relating to, or derived from another individual of the same spe- cies (∼ grafts)

ho·mo·sal·ate \ˌhō-mō-'sa-ˌlāt, ˌhä-\ *n* : a salicylate $C_{16}H_{22}O_3$ that is used in sunscreen lotions to absorb ultravio- let rays and promote tanning

ho·mo·ser·ine \ˌhō-mō-'ser-ˌēn, ˌhä-, -'sir-\ *n* : an amino acid $C_4H_9NO_3$ that is formed in the conversion of methionine to cysteine — see HOMO- CYSTEINE

¹ho·mo·sex·u·al \ˌhō-mə-'sek-shə-wəl\ *adj* **1** : of, relating to, or characterized by a tendency to direct sexual desire toward individuals of one's own sex — compare HETEROSEXUAL 1a **2** : of, relating to, or involving sexual inter- course between individuals of the same sex — compare HETEROSEXUAL 1b — **ho·mo·sex·u·al·ly** *adv*

²homosexual *n* : a homosexual individu- al and esp. a male

ho·mo·sex·u·al·i·ty \ˌhō-mə-ˌsek-shə- 'wa-lə-tē\ *n, pl* **-ties 1** : the quality or state of being homosexual **2** : erotic activity with another of the same sex

ho·mo·trans·plant \ˌhō-mō-'trans- ˌplant, ˌhä-\ *n* : HOMOGRAFT — **ho· motransplant** *vb* — **ho·mo·trans· plan·ta·tion** \-ˌtrans-ˌplan-'tā-shən\ *n*

ho·mo·va·nil·lic acid \-və-'ni-lik-\ *n* : a dopamine metabolite excreted in hu- man urine

ho·mo·zy·go·sis \-zī-'gō-səs\ *n, pl* **-go- ses** \-ˌsēz\ : HOMOZYGOSITY

ho·mo·zy·gos·i·ty \-'gä-sə-tē\ *n, pl* **-ties** : the state of being homozygous

ho·mo·zy·gote \-'zī-ˌgōt\ *n* : a homozy- gous individual

ho·mo·zy·gous \-'zī-gəs\ *adj* : having the two genes at corresponding loci on homologous chromosomes identical for one or more loci — compare HET- EROZYGOUS

hon·ey·bee \'hə-nē-ˌbē\ *n* : a honey=

producing bee (*Apis* and related genera); *esp* : a European bee (*A. mellifera*) introduced worldwide and kept in hives for the honey it produces

hon•ey•comb \'hə-nē-ˌkōm\ *n* : RETICULUM 1

Hong Kong flu \'häŋ-'käŋ-\ *n* : a relatively mild pandemic influenza that first appeared in 1968 and is caused by a variant strain of the influenza virus

hoof \'hüf, 'hüf\ *n, pl* **hooves** \'hüvz, 'hüvz\ *or* **hoofs** : a horny covering that protects the ends of the toes of numerous plant-eating 4-footed mammals (as horses or cattle); *also* : a hoofed foot — **hoofed** \'hüft, 'hüft, 'hüvd, 'hüvd\ *or* **hooved** \'hüvd, 'hüvd\ *adj*

hoof-and-mouth disease *n* : FOOT-AND-MOUTH DISEASE

hook \'hük\ *n* 1 : an instrument used in surgery to take hold of tissue 2 : an anatomical part that resembles a hook

hook•worm \-ˌwərm\ *n* 1 : any of several parasitic nematode worms (family Ancylostomatidae) that have strong buccal hooks or plates for attaching to the host's intestinal lining and that include serious bloodsucking pests 2 : ANCYLOSTOMIASIS

hookworm disease *n* : ANCYLOSTOMIASIS

hoose \'hüz\ *n* : verminous bronchitis of cattle, sheep, and goats caused by larval strongylid roundworms irritating the bronchial tubes — called also *husk*

hor•de•o•lum \hor-'dē-ə-ləm\ *n, pl* **-o•la** \-lə\ : STY

hore•hound \'hōr-ˌhaùnd\ *n* : a European aromatic plant (*Marrubium vulgare*) of the mint family (Labiatae) that is naturalized in the U.S., has a very bitter taste, and is used as a tonic and anthelmintic 2 : an extract or confection made from horehound and used as a remedy for coughs and colds

hor•i•zon•tal \ˌhor-ə-'zänt-ºl, ˌhär-\ *adj* 1 : relating to or being a transverse plane or section of the body 2 : relating to or being transmission (as of a disease) by physical contact or proximity in contrast with inheritance — compare VERTICAL — **hor•i•zon•tal•ly** *adv*

horizontal cell *n* : any of the retinal neurons whose axons pass along a course in the plexiform layer following the contour of the retina and whose dendrites synapse with the rods and cones

horizontal fissure *n* : a fissure of the right lung that begins at the oblique fissure and runs horizontally dividing the lung into superior and middle lobes

horizontal plate *n* : a plate of the palatine bone that is situated horizontally

joins the bone of the opposite side, and forms the back part of the hard palate — compare PERPENDICULAR PLATE 2

hor•mone \'hor-ˌmōn\ *n* 1 : a product of living cells that circulates in body fluids and produces a specific effect on the activity of cells remote from its point of origin; *esp* : one exerting a stimulatory effect on a cellular activity 2 : a synthetic substance that acts like a hormone — **hor•mon•al** \hor-'mōn-ºl\ *adj* — **hor•mon•al•ly** *adv* — **hor•mone-like** *adj*

horn \'hörn\ *n* 1 : one of the hard projections of bone or keratin on the head of many hoofed mammals; *also* : the material of which horns are composed or a similar material 2 : CORNU — **horned** \'hörnd\ *adj*

horn cell *n* : a nerve cell lying in one of the gray columns of the spinal cord

horned rattlesnake *n* : SIDEWINDER

Hor•ner's syndrome \'hor-nərz-\ *n* : a syndrome marked by sinking in of the eyeball, contraction of the pupil, drooping of the upper eyelid, and vasodilation and anhidrosis of the face, and caused by injury to the cervical sympathetic nerve fibers on the affected side

Horner, Johann Friedrich (1831–1886), Swiss ophthalmologist.

horn fly *n* : a small black European dipteran fly (*Haematobia irritans* of the family Muscidae) that has been introduced into No. America where it is a bloodsucking pest of cattle

horny \'hor-nē\ *adj* **horn•i•er; -est** 1 : composed of or resembling tough fibrous material consisting chiefly of keratin : KERATINOUS (~ tissue) 2 : being hard or callous

horny layer *n* : STRATUM CORNEUM

hor•rip•i•la•tion \ho-ˌri-pə-'lā-shən, hä-\ *n* : a bristling of the hair of the head or body (as from disease, terror, or chilliness) : GOOSE BUMPS — **hor•rip•i•late** \-'ri-pə-ˌlāt\ *vb*

horror au•to•tox•i•cus \-ˌo-tō-'täk-sə-kəs\ *n* : SELF-TOLERANCE

horse \'hors\ *n, pl* **horses** *also* **horse** : a large solid-hoofed herbivorous mammal (*Equus caballus* of the family Equidae) domesticated since a prehistoric period

horse bot *n* : HORSE BOTFLY; *specif* : a larva of a horse botfly

horse botfly *n* : a cosmopolitan botfly of the genus *Gasterophilus* (*G. intestinalis*) whose larvae parasitize the stomach lining of the horse

horse-fly \'hors-ˌflī\ *n, pl* **-flies** : any of a family (Tabanidae) of usu. large dipteran flies with bloodsucking females

horse-pox \-ˌpäks\ *n* : a virus disease of horses related to cowpox and marked by a vesiculopustular eruption of the skin

horse-shoe kidney \-ˌshü\ *n* : a congenital partial fusion of the kidneys resulting in a horseshoe shape

Hor·ton's syndrome \'hȯr-tənz-\ *n* : CLUSTER HEADACHE

Horton, Bayard Taylor (1895–1980), American physician.

hosp *abbr* hospital

hos·pice \'häs-pəs\ *n* : a facility or program designed to provide a caring environment for supplying the physical and emotional needs of the terminally ill

hos·pi·tal \'häs-ˌpit-ᵊl\ *n, often attrib* **1** : a charitable institution for the needy, aged, infirm, or young **2 a** : an institution where the sick or injured are given medical or surgical care — when used in British English following a preposition, the article is usu. omitted (came and saw me in ∼ — Robert Graves) **b** : a place for the care and treatment of sick and injured animals

hospital bed *n* : a bed with a frame in three movable sections equipped with mechanical spring parts that permit raising the head end, foot end, or middle as required — called also *Gatch bed*

hos·pi·tal·ism \'häs-(ˌ)pit-ᵊl-ˌi-zəm\ *n* **1 a** : the factors and influences that adversely affect the health of hospitalized persons **b** : the effect of such factors on mental or physical health **2** : the deleterious physical and mental effects on infants and children resulting from their living in institutions without the benefit of a home environment and parents

hos·pi·tal·iza·tion \ˌhäs-(ˌ)pit-ᵊl-ə-'zā-shən\ *n* **1** : the act or process of being hospitalized **2** : the period of stay in a hospital

hospitalization insurance *n* : insurance that provides benefits to cover or partly cover hospital expenses

hos·pi·tal·ize \'häs-(ˌ)pit-ᵊl-ˌīz, häs-'pit-ᵊl-ˌīz\ *vb* **-ized; -iz·ing** : to place in a hospital as a patient

host \'hōst\ *n* **1** : a living animal or plant on or in which a parasite lives — see DEFINITIVE HOST, INTERMEDIATE HOST **2 a** : an individual into which a tissue or part is transplanted from another **b** : an individual in whom an abnormal growth (as a cancer) is proliferating

hos·til·i·ty \hä-'sti-lə-tē\ *n, pl* **-ties** : conflict, opposition, or resistance in thought or principle — **hos·tile** \'häs-tᵊl, -ˌtīl\ *adj*

hot \'hät\ *adj* **hot·ter; hot·test 1** : having heat in a degree exceeding normal body heat **2** : RADIOACTIVE; *esp* : exhibiting a relatively great amount of radioactivity when subjected to radionuclide scanning

hot flash *n* : a sudden brief flushing and sensation of heat caused by dilation of skin capillaries usu. associated

with menopausal endocrine imbalance — called also *hot flush*

hot line *n* : a telephone service by which usu. unidentified callers can talk confidentially about personal problems to a sympathetic listener

hot pack *n* : absorbent material (as squares of gauze) wrung out in hot water, wrapped around the body or a portion of the body, and covered with dry material to hold in the moist heat — compare COLD PACK

hot-water bottle *n* : a usu. rubber bag that has a stopper and is filled with hot water to provide warmth

hourglass stomach *n* : a stomach divided into two communicating cavities by a circular constriction usu. caused by the scar tissue around an ulcer

house-bro·ken \'haus-ˌbrō-kən\ *adj* : trained to excretory habits acceptable in indoor living — used of a household pet — **house-break** \-ˌbrāk\ *vb*

house call *n* : a visit (as by a doctor) to a home to provide medical care

house doctor *n* : a physician in residence at an establishment (as a hotel) or on the premises temporarily in the event of a medical emergency

house-fly \-ˌflī\ *n, pl* **-flies** : a cosmopolitan dipteran fly of the genus *Musca* (*M. domestica*) that is often found about human habitations and may act as a mechanical vector of diseases (as typhoid fever); *also* : any of various flies of similar appearance or habitat

house-maid's knee \'haus-ˌmādz-\ *n* : a swelling over the knee due to an enlargement of the bursa in the front of the patella

house-man \'haus-mən\ *n, pl* **-men** \-mən\ *chiefly Brit* : INTERN

house mouse *n* : a common nearly cosmopolitan mouse of the genus *Mus* (*M. musculus*) that usu. lives and breeds about buildings, is an important laboratory animal, and is an important pest as a consumer of human food and as a vector of diseases

house officer *n* : an intern or resident employed by a hospital

house physician *n* : a physician and esp. a resident employed by a hospital

house staff *n* : the physicians and esp. the interns and residents sometimes along with other health professionals (as physician's assistants and physical therapists) employed by a hospital

house surgeon *n* : a surgeon fully qualified in a specialty and resident in a hospital

Hous·ton's valve \'hü-stənz-\ *n* : any of the usu. three but sometimes four or two permanent transverse crescent-shaped folds of the rectum

Houston, John (1802–1845), British surgeon.

How·ard test \'hau̇-ərd-\ *n* : a test of renal function that involves the catheterization of each ureter so that the urinary output of each kidney can be determined and analyzed separately

Howard, John Eager (1902–1985), American internist and endocrinologist.

How·ell–Jol·ly body \'hau̇-əl-zhȯ-'lē-, -'jä-lē-\ n : one of the basophilic granules that are probably nuclear fragments, that sometimes occur in red blood cells, and that indicate by their appearance in circulating blood that red cells are leaving the marrow while incompletely mature (as in certain anemias)

Howell, William Henry (1860–1945), American physiologist.

Jolly \zhȯ-'lē\, **Justin Marie Jules** (1870–1953), French histologist.

How·ship's lacuna \'hau̇-,ships-\ n : a groove or cavity usu. containing osteoclasts that occurs in bone which is undergoing reabsorption

Howship, John (1781–1841), British anatomist.

HPI abbr history of present illness

HPLC abbr high-performance liquid chromatography

hr abbr [Latin hora] hour — used in writing prescriptions; see QH

hs abbr [Latin hora somni] at bedtime — used esp. in writing prescriptions

HS abbr house surgeon

HSA abbr human serum albumin

HSV abbr herpes simplex virus

ht abbr height

HTLV \,āch-(,)tē-(,)el-'vē\ n : any of several retroviruses (as HIV-1) — often used with a number or Roman numeral to indicate the type and order of discovery (HTLV-III); called also human T-cell leukemia virus, human T-cell lymphotropic virus, human T-lymphotropic virus

HTLV–III n : HIV-1

Hub·bard tank \'hə-bərd-\ n : a large tank in which a patient can easily be assisted in exercises while in the water

Hubbard, Leroy Watkins (1857–1938), American orthopedic surgeon.

hue \'hyü\ n : the one of the three psychological dimensions of color perception that permits them to be classified as red, yellow, green, blue, or an intermediate between any contiguous pair of these colors and that is correlated with the wavelength of the combination of wavelengths comprising the stimulus — compare BRIGHTNESS, SATURATION 4

Huh·ner test \'hyü-nər-\ n : a test used in sterility studies that involves postcoital examination of fluid aspirated from the vagina and cervix to determine the presence or survival of spermatozoa in these areas

Huhner, Max (1873–1947), American surgeon.

¹**hu·man** \'hyü-mən, 'yü-\ adj 1 a : of, relating to, or characteristic of humans (~ chorionic gonadotropin) (~ growth hormone) b : primarily or usu. harbored by, affecting, or attacking humans (~ appendicitis) (the common ~ flea) 2 : being or consisting of humans (the ~ race) 3 : consisting of hominids — **hu·man·ness** n

²**human** n : a bipedal primate mammal of the genus Homo (H. sapiens) : MAN; broadly : any living or extinct member of the family (Hominidae) to which this primate belongs — **hu·man·like** \-,līk\ adj

human being n : HUMAN

human botfly n : a large fly of the genus Dermatobia (D. hominis) that is widely distributed in tropical America and undergoes its larval development subcutaneously in some mammals including humans

human ecology n : the ecology of human communities and populations esp. as concerned with preservation of environmental quality (as of air or water) through proper application of conservation and civil engineering practices

human engineering n : ERGONOMICS

human factors n : ERGONOMICS

human factors engineering n : ERGONOMICS

human immunodeficiency virus n : HIV

human relations n 1 : the social and interpersonal relations between human beings 2 : a course, study, or program designed to develop better interpersonal and intergroup adjustments

human T-cell leukemia virus n : HTLV

human T-cell leukemia virus type III n : HIV-1

human T-cell lym·pho·tro·pic virus \-,lim-fə-'trō-pik-\ n : HTLV

human T-cell lymphotropic virus type III n : HIV-1

human T-lymphotropic virus n : HTLV

human T-lymphotropic virus type III n : HIV-1

hu·mec·tant \hyü-'mek-tənt\ n : a substance (as glycerol or sorbitol) that promotes retention of moisture — **humectant** adj

hu·mer·al \'hyü-mə-rəl\ adj : of, relating to, or situated in the region of the humerus or shoulder

humeral circumflex artery — see ANTERIOR HUMERAL CIRCUMFLEX ARTERY, POSTERIOR HUMERAL CIRCUMFLEX ARTERY

hu·mer·us \'hyü-mə-rəs\ n, pl **hu·meri** \-,rī, -,rē\ : the longest bone of the upper arm or forelimb extending from the shoulder to the elbow, articulating above by a rounded head with the glenoid fossa, having below a broad articular surface divided by a ridge into a medial pulley-shaped portion and a lateral rounded eminence that articulate with the ulna and radius respectively

hu·mid·i·fi·er \hyü-'mi-də-,fī-ər, yü-\ n

: a device for supplying or maintaining humidity

hu·mid·i·fy \-ˌfī\ *vb* **-fied; -fy·ing** : to make humid — **hu·mid·i·fi·ca·tion** \-ˌmi-də-fə-ˈkā-shən\ *n*

hu·mid·i·ty \hyü-ˈmi-də-tē, yü-\ *n, pl* **-ties** : a moderate degree of wetness esp. of the atmosphere — see ABSOLUTE HUMIDITY, RELATIVE HUMIDITY

hu·mor \ˈhyü-mər, ˈyü-\ *n* 1 : a normal functioning bodily semifluid or fluid (as the blood or lymph) 2 : a secretion (as a hormone) that is an excitant of activity

hu·mor·al \ˈhyü-mə-rəl, ˈyü-\ *adj* 1 : of, relating to, proceeding from, or involving a bodily humor (as a hormone) 2 : relating to or being the part of immunity or the immune response that involves antibodies secreted by B cells and circulating in bodily fluids (∼ immunity) — compare CELL-MEDIATED

hu·mour *chiefly Brit var of* HUMOR

hump \ˈhəmp\ *n* : a rounded protuberance; *esp* : HUMPBACK

hump·back \-ˌbak. *for 1 also* -ˈbak\ *n* 1 : a humped or crooked back; *also* : KYPHOSIS 2 : HUNCHBACK 2 — **hump·backed** \-ˌbakt\ *adj*

hunch·back \ˈhənch-ˌbak\ *n* 1 : HUMPBACK 1 2 : a person with a humpback — **hunch·backed** \-ˌbakt\ *adj*

hun·ger \ˈhəŋ-gər\ *n* 1 : a craving, desire, or urgent need for food 2 : an uneasy sensation occasioned normally by the lack of food and resulting directly from stimulation of the sensory nerves of the stomach by the contraction and churning movement of the empty stomach 3 : a weakened disordered condition brought about by prolonged lack of food (die of ∼)

hunger pangs *n pl* : pains in the abdominal region which occur in the early stages of hunger or fasting and are correlated with contractions of the empty stomach or intestines

Hun·ner's ulcer \ˈhə-nərz-\ *n* : a painful ulcer affecting all layers of the bladder wall and usu. associated with inflammation of the wall

Hunner, Guy Leroy (1868–1957), American gynecologist.

Hun·ter's canal \ˈhən-tərz-\ *n* : an aponeurotic canal in the middle third of the thigh through which the femoral artery passes

Hunter, John (1728–1793), British anatomist and surgeon.

Hunter's syndrome *or* **Hunter syndrome** \ˈhən-tər-\ *n* : a mucopolysaccharidosis that is similar to Hurler's syndrome but is inherited as a sex-linked recessive trait and has milder symptoms

Hunter, Charles (*fl* 1917), Canadian physician.

Hun·ting·ton's chorea \ˈhən-tiŋ-tənz-\ *n* : HUNTINGTON'S DISEASE

Huntington, George (1850–1916), American neurologist.

Huntington's disease *n* : a hereditary chorea usu. developing in adult life and progressing to dementia

Hur·ler's syndrome \ˈhər-lərz-, ˈhùr-\ *or* **Hur·ler syndrome** \-lər-\ *n* : a mucopolysaccharidosis that is inherited as an autosomal recessive trait and is characterized by deformities of the skeleton and features, hepatosplenomegaly, restricted joint flexibility, clouding of the cornea, mental deficiency, and deafness — called also *Hurler's disease*

Hur·ler \ˈhùr-ler\, Gertrud (*fl* 1920), German pediatrician.

husk \ˈhəsk\ *n* : HOOSE

Hutch·in·son's teeth \ˈhə-chən-sənz-\ *n* : peg-shaped teeth having a crescent-shaped notch in the cutting edge and occurring esp. in children with congenital syphilis

Hutchinson, Sir Jonathan (1828–1913), British surgeon and pathologist.

Hutchinson's triad *n* : a triad of symptoms that comprises Hutchinson's teeth, interstitial keratitis, and deafness and occurs in children with congenital syphilis

Hux·ley's layer \ˈhəks-lēz-\ *n* : a layer of the inner stratum of a hair follicle composed of one or two layers of horny, flattened, epithelial cells with nuclei and situated between Henle's layer and the cuticle next to the hair

Huxley, Thomas Henry (1825–1895), British biologist.

hy- *or* **hyo-** *comb form* : of, relating to, or connecting with the hyoid bone (*hyo*glossus)

hyal- *or* **hyalo-** *comb form* : glass : glassy : hyaline (*hyal*uronic acid)

¹**hy·a·line** \ˈhī-ə-lən, -ˌlin\ *adj* : transparent or nearly transparent and usu. homogeneous

²**hy·a·line** \-ə-lən\ *n* : any of several translucent nitrogenous substances that collect around cells and are capable of being stained by eosin

hyaline cartilage *n* : translucent bluish white cartilage consisting of cells embedded in an apparently homogeneous matrix, present in joints and respiratory passages, and forming most of the fetal skeleton

hyaline cast *n* : a renal cast of mucoprotein characterized by homogeneity of structure

hyaline degeneration *n* : tissue degeneration chiefly of connective tissues in which structural elements of affected cells are replaced by homogeneous translucent material that stains intensely with acid stains

hyaline membrane disease *n* : a respiratory disease of unknown cause that occurs in newborn premature infants and is characterized by deficiency of the surfactant coating the inner surface of the lungs. by failure of the lungs to expand and contract properly during breathing with resulting collapse, and by the accumulation of a protein-containing film lining the alveoli and their ducts — abbr. *HMD;* called also *respiratory distress syndrome*

hy·a·lin·i·za·tion \ˌhī-ə-lə-nə-ˈzā-shən\ *n* : the process of becoming hyaline or of undergoing hyaline degeneration; *also* : the resulting state — **hy·a·lin·ized** \ˈhī-ə-lə-ˌnīzd\ *adj*

hy·a·li·no·sis \ˌhī-ə-lə-ˈnō-səs\ *n, pl* **-no·ses** \-ˌsēz\ 1 : HYALINE DEGENERATION 2 : a condition characterized by hyaline degeneration

hy·a·li·tis \ˌhī-ə-ˈlī-təs\ *n* 1 : inflammation of the vitreous humor of the eye 2 : inflammation of the hyaloid membrane of the vitreous humor

hyalo- — see HYAL-

hy·a·loid \ˈhī-ə-ˌlȯid\ *adj* : being glassy or transparent ⟨a ~ appearance⟩

hyaloid membrane *n* : a very delicate membrane enclosing the vitreous humor of the eye

hy·a·lo·mere \ˈhī-ˈa-lə-ˌmir\ *n* : the pale portion of a blood platelet that is not refractile — compare CHROMOMERE

Hy·a·lom·ma \ˌhī-ə-ˈlä-mə\ *n* : a genus of Old World ticks that attack wild and domestic mammals and sometimes humans, produce severe lesions by their bites, and often serve as vectors of viral and protozoal diseases (as east coast fever)

hy·a·lo·plasm \ˈhī-ˈa-lə-ˌpla-zəm, ˈhī-ə-lō-\ *n* : CYTOSOL — **hy·a·lo·plas·mic** \ˌhī-ə-lə-ˈplaz-mik, ˌhī-ə-lō-\ *adj*

hy·al·uron·ic acid \ˌhī-ˌyu̇r-ˈä-nik-, -əl-yu̇-\ *n* : a viscous glycosaminoglycan that occurs esp. in the vitreous humor, the umbilical cord, and synovia and as a cementing substance in the subcutaneous tissue

hy·al·uron·i·dase \-ˈrä-nə-ˌdās, -ˌdāz\ *n* : a mucolytic enzyme that facilitates the spread of fluids through tissues by lowering the viscosity of hyaluronic acid and is used esp. to aid in the dispersion of fluids (as local anesthetics) injected subcutaneously for therapeutic purposes — called also *spreading factor*

H–Y antigen *n* : a male histocompatibility antigen determined by genes on the Y chromosome

hy·brid \ˈhī-brəd\ *n* 1 : an offspring of two animals or plants of different races, breeds, varieties, species, or genera 2 : something heterogeneous in origin or composition ⟨artificial ~s of DNA and RNA⟩ ⟨somatic cell ~s of mouse and human cells⟩ — **hybrid** *adj* — **hy·brid·ism** \-brə-ˌdi-zəm\ *n*

hy·brid·ize \ˈhī-brə-ˌdīz\ *vb* **-ized; -iz·ing** : to cause to interbreed or combine so as to produce hybrids — **hy·brid·i·za·tion** \ˌhī-brə-də-ˈzā-shən\ *n*

hy·brid·oma \ˌhī-brə-ˈdō-mə\ *n* : a hybrid cell produced by the fusion of an antibody-producing lymphocyte with a tumor cell and used to culture continuously a specific monoclonal antibody

hy·can·thone \hī-ˈkan-ˌthōn\ *n* : a lucanthone analog $C_{20}H_{24}N_2O_2S$ used to treat schistosomiasis

Hy·co·dan \ˈhī-kə-ˌdan\ *trademark* — used for a preparation of dihydrocodeinone

hy·dan·to·in \hī-ˈdan-tə-wən\ *n* 1 : a crystalline weakly acidic compound $C_3H_4N_2O_2$ with a sweetish taste that is found in beet juice 2 : a derivative of hydantoin (as phenytoin)

hy·dan·to·in·ate \-wə-ˌnāt\ *n* : a salt of hydantoin or of one of its derivatives

hy·da·tid \ˈhī-ə-təd, -ˌtid\ *n* 1 : the larval cyst of a tapeworm of the genus *Echinococcus* that usu. occurs as a fluid-filled sac containing daughter cysts in which scolices develop but that occas. forms a proliferating spongy mass which actively metastasizes in the host's tissues — called also *hydatid cyst*; see ECHINOCOCCUS 2 a : an abnormal cyst or cystic structure; *esp* : HYDATIDIFORM MOLE b : HYDATID DISEASE

hydatid disease *n* : a form of echinococcosis caused by the development of hydatids of a tapeworm of the genus *Echinococcus* (*E. granulosus*) in the tissues esp. of the liver or lungs of humans and some domestic animals (as sheep and dogs)

hy·da·tid·i·form mole \ˌhī-də-ˈti-də-ˌfȯrm-\ *n* : a mass in the uterus consisting of enlarged edematous degenerated placental villi growing in clusters resembling grapes and usu. associated with death of the fetus

hy·da·tid·o·sis \ˌhī-də-ˌti-ˈdō-səs\ *n, pl* **-o·ses** \-ˌsēz\ : ECHINOCOCCOSIS; *specif* : HYDATID DISEASE

Hyd·er·gine \ˈhī-dər-ˌjēn\ *trademark* — used for a preparation of ergoloid mesylates

hydr- *or* **hydro-** *comb form* 1 : water ⟨*hydro*therapy⟩ 2 : an accumulation of fluid in a (specified) bodily part ⟨*hydro*cephalus⟩ ⟨*hydro*nephrosis⟩

hy·drae·mia *chiefly Brit var of* HYDREMIA

hy·dra·gogue \ˈhī-drə-ˌgäg\ *n* : a cathartic that causes copious watery discharges from the bowels

hy·dral·a·zine \hī-ˈdra-lə-ˌzēn\ *n* : an antihypertensive drug $C_8H_8N_4$ used in the form of its hydrochloride and acting to produce peripheral arteriolar dilation by relaxing vascular smooth muscle

hy·dram·ni·os \hī-ˈdram-nē-ˌäs\ *n* : excessive accumulation of the amniotic fluid — called also *polyhydramnios* — **hy·dram·ni·ot·ic** \hī-ˌdram-nē-ˈä-tik\ *adj*

hy·dran·en·ceph·a·ly \ˌhī-ˌdra-nen-ˈse-fə-lē\ *n, pl* **-lies** : a congenital defect of the brain in which fluid-filled cavities take the place of the cerebral hemispheres

hy·drar·gy·rism \hi-ˈdrär-jə-ˌri-zəm\ *n* : MERCURIALISM

hy·drar·thro·sis \ˌhi-(ˌ)drär-ˈthrō-səs\ *n, pl* **-thro·ses** \-ˌsēz\ : a watery effusion into a joint cavity

hy·dras·ti·nine \hi-ˈdras-tə-ˌnēn, -nən\ *n* : a crystalline base $C_{11}H_{13}NO_3$ useful in controlling uterine hemorrhage

¹**hy·drate** \ˈhi-ˌdrāt\ *n* 1 : a compound or complex ion formed by the union of water with some other substance 2 : HYDROXIDE

²**hydrate** *vb* **hy·drat·ed; hy·drat·ing** 1 : to cause to take up or combine with water or the elements of water 2 : to become a hydrate

hy·dra·tion \hi-ˈdrā-shən\ *n* 1 : the act or process of combining or treating with water: as **a** : the introduction of additional fluid into the body **b** : a chemical reaction in which water takes part with the formation of only one product 2 : the quality or state of being hydrated; *esp* : the condition of having adequate fluid in the cerebral tissues

hy·dra·zide \ˈhi-drə-ˌzīd\ *n* : any of a class of compounds resulting from the replacement by an acid group of hydrogen in hydrazine or in one of its derivatives

hy·dra·zine \ˈhi-drə-ˌzēn\ *n* : a colorless fuming corrosive strongly reducing liquid base N_2H_4 used in the production of numerous materials (as pharmaceuticals and plastics): *also* : an organic base derived from this

hy·dra·zone \ˈhi-drə-ˌzōn\ *n* : any of a class of compounds containing the grouping >C=NNHR

hy·dre·mia \hi-ˈdrē-mē-ə\ *n* : an abnormally watery state of the blood — **hy·dre·mic** \-mik\ *adj*

hy·dren·ceph·a·ly \ˌhi-dren-ˈse-fə-lē\ *n, pl* **-lies** : HYDROCEPHALUS

hydro- — see HYDR-

hy·droa \hi-ˈdrō-ə\ *n* : an itching usu. vesicular eruption of the skin: *esp* : one induced by exposure to light

hy·dro·bro·mide \ˌhi-drō-ˈbrō-ˌmīd\ *n* : a chemical complex composed of an organic compound in association with hydrogen bromide

hy·dro·car·bon \-ˈkär-bən\ *n* : an organic compound (as benzene) containing only carbon and hydrogen and often occurring esp. in petroleum, natural gas, and coal

hy·dro·cele \ˈhi-drə-ˌsēl\ *n* : an accumulation of serous fluid in a sacculated cavity (as the scrotum)

hy·dro·ce·lec·to·my \ˌhi-drə-sē-ˈlek-tə-mē\ *n, pl* **-mies** : surgical removal of a hydrocele

¹**hy·dro·ce·phal·ic** \ˌhi-drō-sə-ˈfa-lik\ *adj* : relating to, characterized by, or affected with hydrocephalus

²**hydrocephalic** *n* : an individual affected with hydrocephalus

hy·dro·ceph·a·lus \-ˈse-fə-ləs\ *n, pl* **-li** \-ˌlī\ : an abnormal increase in the amount of cerebrospinal fluid within the cranial cavity that is accompanied by expansion of the cerebral ventricles and enlargement of the skull

hy·dro·ceph·a·ly \-ˈse-fə-lē\ *n, pl* **-lies** : HYDROCEPHALUS

hy·dro·chlo·ric acid \ˌhi-drə-ˈklôr-ik-\ : an aqueous solution of hydrogen chloride HCl that is a strong corrosive irritating acid and is normally present in dilute form in gastric juice — called also *muriatic acid*

hy·dro·chlo·ride \-ˈklôr-ˌīd\ *n* : a chemical complex composed of an organic base (as an alkaloid) in association with hydrogen chloride

hy·dro·chlo·ro·thi·a·zide \-ˌklôr-ə-ˈthī-ə-ˌzīd\ *n* : a diuretic and antihypertensive drug $C_7H_8ClN_3O_4S_2$ — see HYDRODIURIL, ORETIC

hy·dro·cho·le·re·sis \-ˌkō-lər-ˈē-səs, -ˌkä-\ *n, pl* **-re·ses** \-ˌsēz\ : increased production of watery liver bile without necessarily increased secretion of bile solids — compare CHOLERESIS

¹**hy·dro·cho·le·ret·ic** \-ˈe-tik\ *adj* : of, relating to, or characterized by hydrocholeresis

²**hydrocholeretic** *n* : an agent that produces hydrocholeresis

hy·dro·co·done \ˌhi-drō-ˈkō-ˌdōn\ *n* : DIHYDROCODEINONE

hy·dro·cor·ti·sone \-ˈkor-tə-ˌsōn, -ˌzōn\ *n* : a glucocorticoid $C_{21}H_{30}O_5$ of the adrenal cortex that is a derivative of cortisone and is used in the treatment of rheumatoid arthritis — called also *cortisol*

hy·dro·cy·an·ic acid \ˌhi-drō-sī-ˈa-nik-\ *n* : an aqueous solution of hydrogen cyanide HCN that is an extremely poisonous weak acid used esp. in fumigating — called also *prussic acid*

Hy·dro·di·ur·il \-ˈdī-yə-ˌril\ *trademark* — used for a preparation of hydrochlorothiazide

hy·dro·dy·nam·ics \ˌhi-drō-dī-ˈna-miks\ *n* : a science that deals with the motion of fluids and the forces acting on moving bodies immersed in fluids — **hy·dro·dy·nam·ic** \-mik\ *adj*

hy·dro·flu·me·thi·a·zide \-ˌflü-mə-ˈthī-ə-ˌzīd\ *n* : a diuretic and antihypertensive drug $C_8H_8F_3N_3O_4S_2$ — see SALURON

hy·dro·gel \ˈhi-drə-ˌjel\ *n* : a gel in which the liquid is water

hy·dro·gen \ˈhi-drə-jən\ *n* : a nonmetallic element that is the simplest and lightest of the elements and is normally a colorless odorless highly flammable gas, having two atoms in a molecule — symbol *H*; see ELEMENT table — **hy·drog·e·nous** \hi-ˈdrä-jə-nəs\ *adj*

hy·dro·ge·nate \hi-ˈdrä-jə-ˌnāt, ˈhi-drə-jə-\ *vb* **-nat·ed; -nat·ing** : to add hydrogen to the molecule of (an unsaturated organic compound) — **hydrogenation** \hī-ˌdrä-jə-ˈnā-shən, ˌhī-drə-jə-\ n

hydrogen bond n : a linkage consisting of a hydrogen atom bonded between two negatively charged atoms (as fluorine, oxygen, or nitrogen) with one side of the linkage being a covalent bond and the other being electrostatic in nature; also : the electrostatic bond in this linkage

hydrogen bromide n : a colorless irritating gas HBr that fumes in moist air and yields a strong acid resembling hydrochloric acid when dissolved in water

hydrogen chloride n : a colorless pungent poisonous gas HCl that fumes in moist air and yields hydrochloric acid when dissolved in water

hydrogen cyanide n 1 : a poisonous usu. gaseous compound HCN that has the odor of bitter almonds 2 : HYDROCYANIC ACID

hydrogen peroxide n : an unstable compound H_2O_2 used esp. as an oxidizing and bleaching agent and as an antiseptic

hy·dro·lase \ˈhī-drə-ˌlās, -ˌlāz\ n : a hydrolytic enzyme (as an esterase)

hy·drol·o·gy \hī-ˈdrä-lə-jē\ n, pl -gies : the body of medical knowledge and practice concerned with the therapeutic use of bathing and water

hy·dro·ly·sate \hī-ˈdrä-lə-ˌsāt, ˌhī-drə-ˈlī-\ or **hy·dro·ly·zate** \-ˌzāt\ n : a product of hydrolysis

hy·drol·y·sis \hī-ˈdrä-lə-səs, ˌhī-drə-ˈlī-\ n : a chemical process of decomposition involving splitting of a bond and addition of the elements of water — **hy·dro·lyt·ic** \ˌhī-drə-ˈli-tik\ adj — **hy·dro·lyze** \ˈhī-drə-ˌlīz\ vb — **hy·dro·lyz·able** \ˌhī-drə-ˈlī-zə-bəl\ adj

hy·dro·me·tro·col·pos \ˌhī-drō-ˌmē-trō-ˈkäl-ˌpäs\ n : an accumulation of watery fluid in the uterus and vagina

hy·dro·mor·phone \ˈmȯr-ˌfōn\ n : a morphine derivative $C_{17}H_{19}NO_3$ used as an analgesic in the form of its hydrochloride salt

hy·dro·ne·phro·sis \-ni-ˈfrō-səs\ n, pl -phro·ses \-ˌsēz\ : cystic distension of the kidney caused by the accumulation of urine in the renal pelvis as a result of obstruction to outflow and accompanied by atrophy of the kidney structure and cyst formation — **hy·dro·ne·phrot·ic** \-ni-ˈfrä-tik\ adj

hy·drop·a·thy \hī-ˈdrä-pə-thē\ n, pl -thies : a method of treating disease by copious and frequent use of water both externally and internally — compare HYDROTHERAPY — **hy·dro·path·ic** \ˌhī-drə-ˈpa-thik\ adj

hy·dro·pe·nia \ˌhī-drə-ˈpē-nē-ə\ n : a condition in which the body is deficient in water — **hy·dro·pe·nic** \-ˈpē-nik\ adj

hy·dro·peri·car·di·um \ˌhī-drō-per-ə-

ˈkär-dē-əm\ n, pl -dia \-dē-ə\ : an excess of watery fluid in the pericardial cavity

hy·dro·phil·ic \-ˈfi-lik\ adj : of, relating to, or having a strong affinity for water (~ colloids) — compare LIPOPHILIC — **hy·dro·phi·lic·i·ty** \-ˌfi-ˈli-sə-tē\ n

hy·dro·pho·bia \ˌhī-drə-ˈfō-bē-ə\ n 1 : a morbid dread of water 2 : RABIES

hy·dro·pho·bic \-ˈfō-bik\ adj 1 : of, relating to, or suffering from hydrophobia 2 : resistant to or avoiding wetting (a ~ lens) 3 : of, relating to, or having a lack of affinity for water (~ colloids) — **hy·dro·pho·bic·i·ty** \-ˌfō-ˈbi-sə-tē\ n

hy·droph·thal·mos \ˌhī-dräf-ˈthal-mäs\ n : general enlargement of the eyeball due to a watery effusion within it

hy·drop·ic \hī-ˈdrä-pik\ adj 1 : exhibiting hydrops; esp : EDEMATOUS 2 : characterized by swelling and taking up of fluid — used of a type of cellular degeneration

hy·dro·pneu·mo·tho·rax \ˌhī-drə-ˌnü-mə-ˈthȯr-ˌaks, -ˌnyü-\ n, pl -tho·rax·es or -tho·ra·ces \-ˈthȯr-ə-ˌsēz\ : the presence of gas and serous fluid in the pleural cavity

hy·drops \ˈhī-ˌdräps\ n, pl **hy·drop·ses** \-ˌdräp-ˌsēz\ 1 : EDEMA 2 : distension of a hollow organ with fluid 3 : HYDROPS FETALIS

hydrops fe·tal·is \-fē-ˈta-ləs\ n : serious and extensive edema of the fetus (as in erythroblastosis fetalis)

hy·dro·qui·none \ˌhī-drō-kwi-ˈnōn, -ˈkwi-ˌnōn\ n : a bleaching agent $C_6H_6O_2$ used topically to remove pigmentation from hyperpigmented areas of skin (as a lentigo or freckle)

hy·dro·sal·pinx \-ˈsal-(ˌ)piŋks\ n, pl -sal·pin·ges \-sal-ˈpin-(ˌ)jēz\ : abnormal distension of one or both fallopian tubes with fluid usu. due to inflammation

hy·dro·ther·a·py \ˌhī-drō-ˈther-ə-pē\ n, pl -pies : the therapeutic use of water (as in a whirlpool bath) — compare HYDROPATHY — **hy·dro·ther·a·peu·tic** \-ˌther-ə-ˈpyü-tik\ adj

hy·dro·tho·rax \ˌhī-drō-ˈthȯr-ˌaks, n, pl -tho·rax·es or -tho·ra·ces \-ˈthȯr-ə-ˌsēz\ : an excess of serous fluid in the pleural cavity; esp : an effusion resulting from failing circulation (as in heart disease)

hy·dro·ure·ter \ˌhī-drō-ˈyür-ə-tər, -yü-ˈrē-tər\ n : abnormal distension of the ureter with urine

hydrous wool fat \ˈhī-drəs-\ n : LANOLIN

hy·drox·ide \hī-ˈdräk-ˌsīd\ n 1 : the anion OH^- consisting of one atom of hydrogen and one of oxygen — called also hydroxide ion 2 a : an ionic compound of hydroxide with an element or group b : any of various hydrated oxides

hy·droxo·co·bal·amin \hī-ˈdräk-(ˌ)sō-kō-ˈba-lə-mən\ n : a member C_{62}

$H_{89}CoN_{13}O_{15}P$ of the vitamin B_{12} group used in treating and preventing vitamin B_{12} deficiency

hy·droxy \hī-'dräk-sē\ *adj* : being or containing hydroxyl; *esp* : containing hydroxyl in place of a hydrogen — often used in combination ⟨*hydroxy-butyric* acid⟩

hy·droxy·am·phet·amine \hī-ˌdräk-sē-am-'fe-tə-ˌmēn, -mən\ *n* : a sympathomimetic drug $C_9H_{13}NO$ used esp. as a decongestant and mydriatic

hydroxyanisole — see BUTYLATED HYDROXYANISOLE

hy·droxy·ap·a·tite \hī-ˌdräk-sē-'a-pə-ˌtīt\ *n* : a complex phosphate of calcium $Ca_5(PO_4)_3OH$ that is the chief structural element of bone

hy·droxy·ben·zo·ic acid \-ben-'zō-ik-\ *n* : SALICYLIC ACID

hy·droxy·bu·ty·rate \-'byü-tə-ˌrāt\ *n* : a salt or ester of hydroxybutyric acid

hy·droxy·bu·tyr·ic acid \-byü-'tir-ik-\ *n* : a derivative $C_4H_8O_3$ of butyric acid that is excreted in urine in increased quantities in diabetes — called also *oxybutyric acid*

hy·droxy·chlor·o·quine \-'klōr-ə-ˌkwēn, -ˌkwin\ *n* : a drug $C_{18}H_{26}ClN_3O$ derived from quinoline that is administered as the sulfate and is used in the treatment of malaria, rheumatoid arthritis, and lupus erythematosus — see PLAQUENIL

25-hy·droxy·cho·le·cal·cif·er·ol \'twen-tē-'fīv-hī-ˌdräk-sē-ˌkō-lə-(ˌ)kal-'sif-ə-ˌról, -ˌról\ *n* : a sterol $C_{27}H_{44}O_2$ that is a metabolite of cholecalciferol formed in the liver and is the circulating form of vitamin D

17-hy·droxy·cor·ti·co·ste·roid \-ˌse-vən-'tēn-hī-ˌdräk-sē-ˌkört-i-kō-'stir-ˌoid, -'ster-\ *n* : any of several adrenocorticosteroids (as hydrocortisone) with an —OH group and an $HOCH_2CO$ group attached to carbon 17 of the fused ring structure of the steroid

hy·droxy·di·one sodium suc·ci·nate \hī-ˌdräk-sē-'dī-ˌōn . . . 'sək-sə-ˌnāt\ *n* : a steroid $C_{25}H_{35}NaO_6$ given intravenously as a general anesthetic

6-hy·droxy·do·pa·mine \'siks-hī-ˌdräk-sē-'dō-pə-ˌmēn\ *n* : an isomer of norepinephrine that is taken up by catecholaminergic nerve fibers and causes the degeneration of their terminals

5-hy·droxy·in·dole·ace·tic acid \'fīv-hī-ˌdräk-sē-in-(ˌ)dō-lə-'sē-tik-\ *n* : a metabolite $C_{10}H_9NO_3$ of serotonin that is present in cerebrospinal fluid and in urine

hy·drox·yl \hī-'dräk-səl\ *n* **1** : the chemical group or ion OH that consists of one atom of hydrogen and one of oxygen and is neutral or positively charged **2** : HYDROXIDE 1

hy·drox·yl·ap·a·tite \hī-ˌdräk-sə-'la-pə-ˌtīt\ *var of* HYDROXYAPATITE

hy·drox·y·lase \hī-'dräk-sə-ˌlās, -ˌlāz\ *n* : any of a group of enzymes that cat-

alyze oxidation reactions in which one of the two atoms of molecular oxygen is incorporated into the substrate and the other is used to oxidize NADH or NADPH

hy·droxy·ly·sine \hī-ˌdräk-sē-'lī-ˌsēn\ *n* : an amino acid $C_6H_{14}N_2O_3$ that is found esp. in collagen

hy·droxy·pro·ges·ter·one \hī-ˌdräk-sē-prō-'jes-tə-ˌrōn\ *or* 17α**-hydroxy-progesterone** \ˌse-vən-'tēn-'al-fə-\ *n* : a synthetic derivative $C_{21}H_{30}O_3$ of progesterone used esp. as the caproate in progestational therapy (as for amenorrhea)

hy·droxy·pro·line \-'prō-ˌlēn\ *n* : an amino acid $C_5H_9NO_3$ that occurs naturally as a constituent of collagen

8-hy·droxy·quin·o·line \'āt-hī-ˌdräk-sē-'kwin-ᵊl-ˌēn\ *n* : a derivative C_9H_7-NO of quinoline used esp. in the form of its sulfate as a disinfectant, topical antiseptic, antiperspirant, and deodorant — called also *oxyquinoline*

hy·droxy·ste·roid \-'stir-ˌoid, -'ster-\ *n* : any of several ketosteroids (as androsterone) found esp. in urine

hydroxytoluene — see BUTYLATED HYDROXYTOLUENE

5-hy·droxy·tryp·ta·mine \'fīv-hī-ˌdräk-sē-'trip-tə-ˌmēn\ *n* : SEROTONIN

hy·droxy·urea \-yü-'rē-ə\ *n* : an antineoplastic drug $CH_4N_2O_2$ used to treat some forms of leukemia

hy·droxy·zine \hī-'dräk-sə-ˌzēn\ *n* : a compound $C_{21}H_{27}ClN_2O_2$ that is administered usu. in the form of the hydrochloride or the pamoate and is used as an antihistamine and tranquilizer — see VISTARIL

hy·giene \'hī-ˌjēn\ *n* **1** : a science of the establishment and maintenance of health — see MENTAL HYGIENE 2 : conditions or practices (as of cleanliness) conducive to health — **hy·gien·ic** \hī-jē-'e-nik, hī-'je-, hī-'jē-\ *adj* — **hy·gien·i·cal·ly** *adv*

hy·gien·ics \-iks\ *n* : HYGIENE 1

hy·gien·ist \hī-'jē-nist, -'je-; 'hī-ˌjē-\ *n* : a specialist in hygiene; *esp* : one skilled in a specified branch of hygiene — see DENTAL HYGIENIST

hy·gro·ma \hī-'grō-mə\ *n, pl* **-mas** *or* **-ma·ta** \-mə-tə\ : a cystic tumor of lymphatic origin

hy·grom·e·ter \hī-'grä-mə-tər\ *n* : any of several instruments for measuring the humidity of the atmosphere — **hy·gro·met·ric** \ˌhī-grə-'me-trik\ *adj*

hy·gro·my·cin B \ˌhī-grə-'mis-ᵊn-'bē\ *n* : an antibiotic $C_{20}H_{37}N_3O_{13}$ obtained from a bacterium of the genus *Streptomyces* (*S. hygroscopicus*) and used as an anthelmintic in swine and chickens

hy·gro·scop·ic \ˌhī-grə-'skä-pik\ *adj* : readily taking up and retaining moisture ⟨glycerol is ∼⟩

Hy·gro·ton \'hī-grə-ˌtän\ *trademark* — used for a preparation of chlorthalidone

hy·men \\'hī-mən\\ n : a fold of mucous membrane partly or wholly closing the orifice of the vagina — **hy·men·al** \\-mən-əl\\ adj

hymen- or **hymeno-** comb form : hymen : membrane ⟨hymenectomy⟩ ⟨hymenotomy⟩

hy·men·ec·to·my \\,hī-mə-'nek-tə-mē\\ n, pl -mies : surgical removal of the hymen

Hy·me·nol·e·pis \\,hī-mə-'nä-lə-pəs\\ n : a genus of small taenioid tapeworms (family Hymenolepididae) that are parasites of mammals and birds and include one (H. nana) that is an intestinal parasite of humans

hy·me·nop·ter·an \\,hī-mə-'näp-tə-rən\\ n : any of an order (Hymenoptera) of highly specialized and often colonial insects (as bees, wasps, and ants) that have usu. four thin transparent wings and the abdomen on a slender stalk — **hymenopteran** adj — **hy·me·nop·ter·ous** \\-tə-rəs\\ adj

hy·me·nop·ter·ism \\-'näp-tə-,ri-zəm\\ n : poisoning resulting from the bite or sting of a hymenopteran insect

hy·men·ot·o·my \\,hī-mə-'nä-tə-mē\\ n, pl -mies : surgical incision of the hymen

hyo- — see HY-

hyo·glos·sal \\,hī-ō-'gläs-əl, -'glós-\\ adj : of, relating to, or connecting the tongue and hyoid bone

hyo·glos·sus \\-'glä-səs, -'glò-\\ n, pl -si \\-,sī, -,sē\\ : a flat muscle on each side of the tongue

hy·oid \\'hī-,òid\\ adj : of or relating to the hyoid bone

hyoid bone n : a bone or complex of bones situated at the base of the tongue and supporting the tongue and its muscles — called also hyoid

hyo·man·dib·u·lar \\,hī-ō-man-'di-byù-lər\\ n : a bone or cartilage that forms the columella or stapes of the ear of higher vertebrates — **hyomandibular** adj

hyo·scine \\'hī-ə-,sēn\\ n : SCOPOLAMINE; esp : the levorotatory form of scopolamine

hyo·scy·a·mine \\,hī-ə-'sī-ə-,mēn\\ n : a poisonous crystalline alkaloid $C_{17}H_{23}NO_3$ of which atropine is a racemic mixture; esp : its levorotatory form found esp. in the plants belladonna and henbane and used similarly to atropine

hyo·scy·a·mus \\-məs\\ n 1 cap : a genus of poisonous Eurasian herbs of the nightshade family (Solanaceae) that includes the henbane (H. niger) 2 : the dried leaves of the henbane containing the alkaloids hyoscyamine and scopolamine and used as an antispasmodic and sedative

Hyo·stron·gy·lus \\-'strän-jə-ləs\\ n : a genus of nematode worms (family Trichostrongylidae) that includes the common small red stomach worm (H. rubidus) of swine

¹hyp·acu·sic \\,hī-pə-'kü-sik, ,hī-, -'kyü-\\ adj : affected with hypoacusis

²hypacusic n : one affected with hypoacusis

hyp·acu·sis \\-'kü-səs, -'kyü-\\ n : HYPOACUSIS

hyp·aes·the·sia Brit var of HYPESTHESIA

hyp·al·ge·sia \\,hī-,pal-'jē-zhə, ,hī-pal-, -zē-ə, -zhē-ə\\ n : diminished sensitivity to pain — **hyp·al·ge·sic** \\-'jē-zik, -sik\\ adj

Hy·paque \\'hī-,pāk\\ trademark — used for a diatrizoate preparation for use in radiographic diagnosis

hyper- prefix 1 : excessively ⟨hypersensitive⟩ 2 : excessive ⟨hyperemia⟩ ⟨hypertension⟩

hy·per·acid·i·ty \\,hī-pə-rə-'si-də-tē\\ n, pl -ties : the condition of containing more than the normal amount of acid — **hy·per·ac·id** \\,hī-pə-'ra-səd\\ adj

¹hy·per·ac·tive \\,hī-pə-'rak-tiv\\ adj : affected with or exhibiting hyperactivity; broadly : more active than is usual or desirable

²hyperactive n : one who is hyperactive

hy·per·ac·tiv·i·ty \\,hī-pə-,rak-'ti-və-tē\\ n, pl -ties : a state or condition of being excessively or pathologically active; esp : ATTENTION DEFICIT DISORDER

hy·per·acu·sis \\,hī-pə-rə-'kü-səs, -'kyü-\\ n : abnormally acute hearing

hy·per·acute \\,hī-pə-rə-'kyüt\\ adj : extremely or excessively acute ⟨~ hearing⟩

hy·per·adren·a·lin·ae·mia chiefly Brit var of HYPERADRENALINEMIA

hy·per·adren·a·lin·emia \\,hī-pə-rə-,dren-əl-ə-'nē-mē-ə\\ n : the presence of an excess of adrenal hormones (as epinephrine) in the blood

hy·per·ad·re·no·cor·ti·cism \\,hī-pə-rə-,drē-nō-'kòr-tə-,si-zəm\\ n : the presence of an excess of adrenocortical products in the body

hy·per·ae·mia, hy·per·aes·the·sia chiefly Brit var of HYPEREMIA, HYPERESTHESIA

hy·per·ag·gres·sive \\,hī-pə-rə-'gre-səv\\ adj : extremely or excessively aggressive ⟨~ patients⟩

hy·per·al·do·ste·ron·ae·mia chiefly Brit var of HYPERALDOSTERONEMIA

hy·per·al·do·ste·ron·emia \\,hī-pə-ral-,däs-tə-,rō-'nē-mē-ə, -,ral-dō-stə-,rō-\\ n : the presence of an excess of aldosterone in the blood

hy·per·al·do·ste·ron·ism \\,hī-pə-ral-'däs-tə-,rō-,ni-zəm, -,ral-dō-stə-'rō-\\ n : ALDOSTERONISM

hy·per·al·ge·sia \\,hī-pə-ral-'jē-zhə, -zē-ə, -zhē-ə\\ n : increased sensitivity to pain or enhanced intensity of pain sensation — **hy·per·al·ge·sic** \\-'jē-zik, -sik\\ adj

hy·per·al·i·men·ta·tion \\,hī-pə-ra-lə-mən-'tā-shən\\ n : the administration of nutrients by intravenous feeding

hy·per·ami·no·ac·id·uria \\,hī-pə-rə-,mē-nō-,a-sə-'dúr-ē-ə, -'dyúr-\\ n : the presence of an excess of amino acids in the urine

hy·per·am·mo·nae·mia *also* **hy·per·am·mon·i·ae·mia** *chiefly Brit var of* HYPERAMMONEMIA

hy·per·am·mo·ne·mia \ˌhī-pə-ˌra-mə-ˈnē-mē-ə\ *also* **hy·per·am·mon·i·emia** \ˌhī-pə-rə-ˌmō-nē-ˈyē-mē-ə\ *n* : the presence of an excess of ammonia in the blood — **hy·per·am·mo·ne·mic** \ˌhī-pe-ˌra-mə-ˈnē-mik\ *adj*

hy·per·am·y·las·ae·mia *chiefly Brit var of* HYPERAMYLASEMIA

hy·per·am·y·las·emia \ˌhī-pə-ˌra-mə-ˌlā-ˈsē-mē-ə\ *n* : the presence of an excess of amylase in the blood

hy·per·arous·al \ˌhī-pə-rə-ˈrau-zəl\ *n* : excessive arousal

hy·per·bar·ic \ˌhī-pər-ˈbar-ik\ *adj* **1** : having a specific gravity greater than that of cerebrospinal fluid — used of solutions for spinal anesthesia; compare HYPOBARIC **2** : of, relating to, or utilizing greater than normal pressure esp. of oxygen (a ~ chamber) ⟨~ medicine⟩ — **hy·per·bar·i·cal·ly** *adv*

hy·per·be·ta·li·po·pro·tein·emia \-ˌbā-tə-ˌli-pō-ˌprō-tē-ˈnē-mē-ə, -ˌli-, -ˌprō-tē-ə-\ *n* : the presence of excess LDLs in the blood

hy·per·bil·i·ru·bin·emia \-ˌbi-lē-ˌrü-bi-ˈnē-mē-ə\ *n* : the presence of an excess of bilirubin in the blood — called also *bilirubinemia*

hy·per·cal·cae·mia *chiefly Brit var of* HYPERCALCEMIA

hy·per·cal·ce·mia \ˌhī-pər-ˌkal-ˈsē-mē-ə\ *n* : the presence of an excess of calcium in the blood — **hy·per·cal·ce·mic** \-ˈsē-mik\ *adj*

hy·per·cal·ci·uria \-ˌkal-sē-ˈyùr-ē-ə\ *also* **hy·per·cal·cin·uria** \-ˌkal-sə-ˈnùr-ē-ə\ *n* : the presence of an excess amount of calcium in the urine

hy·per·cap·nia \-ˈkap-nē-ə\ *n* : the presence of an excess of carbon dioxide in the blood — **hy·per·cap·nic** \-nik\ *adj*

hy·per·car·bia \-ˈkär-bē-ə\ *n* : HYPERCAPNIA

hy·per·cel·lu·lar·i·ty \-ˌsel-yə-ˈlar-ə-tē\ *n, pl* **-ties** : the presence of an abnormal excess of cells (as in bone marrow) — **hy·per·cel·lu·lar** \-ˈsel-yə-lər\ *adj*

hy·per·ce·men·to·sis \-ˌsē-mən-ˈtō-səs\ *n, pl* **-to·ses** \-ˌsēz\ : excessive formation of cementum at the root of a tooth

hy·per·chlor·ae·mia *chiefly Brit var of* HYPERCHLOREMIA

hy·per·chlor·emia \-ˌklōr-ˈē-mē-ə\ *n* : the presence of excess chloride ions in the blood — **hy·per·chlor·emic** \-ˈē-mik\ *adj*

hy·per·chlor·hy·dria \-ˌklōr-ˈhī-drē-ə\ *n* : the presence of a greater than typical proportion of hydrochloric acid in gastric juice — compare ACHLORHYDRIA, HYPOCHLORHYDRIA

hy·per·cho·les·ter·ol·emia \ˌhī-pər-kə-ˌles-tə-rə-ˈlē-mē-ə\ *or* **hy·per·cho·les·ter·emia** \-tə-ˈrē-mē-ə\ *n* : the presence of excess cholesterol in the blood — **hy·per·cho·les·ter·ol·emic** \-tə-rə-ˈlē-mik\ *or* **hy·per·cho·les·ter·emic** \-tə-ˈrē-mik\ *adj*

hy·per·chro·ma·sia \-krō-ˈmā-zhə, -zē-ə, -zhē-ə\ *n* : HYPERCHROMATISM

hy·per·chro·ma·tism \-ˈkrō-mə-ˌti-zəm\ *n* : the development of excess chromatin or of excessive nuclear staining esp. as a part of a pathological process — **hy·per·chro·mat·ic** \-ˌkrō-ˈma-tik\ *adj*

hy·per·chro·mia \-ˈkrō-mē-ə\ *n* **1** : excessive pigmentation (as of the skin) **2** : a state of the red blood cells marked by increase in the hemoglobin content — **hy·per·chro·mic** \-ˈkrō-mik\ *adj*

hyperchromic anemia *n* : an anemia with increase of hemoglobin in individual red blood cells and reduction in the number of red blood cells — compare HYPOCHROMIC ANEMIA; see PERNICIOUS ANEMIA

hy·per·chy·lo·mi·cro·ne·mia \ˌhī-pər-ˌkī-lō-ˌmī-krō-ˈnē-mē-ə\ *n* : the presence of excess chylomicrons in the blood

hy·per·co·ag·u·la·bil·i·ty \-ˌkō-ˌa-gyə-lə-ˈbil-ə-tē\ *n, pl* **-ties** : excessive coagulability — **hy·per·co·ag·u·la·ble** \-ˈa-gyə-lə-bəl\ *adj*

hy·per·cor·ti·sol·ism \-ˈkȯr-ti-ˌsō-ˌli-zəm, -ˌsō-\ *n* : hyperadrenocorticism produced by excess hydrocortisone in the body

hy·per·cu·prae·mia *chiefly Brit var of* HYPERCUPREMIA

hy·per·cu·pre·mia \-kü-ˈprē-mē-ə, -kyü-\ *n* : the presence of an excess of copper in the blood

hy·per·cy·thae·mia *chiefly Brit var of* HYPERCYTHEMIA

hy·per·cy·the·mia \-sī-ˈthē-mē-ə\ *n* : the presence of an excess of red blood cells in the blood — **hy·per·cy·the·mic** \-ˈthē-mik\ *adj*

hy·per·dip·loid \-ˈdi-ˌplȯid\ *adj* : having slightly more than the diploid number of chromosomes

hy·per·eme·sis \-ˈe-mə-səs, -ˌi-ˈmē-\ *n, pl* **-eme·ses** \-ˌsēz\ : excessive vomiting

hyperemesis grav·i·dar·um \-ˌgra-və-ˈdar-əm\ *n* : excessive vomiting during pregnancy

hy·per·emia \ˌhī-pə-ˈrē-mē-ə\ *n* : excess of blood in a body part : CONGESTION — **hy·per·emic** \-mik\ *adj*

hy·per·en·dem·ic \-ˌen-ˈde-mik, -in-\ *adj* **1** : exhibiting a high and continued incidence — used chiefly of human diseases **2** : marked by hyperendemic disease — used of geographic areas — **hy·per·en·de·mic·i·ty** \-ˌen-də-ˈmi-sə-tē\ *n*

hy·per·er·gic \ˌhī-pər-ˈər-jik\ *adj* : characterized by or exhibiting a greater than normal sensitivity to an allergen — **hy·per·er·gy** \'hī-pər-₁ər-jē\ n

hy·per·es·the·sia \₁hī-pər-es-'thē-zhə, -zhē-ə\ n : unusual or pathological sensitivity of the skin or of a particular sense to stimulation — **hy·per·es·thet·ic** \-'the-tik\ adj

hy·per·es·trin·ism \-'es-trə-₁ni-zəm\ n : a condition marked by the presence of excess estrins in the body

hy·per·es·tro·gen·ism \-'es-trə-jə-₁ni-zəm\ n : a condition marked by the presence of excess estrogens in the body

hy·per·ex·cit·abil·i·ty \₁hī-pər-ik-₁sī-tə-'bil-ə-tē\ n, pl -ties : the state or condition of being unusually or excessively excitable — **hy·per·ex·cit·ed** \-ik-'sī-təd\ adj — **hy·per·ex·cite·ment** n

hy·per·ex·tend \₁hī-pər-ik-'stend\ vb : to extend so that the angle between bones of a joint is greater than normal (a ~ed elbow) — **hy·per·ex·ten·sion** \-'sten-chən\ n

hy·per·ex·ten·si·ble \-ik-'sten-sə-bəl\ adj : having the capacity to be hyperextended or stretched to a greater than normal degree (~ joints) — **hy·per·ex·ten·si·bil·i·ty** \-sten-sə-'bi-lə-tē\ n

hy·per·flex \'hī-pər-₁fleks\ vb : to flex so that the angle between the bones of a joint is smaller than normal — **hy·per·flex·ion** \-flek-shən\ n

hy·per·func·tion \-₁fəŋk-shən\ n : excessive or abnormal activity (cardiac ~) — **hy·per·func·tion·al** \-shə-nəl\ adj — **hy·per·func·tion·ing** n

hy·per·gam·ma·glob·u·lin·ae·mia chiefly Brit var of HYPERGAMMAGLOBULINEMIA

hy·per·gam·ma·glob·u·lin·emia \₁hī-pər-₁ga-mə-₁glä-byə-lə-'nē-mē-ə\ n : the presence of an excess of gamma globulins in the blood — **hy·per·gam·ma·glob·u·lin·emic** \-'nē-mik\ adj

hy·per·gas·trin·ae·mia chiefly Brit var of HYPERGASTRINEMIA

hy·per·gas·trin·emia \-₁gas-trə-'nē-mē-ə\ n : the presence of an excess of gastrin in the blood — **hy·per·gas·trin·emic** \-'nē-mik\ adj

hy·per·glob·u·lin·ae·mia chiefly Brit var of HYPERGLOBULINEMIA

hy·per·glob·u·lin·emia \₁hī-pər-₁glä-byə-lə-'nē-mē-ə\ n : the presence of excess globulins in the blood — **hy·per·glob·u·lin·emic** \-'nē-mik\ adj

hy·per·gly·ce·mia \₁hī-pər-glī-'sē-mē-ə\ n : an excess of sugar in the blood — **hy·per·gly·ce·mic** \-mik\ adj

hyperglycemic factor n : GLUCAGON

hy·per·gly·ci·nae·mia chiefly Brit var of HYPERGLYCINEMIA

hy·per·gly·ci·ne·mia \₁hī-pər-₁glī-sə-'nē-mē-ə\ n : a hereditary disorder characterized by the presence of excess glycine in the blood

hy·per·go·nad·ism \₁hī-pər-'gō-₁na-di-zəm\ n : excessive hormonal secretion by the gonads

hy·per·hi·dro·sis \-hi-'drō-səs, -hī-\ also **hy·peri·dro·sis** \-i-'drō-\ n, pl -dro·ses \-₁sēz\ : generalized or localized excessive sweating — compare HYPOHIDROSIS

hy·per·hy·dra·tion \-hī-'drā-shən\ n : an excess of water in the body

hy·per·i·cism \hī-'per-ə-₁si-zəm\ n : a severe dermatitis of domestic animals due to photosensitivity resulting from eating Saint-John's-wort — compare FAGOPYRISM

hy·per·im·mune \₁hī-pər-i-'myün\ adj : exhibiting an unusual degree of immunization: **a** of a serum : containing exceptional quantities of antibody **b** of an antibody : having the characteristics of a blocking antibody

hy·per·im·mu·nize \-'i-myə-₁nīz\ vb -nized; -niz·ing : to induce a high level of immunity or of circulating antibodies in — **hy·per·im·mu·ni·za·tion** \-₁i-myə-nə-'zā-shən\ n

hy·per·in·fec·tion \-in-'fek-shən\ n : repeated reinfection with larvae produced by parasitic worms already in the body — compare AUTOINFECTION

hy·per·in·fla·tion \-in-'flā-shən\ n : excessive inflation (as of the lungs)

hy·per·in·su·lin·emia \-in-sə-lə-'nē-mē-ə\ n : the presence of excess insulin in the blood — **hy·per·in·su·lin·emic** \-mik\ adj

hy·per·in·su·lin·ism \-'in-sə-lə-₁ni-zəm\ n : the presence of excess insulin in the body resulting in hypoglycemia

hy·per·ir·ri·ta·bil·i·ty \-ir-₁a-tə-'bi-lə-tē\ n, pl -ties : abnormally great or uninhibited response to stimuli — **hy·per·ir·ri·ta·ble** \-'ir-ə-tə-bəl\ adj

hy·per·ka·lae·mia chiefly Brit var of HYPERKALEMIA

hy·per·ka·le·mia \-kā-'lē-mē-ə\ n : the presence of an abnormally high concentration of potassium in the blood — called also hyperpotassemia — **hy·per·ka·le·mic** \-'lē-mik\ adj

hy·per·ke·ra·ti·ni·za·tion \-₁ker-ə-tə-nə-'zā-shən, -kə-₁rat-ᵊn-ə-\ n : HYPERKERATOSIS

hy·per·ke·ra·to·sis \-₁ker-ə-'tō-səs\ n, pl -to·ses \-'tō-₁sēz\ **1** : hypertrophy of the stratum corneum of the skin **2** : any of various conditions marked by hyperkeratosis — **hy·per·ke·ra·tot·ic** \-'tät-ik\ adj

hy·per·ke·to·ne·mia \-₁kē-tə-'nē-mē-ə\ n : KETONEMIA 1

hy·per·ki·ne·sia \-kə-'nē-zhə, -kī-, -zhē-ə\ n : HYPERKINESIS

hy·per·ki·ne·sis \-'nē-səs\ n **1** : abnormally increased and sometimes uncontrollable activity or muscular movements **2** : a condition esp. of childhood characterized by hyperactivity

hy·per·ki·net·ic \-kə-'ne-tik, -kī-\ *adj* : of, relating to, or affected with hyperkinesis or hyperactivity

hy·per·lex·ia \-'lek-sē-ə\ *n* : precocious reading ability in a retarded child — **hy·per·lex·ic** \-sik\ *adj*

hy·per·li·pe·mia \,hī-pər-lī-'pē-mē-ə\ *n* : the presence of excess fat or lipids in the blood — **hy·per·li·pe·mic** \-mik\ *adj*

hy·per·lip·id·ae·mia *chiefly Brit var of* HYPERLIPIDEMIA

hy·per·lip·id·emia \-,li-pə-'dē-mē-ə\ *n* : HYPERLIPEMIA — **hy·per·lip·id·emic** \-mik\ *adj*

hy·per·li·po·pro·tein·ae·mia *chiefly Brit var of* HYPERLIPOPROTEINEMIA

hy·per·li·po·pro·tein·emia \-,li-pə-,prō-tē-'nē-mē-ə, -,lī-\ *n* : the presence of excess lipoprotein in the blood

hy·per·lu·cent \-'lüs-ənt\ *adj* : being excessively radiolucent (a ~ lung) — **hy·per·lu·cen·cy** \-'lüs-ən-sē\ *n*

hy·per·mag·ne·sae·mia *chiefly Brit var of* HYPERMAGNESEMIA

hy·per·mag·ne·se·mia \-,mag-ni-'sē-mē-ə\ *n* : the presence of excess magnesium in the blood serum

hy·per·men·or·rhea \-,me-nə-'rē-ə\ *n* : abnormally profuse or prolonged menstrual flow — compare MENORRHAGIA

hy·per·me·tab·o·lism \-mə-'ta-bə-,li-zəm\ *n* : metabolism at an increased or excessive rate — **hy·per·meta·bol·ic** \-,me-tə-'bä-lik\ *adj*

hy·per·me·tria \-'mē-trē-ə\ *n* : a condition of cerebellar dysfunction in which voluntary muscular movements tend to result in the movement of bodily parts (as the arm and hand) beyond the intended goal

hy·per·me·tro·pia \,hī-pər-mi-'trō-pē-ə\ *n* : HYPEROPIA — **hy·per·me·tro·pic** \-'trō-pik, -'trä-\ *adj*

hy·perm·ne·sia \,hī-(,)pərm-'nē-zhə, -zhē-ə\ *n* : abnormally vivid or complete memory or recall of the past (as at times of extreme danger) — **hy·perm·ne·sic** \-'nē-zik, -sik\ *adj*

hy·per·mo·bil·i·ty \,hī-pər-mō-'bi-lə-tē\ *n, pl* -ties : an increase in the range of movement of which a bodily part and esp. a joint is capable — **hy·per·mo·bile** \-'mō-bəl, -,bil, -,bēl\ *adj*

hy·per·mo·til·i·ty \,hī-pər-mō-'ti-lə-tē\ *n, pl* -ties : abnormal or excessive movement; *specif* : excessive motility of all or part of the gastrointestinal tract — compare HYPERPERISTALSIS, HYPOMOTILITY — **hy·per·mo·tile** \-'mōt-əl, -'mō-,til\ *adj*

hy·per·na·trae·mia *chiefly Brit var of* HYPERNATREMIA

hy·per·na·tre·mia \-nā-'trē-mē-ə\ *n* : the presence of an abnormally high concentration of sodium in the blood — **hy·per·na·tre·mic** \-mik\ *adj*

hy·per·neph·roid \-'ne-,froid\ *adj* : resembling the adrenal cortex in histological structure (~ tumors)

hy·per·ne·phro·ma \-ni-'frō-mə\ *n, pl* -mas *or* -ma·ta \-mə-tə\ : a tumor of the kidney resembling the adrenal cortex in its histological structure

hy·per·oes·trin·ism, hy·per·oes·tro·gen·ism *chiefly Brit var of* HYPERESTRINISM, HYPERESTROGENISM

hy·per·ope \'hī-pər-,ōp\ *n* : a person affected with hyperopia

hy·per·opia \,hī-pər-'ō-pē-ə\ *n* : a condition in which visual images come to a focus behind the retina of the eye and vision is better for distant than for near objects — called also *farsightedness, hypermetropia* — **hy·per·opic** \-'ō-pik, -'ä-\ *adj*

hy·per·os·mia \-,hī-pər-'äz-mē-ə\ *n* : extreme acuteness of the sense of smell

hy·per·os·mo·lal·i·ty \-,äz-mō-'la-lə-tē\ *n, pl* -ties : the condition esp. of a bodily fluid of having abnormally high osmolality

hy·per·os·mo·lar·i·ty \-'lar-ə-tē\ *n, pl* -ties : the condition esp. of a bodily fluid of having abnormally high osmolarity — **hy·per·os·mo·lar** \-,äz-'mō-lər\ *adj*

hy·per·os·mot·ic \-,äz-'mä-tik\ *adj* : HYPERTONIC 2

hy·per·os·to·sis \-,äs-'tō-səs\ *n, pl* -to·ses \-,sēz\ : excessive growth or thickening of bone tissue — **hy·per·os·tot·ic** \-'tä-tik\ *adj*

hy·per·ox·al·uria \-,äk-sə-'lùr-ē-ə\ *n* : the presence of excess oxalic acid or oxalates in the urine

hy·per·ox·ia \-'äk-sē-ə\ *n* : a bodily condition characterized by a greater oxygen content of the tissues and organs than normally exists at sea level

hy·per·para·thy·roid·ism \,hī-pər-,par-ə-'thī-,rȯi-,di-zəm\ *n* : the presence of excess parathyroid hormone in the body resulting in disturbance of calcium metabolism

hy·per·path·ia \-'pa-thē-ə\ *n* 1 : disagreeable or painful sensation in response to a normally innocuous stimulus (as touch) 2 : a condition in which the sensations of hyperpathia occur — **hy·per·path·ic** \-thik\ *adj*

hy·per·peri·stal·sis \-,per-ə-'stȯl-səs, -'stäl-, -'stal-\ *n, pl* -stal·ses \-,sēz\ : excessive or excessively vigorous peristalsis — compare HYPERMOTILITY

hy·per·pha·gia \-'fā-jə, -jē-ə\ *n* : abnormally increased appetite for food frequently associated with injury to the hypothalamus — compare POLYPHAGIA — **hy·per·phag·ic** \-'fa-jik\ *adj*

hy·per·phe·nyl·al·a·nin·ae·mia *chiefly Brit var of* HYPERPHENYLALANINEMIA

hy·per·phe·nyl·al·a·nin·emia \-,fen-əl-,a-lə-nə-'nē-mē-ə, -,fēn-\ *n* : the presence of excess phenylalanine in the blood (as in phenylketonuria) — hyper·phe·nyl·al·a·nin·emic \-'nē-mik\ adj

hy·per·pho·ria \-'fōr-ē-ə\ n : latent strabismus in which one eye deviates upward in relation to the other

hy·per·phos·pha·tae·mia chiefly Brit var of HYPERPHOSPHATEMIA

hy·per·phos·pha·te·mia \-ıfäs-fə-'tē-mē-ə\ n : the presence of excess phosphate in the blood

hy·per·phos·pha·tu·ria \-ıfäs-fə-'tùr-ē-ə, -'tyùr-\ n : the presence of excess phosphate in the urine

hy·per·pi·e·sia \-ıpī-'ē-zhə, -zhē-ə\ n : HYPERTENSION; esp : ESSENTIAL HYPERTENSION

hy·per·pig·men·ta·tion \-ıpig-mən-'tā-shən, -ımen-\ n : excess pigmentation in a bodily part or tissue (as the skin) — hy·per·pig·ment·ed \-'pig-mən-təd, -ımen-\ adj

hy·per·pi·tu·ita·rism \-pə-'tü-ə-tə-ıri-zəm, -'tyü-, -ıtri-zəm\ n : excessive production of growth hormones by the pituitary gland — hy·per·pi·tu·itary \-pə-'tü-ə-ıter-ē, -'tyü-\ adj

hy·per·pla·sia \ıhī-pər-'plā-zhə, -zhē-ə\ n : an abnormal or unusual increase in the elements composing a part (as cells composing a tissue) — hy·per·plas·tic \-'plas-tik\ adj

hy·per·ploid \'hī-pər-ıplóid\ adj : having a chromosome number slightly greater than an exact multiple of the haploid number — hy·per·ploi·dy \-ıplóid-ē\ n

hy·perp·nea \ıhī-pərp-'nē-ə, -ıpər-\ n : abnormally rapid or deep breathing — hy·perp·ne·ic \-'nē-ik\ adj

hy·perp·noea chiefly Brit var of HYPERPNEA

hy·per·po·lar·ize \ıhī-pər-'pō-lə-ırīz\ vb -ized; -iz·ing 1 : to produce an increase in potential difference across (a biological membrane) 2 : to undergo or produce an increase in potential difference across something — hy·per·po·lar·i·za·tion \-ıpō-lə-rə-'zā-shən\ n

hy·per·po·tas·sae·mia chiefly Brit var of HYPERPOTASSEMIA

hy·per·po·tas·se·mia \-pə-ıta-'sē-mē-ə\ n : HYPERKALEMIA — hy·per·po·tas·se·mic \-'sē-mik\ adj

hy·per·pro·duc·tion \-prə-'dək-shən, -prō-\ n : excessive production

hy·per·pro·lac·tin·ae·mia chiefly Brit var of HYPERPROLACTINEMIA

hy·per·pro·lac·tin·e·mia \-ıprō-ılak-tə-'nē-mē-ə\ n : the presence of an abnormally high concentration of prolactin in the blood — hy·per·pro·lac·tin·emic \-'nē-mik\ adj

hy·per·pro·lin·ae·mia chiefly Brit var of HYPERPROLINEMIA

hy·per·pro·lin·e·mia \-ıprō-lə-'nē-mē-ə\ n : a hereditary metabolic disorder characterized by an abnormally high concentration of proline in the blood and often associated with mental retardation

hy·per·py·rex·ia \-pī-'rek-sē-ə\ n : exceptionally high fever

hy·per·re·ac·tive \-rē-'ak-tiv\ adj : having or showing abnormally high sensitivity to stimuli — hy·per·re·ac·tiv·i·ty \-(ı)rē-ak-'ti-və-tē\ n

hy·per·re·flex·ia \-rē-'flek-sē-ə\ n : overactivity of physiological reflexes

hy·per·re·nin·ae·mia chiefly Brit var of HYPERRENINEMIA

hy·per·re·nin·e·mia \-ırē-nə-'nē-mē-ə, -ıre-\ n : the presence of an abnormally high concentration of renin in the blood

hy·per·re·spon·sive \-ri-'spän-siv\ adj : characterized by an abnormal degree of responsiveness (as to a physical stimulus) — hy·per·re·spon·siv·i·ty \-ri-ıspän-'si-və-tē\ n

hy·per·sal·i·va·tion \-ısa-lə-'vā-shən\ n : excessive salivation

hy·per·se·cre·tion \-si-'krē-shən\ n : excessive production of a bodily secretion — hy·per·se·crete \-si-'krēt\ vb — hy·per·se·cre·to·ry \-'sē-krə-ıtor-ē, -si-'krē-tə-rē\ adj

hy·per·sen·si·tive \ıhī-pər-'sen-sə-tiv\ adj 1 : excessively or abnormally sensitive 2 : abnormally susceptible physiologically to a specific agent (as a drug) — hy·per·sen·si·tive·ness n — hy·per·sen·si·tiv·i·ty \-ısen-sə-'ti-və-tē\ n — hy·per·sen·si·ti·za·tion \-ısen-sə-tə-'zā-shən\ n — hy·per·sen·si·tize \-'sen-sə-ıtīz\ vb

hy·per·sex·u·al \-'sek-shə-wəl\ adj : exhibiting unusual or excessive concern with or indulgence in sexual activity — hy·per·sex·u·al·i·ty \-ısek-shə-'wa-lə-tē\ n

hy·per·sid·er·ae·mia chiefly Brit var of HYPERSIDEREMIA

hy·per·sid·er·emia \-ısi-də-'rē-mē-ə\ n : the presence of an abnormally high concentration of iron in the blood — hy·per·sid·er·emic \-mik\ adj

hy·per·som·nia \-'säm-nē-ə\ n 1 : sleep of excessive depth or duration 2 : the condition of sleeping for excessive periods at intervals with intervening periods of normal duration of sleeping and waking — compare NARCOLEPSY

hy·per·sple·nism \-'splē-ıni-zəm, -'sple-\ n : a condition marked by excessive destruction of one or more kinds of blood cells in the spleen

hy·per·sthen·ic \ıhī-pərs-'the-nik\ adj : of, relating to, or characterized by excessive muscle tone

hy·per·sus·cep·ti·ble \-sə-'sep-tə-bəl\ adj : HYPERSENSITIVE — hy·per·sus·cep·ti·bil·i·ty \-ısep-tə-'bi-lə-tē\ n

hy·per·tel·or·ism \-'te-lə-ıri-zəm\ n : excessive width between two bodily parts or organs (as the eyes)

hy·per·tense \ıhī-pər-'tens\ adj : excessively tense (a ~ emotional state)

Hy·per·ten·sin \-'ten-sən\ trademark — used for a preparation of the amide of angiotensin hy·per·ten·sin·ase \-ˈten-sə-ˌnās, -ˌnāz\ n : ANGIOTENSINASE

hy·per·ten·sin·o·gen \-ˌten-ˈsi-nə-jən, -ˌjen\ n : ANGIOTENSINOGEN

hy·per·ten·sion \ˌhī-pər-ˈten-chən\ n 1 : abnormally high arterial blood pressure: **a** : such blood pressure occurring without apparent or determinable prior organic changes in the tissues possibly because of hereditary tendency, emotional tensions, faulty nutrition, or hormonal influence **b** : such blood pressure with demonstrable organic changes (as in nephritis, diabetes, and hyperthyroidism) 2 : a systemic condition resulting from hypertension that is either symptomless or is accompanied by nervousness, dizziness, or headache

¹hy·per·ten·sive \-ˈten-siv\ adj : marked by a rise in blood pressure : suffering or caused by hypertension

²hypertensive n : a person affected with hypertension

hy·per·ther·mia \-ˈthər-mē-ə\ n : exceptionally high fever esp. when induced artificially for therapeutic purposes — hy·per·ther·mic \-mik\ adj

hy·per·thy·roid \-ˈthī-ˌrȯid\ adj : of, relating to, or affected with hyperthyroidism (a ~ state)

hy·per·thy·roid·ism \-ˌrȯi-ˌdi-zəm\ n : excessive functional activity of the thyroid gland; also : the resulting condition marked esp. by increased metabolic rate, enlargement of the thyroid gland, rapid heart rate, and high blood pressure — called also thyrotoxicosis; see GRAVES' DISEASE

hy·per·to·nia \ˌhī-pər-ˈtō-nē-ə\ n : HYPERTONICITY

hy·per·ton·ic \-ˈtä-nik\ adj 1 : exhibiting excessive tone or tension (a ~ bladder) 2 : having a higher osmotic pressure than a surrounding medium or a fluid under comparison — compare HYPOTONIC 2, ISOSMOTIC

hy·per·to·nic·i·ty \-tə-ˈni-sə-tē\ n, pl -ties : the quality or state of being hypertonic

hy·per·to·nus \-ˈtō-nəs\ n : HYPERTONICITY

hy·per·tri·cho·sis \-tri-ˈkō-səs\ n, pl -cho·ses \-ˌsēz\ : excessive growth of hair

hy·per·tri·glyc·er·i·dae·mia chiefly Brit var of HYPERTRIGLYCERIDEMIA

hy·per·tri·glyc·er·i·de·mia \-ˌtrī-ˌgli-sə-ˌrī-ˈdē-mē-ə\ n : the presence of an excess of triglycerides in the blood — hy·per·tri·glyc·er·i·de·mic \-ˈdē-mik\ adj

hypertrophic arthritis n : OSTEOARTHRITIS

hy·per·tro·phy \hī-ˈpər-trə-fē\ n, pl -phies : excessive development of an organ or part; specif : increase in bulk (as by thickening of muscle fibers) without multiplication of parts — hy·per·tro·phic \ˌhī-pər-ˈtrō-fik\ adj — hypertrophy vb

hy·per·tro·pia \ˌhī-pər-ˈtrō-pē-ə\ n : elevation of the line of vision of one eye above that of the other : upward strabismus

hy·per·uri·ce·mia \ˌhī-pər-ˌyu̇r-ə-ˈsē-mē-ə\ n : excess uric acid in the blood (as in gout) — called also uricemia — hy·per·uri·ce·mic \-ˈsē-mik\ adj

hy·per·uri·cos·uria \-ˌyu̇r-i-kō-ˈshu̇r-ē-ə, -ˈsyu̇r-\ n : the excretion of excessive amounts of uric acid in the urine

hy·per·ven·ti·late \-ˈvent-ᵊl-ˌāt\ vb -lat·ed; -lat·ing : to breathe rapidly and deeply : undergo hyperventilation

hy·per·ven·ti·la·tion \-ˌvent-ᵊl-ˈā-shən\ n : excessive rate and depth of respiration leading to abnormal loss of carbon dioxide from the blood — called also overventilation

hy·per·vis·cos·i·ty \-vis-ˈkä-sə-tē\ n, pl -ties : excessive viscosity (as of the blood)

hy·per·vi·ta·min·osis \-ˌvī-tə-mə-ˈnō-səs\ n, pl -oses \-ˌsēz\ : an abnormal state resulting from excessive intake of one or more vitamins

hy·per·vo·lae·mia chiefly Brit var of HYPERVOLEMIA

hy·per·vol·emia \-və-ˈlē-mē-ə\ n : an excessive volume of blood in the body — hy·per·vol·emic \-ˈlē-mik\ adj

hyp·es·the·sia \ˌhī-pes-ˈthē-zhə, ˌhi-, -zhē-ə\ n : impaired or decreased tactile sensibility — hyp·es·thet·ic \-ˈthe-tik\ adj

hy·phae·ma chiefly Brit var of HYPHEMA

hy·phe·ma \hī-ˈfē-mə\ n : a hemorrhage in the anterior chamber of the eye

hypn- or hypno- comb form 1 : sleep (hypnagogic) 2 : hypnotism (hypnotherapy)

hyp·na·go·gic also hyp·no·go·gic \ˌhip-nə-ˈgä-jik, -ˈgō-\ adj : of, relating to, or associated with the drowsiness preceding sleep (~ hallucinations) — compare HYPNOPOMPIC

hyp·no·anal·y·sis \ˌhip-nō-ə-ˈna-lə-səs\ n, pl -y·ses \-ˌsēz\ : the treatment of mental disease by hypnosis and psychoanalytic methods

hyp·no·pom·pic \ˌhip-nə-ˈpäm-pik\ adj : associated with the semiconsciousness preceding waking (~ illusions) — compare HYPNAGOGIC

hyp·no·sis \hip-ˈnō-səs\ n, pl -no·ses \-ˌsēz\ 1 : a state that resembles sleep but is induced by a person whose suggestions are readily accepted by the subject 2 : any of various conditions that resemble sleep 3 : HYPNOTISM 1

hyp·no·ther·a·pist \ˌhip-nō-ˈther-ə-pist\ n : a specialist in hypnotherapy

hyp·no·ther·a·py \-ˈther-ə-pē\ n, pl -pies 1 : the treatment of disease by hypnotism 2 : psychotherapy that facilitates suggestion, reeducation, or analysis by means of hypnosis

¹hyp·not·ic \hip-ˈnä-tik\ adj 1 : tending to produce sleep : SOPORIFIC 2 : of or

relating to hypnosis or hypnotism — **hyp·not·i·cal·ly** *adv*

²**hypnotic** *n* **1 :** a sleep-inducing agent **:** SOPORIFIC **2 :** one that is or can be hypnotized

hyp·no·tism \\'hip-nə-₊ti-zəm\ *n* **1 :** the study or act of inducing hypnosis — compare MESMERISM **2 :** HYPNOSIS **1**

hyp·no·tist \-tist\ *n* **:** an expert in hypnotism **:** a person who induces hypnosis

hyp·no·tize \-₊tīz\ *vb* -**tized;** -**tiz·ing :** to induce hypnosis in — **hyp·no·tiz·abil·i·ty** \₊hip-nə-₊tī-zə-'bi-lə-tē\ *n* — **hyp·no·tiz·able** \'hip-nə-₊tī-zə-bəl\ *adj*

¹**hy·po** \'hī-(₊)pō\ *n, pl* **hypos :** HYPOCHONDRIA

²**hypo** *n, pl* **hypos 1 :** HYPODERMIC SYRINGE **2 :** HYPODERMIC INJECTION

hypo- *or* **hyp-** *prefix* **1 :** under **:** beneath **:** down *(hypoblast) (hypodermic)* **2 :** less than normal or normally *(hypesthesia) (hypotension)*

hy·po·acid·i·ty \₊hī-pō-ə-'si-də-tē\ *n, pl* -**ties :** abnormally low acidity ⟨gastric ∼⟩

hy·po·ac·tive \-'ak-tiv\ *adj* **:** less than normally active ⟨∼ children⟩ ⟨∼ bowel sounds⟩ — **hy·po·ac·tiv·i·ty** \-ak-'ti-və-tē\ *n*

hy·po·acu·sis \-ə-'kü-səs, -'kyü-\ *n* **:** partial loss of hearing — called also *hypacusis*

hy·po·adren·al·ism \-ə-'dren-əl-₊i-zəm\ *n* **:** abnormally decreased activity of the adrenal glands; *specif* **:** HYPOADRENOCORTICISM

hy·po·ad·re·no·cor·ti·cism \-ə-₊drē-nō-'kor-tə-₊si-zəm\ *n* **:** abnormally decreased activity of the adrenal cortex (as in Addison's disease)

hy·po·aes·the·sia \₊hī-pō-es-'thē-zhə, ₊hī-, -zhē-ə\ *Brit var of* HYPESTHESIA

hy·po·al·bu·min·ae·mia *chiefly Brit var of* HYPOALBUMINEMIA

hy·po·al·bu·min·emia \-al-'byü-mə-'nē-mē-ə\ *n* **:** hypoproteinemia marked by reduction in serum albumins — **hy·po·al·bu·min·emic** \-'nē-mik\ *adj*

hy·po·al·ge·sia \-al-'jē-zhə, -zhē-ə, -zē-ə\ *n* **:** decreased sensitivity to pain

hy·po·al·ler·gen·ic \-₊a-lər-'je-nik\ *adj* **:** having little likelihood of causing an allergic response ⟨∼ food⟩

hy·po·ami·no·ac·id·emia \-ə-₊mē-nō-₊a-sə-'dē-mē-ə\ *n* **:** the presence of abnormally low concentrations of amino acids in the blood

hy·po·bar·ic \-'bar-ik\ *adj* **:** having a specific gravity less than that of cerebrospinal fluid — used of solutions for spinal anesthesia; compare HYPERBARIC **1**

hy·po·bar·ism \-'bar-₊i-zəm\ *n* **:** a condition which occurs when the ambient pressure is lower than the pressure of gases within the body and which may be marked by the distension of bodily cavities and the release of gas bubbles within bodily tissues

hy·po·blast \'hī-pə-₊blast\ *n* **:** the endo-

derm of an embryo — **hy·po·blas·tic** \₊hī-pə-'blas-tik\ *adj*

hy·po·cal·cae·mia *chiefly Brit var of* HYPOCALCEMIA

hy·po·cal·ce·mia \₊hī-pō-kal-'sē-mē-ə\ *n* **:** a deficiency of calcium in the blood — **hy·po·cal·ce·mic** \-mik\ *adj*

hy·po·cal·ci·fi·ca·tion \-₊kal-sə-fə-'kā-shən\ *n* **:** decreased or deficient calcification (as of tooth enamel)

hy·po·cap·nia \-'kap-nē-ə\ *n* **:** a deficiency of carbon dioxide in the blood — **hy·po·cap·nic** \-nik\ *adj*

hy·po·chlor·ae·mia *chiefly Brit var of* HYPOCHLOREMIA

hy·po·chlor·emia \₊hī-pō-klōr-'ē-mē-ə\ *n* **:** abnormal decrease of chlorides in the blood — **hy·po·chlor·emic** \-klōr-'ē-mik\ *adj*

hy·po·chlor·hy·dria \-klōr-'hī-drē-ə\ *n* **:** deficiency of hydrochloric acid in the gastric juice — compare ACHLORHYDRIA, HYPERCHLORHYDRIA — **hy·po·chlor·hy·dric** \-'hī-drik\ *adj*

hy·po·chlo·rite \₊hī-pə-'klōr-₊īt\ *n* **:** a salt or ester of hypochlorous acid

hy·po·chlo·rous acid \-'klōr-əs-\ *n* **:** an unstable strongly oxidizing but weak acid HClO obtained in solution along with hydrochloric acid by reaction of chlorine with water and used esp. in the form of salts as an oxidizing agent, bleaching agent, disinfectant and chlorinating agent

hy·po·cho·les·ter·ol·emia \₊hī-pō-kə-₊les-tə-rə-'lē-mē-ə\ *or* **hy·po·cho·les·ter·emia** \-tə-'rē-mē-ə\ *n* **:** an abnormal deficiency of cholesterol in the blood — **hy·po·cho·les·ter·ol·emic** \-'lē-mik\ *or* **hy·po·cho·les·ter·emic** \-'rē-mik\ *adj*

hy·po·chon·dria \₊hī-pə-'kän-drē-ə\ *n* **:** extreme depression of mind or spirits often centered on imaginary physical ailments; *specif* **:** HYPOCHONDRIASIS

¹**hy·po·chon·dri·ac** \-drē-₊ak\ *adj* **1 :** HYPOCHONDRIACAL **2 a :** situated below the costal cartilages **b :** of, relating to, or being the two abdominal regions lying on either side of the epigastric region and above the lumbar regions

²**hypochondriac** *n* **:** a person affected by hypochondria or hypochondriasis

hy·po·chon·dri·a·cal \-kən-'drī-ə-kəl, -₊kän-\ *adj* **:** affected with or produced by hypochondria

hy·po·chon·dri·a·sis \-'drī-ə-səs\ *n, pl* -**a·ses** \-₊sēz\ **:** morbid concern about one's health esp. when accompanied by delusions of physical disease

hy·po·chon·dri·um \-'kän-drē-əm\ *n, pl* -**dria** \-drē-ə\ **:** either hypochondriac region of the body

hy·po·chro·mia \-'krō-mē-ə\ *n* **1 :** deficiency of color or pigmentation **2 :** deficiency of hemoglobin in the red blood cells (as in nutritional anemia) — **hy·po·chro·mic** \-'krō-mik\ *adj*

hypochromic anemia *n* **:** an anemia marked by deficient hemoglobin and usu. microcytic red blood cells — compare HYPERCHROMIC ANEMIA

hy·po·co·ag·u·la·bil·i·ty \hī-pō-kō-₁a-gyə-lə-'bi-lə-tē\ n, pl **-ties** : decreased or deficient coagulability of blood — **hy·po·co·ag·u·la·ble** \-kō-'a-gyə-lə-bəl\ adj

hy·po·com·ple·men·tae·mia chiefly Brit var of HYPOCOMPLEMENTEMIA

hy·po·com·ple·men·te·mia \-₁käm-plə-(₁)men-'tē-mē-ə\ n : an abnormal deficiency of complement in the blood — **hy·po·com·ple·men·te·mic** \-'tē-mik\ adj

hy·po·cu·prae·mia chiefly Brit var of HYPOCUPREMIA

hy·po·cu·pre·mia \-kü-'prē-mē-ə, -kyü-\ n : an abnormal deficiency of copper in the blood

hy·po·cu·pro·sis \-kü-'prō-səs, -kyü-\ n, pl **-pro·ses** \-₁sēz\ : HYPOCUPREMIA

hy·po·der·ma \₁hī-pə-'dər-mə\ n **1** cap : a genus (family Hypodermatidae) of dipteran flies that have parasitic larvae and include the common cattle grub (H. lineatum) **2** : any insect or maggot of the genus Hypoderma

hy·po·der·ma·to·sis \₁dər-mə-'tō-səs\ n : infestation with maggots of flies of the genus Hypoderma

hy·po·der·mi·a·sis \-₁dər-'mī-ə-səs\ n, pl **-a·ses** \-₁sēz\ : HYPODERMATOSIS

¹hy·po·der·mic \₁hī-pə-'dər-mik\ adj **1** : of or relating to the parts beneath the skin **2** : adapted for use in or administered by injection beneath the skin — **hy·po·der·mi·cal·ly** adv

²hypodermic n **1** : HYPODERMIC INJECTION **2** : HYPODERMIC SYRINGE

hypodermic injection n : an injection made into the subcutaneous tissues

hypodermic needle n **1** : NEEDLE 2 **2** : a hypodermic syringe complete with needle

hypodermic syringe n : a small syringe used with a hollow needle for injection of material into or beneath the skin

hy·po·der·mis \₁hī-pə-'dər-məs\ n : SUPERFICIAL FASCIA

hy·po·der·moc·ly·sis \-dər-'mä-klə-səs\ n, pl **-ly·ses** \-₁sēz\ : subcutaneous injection of fluids (as saline solution)

hy·po·dip·loid \₁hī-pō-'di-₁plȯid\ adj : having slightly fewer than the diploid number of chromosomes — **hy·po·dip·loi·dy** \-₁plȯi-dē\ n

hy·po·don·tia \-'dän-chə, -chē-ə\ n : an esp. congenital condition marked by a less than normal number of teeth : partial anodontia — **hy·po·don·tic** \-'dän-tik\ adj

hy·po·dy·nam·ic \-dī-'na-mik\ adj : marked by or exhibiting a decrease in strength or power (the ~ heart)

hy·po·es·the·sia \₁hī-pō-es-'thē-zhə, -zhē-ə, -zē-ə\ var of HYPESTHESIA

hy·po·fer·rae·mia chiefly Brit var of HYPOFERREMIA

hy·po·fer·re·mia \₁hī-pō-fə-'rē-mē-ə\ n : an abnormal deficiency of iron in the blood — **hy·po·fer·re·mic** \-'rē-mik\ adj

hy·po·fi·brin·o·gen·ae·mia chiefly Brit var of HYPOFIBRINOGENEMIA

hy·po·fi·brin·o·gen·emia \-fī-₁bri-nə-jə-'nē-mē-ə\ n : an abnormal deficiency of fibrinogen in the blood

hy·po·func·tion \'hī-pō-₁fəŋk-shən\ n : decreased or insufficient function esp. of an endocrine gland

hy·po·gam·ma·glob·u·lin·emia \-₁ga-mə-₁glä-byə-lə-'nē-mē-ə\ n : a deficiency of gamma globulins in the blood — **hy·po·gam·ma·glob·u·lin·emic** \-'nē-mik\ adj

hy·po·gas·tric \₁hī-pə-'gas-trik\ adj **1** : of or relating to the lower median abdominal region **2** : relating to or situated along or near the internal iliac arteries or the internal iliac veins

hypogastric artery n : ILIAC ARTERY 3

hypogastric nerve n : a nerve or several parallel nerve bundles situated dorsal and medial to the common and the internal iliac arteries

hypogastric plexus n : the sympathetic nerve plexus that supplies the pelvic viscera

hypogastric vein n : ILIAC VEIN c

hy·po·gas·tri·um \₁hī-pə-'gas-trē-əm\ n, pl **-tria** \-trē-ə\ : the hypogastric region of the abdomen

hy·po·gen·i·tal·ism \-'je-nə-tə-₁li-zəm\ n : subnormal development of genital organs : genital infantilism

hy·po·geu·sia \-'gü-sē-ə, -'jü-, -zē-ə\ n : decreased sensitivity to taste (idiopathic ~)

hy·po·glos·sal \₁hī-pə-'glä-səl\ adj : of or relating to the hypoglossal nerves

hypoglossal nerve n : either of the 12th and final pair of cranial nerves which are motor nerves arising from the medulla oblongata and supplying muscles of the tongue and hyoid apparatus — called also hypoglossal, twelfth cranial nerve

hypoglossal nucleus n : a nucleus in the floor of the fourth ventricle of the brain that is the origin of the hypoglossal nerve

hy·po·glos·sus \-'glä-səs\ n, pl **-glos·si** \-₁sī, -₁sē\ : HYPOGLOSSAL NERVE

hy·po·gly·ce·mia \₁hī-pō-glī-'sē-mē-ə\ n : abnormal decrease of sugar in the blood

¹hy·po·gly·ce·mic \-'sē-mik\ adj **1** : of, relating to, caused by, or affected with hypoglycemia **2** : producing a decrease in the level of sugar in the blood (~ drugs)

²hypoglycemic n **1** : one affected with hypoglycemia **2** : an agent that lowers the level of sugar in the blood

hy·po·go·nad·al \-gō-'nad-əl\ adj **1** : relating to or affected with hypogonadism **2** : marked by or exhibiting deficient development of secondary sexual characteristics

hy·po·go·nad·ism \-'gō-₁na-₁di-zəm\ n : functional incompetence of the gonads esp. in the male **2** : a condition (as Klinefelter's syndrome) involving gonadal incompetence

hy·po·go·nad·o·trop·ic \-gō-ˌna-də-ˈträ-pik\ *or* **hy·po·go·nad·o·tro·phic** \-ˈtrō-fik, -ˈträ-\ *adj* : characterized by a deficiency of gonadotropins

hy·po·hi·dro·sis \-hi-ˈdrō-səs, -hī-\ *n, pl* **-dro·ses** \-ˌsēz\ : abnormally diminished sweating — compare HYPERHIDROSIS

hy·po·his·ti·di·ne·mia \-ˌhis-tə-də-ˈnē-mē-ə\ *n* : a low concentration of histidine in the blood that is characteristic of rheumatoid arthritis — **hy·po·his·ti·di·ne·mic** \-ˈnē-mik\ *adj*

hy·po·in·su·lin·emia \-ˌin-sə-lə-ˈnē-mē-ə\ *n* : an abnormally low concentration of insulin in the blood — **hy·po·in·su·lin·emic** \-ˈnē-mik\ *adj*

hy·po·ka·lae·mia *chiefly Brit var of* HYPOKALEMIA

hy·po·ka·le·mia \-kā-ˈlē-mē-ə\ *n* : a deficiency of potassium in the blood — called also *hypopotassemia* — **hy·po·ka·le·mic** \-ˈlē-mik\ *adj*

hy·po·ki·ne·sia \-kə-ˈnē-zhə, -kī-, -zhē-ə\ *n* : abnormally decreased muscular movement — compare HYPERKINESIS

hy·po·ki·ne·sis \-ˈnē-səs\ *n, pl* **-ne·ses** \-ˌsēz\ : HYPOKINESIA

hy·po·ki·net·ic \-ˈne-tik\ *adj* : characterized by, associated with, or caused by decreased motor activity ⟨∼ hypoxia⟩

hy·po·lip·id·ae·mia *chiefly Brit var of* HYPOLIPIDEMIA

hy·po·lip·id·emia \-ˌli-pə-ˈdē-mē-ə\ *n* : a deficiency of lipids in the blood — **hy·po·lip·id·emic** \-ˈdē-mik\ *adj*

hy·po·mag·ne·sae·mia *chiefly Brit var of* HYPOMAGNESEMIA

hy·po·mag·ne·se·mia \-hī-pə-ˌmag-nə-ˈsē-mē-ə\ *n* : a deficiency of magnesium in the blood — **hy·po·mag·ne·se·mic** \-mik\ *adj*

hy·po·mag·ne·sia \-mag-ˈnē-shə, -zhə\ *n* : GRASS TETANY

hy·po·ma·nia \-ˈpō-ˌmā-nē-ə, -ˈmā-nē-ə, -nyə\ *n* : a mild mania esp. when part of a manic-depressive cycle

¹**hy·po·man·ic** \-ˈma-nik\ *adj* : of, relating to, or affected with hypomania

²**hypomanic** *n* : one affected with hypomania

hy·po·men·or·rhea \-ˌme-nə-ˈrē-ə\ *n* : decreased menstrual flow

hy·po·me·tab·o·lism \ˌhī-pō-mə-ˈta-bə-ˌli-zəm\ *n* : a condition (as in myxedema) marked by an abnormally low metabolic rate — **hy·po·meta·bol·ic** \-ˌme-tə-ˈbä-lik\ *adj*

hy·po·me·tria \-ˈmē-trē-ə\ *n* : a condition of cerebellar dysfunction in which voluntary muscular movements tend to result in the movement of bodily parts (as the arm and hand) short of the intended goal — compare HYPERMETRIA

hy·po·min·er·al·ized \-ˈmi-nə-rə-ˌlīzd\ *adj* : relating to or characterized by a deficiency of minerals ⟨∼ defects in tooth enamel⟩

hy·po·mo·til·i·ty \ˌhī-pō-mō-ˈti-lə-tē\ *n, pl* **-ties** : abnormal deficiency of movement; *specif* : decreased motility of all or part of the gastrointestinal tract — compare HYPERMOTILITY

hy·po·na·trae·mia *chiefly Brit var of* HYPONATREMIA

hy·po·na·tre·mia \-nā-ˈtrē-mē-ə\ *n* : deficiency of sodium in the blood — **hy·po·na·tre·mic** \-mik\ *adj*

hy·po·os·mo·lal·i·ty \-ˌäz-mō-ˈla-lə-tē, -ˌäs-\ *var of* HYPOSMOLALITY

hy·po·os·mot·ic \-ˌäz-ˈmä-tik\ *adj* : HYPOTONIC 2

hy·po·para·thy·roid·ism \-ˌpar-ə-ˈthī-ˌroi-ˌdi-zəm\ *n* : deficiency of parathyroid hormone in the body; *also* : the resultant abnormal state marked by low serum calcium and a tendency to chronic tetany — **hy·po·para·thy·roid** \-ˈthī-ˌroid\ *adj*

hy·po·per·fu·sion \ˌhī-pō-pər-ˈfyü-zhən\ *n* : decreased blood flow through an organ ⟨cerebral ∼⟩

hy·po·phar·ynx \-ˈfar-iŋks\ *n, pl* **-pha·ryn·ges** \-fər-(ˌ)jēz\ *also* **-phar·ynx·es** : the laryngeal part of the pharynx extending from the hyoid bone to the lower margin of the cricoid cartilage — **hy·po·pha·ryn·geal** \-ˌfar-ən-ˈjē-əl; -fə-ˈrin-jəl, -jē-əl\ *adj*

hy·po·phos·pha·tae·mia *chiefly Brit var of* HYPOPHOSPHATEMIA

hy·po·phos·pha·ta·sia \ˌhī-pō-ˌfäs-fə-ˈtā-zhə, -zhē-ə\ *n* : a congenital metabolic disorder characterized by a deficiency of alkaline phosphatase and usu. resulting in demineralization of bone

hy·po·phos·pha·te·mia \-ˌfäs-fə-ˈtē-mē-ə\ *n* : deficiency of phosphates in the blood — **hy·po·phos·pha·te·mic** \-ˈtē-mik\ *adj*

hy·po·phy·se·al *also* **hy·po·phy·si·al** \(ˌ)hī-ˌpä-fə-ˈsē-əl, ˌhī-pə-fə-, -ˈzē-; ˌhī-pə-ˈfi-zē-əl\ *adj* : of or relating to the hypophysis

hypophyseal fossa *n* : the depression in the sphenoid bone that contains the hypophysis

hy·poph·y·sec·to·mize \(ˌ)hī-ˌpä-fə-ˈsek-tə-ˌmīz\ *vb* **-mized; -miz·ing** : to remove the pituitary gland from

hy·poph·y·sec·to·my \-mē\ *n, pl* **-mies** : surgical removal of the pituitary gland

hy·po·phys·io·tro·pic \ˌhī-pō-ˌfi-zē-ō-ˈtrō-pik, -ˈträ-\ *or* **hy·po·phys·io·tro·phic** \-ˈtrō-fik\ *adj* : acting on or stimulating the hypophysis ⟨∼ hormones⟩

hy·poph·y·sis \hī-ˈpä-fə-səs\ *n, pl* **-y·ses** \-ˌsēz\ : PITUITARY GLAND

hypophysis ce·re·bri \-sə-ˈrē-ˌbrī, -ˈser-ə-\ *n* : PITUITARY GLAND

hy·po·pig·men·ta·tion \ˌhī-pō-ˌpig-mən-ˈtā-shən, -ˌmen-\ *n* : diminished pigmentation in a bodily part or tissue (as the skin) — **hy·po·pig·ment·ed** \-ˈpig-mən-təd, -ˌmen-\ *adj*

hy·po·pi·tu·ita·rism \ˌhī-pō-pə-ˈtü-ə-tə-ˌri-zəm, -ˈtyü-\ *n* : deficient production of growth hormones by the pituitary gland — **hy·po·pi·tu·itary** \-ˈtü-ə-ˌter-ē, -ˈtyü-\ *adj*

hy·po·pla·sia \-ˈplā-zhə, -zhē-ə\ *n* : a condition of arrested development in which an organ or part remains below the normal size or in an immature state — **hy·po·plas·tic** \-ˈplas-tik\ *adj*

hypoplastic anemia *n* : APLASTIC ANEMIA

hypoplastic left heart syndrome *n* : a congenital malformation of the heart in which the left side is underdeveloped resulting in insufficient blood flow

hy·po·pnea \ˌhī-pō-ˈnē-ə\ *n* : abnormally slow or esp. shallow respiration

hy·po·pnoea *chiefly Brit var of* HYPOPNEA

hy·po·po·tas·sae·mia *chiefly Brit var of* HYPOPOTASSEMIA

hy·po·po·tas·se·mia \-pə-ˌta-ˈsē-mē-ə\ *n* : HYPOKALEMIA — **hy·po·po·tas·se·mic** \-ˈsē-mik\ *adj*

hy·po·pro·tein·ae·mia *chiefly Brit var of* HYPOPROTEINEMIA

hy·po·pro·tein·emia \-ˌprō-tə-ˈnē-mē-ə, -ˌprō-ˌtē-, -ˌprō-tē-ə-\ *n* : abnormal deficiency of protein in the blood — **hy·po·pro·tein·emic** \-ˈnē-mik\ *adj*

hy·po·pro·throm·bin·ae·mia *chiefly Brit var of* HYPOPROTHROMBINEMIA

hy·po·pro·throm·bin·emia \-prō-ˈthräm-bə-ˈnē-mē-ə\ *n* : deficiency of prothrombin in the blood usu. due to vitamin K deficiency or liver disease and resulting in delayed clotting of blood or spontaneous bleeding (as from the nose) — **hy·po·pro·throm·bin·emic** \-ˈnē-mik\ *adj*

hy·po·py·on \hī-ˈpō-pē-ˌän\ *n* : an accumulation of white blood cells in the anterior chamber of the eye

hy·po·re·ac·tive \ˌhī-pō-rē-ˈak-tiv\ *adj* : having or showing abnormally low sensitivity to stimuli — **hy·po·re·ac·tiv·ity** \-(ˌ)rē-ˌak-ˈti-və-tē\ *n*

hy·po·re·flex·ia \-rē-ˈflek-sē-ə\ *n* : underactivity of bodily reflexes

hy·po·re·spon·sive \-ri-ˈspän-siv\ *adj* : characterized by a diminished degree of responsiveness (as to a physical or emotional stimulus) — **hy·po·re·spon·sive·ness** *n*

hypos *pl of* HYPO

hy·po·sal·i·va·tion \-ˌsa-lə-ˈvā-shən\ *n* : diminished salivation

hy·po·se·cre·tion \ˌhī-pō-si-ˈkrē-shən\ *n* : production of a bodily secretion at an abnormally slow rate or in abnormally small quantities

hy·po·sen·si·tive \-ˈsen-sə-tiv\ *adj* : exhibiting or marked by deficient response to stimulation — **hy·po·sen·si·tiv·ity** \-ˌsen-sə-ˈti-və-tē\ *n*

hy·po·sen·si·ti·za·tion \-ˌsen-sə-tə-ˈzā-shən\ *n* : the state or process of being reduced in sensitivity esp. to an allergen : DESENSITIZATION — **hy·po·sen·si·tize** \-ˈsen-sə-ˌtīz\ *vb*

hy·pos·mia \hī-ˈpäz-mē-ə, hi-\ *n* : impairment of the sense of smell

hy·pos·mo·lal·i·ty \ˌhī-ˌpäz-mō-ˈla-lə-tē\ *n, pl* **-ties** : the condition esp. of a bodily fluid of having abnormally low osmolality

hy·pos·mo·lar·i·ty \ˌhī-ˌpäz-mō-ˈlar-ə-tē\ *n, pl* **-ties** : the condition esp. of a bodily fluid of having abnormally low osmolarity — **hy·pos·mo·lar** \ˌhī-ˈpäz-ˈmō-lər\ *adj*

hy·pos·mot·ic \-ˌpäz-ˈmä-tik\ *var of* HYPOOSMOTIC

hy·po·spa·di·as \ˌhī-pə-ˈspā-dē-əs\ *n* : an abnormality of the penis in which the urethra opens on the underside

Hy·po·spray \ˈhī-pō-ˌsprā\ *trademark* — used for a device with a spring and plunger for administering a medicated solution by forcing it in extremely fine jets through the unbroken skin

hy·pos·ta·sis \hī-ˈpäs-tə-səs\ *n, pl* **-ta·ses** \-ˌsēz\ : the settling of blood in relatively lower parts of an organ or the body due to impaired or absent circulation — **hy·po·stat·ic** \ˌhī-pə-ˈsta·tik\ *adj*

hypostatic pneumonia *n* : pneumonia that usu. results from the collection of fluid in the dorsal region of the lungs and occurs esp. in those (as the bedridden or elderly) confined to a supine position for extended periods

hy·po·sthe·nia \ˌhī-pəs-ˈthē-nē-ə\ *n* : lack of strength : bodily weakness — **hy·po·sthen·ic** \ˌhī-pəs-ˈthe-nik\ *adj*

hy·po·sthe·nu·ria \hī-ˌpäs-thə-ˈnur-ē-ə, -ˈnyur-\ *n* : the secretion of urine of low specific gravity due to inability of the kidney to concentrate the urine normally

hy·po·ten·sion \ˌhī-pō-ˈten-chən\ *n* 1 : abnormally low pressure of the blood — called also *low blood pressure* 2 : abnormally low pressure of the intraocular fluid

¹hy·po·ten·sive \-ˈten-siv\ *adj* 1 : characterized by or due to hypotension (~ shock) 2 : causing low blood pressure or a lowering of blood pressure (~ drugs)

²hypotensive *n* : one with hypotension

hy·po·tha·lam·ic \ˌhī-pō-thə-ˈla-mik\ *adj* : of or relating to the hypothalamus — **hy·po·tha·lam·i·cal·ly** *adv*

hypothalamic releasing factor *n* : any hormone that is secreted by the hypothalamus and stimulates the pituitary gland directly to secrete a hormone — called also *hypothalamic releasing hormone, releasing factor*

hypothalamo- *comb form* : hypothalamus (*hypothalamotomy*)

hy·po·thal·a·mot·o·my \ˌhī-pō-ˌtha-lə-ˈmä-tə-mē\ *n, pl* **-mies** : psychosurgery in which lesions are made in the hypothalamus

hy·po·thal·a·mus \-ˈtha-lə-məs\ *n, pl* **-mi** \-ˌmī\ : a basal part of the diencephalon that lies beneath the thalamus on each side. forms the floor of the third ventricle. and includes vital autonomic regulatory centers

hy·po·the·nar eminence \ˌhī-pō-ˈthē-ˌnär-, -nər-; hī-ˈpä-thə-, -nər-\ n : the prominent part of the palm of the hand above the base of the little finger

hypothenar muscle n : any of four muscles located in the area of the hypothenar eminence: **a** : ABDUCTOR DIGITI MINIMI **b** : FLEXOR DIGITI MINIMI BREVIS **c** : PALMARIS BREVIS **d** : OPPONENS DIGITI MINIMI

hy·po·ther·mia \-ˈthər-mē-ə\ n : subnormal temperature of the body — **hy·po·ther·mic** \-mik\ adj

hy·po·thy·reo·sis \ˌhī-pō-ˌthī-rē-ˈō-səs\ n : HYPOTHYROIDISM

hy·po·thy·roid·ism \ˌhī-pō-ˈthī-ˌrȯi-ˌdiz-əm\ n : deficient activity of the thyroid gland; also : a resultant bodily condition characterized by lowered metabolic rate and general loss of vigor — **hy·po·thy·roid** \-ˌrȯid\ adj

hy·po·thy·ro·sis \-ˌthī-ˈrō-səs\ n : HYPOTHYROIDISM

hy·po·thy·rox·in·ae·mia chiefly Brit var of HYPOTHYROXINEMIA

hy·po·thy·rox·in·emia \ˌhī-pō-thī-ˌräk-sə-ˈnē-mē-ə\ n : the presence of an abnormally low concentration of thyroxine in the blood — **hy·po·thy·rox·in·emic** \-ˈnē-mik\ adj

hy·po·to·nia \ˌhī-pə-ˈtō-nē-ə, -pō-\ n **1** : abnormally low pressure of the intraocular fluid **2** : the state of having hypotonic muscle tone

hy·po·ton·ic \ˌhī-pə-ˈtä-nik, -pō-\ adj **1** : having deficient tone or tension **2** : having a lower osmotic pressure than a surrounding medium or a fluid under comparison — compare HYPERTONIC 2, ISOSMOTIC

hy·po·to·nic·i·ty \-tə-ˈni-sə-tē\ n, pl -ties **1** : the state or condition of having hypotonic osmotic pressure **2** : HYPOTONIA 2

hy·pot·o·ny \hī-ˈpä-tə-nē\ n, pl -onies : HYPOTONIA

hy·po·tri·cho·sis \-tri-ˈkō-səs\ n, pl -cho·ses \-ˌsēz\ : congenital deficiency of hair

hy·pot·ro·phy \hī-ˈpä-trə-fē\ n, pl -phies : subnormal growth

hy·po·tym·pa·num \ˌhī-pō-ˈtim-pə-nəm\ n, pl -na \-nə\ also -nums : the lower part of the middle ear — compare EPITYMPANUM

hy·po·uri·ce·mia \-ˌyūr-ə-ˈsē-mē-ə\ n : deficient uric acid in the blood — **hy·po·uri·ce·mic** \-ˈsē-mik\ adj

hy·po·ven·ti·la·tion \-ˌvent-ᵊl-ˈā-shən\ n : deficient ventilation of the lungs that results in reduction in the oxygen content or increase in the carbon dioxide content of the blood or both — **hy·po·ven·ti·lat·ed** \-ˈvent-ᵊl-ˌā-təd\ adj

hy·po·vi·ta·min·osis \-ˌvī-tə-mə-ˈnō-səs\ n : AVITAMINOSIS — **hy·po·vi·ta·min·ot·ic** \-ˈnä-tik\ adj

hy·po·vo·lae·mia chiefly Brit var of HYPOVOLEMIA

hy·po·vo·le·mia \-və-ˈlē-mē-ə\ n : decrease in the volume of the circulating blood — **hy·po·vo·le·mic** \-ˈlē-mik\ adj

hy·pox·ae·mia chiefly Brit var of HYPOXEMIA

hy·po·xan·thine \hī-pō-ˈzan-ˌthēn\ n : a purine base $C_5H_4N_4O$ of plant and animal tissues that is an intermediate in uric acid synthesis

hypoxanthine–guanine phosphoribosyltransferase n : an enzyme that conserves hypoxanthine in the body by limiting its conversion to uric acid and that is lacking in Lesch-Nyhan syndrome — called also *hypoxanthine phosphoribosyltransferase*

hyp·ox·emia \ˌhī-ˌpäk-ˈsē-mē-ə, -hī-\ n : deficient oxygenation of the blood — **hyp·ox·emic** \-mik\ adj

hyp·ox·ia \hī-ˈpäk-sē-ə, hi-\ n : a deficiency of oxygen reaching the tissues of the body — **hyp·ox·ic** \-sik\ adj

hyps- or **hypsi-** or **hypso-** comb form : high ⟨hypsarrhythmia⟩

hyps·ar·rhyth·mia or **hyps·arhyth·mia** \ˌhips-ā-ˈrith-mē-ə\ n : an abnormal encephalogram that is characterized by slow waves of high voltage and a disorganized arrangement of spikes, occurs esp. in infants, and is indicative of a condition that leads to severe mental retardation if left untreated

hyster- or **hystero-** comb form **1** : womb ⟨hysterotomy⟩ **2** : hysteria ⟨hysteroid⟩

hys·ter·ec·to·my \ˌhis-tə-ˈrek-tə-mē\ n, pl -mies : surgical removal of the uterus — **hys·ter·ec·to·mized** \-tə-ˌmīzd\ adj

hys·te·ria \hi-ˈster-ē-ə, -ˈstir-\ n **1** : a psychoneurosis marked by emotional excitability and disturbances of the psychic, sensory, vasomotor, and visceral functions without an organic basis **2** : behavior exhibiting overwhelming or unmanageable fear or emotional excess

hys·ter·ic \hi-ˈster-ik\ n : one subject to or affected with hysteria

hys·ter·i·cal \-ˈster-i-kəl\ also **hys·ter·ic** \-ˈster-ik\ adj : of, relating to, or marked by hysteria — **hys·ter·i·cal·ly** adv

hysterical personality n : a personality characterized by superficiality, egocentricity, vanity, dependence, and manipulativeness, by dramatic, reactive, and intensely expressed emotional behavior, and often by disturbed interpersonal relationships

hys·ter·ics \-iks\ n sing or pl : a fit of uncontrollable laughter or crying : HYSTERIA

hystericus — see GLOBUS HYSTERICUS

hys·ter·o·gram \ˈhis-tə-rō-ˌgram\ n : a roentgenogram made of the uterus

hys·ter·og·ra·phy \ˌhis-tə-ˈrä-grə-fē\ n,

pl **-phies** : examination of the uterus by roentgenography after the injection of an opaque medium

hys·ter·oid \'his-tə-ˌrȯid\ *adj* : resembling or tending toward hysteria

hys·ter·o·plas·ty \'his-tə-rō-ˌplas-tē\ *n, pl* **-ties** : plastic surgery of the uterus

hys·ter·or·rha·phy \ˌhis-tə-'rȯr-ə-fē\ *n, pl* **-phies** : a suturing of an incised or ruptured uterus

hys·ter·o·sal·pin·go·gram \ˌhis-tə-rō-ˌsal-'piŋ-gə-ˌgram\ *n* : a roentgenogram made by hysterosalpingography

hys·ter·o·sal·pin·gog·ra·phy \-ˌsal-ˌpiŋ-'gä-gre-fē\ *n, pl* **-phies** : examination of the uterus and fallopian tubes by roentgenography after injection of an opaque medium — called also *uterosalpingography*

hys·ter·o·sal·pin·gos·to·my \-'gäs-tə-mē\

n, pl **-mies** : surgical establishment of an anastomosis between the uterus and an occluded fallopian tube

hys·ter·o·scope \'his-tə-rō-ˌskōp\ *n* : an instrument used in inspection of the uterus — **hys·ter·o·scop·ic** \ˌhis-tə-rō-'skä-pik\ *adj* — **hys·ter·os·co·py** \ˌhis-tə-'räs-kə-pē\ *n*

hys·ter·o·sto·ma·to·my \ˌhis-tə-rō-ˌstō-'ma-tə-mē\ *n, pl* **-mies** : surgical incision of the uterine cervix

hys·ter·ot·o·my \ˌhis-tə-'rä-tə-mē\ *n, pl* **-mies** : surgical incision of the uterus: *esp* : CESAREAN SECTION

hystrix — see ICHTHYOSIS HYSTRIX GRAVIOR

H zone \'āch-ˌzōn\ *n* : a narrow and less dense zone of myosin filaments bisecting the A band in striated muscle — compare M LINE

I

i *abbr* incisor

I *symbol* iodine

-i·a·sis \'ī-ə-səs\ *n suffix, pl* **-i·a·ses** \-ˌsēz\ : disease having characteristics of or produced by (something specified) (amebi*asis*) (onchocerci*asis*) (ancylostomi*asis*)

-i·at·ric \ē-'a-trik\ *also* \-'a-tri·cal \-tri-kəl\ *adj comb form* : of or relating to (such) medical treatment or healing (pediatric)

-i·at·rics \ē-'a-triks\ *n pl comb form* : medical treatment (pediatrics)

-i·a·trist \'ī-ə-trəst\ *n comb form* : physician : healer (psychiatrist) (podiatrist)

iatro- *comb form* : physician : medicine : healing (iatrogenic)

iat·ro·gen·ic \(ˌ)ī-ˌa-trə-'je-nik\ *adj* : induced inadvertently by a physician or surgeon or by medical treatment or diagnostic procedures (~ rash) — **iat·ro·gen·e·sis** \-'je-nə-səs\ *n* — **iat·ro·gen·i·cal·ly** *adv*

-i·a·try \'ī-ə-trē\ *n comb form, pl* **-iatries** : medical treatment : healing (podiatry) (psychiatry)

I band \'ī-\ *n* : a pale band across a striated muscle fiber that consists of actin and is situated between two A bands — called also *isotropic band*

ibo·te·nic acid \ˌī-bō-'tē-nik-\ *n* : a neurotoxic compound $C_5H_6N_2O_4$ found esp. in fly agaric

ibu·pro·fen \ˌī-byü-'prō-fən\ *n* : a nonsteroidal anti-inflammatory drug $C_{13}H_{18}O_2$ used in over-the-counter preparations to relieve pain and fever and in prescription strength esp. to relieve the symptoms of rheumatoid arthritis and degenerative arthritis — see MOTRIN

ice bag *n* : a waterproof bag to hold ice for local application of cold to the body

ice pack *n* : crushed ice placed in a container (as an ice bag) or folded in a towel and applied to the body

ich·tham·mol \'ik-thə-ˌmȯl, -ˌmōl\ *n* : a brownish black viscous tarry liquid prepared from a distillate of some hydrocarbon-containing rocks and used as an antiseptic and emollient — see ICHTHYOL

ichthy- *or* **ichthyo-** *comb form* : fish (ichthyosarcotoxism)

Ich·thy·ol \'ik-thē-ˌȯl, -ˌōl\ *trademark* — used for a preparation of ichthammol

ich·thyo·sar·co·tox·ism \ˌik-thē-ō-ˌsär-kə-'täk-ˌsi-zəm\ *n* : poisoning caused by the ingestion of fish whose flesh contains a toxic substance

ich·thy·o·si·form \ˌik-thē-'ō-sə-ˌfȯrm\ *adj* : resembling ichthyosis or that of ichthyosis (~ erythroderma)

ich·thy·o·sis \ˌik-thē-'ō-səs\ *n, pl* **-o·ses** \-ˌsēz\ : any of several congenital diseases of hereditary origin characterized by rough, thick, and scaly skin — **ich·thy·ot·ic** \-'ä-tik\ *adj*

ichthyosis hys·trix gra·vi·or \-'his-triks-'gra-vē-ˌȯr, -'grä-\ *n* : a rare hereditary abnormality characterized by the formation of brown, verrucose, and often linear lesions of the skin

ichthyosis vul·gar·is \-ˌvəl-'gar-əs\ *n* : the common hereditary form of ichthyosis

ICN *abbr* International Council of Nurses

-ics \iks\ *n sing or pl suffix* **1** : study : knowledge : skill : practice (optics) (pediatrics) **2** : characteristic actions or activities (hysterics) **3** : characteristic qualities, operations, or phenomena (acoustics) (phonetics)

ICSH *abbr* interstitial-cell stimulating hormone

ICT *abbr* insulin coma therapy

ic·tal \'ik-təl\ *adj* : of, relating to, or caused by ictus

icter- *or* **ictero-** *comb form* : jaundice ⟨*icterogenic*⟩

ic·ter·ic \ik-'ter-ik\ *adj* : of, relating to, or affected with jaundice

icteric index *n* : ICTERUS INDEX

ic·ter·o·gen·ic \ik-tə-rō-'je-nik, ik-ter-ə-\ *adj* : causing or tending to cause jaundice ⟨∼drugs⟩

ic·ter·us \'ik-tə-rəs\ *n* : JAUNDICE

icterus gra·vis \-'gra-vəs, -'grä-\ *n* : ICTERUS GRAVIS NEONATORUM

icterus gravis neo·na·tor·um \-nē-ō-nā-'tōr-əm\ *n* : severe jaundice in a newborn child due esp. to erythroblastosis fetalis

icterus index *n* : a figure representing the amount of bilirubin in the blood as determined by comparing the color of a sample of test serum with a set of color standards ⟨an *icterus index* of 15 or above indicates active jaundice⟩ — called also *icteric index*

icterus neo·na·tor·um \-nē-ō-nā-'tōr-əm\ *n* : jaundice in a newborn

ic·tus \'ik-təs\ *n* 1 : a beat or pulsation esp. of the heart 2 : a sudden attack or seizure esp. of stroke

ICU *abbr* intensive care unit

¹id \'id\ *n* : the one of the three divisions of the psyche in psychoanalytic theory that is completely unconscious and is the source of psychic energy derived from instinctual needs and drives — compare EGO, SUPEREGO

²id *n* : a skin rash that is an allergic reaction to an agent causing an infection ⟨a syphilitic ∼⟩

ID *abbr* intradermal

¹-id \əd, (,)id\ *also* **-ide** \'īd\ *n suffix* : skin rash caused by (something specified) ⟨syphil*id*⟩

²-id *n suffix* : structure, body, or particle of a (specified) kind ⟨chromat*id*⟩

-i·da \ə-də\ *n pl suffix* : animals that are or have the form of — in names of higher taxa (as orders and classes) ⟨Arachn*ida*⟩ — **-i·dan** \ə-dən, əd-ᵊn\ *n or adj suffix*

-i·dae \ə-ˌdē\ *n pl suffix* : members of the family of — in names of zoological families ⟨Homin*idae*⟩ ⟨Ixod*idae*⟩

IDDM *abbr* insulin-dependent diabetes mellitus

idea \ī-'dē-ə\ *n* : something imagined or pictured in the mind

idea of reference *n* : a delusion that the remarks one overhears and people one encounters seem to be concerned with and usu. hostile to oneself — called also *delusion of reference*

ide·ation \ī-dē-'ā-shən\ *n* : the capacity for or the act of forming or entertaining ideas ⟨suicidal ∼⟩ — **ide·ation·al** \-shə-nəl\ *adj*

idée fixe \(,)ē-ˌdā-'fēks\ *n, pl* **idées fixes** *same or* -'fēk-səz\ : a usu. delusional idea that dominates the whole mental life during a prolonged period (as in certain mental disorders) — called also *fixed idea*

iden·ti·cal \ī-'den-ti-kəl\ *adj* : MONOZYGOTIC

iden·ti·fi·ca·tion \ī-ˌden-tə-fə-'kā-shən\ *n* 1 : psychological orientation of the self in regard to something (as a person or group) with a resulting feeling of close emotional association 2 : a largely unconscious process whereby an individual models thoughts, feelings, and actions after those attributed to an object that has been incorporated as a mental image — **iden·ti·fy** \ī-'den-tə-ˌfī\ *vb*

iden·ti·ty \ī-'den-tə-tē\ *n, pl* **-ties** 1 : the distinguishing character or personality of an individual 2 : the relation established by psychological identification

identity crisis *n* : personal psychosocial conflict esp. in adolescence that involves confusion about one's social role and often a sense of loss of continuity to one's personality

ideo·mo·tor \ī-dē-ə-'mō-tər, ˌi-\ *adj* 1 : not reflex but motivated by an idea ⟨∼ muscular activity⟩ 2 : of, relating to, or concerned with ideomotor activity

ID₅₀ *symbol* — used for the dose of an infectious organism required to produce infection in 50% of the experimental subjects

idio- *comb form* 1 : one's own : personal : separate : distinct ⟨*idiotype*⟩ ⟨*idiosyncrasy*⟩ 2 : self-produced : arising within ⟨*idiopathic*⟩ ⟨*idioventricular*⟩

id·i·o·cy \'i-dē-ə-sē\ *n, pl* **-cies** : extreme mental retardation commonly due to incomplete or abnormal development of the brain

id·io·path·ic \ˌi-dē-ə-'pa-thik\ *adj* : arising spontaneously or from an obscure or unknown cause : PRIMARY ⟨∼ epilepsy⟩ ⟨∼ hypertension⟩ ⟨∼ thrombocytopenic purpura⟩ — **id·io·path·i·cal·ly** *adv*

id·io·syn·cra·sy \ˌi-dē-ə-'siŋ-krə-sē\ *n, pl* **-sies** 1 : a peculiarity of physical or mental constitution or temperament 2 : individual hypersensitiveness (as to a food) — **id·io·syn·crat·ic** \ˌi-dē-ō-sin-'kra-tik\ *adj*

id·i·ot \'i-dē-ət\ *n* : a person affected with idiocy; *esp* : a feebleminded person having a mental age not exceeding three years and requiring complete custodial care — **idiot** *adj*

idiot sa·vant \'ē-ˌdyō-sä-'väⁿ *n, pl* **idiots savants** *or* **idiot savants** *same or* -'väⁿz\ : a mentally defective person who exhibits exceptional skill or brilliance in some limited field

id·io·type \'i-dē-ə-ˌtīp\ *n* : the molecular structure and conformation in the variable region of an antibody that confers its antigenic specificity — compare ALLOTYPE, ISOTYPE — **id·io·typ·ic** \ˌi-dē-ə-'ti-pik\ *adj*

id·io·ven·tric·u·lar \ˌi-dē-ō-ven-'tri-kyə-**

lər, -vən\ *adj* : of, relating to, associated with, or arising in the ventricles of the heart independently of the atria

idox·uri·dine \ i-'däks-'yur-ə-ˌdēn\ *n* : a drug C₉H₁₁IN₂O₅ used to treat keratitis caused by the herpesviruses producing herpes simplex — abbr. *IDU*; called also *iododeoxyuridine*, *IUDR*

-i·dro·sis \i-'drō-səs\ *n comb form*, *pl* **-i·dro·ses** \-ˌsēz\ : a specified form of sweating (chrom*idrosis*) (brom*idrosis*)

IDU *abbr* idoxuridine

IF *abbr* interferon

IFN *abbr* interferon

Ig *abbr* immunoglobulin

IgA \ˌi-(ˌ)jē-'ā\ *n* : a class of antibodies found in external bodily secretions (as saliva, tears, and sweat) — called also *immunoglobulin A*

IgD \ˌi-(ˌ)jē-'dē\ *n* : a minor class of antibodies of undetermined function — called also *immunoglobulin D*

IgE \ˌi-(ˌ)jē-'ē\ *n* : a class of antibodies that function esp. in allergic reactions — called also *immunoglobulin E*

IgG \ˌi-(ˌ)jē-'jē\ *n* : a class of antibodies including those most commonly circulating in the blood and active esp. against bacteria, viruses, and proteins foreign to the body — called also *immunoglobulin G*

IgM \ˌi-(ˌ)jē-'em\ *n* : a class of antibodies of high molecular weight including those appearing early in the immune response to be replaced later by IgG of lower molecular weight — called also *immunoglobulin M*

il *symbol* illinium

il- — see IN-

ile- *also* **ileo-** *comb form* **1** : ileum (*ile-itis*) **2** : ileal and (*ileocecal*)

ilea *pl of* ILEUM

il·e·al \'i-lē-əl\ *also* **il·e·ac** \-ˌak\ *adj* : of, relating to, or affecting the ileum

il·e·itis \ˌi-lē-'i-təs\ *n*, *pl* **-it·i·des** \-'i-tə-ˌdēz\ : inflammation of the ileum — see REGIONAL ILEITIS

il·eo·ce·cal \ˌi-lē-ō-'sē-kəl\ *adj* : of, relating to, or connecting the ileum and cecum

ileocecal valve *n* : the valve formed by two folds of mucous membrane at the opening of the ileum into the large intestine — called also *Bauhin's valve*

il·eo·col·ic \-'kō-lik, -'kä-\ *adj* : relating to, situated near, or involving the ileum and the colon

ileocolic artery *n* : a branch of the superior mesenteric artery that supplies the terminal part of the ileum and the beginning of the colon

il·eo·co·li·tis \ˌi-lē-ō-kō-'lī-təs\ *n* : inflammation of the ileum and colon

il·eo·co·los·to·my \-kə-'läs-tə-mē\ *n*, *pl* **-mies** : a surgical operation producing an artificial opening connecting the ileum and the colon

il·eo·cy·to·plas·ty \-'sī-tə-ˌplas-tē\ *n*, *pl* **-ties** : a surgical operation that in-

volves anastomosing a segment of the ileum to the bladder esp. in order to increase bladder capacity and preserve the function of the kidneys and ureters

il·e·o·il·e·al \-'i-lē-əl\ *adj* : relating to or involving two different parts of the ileum (an ∼ anastomosis)

il·eo·proc·tos·to·my \-ˌpräk-'täs-tə-mē\ *n*, *pl* **-mies** : a surgical operation producing a permanent artificial opening connecting the ileum and rectum

il·e·os·to·my \ˌi-lē-'äs-tə-mē\ *n*, *pl* **-mies** **1** : surgical formation of an artificial anus by connecting the ileum to an opening in the abdominal wall **2** : the artificial opening made by ileostomy

ileostomy bag *n* : a container designed to receive feces discharged through an ileostomy

Iletin \'i-lə-tən\ *trademark* — used for a preparation of insulin

il·e·um \'i-lē-əm\ *n*, *pl* **il·ea** \-lē-ə\ : the last division of the small intestine extending between the jejunum and large intestine

il·e·us \'i-lē-əs\ *n* : obstruction of the bowel; *specif* : a condition that is commonly marked by a painful distended abdomen, vomiting of dark or fecal matter, toxemia, and dehydration and that results when the intestinal contents back up because peristalsis fails although the lumen is not occluded — compare VOLVULUS

ilia *pl of* ILIUM

il·i·ac \'i-lē-ˌak\ *adj* **1** : of, relating to, or located near the ilium (the ∼ bone) **2** : of or relating to either of the lowest lateral abdominal regions

iliac artery *n* **1** : either of the large arteries supplying blood to the lower trunk and hind limbs and arising by bifurcation of the aorta to form one vessel for each side of the body — called also *common iliac artery* **2** : the outer branch of the common iliac artery on either side of the body that becomes the femoral artery — called also *external iliac artery* **3** : the inner branch of the common iliac artery on either side of the body that supplies blood chiefly to the pelvic and gluteal areas — called also *hypogastric artery, internal iliac artery*

iliac crest *n* : the thick curved upper border of the ilium

iliac fossa *n* : the inner concavity of the ilium

iliac node *n* : any of the lymph nodes grouped around the iliac arteries and the iliac veins — see EXTERNAL ILIAC NODE, INTERNAL ILIAC NODE

iliac spine *n* : any of four projections on the ilium: **a** : ANTERIOR INFERIOR ILIAC SPINE **b** : ANTERIOR SUPERIOR ILIAC SPINE **c** : POSTERIOR INFERIOR ILIAC SPINE **d** : POSTERIOR SUPERIOR ILIAC SPINE

ili·a·cus \i-'lī-ə-kəs\ *n*, *pl* **ili·a·ci** \-ə-ˌsī\ : a muscle of the iliac region of the abdomen that flexes the thigh or bends the pelvis and lumbar region forward

iliac vein *n* : any of several veins on each side of the body corresponding to and accompanying the iliac arteries: **a** : either of two veins of which one is formed on each side of the body by the union of the external and internal iliac veins and which unite to form the inferior vena cava — called also *common iliac vein* **b** : a vein that drains the leg and lower part of the anterior abdominal wall, is an upward continuation of the femoral vein, and unites with the internal iliac vein — called also *external iliac vein* **c** : a vein that drains the pelvis and gluteal and perineal regions and that unites with the external iliac vein to form the common iliac vein — called also *hypogastric vein, internal iliac vein*

il·i·al \'i-lē-əl\ *var of* ILIAC

ilio- *comb form* : iliac and ⟨*ilio*inguinal⟩

il·io·coc·cy·geus \ˌi-lē-ō-käk-ˈsi-jəs, -jē-əs\ *n* : a muscle of the pelvis that is a subdivision of the levator ani and helps support the pelvic viscera — compare PUBOCOCCYGEUS

il·io·cos·ta·lis \-käs-ˈtā-ləs\ *n* : the lateral division of the sacrospinalis muscle that helps to keep the trunk erect and consists of three parts: **a** : ILIOCOSTALIS CERVICIS **b** : ILIOCOSTALIS LUMBORUM **c** : ILIOCOSTALIS THORACIS

iliocostalis cer·vi·cis \-ˈsər-və-səs\ *n* : a muscle that extends from the ribs to the cervical transverse processes and acts to draw the neck to the same side and to elevate the ribs

iliocostalis dor·si \-ˈdȯr-ˌsī\ *n* : ILIOCOSTALIS THORACIS

iliocostalis lum·bor·um \-ˌləm-ˈbȯr-əm\ *n* : a muscle that extends from the ilium to the lower ribs and acts to draw the trunk to the same side or to depress the ribs

iliocostalis tho·ra·cis \-thə-ˈrā-səs\ *n* : a muscle that extends from the lower to the upper ribs and acts to draw the trunk to the same side and to approximate the ribs

il·io·fem·o·ral \ˌi-lē-ō-ˈfe-mə-rəl\ *adj* **1** : of or relating to the ilium and the femur **2** : relating to or involving an iliac vein and a femoral vein ⟨∼ bypass graft⟩

iliofemoral ligament *n* : a ligament that extends from the anterior inferior iliac spine to the intertrochanteric line of the femur and divides below into two branches — called also *Y ligament*

il·io·hy·po·gas·tric nerve \ˌi-lē-ō-ˌhī-pə-ˈgas-trik-\ *n* : a branch of the first lumbar nerve distributed to the skin of the lateral part of the buttocks, the skin of the pubic region, and the muscles of the anterolateral abdominal wall

il·io·in·gui·nal \-ˈiŋ-gwən-əl\ *adj* : of, re-

lating to, or affecting the iliac and inguinal regions

ilioinguinal nerve *n* : a branch of the first lumbar nerve distributed to the muscles of the anterolateral wall of the abdomen, the skin of the proximal and medial part of the thigh, the base of the penis and the scrotum in the male, and the mons veneris and labia majora in the female

il·io·lum·bar artery \ˌi-lē-ō-ˈləm-bər-, -ˌbär-\ *n* : a branch of the internal iliac artery that supplies muscles in the lumbar region and the iliac fossa

iliolumbar ligament *n* : a ligament connecting the transverse process of the last lumbar vertebra with the iliac crest

il·io·pec·tin·e·al eminence \ˌi-lē-ō-pek-ˈti-nē-əl-\ *n* : a ridge on the hipbone marking the junction of the ilium and the pubis

iliopectineal line *n* : a line or ridge on the inner surface of the hipbone marking the border between the true and false pelvis

il·io·pso·as \ˌi-lē-ō-ˈsō-əs, -lē-ˈäp-sō-əs\ *n* : a muscle consisting of the iliacus and psoas major muscles

iliopsoas tendon *n* : the tendon that is common to the iliacus and psoas major

il·io·tib·i·al \ˌi-lē-ō-ˈti-bē-əl\ *adj* : of or relating to the ilium and the tibia

iliotibial band *n* : a fibrous thickening of the fascia lata that extends from the iliac crest down the lateral part of the thigh to the lateral condyle of the tibia — called also *iliotibial tract*

il·i·um \'i-lē-əm\ *n, pl* **il·ia** \-lē-ə\ : the dorsal, upper, and largest one of the three bones composing either lateral half of the pelvis that is broad and expanded above and narrower below where it joins with the ischium and pubis to form part of the acetabulum

¹**ill** \'il\ *adj* **worse** \'wərs\ *also* **ill·er**; **worst** \'wərst\ **1** : affected with some ailment : not in good health ⟨incurably ∼⟩ ⟨emotionally ∼⟩ **2** : affected with nausea often to the point of vomiting

²**ill** *n* : AILMENT, SICKNESS

il·lin·i·um \i-ˈli-nē-əm\ *n* : PROMETHIUM

ill·ness \'il-nəs\ *n* : an unhealthy condition of body or mind : SICKNESS

il·lu·sion \i-ˈlü-zhən\ *n* **1** : perception of something objectively existing in such a way as to cause misinterpretation of its actual nature; *esp* : OPTICAL ILLUSION **2** : HALLUCINATION 1 **3** : a pattern capable of reversible perspective

IL-1 *abbr* interleukin-1

Il·o·sone \'i-lə-ˌsōn\ *trademark* — used for a preparation of a salt of erythromycin

Il·o·ty·cin \ˌi-lə-ˈtī-sən\ *trademark* — used for a preparation of erythromycin

IL-2 *abbr* interleukin-2

IM *abbr* intramuscular: intramuscularly

im- — see IN-

¹**im·age** \'i-mij\ *n* : a mental picture or impression of something: as **a** : an idealized conception of a person and esp. a parent that is formed by an infant or child, is retained in the unconscious, and influences behavior in later life — called also *imago* **b** : the memory of a perception in psychology that is modified by subsequent experience; *also* : the representation of the source of a stimulus on a receptor mechanism

²**image** *vb* **im·aged; im·ag·ing 1** : to call up a mental picture of **2** : to create a representation of: *also* : to form an image of

image intensifier *n* : a device used esp. for diagnosis in radiology that provides a more intense image for a given amount of radiation than can be obtained by the usual fluorometric methods — **image intensification** *n*

im·ag·ery \'i-mij-rē, -mi-jə-\ *n, pl* **-eries** : mental images; *esp* : the products of imagination (psychotic ~)

im·ag·ing *n* : the action or process of producing an image esp. of a part of the body by radiographic techniques (diagnostic ~) (cardiac ~) — see MAGNETIC RESONANCE IMAGING

ima·go \i-'mā-(ₐ)gō, -'mä-\ *n, pl* **imagoes** *or* **ima·gi·nes** \-'mā-gə-ˌnēz, -'mä-\ : IMAGE a

im·bal·ance \(ₐ)im-'ba-ləns\ *n* : lack of balance : the state of being out of equilibrium or out of proportion: as **a** : loss of parallel relation between the optical axes of the eyes caused by faulty action of the extrinsic muscles and often resulting in diplopia **b** : absence of biological equilibrium (a vitamin ~) — **im·bal·anced** \-lənst\ *adj*

im·be·cile \'im-bə-səl, -ˌsil\ *n* : a mentally retarded person having a mental age of three to seven years and requiring help in routine personal care — **imbecile** *or* **im·be·cil·ic** \ˌim-bə-'si-lik\ *adj* — **im·be·cil·i·ty** \ˌim-bə-'si-lə-tē\ *n*

im·bed \im-'bed\ *var of* EMBED

im·bri·ca·tion \ˌim-brə-'kā-shən\ *n* : an overlapping esp. of successive layers of tissue in the surgical closure of a wound — **im·bri·cate** \'im-brə-ˌkāt\ *vb*

im·id·az·ole \ˌi-mə-'da-ˌzōl\ *n* **1** : a white crystalline heterocyclic base $C_3H_4N_2$ that is an antimetabolite related to histidine **2** : any of a large class of derivatives of imidazole including histidine and histamine

im·id·az·o·line \ˌi-mə-'da-zə-ˌlēn\ *n* : any of three derivatives $C_3H_6N_2$ of imidazole with adrenergic blocking activity

im·i·no·gly·cin·uria \ˌi-mə-ˌnō-ˌglī-sə-'nūr-ē-ə, -'nyūr-\ *n* : an abnormal inherited condition of the kidney associated esp. with hyperprolinemia and characterized by the presence of proline, hydroxyproline, and glycine in the urine

imip·ra·mine \i-'mi-prə-ˌmēn\ *n* : a tricyclic antidepressant drug $C_{19}H_{24}N_2$ administered esp. in the form of its hydrochloride — see TOFRANIL

im·ma·ture \ˌi-mə-'tùr, -'tyùr, -'chùr\ *adj* : lacking complete growth, differentiation, or development — **im·ma·ture·ly** *adv* — **im·ma·tu·ri·ty** \-'tùr-ə-, -'tyùr-, -'chùr-\ *n*

im·me·di·ate \i-'mē-dē-ət\ *adj* **1** : acting or being without the intervention of another object, cause, or agency : being direct (the ~ cause of death) **2** : present to the mind independently of other states or factors (~ awareness)

immediate auscultation *n* : auscultation performed without a stethoscope by laying the ear directly against the patient's body

immediate hypersensitivity *n, pl* **-ties** : hypersensitivity in which exposure to an antigen produces an immediate or almost immediate reaction

immersion foot *n* : a painful condition of the feet marked by inflammation and stabbing pain and followed by discoloration, swelling, ulcers, and numbness due to prolonged exposure to moist cold usu. without actual freezing

im·mo·bile \i-'mō-bəl, -ˌbēl, -ˌbīl\ *adj* **1** : incapable of being moved **2** : not moving (keep the patient ~) — **im·mo·bil·i·ty** \ˌi-mō-'bi-lə-tē\ *n*

im·mo·bi·lize \i-'mō-bə-ˌlīz\ *vb* **-ized; -iz·ing** : to make immobile; *esp* : to fix (as a body part) so as to reduce or eliminate motion usu. by means of a cast or splint, by strapping, or by strict bed rest — **im·mo·bi·li·za·tion** \ˌi-ˌmō-bə-lə-'zā-shən\ *n*

im·mune \i-'myün\ *adj* **1** : not susceptible or responsive; *esp* : having a high degree of resistance to a disease **2 a** : having or producing antibodies or lymphocytes capable of reacting with a specific antigen (an ~ serum) **b** : produced by, involved in, or concerned with immunity or an immune response (~ agglutinins)

immune complex *n* : any of various molecular complexes formed in the blood by combination of an antigen and an antibody that tend to accumulate in bodily tissue and are associated with various pathological conditions (as glomerulonephritis and systemic lupus erythematosus)

immune globulin *n* : globulin from the blood of a person or animal immune to a particular disease — called also *immune serum globulin*

immune response *n* : a bodily response to an antigen that occurs when lymphocytes identify the antigenic molecule as foreign and induce the for-

mation of antibodies and lymphocytes capable of reacting with it and
rendering it harmless — called also
immune reaction

immune serum *n* : ANTISERUM

immune system *n* : the bodily system
that protects the body from foreign
substances, cells, and tissues by producing the immune response and that
includes esp. the thymus, spleen,
lymph nodes, special deposits of lymphoid tissue (as in the gastrointestinal
tract and bone marrow), lymphocytes
including the B cells and T cells, and
antibodies

immune therapy *n* : IMMUNOTHERAPY

im·mu·ni·ty \i-'myü-nə-tē\ *n, pl* **-ties**
: the quality or state of being immune;
esp : a condition of being able to resist a particular disease esp. through
preventing development of a pathogenic microorganism or by counteracting the effects of its products —
see ACQUIRED IMMUNITY, ACTIVE IM-
MUNITY, NATURAL IMMUNITY, PAS-
SIVE IMMUNITY

im·mu·ni·za·tion \i-myə-nə-'zā-shən\ *n*
: the creation of immunity usu.
against a particular disease; *esp* : treatment of an organism for the purpose
of making it immune to subsequent
attack by a particular pathogen — **im·
mu·nize** \'i-myə-ˌnīz\ *vb*

immuno- *comb form* **1** : physiological
immunity (*immunology*) **2** : immunologic (*immunochemistry*) : immunologically (*immunocompromised*) : immunology and (*immunogenetics*)

im·mu·no·ad·sor·bent \ˌi-myə-nō-ad-
'sor-bənt, i-ˌmyü-nō-, -'zor-\ *n* : IM-
MUNOSORBENT — **immunoadsorbent**
adj

im·mu·no·as·say \-'as-ˌā, -a-'sā\ *n* : the
identification of a substance (as a
protein) based on its capacity to act
as an antigen — **immunoassay** *vb* —
im·mu·no·as·say·able \-a-'sā-ə-bəl\ *adj*

im·mu·no·bi·ol·o·gy \-bī-'ä-lə-jē\ *n, pl*
-gies : a branch of biology concerned
with the physiological reactions characteristic of the immune state — **im·
mu·no·bi·o·log·i·cal** \-ˌbī-ə-'lä-ji-kəl\
or **im·mu·no·bi·o·log·ic** \-'lä-jik\ *adj* —
im·mu·no·bi·ol·o·gist \-bī-'ä-lə-jist\ *n*

im·mu·no·blast \i-'myü-nō-ˌblast, 'i-
myə-nō-\ *n* : a cell formed by transformation of a T cell after antigenic
stimulation and giving rise to a population of T cells with specificity
against the stimulating antigen — **im·
mu·no·blas·tic** \ˌi-myə-nō-'blas-tik,
i-ˌmyü-nō-\ *adj*

im·mu·no·blot \-ˌblät\ *n* : a blot in
which a radioactively labeled antibody is used as the molecular probe
— **im·mu·no·blot·ting** *n*

im·mu·no·chem·is·try \-'ke-mə-strē\ *n,
pl* **-tries** : a branch of chemistry that
deals with the chemical aspects of immunology — **im·mu·no·chem·i·cal**
\-'ke-mə-kəl\ *adj* — **im·mu·no·chem-**

i·cal·ly *adv* — **im·mu·no·chem·ist**
\-'ke-mist\ *n*

im·mu·no·che·mo·ther·a·py \-ˌkē-mō-
'ther-ə-pē\ *n, pl* **-pies** : the combined
use of immunotherapy and chemotherapy in the treatment or control of
disease

im·mu·no·com·pe·tence \-'käm-pə-təns\
n : the capacity for a normal immune
response — **im·mu·no·com·pe·tent**
\-tənt\ *adj*

im·mu·no·com·pro·mised \-'käm-prə-
ˌmīzd\ *adj* : having the immune system impaired or weakened (as by
drugs or illness)

im·mu·no·cyte \i-'myü-nō-ˌsīt, 'i-myə-
nō-\ *n* : a cell (as a lymphocyte) that
has an immunologic function

im·mu·no·cy·to·chem·is·try \ˌi-myə-nō-
ˌsī-tō-'ke-mə-strē, i-ˌmyü-nō-\ *n, pl*
-tries : the application of biochemistry to cellular immunology — **im·mu·
no·cy·to·chem·i·cal** \-'ke-mi-kəl\ *adj*

im·mu·no·de·fi·cien·cy \-di-'fi-shən-sē\
n, pl **-cies** : inability to produce a normal complement of antibodies or immunologically sensitized T cells esp.
in response to specific antigens — see
AIDS — **im·mu·no·de·fi·cient** \-shənt\
adj

im·mu·no·de·pres·sion \-di-'pre-shən\ *n*
: IMMUNOSUPPRESSION — **im·mu·no·
de·pres·sant** \-di-'pres-ənt\ *n*

im·mu·no·di·ag·no·sis \-ˌdī-ig-'nō-səs\
n, pl **-no·ses** \-ˌsēz\ : diagnosis (as of
cancer) by immunological methods —
im·mu·no·di·ag·nos·tic \-'näs-tik\ *adj*

im·mu·no·dif·fu·sion \-di-'fyü-zhən\ *n*
: any of several techniques for obtaining a precipitate between an antibody
and its specific antigen by suspending
one in a gel and letting the other migrate through it from a well or by letting both antibody and antigen
migrate through the gel from separate
wells to form an area of precipitation

im·mu·no·elec·tro·pho·re·sis \-ə-ˌlek-trə-
fə-'rē-səs\ *n, pl* **-re·ses** \-ˌsēz\ : electrophoretic separation of proteins
followed by identification by the formation of precipitates through specific immunologic reactions — **im·mu·
no·elec·tro·pho·ret·ic** \-'re-tik\ *adj* —
im·mu·no·elec·tro·pho·ret·i·cal·ly *adv*

im·mu·no·flu·o·res·cence \-ˌflō-'res-ᵊns,
-flü-\ *n* : the labeling of antibodies or
antigens with fluorescent dyes esp.
for the purpose of demonstrating the
presence of a particular antigen or
antibody in a tissue preparation or
smear — **im·mu·no·flu·o·res·cent** \-ᵊnt\
adj

im·mu·no·gen \i-'myü-nə-jən, 'i-myə-
nə-, -ˌjen\ *n* : an antigen that pro-
vokes an immune response

im·mu·no·ge·net·ics \-jə-'ne-tiks\ *n* : a
branch of immunology concerned
with the interrelations of heredity,
disease, and the immune system and
its components (as antibodies) — **im·
mu·no·ge·net·ic** \-tik\ *adj* — **im·mu·no-**

ge·net·i·cal·ly *adv* — im·mu·no·ge·net·i·cist \-jə-'ne-tə-sist\ *n*

im·mu·no·gen·ic \,i-myə-nō-'jen-ik, i-,myü-nō-\ *adj* : relating to or producing an immune response ⟨∼ substances⟩ — im·mu·no·gen·i·cal·ly *adv* — im·mu·no·ge·nic·i·ty \-jə-'ni-sə-tē\ *n*

im·mu·no·glob·u·lin \-'glä-byə-lən\ *n* : ANTIBODY — abbr. *Ig*

immunoglobulin A *n* : IGA

immunoglobulin D *n* : IGD

immunoglobulin E *n* : IGE

immunoglobulin G *n* : IGG

immunoglobulin M *n* : IGM

im·mu·no·he·ma·tol·o·gy \-,hē-mə-'tä-lə-jē\ *n, pl* -gies : a branch of immunology that deals with the immunologic properties of blood — im·mu·no·he·ma·to·log·ic \-,hē-mə-tə-'lä-jik\ *or* im·mu·no·he·ma·to·log·i·cal \-ji-kəl\ *adj* — im·mu·no·he·ma·tol·o·gist \-,hē-mə-'tä-lə-jist\ *n*

im·mu·no·his·to·chem·i·cal \-,his-tō-'ke-mi-kəl\ *adj* : of or relating to the application of histochemical and immunologic methods to chemical analysis of living cells and tissues — im·mu·no·his·to·chem·i·cal·ly *adv* — im·mu·no·his·to·chem·is·try \-'ke-mə-strē\ *n*

im·mu·no·his·to·log·i·cal \-,his-tə-'lä-ji-kəl\ *also* im·mu·no·his·to·log·ic \-'lä-jik\ *adj* : of or relating to the application of immunologic methods to histology — im·mu·no·his·tol·o·gy \-hi-'stä-lə-jē\ *n*

immunological surveillance *n* : IMMUNOSURVEILLANCE

im·mu·nol·o·gist \,i-myə-'nä-lə-jist\ *n* : a specialist in immunology

im·mu·nol·o·gy \,i-myə-'nä-lə-jē\ *n, pl* -gies : a science that deals with the immune system and the cell-mediated and humoral aspects of immunity and immune responses — im·mu·no·log·ic \-nə-'lä-jik\ *or* im·mu·no·log·i·cal \-ji-kəl\ *adj* — im·mu·no·log·i·cal·ly *adv*

im·mu·no·mod·u·la·tor \-,i-myə-nō-'mä-jə-,lā-tər, i-,myü-nō-\ *n* : a substance that affects the functioning of the immune system — im·mu·no·mod·u·la·to·ry \-'mä-jə-lə-,tōr-ē\ *adj*

im·mu·no·patho·gen·e·sis \-,pa-thə-'je-nə-səs\ *n, pl* -e·ses \-,sēz\ : the development of disease as affected by the immune system

im·mu·no·pa·thol·o·gist \-pə-'thä-lə-jist, -pa-\ *n* : a specialist in immunopathology

im·mu·no·pa·thol·o·gy \-pə-'thä-lə-jē, -pa-\ *n, pl* -gies : a branch of medicine that deals with immune responses associated with disease — im·mu·no·path·o·log·ic \-,pa-thə-'lä-jik\ *or* im·mu·no·path·o·log·i·cal \-ji-kəl\ *adj*

im·mu·no·pre·cip·i·ta·tion \-,pri-,si-pə-'tā-shən\ *n* : precipitation of a complex of an antibody and its specific antigen — im·mu·no·pre·cip·i·tate \-'si-pə-,tət, -,tāt\ *n* — im·mu·no·pre·cip·i·tate \-,tāt\ *vb*

im·mu·no·pro·phy·lax·is \-,prō-fə-'lak-səs, -,prä-\ *n, pl* -lax·es \-,sēz\ : the prevention of disease by the production of active or passive immunity

im·mu·no·ra·dio·met·ric assay \-,rā-dē-ō-'me-trik-\ *n* : immunoassay of a substance by combining it with a radioactively labeled antibody

im·mu·no·re·ac·tive \-,rē-'ak-tiv\ *adj* : reacting to particular antigens or haptens ⟨serum ∼ insulin⟩ ⟨∼ lymphocytes⟩ — im·mu·no·re·ac·tion \-'ak-shən\ *n* — im·mu·no·re·ac·tiv·i·ty \-(,)rē-,ak-'ti-və-tē\ *n*

im·mu·no·reg·u·la·to·ry \-'re-gyə-lə-,tōr-ē\ *adj* : of or relating to the regulation of the immune system ⟨∼ T cells⟩ — im·mu·no·reg·u·la·tion \-,re-gyə-'lā-shən\ *n*

im·mu·no·sor·bent \-'sor-bənt, -'zor-\ *adj* : relating to or using a substrate consisting of a specific antibody or antigen chemically combined with an insoluble substance (as cellulose) to selectively remove the corresponding specific antigen or antibody from solution — immunosorbent *n*

im·mu·no·stim·u·lant \-'sti-myə-lənt\ *n* : an agent that stimulates an immune response — immunostimulant *adj* — im·mu·no·stim·u·la·tion \-,sti-myə-'lā-shən\ *n*

im·mu·no·sup·pres·sion \-sə-'pre-shən\ *n* : suppression (as by drugs) of natural immune responses — im·mu·no·sup·press \-sə-'pres\ *vb* — im·mu·no·sup·pres·sant \-'pre-sənt\ *n or adj* — im·mu·no·sup·pres·sive \-'pre-səv\ *adj*

im·mu·no·sur·veil·lance \-sər-'vā-lən s\ *n* : a monitoring process of the immune system which detects and destroys neoplastic cells and which tends to break down in immunosuppressed individuals — called also *immunological surveillance*

im·mu·no·ther·a·py \-'ther-ə-pē\ *n, pl* -pies : treatment of or prophylaxis against disease by attempting to produce active or passive immunity — called also *immune therapy* — im·mu·no·ther·a·peu·tic \-,ther-ə-'pyü-tik\ *adj*

IMP \,ī-(,)em-'pē\ *n* : INOSINIC ACID

im·pact·ed \im-'pak-təd\ *adj* **1 a** : blocked by material (as feces) that is firmly packed or wedged in position ⟨an ∼ colon⟩ **b** : wedged or lodged in a bodily passage ⟨an ∼ mass of feces⟩ **2** : characterized by broken ends of bone driven together ⟨an ∼ fracture⟩ **3** *of a tooth* : wedged between the jawbone and another tooth ⟨an ∼ wisdom tooth⟩ — im·pac·tion \im-'pak-shən\ *n*

impaction fracture *n* : a fracture that is impacted

im·paired \im-'pard\ *adj* : being in a less than perfect or whole condition: as **a** : handicapped or functionally defective — often used in combination ⟨hearing-*impaired*⟩ **b** *chiefly Canad* : intoxicated by alcohol or narcotics ⟨driving while ~⟩ — **im·pair·ment** \-ˈpar-mənt\ *n*

im·pal·pa·ble \(ˌ)im-ˈpal-pə-bəl\ *adj* : incapable of being felt by touch

im·ped·ance \im-ˈpēd-ᵊns\ *n* : opposition to blood flow in the circulatory system

im·ped·i·ment \im-ˈpe-də-mənt\ *n* : something that impedes: *esp* : an organic obstruction to speech

imperfecta — see AMELOGENESIS IMPERFECTA, OSTEOGENESIS IMPERFECTA, OSTEOGENESIS IMPERFECTA CONGENITA, OSTEOGENESIS IMPERFECTA TARDA

im·per·fect fungus \(ˌ)im-ˈpər-fikt-\ *n* : any of various fungi (order Fungi Imperfecti syn. Deuteromycetes) of which only the asexual spore-producing stage is known

im·per·fo·rate \(ˌ)im-ˈpər-fə-rət, -ˌrāt\ *adj* : having no opening or aperture; *specif* : lacking the usual or normal opening ⟨an ~ hymen⟩ ⟨an ~ anus⟩

im·pe·ri·al gallon \im-ˈpir-ē-əl-\ *n* : GALLON 2

im·per·me·able \(ˌ)im-ˈpər-mē-ə-bəl\ *adj* : not permitting passage (as of a fluid) through its substance — **im·per·me·abil·i·ty** \-mē-ə-ˈbi-lə-tē\ *n*

im·pe·ti·gin·ized \ˌim-pə-ˈti-jə-ˌnīzd\ *adj* : affected with impetigo on top of an underlying dermatologic condition

im·pe·tig·i·nous \ˌim-pə-ˈti-jə-nəs\ *adj* : of, relating to, or resembling impetigo ⟨~ skin lesions⟩

im·pe·ti·go \ˌim-pə-ˈtē-(ˌ)gō, -ˈtī-\ *n* : an acute contagious staphylococcal or streptococcal skin disease characterized by vesicles, pustules, and yellowish crusts

impetigo con·ta·gi·o·sa \-kən-ˌtā-jē-ˈō-sə\ *n*

im·plant \ˈim-ˌplant\ *n* : something (as a graft, a small container of radioactive material for treatment of cancer, or a pellet containing hormones to be gradually absorbed) that is implanted esp. in tissue — **im·plant** \im-ˈplant\ *vb* — **im·plant·able** \-ˈplan-tə-bəl\ *adj*

im·plan·ta·tion \ˌim-ˌplan-ˈtā-shən\ *n* : the act or process of implanting or the state of being implanted: as **a** : the placement of a natural or artificial tooth in an artificially prepared socket in the jawbone **b** *in placental mammals* : the process of attachment of the embryo to the maternal uterine wall — called also *nidation* **c** : medical treatment by the insertion of an implant

im·plant·ee \ˌim-ˌplan-ˈtē\ *n* : the recipient of an implant

im·plan·tol·o·gist \ˌim-ˌplan-ˈtä-lə-jist\ *n* : a dentist who specializes in implantology

im·plan·tol·o·gy \-ˈtä-lə-jē\ *n, pl* **-gies** : a branch of dentistry dealing with dental implantation

im·plo·sion therapy \im-ˈplō-zhən-\ *n* : IMPLOSIVE THERAPY

im·plo·sive therapy \im-ˈplō-siv-\ *n* : psychotherapy esp. for treating phobias in which the patient is directly confronted with what he or she fears

imported fire ant *n* : either of two mound-building So. American fire ants of the genus *Solenopsis* (*S. invicta* and *S. richteri*) that have been introduced into the southeastern U.S. and can inflict stings requiring medical attention

im·po·tence \ˈim-pə-təns\ *n* : the quality or state of being impotent; *esp* : an abnormal physical or psychological state of a male characterized by inability to copulate because of failure to have or maintain an erection

im·po·ten·cy \-tən-sē\ *n, pl* **-cies** : IMPOTENCE

im·po·tent \ˈim-pə-tənt\ *adj* **1** : not potent **2** : unable to engage in sexual intercourse because of inability to have and maintain an erection; *broadly* : STERILE — usu. used of males

im·preg·nate \im-ˈpreg-ˌnāt, ˈim-ˌ\ *vb* **-nat·ed; -nat·ing 1 a** : to make pregnant **b** : to introduce sperm cells into : FERTILIZE **2** : to cause to be filled, imbued, permeated, or saturated — **im·preg·na·tion** \(ˌ)im-ˌpreg-ˈnā-shən\ *n*

im·pres·sion \im-ˈpre-shən\ *n* : an imprint in plastic material of the surfaces of the teeth and adjacent portions of the jaw from which a likeness may be produced in dentistry

im·print·ing \ˈim-ˌprint-iŋ, im-ˈ\ *n* : a rapid learning process that takes place early in the life of a social animal and establishes a behavior pattern (as recognition of and attraction to its own kind or a substitute) — **imprint** *vb*

im·pulse \ˈim-ˌpəls\ *n* **1** : a wave of excitation transmitted through tissues and esp. nerve fibers and muscles that results in physiological activity or inhibition **2** : a sudden spontaneous inclination or incitement to some usu. unpremeditated action — **im·pul·sive** \im-ˈpəl-siv\ *adj*

Im·u·ran \ˈi-myə-ˌran\ *trademark* — used for a preparation of azathioprine

in *abbr* inch

In *symbol* indium

¹in- or **il-** or **im-** or **ir-** *prefix* : not — usu. *il-* before *l* (*illegitimate*) and *im-* before *b, m,* or *p* (*imbalance*) (*immobile*) (*impalpable*) and *ir-* before *r* (*irreducible*) and *in-* before other sounds (*inoperable*)

²in- or **il-** or **im-** or **ir-** *prefix* : in : within : into : toward : on (*irradiation*) — usu. *il-* before *l, im-* before *b, m,* or *p, ir-* before *r,* and *in-* before other sounds

-in \ən,ᵊn, ˌin\ *n suffix* **1 a** : neutral

chemical compound ⟨insul*in*⟩ b : enzyme ⟨pancreat*in*⟩ c : antibiotic ⟨penicill*in*⟩ 2 : pharmaceutical product ⟨niac*in*⟩

in·ac·ti·vate \(ͺ)i-ˈnak-tə-ͺvāt\ *vb* **-vated; -vat·ing** : to make inactive: as a : to destroy certain biological activities of (~ the complement of normal serum by heat) b : to cause (as an infective agent) to lose disease-producing capacity (~ bacteria) — **in·ac·ti·va·tion** \i-ͺnak-tə-ˈvā-shən\ *n*

in·ac·tive \i-ˈnak-tiv\ *adj* : not active: as a : marked by deliberate or enforced absence of activity or effort (forced by illness to lead an ~ life) b *of a disease* : not progressing or fulminating : QUIESCENT c : chemically inert (~ charcoal) d : biologically inert esp. because of the loss of some quality (as infectivity or antigenicity) — **in·ac·tiv·i·ty** \i-ͺnak-ˈti-və-tē\ *n*

in·ad·e·quate \i-ˈna-də-kwət\ *adj* : not adequate; *specif* : lacking the capacity for psychological maturity or adequate social adjustment

in·a·ni·tion \ͺi-nə-ˈni-shən\ *n* : the exhausted condition that results from lack of food and water

in·ap·pe·tence \i-ˈna-pə-təns\ *n* : loss or lack of appetite

in·ap·pro·pri·ate \ͺi-nə-ˈprō-prē-ət\ *adj* : ABNORMAL 1

in·born \ˈin-ˈbórn\ *adj* : HEREDITARY, INHERITED (~ errors of metabolism)

in·breed·ing \ˈin-ͺbrē-diṇ\ *n* : the interbreeding of closely related individuals — **in·bred** \-ˈbred\ *adj* — **in·breed** \-ͺbrēd\ *vb* — compare OUTBREEDING

in·ca·pac·i·tant \ͺin-kə-ˈpa-sə-tənt\ *n* : a chemical or biological agent (as tear gas) used to temporarily incapacitate people or animals (as in war or a riot)

in·car·cer·at·ed \in-ˈkär-sə-ͺrā-təd\ *adj*, *of a hernia* : constricted but not strangulated

in·car·cer·a·tion \in-ͺkär-sə-ˈrā-shən\ *n* 1 : a confining or state of being confined 2 : abnormal retention or confinement of a body part; *specif* : a constriction of the neck of a hernial sac so that the hernial contents become irreducible

in·cest \ˈin-ͺsest\ *n* : sexual intercourse between persons so closely related that they are forbidden by law to marry; *also* : the statutory crime of such a relationship — **in·ces·tu·ous** \in-ˈses-chə-wəs\ *adj*

inch \ˈinch\ *n* : a unit of length equal to ¹⁄₃₆ yard or 2.54 centimeters

in·ci·dence \ˈin-sə-dəns, -ͺdens\ *n* : rate of occurrence or influence; *esp* : the rate of occurrence of new cases of a particular disease in a population being studied — compare PREVALENCE

in·cip·i·ent \in-ˈsi-pē-ənt\ *adj* : beginning to come into being or to become apparent (the ~ stage of a fever)

in·ci·sal \in-ˈsī-zəl\ *adj* : relating to, be-

ing, or involving the cutting edge or surface of a tooth (as an incisor)

in·cise \in-ˈsīz, -ˈsīs\ *vb* **in·cised; in·cis·ing** : to cut into : to make an incision in (*incised* the swollen tissue)

incised *adj*, *of a cut or wound* : made with or as if with a sharp knife or scalpel : clean and well-defined

in·ci·sion \in-ˈsi-zhən\ *n* 1 : a cut or wound of body tissue made esp. in surgery 2 : an act of incising something — **in·ci·sion·al** \-zhə-nəl\ *adj*

in·ci·sive \in-ˈsī-siv\ *adj* : INCISAL; *also* : of, relating to, or situated near the incisors

incisive canal *n* : a narrow branched passage that extends from the floor of the nasal cavity to the incisive fossa and transmits the nasopalatine nerve and a branch of the greater palatine artery

incisive fossa *n* : a depression on the front of the maxillary bone above the incisor teeth

in·ci·sor \in-ˈsī-zər\ *n* : a front tooth adapted for cutting; *esp* : any of the eight cutting human teeth that are located between the canines with four in the lower and four in the upper jaw

in·ci·su·ra \ͺin-ͺsī-ˈzhúr-ə, -sə-\ *n*, *pl* **in·ci·su·rae** \-ͺē, -ͺī\ 1 : a notch, cleft, or fissure of a body part or organ 2 : a downward notch in the curve recording aortic blood pressure that occurs between systole and diastole and is caused by backward flow of blood for a short time before the aortic valve closes

incisura an·gu·lar·is \-ͺaṇ-gyə-ˈlar-əs\ *n* : a notch or bend in the lesser curvature of the stomach near its pyloric end

in·cli·na·tion \ͺin-klə-ˈnā-shən\ *n* : a deviation from the true vertical or horizontal; *esp* : the deviation of the long axis of a tooth or of the slope of a cusp from the vertical

in·clu·sion \in-ˈklü-zhən\ *n* : something that is included; *esp* : a passive usu. temporary product of cell activity (as a starch grain) within the cytoplasm or nucleus

inclusion blennorrhea *n* : INCLUSION CONJUNCTIVITIS

inclusion body *n* : an inclusion, abnormal structure, or foreign cell within a cell; *specif* : an intracellular body that is characteristic of some virus diseases and that is the site of virus multiplication

inclusion conjunctivitis *n* : an infectious disease esp. of newborn infants characterized by acute conjunctivitis and the presence of large inclusion bodies and caused by a chlamydia (*C. trachomatis*)

inclusion disease *n* : CYTOMEGALIC INCLUSION DISEASE

in·co·her·ent \ͺin-kō-ˈhir-ənt, -ˈher-\ *adj* : lacking clarity or intelligibility usu. by reason of some emotional

stress ⟨∼ speech⟩ — in·co·her·ence
\-əns\ n — in·co·her·ent·ly adv
in·com·pat·i·ble \ˌin-kəm-ˈpa-tə-bəl\
adj 1 : unsuitable for use together because of chemical interaction or antagonistic physiological effects ⟨∼
drugs⟩ 2 of blood or serum : unsuitable for use in a particular transfusion because of the presence of agglutinins that act against the recipient's
red blood cells — in·com·pat·i·bil·i-
ty \-ˌpa-tə-ˈbi-lə-tē\ n
in·com·pe·tence \in-ˈkäm-pə-təns\ n 1
: lack of legal qualification 2 : inability of an organ or part to perform its
function adequately — in·com·pe·tent
\-tənt\ adj
in·com·pe·ten·cy \-tən-sē\ n, pl -cies : IN-
COMPETENCE
in·com·plete \ˌin-kəm-ˈplēt\ adj 1 of insect metamorphosis : having no pupal
stage between the immature stages
and the adult with the young insect
usu. resembling the adult — compare
COMPLETE 1 2 of a bone fracture : not
broken entirely across — compare
COMPLETE 2
incomplete dominance n : the property
of being expressed or inherited as a
semidominant gene or trait
in·con·stant \in-ˈkän-stənt\ adj : not always present ⟨an ∼ muscle⟩
in·con·ti·nence \in-ˈkänt-ᵊn-əns\ n 1
: inability or failure to restrain sexual
appetite 2 : inability of the body to
control the evacuative functions —
in·con·ti·nent \-ᵊnt\ adj
in·co·or·di·na·tion \ˌin-kō-ˌȯrd-ᵊn-ˈā-
shən\ n : lack of coordination esp. of
muscular movements resulting from
loss of voluntary control
in·cre·men·tal lines \ˌin-krə-ˈment-ᵊl-,
ˌin-\ n pl : lines seen in a tooth in section showing the periodic depositions
of dentin, enamel, and cementum occurring during growth
incremental lines of Ret·zi·us \-ˈret-sē-
əs\ n pl : incremental lines in the
enamel of a tooth
   Retzius, Magnus Gustaf (1842–1919),
   Swedish anatomist and anthropologist.
in·crus·ta·tion \ˌin-ˌkrəs-ˈtā-shən\ n 1
: the act of encrusting : the state of
being encrusted 2 : a crust or hard
coating
in·cu·bate \ˈiŋ-kyə-ˌbāt, ˈin-\ vb -bat-
ed; -bat·ing 1 : to maintain (as embryos or bacteria) under conditions favorable for hatching or development
2 : to undergo incubation
in·cu·ba·tion \ˌiŋ-kyə-ˈbā-shən, ˌin-\ n
1 : the act or process of incubating 2
: INCUBATION PERIOD
incubation period n : the period between the infection of an individual
by a pathogen and the manifestation
of the disease it causes
in·cu·ba·tor \ˈiŋ-kyə-ˌbā-tər, ˈin-\ n
: one that incubates; esp : an apparatus with a chamber used to provide

controlled environmental conditions
esp. for the cultivation of microorganisms or the care and protection of
premature or sick babies
in·cur·able \in-ˈkyur-ə-bəl\ adj : impossible to cure — in·cur·ably \-blē\ adv
in·cus \ˈiŋ-kəs\, n, pl in·cu·des \iŋ-ˈkyü-
(ˌ)dēz, ˈiŋ-kyə-ˌdēz\ : the middle
bone of a chain of three small bones
in the ear — called also anvil
IND \ˌī-(ˌ)en-ˈdē\ abbr investigational
new drug
in·dane·di·one \ˌin-dān-ˈdī-ˌōn\ or in-
dan·di·one \in-dan-\ n : any of a group
of synthetic anticoagulants
indecent assault n : a sexually aggressive act or series of acts exclusive of
rape committed against another person without consent
indecent exposure n : intentional exposure of part of one's body (as the genitalia) in a place where such exposure
is likely to be an offense against the
generally accepted standards of decency in a community
independent assortment n : formation
of random combinations of chromosomes in meiosis and of genes on different pairs of homologous chromosomes by the passage at random of
one of each diploid pair of homologous chromosomes into each gamete
independently of each other pair
In·der·al \ˈin-də-ˌral\ trademark —
used for a preparation of propranolol
in·de·ter·mi·nate \ˌin-di-ˈtər-mə-nət\
adj : relating to, being, or undergoing
indeterminate cleavage ⟨an ∼ egg⟩
indeterminate cleavage n : cleavage in
which all the early divisions produce
cells with the potencies of the entire
zygote — compare DETERMINATE
CLEAVAGE
in·dex \ˈin-ˌdeks\ n, pl in·dex·es or in-
di·ces \-də-ˌsēz\ 1 : a ratio or other
number derived from a series of observations and used as an indicator or
measure (as of a condition, property,
or phenomenon) 2 : the ratio of one
dimension of a thing (as an anatomical structure) to another dimension —
see CEPHALIC INDEX, CRANIAL INDEX
index case n : a case of a disease or condition which is discovered first and
which leads to the discovery of others in a family or group; also : the
first case of a contagious disease
index finger n : FOREFINGER
index of refraction n : the ratio of the
speed of radiation (as light) in one
medium to that in another medium —
called also refractive index
Indian hemp n : HEMP 1
indica — see CANNABIS INDICA
in·di·can \ˈin-də-ˌkan\ n : an indigo-
forming substance $C_8H_7NO_4S$ found
as a salt in urine and other animal fluids; also : its potassium salt C_8H_6-
KNO_4S
in·di·cate \ˈin-də-ˌkāt\ vb -cat·ed; -cat-
ing 1 : to be a fairly certain symptom

of : show the presence or existence of 2 : to call for esp. as treatment for a particular condition (radical surgery is *indicated*)

in-di-ca-tion \,in-də-'kā-shən\ *n* 1 : a symptom or particular circumstance that indicates the advisability or necessity of a specific medical treatment or procedure 2 : something that is indicated as advisable or necessary

in-di-ca-tor \'in-də-,kā-tər\ *n* : a substance (as a dye) used to show visually usu. by its capacity for color change the condition of a solution with respect to the presence of free acid or alkali or some other substance

indices *pl of* INDEX

indicis — see EXTENSOR INDICIS, EXTENSOR INDICIS PROPRIUS

in-dig-e-nous \in-'di-jə-nəs\ *adj* : having originated in and being produced, growing, or living naturally in a particular region or environment ⟨a disease ~ to the tropics⟩

in-di-gest-ible \,in-(,)dī-'jes-tə-bəl, -də-\ *adj* : not digestible : not easily digested — **in-di-gest-ibil-i-ty** \-,jes-tə-'bi-lə-tē\ *n*

in-di-ges-tion \-'jes-chən\ *n* 1 : inability to digest or difficulty in digesting food : incomplete or imperfect digestion of food 2 : a case or attack of indigestion

in-di-go car-mine \'in-di-,gō-'kär-mən, -,mīn\ *n* : a soluble blue dye $C_{16}H_8N_2Na_2O_8S_2$ that is used chiefly as a biological stain and food color and since it is rapidly excreted by the kidneys is used as a dye to mark ureteral structures (as in cystoscopy and catheterization)

in-dis-posed \,in-di-'spōzd\ *adj* : being usu. temporarily in poor physical health : slightly ill — **in-dis-po-si-tion** \(,)in-,dis-pə-'zi-shən\ *n*

in-di-um \'in-dē-əm\ *n* : a malleable fusible silvery metallic element — abbr. *In*; see ELEMENT table

individual psychology *n* : a modification of psychoanalysis developed by the Austrian psychologist Alfred Adler emphasizing feelings of inferiority and a desire for power as the primary motivating forces in human behavior

in-di-vid-u-a-tion \,in-də-,vi-jə-'wā-shən\ *n* : the process in the analytic psychology of C. G. Jung by which the self is formed by integrating elements of the conscious and unconscious mind — **in-di-vid-u-ate** \-'vi-jə-,wāt\ *vb*

In-do-cin \'in-də-sən\ *trademark* — used for a preparation of indomethacin

in-do-cy-a-nine green \,in-dō-'sī-ə-,nēn-, -nən-\ *n* : a green dye $C_{43}H_{47}N_2NaO_6S_2$ used esp. in testing liver blood flow and cardiac output

In-do-klon \'in-də-,klän\ *trademark* — used for a preparation of flurothyl

in-dole \'in-,dōl\ *n* : a crystalline compound C_8H_7N that is found in the in-

testines and feces as a decomposition product of proteins containing tryptophan; *also* : a derivative of indole

in-dole-ace-tic acid \,in-,dōl-ə-,sē-tik-\ *n* : a compound $C_{10}H_9NO_2$ formed from tryptophan in plants and animals that is present in small amounts in normal urine and acts as a growth hormone in plants

in-do-lent \'in-də-lənt\ *adj* 1 : causing little or no pain ⟨an ~ tumor⟩ 2 a : growing or progressing slowly ⟨an ~ disease⟩ b : slow to heal ⟨an ~ ulcer⟩ — **in-do-lence** \-ləns\ *n*

in-do-meth-a-cin \,in-dō-'me-thə-sən\ *n* : a nonsteroidal drug $C_{19}H_{16}ClNO_4$ with anti-inflammatory, analgesic, and antipyretic properties used esp. in treating arthritis — see INDOCIN

in-duce \in-'düs, -'dyüs\ *vb* **in-duced; in-duc-ing** 1 : to cause or bring about: as a : to cause to form through embryonic induction b : to cause or initiate by artificial means ⟨*induced* labor⟩ 2 : to produce anesthesia in

in-duc-er \-'dü-sər, -'dyü-\ *n* : one that induces; *specif* : a substance that is capable of activating a structural gene by combining with and inactivating a genetic repressor

in-duc-ible \in-'dü-sə-bəl, -'dyü-\ *adj* : capable of being induced; *esp* : formed by a cell in response to the presence of its substrate ⟨~ enzymes⟩ — **in-duc-ibil-i-ty** \in-,dü-sə-'bi-lə-tē, -,dyü-\ *n*

in-duc-tion \in-'dək-shən\ *n* 1 : the act of causing or bringing on or about ⟨~ of labor⟩; *specif* : the establishment of the initial state of anesthesia often with an agent other than that used subsequently to maintain the anesthetic state 2 a : arousal of a part or area (as of the retina) by stimulation of an adjacent part or area b : the sum of the processes by which the fate of embryonic cells is determined and differentiation brought about — **in-duct** \in-'dəkt\ *vb* — **in-duc-tive** \in-'dək-tiv\ *adj* — **in-duc-tive-ly** *adv*

in-duc-tor \in-'dək-tər\ *n* : one that inducts; *esp* : ORGANIZER

in-du-rat-ed \'in-dü-,rā-təd, -dyü-\ *adj* : having become firm or hard esp. by increase of fibrous elements ⟨~ tissue⟩ ⟨an ulcer with an ~ border⟩

in-du-ra-tion \,in-dü-'rā-shən, -dyü-\ *n* 1 : an increase in the fibrous elements in tissue commonly associated with inflammation and marked by loss of elasticity and pliability : SCLEROSIS 2 : a hardened mass or formation — **in-du-ra-tive** \'in-dü-,rā-tiv, -dyü-; in-'dür-ə-tiv, -'dyür-\ *adj*

in-du-si-um gris-e-um \in-,dü-zē-əm-'gri-zē-əm, -'dyü-, -zhē-\ *n* : a thin layer of gray matter over the dorsal surface of the corpus callosum

industrial disease *n* : OCCUPATIONAL DISEASE

in-dwell-ing \'in-,dwe-liŋ\ *adj* : left

within a bodily organ or passage to maintain drainage, prevent obstruction, or provide a route for administration of food or drugs — used of an implanted tube (as a catheter)

in·elas·tic \¡i-nə-ˈlas-tik\ *adj* : not elastic

in·ert \i-ˈnərt\ *adj* **1** : lacking the power to move **2** : deficient in active properties; *esp* : lacking a usual or anticipated chemical or biological action (an ~ drug) — **in·ert·ness** *n*

inert gas *n* : NOBLE GAS

in·er·tia \i-ˈnər-shə\ *n* : lack of activity or movement — used esp. of the uterus in labor when its contractions are weak or irregular

in ex·tre·mis \¡in-ik-ˈstrē-məs, -ˈstrā-\ *adv* : at the point of death

in·fan·cy \ˈin-fən-sē\ *n, pl* **-cies** **1** : early childhood **2** : the legal status of an infant

in·fant \ˈin-fənt\ *n* **1 a** : a child in the first year of life : BABY **b** : a child several years of age **2** : a person who is not of full age : MINOR — **infant** *adj*

in·fan·ti·cide \in-ˈfan-tə-ˌsīd\ *n* : the killing of an infant — **in·fan·ti·ci·dal** \-ˌfan-tə-ˈsīd-ᵊl\ *adj*

in·fan·tile \ˈin-fən-ˌtīl, -ˌtēl, -(ˌ)til\ *adj* **1** : of, relating to, or occurring in infants or infancy (~ eczema) **2** : suitable to or characteristic of an infant; *esp* : very immature

infantile amaurotic idiocy *n* **1** : TAY-SACHS DISEASE **2** : SANDHOFF'S DISEASE

infantile autism *n* : a severe autism that first occurs before 30 months of age — called also *Kanner's syndrome*

infantile paralysis *n* : POLIOMYELITIS

infantile scurvy *n* : acute scurvy during infancy caused by malnutrition — called also *Barlow's disease*

in·fan·til·ism \ˈin-fən-ˌtī-ˌli-zəm, -tə-; in-ˈfant-ᵊl-ˌi-\ *n* : retention of childish physical, mental, or emotional qualities in adult life; *esp* : failure to attain sexual maturity

infantum — see ROSEOLA INFANTUM

in·farct \ˈin-ˌfärkt, in-ˈ\ *n* : an area of necrosis in a tissue or organ resulting from obstruction of the local circulation by a thrombus or embolism — **in·farct·ed** \in-ˈfärk-təd\ *adj*

in·farc·tion \in-ˈfärk-shən\ *n* **1** : the process of forming an infarct **2** : INFARCT

in·fect \in-ˈfekt\ *vb* **1** : to contaminate with a disease-producing substance or agent (as bacteria) **2 a** : to communicate a pathogen or a disease to **b** *of a pathogenic organism* : to invade (an individual or organ) usu. by penetration — compare INFEST

in·fec·tant \in-ˈfek-tənt\ *n* : an agent of infection (as a bacterium or virus)

in·fec·tion \in-ˈfek-shən\ *n* **1** : an infective agent or material contaminated with an infective agent **2 a** : the state produced by the establishment of an infective agent in or on a suitable host

b : a disease resulting from infection : INFECTIOUS DISEASE **3** : an act or process of infecting; *also* : the establishment of a pathogen in its host after invasion

infectiosum — see ERYTHEMA INFECTIOSUM

in·fec·tious \in-ˈfek-shəs\ *adj* **1** : capable of causing infection **2** : communicable by invasion of the body of a susceptible organism — compare CONTAGIOUS 1 — **in·fec·tious·ly** *adv* — **in·fec·tious·ness** *n*

infectious abortion *n* : CONTAGIOUS ABORTION

infectious anemia *n* **1** : EQUINE INFECTIOUS ANEMIA **2** : FELINE INFECTIOUS ANEMIA

infectious bovine rhinotracheitis *n* : a disease of cattle caused by a virus serologically related to the virus causing herpes simplex in humans

infectious coryza *n* : an acute infectious respiratory disease of chickens that is caused by a bacterium of the genus *Haemophilus* (*H. paragallinarum* syn. *H. gallinarum*) and is characterized by catarrhal inflammation of the mucous membranes of the nasal passages and sinuses frequently with conjunctivitis and subcutaneous edema of the face and wattles and sometimes with pneumonia

infectious disease *n* : a disease caused by the entrance into the body of organisms (as bacteria) which grow and multiply there — see COMMUNICABLE DISEASE, CONTAGIOUS DISEASE

infectious enterohepatitis *n* : BLACKHEAD 2

infectious hepatitis *n* : HEPATITIS A

infectious jaundice *n* **1** : HEPATITIS A **2** : WEIL'S DISEASE

infectious laryngotracheitis *n* : a severe highly contagious and often fatal disease of chickens and pheasants that affects chiefly adult birds, is caused by a herpesvirus, and is characterized by inflammation of the trachea and larynx often marked by local necrosis and hemorrhage and by the formation of purulent or cheesy exudate interfering with breathing

infectious mononucleosis *n* : an acute infectious disease associated with Epstein-Barr virus and characterized by fever, swelling of lymph nodes, and lymphocytosis — called also *glandular fever, kissing disease, mono*

in·fec·tive \in-ˈfek-tiv\ *adj* : producing or capable of producing infection : INFECTIOUS

in·fec·tiv·i·ty \ˌin-ˌfek-ˈti-və-tē\ *n, pl* **-ties** : the quality of being infective : the ability to produce infection; *specif* : a tendency to spread rapidly from host to host — compare VIRULENCE b

in·fec·tor \in-ˈfek-tər\ *n* : one that infects

in·fe·ri·or \in-ᵊfir-ē-ər\ adj 1 : situated below and closer to the feet than another and esp. another similar part of an upright body esp. of a human being — compare SUPERIOR 1 2 : situated in a more posterior or ventral position in the body of a quadruped — compare SUPERIOR 2

inferior alveolar artery n : a branch of the maxillary artery that is distributed to the mucous membrane of the mouth and to the teeth of the lower jaw — called also mandibular artery, inferior dental artery

inferior alveolar nerve n : a branch of the mandibular nerve that is distributed to the teeth of the lower jaw and to the skin of the chin and the skin and mucous membrane of the lower lip — called also inferior alveolar, inferior dental nerve

inferior alveolar vein n : the vein accompanying the inferior alveolar artery

inferior articular process n : ARTICULAR PROCESS b

inferior cerebellar peduncle n : CEREBELLAR PEDUNCLE c

inferior colliculus n : either member of the posterior and lower pair of corpora quadrigemina that are situated next to the pons and together constitute one of the lower centers for hearing — compare SUPERIOR COLLICULUS

inferior concha n : NASAL CONCHA a

inferior constrictor n : a muscle of the pharynx that acts to constrict part of the pharynx in swallowing — called also constrictor pharyngis inferior, inferior pharyngeal constrictor muscle; compare MIDDLE CONSTRICTOR, SUPERIOR CONSTRICTOR

inferior dental artery n : INFERIOR ALVEOLAR ARTERY

inferior dental nerve n : INFERIOR ALVEOLAR NERVE

inferior extensor retinaculum n : EXTENSOR RETINACULUM 1a

inferior ganglion n 1 : the lower and larger of the two sensory ganglia of the glossopharyngeal nerve — called also petrosal ganglion; compare SUPERIOR GANGLION 1 2 : the lower of the two ganglia of the vagus nerve that forms a swelling just beyond the exit of the nerve from the jugular foramen — called also inferior vagal ganglion, nodose ganglion; compare SUPERIOR GANGLION 2

inferior gluteal artery n : GLUTEAL ARTERY b

inferior gluteal nerve n : GLUTEAL NERVE b

inferior hemorrhoidal artery n : RECTAL ARTERY a

inferior hemorrhoidal vein n : RECTAL VEIN a

inferior horn n : the cornu in the lateral ventricle of each cerebral hemisphere that curves downward into the temporal lobe — compare ANTERIOR HORN 2, POSTERIOR HORN 2

in·fe·ri·or·i·ty \(ˌ)in-ˌfir-ē-ᵊôr-ə-tē, -ᵊär-\ n, pl -ties : a condition or state of being or having a sense of being inferior or inadequate esp. with respect to one's apparent equals or to the world at large

inferiority complex n : an acute sense of personal inferiority resulting either in timidity or through overcompensation in exaggerated aggressiveness

inferior laryngeal artery n : LARYNGEAL ARTERY a

inferior laryngeal nerve n 1 : LARYNGEAL NERVE b — called also inferior laryngeal 2 : any of the terminal branches of the inferior laryngeal nerve

inferior longitudinal fasciculus n : a band of association fibers in each cerebral hemisphere that connects the occipital and temporal lobes

in·fe·ri·or·ly adv : in a lower position

inferior maxillary bone n : JAW Ib

inferior maxillary nerve n : MANDIBULAR NERVE

inferior meatus n : a space extending along the lateral wall of the nasal cavity between the inferior nasal concha and the floor of the nasal cavity — compare MIDDLE MEATUS, SUPERIOR MEATUS

inferior mesenteric artery n : MESENTERIC ARTERY a

inferior mesenteric ganglion n : MESENTERIC GANGLION a

inferior mesenteric plexus n : MESENTERIC PLEXUS a

inferior mesenteric vein n : MESENTERIC VEIN a

inferior nasal concha n : NASAL CONCHA a

inferior nuchal line n : NUCHAL LINE c

inferior oblique n : OBLIQUE b(2)

inferior olive n : a large gray nucleus that forms the interior of the olive on each side of the medulla oblongata — called also inferior olivary nucleus; see ACCESSORY OLIVARY NUCLEUS; compare SUPERIOR OLIVE

inferior ophthalmic vein n : OPHTHALMIC VEIN b

inferior orbital fissure n : ORBITAL FISSURE b

inferior pancreaticoduodenal artery n : PANCREATICODUODENAL ARTERY a

inferior pectoral nerve n : PECTORAL NERVE b

inferior peroneal retinaculum n : PERONEAL RETINACULUM b

inferior petrosal sinus n : PETROSAL SINUS b

inferior pharyngeal constrictor muscle n : INFERIOR CONSTRICTOR

inferior phrenic artery n : PHRENIC ARTERY b

inferior phrenic vein n : PHRENIC VEIN b

inferior radioulnar joint n : DISTAL RADIOULNAR JOINT

inferior ramus n : RAMUS b(2), c
inferior rectal artery n : RECTAL ARTERY a
inferior rectal vein n : RECTAL VEIN a
inferior rectus n : RECTUS 2d
inferior sagittal sinus n : SAGITTAL SINUS b
inferior temporal gyrus n : TEMPORAL GYRUS c
inferior thyroarytenoid ligament n : VOCAL LIGAMENT
inferior thyroid artery n : THYROID ARTERY b
inferior turbinate n : NASAL CONCHA a
inferior turbinate bone also **inferior tur·bi·nat·ed bone** \-ˈtər-bə-ˌnā-təd-\ n : NASAL CONCHA a
inferior ulnar collateral artery n : a small artery that arises from the brachial artery just above the elbow and branches to anastomose with other arteries in the region of the elbow — compare SUPERIOR ULNAR COLLATERAL ARTERY
inferior vagal ganglion n : INFERIOR GANGLION 2
inferior vena cava n : a vein that is the largest vein in the human body, is formed by the union of the two common iliac veins at the level of the fifth lumbar vertebra, and returns blood to the right atrium of the heart from bodily parts below the diaphragm
inferior vermis n : VERMIS 1b
inferior vesical n : VESICAL ARTERY b
inferior vesical artery n : VESICAL ARTERY b
inferior vestibular nucleus n : the one of the four vestibular nuclei on each side of the medulla oblongata that sends fibers down both sides of the spinal cord to synapse with motoneurons of the ventral roots
inferior vocal cords n pl : TRUE VOCAL CORDS
infero- comb form : below and (inferomedial)
in·fe·ro·me·di·al \ˌin-fə-rō-ˈmē-dē-əl\ adj : situated below and in the middle
in·fer·tile \in-ˈfərt-əl\ adj : not fertile : BARREN — compare STERILE 1 — **in·fer·til·i·ty** \ˌin-(ˌ)fər-ˈti-lə-tē\ n
in·fest \in-ˈfest\ vb : to live in or on as a parasite — compare INFECT — **in·fes·tant** \in-ˈfes-tənt\ n — **in·fes·ta·tion** \ˌin-ˌfes-ˈtā-shən\ n
in·fib·u·la·tion \(ˌ)in-ˌfi-byə-ˈlā-shən\ n : an act or practice of fastening by ring, clasp, or stitches the labia majora in girls and the prepuce in boys in order to prevent sexual intercourse
in·fil·trate \in-ˈfil-ˌtrāt, ˈin-(ˌ)fil-\ n : something that passes or is caused to pass into or through something by permeating or filtering; esp : a substance that passes into the bodily tissues and forms an abnormal accumulation ⟨a lung ∼⟩ — **infiltrate** vb — **in·fil·tra·tion** \ˌin-(ˌ)fil-ˈtrā-shən\ n — **in·fil·tra·tive** \ˈin-fil-ˌtrā-tiv, in-ˈfil-trə-\ adj

infiltration anesthesia n : anesthesia of an operative site accomplished by local injection of anesthetics
in·firm \in-ˈfərm\ adj : of poor or deteriorated vitality; esp : feeble from age
in·fir·ma·ry \in-ˈfər-mə-rē\ n, pl -ries : a place where the infirm or sick are lodged for care and treatment
in·fir·mi·ty \in-ˈfər-mə-tē\ n, pl -ties : the quality or state of being infirm; esp : an unsound, unhealthy, or debilitated state
in·flame \in-ˈflām\ vb **in·flamed**; **in·flam·ing** 1 : to cause inflammation in (bodily tissue) 2 : to become affected with inflammation
in·flam·ma·tion \ˌin-flə-ˈmā-shən\ n : a local response to cellular injury that is marked by capillary dilatation, leukocytic infiltration, redness, heat, pain, swelling, and often loss of function and that serves as a mechanism initiating the elimination of noxious agents and of damaged tissue — **in·flam·ma·to·ry** \in-ˈfla-mə-ˌtōr-ē\ adj
inflammatory bowel disease n : an inflammatory disease of the bowel: a : CROHN'S DISEASE b : ULCERATIVE COLITIS
in·flu·en·za \ˌin-(ˌ)flü-ˈen-zə\ n 1 a : an acute highly contagious virus disease that is caused by various strains of an orthomyxovirus belonging to three major types and that is characterized by sudden onset, fever, prostration, severe aches and pains, and progressive inflammation of the respiratory mucous membrane — often used with the letter A, B, or C to denote disease caused by a strain of virus of one of the three major types b : any human respiratory infection of undetermined cause — not used technically 2 : any of numerous febrile usu. virus diseases of domestic animals marked esp. by respiratory symptoms — **in·flu·en·zal** \-zəl\ adj
influenza vaccine n : a vaccine against influenza; specif : a mixture of strains of inactivated influenza virus from chick embryo culture
informed consent n : consent to surgery by a patient or to participation in a medical experiment by a subject after achieving an understanding of what is involved
infra- prefix 1 : below (infrahyoid) 2 : below in a scale or series (infrared)
in·fra·car·di·ac \ˌin-frə-ˈkär-dē-ˌak\ adj : situated below the heart
in·fra·cla·vic·u·lar \ˌin-frə-klə-ˈvi-kyə-lər\ adj : situated or occurring below the clavicle
in·fra·dia·phrag·mat·ic \ˌin-frə-ˌdī-ə-frəˈma-tik, -ˌfrag-\ adj : situated, occurring, or performed below the diaphragm (an ∼ abscess)
in·fra·gle·noid tubercle \ˌin-frə-ˈglē-ˌnoid-, -ˈgle-\ n : a tubercle on the scapula for the attachment of the long head of the triceps muscle

in·fra·hy·oid \ˌin-frə-ˈhī-ˌȯid\ adj : situated below the hyoid bone

infrahyoid muscle n : any of four muscles on each side that are situated next to the larynx and comprise the sternohyoid, sternothyroid, thyrohyoid, and omohyoid muscles

in·fra·mam·ma·ry \ˌin-frə-ˈma-mə-rē\ adj : situated or occurring below the mammary gland (~ pain)

in·fra·or·bit·al \ˌin-frə-ˈȯr-bət-ᵊl\ adj : situated beneath the orbit

infraorbital artery n : a branch or continuation of the maxillary artery that runs along the infraorbital groove with the infraorbital nerve and passes through the infraorbital foramen to give off branches which supply the face just below the eye

infraorbital fissure n : ORBITAL FISSURE b

infraorbital foramen n : an opening in the maxillary bone just below the lower rim of the orbit that gives passage to the infraorbital artery, nerve, and vein

infraorbital groove n : a groove in the middle of the posterior part of the bony floor of the orbit that gives passage to the infraorbital artery, vein, and nerve

infraorbital nerve n : a branch of the maxillary nerve that divides into branches distributed to the skin of the upper part of the cheek, the upper lip, and the lower eyelid

infraorbital vein n : a vein that drains the inferior structures of the orbit and the adjacent area of the face and that empties into the pterygoid plexus

in·fra·pa·tel·lar \ˌin-frə-pə-ˈte-lər\ adj : situated below the patella or its ligament

in·fra·red \ˌin-frə-ˈred\ adj 1 : lying outside the visible spectrum at its red end — used of radiation of wavelengths longer than those of visible light 2 : relating to, producing, or employing infrared radiation (~ therapy) — **infrared** n

in·fra·re·nal \ˌin-frə-ˈrēn-ᵊl\ adj : situated or occurring below the kidneys

in·fra·spi·na·tus \ˌin-frə-spī-ˈnā-təs\ n, pl -na·ti \-ˈnā-ˌtī\ : a muscle that occupies the chief part of the infraspinous fossa of the scapula and rotates the arm laterally

in·fra·spi·nous \ˌin-frə-ˈspī-nəs\ adj : lying below a spine; esp : lying below the spine of the scapula

infraspinous fossa n : the part of the dorsal surface of the scapula below the spine of the scapula

in·fra·tem·po·ral \ˌin-frə-ˈtem-pə-rəl\ adj : situated below the temporal fossa

infratemporal crest n : a transverse ridge on the outer surface of the greater wing of the sphenoid bone that divides it into a superior portion that contributes to the formation of

the temporal fossa and an inferior portion that contributes to the formation of the infratemporal fossa

infratemporal fossa n : a fossa that is bounded above by the plane of the zygomatic arch, laterally by the ramus of the mandible, and medially by the pterygoid plate, and that contains the masseter and pterygoid muscles and the mandibular nerve

in·fra·ten·to·ri·al \ˌin-frə-ten-ˈtōr-ē-əl\ adj : occurring or made below the tentorium cerebelli (~ burr holes)

in·fun·dib·u·lar \ˌin-(ˌ)fən-ˈdi-byə-lər\ adj : of, relating to, affecting, situated near, or having an infundibulum

infundibular process n : NEURAL LOBE

infundibular recess n : a funnel-shaped downward prolongation of the floor of the third ventricle of the brain

in·fun·dib·u·lo·pel·vic ligament \ˌin-fən-ˌdi-byə-lō-ˈpel-vik-\ n : SUSPENSORY LIGAMENT OF THE OVARY

in·fun·dib·u·lum \ˌin-(ˌ)fən-ˈdi-byə-ləm\ n, pl -la \-lə\ : any of various conical or dilated organs or parts: as a : the hollow conical process of gray matter that constitutes the stalk of the neurohypophysis by which the pituitary gland is continuous with the brain b : any of the small spaces having walls beset with air sacs in which the bronchial tubes terminate in the lungs c : CONUS ARTERIOSUS d : the abdominal opening of a fallopian tube

in·fu·sion \in-ˈfyü-zhən\ n 1 : the introducing of a solution (as of salt) esp. into a vein; also : the solution so used 2 a : the steeping or soaking usu. in water of a substance (as a plant drug) in order to extract its soluble constituents or principles — compare DECOCTION 1 b : the liquid extract obtained by this process — **in·fuse** \in-ˈfyüz\ vb

infusion pump n : a device that releases a measured amount of a substance in a specific period of time

in·ges·ta \in-ˈjes-tə\ n pl : material taken into the body by way of the digestive tract

in·gest·ible \in-ˈjes-tə-bəl\ adj : capable of being ingested (~ capsules)

in·ges·tion \in-ˈjes-chən\ n : the taking of material (as food) into the digestive system — **in·gest** \-ˈjest\ vb — **in·gest·ive** \in-ˈjes-tiv\ adj

in·grow·ing \ˈin-ˌgrō-iŋ\ adj : INGROWN

in·grown \ˈin-ˌgrōn\ adj : grown in; specif : having the normally free tip or edge embedded in the flesh (an ~ toenail)

in·growth \ˈin-ˌgrōth\ n 1 : a growing inward (as to fill a void) (~ of cells) 2 : something that grows in or into a space (lymphoid ~s)

in·gui·nal \ˈiŋ-gwən-ᵊl\ adj 1 : of, relating to, or situated in the region of the groin 2 : ILIAC 2

inguinal canal n 1 : a passage in the male through which the testis descends into the scrotum and in which the spermatic cord lies **2** : a passage in the female accommodating the round ligament

inguinale — see GRANULOMA INGUINALE, LYMPHOGRANULOMA INGUINALE

inguinal hernia *n* : a hernia into the inguinal canal

inguinal ligament *n* : the thickened lower border of the aponeurosis of the external oblique muscle of the abdomen — called also *Poupart's ligament*

inguinal node *n* : any of the superficial lymph nodes of the groin

inguinal ring *n* : either of two openings in the fasciae of the abdominal muscles on each side of the body that are the inlet and outlet of the inguinal canal, give passage to the spermatic cord in the male and the round ligament in the female, and are a frequent site of hernia formation: **a** : DEEP INGUINAL RING **b** : SUPERFICIAL INGUINAL RING

INH *abbr* isoniazid

¹**in·hal·ant** \in-ˈhā-lənt\ *n* : something (as an allergen) that is inhaled

²**inhalant** *adj* : used for inhaling or constituting an inhalant ⟨~ anesthetics⟩

in·ha·la·tion \ˌin-hə-ˈlā-shən, ˌin-əl-ˈā-\ *n* **1** : the act or an instance of inhaling; *specif* : the action of drawing air into the lungs by means of a complex of essentially reflex actions **2** : material (as medication) to be taken in by inhaling — **in·ha·la·tion·al** \-shə-nəl\ *adj*

inhalation therapist *n* : a specialist in inhalation therapy

inhalation therapy *n* : the therapeutic use of inhaled gases and esp. oxygen (as in the treatment of respiratory disease)

in·ha·la·tor \ˈin-hə-ˌlā-tər, ˈin-əl-ˌā-\ *n* : a device providing a mixture of oxygen and carbon dioxide for breathing that is used esp. in conjunction with artificial respiration — compare INHALER

in·hale \in-ˈhāl\ *vb* **in·haled; in·hal·ing** : to breathe in

inhalent *var of* INHALANT

in·hal·er \in-ˈhā-lər\ *n* : a device by means of which usu. medicinal material is inhaled — compare INHALATOR

in·her·it \in-ˈher-ət\ *vb* : to receive from a parent or ancestor by genetic transmission — **in·her·it·able** \in-ˈher-ə-tə-bəl\ *adj* — **in·her·it·abil·i·ty** \-ˌher-ə-tə-ˈbi-lə-tē\ *n*

in·her·i·tance \in-ˈher-ə-təns\ *n* **1** : the reception of genetic qualities by transmission from parent to offspring **2** : the sum total of genetic characters or qualities transmitted from parent to offspring — compare PHENOTYPE

in·hib·in \in-ˈhi-bən\ *n* : a hormone that is secreted by Sertoli cells in the male and granulosa cells in the female and

that inhibits the secretion of follicle-stimulating hormone

in·hib·it \in-ˈhi-bət\ *vb* **1 a** : to restrain from free or spontaneous activity esp. through the operation of inner psychological or external social constraints **b** : to check or restrain the force or vitality of ⟨~ aggressive tendencies⟩ **2 a** : to reduce or suppress the activity of ⟨~ a nerve⟩ **b** : to retard or prevent the formation of **c** : to retard, interfere with, or prevent (a process or reaction) ⟨~ ovulation⟩ — **in·hib·i·tor** \in-ˈhi-bə-tər\ *n* — **in·hib·i·to·ry** \in-ˈhi-bə-ˌtōr-ē\ *adj*

in·hib·it·able \-bə-tə-bəl\ *adj* : capable of being inhibited

in·hi·bi·tion \ˌin-hə-ˈbi-shən, ˌi-nə-\ *n* : the act or an instance of inhibiting or the state of being inhibited: as **a** (1) : a restraining of the function of a bodily organ or an agent (as an enzyme) ⟨~ of the heartbeat⟩ (2) : interference with or retardation or prevention of a process or activity ⟨~ of bacterial growth⟩ **b** (1) : a desirable restraint or check upon the free or spontaneous instincts or impulses of an individual guided or directed by social and cultural forces (2) : a neurotic restraint upon a normal or beneficial impulse or activity caused by psychological inner conflicts or by sociocultural forces

inhibitory postsynaptic potential *n* : increased negativity of the membrane potential of a neuron on the postsynaptic side of a nerve synapse that is caused by a neurotransmitter and that tends to inhibit the neuron — abbr. *IPSP*

in·i·en·ceph·a·lus \ˌi-nē-in-ˈse-fə-ləs\ *n* : a teratological fetus with a fissure in the occiput through which the brain protrudes — **in·i·en·ceph·a·ly** \-lē\ *n*

in·i·on \ˈi-nē-ˌän, -ən\ *n* : OCCIPITAL PROTUBERANCE a

initiation codon *n* : a codon that stimulates the binding of a transfer RNA which starts protein synthesis — called also *initiator codon*; compare TERMINATOR

ini·ti·a·tor \i-ˈni-shē-ˌā-tər\ *n* **1** : a substance that initiates a chemical reaction **2** : a substance that produces an irreversible change in bodily tissue causing it to respond to other substances which promote the growth of tumors

in·ject \in-ˈjekt\ *vb* : to introduce a fluid into (a living body); *also* : to treat (an individual) with injections

¹**in·ject·able** \-ˈjek-tə-bəl\ *adj* : capable of being injected ⟨~ medications⟩

²**injectable** *n* : an injectable substance (as a drug)

in·jec·tion \in-ˈjek-shən\ *n* **1 a** : the act or an instance of injecting a drug or other substance into the body **b** : a solution (as of a drug) intended for injection (as by catheter or hypodermic syringe) either under or through the skin or into the tissues, a vein, or a body cavity **2** : the state of being injected : CONGESTION — see CIRCUMCORNEAL INJECTION

in·jure \'in-jər\ vb **in·jured; in·jur·ing 1** : to inflict bodily hurt on **2** : to impair the soundness of — **in·ju·ri·ous** \in-'jur-ē-əs\ adj — **in·ju·ri·ous·ly** adv

in·ju·ry \'in-jə-rē\ n, pl **-ries** : hurt, damage, or loss sustained

injury potential n : the difference in electrical potential between the injured and uninjured parts of a nerve or muscle

inkblot test n : any of several psychological tests (as a Rorschach test) based on the interpretation of irregular figures (as blots of ink)

in·lay \'in-ılā\ n **1** : a tooth filling shaped to fit a cavity and then cemented into place **2** : a piece of tissue (as bone) laid into the site of missing tissue to cover a defect

in·let \'in-ılet, -lət\ n : the upper opening of a bodily cavity; esp : that of the cavity of the true pelvis bounded by the pelvic brim

in·mate \'in-ımāt\ n : a person confined (as in a psychiatric hospital) esp. for a long time

in·nards \'i-nərdz\ n pl : the internal organs of a human being or animal; esp : VISCERA

in·nate \i-'nāt, 'i-ı\ adj : existing in, belonging to, or determined by factors present in an individual from birth : INBORN (~ behavior) — **in·nate·ly** adv — **in·nate·ness** n

inner cell mass n : the portion of the blastocyst of an embryo that is destined to become the embryo proper

inner-directed adj : directed in thought and action by one's own scale of values as opposed to external norms — **inner-direction** n

inner ear n : the essential organ of hearing and equilibrium that is located in the temporal bone, is innervated by the auditory nerve, and includes the vestibule, the semicircular canals, and the cochlea — called also internal ear

in·ner·vate \i-'nər-ıvāt, 'i-(ı)nər-\ vb **-vat·ed; -vat·ing 1** : to supply with nerves **2** : to arouse or stimulate (a nerve or an organ) to activity — **in·ner·va·tion** \ıi-(ı)nər-'vā-shən, ıi-ınər-\ n

in·no·cent \'i-nə-sənt\ adj : lacking capacity to injure : BENIGN (an ~ tumor) (~ heart murmurs)

innominata — see SUBSTANTIA INNOMINATA

in·nom·i·nate artery \i-'nä-mə-nət-\ n : BRACHIOCEPHALIC ARTERY

innominate bone n : HIPBONE

innominate vein n : BRACHIOCEPHALIC VEIN

ino- comb form : fiber : fibrous (inotropic)

in·oc·u·lant \i-'nä-kyə-lənt\ n : INOCULUM

in·oc·u·late \-ılāt\ vb **-lat·ed; -lat·ing 1** : to communicate a disease to (an organism) by inserting its causative agent into the body **2** : to introduce (as a microorganism) into a suitable situation for growth **3** : to introduce immunologically active material (as an antibody or antigen) into esp. in order to treat or prevent a disease

in·oc·u·la·tion \i-ınä-kyə-'lā-shən\ n **1** : the act or process or an instance of inoculating: as **a** : the introduction of a pathogen or antigen into a living organism to stimulate the production of antibodies **b** : the introduction of a vaccine or serum into a living organism to confer immunity **2** : INOCULUM

in·oc·u·lum \i-'nä-kyə-ləm\ n, pl **-la** \-lə\ : material used for inoculation

in·op·er·a·ble \i-'nä-pə-rə-bəl\ adj : not treatable or remediable by surgery (~ cancer) — **in·op·er·a·bil·i·ty** \i-ınä-pə-rə-'bi-lə-tē\ n

in·or·gan·ic \ıin-òr-'ga-nik\ adj **1** : being or composed of matter other than plant or animal (an ~ heart) **2** : of, relating to, or dealt with by a branch of chemistry concerned with substances not usu. classed as organic — **in·or·gan·i·cal·ly** adv

in·or·gas·mic \ıin-òr-'gaz-mik\ adj : not experiencing or having experienced orgasm

ino·sin·ate \i-'nō-si-ınāt\ n : a salt or ester of inosinic acid

ino·sine \'i-nə-ısēn, 'ī-, -sən\ n : a crystalline nucleoside $C_{10}H_{12}N_4O_5$

ino·sin·ic acid \ıi-nə-'si-nik-, ıī-\ n : a nucleotide $C_{10}H_{13}N_4O_8P$ that is found in muscle and is formed by deamination of AMP — called also IMP

ino·si·tol \i-'nō-sə-ıtòl, ī-, -ıtōl\ n : any of several stereoisomeric cyclic alcohols $C_6H_{12}O_6$; esp : MYOINOSITOL

ino·tro·pic \ıē-nə-'trō-pik, ıi-, -'trä-\ adj : relating to or influencing the force of muscular contractions

in·pa·tient \'in-ıpā-shənt\ n : a hospital patient who receives lodging and food as well as treatment — compare OUTPATIENT

in·quest \'in-ıkwest\ n : a judicial or official inquiry esp. before a jury to determine the cause of a violent or unexpected death (a coroner's ~)

in·sane \(ı)in-'sān\ adj **1** : mentally disordered : exhibiting insanity **2** : used by, typical of, or intended for insane persons — **in·sane·ly** adv

in·san·i·tary \(ı)in-'sa-nə-ıter-ē\ adj : unclean enough to endanger health

in·san·i·ty \in-'sa-nə-tē\ n, pl **-ties 1 a** : a deranged state of the mind usu. occurring as a specific disorder (as schizophrenia) and usu. excluding such states as mental retardation, psychoneurosis, and various character disorders **b** : a mental disorder **2** : such unsoundness of mind or lack of understanding as prevents one from having the mental capacity required by law to enter into a particular relationship, status, or transaction or as removes one from criminal or civil responsibility

in·scrip·tion \in-ˈskrip-shən\ n : the part of a medical prescription that contains the names and quantities of the drugs to be compounded

in·sect \ˈin-ˌsekt\ n : any of a class (Insecta) of arthropods with well-defined head, thorax, and abdomen, three pairs of legs, and typically one or two pairs of wings — **insect** adj

in·sec·ti·cide \in-ˈsek-tə-ˌsīd\ n : an agent that destroys insects — **in·sec·ti·cid·al** \(ˌ)in-ˌsek-tə-ˈsīd-ᵊl\ adj

in·se·cu·ri·ty \ˌin-si-ˈkyúr-ə-tē\ n, pl -ties : a feeling of apprehensiveness and uncertainty : lack of assurance or stability — **in·se·cure** \-ˈkyúr\ adj

in·sem·i·nate \in-ˈse-mə-ˌnāt\ vb -nat·ed; -nat·ing : to introduce semen into the genital tract of (a female) — **in·sem·i·na·tion** \-ˌse-mə-ˈnā-shən\ n

in·sem·i·na·tor \-ˌnā-tər\ n : one that inseminates cattle artificially

in·sen·si·ble \(ˌ)in-ˈsen-sə-bəl\ adj 1 : incapable or bereft of feeling or sensation: as a : UNCONSCIOUS b : lacking sensory perception or ability to react c : lacking emotional response : APATHETIC 2 : not perceived by the senses (~ perspiration) — **in·sen·si·bil·i·ty** \(ˌ)in-ˌsen-sə-ˈbi-lə-tē\ n

in·sert \in-ˈsərt\ vb, of a muscle : to be in attachment to the part to be moved

inserted adj : attached by natural growth (as a muscle or tendon)

in·ser·tion \in-ˈsər-shən\ n 1 : the part of a muscle by which it is attached to the part to be moved — compare ORIGIN 2 2 : the mode or place of attachment of an organ or part 3 a : a section of genetic material inserted into an existing gene sequence b : the mutational process producing a genetic insertion — **in·ser·tion·al** \-shə-nəl\ adj

in·sid·i·ous \in-ˈsi-dē-əs\ adj : developing so gradually as to be well established before becoming apparent (an ~ disease) — **in·sid·i·ous·ly** adv

in·sight \ˈin-ˌsīt\ n 1 : understanding or awareness of one's mental or emotional condition; esp : recognition that one is mentally ill 2 : immediate and clear understanding (as seeing the solution to a problem or the means to reaching a goal) that takes place without recourse to overt trial-and-error behavior — **in·sight·ful** \ˈin-ˌsīt-fəl, in-ˈ\ adj — **in·sight·ful·ly** adv

insipidus — see DIABETES INSIPIDUS

in si·tu \in-ˈsī-(ˌ)tü, -ˈsi-, -ˈsē-, -(ˌ)tyü, -(ˌ)chü\ adv or adj : in the natural or original position

in·som·nia \in-ˈsäm-nē-ə\ n : prolonged and usu. abnormal inability to obtain adequate sleep

¹**in·som·ni·ac** \-nē-ˌak\ n : one affected with insomnia

²**insomniac** adj : affected with insomnia

in·spec·tion \in-ˈspek-shən\ n : visual observation of the body in the course of a medical examination — compare PALPATION 2 — **in·spect** \in-ˈspekt\ vb

in·spi·ra·tion \ˌin-spə-ˈrā-shən\ n : the drawing of air into the lungs — **in·spi·ra·to·ry** \in-ˈspī-rə-ˌtōr-ē, ˈin-spə-rə-\ adj

inspiratory capacity n : the total amount of air that can be drawn into the lungs after normal expiration

inspiratory reserve volume n : the maximal amount of additional air that can be drawn into the lungs by determined effort after normal inspiration — compare EXPIRATORY RESERVE VOLUME

in·spire \in-ˈspīr\ vb in·spired; in·spir·ing : to draw in by breathing : breathe in : INHALE

in·spis·sat·ed \in-ˈspi-sā-təd, ˈin-spə-ˌsā-\ adj : made or having become thickened in consistency

in·sta·bil·i·ty \in-stə-ˈbi-lə-tē\ n, pl -ties : lack of emotional or mental stability

in·step \ˈin-ˌstep\ n : the arched middle portion of the human foot in front of the ankle joint; esp : its upper surface

in·still \in-ˈstil\ vb in·stilled; in·still·ing : to cause to enter esp. drop by drop (~ medication into the infected eye) — **in·stil·la·tion** \ˌin-stə-ˈlā-shən\ n

in·stinct \ˈin-ˌstiŋkt\ n 1 : a largely inheritable and unalterable tendency of an organism to make a complex and specific response to environmental stimuli without involving reason 2 : behavior that is mediated by reactions below the conscious level — **in·stinc·tive** \in-ˈstiŋk-tiv\ adj — **in·stinc·tive·ly** adv — **in·stinc·tu·al** \in-ˈstiŋk-chə-wəl\ adj

in·sti·tu·tion·al·ize \ˌin-stə-ˈtü-shə-nə-ˌlīz, -ˈtyü-\ vb 1 : to place in or commit to the care of a specialized institution (as for the mentally ill) 2 : to accustom (a person) so firmly to the care and supervised routine of an institution as to make incapable of managing a life outside — **in·sti·tu·tion·al·iza·tion** \-ˌtü-shə-nə-lə-ˈzā-shən, -ˌtyü-\ n

in·stru·men·tal \ˌin-strə-ˈmen-təl\ adj : OPERANT (~ conditioning)

in·stru·men·ta·tion \ˌin-strə-mən-ˈtā-shən, -ˌmen-\ n : a use of or operation with instruments

in·suf·fi·cien·cy \ˌin-sə-ˈfi-shən-sē\ n, pl -cies : the quality or state of not being sufficient: as a : lack of adequate supply of something b : lack of physical power or capacity; esp : inability of an organ or bodily part to function normally — compare AORTIC REGURGITATION — **in·suf·fi·cient** \-shənt\ adj

in·suf·fla·tion \ˌin-sə-ˈflā-shən\ n : the act of blowing something (as a gas) into a body cavity (as the uterus) — **in·suf·flate** \'in-sə-ˌflāt, in-'sə-ˌflāt\ *vb* — **in·suf·fla·tor** \'in-sə-ˌflā-tər, in-'sə-ˌflā-tər\ *n*

in·su·la \'in-sü-lə, -syü-, -shü-\ *n, pl* **in·su·lae** \-ˌlē, -ˌlī\ : the lobe in the center of the cerebral hemisphere that is situated deeply between the lips of the fissure of Sylvius — called also *central lobe, island of Reil*

in·su·lar \-lər\ *adj* : of or relating to an island of cells or tissue (as the islets of Langerhans or the insula)

in·su·lin \'in-sə-lən\ *n* : a protein pancreatic hormone secreted by the islets of Langerhans that is essential esp. for the metabolism of carbohydrates and is used in the treatment and control of diabetes mellitus — see ILETIN

in·su·lin·ae·mia *chiefly Brit var of* INSULINEMIA

in·su·lin·ase \-lə-ˌnās, -ˌnāz\ *n* : an enzyme found esp. in liver that inactivates insulin

insulin–dependent diabetes mellitus *n* : a form of diabetes mellitus that usu. develops during childhood or adolescence and is characterized by a severe deficiency in insulin secretion resulting from atrophy of the islets of Langerhans and causing hyperglycemia and a marked tendency toward ketoacidosis — abbr. *IDDM*; called also *juvenile diabetes, juvenile-onset diabetes, insulin-dependent diabetes, type I diabetes*

in·su·lin·emia \ˌin-sə-lə-'nē-mē-ə\ *n* : the presence of an abnormally high concentration of insulin in the blood

in·su·lin·o·ma \ˌin-sə-lə-'nō-mə\ *n, pl* **-mas** *or* **-ma·ta** \-mə-tə\ : a usu. benign insulin-secreting tumor of the islets of Langerhans

in·su·li·no·tro·pic \ˌin-sə-ˌli-nə-'trō-pik, -'trä-\ *adj* : stimulating or affecting the production and activity of insulin ⟨an ~ hormone⟩

insulin shock *n* : hypoglycemia associated with the presence of excessive insulin in the system and characterized by progressive development of coma

in·su·lo·ma \ˌin-sə-'lō-mə\ *n, pl* **-mas** *or* **-ma·ta** \-mə-tə\ : INSULINOMA

in·sult \'in-ˌsəlt\ *n* **1** : injury to the body or one of its parts **2** : something that causes or has a potential for causing insult to the body — **insult** *vb*

in·tact \in-'takt\ *adj* **1** : physically and functionally complete **2** : mentally unimpaired — **in·tact·ness** *n*

in·te·gra·tion \ˌin-tə-'grā-shən\ *n* **1** : coordination of mental processes into a normal effective personality or with the individual's environment **2** : the process by which the different parts of an organism are made a functional and structural whole esp. through the activity of the nervous system and of hormones — **in·te·grate** \'in-tə-ˌgrāt\ *vb* — **in·te·gra·tive** \'in-tə-ˌgrā-tiv\ *adj*

in·teg·ri·ty \in-'te-grə-tē\ *n, pl* **-ties** : an unimpaired condition ⟨~ of brain function⟩

in·teg·u·ment \in-'te-gyə-mənt\ *n* : an enveloping layer (as a skin or membrane) of an organism or one of its parts — **in·teg·u·men·ta·ry** \-'men-tə-rē\ *adj*

in·tel·lec·tu·al·ize \ˌint-ᵊl-'ek-chə-wə-ˌlīz\ *vb* **-ized; -iz·ing** : to avoid conscious recognition of the emotional basis of (an act or feeling) by substituting a superficially plausible explanation — **in·tel·lec·tu·al·iza·tion** \-ˌek-chə-wə-lə-'zā-shən\ *n*

in·tel·li·gence \in-'te-lə-jəns\ *n* **1 a** : the ability to learn or understand or to deal with new or trying situations **b** : the ability to apply knowledge to manipulate one's environment or to think abstractly as measured by objective criteria (as tests) **2** : mental acuteness — **in·tel·li·gent** \-jənt\ *adj* — **in·tel·li·gent·ly** *adv*

intelligence quotient *n* : a number used to express the apparent relative intelligence of a person that is the ratio multiplied by 100 of the mental age as reported on a standardized test to the chronological age — called also *IQ*

intelligence test *n* : a test designed to determine the relative mental capacity of a person

intensifying screen *n* : a fluorescent screen placed next to an X-ray photographic film in order to intensify the image initially produced on the film by the action of X rays

in·ten·si·ty \in-'ten-sə-tē\ *n, pl* **-ties** : SATURATION 4

in·ten·sive \in-'ten-siv\ *adj* : of, relating to, or marked by intensity; *esp* : involving the use of large doses or substances having great therapeutic activity — **in·ten·sive·ly** *adv*

intensive care *adj* : having special medical facilities, services, and monitoring devices to meet the needs of gravely ill patients ⟨an *intensive care* unit⟩ — **intensive care** *n*

in·ten·tion \in-'ten-chən\ *n* : a process or manner of healing of incised wounds — see FIRST INTENTION, SECOND INTENTION

intention tremor *n* : a slow tremor of the extremities that increases on attempted voluntary movement and is observed in certain diseases (as multiple sclerosis) of the nervous system

inter- *comb form* : between : among ⟨*intercellular*⟩ ⟨*intercostal*⟩

in·ter·al·ve·o·lar \ˌin-tə-ral-'vē-ə-lər\ *adj* : situated between alveoli esp. of the lungs

in·ter·atri·al septum \ˌin-tər-'ā-trē-əl-\ *n* : the wall separating the right and left atria of the heart — called also *atrial septum*

in·ter·au·ral \-'ȯr-əl\ *adj* **1** : situated between or connecting the ears **2** : of or relating to sound reception and perception by each ear considered separately

in·ter·body \'in-tər-ˌbä-dē\ adj : performed between the bodies of two contiguous vertebrae (an ~ fusion)

in·ter·breed \ˌin-tər-'brēd\ -'bred \-'bred\ vb -bred \-'bred\; -breed·ing : to breed together: as **a** : CROSSBREED **b** : to breed within a closed population

in·ter·ca·lat·ed disk \in-'tər-kə-ˌlā-təd-\ n : any of the apparent striations across cardiac muscle that are actually membranes separating adjacent cells

intercalated duct n : a duct from a tubule or acinus of the pancreas that drains into an intralobular duct

in·ter·cap·il·lary \ˌin-tər-'ka-pə-ˌler-ē\ adj : situated between capillaries (~ thrombi)

in·ter·car·pal \-'kär-pəl\ adj : situated between, occurring between, or connecting carpal bones

in·ter·cav·ern·ous \-'ka-vər-nəs\ adj : situated between and connecting the cavernous sinuses behind and in front of the pituitary gland (~ sinus)

in·ter·cel·lu·lar \-'sel-yə-lər\ adj : occurring between cells (~ spaces) — **in·ter·cel·lu·lar·ly** adv

in·ter·con·dy·lar \-'kän-də-lər\ adj : situated between two condyles

in·ter·con·dy·loid \-'kän-də-ˌloid\ adj : INTERCONDYLAR

¹in·ter·cos·tal \ˌin-tər-'käs-təl\ adj : situated or extending between the ribs (~ spaces) (~ muscles)

²intercostal n : an intercostal part or structure (as a muscle or nerve)

intercostal artery n : any of the arteries supplying or lying in the intercostal spaces: **a** : any of the arteries branching in front directly from the internal thoracic artery — called also *anterior intercostal artery* **b** : any of the arteries that branch from the costocervical trunk of the subclavian artery — called also *posterior intercostal artery*

intercostal muscle n : any of the short muscles that extend between the ribs and serve to move the ribs in respiration: **a** : any of 11 muscles on each side between the vertebrae and the junction of the ribs and their cartilages — called also *external intercostal muscle* **b** : any of 11 muscles on each side between the sternum and the line on a rib marking an insertion of the iliocostalis — called also *internal intercostal muscle*

intercostal nerve n : any of 11 nerves on each side of which each is an anterior division of a thoracic nerve lying between a pair of adjacent ribs

intercostal vein n : any of the veins of the intercostal spaces — see SUPERIOR INTERCOSTAL VEIN

in·ter·cos·to·bra·chi·al nerve \ˌin-tər-ˌkäs-tō-ˌbrā-kē-əl-\ n : a branch of the second intercostal nerve that supplies

the skin of the inner and back part of the upper half of the arm

in·ter·course \'int-ər-ˌkörs\ n : physical sexual contact between individuals that involves the genitalia of at least one person; *esp* : SEXUAL INTERCOURSE 1

in·ter·cris·tal \ˌin-tər-'kris-təl\ adj : measured between two crests (as of bone)

in·ter·crit·i·cal \-'kri-ti-kəl\ adj : being in the period between attacks (~ gout)

in·ter·cur·rent \-'kər-ənt\ adj : occurring during and modifying the course of another disease

in·ter·den·tal \-'dent-əl\ adj : situated or intended for use between the teeth — **in·ter·den·tal·ly** \-əl-ē\ adv

interdental papilla n : the triangular wedge of gingiva between two adjacent teeth — called also *gingival papilla*

in·ter·dig·i·tal \-'di-jə-təl\ adj : occurring between digits (~ neuroma)

in·ter·dig·i·tate \-'di-jə-ˌtāt\ vb -tat·ed; -tat·ing : to become interlocked like the fingers of folded hands — **in·ter·dig·i·ta·tion** \-ˌdij-ə-'tā-shən\ n

in·ter·fere \ˌin-tər-'fir\ vb -fered; -fer·ing : to be inconsistent with and disturb the performance of previously learned behavior

in·ter·fer·ence \-'fir-əns\ n **1** : partial or complete inhibition or sometimes facilitation of other genetic crossovers in the vicinity of a chromosomal locus where a preceding crossover has occurred **2** : the disturbing effect of new learning on the performance of previously learned behavior with which it is inconsistent — compare NEGATIVE TRANSFER **3** : prevention of typical growth and development of a virus in a suitable host by the presence of another virus in the same host individual

in·ter·fer·on \ˌin-tər-'fir-ˌän\ n : any of a group of heat-stable soluble basic antiviral glycoproteins of low molecular weight that are produced usu. by cells exposed to the action of a virus, sometimes to the action of another intracellular parasite (as a bacterium), or experimentally to the action of some chemicals, and that include some used medically as antiviral or antineoplastic agents

in·ter·fi·bril·lar \-'fi-brə-lər, -'fī-\ or **in·ter·fi·bril·lary** \-'fi-brə-ˌler-ē, -'fī\ adj : situated between fibrils

in·ter·gen·ic \-'jē-nik\ adj : occurring between genes : involving more than one gene

in·ter·glob·u·lar \-'glä-byə-lər\ adj : resulting from or situated in an area of faulty dentin formation (~ dentin)

in·ter·hemi·spher·ic \-ˌhe-mə-'sfir-ik, -'sfer-\ *also* **in·ter·hemi·spher·al** \-əl\ adj : extending or occurring between hemispheres (as of the cerebrum)

in·ter·ic·tal \-ˈik-təl\ *adj* : occurring between seizures (as of epilepsy)

in·ter·ki·ne·sis \-kə-ˈnē-səs, -kī-\ *n, pl* **-ne·ses** \-ˌsēz\ : the period between the first and second meiotic divisions

in·ter·leu·kin \ˌin-tər-ˈlü-kən\ *n* : any of several compounds of low molecular weight that are produced by lymphocytes, macrophages, and monocytes and that function esp. in regulation of the immune system and esp. cell-mediated immunity

interleukin-1 \-ˈwən\ *n* : an interleukin produced esp. by monocytes and macrophages that regulates cell-mediated and humoral immune responses by activating lymphocytes and mediates other biological processes (as the onset of fever) usu. associated with infection and inflammation — abbr. *IL-1*

interleukin-2 \-ˈtü\ *n* : an interleukin produced by antigen-stimulated helper T cells in the presence of interleukin-1 that induces proliferation of immune cells (as T cells and B cells) and is used experimentally esp. in treating certain cancers — abbr. *IL-2*

in·ter·lo·bar \ˌint-ər-ˈlō-bər, -ˌbär\ *adj* : situated between the lobes of an organ or structure

interlobar artery *n* : any of various secondary branches of the renal arteries that branch to form the arcuate arteries

interlobar vein *n* : any of the veins of the kidney that are formed by convergence of arcuate veins and empty into the renal veins or their branches

in·ter·lob·u·lar \-ˈlä-byə-lər\ *adj* : lying between, connecting, or transporting the secretions of lobules

interlobular artery *n* : any of the branches of an arcuate artery that pass radially in the cortex of the kidney toward the surface

interlobular vein *n* : any of the veins in the cortex of the kidney that empty into the arcuate veins

in·ter·max·il·lary \-ˈmak-sə-ˌler-ē\ *adj* 1 : lying between maxillae; *esp* : joining the two maxillary bones (~ suture) 2 : of or relating to the premaxillae

intermedia — see MASSA INTERMEDIA, PARS INTERMEDIA

intermediary metabolism *n* : the intracellular process by which nutritive material is converted into cellular components

intermediate cuneiform bone *n* : CUNEIFORM BONE 1b — called also INTERMEDIATE CUNEIFORM

intermediate host *n* 1 : a host which is normally used by a parasite in the course of its life cycle and in which it may multiply asexually but not sexually — compare DEFINITIVE HOST 2 a : RESERVOIR 2 b : VECTOR 1

intermediate metabolism *n* : INTERMEDIARY METABOLISM

intermediate temporal artery *n* : TEMPORAL ARTERY 3b

in·ter·me·din \ˌin-tər-ˈmēd-ᵊn\ *n* : MELANOCYTE-STIMULATING HORMONE

in·ter·me·dio·lat·er·al \ˌin-tər-ˌmē-dē-ō-ˈla-tə-rəl\ *adj* : of, relating to, or being the lateral column of gray matter in the spinal cord

intermedium — see STRATUM INTERMEDIUM

intermedius — see NERVUS INTERMEDIUS, VASTUS INTERMEDIUS

in·ter·men·stru·al \-ˈmen-strə-wəl\ *adj* : occurring between menstrual periods (~ pain)

in·ter·mis·sion \ˌin-tər-ˈmi-shən\ *n* : the space of time between two paroxysms of a disease — compare REMISSION

in·ter·mit·tent \-ˈmit-ᵊnt\ *adj* : coming and going at intervals : not continuous (~ fever) — **in·ter·mit·tence** \-ᵊns\ *n*

intermittent claudication *n* : cramping pain and weakness in the legs and esp. the calves on walking that disappears after rest and is usu. associated with inadequate blood supply to the muscles

intermittent positive pressure breathing *n* : enforced periodic inflation of the lungs by the intermittent application of an increase of pressure to a reservoir of air (as in a bag) supplying the lungs — abbr. *IPPB*

in·ter·mus·cu·lar \-ˈməs-kyə-lər\ *adj* : lying between and separating muscles (~ fat)

in·tern \ˈin-ˌtərn\ *n* : a physician gaining supervised practical experience in a hospital after graduating from medical school — **intern** *vb*

interna — see THECA INTERNA

in·ter·nal \in-ˈtərn-ᵊl\ *adj* 1 a : situated near the inside of the body b : situated on the side toward the midsagittal plane of the body (the ~ surface of the lung) 2 : present or arising within an organism or one of its parts (~ stimulus) 3 : applied or intended for application through the stomach by being swallowed (an ~ remedy) — **in·ter·nal·ly** *adv*

internal acoustic meatus *n* : INTERNAL AUDITORY MEATUS

internal anal sphincter *n* : ANAL SPHINCTER b

internal auditory artery *n* : a long slender artery that arises from the basilar artery or one of its branches and is distributed to the inner ear — called also *internal auditory, labyrinthine artery*

internal auditory meatus *n* : a short canal in the petrous portion of the temporal bone through which pass the facial and auditory nerves and the nervus intermedius — called also *internal acoustic meatus, internal auditory canal*

internal capsule *n* : CAPSULE 1b(1)

internal carotid artery *n* : the inner branch of the carotid artery that supplies the brain, eyes, and other internal structures of the head — called also *internal carotid*

internal ear *n* : INNER EAR

internal iliac artery *n* : ILIAC ARTERY 3

internal iliac node *n* : any of the lymph nodes grouped around the internal iliac artery and the internal iliac vein — compare EXTERNAL ILIAC NODE

internal iliac vein *n* : ILIAC VEIN c

internal inguinal ring *n* : DEEP INGUINAL RING

internal intercostal muscle *n* : INTERCOSTAL MUSCLE b — called also *internal intercostal*

in·ter·nal·ize \in-ˈtərn-əl-ˌīz\ *vb* **-ized; -iz·ing** : to incorporate (as values) within the self as conscious or subconscious guiding principles through learning or socialization — **in·ter·nal·iza·tion** \-ˌtərn-əl-ə-ˈzā-shən\ *n*

internal jugular vein *n* : JUGULAR VEIN a — called also *internal jugular*

internal malleolus *n* : MALLEOLUS b

internal mammary artery *n* : INTERNAL THORACIC ARTERY

internal maxillary artery *n* : MAXILLARY ARTERY

internal medicine *n* : a branch of medicine that deals with the diagnosis and treatment of nonsurgical diseases

internal oblique *n* : OBLIQUE a(2)

internal occipital crest *n* : OCCIPITAL CREST b

internal occipital protuberance *n* : OCCIPITAL PROTUBERANCE b

internal os *n* : the opening of the cervix into the body of the uterus

internal pterygoid muscle *n* : PTERYGOID MUSCLE b

internal pudendal artery *n* : a branch of the internal iliac artery that is distributed esp. to the external genitalia and the perineum — compare EXTERNAL PUDENDAL ARTERY

internal pudendal vein *n* : any of several veins that receive blood from the external genitalia and the perineum and unite to form a single vein that empties into the internal iliac vein

internal respiration *n* : the exchange of gases (as oxygen and carbon dioxide) between the cells of the body and the blood — compare EXTERNAL RESPIRATION

internal spermatic artery *n* : TESTICULAR ARTERY

internal thoracic artery *n* : a branch of the subclavian artery of each side that runs down along the anterior wall of the thorax — called also *internal mammary artery*

internal thoracic vein *n* : a vein of the trunk on each side of the body that accompanies the corresponding internal thoracic artery and empties into the brachiocephalic vein

In·ter·na·tion·al System of Units \ˌint-ər-ˈnash-nəl-, -ən-ᵊl-\ *n* : a system of units based on the metric system and developed and refined by international convention esp. for scientific work

international unit *n* : a quantity of a biologic (as a vitamin) that produces a particular biological effect agreed upon as an international standard

in·terne, in·terne·ship *var of* INTERN, INTERNSHIP

in·ter·neu·ron \ˌin-tər-ˈnü-ˌrän, -ˈnyü-\ *n* : INTERNUNCIAL NEURON — **in·ter·neu·ro·nal** \-ˈnür-ən-ᵊl, -ˈnyur-ən-, -ˌnyü-ˈrōn-\ *adj*

in·ter·nist \ˈin-tər-nist\ *n* : a specialist in internal medicine esp. as distinguished from a surgeon

in·tern·ship \ˈin-ˌtərn-ˌship\ *n* **1** : the state or position of being an intern 2 a : a period of service as an intern b : the phase of medical training covered during such service

in·ter·nun·ci·al \ˌint-ər-ˈnən-sē-əl, -ˈnün-\ *adj* : of, relating to, or being internuncial neurons (~ fibers)

internuncial neuron *n* : a nerve fiber intercalated in the path of a reflex arc in the central nervous system and tending to modify the arc and coordinate it with other bodily activities — called also *interneuron, internuncial*

internus — see MEATUS ACUSTICUS INTERNUS, OBLIQUUS INTERNUS ABDOMINIS, OBTURATOR INTERNUS, SPHINCTER ANI INTERNUS, VASTUS INTERNUS

in·ter·oc·clu·sal \-ə-ˈklü-səl, -zəl\ *adj* : situated or occurring between the occlusal surfaces of opposing teeth (~ clearance)

in·tero·cep·tive \ˌin-tə-rō-ˈsep-tiv\ *adj* : of, relating to, or being stimuli arising within the body and esp. in the viscera

in·tero·cep·tor \-tər\ *n* : a sensory receptor excited by interoceptive stimuli — compare EXTEROCEPTOR

in·ter·os·se·ous \ˌin-tər-ˈä-sē-əs\ *adj* : situated between bones

interosseous artery — see COMMON INTEROSSEOUS ARTERY

interosseous membrane *n* : either of two thin strong sheets of fibrous tissue: a : one extending between and connecting the shafts of the radius and ulna b : one extending between and connecting the shafts of the tibia and fibula

interosseous muscle *n* : INTEROSSEUS

in·ter·os·se·us \ˌin-tər-ˈä-sē-əs\ *n, pl* **-sei** \-sē-ˌī\ : any of various small muscles arising from the metacarpals and metatarsals and inserted into the bases of the first phalanges: a : DORSAL INTEROSSEUS b : PALMAR INTEROSSEUS c : PLANTAR INTEROSSEUS

interosseus dorsalis *n, pl* **interossei dorsales** : DORSAL INTEROSSEUS

interosseus palmaris *n, pl* **interossei palmares** : PALMAR INTEROSSEUS

interosseus plantaris *n, pl* **interossei plantares** : PLANTAR INTEROSSEUS

in·ter·par·ox·ys·mal \-ˌpar-ək-ˈsiz-məl, -pə-ˈräk-\ *adj* : occurring between paroxysms

in·ter·pe·dun·cu·lar nucleus \ˌin-tər-pi-ˈdəŋ-kyə-lər-\ *n* : a mass of nerve cells lying between the cerebral peduncles in the midsagittal plane just dorsal to the pons — called also *interpeduncular ganglion*

in·ter·per·son·al \-ˈpərs-ⁿn-əl\ *adj* : being, relating to, or involving relations between persons ⟨~ therapy⟩ — **in·ter·per·son·al·ly** *adv*

in·ter·pha·lan·ge·al \ˌin-tər-ˌfā-lən-ˈjē-əl, -ˌfa-; -fə-ˈlan-jē-əl, -fā-\ *adj* : situated or occurring between phalanges; *also* : of or relating to an interphalangeal joint

in·ter·phase \ˈin-tər-ˌfāz\ *n* : the interval between the end of one mitotic or meiotic division and the beginning of another — called also *resting stage*

in·ter·po·lat·ed \in-ˈtər-pə-ˌlā-təd\ *adj* : occurring between normal heartbeats without disturbing the succeeding beat or the basic rhythm of the heart

in·ter·pris·mat·ic \ˌin-tər-priz-ˈma-tik\ *adj* : situated or occurring between prisms esp. of enamel

in·ter·prox·i·mal \-ˈpräk-sə-məl\ *adj* : situated, occurring, or used in the areas between adjoining teeth ⟨~ space⟩

in·ter·pu·pil·lary \-ˈpyü-pə-ˌler-ē\ *adj* : extending between the pupils of the eyes; *also* : extending between the centers of a pair of spectacle lenses ⟨~ distance⟩

in·ter·ra·dic·u·lar \-rə-ˈdi-kyə-lər\ *adj* : situated between the roots of a tooth

interruptus — see COITUS INTERRUPTUS

in·ter·scap·u·lar \ˌin-tər-ˈska-pyə-lər\ *adj* : of, relating to, situated in, or occurring in the region between the scapulae

in·ter·sen·so·ry \-ˈsens-ə-rē\ *adj* : involving two or more sensory systems

in·ter·sep·tal \-ˈsept-ᵊl\ *adj* : situated between septa

in·ter·sex \ˈin-tər-ˌseks\ *n* : an intersexual individual

in·ter·sex·u·al \ˌin-tər-ˈsek-shə-wəl\ *adj* **1** : existing between sexes ⟨~ hostility⟩ **2** : intermediate in sexual characters between a typical male and a typical female — **in·ter·sex·u·al·i·ty** \-ˌsek-shə-ˈwa-lə-tē\ *n*

in·ter·space \ˈin-tər-ˌspās\ *n* : the space between two related body parts whether void or filled by another kind of structure

in·ter·spi·na·lis \ˌint-ər-ˌspī-ˈna-ləs, -ˈnä-\ *n*, *pl* **-na·les** \-ˌlēz\ : any of various short muscles that have their origin on the superior surface of the spinous process of one vertebra and their insertion on the inferior surface of the contiguous vertebra above

in·ter·spi·nal ligament \ˌin-tər-ˈspin-ᵊl-\ *n* : any of the thin membranous ligaments that connect the spinous processes of contiguous vertebrae — called also *interspinous ligament*

in·ter·stim·u·lus \-ˈstim-yə-ləs\ *adj* : of, relating to, or being the interval between the presentation of two discrete stimuli

in·ter·sti·tial \-ˈsti-shəl\ *adj* **1** : situated within but not restricted to or characteristic of a particular organ or tissue — used esp. of fibrous tissue **2** : affecting the interstitial tissues of an organ or part ⟨~ hepatitis⟩ **3** : occurring in the part of a fallopian tube in the wall of the uterus ⟨~ pregnancy⟩ — **in·ter·sti·tial·ly** *adv*

interstitial cell *n* : a cell situated between the germ cells of the gonads; *esp* : LEYDIG CELL

interstitial cell of Leydig *n* : LEYDIG CELL

interstitial-cell stimulating hormone *n* : LUTEINIZING HORMONE

interstitial cystitis *n* : a chronic idiopathic cystitis characterized by painful inflammation of the subepithelial connective tissue and often accompanied by Hunner's ulcer

interstitial keratitis *n* : a chronic progressive keratitis of the corneal stroma often resulting in blindness and frequently associated with congenital syphilis

interstitial pneumonia *n* : any of several chronic lung diseases of unknown etiology that affect interstitial tissues of the lung

in·ter·sti·tium \ˌin-tər-ˈsti-shē-əm\ *n*, *pl* **-tia** \-ē-ə\ : interstitial tissue

in·ter·sub·ject \ˈin-tər-ˌsəb-jekt\ *adj* : occurring between subjects in an experiment ⟨~ variability⟩

in·ter·tar·sal \ˌin-tər-ˈtär-səl\ *adj* : situated, occurring, or performed between tarsal bones ⟨~ joint⟩ ⟨~ arthrotomy⟩

in·ter·trans·ver·sar·ii \-ˌtrans-vər-ˈser-ē-ˌī\ *n pl* : a series of small muscles connecting the transverse processes of contiguous vertebrae

in·ter·tri·go \-ˈtrī-ˌgō\ *n* : inflammation produced by chafing of adjacent areas of skin — **in·ter·trig·i·nous** \-ˈtri-jə-nəs\ *adj*

in·ter·tro·chan·ter·ic \-ˌtrō-kən-ˈter-ik, -ˌkan-\ *adj* : situated, performed, or occurring between trochanters ⟨~ fractures⟩

intertrochanteric line *n* : a line on the anterior surface of the femur that runs obliquely from the greater trochanter to the lesser trochanter

in·ter·tu·ber·cu·lar groove \ˌin-tər-tü-ˈbər-kyə-lər-, -tyü-\ *n* : BICIPITAL GROOVE

intertubercular line *n* : an imaginary line passing through the iliac crests of the hipbones that separates the umbilical and lumbar regions of the abdomen from the hypogastric and iliac regions

in·ter·ven·tion \ˌin-tər-ˈven-chən\ n
: the act or fact of interfering with a
condition to modify it or with a process to change its course — **in·ter-
ven·tion·al** \-ˈven-chə-nəl\ adj

in·ter·ven·tric·u·lar \-ven-ˈtri-kyə-lər\
adj : situated between ventricles ⟨~
septal defect⟩

interventricular foramen n : the opening from each lateral ventricle into
the third ventricle of the brain —
called also *foramen of Monro*

interventricular groove n : INTERVEN-
TRICULAR SULCUS

interventricular septum n : the curved
slanting wall that separates the right
and left ventricles of the heart

interventricular sulcus n : either of the
anterior and posterior grooves on the
surface of the heart that lie over the
interventricular septum and join at
the apex

in·ter·ver·te·bral \ˌin-tər-ˈvər-tə-brəl,
-(ˌ)vər-ˈtē-\ adj : situated between
vertebrae — **in·ter·ver·te·bral·ly** adv

intervertebral disk n : any of the tough
elastic disks that are interposed between the centra of adjoining vertebrae

intervertebral foramen n : any of the
openings that give passage to the spinal nerves from the vertebral canal

in·tes·ti·nal \in-ˈtes-tən-əl\ adj 1 a : affecting or occurring in the intestine b
: living in the intestine ⟨the ~ flora⟩ 2
: of, relating to, or being the intestine
⟨the ~ canal⟩ — **in·tes·ti·nal·ly** adv

intestinal artery n : any of 12 to 15 arteries that arise from the superior
mesenteric artery and supply the jejunum and ileum

intestinal flu n : an acute usu. transitory attack of gastroenteritis that is
marked by nausea, vomiting, diarrhea, and abdominal cramping and is
typically caused by a virus (as the
Norwalk virus) or a bacterium (as
Escherichia coli) — not usu. used
technically

intestinal gland n : CRYPT OF LIEBER-
KÜHN

intestinal juice n : a fluid that is secreted in small quantity by the crypts of
Lieberkühn of the small intestine —
called also *succus entericus*

intestinal lipodystrophy n : WHIPPLE'S
DISEASE

in·tes·tine \in-ˈtes-tən\ n : the tubular
portion of the alimentary canal that
lies posterior to the stomach from
which it is separated by the pyloric
sphincter and consists of a slender
but long anterior part made up of duodenum, jejunum, and ileum and a
broader shorter posterior part made
up of cecum, colon, and rectum — often used in pl.; see LARGE INTESTINE,
SMALL INTESTINE

in·ti·ma \ˈin-tə-mə\ n, pl **-mae** \-ˌmē,
-ˌmī\ or **-mas** : the innermost coat of
an organ (as a blood vessel) consist-

ing usu. of an endothelial layer
backed by connective tissue and elastic tissue — called also *tunica intima*
— **in·ti·mal** \-məl\ adj

in·tol·er·ance \(ˌ)in-ˈtä-lə-rəns\ n 1
: lack of an ability to endure ⟨an ~ to
light⟩ 2 : exceptional sensitivity (as to
a drug) — **in·tol·er·ant** \-rənt\ adj

in·tox·i·cant \in-ˈtäk-si-kənt\ n : something that intoxicates; esp : an alcoholic drink — **intoxicant** adj

in·tox·i·cate \-sə-ˌkāt\ vb **-cat·ed; -cat·**
ing 1 : POISON 2 : to excite or stupefy
by alcohol or a drug esp. to the point
where physical and mental control is
markedly diminished

in·tox·i·cat·ed \-ˌkā-təd\ adj : affected
by an intoxicant and esp. by alcohol

in·tox·i·ca·tion \in-ˌtäk-sə-ˈkā-shən\ n 1
: an abnormal state that is essentially
a poisoning ⟨intestinal ~⟩ 2 : the condition of being drunk or inebriated

in·tra- \in-trə, -(ˌ)trä\ prefix 1 a : within ⟨intracerebellar⟩ b : during ⟨intra-
operative⟩ c : between layers of
⟨intradermal⟩ 2 : INTRO- ⟨an intramuscular injection⟩

in·tra-ab·dom·i·nal \ˌin-trə-ab-ˈdä-
mən-əl\ adj : situated within, occurring within, or administered by
entering the abdomen ⟨an ~ injec-
tion⟩

in·tra-al·ve·o·lar \ˌin-trə-al-ˈvē-ə-lər\
adj : situated or occurring within an
alveolus

in·tra-am·ni·ot·ic \-ˌam-nē-ˈä-tik\ adj
: situated within, occurring within, or
administered by entering the amnion
— **in·tra-am·ni·ot·i·cal·ly** adv

in·tra-aor·tic \-ā-ˈor-tik\ adj 1 : situated or occurring within the aorta 2 : of,
relating to, or used in intra-aortic balloon counterpulsation

intra-aortic balloon counterpulsation n
: counterpulsation in which cardiocir-
culatory assistance is provided by a
balloon inserted in the thoracic aorta
which is inflated during diastole and
deflated just before systole

in·tra-ar·te·ri·al \- är-ˈtir-ē-əl\ adj : situated or occurring within, adminis-
tered into, or involving entry by way
of an artery ⟨an ~ catheter⟩ — **in-
tra-ar·te·ri·al·ly** adv

in·tra-ar·tic·u·lar \-är-ˈti-kyə-lər\ adj
: situated within, occurring within, or
administered by entering a joint — **in-
tra-ar·tic·u·lar·ly** adv

in·tra-atri·al \-ˈā-trē-əl\ adj : situated
or occurring within an atrium esp. of
the heart ⟨an ~ block⟩

in·tra·can·a·lic·u·lar \-ˌkan-əl-ˈi-kyə-
lər\ adj : situated or occurring within
a canaliculus ⟨~ biliary stasis⟩

in·tra·cap·su·lar \-ˈkap-sə-lər\ adj 1
: situated or occurring within a capsule 2 of a cataract operation : involving removal of the entire lens and
its capsule — compare EXTRACAPSU-
LAR 2

in·tra·car·di·ac \-ˈkär-dē-ˌak\ also **in-**

tra·car·di·al \-dē-əl\ *adj* : situated within, occurring within, introduced into, or involving entry into the heart

in·tra·ca·rot·id \-kə-ˈrä-təd\ *adj* : situated within, occurring within, or administered by entering a carotid artery

in·tra·cav·i·tary \-ˈka-və-₃ter-ē\ *adj* : situated or occurring within a body cavity; *esp* : of, relating to, or being treatment (as of cancer) characterized by the insertion of esp. radioactive substances in a cavity

in·tra·cel·lu·lar \-ˈsel-yə-lər\ *adj* : existing, occurring, or functioning within a cell ⟨~ parasites⟩ — **in·tra·cel·lu·lar·ly** *adv*

in·tra·cere·bel·lar \-₃ser-ə-ˈbe-lər\ *adj* : situated or occurring within the cerebellum

in·tra·ce·re·bral \-sə-ˈrē-brəl, -ˈser-ə-\ *adj* : situated within, occurring within, or administered by entering the cerebrum ⟨~ injections⟩ ⟨~ bleeding⟩ — **in·tra·ce·re·bral·ly** *adv*

in·tra·cis·ter·nal \-sis-ˈtər-nəl\ *adj* : situated within, occurring within, or administered by entering a cisterna ⟨an ~ injection⟩ — **in·tra·cis·ter·nal·ly** *adv*

in·tra·co·ro·nal \-ˈkór-ən-ᵊl, -ˈkär-; -kə-ˈrōn-ᵊl\ *adj* : situated or made within the crown of a tooth

in·tra·co·ro·nary \-ˈkór-ə-₃ner-ē, -ˈkär-\ *adj* : situated within, occurring within, or administered by entering the heart

in·tra·cor·ti·cal \-ˈkór-ti-kəl\ *adj* : situated or occurring within a cortex and esp. the cerebral cortex ⟨~ injection⟩

in·tra·cra·ni·al \-ˈkrā-nē-əl\ *adj* : situated or occurring within the cranium ⟨~ pressure⟩; *also* : affecting or involving intracranial structures — **in·tra·cra·ni·al·ly** *adv*

in·trac·ta·ble \(ˌ)in-ˈtrak-tə-bəl\ *adj* 1 : not easily managed or controlled (as by antibiotics or psychotherapy) 2 : not easily relieved or cured ⟨~ pain⟩ — **in·trac·ta·bil·i·ty** \(ˌ)in-₃trak-tə-ˈbi-lə-tē\ *n*

in·tra·cu·ta·ne·ous \₃in-trə-kyù-ˈtā-nē-əs, -(₃)trā-\ *adj* : INTRADERMAL ⟨~ lesions⟩ — **in·tra·cu·ta·ne·ous·ly** *adv*

intracutaneous test *n* : INTRADERMAL TEST

in·tra·cy·to·plas·mic \-₃sī-tə-ˈplaz-mik\ *adj* : lying or occurring within the cytoplasm

in·tra·der·mal \-ˈdər-məl\ *adj* : situated, occurring, or done within or between the layers of the skin; *also* : administered by entering the skin ⟨~ injections⟩ — **in·tra·der·mal·ly** *adv*

intradermal test *n* : a test for immunity or hypersensitivity made by injecting a minute amount of diluted antigen into the skin — called also *intracutaneous test*; compare PATCH TEST, SCRATCH TEST

in·tra·duc·tal \₃in-trə-ˈdəkt-ᵊl\ *adj* : situated within, occurring within, or introduced into a duct ⟨~ carcinoma⟩

in·tra·du·o·de·nal \-₃dü-ə-ˈdēn-ᵊl, -dyü-, ˈäd-ᵊn-əl\ *adj* : situated in or introduced into the duodenum

in·tra·du·ral \-ˈdùr-əl, -ˈdyùr-\ *adj* : situated, occurring, or performed within or between the membranes of the dura mater

in·tra·epi·der·mal \-₃e-pə-ˈdər-məl\ *adj* : located or occurring within the epidermis

in·tra·epi·the·li·al \-₃e-pə-ˈthē-lē-əl\ *adj* : occurring in or situated among the cells of the epithelium

in·tra·eryth·ro·cyt·ic \-i-₃ri-thrə-ˈsi-tik\ *adj* : situated or occurring within the red blood cells

in·tra·fa·mil·ial \-fə-ˈmil-yəl\ *adj* : occurring within a family ⟨~ conflict⟩

in·tra·fol·lic·u·lar \-fə-ˈli-kyə-lər, -fä-\ *adj* : situated within a follicle

in·tra·fu·sal \-ˈfyü-zəl\ *adj* : situated within a muscle spindle ⟨~ muscle fibers⟩ — compare EXTRAFUSAL

in·tra·gen·ic \-ˈje-nik\ *adj* : being or occurring within a gene

in·tra·he·pat·ic \-hi-ˈpa-tik\ *adj* : situated or occurring within or originating in the liver ⟨~ cholestasis⟩

in·tra·le·sion·al \-ˈlē-zhən-ᵊl\ *adj* : introduced into or performed within a lesion ⟨~ injection⟩ — **in·tra·le·sion·al·ly** *adv*

in·tra·lo·bar \-ˈlō-bər, -₃bär\ *adj* : situated within a lobe

in·tra·lob·u·lar \-ˈlä-byə-lər\ *adj* : situated or occurring within a lobule (as of the liver or pancreas)

intralobular vein *n* : CENTRAL VEIN

in·tra·lu·mi·nal \-ˈlü-mən-ᵊl\ *adj* : situated within, occurring within, or introduced into the lumen

in·tra·mam·ma·ry \-ˈma-mə-rē\ *adj* : situated or introduced within the mammary tissue ⟨~ infusion⟩

in·tra·med·ul·lary \-ˈmed-ᵊl-₃er-ē, -ˈmej-ᵊl-; -₃me-də-lə-rē\ *adj* : situated or occurring within a medulla; *esp* : involving use of the marrow space of a bone for support ⟨~ pinning of a fracture⟩

in·tra·mem·brane \-ˈmem-₃brān\ *adj* : INTRAMEMBRANOUS 2

in·tra·mem·bra·nous \-ˈmem-brə-nəs\ *adj* 1 : relating to, formed by, or being ossification of a membrane ⟨~ bone development⟩ 2 : situated within a membrane

in·tra·mi·to·chon·dri·al \-₃mī-tə-ˈkän-drē-əl\ *adj* : situated or occurring within mitochondria ⟨~ inclusions⟩

in·tra·mu·co·sal \-myü-ˈkō-zəl\ *adj* : situated within, occurring within, or administered by entering a mucous membrane

in·tra·mu·ral \-ˈmyùr-əl\ *adj* : situated or occurring within the substance of the walls of an organ ⟨~ infarction⟩

in·tra·mus·cu·lar \-ˈməs-kyə-lər\ *adj* : situated within, occurring within, or administered by entering a muscle — **in·tra·mus·cu·lar·ly** adv

in·tra·myo·car·di·al \-ˌmī-ə-ˈkär-dē-əl\ adj : situated within, occurring within, or administered by entering the myocardium (an ~ injection)

in·tra·na·sal \-ˈnā-zəl\ adj : lying within or administered by way of the nasal structures — **in·tra·na·sal·ly** adv

in·tra·neu·ral \-ˈnùr-əl, -ˈnyùr-\ adj : situated within, occurring within, or administered by entering a nerve or nervous tissue — **in·tra·neu·ral·ly** adv

in·tra·neu·ro·nal \-ˈnùr-ən-əl, -nù-ˈrōn-əl, -nyù-\ adj : situated or occurring within a neuron (excess ~ sodium)

in·tra·nu·cle·ar \-ˈnü-klē-ər, -ˈnyü-\ adj : situated or occurring within a nucleus (cells with prominent ~ inclusions)

in·tra·oc·u·lar \ˌin-trə-ˈä-kyə-lər\ adj : implanted in, occurring within, or administered by entering the eyeball — **in·tra·oc·u·lar·ly** adv

intraocular pressure n : the pressure within the eyeball that gives it a round firm shape and is caused by the aqueous and vitreous humors — called also *intraocular tension*

in·tra·op·er·a·tive \ˌin-trə-ˈä-pə-rə-tiv\ adj : occurring, carried out, or encountered in the course of surgery (~ irradiation) (~ infarction) — **in·tra·op·er·a·tive·ly** adv

in·tra·oral \-ˈōr-əl, -ˈär-\ adj : situated, occurring, or performed within the mouth (~ treatments)

in·tra·os·se·ous \-ˈä-sē-əs\ adj : situated within, occurring within, or administered by entering a bone (~ vasculature) (~ anesthesia)

in·tra·ovu·lar \-ˈä-vyə-lər, -ˈō-\ adj : situated or occurring within the ovum

in·tra·pan·cre·at·ic \-ˌpan-krē-ˈa-tik, -ˌpan-\ adj : situated or occurring within the pancreas

in·tra·pa·ren·chy·mal \-pə-ˈreŋ-kə-məl, -ˌpar-ən-ˈkī-\ adj : situated or occurring within the parenchyma of an organ

in·tra·par·tum \-ˈpär-təm\ adj : occurring chiefly with reference to a mother during the act of birth (~ complications)

in·tra·pel·vic \-ˈpel-vik\ adj : situated or performed within the pelvis

in·tra·peri·car·di·al \-ˌper-ə-ˈkär-dē-əl\ adj : situated within or administered by entering the pericardium

in·tra·per·i·to·ne·al \ˌin-trə-ˌper-ət-ən-ˈē-əl\ adj : situated within or administered by entering the peritoneum — **in·tra·per·i·to·ne·al·ly** adv

in·tra·pleu·ral \-ˈplùr-əl\ adj : situated within, occurring within, or administered by entering the pleura or pleural cavity — **in·tra·pleu·ral·ly** adv

intrapleural pneumonolysis n : PNEUMONOLYSIS b

in·tra·psy·chic \ˌin-trə-ˈsī-kik\ adj : being or occurring within the psyche, mind, or personality

in·tra·pul·mo·nary \-ˈpùl-mə-ˌner-ē, -ˈpəl-\ also **in·tra·pul·mon·ic** \-ˌpùl-ˈmä-nik, -ˌpəl-\ adj : situated within, occurring within, or administered by entering the lungs — **in·tra·pul·mo·nar·i·ly** \-ˌpùl-mə-ˈner-ə-ˌlē\ adv

in·tra·rec·tal \-ˈrekt-əl\ adj : situated within, occurring within, or administered by entering the rectum

in·tra·re·nal \-ˈrēn-əl\ adj : situated within, occurring within, or administered by entering the kidney — **in·tra·re·nal·ly** adv

in·tra·ret·i·nal \-ˈret-ən-əl\ adj : situated or occurring within the retina

in·tra·scro·tal \-ˈskrōt-əl\ adj : situated or occurring within the scrotum

in·tra·spi·nal \-ˈspin-əl\ adj : situated within, occurring within, or introduced into the spine and esp. the vertebral canal (~ nerve terminals)

in·tra·splen·ic \-ˈsple-nik\ adj : situated within or introduced into the spleen — **in·tra·splen·i·cal·ly** adv

in·tra·the·cal \-ˈthē-kəl\ adj : introduced into or occurring in the space under the arachnoid membrane of the brain or spinal cord — **in·tra·the·cal·ly** adv

in·tra·tho·rac·ic \-thə-ˈra-sik\ adj : situated, occurring, or performed within the thorax (~ pressure)

in·tra·thy·roi·dal \-thī-ˈroid-əl\ adj : situated or occurring within the thyroid

in·tra·tra·che·al \-ˈträ-kē-əl\ adj : occurring within or introduced into the trachea — **in·tra·tra·che·al·ly** adv

in·tra·uter·ine \-ˈyü-tə-rən, -ˌrīn\ adj : of, situated in, used in, or occurring within the uterus; also : involving or occurring during the part of development that takes place in the uterus

intrauterine contraceptive device n : INTRAUTERINE DEVICE

intrauterine device n : a device inserted and left in the uterus to prevent effective conception — called also *IUCD*, *IUD*

in·tra·vag·i·nal \-ˈva-jən-əl\ adj : situated within, occurring within, or introduced into the vagina — **in·tra·vag·i·nal·ly** adv

in·tra·vas·cu·lar \ˌin-trə-ˈvas-kyə-lər\ adj : situated in, occurring in, or administered by entry into a blood vessel — **in·tra·vas·cu·lar·ly** adv

in·tra·ve·nous \ˌin-trə-ˈvē-nəs\ adj **1** : situated within, performed within, occurring within, or administered by entering a vein (an ~ feeding) **2** : used in intravenous procedures — **in·tra·ve·nous·ly** adv

intravenous pyelogram n : a pyelogram in which roentgenographic visualization is obtained after intravenous administration of a radiopaque medium which collects in the kidneys

in·tra·ven·tric·u·lar \ˌin-trə-ven-ˈtri-kyə-lər\ adj : situated within, occurring within, or administered into a ventricle — **in·tra·ven·tric·u·lar·ly** *adv*

in·tra·ver·te·bral \-(₁)vər-ᵗtē-brəl, -ᵗvər-tə-\ *adj* : situated within a vertebra

in·tra·ves·i·cal \-ᵗve-si-kəl\ *adj* : situated or occurring within the bladder

in·tra·vi·tal \-ᵗvīt-ᵊl\ *adj* 1 : performed upon or found in a living subject 2 : having or utilizing the property of staining cells without killing them — compare SUPRAVITAL — **in·tra·vi·tal·ly** *adv*

in·tra·vi·tam \-ᵗvī-₁tam, -ᵗwē-₁täm\ *adj* : INTRAVITAL

in·tra·vit·re·al \-ᵗvi-trē-əl\ *adj* : INTRA-VITREOUS (∼ injection)

in·tra·vit·re·ous \-trē-əs\ *adj* : situated within, occurring within, or introduced into the vitreous humor (∼ hemorrhage)

in·trin·sic \in-ᵗtrin-zik, -sik\ *adj* 1 : originating or due to causes or factors within a body, organ, or part (∼ asthma) 2 : originating and included wholly within an organ or part (∼ muscles) — compare EXTRINSIC 2

intrinsic factor *n* : a substance produced by the normal gastrointestinal mucosa that facilitates absorption of vitamin B_{12}

intro- *prefix* 1 : in : into (*intro*jection) 2 : inward : within (*intro*vert) — compare EXTRO-

in·troi·tus \in-ᵗtrō-ə-təs\ *n, pl* **introitus** : the vaginal opening — **in·troi·tal** \in-ᵗtrō-ət-ᵊl\ *adj*

in·tro·ject \in-trə-ᵗjekt\ *vb* 1 : to incorporate (attitudes or ideas) into one's personality unconsciously 2 : to turn toward oneself (the love felt for another) or against oneself (the hostility felt toward another) — **in·tro·jec·tion** \-ᵗjek-shən\ *n*

in·tro·mis·sion \in-trə-ᵗmi-shən\ *n* : the insertion or period of insertion of the penis in the vagina in copulation

in·tron \ᵗin-₁trän\ *n* : a polynucleotide sequence in a nucleic acid that does not code information for protein synthesis and is removed before translation of messenger RNA — compare EXON

In·tro·pin \ᵗin-trə-₁pin\ *trademark* — used for a preparation of the hydrochloride of dopamine

in·tro·spec·tion \in-trə-ᵗspek-shən\ *n* : an examination of one's own thoughts and feelings — **in·tro·spec·tive** \-tiv\ *adj*

in·tro·ver·sion \in-trə-ᵗvər-zhən, -shən\ *n* 1 : the act of directing one's attention toward or getting gratification from one's own interests, thoughts, and feelings 2 : the state or tendency toward being wholly or predominantly concerned with and interested in one's own mental life — compare EXTROVERSION

in·tro·vert \ᵗin-trə-₁vərt\ *n* : one whose personality is characterized by intro-

version: *broadly* : a reserved or shy person — compare EXTROVERT — **in·tro·vert·ed** \ᵗin-trə-₁vər-təd\ *also* **in·tro·vert** \ᵗin-trə-₁vərt\ *adj*

in·tu·ba·tion \in-tü-ᵗbā-shən, -tyü-\ *n* : the introduction of a tube into a hollow organ (as the trachea or intestine) to keep it open or restore its patency if obstructed — compare EXTUBATION — **in·tu·bate** \ᵗin-tü-₁bāt, -tyü-\ *vb*

in·tu·mes·cence \in-tü-ᵗmes-ᵊns, -tyü-\ *n* 1 a : the action or process of becoming enlarged or swollen b : the state of being swollen 2 : something (as a tumor) that is swollen or enlarged

in·tus·sus·cep·tion \in-tə-sə-ᵗsep-shən\ *n* : INVAGINATION; *esp* : the slipping of a length of intestine into an adjacent portion usu. producing obstruction — **in·tus·sus·cept** \in-tə-sə-ᵗsept\ *vb*

in·u·lin \ᵗin-yə-lən\ *n* : a tasteless white polysaccharide found esp. dissolved in the sap of the roots and rhizomes of composite plants and used as a source of levulose and as a diagnostic agent in a test for kidney function

in·unc·tion \i-ᵗnəŋk-shən\ *n* 1 : the rubbing of an ointment into the skin for therapeutic purposes 2 : OINTMENT, UNGUENT

in utero \in-ᵗyü-tə-₁rō\ *adv or adj* : in the uterus : before birth

in·vade \in-ᵗvād\ *vb* **in·vad·ed; in·vad·ing** 1 : to enter and spread within either normally (as in development) or abnormally (as in infection) often with harmful effects 2 : to affect injuriously and progressively

in·vag·i·na·tion \in-₁va-jə-ᵗnā-shən\ *n* 1 : an act or process of folding in so that an outer surface becomes an inner surface: as a : the formation of a gastrula by an infolding of part of the wall of the blastula b : intestinal intussusception 2 : an invaginated part — **in·vag·i·nate** \in-ᵗva-jə-₁nāt\ *vb*

¹**in·va·lid** \ᵗin-və-ləd\ *adj* 1 : suffering from disease or disability : SICKLY 2 : of, relating to, or suited to one that is sick (an ∼ chair)

²**invalid** *n* : one that is sickly or disabled

³**in·va·lid** \ᵗin-və-ləd, -₁lid\ *vb* 1 : to remove from active duty by reason of sickness or disability (was ∼*ed* out of the army) 2 : to make sickly or disabled

in·va·lid·ism \ᵗin-və-lə-₁di-zəm\ *n* : a chronic condition of being an invalid

in·va·sion \in-ᵗvā-zhən\ *n* : the act of invading: as a : the penetration of the body of a host by a microorganism b : the spread and multiplication of a pathogenic microorganism or of malignant cells in the body of a host

in·va·sive \-siv, -ziv\ *adj* 1 : tending to spread; *esp* : tending to invade healthy tissue (∼ cancer cells) 2 : involving entry into the living body (as by incision or by insertion of an instrument) (∼ diagnostic techniques) — **in·va·sive·ness** *n*

in·ven·to·ry \'in-vən-ˌtọr-ē\ *n, pl* **-ries** 1 : a questionnaire designed to provide an index of individual interests or personality traits 2 : a list of traits, preferences, attitudes, interests, or abilities that is used in evaluating personal characteristics or skills

in·ver·sion \in-'vər-zhən, -shən\ *n* 1 : a reversal of position, order, form, or relationship: as a : a dislocation of a bodily structure in which it is turned partially or wholly inside out (∼ of the uterus) b : the condition (as of the foot) of being turned or rotated inward — compare EVERSION 2 c : a breaking off of a chromosome section and its subsequent reattachment in inverted position; *also* : a chromosomal section that has undergone this process 2 : HOMOSEXUALITY — **in·vert** \in-'vərt\ *vb*

inversus — see SITUS INVERSUS

in·vert·ase \in-'vər-ˌtās, 'in-vər-, -ˌtāz\ *n* : an enzyme found in many microorganisms and plants and in animal intestines that catalyzes the hydrolysis of sucrose — called also *saccharase, sucrase*

¹in·ver·te·brate \(ˌ)in-'vər-tə-brət, -ˌbrāt\ *n* : an animal having no backbone or internal skeleton

²invertebrate *adj* : lacking a spinal column; *also* : of or relating to invertebrate animals

in·vest \in-'vest\ *vb* : to envelop or cover completely (the pleura ∼s the lung)

in·ves·ti·ga·tion·al new drug \in-ˌves-ti-'gā-shə-nəl-\ *n* : a drug that has not been approved for general use by the Food and Drug Administration but is under investigation in clinical trials regarding its safety and efficacy first by clinical investigators and then by practicing physicians using subjects who have given informed consent to participate — abbr. *IND*; called also *investigational drug*

in·vest·ment \-mənt\ *n* : an external covering of a cell, part, or organism

in·vi·a·ble \(ˌ)in-'vī-ə-bəl\ *adj* : incapable of surviving esp. because of a deleterious genetic constitution — **in·vi·a·bil·i·ty** \-ˌvī-ə-'bil-ə-tē\ *n*

in vi·tro \in-'vē-(ˌ)trō, -'vi-\ *adv or adj* : outside the living body and in an artificial environment

in vi·vo \in-'vē-(ˌ)vō\ *adv or adj* 1 : in the living body of a plant or animal 2 : in a real-life situation

in·vo·lu·crum \in-və-'lü-krəm\ *n, pl* **-cra** \-krə\ : a formation of new bone about a sequestrum (as in osteomyelitis)

in·vol·un·tary \(ˌ)in-'vä-lən-ˌter-ē\ *adj* : not subject to control of the will : REFLEX (∼ contractions)

involuntary muscle *n* : muscle governing reflex functions and not under direct voluntary control; *esp* : SMOOTH MUSCLE

in·vo·lute \in-və-'lüt\ *vb* **-lut·ed; -lut·ing** 1 : to return to a former condition 2 : to become cleared up

in·vo·lu·tion \in-və-'lü-shən\ *n* 1 a : an inward curvature or penetration b : the formation of a gastrula by ingrowth of cells formed at the dorsal lip 2 : a shrinking or return to a former size (∼ of the uterus after pregnancy) 3 : the regressive alterations of a body or its parts characteristic of the aging process; *specif* : decline marked by a decrease of bodily vigor and in women by menopause

in·vo·lu·tion·al \in-və-'lü-shə-nəl\ *adj* 1 : of or relating to involutional melancholia 2 : of or relating to the climacterium and its associated bodily and psychic changes

involutional melancholia *n* : a depression that occurs at the time of menopause or the climacteric and is usu. characterized by somatic and nihilistic delusions — called also *involutional psychosis*

in·volve \in-'välv, -'vȯlv\ *vb* **in·volved; in·volv·ing** : to affect with a disease or condition : include in an area of damage, trauma, or insult (herpes *involved* the trigeminal nerve) — **in·volve·ment** \-mənt\ *n*

Iod·amoe·ba \(ˌ)ī-ō-də-'mē-bə\ *n* : a genus of amebas commensal in the intestine of mammals including humans

io·dide \'ī-ə-ˌdīd\ *n* : a compound of iodine usu. with a more electrically positive element or radical

io·dine \'ī-ə-ˌdīn, -dən, -ˌdēn\ *n* 1 : a nonmetallic halogen element used in medicine (as in antisepsis and in the treatment of goiter and cretinism) 2 : a tincture of iodine used esp. as a topical antiseptic — symbol *I*; see ELEMENT table

iodine–131 *n* : a heavy radioactive isotope of iodine that has the mass number 131 and a half-life of eight days, gives off beta and gamma rays, and is used esp. in the form of its sodium salt in the diagnosis of thyroid disease and the treatment of goiter

iodine–125 *n* : a light radioactive isotope of iodine that has a mass number of 125 and a half-life of 60 days, gives off soft gamma rays, and is used as a tracer in thyroid studies and as therapy in hyperthyroidism

io·dip·amide \ˌī-ō-'di-pə-ˌmīd\ *n* : a radiopaque substance $C_{20}H_{14}I_6N_2O_6$ used as the sodium or meglumine salts esp. in cholecystography

io·dism \'ī-ə-ˌdi-zəm\ *n* : an abnormal local and systemic condition resulting from overdosage with, prolonged use of, or sensitivity to iodine or iodine compounds and marked by ptyalism, coryza, frontal headache, emaciation, and skin eruptions

io·dize \'ī-ə-ˌdīz\ *vb* **io·dized; io·diz·ing** : to treat with iodine or an iodide (*iodized* salt)

io·do·chlor·hy·droxy·quin \ī-ₜō-də-ₜklōr-hi-¹dräk-sē-ₜkwin, ī-ₜä-də-\ *n* : an antimicrobial and mildly irritant drug C_9H_5ClINO formerly used esp. as an antidiarrheal but now used mainly as an antiseptic

io·do·de·oxy·uri·dine \ī-ₜō-də-ₜdē-ₜäk-sē-¹yür-ə-ₜdēn\ *or* 5-**io·do·de·oxy·uri·dine** \ⁱfīv-\ *n* : IDOXURIDINE

io·do·form \ī-¹ō-də-ₜfòrm, -¹ä-\ *n* : a yellow crystalline volatile compound CHI_3 that is used as an antiseptic dressing

iodohippurate — see SODIUM IODOHIPPURATE

io·do·hip·pur·ate sodium \ī-ₜō-də-¹hi-pyə-ₜrāt-, ī-ₜä-, -hi-¹pyür-ₜāt-\ *n* : HIPPURAN

io·do·phor \ī-¹ō-də-ₜfòr, ī-¹ä-\ *n* : a complex of iodine and a surface-active agent that releases iodine gradually and serves as a disinfectant

io·dop·sin \ī-ə-¹däp-sən\ *n* : a photosensitive violet pigment in the retinal cones that is similar to rhodopsin but more labile, is formed from vitamin A, and is important in photopic vision

io·do·pyr·ac·et \ī-ₜō-də-¹pir-ə-ₜset, ī-ₜä-\ *n* : a salt $C_8H_{19}I_2N_2O_3$ used as a radiopaque medium esp. in urography — see DIODRAST

io·do·quin·ol \ī-ₜō-də-¹kwi-ₜnòl, -ₜä-, -ₜnòl\ *n* : a drug $C_9H_5I_2NO$ used esp. in the treatment of amebic dysentery — called also *diiodohydroxyquin, diiodohydroxyquinoline*

ion \¹ī-ₜän, -ən\ *n* : an electrically charged particle, atom, or group of atoms — **ion·ic** \ī-¹ä-nik\ *adj* — **ion·i·cal·ly** *adv*

ion·ize \¹ī-ə-ₜnīz\ *vb* **ion·ized; ion·iz·ing** 1 : to convert wholly or partly into ions 2 : to become ionized — **ion·iz·able** \ī-ə-¹nī-zə-bəl\ *adj* — **ion·iza·tion** \ₜī-ə-nə-¹zā-shən\ *n*

ion·o·phore \ī-¹ä-nə-ₜfòr\ *n* : a compound that facilitates transmission of an ion (as of calcium) across a lipid barrier (as in a cell membrane) by combining with the ion or by increasing the permeability of the barrier to it — **io·noph·or·ous** \ī-ə-¹nä-fə-rəs\ *adj*

ion·to·pho·re·sis \(ₜ)ī-ₜän-tə-fə-¹rē-səs\ *n, pl* **-re·ses** \-ₜsēz\ : the introduction of an ionized substance (as a drug) through intact skin by the application of a direct electric current — **ion·to·pho·ret·ic** \-¹re-tik\ *adj* — **ion·to·pho·ret·i·cal·ly** *adv*

io·pa·no·ic acid \ī-ə-pə-¹nō-ik-\ *n* : a crystalline powder $C_{11}H_{12}I_3NO_2$ used as a radiopaque medium in cholecystography

io·phen·dyl·ate \ī-ə-¹fen-də-ₜlāt\ *n* : a radiopaque liquid $C_{19}H_{29}IO_2$ used esp. in myelography

io·thal·a·mate \ī-ə-¹tha-lə-ₜmāt\ *n* : any of several salts of iothalamic acid that are administered by injection as radiopaque media

io·tha·lam·ic acid \ī-ə-thə-¹la-mik-\ *n*

: a white odorless powder $C_{11}H_9$-$I_3N_2O_4$ used as a radiopaque medium

IP *abbr* intraperitoneal; intraperitoneally

ip·e·cac \¹i-pi-ₜkak\ *or* **ipe·ca·cu·an·ha** \ₜi-pi-ₜka-kü-¹a-nə\ *n* 1 : the dried rhizome and roots of either of two tropical American plants (*Cephaelis acuminata* and *C. ipecacuanha*) of the madder family (Rubiaceae) used esp. as a source of emetine 2 : an emetic and expectorant drug that contains emetine and is prepared from ipecac esp. as a syrup for use in treating accidental poisoning

ipo·date \¹ī-pə-ₜdāt\ *n* : a compound $C_{12}H_{13}I_3N_2O_2$ that is administered as the sodium or calcium salt for use as a radiopaque medium in cholecystography and cholangiography

IPPB *abbr* intermittent positive pressure breathing

ipro·ni·a·zid \ₜī-prə-¹nī-ə-zəd\ *n* : a derivative $C_9H_{13}N_3O$ of isoniazid that is a monoamine oxidase inhibitor used as an antidepressant and formerly used in treating tuberculosis — see MARSILID

ip·si·lat·er·al \ip-si-¹la-tə-rəl\ *adj* : situated or appearing on or affecting the same side of the body — compare CONTRALATERAL — **ip·si·lat·er·al·ly** *adv*

IPSP *abbr* inhibitory postsynaptic potential

IQ \ₜī-¹kyü\ *n* : INTELLIGENCE QUOTIENT

Ir *symbol* iridium

IR *abbr* infrared

ir- — see IN-

irid- *or* **irido-** *comb form* 1 : iris of the eye (*iridectomy*) 2 : iris and (*iridocyclitis*)

iri·dec·to·my \ₜir-ə-¹dek-tə-mē, ₜīr-\ *n, pl* **-mies** : the surgical removal of part of the iris of the eye

iri·den·clei·sis \ₜir-ə-den-¹klī-səs, ₜīr-\ *n, pl* **-clei·ses** \-ₜsēz\ : a surgical procedure esp. for relief of glaucoma in which a small portion of the iris is implanted in a corneal incision to facilitate drainage of aqueous humor

irides *pl of* IRIS

irid·ic \ī-¹ri-dik, i-\ *adj* : of or relating to the iris of the eye

iridis — see HETEROCHROMIA IRIDIS, RUBEOSIS IRIDIS

irid·i·um \ir-¹i-dē-əm\ *n* : a silver-white brittle metallic element of the platinum group — symbol *Ir*; see ELEMENT table

irido·cy·cli·tis \ₜir-ə-dō-sī-¹klī-təs, ₜīr-, -si-\ *n* : inflammation of the iris and the ciliary body

iri·do·di·al·y·sis \ₜir-ə-dō-dī-¹a-lə-səs, ₜīr-\ *n, pl* **-y·ses** \-ₜsēz\ : separation of the iris from its attachments to the ciliary body

ir·i·dol·o·gy \ₜī-rə-¹dä-lə-jē\ *n, pl* **-gies** : the study of the iris of the eye for indications of bodily health and disease — **ir·i·dol·o·gist** \-jist\ n

irid·o·ple·gia \,ir-ə-dō-ˈplē-jə, ,ir-, -jē-ə\ n : paralysis of the sphincter of the iris

irid·ot·o·my \,ir-ə-ˈdä-tə-mē, ,ir-\ n, pl **-mies** : incision of the iris

iris \ˈi-rəs\ n, pl **iris·es** or **iri·des** \ˈi-rə-,dēz, ˈir-ə-\ : the opaque muscular contractile diaphragm that is suspended in the aqueous humor in front of the lens of the eye, is perforated by the pupil and is continuous peripherally with the ciliary body, has a deeply pigmented posterior surface which excludes the entrance of light except through the pupil and a colored anterior surface which determines the color of the eyes

iris bom·bé \-bäm-ˈbā\ n : a condition in which the iris is bowed forward by an accumulation of fluid between the iris and the lens

Irish moss n : the dried and bleached plants of a red alga (esp. *Chondrus crispus*) used as an agent for thickening or emulsifying or as a demulcent; *also* : the red alga itself

iri·tis \i-ˈri-təs\ n : inflammation of the iris of the eye

iron \ˈi̇rn, ˈi-ərn\ n 1 : a heavy malleable ductile magnetic silver-white metallic element vital to biological processes (as in transport of oxygen in the body) — symbol *Fe*; see ELEMENT table 2 : iron chemically combined (~ in the blood) — **iron** *adj*

iron–deficiency anemia n : anemia that is caused by a deficiency of iron and characterized by hypochromic microcytic red blood cells

iron lung n : a device for artificial respiration in which rhythmic alternations in the air pressure in a chamber surrounding a patient's chest force air into and out of the lungs esp. when the nerves governing the chest muscles fail to function because of poliomyelitis — called also *Drinker respirator*

ir·ra·di·ate \i-ˈrā-dē-,āt\ vb **-at·ed; -at·ing** : to affect or treat by radiant energy (as heat); *specif* : to treat by exposure to radiation (as ultraviolet light or gamma rays) — **ir·ra·di·a·tor** \-,ā-tər\ n

ir·ra·di·a·tion \ir-,ā-dē-ˈā-shən\ n 1 : the radiation of a physiologically active agent from a point of origin within the body; *esp* : the spread of a nervous impulse beyond the usual conduction path 2 a : exposure to radiation (as ultraviolet light, X rays, or alpha rays) b : application of radiation (as X rays or gamma rays) esp. for therapeutic purposes

ir·re·duc·ible \ir-i-ˈdü-sə-bəl, -ˈdyü-\ adj : impossible to bring into a desired or normal position or state (an ~ hernia)

ir·reg·u·lar \i-ˈre-gyə-lər\ adj 1 : lacking perfect symmetry of form : not straight, smooth, even, or regular (~ teeth) 2 a : lacking continuity or regularity of occurrence, activity, or function (~ breathing) b *of a physiological function* : failing to occur at regular or normal intervals c *of an individual* : failing to defecate at regular or normal intervals — **ir·reg·u·lar·i·ty** \i-,re-gyə-ˈlar-ə-tē\ n — **ir·reg·u·lar·ly** *adv*

ir·re·me·di·a·ble \ir-i-ˈmē-dē-ə-bəl\ adj : impossible to remedy or cure

ir·re·vers·ible \ir-i-ˈvər-sə-bəl\ adj, *of a pathological process* : of such severity that recovery is impossible (~ brain damage) — **ir·re·vers·ibil·i·ty** \-,vər-sə-ˈbi-lə-tē\ n — **ir·re·vers·ibly** \-ˈvər-sə-blē\ adv

ir·ri·gate \ˈir-ə-,gāt\ vb **-gat·ed; -gat·ing** : to flush (a body part) with a stream of liquid (as in removing a foreign body or medication) — **ir·ri·ga·tion** \,ir-ə-ˈgā-shən\ n — **ir·ri·ga·tor** \ˈir-ə-,gā-tər\ n

ir·ri·ta·bil·i·ty \,ir-ə-tə-ˈbi-lə-tē\ n, pl **-ties** 1 : the property of protoplasm and of living organisms that permits them to react to stimuli 2 a : quick excitability to annoyance, impatience, or anger b : abnormal or excessive excitability of an organ or part of the body (as the stomach or bladder) — **ir·ri·ta·ble** \ˈir-ə-tə-bəl\ adj

irritable bowel syndrome n : a functional commonly psychosomatic disorder of the colon characterized by the secretion and passage of large amounts of mucus, by constipation alternating with diarrhea, and by cramping abdominal pain — called also *irritable colon, irritable colon syndrome, mucous colitis, spastic colon*

ir·ri·tant \ˈir-ə-tənt\ adj : causing irritation; *specif* : tending to produce inflammation — **irritant** n

ir·ri·tate \ˈir-ə-,tāt\ vb **-tat·ed; -tat·ing** 1 : to provoke impatience, anger, or displeasure in 2 : to cause (an organ or tissue) to be irritable : produce irritation in 3 : to produce excitation in (as a nerve) : cause (as a muscle) to contract — **ir·ri·ta·tion** \,ir-ə-ˈtā-shən\ n

ir·ri·ta·tive \ˈir-ə-,tā-tiv\ adj 1 : serving to excite : IRRITATING (an ~ agent) 2 : accompanied with or produced by irritation (~ coughing)

is- or **iso-** *comb form* 1 : equal : homogeneous : uniform (isosmotic) 2 : for or from different individuals of the same species (isoagglutinin)

isch·ae·mia *chiefly Brit var of* ISCHEMIA

isch·emia \is-ˈkē-mē-ə\ n : localized tissue anemia due to obstruction of the inflow of arterial blood (as by the narrowing of arteries by spasm or disease) — **isch·emic** \-mik\ adj — **isch·emi·cal·ly** adv

ischi- or **ischio-** *comb form* 1 : ischium

⟨*ischi*ectomy⟩ 2 : ischial and ⟨*ischio*-rectal⟩

ischia *pl of* ISCHIUM

is·chi·al \'is-kē-əl\ *adj* : of, relating to, or situated near the ischium

ischial spine *n* : a thin pointed triangular eminence that projects from the dorsal border of the ischium and gives attachment to the gemellus superior on its external surface and to the coccygeus, levator ani, and pelvic fascia on its internal surface

ischial tuberosity *n* : a bony swelling on the posterior part of the superior ramus of the ischium that gives attachment to various muscles and bears the weight of the body in sitting

is·chi·ec·to·my \,is-kē-'ek-tə-mē\ *n, pl* **-mies** : surgical removal of a segment of the hipbone including the ischium

is·chio·cav·er·no·sus \,is-kē-ō-,ka-vər-'nō-səs\ *n, pl* **-no·si** \-,sī\ : a muscle on each side that arises from the ischium near the crus of the penis or clitoris and is inserted on the crus near the pubic symphysis

is·chio·coc·cy·geus \-käk-'si-jē-əs\ *n, pl* **-cy·gei** \-jē-,ī, -ē\ : COCCYGEUS

is·chio·fem·o·ral \-'fe-mə-rəl\ *adj* : of, relating to, or being an accessory ligament of the hip joint passing from the ischium below the acetabulum to blend with the articular capsule

is·chio·pu·bic ramus \,is-kē-ō-'pyü-bik-\ *n* : the flattened inferior projection of the hipbone below the obturator foramen consisting of the united inferior rami of the pubis and ischium

is·chio·rec·tal \,is-kē-ō-'rekt-əl\ *adj* : of, relating to, or adjacent to both ischium and rectum (pelvic ∼ abscess)

is·chi·um \'is-kē-əm\ *n, pl* **is·chia** \-ə\ : the dorsal and posterior of the three principal bones composing either half of the pelvis consisting in humans of a thick portion, a large rough eminence on which the body rests when sitting, and a forwardly directed ramus which joins that of the pubis

Ishi·ha·ra \,i-shē-'här-ə\ *adj* : of, relating to, or used in an Ishihara test

Ishihara, Shinobu (1879–1963), Japanese ophthalmologist.

Ishihara test *n* : a widely used test for color blindness that consists of a set of plates covered with colored dots which the test subject views in order to find a number composed of dots of one color which a person with various defects of color vision will confuse with surrounding dots of color

is·land \'ī-lənd\ *n* : an isolated anatomical structure, tissue, or group of cells

island of Lang·er·hans \-'läŋ-ər-,hänz, -,häns\ *n* : ISLET OF LANGERHANS

island of Reil \-'rīl\ *n* : INSULA

Reil, Johann Christian (1759–1813), German anatomist.

is·let \'ī-lət\ *n* : ISLET OF LANGERHANS

islet cell *n* : one of the endocrine cells making up an islet of Langerhans

islet of Lang·er·hans \-'läŋ-ər-,hänz, -,häns\ *n* : any of the groups of small slightly granular endocrine cells that form anastomosing trabeculae among the tubules and alveoli of the pancreas and secrete insulin and glucagon — called also *islet*

Langerhans, Paul (1847–1888), German pathologist.

-ism \,i-zəm\ *n suffix* **1** : act, practice, or process ⟨hypnot*ism*⟩ **2 a** : state, condition, or property ⟨polymor-ph*ism*⟩ **b** : abnormal state or condition resulting from excess of a (specified) thing or marked by resemblance to a (specified) person or thing ⟨alcohol*ism*⟩ ⟨morphin*ism*⟩ ⟨mongol*ism*⟩

iso- — see IS-

iso·ag·glu·ti·na·tion \,ī-(,)sō-ə-,glüt-ᵊn-'ā-shən\ *n* : agglutination of an agglutinogen of one individual by the serum of another of the same species

iso·ag·glu·ti·nin \-ə-'glüt-ᵊn-ən\ *n* : an antibody produced by one individual that causes agglutination of cells (as red blood cells) of other individuals of the same species

iso·ag·glu·tin·o·gen \-ə-glü-'ti-nə-jən\ *n* : an antigenic substance capable of provoking formation of or reacting with an isoagglutinin

iso·al·lox·a·zine \-ə-'läk-sə-,zēn\ *n* : a yellow solid $C_{10}H_6N_4O_2$ that is the precursor of various flavins (as riboflavin)

iso·am·yl nitrite \,ī-sō-'a-məl-\ *n* : AMYL NITRITE

iso·an·ti·body \,ī-(,)sō-'an-ti-,bä-dē\ *n, pl* **-bod·ies** : ALLOANTIBODY

iso·an·ti·gen \-'an-ti-jən\ *n* : ALLOANTIGEN

iso·bor·nyl thio·cyan·o·ace·tate \,ī-sō-'bȯr-nil-,thī-ō-,sī-a-nō-'a-sə-,tāt, -sī-,a-nō-\ *n* : a yellow oily liquid $C_{13}H_{19}N_2OS$ used as a pediculicide

iso·bu·tyl nitrite \,ī-sō-'byüt-ᵊl-\ *n* : a colorless pungent liquid $C_4H_9NO_2$ inhaled by drug abusers for its stimulating effects which are similar to those of amyl nitrite — called also *butyl nitrite*

iso·car·box·az·id \-,kär-'bäk-sə-zəd\ *n* : a hydrazide monoamine oxidase inhibitor $C_{12}H_{13}N_3O_2$ used as an antidepressant — see MARPLAN

iso·chro·mo·some \-'krō-mə-,sōm, -,zōm\ *n* : a chromosome produced by transverse splitting of the centromere so that both arms are from the same side of the centromere, are of equal length, and possess identical genes

iso·cit·rate \,ī-sō-'si-,trāt\ *n* : any salt or ester of isocitric acid; *also* : ISOCITRIC ACID

isocitrate de·hy·dro·ge·nase \-dē-(,)hī-'drä-je-,nās, -'hī-drə-jə-, -,nāz\ *n* : either of two enzymes which catalyze the oxidation of isocitric acid (as in the Krebs cycle) — called also *iso-citric dehydrogenase*

iso·cit·ric acid \ˌī-sə-ˈsi-trik-\ *n* : a crystalline isomer of citric acid that occurs esp. as an intermediate stage in the Krebs cycle

isocitric dehydrogenase *n* : ISOCITRATE DEHYDROGENASE

iso·dose \ˈī-sə-ˌdōs\ *adj* : of or relating to points or zones in a medium that receive equal doses of radiation

iso·elec·tric \ˌī-sō-i-ˈlek-trik\ *adj* : being the pH at which the electrolyte will not migrate in an electrical field ⟨the ~ point of a protein⟩

isoelectric focusing *n* : an electrophoretic technique for separating proteins by causing them to migrate under the influence of an electric field through a medium (as a gel) having a pH gradient to locations with pH values corresponding to their isoelectric points

iso·en·zyme \ˌī-sō-ˈen-ˌzīm\ *n* : any of two or more chemically distinct but functionally similar enzymes — called also *isozyme* — **iso·en·zy·mat·ic** \ˌī-sō-ˌen-zə-ˈma-tik, -zī-\ *adj* — **iso·en·zy·mic** \-en-ˈzī-mik\ *adj*

iso·eth·a·rine \ˈī-e-thə-ˌrēn\ *n* : an adrenergic drug $C_{13}H_{21}NO_3$ used as a bronchodilator

iso·fluro·phate \-ˈflur-ə-ˌfāt\ *n* : a volatile irritating liquid ester $C_6H_{14}FO_3P$ that acts as a nerve gas by inhibiting cholinesterases and as a miotic and that is used chiefly in treating glaucoma — called also *DFP, diisopropyl fluorophosphate*

iso·ge·ne·ic \ˌī-sō-jə-ˈnē-ik, -ˈnā-\ *adj* : SYNGENEIC ⟨an ~ graft⟩

iso·gen·ic \-ˈje-nik\ *adj* : characterized by essentially identical genes

iso·graft \ˈī-sə-ˌgraft\ *n* : a homograft between genetically identical or nearly identical individuals — **isograft** *vb*

iso·hem·ag·glu·ti·nin \-ˌhē-mə-ˈglüt-ᵊn-ən\ *n* : a hemagglutinin causing isoagglutination

iso·hy·dric shift \ˌī-sō-ˈhī-drik-\ *n* : the set of chemical reactions in a red blood cell by which oxygen is released to the tissues and carbon dioxide is taken up while the blood remains at constant pH

iso·im·mu·ni·za·tion \ˌī-sō-ˌi-myə-nə-ˈzā-shən\ *n* : production by an individual of antibodies against constituents of the tissues of another individual of the same species (as when transfused with blood from one belonging to a different blood group)

¹iso·late \ˈī-sə-ˌlāt\ *vb* **-lat·ed; -lat·ing** : to set apart from others: as a : to separate (one with a contagious disease) from others not similarly infected b : to separate (as a chemical compound) from all other substances : obtain pure or in a free state

²iso·late \ˈī-sə-lət, -ˌlāt\ *n* 1 : an individual (as a single organism), viable part

of an organism (as a cell), or a strain that has been isolated (as from diseased tissue): *also* : a pure culture produced from such an isolate 2 : a socially withdrawn individual

iso·la·tion \ˌī-sə-ˈlā-shən\ *n* 1 : the action of isolating or condition of being isolated ⟨put the patient in ~⟩ 2 : a psychological defense mechanism consisting of the separating of ideas or memories from the emotions connected with them

Iso·lette \ˌī-sə-ˈlet\ *trademark* — used for an incubator for premature infants that provides controlled temperature and humidity and an oxygen supply

iso·leu·cine \ˌī-sō-ˈlü-ˌsēn\ *n* : a crystalline essential amino acid $C_6H_{13}NO_2$ isomeric with leucine

isol·o·gous \ī-ˈsä-lə-gəs\ *adj* : SYNGENEIC

iso·mer \ˈī-sə-mər\ *n* : any of two or more compounds, radicals, ions, or nuclides that contain the same number of atoms of the same elements but differ in structural arrangement and properties — **iso·mer·ic** \ˌī-sə-ˈmer-ik\ *adj* — **isom·er·ism** \ī-ˈsä-mə-ˌri-zəm\ *n*

iso·me·thep·tene \ˌī-sō-me-ˈthep-ˌtēn\ *n* : a vasoconstrictive and antispasmodic drug $C_9H_{19}N$ administered as the hydrochloride or mucate

iso·met·ric \ˌī-sə-ˈme-trik\ *adj* : of, relating to, involving, or being muscular contraction (as in isometrics) against resistance, without significant shortening of muscle fibers, and with marked increase in muscle tone — compare ISOTONIC 2 — **iso·met·ri·cal·ly** *adv*

iso·met·rics \ˌī-sə-ˈme-triks\ *n sing or pl* : isometric exercise or an isometric system of exercises

iso·ni·a·zid \ˌī-sə-ˈnī-ə-zəd\ *n* : a crystalline compound $C_6H_7N_3O$ used in treating tuberculosis

isonicotinic acid hydrazide *n* : ISONIAZID

iso·nip·e·caine \ˌī-sō-ˈni-pə-ˌkān\ *n* : MEPERIDINE

Iso·nor·in \ˌī-sə-ˈnȯr-ən\ *trademark* — used for a preparation of isoproterenol

iso·os·mot·ic \ˌī-sō-äz-ˈmä-tik\ *adj* : ISOSMOTIC

Iso·paque \ˌī-sō-ˈpāk\ *trademark* — used for a preparation of metrizoate sodium

iso·peri·stal·tic \ˌī-sō-ˌper-ə-ˈstȯl-tik, -ˈstäl-, -ˈstal-\ *adj* : performed or arranged so that the grafted or anastomosed parts exhibit peristalsis in the same direction ⟨~ gastroenterostomy⟩ — **iso·peri·stal·ti·cal·ly** *adv*

iso·phane \ˈī-sō-ˌfān\ *adj* : of, relating to, or being a ratio of protamine to insulin equal to that in a solution made by mixing equal parts of a solution of the two in which all the protamine precipitates and a solution of the two in which all the insulin precipitates

iso·phane insulin n : an isophane mixture of protamine and insulin — called also *isophane*

iso·preg·nen·one \-'preg-ne-₁nōn\ n : DYDROGESTERONE

iso·pren·a·line \₁ī-sə-'pren-ᵊl-ən\ n : ISOPROTERENOL

iso·pro·pa·mide iodide \₁ī-sō-'prō-pə-₁mēd-\ n : an anticholinergic C₂₃H₃₃IN₂O used esp. for its antispasmodic and antisecretory effect on the gastrointestinal tract — called also *isopropamide*

iso·pro·pa·nol \-'prō-pə-₁nȯl, -₁nōl\ n : ISOPROPYL ALCOHOL

iso·pro·pyl alcohol \₁ī-sə-'prō-pəl-\ n : a volatile flammable alcohol C₃H₈O used as a rubbing alcohol — called also *isopropanol*

iso·pro·pyl·ar·te·re·nol \₁ī-sə-₁prō-pə-₁lär-tə-'rē-₁nȯl, -₁nōl\ n : ISOPROTERENOL

isopropyl my·ris·tate \-mə-'ris-₁tāt\ n : an ester C₁₇H₃₄O₂ of isopropyl alcohol that is used as an emollient to promote absorption through the skin

iso·pro·ter·e·nol \₁ī-sə-prō-'ter-ə-₁nȯl, -nȯl\ n : a drug C₁₁H₁₇NO₃ used in the treatment of asthma — called also *isoprenaline, isopropylarterenol*; see ISONORIN, ISUPREL

isop·ter \ī-'säp-tər\ n : a contour line in a representation of the visual field around the points representing the macula lutea that passes through the points of equal visual acuity

Isor·dil \'ī-sȯr-₁dil\ *trademark* — used for a preparation of isosorbide dinitrate

is·os·mot·ic \₁ī-₁säz-'mä-tik, -₁säs-\ adj : of, relating to, or exhibiting equal osmotic pressure ⟨∼ solutions⟩ — compare HYPERTONIC 2, HYPOTONIC 2 — **is·os·mot·i·cal·ly** adv

iso·sor·bide \₁ī-sō-'sȯr-₁bīd\ n 1 : a diuretic C₆H₁₀O₄ 2 : ISOSORBIDE DINITRATE

isosorbide di·ni·trate \-dī-'nī-₁trāt\ n : a coronary vasodilator C₆H₈N₂O₈ used esp. in the treatment of angina pectoris — see ISORDIL

Isos·po·ra \ī-'säs-pə-rə\ n : a genus of coccidian protozoans closely related to the genus *Eimeria* and including the only coccidian (*I. hominis*) known to be parasitic in humans

isothiocyanate — see ALLYL ISOTHIOCYANATE

iso·thio·pen·dyl \₁ī-sō-₁thī-ō-'pen-₁dil\ n : an antihistaminic drug C₁₆H₁₉N₃S

iso·ton·ic \₁ī-sə-'tä-nik\ adj 1 : ISOSMOTIC — used of solutions 2 : of, relating to, or being muscular contraction in the absence of significant resistance, with marked shortening of muscle fibers, and without great increase in muscle tone — compare ISOMETRIC — **iso·ton·i·cal·ly** adv — **iso·to·nic·i·ty** \-tō-'ni-sə-tē\ n

iso·tope \'ī-sə-₁tōp\ n 1 : any of two or more species of atoms of a chemical element with the same atomic number but that differ in the number of neutrons in an atom and have different physical properties 2 : NUCLIDE — **iso·to·pic** \₁ī-sə-'tä-pik, -'tō-\ adj — **iso·to·pi·cal·ly** adv

iso·trans·plant \₁ī-sō-'trans-₁plant\ n : a graft between syngeneic individuals

iso·tret·i·no·in \₁ī-sō-'tre-tə-₁nō-ən\ n : a synthetic vitamin A derivative C₂₀H₂₈O₂ that inhibits sebaceous gland function and keratinization and that is used in the treatment of acne but is contraindicated in pregnancy because of implication as a cause of birth defects — see ACCUTANE

isotropic band n : I BAND

iso·type \'ī-sə-₁tīp\ n : any of the categories of antibodies determined by their physicochemical properties (as molecular weight) and antigenic characteristics that occur in all individuals of a species — compare ALLOTYPE, IDIOTYPE — **iso·typ·ic** \₁ī-sə-'ti-pik\ adj

iso·va·ler·ic acid \₁ī-sō-və-'lir-ik-, -'ler-\ n : a liquid acid C₅H₁₀O₂ that has a disagreeable odor

isovaleric ac·i·de·mia \-₁a-sə-'dē-mē-ə\ n : a metabolic disorder characterized by the presence of an abnormally high concentration of isovaleric acid in the blood causing acidosis, coma, and an unpleasant body odor

iso·vol·ume \'ī-sə-₁väl-yəm, -(₁)yüm\ adj : ISOVOLUMETRIC

iso·vol·u·met·ric \₁ī-sə-₁väl-yü-'me-trik\ adj : of, relating to, or characterized by unchanging volume; *esp* : relating to or being an early phase of ventricular systole in which the cardiac muscle exerts increasing pressure on the contents of the ventricle without significant change in the muscle fiber length and the ventricular volume remains constant

iso·vo·lu·mic \-və-'lü-mik\ adj : ISOVOLUMETRIC

is·ox·az·o·lyl \(₁)ī-₁säk-'sa-zə-₁lil\ adj : relating to or being any of a group of semisynthetic penicillins (as oxacillin and cloxacillin) that are resistant to penicillinase, stable in acids, and active against gram-positive bacteria

is·ox·su·prine \ī-'säk-sə-₁prēn\ n : a sympathomimetic drug C₁₈H₂₃NO₃ used chiefly as a vasodilator

iso·zyme \'ī-sə-₁zīm\ n : ISOENZYME — **iso·zy·mic** \₁ī-sə-'zī-mik\ adj

is·sue \'i-(₁)shü\ n : a discharge (as of blood) from the body that is caused by disease or other physical disorder or that is produced artificially; *also* : an incision made to produce such a discharge

isth·mus \'is-məs\ n : a contracted anatomical part or passage connecting two larger structures or cavities: as a : an embryonic constriction separating the midbrain from the hindbrain b : the lower portion of the uterine corpus — **isth·mic** \'is-mik\ *adj*

isthmus of the fauces *n* : FAUCES

Isu·prel \'i-sù-ˌprel\ *trademark* — used for a preparation of isoproterenol

itai–itai \i-ˌtī-i-ˌtī\ *n* : an extremely painful condition caused by poisoning following the ingestion of cadmium and characterized by bone decalcification — called also *itai-itai disease*

itch \'ich\ *n* **1** : an uneasy irritating sensation in the upper surface of the skin usu. held to result from mild stimulation of pain receptors 2 : a skin disorder accompanied by an itch: *esp* : a contagious eruption caused by an itch mite of the genus *Sarcoptes* (*S. scabiei*) that burrows in the skin and causes intense itching — **itch** *vb* — **itch·i·ness** \'i-chē-nəs\ *n* — **itchy** \'i-chē\ *adj*

¹**itching** *adj* : having, producing, or marked by an uneasy sensation in the skin (an ~ skin eruption)

²**itching** *n* : ITCH 1

itch mite *n* : any of several minute parasitic mites that burrow into the skin and cause itch; *esp* : a mite of any of several varieties of a species of the genus *Sarcoptes* (*S. scabiei*) that causes the itch

-ite \ˌīt\ *n suffix* **1** : substance produced through some (specified) process (catabol*ite*) 2 : segment or constituent part of a body or of a bodily part (somite) (dendr*ite*)

-it·ic \'i-tik\ *adj suffix* : of, resembling, or marked by — in adjectives formed from nouns usu. ending in *-ite* (dendr*itic*) and *-itis* (bronch*itic*)

-i-tis \'ī-təs\ *n suffix, pl* **-i-tis-es** *also* **-it-i-des** \'i-tə-ˌdēz\ *or* **-i-tes** \'ī-(ˌ)tēz\

: disease usu. inflammatory of a (specified) part or organ : inflammation of (laryng*itis*) (appendic*itis*) (bronch*itis*)

ITP *abbr* idiopathic thrombocytopenic purpura

IU *abbr* : international unit

IUCD \ˌi-(ˌ)yü-(ˌ)sē-'dē\ *n* : INTRAUTERINE DEVICE

IUD \ˌi-(ˌ)ü-'dē\ *n* : INTRAUTERINE DEVICE

IUDR \ˌi-(ˌ)yü-(ˌ)dē-'är\ *n* : IDOXURIDINE

¹**IV** \'ī-'vē\ *n, pl* **IVs** : an apparatus used to administer an intravenous injection or feeding: *also* : such an injection or feeding

²**IV** *abbr* **1** intravenous; intravenously 2 intraventricular

iver·mec·tin \ˌi-vər-'mek-tən\ *n* : a drug mixture of two structurally similar semisynthetic lactones that is used in veterinary medicine as an anthelmintic, acaricide, and insecticide and in human medicine to treat onchocerciasis

IVF *abbr* in vitro fertilization

IVP *abbr* intravenous pyelogram

Ix·o·des \ik-'sō-(ˌ)dēz\ *n* : a widespread genus of ixodid ticks (as the deer tick) many of which are bloodsucking parasites of humans and animals, and sometimes cause paralysis or other severe reactions

ix·od·i·cide \ik-'sä-di-ˌsīd, -'sō-\ *n* : an agent that destroys ticks

ix·o·did \ik-'sä-did, -'sō-\ *adj* : of or relating to a family (Ixodidae) of ticks (as the deer tick, American dog tick, and lone star tick) having a hard outer shell and feeding on two or three hosts during the life cycle — **ixodid** *n*

J

jaag·siek·te *also* **jaag·ziek·te** \'yäg-ˌsēk-tə, -ˌzēk-\ *n* : a chronic contagious pneumonia of sheep and sometimes goats that is caused by a virus

jack·et \'ja-kət\ *n* **1** : a rigid covering that envelops the upper body and provides support, correction, or restraint 2 : JACKET CROWN

jacket crown *n* : an artificial crown that is placed over the remains of a natural tooth

jack·so·ni·an \jak-'sō-nē-ən\ *adj, often cap* : of, relating to, associated with, or resembling Jacksonian epilepsy

    Jack·son \'jak-sən\, **John Hughlings** (1835–1911), British neurologist.

Jacksonian epilepsy *n* : epilepsy that is characterized by progressive spreading of the abnormal movements or sensations from a focus affecting a muscle group on one side of the body to adjacent muscles or by becoming generalized and that corresponds to

the spread of epileptic activity in the motor cortex

Ja·cob·son's nerve \'jä-kəb-sənz-\ *n* : TYMPANIC NERVE

    Jacobson \'yä-kóp-sən\, **Ludwig Levin** (1783–1843), Danish anatomist.

Jacobson's organ *n* : a slender canal in the nasal mucosa that ends in a blind pouch, has an olfactory function, and is rudimentary in adult humans — called also *vomeronasal organ*

jac·ti·ta·tion \ˌjak-tə-'tā-shən\ *n* : a tossing to and fro or jerking and twitching of the body or its parts : excessive restlessness esp. in certain psychiatric disorders — **jac·ti·tate** \'jak-tə-ˌtāt\ *vb*

Jaf·fé reaction \yä-'fā-, zhä-\ *also* **Jaffé's reaction** \-'fāz-\ *n* : a reaction between creatinine and picric acid in alkaline solution that results in the formation of a red compound and is used to determine creatinine (as in creatinuria)

Jaffé \ yä-ʹfā\, **Max** (1841–1911), German biochemist.

jag·siek·te *or* **jag·ziek·te** *var of* JAAG-SIEKTE

jail fever \ʹjāl-\ *n* : TYPHUS a

jake leg \ʹjāk-\ *n* : a paralysis caused by drinking improperly distilled or contaminated liquor

Ja·kob–Creutz·feldt disease \ʹyä-(₊)kōb-ʹkroits-₊felt-\ *n* : CREUTZ-FELDT-JAKOB DISEASE

jal·ap \ʹja-ləp, ʹjä-\ *n* **1** : the dried tuberous root of a Mexican plant (*Ipomoea purga*) of the morning-glory family (Convolvulaceae); *also* : a powdered purgative drug prepared from it that contains resinous glycosides **2** : a plant yielding jalap

JAMA *abbr* Journal of the American Medical Association

ja·mais vu \₊zhä-₊me-ʹvǖ, ₊jä-mä-ʹvü\ *n* : a disorder of memory characterized by the illusion that the familiar is being encountered for the first time — compare AMNESIA, PARAMNESIA b

James·town weed \ʹjāmz-taún-\ *n* : JIMSONWEED

jani·ceps \ʹja-nə-₊seps, ʹjā-\ *n* : a malformed double fetus joined at the thorax and skull and having two equal faces looking in opposite directions

Japanese B encephalitis *n* : an encephalitis that occurs epidemically esp. in Japan in the summer, is caused by an arbovirus, and usu. produces a subclinical infection

japonica — see SCHISTOSOMIASIS JAPONICA

jar·gon \ʹjär-gən\ *n* : gibberish or babbling speech associated with aphasia, extreme mental retardation, or a severe mental illness

Ja·risch–Herx·hei·mer reaction \ʹyä-rish-ʹherks-₊hi-mər-\ *n* : an increase in the symptoms of a spirochetal disease (as syphilis, Lyme disease, or relapsing fever) occurring in some persons when treatment with spirocheticidal drugs is started — called also *Herxheimer reaction*

  Jarisch, Adolf (1850–1902), Austrian dermatologist.

  Herxheimer, Karl (1861–1944), German dermatologist.

jaun·dice \ʹjón-dəs, ʹjän-\ *n* **1** : a yellowish pigmentation of the skin, tissues, and certain body fluids caused by the deposition of bile pigments that follows interference with normal production and discharge of bile (as in certain liver diseases) or excessive breakdown of red blood cells (as after internal hemorrhage or in various hemolytic states) **2** : any disease or abnormal condition (as hepatitis A or leptospirosis) that is characterized by jaundice — **jaun·diced** \-dəst\ *adj*

jaw \ʹjó\ *n* **1** : either of two complex cartilaginous or bony structures in most vertebrates that border the mouth, support the soft parts enclosing it, and usu. bear teeth on their oral margin: **a** : an upper structure more or less firmly fused with the skull — called also *upper jaw, maxilla* **b** : a lower structure that consists of a single bone or of completely fused bones and that is hinged, movable, and articulated by a pair of condyles with the temporal bone of either side — called also *inferior maxillary bone, lower jaw, mandible* **2** : the parts constituting the walls of the mouth and serving to open and close it — usu. used in pl.

jaw·bone \ʹjó-₊bōn\ *n* : JAW 1: *esp* : MANDIBLE

jawed \ʹjód\ *adj* : having jaws — usu. used in combination (square-*jawed*)

JCAH *abbr* Joint Commission on Accreditation of Hospitals

J chain \ʹjā-\ *n* : a relatively short polypeptide chain with a high number of cysteine residues that is found in antibodies of the IgM and IgA classes

jejun- *or* **jejuno-** *comb form* **1** : jejunum (*jejunitis*) **2** : jejunum and (*jejunoileitis*)

je·ju·nal \ji-ʹjün-ᵊl\ *adj* : of or relating to the jejunum

je·ju·ni·tis \₊je-jü-ʹnī-təs\ *n* : inflammation of the jejunum

je·ju·no·il·e·al bypass \ji-₊jü-nō-ʹi-lē-əl-\ *n* : a surgical bypass operation performed esp. to reduce absorption in the small intestine that involves joining the first part of the jejunum with the more distal segment of the ileum

je·ju·no·il·e·it·is \ji-₊jü-nō-₊i-lē-ʹī-təs, ₊je-jü-nō-\ *n* : inflammation of the jejunum and the ileum

je·ju·no·il·e·os·to·my \ji-₊jü-nō-₊i-lē-ʹäs-tə-mē, ₊je-jü-nō-\ *n, pl* **-mies** : the formation of an anastomosis between the jejunum and the ileum

je·ju·nos·to·my \ji-₊jü-ʹnäs-tə-mē, ₊je-jü-\ *n, pl* **-mies 1** : the surgical formation of an opening through the abdominal wall into the jejunum **2** : the opening made by jejunostomy

je·ju·num \ji-ʹjü-nəm\ *n, pl* **je·ju·na** \-nə\ : the section of the small intestine that comprises the first two fifths beyond the duodenum and that is larger, thicker-walled, and more vascular and has more circular folds and fewer Peyer's patches than the ileum

jel·ly \ʹje-lē\ *n, pl* **jellies** : a semisolid gelatinous substance: as **a** : a medicated preparation usu. intended for local application (ephedrine ∼) **b** : a jellylike preparation used in electrocardiography to obtain better conduction of electricity (electrode ∼)

jel·ly·fish \-₊fish\ *n* : a free-swimming marine sexually reproducing coelenterate of either of two classes (Hydrozoa and Scyphozoa) that has a nearly transparent saucer-shaped body and marginal tentacles studded with stinging cells

je·quir·i·ty bean \jə-ˈkwir-ə-tē-\ *n* 1 : the poisonous scarlet and black seed of the rosary pea 2 : ROSARY PEA 1

jerk \ˈjərk\ *n* : an involuntary spasmodic muscular movement due to reflex action; *esp* : one induced by an external stimulus — see KNEE JERK

jet fa·tigue \ˈjet-fə-ˌtēg\ *n* : JET LAG

jet in·jec·tor \-in-ˈjek-tər\ *n* : a device used to inject subcutaneously a fine stream of fluid under high pressure without puncturing the skin — **jet in·jec·tion** \-ˈjek-shən\ *n*

jet lag \ˈjet-ˌlag\ *n* : a condition that is characterized by various psychological and physiological effects (as fatigue and irritability), occurs following long flight through several time zones, and prob. results from disruption of circadian rhythms in the human body — called also *jet fatigue* — **jet-lagged** *adj*

jig·ger \ˈji-gər\ *n* : CHIGGER

jim·son·weed \ˈjim-sən-ˌwēd\ *n* : a poisonous tall annual weed of the genus *Datura* (*D. stramonium*) with rank-smelling foliage, large white or violet trumpet-shaped flowers, and globe-shaped prickly fruits that is a source of stramonium — called also *Jamestown weed*

jit·ters \ˈji-tərz\ *n pl* : a state of extreme nervousness or nervous shaking — **jit·ter** \-tər\ *vb* — **jit·teri·ness** \-tə-rē-nəs\ *n* — **jit·tery** *adj*

JND *abbr* just noticeable difference

jock itch \ˈjäk-\ *n* : ringworm of the crotch : TINEA CRURIS — called also *jockey itch*

jock·strap \ˈjäk-ˌstrap\ *n* : ATHLETIC SUPPORTER

John·e's bacillus \ˈyō-ˌnēz-\ *n* : a bacillus of the genus *Mycobacterium* (*M. paratuberculosis*) that causes Johne's disease

    Johne \ˈyō-nə\, **Heinrich Albert** (1839–1910), German bacteriologist.

John·e's disease \ˈyō-nəz-\ *n* : a chronic often fatal enteritis esp. of cattle that is caused by Johne's bacillus — called also *paratuberculosis*

john·ny *also* **john·nie** \ˈjä-nē\ *n, pl* **john·nies** : a short-sleeved collarless gown with an opening in the back for wear by persons (as hospital patients) undergoing medical examination or treatment

joint \ˈjȯint\ *n* : the point of contact between skeletal elements whether movable or rigidly fixed together with the surrounding and supporting parts (as membranes, tendons, ligaments) — **out of joint** *of a bone* : having the head slipped from its socket

joint capsule *n* : ARTICULAR CAPSULE

joint·ed \ˈjȯin-təd\ *adj* : having joints

joint ill *n* : NAVEL ILL

joint mouse \-ˈmau̇s\ *n* : a loose frag-

ment (as of cartilage) within a synovial space

joule \ˈjül\ *n* : the absolute mks unit of work or energy equal to 10^7 ergs or approximately 0.7375 foot-pounds

    Joule, James Prescott (1818–1889), British physicist.

¹ju·gal \ˈjü-gəl\ *adj* : MALAR

²jugal *n* : ZYGOMATIC BONE — called also *jugal bone*

¹jug·u·lar \ˈjä-gyə-lər, ˈjü-\ *adj* 1 : of or relating to the throat or neck 2 : of or relating to the jugular vein ⟨~ pulsations⟩

²jugular *n* : JUGULAR VEIN

jugulare — see GLOMUS JUGULARE

jugular foramen *n* : a large irregular opening from the posterior cranial fossa that is bounded anteriorly by the petrous part of the temporal bone and posteriorly by the jugular notch of the occipital bone and that transmits the inferior petrosal sinus, the glossopharyngeal, vagus, and accessory nerves, and the internal jugular vein

jugular fossa *n* : a depression on the basilar surface of the petrous portion of the temporal bone that contains a dilation of the internal jugular vein

jugular ganglion *n* : SUPERIOR GANGLION

jugular notch \-ˈnäch\ *n* 1 : SUPRASTERNAL NOTCH 2 **a** : a notch in the inferior border of the occipital bone behind the jugular process that forms the posterior part of the jugular foramen **b** : a notch in the petrous portion of the temporal bone that corresponds to the jugular notch of the occipital bone and with it makes up the jugular foramen

jugular process *n* : a quadrilateral or triangular process of the occipital bone on each side that articulates with the temporal bone and is situated lateral to the condyle of the occipital bone on each side articulating with the atlas

jugular trunk *n* : either of two major lymph vessels of which one lies on each side of the body and drains the head and neck

jugular vein *n* : any of several veins of each side of the neck: as **a** : a vein that collects the blood from the interior of the cranium, the superficial part of the face, and the neck, runs down the neck on the outside of the internal and common carotid arteries, and unites with the subclavian vein to form the innominate vein — called also *internal jugular vein* **b** : a smaller and more superficial vein that collects most of the blood from the exterior of the cranium and deep parts of the face and opens into the subclavian vein — called also *external jugular vein* **c** : a vein that commences near the hyoid bone and joins the terminal part of the external jugular vein or the subclavian vein — called also *anterior jugular vein*

juice \'jüs\ *n* : a natural bodily fluid (as blood, lymph, or a secretion) — see GASTRIC JUICE, PANCREATIC JUICE

junc·tion \'jəŋk-shən\ *n* : a place or point of meeting — see NEUROMUSCULAR JUNCTION — **junc·tion·al** \-shə-nəl\ *adj*

junctional nevus *n* : a nevus that develops at the junction of the dermis and epidermis and is potentially cancerous

junctional rhythm *n* : a cardiac rhythm resulting from impulses coming from a locus of tissue in the area of the atrioventricular node

junctional tachycardia *n* : tachycardia associated with the generation of impulses in a locus in the region of the atrioventricular node

Jung·ian \'yŭŋ-ē-ən\ *adj* : of, relating to, or characteristic of C. G. Jung or his psychological doctrines which stress the opposition of introversion and extroversion and the concept of mythology and cultural and racial inheritance in the psychology of individuals — **Jungian** *n*

Jung \'yŭŋ\, **Carl Gustav (1875–1961),** Swiss psychologist and psychiatrist.

jungle fever *n* : a severe form of malaria or yellow fever — compare JUNGLE YELLOW FEVER

jungle rot *n* : any of various esp. pyogenic skin infections contracted in tropical environments

jungle yellow fever *n* : yellow fever endemic in or near forest or jungle areas in Africa and So. America and transmitted by mosquitoes (esp. genus *Haemagogus*) other than members of the genus *Aedes*

ju·ni·per \'jü-nə-pər\ *n* : an evergreen shrub or tree (genus *Juniperus*) of the cypress family (Cupressaceae)

juniper tar *n* : a dark tarry liquid used locally in treating skin diseases and obtained by distillation from the wood of a Eurasian juniper (*Junip-*

erus oxycedrus) — called also *cade oil, juniper tar oil*

just noticeable difference *n* : the minimum amount of change in a physical stimulus required for a subject to detect reliably a difference in the level of stimulation

jus·to ma·jor \'jəs-tō-'mā-jər\ *adj, of pelvic dimensions* : greater than normal

justo mi·nor \-'mī-nər\ *adj, of pelvic dimensions* : smaller than normal

ju·ve·nile \'jü-və-ˌnīl, -nəl\ *adj* 1 : physiologically immature or undeveloped 2 : reflecting psychological or intellectual immaturity — **juvenile** *n*

juvenile amaurotic idiocy *n* : SPIELMEYER-VOGT DISEASE

juvenile delinquency *n* 1 : conduct by a juvenile characterized by antisocial behavior that is beyond parental control and therefore subject to legal action 2 : a violation of the law committed by a juvenile and not punishable by death or life imprisonment — **juvenile delinquent** *n*

juvenile diabetes *n* : INSULIN-DEPENDENT DIABETES MELLITUS

juvenile–onset diabetes *n* : INSULIN-DEPENDENT DIABETES MELLITUS

juxta- *comb form* : situated near (*juxta*glomerular)

jux·ta·ar·tic·u·lar \ˌjək-stə-är-'ti-kyə-lər\ *adj* : situated near a joint

jux·ta·glo·mer·u·lar \-glə-'mer-yə-lər, -glō-, -ə-lər\ *adj* : situated near a kidney glomerulus

juxtaglomerular apparatus *n* : a functional unit near a kidney glomerulus that controls renin release and is composed of juxtaglomerular cells and a macula densa

juxtaglomerular cell *n* : any of a group of cells that are situated in the wall of each afferent arteriole of a kidney glomerulus near its point of entry adjacent to a macula densa and that produce and secrete renin

jux·ta·med·ul·lary \ˌjək-stə-'med-əl-ˌer-ē, -'mej-ə-l-; -mə-'də-lə-rē\ *adj* : situated or occurring near the edge of the medulla of the kidney

K

K *symbol* [New Latin *kalium*] potassium

Kahn test \'kän-\ *n* : a serum-precipitation reaction for the diagnosis of syphilis — called also *Kahn, Kahn reaction*

Kahn, **Reuben Leon** (*b* 1887), American immunologist.

kai·nic acid \'kī-nik-, 'kā-\ *n* : the neurotoxic active principle $C_{10}H_{15}NO_4$ from a dried red alga (*Digenia simplex*) used as an ascaricide

kala–azar \'kä-lə-ə-'zär, 'ka-\ *n* : a severe infectious disease chiefly of Asia

marked by fever, progressive anemia, leukopenia, and enlargement of the spleen and liver and caused by a flagellate of the genus *Leishmania* (*L. donovani*) that is transmitted by the bite of sand flies and proliferates in reticuloendothelial cells — called also *dumdum fever*; see LEISHMANDONOVAN BODY

ka·li·ure·sis \ˌkä-lē-yù-'rē-səs, ˌka-\ *n, pl* **-ure·ses** \-ˌsēz\ : excretion of potassium in the urine esp. in excessive amounts — **ka·li·uret·ic** \-'re-tik\ *adj*

kal·li·din \'ka-lə-din\ *n* : either of two

vasodilator kinins formed from blood plasma globulin by the action of kallikrein

kal·li·kre·in \ˌka-lə-ʰkrē-ən, kə-ʰli-krē-ən\ *n* : a hypotensive proteinase that liberates kinins from blood plasma proteins and is used therapeutically for vasodilation

Kall·mann's syndrome \ʰkȯl-mənz-\ *n* : a hereditary condition marked by hypogonadism caused by a deficiency of gonadotropins and anosmia caused by failure of the olfactory lobes to develop

    Kallmann, Franz Josef (1897–1965), American geneticist and psychiatrist.

kal·ure·sis \ˌkā-lù-ʰrē-səs, ˌka-, -lyù-\ *var of* KALIURESIS

ka·ma·la \ʰkä-mə-lə\ *n* : an orange red cathartic powder derived from the fruit of an East Indian tree (*Mallotus philippinensis*) of the spurge family (Euphorbiaceae) and used as a vermifuge chiefly in veterinary practice

kana·my·cin \ˌka-nə-ʰmīs-ᵊn\ *n* : a broad-spectrum antibiotic from a Japanese soil bacterium of the genus *Streptomyces* (*S. kanamyceticus*)

Kan·ner's syndrome \ʰka-nərz-\ *n* : INFANTILE AUTISM

    Kanner, Leo (1894–1981), American psychiatrist.

Kan·trex \ʰkan-ˌtreks\ *trademark* — used for a preparation of kanamycin

ka·olin \ʰkā-ə-lin\ *n* : a fine usu. white clay that is used in medicine esp. as an adsorbent in the treatment of diarrhea (as in food poisoning or dysentery)

Kao·pec·tate \ˌkā-ō-ʰpek-ˌtāt\ *trademark* — used for a preparation of kaolin used as an antidiarrheal

Ka·po·si's sarcoma \ʰka-pə-zēz-, kə-ʰpō-, -sēz-\ *n* : a neoplastic disease affecting esp. the skin and mucous membranes, characterized usu. by the formation of pink to reddish-brown or bluish tumorous plaques, macules, papules, or nodules esp. on the lower extremities, and formerly limited primarily to elderly men in whom it followed a benign course but now being a major and sometimes fatal disease associated with immunodeficient individuals with AIDS — abbr. *KS*

    Kaposi \ʰkȯ-pō-sē\, **Moritz (1837–1902)**, Hungarian dermatologist.

kap·pa chain *or* **κ chain** \ʰka-pə-\ *n* : a polypeptide chain of one of the two types of light chain that are found in antibodies and can be distinguished antigenically and by the sequence of amino acids in the chain — compare LAMBDA CHAIN

ka·ra·ya gum \kə-ʰrī-ə-\ *n* : any of several laxative vegetable gums obtained from tropical Asian trees (genera *Sterculia* of the family Sterculiaceae and *Cochlospermum* of the family Bixaceae) — called also *gum karaya, karaya, sterculia gum*

ka·rez·za \kä-ʰret-sə\ *n* : COITUS RESERVATUS

Kar·ta·ge·ner's syndrome \kär-ʰtä-gə-nərz-, ˌkär-tə-ʰgä-nərz-\ *n* : an abnormal condition inherited as an autosomal recessive trait and characterized by situs inversus, abnormalities in the protein structure of cilia, and chronic bronchiectasis and sinusitis

    Kartagener, Manes (b 1897), Swiss physician.

kary- *or* **karyo-** *also* **cary-** *or* **caryo-** *comb form* : nucleus of a cell (*karyokinesis*) (*karyotype*)

kary·oga·my \ˌkar-ē-ʰä-gə-mē\ *n, pl* **-mies** : the fusion of cell nuclei (as in fertilization)

karyo·gram \ʰkar-ē-ō-ˌgram\ *n* : KARYOTYPE; *esp* : a diagrammatic representation of the chromosome complement of an organism

karyo·ki·ne·sis \ˌkar-ē-ō-kə-ʰnē-səs, -ki-\ *n, pl* **-ne·ses** \-ˌsēz\ **1** : the nuclear phenomena characteristic of mitosis **2** : the whole process of mitosis — compare CYTOKINESIS — **karyo·ki·net·ic** \-ʰne-tik\ *adj*

kary·ol·o·gy \ˌkar-ē-ʰä-lə-jē\ *n, pl* **-gies 1** : the minute cytological characteristics of the cell nucleus esp. with regard to the chromosomes of a single cell or of the cells of an organism or group of organisms **2** : a branch of cytology concerned with the karyology of cell nuclei — **karyo·log·i·cal** \-ē-ə-ʰlä-ji-kəl\ *also* **karyo·log·ic** \-jik\ *adj* — **karyo·log·i·cal·ly** *adv*

karyo·lymph \ʰkar-ē-ō-ˌlimf\ *n* : NUCLEAR SAP

kary·ol·y·sis \ˌkar-ē-ʰä-lə-səs\ *n, pl* **-y·ses** \-ˌsēz\ : dissolution of the cell nucleus with loss of its affinity for basic stains sometimes occurring normally but usu. in necrosis — compare KARYORRHEXIS

karyo·plasm \ʰkar-ē-ō-ˌpla-zəm\ *n* : NUCLEOPLASM

karyo·pyk·no·sis \ˌkar-ē-(ˌ)ō-pik-ʰnō-səs\ *n* : shrinkage of the cell nuclei of epithelial cells (as of the vagina) with breakup of the chromatin into unstructured granules — **karyo·pyk·not·ic** \-ʰnä-tik\ *adj*

karyopyknotic index *n* : an index that is calculated as the percentage of epithelial cells with karyopyknotic nuclei exfoliated from the vagina and is used in the hormonal evaluation of a patient

kary·or·rhex·is \ˌkar-ē-ō-ʰrek-səs\ *n, pl* **-rhex·es** \-ˌsēz\ : a degenerative cellular process involving fragmentation of the nucleus and the breakup of the chromatin into unstructured granules — compare KARYOLYSIS

karyo·some \ʰkar-ē-ə-ˌsōm\ *n* : a mass of chromatin in a cell nucleus that resembles a nucleolus

karyo·type \ʰkar-ē-ə-ˌtīp\ *n* : the chromosomal characteristics of a cell; *also* : the chromosomes themselves or a representation of them — **karyo·typ·ic** \,kar-ē-ə-'ti-pik\ *adj* — **karyo·typ·i·cal·ly** *adv*

²**karyotype** *vb* **-typed; -typ·ing** : to determine the karyotype of

karyo·typ·ing \-,tīp-iŋ\ *n* : the action or process of studying karyotypes or of making representations of them

Ka·ta·ya·ma \,kä-tə-'yä-mə\ *n* : a genus of Asian freshwater snails (family Bulimidae) including important intermediate hosts of human trematode worms of the genus *Schistosoma* (as *S. japonicum*)

Ka·wa·sa·ki disease \,kä-wə-'sä-kē-\ *n* : an acute febrile disease affecting young children that is characterized by erythema of the conjunctivae and of the mucous membranes of the upper respiratory tract, erythema and edema of the hands and feet, a rash followed by desquamation, and cervical lymphadenopathy — called also *Kawasaki syndrome, mucocutaneous lymph node disease, mucocutaneous lymph node syndrome*

Kawasaki, Tomisaku (*fl* 1961), Japanese pediatrician.

Kay·ser–Flei·scher ring \'kī-zər-'flī-shər-\ *n* : a brown or greenish brown ring of copper deposits around the cornea that is characteristic of Wilson's disease

Kayser, Bernhard (1869–1954) and Fleischer, Bruno Otto (*b* 1874), German ophthalmologists.

kb *abbr* kilobase

ked \'ked\ *n* : SHEEP KED

Ke·gel exercises \'kā-gəl-, 'kē-\ *n pl* : repetitive contractions by a woman of the muscles that are used to stop the urinary flow in urination in order to increase the tone of the pubococcygeal muscle esp. to control incontinence or to enhance sexual responsiveness during intercourse

Kegel, Arnold Henry (*b* 1894), American physician.

Kell \'kel\ *adj* : of, relating to, or being a group of allelic red-blood-cell antigens of which some are important causes of transfusion reactions and some forms of erythroblastosis fetalis

Kell, medical patient.

Kel·ler \'ke-lər\ *adj* : relating to or being an operation to correct hallux valgus by excision of the proximal part of the proximal phalanx of the big toe with resulting shortening of the toe

Keller, William Lorden (1874–1959), American surgeon.

ke·loid \'kē-,loid\ *n* : a thick scar resulting from excessive growth of fibrous tissue and occurring esp. after burns or radiation injury — **keloid** *adj* — **ke·loi·dal** \kē-'loid-ᵊl\ *adj*

kelp \'kelp\ *n* : any of various seaweeds that are large brown algae (or-

ders Laminariales and Fucales) and esp. laminarias

kel·vin \'kel-vin\ *n* : a unit of temperature equal to ¹/₂₇₃.₁₆ of the Kelvin scale temperature of the triple point of water and equal to the Celsius degree

Thom·son \'täm-sən\, Sir William (1st Baron Kelvin of Largs) (1824–1907), British physicist.

Kelvin *adj* : relating to, conforming to, or being a temperature scale according to which absolute zero is 0 K, the equivalent of −273.15°C

Ken·a·cort \'ke-nə-,kȯrt\ *trademark* — used for a preparation of triamcinolone

kennel cough *n* : tracheobronchitis of dogs or cats

Ken·ny method \'ke-nē-\ *n* : a method of treating poliomyelitis consisting basically of application of hot fomentations and rehabilitation of muscular activity by passive movement and then guided active coordination — called also *Kenny treatment*

Kenny, Elizabeth (1880–1952), Australian nurse.

ker·a·sin \'ker-ə-sən\ *n* : a cerebroside $C_{48}H_{93}NO_8$ that occurs esp. in Gaucher's disease

ker·a·tan sulfate \'ker-ə-,tan-\ *n* : any of several sulfated glycosaminoglycans that have been found esp. in the cornea, cartilage, and bone

ker·a·tec·to·my \,ker-ə-'tek-tə-mē\ *n, pl* **-mies** : surgical excision of part of the cornea

ke·rat·ic precipitates \kə-'ra-tik-\ *n pl* : accumulations on the posterior surface of the cornea esp. of macrophages and epithelial cells that occur in chronic inflammatory conditions — called also *keratitis punctata*

ker·a·tin \'ker-ət-ᵊn\ *n* : any of various sulfur-containing fibrous proteins that form the chemical basis of horny epidermal tissues (as hair and nails)

ke·ra·ti·ni·za·tion \,ker-ə-tə-nə-'zā-shən, kə-,rat-ᵊn-ə-\ *n* : conversion into keratin or keratinous tissue — **ke·ra·ti·nize** \'ker-ə-tə-,nīz, kə-'rat-ᵊn-,īz\ *vb*

ke·ra·ti·no·cyte \kə-'rat-ᵊn-ə-,sīt, ,ker-ə-'ti-nə-\ *n* : an epidermal cell that produces keratin

ke·ra·ti·nous \kə-'rat-ᵊn-əs, ,ker-ə-'tī-nəs\ *adj* : composed of or containing keratin : HORNY

ker·a·ti·tis \,ker-ə-'tī-təs\ *n, pl* **-tit·i·des** \-'ti-tə-,dēz\ : inflammation of the cornea of the eye characterized by burning or smarting, blurring of vision, and sensitiveness to light and caused by infectious or noninfectious agents — compare KERATOCONJUNCTIVITIS

keratitis punc·ta·ta \-,pəŋk-'tä-tə, -'tā-\ *n* : KERATIC PRECIPITATES

ker·a·to·ac·an·tho·ma \,ker-ə-tō-,a-,kan-'thō-mə\ *n, pl* **-mas** *or* **-ma·ta**

\-mə-tə\ : a rapidly growing skin tumor that occurs esp. in elderly individuals, resembles a carcinoma of squamous epithelial cells but does not spread, and tends to heal spontaneously with some scarring if left untreated

ker·a·to·con·junc·ti·vi·tis \'ker-ə-(₁)tō-kən-₁jəŋk-tə-'vi-təs\ n : combined inflammation of the cornea and conjunctiva; esp : EPIDEMIC KERATOCONJUNCTIVITIS — compare KERATITIS

keratoconjunctivitis sic·ca \-'si-kə\ n : a condition associated with reduction in lacrimal secretion and marked by redness of the conjunctiva, by itching and burning of the eye, and usu. by filaments of desquamated epithelial cells adhering to the cornea

ker·a·to·co·nus \₁ker-ə-tō-'kō-nəs\ n : cone-shaped protrusion of the cornea

ker·a·to·der·ma \-'dər-mə\ n : a horny condition of the skin

keratoderma blen·nor·rhag·i·cum \-₁ble-nō-'ra-ji-kəm\ n : KERATOSIS BLENNORRHAGICA

ker·a·to·der·mia \₁ker-ə-tō-'dər-mē-ə\ n : KERATODERMA

ker·a·to·hy·a·lin \-'hi-ə-lən\ also **ker·a·to·hy·a·line** \-lən, -₁lēn\ n : a colorless translucent protein that occurs esp. in granules of the stratum granulosum of the epidermis

ker·a·tol·y·sis \₁ker-ə-'tä-lə-səs\ n, pl -y·ses \-₁sēz\ 1 : the process of breaking down or dissolving keratin 2 : a skin disease marked by peeling of the horny layer of the epidermis

¹**ker·a·to·lyt·ic** \₁ker-ə-tō-'li-tik\ adj : relating to or causing keratolysis

²**keratolytic** n : a keratolytic agent

ker·a·to·ma·la·cia \₁ker-ə-tō-mə-'lā-shə, -sē-ə\ n : a softening and ulceration of the cornea of the eye resulting from severe systemic deficiency of vitamin A — compare XEROPHTHALMIA

ker·a·tome \'ker-ə-₁tōm\ n : a surgical instrument used for making an incision in the cornea in cataract operations

ker·a·tom·e·ter \₁ker-ə-'tä-mə-tər\ n : an instrument for measuring the curvature of the cornea

ker·a·tom·e·try \₁ker-ə-'tä-mə-trē\ n, pl -tries : measurement of the form and curvature of the cornea — **ker·a·to·met·ric** \-tō-'me-trik\ adj

ker·a·to·mil·eu·sis \₁ker-ət-ō-mi-'lü-səs, -'lyü-\ n : keratoplasty in which a piece of the cornea is removed, frozen, shaped to correct refractive error, and reinserted

ker·a·top·a·thy \₁ker-ə-'tä-pə-thē\ n, pl -thies : any noninflammatory disease of the eye — see BAND KERATOPATHY

ker·a·to·pha·kia \₁ker-ə-tō-'fā-kē-ə\ n : keratoplasty in which corneal tissue from a donor is frozen, shaped, and

inserted into the cornea of a recipient

ker·a·to·plas·ty \'ker-ə-tō-₁plas-tē\ n, pl -ties : plastic surgery on the cornea; esp : corneal grafting

ker·a·to·pros·the·sis \₁ker-ə-tō-präs-'thē-səs, -'präs-thə-\ n, pl -the·ses \-₁sēz\ : a plastic replacement for an opacified inner part of a cornea

ker·a·to·scope \'ker-ə-tō-₁skōp\ n : an instrument for examining the cornea esp. to detect irregularities of its anterior surface

ker·a·to·sis \₁ker-ə-'tō-səs\ n, pl -to·ses \-₁sēz\ 1 : a disease of the skin marked by overgrowth of horny tissue 2 : an area of the skin affected with keratosis — **ker·a·tot·ic** \-'tä-tik\ adj

keratosis blen·nor·rhag·i·ca \-₁ble-nō-'ra-ji-kə\ n : a disease that is characterized by a scaly rash esp. on the palms and soles and is associated esp. with Reiter's syndrome — called also keratoderma blennorrhagicum

keratosis fol·lic·u·lar·is \-₁fä-lə-kyə-'ler-əs\ n : DARIER'S DISEASE

keratosis pi·lar·is \-pi-'ler-əs\ n : a condition marked by the formation of hard conical elevations in the openings of the sebaceous glands esp. of the thighs and arms that resemble permanent goose bumps

ker·a·tot·o·mist \₁ker-ə-'tä-tə-mist\ n : a surgeon who performs keratotomies

ker·a·tot·o·my \-mē\ n, pl -mies : incision of the cornea

ke·ri·on \'kir-ē-₁än\ n : inflammatory ringworm of the hair follicles of the beard and scalp usu. accompanied by secondary bacterial infection

ker·nic·ter·us \₁kar-'nik-tə-rəs\ n : a condition marked by the deposit of bile pigments in the nuclei of the brain and spinal cord and by degeneration of nerve cells that occurs usu. in infants as a part of the syndrome of erythroblastosis fetalis — **ker·nic·ter·ic** \-rik\ adj

Ker·nig sign \'ker-nig-\ or **Kernig's sign** \'ker-nigz-\ n : an indication usu. present in meningitis that consists of pain and resistance on attempting to extend the leg at the knee with the thigh flexed at the hip

Kernig, Vladimir Mikhailovich (1840–1917), Russian physician.

ket·a·mine \'kē-tə-₁mēn\ n : a general anesthetic that is administered intravenously and intramuscularly in the form of its hydrochloride $C_{13}H_{16}$CINO·HCl

ke·thox·al \kē-'thäk-səl\ n : an antiviral agent $C_6H_{12}O_4$

ke·to \'kē-(₁)tō\ adj : of or relating to a ketone; also : containing a ketone group

keto acid n : a compound that is both a ketone and an acid

ke·to·ac·i·do·sis \₁kē-tō-₁a-sə-'dō-səs\ n, pl -do·ses \-₁sēz\ : acidosis accompanied by ketosis (diabetic ~)

ke·to·co·na·zole \ˌkē-tō-ˈkō-nə-ˌzōl\ *n* : a broad-spectrum antifungal agent used to treat chronic internal and cutaneous disorders

ke·to·gen·e·sis \ˌkē-tō-ˈje-nə-səs\ *n, pl* **-e·ses** \-ˌsēz\ : the production of ketone bodies (as in diabetes) — **ke·to·gen·ic** \-ˈje-nik\ *adj*

ketogenic diet *n* : a diet supplying a large amount of fat and minimal amounts of carbohydrate and protein

ke·to·glu·tar·ic acid \ˌkē-tō-glü-ˈtar-ik-\ *n* : either of two crystalline keto derivatives $C_5H_6O_5$ of glutaric acid; *esp* : ALPHA-KETOGLUTARIC ACID

α–ketoglutaric acid *var of* ALPHA-KETOGLUTARIC ACID

ke·to·nae·mia *chiefly Brit var of* KETONEMIA

ke·tone \ˈkē-ˌtōn\ *n* : an organic compound (as acetone) with a CO group attached to two carbon atoms

ketone body *n* : any of the three compounds acetoacetic acid, acetone, and hydroxybutyric acid which are normal intermediates in lipid metabolism and accumulate in the blood and urine in abnormal amounts in conditions of impaired metabolism (as diabetes mellitus) — called also *acetone body*

ke·to·ne·mia \ˌkē-tə-ˈnē-mē-ə\ *n* 1 : a condition marked by an abnormal increase of ketone bodies in the circulating blood — called also *hyperketonemia* 2 : KETOSIS 2 — **ke·to·ne·mic** \-ˈnē-mik\ *adj*

ke·ton·uria \ˌkē-tə-ˈnùr-ē-ə, -ˈnyùr-\ *n* : the presence of excess ketone bodies in the urine in conditions (as diabetes mellitus and starvation acidosis) involving reduced or disturbed carbohydrate metabolism — called also *acetonuria*

ke·tose \ˈkē-ˌtōs, -ˌtōz\ *n* : a sugar (as fructose) containing one ketone group per molecule

ke·to·sis \kē-ˈtō-səs\ *n, pl* **-to·ses** \-ˌsēz\ 1 : an abnormal increase of ketone bodies in the body in conditions of reduced or disturbed carbohydrate metabolism (as in uncontrolled diabetes mellitus) — compare ACIDOSIS, ALKALOSIS 2 : a nutritional disease esp. of cattle that is marked by reduction of blood sugar and the presence of ketone bodies in the blood, tissues, milk, and urine — **ke·tot·ic** \-ˈtä-tik\ *adj*

ke·to·ste·roid \ˌkē-tō-ˈstir-ˌòid, -ˈster-\ *n* : a steroid (as cortisone or estrone) containing a ketone group; *esp* : 17-KETOSTEROID

17–ketosteroid *n* : any of the ketosteroids (as androsterone, dehydroepiandrosterone, and estrone) that have the keto group attached to carbon atom 17 of the steroid ring structure, are present in normal human urine, and may be an indication of a tumor

of the adrenal cortex or ovary when present in excess

Ke·ty method \ˈkē-tē-\ *n* : a method of determining coronary blood flow by measurement of nitrous oxide levels in the blood of a patient breathing nitrous oxide

Kety, Seymour Solomon (*b* 1915), American physiologist.

kg *abbr* kilogram

khel·lin \ˈke-lən\ *n* : a crystalline compound $C_{14}H_{12}O_5$ obtained from the fruit of a Middle Eastern plant (*Ammi visnaga*) of the carrot family (Umbelliferae) and used esp. as a coronary vasodilator

kid·ney \ˈkid-nē\ *n, pl* **kidneys** : one of a pair of vertebrate organs situated in the body cavity near the spinal column that excrete waste products of metabolism. in humans are bean-shaped organs about 4½ inches (11½ centimeters) long lying behind the peritoneum in a mass of fatty tissue, and consist chiefly of nephrons by which urine is secreted, collected, and discharged into the pelvis of the kidney whence it is conveyed by the ureter to the bladder — compare MESONEPHROS, METANEPHROS, PRONEPHROS

kidney stone *n* : a calculus in the kidney — called also *renal calculus*

kidney worm *n* : any of several nematode worms parasitic in the kidneys: as **a** : GIANT KIDNEY WORM **b** : a common worm of the genus *Stephanurus* (*S. dentatus*) that is related to the gapeworm and is parasitic in the kidneys, lungs, and other viscera of the hog in warm regions

Kien·böck's disease \ˈkēn-ˌbeks-\ *n* : osteochondrosis affecting the lunate bone

Kien·böck \ˈkēn-ˌbœk\, **Robert** (1871–1953), Austrian roentgenologist.

killer bee *n* : AFRICANIZED BEE

killer cell *n* : a T cell that functions in cell-mediated immunity by destroying a cell (as a tumor cell) having a specific antigenic molecule on its surface by causing lysis of the cell or by releasing a nonspecific toxin — called also *killer T cell*

ki·lo·base \ˈki-lə-ˌbās\ *n* : a unit of measure of the length of a nucleic-acid chain (as of DNA or RNA) that equals one thousand base pairs

ki·lo·cal·o·rie \-ˌka-lə-rē\ *n* : CALORIE 1b

ki·lo·gram \ˈki-lə-ˌgram, ˈkē-\ *n* 1 : the basic metric unit of mass and weight that is nearly equal to 1000 cubic centimeters of water at its maximum density 2 : the weight of a kilogram mass under earth's gravity

kilogram calorie *n* : CALORIE 1b

ki·lo·joule \ˈki-lə-ˌjül\ *n* : 1000 joules

ki·lo·me·ter \ˈki-lə-ˌmē-tər, kə-ˈlä-mə-tər\ *n* : 1000 meters

ki·lo·rad \ˈki-lə-ˌrad\ *n* : 1000 rads

ki·lo·volt \-ˌvōlt\ *n* : a unit of potential difference equal to 1000 volts

kin- *or* **kine-** *or* **kino-** *or* **cin-** *or* **cino-** *comb form* : motion : action ⟨*kines*thesia⟩

kin·aes·the·sia *chiefly Brit var of* KINES-THESIA

ki·nase \ˈkī-ˌnās, -ˌnāz\ *n* : an enzyme that catalyzes the transfer of phosphate groups from a high-energy phosphate-containing molecule (as ATP or ADP) to a substrate — called also *phosphokinase*

ki·ne·mat·ics \ˌkī-nə-ˈma-tiks, ˌki-\ *n* 1 : a science that deals with aspects of motion apart from considerations of mass and force 2 : the properties and phenomena of an object or system in motion of interest to kinematics ⟨the ~ of the human ankle joint⟩ — **ki·ne·mat·ic** \-tik\ *or* **ki·ne·mat·i·cal** \-ti-kəl\ *adj*

ki·ne·plas·ty \ˈkī-nə-ˌplas-tē, ˈkī-\ *var of* CINEPLASTY

kinesi- *or* **kinesio-** *comb form* : movement ⟨*kinesio*logy⟩

-ki·ne·sia \kə-ˈnē-zhə, kī-, -zhē-ə\ *n comb form* : movement : motion ⟨hyper*kinesia*⟩

ki·ne·si·ol·o·gy \kə-ˌnē-sē-ˈä-lə-jē, kī-, -zē-\ *n, pl* **-gies** : the study of the principles of mechanics and anatomy in relation to human movement — **ki·ne·si·o·log·ic** \-ō-ˈlä-jik\ *or* **ki·ne·si·o·log·i·cal** \-i-kəl\ *adj* — **ki·ne·si·ol·o·gist** \kə-ˌnē-sē-ˈä-lə-jist, kī-, -zē-\ *n*

ki·ne·sis \kə-ˈnē-səs, kī-\ *n, pl* **ki·ne·ses** \-ˌsēz\ : a movement that lacks directional orientation and depends upon the intensity of stimulation

-ki·ne·sis \kə-ˈnē-sis, kī-\ *n, pl* **-ki·ne·ses** \-ˌsēz\ 1 : division ⟨karyo*kinesis*⟩ 2 : production of motion ⟨psycho*kinesis*⟩ ⟨tele*kinesis*⟩

kin·es·the·sia \ˌki-nəs-ˈthē-zhə, ˌkī-, -zhē-ə\ *or* **kin·es·the·sis** \-ˈthē-səs\ *n, pl* **-the·sias** *or* **-the·ses** \-ˌsēz\ : a sense mediated by end organs located in muscles, tendons, and joints and stimulated by bodily movements and tensions; *also* : sensory experience derived from this sense — see MUSCLE SENSE — **kin·es·thet·ic** \-ˈthe-tik\ *adj* — **kin·es·thet·i·cal·ly** *adv*

kinet- *or* **kineto-** *comb form* : movement : motion ⟨*kineto*chore⟩

ki·net·ic \kə-ˈne-tik, kī-\ *adj* : of or relating to the motion of material bodies and the forces and energy associated therewith — **ki·net·i·cal·ly** *adv*

ki·net·ics \kə-ˈne-tiks, kī-\ *n sing or pl* 1 a : a science that deals with the effects of forces upon the motions of material bodies or with changes in a physical or chemical system b : the rate of change in such a system 2 : the mechanism by which a physical or chemical change is effected

ki·net·o·chore \kə-ˈne-tə-ˌkōr, kī-\ *n* : CENTROMERE

king co·bra \-ˈkō-brə\ *n* : a large cobra

(*Ophiophagus hannah*) of southeastern Asia and the Philippines — called also *hamadryad*

king·dom \ˈkiŋ-dəm\ *n* : any of the three primary divisions of lifeless material, plants, and animals into which natural objects are grouped; *also* : a biological category (as Protista) that ranks above the phylum

king's evil *n, often cap K & E* : SCROFULA

ki·nin \ˈkī-nən\ *n* : any of various polypeptide hormones that are formed locally in the tissues and cause dilation of blood vessels and contraction of smooth muscle

ki·ni·nase \ˈkī-nə-ˌnās, -ˌnāz\ *n* : an enzyme in blood that destroys a kinin

ki·nin·o·gen \kī-ˈni-nə-jən\ *n* : an inactive precursor of a kinin — **ki·nin·o·gen·ic** \(ˌ)kī-ˌni-nə-ˈje-nik\ *adj*

kino- — see KIN-

ki·no·cil·i·um \ˌkī-nō-ˈsi-lē-əm\ *n, pl* **-cil·ia** \-lē-ə\ : a motile cilium; *esp* : one that occurs alone at the end of a sensory hair cell of the inner ear among numerous nonmotile stereocilia

Kirsch·ner wire \ˈkərsh-nər-\ *n* : metal wire inserted through bone and used to achieve internal traction or immobilization of bone fractures

Kirschner, Martin (1879–1942), German surgeon.

kissing bug *n* : CONENOSE

kissing disease *n* : INFECTIOUS MONONUCLEOSIS

kiss of life *n, chiefly Brit* : artificial respiration by the mouth-to-mouth method

kleb·si·el·la \ˌkleb-zē-ˈe-lə\ *n* 1 *cap* : a genus of nonmotile gram-negative rod-shaped and frequently encapsulated bacteria (family Enterobacteriaceae) 2 : any bacterium of the genus *Klebsiella*

Klebs \ˈkleps\, **(Theodor Albrecht) Edwin (1834–1913),** German bacteriologist.

Klebs–Löff·ler bacillus \ˈkleps-ˈlef-lər-, ˈklebz-\ *n* : a bacterium of the genus *Corynebacterium* (*C. diphtheriae*) that causes human diphtheria

Löff·ler \ˈlœf-lər\, **Friedrich August Johannes (1852–1915),** German bacteriologist.

klee·blatt·schä·del \ˈklā-ˌblät-ˌshäd-ᵊl\ *n* : CLOVERLEAF SKULL

Klein·ian \ˈklī-nē-ən\ *adj* : of, relating to, or according to the psychoanalytic theories or practices of Melanie Klein — **Kleinian** *n*

Klein \ˈklīn\, **Melanie (1882–1960),** Austrian psychoanalyst.

klept- *or* **klepto-** *comb form* : stealing : theft ⟨*klepto*mania⟩

klep·to·lag·nia \ˌklep-tə-ˈlag-nē-ə\ *n* : sexual arousal and gratification produced by committing an act of theft

klep·to·ma·nia \ˌklep-tə-ˈmā-nē-ə, -nyə\ *n* : a persistent neurotic impulse to steal esp. without economic motive

klep·to·ma·ni·ac \-nē-ˌak\ n : an individual exhibiting kleptomania

Kline·fel·ter's syndrome \ˈklīn-ˌfel-tərz-\ also **Kline·fel·ter syndrome** \-tər-\ n : an abnormal condition in a male characterized by two X chromosomes and one Y chromosome, infertility, and smallness of the testicles

Klinefelter, Harry Fitch (b 1912), American physician.

Kline reaction \ˈklīn-\ n : KLINE TEST

Kline test n : a rapid precipitation test for the diagnosis of syphilis

Kline, Benjamin Schoenbrun (b 1886), American pathologist.

Klip·pel–Feil syndrome \kli-ˈpel-ˈfīl-\ n : congenital fusion of the cervical vertebrae resulting in a short and relatively immobile neck

Klip·pel \klē-ˈpel\, **Maurice** (1858–1942) and **Feil** \ˈfāl\, **André** (b 1884), French neurologists.

Klump·ke's paralysis \ˈklümp-kēz-\ n : atrophic paralysis of the forearm and the hand due to injury to the eighth cervical and first thoracic nerves

Dé·jé·rine–Klump·ke \dā-zhā-ˌrēn-klüm-ˈkē\, **Augusta** (1859–1927), French neurologist.

km abbr kilometer

knee \ˈnē\ n 1 : a joint in the middle part of the leg that is the articulation between the femur, tibia, and patella — called also *knee joint* 2 : the part of the leg that includes this joint — **kneed** \ˈnēd\ adj

knee–cap \ˈnē-ˌkap\ n : PATELLA

knee jerk n : an involuntary forward jerk or kick produced by a light blow or sudden strain upon the patellar ligament of the knee that causes a reflex contraction of the quadriceps muscle — called also *patellar reflex*

knee joint n : KNEE 1

Kne·mi·do·kop·tes \ˌnē-mə-dō-ˈkäp-(ˌ)tēz\ n : a genus of itch mites (family Sarcoptidae) that attack birds

knife \ˈnīf\ n, pl **knives** \ˈnīvz\ 1 : any of various instruments used in surgery primarily to sever tissues: as a : a cutting instrument consisting of a sharp blade attached to a handle b : an instrument that cuts by means of an electrical current 2 : SURGERY 3 — usu. used in the phrase *under the knife* (went under the ~ this morning)

knit \ˈnit\ vb **knit** or **knit·ted**; **knit·ting** : to grow or cause to grow together (a fracture that *knitted* slowly)

knock–knee \ˈnäk-ˈnē\ n : a condition in which the legs curve inward at the knees — called also *genu valgum* — **knock–kneed** \-ˌnēd\ adj

knot \ˈnät\ n 1 : an interlacing of the parts of one or more flexible bodies (as threads or sutures) in a lump to prevent their spontaneous separation — see SURGEON'S KNOT 2 : a usu. firm

or hard lump or swelling or protuberance in or on a part of the body or a bone or process — compare SURFER'S KNOT — **knot** vb

knuck·le \ˈnə-kəl\ n 1 a : the rounded prominence formed by the ends of the two adjacent bones at a joint — used esp. of those at the joints of the fingers b : the joint of a knuckle 2 : a sharply flexed loop of intestines incarcerated in a hernia

Koch·er's forceps \ˈkō-kərz-\ n : a strong forceps for controlling bleeding in surgery having serrated blades with interlocking teeth at the tips

Kocher \ˈkō-kər\, **Emil Theodor** (1841–1917), Swiss surgeon.

Koch's bacillus \ˈköks-, ˈkä-chəz-\ or **Koch bacillus** \ˈkök-, ˈkäch-\ n : a bacillus of the genus *Mycobacterium* (*M. tuberculosis*) that causes human tuberculosis

Koch \ˈkök\, **(Heinrich Hermann) Robert** (1843–1910), German bacteriologist.

Koch's postulates n pl : a statement of the steps required to establish a microorganism as the cause of a disease: (1) it must be found in all cases of the disease; (2) it must be isolated from the host and grown in pure culture; (3) it must reproduce the original disease when introduced into a susceptible host; (4) it must be found present in the experimental host so infected — called also *Koch's laws*

Koch–Weeks bacillus \-ˈwēks-\ n : a bacterium of the genus *Haemophilus* (*H. aegyptius*) associated with an infectious form of human conjunctivitis

Weeks, John Elmer (1853–1949), American ophthalmologist.

Koch–Weeks conjunctivitis n : conjunctivitis caused by the Koch-Weeks bacillus

koil·onych·ia \ˌkȯi-lō-ˈni-kē-ə\ n : abnormal thinness and concavity of fingernails occurring esp. in hypochromic anemias — called also *spoon nails*

Kop·lik's spots \ˈkä-pliks-\ or **Kop·lik spots** \-plik-\ n pl : small bluish white dots surrounded by a reddish zone that appear on the mucous membrane of the cheeks and lips before the appearance of the skin eruption in a case of measles

Koplik, Henry (1858–1927), American pediatrician.

Korean hemorrhagic fever n : a hemorrhagic fever that is endemic to Korea, Manchuria, and Siberia, is caused by a hantavirus, and is characterized by acute renal failure in addition to the usual symptoms of the hemorrhagic fevers

Ko·rot·koff sounds also **Ko·rot·kow sounds** or **Ko·rot·kov sounds** \kō-ˈröt-kȯf-\ n pl : arterial sounds heard through a stethoscope applied to the brachial artery distal to the cuff of a sphygmomanometer that change with varying cuff pressure and that are used to determine systolic and diastolic blood pressure

Ko·rot·koff, Nikolai Sergieyevich (*b* 1874), Russian physician.

Kor·sa·koff's psychosis \'kȯr-sə-ˌkȯfs-\ *n* : an abnormal mental condition that is usu. a sequel of chronic alcoholism, is often associated with polyneuritis, and is characterized by an impaired ability to acquire new information and by an irregular memory loss for which the patient often attempts to compensate through confabulation

Korsakoff (*or* **Korsakov**), **Sergei Sergeyevich** (1853–1900), Russian psychiatrist.

Korsakoff's syndrome *or* **Korsakoff syndrome** *n* : KORSAKOFF'S PSYCHOSIS

Kr *symbol* krypton

Krab·be's disease \'kra-bēz-\ *n* : a rapidly progressive demyelinating familial leukoencephalopathy with onset in infancy characterized by irritability followed by tonic convulsions, quadriplegia, blindness, deafness, dementia, and death

Krabbe \'krä-bə\, **Knud H.** (1885–1961), Danish neurologist.

krad \'kā-ˌrad\ *n, pl* **krad** *also* **krads** : KILORAD

krait \'krīt\ *n* : any of a genus (*Bungarus*) of brightly banded extremely venomous nocturnal elapid snakes of Pakistan, India, southeastern Asia, and adjacent islands

krau·ro·sis \krȯ-'rō-səs\ *n, pl* **-ro·ses** \-ˌsēz\ : atrophy and shriveling of the skin or mucous membrane esp. of the vulva where it is often a precancerous lesion — **krau·rot·ic** \-'rä-tik\ *adj*

kraurosis vul·vae \-'vȯl-vē\ *n* : kraurosis of the vulva

Krau·se's corpuscle \'kraú-zəz-\ *n* : any of various rounded sensory end organs occurring in mucous membranes (as of the conjunctiva or genitals) — called also *corpuscle of Krause*

Krause, Wilhelm Johann Friedrich (1833–1910), German anatomist.

Krause's end–bulb *n* : KRAUSE'S CORPUSCLE

kre·bi·o·zen \krə-'bī-ə-zən\ *n* : a drug used in the treatment of cancer esp. in the 1950's that was of unproved effectiveness, is not now used in the U.S., and was of undisclosed formulation but was reported to contain creatine

Krebs cycle \'krebz-\ *n* : a sequence of reactions in the living organism in which oxidation of acetic acid or acetyl equivalent provides energy for storage in phosphate bonds (as in ATP) — called also *citric acid cycle, tricarboxylic acid cycle*

Krebs, Sir Hans Adolf (1900–1981), German-British biochemist.

Kru·ken·berg tumor \'krü-kən-ˌbərg-\ *n* : a metastatic ovarian tumor of mucin-producing epithelial cells usu. derived from a primary gastrointestinal tumor

Kru·ken·berg \-ˌberk\, **Friedrich Ernst** (1871–1946), German pathologist.

kryp·ton \'krip-ˌtän\ *n* : a colorless relatively inert gaseous element — symbol *Kr*; see ELEMENT table

KS *abbr* Kaposi's sarcoma

KUB *abbr* kidney, ureter, and bladder

Kupf·fer cell \'kúp-fər-\ *also* **Kupf·fer's cell** \-fərz-\ *n* : a fixed macrophage of the walls of the liver sinusoids that is stellate with a large oval nucleus and the cytoplasm commonly packed with fragments resulting from phagocytic action

Kupffer, Karl Wilhelm von (1829–1902), German anatomist.

ku·ru \'kü-ˌrü, 'kúr-ü\ *n* : a rare progressive fatal encephalopathy that is caused by a slow virus, resembles Creutzfeldt-Jakob disease, occurs among tribesmen in eastern New Guinea, and is characterized esp. by spongiform changes and proliferation of astrocytes in the brain — called also *laughing death, laughing sickness*

Kuss·maul breathing \'kús-ˌmaúl-\ *n* : abnormally slow deep respiration characteristic of air hunger and occurring esp. in acidotic states — called also *Kussmaul respiration*

Kussmaul, Adolf (1822–1902), German physician.

Kveim test \'kvām-\ *n* : an intradermal test for sarcoidosis in which an antigen prepared from the lymph nodes or spleen of human sarcoidosis patients is injected intracutaneously and which is positive when an infiltrated area, papule, nodule, or superficial necrosis appears around the site of injection or a skin biopsy yields typical tubercles and giant cell formations upon histological examination

Kveim, Morten Ansgar (*b* 1892), Norwegian physician.

kwa·shi·or·kor \ˌkwä-shē-'ȯr-kȯr, -ȯr-'kȯr\ *n* : severe malnutrition in infants and children that is characterized by failure to grow and develop, changes in the pigmentation of the skin and hair, edema, fatty degeneration of the liver, anemia, and apathy and is caused by a diet excessively high in carbohydrate and extremely low in protein — compare PELLAGRA

Kwell \'kwel\ *trademark* — used for a preparation of lindane

Kya·sa·nur For·est disease \ˌkya-sə-'nùr-'fȯr-əst-\ *n* : a disease caused by a flavivirus that is characterized by fever, headache, diarrhea, and intestinal bleeding and is transmitted by immature ticks of the genus *Haemaphysalis*

ky·mo·gram \'kī-mə-ˌgram\ *n* : a record made by a kymograph

ky·mo·graph \-ˌgraf\ *n* : a device which graphically records motion or pressure: *esp* : a recording device including an electric motor or clockwork that drives a usu. slowly revolving drum which carries a roll of plain or smoked paper and also having an arrangement for tracing on the paper by means of a stylus a graphic record of motion or pressure (as of the organs of speech, blood pressure, or respira-tion) often in relation to particular intervals of time — **ky·mo·graph·ic** \ˌkī-mə-'gra-fik\ *adj* — **ky·mog·ra·phy** \kī-'mä-grə-fē\ *n*

ky·pho·sco·li·o·sis \ˌkī-fō-ˌskō-lē-'ō-səs\ *n*, *pl* **-o·ses** \-ˌsēz\ : backward and lateral curvature of the spine

ky·pho·sis \kī-'fō-səs\ *n*, *pl* **-pho·ses** \-ˌsēz\ : exaggerated backward curvature of the thoracic region of the spinal column — compare LORDOSIS, SCOLIOSIS — **ky·phot·ic** \-'fä-tik\ *adj*

L

L *abbr* lumbar — used esp. with a number from 1 to 5 to indicate a vertebra or segment of the spinal cord in the lumbar region

l- *prefix* 1 \ˌel-(ˌ)vō, ˌel, 'el\ : levorotatory ⟨*l*-tartaric acid⟩ 2 \ˌel, 'el\ : having a similar configuration at a selected carbon atom to the configuration of levorotatory glyceraldehyde — usu. printed as a small capital ⟨L-fructose⟩

La *symbol* lanthanum

lab \'lab\ *n* : LABORATORY

¹la·bel \'lā-bəl\ *n* : material used in isotopic labeling

²label *vb* **la·beled** *or* **la·belled**; **la·bel·ing** *or* **la·bel·ling** 1 : to distinguish (an element or atom) by using a radioactive isotope or an isotope of unusual mass for tracing through chemical reactions or biological processes 2 : to distinguish (as a compound or cell) by introducing a traceable constituent (as a dye or labeled atom)

la·bet·a·lol \lə-'be-tə-ˌlōl, -ˌlōl\ *n* : a beta-adrenergic blocking agent used as the hydrochloride C₁₉H₂₄O₃·HCl

labia *pl of* LABIUM

la·bi·al \'lā-bē-əl\ *adj* : of, relating to, or situated near the lips or labia — **la·bi·al·ly** *adv*

labial artery *n* : either of two branches of the facial artery of which one is distributed to the upper and one to the lower lip

labial gland *n* : one of the small tubular mucous and serous glands lying beneath the mucous membrane of the lips

labialis — see HERPES LABIALIS

la·bia ma·jo·ra \'lā-bē-ə-mə-'jōr-ə\ *n pl* : the outer fatty folds of the vulva bounding the vestibule

labia mi·no·ra \-mə-'nōr-ə\ *n pl* : the inner highly vascular largely connective-tissue folds of the vulva bounding the vestibule — called also *nymphae*

labii — see LEVATOR LABII SUPERIORIS, LEVATOR LABII SUPERIORIS ALAEQUE NASI, QUADRATUS LABII SUPERIORIS

la·bile \'lā-ˌbīl, -bəl\ *adj* : readily or frequently changing: as **a** : readily or continually undergoing chemical, physical, or biological change or breakdown **b** : characterized by wide fluctuations (as in blood pressure or glucose tolerance) ⟨~ hypertension⟩ **c** : emotionally unstable — **la·bil·i·ty** \lā-'bi-lə-tē\ *n*

labile factor *n* : FACTOR V

labio- *comb form* : labial and ⟨*labio*lingual⟩

la·bio·buc·cal \ˌlā-bē-ō-'bə-kəl\ *adj* : of, relating to, or lying against the inner surface of the lips and cheeks; *also* : administered to labio-buccal tissue

la·bio·glos·so·pha·ryn·geal \ˌlā-bē-ō-ˌglä-sō-ˌfar-ən-'jē-əl, -ˌglō-, -fə-'rin-jəl, -jē-əl\ *adj* : of, relating to, or affecting the lips, tongue, and pharynx

la·bio·lin·gual \-'liŋ-gwəl, -gyə-wəl\ *adj* 1 : of or relating to the lips and the tongue 2 : of or relating to the labial and lingual aspects of a tooth — **la·bio·lin·gual·ly** *adv*

la·bio·scro·tal \-'skrōt-ᵊl\ *adj* : relating to or being a swelling or ridge on each side of the embryonic rudiment of the penis or clitoris which develops into one of the scrotal sacs in the male and one of the labia majora in the female

la·bi·um \'lā-bē-əm\ *n*, *pl* **la·bia** \-ə\ : any of the folds at the margin of the vulva — compare LABIA MAJORA, LABIA MINORA

la·bor \'lā-bər\ *n* : the physical activities involved in parturition consisting essentially of a prolonged series of involuntary contractions of the uterine musculature together with both reflex and voluntary contractions of the abdominal wall; *also* : the period of time during which such labor takes place — **labor** *vb*

lab·o·ra·to·ry \'la-brə-ˌtōr-ē\ *n*, *pl* **-ries** *often attrib* : a place equipped for experimental study in a science or for testing and analysis

la·bored \'lā-bərd\ *adj* : produced or performed with difficulty or strain ⟨~ breathing⟩

labor room *n* : a hospital room where a

woman in labor is kept before being taken to the delivery room

la·brum \ˈlā-brəm\ *n* : a fibrous ring of cartilage attached to the rim of a joint; *esp* : GLENOID LABRUM

lab·y·rinth \ˈla-bə-ˌrinth\ *n* : a tortuous anatomical structure; *esp* : the internal ear or its bony or membranous part — see BONY LABYRINTH, MEMBRANOUS LABYRINTH

lab·y·rin·thec·to·my \ˌlab-ə-ˌrin-ˈthek-tə-mē\ *n, pl* -**mies** : surgical removal of the labyrinth of the ear

lab·y·rin·thine \-ˈrin-thən, -ˌthīn, -ˌthēn\ *adj* : of, relating to, affecting, or originating in the internal ear ⟨human ∼ lesions⟩

labyrinthine artery *n* : INTERNAL AUDITORY ARTERY

labyrinthine sense *n* : a complex sense concerned with the perception of bodily position and motion, mediated by end organs in the vestibular apparatus and the semicircular canals, and stimulated by alterations in the pull of gravity and by head movements

lab·y·rin·thi·tis \ˌla-bə-rin-ˈthī-təs\ *n* : inflammation of the labyrinth of the internal ear

lab·y·rin·thot·o·my \ˌla-bə-rin-ˈthä-tə-mē\ *n, pl* -**mies** : surgical incision into the labyrinth of the internal ear

lac·er·a·tion \ˌla-sə-ˈrā-shən\ *n* **1** : the act of making a rough or jagged wound or tear **2** : a torn and ragged wound — **lac·er·ate** \ˈla-sə-ˌrāt\ *vb*

lacerum — see FORAMEN LACERUM

Each boldface word in the list below is a variant of the word to its right in small capitals.

lachrymal	LACRIMAL
lachrymation	LACRIMATION
lachrymator	LACRIMATOR
lachrymatory	LACRIMATORY

lac operon \ˈlak-\ *n* : the operon which controls lactose metabolism and has been isolated from one of the colon bacilli of the genus *Escherichia* (*E. coli*)

¹lac·ri·mal \ˈla-krə-məl\ *adj* **1** : of, relating to, associated with, located near, or constituting the glands that produce tears **2** : of or relating to tears ⟨∼ effusions⟩

²lacrimal *n* : a lacrimal anatomical part (as a lacrimal bone)

lacrimal apparatus *n* : the bodily parts which function in the production of tears including the lacrimal glands, lacrimal ducts, lacrimal sacs, nasolacrimal ducts, and lacrimal puncta

lacrimal artery *n* : a large branch of the ophthalmic artery that arises near the optic foramen and supplies the lacrimal gland

lacrimal bone *n* : a small thin bone making up part of the front inner wall of each orbit and providing a groove for the passage of the lacrimal ducts

lacrimal canal *n* : LACRIMAL DUCT 1

lacrimal canaliculus *n* : LACRIMAL DUCT 1

lacrimal caruncle *n* : a small reddish follicular elevation at the medial angle of the eye

lacrimal duct *n* **1** : a short canal leading from a minute orifice on a small elevation at the medial angle of each eyelid to the lacrimal sac — called also *lacrimal canal*, *lacrimal canaliculus* **2** : any of several small ducts that carry tears from the lacrimal gland to the fornix of the conjunctiva

lacrimal gland *n* : an acinous gland that is about the size and shape of an almond, secretes tears, and is situated laterally and superiorly to the bulb of the eye in a shallow depression on the inner surface of the frontal bone — called also *tear gland*

lacrimal nerve *n* : a small branch of the ophthalmic nerve that enters the lacrimal gland with the lacrimal artery and supplies the lacrimal gland and the adjacent conjunctiva and the skin of the upper eyelid

lacrimal punc·tum \-ˈpəŋk-təm\ *n* : the opening of either the upper or the lower lacrimal duct at the inner canthus of the eye

lacrimal sac *n* : the dilated oval upper end of the nasolacrimal duct that is situated in a groove formed by the lacrimal bone and the frontal process of the maxilla, is closed at its upper end, and receives the lacrimal ducts

lac·ri·ma·tion \ˌla-krə-ˈmā-shən\ *n* : the secretion of tears; *specif* : abnormal or excessive secretion of tears due to local or systemic disease

lac·ri·ma·tor \ˈla-krə-ˌmā-tər\ *n* : a tear-producing substance (as tear gas)

lac·ri·ma·to·ry \ˈla-kri-mə-ˌtōr-ē\ *adj* : of, relating to, or prompting tears

lact- *or* **lacti-** *or* **lacto-** *comb form* **1** : milk ⟨*lacto*genesis⟩ **2 a** : lactic acid ⟨*lactate*⟩ **b** : lactose ⟨*lactase*⟩

lact·aci·de·mia \ˌlak-ˌta-sə-ˈdē-mē-ə\ *n* : the presence of excess lactic acid in the blood

lact·al·bu·min \ˌlak-ˌtal-ˈbyü-mən\ *n* : an albumin that is found in milk and is similar to serum albumin; *esp* : a protein fraction from whey

lac·tam \ˈlak-ˌtam\ *n* : any of a class of amides of amino carboxylic acids that are characterized by the grouping −CONH− in a ring and that include many antibiotics

β-lactam *var of* BETA-LACTAM

β-lactamase *var of* BETA-LACTAMASE

lac·tase \ˈlak-ˌtās, -ˌtāz\ *n* : an enzyme that hydrolyzes lactose to glucose and galactose and occurs esp. in the intestines of young mammals and in yeasts

¹lac·tate \ˈlak-ˌtāt\ *n* : a salt or ester of lactic acid

²**lactate** *vb* **lac·tat·ed; lac·tat·ing** : to secrete milk

lactate dehydrogenase *n* : any of a group of isoenzymes that catalyze reversibly the conversion of pyruvic acid to lactic acid, are found esp. in the liver, kidneys, striated muscle, and the myocardium, and tend to accumulate in the body when these organs or tissues are diseased or injured — called also *lactic dehydrogenase*

lac·ta·tion \lak-'tā-shən\ *n* 1 : the secretion and yielding of milk by the mammary gland 2 : one complete period of lactation extending from about the time of parturition to weaning

lactation tetany *n* : MILK FEVER 1

¹**lac·te·al** \'lak-tē-əl\ *adj* 1 : relating to, consisting of, producing, or resembling milk (~ fluid) 2 a : conveying or containing a milky fluid (as chyle) (a ~ channel) b : of or relating to the lacteals (impaired ~ function)

²**lacteal** *n* : any of the lymphatic vessels arising from the villi of the small intestine and conveying chyle to the thoracic duct

lacti- — see LACT-

lac·tic acid \'lak-tik-\ *n* : an organic acid $C_3H_6O_3$ that is known in three optically isomeric forms: **a** *or* D-**lactic acid** \'dē-\ : the dextrorotatory form present normally in blood and muscle tissue as a product of the metabolism of glucose and glycogen **b** *or* L-**lactic acid** \'el-\ : the levorotatory form obtained by biological fermentation of sucrose **c** *or* DL-**lactic acid** \'dē-'el-\ : the racemic form present in food products and made usu. by bacterial fermentation

lactic acidosis *n* : a condition characterized by the accumulation of lactic acid in bodily tissues

lactic dehydrogenase *n* : LACTATE DEHYDROGENASE

lac·tif·er·ous duct \lak-'ti-fə-rəs-\ *n* : any of the milk-carrying ducts of the mammary gland that open on the nipple

lactiferous sinus *n* : an expansion in a lactiferous duct at the base of the nipple in which milk accumulates

lacto- — see LACT-

lac·to·ba·cil·lus \lak-tō-bə-'si-ləs\ *n* 1 *cap* : a genus of gram-positive nonmotile lactic-acid-forming bacteria (family Lactobacillaceae) 2 *pl* -**li** \-ˌī *also* -ˌē\ : any bacterium of the genus Lactobacillus

lac·to·fer·rin \ˌlak-tō-'fer-ən\ *n* : a red iron-binding protein synthesized by neutrophils and glandular epithelial cells, found in many human secretions (as tears and milk), and retarding bacterial and fungal growth

lac·to·fla·vin \ˌlak-tō-'flā-vən\ *n* : RIBOFLAVIN

lac·to·gen \'lak-tə-jən, -ˌjen\ *n* : any hormone (as prolactin) that stimulates the production of milk

lac·to·gen·e·sis \ˌlak-tō-'je-nə-səs\ *n*, *pl* -**e·ses** \-ˌsēz\ : initiation of lactation

lac·to·gen·ic \ˌlak-tō-'je-nik\ *adj* : stimulating lactation

lactogenic hormone *n* : LACTOGEN; *esp* : PROLACTIN

lac·tone \'lak-ˌtōn\ *n* : any of various cyclic esters formed from acids containing one or more OH groups

lac·to-ovo-veg·e·tar·i·an \ˌlak-tō-ˌō-vō-ˌve-jə-'ter-ē-ən\ *n* : a vegetarian whose diet includes milk, eggs, vegetables, fruits, grains, and nuts — compare LACTO-VEGETARIAN — **lacto–ovo–vegetarian** *adj*

lac·to·per·ox·i·dase \ˌlak-tō-pə-'räk-sə-ˌdās, -ˌdāz\ *n* : a peroxidase that is found in milk and saliva and is used to catalyze the addition of iodine to tyrosine-containing proteins (as thyroglobulin)

lac·tose \'lak-ˌtōs, -ˌtōz\ *n* : a disaccharide sugar $C_{12}H_{22}O_{11}$ that is present in milk, yields glucose and galactose upon hydrolysis, yields esp. lactic acid upon fermentation, and is used chiefly in foods, medicines, and culture media (as for the manufacture of penicillin) — called also *milk sugar*

lac·tos·uria \ˌlak-tō-'shùr-ē-ə, -'syùr-\ *n* : the presence of lactose in the urine

lac·to·veg·e·tar·i·an \ˌlak-tō-ˌve-jə-'ter-ē-ən\ *n* : a vegetarian whose diet includes milk, vegetables, fruits, grains, and nuts — compare LACTO-OVO-VEGETARIAN — **lacto–vegetarian** *adj*

lac·tu·lose \'lak-tyù-ˌlōs, -tù-, -ˌlōz\ *n* : a cathartic disaccharide $C_{12}H_{22}O_{11}$ used to treat chronic constipation and disturbances of function in the central nervous system accompanying severe liver disease

la·cu·na \lə-'kü-nə, -'kyü-\ *n*, *pl* **la·cu·nae** \-ˌnē, -ˌnī\ : a small cavity, pit, or discontinuity in an anatomical structure: as **a** : one of the follicles in the mucous membrane of the urethra **b** : one of the minute cavities in bone or cartilage occupied by the osteocytes — **la·cu·nar** \-nər\ *adj*

Laen·nec's cirrhosis *or* **Laën·nec's cirrhosis** \'lā-neks-\ *n* : hepatic cirrhosis in which increased connective tissue spreads out from the portal spaces compressing and distorting the lobules, causing impairment of liver function, and ultimately producing the typical hobnail liver — called also *portal cirrhosis*

Laennec, René–Théophile–Hyacinthe (1781–1826), French physician.

la·e·trile \'lā-ə-(ˌ)tril\ *n*, *often cap* : a drug derived esp. from pits of the apricot (*Prunus armeniaca* of the rose family, Rosaceae) that contains amygdalin and has been used in the treatment of cancer although of unproved effectiveness

laev- *or* **laevo-** *Brit var of* LEV-lae•vo•car•dia, lae•vo•do•pa *Brit var of* LEVOCARDIA, LEVODOPA

La•fo•ra body \lä-'för-ə-\ *n* : any of the cytoplasmic inclusion bodies found in neurons of parts of the central nervous system in myoclonic epilepsy and consisting of a complex of glyco-protein and glycosaminoglycan

Lafora, Gonzalo Rodriguez (*b* 1886), Spanish neurologist.

Lafora's disease *n* : MYOCLONIC EPILEPSY

-lag•nia \'lag-nē-ə\ *comb form* : lust (kleptolagnia) (urolagnia)

lag•oph•thal•mos *or* lag•oph•thal•mus \la-'gäf-'thal-məs\ *n* : pathological incomplete closure of the eyelids : inability to close the eyelids fully

la grippe \lä-'grip\ *n* : INFLUENZA

LAK \'lak; ̣el-(ˌ)ä-'kä\ *n* : LYMPHO-KINE-ACTIVATED KILLER CELL

LAK cell *n* : LYMPHOKINE-ACTIVATED KILLER CELL

lake \'läk\ *vb* laked; lak•ing : to undergo or cause (blood) to undergo a physiological change in which the hemoglobin becomes dissolved in the plasma

-la•lia \'lä-lē-ə\ *n comb form* : speech disorder (of a specified type) (echolalia)

lal•la•tion \la-'lä-shən\ *n* 1 : infantile speech whether in infants or in older speakers (as by mental retardation) 2 : a defective articulation of the letter *l*, the substitution of \l\ for another sound, or the substitution of another sound for \l\ — compare LAMBDACISM

La•maze \lə-'mäz\ *adj* : relating to or being a method of childbirth that involves psychological and physical preparation by the mother in order to suppress pain and facilitate delivery without drugs

Lamaze, Fernand (1890–1957), French obstetrician.

lamb•da \'lam-də\ *n* 1 : the point of junction of the sagittal and lambdoid sutures of the skull 2 : PHAGE LAMBDA

lambda chain *or* λ chain *n* : a polypeptide chain of one of the two types of light chain that are found in antibodies and can be distinguished antigenically and by the sequence of amino acids in the chain — compare KAPPA CHAIN

lamb•da•cism \'lam-də-ˌsi-zəm\ *n* : a defective articulation of \l\, the substitution of other sounds for it, or the substitution of \l\ for another sound — compare LALLATION 2

lambda phage *n* : PHAGE LAMBDA

lamb•doid \'lam-ˌdöid\ *or* lamb•doi•dal \ˌlam-'döid-ºl\ *adj* : of, relating to, or being the suture shaped like the Greek letter lambda (λ) that connects the occipital and parietal bones

lam•bli•a•sis \lam-'blī-ə-səs\ *n, pl* -a•ses \-ˌsēz\ : GIARDIASIS

Lambl \'lämb-ºl\, Wilhelm Dusan (1824–1895), Austrian physician.

lame \'läm\ *adj* lam•er; lam•est : having a body part and esp. a limb so disabled as to impair freedom of movement : physically disabled — lame•ly *adv* — lame•ness *n*

la•mel•la \lə-'me-lə\ *n, pl* la•mel•lae \-ˌlē, -ˌlī\ *also* lamellas 1 : an organ, process, or part resembling a plate: as a : one of the bony concentric layers surrounding the Haversian canals in bone b (1) : one of the incremental layers of cementum laid down in a tooth (2) : a thin sheetlike organic structure in the enamel of a tooth extending inward from a surface crack 2 : a small medicated disk prepared from gelatin and glycerin for use esp. in the eyes — la•mel•lar \lə-'me-lər\ *adj* — lam•el•lat•ed \'la-mə-ˌlä-təd\ *adj*

lamellar ichthyosis *n* : a rare inherited form of ichthyosis characterized by large coarse scales

lamin- *or* lamini- *or* lamino- *comb form* : lamina (laminitis) (laminograph)

lam•i•na \'la-mə-nə\ *n, pl* -nae \-ˌnē, -ˌnī\ *or* -nas : a thin plate or layer esp. of an anatomical part

lamina cri•bro•sa \-kri-'brō-sə\ *n, pl* laminae cri•bro•sae \-ˌsē-, -ˌsī\ : any of several anatomical structures having the form of a perforated plate: as a : CRIBRIFORM PLATE 1 b : the part of the sclera of the eye penetrated by the fibers of the optic nerve c : a perforated plate that closes the internal auditory meatus

lamina du•ra \-'dúr-ə, -'dyúr-\ *n* : the thin hard layer of bone that lines the socket of a tooth and that appears as a dark line in radiography

lam•i•na•gram, lam•i•na•graph *var of* LAMINOGRAM, LAMINOGRAPH

lamina pro•pria \-'prō-prē-ə\ *n, pl* laminae pro•pri•ae \-ˌprē-ˌē, -ˌī\ : a highly vascular layer of connective tissue under the basement membrane lining a layer of epithelium

lam•i•nar \'la-mə-nər\ *adj* : arranged in, consisting of, or resembling laminae

lam•i•nar•ia \ˌla-mə-'nar-ē-ə\ *n* : any of a genus (Laminaria) of kelps of which some have been used to dilate the cervix in performing an abortion

lamina spi•ral•is \-spə-'ra-ləs, -'rä-\ *n* : SPIRAL LAMINA

lam•i•nat•ed \'la-mə-ˌnä-təd\ *adj* : composed or arranged in layers or laminae (~ membranes)

lamina ter•mi•nal•is \-ˌtər-mi-'na-ləs, -'nä-\ *n* : a thin layer of gray matter in the telencephalon that extends backward from the corpus callosum above the optic chiasma and forms the median portion of the rostral wall of the third ventricle of the cerebrum

lam•i•na•tion \ˌla-mə-'nä-shən\ *n* : a laminated structure or arrangement

lam•i•nec•to•my \ˌla-mə-'nek-tə-mē\ *n*,

pl **-mies** : surgical removal of the posterior arch of a vertebra

lamini- *or* **lamino-** — see LAMIN-

lam·i·nin \'la-mə-nən\ *n* : a glycoprotein that is a component of connective tissue basement membrane and that promotes cell adhesion

lam·i·ni·tis \,la-mə-'nī-təs\ *n* : inflammation of a lamina esp. in the hoof of a horse, cow, or goat that is typically caused by excessive ingestion of a dietary substance (as carbohydrate) — called also *founder*

lam·i·no·gram \'la-mə-nə-,gram\ *n* : a roentgenogram of a layer of the body made by means of a laminograph: *broadly* : TOMOGRAM

lam·i·no·graph \-,graf\ *n* : an X-ray machine that makes roentgenography of body tissue possible at any desired depth: *broadly* : TOMOGRAPH — **lam·i·no·graph·ic** \,la-mə-nə-'gra-fik\ *adj* — **lam·i·nog·ra·phy** \,la-mə-'nä-grə-fē\ *n*

lam·i·not·o·my \,la-mə-'nä-tə-mē\ *n, pl* **-mies** : surgical division of a vertebral lamina

lamp \'lamp\ *n* : any of various devices for producing light or heat — see SLIT LAMP

lam·pas \'lam-pəs\ *n* : a congestion of the mucous membrane of the hard palate just posterior to the incisor teeth of the horse due to irritation and bruising from harsh coarse feeds

lam·siek·te \'lam-,sēk-tə, 'läm-\ *or* **lam·ziek·te** \-,zēk-\ *n* : botulism of phophorus-deficient cattle esp. in southern Africa due to ingestion of bones and carrion containing clostridial toxins

la·nat·o·side \lə-'na-tə-,sīd\ *n* : any of three poisonous crystalline cardiac steroid glycosides occurring in the leaves of a foxglove (*Digitalis lanata*): **a** : the glycoside $C_{49}H_{76}O_{19}$ yielding digitoxin, glucose, and acetic acid on hydrolysis — called also *digilanid A, lanatoside A* **b** : the glycoside $C_{49}H_{76}O_{20}$ yielding gitoxin, glucose, and acetic acid on hydrolysis — called also *digilanid B, lanatoside B* **c** : the bitter glycoside $C_{49}H_{76}O_{20}$ yielding digoxin, glucose, and acetic acid on hydrolysis and used similarly to digitalis — called also *digilanid C, lanatoside C*

¹**lance** \'lans\ *n* : LANCET

²**lance** *vb* **lanced; lanc·ing** : to open with a lancet : make an incision in or into 〈~ a boil〉 〈~ a vein〉

Lance·field group \'lans-,fēld-\ *also* **Lance·field's group** \-,fēldz-\ *n* : one of the serologically distinguishable groups (as group A, group B) into which streptococci can be divided

Lancefield, Rebecca Craighill (1895–1981), American bacteriologist.

lan·cet \'lan-sət\ *n* : a sharp-pointed and commonly two-edged surgical instrument used to make small incisions (as in a vein or a boil)

lancet fluke *n* : a small liver fluke of the genus *Dicrocoelium* (*D. dendriticum*) widely distributed in sheep and cattle and rarely infecting humans

lan·ci·nat·ing \'lan-sə-,nā-tiŋ\ *adj* : characterized by piercing or stabbing sensations 〈~ pain〉

land·mark \'land-,märk\ *n* : an anatomical structure used as a point of orientation in locating other structures

Lan·dolt ring \'län-,dōlt-\ *n* : one of a series of incomplete rings or circles used in some eye charts to determine visual discrimination or acuity

Landolt, Edmond (1846–1926), French ophthalmologist.

Lan·dry's paralysis \'lan-drēz-\ *n* : GUILLAIN-BARRÉ SYNDROME

Landry, Jean-Baptiste-Octave (1826–1865), French physician.

Lang·er·hans cell \'läŋ-ər-,häns-\ *n* : a dendritic cell of the interstitial spaces of the epidermis

P. Langerhans — see ISLET OF LANGERHANS

Lang·hans cell \'läŋ-,häns-\ *n* : any of the cells of cuboidal epithelium that make up the cytotrophoblast

Langhans, Theodor (1839–1915), German pathologist and anatomist.

Langhans giant cell *n* : any of the large cells found in the lesions of some granulomatous conditions (as leprosy) and containing a number of peripheral nuclei arranged in a circle or in the shape of a horseshoe

lan·o·lin \'lan-ə-lən\ *n* : wool grease that can be absorbed by the skin, contains from 25% to 30% water, and is used chiefly in ointments and cosmetics — called also *hydrous wool fat*

Lan·ox·in \la-'näk-sən\ *trademark* — used for a preparation of digoxin

lan·tha·num \'lan-thə-nəm\ *n* : a white soft malleable metallic element — symbol *La*; see ELEMENT table

la·nu·go \lə-'nü-(,)gō, -'nyü-\ *n* : a dense cottony or downy growth; *specif* : the soft downy hair that covers the fetus

lap *abbr* laparotomy

lap·a·ro·scope \'la-pə-rə-,skōp\ *n* : a fiberoptic instrument that is inserted through an incision in the abdominal wall and is used to examine visually the interior of the peritoneal cavity — called also *peritoneoscope*

lap·a·ros·co·pist \,la-pə-'räs-kə-pist\ *n* : a physician or surgeon who performs laparoscopies

lap·a·ros·co·py \-pē\ *n, pl* **-pies 1** : visual examination of the abdomen by means of a laparoscope **2** : an operation involving laparoscopy; *esp* : one for sterilization of the female or for removal of ova that involves use of a laparoscope to guide surgical procedures within the abdomen — **lap·a-**

ro·scop·ic \-rə-ˈskä-pik\ *adj* — **lap·a·ro·scop·i·cal·ly** *adv*

lap·a·rot·o·my \ˌla-pə-ˈrä-tə-mē\ *n, pl* **-mies** : surgical section of the abdominal wall

La·place's law \lä-ˈplä-səz-\ *n* : LAW OF LAPLACE

Lar·gac·til \lär-ˈgak-til\ *trademark* — used for a preparation of chlorpromazine

large bowel *n* : LARGE INTESTINE

large calorie *n* : CALORIE 1b

large intestine *n* : the more terminal division of the intestine that is wider and shorter than the small intestine, typically divided into cecum, colon, and rectum, and concerned esp. with the resorption of water and the formation of feces

Lar·gon \ˈlär-ˌgän\ *trademark* — used for a preparation of propiomazine

lark·spur \ˈlärk-ˌspər\ *n* : DELPHINIUM 2

Lar·o·tid \ˈlar-ə-ˌtid\ *trademark* — used for a preparation of amoxicillin

Lar·sen's syndrome \ˈlär-sənz-\ *n* : a syndrome characterized by cleft palate, flattened facies, multiple congenital joint dislocations and deformities of the foot

Larsen, Loren Joseph (*b* 1914), American orthopedic surgeon.

lar·va \ˈlär-və\ *n, pl* **lar·vae** \-(ˌ)vē, -ˌvī\ *also* **larvas** : the immature, wingless, and often wormlike feeding form that hatches from the egg of many insects — **lar·val** \-vəl\ *adj*

lar·va·cide *var of* LARVICIDE

larval mi·grans \-ˈmī-ˌgranz\ *n* : CREEPING ERUPTION

larva migrans *n, pl* **larvae mi·gran·tes** \-ˌmī-ˈgran-ˌtēz\ : CREEPING ERUPTION

lar·vi·cide \ˈlär-və-ˌsīd\ *n* : an agent for killing larvae — **lar·vi·cid·al** \ˌlär-və-ˈsīd-ᵊl\ *adj* — **lar·vi·cid·al·ly** *adv*

laryng- *or* **laryngo-** *comb form* **1** : larynx (*laryngitis*) **2 a** : laryngeal (*laryngospasm*) **b** : laryngeal and (*laryngopharyngeal*)

¹la·ryn·geal \lə-ˈrin-jəl, -jē-əl; ˌlar-ən-ˈjē-əl\ *adj* : of, relating to, affecting, or used on the larynx — **la·ryn·geal·ly** *adv*

²laryngeal *n* : an anatomical part (as a nerve or artery) that supplies or is associated with the larynx

laryngeal artery *n* : either of two arteries supplying blood to the larynx: **a** : a branch of the inferior thyroid artery that supplies the muscles and mucous membranes of the dorsal part of the larynx — called also *inferior laryngeal artery* **b** : a branch of the superior thyroid artery or sometimes of the external carotid artery that supplies the muscles, mucous membranes, and glands of the larynx — called also *superior laryngeal artery*

laryngeal nerve *n* : either of two branches of the vagus nerve supplying the larynx: **a** : one that arises from the ganglion of the vagus situated below the jugular foramen and supplies the cricothyroid muscle — called also *superior laryngeal nerve* **b** : one that arises below the larynx and supplies all the muscles of the thyroid except the cricothyroid — called also *inferior laryngeal nerve, recurrent laryngeal nerve;* see INFERIOR LARYNGEAL NERVE 2

lar·yn·gec·to·mee \ˌlar-ən-ˌjek-tə-ˈmē\ *n* : a person who has undergone laryngectomy

lar·yn·gec·to·my \-ˈjek-tə-mē\ *n, pl* **-mies** : surgical removal of all or part of the larynx — **lar·yn·gec·to·mized** \-tə-ˌmīzd\ *adj*

lar·yn·gis·mus stri·du·lus \ˌlar-ən-ˌjiz-məs-ˈstri-jə-ləs\ *n, pl* **lar·yn·gis·mi strid·u·li** \-ˌmī-ˈstri-jə-ˌlī\ : a sudden spasm of the larynx that occurs in children esp. in rickets and is marked by difficult breathing with prolonged noisy inspiration — compare LARYNGOSPASM

lar·yn·gi·tis \ˌlar-ən-ˈjī-təs\ *n, pl* **-git·i·des** \-ˈji-tə-ˌdēz\ : inflammation of the larynx

laryngo- — see LARYNG-

la·ryn·go·cele \lə-ˈrin-gə-ˌsēl\ *n* : an air-containing evagination of laryngeal mucous membrane having its opening communicating with the ventricle of the larynx

la·ryn·go·fis·sure \lə-ˌrin-gō-ˈfi-shər\ *n* : surgical opening of the larynx by an incision through the thyroid cartilage esp. for the removal of a tumor

la·ryn·gog·ra·phy \ˌlar-ən-ˈgä-grə-fē\ *n, pl* **-phies** : X-ray depiction of the larynx after use of a radiopaque material

laryngol *abbr* laryngological

la·ryn·go·log·i·cal \lə-ˌrin-gə-ˈlä-ji-kəl\ *also* **la·ryn·go·log·ic** \-ˈlä-jik\ *adj* : of or relating to laryngology or the larynx

lar·yn·gol·o·gist \ˌlar-ən-ˈgä-lə-jist\ *n* : a physician specializing in laryngology

lar·yn·gol·o·gy \ˌlar-ən-ˈgä-lə-jē\ *n, pl* **-gies** : a branch of medicine dealing with diseases of the larynx and nasopharynx

la·ryn·go·pha·ryn·ge·al \lə-ˌrin-gō-ˌfar-ən-ˈjē-əl, -fə-ˈrin-jəl, -jē-əl\ *adj* : of or common to both the larynx and the pharynx (~ cancer)

la·ryn·go·phar·yn·gi·tis \-ˌfar-ən-ˈjī-təs\ *n, pl* **-git·i·des** \-ˈji-tə-ˌdēz\ : inflammation of both the larynx and the pharynx

la·ryn·go·phar·ynx \-ˈfar-iŋks\ *n* : the lower part of the pharynx lying behind or adjacent to the larynx — compare NASOPHARYNX

la·ryn·go·plas·ty \lə-ˈrin-gə-ˌplas-tē\ *n, pl* **-ties** : plastic surgery to repair laryngeal defects

la·ryn·go·scope \lə-ˈrin-gə-ˌskōp, -ˈrin-jə-\ *n* : an instrument for examining the interior of the larynx — **la·ryn·**

go·scop·ic \-'riŋ-gə-'skä-pik. -'rin-jə-\ or la·ryn·go·scop·i·cal \-pi-kəl\ *adj*

lar·yn·gos·co·py \,lar-ən-'gäs-kə-pē\ *n, pl* -pies : examination of the interior of the larynx (as with a laryngoscope)

la·ryn·go·spasm \lə-'riŋ-gə-,spa-zəm\ *n* : spasmodic closure of the larynx — compare LARYNGISMUS STRIDULUS

lar·yn·got·o·my \,lar-ən-'gä-tə-mē\ *n, pl* -mies : surgical incision of the larynx

la·ryn·go·tra·che·al \lə-,riŋ-gō-'trā-kē-əl\ *adj* : of or common to the larynx and trachea (~ stenosis)

la·ryn·go·tra·che·itis \-,trā-kē-'ī-təs\ *n* : inflammation of both larynx and trachea — see INFECTIOUS LARYN-GOTRACHEITIS

la·ryn·go·tra·cheo·bron·chi·tis \-,trā-kē-ō-,brän-'ki-təs, -,brän-\ *n, pl* -chit·ides \-'ki-tə-,dēz\ : inflammation of the larynx, trachea, and bronchi

lar·ynx \'lar-iŋks\ *n, pl* la·ryn·ges \lə-'rin-(,)jēz\ *or* lar·ynx·es : the modified upper part of the respiratory passage that is bounded above by the glottis, is continuous below with the trachea, has a complex cartilaginous or bony skeleton capable of limited motion through the action of associated muscles, and has a set of elastic vocal cords that play a major role in sound production and speech — called also *voice box*

la·ser \'lā-zər\ *n* : a device that utilizes the natural oscillations of atoms or molecules between energy levels for generating coherent electromagnetic radiation in the ultraviolet, visible, or infrared regions of the spectrum

lash \'lash\ *n* : EYELASH

La·six \'lā-ziks, -siks\ *trademark* — used for a preparation of furosemide

L-as·par·a·gi·nase \'el-as-'par-ə-jə-,nās, -,nāz\ *n* : an enzyme that breaks down the physiologically commoner form of asparagine, is obtained esp. from bacteria, and is used esp. to treat leukemia

Las·sa fever \'la-sə-\ *n* : a disease esp. of Africa that is caused by an arenavirus and is characterized by a high fever, headaches, mouth ulcers, muscle aches, small hemorrhages under the skin, heart and kidney failure, and a high mortality rate

Lassa virus *n* : an arenavirus that is the causative agent of Lassa fever

las·si·tude \'la-sə-,tüd, -,tyüd\ *n* : a condition of weariness, debility, or fatigue

lat \'lat\ *n* : LATISSIMUS DORSI — usu. used in pl.

lata — see FASCIA LATA

latae — see FASCIA LATA, TENSOR FASCIAE LATAE

la·tah \'lä-tə\ *n* : a neurotic condition marked by automatic obedience, echolalia, and echopraxia observed esp. among Malays

la·ten·cy \'lāt-ᵊn-sē\ *n, pl* -cies 1 : the quality or state of being latent; *esp*

: the state or period of living or developing in a host without producing symptoms — used of an infective agent or disease 2 : LATENCY PERIOD 1 3 : the interval between stimulation and response — called also *latent period*

latency period *n* 1 : a stage of personality development that extends from about the age of five to the beginning of puberty and during which sexual urges often appear to lie dormant — called also *latency* 2 : LATENT PERIOD

la·tent \'lāt-ᵊnt\ *adj* : existing in hidden or dormant form: as a : present or capable of living or developing in a host without producing visible symptoms of disease (a ~ virus) b : not consciously expressed (~ anxiety) c : relating to or being the latent content of a dream or thought — la·tent·ly *adv*

latent content *n* : the underlying meaning of a dream or thought that is expressed in psychoanalysis by interpretation of its symbols or by free association — compare MANIFEST CONTENT

latent learning *n* : learning that is not demonstrated by behavior at the time it is held to take place but that is inferred to exist based on a greater than expected number of favorable or desired responses at a later time when reinforcement is given

latent period *n* 1 : the period between exposure to a disease-causing agent or process and the appearance of symptoms 2 : LATENCY 3

lat·er·al \'la-tə-rəl, -tral\ *adj* : of or relating to the side: *esp, of a body part* : lying at or extending toward the right or left side : lying away from the median axis of the body

lateral arcuate ligament *n* : a fascial band that extends from the tip of the transverse process of the first lumbar vertebra to the twelfth rib and provides attachment for part of the diaphragm — compare MEDIAL ARCUATE LIGAMENT, MEDIAN ARCUATE LIGAMENT

lateral brachial cutaneous nerve *n* : a continuation of the posterior branch of the axillary nerve that supplies the skin of the lateral aspect of the upper arm over the distal part of the deltoid muscle and the adjacent head of the triceps brachii

lateral collateral ligament *n* : a ligament that connects the lateral epicondyle of the femur with the lateral side of the head of the fibula and that helps to stabilize the knee by preventing lateral dislocation — called also *fibular collateral ligament*; compare MEDIAL COLLATERAL LIGAMENT

lateral column *n* 1 : a lateral extension of the gray matter in each lateral half of the spinal cord present in the thoracic and upper lumbar regions — called also *lateral horn*; compare

DORSAL HORN. VENTRAL HORN 2 : LATERAL FUNICULUS

lateral condyle *n* : a condyle on the outer side of the lower extremity of the femur: *also* : a corresponding eminence on the upper part of the tibia that articulates with the lateral condyle of the femur — compare MEDIAL CONDYLE

lateral cord *n* : a cord of nerve tissue that is formed by union of the superior and middle trunks of the brachial plexus and that forms one of the two roots of the median nerve — compare MEDIAL CORD. POSTERIOR CORD

lateral corticospinal tract *n* : a band of nerve fibers that descends in the posterolateral part of each side of the spinal cord and consists mostly of fibers arising in the motor cortex of the contralateral side of the brain

lateral cricoarytenoid *n* : CRICOARYTENOID 1

lateral cuneiform bone *n* : CUNEIFORM BONE 1c — called also *lateral cuneiform*

lateral decubitus *n* : a position in which a patient lies on his or her side and which is used esp. in radiography and in making a lumbar puncture

lateral epicondyle *n* : EPICONDYLE a

lateral femoral circumflex artery *n* : an artery that branches from the deep femoral artery or from the femoral artery itself and that supplies the muscles of the lateral part of the thigh and hip joint — compare MEDIAL FEMORAL CIRCUMFLEX ARTERY

lateral femoral circumflex vein *n* : a vein accompanying the lateral femoral circumflex artery and emptying into the femoral vein — compare MEDIAL FEMORAL CIRCUMFLEX VEIN

lateral femoral cutaneous nerve *n* : a nerve that arises from the lumbar plexus and that supplies the anterior and lateral aspects of the thigh down to the knee — compare POSTERIOR FEMORAL CUTANEOUS NERVE

lateral fissure *n* : FISSURE OF SYLVIUS

lateral funiculus *n* : a longitudinal division on each side of the spinal cord comprising white matter between the dorsal and ventral roots — compare ANTERIOR FUNICULUS. POSTERIOR FUNICULUS

lateral gastrocnemius bursa *n* : a bursa of the knee joint that is situated between the lateral head of the gastrocnemius muscle and the joint capsule

lateral geniculate body *n* : a part of the metathalamus that is the terminus of most fibers of the optic tract and receives nerve impulses from the retinas which are relayed to the visual area by way of the geniculocalcarine tracts — compare MEDIAL GENICULATE BODY

lateral geniculate nucleus *n* : a nucleus of the lateral geniculate body

lateral horn *n* : LATERAL COLUMN 1

lateral inhibition *n* : a visual process in which the firing of a retinal cell inhibits the firing of surrounding retinal cells and which is held to enhance the perception of areas of contrast

lateralis — see RECTUS LATERALIS, VASTUS LATERALIS

lat·er·al·i·ty \la-tə-ˈra-lə-tē\ *n, pl* **-ties** : preference in use of homologous parts on one lateral half of the body over those on the other : dominance in function of one of a pair of lateral homologous parts

lat·er·al·i·za·tion \ˌla-tə-rə-lə-ˈzā-shən, ˌla-trə-lə-\ *n* : localization of function or activity (as of verbal processes in the brain) on one side of the body in preference to the other — **lat·er·al·ize** \ˈla-tə-rə-ˌlīz, -trə-\ *vb*

lateral lemniscus *n* : a band of nerve fibers that arises in the cochlear nuclei and terminates in the inferior colliculus and the lateral geniculate body of the opposite side of the brain

lateral ligament *n* : any of various ligaments (as the lateral collateral ligament of the knee) that are in a lateral position or that prevent lateral dislocation of a joint

lateral malleolus *n* : MALLEOLUS a

lateral meniscus *n* : MENISCUS a(1)

lateral nucleus *n* : any of a group of nuclei of the thalamus situated in the dorsolateral region extending from its anterior to posterior ends

lateral pectoral nerve *n* : PECTORAL NERVE a

lateral plantar artery *n* : PLANTAR ARTERY a

lateral plantar nerve *n* : PLANTAR NERVE a

lateral plantar vein *n* : PLANTAR VEIN a

lateral popliteal nerve *n* : COMMON PERONEAL NERVE

lateral pterygoid muscle *n* : PTERYGOID MUSCLE a

lateral pterygoid nerve *n* : PTERYGOID NERVE a

lateral pterygoid plate *n* : PTERYGOID PLATE a

lateral rectus *n* : RECTUS 2b

lateral reticular nucleus *n* : a nucleus of the reticular formation that receives fibers esp. from the dorsal horn of the spinal cord and sends axons to the cerebellum on the same side of the body

lateral sacral artery *n* : either of two arteries on each side which arise from the posterior division of the internal iliac artery and supply muscles and skin in the area

lateral sacral crest *n* : SACRAL CREST b

lateral sacral vein *n* : any of several veins that accompany the corresponding lateral sacral arteries and empty into the internal iliac veins

lateral semilunar cartilage *n* : MENISCUS a(1)

lateral spinothalamic tract *n* : SPINOTHALAMIC TRACT b

lateral sulcus *n* : FISSURE OF SYLVIUS

lateral thoracic artery *n* : THORACIC ARTERY 1b

lateral umbilical ligament *n* : MEDIAL UMBILICAL LIGAMENT

lateral ventricle *n* : an internal cavity in each cerebral hemisphere that consists of a central body and three cornua — see ANTERIOR HORN 2, INFERIOR HORN, POSTERIOR HORN 2

lateral vestibular nucleus *n* : the one of the four vestibular nuclei on each side of the medulla oblongata that sends fibers down the same side of the spinal cord through the vestibulospinal tract — called also *Deiters' nucleus*

latex agglutination test *n* : a test for a specific antibody and esp. rheumatoid factor in which the corresponding antigen is adsorbed on spherical polystyrene latex particles which undergo agglutination upon addition of the specific antibody — called also *latex fixation test, latex test*

lath-y-rism \'la-thə-ˌri-zəm\ *n* : a diseased condition of humans and domestic animals that results from poisoning by a substance found in some legumes (genus *Lathyrus* and esp. *L. sativus*) and is characterized esp. by spastic paralysis of the hind or lower limbs — **lath-y-rit-ic** \ˌla-thə-'ri-tik\ *adj*

lath-y-ro-gen \'la-thə-rə-jən, -ˌjen\ *n* : any of a group of compounds that tend to cause lathyrism and inhibit the formation of links between chains of collagen

la-tis-si-mus dor-si \lə-'ti-sə-məs-'dòr-ˌsī\ *n, pl* **la-tis-si-mi dorsi** \-ˌmī-\ : a broad flat superficial muscle of the lower part of the back that extends, adducts, and rotates the arm medially and draws the shoulder downward and backward

Lat-ro-dec-tus \ˌla-trō-'dek-təs\ *n* : a genus of nearly cosmopolitan spiders (family Theridiidae) that includes most of the well-known venomous spiders (as the black widow, *L. mactans*)

lats \'lats\ *pl of* LAT

LATS *abbr* long-acting thyroid stimulator

laud-able pus \'lò-də-bəl-\ *n* : pus discharged freely (as from a wound) and formerly supposed to facilitate the elimination of unhealthy humors from the injured body

lau-da-num \'lòd-nəm, -ᵊn-əm\ *n* 1 : any of various formerly used preparations of opium 2 : a tincture of opium

laughing death *n* : KURU

laughing gas *n* : NITROUS OXIDE

laughing sickness *n* : KURU

Lau-rence–Moon–Biedl syndrome \'lòr-əns-'mün-'bēd-ᵊl-, 'lär-\ *n* : an inherited disorder affecting esp. males and characterized by obesity, mental retardation, the presence of extra fingers or toes, subnormal development of the genital organs, and sometimes by retinitis pigmentosa

Laurence, John Zachariah (1830–1874), British physician.

Moon, Robert Charles (1844–1914), American ophthalmologist.

Biedl, Artur (1869–1933), German physician.

lau-ryl \'lòr-əl, 'lär-\ *n* : the chemical group $C_{12}H_{25}$— having a valence of one — see SODIUM LAURYL SULFATE

LAV \ˌel-(ˌ)ā-'vē\ *n* : HIV-1

la-vage \lə-'väzh, 'la-vij\ *n* : the act or action of washing; *esp* : the therapeutic washing out of an organ — lavage *vb*

law of dominance *n* : MENDEL'S LAW 3

law of independent assortment *n* : MENDEL'S LAW 2

law of La-place \-lä-'pläs\ *n* : a law in physics that in medicine is applied in the physiology of blood flow: under equilibrium conditions the pressure tangent to the circumference of a vessel storing or transmitting fluid equals the product of the pressure across the wall and the radius of the vessel for a sphere and half this for a tube — called also *Laplace's law*

Laplace, Pierre–Simon (1749–1827), French astronomer and mathematician.

law of segregation *n* : MENDEL'S LAW 1

law-ren-ci-um \lò-'ren-sē-əm\ *n* : a short-lived radioactive element that is produced artificially from californium — symbol *Lr*; see ELEMENT table

Law-rence \'lòr-əns, 'lär-, **Ernest Orlando (1901–1958),** American physicist.

lax \'laks\ *adj* 1 *of the bowels* : LOOSE 3 2 : having loose bowels

lax-a-tion \lak-'sā-shən\ *n* : a bowel movement

¹**lax-a-tive** \'lak-sə-tiv\ *adj* 1 : having a tendency to loosen or relax; *specif* : relieving constipation 2 : LAX 2 — **lax-a-tive-ly** *adv*

²**laxative** *n* : a usu. mild laxative drug

lax-i-ty \'lak-sə-tē\ *n, pl* **-ties** : the quality or state of being loose ⟨a certain ~ of the bowels⟩ ⟨ligamentous ~⟩

la-zar \'la-zər, 'lā\ *n* : LEPER

laz-a-ret-to \ˌla-zə-'re-(ˌ)tō\ *or* **laz-a-ret** \-'re, -'rē\ *n, pl* **-rettos** *or* **-rets** 1 *usu* lazaretto : an institution (as a hospital) for those with contagious diseases 2 : a building or a ship used for detention in quarantine

lazy eye *n* : AMBLYOPIA; *also* : an eye affected with amblyopia

lazy-eye blindness *n* : AMBLYOPIA

lb *abbr* pound

LC *abbr* liquid chromatography

L chain *n* : LIGHT CHAIN

LD *abbr* 1 learning disabled; learning disability 2 lethal dose

LD50 *or* **LD₅₀** \ˌel-(ˌ)dē-'fif-tē\ *n* : the amount of a toxic agent (as a poison, virus. or radiation) that is sufficient to kill 50% of a population of animals usu. within a certain time — called also *median lethal dose*

LDH *abbr* lactate dehydrogenase: lactic dehydrogenase

LDL \ˌel-(ˌ)dē-ˈel\ *n* : a lipoprotein of blood plasma that is composed of a moderate proportion of protein with little triglyceride and a high proportion of cholesterol and that is associated with increased probability of developing atherosclerosis — called also *beta-lipoprotein*, *low-density lipoprotein*; compare HDL. VLDL

L-do·pa \ˈel-ˈdō-pə\ *n* : the levoratory form of dopa that is obtained esp. from broad beans or prepared synthetically, stimulates the production of dopamine in the brain, and is used in treating Parkinson's disease — called also *levodopa*

LE *abbr* lupus erythematosus

¹lead \ˈlēd\ *n* : a flexible or solid insulated conductor connected to or leading out from an electrical device (as an electroencephalograph)

²lead \ˈled\ *n, often attrib* : a heavy soft malleable bluish white metallic element found mostly in combination and used esp. in pipes, cable sheaths, batteries, solder, type metal, and shields against radioactivity — symbol *Pb*; see ELEMENT table

lead acetate \ˈled-\ *n* : a poisonous soluble lead salt $PbC_4H_6O_4 \cdot 3H_2O$ used in medicine esp. formerly as an astringent

lead arsenate *n* : an arsenate of lead; *esp* : an acid salt $PbHAsO_4$ or a basic salt $Pb_3(AsO_4)_2$ or a mixture of the two used as an insecticide

lead palsy *n* : localized paralysis caused by lead poisoning esp. of the extensor muscles of the forearm

lead poisoning *n* : chronic intoxication that is produced by the absorption of lead into the system and is characterized by severe colicky pains, a dark line along the gums, and local muscular paralysis — called also *plumbism*, *saturnism*

leaf·let \ˈlē-flət\ *n* : a leaflike organ, structure, or part; *esp* : any of the flaps of the biscuspid valve or the tricuspid valve

learn·ing \ˈlər-niŋ\ *n* : the process of acquiring a modification in a behavioral tendency by experience (as exposure to conditioning); *also* : the modified behavioral tendency itself — **learn** \ˈlərn\ *vb*

learning disabled *adj* : having difficulty in learning a basic scholastic skill and esp. reading, writing, or arithmetic because of a psychological or organic disorder (as dyslexia or attention deficit disorder) that interferes with the learning process — **learning disability**

least splanchnic nerve \ˈlēst-\ *n* : SPLANCHNIC NERVE c

Le·boy·er \lə-boi-ˈā\ *adj* : of or relating to a method of childbirth designed to reduce trauma for the newborn esp. by avoiding use of forceps and bright lights in the delivery room and by giving the newborn a warm bath

Leboyer, Frédéric (*b* 1918), French obstetrician.

LE cell \ˈel-ˈē-ˌsel\ *n* : a polymorphonuclear leukocyte that is found esp. in patients with lupus erythematosus — called also *lupus erythematosus cell*

lecith- or **lecitho-** *comb form* : yolk of an egg (*lecith*al) (*ovolecith*in)

lec·i·thal \ˈle-sə-thəl\ *adj* : having a yolk — often used in combination

lec·i·thin \ˈle-sə-thən\ *n* : any of several waxy hygroscopic phospholipids that are widely distributed in animals and plants, form colloidal solutions in water, and have emulsifying, wetting, and antioxidant properties; *also* : a mixture of or a substance rich in lecithins — called also *phosphatidylcholine*

lec·i·thin·ase \-thə-ˌnās, -ˌnāz\ *n* : PHOSPHOLIPASE

lec·tin \ˈlek-tin\ *n* : any of a group of proteins esp. of plants that are not antibodies and do not originate in an immune system but bind specifically to carbohydrate-containing receptors on cell surfaces (as of red blood cells)

leech \ˈlēch\ *n* : any of numerous carnivorous or bloodsucking usu. freshwater annelid worms (class Hirudinea) that have typically a flattened segmented lance-shaped body with a sucker at each end — see MEDICINAL LEECH

LE factor \ˌel-ˈē-\ *n* : an antibody found in the serum esp. of patients with systemic lupus erythematosus

left *adj* : of, relating to, or being the side of the body in which the heart is mostly located; *also* : located nearer to this side than to the right

left atrioventricular valve *n* : BICUSPID VALVE

left colic flexure *n* : SPLENIC FLEXURE

left gastric artery *n* : GASTRIC ARTERY 1

left gastroepiploic artery *n* : GASTROEPIPLOIC ARTERY b

left-hand \ˈleft-ˈhand\ *adj* 1 : situated on the left 2 : LEFT-HANDED

left hand *n* 1 : the hand on a person's left side 2 : the left side

left-hand·ed \ˈleft-ˈhan-dəd\ *adj* 1 : using the left hand habitually or more easily than the right 2 : relating to, designed for, or done with the left hand 3 : having a direction contrary to that of movement of the hands of a watch viewed from in front 4 : LEVOROTATORY — **left-handed** *adv* — **left-handed·ness** *n*

left heart *n* : the left atrium and ventricle : the half of the heart that receives oxygenated blood from the pulmonary circulation and passes it to the aorta

left lymphatic duct *n* : THORACIC DUCT

left pulmonary artery *n* : PULMONARY ARTERY C

left subcostal vein *n* : SUBCOSTAL VEIN b

leg \'leg\ *n* : a limb of an animal used esp. for supporting the body and for walking: as a : either of the two lower human limbs that extend from the top of the thigh to the foot and esp. the part between the knee and the ankle b : any of the rather generalized appendages of an arthropod used in walking and crawling — **leg•ged** \'le-gəd, 'legd\ *adj*

legal age *n* : the age at which a person enters into full adult legal rights and responsibilities (as of making contracts or wills)

legal blindness *n* : blindness as recognized by law which in most states of the U.S. means that the better eye using the best possible methods of correction has visual acuity of 20/200 or worse or that the visual field is restricted to 20 degrees or less — **legal•ly blind** *adj*

legal medicine *n* : FORENSIC MEDICINE

Legg-Cal•vé-Per•thes disease \'leg-,kal-'vā-'pər-,tēz-\ *n* : osteochondritis affecting the bony knob at the upper end of the femur — called also *Perthes disease*

Legg, Arthur Thornton (1874–1939), American orthopedic surgeon.

Calvé, Jacques (1875–1954), French surgeon.

Perthes, Georg Clemens (1869–1927), German surgeon.

Legg-Perthes disease *n* : LEGG-CALVÉ-PERTHES DISEASE

Le•gion•el•la \,lē-jə-'ne-lə\ *n* : a genus of gram-negative rod-shaped bacteria (family Legionellaceae) that includes the causative agent (*L. pneumophila*) of Legionnaires' disease

le•gion•el•lo•sis \,lē-jə-,ne-'lō-səs\ *n* : LEGIONNAIRES' DISEASE

Le•gion•naires' bacillus \,lē-jə-'narz-\ *n* : a bacterium of the genus *Legionella* (*L. pneumophila*) that causes Legionnaires' disease

Legionnaires' disease *also* **Legionnaire's disease** *n* : a lobar pneumonia caused by a bacterium of the genus *Legionella* (*L. pneumophila*)

le•gume \'le-,gyüm, li-'gyüm\ *n* : any of a large family (Leguminosae) of plants having fruits that are dry pods and split when ripe and including important food and forage plants (as beans and clover); *also* : the part (as seeds or pods) of a legume used as food — **le•gu•mi•nous** \li-'gyü-mə-nəs, le-\ *adj*

leio- *or* **lio-** *comb form* : smooth ⟨*leiomyoma*⟩

leio•myo•blas•to•ma \,lī-ō-,mī-ō-blas-'tō-mə\ *n, pl* **-mas** *or* **-ma•ta** \-mə-tə\

: LEIOMYOMA; *esp* : one resembling epithelium

leio•my•o•ma \,lī-ō-mī-'ō-mə\ *n, pl* **-mas** *or* **-ma•ta** \-mə-tə\ : a tumor consisting of smooth muscle fibers — **leio•my•o•ma•tous** \-mə-təs\ *adj*

leio•myo•sar•co•ma \,lī-ō-,mī-ō-sär-'kō-mə\ *n, pl* **-mas** *or* **-ma•ta** \-mə-tə\ : a sarcoma composed in part of smooth muscle cells

Leish•man–Don•o•van body \'lēsh-mən-'dä-nə-vən-\ *n* : a protozoan of the genus *Leishmania* (esp. *L. donovani*) in its nonmotile stage that is found esp. in cells of the skin, spleen, and liver of individuals affected with leishmaniasis and esp. kala-azar — compare DONOVAN BODY

Leishman, Sir William Boog (1865–1926), British bacteriologist.

Donovan, Charles (1863–1951), British surgeon.

leish•man•ia \lēsh-'ma-nē-ə, -'mä-\ *n* 1 *cap* : a genus of flagellate protozoans (family Trypanosomatidae) that are parasitic in the tissues of vertebrates and include one (*L. donovani*) causing kala-azar and another (*L. tropica*) causing oriental sore 2 : any protozoan of the genus *Leishmania; broadly* : a protozoan resembling the leishmanias that is included in the family (Trypanosomatidae) to which they belong — **leish•man•i•al** \-nē-əl\ *adj*

leish•man•i•a•sis \,lēsh-mə-'nī-ə-səs\ *n, pl* **-a•ses** \-,sēz\ : infection with or disease (as kala-azar or oriental sore) caused by leishmanias

lem•nis•cus \lem-'nis-kəs\ *n, pl* **-nis•ci** \-'nis-,kī, -,kē; -'ni-,sī\ : a band of fibers and esp. nerve fibers — called also *fillet*; see LATERAL LEMNISCUS, MEDIAL LEMNISCUS — **lem•nis•cal** \-'nis-kəl\ *adj*

len•i•tive \'le-nə-tiv\ *adj* : alleviating pain or harshness — **lenitive** *n*

lens *also* **lense** \'lenz\ *n* 1 : a curved piece of glass or plastic used singly or combined in eyeglasses or an optical instrument (as a microscope) for forming an image; *also* : a device for focusing radiation other than light 2 : a highly transparent biconvex lens-shaped or nearly spherical body in the eye that focuses light rays entering the eye typically onto the retina and that lies immediately behind the pupil — **lensed** *adj* — **lens•less** *adj*

lens•om•e•ter \len-'zä-mə-tər\ *n* : an instrument used to determine the optical properties (as the focal length and axis) of ophthalmic lenses

Lente insulin \'len-tā-\ *n* : a suspension of insulin for injection in a buffered solution containing zinc chloride in which forms of insulin which are relatively slowly and rapidly absorbed are in the approximate ratio of 3:7

len•ti•co•nus \,len-tə-'kō-nəs\ *n* : a rare abnormal and usu. congenital condition of the lens of the eye in which the surface is conical esp. on the posteri- or side

len·tic·u·lar \len-ˈti-kyə-lər\ *adj* **1** : having the shape of a double-convex lens **2** : of or relating to a lens esp. of the eye **3** : relating to or being the lentiform nucleus of the brain

lenticular nucleus *n* : LENTIFORM NUCLEUS

lenticular process *n* : the tip of the long process of the incus which articulates with the stapes

lentiform nucleus *n* : the one of the four basal ganglia in each cerebral hemisphere that comprises the larger and external nucleus of the corpus striatum — called also *lenticular nucleus*

len·ti·go \len-ˈtī-(ˌ)gō, -ˈtē-\ *n, pl* **len·tig·i·nes** \len-ˈti-jə-ˌnēz\ **1** : a small melanotic spot in the skin in which the formation of pigment is unrelated to exposure to sunlight and which is potentially malignant; *esp* : NEVUS — compare FRECKLE **2** : FRECKLE

lentigo ma·lig·na \-mə-ˈlig-nə\ *n* : a precancerous lesion on the skin esp. in areas exposed to the sun (as the face) that is flat, mottled, and brownish with an irregular outline and grows slowly over a period of years

lentigo se·nil·is \-sə-ˈni-ləs\ *n* : flat spots evenly colored with darker pigment that occur on the exposed skin esp. of persons aged 50 and over — see LIVER SPOTS

len·ti·vi·rus \ˈlen-tə-ˌvī-rəs\ *n* : any of a group of retroviruses that cause slowly progressive often fatal diseases (as AIDS)

le·on·ti·a·sis os·sea \ˌlē-ən-ˈtī-ə-səs-ˈä-sē-ə\ *n* : an overgrowth of the bones of the head producing enlargement and distortion of the face

lep·er \ˈle-pər\ *n* : an individual affected with leprosy

LE phenomenon \ˌel-ˈē-\ *n* : the process which a leukocyte undergoes in becoming a lupus erythematosus cell

lep·ra \ˈle-prə\ *n* : LEPROSY

lep·re·chaun·ism \ˈle-prə-ˌkä-ˌni-zəm, -ˌkô-\ *n* : a rare genetically-determined disorder characterized by mental and physical retardation, by endocrine disorders, by hirsutism, and esp. by a facies marked by large wide-set eyes and large low-set ears

lep·rol·o·gist \le-ˈprä-lə-jist\ *n* : a specialist in the study of leprosy and its treatment — **lep·rol·o·gy** \-jē\ *n*

lep·ro·ma \le-ˈprō-mə\ *n, pl* **-mas** or **-ma·ta** \-mə-tə\ : a nodular lesion of leprosy

le·pro·ma·tous \lə-ˈprä-mə-təs, -ˈprō-\ *adj* : of, relating to, characterized by, or affected with lepromas or lepromatous leprosy ⟨~ patients⟩

lepromatous leprosy *n* : the one of the two major forms of leprosy that is characterized by the formation of lep-

romas, the presence of numerous Hansen's bacilli in the lesions, and a negative skin reaction to lepromin and that remains infectious to others until treated — compare TUBERCULOID LEPROSY

lep·ro·min \le-ˈprō-mən\ *n* : an extract of human leprous tissue used in a skin test for leprosy infection

lep·ro·sar·i·um \ˌle-prə-ˈser-ē-əm\ *n, pl* **-i·ums** or **-ia** \-ē-ə\ : a hospital for leprosy patients

lep·ro·ser·ie *also* **lep·ro·sery** \ˈle-prə-ˌser-ē\ *n, pl* **-series** : LEPROSARIUM

lep·ro·stat·ic \ˌle-prə-ˈsta-tik\ *n* : an agent that inhibits the growth of Hansen's bacillus

lep·ro·sy \ˈle-prə-sē\ *n, pl* **-sies** : a chronic disease caused by infection with an acid-fast bacillus of the genus *Mycobacterium* (*M. leprae*) and characterized by the formation of nodules on the surface of the body and esp. on the face or by the appearance of tuberculoid macules on the skin that enlarge and spread and are accompanied by loss of sensation followed sooner or later in both types if not treated by involvement of nerves with eventual paralysis, wasting of muscle, and production of deformities and mutilations — called also *Hansen's disease*, *lepra*; see LEPROMATOUS LEPROSY, TUBERCULOID LEPROSY

lep·rot·ic \le-ˈprä-tik\ *adj* : of, caused by, or infected with leprosy

lep·rous \ˈle-prəs\ *adj* **1** : infected with leprosy **2** : of, relating to, or associated with leprosy or a leper

-lep·sy \ˌlep-sē\ *n comb form, pl* **-lep·sies** : taking : seizure ⟨narco*lepsy*⟩

lept- or **lepto-** *comb form* : small : weak : thin : fine ⟨*lepto*meninges⟩ ⟨*lepto*tene⟩

lep·ta·zol \ˈlep-tə-ˌzôl, -ˌzōl\ *n, chiefly Brit* : PENTYLENETETRAZOL

lep·to \ˈlep-ˌtō\ *n* : LEPTOSPIROSIS

lep·to·me·nin·ges \ˌlep-tō-mə-ˈnin-(ˌ)jēz\ *n pl* : the pia mater and the arachnoid considered together as investing the brain and spinal cord — called also *pia-arachnoid* — **lep·to·men·in·ge·al** \-ˌme-nən-ˈjē-əl\ *adj*

lep·to·men·in·gi·tis \-ˌme-nən-ˈji-təs\ *n, pl* **-git·i·des** \-ˈji-tə-ˌdēz\ : inflammation of the pia mater and the arachnoid membrane

lep·to·ne·ma \ˌlep-tə-ˈnē-mə\ *n* : a chromatin thread or chromosome at the leptotene stage of meiotic prophase

lep·to·phos \ˈlep-tō-ˌfäs\ *n* : an organophosphorus pesticide $C_{13}H_{10}BrCl_2O_2PS$ that has been associated with the occurrence of neurological damage in individuals exposed to it esp. in the early and mid 1970s

lep·to·spi·ra \ˌlep-tō-ˈspī-rə\ *n* **1** *cap* : a genus of extremely slender aerobic spirochetes (family Treponemataceae) that are free-living or parasitic in mammals and include a number of important pathogens (as *L. icterohaemorrhagiae* of Weil's disease or *L. canicola* of canicola fever) 2 *pl* -ra or -ras or -rae \-ˌrē\ : LEPTOSPIRE

lep·to·spire \'lep-tə-ˌspīr\ *n* : any spirochete of the genus *Leptospira* — called also *leptospira* — **lep·to·spi·ral** \ˌlep-tə-'spī-rəl\ *adj*

lep·to·spi·ro·sis \ˌlep-tə-spī-'rō-səs\ *n*, *pl* -ro·ses \-ˌsēz\ : any of several diseases of humans and domestic animals that are caused by infection with spirochetes of the genus *Leptospira* — called also *lepto*; see WEIL'S DISEASE

lep·to·tene \'lep-tə-ˌtēn\ *n* : a stage of meiotic prophase immediately preceding synapsis in which the chromosomes appear as fine discrete threads — **leptotene** *adj*

Le·riche's syndrome \lə-'rēsh-əz-\ : occlusion of the descending continuation of the aorta in the abdomen typically resulting in impotence, the absence of a pulse in the femoral arteries, and weakness and numbness in the lower back, buttocks, hips, thighs, and calves

Leriche, René (1879–1955), French surgeon.

¹**les·bi·an** \'lez-bē-ən\ *adj*, *often cap* : of or relating to homosexuality between females

²**lesbian** *n*, *often cap* : a female homosexual — called also *sapphic*, *sapphist*

les·bi·an·ism \'lez-bē-ə-ˌni-zəm\ *n* : female homosexuality — called also *sapphism*

Lesch–Ny·han syndrome \'lesh-'nī-ən-\ *n* : a rare and usu. fatal genetic disorder of male children that is transmitted as a recessive trait linked to the X chromosome and that is characterized by hyperuricemia, mental retardation, spasticity, compulsive biting of the lips and fingers, and a deficiency of hypoxanthine-guanine phosphoribosyltransferase — called also *Lesch-Nyhan disease*

Lesch, Michael (*b* 1939) and Nyhan, William Leo (*b* 1926), American pediatricians.

¹**le·sion** \'lē-zhən\ *n* : an abnormal change in structure of an organ or part due to injury or disease; *esp* : one that is circumscribed and well defined — **le·sioned** \-zhənd\ *adj*

²**lesion** *vb* : to produce lesions in

les·ser cornu \'les-ər-\ *n* : CERATOHYAL

lesser curvature *n* : the boundary of the stomach that in humans forms a relatively short concave curve on the right from the opening for the esophagus to the opening into the duodenum — compare GREATER CURVATURE

lesser multangular *n* : TRAPEZOID — called also *lesser multangular bone*

lesser occipital nerve *n* : OCCIPITAL NERVE b

lesser omentum *n* : a part of the peritoneum attached to the liver and to the lesser curvature of the stomach and supporting the hepatic vessels — compare GREATER OMENTUM

lesser petrosal nerve *n* : the continuation of the tympanic nerve beyond the inferior ganglion of the glossopharyngeal nerve that terminates in the otic ganglion which it supplies with preganglionic parasympathetic fibers

lesser sciatic foramen *n* : SCIATIC FORAMEN b

lesser sciatic notch *n* : SCIATIC NOTCH b

lesser splanchnic nerve *n* : SPLANCHNIC NERVE b

lesser trochanter *n* : TROCHANTER b

lesser tubercle *n* : a prominence on the upper anterior part of the end of the humerus that serves as the insertion for the subscapularis — compare GREATER TUBERCLE

lesser wing *n* : an anterior triangular process on each side of the sphenoid bone in front of and much smaller than the corresponding greater wing — compare GREATER WING

¹**le·thal** \'lē-thəl\ *adj* : of, relating to, or causing death ⟨a ~ injury⟩; *also* : capable of causing death ⟨~ chemicals⟩ ⟨a ~ dose⟩ — **le·thal·i·ty** \lē-'tha-lə-tē\ *n* — **le·thal·ly** *adv*

²**lethal** *n* 1 : an abnormality of genetic origin causing the death of the organism possessing it usu. before maturity 2 : LETHAL GENE

lethal gene *n* : a gene that in some (as homozygous) conditions may prevent development or cause the death of an organism or its germ cells — called also *lethal factor*, *lethal mutant*, *lethal mutation*

lethargica — see ENCEPHALITIS LETHARGICA

leth·ar·gy \'le-thər-jē\ *n*, *pl* -gies 1 : abnormal drowsiness 2 : the quality or state of being lazy, sluggish, or indifferent — **lethargic** *adj*

Let·ter·er–Si·we disease \'le-tər-ər-'sē-və-\ *n* : an acute disease of children characterized by fever, hemorrhages, and other evidences of a disturbance in the reticuloendothelial system and by severe bone lesions esp. of the skull

Letterer, Erich (*b* 1895), German physician.

Siwe, Sture August (*b* 1897), Swedish pediatrician.

Leu *abbr* leucine

leuc- or **leuco-** *chiefly Brit var of* LEUK-

leu·cine \'lü-ˌsēn\ *n* : a white crystalline essential amino acid $C_6H_{13}NO_2$ obtained by the hydrolysis of most dietary proteins

leucine aminopeptidase *n* : an aminopeptidase that is found in all bodily tissues and is increased in the serum in some conditions or diseases (as pancreatic carcinoma)

leucine-en·keph·a·lin \-en-ˈke-fə-lən\ *n* : a pentapeptide having a terminal leucine residue that is one of the two enkephalins occurring naturally in the brain — called also *Leu‑enkephalin*

leu·ci·no·sis \ˌlü-sə-ˈnō-səs\ *n, pl* **-no·ses** \-ˌsēz\ *or* **-no·sis·es** : a condition characterized by an abnormally high concentration of leucine in bodily tissues and the presence of leucine in the urine

leucocyt- *or* **leucocyto-** *chiefly Brit var of* LEUKOCYT-

leu·co·cy·to·zo·on \ˌlü-kō-ˌsī-tə-ˈzō-ˌän, -ən\ *n* **1** *cap* : a genus of sporozoans parasitic in birds **2** *pl* **-zoa** \-ˈzō-ə\ : any sporozoan of the genus *Leucocytozoon*

leu·co·cy·to·zoo·no·sis \-ˌzō-ə-ˈnō-səs\ *n, pl* **-no·ses** \-ˌsēz\ : infection by or a disease caused by infection by sporozoans of the genus *Leucocytozoon*

leu·co·vo·rin \ˈlü-ˈkä-və-rin\ *n* : CITROVORUM FACTOR

Leu-en·keph·a·lin \ˌlü-en-ˈke-fə-lin\ *n* : LEUCINE-ENKEPHALIN

leuk- *or* **leuko-** *comb form* **1** : white : colorless : weakly colored (*leuko*cyte) (*leuk*orrhea) **2** : leukocyte (*leuk*emia) **3** : white matter of the brain (*leuko*encephalopathy)

leu·kae·mia, leu·kae·mic *chiefly Brit var of* LEUKEMIA, LEUKEMIC

leu·ka·phe·re·sis \ˌlü-kə-fə-ˈrē-səs\ *n, pl* **-phe·re·ses** \-ˌsēz\ : a procedure by which the leukocytes are removed from a donor's blood which is then transfused back into the donor — called also *leukopheresis*

leu·ke·mia \lü-ˈkē-mē-ə\ *n* : an acute or chronic disease characterized by an abnormal increase in the number of white blood cells in bodily tissues with or without a corresponding increase of those in the circulating blood — see MONOCYTIC LEUKEMIA, MYELOGENOUS LEUKEMIA

¹leu·ke·mic \lü-ˈkē-mik\ *adj* **1** : of, relating to, or affected by leukemia **2** : characterized by an increase in white blood cells (~ blood)

²leukemic *n* : a person affected with leukemia

leu·ke·mo·gen·e·sis \ˌlü-ˌkē-mə-ˈje-nə-səs\ *n, pl* **-e·ses** \-ˌsēz\ : induction or production of leukemia — **leu·ke·mo·gen·ic** \-ˈjen-ik\ *adj*

leu·ke·moid \ˈlü-ˈkē-ˌmöid\ *adj* : resembling leukemia

leuko- — see LEUK-

leu·ko·ag·glu·ti·nin \ˌlü-kō-ə-ˈglüt-ᵊn-ən\ *n* : an antibody that agglutinates leukocytes — compare HEMAGGLUTININ

leukocyt- *or* **leukocyto-** *comb form* : leukocyte (*leukocyto*sis)

leu·ko·cyte \ˈlü-kə-ˌsīt\ *n* **1** : WHITE BLOOD CELL **2** : a cell (as a macro-phage) of the tissues comparable to or derived from a leukocyte

leu·ko·cyt·ic \ˌlü-kə-ˈsi-tik\ *adj* **1** : of, relating to, or involving leukocytes **2** : characterized by an excess of leukocytes

leu·ko·cy·to·sis \ˌlü-kə-sī-ˈtō-səs, -kə-sə-\ *n, pl* **-to·ses** \-ˌsēz\ : an increase in the number of leukocytes in the circulating blood that occurs normally (as after meals) or abnormally (as in some infections) — **leu·ko·cy·tot·ic** \-ˈtä-tik\ *adj*

leu·ko·der·ma \ˌlü-kə-ˈdər-mə\ *n* : a skin abnormality that is characterized by a usu. congenital lack of pigment in spots or bands and produces a patchy whiteness — compare VITILIGO

leu·ko·dys·tro·phy \ˌlü-kō-ˈdis-trə-fē\ *n, pl* **-phies** : any of several genetically determined diseases characterized by degeneration of the white matter of the brain

leu·ko·en·ceph·a·lop·a·thy \-in-ˌse-fə-ˈlä-pə-thē\ *n, pl* **-thies** : any of various diseases (as leukodystrophy) affecting the brain's white matter

leuk·onych·ia \ˌlü-kō-ˈni-kē-ə\ *n* : a white spotting, streaking, or discoloration of the fingernails caused by injury or ill health

leu·ko·pe·nia \ˌlü-kō-ˈpē-nē-ə\ *n* : a condition in which the number of leukocytes circulating in the blood is abnormally low and which is most commonly due to a decreased production of new cells in conjunction with various infectious diseases, as a reaction to various drugs or other chemicals, or in response to irradiation — **leu·ko·pe·nic** \-ˈpē-nik\ *adj*

leu·ko·phe·re·sis \-fə-ˈrē-səs\ *n, pl* **-re·ses** \-ˌsēz\ : LEUKAPHERESIS

leu·ko·pla·kia \ˌlü-kō-ˈplā-kē-ə\ *n* : a condition commonly considered precancerous in which thickened white patches of epithelium occur on the mucous membranes esp. of the mouth, vulva, and renal pelvis; *also* : a lesion or lesioned area of leukoplakia — **leu·ko·pla·kic** \-ˈplā-kik\ *adj*

leu·ko·poi·e·sis \-pöi-ˈē-səs\ *n, pl* **-e·ses** \-ˌsēz\ : the formation of white blood cells — **leu·ko·poi·et·ic** \-ˈe-tik\ *adj*

leu·kor·rhea \ˌlü-kə-ˈrē-ə\ *n* : a white, yellowish, or greenish white viscid discharge from the vagina resulting from inflammation or congestion of the uterine or vaginal mucous membrane — **leu·kor·rhe·al** \-ˈrē-əl\ *adj*

leu·ko·sar·co·ma \ˌlü-kō-sär-ˈkō-mə\ *n, pl* **-mas** *or* **-ma·ta** \-mə-tə\ : lymphosarcoma accompanied by leukemia — **leu·ko·sar·co·ma·to·sis** \-ˌsär-kō-mə-ˈtō-səs\ *n*

leu·ko·sis \lü-ˈkō-səs\ *n, pl* **-ko·ses** \-ˌsēz\ : LEUKEMIA; *esp* : any of various leukemic diseases of poultry — **leu·kot·ic** \-ˈkä-tik\ *adj*

leu·ko·tac·tic \ˌlü-kō-ˈtak-tik\ *adj* : tending to attract leukocytes

leu·ko·tome \ˈlü-kə-ˌtōm\ *n* : a cannula through which a wire is inserted and used to cut the white matter in the brain in lobotomy

leu·kot·o·my \lü-ˈkä-tə-mē\ *n, pl* **-mies** : LOBOTOMY

leu·ko·tox·in \ˌlü-kō-ˈtäk-sən\ *n* : a substance specif. destructive to leukocytes

leu·ko·tri·ene \ˌlü-kə-ˈtrī-ˌēn\ *n* : any of a group of eicosanoids that are generated in basophils, mast cells, macrophages, and human lung tissue by lipoxygenase-catalyzed oxygenation esp. of arachidonic acid and that participate in allergic responses (as bronchoconstriction in asthma) — see SLOW-REACTING SUBSTANCE OF ANAPHYLAXIS

leu·ro·cris·tine \ˌlür-ō-ˈkris-ˌtēn\ *n* : VINCRISTINE

lev- *or* **levo-** *comb form* : left : on the left side : to the left (*levo*cardia)

lev·al·lor·phan \ˌle-və-ˈlor-ˌfan, -fən\ *n* : a drug $C_{19}H_{25}NO$ related to morphine that is used to counteract morphine poisoning

le·vam·i·sole \lə-ˈva-mə-ˌsōl\ *n* : an anthelmintic drug $C_{11}H_{12}N_2S$ administered in the form of its hydrochloride that also possesses immunostimulant properties and is used esp. in the treatment of colon cancer

Le·vant storax \lə-ˈvant-\ *n* : STORAX 1

lev·ar·ter·e·nol \ˌle-vär-ˈtir-ə-ˌnol, -ˈter-, -ˌnōl\ *n* : levorotatory norepinephrine

le·va·tor \li-ˈvā-tər\ *n, pl* **le·va·to·res** \ˌle-və-ˈtōr-(ˌ)ēz\ *or* **le·va·tors** \li-ˈvā-tərz\ : a muscle that serves to raise a body part — compare DEPRESSOR a

levator an·gu·li oris \-ˈaŋ-gyə-ˌlī-ˈor-əs\ *n* : a facial muscle that arises from the maxilla, inclines downward to be inserted into the corner of the mouth, and draws the lips up and back — called also *caninus*

levator ani \-ˈā-ˌnī\ *n* : a broad thin muscle that is attached in a sheet to each side of the inner surface of the pelvis and descends to form the floor of the pelvic cavity where it supports the viscera and surrounds structures which pass through it and inserts into the sides of the apex of the coccyx, the margins of the anus, the side of the rectum, and the central tendinous point of the perineum — see ILIOCOCCYGEUS, PUBOCOCCYGEUS

le·va·to·res cos·ta·rum \ˌkäs-ˈtär-əm, -ˈtär-\ *n pl* : a series of 12 muscles on each side that arise from the transverse processes of the seventh cervical and upper 11 thoracic vertebrae, that insert into the ribs, and that raise the ribs increasing the volume of the thoracic cavity and extend, bend, and rotate the spinal column

levator la·bii su·pe·ri·or·is \-ˈlā-bē-ˌī-sù-

ˌpir-ē-ˈor-əs\ *n* : a facial muscle arising from the lower margin of the orbit and inserting into the muscular substance of the upper lip which it elevates — called also *quadratus labii superioris*

levator labii superioris alae·que na·si \-ā-ˈlē-kwē-ˈnā-ˌzī\ *n* : a muscle that arises from the nasal process of the maxilla, that passes downward and laterally, that divides into a part inserting into the alar cartilage and one inserting into the upper lip, and that dilates the nostril and raises the upper lip

levator pal·pe·brae su·pe·ri·or·is \-ˌpal-ˈpē-ˌbrē-sù-ˌpir-ē-ˈor-əs\ *n* : a thin flat extrinsic muscle of the eye arising from the lesser wing of the sphenoid bone and inserting into the tarsal plate of the skin of the upper eyelid which it raises

levator pros·ta·tae \-ˈpräs-tə-ˌtē\ *n* : a part of the pubococcygeus comprising the more medial and ventral fasciculi that insert into the tissue in front of the anus and serve to support and elevate the prostate gland

levator scap·u·lae \-ˈska-pyə-ˌlē\ *n* : a back muscle that arises in the transverse processes of the first four cervical vertebrae and descends to insert into the vertebral border of the scapula which it elevates

levator ve·li pal·a·ti·ni \-ˈvē-ˌlī-ˌpa-lə-ˈtī-ˌnī\ *n* : a muscle arising from the temporal bone and the cartilage of the eustachian tube and descending to insert into the midline of the soft palate which it elevates esp. to close the nasopharynx while swallowing is taking place

Le·Veen shunt \lə-ˈvēn-ˈshənt\ *n* : a plastic tube that passes from the jugular vein to the peritoneal cavity where a valve permits absorption of ascitic fluid which is carried back to venous circulation by way of the superior vena cava

LeVeen, Harry Henry (*b* 1916), American surgeon.

Le·vin tube \lə-ˈvēn-, lə-ˈvin-\ *n* : a tube designed to be passed into the stomach or duodenum through the nose

Levin, Abraham Louis (1880–1940), American physician.

le·vo \ˈlē-(ˌ)vō\ *adj* : LEVOROTATORY

levo- — see LEV-

le·vo·car·dia \ˌlē-və-ˈkär-dē-ə\ *n* : normal position of the heart when associated with situs inversus of other abdominal viscera and usu. with structural defects of the heart itself

le·vo·di·hy·droxy·phe·nyl·al·a·nine \ˌlē-vō-ˌdī-hī-ˌdräk-sē-ˌfen-əl-ˈa-lə-ˌnēn, -ˌfēn-\ *n* : L-DOPA

le·vo·do·pa \ˈle-və-ˌdō-pə, ˌlē-və-ˈdō-pə\ *n* : L-DOPA

Le·vo-Dro·mo·ran \ˌlē-vō-ˈdrō-mə-

.ran\ *trademark* — used for a preparation of levorphanol

le·vo·nor·ges·trel \ˌlē-və-nȯr-ˈjes-trəl\ *n* : the levorotatory form of norgestrel used in oral contraceptives and contraceptive implants — see NORPLANT

Levo-phed \ˈle-və-ˌfed\ *trademark* — used for a preparation of norepinephrine

Le·vo·prome \ˈlē-və-ˌprōm\ *trademark* — used for a preparation of methotrimeprazine

le·vo·pro·poxy·phene \ˌlē-və-ˌprō-ˈpäk-si-ˌfēn\ *n* : a drug $C_{22}H_{29}NO_2$ used esp. in the form of the napsylate as an antitussive

le·vo·ro·ta·to·ry \-ˈrō-tə-ˌtōr-ē\ *or* **le·vo·ro·ta·ry** \-ˈrō-tə-rē\ *adj* : turning toward the left or counterclockwise; *esp* : rotating the plane of polarization of light to the left — compare DEXTROROTATORY

lev·or·pha·nol \le-ˈvȯr-fə-ˌnȯl\ *n* : an addictive drug $C_{17}H_{23}NO$ used esp. in the form of the tartrate as a potent analgesic with properties similar to morphine — see LEVO-DROMORAN

le·vo·thy·rox·ine \ˌlē-vō-thī-ˈräk-ˌsēn, -sən\ *n* : the levorotatory isomer of thyroxine that is administered in the form of the sodium salt for treatment of hypothyroidism

lev·u·lose \ˈle-vyə-ˌlōs, -ˌlōz\ *n* : FRUCTOSE 2

lev·u·los·uria \ˌle-vyə-lō-ˈsyúr-ē-ə, -ˈshúr\ *n* : the presence of fructose in the urine

Lew·is blood group \ˈlü-əs-\ *n* : any of a system of blood groups controlled by a pair of dominant-recessive alleles and characterized by antigens which are adsorbed onto the surface of red blood cells and tend to interreact with the antigens produced by secretors although they are genetically independent of them

    Lewis, H. D. G., British hospital patient.

lew·is·ite \ˈlü-ə-ˌsīt\ *n* : a colorless or brown vesicant liquid $C_2H_2AsCl_3$ developed as a poison gas for war use

    Lewis, Winford Lee (1878–1943), American chemist.

-lex·ia \ˈlek-sē-ə\ *n comb form* : reading (of such) a kind or with (such) an impairment (dys*lexia*)

Ley·dig cell \ˈlī-dig-\ *also* **Ley·dig's cell** \-digz-\ *n* : an interstitial cell of the testis usu. considered the chief source of testicular androgens and perhaps other hormones — called also *cell of Leydig, interstitial cell of Leydig*

    Leydig, Franz von (1821–1908), German anatomist.

L–form \ˈel-ˌfȯrm\ *n* : a variant form of some bacteria that usu. lacks a cell wall — called also *L-phase*

LH *abbr* luteinizing hormone

LHRH *abbr* luteinizing hormone‐releasing hormone

Li *symbol* lithium

lib — see AD LIB

li·bi·do \lə-ˈbē-(ˌ)dō, -ˈbī-, ˈli-bə-ˌdō\ *n, pl* **-dos** 1 : emotional or psychic energy that in psychoanalytic theory is derived from primitive biological urges and that is usu. goal-directed 2 : sexual drive — **li·bid·i·nal** \lə-ˈbid-ᵊn-əl\ *adj*

libitum — see AD LIBITUM

Lib·man–Sacks endocarditis \ˈlib-mən-ˈsaks-\ *n* : a noninfectious form of verrucous endocardititis associated with systemic lupus erythematosus — called also *Libman-Sacks disease, Libman-Sacks syndrome*

    Libman, Emanuel (1872–1946) and Sacks, Benjamin (*b* 1896), American physicians.

li·brary \ˈli-ˌbrer-ē\ *n* : a collection of sequences of DNA and esp. recombinant DNA that are maintained in a suitable cellular environment and that represent the genetic material of a particular organism or tissue

Lib·ri·um \ˈli-brē-əm\ *trademark* — used for a preparation of chlordiazepoxide

lice *pl of* LOUSE

licensed practical nurse *n* : a person who has undergone training and obtained a license (as from a state) to provide routine care for the sick — called also *LPN*

licensed vocational nurse *n* : a licensed practical nurse authorized by license to practice in the states of California or Texas — called also *LVN*

li·chen \ˈlī-kən\ *n* 1 : any of several skin diseases characterized by the eruption of flat papules; *esp* : LICHEN PLANUS 2 : any of numerous complex plants (group Lichenes) made up of an alga and a fungus growing in symbiotic association on a solid surface (as a rock)

li·chen·i·fi·ca·tion \lī-ˌke-nə-fə-ˈkā-shən, ˌli-kə-\ *n* : the process by which skin becomes hardened and leathery or lichenoid usu. as a result of chronic irritation; *also* : a patch of skin so modified — **li·chen·i·fied** \lī-ˈke-nə-ˌfīd, ˈli-kə-\ *adj*

li·chen·oid \ˈlī-kə-ˌnȯid\ *adj* : resembling lichen (a ~ eruption)

lichenoides — see PITYRIASIS LICHENOIDES ET VARIOLIFORMIS ACUTA

lichen pla·nus \-ˈplā-nəs\ *n* : a skin disease characterized by an eruption of wide flat papules covered by a horny glazed film, marked by intense itching, and often accompanied by lesions on the oral mucosa

lichen scle·ro·sus et atro·phi·cus \-sklə-ˈrō-səs-et-ˌā-ˈtrō-fi-kəs\ *n* : a chronic skin disease that is characterized by the eruption of flat white hardened papules with central hair follicles often having black keratotic plugs

lichen sim·plex chron·i·cus \-ˈsim-ˌpleks-ˈkrä-ni-kəs\ *n* : dermatitis marked by one or more clearly defined patches produced by chronic rubbing of the skin

lic·o·rice \'li-kə-rish, -ris\ n : GLYCYRRHIZA

licorice root n : GLYCYRRHIZA

lid \'lid\ n : EYELID

li·do·caine \'lī-də-ˌkān\ n : a crystalline compound $C_{14}H_{22}N_2O$ that is used in the form of its hydrochloride as a local anesthetic — called also *lignocaine;* see XYLOCAINE

Lie·ber·mann–Bur·chard reaction \'lē-bər-mən-'bùr-ˌkärt-\ n : a test for unsaturated steroids (as cholesterol) and for terpenes having the formula $C_{30}H_{48}$ — called also *Liebermann–Burchard test*

Liebermann, Carl Theodore (1842–1914), German chemist. H. Burchard may have been one of his many student-research assistants.

lie detector \'lī-di-ˌtek-tər\ n : an instrument for detecting physiological evidence (as changes in pulse or blood pressure) of the tension that accompanies lying

li·en \'lī-ən, 'lī-ˌen\ n : SPLEEN — **li·en·al** \-əl\ adj

lienal vein n : SPLENIC VEIN

life \'līf\ n, pl **lives** \'līvz\ 1 a : the quality that distinguishes a vital and functional plant or animal from a dead body b : a state of living characterized by capacity for metabolism, growth, reaction to stimuli, and reproduction 2 a : the sequence of physical and mental experiences that make up the existence of an individual b : a specific aspect or aspect of the process of living ⟨sex ∼⟩ ⟨adult ∼⟩ — **life·less** \'līf-ləs\ adj

life cycle n : the series of stages in form and functional activity through which an organism passes between successive recurrences of a specified primary stage

life expectancy n : an expected number of years of life based on statistical probability

¹life·sav·ing \'līf-ˌsā-viŋ\ adj : designed for or used in saving lives ⟨∼ drugs⟩

²lifesaving n : the skill or practice of saving or protecting the lives esp. of drowning persons

life science n : a branch of science (as biology, medicine, anthropology, or sociology) that deals with living organisms and life processes — usu. used in pl. — **life scientist** n

life space n : the physical and psychological environment of an individual or group

life span \'līf-ˌspan\ n 1 : the duration of existence of an individual 2 : the average length of life of a kind of organism or of a material object

life-sup·port \'līf-sə-ˌpòrt\ adj : providing support necessary to sustain life: esp : of, relating to, or being a life-support system ⟨∼ equipment⟩

life support n : medical life-support equipment (the patient was placed on *life support*)

life-support system n : a system that provides all or some of the items (as oxygen, food, water, and disposition of carbon dioxide and body wastes) necessary for maintaining life or health

lift \'lift\ n : FACE-LIFT — **lift** vb

lig·a·ment \'li-gə-mənt\ n 1 : a tough band of tissue that serves to connect the articular extremities of bones or to support or retain an organ in place and is usu. composed of coarse bundles of dense white fibrous tissue parallel or closely interlaced, pliant, and flexible, but not extensible 2 : any of various folds or bands of pleura, peritoneum, or mesentery connecting parts or organs

ligament of the ovary n : a rounded cord of fibrous and muscular tissue extending from each superior angle of the uterus to the inner extremity of the ovary of the same side — called also *ovarian ligament;* see SUSPENSORY LIGAMENT OF THE OVARY

ligament of Treitz \-'trits\ n : a band of smooth muscle extending from the junction of the duodenum and jejunum to the left crus of the diaphragm and functioning as a suspensory ligament

Treitz, Wenzel (1819–1872), Austrian physician.

ligament of Zinn \-'zin, -'tsin\ n : the common tendon of the inferior rectus and the internal rectus muscles of the eye — called also *tendon of Zinn*

Zinn \'tsin\, Johann Gottfried (1727–1759), German anatomist and botanist.

lig·a·men·tous \ˌli-gə-'men-təs\ adj 1 : of or relating to a ligament 2 : forming or formed of a ligament

lig·a·men·tum \ˌli-gə-'men-təm\ n, pl **-ta** \-tə\ : LIGAMENT

ligamentum ar·te·ri·o·sum \-är-ˌtir-ē-'ō-səm\ n : a cord of tissue that connects the pulmonary trunk and the aorta and that is the vestige of the ductus arteriosus

ligamentum fla·vum \-'flā-vəm\ n, pl **ligamenta fla·va** \-və\ : any of a series of ligaments of yellow elastic tissue connecting the laminae of adjacent vertebrae from the axis to the sacrum

ligamentum nu·chae \-'nü-ˌkē, -'nyü-, -ˌkī\ n, pl **ligamenta nuchae** : a medium ligament of the back of the neck that is rudimentary in humans but highly developed and composed of yellow elastic tissue in many quadrupeds where it assists in supporting the head

ligamentum te·res \-'tē-ˌrēz\ n : ROUND LIGAMENT; esp : ROUND LIGAMENT 1

ligamentum ve·no·sum \-vē-'nō-səm\ n : a cord of tissue connected to the liver that is the vestige of the ductus venosus

li·gase \'lī-ˌgās, -ˌgāz\ *n* : SYNTHETASE

li·ga·tion \lī-'gā-shən\ *n* **1 a** : the surgical process of tying up an anatomical channel (as a blood vessel) **b** : the process of joining together chemical chains (as of DNA or protein) **2** : something that binds : LIGATURE — **li·gate** \'lī-ˌgāt, lī-'\ *vb*

lig·a·ture \'li-gə-ˌchùr, -chər, -ˌtyùr\ *n* **1** : something that is used to bind; *specif* : a filament (as a thread) used in surgery (as for tying blood vessels) **2** : the action or result of binding or tying — **ligature** *vb*

light \'līt\ *n* **1 a** : the sensation aroused by stimulation of the visual receptors **b** : an electromagnetic radiation in the wavelength range including infrared, visible, ultraviolet, and X rays and traveling in a vacuum with a speed of about 186,281 miles (300,000 kilometers) per second; *specif* : the part of this range that is visible to the human eye **2** : a source of light

light adaptation *n* : the adjustments including narrowing of the pupillary opening and decrease in rhodopsin by which the retina of the eye is made efficient as a visual receptor under conditions of strong illumination — compare DARK ADAPTATION — **light-adapt·ed** \'līt-ə-ˌdap-təd\ *adj*

light chain *n* : either of the two smaller of the four polypeptide chains that are subunits of antibodies — called also *L chain*; compare HEAVY CHAIN

light·en·ing \'līt-ᵊn-iŋ\ *n* : a sense of decreased weight and abdominal tension felt by a pregnant woman on descent of the fetus into the pelvic cavity prior to labor

light-head·ed \'līt-'he-dəd\ *adj* : mentally disordered : DIZZY — **light-head·ed·ness** *n*

light microscope *n* : an ordinary microscope that uses light as distinguished from an electron microscope — **light microscopy** *n*

light·ning pains \'līt-niŋ-\ *n pl* : intense shooting or lancinating pains occurring in tabes dorsalis

lig·no·caine \'lig-na-ˌkān\ *n, Brit* : LIDOCAINE

limb \'lim\ *n* **1** : one of the projecting paired appendages of an animal body concerned esp. with movement and grasping; *esp* : a human leg or arm **2** : a branch or arm of something (as an anatomical part)

lim·bal \'lim-bəl\ *adj* : of or relating to the limbus (a ~ incision)

limb bud *n* : a proliferation of embryonic tissue shaped like a mound from which a limb develops

lim·ber·neck \'lim-bər-ˌnek\ *n* : a botulism of birds (esp. poultry) characterized by paralysis of the neck muscles and pharynx

lim·bic \'lim-bik\ *adj* : of, relating to, or

being the limbic system of the brain

limbic lobe *n* : the marginal medial portion of the cortex of a cerebral hemisphere

limbic system *n* : a group of subcortical structures (as the hypothalamus, the hippocampus, and the amygdala) of the brain that are concerned esp. with emotion and motivation

lim·bus \'lim-bəs\ *n* : a border distinguished by color or structure; *esp* : the marginal region of the cornea of the eye by which it is continuous with the sclera

lime \'līm\ *n* : a caustic powdery white solid that consists of the oxide of calcium often together with magnesia

li·men \'lī-mən\ *n* : THRESHOLD

lim·i·nal \'li-mə-nəl\ *adj* **1** : of or relating to a sensory threshold **2** : barely perceptible

limp \'limp\ *vb* **1** : to walk lamely; *esp* : to walk favoring one leg **2** : to go unsteadily — **limp** *n*

Lin·co·cin \liŋ-'kō-sən\ *trademark* — used for a preparation of lincomycin

lin·co·my·cin \ˌliŋ-kə-'mīs-ᵊn\ *n* : an antibiotic obtained from an actinomycete of the genus *Streptomyces* (*S. lincolnensis*) and effective esp. against gram-positive bacteria

linc·tus \'liŋk-təs\ *n, pl* **linc·tus·es** : a syrupy or sticky preparation containing medicaments exerting a local action on the mucous membrane of the throat

lin·dane \'lin-ˌdān\ *n* : an insecticide consisting of not less than 99 percent gamma benzene hexachloride that is biodegraded very slowly

Lin·dau's disease \'lin-ˌdaùz-\ *n* : VON HIPPEL-LINDAU DISEASE

line \'līn\ *n* : a strain produced and maintained esp. by selective breeding or biological culture

lin·ea al·ba \ˌli-nē-ə-'al-bə\ *n, pl* **lin·e·ae al·bae** \'li-nē-ˌē-'al-ˌbē\ : a median vertical tendinous line on the abdomen formed of fibers from the aponeuroses of the two rectus abdominis muscles and extending from the xiphoid process to the pubic symphysis

linea as·pe·ra \-'as-pə-rə\ *n, pl* **lineae as·pe·rae** \-ˌrē\ : a longitudinal ridge on the posterior surface of the middle third of the femur

lineae al·bi·can·tes \-ˌal-bə-'kan-ˌtēz\ *pl* : whitish marks in the skin esp. of the abdomen and breasts that often follow pregnancy

linea semi·lu·nar·is \-ˌse-mi-lü-'nar-əs\ *n, pl* **lineae semi·lu·nar·es** \-'nar-ˌēz\ : a curved line on the ventral abdominal wall parallel to the midline and halfway between it and the side of the body that marks the lateral border of the rectus abdominis muscle — called also *semilunar line*

line of sight *n* : a line from an observer's eye to a distant point

line of vision *n* : a straight line joining the fovea of the eye with the fixation point

linguae — see LONGITUDINALIS LINGUAE

lin·gual \'liŋ-gwəl, -gyə-wəl\ *adj* **1** : of, relating to, or resembling the tongue **2** : lying near or next to the tongue; *esp* : relating to or being the surface of tooth next to the tongue

lingual artery *n* : an artery arising from the external carotid artery between the superior thyroid and facial arteries and supplying the tongue

lingual gland *n* : any of the mucous, serous, or mixed glands that empty their secretions onto the surface of the tongue

lin·gual·ly \'liŋ-gwə-lē\ *adv* : toward the tongue (a tooth displaced ~)

lingual nerve *n* : a branch of the mandibular division of the trigeminal nerve supplying the anterior two thirds of the tongue and responding to stimuli of pressure, touch, and temperature

lingual tonsil *n* : a variable mass or group of small nodules of lymphoid tissue lying at the base of the tongue just anterior to the epiglottis

lin·gu·la \'liŋ-gyə-lə\ *n, pl* **lin·gu·lae** \-ˌlē\ : a tongue-shaped process or part: as **a** : a ridge of bone in the angle between the body and the greater wing of the sphenoid **b** : an elongated prominence of the superior vermis of the cerebellum **c** : a dependent projection of the upper lobe of the left lung — **lin·gu·lar** \-lər\ *adj*

lin·i·ment \'li-nə-mənt\ *n* : a liquid or semifluid preparation that is applied to the skin as an anodyne or a counterirritant — called also *embrocation*

li·ni·tis plas·ti·ca \lə-'nī-təs-'plas-ti-kə\ *n* : carcinoma of the stomach characterized by thickening and diffuse infiltration of the wall rather than localization of the tumor in a discrete lump

link·age \'liŋ-kij\ *n* : the relationship between genes on the same chromosome that causes them to be inherited together — compare MENDEL'S LAW 2

linkage group *n* : a set of linked genes at different loci on the same chromosome

linked \'liŋkt\ *adj* : marked by linkage (~ genes)

Li·nog·na·thus \li-'näg-nə-thəs\ *n* : a genus of sucking lice including parasites of several domestic mammals

lio- — see LEIO-

li·o·thy·ro·nine \ˌlī-ō-'thī-rə-ˌnēn\ *n* : TRIIODOTHYRONINE

lip \'lip\ *n* **1** : either of the two fleshy folds which surround the mouth and organs of speech essential to certain articulations; *also* : the pink or reddish margin of the human lip composed of nonglandular mucous

membrane **2** : an edge of a wound **3** : either of a pair of fleshy folds surrounding an orifice **4** : an anatomical part or structure (as a labium) resembling a lip — **lip·like** \'lip-ˌlīk\ *adj*

lip- *or* **lipo-** *comb form* : fat : fatty tissue : fatty (*lipoid*) (*lipoprotein*)

li·pae·mia *chiefly Brit var of* LIPEMIA

li·pase \'lī-ˌpās, 'li-, -ˌpāz\ *n* : an enzyme that hydrolyzes glycerides

li·pec·to·my \li-'pek-tə-mē, lī-\ *n, pl* **-mies** : the excision of subcutaneous fatty tissue esp. as a cosmetic surgical procedure

li·pe·mia \li-'pē-mē-ə\ *n* : the presence of an excess of fats or lipids in the blood; *specif* : HYPERCHOLESTEROLEMIA — **li·pe·mic** \-mik\ *adj*

lip·id \'li-pəd\ *also* **lip·ide** \-ˌpīd\ *n* : any of various substances that are soluble in nonpolar organic solvents, that with proteins and carbohydrates constitute the principal structural components of living cells, and that include fats, waxes, phospholipids, cerebrosides, and related and derived compounds — **li·pid·ic** \li-'pi-dik\ *adj*

lip·i·do·sis \li-pə-'dō-səs\ *n, pl* **-do·ses** \-ˌsēz\ : a disorder of fat metabolism esp. involving the deposition of fat in an organ (as the liver or spleen) — called also *lipoidosis*; compare LIPODYSTROPHY

li·po·at·ro·phy \li-pō-'a-trə-fē\ *n, pl* **-phies** : an allergic reaction to insulin medication that is manifested as a loss of subcutaneous fat — **li·po·atro·phic** \-(ˌ)ā-'trō-fik\ *adj*

li·po·chon·dro·dys·tro·phy \-ˌkän-drə-'dis-trə-fē\ *n, pl* **-phies** : MUCOPOLYSACCHARIDOSIS; *esp* : HURLER'S SYNDROME

li·po·chrome \'li-pə-ˌkrōm, 'lī-\ *n* : any of the naturally occurring pigments soluble in fats or in solvents for fats; *esp* : CAROTENOID

li·po·dys·tro·phy \ˌli-pō-'dis-trə-fē, ˌlī-\ *n, pl* **-phies** : a disorder of fat metabolism esp. involving loss of fat from or deposition of fat in tissue — compare LIPIDOSIS

li·po·fi·bro·ma \ˌli-pō-fī-'brō-mə, ˌlī-\ *n, pl* **-mas** *also* **-ma·ta** \-mə-tə\ : a lipoma containing fibrous tissue

li·po·fus·cin \ˌli-pə-'fəs-ən, ˌli-, -'fyü-s²n\ *n* : a dark brown lipochrome found esp. in the tissue (as of the heart) of the aged

li·po·fus·cin·o·sis \-ˌfə-sə-'nō-səs, -ˌfyü-\ *n* : any condition characterized by disordered storage of lipofuscins

li·po·gen·e·sis \-'je-nə-səs\ *n, pl* **-e·ses** \-ˌsēz\ **1** : formation of fat in the living body esp. when excessive or abnormal **2** : the formation of fatty acids from acetyl coenzyme A in the living body

li·po·ic acid \li-'pō-ik-, lī-\ *n* : any of several microbial growth factors; *esp* : a crystalline compound $C_8H_{14}O_2S_2$

that is essential for the oxidation of alpha-keto acids (as pyruvic acid) in metabolism

li·poid \\'li-ˌpȯid, 'li-\ *or* **li·poi·dal** \li-'pȯid-ᵊl\ *adj* : resembling fat

²**lipoid** *n* : LIPID

lip·oi·di·ca — see NECROBIOSIS LIPOIDICA, NECROBIOSIS LIPOIDICA DIABETICORUM

li·poid·o·sis \ˌli-ˌpȯi-'dō-səs, ˌlī-\ *n, pl* -o·ses \-ˌsēz\ : LIPIDOSIS

li·pol·y·sis \li-'pä-lə-səs, lī-\ *n, pl* -y·ses \-ˌsēz\ : the hydrolysis of fat — **li·po·lyt·ic** \ˌli-pə-'li-tik, ˌlī-\ *adj*

li·po·ma \li-'pō-mə, lī-\ *n, pl* -mas *or* -ma·ta \-mə-tə\ : a tumor of fatty tissue — **li·po·ma·tous** \-mə-təs\ *adj*

li·po·ma·to·sis \ˌli-ˌpō-mə-'tō-səs, ˌlī-\ *n, pl* -to·ses \-ˌsēz\ : any of several abnormal conditions marked by local or generalized deposits of fat or replacement of other tissue by fat; *specif* : the presence of multiple lipomas

li·po·phil·ic \ˌli-pə-'fi-lik, ˌlī-\ *adj* : having an affinity for lipids (as fats) (a ~ metabolite) — compare HYDROPHILIC — **li·po·phil·ic·i·ty** \-fi-'li-sə-tē\ *n*

li·po·poly·sac·cha·ride \ˌli-pō-ˌpä-li-'sakə-ˌrīd, ˌlī-\ *n* : a large molecule consisting of lipids and sugars joined by chemical bonds

li·po·pro·tein \-'prō-ˌtēn\ *n* : any of a large class of conjugated proteins composed of a complex of protein and lipid and separable on the basis of solubility and mobility properties — see HDL, LDL, VLDL

li·po·sar·co·ma \-sär-'kō-mə\ *n, pl* -mas *or* -ma·ta \-mə-tə\ : a sarcoma arising from immature fat cells of the bone marrow

li·po·some \'li-pə-ˌsōm, 'lī-\ *n* 1 : one of the fatty droplets in the cytoplasm of a cell 2 : a vesicle composed of one or more concentric phospholipid bilayers and used medically esp. to deliver a drug into the body — **li·po·so·mal** \ˌli-pə-'sō-məl, ˌlī-\ *adj*

li·po·suc·tion \-ˌsək-shən\ *n* : surgical removal of local fat deposits (as in the thighs) esp. for cosmetic purposes by applying suction through a small tube inserted into the body

li·po·tro·pin \ˌli-pə-'trō-pən, ˌlī-\ *n* : either of two protein hormones of the anterior part of the pituitary gland that function in the mobilization of fat reserves; *esp* : BETA-LIPOTROPIN

li·pox·y·gen·ase \li-'päk-sə-jə-ˌnās, lī-, -ˌnāz\ *n* : a crystallizable enzyme that catalyzes the oxidation primarily of unsaturated fatty acids or unsaturated fats by oxygen

Lippes loop \'li-pēz-\ *n* : an S-shaped plastic intrauterine device

    Lippes, Jack (*b* 1924), American obstetrician and gynecologist.

Li·quae·min \'li-kwə-ˌmin\ *trademark* — used for a preparation of heparin

liq·ue·fac·tion \ˌli-kwə-'fak-shən\ *n* 1 : the process of making or becoming

liquid 2 : the state of being liquid

¹**liq·uid** \'lik-wəd\ *adj* 1 : flowing freely like water 2 : neither solid nor gaseous : characterized by free movement of the constituent molecules among themselves but without the tendency to separate (~ mercury)

²**liquid** *n* : a liquid substance

liq·uid·am·bar \ˌli-kwə-'dam-bər\ *n* 1 *cap* : a genus of trees of the witch hazel family (Hamamelidaceae) 2 : STORAX 2

liquid chromatography *n* : chromatography in which the mobile phase is a liquid

liquid protein diet *n* : a reducing diet consisting of high-protein liquids

Li·qui·prin \'li-kwə-ˌprin\ *trademark* — used for a preparation of acetaminophen

li·quor \'li-kər\ *n* : a liquid substance (as a medicinal solution) — compare TINCTURE

li·quor am·nii \'lī-ˌkwȯr-'am-nē-ˌī, 'li-\ *n* : AMNIOTIC FLUID

liquor fol·li·cu·li \-'fä-'li-kyə-ˌlī\ *n* : the fluid surrounding the ovum in the ovarian follicle

li·quo·rice *chiefly Brit var of* LICORICE

li·sin·o·pril \lī-'si-nə-ˌpril, li-\ *n* : an antihypertensive drug $C_{21}H_{31}N_3O_5$·$2H_2O$ that is an ACE inhibitor — see PRINIVIL, ZESTRIL

lisp \'lisp\ *vb* 1 : to pronounce the sibilants \s\ and \z\ imperfectly esp. by giving them the sounds \th\ and \th\ 2 : to speak with a lisp — **lisp** *n* — **lisp·er** \'lis-pər\ *n*

liss- *or* **lisso-** *comb form* : smooth ⟨*lis·sencephaly*⟩

lis·sen·ceph·a·ly \ˌli-sen-'se-fə-lē\ *n, pl* -lies : the condition of having a smooth cerebrum without convolutions — **lis·sen·ce·phal·ic** \-sə-'fa-lik\ *adj*

lis·te·ria \li-'stir-ē-ə\ *n* 1 *cap* : a genus of small gram-positive flagellated rod-shaped bacteria (family Corynebacteriaceae) including one (*L. monocytogenes*) that causes infectious mononucleosis 2 : any bacterium of the genus *Listeria* \li-'stir-ē-ə\ *adj* — **lis·te·ri·al** \li-'stir-ē-əl\ *adj* — **lis·te·ric** \-ik\ *adj*

    Lis·ter \'lis-tər\, **Joseph** (1827–1912), British surgeon and medical scientist.

lis·te·ri·o·sis \(ˌ)li-ˌstir-ē-'ō-səs\ *n, pl* -ri·o·ses \-ˌsēz\ : a serious commonly fatal disease of a great variety of mammals and birds and occas. humans caused by a bacterium of the genus *Listeria* (*L. monocytogenes*) and taking the form of a severe encephalitis accompanied by disordered movements usu. ending in paralysis, fever, and monocytosis — see CIRCLING DISEASE

li·ter \'lē-tər\ *n* : a metric unit of capacity equal to the volume of one kilogram of water at 4°C (39°F) and at standard atmospheric pressure of 760 millimeters of mercury

lith- *or* **litho-** *comb form* : calculus ⟨*li-thiasis*⟩ ⟨*lithotripsy*⟩

-lith \lith\ *n comb form* : calculus ⟨uro-*lith*⟩

li·thi·a·sis \li-ˈthī-ə-səs\ *n, pl* **-a·ses** \-ˌsēz\ : the formation of stony concretions in the body (as in the urinary tract or gallbladder) — often used in combination ⟨chole*lithiasis*⟩

lith·i·um \ˈli-thē-əm\ *n* **1** : a soft silver-white element that is the lightest metal known — symbol *Li;* see ELEMENT table **2** : a lithium salt and esp. lithium carbonate used in psychiatric medicine

lithium carbonate *n* : a crystalline salt Li_2CO_3 used in medicine in the treatment of mania and hypomania in manic-depressive psychosis

lith·o·gen·ic \ˌli-thə-ˈje-nik\ *adj* : of, promoting, or undergoing the formation of calculi ⟨a ~ diet⟩ — **lith·o·gen·e·sis** \-ˈje-nə-səs\ *n*

lith·o·la·paxy \li-ˈthä-lə-ˌpak-sē, ˈli-thə-lə-\ *n, pl* **-pax·ies** : LITHOTRIPSY

lith·o·pe·di·on \ˌli-thə-ˈpē-dē-ˌän\ *n* : a fetus calcified in the body of the mother

li·thot·o·my \li-ˈthä-tə-mē\ *n, pl* **-mies** : surgical incision of the urinary bladder for removal of a stone

lith·o·trip·sy \ˈli-thə-ˌtrip-sē\ *n, pl* **-sies** : the breaking (as by shock waves or crushing with a surgical instrument) of a stone in the urinary system into pieces small enough to be voided or washed out — called also *litholapaxy*

lith·o·trip·ter *also* **lith·o·trip·tor** \ˈli-thə-ˌtrip-tər\ *n* : a device for performing lithotripsy; *esp* : a noninvasive device that pulverizes stones by focusing shock waves on a patient immersed in a water bath

lit·mus \ˈlit-məs\ *n* : a coloring matter from lichens that turns red in acid solutions and blue in alkaline solutions and is used as an acid-base indicator

litmus paper *n* : paper colored with litmus and used as an acid-base indicator

li·tre \ˈlē-tər\ *chiefly Brit var of* LITER

lit·ter \ˈli-tər\ *n* **1** : a device (as a stretcher) for carrying a sick or injured person **2** : the offspring at one birth of a multiparous animal

²litter *vb* : to give birth to young

little finger *n* : the fourth and smallest finger of the hand counting the forefinger as the first

Little League elbow *n* : inflammation of the medial epicondyle and adjacent tissues of the elbow esp. in preteen and teenage baseball players who make too strenuous use of the muscles of the forearm — called also *Little Leaguer's elbow*

little toe *n* : the outermost and smallest digit of the foot

live birth \ˈlīv-\ *n* : birth in such a state

that acts of life are manifested after the extrusion of the whole body — compare STILLBIRTH

live–born \ˈlīv-ˈbȯrn\ *adj* : born alive — compare STILLBORN

li·ve·do re·tic·u·lar·is \li-ˈvē-dō-ri-ˌti-kyə-ˈlar-əs\ *n* : a condition of the peripheral blood vessels characterized by reddish blue mottling of the skin esp. of the extremities usu. upon exposure to cold

liv·er \ˈli-vər\ *n* : a large very vascular glandular organ of vertebrates that secretes bile and causes important changes in many of the substances contained in the blood which passes through it (as by converting sugars into glycogen which it stores up until required and by forming urea) and that in humans is the largest gland in the body, weighs from 40 to 60 ounces (1100 to 1700 grams), is a dark red color, and occupies the upper right portion of the abdominal cavity immediately below the diaphragm

liver cell *n* : HEPATOCYTE

liver fluke *n* : any of various trematode worms that invade the mammalian liver; *esp* : one of the genus *Fasciola* (*F. hepatica*) that is a major parasite of the liver, bile ducts, and gallbladder of cattle and sheep, causes fascioliasis in humans, and uses snails of the genus *Lymnaea* as an intermediate host — see CHINESE LIVER FLUKE

liver rot *n* : a disease caused by liver flukes esp. in sheep and cattle and marked by great local damage to the liver — see DISTOMATOSIS; compare BLACK DISEASE

liver spots *n pl* : spots of darker pigmentation (as lentigo senilis or those of chloasma and tinea versicolor) on the skin

lives *pl of* LIFE

liv·id \ˈli-vəd\ *adj* : discolored by bruising : BLACK-AND-BLUE — **li·vid·i·ty** \li-ˈvi-də-tē\ *n*

living will *n* : a document in which the signer requests to be allowed to die rather than be kept alive by artificial means in the event of becoming disabled beyond a reasonable expectation of recovery

LLQ *abbr* left lower quadrant (abdomen)

Loa \ˈlō-ə\ *n* : a genus of African filarial worms (family Dipetalonematidae) that infect the subcutaneous tissues and blood, include the eye worm (*L. loa*) causing Calabar swellings, are transmitted by the bite of flies of the genus *Chrysops*, and are associated with some allergic manifestations (as hives)

load \ˈlōd\ *n* **1** : BURDEN (the worm ~ in rats) **2** : the decrease in capacity for survival of the average individual in a population due to the presence of deleterious genes in the gene pool

load·ing \ˈlō-diŋ\ *n* **1** : administration of

a factor or substance to the body or a bodily system in sufficient quantity to test capacity to deal with it **2** : the relative contribution of each component factor in a psychological test or in an experimental, clinical, or social situation

lo·ai·a·sis \ˌlō-ə-ˈī-ə-səs\ *n, pl* **-a·ses** \-ˌsēz\ : infestation with or disease caused by an eye worm of the genus *Loa* (*L. loa*) that migrates through the subcutaneous tissue and across the cornea of the eye — compare CALABAR SWELLING

loa loa \ˈlō-ə-ˈlō-ə\ *n* : LOAIASIS

lob- *or* **lobi-** *or* **lobo-** *comb form* : lobe ⟨*lobectomy*⟩ ⟨*lobotomy*⟩

lo·bar \ˈlō-bər, -ˌbär\ *adj* : of or relating to a lobe

lobar pneumonia *n* : acute pneumonia involving one or more lobes of the lung characterized by sudden onset, chill, fever, difficulty in breathing, cough, and blood-stained sputum, marked by consolidation, and normally followed by resolution and return to normal of the lung tissue

lobe \ˈlōb\ *n* : a curved or rounded projection or division: as **a** : a more or less rounded projection of a body organ or part (∼ of the ear) **b** : a division of a body organ marked off by a fissure on the surface (as of the brain, lungs, or liver) — **lobed** \ˈlōbd\ *adj*

lo·bec·to·my \lō-ˈbek-tə-mē\ *n, pl* **-mies** : surgical removal of a lobe of an organ (as a lung) or gland (as the thyroid); *specif* : excision of a lobe of the lung — compare LOBOTOMY

lo·be·line \ˈlō-bə-ˌlēn\ *n* : an alkaloid $C_{22}H_{27}NO_2$ that is obtained from an American herb (*Lobelia inflata* of the family Lobeliaceae) and is used esp. in nonprescription drugs as a smoking deterrent

lobi-, lobo- — see LOB-

lo·bot·o·my \lō-ˈbä-tə-mē\ *n, pl* **-mies** : surgical severance of nerve fibers connecting the frontal lobes to the thalamus for the relief of some mental disorders — called also *leukotomy*; compare LOBECTOMY — **lo·bot·o·mize** \-ˌmīz\ *vb*

lobster claw \ˈläb-stər-ˌklȯ\ *n* : an incompletely dominant genetic anomaly marked by variable reduction of the skeleton of the extremities and cleaving of the hands and feet into two segments

lob·u·lar \ˈlä-byə-lər\ *adj* : of, relating to, affecting, or resembling a lobule

lob·u·lat·ed \ˈlä-byə-ˌlā-təd\ *adj* : made up of, provided with, or divided into lobules (a ∼ tumor) — **lob·u·la·tion** \ˌlä-byə-ˈlā-shən\ *n*

lob·ule \ˈlä-ˌbyül\ *n* **1** : a small lobe (the ∼ of the ear) **2** : a subdivision of a lobe; *specif* : one of the small masses of tissue of which various organs (as the liver) are made up

lob·u·lus \ˈlä-byə-ləs\ *n, pl* **lob·u·li** \-ˌlī\ **1** : LOBE **2** : LOBULE

¹lo·cal \ˈlō-kəl\ *adj* : involving or affecting only a restricted part of the organism : TOPICAL — compare SYSTEMIC a — **lo·cal·ly** *adv*

²local *n* : LOCAL ANESTHETIC; *also* : LOCAL ANESTHESIA

local anesthesia *n* : loss of sensation in a limited and usu. superficial area esp. from the effect of a local anesthetic

local anesthetic *n* : an anesthetic for topical and usu. superficial application

lo·cal·ize \ˈlō-kə-ˌlīz\ *vb* **-ized; -iz·ing 1** : to make local; *esp* : to fix in or confine to a definite place or part **2** : to accumulate in or be restricted to a specific or limited area — **lo·cal·iza·tion** \ˌlō-kə-lə-ˈzā-shən\ *n*

lo·chia \ˈlō-kē-ə, ˈlä-\ *n, pl* **lochia** : a discharge from the uterus and vagina following delivery — **lo·chi·al** \-əl\ *adj*

loci *pl of* LOCUS

locked \ˈläkt\ *adj, of the knee joint* : having a restricted mobility and incapable of complete extension

lock-jaw \ˈläk-ˌjȯ\ *n* : an early symptom of tetanus characterized by spasm of the jaw muscles and inability to open the jaws; *also* : TETANUS 1a

lo·co·ism \ˈlō-kō-ˌi-zəm\ *n* **1** : a disease of horses, cattle, and sheep caused by chronic poisoning with locoweeds and characterized by motor and sensory nerve damage resulting in peculiarities of gait, impairment of vision, lassitude or extreme excitement, emaciation, and ultimately paralysis and death if not controlled **2** : any of several intoxications of domestic animals (as selenosis) that are sometimes confused with locoweed poisoning

lo·co·mo·tion \ˌlō-kə-ˈmō-shən\ *n* : an act or the power of moving from place to place : progressive movement (as of an animal body) — **lo·co·mo·tor** \ˌlō-kə-ˈmō-tər\ *adj* — **lo·co·mo·to·ry** \ˌlō-kə-ˈmō-tə-rē\ *adj*

locomotor ataxia *n* : TABES DORSALIS

lo·co·weed \ˈlō-(ˌ)kō-ˌwēd\ *n* : any of several leguminous plants (genera *Astragalus* and *Oxytropis*) of western No. America that cause locoism

loc·u·lus \ˈlä-kyə-ləs\ *n, pl* **-li** \-ˌlī, -ˌlē\ : a small chamber or cavity esp. in a plant or animal body — **loc·u·lat·ed** \ˈlä-kyə-ˌlā-təd\ *adj* — **loc·u·la·tion** \ˌlä-kyə-ˈlā-shən\ *n*

lo·cum te·nens \ˌlō-kəm-ˈtē-ˌnenz, -ˌnänz\ *n, pl* **locum te·nen·tes** \-ti-ˈnen-ˌtēz\ : a medical practitioner who temporarily takes the place of another

lo·cus \ˈlō-kəs\ *n, pl* **lo·ci** \ˈlō-ˌsī, -ˌkī, -ˌkē\ **1** : a place or site of an event, activity, or thing **2** : the position in a chromosome of a particular gene or allele

lo·cus coe·ru·le·us *also* **lo·cus ce·ru·le·us** \ˌlō-kəs-si-ˈrü-lē-əs\ *n, pl* **loci coe·ru·lei** *also* **loci ce·ru·lei** \-ˈlē-ˌī\ : a blue area of the brain stem with many norepinephrine-containing neurons

Loef·fler's syndrome \ˈle-flərz-\ *n* : a mild pneumonitis marked by transitory pulmonary infiltration and eosinophilia and usu. considered to be basically an allergic reaction — called also *Loeffler's pneumonia*

Löf·fler \ˈꟸœ-fler\, **Wilhelm** (*b* 1887), Swiss physician.

log- *or* **logo-** *comb form* : word : thought : speech : discourse ⟨*logorrhea*⟩

log·o·pe·dics \ˌlȯ-gə-ˈpē-diks, ˌlä-\ *n sing or pl* : the scientific study and treatment of speech defects

log·or·rhea \ˌlȯ-gə-ˈrē-ə, ˌlä-\ *n* : pathologically excessive and often incoherent talkativeness or wordiness

log·or·rhoea *chiefly Brit var of* LOGORRHEA

log·o·ther·a·py \ˌlȯ-gə-ˈther-ə-pē, ˌlä-\ *n, pl* **-pies** : a highly directive existential psychotherapy that emphasizes the importance of meaning in the patient's life esp. as gained through spiritual values

-l·o·gy \l-ə-jē\ *n comb form, pl* **-logies** : doctrine : theory : science ⟨physio*logy*⟩

loi·a·sis \ˌlō-ī-ə-səs\ *var of* LOAIASIS

loin \ˈlȯin\ *n* **1** : the part of the body on each side of the spinal column between the hipbone and the false ribs 2 *pl* **a** : the upper and lower abdominal regions and the region about the hips **b** (1) : the pubic region (2) : the generative organs — not usu. used technically in senses 2a, b

loin disease *n* : aphosphorosis of cattle often complicated by botulism

Lo·mo·til \ˈlō-mə-ˌtil, lō-ˈmōt-ᵊl\ *trademark* — used for a preparation of diphenoxylate

lo·mus·tine \lō-ˈməs-ˌtēn\ *n* : an antineoplastic drug $C_9H_{16}ClN_3O_2$ used esp. in the treatment of brain tumors and Hodgkin's disease

lone star tick *n* : a No. American ixodid tick of the genus *Amblyomma* (*A. americanum*) that is a vector of Rocky Mountain spotted fever

long–acting thyroid stimulator *n* : a protein that often occurs in the plasma of patients with Graves' disease and may be an IgG immunoglobulin — abbr. *LATS*

long bone *n* : any of the elongated bones supporting a limb and consisting of an essentially cylindrical shaft that contains marrow and ends in enlarged heads for articulation with other bones

long ciliary nerve *n* : any of two or three nerves that are given off by the nasociliary nerve and are distributed to the iris and cornea — compare SHORT CILIARY NERVE

long head *n* : the longest of the three heads of the triceps muscle that arises from the infraglenoid tubercle of the scapula

longi *pl of* LONGUS

lon·gis·si·mus \län-ˈji-si-məs\ *n, pl* **lon·gis·si·mi** \-ˌmī\ : the intermediate division of the sacrospinalis muscle that consists of the longissimus capitis, longissimus cervicis, and longissimus thoracis: *also* : any of these three muscles

longissimus cap·i·tis \-ˈka-pi-təs\ *n* : a muscle that arises by tendons from the upper thoracic and lower cervical vertebrae, is inserted into the posterior margin of the mastoid process, and extends the head and bends and rotates it to one side — called also *trachelomastoid muscle*

longissimus cer·vi·cis \-ˈsər-vi-səs\ *n* : a muscle medial to the longissimus thoracis that arises by long thin tendons from the transverse processes of the upper four or five thoracic vertebrae, is inserted by similar tendons into the transverse processes of the second to sixth cervical vertebrae, and extends the spinal column and bends it to one side

longissimus dor·si \-ˈdȯr-sī\ *n* : LONGISSIMUS THORACIS

longissimus tho·ra·cis \-ˈthȯr-ə-səs, -thō-ˈrā-səs\ *n* : a muscle that arises as the middle and largest division of the sacrospinalis muscle, that is attached by some of its fibers to the lumbar vertebrae, that is inserted into all the thoracic vertebrae and the lower 9 or 10 ribs and that depresses the ribs and with the longissimus cervicis extends the spinal column and bends it to one side

lon·gi·tu·di·nal \ˌlän-jə-ˈtüd-ᵊn-əl, -ˈtyüd-\ *adj* **1** : of, relating to, or occurring in the lengthwise dimension ⟨a ~ bone fracture⟩ **2** : extending along or relating to the anteroposterior axis of a body or part **3** : involving the repeated observation or examination of a set of subjects over time with respect to one or more study variables — **lon·gi·tu·di·nal·ly** *adv*

longitudinal fissure *n* : the deep groove that divides the cerebrum into right and left hemispheres

lon·gi·tu·di·na·lis linguae \ˌlän-jə-ˌtüd-ə-ˈnā-ləs-, -ˌtyü-\ *n* : either of two bands of muscle comprising the intrinsic musculature of the tongue — called also *longitudinalis*

long–nosed cattle louse *n* : a sucking louse of the genus *Linognathus* (*L. vituli*) that feeds on cattle

long posterior ciliary artery *n* : either of usu. two arteries of which one arises from the ophthalmic artery on each side of the optic nerve, passes forward along the optic nerve, enters the sclera, and at the junction of the ciliary process and the iris divides into upper and lower branches which form a ring of arteries around the iris — compare SHORT POSTERIOR CILIARY ARTERY

long saphenous vein *n* : SAPHENOUS VEIN a

long·sight·ed \'loŋ-'sī-təd\ *adj* : FARSIGHTED — **long·sight·ed·ness** *n*

long–term memory *n* : memory that involves the storage and recall of information over a long period of time (as days, weeks, or years)

lon·gus \'loŋ-gəs\ *n, pl* **lon·gi** \-ˌgī\ : a long structure (as a muscle) in the body — see ABDUCTOR POLLICIS LONGUS, ADDUCTOR LONGUS, EXTENSOR CARPI RADIALIS LONGUS, EXTENSOR DIGITORUM LONGUS, EXTENSOR HALLUCIS LONGUS, EXTENSOR POLLICIS LONGUS, FLEXOR DIGITORUM LONGUS, FLEXOR HALLUCIS LONGUS, FLEXOR POLLICIS LONGUS, PALMARIS LONGUS, PERONEUS LONGUS

longus cap·i·tis \-'ka-pi-təs\ *n* : a muscle of either side of the front and upper portion of the neck that arises from the third to sixth cervical vertebrae, is inserted into the basilar portion of the occipital bone, and bends the neck forward

Lon·i·ten \'lä-ni-tən\ *trademark* — used for a preparation of minoxidil

loop — see LIPPES LOOP

loop of Hen·le \-'hen-lē\ *n* : the U-shaped part of a nephron that lies between and is continuous with the proximal and distal convoluted tubules, that leaves the cortex of the kidney descending into the medullary tissue and then bending back and re-entering the cortex, and that functions in water resorption — called also *Henle's loop*

F. G. J. Henle — see HENLE'S LAYER

loose \'lüs\ *adj* **loos·er; loos·est** 1 a (1) : having worked partly free from attachments ⟨a ~ tooth⟩ (2) : having relative freedom of movement b : produced freely and accompanied by raising of mucus ⟨a ~ cough⟩ 2 : not dense, close, or compact in structure or arrangement ⟨~ connective tissue⟩ 3 : lacking in restraint or power of restraint ⟨~ bowels⟩ 4 : not tightly drawn or stretched — **loosely** *adv* — **loose·ness** *n*

lor·az·e·pam \lȯr-'a-zə-ˌpam\ *n* : an anxiolytic benzodiazepine $C_{15}H_{10}$ $Cl_2N_2O_2$ — see ATIVAN

lor·do·sis \lȯr-'dō-səs\ *n* : exaggerated forward curvature of the lumbar and cervical regions of the spinal column — compare KYPHOSIS, SCOLIOSIS — **lor·dot·ic** \-'dä-tik\ *adj*

lo·tion \'lō-shən\ *n* 1 : a liquid usu. aqueous medicinal preparation containing one or more insoluble substances and applied externally for skin disorders 2 : a liquid cosmetic preparation usu. containing alcohol

and a cleansing, softening, or astringent agent and applied to the skin

Lo·tri·min \'lō-trə-min\ *trademark* — used for a preparation of clotrimazole

Lou Geh·rig's disease \'lü-'ger-igz-\ *n* : AMYOTROPHIC LATERAL SCLEROSIS

Gehrig, Lou (1903–1941), American baseball player.

loupe \'lüp\ *n* : a magnifying lens worn esp. by surgeons performing microsurgery; *also* : two such lenses mounted on a single frame

loup·ing ill \'lau̇-piŋ-, 'lō-\ *n* : a tick-borne disease of sheep and other domestic animals that is caused by a flavivirus and is related to or identical with the Russian spring-summer encephalitis of humans

louse \'lau̇s\ *n, pl* **lice** \'līs\ : any of the small wingless usu. flattened insects that are parasitic on warm-blooded animals and constitute two orders (Anoplura and Mallophaga)

louse–borne typhus *n* : TYPHUS a

lousy \'lau̇-zē\ *adj* **lous·i·er; -est** : infested with lice — **lous·i·ness** \'lau̇-zē-nəs\ *n*

lov·a·stat·in \'lō-və-ˌsta-tən, 'lə-\ *n* : a drug $C_{24}H_{36}O_5$ that decreases the level of cholesterol in the blood stream by inhibiting the liver enzyme that controls cholesterol synthesis and is used in the treatment of hypercholesterolemia

love object *n* : a person on whom affection is centered or on whom one is dependent for affection or needed help

low \'lō\ *adj* : having a relatively less complex organization : not greatly differentiated or developed phylogenetically — usu. used in the comparative degree of less advanced types of plants and animals ⟨the ~*er* vertebrates⟩; compare HIGH 1

low–back \'lō-'bak\ *adj* : of, relating to, suffering, or being pain in the lowest portion of the back ⟨~ pain⟩

low blood pressure *n* : HYPOTENSION 1

low–density lipoprotein *n* : LDL

low·er \'lō-ər\ *n* : the lower member of a pair; *esp* : a lower denture

lower jaw *n* : JAW 1b

lower respiratory *adj* : of, relating to, or affecting the lower respiratory tract ⟨*lower respiratory* infections⟩

lower respiratory tract *n* : the part of the respiratory system including the larynx, trachea, bronchi, and lungs — compare UPPER RESPIRATORY TRACT

lowest splanchnic nerve *n* : SPLANCHNIC NERVE c

low forceps *n* : a procedure for delivery of an infant by the use of forceps when the head is visible at the outlet of the birth canal — called also *outlet forceps;* compare HIGH FORCEPS, MID-FORCEPS

low–grade \'lō-'grād\ *adj* : being near that extreme of a specified range which is lowest, least intense, or least competent ⟨a ~ fever⟩ ⟨a ~ infection⟩ — compare HIGH-GRADE

low–power *adj* : of, relating to, or being a lens that magnifies an image a relatively small number of times and esp. 10 times — compare HIGH-POWER

low–salt diet *n* : LOW-SODIUM DIET

low–sodium diet *n* : a diet restricted to foods naturally low in sodium content and prepared without added salt that is used esp. in the management of certain circulatory or kidney disorders

low vision *n* : impaired vision in which there is a significant reduction in visual function that cannot be corrected by conventional glasses but which may be improved with special aids or devices

Lox·os·ce·les \läk-ˈsä-sə-ˌlēz\ *n* : a genus of spiders (family Loxoscelidae) native to So. America that includes the brown recluse spider (*L. reclusa*)

lox·os·ce·lism \läk-ˈsä-sə-ˌli-zəm\ *n* : a painful condition resulting from the bite of a spider of the genus *Loxosceles* and esp. the brown recluse spider (*L. reclusa*) that is characterized esp. by local necrosis of tissue

loz·enge \ˈläz-ᵊnj\ *n* : a small usu. sweetened solid piece of medicated material that is designed to be held in the mouth for slow dissolution and often contains a demulcent — called also *pastille, troche*

L–PAM \ˈel-ˌpam\ *n* : MELPHALAN

L–phase \ˈel-ˌfāz\ *n* : L-FORM

LPN \ˌel-(ˌ)pē-ˈen\ *n* : LICENSED PRACTICAL NURSE

Lr *symbol* lawrencium

LSD \ˌel-(ˌ)es-ˈdē\ *n* : an organic compound $C_{20}H_{25}N_3O$ that induces psychotic symptoms similar to those of schizophrenia — called also *acid, lysergic acid diethylamide, lysergide*

LSD–25 *n* : LSD

LTH *abbr* luteotropic hormone

Lu *symbol* lutetium

lubb–dupp *also* **lub–dup** *or* **lub–dub** \ˈləb-ˈdəp, -ˈdəb\ *n* : the characteristic sounds of a normal heartbeat as heard in auscultation

lu·can·thone \lü-ˈkan-ˌthōn\ *n* : an antischistosomal drug $C_{20}H_{24}N_2OS$ administered in the form of its hydrochloride — called also *miracil D*

lu·cid \ˈlü-səd\ *adj* : having, showing, or characterized by an ability to think clearly and rationally — **lu·cid·i·ty** \lü-ˈsi-də-tē\ *n*

lucid interval *n* : a temporary period of rationality between periods of insanity or delirium

lucidum — see STRATUM LUCIDUM

Lu·cil·ia \lü-ˈsi-lē-ə\ *n* : a genus of blowflies whose larvae are sometimes the cause of intestinal myiasis and infest open wounds

lüc·ken·schä·del \ˈlük-kən-ˌshäd-ᵊl\ *n* : a

condition characterized by incomplete ossification of the bones of the skull

Lud·wig's angina \ˈlüd-(ˌ)vigz-\ *n* : an acute streptococcal or sometimes staphylococcal infection of the deep tissues of the floor of the mouth and adjoining parts of the neck and lower jaw marked by severe rapid swelling that may close the respiratory passage and accompanied by chills and fever

Ludwig, Wilhelm Friedrich von (1790–1865), German surgeon.

Lu·er syringe \ˈlü-ər-\ *n* : a glass syringe with a glass piston that has the apposing surfaces ground and that is used esp. for hypodermic injection

Luer (*d* 1883), German instrument maker.

lu·es \ˈlü-(ˌ)ēz\ *n, pl* lues : SYPHILIS

lu·et·ic \lü-ˈe-tik\ *adj* : SYPHILITIC

Lu·gol's solution \lü-ˈgölz-\ *n* : any of several deep brown solutions of iodine and potassium iodide in water or alcohol — called also *Lugol's iodine, Lugol's iodine solution*

Lugol, Jean Guillaume Auguste (1786–1851), French physician.

lumb- *or* **lumbo-** *comb form* : lumbar and ⟨*lumbo*sacral⟩

lum·ba·go \ˌləm-ˈbā-(ˌ)gō\ *n* : usu. painful rheumatism involving muscular and fibrous tissue of the lower back region

lum·bar \ˈləm-bər, -ˌbär\ *adj* 1 : of, relating to, or constituting the loins or the vertebrae between the thoracic vertebrae and sacrum 2 : of, relating to, or being the abdominal region lying on either side of the umbilical region and above the corresponding iliac region

lumbar artery *n* : any artery of the usu. four pairs that arise from the back of the aorta opposite the lumbar vertebrae and supply the muscles of the loins, the skin of the sides of the abdomen, and the spinal cord

lumbar nerve *n* : any nerve of the five pairs of spinal nerves of the lumbar region of which one on each side passes out below each lumbar vertebra and the upper four unite by connecting branches into a lumbar plexus

lumbar plexus *n* : a plexus embedded in the psoas major and formed by the anterior or ventral divisions of the four upper lumbar nerves of which the first is usu. supplemented by a communication from the twelfth thoracic nerve

lumbar puncture *n* : puncture of the subarachnoid space in the lumbar region of the spinal cord to withdraw cerebrospinal fluid or inject anesthetic drugs — called also *spinal tap*

lumbar vein *n* : any vein of the four pairs collecting blood from the muscles and integument of the loins, the walls of the abdomen, and adjacent parts and emptying into the dorsal part of the inferior vena cava — see ASCENDING LUMBAR VEIN

lumbar vertebra *n* : any of the five vertebrae situated between the thoracic vertebrae above and the sacrum below

lumbo- — see LUMB-

lum·bo·dor·sal fascia \ˌləm-bō-ˈdȯr-səl-\ *n* : a large fascial band on each side of the back extending from the iliac crest and the sacrum to the ribs and the intermuscular septa of the muscles of the neck

lumborum — see ILIOCOSTALIS LUMBORUM, QUADRATUS LUMBORUM

lum·bo·sa·cral \ˌləm-bō-ˈsa-krəl, -ˈsā-\ *adj* : of, relating to, or being the lumbar and sacral regions or parts

lumbosacral joint *n* : the joint between the fifth lumbar vertebra and the sacrum

lumbosacral plexus *n* : a network of nerves comprising the lumbar plexus and the sacral plexus

lumbosacral trunk *n* : a nerve trunk that is formed by the fifth lumbar nerve and a smaller branch of the fourth lumbar nerve and that connects the lumbar plexus to the sacral plexus

lum·bri·ca·lis \ˌləm-brə-ˈkā-ləs\ *n, pl* **-les** \-ˌlēz\ 1 : any of the four small muscles of the palm of the hand that arise from tendons of the flexor digitorum profundus, are inserted at the base of the digit to which the tendon passes, and flex the proximal phalanx and extend the two distal phalanges of each finger 2 : any of four small muscles of the foot homologous to the lumbricales of the hand that arise from tendons of the flexor digitorum longus and are inserted into the first phalanges of the four small toes of which they flex the proximal phalanges and extend the two distal phalanges — **lum·bri·cal** \ˈləm-bri-kəl\ *adj*

lu·men \ˈlü-mən\ *n, pl* **lu·mi·na** \-mə-nə\ *or* **lumens** 1 : the cavity of a tubular organ (the ~ of a blood vessel) 2 : the bore of a tube (as of a catheter) — **lu·mi·nal** *also* **lu·me·nal** \ˈlü-mən-ᵊl\ *adj*

Lu·mi·nal \ˈlü-mə-ˌnal, -ˌnȯl\ *trademark* — used for a preparation of phenobarbital

lump \ˈləmp\ *n* 1 : a piece or mass of indefinite size and shape 2 : an abnormal swelling

lump·ec·to·my \ˌləm-ˈpek-tə-mē\ *n, pl* **-mies** : excision of a breast tumor with a limited amount of associated tissue — called also *tylectomy*

lumpy jaw \ˈləm-pē\ *also* **lump jaw** *n* : ACTINOMYCOSIS; *esp* : actinomycosis of the head in cattle

lu·na·cy \ˈlü-nə-sē\ *n, pl* **-cies** : any of various forms of insanity

lu·nar caustic \ˈlü-nər-, -ˌnär-\ *n* : silver nitrate esp. when fused and molded into sticks or small cones for use as a caustic

lu·nate bone \ˈlü-ˌnāt-\ *n* : a crescent-shaped bone that is the middle bone in the proximal row of the carpus between the scaphoid bone and the triquetral bone and that has a deep concavity on the distal surface articulating with the capitate — called also *lunate, semilunar bone*

lunate sulcus *n* : a sulcus of the cerebrum on the lateral part of the occipital lobe that marks the front boundary of the visual area

¹**lu·na·tic** \ˈlü-nə-ˌtik\ *adj* : INSANE; *also* : used for the care of insane individuals

²**lunatic** *n* : an insane individual

lung \ˈləŋ\ *n* 1 : one of the usu. two compound saccular organs that constitute the basic respiratory organ of air-breathing vertebrates, that normally occupy the entire lateral parts of the thorax and consist essentially of an inverted tree of intricately branched bronchioles communicating with thin-walled terminal alveoli swathed in a network of delicate capillaries where the actual gaseous exchange of respiration takes place, and that in humans are somewhat flattened with a broad base resting against the diaphragm and have the right lung divided into three lobes and the left into two lobes 2 : a mechanical device for regularly introducing fresh air into and withdrawing stale air from the lungs : RESPIRATOR — see IRON LUNG — **lunged** *adj*

lung·er \ˈləŋ-ər\ *n* : one affected with a chronic disease of the lungs; *esp* : one who is tubercular

lung fluke *n* : a fluke invading the lungs; *esp* : either of two Old World forms of the genus *Paragonimus* (*P. westermanii* and *P. kellicotti*) that produce lesions in humans which are comparable to those of tuberculosis and that are acquired by eating inadequately cooked freshwater crustaceans which act as intermediate hosts

lung·worm \ˈləŋ-ˌwərm\ *n* : any of various nematodes (esp. genera *Dictyocaulus* and *Metastrongylus* of the family Metastrongylidae) that infest the lungs and air passages of mammals

lu·nu·la \ˈlü-nyə-lə\ *n, pl* **-lae** \-ˌlē *also* -ˌlī\ : a crescent-shaped body part: as **a** : the whitish mark at the base of a fingernail — called also *half-moon* **b** : the crescentic unattached border of a semilunar valve

lu·nule \ˈlü-ˌnyül\ *n* : LUNULA

lu·pine *also* **lu·pin** \ˈlü-pən\ *n* : any of a genus (*Lupinus*) of leguminous herbs some of which cause lupinosis

lu·pi·no·sis \ˌlü-pə-ˈnō-səs\ *n, pl* **-no·ses** \-ˌsēz\ : acute liver atrophy of domestic animals (as sheep) due to poisoning by ingestion of various lupines

lu·poid hepatitis \'lü-ˌpȯid-\ *n* : chronic active hepatitis associated with lupus erythematosus

lu·pus \'lü-pəs\ *n* : any of several diseases (as lupus vulgaris or systemic lupus erythematosus) characterized by skin lesions

lupus band test *n* : a test to determine the presence of antibodies and complement deposits at the junction of the dermal and epidermal skin layers of patients with systemic lupus erythematosus

lupus er·y·the·ma·to·sus \-ˌer-ə-ˌthē-mə-'tō-səs\ *n* : a disorder characterized by skin inflammation; *esp* : SYSTEMIC LUPUS ERYTHEMATOSUS

lupus erythematosus cell *n* : LE CELL

lupus ne·phri·tis \-ni-'frī-təs\ *n* : glomerulonephritis associated with systemic lupus erythematosus that is typically characterized by proteinuria and hematuria and that often leads to renal failure

lupus vul·gar·is \-ˌvəl-'gar-əs\ *n* : a tuberculous disease of the skin marked by formation of soft brownish nodules with ulceration and scarring

LUQ *abbr* left upper quadrant (abdomen)

Lur·ide \'lur-ˌīd\ *trademark* — used for a preparation of sodium fluoride

lute- *or* **luteo-** *comb form* : corpus luteum (*lute*al) (*luteo*lysis)

lutea — see MACULA LUTEA

lu·te·al \'lü-tē-əl\ *adj* : of, relating to, characterized by, or involving the corpus luteum (~ activity)

lu·te·cium *var of* LUTETIUM

lu·tein \'lü-tē-ən, 'lü-ˌtēn\ *n* : an orange xanthophyll $C_{40}H_{56}O_2$ occurring in plants usu. with carotenes and chlorophylls and in animal fat, egg yolk, and the corpus luteum

lu·tein·i·za·tion \ˌlü-tē-ə-nə-'zā-shən, ˌlü-ˌtē-\ *n* : the process of forming corpora lutea — **lu·tein·ize** \'lü-tē-ə-ˌnīz, 'lü-ˌtē-ˌnīz\ *vb*

luteinizing hormone *n* : a hormone of the adenohypophysis of the pituitary gland that in the female stimulates the development of the corpora lutea and together with follicle-stimulating hormone the secretion of progesterone and in the male the development of interstitial tissue in the testis and the secretion of testosterone — *abbr. LH*; called also *interstitial-cell stimulating hormone, lutropin*

luteinizing hormone–releasing factor *n* : GONADOTROPIN-RELEASING HORMONE

luteinizing hormone–releasing hormone *n* : GONADOTROPIN-RELEASING HORMONE

lu·te·ol·y·sis \ˌlü-tē-'ä-lə-səs\ *n, pl* **-y·ses** \-ˌsēz\ : regression of the corpus luteum — **lu·teo·lyt·ic** \ˌlü-tē-ə-'li-tik\ *adj*

lu·te·oma \ˌlü-tē-'ō-mə\ *n, pl* **-mas** *or* **-ma·ta** \-mə-tə\ : an ovarian tumor de-

rived from a corpus luteum — **lu·te·o·ma·tous** \-mə-təs\ *adj*

lu·teo·tro·pic \ˌlü-tē-ə-'trō-pik, -'trä-\ *or* **lu·teo·tro·phic** \-'trō-fik, -'trä-\ *adj* : acting on the corpora lutea

luteotropic hormone *n* : PROLACTIN

lu·teo·tro·pin \ˌlü-tē-ə-'trō-pən\ *or* **lu·teo·tro·phin** \-fən\ *n* : PROLACTIN

lu·te·tium \lü-'tē-shē-əm, -shəm\ *n* : a metallic element — symbol *Lu*; see ELEMENT table

luteum — see CORPUS LUTEUM

lu·tro·pin \lü-'trō-pən\ *n* : LUTEINIZING HORMONE

lux·a·tion \ˌlək-'sā-shən\ *n* : dislocation of an anatomical part — **lux·ate** \'lək-ˌsāt\ *vb*

LVN \ˌel-(ˌ)vē-'en\ *n* : LICENSED VOCATIONAL NURSE

ly·can·thro·py \lī-'kan-thrə-pē\ *n, pl* **-pies** : a delusion that one has become or has assumed the characteristics of a wolf

Ly·ell's syndrome \'lī-əlz-\ *n* : TOXIC EPIDERMAL NECROLYSIS

Lyell, Alan (*fl* 1950–1972), British dermatologist.

ly·ing-in \ˌlī-iŋ-'in\ *n, pl* **lyings-in** *or* **lying-ins** : the state attending and consequent to childbirth : CONFINEMENT

Lyme disease \'līm-\ *n* : an acute inflammatory disease that is usu. characterized initially by the skin lesion erythema chronicum migrans and by fatigue, fever, and chills and if left untreated may later manifest itself in cardiac and neurological disorders, joint pain, and arthritis and that is caused by a spirochete of the genus *Borrelia* (*B. burgdorferi*) transmitted by the bite of a tick esp. of the genus *Ixodes* (*I. scapularis* in the eastern and midwestern U.S., *I. pacificus* in the Pacific northwestern U.S., and *I. ricinus* in Europe) — called also *Lyme arthritis*

Lym·naea \lim-'nē-ə, 'lim-nē-ə\ *n* : a genus of snails (family Lymnaeidae) including some medically important intermediate hosts of flukes — compare FOSSARIA, GALBA

lymph \'limf\ *n* : a pale coagulable fluid that bathes the tissues, passes into lymphatic channels and ducts, is discharged into the blood by way of the thoracic duct, and consists of a liquid portion resembling blood plasma and containing white blood cells but normally no red blood cells — see CHYLE

lymph- *or* **lympho-** *comb form* : lymph : lymphatic tissue (*lymph*edema) (*lympho*granuloma)

lymph·ad·e·nec·to·my \ˌlim-ˌfad-ᵊn-'ek-tə-mē\ *n, pl* **-mies** : surgical removal of a lymph node

lymph·ad·e·ni·tis \ˌlim-ˌfad-ᵊn-'ī-təs\ *n* : inflammation of lymph nodes — **lymph·ad·e·nit·ic** \-'i-tik\ *adj*

lymph·ad·e·nop·a·thy \ˌlim-ˌfad-ᵊn-'ä-pə-thē\ *n, pl* **-thies** : abnormal enlargement of the lymph nodes — **lymph-ad-e-no-path-ic** \lim-ıfad-ᵊn-ō-'pa-thik\ *adj*

lymphadenopathy—associated virus *n* : HIV-I

lymph-ad-e-no-sis \lim-ıfad-ᵊn-'ō-səs\ *n, pl* **-no-ses** \-ısēz\ : any of certain abnormalities or diseases affecting the lymphatic system: as **a** : leukosis involving lymphatic tissues **b** : LYMPHOCYTIC LEUKEMIA

lymphangi- *or* **lymphangio-** *comb form* : lymphatic vessels (*lymphangiography*)

lymph-an-gi-ec-ta-sia \lim-ıfan-jē-ek-'tā-zhə, -zhē-ə\ *or* **lymph-an-gi-ec-ta-sis** \-'ek-tə-səs\ *n, pl* **-ta-sias** *or* **-ta-ses** \-ısēz\ : dilatation of the lymphatic vessels

lymph-an-gio-gram \(ı)lim-'fan-jē-ə-ıgram\ *n* : an X-ray picture made by lymphangiography

lymph-an-gi-og-ra-phy \ılim-ıfan-jē-'ä-grə-fē\ *n, pl* **-phies** : X-ray depiction of lymphatic vessels and lymph nodes after use of a radiopaque material — called also *lymphography* — **lymph-an-gio-graph-ic** \ılim-ıfan-jē-ə-'gra-fik\ *adj*

lymph-an-gi-o-ma \ılim-ıfan-jē-'ō-mə\ *n, pl* **-mas** *or* **-ma-ta** \-mə-tə\ : a tumor formed of dilated lymphatic vessels

lymph-an-gio-sar-co-ma \ılim-ıfan-jē-ō-(ı)sär-'kō-mə\ *n, pl* **-mas** *or* **-ma-ta** \-mə-tə\ : a sarcoma arising from the endothelial cells of lymphatic vessels

lymph-an-gi-ot-o-my \ılim-ıfan-jē-'ä-tə-mē\ *n, pl* **-mies** : incision of a lymphatic vessel

lym-phan-gi-tis \ılim-ıfan-'jī-təs\ *n, pl* **-git-i-des** \-'ji-tə-ıdēz\ : inflammation of the lymphatic vessels

¹**lym-phat-ic** \lim-'fa-tik\ *adj* **1** : of, relating to, or produced by lymph, lymphoid tissue, or lymphocytes **2** : conveying lymph — **lym-phat-i-cal-ly** *adv*

²**lymphatic** *n* : a vessel that contains or conveys lymph, that originates as an interfibrillar or intercellular cleft or space in a tissue or organ, and that if small has no distinct walls or walls composed only of endothelial cells and if large resembles a vein in structure — called also *lymphatic vessel, lymph vessel*; see THORACIC DUCT

lymphatic capillary *n* : any of the smallest lymphatic vessels that are blind at one end and collect lymph in organs and tissues — called also *lymph capillary*

lymphatic duct *n* : any of the lymphatic vessels that are part of the system collecting lymph from the lymphatic capillaries and pouring it into the subclavian veins by way of the right lymphatic duct and the thoracic duct — called also *lymph duct*

lymphatic leukemia *n* : LYMPHOCYTIC LEUKEMIA

lym-phat-i-co-ve-nous \lim-ıfa-ti-kō-'vē-nəs\ *adj* : of, relating to, or connecting the veins and lymphatic vessels

lymphatic vessel *n* : LYMPHATIC

lymph capillary *n* : LYMPHATIC CAPILLARY

lymph duct *n* : LYMPHATIC DUCT

lymph-ede-ma \lim-fi-'dē-mə\ *n* : edema due to faulty lymphatic drainage — **lymph-edem-a-tous** \lim-fi-'de-mə-təs\ *adj*

lymph follicle *n* : LYMPH NODE; *esp* : LYMPH NODULE

lymph gland *n* : LYMPH NODE

lymph node *n* : any of the rounded masses of lymphoid tissue that are surrounded by a capsule of connective tissue, are distributed along the lymphatic vessels, and contain numerous lymphocytes which filter the flow of lymph passing through the node — called also *lymph gland*

lymph nodule *n* : a small simple lymph node

lympho- — see LYMPH-

lym-pho-blast \'lim-fə-ıblast\ *n* : a lymphocyte that has enlarged following stimulation by an antigen, has the capacity to recognize the stimulating antigen, and is undergoing proliferation and differentiation either to an effector state in which it functions to eliminate the antigen or to a memory state in which it functions to recognize the future reappearance of the antigen — **lym-pho-blas-tic** \ılim-fə-'blas-tik\ *adj*

lymphoblastic leukemia *n* : lymphocytic leukemia characterized by an abnormal increase in the number of lymphoblasts

lym-pho-blas-toid \ılim-fə-'blas-ıtöid\ *adj* : resembling a lymphoblast

lym-pho-blas-to-ma \ılim-fə-ıblas-'tō-mə\ *n, pl* **-mas** *or* **-ma-ta** \-mə-tə\ : any of several diseases of lymph nodes marked by the formation of tumorous masses composed of mature or immature lymphocytes

lym-pho-blas-to-sis \-ıblas-'tō-səs\ *n, pl* **-to-ses** \-ısēz\ : the presence of lymphoblasts in the peripheral blood

lym-pho-cele \'lim-fə-ısēl\ *n* : a cyst containing lymph

lym-pho-cyte \'lim-fə-ısīt\ *n* : any of the colorless weakly motile cells originating from stem cells and differentiating in lymphoid tissue (as of the thymus or bone marrow) that are the typical cellular elements of lymph, include the cellular mediators of immunity, and constitute 20 to 30 percent of the leukocytes of normal human blood — see B CELL, T CELL — **lym-pho-cyt-ic** \ılim-fə-'si-tik\ *adj*

lymphocyte transformation *n* : a transformation caused in lymphocytes by a mitosis-inducing agent (as phytohemagglutinin) or by a second exposure to an antigen and characterized by an increase in size and in the amount of cytoplasm, by visibility of nucleoli in the nucleus, and after about 72 hours by a marked resemblance to blast cells

lym·pho·cyt·ic cho·rio·men·in·gi·tis \-ˌkȯr-ē-ō-ˌme-nən-ˈjī-təs\ *n* : an acute disease caused by an arenavirus, characterized by fever, nausea and vomiting, headache, stiff neck, and slow pulse, and transmitted esp. by rodents

lymphocytic leukemia *n* : leukemia marked by proliferation of lymphoid tissue, abnormal increase of leukocytes in the circulating blood, and enlarged lymph nodes — called also *lymphatic leukemia, lymphoid leukemia*; see LYMPHOBLASTIC LEUKEMIA

lym·pho·cy·to·pe·nia \ˌlim-fō-ˌsī-tə-ˈpē-nē-ə\ *n* : a decrease in the normal number of lymphocytes in the circulating blood

lym·pho·cy·to·poi·e·sis \-ˌpȯi-ˈē-səs\ *n, pl* **-e·ses** \-ˌsēz\ : formation of lymphocytes usu. in the lymph nodes

lym·pho·cy·to·sis \ˌlim-fə-ˌsī-ˈtō-səs, -fə-sə-\ *n, pl* **-to·ses** \-ˌsēz\ : an increase in the number of lymphocytes in the blood usu. associated with chronic infections or inflammations — compare GRANULOCYTOSIS, MONOCYTOSIS

lym·pho·cy·to·tox·ic \ˌlim-fə-ˌsī-tə-ˈtäk-sik\ *adj* 1 : being or relating to toxic effects on lymphocytes 2 : being toxic to lymphocytes — **lym·pho·cy·to·tox·ic·i·ty** \-ˌtäk-ˈsi-sə-tē\ *n*

lym·pho·ge·nous \lim-ˈfä-jə-nəs\ *also* **lym·pho·gen·ic** \ˌlim-fə-ˈje-nik\ *adj* 1 : producing lymph or lymphocytes 2 : arising, resulting from, or spread by way of lymphocytes or lymphatic vessels

lym·pho·gran·u·lo·ma \ˌlim-fō-ˌgran-yə-ˈlō-mə\ *n, pl* **-mas** *or* **-ma·ta** \-mə-tə\ 1 : a nodular swelling of a lymph node 2 : LYMPHOGRANULOMA VENEREUM — **lym·pho·gran·u·lo·ma·tous** \-ˈlō-mə-təs\ *adj*

lymphogranuloma in·gui·na·le \-ˌiŋ-gwə-ˈnä-lē, -ˈna-, -ˈnä-\ *n* : LYMPHOGRANULOMA VENEREUM

lym·pho·gran·u·lo·ma·to·sis \-ˌlō-mə-ˈtō-səs\ *n, pl* **-to·ses** \-ˌsēz\ : the development of benign or malignant lymphogranulomas in various parts of the body; *also* : a condition characterized by lymphogranulomas

lymphogranuloma ve·ne·re·um \-və-ˈnir-ē-əm\ *n* : a contagious venereal disease that is caused by various strains of a bacterium of the genus *Chlamydia* (*C. trachomatis*) and is marked by swelling and ulceration of lymphatic tissue in the iliac and inguinal regions — called also *lymphogranuloma inguinale, lymphopathia venereum*

lym·phog·ra·phy \lim-ˈfä-grə-fē\ *n, pl*

-phies : LYMPHANGIOGRAPHY — **lym·pho·graph·ic** \ˌlim-fə-ˈgra-fik\ *adj*

lym·phoid \ˈlim-ˌfȯid\ *adj* 1 : of, relating to, or being tissue (as the lymph nodes or thymus) containing lymphocytes 2 : of, relating to, or resembling lymph

lymphoid cell *n* : any of the cells responsible for the production of immunity mediated by cells or antibodies and including lymphocytes, lymphoblasts, and plasma cells

lymphoid leukemia *n* : LYMPHOCYTIC LEUKEMIA

lym·pho·kine \ˈlim-fə-ˌkīn\ *n* : any of various substances (as interleukin-2) of low molecular weight that are not antibodies, are secreted by T cells in response to stimulation by antigens, and have a role (as the activation of macrophages or the enhancement or inhibition of antibody production) in cell-mediated immunity

lym·pho·kine–activated killer cell *n* : a lymphocyte that has been turned into a cancer-killing cell by being cultured with interleukin-2 — called also *LAK*

lym·pho·ma \lim-ˈfō-mə\ *n, pl* **-mas** *or* **-ma·ta** \-mə-tə\ : a usu. malignant tumor of lymphoid tissue — **lym·pho·ma·tous** \-mə-təs\ *adj*

lym·pho·ma·toid \lim-ˈfō-mə-ˌtȯid\ *adj* : characterized by or resembling lymphomas (a ~ tumor)

lymphomatosa — see STRUMA LYMPHOMATOSA

lym·pho·ma·to·sis \ˌlim-ˌfō-mə-ˈtō-səs\ *n, pl* **-to·ses** \-ˌsēz\ : the presence of multiple lymphomas in the body

lym·pho·path·ia ve·ne·re·um \ˌlim-fə-ˌpa-thē-ə-və-ˈnir-ē-əm\ *n* : LYMPHOGRANULOMA VENEREUM

lym·pho·pe·nia \ˌlim-fə-ˈpē-nē-ə\ *n* : reduction in the number of lymphocytes circulating in the blood — **lym·pho·pe·nic** \-ˈpē-nik\ *adj*

lym·pho·poi·e·sis \ˌlim-fə-pȯi-ˈē-səs\ *n, pl* **-e·ses** \-ˌsēz\ : the formation of lymphocytes or lymphatic tissue — **lym·pho·poi·et·ic** \-pȯi-ˈe-tik\ *adj*

lym·pho·pro·lif·er·a·tive \ˌlim-fō-prə-ˈli-fə-ˌrā-tiv, -rə-tiv\ *adj* : of or relating to the proliferation of lymphoid tissue (~ syndrome)

lym·pho·re·tic·u·lar \ˌlim-fō-ri-ˈti-kyə-lər\ *adj* : RETICULOENDOTHELIAL

lymphoreticular system *n* : RETICULOENDOTHELIAL SYSTEM

lym·pho·sar·co·ma \ˌlim-fō-sär-ˈkō-mə\ *n, pl* **-mas** *or* **-ma·ta** \-mə-tə\ : a malignant lymphoma that tends to metastasize freely

lym·pho·tox·in \ˌlim-fō-ˈtäk-sən\ *n* : a lymphokine that lyses various cells and esp. tumor cells — **lym·pho·tox·ic** \-ˈtäk-sik\ *adj*

lymph vessel *n* : LYMPHATIC

Ly·on hypothesis \ˈlī-ən-\ *n* : a hypothesis explaining why the phenotypic effect of the X chromosome is the same in the mammalian female which has two X chromosomes as it is in the male which has only one X chromosome: one of each two somatic X chromosomes in mammalian females is selected at random and inactivated early in embryonic development

Lyon, Mary Frances (*b* 1925), British geneticist.

ly·oph·i·lize \lī-'ä-fə-₁līz\ *vb* -lized; -liz·ing : FREEZE–DRY — **ly·oph·i·li·za·tion** *n*

ly·pres·sin \lī-'pres-ʰn\ *n* : a lysine-containing vasopressin $C_{46}H_{65}N_{13}O_{12}S_2$ used esp. as a nasal spray in the control of diabetes insipidus

lys- *or* **lysi-** *or* **lyso-** *comb form* : lysis ⟨*lysin*⟩ ⟨*lysolecithin*⟩

lyse \'līs, 'līz\ *vb* **lysed; lys·ing** : to cause to undergo lysis : produce lysis in

ly·ser·gic acid \lə-'sər-jik-, ₁lī-\ *n* : a crystalline acid $C_{16}H_{16}N_2O_2$ from ergot alkaloids; *also* : LSD

lysergic acid di·eth·yl·am·ide \-₁dī-e-thə-'la-₁mid\ *n* : LSD

ly·ser·gide \lə-'sər-₁jid, li-\ *n* : LSD

lysi- — see LYS-

ly·sin \'līs-ʰn\ *n* : a substance (as an antibody) capable of causing lysis

ly·sine \'lī-₁sēn\ *n* : a crystalline essential amino acid $C_6H_{14}N_2O_2$ obtained from the hydrolysis of various proteins

ly·sis \'lī-səs\ *n, pl* **ly·ses** \-₁sēz\ **1** : the gradual decline of a disease process (as fever) — compare CRISIS 1 **2** : a process of disintegration or dissolution (as of cells)

-ly·sis \l-ə-səs, 'lī-səs\ *n comb form, pl* **-ly·ses** \l-ə-₁sēz\ **1** : decomposition ⟨hydro*lysis*⟩ **2** : disintegration : breaking down ⟨auto*lysis*⟩ **3 a** : relief or reduction ⟨neuro*lysis*⟩ **b** : detachment ⟨epidermo*lysis*⟩

lyso- — see LYS-

ly·so·gen \'lī-sə-jən\ *n* : a lysogenic bacterium or bacterial strain

ly·so·gen·ic \₁lī-sə-'je-nik\ *adj* **1** : harboring a prophage as hereditary material ⟨∼ bacteria⟩ **2** : TEMPERATE — **ly·sog·e·ny** \lī-'sä-jə-nē\ *n*

Ly·sol \'lī-₁sȯl, -₁sōl\ *trademark* — used for a disinfectant consisting of a brown emulsified solution containing cresols

ly·so·lec·i·thin \₁lī-sə-'le-sə-thən\ *n* : LYSOPHOSPHATIDYLCHOLINE

ly·so·phos·pha·ti·dyl·cho·line \₁lī-sō-₁fäs-fə-₁tīd-ʰl-'kō-₁lēn, -(₁)fäs-₁fa-təd-ʰl-\ *n* : a hemolytic substance produced by the removal of a fatty acid group (as by the action of cobra venom) from a lecithin

ly·so·some \'lī-sə-₁sōm\ *n* : a saclike cellular organelle that contains various hydrolytic enzymes — **ly·so·som·al** \₁lī-sə-'sō-məl\ *adj* — **ly·so·so·mal·ly** *adv*

ly·so·zyme \'lī-sə-₁zīm\ *n* : a basic bacteriolytic protein that hydrolyzes peptidoglycon and is present in egg white and in saliva and tears — called also *muramidase*

-lyte \₁līt\ *n comb form* : substance capable of undergoing (such) decomposition ⟨electro*lyte*⟩

lyt·ic \'li-tik\ *adj* : of or relating to lysis or a lysin; *also* : productive of or effecting lysis (as of cells) ⟨∼ viruses⟩ — **lyt·i·cal·ly** *adv*

-lyt·ic \'li-tik\ *adj suffix* : of, relating to, or effecting (such) decomposition ⟨hydro*lytic*⟩

M

m *abbr* **1** meter **2** molar **3** molarity **4** mole **5** muscle

M *abbr* [Latin *misce*] mix — used in writing prescriptions

MA *abbr* mental age

McArdle's disease, McBurney's point — see entries alphabetized as MC-

Mace \'mās\ *trademark* — used for a temporarily disabling liquid that when sprayed in the face of a person causes tears, dizziness, immobilization, and sometimes nausea

¹mac·er·ate \'ma-sə-₁rāt\ *vb* -at·ed; -at·ing : to soften (as tissue) by steeping or soaking so as to separate into constituent elements — **mac·er·at·ed** \-₁rā-təd\ *adj* — **mac·er·a·tion** \₁ma-sə-'rā-shən\ *n*

²mac·er·ate \-rət\ *n* : a product of macerating : something prepared by maceration — compare HOMOGENATE

Ma·chu·po virus \mä-'chü-pō-\ *n* : an arenavirus associated with hemorrhagic fever in Bolivia

mackerel shark *n* : any of a family (Lamnidae) of large aggressive sharks that include the great white shark

Mac·leod's syndrome \mə-'klaủdz-\ *n* : abnormally increased translucence of one lung usu. accompanied by reduction in ventilation and in perfusion with blood

Macleod, William Mathieson (1911–1977), British physician.

macr- *or* **macro-** *comb form* : large ⟨*macro*molecule⟩ ⟨*macro*cyte⟩

Mac·ra·can·tho·rhyn·chus \₁ma-krə-₁kan-thə-'riŋ-kəs\ *n* : a genus of intestinal worms (phylum Acanthocephala) that include the common acanthocephalan (*M. hirudinaceus*) of swine

Mac·rob·del·la \₁ma-₁kräb-'de-lə\ *n* : a genus of large blood-sucking leeches including one (*M. decora*) that has been used medicinally

mac·ro·bi·ot·ic \₁ma-krō-bī-'ä-tik, -bē-\

adj : of, relating to, or being an extremely restricted diet (as one containing chiefly whole grains)

mac·ro·bi·ot·ics \-tiks\ *n* : a macrobiotic dietary system

mac·ro·ceph·a·lous \ma-krō-ˈse-fə-ləs\ *or* **mac·ro·ce·phal·ic** \-sə-ˈfa-lik\ *adj* : having or being an exceptionally large head or cranium — **mac·ro·ceph·a·ly** \-ˈse-fə-lē\ *n*

mac·ro·cy·clic \ma-krō-ˈsi-klik, -ˈsī-\ *adj* : containing or being a chemical ring that consists usu. of 15 or more atoms (a ~ antibiotic) — **macrocyclic** *n*

mac·ro·cyte \ˈma-krə-ˌsīt\ *n* : an exceptionally large red blood cell occurring chiefly in anemias (as pernicious anemia) — called also **megalocyte**

mac·ro·cyt·ic \ma-krə-ˈsi-tik\ *adj* : of or relating to macrocytes; *specif* : of an anemia : characterized by macrocytes in the blood

mac·ro·cy·to·sis \ma-krə-sī-ˈtō-səs\ *n, pl* **-to·ses** \-ˌsēz\ : the occurrence of macrocytes in the blood

mac·ro·ga·mete \ma-krō-gə-ˈmēt, -ˈga-ˌmēt\ *n* : the larger and usu. female gamete of a heterogamous organism — compare MICROGAMETE

mac·ro·ga·me·to·cyte \-gə-ˈmē-tə-ˌsīt\ *n* : a gametocyte producing macrogametes

mac·ro·gen·i·to·so·mia \ma-krō-ˌje-ni-tə-ˈsō-mē-ə\ *n* : premature excessive development of the external genitalia

mac·ro·glia \ma-ˈkrä-glē-ə, ˌma-krō-ˈglī-ə\ *n* : neuroglia made up of astrocytes — **mac·ro·gli·al** \-əl\ *adj*

mac·ro·glob·u·lin \ˌma-krō-ˈglä-byə-lən\ *n* : a highly polymerized globulin (as IgM) of high molecular weight

mac·ro·glob·u·lin·ae·mia *chiefly Brit var of* MACROGLOBULINEMIA

mac·ro·glob·u·lin·emia \-ˌglä-byə-lə-ˈnē-mē-ə\ *n* : a disorder characterized by increased blood serum viscosity and the presence of macroglobulins in the serum — **mac·ro·glob·u·lin·emic** \-mik\ *adj*

mac·ro·glos·sia \ˌma-krō-ˈglä-sē-ə, -ˈglo-\ *n* : pathological and commonly congenital enlargement of the tongue

mac·ro·lide \ˈma-krə-ˌlīd\ *n* : any of several antibiotics that are produced by actinomycetes of the genus *Streptomyces*

mac·ro·mol·e·cule \ˌma-krō-ˈmä-li-ˌkyül\ *n* : a large molecule (as of a protein) built up from smaller chemical structures — compare MICROMOLECULE — **mac·ro·mo·lec·u·lar** \-mə-ˈle-kyə-lər\ *adj*

mac·ro·nu·tri·ent \-ˈnü-trē-ənt, ˈnyü-\ *n* : a chemical element or substance (as protein, carbohydrate, or fat) required in relatively large quantities in nutrition

mac·ro·phage \ˈma-krə-ˌfāj, -ˌfäzh\ *n* : a phagocytic tissue cell of the reticuloendothelial system that may be fixed or freely motile, is derived from a monocyte, and functions in the protection of the body against infection and noxious substances — called also **histiocyte** — **mac·ro·phag·ic** \ˌma-krə-ˈfa-jik\ *adj*

mac·ro·scop·ic \ˌma-krə-ˈskä-pik\ *adj* : large enough to be observed by the naked eye — compare MICROSCOPIC 2, SUBMICROSCOPIC, ULTRAMICROSCOPIC 1 — **mac·ro·scop·i·cal·ly** *adv*

mac·ro·so·mia \ˌma-krə-ˈsō-mē-ə\ *n* : GIGANTISM — **mac·ro·so·mic** \-ˈsō-mik\ *adj*

mac·ro·struc·ture \ˈma-krō-ˌstrək-chər\ *n* : the structure (as of a body part) revealed by visual examination with little or no magnification — **mac·ro·struc·tur·al** \ˌma-krō-ˈstrək-chə-rəl, -shə-rəl\ *adj*

macul- *or* **maculo-** *comb form* : macule : macular and (*maculo*papular)

mac·u·la \ˈma-kyə-lə\ *n, pl* **-lae** \-ˌlē, -ˌlī\ *also* **-las 1** : any spot or blotch; *esp* : MACULE 2 **2** : an anatomical structure having the form of a spot differentiated from surrounding tissues: as **a** : MACULA ACUSTICA **b** : MACULA LUTEA

macula acus·ti·ca \-ə-ˈküs-ti-kə\ *n, pl* **maculae acus·ti·cae** \-ti-ˌsē\ : either of two small areas of sensory hair cells in the ear that are covered with gelatinous material on which are located crystals or concretions of calcium carbonate and that are associated with the perception of equilibrium: **a** : one located in the saccule **b** : one located in the utricle

macula den·sa \-ˈden-sə\ *n* : a group of modified epithelial cells in the distal convoluted tubule of the kidney that control renin release by relaying information about the sodium concentration in the fluid passing through the convoluted tubule to the renin-producing juxtaglomerular cells of the afferent arteriole

macula lu·tea \-ˈlü-tē-ə\ *n, pl* **maculae lu·te·ae** \-tē-ˌē, -tē-ˌī\ : a small yellowish area lying slightly lateral to the center of the retina that constitutes the region of maximum visual acuity and is made up almost wholly of retinal cones

mac·u·lar \ˈma-kyə-lər\ *adj* **1** : of, relating to, or characterized by a spot or spots (a ~ skin rash) **2** : of, relating to, affecting, or mediated by the macula lutea (~ vision)

macular degeneration *n* : a loss of central vision in both eyes produced by pathological changes in the macula lutea and characterized by spots of pigmentation or other abnormalities

mac·ule \ˈma-(ˌ)kyül\ *n* **1** : MACULA 2 **2** : a patch of skin that is altered in color or hue usu. not elevated and that is a characteristic feature of various diseases (as smallpox)

maculo- — see MACUL-

mac·u·lo·pap·u·lar \ma-kyə-(ˌ)lō-ˈpa-pyə-lər\ *adj* : combining the characteristics of macules and papules ⟨a ∼ rash⟩ ⟨a ∼ lesion⟩

mac·u·lo·pap·ule \-ˈpa-(ˌ)pyül\ *n* : a maculopapular elevation of the skin

mad \ˈmad\ *adj* **mad·der; mad·dest** 1 : arising from, indicative of, or marked by mental disorder 2 : affected with rabies : RABID

mad itch *n* : PSEUDORABIES

mad·ness \ˈmad-nəs\ *n* 1 : INSANITY 2 : any of several ailments of animals marked by frenzied behavior: *specif* : RABIES

Ma·du·ra foot \ˈma-dyu̇r-ə-, -du̇r-; mə-ˈ\ *n* : maduromycosis of the foot

mad·u·ro·my·co·sis \ˌma-dyu̇-rō-mī-ˈkō-səs, -du̇-\ *n, pl* **-co·ses** \-ˌsēz\ : a destructive chronic disease usu. restricted to the feet, marked by swelling and deformity resulting from the formation of granulomatous nodules and caused esp. by an aerobic form of actinomycetes and sometimes by fungi — compare NOCARDIOSIS — **mad·u·ro·my·cot·ic** \-ˈkä-tik\ *adj*

maf·e·nide \ˈma-fə-ˌnid\ *n* : a sulfonamide C₇H₁₀N₂O₂S applied topically as an antibacterial ointment esp. in the treatment of burns — see SULFA-MYLON

mag·got \ˈma-gət\ *n* : a soft-bodied legless grub that is the larva of a dipteran fly (as the housefly) and develops usu. in decaying organic matter or as a parasite in plants or animals

magic bullet *n* : a substance or therapy capable of destroying pathogenic agents (as bacteria or cancer cells) without deleterious side effects

magic mushroom *n* : any fungus containing hallucinogenic alkaloids (as psilocybin)

mag·ma \ˈmag-mə\ *n* : a suspension of a large amount of precipitated material (as in milk of magnesia or milk of bismuth) in a small volume of a watery vehicle

magma — see CISTERNA MAGNA

Mag·na·my·cin \ˌmag-nə-ˈmīs-ᵊn\ *trademark* — used for a preparation of carbomycin

mag·ne·sia \mag-ˈnē-shə, -ˈnē-zhə\ *n* : MAGNESIUM OXIDE

magnesia magma *n* : MILK OF MAGNESIA

mag·ne·sium \mag-ˈnē-zē-əm, -zhəm\ *n* : a silver-white light malleable ductile metallic element that occurs abundantly in nature (as in bones) — symbol *Mg*; see ELEMENT table

magnesium carbonate *n* : a carbonate of magnesium; *esp* : the very white crystalline salt MgCO₃ used as an antacid and laxative

magnesium chloride *n* : a bitter crystalline salt MgCl₂ used esp. to replenish body electrolytes

magnesium citrate *n* : a crystalline salt used in the form of a lemony acidulous effervescent solution as a saline laxative

magnesium hydroxide *n* : a slightly alkaline crystalline compound Mg(OH)₂ used as an antacid and laxative — see MILK OF MAGNESIA

magnesium oxide *n* : a white compound MgO used as an antacid and mild laxative

magnesium si·li·cate \-ˈsi-lə-ˌkāt, -kət\ *n* : a silicate that is approximately Mg₂Si₃O₈·nH₂O used chiefly in medicine as a gastric antacid adsorbent and coating (as in the treatment of ulcers)

magnesium sulfate *n* : a sulfate of magnesium MgSO₄ that occurs in nature and serves as the basis of Epsom salts

magnetic field *n* : the portion of space near a magnetic body or a current-carrying body in which the magnetic forces due to the body or current can be detected

magnetic resonance *n* : the absorption of energy exhibited by particles (as atomic nuclei or electrons) in a static magnetic field when the particles are exposed to electromagnetic radiation of certain frequencies — see NUCLEAR MAGNETIC RESONANCE

magnetic resonance imaging *n* : a noninvasive diagnostic technique that produces computerized images of internal body tissues and is based on nuclear magnetic resonance of atoms within the body induced by the application of radio waves — abbr. *MRI*

mag·ne·to·en·ceph·a·log·ra·phy \ˌmag-ˌnē-tō-in-ˌse-fə-ˈlä-grə-fē\ *n, pl* **-phies** : the process of detecting and recording the magnetic field of the brain

mag·ni·fi·ca·tion \ˌmag-nə-fə-ˈkā-shən\ *n* : the apparent enlargement of an object by an optical instrument that is the ratio of the dimensions of an image formed by the instrument to the corresponding dimensions of the object — called also *power* — **mag·ni·fy** \ˈmag-nə-ˌfī\ *vb*

mag·no·cel·lu·lar \ˌmag-nō-ˈsel-yə-lər\ *adj* : having or consisting of large cells ⟨∼ hypothalamic nuclei⟩

magnum — see FORAMEN MAGNUM

magnus — see ADDUCTOR MAGNUS

maid·en·head \ˈmād-ᵊn-ˌhed\ *n* : HYMEN

maim \ˈmām\ *vb* 1 : to commit the felony of mayhem upon 2 : to wound seriously : MUTILATE, DISABLE

main·line \ˈmān-ˌlīn\ *vb* **-lined; -lining** *slang* : to inject a narcotic drug (as heroin) into a vein

main·stream \-ˌstrēm\ *adj* : relating to or being tobacco smoke that is drawn (as from a cigarette) directly into the mouth of the smoker and is usu. inhaled into the lungs — compare SIDE-STREAM

main·te·nance \ˈmānt-ᵊn-əns\ *adj* : designed or adequate to maintain a patient in a stable condition : serving to maintain a gradual process of healing or to prevent a relapse (a ~ dose) (~ chemotherapy)

ma·jor \'mā-jər\ *adj* : involving grave risk : SERIOUS (a ~ illness) (a ~ operative procedure) — compare MINOR

majora — see LABIA MAJORA

major histocompatibility complex *n* : a group of genes that function esp. in determining the histocompatibility antigens found on cell surfaces and that in humans comprise the alleles occurring at four loci on the short arm of chromosome 6 — abbr. *MHC*

major labia *n pl* : LABIA MAJORA

major–medical *adj* : of, relating to, or being a form of insurance designed to pay all or part of the medical bills of major illnesses usu. after deduction of a fixed initial sum

major surgery *n* : surgery involving a risk to the life of the patient; *specif* : an operation upon an organ within the cranium, chest, abdomen, or pelvic cavity — compare MINOR SURGERY

mal \'māl, 'mal\ *n* : DISEASE, SICKNESS

mal- *comb form* **1** : bad (*mal*practice) **2 a** : abnormal (*mal*formation) **b** : abnormally (*mal*formed) **3 a** : inadequate (*mal*adjustment) **b** : inadequately (*mal*nourished)

mal·ab·sorp·tion \,ma-ləb-'sȯrp-shən, -'zȯrp-\ *n* : faulty absorption of nutrient materials from the alimentary canal — **mal·ab·sorp·tive** \-tiv\ *adj*

malabsorption syndrome *n* : a syndrome resulting from malabsorption that is typically characterized by weakness, diarrhea, muscle cramps, edema, and loss of weight

malac- *or* **malaco-** *comb form* : soft (*malaco*plakia)

ma·la·cia \mə-'lā-shə, -shē-ə\ *n* : abnormal softening of a tissue — often used in combination (osteo*malacia*) — **ma·lac·ic** \-sik\ *adj*

mal·a·co·pla·kia \,ma-lə-kō-'plā-kē-ə\ *n* : inflammation of the mucous membrane of a hollow organ (as the urinary bladder) characterized by the formation of soft granulomatous lesions

mal·ad·ap·ta·tion \,mal-,a-,dap-'tā-shən\ *n* : poor or inadequate adaptation (psychological ~) — **mal·adap·tive** \,ma-lə-'dap-tiv\ *adj* — **mal·adap·tive·ly** *adv*

mal·a·die de Ro·ger \,ma-lə-'dē-də-rō-'zhā\ *n* : a small usu. asymptomatic ventricular septal defect

Roger, Henri–Louis (1809–1891), French physician.

mal·ad·just·ment \,ma-lə-'jəst-mənt\ *n* : poor, faulty, or inadequate adjustment — **mal·ad·just·ed** \-'jəs-təd\ *adj*

mal·ad·min·is·tra·tion \,ma-ləd-,mi-nə-'strā-shən\ *n* : incorrect administration (as of a drug)

mal·a·dy \'ma-lə-dē\ *n, pl* **-dies** : DISEASE, SICKNESS (a fatal ~)

mal·aise \mə-'lāz, ma-, -'lez\ *n* : an indefinite feeling of debility or lack of health often indicative of or accompanying the onset of an illness

mal·a·ko·pla·kia *var of* MALACOPLAKIA

mal·align·ment \,ma-lə-'līn-mənt\ *n* : incorrect or imperfect alignment (as of teeth) — **mal·aligned** \-'līnd\ *adj*

ma·lar \'mā-lər, -,lär\ *adj* : of or relating to the cheek, the side of the head, or the zygomatic bone

malar bone *n* : ZYGOMATIC BONE — called also *malar*

malari- *or* **malario-** *comb form* : malaria (*malario*logy)

ma·lar·ia \mə-'ler-ē-ə\ *n* **1** : an acute or chronic disease caused by the presence of sporozoan parasites of the genus *Plasmodium* in the red blood cells, transmitted from an infected to an uninfected individual by the bite of anopheline mosquitoes, and characterized by periodic attacks of chills and fever that coincide with mass destruction of blood cells and the release of toxic substances by the parasite at the end of each reproductive cycle — see FALCIPARUM MALARIA, VIVAX MALARIA **2** : any of various diseases of birds and mammals that are more or less similar to malaria of human beings and are caused by blood protozoans — **ma·lar·i·al** \-əl\ *adj*

ma·lar·i·ae malaria \mə-'ler-ē-,ē-\ *n* : malaria caused by a malaria parasite (*Plasmodium malariae*) and marked by recurrence of paroxysms at 72-hour intervals — called also *quartan malaria*

malarial mosquito *or* **malaria mosquito** *n* : a mosquito of the genus *Anopheles* (esp. *A. quadrimaculatus*) that transmits the malaria parasite

malaria parasite *n* : a protozoan of the sporozoan genus *Plasmodium* that is transmitted to humans or to certain other mammals or birds by the bite of a mosquito in which its sexual reproduction takes place, that multiplies asexually in the vertebrate host by schizogony in the red blood cells or in certain tissue cells, and that causes destruction of red blood cells and the febrile disease malaria — see MEROZOITE, PHANEROZITE, SCHIZONT, SPOROZOITE

ma·lar·i·ol·o·gy \mə-,ler-ē-'ä-lə-jē\ *n, pl* **-gies** : the scientific study of malaria — **ma·lar·i·ol·o·gist** \-jist\ *n*

ma·lar·i·ous \mə-'ler-ē-əs\ *adj* : characterized by the presence of or infected with malaria (~ regions)

ma·late \'ma-,lāt, 'mā-\ *n* : a salt or ester of malic acid

mal·a·thi·on \,ma-lə-'thī-ən, -,än\ *n* : an insecticide $C_{10}H_{19}O_6PS_2$ with a lower mammalian toxicity than parathion

mal de mer \ˌmal-də-ˈmer\ n : SEASICK-NESS

mal·des·cent \ˌmal-di-ˈsent\ n : an improper or incomplete descent of a testis into the scrotum — **mal·des·cend·ed** \-ˈsen-dəd\ adj

mal·de·vel·op·ment \ˌmal-di-ˈve-ləp-mənt\ n : abnormal growth or development : DYSPLASIA

¹**male** \ˈmāl\ n : an individual that produces small usu. motile gametes (as sperm or spermatozoa) which fertilize the eggs of a female

²**male** adj : of, relating to, or being the sex that produces gametes which fertilize the eggs of a female

ma·le·ate \ˈmā-lē-ˌāt, -lē-ət\ n : a salt or ester of maleic acid

male bonding n : bonding between males through shared activities excluding females

male climacteric n : CLIMACTERIC 2

ma·le·ic acid \mə-ˈlē-ik-, -ˈlā-\ n : an isomer of fumaric acid

male menopause n : CLIMACTERIC 2

male–pattern baldness n : typical hereditary baldness in the male characterized by loss of hair on the crown and temples

mal·for·ma·tion \ˌmal-fȯr-ˈmā-shən\ n : irregular, anomalous, abnormal, or faulty formation or structure — **mal·formed** \(ˌ)mal-ˈfȯrmd\ adj

mal·func·tion \(ˌ)mal-ˈfaŋk-shən\ vb : to function imperfectly or badly : fail to operate in the normal or usual manner — **malfunction** n

ma·lic acid \ˈma-lik, ˈmā-\ n : any of three optical isomers of an acid C₄H₆O₅; esp : the one formed as an intermediate in the Krebs cycle

maligna — see LENTIGO MALIGNA

ma·lig·nan·cy \mə-ˈlig-nən-sē\ n, pl -cies 1 : the quality or state of being malignant 2 a : exhibition (as by a tumor) of malignant qualities : VIRULENCE b : a malignant tumor

ma·lig·nant \-nənt\ adj 1 : tending to produce death or deterioration; esp : tending to infiltrate, metastasize, and terminate fatally ⟨~ tumor⟩ — compare BENIGN 1 2 : of unfavorable prognosis : not responding favorably to treatment

malignant catarrhal fever n : an acute infectious often fatal disease esp. of cattle and deer that is caused by one or more herpesviruses and is characterized by fever, depression, enlarged lymph nodes, discharge from the eyes and nose, and lesions affecting most organ systems — called also *catarrhal fever, malignant catarrh*

malignant edema n : an acute often fatal toxemia of wild and domestic animals that follows wound infection by an anaerobic toxin-producing bacterium of the genus *Clostridium* (*C. septicum*) and is characterized by anorexia, intoxication, fever, and soft

fluid-filled swellings — compare BLACK DISEASE, BRAXY

malignant hypertension n : essential hypertension characterized by acute onset, severe symptoms, rapidly progressive course, and poor prognosis

malignant hyperthermia n : a rare inherited condition characterized by a rapid, extreme, and often fatal rise in body temperature following the administration of general anesthesia

malignant malaria n : FALCIPARUM MALARIA

malignant malnutrition n : KWASHIORKOR

malignant pustule n : localized anthrax of the skin taking the form of a pimple surrounded by a zone of edema and hyperemia and tending to become necrotic and ulcerated

malignant tertian malaria n : FALCIPARUM MALARIA

malignant transformation n : the transformation that a cell undergoes to become a rapidly dividing tumor-producing cell

ma·lig·ni·za·tion \mə-ˌlig-nə-ˈzā-shən\ n : a process or instance of becoming malignant ⟨~ of a tumor⟩

ma·lin·ger \mə-ˈliŋ-gər\ vb -gered; -gering : to pretend or exaggerate incapacity or illness so as to avoid duty or work — **ma·lin·ger·er** \-ər\ n

mal·le·o·lar \mə-ˈlē-ə-lər\ adj : of or relating to a malleolus of the ankle

mal·le·o·lus \mə-ˈlē-ə-ləs\ n, pl -li \-ˌlī\ : an expanded projection or process at the distal extremity of each bone of the leg: **a** : the expanded lower extremity of the fibula situated on the lateral side of the leg at the ankle — called also *external malleolus, lateral malleolus* **b** : a strong pyramid-shaped process of the tibia that projects distally on the medial side of its lower extremity at the ankle — called also *internal malleolus, medial malleolus*

mal·let finger \ˈma-lət-\ n : involuntary flexion of the distal phalanx of a finger caused by avulsion of the extensor tendon

mal·le·us \ˈma-lē-əs\ n, pl **mal·lei** \-lē-ˌī, -lē-ˌē\ : the outermost of the three auditory ossicles of the middle ear consisting of a head, neck, short process, long process, and handle with the short process and handle being fastened to the tympanic membrane and the head articulating with the head of the incus — called also *hammer*

mal·nour·ished \(ˌ)mal-ˈnər-isht\ adj : UNDERNOURISHED

mal·nour·ish·ment \-ˈnər-ish-mənt\ n : MALNUTRITION

mal·nu·tri·tion \ˌmal-nü-ˈtri-shən, -nyü-\ n : faulty nutrition due to inadequate or unbalanced intake of nutrients or their impaired assimilation or utilization — **mal·nu·tri·tion·al** \-ᵊl\ adj

mal·oc·clu·sion \ˌma-lə-ˈklü-zhən\ n

: improper occlusion; *esp* : abnormality in the coming together of teeth — **mal·oc·clu·ded** \-'klü-dəd\ *adj*

Mal·pi·ghi·an body \mal-'pi-gē-ən-, -'pē-\ *n* : RENAL CORPUSCLE; *also* : MALPIGHIAN CORPUSCLE 2

Malpighi \mäl-'pē-gē\, **Marcello** (1628–1694), Italian anatomist.

Malpighian corpuscle *n* 1 : RENAL CORPUSCLE 2 : any of the small masses of adenoid tissue formed around the branches of the splenic artery in the spleen

Malpighian layer *n* : the deeper part of the epidermis consisting of cells whose protoplasm has not yet changed into horny material — called also *stratum germinativum*

Malpighian pyramid *n* : RENAL PYRAMID

mal·posed \mal-'pōzd\ *adj* : characterized by malposition (~ teeth)

mal·po·si·tion \mal-pə-'zi-shən\ *n* : wrong or faulty position

mal·prac·tice \(,)mal-'prak-təs\ *n* : a dereliction of professional duty or a failure to exercise an accepted degree of professional skill or learning by a physician rendering professional services which results in injury, loss, or damage — **malpractice** *vb*

mal·pre·sen·ta·tion \mal-,prē-zen-'tā-shən, -,pre-\ *n* : abnormal presentation of the fetus at birth

mal·ro·ta·tion \mal-rō-'tā-shən\ *n* : improper rotation of a bodily part and esp. of the intestines — **mal·ro·ta·ted** \-'rō-,tāt-əd\ *adj*

Mal·ta fever \'mȯl-tə-\ *n* : BRUCELLOSIS a

malt·ase \'mȯl-,tās, -,tāz\ *n* : an enzyme that catalyzes the hydrolysis of maltose to glucose

malt·ose \'mȯl-,tōs, -,tōz\ *n* : a crystalline dextrorotatory sugar $C_{12}H_{22}O_{11}$ formed esp. from starch by amylase (as in saliva)

mal·union \mal-'yün-yən\ *n* : incomplete or faulty union (as of the fragments of a fractured bone)

mam·ba \'mäm-bə, 'mam-\ *n* : any of several venomous elapid snakes (genus *Dendroaspis*) of sub-Saharan Africa

mam·il·la·ry, mam·il·lat·ed, mam·il·lo·tha·lam·ic tract *var of* MAMMILLARY, MAMMILLATED, MAMMILLOTHALAMIC TRACT

mamm- *or* **mamma-** *or* **mammi-** *or* **mammo-** *comb form* : breast ⟨*mammogram*⟩

mam·ma \'ma-mə\ *n, pl* **mam·mae** \'ma-,mē, -,mī\ : a mammary gland and its accessory parts

mam·mal \'ma-məl\ *n* : any of a class (Mammalia) of warm-blooded higher vertebrates (as dogs, cats, and humans) that nourish their young with milk secreted by mammary glands and have the skin more or less covered by hair — **mam·ma·li·an** \mə-'mā-lē-ən, ma-\ *adj or n*

mam·ma·plas·ty \'ma-mə-,plas-tē\ *n, pl* **-ties** : plastic surgery of the breast

¹**mam·ma·ry** \'ma-mə-rē\ *adj* : of, relating to, lying near, or affecting the mammae

²**mammary** *n, pl* **-aries** : MAMMARY GLAND

mammary artery — see INTERNAL THORACIC ARTERY

mammary gland *n* : any of the large compound sebaceous glands that in female mammals are modified to secrete milk, are situated ventrally in pairs, and usu. terminate in a nipple

mam·mil·la·ry \'ma-mə-,ler-ē, ma-'mil-ə-rē\ *adj* 1 : of, relating to, or resembling the breasts 2 : studded with breast-shaped protuberances

mammillary body *n* : either of two small rounded eminences on the underside of the brain behind the tuber cinereum

mam·mil·lat·ed \'ma-mə-,lā-təd\ *adj* 1 : having nipples or small protuberances 2 : having the form of a bluntly rounded protuberance

mam·mil·lo·tha·lam·ic tract \mə-,mi-lō-thə-'la-mik-\ *n* : a bundle of nerve fibers that runs from the mammillary body to the anterior nucleus of the thalamus — called also *mammillothalamic fasciculus*

mammo- — see MAMM-

mam·mo·gram \'ma-mə-,gram\ *n* : a photograph of the breasts made by X rays

mam·mo·graph \-,graf\ *n* : MAMMOGRAM

mam·mog·ra·phy \ma-'mä-grə-fē\ *n, pl* **-phies** : X-ray examination of the breasts (as for early detection of cancer) — **mam·mo·graph·ic** \,ma-mə-'gra-fik\ *adj*

mam·mo·plas·ty \'ma-mə-,plas-tē\ *n, pl* **-ties** : plastic surgery of the breast

mam·mo·tro·pin \,ma-mə-'trōp-ən\ *n* : PROLACTIN

man \'man\ *n, pl* **men** \'men\ : a bipedal primate mammal of the genus *Homo* (*H. sapiens*) that is anatomically related to the family (Pongidae) of larger more advanced apes but is distinguished esp. by notable development of the brain with a resultant capacity for articulate speech and abstract reasoning, is usu. considered to form a variable number of freely interbreeding races, and is the sole representative of a natural family (Hominidae); *broadly* : any living or extinct member of this family

managed care *n* : a system of providing health care through managed programs (as HMOs or PPOs) that is designed esp. to control costs

man·age·ment \'ma-nij-mənt\ *n* : the whole system of care and treatment of a disease or a sick individual — **man·age** \'ma-nij\ *vb*

Man·del·amine \man-ˈde-lə-mēn\ *trade-mark* — used for a preparation of the mandelate of methenamine

man·del·ate \ˈman-də-ˌlāt\ *n* : a salt or ester of mandelic acid

man·del·ic acid \man-ˈde-lik-\ *n* : an acid $C_8H_8O_3$ that is used chiefly in the form of its salts as a bacteriostatic agent for genitourinary tract infections

man·di·ble \ˈman-də-bəl\ *n* 1 : JAW 1; *esp* : JAW 1b 2 : the lower jaw with its investing soft parts — **man·dib·u·lar** \man-ˈdi-byə-lər\ *adj*

mandibul- *or* **mandibuli-** *or* **mandibulo-** *comb form* : mandibular and ⟨*man-dibulo*facial dysostosis⟩

mandibular arch *n* : the first branchial arch of the vertebrate embryo from which in humans are developed the lower lip, the mandible, the masticatory muscles, and the anterior part of the tongue

mandibular artery *n* : INFERIOR ALVEOLAR ARTERY

mandibular canal *n* : a bony canal within the mandible that gives passage to blood vessels and nerves supplying the lower teeth

mandibular foramen *n* : the opening on the medial surface of the ramus of the mandible that leads into the mandibular canal and transmits blood vessels and nerves supplying the lower teeth

mandibular fossa *n* : GLENOID FOSSA

mandibular nerve *n* : the one of the three major branches or divisions of the trigeminal nerve that supplies sensory fibers to the lower jaw, the floor of the mouth, the anterior two-thirds of the tongue, and the lower teeth and motor fibers to the muscles of mastication — called also *inferior maxillary nerve*; compare MAXILLARY NERVE, OPHTHALMIC NERVE

mandibuli-, mandibulo- — see MANDIBUL-

man·di·bu·lo·fa·cial dysostosis \man-ˌdi-byə-lō-ˈfā-shəl-\ *n* : a dysostosis of the face and lower jaw inherited as an autosomal dominant trait and characterized by bilateral malformations, deformities of the outer and middle ear, and a usu. smaller lower jaw — called also *Treacher Collins syndrome*

man·eat·er \ˈman-ˌē-tər\ *n* : one (as a great white shark) having an appetite for human flesh — **man·eat·ing** *adj*

man-eater shark *n* : MACKEREL SHARK; *esp* : GREAT WHITE SHARK

man-eating shark *n* : MAN-EATER SHARK

ma·neu·ver \mə-ˈnü-vər, -ˈnyü-\ *n* 1 : a movement, procedure, or method performed to achieve a desired result and esp. to restore a normal physiological state or to promote normal function — see HEIMLICH MANEUVER, VALSALVA MANEUVER 2 : a manipulation to accomplish a change of position; *specif* : a rotation or other movement applied to a fetus within the uterus to alter its position and facilitate delivery — see SCANZONI MANEUVER

man·ga·nese \ˈmaŋ-gə-ˌnēz, -ˌnēs\ *n* : a grayish white usu. hard and brittle metallic element — symbol *Mn*; see ELEMENT table

mange \ˈmānj\ *n* : any of various more or less severe, persistent, and contagious skin diseases that are marked esp. by eczematous inflammation and loss of hair and that affect domestic animals or sometimes humans; *esp* : a skin disease caused by a minute parasitic mite of *Sarcoptes*, *Psoroptes*, *Chorioptes*, or related genera that burrows in or lives on the skin or by one of the genus *Demodex* that lives in the hair follicles or sebaceous glands — see CHORIOPTIC MANGE, DEMODECTIC MANGE, SARCOPTIC MANGE, SCABIES

mange mite *n* : any of the small parasitic mites that infest the skin of animals and cause mange

man·go fly \ˈmaŋ-gō-\ *n* : any of various horseflies of the genus *Chrysops* that are vectors of filarial worms

man·gy \ˈmān-jē\ *adj* **man·gi·er; -est** 1 : infected with mange ⟨a ∼ dog⟩ 2 : relating to, characteristic of, or resulting from mange ⟨a ∼ itch⟩

ma·nia \ˈmā-nē-ə, -nyə\ *n* : excitement of psychotic proportions manifested by mental and physical hyperactivity, disorganization of behavior, and elevation of mood; *specif* : the manic phase of manic-depressive psychosis

ma·ni·ac \ˈmā-nē-ˌak\ *n* : an individual affected with or exhibiting madness — **ma·ni·a·cal** \mə-ˈnī-ə-kəl\ *also* **ma·ni·ac** \ˈmā-nē-ak\ *adj*

¹**man·ic** \ˈma-nik\ *adj* : affected with, relating to, or resembling mania — **man·i·cal·ly** *adv*

²**manic** *n* : an individual affected with mania

manic-depression *n* : MANIC-DEPRESSIVE PSYCHOSIS

¹**manic-depressive** *adj* : characterized by mania, by psychotic depression, or by alternating mania and depression

²**manic-depressive** *n* : a manic-depressive person

manic-depressive psychosis *n* : a major mental disorder characterized by manic-depressive episodes — called also *manic-depressive reaction*

man·i·fes·ta·tion \ˌma-nə-fə-ˈstā-shən, -fe-\ *n* : a perceptible, outward, or visible expression (as of a disease or abnormal condition)

manifest content *n* : the content of a dream as it is recalled by the dreamer in psychoanalysis — compare LATENT CONTENT

ma·nip·u·late \mə-ˈni-pyə-ˌlāt\ *vb* **-lat-**

ed; **-lat·ing 1** : to treat or operate with the hands or by mechanical means esp. in a skillful manner (~ the fragments of a broken bone into correct position) **2** : to control or play upon by artful, unfair, or insidious means esp. to one's own advantage — **ma·nip·u·la·tive** \mə-'ni-pyə-₁lā-tiv, -lə-\ *adj* — **ma·nip·u·la·tive·ness** *n*

ma·nip·u·la·tion \mə-₁ni-pyə-'lā-shən\ *n* **1** : the act, process, or an instance of manipulating esp. a body part by manual examination and treatment; *esp* : adjustment of faulty structural relationships by manual means (as in the reduction of fractures or dislocations) **2** : the condition of being manipulated

man·ner·ism \'ma-nə-₁ri-zəm\ *n* : a characteristic and often unconscious mode or peculiarity of action, bearing, or treatment; *esp* : any pointless and compulsive activity performed repeatedly

man·ni·tol \'ma-nə-₁tȯl, -₁tōl\ *n* : a slightly sweet crystalline alcohol $C_6H_{14}O_6$ found in many plants and used esp. as a diuretic and in testing kidney function

mannitol hexa·ni·trate \-₁hek-sə-'nī-₁trāt\ *n* : an explosive crystalline ester $C_6H_8(NO_3)_6$ made from mannitol and used mixed with a carbohydrate (as lactose) in the treatment of angina pectoris and vascular hypertension

man·nose \'ma-₁nōs, -₁nōz\ *n* : an aldose $C_6H_{12}O_6$ found esp. in plants

man·nos·i·do·sis \mə-₁nō-sə-'dō-səs\ *n, pl* **-do·ses** \-₁sēz\ : a rare inherited metabolic disease characterized by deficiency of an enzyme catalyzing the metabolism of mannose with resulting accumulation of mannose in the body and marked esp. by facial and skeletal deformities and by mental retardation

ma·noeu·vre *chiefly Brit var of* MANEUVER

ma·nom·e·ter \mə-'nä-mə-tər\ *n* **1** : an instrument for measuring the pressure of gases and vapors **2** : SPHYGMOMANOMETER — **mano·met·ric** \₁ma-nə-'me-trik\ *adj* — **mano·met·ri·cal·ly** *adv* — **ma·nom·e·try** \mə-'nä-mə-trē\ *n*

Man·son·el·la \₁man-sə-'ne-lə\ *n* : a genus of filarial worms (family Dipetalonematidae) including one (*M. ozzardi*) that is common and apparently nonpathogenic in human visceral fat and mesenteries in So. and Central America

Man·son \'man-sən\, **Sir Patrick (1844–1922)**, British parasitologist.

mansoni — see SCHISTOSOMIASIS MANSONI

Man·son's disease \'man-sənz-\ *n* : SCHISTOSOMIASIS MANSONI

man·tle \'mant-ᵊl\ *n* **1** : something that covers, enfolds, or envelops **2** : CEREBRAL CORTEX

Man·toux test \man-'tü-, ₁män-\ *n* : an intradermal test for hypersensitivity to tuberculin that indicates past or present infection with tubercle bacilli — compare TUBERCULIN TEST

Mantoux, Charles (1877–1947), French physician.

ma·nu·bri·um \mə-'nü-brē-əm, -'nyü-\ *n, pl* **-bria** \-brē-ə\ *also* **-bri·ums** : an anatomical process or part shaped like a handle: as **a** : the cephalic segment of the sternum that is a somewhat triangular flattened bone with anterolateral borders which articulate with the clavicles **b** : the process of the malleus of the ear

ma·nus \'mā-nəs, 'mä-\ *n, pl* **ma·nus** \-nəs, -₁nüs\ : the distal segment of the vertebrate forelimb from the carpus to the end of the limb

many·plies \'me-nē-₁plīz\ *n* : OMASUM

MAO *abbr* monoamine oxidase

MAOI *abbr* monoamine oxidase inhibitor

Mao·late \'mā-ō-₁lāt\ *trademark* — used for a preparation of chlorphenesin carbamate

¹**map** \'map\ *n* : the arrangement of genes on a chromosome — called also *genetic map*

²**map** *vb* **mapped; map·ping 1** : to locate (a gene) on a chromosome **2** *of a gene* : to be located (a repressor ~s near the corresponding structural gene)

maple syrup urine disease *n* : a hereditary aminoaciduria caused by a deficiency of decarboxylase leading to high concentrations of valine, leucine, isoleucine, and alloisoleucine in the blood, urine, and cerebrospinal fluid and characterized by an odor of maple syrup to the urine, vomiting, hypertonicity, severe mental retardation, seizures, and eventually death unless the condition is treated with dietary measures

ma·pro·ti·line \mə-'prō-tə-₁lēn\ *n* : an antidepressant drug used in the form of its hydrochloride $C_{20}H_{23}N \cdot HCl$ to relieve major depression (as in manic-depressive psychosis) and anxiety associated with depression

ma·ras·mus \mə-'raz-məs\ *n* : a condition of chronic undernourishment occurring esp. in children and usu. caused by a diet deficient in calories and proteins but sometimes by disease (as congenital syphilis) or parasitic infection — **ma·ras·mic** \-mik\ *adj*

marble bone disease *n* : OSTEOPETROSIS

Mar·bor·an \'mär-bə-₁ran\ *trademark* — used for a preparation of methisazone

Mar·burg disease \'mär-bərg-\ *n* : GREEN MONKEY DISEASE

Marburg virus *n* : an African RNA arbovirus that causes green monkey disease

march \'märch\ *n* : the progression of epileptic activity through the motor centers of the cerebral cortex that is manifested in localized convulsions in first one and then an adjacent part of the body

Mar·ek's disease \'mar-iks-\ *n* : a highly contagious viral disease of poultry that is characterized esp. by proliferation of lymphoid cells and is caused by a herpesvirus

Marek, Jozsef (1867–1952), Hungarian veterinarian.

Ma·rey's law \mə-'rāz-\ *n* : a statement in physiology: heart rate is related inversely to arterial blood pressure

Marey, Étienne–Jules (1830–1904), French physiologist.

Mar·e·zine \'mar-ə-ˌzēn\ *trademark* — used for a preparation of the hydrochloride of cyclizine

Mar·fan's syndrome \'mär-ˌfanz-\ *or* **Mar·fan syndrome** \-ˌfan-\ *n* : a disorder of connective tissue inherited as a simple dominant and characterized by abnormal elongation of the long bones and often by ocular and circulatory defects

Marfan \mär-'fäⁿ\, **Antonin Bernard Jean** (1858–1942), French pediatrician.

mar·gin \'mär-jən\ *n* 1 : the outside limit or edge of something (as a bodily part or a wound) 2 : the part of consciousness at a particular moment that is felt only vaguely and dimly — **mar·gin·al** \'mär-jə-nəl\ *adj*

mar·gin·ation \ˌmär-jə-'nā-shən\ *n* 1 : the act or process of forming a margin; *specif* : the adhesion of white blood cells to the walls of damaged blood vessels 2 : the action of finishing a dental restoration or a filling for a cavity (∼ of an amalgam with a bur)

Ma·rie–Strüm·pell's disease *also* **Ma·rie–Strüm·pell's disease** \mä-'rē-'strüm-pəl(z)-\ *n* : ANKYLOSING SPONDYLITIS

Marie, Pierre (1853–1940), French neurologist.

Strümpell \'shtruem-pəl\, **Ernst Adolf Gustav Gottfried von** (1853–1925), German neurologist.

mari·jua·na *also* **mari·hua·na** \ˌmar-ə-'wä-nə, -'hwä-\ *n* 1 : HEMP 1 2 : the dried leaves and flowering tops of the pistillate hemp plant that yield THC and are sometimes smoked in cigarettes for their intoxicating effect — compare BHANG, CANNABIS, HASHISH

mark \'märk\ *n* : an impression or trace made or occurring on something — see BIRTHMARK, STRAWBERRY MARK

mark·er \'mär-kər\ *n* 1 : something that serves to characterize or distinguish ⟨a surface ∼ on a cell that acts as an antigen⟩ 2 : GENETIC MARKER — called also *marker gene*

Ma·ro·teaux–La·my syndrome \mär-ō-'tō-lä-'mē-\ *n* : a mucopolysaccharidosis that is inherited as an autosomal recessive trait and that is similar to Hurler's syndrome except that

intellectual development is not retarded

Maroteaux, Pierre (*b* 1926), French physician.

Lamy, Maurice Emile Joseph (*b* 1895), French physician.

Mar·plan \'mär-ˌplan\ *trademark* — used for a preparation of isocarboxazid

mar·row \'mar-(ˌ)ō\ *n* 1 : a soft highly vascular modified connective tissue that occupies the cavities and cancellous part of most bones and occurs in two forms: **a** : a whitish or yellowish marrow consisting chiefly of fat cells and predominating in the cavities of the long bones — called also *yellow marrow* **b** : a reddish marrow containing little fat, being the chief seat of red blood cell and blood granulocyte production, and occurring in the normal adult only in cancellous tissue esp. in certain flat bones — called also *red marrow* 2 : the substance of the spinal cord

Mar·seilles fever \mär-'sā-\ *n* : BOUTONNEUSE FEVER

Mar·si·lid \'mär-sə-lid\ *trademark* — used for a preparation of iproniazid

mar·su·pi·al·ize \mär-'sü-pē-ə-ˌlīz\ *vb* **-ized; -iz·ing** : to open (as the bladder or a cyst) and sew by the edges to the abdominal wound to permit further treatment (as of an enclosed tumor) or to discharge pathological matter (as from a hydatid cyst) — **mar·su·pi·al·i·za·tion** \-ˌsü-pē-ə-li-'zā-shən\ *n*

mas·cu·line \'mas-kyə-lən\ *adj* 1 : MALE 2 : having the qualities distinctive of or appropriate to a male 3 : having a mannish bearing or quality — **mas·cu·lin·i·ty** \ˌmas-kyə-'li-nə-tē\ *n*

mas·cu·lin·ize \'mas-kyə-lə-ˌnīz\ *vb* **-ized; -iz·ing** : to give a preponderantly masculine character to; *esp* : to cause (a female) to take on male characteristics — **mas·cu·lin·i·za·tion** \ˌmas-kyə-lə-nə-'zā-shən\ *n*

MASH *abbr* mobile army surgical hospital

¹**mask** \'mask\ *n* 1 : a protective covering for the face 2 **a** : a device covering the mouth and nose to facilitate inhalation **b** : a comparable device to prevent exhalation of infective material **c** : a cosmetic preparation for the skin of the face that produces a tightening effect as it dries

²**mask** *vb* 1 : to modify or reduce the effect or activity of (as a process or a reaction) 2 : to raise the audibility threshold of (a sound) by the simultaneous presentation of another sound

masked *adj* : failing to present or produce the usual symptoms : not obvious : LATENT ⟨a ∼ fever⟩

mas·och·ism \'ma-sə-ˌki-zəm, 'ma-zə-, 'mä-sə-\ *n* : a sexual perversion characterized by pleasure in being subjected to pain or humiliation esp. by a love object — compare ALGO-

LAGNIA, SADISM — **mas·och·is·tic** \ˌma-sə-ˈkis-tik, ˌma-zə-, ˌmä-sə-\ *adj* — **mas·och·is·ti·cal·ly** *adv*

Sa·cher-Ma·soch \ˈzä-kər-ˈmä-ˌzòk\, **Leopold von** (1836–1895), Austrian novelist.

mas·och·ist \-kist\ *n* : an individual who is given to masochism

mass \ˈmas\ *n* **1** : the property of a body that is a measure of its inertia, that is commonly taken as a measure of the amount of material it contains and causes it to have weight in a gravitational field **2** : a homogeneous pasty mixture compounded for making pills, lozenges, and plasters

mas·sage \mə-ˈsäzh, -ˈsäj\ *n* : manipulation of tissues (as by rubbing, stroking, kneading, or tapping) with the hand or an instrument for therapeutic purposes — **massage** *vb*

mas·sa in·ter·me·dia \ˈma-sə-ˌin-tər-ˈmē-dē-ə\ *n* : an apparently functionless mass of gray matter in the midline of the third ventricle that is found in many but not all human brains and is formed when the surfaces of the thalami protruding inward from opposite sides of the third ventricle make contact and fuse

mas·se·ter \mə-ˈsē-tər, ma-\ *n* : a large muscle that raises the lower jaw and assists in mastication, arises from the zygomatic arch and the zygomatic process of the temporal bone, and is inserted into the mandibular ramus and gonial angle — **mas·se·ter·ic** \ˌma-sə-ˈter-ik\ *adj*

mas·seur \ma-ˈsər, mə-\ *n* : a man who practices massage

mas·seuse \-ˈsərz, -ˈsüz\ *n* : a woman who practices massage

mas·sive \ˈma-siv\ *adj* **1** : large in comparison to what is typical — used esp. of medical dosage or of an infective agent ⟨a ~ dose of penicillin⟩ **2** : being extensive and severe — used of a pathologic condition ⟨a ~ hemorrhage⟩

mass number *n* : an integer that approximates the mass of an isotope and designates the total number of protons and neutrons in the nucleus ⟨the symbol for carbon of *mass number* 14 is ^{14}C or C^{14}⟩

mas·so·ther·a·py \ˌma-sō-ˈther-ə-pē\ *n*, *pl* **-pies** : the practice of massage for remedial or hygienic purposes

mass spectrometry *n* : an instrumental method for identifying the chemical constitution of a substance by means of the separation of gaseous ions according to their differing mass and charge — **mass spectrometer** *n* — **mass spectrometric** *adj*

mass spectroscopy *n* : MASS SPECTROMETRY — **mass spectroscope** *n* — **mass spectroscopic** *adj*

mast- *or* **masto-** *comb form* : breast : nipple : mammary gland ⟨*mastitis*⟩

mas·tal·gia \mas-ˈtal-jə\ *n* : MASTODYNIA

mast cell \ˈmast-\ *n* : a large cell that occurs esp. in connective tissue and has basophilic granules containing substances (as histamine and heparin) which mediate allergic reactions

mas·tec·to·mee \ma-ˌstek-tə-ˈmē\ *n* : a person who has had a mastectomy

mas·tec·to·my \ma-ˈstek-tə-mē\ *n*, *pl* **-mies** : excision or amputation of a mammary gland and usu. associated tissue

master gland *n* : PITUITARY GLAND

-mas·tia \ˈmas-tē-ə\ *n comb form* : condition of having (such or so many) breasts or mammary glands ⟨gynecomastia⟩

mas·ti·cate \ˈmas-tə-ˌkāt\ *vb* **-cat·ed**; **-cat·ing 1** : to grind, crush, and chew (food) with or as if with the teeth in preparation for swallowing **2** : to soften or reduce to pulp by crushing or kneading — **mas·ti·ca·tion** \ˌmas-tə-ˈkā-shən\ *n* — **mas·ti·ca·to·ry** \ˈmas-ti-kə-ˌtōr-ē\ *adj*

mas·ti·tis \ma-ˈstī-təs\ *n*, *pl* **-tit·i·des** \-ˈti-tə-ˌdēz\ : inflammation of the mammary gland or udder usu. caused by infection — see BLUE BAG, BOVINE MASTITIS, GARGET — **mas·tit·ic** \ma-ˈsti-tik\ *adj*

masto- — see MAST-

mas·to·cy·to·ma \ˌmas-tə-ˌsī-ˈtō-mə\ *n*, *pl* **-mas** *or* **-ma·ta** \-mə-tə\ : a tumorous mass produced by proliferation of mast cells

mas·to·cy·to·sis \-ˈtō-səs\ *n*, *pl* **-to·ses** \-ˌsēz\ : excessive proliferation of mast cells in the tissues

mas·to·dyn·ia \ˌmas-tə-ˈdī-nē-ə\ *n* : pain in the breast — called also *mastalgia*

¹mas·toid \ˈmas-ˌtòid\ *adj* : of, relating to, or being the mastoid process; *also* : occurring in the region of the mastoid process

²mastoid *n* : a mastoid bone or process

mastoid air cell *n* : MASTOID CELL

mastoid antrum *n* : TYMPANIC ANTRUM

mastoid cell *n* : one of the small cavities in the mastoid process that develop after birth and are filled with air — called also *mastoid air cell*

mas·toid·ec·to·my \ˌmas-ˌtòi-ˈdek-tə-mē\ *n*, *pl* **-mies** : surgical removal of the mastoid cells or of the mastoid process of the temporal bone

mas·toid·itis \ˌmas-ˌtòi-ˈdī-təs\ *n*, *pl* **-it·i·des** \-ˈdi-tə-ˌdēz\ : inflammation of the mastoid and esp. of the mastoid cells

mas·toid·ot·o·my \ˌmas-ˌtòi-ˈdä-tə-mē\ *n*, *pl* **-mies** : incision of the mastoid

mastoid process *n* : the process of the temporal bone behind the ear that is well developed and of somewhat conical form in adults but inconspicuous in children

mas·top·a·thy \ma-ˈstä-pə-thē\ *n*, *pl*

-thies : a disorder of the breast; *esp* : a painful disorder of the breast

mas·tot·o·my \ma-ˈstä-tə-mē\ *n, pl* -mies : incision of the breast

mas·tur·ba·tion \ˌmas-tər-ˈbā-shən\ *n* : erotic stimulation esp. of one's own genital organs commonly resulting in orgasm and achieved by manual or other bodily contact exclusive of sexual intercourse, by instrumental manipulation, occasionally by sexual fantasies, or by various combinations of these agencies — called also *onanism, self-abuse* — mas·tur·bate \ˈmas-tər-ˌbāt\ *vb* — mas·tur·ba·tor \-ˌbā-tər\ *n*

mas·tur·ba·tory \ˈmas-tər-bə-ˌtōr-ē\ *adj* : of, relating to, or associated with masturbation (~ fantasies)

mate *vb* mated; mat·ing 1 : to pair or join for breeding 2 : COPULATE

ma·te·ria al·ba \mə-ˈtir-ē-ə-ˈal-bə\ *n pl* : a soft whitish deposit of epithelial cells, white blood cells, and microorganisms esp. at the gumline

materia med·i·ca \-ˈme-di-kə\ *n* 1 : substances used in the composition of medical remedies : DRUGS, MEDICINE 2 a : a branch of medical science that deals with the sources, nature, properties, and preparation of drugs b : a treatise on materia medica

ma·ter·nal \mə-ˈtərn-əl\ *adj* 1 : of, relating to, belonging to, or characteristic of a mother (~ instinct) 2 a : related through a mother b : inherited or derived from the female parent (~ genes) — ma·ter·nal·ly *adv*

maternal inheritance *n* : inheritance of characters transmitted through the cytoplasm of the egg

maternal rubella *n* : German measles in a pregnant woman that may cause developmental anomalies in the fetus when occurring during the first trimester

¹ma·ter·ni·ty \mə-ˈtər-nə-tē\ *n, pl* -ties : a hospital facility designed for the care of women before and during childbirth and for the care of newborn babies

²maternity *adj* : of, relating to pregnancy or the period close to and including childbirth

ma·ter·no·fe·tal \me-ˌtər-nō-ˈfēt-əl\ *adj* : involving a fetus and its mother (the human ~ interface)

ma·tri·cide \ˈma-trə-ˌsīd, ˈmā-\ *n* : murder of a mother by her son or daughter

ma·trix \ˈmā-triks\ *n, pl* ma·tri·ces \ˈmā-trə-ˌsēz, ˈma-\ *or* matrixes 1 a : the intercellular substance in which tissue cells (as of connective tissue) are embedded b : the thickened epithelium at the base of a fingernail or toenail from which new nail substance develops — called also *nail bed, nail matrix* 2 : a mass by which something is enclosed or in which something is embedded 3 a : a strip or

band placed so as to serve as a retaining outer wall of a tooth in filling a cavity b : a metal or porcelain pattern in which an inlay is cast or fused

mat·ter \ˈma-tər\ *n* 1 : material (as feces or urine) discharged or for discharge from the living body 2 : material discharged by suppuration : PUS

mattress suture *n* : a surgical stitch in which the suture is passed back and forth through both edges of a wound so that the needle is reinserted each time on the side of exit and passes through to the side of insertion

mat·u·rate \ˈma-chə-ˌrāt\ *vb* -rat·ed; -rat·ing : MATURE

mat·u·ra·tion \ˌma-chə-ˈrā-shən\ *n* 1 a : the process of becoming mature b : the emergence of personal and behavioral characteristics through growth processes c : the final stages of differentiation of cells, tissues, or organs d : the achievement of intellectual or emotional maturity 2 a : the entire process by which diploid gamete-producing cells are transformed into haploid gametes that includes both meiosis and physiological and structural changes fitting the gamete for its future role b : SPERMIOGENESIS 2 — mat·u·ra·tion·al \ˌma-chə-ˈrā-shə-nəl\ *adj*

ma·ture \mə-ˈtür, -ˈtyür, -ˈchür\ *adj* ma·tur·er; -est 1 : having completed natural growth and development 2 : having undergone maturation — mature *vb*

ma·tu·ri·ty \mə-ˈtür-ə-tē, -ˈtyür-, -ˈchür-\ *n, pl* -ties : the quality or state of being mature; *esp* : full development

maturity–onset diabetes *n* : NON-INSULIN-DEPENDENT DIABETES MELLITUS

max *abbr* maximum

Max·ib·o·lin \ˌmak-ˈsi-bə-lin, ˌmak-si-ˈbō-lin\ *trademark* — used for a preparation of ethylestrenol

maxill- *or* maxilli- *or* maxillo- *comb form* 1 : maxilla (maxillectomy) 2 : maxillary and (maxillofacial)

max·il·la \mak-ˈsi-lə\ *n, pl* max·il·lae \-ˈsi-(ˌ)lē, -ˌlī\ *or* maxillas 1 : JAW 1a 2 a : an upper jaw esp. of humans or other mammals in which the bony elements are closely fused b : either of two membrane bone elements of the upper jaw that lie lateral to the premaxillae and bear most of the teeth

¹max·il·lary \ˈmak-sə-ˌler-ē\ *adj* : of, relating to, being, or associated with a maxilla (~ blood vessels)

²maxillary *n, pl* -lar·ies 1 : MAXILLA 2b 2 : a maxillary part (as a nerve or blood vessel)

maxillary air sinus *n* : MAXILLARY SINUS

maxillary artery *n* : an artery supplying the deep structures of the face (as the nasal cavities, palate, tonsils, and pharynx) and sending a branch to the meninges of the brain — called also *internal maxillary artery;* compare FACIAL ARTERY

maxillary bone *n* : MAXILLA 2b

maxillary nerve *n* : the one of the three major branches or divisions of the trigeminal nerve that supplies sensory fibers to the skin areas of the middle part of the face, the upper jaw and its teeth, and the mucous membranes of the palate, nasal cavities, and nasopharynx — called also *maxillary division;* compare MANDIBULAR NERVE, OPHTHALMIC NERVE

maxillary process *n* : a triangular embryonic process that grows out from the dorsal end of the mandibular arch on each side and forms the lateral part of the upper lip, the cheek, and the upper jaw except the premaxilla

maxillary sinus *n* : an air cavity in the body of the maxilla that communicates with the middle meatus of the nose — called also *antrum of Highmore*

maxillary vein *n* : a short venous trunk of the face that is formed by the union of veins from the pterygoid plexus and that joins with the superficial temporal vein to form a vein which contributes to the formation of the external jugular vein

max·il·lec·to·my \ˌmak-sə-ˈlek-tə-mē\ *n, pl* **-mies** : surgical removal of the maxilla

maxilli-, maxillo- — see MAXILL-

max·il·lo·fa·cial \mak-ˌsi-(ˌ)lō-ˈfā-shəl, ˌmak-sə-(ˌ)lō-\ *adj* : of, relating to, treating, or affecting the maxilla and the face (~ lesions)

max·i·mal \ˈmak-sə-məl\ *adj* 1 : most complete or effective (~ vasodilation) 2 : being an upper limit — **max·i·mal·ly** *adv*

max·i·mum \ˈmak-sə-məm\ *n, pl* **max·i·ma** \-sə-mə\ *or* **maximums** 1 a : the greatest quantity or value attainable or attained b : the period of highest, greatest, or utmost development 2 : an upper limit allowed (as by a legal authority) or allowable (as by the circumstances of a particular case) — **maximum** *adj*

maximum permissible concentration *n* : the maximum concentration of radioactive material in body tissue that is regarded as acceptable and not producing significant deleterious effects on the human organism — abbr. *MPC*

maximum permissible dose *n* : the amount of ionizing radiation a person may be exposed to supposedly without being harmed

Max·i·pen \ˈmak-si-ˌpen\ *trademark* — used for a preparation of the potassium salt of phenethicillin

may·ap·ple \ˈmā-ˌap-əl\ *n, often cap* : a No. American herb of the genus *Podophyllum* (*P. peltatum*) having a poisonous rootstock and rootlets that are a source of the drug podophyllum

Ma·ya·ro virus \mä-ˈyä-rō-\ *n* : a So. American togavirus that is the causative agent of a febrile disease

may·hem \ˈmā-ˌhem, ˈmā-əm\ *n* 1 : willful and permanent deprivation of a bodily member resulting in impairment of a person's fighting ability and constituting a grave felony under English common law 2 : willful and permanent crippling, mutilation, or disfiguring of any part of the body constituting a grave felony under modern statutes and in some jurisdictions requiring a specific intent as distinguished from general malice

may·tan·sine \ˈmā-ˌtan-ˌsēn\ *n* : an antineoplastic agent $C_{34}H_{46}ClN_3O_{10}$ isolated from several members of a genus (*Maytenus* of the family Celastraceae) of tropical American shrubs and trees

maz- or mazo- comb form : breast (*mazoplasia*)

ma·zin·dol \ˈmā-zin-ˌdōl\ *n* : an adrenergic drug $C_{16}H_{13}ClN_2O$ used as an appetite suppressant

ma·zo·pla·sia \ˌmā-zə-ˈplā-zhə, -zhē-ə\ *n* : a degenerative condition of breast tissue

Maz·zi·ni test \mə-ˈzē-nē-\ *n* : a flocculation test for the diagnosis of syphilis

Mazzini, Louis Yolando (1894–1973), American serologist.

MB *abbr* [New Latin *medicinae baccalaureus*] bachelor of medicine

M band \ˈem-ˌband\ *n* : M LINE

MBD *abbr* minimal brain dysfunction

mc *abbr* millicurie

MC *abbr* 1 medical corps 2 [New Latin *magister chirurgiae*] master of surgery

Mc·Ar·dle's disease \mə-ˈkärd-ᵊlz-\ *n* : glycogenosis that is due to a deficiency of muscle phosphorylase and affects skeletal muscle — called also *McArdle's syndrome*

McArdle, Brian (*fl* 1936–1972), British physician.

MCAT *abbr* Medical College Admissions Test

Mc·Bur·ney's point \mək-ˈbər-nēz-\ *n* : a point on the abdominal wall that lies between the navel and the right anterior superior iliac spine and that is the point where most pain is elicited by pressure in acute appendicitis

McBurney, Charles (1845–1913), American surgeon.

mcg *abbr* microgram

MCh *abbr* [New Latin *magister chirurgiae*] master of surgery

MCH *abbr* 1 maternal and child health 2 mean corpuscular hemoglobin (concentration)

MCHC *abbr* mean corpuscular hemoglobin concentration

mCi *abbr* millicurie

MCV *abbr* mean corpuscular volume

Md *symbol* mendelevium

¹MD \ˌem-ˈdē\ *n* 1 [Latin *medicinae*

doctor] : an earned academic degree conferring the rank and title of doctor of medicine 2 : a person who has a doctor of medicine

²**MD** *abbr* muscular dystrophy

MDMA \₁em-(₁)dē-(₁)em-¹ā\ *n* : ECSTASY 2

MDR *abbr* minimum daily requirement

MDS *abbr* master of dental surgery

ME *abbr* medical examiner

meadow mushroom *n* : a common edible brown-spored mushroom (*Agaricus campestris*) that occurs naturally in moist open organically rich soil and is often cultivated

mean corpuscular hemoglobin concentration *n* : the number of grams of hemoglobin per unit volume and usu. 100 ml of packed red blood cells that is found by multiplying the number of grams of hemoglobin per unit volume of the original blood sample of whole blood by 100 and dividing by the hematocrit — abbr. *MCHC*

mean corpuscular volume *n* : the volume of the average red blood cell in a given blood sample that is found by multiplying the hematocrit by 10 and dividing by the estimated number of red blood cells — abbr. *MCV*

mea·sle \¹mē-zəl\ *n* : CYSTICERCUS; *specif* : one found in the muscles of a domesticated mammal — compare TAENIA 1

mea·sles \¹mē-zəlz\ *n sing or pl* 1 a : an acute contagious disease caused by a paramyxovirus, commencing with catarrhal symptoms, conjunctivitis, cough, and Koplik's spots on the oral mucous membrane, and marked by the appearance on the third or fourth day of an eruption of distinct red circular spots which coalesce in a crescentic form, are slightly raised, and after the fourth day of the eruption gradually decline — called also *rubeola* b : any of various eruptive diseases (as German measles) 2 : infestation with or disease caused by larval tapeworms in the muscles and tissues; *specif* : infestation of cattle and swine with cysticerci of tapeworms that as adults parasitize humans — see MEASLE

mea·sly \¹mē-zə-lē, ¹mēz-lē\ *adj* **mea·sli·er; -est** 1 : infected with measles 2 a : containing larval tapeworms b : infected with trichinae

meat- *or* **meato-** *comb form* : meatus ⟨*meato*plasty⟩

me·a·tal \mē-¹āt-ᵊl\ *adj* : of, relating to, or forming a meatus

me·a·to·plas·ty \mē-¹a-tə-₁plast-ē\ *n, pl* **-ties** : plastic surgery of a meatus (urethral ∼)

me·a·tot·o·my \₁mē-ə-¹tä-tə-mē\ *n, pl* **-mies** : incision of the urethral meatus esp. to enlarge it

me·atus \mē-¹ā-təs\ *n, pl* **me·atus·es** \-tə-səz\ *or* **me·atus** \-¹ā-təs, -₁tüs\ : a natural body passage : CANAL, DUCT

meatus acus·ti·cus ex·ter·nus \-ə-¹küs-ti-kəs-ek-¹stər-nəs\ *n* : EXTERNAL AUDITORY MEATUS

meatus acusticus in·ter·nus \-in-¹tər-nəs\ *n* : INTERNAL AUDITORY MEATUS

me·ban·a·zine \me-¹ba-nə-₁zēn\ *n* : a monoamine oxidase inhibitor C₈H₁₂N₂ used as an antidepressant

Meb·a·ral \¹me-bə-₁ral\ *trademark* — used for a preparation of mephobarbital

me·ben·da·zole \me-¹ben-də-₁zōl\ *n* : a broad-spectrum anthelmintic agent C₁₆H₁₃N₃O₃

me·bu·ta·mate \me-¹byü-tə-₁māt\ *n* : a central nervous system depressant C₁₀H₂₀N₂O₄ used to treat mild hypertension

mec·a·myl·a·mine \₁me-kə-¹mi-lə-₁mēn\ *n* : a drug that is used orally in the form of its hydrochloride C₁₁H₂₁N·HCl as a ganglionic blocking agent to effect a rapid lowering of severely elevated blood pressure

me·chan·i·cal \mi-¹ka-ni-kəl\ *adj* : caused by, resulting from, or relating to physical as opposed to biological or chemical processes or change (∼ injury) (∼ asphyxiation) — **me·chan·i·cal·ly** *adv*

mechanical heart *n* : a mechanism designed to maintain the flow of blood to the tissues of the body esp. during a surgical operation on the heart

mech·a·nism \¹me-kə-₁ni-zəm\ *n* 1 : a piece of machinery 2 a : a bodily process or function (the ∼ of healing) b : the combination of mental processes by which a result is obtained (psychological ∼s) 3 : the fundamental physical or chemical processes involved in or responsible for an action, reaction, or other natural phenomenon — **mech·a·nis·tic** \₁me-kə-¹nis-tik\ *adj*

mech·a·no·chem·is·try \₁me-kə-nō-¹ke-mə-strē\ *n, pl* **-tries** : chemistry that deals with the conversion of chemical energy into mechanical work (as in the contraction of a muscle) — **mech·a·no·chem·i·cal** \-¹ke-mi-kəl\ *adj*

mech·a·no·re·cep·tor \-ri-¹sep-tər\ *n* : a neural end organ (as a tactile receptor) that responds to a mechanical stimulus (as a change in pressure) — **mech·a·no·re·cep·tion** \-¹sep-shən\ *n* — **mech·a·no·re·cep·tive** \-¹sep-tiv\ *adj*

mech·a·no·sen·so·ry \-¹sen-sə-rē\ *adj* : of or relating to the sensing of mechanical stimuli (∼ nerve terminals)

mech·lor·eth·amine \₁me-₁klōr-¹e-thə-₁mēn\ *n* : a nitrogen mustard C₅H₁₁Cl₂N used in the form of its hydrochloride in palliative treatment of some neoplastic diseases

Mech·o·lyl \¹me-kə-₁lil\ *trademark* — used for a preparation of methacholine

Me·cis·to·cir·rus \mə-₁sis-tō-¹sir-əs\ *n* : a genus of nematode worms (family Trichostrongylidae) including a common parasite (*M. digitatus*) of the abomasum of domesticated ruminants and the stomach of swine

Meck·el–Gru·ber syndrome \'me-kəl-'grü-bər-\ n : a syndrome inherited as an autosomal recessive trait and typically characterized by occipital encephalocele, microcephaly, cleft palate, polydactyly, and polycystic kidneys — called also *Meckel's syndrome*

Meckel, Johann Friedrich, the Younger (1781–1833), German anatomist.

Gruber, Georg Benno Otto (*b* 1884), German pathologist.

Meck·el's cartilage \'me-kəlz-\ n : the cartilaginous bar of the embryonic mandibular arch of which the distal end ossifies to form the malleus

J. F. Meckel the Younger — see MECKEL-GRUBER SYNDROME

Meckel's diverticulum n : the proximal part of the omphalomesenteric duct when persistent as a blind fibrous tube connected with the lower ileum

J. F. Meckel the Younger — see MECKEL-GRUBER SYNDROME

Meckel's ganglion n : PTERYGOPALATINE GANGLION

Meckel, Johann Friedrich, the Elder (1724–1774), German anatomist.

mec·li·zine \'me-klə-ˌzēn\ n : a drug $C_{25}H_{27}ClN_2$ used usu. in the form of its hydrochloride to treat nausea and vertigo — see ANTIVERT

mec·lo·fen·a·mate sodium \ˌme-klō-'fe-nə-ˌmāt-\ n : a mild analgesic and anti-inflammatory drug $C_{14}H_{10}Cl_2N-NaO_2 \cdot H_2O$ used orally to treat rheumatoid arthritis and osteoarthritis — called also *meclofenamate*

mec·lo·zine \'me-klō-ˌzēn\ *Brit var of* MECLIZINE

me·co·ni·um \mi-'kō-nē-əm\ n : a dark greenish mass of desquamated cells, mucus, and bile that accumulates in the bowel of a fetus and is discharged shortly after birth

meconium ileus n : congenital intestinal obstruction by inspissated meconium that is often associated with cystic fibrosis of newborn infants

med \'med\ *adj* : MEDICAL (~ school)

me·daz·e·pam \me-'da-zə-ˌpam\ n : a drug $C_{16}H_{15}ClN_2$ used in the form of its hydrochloride as a tranquilizer

med·e·vac \'me-də-ˌvak\ n 1 : emergency evacuation of the sick or wounded (as from a combat area) 2 : a helicopter used for medevac — **medevac** *vb*

medi- *or* **medio-** *comb form* : middle ⟨*medio*lateral⟩

¹**media** *pl of* MEDIUM

²**me·dia** \'mē-dē-ə\ n, *pl* **me·di·ae** \-dē-ˌē\ : the middle coat of the wall of a blood or lymph vessel consisting chiefly of circular muscle fibers — called also *tunica media*

media — see AERO-OTITIS MEDIA, OTITIS MEDIA, SCALA MEDIA, SEROUS OTITIS MEDIA

me·di·ad \'mē-dē-ˌad\ *adv* : toward the median line or plane of a body or part

me·di·al \'mē-dē-əl\ *adj* 1 : lying or extending in the middle; *esp. of a body part* : lying or extending toward the median axis of the body (the ~ surface of the tibia) 2 : of or relating to the media of a blood vessel — **me·di·al·ly** *adv*

medial arcuate ligament n : an arched band of fascia that covers the upper part of the psoas major muscle, extends from the body of the first or second lumbar vertebra to the transverse process of the first and sometimes also the second lumbar vertebra, and provides attachment for part of the lumbar portion of the diaphragm — compare LATERAL ARCUATE LIGAMENT

medial collateral ligament n : a ligament that connects the medial epicondyle of the femur with the medial condyle and medial surface of the tibia and that helps to stabilize the knee by preventing lateral dislocation — called also *tibial collateral ligament*; compare LATERAL COLLATERAL LIGAMENT

medial condyle n : a condyle on the inner side of the lower extremity of the femur; *also* : a corresponding eminence on the upper part of the tibia that articulates with the medial condyle of the femur — compare LATERAL CONDYLE

medial cord n : a cord of nerve tissue that is continuous with the anterior division of the inferior trunk of the brachial plexus and that is one of the two roots forming the median nerve — compare LATERAL CORD, POSTERIOR CORD

medial cuneiform bone n : CUNEIFORM BONE 1a — called also *medial cuneiform*

medial epicondyle n : EPICONDYLE b

medial femoral circumflex artery n : an artery that branches from the deep femoral artery or from the femoral artery itself and that supplies the muscles of the medial part of the thigh and hip joint — compare LATERAL FEMORAL CIRCUMFLEX ARTERY

medial femoral circumflex vein n : a vein accompanying the medial femoral circumflex artery and emptying into the femoral vein or sometimes into one of its tributaries corresponding to the deep femoral artery — compare LATERAL FEMORAL CIRCUMFLEX VEIN

medial forebrain bundle n : a prominent tract of nerve fibers that connects the subcallosal area of the cerebral cortex with the lateral areas of the hypothalamus and that has fibers passing to the tuber cinereum, the brain stem, and the mammillary bodies

medial geniculate body n : a part of the

metathalamus consisting of a small oval tubercle situated between the pulvinar, colliculi, and cerebral peduncle that receives nerve impulses from the inferior colliculus and relays them to the auditory area — compare LATERAL GENICULATE BODY

medialis — see RECTUS MEDIALIS, VASTUS MEDIALIS

medial lemniscus *n* : a band of nerve fibers that transmits proprioceptive impulses from the spinal cord to the thalamus

medial longitudinal fasciculus *n* : any of four longitudinal bundles of white matter of which there are two on each side that extend from the midbrain to the upper parts of the spinal cord where they are located close to the midline ventral to the gray commissure and that are composed of fibers esp. from the vestibular nuclei

medial malleolus *n* : MALLEOLUS b

medial meniscus *n* : MENISCUS a(2)

medial pectoral nerve *n* : PECTORAL NERVE b

medial plantar artery *n* : PLANTAR ARTERY b

medial plantar nerve *n* : PLANTAR NERVE b

medial plantar vein *n* : PLANTAR VEIN b

medial popliteal nerve *n* : TIBIAL NERVE

medial pterygoid muscle *n* : PTERYGOID MUSCLE b

medial pterygoid nerve *n* : PTERYGOID NERVE b

medial pterygoid plate *n* : PTERYGOID PLATE b

medial rectus *n* : RECTUS 2c

medial semilunar cartilage *n* : MENISCUS a(2)

medial umbilical ligament *n* : a fibrous cord sheathed in peritoneum and extending from the pelvis to the umbilicus that is a remnant of part of the umbilical artery in the fetus — called also *lateral umbilical ligament*

medial vestibular nucleus *n* : the one of the four vestibular nuclei on each side of the medulla oblongata that sends ascending fibers to the oculomotor and trochlear nuclei in the cerebrum on the opposite side of the brain and sends descending fibers down both sides of the spinal cord to synapse with motoneurons of the ventral roots

¹**me·di·an** \ˈmē-dē-ən\ *n* : a medial part (as a vein or nerve)

²**median** *adj* : situated in the middle; *specif* : lying in a plane dividing a bilateral animal into right and left halves

median an·te·bra·chi·al vein \-ˌan-ti-ˈbrā-kē-əl-\ *n* : a vein usu. present in the forearm that drains the plexus of veins in the palm of the hand and that runs up the little finger side of the forearm

median arcuate ligament *n* : a tendinous arch that lies in front of the aorta and that connects the attachments

of the lumbar portion of the diaphragm to the lumbar vertebrae on each side — compare LATERAL ARCUATE LIGAMENT

median cubital vein *n* : a continuation of the cephalic vein of the forearm that passes obliquely toward the inner side of the arm in the bend of the elbow to join with the ulnar veins in forming the basilic vein and is often selected for venipuncture

median eminence *n* : a raised area in the floor of the third ventricle of the brain produced by the infundibulum of the hypothalamus

median lethal dose *n* : LD50

median nerve *n* : a nerve that arises by two roots from the brachial plexus and passes down the middle of the front of the arm

median nuchal line *n* : OCCIPITAL CREST a

median plane *n* : MIDSAGITTAL PLANE

median sacral crest *n* : SACRAL CREST a

median sacral vein *n* : an unpaired vein that accompanies the middle sacral artery and usu. empties into the left common iliac vein

median umbilical ligament *n* : a fibrous cord extending from the urinary bladder to the umbilicus that is the remnant of the fetal urachus

me·di·as·ti·nal \ˌmē-dē-ə-ˈstī-nəl\ *adj* : of or relating to a mediastinum

me·di·as·ti·ni·tis \ˌmē-dē-ˌas-tə-ˈnī-təs\ *n, pl* **-nit·i·des** \-ˈni-tə-ˌdēz\ : inflammation of the tissues of the mediastinum

me·di·as·tin·o·scope \ˌmē-dē-ə-ˈsti-nə-ˌskōp\ *n* : an optical instrument used in mediastinoscopy

me·di·as·ti·nos·co·py \ˌmē-dē-ˌas-tə-ˈnäs-kə-pē\ *n, pl* **-pies** : examination of the mediastinum through an incision above the sternum

me·di·as·ti·not·o·my \ˌmē-dē-ˌas-tə-ˈnä-tə-mē\ *n, pl* **-mies** : surgical incision into the mediastinum

me·di·as·ti·num \ˌmē-dē-ə-ˈstī-nəm\ *n, pl* **-na** \-nə\ **1** : the space in the chest between the pleural sacs of the lungs that contains all the viscera of the chest except the lungs and pleurae; *also* : this space with its contents **2** : MEDIASTINUM TESTIS

mediastinum testis *n* : a mass of connective tissue at the back of the testis that is continuous externally with the tunica albuginea and internally with the interlobular septa and encloses the rete testis

¹**me·di·ate** \ˈmē-dē-ət\ *adj* **1** : occupying a middle position **2** : acting through an intervening agency : exhibiting indirect causation, connection, or relation

²**me·di·ate** \ˈmē-dē-ˌāt\ *vb* **-at·ed; -at·ing** : to transmit or carry (as a physical process or effect) as intermediate mechanism or agency — **me·di·a·tion** \ˌmē-dē-ˈā-shən\ *n*

me·di·a·tor \\'mē-dē-ˌā-tər\\ n : one that mediates; *esp* : a mediating agent (as an enzyme or hormone) in a chemical or biological process

med·ic \\'me-dik\\ n : one engaged in medical work; *esp* : CORPSMAN

medica — see MATERIA MEDICA

med·i·ca·ble \\'me-di-kə-bəl\\ adj : CURABLE, REMEDIABLE

med·ic·aid \\'me-di-ˌkād\\ n, often cap : a program of medical aid designed for those unable to afford regular medical service and financed jointly by the state and federal governments

¹med·i·cal \\'me-di-kəl\\ adj 1 : of, relating to, or concerned with physicians or the practice of medicine often as distinguished from surgery 2 : requiring or devoted to medical treatment — **med·i·cal·ly** adv

²medical n : a medical examination

medical examiner n 1 : a usu. appointed public officer who must be a person trained in medicine and whose functions are to make postmortem examinations of the bodies of persons dead by violence or suicide or under circumstances suggesting crime, to investigate the cause of their deaths, to conduct autopsies, and sometimes to initiate inquests 2 : a physician employed to make medical examinations (as of applicants for military service or of claimants of workers' compensation) 3 : a physician appointed to examine and license candidates for the practice of medicine in a political jurisdiction (as a state)

medical jurisprudence n : FORENSIC MEDICINE

medical psychology n : theories of personality and behavior not necessarily derived from academic psychology that provide a basis for psychotherapy in psychiatry and in general medicine

medical record n : a record of a person's illnesses and their treatment

medical tran·scrip·tion·ist \\-tran-ˈskrip-shə-nist\\ n : a typist who transcribes dictated medical reports

me·di·ca·ment \\mi-ˈdi-kə-mənt, ˈme-di-kə-\\ n : a substance used in therapy — **med·i·ca·men·tous** \\ˌmi-ˌdi-kə-ˈmen-təs, ˌme-di-kə-\\ adj

med·i·cant \\'me-di-kənt\\ n : a medicinal substance

med·i·care \\'me-di-ˌkar\\ n, often cap : a government program of medical care esp. for the elderly

med·i·cate \\'me-də-ˌkāt\\ vb -cat·ed; -cat·ing 1 : to treat medicinally 2 : to impregnate with a medicinal substance (*medicated* soap)

med·i·ca·tion \\ˌme-də-ˈkā-shən\\ n 1 : the act or process of medicating 2 : a medicinal substance : MEDICAMENT

¹me·dic·i·nal \\mə-ˈdis-ⁿn-əl\\ adj : of, relating to, or being medicine : tending or used to cure disease or relieve pain — **me·dic·i·nal·ly** adv

²medicinal n : a medicinal substance : MEDICINE

medicinal leech n : a large European freshwater leech of the genus *Hirudo* (*H. medicinalis*) that is a source of hirudin, is now sometimes used to drain blood (as from a hematoma), and was formerly used to bleed patients thought to have excess blood

med·i·cine \\'me-də-sən\\ n 1 : a substance or preparation used in treating disease 2 a : the science and art dealing with the maintenance of health and the prevention, alleviation, or cure of disease b : the branch of medicine concerned with the nonsurgical treatment of disease

medicine cabinet n : CHEST 1

medicine chest n : CHEST 1

medicine dropper n : DROPPER

med·i·co \\'me-di-ˌkō\\ n, pl -cos : a medical practitioner : PHYSICIAN; *also* : a medical student

medico- comb form : medical : medical and (*medico*legal)

med·i·co·le·gal \\ˌme-di-kō-ˈlē-gəl\\ adj : of or relating to both medicine and law

Med·i·nal \\'me-di-ˌnal\\ trademark — used for a preparation of the sodium salt of barbital

Me·di·na worm \\mə-ˈdē-nə-\\ n : GUINEA WORM

medio- — see MEDI-

me·dio·car·pal \\ˌmē-dē-ō-ˈkär-pəl\\ adj : located between the two rows of the bones of the carpus (the ~ joint)

me·dio·lat·er·al \\-ˈla-tə-rəl\\ adj : relating to, extending along, or being a direction or axis from side to side or from median to lateral — **me·dio·lat·er·al·ly** adv

Med·i·ter·ra·nean anemia \\ˌme-də-tə-ˈrā-nē-ən-\\ n : THALASSEMIA

Mediterranean fever n : any of several febrile conditions often endemic in parts of the Mediterranean region; *specif* : BRUCELLOSIS a

me·di·um \\'mē-dē-əm\\ n, pl **mediums** or **me·dia** \\-dē-ə\\ 1 : a means of effecting or conveying something 2 pl **media** : a nutrient system for the artificial cultivation of cells or organisms and esp. bacteria

medius — see CONSTRICTOR PHARYNGIS MEDIUS, GLUTEUS MEDIUS, PEDUNCULUS CEREBELLARIS MEDIUS, SCALENUS MEDIUS

med·i·vac var of MEDEVAC

MED·LARS \\'med-ˌlärz\\ n : a computer system for the storage and retrieval of bibliographical information concerning medical literature

MED·LINE \\'med-ˌlīn\\ n : a system providing rapid access to MEDLARS through a direct telephone linkage

med·ro·ges·tone \\ˌme-drō-ˈjes-ˌtōn\\ n : a synthetic progestin $C_{23}H_{32}O_2$ that has been used in the treatment of fibroid uterine tumors

Med·rol \\'me-ˌdrōl\\ trademark — used

for a preparation of methylprednisolone

me·drox·y·pro·ges·ter·one acetate \me-ˌdräk-sē-prō-ˈjes-tə-ˌrōn\ n : a synthetic steroid progestational hormone $C_{24}H_{34}O_4$ that is used orally to treat secondary amenorrhea and abnormal uterine bleeding due to hormonal imbalance and parenterally in the palliative treatment of endometrial and renal carcinoma — called also *medroxyprogesterone*; see DEPO-PROVERA

me·dul·la \mə-ˈdə-lə, -ˈdù-\ n, pl **-las** or **-lae** \-(ˌ)lē, -ˌlī\ **1** pl **medullae a** : MARROW 1 b : MEDULLA OBLONGATA **2 a** : the inner or deep part of an organ or structure **b** : MYELIN SHEATH

medulla ob·lon·ga·ta \-ˌä-ˌblȯŋ-ˈgä-tə\ n, pl **medulla oblongatas** or **medullae oblongatae** \-ˈgä-ˌtē..-ˌtī\: the somewhat pyramidal last part of the vertebrate brain developed from the posterior portion of the hindbrain and continuous posteriorly with the spinal cord, enclosing the fourth ventricle, and containing nuclei associated with most of the cranial nerves, major fiber tracts and decussations that link spinal with higher centers, and various centers mediating the control of involuntary vital functions (as respiration)

medullaris — see CONUS MEDULLARIS

med·ul·lary \ˈmed-ᵊl-ˌer-ē. ˈme-jə-ˌler-ē; mə-ˈdə-lə-rē\ adj **1 a** : of or relating to the medulla of any body part or organ **b** : containing, consisting of, or resembling marrow **c** : of or relating to the medulla oblongata or the spinal cord **d** : of, relating to, or formed of the dorsally located embryonic ectoderm destined to sink below the surface and become neural tissue **2** : resembling marrow in consistency — used of cancers

medullary canal n : the marrow cavity of a bone

medullary cavity n : MEDULLARY CANAL

medullary cystic disease n : a progressive familial kidney disease that is characterized by renal medullary cysts and that manifests itself in anemia and uremia

medullary fold n : NEURAL FOLD

medullary groove n : NEURAL GROOVE

medullary plate n : the longitudinal dorsal zone of epiblast in the early vertebrate embryo that constitutes the primordium of the neural tissue

medulla spi·na·lis \-ˌspī-ˈnä-ləs\ n : SPINAL CORD

med·ul·lat·ed \ˈmed-ᵊl-ˌā-təd, ˈme-jə-ˌlā-\ adj **1** : MYELINATED **2** : having a medulla — used of fibers other than nerve fibers

med·ul·lec·to·my \ˌmed-ᵊl-ˈek-tə-mē, ˌme-jə-ˈlek-\ n, pl **-mies** : surgical excision of a medulla (as of the adrenal glands)

me·dul·lin \me-ˈdə-lən, ˈmed-ᵊl-in, ˈme-jə-lin\ n : a renal prostaglandin effective in reducing blood pressure

me·dul·lo·blas·to·ma \mə-ˌdə-lō-ˌblas-ˈtō-mə\ n, pl **-tomas** also **-toma·ta** \-ˈtō-mə-tə\: a malignant tumor of the central nervous system arising in the cerebellum esp. in children

mef·e·nam·ic acid \ˌme-fə-ˈna-mik-\ n : a drug $C_{15}H_{15}NO_2$ used as an anti-inflammatory

mega- or **meg-** comb form **1** : great : large ⟨*mega*colon⟩ ⟨*mega*dose⟩ **2** : million : multiplied by one million ⟨*mega*curie⟩

mega·co·lon \ˈme-gə-ˌkō-lən\ n : great often congenital dilation of the colon — see HIRSCHSPRUNG'S DISEASE

mega·cu·rie \ˈme-gə-ˌkyùr-ē, -ˌkyù-ˈrē\ n : one million curies

mega·dose \-ˌdōs\ n : a large dose (as of a vitamin) — **mega·dos·ing** \-ˌdō-siŋ\ n

mega·esoph·a·gus \ˌme-gə-i-ˈsä-fə-gəs\ n, pl **-gi** \-ˌgī. -ˌjī\ : enlargement and hypertrophy of the lower portion of the esophagus

mega·karyo·blast \ˌme-gə-ˈkar-ē-ō-ˌblast\ n : a large cell with large reticulate nucleus that gives rise to megakaryocytes

mega·karyo·cyte \ˌme-gə-ˈkar-ē-ō-ˌsīt\ n : a large cell that has a lobulated nucleus, is found esp. in the bone marrow, and is considered to be the source of blood platelets — **mega·karyo·cyt·ic** \-ˌkar-ē-ō-ˈsi-tik\ adj

megal- or **megalo-** comb form **1** : large ⟨*megalo*cyte⟩ ; abnormally large ⟨*megalo*cephaly⟩ **2** : grandiose ⟨*megalo*mania⟩

mega·lo·blast \ˈme-gə-lō-ˌblast\ n : a large erythroblast that appears in the blood esp. in pernicious anemia — **mega·lo·blas·tic** \ˌme-gə-lō-ˈblas-tik\ adj

megaloblastic anemia n : an anemia (as pernicious anemia) characterized by the presence of megaloblasts in the circulating blood

mega·lo·ceph·a·ly \ˌme-gə-lō-ˈse-fə-lē\ n, pl **-lies** : largeness and esp. abnormal largeness of the head

mega·lo·cyte \ˈme-gə-lə-ˌsīt\ n : MACROCYTE — **mega·lo·cyt·ic** \ˌme-gə-lə-ˈsi-tik\ adj

mega·lo·ma·nia \ˌme-gə-lō-ˈmā-nē-ə, -nyə\ n : a delusional mental disorder that is marked by infantile feelings of personal omnipotence and grandeur — **mega·lo·ma·ni·a·cal** \-mə-ˈnī-ə-kəl\ or **megalomaniac** also **mega·lo·man·ic** \-ˈma-nik\ adj — **mega·lo·ma·ni·a·cal·ly** adv

mega·lo·ma·ni·ac \-ˈmā-nē-ˌak\ n : an individual affected with or exhibiting megalomania

-megaly \ˈme-gə-lē\ n comb form, pl **-lies** : abnormal enlargement (of a specified part) ⟨hepato*megaly*⟩ ⟨spleno*megaly*⟩

mega·rad \'me-gə-ˌrad\ *n* : one million rads

mega·vi·ta·min \ˌme-gə-'vī-tə-mən\ *adj* : relating to or consisting of very large doses of vitamins

mega·vi·ta·mins \-mənz\ *n pl* : a large quantity of vitamins

me·ges·trol acetate \me-'jes-ˌtról-\ *n* : a synthetic progestational hormone $C_{24}H_{32}O_4$ used in palliative treatment of advanced carcinoma of the breast and in endometriosis

Meg·i·mide \'me-gə-ˌmīd\ *trademark* — used for a preparation of bemegride

meg·lu·mine \'me-glù-ˌmēn, me-'glü-\ *n* : a crystalline base $C_7H_{17}NO_5$ used to prepare salts used in radiopaque and therapeutic substances — see IODIPAMIDE

me·grim \'mē-grəm\ *n* 1 a : MIGRAINE b : VERTIGO 2 : any of numerous diseases of animals marked by disturbance of equilibrium and abnormal gait and behavior — usu. used in pl.

mei·bo·mian gland \mī-'bō-mē-ən-\ *n, often cap M* : one of the long sebaceous glands of the eyelids that discharge a fatty secretion which lubricates the eyelids — called also *tarsal gland;* see CHALAZION

    Mei·bom \'mī-ˌbōm\, **Heinrich** (1638–1700), German physician.

mei·o·sis \mī-'ō-səs\ *n, pl* **mei·o·ses** \-ˌsēz\ : the cellular process that results in the number of chromosomes in gamete-producing cells being reduced to one half and that involves a reduction division in which one of each pair of homologous chromosomes passes to each daughter cell and a mitotic division — compare MITOSIS 1 — **mei·ot·ic** \mī-'ä-tik\ *adj* — **mei·ot·i·cal·ly** *adv*

Meiss·ner's corpuscle \'mīs-nərz-\ *n* : any of the small elliptical tactile end organs in hairless skin containing numerous transversely placed tactile cells and fine flattened nerve endings

    Meissner, Georg (1829–1905), German anatomist and physiologist.

Meissner's plexus *n* : a plexus of ganglionated nerve fibers lying between the muscular and mucous coats of the intestine — compare MYENTERIC PLEXUS

mel \'mel\ *n* : a subjective unit of tone pitch equal to 1/1000 of the pitch of a tone having a frequency of 1000 cycles — used esp. in audiology

me·lae·na *chiefly Brit var of* MELENA

melan- *or* **melano-** *comb form* 1 : black : dark ⟨*melan*in⟩ ⟨*melan*oma⟩ 2 : melanin ⟨*melan*ogenesis⟩

mel·an·cho·lia \ˌme-lən-'kō-lē-ə\ *n* : a mental condition characterized by extreme depression, bodily complaints, and often hallucinations and delusions; *esp* : MANIC-DEPRESSIVE PSYCHOSIS

mel·an·cho·li·ac \-lē-ˌak\ *n* : an individual affected with melancholia

¹mel·an·chol·ic \ˌme-lən-'kä-lik\ *adj* 1 : of, relating to, or subject to melancholy : DEPRESSED 2 : of or relating to melancholia

²melancholic *n* 1 : a melancholy person 2 : MELANCHOLIAC

mel·an·choly \'me-lən-ˌkä-lē\ *n, pl* **-chol·ies** 1 : MELANCHOLIA 2 : depression or dejection of spirits — **melancholy** *adj*

mel·a·nin \'me-lə-nən\ *n* 1 : any of various dark brown or black pigments of animal or plant structures (as skin or hair) 2 : any of various pigments that are similar to the natural melanins and are obtained esp. by enzymatic oxidation of tyrosine or dopa

mel·a·nism \'me-lə-ˌni-zəm\ *n* 1 : an increased amount of black or nearly black pigmentation (as of skin, feathers, or hair) of an individual or kind of organism 2 : intense human pigmentation in skin, eyes, and hair — **mel·a·nis·tic** \ˌme-lə-'nis-tik\ *adj*

mel·a·nize \'me-lə-ˌnīz\ *vb* **-nized; -niz·ing** : to convert into or infiltrate with melanin ⟨*melanized* cell granules⟩ — **mel·a·ni·za·tion** \ˌme-lə-nə-'zā-shən\ *n*

melano- — see MELAN-

me·la·no·blast \mə-'la-nə-ˌblast, 'me-lə-nō-\ *n* : a cell that is a precursor of a melanocyte

me·la·no·blas·to·ma \mə-ˌla-nə-blas-'tō-mə, ˌme-lə-nō-\ *n, pl* **-mas** *or* **-ma·ta** \-mə-tə\ : a malignant tumor derived from melanoblasts

mel·a·no·car·ci·no·ma \-ˌkärs-ᵊn-'ō-mə\ *n, pl* **-mas** *or* **-ma·ta** \-mə-tə\ : a melanoma believed to be of epithelial origin

me·la·no·cyte \mə-'la-nə-ˌsīt, 'me-lə-nō-\ *n* : an epidermal cell that produces melanin

melanocyte–stimulating hormone *n* : either of two vertebrate hormones of the pituitary gland that darken the skin by stimulating melanin dispersion in pigment-containing cells — abbr. *MSH;* called also *intermedin, melanophore-stimulating hormone, melanotropin*

me·la·no·cyt·ic \mə-ˌla-nə-'si-tik, ˌme-lə-nō-\ *adj* : similar to or characterized by the presence of melanocytes

me·la·no·cy·to·ma \-sī-'tō-mə\ *n, pl* **-mas** *or* **-ma·ta** \-mə-tə\ : a benign tumor composed of melanocytes

mel·a·no·der·ma \ˌme-lə-nō-'dər-mə, mə-ˌla-\ *n* : abnormally intense pigmentation of the skin

me·la·no·gen·e·sis \mə-ˌla-nə-'je-nə-səs, ˌme-lə-nō-\ *n, pl* **-e·ses** \-ˌsēz\ : the formation of melanin

me·la·no·gen·ic \-'je-nik\ *adj* 1 : of, relating to, or characteristic of melanogenesis 2 : producing melanin

mel·a·no·ma \ˌme-lə-'nō-mə\ *n, pl* **-mas** *also* **-ma·ta** \-mə-tə\ 1 : a benign or malignant skin tumor containing dark pigment 2 : a tumor of high malignancy that starts in melanocytes of normal skin or moles and metastasizes rapidly and widely — called also *melanosarcoma*

me·la·no·phage \mə-ˈla-nə-ˌfāj, ˈme-lə-nə-\ *n* : a melanin-containing cell which obtains the pigment by phagocytosis

me·la·no·phore–stimulating hormone \mə-ˈla-nō-ˌfōr-, ˈme-lə-nə-\ *n* : MELANOCYTE-STIMULATING HORMONE

me·la·no·sar·co·ma \-sär-ˈkō-mə\ *n, pl* **-mas** *or* **-ma·ta** \-mə-tə\ : MELANOMA 2

mel·a·no·sis \ˌme-lə-ˈnō-səs\ *n, pl* **-no·ses** \-ˈnō-ˌsēz\ : a condition characterized by abnormal deposition of melanins or sometimes other pigments in the tissues of the body

melanosis co·li \-ˈkō-ˌlī\ *n* : dark brownish black pigmentation of the mucous membrane of the colon due to the deposition of pigment in macrophages

me·la·no·some \mə-ˈla-nə-ˌsōm, ˈme-lə-nō-\ *n* : a melanin-producing granule in a melanocyte — **me·la·no·som·al** \mə-ˌla-nə-ˈsō-məl, ˌme-lə-nō-\ *adj*

mel·a·not·ic \ˌme-lə-ˈnä-tik\ *adj* : having or characterized by black pigmentation (a ~ sarcoma)

me·la·no·tro·pin \ˌme-lə-nə-ˈtrō-pən, ˌme-lə-nō-\ *n* : MELANOCYTE-STIMULATING HORMONE

me·lar·so·prol \mə-ˈlar-sə-ˌprōl\ *n* : a drug $C_{12}H_{15}AsN_6OS_2$ used in the treatment of trypanosomiasis esp. in advanced stages

me·las·ma \mə-ˈlaz-mə\ *n* : a dark pigmentation of the skin (as in Addison's disease) — **me·las·mic** \-mik\ *adj*

mel·a·to·nin \ˌme-lə-ˈtō-nən\ *n* : a vertebrate hormone $C_{13}H_{16}N_2O_2$ that is derived from serotonin, is secreted by the pineal gland especially in response to darkness, and has been linked to the regulation of circadian rhythms

me·le·na \mə-ˈlē-nə\ *n* : the passage of dark tarry stools containing decomposing blood that is usu. an indication of bleeding in the upper part of the alimentary canal — compare HEMATOCHEZIA

mel·en·ges·trol acetate \ˌme-lən-ˈjes-ˌtrōl-, -ˌtrōl-\ *n* : a progestational and antineoplastic agent $C_{25}H_{32}O_4$ that has been used as a growth-stimulating feed additive for beef cattle

-me·lia \ˈmē-lē-ə\ *n comb form* : condition of the limbs (micromelia) (hemimelia)

mel·i·oi·do·sis \ˌme-lē-ˌȯi-ˈdō-səs\ *n, pl* **-do·ses** \-ˌsēz\ : a highly fatal bacterial disease closely related to glanders that occurs naturally in rodents of southeastern Asia but is readily transmitted to other mammals and humans by the rat flea or under certain conditions by dissemination in air of the causative bacterium of the genus *Pseudomonas* (*P. pseudomallei*)

me·lit·tin \mə-ˈlit-ᵊn\ *n* : a toxic protein in bee venom that causes localized pain and inflammation

Mel·la·ril \ˈme-lə-ˌril\ *trademark* — used for a preparation of thioridazine

mellitus — see DIABETES MELLITUS, INSULIN-DEPENDENT DIABETES MELLITUS, NON-INSULIN-DEPENDENT DIABETES MELLITUS

Me·loph·a·gus \mə-ˈlä-fə-gəs\ *n* : a genus of wingless flies (family Hippoboscidae) that includes the sheep ked (*M. ovinus*)

melo·rhe·os·to·sis \ˌme-lə-ˌrē-ä-ˈstō-səs\ *n, pl* **-to·ses** \-ˌsēz\ *or* **-tosises** : an extremely rare form of osteosclerosis characterized by asymmetrical or local enlargement and sclerotic changes in the long bones of one extremity

Mel·ox·ine \mə-ˈläk-ˌsēn\ *trademark* — used for a preparation of methoxsalen

mel·pha·lan \ˈmel-fə-ˌlan\ *n* : an antineoplastic drug $C_{13}H_{18}Cl_2N_2O_2$ that is a derivative of nitrogen mustard and is used esp. in the treatment of multiple myeloma — called also *L-PAM, phenylalanine mustard, sarcolysin*

melting point *n* : the temperature at which a solid melts

-melus \mə-ləs\ *n comb form* : one having a (specified) abnormality of the limbs (phocomelus)

mem·ber \ˈmem-bər\ *n* : a body part or organ: as **a** : LIMB **b** : PENIS

membran- *or* **membrani-** *or* **membrano-** *comb form* : membrane (membranoproliferative glomerulonephritis)

mem·bra·na \mem-ˈbrā-nə, -ˈbrä-\ *n, pl* **mem·bra·nae** \-ˌnē, -ˌnī\ : MEMBRANE

membrana nic·ti·tans \-ˈnik-tə-ˌtanz\ *n* : NICTITATING MEMBRANE

mem·brane \ˈmem-ˌbrān\ *n* **1** : a thin soft pliable sheet or layer esp. of animal or plant origin **2** : a limiting protoplasmic surface or interface — see NUCLEAR MEMBRANE, PLASMA MEMBRANE — **mem·braned** \ˈmem-ˌbränd\ *adj*

membrane bone *n* : a bone that ossifies directly in connective tissue without previous existence as cartilage

membrane of Descemet *n* : DESCEMET'S MEMBRANE

membrane potential *n* : the difference in electrical potential between the interior of a cell and the interstitial fluid beyond the membrane

mem·bra·no·pro·lif·er·a·tive glomerulonephritis \mem-ˌbrā-nō-prə-ˈli-fə-rə-tiv-\ *n* : a slowly progressive chronic glomerulonephritis characterized by proliferation of mesangial cells and irregular thickening of glomerular capillary walls and narrowing of the capillary lumina

mem·bra·nous \ˈmem-brə-nəs\ *adj* **1** : of, relating to, or resembling membranes **2** : characterized or accompanied by the formation of a usu. abnormal membrane or membranous layer (~ gastritis) — **mem·bra·nous·ly** *adv*

membranous glomerulonephritis *n* : a form of glomerulonephritis characterized by thickening of glomerular capillary basement membranes and nephrotic syndrome

membranous labyrinth *n* : the sensory structures of the inner ear including the receptors of the labyrinthine sense and the cochlea — see BONY LABYRINTH

membranous urethra *n* : the part of the male urethra that is situated between the layers of the urogenital diaphragm and that connects the parts of the urethra passing through the prostate gland and the penis

mem·o·ry \'mem-rē, 'me-mə-\ *n, pl* **-ries 1** : the power or process of reproducing or recalling what has been learned and retained esp. through associative mechanisms **2** : the store of things learned and retained from an organism's activity or experience as indicated by modification of structure or behavior or by recall and recognition

memory trace *n* : ENGRAM

men *pl of* MAN

men- *or* **meno-** *comb form* : menstruation (*meno*pause) (*meno*rrhagia)

men·a·di·one \me-nə-'dī-ˌōn, -dī-'\ *n* : a yellow crystalline compound $C_{11}H_8O_2$ with the biological activity of natural vitamin K — called also *vitamin K_3*

me·naph·thone \mə-'naf-ˌthōn\ *n, Brit* : MENADIONE

men·a·quin·one \ˌme-nə-'kwi-ˌnōn\ *n* : VITAMIN K 1b; *also* : a synthetic derivative of vitamin K_2

men·ar·che \'me-ˌnär-kē\ *n* : the beginning of the menstrual function; *esp* : the first menstrual period of an individual — **men·ar·che·al** \ˌme-'när-kē-əl\ *or* **men·ar·chal** \-kəl\ *adj*

¹**mend** \'mend\ *vb* **1** : to restore to health : CURE **2** : to improve in health; *also* : HEAL

²**mend** *n* : an act of mending or repair — **on the mend** : getting better or improving esp. in health

men·de·le·vi·um \ˌmen-də-'lē-vē-əm, -'lā-\ *n* : a radioactive element that is artificially produced — symbol *Md* or *Mv*; see ELEMENT table

Men·de·lian \men-'dē-lē-ən, -'dēl-yən\ *adj* : of, relating to, or according with Mendel's laws or Mendelism — **Mendelian** *n*

Men·del \'mend-ᵊl\, **Gregor Johann (1822–1884),** Austrian botanist and geneticist.

Mendelian factor *n* : GENE

Mendelian inheritance *n* : PARTICULATE INHERITANCE

Men·del·ism \'mend-ᵊl-ˌi-zəm\ *n* : the principles or the operations of Mendel's laws; *also* : PARTICULATE INHERITANCE

Men·del's law \'men-dᵊlz-\ *n* **1** : a principle in genetics: hereditary units occur in pairs that separate during gamete formation so that every gamete receives but one member of a pair — called also *law of segregation* **2** : a principle in genetics limited and modified by the subsequent discovery of the phenomenon of linkage: the different pairs of hereditary units are distributed to the gametes independently of each other, the gametes combine at random, and the various combinations of hereditary pairs occur in the zygotes according to the laws of chance — called also *law of independent assortment* **3** : a principle in genetics proved subsequently to be subject to many limitations: because one of each pair of hereditary units dominates the other in expression, characters are inherited as alternatives on an all or nothing basis — called also *law of dominance*

men·go·vi·rus \'meŋ-gō-ˌvī-rəs\ *n* : an enterovirus that causes encephalomyocarditis and has been found esp. in rodents and primates

Mé·nière's disease \mən-'yerz-, 'men-yərz-\ *n* : a disorder of the membranous labyrinth of the inner ear that is marked by recurrent attacks of dizziness, tinnitus, and deafness — called also *Ménière's syndrome*

Ménière, Prosper (1799–1862), French physician.

mening- *or* **meningo-** *also* **meningi-** *comb form* **1** : meninges (*meningo*coccus) (*meningi*tis) **2** : meninges and (*meningo*encephalitis)

men·in·ge·al \ˌme-nən-'jē-əl\ *adj* : of, relating to, or affecting the meninges

meningeal artery *n* : any of several arteries supplying the meninges of the brain and neighboring structures; *esp* : MIDDLE MENINGEAL ARTERY

meningeal vein *n* : any of several veins draining the meninges of the brain and neighboring structures

meninges *pl of* MENINX

me·nin·gi·o·ma \mə-ˌnin-jē-'ō-mə\ *n, pl* **-o·mas** *or* **-o·ma·ta** \-'ō-mə-tə\ : a slowgrowing encapsulated tumor arising from the meninges and often causing damage by pressing upon the brain and adjacent parts

men·in·gism \'me-nən-ˌji-zəm, mə-'nin-\ *n* : MENINGISMUS

men·in·gis·mus \ˌme-nən-'jiz-məs\ *n, pl* **-gis·mi** \-ˌmī\ : a state of meningeal irritation with symptoms suggesting meningitis that often occurs at the onset of acute febrile diseases esp. in children

men·in·gi·tis \ˌme-nən-'jī-təs\ *n, pl* **-git·i·des** \-'ji-tə-ˌdēz\ **1** : inflammation of the meninges and esp. of the pia mater and the arachnoid **2** : a usu. bacterial disease in which inflammation of the meninges occurs — **men·in·git·ic** \-'jit-ik\ *adj*

me·nin·go·cele \me-'niŋ-gə-₁sēl, mə-'nin-jə-\ *n* : a protrusion of meninges through a defect in the skull or spinal column forming a cyst filled with cerebrospinal fluid

me·nin·go·coc·cae·mia *chiefly Brit var of* MENINGOCOCCEMIA

me·nin·go·coc·ce·mia \mə-₁niŋ-gō-käk-'sē-mē-ə, -₁nin-jə-\ *n* : an abnormal condition characterized by the presence of meningococci in the blood

me·nin·go·coc·cus \mə-₁niŋ-gə-'kä-kəs, -₁nin-jə-\ *n, pl* **-coc·ci** \-'kä-₁kī, -₁kē; -'käk-₁sī, -₁sē\ : a bacterium of the genus *Neisseria* (*N. meningitidis*) that causes cerebrospinal meningitis — **me·nin·go·coc·cal** \-'kä-kəl\ *also* **me·nin·go·coc·cic** \-'kä-kik, -'käk-sik\ *adj*

me·nin·go·coele *var of* MENINGOCELE

me·nin·go·en·ceph·a·li·tis \-in-₁se-fə-'lī-təs\ *n, pl* **-lit·i·des** \-'li-tə-₁dēz\ : inflammation of the brain and meninges — **me·nin·go·en·ceph·a·lit·ic** \mə-nin-(₁)gō-ən-₁se-fə-'li-tik, -₁nin-(₁)jō-\ *adj*

me·nin·go·en·ceph·a·lo·cele \-in-'se-fə-lō-₁sēl\ *n* : a protrusion of meninges and brain through a defect in the skull

me·nin·go·en·ceph·a·lo·my·eli·tis \-in-₁se-fə-lō-₁mī-ə-'lī-təs, *n, pl* **-elit·i·des** \-ə-'li-tə-₁dēz\ : inflammation of the meninges, brain, and spinal cord

me·nin·go·my·elo·cele \-'mī-ə-lō-₁sēl\ *n* : a protrusion of meninges and spinal cord through a defect in the spinal column

me·nin·go·vas·cu·lar \-'vas-kyə-lər\ *adj* : of, relating to, or affecting the meninges and the cerebral blood vessels

me·ninx \'mē-niŋks, 'me-\ *n, pl* **me·nin·ges** \mə-'nin-(₁)jēz\ : any of the three membranes that envelop the brain and spinal cord and include the arachnoid, dura mater, and pia mater

me·nis·cal \mə-'nis-kəl\ *adj* : of or relating to a meniscus (a ~ tear)

men·is·cec·to·my \₁me-ni-'sek-tə-mē\ *n, pl* **-mies** : surgical excision of a meniscus of the knee or temporomandibular joint

me·nis·cus \mə-'nis-kəs\ *n, pl* **me·nis·ci** \-'nis-₁kī, -₁kē; -'nī-₁sī\ *also* **me·nis·cus·es** : a fibrous cartilage within a joint: **a** : either of two crescent-shaped lamellae of fibrocartilage that border and partly cover the articulating surfaces of the tibia and femur at the knee: SEMILUNAR CARTILAGE: (1) : one mostly between the lateral condyles of the tibia and femur — called also *lateral meniscus, lateral semilunar cartilage* (2) : one mostly between the medial condyles of the tibia and femur — called also *medial meniscus, medial semilunar cartilage* **b** : a thin oval ligament of the temporomandibular joint that is situated between the condyle of the mandible

and the mandibular fossa and separates the joint into two cavities

meno·met·ror·rha·gia \₁me-nō-₁mē-trə-'rä-jə, -'rä-, -jē-ə, -zhə\ *n* : a combination of menorrhagia and metrorrhagia

meno·pause \'me-nə-₁pöz, 'mē-\ *n* 1 : the period of natural cessation of menstruation occurring usu. between the ages of 45 and 50 2 : CLIMACTERIC — **meno·paus·al** \₁me-nə-'pö-zəl, ₁mē-\ *adj*

Men·o·pon \'me-nə-₁pän\ *n* : a genus of biting lice that includes the shaft louse (*M. gallinae*) of poultry

men·or·rha·gia \₁me-nə-'rä-jə, -'rä-, -jē-ə, -zhə\ *n* : abnormally profuse menstrual flow — compare HYPERMENORRHEA, METRORRHAGIA — **men·or·rhag·ic** \-'ra-jik\ *adj*

men·or·rhea \₁me-nə-'rē-ə\ *n* : normal menstrual flow

men·or·rhoea *chiefly Brit var of* MENORRHEA

men·ses \'men-₁sēz\ *n sing or pl* : the menstrual flow

men·stru·al \'men-strə-wəl\ *adj* : of or relating to menstruation — **men·stru·al·ly** *adv*

menstrual cycle *n* : the whole cycle of physiologic changes from the beginning of one menstrual period to the beginning of the next

menstrual extraction *n* : a procedure for shortening the menstrual period or for early termination of pregnancy by withdrawing the uterine lining and a fertilized egg if present by means of suction

men·stru·a·tion \₁men-strə-'wä-shən\ *n* : a discharging of blood, secretions, and tissue debris from the uterus that recurs in nonpregnant human and other primate females of breeding age at approximately monthly intervals and that is considered to represent a readjustment of the uterus to the nonpregnant state following proliferative changes accompanying the preceding ovulation; *also* : PERIOD 1b — **men·stru·ate** \'men-strə-₁wāt\ *vb* — **men·stru·ous** \'men-strə-wəs\ *adj*

men·stru·um \'men-strə-wəm\ *n, pl* **-struums** *or* **-strua** \-strə-wə\ : a substance that dissolves a solid or holds it in suspension : SOLVENT

menta *pl of* MENTUM

¹**men·tal** \'ment-ᵊl\ *adj* 1 **a** : of or relating to the mind; *specif* : of or relating to the total emotional and intellectual response of an individual to external reality **b** : of or relating to intellectual activity as contrasted with emotional activity 2 **a** : of, relating to, or affected by a psychiatric disorder **b** : intended for the care or treatment of persons affected by psychiatric disorders (~ hospitals) — **men·tal·ly** *adv*

²**mental** *adj* : of or relating to the chin : GENIAL

mental age *n* : a measure used in psychological testing that expresses an individual's mental attainment in terms of the number of years it takes an average child to reach the same level

mental artery n : a branch of the inferior alveolar artery on each side that emerges from the mental foramen and supplies blood to the chin — called also *mental branch*

mental capacity n 1 : sufficient understanding and memory to comprehend in a general way the situation in which one finds oneself and the nature, purpose, and consequence of any act or transaction into which one proposes to enter 2 : the degree of understanding and memory the law requires to uphold the validity of or to charge one with responsibility for a particular act or transaction

mental competence n : MENTAL CAPACITY

mental deficiency n : MENTAL RETARDATION

mental disorder n : MENTAL ILLNESS

mental foramen n : a foramen for the passage of blood vessels and a nerve on the outside of the lower jaw on each side near the chin

mental health n : the condition of being sound mentally and emotionally that is characterized by the absence of mental illness (as neurosis or psychosis) and by adequate adjustment esp. as reflected in feeling comfortable about oneself, positive feelings about others, and ability to meet the demands of life; *also* : the field of mental health : MENTAL HYGIENE

mental hygiene n : the science of maintaining mental health and preventing the development of mental illness

mental illness n : a mental or bodily condition marked primarily by sufficient disorganization of personality, mind, and emotions to seriously impair the normal psychological functioning of the individual — called also *mental disorder*

mental incapacity n 1 : an absence of mental capacity 2 : an inability through mental illness or mental retardation to carry on the everyday affairs of life or to care for one's person or property with reasonable discretion

mental incompetence n : MENTAL INCAPACITY

men·ta·lis \men-ᵗtā-lis\ n, pl **men·ta·les** \-ˌlēz\ : a muscle that originates in the incisive fossa of the mandible, inserts in the skin of the chin, and raises the chin and pushes up the lower lip

men·tal·i·ty \men-ᵗta-lə-tē\ n, pl **-ties** 1 : mental power or capacity 2 : mode or way of thought

mental nerve n : a branch of the inferior alveolar nerve that emerges from the bone of the mandible near the mental

protuberance and divides into branches which are distributed to the skin of the chin and to the skin and mucous membranes of the lower lip

mental protuberance n : the bony protuberance at the front of the lower jaw forming the chin

mental retardation n : subaverage intellectual ability that is equivalent to or less than an IQ of 70, is present from birth or infancy, and is manifested esp. by abnormal development, by learning difficulties, and by problems in social adjustment — **mentally retarded** adj

mental spine n : either of two small elevations on the inner surface of each side of the symphysis of the lower jaw of which the superior one on each side provides attachment for the genioglossus and the inferior for the geniohyoid muscle

mental test n : any of various standardized procedures applied to an individual in order to ascertain ability or evaluate behavior

mental tubercle n : a prominence on each side of the mental protuberance of the mandible — called also *genial tubercle*

men·ta·tion \men-ᵗtā-shən\ n : mental activity (unconscious ~)

men·thol \ᵗmen-ˌthȯl, -ˌthōl\ n : a crystalline alcohol $C_{10}H_{20}O$ that occurs esp. in mint oils, has the odor and cooling properties of peppermint, and is used in flavoring and in medicine (as locally to relieve pain, itching, and nasal congestion)

men·tho·lat·ed \ᵗmen-thə-ˌlā-təd\ adj : containing or impregnated with menthol (a ~ salve)

mentis — see COMPOS MENTIS, NON COMPOS MENTIS

men·tum \ᵗmen-təm\ n, pl **men·ta** \-tə\ : CHIN

Me·o·nine \ᵗmē-ə-ˌnīn\ trademark — used for a preparation of methionine

mep·a·crine \ᵗme-pə-ˌkrēn, -krən\ n, chiefly Brit : QUINACRINE

mep·a·zine \ᵗme-pə-ˌzēn\ n : a phenothiazine tranquilizer $C_{19}H_{22}N_2S$ administered in the form of the acetate or hydrochloride

me·pen·zo·late bromide \mə-ᵗpen-zə-ˌlāt-\ n : an anticholinergic drug $C_{21}H_{26}BrNO_3$

me·per·i·dine \mə-ᵗper-ə-ˌdēn\ n : a synthetic narcotic drug $C_{15}H_{21}NO_2$ used in the form of its hydrochloride as an analgesic, sedative, and antispasmodic — called also *isonipecaine, pethidine*

me·phen·e·sin \mə-ᵗfe-nə-sin\ n : a crystalline compound $C_{10}H_{14}O_3$ used chiefly in the treatment of neuromuscular conditions — called also *myanesin*

meph·en·ox·a·lone \ˌme-fə-ᵗnäk-sə-ˌlōn\ n : a tranquilizing drug $C_{11}H_{13}NO_4$

me·phen·ter·mine \mə-ˈfen-tər-ˌmēn\ *n* : an adrenergic drug $C_{11}H_{17}N$ administered often in the form of the sulfate as a vasopressor and nasal decongestant

me·phen·y·to·in \mə-ˈfe-ni-ˌtō-in\ *n* : an anticonvulsant drug $C_{12}H_{14}N_2O_2$ — see MESANTOIN

mepho·bar·bi·tal \ˌme-fō-ˈbär-bə-ˌtäl\ *n* : a crystalline barbiturate $C_{13}H_{14}N_2O_3$ used as a sedative and in the treatment of epilepsy

Mephy·ton \ˈme-fə-ˌtän\ *trademark* — used for a preparation of vitamin K_1

me·piv·a·caine \me-ˈpi-və-ˌkān\ *n* : a drug $C_{15}H_{22}N_2O$ used esp. in the form of the hydrochloride as a local anesthetic

Me·prane \ˈmē-ˌprän\ *trademark* — used for a preparation of promethestrol

mep·ro·bam·ate \ˌme-prō-ˈba-ˌmāt, mə-ˈprō-bə-ˌmāt\ *n* : a bitter carbamate $C_9H_{18}N_2O_4$ used as a tranquilizer — see MEPROSPAN, MILTOWN

Mep·ro·span \ˈme-prō-ˌspan\ *trademark* — used for a preparation of meprobamate

¹mer- *or* **mero-** *comb form* : thigh ⟨*meralgia*⟩

²mer- *or* **mero-** *comb form* : part : partial ⟨*meroblastic*⟩

me·ral·gia \mə-ˈral-jə, -jē-ə\ *n* : pain esp. of a neuralgic kind in the thigh

meralgia par·es·thet·i·ca *Brit var of* MERALGIA PARESTHETICA

meralgia par·es·thet·i·ca \-ˌpar-əs-ˈthe-ti-kə\ *n* : an abnormal condition characterized by pain and paresthesia in the outer surface of the thigh

mer·al·lu·ride \mə-ˈral-yə-ˌrīd, -rid\ *n* : a diuretic consisting of a chemical combination of an organic mercurial compound $C_9H_{16}HgN_2O_6$ and theophylline and administered chiefly by injection as an aqueous solution of its sodium salt — see MERCUHYDRIN

mer·bro·min \ˌmər-ˈbrō-mən\ *n* : a green crystalline mercurial compound $C_{20}H_8Br_2HgNa_2O_6$ used as a topical antiseptic and germicide in the form of its red solution — see MERCUROCHROME

mer·cap·tom·er·in \(ˌ)mər-ˌkap-ˈtä-mə-rən\ *n* : a mercurial diuretic related chemically to mercurophylline and administered by injection of an aqueous solution of its sodium salt $C_{16}H_{25}HgNNa_2O_6S$

mer·cap·to·pu·rine \(ˌ)mər-ˌkap-tə-ˈpyu̇r-ˌēn\ *n* : an antimetabolite $C_5H_4N_4S$ that interferes esp. with the metabolism of purine bases and the biosynthesis of nucleic acids and that is sometimes useful in the treatment of acute leukemia

Mer·cu·hy·drin \ˌmər-kyū-ˈhī-drən\ *trademark* — used for a preparation of meralluride

mer·cu·mat·i·lin \ˌmər-kyū-ˈmat-əl-ən, mər-ˌkyü-mə-ˈti-lən\ *n* : a mercurial diuretic consisting of a mercury= containing acid $C_{14}H_{14}HgO_6$ and theophylline that is often administered in the form of the sodium salt

¹mer·cu·ri·al \(ˌ)mər-ˈkyu̇r-ē-əl\ *adj* : of, relating to, containing, or caused by mercury ⟨~ salves⟩

²mercurial *n* : a pharmaceutical or chemical containing mercury

mer·cu·ri·al·ism \(ˌ)mər-ˈkyu̇r-ē-ə-ˌli-zəm\ *n* : chronic poisoning with mercury (as from industrial contacts with the metal or its fumes) — called also *hydrargyrism*

mer·cu·ric chloride \(ˌ)mər-ˌkyu̇r-ik-\ *n* : a heavy crystalline poisonous compound $HgCl_2$ used as a disinfectant and fungicide — called also *bichloride of mercury, corrosive sublimate, mercury bichloride*

mercuric cyanide *n* : the mercury cyanide $Hg(CN)_2$ which has been used as an antiseptic

mercuric iodide *n* : a red crystalline poisonous salt HgI_2 which has been used as a topical antiseptic

mercuric oxide *n* : either of two forms of a slightly water-soluble crystalline poisonous compound HgO which has been used in antiseptic ointments

Mer·cu·ro·chrome \(ˌ)mər-ˈkyu̇r-ə-ˌkrōm\ *trademark* — used for a preparation of merbromin

mer·cu·ro·phyl·line \ˌmər-kyə-rō-ˈfi-ˌlēn, -lən\ *n* : a diuretic consisting of a chemical combination of an organic mercurial compound or its sodium salt $C_{14}H_{24}HgNNaO_5$ and theophylline — see MERCUZANTHIN

mer·cu·rous chloride \ˌmər-ˈkyu̇r-əs-, ˈmər-kyə-rəs-\ *n* : CALOMEL

mer·cu·ry \ˈmər-kyə-rē\ *n, pl* **-ries** **1** : a heavy silver-white poisonous metallic element that is liquid at ordinary temperatures — symbol *Hg*; called also *quicksilver*; see ELEMENT table **2** : a pharmaceutical preparation containing mercury or a compound of it

mercury bi·chlo·ride \-ˌbī-ˈklōr-ˌīd\ *n* : MERCURIC CHLORIDE

mercury chloride *n* : a chloride of mercury: as **a** : CALOMEL **b** : MERCURIC CHLORIDE

mercury–vapor lamp *n* : an electric lamp in which the discharge takes place through mercury vapor and which has been used therapeutically as a source of ultraviolet radiation

Mer·cu·zan·thin \ˌmər-kyū-ˈzan-thən\ *trademark* — used for a preparation of mercurophylline

mercy killing *n* : EUTHANASIA

-mere \ˌmir\ *n comb form* : part : segment ⟨*blastomere*⟩ ⟨*centromere*⟩

mer·eth·oxy·ll·ine procaine \ˌmər-e-ˌthäk-sə-ˌlin-\ *n* : a mercurial diuretic $C_{15}H_{19}HgNO_6 \cdot C_{13}H_{20}N_2O_2$

me·rid·i·an \mə-ˈri-dē-ən\ *n* **1** : an imaginary circle or closed curve on the surface of a sphere or globe= shaped body (as the eyeball) that lies in a plane passing through the poles **2** : any of the pathways along which the body's vital energy flows according to the theory of acupuncture — **meridian** *adj* — **me·rid·i·o·nal** \mə-ˈri-dē-ən-ᵊl\ *adj*

Mer·kel–Ran·vier corpuscle \ˈmer-kəl-ˌrän-ˈvyā-\ *n* : MERKEL'S DISK
   Merkel, Friedrich Siegmund (1845–1919), German anatomist.
   Ranvier, Louis-Antoine (1835–1922), French histologist.

Mer·kel's disk \ˈmer-kəlz-\ *n* : a touch receptor of the deep layers of the skin consisting of a flattened or cupped body associated peripherally with a large modified epithelial cell and centrally with an efferent nerve fiber — called also *Merkel's cell, Merkel's corpuscle*

mero- — see MER-

mero·blas·tic \ˌmer-ə-ˈblas-tik\ *adj* : characterized by or being incomplete cleavage as a result of the presence of an impeding mass of yolk material (as in the eggs of birds, class Aves) — compare HOLOBLASTIC — **mero·blas·ti·cal·ly** *adv*

mero·crine \ˈmer-ə-krən, -ˌkrīn, -ˌkrēn\ *adj* : producing a secretion that is discharged without major damage to the secreting cells (~ glands); *also* : of or produced by a merocrine gland (a ~ secretion) — compare APOCRINE, ECCRINE, HOLOCRINE

mero·my·o·sin \ˌmer-ə-ˈmī-ə-sən\ *n* : either of two structural subunits of myosin that are obtained esp. by tryptic digestion

mero·zo·ite \ˌmer-ə-ˈzō-ˌīt\ *n* : a small ameboid sporozoan trophozoite (as of a malaria parasite) produced by schizogony that is capable of initiating a new sexual or asexual cycle of development

mer·sal·yl \(ˌ)mər-ˈsa-lil\ *n* : an organic mercurial $C_{13}H_{16}HgNNaO_6$ administered by injection in combination with theophylline as a diuretic

Mer·thi·o·late \(ˌ)mər-ˈthī-ə-ˌlāt, -lət\ *trademark* — used for a preparation of thimerosal

mes- *or* **meso-** *comb form* **1 a** : mid : in the middle ⟨*meso*derm⟩ **b** : mesentery or membrane supporting a (specified) part ⟨*meso*appendix⟩ ⟨*meso*colon⟩ **2** : intermediate (as in size or type) ⟨*meso*morph⟩

mes·an·gi·um \me-ˈsan-jē-əm, mē-\ *n*, *pl* **-gia** \-jē-ə\ : a thin membrane that gives support to the capillaries surrounding the tubule of a nephron — **mes·an·gi·al** \-jē-əl\ *adj*

Mes·an·to·in \me-ˈsan-tō-in\ *trademark* — used for a preparation of mephenytoin

mes·aor·ti·tis \ˌme-ˌsā-ȯr-ˈtī-təs, ˌmē-\ *n*, *pl* **-tit·i·des** \-ˈti-tə-ˌdēz\ : inflammation of the middle layer of the aorta

mes·ar·ter·i·tis \-ˌsär-tə-ˈrī-təs\ *n*, *pl* **-it-**

i·des \-ˈri-tə-ˌdēz\ : inflammation of the middle layer of an artery

mes·cal \me-ˈskal, mə-\ *n* **1** : a small cactus (*Lophophora williamsii*) with rounded stems covered with jointed tubercles that are used as a stimulant and antispasmodic esp. among the Mexican Indians **2** : a usu. colorless Mexican liquor distilled esp. from the central leaves of any of various fleshy-leaved agaves (genus *Agave* of the family Agavaceae); *also* : a plant from which mescal is produced

mescal button *n* : one of the dried discoid tops of the mescal

mes·ca·line \ˈmes-kə-lən, -ˌlēn\ *n* : a hallucinatory crystalline alkaloid $C_{11}H_{17}NO_3$ that is the chief active principle in mescal buttons

mes·en·ceph·a·lon \ˌme-zən-ˈse-fə-ˌlän, ˌmē-, -sən-, -lən\ *n* : MIDBRAIN — **mes·en·ce·phal·ic** \-zen-sə-ˈfa-lik, -sen-\ *adj*

mes·en·chyme \ˈme-zən-ˌkīm, ˈmē-, -sən-\ *n* : loosely organized undifferentiated mesodermal cells that give rise to such structures as connective tissues, blood, lymphatics, bone, and cartilage — **mes·en·chy·mal** \me-zən-ˈkī-məl, ˌmē-, -sən-\ *adj* — **mes·en·chy·ma·tous** \-mə-təs\ *adj*

mes·en·chy·mo·ma \ˌme-zən-kī-ˈmō-mə, ˌmē-, -sən-\ *n*, *pl* **-mas** *or* **-ma·ta** \-mə-tə\ : a benign or malignant tumor consisting of a mixture of at least two types of embryonic connective tissue

¹mes·en·ter·ic \ˌme-zən-ˈter-ik, -sən-\ *adj* : of, relating to, or located in or near a mesentery

²mesenteric *n* : a mesenteric part; *esp* : MESENTERIC ARTERY

mesenteric artery *n* : either of two arteries arising from the aorta and passing between the two layers of the mesentery to the intestine: **a** : one that arises just above the bifurcation of the abdominal aorta into the common iliac arteries and supplies the left half of the transverse colon, the descending colon, the sigmoid colon, and most of the rectum — called also *inferior mesenteric artery* **b** : a large artery that arises from the aorta just below the celiac artery at the level of the first lumbar vertebra and supplies the greater part of the small intestine, the cecum, the ascending colon, and the right half of the transverse colon — called also *superior mesenteric artery*

mesenteric ganglion *n* : either of two ganglionic masses of the sympathetic nervous system associated with the corresponding mesenteric plexus: **a** : a variable amount of massed ganglionic tissue of the inferior mesenteric plexus near the origin of the inferior mesenteric artery — called also *inferior mesenteric ganglion* **b** : a usu. discrete ganglionic mass of the superior mesenteric plexus near the origin of the superior mesenteric artery — called also *superior mesenteric ganglion*

mesenteric node *n* : any of the lymphatic glands of the mesentery — called also *mesenteric gland, mesenteric lymph node*

mesenteric plexus *n* : either of two plexuses of the sympathetic nervous system lying mostly in the mesentery in close proximity to and distributed to the same structures as the corresponding mesenteric arteries: **a** : one associated with the inferior mesenteric artery — called also *inferior mesenteric plexus* **b** : a subdivision of the celiac plexus that is associated with the superior mesenteric artery — called also *superior mesenteric plexus*

mesenteric vein *n* : either of two veins draining the intestine, passing between the two layers of the mesentery, and associated with the corresponding mesenteric arteries: **a** : one that is a continuation of the superior rectal vein, that returns blood from the rectum, the sigmoid colon, and the descending colon, that accompanies the inferior mesenteric artery, and that usu. empties into the splenic vein — called also *inferior mesenteric vein* **b** : one that drains blood from the small intestine, the cecum, the ascending colon, and the transverse colon, that accompanies the superior mesenteric artery, and that joins with the splenic vein to form the portal vein — called also *superior mesenteric vein*

mes·en·tery \'me-zən-₁ter-ē, -sən-\ *n, pl* **-ter·ies** 1 : one or more vertebrate membranes that consist of a double fold of the peritoneum and invest the intestines and their appendages and connect them with the dorsal wall of the abdominal cavity; *specif* : such membranes connected with the jejunum and ileum in humans 2 : a fold of membrane comparable to a mesentery and supporting a viscus (as the heart) that is not a part of the digestive tract

mesh \'mesh\ *n* : a flexible netting of fine wire used in surgery esp. in the repair of large hernias and other body defects

me·si·al \'mē-zē-əl, -sē-\ *adj* 1 : being or located in the middle or a median part ⟨the ~ aspect of the metacarpal head⟩ 2 : situated in or near or directed toward the median plane of the body ⟨the heart is ~ to the lungs⟩ — compare DISTAL 1b 3 : of, relating to, or being the surface of a tooth that is next to the tooth in front of it or that is closest to the middle of the front of the jaw — compare DISTAL 1c, PROXIMAL 1b — **me·si·al·ly** *adv*

mesio- *comb form* : mesial and ⟨*mesiodistal*⟩ ⟨*mesiobuccal*⟩

me·sio·buc·cal \₁mē-zē-ō-'bək-əl, -sē-\ *adj* : of or relating to the mesial and buccal surfaces of a tooth — **me·sio·buc·cal·ly** *adv*

me·sio·clu·sion *also* **me·si·oc·clu·sion** \₁mē-zē-ə-'klü-zhən, -sē-\ *n* : malocclusion characterized by mesial displacement of one or more of the lower teeth

me·sio·dis·tal \₁mē-zē-ō-'dist-əl\ *adj* : of or relating to the mesial and distal surfaces of a tooth; *esp* : relating to, lying along, containing, or being a diameter joining the mesial and distal surfaces — **me·sio·dis·tal·ly** *adv*

me·sio·lin·gual \-'liŋ-gwəl\ *adj* : of or relating to the mesial and lingual surfaces of a tooth — **me·sio·lin·gual·ly** *adv*

mes·mer·ism \'mez-mə-₁ri-zəm, 'mes-\ *n* : hypnotic induction by the practices of F. A. Mesmer; *broadly* : HYPNOTISM — **mes·mer·ist** \-rist\ *n* — **mes·mer·ize** \-₁rīz\ *vb*

    Mes·mer \'mes-mər\, Franz *or* Friedrich Anton (1734–1815), German physician.

meso- — see MES-

me·so·ap·pen·dix \₁me-zō-ə-'pen-diks, ₁mē-, -sō-\ *n, pl* **-dix·es** *or* **-di·ces** \-də-₁sēz\ : the mesentery of the vermiform appendix — **me·so·ap·pen·di·ce·al** \-₁pen-də-'sē-əl\ *adj*

me·so·blast \'me-zə-₁blast, 'mē-, -sə-\ *n* : the embryonic cells that give rise to mesoderm; *broadly* : MESODERM — **me·so·blas·tic** \₁me-zō-'blas-tik, ₁mē-, -sō-\ *adj*

me·so·car·di·um \₁me-zō-'kär-dē-əm, ₁mē-, -sō-\ *n* 1 : the transitory mesentery of the embryonic heart 2 : either of two tubular prolongations of the epicardium that enclose the aorta and pulmonary trunk and the venae cavae and pulmonary veins

Me·so·ces·toi·des \₁ses-'tȯi-(₁)dēz\ *n* : a genus (family Mesocestoididae) of tapeworms having the adults parasitic in mammals and birds and a slender threadlike contractile larva free in cavities or encysted in tissues of mammals, birds, and sometimes reptiles

me·so·co·lon \₁me-zə-'kō-lən, ₁mē-, -sə-\ *n* : a mesentery joining the colon to the dorsal abdominal wall

me·so·derm \'me-zə-₁dərm, 'mē-, -sə-\ *n* : the middle of the three primary germ layers of an embryo that is the source esp. of bone, muscle, connective tissue, and dermis; *broadly* : tissue derived from this germ layer — **me·so·der·mal** \₁me-zə-'dər-məl, ₁mē-, -sə-\ — **me·so·der·mal·ly** *adv*

me·so·duo·de·num \₁me-zə-₁dü-ə-'dē-nəm, ₁mē-, -sə-, -₁dyü-; -dü-'äd-ᵊn-əm, -dyü-\, *n, pl* **-de·na** \-ə-'dē-nə, -'äd-ᵊn-ə\ *or* **-de·nums** : the mesentery of the duodenum usu. not persisting in adult life in humans and other mammals in which the developing intestine undergoes a counterclockwise rotation

me·so·gas·tri·um \-ˈgas-trē-əm\ *n, pl* **-tria** \-trē-ə\ 1 : a ventral mesentery of the embryonic stomach that persists as the falciform ligament and the lesser omentum — called also *ventral mesogastrium* 2 : a dorsal mesentery of the embryonic stomach that gives rise to ligaments between the stomach and spleen and the spleen and kidney — called also *dorsal mesogastrium*

me·so·ino·si·tol \ˌme-zō-i-ˈnō-sə-ˌtōl, ˌmē-, -ˌī-ˈnō-, -ˌtōl\ *n* : MYOINOSITOL

me·so·morph \ˈme-zə-ˌmorf, ˈmē-, -sə-\ *n* : a mesomorphic body or person

me·so·mor·phic \ˌme-zə-ˈmor-fik, ˌmē-, -sə-\ *adj* 1 : of or relating to the component in W. H. Sheldon's classification of body types that measures esp. the degree of muscularity and bone development 2 : having a husky muscular body build — compare ECTOMORPHIC 1, ENDOMORPHIC 1 — **me·so·mor·phy** \ˈme-zə-ˌmor-fē, ˈmē-, -sə-\ *n*

me·so·neph·ric \ˌme-zə-ˈne-frik, ˌmē-, -sə-\ *adj* : of or relating to the mesonephros

mesonephric duct *n* : WOLFFIAN DUCT

me·so·ne·phro·ma \-ni-ˈfrō-mə\ *n, pl* **-mas** *or* **-ma·ta** \-mə-tə\ : a benign or malignant tumor esp. of the female genital tract held to be derived from the mesonephros

me·so·neph·ros \ˌme-zə-ˈne-frəs, ˌmē-, -sə-, -ˌfräs\ *n, pl* **-neph·roi** \-ˈne-ˌfroi\ : either member of the second and midmost of the three paired vertebrate renal organs that functions in adult fishes and amphibians but functions only in the embryo of reptiles, birds, and mammals in which it is replaced by a metanephros in the adult — called also *Wolffian body;* compare PRONEPHROS

Mes·o·pin \ˈme-sə-pin\ *trademark* — used for a preparation of a semisynthetic quaternary antimuscarinic bromide $C_{17}H_{24}BrNO_3$ of homatropine

me·sor·chi·um \mə-ˈzor-kē-əm\ *n, pl* **-chia** \-kē-ə\ : the fold of peritoneum that attaches the testis to the dorsal wall in the fetus

me·so·rec·tum \ˌme-zə-ˈrek-təm, ˌmē-, -sə-\ *n, pl* **-tums** *or* **-ta** \-tə\ : the mesentery that supports the rectum

mes·orid·a·zine \ˌme-zō-ˈri-də-ˌzēn, ˌmē-, -sō-\ *n* : a phenothiazine tranquilizer $C_{21}H_{26}N_2OS_2$ used in the treatment of schizophrenia, organic brain disorders, alcoholism, and psychoneuroses

me·so·sal·pinx \ˌme-zō-ˈsal-(ˌ)pinks, ˌmē-, -sō-\ *n, pl* **-sal·pin·ges** \-sal-ˈpin-(ˌ)jēz\ : a fold of the broad ligament

investing and supporting the fallopian tube

me·so·sig·moid \-ˈsig-ˌmoid\ *n* : the mesentery of the sigmoid part of the descending colon

me·so·ster·num \ˌme-zə-ˈstər-nəm, ˌmē-, -sə-\ *n, pl* **-ster·na** \-nə\ : GLADIOLUS

me·so·ten·don \-ˈten-dən\ *n* : a fold of synovial membrane connecting a tendon to its synovial sheath

me·so·the·li·o·ma \ˌme-zə-ˌthē-lē-ˈō-mə, ˌmē-, -sə-\ *n, pl* **-mas** *or* **-ma·ta** \-mə-tə\ : a tumor derived from mesothelial tissue (as that lining the peritoneum or pleura)

me·so·the·li·um \-ˈthē-lē-əm\ *n, pl* **-lia** \-lē-ə\ : epithelium derived from mesoderm that lines the body cavity of a vertebrate embryo and gives rise to epithelia (as of the peritoneum, pericardium, and pleurae), striated muscle, heart muscle, and several minor structures — **me·so·the·li·al** \-lē-əl\ *adj*

mes·ovar·i·um \-ˈvar-ē-əm\ *n, pl* **-ovar·ia** \-ē-ə\ : the mesentery uniting the ovary with the body wall

mes·ox·a·lyl·urea \-ˌäk-sə-li-ˈlur-ē-ə, -ˌlil-ˈyūr-\ *n* : ALLOXAN

mes·sen·ger \ˈme-sᵊn-jər\ *n* 1 : a substance (as a hormone) that mediates a biological effect — see SECOND MESSENGER 2 : MESSENGER RNA

messenger RNA *n* : an RNA produced by transcription that carries the code for a particular protein from the nuclear DNA to a ribosome in the cytoplasm and acts as a template for the formation of that protein — called also *mRNA;* compare TRANSFER RNA

mes·ter·o·lone \me-ˈster-ə-ˌlōn\ *n* : an androgen $C_{20}H_{32}O_2$ used in the treatment of male infertility

Mes·ti·non \ˈmes-tə-ˌnän\ *trademark* — used for a preparation of pyridostigmine

mes·tra·nol \ˈmes-trə-ˌnol, -ˌnōl\ *n* : a synthetic estrogen $C_{21}H_{26}O_2$ used in oral contraceptives — see ENOVID

mes·y·late \ˈme-si-ˌlāt\ *n* : any of the salts or esters of an acid CH_4SO_3 including some in which it is combined with a drug — see ERGOLOID MESYLATES

Met *abbr* methionine

meta- *or* **met-** *prefix* 1 : situated behind or beyond ⟨*met*encephalon⟩ 2 : change in : transformation of ⟨*meta*plasia⟩

met·a·bol·ic \ˌme-tə-ˈbä-lik\ *adj* 1 : of, relating to, or based on metabolism 2 : VEGETATIVE 1a(2) — used esp. of a cell nucleus that is not dividing — **met·a·bol·i·cal·ly** *adv*

metabolic acidosis *n* : acidosis resulting from excess acid due to abnormal metabolism, excessive acid intake, or renal retention or from excessive loss of bicarbonate (as in diarrhea)

metabolic alkalosis *n* : alkalosis resulting from excessive alkali intake or excessive acid loss (as from vomiting)

metabolic pathway *n* : PATHWAY 2

metabolic rate *n* : metabolism per unit time esp. as estimated by food consumption, energy released as heat, or oxygen used in metabolic processes — see BASAL METABOLIC RATE

me·tab·o·lism \mə-'ta-bə-ˌli-zəm\ *n* 1 : the sum of the processes in the buildup and destruction of protoplasm; *specif* : the chemical changes in living cells by which energy is provided for vital processes and activities and new material is assimilated — see ANABOLISM, CATABOLISM 2 : the sum of the processes by which a particular substance is handled (as by assimilation and incorporation or by detoxification and excretion) in the living body

me·tab·o·lite \-ˌlīt\ *n* 1 : a product of metabolism: **a** : a metabolic waste usu. more or less toxic to the organism producing it : EXCRETION **b** : a product of one metabolic process that is essential to another such process in the same organism **c** : a metabolic waste of one organism that is markedly toxic to another : ANTIBIOTIC 2 : a substance essential to the metabolism of a particular organism or to a particular metabolic process

me·tab·o·lize \-ˌlīz\ *vb* **-lized; -liz·ing** : to subject to metabolism — **me·tab·o·liz·able** \-ˌta-bə-ˈlī-zə-bəl\ *adj*

¹meta·car·pal \ˌme-tə-ˈkär-pəl\ *adj* : of, relating to, or being the metacarpus or a metacarpal

²metacarpal *n* : any bone of the metacarpus of the human hand or the front foot in quadrupeds

meta·car·po·pha·lan·ge·al \ˌme-tə-ˌkär-pō-ˌfā-lən-ˈjē-əl, -ˌfa-, -fə-ˈlan-jē-əl\ *adj* : of, relating to, or involving both the metacarpus and the phalanges

meta·car·pus \-ˈkär-pəs\ *n* : the part of the human hand or the front foot in quadrupeds between the carpus and the phalanges that contains five more or less elongated bones when all the digits are present (as in humans) but is modified in many animals by the loss or reduction of some bones or the fusing of adjacent bones

meta·cen·tric \ˌme-tə-ˈsen-trik\ *adj* : having the centromere medially situated so that the two chromosomal arms are of roughly equal length — compare ACROCENTRIC, TELOCENTRIC — **metacentric** *n*

meta·cer·car·ia \ˌme-tə-(ˌ)sər-ˈkar-ē-ə\ *n, pl* **-i·ae** \-ē-ˌē\ : a tailless encysted late larva of a digenetic trematode that is usu. the form which is infective for the definitive host — **meta·cer·car·i·al** \-ē-əl\ *adj*

meta·ces·tode \-ˈses-ˌtōd\ *n* : a stage of a tapeworm occurring in an intermediate host : a larval tapeworm

metachromatic leukodystrophy *n* : a hereditary neurological disorder of lipid metabolism characterized by the accumulation of cerebroside sulfates, loss of myelin in the central nervous system, and progressive deterioration of mental and motor activity

me·tach·ro·nous \mə-ˈta-krə-nəs\ *adj* : occurring or starting at different times (~ cancers)

meta·cre·sol \ˌme-tə-ˈkrē-ˌsȯl, -ˌsōl\ *n* : an isomer of cresol that has antiseptic properties

meta·cryp·to·zo·ite \-ˌkrip-tō-ˈzō-ˌīt\ *n* : a member of a second or subsequent generation of tissue-dwelling forms of a malaria parasite derived from the sporozoite without intervening generations of blood parasites — compare CRYPTOZOITE

Meta·gon·i·mus \-ˈgä-nə-məs\ *n* : a genus of small intestinal flukes (family Heterophyidae) that includes one (*M. yokogawai*) common in humans, dogs, and cats in parts of eastern Asia as a result of the eating of raw fish containing the larva

Meta·hy·drin \-ˈhī-drin\ *trademark* — used for a preparation of trichlormethiazide

metall- *or* **metallo-** *comb form* : containing a metal atom or ion in the molecule (*metallo*porphyrin)

me·tal·lo·en·zyme \mə-ˌta-lō-ˈen-ˌzīm\ *n* : an enzyme consisting of a protein linked with a specific metal

met·al·loid \ˈmet-əl-ˌȯid\ *n* : an element (as boron, silicon, or arsenic) intermediate in properties between the typical metals and nonmetals

me·tal·lo·por·phy·rin \-ˈpȯr-fə-rən\ *n* : a compound (as heme) formed from a porphyrin and a metal ion

me·tal·lo·pro·tein \-ˈprō-ˌtēn, -ˈprōt-ē-ən\ *n* : a conjugated protein in which the prosthetic group is a metal

me·tal·lo·thio·ne·in \-ˌthī-ə-ˈnē-ən\ *n* : a metal-binding protein involved in the storage of copper in the liver

meta·mere \ˈme-tə-ˌmir\ *n* : any of a linear series of primitively similar segments into which the body of a higher invertebrate or vertebrate is divisible and which are usu. clearly distinguishable in the embryo, identifiable in somewhat modified form in various invertebrates (as annelid worms), and detectable in the adult higher vertebrate only in specialized segmentally arranged structures (as cranial and spinal nerves or vertebrae) : SOMITE — **meta·mer·ic** \ˌme-tə-ˈmer-ik\ *adj*

Met·a·mine \ˈme-tə-ˌmēn\ *trademark* — used for a preparation of the phosphate of trolnitrate

meta·mor·phic \ˌme-tə-ˈmȯr-fik\ *adj* : of or relating to metamorphosis

meta·mor·pho·sis \ˌme-tə-ˈmȯr-fə-səs\ *n, pl* **-pho·ses** \-ˌsēz\ 1 : change of physical form, structure, or substance 2 : a marked and more or less abrupt developmental change in the form or structure of an animal (as a butterfly or a frog) occurring subsequent to birth or hatching — **meta-mor-phose** \-ˌfōz, -ˌfōs\ *vb*

Met-a-mu-cil \ˌme-tə-ˈmyüs-əl\ *trademark* — used for a laxative preparation of a hydrophilic mucilloid from the husk of psyllium seed

meta-my-elo-cyte \ˌme-tə-ˈmī-ə-lə-ˌsīt\ *n* : any of the most immature granulocytes present in normal blood that are distinguished by typical cytoplasmic granulation in combination with a simple kidney-shaped nucleus

Me-tan-dren \me-ˈtan-drən\ *trademark* — used for a preparation of methyltestosterone

meta-neph-ric \ˌme-tə-ˈne-frik\ *adj* : of or relating to the metanephros

meta-neph-rine \-ˈne-ˌfrēn\ *n* : a catabolite of epinephrine that is found in the urine and some tissues

meta-neph-ro-gen-ic \-ˌne-frə-ˈje-nik\ *adj* : giving rise to the metanephroi

meta-neph-ros \-ˈne-frəs, -ˌfräs\ *n, pl* **-neph-roi** \-ˈne-ˌfrȯi\ : either member of the final and most caudal pair of the three successive pairs of vertebrate renal organs that functions as a permanent adult kidney in reptiles, birds, and mammals but is not present at all in lower forms — compare MESONEPHROS, PRONEPHROS

meta-phase \ˈme-tə-ˌfāz\ *n* : the stage of mitosis and meiosis in which the chromosomes become arranged in the equatorial plane of the spindle

metaphase plate *n* : a section in the equatorial plane of the metaphase spindle having the chromosomes oriented upon it

Met-a-phen \ˈme-tə-fən\ *trademark* — used for a preparation of nitromersol

me-taph-y-se-al *also* **me-taph-y-si-al** \ˌme-ˌta-fə-ˈsē-əl, -ˈzē-, ˌme-tə-ˈfi-zē-əl\ *adj* : of or relating to a metaphysis

me-taph-y-sis \mə-ˈta-fə-səs\ *n, pl* **-y-ses** \-ˌsēz\ : the transitional zone at which the diaphysis and epiphysis of a bone come together

meta-pla-sia \ˌme-tə-ˈplā-zhə, -zhē-ə\ *n* **1** : transformation of one tissue into another (~ of cartilage into bone) **2** : abnormal replacement of cells of one type by cells of another — **meta-plas-tic** \-ˈplas-tik\ *adj*

meta-pro-ter-e-nol \-prō-ˈter-ə-ˌnȯl, -ˌnȯl\ *n* : a beta-adrenergic bronchodilator $C_{11}H_{17}NO_3$ that is used in the treatment of bronchial asthma and reversible bronchospasm associated with bronchitis and emphysema and that is administered as the sulfate — see ALUPENT

meta-ram-i-nol \ˌme-tə-ˈra-mə-ˌnȯl, -ˌnȯl\ *n* : a sympathomimetic drug $C_9H_{13}NO_2$ used esp. as a vasoconstrictor

met-ar-te-ri-ole \ˌmet-ˌär-ˈtir-ē-ˌōl\ *n* : any of the delicate blood vessels that branch from the smallest arteri-

oles and connect with the capillary bed — called also *precapillary*

me-tas-ta-sis \mə-ˈtas-tə-səs\ *n, pl* **-ta-ses** \-ˌsēz\ : change of position, state, or form: as **a** : transfer of a disease-producing agency (as cancer cells or bacteria) from an original site of disease to another part of the body with development of a similar lesion in the new location **b** : a secondary metastatic growth of a malignant tumor — **me-tas-ta-size** \mə-ˈtas-tə-ˌsīz\ *vb* — **met-a-stat-ic** \ˌme-tə-ˈsta-tik\ *adj*

Meta-stron-gy-lus \ˌme-tə-ˈsträn-jə-ləs\ *n* : a genus of nematode worms (family Metastrongylidae) parasitizing as adults the lungs and sometimes other organs of mammals

¹meta-tar-sal \ˌme-tə-ˈtär-səl\ *adj* : of, relating to, or being the part of the human foot or of the hind foot in quadrupeds between the tarsus and the phalanges

²metatarsal *n* : a metatarsal bone

meta-tar-sal-gia \-ˌtär-ˈsal-jə, -jē-ə\ *n* : a cramping burning pain below and between the metatarsal bones where they join the toe bones — see MORTON'S TOE

meta-tar-sec-to-my \-ˌtär-ˈsek-tə-mē\ *n, pl* **-mies** : surgical removal of the metatarsus or a metatarsal bone

meta-tar-so-pha-lan-ge-al joint \-ˌtär-sō-ˌfā-lən-ˈjē-əl-, -ˌfa-, -fə-ˈlan-jē-\ *n* : any of the joints between the metatarsals and the phalanges

meta-tar-sus \ˌme-tə-ˈtär-səs\ *n* : the part of the human foot or of the hind foot in quadrupeds that is between the tarsus and phalanges, contains when all the digits are present (as in humans) five more or less elongated bones but is modified in many animals with loss or reduction of some bones or fusing of others, and in humans forms the instep

meta-thal-a-mus \-ˈtha-lə-məs\ *n, pl* **-mi** \-ˌmī\ : the part of the diencephalon on each side that comprises the lateral and medial geniculate bodies

met-ax-a-lone \mə-ˈtak-sə-ˌlōn\ *n* : a drug $C_{12}H_{15}NO_3$ used as a skeletal muscle relaxant

meta-zo-an \ˌme-tə-ˈzō-ən\ *n* : any of a group (Metazoa) that comprises all animals having the body composed of cells differentiated into tissues and organs and usu. a digestive cavity lined with specialized cells — **metazoan** *adj*

met-en-ceph-a-lon \ˌmet-ˌen-ˈse-fə-ˌlän, -lən\ *n* : the anterior segment of the developing vertebrate hindbrain or the corresponding part of the adult brain composed of the cerebellum and pons — **met-en-ce-phal-ic** \-ˌen-sə-ˈfa-lik\ *adj*

Met-en-keph-a-lin \ˌme-ten-ˈke-fə-lin\ *n* : METHIONINE-ENKEPHALIN

me-te-or-ism \ˈmē-tē-ə-ˌri-zəm\ *n* : gaseous distension of the stomach or intestine — see TYMPANITES

me·ter \'mē-tər\ *n* : the basic metric unit of length that is equal to 39.37 inches

-meter *n comb form* : instrument or means for measuring (calori*meter*)

meter–kilogram–second *adj* : MKS

meth \'meth\ *n* : METHAMPHETAMINE

meth- *or* **metho-** *comb form* : methyl (*metho*amphetamine)

metha·cho·line \₁me-thə-'kō-₁lēn\ *n* : a parasympathomimetic drug $C_8H_{19}NO_3$ administered in the form of its crystalline chloride or bromide — see MECHOLYL

metha·cy·cline \₁me-thə-'sī-₁klēn\ *n* : a semisynthetic tetracycline $C_{22}H_{22}N_2O_8$ with longer duration of action than most other tetracyclines and used in the treatment of gonorrhea esp. in penicillin-sensitive subjects

meth·a·done \'me-thə-₁dōn\ *also* **meth·a·don** \-₁dän\ *n* : a synthetic addictive narcotic drug $C_{21}H_{27}NO$ used esp. in the form of its hydrochloride for the relief of pain and as a substitute narcotic in the treatment of heroin addiction — called also *amidone*

met·hae·mo·glo·bi·nae·mia *chiefly Brit var of* METHEMOGLOBINEMIA

meth·am·phet·amine \₁me-tham-'fe-tə-₁mēn, -tham-, -mən\ *n* : an amine $C_{10}H_{15}N$ used medically in the form of its crystalline hydrochloride esp. in the treatment of obesity and often used illicitly as a stimulant — called also *methedrine*

meth·an·dro·sten·o·lone \₁me-₁than-drō-'ste-nə-₁lōn\ *n* : an anabolic steroid $C_{20}H_{28}O_2$

meth·a·nol \'me-thə-₁nȯl, -₁nōl\ *n* : a light volatile pungent flammable poisonous liquid alcohol CH_3OH used esp. as a solvent, antifreeze, or denaturant for ethyl alcohol and in the synthesis of other chemicals — called also *methyl alcohol, wood alcohol*

meth·an·the·line \me-'than-thə-₁lēn, -lən\ *n* : an anticholinergic drug usu. administered in the form of its crystalline bromide $C_{21}H_{26}BrNO_3$ in the treatment of peptic ulcers — see BANTHINE

meth·a·phen·i·lene \₁me-thə-'fen-ᵊl-₁ēn\ *n* : an antihistamine drug $C_{15}H_{20}N_2S$ usu. administered in the form of its hydrochloride

meth·a·pyr·i·lene \-'pir-ə-₁lēn\ *n* : an antihistamine drug $C_{14}H_{19}N_3S$ widely used in the form of its fumarate or hydrochloride as a mild sedative in proprietary sleep-inducing drugs

meth·aqua·lone \me-'tha-kwə-₁lōn\ *n* : a sedative and hypnotic nonbarbiturate drug $C_{16}H_{14}N_2O$ that is habit-forming — see QUAALUDE

meth·ar·bi·tal \me-'thär-bə-₁tȯl, -₁täl\ *n* : an anticonvulsant barbiturate $C_9H_{14}N_2O_3$

meth·a·zol·amide \₁me-thə-'zō-lə-₁mīd\

n : a sulfonamide $C_5H_8N_4O_3S_2$ that inhibits the production of carbonic anhydrase, reduces intraocular pressure, and is used in the treatment of glaucoma — see NEPTAZANE

meth·dil·a·zine \meth-'di-lə-₁zēn, -'dī-lə-₁zēn\ *n* : a phenothiazine antihistamine $C_{18}H_{20}N_2S$ used in the form of its hydrochloride as an antipruritic

meth·e·drine \'me-thə-drən, -₁drēn\ *n* : METHAMPHETAMINE

met·hem·al·bu·min \₁met-₁hē-mal-'byü-mən\ *n* : an albumin complex with hematin found in plasma during diseases (as blackwater fever) that are associated with extensive hemolysis

met·he·mo·glo·bin \(₁)met-'hē-mə-₁glō-bin\ *n* : a soluble brown crystalline basic blood pigment that is found in normal blood in much smaller amounts than hemoglobin, that is formed from blood, hemoglobin, or oxyhemoglobin by oxidation, and that differs from hemoglobin in containing ferric iron and in being unable to combine reversibly with molecular oxygen — called also *ferrihemoglobin*

met·he·mo·glo·bi·ne·mia \₁met-₁hē-mə-₁glō-bə-'nē-mē-ə\ *n* : the presence of methemoglobin in the blood due to conversion of part of the hemoglobin to this inactive form

me·the·na·mine \mə-'thē-nə-₁mēn, -mən\ *n* : a crystalline compound $C_6H_{12}N_4$ used in medicine as a urinary antiseptic esp. in cystitis and pyelitis — called also *hexamethylenetetramine, hexamine*; see MANDELAMINE, UROTROPIN

me·the·no·lone \mə-'thē-nə-lōn, me-'the-\ *n* : a hormone $C_{20}H_{30}O_2$ that is an anabolic steroid

Meth·er·gine \'me-thər-jən\ *trademark* — used for a preparation of methylergonovine

meth·i·cil·lin \₁me-thə-'si-lən\ *n* : a semisynthetic penicillin $C_{17}H_{19}N_2O_6NaS$ that is esp. effective against penicillinase-producing staphylococci

meth·i·ma·zole \me-'thī-mə-₁zȯl, mə-\ *n* : a drug $C_4H_6N_2S$ used to inhibit activity of the thyroid gland

meth·io·dal sodium \mə-'thī-ə-₁dal-\ *n* : a crystalline salt CH_2ISO_3Na used as a radiopaque contrast medium in intravenous urography

me·thi·o·nine \mə-'thī-ə-₁nēn\ *n* : a crystalline sulfur-containing essential amino acid $C_5H_{11}NO_2S$ that occurs in the L-form as a constituent of many proteins (as casein and egg albumin) and that is used as a dietary supplement and in the treatment of fatty infiltration of the liver — see MEONINE

methionine–en·keph·a·lin \-en-'kə-fə-lin\ *n* : a pentapeptide having a terminal methionine residue that is one of the two enkephalins occurring naturally in the brain — called also *Met=enkephalin*

meth·is·a·zone \me-ˈthi-sə-ˌzōn\ *n* : an antiviral drug $C_{10}H_{10}N_4OS$ that has been used in the preventive treatment of smallpox — see MARBORAN

Meth·i·um \ˈme-thē-əm\ *trademark* — used for a preparation of hexamethonium in its chloride form $C_{12}H_{30}Cl_2N_2$

me·thix·ene \me-ˈthik-ˌsēn\ *n* : an anticholinergic drug $C_{20}H_{23}NS$ used as an antispasmodic in the treatment of functional bowel hypermotility and spasm — see TREST

metho- — see METH-

meth·o·car·ba·mol \ˌme-thə-ˈkär-bə-ˌmól\ *n* : a skeletal muscle relaxant drug $C_{11}H_{15}NO_5$

meth·o·hex·i·tal \ˌme-thə-ˈhek-sə-ˌtòl, -ˌtal\ *n* : a barbiturate with a short period of action usu. used in the form of its sodium salt $C_{14}H_{17}N_2NaO_3$ as an intravenous general anesthetic

meth·o·trex·ate \-ˈtrek-ˌsāt\ *n* : a toxic anticancer drug $C_{20}H_{22}N_8O_5$ that is an analog of folic acid and an antimetabolite — called also *amethopterin*

meth·o·tri·mep·ra·zine \-ˌtrī-ˈme-prə-ˌzēn\ *n* : a nonnarcotic analgesic and tranquilizer $C_{19}H_{24}N_2OS$ — see LEVOPROME

me·thox·amine \me-ˈthäk-sə-ˌmēn, -mən\ *n* : a sympathomimetic amine $C_{11}H_{17}NO_3$ used in the form of its hydrochloride esp. to raise or maintain blood pressure (as during surgery) by its vasoconstrictor effects — see VASOXYL

me·thox·sa·len \me-ˈthäk-sə-lən\ *n* : a drug $C_{12}H_8O_4$ used to increase the production of melanin in the skin upon exposure to ultraviolet light and in the treatment of vitiligo — called also *xanthotoxin*; see MELOXINE

me·thoxy·flu·rane \me-ˌthäk-sē-ˈflür-ˌān\ *n* : a potent nonexplosive inhalational general anesthetic $C_3H_4Cl_2F_2O$

8-meth·oxy·psor·a·len \ˈāt-ˌme-ˌthäk-sē-ˈsòr-ə-lən\ *n* : METHOXSALEN

meth·sco·pol·amine \ˌme-thə-skō-ˈpä-lə-ˌmēn, -mən\ *n* : an anticholinergic derivative of scopolamine that is usu. used in the form of its bromide $C_{18}H_{24}BrNO_4$ for its inhibitory effect on gastric secretion and gastrointestinal motility esp. in the treatment of peptic ulcer and gastric disorders — see PAMINE

meth·sux·i·mide \-ˈsək-si-ˌmid\ *n* : an anticonvulsant drug $C_{12}H_{13}NO_2$ used esp. in the control of petit mal seizures

meth·y·clo·thi·a·zide \ˌme-thē-ˌklō-ˈthī-ə-ˌzīd\ *n* : a thiazide drug $C_9H_{11}Cl_2N_3O_4S_2$ used as a diuretic and antihypertensive agent

meth·yl \ˈme-thəl, *Brit also* ˈmē-ˌthīl\ *n* : an alkyl group CH_3 that occurs esp.

in combination in many compounds

meth·yl·al \ˈme-thə-ˌlal\ *n* : a volatile flammable liquid $C_3H_8O_2$ used as a hypnotic and anesthetic

methyl alcohol *n* : METHANOL

me·thyl·am·phet·amine \ˌme-thəl-am-ˈfe-tə-ˌmēn\ *n* : METHAMPHETAMINE

meth·yl·ate \ˈme-thə-ˌlāt\ *vb* **-at·ed; -at·ing 1** : to impregnate or mix with methanol **2** : to introduce the methyl group into — **meth·yl·a·tion** \ˌme-thə-ˈlā-shən\ *n*

methylated spirit *n* : ethyl alcohol denatured with methanol — often used in pl. with a sing. verb

meth·yl·ben·ze·tho·ni·um chloride \ˌme-thəl-ˌben-zə-ˌthō-nē-əm-\ *n* : a quaternary ammonium salt $C_{28}H_{44}ClNO_2$ used as a bactericide and antiseptic esp. in the treatment of diaper rash — called also *methylbenzethonium*

meth·yl·cel·lu·lose \ˌme-thəl-ˈsel-yə-ˌlōs, -ˌlōz\ *n* : any of various gummy products of cellulose methylation that swell in water and are used as bulk laxatives

meth·yl·cho·lan·threne \-kə-ˈlan-ˌthrēn\ *n* : a potent carcinogenic hydrocarbon $C_{21}H_{16}$ obtained from certain bile acids and cholesterol as well as synthetically

meth·yl·do·pa \-ˈdō-pə\ *n* : a drug $C_{10}H_{13}NO_4$ used to lower blood pressure

meth·y·lene blue \ˈme-thə-ˌlēn-, -lən-\ *n* : a basic thiazine dye $C_{16}H_{18}ClN_3S \cdot 3H_2O$ used in the treatment of methemoglobinemia and as an antidote in cyanide poisoning

meth·yl·er·go·no·vine \ˌme-thəl-ˌər-gə-ˈnō-ˌvēn\ *n* : an oxytocic drug $C_{20}H_{25}N_3O_2$ used similarly to ergonovine usu. in the form of its maleate salt — see METHERGINE

meth·yl·glu·ca·mine \-ˈglü-kə-ˌmēn\ *n* : MEGLUMINE

meth·yl·hex·ane·amine \ˌme-thəl-ˌhek-sā-ˈna-mēn\ *n* : an amine base $C_7H_{17}N$ used as a local vasoconstrictor of nasal mucosa in the treatment of nasal congestion

meth·yl·iso·cy·a·nate \-ˌī-sō-ˈsī-ə-ˌnāt\ *n* : an extremely toxic chemical CH_3NCO that is used esp. in the manufacture of pesticides and was the cause of numerous deaths and injuries in a leak at a chemical plant in Bhopal, India, in 1984 — abbr. *MIC*

meth·yl·ma·lon·ic acid \ˌme-thəl-mə-ˈlä-nik-\ *n* : a structural isomer of succinic acid present in minute amounts in healthy human urine but excreted in large quantities in the urine of individuals with a vitamin B_{12} deficiency

methylmalonic aciduria *n* : a metabolic defect which is controlled by an autosomal recessive gene and in which methylmalonic acid is not converted to succinic acid with chronic metabolic acidosis resulting

meth·yl mer·cap·tan \'me-thəl-mər-'kap-ˌtan\ *n* : a pungent gas CH_4S produced in the intestine by the decomposition of certain proteins and responsible for the characteristic odor of fetor hepaticus

meth·yl·mer·cury \ˌme-thəl-'mər-kyə-rē\ *n, pl* **-cu·ries** : any of various toxic compounds of mercury containing the complex CH_3Hg- that often occur as pollutants formed as industrial by-products or pesticide residues, tend to accumulate in living organisms (as fish) esp. in higher levels of a food chain, are rapidly and easily absorbed through the human intestinal wall, and cause neurological dysfunction in humans — see MINAMATA DISEASE

meth·yl·mor·phine \ˌme-thəl-'mȯr-ˌfēn\ *n* : CODEINE

meth·yl·para·ben \ˌme-thəl-'par-ə-ˌben\ *n* : a crystalline compound $C_8H_8O_3$ used as an antifungal preservative (as in pharmaceutical ointments and cosmetic creams)

meth·yl·para·fy·nol \-ˌpar-ə-'fī-ˌnȯl\ *n* : a sedative and hypnotic drug $C_6H_{10}O$

methyl parathion *n* : a potent synthetic organophosphate insecticide $C_8H_{10}NO_5PS$ that is more toxic than parathion

meth·yl·phe·ni·date \ˌme-thəl-'fe-nə-ˌdāt, -'fē-\ *n* : a mild stimulant $C_{14}H_{19}NO_2$ of the central nervous system used in the form of its hydrochloride to treat narcolepsy and hyperkinetic behavior disorders in children — see RITALIN

meth·yl·pred·nis·o·lone \-pred-'ni-sə-ˌlōn\ *n* : a glucocorticoid $C_{22}H_{30}O_5$ that is a derivative of prednisolone and is used as an anti-inflammatory agent; *also* : any of several of its salts (as an acetate) used similarly — see MEDROL

methyl salicylate *n* : a liquid ester $C_8H_8O_3$ that is obtained from the leaves of a wintergreen (*Gaultheria procumbens*) or the bark of a birch (*Betula lenta*), but is usu. made synthetically, and that is used as a flavoring and a counterirritant — see OIL OF WINTERGREEN

methylsulfate — see PENTAPIPERIDE METHYLSULFATE

meth·yl·tes·tos·ter·one \-te-'stäs-tə-ˌrōn\ *n* : a synthetically prepared crystalline compound $C_{20}H_{30}O_2$ administered orally in cases of male sex hormone deficiency — see METANDREN

meth·yl·thio·ura·cil \-ˌthī-ō-'yùr-ə-ˌsil\ *n* : a crystalline compound $C_5H_6N_2OS$ used in the suppression of hyperactivity of the thyroid

α-meth·yl·ty·ro·sine \ˌal-fə-ˌme-thəl-'tī-rə-ˌsēn\ *n* : a compound $C_{10}H_{13}NO_3$ that inhibits the synthesis of catecholamines but not of serotonin

meth·yl·xan·thine \ˌme-thəl-'zan-ˌthēn\ *n* : a methylated xanthine derivative (as caffeine, theobromine, or theophylline)

meth·y·pry·lon \ˌme-thə-'prī-ˌlän\ *n* : a sedative and hypnotic drug $C_{10}H_{17}NO_2$

meth·y·ser·gide \ˌme-thə-'sər-ˌjīd\ *n* : a serotonin antagonist $C_{21}H_{27}N_3O_2$ used in the form of its maleate esp. in the treatment and prevention of migraine headaches

Met·i·cor·te·lone \ˌme-ti-'kȯr-tə-ˌlōn\ *trademark* — used for a preparation of prednisolone

met·o·clo·pra·mide \ˌme-tə-'klō-prə-ˌmīd\ *n* : an antiemetic drug $C_{14}H_{22}ClN_3O_2$ administered as the hydrochloride

met·o·cur·ine iodide \ˌme-tə-'kyùr-ˌēn-\ *n* : a crystalline iodine-containing powder $C_{40}H_{48}I_2N_2O_6$ that is derived from the dextrorotatory form of tubocurarine and is a potent skeletal muscle relaxant — called also *metocurine*; see METUBINE

me·to·la·zone \me-'tō-lə-ˌzōn\ *n* : a diuretic and antihypertensive drug $C_{16}H_{16}ClN_3O_3S$

me·top·ic \me-'tä-pik\ *adj* : of or relating to the forehead : FRONTAL; *esp* : of, relating to, or being a suture uniting the frontal bones in the fetus and sometimes persistent after birth

met·o·pim·a·zine \ˌme-tə-'pi-mə-ˌzēn\ *n* : an antiemetic drug $C_{22}H_{27}N_3O_3S_2$

Met·o·pir·one \ˌme-tə-'pir-ˌōn\ *trademark* — used for a preparation of metyrapone

Me·to·pi·um \mə-'tō-pē-əm\ *n* : a genus of trees and shrubs of the cashew family (Anacardiaceae) that includes the poisonwood (*M. toxiferum*)

met·o·pon \'me-tə-ˌpän\ *n* : a narcotic drug $C_{18}H_{21}NO_3$ that is derived from morphine and is used in the form of the hydrochloride to relieve pain

me·to·pro·lol \me-'tō-prə-ˌlȯl, -ˌlōl\ *n* : a beta-blocker $C_{15}H_{25}NO_3$ used in the treatment of hypertension

metr- *or* **metro-** *comb form* : uterus (*metritis*)

-me·tra \'mē-trə\ *n comb form* : a (specified) condition of the uterus (hemato*metra*)

Met·ra·zol \'me-trə-ˌzȯl, -ˌzōl\ *trademark* — used for pentylenetetrazol

me·tre *chiefly Brit var of* METER

met·ric \'me-trik\ *adj* : of, relating to, or using the metric system — **met·ri·cal·ly** *adv*

-met·ric \'me-trik\ *or* **-met·ri·cal** \'me-tri-kəl\ *adj comb form* 1 : of, employing, or obtained by (such) a meter (calori*metric*) 2 : of or relating to (such) an art, process, or science of measuring (psycho*metric*)

metric system *n* : a decimal system of weights and measures based on the meter and on the kilogram — compare CGS, MKS

me·tri·tis \mə-ˈtrī-təs\ n : inflammation of the uterus

-met·ri·um \ˈmē-trē-əm\ n comb form : part or layer of the uterus (endometrium)

me·triz·a·mide \me-ˈtri-za-ˌmīd\ n : a radiopaque medium $C_{18}H_{22}I_3N_3O_8$

met·ri·zo·ate sodium \ˌme-tri-ˈzō-ˌāt-\ n : a radiopaque medium $C_{12}H_{10}I_3$-N_2NaO_4 — see ISOPAQUE

met·ro·ni·da·zole \ˌme-trə-ˈnī-də-ˌzōl\ n : a drug $C_6H_9N_3O_3$ used esp. in treating vaginal trichomoniasis

me·tror·rha·gia \ˌmē-trə-ˈrā-jə, -jē-ə, -zhə; -ˈrā-\ n : profuse uterine bleeding esp. between menstrual periods — compare MENORRHAGIA — me·tror·rhag·ic \-ˈra-jik\ adj

-me·try \mə-trē\ n comb form : art, process, or science of measuring (something specified) (audiometry)

Me·tu·bine \me-ˈtü-ˌbēn, -ˈtyü-\ trademark — used for a preparation of metocurine iodide

me·tu·re·de·pa \mə-ˌtür-ə-ˈde-pə, ˌme-tyə-rə-\ n : an antineoplastic drug $C_{11}H_{22}N_3O_3P$

Met·y·caine \ˈme-tə-ˌkān\ trademark — used for a preparation of the hydrochloride of piperocaine

me·tyr·a·pone \mə-ˈtir-ə-ˌpōn, -ˈtir-\ n : a metabolic hormone $C_{14}H_{14}N_2O$ that inhibits biosynthesis of cortisol and corticosterone and is used to test for normal functioning of the pituitary gland — see METOPIRONE

me·ze·re·um \mə-ˈzir-ē-əm\ n : the dried bark of various European shrubs (genus *Daphne* and esp. *D. mezereum* of the family Thymelaeaceae) used externally as a vesicant and irritant

mg abbr milligram

Mg symbol magnesium

MHC abbr major histocompatibility complex

MI abbr 1 mitral incompetence; mitral insufficiency 2 myocardial infarction

mi·an·ser·in \mī-ˈan-sər-in\ n : a drug $C_{18}H_{20}N_2$ administered in the form of its hydrochloride as a serotonin inhibitor and antihistamine

MIC abbr 1 methylisocyanate 2 minimal inhibitory concentration; minimum inhibitory concentration

mice pl of MOUSE

mi·con·a·zole \mī-ˈkä-nə-ˌzōl\ n : an antifungal agent administered esp. in the form of its nitrate $C_{18}H_{14}Cl_4$-$N_2O·HNO_3$

micr- or **micro-** comb form 1 a : small : minute (microaneurysm) b : used for or involving minute quantities or variations (microanalysis) 2 a : using microscopy (microdissection) : used in microscopy (microneedle) b : revealed by or having its structure discernible only by microscopical examination (microorganism) 3 : abnormally small (microcyte)

micra pl of MICRON

mi·cren·ceph·a·ly \ˌmī-ˌkren-ˈse-fə-lē\ n, pl -lies : the condition of having an abnormally small brain

mi·cro·ab·scess \ˈmī-krō-ˌab-ses\ n : a very small abscess

mi·cro·ad·e·no·ma \ˌmī-krō-ˌad-ən-ˈō-mə\ n, pl -mas or -ma·ta \-mə-tə\ : a very small adenoma

mi·cro·ag·gre·gate \-ˈa-gri-gət\ n : an aggregate of microscopic particles (as of fibrin) formed esp. in stored blood

mi·cro·anal·y·sis \ˌmī-krō-ə-ˈna-lə-səs\ n, pl -y·ses \-ˌsēz\ : chemical analysis on a small or minute scale that usu. requires special, very sensitive, or small-scale apparatus — mi·cro·an·a·lyt·ic \-ˌan-əl-ˈi-tik\ or mi·cro·an·a·lyt·i·cal \-ˈi-ti-kəl\ adj

mi·cro·anat·o·my \-ə-ˈna-tə-mē\ n, pl -mies : HISTOLOGY — mi·cro·ana·tom·i·cal \-ˌa-nə-ˈtä-mi-kəl\ adj

mi·cro·an·eu·rysm also **mi·cro·an·eu·rism** \-ˈa-nyə-ˌri-zəm\ n : a saccular enlargement of the venous end of a retinal capillary associated esp. with diabetic retinopathy — mi·cro·an·eu·rys·mal \-ˌa-nyə-ˈriz-məl\ adj

mi·cro·an·gi·og·ra·phy \-ˌan-jē-ˈä-grə-fē\ n, pl -phies : minutely detailed angiography — mi·cro·an·gio·graph·ic \-ˌan-jē-ə-ˈgra-fik\ adj

mi·cro·an·gi·op·a·thy \-ˈä-pə-thē\ n, pl -thies : a disease of very fine blood vessels (thrombotic ~) — mi·cro·an·gio·path·ic \-ˌan-jē-ə-ˈpa-thik\ adj

mi·cro·ar·te·ri·og·ra·phy \-ˌär-ˌtir-ē-ˈä-grə-fē\ n, pl -phies : minutely detailed arteriography

mi·crobe \ˈmī-ˌkrōb\ n : MICROORGANISM, GERM — used esp. of pathogenic bacteria

mi·cro·bi·al \mī-ˈkrō-bē-əl\ adj : of, relating to, caused by, or being microbes (~ infection) (~ agents)

mi·cro·bic \mī-ˈkrō-bik\ adj : MICROBIAL

mi·cro·bi·cide \mī-ˈkrō-bə-ˌsīd\ n : an agent that destroys microbes — mi·cro·bi·ci·dal \mī-ˌkrō-bə-ˈsīd-əl\ adj

mi·cro·bi·ol·o·gy \ˌmī-krō-bī-ˈä-lə-jē\ n, pl -gies : a branch of biology dealing esp. with microscopic forms of life (as bacteria, protozoa, viruses, and fungi) — mi·cro·bi·o·log·i·cal \ˌmī-krō-ˌbī-ə-ˈlä-ji-kəl\ also mi·cro·bi·o·log·ic \-ˈlä-jik\ adj — mi·cro·bi·o·log·i·cal·ly \-ˈlä-ji-k(ə-)lē\ adv — mi·cro·bi·ol·o·gist \-jist\ n

mi·cro·body \ˈmī-krō-ˌbä-dē\ n, pl -bod·ies : PEROXISOME

mi·cro·cap·sule \ˈmī-krō-ˌkap-səl, -(ˌ)sül\ n : a tiny capsule containing material (as a medicine) that is released when the capsule is broken, melted, or dissolved

¹mi·cro·ce·phal·ic \ˌmī-krō-sə-ˈfa-lik\ adj : having a small head; specif : having an abnormally small head

²microcephalic n : an individual with an abnormally small head

mi·cro·ceph·a·lus \-ˈse-fə-ləs\ n, pl -li \-ˌlī\ : MICROCEPHALY

mi·cro·ceph·a·ly \-'se-fə-lē\ n, pl -lies : a condition of abnormal smallness of the head usu. associated with mental defects

mi·cro·cir·cu·la·tion \-ˌsər-kyə-'lā-shən\ n : blood circulation in the microvascular system: also : the microvascular system itself — mi·cro·cir·cu·la·to·ry \-'sər-kyə-lə-ˌtōr-ē\ adj

mi·cro·coc·cus \ˌmī-krō-'kä-kəs\ n 1 cap : a genus of nonmotile gram-positive spherical bacteria (family Micrococcaceae) that occur in tetrads or irregular clusters and include nonpathogenic forms found on human and animal skin 2 pl -coc·ci \-'kä-ˌkī, -'käk-ˌsī\ : a small spherical bacterium: esp : any bacterium of the genus Micrococcus — mi·cro·coc·cal \ˌmī-krō-'kä-kəl\ adj

mi·cro·cul·ture \'mī-krō-ˌkəl-chər\ n : a microscopic culture of cells or organisms (a ∼ of lymphocytes) — mi·cro·cul·tur·al \ˌmī-krō-'kəlch-(ə-)rəl\ adj

mi·cro·cu·rie \'mī-krō-ˌkyūr-ē, ˌmī-krō-kyū-'rē\ n : a unit of quantity or of radioactivity equal to one millionth of a curie

mi·cro·cyte \'mī-krə-ˌsīt\ n : an abnormally small red blood cell present esp. in some anemias

mi·cro·cyt·ic \ˌmī-krə-'si-tik\ adj : of, relating to, being, or characterized by the presence of microcytes

microcytic anemia n : an anemia characterized by the presence of microcytes in the blood

mi·cro·cy·to·sis \-sī-'tō-səs\ n, pl -to·ses \-ˌsēz\ : decrease in the size of red blood cells

mi·cro·cy·to·tox·ic·i·ty test \-ˌsī-tō-ˌtäk-'si-sə-tē\ n : a procedure using microscopic quantities of materials (as complement and lymphocytes in cell-mediated immunity) to determine cytotoxicity (as to cancer cells or cells of transplanted tissue) — called also microcytotoxicity assay

mi·cro·dis·sec·tion \ˌmī-krō-di-'sek-shən, -dī-\ n : dissection under the microscope: specif : dissection of cells and tissues by means of fine needles that are precisely manipulated by levers — mi·cro·dis·sect·ed \-'sek-təd\ adj

mi·cro·dose \'mī-krō-ˌdōs\ n : an extremely small dose

mi·cro·do·sim·e·try \ˌmī-krō-dō-'si-mə-trē\ n, pl -tries : dosimetry involving microdoses of radiation or minute amounts of radioactive materials

mi·cro·drop \'mī-krō-ˌdräp\ n : a very small drop or minute droplet (as 0.1 to 0.01 of a drop)

mi·cro·drop·let \-ˌdrä-plət\ n : MICRODROP

mi·cro·elec·trode \ˌmī-krō-i-'lek-ˌtrōd\ n : a minute electrode; specif : one that is inserted in a living biological cell or tissue in studying its electrical characteristics

mi·cro·elec·tro·pho·re·sis \-ˌlek-trə-fə-'rē-səs\ n, pl -re·ses \-ˌsēz\ : electrophoresis in which the movement of single particles is observed in a microscope — mi·cro·elec·tro·pho·ret·ic \-'re-tik\ adj — mi·cro·elec·tro·pho·ret·i·cal·ly adv

mi·cro·el·e·ment \ˌmī-krō-'e-lə-mənt\ n : TRACE ELEMENT

mi·cro·em·bo·lus \-'em-bə-ləs\ n, pl -li \-ˌlī\ : an extremely small embolus

mi·cro·en·cap·su·late \in-'kap-sə-ˌlāt\ vb -lat·ed; -lat·ing : to enclose in a microcapsule — mi·cro·en·cap·su·la·tion \-in-ˌkap-sə-'lā-shən\ n

mi·cro·en·vi·ron·ment \-in-'vī-rən-mənt, -'vī-ərn-\ n : a small usu. distinctly specialized and effectively isolated habitat — called also microhabitat — mi·cro·en·vi·ron·men·tal \-ˌvī-rən-'ment-əl\ adj

mi·cro·fi·bril \-'fī-brəl, -'fi-\ n : an extremely fine fibril — mi·cro·fi·bril·lar \-brə-lər\ adj

mi·cro·fil·a·ment \ˌmī-krō-'fi-lə-mənt\ n : any of the minute actin-containing protein filaments that are widely distributed in the cytoplasm of eukaryotic cells, help maintain their structural framework, and play a role in the movement of cell components — mi·cro·fil·a·men·tous \-ˌfi-lə-'men-təs\ adj

mi·cro·fil·a·rae·mia chiefly Brit var of MICROFILAREMIA

mi·cro·fil·a·re·mia \-ˌfi-lə-'rē-mē-ə\ n : the presence of microfilariae in the blood of one affected with some forms of filariasis

mi·cro·fi·lar·ia \ˌmī-krō-fə-'lar-ē-ə\ n, pl -i·ae \-ē-ē\ : a minute larval filaria — mi·cro·fi·lar·i·al \-ē-əl\ adj

mi·cro·flo·ra \ˌmī-krə-'flōr-ə\ n : a small or strictly localized flora (intestinal ∼) — mi·cro·flo·ral \-əl\ adj

mi·cro·fluo·rom·e·try \-ˌflū-'rä-mə-trē\ n, pl -tries : the detection and measurement of the fluorescence produced by minute quantities of materials (as in cells) — mi·cro·fluo·rom·e·ter \-'rä-mə-tər\ n — mi·cro·fluo·ro·met·ric \-rə-'me-trik\ adj

mi·cro·ga·mete \-'ga-ˌmēt, -gə-'mēt\ n : the smaller and usu. male gamete of an organism producing two types of gametes — compare MACROGAMETE

mi·cro·ga·me·to·cyte \-gə-'mē-tə-ˌsīt\ n : a gametocyte producing microgametes

mi·crog·lia \mī-'krä-glē-ə\ n : neuroglia consisting of small cells with few processes that are scattered throughout the central nervous system, have a phagocytic function as part of the reticuloendothelial system, and are now usu. considered to be of mesodermal origin — mi·crog·li·al \-glē-əl\ adj

β₂-mi·cro·glob·u·lin \ˌbā-tə-ˌtü-ˌmī-krō-'glä-byə-lən\ n : a beta globulin of low molecular weight that is present at a low level in plasma, is normally excreted in the urine, is homologous in structure to part of an antibody, and forms a subunit of histocompatibility antigens

mi·cro·glos·sia \mī-krō-ˈglä-sē-ə, -ˈglō-\ n : abnormal smallness of the tongue

mi·cro·gna·thia \mī-krō-ˈnä-thē-ə, -ˈna-, mī-kräg-\ n : abnormal smallness of one or both jaws

mi·cro·gram \ˈmī-krə-gram\ n : one millionth of a gram

mi·cro·graph \-ˌgraf\ n : a graphic reproduction (as a photograph) of the image of an object formed by a microscope — **micrograph** vb

mi·cro·hab·i·tat \mī-krō-ˈha-bə-ˌtat\ n : MICROENVIRONMENT

mi·cro·he·ma·to·crit \-hi-ˈma-tə-ˌkrit\ n 1 : a procedure for determining the ratio of the volume of packed red blood cells to the volume of whole blood by centrifuging a minute quantity of blood in a capillary tube coated with heparin 2 : a hematocrit value obtained by microhematocrit ⟨a ∼ of 37%⟩

mi·cro·in·farct \-in-ˈfärkt\ n : a very small infarct

mi·cro·in·jec·tion \mī-krō-in-ˈjek-shən\ n : injection under the microscope; specif : injection into cells or tissues by means of a fine mechanically controlled capillary tube — **mi·cro·in·ject** \-in-ˈjekt\ vb

mi·cro·in·va·sive \-in-ˈvā-siv\ adj : of, relating to, or characterized by very slight invasion into adjacent tissues by malignant cells of a carcinoma in situ — **mi·cro·in·va·sion** \-ˈvā-zhən\ n

mi·cro·ion·to·pho·re·sis \-(ˌ)ī-ˌän-tə-fə-ˈrē-səs\ n, pl -re·ses \-ˌsēz\ : a process for observing or recording the effect of an ionized substance on nerve cells that involves inserting a double micropipette into the brain close to a nerve cell, injecting an ionized fluid through one barrel of the pipette, and using a concentrated saline solution in the other tube as an electrical conductor to pick up and transmit back to an oscilloscope any change in neural activity — **mi·cro·ion·to·pho·ret·ic** \-ˈre-tik\ adj — **mi·cro·ion·to·pho·ret·i·cal·ly** adv

mi·cro·li·ter \ˈmī-krō-ˈlē-tər\ n : a unit of capacity equal to one millionth of a liter

mi·cro·lith \ˈmī-krō-ˌlith\ n : a microscopic calculus or concretion — compare GRAVEL 1

mi·cro·li·thi·a·sis \mī-krō-li-ˈthī-ə-səs\ n, pl -a·ses \-ˌsēz\ : the formation or presence of microliths or gravel

mi·cro·ma·nip·u·la·tion \mī-krō-mə-ni-pyə-ˈlā-shən\ n : the technique or practice of microdissection and microinjection — **mi·cro·ma·nip·u·late** \-ˈni-pyə-ˌlāt\ vb — **mi·cro·ma·nip·u·la·tor** \-ˈni-pyə-ˌlā-tər\ n

mi·cro·mas·tia \-ˈmas-tē-ə\ n : postpubertal immaturity and abnormal smallness of the breasts

mi·cro·me·lia \-ˈmē-lē-ə\ n : a condition characterized by abnormally small and imperfectly developed extremities — **mi·cro·me·lic** \-ˈmē-lik\ adj

mi·cro·me·tas·ta·sis \mī-krō-mə-ˈtas-tə-səs\ n, pl -ta·ses \-ˌsēz\ : the spread of cancer cells from a primary site and the formation of microscopic tumors at secondary sites — **mi·cro·met·a·stat·ic** \-me-tə-ˈsta-tik\ adj

mi·cro·me·ter \ˈmī-krō-ˌmē-tər\ n : a unit of length equal to one millionth of a meter — called also micron, mu

mi·cro·meth·od \ˈmī-krō-ˌme-thəd\ n : a method (as of microanalysis) that requires only very small quantities of material or that involves the use of the microscope

mi·cro·mi·cro·cu·rie \ˌmī-krō-ˈmī-krō-ˌkyür-ē\ n : one millionth of a microcurie

mi·cro·mol·e·cule \-ˈmä-lə-ˌkyül\ n : a molecule (as of an amino acid or a fatty acid) of relatively low molecular weight — compare MACROMOLECULE — **mi·cro·mo·lec·u·lar** \-mə-ˈle-kyə-lər\ adj

mi·cro·mono·spo·ra \-ˌmä-nə-ˈspór-ə\ n 1 cap : a genus of actinomycetes that includes several antibiotic-producing forms (as M. purpurea, the source of gentamicin) 2 pl -rae \-ˌrē\ : any bacterium of the genus Micromonospora

mi·cron \ˈmī-ˌkrän\ n, pl microns also mi·cra \-krə\ : MICROMETER

mi·cro·nee·dle \ˈmī-krō-ˌnēd-ᵊl\ n : a needle for micromanipulation

mi·cro·nod·u·lar \ˌmī-krō-ˈnä-jə-lər\ adj : characterized by the presence of extremely small nodules

mi·cro·nu·tri·ent \-ˈnü-trē-ənt, -ˈnyü-\ n : a mineral or organic compound (as a vitamin) essential in minute amounts to the growth and health of an animal — compare TRACE ELEMENT

mi·cro·or·gan·ism \-ˈór-gə-ˌni-zəm\ n : an organism of microscopic or ultramicroscopic size — **mi·cro·or·gan·is·mal** \-ˌór-gə-ˈniz-məl\ adj

mi·cro·par·a·site \mī-krō-ˈpar-ə-ˌsīt\ n : a parasitic microorganism — **mi·cro·par·a·sit·ic** \-ˌpar-ə-ˈsi-tik\ adj

mi·cro·pe·nis \-ˈpē-nəs\ n, pl -pe·nes \-(ˌ)nēz\ or -pe·nis·es : MICROPHALLUS

mi·cro·per·fu·sion \-pər-ˈfyü-zhən\ n : an act or instance of forcing a fluid through a small organ or tissue by way of a tubule or blood vessel — **mi·cro·per·fused** \-ˈfyüzd\ adj

mi·cro·phage \ˈmī-krə-ˌfāj\ n : a small phagocyte

mi·cro·pha·kia \mī-krō-ˈfā-kē-ə\ n : abnormal smallness of the lens of the eye

mi·cro·phal·lus \-ˈfa-ləs\ n : smallness of the penis esp. to an abnormal degree — called also micropenis

mi·cro·phon·ic \ˌmī-krō-ˈfä-nik\ n : an electrical potential arising in the cochlea when the mechanical energy of a sound stimulus is transformed to electrical energy as the action potential of the transmitting nerve — **mi-crophonic** *adj*

mi-cro-pho-to-graph \-'fō-tə-ˌgraf\ : PHOTOMICROGRAPH — **mi-cro-pho-tog-ra-phy** \-fə-'tä-grə-fē\ *n*

mi-croph-thal-mia \ˌmī-ˌkräf-'thal-mē-ə\ *n* : abnormal smallness of the eye usu. occurring as a congenital anomaly

mi-croph-thal-mic \-'thal-mik\ *adj* : exhibiting microphthalmia : having small eyes

mi-croph-thal-mos \-məs, -ˌmäs\ *or* **mi-croph-thal-mus** \-'thal-məs\ *n, pl* **-moi** \-ˌmoi\ *or* **-mi** \-ˌmē\ : MICROPHTHALMIA

mi-cro-pi-pette *or* **mi-cro-pi-pet** \-pī-'pet\ *n* 1 : a pipette for the measurement of minute volumes 2 : a small and extremely fine-pointed pipette used in making microinjections — **micropipette** *vb*

mi-cro-probe \'mī-krō-ˌprōb\ *n* : a device for microanalysis that operates by exciting radiation in a minute area or volume of material so that the composition may be determined from the emission spectrum

mi-crop-sia \mī-'kräp-sē-ə\ *also* **mi-crop-sy** \'mī-ˌkräp-sē\ *n, pl* **-sias** *also* **-sies** : a pathological condition in which objects appear to be smaller than they are in reality

mi-cro-punc-ture \ˌmī-krō-'pəŋk-chər\ *n* : an extremely small puncture (as of a nephron); *also* : an act of making a micropuncture

mi-cro-pyle \'mī-krə-ˌpīl\ *n* : a differentiated area of surface in an egg through which a sperm enters — **mi-cro-py-lar** \ˌmī-krə-'pī-lər\ *adj*

mi-cro-ra-dio-gram \ˌmī-krō-'rā-dē-ə-ˌgram\ *n* : MICRORADIOGRAPH

mi-cro-ra-dio-graph \-ˌgraf\ *n* : an X-ray photograph prepared by microradiography

mi-cro-ra-di-og-ra-phy \-ˌrā-dē-'ä-grə-fē\ *n, pl* **-phies** : radiography in which an X-ray photograph is prepared showing minute internal structure — **mi-cro-ra-dio-graph-ic** \-ˌrā-dē-ə-'gra-fik\ *adj*

mi-cro-scis-sors \'mī-krō-ˌsi-zərz\ *n sing or pl* : extremely small scissors for use in microsurgery

mi-cro-scope \'mī-krə-ˌskōp\ *n* : an instrument for making enlarged images of minute objects usu. using light; *esp* : COMPOUND MICROSCOPE — see ELECTRON MICROSCOPE, LIGHT MICROSCOPE, PHASE-CONTRAST MICROSCOPE, POLARIZING MICROSCOPE, ULTRAVIOLET MICROSCOPE

mi-cro-scop-ic \ˌmī-krə-'skä-pik\ *also* **mi-cro-scop-i-cal** \-pi-kəl\ *adj* 1 : of, relating to, or conducted with the microscope or microscopy 2 : so small or fine as to be invisible or indistin-

guishable without the use of a microscope — compare MACROSCOPIC, SUBMICROSCOPIC, ULTRAMICROSCOPIC 1 — **mi-cro-scop-i-cal-ly** *adv*

microscopic anatomy *n* : HISTOLOGY

mi-cros-co-py \mī-'kräs-kə-pē\ *n, pl* **-pies** : the use of or investigation with the microscope — **mi-cros-co-pist** \-pist\ *n*

mi-cro-sec-ond \'mī-krō-ˌse-kənd, -kənt\ *n* : one millionth of a second

mi-cro-sec-tion \-ˌsek-shən\ *n* : a thin section (as of tissue) prepared for microscopic examination — **microsec-tion** *vb*

mi-cro-slide \'mī-krō-ˌslīd\ *n* : a slip of glass on which a preparation is mounted for microscopic examination

mi-cro-some \'mī-krə-ˌsōm\ *n* 1 : any of various minute cellular structures (as a ribosome) 2 : a particle in a particulate fraction that is obtained by heavy centrifugation of broken cells and consists of various amounts of ribosomes, fragmented endoplasmic reticulum, and mitochondrial cristae — **mi-cro-som-al** \ˌmī-krə-'sō-məl\ *adj*

mi-cro-so-mia \ˌmī-krə-'sō-mē-ə\ *n* : abnormal smallness of the body

mi-cro-sphe-ro-cy-to-sis \ˌsfir-ō-sī-'tō-səs, -ˌsfer-\ *n, pl* **-to-ses** \-'tō-ˌsēz\ : spherocytosis esp. when marked by very small spherocytes

mi-cro-spo-rum \mī-'kräs-pə-rəm\ *n* 1 *cap* : a genus of fungi (family Moniliaceae) producing both small, nearly oval single-celled spores and large spindle-shaped multicellular spores with a usu. rough outer wall and including several that cause ringworm, tinea capitis, and tinea corporis 2 *pl* **-ra** : any fungus of the genus *Microsporum*

mi-cro-struc-ture \'mī-krō-ˌstrək-chər\ *n* : microscopic structure (as of a cell) — **mi-cro-struc-tur-al** \ˌmī-krō-'strək-chə-rəl, -'strək-shrəl\ *adj*

mi-cro-sur-gery \ˌmī-krō-'sər-jə-rē\ *n, pl* **-ger-ies** : minute dissection or manipulation (as by a micromanipulator or laser beam) of living structures or tissue — **mi-cro-sur-geon** \'mī-krō-ˌsər-jən\ *n* — **mi-cro-sur-gi-cal** \ˌmī-krō-'sər-ji-kəl\ *adj* — **mi-cro-sur-gi-cal-ly** *adv*

mi-cro-sy-ringe \-sə-'rinj\ *n* : a hypodermic syringe equipped for the precise measurement and injection of minute quantities of fluid

mi-cro-tech-nique \ˌmī-krō-tek-'nēk\ *also* **mi-cro-tech-nic** \'mī-krō-ˌtek-nik, ˌmī-krō-tek-'nēk\ *n* : any of various methods of handling and preparing material for microscopic observation and study

mi-cro-throm-bus \-'thräm-bəs\ *n, pl* **-bi** \-ˌbī\ : a very small thrombus

mi-cro-tia \mī-'krō-shə, -shē-ə\ *n* : abnormal smallness of the external ear

mi-cro-tome \'mī-krə-ˌtōm\ *n* : an instrument for cutting sections (as of organic tissues) for microscopic examination — **microtome** *vb*

mi·cro·trau·ma \·¹mī-krō-¹traù-mə. -¡trò-\ *n* : a very slight injury or lesion

mi·cro·tu·bule \·¹mī-krō-¹tü-¡byül. -¹tyü-\ *n* : any of the minute tubules in eukaryotic cytoplasm that are composed of the protein tubulin and form an important component of the cytoskeleton, mitotic spindle, cilia, and flagella — **mi·cro·tu·bu·lar** \-byə-lər\ *adj*

mi·cro·unit \¹mī-krō-¡yü-nət\ *n* : one millionth of a standard unit and esp. an international unit (~s of insulin)

mi·cro·vas·cu·lar \-¹vas-kyə-lər\ *adj* : of, relating to, or constituting the part of the circulatory system made up of minute vessels (as venules or capillaries) that average less than 0.3 millimeters in diameter — **mi·cro·vas·cu·la·ture** \-lə-¡chùr. -¡tyùr\ *n*

mi·cro·ves·i·cle \-¹ve-si-kəl\ *n* : a very small vesicle

mi·cro·ves·sel \-¹ve-səl\ *n* : a blood vessel (as a capillary, arteriole, or venule) of the microcirculatory system

mi·cro·vil·lus \-¹vi-ləs\ *n, pl* **-vil·li** \-¡lī\ : a microscopic projection of a tissue, cell, or cell organelle; *esp* : any of the fingerlike outward projections of some cell surfaces — **mi·cro·vil·lar** \-¹vi-lər\ *adj* — **mi·cro·vil·lous** \-¹vi-ləs\ *adj*

mi·cro·wave \¹mī-krō-¡wāv\ *n, often attrib* : a comparatively short electromagnetic wave; *esp* : one between about 1 millimeter and 1 meter in wavelength

microwave sickness *n* : a condition of impaired health reported esp. in the Russian medical literature that is characterized by headaches, anxiety, sleep disturbances, fatigue, and difficulty in concentrating and by changes in the cardiovascular and central nervous systems and that is held to be caused by prolonged exposure to low-intensity microwave radiation

Mi·cru·rus \mī-¹krür-əs\ *n* : a genus of small venomous elapid snakes comprising the American coral snakes

mic·tu·ri·tion \¡mik-chə-¹ri-shən. ¡mik-tyü-\ *n* : URINATION — **mic·tu·rate** \¹mik-chə-¡rāt. -¡tyü-\ *vb*

MID *abbr* minimal infective dose

mid·ax·il·lary line \¡mid-¹ak-sə-¡ler-ē-\ *n* : an imaginary line through the axilla parallel to the long axis of the body and midway between its ventral and dorsal surfaces

mid·brain \¹mid-¡brān\ *n* : the middle of the three primary divisions of the developing vertebrate brain or the corresponding part of the adult brain that includes a ventral part containing the cerebral peduncles and a dorsal tectum containing the corpora quadrigemina and that surrounds the aqueduct of Sylvius connecting the third and fourth ventricles — called also *mesencephalon*

mid·cla·vic·u·lar line \-kla-¹vi-kyə-lər-. -klə-\ *n* : an imaginary line parallel to the long axis of the body and passing through the midpoint of the clavicle on the ventral surface of the body

middle age *n* : the period of life from about 40 to about 60 — **mid·dle-aged** \¡mid-əl-¹ājd\ *adj* — **mid·dle-ag·er** \-¹ā-jər\ *n*

middle cerebellar peduncle *n* : CEREBELLAR PEDUNCLE b

middle cerebral artery *n* : CEREBRAL ARTERY b

middle concha *n* : NASAL CONCHA b

middle constrictor *n* : a fan-shaped muscle of the pharynx that arises from the ceratohyal and thyrohyal of the hyoid bone and from the stylohyoid ligament, inserts into the median line at the back of the pharynx, and acts to constrict part of the pharynx in swallowing — called also *constrictor pharyngis medius, middle pharyngeal constrictor muscle*; compare INFERIOR CONSTRICTOR, SUPERIOR CONSTRICTOR

middle ear *n* : the intermediate portion of the ear of higher vertebrates consisting typically of a small air-filled membrane-lined chamber in the temporal bone continuous with the nasopharynx through the eustachian tube, separated from the external ear by the tympanic membrane and from the inner ear by fenestrae, and containing a chain of three ossicles that extends from the tympanic membrane to the oval window and transmits vibrations to the inner ear — called also *tympanic cavity*; compare INCUS, MALLEUS, STAPES

middle finger *n* : the midmost of the five digits of the hand

middle hemorrhoidal artery *n* : RECTAL ARTERY b

middle hemorrhoidal vein *n* : RECTAL VEIN b

middle meatus *n* : a curved anteroposterior passage in each nasal cavity that is situated below the middle nasal concha and extends along the entire superior border of the inferior nasal concha — compare INFERIOR MEATUS, SUPERIOR MEATUS

middle meningeal artery *n* : a branch of the first portion of the maxillary artery that is the largest artery supplying the dura mater, enters the cranium through the foramen spinosum, and divides into anterior and posterior branches in a groove in the greater wing of the sphenoid bone

middle nasal concha *n* : NASAL CONCHA b

middle peduncle *n* : CEREBELLAR PEDUNCLE b

middle pharyngeal constrictor muscle *n* : MIDDLE CONSTRICTOR

middle rectal artery *n* : RECTAL ARTERY b

middle rectal vein *n* : RECTAL VEIN b

middle sacral artery *n* : a small artery that arises from the back of the abdominal part of the aorta just before it forks into the two common iliac arteries and that descends near the midline in front of the fourth and fifth lumbar vertebrae, the sacrum, and the coccyx to the glomus coccygeum

middle temporal artery *n* : TEMPORAL ARTERY 2b

middle temporal gyrus *n* : TEMPORAL GYRUS b

middle temporal vein *n* : TEMPORAL VEIN a(2)

middle turbinate *n* : NASAL CONCHA b

middle turbinate bone *also* **middle turbinated bone** *n* : NASAL CONCHA b

mid·dor·sal \(ˌ)mid-ˈdȯr-səl\ *adj* : of, relating to, or situated in the middle part or median line of the back

mid·epi·gas·tric \-ˌe-pi-ˈgas-trik\ *adj* : of, relating to, or located in the middle of the epigastric region of the abdomen ⟨∼ tenderness⟩

mid·for·ceps \-ˈfȯr-səps, -ˌseps\ *n* : a procedure for delivery of an infant by the use of forceps after engagement has occurred but before the head has reached the lower part of the birth canal — compare HIGH FORCEPS, LOW FORCEPS

midge \ˈmij\ *n* : any of numerous tiny dipteran flies (esp. families Ceratopogonidae, Cecidomyiidae, and Chironomidae) many of which are capable of giving painful bites and some of which are vectors or intermediate hosts of parasites of humans and various other vertebrates — see BITING MIDGE

midg·et \ˈmi-jət\ *n* : a very small person; *specif* : a person of unusually small size who is physically well-proportioned

midg·et·ism \ˈmi-jə-ˌti-zəm\ *n* : the state of being a midget

mid·gut \ˈmid-ˌgət\ *n* : the middle part of the alimentary canal of a vertebrate embryo that in humans gives rise to the more distal part of the duodenum and to the jejunum, ileum, cecum and appendix, ascending colon, and much of the transverse colon

mid–life \(ˌ)mid-ˈlīf\ *n* : MIDDLE AGE

mid–life crisis *n* : a period of emotional turmoil in middle age caused by the realization that one is no longer young and characterized esp. by a strong desire for change

mid·line \ˈmid-ˌlīn, mid-ˈlīn\ *n* : a median line: *esp* : the median line or median plane of the body or some part of the body

mid·preg·nan·cy \(ˌ)mid-ˈpreg-nən-sē\ *n*, *pl* -cies : the middle period of a term of pregnancy

mid·riff \ˈmi-drif\ *n* 1 : DIAPHRAGM 1 2 : the mid-region of the human torso

mid·sag·it·tal \(ˌ)mid-ˈsa-jət-əl\ *adj* : median and sagittal

midsagittal plane *n* : the median vertical longitudinal plane that divides a bilaterally symmetrical animal into right and left halves — called also *median plane*

mid·sec·tion \ˈmid-ˌsek-shən\ *n* : a section midway between the extremes: *esp* : MIDRIFF 2

mid·stream \ˌmid-ˈstrēm\ *adj* : of, relating to, or being urine passed during the middle of an act of urination and not at the beginning or end ⟨a ∼ specimen⟩

mid·tar·sal \-ˈtär-səl\ *adj* : of, relating to, or being the articulation between the two rows of tarsal bones

midtarsal amputation *n* : amputation of the forepart of the foot through the midtarsal joint

mid·tri·mes·ter \-(ˌ)trī-ˈmes-tər\ *adj* : of, performed during, or occurring during the fourth through sixth months of human pregnancy

mid·ven·tral \-ˈven-trəl\ *adj* : of, relating to, or being the middle of the ventral surface — **mid·ven·tral·ly** *adv*

mid·wife \ˈmid-ˌwif\ *n* : one who assists women in childbirth — see NURSE-MIDWIFE

mid·wife·ry \mid-ˈwi-fə-rē, -ˈwī-; ˈmid-ˌwī-\ *n*, *pl* -ries : the art or act of assisting at childbirth; *also* : OBSTETRICS

mi·fep·ris·tone \mi-ˈfe-pri-ˌstōn\ *n* : RU 486

mi·graine \ˈmī-ˌgrān\ *n* 1 : a condition that is marked by recurrent usu. unilateral severe headache often accompanied by nausea and vomiting and followed by sleep, that tends to occur in more than one member of a family, and that is of uncertain origin though attacks appear to be precipitated by dilatation of intracranial blood vessels 2 : an episode or attack of migraine ⟨suffers from ∼s⟩ — called also *sick headache* — **mi·grain·ous** \-ˈgrā-nəs\ *adj*

mi·grain·eur \ˌmē-gre-ˈnər\ *n* : a person who experiences migraines

mi·grain·oid \ˈmī-ˌgrā-ˌnȯid, mī-ˈgrā-\ *adj* : resembling migraine

migrans — see ERYTHEMA CHRONICUM MIGRANS, LARVAL MIGRANS, LARVA MIGRANS

migrantes — see LARVA MIGRANS

mi·grate \ˈmī-ˌgrāt, mī-ˈ\ *vb* **mi·grat·ed; mi·grat·ing** : to move from one place to another: as **a** : to move from one site to another in a host organism esp. as part of a life cycle **b** *of an atom or group* : to shift position within a molecule — **mi·gra·tion** \mī-ˈgrā-shən\ *n* — **mi·gra·to·ry** \ˈmī-grə-ˌtȯr-ē\ *adj*

migration inhibitory factor *n* : a lymphokine that inhibits the migration of macrophages away from the site of interaction between lymphocytes and antigens

mi·ka·my·cin \ˌmī-kə-ˈmī-sən\ *n* : an antibiotic complex isolated from a bacterium of the genus *Streptomyces* (*S. mitakaensis*)

Mi·ku·licz resection \ˈme-kü-ˌlich-\ *n* : an operation for removal of part of the intestine and esp. the colon in stages that involves bringing the diseased portion out of the body, closing the wound around the two parts of the loop which have been sutured together, and cutting off the diseased part leaving a double opening which is later joined by crushing the common wall and closed from the exterior

Mikulicz–Ra·dec·ki \-ra-ˈdet-skē\, **Johann von (1850–1905),** Polish surgeon.

Mi·ku·licz's disease \-ˌli-chəz-\ *n* : abnormal enlargement of the lacrimal and salivary glands

Mikulicz's syndrome *n* : Mikulicz's disease esp. when occurring as a complication of another disease (as leukemia or sarcoidosis)

mild \ˈmī(ə)ld\ *adj* 1 : moderate in action or effect (a ~ drug) 2 : not severe

mil·dew \ˈmil-ˌdü, -ˌdyü\ *n* 1 : a superficial usu. whitish growth produced esp. on organic matter or living plants by fungi (as of the families Erysiphaceae and Peronosporaceae) 2 : a fungus producing mildew

mild silver protein *n* : SILVER PROTEIN a

mil·i·a·ria \ˌmil-lē-ˈar-ē-ə\ *n* : an inflammatory disorder of the skin characterized by redness, eruption, burning or itching, and the release of sweat in abnormal ways (as by the eruption of vesicles) due to blockage of the ducts of the sweat glands; *esp* : PRICKLY HEAT — **mil·i·ar·i·al** \-əl\ *adj*

miliaria crys·tal·li·na \-ˌkris-tə-ˈlē-nə\ *n* : SUDAMINA

mil·i·ary \ˈmi-lē-ˌer-ē\ *adj* 1 : resembling or suggesting a small seed or many small seeds (a ~ aneurysm) (~ tubercles) 2 : characterized by the formation of numerous small lesions (~ pneumonia)

miliary tuberculosis *n* : acute tuberculosis in which minute tubercles are formed in one or more organs of the body by tubercle bacilli usu. spread by way of the blood

Mil·i·bis \ˈmi-li-bis\ *trademark* — used for a preparation of glycobiarsol

mi·lieu \mēl-ˈyə(r), -ˈyü; ˈmēl-ˌyü, mē-ˈlyœ\ *n, pl* **milieus** *or* **mi·lieux** *same or* -ˈyə(r)z, -ˈyüz; -ˌyüz, -ˈlyœz\ : ENVIRONMENT

milieu therapy *n* : manipulation of the environment of a mental patient for therapeutic purposes

mil·i·um \ˈmi-lē-əm\ *n, pl* **mil·ia** \-lē-ə\ : a small pearly firm noninflammatory elevation of the skin (as of the face) due to retention of keratin in an oil gland duct blocked by a thin layer

of epithelium — called also *whitehead;* compare BLACKHEAD 1

¹**milk** \ˈmilk\ *n* : a fluid secreted by the mammary glands of females for the nourishment of their young; *esp* : cow's milk used as a food by humans

²**milk** *vb* : to draw off the milk of

milk·er's nodules \ˈmil-kərz-\ *n* : a mild virus infection characterized by reddish blue nodules on the hands, arms, face, or neck acquired by direct contact with the udders of cows infected with a virus similar to that causing cowpox — called also *paravaccinia, pseudocowpox*

milk fever *n* 1 : a febrile disorder following parturition 2 : a disease of newly lactating cows, sheep, or goats that is caused by excessive drain on the body mineral reserves during the establishment of the milk flow — called also *parturient paresis;* compare GRASS TETANY

milk leg *n* : postpartum thrombophlebitis of a femoral vein — called also *phlegmasia alba dolens*

Milk·man's syndrome \ˈmilk-mənz-\ *n* : an abnormal condition marked by porosity of bone and tendency to spontaneous often symmetrical fractures

Milkman, Louis Arthur (1895–1951), American roentgenologist.

milk of bismuth *n* : a thick white suspension in water of the hydroxide of bismuth and bismuth subcarbonate that is used esp. in the treatment of diarrhea

milk of magnesia *n* : a milk-white suspension of magnesium hydroxide in water used as an antacid and laxative — called also *magnesia magma*

milk sickness *n* : an acute disease characterized by weakness, vomiting, and constipation and caused by eating dairy products or meat from cattle affected with trembles

milk sugar *n* : LACTOSE

milk tooth *n* : a temporary tooth of a young mammal; *esp* : one of the human dentition including four incisors, two canines, and four molars in each jaw which fall out during childhood and are replaced by the permanent teeth — called also *baby tooth, deciduous tooth, primary tooth*

Mil·ler–Ab·bott tube \ˈmi-lər-ˈa-bət-\ *n* : a double-lumen balloon-tipped rubber tube used for the purpose of decompression in treating intestinal obstruction

Miller, Thomas Grier (*b* 1886) and Abbott, William Osler (1902–1943), American physicians.

milli- *comb form* : thousandth — used esp. in terms belonging to the metric system (*millirad*)

mil·li·bar \ˈmi-lə-ˌbär\ *n* : a unit of atmospheric pressure equal to 1/1000 bar or 1000 dynes per square centimeter

mil·li·cu·rie \ˌmi-lə-ˈkyùr-(ˌ)ē. -kyü-ˈrē\ n : one thousandth of a curie

mil·li·gram \ˈmi-lə-ˌgram\ n : one thousandth of a gram

mil·li·li·ter \-ˌlē-tər\ n : one thousandth of a liter

mil·li·me·ter \-ˌmē-tər\ n : one thousandth of a meter

mil·li·mi·cron \ˌmi-lə-ˈmī-ˌkrän\ n : NANOMETER

mil·li·os·mol or **mil·li·os·mole** \ˌmi-lē-ˈäz-ˌmōl, -ˈäs-\ n : one thousandth of an osmol

mil·li·pede \ˈmi-lə-ˌpēd\ n : any of a class (Diplopoda) of arthropods having usu. a cylindrical segmented body, two pairs of legs on most segments, and including some forms that secrete toxic substances causing skin irritation but that unlike centipedes possess no poison fangs

mil·li·rad \-ˌrad\ n : one thousandth of a rad

mil·li·rem \-ˌrem\ n : one thousandth of a rem

mil·li·roent·gen \ˌmi-lə-ˈrent-gən. -ˈrənt-, -jən; -ˈren-chən. -ˈrən-\ n : one thousandth of a roentgen

mil·li·unit \ˈmi-lə-ˌyü-nət\ n : one thousandth of a standard unit and esp. of an international unit

Mi·lon·tin \mi-ˈlän-tin\ trademark — used for a preparation of phensuximide

Mil·roy's disease \ˈmil-ˌròiz-\ n : a hereditary lymphedema esp. of the legs
Milroy, William Forsyth (1855–1942), American physician.

Mil·town \ˈmil-ˌtaùn\ trademark — used for a preparation of meprobamate

Mil·wau·kee brace \mil-ˈwò-kē-, -ˈwä-\ n : an orthopedic brace that extends from the pelvis to the neck and is used esp. in the treatment of scoliosis

mi·met·ic \mə-ˈme-tik, mī-\ adj : simulating the action or effect of — usu. used in combination ⟨sympathomimetic drugs⟩

mim·ic \ˈmi-mik\ vb **mim·icked** \-mikt\ : **mim·ick·ing** : to imitate or resemble closely: as **a** : to imitate the symptoms of **b** : to produce an effect and esp. a physiological effect similar to — **mimic** n — **mim·ic·ry** \ˈmi-mi-krē\ n

min abbr minim

Min·a·ma·ta disease \ˌmi-nə-ˈmä-tə-\ n : a toxic neuropathy caused by the ingestion of methylmercury compounds (as in contaminated seafood) and characterized by impairment of cerebral functions, constriction of the visual field, and progressive weakening of muscles

mind \ˈmīnd\ n **1** : the element or complex of elements in an individual that feels, perceives, thinks, wills, and esp. reasons **2** : the conscious mental events and capabilities in an organism **3** : the organized conscious and unconscious adaptive mental activity of an organism

mind–set \ˈmīnd-ˌset\ n : a mental inclination, tendency, or habit

¹min·er·al \ˈmi-nə-rəl\ n : a solid homogeneous crystalline chemical element or compound that results from the inorganic processes of nature

²mineral adj **1** : of or relating to minerals; also : INORGANIC **2** : impregnated with mineral substances

min·er·al·ize \ˈmi-nə-rə-ˌlīz\ vb **-ized**; **-iz·ing** : to impregnate or supply with minerals or an inorganic compound — **min·er·al·i·za·tion** \ˌmi-nə-rəl-ə-ˈzā-shən\ n

min·er·al·o·cor·ti·coid \ˌmi-nə-rə-lō-ˈkòr-tə-ˌkòid\ n : a corticosteroid (as aldosterone) that affects chiefly the electrolyte and fluid balance in the body — compare GLUCOCORTICOID

mineral oil n : a transparent oily liquid obtained usu. by distilling petroleum and used in medicine esp. for treating constipation

min·er's asthma \ˈmī-nərz-\ n : PNEUMOCONIOSIS

miner's elbow n : bursitis of the elbow that tends to occur in miners who work in small tunnels and rest their weight on their elbows

miner's phthisis n : an occupational respiratory disease (as pneumoconiosis or anthracosilicosis) of miners

mini·lap·a·rot·o·my \ˌmi-nē-ˌla-pə-ˈrä-tə-mē\ n, pl **-mies** : a ligation of the Fallopian tubes performed through a small incision in the abdominal wall

min·im \ˈmi-nəm\ n : either of two units of capacity equal to ¹⁄₆₀ fluid dram: **a** : a U.S. unit of liquid capacity equivalent to 0.003760 cubic inch or 0.061610 milliliter **b** : a British unit of liquid capacity and dry measure equivalent to 0.003612 cubic inch or 0.059194 milliliter

minimae — see VENAE CORDIS MINIMAE

min·i·mal \ˈmi-nə-məl\ adj : relating to or being a minimum : constituting the least possible with respect to size, number, degree, or certain stated conditions

minimal brain damage n : ATTENTION DEFICIT DISORDER

minimal brain dysfunction n : ATTENTION DEFICIT DISORDER — abbr. MBD

minimal infective dose n : the smallest quantity of infective material that regularly produces infection — abbr. MID

minimal inhibitory concentration n : the smallest concentration of an antibiotic that regularly inhibits growth of a bacterium in vitro — abbr. MIC

minimi — see ABDUCTOR DIGITI MINIMI, EXTENSOR DIGITI MINIMI, FLEXOR DIGITI MINIMI BREVIS, GLUTEUS MINIMUS, OPPONENS DIGITI MINIMI

min·i·mum \ˈmi-nə-məm\ n, pl **-i·ma** \-mə\ or **-i·mums 1** : the least quantity assignable. admissible. or possible **2** : the lowest degree or amount of variation (as of temperature) reached or recorded — **minimum** *adj*

minimum dose : the smallest dose of a medicine or drug that will produce an effect

minimum inhibitory concentration *n* : MINIMAL INHIBITORY CONCENTRATION

minimum lethal dose *n* : the smallest dose experimentally found to kill any one animal of a test group

minimus — see GLUTEUS MINIMUS

mini-pill \'mi-nē-ˌpill\ *n* : a contraceptive pill that is intended to minimize side effects. contains a very low dose of a progestogen and esp. norethindrone but no estrogen. and is taken daily

Mini-press \-ˌpres\ *trademark* — used for a preparation of prazosin

Min·ne·so·ta Mul·ti·pha·sic Personality Inventory \ˌmi-nə-ˈsō-tə-ˌməl-ti-ˈfā-zik-. -ˌməl-ˌtī-\ *n* : a test of personal and social adjustment based on a complex scaling of the answers to an elaborate true or false test

Mi·no·cin \mi-ˈnō-sin\ *trademark* — used for a preparation of minocycline

min·o·cy·cline \ˌmi-nō-ˈsi-klēn\ *n* : a broad-spectrum tetracycline antibiotic $C_{23}H_{27}N_3O_7$

¹mi·nor \'mī-nər\ *adj* : not serious or involving risk to life (~ illness) (a ~ operation) — compare MAJOR

²minor *n* : a person of either sex under the age of legal qualification for adult rights and responsibilities that has traditionally been 21 in the U.S. but is now 18 in many states or sometimes less under certain circumstances (as marriage or pregnancy)

minora — see LABIA MINORA

minor surgery *n* : surgery involving little risk to the life of the patient; *specif* : an operation on the superficial structures of the body or a manipulative procedure that does not involve a serious risk — compare MAJOR SURGERY

min·ox·i·dil \mi-ˈnäk-sə-ˌdil\ *n* : a peripheral vasodilator $C_9H_{15}N_5O$ used orally to treat hypertension and topically in a propylene glycol solution to promote hair regrowth in male-pattern baldness — see ROGAINE

minute volume *n* : CARDIAC OUTPUT

mi·o·sis \mī-ˈō-səs, mē-\ *n, pl* **mi·o·ses** \-ˌsēz\ : excessive smallness or contraction of the pupil of the eye

¹mi·ot·ic \-ˈä-tik\ *n* : an agent that causes miosis

²miotic *adj* : relating to or characterized by miosis

mi·ra·cid·i·um \ˌmir-ə-ˈsi-dē-əm, mī-rə-\ *n, pl* **-cid·ia** \-dē-ə\ : the free-swimming ciliated first larva of a digenetic trematode that seeks out and penetrates a suitable snail intermediate host in which it develops into a

sporocyst — **mi·ra·cid·i·al** \-dē-əl\ *adj*

mir·a·cil D \'mir-ə-ˌsil-ˈdē\ *n* : LUCANTHONE

mir·a·cle drug \'mir-ə-kəl\ *n* : a drug usu. newly discovered that elicits a dramatic response in a patient's condition — called also *wonder drug*

mi·rage \mə-ˈräzh\ *n* : an optical effect that is sometimes seen at sea. in the desert. or over a hot pavement. that may have the appearance of a pool of water or a mirror in which distant objects are seen inverted. and that is caused by the bending or reflection of rays of light by a layer of heated air of varying density

mi·rex \'mī-ˌreks\ *n* : an organochlorine insecticide $C_{10}Cl_{12}$ formerly used esp. against ants that is a suspected carcinogen

mirror writing *n* : backward writing resembling in slant and order of letters the reflection of ordinary writing in a mirror

mis- *prefix* : badly : wrongly (*misdiagnose*)

mis·car·riage \mis-ˈkar-ij\ *n* : spontaneous expulsion of a human fetus before it is viable and esp. between the 12th and 28th weeks of gestation — compare ABORTION 1a — **mis·car·ry** \(ˌ)mis-ˈkar-ē\ *vb*

mis·di·ag·nose \(ˌ)mis-ˈdī-ig-ˌnōs, -ˌnōz\ *vb* **-nosed; -nos·ing** : to diagnose incorrectly — **mis·di·ag·no·sis** \(ˌ)mis-ˌdī-ig-ˈnō-səs\ *n*

mi·sog·y·nist \mə-ˈsä-jə-nist\ *n* : one who hates women — **misogynist** *adj* — **mi·sog·y·ny** \mə-ˈsä-jə-nē\ *n*

mi·so·pros·tol \ˌmi-sō-ˈpräs-ˌtōl. -ˌtȯl\ *n* : a prostaglandin analog $C_{22}H_{38}O_5$ used to prevent stomach ulcers occurring esp. as a side effect of drugs used to treat arthritis

missed abortion \'mist-\ *n* : an intrauterine death of a fetus that is not followed by its immediate expulsion

missed labor *n* : a retention of a fetus in the uterus beyond the normal period of pregnancy

¹mis·sense \'mis-ˌsens\ *adj* : relating to or being a genetic mutation involving alteration of one or more codons so that different amino acids are determined — compare ANTISENSE. NONSENSE

²missense *n* : missense genetic mutation

missionary position *n* : a coital position in which the female lies on her back with the male on top and with his face opposite hers

mit- *or* **mito-** *comb form* **1** : thread (*mitochondrion*) **2** : mitosis (*mitogenesis*)

mite \'mīt\ *n* : any of numerous small to very minute acarid arachnids that include parasites of insects and vertebrates some of which are important disease vectors. parasites of plants. pests of various stored products. and free-living aquatic and terrestrial forms — see ITCH MITE

mith·ra·my·cin \ˌmi-thrə-ˈmīs-ᵊn\ *n* : PLICAMYCIN

mith·ri·da·tism \ˌmi-thrə-ˈdā-ˌti-zəm\ *n* : tolerance to a poison acquired by taking gradually increased doses of it

Mith·ra·da·tes VI Eu·pa·tor \ˌmi-thrə-ˈdā-tēz-ˈsiks-ˈyü-pə-ˌtōr\, (*d* 63 BC), king of Pontus.

mi·ti·cide \ˈmi-tə-ˌsīd\ *n* : an agent used to kill mites — **mi·ti·cid·al** \ˌmi-tə-ˈsīd-ᵊl\ *adj*

mi·to·chon·dri·on \ˌmī-tə-ˈkän-drē-ən\ *n, pl* **-dria** \-drē-ə\ : any of various round or long cellular organelles of most eukaryotes that are found outside the nucleus, produce energy for the cell through cellular respiration, and are rich in fats, proteins, and enzymes — **mi·to·chon·dri·al** \-drē-əl\ *adj* — **mi·to·chon·dri·al·ly** *adv*

mi·to·gen \ˈmi-tə-jən\ *n* : a substance that induces mitosis

mi·to·gen·e·sis \ˌmi-tə-ˈje-nə-səs\ *n, pl* **-e·ses** \-ˌsēz\ : the production of cell mitosis

mi·to·gen·ic \-ˈje-nik\ *adj* : of, producing, or stimulating mitosis

mi·to·my·cin \ˌmi-tə-ˈmīs-ᵊn\ *n* : a complex of antibiotic substances which is produced by a Japanese bacterium of the genus *Streptomyces* (*S. caespitosus*) and one form of which inhibits DNA synthesis and is used as an antineoplastic agent

mi·to·sis \mi-ˈtō-səs\ *n, pl* **-to·ses** \-ˌsēz\ 1 : a process that takes place in the nucleus of a dividing cell, involves typically a series of steps consisting of prophase, metaphase, anaphase, and telophase, and results in the formation of two new nuclei each having the same number of chromosomes as the parent nucleus — compare MEIOSIS 2 : cell division in which mitosis occurs — **mi·tot·ic** \-ˈtä-tik\ *adj* — **mi·tot·i·cal·ly** *adv*

mitotic index *n* : the number of cells per thousand cells actively dividing at a particular time

mi·tral \ˈmī-trəl\ *adj* : of, relating to, being, or adjoining a mitral valve or orifice

mitral cell *n* : any of the pyramidal cells of the olfactory bulb about which terminate numerous fibers from the olfactory cells of the nasal mucosa

mitral insufficiency *n* : inability of the mitral valve to close perfectly permitting blood to flow back into the atrium and leading to varying degrees of heart failure — called also *mitral incompetence*

mitral orifice *n* : the left atrioventricular orifice

mitral regurgitation *n* : backward flow of blood into the atrium due to mitral insufficiency

mitral stenosis *n* : a condition usu. the result of disease in which the mitral valve is abnormally narrow

mitral valve *n* : BICUSPID VALVE

mit·tel·schmerz \ˈmi-tᵊl-ˌshmertz\ *n* : abdominal pain occurring between the menstrual periods and usu. considered to be associated with ovulation

mixed \ˈmikst\ *adj* 1 : combining features or exhibiting symptoms of more than one condition or disease (a ~ tumor) 2 : producing more than one kind of secretion (~ salivary glands)

mixed connective tissue disease *n* : a syndrome characterized by symptoms of various rheumatic diseases (as systemic lupus erythematosus, scleroderma, and polymyositis) and by high concentrations of antibodies to extractable nuclear antigens

mixed glioma *n* : a glioma consisting of more than one cell type

mixed nerve *n* : a nerve containing both sensory and motor fibers

mix·ture \ˈmiks-chər\ *n* : a product of mixing: as a : a portion of matter consisting of two or more components in varying proportions that retain their own properties b : an aqueous liquid medicine; *specif* : a preparation in which insoluble substances are suspended in watery fluids by the addition of a viscid material (as gum, sugar, or glycerol)

mks \ˌem-ˌkā-ˈes\ *adj, often cap M&K&S* : of, relating to, or being a system of units based on the meter, the kilogram, and the second (~ system) (~ units)

ml *abbr* milliliter

MLD *abbr* 1 median lethal dose 2 minimum lethal dose

M line \ˈem-ˌlīn\ *n* : a thin dark line across the center of the H zone of a striated muscle fiber — called also *M band*

MLT *abbr* medical laboratory technician

mm *abbr* millimeter

M-mode \ˈem-ˌmōd\ *adj* : of, relating to, or being an ultrasonographic technique that is used for studying the movement of internal body structures

MMPI *abbr* Minnesota Multiphasic Personality Inventory

MMR *abbr* measles-mumps-rubella (vaccine)

Mn *symbol* manganese

MN *abbr* master of nursing

-m·ne·sia \m-ˈnē-zhə\ *n comb form* : a (specified) type or condition of memory (param*nesia*)

Mo *symbol* molybdenum

MO *abbr* medical officer

mo·bile \ˈmō-bəl, -ˌbil\ *adj* : capable of moving or being moved about readily; *specif* : characterized by an extreme degree of fluidity — **mo·bil·i·ty** \mō-ˈbi-lə-tē\ *n*

mo·bi·lize \ˈmō-bə-ˌlīz\ *vb* **-lized; -lizing** 1 : to put into movement or circulation : make mobile; *specif* : to release (something stored in the body) for body use 2 : to assemble (as resources) and make ready for use 3 : to separate (an organ or part) from associated structures so as to make more accessible for operative procedures 4 : to develop to a state of acute activity — **mo·bi·li·za·tion** \ˌmō-bə-lə-ˈzā-shən\ *n*

Mö·bi·us syndrome \ˈmü-bē-əs-, ˈmœ-\ *n* : congenital bilateral paralysis of the facial muscles associated with other neurological disorders

Möbius, Paul Julius (1853–1907), German neurologist.

moc·ca·sin \ˈmä-kə-sən\ *n* 1 : WATER MOCCASIN 2 : a snake (as of the genus *Natrix*) resembling a water moccasin

mo·dal·i·ty \mō-ˈda-lə-tē\ *n, pl* **-ties** 1 : one of the main avenues of sensation (as vision) 2 a : a usu. physical therapeutic agency b : an apparatus for applying a modality

¹**mod·el** \ˈmäd-əl\ *n* 1 a : a pattern of something to be made b : a cast of a tooth or oral cavity 2 : something (as a similar object or a construct) used to help visualize or explore something else (as the living human body) that cannot be directly observed or experimented on — see ANIMAL MODEL

²**model** *vb* **mod·eled** *or* **mod·elled; mod·el·ing** *or* **mod·el·ling** : to produce (as by computer) a representation or simulation of

mod·er·ate \ˈmä-də-rət\ *adj* : not severe in effect : not seriously or permanently disabling or incapacitating

Mod·er·il \ˈmä-də-ˌril\ *trademark* — used for a preparation of rescinnamine

modified radical mastectomy *n* : a mastectomy that is similar to the radical mastectomy but does not include removal of the pectoral muscles

mod·i·fi·er \ˈmä-də-ˌfī-ər\ *n* 1 : one that modifies 2 : a gene that modifies the effect of another

mod·i·fy \ˈmä-də-ˌfī\ *vb* **-fied; -fy·ing** : to make a change in (∼ behavior by the use of drugs) — **mod·i·fi·ca·tion** \ˌmä-də-fə-ˈkā-shən\ *n*

mo·di·o·lar \mə-ˈdī-ə-lər\ *adj* : of or relating to the modiolus of the ear

mo·di·o·lus \mə-ˈdī-ə-ləs\ *n, pl* **-li** \-ˌlī\ : a central bony column in the cochlea of the ear

mod·u·late \ˈmä-jə-ˌlāt\ *vb* **-lat·ed; -lat·ing** : to adjust to or keep in proper measure or proportion (∼ an immune response) (∼ cell activity) — **mod·u·la·tion** \ˌmä-jə-ˈlā-shən\ *n* — **mod·u·la·tor** \ˈmä-jə-ˌlā-tər\ *n* — **mod·u·la·to·ry** \-lə-ˌtōr-ē\ *adj*

Moe·bi·us syndrome *var of* MÖBIUS SYNDROME

Mohs' technique \ˈmōz-\ *n* : a chemosurgical technique for the removal of skin malignancies in which excision is made to a depth at which the tissue is microscopically free of cancer — called also *Mohs' chemosurgery*

Mohs, Frederic Edward (*b* 1910), American surgeon.

moist \ˈmöist\ *adj* 1 : slightly or moderately wet 2 a : marked by a discharge or exudation of liquid (∼ eczema) b : suggestive of the presence of liquid — used of sounds heard in auscultation (∼ rales)

moist gangrene *n* : gangrene that develops in the presence of combined arterial and venous obstruction, is usu. accompanied by an infection, and is characterized by a watery discharge usu. of foul odor

mol *var of* ³MOLE

mol·al \ˈmō-ləl\ *adj* : of, relating to, or containing a mole of solute per 1000 grams of solvent (a ∼ solution) — **mo·lal·i·ty** \mō-ˈla-lə-tē\ *n*

¹**mo·lar** \ˈmō-lər\ *n* : a tooth with a rounded or flattened surface adapted for grinding; *specif* : one of the mammalian teeth behind the incisors and canines sometimes including the premolars but more exactly restricted to the three posterior pairs in each adult human jaw on each side which are not preceded by milk teeth

²**molar** *adj* 1 a : pulverizing by friction (∼ teeth) b : of, relating to, or located near the molar teeth (∼ gland) 2 : of, relating to, possessing the qualities of, or characterized by a uterine mole (∼ pregnancy)

³**molar** *adj* 1 : of or relating to a mole of a substance (the ∼ volume of a gas) 2 : containing one mole of solute in one liter of solution — **mo·lar·i·ty** \mō-ˈlar-ə-tē\ *n*

¹**mold** \ˈmōld\ *n* : a cavity in which a fluid or malleable substance is shaped

²**mold** *vb* : to give shape to esp. in a mold

³**mold** *vb* : to become moldy

⁴**mold** *n* 1 : a superficial often woolly growth produced esp. on damp or decaying organic matter or on living organisms 2 : a fungus (as of the order Mucorales) that produces mold

mold·ing \ˈmōl-diŋ\ *n* : the shaping of the fetal head to allow it to pass through the birth canal during parturition

moldy \ˈmōl-dē\ *adj* **mold·i·er; -est** : covered with a mold-producing fungus (∼ bread)

¹**mole** \ˈmōl\ *n* : a pigmented spot, mark, or small permanent protuberance on the human body; *esp* : NEVUS

²**mole** *n* : an abnormal mass in the uterus: a : a blood clot containing a degenerated fetus and its membranes b : HYDATIDIFORM MOLE

³**mole** \ˈmōl\ *n* : the base unit in the International System of Units for the amount of pure substance that contains the same number of elementary entities as there are atoms in exactly 12 grams of the isotope carbon 12

mo·lec·u·lar \mə-ˈle-kyə-lər\ *adj* : of,

relating to. or produced by molecules — **mo·lec·u·lar·ly** *adv*

molecular biology *n* : a branch of biology dealing with the ultimate physicochemical organization of living matter and esp. with the molecular basis of inheritance and protein synthesis — **molecular biologist** *n*

molecular formula *n* : a chemical formula (as $C_6H_{12}O_6$ for glucose) that is based on both analysis and molecular weight and gives the total number of atoms of each element in a molecule — see STRUCTURAL FORMULA

molecular genetics *n pl* : a branch of genetics dealing with the structure and activity of genetic material at the molecular level

molecular weight *n* : the mass of a molecule that may be calculated as the sum of the atomic weights of its constituent atoms

mol·e·cule \'mä-li-ıkyül\ *n* : the smallest particle of a substance that retains all the properties of the substance and is composed of one or more atoms

mol·in·done \mō-'lin-ıdōn\ *n* : a drug $C_{16}H_{24}N_2O_2$ used in the form of the hydrochloride as an antipsychotic agent

mol·lus·ci·cide \mə-'ləs-kə-ısīd, -'lə-si-ısīd\ *n* : an agent for destroying mollusks (as snails) — **mol·lus·ci·cid·al** \-ıləs-kə-'sīd-ᵊl, -ılə-si-'sīd-\ *adj*

mol·lus·cum \mə-'ləs-kəm\ *n, pl* **-ca** \-kə\ : any of several skin diseases marked by soft pulpy nodules: *esp* : MOLLUSCUM CONTAGIOSUM

molluscum body *n* : any of the rounded cytoplasmic bodies found in the central opening of the nodules characteristic of molluscum contagiosum

molluscum con·ta·gio·sum \-ıkan-ıtā-jē-'ō-səm\ *n, pl* **mollusca con·ta·gi·o·sa** \-sə\ : a mild chronic disease of the skin caused by a poxvirus and characterized by the formation of small nodules with a central opening and contents resembling curd

mol·lusk *or* **mol·lusc** \'mä-ləsk\ *n* : any of a large phylum (Mollusca) of invertebrate animals (as snails) that have a soft unsegmented body lacking segmented appendages and commonly protected by a calcareous shell — **mol·lus·can** *also* **mol·lus·kan** \mə-'leskən, mä-\ *adj*

molt \'mōlt\ *vb* : to shed hair, feathers, shell, horns, or an outer layer periodically — **molt** *n*

mo·lyb·de·num \mə-'lib-də-nəm\ *n* : a metallic element that is a trace element in plant and animal metabolism — symbol *Mo*; see ELEMENT table

mom·ism \'mä-ımi-zəm\ *n* : an excessive popular adoration and sentimentalizing of mothers that is held to be oedipal in nature

mon- *or* **mono-** *comb form* **1** : one : single (*mono*filament) **2** : affecting a single part (*mono*plegia)

mon·ar·tic·u·lar \ımä-när-'ti-kyə-lər\ *var of* MONOARTICULAR

mon·au·ral \(ı)mä-'nòr-əl\ *adj* : of, relating to, affecting, or designed for use with one ear (~ hearing aid systems) — **mon·au·ral·ly** *adv*

Mönck·e·berg's sclerosis \'müŋ-kə-ıbərgz-, 'meŋ-\ *n* : arteriosclerosis characterized by the formation of calcium deposits in the mediae of esp. the peripheral arteries
  Mönck·e·berg \'mœŋ-kə-ıberk\. **Johann Georg** (1877–1925), German pathologist.

Monday morning disease *n* : azoturia of horses caused by heavy feeding during a period of inactivity — called also *Monday disease*

mo·nen·sin \mō-'nen-sən\ *n* : an antibiotic $C_{36}H_{62}O_{11}$ obtained from a bacterium of the genus *Streptomyces* (*S. cinnamonensis*) and used as an antiprotozoal. antibacterial. and antifungal agent and as an additive to cattle feed

mo·ne·ran \mə-'nir-ən\ *n* : PROKARYOTE — **moneran** *adj*

mon·es·trous \(ı)mä-'nes-trəs\ *adj* : experiencing estrus once each year or breeding season

Mon·gol \'mäŋ-gəl, 'män-ıgōl, 'mäŋ-\ *n, often not cap* : one affected with Down's syndrome

Mon·go·lian \mäŋ-'gōl-yən, mäŋ-, -'gō-lē-ən\ *adj* : MONGOLOID

Mongolian spot *n* : a bluish pigmented area near the base of the spine that is present at birth esp. in Asian, southern European, American Indian, and black infants and that usu. disappears during childhood

mon·gol·ism \'mäŋ-gə-ıli-zəm\ *n* : DOWN'S SYNDROME

Mon·gol·oid \'mäŋ-gə-ılòid\ *adj, often not cap* : of, relating to, or affected with Down's syndrome — **Mongoloid** *n, often not cap*

mo·nie·zia \ımä-nē-'e-zē-ə\ *n* **1** *cap* : a genus of tapeworms (family Anoplocephalidae) parasitizing the intestine of various ruminants **2** : any tapeworm of the genus *Moniezia*
  Moniez \mon-'yā\. **Romain–Louis** (1852–1936), French parasitologist.

mo·ni·le·thrix \mə-'ni-lə-ıthriks\ *n, pl* **mon·i·let·ri·ches** \ımä-nə-'le-trə-ıkēz\ : a disease of the hair in which each hair appears as if strung with small beads or nodes

mo·nil·ia \mə-'ni-lē-ə\ *n, pl* **monilias** *or* **monilia** *also* **mo·nil·i·ae** \-lē-ıē\ **1** : any fungus of the genus *Candida* **2** *pl* **mo·nilias** : CANDIDIASIS

Mo·nil·ia \mə-'ni-lē-ə\ *n, syn of* CANDIDA

mo·nil·i·al \mə-'ni-lē-əl\ *adj* : of, relating to, or caused by a fungus of the genus *Candida* (~ vaginitis) mo·ni·li·a·sis \ˌmō-nə-ˈlī-ə-səs, ˌmä-\ n, pl -a·ses \-ˌsēz\ : CANDIDIASIS

mo·nil·iid \mə-ˈni-lē-əd\ n : a secondary commonly generalized dermatitis resulting from hypersensitivity developed in response to a primary focus of infection with a fungus of the genus *Candida*

¹mon·i·tor \ˈmä-nə-tər\ n : one that monitors; *esp* : a device for observing or measuring a biologically important condition or function (a heart ~)

²monitor vb 1 : to watch, observe, or check closely or continuously (~ a patient's vital signs) 2 : to test for intensity of radiations esp. if due to radioactivity

mon·key \ˈmən-kē\ n : a nonhuman primate mammal with the exception of the smaller more primitive primates (as the lemurs, family Lemuridae)

mono \ˈmä-(ˌ)nō\ n : INFECTIOUS MONONUCLEOSIS

mono- — see MON-

monoacetate — see RESORCINOL MONOACETATE

mono·am·ine \ˌmä-nō-ə-ˈmēn, -ˈa-ˌmēn\ n : an amine RNH₂ that has one organic substituent attached to the nitrogen atom; *esp* : one (as serotonin) that is functionally important in neural transmission

monoamine oxidase n : an enzyme that deaminates monoamines oxidatively and that functions in the nervous system by breaking down monoamine neurotransmitters oxidatively

monoamine oxidase inhibitor n : any of various antidepressant drugs which increase the concentration of monoamines in the brain by inhibiting the action of monoamine oxidase

mono·am·in·er·gic \ˌmä-nō-ˌa-mə-ˈnər-jik\ adj : liberating or involving monoamines (as serotonin or norepinephrine) in neural transmission (~ neurons) (~ mechanisms)

mono·ar·tic·u·lar \ˌmä-nō-är-ˈti-kyə-lər\ adj : affecting only one joint of the body (~ arthritis)

mono·ben·zone \ˌmä-nō-ˈben-ˌzōn\ n : a drug C₁₃H₁₂O₂ applied topically as a melanin inhibitor in the treatment of hyperpigmentation

mono·blast \ˈmä-nō-ˌblast\ n : a motile cell of the spleen and bone marrow that gives rise to the monocyte of the circulating blood

mono·cho·ri·on·ic \ˌmä-nō-ˌkōr-ē-ˈä-nik\ *also* mono·cho·ri·al \-ˈkōr-ē-əl\ adj, of twins : sharing or developed with a common chorion

mono·chro·ma·cy \-ˈkrō-mə-sē\ n pl -cies : MONOCHROMATISM

mono·chro·mat \ˈmä-nō-krō-ˌmat, ˌmä-ˈ\ n : a person who is completely color-blind

mono·chro·mat·ic \ˌmä-nō-krō-ˈma-tik\ adj 1 : having or consisting of one color or hue 2 : consisting of radiation of a single wavelength or of a very small range of wavelengths 3 : of, relating to, or exhibiting monochromatism

mono·chro·ma·tism \-ˈkrō-mə-ˌti-zəm\ n : complete color blindness in which all colors appear as shades of gray — called also *monochromacy*

mon·o·cle \ˈmä-ni-kəl\ n : an eyeglass for one eye

¹mono·clo·nal \ˌmä-nō-ˈklōn-ᵊl\ adj : produced by, being, or composed of cells derived from a single cell (a ~ tumor); *esp* : relating to or being an antibody derived from a single cell in large quantities for use against a specific antigen (as a cancer cell)

²monoclonal n : a monoclonal antibody

mono·crot·ic \-ˈkrä-tik\ adj, of the pulse : having a simple beat and forming a smooth single-crested curve on a sphygmogram — compare DICROTIC 1

mon·oc·u·lar \mä-ˈnä-kyə-lər, mə-\ adj 1 : of, involving, or affecting a single eye (~ vision) (a ~ cataract) 2 : suitable for use with only one eye (a ~ microscope) — mon·oc·u·lar·ly adv

mono·cyte \ˈmä-nə-ˌsīt\ n : a large leukocyte with finely granulated chromatin dispersed throughout the nucleus that is formed in the bone marrow, enters the blood, and migrates into the connective tissue where it differentiates into a macrophage — mono·cyt·ic \ˌmä-nə-ˈsi-tik\ adj

monocytic leukemia n : leukemia characterized by the presence of large numbers of monocytes in the circulating blood

mono·cy·to·sis \ˌmä-nō-sī-ˈtō-səs\ n, pl -to·ses \-ˌsēz\ : an abnormal increase in the number of monocytes in the circulating blood — compare GRANULOCYTOSIS, LYMPHOCYTOSIS

mono·fac·to·ri·al \-fak-ˈtōr-ē-əl\ adj : MONOGENIC

mono·fil·a·ment \-ˈfi-lə-mənt\ n : a single untwisted synthetic filament (as of nylon) used to make surgical sutures

mo·nog·a·mist \mə-ˈnä-gə-mist\ n : one who practices or upholds monogamy

mo·nog·a·my \-mē\ n, pl -mies : the state or custom of being married to one person at a time or of having only one mate at a time — mo·nog·a·mous \mə-ˈnä-gə-məs\ *also* mono·gam·ic \ˌmä-nə-ˈga-mik\ adj

mono·gas·tric \ˌmä-nō-ˈgas-trik\ adj : having a stomach with only a single compartment (as in humans)

mono·gen·ic \-ˈje-nik, -ˈjē-\ adj : of, relating to, or controlled by a single gene and esp. by either of an allelic pair — mono·gen·i·cal·ly adv

mono·graph \ˈmä-nə-ˌgraf\ n 1 : a learned detailed thoroughly documented treatise covering exhaustively a small area of a field of learning 2 : a description (as in a pharmacopoeia or formulary) of the name, chemical formula, and uniform method for determining the strength and purity of a drug — **monograph** *vb*

mono•iodo•ty•ro•sine \,mä-nō-ī-,ō-də-ˈtī-rə-,sēn, -i-,ä-\ *n* : an iodine-containing tyrosine $C_9H_{10}INO_3$ that is produced in the thyroid gland and that combines with diiodotyrosine to form triiodothyronine

mono•lay•er \ˈmä-nō-,lā-ər\ *n* : a single continuous layer or film that is one cell or molecule in thickness

mono•ma•nia \,mä-nō-ˈmā-nē-ə, -nyə\ *n* : mental illness esp. when limited in expression to one idea or area of thought — **mono•ma•ni•a•cal** \-mə-ˈnī-ə-kəl\ *adj*

mono•ma•ni•ac \-nē-,ak\ *n* : an individual affected by monomania

mono•me•lic \-ˈmē-lik\ *adj* : relating to or affecting only one limb

mono•mer \ˈmä-nə-mər\ *n* : a chemical compound that can undergo polymerization — **mono•mer•ic** \,mä-nə-ˈmer-ik, ,mō-\ *adj*

mono•neu•ri•tis \,mä-nō-nù-ˈrī-təs, -nyù-\ *n, pl* **-rit•i•des** \-ˈri-tə-,dēz\ *or* **-ri•tis•es** : neuritis of a single nerve

mononeuritis mul•ti•plex \-ˈməl-ti-,pleks\ *n* : neuritis that affects several separate nerves — called also *mono-neuropathy multiplex*

mono•neu•rop•a•thy \-nù-ˈrä-pə-thē, -nyù-\ *n, pl* **-thies** : a nerve disease affecting only a single nerve

¹**mono•nu•cle•ar** \,mä-nō-ˈnü-klē-ər, -ˈnyü-\ *adj* : having only one nucleus

²**mononuclear** *n* : a mononuclear cell; *esp* : MONOCYTE

mono•nu•cle•at•ed \-ˈnü-klē-,ā-təd, -ˈnyü-\ *also* **mono•nu•cle•ate** \-klē-ət, -,āt\ *adj* : MONONUCLEAR

mono•nu•cle•o•sis \-,nü-klē-ˈō-səs, -,nyü-\ *n* : an abnormal increase of mononuclear leukocytes in the blood; *specif* : INFECTIOUS MONONUCLEOSIS

mono•nu•cle•o•tide \-ˈnü-klē-ə-,tīd, -ˈnyü-\ *n* : a nucleotide that is derived from one molecule each of a nitrogenous base, a sugar, and a phosphoric acid

mono•pha•sic \-ˈfā-zik\ *adj* **1** : having a single phase; *specif* : relating to or being a record of a nerve impulse that is negative or positive but not both ⟨a ∼ action potential⟩ — compare DIPHASIC b, POLYPHASIC 1 **2** : having a single period of activity followed by a period of rest in each 24 hour period

mono•phos•phate \-ˈfäs-,fāt\ *n* : a phosphate containing a single phosphate group

mono•ple•gia \-ˈplē-jə, -jē-ə\ *n* : paralysis affecting a single limb, body part, or group of muscles — **mono•ple•gic** \-jik\ *adj*

mono•ploid \ˈmä-nō-,plȯid\ *adj* : HAPLOID

mono•po•lar \,mä-nō-ˈpō-lər\ *adj* : UNIPOLAR

mon•or•chid \mä-ˈnȯr-kəd\ *n* : an individual who has only one testis or only

one descended into the scrotum — compare CRYPTORCHID — **monorchid** *adj*

mon•or•chid•ism \-kə-,di-zəm\ *also* **mon•or•chism** \mä-ˈnȯr-,ki-zəm\ *n* : the quality or state of being monorchid — compare CRYPTORCHIDISM

mono•sac•cha•ride \,mä-nō-ˈsa-kə-,rīd\ *n* : a sugar not decomposable to simpler sugars by hydrolysis — called also *simple sugar*

mono•so•di•um glu•ta•mate \,mä-nō-ˈsō-dē-əm-ˈglü-tə-,māt\ *n* : a crystalline salt $C_5H_8O_4NaN$ used to enhance the flavor of food and medicinally to reduce ammonia levels in blood and tissues in ammoniacal azotemia (as in hepatic insufficiency) — abbr. *MSG*; called also *sodium glutamate*; see CHINESE RESTAURANT SYNDROME

monosodium urate *n* : a salt of uric acid that precipitates out in cartilage as tophi in gout

mono•some \ˈmä-nō-,sōm\ *n* **1** : a chromosome lacking a synaptic mate: *esp* : an unpaired X chromosome **2** : a single ribosome

mono•so•mic \,mä-nə-ˈsō-mik\ *adj* : having one less than the diploid number of chromosomes — **mono•so•my** \ˈmä-nə-,sō-mē\ *n*

mono•spe•cif•ic \,mä-nō-spə-ˈsi-fik\ *adj* : specific for a single antigen or receptor site on an antigen — **mono•spec•i•fic•i•ty** \-,spe-sə-ˈfi-sə-tē\ *n*

mono•sper•mic \-ˈspər-mik\ *adj* : involving or resulting from a single sperm cell ⟨∼ fertilization⟩

mono•sper•my \ˈmä-nō-,spər-mē\ *n, pl* **-mies** : the entry of a single fertilizing sperm into an egg — compare POLYSPERMY

mon•os•tot•ic \,mä-,näs-ˈtä-tik\ *adj* : relating to or affecting a single bone

mono•symp•tom•at•ic \,mä-nō-,simp-tə-ˈma-tik\ *adj* : exhibiting or manifested by a single principal symptom

mono•syn•ap•tic \,mä-nō-sə-ˈnap-tik\ *adj* : having or involving a single neural synapse — **mono•syn•ap•ti•cal•ly** *adv*

mono•un•sat•u•rate \-,ən-ˈsa-chə-rət\ *n* : a monounsaturated oil or fatty acid

mono•un•sat•u•rat•ed \-,ən-ˈsa-chə-,rā-təd\ *adj, of an oil or fatty acid* : containing one double or triple bond per molecule — compare POLYUNSATURATED

mono•va•lent \,mä-nə-ˈvā-lənt\ *adj* **1** : having a chemical valence of one **2** : containing antibodies specific for or antigens of a single strain of a microorganism ⟨a ∼ vaccine⟩

mon•ovu•lar \(,)mä-ˈnä-vyə-lər, -ˈnō-\ *adj* : MONOZYGOTIC ⟨∼ twins⟩

mon•ox•ide \mə-ˈnäk-,sīd\ *n* : an oxide containing one atom of oxygen per molecule — see CARBON MONOXIDE

mono•zy•got•ic \,mä-nō-zī-ˈgä-tik\ *adj* : derived from a single egg ⟨∼ twins⟩ — **mono•zy•gos•i•ty** \-ˈgä-sə-tē\ *n* — **mono•zy•gote** \-ˈzī-,gōt\ *n*

monozygous • morning sickness

432

mono·zy·gous \ˌmä-nō-ˈzī-gəs, (ˌ)mä-ˈnä-zə-gəs\ *adj* : MONOZYGOTIC

mons \ˈmänz\ *n, pl* **mon·tes** \ˈmän-ˌtēz\ : a body part or area raised above or demarcated from surrounding structures (as the papilla of mucosa through which the ureter enters the bladder)

mons pubis *n, pl* **montes pubis** : a rounded eminence of fatty tissue upon the pubic symphysis esp. of the human female

mon·ster \ˈmän-stər\ *n* : an animal or plant of abnormal form or structure; *esp* : a fetus or offspring with a major developmental abnormality

mon·stros·i·ty \män-ˈsträ-sə-tē\ *n, pl* **-ties 1 a** : a malformation of a plant or animal **b** : MONSTER **2** : the quality or state of deviating greatly from the natural form or character — **mon·strous** \ˈmän-strəs\ *adj*

mons ve·ne·ris \-ˈve-nə-rəs\ *n, pl* **mon·tes veneris** : the mons pubis of a female

Mon·teg·gia fracture \män-ˈte-jə-\ *or* **Mon·teg·gia's fracture** \-ˈte-jəz-\ *n* : a fracture in the proximal part of the ulna with dislocation of the head of the radius

    Monteggia, Giovanni Battista (1762–1815), Italian surgeon.

Mon·te·zu·ma's revenge \ˌmän-tə-ˈzü-məz-\ *n* : diarrhea contracted in Mexico esp. by tourists

    Montezuma II (1466–1520), Mexican emperor.

Mont·gom·ery's gland \(ˌ)mənt-ˈgəm-rēz-, mänt-ˈgäm-\ *n* : an apocrine gland in the areola of the mammary gland

    Montgomery, William Fetherston (1797–1859), British obstetrician.

month·lies \ˈmənth-lēz\ *n pl* : a menstrual period

mon·tic·u·lus \män-ˈtik-yə-ləs\ *n* : the median dorsal ridge of the cerebellum formed by the vermis

mood \ˈmüd\ *n* : a conscious state of mind or predominant emotion : affective state : FEELING 3 (~ disorders such as mania and depression)

moon \ˈmün\ *n* : LUNULA 2

moon blindness *n* : a recurrent inflammation of the eye of the horse — called also *periodic ophthalmia*

moon face *n* : the full rounded facies characteristic of hyperadrenocorticism — called also *moon facies*

Moon's molar *or* **Moon molar** *n* : a first molar tooth which has become dome-shaped due to malformation by congenital syphilis; *also* : MULBERRY MOLAR

    Moon, Henry (1845–1892), British surgeon.

MOPP \ˌem-(ˌ)ō-(ˌ)pē-ˈpē\ *n* : a combination of four drugs including mechlorethamine, vincristine, procarbazine, and prednisone that is

used in the treatment of some forms of cancer (as Hodgkin's disease)

Mor·ax–Ax·en·feld bacillus \ˈmȯr-ˌaks-ˈäk-sən-ˌfeld-\ *n* : a rod-shaped bacterium of the genus *Moraxella* (*M. lacunata*) that causes Morax-Axenfeld conjunctivitis

    Morax, Victor (1866–1935), French ophthalmologist.
    Axenfeld, Karl Theodor Paul Polykarpos (1867–1930), German ophthalmologist.

Morax–Axenfeld conjunctivitis *n* : a chronic conjunctivitis caused by a rod-shaped bacterium of the genus *Moraxella* (*M. lacunata*) and now occurring rarely but formerly more prevalent in persons living under poor hygienic conditions

Mor·ax·el·la \ˌmȯr-ak-ˈse-lə\ *n* : a genus of short rod-shaped gram-negative bacteria (family Neisseriaceae) that includes the causative agent (*M. lacunata*) of Morax-Axenfeld conjunctivitis

mor·bid \ˈmȯr-bəd\ *adj* **1 a** : of, relating to, or characteristic of disease **b** : affected with or induced by disease (a ~ condition) **c** : productive of disease (~ substances) **2** : abnormally susceptible to or characterized by gloomy or unwholesome feelings

mor·bid·i·ty \mȯr-ˈbi-də-tē\ *n, pl* **-ties 1** : a diseased state or symptom **2** : the incidence of disease : the rate of sickness (as in a specified community or group) — compare MORTALITY 2

mor·bil·li \mȯr-ˈbi-ˌlī\ *n pl* : MEASLES 1

mor·bil·li·form \mȯr-ˈbi-lə-ˌfȯrm\ *adj* : resembling the eruption of measles (a ~ pruritic rash)

mor·bus \ˈmȯr-bəs\ *n, pl* **mor·bi** \-ˌbī\ : DISEASE — see CHOLERA MORBUS

mor·cel·la·tion \ˌmȯr-sə-ˈlā-shən\ *n* : division and removal in small pieces (as of a tumor)

mor·gan \ˈmȯr-gən\ *n* : a unit of inferred distance between genes on a chromosome that is used in constructing genetic maps and is equal to the distance for which the frequency of crossing-over between specific pairs of genes is 100 percent

    Morgan, Thomas Hunt (1866–1945), American geneticist.

morgue \ˈmȯrg\ *n* : a place where the bodies of persons found dead are kept until identified and claimed by relatives or are released for burial

mor·i·bund \ˈmȯr-ə-(ˌ)bənd, ˈmär-\ *adj* : being in the state of dying : approaching death

morning-after pill *n* : an oral drug usu. containing high doses of estrogen that interferes with pregnancy by blocking implantation of a fertilized egg in the human uterus

morning sickness *n* : nausea and vomiting that occurs on rising in the morning esp. during the earlier months of pregnancy

mo·ron \'mōr-,än\ n : a mentally retarded person who has a potential mental age of between 8 and 12 years and is capable of doing routine work under supervision

Moro reflex \'mōr-ō-\ n : a reflex reaction of infants upon being startled (as by a loud noise or a bright light) that is characterized by extension of the arms and legs away from the body and to the side and then by drawing them together as if in an embrace

    Moro, Ernst (1874–1951), German pediatrician.

Moro test n : a diagnostic skin test formerly used to detect infection or past infection by the tubercle bacillus and involving the rubbing of an ointment containing tuberculin directly on the skin with the appearance of reddish papules after one or two days indicating a positive result

morph- or **morpho-** comb form : form : shape : structure : type (morphology)

-morph \,mȯrf\ n comb form : one having (such) a form (ectomorph)

mor·phea \mȯr-'fē-ə\ n, pl **mor·phe·ae** \-'fē-,ē\ : localized scleroderma

mor·phia \'mȯr-fē-ə\ n : MORPHINE

-mor·phic \'mȯr-fik\ adj comb form : having (such) a form (endomorphic)

mor·phine \'mȯr-,fēn\ n : a bitter crystalline addictive narcotic base $C_{17}H_{19}NO_3$ that is the principal alkaloid of opium and is used in the form of a soluble salt (as a hydrochloride or a sulfate) as an analgesic and sedative

mor·phin·ism \'mȯr-,fē-,ni-zəm, -fə-\ n : a disordered condition of health produced by habitual use of morphine

mor·phi·no·mi·met·ic \,mȯr-fē-nə-mə-'me-tik, -fə-, -mī-\ adj : resembling opiates in their affinity for opiate receptors in the brain (the enkephalins are ~ pentapeptides)

-mor·phism \'mȯr-,fi-zəm\ n comb form : quality or state of having (such) a form (polymorphism)

mor·pho·dif·fer·en·ti·a·tion \,mȯr-fō-,di-fə-,ren-chē-'ā-shən\ n : structure or organ differentiation (as in tooth development)

mor·phoea Brit var of MORPHEA

mor·pho·gen \'mȯr-fə-jən, -,jen\ n : a diffusible chemical substance that exerts control over morphogenesis esp. by forming a gradient in concentration

mor·pho·gen·e·sis \,mȯr-fə-'je-nə-səs\ n, pl **-e·ses** \-,sēz\ : the formation and differentiation of tissues and organs — compare ORGANOGENESIS

mor·pho·ge·net·ic \-jə-'ne-tik\ adj : relating to or concerned with the development of normal organic form — **mor·pho·ge·net·i·cal·ly** adv

mor·pho·gen·ic \-'je-nik\ adj : MORPHOGENETIC

mor·pho·log·i·cal \,mȯr-fə-'lä-ji-kəl\ also **mor·pho·log·ic** \-'lä-jik\ adj : of, relating to, or concerned with form or structure — **mor·pho·log·i·cal·ly** adv

mor·phol·o·gy \mȯr-'fä-lə-jē\ n, pl **-gies** 1 : a branch of biology that deals with the form and structure of animals and plants esp. with respect to the forms, relations, metamorphoses, and phylogenetic development of organs apart from their functions — see ANATOMY 1; compare PHYSIOLOGY 1 2 : the form and structure of an organism or any of its parts — **mor·phol·o·gist** \-jist\ n

-mor·phous \'mȯr-fəs\ adj comb form : having (such) a form (polymorphous)

-mor·phy \,mȯr-fē\ n comb form, pl **-phies** : quality or state of having (such) a form (mesomorphy)

Mor·quio's disease \'mȯr-kē-,ōz-\ n : an autosomal recessive mucopolysaccharidosis characterized by excretion of keratan sulfate in the urine, dwarfism, a short neck, protruding sternum, kyphosis, a flat nose, prominent upper jaw, and a waddling gait

    Morquio, Luis (1867–1935), Uruguayan physician.

mor·tal \'mȯrt-ᵊl\ adj 1 : having caused or being about to cause death : FATAL (a ~ injury) 2 : of, relating to, or connected with death (~ agony)

mor·tal·i·ty \mȯr-'ta-lə-tē\ n, pl **-ties** 1 : the quality or state of being mortal 2 a : the number of deaths in a given time or place b : the proportion of deaths to population : DEATH RATE — called also mortality rate; compare FERTILITY 2, MORBIDITY 2

mor·tar \'mȯr-tər\ n : a strong vessel in which material is pounded or rubbed with a pestle

mor·ti·cian \mȯr-'ti-shən\ n : UNDERTAKER

mor·ti·fi·ca·tion \,mȯr-tə-fə-'kā-shən\ n : local death of tissue in the animal body : NECROSIS, GANGRENE

mortis — see ALGOR MORTIS, RIGOR MORTIS

Mor·ton's toe \'mȯrt-ᵊnz-\ n : metatarsalgia that is caused by compression of a branch of the plantar nerve between the heads of the metatarsal bones and tends to occur when the second toe is longer than the big toe — called also Morton's disease, Morton's foot

    Morton, Thomas George (1835–1903), American surgeon.

mor·tu·ary \'mȯr-chə-,wer-ē\ n, pl **-ar·ies** : a place in which dead bodies are kept and prepared for burial or cremation

mor·u·la \'mȯr-yù-lə, 'mär-\ n, pl **-lae** \-,lē, -,lī\ : a globular solid mass of blastomeres formed by cleavage of a zygote that typically precedes the blastula — compare GASTRULA —

mor·u·la·tion \ˌmȯr-yü-ˈlā-shən. -ˈmär-\ n

¹mo·sa·ic \mō-ˈzā-ik\ n : an organism or one of its parts composed of cells of more than one genotype : CHIMERA

²mosaic adj 1 : exhibiting mosaicism 2 : DETERMINATE — **mo·sa·i·cal·ly** adv

mo·sa·i·cism \mō-ˈzā-ə-ˌsi-zəm\ n : the condition of possessing cells of two or more different genetic constitutions

mos·qui·to \mə-ˈskē-tō\ n, pl **-toes** also **-tos** : any of numerous dipteran flies (family Culicidae) that have a rather narrow abdomen and usu. a long slender rigid proboscis, that have in the male broad feathery antennae and mouthparts not fitted for piercing and in the female slender antennae and a set of needlelike organs in the proboscis with which they puncture the skin of animals to suck the blood, and that in some species are the only vectors of certain diseases — see AEDES. ANOPHELES, CULEX

mosquito forceps n : a very small surgical forceps — called also *mosquito clamp*

mossy fiber n : any of the complexly ramifying nerve fibers that surround some nerve cells of the cerebellar cortex

moth·er \ˈmə-thər\ n : a female parent

mother cell n : a cell that gives rise to other cells usu. of a different sort

mo·tile \ˈmōt-ᵊl. ˈmō-ˌtīl\ adj : exhibiting or capable of movement

mo·til·i·ty \mō-ˈti-lə-tē\ n, pl **-ties** : the quality or state of being motile : CONTRACTILITY (gastrointestinal ~)

mo·tion \ˈmō-shən\ n 1 : an act, process, or instance of changing place : MOVEMENT 2 a : an evacuation of the bowels b : the matter evacuated — often used in pl. (blood in the ~s)

motion sickness n : sickness induced by motion (as in travel by air. car. or ship) and characterized by nausea

mo·ti·vate \ˈmō-tə-ˌvāt\ vb **-vat·ed; -vat·ing** : to provide with a motive or serve as a motive for — **mo·ti·va·tion** \ˌmō-tə-ˈvā-shən\ n — **mo·ti·va·tion·al** \-shnəl. -shən-ᵊl\ adj — **mo·ti·va·tion·al·ly** adv

mo·tive \ˈmō-tiv\ n : something (as a need or desire) that causes a person to act

moto- comb form : motion : motor (*motoneuron*)

mo·to·neu·ron \ˌmō-tō-ˈnü-ˌrän. -ˈnyü-\ n : a neuron that passes from the central nervous system or a ganglion toward or to a muscle and conducts an impulse that causes movement — called also *motor neuron*; compare ASSOCIATIVE NEURON. SENSORY NEURON — **mo·to·neu·ro·nal** \-ˈnür-ən-ᵊl. -ˈnyür-: -nü-ˈrōn-. -nyü-\ adj

mo·tor \ˈmō-tər\ adj 1 : causing or imparting motion 2 : of. relating to. or being a motoneuron or a nerve con-

taining motoneurons ⟨~ fibers⟩ 3 : of. relating to. concerned with. or involving muscular movement

motor aphasia n : the inability to speak or to organize the muscular movements of speech — called also *Broca's aphasia*

motor area n : any of various areas of cerebral cortex believed to be associated with the initiation. coordination. and transmission of motor impulses to lower centers; *specif* : a region immediately anterior to the central sulcus having an unusually thick zone of cortical gray matter and communicating with lower centers chiefly through the corticospinal tracts — see PRECENTRAL GYRUS

motor center n : a nervous center that controls or modifies (as by inhibiting or reinforcing) a motor impulse

motor cortex n : the cortex of a motor area; *also* : the motor areas as a functional whole

motor end plate n : the terminal arborization of a motor axon on a muscle fiber

mo·tor·ic \mō-ˈtȯr-ik. -ˈtär-\ adj : MOTOR 3 (~ and verbal behavior) — **mo·tor·i·cal·ly** adv

motor neuron n : MOTONEURON

motor paralysis n : paralysis of the voluntary muscles

motor root n : a nerve root containing only motor fibers; *specif* : the ventral root of a spinal nerve

motor unit n : a motor neuron together with the muscle fibers on which it acts

Mo·trin \ˈmō-trən\ trademark — used for a preparation of ibuprofen

mottled enamel n : spotted tooth enamel caused by drinking water containing excessive fluorides during the time the teeth are calcifying

mou·lage \mü-ˈläzh\ n : a mold of a lesion or defect used as a guide in applying medical treatment (as in radiotherapy) or in performing reconstructive surgery esp. on the face

mould, moulding, mouldy *chiefly Brit var of* MOLD. MOLDING, MOLDY

moult *chiefly Brit var of* MOLT

mount \ˈmaunt\ n 1 : a glass slide with its accessories on which objects are placed for examination with a microscope 2 : a specimen mounted on a slide for microscopic examination — **mount** vb

mountain fever n : any of various febrile diseases occurring in mountainous regions

mountain sickness n : altitude sickness experienced esp. above 10.000 feet (about 3000 meters) and caused by insufficient oxygen in the air

mouse \ˈmaus\ n, pl **mice** \ˈmīs\ 1 : any of numerous small rodents (as of the genus *Mus*) with pointed snout. rather small ears. elongated body. and slender hairless or sparsely haired tail **2** : a dark-colored swelling caused by a blow; *specif* : BLACK EYE

mouse·pox \'maús-ˌpäks\ *n* : a highly contagious disease of mice that is caused by a poxvirus — called also *ectromelia*

mouth \'maúth\ *n, pl* **mouths** \'maúthz\ : the natural opening through which food passes into the animal body and which in vertebrates is typically bounded externally by the lips and internally by the pharynx and encloses the tongue, gums, and teeth

mouth breather *n* : a person who habitually inhales and exhales through the mouth rather than through the nose

mouth-to-mouth *adj* : of, relating to, or being a method of artificial respiration in which the rescuer's mouth is placed tightly over the victim's mouth in order to force air into the victim's lungs by blowing forcefully enough every few seconds to inflate them (∼ resuscitation)

mouth·wash \'maúth-ˌwósh, -ˌwäsh\ *n* : a liquid preparation (as an antiseptic solution) for cleansing the mouth and teeth — called also *collutorium*

move \'müv\ *vb* **moved; mov·ing 1** : to go or pass from one place to another **2** *of the bowels* : to eject fecal matter : EVACUATE

move·ment \'müv-mənt\ *n* **1** : the act or process of moving **2 a** : an act of voiding the bowels **b** : matter expelled from the bowels at one passage : STOOL

moxa \'mäk-sə\ *n* : a soft woolly mass prepared from the young leaves of various wormwoods of eastern Asia and used esp. in Japanese popular medicine as a cautery by being ignited on the skin

mox·i·bus·tion \ˌmäk-si-'bəs-chən\ *n* : the use of a moxa as a cautery by igniting it on the skin

MPC *abbr* maximum permissible concentration

MPH *abbr* master of public health

M phase \'em-ˌfāz\ *n* : the period in the cell cycle during which cell division takes place — compare G₁ PHASE, G₂ PHASE, S PHASE

MRI *abbr* magnetic resonance imaging

mRNA \ˌem-(ˌ)är-(ˌ)en-'ā\ *n* : MESSENGER RNA

MS *abbr* multiple sclerosis

MSG *abbr* monosodium glutamate

MSH *abbr* melanocyte-stimulating hormone

MSN *abbr* master of science in nursing

M substance \'em-ˌ\ *n* : a protein that is an antigen tending to occur on the surface of beta-hemolytic bacteria belonging to the genus *Streptococcus* and placed in a particular group (Lancefield group A) and that is closely associated with high virulence (as for scarlet fever)

MSW *abbr* master of social work

MT *abbr* medical technologist

mu \'myü, 'mü\ *n, pl* **mu** : MICROMETER

muc- or **muci-** or **muco-** *comb form* **1** : mucus ⟨*mucin*⟩ ⟨*mucoprotein*⟩ **2** : mucous and ⟨*mucopurulent*⟩

mu·cate \'myü-ˌkāt\ *n* : a salt or ester of a crystalline acid C₆H₁₀O₈

mu·ci·lage \'myü-sə-lij\ *n* **1** : a gelatinous substance of various plants (as legumes or seaweeds) that contains protein and polysaccharides and is similar to plant gums **2** : an aqueous usu. viscid solution (as of a gum) used in pharmacy as an excipient and in medicine as a demulcent — **mu·ci·lag·i·nous** \ˌmyü-sə-'la-jə-nəs\ *adj*

mu·cil·loid \'myü-sə-ˌlóid\ *n* : a mucilaginous substance

mu·cin \'myüs-ᵊn\ *n* : any of a group of mucoproteins that are found in various human and animal secretions and tissues (as in saliva, the lining of the stomach, and the skin) and that are white or yellowish powders when dry and viscid when moist (gastric ∼)

mu·cin·o·gen \myü-'si-nə-jən, -ˌjen\ *n* : any of various substances which undergo conversion into mucins

mu·ci·nous \'myüs-ᵊn-əs\ *adj* : of, relating to, resembling, or containing mucin (∼ fluid) (∼ carcinoma)

muco- — see MUC-

mu·co·buc·cal fold \ˌmyü-kō-'bə-kəl-\ *n* : the fold formed by the oral mucosa where it passes from the mandible or maxilla to the cheek

mu·co·cele \'myü-kə-ˌsēl\ *n* : a swelling like a sac that is due to distension of a hollow organ or cavity with mucus ⟨a ∼ of the appendix⟩; *specif* : a dilated lacrimal sac

mu·co·cil·i·ary \ˌmyü-kō-'si-lē-ˌer-ē\ *adj* : of, relating to, or involving cilia of the mucous membranes of the respiratory system

mu·co·cu·ta·ne·ous \ˌmyü-kō-kyü-'tā-nē-əs\ *adj* : made up of or involving both typical skin and mucous membrane (∼ candidiasis)

mucocutaneous lymph node disease *n* : KAWASAKI DISEASE

mucocutaneous lymph node syndrome *n* : KAWASAKI DISEASE

mu·co·epi·der·moid \ˌmyü-kō-ˌe-pə-'dər-ˌmóid\ *adj* : of, relating to, or consisting of both mucous and squamous epithelial cells; *esp* : being a tumor of the salivary glands made up of mucous and epithelial elements (∼ carcinoma)

mu·co·gin·gi·val \-'jin-jə-vəl\ *adj* : of, relating to, or being the junction between the oral mucosa and the gingiva (the ∼ line)

¹mu·coid \'myü-ˌkóid\ *adj* : resembling mucus

²mucoid *n* : MUCOPROTEIN

mu·co·lyt·ic \ˌmyü-kə-'li-tik\ *adj* : hydrolyzing mucopolysaccharides : tending to break down or lower the viscosity of mucin-containing body secretions or components

Mu·co·myst \'myü-kə-ˌmist\ *trademark* — used for a preparation of acetyl-cysteine

mu·co·pep·tide \ˌmyü-kō-'pep-ˌtīd\ n : PEPTIDOGLYCAN

mu·co·peri·os·te·um \-ˌper-ē-'äs-tē-əm\ n : a periosteum backed with mucous membrane (as that of the palatine surface of the mouth) — **mu·co·peri·os·te·al** \-'äs-tē-əl\ adj

mu·co·poly·sac·cha·ride \ˌmyü-kō-ˌpä-li-'sa-kə-ˌrīd\ n : GLYCOSAMINOGLYCAN

mu·co·poly·sac·cha·ri·do·sis \-ˌsa-kə-rī-'dō-səs\ n, pl **-do·ses** \-ˌsēz\ : any of a group of genetically determined disorders (as Hunter's syndrome and Hurler's syndrome) of glycosaminoglycan metabolism that are characterized by the accumulation of glycosaminoglycans in the tissues and their excretion in the urine — called also *gargoylism, lipochondrodystrophy*

mu·co·pro·tein \ˌmyü-kə-'prō-ˌtēn\ n : any of a group of various complex conjugated proteins (as mucins) that contain glycosaminoglycans (as chondroitin sulfate) combined with amino acid units or polypeptides and that occur in body fluids and tissues — called also *mucoid*; compare GLYCOPROTEIN

mu·co·pu·ru·lent \-'pyür-yə-lənt\ adj : containing both mucus and pus (∼ discharge)

mu·co·pus \'myü-ˌkōr\ n : mucus mixed with pus

mu·cor \'myü-ˌkōr\ n 1 cap : a genus (family Mucoraceae) of molds including several (as *M. corymbifer*) causing infections in humans and animals 2 : any mold of the genus *Mucor*

mu·cor·my·co·sis \ˌmyü-kər-mī-'kō-səs\ n, pl **-co·ses** \-ˌsēz\ : mycosis caused by fungi of the genus *Mucor* usu. primarily involving the lungs and invading other tissues by means of metastatic lesions — **mu·cor·my·cot·ic** \-'kä-tik\ adj

mu·co·sa \myü-'kō-zə\ n, pl **-sae** \-(ˌ)zē, -ˌzī\ or **-sas** : MUCOUS MEMBRANE — **mu·co·sal** \-zəl\ adj

mucosae — see MUSCULARIS MUCOSAE

mucosal disease n : a virus disease of cattle characterized by fever, diarrhea, loss of appetite, dehydration, and excessive salivation

mu·co·si·tis \ˌmyü-kə-'sī-təs\ n : inflammation of a mucous membrane

mu·co·stat·ic \ˌmyü-kō-'sta-tik\ adj 1 : of, relating to, or representing the mucosal tissues of the jaws as they are in a state of rest 2 : stopping the secretion of mucus

mu·cous \'myü-kəs\ adj 1 : covered with or as if with mucus (a ∼ surface) 2 : of, relating to, or resembling mucus (a ∼ secretion) 3 : secreting or containing mucus (∼ glands)

mucous cell n : a cell that secretes mucus

mucous colitis n : IRRITABLE BOWEL SYNDROME: *esp* : irritable bowel syndrome characterized by the passage of unusually large amounts of mucus in mucous glands: *specif* : one that lines body passages and cavities which communicate directly or indirectly with the exterior (as the alimentary, respiratory, and genitourinary tracts), that functions in protection, support, nutrient absorption, and secretion of mucus, enzymes, and salts, and that consists of a deep vascular connective-tissue stroma and a superficial epithelium — compare SEROUS MEMBRANE

mu·co·vis·ci·do·sis \ˌmyü-kō-ˌvi-sə-'dō-səs\ n, pl **-do·ses** \-ˌsēz\ : CYSTIC FIBROSIS

mu·cus \'myü-kəs\ n : a viscid slippery secretion that is usu. rich in mucins and is produced by mucous membranes which it moistens and protects

mud bath n : an immersion of the body or a part of it in mud (as for the alleviation of rheumatism or gout)

mud fever n 1 : a chapped inflamed condition of the skin of the legs and belly of a horse due to irritation from mud or drying resulting from washing off mud spatters and closely related or identical in nature to grease heel 2 : a mild leptospirosis that occurs chiefly in European agricultural and other workers in wet soil, is caused by infection with a spirochete of the genus *Leptospira* (*L. grippotyphosa*) present in native field mice, and is marked by fever and headache without accompanying jaundice

Muel·le·ri·an duct var of MÜLLERIAN DUCT

Muel·le·ri·us \myü-'lir-ē-əs\ n : a genus of lungworms (family Metastrongylidae) that include forms (as *M. capillaris* syn. *M. minutissimus*) infecting the lungs of sheep and goats and having larval stages in various snails and slugs

Mül·ler \'mue-lər\, **Fritz (Johann Friedrich Theodor) (1822–1897)**, German zoologist.

mulberry molar n : a first molar tooth whose occlusal surface is pitted due to congenital syphilis with nodules replacing the cusps — see MOON'S MOLAR

mules·ing \'myül-ziŋ\ n : the use of Mules operation to reduce the occurrence of blowfly strike

Mules operation \'myülz-\ n : removal of excess loose skin from either side of the crutch of a sheep to reduce the incidence of blowfly strike

Mules, J. H. W., Australian sheep rancher.

Mül·ler cell \'myü-lər-, 'mi-, 'mə-\ *also* **Mül·ler's cell** \-lərz-\ *n* : FIBER OF MÜLLER

Mül·ler \'mue-lər, 'myü-\, **Heinrich** (1820–1864), German anatomist.

Mül·le·ri·an duct \myə-'lir-ē-ən-, mi-, mə-\ *n* : either of a pair of ducts parallel to the Wolffian ducts and giving rise in the female to the oviducts — called also *paramesonephric duct*

Mül·ler \'mue-lər, 'myü-\, **Johannes Peter** (1801–1858), German physiologist and anatomist.

Müllerian tubercle *n* : an elevation on the wall of the embryonic urogenital sinus where the Müllerian ducts enter

¹mult·an·gu·lar \məl-'taŋ-gyə-lər\ *adj* : having many angles (a ~ bone)

²multangular *n* : a multangular bone — see TRAPEZIUM, TRAPEZOID

multi- *comb form* **1 a** : many : multiple : much (*multineuronal*) **b** : consisting of, containing, or having more than two (*multinucleate*) **c** : more than one (*multiparous*) **2** : affecting many parts (*multiglandular*)

mul·ti·an·gu·lar \məl-tē-'aŋ-gyə-lər, mə̄l-əti-\ *adj* : MULTANGULAR

mul·ti·cel·lu·lar \-'sel-yə-lər\ *adj* : having or consisting of many cells — **mul·ti·cel·lu·lar·i·ty** \-ısel-yə-'lar-ə-tē\ *n*

mul·ti·cen·ter \-'sen-tər\ *adj* : involving more than one medical or research institution (a ~ clinical study)

mul·ti·cen·tric \-'sen-trik\ *adj* : having multiple centers of origin (a ~ tumor)

mul·ti·ceps \'məl-tə-ıseps\ *n* **1** *cap* : a genus of taeniid tapeworms that have a coenurus larva parasitic in ruminants, rodents, and rarely humans and that include the parasite of gid (*M. multiceps*) and other worms typically parasitic on carnivores **2** : COENURUS

mul·ti·clo·nal \ıməl-tē-'klō-nəl, -ıtī-\ *adj* : POLYCLONAL

mul·ti·cus·pid \-'kəs-pəd\ *adj* : having several cusps (a ~ tooth)

mul·ti·cys·tic \-'sis-tik\ *adj* : POLYCYSTIC

mul·ti·dose \'məl-tē-ıdōs, -ıtī-\ *adj* : utilizing or containing more than one dose

mul·ti·drug \-ıdrəg\ *adj* : utilizing or relating to more than one drug (~ therapy)

mul·ti·en·zyme \ıməl-tē-'en-ızīm, -ıtī-\ *adj* : composed of or involving two or more enzymes that function in a biosynthetic pathway (~ complex)

mul·ti·fac·to·ri·al \-fak-'tōr-ē-əl\ *adj* **1** : having characters or a mode of inheritance dependent on a number of genes at different loci **2** *or* **mul·ti·fac·tor** \-'fak-tər\ : having, involving, or produced by a variety of elements or causes (a ~ study) (a disease with a ~ etiology) — **mul·ti·fac·to·ri·al·ly** *adv*

mul·tif·i·dus \ıməl-'ti-fə-dəs\ *n*, *pl* **-di** \-ıdī\ : a muscle of the fifth and deep-

est layer of the back filling up the groove on each side of the spinous processes of the vertebrae from the sacrum to the skull and consisting of many fasciculi that pass upward and inward to the spinous processes and help to erect and rotate the spine

mul·ti·fo·cal \ıməl-tē-'fō-kəl\ *adj* **1** : having more than one focal length (~ lenses) **2** : arising from or occurring in more than one focus or location (~ convulsions)

multifocal leukoencephalopathy — see PROGRESSIVE MULTIFOCAL LEUKOENCEPHALOPATHY

mul·ti·form \'məl-ti-ıfòrm\ *adj* : having or occurring in many forms

multiforme — see ERYTHEMA MULTIFORME, GLIOBLASTOMA MULTIFORME

mul·ti·gene \ıməl-tē-'jēn, -ıtī-\ *adj* : relating to or determined by a group of genes which were originally copies of the same gene but evolved by mutation to become different from each other

mul·ti·gen·ic \-'je-nik, -'jē-\ *adj* : MULTIFACTORIAL 1

mul·ti·glan·du·lar \-'glan-jə-lər\ *adj* : POLYGLANDULAR

mul·ti·grav·i·da \-'gra-vi-də\ *n* : a woman who has been pregnant more than once — compare MULTIPARA

mul·ti·han·di·capped \ıməl-tē-'han-di-ıkapt, -ıtī-\ *adj* : affected by more than one handicap (~ children)

mul·ti·hos·pi·tal \-'häs-ıpit-ə̄l\ *adj* : involving or affiliated with more than one hospital

mul·ti·lobed \-'lōbd\ *adj* : having two or more lobes

mul·ti·loc·u·lar \-'lä-kyə-lər\ *adj* : having or divided into many small chambers or vesicles (a ~ cyst)

mul·ti·mam·mate mouse \-'ma-ımāt-\ *n* : any of several common African rodents of the genus *Rattus* that have 12 rather than the usual five or six mammae on each side, are vectors of disease, and are used in medical research — called also *multimammate rat*

mul·ti·mo·dal \-'mōd-ə̄l\ *adj* : relating to, having, or utilizing more than one mode or modality (as of stimulation or treatment)

mul·ti·neu·ro·nal \-'nùr-ən-ə̄l, -'nyùr-; -nù-'rōn-, -nyù-\ *adj* : made up of or involving more than one neuron (~ circuits)

mul·ti·nod·u·lar \-'nä-jə-lər\ *adj* : having many nodules (~ goiter)

mul·ti·nu·cle·ate \-'nü-klē-ət, -'nyü-\ *or* **mul·ti·nu·cle·at·ed** \-klē-ıā-təd\ *adj* : having more than two nuclei

mul·ti·or·gas·mic \-ıòr-'gaz-mik\ *adj* : experiencing one orgasm after another with little or no recovery period between them

mul·tip·a·ra \məl-'ti-pə-rə\ *n* : a woman who has borne more than one child — compare MULTIGRAVIDA

mul·ti·par·i·ty \,məl-ti-'par-ə-tē\ n, pl **-ties** 1 : the production of two or more young at a birth 2 : the condition of having borne a number of children

mul·tip·a·rous \məl-'ti-pər-əs\ adj 1 : producing many or more than one at a birth 2 : having experienced one or more previous parturitions — compare PRIMIPAROUS

mul·ti·ple \'məl-tə-pəl\ adj 1 : consisting of, including, or involving more than one (~ births) 2 : affecting many parts of the body at once

multiple allele n : an allele of a genetic locus having more than two allelic forms within a population

multiple factor n : POLYGENE

multiple myeloma n : a disease of bone marrow that is characterized by the presence of numerous myelomas in various bones of the body — called also *myelomatosis*

multiple personality n : an hysterical neurosis in which the personality becomes dissociated into two or more distinct but complex and socially and behaviorally integrated parts each of which becomes dominant and controls behavior from time to time to the exclusion of the others — called also *alternating personality;* compare SPLIT PERSONALITY

multiple sclerosis n : a demyelinating disease marked by patches of hardened tissue in the brain or the spinal cord and associated esp. with partial or complete paralysis and jerking muscle tremor

multiplex — see ARTHROGRYPOSIS MULTIPLEX CONGENITA, MONONEURITIS MULTIPLEX, PARAMYOCLONUS MULTIPLEX

mul·ti·po·lar \,məl-tē-'pō-lər, -'tī-\ adj 1 : having several poles (~ mitoses) 2 : having several dendrites (~ nerve cells) — **mul·ti·po·lar·i·ty** \-pō-'lar-ə-tē\ n

mul·ti·po·tent \,məl-'ti-pə-tənt\ adj : having power to do many things

mul·ti·po·ten·tial \,məl-tē-pə-'ten-chəl, -'tī-\ adj : having the potential of becoming any of several mature cell types (~ stem cell)

mul·ti·re·sis·tant \-ri-'zis-tənt\ adj : biologically resistant to several toxic agents

mul·ti·spe·cial·ty \-'spe-shəl-tē\ adj : providing service in or staffed by members of several medical specialties (~ health center)

mul·ti·syn·ap·tic \-sə-'nap-tik\ adj : relating to or consisting of more than one synapse (~ pathways)

mul·ti·sys·tem \-'sis-təm\ also **mul·ti·sys·te·mic** \-sis-'tē-mik\ adj : relating to, consisting of, or involving more than one bodily system

¹mul·ti·va·lent \-'vā-lənt\ adj 1 : represented more than twice in the somatic chromosome number (~ chromosomes) 2 : POLYVALENT

²multivalent n : a multivalent group of chromosomes

¹mul·ti·vi·ta·min \-'vī-tə-mən, -'vi-\ adj : containing several vitamins and esp. all known to be essential to health ⟨a ~ formula⟩

²multivitamin n : a multivitamin preparation

mum·mi·fy \'mə-mi-fī\ vb **-fied; -fy·ing** : to dry up and shrivel like a mummy ⟨a *mummified* fetus⟩ — **mum·mi·fi·ca·tion** \,mə-mi-fə-'kā-shən\ n

mumps \'məmps\ n sing or pl : an acute contagious disease caused by a paramyxovirus and marked by fever and by swelling esp. of the parotid gland — called also *epidemic parotitis*

Mun·chau·sen syndrome \'mən-,chaù-zən-\ or **Mun·chau·sen's syndrome** \-zənz-\ n : a condition characterized by the feigning of the symptoms of a disease or injury in order to undergo diagnostic tests, hospitalization, or medical or surgical treatment

Münch·hau·sen \'muenk-,haù-zən\, Karl Friedrich Hieronymous, Freiherr von (1720–1797), German soldier.

mu·ral \'myùr-əl\ adj : attached to and limited to a wall or a cavity (~ thrombus) (~ abscess)

mu·ram·i·dase \myù-'ra-mə-,dās, -,dāz\ n : LYSOZYME

mu·rein \'myùr-ē-ən, 'myùr-,ēn\ n : PEPTIDOGLYCAN

mu·ri·at·ic acid \myùr-ē-'a-tik-\ n : HYDROCHLORIC ACID

mu·rid \'myùr-id\ n : any of a large family (Muridae) of relatively small rodents including various Old World forms such as the house mouse and the common rats) — **murid** adj

¹mu·rine \'myùr-,īn\ adj 1a : of or relating to the genus *Mus* or its subfamily (Murinae) that includes most of the rats and mice which habitually live in intimate association with humans (~ rodents) b : of, relating to, or produced by the house mouse (a ~ odor) 2 : affecting or transmitted by rats or mice (~ rickettsial diseases)

²murine n : a murine animal

murine typhus n : a mild febrile disease that is marked by headache and rash, is caused by a rickettsial bacterium of the genus *Rickettsia* (*R. typhi*), is widespread in nature in rodents, and is transmitted to humans by a flea — called also *endemic typhus*

mur·mur \'mər-mər\ n : an atypical sound of the heart indicating a functional or structural abnormality — called also *heart murmur*

Mus \'məs\ n : a genus of rodents (family Muridae) that includes the house mouse (*M. musculus*) and a few related small forms

Mus·ca \'məs-kə\ n : a genus of flies (family Muscidae) that is now restricted to the common housefly (*M. domestica*) and closely related flies

mus·cae vo·li·tan·tes \\'məs-ˌkē-ˌvä-lə-'tan-ˌtēz, 'mə-ˌsē-\ *n pl* : spots before the eyes due to cells and cell fragments in the vitreous humor and lens — compare FLOATER

mus·ca·rine \\'məs-kə-ˌrēn\ *n* : a toxic ammonium base [$C_9H_{20}NO_2$]⁺ that is biochemically related to acetylcholine, is found esp. in fly agaric, acts directly on smooth muscle, and when ingested produces profuse salivation and sweating, abdominal colic with evacuation of bowels and bladder, contracted pupils and blurring of vision, excessive bronchial secretion, bradycardia, and respiratory depression

mus·ca·rin·ic \ˌməs-kə-'ri-nik\ *adj* : relating to, resembling, producing, or mediating the parasympathetic effects (as a slowed heart rate and increased activity of smooth muscle) produced by muscarine (~ receptors) — compare NICOTINIC

mus·cle \\'mə-səl\ *n, often attrib* 1 : a body tissue consisting of long cells that contract when stimulated and produce motion — see CARDIAC MUSCLE, SMOOTH MUSCLE, STRIATED MUSCLE 2 : an organ that is essentially a mass of muscle tissue attached at either end to a fixed point and that by contracting moves or checks the movement of a body part — see AGONIST 1, ANTAGONIST a, SYNERGIST 2

mus·cle-bound \\'mə-səl-ˌbaúnd\ *adj* : having some of the muscles tense and enlarged and of impaired elasticity sometimes as a result of excessive exercise

muscle fiber *n* : any of the elongated cells characteristic of muscle

muscle sense *n* : the part of kinesthesia mediated by end organs located in muscles

muscle spasm *n* : persistent involuntary hypertonicity of one or more muscles usu. of central origin and commonly associated with pain and excessive irritability

muscle spindle *n* : a sensory end organ in a muscle that is sensitive to stretch in the muscle, consists of small striated muscle fibers richly supplied with nerve fibers, and is enclosed in a connective tissue sheath — called also *stretch receptor*

muscle tone *n* : TONUS 2

muscul- *or* **musculo-** *comb form* 1 : muscle (*muscular*) 2 : muscular and (*musculo*skeletal)

mus·cu·lar \\'məs-kyə-lər\ *adj* 1 a : of, relating to, or constituting muscle b : of, relating to, or performed by the muscles 2 : having well-developed musculature — **mus·cu·lar·ly** *adv*

muscular coat *n* : an outer layer of smooth muscle surrounding a hollow or tubular organ (as the bladder, esophagus, large intestine, small intestine, stomach, ureter, uterus, and

vagina) that often consists of an inner layer of circular fibers serving to narrow the lumen of the organ and an outer layer of longitudinal fibers serving to shorten its length — called also *muscularis externa, tunica muscularis*

muscular dystrophy *n* : any of a group of hereditary diseases characterized by progressive wasting of muscles

mus·cu·la·ris \ˌməs-kyə-'lar-is\ *n* 1 : the smooth muscular layer of the wall of various more or less contractile organs (as the bladder) 2 : the thin layer of smooth muscle that forms part of a mucous membrane (as in the esophagus)

muscularis ex·ter·na \-eks-'tər-nə\ *n* : MUSCULAR COAT

muscularis mu·co·sae \-myü-'kō-sē\ *also* **muscularis mu·co·sa** \-sə\ *n* : MUSCULARIS 2

mus·cu·lar·i·ty \ˌməs-kyə-'lar-ə-tē\ *n, pl* **-ties** : the quality or state of being muscular

mus·cu·la·ture \\'məs-kyə-lə-ˌchür, -chər, -ˌtyúr\ *n* : the muscles of all or a part of the body

mus·cu·li pec·ti·na·ti \\'məs-kyə-ˌli-ˌpek-ti-'nā-ˌti\ *n pl* : small muscular ridges on the inner wall of the auricular appendage of the left and the right atria of the heart

musculo- — see MUSCUL-

mus·cu·lo·cu·ta·ne·ous \ˌməs-kyə-lō-kyü-'tā-nē-əs\ *adj* : of, relating to, supplying, or consisting of both muscle and skin

musculocutaneous nerve *n* 1 : a large branch of the brachial plexus supplying various parts of the upper arm (as flexor muscles) and forearm (as the skin) 2 : SUPERFICIAL PERONEAL NERVE

mus·cu·lo·fas·cial \-'fa-shəl, -shē-əl\ *adj* : relating to or consisting of both muscular and fascial tissue

mus·cu·lo·fi·brous \-'fī-brəs\ *adj* : relating to or consisting of both muscular and fibrous connective tissue

mus·cu·lo·mem·bra·nous \-'mem-brə-nəs\ *adj* : relating to or consisting of both muscle and membrane

mus·cu·lo·phren·ic artery \-'fre-nik-\ *n* : a branch of the internal thoracic artery that gives off branches to the seventh, eighth, and ninth intercostal spaces as anterior intercostal arteries, to the pericardium, to the diaphragm, and to the abdominal muscles — called also *musculophrenic, musculophrenic branch*

musculorum — see DYSTONIA MUSCULORUM DEFORMANS

mus·cu·lo·skel·e·tal \ˌməs-kyə-lō-'skel-ət-ᵊl\ *adj* : of, relating to, or involving both musculature and skeleton

mus·cu·lo·ten·di·nous \-'ten-də-nəs\ *adj* : of, relating to, or affecting muscular and tendinous tissue (~ injuries)

musculotendinous cuff *n* : ROTATOR CUFF

mus·cu·lus \'məs-kyə-ləs\ *n, pl* **-li** \-₁lī\ : MUSCLE

mush·room \'məsh-₁rüm, -₁rüm\ *n* **1** : an enlarged complex fleshy fruiting body of a fungus (as most members of the class Basidiomycetes) that arises from an underground mycelium and consists typically of a stem bearing a spore-bearing structure; *esp* : one that is edible — compare TOADSTOOL **2** : FUNGUS 1

mu·si·co·gen·ic \₁myü-zi-kō-'je-nik\ *adj* : of, relating to, or being epileptic seizures precipitated by music

music therapy *n* : the treatment of disease (as mental illness) by means of music — **music therapist** *n*

mussel poisoning *n* : a toxic reaction following the eating of mussels; *esp* : a severe often fatal intoxication following the consumption of mussels that have fed on red tide flagellates and esp. gonyaulax and stored up a dangerous alkaloid in their tissues

mus·tard \'məs-tərd\ *n* **1** : a pungent yellow condiment consisting of the pulverized seeds of either of two herbs (*Brassica nigra* and *B. hirta* of the family Cruciferae, the mustard family) either dry or made into a paste and serving as a stimulant and diuretic or in large doses as an emetic and as a counterirritant when applied to the skin as a poultice **2 a** : MUSTARD GAS **b** : NITROGEN MUSTARD

mustard gas *n* : an irritant oily liquid $C_4H_8Cl_2S$ that is a war gas, causes blistering, attacks the eyes and lungs, and is a systemic poison

mustard oil *n* **1** : a colorless to pale yellow pungent irritating essential oil that is obtained by distillation from mustard seeds, that consists largely of allyl isothiocyanate, and that is used esp. in liniments and medicinal plasters **2** : ALLYL ISOTHIOCYANATE

mustard plaster *n* : a counterirritant and rubefacient plaster containing powdered mustard — called also *mustard paper*

mu·ta·gen \'myü-tə-jən\ *n* : a substance (as mustard gas or various radiations) that tends to increase the frequency or extent of mutation

mu·ta·gen·e·sis \₁myü-tə-'je-nə-səs\ *n, pl* **-eses** \-₁sēz\ : the occurrence or induction of mutation — **mu·ta·gen·ic** \-'je-nik\ *adj* — **mu·ta·ge·nic·i·ty** \-jə-'ni-sə-tē\ *n*

mu·ta·gen·ize \'myü-tə-jə-₁nīz\ *vb* **-ized; -iz·ing** : MUTATE

¹mu·tant \'myüt-ᵊnt\ *adj* : of, relating to, or produced by mutation

²mutant *n* : a mutant individual

mu·ta·tion \myü-'tā-shən\ *n* **1** : a relatively permanent change in hereditary material involving either a physical change in chromosome relations or a biochemical change in the codons that make up genes; *also* : the process of producing a mutation **2** : an individual, strain, or trait resulting from mutation — **mu·tate** \'myü-₁tāt, myü-'\ *vb* — **mu·ta·tion·al** \-shə-nəl\ *adj* — **mu·ta·tion·al·ly** *adv*

¹mute \'myüt\ *adj* **mut·er; mut·est** : unable to speak : DUMB — **mute·ness** *n*

²mute *n* : a person who cannot or does not speak

mu·ti·late \'myüt-ᵊl-₁āt\ *vb* **-lat·ed; -lat·ing** : to cut off or permanently destroy a limb or essential part of; *also* : CASTRATE — **mu·ti·la·tion** \₁myüt-ᵊl-'ā-shən\ *n*

mut·ism \'myü-₁ti-zəm\ *n* : the condition of being mute whether from physical, functional, or psychological cause

¹muz·zle \'mə-zəl\ *n* **1** : the projecting jaws and nose of an animal **2** : a fastening or covering for the mouth of an animal used to prevent eating or biting

²muzzle *vb* **muz·zled; muz·zling** : to fit with a muzzle

Mv *symbol* mendelevium

my- *or* **myo-** *comb form* **1 a** : muscle (*my*asthenia) (*myo*globin) **b** : muscular and (*myo*neural) **2** : myoma and (*myo*edema)

my·al·gia \mī-'al-jē, -jē-ə\ *n* : pain in one or more muscles — **my·al·gic** \-jik\ *adj*

My·am·bu·tol \mī-'am-byü-₁tól, -₁tōl\ *trademark* — used for a preparation of ethambutol

my·an·e·sin \mī-'a-nə-sən\ *n* : MEPHENESIN

my·as·the·nia \₁mī-əs-'thē-nē-ə\ *n* : muscular debility — **my·as·then·ic** \-'the-nik\ *adj*

myasthenia gra·vis \-'gra-vis, -'grä-\ *n* : a disease characterized by progressive weakness of voluntary muscles without atrophy or sensory disturbance and caused by an autoimmune attack on acetylcholine receptors at neuromuscular junctions

my·a·to·nia \₁mī-ə-'tō-nē-ə\ *n* : lack of muscle tone : muscular flabbiness

myc- *or* **myco-** *comb form* : fungus (*my*celium) (*myco*logy) (*myc*osis)

my·ce·li·um \mī-'sē-lē-əm\ *n, pl* **-lia** \-lē-ə\ : the mass of interwoven filaments that forms esp. the vegetative body of a fungus and is often submerged in another body (as of soil or organic matter or the tissues of a host); *also* : a similar mass of filaments formed by some bacteria (as of the genus *Streptomyces*) — **my·ce·li·al** \-lē-əl\ *adj*

-my·ces \'mī-₁sēz\ *n comb form* : fungus (*Streptomyces*)

mycet- *or* **myceto-** *comb form* : fungus (*myceto*ma)

-my·cete \'mī-₁sēt, ₁mī-'sēt\ *n comb form* : fungus (actino*mycete*)

my·ce·tis·mus \₁mī-sə-'tiz-məs\ *n, pl* **-mi** \-₁mī\ : mushroom poisoning

my·ce·to·ma \ˌmī-sə-ˈtō-mə\ *n, pl* **-mas** *or* **-ma·ta** \-mə-tə\ **1** : a condition marked by invasion of the deep subcutaneous tissues with fungi or actinomycetes: **a** : MADUROMYCOSIS **b** : NOCARDIOSIS **2** : a tumorous mass occurring in mycetoma — **my·ce·to·ma·tous** \-mə-təs\ *adj*

-my·cin \ˈmīs-ᵊn\ *n comb form* : substance obtained from a fungus (erythro**mycin**)

my·co·bac·te·ri·o·sis \ˌmī-kō-bak-ˌtir-ē-ˈō-səs\ *n, pl* **-o·ses** \-ˌsēz\ : a disease caused by bacteria of the genus *Mycobacterium*

my·co·bac·te·ri·um \-bak-ˈtir-ē-əm\ *n* **1** *cap* : a genus of nonmotile acid-fast aerobic bacteria (family Mycobacteriaceae) that include the causative agents of tuberculosis (*M. tuberculosis*) and leprosy (*M. leprae*) as well as numerous purely saprophytic forms **2** *pl* **-ria** : any bacterium of the genus *Mycobacterium* or a closely related genus — **my·co·bac·te·ri·al** \-ē-əl\ *adj*

my·col·o·gy \mī-ˈkä-lə-jē\ *n, pl* **-gies** **1** : a branch of biology dealing with fungi **2** : fungal life — **my·co·log·i·cal** \ˌmī-kə-ˈläj-i-kəl\ *adj* — **my·col·o·gist** \mī-ˈkä-lə-jist\ *n*

my·co·my·cin \ˌmī-kə-ˈmīs-ᵊn\ *n* : an antibiotic acid $C_{13}H_{10}O_2$ obtained from an actinomycete of the genus *Nocardia* (*N. acidophilus*)

my·co·phe·no·lic acid \ˌmī-kō-fi-ˈnō-lik-, -ˈnä-\ *n* : a crystalline antibiotic $C_{17}H_{20}O_6$ obtained from fungi of the genus *Penicillium*

my·co·plas·ma \ˌmī-kō-ˈplaz-mə\ *n* **1** *cap* : a genus of minute pleomorphic gram-negative chiefly nonmotile prokaryotic microorganisms (family Mycoplasmataceae) without cell walls that are intermediate in some respects between viruses and bacteria and are mostly parasitic usu. in mammals — see PLEUROPNEUMONIA **2 2** *pl* **-mas** *or* **-ma·ta** \-mə-tə\ : any microorganism of the genus *Mycoplasma* or of the family (Mycoplasmataceae) to which it belongs — called also *pleuropneumonia-like organism, PPLO* — **my·co·plas·mal** \-məl\ *adj*

my·co·sis \mī-ˈkō-səs\ *n, pl* **my·co·ses** \-ˌsēz\ : infection with or disease caused by a fungus — **my·cot·ic** \-ˈkä-tik\ *adj*

mycosis fun·goi·des \-fəŋ-ˈgòi-ˌdēz\ *n* : a form of lymphoma characterized by a chronic, patchy, red, scaly, irregular and often eczematous dermatitis that progresses over a period of years to form elevated plaques and then tumors

my·co·stat \ˈmī-kə-ˌstat\ *n* : an agent that inhibits the growth of molds — **my·co·stat·ic** \ˌmī-kə-ˈsta-tik\ *adj*

My·co·stat·in \ˈmī-kə-ˌsta-tən\ *trademark* — used for a preparation of nystatin

my·cot·ic \mī-ˈkä-tik\ *adj* : of, relating to, or characterized by mycosis

my·co·tox·ic \ˌmī-kō-ˈtäk-sik\ *adj* : of, relating to, or caused by a mycotoxin — **my·co·tox·ic·i·ty** \-täk-ˈsi-sə-tē\ *n*

my·co·tox·i·co·sis \ˌmī-kō-ˌtäk-sə-ˈkō-səs\ *n, pl* **-co·ses** \-ˈkō-ˌsēz\ : poisoning caused by a mycotoxin

my·co·tox·in \-ˈtäk-sən\ *n* : a poisonous substance produced by a fungus and esp. a mold — see AFLATOXIN

My·dri·a·cyl \mə-ˈdrī-ə-ˌsil\ *trademark* — used for a preparation of tropicamide

myd·ri·a·sis \mə-ˈdrī-ə-səs\ *n, pl* **-a·ses** \-ˌsēz\ : a long-continued or excessive dilatation of the pupil of the eye

¹**myd·ri·at·ic** \ˌmi-drē-ˈa-tik\ *adj* : causing or involving dilatation of the pupil of the eye

²**mydriatic** *n* : a drug that produces dilatation of the pupil of the eye

my·ec·to·my \mī-ˈek-tə-mē\ *n, pl* **-mies** : surgical excision of part of a muscle

myel- *or* **myelo-** *comb form* : marrow: as **a** : bone marrow (*myelo*cyte) **b** : spinal cord (*myelo*dysplasia)

my·el·en·ceph·a·lon \ˌmī-ə-len-ˈse-fə-ˌlän, -ən\ *n* : the posterior part of the developing vertebrate hindbrain or the corresponding part of the adult brain composed of the medulla oblongata — **my·el·en·ce·phal·ic** \-ˌlen-sə-ˈfa-lik\ *adj*

-my·e·lia \ˌmī-ˈē-lē-ə\ *n comb form* : a (specified) condition of the spinal cord (hemato*myelia*) (syringo*myelia*)

my·e·lin \ˈmī-ə-lən\ *n* : a soft white somewhat fatty material that forms a thick myelin sheath about the protoplasmic core of a myelinated nerve fiber — **my·e·lin·ic** \ˌmī-ə-ˈli-nik\ *adj*

my·e·lin·at·ed \ˈmī-ə-lə-ˌnā-təd\ *adj* : having a myelin sheath

my·e·li·na·tion \ˌmī-ə-lə-ˈnā-shən\ *n* **1** : the process of acquiring a myelin sheath **2** : the condition of being myelinated

my·e·lin·i·za·tion \ˌmī-ə-ˌli-nə-ˈzā-shən\ *n* : MYELINATION

my·e·li·nol·y·sis \ˌmī-ə-ˈnä-lə-səs\ — see CENTRAL PONTINE MYELINOLYSIS

myelin sheath *n* : a layer of myelin surrounding some nerve fibers

my·e·li·tis \ˌmī-ə-ˈlī-təs\ *n, pl* **my·elit·i·des** \-ˈli-tə-ˌdēz\ : inflammation of the spinal cord or of the bone marrow — **my·e·lit·ic** \-ˈli-tik\ *adj*

my·e·lo·blast \ˈmī-ə-lə-ˌblast\ *n* : a large mononuclear nongranular bone-marrow cell; *esp* : one that is a precursor of a myelocyte — **my·e·lo·blas·tic** \ˌmī-ə-lə-ˈblas-tik\ *adj*

myeloblastic leukemia *n* : MYELOGENOUS LEUKEMIA

my·e·lo·blas·to·sis \ˌmī-ə-lō-blas-ˈtō-səs\ *n, pl* **-to·ses** \-ˌsēz\ : the presence of an abnormally large number of myeloblasts in the tissues, organs, or circulating blood

my·e·lo·cele \ˈmī-ə-lə-ˌsēl\ *n* : spina bifida in which the neural tissue of the

myelocyte • myenteric plexus

spinal cord is exposed — compare MYELOMENINGOCELE

my·elo·cyte \'mī-ə-lə-ˌsīt\ *n* : a bone-marrow cell; *esp* : a motile cell with cytoplasmic granules that gives rise to the blood granulocytes and occurs abnormally in the circulating blood (as in myelogenous leukemia) — **my·elo·cyt·ic** \ˌmī-ə-lə-'si-tik\ *adj*

myelocytic leukemia *n* : MYELOGENOUS LEUKEMIA

my·elo·cy·to·ma \-sī-'tō-mə\ *n, pl* -**mas** *or* -**ma·ta** \-mə-tə\ : a tumor esp. of fowl in which the typical cellular element is a myelocyte or a cell of similar differentiation

my·elo·cy·to·sis \-sī-'tō-səs\ *n, pl* -**to·ses** \-ˌsēz\ : the presence of excess numbers of myelocytes esp. in the blood or bone marrow

my·elo·dys·pla·sia \-dis-'plā-zhə, -zhē-ə\ *n* : a developmental anomaly of the spinal cord — **my·elo·dys·plas·tic** \-'plas-tik\ *adj*

my·elo·fi·bro·sis \ˌmī-ə-lō-fī-'brō-səs\ *n, pl* -**bro·ses** \-ˌsēz\ : an anemic condition in which bone marrow becomes fibrotic and the liver and spleen usu. exhibit a development of blood cell precursors — **my·elo·fi·brot·ic** \-'brä-tik\ *adj*

my·elog·e·nous \ˌmī-ə-'lä-jə-nəs\ *also* **my·elo·gen·ic** \ˌmī-ə-lə-'je-nik\ *adj* : of, relating to, originating in, or produced by the bone marrow

myelogenous leukemia *n* : leukemia characterized by proliferation of myeloid tissue (as of the bone marrow and spleen) and an abnormal increase in the number of granulocytes, myelocytes, and myeloblasts in the circulating blood — called also *granulocytic leukemia, myeloblastic leukemia, myelocytic leukemia, myeloid leukemia*

my·elo·gram \'mī-ə-lə-ˌgram\ *n* 1 : a differential study of the cellular elements present in bone marrow usu. made on material obtained by sternal biopsy 2 : a roentgenogram of the spinal cord made by myelography

my·elo·graph·ic \ˌmī-ə-lə-'gra-fik\ *adj* : of, relating to, or by means of a myelogram or myelography — **my·elo·graph·i·cal·ly** *adv*

my·elog·ra·phy \ˌmī-ə-'lä-grə-fē\ *n, pl* -**phies** : roentgenographic visualization of the spinal cord after injection of a contrast medium into the spinal subarachnoid space

my·eloid \'mī-ə-ˌloid\ *adj* 1 : of or relating to the spinal cord 2 : of, relating to, or resembling bone marrow

myeloid leukemia *n* : MYELOGENOUS LEUKEMIA

my·elo·li·po·ma \ˌmī-ə-lō-li-'pō-mə, -li-\ *n, pl* -**mas** *or* -**ma·ta** \-mə-tə\ : a benign tumor esp. of the adrenal glands that consists of fat and hematopoietic tissue

my·elo·ma \ˌmī-ə-'lō-mə\ *n, pl* -**mas** *or* -**ma·ta** \-mə-tə\ : a primary tumor of the bone marrow formed of any one of the bone marrow cells (as myelocytes or plasma cells) and usu. involving several different bones at the same time — see MULTIPLE MYELOMA

my·elo·ma·to·sis \ˌmī-ə-lō-mə-'tō-səs\ *n, pl* -**to·ses** \-ˌsēz\ : MULTIPLE MYELOMA

my·elo·me·nin·go·cele \ˌmī-ə-lō-mə-'nin-gə-ˌsēl, -mə-'nin-jə-\ *n* : spina bifida in which neural tissue and the investing meninges protrude from the spinal column forming a sac under the skin — compare MYELOCELE

my·elo·mono·cyt·ic \-ˌmä-nə-'si-tik\ *adj* : relating to or being a blood cell that has the characteristics of both monocytes and granulocytes

myelomonocytic leukemia *n* : a kind of monocytic leukemia in which the cells resemble granulocytes

my·elop·a·thy \ˌmī-ə-'lä-pə-thē\ *n, pl* -**thies** : any disease or disorder of the spinal cord or bone marrow — **my·elo·path·ic** \ˌmī-ə-lō-'pa-thik\ *adj*

my·elo·phthi·sic anemia \ˌmī-ə-lō-'ti-zik-, -'ti-sik-\ *n* : anemia in which the blood-forming elements of the bone marrow are unable to reproduce normal blood cells and which is commonly caused by specific toxins or by overgrowth of tumor cells

my·elo·poi·e·sis \ˌmī-ə-lō-(ˌ)pȯi-'ē-səs\ *n, pl* -**poi·e·ses** \-'ē-ˌsēz\ 1 : production of marrow or marrow cells 2 : production of blood cells in bone marrow; *esp* : formation of blood granulocytes — **my·elo·poi·et·ic** \-(ˌ)pȯi-'e-tik\ *adj*

my·elo·pro·lif·er·a·tive \ˌmī-ə-lō-prə-'li-fə-ˌrā-tiv, -rə-\ *adj* : of, relating to, or being a disorder (as leukemia) marked by excessive proliferation of bone marrow elements and esp. blood cell precursors

my·elo·sis \ˌmī-ə-'lō-səs\ *n, pl* -**elo·ses** \-ˌsēz\ 1 : the proliferation of marrow tissue to produce the changes in cell distribution typical of myelogenous leukemia 2 : MYELOGENOUS LEUKEMIA

my·elo·sup·pres·sion \ˌmī-ə-lō-sə-'preshən\ *n* : suppression of the bone marrow's production of blood cells and platelets — **my·elo·sup·pres·sive** \-sə-'pre-siv\ *adj*

my·elot·o·my \ˌmī-ə-'lä-tə-mē\ *n, pl* -**mies** : surgical incision of the spinal cord; *esp* : section of crossing nerve fibers at the midline of the spinal cord and esp. of sensory fibers for the relief of intractable pain

my·elo·tox·ic \ˌmī-ə-lō-'täk-sik\ *adj* : destructive to bone marrow or any of its elements (a ~ agent) — **my·elo·tox·ic·i·ty** \-täk-'si-sə-tē\ *n*

my·en·ter·ic \ˌmī-ən-'ter-ik\ *adj* : of or relating to the muscular coat of the intestinal wall

myenteric plexus *n* : a network of nerve

fibers and ganglia between the longitudinal and circular muscle layers of the intestine — called also *Auerbach's plexus;* compare MEISSNER'S PLEXUS

myenteric plexus of Auerbach *n* : MYENTERIC PLEXUS

myenteric reflex *n* : a reflex that is responsible for the wave of peristalsis moving along the intestine and that involves contraction of the digestive tube above and relaxation below the place where it is stimulated by an accumulated mass of food

my·ia·sis \mī-ˈī-ə-səs, mē-\ *n, pl* **my·ia·ses** \-ˌsēz\ : infestation with fly maggots

myl- *or* **mylo-** *comb form* : molar (*mylohyoid*)

My·lan·ta \mī-ˈlan-tə\ *trademark* — used for an antacid and antiflatulent preparation

Myl·er·an \ˈmi-lə-ˌran\ *trademark* — used for a preparation of busulfan

My·li·con \ˈmi-lə-ˌkän\ *trademark* — used for a preparation of simethicone

my·lo·hy·oid \ˌmī-lō-ˈhī-ˌoid\ *adj* : of, indicating, or adjoining the mylohyoid muscle

my·lo·hy·oi·de·us \-hī-ˈoi-dē-əs\ *n, pl* **-dei** \-dē-ˌī\ : MYLOHYOID MUSCLE

mylohyoid line *n* : a ridge on the inner side of the bone of the lower jaw giving attachment to the mylohyoid muscle and to the superior constrictor of the pharynx — called also *mylohyoid ridge*

mylohyoid muscle *n* : a flat triangular muscle on each side of the mouth that is located above the anterior belly of the digastric muscle, extends from the inner surface of the mandible to the hyoid bone, and with its mate on the opposite side forms the floor of the mouth — called also *mylohyoid, mylohyoideus*

myo- — see MY-

myo·blast \ˈmī-ə-ˌblast\ *n* : an undifferentiated cell capable of giving rise to muscle cells

myo·blas·to·ma \ˌmī-ə-(ˌ)blas-ˈtō-mə\ *n, pl* **-mas** *or* **-ma·ta** \-mə-tə\ : a tumor that is composed of cells resembling primitive myoblasts and is associated with striated muscle

myo·car·di·al \ˌmī-ə-ˈkär-dē-əl\ *adj* : of, relating to, or involving the myocardium — **myo·car·di·al·ly** *adv*

myocardial infarction *n* : infarction of the myocardium that results typically from coronary occlusion — compare ANGINA PECTORIS, CORONARY INSUFFICIENCY, HEART FAILURE 1

myocardial insufficiency *n* : inability of the myocardium to perform its function : HEART FAILURE

myo·car·di·op·a·thy \-kär-dē-ˈä-pə-thē\ *n, pl* **-thies** : disease of the myocardium

myo·car·di·tis \ˌmī-ə-(ˌ)kär-ˈdī-təs\ *n* : inflammation of the myocardium

myo·car·di·um \ˌmī-ə-ˈkär-dē-əm\ *n, pl* **-dia** \-dē-ə\ : the middle muscular layer of the heart wall

Myo·chry·sine \ˌmī-ō-ˈkrī-ˌsēn, -ˌsən\ *trademark* — used for a preparation of gold sodium thiomalate

myo·clo·nia \ˌmī-ə-ˈklō-nē-ə\ *n* : MYOCLONUS

myo·clon·ic \ˌmī-ə-ˈklä-nik\ *adj* : of, relating to, characterized by, or being myoclonus (~ seizures)

myoclonic epilepsy *n* : an inherited form of epilepsy characterized by myoclonic seizures, progressive mental deterioration, and the presence of Lafora bodies in parts of the central nervous system — called also *Lafora's disease, myoclonus epilepsy*

myo·oc·lo·nus \mī-ˈä-klə-nəs\ *n* : irregular involuntary contraction of a muscle usu. resulting from functional disorder of controlling motoneurons; *also* : a condition characterized by myoclonus

myo·cyte \ˈmī-ə-ˌsīt\ *n* : a contractile cell; *specif* : a muscle cell

myo·ede·ma \ˌmī-ō-i-ˈdē-mə\ *n, pl* **-mas** *or* **-ma·ta** \-mə-tə\ : the formation of a lump in a muscle when struck a slight blow that occurs in states of exhaustion or in certain diseases

myo·elec·tric \ˌmī-ō-i-ˈlek-trik\ *also* **myo·elec·tri·cal** \-tri-kəl\ *adj* : of, relating to, or utilizing electricity generated by muscle

myo·epi·the·li·al \-ˌe-pə-ˈthē-lē-əl\ *adj* : of, relating to, or being large contractile cells of epithelial origin which are located at the base of the secretory cells of various glands (as the salivary and mammary glands)

myo·epi·the·li·o·ma \-ˌe-pə-ˌthē-lē-ˈō-mə\ *n, pl* **-mas** *or* **-ma·ta** \-mə-tə\ : a tumor arising from myoepithelial cells esp. of the sweat glands

myo·epi·the·li·um \-ˌe-pə-ˈthē-lē-əm\ *n, pl* **-lia** : tissue made up of myoepithelial cells

myo·fas·cial \-ˈfa-shəl, -shē-əl\ *adj* : of or relating to the fasciae of muscles

myo·fi·bril \ˌmī-ō-ˈfī-brəl, -ˈfi-\ *n* : one of the longitudinal parallel contractile elements of a muscle cell that are composed of myosin and actin — **myo·fi·bril·lar** \-brə-lər\ *adj*

myo·fi·bro·blast \-ˈfī-brə-ˌblast, -ˈfi-\ *n* : a fibroblast that has developed some of the functional and structural characteristics (as the presence of myofilaments) of smooth muscle cells

myo·fil·a·ment \-ˈfi-lə-mənt\ *n* : one of the individual filaments of actin or myosin that make up a myofibril

myo·func·tion·al \-ˈfəŋk-shə-nəl\ *adj* : of, relating to, or concerned with muscle function esp. in the treatment of orthodontic problems

myo·gen·e·sis \ˌmī-ə-ˈje-nə-səs\ *n, pl* **-e·ses** \-ˌsēz\ : the development of muscle tissue

myo·gen·ic \ˌmī-ə-ˈje-nik\ *also* **myog-**

e·nous \'mī-'ä-jə-nəs\ *adj* 1 : originating in muscle (∼ pain) 2 : taking place or functioning in ordered rhythmic fashion because of inherent properties of cardiac muscle rather than by reason of specific neural stimuli (a ∼ heartbeat) — compare NEUROGENIC 2b — **my·o·ge·nic·i·ty** \-jə-'ni-sə-tē\ *n*

myo·glo·bin \mī-ə-'glō-bən, 'mī-ə-,\ *n* : a red iron-containing protein pigment in muscles that is similar to hemoglobin

myo·glo·bin·uria \-,glō-bi-'nùr-ē-ə, -'nyùr-\ *n* : the presence of myoglobin in the urine

myo·gram \'mī-ə-,gram\ *n* : a graphic representation of the phenomena (as intensity) of muscular contractions

myo·graph \-,graf\ *n* : an apparatus for producing myograms

myoid \'mī-,òid\ *adj* : resembling muscle

myo·ino·si·tol \,mī-ō-i-'nō-sə-,tòl, -,tōl\ *n* : a biologically active inositol that is a component of the vitamin B complex — called also *mesoinositol*

myom- or **myomo-** *comb form* : myoma ⟨*myomectomy*⟩

myo·ma \mī-'ō-mə\ *n, pl* **-mas** or **-mata** \-mə-tə\ : a tumor consisting of muscle tissue

myo·mec·to·my \,mī-ə-'mek-tə-mē\ *n, pl* **-mies** : surgical excision of a myoma

myo·me·tri·tis \-mə-'trī-təs\ *n* : inflammation of the uterine myometrium

myo·me·tri·um \,mī-ə-'mē-trē-əm\ *n* : the muscular layer of the wall of the uterus — **myo·me·tri·al** \-'mē-trē-əl\ *adj*

myo·ne·cro·sis \-nə-'krō-səs, -ne-\ *n, pl* **-cro·ses** \-,sēz\ : necrosis of muscle

myo·neu·ral \,mī-ə-'nùr-əl, -'nyùr-\ *adj* : of, relating to, or connecting muscles and nerves (∼ effects)

myoneural junction *n* : NEUROMUSCULAR JUNCTION

myo·path·ic \,mī-ə-'pa-thik\ *adj* 1 : involving abnormality of the muscles (∼ syndrome) 2 : of or relating to myopathy (∼ dystrophy)

my·op·a·thy \mī-'ä-pə-thē\ *n, pl* **-thies** : a disorder of muscle tissue or muscles

my·ope \'mī-,ōp\ *n* : a myopic person — called also *myopic*

myo·peri·car·di·tis \,mī-ō-,per-ə-,kär-'dī-təs\ *n, pl* **-dit·i·des** \-'di-tə-,dēz\ : inflammation of both the myocardium and pericardium

my·o·pia \mī-'ō-pē-ə\ *n* : a condition in which the visual images come to a focus in front of the retina of the eye because of defects in the refractive media of the eye or of abnormal length of the eyeball resulting esp. in defective vision of distant objects — called also *nearsightedness*; compare ASTIGMATISM 2, EMMETROPIA

¹**my·o·pic** \-'ō-pik, -'ä-\ *adj* : affected by

myopia : of, relating to, or exhibiting myopia — **my·o·pi·cal·ly** *adv*

²**myopic** *n* : MYOPE

myo·plasm \'mī-ə-,pla-zəm\ *n* : the contractile portion of muscle tissue — compare SARCOPLASM — **myo·plas·mic** \,mī-ə-'plaz-mik\ *adj*

¹**myo·re·lax·ant** \,mī-ō-ri-'lak-sənt\ *n* : a drug that causes relaxation of muscle

²**myorelaxant** *adj* : relating to or causing relaxation of muscle (∼ effects) — **myo·re·lax·ation** \-,rē-,lak-'sä-shən, -,ri-,lak-\ *n*

myo·sar·co·ma \-sär-'kō-mə\ *n, pl* **-mas** or **-ma·ta** \-mə-tə\ : a sarcomatous myoma

myo·sin \'mī-ə-sən\ *n* : a fibrous globulin of muscle that can split ATP and that reacts with actin to form actomyosin

myo·sis *var of* MIOSIS

myo·si·tis \,mī-ə-'sī-təs\ *n* : muscular discomfort or pain

myositis os·sif·i·cans \-ä-'si-fə-,kanz\ *n* : myositis accompanied by ossification of muscle tissue or bony deposits in the muscles

myo·tat·ic reflex \,mī-ə-'ta-tik-\ *n* : STRETCH REFLEX

my·ot·ic *var of* MIOTIC

myo·tome \'mī-ə-,tōm\ *n* 1 : the portion of an embryonic somite from which skeletal musculature is produced 2 : an instrument for myotomy — **myo·to·mal** \,mī-ə-'tō-məl\ *adj*

my·ot·o·my \mī-'ä-tə-mē\ *n, pl* **-mies** : incision or division of a muscle

myo·to·nia \,mī-ə-'tō-nē-ə\ *n* : tonic spasm of one or more muscles; *also* : a condition characterized by such spasms — **myo·ton·ic** \-'tä-nik\ *adj*

myotonia con·gen·i·ta \-kän-'je-nə-tə\ *n* : an inherited condition that is characterized by delay in the ability to relax muscles after forceful contractions but not by wasting of muscle — called also *Thomsen's disease*

myotonia dys·tro·phi·ca \-dis-'trä-fi-kə, -'trō-\ *n* : MYOTONIC DYSTROPHY

myotonic dystrophy *n* : an inherited condition characterized by delay in the ability to relax muscles after forceful contraction, wasting of muscles, the formation of cataracts, premature baldness, atrophy of the gonads, and often mental deficiency

my·ot·o·nus \mī-'ä-tə-nəs\ *n* : sustained spasm of a muscle or muscle group

myo·trop·ic \,mī-ə-'trä-pik, -'trō-\ *adj* : affecting or tending to invade muscles (a ∼ infection)

myo·tube \'mī-ə-,tüb, -,tyüb\ *n* : a developmental stage of a muscle fiber

myring- or **myringo-** *comb form* : tympanic membrane ⟨*myringotomy*⟩

myr·in·go·plas·ty \mə-'riŋ-gə-,plas-tē\ *n, pl* **-ties** : a plastic operation for the repair of perforations in the tympanic membrane

myr·in·got·o·my \,mir-ən-'gä-tə-mē\ *n, pl* **-mies** : incision of the tympanic membrane — called also *tympanoto-my*

my·ris·tate \mi-ˈris-ˌtāt\ — see ISOPRO-PYL MYRISTATE

myx- *or* **myxo-** *comb form* **1** : mucus (*myxoma*) **2** : myxoma (*myxosarcoma*)

myx·ede·ma \ˌmik-sə-ˈdē-mə\ *n* : severe hypothyroidism characterized by firm inelastic edema, dry skin and hair, and loss of mental and physical vigor — **myx·ede·ma·tous** \-ˈde-mə-təs, -ˈdē\ *adj*

myx·oid \ˈmik-ˌsȯid\ *adj* : resembling mucus

myx·o·ma \mik-ˈsō-mə\ *n, pl* **-mas** *or* **-ma·ta** \-mə-tə\ : a soft tumor made up of gelatinous connective tissue resembling that found in the umbilical

cord — **myx·o·ma·tous** \-mə-təs\ *adj*

myx·o·ma·to·sis \mik-ˌsō-mə-ˈtō-səs\ *n, pl* **-to·ses** \-ˌsēz\ : a condition characterized by the presence of myxomas in the body; *specif* : a severe disease of rabbits that is caused by a poxvirus, is transmitted by mosquitos, biting flies, and direct contact, and has been used in the biological control of wild rabbit populations

myxo·sar·co·ma \-sär-ˈkō-mə\ *n, pl* **-mas** *or* **-ma·ta** \-mə-tə\ : a sarcoma with myxomatous elements

myxo·vi·rus \ˈmik-sə-ˌvī-rəs\ *n* : any of a group of rather large RNA-containing viruses that includes the orthomyxoviruses and the paramyxoviruses — **myxo·vi·ral** \ˌmik-sə-ˈvī-rəl\ *adj*

N

n \ˈen\ *n, pl* **n's** *or* **ns** \ˈenz\ : the haploid or gametic number of chromosomes — compare X

N *symbol* nitrogen — usu. italicized when used as a prefix (*N*-allylnormorphine)

Na *symbol* sodium

NA *abbr* **1** Nomina Anatomica **2** nurse's aide

na·bo·thi·an cyst \nə-ˈbō-thē-ən-\ *n* : a mucous gland of the uterine cervix esp. when occluded and dilated — called also **nabothian follicle**

Na·both \ˈnä-ˌbōt\, **Martin** (1675–1721), German anatomist and physician.

NAD \ˌen-(ˌ)ā-ˈdē\ *n* : a coenzyme $C_{21}H_{27}N_7O_{14}P_2$ of numerous dehydrogenases that occurs in most cells and plays an important role in all phases of intermediary metabolism as an oxidizing agent or when in the reduced form as a reducing agent for various metabolites — called also *nicotinamide adenine dinucleotide, diphosphopyridine nucleotide*

NADH \ˌen-(ˌ)ā-(ˌ)dē-ˈāch\ *n* : the reduced form of NAD

na·do·lol \nā-ˈdō-ˌlȯl, -ˌlōl\ *n* : a beta-blocker $C_{17}H_{27}NO_4$ used in the treatment of hypertension and angina pectoris

NADP \ˌen-(ˌ)ā-(ˌ)dē-ˈpē\ *n* : a coenzyme $C_{21}H_{28}N_7O_{17}P_3$ of numerous dehydrogenases (as that acting on glucose-6-phosphate) that occurs esp. in red blood cells and plays a role in intermediary metabolism similar to NAD but acting often on different metabolites — called also *nicotinamide adenine dinucleotide phosphate, TPN, triphosphopyridine nucleotide*

NADPH \ˌen-(ˌ)ā-(ˌ)dē-(ˌ)pē-ˈāch\ *n* : the reduced form of NADP

nae·paine \ˈnē-ˌpān\ *n* : a drug $C_{14}H_{22}N_2O_2$ used in the form of its

hydrochloride as a local anesthetic

nae·void, nae·vus *chiefly Brit var of* NEVOID, NEVUS

naf·cil·lin \naf-ˈsil-lən\ *n* : a semisynthetic penicillin $C_{21}H_{22}N_2O_5S$ that is resistant to penicillinase and is used esp. in the form of its sodium salt as an antibiotic

naf·ox·i·dine \na-ˈfäk-sə-ˌdēn\ *n* : an antiestrogen administered in the form of its hydrochloride $C_{29}H_{31}NO_2 \cdot HCl$

na·ga·na \nə-ˈgä-nə\ *n* : a highly fatal disease of domestic animals in tropical Africa caused by a flagellated protozoan of the genus *Trypanosoma* and transmitted by tsetse and possibly other biting flies; *broadly* : trypanosomiasis of domestic animals

nail \ˈnāl\ *n* **1** : a horny sheath of thickened and condensed epithelial stratum lucidum that grows out from a vascular matrix of cutis and protects the upper surface of the end of each finger and toe — called also **nail plate** **2** : a rod (as of metal) used to fix the parts of a broken bone in normal relation (medullary ~)

nail bed *n* : MATRIX 1b

nail-biting *n* : habitual biting at the fingernails usu. being symptomatic of emotional tensions and frustrations

nail fold *n* : the fold of the cutis at the margin of a fingernail or toenail

nail·ing \ˈnā-liŋ\ *n* : the act or process of fixing the parts of a broken bone by means of a nail (intramedullary ~)

nail matrix *n* : MATRIX 1b

nail plate *n* : NAIL 1

na·ive *or* **na·ïve** \nä-ˈēv\ *adj* **na·iv·er; -est** : not previously subjected to experimentation or a particular experimental situation (made the test with ~ rats); *also* : not having previously used a particular drug (as marijuana)

Na·ja \ˈnä-jə\ *n* : a genus of elapid snakes comprising the true cobras

na·ked \ˈnā-kəd\ *adj* : lacking some

natural external covering (as of hair or myelin) — used of the animal body or one of its parts (∼ nerve endings)

na·li·dix·ic acid \ˌnā-lə-ˈdik-sik-\ n : an antibacterial agent $C_{12}H_{12}N_2O_3$ that is used esp. in the treatment of genitourinary infections — see NEGGRAM

Nal·line \ˈna-ˌlēn\ trademark — used for a preparation of nalorphine

na·lor·phine \na-ˈlȯr-ˌfēn\ n : a white crystalline compound $C_{19}H_{21}NO_3$ that is derived from morphine and is used in the form of its hydrochloride as a respiratory stimulant to counteract poisoning by morphine and similar narcotic drugs — called also N-allylnormorphine; see NALLINE

nal·ox·one \na-ˈläk-ˌsōn, ˈna-lək-ˌsōn\ n : a potent antagonist $C_{19}H_{21}NO_4$ of narcotic drugs and esp. morphine that is administered esp. in the form of its hydrochloride — see NARCAN

nal·trex·one \nal-ˈtrek-ˌsōn\ n : a synthetic opiate antagonist $C_{20}H_{23}NO_4$ used esp. to maintain detoxified opiate addicts in a drug-free state

nan- or **nano-** comb form : dwarf ⟨nanocephalic⟩

nan·dro·lone \ˈnan-drə-ˌlōn\ n : a synthetic androgen $C_{18}H_{26}O_2$ used as an anabolic steroid

na·nism \ˈna-ˌni-zəm, ˈnā-\ n : the condition of being abnormally or exceptionally small in stature : DWARFISM

nano- comb form : one billionth (10^{-9}) part of ⟨nanosecond⟩

nano·ce·phal·ic \ˌna-nō-si-ˈfa-lik\ adj : having an abnormally small head

nano·cu·rie \ˈna-nō-ˌkyur-ē, -kyu-ˈrē\ n : one billionth of a curie

nano·gram \-ˌgram\ n : one billionth of a gram

nano·me·ter \-ˌmē-tər\ n : one billionth of a meter — abbr. nm

nano·sec·ond \-ˌse-kənd, -kənt\ n : one billionth of a second — abbr. ns, nsec

nape \ˈnāp, ˈnap\ n : the back of the neck

na·phaz·o·line \nə-ˈfa-zə-ˌlēn\ n : a base $C_{14}H_{14}N_2$ used locally in the form of its bitter crystalline hydrochloride esp. to relieve nasal congestion

naph·tha·lene \ˈnaf-thə-ˌlēn\ n : a crystalline aromatic hydrocarbon $C_{10}H_8$

naphthoate — see PAMAQUINE NAPHTHOATE

naph·thol \ˈnaf-ˌthȯl, -ˌthōl\ n : either of two isomeric derivatives $C_{10}H_8O$ of naphthalene

naph·tho·qui·none also **naph·tha·qui·none** \ˌnaf-thō-kwi-ˈnōn, -ˌkwi-ˈnōn\ n : any of three isomeric yellow to red crystalline compounds $C_{10}H_6O_2$; esp : one that occurs naturally in the form of derivatives (as vitamin K)

naph·thyl·amine \naf-ˈthi-lə-ˌmēn\ n : either of two isomeric crystalline bases $C_{10}H_9N$ that are used esp. in synthesizing dyes; esp : one (β-naphthylamine) with the amino group

in the beta position that has been demonstrated to cause bladder cancer in individuals exposed to it while working in the dye industry

Naph·ur·ide \ˈna-fyū-ˌrīd\ trademark — used for a preparation of suramin

nap·kin \ˈnap-kən\ n : SANITARY NAPKIN

na·prap·a·thy \nə-ˈpra-pə-thē\ n, pl -thies : a system of treatment by manipulation of connective tissue and adjoining structures (as ligaments, joints, and muscles) and by dietary measures that is held to facilitate the recuperative and regenerative processes of the body

Na·pro·syn \nə-ˈprōs-ᵊn\ trademark — used for a preparation of naproxen

na·prox·en \nə-ˈpräk-sᵊn\ n : an antiinflammatory analgesic antipyretic drug $C_{14}H_{14}O_3$ used esp. to treat arthritis — see NAPROSYN

nap·syl·ate \ˈnap-sə-ˌlāt\ n : a salt or ester of either of two crystalline acids $C_{10}H_7SO_3H$

Naqua \ˈna-kwə\ trademark — used for a preparation of trichlormethiazide

narc- or **narco-** comb form 1 : numbness : stupor ⟨narcosis⟩ 2 : deep sleep ⟨narcolepsy⟩

Nar·can \ˈnär-ˌkan\ trademark — used for a preparation of naloxone

nar·cis·sism \ˈnär-sə-ˌsi-zəm\ n 1 : love of or sexual desire for one's own body 2 : the state or stage of development in which there is considerable erotic interest in one's own body and ego and which in abnormal forms persists through fixation or reappears through regression — **nar·cis·sist** \-sist\ n — **nar·cis·sis·tic** \ˌnär-sə-ˈsis-tik\ adj

nar·co·anal·y·sis \ˌnär-kō-ə-ˈna-lə-səs\ n, pl -y·ses \-ˌsēz\ : psychotherapy that is performed under sedation for the recovery of repressed memories together with the emotion accompanying the experience and that is designed to facilitate an acceptable integration of the experience in the patient's personality

nar·co·lep·sy \ˈnär-kə-ˌlep-sē\ n, pl -sies : a condition characterized by brief attacks of deep sleep — compare HYPERSOMNIA 2

¹**nar·co·lep·tic** \ˌnär-kə-ˈlep-tik\ adj : of, relating to, or affected with narcolepsy

²**narcoleptic** n : an individual who is subject to attacks of narcolepsy

nar·co·sis \när-ˈkō-səs\ n, pl -co·ses \-ˌsēz\ : a state of stupor, unconsciousness, or arrested activity produced by the influence of narcotics or other chemicals

nar·co·syn·the·sis \ˌnär-kō-ˈsin-thə-səs\ n, pl -the·ses \-ˌsēz\ : narcoanalysis which has as its goal a reintegration of the patient's personality

¹**nar·cot·ic** \när-ˈkä-tik\ n 1 : a drug (as opium) that in moderate doses dulls

the senses, relieves pain, and induces profound sleep but in excessive doses causes stupor, coma, or convulsions **2** : a drug (as marijuana or LSD) subject to restriction similar to that of addictive narcotics whether physiologically addictive and narcotic or not

²**narcotic** *adj* **1** : having the properties of or yielding a narcotic **2** : of, induced by, or concerned with narcotics **3** : of, involving, or intended for narcotic addicts

nar·co·ti·za·tion \ˌnär-kə-tə-'zā-shən\ *n* : the act or process of inducing narcosis

nar·co·tize \'när-kə-ˌtīz\ *vb* **-tized; -tiz·ing 1** : to treat with or subject to a narcotic **2** : to put into a state of narcosis

Nar·dil \'när-ˌdil\ *trademark* — used for a preparation of phenelzine

na·res \'nar-ˌēz\ *n pl* : the pair of openings of the nose

narrow–angle glaucoma *n* : CLOSED-ANGLE GLAUCOMA

narrow–spectrum *adj* : effective against only a limited range of organisms — compare BROAD-SPECTRUM

nas- *or* **naso-** *also* **nasi-** *comb form* **1** : nose : nasal (*naso*pharyngoscope) **2** : nasal and (*naso*tracheal)

¹**na·sal** \'nā-zəl\ *n* : a nasal part (as a bone)

²**nasal** *adj* : of or relating to the nose — **na·sal·ly** *adv*

nasal bone *n* : either of two bones of the skull of vertebrates above the fishes that lie in front of the frontal bones and in humans are oblong in shape forming by their junction the bridge of the nose and partly covering the nasal cavity

nasal cavity *n* : the vaulted chamber that lies between the floor of the cranium and the roof of the mouth of higher vertebrates extending from the external nares to the pharynx, being enclosed by bone or cartilage and usu. incompletely divided into lateral halves by the septum of the nose, and having its walls lined with mucous membrane that is rich in venous plexuses and ciliated in the lower part which forms the beginning of the respiratory passage and warms and filters the inhaled air and that is modified as sensory epithelium in the upper olfactory part

nasal concha *n* : any of three thin bony plates on the lateral wall of the nasal fossa on each side with or without their covering of mucous membrane: **a** : a separate curved bony plate that is the largest of the three and separates the inferior and middle meatuses of the nose — called also *inferior concha, inferior nasal concha, inferior turbinate, inferior turbinate bone* **b** : the lower of two thin bony processes of the ethmoid bone on the lateral wall of each nasal fossa that sepa-

rates the superior and middle meatuses of the nose — called also *middle concha, middle nasal concha, middle turbinate, middle turbinate bone* **c** : the upper of two thin bony processes of the ethmoid bone on the lateral wall of each nasal fossa that forms the upper boundary of the superior meatus of the nose — called also *superior concha, superior nasal concha, superior turbinate, superior turbinate bone*

nasal fossa *n* : either lateral half of the nasal cavity

na·sa·lis \nā-'zā-ləs, -'sā-\ *n* : a small muscle on each side of the nose that constricts the nasal aperture

nasal nerve *n* : NASOCILIARY NERVE

nasal notch *n* : the rough surface on the anterior lower border of the frontal bone between the orbits which articulates with the nasal bones and the maxillae

nasal process *n* : FRONTAL PROCESS 1

nasal septum *n* : the bony and cartilaginous partition between the nasal passages

nasal spine *n* : any of several median bony processes adjacent to the nasal passages: as **a** : ANTERIOR NASAL SPINE **b** : POSTERIOR NASAL SPINE

nasi — *see* ALA NASI, LEVATOR LABII SUPERIORIS ALAEQUE NASI

nasi- — *see* NAS-

na·si·on \'nā-zē-ˌän\ *n* : the middle point of the nasofrontal suture

Na·smyth's membrane \'nā-smiths-\ *n* : the thin cuticular remains of the enamel organ which surrounds the enamel of a tooth during its fetal development and for a brief period after birth

Nasmyth, Alexander (*d* 1848), British anatomist and dentist.

naso- — *see* NAS-

na·so·cil·i·ary \ˌnā-zō-'si-lē-ˌer-ē\ *adj* : nasal and ciliary

nasociliary nerve *n* : a branch of the ophthalmic nerve distributed in part to the ciliary ganglion and in part to the mucous membrane and skin of the nose — called also *nasal nerve*

na·so·fron·tal \-'frənt-əl\ *adj* : of or relating to the nasal and frontal bones

nasofrontal suture *n* : the cranial suture between the nasal and frontal bones

na·so·gas·tric \-'gas-trik\ *adj* : of, relating to, being, or performed by intubation of the stomach by way of the nasal passages (insertion of a ~ tube)

na·so·la·bi·al \-'lā-bē-əl\ *adj* : of, relating to, located between, or occurring between the nose and the lips

na·so·lac·ri·mal *also* **na·so·lach·ry·mal** \-'la-krə-məl\ *adj* : of or relating to the lacrimal apparatus and nose

nasolacrimal duct *n* : a duct that transmits tears from the lacrimal sac to the inferior meatus of the nose

na·so·max·il·lary \-'mak-sə-ˌler-ē\ *adj* : of, relating to, or located between the nasal bone and the maxilla ⟨~ fracture⟩

na·so·pal·a·tine \-ˈpal-ə-ˌtīn\ adj : of, relating to, or connecting the nose and the palate

nasopalatine nerve n : a parasympathetic and sensory nerve that arises in the sphenopalatine ganglion, passes through the sphenopalatine foramen, across the roof of the nasal cavity to the nasal septum, and obliquely downward to and through the incisive canal, and innervates esp. the glands and mucosa of the nasal septum and the anterior part of the hard palate

na·so·pha·ryn·ge·al \ˌnā-zō-fə-ˈrin-jəl, -jē-əl; -ˌfar-ən-ˈjē-əl\ adj : of, relating to, or affecting the nose and pharynx or the nasopharynx

nasopharyngeal tonsil n : PHARYNGEAL TONSIL

na·so·pha·ryn·go·scope \-fə-ˈrin-gə-ˌskōp\ n : an instrument equipped with an optical system and used in examining the nasal passages and pharynx — **na·so·pha·ryn·go·scop·ic** \-fə-ˌrin-gə-ˈskä-pik\ adj — **na·so·pharyn·gos·co·py** \-ˌfar-ən-ˈgäs-kə-pē\ n

na·so·phar·ynx \-ˈfar-iŋks\ n, pl -pha·ryn·ges \-fə-ˈrin-(ˌ)jēz\ also -phar·ynx·es : the upper part of the pharynx continuous with the nasal passages — compare LARYNGOPHARYNX

na·so·tra·che·al \-ˈträ-kē-əl\ adj : of, relating to, being, or performed by means of intubation of the trachea by way of the nasal passage

na·tal \ˈnāt-əl\ adj : of or relating to birth (the ~ death rate)

na·tal·i·ty \nā-ˈta-lə-tē, nə-\ n, pl -ties : BIRTHRATE

na·tes \ˈnā-ˌtēz\ n pl : BUTTOCKS

National Formulary n : a periodically revised book of officially established and recognized drug names and standards — abbr. NF

na·tri·ure·sis \ˌnā-trē-yū-ˈrē-səs\ n : excessive loss of cations and esp. sodium in the urine — **na·tri·uret·ic** \-ˈretik\ adj or n

natural childbirth n : a system of managing childbirth in which the mother receives preparatory education in order to remain conscious during and assist in delivery with minimal or no use of drugs or anesthetics

natural family planning n : a method of birth control that involves abstention from sexual intercourse during the period of ovulation which is determined through observation and measurement of bodily symptoms (as cervical mucus and body temperature)

natural food n : food that has undergone minimal processing and contains no preservatives or artificial additives (as synthetic flavorings)

natural history n : the natural development of something (as an organism or disease) over a period of time

natural immunity n : immunity that is possessed by a group (as a race, strain, or species) and occurs in an individual as part of its natural biologic makeup and that is sometimes considered to include that acquired passively in utero or from mother's milk or actively by exposure to infection — compare ACQUIRED IMMUNITY, ACTIVE IMMUNITY, PASSIVE IMMUNITY

natural killer cell n : a large granular lymphocyte capable of killing a tumor or microbial cell without prior exposure to the target cell and without having it presented with or marked by a histocompatibility antigen

na·tu·ro·path \ˈnā-chə-rə-ˌpath, nə-ˈtyùr-ə-\ n : a practitioner of naturopathy

na·tu·rop·a·thy \ˌnā-chə-ˈrä-pə-thē\ n, pl -thies : a system of treatment of disease that avoids drugs and surgery and emphasizes the use of natural agents (as air, water, and sunshine) and physical means (as manipulation and electrical treatment) — **na·tu·ro·path·ic** \ˌnā-chə-rə-ˈpa-thik, nə-ˌtyùr-ə-\ adj

nau·sea \ˈnó-zē-ə, -sē-ə; ˈnó-zhə, -shə\ n : a stomach distress with distaste for food and an urge to vomit

nau·se·ant \ˈnó-zhənt, -zhē-ənt, -shənt, -shē-ənt\ adj : inducing nausea : NAUSEATING

nau·se·ate \ˈnó-zē-ˌāt, -zhē-, -sē-, -shē-\ vb -at·ed; -at·ing : to affect or become affected with nausea

nau·seous \ˈnó-shəs, ˈnó-zē-əs\ adj 1 : causing nausea 2 : affected with nausea

Nav·ane \ˈna-ˌvān\ trademark — used for a preparation of thiothixene

na·vel \ˈnā-vəl\ n : a depression in the middle of the abdomen that marks the point of former attachment of the umbilical cord to the embryo — called also umbilicus

navel ill n : a serious septicemia of newborn animals caused by pus-producing bacteria entering the body through the umbilical cord or opening — called also joint ill

¹**na·vic·u·lar** \nə-ˈvi-kyə-lər\ n : a navicular bone: a : the one of the seven tarsal bones of the human foot that is situated on the big-toe side between the talus and the cuneiform bones — called also scaphoid b : SCAPHOID 2

²**navicular** adj 1 : resembling or having the shape of a boat (a ~ bone) 2 : of, relating to, or involving a navicular bone (~ fractures)

navicular disease n : inflammation of the navicular bone and forefoot of the horse

navicular fossa n : the dilated terminal portion of the urethra in the glans penis

navicularis — see FOSSA NAVICULARIS

Nb symbol niobium

NBRT abbr National Board for Respiratory Therapy

NCI *abbr* National Cancer Institute

Nd *symbol* neodymium

NDT *abbr* neurodevelopmental treatment

Ne *symbol* neon

ne- *or* **neo-** *comb form* **1** : new : recent ⟨*neo*natal⟩ **2** : an abnormal new formation ⟨*neo*plasm⟩ **3** : new chemical compound isomeric with or otherwise related to (such) a compound ⟨*neo*stigmine⟩

near point *n* : the point nearest the eye at which an object is accurately focused on the retina when the maximum degree of accommodation is employed — compare FAR POINT

near·sight·ed \'nir-ˌsī-təd\ *adj* : able to see near things more clearly than distant ones : MYOPIC — **near·sight·ed·ly** *adv*

near·sight·ed·ness *n* : MYOPIA

neb·u·li·za·tion \ˌne-byə-lə-'zā-shən\ *n* **1** : reduction of a medicinal solution to a fine spray **2** : treatment (as of respiratory diseases) by means of a fine spray — **neb·u·lize** \'ne-byə-ˌlīz\ *vb*

neb·u·liz·er \-ˌlī-zər\ *n* : ATOMIZER; *specif* : an atomizer equipped to produce an extremely fine spray for deep penetration of the lungs

Ne·ca·tor \nə-'kā-tər\ *n* : a genus of common hookworms that include internal parasites of humans and various other mammals, and that are prob. of African origin though first identified in No. America — compare ANCYLOSTOMA

neck \'nek\ *n* **1 a** : the usu. narrowed part of an animal that connects the head with the body; *specif* : the cervical region of a vertebrate **b** : the part of a tapeworm immediately behind the scolex from which new proglottids are produced **2** : a relatively narrow part suggestive of a neck: as **a** : a narrow part of a bone (the ∼ of the femur) **b** : CERVIX 2 **c** : the part of a tooth between the crown and the root

necr- *or* **necro-** *comb form* **1 a** : those that are dead : the dead : corpses ⟨*necro*philia⟩ **b** : one that is dead : corpse ⟨*necro*psy⟩ **2** : death : conversion to dead tissue : atrophy ⟨*necro*sis⟩

nec·ro \'ne-(ˌ)krō\ *n* : NECROTIC ENTERITIS

nec·ro·bac·il·lo·sis \ˌne-krō-ˌba-sə-'lō-səs\ *n, pl* **-lo·ses** \-ˌsēz\ : any of several infections or diseases (as bullnose or calf diphtheria) that are either localized (as in foot rot) or disseminated through the body of the infected animal and that are characterized by inflammation and ulcerative or necrotic lesions from which a bacterium of the genus *Fusobacterium* (*F. necrophorum* syn. *Sphaerophorus necrophorus*) has been isolated — see QUITTOR

nec·ro·bi·o·sis \-bī-'ō-səs\ *n, pl* **-o·ses** \-ˌsēz\ : death of a cell or group of cells within a tissue whether normal (as in various epithelial tissues) or part of a pathologic process — compare NECROSIS

nec·ro·bi·o·sis li·poid·i·ca \-li-'pȯi-di-kə\ *n* : a disease of the skin that is characterized by the formation of multiple necrobiotic lesions esp. on the legs and that is often associated with diabetes mellitus

necrobiosis lipoidica dia·bet·i·co·rum \-ˌdī-ə-ˌbe-ti-'kȯr-əm\ *n* : NECROBIOSIS LIPOIDICA

nec·ro·bi·ot·ic \ˌne-krə-bī-'ä-tik\ *adj* : of, relating to, or being in a state of necrobiosis

nec·ro·phile \'ne-krə-ˌfīl\ *n* : one that is affected with necrophilia

nec·ro·phil·ia \ˌne-krə-'fi-lē-ə\ *n* : obsession with and usu. erotic interest in or stimulation by corpses

nec·ro·phil·i·ac \-'fi-lē-ˌak\ *adj* : of, relating to, or affected with necrophilia

necrophiliac *n* : NECROPHILE

nec·ro·phil·ic \-'fi-lik\ *adj* : NECROPHILIAC

necrop·sy \'ne-ˌkräp-sē\ *n, pl* **-sies** : AUTOPSY

necropsy *vb* **-sied; -sy·ing** : AUTOPSY

ne·crose \'ne-ˌkrōs, -ˌkrōz, ne-'krōz\ *vb* **ne·crosed; ne·ros·ing** : to undergo or cause to undergo necrosis

ne·cro·sis \nə-'krō-sis, ne-\ *n, pl* **ne·cro·ses** \-ˌsēz\ : death of living tissue; *specif* : death of a portion of tissue differentially affected by local injury (as loss of blood supply, corrosion, burning, or the local lesion of a disease) — compare *necrobiosis*

nec·ro·sper·mia \ˌne-krə-'spər-mē-ə\ *n* : a condition in which the spermatozoa in seminal fluid are dead or motionless

ne·crot·ic \nə-'krä-tik, ne-\ *adj* : affected with, characterized by, or producing necrosis (a ∼ gall bladder)

necrotic enteritis *n* : a serious infectious disease of young swine caused by a bacterium of the genus *Salmonella* (*S. cholerae-suis*) — called also *necro*; see PARATYPHOID

necrotic rhinitis *n* : BULLNOSE

nec·ro·tiz·ing \'ne-krə-ˌtī-ziŋ\ *adj* : causing, associated with, or undergoing necrosis (∼ infections) (∼ tissue)

necrotizing angiitis *n* : an inflammatory condition of the blood vessels characterized by necrosis of vascular tissue

necrotizing papillitis *n* : necrosis of the papillae of the kidney — called also *necrotizing renal papillitis*

nee·dle \'nēd-ᵊl\ *n* **1** : a small slender usu. steel instrument designed to carry sutures when sewing tissues in surgery **2** : a slender hollow instrument for introducing material into or removing material from the body parenterally

needle *vb* **nee·dled; nee·dling** : to punc-

ture. operate on. or inject with a needle

needle aspiration biopsy *n* : a needle biopsy in which tissue is removed by
aspiration into a syringe

needle biopsy *n* : a biopsy esp. of deep
tissues done with a hollow needle

nee·dle·stick \'nēd-əl-ˌstik\ *n* : an accidental puncture of the skin with an
unsterile instrument (as a syringe) —
called also *needlestick injury*

neg·a·tive \'ne-gə-tiv\ *adj* 1 : marked by
denial, prohibition, or refusal 2
: marked by features (as hostility or
withdrawal) opposing constructive
treatment or development 3 : being,
relating to, or charged with electricity
of which the electron is the elementary unit 4 : not affirming the presence
of the organism or condition in question (a ~ TB test) — **neg·a·tive·ly** *adv*
— **neg·a·tiv·i·ty** \ˌne-gə-'ti-və-tē\ *n*

negative feedback *n* : feedback that
tends to stabilize a process by reducing its rate or output when its effects
are too great

negative pressure *n* : pressure that is
less than existing atmospheric pressure

negative reinforcement *n* : psychological reinforcement by removal of an
unpleasant stimulus when a desired
response occurs

negative transfer *n* : the impeding of
learning or performance in a situation
by the carry-over of learned responses from another situation — compare
INTERFERENCE 2

neg·a·tiv·ism \'ne-gə-ti-ˌvi-zəm\ *n* 1 : an
attitude of mind marked by skepti-
cism about nearly everything af-
firmed by others 2 : a tendency to
refuse to do, to do the opposite of, or
to do something at variance with
what is asked — **neg·a·tiv·ist·ic** \ˌne-
gə-ti-'vis-tik\ *adj*

Neg-Gram \'neg-ˌgram\ *trademark* —
used for a preparation of nalidixic
acid

Ne·gri body \'nā-grē-\ *n* : an inclusion
body found in the nerve cells in rabies
Negri, **Adelchi** (1876–1912), Italian
physician and pathologist.

Neis·se·ria \nī-'sir-ē-ə\ *n* : a genus (family Neisseriaceae) of parasitic bacteria that grow in pairs and occas.
tetrads and include the gonococcus
(*N. gonorrhoeae*) and meningococcus (*N. meningitidis*)
Neis·ser \'nī-sər\, **Albert Ludwig
Sigesmund** (1855–1916), German dermatologist.

neis·se·ri·an \nī-'sir-ē-ən\ *or* **neis·se·
ri·al** \-ē-əl\ *adj* : of, relating to, or
caused by bacteria of the genus
Neisseria (~ culture) (~ infection)

nemat- *or* **nemato-** *comb form* 1
: thread (*nematocyst*) 2 : nematode
(*nematology*)

ne·ma·to·cide *or* **ne·ma·ti·cide** \'ne-mə-
tə-ˌsīd, ni-'ma-tə-\ *n* : a substance or

preparation used to destroy nematodes — **ne·ma·to·cid·al** *also* **ne·ma·
ti·cid·al** \ˌne-mə-tə-'sīd-əl, ni-ˌma-tə-\
adj

ne·ma·to·cyst \'ne-mə-tə-ˌsist, ni-'ma-
tə-\ *n* : one of the minute stinging organelles of various coelenterates

nem·a·tode \'ne-mə-ˌtōd\ *n* : any of a
phylum (Nematoda) of elongated cylindrical worms parasitic in animals
or plants or free-living in soil or water

Nem·a·to·di·rus \ˌne-mə-tə-'dī-rəs\ *n* : a
genus of reddish strongylid nematode
worms parasitic in the small intestine
of ruminants and sometimes other
mammals

nem·a·tol·o·gy \ˌne-mə-'tä-lə-jē\ *n, pl*
-gies : a branch of zoology that deals
with nematodes — **nem·a·tol·o·gist**
\-jist\ *n*

Nem·bu·tal \'nem-byə-ˌtȯl\ *trademark*
— used for the sodium salt of pentobarbital

neo- — see NE-

Neo-Ant·er·gan \ˌnē-ō-'an-'tər-gən\
trademark — used for a preparation
of pyrilamine

neo·ars·phen·a·mine \ˌnē-ō-ärs-'fe-nə-
ˌmēn\ *n* : a yellow powder
$C_{13}H_{13}As_2N_2NaO_4S$ similar to arsphenamine in structure and use —
called also *neosalvarsan*

neo·cer·e·bel·lum \ˌnē-ō-ˌser-ə-'bel-
əm\ *n, pl* **-bellums** *or* **-bel·la** : the part
of the cerebellum associated with the
cerebral cortex in the integration of
voluntary limb movements and comprising most of the cerebellar hemispheres and the superior vermis —
compare PALEOCEREBELLUM — **neo·
cer·e·bel·lar** \ˌnē-ō-ˌser-ə-'bel-ər\ *adj*

neo·cin·cho·phen \ˌnē-ō-'siŋ-kə-ˌfen\ *n*
: a white crystalline compound
$C_{19}H_{17}NO_2$ used as an analgesic and
in the treatment of gout

neo·cor·tex \ˌnē-ō-'kȯr-ˌteks\ *n, pl*
-cor·ti·ces \-'kȯr-tə-ˌsēz\ *or* **-cortexes**
: the dorsal region of the cerebral cortex that is unique to mammals — **neo·
cor·ti·cal** \-'kȯr-ti-kəl\ *adj*

neo·dym·i·um \ˌnē-ō-'di-mē-əm\ *n* : a
yellow metallic element — symbol
Nd; see ELEMENT table

¹neo-Freud·ian \-'frȯi-dē-ən\ *adj, often
cap N* : of or relating to a school of
psychoanalysis that differs from
Freudian orthodoxy in emphasizing
the importance of social and cultural
factors in the development of an individual's personality

²neo-Freudian *n, often cap N* : a member of or advocate of a neo-Freudian
school of psychoanalysis
S. Freud — see FREUDIAN

Neo·het·ra·mine \ˌnē-ō-'he-trə-ˌmēn\
trademark — used for a preparation
of thonzylamine

ne·ol·o·gism \nē-'ä-lə-ˌji-zəm\ *n* 1 : a
new word, usage, or expression 2 : a
word coined by a psychotic that is
meaningless except to the coiner

neo·my·cin \nē-ə-ˈmīs-ᵊn\ n : a broad-spectrum highly toxic antibiotic or mixture of antibiotics produced by a bacterium of the genus *Streptomyces* (*S. fradiae*) and used to treat local infections

ne·on \ˈnē-ˌän\ n : a colorless odorless primarily inert gaseous element — symbol *Ne*; see ELEMENT table

neo·na·tal \nē-ō-ˈnāt-ᵊl\ adj : of, relating to, or affecting the newborn and esp. the human infant during the first month after birth — compare PRENATAL, POSTNATAL — **neo·na·tal·ly** adv

ne·o·nate \ˈnē-ə-ˌnāt\ n : a newborn child; esp : a child less than a month old

neo·na·tol·o·gist \nē-ə-nā-ˈtä-lə-jist\ n : a specialist in neonatology

neo·na·tol·o·gy \-jē\ n, pl -gies : a branch of medicine concerned with the care, development, and diseases of newborn infants

neonatorum — see ICTERUS GRAVIS NEONATORUM, ICTERUS NEONATORUM, OPHTHALMIA NEONATORUM, SCLEREMA NEONATORUM

neo·pal·li·um \nē-ō-ˈpa-lē-əm\ n, pl **-lia** \-lē-ə\ : the part of the cerebral cortex that develops from the area between the piriform lobe and the hippocampus, comprises the nonolfactory region of the cortex, and attains its maximum development in humans where it makes up the greater part of the cerebral hemisphere on each side — compare ARCHIPALLIUM

neo·pho·bia \nē-ə-ˈfō-bē-ə\ n : dread of or aversion to novelty

neo·pla·sia \nē-ə-ˈplā-zh-ə, -zhē-ə\ n 1 : the process of tumor formation 2 : a tumorous condition of the body

neo·plasm \ˈnē-ə-ˌpla-zəm\ n : a new growth of tissue serving no physiological function : TUMOR — compare CANCER 1

neo·plas·tic \nē-ə-ˈplas-tik\ adj : of, relating to, or constituting a neoplasm or neoplasia — **neo·plas·ti·cal·ly** adv

neo·sal·var·san \nē-ō-ˈsal-vər-ˌsan\ n : NEOARSPHENAMINE

neo·stig·mine \nē-ə-ˈstig-ˌmēn\ n : a cholinergic drug used in the form of its bromide $C_{12}H_{19}BrN_2O_2$ or a sulfate derivative $C_{13}H_{22}N_2O_6S$ esp. in the treatment of some ophthalmic conditions and in the diagnosis and treatment of myasthenia gravis — see PROSTIGMIN

neo·stri·a·tum \nē-ō-(ˌ)strī-ˈā-təm\ n, pl **-tums** or **-ta** \-tə\ : the evolutionarily older part of the corpus striatum consisting of the caudate nucleus and putamen — **neo·stri·a·tal** \-ˈāt-ᵊl\ adj

Neo-Syn·eph·rine \nē-ō-si-ˈne-frən, -frēn\ trademark — used for a preparation of phenylephrine

Neo·thyl·line \nē-ə-ˈthi-lən\ trademark — used for a preparation of dyphylline

neo·vas·cu·lar·i·za·tion \-ˌvas-kyə-lə-rə-ˈzā-shən\ n : vascularization esp. in abnormal quantity (as in some conditions of the retina) or in abnormal tissue (as a tumor) — **neo·vas·cu·lar** \nē-ō-ˈvas-kyə-lər\ adj — **neo·vas·cu·lar·i·ty** \-ˌvas-kyə-ˈlar-ə-tē\ n

neph·e·lom·e·ter \ne-fə-ˈlä-mə-tər\ n : an instrument for measuring turbidity (as to determine the number of bacteria suspended in a fluid) — **neph·e·lo·met·ric** \-ˌne-fə-lō-ˈme-trik\ adj — **neph·e·lom·e·try** \-ˈläm-ə-trē\ n

nephr- or **nephro-** comb form : kidney ⟨nephrectomy⟩ ⟨nephrology⟩

ne·phrec·to·my \ni-ˈfrek-tə-mē\ n, pl **-mies** : the surgical removal of a kidney — **ne·phrec·to·mize** \-ˌmīz\ vb

neph·ric \ˈne-frik\ adj : RENAL

ne·phrit·ic \ni-ˈfri-tik\ adj 1 : RENAL 2 : of, relating to, or affected with nephritis

ne·phri·tis \ni-ˈfrī-təs\ n, pl **ne·phrit·i·des** \-ˈfri-tə-ˌdēz\ : acute or chronic inflammation of the kidney affecting the structure (as of the glomerulus or parenchyma) and caused by infection, degenerative process, or vascular disease — compare NEPHROSCLEROSIS, NEPHROSIS

neph·ri·to·gen·ic \ne-frə-tə-ˈje-nik, ni-ˌfri-tə-\ adj : causing nephritis

neph·ro·blas·to·ma \ne-frō-blas-ˈtō-mə\ n, pl **-mas** or **-ma·ta** \-mə-tə\ : WILMS' TUMOR

neph·ro·cal·ci·no·sis \ne-frō-ˌkal-si-ˈnō-səs\ n, pl **-no·ses** \-ˌsēz\ : a condition marked by calcification of the tubules of the kidney

neph·ro·gen·ic \ne-frə-ˈje-nik\ adj 1 : originating in the kidney : caused by factors originating in the kidney ⟨~ hypertension⟩ 2 : developing into or producing kidney tissue

neph·ro·gram \ˈne-frə-ˌgram\ n : an X ray of the kidney

ne·phrog·ra·phy \ni-ˈfrä-grə-fē\ n, pl **-phies** : roentgenography of the kidney

-nephroi pl of -NEPHROS

neph·ro·lith·i·a·sis \ne-frō-li-ˈthī-ə-səs\ n, pl **-a·ses** \-ˌsēz\ : a condition marked by the presence of renal calculi

neph·ro·li·thot·o·my \-li-ˈthä-tə-mē\ n, pl **-mies** : the surgical operation of removing a calculus from the kidney

ne·phrol·o·gist \ni-ˈfrä-lə-jist\ n : a specialist in nephrology

ne·phrol·o·gy \ni-ˈfrä-lə-jē\ n, pl **-gies** : a medical specialty concerned with the kidneys and esp. with their structure, functions, or diseases

ne·phro·ma \ni-ˈfrō-mə\ n, pl **-mas** also **-ma·ta** \-mə-tə\ : a malignant tumor of the renal cortex

neph·ron \ˈne-ˌfrän\ n : a single excretory unit of the vertebrate kidney typically consisting of a Malpighian corpuscle, proximal convoluted tubule, loop of Henle, distal convoluted tubule, collecting tubule, and vascular and supporting tissues and discharging by way of a renal papilla into the renal pelvis

ne·phrop·a·thy \ni-ˈfräp-ə-thē\ *n, pl* **-thies** : an abnormal state of the kidney; *esp* : one associated with or secondary to some other pathological process — **neph·ro·path·ic** \ˌne-frə-ˈpa-thik\ *adj*

neph·ro·pexy \ˈne-frə-ˌpek-sē\ *n, pl* **-pex·ies** : surgical fixation of a floating kidney

neph·rop·to·sis \ˌne-ˌfräp-ˈtō-səs\ *n, pl* **-to·ses** \-ˌsēz\ : abnormal mobility of the kidney : floating kidney

ne·phror·rha·phy \ne-ˈfrȯr-ə-fē\ *n, pl* **-phies** 1 : the fixation of a floating kidney by suturing it to the posterior abdominal wall 2 : the suturing of a kidney wound

-neph·ros \ˈne-frəs, -ˌfräs\ *n comb form, pl* **-neph·roi** \ˈne-ˌfrȯi\ : kidney ⟨*pronephros*⟩

neph·ro·scle·ro·sis \ˌne-frō-sklə-ˈrō-səs\ *n, pl* **-ro·ses** \-ˌsēz\ : hardening of the kidney; *specif* : a condition that is characterized by sclerosis of the renal arterioles with reduced blood flow and contraction of the kidney, that is associated usu. with hypertension, and that terminates in renal failure and uremia — compare NEPHRITIS — **neph·ro·scle·rot·ic** \-ˈrä-tik\ *adj*

ne·phro·sis \ni-ˈfrō-səs\ *n, pl* **ne·phro·ses** \-ˌsēz\ *n* : a noninflammatory disease of the kidneys chiefly affecting function of the nephrons; *esp* : NEPHROTIC SYNDROME — compare NEPHRITIS

ne·phros·to·gram \ni-ˈfräs-tə-ˌgram\ *n* : a roentgenogram of the renal pelvis after injection of a radiopaque substance through an opening formed by nephrostomy

ne·phros·to·my \ni-ˈfräs-tə-mē\ *n, pl* **-mies** : the surgical formation of an opening between a renal pelvis and the outside of the body

ne·phrot·ic \ni-ˈfrä-tik\ *adj* : of, relating to, affected by, or associated with nephrosis ⟨~ edema⟩ ⟨a ~ patient⟩

nephrotic syndrome *n* : an abnormal condition that is marked by deficiency of albumin in the blood and its excretion in the urine due to altered permeability of the glomerular basement membranes (as by a toxic chemical agent)

neph·ro·to·mo·gram \ˌne-frō-ˈtō-mə-ˌgram\ *n* : a roentgenogram made by nephrotomography

neph·ro·to·mog·ra·phy \-tō-ˈmä-grə-fē\ *n, pl* **-phies** : tomographic visualization of the kidney usu. combined with intravenous nephrography — **neph·ro·to·mo·graph·ic** \-ˌtō-mə-ˈgra-fik\ *adj*

ne·phrot·o·my \ni-ˈfrä-tə-mē\ *n, pl* **-mies** : surgical incision of a kidney (as for the extraction of a stone)

neph·ro·tox·ic \ˌne-frə-ˈtäk-sik\ *adj*

: poisonous to the kidney ⟨~ drugs⟩; *also* : resulting from or marked by poisoning of the kidney ⟨~ effects⟩ — **neph·ro·tox·ic·i·ty** \-ˌtäk-ˈsi-sə-tē\ *n*

neph·ro·tox·in \-ˈtäk-sən\ *n* : a cytotoxin that is destructive to kidney cells

Nep·ta·zane \ˈnep-tə-ˌzān\ *trademark* — used for a preparation of methazolamide

nep·tu·ni·um \nep-ˈtü-nē-əm, -ˈtyü-\ *n* : a radioactive metallic element — symbol *Np*; see ELEMENT table

nerve \ˈnərv\ *n* 1 : any of the filamentous bands of nervous tissue that connect parts of the nervous system with the other organs, conduct nervous impulses, and are made up of axons and dendrites together with protective and supportive structures and that for the larger nerves have the fibers gathered into funiculi surrounded by a perineurium and the funiculi enclosed in a common epineurium 2 *pl* : a state or condition of nervous agitation or irritability 3 : the sensitive pulp of a tooth

nerve block *n* 1 : an interruption of the passage of impulses through a nerve (as with pressure or narcotization) — called also *nerve blocking* 2 : BLOCK ANESTHESIA

nerve cell *n* : NEURON; *also* : CELL BODY

nerve center *n* : CENTER

nerve cord *n* : the dorsal tubular cord of nervous tissue above the notochord that in vertebrates includes or develops an anterior enlargement comprising the brain and a more posterior part comprising the spinal cord with the two together making up the central nervous system

nerve deafness *n* : hearing loss or impairment resulting from injury to or loss of function of the organ of Corti or the auditory nerve — called also *perceptive deafness*; compare CENTRAL DEAFNESS, CONDUCTION DEAFNESS

nerve ending *n* : the structure in which the distal end of the axon of a nerve fiber terminates

nerve fiber *n* : any of the processes (as axons or dendrites) of a neuron

nerve gas *n* : an organophosphate chemical weapon that interferes with normal nerve transmission and induces intense bronchial spasm with resulting inhibition of respiration

nerve growth factor *n* : a protein that promotes development of the sensory and sympathetic nervous systems and is required for maintenance of sympathetic neurons — abbr. *NGF*

nerve impulse *n* : the progressive physicochemical change in the membrane of a nerve fiber that follows stimulation and serves to transmit a record of sensation from a receptor or an instruction to act to an effector — called also *nervous impulse*

nerve of Her·ing \-ˈher-iŋ\ *n* : a nerve

that arises from the main trunk of the glossopharyngeal nerve and runs along the internal carotid artery to supply afferent fibers esp. to the baroreceptors of the carotid sinus

Hering, Heinrich Ewald (1866–1948), German physiologist.

nerve sheath n : NEURILEMMA

nerve trunk n : a bundle of nerve fibers enclosed in a connective tissue sheath

nervi pl of NERVUS

nerv·ing \'nər-viŋ\ n : the removal of part of a nerve trunk in chronic inflammation in order to cure lameness (as of a horse) by destroying sensation in the parts supplied

nervosa — see ANOREXIA NERVOSA, PARS NERVOSA

ner·vous \'nər-vəs\ adj 1 : of, relating to, or composed of neurons ⟨the ∼ layer of the eye⟩ 2 a : of or relating to the nerves; also : originating in or affected by the nerves ⟨∼ energy⟩ b : easily excited or irritated — **ner·vous·ly** adv — **ner·vous·ness** n

nervous breakdown n : an attack of mental or emotional disorder esp. when of sufficient severity to require hospitalization

nervous impulse n : NERVE IMPULSE

nervous system n : the bodily system that in vertebrates is made up of the brain and spinal cord, nerves, ganglia, and parts of the receptor organs and that receives and interprets stimuli and transmits impulses to the effector organs — see CENTRAL NERVOUS SYSTEM; AUTONOMIC NERVOUS SYSTEM, PERIPHERAL NERVOUS SYSTEM

ner·vus \'nər-vəs, 'ner-\ n, pl **ner·vi** \'nər-ˌvī, 'ner-ˌvē\ : NERVE 1

nervus er·i·gens \-'er-i-ˌjenz\ n, pl **nervi er·i·gen·tes** \-ˌer-i-'jen-(ˌ)tēz\ : PELVIC SPLANCHNIC NERVE

nervus in·ter·me·di·us \-ˌin-tər-'mē-dē-əs\ n : the branch of the facial nerve that contains sensory and parasympathetic fibers and that supplies the anterior tongue and parts of the palate and fauces — called also *glosso·palatine nerve*

nervus ra·di·a·lis \-ˌrā-dē-'ā-ləs\ n, pl **nervi ra·di·a·les** \-(ˌ)lēz\ : RADIAL NERVE

nervus ter·mi·na·lis \-ˌtər-mə-'nā-ləs\ n, pl **nervi ter·mi·na·les** \-(ˌ)lēz\ : a group of ganglioned nerve fibers that arise where the nerve tract leading from the olfactory bulb joins the temporal lobe and that pass anteriorly along this tract and the olfactory bulb through the cribriform plate to the nasal mucosa — called also *terminal nerve*

Nes·a·caine \'ne-sə-ˌkān\ *trademark* — used for a preparation of chloroprocaine

neth·a·lide \'ne-thə-ˌlīd\ n : PRONETHALOL

net·tle \'net-ᵊl\ n 1 : any plant of the genus *Urtica* 2 : any of various prickly or stinging plants other than one of the genus *Urtica*

nettle rash n : an eruption on the skin caused by or resembling the condition produced by stinging with nettles : URTICARIA

neur- or **neuro-** comb form 1 : nerve ⟨neural⟩ ⟨neurology⟩ 2 : neural : neural and ⟨neuromuscular⟩

neu·ral \'nùr-əl, -'nyùr-\ adj 1 : of, relating to, or affecting a nerve or the nervous system 2 : situated in the region of or on the same side of the body as the brain and spinal cord : DORSAL — compare HEMAL 2 — **neu·ral·ly** adv

neural arch n : the cartilaginous or bony arch enclosing the spinal cord on the dorsal side of a vertebra — called also *vertebral arch*

neural canal n 1 : VERTEBRAL CANAL 2 : the cavity or system of cavities in a vertebrate embryo that form the central canal of the spinal cord and the ventricles of the brain

neural crest n : the ridge of one of the folds forming the neural tube that gives rise to the spinal ganglia and various structures of the autonomic nervous system — called also *neural ridge;* compare NEURAL PLATE

neural fold n : the lateral longitudinal fold on each side of the neural plate that by folding over and fusing with the opposite fold gives rise to the neural tube

neu·ral·gia \nù-'ral-jə, nyù-\ n : acute paroxysmal pain radiating along the course of one or more nerves usu. without demonstrable changes in the nerve structure — compare NEURITIS — **neu·ral·gic** \-jik\ adj

neural groove n : the median dorsal longitudinal groove formed in the vertebrate embryo by the neural plate after the appearance of the neural folds — called also *medullary groove*

neural lobe n : the expanded distal portion of the neurohypophysis — called also *infundibular process, pars nervosa*

neural plate n : a thickened plate of ectoderm along the dorsal midline of the early embryo that gives rise to the neural tube and crests

neural ridge n : NEURAL CREST

neural tube n : the hollow longitudinal dorsal tube that is formed by infolding and subsequent fusion of the opposite ectodermal folds in the vertebrate embryo and gives rise to the brain and spinal cord

neur·amin·ic acid \ˌnùr-ə-'mi-nik-, ˌnyùr-\ n : an amino acid $C_9H_{17}NO_8$ of carbohydrate character occurring in the form of acyl derivatives

neur·amin·i·dase \ˌnùr-ə-'mi-nə-ˌdās,

nyür-, -ˌdāz *n* : a hydrolytic enzyme that is produced by some bacteria and viruses, splits mucoproteins by breaking a glucoside bond, and occurs as a cell-surface antigen of the influenza virus

neur·a·prax·ia \ˌnur-ə-ˈprak-sē-ə, ˌnyür-, -(ˌ)ā-ˈ\ *n* : an injury to a nerve that interrupts conduction causing temporary paralysis but not degeneration and that is followed by a complete and rapid recovery

neur·as·the·nia \ˌnur-əs-ˈthē-nē-ə, ˌnyür-\ *n* : an emotional and psychic disorder that is characterized esp. by easy fatigability and often by lack of motivation, feelings of inadequacy, and psychosomatic symptoms

¹**neur·as·then·ic** \-ˈthe-nik\ *adj* : of, relating to, or having neurasthenia

²**neurasthenic** *n* : a person affected with neurasthenia

neur·ax·is \nur-ˈak-səs, nyür-\ *n, pl* **neur·ax·es** \-ˌsēz\ : CENTRAL NERVOUS SYSTEM

neu·rec·to·my \nù-ˈrek-tə-mē, nyù-\ *n, pl* **-mies** : the surgical excision of part of a nerve

neu·ri·lem·ma \ˌnur-ə-ˈle-mə, ˌnyür-\ *n* : the plasma membrane surrounding a Schwann cell of a myelinated nerve fiber and separating layers of myelin — **neu·ri·lem·mal** \-ˈle-məl\ *adj*

neu·ri·lem·mo·ma *or* **neu·ri·le·mo·ma** \-lə-ˈmō-mə\ *n, pl* **-mas** *or* **-ma·ta** \-mə-tə\ : a tumor of the myelinated sheaths of nerve fibers that consist of Schwann cells in a matrix — called also *neurinoma, schwannoma*

neu·ri·no·ma \nur-ə-ˈnō-mə, nyur-\ *n, pl* **-mas** *or* **-ma·ta** \-mə-tə\ : NEURILEMMOMA

neu·rite \ˈn(y)ù-ˌrīt\ *n* : AXON; *also* : DENDRITE

neu·ri·tis \nù-ˈrī-təs, nyù-\ *n, pl* **-rit·i·des** \-ˈri-tə-ˌdēz\ *or* **-ri·tis·es** : an inflammatory or degenerative lesion of a nerve marked esp. by pain, sensory disturbances, and impaired or lost reflexes — compare NEURALGIA — **neu·rit·ic** \-ˈri-tik\ *adj*

neu·ro \ˈnù-ˌrō, ˈnyu-\ *adj* : NEUROLOGICAL

neuro- — see NEUR-

neu·ro·ac·tive \ˌnur-ō-ˈak-tiv, ˌnyur-\ *adj* : stimulating neural tissue

neu·ro·anat·o·my \-ə-ˈna-tə-mē\ *n, pl* **-mies** : the anatomy of nervous tissue and the nervous system — **neu·ro·ana·tom·i·cal** \-ˌa-nə-ˈtä-mi-kəl\ *also* **neu·ro·ana·tom·ic** \-mik\ *adj* — **neu·ro·anat·o·mist** \-mist\ *n*

neu·ro·ar·throp·a·thy \-är-ˈthrä-pə-thē\ *n, pl* **-thies** : a joint disease (as Charcot's joint) that is associated with a disorder of the nervous system

neu·ro·be·hav·ior·al \-bi-ˈhā-vyə-rəl\ *adj* : of or relating to the relationship between the action of the nervous system and behavior

neu·ro·bi·ol·o·gy \-bī-ˈä-lə-jē\ *n, pl* **-gies** : a branch of biology that deals with the anatomy, physiology, and pathology of the nervous system — **neu·ro·bi·o·log·i·cal** \-ˌbī-ə-ˈlä-ji-kəl\ *adj* — **neu·ro·bi·ol·o·gist** \-bī-ˈä-lə-jist\ *n*

neu·ro·blast \ˈnur-ə-ˌblast, ˈnyür-\ *n* : a cellular precursor of a nerve cell; *esp* : an undifferentiated embryonic nerve cell — **neu·ro·blas·tic** \ˌnur-ə-ˈblas-tik, ˌnyür-\ *adj*

neu·ro·blas·to·ma \ˌnur-ō-blas-ˈtō-mə, ˌnyür-\ *n, pl* **-mas** *or* **-ma·ta** \-mə-tə\ : a malignant tumor formed of embryonic ganglion cells

neu·ro·cen·trum \-ˈsen-trəm\ *n, pl* **-trums** *or* **-tra** \-trə\ : either of the two dorsal elements of a vertebra that unite to form a neural arch from which the vertebral spine is developed — **neu·ro·cen·tral** \-ˈsen-trəl\ *adj*

neu·ro·chem·is·try \-ˈke-mə-strē\ *n, pl* **-tries 1** : the study of the chemical makeup and activities of nervous tissue **2** : chemical processes and phenomena related to the nervous system — **neu·ro·chem·i·cal** \-ˈke-mi-kəl\ *adj or n* — **neu·ro·chem·ist** \-mist\ *n*

neu·ro·cir·cu·la·to·ry \-ˈsər-kyə-lə-ˌtōr-ē\ *adj* : of or relating to the nervous and circulatory systems

neurocirculatory asthenia *n* : a condition marked by shortness of breath, fatigue, rapid pulse, and heart palpitation sometimes with extra beats that occurs chiefly with exertion and is not due to physical disease of the heart — called also *cardiac neurosis, effort syndrome, soldier's heart*

neu·ro·cra·ni·um \-ˈkrā-nē-əm\ *n, pl* **-ni·ums** *or* **-nia** \-nē-ə\ : the portion of the skull that encloses and protects the brain — **neu·ro·cra·ni·al** \-nē-əl\ *adj*

neu·ro·cu·ta·ne·ous \-kyü-ˈtā-nē-əs\ *adj* : of, relating to, or affecting the skin and nerves

neu·ro·cy·to·ma \-sī-ˈtō-mə\ *n, pl* **-mas** *or* **-ma·ta** \-mə-tə\ : any of various tumors of nerve tissue arising in the central or sympathetic nervous system

neu·ro·de·gen·er·a·tive \-di-ˈje-nə-rə-tiv, -ˌrā-\ *adj* : relating to or characterized by degeneration of nervous tissue — **neu·ro·de·gen·er·a·tion** \-ˌje-nə-ˈrā-shən\ *n*

neu·ro·der·ma·ti·tis \-ˌdər-mə-ˈtī-təs\ *n, pl* **-ti·tis·es** *or* **-tit·i·des** \-ˈti-tə-ˌdēz\ : a chronic allergic disorder of the skin characterized by patches of an itching lichenoid eruption and occurring esp. in persons of nervous and emotional instability

neu·ro·de·vel·op·ment \-di-ˈve-ləp-mənt\ *n* : the development of the nervous system — **neu·ro·de·vel·op·men·tal** \-ˌve-ləp-ˈment-ᵊl\ *adj*

neu·ro·di·ag·nos·tic \-ˌdī-ig-ˈnäs-tik\ *adj* : of or relating to the diagnosis of diseases of the nervous system

neu·ro·dy·nam·ic \-ˌdī-ˈna-mik\ *adj* : of,

relating to, or involving communication between different parts of the nervous system — **neu·ro·dy·nam·ics** \-miks\ n

neu·ro·ec·to·derm \-'ek-tə-ˌdərm\ n : embryonic ectoderm that gives rise to nervous tissue — **neu·ro·ec·to·der·mal** \-ˌek-tə-'dər-məl\ adj

neu·ro·ef·fec·tor \-i-'fek-tər, -ˌtȯr\ adj : of, relating to, or involving both neural and effector components

neu·ro·elec·tric \-i-'lek-trik\ also **neu·ro·elec·tri·cal** \-tri-kəl\ adj : of or relating to the electrical phenomena (as potentials or signals) generated by the nervous system

neu·ro·en·do·crine \-'en-də-krən, -ˌkrīn, -ˌkrēn\ adj 1 : of, relating to, or being a hormonal substance that influences the activity of nerves 2 : of, relating to, or functioning in neurosecretion

neu·ro·en·do·cri·nol·o·gy \-ˌen-də-kri-'nä-lə-jē, -(ˌ)krī-\ n, pl -gies : a branch of biology dealing with neurosecretion and the physiological interaction between the central nervous system and the endocrine system — **neu·ro·en·do·cri·no·log·i·cal** \-kri-nəl-'äj-i-kəl, -ˌkrī-, -ˌkrē-\ also **neu·ro·en·do·cri·no·log·ic** \-nə-'lä-jik\ adj — **neu·ro·en·do·cri·nol·o·gist** \-'nä-lə-jist\ n

neu·ro·ep·i·the·li·al \ˌnür-ō-ˌe-pə-'thē-lē-əl, ˌnyür-\ adj 1 : of or relating to neuroepithelium 2 : having qualities of both neural and epithelial cells

neu·ro·epi·the·li·o·ma \-ˌthē-lē-'ō-mə\ n, pl -mas or -ma·ta \-mə-tə\ : a neurocytoma or glioma esp. of the retina

neu·ro·epi·the·li·um \-'thē-lē-əm\ n, pl -lia \-lē-ə\ 1 : the part of the embryonic ectoderm that gives rise to the nervous system 2 : the modified epithelium of an organ of special sense

neu·ro·fi·bril \ˌnür-ō-'fī-brəl, ˌnyür-, -'fī-\ n : a fine proteinaceous fibril that is found in cytoplasm (as of a neuron) and is capable of conducting excitation — **neu·ro·fi·bril·lary** \-brə-ˌler-ē\ also **neu·ro·fi·bril·lar** \-brə-lər\ adj

neurofibrillary tangle n : an abnormality of the cytoplasm of the pyramidal cells of the hippocampus and neurons of the cerebral cortex that occurs esp. in Alzheimer's disease and appears under the light microscope after impregnation and staining with silver as arrays of parallel thick coarse argentophil fibers

neu·ro·fi·bro·ma \-fī-'brō-mə\ n, pl -mas also -ma·ta \-mə-tə\ : a fibroma composed of nervous and connective tissue and produced by proliferation of Schwann cells

neu·ro·fi·bro·ma·to·sis \-fī-ˌbrō-mə-'tō-səs\ n, pl -to·ses \-ˌsēz\ : a disorder inherited as an autosomal dominant and characterized by brown spots on the skin, neurofibromas of peripheral nerves, and deformities of subcutane-

ous tissues and bone — abbr. NF; called also Recklinghausen's disease, von Recklinghausen's disease

neu·ro·fi·bro·sar·co·ma \-ˌfī-brō-sär-'kō-mə\ n, pl -mas or -ma·ta \-mə-tə\ : a malignant neurofibroma

neu·ro·fil·a·ment \-'fil-ə-mənt\ n : a microscopic filament of protein that is found in the cytoplasm of neurons and that with neurotubules makes up the structure of neurofibrils — **neu·ro·fil·a·men·tous** \-ˌfil-ə-'men-təs\ adj

neu·ro·gen·e·sis \ˌnür-ə-'je-nə-səs, ˌnyür-\ n, pl -e·ses \-ˌsēz\ : development of nerves, nervous tissue, or the nervous system

neu·ro·ge·net·ics \-jə-'ne-tiks\ n : a branch of genetics dealing with the nervous system and esp. with its development

neu·ro·gen·ic \ˌnür-ō-'je-nik, ˌnyür-\ also **neu·rog·e·nous** \nü-'rä-jə-nəs, nyü-\ adj 1 a : originating in nervous tissue (a ~ tumor) b : induced, controlled, or modified by nervous factors; esp : disordered because of abnormally altered neural relations (the ~ kidney) 2 a : constituting the neural component of a bodily process (~ factors in disease) b : taking place or viewed as taking place in ordered rhythmic fashion under the control of a network of nerve cells scattered in the cardiac muscle (a ~ heartbeat) — compare MYOGENIC 2 — **neu·ro·gen·i·cal·ly** adv

neu·rog·lia \nü-'rō-glē-ə, nyü-, -'rä-; ˌnür-ə-'glē-ə, ˌnyür-, -'gli-\ n : supporting tissue that is intermingled with the essential elements of nervous tissue esp. in the brain, spinal cord, and ganglia, is of ectodermal origin, and is composed of a network of fine fibrils and of flattened stellate cells with numerous radiating fibrillar processes — see MICROGLIA — **neu·rog·li·al** \-əl\ adj

neu·ro·his·tol·o·gy \ˌnür-ō-hi-'stä-lə-jē, ˌnyür-\ n, pl -gies : a branch of histology concerned with the nervous system — **neu·ro·his·to·log·i·cal** \-ˌhis-tə-'lä-ji-kəl\ also **neu·ro·his·to·log·ic** \-'lä-jik\ adj — **neu·ro·his·tol·o·gist** \-hi-'stä-lə-jist\ n

neu·ro·hor·mon·al \-hȯr-'mōn-ᵊl\ adj 1 : involving both neural and hormonal mechanisms 2 : of, relating to, or being a neurohormone

neu·ro·hor·mone \-'hȯr-ˌmōn\ n : a hormone (as acetylcholine or norepinephrine) produced by or acting on nervous tissue

neu·ro·hu·mor \-'hyü-mər, -'yü-\ n : NEUROHORMONE; esp : NEUROTRANSMITTER — **neu·ro·hu·mor·al** \-mə-rəl\ adj

neu·ro·hy·po·phy·se·al or **neu·ro·hy·po·phys·i·al** \-(ˌ)hī-ˌpä-fə-'sē-əl, -ˌhī-pə-fə-, -ˌzē-; -ˌhī-pə-'fi-zē-əl\ adj : of, relating to, or secreted by the neurohypophysis (~ hormones)

neu·ro·hy·poph·y·sis \-hī-ˈpä-fə-səs\ *n* : the portion of the pituitary gland that is derived from the embryonic brain, is composed of the infundibulum and neural lobe, and is concerned with the secretion of various hormones — called also *posterior pituitary gland*

neu·ro·im·mu·nol·o·gy \-ˌi-myə-ˈnä-lə-jē\ *n, pl* **-gies** : a branch of immunology that deals esp. with the interrelationships of the nervous system and immune responses and autoimmune disorders

neu·ro·lem·mo·ma *var of* NEURILEMMOMA

neu·ro·lept·an·al·ge·sia \-ˌlep-ˌtan-ᵊl-ˈjē-zhə, -zhē-ə, -zē-ə\ *also* **neu·ro·lep·to·an·al·ge·sia** \-ˌlep-tō-ˌan-ᵊl-\ *n* : joint administration of a tranquilizing drug and an analgesic esp. for relief of surgical pain — **neu·ro·lept·an·al·ge·sic** \-ˈjē-zik, -sik\ *adj*

neu·ro·lep·tic \-ˈlep-tik\ *n* : any of the powerful tranquilizers (as the phenothiazines or butyrophenones) used esp. to treat psychosis and believed to act by blocking dopamine nervous receptors — called also *antipsychotic* — **neuroleptic** *adj*

neu·ro·lin·guis·tics \-liŋ-ˈgwis-tiks\ *n* : the study of the relationships between the human nervous system and language esp. with respect to the correspondence between disorders of language and the nervous system — **neu·ro·lin·guis·tic** \-tik\ *adj*

neu·rol·o·gist \nù-ˈrä-lə-jist, nyù-\ *n* : one specializing in neurology; *esp* : a physician skilled in the diagnosis and treatment of disease of the nervous system

neu·rol·o·gy \-jē\ *n, pl* **-gies** : the scientific study of the nervous system esp. in respect to its structure, functions, and abnormalities — **neu·ro·log·i·cal** \ˌnùr-ə-ˈlä-ji-kəl, ˌnyùr-\ *or* **neu·ro·log·ic** \-jik\ *adj* — **neu·ro·log·i·cal·ly** *adv*

neu·rol·y·sis \nù-ˈrä-lə-səs, nyù-\ *n, pl* **-y·ses** \-ˌsēz\ **1** : the breaking down of nerve substance (as from disease or exhaustion) **2** : the operation of freeing a nerve from adhesions — **neu·ro·lyt·ic** \ˌnùr-ə-ˈli-tik, ˌnyùr-\ *adj*

neu·ro·ma \nù-ˈrō-mə, nyù-\ *n, pl* **-mas** *or* **-ma·ta** \-mə-tə\ **1** : a tumor or mass growing from a nerve and usu. consisting of nerve fibers **2** : a mass of nerve tissue in an amputation stump resulting from abnormal regrowth of the stumps of severed nerves — called also *amputation neuroma*

neu·ro·mod·u·la·tor \ˌnùr-ō-ˈmä-jə-ˌlā-tər, ˌnyùr-\ *n* : something (as a polypeptide) that potentiates or inhibits the transmission of a nerve impulse but is not the actual means of transmission itself — **neu·ro·mod·u·la·to·ry** \-lə-ˌtōr-ē\ *adj*

neu·ro·mo·tor \-ˈmō-tər\ *adj* : relating to efferent nervous impulses

neu·ro·mus·cu·lar \-ˈməs-kyə-lər\ *adj* : of or relating to nerves and muscles; *esp* : jointly involving nervous and muscular elements

neuromuscular junction *n* : the junction of an efferent nerve fiber and the muscle fiber plasma membrane — called also *myoneural junction*

neuromuscular spindle *n* : MUSCLE SPINDLE

neu·ro·my·eli·tis \ˌnùr-ō-ˌmī-ə-ˈlī-təs, ˌnyùr-\ *n* **1** : inflammation of the medullary substance of the nerves **2** : inflammation of both spinal cord and nerves

neu·ro·my·op·a·thy \-ˌmī-ˈä-pə-thē\ *n, pl* **-thies** : a disease of nerves and associated muscle tissue

neu·ron \ˈnù-ˌrän, ˈnyù-\ *also* **neu·rone** \-ˌrōn\ *n* : one of the cells that constitute nervous tissue, that have the property of transmitting and receiving nervous impulses, and that possess cytoplasmic processes which are highly differentiated frequently as multiple dendrites or usu. as solitary axons and which conduct impulses toward and away from the nerve cell body — **neu·ro·nal** \ˈnù-rən-ᵊl, ˈnyù-; nù-ˈrōn-ᵊl, nyù-\ *also* **neu·ron·ic** \nù-ˈrä-nik, nyù-\ *adj*

neu·ro·neu·ro·nal \ˌnùr-ō-ˈnù-rən-ᵊl, ˌnyùr-ō-ˈnyù-; ˌnùr-ō-nù-ˈrōn-ᵊl, ˌnyùr-ō-nyù-\ *adj* : between nerve cells or nerve fibers

neu·ron·i·tis \ˌnùr-ō-ˈnī-təs, ˌnyùr-\ *n* : inflammation of neurons; *esp* : neuritis involving nerve roots and nerve cells within the spinal cord

neu·ro·no·tro·pic \-ˈtrō-pik, -ˈträ-\ *adj* : having an affinity for neurons : NEUROTROPIC

neu·ro·oph·thal·mol·o·gy \-ˌäf-thəl-ˈmä-lə-jē, -ˌäp-\ *n, pl* **-gies** : the neurological study of the eye — **neu·ro·oph·thal·mo·log·ic** \-mə-ˈlä-jik\ *or* **neu·ro·oph·thal·mo·log·i·cal** \-ˈlä-ji-kəl\ *adj*

neu·ro·otol·o·gy \-ō-ˈtä-lə-jē\ *n, pl* **-gies** : the neurological study of the ear — **neu·ro·oto·log·ic** \-ō-tə-ˈlä-jik\ *or* **neu·ro·oto·log·i·cal** \-ˈlä-ji-kəl\ *adj*

neu·ro·par·a·lyt·ic \-ˌpar-ə-ˈli-tik\ *adj* : of, relating to, causing, or characterized by paralysis or loss of sensation due to a lesion in a nerve

neu·ro·path·ic \ˌnùr-ə-ˈpa-thik, ˌnyùr-\ *adj* : of, relating to, characterized by, or being a neuropathy — **neu·ro·path·i·cal·ly** *adv*

neu·ro·patho·gen·e·sis \-ˌpa-thə-ˈje-nə-səs\ *n, pl* **-e·ses** \-ˌsēz\ : the pathogenesis of a nervous disease

neu·ro·patho·gen·ic \-je-nik\ *adj* : causing or capable of causing disease of nervous tissue (~ viruses)

neu·ro·pa·thol·o·gist \ˌnùr-ō-pə-ˈthä-lə-jist, ˌnyùr-\ *n* : a specialist in neuropathology

neu·ro·pa·thol·o·gy \-pə-'thä-lə-jē, -pa-\ *n, pl* **-gies** : pathology of the nervous system — **neu·ro·path·o·log·ic** \-ˌpa-thə-'lä-jik\ *or* **neu·ro·path·o·log·i·cal** \-ji-kəl\ *adj*

neu·rop·a·thy \nú-'rä-pə-thē, nyú-\ *n, pl* **-thies** : an abnormal and usu. degenerative state of the nervous system or nerves; *also* : a systemic condition (as muscular atrophy) that stems from a neuropathy

neu·ro·pep·tide \ˌnúr-ō-'pep-ˌtīd, ˌnyúr-\ *n* : an endogenous peptide (as an endorphin or an enkephalin) that influences neural activity or functioning

neu·ro·phar·ma·col·o·gist \-ˌfär-mə-'kä-lə-jist\ *n* : a specialist in neuropharmacology

neu·ro·phar·ma·col·o·gy \-ˌfär-mə-'kä-lə-jē\ *n, pl* **-gies** 1 : a branch of medical science dealing with the action of drugs on and in the nervous system 2 : the properties and reactions of a drug on and in the nervous system — **neu·ro·phar·ma·co·log·i·cal** \-kə-'lä-ji-kəl\ *also* **neu·ro·phar·ma·co·log·ic** \-jik\ *adj*

neu·ro·phy·sin \-'fī-sᵊn\ *n* : any of several brain hormones that bind with and carry either oxytocin or vasopressin

neu·ro·phys·i·ol·o·gist \-ˌfī-zē-'ä-lə-jist\ *n* : a specialist in neurophysiology

neu·ro·phys·i·ol·o·gy \-ˌfī-zē-'ä-lə-jē\ *n, pl* **-gies** : physiology of the nervous system — **neu·ro·phys·i·o·log·i·cal** \-zē-ə-'lä-ji-kəl\ *also* **neu·ro·phys·i·o·log·ic** \-jik\ *adj* — **neu·ro·phys·i·o·log·i·cal·ly** *adv*

neu·ro·pil \'núr-ō-ˌpil, 'nyúr-\ *also* **neu·ro·pile** \-ˌpīl\ *n* : a fibrous network of delicate unmyelinated nerve fibers found in concentrations of nervous tissue esp. in parts of the brain where it is highly developed — **neu·ro·pi·lar** \ˌnúr-ō-'pī-lər, ˌnyúr-\ *adj*

neu·ro·psy·chi·a·trist \ˌnúr-ō-sə-'kī-ə-trist, ˌnyúr-, -sī-\ *n* : a specialist in neuropsychiatry

neu·ro·psy·chi·a·try \-sə-'kī-ə-trē, -sī-\ *n, pl* **-tries** : a branch of medicine concerned with both neurology and psychiatry — **neu·ro·psy·chi·at·ric** \-ˌsī-kē-'a-trik\ *adj* — **neu·ro·psy·chi·at·ri·cal·ly** *adv*

neu·ro·psy·chol·o·gist \-sī-'kä-lə-jist\ *n* : a specialist in neuropsychology

neu·ro·psy·chol·o·gy \-jē\ *n, pl* **-gies** : a science concerned with the integration of psychological observations on behavior and the mind with neurological observations on the brain and nervous system — **neu·ro·psy·cho·log·i·cal** \-sī-kə-'lä-ji-kəl\ *adj* — **neu·ro·psy·cho·log·i·cal·ly** *adv*

neu·ro·psy·cho·phar·ma·col·o·gy \-sī-kō-ˌfär-mə-'kä-lə-jē\ *n, pl* **-gies** : a branch of medical science combining neuropharmacology and psychopharmacology

neu·ro·ra·di·ol·o·gist \-ˌrā-dē-'ä-lə-jist\ *n* : a specialist in neuroradiology

neu·ro·ra·di·ol·o·gy \-ˌrā-dē-'ä-lə-jē\ *n, pl* **-gies** : radiology of the nervous system — **neu·ro·ra·dio·log·i·cal** \-dē-ə-'lä-ji-kəl\ *also* **neu·ro·ra·dio·log·ic** \-jik\ *adj*

neu·ro·ret·i·ni·tis \-ˌret-ᵊn-'ī-təs\ *n, pl* **-nit·i·des** \-'ni-tə-ˌdēz\ : inflammation of the optic nerve and the retina

neu·ror·rha·phy \nú-'rór-ə-fē, nyú-\ *n, pl* **-phies** : the surgical suturing of a divided nerve

neu·ro·sci·ence \ˌnúr-ō-'sī-əns, ˌnyúr-\ *n* : a branch (as neurophysiology) of biology that deals with the anatomy, physiology, biochemistry, or molecular biology of nerves and nervous tissue and esp. their relation to behavior and learning — **neu·ro·sci·en·tif·ic** \-ˌsī-ən-'ti-fik\ *adj* — **neu·ro·sci·en·tist** \-'sī-ən-tist\ *n*

neu·ro·se·cre·tion \-si-'krē-shən\ *n* 1 : the process of producing a secretion by nerve cells 2 : a secretion produced by neurosecretion — **neu·ro·se·cre·to·ry** \-'sē-krə-ˌtór-ē\ *adj*

neu·ro·sen·so·ry \-'sen-sə-rē\ *adj* : of or relating to afferent nerves

neu·ro·sis \nú-'rō-səs, nyú-\ *n, pl* **-ro·ses** \-ˌsēz\ : a mental and emotional disorder that affects only part of the personality, is accompanied by a less distorted perception of reality than in a psychosis, does not result in disturbance of the use of language, and is accompanied by various physical, physiological, and mental disturbances (as visceral symptoms or phobias)

neu·ro·stim·u·la·tor \ˌnúr-ō-'sti-myə-ˌlā-tər, ˌnyúr-\ *n* : a device that provides electrical stimulation to nerves

neu·ro·sur·geon \-'sər-jən\ *n* : a surgeon specializing in neurosurgery

neu·ro·sur·gery \-'sər-jə-rē\ *n, pl* **-gies** : surgery of nervous structures (as nerves, the brain, or the spinal cord) — **neu·ro·sur·gi·cal** \-'sər-ji-kəl\ *adj* — **neu·ro·sur·gi·cal·ly** *adv*

neu·ro·syph·i·lis \-'si-fə-ləs\ *n* : syphilis of the central nervous system — **neu·ro·syph·i·lit·ic** \-ˌsi-fə-'li-tik\ *adj*

neu·ro·ten·di·nous spindle \-'ten-di-nəs-\ *n* : GOLGI TENDON ORGAN

neu·ro·ten·sin \-'ten-sən\ *n* : a protein composed of 13 amino acid residues that causes hypertension and vasodilation and is present in the brain

¹**neu·rot·ic** \nú-'rä-tik, nyú-\ *adj* **1 a** : of, relating to, or involving the nerves ⟨a ~ disorder⟩ **b** : being a neurosis : NERVOUS 2 : affected with, relating to, or characterized by neurosis — **neu·rot·i·cal·ly** *adv*

²**neurotic** *n* **1** : one affected with a neurosis **2** : an emotionally unstable individual

neu·rot·i·cism \-'rä-tə-ˌsi-zəm\ *n* : a neurotic character, condition, or trait

neu·ro·tol·o·gy \ˌnúr-ō-'tä-lə-jē, ˌnyúr-\ *var of* NEURO-OTOLOGY

neu·rot·o·my \-'rä-tə-mē\ n, pl -mies 1 : the dissection or cutting of nerves 2 : the division of a nerve (as to relieve neuralgia)

neu·ro·tox·ic \₁nùr-ō-'täk-sik, ₁nyùr-\ adj : toxic to the nerves or nervous tissue — **neu·ro·tox·ic·i·ty** \-₁täk-'sis-sə-tē\ n

neu·ro·tox·i·col·o·gist \-₁täk-sə-'kä-lə-jist\ n : a specialist in the study of neurotoxins and their effects

neu·ro·tox·i·col·o·gy \-jē\ n, pl -gies : the study of neurotoxins and their effects — **neu·ro·tox·i·co·log·i·cal** \-kə-'lä-jə-kəl\ adj

neu·ro·tox·in \-'täk-sən\ n : a poisonous protein complex that acts on the nervous system

neu·ro·trans·mis·sion \-trans-'mi-shən, -tranz-\ n : the transmission of nerve impulses across a synapse

neu·ro·trans·mit·ter \-trans-'mi-tər, -tranz-\ ; -'trans-₁mi-, -'tranz-\ n : a substance (as norepinephrine or acetylcholine) that transmits nerve impulses across a synapse

neu·ro·troph·ic \-'trä-fik, -'trō-\ adj 1 : relating to or dependent on the influence of nerves on the nutrition of tissue 2 : NEUROTROPIC

neu·ro·tro·pic \-'trä-pik\ adj : having an affinity for or localizing selectively in nerve tissue (~ viruses) — compare PANTROPIC — **neu·rot·ro·pism** \nù-'rä-trə-₁pi-zəm, nyù-\ n

neu·ro·tu·bule \₁nùr-ō-'tü-₁byùl, ₁nyùr-ō-'tyù-\ n : one of the tubular elements sometimes considered to be a fundamental part of the nerve-cell axon

neu·ro·vas·cu·lar \-'vas-kyə-lər\ adj : of, relating to, or involving both nerves and blood vessels

neu·ro·vir·u·lence \-'vir-yə-ləns, -'vir-ə-\ n : the tendency or capacity of a microorganism to attack the nervous system — **neu·ro·vir·u·lent** \-lənt\ adj

neu·ru·la \'nùr-yù-lə, 'nyùr-, -ù-lə\ n, pl -lae \-₁lē\ or -las : an early vertebrate embryo which follows the gastrula and in which nervous tissue begins to differentiate — **neu·ru·la·tion** \₁nùr-yù-'lä-shən, ₁nyùr-, -ù-'lä-\ n

¹**neu·ter** \'nü-tər, 'nyü-\ n : a spayed or castrated animal (as a cat)

²**neuter** vb : CASTRATE, ALTER

neu·tral \'nü-trəl, 'nyü-\ adj 1 : not decided or pronounced as to characteristics 2 : neither acid nor basic : neither acid nor alkaline; specif : having a pH value of 7.0 3 : not electrically charged

neutral fat n : TRIGLYCERIDE

neu·tral·ize \'nü-trə-₁līz, 'nyü-\ vb -ized; -iz·ing 1 : to make chemically neutral 2 : to counteract the activity or effect of : make ineffective 3 : to make electrically inert by combining equal positive and negative quantities — **neu·tral·i·za·tion** \₁nü-trə-lə-'zā-shən, ₁nyü-\ n

neutro- comb form 1 : neutral (neutrophil) 2 : neutrophil (neutropenia)

neu·tron \'nü-₁trän, 'nyü-\ n : an uncharged atomic particle that is nearly equal in mass to the proton

neu·tro·pe·nia \₁nü-trə-'pē-nē-ə, ₁nyü-\ n : leukopenia in which the decrease in white blood cells is chiefly in neutrophils — **neu·tro·pe·nic** \-'pē-nik\ adj

¹**neu·tro·phil** \'nü-trə-₁fil, 'nyü-\ or **neu·tro·phil·ic** \₁nü-trə-'fi-lik, ₁nyü-\ adj : staining to the same degree with acid or basic dyes (~ granulocytes)

²**neutrophil** n : a granulocyte that is the chief phagocytic white blood cell of the blood

neu·tro·phil·ia \₁nü-trə-'fi-lē-ə, ₁nyü-\ n : leukocytosis in which the increase in white blood cells is chiefly in neutrophils

ne·void \'nē-₁vòid\ adj : resembling a nevus (a ~ tumor); also : accompanied by nevi or similar superficial lesions

ne·vus \'nē-vəs\ n, pl **ne·vi** \₁vī\ : a congenital pigmented area on the skin : BIRTHMARK, MOLE; esp : a tumor made up chiefly of blood vessels — see BLUE NEVUS

nevus flam·me·us \-'fla-mē-əs\ n : PORT-WINE STAIN

¹**new·born** \'nü-₁bórn, 'nyü-\ adj 1 : recently born 2 : affecting or relating to the newborn

²**newborn** \-₁bórn\ n, pl **newborn** or **newborns** : a newborn individual : NEONATE

New·cas·tle disease \'nü-₁ka-səl-, 'nyü-; nü-'ka-səl-, ₁nyü-\ n : a disease of domestic fowl and other birds caused by a paramyxovirus and resembling bronchitis or coryza

new drug n : a drug that has not been declared safe and effective by qualified experts under the conditions prescribed, recommended, or suggested in the label and that may be a new chemical formula or an established drug prescribed for use in a new way

New Latin n : Latin as used since the end of the medieval period esp. in scientific description and classification

new·ton \'nü-tən, 'nyü-\ n : the unit of force in the metric system equal to the force required to impart an acceleration of one meter per second per second to a mass of one kilogram

NF abbr 1 National Formulary 2 neurofibromatosis

ng abbr nanogram

NG abbr nasogastric

n'ga·na \nə-'gä-nə\ var of NAGANA

NGF abbr nerve growth factor

NGU abbr nongonococcal urethritis

NHS abbr National Health Service

Ni symbol nickel

ni·a·cin \'nī-ə-sən\ n : a crystalline acid $C_6H_5NO_2$ that is a member of the vitamin B complex occurring usu. in the form of a complex of niacinamide in various animal and plant parts (as blood, liver, yeast, bran, and legumes) and is effective in preventing and treating human pellagra and blacktongue of dogs — called also *nicotinic acid*

ni·a·cin·amide \ˌnī-ə-ˈsi-nə-ˌmīd\ *n* : a bitter crystalline basic amide C_6H_6-N_2O that is a member of the vitamin B complex and is formed from and converted to niacin in the living organism, that occurs naturally usu. as a constituent of coenzymes, and that is used similarly to niacin — called also *nicotinamide*

ni·al·amide \nī-ˈa-lə-ˌmīd\ *n* : a synthetic antidepressant drug $C_{16}H_{18}$-N_4O_2 that is an inhibitor of monoamine oxidase

nick \ˈnik\ *n* : a break in one strand of two-stranded DNA caused by a missing phosphodiester bond — **nick** *vb*

nick·el \ˈni-kəl\ *n* : a silver-white hard malleable ductile metallic element — symbol *Ni*; see ELEMENT table

nick·ing \ˈni-kiŋ\ *n* : localized constriction of a retinal vein by the pressure from an artery crossing it seen esp. in arterial hypertension

nicotin- *or* **nicotino-** *comb form* 1 : nicotine (*nicotinic*) 2 : nicotinic acid (*nicotinamide*)

nic·o·tin·amide \ˌni-kə-ˈtē-nə-ˌmīd, -ˈti-\ *n* : NIACINAMIDE

nicotinamide adenine dinucleotide *n* : NAD

nicotinamide adenine dinucleotide phosphate *n* : NADP

nic·o·tine \ˈni-kə-ˌtēn\ *n* : a poisonous alkaloid $C_{10}H_{14}N_2$ that is the chief active principle of tobacco
   Ni·cot \nē-ˈkō\, Jean (1530?–1600), French diplomat.

nic·o·tin·ic \ˌni-kə-ˈtē-nik, -ˈti-\ *adj* : relating to, resembling, producing, or mediating the effects that are produced by acetylcholine liberated by nerve fibers at autonomic ganglia and at the neuromuscular junctions of voluntary muscle and that are mimicked by nicotine which increases activity in small doses and inhibits it in larger doses ⟨∼ receptors⟩ — compare MUSCARINIC

nicotinic acid *n* : NIACIN

nictitans — see MEMBRANA NICTITANS

nic·ti·ta·ting membrane \ˈnik-tə-ˌtā-tiŋ-\ *n* : a thin membrane found in many vertebrate animals at the inner angle or beneath the lower lid of the eye and capable of extending across the eyeball — called also *membrana nictitans, third eyelid*

ni·da·tion \nī-ˈdā-shən\ *n* 1 : the development of the epithelial membrane lining the inner surface of the uterus following menstruation 2 : IMPLANTATION b

NIDDM *abbr* non-insulin-dependent diabetes mellitus

ni·dus \ˈnī-dəs\ *n, pl* **ni·di** \-ˌdī\ *or* **ni·dus·es** 1 : a place or substance in tissue where the germs of a disease or other organisms lodge and multiply 2 : a place where something originates or is fostered or develops

Nie·mann–Pick disease \ˈnē-ˌmän-ˈpik-\ *n* : an error in lipid metabolism that is inherited as an autosomal recessive trait, is characterized by accumulation of phospholipid in macrophages of the liver, spleen, lymph glands, and bone marrow, and leads to gastrointestinal disturbances, malnutrition, enlargement of the spleen, liver, and lymph nodes, and abnormalities of the blood-forming organs
   Niemann, Albert (1880–1921) and Pick, Ludwig (1868–1944), German physicians.

ni·fed·i·pine \nī-ˈfe-də-ˌpēn\ *n* : a calcium channel blocker $C_{17}H_{18}N_2O_6$ that is a coronary vasodilator used esp. in the treatment of angina pectoris — see PROCARDIA

night blindness *n* : reduced visual capacity in faint light (as at night) — called also *nyctalopia* — **night-blind** \ˈnīt-ˌblīnd\ *adj*

night·mare \ˈnīt-ˌmar\ *n* : a frightening dream accompanied by a sense of oppression or suffocation that usu. awakens the sleeper

night·shade \ˈnīt-ˌshād\ *n* 1 : any plant of the genus *Solanum* (family Solanaceae, the nightshade family) which includes some poisonous weeds, various ornamental garden plants, and important crop plants (as the potato and eggplant) 2 : BELLADONNA 1

night sweat *n* : profuse sweating during sleep that is sometimes a symptom of febrile disease

night terrors *n pl* : a sudden awakening in dazed terror occurring in children and often preceded by a sudden shrill cry uttered in sleep — called also *pavor nocturnus*

night vision *n* : ability to see in dim light (as provided by moon and stars)

ni·gra \ˈnī-grə\ *n* : SUBSTANTIA NIGRA — **ni·gral** \-grəl\ *adj*

nigricans — see ACANTHOSIS NIGRICANS

ni·gro·stri·a·tal \ˌnī-grō-strī-ˈāt-ᵊl\ *adj* : of, relating to, or joining the corpus striatum and the substantia nigra

NIH *abbr* National Institutes of Health

ni·hi·lism \ˈnī-ə-ˌli-zəm, ˈnē-, -hə-\ *n* 1 : NIHILISTIC DELUSION 2 : skepticism as to the value of a drug or method of treatment (therapeutic ∼) — **ni·hi·lis·tic** \ˌnī-ə-ˈlis-tik, ˌnē-, -hə-\ *adj*

nihilistic delusion *n* : the belief that oneself, a part of one's body, or the real world does not exist or has been destroyed

nik·eth·amide \ni-ˈke-thə-ˌmīd\ *n* : a

bitter viscous liquid or crystalline compound $C_{10}H_{14}N_2O$ used chiefly in aqueous solution as a respiratory stimulant

NIMH *abbr* National Institute of Mental Health

ni·mo·di·pine \ni-ꞌmō-də-ꞏpēn\ *n* : a calcium channel blocker $C_{21}H_{26}N_2O_7$ used as a cerebral vasodilator

ninth cranial nerve *n* : GLOSSOPHARYNGEAL NERVE

ni·o·bi·um \nī-ꞌō-bē-əm\ *n* : a lustrous ductile metallic element — symbol *Nb*; see ELEMENT table

NIOSH *abbr* National Institute of Occupational Safety and Health

nip·per \ꞌni-pər\ *n* : an incisor of a horse; *esp* : one of the middle four incisors — compare DIVIDER

nip·ple \ꞌni-pəl\ *n* 1 : the protuberance of a mammary gland upon which in the female the lactiferous ducts open and from which milk is drawn 2 : an artificial teat through which a bottle-fed infant nurses

Ni·pride \ꞌnī-ꞏprid\ *trademark* — used for a preparation of sodium nitroprusside

ni·sin \ꞌnī-sən\ *n* : a polypeptide antibiotic that is produced by a bacterium of the genus *Streptococcus* (*S. lactis*) and is used as a food preservative esp. for cheese and canned fruits and vegetables

Nissl bodies \ꞌni-səl-\ *n pl* : discrete granular bodies of variable size that occur in the perikaryon and dendrites but not the axon of neurons and are composed of RNA and polyribosomes — called also *Nissl granules*, *tigroid substance*

Nissl, Franz (1860–1919), German neurologist.

Nissl substance *n* : the nucleoprotein material of Nissl bodies — called also *chromidial substance*

nit \ꞌnit\ *n* : the egg of a louse or other parasitic insect; *also* : the insect itself when young

ni·trate \ꞌnī-ꞏtrāt, -trət\ *n* : a salt or ester of nitric acid

ni·tric acid \ꞌnī-trik-\ *n* : a corrosive liquid inorganic acid HNO_3

ni·trite \ꞌnī-ꞏtrīt\ *n* : a salt or ester of nitrous acid

ni·tri·toid \ꞌnī-trə-ꞏtȯid\ *adj* : resembling a nitrite or a reaction characterized esp. by flushing and faintness that is caused by a nitrite (a severe ~ crisis may follow arsphenamine injection)

ni·tro·ben·zene \ꞏnī-trō-ꞌben-ꞏzēn, -benꞏ\ *n* : a poisonous yellow insoluble oil $C_6H_5NO_2$

ni·tro·fu·ran \ꞏnī-trō-ꞌfyu̇r-ꞏan, -fyu̇-ꞌran\ *n* : any of several compounds containing a nitro group that are used as bacteria-inhibiting agents

ni·tro·fu·ran·to·in \-fyu̇-ꞌran-tō-in\ *n* : a nitrofuran derivative $C_8H_6N_4O_5$ that is a broad-spectrum antimicrobial

agent used esp. in treating urinary tract infections

ni·tro·fu·ra·zone \-ꞌfyu̇r-ə-ꞏzōn\ *n* : a pale yellow crystalline compound $C_6H_6N_4O_4$ used chiefly externally as a bacteriostatic or bactericidal dressing (as for wounds and infections)

ni·tro·gen \ꞌnī-trə-jən\ *n* : a common nonmetallic element that in the free form is normally a colorless odorless tasteless insoluble inert gas containing two atoms per molecule and comprising 78 percent of the atmosphere by volume and that in the combined form is a constituent of biologically important compounds (as proteins, nucleic acids, alkaloids) — symbol *N*; see ELEMENT table

nitrogen balance *n* : the difference between nitrogen intake and nitrogen excretion in the animal body such that a greater intake results in a positive balance and an increased excretion causes a negative balance

nitrogen base *or* **nitrogenous base** *n* : a nitrogen-containing molecule with basic properties; *esp* : one that is a purine or pyrimidine

nitrogen dioxide *n* : a poisonous strongly oxidizing reddish brown gas NO_2

nitrogen mustard *n* : any of various toxic blistering compounds analogous to mustard gas but containing nitrogen instead of sulfur; *esp* : an amine $C_5H_{11}Cl_2N$ used in the form of its hydrochloride in treating neoplastic diseases (as Hodgkinꞌs disease and leukemia)

nitrogen narcosis *n* : a state of euphoria and exhilaration that occurs when nitrogen in normal air enters the bloodstream at approximately seven times atmospheric pressure (as in deepwater diving) — called also *rapture of the deep*

ni·trog·e·nous \nī-ꞌträj-ə-nəs\ *adj* : of, relating to, or containing nitrogen in combined form (as in proteins)

ni·tro·glyc·er·in *or* **ni·tro·glyc·er·ine** \ꞏnī-trə-ꞌgli-sə-rən\ *n* : a heavy oily explosive poisonous liquid $C_3H_5N_3O_9$ used in medicine as a vasodilator (as in angina pectoris)

ni·tro·mer·sol \ꞏnī-trō-ꞌmər-ꞏsȯl, -ꞏsōl\ *n* : a brownish yellow to yellow solid organic mercurial $C_7H_5HgNO_3$ used chiefly in the form of a solution of its sodium salt as an antiseptic and disinfectant — see METAPHEN

nitroprusside — see SODIUM NITROPRUSSIDE

ni·tro·sa·mine \nī-ꞌtrō-sə-ꞏmēn\ *n* : any of various neutral compounds which are characterized by the grouping NNO and some of which are powerful carcinogens

ni·tro·so·di·meth·yl·amine \nī-ꞏtrō-sō-ꞏdī-ꞏme-thə-ꞌla-ꞏmēn, -ə-ꞌmēn\ *n* : DIMETHYLNITROSAMINE

ni·tro·so·urea \-yu̇-ꞌrē-ə\ *n* : any of a group of lipid-soluble drugs that function as alkylating agents, have the ability to enter the central nervous system. and are effective in the treatment of some brain tumors and meningeal leukemias

ni·trous oxide \\'nī-trəs-\ *n* : a colorless gas N_2O that when inhaled produces loss of sensibility to pain preceded by exhilaration and sometimes laughter and is used esp. as an anesthetic in dentistry — called also *laughing gas*

NK cell \\en-'kā-\ *n* : NATURAL KILLER CELL

nm *abbr* nanometer

NMR *abbr* nuclear magnetic resonance

No *symbol* nobelium

no·bel·i·um \nō-'be-lē-əm\ *n* : a radioactive element produced artificially — symbol *No*; see ELEMENT table

No·bel \nō-'bel\. **Alfred Bernhard** (1833–1896). Swedish inventor and philanthropist.

no·ble gas \\'nō-bəl-\ *n* : any of a group of rare gases that include helium, neon, argon, krypton, xenon, and sometimes radon and that exhibit great stability and extremely low reaction rates — called also *inert gas*

no·car·dia \nō-'kär-dē-ə\ *n* 1 *cap* : a genus of aerobic actinomycetes (family Actinomycetaceae) that include various pathogens as well as some soil-dwelling saprophytes 2 : any actinomycete of the genus *Nocardia* — **no·car·di·al** \-əl\ *adj*

No·card \nō-'kär\. **Edmond–Isidore–Etienne** (1850–1903), French veterinarian and biologist.

no·car·di·o·sis \nō-ıkär-dē-'ō-səs\ *n, pl* **-o·ses** \-ısēz\ : actinomycosis caused by actinomycetes of the genus *Nocardia* and characterized by production of spreading granulomatous lesions — compare MADUROMYCOSIS

noci- *comb form* : pain (*nociceptor*)

no·ci·cep·tive \ınō-si-'sep-tiv\ *adj* 1 *of a stimulus* : causing pain or injury 2 : of, induced by, or responding to a nociceptive stimulus — used esp. of receptors or protective reflexes

no·ci·cep·tor \-'sep-tər\ *n* : a receptor for injurious or painful stimuli : a pain sense organ

noc·tu·ria \näk-'túr-ē-ə, -'tyùr-\ *n* : urination at night esp. when excessive

noc·tur·nal \näk-'tərn-əl\ *adj* 1 : of. relating to, or occurring at night (~ myoclonus) 2 : characterized by nocturnal activity

nocturnal emission *n* : an involuntary discharge of semen during sleep often accompanied by an erotic dream — see WET DREAM

nocturnus — see PAVOR NOCTURNUS

noc·u·ous \\'nä-kyə-wəs\ *adj* : likely to cause injury (a ~ stimulus)

nod·al \\'nōd-əl\ *adj* : being. relating to. or located at or near a node — **nod·al·ly** *adv*

node \\'nōd\ *n* 1 : a pathological swelling or enlargement (as of a rheumatic joint) 2 : a body part resembling a knot: *esp* : a discrete mass of one kind of tissue enclosed in tissue of a different kind — see ATRIOVENTRICULAR NODE, LYMPH NODE

node of Ran·vier \-ırän-vē-'ā\ *n* : a constriction in the myelin sheath of a myelinated nerve fiber

L.–A. Ranvier — see MERKEL–RANVIER CORPUSCLE

nodosa — see PERIARTERITIS NODOSA, POLYARTERITIS NODOSA

no·dose ganglion \\'nō-ıdōs-\ *n* : INFERIOR GANGLION 2

nodosum — see ERYTHEMA NODOSUM

nod·u·lar \\'nä-jə-lər\ *adj* : of. relating to. characterized by, or occurring in the form of nodules (~ lesions) — **nod·u·lar·i·ty** \ınä-jə-'lar-ə-tē\ *n*

nodular disease *n* : infestation with or disease caused by nodular worms of the genus *Oesophagostomum* — called also *nodule worm disease*

nodular worm *n* : any of several nematode worms of the genus *Oesophagostomum* that are parasitic in the large intestine of ruminants and swine — called also *nodule worm*

nod·ule \\'nä-(ı)jül\ *n* : a small mass of rounded or irregular shape: as a : a small abnormal knobby bodily protuberance (as a tumorous growth or a calcification near an arthritic joint) b : the nodulus of the cerebellum

nod·u·lus \\'nä-jə-ləs\ *n, pl* **nod·u·li** \-ılī\ : NODULE: *esp* : a prominence on the inferior surface of the cerebellum forming the anterior end of the vermis

noire — see TACHE NOIRE

noise pollution *n* : environmental pollution consisting of annoying or harmful noise (as of automobiles or jet airplanes) — called also *sound pollution*

no·ma \\'nō-mə\ *n* : a spreading invasive gangrene chiefly of the lining of the cheek and lips that is usu. fatal and occurs most often in persons severely debilitated by disease or profound nutritional deficiency — see CANCRUM ORIS

no·men·cla·ture \\'nō-mən-ıklā-chər\ *n* : a system of terms used in a particular science; *esp* : an international system of standardized New Latin names used in biology for kinds and groups of kinds of animals and plants — see BINOMIAL NOMENCLATURE — **no·men·cla·tur·al** \ınō-mən-'klā-chə-rəl\ *adj*

No·mi·na An·a·tom·i·ca \\'nä-mi-nə-ıa-nə-'tä-mi-kə, 'nō-\ *n* : the Latin anatomical nomenclature that was prepared by revising the Basle Nomina Anatomica, adopted in 1955 at the Sixth International Congress of Anatomists. and modified at subsequent Congresses — abbr. *NA*

no·mo·top·ic \ınä-mə-'tō-pik, ınō-,

-'tä-\ *adj* : occurring in the normal place

-**no•my** \n-ə-mē\ *n comb form, pl* -**nomies** : system of laws or sum of knowledge regarding a (specified) field ⟨taxonomy⟩

non- *prefix* : not : reverse of : absence of ⟨nonallergic⟩

non•ab•sorb•able \₁nän-əb-'sȯr-bə-bəl, -'zȯr-\ *adj* : not capable of being absorbed ⟨~ silk sutures⟩

non•ac•id \'-'a-səd\ *adj* : not acid : being without acid properties

non•adap•tive \₁nän-ə-'dap-tiv\ *adj* : not serving to adapt the individual to the environment ⟨~ traits⟩

non•ad•dict \'-'a-dikt\ *n* : a person who is not addicted to a drug

non•ad•dict•ing \-ə-'dik-tiŋ\ *adj* : not causing addiction

non•ad•dic•tive \-ə-'dik-tiv\ *adj* : NON-ADDICTING

non•al•le•lic \₁nän-ə-'lē-lik, -'le-\ *adj* : not behaving as alleles toward one another ⟨~ genes⟩

non•al•ler•gen•ic \-ə-lər-'je-nik\ *adj* : not causing an allergic reaction

non•al•ler•gic \-ə-'lər-jik\ *adj* : not allergic ⟨~ individuals⟩ ⟨a ~ reaction⟩

non•am•bu•la•to•ry \-'am-byə-lə-₁tȯr-ē\ *adj* : not able to walk about ⟨~ patients⟩

non–A, non–B hepatitis \₁nän-'ā-₁nän-'bē-\ *n* : hepatitis clinically and immunologically similar to hepatitis A and hepatitis B but caused by different viruses

non•an•ti•bi•ot•ic \- an-tē-bī-'ä-tik, -₁an-₁tī-\ *adj* : not antibiotic

non•an•ti•gen•ic \-₁an-ti-'je-nik\ *adj* : not antigenic ⟨~ materials⟩

non•ar•tic•u•lar \₁nän-är-'ti-kyə-lər\ *adj* : affecting or involving soft tissues (as muscles and connective tissues) rather than joints ⟨~ rheumatic disorders⟩

non•as•so•cia•tive \-ə-'sō-shē-₁ā-tiv, -sē-₁ā-tiv, -shə-tiv\ *adj* : relating to or being learning (as habituation and sensitization) that is not associative learning

non•bac•te•ri•al \-bak-'tir-ē-əl\ *adj* : not of, relating to, caused by, or being bacteria ⟨~ pneumonia⟩

non•bar•bi•tu•rate \-bär-'bi-chə-rət, -₁rāt\ *adj* : not derived from barbituric acid

non•bio•log•i•cal \-₁bī-ə-'lä-ji-kəl\ *adj* : not biological

non•can•cer•ous \-'kan-sə-rəs\ *adj* : not affected with or being cancer

non•car•ci•no•gen•ic \-₁kär-₁si-nə-'je-nik, -₁kärs-ⁿə-ə-\ *adj* : not causing cancer — **non•car•ci•no•gen** \-kär-'si-nə-jən, -'kärs-ⁿə-ə-jen\ *n*

non•car•di•ac \-'kär-dē-₁ak\ *adj* : not cardiac: as **a** : not affected with heart disease **b** : not relating to the heart or heart disease ⟨~ disorders⟩

non•cel•lu•lar \-'sel-yə-lər\ *adj* : not made up of or divided into cells

non•chro•mo•som•al \-₁krō-mə-'sō-məl\ *adj* **1** : not situated on a chromosome ⟨~ DNA⟩ **2** : not involving chromosomes ⟨~ mutations⟩

non•cod•ing \-'kō-diŋ\ *adj* : not specifying the genetic code ⟨~ DNA⟩

non•co•ital \-'kō-ət-ᵊl, -kō-'ēt-\ *adj* : not involving heterosexual copulation

non•com•mu•ni•ca•ble \-kə-'myü-ni-kə-bəl\ *adj* : not capable of being communicated; *specif* : not transmissible by direct contact ⟨a ~ disease⟩

non•com•pli•ance \-kəm-'plī-əns\ *n* : failure or refusal to comply (as in the taking of prescribed medication) — **non•com•pli•ant** \-ənt\ *adj*

non com•pos men•tis \₁nän-'käm-pəs-'men-təs, ₁nōn-\ *adj* : not of sound mind

non•con•scious \-'kän-chəs\ *adj* : not conscious

non•con•ta•gious \₁nän-kən-'tā-jəs\ *adj* : not contagious

non•con•trac•tile \-kən-'trakt-ᵊl, -₁īl\ *adj* : not contractile ⟨~ fibers⟩

non•con•vul•sive \-kən-'vəl-siv\ *adj* : not convulsive ⟨~ seizures⟩

non•cor•o•nary \-'kȯr-ə-₁ner-ē, -'kär-\ *adj* : not affecting, affected with disease of, or involving the coronary vessels of the heart

non•de•form•ing \-di-'fȯr-miŋ\ *adj* : not causing deformation

¹non•di•a•bet•ic \-₁dī-ə-'be-tik\ *adj* : not affected with diabetes

²nondiabetic *n* : an individual not affected with diabetes

non•di•a•lyz•able \-₁dī-ə-'lī-zə-bəl\ *adj* : not dialyzable

non•di•rec•tive \₁nän-də-'rek-tiv, -(₁)dī-\ *adj* : of, relating to, or being psychotherapy, counseling, or interviewing in which the counselor refrains from interpretation or explanation but encourages the client (as by repeating phrases) to talk freely

non•dis•junc•tion \-dis-'jəŋk-shən\ *n* : failure of homologous chromosomes or sister chromatids to separate subsequent to metaphase in meiosis or mitosis so that one daughter cell has both and the other neither of the chromosomes

non•dis•sem•i•nat•ed \-di-'se-mə-₁nā-təd\ *adj* : not disseminated ⟨~ lupus erythematosus⟩

non•di•vid•ing \-də-'vī-diŋ\ *adj* : not undergoing cell division

non•drug \(₁)nän-'drəg\ *adj* : not relating to, being, or employing drugs

non•elas•tic \-ₑ-'las-tik\ *adj* : not elastic ⟨~ fibrous tissue⟩

non•emer•gency \-i-'mər-jən-sē\ *adj* : not being or requiring emergency care ⟨~ surgery⟩ ⟨~ patients⟩

non•en•zy•mat•ic \-₁en-zə-'ma-tik\ *or* **non•en•zy•mic** \-en-'zī-mik\ *also* **non•en•zyme** \-'en-₁zīm\ *adj* : not involving the action of enzymes

non•es•sen•tial \-i-'sen-chəl\ *adj* : being a nonessential amino acid

nonessential amino acid *n* : any of various amino acids which are required for normal health and growth, whose carbon chains can be synthesized within the body or which can be derived in the body from essential amino acids, and which include alanine, asparagine, aspartic acid, cystine, glutamic acid, glutamine, glycine, proline, serine, and tyrosine

non·fat \-ˈnän-ˈfat\ *adj* : lacking fat solids : having fat solids removed (∼ milk)

non·fa·tal \-ˈfāt-əl\ *adj* : not fatal

non·fe·brile \-ˈfe-ˌbrīl, -ˈfē-\ *adj* : not febrile (∼ illnesses)

non·flag·el·lat·ed \-ˈfla-jə-ˌlā-təd\ *adj* : not having flagella

non·func·tion·al \-ˈfeŋk-shə-nəl\ *adj* : not performing or able to perform a regular function (a ∼ muscle)

non·ge·net·ic \-jə-ˈne-tik\ *adj* : not genetic (∼ diseases)

non·glan·du·lar \-ˈglan-jə-lər\ *adj* : not glandular (the ∼ mucosa)

non·gono·coc·cal \-ˌgä-nə-ˈkä-kəl\ *adj* : not caused by a gonococcus (∼ urethritis)

non·gran·u·lar \-ˈgra-nyə-lər\ *adj* : not granular; *esp* : characterized by or being cytoplasm which does not contain granules (∼ white blood cells)

non·grav·id \-ˈgra-vid\ *adj* : not pregnant

non·heme \-ˈhēm\ *adj* : not containing or being iron that is bound in a porphyrin ring like that of heme

non·he·mo·lyt·ic \-ˌhē-mə-ˈli-tik\ *adj* : not causing or characterized by hemolysis (a ∼ streptococcus)

non·hem·or·rhag·ic \-ˌhe-mə-ˈra-jik\ *adj* : not causing or associated with hemorrhage (∼ shock)

non·he·red·i·tary \-hə-ˈre-də-ˌter-ē\ *adj* : not hereditary

non·her·i·ta·ble \-ˈher-ə-tə-bəl\ *adj* : not heritable (∼ diseases)

non·his·tone \-ˈhis-ˌtōn\ *adj* : relating to or being any of the eukaryotic proteins (as DNA polymerase) that form complexes with DNA but are not considered histones

non–Hodg·kin's lymphoma \-ˈhäj-kinz-\ *n* : any of the numerous malignant lymphomas (as Burkitt's lymphoma) that are not classified as Hodgkin's disease and that usu. have malignant cells derived from B cells or T cells

non·ho·mol·o·gous \-hō-ˈmä-lə-gəs, -hə-\ *adj* : being of unlike genic constitution — used of chromosomes of one set containing nonallelic genes

non·hor·mo·nal \-hȯr-ˈmōn-əl\ *adj* : not hormonal

non·hos·pi·tal \-ˈhäs-ˌpit-əl\ *adj* : not relating to, associated with, or occurring within a hospital (∼ clinics)

non·hos·pi·tal·ized \-ˈhäs-ˌpit-əl-ˌīzd\ *adj* : not hospitalized (∼ patients)

non·iden·ti·cal \-(ˌ)ī-ˈden-ti-kəl\ *adj* : not identical; *esp* : FRATERNAL

non·im·mune \-i-ˈmyün\ *adj* : not immune

non·in·fect·ed \-in-ˈfek-təd\ *adj* : not having been subjected to infection

non·in·fec·tious \-in-ˈfek-shəs\ *adj* : not infectious (∼ endocarditis)

non·in·fec·tive \-tiv\ *adj* : not infective (∼ leukemia)

non·in·flam·ma·to·ry \-in-ˈfla-mə-ˌtōr-ē\ *adj* : not inflammatory

non·in·sti·tu·tion·al·ized \-in-stə-ˈtü-shə-nə-ˌlīzd, -ˈtyü-\ *adj* : not institutionalized

non–insulin–dependent diabetes mellitus *n* : a common form of diabetes mellitus that develops esp. in adults and most often in obese individuals and that is characterized by hyperglycemia resulting from impaired insulin utilization coupled with the body's inability to compensate with increased insulin production — abbr. *NIDDM*; called also *adult-onset diabetes, maturity-onset diabetes, non-insulin-dependent diabetes, type II diabetes*

non·in·va·sive \-in-ˈvā-siv, -ziv\ *adj* 1 : not tending to spread; *specif* : not tending to infiltrate and destroy healthy tissue (∼ cancer of the bladder) 2 : not involving penetration (as by surgery) of the skin of the intact organism (∼ diagnostic techniques) — **non·in·va·sive·ly** *adv* — **non·in·va·sive·ness** *n*

non·ir·ra·di·at·ed \-i-ˈrā-dē-ˌā-təd\ *adj* : not having been exposed to radiation

non·ke·tot·ic \-kē-ˈtä-tik\ *adj* : not associated with ketosis (∼ diabetes)

non·liv·ing \-ˈli-viŋ\ *adj* : not having or characterized by life

non·lym·pho·cyt·ic \-ˌlim-fə-ˈsi-tik\ *adj* : not lymphocytic; *esp* : being or relating to a form of leukemia other than lymphocytic leukemia

non·ma·lig·nant \-mə-ˈlig-nənt\ *adj* : not malignant (a ∼ tumor)

non·med·ul·lat·ed \-ˈmed-əl-ˌā-təd, -ˈme-jə-ˌlā-\ *adj* : UNMYELINATED

non·met·al \-ˈmet-əl\ *n* : a chemical element (as carbon) that lacks the characteristics of a metal — **non·me·tal·lic** \-mə-ˈta-lik\ *adj*

non·mi·cro·bi·al \-mī-ˈkrō-bē-əl\ *adj* : not microbial (∼ diseases)

non·mo·tile \-ˈmōt-əl, -ˈmō-ˌtīl\ *adj* : not motile (∼ gametes)

non·my·elin·at·ed \-ˈmī-ə-lə-ˌnā-təd\ *adj* : UNMYELINATED

non·nar·cot·ic \-när-ˈkä-tik\ *adj* : not narcotic (∼ analgesics)

non·neo·plas·tic \-ˌnē-ə-ˈplas-tik\ *adj* : not being or caused by neoplasms (∼ diseases)

non·ner·vous \-ˈnər-vəs\ *adj* : not nervous (∼ tissue)

non·nu·cle·at·ed \-ˈnü-klē-ˌā-təd, -ˈnyü-\ *adj* : not nucleated (∼ bacterial cells)

non·nu·tri·tive \-ˈnü-trə-tiv, -ˈnyü-\ *adj* : not relating to or providing nutrition

non·obese \-ō-'bēs\ *adj* : not obese

non·ob·struc·tive \-əb-'strək-tiv\ *adj* : not causing or characterized by obstruction (as of a bodily passage)

non·oc·clu·sive \-ə-'klü-siv\ *adj* : not causing or characterized by occlusion

non·of·fi·cial \-ə-'fi-shəl\ *adj* : not described in the current *U.S. Pharmacopeia* and *National Formulary* and never having been described therein — compare OFFICIAL

non·ol·fac·to·ry \-äl-'fak-tə-rē, -ōl-\ *adj* : not olfactory

non·or·gas·mic \-ȯr-'gaz-mik\ *adj* : not capable of experiencing orgasm

no·nox·y·nol-9 \nä-'näk-sə-₊nȯl-'nīn, -₊nōl-\ *n* : a spermicide used in contraceptive products that consists of a mixture of compounds having the general formula $C_{15}H_{23}(OCH_2CH_2)_n$-OH with an average of nine ethylene oxide groups per molecule

non·par·a·sit·ic \-₊par-ə-'si-tik\ *adj* : not parasitic; *esp* : not caused by parasites (~ diseases)

non·patho·gen·ic \-₊pa-thə-'je-nik\ *adj* : not capable of inducing disease — compare AVIRULENT

non·per·sis·tent \-pər-'sis-tənt\ *adj* : not persistent; *esp* : decomposed rapidly by environmental action (~ insecticides)

non·phy·si·cian \-fə-'zi-shən\ *n* : a person who is not a legally qualified physician

non·pig·ment·ed \-'pig-mən-təd\ *adj* : not pigmented

non·poi·son·ous \-'pȯi-zə-nəs\ *adj* : not poisonous

non·po·lar \-'pō-lər\ *adj* : not polar; *esp* : not having or requiring the presence of electrical poles (~ molecules)

non·preg·nant \-'preg-nənt\ *adj* : not pregnant

non·pre·scrip·tion \-pri-'skrip-shən\ *adj* : available for purchase without a doctor's prescription (~ drugs)

non·pro·duc·tive \-prə-'dək-tiv\ *adj, of a cough* : not effective in raising mucus or exudate from the respiratory tract — DRY 2

non·pro·pri·etary \-prə-'prī-ə-₊ter-ē\ *adj* : not proprietary (a drug's ~ name)

non·pro·tein \-'prō-₊tēn\ *adj* : not being or derived from protein (the ~ part of an enzyme)

non·psy·chi·at·ric \-₊sī-kē-'a-trik\ *adj* : not psychiatric

non·psy·chi·a·trist \-sə-'kī-ə-trist, -sī-\ *adj* : not specializing in psychiatry (~ physicians) — **nonpsychiatrist** *n*

non·psy·chot·ic \-sī-'kä-tik\ *adj* : not psychotic (~ emotional disorders)

non·ra·dio·ac·tive \-₊rā-dē-ō-'ak-tiv\ *adj* : not radioactive

non·re·ac·tive \-rē-'ak-tiv\ *adj* : not reactive; *esp* : not exhibiting a positive reaction in a particular laboratory test (40% of the serums were ~)

non·re·nal \-'rēn-əl\ *adj* : not renal; *esp*

: not resulting from dysfunction of the kidneys (~ alkalosis)

non·rheu·ma·toid \-'rü-mə-₊tȯid\ *adj* : not relating to, affected with, or being rheumatoid arthritis

non·rhyth·mic \-'rith-mik\ *adj* : not rhythmic (~ contractions)

¹non·schizo·phren·ic \-₊skit-sə-'fre-nik\ *adj* : not relating to, affected with, or having schizophrenia (~ patients)

²nonschizophrenic *n* : a nonschizophrenic individual

non·se·cre·tor \-si-'krē-tər\ *n* : an individual of blood group A, B, or AB who does not secrete the antigens characteristic of these blood groups in bodily fluids (as saliva)

non·se·cre·to·ry \-'sē-krə-₊tȯr-ē\ *adj* : not secretory (~ cells)

non·se·lec·tive \-sə-'lek-tiv\ *adj* : not selective; *esp* : not limited (as to a single body part or organism) in action or effect (~ anti-infective agents)

non·self \nän-'self\ *n* : material that is foreign to the body of an organism — **nonself** *adj*

¹non·sense \'nän-₊sens, -səns\ *n* : genetic information consisting of one or more codons that do not code for any amino acid and usu. cause termination of the molecular chain in protein synthesis — compare ANTISENSE, MISSENSE

²nonsense *adj* : consisting of one or more codons that are genetic nonsense

non·sen·si·tive \-'sen-sə-tiv\ *adj* : not sensitive

non·sex·u·al \-'sek-shə-wəl\ *adj* : not sexual (~ reproduction)

non·spe·cif·ic \-spi-'si-fik\ *adj* : not specific: as **a** : not caused by a specific agent (~ enteritis) **b** : having a general purpose or effect — **non·spe·cif·i·cal·ly** *adv*

non·ste·roi·dal \-stə-'rȯid-əl\ *also* **non·ste·roid** \-'stir-₊ȯid, -'ster-\ *adj* : of, relating to, or being a compound and esp. a drug that is not a steroid — see NSAID — **nonsteroid** *n*

nonstriated muscle *n* : SMOOTH MUSCLE

non·sug·ar \-'shù-gər\ *n* : a substance that is not a sugar; *esp* : AGLYCONE

non·sur·gi·cal \-'sər-ji-kəl\ *adj* : not surgical (~ hospital care) — **non·sur·gi·cal·ly** *adv*

non·sys·tem·ic \-sis-'te-mik\ *adj* : not systemic

non·tast·er \-'tā-stər\ *n* : a person unable to taste the chemical phenylthiocarbamide

non·thera·peu·tic \-₊ther-ə-'pyü-tik\ *adj* : not relating to or being therapy

non·throm·bo·cy·to·pe·nic \-₊thräm-bə-₊sī-tə-'pē-nik\ *adj* : not relating to, affected with, or associated with thrombocytopenia (~ purpura)

non·tox·ic \-'täk-sik\ *adj* **1** : not toxic **2** *of goiter* : not associated with hyperthyroidism

non-trop-i-cal sprue \-ʹträ-pi-kəl-\ n
: CELIAC DISEASE

non-union \-ʹyün-yən\ n : failure of the
fragments of a broken bone to knit together

non-vas-cu-lar \-ʹvas-kyə-lər\ adj
: lacking blood vessels or a vascular
system ⟨a ~ layer of the skin⟩

non-ven-om-ous \-ʹve-nə-məs\ adj : not
venomous

non-vi-a-ble \-ʹvī-ə-bəl\ adj : not capable of living, growing, or developing
and functioning successfully

NOPHN abbr National Organization
for Public Health Nursing

nor-adren-a-line also **nor-adren-a-lin**
\ˌnȯr-ə-ʹdren-ᵊl-ən\ n : NOREPINEPH-
RINE

nor-ad-ren-er-gic \ˌnȯr-ˌa-drə-ʹnər-jik\
adj : liberating, activated by, or involving norepinephrine in the transmission of nerve impulses — compare ADRENERGIC 1, CHOLINERGIC 1

nor-epi-neph-rine \ˌnȯr-ˌe-pə-ʹne-frən,
-ˌfrēn\ n : a catecholamine $C_8H_{11}NO_3$
that is the chemical means of transmission across synapses in postganglionic neurons of the sympathetic
nervous system and in some parts of
the central nervous system, is a vasopressor hormone of the adrenal medulla, and is a precursor of
epinephrine in its major biosynthetic
pathway — called also noradrena-
line; see LEVOPHED

nor-eth-in-drone \nȯ-ʹre-thən-ˌdrōn\ n
: a synthetic progestational hormone
$C_{20}H_{26}O_2$ used in oral contraceptives
often in the form of its acetate

nor-ethis-ter-one \ˌnȯr-ə-ʹthis-tə-ˌrōn\
n, chiefly Brit : NORETHINDRONE

nor-ethyn-o-drel \ˌnȯr-ə-ʹthi-nə-ˌdrəl\ n
: a progesterone derivative $C_{20}H_{26}O_2$
used in oral contraceptives and clinically in the treatment of abnormal
uterine bleeding and the control of
menstruation — see ENOVID

nor-ges-trel \nȯr-ʹjes-trel\ n : a synthetic progestogen $C_{21}H_{28}O_2$ having two
optically active forms of which the biologically active levorotatory form is
used in oral contraceptives — see
LEVONORGESTREL

norm \ʹnȯrm\ n : an established standard or average: as a : a set standard
of development or achievement usu.
derived from the average or median
achievement of a large group b : a
pattern or trait taken to be typical in
the behavior of a social group

norm- or **normo-** comb form : normal
⟨normoblast⟩ ⟨normotensive⟩

¹**nor-mal** \ʹnȯr-məl\ adj 1 a : according
with, constituting, or not deviating
from a norm, rule, or principle b
: conforming to a type, standard, or
regular pattern 2 : occurring naturally
and not because of disease, inoculation, or any experimental treatment
⟨~ immunity⟩ 3 a : of, relating to, or
characterized by average intelligence

or development b : free from mental
disorder : SANE c : characterized by
balanced well-integrated functioning
of the organism as a whole — nor-
mal-ize \ʹnȯr-mə-ˌlīz\ vb — nor-mal-
ly \ʹnȯr-mə-lē\ adv

²**normal** n : a subject who is normal

nor-meta-neph-rine \ˌnȯr-ˌme-tə-ʹne-
frən, -ˌfrēn\ n : a metabolite of norepinephrine $C_9H_{13}NO_3$ found esp. in
the urine

nor-mo-ac-tive \ˌnȯr-mō-ʹak-tiv\ adj
: normally active

nor-mo-blast \ʹnȯr-mə-ˌblast\ n : an immature red blood cell containing hemoglobin and a pyknotic nucleus and
normally present in bone marrow but
appearing in the blood in many
anemias — compare ERYTHROBLAST
— **nor-mo-blas-tic** \ˌnȯr-mə-ʹblas-tik\
adj

nor-mo-cal-cae-mia chiefly Brit var of
NORMOCALCEMIA

nor-mo-cal-ce-mia \ˌnȯr-mō-kal-ʹsē-
mē-ə\ n : the presence of a normal
concentration of calcium in the blood
— **nor-mo-cal-ce-mic** \-mik\ adj

nor-mo-chro-mia \ˌnȯr-mə-ʹkrō-mē-ə\ n
: the color of red blood cells that contain a normal amount of hemoglobin
— **nor-mo-chro-mic** \-ʹkrō-mik\ adj

normochromic anemia n : an anemia
marked by reduced numbers of normochromic red blood cells in the circulating blood

nor-mo-cyte \ʹnȯr-mə-ˌsīt\ n : a red
blood cell that is normal in size and in
hemoglobin content

nor-mo-cyt-ic \ˌnȯr-mə-ʹsi-tik\ adj
: characterized by red blood cells that
are normal in size and usu. also in hemoglobin content ⟨~ blood⟩

normocytic anemia n : an anemia
marked by reduced numbers of normal red blood cells in the circulating
blood

nor-mo-gly-ce-mia \ˌnȯr-mō-glī-ʹsē-
mē-ə\ n : the presence of a normal
concentration of glucose in the blood
— **nor-mo-gly-ce-mic** \-mik\ adj

nor-mo-ka-le-mic \ˌnȯr-mō-kā-ʹlē-mik\
adj : having or characterized by a
normal concentration of potassium in
the blood

nor-mo-ten-sive \ˌnȯr-mō-ʹten-siv\ adj
: having blood pressure typical of the
group to which one belongs

nor-mo-ther-mia \-ʹthər-mē-ə\ n : normal body temperature — **nor-mo-
ther-mic** \-mik\ adj

nor-mo-vo-lae-mia chiefly Brit var of
NORMOVOLEMIA

nor-mo-vol-emia \ˌnȯr-mō-ˌvä-ʹlē-
mē-ə\ n : a normal volume of blood in
the body — **nor-mo-vol-emic** \-mik\
adj

Nor-plant \ʹnȯr-ˌplant\ trademark —
used for contraceptive implants of encapsulated levonorgestrel

North American blastomycosis n : blastomycosis that involves esp. the skin,

lymph nodes, and lungs and that is caused by infection with a fungus of the genus *Blastomyces* (*B. dermatitidis*) — called also *Gilchrist's disease*

Northern blot *n* : a blot consisting of a sheet of a cellulose derivative that contains spots of RNA for identification by a suitable molecular probe — compare SOUTHERN BLOT, WESTERN BLOT — **Northern blotting** *n*

northern cattle grub *n* : an immature form or adult of a warble fly of the genus *Hypoderma* (*H. bovis*) — called also *cattle grub*

northern fowl mite *n* : a parasitic mite (*Ornithonyssus sylviarum*) that is a pest of birds and esp. poultry and pigeons

northern rat flea *n* : a common and widely distributed flea of the genus *Nosopsyllus* (*N. fasciatus*) that is parasitic on rats and transmits murine typhus and possibly plague

nor·trip·ty·line \nȯr-ˈtrip-tə-ˌlēn\ *n* : a tricyclic antidepressant $C_{19}H_{21}N$ used in the form of its hydrochloride — see AVENTYL

Norwalk virus \ˈnȯr-ˌwȯk-\ *n* : a parvovirus that causes an infectious human gastroenteritis — called also *Norwalk agent*

Nor·way rat \ˈnȯr-ˌwā-\ *n* : BROWN RAT

nos- or **noso-** *comb form* : disease (*nosology*)

nose \ˈnōz\ *n* **1 a** : the part of the face that bears the nostrils and covers the anterior part of the nasal cavity; *broadly* : this part together with the nasal cavity **b** : the anterior part of the head above or projecting beyond the muzzle **2** : the sense of smell : OLFACTION **3** : OLFACTORY ORGAN

nose·bleed \-ˌblēd\ *n* : an attack of bleeding from the nose — called also *epistaxis*

nose botfly *n* : a botfly of the genus *Gasterophilus* (*G. haemorrhoidalis*) that is parasitic in the larval stage esp. on horses and mules — called also *nose fly*

nose job *n* : RHINOPLASTY

nose·piece \ˈnōz-ˌpēs\ *n* : the bridge of a pair of eyeglasses

nos·o·co·mi·al \ˌnä-sə-ˈkō-mē-əl\ *adj* : originating or taking place in a hospital (~ infection)

no·sol·o·gy \nō-ˈsä-lə-jē, -ˈzä-\ *n, pl* **-gies 1** : a classification or list of diseases **2** : a branch of medical science that deals with classification of diseases — **no·so·log·i·cal** \ˌnō-sə-ˈlä-ji-kəl\ *or* **no·so·log·ic** \-jik\ *adj* — **no·so·log·i·cal·ly** *adv* — **no·sol·o·gist** \nō-ˈsä-lə-jist\ *n*

Nos·o·psyl·lus \ˌnä-sə-ˈsi-ləs\ *n* : a genus of fleas that includes the northern rat flea (*N. fasciatus*)

nos·tril \ˈnäs-trəl\ *n* **1** : either of the external nares; *broadly* : either of the nares with the adjoining passage on

the same side of the nasal septum **2** : either fleshy lateral wall of the nose

nos·trum \ˈnäs-trəm\ *n* : a medicine of secret composition recommended by its preparer but usu. without scientific proof of its effectiveness

not- or **noto-** *comb form* : back : back part (*notochord*)

notch \ˈnäch\ *n* : a V-shaped indentation (as on a bone) — see ACETABULAR NOTCH, SCIATIC NOTCH, VERTEBRAL NOTCH — **notched** \ˈnächt\ *adj*

no·ti·fi·able \ˌnō-tə-ˈfī-ə-bəl\ *adj* : required by law to be reported to official health authorities (a ~ disease)

no·ti·fy \ˈnō-tə-ˌfī\ *vb* **-fied; -fy·ing** : to report the occurrence of (a communicable disease or an individual suffering from such disease) in a community to public-health or other authority — **no·ti·fi·ca·tion** \ˌnō-tə-fə-ˈkā-shən\ *n*

no·to·chord \ˈnō-tə-ˌkȯrd\ *n* : a longitudinal flexible rod of cells that in all vertebrates and some more primitive forms provides the supporting axis of the body, that is almost obliterated in the adult of higher vertebrates as the body develops, and that arises as an outgrowth from dorsal lip of the blastopore extending forward between epiblast and hypoblast in the middorsal line — **no·to·chord·al** \ˌnō-tə-ˈkȯrd-ᵊl\ *adj*

No·to·ed·res \ˌnō-tō-ˈe-ˌdrēz\ *n* : a genus of mites (family Sarcoptidae) containing mange mites that attack various mammals including occas. but rarely seriously humans usu. through contact with cats

nour·ish \ˈnər-ish\ *vb* : to furnish or sustain with nutriment

nour·ish·ing *adj* : giving nourishment : NUTRITIOUS

nour·ish·ment \ˈnər-ish-mənt\ *n* **1** : FOOD 1, NUTRIMENT **2** : the act of nourishing or the state of being nourished

no·vo·bi·o·cin \ˌnō-və-ˈbī-ə-sən\ *n* : a highly toxic antibiotic $C_{31}H_{36}N_2O_{11}$ used in some serious cases of staphylococcal and urinary tract infection

No·vo·cain \ˈnō-və-ˌkān\ *trademark* — used for a preparation containing the hydrochloride of procaine

no·vo·caine \-ˌkān\ *n* : PROCAINE; *also* : its hydrochloride

noxa \ˈnäk-sə\ *n, pl* **nox·ae** \-ˌsē, -ˌsī\ : something that exerts a harmful effect on the body

nox·ious \ˈnäk-shəs\ *adj* : physically harmful or destructive to living beings

Np *symbol* neptunium

NP *abbr* neuropsychiatric; neuropsychiatry

NPN *abbr* nonprotein nitrogen

NR *abbr* no refill

NREM sleep \ˈen-ˌrem-\ *n* : SLOW-WAVE SLEEP

ns *abbr* nanosecond

NSAID \'en-₁sed, -₁säd\ *n* : a nonste-roidal anti-inflammatory drug (as ibu-profen)

nsec *abbr* nanosecond

NSU *abbr* nonspecific urethritis

nu·chae \'nü-kē, 'nyü-\ — see LIGA-MENTUM NUCHAE

nu·chal \'nü-kəl, 'nyü-\ *adj* : of, relat-ing to, or lying in the region of the nape

nuchal line *n* : any of several ridges on the outside of the skull: as **a** : one on each side that extends laterally in a curve from the external occipital pro-tuberance to the mastoid process of the temporal bone — called also *su-perior nuchal line* **b** : OCCIPITAL CREST **a c** : one on each side that extends lat-erally from the middle of the external occipital crest below and roughly par-allel to the superior nuchal line — called also *inferior nuchal line*

nucle- *or* **nucleo-** *comb form* **1** : nucleus ⟨*nucle*on⟩ ⟨*nucleo*plasm⟩ **2** : nucleic acid ⟨*nucleo*protein⟩

nu·cle·ar \'nü-klē-ər, 'nyü-\ *adj* **1** : of, relating to, or constituting a nucleus **2** : of, relating to, or utilizing the atomic nucleus, atomic energy, the atomic bomb, or atomic power

nuclear family *n* : a family group that consists only of father, mother, and children — see EXTENDED FAMILY

nuclear fission *n* : FISSION 2

nuclear magnetic resonance *n* **1** : the magnetic resonance of an atomic nu-cleus **2** : chemical analysis that uses nuclear magnetic resonance esp. to study molecular structure — *abbr.* *NMR;* see MAGNETIC RESONANCE IM-AGING

nuclear medicine *n* : a branch of med-icine dealing with the use of radioac-tive materials in the diagnosis and treatment of disease

nuclear membrane *n* : a double mem-brane enclosing a cell nucleus and having its outer part continuous with the endoplasmic reticulum

nuclear sap *n* : the clear homogeneous ground substance of a cell nucleus — called also *karyolymph*

nu·cle·ase \'nü-klē-₁ās, 'nyü-, -₁āz\ *n* : any of various enzymes that pro-mote hydrolysis of nucleic acids

nu·cle·at·ed \-ā-təd\ *or* **nu·cle·ate** \-klē-ət\ *adj* : having a nucleus or nuclei ⟨∼ cells⟩

nucleic acid \nü-'klē-ik-, nyü-, -'klā-\ *n* : any of various acids (as an RNA or a DNA) composed of nucleotide chains

nu·cle·in \'nü-klē-in, 'nyü-\ *n* **1** : NU-CLEOPROTEIN **2** : NUCLEIC ACID

nucleo- — see NUCLE-

nu·cle·o·cap·sid \₁nü-klē-ō-'kap-səd, ₁nyü-\ *n* : the nucleic acid and sur-rounding protein coat of a virus

nu·cle·o·cy·to·plas·mic \-₁sī-tə-'plaz-mik\ *adj* : of or relating to the nucleus and cytoplasm

nu·cle·o·his·tone \-'his-₁tōn\ *n* : a nu-cleoprotein in which the protein is a histone

nu·cle·oid \'nü-klē-₁óid, 'nyü-\ *n* : the DNA-containing area of a prokaryot-ic cell (as a bacterium)

nucleol- *or* **nucleolo-** *comb form* : nucle-olus ⟨*nucleol*ar⟩

nu·cle·o·lar \nü-'klē-ə-lər, nyü-, ₁nü-klē-'ō-lər, ₁nyü-\ *adj* : of, relating to, or constituting a nucleolus ⟨∼ pro-teins⟩

nucleolar organizer *n* : NUCLEOLUS OR-GANIZER

nu·cle·o·lus \nü-'klē-ə-ləs, nyü-\ *n, pl* **-li** \-₁lī\ : a spherical body of the nucleus of most eukaryotes that becomes en-larged during protein synthesis, is as-sociated with a nucleolus organizer, and contains the DNA templates for ribosomal RNA

nucleolus organizer *n* : the specific part of a chromosome with which a nucle-olus is associated esp. during its reor-ganization after nuclear division — called also *nucleolar organizer*

nu·cle·on \'nü-klē-₁än, 'nyü-\ *n* : a pro-ton or neutron esp. in the atomic nu-cleus

nu·cle·o·phil·ic \₁nü-klē-ə-'fi-lik, ₁nyü-\ *adj* : having an affinity for atomic nu-clei : electron-donating

nu·cle·o·plasm \'nü-klē-ə-₁pla-zəm, 'nyü-\ *n* : the protoplasm of a nucleus; *esp* : NUCLEAR SAP

nu·cle·o·pro·tein \₁nü-klē-ō-'prō-₁tēn, ₁nyü-\ *n* : a compound that consists of a protein (as a histone) conjugated with a nucleic acid (as a DNA) and that is the principal constituent of the hereditary material in chromosomes

nu·cle·o·side \'nü-klē-ə-₁sīd, 'nyü-\ *n* : a compound (as guanosine or adeno-sine) that consists of a purine or py-rimidine base combined with de-oxyribose or ribose and is found esp. in DNA or RNA — compare NUCLE-OTIDE

nu·cle·o·some \-₁sōm\ *n* : any of the re-peating globular subunits of chroma-tin that consist of a complex of DNA and histone — **nu·cle·o·so·mal** \₁nü-klē-ə-'sō-məl, ₁nyü-\ *adj*

nu·cle·o·tide \'nü-klē-ə-₁tīd, 'nyü-\ *n* : any of several compounds that con-sist of a ribose or deoxyribose sugar joined to a purine or pyrimidine base and to a phosphate group and that are the basic structural units of RNA and DNA — compare NUCLEOSIDE

nu·cle·us \'nü-klē-əs, 'nyü-\ *n, pl* **nu·clei** \-klē-₁ī\ *also* **nu·cle·us·es 1** : a cel-lular organelle of eukaryotes that is essential to cell functions (as repro-duction and protein synthesis), is composed of nuclear sap and a nucleoprotein-rich network from which chromosomes and nucleoli arise, and is enclosed in a definite membrane **2** : a mass of gray matter or group of nerve cells in the central nervous system **3** : the positively charged central portion of an atom that comprises nearly all of the atomic mass and that consists of protons and neutrons except in hydrogen which consists of one proton only

nucleus ac·cum·bens \-ə-'kəm-bənz\ : a nucleus forming the floor of the caudal part of the anterior prolongation of the lateral ventricle of the brain

nucleus am·big·u·us \-am-'bi-gyə-wəs\ *n* : an elongated nucleus in the medulla oblongata that is a continuation of a group of cells in the ventral horn of the spinal cord and gives rise to the motor fibers of the glossopharyngeal, vagus, and accessory nerves supplying striated muscle of the larynx and pharynx

nucleus cu·ne·a·tus \-ˌkyü-nē-'ā-təs\ *n* : the nucleus in the medulla oblongata in which the fibers of the fasciculus cuneatus terminate and synapse with a component of the medial lemniscus — called also *cuneate nucleus*

nucleus grac·i·lis \-'gra-sə-ləs\ *n* : a nucleus in the posterior part of the medulla oblongata in which the fibers of the fasciculus gracilis terminate

nucleus pul·po·sus \-ˌpəl-'pō-səs\ *n, pl* **nuclei pul·po·si** \-ˌsī\ : an elastic pulpy mass lying in the center of each intervertebral fibrocartilage

nu·clide \'nü-ˌklīd, 'nyü-\ *n* : a species of atom characterized by the constitution of its nucleus and hence by the number of protons, the number of neutrons, and the energy content

null cell \'nəl-\ *n* : a lymphocyte in the blood that does not have on its surface the receptors typical of either mature B cells or T cells

nul·li·grav·i·da \ˌnə-lə-'gra-və-də\ *n* : a woman who has never been pregnant

nul·lip·a·ra \ˌnə-'li-pə-rə\ *n, pl* **-ras** *also* **-rae** \-ˌrē\ : a woman who has never borne a child

nul·lip·a·rous \ˌnə-'li-pə-rəs\ *adj* : of, relating to, or being a female that has not borne offspring — **nul·li·par·i·ty** \ˌnə-lə-'par-ə-tē\ *n*

numb \'nəm\ *adj* : devoid of sensation esp. as a result of cold or anesthesia — **numb·ness** *n*

num·mu·lar \'nə-myə-lər\ *adj* **1** : circular or oval in shape ⟨∼ lesions⟩ **2** : characterized by circular or oval lesions or drops ⟨∼ dermatitis⟩

Nu·per·caine \'nü-pər-ˌkān, 'nyü-\ *trademark* — used for a preparation of dibucaine

¹**nurse** \'nərs\ *n* **1** : a woman who suckles an infant not her own : WET NURSE **2** : a person who is skilled or trained in caring for the sick or infirm esp. under the supervision of a physician

²**nurse** *vb* **nursed; nurs·ing 1 a** : to nourish at the breast : SUCKLE **b** : to take

nourishment from the breast : SUCK **2 a** : to care for and wait on (as an injured or infirm person) **b** : to attempt a cure of (as an ailment) by care and treatment

nurse-anes·the·tist \-ə-'nes-thə-tist\ *n* : a registered nurse who has completed two years of additional training in anesthesia and is qualified to serve as an anesthetist under the supervision of a physician

nurse clinician *n* : NURSE-PRACTITIONER

nurse-midwife *n, pl* **nurse-midwives** : a registered nurse who has received additional training as a midwife, delivers infants, and provides antepartum and postpartum care — **nurse-midwifery** *n*

nurse-practitioner *n* : a registered nurse who through advanced training is qualified to assume some of the duties and responsibilities formerly assumed only by a physician — called also *nurse clinician*

nurs·ery \'nər-sə-rē\ *n, pl* **-er·ies** : the department of a hospital where newborn infants are cared for

nurse's aide *n* : a worker who assists trained nurses in a hospital by performing general services

nurs·ing \'nər-siŋ\ *n* **1** : the profession of a nurse ⟨schools of ∼⟩ **2** : the duties of a nurse

nursing bottle *n* : a bottle with a rubber nipple used in supplying food to infants

nursing home *n* : a privately operated establishment where maintenance and personal or nursing care are provided for persons (as the aged or the chronically ill) who are unable to care for themselves properly — compare REST HOME

nur·tur·ance \'nər-chə-rəns\ *n* : affectionate care and attention — **nur·tur·ant** \-rənt\ *adj*

Nu·tra·Sweet \'nü-trə-ˌswēt, 'nyü-\ *trademark* — used for a preparation of aspartame

¹**nu·tri·ent** \'nü-trē-ənt, 'nyü-\ *adj* : furnishing nourishment

²**nutrient** *n* : a nutritive substance or ingredient

nu·tri·ment \'nü-trə-mənt, 'nyü-\ *n* : something that nourishes or promotes growth and repairs the natural wastage of organic life

nu·tri·tion \nü-'tri-shən, nyü-\ *n* : the act or process of nourishing or being nourished; *specif* : the sum of the processes by which an animal or plant takes in and utilizes food substances — **nu·tri·tion·al** \-'tri-shə-nəl\ *adj* — **nu·tri·tion·al·ly** *adv*

nutritional anemia *n* : anemia (as hypochromic anemia) that results from inadequate intake or assimilation of materials essential for the production of red blood cells and hemoglobin — called also *deficiency anemia*

nu·tri·tion·ist \-ˈtri-shə-nist\ *n* : a specialist in the study of nutrition

nu·tri·tious \nü-ˈtri-shəs. nyü-\ *adj* : providing nourishment

nu·tri·tive \ˈnü-trə-tiv. ˈnyü-\ *adj* 1 : of or relating to nutrition 2 : NOURISHING

nu·tri·ture \ˈnü-trə-ˌchúr. ˈnyü-. -chər\ *n* : bodily condition with respect to nutrition and esp. with respect to a given nutrient (as zinc)

nux vom·i·ca \ˈnəks-ˈvä-mi-kə\ *n, pl* **nux vomica** 1 : the poisonous seed of an Asian tree of the genus *Strychnos* (*S. nux-vomica*) that contains the alkaloids strychnine and brucine 2 : a drug containing nux vomica

nyc·ta·lo·pia \ˌnik-tə-ˈlō-pē-ə\ *n* : NIGHT BLINDNESS

ny·li·dron \ˈni-li-drən\ *n* : a synthetic adrenergic drug $C_{19}H_{25}NO_2$ that acts as a peripheral vasodilator and is usually administered in the form of its hydrochloride

nymph \ˈnimf\ *n* 1 : any of various insects in an immature stage and esp. a late larva (as of a true bug) in which rudiments of the wings and genitalia are present; *broadly* : any insect larva that differs chiefly in size and degree of differentiation from the adult 2 : a mite or tick in the first eight-legged form that immediately follows the last larval molt — **nymph·al** \ˈnim-fəl\ *adj*

nymph- *or* **nympho-** *also* **nymphi-** *comb form* : nymph : nymphae (*nymphomania*)

nym·phae \ˈnim-(ˌ)fē\ *n pl* : LABIA MINORA

nym·pho \ˈnim-(ˌ)fō\ *n, pl* **nymphos** : NYMPHOMANIAC

nym·pho·ma·nia \ˌnim-fə-ˈmā-nē-ə. -nyə\ *n* : excessive sexual desire by a female — compare SATYRIASIS

¹**nym·pho·ma·ni·ac** \-nē-ˌak\ *n* : one affected with nymphomania

²**nymphomaniac** *or* **nym·pho·ma·ni·a·cal** \-mə-ˈnī-ə-kəl\ *adj* : of. affected with. or characterized by nymphomania

nys·tag·mus \ni-ˈstag-məs\ *n* : a rapid involuntary oscillation of the eyeballs occurring normally with dizziness during and after bodily rotation or abnormally after injuries

nys·ta·tin \ˈnis-tət-ən\ *n* : an antibiotic that is derived from a soil actinomycete of the genus *Streptomyces* (*S. noursei*) and is used esp. in the treatment of candidiasis

O

¹**O** *abbr* [Latin *octarius*] pint — used in writing prescriptions

²**O** *symbol* oxygen

o- *or* **oo-** *comb form* : egg : ovum (*oocyte*)

O antigen \ˈō-\ *n* : an antigen that occurs in the body of a gram-negative bacterial cell — compare H ANTIGEN

oat-cell \ˈōt-ˌsel\ *adj* : of. relating to, or being a highly malignant form of cancer esp. of the lungs that is characterized by rapid proliferation of small anaplastic cells (∼ carcinomas)

oath — see HIPPOCRATIC OATH

OB *abbr* 1 obstetric 2 obstetrician 3 obstetrics

obese \ō-ˈbēs\ *adj* : excessively fat

obe·si·ty \ō-ˈbē-sə-tē\ *n, pl* **-ties** : a condition characterized by excessive bodily fat

obex \ˈō-ˌbeks\ *n* : a thin triangular lamina of gray matter in the roof of the fourth ventricle of the brain

ob-gyn \ˌō-(ˌ)bē-ˈjin. -(ˌ)jē-(ˌ)wī-ˈen\ *n, pl* **ob-gyns** : a physician who specializes in obstetrics and gynecology

OB–GYN *abbr* obstetrics-gynecology

ob·jec·tive \əb-ˈjek-tiv. äb-\ *adj* 1 : of. relating to, or being an object. phenomenon. or condition in the realm of sensible experience independent of individual thought and perceptible by all observers (∼ reality) 2 : perceptible to persons other than the affected individual (an ∼ symptom of disease) — compare SUBJECTIVE 2b — **ob·jec·tive·ly** *adv*

ob·li·gate \ˈä-bli-gət. -ˌgät\ *adj* 1 : restricted to one particularly characteristic mode of life or way of functioning 2 : biologically essential for survival — **ob·li·gate·ly** *adv*

oblig·a·to·ry \ə-ˈbli-gə-ˌtōr-ē. ä-\ *adj* : OBLIGATE 1

¹**oblique** \ō-ˈblēk. ə-. -ˈblik\ *adj* 1 : neither perpendicular nor parallel : being on an incline 2 : situated obliquely and having one end not inserted on bone (∼ muscles) — **oblique·ly** *adv*

²**oblique** *n* : any of several oblique muscles: as a : either of two flat muscles on each side that form the middle and outer layers of the lateral walls of the abdomen and that act to compress the abdominal contents and to assist in expelling the contents of various visceral organs (as in urination and expiration): (1) : one that forms the outer layer of the lateral abdominal wall — called also *external oblique*, *obliquus externus abdominis* (2) : one situated under the external oblique in the lateral and ventral part of the abdominal wall — called also *internal oblique*, *obliquus internus abdominis* b (1) : a long thin muscle that arises just above the margin of the optic foramen. is inserted on the upper part of the eyeball. and moves the eye downward and laterally — called also *superior oblique*, *obliquus superior*

oculi (2) : a short muscle that arises from the orbital surface of the maxilla, is inserted slightly in front of and below the superior oblique, and moves the eye upward and laterally — called also *inferior oblique, obliquus inferior oculi* c (1) : a muscle that arises from the superior surface of the transverse process of the atlas, passes medially upward to insert into the occipital bone, and functions to extend the head and bend it to the side — called also *obliquus capitis superior* (2) : a muscle that arises from the apex of the spinous process of the axis, inserts into the transverse process of the atlas, and rotates the atlas turning the face in the same direction — called also *obliquus capitis inferior*

oblique fissure *n* : either of two fissures of the lungs of which the one on the left side of the body separates the superior lobe of the left lung from the inferior lobe and the one on the right separates the superior and middle lobes of the right lung from the inferior lobe

oblique popliteal ligament *n* : a strong broad flat fibrous ligament that passes obliquely across and strengthens the posterior part of the knee — compare ARCUATE POPLITEAL LIGAMENT

oblique vein of Mar·shall \-ˈmär-shəl\ *n* : OBLIQUE VEIN OF THE LEFT ATRIUM
Marshall, John (1818–1891), British anatomist and surgeon.

oblique vein of the left atrium *n* : a small vein that passes obliquely down the posterior surface of the left atrium and empties into the coronary sinus — called also *oblique vein, oblique vein of left atrium*

ob·li·quus \ō-ˈbli-kwəs\ *n, pl* **ob·li·qui** \-ˌkwī\ : OBLIQUE

obliquus cap·i·tis inferior \-ˈka-pə-təs-\ *n* : OBLIQUE c(2)

obliquus capitis superior *n* : OBLIQUE c(1)

obliquus externus ab·dom·i·nis \-ab-ˈdä-mə-nəs\ *n* : OBLIQUE a(1)

obliquus inferior *n* : OBLIQUE b(2)

obliquus inferior oc·u·li \ˈä-kyü-ˌlī, -ˌlē\ *n* : OBLIQUE b(2)

obliquus internus ab·dom·i·nis \-ab-ˈdä-mə-nəs\ *n* : OBLIQUE a(2)

obliquus superior *n* : OBLIQUE b(1)

obliquus superior oc·u·li \-ˈä-kyü-ˌlī, -ˌlē\ *n* : OBLIQUE b(1)

obliterans — see ARTERIOSCLEROSIS OBLITERANS, ENDARTERITIS OBLITERANS, THROMBOANGIITIS OBLITERANS

oblit·er·ate \ə-ˈbli-tə-ˌrāt, ō-\ *vb* **-at·ed; -at·ing** : to cause to disappear (as a bodily part or a scar) or collapse (as a duct conveying body fluid) — **oblit·er·a·tion** \-ˌbli-tə-ˈrā-shən\ *n* — **oblit·er·a·tive** \ə-ˈbli-tə-ˌrā-tiv, ō-, -rə-\ *adj*

obliterating endarteritis *n* : ENDARTERITIS OBLITERANS

ob·lon·ga·ta \ˌä-blöŋ-ˈgä-tə\ *n, pl* **-tas** *or* **-tae** \-ˌtē\ : MEDULLA OBLONGATA

OBS *abbr* 1 obstetrician 2 obstetrics

ob·ser·va·tion \ˌäb-sər-ˈvā-shən, -zər-\ *n* 1 : the noting of a fact or occurrence (as in nature) often involving the measurement of some magnitude with suitable instruments; *also* : a record so obtained 2 : close watch or examination (as to monitor or diagnose a condition) (postoperative ∼)

ob·sess \əb-ˈses, äb-\ *vb* 1 : to preoccupy intensely or abnormally (∼ed with success) 2 : to engage in obsessive thinking (solve problems rather than ∼ about them — Carol Tavris)

ob·ses·sion \äb-ˈse-shən, əb-\ *n* : a persistent disturbing preoccupation with an often unreasonable idea or feeling; *also* : something that causes such preoccupation — compare COMPULSION, PHOBIA — **ob·ses·sion·al** \-ˈse-shə-nəl\ *adj*

obsessional neurosis *n* : an obsessive-compulsive neurosis in which obsessive thinking predominates with little need to perform compulsive acts

¹**ob·ses·sive** \äb-ˈse-siv, əb-\ *adj* : of, relating to, causing, or characterized by obsession : deriving from obsession (∼ behavior) — **ob·ses·sive·ly** *adv* — **ob·ses·sive·ness** *n*

²**obsessive** *n* : an obsessive individual

¹**obsessive–compulsive** *adj* : relating to or characterized by recurring obsessions and compulsions esp. as symptoms of an obsessive-compulsive disorder

²**obsessive–compulsive** *n* : a person affected with an obsessive-compulsive disorder

obsessive–compulsive disorder *n* : a psychoneurotic disorder in which the patient is beset with obsessions or compulsions or both and suffers extreme anxiety or depression through failure to think the obsessive thoughts or perform the compelling acts — called also *obsessive-compulsive neurosis, obsessive-compulsive reaction*

ob·stet·ric \əb-ˈste-trik, äb-\ *or* **ob·stet·ri·cal** \-tri-kəl\ *adj* : of, relating to, or associated with childbirth or obstetrics — **ob·stet·ri·cal·ly** *adv*

obstetric forceps *n* : a forceps for grasping the fetal head or other part to facilitate delivery in difficult labor

ob·ste·tri·cian \ˌäb-stə-ˈtri-shən\ *n* : a physician or veterinarian specializing in obstetrics

ob·stet·rics \əb-ˈste-triks, äb-\ *n sing or pl* : a branch of medical science that deals with birth and with its antecedents and sequels

ob·sti·pa·tion \ˌäb-stə-ˈpā-shən\ *n* : severe and intractable constipation

ob·struct \əb-ˈstrəkt, äb-\ *vb* : to block or close up by an obstacle

ob·struc·tion \əb-ˈstrək-shən, äb-\ *n* **1 a** : an act of obstructing **b** : a condition of being clogged or blocked (intestinal $\sim$) 2 : something that obstructs — **ob·struc·tive** \-tiv\ *adj*

obstructive jaundice *n* : jaundice due to obstruction of the biliary passages (as by gallstones or tumor)

ob·tund \äb-ˈtənd\ *vb* : to reduce the intensity or sensitivity of : make dull (~ed reflexes) (agents that ~ pain) — **ob·tun·da·tion** \⸴äb-(⸴)tən-ˈdā-shən\ *n*

ob·tu·ra·tor \ˈäb-tyə-⸴rā-tər, -tə-\ *n* 1 a : either of two muscles arising from the obturator membrane and adjacent bony surfaces: (1) : OBTURATOR EXTERNUS (2) : OBTURATOR INTERNUS b : OBTURATOR NERVE 2 a : a prosthetic device that closes or blocks up an opening (as a fissure in the palate) b : a device that blocks the opening of an instrument (as a sigmoidoscope) that is being introduced into the body

obturator artery *n* : an artery that arises from the internal iliac artery or one of its branches, passes out through the obturator canal, and divides into two branches which are distributed to the muscles and fasciae of the hip and thigh

obturator canal *n* : the small patent opening of the obturator foramen through which nerves and vessels pass

obturator ex·ter·nus \-ek-ˈstər-nəs\ *n* : a flat triangular muscle that arises esp. from the medial side of the obturator foramen and from the medial part of the obturator membrane, that inserts by a tendon into the trochanteric fossa of the femur, and that acts to rotate the thigh laterally

obturator foramen *n* : an opening that is the largest foramen in the human body and is situated between the ischium and pubis of the hipbone

obturator in·ter·nus \-in-ˈtər-nəs\ *n* : a muscle that arises from the margin of the obturator foramen and from the obturator membrane, that inserts into the greater trochanter of the femur, and that acts to rotate the thigh laterally when it is extended and to abduct it in the flexed position

obturator membrane *n* : a firm fibrous membrane covering most of the obturator foramen except for the obturator canal

obturator nerve *n* : a branch of the lumbar plexus that arises from the second, third, and fourth lumbar nerves and that supplies the hip and knee joints, the adductor muscles of the thigh, and the skin

obturator vein *n* : a tributary of the internal iliac vein that accompanies the obturator artery

occipit- or **occipito-** *comb form* : occipital and ⟨*occipito*temporal⟩

occipita *pl of* OCCIPUT

¹**oc·cip·i·tal** \äk-ˈsi-pət-ᵊl\ *adj* : of, relating to, or located within or near the occiput or the occipital bone

²**occipital** *n* : OCCIPITAL BONE

occipital artery *n* : an artery that arises from the external carotid artery, ascends within the superficial fascia of the scalp, and supplies or gives off branches supplying structures and esp. muscles of the back of the neck and head

occipital bone *n* : a compound bone that forms the posterior part of the skull and surrounds the foramen magnum, bears the condyles for articulation with the atlas, is composed of four united elements, is much curved and roughly trapezoidal in outline, and ends in front of the foramen magnum in the basilar process

occipital condyle *n* : an articular surface on the occipital bone by which the skull articulates with the atlas

occipital crest *n* : either of the two ridges on the occipital bone: **a** : a median ridge on the outer surface of the occipital bone that with the external occipital protuberance gives attachment to the ligamentum nuchae — called also *external occipital crest, median nuchal line* **b** : a median ridge similarly situated on the inner surface of the occipital bone that bifurcates near the foramen magnum to give attachment to the falx cerebelli — called also *internal occipital crest*

occipital fontanel *n* : a triangular fontanel at the meeting of the sutures between the parietal and occipital bones

oc·cip·i·ta·lis \äk-⸴si-pə-ˈtā-ləs\ *n* : the posterior belly of the occipitofrontalis that arises from the lateral two-thirds of the superior nuchal lines and from the mastoid part of the temporal bone, inserts into the galea aponeurotica, and acts to move the scalp

occipital lobe *n* : the posterior lobe of each cerebral hemisphere that bears the visual areas and has the form of a 3-sided pyramid

occipital nerve *n* : either of two nerves that arise mostly from the second cervical nerve: **a** : one that innervates the scalp at the top of the head — called also *greater occipital nerve* **b** : one that innervates the scalp esp. in the lateral area of the head behind the ear — called also *lesser occipital nerve*

occipital protuberance *n* : either of two prominences on the occipital bone: **a** : a prominence on the outer surface of the occipital bone midway between the upper border and the foramen magnum — called also *external occipital protuberance, inion* **b** : a prominence similarly situated on the inner surface of the occipital bone — called also *internal occipital protuberance*

occipital sinus *n* : a single or paired venous sinus that arises near the margin of the foramen magnum by the union of several small veins and empties into the confluence of sinuses or sometimes into one of the transverse sinuses

occipito- — see OCCIPIT-

oc·cip·i·to·fron·ta·lis \äk-ˌsi-pə-tō-frən-ˈtā-ləs\ n : a fibrous and muscular sheet on each side of the vertex of the skull that extends from the eyebrow to the occiput, that is composed of the frontalis muscle in front and the occipitalis muscle in back with the galea aponeurotica in between, and that acts to draw back the scalp to raise the eyebrow and wrinkle the forehead — called also *epicranius*

oc·cip·i·to·pa·ri·etal \-pə-ˈrī-ət-ᵊl\ adj : of or relating to the occipital and parietal bones of the skull

oc·cip·i·to·tem·po·ral \-ˈtem-pə-rəl\ adj : of, relating to, or distributed to the occipital and temporal lobes of a cerebral hemisphere (the ∼ cortex)

oc·ci·put \ˈäk-sə-(ˌ)pət\ n, pl **occiputs** or **oc·cip·i·ta** \äk-ˈsi-pə-tə\ : the back part of the head or skull

oc·clude \ə-ˈklüd, ä-\ vb **oc·clud·ed**; **oc·clud·ing** 1 : to close up or block off : OBSTRUCT 2 : to bring (upper and lower teeth) into occlusion 3 : SORB

occlus- or **occluso-** : occlusion (*occlusal*)

oc·clu·sal \ə-ˈklü-səl, ä-, -zəl\ adj : of, relating to, or being the grinding or biting surface of a tooth; *also* : of or relating to occlusion of the teeth (∼ abnormalities) — **oc·clu·sal·ly** adv

occlusal disharmony n : a condition in which incorrect positioning of one or more teeth causes an abnormal increase in or change of direction of the force applied to one or more teeth when the upper and lower teeth are occluded

occlusal plane n : an imaginary plane formed by the occlusal surfaces of the teeth when the jaw is closed

oc·clu·sion \ə-ˈklü-zhən\ n 1 : the act of occluding or the state of being occluded : a shutting off or obstruction of something (a coronary ∼); *esp* : a blocking of the central passage of one reflex by the passage of another 2 a : the bringing of the opposing surfaces of the teeth of the two jaws into contact; *also* : the relation between the surfaces when in contact b : the transient approximation of the edges of a natural opening (∼ of the eyelids) — **oc·clu·sive** \-siv\ adj

occlusive dressing n : a dressing that seals a wound to protect against infection

oc·cult \ə-ˈkəlt, ˈä-ˌkəlt\ adj : not manifest or detectable by clinical methods alone (∼ carcinoma); *also* : not present in macroscopic amounts (∼ blood in a stool specimen) — compare GROSS 2

occulta — see SPINA BIFIDA OCCULTA

oc·cu·pa·tion·al \ˌä-kyə-ˈpā-shə-nəl\ adj : relating to or being an occupational disease (∼ deafness) — **oc·cu·pa·tion·al·ly** adv

occupational disease n : an illness caused by factors arising from one's occupation — called also *industrial disease*

occupational medicine n : a branch of medicine concerned with the prevention and treatment of occupational diseases

occupational therapist n : a person trained in or engaged in the practice of occupational therapy

occupational therapy n : therapy by means of activity; *esp* : creative activity prescribed for its effect in promoting recovery or rehabilitation — compare RECREATIONAL THERAPY

och·ra·tox·in \ˌō-krə-ˈtäk-sən\ n : a mycotoxin produced by a fungus of the genus *Aspergillus* (*A. ochraceus*)

ochro·no·sis \ˌō-krə-ˈnō-səs\ n, pl **-no·ses** \-ˌsēz\ : a condition often associated with alkaptonuria and marked by pigment deposits in cartilages, ligaments, and tendons — **ochro·not·ic** \-ˈnä-tik\ adj

oc·ta·pep·tide \ˌäk-tə-ˈpep-ˌtīd\ n : a protein fragment or molecule (as oxytocin) that consists of eight amino acids linked in a polypeptide chain

ocul- or **oculo-** comb form 1 : eye (*oculomotor*) 2 : ocular and (*oculo*cutaneous)

oc·u·lar \ˈä-kyə-lər\ adj : of or relating to the eye (∼ muscles) (∼ diseases)

oc·u·lar·ist \ˈä-kyə-lə-rist\ n : a person who makes and fits artificial eyes

oculi — see OBLIQUUS INFERIOR OCULI, OBLIQUUS SUPERIOR OCULI, ORBICULARIS OCULI, RECTUS OCULI

oc·u·list \ˈä-kyə-list\ n 1 : OPHTHALMOLOGIST 2 : OPTOMETRIST

oc·u·lo·cu·ta·ne·ous \ˌä-kyə-(ˌ)lō-kyù-ˈtā-nē-əs\ adj : relating to or affecting both the eyes and the skin

oc·u·lo·gy·ric crisis \ˌä-kyə-lō-ˈjī-rik-\ n : a spasmodic attack that occurs in some nervous diseases and is marked by fixation of the eyeballs in one position usu. upward — called also *oculogyric spasm*

oc·u·lo·mo·tor \ˌä-kyə-lə-ˈmō-tər\ adj 1 : moving or tending to move the eyeball 2 : of or relating to the oculomotor nerve

oculomotor nerve n : either nerve of the third pair of cranial nerves that are motor nerves with some associated autonomic fibers, arise from the midbrain, and supply most muscles of the eye with motor fibers and the ciliary body and iris with autonomic fibers by way of the ciliary ganglion — called also *third cranial nerve*

oculomotor nucleus n : a nucleus that is situated under the aqueduct of Sylvius rostral to the trochlear nucleus and is the source of the motor fibers of the oculomotor nerve

oc·u·lo·plas·tic \ˌä-kyə-lō-ˈplas-tik\ adj

: of, relating to, or being plastic surgery of the eye and associated structures

od *abbr* [Latin *omnes dies*] every day — used in writing prescriptions

¹OD \(ˌ)ō-ˈdē\ *n* **1** : an overdose of a narcotic **2** : one who has taken an OD

²OD *vb* **OD'd** *or* **ODed**; **OD'·ing**; **OD's** : to become ill or die of an OD

³OD *abbr* **1** doctor of optometry **2** [Latin *oculus dexter*] right eye — used in writing prescriptions

Oddi — see SPHINCTER OF ODDI

odont- *or* **odonto-** *comb form* : tooth (*odont*itis) (*odonto*blast)

odon·tal·gia \ˌō-ˌdän-ˈtal-jə, -jē-ə\ *n* : TOOTHACHE — **odon·tal·gic** \-jik\ *adj*

-odon·tia \ə-ˈdän-chə, -chē-ə\ *n comb form* : form, condition, or mode of treatment of the teeth (ortho*dontia*)

odon·ti·tis \ˌō-ˈtī-təs\ *n, pl* **odon·tit·i·des** \-ˈti-tə-ˌdēz\ : inflammation of a tooth

odon·to·blast \ō-ˈdän-tə-ˌblast\ *n* : one of the elongated radially arranged outer cells of the dental pulp that secrete dentin — **odon·to·blas·tic** \-ˌdän-tə-ˈblas-tik\ *adj*

odon·to·gen·e·sis \ō-ˌdän-tə-ˈje-nə-səs\ *n, pl* **-e·ses** \-ˌsēz\ : the formation and development of teeth

odon·to·gen·ic \ō-ˌdän-tə-ˈje-nik\ *adj* **1** : forming or capable of forming teeth (~ tissues) **2** : containing or arising from odontogenic tissues (~ tumors)

odon·toid process \ō-ˈdän-ˌtȯid-\ *n* : a toothlike process that projects from the anterior end of the centrum of the axis in the spinal column and serves as a pivot on which the atlas rotates — called also *dens*

odon·tol·o·gist \(ˌ)ō-ˌdän-ˈtä-lə-jist\ *n* : a specialist in odontology

odon·tol·o·gy \(ˌ)ō-ˌdän-ˈtä-lə-jē\ *n, pl* **-gies** : a science dealing with the teeth, their structure and development, and their diseases — **odon·to·log·i·cal** \-ˌdänt-əl-ˈä-ji-kəl\ *adj*

odon·to·ma \(ˌ)ō-ˌdän-ˈtō-mə\ *n, pl* **-mas** *also* **-ma·ta** \-mə-tə\ : a tumor originating from a tooth and containing dental tissue (as enamel, dentin, or cementum)

odon·tome \ō-ˈdän-ˌtōm\ *n* : ODONTOMA

odor \ˈō-dər\ *n* **1** : a quality of something that affects the sense of smell **2** : a sensation resulting from adequate chemical stimulation of the receptors for the sense of smell — **odored** *adj* — **odor·less** *adj*

odour *chiefly Brit var of* ODOR

-o·dyn·ia \ə-ˈdi-nē-ə\ *n comb form* : pain (pleur*odynia*)

odyno·pha·gia \ˌō-ˌdi-nə-ˈfā-jə, -jē-ə\ *n* : pain produced by swallowing

oe·de·ma *chiefly Brit var of* EDEMA

oe·di·pal \ˈe-də-pəl, ˈē-\ *adj, often cap* : of, relating to, or resulting from the Oedipus complex — **oe·di·pal·ly** *adv, often cap*

¹Oe·di·pus \-pəs\ *adj* : OEDIPAL

²Oedipus *n* : OEDIPUS COMPLEX

Oedipus complex *n* : the positive libidinal feelings of a child toward the parent of the opposite sex and hostile or jealous feelings toward the parent of the same sex that may be a source of adult personality disorder when unresolved — used esp. of the male child; see ELECTRA COMPLEX

oesophag- *or* **oesophago-** *chiefly Brit var of* ESOPHAG-

oe·soph·a·ge·al, oe·soph·a·gec·to·my, oe·soph·a·go·gas·trec·to·my, oe·soph·a·go·plas·ty, oe·soph·a·gus *chiefly Brit var of* ESOPHAGEAL, ESOPHAGECTOMY, ESOPHAGOGASTRECTOMY, ESOPHAGOPLASTY, ESOPHAGUS

oe·soph·a·go·sto·mi·a·sis \i-ˌsä-fə-(ˌ)gō-stə-ˈmī-ə-səs, -ˌsēz\ *n, pl* **-a·ses** \-ˌsēz\ : infestation with or disease caused by nematode worms of the genus *Oesophagostomum* : NODULAR DISEASE

Oe·soph·a·gos·to·mum \i-ˌsä-fə-ˈgäs-tə-məm\ *n* : a genus of strongylid nematode worms comprising the nodular worms of ruminants and swine and other worms affecting primates including humans esp. in Africa

oestr- *or* **oestro-** *chiefly Brit var of* ESTR-

oes·tra·di·ol \ˌes-trə-ˈdī-ˌȯl, -ˌōl\, **oes·tro·gen** \ˈē-strə-jən\, **oes·trus** \ˈē-strəs\ *chiefly Brit var of* ESTRADIOL, ESTROGEN, ESTRUS

Oes·trus \ˈes-trəs, ˈēs-\ *n* : a genus (family Oestridae) of dipteran flies including the sheep botfly (*O. ovis*)

of·fi·cial \ə-ˈfi-shəl\ *adj* : prescribed or recognized as authorized; *specif* : described by the *U.S. Pharmacopeia* or the *National Formulary* — compare NONOFFICIAL, UNOFFICIAL — **of·fi·cial·ly** *adv*

¹of·fic·i·nal \ə-ˈfis-ə̇n-əl, ȯ-, ä-; ˌȯ-fə-ˈsin-əl, ˌä-\ *adj* **1 a** : available without special preparation or compounding (~ medicine) **b** : OFFICIAL **2** : of a plant : MEDICINAL (~ rhubarb)

²officinal *n* : an officinal drug, medicine, or plant

off·spring \ˈȯf-ˌspriŋ\ *n, pl* **offspring** *also* **offsprings** : the progeny of an animal or plant

ohm \ˈōm\ *n* : a unit of electrical resistance equal to the resistance of a circuit in which a potential difference of one volt produces a current of one ampere

oid·i·um \ō-ˈi-dē-əm\ *n* **1** *cap* : a genus (family Moniliaceae) of imperfect fungi including many which are now considered to be asexual spore-producing stages of various powdery mildews **2** *pl* **oid·ia** \-dē-ə\ : any fungus of the genus *Oidium*

oil \ˈȯil\ *n* **1** : any of numerous fatty or greasy liquid substances obtained from plants, animals, or minerals and used for fuel, food, medicines, and manufacturing **2** : a substance (as a cosmetic preparation) of oily consistency — **oil** *adj*

oil gland *n* : a gland (as of the skin) that produces an oily secretion; *specif* : SEBACEOUS GLAND

oil of wintergreen *n* : a preparation of methyl salicylate obtained by distilling the leaves of wintergreen (*Gaultheria procumbens*) — called also *wintergreen oil*

oily \\'ȯi-lē\ *adj* **oil·i·er; -est 1** : of, relating to, or consisting of oil **2** : excessively high in naturally secreted oils (~ hair) (~ skin)

oint·ment \\'ȯint-mənt\ *n* : a salve or unguent for application to the skin; *specif* : a semisolid medicinal preparation usu. having a base of fatty or greasy material

-ol \ȯl, ōl\ *n suffix* : chemical compound (as an alcohol or phenol) containing hydroxyl (glycerol)

OL *abbr* [Latin *oculus laevus*] left eye — used in writing prescriptions

ole- *or* **oleo-** *also* **olei-** *comb form* : oil (olein)

olea *pl of* OLEUM

ole·an·der \\'ō-lē-ˌan-dər, ˌō-lē-'\ *n* : a poisonous evergreen shrub (*Nerium oleander*) of the dogbane family (Apocynaceae) with fragrant white to red flowers that contains the cardiac glycoside oleandrin

ole·an·do·my·cin \ˌō-lē-ˌan-də-'mīs-ᵊn\ *n* : an antibiotic $C_{35}H_{61}NO_{12}$ produced by a bacterium of the genus *Streptomyces* (*S. antibioticus*)

ole·an·drin \ō-lē-'an-drən\ *n* : a poisonous crystalline glycoside $C_{32}H_{48}O_9$ found in oleander leaves and resembling digitalis in its action

ole·ate \\'ō-lē-ˌāt\ *n* **1** : a salt or ester of oleic acid **2** : a liquid or semisolid preparation of a medicinal dissolved in an excess of oleic acid

olec·ra·non \ō-'le-krə-ˌnän\ *n* : the large process of the ulna that projects behind the elbow joint, forms the bony prominence of the elbow, and receives the insertion of the triceps muscle

olecranon fossa *n* : the fossa at the distal end of the humerus into which the olecranon fits when the arm is in full extension — compare CORONOID FOSSA

ole·ic acid \ō-'lē-ik-, -'lā-\ *n* : a monounsaturated fatty acid $C_{18}H_{34}O_2$ found in natural fats and oils

ole·in \\'ō-lē-ən\ *n* : an ester of glycerol and oleic acid

oleo- — see OLE-

oleo·res·in \ˌō-lē-ō-'rez-ᵊn\ *n* **1** : a natural plant product (as turpentine) containing chiefly essential oil and resin **2** : a preparation consisting essentially of oil holding resin in solution — **oleo·res·in·ous** \-'rez-ᵊn-əs\ *adj*

oleo·tho·rax \-'thōr-ˌaks\ *n, pl* **-tho·rax·es** *or* **-tho·ra·ces** \-'thōr-ə-ˌsēz\ : a state in which oil is present in the pleural cavity usu. as a result of injection — compare PNEUMOTHORAX

ole·um \\'ō-lē-əm\ *n, pl* **olea** \-lē-ə\ : OIL

ol·fac·tion \äl-'fak-shən, ōl-\ *n* **1** : the sense of smell **2** : the act or process of smelling

ol·fac·to·ry \äl-'fak-tə-rē, ōl-\ *adj* : of, relating to, or connected with the sense of smell

olfactory area *n* **1** : the sensory area for olfaction lying in the hippocampal gyrus **2** : the area of nasal mucosa in which the olfactory organ is situated

olfactory bulb *n* : a bulbous anterior projection of the olfactory lobe that is the place of termination of the olfactory nerves

olfactory cell *n* : a sensory cell specialized for the reception of sensory stimuli caused by odors; *specif* : one of the spindle-shaped neurons buried in the nasal mucous membrane of vertebrates — see OLFACTORY ORGAN

olfactory epithelium *n* : the nasal mucosa containing olfactory cells

olfactory gland *n* : GLAND OF BOWMAN

olfactory gyrus *n* : either a lateral or a medial gyrus on each side of the brain by which the olfactory tract on the corresponding side communicates with the olfactory area

olfactory lobe *n* : a lobe of the brain that rests on the lower surface of a temporal lobe and projects forward from the anterior lower part of each cerebral hemisphere and that consists of an olfactory bulb, an olfactory tract, and an olfactory trigone

olfactory nerve *n* : either of the pair of nerves that are the first cranial nerves, that serve to conduct sensory stimuli from the olfactory organ to the brain, and that arise from the olfactory cells and terminate in the olfactory bulb — called also *first cranial nerve*

olfactory organ *n* : an organ of chemical sense that receives stimuli interpreted as odors, that lies in the walls of the upper part of the nasal cavity, and that forms a mucous membrane continuous with the rest of the lining of the nasal cavity

olfactory pit *n* : a depression on the head of an embryo that becomes converted into a nasal passage

olfactory tract *n* : a tract of nerve fibers in the olfactory lobe on the inferior surface of the frontal lobe of the brain that passes from the olfactory bulb to the olfactory trigone

olfactory trigone *n* : a triangular area of gray matter on each side of the brain forming the junction of an olfactory tract with a cerebral hemisphere near the optic chiasma

olig- *or* **oligo-** *comb form* **1** : few (oligopeptide) **2** : deficiency : insufficiency (oliguria)

ol·i·gae·mia *chiefly Brit var of* OLI-GEMIA

oli·ge·mia \ä-lə-ˈgē-mē-ə, -ˈjē-\ *n* : a condition in which the total volume of the blood is reduced — **ol·i·ge·mic** \-ˈmik\ *adj*

oli·go·dac·tyl·ism \ä-li-gō-ˈdak-tə-ˌli-zəm, ə-ˌli-gō-\ *also* **oli·go·dac·tyly** \-lē\ *n, pl* **-tyl·isms** *also* **-tylies** : the presence of fewer than five digits on a hand or foot

oli·go·den·dro·cyte \-ˈden-drə-ˌsīt\ *n* : a neuroglial cell resembling an astrocyte but smaller with few and slender processes having few branches

oli·go·den·drog·lia \ä-li-gō-den-ˈdrä-glē-ə, ˌō-li-, -ˈdrō-\ *n* : neuroglia made up of oligodendrocytes that is held to function in myelin formation in the central nervous system — **oli·go·den·drog·li·al** \-lē-əl\ *adj*

oli·go·den·dro·gli·o·ma \-ˌden-drō-glī-ˈō-mə\ *n, pl* **-mas** *or* **-ma·ta** \-mə-tə\ : a tumor of the nervous system composed of oligodendroglia

oli·go·hy·dram·ni·os \-ˌhī-ˈdram-nē-ˌäs\ *n* : deficiency of amniotic fluid sometimes resulting in an embryonic defect through adherence between embryo and amnion

oli·go·men·or·rhea \-ˌme-nə-ˈrē-ə\ *n* : abnormally infrequent or scanty menstrual flow

oli·go·men·or·rhoea *chiefly Brit var of* OLIGOMENORRHEA

oli·go·nu·cle·o·tide \-ˈnü-klē-ə-ˌtīd, -ˈnyü-\ *n* : a chain of up to 20 nucleotides

oli·go·pep·tide \ä-li-gō-ˈpep-ˌtīd, ˌō-li-\ *n* : a protein fragment or molecule that usu. consists of less than 25 amino acid residues linked in a polypeptide chain

oli·go·phre·nia \-ˈfrē-nē-ə\ *n* : MENTAL RETARDATION

oli·go·sper·mia \-ˈspər-mē-ə\ *n* : deficiency of sperm in the semen — **oli·go·sper·mic** \-mik\ *adj*

oli·gu·ria \ä-lə-ˈgür-ē-ə, -ˈgyur-\ *n* : reduced excretion of urine — **ol·i·gur·ic** \-ik\ *adj*

ol·i·vary \ˈä-lə-ˌver-ē\ *adj* **1** : shaped like an olive **2** : of, relating to, situated near, or comprising one or more of the olives, inferior olives, or superior olives (the ∼ complex) (∼ fibers)

olivary nucleus *n* **1** : INFERIOR OLIVE **2** : SUPERIOR OLIVE

ol·ive \ˈä-liv\ *n* : an oval eminence on each ventrolateral aspect of the medulla oblongata that contains the inferior olive of the same side — called also *olivary body*

olive oil *n* : a pale yellow to yellowish green oil obtained from the pulp of olives (from the olive tree, *Olea europaea* of the family Oleaceae) usu. by expressing and used chiefly as a salad oil and in cooking, in toilet soaps, and as an emollient

ol·i·vo·cer·e·bel·lar tract \ˌä-li-vō-ˌser-ə-ˈbe-lər-\ *n* : a tract of fibers that arises in the olive on one side, crosses to the olive on the other, and enters the cerebellum by way of the inferior cerebellar peduncle

ol·i·vo·pon·to·cer·e·bel·lar atrophy \-ˌpän-tō-ˌser-ə-ˈbe-lər-\ *n* : an inherited disease esp. of mid to late life that is characterized by ataxia, hypotonia, dysarthria, and degeneration of the cerebellar cortex, middle cerebellar peduncles, and inferior olives — called also *olivopontocerebellar degeneration*

ol·i·vo·spi·nal tract \-ˈspīn-ᵊl-\ *n* : a tract of fibers on the peripheral aspect of the ventral side of the cervical part of the spinal cord that communicates with the inferior olive

-o·ma \ˈō-mə\ *n suffix, pl* **-o·mas** \-məz\ *or* **-o·ma·ta** \-mə-tə\ : tumor (adenoma) (fibroma)

oma·sum \ō-ˈmā-səm\ *n, pl* **oma·sa** \-sə\ : the third chamber of the ruminant stomach that is situated between the reticulum and the abomasum — called also *manyplies, psalterium* — **oma·sal** \-səl\ *adj*

omega-3 \ō-ˈme-gə-ˈthrē, -ˈmä-\ *adj* : being or composed of polyunsaturated fatty acids that have the final double bond in the hydrocarbon chain between the third and fourth carbon atoms from the end of the molecule opposite that of the carboxylic acid group and that are found esp. in fish, fish oils, vegetable oils, and green leafy vegetables — **omega-3** *n*

oment- *or* **omento-** *comb form* : omentum (omentectomy) (omentopexy)

omen·tec·to·my \ˌō-men-ˈtek-tə-mē\ *n, pl* **-mies** : excision or resection of all or part of an omentum — called also *epiploectomy*

omen·to·pexy \ō-ˈmen-tə-ˌpek-sē\ *n, pl* **-pex·ies** : the operation of suturing the omentum esp. to another organ

omen·to·plas·ty \-ˌplas-tē\ *n, pl* **-ties** : the use of a piece or flap of tissue from an omentum as a graft

omen·tor·rha·phy \ˌō-men-ˈtȯr-ə-fē\ *n, pl* **-phies** : surgical repair of an omentum by suturing

omen·tum \ō-ˈmen-təm\ *n, pl* **-ta** \-tə\ *or* **-tums** : a fold of peritoneum connecting or supporting abdominal structures (as the viscera) — see GREATER OMENTUM, LESSER OMENTUM — **omen·tal** \-ˈment-ᵊl\ *adj*

om·ni·fo·cal \ˌäm-ni-ˈfō-kəl\ *adj* : of, relating to, or being a bifocal eyeglass that is so ground as to permit smooth transition from one correction to the other

omo·hy·oi·de·us \-hi-ˈȯi-dē-əs\ *n, pl* **-dei** \-dē-ˌī\ : OMOHYOID MUSCLE

omo·hy·oid muscle \ˌō-mō-ˈhī-ˌȯid-\ *n* : a muscle that arises from the upper border of the scapula, is inserted in the body of the hyoid bone, and acts to draw the hyoid bone in a caudal direction — called also *omohyoid*

om·phal- *or* **omphalo-** *comb form* **1** : umbilicus ⟨*omphal*itis⟩ **2** : umbilical and ⟨*omphalo*mesenteric duct⟩

om·pha·lec·to·my \ˌäm-fə-ˈlek-tə-mē\ *n, pl* **-mies** : surgical excision of the umbilicus — called also *umbilectomy*

om·phal·ic \(ˌ)äm-ˈfa-lik\ *adj* : of or relating to the umbilicus

om·pha·li·tis \ˌäm-fə-ˈli-təs\ *n, pl* **-lit·i·des** \-ˈli-tə-ˌdēz\ : inflammation of the umbilicus

om·pha·lo·cele \äm-ˈfa-lə-ˌsēl, ˈäm-fə-lə-\ *n* : protrusion of abdominal contents through an opening at the umbilicus occurring esp. as a congenital defect

om·pha·lo·mes·en·ter·ic duct \ˌäm-fə-lō-ˌmez-ᵊn-ˈter-ik-, -ˌmes-\ *n* : the duct by which the yolk sac or umbilical vesicle remains connected with the alimentary tract of the vertebrate embryo — called also *vitelline duct, yolk stalk*

om·pha·lo·phle·bi·tis \-fli-ˈbī-təs\ *n, pl* **-bit·i·des** \-ˈbi-tə-ˌdēz\ : a condition (as navel ill) characterized by or resulting from inflammation and infection of the umbilical vein

onan·ism \ˈō-nə-ˌni-zəm\ *n* **1** : MASTURBATION **2** : COITUS INTERRUPTUS — **onan·is·tic** \ˌō-nə-ˈnis-tik\ *adj*

onan·ist \ˈō-nə-nist\ *n* : one that practices onanism

On·cho·cer·ca \ˌäŋ-kə-ˈsər-kə\ *n* : a genus of long slender filarial worms (family Dipetalonematidae) that are parasites of mammalian subcutaneous and connective tissues

on·cho·cer·ci·a·sis \ˌäŋ-kō-ˌsər-ˈkī-ə-səs\ *n, pl* **-a·ses** \-ˌsēz\ : infestation with or disease caused by filarial worms of the genus *Onchocerca; esp* : a human disease caused by a worm (*O. volvulus*) that is native to Africa but now present in parts of tropical America and is transmitted by several blackflies — called also *river blindness*

on·cho·sphere *var of* ONCOSPHERE

onco- *or* **oncho-** *comb form* **1** : tumor ⟨*onco*logy⟩ **2** : bulk : mass ⟨*onco*sphere⟩

on·co·cyte \ˈäŋ-kō-ˌsīt\ *n* : an acidophilic granular cell esp. of the parotid gland

on·co·cy·to·ma \ˌäŋ-kō-sī-ˈto-mə\ *n, pl* **-mas** *or* **-ma·ta** \-mə-tə\ : a tumor (as of the parotid gland) consisting chiefly or entirely of oncocytes

on·co·fe·tal \-ˈfēt-ᵊl\ *adj* : of, relating to, or occurring in both tumorous and fetal tissues

on·co·gene \ˈäŋ-kō-ˌjēn\ *n* : a gene having the potential to cause a normal cell to become cancerous

on·co·gen·e·sis \ˌäŋ-kō-ˈje-nə-səs\ *n, pl* **-e·ses** \-ˌsēz\ : the induction or formation of tumors

on·co·gen·ic \-ˈje-nik\ *adj* **1** : relating to

tumor formation **2** : tending to cause tumors — **on·co·gen·i·cal·ly** *adv* — **on·co·ge·nic·i·ty** \-jə-ˈni-sə-tē\ *n*

on·col·o·gist \än-ˈkä-lə-jəst, äŋ-\ *n* : a specialist in oncology

on·col·o·gy \än-ˈkä-lə-jē, äŋ-\ *n, pl* **-gies** : the study of tumors — **on·co·log·i·cal** \ˌäŋ-kə-ˈlä-ji-kəl\ *also* **on·co·log·ic** \-jik\ *adj*

on·col·y·sis \-ˈkä-lə-səs\ *n, pl* **-y·ses** \-ˌsēz\ : the destruction of tumor cells — **on·co·lyt·ic** \ˌäŋ-kə-ˈli-tik\ *adj* — **on·co·lyt·i·cal·ly** *adv*

on·cor·na·vi·rus \ˌäŋ-ˌkȯr-nə-ˈvī-rəs\ *n* : any of a group of RNA-containing viruses that produce tumors

on·co·sphere \ˈäŋ-kō-ˌsfir\ *n* : an embryo of a tapeworm (order Cyclophyllidea) that has six hooks and is in the earliest differentiated stage

on·cot·ic pressure \(ˌ)äŋ-ˈkä-tik-, (ˌ)än-\ *n* : the pressure exerted by plasma proteins on the capillary wall

On·co·vin \ˈäŋ-kō-ˌvin\ *trademark* — used for a preparation of vincristine

one-egg *adj* : MONOZYGOTIC ⟨~ twins⟩

on·lay \ˈon-ˌlā, ˈän-\ *n* **1** : a metal covering attached to a tooth to restore one or more of its surfaces **2** : a graft applied to the surface of a tissue (as bone)

on·set \ˈon-ˌset, ˈän-\ *n* : the initial existence or symptoms of a disease

ont- *or* **onto-** *comb form* : organism ⟨*ont*ogeny⟩

-ont \ˌänt\ *n comb form* : cell : organism ⟨schiz*ont*⟩

on·to·gen·e·sis \ˌän-tə-ˈje-nə-səs\ *n, pl* **-gen·e·ses** \-ˌsēz\ : ONTOGENY

on·to·ge·net·ic \-jə-ˈne-tik\ *adj* : of, relating to, or appearing in the course of ontogeny ⟨~ variation⟩ — **on·to·ge·net·i·cal·ly** *adv*

on·tog·e·ny \än-ˈtä-jə-nē\ *n, pl* **-nies** : the development or course of development of an individual organism — called also *ontogenesis;* compare PHYLOGENY 2

onych- *or* **onycho-** *comb form* : nail of the finger or toe ⟨*onych*olysis⟩

on·ych·ec·to·my \ˌä-ni-ˈkek-tə-mē\ *n, pl* **-mies** : surgical excision of a fingernail or toenail

onych·ia \ō-ˈni-kē-ə\ *n* : inflammation of the matrix of a nail often leading to suppuration and loss of the nail

-onych·ia \ə-ˈni-kē-ə\ *n comb form* : condition of the nails of the fingers or toes ⟨leuk*onychia*⟩

-onych·i·um \ə-ˈni-kē-əm\ *n comb form* : fingernail : toenail : region of the fingernail or toenail ⟨epo*nychium*⟩

on·y·cho·gry·po·sis \ˌä-ni-kō-gri-ˈpō-səs\ *n, pl* **-po·ses** \-ˌsēz\ : an abnormal condition of the nails characterized by marked hypertrophy and increased curvature

on·y·chol·y·sis \ˌä-nə-ˈkä-lə-səs\ *n, pl* **-y·ses** \-ˌsēz\ : a loosening of a nail from the nail bed beginning at the free edge and proceeding to the root

on·y·cho·ma·de·sis \ˌä-ni-kō-mə-ˈdē-səs\ *n, pl* **-de·ses** \-ˌsēz\ : loosening and shedding of the nails

on·y·cho·my·co·sis \-mī-ˈkō-səs\ *n, pl* **-co·ses** \-ˌsēz\ : a fungal disease of the nails

oo- — see O-

oo·cy·e·sis \ˌō-ə-sī-ˈē-səs\ *n, pl* **-e·ses** \-ˌsēz\ : extrauterine pregnancy in an ovary

oo·cyst \ˈō-ə-ˌsist\ *n* : ZYGOTE; *specif* : a sporozoan zygote undergoing sporogenous development

oo·cyte \ˈō-ə-ˌsīt\ *n* : an egg before maturation : a female gametocyte

oo·gen·e·sis \ˌō-ə-ˈje-nə-səs\ *n, pl* **-e·ses** \-ˌsēz\ : formation and maturation of the egg — called also *ovogenesis*

oo·go·ni·um \ˌō-ə-ˈgō-nē-əm\ *n* : a descendant of a primordial germ cell that gives rise to oocytes — **oo·go·ni·al** \-nē-əl\ *adj*

oophor- or **oophoro-** *comb form* : ovary ⟨*oophoro*rectomy⟩

oo·pho·rec·to·my \ˌō-ə-fə-ˈrek-tə-mē\ *n, pl* **-mies** : OVARIECTOMY — **oo·pho·rec·to·mize** \-ˌmīz\ *vb*

oo·pho·ri·tis \ˌō-ə-fə-ˈrī-təs\ *n* : inflammation of one or both ovaries

oophorus — see CUMULUS OOPHORUS

oo·plasm \ˈō-ə-ˌpla-zəm\ *n* : the cytoplasm of an egg — **oo·plas·mic** \-ˈplaz-mik\ *adj*

oo·tid \ˈō-ə-ˌtid\ *n* : an egg cell after meiosis — compare SPERMATID

opac·i·fi·ca·tion \ō-ˌpa-sə-fə-ˈkā-shən\ *n* : an act or the process of becoming or rendering opaque ⟨~ of the cornea⟩ — **opac·i·fy** \ō-ˈpa-sə-ˌfī\ *vb*

opac·i·ty \ō-ˈpa-sə-tē\ *n, pl* **-ties** 1 : the quality or state of a body that makes it impervious to the rays of light; *broadly* : the relative capacity of matter to obstruct by absorption or reflection the transmission of radiant energy 2 : an opaque spot in a normally transparent structure (as the lens of the eye)

opaque \ō-ˈpāk\ *adj* : exhibiting opacity : not allowing passage of radiant energy

OPD *abbr* outpatient department

¹**open** \ˈō-pən\ *adj* 1 a : not covered, enclosed, or scabbed over b : not involving or encouraging a covering (as by bandages or overgrowth of tissue) or enclosure ⟨~ treatment of burns⟩ c : shedding the infective agent to the exterior ⟨~ tuberculosis⟩ — compare CLOSED 2 d : relating to or being a compound fracture 2 a : unobstructed by congestion ⟨~ sinuses⟩ b : not constipated ⟨~ bowels⟩ 3 : using a minimum of physical restrictions and custodial restraints on the freedom of movement of the patients or inmates

²**open** *vb* **opened; open·ing** 1 : to make available for entry or passage by removing (as a cover) or clearing away (as an obstruction); *specif* : to free (a body passage) of an occluding agent 2 : to make one or more openings in ⟨~ed the boil⟩

open–angle glaucoma *n* : a progressive form of glaucoma in which the drainage channel for the aqueous humor composed of the attachment at the edge of the iris and the junction of the sclera and cornea remains open and in which serious reduction in vision occurs only in the advanced stages of the disease due to tissue changes along the drainage channel — compare CLOSED-ANGLE GLAUCOMA

open chain *n* : an arrangement of atoms represented in a structural formula by a chain whose ends are not joined so as to form a ring

open–heart *adj* : of, relating to, or performed on a heart temporarily relieved of circulatory function and surgically opened for inspection and treatment ⟨~ surgery⟩

open reduction *n* : realignment of a fractured bone after incision into the fracture site

op·er·a·ble \ˈä-pə-rə-bəl\ *adj* 1 : fit, possible, or desirable to use 2 : likely to result in a favorable outcome upon surgical treatment — **op·er·a·bil·i·ty** \ˌä-pə-rə-ˈbi-lə-tē\ *n*

¹**op·er·ant** \ˈä-pə-rənt\ *adj* : of, relating to, or being an operant or operant conditioning ⟨~ behavior⟩ — compare RESPONDENT — **op·er·ant·ly** *adv*

²**operant** *n* : behavior that operates on the environment to produce rewarding and reinforcing effects

operant conditioning *n* : conditioning in which the desired behavior or increasingly closer approximations to it are followed by a rewarding or reinforcing stimulus — compare CLASSICAL CONDITIONING

op·er·ate \ˈä-pə-ˌrāt\ *vb* **-at·ed; -at·ing** : to perform surgery

op·er·at·ing *adj* : of, relating to, or used for operations

op·er·a·tion \ˌä-pə-ˈrā-shən\ *n* : a procedure carried out on a living body usu. with instruments esp. for the repair of damage or the restoration of health

op·er·a·tive \ˈä-pə-rə-tiv, -ˌrā-\ *adj* : of, relating to, involving, or resulting from an operation

op·er·a·tor \ˈä-pə-ˌrā-tər\ *n* 1 : one (as a dentist or surgeon) who performs surgical operations 2 : a binding site in a DNA chain at which a genetic repressor binds to inhibit the initiation of transcription of messenger RNA by one or more nearby structural genes — called also *operator gene*; compare OPERON

op·er·a·to·ry \ˈä-pə-rə-ˌtōr-ē\ *n, pl* **-ries** : a working space (as of a dentist or surgeon) : SURGERY

oper·cu·lum \ō-ˈpər-kyə-ləm\ *n, pl* **-la** \-lə\ *also* **-lums** : any of several parts of the cerebrum bordering the fissure of Sylvius and concealing the insula

operon • opium

op·er·on \'ä-pə-ˌrän\ *n* : a group of closely linked genes that produces a single messenger RNA molecule in transcription and that consists of structural genes and regulating elements (as an operator and promoter)

ophthalm- *or* **ophthalmo-** *comb form* : eye ⟨*ophthalmology*⟩ : eyeball ⟨*ophthalmo*dynamometry⟩

oph·thal·mia \äf-ˈthal-mē-ə, äp-\ *n* : inflammation of the conjunctiva or the eyeball

-oph·thal·mia \ˌäf-ˈthal-mē-ə, ˌäp-\ *n comb form* : condition of having (such) eyes ⟨micr*ophthalmia*⟩

ophthalmia neo·na·to·rum \-ˌnē-ə-nə-ˈtōr-əm\ *n* : acute inflammation of the eyes of a newborn from infection during passage through the birth canal

oph·thal·mic \äf-ˈthal-mik, äp-\ *adj* 1 : of, relating to, or situated near the eye 2 : supplying or draining the eye or structures in the region of the eye

ophthalmic artery *n* : a branch of the internal carotid artery following the optic nerve through the optic foramen into the orbit and supplying the eye and adjacent structures

ophthalmic nerve *n* : the one of the three major branches or divisions of the trigeminal nerve that supply sensory fibers to the lacrimal gland, eyelids, ciliary muscle, nose, forehead, and adjoining parts — called also *ophthalmic, ophthalmic division*; compare MANDIBULAR NERVE, MAXILLARY NERVE

ophthalmic vein *n* : either of two veins that pass from the orbit: **a** : one that begins at the inner angle of the orbit and empties into the cavernous sinus — called also *superior ophthalmic vein* **b** : one that drains a venous network in the floor and medial wall of the orbit and divides into two parts of which one joins the pterygoid plexus of veins and the other empties into the cavernous sinus — called also *inferior ophthalmic vein*

ophthalmo- — see OPHTHALM-

oph·thal·mo·dy·na·mom·e·try \äf-ˌthal-mō-ˌdī-nə-ˈmä-mə-trē, äp-\ *n, pl* **-tries** : measurement of the arterial blood pressure in the retina

oph·thal·mol·o·gist \ˌäf-thəl-ˈmä-lə-jist, ˌäp-, -thal-\ *n* : a physician who specializes in ophthalmology — compare OPTICIAN 2, OPTOMETRIST

oph·thal·mol·o·gy \-jē\ *n, pl* **-gies** : a branch of medical science dealing with the structure, functions, and diseases of the eye — **oph·thal·mo·log·ic** \-mə-ˈlä-jik\ *or* **oph·thal·mo·log·i·cal** \-ji-kəl\ *adj* — **oph·thal·mo·log·i·cal·ly** *adv*

oph·thal·mom·e·ter \-ˈmä-mə-tər\ *n* : an instrument for measuring the eye; *specif* : KERATOMETER

oph·thal·mo·ple·gia \-ˈplē-jə, -jē-ə\ *n* : paralysis of some or all of the muscles of the eye — **oph·thal·mo·ple·gic** \-jik\ *adj*

oph·thal·mo·scope \äf-ˈthal-mə-ˌskōp\ *n* : an instrument for viewing the interior of the eye consisting of a concave mirror with a hole in the center through which the observer examines the eye, a source of light that is reflected into the eye by the mirror, and lenses in the mirror which can be rotated into the opening in the mirror — **oph·thal·mo·scop·ic** \äf-ˌthal-mə-ˈskä-pik\ *adj*

oph·thal·mos·co·py \ˌäf-thal-ˈmäs-kə-pē\ *n, pl* **-pies** : examination of the eye with an ophthalmoscope

-opia \'ō-pē-ə\ *n comb form* 1 : condition of having (such) vision ⟨dipl*opia*⟩ 2 : condition of having (such) a visual defect ⟨hyper*opia*⟩

¹opi·ate \'ō-pē-ət, -ˌāt\ *n* 1 : a preparation (as morphine, heroin, and codeine) containing or derived from opium and tending to induce sleep and to alleviate pain 2 : a synthetic drug capable of producing or sustaining addiction similar to that characteristic of morphine and cocaine : a narcotic or opioid peptide — used esp. in modern law

²opiate *adj* 1 : of, relating to, or being opium or an opium derivative 2 : of, relating to, binding, or being an opiate ⟨~ receptors⟩

opin·ion \ə-ˈpin-yən\ *n* : a formal expression of judgment or advice by an expert ⟨wanted a second ~⟩

opi·oid \'ō-pē-ˌoid\ *adj* 1 : possessing some properties characteristic of opiate narcotics but not derived from opium 2 : of, involving, or induced by an opioid substance or an opioid peptide

opioid peptide *n* : any of a group of endogenous neural polypeptides (as an endorphin or enkephalin) that bind esp. to opiate receptors and mimic some of the pharmacological properties of opiates — called also *opioid*

opisth- *or* **opistho-** *comb form* : dorsal : posterior ⟨*opisthotonos*⟩

opis·thor·chi·a·sis \ə-ˌpis-thōr-ˈkī-ə-səs\ *n* : infestation with or disease caused by liver flukes of the genus *Opisthorchis*

Op·is·thor·chis \ˌä-pəs-ˈthōr-kəs\ *n* : a genus of digenetic trematode worms (family Opisthorchiidae) including several that are casual or incidental parasites of the human liver

op·is·thot·o·nos \ˌä-pəs-ˈthät-ᵊn-əs\ *n* : a condition of spasm of the muscles of the back, causing the head and lower limbs to bend backward and the trunk to arch forward

opi·um \'ō-pē-əm\ *n* : a highly addictive drug that consists of the dried milky juice from the seed capsules of the opium poppy, that is a stimulant narcotic causing coma or death if the dose is excessive, that was formerly used in medicine to soothe pain, and that is smoked as an intoxicant

opium poppy *n* : a Eurasian poppy (*Papaver somniferum*) that is the source of opium

op·po·nens \ə-'pō-nenz\ *n, pl* **-nen·tes** \ä-pə-'nen-(,)tēz\ *or* **-nens** : any of several muscles of the hand or foot that tend to draw one of the lateral digits across the palm or sole toward the others

opponens dig·i·ti min·i·mi \-'di-jə-ti-'mi-nə-,mī\ *n* : a triangular muscle of the hand that arises from the hamate and adjacent flexor retinaculum, is inserted along the ulnar side of the metacarpal of the little finger, and functions to abduct, flex, and rotate the fifth metacarpal in opposing the little finger and thumb

opponens pol·li·cis \-'pä-lə-səs\ *n* : a small triangular muscle of the hand that is located below the abductor pollicis brevis, arises from the trapezium and the flexor retinaculum of the hand, is inserted along the radial side of the metacarpal of the thumb, and functions to abduct, flex, and rotate the metacarpal of the thumb in opposing the thumb and fingers

op·po·nent \ə-'pō-nənt\ *n* : a muscle that opposes or counteracts and limits its action of another

op·por·tun·ist \,ä-pər-'tü-nist, -'tyü-\ *n* : an opportunistic microorganism

op·por·tu·nist·ic \-tü-'nis-tik, -tyü-\ *adj* **1** : of, relating to, or being a microorganism that is usu. harmless but can become pathogenic when the host's resistance to disease is impaired **2** : of, relating to, or being a disease caused by an opportunistic organism

op·pos·able \ə-'pō-zə-bəl\ *adj* : capable of being placed against one or more of the remaining digits of a hand or foot (an ~ thumb)

-op·sia \'äp-sē-ə\ *n comb form, pl* **-opsias** : vision of a (specified) kind or condition (hemian*opsia*)

op·sin \'äp-sən\ *n* : any of various colorless proteins that in combination with retinal or a related prosthetic group form a visual pigment (as rhodopsin) in a reaction which is reversed by light

op·so·nin \'äp-sə-nən\ *n* : an antibody of blood serum that makes foreign cells more susceptible to the action of the phagocytes — **op·son·ic** \äp-'sä-nik\ *adj*

op·son·iza·tion \,äp-sə-nə-'zā-shən, -,nī-'zā-\ *n* : the process of modifying (as a bacterium) by the action of opsonins — **op·son·ize** \'äp-sə-,nīz\ *vb*

-op·sy \,äp-sē, əp-\ *n comb form, pl* **-opsies** : examination (biopsy) (necropsy)

opt *abbr* optical

¹op·tic \'äp-tik\ *adj* **1** : of or relating to vision (~ phenomena) **2 a** : of or relating to the eye : OCULAR **b** : affecting the eye or an optic structure

²optic *n* : any of the lenses, prisms, or mirrors of an optical instrument

op·ti·cal \'äp-ti-kəl\ *adj* **1** : of or relating to the science of optics **2 a** : of or relating to vision : VISUAL **b** : designed to aid vision **3** : of, relating to, or utilizing light (~ microscopy) — **op·ti·cal·ly** *adv*

optical activity *n* : ability to rotate the plane of vibration of polarized light to the right or left

optical axis *n* : a straight line perpendicular to the front of the cornea of the eye and extending through the center of the pupil — called also *optic axis*

optical illusion *n* : visual perception of a real object in such a way as to misinterpret its actual nature

optically active *adj* : capable of rotating the plane of vibration of polarized light to the right or left : either dextrorotatory or levorotatory — used of compounds, molecules, or atoms

optic atrophy *n* : degeneration of the optic nerve

optic axis *n* : OPTICAL AXIS

optic canal *n* : OPTIC FORAMEN

optic chiasma *n* : the X-shaped partial decussation on the undersurface of the hypothalamus through which the optic nerves are continuous with the brain — called also *optic chiasm*

optic cup *n* : the optic vesicle after invaginating to form a 2-layered cup from which the retina and pigmented layer of the eye will develop — called also *eyecup*

optic disk *n* : BLIND SPOT

optic foramen *n* : the passage through the orbit of the eye in the lesser wing of the sphenoid bone that is traversed by the optic nerve and ophthalmic artery — called also *optic canal;* see CHIASMATIC GROOVE

op·ti·cian \äp-'ti-shən\ *n* **1** : a maker of or dealer in optical items and instruments **2** : a person who reads prescriptions for visual correction, orders lenses, and dispenses eyeglasses and contact lenses — compare OPHTHALMOLOGIST, OPTOMETRIST

op·ti·cian·ry \-rē\ *n, pl* **-ries** : the profession or practice of an optician

optic lobe *n* : SUPERIOR COLLICULUS

optic nerve *n* : either of the pair of sensory nerves that comprise the second pair of cranial nerves, arise from the ventral part of the diencephalon, form an optic chiasma before passing to the eye and spreading over the anterior surface of the retina, and conduct visual stimuli to the brain — called also *second cranial nerve*

op·tics \'äp-tiks\ *n sing or pl* **1** : a science that deals with the nature and properties of light **2** : optical properties

optic stalk *n* : the constricted part of the optic vesicle by which it remains continuous with the embryonic forebrain

optic tectum *n* : SUPERIOR COLLICULUS

optic tract *n* : the portion of each optic nerve between the optic chiasma and the diencephalon proper

optic vesicle *n* : an evagination of each lateral wall of the embryonic vertebrate forebrain from which the nervous structures of the eye develop

opto- *comb form* **1** : vision (*optometry*) **2** : optic : optic and (*optokinetic*)

op·to·ki·net·ic \ˌäp-tō-kə-ˈne-tik, -ˌkī-\ *adj* : of, relating to, or involving movements of the eyes (∼ nystagmus)

op·tom·e·trist \äp-ˈtä-mə-trist\ *n* : a specialist licensed to practice optometry — compare OPHTHALMOLOGIST, OPTICIAN 2

op·tom·e·try \-trē\ *n, pl* **-tries** : the art or profession of examining the eye for defects and faults of refraction and prescribing corrective lenses or exercises but not drugs or surgery — **op·to·met·ric** \ˌäp-tə-ˈme-trik\ *adj*

OPV *abbr* oral polio vaccine

OR *abbr* operating room

ora *pl of* [2]OS

orad \ˈōr-ˌad\ *adv* : toward the mouth or oral region

orae serratae *pl of* ORA SERRATA

oral \ˈōr-əl, ˈär-\ *adj* **1 a** : of, relating to, or involving the mouth : BUCCAL (the ∼ mucous membrane) **b** : given or taken through or by way of the mouth (∼ contraceptives) **c** : acting on the mouth **2 a** : of, relating to, or characterized by the first stage of psychosexual development in psychoanalytic theory during which libidinal gratification is derived from intake (as of food), by sucking, and later by biting **b** : of, relating to, or characterized by personality traits of passive dependence and aggressiveness — compare ANAL 2, GENITAL 3, PHALLIC 2 — **oral·ly** *adv*

oral cavity *n* : the cavity of the mouth; *esp* : the part of the mouth behind the gums and teeth that is bounded above by the hard and soft palates and below by the tongue and by the mucous membrane connecting it with the inner part of the mandible

oral sex *n* : oral stimulation of the genitals : CUNNILINGUS : FELLATIO

oral surgeon *n* : a specialist in oral surgery

oral surgery *n* **1** : a branch of dentistry that deals with the diagnosis and treatment of oral conditions requiring surgical intervention **2** : a branch of surgery that deals with conditions of the jaws and mouth structures requiring surgery

ora ser·ra·ta \ˌōr-ə-sə-ˈrä-tə, -ˈrä-\ *n, pl* **orae ser·ra·tae** \ˌōr-ē-sə-ˈrä-tē\ : the dentate border of the retina

or·bi·cu·lar·is oculi \ˌòr-ə-sə-ˈä-kyə-ˈlar-əs-ˈä-kyü-ˌlī-,-ˌlē\ *n, pl* **or·bi·cu·lar·es**

oculi \-ˈlar-(ˌ)ēz-\ : the muscle encircling the opening of the orbit and functioning to close the eyelids

or·bic·u·lar·is oris \-ˈôr-əs, *n, pl* **orbicu·lar·es oris** : a muscle made up of several layers of fibers passing in different directions that encircles the mouth and controls most movements of the lips

or·bic·u·lus cil·i·ar·is \-ˌsi-lē-ˈer-əs\ *n* : a circular tract in the eye that extends from the ora serrata forward to the posterior part of the ciliary processes — called also *ciliary ring, pars plana*

or·bit \ˈòr-bət\ *n* : the bony cavity perforated for the passage of nerves and blood vessels that occupies the lateral front of the skull immediately beneath the frontal bone on each side and encloses and protects the eye and its appendages — called also *eye socket, orbital cavity* — **or·bit·al** \-ˀl\ *adj*

orbital fissure *n* : either of two openings transmitting nerves and blood vessels to or from the orbit: **a** : one situated superiorly between the greater wing and the lesser wing of the sphenoid bone — called also *superior orbital fissure, supraorbital fissure* **b** : one situated inferiorly between the greater wing of the sphenoid bone and the maxilla — called also *inferior orbital fissure, infraorbital fissure, sphenomaxillary fissure*

orbital plate *n* **1** : the part of the frontal bone forming most of the top of the orbit **2** : a thin plate of bone forming the lateral wall enclosing the ethmoidal air cells and forming part of the side of the orbit next to the nose

or·bi·tot·o·my \ˌòr-bə-ˈtä-tə-mē\ *n, pl* **-mies** : incision of the orbit

or·bi·vi·rus \ˈòr-bi-ˌvī-rəs\ *n* : any of a group of reoviruses that include the causative agents of Colorado tick fever and bluetongue of sheep

or·chi·dec·to·my \ˌòr-kə-ˈdek-tə-mē\ *n, pl* **-mies** : ORCHIECTOMY

-or·chi·dism \ˈòr-kə-ˌdi-zəm\ *also* **-or·chism** \ˈòr-ˌki-zəm\ *n comb form* : a (specified) form or condition of the testes (cryptorchidism)

or·chi·do·pexy \ˈòr-kə-dō-ˌpek-sē\ *n, pl* **-pex·ies** : surgical fixation of a testis — called also *orchiopexy*

or·chi·ec·to·my \ˌòr-kē-ˈek-tə-mē\ *n, pl* **-mies** : surgical excision of a testis or of both testes — called also *orchidectomy*

or·chi·o·pexy \ˈòr-kē-ō-ˌpek-sē\ *n, pl* **-pex·ies** : ORCHIDOPEXY

or·chi·tis \òr-ˈkī-təs\ *n* : inflammation of a testis — **or·chit·ic** \òr-ˈki-tik\ *adj*

[1]**or·der** \ˈòr-dər\ *vb* **or·dered; or·der·ing** : to give a prescription for : PRESCRIBE

[2]**order** *n* : a category of taxonomic classification ranking above the family and below the class

or·der·ly \-lē\ *n, pl* **-lies** : a hospital attendant who does routine or heavy work (as cleaning, carrying supplies, or moving patients)

Oret·ic \ȯr-ˈe-tik\ *trademark* — used for a preparation of hydrochlorothiazide

-o·rex·ia \ə-ˈrek-sē-ə, ə-ˈrek-shə\ *n comb form* : appetite ⟨ano*rexia*⟩

or·gan \ˈȯr-gən\ *n* : a differentiated structure (as a heart or kidney) consisting of cells and tissues and performing some specific function in an organism

organ- *or* **organo-** *comb form* 1 : organ ⟨*organelle*⟩ ⟨*organogenesis*⟩ 2 : organic ⟨*organo*phosphorus⟩

or·gan·elle \ˌȯr-gə-ˈnel\ *n* : a specialized cellular part (as a mitochondrion, lysosome, or ribosome) that is analogous to an organ

or·gan·ic \ȯr-ˈga-nik\ *adj* 1 a : of, relating to, or arising in a bodily organ b : affecting the structure of the organism ⟨an ~ disease⟩ — compare FUNCTIONAL 1b 2 a : of, relating to, or derived from living organisms b (1) : of, relating to, or containing carbon compounds (2) : relating to, being, or dealt with by a branch of chemistry concerned with the carbon compounds of living beings and most other carbon compounds — **or·gan·i·cal·ly** *adv*

organic brain syndrome *n* : any mental disorder (as senile dementia) resulting from or associated with organic changes in brain tissue — called also *organic brain disorder, organic mental syndrome*

or·gan·ism \ˈȯr-gə-ˌni-zəm\ *n* : an individual constituted to carry on the activities of life by means of organs separate in function but mutually dependent : a living being — **or·gan·is·mic** \ˌȯr-gə-ˈniz-mik\ *also* **or·gan·is·mal** \-məl\ *adj* — **or·gan·is·mi·cal·ly** *adv*

or·ga·ni·za·tion \ˌȯr-gə-nə-ˈzā-shən\ *n* : the formation of fibrous tissue from a clot or exudate by invasion of connective tissue cells and capillaries from adjoining tissues — **or·ga·nize** \ˈȯr-gə-ˌnīz\ *vb*

or·ga·niz·er \ˈȯr-gə-ˌnī-zər\ *n* : a region of a developing embryo (as part of the dorsal lip of the blastopore) or a substance produced by such a region that is capable of inducing a specific type of development in undifferentiated tissue — called also *inductor*

organo- — see ORGAN-

or·gano·chlo·rine \ˌȯr-ˌga-nə-ˈklȯr-ˌēn, -ən\ *adj* : of, relating to, or belonging to the chlorinated hydrocarbon pesticides (as aldrin, DDT, or dieldrin) — **organochlorine** *n*

organ of Cor·ti \-ˈkȯr-tē\ *n* : a complex epithelial structure in the cochlea that in mammals is the chief part of the ear by which sound is directly perceived

Corti, Alfonso Giacomo Gaspare (1822–1876), Italian anatomist.

organ of Ro·sen·mül·ler \-ˈrō-zən-ˌmyü-lər\ *n* : EPOOPHORON

Rosenmüller, Johann Christian (1771–1820), German anatomist.

or·gano·gen·e·sis \ˌȯr-gə-nō-ˈje-nə-səs, ȯr-ˌga-nə-\ *n, pl* **-e·ses** \-ˌsēz\ : the origin and development of bodily organs — compare MORPHOGENESIS — **or·gano·ge·net·ic** \-jə-ˈne-tik\ *adj*

or·gan·oid \ˈȯr-gə-ˌnȯid\ *adj* : resembling an organ in structural appearance or qualities — used esp. of abnormal masses (as tumors)

or·gan·o·lep·tic \ˌȯr-gə-nō-ˈlep-tik, ȯr-ˌga-nə-\ *adj* 1 : being, affecting, or relating to qualities (as taste, color, and odor) of a substance (as a food) that stimulate the sense organs 2 : involving use of the sense organs

or·gan·ol·o·gy \ˌȯr-gə-ˈnä-lə-jē\ *n, pl* **-gies** : the study of the organs of plants and animals

or·gano·mer·cu·ri·al \ȯr-ˌga-nō-(ˌ)mər-ˈkyùr-ē-əl\ *n* : an organic compound or a pharmaceutical preparation containing mercury — **organomercurial** *adj*

or·gano·phos·phate \ȯr-ˌga-nə-ˈfäs-ˌfāt\ *n* : an organophosphorus pesticide — **organophosphate** *adj*

or·gano·phos·pho·rus \-ˈfäs-fə-rəs\ *also* **or·gano·phos·pho·rous** \-fäs-ˈfȯr-əs\ *adj* : of, relating to, or being a phosphorus-containing organic pesticide (as malathion) that acts by inhibiting cholinesterase — **organophosphorus** *n*

or·gasm \ˈȯr-ˌga-zəm\ *n* : the climax of sexual excitement that is usu. accompanied in the male by ejaculation — **or·gas·mic** \ȯr-ˈgaz-mik\ *also* **or·gas·tic** \-ˈgas-tik\ *adj*

ori- *comb form* : mouth ⟨*orifice*⟩

ori·ent \ˈȯr-ē-ˌent\ *vb* : to acquaint with or adjust according to the existing situation or environment

oriental rat flea *n* : a flea of the genus *Xenopsylla* (*X. cheopis*) that is widely distributed on rodents and is a vector of plague

oriental sore *n* : a skin disease caused by a protozoan of the genus *Leishmania* (*L. tropica*) that is marked by persistent granulomatous and ulcerating lesions and occurs widely in Asia and in tropical regions

ori·en·ta·tion \ˌȯr-ē-ən-ˈtā-shən, -ˌen-\ *n* 1 a : the act or process of orienting or of being oriented b : the state of being oriented 2 : change of position by organs, organelles, or organisms in response to external stimulus 3 : awareness of the existing situation with reference to time, place, and identity of persons — **ori·en·ta·tion·al** \-shə-nəl\ *adj*

oriented *adj* : having psychological orientation ⟨the patient was alert and ~⟩

or·i·fice \ˈȯr-ə-fəs, ˈär-\ *n* : an opening

through which something may pass — **ori•fi•cial** \ˌȯr-ə-ˈfi-shəl, ˌär-\ *adj*

or•i•gin \ˈȯr-ə-jən, ˈär-\ *n* **1** : the point at which something begins or rises or from which it derives **2** : the more fixed, central, or larger attachment of a muscle — compare INSERTION 1

oris — see CANCRUM ORIS, LEVATOR ANGULI ORIS, ORBICULARIS ORIS

Or•mond's disease \ˈȯr-ˌmändz-\ *n* : RETROPERITONEAL FIBROSIS

Ormond, John Kelso (b 1886), American urologist.

or•ni•thine \ˈȯr-nə-ˌthēn\ *n* : a crystalline amino acid $C_5H_{12}N_2O_2$ that functions esp. in urea production

Or•ni•thod•o•ros \ˌȯr-nə-ˈthä-də-rəs\ *n* : a genus of ticks (family Argasidae) containing forms that act as carriers of relapsing fever as well as Q fever

or•ni•tho•sis \ˌȯr-nə-ˈthō-səs\ *n, pl* **-tho•ses** \-ˌsēz\ : PSITTACOSIS; *esp* : a form of the disease occurring in or originating in birds (as the turkeys and pigeons) that do not belong to the family (Psittacidae) containing the parrots

oro- *comb form* **1** : mouth (*oropharynx*) **2** : oral and (*orofacial*) (*oronasal*)

oro•an•tral \ˌȯr-ō-ˈan-trəl\ *adj* : of, relating to, or connecting the mouth and the maxillary sinus

oro•fa•cial \-ˈfā-shəl\ *adj* : of or relating to the mouth and face

oro•na•sal \-ˈnā-zəl\ *adj* : of or relating to the mouth and nose; *esp* : connecting the mouth and the nasal cavity

oro•pha•ryn•geal \-ˌfar-ən-ˈjē-əl, -fə-ˈrin-jəl, -jē-əl\ *adj* **1** : of or relating to the oropharynx **2** : of or relating to the mouth and pharynx

oropharyngeal airway *n* : a tube used to provide free passage of air between the mouth and pharynx of an unconscious person

oro•phar•ynx \-ˈfar-iŋks\ *n, pl* **-pha•ryn•ges** \-fə-ˈrin-(ˌ)jēz\ *also* **-phar•ynx•es** : the part of the pharynx that is below the soft palate and above the epiglottis and is continuous with the mouth

oro•so•mu•coid \ˌȯr-ə-sō-ˈmyü-ˌkȯid\ *n* : a plasma glycoprotein believed to be associated with inflammation

oro•tra•che•al \ˌȯr-ō-ˈtrā-kē-əl\ *adj* : relating to or being intubation of the trachea by way of the mouth

Oroya fever \ȯr-ˈȯi-ə-\ *n* : the acute first stage of bartonellosis characterized by high fever and severe anemia

orphan drug *n* : a drug that is not developed or marketed because its extremely limited use (as in the treatment of a rare disease) makes it unprofitable

or•phen•a•drine \ȯr-ˈfe-nə-drən, -ˌdrēn\ *n* : a drug $C_{18}H_{23}NO$ used in the form of the citrate and the hydrochloride as a muscle relaxant and antispasmodic

orth- *or* **ortho-** *comb form* : correct : corrective (*orthodontia*)

or•tho•caine \ˈȯr-thə-ˌkān\ *n* : a white crystalline powder $C_8H_9NO_3$ used as a local anesthetic

or•tho•chro•mat•ic \ˌȯr-thə-krō-ˈma-tik\ *adj* : staining in the normal way (~ tissue) (an ~ erythroblast)

orth•odon•tia \ˌȯr-thə-ˈdän-chə, -chē-ə\ *n* : ORTHODONTICS

orth•odon•tics \-ˈdän-tiks\ *n* : a branch of dentistry dealing with irregularities of the teeth and their correction (as by means of braces) — **orth•odon•tic** \-tik\ *adj* — **or•tho•don•ti•cal•ly** *adv*

orth•odon•tist \ˌȯr-thə-ˈdän-tist\ *n* : a specialist in orthodontics

orthodox sleep *n* : SLOW-WAVE SLEEP

or•tho•drom•ic \ˌȯr-thə-ˈdrä-mik\ *adj* : of, relating to, or inducing nerve impulses along an axon in the normal direction

or•thog•nath•ic \ˌȯr-thag-ˈna-thik, -ˌthäg-\ *adj* : correcting deformities of the jaw and the associated malocclusion (~ surgery)

or•tho•my•xo•vi•rus \ˌȯr-thō-ˈmik-sə-ˌvī-rəs\ *n* : any of a group of RNA-containing viruses that cause influenza and are smaller than the related paramyxoviruses

or•tho•pae•dic, or•tho•pae•dics, or•tho•pae•dist *chiefly Brit var of* ORTHOPEDIC, ORTHOPEDICS, ORTHOPEDIST

or•tho•pe•dic \ˌȯr-thə-ˈpē-dik\ *adj* **1** : of, relating to, or employed in orthopedics **2** : marked by deformities or crippling — **or•tho•pe•di•cal•ly** *adv*

or•tho•pe•dics \-ˈpē-diks\ *n sing or pl* : a branch of medicine concerned with the correction or prevention of skeletal deformities

or•tho•pe•dist \-ˈpē-dist\ *n* : one who practices orthopedics

or•tho•phos•phor•ic acid \ˌȯr-thə-fäs-ˈfȯr-ik-, -ˌfär-; -ˌfäs-fə-rik-\ *n* : PHOSPHORIC ACID 1

or•thop•nea \ȯr-ˈthäp-nē-ə, ˌȯr-ˌthäp-ˈnē-ə\ *n* : inability to breathe except in an upright position (as in congestive heart failure) — **or•thop•ne•ic** \-ik\ *adj*

or•thop•noea *chiefly Brit var of* ORTHOPNEA

or•tho•psy•chi•a•trist \ˌȯr-thə-sə-ˈkī-ə-trəst, -(ˌ)sī-\ *n* : a specialist in orthopsychiatry

or•tho•psy•chi•a•try \-sə-ˈkī-ə-trē, -(ˌ)sī-\ *n, pl* **-tries** : prophylactic psychiatry concerned esp. with incipient mental and behavioral disorders in youth — **or•tho•psy•chi•at•ric** \-ˌsī-kē-ˈa-trik\ *adj*

or•thop•tics \ȯr-ˈthäp-tiks\ *n sing or pl* : the treatment or the art of treating defective visual habits, defects of binocular vision, and muscle imbalance (as strabismus) by reeducation of visual habits, exercise, and visual training — **or•thop•tic** \-tik\ *adj*

or•thop•tist \-tist\ *n* : a person who is

trained in or practices orthoptics

or·tho·sis \or-ˈthō-səs\ *n, pl* **or·tho·ses** \-ˌsēz\ : ORTHOTIC

or·tho·stat·ic \ˌor-thə-ˈsta-tik\ *adj* : of, relating to, or caused by erect posture ⟨~ hypotension⟩

orthostatic albuminuria *n* : albuminuria that occurs only when a person is in an upright position

¹**or·thot·ic** \or-ˈthä-tik\ *adj* **1** : of or relating to orthotics **2** : designed for the support of weak or ineffective joints or muscles ⟨~ devices⟩

²**orthotic** *n* : a support or brace for weak or ineffective joints or muscles — called also *orthosis*

or·thot·ics \-tiks\ *n* : a branch of mechanical and medical science that deals with the support and bracing of weak or ineffective joints or muscles

or·thot·ist \-tist\ *n* : a person who practices orthotics

or·tho·top·ic \ˌor-thə-ˈtä-pik\ *adj* : of or relating to the grafting of tissue in a natural position ⟨~ transplant⟩ — **or·tho·top·i·cal·ly** *adv*

or·tho·volt·age \ˈor-thō-ˌvōl-tij\ *n* : X-ray voltage of about 150 to 500 kilovolts

¹**os** \ˈäs\ *n, pl* **os·sa** \ˈä-sə\ : BONE

²**os** \ˈäs\ *n, pl* **ora** \ˈōr-ə\ : ORIFICE

Os *symbol* osmium

OS *abbr* [Latin *oculus sinister*] left eye — used in writing prescriptions

os cal·cis \ˈkal-səs\ *n, pl* **ossa calcis** : CALCANEUS

os·cil·late \ˈä-sə-ˌlāt\ *vb* **-lat·ed; -lat·ing 1** : to swing backward and forward like a pendulum **2** : to move or travel back and forth between two points — **os·cil·la·tion** \ˌä-sə-ˈlā-shən\ *n* — **os·cil·la·tor** \ˈä-sə-ˌlā-tər\ *n* — **os·cil·la·to·ry** \ˈä-sə-lə-ˌtōr-ē\ *adj*

os·cil·lo·scope \ä-ˈsi-lə-ˌskōp, ə-\ *n* : an instrument in which the variations in a fluctuating electrical quantity appear temporarily as a visible waveform on the fluorescent screen of a cathode-ray tube — called also *cathode-ray oscilloscope* — **os·cil·lo·scop·ic** \ä-ˌsi-lə-ˈskä-pik, ˌä-sə-lə-\ *adj*

os cox·ae \-ˈkäk-ˌsē\ *n, pl* **ossa coxae** : HIPBONE

-ose \ˌōs\ *n suffix* : carbohydrate; *esp* : sugar ⟨fructose⟩ ⟨pentose⟩

Os·good–Schlat·ter's disease \ˈäz-ˌgud-ˈshlä-tərz-\ *n* : an osteochondritis of the tuberosity of the tibia that occurs esp. among adolescent males

Osgood, Robert Bayley (1873–1956), American orthopedic surgeon.

Schlatter, Carl (1864–1934), Swiss surgeon.

-o·side \ə-ˌsīd\ *n suffix* : glycoside or similar compound ⟨ganglioside⟩

-o·sis \ˈō-səs\ *n suffix, pl* **-o·ses** \ˈō-ˌsēz\ *or* **-o·sis·es 1 a** : action : process : condition ⟨hypnosis⟩ **b** : abnormal or diseased condition ⟨leukosis⟩ **2** : increase : formation ⟨leukocytosis⟩

os·mic acid \ˈäz-mik-\ *n* : OSMIUM TETROXIDE

os·mi·um \ˈäz-mē-əm\ *n* : a hard brittle blue-gray or blue-black polyvalent metallic element — symbol *Os;* see ELEMENT table

osmium tetroxide *n* : a crystalline compound OsO_4 that is an oxide of osmium used as a biological fixative and stain (as for fatty substances in cytology)

osmo- *comb form* : osmosis : osmotic ⟨osmoregulation⟩

os·mol *or* **os·mole** \ˈäz-ˌmōl, ˈäs-\ *n* : a standard unit of osmotic pressure based on a one molal concentration of an ion in a solution

os·mo·lal·i·ty \ˌäz-mō-ˈla-lə-tē, ˌäs-\ *n, pl* **-ties** : the concentration of an osmotic solution esp. when measured in osmols or milliosmols per 1000 grams of solvent — **os·mo·lal** \äz-ˈmō-ləl, äs-\ *adj*

os·mo·lar·i·ty \ˌäz-mō-ˈlar-ə-tē, ˌäs-\ *n, pl* **-ties** : the concentration of an osmotic solution esp. when measured in osmols or milliosmols per liter of solution — **os·mo·lar** \äz-ˈmō-lər, äs-\ *adj*

os·mo·re·cep·tor \ˌäz-mō-ri-ˈsep-tər\ *n* : any of a group of cells sensitive to plasma osmolality that are held to exist in the brain and to regulate water balance in the body by controlling thirst and the release of vasopressin

os·mo·reg·u·la·to·ry \-ˈre-gyə-lə-ˌtōr-ē\ *adj* : of, relating to, or concerned with the maintenance of constant osmotic pressure — **os·mo·reg·u·la·tion** \ˌäz-mō-ˌre-gyə-ˈlā-shən, ˌäs-\ *n*

os·mo·sis \äz-ˈmō-səs, äs-\ *n, pl* **os·mo·ses** \-ˌsēz\ : movement of a solvent through a semipermeable membrane (as of a living cell) into a solution of higher solute concentration that tends to equalize the concentrations of solute on the two sides of the membrane — **os·mot·ic** \-ˈmä-tik\ *adj* — **os·mot·i·cal·ly** *adv*

osmotic pressure *n* : the pressure produced by or associated with osmosis and dependent on molar concentration and absolute temperature: as **a** : the maximum pressure that develops in a solution separated from a solvent by a membrane permeable only to the solvent **b** : the pressure that must be applied to a solution to just prevent osmosis

ossa *pl of* ¹OS

os·se·ous \ˈä-sē-əs\ *adj* : of, relating to, or composed of bone — **os·se·ous·ly** *adv*

osseous labyrinth *n* : BONY LABYRINTH

ossi- *comb form* : bone ⟨ossify⟩

os·si·cle \ˈä-si-kəl\ *n* : a small bone or bony structure; *esp* : any of three small bones of the middle ear including the malleus, incus, and stapes — **os·sic·u·lar** \ä-ˈsi-kyə-lər\ *adj*

ossificans — see MYOSITIS OSSIFICANS

os·si·fi·ca·tion \ˌä-sə-fə-ˈkā-shən\ *n* **1 a** : the process of bone formation usu. beginning at particular centers in each prospective bone and involving the activities of special osteoblasts that segregate and deposit inorganic bone substance about themselves — compare CALCIFICATION a **b** : an instance of this process **2 a** : the condition of being altered into a hard bony substance (∼ of the muscular tissue) **b** : a mass or particle of ossified tissue ; a calcareous deposit in the tissues (∼s in the aortic wall) — **os·si·fy** \ˈä-sə-ˌfī\ *vb*

ossium — see FRAGILITAS OSSIUM

oste- *or* **osteo-** *comb form* : bone (*osteal*) (*osteomyelitis*)

os·te·al \ˈäs-tē-əl\ *adj* : of, relating to, or resembling bone; *also* : affecting or involving bone or the skeleton

os·te·ec·to·my \ˌäs-tē-ˈek-tə-mē\ *n, pl* **-mies** : surgical removal of all or part of a bone

os·te·itis \ˌäs-tē-ˈī-təs\ *n, pl* **-it·i·des** \-ˈi-tə-ˌdēz\ : inflammation of bone — called also *ostitis* — **os·te·it·ic** \-ˈi-tik\ *adj*

osteitis de·for·mans \-di-ˈfȯr-ˌmanz\ *n* : PAGET'S DISEASE 2

osteitis fi·bro·sa \-fī-ˈbrō-sə\ *n* : a disease of bone that is characterized by fibrous degeneration of the bone and the formation of cystic cavities and that results in deformities of the affected bones and sometimes in fracture — called also *osteodystrophia fibrosa*

osteitis fibrosa cys·ti·ca \-ˈsis-tə-kə\ *n* : OSTEITIS FIBROSA

osteitis fibrosa cystica gen·er·al·is·ta \-ˌje-nə-rə-ˈlis-tə\ *n* : OSTEITIS FIBROSA

os·teo·ar·thri·tis \ˌäs-tē-ō-är-ˈthrī-təs\ *n, pl* **-thrit·i·des** \-ˈthri-tə-ˌdēz\ : arthritis of middle age characterized by degenerative and sometimes hypertrophic changes in the bone and cartilage of one or more joints and a progressive wearing down of apposing joint surfaces with consequent distortion of joint position usu. without bony stiffening — called also *degenerative arthritis*, *degenerative joint disease*, *hypertrophic arthritis*; compare RHEUMATOID ARTHRITIS — **os·teo·ar·thrit·ic** \-ˈthri-tik\ *adj*

os·teo·ar·throp·a·thy \-är-ˈthrä-pə-thē\ *n, pl* **-thies** : a disease of joints or bones; *specif* : a condition marked by enlargement of the terminal phalanges, thickening of the joint surfaces, and curving of the nails and sometimes associated with chronic disease of the lungs — called also *acropachy*

os·teo·ar·thro·sis \-är-ˈthrō-sis\ *n* : OSTEOARTHRITIS — **os·teo·ar·throt·ic** \-ˈthrä-tik\ *adj*

os·teo·ar·tic·u·lar \-är-ˈti-kyə-lər\ *adj* : relating to, involving, or affecting bones and joints (∼ diseases)

os·teo·blast \ˈäs-tē-ə-ˌblast\ *n* : a bone-forming cell

os·teo·blas·tic \ˌäs-tē-ə-ˈblas-tik\ *adj* **1** : relating to or involving the formation of bone **2** : composed of or being osteoblasts

os·teo·blas·to·ma \-bla-ˈstō-mə\ *n, pl* **-mas** *or* **-ma·ta** \-mə-tə\ : a benign tumor of bone

os·teo·car·ti·lag·i·nous \-ˌkärt-ə-ˈla-jə-nəs\ *adj* : relating to or composed of bone and cartilage (an ∼ nodule)

osteochondr- *or* **osteochondro-** *comb form* : bone and cartilage (*osteochondritis*)

os·teo·chon·dral \-ˈkän-drəl\ *adj* : relating to or composed of bone and cartilage

os·teo·chon·dri·tis \-kän-ˈdrī-təs\ *n* : inflammation of bone and cartilage

osteochondritis dis·se·cans \-ˈdi-sə-ˌkanz\ *n* : partial or complete detachment of a fragment of bone and cartilage at a joint

os·teo·chon·dro·dys·pla·sia \-ˌkän-drō-ˌdis-ˈplā-zhə, -zhē-ə\ *n* : abnormal growth or development of cartilage and bone

os·teo·chon·dro·ma \-ˌkän-ˈdrō-mə\ *n, pl* **-mas** *or* **-ma·ta** \-mə-tə\ : a benign tumor containing both bone and cartilage and usu. occurring near the end of a long bone

os·teo·chon·dro·sis \-ˌkän-ˈdrō-səs\ *n, pl* **-dro·ses** \-ˌsēz\ : a disease esp. of children and young animals in which an ossification center esp. in the epiphyses of long bones undergoes degeneration followed by calcification — **os·teo·chon·drot·ic** \-ˈdrä-tik\ *adj*

os·teo·clast \ˈäs-tē-ə-ˌklast\ *n* : any of the large multinucleate cells closely associated with areas of bone resorption (as in a fracture that is healing) — compare CHONDROCLAST — **os·teo·clas·tic** \ˌäs-tē-ə-ˈklas-tik\ *adj*

os·teo·clas·to·ma \ˌäs-tē-ō-kla-ˈstō-mə\ *n, pl* **-mas** *or* **-ma·ta** \-mə-tə\ : GIANT-CELL TUMOR

os·teo·cyte \ˈäs-tē-ə-ˌsīt\ *n* : a cell that is characteristic of adult bone and is isolated in a lacuna of the bone substance

os·teo·dys·tro·phia fi·bro·sa \ˌäs-tē-ō-di-ˈstrō-fē-ə-fī-ˈbrō-sə\ *n* : OSTEITIS FIBROSA

os·teo·dys·tro·phy \-ˈdis-trə-fē\ *n, pl* **-phies** : defective ossification of bone usu. associated with disturbed calcium and phosphorus metabolism

os·teo·gen·e·sis \ˌäs-tē-ə-ˈje-nə-səs\ *n, pl* **-e·ses** \-ˌsēz\ : development and formation of bone

osteogenesis im·per·fec·ta \-ˌim-pər-ˈfek-tə\ *n* : a hereditary disease marked by extreme brittleness of the long bones and a bluish color of the whites of the eyes — called also *fragilitas ossium*, *osteopsathyrosis*

osteogenesis imperfecta con·gen·i·ta

\-kən-ˈje-nə-tə\ *n* : a severe and often fatal form of osteogenesis imperfecta characterized by usu. multiple fractures in utero

osteogenesis imperfecta tar·da \-ˈtär-də\ *n* : a less severe form of osteogenesis imperfecta which is not apparent at birth

os·teo·gen·ic \ˌäs-tē-ə-ˈje-nik\ *also* **os·teo·ge·net·ic** \-jə-ˈne-tik\ *adj* **1** : of, relating to, or functioning in osteogenesis; *esp* : producing bone **2** : originating in bone

osteogenic sarcoma *n* : OSTEOSARCOMA

¹**os·te·oid** \ˈäs-tē-ˌoid\ *adj* : resembling bone (~ tissue)

²**osteoid** *n* : uncalcified bone matrix

osteoid osteoma *n* : a small benign painful tumor of bony tissue occurring esp. in the extremities of children and young adults

os·te·ol·o·gy \ˌäs-tē-ˈä-lə-jē\ *n, pl* **-gies 1** : a branch of anatomy dealing with the bones **2** : the bony structure of an organism — **os·te·o·log·i·cal** \ˌäs-tē-ə-ˈlä-ji-kəl\ *adj* — **os·te·ol·o·gist** \ˌäs-tē-ˈä-lə-jist\ *n*

os·te·ol·y·sis \ˌäs-tē-ˈä-lə-səs\ *n, pl* **-y·ses** \-ˌsēz\ : dissolution of bone esp. when associated with resorption — **os·te·o·lyt·ic** \ˌäs-tē-ə-ˈli-tik\ *adj*

os·te·o·ma \ˌäs-tē-ˈō-mə\ *n, pl* **-mas** *or* **-ma·ta** \-mə-tə\ : a benign tumor composed of bone tissue

os·teo·ma·la·cia \ˌäs-tē-ō-mə-ˈlā-shə, -shē-ə\ *n* : a disease of adults that is characterized by softening of the bones and is analogous to rickets in the immature — **os·teo·ma·la·cic** \-ˈlā-sik\ *adj*

os·teo·my·eli·tis \-ˌmī-ə-ˈlī-təs\ *n, pl* **-eli·ti·des** \-ə-ˈli-tə-ˌdēz\ : an infectious inflammatory disease of bone often of bacterial origin that is marked by local death and separation of tissue — **os·teo·my·elit·ic** \-ˈli-tik\ *adj*

os·te·on \ˈäs-tē-ˌän\ *n* : HAVERSIAN SYSTEM — **os·te·on·al** \ˌäs-tē-ˈän-əl, -ˈōn-\ *adj*

os·teo·ne·cro·sis \ˌäs-tē-ō-nə-ˈkrō-səs\ *n, pl* **-cro·ses** \-ˌsēz\ : necrosis of bone

os·teo·path \ˈäs-tē-ə-ˌpath\ *n* : a practitioner of osteopathy

os·te·op·a·thy \ˌäs-tē-ˈä-pə-thē\ *n, pl* **-thies 1** : a disease of bone **2** : a system of medical practice based on a theory that diseases are due chiefly to loss of structural integrity which can be restored by manipulation of the parts supplemented by therapeutic measures (as use of medicine or surgery) — **os·teo·path·ic** \ˌäs-tē-ə-ˈpa-thik\ *adj* — **os·teo·path·i·cal·ly** *adv*

os·teo·pe·nia \ˌäs-tē-ō-ˈpē-nē-ə\ *n* : reduction in bone volume to below normal levels esp. due to inadequate replacement of bone lost to normal lysis — **os·teo·pe·nic** \-nik\ *adj*

os·teo·pe·tro·sis \-pə-ˈtrō-səs\ *n, pl* **-tro·ses** \-ˌsēz\ : a rare hereditary disease characterized by extreme density and hardness and abnormal fragility of the bones with partial or complete obliteration of the marrow cavities — called also *Albers-Schönberg disease* — **os·teo·pe·trot·ic** \-pə-ˈträ-tik\ *adj*

os·teo·phyte \ˈäs-tē-ə-ˌfīt\ *n* : a pathological bony outgrowth — **os·teo·phyt·ic** \ˌäs-tē-ə-ˈfi-tik\ *adj*

os·teo·plas·tic \ˌäs-tē-ə-ˈplas-tik\ *adj* : of, relating to, or being osteoplasty

osteoplastic flap *n* : a surgically excised portion of the skull folded back on a hinge of skin to expose the underlying tissues (as in a craniotomy)

os·teo·plas·ty \ˈäs-tē-ə-ˌplas-tē\ *n, pl* **-ties** : plastic surgery on bone; *esp* : replacement of lost bone tissue or reconstruction of defective bony parts

os·teo·poi·ki·lo·sis \ˌäs-tē-ō-ˌpòi-kə-ˈlō-səs\ *n* : an asymptomatic hereditary bone disorder characterized by numerous sclerotic foci giving the bones a mottled or spotted appearance

os·teo·po·ro·sis \ˌäs-tē-ō-pə-ˈrō-səs\ *n, pl* **-ro·ses** \-ˌsēz\ : a condition that affects esp. older women and is characterized by decrease in bone mass with decreased density and enlargement of bone spaces producing porosity and fragility — **os·teo·po·rot·ic** \-ˈrä-tik\ *adj*

os·te·op·sath·y·ro·sis \ˌäs-tē-äp-ˌsa-thə-ˈrō-səs\ *n, pl* **-ro·ses** \-ˌsēz\ : OSTEOGENESIS IMPERFECTA

os·teo·ra·dio·ne·cro·sis \ˌäs-tē-ō-ˌrä-dē-ō-nə-ˈkrō-səs\ *n, pl* **-cro·ses** \-ˌsēz\ : necrosis of bone following irradiation

os·teo·sar·co·ma \-sär-ˈkō-mə\ *n, pl* **-mas** *or* **-ma·ta** \-mə-tə\ : a sarcoma derived from bone or containing bone tissue — called also *osteogenic sarcoma*

os·teo·scle·ro·sis \-sklə-ˈrō-səs\ *n, pl* **-ro·ses** \-ˌsēz\ : abnormal hardening of bone or of bone marrow — **os·teo·scle·rot·ic** \-ˈrä-tik\ *adj*

os·teo·syn·the·sis \-ˈsin-thə-səs\ *n, pl* **-the·ses** \-ˌsēz\ : the operation of uniting the ends of a fractured bone by mechanical means (as a wire)

os·teo·tome \ˈäs-tē-ə-ˌtōm\ *n* : a chisel without a bevel that is used for cutting bone

os·te·ot·o·my \ˌäs-tē-ˈä-tə-mē\ *n, pl* **-mies** : a surgical operation in which a bone is divided or a piece of bone is excised (as to correct a deformity)

Os·ter·ta·gia \ˌäs-tər-ˈtä-jə, -jē-ə\ *n* : a genus of nematode worms (family Trichostrongylidae) parasitic in the abomasum of ruminants

os·ti·tis \äs-ˈtī-təs\ *n* : OSTEITIS

os·ti·um \ˈäs-tē-əm\ *n, pl* **os·tia** \-tē-ə\ : a mouthlike opening in a bodily part (as a fallopian tube or a blood vessel) — **os·ti·al** \ˈäs-tē-əl\ *adj*

os·to·mate \ˈäs-tə-ˌmāt\ *n* : a person who has undergone an ostomy

os·to·my \ˈäs-tə-mē\ n, pl **-mies** : an operation (as a colostomy, ileostomy, or urostomy) to create an artificial passage for bodily elimination

-os·to·sis \äs-ˈtō-səs\ n comb form, pl **-os·to·ses** \-ˌsēz\ or **-os·to·sis·es** : ossification of a (specified) part or to a (specified) degree ⟨hyper*ostosis*⟩

OT abbr 1 occupational therapist 2 occupational therapy

ot- or **oto-** comb form 1 : ear ⟨*otitis*⟩ 2 : ear and ⟨*otolaryngology*⟩

otal·gia \ō-ˈtal-jə, -jē-ə\ n : EARACHE

other–directed adj : directed in thought and action primarily by external norms rather than by one's own scale of values — compare INNER–DIRECTED

otic \ˈō-tik\ adj : of, relating to, or located in the region of the ear

¹**-ot·ic** \ˈä-tik\ adj suffix 1 a : of, relating to, or characterized by a (specified) action, process, or condition ⟨symbi*otic*⟩ b : having an abnormal or diseased condition of a (specified) kind ⟨epiz*ootic*⟩ 2 : showing an increase or a formation of ⟨leukocyt*ic*⟩

²**-otic** \ˈō-tik\ adj comb form : having (such) a relationship to the ear ⟨dich*otic*⟩

otic ganglion n : a small parasympathetic ganglion that is associated with the mandibular nerve and sends postganglionic fibers to the parotid gland by way of the auriculotemporal nerve

oti·tis \ō-ˈtī-təs\ n, pl **otit·i·des** \ō-ˈti-tə-ˌdēz\ : inflammation of the ear — **otit·ic** \-ˈti-tik\ adj

otitis ex·ter·na \-ek-ˈstər-nə\ n : inflammation of the external ear

otitis in·ter·na \-in-ˈtər-nə\ n : inflammation of the inner ear

otitis me·dia \-ˈmē-dē-ə\ n : inflammation of the middle ear marked by pain, fever, dizziness, and abnormalities of hearing — see SEROUS OTITIS MEDIA

oto- — see OT-

Oto·bi·us \ō-ˈtō-bē-əs\ n : a genus of ticks (family Argasidae) that includes the spinose ear tick (*O. megnini*) of southwestern U.S. and Mexico

oto·co·nia \ō-tə-ˈkō-nē-ə\ n pl : small crystals of calcium carbonate in the saccule and utricle of the ear that under the influence of acceleration in a straight line cause stimulation of the hair cells by their movement relative to the gelatinous supporting substrate containing the embedded cilia of the hair cells — called also *statoconia*

Oto·dec·tes \ō-tə-ˈdek-ˌtēz\ n : a genus of mites that includes one (*O. cynotis*) causing otodectic mange — **oto·dec·tic** \-ˈdek-tik\ adj

otodectic mange n : ear mange caused by a mite (*O. cynotis*) of the genus *Otodectes*

oto·lar·yn·gol·o·gist \ˌō-tō-ˌlar-ən-ˈgä-lə-jist\ n : a specialist in otorhino-

laryngology — called also *otorhinolaryngologist*

oto·lar·yn·gol·o·gy \-jē\ n, pl **-gies** : a medical specialty concerned esp. with the ear, nose, and throat — called also *otorhinolaryngology* — **oto·lar·yn·go·log·i·cal** \-ˌlar-ən-gə-ˈlä-ji-kəl\ adj

oto·lith \ˈōt-ə-ˌlith\ n : a calcareous concretion in the internal ear composed of masses of otoconia — called also *statolith* — **oto·lith·ic** \ˌōt-ə-ˈli-thik\ adj

otol·o·gist \ō-ˈtä-lə-jist\ n : a specialist in otology

otol·o·gy \-jē\ n, pl **-gies** : a science that deals with the ear and its diseases — **oto·log·ic** \ˌō-tə-ˈlä-jik\ also **oto·log·i·cal** \-ˈlä-ji-kəl\ adj — **oto·log·i·cal·ly** adv

oto·my·co·sis \ˌō-tō-mī-ˈkō-səs\ n, pl **-co·ses** \-ˌsēz\ : disease of the ear produced by the growth of fungi in the external auditory meatus

oto·plas·ty \ˈō-tə-ˌplas-tē\ n, pl **-ties** : plastic surgery of the external ear

oto·rhi·no·lar·yn·gol·o·gist \ˌō-tō-ˌrī-nō-ˌlar-ən-ˈgä-lə-jist\ n : OTOLARYNGOLOGIST

oto·rhi·no·lar·yn·gol·o·gy \-jē\ n, pl **-gies** : OTOLARYNGOLOGY — **oto·rhi·no·lar·yn·go·log·i·cal** \-ˌgä-lə-ˈlä-ji-kəl\ adj

otor·rhea \ˌō-tə-ˈrē-ə\ n : a discharge from the external ear

otor·rhoea chiefly Brit var of OTORRHEA

oto·scle·ro·sis \ˌō-tō-sklə-ˈrō-səs\ n, pl **-ro·ses** \-ˌsēz\ : growth of spongy bone in the inner ear where it gradually obstructs the oval window or round window or both and causes progressively increasing deafness — **oto·scle·rot·ic** \-sklə-ˈrä-tik\ adj

oto·scope \ˈō-tə-ˌskōp\ n : an instrument fitted with lighting and magnifying lens systems and used to facilitate visual examination of the auditory canal and ear drum — **oto·scop·ic** \ˌō-tə-ˈskä-pik\ adj — **otos·co·py** \ō-ˈtäs-kə-pē\ n

oto·tox·ic \ˌō-tə-ˈtäk-sik\ adj : producing, involving, or being adverse effects on organs or nerves involved in hearing or balance — **oto·tox·ic·i·ty** \-ˌtäk-ˈsi-sə-tē\ n

OTR abbr registered occupational therapist

oua·bain \wä-ˈbā-ən, ˈwä-ˌbän\ n : a poisonous glycoside $C_{29}H_{44}O_{12}$ used medically like digitalis

ounce \ˈau̇ns\ n 1 a : a unit of troy weight equal to $\frac{1}{12}$ troy pound or 31.103 grams b : a unit of avoirdupois weight equal to $\frac{1}{16}$ avoirdupois pound or 28.350 grams 2 : FLUID OUNCE

out·breed·ing \ˈau̇t-ˌbrē-diŋ\ n : breeding between individuals or stocks that are relatively unrelated — compare INBREEDING — **out·bred** \-ˌbred\ adj — **out·breed** \-ˌbrēd\ vb

out·cross \ˈau̇t-ˌkrȯs\ n 1 : a cross between relatively unrelated individuals **2** : the progeny of an outcross — **out-cross** *vb*

outer ear *n* : the outer visible portion of the ear that collects and directs sound waves toward the tympanic membrane by way of a canal which extends inward through the temporal bone

out·growth \ˈaut-ˌgrōth\ *n* **1** : the process of growing out **2** : something that grows directly out of something else ⟨an ∼ of hair⟩ ⟨a deformed ∼⟩

out·let \ˈaut-ˌlet, -lət\ *n* **1** : an opening or a place through which something is let out ⟨the pelvic ∼⟩ **2** : a means of release or satisfaction for an emotion or impulse

outlet forceps *n* : LOW FORCEPS

out-of-body *adj* : relating to or involving a feeling of separation from one's body and of being able to view oneself and others from an external perspective ⟨an ∼ experience⟩

out·pa·tient \ˈaut-ˌpā-shənt\ *n* : a patient who is not hospitalized overnight but who visits a hospital, clinic, or associated facility for diagnosis or treatment — compare INPATIENT

out·pock·et·ing \ˈaut-ˌpä-kə-tiŋ\ *n* : EVAGINATION 2

out·pouch·ing \-ˌpau-chiŋ\ *n* : EVAGINATION 2

out·put \ˈaut-ˌput\ *n* : the amount of energy or matter discharged usu. within a specified time by a bodily system or organ ⟨renal ∼⟩ ⟨urinary ∼⟩ — see CARDIAC OUTPUT

ov- *or* **ovi-** *or* **ovo-** *comb form* : egg ⟨*ovicide*⟩ : ovum ⟨*oviduct*⟩ ⟨*ovogenesis*⟩

ova *pl of* OVUM

ovale — see FORAMEN OVALE

ova·le malaria \ō-ˈvä-lē-\ *n* : a relatively mild form of malaria caused by a protozoan of the genus *Plasmodium* (*P. ovale*) that is characterized by tertian chills and febrile paroxysms and that usu. ends spontaneously

ovalis — see FENESTRA OVALIS, FOSSA OVALIS

oval window *n* : an oval opening between the middle ear and the vestibule having the base of the stapes or columella attached to its membrane — called also *fenestra ovalis, fenestra vestibuli*

ovari- *or* **ovario-** *also* **ovar-** *comb form* **1** : ovary ⟨*ovariectomy*⟩ ⟨*ovariotomy*⟩ **2** : ovarian and ⟨*ovariohysterectomy*⟩

ovar·i·an \ō-ˈvar-ē-ən\ *also* **ovar·i·al** \-ē-əl\ *adj* : of, relating to, affecting, or involving an ovary

ovarian artery *n* : either of two arteries in the female that arise from the aorta below the renal arteries with one on each side, and are distributed to the ovaries with branches supplying the ureters, the fallopian tubes, the labia majora, and the groin

ovarian follicle *n* : FOLLICLE 3

ovarian ligament *n* : LIGAMENT OF THE OVARY

ovarian vein *n* : either of two veins in the female with one on each side that drain a venous plexus in the broad ligament of the same side and empty on the right into the inferior vena cava and on the left into the left renal vein

ovari·ec·to·my \ˌō-ˌvar-ē-ˈek-tə-mē\ *n*, *pl* **-mies** : the surgical removal of an ovary — called also *oophorectomy* — **ovari·ec·to·mize** \ō-ˌvar-ē-ˈek-tə-ˌmīz\ *vb*

ovar·io·hys·ter·ec·to·my \ō-ˌvar-ē-ō-ˌhis-tə-ˈrek-tə-mē\ *n*, *pl* **-mies** : surgical removal of the ovaries and of the uterus

ovar·i·ot·o·my \ō-ˌvar-ē-ˈä-tə-mē\ *n*, *pl* **-mies** **1** : surgical incision of an ovary **2** : OVARIECTOMY

ova·ry \ˈō-və-rē\ *n*, *pl* **-ries** : one of the typically paired essential female reproductive organs that produce eggs and female sex hormones, that occur in the adult human as oval flattened bodies about one and a half inches (four centimeters) long suspended from the dorsal surface of the broad ligament of either side, that arise from the mesonephros, and that consist of a vascular fibrous stroma enclosing developing egg cells

over·achiev·er \ˌō-vər-ə-ˈchē-vər\ *n* : one who achieves success over and above the standard or expected level esp. at an early age — **overachieve** *vb*

over·ac·tive \ˌō-vər-ˈak-tiv\ *adj* : excessively or abnormally active ⟨∼ glands⟩ — **over·ac·tiv·i·ty** \-ˌak-ˈti-və-tē\ *n*

over·bite \ˈō-vər-ˌbīt\ *n* : the projection of the upper anterior teeth over the lower when the jaws are in the position they occupy in occlusion — compare OVERJET

over·breathe \ˌō-vər-ˈbrēth\ *vb* **-breathed; -breath·ing** : HYPERVENTILATE

over·com·pen·sa·tion \-ˌkäm-pən-ˈsā-shən, -ˌpen-\ *n* : excessive compensation; *specif* : excessive reaction to a feeling of inferiority, guilt, or inadequacy leading to an exaggerated attempt to overcome the feeling — **over·com·pen·sate** \ˈkäm-pən-ˌsāt\ *vb*

over·dis·ten·sion *or* **over·dis·ten·tion** \-dis-ˈten-chən\ *n* : excessive distension ⟨gastric ∼⟩ ⟨∼ of the alveoli⟩ — **over·dis·tend·ed** \-dis-ˈten-dəd\ *adj*

over·dose \ˈō-vər-ˌdōs\ *n* : too great a dose ⟨as of a therapeutic agent⟩; *also* : a lethal or toxic amount ⟨as of a drug⟩ — **over·dos·age** \ō-vər-ˈdō-sij\ *n* — **over·dose** \ˌō-vər-ˈdōs\ *vb*

over·eat \ˌō-vər-ˈēt\ *vb* **over·ate** \-ˈāt\; **over·eat·en** \-ˈēt-ᵊn\; **over·eat·ing** : to eat to excess — **over·eat·er** *n*

overeating disease *n* : ENTEROTOXEMIA

over·ex·ert \-ig-ˈzərt\ *vb* : to exert (oneself) too much — **over·ex·er·tion** \-ˈzər-shən\ *n*

over·ex·pose \ˌō-vər-ik-ˈspōz\ vb -posed; -pos·ing : to expose excessively (skin *overexposed* to sunlight) — **over·ex·po·sure** \-ˈspō-zhər\ n

over·ex·tend \-ik-ˈstend\ vb : to extend too far (~ the back) — **over·ex·ten·sion** \-ik-ˈsten-chən\ n

over·fa·tigue \-fə-ˈtēg\ n : excessive fatigue esp. when carried beyond the recuperative capacity of the individual

over·feed \-ˈfēd\ vb -fed \-ˈfed\; -feed·ing : to feed or eat to excess

over·growth \ˈō-vər-ˌgrōth\ n 1 a : excessive growth or increase in numbers b : HYPERTROPHY, HYPERPLASIA 2 : something (as cells or tissue) grown over something else

over·hang \ˈō-vər-ˌhaŋ\ n : a portion of a filling that extends beyond the normal contour of a tooth

over·hy·dra·tion \ˌō-vər-hī-ˈdrā-shən\ n : a condition in which the body contains an excessive amount of fluids

over·jet \ˈō-vər-ˌjet\ n : displacement of the mandibular teeth sideways when the jaws are held in the position they occupy in occlusion — compare OVERBITE

over·med·i·cate \-ˈme-di-ˌkāt\ vb -cat·ed; -cat·ing : to administer too much medication to : to prescribe too much medication for — **over·med·i·ca·tion** \-ˌme-di-ˈkā-shən\ n

over·nu·tri·tion \ˌō-vər-nü-ˈtri-shən, -nyü-\ n : excessive food intake esp. when viewed as a factor in pathology

over·pre·scribe \-pri-ˈskrīb\ vb -scribed; -scrib·ing : to prescribe excessive or unnecessary medication — **over·pre·scrip·tion** \-pri-ˈskrip-shən\ n

over·reach \-ˈrēch\ vb, of a horse : to strike the toe of the hind foot against the heel or quarter of the forefoot

over·se·da·tion \-si-ˈdā-shən\ n : excessive sedation

over·shot \ˈō-vər-ˌshät\ adj 1 : having the upper jaw extending beyond the lower 2 : projecting beyond the lower jaw

over·stim·u·la·tion \ˌō-vər-ˌsti-myə-ˈlā-shən\ n : excessive stimulation (~ of the pancreas) — **over·stim·u·late** \-ˈsti-myə-ˌlāt\ vb

overt \ō-ˈvərt, ˈō-ˌvərt\ adj : open to view : readily perceived

over-the-coun·ter adj : sold lawfully without prescription (~ drugs)

over·ven·ti·la·tion \ˌō-vər-ˌvent-əl-ˈā-shən\ n : HYPERVENTILATION

over·weight \-ˈwāt\ n 1 : bodily weight in excess of the normal for one's age, height, and build 2 : an individual of more than normal weight — **overweight** adj

over·work \-ˈwərk\ vb : to cause to work too hard, too long, or to exhaustion

ovi- — see OV-

ovi·cide \ˈō-və-ˌsīd\ n : an agent that kills eggs; esp : an insecticide effective against the egg stage — **ovi·cid·al** \ˌō-və-ˈsīd-əl\ adj

ovi·du·cal \ˌō-və-ˈdü-kəl, -ˈdyü-\ adj : OVIDUCTAL

ovi·duct \ˈō-və-ˌdəkt\ n : a tube that serves exclusively or esp. for the passage of eggs from an ovary

ovi·duc·tal \ˌō-və-ˈdəkt-əl\ adj : of, relating to, or affecting an oviduct (~ surgery)

ovine \ˈō-ˌvīn\ adj : of, relating to, or resembling sheep (~ growth hormone)

ovip·a·rous \ō-ˈvi-pə-rəs\ adj : producing eggs that develop and hatch outside the maternal body — compare OVOVIVIPAROUS, VIVIPAROUS — **ovi·par·i·ty** \ˌō-və-ˈpar-ə-tē\ n

ovi·pos·it \ˌō-və-pə-ˈzət, ˌō-və-ˈ\ vb : to lay eggs — used esp. of insects — **ovi·po·si·tion** \ˌō-və-pə-ˈzi-shən\ n — **ovi·po·si·tion·al** \-ˈzi-shə-nəl\ adj

ovi·pos·i·tor \ˈō-və-ˌpä-zə-tər, ˌō-və-ˈ\ n : a specialized organ (as of an insect) for depositing eggs

ovo- — see OV-

ovo·gen·e·sis \ˌō-və-ˈje-nə-səs\ n, pl -e·ses \-ˌsēz\ : OOGENESIS

ovoid \ˈō-ˌvȯid\ adj : shaped like an egg (an ~ tumor)

ovo·lec·i·thin \ˌō-və-ˈle-sə-thən\ n : lecithin obtained from egg yolk

ovo·mu·coid \-ˈmyü-ˌkȯid\ n : a mucoprotein present in egg white

ovo·plasm \ˈō-və-ˌpla-zəm\ n : the cytoplasm of an unfertilized egg

ovo·tes·tis \ˌō-və-ˈtes-təs\ n, pl -tes·tes \-ˌtēz\ : a hermaphrodite gonad

ovo·vi·tel·lin \ˌō-və-vī-ˈte-lən\ n : VITELLIN

ovo·vi·vip·a·rous \ˌō-və-ˌvī-ˈvi-pə-rəs\ adj : producing eggs that develop within the maternal body — compare OVIPAROUS, VIVIPAROUS — **ovo·vi·vi·par·i·ty** \-ˌvī-və-ˈpar-ə-tē, -ˌvi-\ n

ovu·lar \ˈä-vyə-lər, ˈō-\ adj : of or relating to an ovule or ovum

ovu·la·tion \ˌä-vyə-ˈlā-shən, ˌō-\ n : the discharge of a mature ovum from the ovary — **ovu·late** \ˈä-vyə-ˌlāt\ vb — **ovu·la·to·ry** \ˈä-vyə-lə-ˌtōr-ē, ˈō-\ adj

ovule \ˈä-ˌvyül, ˈō-\ n 1 : an outgrowth of the ovary of a seed plant that after fertilization develops into a seed 2 : a small egg; esp : one in an early stage of growth

ovum \ˈō-vəm\ n, pl ova \-və\ : a female gamete : MACROGAMETE; esp : a mature egg that has undergone reduction, is ready for fertilization, and takes the form of a relatively large inactive gamete providing a comparatively great amount of reserve material and contributing most of the cytoplasm of the zygote

ox \ˈäks\ n, pl ox·en \ˈäk-sən\ also ox : a domestic bovine mammal (*Bos taurus* of the subfamily Bovinae); also : an adult male castrated domestic ox

ox·a·cil·lin \ˌäk-sə-ˈsi-lən\ n : a semi-synthetic penicillin that is esp. effective in the control of infections caused by penicillin-resistant staphylococci

¹ox·a·late \'äk-sə-ˌlāt\ n : a salt or ester of oxalic acid

²oxalate vb **-lat·ed; -lat·ing** : to add an oxalate to (blood or plasma) to prevent coagulation

ox·al·ic acid \(ˌ)äk-ˌsa-lik-\ n : a poisonous strong acid (COOH)₂ or H₂C₂O₄ that occurs in various plants as oxalates

ox·a·lo·ace·tic acid \ˌäk-sə-lō-ə-'sē-tik-\ also **ox·al·ace·tic acid** \ˌäk-sə-lə-'sē-tik-\ n : a crystalline acid C₄H₄O₅ that is formed by reversible oxidation of malic acid (as in carbohydrate metabolism via the Krebs cycle) and in reversible transamination reactions (as from aspartic acid)

ox·a·lo·sis \ˌäk-sə-'lō-səs\ n : an abnormal condition characterized by hyperoxaluria and the formation of calcium oxalate deposits in tissues throughout the body

ox·an·a·mide \äk-'sa-nə-ˌmīd\ n : a tranquilizing drug C₈H₁₅NO₂

ox·an·dro·lone \äk-'san-drə-ˌlōn\ n : an anabolic agent C₁₉H₃₀O₃

ox·a·pro·zin \ˌäk-sə-'prō-zən\ n : an anti-inflammatory drug C₁₈H₁₅NO₃

ox·az·e·pam \äk-'sa-zə-ˌpam\ n : a benzodiazepine tranquilizer C₁₅H₁₁ClN₂O₂

ox·a·zol·i·dine \ˌäk-sə-'zō-lə-ˌdēn, -'zä-\ n : the heterocyclic compound C₃H₇NO; also : an anticonvulsant derivative (as trimethadione) of this compound

ox·i·dase \'äk-sə-ˌdās, -ˌdāz\ n : any of various enzymes that catalyze oxidations; esp : one able to react directly with molecular oxygen

ox·i·da·tion \ˌäk-sə-'dā-shən\ n 1 : the act or process of oxidizing 2 : the state or result of being oxidized — **ox·i·da·tive** \'äk-sə-ˌdā-tiv\ adj — **ox·i·da·tive·ly** adv

oxidation–reduction n : a chemical reaction in which one or more electrons are transferred from one atom or molecule to another — called also **redox**

oxidative phosphorylation n : the synthesis of ATP by phosphorylation of ADP for which energy is obtained by electron transport and which takes place in the mitochondria during aerobic respiration

ox·ide \'äk-ˌsīd\ n : a binary compound of oxygen with an element or chemical group

ox·i·dize \'äk-sə-ˌdīz\ vb **-dized; -diz·ing** 1 : to combine with oxygen 2 : to dehydrogenate esp. by the action of oxygen 3 : to change (a compound) by increasing the proportion of the part tending to attract electrons or change (an element or ion) from a lower to a higher positive valence : remove one or more electrons from (an atom, ion, or molecule) — **ox·i·diz·able** \ˌäk-sə-'dī-zə-bəl\ adj

oxidized cellulose n : an acid degradation product of cellulose that is usu. obtained by oxidizing cotton or gauze with nitrogen dioxide, is a useful hemostatic (as in surgery), and is absorbed by body fluids (as when used to pack wounds)

oxidizing agent n : a substance that oxidizes something esp. chemically (as by accepting electrons) — compare REDUCING AGENT

oxi·do·re·duc·tase \ˌäk-sə-dō-ri-'dək-ˌtās, -ˌtāz\ n : an enzyme that catalyzes an oxidation-reduction reaction

ox·im·e·ter \äk-'si-mə-tər\ n : an instrument for measuring continuously the degree of oxygen saturation of the circulating blood — **ox·i·met·ric** \ˌäk-sə-'me-trik\ adj — **ox·im·e·try** \äk-'si-mə-trē\ n

oxo·phen·ar·sine \ˌäk-sə-fe-'när-ˌsēn, -sən\ n : an arsenical used in the form of its white powdery hydrochloride C₆H₆AsNO₂·HCl esp. in the treatment of syphilis

oxo·trem·o·rine \ˌäk-sō-'tre-mə-ˌrēn, -rən\ n : a cholinergic agent C₁₂H₁₈N₂O that induces tremors

ox·pren·o·lol \äks-'pre-nə-ˌlól\ n : a beta-adrenergic blocking agent C₁₅H₂₃NO₃ used in the form of the hydrochloride as a coronary vasodilator

ox·tri·phyl·line \ˌäks-tri-'fi-ˌlēn, -'tri-fə-lēn\ n : the choline salt C₁₂H₂₁N₅O₃ of theophylline used chiefly as a bronchodilator

ox warble n : the maggot of either the common cattle grub or the northern cattle grub

oxy \'äk-sē\ adj : containing oxygen or additional oxygen — often used in combination (oxyhemoglobin)

oxy- comb form 1 : sharp : pointed : acute (oxycephaly) 2 : quick (oxytocic) 3 : acid (oxyntic)

oxy·ben·zone \ˌäk-sē-'ben-ˌzōn\ n : a sunscreening agent C₁₄H₁₂O₃

oxy·bu·tyr·ic acid \-byü-'tir-ik-\ n : HYDROXYBUTYRIC ACID

oxy·ceph·a·ly \-'se-fə-lē\ n, pl **-lies** : congenital deformity of the skull due to early synostosis of the parietal and occipital bones with compensating growth in the region of the anterior fontanel resulting in a pointed or pyramidal skull — called also acrocephaly, turricephaly — **oxy·ce·phal·ic** \-si-'fa-lik\ adj

oxy·chlo·ro·sene \-'klōr-ə-ˌsēn\ n : a topical antiseptic C₂₀H₃₄O₃S·HOCl

oxy·co·done \-'kō-ˌdōn\ n : a narcotic analgesic C₁₈H₂₁NO₄ used esp. in the form of the hydrochloride

oxy·gen \'äk-si-jən\ n : an element that is found free as a colorless tasteless odorless gas in the atmosphere of which it forms about 21 percent or combined in water, is active in physiological processes, and is involved esp. in combustion processes — symbol O; see ELEMENT table

oxy·gen·ate \'äk-si-jə-ˌnāt, äk-'si-jə-\

vb **-at·ed; -at·ing** : to impregnate, combine, or supply with oxygen ⟨*oxygenated* blood⟩ — **ox·y·gen·ation** \ˌäk-si-jə-ˈnā-shən, ˌäk-ˌsi-jə-\ *n*

ox·y·gen·ator \ˈäk-si-jə-ˌnā-tər, ˌäk-ˈsi-jə-\ *n* : one that oxygenates; *specif* : an apparatus that oxygenates the blood extracorporeally (as during open-heart surgery)

oxygen capacity *n* : the amount of oxygen which a quantity of blood is able to absorb

oxygen debt *n* : a cumulative deficit of oxygen available for oxidative metabolism that develops during periods of intense bodily activity and must be made good when the body returns to rest

oxygen mask *n* : a device worn over the nose and mouth through which oxygen is supplied from a storage tank

oxygen tent *n* : a canopy which can be placed over a bedridden person and within which a flow of oxygen can be maintained

oxy·he·mo·glo·bin \ˌäk-si-ˈhē-mə-ˌglō-bən\ *n* : hemoglobin loosely combined with oxygen that it releases to the tissues

oxy·mor·phone \-ˈmȯr-ˌfōn\ *n* : a semisynthetic narcotic analgesic drug used in the form of its hydrochloride $C_{17}H_{19}NO_4 \cdot HCl$ and having uses, activity, and side effects like those of morphine

oxy·myo·glo·bin \ˌäk-si-ˈmī-ə-ˌglō-bən\ *n* : a pigment formed by the combination of myoglobin with oxygen

ox·yn·tic \äk-ˈsin-tik\ *adj* : secreting acid — used esp. of the parietal cells of the gastric glands

oxy·phen·bu·ta·zone \ˌäk-sē-ˌfen-ˈbyüt-ə-ˌzōn\ *n* : a phenylbutazone derivative $C_{19}H_{20}N_2O_3$ used for its antiinflammatory, analgesic, and antipyretic effects

oxy·phen·cy·cli·mine \-ˈsī-klə-ˌmēn\ *n* : an anticholinergic drug $C_{20}H_{28}N_2O_3$ with actions similar to atropine usu. used in the form of its hydrochloride as an antispasmodic esp. in the treatment of peptic ulcer

oxy·quin·o·line \-ˈkwin-ᵊl-ˌēn\ *n* : 8-HYDROXYQUINOLINE

Oxy·spi·ru·ra \ˌäk-si-ˌspī-ˈrür-ə\ *n* : a genus of nematode worms (family Thelaziidae) comprising the eye worms of birds and esp. domestic poultry

oxy·tet·ra·cy·cline \-ˌte-trə-ˈsī-ˌklēn\ *n* : a yellow crystalline broad-spectrum antibiotic $C_{22}H_{24}N_2O_9$ produced by a soil actinomycete of the genus *Streptomyces* (*S. rimosus*) — see TERRAMYCIN

¹**oxy·to·cic** \ˌäk-si-ˈtō-sik\ *adj* : hastening parturition; *also* : inducing contraction of uterine smooth muscle

²**oxytocic** *n* : a substance that stimulates contraction of uterine smooth muscle or hastens childbirth

oxy·to·cin \-ˈtōs-ᵊn\ *n* : a postpituitary octapeptide hormone $C_{43}H_{66}N_{12}O_{12}S_2$ that stimulates esp. the contraction of uterine muscle and the secretion of milk — see PITOCIN

oxy·uri·a·sis \ˌäk-si-yù-ˈrī-ə-səs\ *n, pl* **-a·ses** \-ˌsēz\ : infestation with or disease caused by pinworms (as of the genera *Enterobius* and *Oxyuris*)

oxy·urid \ˌäk-sē-ˈyùr-əd\ *n* : any of a family (Oxyuridae) of nematode worms that are chiefly parasites of the vertebrate intestinal tract — see PINWORM — **oxyurid** *adj*

oxy·uris \-ˈyùr-əs\ *n* 1 *cap* : a genus of parasitic nematodes (family Oxyuridae) 2 : any nematode worm of the genus *Oxyuris* or a related genus (as *Enterobius*) : PINWORM

oz *abbr* ounce; ounces

oze·na \ō-ˈzē-nə\ *n* : a chronic disease of the nose accompanied by a fetid discharge and marked by atrophic changes in the nasal structures

ozone \ˈō-ˌzōn\ *n* : a very reactive form of oxygen containing three atoms per molecule that is a bluish irritating gas of pungent odor, that is formed naturally in the atmosphere by a photochemical reaction and is a major air pollutant in the lower atmosphere but a beneficial component of the upper atmosphere, and that is used for oxidizing, bleaching, disinfecting, and deodorizing

P

¹**P** *abbr* 1 parental 2 pressure 3 pulse
²**P** *symbol* phosphorus

p- *abbr* para- ⟨*p*-dichlorobenzene⟩

Pa *symbol* protactinium

PA *n* : PHYSICIAN'S ASSISTANT

PA *abbr* pernicious anemia

PABA \ˈpa-bə, ˌpē-ˌā-ˈbē-ˌā\ *n* : PARAAMINOBENZOIC ACID

pab·u·lum \ˈpa-byə-ləm\ *n* : FOOD; *esp* : a suspension or solution of nutrients in a state suitable for absorption

PAC *abbr* physician's assistant, certified

pac·chi·o·ni·an body \ˌpa-kē-ˈō-nē-ən-\ *n* : ARACHNOID GRANULATION

Pac·chi·o·ni \ˌpä-kē-ˈō-nē\ **Antonio** (1665–1726), Italian anatomist.

pace·mak·er \ˈpās-ˌmā-kər\ *n* 1 : a body part (as the sinoatrial node of the heart) that serves to establish and maintain a rhythmic activity 2 : an electrical device for stimulating or steadying the heartbeat or reestablishing the rhythm of an arrested heart — called also *pacer*

pace·mak·ing \-mā-kiŋ\ *n* : the act or process of serving as a pacemaker

pac·er \'pā-sər\ *n* : PACEMAKER 2

pachy- *comb form* : thick (*pachytene*)

pachy·men·in·gi·tis \,pa-kē-,me-nən-'jī-təs\ *n, pl* **-git·i·des** \-'ji-tə-,dēz\ : inflammation of the dura mater

pachy·me·ninx \-'mē-niŋks, -'me-\ *n, pl* **-me·nin·ges** \-mə-'nin-(,)jēz\ : DURA MATER

pachy·o·nych·ia \,pa-kē-ō-'ni-kē-ə\ *n* : extreme usu. congenital thickness of the nails

pachy·tene \'pa-ki-,tēn\ *n* : the stage of meiotic prophase which immediately follows the zygotene and in which the paired chromosomes are thickened and visibly divided into chromatids — **pachytene** *adj*

pac·i·fi·er \'pa-sə-,fī-ər\ *n* 1 : a usu. nipple-shaped device for babies to suck or bite on 2 : TRANQUILIZER

pac·ing \'pā-siŋ\ *n* : the act or process of regulating or changing the timing or intensity of cardiac contractions (as by an artificial pacemaker)

Pa·cin·i·an corpuscle \pə-'si-nē-ən-\ *also* **Pa·ci·ni's corpuscle** \pə-'chē-nēz-\ *n* : an oval capsule that terminates some sensory nerve fibers esp. in the skin of the hands and feet

   Pacini, Filippo (1812–1883), Italian anatomist.

¹pack \'pak\ *n* 1 : a container shielded with lead or mercury for holding radium in large quantities esp. for therapeutic application 2 a : absorbent material saturated with water or other liquid for therapeutic application to the body or a body part b : a folded square or compress of gauze or other absorbent material used esp. to maintain a clear field in surgery, to plug cavities, to check bleeding by compression, or to apply medication

²pack *vb* : to cover or surround with a pack; *specif* : to envelop (a patient) in a wet or dry sheet or blanket

packed cell volume *n* : the percentage of the total volume of a blood sample that is represented by the centrifuged red blood cells in it — abbr. **PCV**

pack·ing \'pa-kiŋ\ *n* 1 : the therapeutic application of a pack 2 : the material used in packing

pad \'pad\ *n* 1 : a usu. square or rectangular piece of often folded typically absorbent material (as gauze) fixed in place over some part of the body as a dressing or other protective covering 2 : a part of the body or of an appendage that resembles or is suggestive of a cushion : a thick fleshy resilient part: as a : the sole of the foot or underside of the toes of an animal (as a dog) that is typically thickened so as to form a cushion b : the underside of the extremities of the fingers; *esp* : the ball of the thumb

pad·i·mate A \'pa-di-,māt-'ā\ *n* : a sunscreen $C_{14}H_{21}NO_2$

paed- *or* **paedo-** *chiefly Brit var of* PED-

pae·di·a·trics, pae·do·don·tics, pae·do·phil·ia *chiefly Brit var of* PEDIATRICS, PEDODONTICS, PEDOPHILIA

PAF *abbr* platelet-activating factor

Pag·et's disease \'pa-jəts-\ *n* 1 : an eczematous inflammatory condition esp. of the nipple and areola that is the epidermal manifestation of an underlying carcinoma 2 : a chronic disease of bones characterized by their great enlargement and rarefaction with bowing of the long bones and deformation of the flat bones — called also *osteitis deformans*

   Pag·et \'pa-jət\ **Sir James** (1814–1899), British surgeon.

pa·go·pha·gia \,pā-gə-'fā-jə, -jē-ə\ *n* : the compulsive eating of ice that is a common symptom of a lack of iron

-pa·gus \pə-gəs\ *n comb form, pl* **-pa·gi** \pə-,jī, -,gī\ : congenitally united twins with a (specified) type of fixation (cranio*pagus*)

¹PAH \,pē-(,)ā-'āch\ *n* : POLYCYCLIC AROMATIC HYDROCARBON

²PAH *abbr* 1 para-aminohippurate; para-aminohippuric acid 2 polynuclear aromatic hydrocarbon

¹pain \'pān\ *n* 1 a : a usu. localized physical suffering associated with bodily disorder (as a disease or an injury); *also* : a basic bodily sensation that is induced by a noxious stimulus, is received by naked nerve endings, is characterized by physical discomfort (as pricking, throbbing, or aching), and typically leads to evasive action b : acute mental or emotional suffering or distress 2 **pains** *pl* : the protracted series of involuntary contractions of the uterine musculature that constitute the major factor in parturient labor and that are often accompanied by considerable pain — **pain·ful** \-fəl\ *adj* — **pain·ful·ly** *adv* — **pain·less** \-ləs\ *adj* — **pain·less·ly** *adv*

²pain *vb* : to cause or experience pain

pain·kill·er \-,kil-lər\ *n* : something (as a drug) that relieves pain — **pain·kill·ing** *adj*

pain spot *n* : one of many small localized areas of the skin that respond to stimulation (as by pricking or burning) by giving a sensation of pain

paint·er's colic \'pān-tərz-\ *n* : intestinal colic associated with obstinate constipation due to chronic lead poisoning

pair–bond *n* : a monogamous relationship — **pair–bond·ing** *n*

paired–associate learning *n* : the learning of items (as syllables, digits, or words) in pairs so that one member of the pair evokes recall of the other — compare ASSOCIATIVE LEARNING

palae- *or* **palaeo-** *chiefly Brit var of* PALE-

pal·ae·o·cer·e·bel·lum, pal·ae·o·pa·thol·ogy *chiefly Brit var of* PALEOCEREBELLUM, PALEOPATHOLOGY

pal·a·tal \'pa-lət-əl\ *adj* : of, relating to, forming, or affecting the palate — **pal·a·tal·ly** *adv*

palatal bar *n* : a connector extending across the roof of the mouth to join the parts of a maxillary partial denture

palatal process *n* : PALATINE PROCESS

pal·ate \'pa-lət\ *n* : the roof of the mouth separating the mouth from the nasal cavity — see HARD PALATE, SOFT PALATE

palati — see TENSOR PALATI

¹**pal·a·tine** \'pa-lə-ˌtīn\ *adj* : of, relating to, or lying near the palate

²**palatine** *n* : PALATINE BONE

palatine aponeurosis *n* : a thin fibrous lamella attached to the posterior part of the hard palate that supports the soft palate, includes the tendon of the tensor veli palatini, and supports the other muscles of the palate

palatine artery *n* 1 : either of two arteries of each side of the face: **a** : an inferior artery that arises from the facial artery and divides into two branches of which one supplies the soft palate and the palatine glands and the other supplies esp. the tonsils and the eustachian tube — called also *ascending palatine artery* **b** : a superior artery that arises from the maxillary artery and sends branches to the soft palate, the palatine glands, the mucous membrane of the hard palate, and the gums — called also *greater palatine artery* 2 : any of the branches of the palatine arteries

palatine bone *n* : a bone of extremely irregular form on each side of the skull that is situated in the posterior part of the nasal cavity between the maxilla and the pterygoid process of the sphenoid bone and that consists of a horizontal plate which joins the bone of the opposite side and forms the back part of the hard palate and a vertical plate which is extended into three processes and helps to form the floor of the orbit, the outer wall of the nasal cavity, and several adjoining parts — called also *palatine*

palatine foramen *n* : any of several foramina in the palatine bone giving passage to the palatine vessels and nerves — see GREATER PALATINE FORAMEN

palatine gland *n* : any of numerous small mucous glands in the palate opening into the mouth

palatine nerve *n* : any of several nerves arising from the pterygopalatine ganglion and supplying the roof of the mouth, parts of the nose, and adjoining parts

palatine process *n* : a process of the maxilla that projects medially, articulates posteriorly with the palatine

bone, and forms with the corresponding process on the other side the anterior three-fourths of the hard palate — called also *palatal process*

palatine suture *n* : either of two sutures in the hard palate: **a** : a transverse suture lying between the horizontal plates of the palatine bones and the maxillae **b** : a median suture lying between the maxillae in front and continued posteriorly between the palatine bones

palatine tonsil *n* : TONSIL 1a

palatini — see LEVATOR VELI PALATINI, TENSOR VELI PALATINI

palato- *comb form* 1 : palate : of the palate ⟨*palato*plasty⟩ 2 : palatal and ⟨*palato*glossal arch⟩

pal·a·to·glos·sal arch \ˌpa-lə-tō-ˈglä-səl-, -ˌglō-\ *n* : the more anterior of the two ridges of soft tissue at the back of the mouth on each side that curves downward from the side of the uvula to the side of the base of the tongue forming a recess for the palatine tonsil as it diverges from the palatopharyngeal arch and is composed of part of the palatoglossus with its covering of mucous membrane — called also *anterior pillar of the fauces, glossopalatine arch*

pal·a·to·glos·sus \-ˈglä-səs, -ˈglō-ˌglos·si \-(ˌ)sī\ *n, pl* : a thin muscle that arises from the soft palate on each side, contributes to the structure of the palatoglossal arch, and is inserted into the side and dorsum of the tongue — called also *glossopalatinus*

pal·a·to·pha·ryn·ge·al arch \ˌfar-ən-ˈjē-əl-; -fə-ˈrin-jəl-, -jē-əl-\ *n* : the more posterior of the two ridges of soft tissue at the back of the mouth on each side that curves downward from the uvula to the side of the pharynx forming a recess for the palatine tonsil as it diverges from the palatoglossal arch and is composed of part of the palatopharyngeus with its covering of mucous membrane — called also *posterior pillar of the fauces, pharyngopalatine arch*

pal·a·to·pha·ryn·ge·us \ˌfar-ən-ˈjē-əs; -fə-ˈrin-jəs, -jē-əs\ *n* : a longitudinal muscle of the pharynx that arises from the soft palate, contributes to the structure of the palatopharyngeal arch, and is inserted into the thyroid cartilage and the wall of the pharynx

pal·a·to·plas·ty \'pa-lə-tə-ˌplas-tē\ *n, pl* **-ties** : a plastic operation for repair of the palate (as in cleft palate)

pale \'pāl\ *adj* **pal·er; pal·est** : deficient in color or intensity of color ⟨a ~ face⟩ — **pale·ness** \-nəs\ *n*

pale- *or* **paleo-** *comb form* : early : old ⟨*paleo*pathology⟩

pa·leo·cer·e·bel·lum \ˌpā-lē-ō-ˌser-ə-ˈbe-ləm\ *n, pl* **-bel·lums** *or* **-bel·la** \-ˈbe-lə\ : an evolutionarily old part of the cerebellum concerned with maintenance of normal postural relationships and made up chiefly of the anterior lobe of the vermis and of the pyramid — compare NEOCEREBELLUM

pa·leo·pa·thol·o·gy \ˌpā-lē-ō-pə-ˈthä-lə-jē\ *n, pl* **-gies** : a branch of pathology concerned with diseases of former times as determined esp. from fossil or other remains — **pa·leo·pa·thol·o·gist** \-jist\ *n*

pali- *comb form* : pathological state characterized by repetition of a (specified) act (*palilalia*)

pali·la·lia \ˌpa-lə-ˈlā-lē-ə\ *n* : a speech defect marked by abnormal repetition of syllables, words, or phrases

pal·in·drome \ˈpa-lən-ˌdrōm\ *n* : a palindromic sequence of DNA

pal·in·dro·mic \ˌpa-lən-ˈdrō-mik\ *adj* **1** : RECURRENT (~ rheumatism) **2** : of, relating to, or consisting of a double-stranded sequence of DNA in which the order of the nucleotides is the same on each side but running in opposite directions

pal·i·sade worm \ˌpa-lə-ˈsād-\ *n* : BLOODWORM

pal·la·di·um \pə-ˈlā-dē-əm\ *n* : a silver-white ductile malleable metallic element — symbol Pd; see ELEMENT table

pal·li·ate \ˈpa-lē-ˌāt\ *vb* **-at·ed; -at·ing** : to reduce the violence of (a disease) : ease without curing — **pal·li·a·tion** \ˌpa-lē-ˈā-shən\ *n*

¹pal·lia·tive \ˈpa-lē-ˌā-tiv, -lē-yə-\ *adj* : serving to palliate (~ surgery)

²palliative *n* : something that palliates

pal·li·dal \ˈpa-ləd-ᵊl\ *adj* : of, relating to, or involving the globus pallidus

pal·li·dum \ˈpa-lə-dəm\ *n* : GLOBUS PALLIDUS

pallidus — see GLOBUS PALLIDUS

pal·li·um \ˈpa-lē-əm\ *n, pl* **-lia** \-lē-ə\ or **-li·ums** : CEREBRAL CORTEX

pal·lor \ˈpa-lər\ *n* : deficiency of color esp. of the face : PALENESS

palm \ˈpälm, ˈpäm\ *n* : the somewhat concave part of the hand between the bases of the fingers and the wrist — **pal·mar** \ˈpal-mər, ˈpäl-, ˈpä-\ *adj*

palmar aponeurosis *n* : an aponeurosis of the palm of the hand that consists of a superficial longitudinal layer continuous with the tendon of the palmaris longus and of a deeper transverse layer — called also *palmar fascia*

palmar arch *n* : either of two loops of blood vessels in the palm of the hand: **a** : a deeply situated transverse artery that is composed of the terminal part of the radial artery joined to a branch of the ulnar artery and that supplies principally the deep muscles of the hand, thumb, and index finger — called also *deep palmar arch* **b** : a superficial arch that is the continuation of the ulnar artery which anastomoses with a branch derived from the radial artery and that sends branches

mostly to the fingers — called also *superficial palmar arch*

palmar fascia *n* : PALMAR APONEUROSIS

palmar interosseus *n* : any of three small muscles of the palmar surface of the hand each of which arises from, extends along, and inserts on the side of the second, fourth, or fifth finger facing the middle finger and which acts to adduct its finger toward the middle finger, flex its metacarpophalangeal joint, and extend its distal two phalanges — called also *interosseus palmaris*, *palmar interosseous muscle*

pal·mar·is \pal-ˈmar-əs\ *n, pl* **pal·mar·es** \-ˌēz\ : either of two muscles of the palm of the hand: **a** : PALMARIS BREVIS **b** : PALMARIS LONGUS — see PALMAR INTEROSSEUS

palmaris brev·is \-ˈbrev-əs\ *n* : a short transverse superficial muscle of the ulnar side of the palm of the hand that arises from the flexor retinaculum and palmar aponeurosis, inserts into the skin on the ulnar edge of the palm, and functions to tense and stabilize the palm (as in making a fist or catching a ball)

palmaris lon·gus \-ˈlȯŋ-gəs\ *n* : a superficial muscle of the forearm lying on the medial side of the flexor carpi radialis that arises esp. from the medial epicondyle of the humerus, inserts esp. into the palmar aponeurosis, and acts to flex the hand

pal·mi·tate \ˈpal-mə-ˌtāt, ˈpäl-, ˈpä-\ *n* : a salt or ester of palmitic acid

pal·mit·ic acid \(ˌ)pal-ˈmit-ik-, (ˌ)päl-, (ˌ)pä-\ *n* : a waxy crystalline saturated fatty acid $C_{16}H_{32}O_2$ occurring free or in the form of esters (as glycerides) in most fats and fatty oils and in several essential oils and waxes

pal·mi·tin \ˈpal-mə-tən, ˈpäl-, ˈpä-\ *n* : the triglyceride $C_{51}H_{98}O_6$ of palmitic acid that occurs as a solid with stearin and olein in animal fats — called also *tripalmitin*

pal·mo·plan·tar \ˌpal-mō-ˈplan-tər, ˌpäl-, ˌpä-\ *adj* : of, relating to, or affecting both the palms of the hands and the soles of the feet (~ psoriasis)

pal·pa·ble \ˈpal-pə-bəl\ *adj* : capable of being touched or felt; *esp* : capable of being examined by palpation

pal·pa·tion \pal-ˈpā-shən\ *n* **1** : an act of touching or feeling **2** : physical examination in medical diagnosis by pressure of the hand or fingers to the surface of the body esp. to determine the condition (as of size or consistency) of an underlying part or organ (~ of the liver) — compare INSPECTION — **pal·pate** \ˈpal-ˌpāt\ *vb* — **pal·pa·to·ry** \ˈpal-pə-ˌtōr-ē\ *adj*

pal·pe·bra \ˈpal-pə-brə, pal-ˈpē-brə\ *n, pl* **pal·pe·brae** \-ˌbrē\ : EYELID — **pal·pe·bral** \ˈpal-ˌpē-brəl\ *adj*

palpebrae — see LEVATOR PALPEBRAE SUPERIORIS

palpebral fissure n : the space between the margins of the eyelids — called also *rima palpebrarum*

palpebrarum — see RIMA PALPEBRARUM, XANTHELASMA PALPEBRARUM

pal·pi·tate \'pal-pə-ˌtāt\ vb -tat·ed; -tat·ing : to beat rapidly and strongly — used esp. of the heart when its pulsation is abnormally rapid

pal·pi·ta·tion \ˌpal-pə-'tā-shən\ n : a rapid pulsation; esp : an abnormally rapid beating of the heart when excited by violent exertion, strong emotion, or disease

pal·sied \'pol-zēd\ adj : affected with palsy ⟨hands weak and ∼⟩

pal·sy \'pol-zē\ n, pl **pal·sies** 1 : PARALYSIS — used chiefly in combination ⟨oculomotor ∼⟩ — see BELL'S PALSY, CEREBRAL PALSY 2 : a condition that is characterized by uncontrollable tremor or quivering of the body or one or more of its parts — not used technically

Pal·u·drine \'pa-lə-drən\ trademark — used for derivatives of biguanide used as antimalarials

L-PAM \'el-ˌpam\ n : MELPHALAN

2-PAM \ˌtü-ˌpē-ˌā-'em\ n : PRALIDOXIME

pam·a·quine \'pa-mə-ˌkwin, -ˌkwēn\ n : a toxic antimalarial drug $C_{19}H_{29}N_3O$; also : PAMAQUINE NAPHTHOATE — see PLASMOCHIN

pamaquine naph·tho·ate \-'naf-thə-ˌwāt\ n : an insoluble salt $C_{42}H_{45}N_3O_7$ of pamaquine

Pam·ine \'pa-ˌmēn\ trademark — used for a preparation of the bromide salt of methscopolamine

pam·o·ate \'pa-mə-ˌwāt\ n : any of various salts or esters of an acid $C_{23}H_{16}O_6$ — see HYDROXYZINE

pam·pin·i·form plexus \pam-'pi-nə-ˌform-\ n : a venous plexus that is associated with each testicular vein in the male and each ovarian vein in the female — called also *pampiniform venous plexus*

pan- comb form : whole : general ⟨pancarditis⟩ ⟨panleukopenia⟩

pan·car·di·tis \ˌpan-kär-'dī-təs\ n : general inflammation of the heart

Pan·coast's syndrome \'pan-ˌkōsts-\ n : a complex of symptoms associated with Pancoast's tumor which includes Horner's syndrome and neuralgia of the arm resulting from pressure on the brachial plexus

Pancoast, Henry Khunrath (1875–1939), American radiologist.

Pancoast's tumor or **Pancoast tumor** n : a malignant tumor formed at the upper extremity of the lung

pan·cre·as \'paŋ-krē-əs, 'pan-\ n, pl **-cre·as·es** also **-cre·ata** \pan-'krē-ə-tə\ : a large lobulated gland that in humans lies in front of the upper lumbar vertebrae and behind the stomach and is somewhat hammer-shaped and firmly attached anteriorly to the

curve of the duodenum with which it communicates through one or more pancreatic ducts and that consists of (1) tubular acini secreting digestive enzymes which pass to the intestine and function in the breakdown of proteins, fats, and carbohydrates; (2) modified acinar cells that form islets of Langerhans between the tubules and secrete the hormones insulin and glucagon; and (3) a firm connective-tissue capsule that extends supportive strands into the organ

pancreat- or **pancreato-** comb form 1 : pancreas : pancreatic ⟨pancreatectomy⟩ ⟨pancreatin⟩ 2 : pancreas and ⟨pancreatoduodenectomy⟩

pan·cre·atec·to·my \ˌpaŋ-krē-ə-'tek-tə-mē, ˌpan-\ n, pl **-mies** : surgical excision of all or part of the pancreas —

pan·cre·atec·to·mized \ˌpaŋ-krē-ə-'tek-tə-ˌmīzd, ˌpan-\ adj

pan·cre·at·ic \ˌpaŋ-krē-'a-tik, ˌpan-\ adj : of, relating to, or produced in the pancreas ⟨∼ amylase⟩

pancreatic cholera n : VERNER-MORRISON SYNDROME

pancreatic duct n : a duct connecting the pancreas with the intestine: a : the chief duct of the pancreas that runs from left to right through the body of the gland, passes out its neck, and empties into the duodenum either through an opening shared with the common bile duct or through one close to it — called also *duct of Wirsung, Wirsung's duct* b : ACCESSORY PANCREATIC DUCT

pancreatic juice n : a clear alkaline secretion of pancreatic enzymes (as trypsin and lipase) that flows into the duodenum and acts on food already acted on by the gastric juice and saliva

pancreatico- comb form : pancreatic : pancreatic and ⟨pancreaticoduodenal⟩

pan·cre·at·i·co·du·o·de·nal \ˌpaŋ-krē-ə-ti-(ˌ)kō-ˌdü-ə-'dē-nəl, ˌpan-, -ˌdyü-; -dü-'äd-ᵊn-əl, -dyü-\ adj : of or relating to the pancreas and the duodenum

pancreaticoduodenal artery n : either of two arteries that supply the pancreas and duodenum forming an anastomosis giving off numerous branches to these parts: a : one arising from the superior mesenteric artery — called also *inferior pancreaticoduodenal artery* b : one arising from the gastroduodenal artery — called also *superior pancreaticoduodenal artery*

pancreaticoduodenal vein n : any of several veins that drain the pancreas and duodenum accompanying the inferior and superior pancreaticoduodenal arteries

pan·cre·at·i·co·du·o·de·nec·to·my \-ˌdü-ə-ˌdē-'nek-tə-mē, -ˌdyü-; -ˌdü-ˌäd-ᵊn-'ek-tə-mē, -dyü-\ n, pl **-mies** : partial or complete excision of the pancreas and the duodenum — called also *pancreatoduodenectomy*

pan·cre·at·i·co·du·o·de·nos·to·my \-'näs-tə-mē\ *n, pl* **-mies** : surgical formation of an artificial opening connecting the pancreas to the duodenum

pan·cre·at·i·co·je·ju·nos·to·my \-ji-jü-'näs-tə-mē, -je-jü-\ *n, pl* **-mies** : surgical formation of an artificial passage connecting the pancreas to the jejunum

pan·cre·atin \pan-'krē-ə-tən; 'paŋ-krē-, 'pan-\ *n* : a mixture of enzymes from the pancreatic juice; *also* : a preparation containing such a mixture obtained from the pancreas of the domestic swine or ox and used as a digestant

pan·cre·ati·tis \,paŋ-krē-ə-'tī-təs, ,pan-\ *n, pl* **-atit·i·des** \-'ti-tə-,dēz\ : inflammation of the pancreas

pancreato— see PANCREAT-

pan·cre·a·to·du·o·de·nec·to·my \'pan-krē-ə-tō-,dü-ə-,dē-'nek-tə-mē, -,dyü-; -dü-,ad-ə-'nek-tə-mē, -dyü-\ *n, pl* **-mies** : PANCREATICODUODENECTOMY

pan·creo·zy·min \,pan-krē-ō-'zī-mən\ *n* : CHOLECYSTOKININ

pan·cu·ro·ni·um bromide \,pan-kyə-'rō-nē-əm-\ *n* : a neuromuscular blocking agent $C_{35}H_{60}Br_2N_2O_4$ used as a skeletal muscle relaxant — called also *pancuronium*

pan·cy·to·pe·nia \,pan-,sī-tə-'pē-nē-ə\ *n* : an abnormal reduction in the number of red blood cells, white blood cells, and blood platelets in the blood; *also* : a disorder (as aplastic anemia) characterized by such a reduction — **pan·cy·to·pe·nic** \-'pē-nik\ *adj*

¹**pan·dem·ic** \pan-'de-mik\ *adj* : occurring over a wide geographic area and affecting an exceptionally high proportion of the population (~ malaria)

²**pandemic** *n* : a pandemic outbreak of a disease

pan·en·ceph·a·li·tis \,pan-in-,se-fə-'lī-təs\ *n, pl* **-lit·i·des** \-'li-tə-,dēz\ : inflammation of the brain affecting both white and gray matter — see SUBACUTE SCLEROSING PANENCEPHALITIS

pan·en·do·scope \'-en-də-,skōp\ *n* : a cystoscope fitted with an obliquely forward telescopic system that permits wide-angle viewing of the interior of the urinary bladder — **pan·en·do·scop·ic** \-,en-də-'skä-pik\ *adj* — **pan·en·dos·co·py** \-en-'däs-kə-pē\ *n*

Pa·neth cell \'pä-net-\ *n* : any of the granular epithelial cells with large acidophilic nuclei occurring at the base of the crypts of Lieberkühn in the small intestine and appendix

Paneth, Josef (1857–1890), Austrian physiologist.

pang \'paŋ\ *n* : a brief piercing spasm of pain — see BIRTH PANG, HUNGER PANGS

pan·hy·po·pi·tu·ita·rism \(,)pan-,hī-pō-pə-'tü-ə-tə-,ri-zəm, -'tyü-\ *n* : gener-

alized secretory deficiency of the anterior lobe of the pituitary gland; *also* : a disorder (as Simmond's disease) characterized by such deficiency — **pan·hy·po·pi·tu·itary** \-'tü-ə-,ter-ē, -'tyü-\ *adj*

pan·hys·ter·ec·to·my \(,)pan-,his-tə-'rek-tə-mē\ *n, pl* **-mies** : surgical excision of the uterus and uterine cervix

pan·ic \'pa-nik\ *n* : a sudden overpowering fright; *esp* : a sudden unreasoning terror often accompanied by mass flight — **panic** *vb*

panic disorder *n* : ANXIETY NEUROSIS

pan·leu·ko·pe·nia \,pan-,lü-kə-'pē-nē-ə\ *n* : an acute usu. fatal viral epizootic disease esp. of cats that is caused by a parvovirus and is characterized by fever, diarrhea and dehydration, and extensive destruction of white blood cells — called also *cat distemper, cat fever, feline distemper, feline enteritis, feline panleukopenia*

pan·nic·u·li·tis \pə-,ni-kyə-'lī-təs\ *n* 1 : inflammation of the subcutaneous layer of fat 2 : a syndrome characterized by recurring fever and usu. painful inflammatory and necrotic nodules in the subcutaneous tissues esp. of the thighs, abdomen, or buttocks — called also *relapsing febrile nodular nonsuppurative panniculitis, Weber-Christian disease*

pan·nic·u·lus \pə-'ni-kyə-ləs\ *n, pl* **-u·li** \-,lī\ : a sheet or layer of tissue; *esp* : PANNICULUS ADIPOSUS

panniculus ad·i·po·sus \-,a-də-'pō-səs\ *n* : any superficial fascia bearing deposits of fat

pan·nus \'pa-nəs\ *n, pl* **pan·ni** \-,nī\ 1 : a vascular tissue causing a superficial opacity of the cornea and occurring esp. in trachoma 2 : a sheet of inflammatory granulation tissue that spreads from the synovial membrane and invades the joint in rheumatoid arthritis ultimately leading to fibrous ankylosis

pan·oph·thal·mi·tis \(,)pan-,äf-thəl-'mī-təs, -,äp-\ *n* : inflammation involving all the tissues of the eyeball

pan·sys·tol·ic \(,)pan-sis-'tä-lik\ *adj* : persisting throughout systole (a ~ heart murmur)

pant \'pant\ *vb* : to breathe quickly, spasmodically, or in a labored manner

pan·to·caine \'pan-tə-,kān\ *n* : TETRACAINE

pan·to·the·nate \,pan-tə-'the-,nāt, pan-'tä-thə-,nāt\ *n* : a salt or ester of pantothenic acid — see CALCIUM PANTOTHENATE

pan·to·then·ic acid \,pan-tə-'the-nik-\ *n* : a viscous oily acid $C_9H_{17}NO_5$ that belongs to the vitamin B complex, occurs usu. combined (as in coenzyme A) in all living tissues

pan·trop·ic \(,)pan-'trä-pik\ *adj* : affecting various tissues without showing special affinity for one of them ⟨a ~ virus⟩ — compare NEUROTROPIC

pa·pa·in \pə-ˈpā-ən, -ˈpī-\ n : a crystallizable proteinase in the juice of the green fruit of the papaya (*Carica papaya* of the family Caricaceae) obtained usu. as a brownish powder and used chiefly as a tenderizer for meat and in medicine as a digestant

Pa·pa·ni·co·laou smear \pä-pə-ˈnē-kə-ˌlaȯ-, ˌpa-pə-ˈni-kə-\ n : PAP SMEAR **Papanicolaou, George Nicholas (1883–1962), American anatomist and cytologist.**

Papanicolaou test n : PAP SMEAR

Pa·pa·ver \pə-ˈpā-vər, -ˈpä-\ n : a genus (family Papaveraceae) of chiefly bristly hairy herbs that contains the opium poppy (*P. somniferum*)

pa·pav·er·ine \pə-ˈpa-və-ˌrēn, -rən\ n : a crystalline alkaloid $C_{20}H_{21}NO_4$ that is used in the form of its hydrochloride chiefly as an antispasmodic (as in spasm of blood vessels due to a blood clot)

paper chromatography n : chromatography that uses paper strips or sheets as the adsorbent stationary phase through which a solution flows and is used esp. to separate amino acids — compare COLUMN CHROMATOGRAPHY, THIN-LAYER CHROMATOGRAPHY

papill- *or* **papillo-** *comb form* 1 : papilla (*papillitis*) 2 : papillary (*papilledema*) (*papilloma*)

pa·pil·la \pə-ˈpi-lə\ n, pl **pa·pil·lae** \-ˈpi-(ˌ)lē, -ˌlī\ : a small projecting body part similar to a nipple in form: as a : a vascular process of connective tissue extending into and nourishing the root of a hair or developing tooth b : any of the vascular protuberances of the dermal layer of the skin extending into the epidermal layer and often containing tactile corpuscles c : RENAL PAPILLA d : any of the small protuberances on the upper surface of the tongue — see CIRCUMVALLATE PAPILLA, FILIFORM PAPILLA, FUNGIFORM PAPILLA, INTERDENTAL PAPILLA

papilla of Vater n : AMPULLA OF VATER

pap·il·lary \ˈpa-pə-ˌler-ē\ adj : of, relating to, or resembling a papilla : PAPILLOSE

papillary carcinoma n : a carcinoma characterized by a papillary structure

papillary layer n : the superficial layer of the dermis raised into papillae that fit into corresponding depressions on the inner surface of the epidermis

papillary muscle n : one of the small muscular columns attached at one end to the chordae tendineae and at the other to the wall of the ventricle and that maintain tension on the chordae tendineae as the ventricle contracts

pap·il·late \ˈpa-pə-ˌlāt, pə-ˈpi-lət\ adj : covered with or bearing papillae

pap·il·lec·to·my \ˌpa-pə-ˈlek-tə-mē\ n,

pl -**mies** : the surgical removal of a papilla

pap·il·le·de·ma \ˌpa-pə-lə-ˈdē-mə\ n : swelling and protrusion of the blind spot of the eye caused by edema — called also *choked disk*

pap·il·li·tis \ˌpa-pə-ˈlī-təs\ n : inflammation of a papilla; *esp* : inflammation of the optic disk — see NECROTIZING PAPILLITIS

pap·il·lo·ma \ˌpa-pə-ˈlō-mə\ n, pl -**mas** or -**ma·ta** \-mə-tə\ 1 : a benign tumor (as a wart or condyloma) resulting from an overgrowth of epithelial tissue on papillae of vascularized connective tissue (as of the skin) 2 : an epithelial tumor caused by a virus

pap·il·lo·ma·to·sis \-ˌlō-mə-ˈtō-səs\ n, pl -**to·ses** \-ˌsēz\ : a condition marked by the presence of numerous papillomas

pap·il·lo·ma·tous \-ˈlō-mə-təs\ adj 1 : resembling or being a papilloma 2 : marked or characterized by papillomas

pap·il·lo·ma·vi·rus \ˌpa-pə-ˈlō-mə-ˌvī-rəs\ n : any of a group of papovaviruses that cause papillomas

pap·il·lose \ˈpa-pə-ˌlōs\ adj : covered with, resembling, or bearing papillae

pa·po·va·vi·rus \pə-ˈpō-və-ˌvī-rəs\ n : any of a group of viruses that have a capsid composed of 72 capsomers and that are associated with or responsible for various neoplasms (as some warts)

pap·pa·ta·ci fever also **pa·pa·ta·ci fever** \ˌpä-pə-ˈtä-chē-\ or **pa·pa·ta·si fever** \-ˈtä-sē-\ n : SANDFLY FEVER

Pap smear \ˈpap-\ n : a method or a test based on it for the early detection of cancer esp. of the uterine cervix that involves staining exfoliated cells by a special technique which differentiates diseased tissue — called also *Papanicolaou smear, Papanicolaou test, Pap test*

G. N. Papanicolaou — see PAPANICOLAOU SMEAR

pap·u·la \ˈpa-pyə-lə\ n, pl **pap·u·lae** \-ˌlē\ 1 : PAPULE 2 : a small papilla

pap·u·lar \ˈpa-pyə-lər\ adj : consisting of or characterized by papules ⟨a ~ rash⟩ ⟨~ lesions⟩

pap·u·la·tion \ˌpa-pyə-ˈlā-shən\ n 1 : a stage in some eruptive conditions marked by the formation of papules 2 : the formation of papules

pap·ule \ˈpa-(ˌ)pyül\ n : a small solid usu. conical elevation of the skin caused by inflammation, accumulated secretion, or hypertrophy of tissue elements

papulo- *comb form* 1 : papula (*papulopustular*) 2 : papulous and ⟨*papulovesicular*⟩

pap·u·lo·pus·tu·lar \ˌpa-pyə-lō-ˈpəs-chə-lər, -ˈpəs-tyü-\ adj : consisting of both papules and pustules ⟨~ lesions⟩

pap·u·lo·sis \ˌpa-pyə-ˈlō-səs\ n : the condition of having papular lesions

pap·u·lo·ve·sic·u·lar \ˌpa-pyə-lō-və-ˈsi-**

kyə-lər\ *adj* : marked by the presence of both papules and vesicles

pap·y·ra·ceous \ˌpa-pə-ˈrā-shəs\ *adj* : of, relating to, or being one of twin fetuses which has died in the uterus and been compressed to a thinness like paper by the growth of the other

para \ˈpar-ə\ *n, pl* **par·as** *or* **par·ae** \ˈpar-ˌē\ : a woman delivered of a specified number of children — used in combination with a term or figure to indicate the number (multi*para*) (a 36-year-old *para* 5); compare GRAVIDA

para- \ˌpar-ə, ˈpar-ə\ *or* **par-** *prefix* **1** : beside : alongside of : beyond : aside from (*para*thyroid) (*par*enteral) **2 a** : closely related to (*para*ldehyde) **b** : involving substitution at or characterized by two opposite positions that are separated by two carbon atoms in the flat symmetrical ring of six carbon atoms characteristic of benzene (*para*dichlorobenzene) — abbr. *p-* **3 a** : faulty : abnormal (*par*esthesia) **b** : associated in a subsidiary or accessory capacity (*para*medical) **c** : closely resembling : almost (*para*typhoid)

para–ami·no·ben·zo·ic acid \ˈpar-ə-ə-ˌmē-ˌno-ˌben-ˈzō-ik-, ˈpar-ə-ˌa-mə-(ˌ)nō-\ *n* : a colorless para-substituted aminobenzoic acid that is a growth factor of the vitamin B complex — called also PABA

para–ami·no·hip·pu·rate \-ˈhi-pyə-ˌrāt\ *n* : a salt of para-aminohippuric acid

para–ami·no·hip·pu·ric acid \-hi-ˈpyùr-ik-\ *n* : a crystalline acid $C_{19}H_{10}N_2O_3$ used chiefly in the form of its sodium salt in testing kidney function

para–ami·no·sal·i·cyl·ic acid \-ˌsal-ə-ˈsil-ik\ *n* : the white crystalline para-substituted isomer of aminosalicylic acid that is made synthetically and is used in the treatment of tuberculosis

para–aor·tic \ˌpar-ə-ā-ˈȯr-tik\ *adj* : close to the aorta (~ lymph nodes)

para–api·cal \-ˈā-pi-kəl, -ˈa-\ *adj* : close to the apex of the heart

para·ben \ˈpar-ə-ˌben\ *n* : either of two antifungal agents used as preservatives in foods and pharmaceuticals: **a** : METHYLPARABEN **b** : PROPYLPARABEN

para·bi·o·sis \ˌpar-ə-(ˌ)bī-ˈō-səs, -bē-\ *n, pl* **-o·ses** \-ˌsēz\ : the anatomical and physiological union of two organisms either natural or artificially produced — **para·bi·ot·ic** \-ˈä-tik\ *adj* — **para·bi·ot·i·cal·ly** *adv*

para·cen·te·sis \ˌpar-ə-(ˌ)sen-ˈtē-səs, -ˌtē-ˌsēz\ *n, pl* **-te·ses** \-ˌsēz\ : a surgical puncture of a cavity of the body with a trocar, aspirator, or other instrument usu. to draw off any abnormal effusion

para·cen·tral \ˌpar-ə-ˈsen-trəl\ *adj* : lying near a center or central part

para·cen·tric \-ˈsen-trik\ *adj* : being an inversion that occurs in a single arm of one chromosome and does not involve the chromomere — compare PERICENTRIC

para·cer·vi·cal \-ˈsər-və-kəl\ *adj* : located or administered next to the uterine cervix (~ injection)

para·cet·a·mol \ˌpar-ə-ˈsē-tə-ˌmȯl\ *n, Brit* : ACETAMINOPHEN

para·chlo·ro·phe·nol \-ˌklȯr-ə-ˈfē-ˌnȯl, -ˌnōl, -fi-ˈnōl\ *n* : a chlorinated phenol C_6H_5ClO used as a germicide

para·chol·era \-ˈkä-lə-rə\ *n* : a disease clinically resembling Asiatic cholera but caused by a different vibrio

para·coc·cid·i·oi·des \ˌpar-ə-(ˌ)käk-ˌsi-dē-ˈȯi-ˌdēz\ *n* : a genus of imperfect fungi that includes the causative agent (*P. brasiliensis*) of South American blastomycosis

para·coc·cid·i·oi·do·my·co·sis \-(ˌ)käk-ˌsi-dē-ˌȯi-dō-(ˌ)mī-ˈkō-sis\ *n, pl* **-co·ses** \-ˌsēz\ : SOUTH AMERICAN BLASTOMYCOSIS

para·co·lic \-ˈkō-lik, -ˈkä-\ *adj* : adjacent to the colon (~ lymph nodes)

para·cone \ˈpar-ə-ˌkōn\ *n* : the anterior of the three cusps of a primitive upper molar that in higher forms is the principal anterior and external cusp

par·acu·sis \ˌpar-ə-ˈkyü-səs, -ˈkü-\ *n, pl* **-acu·ses** \-ˌsēz\ : a disorder in the sense of hearing

para·den·tal \-ˈdent-ᵊl\ *adj* : adjacent to a tooth (~ infections)

para·di·chlo·ro·ben·zene \ˌpar-ə-ˌdī-ˌklōr-ə-ˈben-ˌzēn, -ˌben-\ *n* : a white crystalline compound $C_6H_4Cl_2$ made by chlorinating benzene and used chiefly as a fumigant against clothes moths — called also *PDB*

para·did·y·mis \-ˈdi-də-məs\ *n, pl* **-y·mi·des** \-mə-ˌdēz\ : a group of coiled tubules situated in front of the lower end of the spermatic cord above the enlarged upper extremity of the epididymis and considered to be a remnant of tubes of the mesonephros

par·a·dox·i·cal \ˌpar-ə-ˈdäk-si-kəl\ *also* **par·a·dox·ic** \-sik\ *adj* : not being the normal or usual kind (~ pulse)

paradoxical sleep *n* : REM SLEEP

paradoxus — see PULSUS PARADOXUS

para·esoph·a·ge·al \-i-ˌsä-fə-ˈjē-əl\ *adj* : adjacent to the esophagus; *esp* : relating to or being a hiatal hernia in which the connection between the esophagus and the stomach remains in its normal location but part or all of the stomach herniates through the hiatus into the thorax

par·aes·the·sia *chiefly Brit var of* PARESTHESIA

par·af·fin \ˈpar-ə-fən\ *n* **1** : a waxy crystalline flammable substance obtained esp. from distillates of wood, coal, or petroleum that is a complex mixture of hydrocarbons and is used in pharmaceuticals and cosmetics **2** : ALKANE — **par·af·fin·ic** \ˌpar-ə-ˈfin-ik\ *adj*

para·fol·lic·u·lar \ˌpar-ə-fə-ˈli-kyə-lər\ *adj* : located in the vicinity of or surrounding a follicle (∼ cells of the thyroid)

para·for·mal·de·hyde \-fȯr-ˈmal-də-ˌhīd, -fər-\ *n* : a white powder $(CH_2O)_x$ that consists of a polymer of formaldehyde and is used esp. as a fungicide

para·fo·vea \-ˈfō-vē-ə\ *n, pl* **-fo·ve·ae** \-ˈfō-vē-ˌē, -vē-ˌī\ : the area surrounding the fovea — **para·fo·ve·al** \-ˈfō-vē-əl\ *adj*

para·gan·gli·o·ma \-ˌgaṅ-glē-ˈō-mə\ *n, pl* **-mas** *or* **-ma·ta** \-mə-tə\ : a ganglioma derived from chromaffin cells — compare PHEOCHROMOCYTOMA

para·gan·gli·on \-ˈgaṅ-glē-ən\ *n, pl* **-glia** \-glē-ə\ : one of numerous collections of chromaffin cells associated with ganglia and plexuses of the sympathetic nervous system and similar in structure to the medulla of the adrenal glands — **para·gan·gli·on·ic** \-ˌgaṅ-glē-ˈä-nik\ *adj*

par·a·gon·i·mi·a·sis \ˌpar-ə-ˌgä-nə-ˈmī-ə-səs\ *n, pl* **-a·ses** \-ˌsēz\ : infestation with or disease caused by a lung fluke of the genus *Paragonimus* (*P. westermanii*) that invades the lung

Par·a·gon·i·mus \ˌpar-ə-ˈgä-nə-məs\ *n* : a genus of digenetic trematodes (family Troglotrematidae) comprising forms normally parasitic in the lungs of mammals including humans

para·gran·u·lo·ma \-ˌgra-nyə-ˈlō-mə\ *n, pl* **-mas** *or* **-ma·ta** \-mə-tə\ 1 : a granuloma esp. of the lymph glands that is characterized by inflammation and replacement of the normal cell structure by an infiltrate 2 : a benign form of Hodgkin's disease in which paragranulomas of the lymph glands are a symptom — called also *Hodgkin's paragranuloma*

para·in·flu·en·za virus \ˌpar-ə-ˌin-flü-ˈen-zə\ *n* : any of several paramyxoviruses that are associated with or responsible for some respiratory infections esp. in children — called also *parainfluenza*

para·ker·a·to·sis \ˌpar-ə-ˌker-ə-ˈtō-səs\ *n, pl* **-to·ses** \-ˌsēz\ : an abnormality of the horny layer of the skin resulting in a disturbance in the process of keratinization

par·al·de·hyde \pa-ˈral-də-ˌhīd, pə-\ *n* : a colorless liquid polymeric modification $C_6H_{12}O_3$ of acetaldehyde used as a hypnotic esp. for controlling insomnia, excitement, delirium, and convulsions (as in delirium tremens and withdrawal from alcohol abuse)

pa·ral·y·sis \pə-ˈra-lə-səs\ *n, pl* **-y·ses** \-ˌsēz\ : complete or partial loss of function esp. when involving the power of motion or of sensation in any part of the body — see HEMIPLEGIA, PARAPLEGIA, PARESIS 1

paralysis agi·tans \-ˈa-jə-ˌtanz\ *n* : PARKINSON'S DISEASE

¹**par·a·lyt·ic** \ˌpar-ə-ˈli-tik\ *adj* 1 : affected with or characterized by paralysis

2 : of, relating to, or resembling paralysis

²**paralytic** *n* : one affected with paralysis

paralytica — see DEMENTIA PARALYTICA

paralytic dementia *n* : GENERAL PARESIS

paralytic ileus *n* : ileus resulting from failure of peristalsis

paralytic rabies *n* : rabies marked by sluggishness and by early paralysis esp. of the muscles of jaw and throat — called also *dumb rabies;* compare FURIOUS RABIES

paralytic shellfish poisoning *n* : food poisoning that results from consumption of shellfish and esp. 2-shelled mollusks (as clams, mussels, or scallops) contaminated with dinoflagellates causing red tide and that is characterized by paresthesia, nausea, vomiting, abdominal cramping, muscle weakness, and sometimes paralysis which may lead to respiratory failure

par·a·lyze \ˈpar-ə-ˌlīz\ *vb* **-lyzed; -lyz·ing** : to affect with paralysis — **par·a·ly·za·tion** \ˌpar-ə-lə-ˈzā-shən\ *n*

para·me·di·an \ˌpar-ə-ˈmē-dē-ən\ *adj* : situated adjacent to the midline

para·med·ic \ˌpar-ə-ˈme-dik\ *also* **para·med·i·cal** \-di-kəl\ *n* 1 : a person who works in a health field in an auxiliary capacity to a physician (as by giving injections and taking X rays) 2 : a specially trained medical technician licensed to provide a wide range of emergency medical services (as defibrillation and the intravenous administration of drugs) before or during transportation to the hospital — compare EMT

para·med·i·cal \ˌpar-ə-ˈme-di-kəl\ *also* **para·med·ic** \-dik\ *adj* : concerned with supplementing the work of highly trained medical professionals

para·me·so·neph·ric duct \-ˌme-zə-ˈne-frik-, -ˌmē-, -sə-\ *n* : MÜLLERIAN DUCT

para·metha·di·one \-ˌme-thə-ˈdī-ˌōn\ *n* : a liquid compound $C_7H_{11}NO_3$ that is a derivative of trimethadione and is used in the treatment of petit mal epilepsy

para·meth·a·sone \-ˈme-thə-ˌzōn\ *n* : a glucocorticoid with few mineralocorticoid side effects that is used for its anti-inflammatory and antiallergic actions esp. as the acetate $C_{24}H_{31}FO_6$

para·me·tri·tis \-mə-ˈtrī-təs\ *n* : inflammation of the parametrium

para·me·tri·um \-ˈmē-trē-əm\ *n, pl* **-tria** \-trē-ə\ : the connective tissue and fat adjacent to the uterus

par·am·ne·sia \ˌpar-am-ˈnē-zhə, -əm-\ *n* : a disorder of memory: as **a** : a condition in which the proper meaning of words cannot be remembered **b** : the illusion of remembering scenes and events when experienced for the first time — called also *déjà vu;* compare JAMAIS VU

para·mo·lar \,par-ə-ᵇmō-lər\ *adj* : of, relating to, or being a supernumerary tooth esp. on the buccal side of a permanent molar or a cusp or tubercle located esp. on the buccal aspect of a molar and representing such a tooth

par·am·y·loid·osis \,par-,a-mə-ᵇlȯi-ᵇdō-səs\ *n, pl* **-oses** \-,sēz\ : amyloidosis characterized by the accumulation of an atypical form of amyloid in the tissues

para·my·oc·lo·nus mul·ti·plex \,par-ə-mī-ᵇä-klə-nəs-ᵇməl-tə-,pleks\ *n* : a nervous disease characterized by clonic spasms with tremor in corresponding muscles on the two sides

para·myo·to·nia \,par-ə-,mī-ə-ᵇtō-nē-ə\ *n* : an abnormal state characterized by tonic muscle spasm

para·myxo·vi·rus \,par-ə-ᵇmik-sə-,vī-rəs\ *n* : any of a group of RNA-containing viruses (as the mumps, measles, and parainfluenza viruses) that are larger than the related orthomyxoviruses

para·na·sal \-ᵇnā-zəl\ *adj* : adjacent to the nasal cavities; *esp* : of, relating to, or affecting the paranasal sinuses

paranasal sinus *n* : any of various sinuses (as the maxillary sinus and frontal sinus) in the bones of the face and head that are lined with mucous membrane derived from and continuous with the lining of the nasal cavity

para·neo·plas·tic \,par-ə-,nē-ə-ᵇplas-tik\ *adj* : caused by or resulting from the presence of cancer in the body but not the physical presence of cancerous tissue in the part or organ affected

para·noia \,par-ə-ᵇnȯi-ə\ *n* 1 : a psychosis characterized by systematized delusions of persecution or grandeur usu. without hallucinations 2 : a tendency on the part of an individual or group toward excessive or irrational suspiciousness and distrustfulness of others

¹**para·noi·ac** \-ᵇnȯi-,ak, -ᵇnȯi-ik\ *also* **para·no·ic** \-ᵇnȯ-ik\ *adj* : of, relating to, affected with, or characteristic of paranoia or paranoid schizophrenia

²**paranoiac** *also* **paranoic** *n* : PARANOID

¹**para·noid** \ᵇpar-ə-,nȯid\ *also* **para·noi·dal** \,par-ə-ᵇnȯid-ᵊl\ *adj* 1 : characterized by or resembling paranoia or paranoid schizophrenia 2 : characterized by suspiciousness, persecutory trends, or megalomania

²**paranoid** *n* : one affected with paranoia or paranoid schizophrenia — called also *paranoiac*

paranoid schizophrenia *n* : schizophrenia characterized esp. by persecutory or grandiose delusions or hallucinations or by delusional jealousy

paranoid schizophrenic *n* : an individu-

al affected with paranoid schizophrenia

para·nor·mal \,par-ə-ᵇnȯr-məl\ *adj* : not understandable in terms of known scientific laws and phenomena — **para·nor·mal·ly** *adv*

para·ol·fac·to·ry \,par-ə-äl-ᵇfak-tə-rē, -ȯl-\ *n* : a small area of the cerebral cortex situated on the medial side of the frontal lobe below the corpus callosum and considered part of the limbic system

para·ox·on \-ᵇäk-,sän\ *n* : a phosphate ester $C_{10}H_{14}NO_6P$ that is formed from parathion in the body and that is a potent anticholinesterase

para·pa·re·sis \,par-ə-pə-ᵇrē-səs, ,par-ə-ᵇpar-ə-səs\ *n, pl* **-re·ses** \-,sēz\ : partial paralysis affecting the lower limbs — **para·pa·ret·ic** \-pə-ᵇre-tik\ *adj*

para·per·tus·sis \-(,)pər-ᵇtə-sis\ *n* : a human respiratory disease closely resembling whooping cough but milder and less often fatal and caused by a different bacterium of the genus *Bordetella* (*B. parapertussis*)

para·pha·ryn·geal space \-ᵇfar-ən-ᵇjē-əl-, -fə-ᵇrin-jəl-, -jē-əl-\ *n* : a space bounded medially by the superior constrictor of the pharynx, laterally by the medial pterygoid muscle, posteriorly by the cervical vertebrae, and below by the muscles arising from the styloid process

par·a·pha·sia \-ᵇfā-zhə, -zhē-ə\ *n* : aphasia in which the patient uses wrong words or uses words or sounds in senseless combinations — **par·a·pha·sic** \-ᵇfā-zik\ *adj*

para·phen·yl·ene·di·amine \-,fen-ᵊl-,ēn-ᵇdī-ə-,mēn\ *n* : a benzene derivative C_6H_8N used esp. in dyeing hair and sometimes causing an allergic reaction

para·phil·ia \-ᵇfil-ē-ə\ *n* : perverted sexual behavior

¹**para·phil·iac** \-ᵇfil-ē-,ak\ *adj* : of, relating to, or characterized by paraphilia

²**paraphiliac** *n* : a person who engages in paraphilia

para·phi·mo·sis \-fī-ᵇmō-səs, -fī-\ *n, pl* **-mo·ses** \-,sēz\ : a condition in which the foreskin is retracted behind the glans penis and cannot be replaced

para·phre·nia \-ᵇfrē-nē-ə\ *n* 1 : the group of paranoid disorders 2 : any of the paranoid disorders; *also* : SCHIZOPHRENIA — **para·phren·ic** \-ᵇfre-nik\ *adj*

para·ple·gia \,par-ə-ᵇplē-jə, -jē-ə\ *n* : paralysis of the lower half of the body with involvement of both legs usu. due to disease of or injury to the spinal cord

¹**para·ple·gic** \-ᵇplē-jik\ *adj* : of, relating to, or affected with paraplegia

²**paraplegic** *n* : an individual affected with paraplegia

para·prax·is \-ᵇprak-səs\ *n, pl* **-prax·es** \-ᵇprak-,sēz\ : a faulty act (as a

Freudian slip) of purposeful behavior

para·pro·tein \-'prō-tēn\ n : any of various abnormal serum globulins with unique physical and electrophoretic characteristics

para·pro·tein·emia \-,prō-tē-'nē-mē-ə. -,prō-tē-ə-'nē-\ n : the presence of a paraprotein in the blood

para·pso·ri·a·sis \-sə-'rī-ə-səs\ n, pl -a·ses \-,sēz\ : a rare skin disease characterized by red scaly patches similar to those of psoriasis but causing no sensations of pain or itch

para·psy·chol·o·gy \,par-ə-(,)sī-'kä-lə-jē\ n, pl -gies : a field of study concerned with the investigation of evidence for paranormal psychological phenomena (as telepathy, clairvoyance, and psychokinesis) — **para·psych·o·log·i·cal** \-,sī-kə-'läj-i-kəl\ adj — **para·psy·chol·o·gist** \-sī-'kä-lə-jist, -sə-\ n

para·quat \'par-ə-,kwät\ n : an herbicide containing a salt of a cation $C_{12}H_{14}N_2$ that is extremely toxic to the liver, kidneys, and lungs if ingested

para·re·nal \,par-ə-'rēn-ᵊl\ adj : adjacent to the kidney

para·ros·an·i·line \,par-ə-,rō-'zan-ᵊl-ən\ n : a white crystalline base $C_{19}H_{19}N_3O$ that is the parent compound of many dyes; also : its red chloride used esp. as a biological stain

para·sag·it·tal \-'saj-ət-ᵊl\ adj : situated alongside of or adjacent to a sagittal location or a sagittal plane

Par·as·ca·ris \(,)par-'as-kə-rəs\ n : a genus of nematode worms (family Ascaridae) including the large roundworm (P. equorum) of the horse

parasit- or **parasito-** also **parasiti-** comb form : parasite (parasitemia) (parasiticide)

para·sit·ae·mia chiefly Brit var of PARASITEMIA

par·a·site \'par-ə-,sīt\ n : an organism living in, with, or on another organism in parasitism

par·a·sit·emia \,par-ə-,sī-'tē-mē-ə\ n : a condition in which parasites are present in the blood — used esp. to indicate the presence of parasites without clinical symptoms (an afebrile ~ of malaria)

par·a·sit·ic \,par-ə-'si-tik\ also **par·a·sit·i·cal** \-ti-kəl\ adj 1 : relating to or having the habit of a parasite : living on another organism 2 : caused by or resulting from the effects of parasites — **par·a·sit·i·cal·ly** adv

par·a·sit·i·cide \-'si-tə-,sīd\ n : an agent that is destructive to parasites — **par·a·sit·i·cid·al** \-,si-tə-'sīd-ᵊl\ adj

par·a·sit·ism \'par-ə-sə-,ti-zəm, -,sī-\ n 1 : an intimate association between organisms of two or more kinds; esp : one in which a parasite obtains benefits from a host which it usu. injures 2 : PARASITOSIS

par·a·sit·ize \-sə-,tīz, -,sī-\ vb **-ized**; **-iz·ing** : to infest or live on or with as a parasite — **par·a·sit·iza·tion** \,par-ə-sə-tə-'zā-shən, -,sī-\ n

parasito- — see PARASIT-

par·a·si·tol·o·gist \-'tä-lə-jist\ n : a specialist in parasitology; esp : one who deals with the worm parasites of animals

par·a·si·tol·o·gy \,par-ə-sə-'tä-lə-jē, -,sī-\ n, pl -gies : a branch of biology dealing with parasites and parasitism esp. among animals — **par·a·si·to·log·i·cal** \-,sit-ᵊl-'äj-i-kəl, -,sīt-\ also **par·a·si·to·log·ic** \-jik\ adj — **par·a·si·to·log·i·cal·ly** adv

par·a·sit·osis \-sə-'tō-səs, -,sī-\ n, pl -o·ses \-,sēz\ : infestation with or disease caused by parasites

para·spe·cif·ic \-spi-'si-fik\ adj : having or being curative actions or properties in addition to the specific one considered medically useful

para·spi·nal \-'spin-ᵊl\ adj : adjacent to the spinal column (~ muscles)

para·ster·nal \-'stər-nəl\ adj : adjacent to the sternum — **para·ster·nal·ly** adv

¹**para·sym·pa·thet·ic** \,par-ə-,sim-pə-'the-tik\ adj : of, relating to, being, or acting on the parasympathetic nervous system (~ drugs)

²**parasympathetic** n 1 : a parasympathetic nerve 2 : PARASYMPATHETIC NERVOUS SYSTEM

parasympathetic nervous system n : the part of the autonomic nervous system that contains chiefly cholinergic fibers, that tends to induce secretion, to increase the tone and contractility of smooth muscle, and to slow the heart rate, and that consists of a cranial part and a sacral part — called also parasympathetic system; compare SYMPATHETIC NERVOUS SYSTEM

¹**para·sym·pa·tho·lyt·ic** \,par-ə-,sim-pə-thō-'li-tik\ adj : tending to oppose the physiological results of parasympathetic nervous activity or of parasympathomimetic drugs — compare SYMPATHOLYTIC

²**parasympatholytic** n : a parasympatholytic substance

¹**para·sym·pa·tho·mi·met·ic** \,par-ə-,sim-pə-(,)thō-mī-'me-tik, -mə-\ adj : simulating parasympathetic nervous action in physiological effect — compare SYMPATHOMIMETIC

²**parasympathomimetic** n : a parasympathomimetic agent (as a drug)

para·sys·to·le \-'sis-tə-(,)lē\ n : an irregularity in cardiac rhythm caused by an ectopic pacemaker in addition to the normal one

para·tax·ic \,par-ə-'tak-sik\ adj : relating to or being thinking in which a cause and effect relationship is attributed to events occurring at about the same time but having no logical relationship

para·ten·on \,par-ə-'te-nən, -(,)nän\ n

: the areolar tissue filling the space between a tendon and its sheath

para·thi·on \par-ə-ˈthī-ən, -ˌän\ n : an extremely toxic sulfur-containing insecticide $C_{10}H_{14}NO_5PS$

para·thor·mone \ˌpar-ə-ˈthȯr-ˌmōn\ n : PARATHYROID HORMONE

¹**para·thy·roid** \-ˈthī-ˌrȯid\ n : PARATHYROID GLAND

²**parathyroid** adj 1 : adjacent to a thyroid gland 2 : of, relating to, or produced by the parathyroid glands

para·thy·roid·ec·to·my \-ˌthī-ˌrȯi-ˈdek-tə-mē\ n, pl -mies : partial or complete excision of the parathyroid glands — **para·thy·roid·ec·to·mized** \-ˈmizd\ adj

parathyroid gland n : any of usu. four small endocrine glands that are adjacent to or embedded in the thyroid gland, are composed of irregularly arranged secretory epithelial cells lying in a stroma rich in capillaries, and produce parathyroid hormone

parathyroid hormone n : a hormone of the parathyroid gland that regulates the metabolism of calcium and phosphorus in the body — abbr. *PTH*; called also *parathormone*

para·thy·ro·trop·ic \ˌpar-ə-ˌthī-rō-ˈträ-pik\ adj : acting on or stimulating the parathyroid glands (a ~ hormone)

para·tra·che·al \-ˈtrā-kē-əl\ adj : adjacent to the trachea

para·tu·ber·cu·lo·sis \-ˌtü-bər-kyə-ˈlō-səs, -tyü-\ n, pl -lo·ses \-ˌsēz\ : JOHNE'S DISEASE

¹**para·ty·phoid** \ˌpar-ə-ˈtī-ˌfȯid, -ˌ(ˌ)tī-ˈ\ adj 1 : resembling typhoid fever 2 : of or relating to paratyphoid or its causative organisms (~ infection)

²**paratyphoid** n : any of numerous salmonelloses (as necrotic enteritis) that resemble typhoid fever and are commonly contracted by eating contaminated food — called also *paratyphoid fever*

para·um·bil·i·cal \-ˌəm-ˈbi-li-kəl\ adj : adjacent to the navel (~ pain)

para·ure·thral \-yü-ˈrē-thrəl\ adj : adjacent to the urethra

paraurethral gland n : any of several small glands that open into the female urethra near its opening and are homologous to glandular tissue in the prostate gland in the male — called also *Skene's gland*

para·vac·cin·ia \-vak-ˈsi-nē-ə\ n : MILKER'S NODULES

para·ven·tric·u·lar nucleus \-ven-ˈtri-kyə-lər-, -vən-\ n : a nucleus in the hypothalamus that produces vasopressin and esp. oxytocin and that innervates the neurohypophysis

para·ver·te·bral \-(ˌ)vər-ˈtē-brəl, -ˈvər-tə-\ adj : situated, occurring, or performed beside or adjacent to the spinal column (~ sympathectomy)

par·e·gor·ic \ˌpar-ə-ˈgȯr-ik, -ˈgär-\ n : camphorated tincture of opium used esp. to relieve pain

pa·ren·chy·ma \pə-ˈreŋ-kə-mə\ n : the essential and distinctive tissue of an organ or an abnormal growth as distinguished from its supportive framework

pa·ren·chy·mal \pə-ˈreŋ-kə-məl, ˌpar-ən-ˈki-məl\ adj : PARENCHYMATOUS

par·en·chy·ma·tous \ˌpar-ən-ˈki-mə-təs, -ˈki-\ adj : of, relating to, made up of, or affecting parenchyma

par·ent \ˈpar-ənt\ n 1 : one that begets or brings forth offspring 2 : the material or source from which something is derived — **parent** adj

pa·ren·tal generation \pə-ˈrent-əl-\ n : a generation of individuals of distinctively different genotypes that are crossed to produce hybrids — see FILIAL GENERATION

¹**par·en·ter·al** \pə-ˈren-tə-rəl\ adj : situated or occurring outside the intestine; esp : introduced otherwise than by way of the intestines — **par·en·ter·al·ly** adv

²**parenteral** n : an agent (as a drug or solution) intended for parenteral administration

par·ent·ing \ˈpar-ənt-iŋ\ n : the raising of a child by his or her parents

pa·re·sis \pə-ˈrē-səs, ˈpar-ə-səs\ n, pl **pa·re·ses** \-ˌsēz\ 1 : slight or partial paralysis 2 : GENERAL PARESIS

par·es·the·sia \ˌpar-es-ˈthē-zhə, -zhē-ə\ n : a sensation of pricking, tingling, or creeping on the skin having no objective cause and usu. associated with injury or irritation of a sensory nerve or nerve root — **par·es·thet·ic** \-ˈthe-tik\ adj

paresthetica — see MERALGIA PARESTHETICA

¹**pa·ret·ic** \pə-ˈre-tik\ adj : of, relating to, or affected with paresis

²**paretic** n : a person affected with paresis

par·gy·line \ˈpär-jə-ˌlēn\ n : a monoamine oxidase inhibitor $C_{11}H_{13}N$ that is used in the form of its hydrochloride esp. as an antihypertensive agent

par·ies \ˈpar-ē-ˌēz\ n, pl **pa·ri·e·tes** \pə-ˈrī-ə-ˌtēz\ : the wall of a cavity or hollow organ — usu. used in pl.

¹**pa·ri·e·tal** \pə-ˈrī-ət-əl\ adj 1 : of or relating to the walls of a part or cavity — compare VISCERAL 2 : of, relating to, or located in the upper posterior part of the head; specif : relating to the parietal bones

²**parietal** n : a parietal part (as a bone)

parietal bone n : either of a pair of membrane bones of the roof of the skull between the frontal and occipital bones that are large and quadrilateral in outline, meet in the sagittal suture, and form much of the top and sides of the cranium

parietal cell n : any of the large oval cells of the gastric mucous membrane that secrete hydrochloric acid and lie between the chief cells and the basement membrane

parietal emissary vein *n* : a vein that passes from the superior sagittal sinus inside the skull through a foramen in the parietal bone to connect with veins of the scalp

parietalis — see DECIDUA PARIETALIS

parietal lobe *n* : the middle division of each cerebral hemisphere that is situated behind the central sulcus, above the fissure of Sylvius, and in front of the parieto-occipital sulcus and that contains an area concerned with bodily sensations

parietal pericardium *n* : the tough thickened membranous outer layer of the pericardium that is attached to the central part of the diaphragm and the posterior part of the sternum — compare EPICARDIUM

parietal peritoneum *n* : the part of the peritoneum that lines the abdominal wall — compare VISCERAL PERITONEUM

parieto- *comb form* : parietal and (*parietotemporal*)

pa·ri·e·to-oc·cip·i·tal \pǝ-ˌrī-ǝ-tō-äk-ˈsi-pǝt-ᵊl\ *adj* : of, relating to, or situated between the parietal and occipital bones or lobes

parieto-occipital sulcus *n* : a fissure near the posterior end of each cerebral hemisphere separating the parietal and occipital lobes — called also *parieto-occipital fissure*

pa·ri·e·to·tem·po·ral \ˈtem-pǝ-rǝl\ *n* : of or relating to the parietal and temporal bones or lobes

Par·i·naud's oc·u·lo·glan·du·lar syn·drome \ˌpär-i-ˈnōz-ˌä-kyǝ-lō-ˈglan-jǝ-lǝr-\ *n* : conjunctivitis that is often unilateral, is usu. characterized by dense local infiltration by lymphoid tissue with tenderness and swelling of the preauricular lymph nodes, and is usu. associated with a bacterial infection (as in cat scratch disease and tularemia) — called also *Parinaud's conjunctivitis*

Parinaud, Henri (1844–1905), French ophthalmologist.

Parinaud's syndrome *n* : paralysis of the upward movements of the two eyes that is associated esp. with a lesion or compression of the superior colliculi of the midbrain

Par·is green \ˈpar-ǝs-\ *n* : a very poisonous copper-based bright green powder $Cu(C_2H_3O_2)_2 \cdot 3Cu(AsO_2)_2$ that is used as an insecticide and pigment

par·i·ty \ˈpar-ǝ-tē\ *n, pl* **-ties** : the state or fact of having borne offspring; *also* : the number of children previously borne

¹par·kin·so·nian \ˌpär-kǝn-ˈsō-nē-ǝn, -nyǝn\ *adj* 1 : of or similar to that of parkinsonism 2 : affected with parkinsonism and esp. Parkinson's disease

Par·kin·son \ˈpär-kǝn-sǝn\, **James (1755–1824),** British surgeon.

²parkinsonian *n* : an individual affected with parkinsonism and esp. Parkinson's disease

par·kin·son·ism \ˈpär-kǝn-sǝ-ˌni-zǝm\ *n* 1 : PARKINSON'S DISEASE 2 : a nervous disorder that resembles Parkinson's disease

Par·kin·son's disease \ˈpär-kǝn-sǝnz-\ *n* : a chronic progressive nervous disease chiefly of later life that is linked to decreased dopamine production in the substantia nigra and is marked by tremor and weakness of resting muscles and by a shuffling gait — called also *paralysis agitans, parkinsonism, Parkinson's, Parkinson's syndrome*

par·odon·tal \ˌpar-ǝ-ˈdänt-ᵊl\ *adj* : PERIODONTAL 2 — **par·odon·tal·ly** *adv*

par·o·mo·my·cin \ˌpar-ǝ-mō-ˈmīs-ᵊn\ *n* : a broad-spectrum antibiotic $C_{23}H_{45}N_5O_{14}$ that is obtained from a bacterium of the genus *Streptomyces* (*S. rimosus paromomycinus*) and is used against intestinal amebiasis esp. in the form of its sulfate

par·onych·ia \ˌpar-ǝ-ˈni-kē-ǝ\ *n* : inflammation of the tissues adjacent to the nail of a finger or toe usu. accompanied by infection and pus formation — compare WHITLOW

par·ooph·o·ron \ˌpar-ō-ˈä-fǝ-ˌrän\ *n* : a group of rudimentary tubules in the broad ligament between the epoophoron and the uterus that constitutes a remnant of the lower part of the mesonephros in the female

par·os·mia \ˌpar-ˈäz-mē-ǝ\ *n* : a distortion of the sense of smell (as when affected with a cold)

¹pa·rot·id \pǝ-ˈrä-tǝd\ *adj* : of, relating to, being, produced by, or located near the parotid gland

²parotid *n* : PAROTID GLAND

parotid duct *n* : the duct of the parotid gland opening on the inner surface of the cheek opposite the second upper molar tooth — called also *Stensen's duct*

parotid gland *n* : a salivary gland that is situated on each side of the face below and in front of the ear, in humans is the largest of the salivary glands, is of pure serous type, and communicates with the mouth by the parotid duct

par·o·ti·tis \ˌpar-ǝ-ˈtī-tǝs\ *n* 1 : inflammation and swelling of one or both parotid glands or other salivary glands (as in mumps) 2 : MUMPS

par·ous \ˈpar-ǝs\ *adj* 1 : having produced offspring 2 : of or characteristic of the parous female

-a·rous \p-ǝ-rǝs\ *adj comb form* : giving birth to : producing (multi*parous*)

par·o·var·i·um \ˌpar-ō-ˈvar-ē-ǝm\ *n* : EPOOPHORON — **par·o·var·i·an** \-ē-ǝn\ *adj*

par·ox·ysm \ˈpar-ǝk-ˌsi-zǝm, pǝ-ˈräk-\ *n* 1 : a sudden attack or spasm (as of a disease) 2 : a sudden recurrence of symptoms or an intensification of existing symptoms — **par·ox·ys·mal** \ˌpar-ək-ˈsiz-məl, pə-ˈräk-\ adj

paroxysmal dyspnea n : CARDIAC ASTHMA

paroxysmal nocturnal hemoglobinuria n : a form of hemolytic anemia that is characterized by an abnormally strong response to the action of complement, by acute episodes of hemolysis esp. at night with hemoglobinuria noted upon urination after awakening, venous occlusion, and often leukopenia and thrombocytopenia

paroxysmal tachycardia n : tachycardia that begins and ends abruptly and that is initiated by a premature supraventricular beat originating in the atrium or in the atrioventricular node or bundle of His or by a premature ventricular beat

par·rot fever \ˈpar-ət-\ n : PSITTACOSIS

pars \ˈpärs\ n, pl **par·tes** \ˈpär-(ˌ)tēz\ : an anatomical part

pars com·pac·ta \-ˈkäm-ˈpak-tə\ n : the large dorsal part of gray matter of the substantia nigra that is next to the tegmentum

pars dis·ta·lis \-di-ˈstä-ləs\ n : the anterior part of the adenohypophysis that is the major secretory part of the gland

pars in·ter·me·dia \-ˌin-tər-ˈmē-dē-ə\ n : a thin slip of tissue fused with the neurohypophysis and representing the remains of the posterior wall of Rathke's pouch

pars ner·vo·sa \-nər-ˈvō-sə\ n : NEURAL LOBE

pars pla·na \-ˈplā-nə\ n : ORBICULUS CILIARIS

pars tu·ber·a·lis \-ˌtü-bə-ˈrä-ləs, -ˌtyü-\ n : a thin plate of cells that is an extension of the adenohypophysis on the ventral or anterior aspect of the infundibulum

partes pl of PARS

parthen- or **partheno-** comb form : virgin : without fertilization (partheno-genesis)

par·the·no·gen·e·sis \ˌpär-thə-nō-ˈje-nə-səs\ n, pl **-e·ses** \-ˌsēz\ : reproduction by development of an unfertilized usu. female gamete that occurs esp. among lower plants and invertebrate animals — **par·the·no·ge·net·ic** \-jə-ˈne-tik\ also **par·the·no·gen·ic** \-ˈje-nik\ adj

par·tial denture \ˈpär-shəl-\ n : a usu. removable artificial replacement of one or more teeth

partial pressure n : the pressure exerted by a (specified) component in a mixture of gases

¹**par·tic·u·late** \pär-ˈti-kyə-lət\ adj : of, relating to, or existing in the form of minute separate particles

²**particulate** n : a particulate substance

particulate inheritance n : inheritance of characters specif. transmitted by genes in accord with Mendel's laws — called also Mendelian inheritance;

compare QUANTITATIVE INHERITANCE

¹**par·tu·ri·ent** \pär-ˈtur-ē-ənt, -ˈtyur-\ adj 1 : bringing forth or about to bring forth young 2 : of or relating to parturition (~ pangs) 3 : typical of parturition (the ~ uterus)

²**parturient** n : a parturient individual

parturient paresis n : MILK FEVER 2

par·tu·ri·tion \ˌpär-tə-ˈri-shən, ˌpär-chə-, ˌpär-tyü-\ n : the action or process of giving birth to offspring — **par·tu·ri·tion·al** \-shə-nəl\ adj

pa·ru·lis \pə-ˈrü-ləs\ n, pl **-li·des** \-lə-ˌdēz\ : an abscess in the gum : GUMBOIL

par·um·bil·i·cal vein \ˌpar-əm-ˈbi-li-kəl-\ n : any of several small veins that connect the veins of the anterior abdominal wall with the portal vein and the internal and common iliac veins

parv- or **parvi-** also **parvo-** comb form : small (parvovirus)

par·vo \ˈpär-ˌvō\ n : PARVOVIRUS 2

par·vo·cel·lu·lar also **par·vi·cel·lu·lar** \ˌpär-və-ˈsel-yə-lər\ adj : of, relating to, or being small cells

par·vo·vi·rus \ˈpär-vō-ˌvī-rəs\ n 1 : any of a group of small single-stranded DNA viruses that include the causative agent of erythema infectiosum 2 : a highly contagious febrile disease of dogs that is caused by a parvovirus, that is spread esp. by contact with infected feces, and that is marked by loss of appetite, lethargy, often bloody diarrhea and vomiting, and sometimes death — called also parvo

¹**PAS** \ˌpē-(ˌ)ā-ˈes\ adj : PERIODIC ACID-SCHIFF

²**PAS** abbr para-aminosalicylic acid

PASA abbr para-aminosalicylic acid

pass \ˈpas\ vb : to emit or discharge from a bodily part and esp. from the bowels : EVACUATE 2, VOID

¹**pas·sage** \ˈpa-sij\ n 1 : the action or process of passing from one place, condition, or stage to another 2 : an anatomical channel (the nasal ~s) 3 : a movement or an evacuation of the bowels 4 a : an act or action of passing something or undergoing a passing (~ of a catheter through the urethra) b : incubation of a pathogen (as a virus) in a tissue culture, a developing egg, or a living organism to increase the amount of pathogen or to alter its characteristics

²**passage** vb **pas·saged**; **pas·sag·ing** : to subject to passage

pas·sive \ˈpa-siv\ adj 1 a (1) : lethargic or lacking in energy or will (2) : tending not to take an active or dominant part b : induced by an outside agency (~ exercise of a paralyzed leg) 2 a : of, relating to, or characterized by a state of chemical inactivity b : not involving expenditure of chemical energy (~ transport across a cell mem brane) — **pas·sive·ly** *adv* — **pas·sive·ness** *n*

passive congestion *n* : congestion caused by obstruction to the return flow of venous blood — called also *passive hyperemia*

passive immunity *n* : immunity acquired by transfer of antibodies (as by injection of serum from an individual with active immunity) — compare ACQUIRED IMMUNITY, NATURAL IMMUNITY — **passive immunization** *n*

passive smoking *n* : the involuntary inhalation of tobacco smoke (as from another's cigarette) esp. by a nonsmoker

passive transfer *n* : a local transfer of skin sensitivity from an allergic to a normal individual by injection of the allergic individual's serum that is used esp. for identifying specific allergens when a high degree of sensitivity is suspected — called also *Prausnitz-Küstner reaction*

pas·siv·i·ty \pa-'si-və-tē\ *n, pl* **-ties** : the quality or state of being passive or submissive

pass out *vb* : to lose consciousness

paste \'pāst\ *n* : a soft plastic mixture or composition; *esp* : an external medicament that has a stiffer consistency than an ointment but is less greasy because of its higher percentage of powdered ingredients

pas·tern \'pas-tərn\ *n* : a part of the foot of an equine extending from the fetlock to the top of the hoof

pas·teu·rel·la \,pas-tə-'re-lə\ *n* **1** *cap* : a genus of gram-negative facultatively anaerobic rod bacteria (family Pasteurellaceae) that include several important pathogens esp. of domestic animals — see HEMORRHAGIC SEPTICEMIA; YERSINIA **2** *pl* **-las** *or* **-lae** \-,lī\ : any bacterium of the genus *Pasteurella*

Pas·teur \pa-'stər, -'stœr\, **Louis** (1822–1895), French chemist and bacteriologist.

pas·teu·rel·lo·sis \,pas-tə-rə-'lō-səs\, *n, pl* **-lo·ses** \-,sēz\ : infection with or disease caused by bacteria of the genus *Pasteurella*

pas·teur·i·za·tion \,pas-chə-rə-'zā-shən, ,pas-tə-\ *n* **1** : partial sterilization of a substance and esp. a liquid (as milk) at a temperature and for a period of exposure that destroys objectionable organisms **2** : partial sterilization of perishable food products (as fruit or fish) with radiation (as gamma rays) — **pas·teur·ize** \'pas-chə-,rīz, 'pas-tə-\ *vb*

Pasteur treatment *n* : a method of aborting rabies by stimulating production of antibodies through successive inoculations with attenuated virus of gradually increasing strength

pas·tille \pas-'tēl\ *also* **pas·til** \'past-əl\ *n* : LOZENGE

past–pointing test \'past-'pȯin-tiŋ-\ *n*

: a test for defective functioning of the vestibular nerve in which a subject is asked to point at an object with eyes open and then closed first after rotation in a chair to the right and then to the left and which indicates an abnormality if the subject does not point to the side of the object in the direction of rotation

PAT *abbr* paroxysmal atrial tachycardia

patch \'pach\ *n* **1 a** : a piece of material (as an adhesive plaster) used medically usu. to cover a wound, repair a defect, or supply medication through the skin — see PATCH GRAFT **b** : a shield worn over the socket of an injured or missing eye **2** : a circumscribed region of tissue (as on the skin or in a section from an organ) that differs from the normal color or composition — **patch** *vb* — **patchy** \'pa-chē\ *adj*

patch graft *n* : a graft of living or synthetic material used to repair a defect in a blood vessel

patch test *n* : a test for determining allergic sensitivity that is made by applying to the unbroken skin small pads soaked with the allergen to be tested and that indicates sensitivity when irritation develops at the point of application — compare INTRADERMAL TEST, SCRATCH TEST

pa·tel·la \pa-'te-lə\ *n, pl* **-lae** \-'te-(,)lē, -,lī\ *or* **-las** : a thick flat triangular movable bone that forms the anterior point of the knee joint, protects the front of the knee joint, and increases the leverage of the quadriceps — called also *kneecap* — **pa·tel·lar** \-lər\ *adj*

patellar ligament *n* : the part of the tendon of the quadriceps that extends from the patella to the tibia — called also *patellar tendon*

patellar reflex *n* : KNEE JERK

patellar tendon *n* : PATELLAR LIGAMENT

pat·el·lec·to·my \,pa-tə-'lek-tə-mē\ *n, pl* **-mies** : surgical excision of the patella

pa·tel·lo·fem·o·ral \pə-,te-lō-'fe-mə-rəl\ *adj* : of or relating to the patella and femur (the ~ articulation)

pa·ten·cy \'pat-ən-sē, 'pāt-\ *n, pl* **-cies** : the quality or state of being open or unobstructed

pa·tent \'pat-ənt-\ **1** : protected by a trademark or a trade name so as to establish proprietary rights analogous to those conveyed by a patent : PROPRIETARY (~ drugs) **2** \'pāt-\ : affording free passage : being open and unobstructed

pa·tent ductus arteriosus \'pāt-ənt-\ *n* : an abnormal condition in which the ductus arteriosus fails to close after birth

pat·ent medicine \'pat-ənt-\ *n* : a packaged nonprescription drug which is protected by a trademark and whose contents are incompletely disclosed; *also* : any drug that is a proprietary

pa·ter·ni·ty test \pə-'tər-nə-tē-\ *n* : a test esp. of DNA or genetic traits to determine whether a given man could be the biological father of a given child — **paternity testing** *n*

¹**path** \'path\ *n, pl* **paths** \'pathz, 'paths\ : PATHWAY 2

²**path** *abbr* pathological; pathology

path- *or* **patho-** *comb form* 1 : pathological (*patho*biology) 2 : pathological state : disease (*patho*gen)

-path \path\ *n comb form* 1 : practitioner of a (specified) system of medicine that emphasizes one aspect of disease or its treatment (naturo*path*) 2 : one affected with a disorder of (such a part or system) (psycho*path*)

-path·ia \'pa-thē-ə\ *n comb form* : -PATHY 2 (hyper*pathia*)

-path·ic \'pa-thik\ *adj comb form* 1 : feeling or affected in a (specified) way (tele*pathic*) 2 : affected by disease of a (specified) part or kind (myo*pathic*) 3 : relating to therapy based on a (specified) unitary theory of disease or its treatment (homeo*pathic*)

Path·i·lon \'pa-thə-,län\ *trademark* — used for a preparation of tridihexethyl chloride

patho·bi·ol·o·gy \,pa-thō-bī-'ä-lə-jē\ *n, pl* **-gies** : PATHOLOGY 1, 2

patho·gen \'pa-thə-jən\ *n* : a specific causative agent (as a bacterium or virus) of disease

patho·gen·e·sis \,pa-thə-'je-nə-səs\ *n, pl* **-e·ses** \-,sēz\ : the origination and development of a disease

patho·ge·net·ic \-jə-'ne-tik\ *adj* 1 : of or relating to pathogenesis 2 : PATHOGENIC 2

patho·gen·ic \-'je-nik\ *adj* 1 : PATHOGENETIC 1 2 : causing or capable of causing disease (~ microorganisms) — **patho·gen·i·cal·ly** *adv*

patho·ge·nic·i·ty \-jə-'ni-sə-tē\ *n, pl* **-ties** : the quality or state of being pathogenic : degree of pathogenic capacity

path·og·no·mic \,pa-thəg-'nä-mik, -thə-\ *adj* : PATHOGNOMONIC

pa·tho·gno·mon·ic \,pa-thəg-nō-'mä-nik, -thə-\ *adj* : distinctively characteristic of a particular disease or condition

pathol *abbr* pathological; pathologist; pathology

patho·log·i·cal \,pa-thə-'lä-ji-kəl\ *also* **patho·log·ic** \-jik\ *adj* 1 : of or relating to pathology (a ~ laboratory) 2 : altered or caused by disease (~ tissue) — **patho·log·i·cal·ly** *adv*

pathological fracture *n* : a fracture of a bone weakened by disease

pathological liar *n* : an individual who habitually tells lies so exaggerated or bizarre that they are suggestive of mental disorder

pa·thol·o·gist \pə-'thä-lə-jist, pa-\ *n* : a specialist in pathology; *specif* : a physician who interprets and diagnoses the changes caused by disease in tissues and body fluids

pa·thol·o·gy \-jē\ *n, pl* **-gies** 1 : the study of the essential nature of diseases and esp. of the structural and functional changes produced by them 2 : the anatomic and physiologic deviations from the normal that constitute disease or characterize a particular disease 3 : a treatise on or compilation of abnormalities

patho·mor·phol·o·gy \,pa-thō-mór-'fä-lə-jē\ *n, pl* **-gies** : morphology of abnormal conditions — **patho·mor·pho·log·i·cal** \-,mór-fə-'lä-ji-kəl\ *or* **patho·mor·pho·log·ic** \-jik\ *adj*

patho·phys·i·ol·o·gy \-,fi-zē-'ä-lə-jē\ *n, pl* **-gies** : the physiology of abnormal states; *specif* : the functional changes that accompany a particular syndrome or disease — **patho·phys·i·o·log·i·cal** \-,fi-zē-ə-'lä-ji-kəl\ *also* **patho·phys·i·o·log·ic** \-jik\ *adj*

path·way \'path-,wā\ *n* 1 : a line of communication over connected neurons extending from one organ or center to another 2 : the sequence of enzyme catalyzed reactions by which an energy-yielding substance is utilized by protoplasm

-pa·thy \pə-thē\ *n comb form, pl* **-pa·thies** 1 : feeling (apathy) (tele*pathy*) 2 : disease of a (specified) part or kind (myo*pathy*) 3 : therapy or system of therapy based on a (specified) unitary theory of disease or its treatment (homeo*pathy*)

pa·tient \'pā-shənt\ *n* 1 : a sick individual esp. when awaiting or under the care and treatment of a physician or surgeon 2 : a client for medical service (as of a physician or dentist)

pat·ri·cide \'pa-trə-,sïd\ *n* : murder of a father by his son or daughter

pat·tern \'pa-tərn\ *n* 1 : a model for making a mold used to form a casting 2 : a reliable sample of traits, acts, tendencies, or other observable characteristics of a person, group, or institution (~s of behavior) 3 : an established mode of behavior or cluster of mental attitudes, beliefs, and values that are held in common by members of a group

pat·tern·ing *n* : physical therapy intended to improve malfunctioning nervous control by means of feedback from muscular activity imposed by an outside source or induced by other muscles

pat·u·lin \'pa-chə-lən\ *n* : a colorless crystalline very toxic antibiotic $C_7H_6O_4$ produced by several molds (as *Aspergillus clavatus* and *Penicillium patulum*)

pat·u·lous \'pa-chə-ləs\ *adj* : spread widely apart : wide open or distended

Paul–Bun·nell test \'pol-'bə-nəl-\ *n* : a test for heterophile antibodies used in the diagnosis of infectious mononucleosis — called also *Paul-Bunnell reaction*

Paul, John Rodman (1893–1971), and **Bunnell, Walls Willard** (1902–1965), American physicians.

paunch \'pȯnch, 'pänch\ *n* : RUMEN

pa·vil·ion \pə-'vil-yən\ *n* : a more or less detached part of a hospital devoted to a special use

Pav·lov·ian \pav-'lȯ-vē-ən, -'lō-; -'lȯ-fē-\ *adj* : of or relating to Ivan Pavlov or to his work and theories

Pav·lov \'pav-lȯf\, **Ivan Petrovich** (1849–1936), Russian physiologist.

pav·or noc·tur·nus \'pa-ˌvȯr-näk-'tər-nəs\ *n* : NIGHT TERRORS

pay—bed \'pā-ˌbed\ *n, Brit* : hospital accommodations and services for which the patient is charged

Pb *symbol* lead

PBB \ˌpē-(ˌ)bē-'bē\ *n* : POLYBROMINATED BIPHENYL

PC *abbr* **1** [Latin *post cibos*] after meals — used in writing prescriptions **2** professional corporation

PCB \ˌpē-(ˌ)sē-'bē\ *n* : POLYCHLORINATED BIPHENYL

PCP \ˌpē-(ˌ)sē-'pē\ *n* : PHENCYCLIDINE

PCP *abbr* Pneumocystis carinii pneumonia

PCR *abbr* polymerase chain reaction

PCV *abbr* packed cell volume

PCWP *abbr* pulmonary capillary wedge pressure

Pd *symbol* palladium

PDB \ˌpē-(ˌ)dē-'bē\ *n* : PARADICHLOROBENZENE

PDGF *abbr* platelet-derived growth factor

PDR *abbr* Physicians' Desk Reference

PE *abbr* physical examination

pearl \'pərl\ *n* **1** : PERLE 2 : one of the rounded concentric masses of squamous epithelial cells characteristic of certain tumors **3** : a miliary leproma of the iris **4** : a rounded abnormal mass of enamel on a tooth

pec \'pek\ *n* : PECTORALIS — usu. used in pl.

pecking order *also* **peck order** *n* : the basic pattern of social organization within a flock of poultry in which each bird pecks another lower in the scale without fear of retaliation and submits to pecking by one of higher rank

pec·tin \'pek-tən\ *n* **1** : any of various water-soluble substances that bind adjacent cell walls in plant tissues and yield a gel which is the basis of fruit jellies **2** : a product containing mostly pectin obtained as a powder or syrup and used chiefly in making jelly and other foods, in pharmaceutical products esp. for the control of diarrhea, and in cosmetics

pectinati — see MUSCULI PECTINATI

pec·tin·e·al line \pek-'ti-nē-əl-\ *n* : a ridge on the posterior surface of the femur that runs downward from the lesser trochanter and gives attachment to the pectineus

pec·tin·e·us \pek-'ti-nē-əs\ *n, pl* **-tin·ei** \-nē-ˌī, -nē-ˌē\ : a flat quadrangular muscle of the upper front and inner aspect of the thigh that arises mostly from the iliopectineal line of the pubis and is inserted along the pectineal line of the femur

¹pec·to·ral \'pek-tə-rəl\ *n* **1** : a pectoral part or organ; *esp* : PECTORALIS **2** : a medicinal substance for treating diseases of the respiratory tract

²pectoral *adj* **1** : of, relating to, or occurring in or on the chest ⟨∼ arch⟩ **2** : relating to or good for diseases of the respiratory tract ⟨a ∼ syrup⟩

pectoral girdle *n* : the bony or cartilaginous arch supporting the forelimbs of a vertebrate that corresponds to the pelvic girdle of the hind limbs — called also *shoulder girdle*

pec·to·ra·lis \ˌpek-tə-'rä-ləs\ *n, pl* **-ra·les** \-ˌlēz\ : either of the muscles that connect the ventral walls of the chest with the bones of the upper arm and shoulder of which in humans there are two on each side: **a** : a larger one that arises from the clavicle, the sternum, the cartilages of most or all of the ribs, and the aponeurosis of the external oblique muscle and is inserted by a strong flat tendon into the posterior bicipital ridge of the humerus — called also *pectoralis major* **b** : a smaller one that lies beneath the larger, arises from the third, fourth, and fifth ribs, and is inserted by a flat tendon into the coracoid process of the scapula — called also *pectoralis minor*

pectoralis major *n* : PECTORALIS a

pectoralis minor *n* : PECTORALIS b

pectoralis muscle *n* : PECTORALIS

pectoral muscle *n* : PECTORALIS

pectoral nerve *n* : either of two nerves that arise from the brachial plexus on each side or from the nerve trunks forming it and that supply the pectoral muscles: **a** : one lateral to the axillary artery — called also *lateral pectoral nerve, superior pectoral nerve* **b** : one medial to the axillary artery — called also *inferior pectoral nerve, medial pectoral nerve*

pec·to·ril·o·quy \ˌpek-tə-'ri-lə-kwē\ *n, pl* **-quies** : the sound of words heard through the chest wall and usu. indicating a cavity or consolidation of lung tissue — compare BRONCHOPHONY

pectoris — see ANGINA PECTORIS

pec·tus ex·ca·va·tum \'pek-təs-ˌek-skə-'vä-təm\ *n* : FUNNEL CHEST

ped- *or* **pedo-** *comb form* : child : children ⟨*pediatrics*⟩

ped·al \'ped-əl, 'pēd-\ *adj* : of or relating to the foot

ped·er·ast \'pe-də-ˌrast\ *n* : one that practices anal intercourse esp. with a boy as a passive partner — **ped·er-**

as·tic \\pe-də-'ras-tik\ *adj* — **ped·er·as·ty** \'ped-ə-ˌras-tē\ *n*

pe·di·at·ric \ˌpē-dē-'a-trik\ *adj* : of or relating to pediatrics

pe·di·a·tri·cian \ˌpē-dē-ə-'tri-shən\ *n* : a specialist in pediatrics

pe·di·at·rics \ˌpē-dē-'a-triks\ *n* : a branch of medicine dealing with the development, care, and diseases of children

ped·i·cle \'pe-di-kəl\ *n* : a basal attachment: as **a** : the basal part of each side of the neural arch of a vertebra connecting the laminae with the centrum **b** : the narrow basal part by which various organs (as kidney or spleen) are continuous with other body structures **c** : the narrow base of a tumor **d** : the part of a pedicle flap left attached to the original site — **ped·i·cled** \-kəld\ *adj*

pedicle flap *n* : a flap which is left attached to the original site by a narrow base of tissue to provide a blood supply during grafting — called also *pedicle graft*

pe·dic·u·li·cide \pi-'di-kyə-lə-ˌsīd\ *n* : an agent for destroying lice

pe·dic·u·lo·sis \pi-ˌdi-kyə-'lō-səs\ *n*, *pl* **-lo·ses** \-ˌsēz\ : infestation with lice

pediculosis cap·i·tis \-'ka-pi-təs\ *n* : infestation of the scalp by head lice

pediculosis cor·po·ris \-'kȯr-pə-rəs\ *n* : infestation by body lice

pediculosis pubis *n* : infestation by crab lice

pe·dic·u·lus \pi-'di-kyə-ləs\ *n* **1** *cap* : a genus of lice (family Pediculidae) that includes the body louse (*P. humanus corporis*) and head louse (*P. humanus capitis*) infesting humans **2** *pl* **pe·dic·u·li** \-ˌlī\ *or* **pediculus** : any louse of the genus *Pediculus*

ped·i·gree \'pe-də-ˌgrē\ *n* : a record of the ancestry of an individual

pedis — see DORSALIS PEDIS, TINEA PEDIS

pedo· — see PED-

pe·do·don·tics \ˌpē-də-'dän-tiks\ *n* : a branch of dentistry that is concerned with the dental care of children — **pe·do·don·tic** *adj*

pe·do·don·tist \ˌpē-də-'dän-tist\ *n* : a specialist in pedodontics

pe·do·phile \'pē-də-ˌfīl\ *n* : an individual affected with pedophilia

pe·do·phil·ia \ˌpē-də-'fi-lē-ə\ *n* : sexual perversion in which children are the preferred sexual object — **pe·do·phil·i·ac** \ˌpē-də-'fi-lē-ˌak\ *or* **pe·do·phil·ic** \-'fi-lik\ *adj*

pe·dun·cle \'pē-ˌdəŋ-kəl, pi-'\ *n* **1** : a band of white matter joining different parts of the brain — see CEREBELLAR PEDUNCLE, CEREBRAL PEDUNCLE **2** : a narrow stalk by which a tumor or polyp is attached — **pe·dun·cu·lar** \pi-'dəŋ-kyə-lər\ *adj*

pe·dun·cu·lat·ed \pi-'dəŋ-kyə-ˌlā-təd\ *also* **pe·dun·cu·late** \-lət\ *adj* : having,

growing on, or being attached by a peduncle (a ~ tumor)

pe·dun·cu·lot·o·my \pi-ˌdəŋ-kyə-'lä-tə-mē\ *n*, *pl* **-mies** : surgical incision of a cerebral peduncle for relief of involuntary movements

pe·dun·cu·lus ce·re·bel·la·ris inferior \pi-ˌdəŋ-kyə-ləs-ˌser-ə-be-'ler-əs-\ *n* : CEREBELLAR PEDUNCLE c

pedunculus cerebellaris me·di·us \-'mē-dē-əs\ *n* : CEREBELLAR PEDUNCLE b

pedunculus cerebellaris superior *n* : CEREBELLAR PEDUNCLE a

peel *n* : the surgical removal of skin blemishes by the application of a caustic chemical and esp. an acid to the skin — called also *chemical peel*

peep·er \'pē-pər\ *n* : VOYEUR

Peep·ing Tom \ˌpē-piŋ-'täm\ *n* : VOYEUR — **Peeping Tom·ism** \-'tä-ˌmi-zəm\ *n*

Peg·a·none \'pe-gə-ˌnōn\ *trademark* — used for a preparation of ethotoin

pe·li·o·sis hepatitis \ˌpe-lē-'ō-səs-, ˌpē-\ *n* : an abnormal condition characterized by the occurrence of numerous small blood-filled cystic lesions throughout the liver

pel·la·gra \pə-'la-grə, -'lä-, -'lā-\ *n* : a disease marked by dermatitis, gastrointestinal disorders, and nervous symptoms and associated with a diet deficient in niacin and protein — compare KWASHIORKOR — **pel·la·grous** \-grəs\ *adj*

pellagra–preventive factor *n* : NIACIN

pel·la·grin \-grən\ *n* : one that is affected with pellagra

pel·let \'pe-lət\ *n* : a usu. small rounded or spherical body; *specif* : a small cylindrical or ovoid compressed mass (as of a hormone) that is implanted subcutaneously for slow absorption into bodily tissues

pel·li·cle \'pe-li-kəl\ *n* : a thin skin or film: as **a** : an outer membrane of some protozoans **b** : a thin layer of salivary glycoproteins coating the surface of the teeth

pellucida — see SEPTUM PELLUCIDUM, ZONA PELLUCIDA

pel·oid \'pe-ˌlȯid\ *n* : mud prepared and used for therapeutic purposes

pel·ta·tin \pel-'tā-tən\ *n* : either of two lactones that occur as glycosides in the rootstock of the mayapple (*Podophyllum peltatum*) and have some antineoplastic activity

pelv- *or* **pelvi-** *or* **pelvo-** *comb form* : pelvis ⟨*pelvic*⟩ ⟨*pelvimetry*⟩

pelves *pl of* PELVIS

¹pel·vic \'pel-vik\ *adj* : of, relating to, or located in or near the pelvis

²pelvic *n* : a pelvic part

pelvic bone *n* : HIPBONE

pelvic brim *n* : the bony ridge in the cavity of the pelvis that marks the boundary between the false pelvis and the true pelvis

pelvic cavity *n* : the cavity of the pelvis comprising in humans a broad upper and a more contracted lower part — compare FALSE PELVIS, TRUE PELVIS

pelvic colon n : SIGMOID FLEXURE

pelvic diaphragm n : the muscular floor of the pelvis

pelvic fascia n : the fascia lining the pelvic cavity

pelvic girdle n : the bony or cartilaginous arch that supports the hind limbs of a vertebrate and that in humans is represented by paired hipbones articulating solidly with the sacrum dorsally and with one another at the pubic symphysis

pelvic inflammatory disease n : inflammation of the female reproductive tract and esp. the fallopian tubes that is caused esp. by sexually transmitted disease, occurs more often in women using intrauterine devices, and is a leading cause of female sterility — abbr. PID

pelvic outlet n : the irregular bony opening bounded by the lower border of the pelvis and closed by muscle and other soft tissues through which the terminal parts of the excretory, reproductive, and digestive systems pass to communicate with the surface of the body

pelvic plexus n : a plexus of the autonomic nervous system that is formed by the hypogastric plexus, by branches from the sacral part of the sympathetic chain, and by the visceral branches of the second, third, and fourth sacral nerves and that is distributed to the viscera of the pelvic region

pelvic splanchnic nerve n : any of the groups of parasympathetic fibers that originate with cells in the second, third, and fourth sacral segments of the spinal cord, pass through the inferior portion of the hypogastric plexus, and supply the descending colon, rectum, anus, bladder, prostate gland, and external genitalia — called also *nervus erigens*

pel·vim·e·ter \pel-'vi-mə-tər\ n : an instrument for measuring the dimensions of the pelvis

pel·vim·e·try \pel-'vi-mə-trē\ n, pl **-tries** : measurement of the pelvis (as by X-ray examination)

pel·vis \'pel-vəs\ n, pl **pel·vis·es** \-və-səz\ or **pel·ves** \-ˌvēz\ 1 : a basin-shaped structure in the skeleton of many vertebrates that in humans is composed of the two hipbones bounding it on each side and in front while the sacrum and coccyx complete it behind 2 : PELVIC CAVITY 3 : RENAL PELVIS

pelvo- — see PELV-

pem·o·line \'pe-mə-ˌlēn\ n : a synthetic drug $C_9H_8N_2O_2$ that is a mild stimulant of the central nervous system

¹pem·phi·goid \'pem-fə-ˌgȯid\ adj : resembling pemphigus

²pemphigoid n : any of several diseases

that resemble pemphigus: esp : BULLOUS PEMPHIGOID

pem·phi·gus \'pem-fi-gəs, pem-'fī-gəs\ n, pl **-gus·es** or **-gi** \-ˌjī\ : any of several diseases characterized by the formation of successive eruptions of large blisters on apparently normal skin and mucous membranes often in association with sensations of itching or burning and with constitutional symptoms

pemphigus er·y·the·ma·to·sus \-ˌer-i-ˌthē-mə-'tō-səs\ n : a relatively benign form of chronic pemphigus that is characterized by the eruption esp. on the face and trunk of lesions resembling those which occur in systemic lupus erythematosus

pemphigus vul·gar·is \-vəl-'gar-əs\ n : a severe and often fatal form of chronic pemphigus

Pen·brit·in \pen-'bri-tən\ trademark — used for a preparation of ampicillin

pen·cil \'pen-səl\ n : a small medicated or cosmetic roll or stick for local applications (a menthol ~)

pe·nec·to·my \pē-'nek-tə-mē\ n, pl **-mies** : surgical removal of the penis

penes pl of PENIS

pen·e·trance \'pe-nə-trəns\ n : the proportion of individuals of a particular genotype that express its phenotypic effect in a given environment — compare EXPRESSIVITY

pen·e·trate \'pe-nə-ˌtrāt\ vb **-trat·ed; -trat·ing** 1 : to pass, extend, pierce, or diffuse into or through something 2 : to insert the penis into the vagina of in copulation — **pen·e·tra·tion** \ˌpe-nə-'trā-shən\ n

pen·flur·i·dol \pen-'flur-i-ˌdȯl\ n : a tranquilizing drug $C_{28}H_{27}ClF_5NO$

-pe·nia \'pē-nē-ə\ n comb form : deficiency of ⟨eosinopenia⟩

pen·i·cil·la·mine \ˌpe-nə-'si-lə-ˌmēn\ n : an amino acid $C_5H_{11}NO_2S$ that is obtained from penicillins and is used esp. to treat cystinuria and metal poisoning (as by copper or lead)

pen·i·cil·lic acid \ˌpe-nə-'si-lik-\ n : a crystalline antibiotic $C_8H_{10}O_4$ produced by several molds of the genera *Penicillium* and *Aspergillus*

pen·i·cil·lin \ˌpe-nə-'si-lən\ n 1 : a mixture of antibiotic relatively nontoxic acids produced esp. by molds of the genus *Penicillium* (as *P. notatum* or *P. chrysogenum*) and having a powerful bacteriostatic effect against various bacteria (as staphylococci, gonococci, pneumococci, hemolytic streptococci, or some meningococci) 2 : any of numerous often hygroscopic and unstable acids (as penicillin G, penicillin O, and penicillin V) that are components of the penicillin mixture or are produced biosynthetically by the use of different strains of molds or different media or are synthesized chemically 3 : a salt or ester of a penicillin acid or a mixture of such salts or esters

pen·i·cil·lin·ase \-ˈsi-lə-ˌnās, -ˌnāz\ *n* : an enzyme found esp. in staphylococcal bacteria that inactivates the penicillins by hydrolyzing them — called also *beta-lactamase*

penicillin F \-ˈef\ *n* : a penicillin $C_{14}H_{20}N_2O_4S$ that was the first of the penicillins isolated in Great Britain

penicillin G \-ˈjē\ *n* : the penicillin $C_{16}H_{18}N_2O_4S$ that constitutes the principal or sole component of most commercial preparations and is used chiefly in the form of stable salts (as the crystalline sodium salt or the crystalline procaine salt) — called also *benzylpenicillin;* see PROCAINE PENICILLIN G

penicillin O \-ˈō\ *n* : a penicillin $C_{13}H_{18}N_2O_3S_2$ that is similar to penicillin G in antibiotic activity

penicillin V \-ˈvē\ *n* : a crystalline acid $C_{16}H_{18}N_2O_5S$ that is similar to penicillin G in antibacterial action and is more resistant to inactivation by gastric acids — called also *phenoxymethyl penicillin*

pen·i·cil·li·o·sis \ˌpe-nə-ˌsi-lē-ˈō-səs\ *n, pl* **-o·ses** \-ˌsēz\ : infection with or disease caused by molds of the genus *Penicillium*

pen·i·cil·li·um \ˌpe-nə-ˈsi-lē-əm\ *n* 1 *cap* : a genus of fungi (family Moniliaceae) comprising the blue molds found chiefly on moist nonliving organic matter (as decaying fruit) and including molds useful in economic fermentation and the production of antibiotics 2 *pl* **-lia** \-lē-ə\ : any mold of the genus *Penicillium*

pen·i·cil·lo·yl–poly·ly·sine \ˌpe-nə-ˈsi-lō-ᵊil-ˌpä-li-ˈlī-ˌsēn\ *n* : a preparation of a penicillic acid and polylysine which is used in a skin test to determine hypersensitivity to penicillin

pen·i·cil·lus \ˌpe-nə-ˈsi-ləs\ *n, pl* **-li** \-ˌlī\ : one of the small straight arteries of the red pulp of the spleen

pe·nile \ˈpē-ˌnīl\ *adj* : of, relating to, or affecting the penis (a ~ prosthesis) (~ lesions)

pe·nis \ˈpē-nəs\ *n, pl* **pe·nes** \ˈpē-(ˌ)nēz\ *or* **pe·nis·es** : a male copulatory organ that in mammals including humans usu. functions as the channel by which urine leaves the body and is typically a cylindrical organ that is suspended from the pubic arch, contains a pair of large lateral corpora cavernosa and a smaller ventromedial corpus cavernosum containing the urethra, and has a terminal glans enclosing the ends of the corpora cavernosa, covered by mucous membrane, and sheathed by a foreskin continuous with the skin covering the body of the organ

penis envy *n* : the supposed coveting of the penis by a young human female which is held in psychoanalytic theory to lead to feelings of inferiority and defensive or compensatory behavior

pen·nate \ˈpe-ˌnāt\ *adj* : having a structure like that of a feather; *esp* : being a muscle in which fibers extend obliquely from either side of a central tendon

pen·ni·form \ˈpe-ni-ˌform\ *adj* : PENNATE

pe·no·scro·tal \ˌpē-nō-ˈskrōt-ᵊl\ *adj* : of or relating to the penis and scrotum

penoscrotal raphe *n* : the ridge on the surface of the scrotum that divides it into two lateral halves and is continued forward on the underside of the penis and backward along the midline of the perineum to the anus

Pen·rose drain \ˈpen-ˌrōz-\ *n* : CIGARETTE DRAIN

Penrose, Charles Bingham (1862–1925), American gynecologist.

pen·ta·chlo·ro·phe·nol \ˌpen-tə-ˌklor-ə-ˈfē-ˌnol, -fi-\ *n* : a crystalline compound C_6Cl_5OH used esp. as a wood preservative, insecticide, and herbicide

pen·ta·eryth·ri·tol tet·ra·ni·trate \-i-ˈrithrə-ˌtol-ˌte-trə-ˈnī-ˌstrāt, -ˌtol-\ *n* : a crystalline ester $C_5H_8N_4O_{12}$ used in the treatment of angina pectoris

pen·ta·gas·trin \ˌpen-tə-ˈgas-trən\ *n* : a pentapeptide $C_{37}H_{49}N_7O_9S$ that stimulates gastric acid secretion

pen·ta·me·tho·ni·um \ˌpen-tə-me-ˈthō-nē-əm\ *n* : an organic ion $[C_{11}H_{28}N_2]^{2+}$ used in the form of its salts (as the bromide and iodide) for its ganglionic blocking activity in the treatment of hypertension

pent·am·i·dine \pen-ˈta-mə-ˌdēn, -dən\ *n* : an antiprotozoal drug used chiefly in the form of its salt $C_{23}H_{36}N_4O_{10}S_2$ to treat protozoal infections (as leishmaniasis) and to prevent Pneumocystis carinii pneumonia in HIV-infected individuals

pen·ta·pep·tide \ˌpen-tə-ˈpep-ˌtīd\ *n* : a polypeptide that contains five amino acid residues

pen·ta·pip·er·ide meth·yl·sul·fate \ˌpen-tə-ˈpi-pər-ˌid-ˌme-thəl-ˈsəl-ˌfāt\ *n* : a synthetic anticholinergic and antisecretory agent $C_{18}H_{27}NO_2 \cdot C_2H_6O_4S$ used esp. in the treatment of peptic ulcer — see QUILENE

pen·ta·quine \ˈpen-tə-ˌkwēn\ *n* : an antimalarial drug $C_{18}H_{27}N_3O$ used esp. in the form of its pale yellow crystalline phosphate

pen·ta·zo·cine \pen-ˈta-zə-ˌsēn\ *n* : an analgesic drug $C_{19}H_{27}NO$ that is less addictive than morphine — see TALWIN

pen·to·bar·bi·tal \ˌpen-tə-ˈbär-bə-ˌtol\ *n* : a granular barbiturate $C_{11}H_{18}N_2O_3$ used esp. in the form of its sodium or calcium salt as a sedative, hypnotic, and antispasmodic

pen·to·bar·bi·tone \-ˌtōn\ *n, Brit* : PENTOBARBITAL

pen·to·lin·i·um tartrate \ˌpen-tə-ˈli-nē-am-\ *n* : a ganglionic blocking agent $C_{23}H_{42}N_2O_{12}$ used as an antihypertensive drug

pen·tose \'pen-₁tōs, -₁tōz\ *n* : any monosaccharide $C_5H_{10}O_5$ (as ribose) that contains five carbon atoms in a molecule

pen·tos·uria \₁pen-tō-'sur-ē-ə, -'syur-\ *n* : the excretion of pentoses in the urine; *specif* : a rare hereditary anomaly characterized by regular excretion of pentoses

Pen·to·thal \'pen-tə-₁thȯl\ *trademark* — used for a preparation of thiopental

pent·ox·i·fyl·line \₁pen-₁täk-'si-fə-₁lēn\ *n* : a methylxanthine derivative $C_{13}H_{18}N_4O_3$ that reduces blood viscosity, increases microcirculatory blood flow, and is used to treat intermittent claudication resulting from occlusive arterial disease — see TRENTAL

pen·tyl·ene·tet·ra·zol \₁pen-ti-₁lēn-'te-trə-₁zȯl, -₁zōl\ *n* : a white crystalline drug $C_6H_{10}N_4$ used as a respiratory and circulatory stimulant and for producing a state of convulsion in treating certain mental disorders — called also *leptazol*; see METRAZOL

pep pill *n* : any of various stimulant drugs (as amphetamine) in pill or tablet form

-pep·sia \'pep-shə, 'pep-sē-ə\ *n comb form* : digestion (dys*pepsia*)

pep·sin \'pep-sən\ *n* 1 : a crystallizable protease that in an acid medium digests most proteins to polypeptides, that is secreted by glands in the mucous membrane of the stomach, and that in combination with dilute hydrochloric acid is the chief active principle of gastric juice 2 : a preparation containing pepsin obtained as a powder or scales from the stomach esp. of the hog and used esp. as a digestant

pep·sin·o·gen \pep-'si-nə-jən\ *n* : a granular zymogen of the gastric glands that is readily converted into pepsin in a slightly acid medium

pept- or **pepto-** *comb form* : protein fragment or derivative (*peptide*)

pep·tic \'pep-tik\ *adj* 1 : relating to or promoting digestion : DIGESTIVE 2 : of, relating to, producing, or caused by pepsin (~ digestion)

peptic ulcer *n* : an ulcer in the wall of the stomach or duodenum resulting from the digestive action of the gastric juice on the mucous membrane when the latter is rendered susceptible to its action (as by psychosomatic or local factors)

pep·ti·dase \'pep-tə-₁dās, -₁dāz\ *n* : an enzyme that hydrolyzes simple peptides or their derivatives

pep·tide \'pep-₁tīd\ *n* : any of various amides that are derived from two or more amino acids by combination of the amino group of one acid with the carboxyl group of another and are usu. obtained by partial hydrolysis of proteins — **pep·tid·ic** \pep-'ti-dik\ *adj*

peptide bond *n* : the chemical bond between carbon and nitrogen in a peptide linkage

peptide linkage *n* : the group CONH having a chemical valence of two that unites the amino acid residues in a peptide

pep·tid·er·gic \₁pep-tī-'dər-jik\ *adj* : being, relating to, releasing, or activated by neurotransmitters that are short peptide chains (~ neurons)

pep·ti·do·gly·can \₁pep-tə-dō-'glī-₁kan\ *n* : a polymer that is composed of polysaccharide and peptide chains and is found esp. in bacterial cell walls — called also *mucopeptide*, *murein*

pep·tone \'pep-₁stōn\ *n* 1 : any of various protein derivatives that are formed by the partial hydrolysis of proteins (as by enzymes of the gastric and pancreatic juices or by acids or alkalies) 2 : a complex water-soluble product containing peptones and other protein derivatives that is obtained by digesting protein (as meat) with an enzyme (as pepsin or trypsin) and is used chiefly in nutrient media in bacteriology

per \'pər\ *prep* : by the means or agency of : by way of : through (blood ~ rectum) — see PER OS

per·acute \₁pər-ə-'kyüt\ *adj* : very acute and violent

per·ceive \pər-'sēv\ *vb* **per·ceived; per·ceiv·ing** : to become aware of through the senses — **per·ceiv·able** \-'sē-və-bəl\ *adj*

per·cept \'pər-₁sept\ *n* : an impression of an object obtained by use of the senses : SENSE-DATUM

per·cep·ti·ble \pər-'sep-tə-bəl\ *adj* : capable of being perceived esp. by the senses — **per·cep·ti·bly** \-blē\ *adv*

per·cep·tion \pər-'sep-shən\ *n* : awareness of the elements of environment through physical sensation (color ~) — compare SENSATION 1a

per·cep·tive \pər-'sep-tiv\ *adj* : responsive to sensory stimulus (a ~ eye) — **per·cep·tive·ly** *adv*

perceptive deafness *n* : NERVE DEAFNESS

per·cep·tu·al \(₁)pər-'sep-chə-wəl, -shə-\ *adj* : of, relating to, or involving perception esp. in relation to immediate sensory experience (auditory ~ deficits) — **per·cep·tu·al·ly** *adv*

per·co·late \'pər-kə-₁lāt, -lət\ *n* : a product of percolation

per·co·la·tion \₁pər-kə-'lā-shən\ *n* 1 : the slow passage of a liquid through a filtering medium 2 : a method of extraction or purification by means of filtration 3 : the process of extracting the soluble constituents of a powdered drug by passage of a liquid through it — **per·co·late** \'pər-kə-₁lāt\ *vb* — **per·co·la·tor** \-₁lā-tər\ *n*

per·cus·sion \pər-'kə-shən\ *n* 1 : the act

or technique of tapping the surface of a body part to learn the condition of the parts beneath by the resulting sound **2** : massage consisting of the striking of a body part with light rapid blows — called also *tapotement* — **per·cuss** \pər-ˈkəs\ *vb*

per·cu·ta·ne·ous \ˌpər-kyü-ˈtā-nē-əs\ *adj* : effected or performed through the skin ⟨∼ absorption⟩ — **per·cu·ta·ne·ous·ly** *adv*

percutaneous transluminal angioplasty *n* : a surgical procedure used to enlarge the lumen of a partly occluded blood vessel (as one with atherosclerotic plaques on the walls) by passing a balloon catheter through the skin, into the vessel, and through the vessel to the site of the lesion where the tip of the catheter is inflated to expand the lumen of the vessel

percutaneous transluminal coronary angioplasty *n* : percutaneous transluminal angioplasty of a coronary artery — called also *PTCA*

per·fo·rate \ˈpər-fə-ˌrāt\ *vb* **-rat·ed; -rat·ing** : to enter, penetrate, or make a hole through ⟨an ulcer ∼s the duodenal wall⟩

per·fo·rat·ed \-ˌrā-təd\ *adj* : characterized by perforation ⟨a ∼ ulcer⟩

per·fo·ra·tion \ˌpər-fə-ˈrā-shən\ *n* **1** : the act or process of perforating; *specif* : the penetration of a body part through accident or disease **2 a** : a rupture in a body part caused esp. by accident or disease **b** : a natural opening in an organ or body part

per·fo·ra·tor \ˈpər-fə-ˌrā-tər\ *n* : one that perforates: as **a** : an instrument used to perforate tissue (as bone) **b** : a nerve or blood vessel forming a connection between a deep system and a superficial one

per·fus·ate \ˌpər-ˈfyü-ˌzāt, -zət\ *n* : a fluid (as a solution pumped through the heart) that is perfused

per·fuse \ˌpər-ˈfyüz\ *vb* **-fused; -fusing 1** : SUFFUSE **2 a** : to cause to flow or spread : DIFFUSE **b** : to force a fluid through ⟨an organ or tissue⟩ esp. by way of the blood vessels

per·fu·sion \-ˈfyü-zhən\ *n* : an act or instance of perfusing; *specif* : the pumping of a fluid through an organ or tissue

per·fu·sion·ist \pər-ˈfyü-zhə-nist\ *n* : a certified medical technician responsible for extracorporeal oxygenation of the blood during open-heart surgery and for the operation and maintenance of equipment (as a heart-lung machine) controlling it

per·hex·i·line \pər-ˈhek-sə-ˌlēn\ *n* : a drug $C_{19}H_{35}N$ used as a coronary vasodilator

peri- *prefix* **1** : near ⟨*peri*menopausal⟩ **2** : enclosing : surrounding ⟨*peri*neurium⟩

peri·anal \ˌper-ē-ˈān-əl\ *adj* : of, relating to, occurring in, or being the tissues surrounding the anus ⟨a ∼ abscess⟩

peri·aor·tic \-ā-ˈȯr-tik\ *adj* : of, relating to, occurring in, or being the tissues surrounding the aorta

peri·api·cal \-ˈā-pi-kəl, -ˈa-\ *adj* : of, relating to, occurring in, affecting, or being the tissues surrounding the apex of the root of a tooth

peri·aq·ue·duc·tal \-ˌa-kwə-ˈdəkt-əl\ *adj* : of, relating to, or being the gray matter which surrounds the aqueduct of Sylvius

peri·ar·te·ri·al \-är-ˈtir-ē-əl\ *adj* : of, relating to, occurring in, or being the tissues surrounding an artery

peri·ar·te·ri·o·lar \-är-ˌtir-ē-ˈō-lər\ *adj* : of, relating to, occurring in, or being the tissues surrounding an arteriole

peri·ar·ter·i·tis no·do·sa \ˌper-ē-ˌär-tə-ˈrī-təs-nō-ˈdō-sə\ *n* : POLYARTERITIS NODOSA

peri·ar·thri·tis \-är-ˈthrī-təs\ *n, pl* **-thrit·i·des** \-ˈthri-tə-ˌdēz\ : inflammation of the structures (as the muscles, tendons, and bursa of the shoulder) around a joint

peri·ar·tic·u·lar \-är-ˈti-kyə-lər\ *adj* : of, relating to, occurring in, or being the tissues surrounding a joint

peri·bron·chi·al \ˌper-ə-ˈbräŋ-kē-əl\ *adj* : of, relating to, occurring in, affecting, or being the tissues surrounding a bronchus ⟨a ∼ growth⟩

peri·cap·il·lary \-ˈka-pə-ˌler-ē\ *adj* : of, relating to, occurring in, or being the tissues surrounding a capillary ⟨∼ infiltration⟩

pericardi- *or* **pericardio-** *or* **pericardo-** *comb form* **1** : pericardium ⟨*peri*cardiectomy⟩ **2** : pericardial and ⟨*pericardio*phrenic artery⟩

peri·car·di·al \ˌper-ə-ˈkär-dē-əl\ *adj* : of, relating to, or affecting the pericardium; *also* : situated around the heart

pericardial cavity *n* : the fluid-filled space between the two layers of the pericardium

pericardial fluid *n* : the serous fluid that fills the pericardial cavity and protects the heart from friction

peri·car·di·ec·to·my \ˌper-ə-ˌkär-dē-ˈek-tə-mē\ *n, pl* **-mies** : surgical excision of the pericardium

peri·car·dio·cen·te·sis \-ˌkär-dē-ō-(ˌ)sen-ˈtē-səs\ *n, pl* **-te·ses** \-ˌsēz\ : surgical puncture of the pericardium esp. to aspirate pericardial fluid

peri·car·dio·phren·ic artery \ˌper-ə-ˌkär-dē-ə-ˈfre-nik-\ *n* : a branch of the internal thoracic artery that descends through the thorax accompanying the phrenic nerve between the pleura and the pericardium to the diaphragm

peri·car·di·os·to·my \ˌper-ə-ˌkär-dē-ˈäs-tə-mē\ *n, pl* **-mies** : surgical formation of an opening into the pericardium

peri·car·di·ot·o·my \-ˈät-ə-mē\ *n, pl*

-mies : surgical incision of the pericardium

peri·car·di·tis \-ˌkär-ˈdī-təs\ *n, pl* **-dit·i·des** \-ˈdi-tə-ˌdēz\ : inflammation of the pericardium — see ADHESIVE PERICARDITIS

peri·car·di·um \ˌper-ə-ˈkär-dē-əm\ *n, pl* **-dia** \-dē-ə\ : the conical sac of serous membrane that encloses the heart and the roots of the great blood vessels of vertebrates and consists of an outer fibrous coat that loosely invests the heart and is prolonged on the outer surface of the great vessels except the inferior vena cava and a double inner serous coat of which one layer is closely adherent to the heart while the other lines the inner surface of the outer coat with the intervening space being filled with pericardial fluid

pericardo- — see PERICARDI-

peri·cel·lu·lar \-ˈsel-yə-lər\ *adj* : of, relating to, occurring in, or being the tissues surrounding a cell

peri·ce·men·ti·tis \-ˌsē-men-ˈtī-təs\ *n* : PERIODONTITIS

peri·ce·men·tum \-si-ˈmen-təm\ *n* : PERIODONTAL MEMBRANE

peri·cen·tric \-ˈsen-trik\ *adj* : of, relating to, or involving the centromere of a chromosome (~ inversion) — compare PARACENTRIC

peri·chol·an·gi·tis \-ˌkō-ˌlan-ˈjī-təs, -ˌkä-\ *n* : inflammation of the tissues surrounding the bile ducts

peri·chon·dri·tis \-ˌkän-ˈdrī-təs\ *n* : inflammation of a perichondrium

peri·chon·dri·um \ˌper-ə-ˈkän-drē-əm\ *n, pl* **-dria** \-drē-ə\ : the membrane of fibrous connective tissue that invests cartilage except at joints — **peri·chon·dri·al** \-drē-əl\ *adj*

peri·co·ro·nal \ˌper-ə-ˈkór-ən-ᵊl, -ˈkär-; -kə-ˈrōn-ᵊl\ *adj* : occurring about or surrounding the crown of a tooth

peri·cor·o·ni·tis \-ˌkór-ə-ˈnī-təs, -ˌkär-\ *n, pl* **-nit·i·des** \-ˈni-tə-ˌdēz\ : inflammation of the gum about the crown of a partially erupted tooth

peri·cyte \ˈper-ə-ˌsīt\ *n* : a cell of the connective tissue about capillaries or other small blood vessels

peri·du·ral \ˌper-i-ˈdúr-əl, -ˈdyúr-\ *adj* : occurring or applied about the dura mater

peridural anesthesia *n* : EPIDURAL ANESTHESIA

peri·fo·cal \ˌper-ə-ˈfō-kəl\ *adj* : of, relating to, occurring in, or being the tissues surrounding a focus (as of infection) — **peri·fo·cal·ly** *adv*

peri·fol·lic·u·lar \ˌper-ə-fə-ˈli-kyə-lər, -fä-\ *adj* : of, relating to, occurring in, or being the tissues surrounding a follicle

peri·hep·a·ti·tis \-ˌhe-pə-ˈtī-təs\ *n, pl* **-tit·i·des** \-ˈti-tə-ˌdēz\ : inflammation of the peritoneal capsule of the liver

peri·kary·on \-ˈkar-ē-ˌän, -ən\ *n, pl* **-karya** \-ē-ə\ : CELL BODY — **peri·kary·al** \-ē-əl\ *adj*

peri·lymph \ˈper-ə-ˌlimf\ *n* : the fluid between the membranous and bony labyrinths of the ear

peri·lym·phat·ic \ˌper-ə-lim-ˈfa-tik\ *adj* : relating to or containing perilymph

peri·men·o·paus·al \ˌper-ē-ˌme-nə-ˈpó-zəl, -ˌmē-\ *adj* : relating to, being in, or occurring in the period around the onset of menopause (~ women) (~ bleeding)

pe·rim·e·ter \pə-ˈri-mə-tər\ *n* : an instrument for examining the discriminative powers of different parts of the retina

peri·me·tri·um \ˌper-ə-ˈmē-trē-əm\ *n, pl* **-tria** \-trē-ə\ : the peritoneum covering the fundus and ventral and dorsal aspects of the uterus

pe·rim·e·try \pə-ˈri-mə-trē\ *n, pl* **-tries** : examination of the eye by means of a perimeter — **peri·met·ric** \ˌper-ə-ˈme-trik\ *adj*

peri·my·si·um \ˌper-ə-ˈmi-zhē-əm, -zē-\ *n, pl* **-sia** \-zhē-ə, -zē-ə\ : the connective-tissue sheath that surrounds a muscle and forms sheaths for the bundles of muscle fibers

peri·na·tal \-ˈnāt-ᵊl\ *adj* : occurring in, concerned with, or being in the period around the time of birth (~ mortality) — **peri·na·tal·ly** *adv*

peri·na·tol·o·gist \ˌper-ə-nā-ˈtä-lə-jist\ *n* : a specialist in perinatology

peri·na·tol·o·gy \-nā-ˈtä-lə-jē\ *n, pl* **-gies** : a branch of medicine concerned with perinatal care

per·i·ne·al \ˌper-ə-ˈnē-əl\ *adj* : of or relating to the perineum

perineal artery *n* : a branch of the internal pudendal artery that supplies the skin of the external genitalia and the superficial parts of the perineum

perineal body *n* : a mass of muscle and fascia that separates the lower end of the vagina and the rectum in the female and the urethra and the rectum in the male

perinei superficialis — see TRANSVERSUS PERINEI SUPERFICIALIS

perineo- *comb form* : perineum (*perineotomy*)

per·i·ne·o·plas·ty \ˌper-i-ˈnē-ō-ˌplas-tē\ *n, pl* **-ties** : plastic surgery of the perineum

per·i·ne·or·rha·phy \ˌper-ə-nē-ˈór-ə-fē\ *n, pl* **-phies** : suture of the perineum usu. to repair a laceration occurring during labor

per·i·ne·ot·o·my \ˌper-ə-nē-ˈä-tə-mē\ *n, pl* **-mies** : surgical incision of the perineum

peri·neph·ric \ˌper-ə-ˈne-frik\ *adj* : PERIRENAL (a ~ abscess)

per·i·ne·um \ˌper-ə-ˈnē-əm\ *n, pl* **-nea** \-ˈnē-ə\ : an area of tissue that marks externally the approximate boundary of the pelvic outlet and gives passage to the urinogenital ducts and rectum; *also* : the area between the anus and the posterior part of the external genitalia esp. in the female

peri·neu·ral \,per-ə-'nùr-əl, -'nyùr-\ *adj* : occurring about or surrounding nervous tissue or a nerve

peri·neu·ri·al \-'nùr-ē-əl, -'nyùr-\ *adj* 1 : of or relating to perineurium 2 : PERINEURAL

peri·neu·ri·um \,per-ə-'nùr-ē-əm, -'nyùr-\ *n, pl* **-ria** \-ē-ə\ : the connective-tissue sheath that surrounds a bundle of nerve fibers

peri·nu·cle·ar \-'nü-klē-ər, -'nyü-\ *adj* : situated around or surrounding the nucleus of a cell (~ structures)

peri·oc·u·lar \,per-ē-'ä-kyə-lər\ *adj* : surrounding the eyeball but within the orbit (~ space)

pe·ri·od \'pir-ē-əd\ *n* 1 a : a portion of time determined by some recurring phenomenon b : a single cyclic occurrence of menstruation 2 : a chronological division

pe·ri·od·ic \,pir-ē-'ä-dik\ *adj* : occurring or recurring at regular intervals

per·iod·ic acid \,pər-(,)ī-'ä-dik-\ *n* : any of the strongly oxidizing iodine-containing acids (as H_5IO_6 or HIO_4)

periodic acid–Schiff \-'shif\ *adj* : relating to, being, or involving a reaction testing for polysaccharides and related substances in which tissue sections are treated with periodic acid and then Schiff's reagent with a reddish violet color indicating a positive test

periodic breathing *n* : abnormal breathing characterized by an irregular respiratory rhythm; *esp* : CHEYNE-STOKES RESPIRATION

periodic ophthalmia *n* : MOON BLINDNESS

periodic table *n* : an arrangement of chemical elements based on their atomic numbers

peri·odon·tal \,per-ē-ō-'dänt-ᵊl\ *adj* 1 : investing or surrounding a tooth 2 : of or affecting the periodontium (~ infection) — **peri·odon·tal·ly** *adv*

periodontal disease *n* : any disease affecting the periodontium

periodontal membrane *n* : the fibrous connective-tissue layer covering the cementum of a tooth and holding it in place in the jawbone — called also *pericementum, periodontal ligament*

peri·odon·tics \,per-ə-'dän-tiks\ *n* : a branch of dentistry that deals with diseases of the supporting and investing structures of the teeth including the gums, cementum, periodontal membranes, and alveolar bone — called also *periodontology*

peri·odon·tist \-'dän-tist\ *n* : a specialist in periodontics — called also *periodontologist*

peri·odon·ti·tis \,per-ē-(,)ō-,dän-'tī-təs\ *n* : inflammation of the periodontium and esp. the periodontal membrane — called also *pericementitis*

periodontis simplex \-'sim-,pleks\ *n* : the common form of chronic periodontitis usu. resulting from local infection and characterized by destruction of the periodontal membrane, formation of pockets around the teeth, and resorption of alveolar bone in a horizontal direction

peri·odon·ti·um \,per-ē-ō-'dän-chē-əm, -chəm\ *n, pl* **-tia** \-chē-ə, -chə\ : the supporting structures of the teeth including the cementum, the periodontal membrane, the bone of the alveolar process, and the gums

peri·odon·to·cla·sia \-ō-,dän-tə-'klā-zhə, -zhē-ə\ *n* : any periodontal disease characterized by destruction of the periodontium

peri·odon·tol·o·gist \,per-ē-ō-,dän-'tä-lə-jist\ *n* : PERIODONTIST

peri·odon·tol·o·gy \-,dän-'tä-lə-jē\ *n, pl* **-gies** : PERIODONTICS

peri·odon·to·sis \,per-ē-ō-,dän-'tō-səs\ *n, pl* **-to·ses** \-,sēz\ : a severe degenerative disease of the periodontium which in the early stages of its pure form is characterized by a lack of clinical evidence of inflammation

peri·op·er·a·tive \,per-ē-'ä-pə-rə-tiv, -,rā-\ *adj* : relating to, occurring in, or being the period around the time of a surgical operation (~ morbidity)

peri·oral \-'ōr-əl, -'är-\ *adj* : of, relating to, occurring in, or being the tissues around the mouth

peri·or·bit·al \-'ōr-bət-ᵊl\ *adj* : of, relating to, occurring in, or being the tissues surrounding or lining the orbit of the eye (~ edema)

periost- *or* **perioste-** *or* **periosteo-** *comb form* : periosteum (*periostitis*)

peri·os·te·al \,per-ē-'äs-tē-əl\ *adj* 1 : situated around or produced external to bone 2 : of, relating to, or involving the periosteum (a ~ sarcoma)

periosteal elevator *n* : a surgical instrument used to separate the periosteum from bone

peri·os·te·um \,per-ē-'äs-tē-əm\ *n, pl* **-tea** \-tē-ə\ : the membrane of connective tissue that closely invests all bones except at the articular surfaces

peri·os·ti·tis \-,äs-'tī-təs\ *n* : inflammation of the periosteum

peri·pan·cre·at·ic \,per-ə-,paŋ-krē-'a-tik, -,pan-\ *adj* : of, relating to, occurring in, or being the tissue surrounding the pancreas

pe·riph·er·al \pə-'ri-fə-rəl\ *adj* 1 : of, relating to, involving, forming, or located near a periphery or surface part (as of the body) 2 : of, relating to, affecting, or being part of the peripheral nervous system (~ nerves) (~ neuropathy) 3 : of, relating to, or being the outer part of the field of vision 4 : of, relating to, or being blood in the systemic circulation (~ blood) — **pe·riph·er·al·ly** *adv*

peripheral nervous system *n* : the part of the nervous system that is outside the central nervous system and comprises the cranial nerves excepting the optic nerve, the spinal nerves, and the autonomic nervous system

peripheral vascular disease *n* : vascular disease (as Raynaud's disease and thromboangiitis obliterans) affecting blood vessels esp. of the extremities

Peri·pla·ne·ta \,per-ē-plə-'nē-tə\ *n* : a genus of large cockroaches that includes the American cockroach (*P. americana*)

peri·plas·mic \,per-ə-'plaz-mik\ *adj* : of, relating to, occurring in, or being the space between the cell wall and the cell membrane

peri·por·tal \,per-ə-'pōrt-ᵊl\ *adj* : of, relating to, occurring in, or being the tissues surrounding a portal vein

peri·rec·tal \-'rek-tᵊl\ *adj* : of, relating to, occurring in, or being the tissues surrounding the rectum ⟨a ~ abscess⟩

peri·re·nal \-'rēn-ᵊl\ *adj* : of, relating to, occurring in, or being the tissues surrounding the kidney ⟨a ~ abscess⟩

peri·stal·sis \,per-ə-'stȯl-səs, -'stal-, -'stȧl-\ *n, pl* **-stal·ses** \-,sēz\ : successive waves of involuntary contraction passing along the walls of a hollow muscular structure (as the esophagus or intestine) and forcing the contents onward — compare SEGMENTATION 2 — **peri·stal·tic** \-tik\ *adj*

peri·ten·di·ni·tis \,per-ə-,ten-də-'nī-təs\ *n* : inflammation of the tissues around a tendon

periton- or **peritone-** or **peritoneo-** *comb form* 1 : peritoneum ⟨*peritonitis*⟩ 2 : peritoneal and ⟨*peritoneovenous* shunt⟩

peri·to·nae·um *chiefly Brit var of* PERITONEUM

peri·to·ne·al \,per-ə-tə-'nē-əl\ *adj* : of, relating to, or affecting the peritoneum — **peri·to·ne·al·ly** *adv*

peritoneal cavity *n* : a space formed when the parietal and visceral layers of the peritoneum spread apart

peri·to·neo·scope \,per-ə-tə-'nē-ə-,skōp\ *n* : LAPAROSCOPE — **peri·to·neo·scop·ic** \-,nē-ə-'skä-pik\ *adj*

peri·to·ne·os·co·py \,per-ə-,tō-nē-'äs-kə-pē\ *n, pl* **-pies** : the study of the abdominal and pelvic cavities by means of the peritoneoscope

peri·to·neo·ve·nous shunt \,per-ə-tə-,nē-ō-'vē-nəs-\ *n* : a shunt between the peritoneum and the jugular vein for relief of peritoneal ascites

peri·to·ne·um \,per-ə-tə-'nē-əm\ *n, pl* **-ne·ums** or **-nea** \-'nē-ə\ : the smooth transparent serous membrane that lines the cavity of the abdomen, is folded inward over the abdominal and pelvic viscera, and consists of an outer layer closely adherent to the walls of the abdomen and an inner layer that folds to invest the viscera — see PARIETAL PERITONEUM, VISCERAL PERITONEUM; compare MESENTERY 1

peri·to·ni·tis \,per-ə-tə-'nī-təs\ *n* : inflammation of the peritoneum

peri·ton·sil·lar abscess \,per-ə-'tän-sə-lər-\ *n* : QUINSY

peri·tu·bu·lar \,per-ə-'tü-byə-lər, -'tyü-\ *adj* : being adjacent to or surrounding a tubule

peritubular capillary *n* : any of a network of capillaries surrounding the renal tubules

peri·um·bi·li·cal \,per-ē-,əm-'bi-li-kəl\ *adj* : situated or occurring adjacent to the navel ⟨~ pain⟩

peri·un·gual \-'əŋ-gwəl, -'ən-\ *adj* : situated or occurring around a fingernail or toenail

peri·ure·thral \-yü-'rē-thrəl\ *adj* : of, relating to, occurring in, or being the tissues surrounding the urethra

peri·vas·cu·lar \,per-ə-'vas-kyə-lər\ *adj* : of, relating to, occurring in, or being the tissues surrounding a blood vessel

peri·vas·cu·li·tis \-,vas-kyə-'lī-təs\ *n* : inflammation of a perivascular sheath ⟨~ in the retina⟩

peri·ve·nous \,per-ə-'vē-nəs\ *adj* : of, relating to, occurring in, or being the tissues surrounding a vein

peri·ven·tric·u·lar \-ven-'tri-kyə-lər\ *adj* : situated or occurring around a ventricle esp. of the brain

peri·vi·tel·line space \,per-ə-vī-'te-lən-, -,lēn-, -,lin-\ *n* : the fluid-filled space between the fertilization membrane and the ovum after the entry of a sperm into the egg

per·i·win·kle \'per-i-,wiŋ-kəl\ *n* : a commonly cultivated shrub (*Catharanthus roseus* syn. *Vinca rosea*) of the dogbane family (Apocynaceae) that is native to the Old World tropics and is the source of several antineoplastic drugs — see VINBLASTINE, VINCRISTINE

perle \'pərl\ *n* 1 : a soft gelatin capsule for enclosing volatile or unpleasant tasting liquids intended to be swallowed 2 : a fragile glass vial that contains a liquid (as amyl nitrite) and that is intended to be crushed and the vapor inhaled

per·lèche \per-'lesh\ *n* : a superficial inflammatory condition of the angles of the mouth often with fissure formation that is caused esp. by infection or avitaminosis

per·ma·nent \'pər-mə-nənt\ *adj* : of, relating to, or being a permanent tooth ⟨~ dentition⟩

permanent tooth *n* : one of the second set of teeth of a mammal that follow the milk teeth, typically persist into old age, and in humans are 32 in number including 4 incisors, 2 canines, and 10 premolars and molars in each jaw

per·me·able \'pər-mē-ə-bəl\ *adj* : capable of being permeated; *esp* : having pores or openings that permit liquids or gases to pass through — **per·me·abil·i·ty** \,pər-mē-ə-'bi-lə-tē\ *n*

per·me·ate \'pər-mē-,āt\ *vb* **-at·ed; -at·ing** : to diffuse through or penetrate something — **per·me·ation** \ˌpər-mē-ˈā-shən\ n

per·mis·sive \pər-ˈmi-siv\ adj : supporting genetic replication (as of a virus)

per·ni·cious \pər-ˈni-shəs\ adj : highly injurious or destructive : tending to a fatal issue : DEADLY ⟨~ disease⟩

pernicious anemia n : a severe hyperchromic anemia marked by a progressive decrease in number and increase in size and hemoglobin content of the red blood cells and by pallor, weakness, and gastrointestinal and nervous disturbances and associated with reduced ability to absorb vitamin B_{12} due to the absence of intrinsic factor — called also *addisonian anemia*

per·nio \ˈpər-nē-ˌō\ n, pl **per·ni·o·nes** \ˌpər-nē-ˈō-(ˌ)nēz\ : CHILBLAIN

pe·ro·me·lia \ˌpē-rə-ˈmē-lē-ə\ n : congenital malformation of the limbs

pe·ro·ne·al \ˌper-ō-ˈnē-əl, pə-ˈrō-nē-\ adj 1 : of, relating to, or located near the fibula 2 : relating to or involving a peroneal part

peroneal artery n : a deeply seated artery running along the back part of the fibular side of the leg to the heel, arising from the posterior tibial artery, and ending in branches near the ankle

peroneal muscle n : PERONEUS

peroneal muscular atrophy n : a chronic inherited progressive muscular atrophy that affects the parts of the legs and feet innervated by the peroneal nerves first and later progresses to the hands and arms — called also *Charcot-Marie-Tooth disease*, *peroneal atrophy*

peroneal nerve n : COMMON PERONEAL NERVE — see DEEP PERONEAL NERVE, SUPERFICIAL PERONEAL NERVE

peroneal retinaculum n : either of two bands of fascia that support and hold in place the tendons of the peroneus longus and peroneus brevis muscles as they pass along the lateral aspect of the ankle: **a** : one that is situated more superiorly — called also *superior peroneal retinaculum* **b** : one that is situated more inferiorly — called also *inferior peroneal retinaculum*

peroneal vein n : any of several veins that drain the muscles in the lateral and posterior parts of the leg, accompany the peroneal artery, and empty into the posterior tibial veins about two-thirds of the way up the leg

per·o·ne·us \ˌper-ə-ˈnē-əs\ n, pl **-nei** \-ˈnē-ˌī\ : any of three muscles of the lower leg: **a** : PERONEUS BREVIS **b** : PERONEUS LONGUS **c** : PERONEUS TERTIUS

peroneus brev·is \-ˈbre-vis\ n : a peroneus muscle that arises esp. from the side of the lower part of the fibula, ends in a tendon that inserts on the tuberosity at the base of the fifth metatarsal bone, and assists in everting and pronating the foot

peroneus lon·gus \-ˈlȯŋ-gəs\ n : a peroneus muscle that arises esp. from the head and side of the fibula, ends in a long tendon that inserts on the side of the first metatarsal bone and the cuneiform bone on the medial side, and aids in everting and pronating the foot

peroneus ter·ti·us \-ˈtər-shē-əs\ n : a branch of the extensor digitorum longus muscle that arises esp. from the lower portion of the fibula, inserts on the dorsal surface of the base of the fifth metatarsal bone, and flexes the foot dorsally and assists in everting it

per·oral \(ˌ)pər-ˈȯr-əl, per-, -ˈär-\ adj : done, occurring, or obtained through or by way of the mouth ⟨~ administration of a drug⟩ ⟨~ infection⟩ — **per·oral·ly** adv

per os \ˌpər-ˈōs\ adv : by way of the mouth ⟨infection *per os*⟩

pe·ro·sis \pə-ˈrō-səs\ n, pl **pe·ro·ses** \-ˌsēz\ : a disorder of poultry that is characterized by leg deformity and can be prevented by additions of choline to the diet — called also *hock disease*, *slipped tendon*

per·ox·i·dase \pə-ˈräk-sə-ˌdās, -ˌdāz\ n : an enzyme that catalyzes the oxidation of various substances by peroxides

per·ox·ide \pə-ˈräk-ˌsīd\ n : an oxide containing a high proportion of oxygen; *esp* : a compound (as hydrogen peroxide) in which oxygen is visualized as joined to oxygen

per·ox·i·some \pə-ˈräk-sə-ˌsōm\ n : a cytoplasmic cell organelle containing enzymes (as catalase) which act esp. in the production and decomposition of hydrogen peroxide — called also *microbody* — **per·ox·i·som·al** \-ˌräk-sə-ˈsō-məl\ adj

per·pen·dic·u·lar plate \ˌpər-pən-ˈdi-kyə-lər-\ n 1 : a flattened bony lamina of the ethmoid bone that is the largest bony part assisting in forming the nasal septum 2 : a long thin vertical bony plate forming part of the palatine bone — compare HORIZONTAL PLATE

per·phen·a·zine \(ˌ)pər-ˈfe-nə-ˌzēn\ n : a phenothiazine tranquilizer $C_{21}H_{26}ClN_3OS$ that is used to control tension, anxiety, and agitation esp. in psychotic conditions

per·rec·tal \ˌpər-ˈrekt-ᵊl\ adj : done or occurring through or by way of the rectum ⟨~ administration⟩ — **per·rec·tal·ly** adv

per rectum adv : by way of the rectum ⟨a solution injected *per rectum*⟩

Per·san·tine \pər-ˈsan-ˌtēn\ trademark — used for a preparation of dipyridamole

persecution complex n : the feeling of being persecuted esp. without basis in reality

per·se·cu·to·ry \'pər-sə-kyü-ˌtōr-ē, pər-'se-kyə-\ *adj* : of, relating to, or being feelings of persecution : PARANOID

per·sev·er·a·tion \pər-ˌse-və-'rā-shən\ *n* : continual involuntary repetition of a mental act usu. exhibited by speech or by some other form of overt behavior — **per·sev·er·ate** \pər-'se-və-ˌrāt\ *vb* — **per·sev·er·a·tive** \pər-'se-və-ˌrā-tiv\ *adj*

per·sis·tent \pər-'sis-tənt\ *adj* 1 : existing or continuing for a long time: as a : effective in the open for an appreciable time usu. through slow formation of a vapor (mustard gas is ~) b : degraded only slowly by the environment (~ pesticides) c : remaining infective for a relatively long time in a vector after an initial period of incubation (~ viruses) 2 : continuing to exist despite interference or treatment (a ~ cough)

per·so·na \pər-'sō-nə, -ˌnä\ *n, pl* **perso·nas** : an individual's social facade or front that esp. in the analytic psychology of C.G. Jung reflects the role in life the individual is playing — compare ANIMA

per·son·al·i·ty \ˌpər-sə-'na-lə-tē\ *n, pl* **-ties** 1 : the complex of characteristics that distinguishes an individual esp. in relationships with others 2 a : the totality of an individual's behavioral and emotional tendencies b : the organization of the individual's distinguishing character traits, attitudes, or habits

personality disorder *n* : a psychopathological condition or group of conditions in which an individual's entire life pattern is considered deviant or nonadaptive although the individual shows neither neurotic symptoms nor psychotic disorganization

personality inventory *n* : any of several tests that attempt to characterize the personality of an individual by objective scoring of replies to a large number of questions concerning the individual's behavior and attitudes — see MINNESOTA MULTIPHASIC PERSONALITY INVENTORY

personality test *n* : any of several tests that consist of standardized tasks designed to determine various aspects of the personality or the emotional status of the individual examined

per·spi·ra·tion \ˌpər-spə-'rā-shən\ *n* 1 : the act or process of perspiring 2 : a saline fluid that is secreted by the sweat glands, that consists chiefly of water containing sodium chloride and other salts, nitrogenous substances (as urea), carbon dioxide, and other solutes, and that serves both as a means of excretion and as a regulator of body temperature through the cooling effect of its evaporation — **per·spire** \pər-'spīr\ *vb*

per·spi·ra·to·ry \pər-'spī-rə-ˌtōr-ē,

'pər-spə-rə-\ *adj* : of, relating to, secreting, or inducing perspiration

per·sua·sion \pər-'swā-zhən\ *n* : a method of treating neuroses consisting essentially in rational conversation and reeducation

Per·thes disease \'pər-ˌtēz-\ *n* : LEGG-CALVÉ-PERTHES DISEASE

Per·to·frane \'pər-tə-ˌfrān\ *trademark* — used for a preparation of desipramine

per·tus·sis \pər-'tə-səs\ *n* : WHOOPING COUGH

peruana — see VERRUGA PERUANA

Peru balsam *n* : BALSAM OF PERU

Peruvian balsam *n* : BALSAM OF PERU

per·ver·sion \pər-'vər-zhən, -shən\ *n* 1 : the action of perverting or the condition of being perverted 2 : a perverted form; *esp* : an aberrant sexual practice esp. when habitual and preferred to normal coitus — **per·verse** \pər-'vərs\ *adj*

¹**per·vert** \pər-'vərt\ *vb* : to cause to engage in perversion or to become perverted

²**per·vert** \'pər-ˌvərt\ *n* : one that has been perverted; *specif* : one given to some form of sexual perversion

perverted *adj* : marked by abnormality or perversion (~ pancreatic function)

pes an·se·ri·nus \ˌpez-ˌan-sə-'rī-nəs\ *n* : the combined tendinous insertion on the medial aspect of the tuberosity of the tibia of the sartorius, gracilis, and semitendinosus muscles

pes ca·vus \-'kā-vəs\ *n* : a foot deformity characterized by an abnormally high arch

pes·sa·ry \'pe-sə-rē\ *n, pl* **-ries** 1 : a vaginal suppository 2 : a device worn in the vagina to support the uterus, remedy a malposition, or prevent conception

pest \'pest\ *n* 1 : an epidemic disease associated with high mortality; *specif* : PLAGUE 2 2 : something resembling a pest in destructiveness; *esp* : a plant or animal detrimental to humans or human concerns

pes·ti·cide \'pes-tə-ˌsīd\ *n* : an agent used to destroy pests — **pes·ti·cid·al** \ˌpes-tə-'sīd-əl\ *adj*

pes·tif·er·ous \pes-'ti-fə-rəs\ *adj* 1 : carrying or propagating infection : PESTILENTIAL (a ~ insect) 2 : infected with a pestilential disease

pes·ti·lence \'pes-tə-ləns\ *n* : a contagious or infectious epidemic disease that is virulent and devastating; *specif* : BUBONIC PLAGUE — **pes·ti·len·tial** \ˌpes-tə-'len-chəl\ *adj*

pes·tis \'pes-təs\ *n* : PLAGUE 2

pes·tle \'pe-səl, 'pes-təl\ *n* : a usu. club-shaped implement for pounding or grinding substances in a mortar

PET *abbr* positron-emission tomography

pe·te·chia \pə-'tē-kē-ə\ *n, pl* **-chi·ae** \-kē-ˌī\ : a minute reddish or purplish spot containing blood that appears in skin or mucous membrane esp. in some infectious diseases (as typhoid fever) — compare ECCHYMOSIS — **pe·te·chi·al** \-kē-əl\ *adj* — **pe·te·chi·a·tion** \pə-ˌtē-kē-ˈā-shən\ *n*

peth·i·dine \ˈpe-thə-ˌdēn, -dən\ *n, chiefly Brit* : MEPERIDINE

pe·tit mal \ˈpe-tē-ˌmal, -ˌmäl\ *n* : epilepsy caused by a usu. inherited dysrhythmia of the electrical pulsations of the brain and characterized by attacks of mild convulsive seizures with transient clouding of consciousness without amnesia and with or without slight movements of the head, eyes, or extremities — compare GRAND MAL

pe·tri dish \ˈpē-trē-\ *n* : a small shallow dish of thin glass or plastic with a loose cover used esp. for cultures in bacteriology

Pe·tri \ˈpā-trē, *Julius Richard* (1852–1921), German bacteriologist.

pe·tris·sage \ˌpā-tri-ˈsäzh\ *n* : massage in which the muscles are kneaded

pet·ro·la·tum \ˌpe-trə-ˈlā-təm, -ˈlä-\ *n* : PETROLEUM JELLY

pe·tro·leum jelly \pə-ˈtrō-lē-əm-ˌje-lē\ *n* : a neutral unctuous odorless tasteless substance obtained from petroleum and used esp. in ointments and dressings

pe·tro·sal \pə-ˈtrō-səl\ *n* : PETROSAL BONE

petrosal bone *n* : the petrous portion of the human temporal bone

petrosal ganglion *n* : INFERIOR GANGLION 1

petrosal nerve *n* : any of several small nerves passing through foramina in the petrous portion of the temporal bone: as **a** : DEEP PETROSAL NERVE **b** : GREATER PETROSAL NERVE **c** : LESSER PETROSAL NERVE

petrosal sinus *n* : either of two venous sinuses on each side of the base of the brain: **a** : a small superior sinus that connects the cavernous and transverse sinuses of the same side — called also *superior petrosal sinus* **b** : a larger inferior sinus that extends from the posterior inferior end of the cavernous sinus through the jugular foramen to join the internal jugular vein of the same side — called also *inferior petrosal sinus*

pe·tro·tym·pan·ic fissure \ˌpe-trō-tim-ˈpa-nik-, -ˌpe-ˌtrō-\ *n* : a narrow transverse slit dividing the glenoid fossa of the temporal bone — called also *Glaserian fissure*

pe·trous \ˈpe-trəs, ˈpē-\ *adj* : of, relating to, or constituting the exceptionally hard and dense portion of the human temporal bone that contains the internal auditory organs and is a pyramidal process wedged in at the base of the skull between the sphenoid and occipital bones

PET scan \ˈpet-\ *n* : a sectional view of the body constructed by positron-emission tomography — **PET scanning** *n*

PET scanner *n* : a medical instrument consisting of integrated X-ray and computing equipment and used for positron-emission tomography

Peutz–Je·ghers syndrome \ˈpœts-ˈjā-gərz-\ *n* : a familial polyposis inherited as an autosomal dominant trait and characterized by numerous polyps in the stomach, small intestine, and colon and by melanin-containing spots on the skin and mucous membranes esp. of the lips and gums

Peutz, J.L.A. (*fl* 1921), Dutch physician.

Jeghers, Harold (*b* 1904), American physician.

-pexy \ˌpek-sē\ *n comb form, pl* **-pex·ies** : fixation : making fast (gastro*pexy*)

Pey·er's patch \ˈpī-ərz-\ *n* : any of numerous large oval patches of closely aggregated nodules of lymphoid tissue in the walls of the small intestines esp. in the ileum that partially or entirely disappear in advanced life and in typhoid fever become the seat of ulcers which may perforate the intestines — called also *Peyer's gland*

Peyer, Johann Conrad (1653–1712), Swiss physician and anatomist.

pey·o·te \pā-ˈō-tē\ *also* **pey·otl** \-ˈōt-əl\ *n* **1** : any of several American cacti (genus *Lophophora*); esp : MESCAL **2** : a stimulant drug derived from mescal buttons

Pey·ro·nie's disease \ˌpā-rə-ˈnēz-, pā-ˈrō-nēz-\ *n* : the formation of fibrous plaques in one or both corpora cavernosa of the penis resulting in distortion or deflection of the erect organ

La Peyronie \lä-pā-rô-ˈnē\, François Gigot de (1678–1747), French surgeon.

pg *abbr* picogram

PG *abbr* prostaglandin

PGA *abbr* pteroylglutamic acid

PGR *abbr* psychogalvanic reaction: psychogalvanic reflex: psychogalvanic response

PGY *abbr* postgraduate year

pH \ˌpē-ˈāch\ *n* : a measure of acidity and alkalinity of a solution that is a number on a scale whose values run from 0 to 14 with 7 representing neutrality, numbers less than 7 increasing acidity, and numbers greater than 7 increasing alkalinity

PHA *abbr* phytohemagglutinin

phac- *or* **phaco-** *comb form* : lens (*phaco*emulsification)

phaco·emul·si·fi·ca·tion \ˌfa-kō-i-ˌməl-sə-fə-ˈkā-shən\ *n* : a cataract operation in which the diseased lens is reduced to a liquid by ultrasonic vibrations and drained out of the eye — **phaco·emul·si·fi·er** \-ˈməl-sə-ˌfī-ər\ *n*

phaco·ma·to·sis \ˌfa-kō-mə-ˈtō-səs\ *n, pl* **-to·ses** \-ˌsēz\ : any of a group of hereditary or congenital diseases (as neurofibromatosis) affecting the central nervous system and characterized by the development of hamartomas

phaeo·chro·mo·cy·to·ma *Brit var of* PHEOCHROMOCYTOMA

phag- *or* **phago-** *comb form* : eating : feeding (*phage*dena)

phage \'fāj, 'fäzh\ *n* : BACTERIOPHAGE

-phage \,fāj, ,fäzh\ *n comb form* : one that eats (bacterio*phage*)

phag·e·de·na \,fa-jə-'dē-nə\ *n* : rapidly spreading destructive ulceration of soft tissue — **phag·e·den·ic** \-'de-nik, -'dē-\ *adj*

phage lambda *n* : a coliphage that can be integrated as a prophage into the DNA of some lysogenic strains of a bacterium of the genus *Escherichia* (*E. coli*) — called also *bacteriophage lambda, lambda, lambda phage*

phage type *n* : a set of strains of a bacterium susceptible to the same bacteriophages

phage–typing *n* : determination of the phage type of a bacterium

-pha·gia \'fā-jə, -jē-ə\ *n comb form* : -PHAGY (dys*phagia*)

phago·cyte \'fa-gə-,sīt\ *n* : a cell (as a white blood cell) that engulfs and consumes foreign material (as microorganisms) and debris — **phago·cyt·ic** \,fa-gə-'si-tik\ *adj*

phago·cy·tize \'fa-gō-,sī-,tiz, -sə-\ *vb* **-tized; -tiz·ing** : PHAGOCYTOSE

phago·cy·tose \,fa-gō-'sī-,tōs, -,tōz\ *vb* **-tosed; -tos·ing** : to consume by phagocytosis — **phago·cy·tos·able** \,fa-gə-sī-'tō-zə-bəl, -sə-, -,tōs-\ *adj*

phago·cy·to·sis \,fa-gə-sī-'tō-səs, -sə-\ *n, pl* **-to·ses** \-,sēz\ : the engulfing and usu. the destruction of particulate matter by phagocytes that serves as an important bodily defense mechanism against infection by microorganisms and against occlusion of mucous surfaces or tissues by foreign particles and tissue debris — **phago·cy·tot·ic** \-'tä-tik\ *adj*

phago·some \'fa-gə-,sōm\ *n* : a membrane-bound vesicle that encloses particulate matter taken into the cell by phagocytosis

-pha·gous \fə-gəs\ *adj comb form* : feeding esp. on a (specified) kind of food (hemato*phagous*)

-pha·gy \f-ə-jē\ *n comb form, pl* **-phagies** : eating : eating of a (specified) type or substance (geo*phagy*)

phak- *or* **phako-** — *see* PHAC-

pha·lan·ge·al \,fā-lən-'jē-əl, ,fa-; fə-'lan-jē-, fā-\ *adj* : of or relating to a phalanx or the phalanges

pha·lan·gec·to·my \,fā-lən-'jek-tə-mē, ,fa-\ *n, pl* **-mies** : surgical excision of a phalanx of a finger or toe

pha·lanx \'fā-,laŋks\ *n, pl* **pha·lan·ges** \fə-'lan-(,)jēz, fā-\ : any of the digital bones of the hand or foot distal to the metacarpus or metatarsus that in humans are three to each finger

and toe with the exception of the thumb and big toe which have only two each

phall- *or* **phallo-** *comb form* : penis (*phall*oplasty)

phal·lic \'fa-lik\ *adj* **1** : of, relating to, or resembling a penis **2** : of, relating to, or characterized by the stage of psychosexual development in psychoanalytic theory during which a child becomes interested in his or her own sexual organs — compare ANAL 2a, GENITAL 3, ORAL 2a

phal·loi·din \fa-'lȯid-ᵊn\ *also* **phal·loi·dine** \fa-'lȯid-ᵊn, 'fa-lȯi-dēn\ *n* : a very toxic crystalline peptide $C_{35}H_{46}N_8O_{10}S·H_2O$ obtained from the death cap mushroom

phal·lo·plas·ty \'fa-lō-,plas-tē\ *n, pl* **-ties** : plastic surgery of the penis or scrotum

phal·lus \'fa-ləs\ *n, pl* **phal·li** \'fa-,lī, -,lē\ *or* **phal·lus·es** **1** : PENIS **2** : the first embryonic rudiment of the penis or clitoris

phan·ero·zo·ite \,fa-nə-rō-'zō-,īt\ *n* : an exoerythrocytic malaria parasite found late in the course of an infection — **phan·ero·zo·it·ic** \-,zō-'i-tik\ *adj*

phan·tasm \'fan-,ta-zəm\ *n* **1** : a figment of the imagination or disordered mind **2** : an apparition of a living or dead person

phan·ta·sy *var of* FANTASY

¹phan·tom \'fan-təm\ *n* **1** : a model of the body or one of its parts **2** : a body of material resembling a body or bodily part in mass, composition, and dimensions and used to measure absorption of radiations

²phantom *adj* : not caused by an anatomical lesion (~ respiratory disorders)

phantom limb *n* : an often painful sensation of the presence of a limb that has been amputated — called also *phantom pain, phantom sensations*

phantom tumor *n* : a swelling (as of the abdomen) suggesting a tumor

Phar. D. *abbr* doctor of pharmacy

pharm *abbr* pharmaceutical; pharmacist; pharmacy

¹phar·ma·ceu·ti·cal \,fär-mə-'sü-ti-kəl\ *also* **phar·ma·ceu·tic** \-tik\ *adj* : of, relating to, or engaged in pharmacy or the manufacture and sale of pharmaceuticals (a ~ company) — **phar·ma·ceu·ti·cal·ly** *adv*

²pharmaceutical *also* **pharmaceutic** *n* : a medicinal drug

phar·ma·ceu·tics \-tiks\ *n* : the science of preparing, using, or dispensing medicines : PHARMACY

phar·ma·cist \'fär-mə-sist\ *n* : a person licensed to engage in pharmacy

pharmaco- *comb form* : medicine : drug (*pharmaco*logy) (*pharmaco*therapy)

phar·ma·co·dy·nam·ics \,fär-mə-kō-dī-'na-miks, -də-\ *n* : a branch of pharmacology dealing with the reactions

phar·ma·co·dy·nam·ic \-mik\ *adj*
phar·ma·co·dy·nam·i·cal·ly *adv*
phar·ma·co·ge·net·ics \-jə-'ne-tiks\ *n*
: the study of the interrelation of hereditary constitution and response to drugs — **phar·ma·co·ge·net·ic** \-tik\ *adj*
phar·ma·cog·no·sist \·fär-mə-'käg-nə-sist\ *n* : a specialist in pharmacognosy
phar·ma·cog·no·sy \·fär-mə-'käg-nə-sē\ *n, pl* -**sies** : a science dealing with the composition, production, use, and history of crude drugs and simples — **phar·ma·cog·nos·tic** \-·käg-'näs-tik\ *or* **phar·ma·cog·nos·ti·cal** \-ti-kəl\ *adj*
phar·ma·co·ki·net·ics \-kō-kə-'ne-tiks, -kō-kī-\ *n* **1** : the study of the bodily absorption, distribution, metabolism, and excretion of drugs **2** : the characteristic interactions of a drug and the body in terms of its absorption, distribution, metabolism, and excretion — **phar·ma·co·ki·net·ic** \-tik\ *adj*
phar·ma·col·o·gist \·fär-mə-'kä-lə-jist\ *n* : a specialist in pharmacology
phar·ma·col·o·gy \·fär-mə-'kä-lə-jē\ *n, pl* -**gies 1** : the science of drugs including materia medica, toxicology, and therapeutics **2** : the properties and reactions of drugs esp. with relation to their therapeutic value — **phar·ma·co·log·i·cal** \-kə-'lä-ji-kəl\ *also* **phar·ma·co·log·ic** \-jik\ *adj* — **phar·ma·co·log·i·cal·ly** *adv*
phar·ma·co·poe·ia *or* **phar·ma·co·pe·ia** \·fär-mə-kə-'pē-ə\ *n* **1** : a book describing drugs, chemicals, and medicinal preparations; *esp* : one issued by an officially recognized authority and serving as a standard **2** : a collection or stock of drugs — **phar·ma·co·poe·ial** *or* **phar·ma·co·pe·ial** \-əl\ *adj*
phar·ma·co·ther·a·peu·tic \-·ther-ə-'pyü-tik\ *adj* : of or relating to pharmacotherapeutics or pharmacotherapy
phar·ma·co·ther·a·peu·tics \-tiks\ *n sing or pl* : the study of the therapeutic uses and effects of drugs
phar·ma·co·ther·a·py \·fär-mə-kō-'ther-ə-pē\ *n, pl* -**pies** : the treatment of disease and esp. mental illness with drugs
phar·ma·cy \'fär-mə-sē\ *n, pl* -**cies 1** : the art, practice, or profession of preparing, preserving, compounding, and dispensing medical drugs **2 a** : a place where medicines are compounded or dispensed (a hospital ~) **b** : DRUGSTORE **3** : PHARMACOPOEIA 2
Pharm. D. *abbr* doctor of pharmacy
pharyng- *or* **pharyngo-** *comb form* **1** : pharynx (*pharyng*itis) **2** : pharyngeal and (*pharyngo*esophageal)
pha·ryn·geal \·far-ən-'jē-əl; fə-'rin-jəl, -jē-əl\ *adj* **1** : relating to or located in the region of the pharynx **2 a** : innervating the pharynx esp. by contributing to the formation of the pharyngeal plexus (the ~ branch of the vagus nerve) **b** : supplying or draining the

pharynx (the ~ branch of the maxillary artery)
pharyngeal aponeurosis *n* : the middle or fibrous coat of the walls of the pharynx
pharyngeal arch *n* : BRANCHIAL ARCH
pharyngeal cavity *n* : the cavity of the pharynx that consists of a part continuous anteriorly with the nasal cavity by way of the nasopharynx, a part opening into the oral cavity by way of the fauces, and a part continuous posteriorly with the esophagus and opening into the larynx by way of the epiglottis
pharyngeal cleft *n* : BRANCHIAL CLEFT
pharyngeal plexus *n* : a plexus formed by branches of the glossopharyngeal, vagus, and sympathetic nerves supplying the muscles and mucous membrane of the pharynx and adjoining parts
pharyngeal pouch *n* : any of a series of evaginations of ectoderm on either side of the pharynx that meet the corresponding external furrows and give rise to the branchial clefts of the vertebrate embryo
pharyngeal tonsil *n* : a mass of lymphoid tissue at the back of the pharynx between the eustachian tubes that is usu. best developed in young children, is commonly atrophied in the adult, and is markedly subject to hypertrophy and adenoid formation esp. in children — called also *nasopharyngeal tonsil*
phar·yn·gec·to·my \·far-ən-'jek-tə-mē\ *n, pl* -**mies** : surgical removal of a part of the pharynx
pharyngis — see CONSTRICTOR PHARYNGIS INFERIOR, CONSTRICTOR PHARYNGIS MEDIUS, CONSTRICTOR PHARYNGIS SUPERIOR
phar·yn·gi·tis \·far-ən-'jī-təs\ *n, pl* -**git·i·des** \-'ji-tə-·dēz\ : inflammation of the pharynx
pharyngo- — see PHARYNG-
pha·ryn·go·epi·glot·tic fold \fə-·riŋ-gō-·e-pə-'glä-tik-\ *n* : either of two folds of mucous membrane extending from the base of the tongue to the epiglottis with one on each side of the midline
pha·ryn·go·esoph·a·ge·al \-i-·sä-fə-'jē-əl\ *adj* : of or relating to the pharynx and the esophagus
pharyngoesophageal diverticulum *n* : ZENKER'S DIVERTICULUM
pha·ryn·go·lar·yn·gec·to·my \fə-·riŋ-gō-·lar-ən-'jek-tə-mē\ *n, pl* -**mies** : surgical excision of the hypopharynx and larynx
pha·ryn·go·pal·a·tine arch \-'pa-lə-·tīn-\ *n* : PALATOPHARYNGEAL ARCH
pha·ryn·go·plas·ty \fə-'riŋ-gō-·plas-tē\ *n, pl* -**ties** : plastic surgery performed on the pharynx
phar·yn·gos·to·my \·far-iŋ-'gäs-tə-mē\ *n, pl* -**mies** : surgical formation of an artificial opening into the pharynx
phar·yn·got·o·my \·far-iŋ-'gä-tə-mē\ *n,*

pl **-mies** : surgical incision into the pharynx

pha·ryn·go·ton·sil·li·tis \fə-ˌriŋ-gō-ˌtän-sə-ˈlī-təs\ *n* : inflammation of the pharynx and the tonsils

pha·ryn·go·tym·pan·ic tube \tim-ˈpa-nik-\ *n* : EUSTACHIAN TUBE

phar·ynx \ˈfar-iŋks\ *n*, *pl* **pha·ryn·ges** \fə-ˈrin-(ˌ)jēz\ *also* **phar·ynx·es** : the part of the alimentary canal situated between the cavity of the mouth and the esophagus and in humans being a conical musculomembranous tube about four and a half inches long that is continuous above with the mouth and nasal passages, communicates through the eustachian tubes with the ears, and extends downward past the opening into the larynx to the lower border of the cricoid cartilage where it is continuous with the esophagus

phase \ˈfāz\ *n* **1** : a particular appearance or state in a regularly recurring cycle of changes **2** : a distinguishable part in a course, development, or cycle (the early ∼s of a disease) **3** : a point or stage in the period of a periodic motion or process (as a light wave or a vibration) in relation to an arbitrary reference or starting point in the period **4** : a homogeneous, physically distinct, and mechanically separable portion of matter present in a nonhomogeneous physicochemical system; *esp* : one of the fundamental states of matter usu. considered to include the solid, liquid, and gaseous forms

phase–contrast microscope *n* : a microscope that translates differences in phase of the light transmitted through or reflected by the object into differences of intensity in the image — **phase–contrast microscopy** *n*

-pha·sia \ˈfā-zhə, -zhē-ə\ *also* **-pha·sy** \fə-sē\ *n comb form*, *pl* **-phasias** *also* **-phasies** : speech disorder of a specified type) (dys*phasia*)

PhD \ˌpē-(ˌ)āch-ˈdē\ *abbr* **1** an earned academic degree conferring the rank and title of doctor of philosophy **2** a person who has a doctor of philosophy

phe·na·caine \ˈfē-nə-ˌkān, ˈfe-\ *n* : a crystalline base $C_{18}H_{22}N_2O_2$ or its hydrochloride used as a local anesthetic

phen·ac·e·tin \fi-ˈnas-ə-tən\ *n* : a compound $C_{10}H_{13}NO_2$ formerly used to ease pain or fever but now withdrawn from use because of its link to high blood pressure, heart attacks, cancer, and kidney disease — called also *acetophenetidin*

phe·naz·o·cine \fi-ˈna-zə-ˌsēn\ *n* : a drug $C_{22}H_{27}NO$ related to morphine that has greater pain-relieving and slighter narcotic effect

phen·a·zone \ˈfe-nə-ˌzōn\ *n* : ANTIPYRINE

phen·cy·cli·dine \ˌfen-ˈsi-klə-ˌdēn,

-ˈsī-, -dən\ *n* : a piperidine derivative $C_{17}H_{25}N$ used esp. as a veterinary anesthetic and sometimes illicitly as a psychedelic drug to induce vivid mental imagery — called also *angel dust, PCP*

phen·el·zine \ˈfen-əl-ˌzēn\ *n* : a monoamine oxidase inhibitor $C_8H_{12}N_2$ that suppresses REM sleep and is used esp. as an antidepressant drug — see NARDIL

Phen·er·gan \fe-ˈnər-ˌgan\ *trademark* — used for a preparation of promethazine

phen·eth·i·cil·lin \fi-ˌne-thə-ˈsi-lən\ *n* : a semisynthetic penicillin $C_{17}H_{20}$-N_2O_5S administered orally in the form of its potassium salt and used esp. in the treatment of less severe infections caused by bacteria that do not produce penicillinase — see MAXIPEN

phen·eth·yl alcohol \fe-ˈne-thəl-\ *n* : PHENYLETHYL ALCOHOL

phen·for·min \fen-ˈfôr-mən\ *n* : a toxic drug $C_{10}H_{15}N_5$ formerly used to treat diabetes but now banned because of its life-threatening side effects

phen·in·di·one \ˌfen-in-ˈdī-ˌōn\ *n* : an anticoagulant drug $C_{15}H_{10}O_2$

phen·ip·ra·zine \fe-ˈni-prə-ˌzēn\ *n* : a monoamine oxidase inhibitor C_9-$H_{14}N_2$

phen·ir·amine \fe-ˈnir-ə-ˌmēn, -mən\ *n* : a drug $C_{16}H_{20}N_2$ used in the form of its maleate as a antihistamine

phen·met·ra·zine \fen-ˈme-trə-ˌzēn\ *n* : a sympathomimetic stimulant C_{11}-$H_{15}NO$ used in the form of its hydrochloride as an appetite suppressant — see PRELUDIN

phe·no·barb \ˈfē-nō-ˌbärb\ *n* : PHENOBARBITAL; *also* : a pill containing phenobarbital

phe·no·bar·bi·tal \ˌfē-nō-ˈbär-bə-ˌtȯl\ *n* : a crystalline barbiturate $C_{12}H_{12}$-N_2O_3 used as a hypnotic and sedative — see LUMINAL

phe·no·bar·bi·tone \-bə-ˌtōn\ *n*, *chiefly Brit* : PHENOBARBITAL

phe·no·copy \ˈfē-nə-ˌkä-pē\ *n*, *pl* **-copies** : a phenotypic variation that is caused by unusual environmental conditions and resembles the normal expression of a genotype other than its own

phe·nol \ˈfē-ˌnōl, -ˌnȯl, fi-ˈ\ *n* **1** : a caustic poisonous crystalline acidic compound C_6H_5OH present in coal tar that is used in the manufacture of some pharmaceuticals and as a topical anesthetic in dilute solution — called also *carbolic, carbolic acid* **2** : any of various acidic compounds analogous to phenol — **phe·no·lic** \fi-ˈnō-lik, -ˈnä-\ *adj*

phe·nol·phtha·lein \ˌfēn-əl-ˈtha-lē-ən, -ˈtha-ˌlēn, -ˈthā-\ *n* : a white or yellowish white crystalline compound $C_{20}H_{14}O_4$ used in analysis as an indicator because its solution is brilliant red in alkalies and is decolorized by acids and in medicine as a laxative

phe·nol red n : PHENOLSULFONPHTHA-LEIN

phe·nol·sul·fon·phtha·lein \fēn-ᵊl-₁səl-ˈfän-ᵊtha-lē-ən, -₁tha-ˈlēn, -ˈthā-\ n : a red crystalline compound $C_{19}H_{14}O_5S$ used chiefly as a test of kidney function and as an acid-base indicator

phenolsulfonphthalein test n : a test in which phenolsulfonphthalein is administered by injection and urine samples are subsequently taken at regular intervals to measure the rate at which it is excreted by the kidneys

phe·nom·e·non \fi-ˈnä-mə-₁nän, -₁nən\ n, pl -na \-nə, -₁nä\ 1 : an observable fact or event 2 a : an object or aspect known through the senses rather than by thought or intuition b : a fact or event of scientific interest susceptible of scientific description and explanation

phe·no·thi·azine \₁fē-nō-ˈthī-ə-₁zēn\ n 1 : a greenish yellow crystalline compound $C_{12}H_9NS$ used as an anthelmintic and insecticide esp. in veterinary practice 2 : any of various phenothiazine derivatives (as chlorpromazine) that are used as tranquilizing agents esp. in the treatment of schizophrenia

phe·no·type \ˈfē-nə-₁tīp\ n : the visible properties of an organism that are produced by the interaction of the genotype and the environment — compare GENOTYPE — **phe·no·typ·ic** \₁fē-nə-ˈti-pik\ also **phe·no·typ·i·cal** \-pi-kəl\ adj — **phe·no·typ·i·cal·ly** adv

phe·noxy·benz·a·mine \fi-₁näk-sē-ˈben-zə-₁mēn\ n : a drug $C_{18}H_{22}ClNO$ that blocks the activity of alpha-receptors and is used in the form of its hydrochloride esp. to produce peripheral vasodilation

phe·noxy·meth·yl penicillin \-ˈmeth-ᵊl-\ n : PENICILLIN V

phen·pro·cou·mon \fen-prō-ˈkü-₁män\ n : an anticoagulant drug $C_{18}H_{16}O_3$

phen·sux·i·mide \fen-ˈsək-si-₁mid\ n : an anticonvulsant drug $C_{11}H_{11}NO_2$ used esp. in the control of petit mal epilepsy — see MILONTIN

phen·ter·mine \ˈfen-tər-₁mēn\ n : a drug $C_{10}H_{15}N$ used often in the form of its hydrochloride as an appetite suppressant

phen·tol·amine \fen-ˈtä-lə-₁mēn, -mən\ n : an adrenergic blocking agent $C_{17}H_{19}N_3O$ that is used esp. in the diagnosis and treatment of hypertension due to pheochromocytoma — see REGITINE

phe·nyl \ˈfen-ᵊl, ˈfēn-\ n : a chemical group C_6H_5 that has a valence of one and is derived from benzene by removal of one hydrogen atom — often used in combination

phe·nyl·al·a·nine \₁fen-ᵊl-ˈa-lə-₁nēn, ₁fēn-\ n : an essential amino acid $C_9H_{11}NO_2$ that is obtained in its levorotatory L form by the hydrolysis of proteins (as lactalbumin), that is essential in human nutrition, and that is converted in the normal body to tyrosine — see PHENYLKETONURIA, PHENYLPYRUVIC ACID

phenylalanine mustard or **L-phenylalanine mustard** \ˈel-\ n : MELPHALAN

phen·yl·bu·ta·zone \₁fen-ᵊl-ˈbyü-tə-₁zōn\ n : a drug $C_{19}H_{20}N_2O_2$ that is used for its analgesic and anti-inflammatory properties esp. in the treatment of arthritis, gout, and bursitis — see BUTAZOLIDIN

phen·yl·eph·rine \₁fen-ᵊl-ˈe-₁frēn, -frən\ n : a sympathomimetic agent $C_9H_{13}NO_2$ that is used in the form of the hydrochloride as a vasoconstrictor, a mydriatic, and by injection to raise the blood pressure — see NEO-SYNEPHRINE

phe·nyl·eth·yl alcohol \₁fen-ᵊl-ˈeth-ᵊl-, ₁fēn-\ n : a fragrant liquid alcohol $C_8H_{10}O$ that is used as an antibacterial agent in ophthalmic solutions with limited effectiveness

phe·nyl·eth·yl·amine \₁fen-ᵊl-₁eth-ᵊl-ˈa-₁mēn, ₁fēn-\ n : a neurotransmitter $C_8H_{11}N$ that is an amine resembling amphetamine in structure and pharmacological properties; also : any of its derivatives

phe·nyl·ke·ton·uria \₁fen-ᵊl-₁kē-tə-ˈnùr-ē-ə, ₁fēn-, -ˈnyùr-\ n : an inherited metabolic disease that is characterized by inability to oxidize a metabolic product of phenylalanine and by severe mental retardation — abbr. PKU; called also phenylpyruvic amentia, phenylpyruvic oligophrenia

¹**phe·nyl·ke·ton·uric** \-ˈnùr-ik, -ˈnyùr-\ n : one affected with phenylketonuria

²**phenylketonuric** adj : of, relating to, or affected with phenylketonuria

phen·yl·mer·cu·ric \₁fen-ᵊl-mər-ˈkyùr-ik\ adj : of, relating to, or being the positively charged ion $C_6H_5Hg^+$

phenylmercuric acetate n : a crystalline salt $C_8H_8HgO_2$ used chiefly as a fungicide and herbicide

phenylmercuric nitrate n : a crystalline basic salt that is a mixture of $C_6H_5HgNO_3$ and C_6H_5HgOH used chiefly as a fungicide and antiseptic

phen·yl·pro·pa·nol·amine \₁fen-ᵊl-₁prō-pə-ˈnō-lə-₁mēn, -ˈnō-; -₁nō-ˈla-₁mēn\ n : a sympathomimetic drug $C_9H_{13}NO$ used in the form of its hydrochloride esp. as a nasal and bronchial decongestant and as an appetite suppressant — abbr. PPA; see PROPADRINE

phe·nyl·py·ru·vic acid \₁fen-ᵊl-pī-ˈrü-vik-, ₁fēn-\ n : a crystalline keto acid $C_9H_8O_3$ found in the urine as a metabolic product of phenylalanine esp. in phenylketonuria

phenylpyruvic amentia n : PHENYLKETONURIA

phenylpyruvic oligophrenia *n* : PHENYL-KETONURIA

phenyl salicylate *n* : a crystalline ester $C_{13}H_{10}O_3$ used as an ingredient of suntan preparations because of its ability to absorb ultraviolet light and also as an analgesic and antipyretic — called also *salol*

phen·yl·thio·car·ba·mide \ˌfen-ᵊl-ˌthī-ō-ˈkär-bə-ˌmīd\ *n* : a compound $C_7H_8N_2S$ that is extremely bitter or tasteless depending on the presence or absence of a single dominant gene in the taster — called also *PTC*

phen·yl·thio·urea \-ˌthī-ō-yü-ˈrē-ə\ *n* : PHENYLTHIOCARBAMIDE

phe·nyt·o·in \fə-ˈni-tə-wən\ *n* : a crystalline anticonvulsant compound $C_{15}H_{12}N_2O_2$ used in the form of its sodium salt in the treatment of epilepsy — called also *diphenylhydantoin*; see DILANTIN

pheo·chro·mo·cy·to·ma \ˌfē-ə-ˌkrō-mə-sə-ˈtō-mə, -si-\ *n, pl* **-mas** or **-ma·ta** \-mə-tə\ : a tumor that is derived from chromaffin cells and is usu. associated with paroxysmal or sustained hypertension

phe·re·sis \fə-ˈrē-səs\ *n, pl* **phe·re·ses** \-ˌsēz\ : removal of blood from a donor's body, separation of a blood component (as plasma or white blood cells), and transfusion of the remaining blood components back into the donor — called also *apheresis*; see PLASMAPHERESIS, PLATELETPHERESIS

pher·o·mone \ˈfer-ə-ˌmōn\ *n* : a chemical substance that is produced by an animal and serves esp. as a stimulus to other individuals of the same species for one or more behavioral responses — **pher·o·mon·al** \ˌfer-ə-ˈmōn-ᵊl\ *adj*

PhG *abbr* graduate in pharmacy

phi·al \ˈfīl\ *n* : VIAL

Phi·a·loph·o·ra \ˌfī-ə-ˈlä-fə-rə\ *n* : a genus (family Dematiaceae) of imperfect fungi of which some forms are important in human mycotic infections (as chromoblastomycosis)

¹-phil \ˌfil\ *or* **-phile** \ˌfīl\ *n comb form* : lover : one having an affinity for or a strong attraction to ⟨acido*phil*⟩

²-phil *or* **-phile** *adj comb form* : loving : having a fondness or affinity for ⟨hemo*phile*⟩

Philadelphia chromosome *n* : an abnormally short chromosome 22 that is found in the hematopoietic cells of persons suffering from chronic myelogenous leukemia and lacks the major part of its long arm which has usu. undergone translocation to chromosome 9

-phil·ia \ˈfī-lē-ə\ *n comb form* 1 : tendency toward ⟨hemo*philia*⟩ 2 : abnormal appetite or liking for ⟨necro*philia*⟩

-phil·i·ac \ˈfī-lē-ˌak\ *n comb form* 1 : one having a tendency toward ⟨hemo*philiac*⟩ 2 : one having an abnor-

mal appetite or liking for ⟨copro*philiac*⟩

-phil·ic \ˈfi-lik\ *adj comb form* : having an affinity for : loving ⟨acido*philic*⟩

phil·trum \ˈfil-trəm\ *n, pl* **phil·tra** \-trə\ : the vertical groove on the median line of the upper lip

phi·mo·sis \fī-ˈmō-səs, fi-\ *n, pl* **phi·mo·ses** \-ˌsēz\ : tightness or constriction of the orifice of the prepuce arising either congenitally or from inflammation, congestion, or other postnatal causes and making it impossible to bare the glans

phi phenomenon \ˈfī-\ *n* : the appearance of motion resulting from an orderly sequence of stimuli (as lights flashed in rapid succession a short distance apart on a sign) without any actual motion being presented to the eye

phleb- *or* **phlebo-** *comb form* : vein ⟨*phleb*itis⟩

phle·bi·tis \fli-ˈbī-təs\ *n, pl* **phle·bit·i·des** \-ˈbi-tə-ˌdēz\ : inflammation of a vein

phle·bo·gram \ˈflē-bə-ˌgram\ *n* 1 : a tracing made with a sphygmograph that records the pulse in a vein 2 : a roentgenogram of a vein after injection of a radiopaque medium

phle·bo·graph \-ˌgraf\ *n* : a sphygmograph adapted for recording the venous pulse

phle·bog·ra·phy \fli-ˈbä-grə-fē\ *n, pl* **-phies** : the process of making phlebograms — **phle·bo·graph·ic** \ˌflē-bə-ˈgra-fik\ *adj*

phle·bo·lith \ˈflē-bə-ˌlith\ *n* : a calculus in a vein usu. resulting from the calcification of an old thrombus

phle·bol·o·gist \fli-ˈbä-lə-jist\ *n* : a specialist in phlebology

phle·bol·o·gy \fli-ˈbä-lə-jē\ *n, pl* **-gies** : a branch of medicine concerned with the veins

phle·bo·throm·bo·sis \ˌflē-bō-thräm-ˈbō-səs\ *n, pl* **-bo·ses** \-ˌsēz\ : venous thrombosis accompanied by little or no inflammation — compare THROMBOPHLEBITIS

phle·bot·o·mist \fli-ˈbä-tə-mist\ *n* : one who practices phlebotomy

phle·bot·o·mize \fli-ˈbä-tə-ˌmīz\ *vb* **-mized; -miz·ing** : to draw blood from : BLEED

phle·bot·o·mus \fli-ˈbä-tə-məs\ *n* 1 *cap* : a genus of small bloodsucking sand flies (family Psychodidae) including one (*P. papatasii*) that is the carrier of sandfly fever and others suspected of carrying other human disease 2 *pl* **-mi** \-ˌmī\ *also* **-mus·es** : any sand fly of the genus *Phlebotomus*

phlebotomus fever *n* : SANDFLY FEVER

phle·bot·o·my \fli-ˈbä-tə-mē\ *n, pl* **-mies** : the letting of blood for transfusion, pheresis, diagnostic testing, or experimental procedures and esp. formerly for the treatment of disease — called also *venesection, venotomy*

phlegm \'flem\ *n* : viscid mucus secreted in abnormal quantity in the respiratory passages

phleg·ma·sia \fleg-'mā-zhə, -zhē-ə\ *n*, *pl* **-siae** \-zhē, -zhē-ē\ : INFLAMMATION

phlegmasia al·ba do·lens \-'al-bə-'dō-.lenz\ *n* : MILK LEG

phlegmasia ce·ru·lea dolens \-sə-'rü-lē-ə-\ *n* : severe thrombophlebitis with extreme pain, edema, cyanosis, and possible ischemic necrosis

phleg·mon \'fleg-.män\ *n* : purulent inflammation and infiltration of connective tissue — compare ABSCESS — **phleg·mon·ous** \'fleg-mə-nəs\ *adj*

phlor·e·tin \'flōr-ət-ən, flə-'rēt-ᵊn\ *n* : a crystalline phenolic ketone $C_{15}H_{14}O_5$ that is a potent inhibitor of transport systems for sugars and anions

phlo·ri·zin or **phlo·rhi·zin** \'flōr-ə-zən, flə-'rīz-ᵊn\ or **phlo·rid·zin** \'flōr-əd-zən, flə-'rid-zən\ *n* : a bitter crystalline glucoside $C_{21}H_{24}O_{10}$ used chiefly in producing experimental diabetes in animals

phlyc·ten·u·lar \flik-'ten-yə-lər\ *adj* : marked by or associated with phlyctenules (~ conjunctivitis)

phlyc·te·nule \flik-'ten-(.)yül; 'flik-tə-.nül, -.nyül\ *n* : a small vesicle or pustule: *esp* : one on the conjunctiva or cornea of the eye

PHN *abbr* public health nurse

-phobe \.fōb\ *n comb form* : one fearing or averse to (something specified) (chromo*phobe*)

pho·bia \'fō-bē-ə\ *n* : an exaggerated and often disabling fear usu. inexplicable to the subject and having sometimes a logical basis but usu. an illogical or symbolic object, class of objects, or situation — compare COMPULSION, OBSESSION

-pho·bia \'fō-bē-ə\ *n comb form* 1 : abnormal fear of (acro*phobia*) 2 : intolerance or aversion for (photo*phobia*)

pho·bic \'fō-bē-.ak\ *n* : PHOBIC

¹pho·bic \'fō-bik\ *adj* : of, relating to, affected with, or constituting phobia

²phobic *n* : one who exhibits a phobia

-pho·bic \'fō-bik\ or **-pho·bous** \f-ə-bəs\ *adj comb form* 1 : having an aversion for or fear of (agora*phobic*) 2 : lacking affinity for (hydro*phobic*)

phobic reaction *n* : a psychoneurosis in which the principal symptom is a phobia

pho·co·me·lia \.fō-kə-'mē-lē-ə\ *n* : a congenital deformity in which the limbs are extremely shortened so that the feet and hands arise close to the trunk — **pho·co·me·lic** \-'mē-lik\ *adj*

pho·co·me·lus \fō-'kä-mə-ləs\ *n*, *pl* **-li** \-.lī\ : an individual exhibiting phocomelia

phon \'fän\ *n* : the unit of loudness on a scale beginning at zero for the faintest audible sound and corresponding to the decibel scale of sound intensity with the number of phons of a given

sound being equal to the decibels of a pure 1000-cycle tone judged by the average listener to be equal in loudness to the given sound

phon- or **phono-** *comb form* : sound : voice : speech : tone (*phonation*)

pho·na·tion \fō-'nā-shən\ *n* : the production of vocal sounds and esp. speech — **pho·nate** \'fō-.nāt\ *vb*

-pho·nia \'fō-nē-ə, 'fōn-yə\ or **-pho·ny** \fə-nē\ *n comb form*, *pl* **-phonias** or **-phonies** : speech disorder (of a specified type esp. relating to phonation) (dys*phonia*)

pho·no·car·dio·gram \.fō-nə-'kär-dē-ə-.gram\ *n* : a record of heart sounds made by means of a phonocardiograph

pho·no·car·dio·graph \-.graf\ *n* : an instrument used for producing a graphic record of heart sounds

pho·no·car·dio·g·ra·phy \-.kär-dē-'ä-grə-fē\ *n*, *pl* **-phies** : the recording of heart sounds by means of a phonocardiograph — **pho·no·car·dio·graph·ic** \-.kär-dē-ə-'gra-fik\ *adj*

phor·bol \'fōr-.bol, -.bōl\ *n* : an alcohol $C_{20}H_{28}O_6$ that is the parent compound of tumor-promoting esters occurring in croton oil

-pho·re·sis \fə-'rē-səs\ *n comb form* : transmission (electro*phoresis*)

pho·ria \'fō-rē-ə\ *n* : any of various tendencies of the lines of vision to deviate from the normal when binocular fusion of the retinal images is prevented

-pho·ria \'fōr-ē-ə\ *n comb form* : bearing : state : tendency (eu*phoria*) (hetero*phoria*)

-phor·ic \'fōr-ik\ *adj comb form* : having (such) a bearing or tendency (thanato*phoric*)

Phor·mia \'fōr-mē-ə\ *n* : a genus of dipteran flies (family Calliphoridae) including one (*C. regina*) causing myiasis in sheep

phos- *comb form* : light (*phosphene*)

phos·gene \'faz-.jēn\ *n* : a colorless gas $COCl_2$ of unpleasant odor that is a severe respiratory irritant and has been used in chemical warfare

phosph- or **phospho-** *comb form* : phosphoric acid : phosphate (*phospholipid*)

phos·pha·gen \'fäs-fə-jən, -.jen\ *n* : any of several phosphate compounds (as phosphocreatine) occurring esp. in muscle and releasing energy on hydrolysis of the phosphate

phos·pha·tase \'fäs-fə-.tās, -.tāz\ *n* : an enzyme that accelerates the hydrolysis and synthesis of organic esters of phosphoric acid and the transfer of phosphate groups to other compounds: **a** : ALKALINE PHOSPHATASE **b** : ACID PHOSPHATASE

phos·phate \'fäs-.fāt\ *n* 1 **a** : a salt or ester of a phosphoric acid **b** : the negatively charged ion PO_4^{3-} having a chemical valence of three and derived from phosphoric acid H_3PO_4 **2** : an organic compound of phosphoric acid in which the acid group is bound to nitrogen or a carboxyl group in a way that permits useful energy to be released (as in metabolism)

phos·pha·tide \'fäs-fə-ˌtīd\ n : PHOSPHOLIPID

phos·pha·tid·ic acid \ˌfäs-fə-'ti-dik-\ n : any of several acids (RCOO)$_2$C$_3$H$_5$OPO$_3$H$_2$ that are formed from phosphatides and yield on hydrolysis two fatty acid molecules RCOOH and one molecule each of glycerol and phosphoric acid

phos·pha·ti·dyl·cho·line \ˌfäs-fə-ˌtīd-ə¹-'kō-ˌlēn, (ˌ)fäs-fa-təd-ə¹-\ n : LECITHIN

phos·pha·ti·dyl·eth·a·nol·amine \-ˌe-thə-'nä-lə-ˌmēn, -'nō-\ n : any of a group of phospholipids that occur esp. in blood plasma and in the white matter of the central nervous system — called also *cephalin*

phos·pha·ti·dyl·ser·ine \-'ser-ˌēn\ n : a phospholipid found in mammalian cells

phos·pha·tu·ria \ˌfäs-fə-'tür-ē-ə, -'tyur-\ n : the excessive discharge of phosphates in the urine

phos·phene \'fäs-ˌfēn\ n : a luminous impression that occurs when the retina undergoes stimulation (as by pressure on the eyeball when the lid is closed)

phospho- — see PHOSPH-

phos·pho·cre·atine \ˌfäs-(ˌ)fō-'krē-ə-ˌtēn\ n : a compound $C_4H_{10}N_3O_5P$ of creatine and phosphoric acid that is found esp. in vertebrate muscle where it is an energy source for muscle contraction — called also *creatine phosphate*

phos·pho·di·es·ter·ase \-dī-'es-tə-ˌrās, -ˌrāz\ n : a phosphatase (as from snake venom) that acts on compounds (as some nucleotides) having two ester groups to hydrolyze only one of the groups

phos·pho·di·es·ter bond \-dī-'es-tər-\ n : a covalent bond in RNA or DNA that holds a polynucleotide chain together by joining a phosphate group at position 5 in the pentose sugar of one nucleotide to the hydroxyl group at position 3 in the pentose sugar of the next nucleotide — called also *phosphodiester linkage*

phos·pho·enol·pyr·uvate \ˌfäs-fō-ə-ˌnōl-pī-'rü-ˌvāt, -nōl-, -ˌpīr-'yü-\ n : a salt or ester of phosphoenolpyruvic acid

phos·pho·enol·pyr·uvic acid \-pī-'rü-vik-, -ˌpīr-'yü-vik-\ n : a phosphate $H_2C=C(OPO_3H_2)COOH$ formed as an intermediate in carbohydrate metabolism

phos·pho·fruc·to·ki·nase \ˌfäs-(ˌ)fō-ˌfrək-tō-'kī-ˌnās, -ˌfrük-, -ˌfruk-, -ˌnāz\ n : an enzyme that functions in carbohydrate metabolism and esp. in

glycolysis by catalyzing the transfer of a second phosphate (as from ATP) to fructose

phos·pho·glu·co·mu·tase \-ˌglü-kō-'myü-ˌtās, -ˌtāz\ n : an enzyme that catalyzes the reversible isomerization of glucose-1-phosphate to glucose-6-phosphate

phos·pho·glu·co·nate \-'glü-kə-ˌnāt\ n : a compound formed by dehydrogenation of glucose-6-phosphate as the first step in a glucose degradation pathway alternative to the Krebs cycle

phosphogluconate dehydrogenase n : an enzyme that catalyzes the oxidative decarboxylation of phosphogluconate with the generation of NADPH

phos·pho·glyc·er·al·de·hyde \-ˌgli-sə-'ral-də-ˌhīd\ n : a phosphate of glyceraldehyde $C_3H_5O_3(H_2PO_3)$ that is formed esp. in anaerobic metabolism of carbohydrates by the splitting of a diphosphate of fructose

phos·pho·ino·si·tide \-i-'nō-sə-ˌtīd\ n : any of a group of inositol-containing derivatives of phosphatidic acid that do not contain nitrogen and are found in the brain

phos·pho·ki·nase \ˌfäs-fō-'kī-ˌnās, -ˌnāz\ n : KINASE

phos·pho·li·pase \-'li-ˌpās, -ˌpāz\ n : any of several enzymes that hydrolyze lecithins or phosphatidylethanolamines — called also *lecithinase*

phos·pho·lip·id \-'li-pəd\ n : any of numerous lipids (as lecithins and sphingomyelin) in which phosphoric acid as well as a fatty acid is esterified to glycerol and which are found in all living cells and in the bilayers of plasma membranes — called also *phosphatide*

phos·pho·lip·in \-'li-pən\ n : PHOSPHOLIPID

phos·pho·mono·es·ter·ase \-ˌmä-nō-'es-tə-ˌrās, -ˌrāz\ n : a phosphatase that acts on esters containing only a single ester group

phos·pho·pro·tein \ˌfäs-fō-'prō-ˌtēn\ n : any of various proteins (as casein) that contain combined phosphoric acid

phosphor- or **phosphoro-** comb form : phosphoric acid (*phosphorolysis*)

phos·pho·ri·bo·syl·pyr·o·phos·phate \ˌfäs-fō-ˌrī-bə-sil-ˌpī-rō-'fäs-ˌfāt\ n : a substance that is formed enzymatically from ATP and the phosphate of ribose and that plays a fundamental role in nucleotide synthesis

phosphoribosyltransferase n — see HYPOXANTHINE-GUANINE PHOSPHORIBOSYLTRANSFERASE

phos·pho·ric \fäs-'för-ik, -'fär-; 'fäs-fə-rik\ adj : of, relating to, or containing phosphorus esp. with a valence higher than in phosphorous compounds

phosphoric acid n **1** : a syrupy or deliquescent acid H_3PO_4 having three replaceable hydrogen atoms — called also *orthophosphoric acid* 2 : a compound consisting of phosphate groups linked directly to each other by oxygen

phos·pho·rol·y·sis \ˌfäs-fə-ˈrä-lə-səs\ *n, pl* **-y·ses** \-ˌsēz\ : a reversible reaction analogous to hydrolysis in which phosphoric acid functions in a manner similar to that of water with the formation of a phosphate (as glucose-1-phosphate in the breakdown of liver glycogen) — **phos·pho·ro·lyt·ic** \-rō-ˈli-tik\ *adj*

phos·pho·rous \ˈfäs-fə-rəs, fäs-ˈfōr-əs\ *adj* : of, relating to, or containing phosphorus esp. with a valence lower than in phosphoric compounds

phos·pho·rus \ˈfäs-fə-rəs\ *n, often attrib* : a nonmetallic element that occurs widely in combined form esp. as inorganic phosphates in minerals, soils, natural waters, bones, and teeth and as organic phosphates in all living cells — symbol *P*; see ELEMENT table

phosphorus 32 *n* : a heavy radioactive isotope of phosphorus having a mass number of 32 and a half-life of 14.3 days that is produced in nuclear reactors and used chiefly in tracer studies (as in biology and in chemical analysis) and in medical diagnosis (as in location of tumors) and therapy (as of polycythemia vera) — symbol P^{32} or ^{32}P

phos·phor·y·lase \ˈfäs-ˈfōr-ə-ˌlāz\ *n* : any of a group of enzymes that catalyze phosphorolysis with the formation of organic phosphates (as glucose-1-phosphate in the breakdown and synthesis of glycogen)

phos·phor·y·la·tion \ˌfäs-ˌfōr-ə-ˈlā-shən\ *n* : the process by which a chemical compound takes up or combines with phosphoric acid or a phosphorus-containing group: *esp* : the enzymatic conversion of carbohydrates into their phosphoric esters in metabolic processes — **phos·phor·y·late** \ˈfäs-ˈfōr-ə-ˌlāt\ *vb* — **phos·phor·y·la·tive** \ˌfäs-ˈfōr-ə-ˈlā-tiv\ *adj*

phos·pho·ryl·cho·line \ˌfäs-fə-ˌril-ˈkō-ˌlēn\ *n* : a hapten used medicinally in the form of its chloride $C_5H_{15}ClNO_4P$ to treat hepatobiliary dysfunction

phos·pho·trans·fer·ase \ˌfäs-fō-ˈtrans-(ˌ)fər-ˌās, -ˌāz\ *n* : any of several enzymes that catalyze the transfer of phosphorus-containing groups from one compound to another

phos·sy jaw \ˈfä-sē-\ *n* : a jawbone destroyed by chronic phosphorus poisoning

phot- *or* **photo-** *comb form* : light : radiant energy ⟨*photo*dermatitis⟩

pho·tic \ˈfō-tik\ *adj* : of, relating to, or involving light esp. in relation to organisms ⟨~ stimulation⟩ — **pho·ti·cal·ly** *adv*

pho·to·ac·ti·va·tion \ˌfō-tō-ˌak-tə-ˈvā-shən\ *n* : the process of activating a

substance by means of radiant energy and esp. light — **pho·to·ac·ti·vate** \-ˈak-tə-ˌvāt\ *vb* — **pho·to·ac·tive** \-ˈak-tiv\ *adj* — **pho·to·ac·tiv·i·ty** \-ˌak-ˈti-və-tē\ *n*

pho·to·ag·ing \ˈfō-tō-ˈā-jiŋ\ *n* : the long-term negative effects on skin (as increased susceptibility to wrinkles and cancer) of exposure to sunlight — **pho·to·aged** \-ˈājd\ *adj*

pho·to·al·ler·gic \ˌfō-tō-ə-ˈlər-jik\ *adj* : of, relating to, caused by, or affected with a photoallergy ⟨~ dermatitis⟩

pho·to·al·ler·gy \-ˈa-lər-jē\ *n, pl* **-gies** : an allergic sensitivity to light

pho·to·bi·ol·o·gy \-(ˌ)bī-ə-lə-jē\ *n, pl* **-gies** : a branch of biology that deals with the effects of radiant energy (as light) on living things — **pho·to·bi·ol·o·gist** \ˌfō-tō-(ˌ)bī-ˈä-lə-jist\ *n*

pho·to·chem·i·cal \ˌfō-tō-ˈke-mi-kəl\ *adj* : of, relating to, or resulting from the chemical action of radiant energy and esp. light ⟨~ smog⟩

pho·to·che·mo·ther·a·py \-ˌkē-mō-ˈther-ə-pē\ *n, pl* **-pies** : treatment esp. for psoriasis in which administration of a photosensitizing drug (as methoxsalen) is followed by exposure to ultraviolet radiation or sunlight

¹**pho·to·chro·mic** \ˌfō-tə-ˈkrō-mik\ *adj* 1 : capable of changing color on exposure to radiant energy (as light) (eyeglasses with ~ lenses) 2 : of, relating to, or utilizing the change of color shown by a photochromic substance (a ~ process) — **pho·to·chro·mism** \-ˈmi-zəm\ *n*

²**photochromic** *n* : a photochromic substance — usu. used in pl.

pho·to·co·ag·u·la·tion \-kō-ˌa-gyə-ˈlā-shən\ *n* : a surgical process of coagulating tissue by means of a precisely oriented high-energy light source (as a laser beam) — **pho·to·co·ag·u·la·tor** \-kō-ˈa-gyə-ˌlā-tər\ *n*

pho·to·con·vul·sive \ˌfō-tō-kən-ˈvəl-siv\ *adj* : of or relating to an abnormal electroencephalogram produced in response to a flickering light

pho·to·der·ma·ti·tis \-ˌdər-mə-ˈtī-təs\ *n, pl* **-ti·tis·es** *or* **-tit·i·des** \-ˈti-tə-ˌdēz\ : any dermatitis caused or precipitated by exposure to light

pho·to·der·ma·to·sis \-ˌdər-mə-ˈtō-səs\ *n, pl* **-to·ses** \-ˌsēz\ : any dermatosis produced by exposure to light

pho·to·dy·nam·ic \-dī-ˈna-mik\ *adj* : of, relating to, or having the property of intensifying or inducing a toxic reaction to light (as the destruction of cancer cells stained with a light-sensitive dye) in a living system

pho·to·flu·o·rog·ra·phy \-(ˌ)flü-ə-ˈrä-grə-fē\ *n, pl* **-phies** : the photography of the image produced on a fluorescent screen by X rays — **pho·to·flu·o·ro·graph·ic** \-ˌflür-ə-ˈgra-fik\ *adj*

pho·to·gen·ic \ˌfō-tə-ˈje-nik\ *adj* 1 : produced or precipitated by light ⟨~ epilepsy) (~ dermatitis) 2 : producing or generating light (~ bacteria)

pho·tom·e·ter \fō-'tä-mə-tər\ n : an instrument for measuring the intensity of light

pho·to·mi·cro·graph \,fō-tə-'mī-krə-,graf\ n : a photograph of a magnified image of a small object — called also *microphotograph* — **pho·to·mi·cro·graph·ic** \-,mī-krə-'gra-fik\ adj — **pho·to·mi·cro·graph·i·cal·ly** \-k(ə-)lē\ adv — **pho·to·mi·crog·ra·phy** \-,mī-'krä-grə-fē\ n

pho·ton \'fō-,tän\ n 1 : a unit of intensity of light at the retina equal to the illumination received per square millimeter of a pupillary area from a surface having a brightness of one candle per square meter — called also *troland* 2 : a quantum of electromagnetic radiation — **pho·ton·ic** \fō-'tä-nik\ adj

pho·to·patch test \'fō-tō-,pach-\ n : a test of the capability of a particular substance to photosensitize a particular human skin in which the substance is applied to the skin under a patch and the area is irradiated with ultraviolet light

pho·to·pho·bia \,fō-tə-'fō-bē-ə\ n 1 : intolerance to light; *esp* : painful sensitiveness to strong light 2 : an abnormal fear of light — **pho·to·pho·bic** \-'fō-bik\ adj

phot·oph·thal·mia \,fōt-,äf-'thal-mē-ə, -,äp-\ n : inflammation of the eye and esp. of the cornea and conjunctiva caused by exposure to light of short wavelength (as ultraviolet light)

phot·opic \fōt-'ō-pik, -'ä-\ adj : relating to or being vision in bright light with light-adapted eyes that is mediated by the cones of the retina

pho·to·pig·ment \'fō-tō-,pig-mənt\ n : a pigment (as a compound in the retina) that undergoes a physical or chemical change under the action of light

pho·top·sia \fō-'täp-sē-ə\ n : the perception of light (as luminous rays or flashes) that is purely subjective and accompanies a pathological condition esp. of the retina or brain

pho·to·re·cep·tor \,fō-tō-ri-'sep-tər\ n : a receptor for light stimuli

pho·to·scan \'fō-tō-,skan\ n : a photographic representation of variation in tissue state (as of the kidney) determined by gamma-ray emission from an injected radioactive substance — **photoscan** vb

pho·to·sen·si·tive \,fō-tō-'sen-sə-tiv\ adj : sensitive or sensitized to the action of radiant energy — **pho·to·sen·si·tiv·i·ty** \-,sen-sə-'ti-və-tē\ n

pho·to·sen·si·tize \-'sen-sə-,tīz\ vb -tized; -tiz·ing : to make sensitive to the influence of radiant energy and esp. light — **pho·to·sen·si·ti·za·tion** \-,sen-sə-tə-'zā-shən\ n — **pho·to·sen·si·tiz·er** n

pho·to·syn·the·sis \-'sin-thə-səs\ n, pl -the·ses \-,sēz\ : the formation of carbohydrates from carbon dioxide and a source of hydrogen (as water) in chlorophyll-containing cells (as of green plants) exposed to light involving a photochemical release of oxygen through the decomposition of water followed by various enzymatic synthetic reactions that usu. do not require the presence of light — **pho·to·syn·the·size** \-'sīz\ vb — **pho·to·syn·thet·ic** \-sin-'the-tik\ adj — **pho·to·syn·thet·i·cal·ly** adv

pho·to·ther·a·py \-'ther-ə-pē\ n, pl -pies : the application of light for therapeutic purposes

pho·to·tox·ic \,fō-tō-'täk-sik\ adj 1 *of a substance ingested or brought into contact with skin* : rendering the skin susceptible to damage (as sunburn or blisters) upon exposure to light and esp. ultraviolet light 2 : induced by a phototoxic substance (a ~ response) — **pho·to·tox·ic·i·ty** \-,täk-'si-sə-tē\ n

phren- *or* **phreno-** *comb form* 1 : mind ⟨*phrenology*⟩ 2 : diaphragm ⟨*phrenic*⟩

phren·em·phrax·is \,fren-em-'frak-səs\ n, pl **-phrax·es** \-,sēz\ : crushing of the phrenic nerve for therapeutic reasons

phreni- *comb form* : phrenic nerve ⟨*phrenicotomy*⟩

-phre·nia \'frē-nē-ə, 'fre-\ n comb form : disordered condition of mental functions ⟨hebe*phrenia*⟩

¹phren·ic \'fre-nik\ adj : of or relating to the diaphragm

²phrenic n : PHRENIC NERVE

phrenic artery n : any of the several arteries supplying the diaphragm: **a** : either of two arising from the thoracic aorta and distributed over the upper surface of the diaphragm — called also *superior phrenic artery* **b** : either of two that arise from the abdominal aorta and that supply the underside of the diaphragm and the adrenal glands — called also *inferior phrenic artery*

phren·i·cec·to·my \,fre-nə-'sek-tə-mē\ n, pl -mies : surgical removal of part of a phrenic nerve to secure collapse of a diseased lung — compare PHRENICOTOMY

phrenic nerve n : a general motor and sensory nerve on each side of the body that arises chiefly from the fourth cervical nerve, passes down through the thorax to the diaphragm, and supplies or gives off branches supplying esp. the pericardium, pleura, and diaphragm — called also *phrenic*

phren·i·cot·o·my \,fre-ni-'kä-tə-mē\ n, pl -mies : surgical division of a phrenic nerve to secure collapse of a diseased lung — compare PHRENICECTOMY

phrenic vein n : any of the veins that drain the diaphragm and accompany the phrenic arteries: **a** : one that accompanies the pericardiophrenic artery and usu. empties into the internal thoracic vein — called also *superior phrenic vein* **b** : any of two or three veins which follow the course of the inferior phrenic arteries and of which the one on the right empties into the inferior vena cava and the one or two on the left empty into the left renal or suprarenal vein or the inferior vena cava — called also *inferior phrenic vein*

phreno- — see PHREN-

phre·nol·o·gy \fri-ˈnä-lə-jē\ n, pl **-gies** : the study of the conformation of the skull based on the belief that it is indicative of mental faculties and character — **phre·nol·o·gist** \fri-ˈnä-lə-jist\ n

phry·no·der·ma \ˌfrī-nə-ˈdər-mə\ n : a rough dry skin eruption marked by keratosis and usu. associated with vitamin A deficiency

PHS abbr Public Health Service

phthal·yl·sul·fa·thi·a·zole \ˌtha-lil-ˌsəl-fə-ˈthī-ə-ˌzōl\ n : a sulfonamide $C_{17}H_{13}N_3O_5S_2$ used in the treatment of intestinal infections

phthi·ri·a·sis \thə-ˈrī-ə-səs, thī-\ n, pl **-a·ses** \-ˌsēz\ : PEDICULOSIS; esp : infestation with crab lice

Phthir·i·us \ˈthir-ē-əs\ n : a genus of lice (family Phthiriidae) containing the crab louse (*P. pubis*)

Phthi·rus \ˈthī-rəs\ n, syn of PHTHIRIUS

phthi·sic \ˈti-zik, ˈtī-sik\ n : PHTHISIS — **phthisic** or **phthi·si·cal** \ˈti-zi-kəl, ˈtī-si-\ adj

phthisio- comb form : phthisis ⟨*phthisiology*⟩

phthis·i·ol·o·gy \ti-zē-ˈä-lə-jē, ˌthī-\ n, pl **-gies** : the care, treatment, and study of tuberculosis — **phthis·i·ol·o·gist** \-jist\ n

phthi·sis \ˈti-səs, ˈthī, ˈti-, ˈthī-ses \-ˌsēz\ : a progressively wasting or consumptive condition; esp : pulmonary tuberculosis

phthisis bul·bi \-ˈbəl-ˌbī\ n : wasting and shrinkage of the eyeball following destructive diseases of the eye (as panophthalmitis)

phy·co·my·cete \ˌfī-kō-ˈmī-ˌsēt, -mī-ˈsēt\ n : any of a group of lower fungi that are in many respects similar to algae and are often grouped in a class (Phycomycetes) or separated into two major taxonomic groups (Mastigomycotina and Zygomycotina)

phy·co·my·co·sis \-ˌmī-ˈkō-səs\ n, pl **-co·ses** \-ˌsēz\ : any mycosis caused by a phycomycete (as of the genera *Rhizopus* and *Mucor*)

phyl- or **phylo-** comb form : tribe : race : phylum ⟨*phylogeny*⟩

phyl·lode \ˈfi-ˌlōd\ adj : having a cross section that resembles a leaf ⟨~ tumors of the breast⟩

phyl·lo·qui·none \ˌfi-lō-kwi-ˈnōn, -ˈkwi-ˌnōn\ n : VITAMIN K 1a

phy·log·e·ny \fī-ˈlä-jə-nē\ n, pl **-nies 1** : the evolutionary history of a kind of organism **2** : the evolution of a genetically related group of organisms as distinguished from the development of the individual organism — compare ONTOGENY — **phy·lo·ge·net·ic** \ˌfī-lō-jə-ˈne-tik\ adj — **phy·lo·ge·net·i·cal·ly** adv

phy·lum \ˈfī-ləm\ n, pl **phy·la** \-lə\ : a major group of animals or in some classifications plants sharing one or more fundamental characteristics that set them apart from all other animals and plants

phys abbr **1** physical **2** physician **3** physiological

phy·sa·lia \fī-ˈsā-lē-ə\ n **1** cap : a genus of large oceanic siphonophores (family Physaliidae) including the Portuguese man-of-wars **2** : any siphonophore of the genus *Physalia*

Phy·sa·lop·tera \ˌfī-sə-ˈläp-tə-rə, ˌfi-\ n : a large genus of nematode worms (family Physalopteridae) parasitic in the digestive tract of various vertebrates including humans

physes pl of PHYSIS

physi- or **physio-** comb form **1** : physical ⟨*physiotherapy*⟩ **2** : physiological : physiological and ⟨*physiopathologic*⟩

phys·i·at·rics \ˌfi-zē-ˈa-triks\ n : PHYSICAL MEDICINE

phys·i·a·trist \ˌfi-zē-ˈa-trist\ n : a physician who specializes in physical medicine

¹phys·ic \ˈfi-zik\ n **1 a** : the art or practice of healing disease **b** : the practice or profession of medicine **2** : a medicinal agent or preparation; esp : PURGATIVE

²physic vb **phys·icked; phys·ick·ing** : to treat with or administer medicine to; esp : PURGE

¹phys·i·cal \ˈfi-zi-kəl\ adj **1** : having material existence : perceptible esp. through the senses and subject to the laws of nature **2** : of or relating to the body — **phys·i·cal·ly** adv

²physical n : PHYSICAL EXAMINATION

physical examination n : an examination of the bodily functions and condition of an individual

physical medicine n : a branch of medicine concerned with the diagnosis and treatment of disease and disability by physical means (as radiation, heat, and electricity)

physical sign n : an indication of bodily condition that can be directly perceived

physical therapist n : a specialist in physical therapy — called also *physiotherapist*

physical therapy n : the treatment of disease by physical and mechanical means (as massage, regulated exercise, water, light, heat, and electricity) — called also *physiotherapy*

phy·si·cian \fə-ˈzi-shən\ n : a person skilled in the art of healing; specif : a doctor of medicine

physician's assistant or **physician assistant** n : a person who is certified to provide basic medical services (as the diagnosis and treatment of common ailments) usu. under the supervision of a licensed physician — called also **PA**

phys·i·co·chem·i·cal \ˌfī-zi-kō-'ke-mi-kəl\ adj : being physical and chemical — **phys·i·co·chem·i·cal·ly** adv

physio— see PHYSI-

phys·i·o·log·i·cal \ˌfi-zē-ə-'lä-ji-kəl\ or **phys·i·o·log·ic** \-jik\ adj 1 : of or relating to physiology 2 : characteristic of or appropriate to an organism's healthy or normal functioning 3 : differing in, involving, or affecting physiological factors (a ∼ strain of bacteria) — **phys·i·o·log·i·cal·ly** adv

physiological chemistry n : a branch of science dealing with the chemical aspects of physiological and biological systems : BIOCHEMISTRY

physiological dead space n : the total dead space in the entire respiratory system including the alveoli — compare ANATOMICAL DEAD SPACE

physiological psychology n : PSYCHO-PHYSIOLOGY

physiological saline n : a solution of a salt or salts that is essentially isotonic with tissue fluids or blood; esp : an approximately 0.9 percent solution of sodium chloride — called also **physiological saline solution, physiological salt solution**

phys·i·ol·o·gy \ˌfi-zē-'ä-lə-jē\ n, pl **-gies** 1 : a branch of biology that deals with the functions and activities of life or of living matter (as organs, tissues, or cells) and of the physical and chemical phenomena involved — compare ANATOMY 1, MORPHOLOGY 1 2 : the organic processes and phenomena of an organism or any of its parts or of a particular bodily process (∼ of the thyroid gland) 3 : a treatise on physiology — **phys·i·ol·o·gist** \-jist\ n

phys·i·o·pa·thol·o·gy \ˌfi-zē-ō-pə-'thä-lə-jē, -pa-\ n, pl **-gies** : a branch of biology or medicine that combines physiology and pathology esp. in the study of altered bodily function in disease — **phys·i·o·path·o·log·ic** \-ˌpathə-'lä-jik\ or **phys·i·o·path·o·log·i·cal** \-ji-kəl\ adj

phys·i·o·ther·a·peu·tic \ˌfi-zē-ō-ˌther-ə-'pyü-tik\ adj : of or relating to physical therapy

phys·i·o·ther·a·pist \-'ther-ə-pist\ n : PHYSICAL THERAPIST

phys·i·o·ther·a·py \ˌfi-zē-ō-'ther-ə-pē\ n, pl **-pies** : PHYSICAL THERAPY

phy·sique \fi-'zēk\ n : the form or structure of a person's body : bodily makeup (a muscular ∼)

phy·sis \'fī-səs\ n, pl **phy·ses** \-ˌsēz\ : GROWTH PLATE

Phy·so·ceph·a·lus \ˌfi-sə-'se-fə-ləs\ n : a genus of nematode worms (family Thelaziidae) including a common par-

asite (P. sexalatus) of the stomach and small intestine of swine

phy·so·stig·mine \ˌfī-sə-'stig-ˌmēn\ n : a crystalline tasteless alkaloid $C_{15}H_{21}N_3O_2$ from an African vine (Physostigma venenosum) of the legume family (Leguminosae) that is used esp. in the form of its salicylate for its anticholinesterase activity — called also **eserine**

phyt- or **phyto-** comb form : plant (phytotoxin)

phy·tan·ic acid \fī-'ta-nik-\ n : a fatty acid that accumulates in the blood and tissues of patients affected with Refsum's disease

-phyte \ˌfīt\ n comb form 1 : plant having a (specified) characteristic or habitat (saprophyte) 2 : pathological growth (osteophyte)

phy·tic acid \ˌfī-tik-\ n : an acid $C_6H_{18}P_6O_{24}$ that occurs in cereal grains and that when ingested interferes with the intestinal absorption of various minerals (as calcium and magnesium)

phy·to·be·zoar \ˌfī-tō-'bē-ˌzȯr\ n : a concretion formed in the stomach or intestine and composed chiefly of undigested compacted vegetable fiber

phy·to·hem·ag·glu·ti·nin \ˌfī-tō-ˌhē-mə-'glüt-ᵊn-ən\ n : a proteinaceous hemagglutinin of plant origin used esp. to induce mitosis (as in lymphocytes) — abbr. **PHA**

phy·to·na·di·one \ˌfī-tō-nə-'dī-ˌōn\ n : VITAMIN K 1a

phy·to·pho·to·der·ma·ti·tis \ˌfī-tō-ˌfō-tō-ˌdər-mə-'tī-təs\ n, pl **-ti·ses** or **-tit·i·des** \-'ti-tə-ˌdēz\ : a bullous eruption occurring on skin that has been exposed to sunlight after being made hypersensitive by contact with any of various plants

phy·to·ther·a·py \ˌfi-tō-'ther-ə-pē\ n, pl **-pies** : the use of vegetable drugs in medicine

phy·to·tox·in \-'täk-sən\ n : a toxin (as ricin) produced by a plant

pia \'pī-ə, 'pē-ə\ n : PIA MATER

pia–arach·noid \ˌpī-ə-ə-'rak-ˌnȯid, ˌpē-\ n : LEPTOMENINGES

Pia·get·ian \ˌpē-ə-'je-tē-ən\ adj : of, relating to, or dealing with Jean Piaget or his writings, theories, or methods esp. with respect to child development

Pia·get \pē-ä-'zhä\, **Jean** (1896–1980), Swiss psychologist.

pi·al \'pī-əl, 'pē-\ adj : of or relating to the pia mater (a ∼ artery)

pia ma·ter \-'mä-tər\ n : the delicate and highly vascular membrane of connective tissue investing the brain and spinal cord, lying internal to the arachnoid and dura mater, dipping down between the convolutions of the brain, and sending an ingrowth into the anterior fissure of the spinal cord — called also **pia**

pi·an \pē-'an, 'pyän\ n : YAWS

pi·blok·to \pi-'blak-(ˌ)tō\ n : a hysteria among Eskimos characterized by excitement and sometimes by mania, usu. followed by depression, and occurring chiefly in winter and usu. to women

pi·ca \'pī-kə\ n : an abnormal craving for and eating of substances (as chalk, ashes, or bones) not normally eaten that occurs in nutritional deficiency states (as aphosphorosis) in humans or animals or in some forms of mental illness — compare GEOPHAGY

¹Pick's disease \'piks-\ n : a dementia marked by progressive impairment of intellect and judgment and transitory aphasia, caused by progressive atrophic changes of the cerebral cortex, and usu. commencing in late middle age

   Pick \'pik\, **Arnold (1851–1924),** Czechoslovakian psychiatrist and neurologist.

²Pick's disease n : pericarditis with adherent pericardium resulting in circulatory disturbances with edema and ascites

   Pick, Friedel (1867–1926), Czechoslovakian physician.

Pick·wick·ian syndrome \pik-'wi-kē-ən-\ n : obesity accompanied by somnolence and lethargy, hypoventilation, hypoxia, and secondary polycythemia

   Pick·wick \'pik-ˌwik\, **Samuel,** literary character.

pico- comb form 1 : one trillionth (10^{-12}) part of ⟨picogram⟩ 2 : very small ⟨picornavirus⟩

pi·co·cu·rie \ˌpē-kō-'kyur-ē, -kyu-'rē\ n : one trillionth of a curie

pi·co·gram \'pē-kō-ˌgram\ n : one trillionth of a gram — abbr. pg

pi·cor·na·vi·rus \pē-ˌkor-nə-'vī-rəs\ n : any of a group of small single-stranded RNA-containing viruses that include the enteroviruses and rhinoviruses

pic·ric acid \'pi-krik-\ n : a bitter toxic explosive yellow crystalline acid $C_6H_3N_3O_7$ — called also trinitrophenol

pic·ro·tox·in \ˌpi-krō-'täk-sən\ n : a poisonous bitter crystalline principle $C_{30}H_{34}O_{13}$ that is found esp. in the berry of an East Indian vine (Anamirta cocculus of the family Menispermaceae) and is a stimulant and convulsant drug administered intravenously as an antidote for poisoning by overdoses of barbiturates

PID abbr pelvic inflammatory disease

pie·dra \pē-'ā-drä\ n : a fungus disease of the hair marked by the formation of small stony nodules along the hair shafts

Pierre Ro·bin syndrome \ˌpyer-rō-'beⁿ-\ n : a congenital defect of the face characterized by micrognathia, abnormal smallness of the tongue,

cleft palate, absence of the gag reflex, and sometimes accompanied by bilateral eye defects, glaucoma, or retinal detachment

   Robin, Pierre (1867–1950), French pediatrician.

pi·geon breast \'pi-jən-\ n : a rachitic deformity of the chest marked by sharp projection of the sternum — **pi·geon–breast·ed** \-'bres-təd\ adj

pigeon chest n : PIGEON BREAST

pigeon–toed \-'tōd\ adj : having the toes turned in

pig·ment \'pig-mənt\ n : a coloring matter in animals and plants esp. in a cell or tissue; also : any of various related colorless substances — **pig·men·tary** \'pig-mən-ˌter-ē\ adj

pigmentary retinopathy n : RETINITIS PIGMENTOSA

pig·men·ta·tion \ˌpig-mən-'tā-shən, -ˌmen-\ n : coloration with or deposition of pigment; esp : an excessive deposition of bodily pigment

pigment cell n : a cell containing a deposition of coloring matter

pig·ment·ed \'pig-ˌmen-təd\ adj : colored by a deposit of pigment

pigmentosa — see RETINITIS PIGMENTOSA

pigmentosum — see XERODERMA PIGMENTOSUM

pig·weed \'pig-ˌwēd\ n : any of several plants of the genus Amaranthus (as A. retroflexus and A. hybridus) producing pollen that is an important hay fever allergen

pil abbr [Latin pilula] pill — used in writing prescriptions

pil- or **pili-** or **pilo-** comb form : hair ⟨pilomotor⟩

pilaris — see KERATOSIS PILARIS, PITYRIASIS RUBRA PILARIS

pile \'pīl\ n 1 : a single hemorrhoid 2 pl : HEMORRHOIDS; also : the condition of one affected with hemorrhoids

pili pl of PILUS

pili — see ARRECTOR PILI MUSCLE

pill \'pil\ n 1 : medicine in a small rounded mass to be swallowed whole 2 often cap : an oral contraceptive — usu. used with the

pil·lar \'pi-lər\ n : a body part likened to a pillar or column (as the margin of the external inguinal ring); specif : PILLAR OF THE FAUCES

pillar of the fauces n : either of two curved folds on each side that bound the fauces and enclose the tonsil — see PALATOGLOSSAL ARCH, PALATOPHARYNGEAL ARCH

pi·lo·car·pine \ˌpī-lə-'kär-ˌpēn\ n : a miotic alkaloid $C_{11}H_{16}N_2O_2$ that is obtained from the dried crushed leaves of two So. American shrubs (Pilocarpus jaborandi and P. microphyllus) of the rue family (Rutaceae) and is used esp. in the treatment of glaucoma

pi·lo·erec·tion \ˌpī-lō-i-'rek-shən\ n : involuntary erection or bristling of hairs due to a sympathetic reflex usu. triggered by cold, shock, or fright or due to a sympathomimetic agent

pi·lo·mo·tor \'pī-lə-ˈmō-tər\ adj : moving or tending to cause movement of the hairs of the skin (~ nerves) (~ erection)

pi·lo·ni·dal \ˌpī-lə-ˈnīd-ᵊl\ adj 1 : containing hair nested in a cyst — used of congenitally anomalous cysts in the sacrococcygeal area that often become infected and discharge through a channel near the anus 2 : of, relating to, involving, or for use on pilonidal cysts, tracts, or sinuses

pi·lo·se·ba·ceous \ˌpī-lō-si-ˈbā-shəs\ : of or relating to hair and the sebaceous glands

pi·lus \'pī-ləs\ n, pl **pi·li** \-ˌlī\ : a hair or a structure (as of a bacterium) resembling a hair

pi·mar·i·cin \pi-ˈmar-ə-sən\ n : an antifungal antibiotic $C_{34}H_{49}NO_{14}$ derived from a bacterium of the genus *Streptomyces* and effective esp. against aspergillus, candida, and mucor infections

pim·o·zide \'pi-mə-ˌzīd\ n : a tranquilizer $C_{28}H_{29}F_2N_3O$

pim·ple \'pim-pəl\ n 1 : a small inflamed elevation of the skin : PAPULE; esp : PUSTULE 2 : a swelling or protuberance like a pimple — **pim·pled** \-pəld\ adj — **pim·ply** adj

pin \'pin\ n 1 : a metal rod driven into or through a fractured bone to immobilize it 2 : a metal rod driven into the root of a reconstructed tooth to provide support for a crown or into the jaw to provide support for an artificial tooth — **pin** vb

pin·do·lol \'pin-də-ˌlȯl, -ˌlōl\ n : a beta-blocker $C_{14}H_{20}N_2O_2$ used in the treatment of hypertension

pi·ne·al \'pi-nē-əl, 'pī-, pī-ˈ\ adj : of, relating to, or being the pineal gland

pi·ne·a·lec·to·my \ˌpi-nē-ə-ˈlek-tə-mē, pī-nē-, ˌpī-\ n, pl **-mies** : surgical removal of the pineal gland — **pi·ne·a·lec·to·mize** \ˌpi-nē-ə-ˈlek-tə-ˌmīz\ vb

pineal gland n : a small body that arises from the roof of the third ventricle and is enclosed by the pia mater and that functions primarily as an endocrine organ — called also *pineal*, *pineal body*, *pineal organ*

pin·e·a·lo·cyte \'pi-nē-ə-lō-ˌsīt\ n : the parenchymatous epithelioid cell of the pineal gland that has prominent nucleoli and long processes ending in bulbous expansions

pin·e·a·lo·ma \ˌpi-nē-ə-ˈlō-mə\ n, pl **-mas** or **-ma·ta** \-mə-tə\ : a tumor of the pineal gland

pineal organ n : PINEAL GLAND

pine–needle oil n : a colorless or yellowish bitter essential oil obtained from the needles of various pines (esp. *Pinus mugo*) and used in medicine chiefly as an inhalant in treating bronchitis

pine tar n : tar obtained from the wood of pine trees (genus *Pinus* and esp. *P. palustris* of the family Pinaceae) and used in soaps and in the treatment of skin diseases

pink disease \'piŋk-\ n : ACRODYNIA

pink·eye \'piŋ-ˌkī\ n : an acute highly contagious conjunctivitis of humans and various domestic animals

pink spot n : the appearance of pulp through the attenuated hard tissue of the crown of a tooth affected with resorption of dentin

pin·na \'pi-nə\ n, pl **pin·nae** \'pi-ˌnē, -ˌnī\ or **pinnas** : the largely cartilaginous projecting portion of the external ear — **pin·nal** \'pin-ᵊl\ adj

pi·no·cy·to·sis \ˌpī-nə-sə-ˈtō-səs, ˌpi-, -ˌsī-\ n, pl **-to·ses** \-ˌsēz\ : the uptake of fluid by a cell by invagination and pinching off of the plasma membrane — **pi·no·cy·tot·ic** \-ˈtä-tik\ or **pi·no·cyt·ic** \-ˈsi-tik\ adj

pins and needles n pl : a pricking tingling sensation in a limb growing numb or recovering from numbness

pint \'pīnt\ n : any of various measures of liquid capacity equal to one-half quart: as **a** : a U.S. measure equal to 16 fluid ounces, 473.176 milliliters, or 28.875 cubic inches **b** : a British measure equal to 20 fluid ounces, 568.26 milliliters, or 34.678 cubic inches

pin·ta \'pin-tə, -tä\ n : a chronic skin disease that is endemic in tropical America, that occurs successively as an initial papule, a generalized eruption, and a patchy loss of pigment, and that is caused by a spirochete of the genus *Treponema* (*T. careteum*) morphologically indistinguishable from the causative agent of syphilis — called also *pinto*

pin·tid \'pin-təd\ n : one of many initially reddish, then brown, slate blue, or black patches on the skin characteristic of the second stage of pinta

pin·worm \'pin-ˌwərm\ n : any of numerous small oxyurid nematode worms that have the tail of the female prolonged into a sharp point and infest the intestines and esp. the cecum of various vertebrates; esp : a worm of the genus *Enterobius* (*E. vermicularis*) that is parasitic in humans

pi·per·a·zine \pi-ˈper-ə-ˌzēn\ n : a crystalline heterocyclic base $C_4H_{10}N_2$ or $C_4H_{10}N_2 \cdot 6H_2O$ used esp. as an anthelmintic

pi·per·i·dine \pī-ˈper-ə-ˌdēn\ n : a liquid heterocyclic base $C_5H_{11}N$ that has a peppery ammoniacal odor

pi·per·o·caine \pī-ˈper-ə-ˌkān\ n : a local anesthetic $C_{16}H_{23}NO_2$ derived from piperidine and benzoic acid and used in the form of its crystalline hydrochloride — see METYCAINE

pi·per·o·nyl bu·tox·ide \pi-ˈper-ə-ˌnil-ˌbyü-ˈtäk-ˌsīd, -nəl-\ n : an insecticide $C_{19}H_{30}O_5$ that has the capacity to alter the pharmacological action of some drugs; *also* : an oily liquid containing this compound that is used chiefly as a synergist (as for pyrethrum insecticides)

pip·er·ox·an \ˌpi-pə-ˈräk-ˌsan\ *n* : an adrenolytic drug $C_{14}H_{19}NO_2$ that has been used in the form of its crystalline hydrochloride to detect pheochromocytoma by the transient fall in blood pressure it produces

pi·pette *or* **pi·pet** \pī-ˈpet\ *n* : a small piece of apparatus which typically consists of a narrow tube into which fluid is drawn by suction (as for dispensing or measurement) and retained by closing the upper end — **pipette** *or* **pipet** *vb*

pir·i·form \ˈpir-ə-ˌfȯrm\ *adj* : having the form of a pear 2 : of or relating to the piriform lobe (the ∼ cortex)

piriform aperture *n* : the anterior opening of the nasal cavities in the skull

piriform area *n* : PIRIFORM LOBE

piriform fossa *n* : PIRIFORM RECESS

pir·i·for·mis \ˌpir-ə-ˈfȯr-mis\ *n* : a muscle that arises from the front of the sacrum, passes out of the pelvis through the greater sciatic foramen, is inserted into the upper border of the greater trochanter of the femur, and rotates the thigh laterally

piriform lobe *n* : the lateral olfactory gyrus and the hippocampal gyrus taken together

piriform recess *n* : a small cavity or pocket between the lateral walls of the pharynx on each side and the upper part of the larynx — called also *piriform fossa, piriform sinus*

Pi·ro·goff's amputation \ˌpir-ə-ˈgȯfs\ *or* **Pi·ro·goff amputation** \-ˈgȯf-\ *n* : amputation of the foot through the articulation of the ankle with retention of part of the calcaneus — compare SYME'S AMPUTATION

Pirogoff, Nikolai Ivanovich (1810–1881), Russian surgeon.

piro·plasm \ˈpir-ə-ˌpla-zəm\ *or* **piro·plas·ma** \ˌpir-ə-ˈplaz-mə\ *n, pl* **piro·plasms** *or* **piro·plas·ma·ta** \ˌpir-ə-ˈplaz-mə-tə\ : BABESIA 2

Piro·plas·ma \ˌpir-ə-ˈplaz-mə\ *n, syn of* BABESIA

piro·plas·mo·sis \ˌpir-ə-ˌplaz-ˈmō-səs\ *n, pl* **-mo·ses** \-ˌsēz\ : infection with or disease that is caused by protozoans of a family (Babesiidae) and esp. of the genus *Babesia* and that includes Texas fever and east coast fever of cattle and babesiosis of mouse

pi·rox·i·cam \pī-ˈräk-sə-ˌkam\ *n* : a nonsteroidal anti-inflammatory drug $C_{15}H_{13}N_3O_4S$ used in the treatment of rheumatic diseases (as osteoarthritis)

Pir·quet test \pir-ˈkā-\ *n* : a tuberculin test made by applying a drop of tuberculin to a scarified spot on the skin — called also *Pirquet reaction*

Pirquet von Ce·se·na·ti·co \pir-ˈkā-

fȯn-ˌchā-se-ˈnä-ti-kō\, Clemens Peter (1874–1929), Austrian physician.

pi·si·form \ˈpī-sə-ˌfȯrm\ *n* : a bone on the little-finger side of the carpus that articulates with the triquetral bone — called also *pisiform bone*

pit \ˈpit\ *n* : a hollow or indentation esp. in a surface of an organism: as a : a natural hollow in the surface of the body b : one of the indented scars left in the skin by a pustular disease : POCKMARK c : a usu. developmental imperfection in the enamel of a tooth that takes the form of a small pointed depression — **pit** *vb*

pitch \ˈpich\ *n* : the property of a sound and esp. a musical tone that is determined by the frequency of the waves producing it : highness or lowness of sound

pitch·blende \ˈpich-ˌblend\ *n* : a brown to black mineral that has a distinctive luster and contains radium

Pi·to·cin \pi-ˈtō-sən\ *trademark* — used for a preparation of oxytocin

pi·tot tube \ˈpē-ˌtō-\ *n, often cap P* : a device that consists of a tube that is used with a manometer to measure the velocity of fluid flow (as in a blood vessel)

Pitot, Henri (1695–1771), French hydraulic engineer.

Pi·tres·sin \pi-ˈtres-ən\ *trademark* — used for a preparation of vasopressin

pitting *n* 1 : the action or process of forming pits (as in acned skin, a tooth, or a dental restoration) 2 : the formation of a depression or indentation in living tissue that is produced by pressure with a finger or blunt instrument and disappears only slowly following release of the pressure in some forms of edema

pitting edema *n* : edema in which pitting results in a depression in the edematous tissue which disappears only slowly

pi·tu·i·cyte \pə-ˈtü-ə-ˌsīt, -ˈtyü-\ *n* : one of the pigmented more or less fusiform cells of the stalk and posterior lobe of the pituitary gland that are usu. considered to be derived from neuroglial cells

¹pi·tu·itary \pə-ˈtü-ə-ˌter-ē, -ˈtyü-\ *adj* 1 : of or relating to the pituitary gland 2 : caused or characterized by secretory disturbances of the pituitary gland (a ∼ dwarf)

²pituitary *n, pl* **-tar·ies** 1 : PITUITARY GLAND 2 : the cleaned, dried, and powdered posterior lobe of the pituitary gland of cattle that is used in the treatment of uterine atony and hemorrhage, shock, and intestinal paresis

pituitary ba·soph·i·lism \-bā-ˈsä-fə-ˌli-zəm\ *n* : CUSHING'S DISEASE

pituitary gland *n* : a small oval endocrine organ that is attached to the infundibulum of the brain and occupies the sella turcica, that consists essentially of an epithelial anterior lobe derived from a diverticulum of the oral cavity and joined to a posterior lobe of nervous origin by a pars intermedia, and that has the several parts associated with various hormones which directly or indirectly affect most basic bodily functions and include substances exerting a controlling and regulating influence on other endocrine organs, controlling growth and development, or modifying the contraction of smooth muscle, renal function, and reproduction — called also *hypophysis, pituitary body*; see NEUROHYPOPHYSIS

pituitary portal system *n* : a portal system supplying blood to the anterior lobe of the pituitary gland through veins connecting the capillaries of the median eminence of the hypothalamus with those of the anterior lobe

Pi·tu·i·trin \pə-'tü-ə-trin, -'tyü-\ *trademark* — used for an aqueous extract of the fresh pituitary gland of cattle

pit viper *n* : any of various mostly New World venomous snakes (as the rattlesnake, copperhead, and water moccasin) that belong to a subfamily (Crotalinae of the family Viperidae) and have a small depression on each side of the head and hollow perforated fangs

pit·y·ri·a·sis \₁pi-tə-'rī-ə-səs\ *n, pl* **pit·y·ri·a·ses** \-₁sēz\ **1** : any of several skin diseases marked by the formation and desquamation of fine scales **2** : a disease of domestic animals marked by dry epithelial scales or scurf

pityriasis li·che·noi·des et var·i·o·li·for·mis acu·ta \₁li-kə-'nói-₁dēz-et-₁var-ē-ō-lə-'fór-mis-ə-'kyü-tə, -'kü-\ *n* : a disease of unknown cause that is characterized by the sudden appearance of polymorphous lesions (as papules, purpuric vesicles, crusts, or ulcerations) resembling chicken pox but tending to persist from a month to as long as years, occurs esp. between the ages of 30 and 50, and is more common in men

pityriasis ro·sea \-'rō-zē-ə\ *n* : an acute benign and self-limited skin eruption of unknown cause that consists of dry, scaly, oval, pinkish or fawn-colored papules, usu. lasts six to eight weeks, and affects esp. the trunk, arms, and thighs

pityriasis ru·bra pi·lar·is \-'rü-brə-pi-'lar-əs\ *n* : a chronic dermatitis characterized by the formation of papular horny plugs in the hair follicles and pinkish macules which tend to spread and become scaly plaques

pityriasis versicolor *n* : TINEA VERSICOLOR

piv·ot \'pi-vət\ *n* : a usu. metallic pin holding an artificial crown to the root of a tooth

pivot joint *n* : an anatomical articulation that consists of a bony pivot in a ring of bone and ligament (as that of the odontoid process and atlas) and that permits rotatory movement only — called also *trochoid*

pivot tooth *n* : an artificial crown attached to the root of a tooth by a usu. metallic pin — called also *pivot crown*

PK \₁pē-'kā\ *n* : PSYCHOKINESIS

PKU *abbr* phenylketonuria

pla·ce·bo \plə-'sē-(₁)bō\ *n, pl* **-bos 1** : a medication prescribed more for the mental relief of the patient than for its actual effect on a disorder **2** : an inert or innocuous substance used esp. in controlled experiments testing the efficacy of another substance (as a drug)

placebo effect *n* : improvement in the condition of a sick person that occurs in response to treatment but cannot be considered due to the specific treatment used

pla·cen·ta \plə-'sen-tə\ *n, pl* **-centas** or **-cen·tae** \-'sen-(₁)tē\ : the vascular organ that unites the fetus to the maternal uterus and mediates its metabolic exchanges through a more or less intimate association of uterine mucosal with chorionic and usu. allantoic tissues permitting exchange of material by diffusion between the maternal and fetal vascular systems but without direct contact between maternal and fetal blood and typically involving the interlocking of fingerlike vascular chorionic villi with corresponding modified areas of the uterine mucosa — see ABLATIO PLACENTAE, ABRUPTIO PLACENTAE — **pla·cen·tal** \-təl\ *adj*

placental barrier *n* : a semipermeable membrane made up of placental tissues and limiting the kind and amount of material exchanged between mother and fetus

placentalis — see DECIDUA PLACENTALIS

placenta pre·via \-'prē-vē-ə\ *n, pl* **placentae pre·vi·ae** \-vē-₁ē\ : an abnormal implantation of the placenta at or near the internal opening of the uterine cervix so that it tends to precede the child at birth usu. causing severe maternal hemorrhage

plac·en·ti·tis \₁plas-ᵊn-'tī-təs\ *n, pl* **-tit·i·des** \-'ti-tə-₁dēz\ : inflammation of the placenta

plac·en·tog·ra·phy \₁plas-ᵊn-'tä-grə-fē\ *n, pl* **-phies** : roentgenographic visualization of the placenta after injection of a radiopaque medium

Plac·i·dyl \'pla-sə-₁dil\ *trademark* — used for a preparation of ethchlorvynol

pla·gio·ceph·a·ly \₁plā-jē-ō-'se-fə-lē\ *n, pl* **-lies** : a malformation of the head marked by an oblique slant to the main axis of the skull and usu. caused by closure of half of the coronal suture

plague \'plāg\ *n* **1** : an epidemic disease

causing a high rate of mortality : PESTILENCE ⟨a ∼ of cholera⟩ 2 : a virulent contagious febrile disease that is caused by a bacterium of the genus *Yersinia* (*Y. pestis* syn. *Pasteurella pestis*), that occurs in bubonic, pneumonic, and septicemic forms, and that is usu. transmitted from rats to humans by the bite of infected fleas (as in bubonic plague) or directly from person to person (as in pneumonic plague) — called also *black death*

plana — see PARS PLANA

plane \'plān\ *n* 1 a : a surface that contains at least three points not all in a straight line and is such that a line drawn through any two points in it lies wholly in the surface b : an imaginary plane used to identify parts of the body or a part of the skull — see FRANKFORT HORIZONTAL PLANE, MIDSAGITTAL PLANE 2 : a stage in surgical anesthesia (maintained a light ∼ of anesthesia with cyclopropane)

plane joint *n* : GLIDING JOINT

plane of polarization *n* : the plane in which electromagnetic radiation vibrates when it is polarized so as to vibrate in a single plane

pla·ni·gram \'plā-nə-ˌgram, 'pla-\ *n* : TOMOGRAM

pla·nig·ra·phy \plə-'ni-grə-fē\ *n, pl* **-phies** : TOMOGRAPHY

Planned Par·ent·hood \'pland-'par-ᵊnt-ˌhud\ *service mark* — used for research and dissemination of information on contraception

Pla·nor·bis \plə-'nȯr-bis\ *n* : a widely distributed genus of snails (family Planorbidae) that includes several intermediate hosts for schistosomes infecting humans

plantae — see QUADRATUS PLANTAE

plan·ta·go \plan-'tā-(ˌ)gō\ *n* 1 *cap* : a large genus of weeds (family Plantaginaceae) including several (*P. psyllium, P. indica,* and *P. ovata*) that have indigestible and mucilaginous seeds used as a mild cathartic — see PSYLLIUM SEED 2 : PLANTAIN

plantago seed *n* : PSYLLIUM SEED

plan·tain \'plant-ᵊn\ *n* : any plant of the genus *Plantago*

plan·tar \'plan-tər, -ˌtär\ *adj* : of, relating to, or typical of the sole of the foot (the ∼ aspect of the foot)

plantar arch *n* : an arterial arch in the sole of the foot formed by the lateral plantar artery and a branch of the dorsalis pedis

plantar artery *n* : either of the two terminal branches into which the posterior tibial artery divides: a : one that is larger and passes laterally and then medially to join with a branch of the dorsalis pedis to form the plantar arch — called also *lateral plantar artery* b : one that is smaller and follows a more medial course as it passes distally supplying or giving off branches

which supply the plantar part of the foot and the toes — called also *medial plantar artery*

plantar cal·ca·neo·na·vic·u·lar ligament \-(ˌ)kal-ˌkā-nē-ō-nə-ˈvi-kyə-lər-\ *n* : an elastic ligament of the sole of the foot that connects the calcaneus and navicular bone and supports the head of the talus — called also *spring ligament*

plantar fascia *n* : a very strong dense fibrous membrane of the sole of the foot that lies beneath the skin and superficial layer of fat and binds together the deeper structures

plantar fasci·itis *n* : inflammation involving the plantar fascia esp. in the area of its attachment to the calcaneus and causing pain under the heel in walking and running

plantar flexion *n* : movement of the foot that flexes the foot or toes downward toward the sole — compare DORSIFLEXION

plantar interosseus *n* : any of three small muscles of the plantar aspect of the foot each of which lies along the plantar side of one of the third, fourth, and fifth toes facing the second toe and acts to flex the proximal phalanx and extend the distal phalanges of its toe and to adduct its toe toward the second toe — called also *interosseus plantaris, plantar interosseous muscle*

plan·tar·is \plan-'tar-əs\ *n, pl* **plan·tar·es** \-'tar-ˌēz\ : a small muscle of the calf of the leg that arises from the lower end of the femur and the posterior ligament of the knee joint, is inserted with the Achilles tendon by a very long slender tendon into the calcaneus, and weakly flexes the leg at the knee and the foot at the ankle — see INTEROSSEUS PLANTARIS, VERRUCA PLANTARIS

plantar nerve *n* : either of two nerves of the foot that are the two terminal branches into which the tibial nerve divides: a : a smaller one that supplies most of the deeper muscles of the foot and the skin on the lateral part of the sole and on the fifth toe as well as on the lateral part of the fourth toe — called also *lateral plantar nerve* b : a larger one that accompanies the medial plantar artery and supplies a number of muscles of the medial part of the foot, the skin on the medial two-thirds of the sole, and the skin on the first to fourth toes — called also *medial plantar nerve*

plantar reflex *n* : a reflex movement of flexing the foot and toes that after the first year is the normal response to tickling of the sole — compare BABINSKI REFLEX

plantar vein *n* : either of two veins that accompany the plantar arteries: a : one accompanying the lateral plantar artery — called also *lateral plan*

plantar wart • -plastic 534

tar vein **b** : one accompanying the medial plantar artery — called also *medial plantar vein*

plantar wart *n* : a wart on the sole of the foot — called also *planter's wart, verruca plantaris*

plan·ti·grade \'plan-tə-₁grād\ *adj* : walking on the sole with the heel touching the ground (bears and humans are ~ animals) — **plantigrade** *n*

pla·num \'plā-nəm\ *n, pl* **pla·na** \-nə\ : a flat surface of bone esp. of the skull

planus — see LICHEN PLANUS

plaque \'plak\ *n* **1 a** : a localized abnormal patch on a body part or surface and esp. on the skin (psoriatic ~) **b** : a film of mucus that harbors bacteria on a tooth **c** : an atherosclerotic lesion **d** : a histopathologic lesion of brain tissue that is characteristic of Alzheimer's disease and consists of a cluster of degenerating nerve endings and dendrites around a core of amyloid **2** : a visibly distinct and esp. a clear or opaque area in a bacterial culture produced by damage to or destruction of cells by a virus

Plaque·nil \'pla-kə-₁nil\ *trademark* — used for a preparation of hydroxychloroquine

-pla·sia \'plā-zhə, -zhē-ə *or* -zē-ə\ *or* **-pla·sy** \₁plā-sē, -plə-sē\ *n comb form, pl* **-plasias** *or* **-plasies** : development : formation (dys*plasia*)

plasm- *or* **plasmo-** *comb form* : plasma (*plasm*apheresis)

-plasm \₁pla-zəm\ *n comb form* : formative or formed material (as of a cell or tissue) (cyto*plasm*) (endo*plasm*)

plas·ma \'plaz-mə\ *n* : the fluid part of blood and lymph that is distinguished from suspended material and that in blood differs from serum essentially in containing the precursor substance of fibrin in addition to the constituents of serum

plasma cell *n* : a lymphocyte that is a mature antibody-secreting B cell

plas·ma·cy·to·ma \₁plaz-mə-sī-'tō-mə\ *n, pl* **-mas** *or* **-ma·ta** \-mə-tə\ : a myeloma composed of plasma cells

plas·ma·cy·to·sis \₁plaz-mə-sī-'tō-səs\ *n, pl* **-to·ses** \-₁sēz\ : the presence of abnormal numbers of plasma cells in the blood

plas·ma·lem·ma \₁plaz-mə-'le-mə\ *n* : PLASMA MEMBRANE

plas·mal·o·gen \plaz-'ma-lə-jən, -₁jen\ *n* : any of a group of phospholipids in which a fatty acid group is replaced by a fatty aldehyde and which include lecithins and phosphatidylethanolamines

plasma membrane *n* : a semipermeable limiting layer of cell protoplasm consisting of three molecular layers of which the inner and outer are composed of protein while the middle layer is composed of a double layer of fat molecules — called also *cell membrane, plasmalemma*

plas·ma·pher·e·sis \₁plaz-mə-fə-'rē-səs, -'fer-ə-səs\ *n, pl* **-e·ses** \-₁sēz\ : a process for obtaining blood plasma without depleting the donor or patient of other blood constituents (as red blood cells) by separating out the plasma from the whole blood and returning the rest to the donor's or patient's circulatory system

plasma thromboplastin an·te·ced·ent \-₁an-tə-'sēd-ənt\ *n* : a clotting factor whose absence is associated with a form of hemophilia — abbr. *PTA*; called also *factor XI*

plasma thromboplastin component *n* : FACTOR IX

plas·mat·ic \plaz-'ma-tik\ *adj* : of, relating to, or occurring in plasma esp. of blood (~ fibrils)

plas·mid \'plaz-mid\ *n* : an extrachromosomal ring of DNA that replicates independently and is found esp. in bacteria — compare EPISOME

plas·min \-min\ *n* : a proteolytic enzyme that dissolves the fibrin in blood clots

plas·min·o·gen \plaz-'mi-nə-jən\ *n* : the precursor of plasmin that is found in blood plasma and serum — called also *profibrinolysin*

plasmo- — see PLASM-

Plas·mo·chin \'plaz-mə-kin\ *trademark* — used for a preparation of pamaquine

plas·mo·cy·to·ma *var of* PLASMACYTOMA

plas·mo·di·al \plaz-'mō-dē-əl\ *adj* : of, relating to, or resembling a plasmodium

plas·mo·di·um \plaz-'mō-dē-əm\ *n* **1** *cap* : a genus of sporozoans (family Plasmodiidae) that includes all the malaria parasites affecting humans **2** *pl* **-dia** : any individual malaria parasite

-plast \₁plast\ *n comb form* : organized particle or granule : cell (chloro*plast*)

plas·ter \'plas-tər\ *n* : a medicated or protective dressing that consists of a film (as of cloth or plastic) spread with a usu. medicated substance

plaster cast *n* : a rigid dressing of gauze impregnated with plaster of paris

plaster of par·is \-'par-is\ *n* : a white powdery slightly hydrated calcium sulfate $CaSO_4 \cdot \frac{1}{2}H_2O$ or $2CaSO_4 \cdot H_2O$ that forms a quick-setting paste with water and is used in medicine chiefly in casts and for surgical bandages

plas·tic \'plas-tik\ *adj* **1** : capable of being deformed continuously and permanently in any direction without breaking or tearing **2** : capable of growth, repair, or differentiation (a ~ tissue) **3** : of, relating to, or involving plastic surgery (~ repair)

-plas·tic \'plas-tik\ *adj comb form* **1** : developing : forming (thrombo*plastic*) **2** : of or relating to (something designated by a term ending in

-plasia, -plasm, or -plasty) (neoplastic)

plas·tic·i·ty \plas-ˈstis-ə-tē\ n, pl **-ties 1** : the quality or state of being plastic; esp : capacity for being molded or altered **2** : the ability to retain a shape attained by pressure deformation **3** : the capacity of organisms with the same genotype to vary in developmental pattern, in phenotype, or in behavior according to varying environmental conditions

plastic surgeon n : a specialist in plastic surgery

plastic surgery n : a branch of surgery concerned with the repair, restoration, or improvement of lost, injured, defective, or misshapen parts of the body chiefly by transfer of tissue

plas·ty \ˈplas-tē\ n, pl **plas·ties** : a surgical procedure for the repair, restoration, or replacement (as by a prosthesis) of a part of the body (quadriceps ∼) (total knee ∼)

-plas·ty \ˌplas-tē\ n comb form, pl **-plas·ties** : plastic surgery (osteoplasty)

-plasy — see -PLASIA

plat- — see PLATY-

¹plate \ˈplāt\ n **1** : a flat thin piece or lamina (as of bone) that is part of the body **2 a** : a flat glass dish used chiefly for culturing microorganisms; esp : PETRI DISH **b** : a culture or culture medium contained in such a dish **3** : a supporting or reinforcing element: as **a** : the part of a denture that fits in the mouth; broadly : DENTURE **b** : a thin flat narrow piece of metal (as stainless steel) that is used to repair a bone defect or fracture

²plate vb **plat·ed; plat·ing 1** : to inoculate and culture (microorganisms or cells) on a plate; also : to distribute (an inoculum) on a plate or plates for cultivation **2** : to repair (as a fractured bone) with metal plates

plate·let \ˈplāt-lət\ n : BLOOD PLATELET

platelet–activating factor n : phospholipid that is produced esp. by mast cells and basophils, causes the aggregation of blood platelets and the release of blood-platelet substances (as histamine or serotonin), and is a mediator of inflammation (as in asthma) — abbr. PAF

platelet–derived growth factor n : a mitogenic growth factor that is found esp. in platelets, consists of two polypeptide chains linked by bonds containing two sulfur atoms each, stimulates cell proliferation (as in connective tissue, smooth muscle, and neuroglia), and plays a role in wound healing — abbr. PDGF

plate·let·phe·re·sis \ˌplāt-lət-ˈfer-ə-səs, -fə-ˈrē-səs\ n, pl **-re·ses** \-ˌsēz\ : pheresis used to collect blood platelets

plat·ing \ˈplāt-iŋ\ n **1** : the spreading of a sample of cells or microorganisms on a nutrient medium in a petri dish **2**

: the immobilization of a fractured bone by securing a metal plate to it

Plat·i·nol \ˈpla-tə-ˌnȯl, -ˌnōl\ trademark — used for a preparation of cisplatin

plat·i·num \ˈplat-ᵊn-əm\ n : a grayish white ductile malleable metallic element used esp. as a catalyst and in alloys (as in dentistry) — symbol Pt; see ELEMENT table

platy- also **plat-** comb form : flat : broad (platypelloid)

platy·ba·sia \ˌpla-ti-ˈbā-sē-ə\ n : a developmental deformity of the base of the skull in which the lower occiput is pushed by the upper cervical spine into the cranial fossa

platy·hel·minth \ˌpla-ti-ˈhel-ˌminth\ n : any of a phylum (Platyhelminthes) of soft-bodied usu. much flattened worms (as the flukes and tapeworms) — called also flatworm — **platy·hel·min·thic** \-ˌhel-ˈmin-thik, -tik\ adj

platy·pel·loid \-ˈpe-ˌlȯid\ adj, of the pelvis : broad and flat — compare ANDROID, ANTHROPOID, GYNECOID

platys·ma \plə-ˈtiz-mə\ n, pl **-ma·ta** \-mə-tə\ also **-mas** : a broad thin layer of muscle that is situated on each side of the neck immediately under the superficial fascia belonging to the group of facial muscles, that is innervated by the facial nerve, and that draws the lower lip and the corner of the mouth to the side and down and when moved forcefully expands the neck and draws its skin upward

play therapy n : psychotherapy in which a child is encouraged to reveal feelings and conflicts in play rather than by verbalization

pleasure principle n : a tendency for individual behavior to be directed toward immediate satisfaction of instinctual drives and immediate relief from pain or discomfort — compare REALITY PRINCIPLE

pled·get \ˈplej-ət\ n : a compress or small flat mass usu. of gauze or absorbent cotton that is laid over a wound or into a cavity to apply medication, exclude air, retain dressings, or absorb the matter discharged

-ple·gia \ˈplē-jə, -jē-ə\ n comb form : paralysis (diplegia)

pleio·tro·pic \ˌplī-ə-ˈtrō-pik, -ˈträ-\ adj : producing more than one genic effect; specif : having multiple phenotypic expressions (a ∼ gene) — **pleiot·ro·py** \plī-ˈä-trə-pē\ n

pleo·cy·to·sis \ˌplē-ō-ˌsī-ˈtō-səs\ n, pl **-to·ses** \-ˌsēz\ : an abnormal increase in the number of cells (as lymphocytes) in the cerebrospinal fluid

pleo·mor·phic \ˌplē-ə-ˈmȯr-fik\ also **pleio·mor·phic** \ˌplī-ə-\ adj : able to assume different forms : POLYMORPHIC (∼ bacteria) (a ∼ sarcoma) — **pleo·mor·phism** \ˌplē-ə-ˈmȯr-ˌfi-zəm\ n

ple·op·tics \plē-ˈäp-tiks\ n : a system of treating amblyopia by retraining visual habits using guided exercises — **ple·op·tic** \-tik\ *adj*

pleth·o·ra \ˈple-thə-rə\ *n* : a bodily condition characterized by an excess of blood and marked by turgescence and a florid complexion — **ple·tho·ric** \plə-ˈthȯr-ik, ple-, -ˈthär-; ˈple-thə-rik\ *adj*

ple·thys·mo·gram \ple-ˈthiz-mə-ˌgram, plə-\ *n* : a tracing made by a plethysmograph

ple·thys·mo·graph \-ˌgraf\ *n* : an instrument for determining and registering variations in the size of an organ or limb resulting from changes in the amount of blood present or passing through it — **ple·thys·mo·graph·ic** \-ˌthiz-mə-ˈgra-fik\ *adj* — **ple·thys·mo·graph·i·cal·ly** *adv* — **pleth·ys·mog·ra·phy** \ˌple-thiz-ˈmä-grə-fē\ *n*

pleur- *or* **pleuro-** *comb form* 1 : pleura ⟨*pleuro*pneumonia⟩ 2 : pleura and ⟨*pleuro*peritoneal⟩

pleu·ra \ˈplu̇r-ə\ *n, pl* **pleu·rae** \ˈplu̇r-ē\ *or* **pleuras** : either of a pair of two-walled sacs of serous membrane each lining one lateral half of the thorax, having an inner layer closely adherent to the corresponding lung, reflected at the root of the lung to form a parietal layer that adheres to the walls of the thorax, the pericardium, upper surface of the diaphragm, and adjacent parts, and containing a small amount of serous fluid that minimizes the friction of respiratory movements

pleu·ral \ˈplu̇r-əl\ *adj* : of or relating to the pleura or the sides of the thorax

pleural cavity *n* : the space that is formed when the two layers of the pleura spread apart — called also *pleural space*

pleural effusion *n* 1 : an exudation of fluid from the blood or lymph into a pleural cavity 2 : an exudate in a pleural cavity

pleural space *n* : PLEURAL CAVITY

pleu·rec·to·my \plu̇-ˈrek-tə-mē\ *n, pl* **-mies** : surgical excision of part of the pleura

pleu·ri·sy \ˈplu̇r-ə-sē\ *n, pl* **-sies** : inflammation of the pleura usu. with fever, painful and difficult respiration, cough, and exudation of fluid or fibrinous material into the pleural cavity — **pleu·rit·ic** \plu̇-ˈri-tik\ *adj*

pleu·ri·tis \plu̇-ˈrī-təs\ *n, pl* **pleu·rit·i·des** \-ˈri-tə-ˌdēz\ : PLEURISY

pleu·ro·dyn·ia \ˌplu̇r-ə-ˈdi-nē-ə\ *n* 1 : a sharp pain in the side usu. located in the intercostal muscles and believed to arise from inflammation of fibrous tissue 2 : EPIDEMIC PLEURODYNIA

pleu·ro·peri·car·di·tis \ˌplu̇r-ō-ˌper-ə-ˌkär-ˈdī-təs\ *n, pl* **-dit·i·des** \-ˈdi-tə-ˌdēz\ : inflammation of the pleura and the pericardium

pleu·ro·peri·to·ne·al \-ˌper-ə-tə-ˈnē-əl\ *adj* : of or relating to the pleura and the peritoneum

pleu·ro·pneu·mo·nia \ˌplu̇r-ō-nu̇-ˈmō-nyə, -nyü-\ *n* 1 : pleurisy accompanied by pneumonia 2 : a highly contagious pneumonia usu. associated with pleurisy of cattle, goats, and sheep that is caused by a microorganism of the genus *Mycoplasma* (esp. *M. mycoides*) 3 : a contagious often fatal respiratory disease esp. of young pigs that is caused by a bacterium of the genus *Haemophilus* (*H. pleuropneumoniae*) 4 : pleurisy of horses that is often accompanied by pneumonia and is caused by various microorganisms

pleuropneumonia–like organism *n* : MYCOPLASMA 2

pleu·ro·pul·mo·nary \ˌplu̇r-ō-ˈpu̇l-mə-ˌner-ē, -ˈpəl-\ *adj* : of or relating to the pleura and the lungs

plex·ec·to·my \plek-ˈsek-tə-mē\ *n, pl* **-mies** : surgical removal of a plexus

plexi·form \ˈplek-sə-ˌfȯrm\ *adj* : of, relating to, or having the form or characteristics of a plexus ⟨~ networks⟩

plexiform layer *n* : either of two reticular layers of the retina consisting of nerve cell processes and situated between layers of ganglion cells and cell bodies

plex·im·e·ter \plek-ˈsi-mə-tər\ *n* : a small hard flat plate (as of ivory) placed in contact with the body to receive the blow in percussion

plex·op·a·thy \plek-ˈsä-pə-thē\ *n, pl* **-thies** : a disease of a plexus

plex·or \ˈplek-sər\ *n* : a small hammer with a rubber head used in medical percussion

plex·us \ˈplek-səs\ *n, pl* **plex·us·es** : a network of anastomosing or interlacing blood vessels or nerves

pli·ca \ˈplī-kə\ *n, pl* **pli·cae** \-ˌkē, -ˌsē\ : a fold or folded part; *esp* : a groove or fold of skin

plicae cir·cu·la·res \-ˌsər-kyə-ˈlar-(ˌ)ēz\ *n pl* : the numerous permanent crescentic folds of mucous membrane found in the small intestine esp. in the lower part of the duodenum and the jejunum — called also *valvulae conniventes*

plica fim·bri·a·ta \-ˌfim-brē-ˈä-tə\ *n, pl* **plicae fim·bri·a·tae** \-ˈä-tē\ : a fold resembling a fringe on the under surface of the tongue on either side of the frenulum

pli·ca·my·cin \ˌplī-kə-ˈmīs-ᵊn\ *n* : an antineoplastic agent $C_{52}H_{76}O_{24}$ produced by three bacteria of the genus *Streptomyces* (*S. argillaceus*, *S. tanashiensis*, and *S. plicatus*) and administered intravenously esp. in the treatment of malignant tumors of the testes or in the treatment of hypercalcemia and hypercalciuria associated with advanced neoplastic disease — called also *mithramycin*

plica semi·lu·na·ris \-ˌse-mi-lü-ˈnar-əs\ *n, pl* **plicae semi·lu·na·res** \-(ˌ)ēz\ : the vertical fold of conjunctiva that occupies the canthus of the eye nearer the nose

pli·ca·tion \plī-ˈkā-shən\ *n* 1 : the tightening of stretched or weakened bodily tissues or channels by folding the excess in tucks and suturing 2 : the folding of one part on and the fastening of it to another (as areas of the bowel freed from adhesions and left without normal serosal covering) — **pli·cate** \ˈplī-ˌkāt\ *vb*

-ploid \ˌploid\ *adj comb form* : having or being a chromosome number that bears (such) a relationship to or is (so many) times the basic chromosome number characteristic of a given plant or animal group (polyploid)

ploi·dy \ˈploi-dē\ *n, pl* **ploi·dies** : degree of repetition of the basic number of chromosomes

plom·bage \pləm-ˈbäzh\ *n* : sustained compression of the sides of a pulmonary cavity against each other to effect closure by pressure exerted by packing (as of paraffin or plastic sponge)

PLSS *abbr* portable life-support system

plug \ˈpləg\ *n* 1 : an obstructing mass of material in a bodily vessel or the opening of a skin lesion (necrotic ∼) (fibrinous ∼) 2 : a filling for a hollow tooth — **plugged** \ˈpləgd\ *adj*

plug·ger \ˈplə-gər\ *n* : a dental instrument used for driving and consolidating filling material in a tooth cavity

plum·bism \ˈpləm-ˌbi-zəm\ *n* : LEAD POISONING; *esp* : chronic lead poisoning

Plum·mer–Vin·son syndrome \ˈplə-mər-ˈvin-sən-\ *n* : a condition that is marked esp. by the growth of a mucous membrane across the esophageal lumen, by difficulty in swallowing, and by hypochromic anemia and that is considered to be due to an iron deficiency

Plummer, Henry Stanley (1874–1936), American physician.
Vinson, Porter Paisley (1890–1959), American surgeon.

plu·ri·po·ten·cy \ˌplúr-ə-ˈpōt-ᵊn-sē\ *n, pl* **-cies** : PLURIPOTENTIALITY

plu·rip·o·tent \plú-ˈri-pə-tənt\ *adj* 1 : not fixed as to developmental potentialities : having developmental plasticity (a ∼ cell) 2 : capable of affecting more than one organ or tissue

plu·ri·po·ten·tial \ˌplúr-ə-pə-ˈten-chəl\ *adj* : PLURIPOTENT

plu·ri·po·ten·ti·al·i·ty \-pə-ˌten-chē-ˈa-lə-tē\ *n, pl* **-ties** : the quality or state of being pluripotent

plu·to·ni·um \plü-ˈtō-nē-əm\ *n* : a radioactive metallic element similar chemically to uranium that undergoes slow disintegration with the emission of a helium nucleus to form uranium 235 — symbol *Pu*; see ELEMENT table

pm *abbr* premolar

Pm *symbol* promethium

PM *abbr* 1 [Latin *post meridiem*] after noon 2 postmortem

PMN *abbr* polymorphonuclear neutrophilic white blood cell

PMS *n* : PREMENSTRUAL SYNDROME

PN *abbr* psychoneurotic

-pnea \p-nē-ə\ *n comb form* : breath : breathing (apnea)

pneum- *or* **pneumo-** *comb form* 1 : air : gas (pneumothorax) 2 : lung (pneumoconiosis) : pulmonary and (pneumogastric) 3 : respiration (pneumograph) 4 : pneumonia (pneumococcus)

pneumat- *or* **pneumato-** *comb form* : air : vapor : gas (pneumatosis)

pneu·mat·ic \nú-ˈma-tik, nyú-\ *adj* : of, relating to, or using gas (as air): as a : moved or worked by air pressure b : adapted for holding or inflated with compressed air c : having air-filled cavities (∼ bone) — **pneu·mat·i·cal·ly** *adv*

pneu·ma·ti·za·tion \ˌnü-mə-tə-ˈzā-shən, ˌnyü-\ *n* : the presence or development of air-filled cavities in a bone (∼ of the temporal bone) — **pneu·ma·tized** \ˈnü-mə-ˌtīzd, ˈnyü-\ *adj*

pneu·ma·to·cele \ˈnü-mə-tō-ˌsēl, ˈnyü-; nyü-ˈma-tə-, nü-\ *n* : a gas-filled cavity or sac occurring esp. in the lung

pneu·ma·to·sis \ˌnü-mə-ˈtō-səs, ˌnyü-\ *n, pl* **-to·ses** \-ˌsēz\ : the presence of air or gas in abnormal places in the body

pneu·ma·tu·ria \ˌnü-mə-ˈtür-ē-ə, ˌnyü-\ *n* : passage of gas in the urine

pneu·mo·coc·cae·mia *chiefly Brit var of* PNEUMOCOCCEMIA

pneu·mo·coc·cal \ˌnü-mə-ˈkä-kəl, ˌnyü-\ *adj* : of, relating to, caused by, or derived from pneumococci (∼ pneumonia) (a ∼ vaccine)

pneu·mo·coc·ce·mia \ˌnü-mə-ˌkäk-ˈsē-mē-ə, ˌnyü-\ *n* : the presence of pneumococci in the circulating blood

pneu·mo·coc·cus \ˌnü-mə-ˈkä-kəs, ˌnyü-\ *n, pl* **-coc·ci** \-ˈkä-ˌkī, -ˈkäk-ˌsī\ : a bacterium of the genus *Streptococcus* (*S. pneumoniae*) that causes an acute pneumonia involving one or more lobes of the lung

pneu·mo·co·lon \ˌnü-mə-ˈkō-lən, ˌnyü-\ *n* : the presence of air in the colon

pneu·mo·co·ni·o·sis \ˌnü-mō-ˌkō-nē-ˈō-səs, ˌnyü-\ *n, pl* **-o·ses** \-ˌsēz\ : a disease of the lungs caused by the habitual inhalation of irritants (as mineral or metallic particles) — called also *miner's asthma, pneumonoconiosis;* see BLACK LUNG, SILICOSIS

pneu·mo·cys·tic pneumonia \ˌnü-mə-ˈsis-tik-, ˌnyü-\ *n* : PNEUMOCYSTIS CARINII PNEUMONIA

Pneu·mo·cys·tis \ˌnü-mə-ˈsis-təs, ˌnyü-\ *n* 1 : a genus of microorganisms of uncertain affiliation that are usu. considered protozoans or sometimes fungi and that include one (*P. carinii*)

causing pneumonia esp. in immuno-compromised individuals **2** : PNEUMO-CYSTIS CARINII PNEUMONIA

Pneu·mo·cys·tis ca·ri·nii pneumonia \-kə-ˈrī-nē-ˌē-\ *n* : a pneumonia that affects individuals whose immunological defenses have been compromised by malnutrition, by other diseases (as cancer or AIDS), or by artificial immunosuppressive techniques (as after organ transplantation), that is caused by a microorganism of the genus *Pneumocystis* (*P. carinii*) which shows up in specially stained preparations of fresh infected lung tissue as cysts containing six to eight oval bodies, and that attacks esp. the interstitium of the lungs with marked thickening of the alveolar septa and of the alveoli — abbr. *PCP*; called also *pneumocystic pneumonia*, *Pneumocystis carinii pneumonitis*

pneu·mo·cys·tog·ra·phy \ˌnü-mə-ˌsi-ˈstä-grə-fē, ˌnyü-\ *n, pl* **-phies** : roentgenography of the urinary bladder after it has been injected with air

pneu·mo·cyte \ˈnü-mə-ˌsīt, ˈnyü-\ *n* : any of the specialized cells that occur in the alveoli of the lungs

pneu·mo·en·ceph·a·li·tis \ˌnü-mō-in-ˌse-fə-ˈlī-təs, ˌnyü-\ *n, pl* **-lit·i·des** \-ˈli-tə-ˌdēz\ : NEWCASTLE DISEASE

pneu·mo·en·ceph·a·lo·gram \-in-ˈse-fə-lə-ˌgram\ *n* : a roentgenogram made by pneumoencephalography

pneu·mo·en·ceph·a·lo·graph \-ˌgraf\ *n* : PNEUMOENCEPHALOGRAM

pneu·mo·en·ceph·a·log·ra·phy \-in-ˌse-fə-ˈlä-grə-fē\ *n, pl* **-phies** : roentgenography of the brain after the injection of air into the ventricles — **pneu·mo·en·ceph·a·lo·graph·ic** \-in-ˌse-fə-lə-ˈgra-fik\ *adj*

pneu·mo·en·ter·i·tis \-ˌen-tə-ˈrī-təs\ *n, pl* **-en·ter·it·i·des** \-ˈri-tə-ˌdēz\ *or* **-en·ter·i·tis·es** : pneumonia combined with enteritis

pneu·mo·gas·tric nerve \ˌnü-mə-ˈgas-trik-, ˌnyü-\ *n* : VAGUS NERVE

pneu·mo·gram \ˈnü-mə-ˌgram, ˈnyü-\ *n* : a record of respiratory movements obtained by pneumography

pneu·mo·graph \ˈnü-mə-ˌgraf, ˈnyü-\ *n* : an instrument for recording the thoracic movements or volume change during respiration

pneu·mog·ra·phy \nü-ˈmä-grə-fē, nyü-\ *n, pl* **-phies 1** : a description of the lungs **2** : roentgenography after the injection of air into a body cavity **3** : the process of making a pneumogram — **pneu·mo·graph·ic** \ˌnü-mə-ˈgra-fik, ˌnyü-\ *adj*

pneu·mol·y·sis \nü-ˈmä-lə-səs, nyü-\ *n, pl* **-y·ses** : PNEUMONOLYSIS

pneu·mo·me·di·as·ti·num \ˌnü-mō-ˌmē-dē-ə-ˈstī-nəm, ˌnyü-\ *n, pl* **-ti·na** \-nə\ **1** : an abnormal state characterized by the presence of gas (as air) in the mediastinum **2** : the induction of pneumomediastinum as an aid to roentgenography

pneu·mo·my·co·sis \-mī-ˈkō-səs\ *n, pl* **-co·ses** \-ˌsēz\ : a fungus disease of the lungs; *esp* : aspergillosis in poultry

pneumon- *or* **pneumono-** *comb form* : lung ⟨*pneumon*ectomy⟩ ⟨*pneumono*centesis⟩

pneu·mo·nec·to·my \ˌnü-mə-ˈnek-tə-mē, ˌnyü-\ *n, pl* **-mies** : surgical excision of an entire lung or of one or more lobes of a lung — compare SEGMENTAL RESECTION

pneu·mo·nia \nü-ˈmō-nyə, nyü-\ *n* : a disease of the lungs characterized by inflammation and consolidation followed by resolution and caused by infection or irritants — see BRONCHO-PNEUMONIA, LOBAR PNEUMONIA, PRIMARY ATYPICAL PNEUMONIA

pneu·mon·ic \nü-ˈmä-nik, nyü-\ *adj* **1** : of, relating to, or affecting the lungs : PULMONARY **2** : of, relating to, or affected with pneumonia

pneumonic plague *n* : plague of an extremely virulent form that is caused by a bacterium of the genus *Pasteurella* (*P. pestis*), involves chiefly the lungs, and usu. is transmitted from person to person by droplet infection — compare BUBONIC PLAGUE

pneu·mo·ni·tis \ˌnü-mə-ˈnī-təs, ˌnyü-\ *n, pl* **-nit·i·des** \-ˈni-tə-ˌdēz\ **1** : a disease characterized by inflammation of the lungs; *esp* : PNEUMONIA **2** : FELINE PNEUMONITIS

pneu·mo·no·cen·te·sis \ˌnü-mə-(ˌ)nō-sen-ˈtē-səs, ˌnyü-\ *n, pl* **-te·ses** \-ˌsēz\ : surgical puncture of a lung for aspiration

pneu·mo·no·co·ni·o·sis \-ˌkō-nē-ˈō-səs\ *n, pl* **-o·ses** \-ˌsēz\ : PNEUMOCONIOSIS

pneu·mo·nol·y·sis \ˌnü-mə-ˈnä-lə-səs, ˌnyü-\ *n, pl* **-y·ses** \-ˌsēz\ : either of two surgical procedures to permit collapse of a lung: **a** : separation of the parietal pleura from the fascia of the chest wall **b** : separation of the visceral and parietal layers of the pleura — called also *intrapleural pneumonolysis*

pneu·mo·nos·to·my \ˌnü-mə-ˈnäs-tə-mē, ˌnyü-\ *n, pl* **-mies** : surgical formation of an artificial opening (as for drainage of an abscess) into a lung

Pneu·mo·nys·sus \ˌnü-mə-ˈni-səs, ˌnyü-\ *n* : a genus of mites (family Halarachnidae) that live in the air passages of mammals and include one (*P. caninum*) found in dogs

pneu·mop·a·thy \nü-ˈmä-pə-thē, nyü-\ *n, pl* **-thies** : any disease of the lungs

pneu·mo·peri·car·di·um \ˌnü-mō-ˌper-ə-ˈkär-dē-əm, ˌnyü-\ *n, pl* **-dia** \-dē-ə\ : an abnormal state characterized by the presence of gas (as air) in the pericardium

pneu·mo·peri·to·ne·um \-ˌper-ə-tə-ˈnē-əm\ *n, pl* **-ne·ums** *or* **-nea** \-ˈnē-ə\ **1** : an abnormal state characterized by the presence of gas (as air) in the peritoneal cavity **2** : the induction of pneumoperitoneum as a therapeutic measure or as an aid to roentgenography

pneu·mo·scle·ro·sis \-sklə-'rō-səs\ *n, pl* **-ro·ses** \-ˌsēz\ : fibrosis of the lungs

pneu·mo·tacho·gram \ˌnü-mō-'tak-ə-ˌgram, -nyü-\ *n* : a record of the velocity of the respiratory function obtained by use of a pneumotachograph

pneu·mo·tacho·graph \-ˌgraf\ *n* : a device or apparatus for measuring the rate of the respiratory function

pneu·mo·tax·ic center \ˌnü-mə-'tak-sik-, -ˌnyü-\ *n* : a neural center in the upper part of the pons that provides inhibitory impulses on inspiration and thereby prevents overdistension of the lungs and helps to maintain alternately recurrent inspiration and expiration

pneu·mo·tho·rax \-'thōr-ˌaks\ *n, pl* **-tho·rax·es** *or* **-tho·ra·ces** \-'thōr-ə-ˌsēz\ **1** : an abnormal state characterized by the presence of gas (as air) in the pleural cavity — see TENSION PNEUMOTHORAX; compare OLEOTHORAX **2** : the induction of pneumothorax as a therapeutic measure to collapse the lung or as an aid to roentgenography

pneu·mo·tro·pic \-'trō-pik, -'trä-\ *adj* : turning, directed toward, or having an affinity for lung tissues — used esp. of infective agents

-pnoea *chiefly Brit var of* -PNEA

po *abbr* per os — used esp. in writing prescriptions

Po *symbol* polonium

pock \'päk\ *n* : a pustule in an eruptive disease (as smallpox)

pock·et \'pä-kət\ *n* : a small cavity or space; *esp* : an abnormal cavity formed in diseased tissue (a gingival ∼) — **pocketing** *n*

pock·mark \'päk-ˌmärk\ *n* : a mark, pit, or depressed scar caused by smallpox or acne — **pock·marked** *adj*

pod- *or* **podo-** *comb form* **1** : foot (*podiatry*) **2** : hoof (*pododermatitis*)

po·dag·ra \pə-'da-grə\ *n* **1** : GOUT **2** : a painful condition of the big toe caused by gout

po·dal·ic \pō-'da-lik\ *adj* : of, relating to, or by means of the feet; *specif* : being an obstetric version in which the fetus is turned so that the feet emerge first in delivery

po·di·a·try \pə-'dī-ə-trē, pō-\ *n, pl* **-tries** : the medical care and treatment of the human foot — called also *chiropody* — **po·di·at·ric** \pō-dē-'a-trik\ *adj* — **po·di·a·trist** \pə-'dī-ə-trist\ *n*

podo·der·ma·ti·tis \ˌpä-dō-ˌdər-mə-'tī-təs\ *n, pl* **-ti·tis·es** *or* **-tit·i·des** \-'ti-tə-ˌdēz\ : a condition (as foot rot) characterized by inflammation of the dermal tissue underlying the horny layers of a hoof

podo·phyl·lin \ˌpä-də-'fil-lən\ *n* : a resin obtained from podophyllum and used in medicine as a caustic

podo·phyl·lo·tox·in \ˌpä-də-ˌfil-ə-'täk-sən\ *n* : a crystalline polycyclic compound $C_{22}H_{22}O_8$ constituting one of the active principles of podophyllum and podophyllin

podo·phyl·lum \-'fil-ləm\ *n* **1** *cap* : a genus of herbs (family Berberidaceae) that have poisonous rootstocks, large palmate leaves, and large fleshy sometimes edible berries **2** *pl* **-phyl·li** \-'fil-ˌī\ *or* **-phyllums** : the dried rhizome and rootlet of the mayapple (*Podophyllum peltatum*) that is used as a caustic or as a source of the more effective podophyllin

podophyllum resin *n* : PODOPHYLLIN

po·go·ni·on \pə-'gō-nē-ən\ *n* : the most projecting median point on the anterior surface of the chin

-poi·e·sis \(ˌ)pȯi-'ē-səs\ *n comb form, pl* **-poi·e·ses** \-'ē-ˌsēz\ : production : formation (lympho*poiesis*)

-poi·et·ic \(ˌ)pȯi-'e-tik\ *adj comb form* : productive : formative (lympho*poietic*)

poi·ki·lo·cyte \'pȯi-ki-lə-ˌsīt, (ˌ)pȯi-'ki-\ *n* : an abnormally formed red blood cell characteristic of various anemias

poi·ki·lo·cy·to·sis \ˌpȯi-ki-lō-sī-'tō-səs\ *n, pl* **-to·ses** \-ˌsēz\ : a condition characterized by the presence of poikilocytes in the blood

poi·ki·lo·der·ma \ˌpȯi-kə-lə-'dər-mə\ *n, pl* **-mas** *or* **-ma·ta** \-mə-tə\ : any of several disorders characterized by patchy discoloration of the skin

poi·ki·lo·ther·mic \-'thər-mik\ *adj* : COLD-BLOODED

¹point \'point\ *n* **1** : a narrowly localized place or area **2** : the terminal usu. sharp or narrowly rounded part of something

²point *vb, of an abscess* : to become distended with pus prior to breaking

pointer — see HIP POINTER

point mutation *n* : mutation due to reorganization within a gene (as by substitution, addition, or deletion of a nucleotide) — called also *gene mutation*

Poi·seuille's law \pwä-'zœiz-\ *n* : a statement in physics that relates the velocity of flow of a fluid (as blood) through a narrow tube (as a capillary) to the pressure and viscosity of the fluid and the length and radius of the tube

Poiseuille, Jean–Léonard–Marie (1797–1869), French physiologist and physician.

¹poi·son \'pȯiz-ᵊn\ *n* **1** : a substance that through its chemical action usu. kills, injures, or impairs an organism **2** : a substance that inhibits the activity of another substance or the course of a reaction or process (a catalyst ∼)

²poison *vb* **poi·soned; poi·son·ing 1** : to

injure or kill with poison **2** : to treat, taint, or impregnate with poison

³**poison** *adj* **1** : POISONOUS ⟨a ~ plant⟩ **2** : impregnated with poison ⟨a ~ arrow⟩

poison dog·wood \-ᵈdȯg-ˌwu̇d\ *n* : POISON SUMAC

poison gas *n* : a poisonous gas or a liquid or a solid giving off poisonous vapors designed (as in chemical warfare) to kill, injure, or disable by inhalation or contact

poison hemlock *n* **1** : a large branching biennial poisonous herb (*Conium maculatum*) of the carrot family (Umbelliferae) with finely divided leaves and white flowers **2** : WATER HEMLOCK

poison ivy *n* **1 a** : a climbing plant of the genus *Rhus* (*R. radicans* syn. *Toxicodendron radicans*) that is esp. common in the eastern and central U.S., that has leaves in groups of three, greenish flowers, and white berries, and that produces an acutely irritating oil causing a usu. intensely itching skin rash **b** : any of several plants closely related to poison ivy; *esp* : POISON OAK **1b 2** : a skin rash produced by poison ivy

poison oak *n* **1** : any of several plants included in the genus *Rhus* or sometimes in the genus *Toxicodendron* that produce an irritating oil like that of poison ivy: **a** : a bushy plant (*R. diversiloba* syn. *T. diversilobum*) of the Pacific coast **b** : a bushy plant (*R. toxicodendron* syn. *T. pubescens*) of the southeastern U.S. **2** : POISON IVY **1a 3** : a skin rash produced by poison oak

poi·son·ous \ᵖpȯiz-ᵊn-əs\ *adj* : having the properties or effects of poison : VENOMOUS

poison su·mac \-ᵈshü-ˌmak, -ᵈsü-\ *n* : an American swamp shrub of the genus *Rhus* (*R. vernix* syn. *Toxicodendron vernix*) that has pinnate leaves, greenish flowers, and greenish white berries and produces an irritating oil — called also *poison dogwood*

poi·son·wood \ᵖpȯiz-ᵊn-ˌwu̇d\ *n* : a caustic or poisonous tree of the genus *Metopium* (*M. toxiferum*) of Florida and the West Indies that has compound leaves, clusters of greenish flowers, and orange-yellow fruits

poke·weed \ᵖpōk-ˌwēd\ *n* : an American perennial herb (*Phytolacca americana* of the family Phytolaccaceae) which has racemose white flowers, dark purple juicy berries, and a poisonous root and from which is obtained a mitogen that has been used to stimulate lymphocyte proliferation

po·lar \ᵖpō-lər\ *adj* **1** : of or relating to one or more poles (as of a spherical body) **2** : exhibiting polarity; *esp* : having a dipole or characterized by molecules having dipoles ⟨a ~ solvent⟩ **3** : being at opposite ends of a

spectrum of symptoms or manifestations ⟨~ types of leprosy⟩

polar body *n* : a cell that separates from an oocyte during meiosis: **a** : one containing a nucleus produced in the first meiotic division — called also *first polar body* : one containing a nucleus produced in the second meiotic division — called also *second polar body*

po·lar·i·ty \pō-ᵈlar-ə-tē, pə-\ *n, pl* **-ties 1** : the quality or condition inherent in a body that exhibits contrasting properties or powers in contrasting parts or directions **2** : attraction toward a particular object or in a specific direction **3** : the particular state either positive or negative with reference to the two poles or to electrification

po·lar·ize \ᵖpō-lə-ˌrīz\ *vb* **-ized; -iz·ing 1** : to vibrate or cause (as light waves) to vibrate in a definite pattern **2** : to give physical polarity to — **po·lar·i·za·tion** \ˌpō-lə-rə-ᵈzā-shən\ *n*

polarizing microscope *n* : a microscope equipped to produce polarized light for examination of a specimen

pole \ᵖpōl\ *n* **1 a** : either of the two terminals of an electric cell or battery **b** : one of two or more regions in a magnetized body at which the magnetism is concentrated **2** : either of two morphologically or physiologically differentiated areas at opposite ends of an axis in an organism, organ, or cell

poli- *or* **polio-** *comb form* : of or relating to the gray matter of the brain or spinal cord ⟨*polio*myelitis⟩

pol·i·clin·ic \ᵖpä-lē-ˌkli-nik\ *n* : a dispensary or department of a hospital at which outpatients are treated — compare POLYCLINIC

po·lio \ᵖpō-lē-ˌō\ *n* : POLIOMYELITIS

po·lio·dys·tro·phy \ˌpō-lē-ō-ᵈdis-trə-fē\ *n, pl* **-phies** : atrophy of the gray matter esp. of the cerebrum

po·lio·en·ceph·a·li·tis \ˌpō-lē-(ˌ)ō-in-ˌse-fə-ᵈlī-təs\ *n, pl* **-lit·i·des** \-ᵈli-tə-ˌdēz\ : inflammation of the gray matter of the brain

po·lio·en·ceph·a·lo·my·eli·tis \-in-ˌse-fə-lō-ˌmī-ə-ᵈlī-təs\ *n, pl* **-elit·i·des** \-ᵈli-tə-ˌdēz\ : inflammation of the gray matter of the brain and the spinal cord

po·lio·my·eli·tis \ˌpō-lē-(ˌ)ō-ˌmī-ə-ᵈlī-təs\ *n, pl* **-elit·i·des** \-ᵈli-tə-ˌdēz\ : an acute infectious virus disease characterized by fever, motor paralysis, and atrophy of skeletal muscles often with permanent disability and deformity and marked by inflammation of nerve cells in the ventral horns of the spinal cord — called also *infantile paralysis*, *polio* — **po·lio·my·elit·ic** \-ᵈli-tik\ *adj*

po·li·o·sis \ˌpō-lē-ᵈō-səs\ *n, pl* **-o·ses** \-ˌsēz\ : loss of color from the hair

polio vaccine *n* : a vaccine intended to confer immunity to poliomyelitis

po·lio·vi·rus \ᵖpō-lē-(ˌ)ō-ˌvī-rəs\ *n* : an

enterovirus that occurs in several antigenically distinct forms and is the causative agent of human poliomyelitis

po·litz·er bag \\'pō-lit-sər-, 'pä-\\ *n* : a soft rubber bulb used to inflate the middle ear by increasing air pressure in the nasopharynx

Politzer, Adam (1835–1920), Austrian otologist.

pol·len \\'pä-lən\\ *n* : a mass of male spores in a seed plant appearing usu. as a fine dust

pol·lex \\'pä-,leks\\ *n, pl* **pol·li·ces** \\'pä-lə-,sēz\\ : the first digit of the forelimb : THUMB

pollicis — see ABDUCTOR POLLICIS BREVIS, ABDUCTOR POLLICIS LONGUS, ADDUCTOR POLLICIS, EXTENSOR POLLICIS BREVIS, EXTENSOR POLLICIS LONGUS, FLEXOR POLLICIS BREVIS, FLEXOR POLLICIS LONGUS, OPPONENS POLLICIS, PRINCEPS POLLICIS

pol·li·ci·za·tion \\,pä-lə-sə-'zā-shən\\ *n* : the reconstruction or replacement of the thumb esp. from part of the forefinger

pol·li·no·sis *or* **pol·le·no·sis** \\,pä-lə-'nō-səs\\ *n, pl* **-no·ses** \\-,sēz\\ : an acute recurrent catarrhal disorder caused by allergic sensitivity to specific pollens

pol·lut·ant \\pə-'lüt-ᵊnt\\ *n* : something that pollutes

pol·lute \\pə-'lüt\\ *vb* **pol·lut·ed; pol·lut·ing** : to contaminate (an environment) esp. with man-made waste — **pol·lut·er** *n* — **pol·lut·ive** \\-'lü-tiv\\ *adj*

pol·lu·tion \\pə-'lü-shən\\ *n* 1 : the action of polluting or the condition of being polluted 2 : POLLUTANT

po·lo·ni·um \\pə-'lō-nē-əm\\ *n* : a radioactive metallic element that emits a helium nucleus to form an isotope of lead — symbol *Po*; see ELEMENT table

poly- *comb form* 1 : many : several : much : MULTI- (*poly*arthritis) 2 : excessive : abnormal : HYPER- (*poly*dactyly)

poly(A) \\,pä-lē-'ā\\ *n* : RNA or a segment of RNA that is composed of a polynucleotide chain consisting entirely of adenine-containing nucleotides and that codes for polylysine when functioning as messenger RNA in protein synthesis — called also *polyadenylate, polyadenylic acid*

poly·acryl·amide \\,pä-lē-ə-'kri-lə-,mīd\\ *n* : a polymer (−CH₂CHCONH₂−)ₓ derived from acrylic acid

polyacrylamide gel *n* : hydrated polyacrylamide that is used esp. to provide a medium for the suspension of a substance to be subjected to gel electrophoresis

poly·ad·en·yl·ate \\,pä-lē-,ad-ᵊn-'i-,lāt\\ *n* : POLY(A) — **poly·ad·en·yl·at·ed** \\-ā-təd\\ *adj* — **poly·ad·en·yl·a·tion** \\-i-'lā-shən\\ *n*

poly·ad·en·yl·ic acid \\-'i-lik-\\ *n* : POLY(A)

poly·an·dry \\'pä-lē-,an-drē\\ *n, pl* **-dries** : the state or practice of having more than one husband or male mate at one time — compare POLYGAMY, POLYGYNY — **poly·an·drous** \\,pä-lē-'an-drəs\\ *adj*

poly·ar·ter·i·tis \\,pä-lē-,är-tə-'rī-təs\\ *n* : POLYARTERITIS NODOSA

polyarteritis nodosa *n* : an acute inflammatory disease that involves all layers of the arterial wall and is characterized by degeneration, necrosis, exudation, and the formation of inflammatory nodules along the outer layer — called also *periarteritis nodosa*

poly·ar·thri·tis \\-är-'thrī-təs\\ *n, pl* **-thrit·i·des** \\-'thri-tə-,dēz\\ : arthritis involving two or more joints

poly·ar·tic·u·lar \\-är-'ti-kyə-lər\\ *adj* : having or affecting many joints ⟨~ arthritis⟩

poly·bro·mi·nat·ed biphenyl \\,pä-lē-'brō-mə-,nā-təd-\\ *n* : any of several compounds that are similar to polychlorinated biphenyls in environmental toxicity and in structure except that various hydrogen atoms are replaced by bromine rather than chlorine — called also *PBB*

poly(C) \\,pä-lē-'sē\\ *n* : POLYCYTIDYLIC ACID

poly·chlo·ri·nat·ed biphenyl \\,pä-lē-'klōr-ə-,nā-təd-\\ *n* : any of several compounds that are produced by replacing hydrogen atoms in biphenyl with chlorine, have various industrial applications, and are poisonous environmental pollutants which tend to accumulate in animal tissues — called also *PCB*

poly·chro·ma·sia \\-krō-'mā-zhə, -zhē-ə\\ *n* : the quality of being polychromatic; *specif* : POLYCHROMATOPHILIA

poly·chro·mat·ic \\-krō-'ma-tik\\ *adj* 1 : showing a variety or a change of colors 2 *of a cell or tissue* : exhibiting polychromatophilia

¹poly·chro·ma·to·phil \\-krō-'ma-tə-,fil, -'krō-mə-tə-\\ *n* : a young or degenerated red blood corpuscle staining with both acid and basic dyes

²polychromatophil *adj* : exhibiting polychromatophilia; *esp* : staining with both acid and basic dyes

poly·chro·mato·phil·ia \\-krō-,ma-tə-'fi-lē-ə\\ *n* : the quality of being stainable with more than one type of stain and esp. with both acid and basic dyes — **poly·chro·mato·phil·ic** \\-krō-,ma-tə-'fi-lik\\ *adj*

poly·clin·ic \\,pä-lē-'kli-nik\\ *n* : a clinic or hospital treating diseases of many sorts — compare POLICLINIC

poly·clo·nal \\,pä-lē-'klōn-ᵊl\\ *adj* : produced by or being cells derived from two or more cells of different ancestry or genetic constitution ⟨~ antibody synthesis⟩

poly·cy·clic \\,pä-lē-'sī-klik, -'si-\\ *adj* : having more than one cyclic component; *esp* : having two or more usu. fused rings in a molecule

poly·cyclic aromatic hydrocarbon *n* : any of a class of hydrocarbon molecules with multiple carbon rings that include numerous carcinogenic substances and environmental pollutants — called also *PAH*

poly·cys·tic \-'sis-tik\ *adj* : having or involving more than one cyst

polycystic kidney disease *n* : either of two hereditary diseases characterized by gradually enlarging bilateral cysts of the kidney which lead to reduced renal functioning

polycystic ovary syndrome *n* : a variable disorder that is marked esp. by amenorrhea, hirsutism, obesity, infertility, and ovarian enlargement and is usu. initiated by an elevated level of luteinizing hormone, androgen, or estrogen which results in an abnormal cycle of gonadotropin release by the pituitary gland — called also *polycystic ovarian disease, polycystic ovarian syndrome, polycystic ovary disease, Stein-Leventhal syndrome*

poly·cy·thae·mia, **poly·cy·thae·mic** *chiefly Brit var of* POLYCYTHEMIA, POLYCYTHEMIC

poly·cy·the·mia \-(₁)sī-'thē-mē-ə\ *n* : a condition marked by an abnormal increase in the number of circulating red blood cells : HYPERCYTHEMIA; *specif* : POLYCYTHEMIA VERA

polycythemia vera \-'vir-ə\ *n* : polycythemia of unknown cause that is characterized by increase in total blood volume and accompanied by nosebleed, distension of the circulatory vessels, and enlargement of the spleen — called also *erythremia, Vaquez's disease; compare* ERYTHROCYTOSIS

poly·cy·the·mic \-pä-lē-(₁)sī-'thē-mik\ *adj* : relating to or involving polycythemia or polycythemia vera

poly·cyt·i·dyl·ic acid \-₁si-tə-'di-lik\ *n* : RNA or a segment of RNA that is composed of a polynucleotide chain consisting entirely of cytosine-containing nucleotides and that codes for a polypeptide chain consisting of proline residues when functioning as messenger RNA in protein synthesis — called also *poly(C);* see POLY I:C

poly·dac·tyl \-'dak-t²l\ *adj* : characterized by polydactyly; *also* : being a gene that determines polydactyly

poly·dac·tyl·ia \-dak-'ti-lē-ə\ *n* : POLYDACTYLY

poly·dac·tyl·ism \-'dakt-²l-₁i-zəm\ *n* : POLYDACTYLY

poly·dac·tyl·ly \-'dak-tə-lē\ *n, pl* **-lies** : the condition of having more than the normal number of toes or fingers

poly·dip·sia \-'dip-sē-ə\ *n* : excessive or abnormal thirst — **poly·dip·sic** \-sik\ *adj*

poly·drug \'pä-lē-'drəg\ *adj* : relating to or affected by addiction to more than one illicit drug 〈~ abuse〉

poly·em·bry·o·ny \₁pä-lē-'em-brē-ə-nē, -(₁)em-'brī-\ *n, pl* **-nies** : the production of two or more embryos from one ovule or egg

poly·en·do·crine \-'en-də-krən, -₁krīn, -₁krēn\ *adj* : relating to or affecting more than one endocrine gland 〈a family history of ~ disorders〉

po·lyg·a·my \pə-'li-gə-mē\ *n, pl* **-mies** : marriage in which a spouse of either sex may have more than one mate at the same time — compare POLYANDRY, POLYGYNY — **po·lyg·a·mous** \-məs\ *adj*

poly·gene \'pä-lē-₁jēn\ *n* : any of a group of nonallelic genes that collectively control the inheritance of a quantitative character or modify the expression of a qualitative character — called also *multiple factor;* compare QUANTITATIVE INHERITANCE

poly·gen·ic \₁pä-lē-'jē-nik, -'je-\ *adj* : of, relating to, or resulting from polygenes : MULTIFACTORIAL

poly·glan·du·lar \-'glan-jə-lər\ *adj* : of, relating to, or involving several glands 〈~ therapy〉

poly·graph \'pä-lē-₁graf\ *n* : an instrument for simultaneously recording variations of several different pulsations (as of the pulse, blood pressure, and respiration); *broadly* : LIE DETECTOR — **poly·graph·ic** \₁pä-lē-'gra-fik\ *adj*

po·lyg·y·ny \pə-'li-jə-nē\ *n, pl* **-nies** : the state or practice of having more than one wife or female mate at one time — compare POLYANDRY, POLYGAMY — **po·lyg·y·nous** \-nəs\ *adj*

poly·hy·dram·ni·os \₁pä-lē-hī-'dram-nē-₁äs\ *n* : HYDRAMNIOS

poly I:C \₁pä-lē-₁ī-'sē\ *n* : a synthetic 2-stranded RNA composed of one strand of polyinosinic acid and one strand of polycytidylic acid that induces interferon formation and has been used experimentally as an anticancer and antiviral agent — called also *poly I:poly C*

poly·ino·sin·ic acid \₁pä-lē-₁i-nə-'si-nik-, -₁ī-nə-\ *n* : RNA or a segment of RNA that is composed of a polynucleotide chain consisting entirely of inosinic acid residues — see POLY I:C

poly I:poly C \₁pä-lē-'ī-₁pä-lē-'sē\ *n* : POLY I:C

poly·ly·sine \₁pä-lē-'lī-₁sēn\ *n* : a protein whose polypeptide chain consists entirely of lysine residues

poly·mer \'pä-lə-mər\ *n* : a chemical compound or mixture of compounds formed by polymerization and consisting essentially of repeating structural units — **poly·mer·ic** \₁pä-lə-'mer-ik\ *adj* — **poly·mer·ism** \pə-'li-mə-₁ri-zəm, 'pä-lə-mə-\ *n*

poly·mer·ase \-mə-₁rās, -₁rāz\ *n* : any of several enzymes that catalyze the formation of DNA or RNA from precursor substances in the presence of preexisting DNA or RNA acting as a template

polymerase chain reaction n : an in vitro technique for rapidly synthesizing large quantities of a given DNA segment that involves separating the DNA into its two complementary strands, binding a primer to each single strand at the end of the given DNA segment where synthesis will start, using DNA polymerase to synthesize two-stranded DNA from each single strand, and repeating the process — abbr. *PCR*

po·ly·mer·i·za·tion \pə-ˌli-mə-rə-ˈzā-shən, ˌpä-lə-mə-rə-\ n : a chemical reaction in which two or more small molecules combine to form larger molecules that contain repeating structural units of the original molecules — compare ASSOCIATION 3 — **po·ly·mer·ize** \pə-ˈli-mə-ˌrīz, ˈpä-lə-mə-\ vb

poly·meth·yl meth·ac·ry·late \ˌpä-lē-ˈme-thəl-me-ˈtha-krə-ˌlāt\ n : a thermoplastic polymeric resin that is used esp. in hard contact lenses and in prostheses to replace bone

poly·mi·cro·bi·al \ˌpä-lē-mī-ˈkrō-bē-əl\ adj : of, relating to, or caused by several types of microorganisms

poly·morph \ˈpä-lē-ˌmorf\ n 1 : a polymorphic organism; *also* : one of the several forms of such an organism 2 : a polymorphonuclear white blood cell

poly·mor·phism \-ˈmor-ˌfi-zəm\ n : the quality or state of being able to assume different forms — **poly·mor·phic** \-ˈmor-fik\ adj

¹**poly·mor·pho·nu·cle·ar** \-ˌmor-fō-ˈnü-klē-ər, -ˈnyü-\ adj, of a white blood cell : having the nucleus complexly lobed; *specif* : being a mature neutrophil with a characteristic distinctly lobed nucleus

²**polymorphonuclear** n : POLYMORPH 2

poly·mor·phous \-ˈmor-fəs\ adj : having, assuming, or occurring in various forms — **poly·mor·phous·ly** adv

polymorphous perverse adj : relating to or exhibiting infantile sexual tendencies in which the genitals are not yet identified as the sole or principal sexual organs nor coitus as the goal of erotic activity

poly·my·al·gia rheu·mat·i·ca \ˌpä-lē-mī-ˈal-jə-rü-ˈma-ti-kə, -jē-ə-\ n : a disorder of the elderly characterized by muscular pain and stiffness in the shoulders and neck and in the pelvic area

poly·myo·si·tis \-ˌmī-ə-ˈsī-təs\ n : inflammation of several muscles at once

poly·myx·in \ˌpä-lē-ˈmik-sən\ n : any of several toxic antibiotics obtained from a soil bacterium of the genus *Bacillus* (*B. polymyxa*) and active against gram-negative bacteria

polymyxin B n : the least toxic of the polymyxins used in the form of its sulfate chiefly in the treatment of some localized, gastrointestinal, or systemic infections

polymyxin E n : COLISTIN

poly·neu·ri·tis \ˌpä-lē-nü-ˈrī-təs, -nyü-\ n, pl **-rit·i·des** \-ˈri-tə-ˌdēz\ or **-ri·tis·es** : neuritis of several peripheral nerves at the same time — **poly·neu·rit·ic** \-ˈri-tik\ adj

poly·neu·ro·pa·thy \-nü-ˈrä-pə-thē, -nyü-\ n, pl **-thies** : a disease of nerves; *esp* : a noninflammatory degenerative disease of nerves usu. caused by toxins (as of lead)

poly·nu·cle·ar \-ˈnü-klē-ər, -ˈnyü-\ adj : chemically polycyclic esp. with respect to the benzene ring — used chiefly of certain hydrocarbons that are important as pollutants and possibly as carcinogens

poly·nu·cle·o·tide \-ˈnü-klē-ə-ˌtīd, -ˈnyü-\ n : a polymeric chain of nucleotides

poly·oma virus \ˌpä-lē-ˈō-mə-\ n : a papovavirus of rodents that is associated with various kinds of tumors — called also *polyoma*

poly·opia \ˌpä-lē-ˈō-pē-ə\ n : perception of more than one image of a single object esp. with one eye

poly·os·tot·ic \ˌpä-lē-ä-ˈstä-tik\ adj : involving or relating to many bones

pol·yp \ˈpä-ləp\ n : a projecting mass of swollen and hypertrophied or tumorous membrane

pol·yp·ec·to·my \ˌpä-li-ˈpek-tə-mē\ n, pl **-mies** : the surgical excision of a polyp

poly·pep·tide \ˌpä-lē-ˈpep-ˌtīd\ n : a molecular chain of amino acids — **poly·pep·tid·ic** \-(ˌ)pep-ˈti-dik\ adj

poly·pha·gia \-ˈfā-jə, -jē-ə\ n : excessive appetite or eating — compare HYPERPHAGIA

poly·phar·ma·cy \-ˈfär-mə-sē\ n, pl **-cies** : the practice of administering many different medicines esp. concurrently for the treatment of the same disease

poly·pha·sic \-ˈfā-zik\ adj 1 : of, relating to, or having more than one phase (∼ evoked potentials) — compare DIPHASIC b, MONOPHASIC 1 2 : having several periods of activity interrupted by intervening periods of rest in each 24 hours (an infant is essentially ∼)

poly·ploid \ˈpä-lē-ˌplȯid\ adj : having or being a chromosome number that is a multiple greater than two of the monoploid number — **poly·ploi·dy** \-ˌplȯi-dē\ n

po·lyp·nea \pä-ˈlip-nē-ə, pə-\ n : rapid or panting respiration — **po·lyp·ne·ic** \-nē-ik\ adj

po·lyp·noea *chiefly Brit* var of POLYPNEA

pol·yp·oid \ˈpä-lə-ˌpȯid\ adj 1 : resembling a polyp (a ∼ intestinal growth) 2 : marked by the formation of lesions suggesting polyps (∼ disease)

pol·yp·o·sis \ˌpä-li-ˈpō-səs\ n, pl **-o-**

ses \-ˌsēz\ : a condition characterized by the presence of numerous polyps

poly·ri·bo·some \ˌpä-lē-ˈrī-bə-ˌsōm\ n : a cluster of ribosomes linked together by a molecule of messenger RNA and forming the site of protein synthesis — called also *polysome* — **poly·ri·bo·som·al** \-ˌrī-bə-ˈsō-məl\ *adj*

poly·sac·cha·ride \-ˈsa-kə-ˌrīd\ n : a carbohydrate that can be decomposed by hydrolysis into two or more molecules of monosaccharides; *esp* : one of the more complex carbohydrates (as cellulose, starch, or glycogen) — called also *glycan*

poly·se·ro·si·tis \-ˌsir-ə-ˈsī-təs\ n : inflammation of several serous membranes (as the pleura, pericardium, and peritoneum) at the same time

poly·some \ˈpä-lē-ˌsōm\ n : POLYRIBOSOME

poly·sor·bate \ˌpä-lē-ˈsȯr-ˌbāt\ n : any of several emulsifiers used in the preparation of some pharmaceuticals and foods — see TWEEN

poly·sper·my \ˈpä-lē-ˌspər-mē\ n, pl -mies : the entrance of several spermatozoa into one egg — compare MONOSPERMY — **poly·sper·mic** \ˌpä-lē-ˈspər-mik\ *adj*

poly·syn·ap·tic \ˌpä-lē-sə-ˈnap-tik\ *adj* : involving two or more synapses in the central nervous system — **poly·syn·ap·ti·cal·ly** *adv*

poly·tene \ˈpä-lē-ˌtēn\ *adj* : relating to, being, or having chromosomes each of which consists of many strands with the corresponding chromomeres in contact — **poly·te·ny** \-ˌtē-nē\ n

poly·tet·ra·flu·o·ro·eth·yl·ene \ˌpä-lē-ˌte-trə-ˌflür-ō-ˈe-thə-ˌlēn\ n : a polymer ($CF_2-CF_2)_n$ that is a resin used to fabricate prostheses — abbr. *PTFE;* see TEFLON

poly·the·lia \ˌpä-lē-ˈthē-lē-ə\ n : the condition of having more than the normal number of nipples

poly·thi·a·zide \-ˈthī-ə-ˌzīd, -zəd\ n : an antihypertensive and diuretic drug $C_{11}H_{13}ClF_3N_3O_4S_3$ — see RENESE

poly(U) \ˌpä-lē-ˈyü\ n : POLYURIDYLIC ACID

poly·un·sat·u·rate \ˌpä-lē-ˌən-ˈsa-chə-rət\ n : a polyunsaturated oil or fatty acid

poly·un·sat·u·rat·ed \-ˌən-ˈsa-chə-ˌrā-təd\ *adj, of an oil or fatty acid* : having in each molecule many chemical bonds in which two or three pairs of electrons are shared by two atoms — compare MONOUNSATURATED

poly·uria \-ˈyùr-ē-ə\ n : excessive secretion of urine

poly·uri·dyl·ic acid \-ˌyùr-ə-ˌdi-lik-\ n : RNA or a segment of RNA that is composed of a polynucleotide chain consisting entirely of uracil-containing nucleotides and that codes for a polypeptide chain consisting of phenylalanine residues when functioning

as messenger RNA in protein synthesis — called also *poly(U)*

poly·va·lent \ˌpä-lē-ˈvā-lənt\ *adj* : effective against, sensitive toward, or counteracting more than one exciting agent (as a toxin or antigen) (a ∼ vaccine) — **poly·va·lence** \-ləns\ n

poly·vi·nyl·pyr·rol·i·done \ˌpä-lē-ˌvīn-əl-pi-ˈrä-lə-ˌdōn\ n : a water-soluble chemically inert solid polymer $(-CH_2CHC_4H_6NO-)_n$ used chiefly in medicine as a vehicle for drugs (as iodine) and esp. formerly as a plasma expander — called also *povidone*

Pompe's disease \ˈpämps-\ n : an often fatal glycogenosis that results from an enzyme deficiency, is characterized by abnormal accumulation of glycogen esp. in the liver, heart, and muscle, and usu. appears during infancy — called also *acid maltase deficiency*

Pompe, J. C. (*fl* 1932), Dutch physician.

pom·pho·lyx \ˈpäm-fə-ˌliks\ n 1 : FLOWERS OF ZINC 2 : a skin disease marked by an eruption of vesicles esp. on the palms and soles

pon·der·al index \ˈpän-də-rəl-\ n : a measure of relative body mass expressed as the ratio of the cube root of body weight to height multiplied by 100

pons \ˈpänz\ n, pl **pon·tes** \ˈpän-ˌtēz\ : a broad mass of chiefly transverse nerve fibers conspicuous on the ventral surface of the brain at the anterior end of the medulla oblongata

pons Va·ro·lii \-və-ˈrō-lē-ˌī, -lē-ˌē\ n, pl **pontes Varolii** : PONS

Va·ro·lio \vä-ˈrō-lē-ō\, **Costanzo** (1543–1575), Italian anatomist.

pon·tic \ˈpän-tik\ n : an artifical tooth on a dental bridge

pon·tile \ˈpän-ˌtīl, -təl\ *adj* : PONTINE

pon·tine \ˈpän-ˌtīn\ *adj* : of or relating to the pons (a study of ∼ lesions)

pontine flexure n : a flexure of the embryonic hindbrain that serves to delimit the developing cerebellum and medulla oblongata

pontine nucleus n : any of various large groups of nerve cells in the basal part of the pons that receive fibers from the cerebral cortex and send fibers to the cerebellum by way of the middle cerebellar peduncles

pontis — see BRACHIUM PONTIS

Pon·to·caine \ˈpän-tə-ˌkān\ *trademark* — used for a preparation of tetracaine

¹**pool** \ˈpül\ *vb, of blood* : to accumulate or become static (as in the veins of a bodily part) (blood ∼ed in his legs)

²**pool** n : a readily available supply: as a : the whole quantity of a particular material present in the body and available for function or the satisfying of metabolic demands — see GENE POOL b : a body product (as blood)

collected from many donors and stored for later use

pop·li·te·al \ˌpä-plə-ˈtē-əl, päp-ˈli-tē-\ *adj* : of or relating to the back part of the leg behind the knee joint

popliteal artery *n* : the continuation of the femoral artery that after passing through the thigh crosses the popliteal space and soon divides into the anterior and posterior tibial arteries

popliteal fossa *n* : POPLITEAL SPACE

popliteal ligament — see ARCUATE POPLITEAL LIGAMENT, OBLIQUE POPLITEAL LIGAMENT

popliteal nerve — see COMMON PERONEAL NERVE, TIBIAL NERVE

popliteal space *n* : a lozenge-shaped space at the back of the knee joint — called also *popliteal fossa*

popliteal vein *n* : a vein formed by the union of the anterior and posterior tibial veins and ascending through the popliteal space to the thigh where it becomes the femoral vein

pop·li·te·us \ˌpä-plə-ˈtē-əs, päp-ˈli-tē-əs\ *n, pl* **-li·tei** \-tē-ˌī\ : a flat muscle that originates from the lateral condyle of the femur, forms part of the floor of the popliteal space, and functions to flex the leg and rotate the femur medially

pop·per \ˈpä-pər\ *n, slang* : a vial of amyl nitrite or isobutyl nitrite esp. when used illicitly as an aphrodisiac

pop·py \ˈpä-pē\ *n, pl* **poppies** : any herb of the genus *Papaver* (family Papaveraceae); *esp* : OPIUM POPPY

pop·u·la·tion \ˌpä-pyə-ˈlā-shən\ *n* **1** : the organisms inhabiting a particular locality **2** : a group of individual persons, objects, or items from which samples are taken for statistical measurement

population genetics *n* : a branch of genetics concerned with gene and genotype frequencies in populations — see HARDY-WEINBERG LAW

por·ce·lain \ˈpȯr-sə-lən\ *n* : a hard, fine-grained, nonporous, and usu. translucent and white ceramic ware that has many uses in dentistry

por·cine \ˈpȯr-ˌsīn\ *adj* : of or derived from swine (~ heterografts)

pore \ˈpȯr\ *n* : a minute opening esp. in an animal or plant; *esp* : one by which matter passes through a membrane

-pore \ˌpȯr\ *n comb form* : opening ⟨blasto*pore*⟩

por·en·ceph·a·ly \ˌpȯr-in-ˈse-fə-lē\ *n, pl* **-lies** : the presence of cavities in the brain — **por·en·ce·phal·ic** \-ˌen-sə-ˈfa-lik\ *adj*

pork tapeworm \ˈpȯrk-\ *n* : a tapeworm of the genus *Taenia* (*T. solium*) that infests the human intestine as an adult, has a cysticercus larva that typically develops in swine, and is contracted by humans through ingestion of the larva in raw or imperfectly cooked pork

po·ro·ceph·a·li·a·sis \ˌpō-rō-ˌse-fə-ˈlī-ə-

səs\ *n, pl* **-a·ses** \-ˌsēz\ : infestation with or disease caused by a tongue worm of the genus *Porocephalus*

Po·ro·ceph·a·lus \-ˈse-fə-ləs\ *n* : a genus of tongue worms (family Porocephalidae) occurring as adults in the lungs of reptiles and as young in various vertebrates including humans

po·ro·sis \pə-ˈrō-səs\ *n, pl* **po·ro·ses** \-ˌsēz\ *or* **porosises** : a condition (as of a bone) characterized by porosity; *specif* : rarefaction (as of bone) with increased translucency to X rays

po·ros·i·ty \pə-ˈrä-sə-tē, pō-, pȯ-\ *n, pl* **-ties 1 a** : the quality or state of being porous **b** : the ratio of the volume of interstices of a material to the volume of its mass **2** : PORE

po·rot·ic \pə-ˈrä-tik\ *adj* : exhibiting or marked by porous structure or osteoporosis

po·rous \ˈpȯr-əs\ *adj* **1** : possessing or full of pores (~ bones) **2** : permeable to liquids

por·pho·bi·lin·o·gen \ˌpȯr-fō-bī-ˈli-nə-jən\ *n* : an acid $C_{10}H_{14}N_2O_4$ having two carboxyl groups per molecule that is derived from pyrrole and is found in the urine in acute porphyria

por·phyr·ia \pȯr-ˈfir-ē-ə\ *n* : any of several usu. hereditary abnormalities of porphyrin metabolism characterized by excretion of excess porphyrins in the urine

por·phy·rin \ˈpȯr-fə-rən\ *n* : any of various compounds with a structure that consists essentially of four pyrrole rings joined by four =C– groups; *esp* : one (as chlorophyll or hemoglobin) containing a central metal atom and usu. having biological activity

por·phy·rin·uria \ˌpȯr-fə-rə-ˈnȯr-ē-ə, -ˈnyȯr-\ *n* : the presence of porphyrin in the urine

por·ta \ˈpȯr-tə\ *n, pl* **por·tae** \-ˌtē\ : an opening in a bodily part where the blood vessels, nerves, or ducts leave and enter : HILUM

por·ta·ca·val \ˌpȯr-tə-ˈkā-vəl\ *adj* : extending from the portal vein to the vena cava (~ anastomosis)

portacaval shunt *n* : a surgical shunt by which the portal vein is made to empty into the inferior vena cava in order to bypass a damaged liver

porta hep·a·tis \-ˈhe-pə-təs\ *n* : the fissure running transversely on the underside of the liver where most of the vessels enter or leave — called also *transverse fissure*

¹por·tal \ˈpȯrt-ᵊl\ *n* : a communicating part or area of an organism: as **a** : PORTAL VEIN **b** : the point at which something enters the body (~s of infection)

²portal *adj* **1** : of or relating to the porta hepatis **2** : of, relating to, or being a portal vein or a portal system

portal cirrhosis *n* : LAENNEC'S CIRRHOSIS

portal hypertension *n* : hypertension in

the hepatic portal system caused by venous obstruction or occlusion that produces splenomegaly and ascites in its later stages

portal system *n* : a system of veins that begins and ends in capillaries — see HEPATIC PORTAL SYSTEM, PITUITARY PORTAL SYSTEM

portal vein *n* : a large vein that is formed by fusion of other veins, that terminates in a capillary network, and that delivers blood to some area of the body other than the heart; *esp* : HEPATIC PORTAL VEIN

por·tio \'pȯr-shē-ˌō, 'pȯr-tē-ˌō\ *n*, *pl* **-ti·o·nes** \ˌpȯr-shē-'ō-ˌnēz\ : a part, segment, or branch (as of an organ or nerve) (the visible ~ of the cervix)

Por·tu·guese man–of–war \'pȯr-chə-ˌgēz-ˌman-əv-'wȯr\ *n*, *pl* **Portuguese man–of–wars** *also* **Portuguese men–of–war** : any siphonophore of the genus *Physalia* including large tropical and subtropical oceanic forms having a crested bladderlike float which bears a colony comprised of three types of individuals on the lower surface with one of the three having stinging tentacles

port–wine stain \'pȯrt-ˌwin-\ *n* : a reddish purple superficial hemangioma of the skin commonly occurring as a birthmark — called also *nevus flammeus, port-wine mark*

¹po·si·tion \pə-'zi-shən\ *n* : a particular arrangement or location; *specif* : an arrangement of the parts of the body considered particularly desirable for some medical or surgical procedure (knee-chest ~) (lithotomy ~) — **po·si·tion·al** \pə-'zi-shə-nəl\ *adj*

²position *vb* : to put in proper position

pos·i·tive \'pä-zə-tiv\ *adj* 1 : being, relating to, or charged with electricity of which the proton is the elementary unit 2 : affirming the presence of that sought or suspected to be present (a ~ test for blood) — **pos·i·tive·ly** *adv* — **pos·i·tive·ness** *n*

positive electron *n* : POSITRON

pos·i·tron \'pä-zə-ˌträn\ *n* : a positively charged particle having the same mass and magnitude of charge as the electron

positron–emission tomography *n* : tomography in which an in vivo, noninvasive, cross-sectional image of regional metabolism is obtained by a usu. color-coded CRT representation of the distribution of gamma radiation given off in the collision of electrons in cells with positrons emitted by radionuclides incorporated into metabolic substances — abbr. *PET*

post- *prefix* 1 : after : later than (*post*operative) (*post*coronary) 2 : behind : posterior to (*post*auricular)

post·abor·tion \ˌpōst-ə-'bȯr-shən\ *adj* : occurring after an abortion

post·ab·sorp·tive \-əb-'sȯrp-tiv\ *adj* : being in or typical of the period following absorption of nutrients from the alimentary canal

post·ad·o·les·cence \ˌad-əl-'es-əns\ *n* : the period following adolescence and preceding adulthood — **post·ad·o·les·cent** \-'nt\ *adj or n*

post·an·es·the·sia \ˌa-nəs-'thē-zhə\ *adj* : POSTANESTHETIC

post·an·es·thet·ic \-'the-tik\ *adj* : occurring in, used in, or being the period following administration of an anesthetic (~ encephalopathy)

post·an·ox·ic \ˌa-'näk-sik\ *adj* : occurring or being after a period of anoxia

post·au·ric·u·lar \-ˌō-'ri-kyə-lər\ *adj* : located or occurring behind the auricle of the ear (a ~ incision)

post·ax·i·al \-'ak-sē-əl\ *adj* : of or relating to the ulnar side of the vertebrate forelimb or the fibular side of the hind limb; *also* : of or relating to the side of an animal or side of one of its limbs that is posterior to the axis of its body or limbs

post·cap·il·lary \-'ka-pə-ˌler-ē\ *adj* : of, relating to, affecting, or being a venule of the circulatory system

post·car·di·ot·o·my \-ˌkär-dē-'ä-tə-mē\ *adj* : occurring or being in the period following open-heart surgery

post·cen·tral \-'sen-trəl\ *adj* : located behind a center or central structure; *esp* : located behind the central sulcus of the cerebral cortex

postcentral gyrus *n* : a gyrus of the parietal lobe located just posterior to the central sulcus, lying parallel to the precentral gyrus of the temporal lobe, and comprising the somesthetic area

post·cho·le·cys·tec·to·my syndrome \-ˌkō-lə-(ˌ)sis-'tek-tə-mē-\ *n* : persistent pain and associated symptoms (as indigestion and nausea) following a cholecystectomy

post·co·i·tal \-'kō-ət-əl, -'ēt-əl; -'kȯit-əl\ *adj* : occurring, existing, or being administered after coitus

post·cor·o·nary \-'kȯr-ə-ˌner-ē, -'kär-\ *adj* 1 : relating to, occurring in, or being the period following a heart attack (~ exercise) 2 : having suffered a heart attack (a ~ patient)

post·dam \ˌpōst-'dam\ *n* : a posterior extension of a full denture to accomplish a complete seal between denture and tissues

post·en·ceph·a·lit·ic \-in-ˌse-fə-'li-tik\ *adj* : occurring after and presumably as a result of encephalitis (~ parkinsonism)

¹pos·te·ri·or \pō-'stir-ē-ər, pä-\ *adj* : situated behind: as **a** : situated at or toward the hind part of the body : CAUDAL **b** : DORSAL — used of human anatomy in which the upright posture makes dorsal and caudal identical

²pos·te·ri·or \pä-'stir-ē-ər, pō-\ *n* : the posterior bodily parts; *esp* : BUTTOCKS

posterior auricular artery *n* : a small branch of the external carotid artery that supplies or gives off branches supplying the back of the ear and the adjacent region of the scalp, the middle ear, tympanic membrane, and mastoid cells — called also *posterior auricular*

posterior auricular vein *n* : a vein formed from venous tributaries in the region behind the ear that joins with the posterior facial vein to form the external jugular vein

posterior brachial cutaneous nerve *n* : a branch of the radial nerve that arises on the medial side of the arm in the axilla and supplies the skin on the dorsal surface almost to the olecranon

posterior cerebral artery *n* : CEREBRAL ARTERY C

posterior chamber *n* : a narrow space in the eye behind the peripheral part of the iris and in front of the suspensory ligament of the lens and the ciliary processes — compare ANTERIOR CHAMBER

posterior column *n* : DORSAL HORN

posterior commissure *n* : a bundle of white matter crossing from one side of the brain to the other just rostral to the superior colliculi and above the opening of the aqueduct of Sylvius into the third ventricle

posterior communicating artery *n* : COMMUNICATING ARTERY b

posterior cord *n* : a cord of nerve tissue that is formed from the posterior divisions of the three trunks of the brachial plexus and that divides into the axillary and radial nerves — compare LATERAL CORD, MEDIAL CORD

posterior cricoarytenoid *n* : CRICOARYTENOID 2

posterior cruciate ligament *n* : CRUCIATE LIGAMENT a(2)

posterior elastic lamina *n* : DESCEMET'S MEMBRANE

posterior facial vein *n* : a vein that is formed in the upper part of the parotid gland behind the mandible by the union of several tributaries and joins with the posterior auricular vein to form the external jugular vein

posterior femoral cutaneous nerve *n* : a nerve that arises from the sacral plexus and is distributed to the skin of the perineum and of the back of the thigh and leg — compare LATERAL FEMORAL CUTANEOUS NERVE

posterior funiculus *n* : a longitudinal division on each side of the spinal cord comprising white matter between the dorsal root and the posterior median sulcus — compare ANTERIOR FUNICULUS, LATERAL FUNICULUS

posterior gray column *n* : DORSAL HORN

posterior horn *n* 1 : DORSAL HORN 2 : the cornu of the lateral ventricle of each cerebral hemisphere that curves backward into the occipital lobe —

compare ANTERIOR HORN 2, INFERIOR HORN

posterior humeral circumflex artery *n* : an artery that branches from the axillary artery in the shoulder, curves around the back of the humerus, and is distributed esp. to the deltoid muscle and shoulder joint — compare ANTERIOR HUMERAL CIRCUMFLEX ARTERY

posterior inferior cerebellar artery *n* : an artery that usu. branches from the vertebral artery and supplies much of the medulla oblongata, the inferior portion of the cerebellum, and part of the floor of the fourth ventricle

posterior inferior iliac spine *n* : a projection on the posterior margin of the ilium that is situated below the posterior superior iliac spine and is separated from it by a notch — called also *posterior inferior spine*

posterior intercostal artery *n* : INTERCOSTAL ARTERY b

posterior lobe *n* 1 : NEUROHYPOPHYSIS 2 : the part of the cerebellum between the primary fissure and the flocculonodular lobe

pos·te·ri·or·ly *adv* : in a posterior direction

posterior median septum *n* : a sheet of neuroglial tissue in the midsagittal plane of the spinal cord that partitions the posterior part of the spinal cord into right and left halves

posterior median sulcus *n* : a shallow groove along the midline of the posterior part of the spinal cord that separates the two posterior funiculi

posterior nares *n pl* : CHOANAE

posterior nasal spine *n* : the nasal spine that is formed by the union of processes of the two palatine bones

posterior pillar of the fauces *n* : PALATOPHARYNGEAL ARCH

posterior pituitary *n* 1 : NEUROHYPOPHYSIS 2 : an extract of the neurohypophysis of domesticated animals for medicinal use — called also *posterior pituitary extract*

posterior pituitary gland *n* : NEUROHYPOPHYSIS

posterior root *n* : DORSAL ROOT

posterior sacrococcygeal muscle *n* : SACROCOCCYGEUS DORSALIS

posterior spinal artery *n* : SPINAL ARTERY b

posterior spinocerebellar tract *n* : SPINOCEREBELLAR TRACT a

posterior superior alveolar artery *n* : a branch of the maxillary artery that supplies the upper molar and bicuspid teeth

posterior superior iliac spine *n* : a projection at the posterior end of the iliac crest — called also *posterior superior spine*

posterior synechia *n* : SYNECHIA b

posterior temporal artery *n* : TEMPORAL ARTERY 3c

posterior tibial artery *n* : TIBIAL ARTERY a

posterior tibial vein *n* : TIBIAL VEIN a

posterior triangle *n* : a triangular region that is a landmark in the neck and has its apex above at the occipital bone — compare ANTERIOR TRIANGLE

posterior ulnar recurrent artery *n* : ULNAR RECURRENT ARTERY b

posterior vein of the left ventricle *n* : a vein that ascends on the surface of the left ventricle facing the diaphragm and that usu. empties into the coronary sinus — called also *posterior vein*

postero- *comb form* : posterior and ⟨*postero*anterior⟩ ⟨*postero*lateral⟩

pos·tero·an·te·ri·or \ˌpäs-tə-rō-an-ˈtir-ē-ər\ *adj* : involving or produced in a direction from the back toward the front (as of the body or an organ)

pos·tero·lat·er·al \ˌpäs-tə-rō-ˈla-tə-rəl\ *adj* : posterior and lateral in position or direction (the ∼ aspect of the leg) — **pos·tero·lat·er·al·ly** *adv*

pos·tero·me·di·al \-ˈmē-dē-əl\ *adj* : located on or near the dorsal midline of the body or a body part

post·ex·po·sure \ˌpōst-ik-ˈspō-zhər\ *adj* : occurring after exposure (as to a virus) ⟨∼ vaccination⟩ — **postexposure** *adv*

post·gan·gli·on·ic \-ˌgaŋ-glē-ˈä-nik\ *adj* : distal to a ganglion; *specif* : of, relating to, or being an axon arising from a cell body within an autonomic ganglion — compare PREGANGLIONIC

post·gas·trec·to·my \-ga-ˈstrek-tə-mē\ *adj* : occurring in, being in, or characteristic of the period following a gastrectomy

postgastrectomy syndrome *n* : dumping syndrome following a gastrectomy

post·hem·or·rhag·ic \-ˌhe-mə-ˈra-jik\ *adj* : occurring after and as the result of a hemorrhage ⟨∼ shock⟩

post·he·pat·ic \-hi-ˈpa-tik\ *adj* : occurring or located behind the liver

post·hep·a·tit·ic \-ˌhe-pə-ˈti-tik\ *adj* : occurring after and esp. as a result of hepatitis ⟨∼ cirrhosis⟩

post·her·pet·ic \-hər-ˈpe-tik\ *adj* : occurring after and esp. as a result of herpes ⟨∼ scars⟩

pos·thi·tis \(ˌ)päs-ˈthī-təs\ *n, pl* **pos·thit·i·des** \-ˈthi-tə-ˌdēz\ : inflammation of the prepuce

post·hyp·not·ic \ˌpōst-hip-ˈnä-tik\ *adj* : of, relating to, or characteristic of the period following a hypnotic trance during which the subject will still carry out suggestions made by the operator during the trance state ⟨∼ suggestion⟩

post·ic·tal \-ˈikt-ᵊl\ *adj* : occurring after a sudden attack (as of epilepsy)

posticus — see TIBIALIS POSTICUS

post·in·farc·tion \-in-ˈfärk-shən\ *adj* 1 : occurring after and esp. as a result of myocardial infarction ⟨∼ ventricu-

lar septal defect⟩ 2 : having suffered myocardial infarction

post·in·fec·tion \-in-ˈfek-shən\ *adj* : relating to, occurring in, or being the period following infection — **postinfection** *adv*

post·ir·ra·di·a·tion \-i-ˌrā-dē-ˈā-shən\ *adj* : occurring after irradiation — **postirradiation** *adv*

post·isch·emic \-is-ˈkē-mik\ *adj* : occurring after and esp. as a result of ischemia ⟨∼ renal failure⟩

post·junc·tion·al \-ˈjəŋk-shə-nəl\ *adj* : of, relating to, occurring on, or located on the muscle fiber side of a neuromuscular junction

post·mas·tec·to·my \-ma-ˈstek-tə-mē\ *adj* 1 : occurring after and esp. as a result of a mastectomy 2 : having undergone mastectomy

post·ma·ture \-mə-ˈchur, -ˈtyūr, -ˈtūr\ *adj* : remaining in the uterus for longer than the normal period of gestation ⟨a ∼ fetus⟩

post·meno·paus·al \ˌpōst-ˌme-nə-ˈpó-zəl\ *adj* 1 : having undergone menopause ⟨∼ women⟩ 2 : occurring after menopause ⟨∼ osteoporosis⟩ — **postmenopausally** *adv*

¹**post·mor·tem** \-ˈmór-təm\ *adj* : done, occurring, or collected after death ⟨∼ tissue specimens⟩

²**postmortem** *n* : AUTOPSY

post—mortem *adv* : after death

postmortem examination *n* : AUTOPSY

post·na·sal \-ˈnā-zəl\ *adj* : lying or occurring posterior to the nose

postnasal drip *n* : flow of mucous secretion from the posterior part of the nasal cavity onto the wall of the pharynx occurring usu. as a chronic accompaniment of an allergic state

post·na·tal \-ˈnāt-ᵊl\ *adj* : occurring or being after birth; *specif* : of or relating to an infant immediately after birth ⟨∼ care⟩ — compare NEONATAL, PRENATAL — **post·na·tal·ly** *adv*

post·ne·crot·ic cirrhosis \-nə-ˈkrä-tik-\ *n* : cirrhosis of the liver following widespread necrosis of liver cells esp. as a result of hepatitis

post·neo·na·tal \-ˌnē-ō-ˈnāt-ᵊl\ *adj* : of, relating to, or affecting the infant usu. from the end of the first month to a year after birth ⟨∼ mortality⟩

post·nor·mal \-ˈnór-məl\ *adj* : having, characterized by, or resulting from a position (as of the mandible) that is distal to the normal position ⟨∼ malocclusion⟩ — compare PRENORMAL — **post·nor·mal·i·ty** \-nór-ˈma-lə-tē\ *n*

post-op \ˈpōst-ˈäp\ *adj* : POSTOPERATIVE — **post-op** *adv*

post·op·er·a·tive \ˌpōst-ˈä-pə-rə-tiv\ *adj* 1 : relating to, occurring in, or being the period following a surgical operation ⟨∼ care⟩ 2 : having undergone a surgical operation ⟨a ∼ patient⟩ — **post·op·er·a·tive·ly** *adv*

post·or·bit·al \-ˈór-bət-ᵊl\ *adj* : situated

or occurring behind the orbit of the eye

post·par·tum \-'pär-təm\ adj 1 : occurring in or being the period following parturition (~ depression) 2 : being in the postpartum period (~ mothers) — **postpartum** adv

post·phle·bit·ic \-flə-'bi-tik\ adj : occurring after and esp. as the result of phlebitis (~ edema)

postphlebitic syndrome n : chronic venous insufficiency with associated pathological manifestations (as pain, edema, stasis dermatitis, varicose veins, and ulceration) following phlebitis of the deep veins of the leg

post·pi·tu·i·tary \-pə-'tü-ə-ter-ē, -'tyü-\ adj : arising in or derived from the posterior lobe of the pituitary gland

post·po·lio \-'pō-lē-ō\ adj : recovered from poliomyelitis; also : affected with post-polio syndrome

post·polio syndrome n : a condition that affects former poliomyelitis patients long after recovery from the disease and that is characterized by muscle weakness, joint and muscle pain, and fatigue

post·pran·di·al \-'pran-dē-əl\ adj : occurring after a meal (~ hypoglycemia) — **post·pran·di·al·ly** adv

post·pu·ber·tal \-'pyü-bərt-ºl\ adj : occurring after puberty

post·pu·bes·cent \-pyü-'bes-ºnt\ adj : occurring or being in the period following puberty : POSTPUBERTAL

post·ra·di·a·tion \-rā-dē-'ā-shən\ adj : occurring after exposure to radiation

postrema — see AREA POSTREMA

post·sple·nec·to·my \-spli-'nek-tə-mē\ adj : occurring after and esp. as a result of a splenectomy (~ sepsis)

post·sur·gi·cal \-'sər-ji-kəl\ adj : POSTOPERATIVE (~ swelling) (~ patient)

post·syn·ap·tic \-pōst-sə-'nap-tik\ adj 1 : occurring after synapsis (a ~ chromosome) 2 : relating to, occurring in, or being part of a nerve cell by which a wave of excitation is conveyed away from a synapse — **post·syn·ap·ti·cal·ly** adv

post·tran·scrip·tion·al \-trans-'krip-shə-nəl\ adj : occurring, acting, or existing after genetic transcription — **post·tran·scrip·tion·al·ly** adv

post·trans·fu·sion \-trans-'fyü-zhən\ adj 1 : caused by transfused blood (~ hepatitis) 2 : occurring after blood transfusion

post·trans·la·tion·al \-trans-'lā-shə-nəl, -shən-ºl\ adj : occurring or existing after genetic translation — **post·trans·la·tion·al·ly** adv

post·trau·mat·ic \pōst-trə-'ma·tik, -trȯ-, -traú-\ adj : occurring after or as a result of trauma (~ epilepsy)

post–traumatic stress disorder n : a psychological reaction that occurs after experiencing a highly stressing event

(as wartime combat, physical violence, or a natural disaster) outside the range of normal human experience and that is usu. characterized by depression, anxiety, flashbacks, recurrent nightmares, and avoidance of reminders of the event — abbr. *PTSD;* called also *delayed-stress disorder, delayed-stress syndrome, posttraumatic stress syndrome;* compare COMBAT FATIGUE

post·treat·ment \-'trēt-mənt\ adj : relating to, typical of, or occurring in the period following treatment (~ examinations) — **posttreatment** adv

pos·tur·al \'päs-chə-rəl\ adj : of, relating to, or involving posture; also : ORTHOSTATIC (~ hypotension)

postural drainage n : drainage of the lungs by placing the patient in an inverted position so that fluids are drawn by gravity toward the trachea

pos·ture \'päs-chər\ n : the position or bearing of the body whether characteristic or assumed for a special purpose (erect ~)

post·vac·ci·nal \-'vak-sən-ºl\ adj : occurring after and esp. as a result of vaccination (~ dermatosis)

post·vac·ci·na·tion \-vak-sə-'nā-shən\ adj : POSTVACCINAL

post·wean·ing \-'wē-niŋ\ adj : relating to, occurring in, or being the period following weaning

pot \'pät\ n : MARIJUANA

po·ta·ble \'pō-tə-bəl\ adj : suitable for drinking (~ water)

po·tas·si·um \pə-'ta-sē-əm\ n : a silverwhite soft low-melting metallic element that occurs abundantly in nature esp. combined in minerals — symbol *K;* see ELEMENT table

potassium alum n : ALUM

potassium aluminum sulfate n : ALUM

potassium an·ti·mo·nyl·tar·trate \-an-tə-mə-nil-'tär-trāt, -nēl-\ n : TARTAR EMETIC

potassium bicarbonate n : a crystalline salt $KHCO_3$ that gives a weakly alkaline reaction in aqueous solution and is sometimes used as an antacid and urinary alkalizer

potassium bromide n : a crystalline salt KBr with a saline taste that is used as a sedative

potassium chlorate n : a crystalline salt $KClO_3$ used esp. in veterinary medicine as a mild astringent

potassium chloride n : a crystalline salt KCl that is used esp. in the treatment of potassium deficiency and occasionally as a diuretic

potassium citrate n : a crystalline salt $K_3C_6H_5O_7$ used chiefly as a systemic and urinary alkalizer and in the treatment of hypokalemia

potassium cyanide n : a very poisonous crystalline salt KCN

potassium hydroxide n : a white solid KOH that dissolves in water to form a strongly alkaline liquid and that is used as a powerful caustic and in the making of pharmaceuticals

potassium iodide *n* : a crystalline salt KI that is very soluble in water and is used in medicine chiefly as an expectorant

potassium nitrate *n* : a crystalline salt KNO_3 that is a strong oxidizing agent and is used in medicine chiefly as a diuretic — called also *saltpeter*

potassium perchlorate *n* : a crystalline salt $KClO_4$ that is sometimes used as a thyroid inhibitor

potassium permanganate *n* : a dark purple salt $KMnO_4$ used as a disinfectant

potassium phosphate *n* : any of various phosphates of potassium; *esp* : a salt K_2HPO_4 used as a saline cathartic

potassium sodium tartrate *n* : ROCHELLE SALT

potassium thiocyanate *n* : a crystalline salt KSCN that has been used as an antihypertensive agent

pot-bel-ly \'pät-₁be-lē\ *n, pl* **-lies** : an enlarged, swollen, or protruding abdomen; *also* : a condition characterized by such an abdomen that is symptomatic of disease or malnourishment

po-ten-cy \'pōt-ⁿn-sē\ *n, pl* **-cies** : the quality or state of being potent : as a : chemical or medicinal strength or efficacy (a drug's ∼) b : the ability to copulate — usu. used of the male c : initial inherent capacity for development of a particular kind (cells with a ∼ for eye formation)

po-tent \'pōt-ⁿnt\ *adj* 1 : having force or power 2 : chemically or medicinally effective (a ∼ vaccine) 3 : able to copulate — usu. used of the male — **po-tent-ly** *adv*

¹**po-ten-tial** \pə-'ten-chəl\ *adj* : existing in possibility : capable of development into actuality — **po-ten-tial-ly** *adv*

²**potential** *n* 1 : something that can develop or become actual 2 a : any of various functions from which the intensity or the velocity at any point in a field may be readily calculated; *specif* : ELECTRICAL POTENTIAL b : POTENTIAL DIFFERENCE

potential difference *n* : the voltage difference between two points that represents the work involved or the energy released in the transfer of a unit quantity of electricity from one point to the other

potential energy *n* : the energy that a piece of matter has because of its position or because of the arrangement of parts

po-ten-ti-ate \pə-'ten-chē-₁āt\ *vb* **-at-ed; -at-ing** : to make effective or active or more effective or more active; *also* : to augment the activity of (as a drug) synergistically — **po-ten-ti-a-tion** \-₁ten-chē-'ā-shən\ *n* — **po-ten-ti-a-tor** \-'ten-chē-₁ā-tər\ *n*

Pott's disease \'päts-\ *n* : tuberculosis of the spine with destruction of bone re-

sulting in curvature of the spine and occas. in paralysis of the lower extremities

Pott, Percivall (1714–1788), British surgeon.

Pott's fracture *n* : a fracture of the lower part of the fibula often accompanied with injury to the tibial articulation so that the foot is dislocated outward

pouch \'pauch\ *n* : an anatomical structure resembling a bag or pocket

pouch of Doug-las \-'də-gləs\ *n* : a deep peritoneal recess between the uterus and the upper vaginal wall anteriorly and the rectum posteriorly — called also *cul-de-sac, cul-de-sac of Douglas, Douglas's cul-de-sac, Douglas's pouch*

Douglas, James (1675–1742), British anatomist.

poul-tice \'pōl-təs\ *n* : a soft usu. heated and sometimes medicated mass spread on cloth and applied to sores or other lesions to supply moist warmth, relieve pain, or act as a counterirritant or antiseptic — called also *cataplasm* — **poultice** *vb*

pound \'paund\ *n, pl* **pounds** *also* **pound** : any of various units of mass and weight: as a : a unit of troy weight equal to 12 troy ounces or 5760 grains or 0.3732417216 kilogram — called also *troy pound* b : a unit of avoirdupois weight equal to 16 avoirdupois ounces or 7000 grains or 0.45359237 kilogram — called also *avoirdupois pound*

Pou-part's ligament \pü-'pärz-\ *n* : INGUINAL LIGAMENT

Poupart, François (1661–1709), French surgeon and naturalist.

po-vi-done \'pō-və-₁dōn\ *n* : POLYVINYLPYRROLIDONE

povidone–iodine *n* : a solution of polyvinylpyrrolidone and iodine used as an antibacterial agent in topical application (as in preoperative prepping or a surgical scrub) — see BETADINE

pow-der \'pau̇-dər\ *n* : a product in the form of discrete usu. fine particles; *specif* : a medicine or medicated preparation in powdered form

power \'pau̇-ər\ *n* : MAGNIFICATION

pox \'päks\ *n, pl* **pox** *or* **pox-es** 1 : a virus disease (as chicken pox) characterized by pustules or eruptions 2 *archaic* : SMALLPOX 3 : SYPHILIS

pox-vi-rus \'päks-₁vi-rəs\ *n* : any of a group of relatively large round, brick-shaped, or ovoid DNA-containing animal viruses (as the causative agent of smallpox) that have a fluffy appearance caused by a covering of tubules and threads

PPA *abbr* phenylpropanolamine

ppb *abbr* parts per billion

PPD *abbr* purified protein derivative

PPLO \₁pē-(₁)pē-(₁)el-'ō\ *n, pl* **PPLO** : MYCOPLASMA

ppm *abbr* parts per million

PPO \ˌpē-ˌ)pē-ˈō\ *n, pl* **PPOs** : an organization providing health care that gives economic incentives to the individual purchaser of a health-care contract to patronize certain physicians, laboratories, and hospitals which agree to supervision and reduced fees — called also *preferred provider organization;* compare HMO

Pr *symbol* praseodymium

practical nurse *n* : a nurse who cares for the sick professionally without having the training or experience required of a registered nurse; *esp* : LICENSED PRACTICAL NURSE

prac·tice *also* **prac·tise** \ˈprak-təs\ *n* **1** : the continuous exercise of a profession **2** : a professional business; *esp* : one constituting an incorporeal property (the doctor sold his ∼ and retired) — **practice** *or* **practise** *vb*

prac·ti·tio·ner \prak-ˈti-shə-nər\ *n* : one who practices a profession and esp. medicine

prac·to·lol \ˈprak-tə-ˌlȯl\ *n* : a beta-blocker $C_{14}H_{22}N_2O_3$ used in the control of arrhythmia

Pra·der–Wil·li syndrome \ˈprä-dər-ˈvil-ē-\ *n* : a genetic disorder characterized by short stature, mental retardation, hypotonia, abnormally small hands and feet, hypogonadism, and uncontrolled appetite leading to extreme obesity

Prader, Andrea (*b* 1919) and Willi, Heinrich (*fl* 1956), Swiss pediatricians.

praecox — see DEMENTIA PRAECOX. EJACULATIO PRAECOX

pral·i·dox·ime \ˌpra-li-ˈdäk-ˌsēm\ *n* : a substance $C_7H_9ClN_2O$ that restores the reactivity of cholinesterase and is used to counteract phosphorylation (as by an organophosphate pesticide) — called also *2-PAM;* see PROTOPAM

pran·di·al \ˈpran-dē-əl\ *adj* : of or relating to a meal

pra·seo·dym·i·um \ˌprä-zē-ō-ˈdi-mē-əm, ˌprä-sē-\ *n* : a yellowish white trivalent metallic element — symbol *Pr;* see ELEMENT table

Praus·nitz–Küst·ner reaction \ˈpraůs-nits-ˈkůst-nər-\ *n* : PASSIVE TRANSFER

Prausnitz, Carl Willy (*b* 1876), German bacteriologist.

Küstner, Heinz (*b* 1897), German gynecologist.

-prax·ia \ˈprak-sē-ə\ *n comb form* : performance of movements (apraxia)

pra·ze·pam \ˈprä-zə-ˌpam\ *n* : a benzodiazepine derivative $C_{19}H_{17}ClN_2O$ used as a tranquilizer

praz·i·quan·tel \ˌpra-zi-ˈkwän-ˌtel\ *n* : an anthelmintic drug $C_{19}H_{24}N_2O_2$ — see BILTRICIDE

pra·zo·sin \ˈprä-zə-ˌsin\ *n* : an antihypertensive peripheral vasodilator $C_{19}H_{21}N_5O_4$ usu. used in the form of its hydrochloride — see MINIPRESS

pre- *prefix* **1 a** : earlier than : prior to : before (prenatal) **b** : in a formative,

incipient, or preliminary stage (precancerous) **2** : in front of (preaxial) (premolar)

pre·ad·mis·sion \ˌprē-əd-ˈmi-shən\ *adj* : occurring in or relating to the period prior to admission (as to a hospital) (∼ physical examination)

pre·ad·o·les·cence \ˌprē-ˌad-ᵊl-ˈes-ᵊns\ *n* : the period of human development just preceding adolescence; *specif* : the period between the approximate ages of 9 and 12 — **pre·ad·o·les·cent** \-ˌad-ᵊl-ˈes-ᵊnt\ *adj or n*

pre·adult \-ə-ˈdəlt, -ˈa-ˌdəlt\ *adj* : occurring or existing prior to adulthood

pre·al·bu·min \-al-ˈbyü-mən, -ˈal-ˌbyü-\ *n* : TRANSTHYRETIN

¹pre·an·es·thet·ic \-ˌa-nəs-ˈthe-tik\ *adj* : used or occurring before administration of an anesthetic (∼ medication)

²preanesthetic *n* : a substance used to induce an initial light state of anesthesia

pre·au·ric·u·lar \-ȯ-ˈri-kyə-lər\ *adj* : situated or occurring anterior to the auricle of the ear (∼ lymph nodes)

pre·ax·i·al \-ˈak-sē-əl\ *adj* : situated in front of an axis of the body

pre·can·cer·ous \-ˈkan-sə-rəs\ *adj* : tending to become cancerous

¹pre·cap·il·lary \-ˈka-pə-ˌler-ē\ *adj* : being on the arterial side of and immediately adjacent to a capillary

²precapillary *n, pl* **-lar·ies** : METARTERIOLE

precapillary sphincter *n* : a sphincter of smooth muscle tissue located at the arterial end of a capillary and serving to control the flow of blood to the tissues

pre·cen·tral \-ˈsen-trəl\ *adj* : situated in front of the central sulcus of the brain

precentral gyrus *n* : the gyrus containing the motor area immediately anterior to the central sulcus

pre·cep·tee \ˌprē-ˌsep-ˈtē\ *n* : one that works for and studies under a preceptor (a ∼ in urology)

pre·cep·tor \pri-ˈsep-tər, ˈprē-ˌ\ *n* : a practicing physician who gives personal instruction, training, and supervision to a medical student or young physician

pre·cep·tor·ship \pri-ˈsep-tər-ˌship, ˈprē-ˌ\ *n* : the state of being a preceptee : a period of training under a preceptor

¹pre·cip·i·tate \pri-ˈsi-pə-ˌtāt\ *vb* **-tat·ed; -tat·ing 1** : to bring about esp. abruptly **2 a** : to separate or cause to separate from solution or suspension **b** : to cause (vapor) to condense and fall or deposit

²pre·cip·i·tate \pri-ˈsi-pə-tət, -ˌtāt\ *n* : a substance separated from a solution or suspension by chemical or physical change usu. as an insoluble amorphous or crystalline solid

precipitated chalk *n* : precipitated calcium carbonate used esp. as an ingre-

dient of toothpastes and tooth powders for its polishing qualities

precipitated sulfur *n* : sulfur obtained
as a pale yellowish or grayish powder
by precipitation and used chiefly in
treating skin diseases

pre·cip·i·ta·tion \pri-₁si-pə-¹tā-shən\ *n* 1
a : the process of forming a precipitate from a solution b : the process of
precipitating or removing solid or liquid particles from a smoke or gas by
electrical means 2 : PRECIPITATE

pre·cip·i·tin \pri-¹si-pə-tən\ *n* : any of
various antibodies which form insoluble precipitates with specific antigens

precipitin test *n* : a serological test using precipitins to detect the presence
of a specific antigen: *specif* : a test
used in criminology for determining
the human or other source of a blood
stain

pre·clin·i·cal \prē-¹kli-ni-kəl\ *adj* 1 : of,
relating to, or concerned with the period preceding clinical manifestations
⟨the ~ stage of a disease of slow on-
set⟩ 2 : of, relating to, or being the period in medical or dental education
preceding the clinical study of medicine or dentistry

pre·co·cious \pri-¹kō-shəs\ *adj* 1 : exceptionally early in development or
occurrence ⟨~ puberty⟩ 2 : exhibiting
mature qualities at an unusually early
age — **pre·co·cious·ly** *adv* — **pre·co-
cious·ness** *n* — **pre·coc·i·ty** \pri-¹kä-sə-
tē\ *n*

pre·cog·ni·tion \₁prē-(₁)käg-²ni-shən\ *n*
: clairvoyance relating to an event or
state not yet experienced — compare
PSYCHOKINESIS, TELEKINESIS — **pre-
cog·ni·tive** \-¹käg-nə-tiv\ *adj*

pre·co·ital \-¹kō-ət-²l, ₁kō-¹ēt-\ *adj* : occurring before coitus

pre·co·ma \-¹kō-mə\ *n* : a stuporous
condition preceding coma ⟨diabetic
~⟩

¹**pre·con·scious** \₁prē-¹kän-chəs\ *adj*
: not present in consciousness but capable of being recalled without en-
countering any inner resistance or
repression — **pre·con·scious·ly** *adv*

²**preconscious** *n* : the preconscious part
of the psyche esp. in psychoanalysis

pre·cor·di·al \-¹kȯr-dē-əl, -¹kȯr-jəl\ *adj* 1
: situated or occurring in front of the
heart 2 : of or relating to the precor-
dium

pre·cor·di·um \-¹kȯr-dē-əm\ *n, pl* **-dia**
\-dē-ə\ : the part of the ventral surface
of the body overlying the heart and
stomach and comprising the epigastrium and the lower median part of
the thorax

pre·cu·ne·us \-¹kyü-nē-əs\ *n, pl* **-nei**
\-nē-₁ī\ : a somewhat rectangular convolution bounding the mesial aspect
of the parietal lobe of the cerebrum
and lying immediately in front of the
cuneus

pre·cur·sor \pri-¹kər-sər, ¹prē-₁\ *n* 1

: one that precedes and indicates the
onset of another ⟨angina may be the
~ of a second infarction⟩ 2 : a substance, cell, or cellular component
from which another substance, cell,
or cellular component is formed esp.
by natural processes

pre·den·tin \₁prē-¹dent-ən\ *or* **pre·den-
tine** \-¹den-₁tēn, -den-¹\ *n* : immature
uncalcified dentin consisting chiefly
of fibrils

pre·di·a·be·tes \₁prē-₁dī-ə-¹bē-tēz, -¹bē-
təs\ *n* : an inapparent abnormal state
that precedes the development of
clinically evident diabetes

¹**pre·di·a·bet·ic** \-¹be-tik\ *n* : a prediabetic individual

²**prediabetic** *adj* : of, relating to, or affected with prediabetes ⟨~ patients⟩

pre·dic·tor \pri-¹dik-tər\ *n* : a preliminary symptom or indication ⟨as of the
development of a disease⟩

pre·di·ges·tion \₁prē-dī-¹jes-chən, -də-\
n : artificial or natural partial digestion of food — **pre·di·gest** \-¹jest\ *vb*

pre·dis·pose \₁prē-di-¹spōz\ *vb* **-posed;
-pos·ing** : to make susceptible — **pre-
dis·po·si·tion** \₁prē-₁dis-pə-¹zi-shən\ *n*

pred·nis·o·lone \pred-¹ni-sə-₁lōn\ *n* : a
glucocorticoid $C_{21}H_{28}O_5$ used often
in the form of an ester or methyl derivative esp. as an anti-inflammatory
drug in the treatment of arthritis —
see METICORTELONE

pred·ni·sone \¹pred-nə-₁sōn, -₁zōn\ *n*
: a glucocorticoid $C_{21}H_{26}O_5$ used as
an anti-inflammatory agent esp. in
the treatment of arthritis, as an antineoplastic agent, and as an immunosuppressant

pre-drug \₁prē-¹drəg\ *adj* : existing or
occurring prior to the administration
of a drug ⟨~ performance level⟩ ⟨~
temperature⟩

pre·eclamp·sia \₁prē-i-¹klamp-sē-ə\ *n* : a
toxic condition developing in late
pregnancy that is characterized by a
sudden rise in blood pressure, excessive gain in weight, generalized edema, albuminuria, severe headache,
and visual disturbances — compare
ECLAMPSIA a, TOXEMIA OF PREGNAN-
CY

¹**pre·eclamp·tic** \-tik\ *adj* : relating to or
affected with preeclampsia ⟨a ~ pa-
tient⟩

²**preeclamptic** *n* : a woman affected with
preeclampsia

pree·mie \¹prē-mē\ *n* : a baby born prematurely

pre·erup·tive \₁prē-i-¹rəp-tiv\ *adj* : occurring or existing prior to an eruption ⟨~ tooth position⟩

pre·ex·po·sure \-ik-¹spō-zhər\ *adj* : of,
relating to, occurring in, or being the
period preceding exposure ⟨as to a
stimulus or a pathogen⟩

preferred provider organization *n* : PPO

pre·fron·tal \₁prē-¹frənt-²l\ *adj* 1 : situated or occurring anterior to a frontal
structure ⟨a ~ bone⟩ 2 : of, relating

to, or constituting the anterior part of the frontal lobe of the brain bounded posteriorly by the ascending frontal convolution

prefrontal lobe n : the anterior part of the frontal lobe made up chiefly of association areas and mediating various inhibitory controls

prefrontal lobotomy n : lobotomy of the white matter in the frontal lobe of the brain — called also *frontal lobotomy*

pre·gan·gli·on·ic \ˌprē-ˌgaŋ-glē-ˈä-nik\ adj : anterior or proximal to a ganglion: *specif* : being, affecting, involving, or relating to a usu. myelinated efferent nerve fiber arising from a cell body in the central nervous system and terminating in an autonomic ganglion — compare POSTGANGLIONIC

pre·gen·i·tal \ˈjen-ət-ᵊl\ adj : of, relating to, or characteristic of the oral, anal, and phallic phases of psychosexual development

preg·nan·cy \ˈpreg-nən-sē\ n, pl -cies 1 : the condition of being pregnant 2 : an instance of being pregnant

pregnancy disease n : a form of ketosis affecting pregnant ewes that is marked by dullness, staggering, and collapse and is esp. frequent in ewes carrying twins or triplets

pregnancy test n : a physiological test to determine the existence of pregnancy in an individual

preg·nane \ˈpreg-ˌnān\ n : a crystalline steroid $C_{21}H_{36}$ that is the parent compound of the corticosteroid and progestational hormones

preg·nane·di·ol \ˌpreg-ˌnān-ˈdī-ˌōl\ n : a crystalline biologically inactive derivative $C_{21}H_{36}O_2$ of pregnane found esp. in the urine of pregnant women

preg·nant \ˈpreg-nənt\ adj : containing unborn young within the body : GRAVID

preg·nen·o·lone \preg-ˈnen-ᵊl-ˌōn\ n : a steroid ketone $C_{21}H_{32}O_2$ that is formed by the oxidation of steroids (as cholesterol) and yields progesterone on dehydrogenation

pre·hos·pi·tal \ˌprē-ˈhäs-(ˌ)pit-ᵊl\ adj : occurring before or during transportation (as of a trauma victim) to a hospital ⟨~ emergency care⟩

pre·im·plan·ta·tion \-ˌim-ˌplan-ˈtā-shən\ adj : of, involving, or being an embryo before uterine implantation

pre·in·cu·ba·tion \ˌprē-ˌiŋ-kyə-ˈbā-shən\ n : incubation (as of a cell or culture) prior to a treatment or process — **pre·in·cu·bate** \-ˈiŋ-kyə-ˌbāt\ vb

pre·in·va·sive \-in-ˈvā-siv\ adj : not yet having become invasive — used of malignant cells or lesions remaining in their original focus

pre·leu·ke·mia \-lü-ˈkē-mē-ə\ n : the stage of leukemia occurring before the disease becomes overt — **pre·leu·ke·mic** \-mik\ adj

pre·load \ˈprē-ˌlōd\ n : the stretched condition of the heart muscle at the end of diastole just before contraction

Pre·lu·din \pri-ˈlüd-ᵊn\ trademark — used for a preparation of phenmetrazine

pre·ma·lig·nant \ˌprē-mə-ˈlig-nənt\ adj : PRECANCEROUS

¹**pre·ma·ture** \ˌprē-mə-ˈchu̇r, -ˈtyu̇r, -ˈtu̇r-\ adj : happening, arriving, existing, or performed before the proper, usual, or intended time; *esp* : born after a gestation period of less than 37 weeks ⟨~ babies⟩ — **pre·ma·ture·ly** adv

²**premature** n : PREEMIE

premature beat n : EXTRASYSTOLE

premature delivery n : expulsion of the human fetus after the 28th week of gestation but before the normal time

premature ejaculation n : ejaculation of semen that occurs prior to or immediately after penetration of the vagina by the penis — called also *ejaculatio praecox*

premature ejaculator n : a man who experiences premature ejaculation

pre·ma·tu·ri·ty \ˌprē-mə-ˈtu̇r-ə-tē, -ˈtyu̇r-, -ˈchu̇r-\ n, pl -ties : the condition of an infant born viable but before its proper time

pre·max·il·la \ˌprē-mak-ˈsi-lə\ n, pl -lae \-lē\ : either member of a pair of bones of the upper jaw situated between and in front of the maxillae that in humans form the median anterior part of the superior maxillary bones

pre·max·il·lary \-ˈmak-sə-ˌler-ē\ adj 1 : situated in front of the maxillary bones 2 : relating to or being the premaxilla

¹**pre·med** \ˈprē-ˌmed\ n : a premedical student or course of study

²**premed** adj : PREMEDICAL

pre·med·i·cal \-ˈme-di-kəl\ adj : preceding and preparing for the professional study of medicine

pre·med·i·ca·tion \ˌme-də-ˈkā-shən\ n : preliminary medication; *esp* : medication to induce a relaxed state preparatory to the administration of an anesthetic — **pre·med·i·cate** \-ˈme-də-ˌkāt\ vb

pre·mei·ot·ic \ˌprē-mī-ˈä-tik\ adj : of, occurring in, or typical of a stage prior to meiosis ⟨~ DNA synthesis⟩

pre·men·ar·chal \ˌprē-me-ˈnär-kəl\ or **pre·men·ar·che·al** \-kē-əl\ adj : of, relating to, or being in the period of life of a female before the first menstrual period occurs

pre·meno·paus·al \-ˌme-nə-ˈpȯ-zəl, -ˌmē-\ adj : of, relating to, or being in the period preceding menopause

pre·men·stru·al \-ˈmen-strə-wəl\ adj : of, relating to, occurring, or being in the period just preceding menstruation ⟨~ women⟩ — **pre·men·stru·al·ly** adv

premenstrual syndrome n : a varying constellation of symptoms manifested by some women prior to menstruation that may include emotional instability, irritability, insomnia, fatigue, anxiety, depression, headache, edema, and abdominal pain — abbr. *PMS*

premenstrual tension *n* : tension occurring as a part of the premenstrual syndrome

pre·men·stru·um \-'men-strə-wəm\ *n, pl* **-stru·ums** *or* **-strua** \-strə-wə\ : the period or physiological state that immediately precedes menstruation

pre·mie \'prē-mē\ *var of* PREEMIE

¹**pre·mo·lar** \,prē-'mō-lər\ *adj* : situated in front of or preceding the molar teeth; *esp* : being or relating to those teeth in front of the true molars and behind the canines

²**premolar** *n* : a premolar tooth that in humans is one of two in each side of each jaw — called also *bicuspid*

pre·mon·i·to·ry \pri-'mä-nə-,tōr-ē\ *adj* : giving warning (a ∼ symptom)

pre·mor·bid \,prē-'mór-bəd\ *adj* : occurring or existing before the occurrence of physical disease or emotional illness (∼ personality)

pre·mor·tem \-'mórt-ᵊm\ *adj* : existing or taking place immediately before death (∼ coronary angiograms)

pre·mo·tor \-'mō-tər\ *adj* : of, relating to, or being the area of the cortex of the frontal lobe lying immediately in front of the motor area of the precentral gyrus

pre·my·cot·ic \,prē-mī-'kä-tik\ *adj* : of, relating to, or being the earliest and nonspecific stage of eczematoid eruptions of mycosis fungoides

pre·na·tal \-'nāt-ᵊl\ *adj* 1 : occurring, existing, or performed before birth (∼ care) (the ∼ period) 2 : providing or receiving prenatal medical care (a ∼ clinic) (a ∼ patient) — compare NEONATAL, POSTNATAL — **pre·na·tal·ly** *adv*

pre·neo·plas·tic \,prē-ə-'plas-tik\ *adj* : existing or occurring prior to the formation of a neoplasm (∼ cells)

pre·nor·mal \-'nór-məl\ *adj* : having, characterized by, or resulting from a position (as of the mandible) that is proximal to the normal position (∼ malocclusion) — compare POSTNORMAL — **pre·nor·mal·i·ty** \-nór-'ma-lə-tē\ *n*

preop \'prē-,äp\ *adj* : PREOPERATIVE

pre·op·er·a·tive \,prē-'ä-pə-rə-tiv, -,rāt-\ *adj* : occurring, performed, or administered before and usu. close to a surgical operation (∼ care) — **pre·op·er·a·tive·ly** *adv*

pre·op·tic \-'äp-tik\ *adj* : situated in front of an optic part or region

preoptic area *n* : a region of the brain that is situated immediately below the anterior commissure, above the optic chiasma, and anterior to the hypothalamus and that regulates certain autonomic activities often with the hypothalamus

preoptic nucleus *n* : any of several groups of nerve cells located in the preoptic area esp. in the lateral and the medial portions

preoptic region *n* : PREOPTIC AREA

pre·ovu·la·to·ry \,prē-'ä-vyə-lə-,tōr-ē, -ō-\ *adj* : occurring or existing in or typical of the period immediately preceding ovulation (∼ oocytes) (a ∼ surge of luteinizing hormone)

¹**prep** \'prep\ *n* : the act or an instance of preparing a patient for a surgical operation

²**prep** *vb* **prepped; prep·ping** : to prepare, for a surgical operation or examination (*prepped* the patient for an appendectomy)

prep·a·ra·tion \,pre-pə-'rā-shən\ *n* : a medicinal substance made ready for use (a ∼ for colds)

prepared chalk *n* : finely ground calcium carbonate that is freed of most of its impurities and used esp. in dentistry for polishing

pre·par·tum \,prē-'pär-təm\ *adj* : ANTEPARTUM

pre·pa·tel·lar bursa \,prē-pə-'te-lər-\ *n* : a synovial bursa situated between the patella and the skin

pre·pa·tent period \-'pāt-ᵊnt-\ *n* : the period between infection with a parasite and the demonstration of the parasite in the body

pre·po·ten·cy \-'pōt-ᵊn-sē\ *n, pl* **-cies** : unusual ability of an individual or strain to transmit its characters to offspring because of homozygosity for numerous dominant genes — **pre·po·tent** \-'pōt-ᵊnt\ *adj*

pre·pran·di·al \-'pran-dē-əl\ *adj* : of, relating to, or suitable for the time just before a meal

pre·preg·nan·cy \-'preg-nən-sē\ *adj* : existing or occurring prior to pregnancy

pre·psy·chot·ic \-sī-'kä-tik\ *adj* : preceding or predisposing to psychosis : possessing recognizable features prognostic of psychosis (∼ behavior)

pre·pu·ber·al \,prē-'pyü-bə-rəl\ *adj* : PREPUBERTAL

pre·pu·ber·tal \-'pyü-bərt-ᵊl\ *adj* : of, relating to, occurring in, or being in the period immediately preceding puberty — **pre·pu·ber·ty** \-bər-tē\ *n*

pre·pu·bes·cent \-,pyü-'bes-ᵊnt\ *adj* : PREPUBERTAL

pre·puce \'prē-,pyüs\ *n* : FORESKIN; *also* : a similar fold investing the clitoris

pre·pu·tial \,prē-'pyü-shəl\ *adj* : of, relating to, or being a prepuce

preputial gland *n* : GLAND OF TYSON

pre·pu·tium clit·or·i·dis \,prē-'pyü-shəm-kli-'tōr-ə-dəs\ *n* : the prepuce which invests the clitoris

pre·py·lo·ric \,prē-pī-'lōr-ik\ *adj* : situated or occurring anterior to the pylorus (∼ ulcers)

pre·re·nal \-'rēn-əl\ *adj* : occurring in the circulatory system before the kidney is reached ⟨∼ disorders⟩

prerenal azotemia *n* : uremia caused by extrarenal factors

pre·rep·li·cat·ive \,prē-'re-pli-,kā-tiv\ *adj* : relating to or being the G₁ phase of the cell cycle

pre·ret·i·nal \-'ret-ᵊn-əl\ *adj* : situated or occurring anterior to the retina

pre·sa·cral \-'sa-krəl, -'sā-\ *adj* : done or effected by way of the anterior aspect of the sacrum ⟨∼ nerve block⟩

presby- *or* **presbyo-** *comb form* : old age ⟨*presby*opia⟩

pres·by·cu·sis \,prez-bi-'kyü-səs, ,pres-\ *n, pl* **-cu·ses** \-,sēz\ : a lessening of hearing acuteness resulting from degenerative changes in the ear that occur esp. in old age

pres·by·ope \'prez-bē-,ōp; 'pres-\ *n* : one affected with presbyopia

pres·by·opia \,prez-bē-'ō-pē-ə, ,pres-\ *n* : a visual condition which becomes apparent esp. in middle age and in which loss of elasticity of the lens of the eye causes defective accommodation and inability to focus sharply for near vision — **pres·by·opic** \-'ō-pik, -'ä-\ *adj*

pre·scribe \pri-'skrīb\ *vb* **pre·scribed; pre·scrib·ing** : to designate the use of as a remedy ⟨∼ a drug⟩

pre·scrip·tion \pri-'skrip-shən\ *n* 1 : a written direction for the preparation, compounding, and administration of a medicine 2 : a prescribed remedy 3 : a written formula for the grinding of corrective lenses for eyeglasses 4 : a written direction for the application of physical therapy measures (as directed exercise or electrotherapy) in cases of injury or disability

prescription drug *n* : a drug that can be obtained only by means of a physician's prescription

pre·se·nile \,prē-'sē-,nīl\ *adj* 1 : of, relating to, occurring in, or being the period immediately preceding the development of senility in an organism or person 2 : prematurely displaying symptoms of senile dementia

presenile dementia *n* : dementia beginning in middle age and progressing rapidly — compare ALZHEIMER'S DISEASE

pre·sent \pri-'zent\ *vb* 1 **a** : to show or manifest ⟨patients who ∼ symptoms of malaria⟩ **b** : to become manifest ⟨Lyme disease often ∼s with erythema chronicum migrans, fatigue, fever, and chills⟩ **c** : to come forward as a patient ⟨he ∼ed with fever and abdominal pain⟩ 2 : to become directed toward the opening of the uterus — used of a fetus or a part of a fetus

pre·sen·ta·tion \,prē-,zen-'tā-shən, ,prez-ᵊn\ *n* 1 : the position in which the fetus lies in the uterus in labor with respect to the mouth of the uterus ⟨face ∼⟩ ⟨breech ∼⟩ 2 : appearance in conscious experience either as a sensory product or as a memory image 3 : a presenting symptom or group of symptoms 4 : a formal oral report of a patient's medical history

presenting *adj* : of, relating to, or being a symptom, condition, or sign which is patent upon initial examination of a patient or which the patient discloses to the physician

pre·ser·va·tive \pri-'zər-və-tiv\ *n* : something that preserves or has the power of preserving; *specif* : an additive used to protect against decay, discoloration, or spoilage ⟨a food ∼⟩

pre·sphe·noid \,prē-'sfē-,noid\ *n* : a bone or cartilage usu. united with the basisphenoid in the adult and in humans forming the anterior part of the body of the sphenoid — **presphenoid** *also* **pre·sphe·noi·dal** \-,sfi-'noid-ᵊl\ *adj*

pres·sor \'pre-,sor, -sər\ *adj* : raising or tending to raise blood pressure ⟨∼ substances⟩; *also* : involving or producing an effect of vasoconstriction

pres·so·re·cep·tor \,pre-sō-ri-'sep-tər\ *n* : a proprioceptor that responds to alteration of blood pressure

pres·sure \'pre-shər\ *n* 1 : the application of force to something by something else in direct contact with it : COMPRESSION 2 : ATMOSPHERIC PRESSURE 3 : a touch sensation aroused by moderate compression of the skin

pressure bandage *n* : a thick pad of gauze or other material placed over a wound and attached firmly so that it will exert pressure

pressure dressing *n* : PRESSURE BANDAGE

pressure point *n* 1 : a region of the body in which the distribution of soft and skeletal parts is such that a static position (as of a part in a cast or of a bedridden person) tends to cause circulatory deficiency and necrosis due to local compression of blood vessels — compare BEDSORE 2 : a point where a blood vessel runs near a bone and can be compressed (as to check bleeding) by the application of pressure against the bone

pressure sore *n* : BEDSORE

pressure suit *n* : an inflatable suit for high-altitude or space flight to protect the body from low pressure

pre·sump·tive \pri-'zəmp-tiv\ *adj* 1 : expected to develop in a particular direction under normal conditions 2 : being the embryonic precursor of ⟨∼ neural tissue⟩

pre·sur·gi·cal \,prē-'sər-ji-kəl\ *adj* : occurring before, performed before, or preliminary to surgery ⟨∼ care⟩

pre·symp·to·mat·ic \-,simp-tə-'ma-tik\ *adj* : relating to, being, or occurring before symptoms appear ⟨∼ diagnosis of a hereditary disease⟩

pre·syn·ap·tic \-sə-'nap-tik\ *adj* : relating to, occurring in, or being part of a nerve cell by which a wave of excitation is conveyed to a synapse (~ terminals) (~ inhibition) (a ~ membrane) — **pre-syn-ap-ti-cal-ly** adv

pre-sys-tol-ic \-sis-ˈtä-lik\ adj : of, relating to, or occurring just before cardiac systole (a ~ murmur)

pre-tec-tal \-ˈtekt-əl\ adj : occurring in or being the transitional zone of the brain stem between the midbrain and the diencephalon that is associated esp. with the analysis and distribution of light impulses

pre-term \-ˈtərm\ adj : of, relating to, being, or born by premature birth (~ infants) (~ labor)

pre-ter-mi-nal \-ˈtər-mə-nəl\ adj 1 : occurring or being in the period prior to death (~ cancer) (a ~ patient) 2 : situated or occurring anterior to an end (as of a nerve)

pre-tib-i-al \-ˈti-bē-əl\ adj : lying or occurring anterior to the tibia

pretibial fever n : a rare infectious disease that is characterized by an eruption in the pretibial region, headache, backache, malaise, chills, and fever and that is caused by a spirochete of the genus *Leptospira* (*L. interrogans autumnalis*)

pretibial myxedema n : myxedema characterized primarily by a mucoid edema in the pretibial area

pre-treat-ment \ˌprē-ˈtrēt-mənt\ n : preliminary or preparatory treatment — **pre-treat** \-ˈtrēt\ vb — **pretreatment** adj

prev-a-lence \ˈpre-və-ləns\ n : the percentage of a population that is affected with a particular disease at a given time — compare INCIDENCE

pre-ven-ta-tive \pri-ˈven-tə-tiv\ adj or n : PREVENTIVE (a ~ drug)

¹**pre-ven-tive** \pri-ˈven-tiv\ n : something (as a drug) used to prevent disease

²**preventive** adj : devoted to or concerned with the prevention of disease

preventive medicine n : a branch of medical science dealing with methods (as vaccination) of preventing the occurrence of disease

pre-ver-te-bral \ˌprē-ˈvər-tə-brəl, -(ˌ)vər-ˈtē-brəl\ adj : situated or occurring anterior to a vertebra or the spinal column (~ muscles)

pre-ves-i-cal space \ˌprē-ˈve-si-kəl-\ n : RETROPUBIC SPACE

previa — see PLACENTA PREVIA

pre-vi-a-ble \-ˈvī-ə-bəl\ adj : not sufficiently developed to survive outside the uterus (a ~ fetus)

pre-vil-lous \-ˈvi-ləs\ adj : relating to, being in, or being the stage of embryonic development before the formation of villi (a ~ human embryo)

pri-a-pism \ˈprī-ə-ˌpi-zəm\ n : an abnormal, more or less persistent, and often painful erection of the penis; esp : one caused by disease rather than sexual desire

Price–Jones curve \ˈprīs-ˈjōnz-\ n : a graph of the frequency distribution of

the diameters of red blood cells in a sample that has been smeared, stained, and magnified for direct observation and counting

Price–Jones, Cecil (1863–1943), British hematologist.

prick-le cell \ˈpri-kəl-\ n : a cell of the stratum spinosum of the skin having numerous intercellular bridges which give the separated cells a prickly appearance in microscopic preparations

prickle cell layer n : STRATUM SPINOSUM

prick-ly heat \ˈpri-klē-\ n : a noncontagious cutaneous eruption of red pimples with intense itching and tingling caused by inflammation around the sweat ducts — called also *heat rash*; see MILIARIA

pril-o-caine \ˈpri-lə-ˌkān\ n : a local anesthetic $C_{13}H_{20}N_2O$ related to lidocaine and used in the form of its hydrochloride as a nerve block for pain esp. in surgery and dentistry

pri-mal scream therapy \ˈprī-məl-\ n : psychotherapy in which the patient recalls and reenacts a particularly disturbing past experience usu. occurring early in life and expresses normally repressed anger or frustration esp. through spontaneous and unrestrained screams, hysteria, or violence — called also *primal scream, primal therapy*

pri-ma-quine \ˈprī-mə-ˌkwēn, ˈprī-, -kwin\ n : an antimalarial drug $C_{15}H_{21}N_3O$ used in the form of its diphosphate

pri-ma-ry \ˈprī-ˌmer-ē, ˈprī-mə-rē\ adj 1 a (1) : first in order of time or development (2) : relating to or being the deciduous teeth and esp. the 20 deciduous teeth in the human set b : arising spontaneously : IDIOPATHIC (~ tumors) 2 : belonging to the first group or order in successive divisions, combinations, or ramifications (~ nerves) 3 : of, relating to, or being the amino acid sequence in proteins — compare SECONDARY 3, TERTIARY 2

primary aldosteronism n : aldosteronism caused by an adrenal tumor — called also *Conn's syndrome*

primary atypical pneumonia n : any of a group of pneumonias (such as Q fever and psittacosis) caused esp. by a virus, mycoplasma, rickettsia, or chlamydia

primary care n : health care provided by a medical professional (as a general practitioner or a pediatrician) with whom a patient has initial contact and by whom the patient may be referred to a specialist for further treatment — called also *primary health care*

primary fissure n : a fissure of the cerebellum that is situated between the culmen and decline and that marks the boundary between the anterior lobe and the posterior lobe

primary health care n : PRIMARY CARE

primary host n : DEFINITIVE HOST
primary hypertension n : ESSENTIAL HYPERTENSION
primary oocyte n : a diploid oocyte that has not yet undergone meiosis
primary spermatocyte n : a diploid spermatocyte that has not yet undergone meiosis
primary syphilis n : the first stage of syphilis that is marked by the development of a chancre and the spread of the causative spirochete in the tissues of the body
primary tooth n : MILK TOOTH
pri·mate \'prī-ˌmāt\ n : any of an order (Primates) of mammals including humans, apes, monkeys, lemurs, and living and extinct related forms
prime mover \'prīm-\ n : AGONIST 1
prim·er \'prī-mər\ n : a molecule (as a short strand of RNA or DNA) whose presence is required for formation of another molecule (as a longer chain of DNA)
pri·mi·done \'prī-mə-ˌdōn\ n : an anticonvulsant phenobarbital derivative $C_{12}H_{14}N_2O_2$ used esp. to control epileptic seizures
pri·mi·grav·id \ˌprī-mə-'gra-vid\ adj : pregnant for the first time
pri·mi·grav·i·da \-'gra-vi-də\ n, pl -i·das or -i·dae \-ˌdē\ : an individual pregnant for the first time
pri·mip·a·ra \prī-'mi-pə-rə\ n, pl -ras or -rae \-ˌrē\ 1 : an individual bearing a first offspring 2 : an individual that has borne only one offspring
pri·mip·a·rous \-rəs\ adj : of, relating to, or being a primipara : bearing young for the first time — compare MULTIPAROUS 2
prim·i·tive \'pri-mə-tiv\ adj 1 : closely approximating an early ancestral type : little evolved 2 : belonging to or characteristic of an early stage of development (~ cells)
primitive streak n : an elongated band of cells that forms along the axis of an embryo early in gastrulation by the movement of lateral cells toward the axis and that develops a groove along its midline through which cells move to the interior of the embryo to form the mesoderm
pri·mor·di·al \prī-'mȯr-dē-əl\ adj : earliest formed in the growth of an individual or organ : PRIMITIVE
pri·mor·di·um \-dē-əm\ n, pl -dia \-dē-ə\ : the rudiment or commencement of a part or organ : ANLAGE
prin·ceps pol·li·cis \'prin-ˌseps-'pä-lə-səs\ n : a branch of the radial artery that passes along the ulnar side of the first metacarpal and divides into branches running along the palmar side of the thumb
prin·ci·ple \'prin-sə-pəl\ n : an ingredient (as a chemical) that exhibits or imparts a characteristic quality (the active ~ of a drug)
Prin·i·vil \'pri-nə-ˌvil\ trademark —

used for a preparation of lisinopril
P–R interval \ˌpē-'är-\ n : the interval between the beginning of the P wave and the beginning of the QRS complex of an electrocardiogram that represents the time between the beginning of the contraction of the atria and the beginning of the contraction of the ventricles
pri·on \'prē-ˌän\ n : a protein particle that lacks nucleic acid and is sometimes held to be the cause of various infectious diseases of the nervous system (as scrapie and Creutzfeldt= Jakob disease)
pri·vate \'prī-vət\ adj 1 : of, relating to, or receiving hospital service in which the patient has more privileges than a semiprivate or ward patient 2 : of, relating to, or being private practice (a ~ practitioner)
private–duty adj : caring for a single patient either in the home or in a hospital (~ nurse)
private practice n 1 : practice of a profession (as medicine) independently and not as an employee 2 : the patients depending on and using the services of a physician in private practice
privileged communication n : a communication between parties in a confidential relation (as between physician and patient) such that the recipient cannot be legally compelled to disclose it as a witness
prn abbr [Latin pro re nata] as needed: as the circumstances require — used in writing prescriptions
pro- prefix 1 a : rudimentary : PROT- (pronucleus) b : being a precursor of (proinsulin) 2 : front : anterior (pronephros) 3 : projecting (prognathous)
pro-abor·tion \ˌprō-ə-'bȯr-shən\ adj : favoring the legalization of abortion — **pro·abor·tion·ist** \-shə-nist\ n
pro·ac·cel·er·in \ˌprō-ak-'se-lə-rən\ n : FACTOR V
pro·ac·tive \-'ak-tiv\ adj : relating to, caused by, or being interference between previous learning and the recall or performance of later learning (~ inhibition of memory)
pro·band \'prō-ˌband\ n : an individual actually being studied (as in a genetic investigation) : SUBJECT 1 — called also propositus
Pro–Ban·thine \ˌprō-'ban-ˌthēn\ trademark — used for a preparation of propantheline bromide
probe \'prōb\ n 1 : a surgical instrument that consists typically of a light slender fairly flexible pointed metal instrument like a small rod that is used typically for locating a foreign body, for exploring a wound or suppurative tract by prodding or piercing, or for penetrating and exploring bodily passages and cavities 2 : a device (as an ultrasound generator) or a substance (as DNA used in genetic

research) used to obtain specific information for diagnostic or experimental purposes — **probe** *vb*

pro·ben·e·cid \prō-'be-nə-səd\ *n* : a drug $C_{13}H_{19}NO_4S$ that acts on renal tubular function and is used to increase the concentration of some drugs (as penicillin) in the blood by inhibiting their excretion and to increase the excretion of urates in gout

pro·bos·cis \prə-'bä-səs, -'bäs-kəs\ *n*, *pl* -bos·cis·es *also* -bos·ci·des \-'bä-sə-ıdēz\ : any of various elongated or extensible tubular processes esp. of the oral region of an invertebrate

pro·cain·amide \prō-'kā-nə-ımīd, -məd; -kā-'na-məd\ *n* : a base $C_{13}H_{21}ON_3$ of an amide related to procaine that is used in the form of its crystalline hydrochloride as a cardiac depressant in the treatment of ventricular and atrial arrhythmias — see PRONESTYL

pro·caine \'prō-ıkān\ *n* : a basic ester $C_{13}H_{20}N_2O_2$ of para-aminobenzoic acid or its crystalline hydrochloride used as a local anesthetic — called also *novocaine*; see NOVOCAIN

procaine penicillin G *n* : a mixture of procaine and penicillin G that provides a low but persistent serum level of penicillin G following intramuscular injection

pro·car·ba·zine \prō-'kär-bə-ızēn, -zən\ *n* : an antineoplastic drug $C_{12}H_{19}N_3O$ that is a monoamine oxidase inhibitor and is used in the form of its hydrochloride esp. in the palliative treatment of Hodgkin's disease

Pro·car·dia \prō-'kär-dē-ə\ *trademark* — used for a preparation of nifedipine

pro·car·y·ote *var of* PROKARYOTE

pro·ce·dure \prə-'sē-jər\ *n* 1 a : a particular way of accomplishing something or of acting b : a step in a procedure 2 : a series of steps followed in a regular definite order

pro·ce·rus \prō-'sir-əs\ *n*, *pl* -ri \-ırī\ *or* -rus·es : a facial muscle that arises from the nasal bone and a cartilage in the side of the nose and that inserts into the skin of the forehead between the eyebrows

pro·cess \'prä-ıses, 'prō-, -səs\ *n* 1 a : a natural progressively continuing operation or development marked by a series of gradual changes that succeed one another in a relatively fixed way and lead toward a particular result or end (the ~ of growth) b : a natural continuing activity or function (such life ~es as breathing) 2 : a part of the mass of an organism or organic structure that projects outward from the main mass (a bone ~)

pro·ces·sus \prō-'se-səs\ *n*, *pl* processus : PROCESS 2

processus vag·i·na·lis \-ıva-jə-'nā-ləs\ *n* : a pouch of peritoneum that is carried into the scrotum by the descent of the testicle and which in the scrotum forms the tunica vaginalis

pro·chlor·per·azine \ıprō-ıklör-'per-ə-ızēn\ *n* : a tranquilizing and antiemetic drug $C_{20}H_{24}ClN_3S$ — see COMPAZINE

pro-choice \prō-'chóis\ *adj* : favoring the legalization of abortion — **pro-choic·er** \-'chói-sər\ *n*

pro·ci·den·tia \ıprō-sə-'den-chə, ıprä-, -chē-ə\ *n* : PROLAPSE; *esp* : severe prolapse of the uterus in which the cervix projects from the vaginal opening

proc·li·na·tion \ıprä-klə-'nā-shən\ *n* : the condition of being inclined forward (~ of the upper incisors)

¹**pro·co·ag·u·lant** \ıprō-kō-'a-gyə-lənt\ *n* : a procoagulant substance

²**procoagulant** *adj* : promoting the coagulation of blood (~ activity)

pro·col·la·gen \-'kä-lə-jən\ *n* : a molecular precursor of collagen

pro·con·ver·tin \-kən-'vərt-³n\ *n* : FACTOR VII

pro·cre·ate \'prō-krē-ıāt\ *vb* -at·ed; -at·ing : to beget or bring forth offspring : PROPAGATE, REPRODUCE — **pro·cre·ation** \ıprō-krē-'ā-shən\ *n* — **pro·cre·ative** \'prō-krē-ıā-tiv\ *adj*

proct- *or* **procto-** *comb form* 1 a : rectum (*proctoscope*) b : rectum and (*proctosigmoidectomy*) 2 : anus and rectum (*proctology*)

proct·al·gia fu·gax \ıpräk-'tal-jə-'fyü-ıgaks, -jē-ə-\ *n* : a condition characterized by the intermittent occurrence of sudden sharp pain in the rectal area

proc·tec·to·my \präk-'tek-tə-mē\ *n*, *pl* -mies : surgical excision of the rectum

proc·ti·tis \präk-'tī-təs\ *n* : inflammation of the anus and rectum

proc·toc·ly·sis \präk-'tä-klə-səs\ *n*, *pl* -ly·ses \-ısēz\ : slow injection of large quantities of a fluid (as a solution of salt) into the rectum in supplementing the liquid intake of the body

proc·to·co·li·tis \ıpräk-tō-kə-'lī-təs\ *n* : inflammation of the rectum and colon

proc·tol·o·gy \präk-'tä-lə-jē\ *n*, *pl* -gies : a branch of medicine dealing with the structure and diseases of the anus, rectum, and sigmoid flexure — **proc·to·log·ic** \ıpräk-tə-'lä-jik\ *or* **proc·to·log·i·cal** \-ji-kəl\ *adj* — **proc·tol·o·gist** \-jist\ *n*

proc·to·pexy \'präk-tə-ıpek-sē\ *n*, *pl* -pex·ies : the suturing of the rectum to an adjacent structure (as the sacrum)

proc·to·plas·ty \'präk-tə-ıplas-tē\ *n*, *pl* -ties : plastic surgery of the rectum and anus

proc·to·scope \'präk-tə-ıskōp\ *n* : an instrument used for dilating and visually inspecting the rectum — **proc·to·scop·ic** \ıpräk-tə-'skä-pik\ *adj* — **proc·to·scop·i·cal·ly** *adv* — **proc·tos·co·py** \präk-'täs-kə-pē\ *n*

proc·to·sig·moid·ec·to·my \ıpräk-tō-

.sig·moi-'dek-tə-mē\ *n, pl* -mies
: complete or partial surgical excision
of the rectum and sigmoid colon

proc·to·sig·moid·itis \-₁sig-₁moi-'dī-təs\
n : inflammation of the rectum and
sigmoid flexure

proc·to·sig·moid·o·scope \-sig-'moi-də-
₁skōp\ *n* : SIGMOIDOSCOPE

proc·to·sig·moid·os·co·py \-₁sig-₁moi-
'däs-kə-pē\ *n, pl* -pies : SIGMOIDOSCO-
PY — **proc·to·sig·moid·o·scop·ic** \-₁moi-
də-'skä-pik\ *adj*

proc·tot·o·my \präk-'tä-tə-mē\ *n, pl*
-mies : surgical incision into the rectum

prod·ro·ma \'prä-drə-mə\ *n, pl* -mas *or*
-ma·ta \'prä-'drō-mə-tə\ : PRODROME

pro·drome \'prō-₁drōm\ *n* : a premon-
itory symptom of disease — **pro·dro-
mal** \₁prō-'drō-məl\ *also* **pro·dro·mic**
\-mik\ *adj*

pro·duc·tive \prə-'dək-tiv, prō-\ *adj*
: raising mucus or sputum (as from
the bronchi) — used of a cough

pro·en·zyme \prō-'en-₁zīm\ *n* : ZYMO-
GEN

pro·eryth·ro·blast \-i-'ri-thrə-₁blast\ *n*
: a hemocytoblast that gives rise to
erythroblasts

pro·es·trus \-'es-trəs\ *n* : a preparatory
period immediately preceding estrus
and characterized by growth of
graafian follicles, increased estrogenic activity, and alteration of uterine
and vaginal mucosa

professional corporation *n* : a corporation organized by one or more licensed individuals (as a doctor or
dentist) esp. for the purpose of providing professional services and obtaining tax advantages — abbr. *PC*

pro·fi·bri·no·ly·sin \₁prō-₁fī-brə-nə-'lis-
ᵊn\ *n* : PLASMINOGEN

pro·file \'prō-₁fil\ *n* 1 : a set of data exhibiting the significant features of
something and often obtained by multiple tests 2 : a graphic representation
of the extent to which an individual or
group exhibits traits as determined by
tests or ratings (a personality ~)

pro·fla·vine \prō-'flā-₁vēn\ *also* **pro-
fla·vin** \-vin\ *n* : a yellow crystalline
mutagenic acridine dye $C_{13}H_{11}N_3$;
also : the orange to brownish red hygroscopic crystalline sulfate used as
an antiseptic esp. for wounds — see
ACRIFLAVINE

pro·found·ly \prə-'faund-lē, prō-\ *adv* 1
: totally or completely (~ deaf persons) 2 : to the greatest possible degree (~ retarded persons)

pro·fun·da artery \prə-'fən-də-\ *n* 1
: DEEP BRACHIAL ARTERY 2 : DEEP
FEMORAL ARTERY

profunda fem·o·ris \-'fe-mə-rəs\ *n*
: DEEP FEMORAL ARTERY

profunda femoris artery *n* : DEEP FEM-
ORAL ARTERY

profundus — see FLEXOR DIGITORUM
PROFUNDUS

pro·gen·i·tor \prō-'je-nə-tər, prə-\ *n* 1

: an ancestor of an individual in a direct line of descent along which some
or all of the ancestral genes could theoretically have passed 2 : a biologically ancestral form

prog·e·ny \'prä-jə-nē\ *n, pl* -nies : offspring of animals or plants

pro·ge·ria \prō-'jir-ē-ə\ *n* : a rare endocrine disorder of childhood characterized by retarded physical growth
simultaneous with premature accelerated senility

pro·ges·ta·gen *var of* PROGESTOGEN

pro·ges·ta·tion·al \₁prō-₁jes-'tā-shə-nəl\
adj : preceding pregnancy or gestation; *esp* : of, relating to, inducing, or
constituting the modifications of the
female mammalian system associated
with ovulation and corpus luteum formation (~ hormones)

pro·ges·ter·one \prō-'jes-tə-₁rōn\ *n* : a
female steroid sex hormone C_{21}-
$H_{30}O_2$ that is secreted by the corpus
luteum to prepare the endometrium
for implantation and later by the placenta during pregnancy to prevent rejection of the developing embryo or
fetus

pro·ges·tin \prō-'jes-tən\ *n* : PROGES-
TERONE; *broadly* : PROGESTOGEN

pro·ges·to·gen \-'jes-tə-jən\ *n* : any of
several progestational steroids (as
progesterone) — **pro·ges·to·gen·ic**
\prə-₁jes-tə-'je-nik\ *adj*

pro·glot·tid \prō-'glä-tid\ *n* : a segment
of a tapeworm containing both male
and female reproductive organs

pro·glot·tis \-'glä-tis\ *n, pl* -glot·ti·des
\-'glä-tə-₁dēz\ : PROGLOTTID

prog·na·thic \präg-'na-thik, -'nā-\ *adj*
: PROGNATHOUS

prog·na·thous \'präg-nə-thəs\ *adj* : having the jaws projecting beyond the upper part of the face — **prog·na·thism**
\'präg-nə-₁thi-zəm. präg-'nā-\ *n*

prog·no·sis \präg-'nō-səs\ *n, pl* -no-
ses \-₁sēz\ 1 : the act or art of foretell-
ing the course of a disease 2 : the
prospect of survival and recovery
from a disease as anticipated from the
usual course of that disease or indicated by special features of the case
— **prog·nos·tic** \präg-'näs-tik\ *adj*

prog·nos·ti·cate \präg-'näs-tə-₁kāt\ *vb*
-cat·ed; -cat·ing : to make a prognosis
about the probable outcome of —
prog·nos·ti·ca·tion \-₁näs-tə-'kā-shən\
n

pro·gres·sive \prə-'gre-siv\ *adj* : increasing in extent or severity (a ~
disease) — **pro·gres·sive·ly** *adv*

**progressive multifocal leukoencepha-
lopathy** *n* : a rare progressive and fatal demyelinating disease of the
central nervous system that occurs in
immunosuppressed individuals prob.
due to loss of childhood immunity to
a papovavirus ubiquitous in human
populations and that is characterized
by hemianopia, hemiplegia, alter-

ations in mental state, and eventually coma

pro·guan·il \prō-ˈgwän-əl\ n : CHLOROGUANIDE

pro·hor·mone \prō-ˈhȯr-ˌmōn\ n : a physiologically inactive precursor of a hormone

pro·in·su·lin \-ˈin-sə-lən\ n : a single-chain pancreatic polypeptide precursor of insulin that gives rise to the double chain of insulin by loss of the middle part of the molecule

pro·ject \prə-ˈjekt\ vb 1 : to attribute or assign (something in one's own mind or a personal characteristic) to a person, group, or object 2 : to connect by sending nerve fibers or processes

pro·jec·tile vomiting \prə-ˈjek-təl-, -ˌtīl-\ n : vomiting that is sudden, usu. without nausea, and so sufficiently vigorous that the vomitus is forcefully projected to a distance

pro·jec·tion \prə-ˈjek-shən\ n 1 a : the act of referring a mental image constructed by the brain from bits of data collected by the sense organs to the actual source of stimulation outside the body b : the attribution of one's own ideas, feelings, or attitudes to other people or to objects; esp : the externalization of blame, guilt, or responsibility as a defense against anxiety 2 : the functional correspondence and connection of parts of the cerebral cortex with parts of the organism (the ~ of the retina upon the visual area)

projection area n : an area of the cerebral cortex having connection through projection fibers with subcortical centers that in turn are linked with peripheral sense or motor organs

projection fiber n : a nerve fiber connecting some part of the cerebral cortex with lower sensory or motor centers — compare ASSOCIATION FIBER

pro·jec·tive \prə-ˈjek-tiv\ adj : of, relating to, or being a technique, device, or test (as the Rorschach test) designed to analyze the psychodynamic constitution of an individual by presenting unstructured or ambiguous material (as blots of ink, pictures, and sentence elements) that will elicit interpretive responses revealing personality structure

pro·kary·ote \prō-ˈkar-ē-ˌōt\ n : a cellular organism (as a bacterium) that does not have a distinct nucleus — compare EUKARYOTE — **pro·kary·ot·ic** \-ˌkar-ē-ˈä-tik\ adj

pro·lac·tin \prō-ˈlak-tən\ n : a protein hormone of the anterior lobe of the pituitary gland that induces and maintains lactation in the postpartum mammalian female — called also luteotropic hormone, luteotropin, mammotropin

pro·la·min or **pro·la·mine** \ˈprō-lə-mən, -ˌmēn\ n : any of various simple proteins found esp. in seeds and insoluble in absolute alcohol or water

pro·lapse \prō-ˈlaps, ˈprō-ˌ\ n : the falling down or slipping of a body part from its usual position or relations (~ of the uterus) — **pro·lapse** \prō-ˈlaps\ vb

pro·life \prō-ˈlīf\ adj : ANTIABORTION

pro·lifer \-ˈlī-fər\ n : a person who opposes the legalization of abortion

pro·lif·er·a·tion \prə-ˌli-fə-ˈrā-shən\ n 1 a : rapid and repeated production of new parts or of offspring (as in a mass of cells by a rapid succession of cell divisions) b : a growth so formed 2 : the action, process, or result of increasing by proliferation — **pro·lif·er·ate** \-ˈli-fə-ˌrāt\ vb — **pro·lif·er·a·tive** \-ˈli-fə-ˌrā-tiv\ adj

proligerus — see DISCUS PROLIGERUS

pro·line \ˈprō-ˌlēn\ n : an amino acid $C_5H_9NO_2$ that can be synthesized by animals from glutamate

Pro·lix·in \prō-ˈlik-sən\ trademark — used for a preparation of fluphenazine

pro·mas·ti·gote \prō-ˈmas-ti-ˌgōt\ n : a flagellated usu. extracellular stage of some protozoans (family Trypanosomatidae and esp. genus Leishmania) characterized by a single anterior flagellum and no undulating membrane; also : a protozoan in this stage

pro·ma·zine \ˈprō-mə-ˌzēn\ n : a tranquilizer $C_{17}H_{20}N_2S$ derived from phenothiazine and administered in the form of its hydrochloride similarly to chlorpromazine — see SPARINE

pro·mega·kary·o·cyte \ˌprō-ˌme-gə-ˈkar-ē-ō-ˌsīt\ n : a cell in an intermediate stage of development between a megakaryoblast and a megakaryocyte

pro·meth·a·zine \prō-ˈme-thə-ˌzēn\ n : a crystalline antihistamine drug $C_{17}H_{20}N_2S$ derived from phenothiazine and used chiefly in the form of its hydrochloride — see PHENERGAN

pro·meth·es·trol \-me-ˈthes-ˌtrȯl\ n : a synthetic estrogen $C_{20}H_{26}O_2$ — see MEPRANE

pro·me·thi·um \prə-ˈmē-thē-əm\ n : a metallic element obtained as a fission product of uranium or from neutron-irradiated neodymium — symbol Pm; called also illinium; see ELEMENT table

prom·i·nence \ˈprä-mə-nəns\ n : an elevation or projection on an anatomical structure (as a bone)

prominens — see VERTEBRA PROMINENS

pro·mis·cu·ous \prə-ˈmis-kyə-wəs\ adj : not restricted to one sexual partner — **pro·mis·cu·ity** \ˌprä-məs-ˈkyü-ə-tē, prə-ˈmis-\ n

pro·mono·cyte \prə-ˈmä-nə-ˌsīt\ n : a cell in an intermediate stage of development between a monoblast and a monocyte

prom·on·to·ry \ˈprä-mən-ˌtȯr-ē\ n, pl

-ries : a bodily prominence: as **a** : the angle of the ventral side of the sacrum where it joins the vertebra **b** : a prominence on the inner wall of the tympanum of the ear

pro·mot·er \prə-'mō-tər\ n 1 : a substance that in very small amounts is able to increase the activity of a catalyst 2 : a binding site in a DNA chain at which RNA polymerase binds to initiate transcription of messenger RNA by one or more nearby structural genes 3 : a chemical believed to promote carcinogenicity or mutagenicity

pro·my·elo·cyte \prō-'mī-ə-lə-ˌsīt\ n : a partially differentiated granulocyte in bone marrow having the characteristic granulations but lacking the specific staining reactions of a mature granulocyte of the blood — pro·my·elo·cyt·ic \-ˌmī-ə-lə-'si-tik\ adj

promyelocytic leukemia n : a leukemia in which the predominant blood cell type is the promyelocyte

pro·na·tion \prō-'nā-shən\ n : rotation of an anatomical part towards the midline: as **a** : rotation of the hand and forearm so that the palm faces backwards or downwards **b** : rotation of the medial bones in the midtarsal region of the foot inward and downward so that in walking the foot tends to come down on its inner margin — pro·nate \'prō-ˌnāt\ vb

pro·na·tor \'prō-ˌnā-tər\ n : a muscle that produces pronation

pronator qua·dra·tus \-kwä-'drā-təs\ n : a deep muscle of the forearm passing transversely from the ulna to the radius and serving to pronate the forearm

pronator te·res \-'tir-ˌēz\ n : a muscle of the forearm arising from the medial epicondyle of the humerus and the coronoid process of the ulna, inserting into the lateral surface of the middle third of the radius, and serving to pronate and flex the forearm

prone \'prōn\ adj : having the front or ventral surface downward; esp : lying facedown — prone adv

pro·neph·ros \prō-'ne-frəs, -ˌfräs\ n, pl -neph·roi \-'ne-ˌfroi\ : either member of the first and most anterior pair of the three paired vertebrate renal organs present but nonfunctional in embryos of reptiles, birds, and mammals — compare MESONEPHROS, METANEPHROS — pro·neph·ric \prō-'ne-frik\ adj

Pro·nes·tyl \prō-'nes-til\ trademark — used for a preparation of the hydrochloride of procainamide

pro·neth·a·lol \prō-'ne-thə-ˌlȯl, -ˌlōl\ n : a drug $C_{15}H_{19}NO$ that is a beta-adrenergic blocking agent — called also nethalide

pron·to·sil \'prän-tə-ˌsil\ n : any of three sulfonamide drugs: **a** : a red azo dye $C_{12}H_{13}N_5O_2S$ that was the first

sulfa drug tested clinically — called also prontosil rubrum **b** : SULFANILAMIDE **c** : AZOSULFAMIDE

pro·nu·cle·us \prō-'nü-klē-əs, -'nyü-\ n, pl -clei \-klē-ˌī\ also -cle·us·es : the haploid nucleus of a male or female gamete (as an egg or sperm) up to the time of fusion with that of another gamete in fertilization — pro·nu·cle·ar \-klē-ər\ adj

Pro·pa·drine \'prō-pə-drən, -ˌdrēn\ trademark — used for a preparation of phenylpropanolamine

prop·a·gate \'prä-pə-ˌgāt\ vb -gat·ed; -gat·ing 1 : to reproduce or cause to reproduce sexually or asexually 2 : to cause to spread or to be transmitted — prop·a·ga·tion \ˌprä-pə-'gā-shən\ n — prop·a·ga·tive \'prä-pə-ˌgā-tiv\ adj

pro·pam·i·dine \prō-'pa-mə-ˌdēn, -dən\ n : an antiseptic drug $C_{17}H_{20}N_4O_2$

pro·pan·o·lol \prō-'pa-nə-ˌlȯl, -ˌlōl\ n : PROPRANOLOL

pro·pan·the·line bromide \prō-'pan-thə-ˌlēn-\ n : an anticholinergic drug $C_{23}H_{30}BrNO_3$ used esp. in the treatment of peptic ulcer — called also propantheline; see PRO-BANTHINE

pro·par·a·caine \prō-'par-ə-ˌkān\ n : a drug $C_{16}H_{26}N_2O_3$ used in the form of its hydrochloride as a topical anesthetic

pro·per·din \prō-'pərd-ᵊn\ n : a serum protein that participates in destruction of bacteria, neutralization of viruses, and lysis of red blood cells

pro·peri·to·ne·al \prō-ˌper-ə-tə-'nē-əl\ adj : lying between the parietal peritoneum and the ventral musculature of the body cavity (~ fat)

pro·phage \'prō-ˌfāj, -ˌfäzh\ n : an intracellular form of a bacteriophage in which it is harmless to the host, is usu. integrated into the hereditary material of the host, and reproduces when the host does

pro·phase \-ˌfāz\ n 1 : the initial stage of mitosis and of the mitotic division of meiosis characterized by the condensation of chromosomes consisting of two chromatids, disappearance of the nucleolus and nuclear membrane, and formation of the mitotic spindle 2 : the initial stage of the first division of meiosis in which the chromosomes become visible, homologous pairs of chromosomes undergo synapsis and crossing-over, chiasmata appear, chromosomes condense with homologues visible as tetrads, and the nuclear membrane and nucleolus disappear and which is divided into the five consecutive stages leptotene, zygotene, pachytene, diplotene, and diakinesis — pro·pha·sic \prō-'fā-zik\ adj

¹pro·phy·lac·tic \ˌprō-fə-'lak-tik, ˌprä-\ adj 1 : guarding from or preventing disease (~ therapy) 2 : tending to prevent or ward off : PREVENTIVE — pro·phy·lac·ti·cal·ly adv

²**prophylactic** *n* : something (as a medicinal preparation) that is prophylactic; *esp* : a device and esp. a condom for preventing venereal infection or contraception

pro·phy·lax·is \ˌprō-fə-ˈlak-səs\ *n, pl* **-lax·es** \-ˈlak-ˌsēz\ : measures designed to preserve health and prevent the spread of disease : protective or preventive treatment

pro·pio·lac·tone \ˌprō-pē-ō-ˈlak-ˌtōn\ *or* β-**pro·pio·lac·tone** \ˌbā-tə-\ *n* : a liquid disinfectant $C_3H_4O_2$

pro·pi·o·ma·zine \ˌprō-pē-ˈō-mə-ˌzēn\ *n* : a substituted phenothiazine $C_{20}H_{24}N_2OS$ used esp. in the form of its hydrochloride as a sedative — see LARGON

pro·pi·o·nate \ˈprō-pē-ə-ˌnāt\ *n* : a salt or ester of propionic acid

pro·pi·oni·bac·te·ri·um \ˌprō-pē-ˌä-nə-bak-ˈtir-ē-əm\ *n* **1** *cap* : a genus of gram-positive nonmotile usu. anaerobic bacteria (family Propionibacteriaceae) including forms found esp. on human skin and in dairy products **2** *pl* **-ria** \-ē-ə\ : any bacterium of the genus *Propionibacterium*

pro·pi·on·ic acid \ˌprō-pē-ˈä-nik-\ *n* : a liquid sharp-odored fatty acid $C_3H_6O_2$

pro·pos·i·ta \prō-ˈpä-zə-tə\ *n, pl* **-i·tae** \-ˌtē\ : a female proband

pro·pos·i·tus \prō-ˈpä-zə-təs\ *n, pl* **-i·ti** \-ˌtī\ : PROBAND

pro·poxy·phene \prō-ˈpäk-sə-ˌfēn\ *n* : an analgesic $C_{22}H_{29}NO_2$ structurally related to methadone but less addicting that is administered in the form of its hydrochloride — called also *dextropropoxyphene*; see DARVON

pro·pran·o·lol \prō-ˈpra-nə-ˌlól, -ˌlōl\ *n* : a beta-blocker $C_{16}H_{21}NO_2$ used in the form of its hydrochloride in the treatment of abnormal heart rhythms and angina pectoris — called also *propanolol*; see INDERAL

propria — see LAMINA PROPRIA, SUBSTANTIA PROPRIA, TUNICA PROPRIA

¹**pro·pri·e·tary** \prə-ˈprī-ə-ˌter-ē\ *n, pl* **-tar·ies** : something that is used, produced, or marketed under exclusive legal right of the inventor or maker; *specif* : a drug (as a patent medicine) that is protected by secrecy, patent, or copyright against free competition as to name, product, composition, or process of manufacture

²**proprietary** *adj* **1** : used, made, or marketed by one having the exclusive legal right ⟨a ~ drug⟩ **2** : privately owned and managed and run as a profit-making organization ⟨a ~ clinic⟩

pro·prio·cep·tion \ˌprō-prē-ō-ˈsep-shən\ *n* : the reception of stimuli produced within the organism — **pro·prio·cep·tive** \-ˈsep-tiv\ *adj*

pro·prio·cep·tor \-ˈsep-tər\ *n* : a sensory receptor located deep in the tissues (as in skeletal or heart muscle) that functions in proprioception

pro·prio·spi·nal \-ˈspīn-ᵊl\ *adj* : distinctively or exclusively spinal ⟨a ~ neuron⟩

proprius — see EXTENSOR DIGITI QUINTI PROPRIUS, EXTENSOR INDICIS PROPRIUS

pro·pto·sis \präp-ˈtō-səs, prō-ˈtō-\ *n, pl* **-pto·ses** \-ˌsēz\ : forward projection or displacement esp. of the eyeball

pro·pyl·ene glycol \ˈprō-pə-ˌlēn-\ *n* : a sweet viscous liquid $C_3H_8O_2$ used esp. as an antifreeze and solvent, in brake fluids, and as a food preservative

pro·pyl gallate \ˈprō-pəl-\ *n* : a white crystalline antioxidant $C_{10}H_{12}O_5$ that is used as a preservative

pro·pyl·hex·e·drine \ˌprō-pəl-ˈhek-sə-ˌdrēn\ *n* : a sympathomimetic drug $C_{10}H_{21}N$ used chiefly as a nasal decongestant

pro·pyl·par·a·ben \-ˈpar-ə-ˌben\ *n* : a crystalline ester $C_{10}H_{12}O_3$ used as a preservative in pharmaceutical preparations

pro·pyl·thio·ura·cil \-ˌthī-ō-ˈyùr-ə-ˌsil\ *n* : a crystalline compound $C_7H_{10}N_2OS$ used as an antithyroid drug in the treatment of goiter

pro·re·nin \prō-ˈrē-nən, ˌrē-\ *n* : the precursor of the kidney enzyme renin

pros- *prefix* : in front ⟨*prosencephalon*⟩

Pros·car \ˈpräs-ˌkär\ *trademark* — used for a preparation of finasteride

pro·sec·tor \prō-ˈsek-tər\ *n* : one who makes dissections for anatomic demonstrations

pros·en·ceph·a·lon \ˌprä-ˌsen-ˈse-fə-ˌlän, -lən\ *n* : FOREBRAIN

prosop- *or* **prosopo-** *comb form* : face ⟨*prosopagnosia*⟩

pros·op·ag·no·sia \ˌprä-sə-pag-ˈnō-zhə\ *n* : a form of agnosia characterized by an inability to recognize faces

pro·spec·tive \prə-ˈspek-tiv\ *adj* : relating to or being a study (as of the incidence of disease) that starts with the present condition of a population of individuals and follows them into the future — compare RETROSPECTIVE

pros·ta·cy·clin \ˌpräs-tə-ˈsī-klən\ *n* : a prostaglandin that is a metabolite of arachidonic acid, inhibits aggregation of platelets, and dilates blood vessels

pros·ta·glan·din \ˌpräs-tə-ˈglan-dən\ *n* : any of various oxygenated unsaturated cyclic fatty acids of animals that have a variety of hormonelike actions (as in controlling blood pressure or smooth muscle contraction)

prostat- *or* **prostato-** *comb form* : prostate gland ⟨*prostatectomy*⟩ ⟨*prostatitis*⟩

prostatae — see LEVATOR PROSTATAE

pros·tate \ˈpräs-ˌtāt\ *n* : PROSTATE GLAND

pros·ta·tec·to·my \ˌpräs-tə-ˈtek-tə-mē\

n, pl **-mies** : surgical removal or resection of the prostate gland

prostate gland *n* : a firm partly muscular partly glandular body that is situated about the base of the mammalian male urethra and secretes an alkaline viscid fluid which is a major constituent of the ejaculatory fluid — called also **prostate**

prostate–specific antigen *n* : a protease that is secreted by the epithelial cells of the prostate and is used in the diagnosis of prostate cancer since its concentration in the blood serum tends to be proportional to the clinical stage of the disease — abbr. *PSA*

pros·tat·ic \prä-ᵇsta-tik\ *adj* : of, relating to, or affecting the prostate gland ⟨∼ cancer⟩

prostatic urethra *n* : the part of the male urethra from the base of the prostate gland where the urethra begins as the outlet of the bladder to the point where it emerges from the apex of the prostate gland

prostatic utricle *n* : a small blind pouch that projects from the wall of the prostatic urethra into the prostate gland

pros·ta·tism \ᵇpräs-tə-₋ti-zəm\ *n* : disease of the prostate gland; *esp* : a disorder resulting from obstruction of the bladder neck by an enlarged prostate gland

pros·ta·ti·tis \₋präs-tə-ᵇtī-təs\ *n* : inflammation of the prostate gland

pros·the·sis \präs-ᵇthē-səs, ᵇpräs-thə-\ *n, pl* **-the·ses** \₋₋sēz\ : an artificial device to replace a missing part of the body ⟨a dental ∼⟩

pros·thet·ic \präs-ᵇthe-tik\ *adj* 1 : of, relating to, or being a prosthesis ⟨a ∼ device⟩; *also* : of or relating to prosthetics ⟨∼ research⟩ 2 : of, relating to, or constituting a nonprotein group of a conjugated protein — **pros·thet·i·cal·ly** *adv*

prosthetic dentistry *n* : PROSTHODONTICS

pros·thet·ics \-tiks\ *n sing or pl* : the surgical and dental specialty concerned with the design, construction, and fitting of prostheses

prosthetic valve endocarditis *n* : endocarditis caused by or involving a surgically implanted prosthetic heart valve — abbr. *PVE*

pros·the·tist \ᵇpräs-thə-tist\ *n* : a specialist in prosthetics

pros·thi·on \ᵇpräs-thē-₋än\ *n* : a point on the alveolar arch midway between the median upper incisor teeth

prosth·odon·tics \₋präs-thə-ᵇdän-tiks\ *n sing or pl* : the dental specialty concerned with the making of artificial replacements for missing parts of the mouth and jaw — called also *prosthetic dentistry* — **prosth·odon·tic** \-tik\ *adj*

prosth·odon·tist \-ᵇdän-tist\ *n* : a specialist in prosthodontics

Pro·stig·min \prō-ᵇstig-mən\ *trademark* — used for a preparation of neostigmine

¹**pros·trate** \ᵇpräs-₋trät\ *adj* : completely overcome ⟨was ∼ from the heat⟩

²**prostrate** *vb* **pros·trat·ed; pros·trat·ing** : to put into a state of extreme bodily exhaustion ⟨*prostrated* by fever⟩

pros·tra·tion \prä-ᵇstrā-shən\ *n* : complete physical or mental exhaustion — see HEAT EXHAUSTION

prot·ac·tin·i·um \₋prō-₋tak-ᵇti-nē-əm\ *n* : a shiny metallic radioelement — symbol *Pa*; see ELEMENT table

prot·amine \ᵇprō-tə-₋mēn\ *n* : any of various strongly basic proteins of relatively low molecular weight that are rich in arginine and are found associated esp. with DNA in place of histone in the sperm cells of various animals (as fish)

protamine zinc insulin *n* : a combination of protamine, zinc, and insulin used in suspension in water for subcutaneous injection in place of insulin because of its prolonged effect — abbr. *PZI*

prot·anom·a·ly \₋prō-tə-ᵇnä-mə-lē\ *n, pl* **-lies** : trichromatism in which an abnormally large proportion of red is required to match the spectrum — compare DEUTERANOMALY, TRICHROMAT — **prot·anom·a·lous** \-ləs\ *adj*

pro·ta·nope \ᵇprō-tə-₋nōp\ *n* : an individual affected with protanopia

prot·an·opia \₋prō-tə-ᵇnō-pē-ə\ *n* : a dichromatism in which the spectrum is seen in tones of yellow and blue with confusion of red and green and reduced sensitivity to monochromatic lights from the red end of the spectrum

prote- *or* **proteo-** *comb form* : protein ⟨*proteo*lysis⟩

pro·te·ase \ᵇprō-tē-₋ās, -₋āz\ *n* : any of numerous enzymes that hydrolyze proteins and are classified according to the most prominent functional group (as serine or cysteine) at the active site — called also *proteinase*

¹**pro·tec·tive** \prə-ᵇtek-tiv\ *adj* : serving to protect the body or one of its parts from disease or injury

²**protective** *n* : a protective agent (as a medicine or a dressing)

pro·tein \ᵇprō-₋tēn\ *n, often attrib* 1 : any of numerous naturally occurring extremely complex substances that consist of amino-acid residues joined by peptide bonds, contain the elements carbon, hydrogen, nitrogen, oxygen, usu. sulfur, and occas. other elements (as phosphorus or iron), and include many essential biological compounds (as enzymes, hormones, or immunoglobulins) 2 : the total nitrogenous material in plant or animal substances; *esp* : CRUDE PROTEIN

pro·tein·aceous \₋prō-tə-ᵇnā-shəs, -₋tē-\ *adj* : of, relating to, resembling, or being protein

pro·tein·ase \'prō-tə-ˌnās, -ˌtē-, -ˌnāz\ n : PROTEASE

protein kinase n : any of a class of allosteric enzymes that are reversibly dissociated in the presence of cyclic AMP yielding a catalytic subunit which catalyzes the phosphorylation of other enzymes by drawing on phosphate from AMP

pro·tein·o·sis \ˌprō-ˌtē-'nō-səs\ n, pl -o·ses \-ˌsēz\ or -o·sis·es : the accumulation of abnormal amounts of protein in bodily tissues — see PULMONARY ALVEOLAR PROTEINOSIS

pro·tein·uria \ˌprō-tə-'nür-ē-ə, -ˌtē-, -'nyür-\ n : the presence of excess protein in the urine — **pro·tein·uric** \-'nür-ik, -'nyür-\ adj

pro·teo·gly·can \ˌprō-tē-ə-'glī-ˌkan\ n : any of a class of glycoproteins of high molecular weight that are found in the extracellular matrix of connective tissue

pro·teo·lip·id \-'li-pəd\ n : any of a class of proteins that contain a considerable percentage of lipid and are soluble in lipids and insoluble in water

pro·te·ol·y·sis \ˌprō-tē-'ä-lə-səs\ n, pl -y·ses \-ˌsēz\ : the hydrolysis of proteins or peptides with formation of simpler and soluble products (as in digestion) — **pro·teo·lyt·ic** \ˌprō-tē-ə-'li-tik\ adj — **pro·teo·lyt·i·cal·ly** adv

pro·te·us \'prō-tē-əs\ n 1 cap : a genus of aerobic usu. motile enterobacteria that are often found in decaying organic matter and include a common causative agent (P. mirabilis) of urinary tract infections 2 pl -tei -ˌī\ : any bacterium of the genus Proteus

pro·throm·bin \prō-'thräm-bən\ n : a plasma protein produced in the liver in the presence of vitamin K and converted into thrombin by the action of various activators (as thromboplastin) in the clotting of blood — **pro·throm·bic** \-bik\ adj

prothrombin time n : the time required for a particular specimen of prothrombin to induce blood-plasma clotting under standardized conditions in comparison with a time of between 11.5 and 12 seconds for normal human blood

pro·ti·re·lin \prō-'tī-rə-lən\ n : THYROTROPIN-RELEASING HORMONE

pro·tist \'prō-ˌtist\ n : any of a major taxonomic group and usu. a kingdom (Protista) of unicellular, colonial, or multicellular eukaryotic organisms including esp. the protozoans and algae — **pro·tis·tan** \prō-'tis-tən\ adj or n

pro·to·col \'prō-tə-ˌkȯl, -ˌkäl\ n 1 : an official account of a proceeding; esp : the notes or records relating to a case, an experiment, or an autopsy 2 : a detailed plan of a scientific or medical experiment or treatment

pro·to·di·as·to·le \ˌprō-tō-dī-'as-tə-lē\ n 1 : the period just before aortic valve closure 2 : the period just after aortic valve closure — **pro·to·di·a·stol·ic** \-ˌdī-ə-'stä-lik\ adj

pro·ton \'prō-ˌtän\ n : an elementary particle that is identical with the nucleus of the hydrogen atom, that along with neutrons is a constituent of all other atomic nuclei, that carries a positive charge numerically equal to the charge of an electron, and that has a mass of 1.673×10^{-24} gram — **pro·ton·ic** \prō-'tä-nik\ adj

pro·to·on·co·gene \ˌprō-tō-'äŋ-kə-ˌjēn\ n : a gene having the potential for change into an active oncogene

Pro·to·pam \'prō-tə-ˌpam\ trademark — used for a preparation of pralidoxime

pro·to·path·ic \ˌprō-tə-'pa-thik\ adj : of, relating to, being, or mediating cutaneous sensory reception that is responsive only to rather gross stimuli — compare EPICRITIC

pro·to·plasm \'prō-tə-ˌpla-zəm\ n 1 : the organized colloidal complex of organic and inorganic substances (as proteins and water) that constitutes esp. the living nucleus, cytoplasm, and mitochondria of the cell 2 : CYTOPLASM — **pro·to·plas·mic** \ˌprō-tə-'plaz-mik\ adj

pro·to·plast \'prō-tə-ˌplast\ n : the nucleus, cytoplasm, and plasma membrane of a cell as distinguished from inert walls and inclusions

pro·to·por·phyr·ia \ˌprō-tō-pȯr-'fir-ē-ə\ n : the presence of protoporphyrin in the blood — see ERYTHROPOIETIC PROTOPORPHYRIA

pro·to·por·phy·rin \ˌprō-tō-'pȯr-fə-rən\ n : a purple porphyrin acid $C_{34}H_{34}N_4O_4$ obtained from hemin or heme by removal of bound iron

Pro·to·stron·gy·lus \-'strän-jə-ləs\ n : a genus of lungworms (family Metastrongylidae) including one (P. rufescens) parasitic esp. in sheep and goats

Pro·to·the·ca \ˌprō-tə-'thē-kə\ n : a genus of microorganisms that include several causing or associated with human infections

pro·to·the·co·sis \-ˌthē-'kō-səs\ n, pl -co·ses \-ˌsēz\ : an infection produced by a microorganism of the genus Prototheca

protozoa pl of PROTOZOON

pro·to·zo·a·ci·dal \ˌprō-tə-ˌzō-ə-'sid-ᵊl\ adj : destroying protozoans

pro·to·zo·al \ˌprō-tə-'zō-əl\ adj : of or relating to protozoans

pro·to·zo·an \-'zō-ən\ n : any of a phylum or subkingdom (Protozoa) of chiefly motile unicellular protists (as amoebas, trypanosomes, sporozoans, and paramecia) that are represented in almost every kind of habitat and include some pathogenic parasites of humans and domestic animals — **protozoan** adj

pro·to·zo·ol·o·gy \-zō-'ä-lə-jē\ n, pl -gies

: a branch of zoology dealing with protozoans — **pro·to·zo·ol·o·gist** \-jist\ n

pro·to·zo·on \ˌprō-tə-ˈzō-ˌän\ n, pl **pro·to·zoa** : PROTOZOAN

pro·tract \prō-ˈtrakt\ vb : to extend forward or outward — compare RETRACT

pro·trac·tion \-ˈtrak-shən\ n 1 : the act of moving an anatomical part forward 2 : the state of being protracted; esp : protrusion of the jaws

pro·trip·ty·line \prō-ˈtrip-tə-ˌlēn\ n : a tricyclic antidepressant drug $C_{19}H_{21}N$ — see VIVACTIL

pro·trude \prō-ˈtrüd\ vb **pro·trud·ed; pro·trud·ing** : to project or cause to project : jut out — **pro·tru·sion** \prō-ˈtrü-zhən\ n

pro·tru·sive \-ˈtrü-siv, -ziv\ adj 1 : thrusting forward 2 : PROTUBERANT

pro·tu·ber·ance \prō-ˈtü-bə-rəns, -ˈtyü-\ n 1 : something that is protuberant (a bony ~) 2 : the quality or state of being protuberant

protuberans — see DERMATOFIBROSARCOMA PROTUBERANS

pro·tu·ber·ant \-rənt\ adj : bulging beyond the surrounding or adjacent surface (a ~ joint) (~ eyes)

proud flesh n : an excessive growth of granulation tissue (as in an ulcer)

pro·ven·tric·u·lus \ˌprō-ven-ˈtri-kyə-ləs\ n, pl **-li** \-ˌlī, -ˌlē\ : the glandular or true stomach of a bird that is situated between the crop and gizzard

pro·vi·rus \ˈprō-ˌvī-rəs\ n : a form of a virus that is integrated into the genetic material of a host cell and by replicating with it can be transmitted from one cell generation to the next without causing lysis — **pro·vi·ral** \prō-ˈvī-rəl\ adj

pro·vi·ta·min \-ˈvī-tə-mən\ n : a precursor of a vitamin convertible into the vitamin in an organism

provitamin A n : a provitamin of vitamin A; esp : CAROTENE

pro·voke \prə-ˈvōk\ vb **pro·voked; pro·vok·ing** : to call forth or induce (a physical reaction) (ipecac ~s vomiting) — **prov·o·ca·tion** \ˌprä-və-ˈkā-shən\ n — **pro·voc·a·tive** \prə-ˈvä-kə-tiv\ adj

prox·e·mics \präk-ˈsē-miks\ n sing or pl : the study of the nature, degree, and effect of the spatial separation individuals naturally maintain (as in various social and interpersonal situations) and of how this separation relates to environmental and cultural factors — **prox·e·mic** \-mik\ adj

prox·i·mad \ˈpräk-sə-ˌmad\ adv : PROXIMALLY

prox·i·mal \ˈpräk-sə-məl\ adj 1 a : situated next to or near the point of attachment or origin or a central point; esp : located toward the center of the body (the ~ end of a bone) — compare DISTAL 1a b : of, relating to, or being the mesial and distal surfaces of

a tooth 2 : sensory rather than physical or social (~ stimuli) — compare DISTAL 2 — **prox·i·mal·ly** adv

proximal convoluted tubule n : the convoluted portion of the vertebrate nephron that lies between Bowman's capsule and the loop of Henle and functions esp. in the resorption of sugar, sodium and chloride ions, and water from the glomerular filtrate — called also *proximal tubule*

proximal radioulnar joint n : a pivot joint between the upper end of the radius and the ring formed by the radial notch of the ulna and its annular ligament that permits rotation of the proximal head of the radius

proximal tubule n : PROXIMAL CONVOLUTED TUBULE

prox·i·mate cause \ˈpräk-sə-mət-\ n : a cause that directly or with no intervening agency produces an effect

Pro·zac \ˈprō-ˌzak\ trademark — used for a preparation of fluoxetine

pru·rig·i·nous \prü-ˈri-jə-nəs\ adj : resembling, caused by, affected with, or being prurigo (~ dermatosis)

pru·ri·go \prü-ˈrī-(ˌ)gō\ n : a chronic inflammatory skin disease marked by a general eruption of small itching papules

pru·rit·ic \prü-ˈri-tik\ adj : of, relating to, or marked by itching

pru·ri·tus \prü-ˈrī-təs\ n : localized or generalized itching due to irritation of sensory nerve endings from organic or psychogenic causes : ITCH

pruritus ani \-ˈā-ˌnī\ n : pruritus of the anal region

pruritus vul·vae \-ˈvəl-vē\ n : pruritus of the vulva

Prus·sian blue \ˈprə-shən-ˈblü\ n : a blue iron-containing dye $Fe_4[Fe(CN)_6]_3 \cdot xH_2O$ used in a test for ferric iron

prus·sic acid \ˈprə-sik-\ n : HYDROCYANIC ACID

PSA abbr prostate-specific antigen

psal·te·ri·um \sȯl-ˈtir-ē-əm\ n, pl **-ria** \-ē-ə\ 1 : OMASUM 2 : HIPPOCAMPAL COMMISSURE

psam·mo·ma \sa-ˈmō-mə\ n, pl **-mas** or **-ma·ta** \-mə-tə\ : a hard fibrous tumor of the meninges of the brain and spinal cord containing calcareous matter — **psam·mo·ma·tous** \sa-ˈmō-mə-təs, -ˈmä-\ adj

pseud- or **pseudo-** comb form : false : spurious (*pseud*arthrosis) (*pseudo*tumor)

pseud·ar·thro·sis \ˌsüd-är-ˈthrō-səs\ n, pl **-thro·ses** \-ˈthrō-ˌsēz\ : an abnormal union formed by fibrous tissue between parts of a bone that has fractured usu. spontaneously due to congenital weakness — called also *false joint*

pseu·do·an·eu·rysm \ˌsü-dō-ˈan-yə-ˌri-zəm\ n : a vascular abnormality (as an elongation or buckling of the aorta) that resembles an aneurysm in roentgenography

pseu·do·ar·thro·sis *var of* PSEUDARTHROSIS

pseu·do·bul·bar \-'bəl-bər\ *adj* : simulating that caused by lesions of the medulla oblongata (~ paralysis)

pseu·do·cho·lin·es·ter·ase \-₁kō-lə-'nes-tə-₁rās, -₁rāz\ *n* : CHOLINESTERASE 2

pseu·do·cow·pox \-'kaú-₁päks\ *n* : MILKER'S NODULES

pseu·do·cy·e·sis \-sī-'ē-səs\ *n, pl* -e·ses \-₁sēz\ : a psychosomatic state that occurs without conception and is marked by some of the physical symptoms (as cessation of menses, enlargement of the abdomen, and apparent fetal movements) and changes in hormonal balance of pregnancy

pseu·do·cyst \'sü-dō-₁sist\ *n* : a cluster of toxoplasmas in an enucleate host cell

pseu·do·de·men·tia \₁sü-dō-di-'men-chə\ *n* : a condition of extreme apathy which outwardly resembles dementia but is not the result of actual mental deterioration

pseu·do·ephed·rine \-i-'fe-drən\ *n* : a crystalline alkaloid $C_{10}H_{15}NO$ that is isomeric with ephedrine and is used for similar purposes esp. in the form of its hydrochloride

pseu·do·gout \-'gaút\ *n* : an arthritic condition which resembles gout but is characterized by the deposition of crystalline salts other than urates in and around the joints

pseu·do·her·maph·ro·dite \-(₁)hər-'ma-frə-₁dīt\ *n* : an individual exhibiting pseudohermaphroditism — **pseu·do·her·maph·ro·dit·ic** \-(₁)hər-₁ma-frə-'di-tik\ *adj*

pseu·do·her·maph·ro·dit·ism \-rə-₁dī-₁ti-zəm\ *n* : the condition of having the gonads of one sex and the external genitalia and other sex organs so variably developed that the sex of the individual is uncertain

pseu·do·hy·per·tro·phic \₁sü-dō-₁hī-pər-'trō-fik\ *adj* : falsely hypertrophic; *specif* : being a form of muscular dystrophy in which the muscles become swollen with deposits of fat and fibrous tissue — **pseu·do·hy·per·tro·phy** \-hī-'pər-trə-fē\ *n*

pseu·do·hy·po·para·thy·roid·ism \-₁hī-pō-₁par-ə-'thī-₁roi-di-zəm\ *n* : a usu. inherited disorder that clinically resembles hypoparathyroidism but results from the body's inability to respond normally to parathyroid hormone rather than from a deficiency of the hormone itself

pseu·do·mem·brane \₁sü-dō-'mem-₁brān\ *n* : FALSE MEMBRANE

pseu·do·mem·bra·nous \-'mem-brə-nəs\ *adj* : characterized by the presence or formation of a false membrane (~ colitis)

pseu·do·mo·nad \-'mō-₁nad, -nəd\ *n* : any bacterium of the genus *Pseudomonas*

pseu·do·mo·nal \-'mō-nəl\ *adj* : of, relating to, or caused by bacteria of the genus *Pseudomonas* (~ infection)

pseu·do·mo·nas \₁sü-dō-'mō-nəs, sü-'dä-mə-nəs\ *n 1 cap* : a genus of gramnegative rod-shaped motile bacteria (family Pseudomonadaceae) including some saprophytes, a few animal pathogens, and numerous important plant pathogens 2 *pl* **pseu·do·mo·na·des** \₁sü-dō-'mō-nə-₁dēz, -'mä-\ : PSEUDOMONAD

pseu·do·neu·rot·ic \-nú-'rä-tik, -nyú-\ *adj* : having or characterized by neurotic symptoms which mask an underlying psychosis (~ schizophrenia)

pseu·do·pa·ral·y·sis \-pə-'ra-lə-səs\ *n, pl* -y·ses \-₁sēz\ : apparent lack or loss of muscular power (as that produced by pain) that is not accompanied by true paralysis

pseu·do·par·kin·son·ism \-'pär-kən-sə-ni-zəm\ *n* : a condition (as one induced by a drug) characterized by symptoms like those of parkinsonism

pseu·do·phyl·lid·e·an \₁sü-dō-fi-'li-dē-ən\ *n* : any of an order (Pseudophyllidea) of tapeworms (as the fish tapeworm of humans) including numerous parasites of fish-eating vertebrates — **pseudophyllidean** *adj*

pseu·do·pod \'sü-də-₁päd\ *n 1* : PSEUDOPODIUM 2 a : a slender extension from the edge of a wheal at the site of injection of an allergen b : one of the slender processes of some tumor cells extending out from the main mass of a tumor

pseu·do·po·di·um \₁sü-də-'pō-dē-əm\ *n, pl* -dia \-dē-ə\ : a temporary protrusion or retractile process of the cytoplasm of a cell (as a unicellular organism or a white blood cell of a higher organism) that functions esp. as an organ of locomotion or in taking up food

pseu·do·pol·yp \'sü-dō-₁pä-ləp\ *n* : a projecting mass of hypertrophied mucous membrane (as in the stomach or colon) resulting from local inflammation

pseu·do·preg·nan·cy \₁sü-dō-'preg-nən-sē\ *n, pl* -cies : a condition which resembles pregnancy: as a : PSEUDOCYESIS b : an anestrous state resembling pregnancy that occurs in various mammals usu. after an infertile copulation — **pseu·do·preg·nant** \-nənt\ *adj*

pseu·do·ra·bies \-₁rā-bēz\ *n* : an acute febrile virus disease of domestic animals (as cattle and swine) marked by cutaneous irritation and intense itching followed by encephalomyelitis and pharyngeal paralysis and commonly terminating in death within 48 hours — called also *mad itch*

pseu·do·sar·co·ma·tous \₁sü-dō-sär-'kō-mə·təs\ *adj* : resembling but not being a true sarcoma ⟨a ~ polyp⟩

pseu·do·strat·i·fied \-ˈstra-tə-ˌfīd\ *adj* : of, relating to, or being an epithelium consisting of closely packed cells which appear to be arranged in layers but all of which are in fact attached to the basement membrane — **pseu·do·strat·i·fi·ca·tion** \-ˌstra-tə-fə-ˈkā-shən\ *n*

pseu·do·tu·ber·cle \-ˈtü-bər-kəl, -ˈtyü-\ *n* : a nodule or granuloma resembling a tubercle of tuberculosis but due to other causes

pseu·do·tu·ber·cu·lo·sis \-ˌtü-ˌbər-kyə-ˈlō-səs, -ˌtyü-\ *n, pl* **-lo·ses** \-ˌsēz\ : 1 : any of several diseases that are characterized by the formation of granulomas resembling tubercular nodules but are not caused by the tubercle bacillus 2 : CASEOUS LYMPHADENITIS

pseu·do·tu·mor \-ˈtü-mər, -ˈtyü-\ *n* : an abnormality (as a temporary swelling) that resembles a tumor — **pseu·do·tu·mor·al** \-mə-rəl\ *adj*

pseudotumor cer·e·bri \-ˈser-ə-ˌbrī\ *n* : an abnormal condition with symptoms (as increased intracranial pressure, headache, and papilledema) which suggest the occurrence of a brain tumor but have a different cause

pseu·do·uri·dine \-ˈyür-ə-ˌdēn\ *n* : a nucleoside $C_9H_{12}O_6N_2$ that is a uracil derivative incorporated as a structural component into transfer RNA

pseu·do·xan·tho·ma elas·ti·cum \ˌsü-dō-zan-ˈthō-mə-i-ˈlas-ti-kəm\ *n* : a chronic degenerative disease of elastic tissues that is marked by the occurrence of small yellowish papules and plaques on areas of abnormally loose skin

¹**psi** \ˈsī\ *adj* : relating to, concerned with, or being parapsychological psychic events or powers ⟨~ phenomena⟩

²**psi** *n* : psi events or phenomena

psi·lo·cin \ˈsī-lə-sən\ *n* : a hallucinogenic tertiary amine $C_{12}H_{16}N_2O$ obtained from a basidiomycetous fungus (*Psilocybe mexicana*)

psi·lo·cy·bin \ˌsī-lə-ˈsī-bən\ *n* : a hallucinogenic indole $C_{12}H_{17}N_2O_4P$ obtained from a basidiomycetous fungus (*Psilocybe mexicana*)

psit·ta·co·sis \ˌsi-tə-ˈkō-səs\ *n, pl* **-co·ses** \-ˌsēz\ : an infectious disease of birds caused by a bacterium of the genus *Chlamydia* (*C. psittaci*), marked by diarrhea and wasting, and transmissible to humans in whom it usu. occurs as an atypical pneumonia accompanied by high fever — called also *parrot fever*; compare ORNITHOSIS — **psit·ta·co·tic** \-ˈkä-tik, -ˈkō-\ *adj*

pso·as \ˈsō-əs\ *n, pl* **psoai** \ˈsō-ˌī\ *or* **pso·ae** \-ˌē\ : either of two internal muscles of the loin: a : PSOAS MAJOR b : PSOAS MINOR

psoas major *n* : the larger of the two psoas muscles that arises from the anterolateral surfaces of the lumbar vertebrae, passes beneath the inguinal ligament to insert with the iliacus into the lesser trochanter of the femur, and serves esp. to flex the thigh

psoas minor *n* : the smaller of the two psoas muscles that arises from the last dorsal and first lumbar vertebrae and inserts into the brim of the pelvis, which functions to flex the trunk and the lumbar spinal column, and which is often absent

psoas muscle *n* : PSOAS

pso·ra·len \ˈsōr-ə-lən\ *n* : a substance $C_{11}H_6O_3$ found in some plants that photosensitizes mammalian skin and has been used in treating psoriasis; *also* : any of various derivatives of psoralen having similar properties

pso·ri·a·si·form \sə-ˈrī-ə-si-ˌform\ *adj* : resembling psoriasis or a psoriatic lesion

pso·ri·a·sis \sə-ˈrī-ə-səs\ *n, pl* **-a·ses** \-ˌsēz\ : a chronic skin disease characterized by circumscribed red patches covered with white scales — **pso·ri·at·ic** \ˌsōr-ē-ˈa-tik\ *adj*

psoriatic arthritis *n* : a severe form of arthritis accompanied by psoriasis — called also *psoriatic arthropathy*

Pso·rop·tes \sə-ˈräp-(ˌ)tēz\ *n* : a genus of mites (family Psoroptidae) living on and irritating the skin of various mammals and resulting in the development of inflammatory skin diseases (as mange)

pso·rop·tic \sə-ˈräp-tik\ *adj* : of, relating to, caused by, or being mites of the genus *Psoroptes* ⟨~ mange⟩

PSRO *abbr* professional standards review organization

psych *abbr* psychology

psych- *or* **psycho-** *comb form* 1 : mind : mental processes and activities ⟨*psychodynamic*⟩ ⟨*psychology*⟩ 2 : psychological methods ⟨*psychoanalysis*⟩ ⟨*psychotherapy*⟩ 3 : brain ⟨*psychosurgery*⟩ 4 : mental and ⟨*psychosomatic*⟩

psych·as·the·nia \ˌsī-kəs-ˈthē-nē-ə\ *n* : a neurotic state characterized esp. by phobias, obsessions, or compulsions that one knows are irrational

psy·che \ˈsī-(ˌ)kē\ *n* : the specialized cognitive, conative, and affective aspects of a psychosomatic unity : MIND; *specif* : the totality of the id, ego, and superego including both conscious and unconscious components

¹**psy·che·del·ic** \ˌsi-kə-ˈde-lik\ *n* : a psychedelic drug (as LSD)

²**psychedelic** *adj* 1 : of, relating to, or being drugs (as LSD) capable of producing abnormal psychic effects (as hallucinations) and sometimes psychic states resembling mental illness 2 : produced by or associated with the

use of psychedelic drugs ⟨a ~ experience⟩ — **psy·che·del·i·cal·ly** *adv*

psy·chi·at·ric \ˌsī-kē-ˈa-trik\ *adj* 1 : relating to or employed in psychiatry ⟨~ disorders⟩ 2 : engaged in the practice of psychiatry : dealing with cases of mental disorder ⟨~ nursing⟩ — **psy·chi·at·ri·cal·ly** *adv*

psy·chi·a·trist \sə-ˈkī-ə-trist, sī-\ *n* : a physician specializing in psychiatry

psy·chi·a·try \-trē\ *n, pl* **-tries** : a branch of medicine that deals with the science and practice of treating mental, emotional, or behavioral disorders esp. as originating in endogenous causes or resulting from faulty interpersonal relationships

¹**psy·chic** \ˈsī-kik\ *also* **psy·chi·cal** \-ki-kəl\ *adj* 1 : of or relating to the psyche : PSYCHOGENIC 2 : sensitive to nonphysical or supernatural forces and influences — **psy·chi·cal·ly** *adv*

²**psychic** *n* : a person apparently sensitive to nonphysical forces

psychic energizer *n* : ANTIDEPRESSANT

psy·cho \ˈsī-(ˌ)kō\ *n, pl* **psychos** : a deranged or psychopathic individual — not used technically — **psycho** *adj*

psycho- — see PSYCH-

psy·cho·acous·tics \ˌsī-kō-ə-ˈkü-stiks\ *n* : a branch of science dealing with hearing, the sensations produced by sounds, and the problems of communication — **psy·cho·acous·tic** \-stik\ *adj*

psy·cho·ac·tive \ˌsī-kō-ˈak-tiv\ *adj* : affecting the mind or behavior ⟨~ drugs⟩

psy·cho·anal·y·sis \ˌsī-kō-ə-ˈna-lə-səs\ *n, pl* **-y·ses** \-ˌsēz\ 1 : a method of analyzing psychic phenomena and treating emotional disorders that is based on the concepts and theories of Sigmund Freud, that emphasizes the importance of free association, dream analysis, and that involves treatment sessions during which the patient is encouraged to talk freely about personal experiences and esp. about early childhood and dreams 2 : a body of empirical findings and a set of theories on human motivation, behavior, and personality development that developed esp. with the aid of psychoanalysis 3 : a school of psychology, psychiatry, and psychotherapy founded by Sigmund Freud and rooted in and applying psychoanalysis — **psy·cho·an·a·lyt·ic** \-ˌan-əl-ˈi-tik\ *also* **psy·cho·an·a·lyt·i·cal** \-ti-kəl\ *adj* — **psy·cho·an·a·lyt·i·cal·ly** *adv* — **psy·cho·an·a·lyze** \-ˈan-əl-ˌīz\ *vb*

psy·cho·an·a·lyst \-ˈan-əl-ist\ *n* : one who practices or adheres to the principles of psychoanalysis; *specif* : a psychotherapist trained at an established psychoanalytic institute

psy·cho·bi·ol·o·gy \-bī-ˈä-lə-jē\ *n, pl* **-gies** : the study of mental functioning and behavior in relation to other biological processes — **psy·cho·bi·o·log·i·cal** \-ˌbī-ə-ˈlä-ji-kəl\ *also* **psy·cho·bi·o·log·ic** \-jik\ *adj* — **psy·cho·bi·ol·o·gist** \-bī-ˈä-lə-jist\ *n*

psy·cho·di·ag·nos·tics \-ˌdī-ig-ˈnäs-tiks\ *n* : a branch of psychology concerned with the use of tests in the evaluation of personality and the determination of factors underlying human behavior — **psy·cho·di·ag·nos·tic** \-tik\ *adj*

psy·cho·dra·ma \ˌsī-kō-ˈdrä-mə, -ˈdra-\ *n* : an extemporized dramatization designed to afford catharsis and social relearning for one or more of the participants from whose life history the plot is abstracted — **psy·cho·dra·mat·ic** \-krə-ˈma-tik\ *adj*

psy·cho·dy·nam·ics \ˌsī-kō-dī-ˈna-miks, -də-\ *n sing* or *pl* 1 : the psychology of mental or emotional forces or processes developing esp. in early childhood and their effects on behavior and mental states 2 : explanation or interpretation (as of behavior or mental states) in terms of mental or emotional forces or processes 3 : motivational forces acting esp. at the unconscious level — **psy·cho·dy·nam·ic** \-mik\ *adj* — **psy·cho·dy·nam·i·cal·ly** *adv*

psy·cho·ed·u·ca·tion·al \-ˌe-jə-ˈkā-shə-nəl\ *adj* : of or relating to the psychological aspects of education; *specif* : relating to or used in the education of children with behavioral disorders or learning disabilities

psy·cho·gal·van·ic reflex \-gal-ˈva-nik-\ *n* : a momentary decrease in the apparent electrical resistance of the skin resulting from activity of the sweat glands in response to mental or emotional stimulation — called also *psychogalvanic reaction, psychogalvanic response*

psy·cho·gen·e·sis \ˌsī-kō-ˈje-nə-səs\ *n, pl* **-e·ses** \-ˌsēz\ 1 : the origin and development of mental functions, traits, or states 2 : development from mental as distinguished from physical origins

psy·cho·gen·ic \-ˈje-nik\ *adj* : originating in the mind or in mental or emotional conflict ⟨~ impotence⟩ ⟨a ~ disorder⟩ — **psy·cho·gen·i·cal·ly** *adv*

psy·cho·ge·ri·at·rics \-ˌjer-ē-ˈa-triks, -ˌjir-\ *n* : a branch of psychiatry concerned with behavioral and emotional disorders among the elderly — **psy·cho·ge·ri·at·ric** \-trik\ *adj*

psy·cho·ki·ne·sis \-kə-ˈnē-səs, -kī-\ *n, pl* **-ne·ses** \-ˌsēz\ : movement of physical objects by the mind without use of physical means — called also *PK*; compare PRECOGNITION, TELEKINESIS — **psy·cho·ki·net·ic** \-ˈne-tik\ *adj*

psy·cho·ki·net·ics \-kə-ˈne-tiks, -kī-\ *n* : a branch of parapsychology that deals with psychokinesis

psychol *abbr* psychologist; psychology

psy·cho·lin·guis·tics \ˌsī-kō-liŋ-ˈgwis-tiks\ *n* : the study of the mental faculties involved in the perception, production, and acquisition of language — **psy·cho·lin·guist** \-ˈliŋ-gwist\

n — **psy·cho·lin·guis·tic** \-liŋ-ˈgwis-tik\ *adj*

psy·cho·log·i·cal \ˌsī-kə-ˈlä-ji-kəl\ *also* **psy·cho·log·ic** \-ˈjik\ *adj* **1 a** : relating to, characteristic of, directed toward, influencing, arising in, or acting through the mind esp. in its affective or cognitive functions ⟨∼ phenomena⟩ **b** : directed toward the will or toward the mind specif. in its conative function ⟨∼ warfare⟩ **2** : relating to, concerned with, deriving from, or used in psychology — **psy·cho·log·i·cal·ly** *adv*

psy·chol·o·gist \sī-ˈkä-lə-jist\ *n* : a specialist in one or more branches of psychology; *esp* : a practitioner of clinical psychology, counseling, or guidance

psy·chol·o·gize \-ˌjīz\ *vb* **-gized; -giz·ing** : to explain, interpret, or speculate in psychological terms

psy·chol·o·gy \-jē\ *n, pl* **-gies 1** : the science of mind and behavior **2 a** : the mental or behavioral characteristics of an individual or group ⟨mob ∼⟩ **b** : the study of mind and behavior in relation to a particular field of knowledge or activity ⟨the ∼ of learning⟩ **3** : a treatise on or a school, system, or branch of psychology

psy·cho·met·ric \ˌsī-kə-ˈme-trik\ *adj* : of or relating to psychometrics — **psy·cho·met·ri·cal·ly** *adv*

psy·cho·me·tri·cian \-mə-ˈtri-shən\ *n* **1** : a person (as a clinical psychologist) who is skilled in the administration and interpretation of objective psychological tests **2** : a psychologist who devises, constructs, and standardizes psychometric tests

psy·cho·met·rics \-ˈme-triks\ *n* **1** : a branch of clinical or applied psychology dealing with the use and application of mental measurement **2** : the technique of mental measurements : the use of quantitative devices for assessing psychological trends

psy·chom·e·trist \sī-ˈkä-mə-trist\ *n* : PSYCHOMETRICIAN

psy·chom·e·try \sī-ˈkä-mə-trē\ *n, pl* **-tries** : PSYCHOMETRICS

psy·cho·mo·tor \ˌsī-kō-ˈmō-tər\ *adj* **1** : of or relating to motor action directly proceeding from mental activity **2** : of or relating to psychomotor epilepsy ⟨∼ seizures⟩

psychomotor epilepsy *n* : epilepsy characterized by partial rather than generalized seizures that typically originate in the temporal lobe and are marked by impairment of consciousness, automatisms, bizarre changes in behavior, hallucinations (as of odors), and perceptual illusions (as visceral sensations)

psy·cho·neu·ro·im·mu·nol·o·gy \-ˌnùr-ō-ˌi-myü-ˈnä-lə-jē, -ˌnyùr-\ *n* : a field of medicine that deals with the influence of emotional states (as stress) and nervous system activity on immune function esp. in relation to their role in affecting the onset and progression of disease

psy·cho·neu·ro·sis \ˌsī-kō-nù-ˈrō-səs, -nyü-\ *n, pl* **-ro·ses** \-ˌsēz\ : NEUROSIS; *esp* : a neurosis based on emotional conflict in which an impulse that has been blocked seeks expression in a disguised response or symptom

¹**psy·cho·neu·rot·ic** \-ˈrä-tik\ *adj* : of, relating to, being, or affected with a psychoneurosis ⟨a ∼ disorder⟩ ⟨a ∼ patient⟩

²**psychoneurotic** *n* : a psychoneurotic individual

psy·cho·path \ˈsī-kō-ˌpath\ *n* : a mentally ill or unstable individual; *esp* : one having a psychopathic personality

psy·cho·path·ic \ˌsī-kō-ˈpa-thik\ *adj* : of, relating to, or characterized by psychopathy or psychopathic personality — **psy·cho·path·i·cal·ly** *adv*

psychopathic personality *n* **1** : an emotionally and behaviorally disordered state characterized by clear perception of reality except for the individual's social and moral obligations and often by the pursuit of immediate personal gratification in criminal acts, drug addiction, or sexual perversion **2** : an individual having a psychopathic personality

psy·cho·pa·thol·o·gist \-pə-ˈthä-lə-jist, -pa-\ *n* : a specialist in psychopathology

psy·cho·pa·thol·o·gy \ˌsī-kō-pə-ˈthä-lə-jē, -pa-\ *n, pl* **-gies 1** : the study of psychological and behavioral dysfunction occurring in mental disorder or in social disorganization **2** : disordered psychological and behavioral functioning (as in mental illness) — **psy·cho·patho·log·i·cal** \-ˌpa-thə-ˈlä-ji-kəl\ *or* **psy·cho·patho·log·ic** \-ˈjik\ *adj* — **psy·cho·patho·log·i·cal·ly** *adv*

psy·chop·a·thy \sī-ˈkä-pə-thē\ *n, pl* **-thies 1** : mental disorder **2** : PSYCHOPATHIC PERSONALITY 1

psy·cho·phar·ma·ceu·ti·cal \ˌsī-kō-ˌfär-mə-ˈsü-ti-kəl\ *n* : a drug having an effect on the mental state of the user

psy·cho·phar·ma·col·o·gy \ˌsī-kō-ˌfär-mə-ˈkä-lə-jē\ *n, pl* **-gies** : the study of the effect of drugs on the mind and behavior — **psy·cho·phar·ma·co·log·ic** \-ˌfär-mə-kə-ˈlä-jik\ *or* **psy·cho·phar·ma·co·log·i·cal** \-ji-kəl\ *adj* — **psy·cho·phar·ma·col·o·gist** \-ˌfär-mə-ˈkä-lə-jist\ *n*

psy·cho·phys·ics \-ˈfi-ziks\ *n* : a branch of psychology concerned with the effect of physical processes (as intensity of stimulation) on mental processes and esp. sensations of an organism — **psy·cho·phys·i·cal** \ˌsī-kō-ˈfi-zi-kəl\ *adj* — **psy·cho·phys·i·cal·ly** *adv* — **psy·cho·phys·i·cist** \-ˈfi-zə-sist\ *n*

psy·cho·phys·i·o·log·i·cal \ˌsī-kō-ˌfi-zē-ə-ˈlä-ji-kəl\ *also* **psy·cho·phys·i·o·log-**

ic \-jik\ *adj* **1** : of or relating to psychophysiology **2** : combining or involving mental and bodily processes

psy·cho·phys·i·ol·o·gy \-ˌfi-zē-ˈä-lə-jē\ *n, pl* **-gies** : a branch of psychology that deals with the effects of normal and pathological physiological processes on mental life — called also *physiological psychology* — **psy·cho·phys·i·ol·o·gist** \-jist\ *n*

psy·cho·sex·u·al \ˌsī-kō-ˈsek-shə-wəl\ *adj* **1** : of or relating to the mental, emotional, and behavioral aspects of sexual development **2** : of or relating to mental or emotional attitudes concerning sexual activity **3** : of or relating to the psychophysiology of sex

psy·cho·sis \sī-ˈkō-səs\ *n, pl* **-cho·ses** \-ˌsēz\ : a serious mental disorder (as schizophrenia) characterized by defective or lost contact with reality often with hallucinations or delusions

psy·cho·so·cial \ˌsī-kō-ˈsō-shəl\ *adj* **1** : involving both psychological and social aspects **2** : relating social conditions to mental health (~ medicine) — **psy·cho·so·cial·ly** *adv*

psy·cho·so·mat·ic \ˌsī-kō-sə-ˈma-tik\ *adj* **1** : of, relating to, concerned with, or involving both mind and body **2 a** : of, relating to, involving, or concerned with bodily symptoms caused by mental or emotional disturbance **b** : exhibiting psychosomatic symptoms — **psy·cho·so·mat·i·cal·ly** *adv*

psy·cho·so·mat·ics \-tiks\ *n* : a branch of medical science dealing with interrelationships between the mind or emotions and the body and esp. with the relation of psychic conflict to somatic symptomatology

psy·cho·sur·geon \-ˈsər-jən\ *n* : a surgeon specializing in psychosurgery

psy·cho·sur·gery \-ˈsər-jə-rē\ *n, pl* **-ger·ies** : cerebral surgery employed in treating psychic symptoms — **psy·cho·sur·gi·cal** \-ˈsər-ji-kəl\ *adj*

psy·cho·syn·the·sis \ˌsī-kō-ˈsin-thə-səs\ *n, pl* **-the·ses** \-ˌsēz\ : a form of psychotherapy combining psychoanalytic techniques with meditation and exercise

psy·cho·ther·a·peu·tics \-tiks\ *n sing or pl* : PSYCHOTHERAPY

psy·cho·ther·a·pist \-ˈther-ə-pist\ *n* : one (as a psychiatrist, clinical psychologist, or psychiatric social worker) who is a practitioner of psychotherapy

psy·cho·ther·a·py \ˌsī-kō-ˈther-ə-pē\ *n, pl* **-pies** **1** : treatment of mental or emotional disorder or maladjustment by psychological means esp. involving verbal communication (as in psychoanalysis, nondirective psychotherapy, reeducation, or hypnosis) **2** : any alteration in an individual's interpersonal environment, relationships, or life situation brought about esp. by a qualified therapist and intended to have the effect of alleviating symptoms of mental or emotional disturbance — **psy·cho·ther·a·peu·tic** \-ˌther-ə-ˈpyü-tik\ *adj* — **psy·cho·ther·a·peu·ti·cal·ly** *adv*

¹psy·chot·ic \sī-ˈkä-tik\ *adj* : of, relating to, marked by, or affected with psychosis — **psy·chot·i·cal·ly** *adv*

²psychotic *n* : a psychotic individual

¹psy·cho·to·mi·met·ic \sī-ˌkä-tō-mə-ˈme-tik, -mī-\ *adj* : of, relating to, involving, or inducing psychotic alteration of behavior and personality (~ drugs) — **psy·cho·to·mi·met·i·cal·ly** *adv*

²psychotomimetic *n* : a psychotomimetic agent (as a drug)

¹psy·cho·tro·pic \ˌsī-kə-ˈtrō-pik\ *adj* : acting on the mind (~ drugs)

²psychotropic *n* : a psychotropic substance (as a drug)

psyl·li·um \ˈsi-lē-əm\ *n* **1** : FLEAWORT **2** : PSYLLIUM SEED

psyllium seed : the seed of a fleawort (esp. *Plantago psyllium*) that has the property of swelling and becoming gelatinous when moist and is used as a mild laxative — called also *plantago seed, psyllium;* see METAMUCIL

pt *abbr* **1** patient **2** pint

Pt *symbol* platinum

PT *abbr* **1** physical therapist **2** physical therapy

PTA *abbr* plasma thromboplastin antecedent

¹PTC \ˌpē-(ˌ)tē-ˈsē\ *n* : PHENYLTHIOCARBAMIDE

²PTC *abbr* plasma thromboplastin component

PTCA \ˌpē-(ˌ)tē-(ˌ)sē-ˈä\ *n* : PERCUTANEOUS TRANSLUMINAL CORONARY ANGIOPLASTY

pter·o·yl·glu·tam·ic acid \ˌter-ō-il-glü-ˈta-mik-\ *n, also abbr. PGA* : FOLIC ACID — abbr. *PGA*

pteryg- or **pterygo-** *comb form* : pterygoid and ⟨*pterygo*maxillary⟩

pte·ryg·i·um \te-ˈri-jē-əm\ *n, pl* **-iums** or **-ia** \-jē-ä\ **1** : a triangular fleshy mass of thickened conjunctiva occurring usu. at the inner side of the eyeball, covering part of the cornea, and causing a disturbance of vision **2** : a forward growth of the cuticle over the nail

¹pter·y·goid \ˈter-ə-ˌgòid\ *adj* : of, relating to, being, or lying in the region of the inferior part of the sphenoid bone

²pterygoid *n* : a pterygoid part (as a pterygoid muscle or nerve)

pterygoid canal *n* : an anteroposterior canal in the base of each medial pterygoid plate of the sphenoid bone that gives passage to the Vidian artery and the Vidian nerve — called also *Vidian canal*

pter·y·goi·de·us \ˌter-ə-ˈgòi-dē-əs\ *n, pl* **-dei** \-dē-ˌī\ : PTERYGOID MUSCLE

pterygoid fossa *n* : a V-shaped depression on the posterior part of each pterygoid process that contains the medial pterygoid muscle and the tensor veli palatini

pterygoid hamulus *n* : a hook-shaped

process forming the inferior extremity of each medial pterygoid plate of the sphenoid bone and providing a support around which the tendon of the tensor veli palatini moves

pter·y·goid muscle *n* : either of two muscles extending from the sphenoid bone to the lower jaw: **a** : a muscle that arises from the greater wing of the sphenoid bone and from the outer surface of the lateral pterygoid plate, is inserted into the condyle of the mandible and the articular disk of the temporomandibular joint, and acts as an antagonist of the masseter, temporalis, and medial pterygoid muscles — called also *external pterygoid muscle, lateral pterygoid muscle* **b** : a muscle that arises from the inner surface of the lateral pterygoid plate and from the palatine and maxillary bones, is inserted into the ramus and the gonial angle, cooperates with the masseter and temporalis in elevating the lower jaw, and controls certain lateral and rotary movements of the jaw — called also *internal pterygoid muscle, medial pterygoid muscle*

pter·y·goid nerve *n* : either of two branches of the mandibular nerve: **a** : one that is distributed to the lateral pterygoid muscle — called also *lateral pterygoid nerve* **b** : one that is distributed to the medial pterygoid muscle, tensor tympani, and tensor veli palatini — called also *medial pterygoid nerve*

pter·y·goid plate *n* : either of two vertical plates making up a pterygoid process of the sphenoid bone: **a** : a broad thin plate that forms the lateral part of the pterygoid process and gives attachment to the lateral pterygoid muscle on its lateral surface and to the medial pterygoid muscle on its medial surface — called also *lateral pterygoid plate* **b** : a long narrow plate that forms the medial part of the pterygoid process and terminates in the pterygoid hamulus — called also *medial pterygoid plate*

pter·y·goid plexus *n* : a plexus of veins draining the region of the pterygoid muscles and emptying chiefly into the facial vein by way of the deep facial vein and into the maxillary vein

pter·y·goid process *n* : a process that extends downward from each side of the sphenoid bone, that consists of the medial and lateral pterygoid plates which are fused above anteriorly and separated below by a fissure whose edges articulate with a process of the palatine bone, and that contains on its posterior aspect the pterygoid and scaphoid fossae which give attachment to muscles

pter·y·go·man·dib·u·lar raphe \ˌter-ə-gō-man-ˈdi-byə-lər-\ *n* : a fibrous seam that descends from the pterygoid hamulus of the medial pterygoid

plate to the mylohyoid line of the mandible and that separates and gives rise to the superior constrictor of the pharynx and the buccinator

pter·y·go·max·il·lary \ˌter-ə-gō-ˈmak-sə-ˌler-ē\ *adj* : of, relating to, or connecting the pterygoid process of the sphenoid bone and the maxilla

pterygomaxillary fissure *n* : a vertical gap between the lateral pterygoid plate of the pterygoid process and the maxilla that gives passage to part of the maxillary artery and vein

pter·y·go·pal·a·tine fossa \ˌter-ə-gō-ˈpa-lə-ˌtin-\ *n* : a small triangular space beneath the apex of the orbit that contains among other structures the pterygopalatine ganglion — called also *pterygomaxillary fossa*

pterygopalatine ganglion *n* : an autonomic ganglion of the maxillary nerve that is situated in the pterygopalatine fossa and that receives preganglionic parasympathetic fibers from the facial nerve and sends postganglionic fibers to the nasal mucosa, palate, pharynx, and orbit — called also *Meckel's ganglion, sphenopalatine ganglion*

PTFE *abbr* polytetrafluoroethylene

PTH *abbr* parathyroid hormone

pto·maine \ˈtō-ˌmān, tō-ˈ\ *n* : any of various organic bases formed by the action of putrefactive bacteria on nitrogenous matter and including some which are poisonous

ptomaine poisoning *n* : food poisoning caused by bacteria or bacterial products — not used technically

pto·sis \ˈtō-səs\ *n, pl* **pto·ses** \-ˌsēz\ : a sagging or prolapse of an organ or part (renal ∼): *esp* : a drooping of the upper eyelid (as from paralysis of the oculomotor nerve) — **ptot·ic** \ˈtä-tik\ *adj*

PTSD *abbr* post-traumatic stress disorder

ptyal- *or* **ptyalo-** *comb form* : saliva (*ptyalism*)

pty·a·lin \ˈtī-ə-lən\ *n* : an amylase found in saliva that converts starch into sugar

pty·a·lism \-ˌli-zəm\ *n* : an excessive flow of saliva

-p·ty·sis \p-tə-səs\ *n comb form, pl* **-pty·ses** \p-tə-ˌsēz\ : spewing : expectoration (hemo*ptysis*)

Pu *symbol* plutonium

pub·ar·che \ˈpyü-ˌbär-kē\ *n* : the beginning of puberty marked by the first growth of pubic hair

pu·ber·al \ˈpyü-bər-əl\ *adj* : PUBERTAL

pu·ber·tal \ˈpyü-bərt-ᵊl\ *adj* : of, relating to, or occurring in puberty

pu·ber·ty \ˈpyü-bər-tē\ *n, pl* **-ties** **1** : the condition of being or the period of becoming first capable of reproducing sexually marked by maturing of the genital organs, development of secondary sex characteristics, and in humans and the higher primates by the first occurrence of menstruation in the female **2** : the age at which puberty occurs being typically between 13 and 16 years in boys and 11 and 14 in girls

¹**pu·bes** \'pyü-(₁)bēz\ *n, pl* **pubes 1** : the hair that appears on the lower part of the hypogastric region at puberty — called also *pubic hair* **2** : the lower part of the hypogastric region : the pubic region

²**pubes** *pl of* PUBIS

pu·bes·cent \pyü-ᵇbes-ᵊnt\ *adj* **1** : arriving at or having reached puberty **2** : of or relating to puberty

pu·bic \'pyü-bik\ *adj* : of, relating to, or situated in or near the region of the pubes or the pubis

pubic arch *n* : the notch formed by the inferior rami of the two conjoined pubic bones as they diverge from the midline

pubic bone *n* : PUBIS

pubic crest *n* : the border of a pubis between its pubic tubercle and the pubic symphysis

pubic hair *n* : PUBES 1

pubic louse *n* : CRAB LOUSE

pubic symphysis *n* : the rather rigid articulation of the two pubic bones in the midline of the lower anterior part of the abdomen — called also *symphysis pubis*

pubic tubercle *n* : a rounded eminence on the upper margin of each pubis near the pubic symphysis

pu·bis \'pyü-bəs\ *n, pl* **pu·bes** \-(₁)bēz\ : the ventral and anterior of the three principal bones composing either half of the pelvis that in humans consists of two rami diverging posteriorly from the region of the pubic symphysis with the superior ramus extending to the acetabulum of which it forms a part and uniting there with the ilium and ischium and the inferior ramus extending below the obturator foramen where it unites with the ischium — called also *pubic bone*

public health *n* : the art and science dealing with the protection and improvement of community health by organized community effort and including preventive medicine and sanitary and social science

public health nurse *n* : VISITING NURSE

pu·bo·cap·su·lar ligament \₁pyü-bō-ᵇkap-sə-lər-\ *n* : PUBOFEMORAL LIGAMENT

pu·bo·coc·cy·geus \-käk-ᵇsi-jəs, -jē-əs\ *n, pl* **-cy·gei** \-ᵇsi-jē-₁ī\ : the inferior subdivision of the levator ani that arises from the dorsal surface of the pubis, that inserts esp. into the coccyx, and that acts to help support the pelvic viscera, to draw the lower end of the rectum toward the pubis, and to constrict the rectum and in the female the vagina — compare ILIOCOCCYGEUS — **pu·bo·coc·cy·geal** \₁pyü-bō-käk-ᵇsi-jəl, -jē-əl\ *adj*

pu·bo·fem·o·ral ligament \₁pyü-bō-ᵇfe-mə-rəl-\ *n* : a ligament of the hip joint that extends from the superior ramus of the pubis to the capsule of the hip joint near the neck of the femur and that acts to prevent excessive extension and abduction of the thigh

pu·bo·pros·tat·ic ligament \₁pyü-bō-präs-ᵇta-tik-\ *n* : any of three strands of pelvic fascia in the male that correspond to the pubovesical ligament in the female and that support the prostate gland and indirectly the bladder

pu·bo·rec·ta·lis \₁pyü-bō-rek-ᵇtā-ləs\ *n* : a band of muscle fibers that is part of the pubococcygeus and acts to hold the rectum and anal canal at right angles to each other except during defecation

pu·bo·vag·i·na·lis \₁pyü-bō-₁va-jə-ᵇnā-ləs\ *n* : the most medial and anterior fasciculi of the pubococcygeal part of the levator ani in the female that correspond to the levator prostatae in the male, pass along the sides of the vagina, insert into the coccyx, and act to constrict the vagina

pu·bo·ves·i·cal ligament \₁pyü-bō-ᵇve-si-kəl-\ *n* : any of three strands of pelvic fascia in the female that correspond to the puboprostatic ligament in the male and that support the bladder

¹**pu·den·dal** \pyü-ᵇdend-ᵊl\ *adj* : of, relating to, occurring in, or lying in the region of the external genital organs

²**pudendal** *n* : a pudendal anatomical part (as the pudendal nerve)

pudendal artery — see EXTERNAL PUDENDAL ARTERY, INTERNAL PUDENDAL ARTERY

pudendal nerve *n* : a nerve that arises from the second, third, and fourth sacral nerves and that supplies the external genitalia, the skin of the perineum, and the anal sphincters

pudendal vein — see INTERNAL PUDENDAL VEIN

pu·den·dum \pyü-ᵇden-dəm\ *n, pl* **-da** \-də\ : the external genital organs esp. of a woman — usu. used in pl.

pu·er·ile \'pyü-ər-əl, -₁īl\ *adj* **1** : marked by or suggesting childishness and immaturity **2** : being respiration that is like that of a child in being louder than normal (~ breathing)

pu·er·per·al \pyü-ᵇər-pə-rəl\ *adj* : of, relating to, or occurring during childbirth or the period immediately following (~ infection) (~ depression)

puerperal fever *n* : an abnormal condition that results from infection of the placental site following delivery or abortion and is characterized in mild form by fever of not over 100.4°F but may progress to a localized endometritis or spread through the uterine wall and develop into peritonitis or pass into the blood stream and produce septicemia — called also *child-bed fever, puerperal sepsis*

pu·er·pe·ri·um \₁pyü-ər-¹pir-ē-əm\ *n, pl* -ria \-ē-ə\ : the period between child-birth and the return of the uterus to its normal size

puff·er \¹pə-fər\ *n* : any of a family (Tetraodontidae) of chiefly tropical marine bony fishes which can distend themselves to a globular form and most of which are highly poisonous — called also *blowfish, globefish, pufferfish*

Pu·lex \¹pyü-₁leks\ *n* : a genus of fleas (family Pulicidae) that includes the most common flea (*P. irritans*) that regularly attacks human beings

¹pull \¹pul\ *vb* 1 : EXTRACT 1 2 : to strain or stretch abnormally ⟨∼ a muscle⟩

²pull *n* : an injury resulting from abnormal straining or stretching ⟨a muscle ∼⟩ ⟨a groin ∼⟩

pul·let disease \¹pul-lət-\ *n* : BLUE COMB

pul·lo·rum disease \pə-¹lōr-əm-\ *n* : a destructive typically diarrheic salmonellosis esp. of the domestic chicken caused by a bacterium of the genus *Salmonella* (*S. pullorum*) — called also *pullorum*

pulmon- *also* pulmoni- *or* pulmono-*comb form* : lung ⟨pulmonologist⟩

pulmonalia — see CORDIA PULMONALIA

pul·mo·nary \¹pul-mə-₁ner-ē, ¹pəl-\ *adj* : relating to, functioning like, associated with, or carried on by the lungs

pulmonary alveolar proteinosis *n* : a chronic disease of the lungs characterized by the filling of the alveoli with proteinaceous material and by the progressive loss of lung function

pulmonary artery *n* : an arterial trunk or either of its two main branches that carry blood to the lungs: a : a large arterial trunk that arises from the conus arteriosus of the right ventricle and branches into the right and left pulmonary arteries — called also *pulmonary trunk* b : a branch of the pulmonary trunk that passes to the right lung where it divides into branches — called also *right pulmonary artery* c : a branch of the pulmonary trunk that passes to the left lung where it divides into branches — called also *left pulmonary artery*

pulmonary capillary wedge pressure *n* : WEDGE PRESSURE — abbr. *PCWP*

pulmonary circulation *n* : the passage of venous blood from the right atrium of the heart through the right ventricle and pulmonary arteries to the lungs where it is oxygenated and its return via the pulmonary veins to enter the left auricle and participate in the systemic circulation

pulmonary edema *n* : abnormal accumulation of fluid in the lungs

pulmonary embolism *n* : embolism of a pulmonary artery or one of its branches

pulmonary ligament *n* : a supporting fold of pleura that extends from the lower part of the lung to the pericardium

pulmonary plexus *n* : either of two nerve plexuses associated with each lung that lie on the dorsal and ventral aspects of the bronchi of each lung

pulmonary stenosis *n* : abnormal narrowing of the orifice between the pulmonary artery and the right ventricle

pulmonary trunk *n* : PULMONARY ARTERY a

pulmonary valve *n* : a valve consisting of three semilunar cusps separating the pulmonary trunk from the right ventricle

pulmonary vein *n* : any of usu. four veins comprising two from each lung that return oxygenated blood from the lungs to the superior part of the left atrium

pulmonary wedge pressure *n* : WEDGE PRESSURE

pulmoni- *or* pulmono- — see PULMON-

pul·mon·ic \₁pul-¹mä-nik, ₁pəl-\ *adj* : PULMONARY ⟨∼ lesions⟩

pulmonic stenosis *n* : PULMONARY STENOSIS

pul·mo·nol·o·gist \₁pul-mə-¹nä-lə-jist, ₁pəl-\ *n* : a specialist in the anatomy, physiology, and pathology of the lungs

pulp \¹pəlp\ *n* : a mass of soft tissue: as a : DENTAL PULP b : the characteristic somewhat spongy tissue of the spleen c : the fleshy portion of the fingertip — pulp·al \¹pəl-pəl\ *adj* — pulp·less *adj*

pulp canal *n* : ROOT CANAL 1

pulp cavity *n* : the central cavity of a tooth containing the dental pulp and made up of the root canal and the pulp chamber

pulp chamber *n* : the part of the pulp cavity lying in the crown of a tooth

pulp·ec·to·my \₁pəl-¹pek-tə-mē\ *n, pl* -mies : the removal of the pulp of a tooth

pulp·i·tis \₁pəl-¹pī-təs\ *n, pl* pulp·it·i·des \-¹pi-tə-₁dēz\ : inflammation of the pulp of a tooth

pulposi, pulposus — see NUCLEUS PULPOSUS

pulp·ot·o·my \₁pəl-¹pä-tə-mē\ *n, pl* -mies : removal in a dental procedure of the coronal portion of the pulp of a tooth in such a manner that the pulp of the root remains intact and viable

pulp stone *n* : a lump of calcified tissue within the dental pulp — called also *denticle*

pulpy kidney \¹pəl-pē-\ *n* : a destructive enterotoxemia of lambs caused by a bacterium of the genus *Clostridium* (*C. perfringens*) — called also *pulpy kidney disease*

pul·sate \¹pəl-₁sāt\ *vb* pul·sat·ed; pul·sat·ing : to exhibit a pulse or pulsation ⟨a *pulsating* artery⟩

pul·sa·tion \₁pəl-¹sā-shən\ *n* : rhythmic throbbing or vibrating (as of an artery); *also* : a single beat or throb — **pul·sa·tile** \'pəl-sət-ᵊl, -sə-ˌtīl\ *adj*

pulse \'pəls\ *n* **1 a** : a regularly recurrent wave of distension in arteries that results from the progress through an artery of blood injected into the arterial system at each contraction of the ventricles of the heart **b** : the palpable beat resulting from such pulse as detected in a superficial artery (as the radial artery); *also* : the number of such beats in a specified period of time (as one minute) ⟨a resting ~ of 70⟩ **2** : PULSATION **3** : a dose of a substance esp. when applied over a short period of time ⟨therapy with intravenous methylprednisolone ~s⟩ — **pulse** *vb* — **pulse·less** \'pəls-ləs\ *adj*

pulse-la·bel \'pəls-ˌlā-bəl\ *vb* **-la·beled** *or* **-la·belled; -la·bel·ing** *or* **-la·bel·ling** : to cause a pulse of a radiolabeled atom or substance to become incorporated into (as a molecule or cell component) ⟨~ed DNA⟩

pulse pressure *n* : the pressure that is characteristic of the arterial pulse and represents the difference between diastolic and systolic pressures of the heart cycle

pulse rate *n* : the rate of the arterial pulse usu. observed at the wrist and stated in beats per minute

pul·sus al·ter·nans \'pəl-səs-ˈȯl-tər-ˌnanz\ *n* : alternation of strong and weak beats of the arterial pulse due to alternate strong and weak ventricular contractions

pul·sus par·a·dox·us \-ˌpar-ə-ˈdäk-səs\ *n* : a pulse that weakens abnormally during inspiration and is symptomatic of various abnormalities (as pericarditis)

pulv *abbr* [Latin *pulvis*] powder — used in writing prescriptions

pul·vi·nar \ˌpəl-ˈvī-nər\ *n* : a rounded prominence on the back of the thalamus

¹pump \'pəmp\ *n* **1** : a device that raises, transfers, or compresses fluids or that attenuates gases esp. by suction or pressure or both **2** : HEART **3** : an act or the process of pumping **4** : a mechanism (as the sodium pump) for pumping atoms, ions, or molecules

²pump *vb* **1** : to raise (as water) with a pump **2** : to draw fluid from with a pump **3** : to transport (as ions) against a concentration gradient by the expenditure of energy

punch-drunk \'pənch-ˌdrəŋk\ *adj* : suffering cerebral injury from many minute brain hemorrhages as a result of repeated head blows received in boxing

puncta *pl of* PUNCTUM

punctata — see KERATITIS PUNCTATA

punc·tate \'pəŋk-ˌtāt\ *adj* : characterized by dots or points ⟨~ skin lesions⟩

punc·tum \'pəŋk-təm\ *n, pl* **punc·ta** \-tə\ : a small area marked off in any way from a surrounding surface — see LACRIMAL PUNCTUM

¹punc·ture \'pəŋk-chər\ *n* **1** : an act of puncturing **2** : a hole, wound, or perforation made by puncturing

²puncture *vb* **punc·tured; punc·tur·ing** : to pierce with or as if with a pointed instrument or object

pu·pa \'pyü-pə\ *n, pl* **pu·pae** \-(ˌ)pē, -ˌpī\ *or* **pupas** : an intermediate usu. quiescent stage of an insect that occurs between the larva and the adult in forms which undergo complete metamorphosis and that is characterized by internal changes by which larval structures are replaced by those typical of the adult — **pu·pal** \'pyü-pəl\ *adj*

pu·pil \'pyü-pəl\ *n* : the contractile usu. round aperture in the iris of the eye — **pu·pil·lary** *also* **pu·pi·lary** \'pyü-pə-ˌler-ē\ *adj*

pupillae — see SPHINCTER PUPILLAE

pupillary reflex *n* : the contraction of the pupil in response to light entering the eye

pupillo- *comb form* : pupil ⟨*pupillo*meter⟩

pu·pil·log·ra·phy \ˌpyü-pə-ˈlä-grə-fē\ *n, pl* **-phies** : the measurement of the reactions of the pupil

pu·pil·lom·e·ter \ˌpyü-pə-ˈlä-mə-tər\ *n* : an instrument for measuring the diameter of the pupil of the eye — **pu·pil·lom·e·try** \-mə-trē\ *n*

pur·ga·tion \ˌpər-ˈgā-shən\ *n* **1** : the act of purging; *specif* : vigorous evacuation of the bowels (as from the action of a cathartic) **2** : administration of or treatment with a purgative

¹pur·ga·tive \'pər-gə-tiv\ *adj* : purging or tending to purge : CATHARTIC — **pur·ga·tive·ly** *adv*

²purgative *n* : a purging medicine : CATHARTIC

¹purge \'pərj\ *vb* **purged; purg·ing** : to have or cause strong and usu. repeated emptying of the bowels

²purge *n* **1** : something that purges; *esp* : PURGATIVE **2** : an act or instance of purging

purified protein derivative *n* : a purified preparation of tuberculin used in a test for tuberculous infection — *abbr* PPD

pu·rine \'pyür-ˌēn\ *n* **1** : a crystalline base $C_5H_4N_4$ that is the parent of compounds of the uric-acid group **2** : a derivative of purine; *esp* : a base (as adenine or guanine) that is a constituent of DNA or RNA

purine base *n* : any of a group of crystalline bases comprising purine and bases derived from it (as adenine) some of which are components of nucleosides and nucleotides

Pur·kin·je cell \pər-ˈkin-jē-\ *n* : any of numerous nerve cells that occupy the middle layer of the cerebellar cortex and are characterized by a large globe-shaped body with massive dendrites directed outward and a single slender axon directed inward

Pur·ky·nĕ (or **Purkinje**) \'pür-kin-je̊, -yȧ\, **Jan Evangelista (1787–1869)**, Bohemian physiologist.

Purkinje fiber n : any of the modified cardiac muscle fibers with few nuclei, granulated central cytoplasm, and sparse peripheral striations that make up Purkinje's network

Purkinje's network n : a network of intracardiac conducting tissue made up of syncytial Purkinje fibers that lie in the myocardium and constitute the bundle of His and other conducting tracts which spread out from the sinoatrial node — called also *Purkinje's system*, *Purkinje's tissue*

pu·ro·my·cin \₁pyür-ə-'mīs-ᵊn\ n : an antibiotic $C_{22}H_{29}N_7O_5$ that is obtained from an actinomycete (*Streptomyces alboniger*) and is used esp. as a potent inhibitor of cellular protein synthesis

pur·pu·ra \'pər-pü-rə, -pyü-\ n : any of several hemorrhagic states characterized by patches of purplish discoloration resulting from extravasation of blood into the skin and mucous membranes — see THROMBOCYTOPENIC PURPURA — **pur·pu·ric** \-pər-'pyür-ik\ adj

purpura hem·or·rhag·i·ca \-₁he-mə-'ra-jə-kə\ n : THROMBOCYTOPENIC PURPURA

purse–string suture n : a surgical suture passed as a running stitch in and out along the edge of a circular wound in such a way that when the ends of the suture are drawn tight the wound is closed like a purse

pu·ru·lence \'pyür-ə-ləns, 'pyür-yə-\ n : the quality or state of being purulent; also : PUS

pu·ru·lent \-lənt\ adj 1 : containing, consisting of, or being pus 2 : accompanied by suppuration

pus \'pəs\ n : thick opaque usu. yellowish white fluid matter formed by suppuration and composed of exudate containing white blood cells, tissue debris, and microorganisms — **pussy** \'pə-sē\ adj

pus·tu·lar \'pəs-chə-lər, 'pəs-tyə-\ adj 1 : of, relating to, or resembling pustules (~ eruptions) 2 : covered with pustules

pus·tule \'pəs-₁chül, -(₁)tyül, -(₁)tül\ n 1 : a small circumscribed elevation of the skin containing pus and having an inflamed base 2 : a small often distinctively colored elevation or spot resembling a blister or pimple

pu·ta·men \pyü-'tā-mən\ n, pl **pu·tam·i·na** \-'ta-mə-nə\ : an outer reddish layer of gray matter in the lentiform nucleus

pu·tre·fac·tion \₁pyü-trə-'fak-shən\ n 1 : the decomposition of organic matter; esp : the typically anaerobic splitting of proteins by bacteria and fungi with the formation of foul-smelling incompletely oxidized products 2 : the state of being putrefied — **pu·tre·fac·tive** \-tiv\ adj — **pu·tre·fy** \'pyü-trə-₁fī\ vb

pu·tres·cine \pyü-'tre-₁sēn\ n : a crystalline slightly poisonous ptomaine $C_4H_{12}N_2$ that is formed by decarboxylation of ornithine, occurs widely but in small amounts in living things, and is found esp. in putrid flesh

pu·trid \'pyü-trəd\ adj 1 : being in a state of putrefaction 2 : of, relating to, or characteristic of putrefaction

PVD abbr peripheral vascular disease

PVE abbr prosthetic valve endocarditis

PVP abbr polyvinylpyrrolidone

P wave \'pē-₁wāv\ n : a deflection in an electrocardiographic tracing that represents atrial activity of the heart — compare QRS COMPLEX, T WAVE

py- or **pyo-** comb form : pus (pyemia) (pyorrhea)

py·ae·mia chiefly Brit var of PYEMIA

py·ar·thro·sis \₁pī-är-'thrō-səs\ n, pl **-thro·ses** \-₁sēz\ : the formation or presence of pus within a joint

pycn- or **pycno-** — see PYKN-

pyc·nic, pyc·no·dys·os·to·sis, pyc·no·sis var of PYKNIC, PYKNODYSOSTOSIS, PYKNOSIS

pyel- or **pyelo-** comb form : renal pelvis (pyelography)

py·eli·tis \₁pī-ə-'lī-təs\ n : inflammation of the lining of the renal pelvis

py·elo·gram \'pī-ə-lə-₁gram\ n : a roentgenogram made by pyelography

py·elog·ra·phy \₁pī-ə-'lä-grə-fē\ n, pl **-phies** : roentgenographic visualization of the renal pelvis after injection of a radiopaque substance through the ureter or into a vein — see RETROGRADE PYELOGRAPHY — **py·elo·graph·ic** \₁pī-ə-lə-'gra-fik\ adj

py·elo·li·thot·o·my \₁pī-ə-lō-li-'thä-tə-mē\ n, pl **-mies** : surgical incision of the pelvis of a kidney for removal of a kidney stone

py·elo·ne·phri·tis \₁pī-ə-lō-ni-'frī-təs\ n, pl **-phrit·i·des** \-'fri-tə-₁dēz\ : inflammation of both the parenchyma of a kidney and the lining of its pelvis esp. due to bacterial infection — **py·elo·ne·phrit·ic** \-'fri-tik\ adj

py·elo·plas·ty \'pī-ə-lə-₁plas-tē\ n, pl **-ties** : plastic surgery of the pelvis of a kidney

py·emia \pī-'ē-mē-ə\ n : septicemia accompanied by multiple abscesses and secondary toxemic symptoms and caused by pus-forming microorganisms (as the bacterium *Staphylococcus aureus*) — **py·emic** \-mik\ adj

Py·emo·tes \₁pī-ə-'mō-tēz\ n : a genus of mites that are usu. ectoparasites of insects but that include one (*P. ventricosus*) which causes grain itch in humans

py·gop·a·gus \pī-'gä-pə-gəs\ n, pl **-gi**

\-ɪgī, -ˌjī\ : a twin fetus joined in the sacral region

pykn- or **pykno-** also **pycn-** or **pycno-** comb form 1 : close : compact : dense : bulky ⟨*pykn*ic⟩ 2 : marked by short stature or shortness of digits ⟨*pykno*dysostosis⟩

¹**pyk-nic** \'pik-nik\ adj : characterized by shortness of stature, broadness of girth, and powerful muscularity — ENDOMORPHIC 2

²**pyknic** n : a person of pyknic build

pyk-no-dys-os-to-sis \ˌpik-nō-ˌdis-ä-'stō-səs\ n, pl **-to-ses** \-ˌsēz\ : a rare condition inherited as an autosomal recessive trait and characterized esp. by short stature, fragile bones, shortness of the fingers and toes, failure of the anterior fontanel to close properly, and a receding chin

pyk-no-lep-sy \'pik-nə-ˌlep-sē\ n, pl **-sies** : a condition marked by epileptiform attacks resembling petit mal

pyk-no-sis \pik-'nō-səs\ n : a degenerative condition of a cell nucleus marked by clumping of the chromosomes, hyperchromatism, and shrinking of the nucleus — **pyk-not-ic** \-'nä-tik\ adj

pyl- or **pyle-** or **pylo-** comb form : portal vein ⟨*pyle*phlebitis⟩

py-le-phle-bi-tis \ˌpī-lə-fli-'bī-təs\ n, pl **-bit-i-des** \-'bi-tə-ˌdēz\ : inflammation of the renal portal vein usu. secondary to intestinal disease and with suppuration

py-lon \'pī-ˌlän, -lən\ n : a simple temporary artificial leg

pylor- or **pyloro-** comb form : pylorus ⟨*pyloro*plasty⟩

py-lo-ric \pī-'lōr-ik, pə-\ adj : of or relating to the pylorus; also : of, relating to, or situated in or near the posterior part of the stomach

pyloric glands n pl : the short coiled tubular glands of the mucous coat of the stomach occurring chiefly near the pyloric end

pyloric sphincter n : the circular fold of mucous membrane containing a ring of muscle fibers that closes the pylorus — called also *pyloric valve*

pyloric stenosis n : narrowing of the pyloric opening (as from congenital malformation)

py-lo-ro-my-ot-o-my \ˌpī-ˌlōr-ō-mī-'ä-tə-mē, pə-ˌlōr-ə-\ n, pl **-mies** : surgical incision of the muscle fibers of the pyloric sphincter for relief of stenosis caused by muscular hypertrophy

py-lo-ro-plas-ty \pī-'lōr-ə-ˌplas-tē\ n **-ties** : a plastic operation on the pylorus (as to enlarge a stricture)

py-lo-ro-spasm \pī-'lōr-ə-ˌspa-zəm\ n : spasm of the pyloric sphincter often associated with other conditions (as an ulcer of the stomach) or occurring in infants and marked by pain and vomiting

py-lo-rus \pī-'lōr-əs, pə-\ n, pl **py-lo-ri** \-'lōr-ˌī, -ˌ(ˌ)ē\ : the opening from the stomach into the intestine — see PYLORIC SPHINCTER

pyo- — see PY-

pyo-der-ma \ˌpī-ə-'dər-mə\ n : a bacterial skin inflammation marked by pus-filled lesions

pyo-gen-ic \ˌpī-ə-'je-nik\ adj : producing pus ⟨~ bacteria⟩; also : marked by pus production ⟨~ meningitis⟩

pyo-me-tra \ˌpī-ō-'mē-trə\ n : an accumulation of pus in the uterine cavity

pyo-myo-si-tis \ˌpī-ō-ˌmī-ə-'sī-təs\ n : infiltrative bacterial inflammation of muscles leading to the formation of abscesses

pyo-ne-phro-sis \-ni-'frō-səs\ n, pl **-phro-ses** \-ˌsēz\ : a collection of pus in the kidney

py-or-rhea \ˌpī-ə-'rē-ə\ n 1 : a discharge of pus 2 : an inflammatory condition of the periodontium that is an advanced form of periodontal disease associated esp. with a discharge of pus from the alveoli and loosening of the teeth in their sockets — **py-or-rhe-ic** \-'rē-ik\ adj

py-or-rhoea chiefly Brit var of PYORRHEA

pyo-sal-pinx \ˌpī-ō-'sal-(ˌ)piŋks\ n, pl **-sal-pin-ges** \-sal-'pin-(ˌ)jēz\ : a collection of pus in an oviduct

pyo-tho-rax \-'thōr-ˌaks\ n, pl **-tho-rax-es** or **-tho-ra-ces** \-'thōr-ə-(ˌ)sēz\ : EMPYEMA

pyr- or **pyro-** comb form 1 : fire : heat ⟨*pyro*mania⟩ 2 : fever ⟨*pyro*gen⟩

pyr-a-mid \'pir-ə-ˌmid\ n 1 : a polyhedron having for its base a polygon and for faces triangles with a common vertex 2 : an anatomical structure resembling a pyramid: as a : RENAL PYRAMID b : either of two large bundles of motor fibers from the cerebral cortex that reach the medulla oblongata and are continuous with the corticospinal tracts of the spinal cord c : a conical projection making up the central part of the inferior vermis of the cerebellum — **py-ram-i-dal** \pə-'ra-məd-əl\ adj

pyramidal cell n : any of numerous large multipolar pyramid-shaped cells in the cerebral cortex

pyramidal decussation n : DECUSSATION OF PYRAMIDS

py-ram-i-da-lis \pə-ˌra-mə-'dā-ləs\ n, pl **-da-les** \-(ˌ)lēz\ or **-dalises** : a small triangular muscle of the lower front part of the abdomen that is situated in front of and in the same sheath with the rectus and functions to tense the linea alba

pyramidal tract n : CORTICOSPINAL TRACT

py-ram-i-dot-o-my \pə-ˌra-mə-'dä-tə-mē\ n, pl **-mies** : a surgical procedure in which a corticospinal tract is severed (as for relief of parkinsonism)

pyr-a-mis \'pir-ə-məs\ n, pl **py-ram-i-des** \pə-'ra-mə-ˌdēz\ : PYRAMID 2

py-ran-tel \pə-'ran-ˌtel\ n : an anthelmintic drug $C_{11}H_{14}N_2S$ administered in the form of its pamoate or tartrate

pyr·a·zin·amide \ˌpir-ə-ˈzi-nə-ˌmīd, -məd\ n : a tuberculostatic drug $C_5H_5N_3O$

py·re·thrin \pī-ˈrē-thrən, -ˈre-\ n : either of two oily liquid esters $C_{21}H_{28}O_3$ and $C_{22}H_{28}O_5$ that have insecticidal properties and are the active components of pyrethrum

py·re·thrum \pī-ˈrē-thrəm, -ˈre-\ n : an insecticide consisting of or derived from the dried heads of any of several Old World chrysanthemums (genus *Chrysanthemum* of the family Compositae)

py·rex·ia \pī-ˈrek-sē-ə\ n : abnormal elevation of body temperature : FEVER — **py·rex·i·al** \-sē-əl\ adj

py·rex·ic \-sik\ adj : PYREXIAL

Pyr·i·ben·za·mine \ˌpir-ə-ˈben-zə-ˌmēn\ trademark — used for a preparation of tripelennamine

pyr·i·dine \ˈpir-ə-ˌdēn\ n : a toxic water-soluble flammable liquid base C_5H_5N of pungent odor

pyridine nucleotide n : a nucleotide characterized by a pyridine derivative as a nitrogen base; esp : NAD

pyr·i·do·stig·mine \ˌpir-ə-dō-ˈstig-ˌmēn\ n : a cholinergic drug that is administered in the form of its bromide $C_9H_{13}BrN_2O_2$ esp. in the treatment of myasthenia gravis — see MESTINON

pyr·i·dox·al \ˌpir-ə-ˈdäk-ˌsal\ n : a crystalline aldehyde $C_8H_9NO_3$ of the vitamin B_6 group that in the form of its phosphate is active as a coenzyme

pyr·i·dox·amine \ˌpir-ə-ˈdäk-sə-ˌmēn\ n : a crystalline amine $C_8H_{12}N_2O_2$ of the vitamin B_6 group that in the form of its phosphate is active as a coenzyme

pyr·i·dox·ine \ˌpir-ə-ˈdäk-ˌsēn, -sən\ n : a crystalline phenolic alcohol $C_8H_{11}NO_3$ of the vitamin B_6 group found esp. in cereals and convertible in the body into pyridoxal and pyridoxamine

pyridoxine hydrochloride n : the hydrochloride salt $C_8H_{11}NO_3 \cdot HCl$ of pyridoxine that is used therapeutically (as in the treatment of pyridoxine deficiency)

py·ri·form, py·ri·for·mis var of PIRIFORM, PIRIFORMIS

pyr·il·amine \ˌpir-ˈil-ə-ˌmēn\ n : an oily liquid base $C_{17}H_{23}N_3O$ or its bitter crystalline maleate $C_{21}H_{27}N_3O_5$ used as an antihistamine drug in the treatment of various allergies — see NEOANTERGAN

py·ri·meth·amine \ˌpī-rə-ˈme-thə-ˌmēn\ n : a folic acid antagonist $C_{12}H_{13}ClN_4$ that is used in the treatment of malaria and of toxoplasmosis and as an immunosuppressive drug

py·rim·i·dine \pī-ˈri-mə-ˌdēn, pə-\ n 1 : a feeble organic base $C_4H_4N_2$ of penetrating odor that is composed of a single six-membered ring having four carbon atoms with nitrogen atoms in positions one and three 2 : a derivative of pyrimidine having its characteristic ring structure; esp : a base (as cytosine, thymine, or uracil) that is a constituent of DNA or RNA

pyrithione zinc n : ZINC PYRITHIONE

pyro- — see PYR-

py·ro·gal·lic acid \ˌpī-rō-ˈga-lik-\ n : PYROGALLOL

py·ro·gal·lol \-ˈga-ˌlȯl, -ˈgȯ-, -ˌlōl\ n : a poisonous bitter crystalline phenol $C_6H_6O_3$ that is used as a topical antimicrobial (as in the treatment of psoriasis)

py·ro·gen \ˈpī-rə-jən\ n : a fever-producing substance

py·ro·gen·ic \ˌpī-rō-ˈje-nik\ adj : producing or produced by fever — **py·ro·ge·nic·i·ty** \-jə-ˈni-sə-tē\ n

py·ro·ma·nia \ˌpī-rō-ˈmā-nē-ə, -nyə\ n : an irresistible impulse to start fires — **py·ro·ma·ni·a·cal** \-mə-ˈnī-ə-kəl\ adj

py·ro·ma·ni·ac \-nē-ˌak\ n : an individual affected with pyromania

py·ro·sis \pī-ˈrō-səs\ n : HEARTBURN

py·rox·y·lin \pī-ˈräk-sə-lin\ n : a flammable mixture of nitrates of cellulose — see COLLODION

pyr·role \ˈpir-ˌōl\ n : a toxic liquid heterocyclic compound C_4H_5N that has a ring consisting of four carbon atoms and one nitrogen atom, and is the parent compound of many biologically important substances (as bile pigments, porphyrins, and chlorophyll); broadly : a derivative of pyrrole

py·ru·vate \pī-ˈrü-ˌvāt\ n : a salt or ester of pyruvic acid

pyruvate kinase n : an enzyme that functions in glycolysis by catalyzing esp. the transfer of phosphate from phosphoenolpyruvate to ADP forming pyruvate and ATP

py·ru·vic acid \pī-ˈrü-vik-\ n : a 3-carbon keto acid $C_3H_4O_3$ that is an intermediate in carbohydrate metabolism and can be formed either from glucose after phosphorylation or from glycogen by glycolysis

py·uria \pī-ˈyu̇r-ē-ə\ n : the presence of pus in the urine; also : a condition (as pyelonephritis) characterized by pus in the urine

PZI abbr protamine zinc insulin

Q

qd *abbr* [Latin *quaque die*] every day — used in writing prescriptions

Q fever *n* : a disease that is characterized by high fever, chills, and muscular pains, is caused by a rickettsial bacterium of the genus *Coxiella* (*C. burnetii*), and is transmitted by raw milk, by droplet infection, or by ticks

qh *or* **qhr** *abbr* [Latin *quaque hora*] every hour — used in writing prescriptions often with a number indicating the hours between doses ⟨*q4h* means every 4 hours; *q6h*, every 6 hours⟩

qid *abbr* [Latin *quater in die*] four times a day — used in writing prescriptions

QRS \ˌkyü-(ˌ)är-ˈes\ *n* : QRS COMPLEX

QRS complex *n* : the series of deflections in an electrocardiogram that represent electrical activity generated by ventricular depolarization prior to contraction of the ventricles — compare P WAVE, T WAVE

qt *abbr* quart

Q–T interval \ˌkyü-ˈtē-\ *n* : the interval from the beginning of the QRS complex to the end of the T wave on an electrocardiogram that represents the time during which contraction of the ventricles occurs

Quaa·lude \ˈkwā-ˌlüd\ *trademark* — used for a preparation of methaqualone

quack \ˈkwak\ *n* : a pretender to medical skill : an ignorant or dishonest practitioner — **quack** *adj* — **quack·ery** \ˈkwa-kə-rē\ *n*

quad·rant \ˈkwä-drənt\ *n* : any of the four more or less equivalent segments into which an anatomic structure may be divided by vertical and horizontal partitioning through its midpoint ⟨pain in the lower right ∼ of the abdomen⟩

quad·rate lobe \ˈkwä-ˌdrāt-\ *n* : a small lobe of the liver on the underside of the right lobe to the left of the fissure for the gallbladder

qua·dra·tus fem·o·ris \kwä-ˈdrā-təs-ˈfe-mə-rəs\ *n* : a small flat muscle of the gluteal region that arises from the ischial tuberosity, inserts into the greater trochanter and adjacent region of the femur, and serves to rotate the thigh laterally

quadratus la·bii su·pe·ri·or·is \-ˈlā-bē-ˌī-sü-ˌpir-ē-ˈor-əs\ *n* : LEVATOR LABII SUPERIORIS

quadratus lum·bor·um \-ləm-ˈbor-əm\ *n* : a quadrilateral-shaped muscle of the abdomen that arises from the iliac crest and the iliolumbar ligament, inserts into the lowest rib and the upper four lumbar vertebrae, and functions esp. to flex the trunk laterally

quadratus plan·tae \-ˈplan-ˌtē\ *n* : a muscle of the sole of the foot that arises by two heads from the calcaneus, inserts into the lateral side of the tendons of the flexor digitorum longus, and aids in flexing the toes

quad·ri·ceps \ˈkwä-drə-ˌseps\ *n* : a large extensor muscle of the front of the thigh divided above into four parts which include the rectus femoris, vastus lateralis, vastus intermedius, and vastus medialis, and which unite in a single tendon to enclose the patella as a sesamoid bone at the knee and insert as the patellar ligament into the tuberosity of the tibia — called also *quadriceps muscle*

quadriceps fem·o·ris \-ˈfe-mə-rəs\ *n* : QUADRICEPS

quadrigemina — see CORPORA QUADRIGEMINA

quad·ri·ple·gia \ˌkwä-drə-ˈplē-jə, -jē-ə\ *n* : paralysis of both arms and both legs — called also *tetraplegia*

¹quad·ri·ple·gic \ˌkwä-drə-ˈplē-jik\ *adj* : of, relating to, or affected with quadriplegia

²quadriplegic *n* : one affected with paralysis of both arms and both legs

quad·ru·ped \ˈkwä-drə-ˌped\ *n* : an animal having four feet — **qua·dru·pe·dal** \kwä-ˈdrü-pəd-ᵊl, ˌkwä-drə-ˈped-\ *adj*

qua·dru·plet \kwä-ˈdrə-plət, -ˈdrü-; ˈkwä-drə-\ *n* : one of four offspring born at one birth

qual·i·ty \ˈkwä-lə-tē\ *n, pl* -ties : the character of an X-ray beam that determines its penetrating power and is dependent upon its wavelength distribution

quality assurance *n* : a program for the systematic monitoring and evaluation of the various aspects of a project, service, or facility to ensure that standards of quality are being met

quan·ti·ta·tive analysis \ˈkwän-tə-ˌtā-tiv-\ *n* : chemical analysis designed to determine the amounts or proportions of the components of a substance

quantitative character *n* : an inherited character that is expressed phenotypically in all degrees of variation between one often indefinite extreme and another : a character determined by polygenes — compare QUANTITATIVE INHERITANCE

quantitative inheritance *n* : genic inheritance of a character (as human skin color) controlled by polygenes — compare PARTICULATE INHERITANCE

quan·tum \ˈkwän-təm\ *n, pl* **quan·ta** \ˈkwän-tə\ **1** : one of the very small increments or parcels into which many forms of energy are subdivided **2** : one of the small molecular packets of a neurotransmitter (as acetylcholine) released into the synaptic cleft in the transmission of a nerve impulse across a synapse — **quan·tal** \-t̩əl\ *adj*

quar·an·tine \'kwȯr-ən-ˌtēn, 'kwär-\
1 a : a term during which a ship arriving in port and suspected of carrying contagious disease is held in isolation from the shore **b** : a regulation placing a ship in quarantine **c** : a place where a ship is detained during quarantine **2 a** : a restraint upon the activities or communication of persons or the transport of goods that is designed to prevent the spread of disease or pests **b** : a place in which those under quarantine are kept — **quar·an·tin·able** *adj* — **quarantine** *vb*

quart \'kwȯrt\ *n* **1** : a British unit of liquid or dry capacity equal to ¼ gallon or 69.355 cubic inches or 1.136 liters **2** : a U.S. unit of liquid capacity equal to ¼ gallon or 57.75 cubic inches or 0.946 liters

quar·tan \'kwȯrt-ᵊn\ *adj* : occurring every fourth day; *specif* : recurring at approximately 72-hour intervals ⟨~ chills and fever⟩ — compare TERTIAN

quartan malaria *n* : MALARIAE MALARIA

quartz \'kwȯrts\ *n* : a silica-containing mineral SiO_2

quas·sia \'kwä-shə, -shē-ə, -sē-ə\ *n* : a drug consisting of the heartwood of various tropical trees (family Simaroubaceae) used in medicine esp. as a remedy for roundworms

qua·ter·na·ry \'kwä-tər-ˌner-ē, kwə-'tər-nə-rē\ *adj* : consisting of, containing, or being an atom united by four bonds to carbon atoms

quaternary ammonium compound *n* : any of numerous strong bases and their salts derived from ammonium by replacement of the hydrogen atoms with organic radicals and important esp. as surface-active agents, disinfectants, and drugs

que·bra·cho \kā-'brä-(ˌ)chō, ki-\ *n* : a tree (*Aspidosperma quebracho*) of the dogbane family (Apocynaceae) which occurs in Argentina and Chile and whose dried bark is used as a respiratory sedative in dyspnea and in asthma

Queck·en·stedt test \'kvek-ᵊn-ˌshtet-\ *n* : a test for spinal blockage of the subarachnoid space in which manual pressure is applied to the jugular vein to elevate venous pressure, which indicates the absence of a block when there is a simultaneous increase in cerebrospinal fluid pressure, and which indicates the presence of a block when cerebrospinal fluid pressure remains the same or almost the same — called also *Queckenstedt sign*

  Queckenstedt, Hans Heinrich Georg (1876–1918), German physician.

quel·lung \'kwe-ləŋ, 'kve-lu̇ŋ\ *n*, *often*

cap : swelling of the capsule of a microorganism after reaction with an antibody (the ~ reaction)

quer·ce·tin \'kwər-sə-tən\ *n* : a yellow crystalline pigment $C_{15}H_{10}O_7$ occurring usu. in the form of glycosides in various plants

quick \'kwik\ *n* : a painfully sensitive spot or area of flesh (as that underlying a fingernail or toenail)

quick·en \'kwi-kən\ *vb* **quick·ened; quick·en·ing** : to reach the stage of gestation at which fetal motion is felt

quickening *n* : the first motion of a fetus in the uterus felt by the mother usu. somewhat before the middle of the period of gestation

quick·sil·ver \'kwik-ˌsil-vər\ *n* : MERCURY 1

qui·es·cent \kwī-'es-ᵊnt, kwē-\ *adj* **1** : being in a state of arrest ⟨~ tuberculosis⟩ **2** : causing no symptoms ⟨~ gallstones⟩ — **qui·es·cence** \-ᵊns\ *n*

Qui·lene \'kwī-ˌlēn\ *trademark* — used for a preparation of pentapiperide methylsulfate

quin- or **quino-** *comb form* **1** : quina : cinchona bark ⟨*quinine*⟩ ⟨*quinoline*⟩ **2** : quinoline ⟨*quinethazone*⟩

qui·na \'kē-nə\ *n* : CINCHONA 2, 3

quin·a·crine \'kwi-nə-ˌkrēn\ *n* : an antimalarial drug derived from acridine and used esp. in the form of its dihydrochloride $C_{23}H_{30}ClN_3O \cdot 2HCl \cdot 2H_2O$ — called also *mepacrine;* see ATABRINE

quin·al·bar·bi·tone \ˌkwi-nal-'bär-bi-ˌtōn\ *n*, *chiefly Brit* : SECOBARBITAL

Quin·cke's disease \'kviŋ-kəz-\ *n* : ANGIOEDEMA

  Quincke, Heinrich Irenaeus (1842–1922), German physician.

Quincke's edema *n* : ANGIOEDEMA

quin·eth·a·zone \ˌkwi-'ne-thə-ˌzōn\ *n* : a diuretic $C_{10}H_{12}ClN_3O_3S$ used in the treatment of edema and hypertension

quin·i·dine \'kwi-nə-ˌdēn, -dən\ *n* : a crystalline dextrorotatory stereoisomer of quinine found in some species of cinchona and used sometimes in place of quinine but chiefly in the form of its sulfate in the treatment of cardiac rhythm irregularities

qui·nine \'kwī-ˌnīn, 'kwi-, -ˌnēn\ *n* **1** : a bitter crystalline alkaloid $C_{20}H_{24}N_2O_2$ from cinchona bark used in medicine **2** : a salt of quinine used as an antipyretic, antimalarial, antiperiodic, and bitter tonic

quin·o·line \'kwin-ᵊl-ˌēn\ *n* **1** : a pungent oily nitrogenous base C_9H_7N that is the parent compound of many alkaloids, drugs, and dyes **2** : a derivative of quinoline

qui·none \kwi-'nōn, 'kwi-ˌ\ *n* **1** : either of two isomeric cyclic crystalline compounds $C_6H_4O_2$ that are extremely irritating to the skin and mucous membranes **2** : any of various usu. yellow, orange, or red compounds structurally related to the quinones and including several that are biologically important as coenzymes, hydrogen acceptors, or vitamins

quin·sy \\'kwin-zē\\ *n, pl* **quin·sies** : an abscess in the connective tissue around a tonsil usu. resulting from bacterial infection and often accompanied by fever, pain, and swelling — called also *peritonsillar abscess*

quint \\'kwint\\ *n* : QUINTUPLET

quinti — see EXTENSOR DIGITI QUINTI PROPRIUS

quin·tu·plet \\kwin-'tə-plət, -'tü-, -'tyü-; 'kwin-tə-\\ *n* : one of five children or offspring born at one birth

qui·nu·cli·di·nyl ben·zi·late \\kwi-'nü-klə-,dēn-°l-'ben-zə-,lāt, -'nyü-\\ *n* : BZ

quit·tor \\'kwi-tər\\ *n* : a purulent inflammation (as a necrobacillosis) of the feet esp. of horses and donkeys

quo·tid·i·an \\kwō-'ti-dē-ən\\ *adj* : occurring every day (∼ fever)

quo·tient \\'kwō-shənt\\ *n* : the numerical ratio usu. multiplied by 100 between a test score and a measurement on which that score might be expected largely to depend — see INTELLIGENCE QUOTIENT

qv *abbr* [Latin *quantum vis*] as much as you will

Q wave \\'kyü-,\\ *n* : the short initial downward stroke of the QRS complex in an electrocardiogram formed during the beginning of ventricular depolarization

R

r *abbr* roentgen

Ra *symbol* radium

rabbit fever *n* : TULAREMIA

ra·bies \\'rā-bēz\\ *n, pl* **rabies** : an acute virus disease of the nervous system of warm-blooded animals that is transmitted with infected saliva usu. through the bite of a rabid animal and is typically characterized by increased salivation, abnormal behavior, and eventual paralysis and death when untreated — called also *hydrophobia* — **ra·bid** \\'ra-bid, 'rā-\\ *adj*

race \\'rās\\ *n* 1 : a division or group (as a subspecies) within a biological species 2 : one of the three, four, or five divisions based on inherited physical characteristics into which human beings are usu. divided

ra·ce·mic \\rā-'sē-mik, rə-\\ *adj* : of, relating to, or constituting a compound or mixture that is composed of equal amounts of dextrorotatory and levorotatory forms of the same compound and is not optically active

ra·ce·mose \\'ra-sə-,mōs; rā-'sē-, rə-\\ *adj* : having or growing in a form like that of a cluster of grapes (∼ aneurysms)

rachi- *or* **rachio-** *comb form* : spine (*rachischisis*)

ra·chis·chi·sis \\rə-'kis-kə-səs\\ *n, pl* **-chises** \\-kə-,sēz\\ : a congenital abnormality (as spina bifida) characterized by a cleft of the vertebral column

ra·chit·ic \\rə-'ki-tik\\ *adj* : of, relating to, or affected by rickets (∼ lesions)

rachitic rosary *n* : BEADING

ra·chi·tis \\rə-'kī-təs\\ *n, pl* **-chit·i·des** \\-'ki-tə-,dēz\\ : RICKETS

¹rad \\'rad\\ *n* : a unit of absorbed dose of ionizing radiation equal to an energy of 100 ergs per gram of irradiated material

²rad *abbr* [Latin *radix*] root — used in writing prescriptions

radi- — see RADIO-

¹ra·di·al \\'rā-dē-əl\\ *adj* 1 : arranged or

having parts arranged like rays 2 : of, relating to, or situated near the radius or the thumb side of the hand or forearm 3 : developing uniformly around a central axis (∼ cleavage of an egg) — **ra·di·al·ly** *adv*

²radial *n* : a body part (as an artery) lying near or following the course of the radius

radial artery *n* : the smaller of the two branches into which the brachial artery divides just below the bend of the elbow and which passes along the radial side of the forearm to the wrist then winds backward around the outer side of the carpus and enters the palm between the first and second metacarpal bones to form the deep palmar arch

radialis — see EXTENSOR CARPI RADIALIS BREVIS, EXTENSOR CARPI RADIALIS LONGUS, FLEXOR CARPI RADIALIS, NERVUS RADIALIS

radial keratotomy *n* : a surgical operation on the cornea for the correction of myopia that involves flattening it by making a series of incisions in a radial pattern resembling the spokes of a wheel

radial nerve *n* : a large nerve that arises from the posterior cord of the brachial plexus and passes spirally down the humerus to the front of the lateral epicondyle where it divides into a superficial branch distributed to the skin of the back of the hand and arm and a deep branch to the underlying extensor muscles — called also *nervus radialis*

radial notch *n* : a narrow depression on the lateral side of the coronoid process of the ulna that articulates with the head of the radius and gives attachment to the annular ligament of the radius

radial tuberosity *n* : an oval eminence on the medial side of the radius distal to the neck where the tendon of the biceps brachii muscle inserts

radial vein *n* : any of several deep veins of the forearm that unite at the elbow with the ulnar veins to form the brachial veins

ra·di·ant energy \ˈrā-dē-ənt-\ *n* : energy traveling as a wave motion; *specif* : the energy of electromagnetic waves

radiata — see CORONA RADIATA

ra·di·ate \ˈrā-dē-ˌāt\ *vb* -at·ed; -at·ing 1 : to issue in or as if in rays : spread from a central point 2 : IRRADIATE

ra·di·ate ligament \ˈrā-dē-ət-ˌ-ˌāt-\ *n* : a branching ligament uniting the front of the head of a rib with the bodies of the two vertebrae and the intervertebral disk between them — called also *stellate ligament*

ra·di·a·tion \ˌrā-dē-ˈā-shən\ *n* 1 : energy radiated in the form of waves or particles 2 **a** : the action or process of radiating **b** (1) : the process of emitting radiant energy in the form of waves or particles (2) : the combined processes of emission, transmission, and absorption of radiant energy 3 : a tract of nerve fibers within the brain; *esp* : one concerned with the distribution of impulses arising from sensory stimuli to the relevant coordinating centers and nuclei

radiation sickness *n* : sickness that results from exposure to radiation and is commonly marked by fatigue, nausea, vomiting, loss of teeth and hair, and in more severe cases by damage to blood-forming tissue with decrease in red and white blood cells and with bleeding

radiation syndrome *n* : RADIATION SICKNESS

radiation therapy *n* : RADIOTHERAPY

¹**rad·i·cal** \ˈra-di-kəl\ *adj* : designed to remove the root of a disease or all diseased tissue (~ surgery) — compare CONSERVATIVE — **rad·i·cal·ly** *adv*

²**radical** *n* : FREE RADICAL; *also* : a group of atoms bonded together that is considered an entity in various kinds of reactions

radical mastectomy *n* : a mastectomy in which the breast tissue, associated skin, nipple, areola, axillary lymph nodes, and pectoral muscles are removed — called also *Halsted radical mastectomy*; compare MODIFIED RADICAL MASTECTOMY

ra·dic·u·lar \rə-ˈdi-kyə-lər, ra-\ *adj* 1 : of, relating to, or involving a nerve root 2 : of, relating to, or occurring at the root of a tooth (a ~ cyst)

ra·dic·u·li·tis \rə-ˌdi-kyə-ˈlī-təs\ *n* : inflammation of a nerve root

ra·dic·u·lop·a·thy \-ˈlä-pə-thē\ *n*, *pl* -thies : any pathological condition of the nerve roots

radii *pl of* RADIUS

radio- *also* **radi-** *comb form* 1 : radiant energy : radiation (*radio*active) (*radi*opaque) 2 : radioactive (*radio*ele-

ment) 3 : radium : X rays (*radio*therapy) 4 : radioactive isotopes esp. as produced artificially (*radio*cobalt)

ra·dio·ac·tiv·i·ty \ˌrā-dē-ō-ak-ˈti-və-tē\ *n*, *pl* -ties : the property possessed by some elements (as uranium) of spontaneously emitting alpha or beta rays and sometimes also gamma rays by the disintegration of the nuclei of atoms — **ra·dio·ac·tive** \-ˈak-tiv\ *adj* — **ra·dio·ac·tive·ly** *adv*

ra·dio·al·ler·go·sor·bent \ˌrā-dē-ō-ə-ˌlər-gō-ˈsȯr-bənt\ *adj* : relating to, involving, or being a radioallergosorbent test (~ testing)

radioallergosorbent test *n* : a radioimmunoassay for specific antibodies of immunoglobulin class IgE in which an insoluble matrix containing allergenic antigens is reacted with a sample of antibody-containing serum and then reacted again with antihuman antibodies against individual IgE antibodies to make specific determinations — abbr. *RAST*

ra·dio·as·say \ˌrā-dē-ō-ˈa-ˌsā, -a-ˈsā\ *n* : an assay based on examination of the sample in terms of radiation components

ra·dio·au·to·gram \-ˈȯ-tə-ˌgram\ *n* : AUTORADIOGRAPH

ra·dio·au·to·graph \-ˈȯ-tə-ˌgraf\ *n* : AUTORADIOGRAPH — **radioautograph** *vb* — **ra·dio·au·to·graph·ic** \-ˌȯ-tə-ˈgra-fik\ *adj* — **ra·dio·au·tog·ra·phy** \-ˈtä-grə-fē\ *n*

ra·dio·bi·ol·o·gy \ˌrā-dē-ō-bī-ˈä-lə-jē\ *n*, *pl* -gies : a branch of biology dealing with the effects of radiation or radioactive materials on biological systems — **ra·dio·bi·o·log·i·cal** \-bī-ə-ˈlä-ji-kəl\ *also* **ra·dio·bi·o·log·ic** \-jik\ *adj* — **ra·dio·bi·o·log·i·cal·ly** *adv* — **ra·dio·bi·ol·o·gist** \-bī-ˈä-lə-jist\ *n*

¹**ra·dio·chem·i·cal** \-ˈke-mi-kəl\ *adj* : of, relating to, being, or using radiochemicals or the methods of radiochemistry (~ analysis) (~ purity)

²**radiochemical** *n* : a chemical prepared with radioactive elements esp. for medical research or application (as for use as a tracer in renal or heart function studies)

ra·dio·chem·is·try \ˌrā-dē-ō-ˈke-mə-strē\ *n*, *pl* -tries : a branch of chemistry dealing with radioactive substances and phenomena including tracer studies — **ra·dio·chem·ist** \-ˈke-mist\ *n*

ra·dio·chro·mato·gram \-krō-ˈma-tə-ˌgram\ *n* : a chromatogram revealing one or more radioactive substances

ra·dio·chro·ma·tog·ra·phy \-ˌkrō-mə-ˈtä-grə-fē\ *n*, *pl* -phies : the process of making a quantitative or qualitative determination of a radioisotope-labeled substance by measuring the radioactivity of the appropriate zone or spot in the chromatogram — **ra·dio·chro·ma·to·graph·ic** \-krə-ˌma-tə-ˈgra-fik, -ˌkrō-mə-\ *adj*

ra·dio·chro·mi·um \-ˈkrō-mē-əm\ n : a radioactive isotope of chromium and esp. chromium with mass number 51

ra·dio·co·balt \-ˈkō-ˌbȯlt\ n : radioactive cobalt; esp : COBALT 60

ra·dio·den·si·ty \-ˈden-sə-tē\ n, pl **-ties** : RADIOPACITY

ra·dio·der·ma·ti·tis \-ˌdər-mə-ˈtī-təs\ n, pl **-ti·tis·es** or **-tit·i·des** \-ˈti-tə-ˌdēz\ : dermatitis resulting from overexposure to sources of radiant energy (as X rays or radium)

ra·dio·di·ag·no·sis \-ˌdī-ig-ˈnō-səs\ n, pl **-no·ses** \-ˌsēz\ : diagnosis by means of radiology — compare RADIOTHERAPY

ra·dio·el·e·ment \-ˈe-lə-mənt\ n : a radioactive element whether formed naturally or produced artificially — compare RADIOISOTOPE

ra·dio·en·zy·mat·ic \-ˌen-zə-ˈma-tik\ adj : of, relating to, or produced by a radioactive enzyme

ra·dio·fre·quen·cy \-ˈfrē-kwən-sē\ n, pl **-cies** : any of the electromagnetic wave frequencies that lie in a range extending from below 3000 hertz to about 300 billion hertz and that include the frequencies used in radio and television transmission — **radiofrequency** adj

ra·dio·gen·ic \ˌrā-dē-ō-ˈje-nik\ adj : produced by radioactivity (∼ tumors)

ra·dio·gram \ˈrā-dē-ō-ˌgram\ n : RADIOGRAPH

ra·dio·graph \-ˌgraf\ n : an X-ray or gamma-ray photograph — **radiograph** vb — **ra·dio·graph·ic** \ˌrā-dē-ō-ˈgra-fik\ adj

ra·di·og·ra·pher \ˌrā-dē-ˈä-grə-fər\ n : one who radiographs; specif : an X-ray technician

ra·di·og·ra·phy \ˌrā-dē-ˈä-grə-fē\ n, pl **-phies** : the art, act, or process of making radiographs

ra·dio·im·mu·no·as·say \ˌrā-dē-ˌō-i-myə-nō-ˈa-ˌsā, -i-ˌmyü-, -a-ˈsā\ n : immunoassay of a substance (as insulin) that has been radioactively labeled — abbr. RIA — **ra·dio·im·mu·no·as·say·able** adj

ra·dio·im·mu·no·elec·tro·pho·re·sis \-i-ˌlek-trə-fə-ˈrē-səs\ n, pl **-re·ses** \-ˌsēz\ : immunoelectrophoresis in which the substances separated in the electrophoretic system are identified by radioactive labels on antigens or antibodies

ra·dio·im·mu·no·log·i·cal \-ˌi-myə-nə-ˈlä-ji-kəl\ also **ra·dio·im·mu·no·log·ic** \-ˈlä-jik\ adj : of, relating to, or involving a radioimmunoassay

ra·dio·io·dide \-ˈī-ə-ˌdīd\ n : an iodide containing radioactive iodine

ra·dio·io·din·ate \-ˈī-ə-də-ˌnāt\ vb **-at·ed; -at·ing** : to treat or label with radioactive iodine — **ra·dio·io·din·ation** \-ˌī-ə-də-ˈnā-shən\ n

ra·dio·io·dine \-ˈī-ə-ˌdīn, -dən, -ˌdēn\ n : radioactive iodine; esp : IODINE-131

ra·dio·iron \-ˈī(-ə)rn\ n : radioactive iron; esp : a heavy isotope having the mass number 59 produced in nuclear reactors or cyclotrons and used in biochemical tracer studies

ra·dio·iso·tope \ˌrā-dē-ō-ˈī-sə-ˌtōp\ n : a radioactive isotope — compare RADIOELEMENT — **ra·dio·iso·to·pic** \-ˌī-sə-ˈtä-pik, -ˈtō-\ adj

ra·dio·la·bel \-ˈlā-bəl\ vb **-la·beled** or **-la·belled; -la·bel·ing** or **-la·bel·ling** : to label with a radioactive atom or substance — **radiolabel** n

ra·di·ol·o·gist \ˌrā-dē-ˈä-lə-jist\ n : a physician specializing in the use of radiant energy for diagnostic and therapeutic purposes

ra·di·ol·o·gy \-jē\ n, pl **-gies 1** : the science of radioactive substances and high-energy radiations **2** : a branch of medicine concerned with the use of radiant energy (as X rays and radium) in the diagnosis and treatment of disease — **ra·dio·log·i·cal** \ˌrā-dē-ə-ˈlä-ji-kəl\ or **ra·dio·log·ic** \ˌrā-dē-ə-ˈlä-jik\ adj — **ra·dio·log·i·cal·ly** \-jik\ adv

ra·dio·lu·cent \ˌrā-dē-ō-ˈlüs-ᵊnt\ adj : partly or wholly permeable to radiation and esp. X rays — compare RADIOPAQUE — **ra·dio·lu·cen·cy** \-ˈlüs-ᵊn-sē\ n

ra·dio·mi·met·ic \-mə-ˈme-tik, -mī-\ adj : producing effects similar to those of radiation (∼ agents)

ra·dio·ne·cro·sis \-nə-ˈkrō-səs, -nē-\ n, pl **-cro·ses** \-ˌsēz\ : ulceration or destruction of tissue resulting from irradiation — **ra·dio·ne·crot·ic** \-ˈkrä-tik\ adj

ra·dio·nu·clide \-ˈnü-ˌklīd, -ˈnyü-\ n : a radioactive nuclide

ra·dio·opac·i·ty \ˌrā-dē-ō-ˈpa-sə-tē\ n, pl **-ties** : the quality or state of being radiopaque

ra·dio·opaque \-ō-ˈpāk\ adj : being opaque to radiation and esp. X rays — compare RADIOLUCENT

ra·dio·phar·ma·ceu·ti·cal \ˌrā-dē-ō-ˌfär-mə-ˈsüti-kəl\ n : a radioactive drug used for diagnostic or therapeutic purposes — **radiopharmaceutical** adj

ra·dio·phar·ma·cy \-ˈfär-mə-sē\ n, pl **-cies** : a branch of pharmacy concerned with radiopharmaceuticals; also : a pharmacy that supplies radiopharmaceuticals — **ra·dio·phar·ma·cist** \-sist\ n

ra·dio·phos·pho·rus \-ˈfäs-fə-rəs\ n : radioactive phosphorus; esp : PHOSPHORUS 32

ra·dio·pro·tec·tive \-prə-ˈtek-tiv\ adj : serving to protect or aiding in protecting against the injurious effect of radiations (∼ drugs) — **ra·dio·pro·tec·tion** \-ˈtek-shən\ n

ra·dio·pro·tec·tor \-ˈtek-tər\ also **ra·dio·pro·tec·tor·ant** \-ˈtek-tə-rənt\ n : a radioprotective chemical agent

ra·dio·re·cep·tor assay \-ri-ˈsep-tər-\ n : an assay for a substance and esp. a hormone in which a mixture of the test sample and a known amount of the radiolabeled substance under test is exposed to a measured quantity of receptors for the substance and the amount in the test sample is determined from the proportion of receptors occupied by radiolabeled molecules of the substance under the assumption that labeled and unlabeled molecules bind to the receptor sites at random

ra·dio·re·sis·tant \-ri-ˈzis-tənt\ *adj* : resistant to the effects of radiant energy ⟨∼ cancer cells⟩ — compare RADIOSENSITIVE — **ra·dio·re·sis·tance** \-təns\ *n*

ra·dio·sen·si·tive \ˌrā-dē-ō-ˈsen-sə-tiv\ *adj* : sensitive to the effects of radiant energy ⟨∼ cancer cells⟩ — compare RADIORESISTANT — **ra·dio·sen·si·tiv·i·ty** \-ˌsen-sə-ˈti-və-tē\ *n*

ra·dio·sen·si·tiz·er \-ˈsen-sə-ˌtī-zər\ *n* : a substance or condition capable of increasing the radiosensitivity of a cell or tissue — **ra·dio·sen·si·ti·za·tion** \-ˌsen-sə-tə-ˈzā-shən\ *n* — **ra·dio·sen·si·tiz·ing** \-ˈsen-sə-ˌtī-ziŋ\ *adj*

ra·dio·so·di·um \-ˈsō-dē-əm\ *n* : radioactive sodium; *esp* : a heavy istope having the mass number 24, produced in nuclear reactors, and used in the form of a salt (as sodium chloride) chiefly in biochemical tracer studies

ra·dio·stron·tium \-ˈstran-chē-əm, -chəm, -tē-əm\ *n* : radioactive strontium; *esp* : STRONTIUM 90

ra·dio·te·lem·e·try \-tə-ˈle-mə-trē\ *n, pl* **-tries 1** : TELEMETRY **2** : BIOTELEMETRY — **ra·dio·tele·met·ric** \-ˌte-lə-ˈme-trik\ *adj*

ra·dio·ther·a·py \ˌrā-dē-ō-ˈther-ə-pē\ *n, pl* **-pies** : the treatment of disease by means of radiation (as X rays) — called also *radiation therapy*; compare RADIODIAGNOSIS — **ra·dio·ther·a·peut·ic** \-ˌther-ə-ˈpyü-tik\ *adj* — **ra·dio·ther·a·pist** \-ˈther-ə-pist\ *n*

ra·dio·tox·ic·i·ty \-täk-ˈsi-sə-tē\ *n, pl* **-ties** : the toxicity of radioactive substances

ra·dio·trac·er \ˈrā-dē-ō-ˌtrā-sər\ *n* : a radioactive tracer

ra·dio·ul·nar \ˌrā-dē-ō-ˈəl-nər\ *adj* : of, relating to, or connecting the radius and ulna

radioulnar joint *n* : any of three joints connecting the radius and ulna at their proximal and distal ends and along their shafts — see INFERIOR RADIOULNAR JOINT

radio wave *n* : an electromagnetic wave having a frequency in the range that extends from about 3000 hertz to about 300 billion hertz and includes the frequencies used for radio and television

ra·di·um \ˈrā-dē-əm\ *n, often attrib* : an intensely radioactive shining white metallic element that emits alpha particles and gamma rays to form radon and is used in the treatment of cancer — symbol *Ra*; see ELEMENT table

ra·di·us \ˈrā-dē-əs\ *n, pl* **ra·dii** \-dē-ˌī\ *also* **ra·di·us·es** : the bone on the thumb side of the forearm that is articulated with the ulna at both ends so as to permit partial rotation about that bone, that bears on its inner aspect somewhat distal to the head a prominence for the insertion of the biceps tendon, and that has the lower end broadened for articulation with the proximal bones of the carpus so that rotation of the radius involves also that of the hand

ra·don \ˈrā-ˌdän\ *n* : a heavy radioactive gaseous element of the group of inert gases formed by disintegration of radium and used similarly to radium in medicine — symbol *Rn*; see ELEMENT table

rag·weed \ˈrag-ˌwēd\ *n* : any of various chiefly No. American weedy herbaceous plants comprising the genus *Ambrosia* and producing highly allergenic pollen: as **a** : an annual weed (*A. artemisiifolia*) with finely divided foliage that is common on open or cultivated ground in much of No. America **b** : a coarse annual (*A. trifida*) with some or all of the leaves usu. deeply 3-cleft or 5-cleft — called also *great ragweed*

Rail·lie·ti·na \ˌrāl-yə-ˈtī-nə\ *n* : a large genus of armed tapeworms (family Davaineidae of the order Cyclophyllidea) having the adults parasitic in birds, rodents, or rarely humans and the larvae in various insects

Rail·liet \ri-ˈyā\, **Louis-Joseph Alcide** (1852–1930), French veterinarian.

rain·bow \ˈrān-ˌbō\ *n, slang* : a drug in a tablet or capsule of several colors; *esp* : a combination of the sodium derivatives of amobarbital and secobarbital in a blue and red capsule

rainbow pill *n, slang* : RAINBOW

rale \ˈral, ˈräl\ *n* : an abnormal sound heard accompanying the normal respiratory sounds on auscultation of the chest — compare RATTLE, RHONCHUS

ram·i·fi·ca·tion \ˌra-mə-fə-ˈkā-shən\ *n* **1** : the act or process of branching; *specif* : the mode of arrangement of branches **2** : a branch or offshoot from a main stock or channel (the ∼ of an artery); *also* : the resulting branched structure — **ram·i·fy** \ˈra-mə-ˌfī\ *vb*

ra·mus \ˈrā-məs\ *n, pl* **ra·mi** \-ˌmī\ : a projecting part, elongated process, or branch: as **a** : the posterior more or less vertical part of the lower jaw on each side which articulates with the skull **b** (1) : the upper more cranial branch of the pubis that extends from the pubic symphysis to the body of the pubis at the acetabulum and forms the cranial part of the obturator foramen — called also *superior ramus* (2) : the thin flat lower branch of the pubis that extends from the pubic symphysis to unite with the ramus of the ischium in forming the inferior rim of the obturator foramen — called also *inferior ramus* **c** : a branch of the ischium that extends down and forward from the ischial tuberosity to unite with the inferior ramus of the pubis in forming the inferior rim of the obturator foramen — called also *inferior ramus* **d** : a branch of a nerve — see RAMUS COMMUNICANS

ramus com·mu·ni·cans \-kə-ˈmyü-nə-ˌkanz\ *n, pl* **rami com·mu·ni·can·tes** \-kə-ˌmyü-nə-ˈkan-ˌtēz\ : any of the bundles of nerve fibers connecting a sympathetic ganglion with a spinal nerve and being divided into two kinds: **a** : one consisting of myelinated preganglionic fibers — called also *white ramus, white ramus communicans* **b** : one consisting of unmyelinated postganglionic fibers — called also *gray ramus*

ran *past of* RUN

rang *past of* RING

ra·nit·i·dine \ra-ˈni-tə-ˌdēn\ *n* : an antihistamine $C_{13}H_{22}N_4O_3S$ that is administered in the form of its hydrochloride to inhibit gastric acid secretion (as in the treatment of duodenal ulcers or Zollinger-Ellison syndrome) — see ZANTAC

ran·u·la \ˈran-yə-lə\ *n* : a cyst formed under the tongue by obstruction of a gland duct

rape \ˈrāp\ *n* **1** : sexual intercourse with a woman by a man without her consent and chiefly by force or deception — see STATUTORY RAPE **2** : unlawful sexual intercourse by force or threat other than by a man with a woman — **rape** *vb*

ra·phe \ˈrā-fē\ *n* : the seamlike union of the two lateral halves of a part or organ (as of the tongue, perineum, or scrotum) having externally a ridge or furrow and internally usu. a fibrous connective tissue septum

raphe nucleus *n* : any of several groups of nerve cells situated along or near the median plane of the tegmentum of the midbrain

rapid eye movement *n* : a rapid movement of the eyes associated esp. with REM sleep — called also *REM*

rapid eye movement sleep *n* : REM SLEEP

rapid plasma reagin test *n* : a flocculation test for syphilis employing the antigen used in the VDRL test with charcoal particles added so that the flocculation can be seen without the aid of a microscope — called also *RPR card test*

rap·ist \ˈrā-pist\ *n* : an individual who commits rape

rap·port \ra-ˈpȯr, rə-\ *n* : confidence of a subject in the operator (as in hypnotism, psychotherapy, or mental testing) with willingness to cooperate

rapture of the deep *n* : NITROGEN NARCOSIS

rap·tus \ˈrap-təs\ *n* : a pathological paroxysm of activity giving vent to impulse or tension (as in an act of violence)

rar·efy *also* **rar·i·fy** \ˈrar-ə-ˌfī\ *vb* **-efied** *also* **-ified; -efy·ing** *also* **-i·fy·ing** : to make or become rare, thin, porous, or less dense : to expand without the addition of matter — **rar·efac·tion** \ˌrar-ə-ˈfak-shən\ *n*

rash \ˈrash\ *n* : an eruption on the body typically with little or no elevation above the surface

RAST *abbr* radioallergosorbent test

rat \ˈrat\ *n* : any of the numerous rodents (family Muridae) of *Rattus* and related genera that include forms (as the brown rat and the black rat) which live in and about human habitations and are destructive pests and vectors of various diseases (as bubonic plague)

rat–bite fever *n* : either of two human febrile diseases usu. transmitted by the bite of a rat: **a** : a septicemia marked by irregular relapsing fever, rashes, muscular pain and arthritis, and great weakness and caused by a bacterium of the genus *Streptobacillus* (*S. moniliformis*) **b** : a disease that is marked by sharp elevation of temperature, swelling of lymph glands, eruption, recurrent inflammation of the bite wound, and muscular pains in the part where the bite wound occurred and that is caused by a bacterium of the genus *Spirillum* (*S. minor* syn. *S. minus*) — called also *sodoku*

rate \ˈrāt\ *n* **1** : a fixed ratio between two things **2** : a quantity, amount, or degree of something measured per unit of something else — see BASAL METABOLIC RATE, DEATH RATE, HEART RATE

rat flea *n* : any of various fleas that occur on rats: as **a** : NORTHERN RAT FLEA **b** : ORIENTAL RAT FLEA

Rath·ke's pouch \ˈrät-kəz-\ *n* : a pouch of ectoderm that grows out from the upper surface of the embryonic stomodeum and gives rise to the adenohypophysis of the pituitary gland — called also *Rathke's pocket*

Rathke, Martin Heinrich (1793–1860), German anatomist.

rat·i·cide \ˈra-tə-ˌsīd\ *n* : a substance used to kill rats

ra·tio \ˈrā-(ˌ)shō, -shē-ˌō\ *n, pl* **ra·tios** : the relationship in quantity, amount, or size between two or more things — see SEX RATIO

ra·tion \ˈra-shən, ˈrā-\ *n* : a food allowance for one day — **ration** *vb*

ra·tio·nal·ize \ˈra-shə-nə-ˌlīz\ *vb* **-ized; -iz·ing** : to attribute (one's actions) to rational and creditable motives without analysis of true and esp. unconscious motives; *also* : to provide plausible but untrue reasons for conduct — **ra·tio·nal·i·za·tion** \₁ra-shə-nə-lə-'zā-shən\ n

rat louse n : a sucking louse (*Polyplax spinulosa*) that is a widely distributed parasite of rats and transmits murine typhus from rat to rat

rat mite n : a widely distributed mite of the genus *Bdellonyssus* (*B. bacoti*) that usu. feeds on rodents but may cause dermatitis in and transmit typhus to humans

rat·tle \'rat-°l\ n : a throat noise caused by air passing through mucus; *specif* : DEATH RATTLE — compare RALE, RHONCHUS

rat·tle·box \-₁bäks\ n : CROTALARIA 2; *esp* : one (*Crotalaria spectabilis*) that is highly toxic to farm animals

rat·tle·snake \-₁snāk\ n : any of the American pit vipers that have a series of horny interlocking joints at the end of the tail which make a sharp rattling sound when vibrated and that comprise the genera *Sistrurus* and *Crotalus* — see DIAMONDBACK RATTLESNAKE, TIGER RATTLESNAKE, TIMBER RATTLESNAKE

Rat·tus \'ra-təs\ n : a genus of rodents (family Muridae) that comprise the common rats

Rau·dix·in \raù-'diks-ən, rò-\ *trademark* — used for a preparation of reserpine

rau·wol·fia \raù-'wùl-fē-ə, rò-\ n 1 a *cap* : a large tropical genus of the dogbane family (Apocynaceae) of somewhat poisonous trees and shrubs yielding emetic and purgative substances **b** : any plant of the genus *Rauwolfia* 2 : a medicinal extract from the root of an Indian rauwolfia (*Rauwolfia serpentina*) used in the treatment of hypertension and mental disorders

Rauwolf, Leonhard (1535–1596), German botanist.

ray·less goldenrod \'rā-ləs-\ n : a shrubby or herbaceous plant (*Haplopappus heterophyllus* syn. *Isocoma wrightii*) of the daisy family (Compositae) that occurs esp. on open saline ground from Texas to Arizona and northern Mexico and causes trembles in cattle

Ray·naud's disease \rā-'nōz-\ n : a vascular disorder marked by recurrent spasm of the capillaries and esp. those of the fingers and toes upon exposure to cold, characterized by pallor, cyanosis and redness in succession, usu. accompanied by pain, and in severe cases progressing to local gangrene

Raynaud, Maurice (1834–1881), French physician.

Raynaud's phenomenon n : the symptoms associated with Raynaud's disease — called also *Raynaud's syndrome*

Rb *symbol* rubidium

RBC *abbr* 1 red blood cells 2 red blood count

RBE *abbr* relative biological effectiveness

rd *abbr* rutherford

RD *abbr* registered dietitian

RDA *abbr* Recommended Daily Allowance

RDS *abbr* respiratory distress syndrome

Re *symbol* rhenium

re·ab·sorb \₁rē-ab-'sórb, -'zórb\ vb : to take up (something previously secreted or emitted) (sugars ~ed in the kidney); *also* : RESORB — **re·ab·sorp·tion** \-'sórp-shən, -'zórp-\ n

re·act \rē-'akt\ vb 1 : to respond to a stimulus 2 : to undergo or cause to undergo chemical reaction

re·ac·tion \rē-'ak-shən\ n 1 : the act or process or an instance of reacting 2 : bodily response to or activity aroused by a stimulus: **a** : an action induced by vital resistance to another action; *esp* : the response of tissues to a foreign substance (as an antigen or infective agent) **b** : depression or exhaustion due to excessive exertion or stimulation **c** : heightened activity succeeding depression or shock **d** : a mental or emotional disorder forming an individual's response to his or her life situation 3 a (1) : chemical transformation or change : the interaction of chemical entities (2) : the state resulting from such a reaction **b** : a process involving change in atomic nuclei

reaction formation n : a psychological defense mechanism in which one form of behavior substitutes for or conceals a diametrically opposed repressed impulse in order to protect against it

reaction time n : the time elapsing between the beginning of the application of a stimulus and the beginning of an organism's reaction to it

re·ac·ti·vate \rē-'ak-tə-₁vāt\ vb -vat·ed; -vat·ing : to cause to be again active or more active: as **a** : to cause (as a repressed complex) to reappear in consciousness or behavior **b** : to cause (a quiescent disease) to become active again in an individual — **re·ac·ti·va·tion** \-₁ak-tə-'vā-shən\ n

re·ac·tive \rē-'ak-tiv\ adj 1 a : of, relating to, or marked by reaction ⟨~ symptoms⟩ **b** : capable of reacting chemically 2 a : readily responsive to a stimulus **b** : occurring as a result of stress or emotional upset esp. from factors outside the organism ⟨~ depression⟩ — **re·ac·tiv·i·ty** \rē-₁ak-'ti-və-tē\ n

re·ac·tor \rē-'ak-tər\ n 1 : one that reacts: as **a** : a chemical reagent **b** : an individual reacting to a stimulus **c** : an individual reacting positively to a foreign substance (as in a test for disease) 2 : a device for the controlled release of nuclear energy

re·agent \rē-'ā-jənt\ n : a substance

used (as in detecting or measuring a component or in preparing a product) because of its chemical or biological activity

re·agin \rē-'ā-jən, -gən\ *n* 1 : a substance in the blood of persons with syphilis responsible for positive serological reactions for syphilis 2 : an antibody in the blood of individuals with some forms of allergy possessing the power of passively sensitizing the skin of normal individuals — **re·agin·ic** \rē-ə-'ji-nik, -'gi-\ *adj*

reality principle *n* : the tendency to defer immediate instinctual gratification so as to achieve longer-range goals or so as to meet external demands — compare PLEASURE PRINCIPLE

reality testing *n* : the psychological process in which acts are explored and their outcomes determined so that the individual will be aware of these consequences when the stimulus to act in a given fashion recurs

ream·er \'rē-mər\ *n* : an instrument used in dentistry to enlarge and clean out a root canal

re·am·pu·ta·tion \rē-ıam-pyə-'tā-shən\ *n* : the second of two amputations performed upon the same member

re·anas·to·mo·sis \rē-ə-ınas-tə-'mō-səs\ *n, pl* **-mo·ses** \-ısēz\ : the reuniting (as by surgery or healing) of a divided vessel

re·at·tach \rē-ə-'tach\ *vb* : to attach again (~ a severed finger) — **re·at·tach·ment** \-mənt\ *n*

re·base \rē-'bās\ *vb* **re·based; re·bas·ing** : to modify the base of (a denture) after an initial period of wear in order to produce a good fit

re·bound \'rē-ıbaund, ri-'\ *n* : a spontaneous reaction; *esp* : a return to a previous state or condition following removal of a stimulus or cessation of treatment

rebound tenderness *n* : a sensation of pain felt when pressure (as to the abdomen) is suddenly removed

re·breathe \rē-'brēth\ *vb* **re·breathed; re·breath·ing** 1 : to breathe (as reconstituted air) again 2 : to inhale previously exhaled air or gases

re·cal·ci·fi·ca·tion \rē-ıkal-sə-fə-'kā-shən\ *n* : the restoration of calcium or calcium compounds to decalcified tissue (as bone or blood) — **re·cal·ci·fied** \-'kal-sə-ıfid\ *adj*

recalcification time *n* : a measure of the time taken for clot formation in recalcified blood

re·cal·ci·trant \ri-'kal-sə-trənt\ *adj* : not responsive to treatment

re·call \ri-'kól, 'rē-ı\ *n* : remembrance of what has been previously learned or experienced — **recall** \ri-'kól\ *vb*

re·can·a·li·za·tion \rē-ıkan-əl-ə-'zā-shən\ *n* : the process of restoring flow to or reuniting an interrupted channel of a bodily tube (as a blood vessel or

vas deferens) — **re·can·a·lize** \-kə-'na-ılīz, -'kan-əl-ıīz\ *vb*

re·cep·tive \ri-'sep-tiv\ *adj* 1 : open and responsive to ideas, impressions, or suggestions 2 *a of a sensory end organ* : fit to receive and transmit stimuli *b* : SENSORY 1 — **re·cep·tive·ness** *n* — **re·cep·tiv·i·ty** \ırē-ısep-'ti-və-tē, ri-\ *n*

re·cep·tor \ri-'sep-tər\ *n* 1 : a cell or group of cells that receives stimuli : SENSE ORGAN 2 : a chemical group or molecule (as a protein) on the cell surface or in the cell interior that has an affinity for a specific chemical group, molecule, or virus 3 : a cellular entity (as a beta-receptor) that is a postulated intermediary between a chemical agent (as a neurohormone) acting on nervous tissue and the physiological or pharmacological response

re·cess \'rē-ıses, ri-'\ *n* : an anatomical depression or cleft : FOSSA

re·ces·sion \ri-'se-shən\ *n* : pathological withdrawal of tissue from its normal position (gingival ~)

¹re·ces·sive \ri-'se-siv\ *adj* 1 : producing little or no phenotypic effect when occurring in heterozygous condition with a contrasting allele (~ genes) 2 : expressed only when the determining gene is in the homozygous condition (~ traits) — **re·ces·sive·ly** *adv* — **re·ces·sive·ness** *n*

²recessive *n* 1 : a recessive character or gene 2 : an organism possessing one or more recessive characters

re·cid·i·vism \ri-'si-də-ıvi-zəm\ *n* : a tendency to relapse into a previous condition or mode of behavior (~ among heroin addicts); *esp* : relapse into criminal behavior — **re·cid·i·vist** \-vist\ *n*

re·ci·pe \'re-sə-(ı)pē\ *n* : PRESCRIPTION 1

re·cip·i·ent \ri-'si-pē-ənt\ *n* : one who receives biological material (as blood or an organ) from a donor

reciprocal inhibition *n* 1 : RECIPROCAL INNERVATION 2 : behavior therapy in which the patient is exposed to anxiety-producing stimuli while in a controlled state of relaxation so that the anxiety response is gradually inhibited

reciprocal innervation *n* : innervation so that the contraction of a muscle or set of muscles (as of a joint) is accompanied by the simultaneous inhibition of an antagonistic muscle or set of muscles

reciprocal translocation *n* : exchange of parts between nonhomologous chromosomes

Reck·ling·hau·sen's disease \'re-klin-ıhau-zənz-\ *n* : NEUROFIBROMATOSIS

Recklinghausen, Friedrich Daniel von (1833–1910), German pathologist.

rec·og·ni·tion \ıre-kəg-'ni-shən\ *n* : the form of memory that consists in knowing or feeling that a present object has been met before

re·com·bi·nant \rē-ˈkäm-bə-nənt\ adj 1 : relating to or exhibiting genetic recombination 2 : relating to or containing recombinant DNA; also : produced by recombinant DNA technology

²**recombinant** n : an individual exhibiting recombination

recombinant DNA n : genetically engineered DNA prepared in vitro by cutting up DNA molecules and splicing together specific DNA fragments usu. from more than one species of organism

re·com·bi·na·tion \ˌrē-ˌkäm-bə-ˈnā-shən\ n : the formation by the processes of crossing-over and independent assortment of new combinations of genes in progeny that did not occur in the parents — **re·com·bi·na·tion·al** adj

Recommended Daily Allowance n : the amount of a substance (as a vitamin or mineral) that is officially recommended for daily consumption by a governmental board of nutrition experts — abbr. **RDA**

re·com·pres·sion \ˌrē-kəm-ˈpre-shən\ n : a renewed heightening of atmospheric pressure esp. as treatment for decompression sickness

re·con·sti·tute \rē-ˈkän-stə-ˌtüt, -ˌtyüt\ vb **-tut·ed; -tut·ing** : to constitute again or anew; esp : to restore to a former condition by adding liquid ⟨reconstituted blood plasma⟩ — **re·con·sti·tu·tion** \ˌkän-stə-ˈtü-shən, -ˈtyü-\ n

re·con·struc·tion \ˌrē-kən-ˈstrək-shən\ n : repair of an organ or part by reconstructive surgery ⟨breast ∼⟩ — **re·con·struct** \ˌrē-kən-ˈstrəkt\ vb

re·con·struc·tive \-ˈstrək-tiv\ adj : of, relating to, or being reconstructive surgery

reconstructive surgery n : surgery to restore function or normal appearance by remaking defective organs or parts

re·cov·er \ri-ˈkə-vər\ vb **re·cov·ered; re·cov·er·ing** : to regain a normal position or condition (as of health) — **re·cov·er·able** \ri-ˈkə-və-rə-bəl\ adj

re·cov·ery \ri-ˈkə-və-rē\ n, pl **-er·ies** : the act of regaining or returning toward a normal or healthy state

recovery room n : a hospital room which is equipped with apparatus for meeting postoperative emergencies and in which surgical patients are kept during the immediate postoperative period for care and recovery from anesthesia — abbr. **RR**

rec·re·a·tion·al therapy \ˌre-krē-ˈā-shə-nəl-\ n : therapy by means of recreational activities engaged in by the patient — compare OCCUPATIONAL THERAPY

re·cru·des·cence \ˌrē-krü-ˈdes-əns\ n : increased severity of a disease after

a remission; also : recurrence of a disease after a brief intermission — compare RELAPSE — **re·cru·desce** \ˌrē-krü-ˈdes\ vb — **re·cru·des·cent** \-ˈdes-ənt\ adj

re·cruit·ment \ri-ˈkrüt-mənt\ n 1 : increase in intensity of a reflex when the initiating stimulus is prolonged without alteration of intensity due to the activation of increasing numbers of motoneurons 2 : an abnormally rapid increase in the sensation of loudness with increasing sound intensity that occurs in deafness of neural original

rect- or **recto-** comb form 1 : rectum ⟨rectal⟩ 2 : rectal and ⟨rectovaginal⟩

recta pl of RECTUM

rec·tal \ˈrekt-ᵊl\ adj : relating to, affecting, or being near the rectum — **rec·tal·ly** adv

rectal artery n : any of three arteries supplying esp. the rectum: **a** : one arising from the internal pudendal artery and supplying the lower part of the rectum and the perineal region — called also inferior hemorrhoidal artery, inferior rectal artery **b** : one arising from the internal iliac artery and supplying the middle part of the rectum — called also middle hemorrhoidal artery, middle rectal artery **c** : one that is a continuation of the inferior mesenteric artery and that supplies the upper part of the rectum — called also superior hemorrhoidal artery, superior rectal artery

rectal vein n : any of three veins that receive blood from the rectal venous plexus: **a** : one draining the lower part of the rectal venous plexus and emptying into the internal pudendal vein — called also inferior hemorrhoidal vein, inferior rectal vein **b** : one draining the bladder, prostate, and seminal vesicle by way of the middle part of the rectal venous plexus and emptying into the internal iliac vein — called also middle hemorrhoidal vein, middle rectal vein **c** : one draining the upper part of the rectal venous plexus and forming the first part of the inferior mesenteric vein — called also superior hemorrhoidal vein, superior rectal vein

rectal venous plexus n : a plexus of veins that surrounds the rectum and empties esp. into the rectal veins — called also rectal plexus

recti pl of RECTUS

recto- — see RECT-

rec·to·cele \ˈrek-tə-ˌsēl\ n : herniation of the rectum through a defect in the intervening fascia into the vagina

rec·to·sig·moid \ˌrek-tō-ˈsig-ˌmoid\ n : the distal part of the sigmoid flexure and the proximal part of the rectum

rec·to·uter·ine pouch \ˌrek-tō-ˈyü-tə-ˌrīn-, -rən-\ n : a sac between the rectum and the uterus that is formed by a folding of the peritoneum — compare RECTOVESICAL POUCH

rec·to·vag·i·nal \-ˈvaj-ən-ᵊl\ *adj* : of, relating to, or connecting the rectum and the vagina (a ~ fistula)

rec·to·ves·i·cal fascia \ˌrek-tō-ˈve-si-kəl-\ *n* : a membrane derived from the pelvic fascia and investing the rectum, bladder, and adjacent parts

rectovesical pouch *n* : a sac between the rectum and the urinary bladder in males that is formed by a folding of the peritoneum — compare RECTO-UTERINE POUCH

rec·tum \ˈrek-təm\ *n, pl* **rectums** *or* **rec·ta** \-tə\ : the terminal part of the intestine from the sigmoid flexure to the anus

rec·tus \ˈrek-təs\ *n, pl* **rec·ti** \-ˌtī\ **1** : any of several straight muscles (as the rectus femoris) **2** : any of four muscles of the eyeball that arise from the border of the optic foramen and run forward to insert into the sclera of the eyeball: **a** : one that inserts into the superior aspect of the sclera — called also *rectus superior, superior rectus* **b** : one that inserts into the lateral aspect of the sclera — called also *lateral rectus, rectus lateralis* **c** : one that inserts into the medial aspect of the sclera — called also *medial rectus, rectus medialis* **d** : one that inserts into the inferior aspect of the sclera — called also *inferior rectus, rectus inferior*

rectus ab·dom·i·nis \-ab-ˈdä-mə-nəs\ *n* : a long flat muscle on either side of the linea alba extending along the whole length of the front of the abdomen, arising from the pubic crest and symphysis, inserted into the cartilages of the fifth, sixth, and seventh ribs, and acting to flex the spinal column, tense the anterior wall of the abdomen, and assist in compressing the contents of the abdomen

rectus ca·pi·tis posterior major \-ˈka-pə-təs-\ *n* : a muscle on each side of the back of the neck that arises from the spinous process of the axis, inserts into the lateral aspect of the inferior nuchal line and the adjacent inferior area of the occipital bone, and acts to extend and rotate the head

rectus capitis posterior minor *n* : a muscle on each side of the back of the neck that arises from the posterior arch of the atlas, inserts esp. into the medial aspect of the inferior nuchal line, and acts to extend the head

rectus fem·o·ris \-ˈfe-mə-rəs\ *n* : a division of the quadriceps muscle lying in the anterior middle region of the thigh, arising from the ilium by two heads, inserted into the tuberosity of the tibia by a narrow flattened tendon, and acting to flex the thigh at the hip and with the rest of the quadriceps to extend the leg at the knee

rectus inferior *n* : RECTUS 2d

rectus lat·e·ra·lis \-ˌla-tə-ˈrā-ləs, -ˈra-\ *n* : RECTUS 2b

rectus me·di·a·lis \-ˌmē-dē-ˈā-ləs, -ˈa-\ *n* : RECTUS 2c

rectus oc·u·li \-ˈä-kyü-ˌlī, -ˌlē\ *n* : RECTUS 2

rectus superior *n* : RECTUS 2a

re·cum·bent \ri-ˈkəm-bənt\ *adj* : lying down (a patient ~ on a stretcher) — **re·cum·ben·cy** \-bən-sē\ *n*

re·cu·per·a·tion \rē-ˌkü-pə-ˈrā-shən, -ˌkyü-\ *n* : restoration to health or strength — **re·cu·per·ate** \ri-ˈkü-pə-ˌrāt\ *vb*

re·cu·per·a·tive \-ˈkü-pə-ˌrā-tiv, -ˈkyü-\ *adj* **1** : of or relating to recuperation (~ powers) **2** : aiding in recuperation : RESTORATIVE (strongly ~ remedies)

re·cur·rence \ri-ˈkər-əns\ *n* **1** : return of symptoms of a disease after a remission **2** : reappearance of a tumor after previous removal — **re·cur** \ri-ˈkər\ *vb*

re·cur·rent \-ˈkər-ənt\ *adj* **1** : running or turning back in a direction opposite to a former course — used of various nerves and branches of vessels in the arms and legs **2** : returning or happening time after time (~ complaints) — **re·cur·rent·ly** *adv*

recurrent fever *n* : RELAPSING FEVER

recurrent laryngeal nerve *n* : LARYNGEAL NERVE b — called also *recurrent laryngeal*

red alga \ˈred-\ *n* : any of a major group (Rhodophyta) of chiefly marine algae that have predominantly red pigmentation — see IRISH MOSS

red–blind *adj* : affected with protanopia

red blindness *n* : PROTANOPIA

red blood cell *n* : any of the hemoglobin-containing cells that carry oxygen to the tissues and are responsible for the red color of blood — called also *erythrocyte, red blood corpuscle, red cell, red corpuscle*; compare WHITE BLOOD CELL

red blood count *n* : a blood count of the red blood cells — abbr. *RBC*

red bone marrow *n* : MARROW 1b

red bug \-ˌbəg\ *n, Southern & Midland* : CHIGGER 2

red cell *n* : RED BLOOD CELL

red corpuscle *n* : RED BLOOD CELL

red devils *n pl, slang* : REDS

red–green blindness *n* : dichromatism in which the spectrum is seen in tones of yellow and blue — called also *red-green color blindness*

re·dia \ˈrē-dē-ə\ *n, pl* **re·di·ae** \-dē-ˌē\ *also* **re·di·as** : a larva produced within the sporocyst of many trematodes that produces another generation of larvae or develops into a cercaria — **re·di·al** \-dē-əl\ *adj*

red·in·te·gra·tion \ri-ˌdin-tə-ˈgrā-shən, re-\ *n* **1** : revival of the whole of a previous mental state when a phase of it recurs **2** : arousal of any response by a part of the complex of stimuli that orig. aroused that response — **red-in·te·gra·tive** \-'din-tə-ˌgrā-tiv\ *adj*

red marrow *n* : MARROW 1b

red nucleus *n* : a nucleus of gray matter in the tegmentum of the midbrain on each side of the middle line that receives fibers from the cerebellum of the opposite side by way of the superior cerebellar peduncle and gives rise to fibers of the rubrospinal tract of the opposite side

red·out \'red-ˌaút\ *n* : a condition in which centripetal acceleration (as that created when an aircraft abruptly enters a dive) drives blood to the head and causes reddening of the visual field and headache — compare BLACKOUT, GRAYOUT

re·dox \'rē-ˌdäks\ *n* : OXIDATION-RE-DUCTION — **redox** *adj*

red pulp *n* : a parenchymatous tissue of the spleen that consists of loose plates or cords infiltrated with red blood cells — compare WHITE PULP

reds *n pl, slang* : red drug capsules containing the sodium salt of secobarbital — called also *red devils*

red tide *n* : seawater discolored by the presence of large numbers of dinoflagellates esp. of the genera *Gonyaulax* and *Gymnodinium* which produce a toxin poisonous esp. to many forms of marine vertebrate life and to humans who consume contaminated shellfish — see PARALYTIC SHELLFISH POISONING; compare SAXITOXIN

re·duce \ri-'düs, -'dyüs\ *vb* **re·duced; re·duc·ing 1** : to correct (as a fracture or a herniated mass) by bringing displaced or broken parts back into their normal positions **2 a** : to combine with or subject to the action of hydrogen **b** (1) : to change (an element or ion) from a higher to a lower oxidation state (2) : to add one or more electrons to (an atom or ion or molecule) **3** : to lose weight by dieting — **re·duc·ible** \-'dü-sə-bəl, -'dyü-\ *adj*

reducing *adj* : causing or facilitating reduction

reducing agent *n* : a substance (as hydrogen) that donates electrons or a share in its electrons to another substance — compare OXIDIZING AGENT

reducing sugar *n* : a sugar (as glucose or lactose) that is capable of reducing a mild oxidizing agent (as Fehling solution) — see BENEDICT'S TEST

re·duc·tase \ri-'dək-ˌtās, -ˌtāz\ *n* : an enzyme that catalyzes chemical reduction

re·duc·tion \ri-'dək-shən\ *n* **1** : the replacement or realignment of a body part in normal position or restoration of a bodily condition to normal **2** : the process of reducing by chemical or electrochemical means **3** : MEIOSIS; *specif* : production of the gametic

chromosome number in the first meiotic division

reduction division *n* : the usu. first division of meiosis in which chromosome reduction occurs; *also* : MEIOSIS

re·dun·dant \ri-'dən-dənt\ *adj* : characterized by or containing an excess or superfluous amount

re·du·pli·ca·tion \ri-ˌdü-pli-'kā-shən, ˌrē-, -ˌdyü-\ *n* : an act or instance of doubling (∼ of the chromosomes)

red water *n* : any of several cattle diseases characterized by hematuria; *esp* : any of several babesioses (as Texas fever) in which hemoglobin liberated by the destruction of red blood cells appears in the urine

red worm *n* : BLOODWORM

Reed–Stern·berg cell \'rēd-'stərn-bərg-\ *n* : a binucleate or multinucleate acidophilic giant cell found in the tissues in Hodgkin's disease

    Reed, Dorothy (1874–1964), American pathologist.

    Sternberg, Carl (1872–1935), Austrian pathologist.

re·ed·u·ca·tion \ˌrē-ˌe-jə-'kā-shən\ *n* **1** : training in the use of muscles in new functions or of prosthetic devices in old functions in order to replace or restore lost functions (neuromuscular ∼) **2** : training to develop new behaviors (as attitudes or habits) to replace others that are considered undesirable — **re·ed·u·cate** \-'e-jə-ˌkāt\ *vb*

reef·er \'rē-fər\ *n* : a marijuana cigarette; *also* : MARIJUANA 2

re·en·try \rē-'en-trē\ *n, pl* **-tries** : a cardiac mechanism that is held to explain certain abnormal heart actions (as tachycardia) and that involves the transmission of a wave of depolarization along an alternate pathway when the original pathway is blocked with return of the impulse along the blocked pathway when the alternate pathway is refractory and then transmission along the open pathway resulting in an abnormality

re·ep·i·the·li·al·i·za·tion \ˌrē-ˌe-pə-ˌthē-lē-ə-li-'zā-shən\ *n* : restoration of epithelium over a denuded area (as a burn site) by natural growth or plastic surgery

re·fer \ri-'fər\ *vb* **re·ferred; re·fer·ring 1** : to regard as coming from or localized in a certain portion of the body or of space **2** : to send or direct for diagnosis or treatment

re·fer·a·ble \'re-fə-rə-bəl, ri-'fər-ə-\ *adj* : capable of being considered in relation to something else (complaints ∼ to the upper left quadrant of the abdomen)

¹ref·er·ence \'re-frəns, -fə-rəns\ *n* — see IDEA OF REFERENCE

²reference *adj* : of known potency and used as a standard in the biological assay of a sample of the same drug of unknown strength

re·fer·ra·ble *var of* REFERABLE

re·fer·ral \ri-ˈfər-əl\ n 1 : the process of directing or redirecting (as a medical case or a patient) to an appropriate specialist or agency for definitive treatment 2 : one that is referred

referred pain n : a pain subjectively localized in one region though due to irritation in another region

¹**re·fill** \rē-ˈfil\ vb : to fill (a prescription) a second or subsequent time — **re·fill·able** adj

²**re·fill** \ˈrē-ˌfil\ n : a prescription compounded and dispensed for a second or subsequent time without an order from the physician

re·flect \ri-ˈflekt\ vb 1 : to bend or fold back : impart a backward curve, bend, or fold to 2 : to push or lay aside (as tissue or an organ) during surgery in order to gain access to the part to be operated on 3 : to throw back light or sound — **re·flec·tion** \ri-ˈflek-shən\ n

¹**re·flex** \ˈrē-ˌfleks\ n 1 : an automatic and often inborn response to a stimulus that involves a nerve impulse passing inward from a receptor to a nerve center and thence outward to an effector (as a muscle or gland) without reaching the level of consciousness — compare HABIT 2 : the process that culminates in a reflex and comprises reception, transmission, and reaction 3 pl : the power of acting or responding with adequate speed

²**reflex** adj 1 : bent, turned, or directed back : REFLECTED 2 : of, relating to, or produced by a reflex without intervention of consciousness

reflex arc n : the complete nervous path that is involved in a reflex

re·flex·ion Brit var of REFLECTION

re·flex·ive \ri-ˈflek-siv\ adj : characterized by habitual and unthinking behavior; also : relating to or consisting of a reflex

re·flex·ly adv : in a reflex manner : by means of reflexes

re·flex·o·gen·ic \ri-ˌflek-sə-ˈje-nik\ adj 1 : causing or being the point of origin of reflexes ⟨a ~ zone⟩ 2 : originating reflexly

re·flex·ol·o·gy \ˌrē-ˌflek-ˈsä-lə-jē\ n, pl -gies 1 : the study and interpretation of behavior in terms of simple and complex reflexes 2 : massage of the feet or hands based on the belief that pressure applied to specific points on these extremities benefits other parts of the body — **re·flex·ol·o·gist** \-jist\ n

re·flux \ˈrē-ˌfləks\ n : a flowing back : REGURGITATION ⟨gastroesophageal ~⟩ ⟨mitral valve ~⟩ — **reflux** adj — **reflux** vb

re·frac·tile \ri-ˈfrak-təl, -ˌtīl\ adj : REFRACTIVE ⟨~ cells⟩

re·frac·tion \ri-ˈfrak-shən\ n 1 : the deflection from a straight path undergone by a light ray or a wave of energy in passing obliquely from one medium (as air) into another (as glass) in which its velocity is different 2 a : the refractive power of the eye b : the act or technique of determining ocular refraction and identifying abnormalities as a basis for the prescription of corrective lenses — **re·fract** \ri-ˈfrakt\ vb

re·frac·tion·ist \-shə-nist\ n : one (as an optometrist) skilled esp. in the determination of errors of refraction in the eye

re·frac·tive \ri-ˈfrak-tiv\ adj 1 : having power to refract ⟨~ lens⟩ 2 : relating to or due to refraction — **re·frac·tive·ly** adv

refractive index n : INDEX OF REFRACTION

re·frac·to·ri·ness \ri-ˈfrak-tə-rē-nəs\ n : the insensitivity to further immediate stimulation that develops in irritable and esp. nervous tissue as a result of intense or prolonged stimulation

re·frac·to·ry \ri-ˈfrak-tə-rē\ adj 1 : resistant to treatment or cure ⟨a ~ fulminating lesion⟩ 2 : unresponsive to stimulus 3 : resistant or not responding to an infectious agent : IMMUNE

refractory period n : the brief period immediately following the response esp. of a muscle or nerve before it recovers the capacity to make a second response — called also refractory phase; see ABSOLUTE REFRACTORY PERIOD, RELATIVE REFRACTORY PERIOD

re·frac·ture \ˈrē-ˈfrak-chər\ vb -tured; -tur·ing : to break along the line of a previous fracture — **refracture** n

Ref·sum's disease \ˈref-səmz-\ n : an autosomal recessive lipidosis characterized by faulty metabolism of phytanic acid resulting in its accumulation in the blood, retinitis pigmentosa, ataxia, deafness, and mental retardation

Refsum, Sigvald Bernhard (b 1907), Norwegian physician.

re·gen·er·a·tion \ri-ˌje-nə-ˈrā-shən, ˌrē-\ n : the renewal, regrowth, or restoration of a body or a bodily part, tissue, or substance after injury or as a normal bodily process ⟨continual ~ of epithelial cells⟩ — compare REGULATION 2a — **re·gen·er·ate** \ri-ˈje-nə-ˌrāt\ vb — **re·gen·er·a·tive** \ri-ˈje-nə-ˌrā-tiv, -rə-\ adj

re·gime \rā-ˈzhēm, ri-ˈjēm\ n : REGIMEN

reg·i·men \ˈre-jə-mən\ n : a systematic plan (as of diet, therapy, or medication) esp. when designed to improve and maintain the health of a patient

re·gion \ˈrē-jən\ n 1 : any of the major subdivisions into which the body or one of its parts is divisible 2 : an indefinite area surrounding a specified body part

re·gion·al \ˈrē-jən-əl\ adj : of, relating to, or affecting a particular bodily region : LOCALIZED

regional anatomy n : a branch of anatomy dealing with regions of the body esp. with reference to diagnosis and treatment of disease or injury — called also *topographic anatomy*

regional anesthesia *n* : anesthesia of a region of the body accomplished by a series of encircling injections of an anesthetic — compare BLOCK ANESTHESIA

regional enteritis *n* : CROHN S DISEASE

regional ileitis *n* : CROHN'S DISEASE

reg·is·tered \'re-ji-stərd\ *adj* : qualified by formal, official, or legal certification or authentication

registered nurse *n* : a graduate trained nurse who has been licensed by a state authority after passing qualifying examinations for registration — called also *RN*

reg·is·trar \'re-ji-ˌsträr\ *n* 1 : an admitting officer at a hospital 2 *Brit* : RESIDENT

reg·is·try \'re-ji-strē\ *n, pl* **-tries** 1 : a place where data, records, or laboratory samples are kept and usu. are made available for research or comparative study ⟨a cancer ∼⟩ 2 : an establishment at which nurses available for employment are listed and through which they are hired

Reg·i·tine \'re-ji-ˌtēn\ *trademark* — used for a preparation of phentolamine

re·gres·sion \ri-'gre-shən\ *n* : a trend or shift toward a lower, less severe, or less perfect state: as a : progressive decline (as in size or severity) of a manifestation of disease ⟨tumor ∼⟩ b (1) : a gradual loss of differentiation and function by a body part esp. as a physiological change accompanying aging ⟨menopausal ∼ of the ovaries⟩ (2) : gradual loss (as in old age) of memories and acquired skills c : reversion to an earlier mental or behavioral level or to an earlier stage of psychosexual development in response to organismic stress or to suggestion — **re·gress** \ri-'gres\ *vb* — **re·gres·sive** \ri-'gre-siv\ *adj*

re·grow \ˌrē-'grō\ *vb* **re·grew** \-'grü\; **re·grown** \-'grōn\; **re·grow·ing** : to continue growth after interruption or injury — **re·growth** \-'grōth\ *n*

reg·u·lar \'re-gyə-lər\ *adj* : conforming to what is usual or normal: as a : recurring or functioning at fixed or normal intervals ⟨∼ bowel movements⟩ b : having menstrual periods or bowel movements at normal intervals — **reg·u·lar·i·ty** \ˌre-gyə-'lar-ə-tē\ *n* — **reg·u·lar·ly** *adv*

reg·u·la·tion \ˌre-gyə-'lā-shən, -gə-\ *n* 1 : the act of fixing or adjusting the time, amount, degree, or rate of something; *also* : the resulting state or condition 2 a : the process of redistributing material (as in an embryo) to restore a damaged or lost part independent of new tissue growth — compare REGENERATION b : the mechanism by which an early em-

bryo maintains normal development 3 : the control of the kind and rate of cellular processes by controlling the activity of individual genes — **reg·u·late** \-ˌlāt\ *vb* — **reg·u·la·to·ry** \-lə-ˌtōr-ē\ *adj*

reg·u·la·tive \'re-gyə-ˌlā-tiv, -lə\ *adj* : INDETERMINATE ⟨∼ eggs⟩

reg·u·la·tor \'re-gyə-ˌlā-tər\ *n* : REGULATORY GENE

regulatory gene *or* **regulator gene** *n* : a gene that regulates the expression of one or more structural genes by controlling the production of a protein (as a genetic repressor) which regulates their rate of transcription

re·gur·gi·tant \rē-'gər-jə-tənt\ *adj* : characterized by, allowing, or being a backward flow (as of blood) ⟨∼ cardiac valves⟩

re·gur·gi·ta·tion \rē-ˌgər-jə-'tā-shən\ *n* 1 : an act of bringing swallowed food back up into the mouth 2 : the backward flow of blood through a defective heart valve — see AORTIC REGURGITATION — **re·gur·gi·tate** \rə-'gər-jə-ˌtāt\ *vb*

re·hab \'rē-ˌhab\ *n, often attrib* : REHABILITATION

re·ha·bil·i·tant \ˌrē-hə-'bi-lə-tənt, ˌrē-ə-\ *n* : an individual undergoing rehabilitation

re·ha·bil·i·ta·tion \ˌrē-hə-ˌbi-lə-'tā-shən, ˌrē-ə-\ *n, often attrib* 1 a : the physical restoration of a sick or disabled person by therapeutic measures and reeducation ⟨∼ after coronary occlusion⟩ b : the process of restoring an individual (as a convict or drug addict) to a useful and constructive place in society through some form of vocational, correctional, or therapeutic retraining 2 : the result of rehabilitation : the state of undergoing or of having undergone rehabilitation — **re·ha·bil·i·tate** \-'bi-lə-ˌtāt\ *vb* — **re·ha·bil·i·ta·tive** \-'bi-lə-ˌtā-tiv\ *adj*

Reh·fuss tube \'rā-fəs\ *n* : a flexible tube that is used esp. for withdrawing gastric juice from the stomach for analysis and that has a syringe at the upper end and an attachment with a slot at the end passing into the stomach

Rehfuss, Martin Emil (1887–1964), American physician.

re·hy·drate \rē-'hī-ˌdrāt\ *vb* **-drat·ed; -drat·ing** : to restore fluid to (something dehydrated); *esp* : to restore body fluid lost in dehydration to ⟨∼ a patient⟩ — **re·hy·dra·tion** \ˌrē-ˌhī-'drā-shən\ *n*

re·im·plan·ta·tion \ˌrē-ˌim-ˌplan-'tā-shən\ *n* 1 : the restoration of a bodily tissue or part (as a tooth) to the site from which it was removed 2 : the implantation of a fertilized egg in the uterus after it has been removed from the body and fertilized in vitro — **re·im·plant** \-im-'plant\ *vb*

re·in·fec·tion \ˌrē-in-'fek-shən\ *n* : infection following recovery from or superimposed on a previous infection of the same type

re·in·force·ment \ˌrē-ən-ˈfōrs-mənt\ n : the action of causing a subject (as a student or an experimental animal) to learn to give or to increase the frequency of a desired response that in classical conditioning involves the repeated presentation of an unconditioned stimulus (as the sight of food) paired with a conditioned stimulus (as the sound of a bell) and that in operant conditioning involves the use of a reward following a correct response or a punishment following an incorrect response; *also* : the reward, punishment, or unconditioned stimulus used in reinforcement — **re·in·force** \-ˈfōrs\ vb

re·in·forc·er \-ˈfōr-sər\ n : a stimulus (as a reward or removal of an electric shock) that increases the probability of a desired response in operant conditioning by being applied or removed following the desired response

re·in·ner·va·tion \ˌrē-ˌi-nər-ˈvā-shən, -in-ˌər-\ n : restoration of function e. p. to a denervated muscle by supplying it with nerves by regrowth or by grafting — **re·in·ner·vate** \-i-ˈnar-ˌvāt, -ˈi-nər-\ vb

re·in·oc·u·la·tion \ˌrē-i-ˌnä-kyə-ˈlā-shən\ n : inoculation a second or subsequent time with the same organism as the original inoculation — **re·in·oc·u·late** \-ˈnä-kyə-ˌlāt\ vb

re·in·te·gra·tion \ˌrē-ˌin-tə-ˈgrā-shən\ n : repeated and renewed integration (as of the personality and mental activity after mental illness) — **re·in·te·grate** \-ˈin-tə-ˌgrāt\ vb

Reiss·ner's membrane \ˈrīs-nərz-\ n : VESTIBULAR MEMBRANE

Reissner, Ernst (1824–1878), German anatomist.

Rei·ter's syndrome \ˈrī-tərz-\ n : a disease that is usu. initiated by infection in genetically predisposed individuals and is characterized usu. by recurrence of arthritis, conjunctivitis, and urethritis — called also *Reiter's disease*

Reiter, Hans Conrad Julius (1881–1969), German bacteriologist.

re·jec·tion \ri-ˈjek-shən\ n 1 : the action of rebuffing, repelling, refusing to hear, or withholding love from another esp. by communicating negative feelings toward and a wish to be free of the other person 2 : the immunological process of sloughing off foreign tissue or an organ (as a transplant) by the recipient organism — **re·ject** \-ˈjekt\ vb — **re·jec·tive** \-ˈjek-tiv\ adj

re·lapse \ri-ˈlaps, ˈrē-ˌ\ n : a recurrence of illness; *esp* : a recurrence of symptoms of a disease after a period of improvement — compare RECRUDESCENCE — **re·lapse** \ri-ˈlaps\ vb

relapsing febrile nodular non·sup·pu·ra·tive panniculitis \-ˌnän-ˈsə-pyə-rə-tiv-, -ˌrā-\ n : PANNICULITIS 2

relapsing fever n : any of several forms of an acute epidemic infectious disease marked by sudden recurring paroxysms of high fever lasting from five to seven days, articular and muscular pains, and a sudden crisis and caused by a spirochete of the genus *Borrelia* transmitted by the bites of lice and ticks and found in the circulating blood

re·late \ri-ˈlāt\ vb **re·lat·ed; re·lat·ing** : to have meaningful social relationships : interact realistically (an inability to ~ to other people)

re·la·tion \ri-ˈlā-shən\ n 1 : the attitude or stance which two or more persons or groups assume toward one another (race ~s) 2 a : the state of being mutually or reciprocally interested (as in social matters) b pl : SEXUAL INTERCOURSE — **re·la·tion·al** \-shə-nəl\ adj

re·la·tion·ship \-shən-ˌship\ n 1 : the state of being related or interrelated (the ~ between diet, cholesterol, and coronary heart disease) 2 a : a state of affairs existing between those having relations or dealings (the doctor-patient ~) b : an emotional attachment between individuals

relative biological effectiveness n : the relative capacity of a particular ionizing radiation to produce a response in a biological system — abbr. *RBE*

relative humidity n : the ratio of the amount of water vapor actually present in the air to the greatest amount possible at the same temperature — compare ABSOLUTE HUMIDITY

relative refractory period n : the period shortly after the firing of a nerve fiber when partial repolarization has occurred and a greater than normal stimulus can stimulate a second response — called also *relative refractory phase*; compare ABSOLUTE REFRACTORY PERIOD

re·lax \ri-ˈlaks\ vb 1 : to slacken or make less tense or rigid (alternately contracting and ~ing their muscles) 2 : to relieve from nervous tension 3 *of a muscle or muscle fiber* : to become inactive and lengthen 4 : to relieve constipation — **re·lax·ation** \ˌrē-ˌlak-ˈsā-shən, ri-ˌlak-\ n

re·lax·ant \ri-ˈlak-sənt\ n : a substance (as a drug) that relaxes; *specif* : one that relieves muscular tension — **relaxant** adj

re·lax·in \ri-ˈlak-sən\ n : a polypeptide sex hormone of the corpus luteum that facilitates birth by causing relaxation of the pelvic ligaments

re·leas·er \ri-ˈlē-sər\ n : a stimulus that serves as the initiator of complex reflex behavior

releasing factor n : HYPOTHALAMIC RELEASING FACTOR

re·li·a·bil·i·ty \ri-ˌlī-ə-ˈbi-lə-tē\ n, pl **-ties**

: the extent to which an experiment, test, or measuring procedure yields the same results on repeated trials — **re·li·able** \ri-ᵊlī-ə-bəl\ adj

re·lief \ri-ᵊlēf\ n : removal or lightening of something oppressive or distressing (~ of pain)

re·lieve \ri-ᵊlēv\ vb **re·lieved; re·liev·ing 1** : to bring about the removal or alleviation of (pain or discomfort) **2** : to emit the contents of the bladder or bowels of (oneself) — **re·liev·er** n

rem \ᵊrem\ n : the dosage of an ionizing radiation that will cause the same biological effect as one roentgen of X-ray or gamma-ray dosage — compare REP

REM \ᵊrem\ n : RAPID EYE MOVEMENT

re·me·di·a·ble \ri-ᵊmē-dē-ə-bəl\ adj : capable of being remedied

re·me·di·al \ri-ᵊmē-dē-əl\ adj : affording a remedy : intended as a remedy (~ surgery)

re·me·di·a·tion \ri-ᵊmē-dē-ᵊā-shən\ n : the act or process of remedying

rem·e·dy \ᵊre-mə-dē\ n, pl **-dies** : a medicine, application, or treatment that relieves or cures a disease — **remedy** vb

re·min·er·al·i·za·tion \ᵊrē-ᵊmi-nə-rə-lə-ᵊzā-shən\ n : the restoring of minerals to demineralized structures or substances (~ of bone) — **re·min·er·al·ize** \-ᵊmi-nə-rə-ᵊlīz\ vb

re·mis·sion \ri-ᵊmi-shən\ n : a state or period during which the symptoms of a disease are abated — compare INTERMISSION

re·mit \ri-ᵊmit\ vb **re·mit·ted; re·mit·ting** : to abate symptoms for a period : go into or be in remission

re·mit·tent \ri-ᵊmit-ᵊnt\ adj : marked by alternating periods of abatement and increase of symptoms (~ fever)

REM sleep n : a state of sleep that recurs cyclically several times during a normal period of sleep and that is characterized by increased neuronal activity of the forebrain and midbrain, by depressed muscle tone, and esp. in humans by dreaming, rapid eye movements, and vascular congestion of the sex organs — called also *paradoxical sleep, rapid eye movement sleep;* compare SLOW-WAVE SLEEP

re·nal \ᵊrēn-ᵊl\ adj : relating to, involving, affecting, or located in the region of the kidneys : NEPHRITIC

renal artery n : either of two branches of the abdominal aorta of which each supplies one of the kidneys and gives off smaller branches to the ureter, adrenal gland, and adjoining structures

renal calculus n : KIDNEY STONE

renal cast n : a cast of a renal tubule consisting of granular, hyaline, albuminoid, or other material formed in and discharged from the kidney in renal disease

renal clearance n : CLEARANCE

renal colic n : the severe pain produced by the passage of a calculus from the kidney through the ureter

renal column n : any of the masses of cortical tissue extending between the sides of the renal pyramids of the kidney as far as the renal pelvis — called also *Bertin's column, column of Bertin*

renal corpuscle n : the part of a nephron that consists of Bowman's capsule with its included glomerulus — called also *Malpighian body, Malpighian corpuscle*

renal glycosuria n : excretion of glucose associated with increased permeability of the kidneys without increased sugar concentration in the blood

renal hypertension n : hypertension that is associated with disease of the kidneys and is caused by kidney damage or malfunctioning

renal osteodystrophy n : a painful rachitic condition of abnormal bone growth that is associated with chronic acidosis, hypocalcemia, hyperplasia of the parathyroid glands, and hyperphosphatemia caused by chronic renal insufficiency — called also *renal rickets*

renal papilla n : the apex of a renal pyramid which projects into the lumen of a calyx of the kidney and through which collecting tubules discharge urine

renal pelvis n : a funnel-shaped structure in each kidney that is formed at one end by the expanded upper portion of the ureter lying in the renal sinus and at the other end by the union of the calyces of the kidney

renal plexus n : a plexus of the autonomic nervous system that arises esp. from the celiac plexus, surrounds the renal artery, and accompanies it into the kidney which it innervates

renal pyramid n : any of the conical masses that form the medullary substance of the kidney, project as the renal papillae into the renal pelvis, and are made up of bundles of straight uriniferous tubules opening at the apex of the conical mass — called also *Malpighian pyramid*

renal rickets n : RENAL OSTEODYSTROPHY

renal sinus n : the main cavity of the kidney that is an expansion behind the hilum and contains the renal pelvis, calyces, and the major renal vessels

renal threshold n : the concentration level up to which a substance (as glucose) in the blood is prevented from passing through the kidneys into the urine

renal tubular acidosis n : decreased ability of the kidneys to excrete hydrogen ions that is associated with a defect in the renal tubules without a defect in the glomeruli and that results in the production of urine deficient in acidity

renal tubule *n* : the part of a nephron that leads away from a glomerulus, that is made up of a proximal convoluted tubule, loop of Henle, and distal convoluted tubule, and that empties into a collecting tubule

renal vein *n* : a short thick vein that is formed in each kidney by the convergence of the interlobar veins, leaves the kidney through the hilum, and empties into the inferior vena cava

Ren·du-Os·ler-Web·er disease \ˈrän-ˈdü-ˈäs-lər-ˈwe-bər-, ˌrän-ˈdyü-\ *n* : HEREDITARY HEMORRHAGIC TELANGIECTASIA

Ren·du \rän-ˈdǣ\, **Henry-Jules-Louis-Marie (1844–1902),** French physician.

Osler, Sir William (1849–1919), American physician.

F. P. Weber — see WEBER-CHRISTIAN DISEASE

Ren·ese \ˈre-ˌnēz\ *trademark* — used for a preparation of polythiazide

reni- *or* **reno-** *comb form* 1 : kidney ⟨*reni*form⟩ 2 : renal and ⟨*reno*vascular⟩

reni·form \ˈrē-nə-ˌförm, ˈre-\ *adj* : suggesting a kidney in outline

re·nin \ˈrē-nən, ˈre-\ *n* : a proteolytic enzyme of the blood that is produced and secreted by the juxtaglomerular cells of the kidney and hydrolyzes angiotensinogen to angiotensin I

ren·nin \ˈre-nən\ *n* : a crystallizable enzyme that coagulates milk, occurs esp. with pepsin in the gastric juice of young animals, and is used in making cheese

re·no·gram \ˈrē-nə-ˌgram\ *n* : a photographic depiction of the course of renal excretion of a radioactively labeled substance — **re·no·graph·ic** \ˌrē-nə-ˈgra-fik\ *adj* — **re·nog·ra·phy** \rē-ˈnä-grə-fē\ *n*

re·no·vas·cu·lar \ˌrē-nō-ˈvas-kyə-lər\ *adj* : of, relating to, or involving the blood vessels of the kidneys ⟨~ hypertension⟩

Ren·shaw cell \ˈren-ˌshȯ-\ *n* : an internuncial neuron in the ventral horn of gray matter of the spinal cord that has an inhibitory effect on motoneurons

Renshaw, Birdsey (1911–1948), American neurologist.

re·op·er·a·tion \ˌrē-ˌä-pə-ˈrā-shən\ *n* : an operation to correct a condition not corrected by a previous operation or to correct the complications of a previous operation — **re·op·er·ate** \-ˈä-pə-ˌrāt\ *vb*

reo·vi·rus \ˈrē-ō-ˌvī-rəs\ *n* : any of a group of double-stranded RNA viruses that lack a lipoprotein envelope, usu. have a capsid consisting of two layers of capsomeres, and include many pathogens of plants or animals

¹**rep** \ˈrep\ *n, pl* **rep** *or* **reps** : the dosage of any ionizing radiation that will develop the same amount of energy upon absorption in human tissues as one roentgen of X-ray or gamma-ray dosage — compare REM

²**rep** *abbr* [Latin *repetatur*] let it be repeated — used in writing prescriptions

re·peat \ri-ˈpēt, ˈrē-ˌ\ *n* : a genetic duplication in which the duplicated parts are adjacent to each other along the chromosome

re·per·fu·sion \ˌrē-pər-ˈfyü-zhən\ *n* : restoration of the flow of blood to a previously ischemic tissue or organ (as the heart) ⟨~ following myocardial infarction⟩

repetition compulsion *n* : an irresistible tendency to repeat an emotional experience or to return to a previous psychological state

replacement therapy *n* : therapy involving the supplying of something (as hormones or blood) lacking from or lost to the system ⟨estrogen *replacement therapy*⟩

re·plan·ta·tion \ˌrē-(ˌ)plan-ˈtā-shən\ *n* : reattachment or reinsertion of a bodily part (as a limb or tooth) after separation from the body — **re·plant** \rē-ˈplant\ *vb*

rep·li·case \ˈre-pli-ˌkās, -ˌkāz\ *n* : a polymerase that promotes synthesis of a particular RNA in the presence of a template of RNA — called also *RNA replicase, RNA synthetase*

rep·li·ca·tion \ˌre-plə-ˈkā-shən\ *n* 1 : the action or process of reproducing or duplicating ⟨~ of DNA⟩ 2 : performance of an experiment or procedure more than once — **rep·li·cate** \ˈre-pli-ˌkāt\ *vb* — **rep·li·cate** \-kət\ *n* — **rep·li·ca·tive** \ˈre-pli-ˌkā-tiv\ *adj*

rep·li·con \ˈre-pli-ˌkän\ *n* : a linear or circular section of DNA or RNA which replicates sequentially as a unit

re·po·lar·i·za·tion \ˌrē-pō-lə-rə-ˈzā-shən\ *n* : restoration of the difference in charge between the inside and outside of the plasma membrane of a muscle fiber or cell following depolarization — **re·po·lar·ize** \-ˈpō-lə-ˌrīz\ *vb*

re·port·able \ri-ˈpȯr-tə-bəl\ *adj* : required by law to be reported ⟨~ diseases⟩

re·po·si·tion \ˌrē-pə-ˈzi-shən\ *vb* : to return to or place in a normal or proper position ⟨~ a dislocated shoulder⟩

re·pos·i·to·ry \ri-ˈpä-zə-ˌtōr-ē\ *adj, of a drug* : designed to act over a prolonged period ⟨~ penicillin⟩

re·press \ri-ˈpres\ *vb* 1 : to exclude from consciousness ⟨~ conflicts⟩ 2 : to inactivate (a gene or formation of a gene product) by allosteric combination at a DNA binding site

re·pressed \ri-ˈprest\ *adj* : subjected to

or marked by repression ⟨a ∼ child⟩ ⟨∼ anger⟩

re·press·ible \ri-ˈpre-sə-bəl\ *adj* : capable of being repressed

re·pres·sion \ri-ˈpre-shən\ *n* **1** : the action or process of repressing ⟨gene ∼⟩ **2 a** : a process by which unacceptable desires or impulses are excluded from consciousness and left to operate in the unconscious — compare SUPPRESSION c **b** : an item so excluded

re·pres·sive \ri-ˈpre-siv\ *adj* : tending to repress or to cause repression

re·pres·sor \ri-ˈpre-sər\ *n* : one that represses; *esp* : a protein that is determined by a regulatory gene, binds to a genetic operator, and inhibits the initiation of transcription of messenger RNA

re·pro·duce \ˌrē-prə-ˈdüs, -ˈdyüs\ *vb* **-duced; -duc·ing 1** : to produce (new individuals of the same kind) by a sexual or asexual process **2** : to achieve (an original result or score) again or anew by repeating an experiment or test

re·pro·duc·tion \ˌrē-prə-ˈdək-shən\ *n* : the act or process of reproducing; *specif* : the process by which plants and animals give rise to offspring — **re·pro·duc·tive** \ˌrē-prə-ˈdək-tiv\ *adj* — **re·pro·duc·tive·ly** *adv*

reproductive system *n* : the system of organs and parts which function in reproduction consisting in the male esp. of the testes, penis, seminal vesicles, prostate, and urethra and in the female esp. of the ovaries, fallopian tubes, uterus, vagina, and vulva

RES *abbr* reticuloendothelial system

res·cin·na·mine \re-ˈsi-nə-ˌmēn, -mən\ *n* : an antihypertensive, tranquilizing, and sedative drug $C_{35}H_{42}N_2O_9$ — see MODERIL

re·sect \ri-ˈsekt\ *vb* : to perform resection on ⟨∼ an ulcer⟩ — **re·sect·abil·i·ty** \ri-ˌsek-tə-ˈbi-lə-tē\ *n* — **re·sect·able** \ri-ˈsek-tə-bəl\ *adj*

re·sec·tion \ri-ˈsek-shən\ *n* : the surgical removal of part of an organ or structure ⟨∼ of the lower bowel⟩ — see WEDGE RESECTION

re·sec·to·scope \ri-ˈsek-tə-ˌskōp\ *n* : an instrument consisting of a tubular fenestrated sheath with a sliding knife within it that is used for surgery within cavities (as of the prostate through the urethra)

re·ser·pine \ri-ˈsər-ˌpēn, ˈre-sər-pən\ *n* : an alkaloid $C_{33}H_{40}N_2O_9$ extracted esp. from the root of rauwolfias and used in the treatment of hypertension, mental disorders, and tension states — see RAUDIXIN, SANDRIL, SERPASIL

reservatus — see COITUS RESERVATUS.

re·serve \ri-ˈzərv\ *n* **1** : something stored or kept available for future use or need ⟨oxygen ∼⟩ — see CARDIAC RESERVE **2** : the capacity of a solution to neutralize alkali or acid when its reaction is shifted from one hydrogen-ion concentration to another — **reserve** *adj*

res·er·voir \ˈre-zər-ˌvwär, -ˌvwȯr\ *n* **1** : a space (as the cavity of a glandular acinus) in which a body fluid is stored **2** : an organism in which a parasite that is pathogenic for some other species lives and multiplies without damaging its host; *also* : a noneconomic organism within which a pathogen of economic or medical importance flourishes without regard to its pathogenicity for the reservoir ⟨rats are ∼s of plague⟩ — compare CARRIER 1a

reservoir host *n* : RESERVOIR 2

res·i·den·cy \ˈre-zəd-ən-sē\ *n, pl* **-cies** : a period of advanced medical training and education that normally follows graduation from medical school and licensing to practice medicine and that consists of supervised practice of a specialty in a hospital and in its outpatient department and instruction from specialists on the hospital staff

res·i·dent \ˈre-zə-dənt\ *n* : a physician serving a residency

¹res·id·u·al \ri-ˈzi-jə-wəl\ *adj* **1** : of, relating to, or being something that remains: as **a** : remaining after a disease or operation ⟨∼ paralysis⟩ **b** : remaining in a body cavity after maximum normal expulsion has occurred ⟨∼ urine⟩ — see RESIDUAL AIR **2 a** : leaving a residue that remains effective for some time after application ⟨∼ insecticides⟩ **b** : of or relating to a residual insecticide ⟨a ∼ spray⟩

²residual *n* **1** : an internal aftereffect of experience or activity that influences later behavior **2** : a residual abnormality (as a scar or limp)

residual air *n* : the volume of air still remaining in the lungs after the most forcible expiration possible and amounting usu. to 60 to 100 cubic inches (980 to 1640 cubic centimeters) — called also *residual volume*; compare SUPPLEMENTAL AIR

residual volume *n* : RESIDUAL AIR

res·i·due \ˈre-zə-ˌdü, -ˌdyü\ *n* : something that remains after a part is taken, separated, or designated; *specif* : a constituent structural unit of a usu. complex molecule ⟨amino acid ∼s in a protein⟩

res·in \ˈrez-ən\ *n* : any of various substances obtained from the gum or sap of some trees and used esp. in various varnishes and plastics and in medicine; *also* : a comparable synthetic product — **res·in·ous** \ˈrez-ən-əs\ *adj*

re·sis·tance \ri-ˈzis-təns\ *n* **1** : power or capacity to resist; *esp* : the inherent ability of an organism to resist harmful influences (as disease, toxic agents, or infection) **2** : a mechanism of ego defense wherein a psychoanalysis patient rejects, denies, or otherwise opposes therapeutic efforts by the analyst **3** : the opposition offered by a body to the passage through it of a steady electric current — **re·sis·tant** *also* **re·sist·ent** \-tənt\ *adj*

re·so·cial·i·za·tion \ˌrē-ˌsō-shə-lə-ˈzā-shən\ *n* : readjustment of an individual (as a mentally or physically handicapped person) to life in society

res·o·lu·tion \ˌre-zə-ˈlü-shən\ *n* **1** : the separating of a chemical compound or mixture into its constituents **2** : the process or capability of making distinguishable the individual parts of an object, closely adjacent optical images, or sources of light **3** : the subsidence of a pathological state (as inflammation) — **re·solve** \ri-ˈzälv, -ˈzȯlv\ *vb*

res·o·nance \ˈrez-ᵊn-əns\ *n* **1** : a quality imparted to voiced sounds by vibration in anatomical resonating chambers or cavities (as the mouth or the nasal cavity) **2** : the sound elicited on percussion of the chest **3 a** : the enhancement of an atomic, nuclear, or particle reaction or a scattering event by excitation of internal motion in the system **b** : MAGNETIC RESONANCE

re·sorb \rē-ˈsȯrb, -ˈzȯrb\ *vb* : to break down and assimilate (something previously differentiated) ⟨~ed bone⟩

res·or·cin \rə-ˈzȯrs-ᵊn\ *n* : RESORCINOL

res·or·cin·ol \-ˌȯl, -ˌōl\ *n* : a crystalline phenol $C_6H_6O_2$ used in medicine as a fungicidal, bactericidal, and keratolytic agent

resorcinol monoacetate *n* : a liquid compound $C_8H_8O_3$ that slowly liberates resorcinol and that is used esp. to treat diseases of the scalp

re·sorp·tion \rē-ˈsȯrp-shən, -ˈzȯrp-\ *n* : the action or process of resorbing something ⟨~ of a tooth root⟩ — **re·sorp·tive** \-tiv\ *adj*

re·spi·ra·ble \ˈres-pə-rə-bəl, ri-ˈspī-rə-\ *adj* : fit for breathing; *also* : capable of being taken in by breathing

res·pi·ra·tion \ˌres-pə-ˈrā-shən\ *n* **1 a** : the placing of air or dissolved gases in intimate contact with the circulating medium (as blood) of a multicellular organism (as by breathing) **b** : a single complete act of breathing (30 ~s per minute) **2** : the physical and chemical processes by which an organism supplies its cells and tissues with the oxygen needed for metabolism and relieves them of the carbon dioxide formed in energy-producing reactions **3** : any of various energy-yielding oxidative reactions in living matter that typically involve transfer of oxygen and production of carbon dioxide and water as end products ⟨cellular ~⟩

res·pi·ra·tor \ˈres-pə-ˌrā-tər\ *n* **1** : a device (as a gas mask) worn over the mouth or nose for protecting the respiratory system **2** : a device for maintaining artificial respiration — called *also* **ventilator**

res·pi·ra·to·ry \ˈres-pə-rə-ˌtōr-ē, ri-ˈspī-rə-\ *adj* **1** : of or relating to respiration ⟨~ diseases⟩ **2** : serving for or functioning in respiration ⟨~ organs⟩

respiratory acidosis *n* : acidosis caused by excessive retention of carbon dioxide due to a respiratory abnormality (as obstructive lung disease)

respiratory alkalosis *n* : alkalosis that is caused by excessive elimination of carbon dioxide due to a respiratory abnormality (as hyperventilation)

respiratory center *n* : a region in the medulla oblongata that regulates respiratory movements

respiratory chain *n* : the metabolic pathway along which electron transport occurs in cellular respiration; *also* : the series of enzymes involved in this pathway

respiratory distress syndrome *n* : HYALINE MEMBRANE DISEASE — abbr. *RDS*; see ADULT RESPIRATORY DISTRESS SYNDROME

respiratory pigment *n* : any of various permanently or intermittently colored conjugated proteins and esp. hemoglobin that function in the transfer of oxygen in cellular respiration

respiratory quotient *n* : the ratio of the volume of carbon dioxide given off in respiration to that of the oxygen consumed — abbr. *RQ*

respiratory syncytial virus *n* : a paramyxovirus that forms syncytia in tissue culture and that is responsible for severe respiratory diseases (as bronchopneumonia and bronchiolitis) in children and esp. in infants — abbr. *RSV*

respiratory system *n* : a system of organs functioning in respiration and consisting esp. of the nose, nasal passages, nasopharynx, larynx, trachea, bronchi, and lungs — called also *respiratory tract*; see LOWER RESPIRATORY TRACT, UPPER RESPIRATORY TRACT

respiratory therapist *n* : a specialist in respiratory therapy

respiratory therapy *n* : the therapeutic treatment of respiratory diseases

respiratory tract *n* : RESPIRATORY SYSTEM

respiratory tree *n* : the trachea, bronchi, and bronchioles

re·spire \ri-ˈspīr\ *vb* **re·spired; re·spir·ing 1** : BREATHE; *specif* : to inhale and exhale air successively **2** *of a cell or tissue* : to take up oxygen and produce carbon dioxide through oxidation

res·pi·rom·e·ter \ˌres-pə-ˈrä-mə-tər\ *n* : an instrument for studying the character and extent of respiration — **res·pi·ro·met·ric** \ˌres-pə-rō-ˈme-trik\ *adj* — **res·pi·rom·e·try** \ˌres-pə-ˈrä-mə-trē\ *n*

re·spond \ri-ˈspänd\ *vb* **1** : to react in response **2** : to show favorable reaction ⟨~ to surgery⟩

re·spon·dent \ri-ˈspän-dənt\ *adj* : relating to or being behavior or responses to a stimulus that are followed by a reward ⟨∼ conditioning⟩ — compare OPERANT

re·spond·er \ri-ˈspän-dər\ *n* : one that responds (as to treatment)

re·sponse \ri-ˈspäns\ *n* : the activity or inhibition of previous activity of an organism or any of its parts resulting from stimulation ⟨a conditioned ∼⟩

re·spon·sive \ri-ˈspän-siv\ *adj* : making a response; *esp* : responding to treatment — **re·spon·sive·ness** *n*

rest \ˈrest\ *n* **1** : a state of repose or sleep; *also* : a state of inactivity or motionlessness — see BED REST **2** : the part of a partial denture that rests on an abutment tooth, distributes stresses, and holds the clasp in position **3** : a firm cushion used to raise or support a portion of the body during surgery ⟨a kidney ∼⟩ — **rest** *vb*

rest home *n* : an establishment that provides housing and general care for the aged or the convalescent — compare NURSING HOME

res·ti·form body \ˈres-tə-ˌfȯrm-\ *n* : CEREBELLAR PEDUNCLE C

rest·ing *adj* **1** : not physiologically active **2** : occurring in or performed on a subject at rest ⟨a ∼ EEG⟩ ⟨a ∼ tremor⟩

resting cell *n* : a living cell with a nucleus that is not undergoing division (as by mitosis)

resting potential *n* : the membrane potential of a cell that is not exhibiting the activity resulting from a stimulus — compare ACTION POTENTIAL

resting stage *n* : INTERPHASE

rest·less \ˈrest-ləs\ *adj* **1** : deprived of rest or sleep **2** : providing no rest

res·to·ra·tion \ˌres-tə-ˈrā-shən\ *n* : the act of restoring or the condition of being restored: as **a** : a returning to a normal or healthy condition **b** : the replacing of missing teeth or crowns; *also* : a dental replacement (as a denture) used for restoration — **re·stor·ative** \ri-ˈstȯr-ə-tiv\ *adj or n*

re·store \ri-ˈstȯr\ *vb* **re·stored; re·stor·ing** : to bring back to or put back into a former or original state ⟨a tooth *restored* with an inlay⟩

Res·to·ril \ˈres-tə-ˌril\ *trademark* — used for a preparation of temazepam

re·straint \ri-ˈstrānt\ *n* : a device (as a straitjacket) that restricts movement

re·stric·tion \ri-ˈstrik-shən\ *n, often attrib* : the breaking of double-stranded DNA into fragments by restriction enzymes ⟨∼ sites⟩

restriction endonuclease *n* : RESTRICTION ENZYME

restriction enzyme *n* : any of various enzymes that break DNA into fragments at specific sites in the interior of the molecule and are often used as tools in molecular analysis

restriction fragment *n* : a segment of DNA produced by the action of a restriction enzyme on a molecule of DNA

restriction fragment length polymorphism *n* : variation in the length of a restriction fragment produced by a specific restriction enzyme acting on DNA from different individuals that usu. results from a genetic mutation (as an insertion or deletion) and that may be used as a genetic marker — called also *RFLP*

rest seat *n* : an area on the surface of a tooth that is specially prepared (as by grinding) for the attachment of a dental rest

re·sus·ci·ta·tion \ri-ˌsə-sə-ˈtā-shən, rē-\ *n* : the act of reviving from apparent death or from unconsciousness — see CARDIOPULMONARY RESUSCITATION — **re·sus·ci·tate** \-ˈsə-sə-ˌtāt\ *vb* — **re·sus·ci·ta·tive** \-ˈsə-sə-ˌtā-tiv\ *adj*

re·sus·ci·ta·tor \ri-ˈsə-sə-ˌtā-tər\ *n* : an apparatus used to restore respiration (as of a partially asphyxiated person)

re·tain·er \ri-ˈtā-nər\ *n* **1** : the part of a dental replacement (as a bridge) by which it is made fast to adjacent natural teeth **2** : a dental appliance used to hold teeth in correct position following orthodontic treatment

re·tar·da·tion \ˌrē-ˌtär-ˈdā-shən, ri-\ *n* **1** : an abnormal slowness of thought or action; *also* : less than normal intellectual competence usu. characterized by an IQ of less than 70 **2** : slowness in development or progress

re·tard·ed \ri-ˈtär-dəd\ *adj* : slow or limited in intellectual or emotional development : characterized by mental retardation

retch \ˈrech\ *vb* : to make an effort to vomit; *also* : VOMIT — **retch** *n*

rete \ˈrē-tē, ˈrä-\ *n, pl* **re·tia** \ˈrē-tē-ə\ **1** : a network esp. of blood vessels or nerves : PLEXUS **2** : an anatomical part resembling or including a network

re·ten·tion \ri-ˈten-chən\ *n* **1** : the act of retaining: as **a** : abnormal retaining of a fluid or secretion in a body cavity **b** : the holding in place of a tooth or dental replacement by means of a retainer **2** : a preservation of the aftereffects of experience and learning that makes recall or recognition possible

re·ten·tive \ri-ˈten-tiv\ *adj* : tending to retain: as **a** : having a good memory ⟨a ∼ mind⟩ **b** : of, relating to, or being a dental retainer

rete peg *n* : any of the inwardly directed prolongations of the Malpighian layer of the epidermis that mesh with the dermal papillae of the skin

rete testis *n, pl* **retia tes·ti·um** \-ˈtes-tē-əm\ : the network of tubules in the mediastinum testis

retia *pl of* RETE

reticul- or reticulo- *comb form* : reticulum ⟨*reticulocyte*⟩

reticula pl of RETICULUM

re·tic·u·lar \ri-'ti-kyə-lər\ adj : of, re-lating to, or forming a network

reticular activating system n : a part of the reticular formation that extends from the brain stem to the midbrain and thalamus with connections distributed throughout the cerebral cortex and that controls the degree of activity of the central nervous system (as in maintaining sleep and wakefulness)

reticular cell n : RETICULUM CELL; esp : RETICULOCYTE

reticular fiber n : any of the thin branching fibers of connective tissue that form an intricate interstitial network ramifying through other tissues and organs

reticular formation n : a mass of nerve cells and fibers situated primarily in the brain stem and functioning upon stimulation esp. in arousal of the organism — called also reticular substance

reticularis — see LIVEDO RETICULARIS, ZONA RETICULARIS

reticular layer n : the deeper layer of the dermis formed of interlacing fasciculi of white fibrous tissue

reticular tissue n : RETICULUM 2a

re·tic·u·late body \ri-'ti-kyə-lət-\ n : a chlamydial cell of a spherical intracellular form that is larger than an elementary body and reproduces by binary fission

re·tic·u·lin \ri-'ti-kyə-lən\ n : a protein substance similar to collagen that is a constituent of reticular tissue

re·tic·u·lo·cyte \ri-'ti-kyə-lō-ˌsīt\ n : an immature red blood cell that appears esp. during regeneration of lost blood and has a fine basophilic reticulum formed of the remains of ribosomes — **re·tic·u·lo·cyt·ic** \ri-ˌti-kyə-lō-'si-tik\ adj

re·tic·u·lo·cy·to·pe·nia \ri-ˌti-kyə-lō-ˌsī-tə-'pē-nē-ə\ n : an abnormal decrease in the number of reticulocytes in the blood

re·tic·u·lo·cy·to·sis \-ˌsī-'tō-səs\ n, pl -to·ses \-ˌsēz\ : an increase in the number of reticulocytes in the blood

re·tic·u·lo·en·do·the·li·al \ri-ˌti-kyə-lō-ˌen-də-'thē-lē-əl\ adj : of, relating to, or being the reticuloendothelial system (~ tissue) (~ cells)

reticuloendothelial system n : a diffuse system of cells arising from mesenchyme and comprising all the phagocytic cells of the body except the circulating white blood cells — called also lymphoreticular system

re·tic·u·lo·en·do·the·li·o·sis \-ˌthē-lē-'ō-səs\ n, pl -o·ses \-ˌsēz\ : any of several disorders characterized by proliferation of reticuloendothelial cells or their derivatives — called also reticulosis

re·tic·u·lo·sar·co·ma \-ˌsär-'kō-mə\ n, pl -mas or -ma·ta \-mə-tə\ : RETICULUM CELL SARCOMA

re·tic·u·lo·sis \ri-ˌti-kyə-'lō-səs\ n, pl -lo·ses \-ˌsēz\ : RETICULOENDOTHELIOSIS

re·tic·u·lo·spi·nal tract \ri-ˌti-kyə-lō-'spī-nᵊl-\ n : a tract of nerve fibers that originates in the reticular formation of the pons and medulla oblongata and descends to the spinal cord

re·tic·u·lum \ri-'ti-kyə-ləm\ n, pl -la \-lə\ 1 : the second compartment of the stomach of a ruminant in which folds of the mucous membrane form hexagonal cells — called also honeycomb; compare ABOMASUM, OMASUM, RUMEN 2 : a reticular structure: as a : the network of interstitial tissue composed of reticular fibers — called also reticular tissue b : the network often visible in fixed protoplasm both of the cell body and the nucleus of many cells

reticulum cell n : any of the branched anastomosing reticuloendothelial cells that form the reticular fibers

reticulum cell sarcoma n : a malignant lymphoma arising from reticulum cells — called also reticulosarcoma

retin- or **retino-** comb form : retina (retinitis) (retinoscopy)

ret·i·na \'ret-ᵊn-ə\ n, pl retinas or ret·i·nae \-ᵊn-ˌē\ : the sensory membrane that lines most of the large posterior chamber of the eye, is composed of several layers including one containing the rods and cones, and functions as the immediate instrument of vision by receiving the image formed by the lens and converting it into chemical and nervous signals which reach the brain by way of the optic nerve

Ret·in-A \ˌret-ᵊn-'ā\ trademark — used for a preparation of retinoic acid

ret·i·nac·u·lum \ˌret-ᵊn-'a-kyə-ləm\ n, pl -la \-lə\ : a connecting or retaining band esp. of fibrous tissue — see EXTENSOR RETINACULUM, FLEXOR RETINACULUM, INFERIOR EXTENSOR RETINACULUM, INFERIOR PERONEAL RETINACULUM, PERONEAL RETINACULUM, SUPERIOR EXTENSOR RETINACULUM, SUPERIOR PERONEAL RETINACULUM

¹**ret·i·nal** \'ret-ᵊn-əl\ adj : of, relating to, involving, or being a retina (a ~ examination) (~ rods)

²**ret·i·nal** \'ret-ᵊn-ˌal, -ˌól\ n : a yellowish to orange aldehyde $C_{20}H_{28}O$ derived from vitamin A that in combination with proteins forms the visual pigments of the retinal rods and cones — called also retinene, retinene₁, vitamin A aldehyde

retinal artery — see CENTRAL ARTERY OF THE RETINA

retinal detachment n : a condition of the eye in which the retina has separated from the choroid — called also detached retina, detachment of the retina

retinal disparity *n* : the slight difference in the two retinal images due to the angle from which each eye views an object

retinal vein — see CENTRAL VEIN OF THE RETINA

ret·i·nene \'ret-ʰn-ˌēn\ *n* : either of two aldehydes derived from vitamin A: **a** : RETINAL **b** : an orange-red crystalline compound $C_{20}H_{26}O$ related to vitamin A_2

retinene₁ \-'wən\ *n* : RETINAL

retinene₂ \-'tü\ *n* : RETINENE b

ret·i·ni·tis \ˌret-ʰn-'ī-təs\ *n*, *pl* **-nit·i·des** \-'i-tə-ˌdēz\ : inflammation of the retina

retinitis pig·men·to·sa \-ˌpig-mən-'tō-sə, -ˌ(ˌ)men-, -zə\ *n* : any of several hereditary progressive degenerative diseases of the eye marked by night blindness in the early stages, atrophy and pigment changes in the retina, constriction of the visual field, and eventual blindness — called also *pigmentary retinopathy*

retinitis pro·lif·er·ans \-prə-'li-fə-ˌranz\ *n* : neovascularization of the retina associated esp. with diabetic retinopathy

retino- — see RETIN-

ret·i·no·blas·to·ma \ˌret-ʰn-ō-ˌblas-'tō-mə\ *n*, *pl* **-mas** *or* **-ma·ta** \-mə-tə\ : a hereditary malignant tumor of the retina that develops during childhood, is derived from retinal germ cells, and is associated with a chromosomal abnormality

ret·i·no·cho·roid·i·tis \-ˌkōr-ˌoi-'dī-təs\ *n* : inflammation of the retina and the choroid

ret·i·no·ic acid \ˌret-ʰn-'ō-ik-\ *n* : an acid $C_{20}H_{28}O_2$ derived from vitamin A and used as a keratolytic esp. in the treatment of acne — called also *tretinoin*; see RETIN-A

ret·i·noid \'ret-ʰn-ˌoid\ *n* : any of various synthetic or naturally occurring analogs of vitamin A — **retinoid** *adj*

ret·i·nol \'ret-ʰn-ˌōl, -ˌōl\ *n* : VITAMIN A a

ret·i·nop·a·thy \ˌret-ʰn-'ä-pə-thē\ *n*, *pl* **-thies** : any of various noninflammatory disorders of the retina including some that cause blindness ⟨diabetic ~⟩

ret·i·no·scope \'ret-ʰn-ə-ˌskōp\ *n* : an apparatus used in retinoscopy

ret·i·nos·co·py \ˌret-ʰn-'äs-kə-pē\ *n*, *pl* **-pies** : a method of determining the state of refraction of the eye by illuminating the retina with a mirror and observing the direction of movement of the retinal illumination and adjacent shadow when the mirror is turned

ret·i·no·tec·tal \ˌret-ʰn-ō-'tek-təl\ *adj* : of, relating to, or being the nerve fibers connecting the retina and the tectum of the midbrain ⟨~ pathways⟩

re·tract \ri-'trakt\ *vb* **1** : to draw back or in ⟨~ the lower jaw⟩ — compare PROTRACT 2 **2** : to use a retractor

re·trac·tion \ri-'trak-shən\ *n* : an act or instance of retracting; *specif* : backward or inward movement of an organ or part

re·trac·tor \ri-'trak-tər\ *n* : one that retracts: as **a** : any of various surgical instruments for holding tissues away from the field of operation **b** : a muscle that draws in an organ or part

retro- *prefix* **1** : backward : back ⟨*retro*flexion⟩ **2** : situated behind ⟨*retro*pubic⟩

ret·ro·bul·bar \ˌre-trō-'bəl-bər, -ˌbär\ *adj* : situated, occurring, or administered behind the eyeball ⟨a ~ injection⟩

retrobulbar neuritis *n* : inflammation of the part of the optic nerve lying immediately behind the eyeball

ret·ro·cli·na·tion \-kli-'nā-shən\ *n* : the condition of being inclined backward

ret·ro·flex·ion \ˌre-trō-'flek-shən\ *n* : the state of being bent back; *specif* : the bending back of the body of the uterus upon the cervix — compare RETROVERSION

ret·ro·gnath·ia \-'na-thē-ə\ *n* : RETROGNATHISM

ret·ro·gnath·ism \ˌre-trō-'na-ˌthi-zəm\ *n* : a condition characterized by recession of one or both of the jaws

ret·ro·grade \'re-trō-ˌgrād\ *adj* **1** : characterized by retrogression **2** : affecting a period immediately prior to a precipitating cause ⟨~ amnesia⟩ **3** : occurring or performed in a direction opposite to the usual direction of conduction or flow ⟨~ catheterization⟩; *esp* : occurring along cell processes toward the cell body ⟨~ axonal transport⟩ — compare ANTEROGRADE 2 — **ret·ro·grade·ly** *adv*

retrograde pyelogram *n* : a roentgenogram of the kidney made by retrograde pyelography

retrograde pyelography *n* : pyelography performed by injection of radio-opaque material through the ureter

ret·ro·gres·sion \ˌre-trō-'gre-shən\ *n* : a reversal in development or condition: as **a** : return to a former and less complex level of development or organization **b** : subsidence or decline of symptoms or manifestations of a disease — **ret·ro·gres·sive** \-'gre-siv\ *adj*

ret·ro·len·tal fibroplasia \ˌre-trō-'lent-ʰl-\ *n* : a disease of the retina that occurs esp. in premature infants of low birth weight and that is characterized by the presence of an opaque fibrous membrane behind the lens of the eye

ret·ro·mo·lar \-'mō-lər\ *adj* : situated or occurring behind the last molar

ret·ro·per·i·to·ne·al \-ˌper-ə-tə-'nē-əl\ *adj* : situated or occurring behind the peritoneum ⟨~ bleeding⟩ ⟨a ~ tumor⟩ — **ret·ro·per·i·to·ne·al·ly** *adv*

retroperitoneal fibrosis *n* : proliferation of fibrous tissue behind the peritoneum often leading to blockage of the ureters — called also *Ormond's disease*

retroperitoneal space n : RETROPERITONEUM

ret·ro·per·i·to·ne·um \-ˌper-ə-tə-ˈnē-əm\ n, pl **-ne·ums** or **-nea** \-ˈnē-ə\ : the space between the peritoneum and the posterior abdominal wall that contains esp. the kidneys and associated structures, the pancreas, and part of the aorta and inferior vena cava

ret·ro·pha·ryn·geal \-ˌfar-ən-ˈjē-əl, -fə-ˈrin-jəl, -jē-əl\ adj : situated or occurring behind the pharynx (a ~ abscess)

ret·ro·pu·bic \ˌre-trō-ˈpyü-bik\ adj **1** : situated or occurring behind the pubis **2** : performed by way of the retropubic space (~ prostatectomy)

retropubic space n : the potential space occurring between the pubic symphysis and the urinary bladder

ret·ro·rec·tal \-ˈrekt-ᵊl\ adj : situated or occurring behind the rectum

ret·ro·spec·tive \-ˈspek-tiv\ adj : relating to or being a study (as of a disease) that starts with the present condition of a population of individuals and collects data about their past history to explain their present condition — compare PROSPECTIVE

ret·ro·ster·nal \-ˈstər-nəl\ adj : situated or occurring behind the sternum

ret·ro·ver·sion \-ˈvər-zhən, -shən\ n : the bending backward of the uterus and cervix out of the normal axis so that the fundus points toward the sacrum and the cervix toward the pubic symphysis — compare RETROFLEXION

Ret·ro·vir \ˈre-trō-ˌvir\ trademark — used for a preparation of azidothymidine

ret·ro·vi·rol·o·gy \ˌre-trō-vī-ˈrä-lə-jē\ n, pl **-gies** : a branch of science concerned with the study of retroviruses — **ret·ro·vi·rol·o·gist** \-jist\ n

ret·ro·vi·rus \ˈre-trō-ˌvī-rəs\ n : any of a group of RNA-containing viruses (as HIV and the Rous sarcoma virus) that produce reverse transcriptase by means of which DNA is produced using their RNA as a template and incorporated into the genome of infected cells and that include numerous tumorigenic viruses — called also *RNA tumor virus* — **ret·ro·vi·ral** \-ˌvī-rəl\ adj

re·tru·sion \ri-ˈtrü-zhən\ n : backward displacement; specif : a condition in which a tooth or the jaw is posterior to its proper occlusal position — **re·trude** \-ˈtrüd\ vb — **re·tru·sive** \-ˈtrü-siv\ adj

reuniens — see DUCTUS REUNIENS

re·up·take \rē-ˈəp-ˌtāk\ n : the reabsorption by a neuron of a neurotransmitter following the transmission of a nerve impulse across a synapse

re·vac·ci·na·tion \ˌrē-ˌvak-sə-ˈnā-shən\ n : vaccination administered some period after an initial vaccination esp. to strengthen or renew immunity — **re·vac·ci·nate** \-ˈvak-sə-ˌnāt\ vb

re·vas·cu·lar·iza·tion \ˌrē-ˌvas-kyə-lə-rə-ˈzā-shən\ n : a surgical procedure for the provision of a new, additional, or augmented blood supply to a body part or organ (myocardial ~)

reverse tran·scrip·tase \ri-ˈvərs-ˌtran-ˈskrip-ˌtās, -ˌtāz\ n : a polymerase esp. of retroviruses that catalyzes the formation of DNA using RNA as a template

reverse transcription n : the process of synthesizing double-stranded DNA using RNA as a template and reverse transcriptase as a catalyst

re·vers·ible \ri-ˈvər-sə-bəl\ adj **1** : capable of going through a series of actions (as changes) either backward or forward **2** : capable of being corrected or undone : not permanent or irrevocable (~ hypertension) — **re·vers·ibly** adv

re·ver·sion \ri-ˈvər-zhən, -shən\ n **1** : an act or the process of returning (as to a former condition) **2** : a return toward an ancestral type or condition : reappearance of an ancestral character — **re·vert** \ri-ˈvərt\ vb

re·ver·tant \ri-ˈvərt-ᵊnt\ n : a mutant gene, individual, or strain that regains a former capability (as the production of a particular protein) by undergoing further mutation (yeast ~s) — **revertant** adj

re·vive \ri-ˈvīv\ vb **re·vived; re·viv·ing 1** : to return or restore to consciousness or life **2** : to restore from a depressed, inactive, or unused state — **re·viv·able** \-ˈvī-və-bəl\ adj

re·ward \ri-ˈwȯrd\ n : a stimulus administered to an organism following a correct or desired response that increases the probability of occurrence of the response — **reward** vb

Reye's syndrome \ˈrīz-, ˈrāz-\ also **Reye syndrome** \ˈrī-, ˈrā-\ n : an often fatal encephalopathy esp. of childhood characterized by fever, vomiting, fatty infiltration of the liver, and swelling of the kidneys and brain

Reye, Ralph Douglas Kenneth (1912–1977), Australian pathologist.

RF abbr rheumatic fever

R factor \ˈär-\ n : a group of genes present in some bacteria that provide a basis for resistance to antibiotics and can be transferred from cell to cell by conjugation

RFLP \ˌär-(ˌ)ef-(ˌ)el-ˈpē\ n : RESTRICTION FRAGMENT LENGTH POLYMORPHISM

¹Rh \ˌär-ˈāch\ adj : of, relating to, or being an Rh factor (~ antigens)

²Rh symbol rhodium

rhabd- or **rhabdo-** comb form : rodlike structure (*rhabdovirus*)

rhab·do·my·ol·y·sis \ˌrab-dō-mī-ˈä-lə-səs\ n, pl -y·ses \-ˌsēz\ : a potentially fatal disease marked by destruction or degeneration of skeletal muscle and often associated with myoglobinuria

rhab·do·my·o·ma \ˌrab-dō-mī-ˈō-mə\ n, pl -mas or -ma·ta \-mə-tə\ : a benign tumor composed of striated muscle fibers (a cardiac ∼)

rhab·do·myo·sar·co·ma \ˌrab-(ˌ)dō-ˌmī-ə-sär-ˈkō-mə\ n, pl -mas or -ma·ta \-mə-tə\ : a malignant tumor composed of striated muscle fibers

rhab·do·virus \-ˌvī-rəs\ n : any of a group of RNA-containing rod- or bullet-shaped viruses found in plants and animals and including the causative agents of rabies and vesicular stomatitis

rha·chi·tis var of RACHITIS

rhag·a·des \ˈra-gə-ˌdēz\ n pl : linear cracks or fissures in the skin occurring esp. at the angles of the mouth or about the anus

rha·phe var of RAPHE

Rh disease n : ERYTHROBLASTOSIS FETALIS

rhe·ni·um \ˈrē-nē-əm\ n : a rare heavy metallic element — symbol Re; see ELEMENT table

rheo- comb form : flow : current ⟨rheobase⟩

rheo·base \ˈrē-ō-ˌbās\ n : the minimal electrical current required to excite a tissue (as nerve or muscle) given indefinitely long time during which the current is applied — compare CHRONAXIE

rhe·sus factor \ˈrē-səs-\ n : RH FACTOR

rheum \ˈrüm\ n : a watery discharge from the mucous membranes esp. of the eyes or nose; also : a condition (as a cold) marked by such discharge — **rheumy** \ˈrü-mē\ adj

¹rheu·mat·ic \rü-ˈma-tik\ adj : of, relating to, characteristic of, or affected with rheumatism ⟨∼ pain⟩ ⟨a ∼ joint⟩

²rheumatic n : a person affected with rheumatism

rheumatica — see POLYMYALGIA RHEUMATICA

rheumatic disease n : any of several diseases (as rheumatic fever or fibrositis) characterized by inflammation and pain in muscles or joints : RHEUMATISM

rheumatic fever n : an acute often recurrent disease occurring chiefly in children and young adults and characterized by fever, inflammation, pain, and swelling in and around the joints, inflammatory involvement of the pericardium and valves of the heart, and often the formation of small nodules chiefly in the subcutaneous tissues and the heart

rheumatic heart disease n : active or inactive disease of the heart that results from rheumatic fever and is characterized by inflammatory changes in the myocardium or scar-

ring of the valves causing reduced functional capacity of the heart

rheu·ma·tism \ˈrü-mə-ˌti-zəm, ˈrü-mə-\ n 1 : any of various conditions characterized by inflammation or pain in muscles, joints, or fibrous tissue ⟨muscular ∼⟩ 2 : RHEUMATOID ARTHRITIS

rheu·ma·toid \-ˌtȯid\ adj : characteristic of or affected with rheumatoid arthritis

rheumatoid arthritis n : a usu. chronic disease that is of unknown cause and is characterized esp. by pain, stiffness, inflammation, swelling, and sometimes destruction of joints — compare OSTEOARTHRITIS

rheumatoid factor n : an autoantibody of high molecular weight that is usu. present in rheumatoid arthritis

rheumatoid spondylitis n : ANKYLOSING SPONDYLITIS

rheu·ma·tol·o·gist \ˌrü-mə-ˈtä-lə-jist, ˌrü-\ n : a specialist in rheumatology

rheu·ma·tol·o·gy \-jē\ n, pl -gies : a medical science dealing with rheumatic diseases

Rh factor \ˌär-ˈāch-\ n : any of one or more genetically determined antigens usu. present in the red blood cells of most persons and of higher animals and capable of inducing intense immunogenic reactions — called also rhesus factor

rhin- or **rhino-** comb form 1 a : nose ⟨rhinitis⟩ ⟨rhinology⟩ b : nose and ⟨rhinotracheitis⟩ 2 : nasal ⟨rhinovirus⟩

rhi·nal \ˈrīn-ᵊl\ adj : of or relating to the nose : NASAL

rhin·en·ceph·a·lon \ˌrī-(ˌ)nen-ˈse-fə-ˌlän, -lən\ n, pl -la \-lə\ : the anterior inferior part of the forebrain that is chiefly concerned with olfaction and that is considered to include the olfactory bulb together with the forebrain olfactory structures receiving fibers directly from it and often esp. formerly the limbic system which is now known to be concerned with emotional states and affect — called also smell brain — **rhin·en·ce·pha·lic** \-ˌri-nen-sə-ˈfa-lik\ adj

rhi·ni·tis \rī-ˈnī-təs\ n, pl -nit·i·des \-ˈni-tə-ˌdēz\ : inflammation of the mucous membrane of the nose ⟨allergic ∼⟩; also : any of various conditions characterized by such inflammation

rhi·no·log·ic \ˌrī-nə-ˈlä-jik\ or **rhi·no·log·i·cal** \-ji-kəl\ adj : of or relating to the nose ⟨∼ disease⟩

rhi·nol·o·gist \rī-ˈnä-lə-jist\ n : a physician who specializes in rhinology

rhi·nol·o·gy \-jē\ n, pl -gies : a branch of medicine that deals with the nose and its diseases

rhi·no·phar·yn·gi·tis \ˌrī-nō-far-ən-ˈjī-təs\ n, pl -git·i·des \-ˈji-tə-ˌdēz\ : inflammation of the mucous membrane of the nose and pharynx

rhi·no·phy·ma \-ˈfī-mə\ n, pl -mas or -ma·ta \-mə-tə\ : a nodular swelling and congestion of the nose in an advanced stage of acne rosacea

rhi·no·plas·ty \'rī-nō-ˌplas-tē\ *n, pl* **-ties** : plastic surgery on the nose usu. for cosmetic purposes — called also *nose job* — **rhi·no·plas·tic** \ˌrī-nō-ˈplas-tik\ *adj*

rhi·no·pneu·mo·ni·tis \ˌrī-nō-ˌnü-mə-ˈnī-təs, -ˌnyü-\ *n* : either of two forms of an acute febrile respiratory disease affecting horses, caused by types of a herpesvirus, characterized esp. by rhinopharyngitis and tracheobronchitis, and sometimes causing abortion in pregnant mares

rhi·nor·rhea \ˌrī-nə-ˈrē-ə\ *n* : excessive mucous secretion from the nose

rhi·nor·rhoea *chiefly Brit var of* RHINORRHEA

rhi·no·scope \'rī-nə-ˌskōp\ *n* : an instrument for examining the cavities and passages of the nose

rhi·nos·co·py \rī-ˈnäs-kə-pē\ *n, pl* **-pies** : examination of the nasal passages — **rhi·no·scop·ic** \ˌrī-nə-ˈskä-pik\ *adj*

rhi·no·spo·rid·i·o·sis \ˌrī-nō-spə-ˌri-dē-ˈō-səs\ *n, pl* **-o·ses** \-ˌsēz\ : a fungal disease of the external mucous membranes (as of the nose) that is characterized by the formation of pinkish red, friable, sessile, or pedunculated polyps and is caused by an ascomycetous fungus (*Rhinosporidium seeberi*)

rhi·not·o·my \rī-ˈnä-tə-mē\ *n, pl* **-mies** : surgical incision of the nose

rhi·no·tra·che·itis \ˌrī-nō-ˌtrā-kē-ˈī-təs\ *n* : inflammation of the nasal cavities and trachea; *esp* : a disease of the upper respiratory system in cats and esp. young kittens that is characterized by sneezing, conjunctivitis with discharge, and nasal discharges — see INFECTIOUS BOVINE RHINOTRACHEITIS

rhi·no·vi·rus \ˌrī-nō-ˈvī-rəs\ *n* : any of a group of picornaviruses that are related to the enteroviruses and are associated with upper respiratory tract disorders (as the common cold)

Rhip·i·ceph·a·lus \ˌri-pə-ˈse-fə-ləs\ *n* : a genus of ixodid ticks that are parasitic on many mammals and some birds and include vectors of serious diseases (as Rocky Mountain spotted fever and east coast fever)

rhi·zo·me·lic \ˌrī-zə-ˈmē-lik\ *adj* : of or relating to the hip and shoulder joints

rhi·zot·o·my \rī-ˈzä-tə-mē\ *n, pl* **-mies** : the operation of cutting the anterior or posterior spinal nerve roots

Rh-neg·a·tive \ˌär-ˌāch-ˈne-gə-tiv\ *adj* : lacking Rh factor in the blood

rhod- *or* **rhodo-** *comb form* : rose : red (*rhodopsin*)

rho·di·um \'rō-dē-əm\ *n* : a white hard ductile metallic element — symbol *Rh*; see ELEMENT table

rho·dop·sin \rō-ˈdäp-sən\ *n* : a red photosensitive pigment in the retinal rods that is important in vision in dim light, is quickly bleached by light to a mixture of opsin and retinal, and is regenerated in the dark — called also *visual purple*

Rho·do·tor·u·la \ˌrō-də-ˈtòr-yə-lə\ *n* : a genus of yeasts (family Cryptococcaceae) including one (*R. rubra* syn. *R. mucilaginosa*) sometimes present in the blood or involved in endocarditis prob. as a secondary infection

rhomb·en·ceph·a·lon \ˌräm-(ˌ)ben-ˈse-fə-ˌlän, -lən\ *n, pl* **-la** \-lə\ : HINDBRAIN

rhom·boi·de·us \räm-ˈbòi-dē-əs\ *n, pl* **-dei** \-dē-ˌī\ : either of two muscles that lie beneath the trapezius muscle and connect the spinous processes of various vertebrae with the medial border of the scapula: **a** : RHOMBOIDEUS MINOR **b** : RHOMBOIDEUS MAJOR

rhomboideus major *n* : a muscle arising from the spinous processes of the second through fifth thoracic vertebrae, inserted into the vertebral border of the scapula, and acting to adduct and laterally rotate the scapula — called also *rhomboid major*

rhomboideus minor *n* : a muscle arising from the inferior part of the ligamentum nuchae and from the spinous processes of the seventh cervical and first thoracic vertebrae, inserted into the vertebral border of the scapula at the base of the bony process terminating in the acromion, and acting to adduct and laterally rotate the scapula — called also *rhomboid minor*

rhomboid fossa *n* : the floor of the fourth ventricle of the brain formed by the dorsal surfaces of the pons and medulla oblongata

rhomboid major *n* : RHOMBOIDEUS MAJOR

rhomboid minor *n* : RHOMBOIDEUS MINOR

rhon·chus \'räŋ-kəs\ *n, pl* **rhon·chi** \'räŋ-ˌkī\ : a whistling or snoring sound heard on auscultation of the chest when the air channels are partly obstructed — compare RALE, RATTLE

rho·ta·cism \'rō-tə-ˌsi-zəm\ *n* : a defective pronunciation of *r*; *esp* : substitution of some other sound for that of *r*

Rh-pos·i·tive \ˌär-ˌāch-ˈpä-zə-tiv\ *adj* : containing Rh factor in the red blood cells

rhus \'rüs\ *n* **1** *cap* : a genus of shrubs and trees of the cashew family (Anacardiaceae) that are native to temperate and warm regions, have compound leaves with three to many leaflets, and include some (as poison ivy, poison oak, and poison sumac) producing irritating oils that cause dermatitis — see TOXICODENDRON **2** *pl* **rhuses** *or* **rhus** : any shrub or tree of the genus *Rhus*

rhus dermatitis *n* : dermatitis caused by contact with various plants of the genus *Rhus* and esp. with the common poison ivy (*R. radicans*)

rhythm \'ri-tḥəm\ *n* **1** : a regularly recurrent quantitative change in a variable biological process: as **a** : the pattern of recurrence of the cardiac cycle ⟨an irregular ∼⟩ **b** : the recurring pattern of physical and functional changes associated with the mammalian and esp. human sexual cycle **2** : RHYTHM METHOD — **rhyth·mic** \'riḥ-mik\ *or* **rhyth·mi·cal** \-mi-kəl\ *adj* — **rhyth·mi·cal·ly** *adv* — **rhyth·mic·i·ty** \riḥ-'mi-sə-tē\ *n*

rhythm method *n* : a method of birth control involving continence during the period of the sexual cycle in which ovulation is most likely to occur — compare SAFE PERIOD

rhyt·i·dec·to·my \ri-tə-'dek-tə-mē\ *n, pl* **-mies** : FACE-LIFT

RIA *abbr* radioimmunoassay

rib \'rib\ *n* : any of the paired curved bony or partly cartilaginous rods that stiffen the lateral walls of the body and protect the viscera and that in humans normally include 12 pairs of which all are articulated with the spinal column at the dorsal end and the first 10 are connected also at the ventral end with the sternum by costal cartilages — see FALSE RIB, FLOATING RIB, TRUE RIB

rib- *or* **ribo-** *comb form* : related to ribose ⟨*ribo*flavin⟩

ri·ba·vi·rin \ri-bə-'vī-rən\ *n* : a synthetic broad-spectrum antiviral drug $C_8H_{12}N_4O_5$ that is a nucleoside resembling guanosine

rib cage *n* : the bony enclosing wall of the chest consisting chiefly of the ribs and the structures connecting them — called also *thoracic cage*

ri·bo·fla·vin \rī-bə-'flā-vən, 'rī-bə-ˌ\ *also* **ri·bo·fla·vine** \-ˌvēn\ *n* : a yellow crystalline compound $C_{17}H_{20}N_4O_6$ that is a growth-promoting member of the vitamin B complex and occurs both free (as in milk) and combined (as in liver) — called also *lactoflavin, vitamin B_2*

riboflavin phosphate *or* **riboflavin 5′-phosphate** \-'fiv-ˈprim-\ *n* : FMN

ri·bo·nu·cle·ase \rī-bō-'nü-klē-ˌās, -ˈnyü-, -ˌāz\ *n* : an enzyme that catalyzes the hydrolysis of RNA — called also *RNase*

ri·bo·nu·cle·ic acid \rī-bō-nü-ˌklē-ik-, -nyü-, -ˌklā-\ *n* : RNA

ri·bo·nu·cleo·pro·tein \-ˌnü-klē-ō-'prō-ˌtēn, -ˌnyü-\ *n* : a nucleoprotein that contains RNA

ri·bo·nu·cle·o·side \-'nü-klē-ə-ˌsīd, -ˈnyü-\ *n* : a nucleoside that contains ribose

ri·bo·nu·cle·o·tide \-ˌtīd\ *n* : a nucleotide that contains ribose and occurs esp. as a constituent of RNA

ri·bose \'rī-ˌbōs, -ˌbōz\ *n* : a pentose $C_5H_{10}O_5$ found esp. in the D-form as a constituent of a number of nucleo-

sides (as adenosine, cytidine, and guanosine) esp. in RNA

ribosomal RNA *n* : RNA that is a fundamental structural element of ribosomes — called also *rRNA*

ri·bo·some \'rī-bə-ˌsōm\ *n* : any of the RNA- and protein-rich cytoplasmic organelles that are sites of protein synthesis — **ri·bo·som·al** \rī-bə-'sō-məl\ *adj*

ri·bo·zyme \-ˌzīm\ *n* : a molecule of RNA that functions as an enzyme (as by catalyzing the cleavage of other RNA molecules)

RICE *abbr* rest, ice, compression, elevation — used esp. for the initial treatment of many esp. minor sports-related injuries (as sprains)

rice-water stool *n* : a watery stool containing white flecks of mucus, epithelial cells, and bacteria and discharged from the bowels in severe forms of diarrhea (as in Asiatic cholera)

ri·cin \'ris-ᵊn, 'rīs-\ *n* : a poisonous protein in the castor bean

rick·ets \'ri-kəts\ *n* : a deficiency disease that affects the young during the period of skeletal growth, is characterized esp. by soft and deformed bones, and is caused by failure to assimilate and use calcium and phosphorus normally due to inadequate sunlight or vitamin D — called also *rachitis*

rick·etts·ae·mia *chiefly Brit var of* RICKETTSEMIA

rick·etts·emia \ri-kət-'sē-mē-ə\ *n* : the abnormal presence of rickettsiae in the blood

Rick·etts, Howard Taylor (1871–1910), American pathologist.

rick·ett·sia \ri-'ket-sē-ə\ *n* **1** *cap* : a genus of rod-shaped, coccoid, or diplococcus-shaped often pleomorphic bacteria (family Rickettsiaceae) that live intracellularly in biting arthropods (as lice or ticks) and when transmitted to humans by the bite of an arthropod host cause a number of serious diseases (as Rocky Mountain spotted fever and typhus) **2** *pl* **-sias** *or* **-si·ae** \-sē-ˌē\ *also* **-sia** : any of an order (Rickettsiales) and esp. a family (Rickettsiaceae) of rod-shaped, coccoid, or diplococcus-shaped, often pleomorphic bacteria — **rick·ett·si·al** \-sē-əl\ *adj*

rick·ett·si·al·pox \ri-ˌket-sē-əl-'päks\ *n* : a disease characterized by fever, chills, headache, backache, and a spotty rash and caused by a bacterium of the genus *Rickettsia* (*R. akari*) transmitted to humans by the bite of a mite of the genus *Allodermanyssus* (*A. sanguineus*) living on rodents (as the house mouse)

rick·ett·si·o·sis \ri-ˌket-sē-'ō-səs\ *n, pl* **-o·ses** \-ˌsēz\ : infection with or disease caused by a rickettsia (a mild ∼)

ridge·ling *or* **ridg·ling** \'rij-liŋ\ *n* **1** : a partially castrated male animal **2** : a male animal having one or both testes retained in the inguinal canal

Rie•del's disease \'rēd-əlz-\ *n* : chronic thyroiditis in which the thyroid gland becomes hard and stony and firmly attached to surrounding tissues

Riedel, Bernhard Moritz Karl Ludwig (1846–1916), German surgeon.

Riedel's struma *n* : RIEDEL'S DISEASE

ri•fam•pin \ri-'fam-pən\ *or* **ri•fam•pi•cin** \ri-'fam-pə-sən\ *n* : a semisynthetic antibiotic $C_{43}H_{58}N_4O_{12}$ that acts against some viruses and bacteria esp. by inhibiting RNA synthesis

rif•a•my•cin \ri-fə-'mis-ən\ *n* : any of several antibiotics that are derived from a bacterium of the genus *Streptomyces* (*S. mediterranei*)

Rift Valley fever *n* : a disease of east African sheep and sometimes cattle that is caused by an arbovirus, is characterized by fever and destructive hepatitis, and is occasionally transmitted to humans in a much-attenuated form

right \'rīt\ *adj* : of, relating to, or being the side of the body which is away from the heart and on which the hand is stronger in most people; *also* : located nearer to this side than to the left — **right** *adv*

right atrioventricular valve *n* : TRICUSPID VALVE

right colic flexure *n* : HEPATIC FLEXURE

right–eyed *adj* : using the right eye in preference (as in using a monocular microscope)

right gastric artery *n* : an artery that arises from the hepatic artery, passes to the left along the lesser curvature of the stomach while giving off a number of branches, and eventually joins a branch of the left gastric artery

right gastroepiploic artery *n* : GASTROEPIPLOIC ARTERY a

right–hand \'rīt-hand\ *adj* 1 : situated on the right 2 : RIGHT-HANDED

right hand *n* 1 : the hand on a person's right side 2 : the right side

right–hand•ed \-'han-dəd\ *adj* 1 : using the right hand habitually or more easily than the left 2 : relating to, designed for, or done with the right hand 3 : having the same direction or course as the movement of the hands of a watch viewed from in front 4 : DEXTROROTATORY — **right–handed** *adv* — **right–hand•ed•ness** *n*

right heart *n* : the right atrium and ventricle : the half of the heart that receives blood from the systemic circulation and passes it into the pulmonary arteries

right lymphatic duct *n* : a short vessel that receives lymph from the right side of the head, neck, and thorax, the right arm, right lung, right side of the heart, and convex surface of the liver and that discharges it into the right subclavian vein at its junction

with the right internal jugular vein

right pulmonary artery *n* : PULMONARY ARTERY b

right subcostal vein *n* : SUBCOSTAL VEIN a

right–to–life *adj* : opposed to abortion — **right–to–lif•er** \rīt-tə-'lī-fər\ *n*

ri•gid•i•ty \rə-'ji-də-tē\ *n, pl* **-ties** : the quality or state of being stiff or devoid of or deficient in flexibility: as a : abnormal stiffness of muscle b : emotional inflexibility and resistance to change — **rig•id** \'ri-jəd\ *adj*

rigidus — see HALLUX RIGIDUS

rig•or \'ri-gər\ *n* 1 a : CHILL 1 b : a tremor caused by a chill 2 a : rigidity or torpor of organs or tissue that prevents response to stimuli b : RIGOR MORTIS

rig•or mor•tis \'ri-gər-'mȯr-təs\ *n* : temporary rigidity of muscles occurring after death

ri•ma \'rī-mə\ *n, pl* **ri•mae** \-mē\ : an anatomical fissure or cleft

rima glot•ti•dis \-'glä-tə-dəs\ *n* : the passage in the glottis between the true vocal cords

rima pal•pe•bra•rum \-pal-pē-'brer-əm\ *n* : PALPEBRAL FISSURE

rin•der•pest \'rin-dər-pest\ *n* : an acute infectious febrile disease of ruminant animals (as cattle) that is caused by a paramyxovirus and is marked by diarrhea and inflammation of mucous membranes

¹ring \'riŋ\ *n* 1 a : a circular band b : an anatomical structure having a circular opening : ANNULUS 2 : an arrangement of atoms represented in formulas or models in a cyclic manner as a closed chain

²ring *vb* **rang** \'raŋ\; **rung** \'rəŋ\; **ring•ing** : to have the sensation of being filled with a humming sound (his ears *rang*)

ring•bone \-bōn\ *n* : a bony outgrowth on the phalangeal bones of a horse's foot that usu. produces lameness

Ring•er's fluid \'riŋ-ərz-\ *n* : RINGER'S SOLUTION

Ringer, Sidney (1835–1910), British physiologist.

Ring•er's solution \'riŋ-ərz-\ *also* **Ringer solution** \'riŋ-ər-\ *n* : a balanced aqueous solution that contains chloride, sodium, potassium, calcium, bicarbonate, and phosphate ions and that is used in physiological experiments to provide a medium essentially isosmotic to many animal tissues

ring•hals \'riŋ-hals\ *n* : a venomous African elapid snake (*Haemachates haemachatus*) that is closely related to the true cobras and that seldom strikes but spits or sprays its venom aiming at the eyes of its victim

ring•worm \'riŋ-wərm\ *n* : any of several contagious diseases of the skin, hair, or nails of humans and domestic animals caused by fungi (as of the genus *Trichophyton*) and characterized by ring-shaped discolored patches on the skin that are covered with vesicles and scales — called also *tinea*

Rin·ne's test \'ri-nəs-\ *or* **Rin·ne test** \'ri-nə-\ *n* : a test for determining a subject's ability to hear a vibrating tuning fork when it is held next to the ear and when it is placed on the mastoid process with diminished hearing acuity through air and somewhat heightened hearing acuity through bone being symptomatic of conduction deafness

Rinne, Heinrich Adolf R. (1819–1868), German otologist.

risk \'risk\ *n* **1** : possibility of loss, injury, disease, or death (hypertension increases the ∼ of stroke) **2** : a person considered in terms of the possible bad effects of a particular course of treatment (a poor surgical ∼) — **at risk** : characterized by high risk or susceptibility (as to disease) (patients *at risk* of developing infections)

risk factor *n* : something which increases risk or susceptibility

ri·so·ri·us \ri-'sōr-ē-əs, -'zōr-\ *n, pl* **-rii** \-ē-ı̄\ : a narrow band of muscle fibers arising from the fascia over the masseter muscle, inserted into the tissues at the corner of the mouth, and acting to retract the angle of the mouth

ris·to·ce·tin \ris-tə-'sēt-ᵊn\ *n* : either of two antibiotics or a mixture of both produced by an actinomycete of the genus *Nocardia* (*N. lurida*)

ri·sus sar·do·ni·cus \'rī-səs-ısär-'dä-ni-kəs, 'rē-\ *n* : a facial expression characterized by raised eyebrows and grinning distortion of the face resulting from spasm of facial muscles esp. in tetanus

Rit·a·lin \'ri-tə-lən\ *trademark* — used for a preparation of methylphenidate

rit·o·drine \'ri-tə-ıdrēn, -drən\ *n* : a drug $C_{17}H_{21}NO_3$ used as a smooth muscle relaxant esp. to inhibit premature labor

Rit·ter's disease \'ri-tərz-\ *n* : STAPHYLOCOCCAL SCALDED SKIN SYNDROME

Ritter von Rittershain, Gottfried (1820–1883), German physician.

rit·u·al \'ri-chə-wəl\ *n* : any act or practice regularly repeated in a set precise manner for relief of anxiety (obsessive-compulsive ∼s)

river blindness *n* : ONCHOCERCIASIS

RLF *abbr* retrolental fibroplasia

RLQ *abbr* right lower quadrant (abdomen)

Rn *symbol* radon

RN \ıär-'en\ *n* : REGISTERED NURSE

RNA \ıär-(ı)en-'ā\ *n* : any of various nucleic acids that contain ribose and uracil as structural components and are associated with the control of cellular chemical activities — called also *ribonucleic acid*; see MESSENGER RNA, RIBOSOMAL RNA, TRANSFER RNA

RNAase *var of* RNASE

RNA polymerase *n* : any of a group of enzymes that promote the synthesis of RNA using DNA or RNA as a template

RNA replicase *n* : REPLICASE

RNase \ıär-ıen-'ā-ıās, -'ā-ıāz\ *n* : RIBONUCLEASE

RNA syn·the·tase \-'sin-thə-ıtās, -ıtāz\ *n* : REPLICASE

RNA tumor virus *n* : RETROVIRUS

roach \'rōch\ *n* : COCKROACH

roar·ing \'rōr-iŋ\ *n* : noisy inhalation in a horse caused by nerve paralysis and muscular atrophy and constituting an unsoundness

Rob·ert·so·ni·an \ırä-bərt-'sō-nē-ən\ *adj* : relating to or being a reciprocal translocation that takes place between certain types of chromosomes and that yields one nonfunctional chromosome having two short arms and one functional chromosome having two long arms of which one arm is derived from each parent chromosome

Rob·ert·son \'rä-bərt-sən\, **William Rees Brebner** (1881–1941), American biologist.

Ro·bi·nul \'rō-bi-ınúl\ *trademark* — used for a preparation of glycopyrrolate

Ro·chelle salt \rō-'shel-\ *n* : a crystalline salt $C_4H_4KNaO_6 \cdot 4H_2O$ that is a mild purgative — called also *potassium sodium tartrate, Seignette salt, sodium potassium tartrate*

rock \'räk\ *n* **1** : a small crystallized mass of crack cocaine **2** : CRACK — called also *rock cocaine*

Rocky Mountain spotted fever *n* : an acute bacterial disease that is characterized by chills, fever, prostration, pains in muscles and joints, and a red purple eruption and that is caused by a bacterium of the genus *Rickettsia* (*R. rickettii*) usu. transmitted by an ixodid tick and esp. by the American dog tick and Rocky Mountain wood tick

Rocky Mountain wood tick *n* : a widely distributed wood tick of the genus *Dermacentor* (*D. andersoni*) of western No. America that is a vector of Rocky Mountain spotted fever and sometimes causes tick paralysis

rod \'räd\ *n* **1** : any of the long rod-shaped photosensitive receptors in the retina responsive to faint light — compare CONE 1 2 : a bacterium shaped like a rod

ro·dent \'rōd-ᵊnt\ *n* : any of an order (Rodentia) of relatively small mammals (as a mouse or a rat) that have in both jaws a single pair of incisors with a chisel-shaped edge — **rodent** *adj*

ro·den·ti·cide \rō-'den-tə-ısīd\ *n* : an agent that kills, repels, or controls rodents

rodent ulcer *n* : a chronic persistent ulcer of the exposed skin and esp. of the face that is destructive locally, spreads slowly, and is usu. a carcinoma derived from basal cells

rod·like \'räd-ˌlīk\ *adj* : resembling a rod ⟨~ bacteria⟩

rod of Cor·ti \-'kȯr-tē\ *n* : any of the minute modified epithelial elements that rise from the basilar membrane of the organ of Corti in two spirally arranged rows so that the free ends of the members incline toward and interlock with corresponding members of the opposite row and enclose the tunnel of Corti

A. G. G. Corti — see ORGAN OF CORTI

¹**roent·gen** \'rent-gən, 'rənt-, -jən, -shən\ *adj* : of, relating to, or using X rays

Rönt·gen *or* Roent·gen \'rœnt-gən\, Wilhelm Conrad (1845–1923), German physicist.

²**roentgen** *n* : the international unit of x-radiation or gamma radiation equal to the amount of radiation that produces in one cubic centimeter of dry air at 0°C (32°F) and standard atmospheric pressure ionization of either sign equal to one electrostatic unit of charge

roent·gen·o·gram \'rent-gə-nə-ˌgram, 'rənt-, -jə-, -shə-\ *n* : a photograph made with X rays

roent·gen·og·ra·phy \ˌrent-gə-'nä-grə-fē, ˌrənt-, -jə-, -shə-\ *n, pl* **-phies** : photography by means of X rays — **roent·gen·o·graph·ic** \-nə-'gra-fik\ *adj* — **roent·gen·o·graph·i·cal·ly** *adv*

roent·gen·ol·o·gist \-'nä-lə-jist\ *n* : a specialist in roentgenology

roent·gen·ol·o·gy \-'nä-lə-jē\ *n, pl* **-gies** : a branch of radiology that deals with the use of X rays for diagnosis or treatment of disease — **roent·gen·o·log·ic** \-nə-'lä-jik\ *or* **roent·gen·o·log·i·cal** \-ji-kəl\ *adj* — **roent·gen·o·log·i·cal·ly** *adv*

roent·gen·o·scope \'rent-gə-nə-ˌskōp, 'rənt-, -jə-, -shə-\ *n* : FLUOROSCOPE — **roent·gen·o·scop·ic** \ˌrent-gə-nə-'skä-pik, ˌrənt-, -jə-, -shə-\ *adj* — **roent·gen·os·co·py** \-'näs-kə-pē\ *n*

roentgen ray *n* : X RAY 1

Ro·gaine \'rō-ˌgān\ *trademark* — used for a preparation of minoxidil

Rog·e·ri·an \rä-'jer-ē-ən\ *adj* : of or relating to the system of therapy or the theory of personality of Carl Rogers

Rog·ers \'rä-jərz\, Carl Ransom (1902–1987), American psychologist.

Ro·lan·dic area \rō-'lan-dik-\ *n* : the motor area of the cerebral cortex lying just anterior to the central sulcus and comprising part of the precentral gyrus

L. Rolando — see FISSURE OF ROLANDO

Rolandic fissure *n* : CENTRAL SULCUS

role *also* **rôle** \'rōl\ *n* : a socially prescribed pattern of behavior usu. de-

termined by an individual's status in a particular society

role model *n* : a person whose behavior in a particular role is imitated by others

role–play \'rōl-ˌplā\ *vb* **1** : ACT OUT 2 : to play a role

rolf \'rȯlf, 'rälf\ *vb, often cap* : to practice Rolfing on — **rolf·er** *n, often cap*

Rolf, Ida P. (1896–1979), American biochemist and physiotherapist.

Rolf·ing \'rȯl-fiŋ, 'räl-\ *service mark* — used for a system of muscle massage intended to serve as both physical and emotional therapy

ro·li·tet·ra·cy·cline \ˌrō-li-ˌte-tra-'sī-ˌklēn\ *n* : a semisynthetic broad-spectrum tetracycline antibiotic $C_{27}H_{33}N_3O_8$ used esp. for parenteral administration in cases requiring high concentrations or when oral administration is impractical

roll·er \'rō-lər\ — see TONGUE ROLLER

roller bandage *n* : a long rolled bandage

Rom·berg's sign \'räm-ˌbərgz-\ *or* **Romberg sign** \-ˌbərg-\ *n* : a diagnostic sign of tabes dorsalis and other diseases of the nervous system consisting of a swaying of the body when the feet are placed close together and the eyes are closed

Romberg, Moritz Heinrich (1795–1873), German pathologist.

Romberg's test *or* **Romberg test** *n* : a test for the presence of Romberg's sign by placing the feet close together and closing the eyes

ron·geur \rōⁿ-'zhər\ *n* : a heavy-duty forceps for removing small pieces of bone or tough tissue

ron·nel \'rän-ᵊl\ *n* : an organophosphate $C_8H_8Cl_3O_3PS$ that is used esp. as a systemic insecticide to protect cattle from pests

rönt·gen *var of* ROENTGEN

roof \'rüf, 'rȯf\ *n, pl* **roofs** \'rüfs, 'rȯfs, 'rüvz, 'rȯvz\ **1** : the vaulted upper boundary of the mouth supported largely by the palatine bones and limited anteriorly by the dental lamina and posteriorly by the uvula and upper part of the fauces **2** : a covering structure of any of various other parts of the body ⟨~ of the skull⟩

room·ing–in \'rü-miŋ-'in, 'rü-\ *n* : an arrangement whereby a newborn infant is kept in the mother's hospital room instead of in a nursery

room temperature *n* : a temperature of from 59° to 77°F (15° to 25°C) which is suitable for human occupancy

root \'rüt, 'rȯt\ *n* **1** : the part of a tooth within the socket; *also* : any of the processes into which this part is often divided **2** : the enlarged basal part of a hair within the skin — called also **hair root 3** : the proximal end of a nerve; *esp* : one or more bundles of nerve fibers joining the cranial and spinal nerves with their respective nuclei and columns of gray matter — see DORSAL ROOT, VENTRAL ROOT 4 : the part of an organ or physical structure by which it is attached to the body (the $\sim$ of the tongue) — **root·less** \-ləs\ *adj*

root canal *n* 1 : the part of the pulp cavity lying in the root of a tooth — called also *pulp canal* 2 : a dental operation to save a tooth by removing the contents of its root canal and filling the cavity with a protective substance

root·ed \'rü-təd, 'rü-\ *adj* 1 : having such or so many roots (single-*rooted* premolars) 2 : having a contracted root nearly closing the pulp cavity and preventing further growth

root·let \'rüt-lət, 'rút-\ *n* : a small root; *also* : one of the ultimate divisions of a nerve root

root planing *n* : the scraping of a bacteria-impregnated layer of cementum from the surface of a tooth root to prevent or treat periodontitis

Ror·schach \'ror-₁shäk\ *adj* : of, relating to, used in connection with, or resulting from the Rorschach test

Rorschach test *n* : a personality and intelligence test in which a subject interprets 10 standard black or colored irregular figures (as blots of ink) in terms that reveal intellectual and emotional factors — called also *Rorschach, Rorschach inkblot test*

   Rorschach, Hermann (1884–1922), Swiss psychiatrist.

ro·sa·cea \rō-'zā-shə, -shē-ə\ *n* : ACNE ROSACEA

rosa — see PITYRIASIS ROSEA

rose ben·gal \-ben-¹gol, -ben-\ *n* : either of two bluish red acid dyes that are derivatives of fluorescein

rose bengal test *n* : a test of liver function by determining the time taken for an injected quantity of rose bengal to be absorbed from the bloodstream

rose cold *n* : ROSE FEVER

rose fever *n* : hay fever occurring in the spring or early summer

ro·se·o·la \₁rō-zē-¹ō-lə, rō-¹zē-ə-lə\ *n* : a rose-colored eruption in spots or a disease marked by such an eruption: *esp* : ROSEOLA INFANTUM — **ro·se·o·lar** \-lər\ *adj*

roseola in·fan·tum \-in-¹fan-təm\ *n* : a mild disease of infants and children characterized by fever lasting three days followed by an eruption of rose-colored spots

ro·sette \rō-'zet\ *n* : a rose-shaped cluster of cells

ros·tral \'räs-trəl, 'rós-\ *adj* 1 : of or relating to a rostrum 2 : situated toward the oral or nasal region: as **a** *of a part of the spinal cord* : SUPERIOR 1 **b** *of a*

part of the brain : anterior or ventral (the $\sim$ pons) — **ros·tral·ly** *adv*

ros·trum \'räs-trəm, 'rós-\ *n*, *pl* **rostrums** or **ros·tra** \-trə\ : a bodily part or process suggesting a bird's bill: as **a** : the reflected anterior portion of the corpus callosum below the genu **b** : the interior median spine of the body of the basisphenoid bone articulating with the vomer

¹**rot** \'rät\ *vb* **rot·ted; rot·ting** : to undergo decomposition from the action of bacteria or fungi

²**rot** *n* 1 : the process of rotting : the state of being rotten 2 : any of several parasitic diseases esp. of sheep marked by necrosis and wasting

ro·ta·tor \'rō-₁tā-tər, rō-'\ *n*, *pl* **rotators** or **ro·ta·to·res** \₁rō-tə-'tor-ēz\ : a muscle that partially rotates a part on its axis; *specif* : any of several small muscles in the dorsal region of the spine arising from the upper and back part of a transverse process and inserted into the lamina of the vertebra above

rotator cuff \-₁kəf\ *n* : a supporting and strengthening structure of the shoulder joint that is made up of part of its capsule blended with tendons of the subscapularis, infraspinatus, supraspinatus, and teres minor muscles as they pass to the capsule or across it to insert on the humerus — called also *musculotendinous cuff*

ro·ta·vi·rus \'rō-tə-₁vī-rəs\ *n* : a reovirus that has a double-layered capsid and a wheel-like appearance and that causes diarrhea esp. in infants

ro·te·none \'rōt-²n-₁ōn\ *n* : a crystalline insecticide $C_{23}H_{22}O_6$ that is of low toxicity for warm-blooded animals and is used esp. in home gardens

rotunda — see FENESTRA ROTUNDA

rotundum — see FORAMEN ROTUNDUM

Rou·get cell \rü-'zhä-\ *n* : any of numerous branching cells adhering to the endothelium of capillaries and regarded as a contractile element in the capillary wall

   Rouget, Charles–Marie–Benjamin (1824–1904), French physiologist and anatomist.

rough \'rəf\ *adj* : having a broken, uneven, or bumpy surface; *specif* : forming or being rough colonies usu. made up of organisms that form chains or filaments and tend to marked decrease in capsule formation and virulence — used of dissociated strains of bacteria; compare SMOOTH

rough·age \'rə-fij\ *n* 1 : FIBER 2; *also* : food (as bran) containing much indigestible material acting as fiber

rou·leau \rü-'lō\ *n*, *pl* **rou·leaux** *same or* -'lōz\ *or* **rouleaus** : a group of red blood corpuscles resembling a stack of coins

round \'raúnd\ *vb* : to go on rounds

round cell *n* : a small lymphocyte or a closely related cell esp. occurring in an area of chronic infection or as the typical cell of some sarcomas

round ligament *n* **1** : a fibrous cord resulting from the obliteration of the umbilical vein of the fetus and passing from the umbilicus to the notch in the anterior border of the liver and along the undersurface of that organ **2** : either of a pair of rounded cords arising from each side of the uterus and traceable through the inguinal canal to the tissue of the labia majora into which they merge

rounds *n pl* : a series of professional calls on hospital patients made by a doctor or nurse — see GRAND ROUNDS

round-shouldered *adj* : having the shoulders stooping or rounded

round window *n* : a round opening between the middle ear and the cochlea that is closed over by a membrane — called also *fenestra cochleae, fenestra rotunda*

round-worm \'raùnd-ˌwərm\ *n* : NEMATODE; *also* : a related round-bodied unsegmented worm (as an acanthocephalan) as distinguished from a flatworm

roup \'rüp, 'raùp\ *n* : TRICHOMONIASIS c

Rous sarcoma \'raùs-\ *n* : a readily transplantable malignant fibrosarcoma of chickens that is caused by a specific carcinogenic retrovirus

Rous, Francis Peyton (1879–1970), American pathologist.

Rous sarcoma virus *n* : the avian retrovirus responsible for Rous sarcoma

route \'rüt, 'raùt\ *n* : a method of transmitting a disease or of administering a remedy

RPh *abbr* registered pharmacist

RPR card test \ˌär-ˌpē-ˌär-ˈkärd-\ *n* : RAPID PLASMA REAGIN TEST

RPT *abbr* registered physical therapist

RQ *abbr* respiratory quotient

RR *abbr* recovery room

RRA *abbr* registered records administrator

-r·rha·gia \'rā-jə, 'rä-, -jē-ə, -zhə, -zhē-ə\ *n comb form* : abnormal or excessive discharge or flow (metrorrhagia) — **-r·rhag·ic** \'rā-jik\ *adj comb form*

-r·rha·phy \r-ə-fē\ *n comb form, pl* **-r·rha·phies** : suture : sewing (nephror-rhaphy)

-r·rhea \'rē-ə\ *n comb form* : flow : discharge (logorrhea) (leukorrhea)

-r·rhex·is \'rek-səs\ *n comb form, pl* **-r·rhex·es** \-ˌsēz\ : rupture (erythrocytorrhexis)

-r·rhoea *chiefly Brit var of* -RRHEA

RRL *abbr* registered records librarian

rRNA \ˌär-ˌär-ˌen-ˈā\ *n* : RIBOSOMAL RNA

RRT *abbr* registered respiratory therapist

RS-T segment \ˌär-ˌes-ˈtē-\ *n* : ST SEGMENT

RSV *abbr* **1** respiratory syncytial virus **2** Rous sarcoma virus

RT *abbr* **1** reaction time **2** recreational therapy **3** respiratory therapist

Ru *symbol* ruthenium

rub \'rəb\ *n* **1** : the application of friction with pressure (an alcohol ~) **2** : a sound heard in auscultation that is produced by the friction of one structure moving against another

rub·ber \'rə-bər\ *n* : CONDOM

rubber dam *n* : a thin sheet of rubber that is stretched around a tooth to keep it dry during dental work or is used in strips to provide drainage in surgical wounds

rubbing alcohol *n* : a cooling and soothing liquid for external application that contains approximately 70 percent denatured ethanol or isopropyl alcohol

¹ru·be·fa·cient \ˌrü-bə-ˈfā-shənt\ *adj* : causing redness of the skin (a ~ cream)

²rubefacient *n* : a substance for external application that produces redness of the skin

ru·bel·la \rü-ˈbe-lə\ *n* : GERMAN MEASLES — see MATERNAL RUBELLA

ru·be·ola \ˌrü-bē-ˈō-lə, rü-ˈbē-ə-lə\ *n* : MEASLES 1a — **ru·be·o·lar** \-lər\ *adj*

ru·be·o·sis \ˌrü-bē-ˈō-səs\ *n, pl* **-o·ses** \-ˈō-ˌsēz\ *or* **-osises** : a condition characterized by abnormal redness; *esp* : RUBEOSIS IRIDIS

rubeosis iri·dis \-ˈi-rə-dəs\ *n* : abnormal redness of the iris resulting from neovascularization and often associated with diabetes

ru·bid·i·um \rü-ˈbi-dē-əm\ *n* : a soft silvery metallic element — symbol *Rb*; see ELEMENT table

Ru·bin test \'rü-bən-\ *n* : a test to determine the patency or occlusion of the fallopian tubes by insufflating them with carbon dioxide

Rubin, Isidor Clinton (1883–1958), American gynecologist.

ru·bor \'rü-ˌbòr\ *n* : redness of the skin (as from inflammation)

rubra — see PITYRIASIS RUBRA PILARIS

ru·bri·cyte \'rü-bri-ˌsīt\ *n* : an immature red blood cell that has a nucleus, is about half the size of developing red blood cells in preceding stages, and has cytoplasm that stains erratically blue, purplish, and gray due to the presence of hemoglobin : polychromatic normoblast

ru·bro·spi·nal \ˌrü-brō-ˈspī-nəl\ *adj* **1** : of, relating to, or connecting the red nucleus and the spinal cord **2** : of, relating to, or constituting a tract of crossed nerve fibers passing from the red nucleus to the spinal cord and relaying impulses from the cerebellum and corpora striata to the motoneurons of the spinal cord

ru·di·ment \'rü-də-mənt\ *n* : an incompletely developed organ or part; *esp* : an organ or part just beginning to develop : ANLAGE

ru·di·men·ta·ry \ˌrü-də-ˈmen-tə-rē\ *adj*

: very imperfectly developed or represented only by a vestige

Ruf·fi·ni's corpuscle \rü-'fē-nēz-\ or **Ruf·fi·ni corpuscle** \-nē-\ n : any of numerous oval sensory end organs occurring in the subcutaneous tissue of the fingers — called also *Ruffini's brush, Ruffini's end organ*

Ruffini, Angelo (1864–1929), Italian histologist and embryologist.

RU 486 \är-(₁)yü-₁fōr-₁ā-tē-'siks\ n : a drug $C_{29}H_{35}NO_2$ taken orally to induce abortion esp. early in pregnancy by blocking the body's use of progesterone — called also *mifepristone*

ru·ga \'rü-gə\ n, pl **ru·gae** \-₁gī, -₁gē, -₁jē\ : an anatomical fold or wrinkle esp. of the viscera — usu. used in pl. ⟨*rugae* of an empty stomach⟩

ru·men \'rü-mən\ n, pl **ru·mi·na** \-mə-nə\ or **rumens** : the large first compartment of the stomach of a ruminant from which food is regurgitated for rumination and in which cellulose is broken down by the action of symbiotic microorganisms — called also *paunch*; compare ABOMASUM, OMASUM, RETICULUM

ru·men·ot·o·my \₁rü-mə-¹nä-tə-mē\ n, pl **-mies** : surgical incision into the rumen

ru·mi·nant \'rü-mə-nənt\ adj : of or relating to a suborder (Ruminantia) of even-toed hoofed mammals (as sheep and oxen) that chew the cud and have a complex usu. 4-chambered stomach — **ruminant** n

ru·mi·na·tion \₁rü-mə-¹nä-shən\ n : the act or process of regurgitating and chewing again previously swallowed food — **ru·mi·nate** \'rü-mə-₁nät\ vb

rump \'rəmp\ n 1 : the upper rounded part of the hindquarters of a quadruped mammal 2 : the seat of the body : BUTTOCKS

Rum·pel–Leede test \'rùm-pel-¹lēd\ n : a test in which the increased bleeding tendency characteristic of various disorders (as scarlet fever and thrombocytopenia) is indicated by the formation of multiple petechiae on the forearm following application of a tourniquet to the upper arm

Rumpel, Theodor (1862–1923), German physician.

Leede, Carl Stockbridge (b 1882), American physician.

run \'rən\ vb ran \'ran\; run; run·ning : to discharge fluid (as pus or serum)

⟨a *running* sore⟩ — **run a fever** or **run a temperature** : to have a fever

rung past part of RING

run·ny \'rə-nē\ adj : running or tending to run ⟨a ∼ nose⟩

runs \'rənz\ n sing or pl : DIARRHEA — used with *the*

ru·pia \'rü-pē-ə\ n : an eruption occurring esp. in tertiary syphilis consisting of vesicles having an inflamed base and filled with serous purulent or bloody fluid which dries up and forms large blackish conical crusts — **ru·pi·al** \-əl\ adj

rup·ture \'rəp-chər\ n 1 : the tearing apart of a tissue ⟨∼ of an intervertebral disk⟩ 2 : HERNIA — **rupture** vb

RUQ abbr right upper quadrant (abdomen)

rush \'rəsh\ n 1 : a rapid and extensive wave of peristalsis along the walls of the intestine ⟨peristaltic ∼⟩ 2 : the immediate pleasurable feeling produced by a drug (as heroin or amphetamine) — called also *flash*

Russian spring–summer encephalitis n : a tick-borne encephalitis of Europe and Asia that is transmitted by ticks of the genus *Ixodes* — see LOUPING ILL

¹**rut** \'rət\ n 1 : sexual excitement in a mammal (as estrus in the female) esp. when periodic 2 : the period during which rut normally occurs — often used with *the*

²**rut** vb **rut·ted; rut·ting** : to be in or enter into a state of rut

ru·the·ni·um \rü-¹thē-nē-əm\ n : a hard brittle grayish rare metallic element — symbol *Ru*; see ELEMENT table

ruth·er·ford \'rə-thər-fərd\ n : a unit strength of a radioactive source corresponding to one million disintegrations per second — abbr. *rd*

Rutherford, Ernest (Baron Rutherford of Nelson) (1871–1937), British physicist.

ru·tin \'rüt-ən\ n : a yellow crystalline glycoside $C_{27}H_{30}O_{16}$ that occurs in various plants (as tobacco) and that is used chiefly for strengthening capillary blood vessels (as in cases of hypertension and radiation injury)

R wave \'är-₁wāv\ n : the positive upward deflection in the QRS complex of an electrocardiogram that follows the Q wave

Rx \₁är-¹eks\ n : a medical prescription

S

¹**S** abbr 1 sacral — used esp. with a number from 1 to 5 to indicate a vertebra or segment of the spinal cord in the sacral region 2 signa — used to introduce the signature in writing a prescription 3 subject 4 svedberg

²**S** symbol sulfur

sa abbr [Latin *secundum artem*] according to art — used in writing prescriptions

S–A abbr sinoatrial

sa·ber shin \'sā-bər-\ n : a tibia that has

a pronounced anterior convexity resembling the curve of a saber and caused by congenital syphilis

Sa·bin vaccine \'sā-bin-\ *n* : a polio vaccine that is taken by mouth and contains weakened live virus — called also *Sabin oral vaccine*

Sabin, Albert Bruce (*b* 1906), American immunologist.

sac \'sak\ *n* : a soft-walled anatomical cavity usu. having a narrow opening or none at all and often containing a special fluid (a synovial ∼) — see AIR SAC, LACRIMAL SAC

sac·cade \sa-'käd\ *n* : a small rapid jerky movement of the eye esp. as it jumps from fixation on one point to another (as in reading) — **sac·cad·ic** \-'kä-dik\ *adj*

sacchar- *or* **sacchari-** *or* **saccharo-** *comb form* : sugar ⟨*saccharide*⟩

sac·cha·rase \'sa-kə-ɹrās, -ɹrāz\ *n* : INVERTASE

sac·cha·ride \'sa-kə-ɹrīd, -rid\ *n* : a simple sugar, combination of sugars, or polymerized sugar : CARBOHYDRATE — see DISACCHARIDE, MONOSACCHARIDE, POLYSACCHARIDE, TRISACCHARIDE

sac·cha·rin \'sa-kə-rin\ *n* : a crystalline compound $C_7H_5NO_3S$ that is unrelated to the carbohydrates, is many times sweeter than sucrose, and is used as a calorie-free sweetener

sac·cha·rine \'sa-kə-rin, -ɹrēn\ *adj* 1 a : of, relating to, or resembling that of sugar (∼ taste) b : yielding or containing sugar (a ∼ fluid) 2 : overly or sickeningly sweet (∼ flavor)

sac·cha·ro·my·ces \ɹsa-kə-rō-'mī-(ɹ)sēz\ *n* 1 *cap* : a genus of usu. unicellular yeasts (family Saccharomycetaceae) that are distinguished by their sparse or absent mycelium and by their facility in reproducing asexually by budding 2 *pl* **saccharomyces** : any yeast of the genus *Saccharomyces*

sac·cu·lar \'sa-kyə-lər\ *adj* : resembling a sac (a ∼ aneurysm)

sac·cu·lat·ed \-ɹlā-təd\ *also* **sac·cu·late** \-ɹlāt, -lət\ *adj* : having or formed of a series of saccular expansions

sac·cu·la·tion \ɹsa-kyə-'lā-shən\ *n* 1 : the quality or state of being sacculated 2 : the process of developing or segmenting into sacculated structures 3 : a sac or sacculated structure; *esp* : one of a linear series of such structures (the ∼s of the colon)

sac·cule \'sa-(ɹ)kyül\ *n* : a little sac; *specif* : the smaller chamber of the membranous labyrinth of the ear

sac·cu·lus \'sa-kyə-ləs\ *n, pl* **-li** \-ɹlī, -ɹlē\ : SACCULE

sac·like \'sak-ɹlīk\ *adj* : having the form of or suggesting a sac

sacr- *or* **sacro-** *comb form* 1 : sacrum (*sacral*) 2 : sacral and (*sacroiliac*)

sacra *pl of* SACRUM

¹**sa·cral** \'sa-krəl, 'sā-\ *adj* : of, relating to, or lying near the sacrum

²**sacral** *n* : a sacral vertebra or sacral nerve

sacral artery — see LATERAL SACRAL ARTERY, MIDDLE SACRAL ARTERY

sacral canal *n* : the part of the vertebral canal lying in the sacrum

sacral cornu *n* : a rounded process on each side of the fifth sacral vertebra

sacral crest *n* : any of several crests or tubercles on the sacrum: as a : one on the midline of the dorsal surface — called also *median sacral crest* b : any of a series of tubercles on each side of the dorsal surface lateral to the sacral foramina that represent the transverse processes of the sacral vertebrae and serve as attachments for ligaments — called also *lateral sacral crest*

sacral foramen *n* : any of 16 openings in the sacrum of which there are four on each side of the dorsal surface giving passage to the posterior branches of the sacral nerves and four on each side of the pelvic surface giving passage to the anterior branches of the sacral nerves

sacral hiatus *n* : the opening into the spinal canal in the midline of the dorsal surface of the sacrum between the laminae of the fifth sacral vertebra

sa·cral·iza·tion \ɹsā-krə-lə-'zā-shən\ *n* : a congenital anomaly in which the fifth lumbar vertebra is fused to the sacrum in varying degrees

sacral nerve *n* : any of the spinal nerves of the sacral region of which there are five pairs and which have anterior and posterior branches passing out through the sacral foramina

sacral plexus *n* : a nerve plexus that lies against the posterior and lateral walls of the pelvis, is formed by the union of the lumbosacral trunk and the first, second, and third sacral nerves, and continues into the thigh as the sciatic nerve

sacral promontory *n* : the inwardly projecting anterior part of the body of the first sacral vertebra

sacral vein — see LATERAL SACRAL VEIN, MEDIAN SACRAL VEIN

sacral vertebra *n* : any of the five fused vertebrae that make up the sacrum

sacro- — see SACR-

sa·cro·coc·cy·geal \ɹsā-krō-käk-'si-jəl, ɹsa-, -jē-əl\ *adj* : of, relating to, affecting, or performed by way of the region of the sacrum and coccyx

sa·cro·coc·cy·geus dor·sa·lis \-käk-'si-jē-əs-ɹdȯr-'sā-ləs\ *n* : an inconstant muscle that sometimes extends from the dorsal part of the sacrum to the coccyx — called also *posterior sacrococcygeal muscle*

sacrococcygeus ven·tra·lis \-ven-'trā-ləs\ *n* : an inconstant muscle that sometimes extends from the ventral surface of the lower sacral vertebrae to the coccyx — called also *anterior sacrococcygeal muscle*

¹sa·cro·il·i·ac \ˌsa-krō-ˈi-lē-ˌak, ˌsā-\ *adj* : of, relating to, affecting, or being the region of the joint between the sacrum and the ilium (~ distress)

²sacroiliac *n* : SACROILIAC JOINT

sacroiliac joint *n* : the joint or articulation between the sacrum and ilium — called also *sacroiliac, sacroiliac articulation*

sa·cro·il·i·itis \ˌsa-krō-ˌi-lē-ˈī-təs, ˌsa-\ *n* : inflammation of the sacroiliac joint or region

sa·cro·spi·na·lis \ˌsā-krō-spī-ˈnā-ləs, ˌsa-krō-spī-ˈna-ləs\ *n* : a muscle that extends the length of the back and neck, that arises from the iliac crest, the sacrum, and the lumbar and two lower thoracic vertebrae, and that splits in the upper lumbar region into the iliocostalis muscles, the longissimus muscles, and the spinalis muscles — called also *erector spinae*

sa·cro·spi·nous ligament \ˌsā-krō-ˈspī-nəs-, ˌsa-\ *n* : a ligament on each side of the body that is attached by a broad base to the lateral margins of the sacrum and coccyx and passes to the ischial spine and that closes off the greater sciatic notch to form the greater sciatic foramen and with the sacrotuberous ligament closes off the lesser sciatic notch to form the lesser sciatic foramen

sa·cro·tu·ber·ous ligament \ˌsā-krō-ˈtü-bə-rəs-, ˌsa-, -ˈtyü-\ *n* : a thin fan-shaped ligament on each side of the body that is attached above to the posterior superior and posterior inferior iliac spines and to the sacrum and coccyx, that passes obliquely downward to insert into the inner margin of the ischial tuberosity, and that with the sacrospinous ligament closes off the lesser sciatic notch to form the lesser sciatic foramen

sa·cro·uter·ine ligament \-ˈyü-tə-ˌrīn-, -rən-\ *n* : UTEROSACRAL LIGAMENT

sa·crum \ˈsa-krəm, ˈsā-\ *n, pl* **sa·cra** \ˈsa-krə, ˈsā-\ : the part of the spinal column that is directly connected with or forms a part of the pelvis by articulation with the ilia and that in humans forms the dorsal wall of the pelvis and consists of five fused vertebrae diminishing in size to the apex at the lower end which bears the coccyx

SAD *abbr* seasonal affective disorder

sad·dle \ˈsad-ᵊl\ *n* : the part of a partial denture that carries an artificial tooth and has connectors for attaching such teeth attached to its ends

saddle block anesthesia *n* : spinal anesthesia confined to the perineum, the buttocks, and the inner aspect of the thighs — called also *saddle block*

saddle joint *n* : a joint (as the carpometacarpal joint of the thumb) with saddle-shaped articular surfaces that are convex in one direction and concave in another and that permit movements in all directions except axial rotation

sad·dle·nose \ˈsad-ᵊl-ˌnōz\ *n* : a nose marked by depression of the bridge resulting from injury or disease

sa·dism \ˈsā-ˌdiz-əm, ˈsa-\ *n* : a sexual perversion in which gratification is obtained by the infliction of physical or mental pain on others (as on a love object) — compare ALGOLAGNIA, MASOCHISM — **sa·dis·tic** \sə-ˈdis-tik, sā-, sa-\ *adj* — **sa·dis·ti·cal·ly** *adv*

Sade \ˈsäd\, **Marquis de (Comte Donatien–Alphonse–François) (1740–1814),** French soldier and writer.

sa·dist \ˈsā-dist, ˈsa-\ *n* : an individual who practices sadism

sa·do·mas·och·ism \ˌsā-(ˌ)dō-ˈma-sə-ˌki-zəm, ˌsa-, -zə-ˌki-\ *n* : the derivation of pleasure from the infliction of physical or mental pain either on others or on oneself — **sa·do·mas·och·is·tic** \-ˌma-sə-ˈkist-ik\ *also* **sadomas·ochist** *adj*

L. von Sacher–Masoch — see MASOCHISM

sa·do·mas·och·ist \-kist\ *n* : an individual who practices sadomasochism

safe \ˈsāf\ *adj* **saf·er; saf·est** : not causing harm or injury; *esp* : having a low incidence of adverse reactions and significant side effects when adequate instructions for use are given and having a low potential for harm under conditions of widespread availability — **safe·ty** \ˈsāf-tē\ *n*

safe period *n* : a portion of the menstrual cycle of the human female during which conception is least likely to occur and which usu. includes several days immediately before and after the menstrual period and the period itself — compare RHYTHM METHOD

safe sex *n* : sexual activity and esp. sexual intercourse in which various measures (as the use of latex condoms or the practice of monogamy) are taken to avoid disease (as AIDS) transmitted by sexual contact

saf·flow·er oil \ˈsa-ˌflau̇-ər-\ *n* : an edible oil that is low in saturated fatty acids, is obtained from the seeds of the safflower (*Carthamus tinctorius*) of the daisy family (Compositae), and is often used in diets low in cholesterol

sag·it·tal \ˈsa-jət-ᵊl\ *adj* **1** : of, relating to, or being the sagittal suture of the skull **2** : of, relating to, situated in, or being the median plane of the body or any plane parallel to it — **sag·it·tal·ly** *adv*

sagittal plane *n* : MIDSAGITTAL PLANE; *also* : any plane parallel to a midsagittal plane : a parasagittal plane

sagittal sinus *n* : either of two venous sinuses of the dura mater: **a** : one passing backward in the convex attached superior margin of the falx cerebri and ending at the internal occipital protuberance by fusion with the transverse sinus — called also *superior sagittal sinus* b : one lying in the posterior two thirds of the concave free inferior margin of the falx cerebri and ending posteriorly by joining the great cerebral vein to form the straight sinus — called also *inferior sagittal sinus*

sagittal suture *n* : the deeply serrated articulation between the two parietal bones in the median plane of the top of the head

sa·go spleen \'sä-(₁)gō-\ *n* : a spleen which is affected with amyloid degeneration and in which the amyloid is deposited in the Malpighian corpuscles which appear in cross section as gray translucent bodies

Saint An·tho·ny's fire \₁sänt-'an-thə-nēz-\ *n* : any of several inflammations or gangrenous conditions (as erysipelas or ergotism) of the skin

Anthony, Saint (*ca* 250–350), Egyptian monk.

Saint–John's–wort \₁sänt-'jänz-₁wərt, -₁wȯrt\ *n* : any of a genus (*Hypericum* of the family Guttiferae) of herbs and shrubs with showy yellow flowers; *esp* : one (*H. perforatum*) of dry soil, roadsides, pastures, and ranges that contains a photodynamic pigment causing dermatitis due to photosensitization in sheep, cattle, horses, and goats when ingested

John the Baptist, Saint (*fl first century A.D.*), Jewish prophet.

Saint Lou·is encephalitis \₁sänt-'lü-is-\ *n* : a No. American viral encephalitis that is transmitted by several mosquitoes of the genus *Culex*

Saint Vi·tus' dance \-'vi-təs-\ *also* **Saint Vitus's dance** \-'vi-tə-səz-\ *n* : CHOREA; *esp* : SYDENHAM'S CHOREA

Vitus, Saint (*d ca* 300), Italian martyr.

sal·abra·sion \₁sal-ə-'brā-zhən\ *n* : a method of removing tattoos from skin in which moist gauze pads saturated with sodium chloride are used to abrade the tattooed area by rubbing

sal am·mo·ni·ac \₁sal-ə-'mō-nē-₁ak\ *n* : AMMONIUM CHLORIDE

sal·bu·ta·mol \sal-'byü-tə-₁mȯl, -₁mōl\ *n* : a xylene derivative $C_{13}H_{21}NO_3$ used as a bronchodilator

salicyl- *or* **salicylo-** *comb form* : related to salicylic acid ⟨*salicyl*amide⟩

sal·i·cyl·amide \₁sal-ə-'si-lə-₁mid\ *n* : the crystalline amide $C_7H_7NO_2$ of salicylic acid that is used chiefly as an analgesic, antipyretic, and antirheumatic

sal·i·cyl·an·il·ide \₁sa-lə-sə-'lan-əl-₁id\ *n* : a crystalline compound $C_{13}H_{11}NO_2$ that is used as a fungicidal agent esp. in the external treatment of tinea capitis caused by a fungus of the genus *Microsporum* (*M. audouini*)

sa·lic·y·late \sə-'li-sə-₁lāt\ *n* : a salt or ester of salicylic acid; *also* : SALICYLIC ACID

sal·i·cyl·azo·sul·fa·pyr·i·dine \₁sa-lə-si-₁lä-zō-₁səl-fə-'pir-ə-₁dēn\ *n* : a sulfonamide $C_{18}H_{14}N_4O_5S$ used in the treatment of chronic ulcerative colitis — called also *sulfasalazine*

sal·i·cyl·ic acid \₁sa-lə-₁si-lik-\ *n* : a crystalline phenolic acid $C_7H_6O_3$ that is used esp. in making pharmaceuticals and dyes, as an antiseptic and disinfectant esp. in treating skin diseases, and in the form of salts and other derivatives as an analgesic and antipyretic — see ASPIRIN

sal·i·cyl·ism \'sa-lə-si-₁li-zəm\ *n* : a toxic condition produced by the excessive intake of salicylic acid or salicylates and marked by ringing in the ears, nausea, and vomiting

¹sa·line \'sā-₁lēn, -₁līn\ *adj* 1 : consisting of or containing salt (a ~ solution) 2 : of, relating to, or resembling salt : SALTY 3 : consisting of or relating to the salts esp. of lithium, sodium, potassium, and magnesium (a ~ cathartic) 4 : relating to or being abortion induced by the injection of a highly concentrated saline solution into the amniotic sac (~ amniocentesis) — **sa·lin·i·ty** \sā-'lin-ət-ē, sə-\ *n*

²saline *n* 1 a : a metallic salt; *esp* : a salt of potassium, sodium, or magnesium with a cathartic action b : an aqueous solution of one or more such salts 2 : a saline solution used in physiology

sa·li·va \sə-'lī-və\ *n* : a slightly alkaline secretion of water, mucin, protein, salts, and often a starch-splitting enzyme (as ptyalin) that is secreted into the mouth by salivary glands, lubricates ingested food, and often begins the breakdown of starches

saliva ejector *n* : a narrow tubular device providing suction to draw saliva, blood, and debris from the mouth of a dental patient in order to maintain a clear operative field

sal·i·vary \'sa-lə-₁ver-ē\ *adj* : of or relating to saliva or the glands that secrete it; *esp* : producing or carrying saliva

salivary gland *n* : any of various glands that discharge a fluid secretion and esp. saliva into the mouth cavity and that in humans comprise large compound racemose glands including the parotid glands, the sublingual glands, and the submandibular glands

sal·i·va·tion \₁sa-lə-'vā-shən\ *n* : the act or process of producing a flow of saliva; *esp* : excessive secretion of saliva often accompanied by soreness of the mouth and gums — **sal·i·vate** \'sa-lə-₁vāt\ *vb*

sal·i·va·to·ry \'sa-lə-və-₁tōr-ē\ *adj* : inducing salivation

Salk vaccine \'sȯk-, 'sȯlk-\ *n* : a vaccine consisting of three strains of poliomyelitis virus grown on embryonated eggs and treated with formaldehyde for inactivation

Salk, Jonas Edward (b 1914), American immunologist.

sal·mo·nel·la \ˌsal-mə-ˈne-lə\ n 1 cap : a genus of aerobic gram-negative rod-shaped usu. motile enterobacteria that are pathogenic for humans and other warm-blooded animals and cause food poisoning, acute gastrointestinal inflammation, typhoid fever, or septicemia 2 pl **-nel·lae** \-ˈne-lē\ or **-nellas** or **-nella** : any bacterium of the genus Salmonella

Salm·on \ˈsa-mən\, **Daniel Elmer** (1850–1914), American veterinarian.

sal·mo·nel·lo·sis \ˌsal-mə-ˌne-ˈlō-səs\ n, pl **-loses** \-ˌsēz\ : infection with or disease caused by bacteria of the genus Salmonella typically marked by gastroenteritis but often complicated by septicemia, meningitis, endocarditis, and various focal lesions (as in the kidneys)

salmon poisoning n : a highly fatal febrile disease of fish-eating dogs and other canine mammals that resembles canine distemper and is caused by a rickettsial bacterium (Neorickettsia helminthoeca) transmitted by encysted larvae of a fluke (Nanophyetus salmincola) ingested with the raw flesh of infested salmon, trout, or salamanders

sal·ol \ˈsa-ˌlȯl, -ˌōl\ n : PHENYL SALICYLATE

salping- or **salpingo-** comb form 1 : fallopian tube (salpingoplasty) 2 : eustachian tube (salpingopharyngeus)

sal·pin·gec·to·my \ˌsal-pən-ˈjek-tə-mē\ n, pl **-mies** : surgical excision of a fallopian tube

sal·pin·gi·tis \ˌsal-pən-ˈjī-təs\ n : inflammation of a fallopian or eustachian tube

sal·pin·gog·ra·phy \ˌsal-pin-ˈgä-grə-fē\ n, pl **-phies** : visualization of a fallopian tube by roentgenography following injection of an opaque medium

sal·pin·gol·y·sis \ˌsal-pin-ˈgä-lə-səs\ n, pl **-yses** : surgical correction of adhesions in a fallopian tube

sal·pin·go-oo·pho·rec·to·my \ˌsal-ˌpin-gō-ˌō-ə-fə-ˈrek-tə-mē\ n, pl **-mies** : surgical excision of a fallopian tube and an ovary

sal·pin·go-oo·pho·ri·tis \-ˌō-ə-fə-ˈrī-təs\ n : inflammation of a fallopian tube and an ovary

sal·pin·go·pha·ryn·ge·us \-fə-ˈrin-jē-əs\ n : a muscle of the pharynx that arises from the inferior part of the eustachian tube near its opening and passes downward to join the posterior part of the palatopharyngeus

sal·pin·go·plas·ty \ˈsal-ˈpin-gə-ˌplas-tē\ n, pl **-ties** : plastic surgery of a fallopian tube

sal·pin·gos·to·my \ˌsal-pin-ˈgäs-tə-mē\ n, pl **-mies** : a surgical opening of a fallopian tube (as to establish patency or facilitate drainage)

¹**salt** \ˈsȯlt\ n 1 a : a crystalline compound NaCl that is the chloride of sodium, is abundant in nature, and is used esp. to season or preserve food — called also sodium chloride b : any of numerous compounds that result from replacement of part or all of the acid hydrogen of an acid by a metal or a group acting like a metal : an ionic crystalline compound 2 pl a : a mineral or saline mixture (as Epsom salts) used as an aperient or cathartic b : SMELLING SALTS — **salty** \ˈsȯl-tē\ adj

²**salt** adj 1 : SALINE 2 : being or inducing the one of the four basic taste sensations that is suggestive of seawater — compare BITTER, SOUR, SWEET

sal·ta·to·ry \ˈsal-tə-ˌtȯr-ē, ˈsȯl-\ adj : proceeding by leaps rather than by gradual transitions ⟨∼ conduction of nerve impulses⟩

salt·pe·ter \ˈsȯlt-ˈpē-tər\ n 1 : POTASSIUM NITRATE 2 : SODIUM NITRATE

¹**sal·uret·ic** \ˌsal-yə-ˈre-tik\ adj : facilitating the urinary excretion of salt and esp. of sodium ion ⟨a ∼ drug⟩

²**saluretic** n : a saluretic agent (as a drug)

Sal·u·ron \ˈsa-lu-ˌrän, -lyü\ trademark — used for a preparation of hydroflumethiazide

sal·vage \ˈsal-vij\ vb **sal·vaged; sal·vag·ing** : to save (an organ, tissue, or patient) by preventive or therapeutic measures ⟨salvaged lung tissue⟩ — **salvage** n

sal·var·san \ˈsal-vər-ˌsan\ n : ARSPHENAMINE

salve \ˈsav, ˈsäv, ˈsalv, ˈsälv\ n : an unctuous adhesive substance for application to wounds or sores

sal vo·la·ti·le \ˌsal-və-ˈlat-ᵊl-ē\ n 1 : AMMONIUM CARBONATE 2 : SMELLING SALTS

sa·mar·i·um \sə-ˈmar-ē-əm\ n : a pale gray lustrous metallic element — symbol Sm; see ELEMENT table

san·a·to·ri·um \ˌsa-nə-ˈtȯr-ē-əm\ n, pl **-riums** or **-ria** \-ē-ə\ 1 : an establishment that provides therapy combined with a regimen (as of diet and exercise) for treatment or rehabilitation 2 a : an institution for rest and recuperation (as of convalescents) b : an establishment for the treatment of the chronically ill ⟨a tuberculosis ∼⟩

sand \ˈsand\ n : gritty particles in various body tissues or fluids

sand crack n : a fissure in the wall of a horse's hoof often causing lameness

sand flea n : CHIGOE 1

sand fly n : any of various small biting dipteran flies (families Psychodidae, Simuliidae, and Ceratopogonidae); esp : any fly of the genus Phlebotomus

sand·fly fever \ˈsand-ˌflī-\ n : a virus disease of brief duration that is characterized by fever, headache, pain in the eyes, malaise, and leukopenia and is transmitted by the bite of a sand fly of the genus Phlebotomus

(*P. papatasii*) — called also *pappataci fever, phlebotomus fever*

Sand·hoff–Jatz·ke·witz disease \-ˈjats-kə-ˌvits-\ *n* : SANDHOFF'S DISEASE

Sand·hoff's disease \ˈsand-ˌhȯfs-\ *or* **Sand·hoff disease** \-ˌhȯf\ *n* : a variant of Tay-Sachs disease in which both hexosaminidase and hexosaminidase B are present in greatly reduced quantities

Sandhoff, K., An·dreae \än-ˈdrä-e\, **U.,** and **Jatzkewitz, H.,** German medical scientists.

San·dril \ˈsan-ˌdril\ *trademark* — used for a preparation of reserpine

sane \ˈsān\ *adj* **san·er; san·est** 1 : free from hurt or disease : HEALTHY 2 : mentally sound; *esp* : able to anticipate and appraise the effect of one's actions 3 : proceeding from a sound mind (~ behavior) — **sane·ly** *adv*

san·guin·e·ous \saŋ-ˈgwi-nē-əs, san-\ *adj* : of, relating to, or containing blood

san·gui·nous \ˈsaŋ-gwə-nəs\ *adj* : SANGUINEOUS

san·i·tar·i·an \ˌsa-nə-ˈter-ē-ən\ *n* : a specialist in sanitary science and public health (milk ~)

san·i·tar·i·um \ˌsa-nə-ˈter-ē-əm\ *n, pl* **-i·ums** *or* **-ia** \-ē-ə\ : SANATORIUM

san·i·tary \ˈsa-nə-ˌter-ē\ *adj* 1 : of or relating to health (~ measures) 2 : of, relating to, or used in the disposal esp. of domestic waterborne waste (~ sewage) 3 : characterized by or readily kept in cleanliness (~ food handling) — **san·i·tar·i·ly** \ˌsa-nə-ˈter-ə-lē\ *adv*

sanitary napkin *n* : a disposable absorbent pad used (as during menstruation) to absorb the flow from the uterus

san·i·ta·tion \ˌsa-nə-ˈtā-shən\ *n* 1 : the act or process of making sanitary 2 : the promotion of hygiene and prevention of disease by maintenance of sanitary conditions (mouth ~)

san·i·tize \ˈsa-nə-ˌtīz\ *vb* **-tized; -tiz·ing** : to make sanitary (as by cleaning or sterilizing) — **san·i·ti·za·tion** \ˌsa-nə-tə-ˈzā-shən\ *n*

san·i·to·ri·um \ˌsa-nə-ˈtōr-ē-əm\ *n, pl* **-ri·ums** *or* **-ria** \-ē-ə\ : SANATORIUM

san·i·ty \ˈsa-nə-tē\ *n, pl* **-ties** : the quality or state of being sane; *esp* : soundness or health of mind

San Joa·quin fever \ˌsan-ˌwä-ˈkēn-\ *n* : COCCIDIOIDOMYCOSIS

San Joaquin valley fever *n* : COCCIDIOIDOMYCOSIS

S–A node \ˌes-ˈā-\ *n* : SINOATRIAL NODE

santa — see YERBA SANTA

sap \ˈsap\ — see CELL SAP, NUCLEAR SAP

sa·phe·no·fem·o·ral \sə-ˌfē-nō-ˈfe-mə-rəl\ *adj* : of or relating to the saphenous and the femoral veins

sa·phe·nous \sə-ˈfē-nəs, ˈsa-fə-nəs\ *adj* : of, relating to, associated with, or being either of the saphenous veins

saphenous nerve *n* : a nerve that is the largest and longest branch of the femoral nerve and supplies the skin over the medial side of the leg

saphenous opening *n* : a passage for the great saphenous vein in the fascia lata of the thigh — called also *fossa ovalis*

saphenous vein *n* : either of two chief superficial veins of the leg: **a** : one originating in the foot and passing up the medial side of the leg and through the saphenous opening to join the femoral vein — called also *great saphenous vein, long saphenous vein* **b** : one originating similarly and passing up the back of the leg to join the popliteal vein at the knee — called also *short saphenous vein, small saphenous vein*

sa·pon·i·fi·ca·tion \sə-ˌpä-nə-fə-ˈkā-shən\ *n* 1 : the hydrolysis of a fat by an alkali with the formation of a soap and glycerol 2 : the hydrolysis esp. by an alkali of an ester into the corresponding alcohol and acid; *broadly* : HYDROLYSIS — **sa·pon·i·fy** \sə-ˈpä-nə-ˌfī\ *vb*

sap·phic \ˈsa-fik\ *adj or n* : LESBIAN

Sap·pho \ˈsa-(ˌ)fō\ (*fl ca* 610 BC–*ca* 580 BC), Greek lyric poet.

sap·phism \ˈsa-ˌfi-zəm\ *n* : LESBIANISM

sap·phist \-fist\ *n* : LESBIAN

sapr- *or* **sapro-** *comb form* : dead or decaying organic matter (*saprophyte*)

sap·ro·phyte \ˈsa-prə-ˌfīt\ *n* : a living thing and esp. a plant living on dead or decaying organic matter

sap·ro·phyt·ic \ˌsa-prə-ˈfi-tik\ *adj* : obtaining food by absorbing dissolved organic material; *esp* : obtaining nourishment osmotically from the products of organic breakdown and decay (meningitis caused by ~ bacteria) — **sap·ro·phyt·i·cal·ly** *adv*

sap·ro·zo·ic \-ˈzō-ik\ *adj* : SAPROPHYTIC — used of animals (as protozoans)

sar·al·a·sin \sä-ˈra-lə-sən\ *n* : an antihypertensive polypeptide used esp. in the form of its acetate in the treatment and diagnosis of hypertension

sarc- *or* **sarco-** *comb form* 1 : flesh (*sarcoid*) 2 : striated muscle (*sarcolemma*)

sar·co·cyst \ˈsär-kə-ˌsist\ *n* : the large intramuscular cyst of a protozoan of the genus *Sarcocystis*

Sar·co·cys·tis \ˌsär-kə-ˈsis-təs\ *n* : a genus of sporozoan protozoans (order Sarcosporidia) that form cysts in vertebrate muscle

¹sar·coid \ˈsär-ˌkȯid\ *adj* : of, relating to, resembling, or being sarcoid or sarcoidosis (~ fibroblastic tissue)

²sarcoid *n* 1 : any of various diseases characterized esp. by the formation of nodules in the skin 2 : a nodule characteristic of sarcoid or of sarcoidosis

sar·coid·o·sis \ˌsär-ˌkȯi-ˈdō-səs\ *n, pl* **-o·ses** \-ˌsēz\ : a chronic disease of unknown cause that is characterized by the formation of nodules resembling true tubercles esp. in the lymph nodes, lungs, bones, and skin — called also *Boeck's sarcoid*

sar·co·lem·ma \ˌsär-kə-ˈle-mə\ *n* : the thin transparent homogeneous sheath enclosing a striated muscle fiber — **sar·co·lem·mal** \-məl\ *adj*

sar·co·ly·sin \ˌsär-kə-ˈli-sən\ *or* **sar·co·ly·sine** \-ˌsēn\ *also* L-**sar·co·ly·sin** \ˈel-\ *or* L-**sar·co·ly·sine** *n* : MELPHALAN

sar·co·ma \sär-ˈkō-mə\ *n, pl* **-mas** *also* **-ma·ta** \-mə-tə\ : a malignant neoplasm arising in tissue of mesodermal origin (as connective tissue, bone, cartilage, or striated muscle) that spreads by extension into neighboring tissue or by way of the bloodstream — compare CANCER 1, CARCINOMA

sarcoma bot·ry·oi·des \-ˌbä-trē-ˈoiˌdēz\ *n* : a malignant tumor of striated muscle that resembles a bunch of grapes and occurs esp. in the urogenital tract of young children

sar·co·ma·to·sis \(ˌ)sär-ˌkō-mə-ˈtō-səs\ *n, pl* **-to·ses** \-ˌsēz\ : a disease characterized by the presence and spread of sarcomas

sar·co·ma·tous \sär-ˈkō-mə-təs\ *adj* : of, relating to, or resembling sarcoma

sar·co·mere \ˈsär-kə-ˌmir\ *n* : any of the repeating structural units of striated muscle fibrils — **sar·co·mer·ic** \ˌsär-kə-ˈmer-ik\ *adj*

Sar·coph·a·ga \sär-ˈkä-fə-gə\ *n* : a genus of dipteran flies (family Sarcophagidae) comprising typical flesh flies

sar·co·plasm \ˈsär-kə-ˌpla-zəm\ *n* : the cytoplasm of a striated muscle fiber — compare MYOPLASM — **sar·co·plas·mic** \ˌsär-kə-ˈplaz-mik\ *adj*

sarcoplasmic reticulum *n* : the endoplasmic reticulum of cardiac muscle and skeletal striated muscle fiber that functions esp. as a storage and release area for calcium

Sar·cop·tes \sär-ˈkäp-(ˌ)tēz\ *n* : a genus of whitish itch mites (family Sarcoptidae)

sar·cop·tic \sär-ˈkäp-tik\ *adj* : of, relating to, caused by, or being itch mites of the genus *Sarcoptes*

sarcoptic mange *n* : a mange caused by mites of the genus *Sarcoptes* that burrow in the skin esp. of the head and face — compare CHORIOPTIC MANGE, DEMODECTIC MANGE

sar·co·sine \ˈsär-kə-ˌsēn, -sən\ *n* : a sweetish crystalline amino acid $C_3H_7NO_2$ formed by the decomposition of creatine or made synthetically

sar·co·some \ˈsär-kə-ˌsōm\ *n* : a mitochondrion of a striated muscle fiber — **sar·co·som·al** \ˌsär-kə-ˈsō-məl\ *adj*

sar·co·spor·id·i·o·sis \ˌsär-kō-spə-ˌri-dē-ˈō-səs\ *n, pl* **-oses** \-ˌsēz\ : infestation with or disease caused by protozoans of the genus *Sarcocystis*

sardonicus — see RISUS SARDONICUS

sa·rin \ˈsär-ən, zä-ˈrēn\ *n* : an extremely toxic chemical warfare agent $C_4H_{10}FO_2P$ — called also *GB*

sar·to·ri·us \sär-ˈtōr-ē-əs\ *n, pl* **-rii** \-ēˌī\ : a muscle that arises from the anterior superior iliac spine, crosses the front of the thigh obliquely to insert on the upper part of the inner surface of the tibia, is the longest muscle in the human body, and acts to flex, abduct, and rotate the thigh laterally at the hip joint and to flex the leg at the knee joint and to rotate it medially in a way that enables one to sit with the heel of one leg on the knee of the opposite leg in a position often attributed to a tailor busy sewing

sas·sa·fras \ˈsa-sə-ˌfras\ *n* 1 : a tall eastern No. American tree (*Sassafras albidum*) of the laurel family (Lauraceae) with mucilaginous twigs and leaves 2 : the dried root bark of the sassafras formerly used as a diaphoretic and flavoring agent but now prohibited for use as a flavoring or food additive because of its carcinogenic properties

sat·el·lite \ˈsat-əl-ˌīt\ *n* 1 : a short segment separated from the main body of a chromosome by a constriction 2 : a bodily structure lying near or associated with another (as a vein accompanying an artery) 3 : a smaller lesion accompanying a main one and situated nearby — **satellite** *adj*

satellite cell *n* : a cell surrounding a ganglion cell

satellite DNA *n* : a fraction of a eukaryotic organism's DNA that differs in density from most of its DNA as determined by centrifugation, that apparently consists of short repetitive nucleotide sequences, that does not undergo transcription, and that in some organisms (as the mouse) is found esp. in centromeric regions

sat·el·lit·osis \ˌsat-əl-i-ˈtō-səs\ *n, pl* **-oses** \-ˌsēz\ : a condition characterized by a grouping of satellite cells around ganglion cells in the brain

sa·ti·ety \sə-ˈtī-ə-tē\ *n, pl* **-ties** : the quality or state of being fed or gratified to or beyond capacity

¹**sat·u·rate** \ˈsa-chə-ˌrāt\ *vb* **-rat·ed; -rat·ing** 1 : to treat, furnish, or charge with something to the point where no more can be absorbed, dissolved, or retained 2 : to cause to combine till there is no further tendency to combine

²**sat·u·rate** \-rət\ *n* : a saturated chemical compound

sat·u·rat·ed \ˈsa-chə-ˌrā-təd\ *adj* 1 : being the most concentrated solution that can persist in the presence of an excess of the dissolved substance 2 : being a compound that does not tend to unite directly with another compound — used esp. of organic compounds containing no double or triple bonds

sat·u·ra·tion \ˌsa-chə-ˈrā-shən\ *n* **1** : the act of saturating : the state of being saturated **2** : conversion of an unsaturated to a saturated chemical compound (as by hydrogenation) **3** : a state of maximum impregnation; *esp* : the presence in air of the most water possible under existent pressure and temperature **4** : the one of the three psychological dimensions of color perception that is related to the purity of the color and that decreases as the amount of white present in the stimulus increases — called also *intensity*; compare BRIGHTNESS, HUE

sat·ur·nine \ˈsa-tər-ˌnīn\ *adj* **1** : of or relating to lead **2** : of, relating to, or produced by the absorption of lead into the system (∼ poisoning)

sat·urn·ism \ˈsa-tər-ˌni-zəm\ *n* : LEAD POISONING

sa·ty·ri·a·sis \ˌsā-tə-ˈrī-ə-səs, ˌsa-\ *n, pl* **-a·ses** \-ˌsēz\ : excessive or abnormal sexual desire in the male — compare NYMPHOMANIA

sau·cer·ize \ˈsȯ-sər-ˌīz\ *vb* **-ized; -izing** : to form a shallow depression by excavation of tissue to promote granulation and healing of (a wound) — **sau·cer·iza·tion** \ˌsȯ-sər-ə-ˈzā-shən\ *n*

sau·na \ˈsau̇-nə, ˈsȯ-nə\ *n* **1** : a Finnish steam bath in which the steam is provided by water thrown on hot stones; *also* : a bathhouse or room used for such a bath **2** : a dry heat bath; *also* : a room or cabinet used for such a bath

saw \ˈsȯ\ *n* : a hand or power tool used to cut hard material (as bone) and equipped usu. with a toothed blade or disk

saxi·tox·in \ˌsak-sə-ˈtäk-sən\ *n* : a potent nonprotein neurotoxin $C_{10}H_{17}$-$N_7O_4·2HCl$ that originates in dinoflagellates of the genus *Gonyaulax* found in red tides and that sometimes occurs in and renders toxic normally edible mollusks which feed on them

Sb *symbol* [Latin *stibium*] antimony

SBS *abbr* sick building syndrome

Sc *symbol* scandium

scab \ˈskab\ *n* **1** : scabies of domestic animals **2** : a hardened covering of dried secretions (as blood, plasma, or pus) that forms over a wound — called also *crust* — **scab** *vb* — **scab·by** \ˈska-bē\ *adj*

scabby mouth *n* : SORE MOUTH 1

sca·bi·cide \ˈskā-bə-ˌsīd\ *n* : a drug that destroys the itch mite causing scabies

sca·bies \ˈskā-bēz\ *n, pl* **scabies** : contagious itch or mange esp. with exudative crusts that is caused by parasitic mites and esp. by a mite of the genus *Sarcoptes* (*S. scabiei*) — **sca·bi·et·ic** \ˌskā-bē-ˈe-tik\ *adj*

scab mite *n* : any of several small mites that cause mange, scabies, or scab; *esp* : one of the genus *Psoroptes*

sca·la \ˈskā-lə\ *n, pl* **sca·lae** \-ˌlē\ : any of the three spirally arranged canals into which the bony canal of the cochlea is partitioned by the vestibular and basilar membranes and which comprise the scala media, scala tympani, and scala vestibuli

scala me·dia \-ˈmē-dē-ə\ *n, pl* **scalae me·di·ae** \-dē-ˌē\ : the spirally arranged canal in the bony canal of the cochlea that contains the organ of Corti, is triangular in cross section, and is bounded by the vestibular membrane above, by the periosteum-lined wall of the cochlea laterally, and by the basilar membrane below — called also *cochlear canal, cochlear duct*

scala tym·pa·ni \-ˈtim-pə-ˌnī, -ˌnē\ *n, pl* **scalae tym·pa·no·rum** \-ˌtim-pə-ˈnȯr-əm\ : the lymph-filled spirally arranged canal in the bony canal of the cochlea that is separated from the scala media by the basilar membrane, communicates at its upper end with the scala vestibuli, and abuts at its lower end upon the membrane that separates the round window from the middle ear

scala ves·tib·u·li \-ve-ˈsti-byə-ˌlī\ *n, pl* **scalae ves·tib·u·lo·rum** \-ve-ˌsti-byə-ˈlō-rəm\ : the lymph-filled spirally arranged canal in the bony canal of the cochlea that is separated from the scala media below by the vestibular membrane, is connected with the oval window, and receives vibrations from the stapes

¹scald \ˈskȯld\ *vb* : to burn with hot liquid or steam (∼ed skin)

²scald *n* : an injury to the body caused by scalding

scalded-skin syndrome *n* : TOXIC EPIDERMAL NECROLYSIS — see STAPHYLOCOCCAL SCALDED SKIN SYNDROME

¹scale \ˈskāl\ *n* **1** : a small thin dry lamina shed (as in many skin diseases) from the skin **2** : a film of tartar encrusting the teeth

²scale *vb* **scaled; scal·ing 1** : to take off or come off in thin layers or scales (∼ tartar from the teeth) **2** : to shed scales or fragmentary surface matter : EXFOLIATE (*scaling* skin)

³scale *n* **1** : a series of marks or points at known intervals used to measure distances (as the height of the mercury in a thermometer) **2** : a graduated series or scheme of rank or order **3** : a graded series of tests or of performances used in rating individual intelligence or achievement

sca·lene \ˈskā-ˌlēn, skā-ˈ\ *n* : SCALENUS — called also *scalene muscle*

sca·le·not·o·my \ˌskā-lə-ˈnä-tə-mē\ *n, pl* **-mies** : surgical severing of one or more scalenus muscles near their insertion on the ribs

sca·le·nus \skā-ˈlē-nəs\ *n, pl* **sca·le·ni** \-ˌnī\ : any of usu. three deeply situated muscles on each side of the neck of which each extends from the transverse processes of two or more cervical vertebrae to the first or second rib: **a** : one arising from the transverse processes of the third to sixth cervical vertebrae, inserting on the scalene tubercle of the first rib, and functioning to bend the neck forward and laterally and to rotate it to the side — called also *scalenus anterior, scalenus anticus* **b** : one arising from the transverse processes of the lower six cervical vertebrae, inserting on the upper surface of the first rib, and functioning similarly to the scalenus anterior — called also *scalenus medius* **c** : one arising from the transverse processes of the fourth to sixth cervical vertebrae, inserting on the outer surface of the second rib, and functioning to raise the second rib and to bend and slightly rotate the neck — called also *scalenus posterior*

scalenus anterior n : SCALENUS a

scalenus an·ti·cus \-an-ᵗtī-kəs\ n : SCALENUS a

scalenus anticus syndrome n : a complex of symptoms including pain and numbness in the region of the shoulder, arm, and neck that is caused by compression of the brachial plexus or subclavian artery or both by the scalenus anticus muscle

scalenus me·di·us \-ᵗmē-dē-əs\ n : SCALENUS b

scalenus posterior n : SCALENUS c

scal·er \ᵗskā-lər\ n : any of various dental instruments for removing tartar from teeth

scalp \ᵗskalp\ n : the part of the integument of the head usu. covered with hair in both sexes

scal·pel \ᵗskal-pəl\ n : a small straight thin-bladed knife used esp. in surgery

scaly \ᵗskā-lē\ adj **scal·i·er**; **-est** : covered with or composed of scale or scales (~ skin) — **scal·i·ness** n

¹**scan** \ᵗskan\ vb **scanned**; **scan·ning** 1 a : to examine esp. systematically with a sensing device (as a beam of radiation) **b** : to move an electron beam over and convert (an image) into variations of electrical properties (as voltage) that convey information electronically 2 : to make a scan of (as the human body) in order to detect the presence or localization of radioactive material

²**scan** n 1 : the act or process of scanning 2 **a** : a depiction (as a photograph) of the distribution of a radioactive material in something (as a bodily organ) **b** : an image of a bodily part produced (as by computer) by combining radiographic data obtained from several angles or sections

scan·di·um \ᵗskan-dē-əm\ n : a white metallic element — symbol Sc; see ELEMENT table

scan·ner \ᵗska-nər\ n : a device (as a CAT scanner) for making scans of the human body

scanning electron micrograph n : a micrograph made by scanning electron microscopy

scanning electron microscope n : an electron microscope in which a beam of focused electrons moves across the object with the secondary electrons produced by the object and the electrons scattered by the object being collected to form a three-dimensional image on a cathode-ray tube — called also *scanning microscope;* compare TRANSMISSION ELECTRON MICROSCOPE — **scanning electron microscopy** n

scanning speech n : speech characterized by regularly recurring pauses between words or syllables

Scan·zo·ni maneuver \skänt-ᵗsō-nē-\ also **Scan·zo·ni's maneuver** \-nēz-\ n : rotation of an abnormally positioned fetus by means of forceps with subsequent reapplication of forceps for delivery

Scanzoni, Friedrich Wilhelm (1821–1891), German obstetrician.

scaph- or **scapho-** comb form : scaphoid (*scaphocephaly*)

sca·pha \ᵗska-fə\ n : an elongated depression of the ear that separates the helix and antihelix

scaph·o·ceph·a·ly \ska-fə-ᵗse-fə-lē\ n, pl **-lies** : a congenital deformity of the skull in which the vault is narrow, elongated, and boat-shaped because of premature ossification of the sagittal suture

¹**scaph·oid** \ᵗska-ᵗfóid\ adj 1 : shaped like a boat : NAVICULAR 2 : characterized by concavity (the ~ abdomen in some serious diseases)

²**scaphoid** n 1 : NAVICULAR a 2 : the largest carpal bone of the proximal row of the wrist that occupies the most lateral position on the thumb side — called also *navicular*

scaphoid bone n : SCAPHOID

scaphoid fossa n : a shallow oval depression that is situated above the pterygoid fossa on the pterygoid process of the sphenoid bone and that provides attachment for the origin of the tensor veli palatini muscle

scapul- or **scapulo-** comb form : scapular and (*scapulohumeral*)

scap·u·la \ᵗska-pyə-lə\ n, pl **-lae** \-lē, -ᵗlī\ or **-las** : either of a pair of large essentially flat and triangular bones lying one in each dorsolateral part of the thorax, being the principal bone of the corresponding half of the pectoral girdle, providing articulation for the humerus, and articulating with the corresponding clavicle — called also *shoulder blade*

scapulae — see LEVATOR SCAPULAE

scap·u·lar \ᵗska-pyə-lər\ adj : of, relating to, or affecting the shoulder or scapula (a ~ fracture)

scapular notch n : a semicircular notch on the superior border of the scapula next to the coracoid process that gives passage to the suprascapular nerve and is converted to a foramen by the suprascapular ligament

scap·u·lo·hu·mer·al \ska-pyə-lō-ˈhyü-mə-rəl\ *adj* : of or relating to the scapula and the humerus

scar \ˈskär\ *n* 1 : a mark left (as in the skin) by the healing of injured tissue 2 : a lasting emotional injury — **scar** *vb*

scar·i·fy \ˈskar-ə-ˌfī\ *vb* **-fied; -fy·ing** : to make scratches or small cuts in (as the skin) \ an area for vaccination) — **scar·i·fi·ca·tion** \ˌskar-ə-fə-ˈkā-shən\ *n*

scar·la·ti·na \ˌskär-lə-ˈtē-nə\ *n* : SCARLET FEVER — **scar·la·ti·nal** \-ˈtēn-ᵊl\ *adj*

scar·la·ti·ni·form \-ˈtē-nə-ˌfȯrm\ *adj* : resembling the rash of scarlet fever

scar·let fever \ˈskär-lət-\ *n* : an acute contagious febrile disease caused by hemolytic bacteria of the genus *Streptococcus* (esp. various strains of *S. pyogenes*) and characterized by inflammation of the nose, throat, and mouth, generalized toxemia, and a red rash — called also *scarlatina*

scarlet red *n* : SUDAN IV

Scar·pa's fascia \ˈskär-pəz-\ *n* : the deep layer of the superficial fascia of the anterior abdominal wall

  Scarpa, Antonio (1752–1832), Italian anatomist and surgeon.

Scarpa's triangle *n* : FEMORAL TRIANGLE

scar tissue *n* : the connective tissue forming a scar and composed chiefly of fibroblasts in recent scars and largely of dense collagenous fibers in old scars

scat·ter·ing \ˈska-tə-riŋ\ *n* : the random change in direction of a beam due to collision of the particles, photons, or waves constituting the radiation with the particles of the medium traversed

ScD *abbr* doctor of science

Schatz·ki ring \ˈshats-kē-\ *or* **Schatz·ki's ring** \-kēz-\ *n* : a local narrowing in the lower part of the esophagus that may cause dysphagia

  Schatzki, Richard (*b* 1901), American radiologist.

sched·ule \ˈske-ˌjül, -jəl; ˈshe-jü-wəl\ *n* 1 : a program or plan that indicates the sequence of each step or procedure; *esp* : REGIMEN 2 *usu cap* : an official list of drugs that are subject to the same legal controls and restrictions — usu. used with a Roman numeral from I to V indicating decreasing potential for abuse or addiction ⟨the Drug Enforcement Administration classifies heroin as a ∼ I drug while the tranquilizer chlordiazepoxide is on ∼ IV⟩

sche·ma \ˈskē-mə\ *n, pl* **sche·ma·ta** \-mə-tə\ *also* **sche·mas** 1 : a nonconscious adjustment of the brain to the afferent impulses indicative of bodily posture that is a prerequisite of appropriate bodily movement and of spatial perception 2 : the organization of experience in the mind or brain that includes a particular organized way of perceiving cognitively and responding to a complex situation or set of stimuli — **sche·mat·ic** \ski-ˈma-tik\ *adj*

scheme \ˈskēm\ *n* : SCHEMA

Scheuer·mann's disease \ˈshȯi-ər-ˌmänz-\ *n* : osteochondrosis of the vertebrae associated in the active state with pain and kyphosis

  Scheuermann, Holger Werfel (1877–1960), Danish orthopedist.

Schick test \ˈshik-\ *n* : a serological test for susceptibility to diphtheria by cutaneous injection of a diluted diphtheria toxin that causes an area of reddening and induration in susceptible individuals

  Schick, Béla (1877–1967), American pediatrician.

Schiff's reagent \ˈshifs-\ *or* **Schiff reagent** \ˈshif-\ *n* : a solution of fuchsin decolorized by treatment with sulfur dioxide that gives a useful test for aldehydes because they restore the reddish violet color of the dye — compare FEULGEN REACTION

  Schiff, Hugo Josef (1834–1915), German chemist.

Schil·der's disease \ˈshil-dərz-\ *n* : a demyelinating X-linked recessive disease of the central nervous system that affects males in childhood and is characterized by progressive blindness, deafness, tonic spasms, and mental deterioration — called also *adrenoleukodystrophy, Schilder's encephalitis*

  Schilder, Paul Ferdinand (1886–1940), Austrian psychiatrist.

Schil·ler's test \ˈshi-lərz-\ *n* : a preliminary test for cancer of the uterine cervix in which the cervix is painted with an aqueous solution of iodine and potassium iodide and which shows up healthy tissue by staining it brown and possibly cancerous tissue as white or yellow

  Schiller, Walter (1887–1960), American pathologist.

Schilling test *n* : a test for gastrointestinal absorption of vitamin B_{12} in which a dose of the radioactive vitamin is taken orally, a dose of the nonradioactive vitamin is given by injection to impede uptake of the absorbed radioactive dose by the liver, and the proportion of the radioactive dose absorbed is determined by measuring the radioactivity of the urine

  Schilling, Robert Frederick (*b* 1919), American hematologist.

schin·dy·le·sis \ˌskin-də-ˈlē-səs\ *n, pl* **-le·ses** \-ˌsēz\ : an articulation in which one bone is received into a groove or slit in another

Schiotz tonometer \ˈshyœts-, ˈshyərts-\

n : a tonometer used to measure intraocular pressure in millimeters of mercury

Schiötz, Hjalmar (1850–1927), Norwegian physician.

-schi·sis \skə-səs\ *n comb form, pl* **-schises** \skə-ˌsēz\ *also* **-schi·ses·es** : breaking up of attachments or adhesions : fissure (gastro*schisis*) (cranio*schisis*)

schisto- *comb form* : cleft : divided (*schistocyte*)

schis·to·cyte \'shis-tə-ˌsīt, 'skis-\ *n* : a hemoglobin-containing fragment of a red blood cell

schis·to·so·ma \ˌshis-tə-'sō-mə, ˌskis-\ *n* **1** *cap* : a genus of elongated digenetic trematode worms (family Schistosomatidae) that parasitize the blood vessels of birds and mammals and cause a destructive human schistosomiasis **2** : any trematode of the genus *Schistosoma* : SCHISTOSOME

schis·to·some \'shis-tə-ˌsōm, 'skis-\ *n* : any trematode worm of the genus *Schistosoma* or broadly of the family (Schistosomatidae) to which it belongs — called also *blood fluke* — **schis·to·so·mal** \ˌshis-tə-'sō-məl, ˌskis-\ *adj*

schistosome dermatitis *n* : SWIMMER'S ITCH

schis·to·so·mi·a·sis \ˌshis-tə-sō-'mī-ə-səs, ˌskis-\ *n, pl* **-a·ses** \-ˌsēz\ : infestation with or disease caused by schistosomes; *specif* : a severe endemic disease of humans in much of Asia, Africa, and So. America that is caused by any of three trematode worms of the genus *Schistosoma* (*S. haematobium, S. mansoni,* and *S. japonicum*) which multiply in snail intermediate hosts and are disseminated into freshwaters as cercariae that bore into the body, migrate through the tissues to the visceral venous plexuses (as of the bladder or intestine) where they attain maturity, and cause much of their injury through hemorrhage and damage to tissues resulting from the passage of the usu. spined eggs to the intestine and bladder — called also *snail fever;* compare SWIMMER'S ITCH

schistosomiasis hae·ma·to·bi·um \-ˌhē-mə-'tō-bē-əm\ *n* : schistosomiasis caused by a schistosome (*Schistosoma haematobium*) occurring over most of Africa and in Asia Minor and predominantly involving infestation of the veins of the urinary bladder

schistosomiasis ja·pon·i·ca \-jə-'pä-ni-kə\ *n* : schistosomiasis caused by a schistosome (*Schistosoma japonicum*) occurring chiefly in eastern Asia and the Pacific islands and predominantly involving infestation of the portal and mesenteric veins

schistosomiasis man·so·ni \-'man-sə-ˌnī\ *n* : schistosomiasis caused by a schistosome (*Schistosoma mansoni*) oc-

curring chiefly in central Africa and eastern So. America and predominantly involving infestation of the mesenteric and portal veins — called also *Manson's disease*

P. Manson — see MANSONELLA

schis·to·som·u·lum \ˌshis-tə-'säm-yə-ləm, ˌskis-\ *n, pl* **-la** \-lə\ : an immature schistosome in the body of the definitive host

schiz- *or* **schizo-** *comb form* **1** : characterized by or involving cleavage (*schizogony*) **2** : schizophrenia (*schizoid*)

schizo- \'skit-(ˌ)sō\ *n, pl* **schiz·os** : SCHIZOPHRENIC

schizo·af·fec·tive \-ə-'fek-tiv\ *adj* : relating to, characterized by, or exhibiting symptoms of both schizophrenia and manic-depressive psychosis

schi·zog·o·ny \ski-'zä-gə-nē, skit-'sä-\ *n, pl* **-nies** : asexual reproduction by multiple segmentation characteristic of sporozoans (as the malaria parasite) — **schiz·o·gon·ic** \ˌskit-sə-'gä-nik\ *or* **schi·zog·o·nous** \ski-'zä-gə-nəs, skit-'sä-\ *adj*

¹**schiz·oid** \'skit-ˌsoid\ *adj* : characterized by, resulting from, tending toward, or suggestive of schizophrenia

²**schizoid** *n* : a schizoid individual

schizoid personality *n* **1** : a personality disorder characterized by shyness, withdrawal, inhibition of emotional expression, and apparent diminution of affect — called also *schizoid personality disorder* **2** : a person with a schizoid personality

schiz·ont \'ski-ˌzänt, 'skit-ˌsänt\ *n* : a multinucleate sporozoan (as a malaria parasite) that reproduces by schizogony

schi·zon·ti·cide \ski-'zän-tə-ˌsīd, skit-'sän-\ *n* : an agent selectively destructive of the schizont of a sporozoan parasite (as of malaria) — **schi·zon·ti·ci·dal** \ski-ˌzän-tə-'sid-əl, skit-ˌsän-\ *adj*

schizo·phrene \'skit-sə-ˌfrēn\ *n* : SCHIZOPHRENIC

schizo·phre·nia \ˌskit-sə-'frē-nē-ə\ *n* : a psychotic disorder characterized by loss of contact with the environment, by noticeable deterioration in the level of functioning in everyday life, and by disintegration of personality expressed as disorder of feeling, thought (as in hallucinations and delusions), and conduct — called also *dementia praecox*

¹**schizo·phren·ic** \-'fre-nik\ *adj* : relating to, characteristic of, or affected with schizophrenia (~ behavior)

²**schizophrenic** *n* : a person affected with schizophrenia — called also *schizo, schizophrene*

schizophrenic reaction *n* : SCHIZOPHRENIA

schiz·o·phren·i·form \ˌskit-sə-'fre-nə-ˌfôrm\ *adj* : being similar to schizophrenia in appearance or manifestations but tending to last usu. more than two weeks and less than six months (~ disorder)

schiz·o·phren·o·gen·ic \\ˌskit-sə-ˌfre-nə-"je-nik\ *adj* : tending to produce schizophrenia (a ~ family environment)

schizos *pl of* SCHIZO

schizo·ty·pal \\skit-sə-"tī-pəl\ *adj* : characterized by, exhibiting, or being patterns of thought, perception, communication, and behavior suggestive of schizophrenia but not of sufficient severity to warrant a diagnosis of schizophrenia (~ personality)

Schlemm's canal \"shlemz-\ *n* : CANAL OF SCHLEMM

Schön·lein–Hen·och \"shœn-līn-"he-nɔk\ *adj* : being a form of purpura that is characterized by swelling and pain of the joints in association with gastrointestinal bleeding and pain
 Schönlein, Johann Lucas (1793–1864), German physician.
 Henoch, Eduard Heinrich (1820–1910), German pediatrician.

Schönlein's disease *n* : Schönlein-Henoch purpura that is characterized esp. by swelling and pain of the joints — compare HENOCH'S PURPURA

Schuff·ner's dots \"shuf-nərz-\ *n pl* : punctate granulations present in red blood cells invaded by the tertian malaria parasite
 Schüff·ner \"shuef-nər\, Wilhelm August Paul (1867–1949), German pathologist.

Schüller–Christian disease *n* : HAND–SCHÜLLER-CHRISTIAN DISEASE

Schwann cell \"shwän-\ *n* : a cell that forms spiral layers around a myelinated nerve fiber between two nodes of Ranvier and forms the myelin sheath consisting of the inner spiral layers from which the protoplasm has been squeezed out
 Schwann \"shvän\, Theodor Ambrose Hubert (1810–1882), German anatomist and physiologist.

schwan·no·ma \shwä-"nō-mə\ *n, pl* **-mas** \-məz\ *or* **-ma·ta** \-mə-tə\ : NEURILEMMOMA

Schwann's sheath *n* : NEURILEMMA

sci·at·ic \sī-"a-tik\ *adj* **1** : of, relating to, or situated near the hip **2** : of, relating to, or caused by sciatica (~ pains)

sci·at·i·ca \sī-"a-ti-kə\ *n* : pain along the course of a sciatic nerve esp. in the back of the thigh caused by compression, inflammation, or reflex mechanisms; *broadly* : pain in the lower back, buttocks, hips, or adjacent parts

sciatic foramen *n* : either of two foramina on each side of the pelvis that are formed by the hipbone, the sacrospinous ligament, and the sacrotuberous ligament: **a** : one giving passage to the piriformis muscle and to the sciatic, superior and inferior gluteal,

and pudendal nerves together with their associated arteries and veins — called also *greater sciatic foramen* **b** : one giving passage to the tendon of the obturator internus muscle and its nerve, to the internal pudendal artery and veins, and to the pudendal nerve — called also *lesser sciatic foramen*

sciatic nerve *n* : either of the pair of largest nerves in the body that arise one on each side from the sacral plexus and that pass out of the pelvis through the greater sciatic foramen and down the back of the thigh to its lower third where division into the tibial and common peroneal nerves occurs

sciatic notch *n* : either of two notches on the dorsal border of the hipbone on each side that when closed off by ligaments form the corresponding sciatic foramina: **a** : a relatively large notch just above the ischial spine that is converted into the greater sciatic foramen by the sacrospinous ligament — called also *greater sciatic notch* **b** : a smaller notch just below the ischial spine that is converted to the lesser sciatic foramen by the sacrospinous ligament and the sacrotuberous ligament — called also *lesser sciatic notch*

SCID *abbr* severe combined immunodeficiency

sci·ence \"sī-əns\ *n* : knowledge or a system of knowledge covering general truths or the operation of general laws esp. as obtained and tested through the scientific method and concerned with the physical world and its phenomena — **sci·en·tif·ic** \ˌsī-ən-"ti-fik\ *adj* — **sci·en·tif·i·cal·ly** *adv*

scientific method *n* : principles and procedures for the systematic pursuit of knowledge involving the recognition and formulation of a problem, the collection of data through observation and experiment, and the formulation and testing of hypotheses

sci·en·tist \"sī-ən-tist\ *n* : one learned in science and esp. natural science : a scientific investigator

scin·ti·gram \"sin-tə-ˌgram\ *n* : a picture produced by scintigraphy

scin·tig·ra·phy \sin-"ti-grə-fē\ *n, pl* **-phies** : a diagnostic technique in which a two-dimensional picture of a bodily radiation source is obtained by the use of radioisotopes (myocardial ~) — **scin·ti·graph·ic** \ˌsin-tə-"gra-fik\ *adj*

scin·til·la·tion \ˌsint-ᵊl-"ā-shən\ *n, often attrib* : a flash of light produced by a phosphorescent substance by an ionizing event — **scin·til·late** \"sint-ᵊl-ˌāt\ *vb*

scintillation counter *n* : a device for detecting and registering individual scintillations (as in radioactive emission) — called also *scintillometer*

scin·til·la·tor \"sint-ᵊl-ˌā-tər\ *n* **1** : a

phosphorescent substance in which scintillations occur (as in a scintillation counter) **2** : a device for sending out scintillations of light **3** : SCINTILLATION COUNTER

scin·til·lom·e·ter \ˌsint-ᵊl-'ä-mə-tər\ *n* : SCINTILLATION COUNTER

scin·ti·scan \'sin-ti-ˌskan\ *n* : a two-dimensional representation of radioisotope radiation from a bodily organ (as the spleen or kidney)

scirrhi *pl of* SCIRRHUS

scir·rhous \'sir-əs. 'skir-\ *adj* : of, relating to, or being a scirrhous carcinoma

scirrhous carcinoma *n* : a hard slow-growing malignant tumor having a preponderance of fibrous tissue

scir·rhus \'sir-əs. 'skir-\ *n, pl* **scir·rhi** \'sir-ˌī. 'skir-. -ˌē\ : SCIRRHOUS CARCINOMA

scler- *or* **sclero-** *comb form* **1** : hard (*scleroderma*) **2** : sclera (*scleritis*)

scle·ra \'skler-ə\ *n* : the dense fibrous opaque white outer coat enclosing the eyeball except the part covered by the cornea — called also *sclerotic, sclerotic coat* — **scler·al** \'skler-əl\ *adj*

sclerae — see SINUS VENOSUS SCLERAE

scle·rec·to·my \sklə-'rek-tə-mē\ *n, pl* **-mies** : surgical removal of a part of the sclera

scle·re·ma neo·na·to·rum \sklə-'rē-mə-ˌnē-ə-nə-'tōr-əm\ *n* : hardening of the cutaneous and subcutaneous tissues in newborn infants

scle·ri·tis \sklə-'rī-təs\ *n* : inflammation of the sclera

scle·ro·cor·ne·al \ˌskler-ō-'kòr-nē-əl\ *adj* : of or involving both sclera and cornea

scle·ro·dac·ty·ly \-'dak-tə-lē\ *n, pl* **-lies** : scleroderma of the fingers and toes

scle·ro·der·ma \ˌskler-ə-'dər-mə\ *n, pl* **-mas** *or* **-ma·ta** \-mə-tə\ : a usu. slowly progressive disease marked by the deposition of fibrous connective tissue in the skin and often in internal organs — **scle·ro·der·ma·tous** \-təs\ *adj*

scle·ro·ma \sklə-'rō-mə\ *n, pl* **-mas** *or* **-ma·ta** \-mə-tə\ : hardening of tissues

scle·ro·pro·tein \ˌskler-ō-'prō-ˌtēn\ *n* : any of a class of fibrous proteins (as collagen and keratin) that are usu. insoluble in aqueous solvents and are resistant to chemical reagents — called also *albuminoid*

scle·rose \sklə-'rōs. -'rōz\ *vb* **-rosed; -ros·ing 1** : to cause sclerosis in **2** : to undergo or become affected with sclerosis

scle·ros·ing *adj* : causing or characterized by sclerosis ⟨∼ agents⟩ — see SUBACUTE SCLEROSING PANENCEPHALITIS

scle·ro·sis \sklə-'rō-səs\ *n, pl* **-ro·ses** \-ˌsēz\ **1** : a pathological condition in which a tissue has become hard and which is produced by overgrowth of fibrous tissue and other changes (as in arteriosclerosis) or by increase in

interstitial tissue and other changes (as in multiple sclerosis) — called also *hardening* **2** : any of various diseases characterized by sclerosis — usu. used in combination; see ARTERIOSCLEROSIS, MULTIPLE SCLEROSIS

scle·ro·stome \'skler-ə-ˌstōm\ *n* : STRONGYLE

sclerosus — see LICHEN SCLEROSUS ET ATROPHICUS

scle·ro·ther·a·py \ˌskler-ō-'ther-ə-pē\ *n, pl* **-pies** : the injection of a sclerosing agent into a varicose vein to create fibrosis which closes the lumen

¹scle·rot·ic \sklə-'rä-tik\ *adj* **1** : being or relating to the sclera (the ∼ layer of the eye) **2** : of, relating to, or affected with sclerosis (a ∼ blood vessel)

²sclerotic *n* : SCLERA

sclerotic coat *n* : SCLERA

scle·ro·tium \sklə-'rō-shəm. -shē-əm\ *n, pl* **-tia** \-shə. -shē-ə\ : a compact mass of hardened mycelium (as an ergot) of a fungus that is stored with reserve food material — **scle·ro·tial** \-shəl\ *adj*

scle·ro·tome \'skler-ə-ˌtōm\ *n* : the ventral and mesial portion of a somite that proliferates mesenchyme which migrates about the notochord to form the axial skeleton and ribs — **scle·ro·tom·ic** \ˌskler-ə-'tō-mik. -'tä-\ *adj*

scle·rot·o·my \sklə-'rä-tə-mē\ *n, pl* **-mies** : surgical cutting of the sclera

ScM *abbr* master of science

SCM *abbr* state certified midwife

sco·lex \'skō-ˌleks\ *n, pl* **sco·li·ces** \'skō-lə-ˌsēz\ *also* **scol·e·ces** \'skä-lə-ˌsēz. 'skō-\ *or* **scolexes** : the head of a tapeworm from which the proglottids are produced by budding

sco·li·o·sis \ˌskō-lē-'ō-səs\ *n, pl* **-o·ses** \-ˌsēz\ : a lateral curvature of the spine — compare KYPHOSIS, LORDOSIS — **sco·li·ot·ic** \-'ä-tik\ *adj*

scoop \'sküp\ *n* : a spoon-shaped surgical instrument used in extracting various materials (as debris and pus)

scope \'skōp\ *n* : any of various instruments for viewing: as **a** : BRONCHOSCOPE **b** : GASTROSCOPE **c** : MICROSCOPE

-scope \ˌskōp\ *n comb form* : means (as an instrument) for viewing or observing (micro*scope*) (laparo*scope*)

-scop·ic \'skä-pik\ *adj comb form* : viewing or observing (laparo*scopic*)

sco·pol·amine \skō-'pä-lə-ˌmēn. -mən\ *n* : a poisonous alkaloid $C_{17}H_{21}NO_4$ found in various plants (as jimsonweed) of the nightshade family (Solanaceae) and used chiefly in the form of its crystalline hydrobromide as a sedative in connection with morphine or other analgesics in surgery and obstetrics. in the prevention of motion sickness, and as the truth serum in lie detector tests — called also *hyoscine*

sco·po·phil·ia \ˌskō-pə-'fil-ē-ə\ *or* **scop·to·phil·ia** \ˌskäp-tə-'fil-ē-ə\ *n* : a desire to look at sexually stimulating scenes esp. as a substitute for actual sexual participation — sco·po·phil·ic or scop·to·phil·ic \-'fil-ik\ adj

sco·po·phil·i·ac or scop·to·phil·i·ac \-'filē-,ak\ n : a person affected with scopophilia — scopophiliac or scoptophiliac adj

-s·co·py \s-kə-pē\ n comb form, pl -sco·pies : viewing : observation (laparoscopy)

scor·bu·tic \skör-'byü-tik\ adj : of, relating to, producing, or affected with scurvy (a ~ diet)

scor·pi·on \'skör-pē-ən\ n : any of an order (Scorpionida) of arachnids that have an elongated body and a narrow segmented tail bearing a venomous stinger at the tip

sco·to·ma \skə-'tō-mə\ n, pl -mas or -ma·ta \-mə-tə\ : a blind or dark spot in the visual field

sco·top·ic \skə-'tō-pik, -'tä-\ adj : relating to or being vision in dim light with dark-adapted eyes which involves only the retinal rods as light receptors

¹scour \'skaủr\ vb, of a domestic animal : to suffer from diarrhea or dysentery (a diet causing cattle to ~)

²scour n sing or pl : diarrhea or dysentery occurring esp. in young domestic animals

scra·pie \'skrā-pē\ n : a usu. fatal disease of the nervous system esp. of sheep that is characterized by twitching, excitability, intense itching, excessive thirst, emaciation, weakness, and finally paralysis and that is caused by a slow virus

scrap·ing \'skrā-pin\ n : material scraped esp. from diseased tissue (as infected skin) for microscopic examination

scratch test n : a test for allergic susceptibility made by rubbing an extract of an allergy-producing substance into small breaks or scratches in the skin — compare INTRADERMAL TEST, PATCH TEST

screen — see SUNSCREEN

screen memory n : a recollection of early childhood that may be falsely recalled or magnified in importance and that masks another memory of deep emotional significance

screw·fly \'skrü-,flī\ n, pl -flies : SCREWWORM FLY

screw·worm \'skrü-,wərm\ n 1 a : a dipteran fly of the genus Cochliomyia (C. hominivorax) of the warmer parts of America whose larva develops in sores or wounds or in the nostrils of mammals including humans; esp : its larva b : SECONDARY SCREWWORM 2 : any of several flies other than the screwworms of the genus Cochliomyia and esp. their larvae which parasitize the flesh of mammals

screwworm fly n : the adult of a screwworm — called also screwfly

scroful- or scrofulo- comb form : scrofula (scrofuloderma)

scrof·u·la \'skrö-fyə-lə, 'skrä-\ n : tuberculosis of lymph nodes esp. in the neck — called also king's evil

scrof·u·lo·der·ma \,skrö-fyə-lō-'dər-mə, ,skrä-\ n : a disease of the skin of tuberculous origin

scrot- or scroti- or scroto- comb form : scrotum (scrotoplasty)

scro·tal \'skröt-əl\ adj 1 : of or relating to the scrotum 2 : lying in or having descended into the scrotum (~ testes)

scro·to·plas·ty \'skrö-tə-,plas-tē\ n, pl -ties : plastic surgery performed on the scrotum

scro·tum \'skrō-təm\ n, pl scro·ta \-tə\ or scrotums : the external pouch that in most mammals contains the testes

scrub \'skrəb\ vb scrubbed; scrub·bing : to clean and disinfect (the hands and forearms) before participating in surgery — scrub n

scrub nurse n : a nurse who assists the surgeon in an operating room

scrub typhus n : TSUTSUGAMUSHI DISEASE

scru·ple \'skrü-pəl\ n : a unit of apothecaries' weight equal to 20 grains or ⅓ dram or 1.296 grams

scurf \'skərf\ n : thin dry scales detached from the epidermis esp. in an abnormal skin condition; specif : DANDRUFF — scurfy \'skər-fē\ adj

scur·vy \'skər-vē\ n, pl scur·vies : a disease that is characterized by spongy gums, loosening of the teeth, and a bleeding into the skin and mucous membranes and that is caused by a lack of vitamin C

Se symbol selenium

seal·ant \'sē-lənt\ n : material used to seal developmental imperfections in teeth (pit and fissure ~s)

seal finger n : a finger rendered swollen and painful by erysipeloid or a similar infection and occurring esp. in individuals handling seals or sealskins

sea·sick·ness \'sē-,sik-nəs\ n : motion sickness experienced on the water — called also mal de mer — seasick adj

sea snake n : any of a family (Hydrophidae) of numerous venomous snakes inhabiting the tropical parts of the Pacific and Indian oceans

seasonal affective disorder n : depression that tends to recur as the days grow shorter during the fall and winter — abbr. SAD

¹seat \'sēt\ n : a part or surface esp. in dentistry on or in which another part or surface rests — see REST SEAT

²seat vb : to provide with or position on a dental seat

seat·worm \-,wərm\ n : a pinworm of the genus Enterobius (E. vermicularis) that is parasitic in humans

sea wasp n : any of various jellyfishes (order or suborder Cubomedusae of the class Scyphozoa) that sting virulently and sometimes fatally

se·ba·ceous \si-'bā-shəs\ adj 1 : secreting sebum **2** : of. relating to, or being fatty material ⟨a ∼ exudate⟩

sebaceous cyst *n* : a cyst filled with sebaceous matter and formed by distension of a sebaceous gland as a result of obstruction of its excretory duct

sebaceous gland *n* : any of the small sacculated glands lodged in the substance of the derma. usu. opening into the hair follicles. and secreting an oily or greasy material composed in great part of fat which softens and lubricates the hair and skin

sebi- *or* **sebo-** *comb form* : fat : grease : sebum ⟨*seborrhea*⟩

seb·or·rhea \se-bə-¹rē-ə\ *n* : abnormally increased secretion and discharge of sebum producing an oily appearance of the skin and the formation of greasy scales

seb·or·rhe·al \se-bə-¹rē-əl\ *adj* : SEBORRHEIC

seb·or·rhe·ic \-¹rē-ik\ *adj* : of. relating to. or characterized by seborrhea ⟨∼ dermatitis⟩

se·bor·rhoea,   se·bor·rhoe·al,   se·bor·rhoe·ic *chiefly Brit var of* SEBORRHEA. SEBORRHEAL, SEBORRHEIC

se·bum \¹sē-bəm\ *n* : fatty lubricant matter secreted by sebaceous glands of the skin

seco·bar·bi·tal \se-kō-¹bär-bə-₁tól\ *n* : a barbiturate $C_{12}H_{18}N_2O_3$ that is used chiefly in the form of its bitter sodium salt as a hypnotic and sedative — called also *quinalbarbitone;* see SECONAL

Sec·o·nal \¹se-kə-₁nól, -₁nal. -nəl\ *trademark* — used for a preparation of secobarbital

sec·ond·ary \¹se-kən-₁der-ē\ *adj* **1** : not first in order of occurrence or development: as **a** : dependent or consequent on another disease ⟨∼ hypertension⟩ **b** : occurring or being in the second stage ⟨∼ symptoms of syphilis⟩ **c** : occurring some time after the original injury ⟨a ∼ hemorrhage⟩ **2** : characterized by or resulting from the substitution of two atoms or groups in a molecule ⟨a ∼ salt⟩ **3** : relating to or being the three-dimensional coiling of the polypeptide chain of a protein esp. in the form of an alpha-helix — compare PRIMARY 3. TERTIARY 2 — **sec·ond·ari·ly** \se-kən-¹der-ə-lē\ *adv*

secondary amenorrhea *n* : cessation of menstruation in a woman who has previously experienced normal menses

secondary dentin *n* : dentin formed following the loss (as by erosion, abrasion, or disease) of original dentin

secondary gain *n* : a benefit (as sympathetic attention) associated with a mental illness

secondary infection *n* : infection occurring at the site of a preexisting infection

secondary oocyte *n* : an oocyte that is produced by division of a primary oocyte in the first meiotic division

secondary screwworm *n* : a screwworm of the genus *Cochliomyia* (*C. macellaria*)

secondary sex characteristic *n* : a physical characteristic (as the breasts of a female) that appears in members of one sex at puberty or in seasonal breeders at the breeding season and is not directly concerned with reproduction — called also *secondary sex character, secondary sexual characteristic*

secondary spermatocyte *n* : a spermatocyte that is produced by division of a primary spermatocyte in the first meiotic division and that divides in the second meiotic division to give spermatids

secondary syphilis *n* : the second stage of syphilis that appears from 2 to 6 months after primary infection. that is marked by lesions esp. in the skin but also in organs and tissues. and that lasts from 3 to 12 weeks

secondary tympanic membrane *n* : a membrane closing the round window and separating the scala tympani from the middle ear

second cranial nerve *n* : OPTIC NERVE

second–degree burn *n* : a burn marked by pain. blistering, and superficial destruction of dermis with edema and hyperemia of the tissues beneath the burn

second in·ten·tion \-in-¹ten-chən\ *n* : healing of an incised wound by granulations that bridge the gap between skin edges — compare FIRST INTENTION

second messenger *n* : a cellular substance (as cyclic AMP) that mediates cell activity by relaying a signal from an extracellular molecule (as of a hormone or neurotransmitter) bound to the cell's surface

second polar body *n* : POLAR BODY b

second wind *n* : recovered full power of respiration after the first exhaustion during exertion due to improved heart action

secret- *or* **secreto-** *comb form* : secretion ⟨*secretin*⟩

se·cre·ta·gogue \si-¹krē-tə-₁gäg\ *n* : a substance that stimulates secretion

se·cre·tin \si-¹krēt-²n\ *n* : an intestinal proteinaceous hormone capable of stimulating secretion by the pancreas and liver

se·cre·tion \si-¹krē-shən\ *n* **1** : the process of segregating, elaborating, and releasing some material either functionally specialized (as saliva) or isolated for excretion (as urine) **2** : a product of secretion formed by an animal or plant; *esp* : one performing a specific useful function in the organism — **se·crete** \si-¹krēt\ *vb* — **se·cre·to·ry** \¹sē-krə-₁tōr-ē, si-¹krē-tə-rē\ *adj*

se·cre·tor \si-¹krē-tər\ *n* : an individual

of blood group A, B, or AB who secretes the antigens characteristic of these blood groups in bodily fluids (as saliva)

-sect \ˌsekt\ *vb comb form* : cut : divide ⟨hemi*sect*⟩ ⟨tran*sect*⟩

sec·tion \'sek-shən\ *n* **1** : the action or an instance of cutting or separating by cutting : *esp* : the action of dividing (as tissues) surgically (abdominal ∼) — see CESAREAN SECTION **2** : a very thin slice (as of tissue) suitable for microscopic examination — **section** *vb*

se·cun·di·grav·id \si-ˌkən-dē-'gra-vəd\ *adj* : pregnant for the second time

se·cun·di·grav·i·da \-'gra-vi-də\ *n, pl* **-das** : a woman in her second pregnancy

sec·un·dines \'se-kən-ˌdēnz, -ˌdīnz; se-'kən-dənz\ *n pl* : AFTERBIRTH

sec·un·dip·a·ra \ˌse-kən-'di-pə-rə\ *n, pl* **-ras** : a woman who has borne children in two separate pregnancies

security blanket *n* : a blanket carried by a child as a protection against anxiety

se·date \si-'dāt\ *vb* **se·dat·ed; se·dat·ing** : to dose with sedatives

se·da·tion \si-'dā-shən\ *n* **1** : the inducing of a relaxed easy state esp. by the use of sedatives **2** : a state resulting from sedation

¹sed·a·tive \'se-də-tiv\ *adj* : tending to calm, moderate, or tranquilize nervousness or excitement

²sedative *n* : a sedative agent or drug

¹sed·i·ment \'se-də-mənt\ *n* : the matter that settles to the bottom of a liquid

²sediment \-ˌment\ *vb* : to deposit as sediment

sed·i·men·ta·tion \ˌse-də-(ˌ)men-'tā-shən\ *n* **1** : the action or process of depositing sediment **2** : the depositing esp. by mechanical means of matter suspended in a liquid

sedimentation rate *n* : the speed at which red blood cells settle to the bottom of a column of citrated blood measured in millimeters deposited per hour and which is used esp. in diagnosing the progress of various abnormal conditions

sed rate \'sed-\ *n* : SEDIMENTATION RATE

¹seed \'sēd\ *n, pl* **seed** *or* **seeds 1 a** : the fertilized ripened ovule of a flowering plant **b** : a propagative animal structure; *esp* : SEMEN **2** : a small usu. glass and gold or platinum capsule used as a container for a radioactive substance (as radium or radon) to be applied usu. interstitially in the treatment of cancer — **seed·ed** \'sē-dəd\ *adj*

²seed *adj* : selected or used to produce a new crop or stock (∼ virus)

Seeing Eye *trademark* — used for a guide dog trained to lead the blind

¹seg·ment \'seg-mənt\ *n* : one of the constituent parts into which a body, entity, or quantity is divided or marked off by or as if by natural boundaries

⟨the affected ∼ of the colon was resected⟩ — **seg·men·tal** \seg-'ment-ᵊl\ *adj* — **seg·men·tal·ly** *adv*

²seg·ment \'seg-ˌment\ *vb* **1** : to cause to undergo segmentation by division or multiplication of cells **2** : to separate into segments

segmental resection *n* : excision of a segment of an organ; *specif* : excision of a portion of a lobe of a lung — called also *segmentectomy*; compare PNEUMONECTOMY

seg·men·ta·tion \ˌseg-(ˌ)men-'tā-shən\ *n* **1** : the act or process of dividing into segments; *esp* : the formation of many cells from a single cell (as in a developing egg) **2** : annular contraction of smooth muscle (as of the intestine) that seems to cut the part affected into segments — compare PERISTALSIS

segmentation cavity *n* : BLASTOCOEL

seg·men·tec·to·my \ˌseg-mən-'tek-tə-mē\ *n, pl* **-mies** : SEGMENTAL RESECTION

seg·ment·ed \'seg-ˌmen-təd, seg-'\ *adj* **1** : having or made up of segments **2** : being a cell in which the nucleus is divided into lobes connected by a fine filament (∼ neutrophils)

seg·re·gant \'se-gri-gənt\ *n* : SEGREGATE

¹seg·re·gate \'se-gri-ˌgāt\ *vb* **-gat·ed; -gat·ing** : to undergo genetic segregation

²seg·re·gate \-gət\ *n* : an individual or class of individuals differing in one or more genetic characters from the parental line usu. because of segregation of genes

seg·re·ga·tion \ˌse-gri-'gā-shən\ *n* : the separation of allelic genes that occurs typically during meiosis

Sei·gnette salt \sen-'yet-\ *or* **Seig·nette's salt** \-'yets-\ *n* : ROCHELLE SALT

Seignette, Pierre (1660–1719), French pharmacist.

sei·zure \'sē-zhər\ *n* : a sudden attack (as of disease) ⟨an epileptic ∼⟩

Sel·dane \'sel-ˌdān\ *trademark* — used for a preparation of terfenadine

se·lec·tion \sə-'lek-shən\ *n* : a natural or artificial process that results or tends to result in the survival and propagation of some individuals or organisms but not of others with the result that the inherited traits of the survivors are perpetuated — compare DARWINISM

se·lec·tive \sə-'lek-tiv\ *adj* **1** : of, relating to, or characterized by selection : selecting or tending to select **2** : highly specific in activity or effect — **se·lec·tive·ly** *adv* — **se·lec·tiv·i·ty** \sə-ˌlek-'ti-və-tē, ˌsē-\ *n*

sel·e·nif·er·ous \ˌse-lə-'ni-fə-rəs\ *adj* : containing or yielding selenium

se·le·ni·um \sə-'lē-nē-əm\ *n* : a nonmetallic element that causes poisoning in range animals when ingested by eating some plants growing in soils in which it occurs in quantity — symbol *Se*; see ELEMENT table

selenium sulfide *n* : the sulfide SeS_2 of selenium usu. in the form of an orange powder that is effective in controlling seborrheic dermatitis and dandruff

sel·e·no·me·thi·o·nine \,se-lə-nō-mə-ᵗthī-ə-,nēn\ *n* : a selenium compound $C_5H_{11}NO_2Se$ that is used as a diagnostic aid in scintigraphy esp. of the pancreas

sel·e·no·sis \,se-lə-ᵗnō-səs\ *n* : poisoning of livestock by selenium due to ingestion of plants grown in seleniferous soils characterized in the acute phase by diffuse necrosis and hemorrhage resulting from capillary damage and in chronic poisoning by degenerative and fibrotic changes esp. of the liver and of the skin and its derivatives — called also *alkali disease;* see BLIND STAGGERS

self \ᵗself\ *n, pl* **selves** \ᵗselvz\ **1** : the union of elements (as body, emotions, thoughts, and sensations) that constitute the individuality and identity of a person **2** : material that is part of an individual organism (ability of the immune system to distinguish ~ from nonself)

self-abuse \,self-ə-ᵗbyüs\ *n* : MASTURBATION

self-ac·tu·al·ize \ᵗself-ᵗak-chə-wə-,līz\ *vb* **-ized; -iz·ing** : to realize fully one's potential — **self-ac·tu·al·iza·tion** \-,ak-chə-wə-lə-ᵗzā-shən\ *n*

self-ad·min·is·ter \-əd-ᵗmi-nə-stər\ *vb* : to administer to oneself (~ed an analgesic) — **self-ad·min·is·tra·tion** \-,mi-nə-ᵗstrā-shən\ *n*

self-anal·y·sis \-ə-ᵗna-lə-səs\ *n, pl* **-y·ses** \-,sēz\ *n* : a systematic attempt by an individual to understand his or her own personality without the aid of another person — **self-an·a·lyt·i·cal** \-,a-nə-ᵗli-ti-kəl\ *or* **self-an·a·lyt·ic** \-tik\ *adj*

self-as·sem·bly \-ə-ᵗsem-blē\ *n, pl* **-blies** : the process by which a complex macromolecule (as collagen) or a supramolecular system (as a virus) spontaneously assembles itself from its components — **self-as·sem·ble** \-bəl\ *vb*

self-aware·ness \-ə-ᵗwer-nəs\ *n* : an awareness of one's own personality or individuality — **self-aware** *adj*

self-care \-ᵗker\ *n* : care for oneself : SELF-TREATMENT

self-con·cept \ᵗself-ᵗkän-,sept\ *n* : the mental image one has of oneself

self-de·struc·tion \-di-ᵗstrək-shən\ *n* : destruction of oneself; *esp* : SUICIDE

self-de·struc·tive \-ᵗstrək-tiv\ *adj* : acting or tending to harm or destroy oneself (~ behavior); *also* : SUICIDAL — **self-de·struc·tive·ly** *adv* — **self-de·struc·tive·ness** *n*

self-ex·am·i·na·tion \-ig-,za-mə-ᵗnā-shən\ *n* : examination of one's body esp. for evidence of disease (~ for detection of breast cancer)

self-hyp·no·sis \,self-hip-ᵗnō-səs\ *n, pl* **-no·ses** \-,sēz\ : hypnosis of oneself : AUTOHYPNOSIS

self-im·age \-ᵗi-mij\ *n* : one's conception of oneself or of one's role

self-in·duced \-in-ᵗdüst, -ᵗdyüst\ *adj* : induced by oneself (a ~ abortion)

self-in·flict·ed \-in-ᵗflik-təd\ *adj* : inflicted by oneself (a ~ wound)

self-lim·it·ed \-ᵗli-mə-təd\ *adj* : limited by one's or its own nature; *specif* : running a definite and limited course (a ~ disease)

self-lim·it·ing *adj* : SELF-LIMITED

self-med·i·ca·tion \-,me-də-ᵗkā-shən\ *n* : medication of oneself esp. without the advice of a physician : SELF-TREATMENT (~ with nonprescription drugs) — **self-med·i·cate** \-ᵗme-də-,kāt\ *vb*

self-mu·ti·la·tion \-,myü-tə-ᵗlā-shən\ *n* : injury or disfigurement of oneself

self-rec·og·ni·tion \-,re-kəg-ᵗni-shən\ *n* : the process by which the immune system of an organism distinguishes between the body's own chemicals, cells, and tissues and those of foreign organisms or agents — compare SELF-TOLERANCE

self-rep·li·cat·ing \-ᵗre-plə-,kā-tiŋ\ *adj* : reproducing itself autonomously (DNA is a ~ molecule) — **self-rep·li·ca·tion** \-,re-plə-ᵗkā-shən\ *n*

self-stim·u·la·tion \-,stim-yə-ᵗlā-shən\ *n* : stimulation of oneself as a result of one's own activity or behavior; *esp* : MASTURBATION — **self-stim·u·la·to·ry** \-ᵗstim-yə-lə-,tōr-ē\ *adj*

self-tol·er·ance \-ᵗtä-lə-rəns\ *n* : the physiological state that exists in a developing organism when its immune system has proceeded far enough in the process of self-recognition to lose the capacity to attack and destroy its own bodily constituents — called also *horror autotoxicus*

self-treat·ment \-ᵗtrēt-mənt\ *n* : medication of oneself or treatment of one's own disease without medical supervision or prescription

sel·la \ᵗse-lə\ *n, pl* **sellas** *or* **sel·lae** \-lē\ : SELLA TURCICA

sellae — see DIAPHRAGMA SELLAE

sel·lar \ᵗse-lər, -,lär\ *adj* : of, relating to, or involving the sella turcica

sel·la tur·ci·ca \ᵗtər-ki-kə, -si-\ *n, pl* **sel·lae tur·ci·cae** \-ki-,kī, -si-,sē\ : a depression in the middle line of the upper surface of the sphenoid bone in which the pituitary gland is lodged

SEM *abbr* **1** scanning electron microscope **2** scanning electron microscopy

se·men \ᵗsē-mən\ *n* : a viscid whitish fluid of the male reproductive tract consisting of spermatozoa suspended in secretions of the accessory glands and esp. of the prostate and Cowper's glands

semi·cir·cu·lar canal \se-mē-ˈsər-kyə-lər-, ˌse-ˌmī-\ *n* : any of the loop-shaped tubular parts of the labyrinth of the ear that together constitute a sensory organ associated with the maintenance of bodily equilibrium, that consist of an inner membranous canal of the membranous labyrinth and a corresponding outer bony canal of the bony labyrinth, and that form a group of three in each ear usu. in planes nearly at right angles to each other — see SEMICIRCULAR DUCT

semicircular duct *n* : any of the three loop-shaped membranous inner tubular parts of the semicircular canals that are about one-fourth the diameter of the corresponding outer bony canals, that communicate at each end with the utricle, and that have near one end an expanded ampulla containing an area of sensory epithelium

semi·co·ma \-ˈkō-mə\ *n* : a semicomatose state from which a person can be aroused

semi·co·ma·tose \-ˈkō-mə-ˌtōs\ *adj* : lethargic and disoriented but not completely comatose (a ~ patient)

semi·con·scious \-ˈkän-chəs\ *adj* : incompletely conscious : imperfectly aware or responsive — **semi·con·scious·ness** *n*

semi·con·ser·va·tive \-kən-ˈsər-və-tiv\ *adj* : relating to or being genetic replication in which a double-stranded molecule of nucleic acid separates into two single strands each of which serves as a template for the formation of a complementary strand that together with the template forms a complete molecule — **semi·con·ser·va·tive·ly** *adv*

semi·dom·i·nant \-ˈdä-mi-nənt\ *adj* : producing an intermediate phenotype in the heterozygous condition

semi·flu·id \-ˈflü-əd\ *adj* : having the qualities of both a fluid and a solid : VISCOUS — **semifluid** *n*

semi·lu·nar \-ˈlü-nər\ *adj* : shaped like a crescent

semilunar bone *n* : LUNATE BONE

semilunar cartilage *n* : MENISCUS a(2)

semilunar cusp *n* : any of the crescentic cusps making up the semilunar valves

semilunares — see LINEA SEMILUNARIS, PLICA SEMILUNARIS

semilunar ganglion *n* : TRIGEMINAL GANGLION

semilunaris — see HIATUS SEMILUNARIS, LINEA SEMILUNARIS, PLICA SEMILUNARIS

semilunar line *n* : LINEA SEMILUNARIS

semilunar lobule *n* : either of a pair of crescent-shaped lobules situated one on each side in the posterior and ventral part of the cerebellum

semilunar notch *n* : the deep depression in the proximal end of the ulna by which it articulates with the trochlea of the humerus at the elbow

semilunar valve *n* **1** : either of two valves of which one is situated at the opening between the heart and the aorta and the other at the opening between the heart and the pulmonary artery, which prevent regurgitation of blood into the ventricles, and each of which is made up of three crescent-shaped cusps **2** : SEMILUNAR CUSP

semi·mem·bra·no·sus \ˌse-mē-ˌmem-brə-ˈnō-səs, ˌse-ˌmī-\ *n, pl* **-no·si** \-ˌsī\ : a large muscle of the inner part and back of the thigh that arises by a thick tendon from the back part of the tuberosity of the ischium, is inserted into the medial condyle of the tibia, and acts to flex the leg and rotate it medially and to extend the thigh

sem·i·nal \ˈse-mən-əl\ *adj* : of, relating to, or consisting of semen

seminal duct *n* : a tube or passage serving esp. or exclusively as an efferent duct of the testis and in humans being made up of the tubules of the epididymis, the vas deferens, and the ejaculatory duct

seminal fluid *n* **1** : SEMEN **2** : the part of the semen that is produced by various accessory glands : semen excepting the spermatozoa

seminal vesicle *n* : either of a pair of glandular pouches that lie one on either side of the male reproductive tract and that in human males secrete a sugar- and protein-containing fluid into the ejaculatory duct

sem·i·nif·er·ous \ˌse-mə-ˈni-fə-rəs\ *adj* : producing or bearing semen

seminiferous tubule *n* : any of the coiled threadlike tubules that make up the bulk of the testis and are lined with a layer of epithelial cells from which the spermatozoa are produced

sem·i·no·ma \ˌse-mi-ˈnō-mə\ *n, pl* **-mas** *or* **-ma·ta** \-mə-tə\ : a malignant tumor of the testis

semi·per·me·able \ˌse-mē-ˈpər-mē-ə-bəl, ˌse-ˌmī-\ *adj* : partially but not freely or wholly permeable; *specif* : permeable to some usu. small molecules but not to other usu. larger particles (a ~ membrane) — **semi·per·me·abil·i·ty** \-ˌpər-mē-ə-ˈbi-lə-tē\ *n*

semi·pri·vate \-ˈprī-vət\ *adj* : of, receiving, or associated with hospital service giving a patient more privileges than a ward patient but fewer than a private patient (a ~ room)

semi·spi·na·lis \-ˌspī-ˈnä-ləs\ *n, pl* **-les** \-ˌlēz\ : any of three muscles of the cervical and thoracic parts of the spinal column: **a** : SEMISPINALIS THORACIS **b** : SEMISPINALIS CERVICIS **c** : SEMISPINALIS CAPITIS

semispinalis cap·i·tis \-ˈka-pi-təs\ *n* : a deep longitudinal muscle of the back that arises esp. from the transverse processes of the upper six or seven thoracic and the seventh cervical vertebrae, is inserted on the outer surface of the occipital bone between two ridges behind the foramen magnum, and acts to extend and rotate the head — called also *complexus*

semispinalis cer·vi·cis \-ˈsər-vi-sis\ *n* : a deep longitudinal muscle of the back that arises from the transverse processes of the upper five or six thoracic vertebrae, is inserted into the cervical spinous processes from the axis to the fifth cervical vertebra, and with the semispinalis thoracis acts to extend the spinal column and rotate it toward the opposite side

semispinalis tho·ra·cis \-thō-ˈrā-səs\ *n* : a deep longitudinal muscle of the back that arises from the transverse processes of the lower five thoracic vertebrae, is inserted into the spinous processes of the upper four thoracic and lower two cervical vertebrae, and with the semispinalis cervicis acts to extend the spinal column and rotate it toward the opposite side

semi·syn·thet·ic \-sin-ˈthe-tik\ *adj* 1 : produced by chemical alteration of a natural starting material (∼ penicillins) 2 : containing both chemically identified and complex natural ingredients (a ∼ diet)

sem·i·ten·di·no·sus \-ˌten-də-ˈnō-səs\ *n, pl* -**no·si** \-ˌsī\ : a fusiform muscle of the posterior and inner part of the thigh that arises from the ischial tuberosity along with the biceps femoris, that is inserted by a long round tendon into the inner surface of the upper part of the shaft of the tibia, and that acts to flex the leg and rotate it medially and to extend the thigh

Sem·li·ki For·est virus \ˈsem-lē-kē-ˈfōr-əst-\ *n* : an arbovirus isolated from mosquitoes in a Ugandan forest and capable of infecting humans

Sen·dai virus \ˈsen-ˌdi-\ *n* : a parainfluenza virus first reported from Japan that infects swine, mice, and humans

se·ne·cio \si-ˈnē-shē-ˌō, -shō\ *n, pl* -**cios** 1 *cap* : a genus of widely distributed plants of the daisy family (Compositae) including some containing various alkaloids which are poisonous to livestock 2 : any plant of the genus *Senecio*

se·ne·ci·o·sis \se-ˌnē-sē-ˈō-səs\ *n, pl* -**o·ses** \-ˌsēz\ : a frequently fatal intoxication esp. of livestock feeding on plants of the genus *Senecio*

se·nes·cence \si-ˈnes-ᵊns\ *n* : the state of being old : the process of becoming old — **se·nes·cent** \-ᵊnt\ *adj*

se·nile \ˈsē-ˌnil\ *adj* 1 : of, relating to, exhibiting, or characteristic of old age; *esp* : exhibiting a loss of mental faculties associated with old age 2 : being a cell that cannot undergo mitosis and is in the stage of declining functional capacities prior to the time of death (a ∼ red blood cell)

senile cataract *n* : a cataract of a type that occurs in the aged and is characterized by an initial opacity in the lens, subsequent swelling of the lens, and final shrinkage with complete loss of transparency

senile dementia *n* : a mental disorder of old age esp. of the degenerative type associated with Alzheimer's disease — called also *senile psychosis*

senile psychosis *n* : SENILE DEMENTIA

senilis — see ARCUS SENILIS, LENTIGO SENILIS

se·nil·i·ty \si-ˈni-lə-tē, se-\ *n, pl* -**ties** : the quality or state of being senile; *specif* : the physical and mental infirmity of old age

se·ni·um \ˈsē-nē-əm\ *n* : the final period in the normal life span

sen·na \ˈse-nə\ *n* 1 : any of a genus (*Cassia*) of leguminous plants; *esp* : one used medicinally 2 : the dried leaflets or pods of various sennas (esp. *Cassia acutifolia* and *C. angustifolia*) used as a purgative

sen·sa·tion \sen-ˈsā-shən, sən-\ *n* 1 a : a mental process (as hearing or smelling) due to immediate bodily stimulation often as distinguished from awareness of the process — compare PERCEPTION b : awareness (as of pain) due to stimulation of a sense organ c : a state of consciousness of a kind usu. due to physical objects or internal bodily changes (a burning ∼ in his chest) 2 : something (as a physical object or pain) that causes or is the object of sensation

¹**sense** \ˈsens\ *n* 1 a : the faculty of perceiving by means of sense organs b : a specialized animal function or mechanism (as sight, hearing, smell, taste, or touch) basically involving a stimulus and a sense organ c : the sensory mechanisms constituting a unit distinct from other functions (as movement or thought) 2 : a particular sensation or kind or quality of sensation (a good ∼ of balance)

²**sense** *vb* **sensed; sens·ing** : to perceive by the senses

sense–da·tum \-ˈdā-təm, -ˈda-, -ˈdä-\ *n, pl* **sense–da·ta** \-tə\ : the immediate private perceived object of sensation as distinguished from the objective material object itself

sense organ *n* : a bodily structure that receives a stimulus (as heat or sound waves) and is affected in such a manner as to initiate a wave of excitation in associated sensory nerve fibers : RECEPTOR

sen·si·bil·i·ty \ˌsen-sə-ˈbi-lə-tē\ *n, pl* -**ties** 1 : ability to receive sensations (tactile ∼) 2 : awareness of and responsiveness toward something

sen·si·ble \ˈsen-sə-bəl\ *adj* 1 : perceptible to the senses or to reason or understanding 2 : capable of receiving sensory impressions (∼ to pain)

sen·si·tive \ˈsen-sə-tiv\ *adj* 1 : SENSORY 2 (∼ nerves) 2 a : receptive to sense impressions b : capable of being stimulated or excited by external agents 3

: highly responsive or susceptible: as **a** : easily hurt or damaged (~ skin); *esp* : easily hurt emotionally **b** : excessively or abnormally susceptible : HYPERSENSITIVE **c** : capable of indicating minute differences — **sen·si·tive·ness** *n* — **sen·si·tiv·i·ty** \ˌsen-sə-ˈti-və-tē\ *n*

sensitivity training *n* : training in a small interacting group that is designed to increase each individual's awareness of his or her own feelings and the feelings of others and to enhance interpersonal relations

sen·si·ti·za·tion \ˌsen-sə-tə-ˈzā-shən\ *n* **1** : the action or process of making sensitive or hypersensitive (allergic ~ of the skin) **2** : the process of becoming sensitive or hypersensitive (as to an antigen); *also* : the resulting state **3** : a form of nonassociative learning characterized by an increase in responsiveness upon repeated exposure to a stimulus — compare HABITUATION 3 — **sen·si·tize** \ˈsen-sə-ˌtīz\ *vb*

sen·si·tiz·er \-ˌtī-zər\ *n* : a substance that sensitizes the skin on first contact so that subsequent contact causes inflammation

sen·sor \ˈsen-ˌsȯr, -sər\ *n* : a device that responds to a physical stimulus (as heat, light, sound, or motion) and transmits a resulting impulse; *also* : SENSE ORGAN

sensori- *also* **senso-** *comb form* : sensory : sensory and ⟨sensorimotor⟩

sen·so·ri·al \sen-ˈsȯr-ē-əl\ *adj* : SENSORY

sen·so·ri·mo·tor \ˌsen-sə-rē-ˈmō-tər\ *adj* : of, relating to, or functioning in both sensory and motor aspects of bodily activity (~ disturbances)

sen·so·ri·neu·ral \-ˈnu̇r-əl, -ˈnyu̇r-\ *adj* : of, relating to, or involving the aspects of sense perception mediated by nerves (~ hearing loss)

sen·so·ri·um \sen-ˈsȯr-ē-əm\ *n*, *pl* **-ri·ums** *or* **-ria** \-ē-ə\ **1** : the parts of the brain or the mind concerned with the reception and interpretation of sensory stimuli; *broadly* : the entire sensory apparatus **2 a** : ability of the brain to receive and interpret sensory stimuli **b** : the state of consciousness judged in terms of this ability

sen·so·ry \ˈsen-sə-rē\ *adj* **1** : of or relating to sensation or the senses **2** : conveying nerve impulses from the sense organs to the nerve centers : AFFERENT (~ nerve fibers)

sensory aphasia *n* : inability to understand spoken, written, or tactile speech symbols that results from a brain lesion

sensory area *n* : an area of the cerebral cortex that receives afferent nerve fibers from lower sensory or motor areas

sensory cell *n* **1** : a peripheral nerve cell (as an olfactory cell) located at a sen-

sory receiving surface and being the primary receptor of a sensory impulse **2** : a nerve cell (as a spinal ganglion cell) transmitting sensory impulses

sensory neuron *n* : a neuron that transmits nerve impulses from a sense organ towards the central nervous system — compare ASSOCIATIVE NEURON, MOTONEURON

sen·ti·nel \ˈsent-ᵊn-əl\ *adj* : being an individual or part of a population potentially susceptible to an infection or infestation that is being monitored for the appearance or recurrence of the causative pathogen or parasite

sep·a·ra·tion \ˌse-pə-ˈrā-shən\ *n* **1** : the process of isolating or extracting from or of becoming isolated from a mixture; *also* : the resulting state **2** : DISLOCATION — see SHOULDER SEPARATION — **sep·a·rate** \ˈse-pə-ˌrāt\ *vb*

separation anxiety *n* : a form of anxiety originally caused by separation from a significant nurturant figure (as a mother) and that is duplicated later in life by usu. sudden and involuntary exposure to novel and potentially threatening situations

sep·a·ra·tor \ˈse-pə-ˌrā-tər\ *n* : a dental appliance for separating adjoining teeth to give access to their surfaces

sep·sis \ˈsep-səs\ *n*, *pl* **sep·ses** \ˈsep-ˌsēz\ : a toxic condition resulting from the spread of bacteria or their products from a focus of infection; *esp* : SEPTICEMIA

sept- *or* **septo-** *also* **septi-** *comb form* : septum ⟨septal⟩ ⟨septoplasty⟩

septa *pl of* SEPTUM

sep·tal \ˈsept-ᵊl\ *adj* : of or relating to a septum (~ defects)

septal cartilage *n* : the cartilage of the nasal septum

septa pellucida *pl of* SEPTUM PELLUCIDUM

sep·tate \ˈsep-ˌtāt\ *adj* : divided by or having a septum — **sep·ta·tion** \sep-ˈtā-shən\ *n*

septa transversa *pl of* SEPTUM TRANSVERSUM

sep·tec·to·my \sep-ˈtek-tə-mē\ *n*, *pl* **-mies** : surgical excision of a septum

sep·tic \ˈsep-tik\ *adj* **1** : of, relating to, or causing putrefaction **2** : relating to, involving, or characteristic of sepsis

septic abortion *n* : abortion caused by or associated with infection by a bacterium esp. of the genus *Clostridium* (*C. perfringens*) or rarely by one of the genus *Mycoplasma* (*M. hominis*)

sep·ti·cae·mia *chiefly Brit var of* SEPTICEMIA

sep·ti·ce·mia \ˌsep-tə-ˈsē-mē-ə\ *n* : invasion of the bloodstream by virulent microorganisms from a focus of infection that is accompanied by chills, fever, and prostration and often by the formation of secondary abscesses in various organs — called also *blood* *poisoning;* see PYEMIA — **sep·ti·ce·mic** \-ˈsē-mik\ *adj*

septic shock *n* : shock produced by usu. gram-negative bacteria that is characterized by hypoperfusion, hyperpyrexia, rigors, impaired cerebral function, and often by decreased cardiac output

septic sore throat *n* : STREP THROAT

septo- — see SEPT-

sep·to·plas·ty \ˈsep-tə-ˌplas-tē\ *n, pl* **-ties** : surgical repair of the nasal septum

sep·tos·to·my \sep-ˈtäs-tə-mē\ *n, pl* **-mies** : the surgical creation of an opening through the interatrial septum

sep·tum \ˈsep-təm\ *n, pl* **sep·ta** \-tə\ : a dividing wall or membrane esp. between bodily spaces or masses of soft tissue; *esp* : NASAL SEPTUM

septum pel·lu·ci·dum \-pə-ˈlü-sə-dəm\ *n, pl* **septa pel·lu·ci·da** \-də\ : the thin double partition extending vertically from the lower surface of the corpus callosum to the fornix and neighboring parts and separating the lateral ventricles of the brain

septum trans·ver·sum \-tranz-ˈvər-səm\ *n, pl* **septa trans·ver·sa** \-sə\ : the diaphragm or the embryonic structure from which it in part develops

sep·tup·let \sep-ˈtə-plət, -ˈtü-plət, -ˈtyü-; ˈsep-tə-\ *n* 1 : one of seven offspring born at one birth 2 *pl* : a group of seven such offspring

se·quel \ˈsē-kwəl, -ˌkwel\ *n* : SEQUELA

se·que·la \si-ˈkwe-lə\ *n, pl* **se·quel·ae** \-(ˌ)lē\ : an aftereffect of disease, injury, procedure, or treatment

¹**se·quence** \ˈsē-kwəns, -ˌkwens\ *n* 1 : a continuous or connected series (as of amino acids in a protein) 2 : a consequence, result, or subsequent development (as of a disease)

²**sequence** *vb* **se·quenced; se·quenc·ing** : to determine the sequence of chemical constituents (as amino-acid residues) in

se·quenc·er \ˈsē-kwən-sər, -ˌkwen-\ *n* : any of various devices for arranging (as informational items) into or separating (as amino acids from protein) in a sequence

¹**se·quen·tial** \si-ˈkwen-chəl\ *adj* 1 : occurring as a sequela of disease or injury 2 : of, relating to, forming, or taken in a sequence

²**sequential** *n* : an oral contraceptive in which the pills taken during approximately the first three weeks contain only estrogen and those taken during the rest of the cycle contain both estrogen and progestogen

se·ques·ter \si-ˈkwes-tər\ *vb* : to hold (as a metallic ion) in solution esp. for the purpose of suppressing undesired chemical or biological activity

se·ques·trant \-trənt\ *n* : a sequestering agent (as citric acid)

se·ques·tra·tion \ˌsē-kwəs-ˈtrā-shən,

ˌse-, si-ˌkwes-\ *n* 1 : the formation of a sequestrum 2 : the process of sequestering or result of being sequestered

se·ques·trec·to·my \ˌsē-ˌkwe-ˈstrek-tə-mē\ *n, pl* **-mies** : the surgical removal of a sequestrum

se·ques·trum \si-ˈkwes-trəm\ *n, pl* **-trums** *also* **-tra** \-trə\ : a fragment of dead bone detached from adjoining sound bone

sera *pl of* SERUM

serial section *n* : any of a series of sections cut in sequence by a microtome from a prepared specimen (as of tissue) — **serially sectioned** *adj* — **serial sectioning** *n*

ser·ine \ˈser-ˌēn\ *n* : a nonessential amino acid $C_3H_7NO_3$ that occurs esp. as a structural part of many proteins and phosphatidylethanolamines

se·ri·ous \ˈsir-ē-əs\ *adj* : having important or dangerous possible consequences (a ~ injury)

sero- *comb form* 1 : serum ⟨*serology*⟩ ⟨*serodiagnosis*⟩ 2 : serous and ⟨*seropurulent*⟩

se·ro·con·ver·sion \ˌsir-ō-kən-ˈvər-zhən, ˌser-\ *n* : the production of antibodies in response to an antigen — **se·ro·con·vert** \-ˈvərt\ *vb*

se·ro·di·ag·no·sis \-ˌdī-ig-ˈnō-səs\ *n, pl* **-no·ses** \-ˌsēz\ : diagnosis by the use of serum (as in the Wassermann test) — **se·ro·di·ag·nos·tic** \-ˈnäs-tik\ *adj*

se·ro·epi·de·mi·o·log·ic \-ˌe-pə-ˌdē-mē-ə-ˈlä-jik\ *or* **se·ro·epi·de·mi·o·log·i·cal** \-ji-kəl\ *adj* : of, relating to, or being epidemiological investigations involving the identification of antibodies to specific antigens in populations of individuals — **se·ro·epi·de·mi·ol·o·gy** \-mē-ˈä-lə-jē\ *n*

se·ro·group \ˈsir-ō-ˌgrüp\ *n* : a group of serotypes having one or more antigens in common

se·rol·o·gist \si-ˈrä-lə-jist\ *n* : a specialist in serology

se·rol·o·gy \si-ˈrä-lə-jē\ *n, pl* **-gies** : a science dealing with serums and esp. their reactions and properties — **se·ro·log·i·cal** \ˌsir-ə-ˈlä-ji-kəl\ *or* **se·ro·log·ic** \-jik\ *adj* — **se·ro·log·i·cal·ly** *adv*

se·ro·neg·a·tive \ˌsir-ō-ˈne-gə-tiv, ˌser-ō-\ *adj* : having or being a negative serum reaction esp. in a test for the presence of an antibody (a ~ patient) — **se·ro·neg·a·tiv·i·ty** \-ˌne-gə-ˈti-və-tē\ *n*

se·ro·pos·i·tive \-ˈpä-zə-tiv\ *adj* : having or being a positive serum reaction esp. in a test for the presence of an antibody (a ~ donor) — **se·ro·pos·i·tiv·i·ty** \-ˌpä-zə-ˈti-və-tē\ *n*

se·ro·prev·a·lence \-ˈpre-və-ləns\ *n* : the frequency of individuals in a population that have a particular element (as antibodies to HIV) in their blood serum

se·ro·pu·ru·lent \-ˈpyür-ə-lənt, -ˈpyüryə-\ *adj* : consisting of a mixture of serum and pus (a ~ exudate)

se·ro·re·ac·tiv·i·ty \-(ˌ)rē-ˌak-ˈti-və-tē\ *n, pl* -ties : reactivity of blood serum — se·ro·re·ac·tion \ˌsir-ō-rē-ˈak-shən, ˌser-\ *n*

se·ro·sa \sə-ˈrō-zə\ *n, pl* -sas *also* -sae \-zē\ : a usu. enclosing serous membrane (the peritoneal ~) — se·ro·sal \-zəl-əd\

se·ro·san·guin·e·ous \ˌsir-ō-san-ˈgwi-nē-əs, ˌser-ō-, -ˌsaŋ-\ *adj* : containing or consisting of both blood and serous fluid (a ~ discharge)

se·ro·si·tis \ˌsir-ō-ˈsī-təs, ˌser-\ *n* : inflammation of one or more serous membranes (peritoneal ~)

se·ro·sur·vey \ˈsir-ō-ˌsər-ˌvā, ˈser-\ *n* : a test of blood serum from a group of individuals to determine seroprevalence (as of antibodies to HIV)

se·ro·ther·a·py \ˌsir-ō-ˈther-ə-pē, ˌser-ō-\ *n, pl* -pies : the treatment of a disease with specific immune serum

se·ro·to·ner·gic \ˌsir-ə-tə-ˈnər-jik\ *or* se·ro·to·nin·er·gic \ˌsir-ə-ˌtō-nə-ˈnər-jik\ *adj* : liberating, activated by, or involving serotonin in the transmission of nerve impulses

se·ro·to·nin \ˌsir-ə-ˈtō-nən, ˌser-\ *n* : a phenolic amine neurotransmitter $C_{10}H_{12}N_2O$ that is a powerful vasoconstrictor and is found esp. in the brain, blood serum, and gastric mucous membrane of mammals — called also *5-hydroxytryptamine*

¹se·ro·type \ˈsir-ə-ˌtīp, ˈser-\ *n* **1** : a group of intimately related microorganisms distinguished by a common set of antigens **2** : the set of antigens characteristic of a serotype

²serotype *vb* -typed; -typ·ing : to determine the serotype of (~ streptococci)

se·rous \ˈsir-əs\ *adj* : of, relating to, producing, or resembling serum; *esp* : having a thin watery constitution

serous cavity *n* : a cavity (as the peritoneal cavity, pleural cavity, or pericardial cavity) that is lined with a serous membrane

serous cell *n* : a cell (as of the parotid gland) that secretes a serous fluid

serous gland *n* : a gland secreting a serous fluid

serous membrane *n* : any of various thin membranes (as the peritoneum, pericardium, or pleurae) that consist of a single layer of thin flat mesothelial cells resting on a connective-tissue stroma, secrete a serous fluid, and usu. line bodily cavities or enclose the organs contained in such cavities — compare MUCOUS MEMBRANE

serous otitis media *n* : a form of otitis media that is characterized by the accumulation of serous exudate in the middle ear

se·ro·var \ˈsir-ə-ˌvär, ˈser-, -ˌvar\ *n* : SEROTYPE 1

Ser·pa·sil \ˈsər-pə-ˌsil\ *trademark* —

used for a preparation of reserpine

ser·pig·i·nous \(ˌ)sər-ˈpi-jə-nəs\ *adj* : slowly spreading; *esp* : healing over in one portion while continuing to advance in another (~ ulcer)

serrata — see ORA SERRATA

ser·rat·ed \sə-ˈrā-təd, ˈser-ˌā-\ *or* ser·rate \ˈser-ˌāt, sə-ˈrāt \ *adj* : notched or toothed on the edge (the ~ sutures of the skull)

Ser·ra·tia \se-ˈrā-shə, -shē-ə\ *n* : a genus of aerobic saprophytic flagellated rod-shaped bacteria (family Enterobacteriaceae) that are now usu. considered serotypes of a single species (*S. marcescens*) which has been implicated in some human opportunistic infections

Ser·ra·ti \se-ˈrä-tē\, Serafino, Italian boatman.

ser·ra·tus \se-ˈrä-təs\ *n, pl* ser·ra·ti \-ˈrä-ˌtī\ : any of three muscles of the thorax that have complex origins but arise chiefly from the ribs or vertebrae: **a** : SERRATUS ANTERIOR **b** : SERRATUS POSTERIOR INFERIOR **c** : SERRATUS POSTERIOR SUPERIOR

serratus anterior *n* : a thin muscular sheet of the thorax that arises from the first eight or nine ribs and from the intercostal muscles between them, is inserted into the ventral side of the medial margin of the scapula, and acts to stabilize the scapula by holding it against the chest wall and to rotate it in raising the arm

serratus posterior inferior *n* : a thin quadrilateral muscle at the junction of the thoracic and lumbar regions that arises chiefly from the spinous processes of the lowest two thoracic and first two or three lumbar vertebrae, is inserted into the lowest four ribs, and acts to counteract the pull of the diaphragm on the ribs to which it is attached

serratus posterior superior *n* : a thin quadrilateral muscle of the upper and dorsal part of the thorax that arises chiefly from the spinous processes of the lowest cervical and the first two or three thoracic vertebrae, is inserted into the second to fifth ribs, and acts to elevate the upper ribs

Ser·to·li cell \ˈser-tə-lē-, ˌser-ˈtō-lē-\ *also* Ser·to·li's cell \-lēz-\ *n* : any of the elongated striated cells in the seminiferous tubules of the testis to which the spermatids become attached and from which they apparently derive nourishment

Sertoli, Enrico (1842–1910), Italian physiologist.

ser·tra·line \ˈsər-trə-ˌlēn\ *n* : an antidepressant drug $C_{17}H_{17}NCl_2$ administered in the form of its hydrochloride and acting to enhance serotonin activity

¹se·rum \ˈsir-əm\ *n, pl* serums *or* se·ra \-ə\ : the watery portion of an animal fluid remaining after coagula-

tion: **a** (1) : the clear yellowish fluid that remains after suspended material (as blood cells), fibrinogen. and fibrin are removed from blood — called also *blood serum* (2) : ANTISERUM **b** : a normal or pathological serous fluid (as in a blister)

²**serum** *adj* : occurring or found in the serum of the blood (~ cholesterol) (~ glutamic-oxaloacetic transaminase)

serum albumin *n* : a crystallizable albumin or mixture of albumins that normally constitutes more than half of the protein in blood serum, that serves to maintain the osmotic pressure of the blood, and that is used in transfusions esp. for the treatment of shock

serum globulin *n* : a globulin or mixture of globulins occurring in blood serum and containing most of the antibodies of the blood

serum hepatitis *n* : HEPATITIS B

serum sickness *n* : an allergic reaction to the injection of foreign serum manifested by hives. swelling, eruption, arthritis, and fever

serv·ice \'sər-vis\ *n* : a branch of a hospital medical staff devoted to a particular specialty (pediatric ~)

service mark *n* : a mark or device used to identify a service (as transportation or insurance) offered to customers — compare TRADEMARK

ses·a·moid \'se-sə-ˌmȯid\ *adj* : of. relating to. or being a nodular mass of bone or cartilage in a tendon esp. at a joint or bony prominence (the patella is the largest ~ bone in the body)

²**sesamoid** *n* : a sesamoid bone or cartilage

ses·a·moid·itis \ˌse-sə-ˌmȯi-'dī-təs\ *n* : inflammation of the navicular bone and adjacent structures in the horse

ses·sile \'se-ˌsīl, -səl\ *adj* **1** : attached directly by a broad base : not pedunculated (a ~ tumor) **2** : firmly attached (as to a cell) : not free to move about

¹**set** \'set\ *vb* **set**; **set·ting** : to restore to normal position or connection when dislocated or fractured (~ a broken bone)

²**set** *n* : a state of psychological preparedness usu. of limited duration for action in response to an anticipated stimulus or situation

Se·tar·ia \se-'tar-ē-ə\ *n* : a genus of filarial worms parasitic as adults in the body cavity of various ungulate mammals (as cattle and deer)

se·ton \'sēt-ᵊn\ *n* : one or more threads or horsehairs or a strip of linen introduced beneath the skin by a knife or needle to provide drainage

set·tle \'set-ᵊl\ *vb* **set·tled**; **set·tling** *of an animal* **1** : IMPREGNATE 1a **2** : CONCEIVE

seventh cranial nerve *n* : FACIAL NERVE

seventh nerve *n* : FACIAL NERVE

severe combined immunodeficiency *n*

: a rare congenital disorder of the immune system that is characterized by inability to produce a normal complement of antibodies and T cells and that results usu. in early death — abbr. *SCID;* called also *severe combined immune deficiency*

¹**sex** \'seks\ *n* **1** : either of the two major forms of individuals that occur in many species and that are distinguished respectively as male or female **2** : the sum of the structural, functional. and behavioral characteristics of living things that are involved in reproduction by two interacting parents and that distinguish males and females **3 a** : sexually motivated phenomena or behavior **b** : SEXUAL INTERCOURSE

²**sex** *vb* : to identify the sex of (~ chicks)

sex cell *n* : GAMETE; *also* : its cellular precursor

sex chromatin *n* : BARR BODY

sex chromosome *n* : a chromosome (as the X chromosome or the Y chromosome in humans) that is concerned directly with the inheritance of sex and that is the seat of factors governing the inheritance of various sex-linked and sex-limited characters

sex gland *n* : GONAD

sex hormone *n* : a hormone (as from the gonads or adrenal cortex) that affects the growth or function of the reproductive organs or the development of secondary sex characteristics

sex-limited *adj* : expressed in the phenotype of only one sex (a ~ character)

sex-linked *adj* **1** : located in a sex chromosome (a ~ gene) **2** : mediated by a sex-linked gene (a ~ character) — **sex-linkage** *n*

sex object *n* : a person regarded esp. exclusively as an object of sexual interest

sex·ol·o·gy \sek-'sä-lə-jē\ *n, pl* **-gies** : the study of sex or of the interaction of the sexes esp. among human beings — **sex·ol·o·gist** \-jist\ *n*

sex ratio *n* : the proportion of males to females in a population esp. as expressed by the number of males per hundred females

sex·tu·plet \sek-'stə-plət, -'stü-, -'styü-; 'sek-stə-\ *n* : any of six offspring born at one birth

sex·u·al \'sek-shə-wəl\ *adj* **1** : of. relating to. or associated with sex or the sexes (~ differentiation) (~ conflict) **2** : having or involving sex (~ reproduction) — **sex·u·al·ly** *adv*

sexual intercourse *n* **1** : heterosexual intercourse involving penetration of the vagina by the penis : COITUS **2** : intercourse involving genital contact between individuals other than penetration of the vagina by the penis

sex·u·al·i·ty \ˌsek-shə-'wa-lə-tē\ *n, pl* **-ties** : the quality or state of being sexual: **a** : the condition of having sex **b** : sexual activity **c** : expression of sexual receptivity or interest esp. when excessive

sexually transmitted disease *n* : any of various diseases transmitted by direct sexual contact that include the classic venereal diseases (as syphilis, gonorrhea, and chancroid) and other diseases (as hepatitis A, hepatitis B, giardiasis, and AIDS) often or sometimes contracted by other than sexual means — called also *STD*

sexual relations *n pl* : COITUS

Se·za·ry syndrome \₁sā-zä-'rē-\ *or* **Se·za·ry's syndrome** \-'rēz-\ *n* : a rare disease that is characterized by the presence in the blood and in the skin of numerous large atypical mononuclear T cells with resultant widespread exfoliation of the skin

    Sézary, Albert (1880–1956), French physician.

SGOT *abbr* serum glutamic-oxaloacetic transaminase

SGPT *abbr* serum glutamic pyruvic transaminase

SH *abbr* serum hepatitis

shad·ow \'sha-(₁)dō\ *n* **1** : a dark outline or image on an X-ray photograph where the X rays have been blocked by a radiopaque mass (as a tumor) **2** : a colorless or scantily pigmented or stained body (as a degenerate cell or empty membrane) only faintly visible under the microscope

shaft \'shaft\ *n* : a long slender cylindrical body or part: as **a** : the cylindrical part of a long bone between the enlarged ends **b** : the part of a hair that is visible above the surface of the skin

shaft louse *n* : a biting louse of the genus *Menopon (M. gallinae)* that commonly infests domestic fowls

shakes \'shāks\ *n sing or pl* **1** : a condition of trembling: *specif* : DELIRIUM TREMENS **2** : MALARIA 1

shaking palsy *n* : PARKINSON'S DISEASE

shal·low \'sha-(₁)lō\ *adj* : displacing comparatively little air (∼ breathing)

shank \'shaŋk\ *n* : the part of the leg between the knee and the ankle in humans or a corresponding part in other vertebrates

shape \'shāp\ *vb* **shaped; shap·ing** : to modify (behavior) by rewarding changes that tend toward a desired response

Shar·pey's fiber \'shär-pēz-\ *n* : any of the thready processes of the periosteum that penetrate the tissue of the superficial lamellae of bones

    Sharpey, William (1802–1880), British anatomist and physiologist.

sheath \'shēth\ *n, pl* **sheaths** \'shēthz, 'shēths\ **1** : an investing cover or case of a plant or animal body or body part: as **a** : the tubular fold of skin into which the penis of many mammals is retracted **b** : the connective tissue of an organ or part that binds together its component elements and holds it in place **2** : CONDOM — **sheathed** *adj*

sheath of Schwann \-'shwän\ *n* : NEURILEMMA

    T. A. H. Schwann — see SCHWANN CELL

shed \'shed\ *vb* **shed; shed·ding** : to give off or out: as **a** : to lose as part of a natural process (∼ the deciduous teeth) **b** : to discharge usu. gradually from the body (∼ a virus in the urine)

Shee·han's syndrome \'shē-ənz-\ *n* : necrosis of the pituitary gland with associated hypopituitarism resulting from postpartum hemorrhage

    Sheehan, Harold Leeming (b 1900), British pathologist.

sheep botfly *n* : a dipteran fly of the genus *Oestrus (O. ovis)* whose larvae parasitize sheep and lodge esp. in the nasal passages, frontal sinuses, and throat

sheep-dip \'shēp-₁dip\ *n* : a liquid preparation of usu. toxic chemicals into which sheep are plunged esp. to destroy parasitic arthropods

sheep ked *n* : a wingless bloodsucking dipteran fly of the genus *Melophagus (M. ovinus)* that feeds chiefly on sheep and is a vector of sheep trypanosomiasis — called also *ked, sheep tick*

sheep pox *n* : a disease of sheep and possibly goats that is caused by a poxvirus related to the one causing smallpox and was formerly epizootic in warmer Old World areas

sheep tick *n* : SHEEP KED

shellfish poisoning — see PARALYTIC SHELLFISH POISONING

shell shock *n* : post-traumatic stress disorder in soldiers as a result of combat experience — **shell-shocked** \'shel-₁shäkt\ *adj*

shi·at·su *also* **shi·at·zu** \shē-'ät-sü\ *n, often cap* : a massage with the fingers applied to those specific areas of the body used in acupuncture — called also *acupressure*

Shi·ga bacillus \'shē-gə-\ *n* : a widely distributed but chiefly tropical bacterium of the genus *Shigella (S. dysenteriae)* that causes dysentery

    Shiga, Kiyoshi (1870–1957), Japanese bacteriologist.

shi·gel·la \shi-'ge-lə\ *n* **1** *cap* : a genus of nonmotile aerobic enterobacteria that form acid but no gas on many carbohydrates and that cause dysenteries in animals and esp. humans **2** *pl* **-gel·lae** \-₁lē\ *also* **-gellas** : any bacterium of the genus *Shigella*

shig·el·lo·sis \₁shi-gə-'lō-səs\ *n, pl* **-lo·ses** \-'lō-₁sēz\ : infection with or dysentery caused by bacteria of the genus *Shigella*

shin \'shin\ *n* : the front part of the leg below the knee

shin·bone \'shin-₁bōn\ *n* : TIBIA

shin·er \'shī-nər\ *n* : BLACK EYE

shin·gles \'shiŋ-gəlz\ *n* : an acute viral inflammation of the sensory ganglia of spinal and cranial nerves associated with a vesicular eruption and neuralgic pain and caused by reactivation of the herpesvirus causing chicken pox — called also *herpes zoster, zona, zoster*

shin·splints \'shin-₋splints\ *n sing or pl* : painful injury to and inflammation of the tibial and toe extensor muscles or their fasciae that is caused by repeated minimal traumas (as by running on a hard surface)

shipping fever *n* : an often fatal febrile disease esp. of young cattle and sheep that occurs under conditions of unusual exposure or exhaustion, is marked by high fever and pneumonia, and is associated with the presence of bacteria (esp. genera *Pasteurella* and *Mycoplasma*) or viruses

shiv·er \'shi-vər\ *vb* : to undergo trembling : experience rapid involuntary muscular twitching esp. in response to cold — **shiver** *n*

shivering *n* **1** : an act or action of one that shivers **2** : a constant abnormal twitching of various muscles in the horse that is prob. due to sensory nerve derangement

shock \'shäk\ *n* **1** : a sudden or violent disturbance in the mental or emotional faculties **2** : a state of profound depression of the vital processes of the body that is characterized by pallor, rapid but weak pulse, rapid and shallow respiration, reduced total blood volume, and low blood pressure and that is caused usu. by severe esp. crushing injuries, hemorrhage, burns, or major surgery **3** : sudden stimulation of the nerves or convulsive contraction of the muscles accompanied by a feeling of concussion that is caused by the discharge of electricity through the body — compare ELECTROSHOCK THERAPY — **shock** *vb*

shock lung *n* : a condition of severe pulmonary edema associated with shock

shock therapy *n* : the treatment of mental disorder by the artificial induction of coma or convulsions through use of drugs or electric current — called also *convulsive therapy, shock treatment;* see ELECTROSHOCK THERAPY

shock treatment *n* : SHOCK THERAPY

shoot \'shüt\ *vb* **shot** \'shät\; **shooting 1** : to give an injection to **2** : to take or administer (as a drug) by hypodermic needle

shoot·ing *adj* : characterized by sudden sharp piercing sensations (∼ pains)

short bone *n* : a bone (as of the tarsus or carpus) that is of approximately equal length in all dimensions

short ciliary nerve *n* : any of 6 to 10 delicate nerve filaments of parasympathetic, sympathetic, and general sensory function that arise in the ciliary ganglion and innervate the smooth muscles and tunics of the eye — compare LONG CILIARY NERVE

shortness of breath *n* : difficulty in drawing sufficient breath : labored breathing

short–nosed cattle louse *n* : a large louse of the genus *Haematopinus* (*H. eurysternus*) that attacks domestic cattle

short posterior ciliary artery *n* : any of 6 to 10 arteries that arise from the ophthalmic artery or its branches and supply the choroid and the ciliary processes — compare LONG POSTERIOR CILIARY ARTERY

short saphenous vein *n* : SAPHENOUS VEIN b

short–sight·ed \'shört-'sī-təd\ *adj* : NEARSIGHTED

short–sight·ed·ness *n* : MYOPIA

short–term memory *n* : memory that involves recall of information for a relatively short time (as a few seconds)

shot \'shät\ *n* : an injection of a drug, immunizing substance, nutrient, or medicament (a flu ∼)

shoul·der \'shōl-dər\ *n* **1** : the laterally projecting part of the body formed of the bones and joints with their covering tissue by which the arm is connected with the trunk **2** : the two shoulders and the upper part of the back — usu. used in pl.

shoulder blade *n* : SCAPULA

shoulder girdle *n* : PECTORAL GIRDLE

shoulder–hand syndrome *n* : pain in and stiffening of the shoulder followed by swelling and stiffening of the hand and fingers often associated with or following myocardial infarction

shoulder joint *n* : the ball-and-socket joint of the humerus and the scapula

shoulder separation *n* : a dislocation of the shoulder at the acromioclavicular joint

show \'shō\ *n* **1** : a discharge of mucus streaked with blood from the vagina at the onset of labor **2** : the first appearance of blood in a menstrual period

shrink \'shriŋk\ *n* : a clinical psychiatrist or psychologist — called also *headshrinker*

shud·der \'shə-dər\ *vb* **shud·dered; shud·der·ing** : to tremble convulsively : SHIVER — **shudder** *n*

shunt \'shənt\ *n* **1** : a passage by which a bodily fluid (as blood) is diverted from one channel, circulatory path, or part to another; *esp* : such a passage established by surgery or occurring as an abnormality (an arteriovenous ∼) **2 a** : a surgical procedure for the establishment of an artificial shunt — see PORTACAVAL SHUNT **b** : a device (as a narrow tube) used to establish an artificial shunt — **shunt** *vb*

¹shut–in \'shət-₋in\ *n* : an invalid confined to home, a room, or bed

²**shut–in** \'shət-ˈin\ *adj* **1** : confined to one's home or an institution by illness or incapacity **2** : tending to avoid social contact : WITHDRAWN (the ~ personality type)

Si *symbol* silicon

SI *abbr* [French *Système International d'Unités*] International System of Units

sial- *or* **sialo-** *comb form* : saliva ⟨*sialolith*⟩ ⟨*sialorrhea*⟩

si·al·ad·e·ni·tis \ˌsī-ə-ˌlad-ᵊn-ˈī-təs\ *n* : inflammation of a salivary gland

si·al·a·gogue \sī-ˈal-ə-ˌgäg\ *n* : an agent that promotes the flow of saliva — called also *sialogogue*

si·al·ic acid \sī-ˈa-lik-\ *n* : any of a group of reducing amido acids that are essentially carbohydrates and are found esp. as components of blood glycoproteins and mucoproteins

si·al·o·ad·e·nec·to·my \ˌsī-ə-lō-ˌad-ᵊn-ˈek-tə-mē\ *n, pl* **-mies** : surgical excision of a salivary gland

si·al·o·gly·co·pro·tein \-ˌglī-kō-ˈprō-ˌtēn\ *n* : a glycoprotein (as of blood) having sialic acid as a component

si·al·o·gogue \sī-ˈa-lə-ˌgäg\ *n* : SIALAGOGUE

si·al·o·gram \sī-ˈa-lə-ˌgram\ *n* : a roentgenogram of the salivary tract made by sialography

si·a·log·ra·phy \ˌsī-ə-ˈlä-grə-fē\ *n, pl* **-phies** : roentgenography of the salivary tract after injection of a radiopaque substance

si·al·o·lith \sī-ˈa-lə-ˌlith\ *n* : a calculus occurring in a salivary gland

si·al·o·li·thi·a·sis \ˌsī-ə-lō-li-ˈthī-ə-səs\ *n, pl* **-ases** \-ˌsēz\ : the formation or presence of a calculus or calculi in a salivary gland

si·al·or·rhea \ˌsī-ə-lə-ˈrē-ə\ *n* : excessive salivation

si·al·or·rhoea *chiefly Brit var of* SIALORRHEA

Si·a·mese twin \ˈsī-ə-ˌmēz-, -ˌmēs-\ *n* : one of a pair of congenitally united twins

sib \ˈsib\ *n* : a brother or sister considered irrespective of sex

sib·i·lant \ˈsi-bə-lənt\ *adj* : characterized by or being a sharp whistling sound ⟨~ breathing⟩ ⟨~ rales⟩

sib·ling \ˈsi-bliŋ\ *n* : SIB; *also* : one of two or more individuals having one common parent

sibling rivalry *n* : competition between siblings esp. for the attention, affection, and approval of their parents

sicca — see KERATOCONJUNCTIVITIS SICCA

sic·ca syndrome \ˈsi-kə-\ *n* : SJÖGREN'S SYNDROME

sick \ˈsik\ *adj* **1 a** : affected with disease or ill health **b** : of, relating to, or intended for use in sickness **c** : affected with nausea : inclined to vomit or being in the act of vomiting **2** : mentally or emotionally unsound or disordered

sick bay *n* : a compartment in a ship used as a dispensary and hospital; *broadly* : a place for the care of the sick or injured

sick·bed \ˈsik-ˌbed\ *n* : the bed upon which one lies sick

sick building syndrome *n* : a set of symptoms (as headache, fatigue, eye irritation, and dizziness) typically affecting workers in modern airtight office buildings that is believed to be caused by indoor pollutants (as formaldehyde fumes, particulate matter, or microorganisms) — abbr. *SBS*

sick call *n* : a scheduled time at which individuals (as soldiers) may report as sick to a medical officer

sick·en \ˈsi-kən\ *vb* : to make or become sick

sick·en·ing *adj* : causing sickness or nausea ⟨a ~ odor⟩

sick headache *n* : MIGRAINE

sick·lae·mia *chiefly Brit var of* SICKLEMIA

¹**sick·le** \ˈsi-kəl\ *n* : a dental scaler with a curved three-sided point

²**sickle** *adj* : of, relating to, or characteristic of sickle-cell anemia or sickle-cell trait ⟨~ hemoglobin⟩

³**sickle** *vb* **sick·led**; **sick·ling** : to change (a red blood cell) into a sickle cell

sick leave *n* **1** : an absence from work permitted because of illness **2** : the number of days per year for which an employer agrees to pay employees who are sick

sickle cell *n* **1** : an abnormal red blood cell of crescent shape **2** : a condition characterized by sickle cells : SICKLE-CELL ANEMIA, SICKLE-CELL TRAIT

sickle–cell anemia *n* : a chronic anemia that occurs primarily in individuals of African descent who are homozygous for the gene controlling hemoglobin S and that is characterized by destruction of red blood cells and by episodic blocking of blood vessels by the adherence of sickle cells to the vascular endothelium which causes the serious complications of the disease (as organ failure)

sickle–cell disease *n* : SICKLE-CELL ANEMIA

sickle–cell trait *n* : a usu. asymptomatic blood condition in which some red blood cells tend to sickle but usu. not enough to produce anemia and which results from heterozygosity for the gene controlling hemoglobin S

sick·le·mia \si-ˈklē-mē-ə\ *n* : SICKLE-CELL TRAIT — **sick·le·mic** \-mik\ *adj*

sick·ler \ˈsi-klər\ *n* : a person with sickle-cell trait or sickle-cell anemia

sick·ly \ˈsi-klē\ *adj* **1** : somewhat unwell; *also* : habitually ailing **2** : produced by or associated with sickness **3** : producing or tending to produce disease **4** : tending to produce nausea ⟨a ~ odor⟩

sick·ness \ˈsik-nəs\ *n* **1** : the condition

of being ill : ill health **2** : a specific disease **3** : NAUSEA

sick-room \\'sik-ṛrüm, -ṛrům\ *n* : a room in which a person is confined by sickness

sick sinus syndrome *n* : a cardiac disorder typically characterized by alternating tachycardia and bradycardia

side \\'sīd\ *n* **1** : the right or left part of the wall or trunk of the body ⟨a pain in the ~⟩ **2** : a lateral half or part of an organ or structure ⟨the right ~ of one leg⟩

side-bone \-ṛbōn\ *n* **1** *or* **sidebones** : abnormal ossification of the cartilages in the lateral posterior part of a horse's hoof (as of a forefoot) often causing lameness — used with a sing. verb **2** : one of the bony structures characteristic of sidebone

side chain *n* : a branched chain of atoms attached to the principal chain or to a ring in a molecule

side effect *n* : a secondary and usu. adverse effect (as of a drug) — called also *side reaction*

sider- *or* **sidero-** *comb form* : iron ⟨*sideropenia*⟩

sid-ero-blast \\'si-də-rə-ṛblast\ *n* : an erythroblast containing cytoplasmic iron granules — **sid-ero-blas-tic** \ṛsi-də-rə-'blas-tik\ *adj*

sid-ero-cyte \\'si-də-rə-ṛsīt\ *n* : an atypical red blood cell containing iron not bound in hemoglobin

sid-ero-pe-nia \ṛsi-də-rə-'pē-nē-ə\ *n* : iron deficiency in the blood serum — **sid-ero-pe-nic** \-'pē-nik\ *adj*

sid-er-o-sis \ṛsi-də-'rō-səs\ *n* **1** : pneumoconiosis occurring in iron workers from inhalation of particles of iron **2** : deposit of iron pigment in a bodily tissue — **sid-er-ot-ic** \ṛsi-də-'rä-tik\ *adj*

side-stream \\'sīd-ṛstrēm\ *adj* : relating to or being tobacco smoke that is emitted from the lighted end of a cigarette or cigar — compare MAINSTREAM

side-wind-er \\'sīd-ṛwīn-dər\ *n* : a small pale-colored rattlesnake of the genus *Crotalus* (*C. cerastes*) of the southwestern U.S. that moves by thrusting its body diagonally forward in a series of S-shaped curves — called also *horned rattlesnake*

SIDS *abbr* sudden infant death syndrome

Sig *abbr* signa — used to introduce the signature in writing a prescription

sight \\'sīt\ *n* **1** : something that is seen **2** : the process, power, or function of seeing; *specif* : the sense by which light stimuli received by the eye are interpreted by the brain in the construction of a representation of the position, shape, brightness, and usu. color of objects in the real world **3 a** : a perception of an object by the eye **b** : the range of vision

sight-ed \\'sī-təd\ *adj* : having sight : not blind

sight-less \\'sīt-ləs\ *adj* : lacking sight : BLIND — **sight-less-ness** *n*

1sig-moid \\'sig-ṃóid\ *adj* **1 a** : curved like the letter C **b** : curved in two directions like the letter S **2** : of, relating to, or being the sigmoid flexure of the intestine ⟨~ lesions⟩

2sigmoid *n* : SIGMOID FLEXURE

sigmoid artery *n* : any of several branches of the inferior mesenteric artery that supply the sigmoid flexure

sigmoid colon *n* : SIGMOID FLEXURE

sig-moid-ec-to-my \ṛsig-ṃói-'dek-tə-mē\ *n, pl* **-mies** : surgical excision of part of the sigmoid flexure

sigmoid flexure *n* : the contracted and crooked part of the colon immediately above the rectum — called also *pelvic colon, sigmoid colon*

sigmoid notch *n* : a curved depression on the upper border of the lower jaw between the coronoid process and the articulatory condyle

sig-moid-o-scope \sig-'ṃói-də-ṛskōp\ *n* : a long hollow tubular instrument designed to be passed through the anus in order to permit inspection, diagnosis, treatment, and photography esp. of the sigmoid flexure — called also *proctosigmoidoscope*

sig-moid-os-co-py \ṛsig-ṃói-'däs-kə-pē\ *n, pl* **-pies** : the process of using a sigmoidoscope — called also *proctosigmoidoscopy* — **sig-moid-o-scop-ic** \-də-'skä-pik\ *adj*

sigmoid sinus *n* : a sinus on each side of the brain that is a continuation of the transverse sinus on the same side, follows an S-shaped course to the jugular foramen, and empties into the internal jugular vein

sigmoid vein *n* : any of several veins that drain the sigmoid flexure and empty into the superior rectal vein

sign \\'sīn\ *n* **1** : one of a set of gestures used to represent language **2** : an objective evidence of disease esp. as observed and interpreted by the physician — compare SYMPTOM; see PHYSICAL SIGN

sig-na \\'sig-nə\ *vb* : write on label — used to introduce the signature in writing a prescription; *abbr* **S, Sig**

signal node *n* : a supraclavicular lymph node which when tumorous is often a secondary sign of gastrointestinal cancer — called also *Virchow's node*

sig-na-ture \\'sig-nə-ṛchůr, -chər, -ṛtyůr, -ṛtůr\ *n* : the part of a medical prescription which contains the directions to the patient

sign language *n* : a system of communicating by means of conventional chiefly manual gestures that is used esp. by the deaf; *esp* : DACTYLOLOGY

Si-las-tic \si-'las-tik\ *trademark* — used for a soft pliable plastic

si-lent \\'sī-lənt\ *adj* **1** : not exhibiting the usual signs or symptoms of presence ⟨a ∼ infection⟩ **2** : yielding no detectable response to stimulation — used esp. of an association area of the brain ⟨∼ cortex⟩ **3** : having no detectable function or effect ⟨∼ genes⟩ — **si·lent·ly** adv

silic- or **silico-** comb form **1** : relating to or containing silicon or its compounds ⟨silicone⟩ **2** : silicosis and ⟨silicotuberculosis⟩

sil·i·ca \'si-li-kə\ n : the dioxide of silicon SiO_2

silica gel n : colloidal silica resembling coarse white sand in appearance but possessing many fine pores and therefore extremely adsorbent

silicate cement n : a dental cement used in restorations

sil·i·con \'si-li-kən, -ˌkän\ n : a nonmetallic element that occurs combined as the most abundant element next to oxygen in the earth's crust — symbol Si; see ELEMENT table

silicon dioxide n : SILICA

sil·i·cone \'si-lə-ˌkōn\ n : any of various polymeric organic silicon compounds some of which have been used as surgical implants

sil·i·co·sis \ˌsi-lə-'kō-səs\ n, pl **-co·ses** \-ˌsēz\ : pneumoconiosis characterized by massive fibrosis of the lungs resulting in shortness of breath and caused by prolonged inhalation of silica dusts

¹sil·i·cot·ic \ˌsi-lə-'kä-tik\ adj : relating to, caused by, or affected with silicosis ⟨∼ patients⟩ ⟨∼ lungs⟩

²silicotic n : an individual affected with silicosis

sil·i·co·tu·ber·cu·lo·sis \ˌsi-li-kō-tú-ˌbər-kyə-'lō-səs, -tyū-\ n, pl **-lo·ses** \-ˌsēz\ : silicosis and tuberculosis in the same lung

silk \'silk\ n **1** : a lustrous tough elastic fiber produced by silkworms **2** : strands of silk thread of various thicknesses used as suture material in surgery ⟨surgical ∼⟩

sil·ver \'sil-vər\ n : a white metallic element that has the highest thermal and electric conductivity of any substance — symbol Ag; see ELEMENT table

silver iodide n : a compound AgI that darkens on exposure to light and is used in medicine as a local antiseptic

silver nitrate n : an irritant compound $AgNO_3$ used in medicine esp. as an antiseptic and caustic

silver protein n : any of several colloidal light-sensitive preparations of silver and protein used in aqueous solution on mucous membranes as antiseptics and classified by their efficacy and irritant properties: as **a** : a preparation containing 19 to 23 percent of silver — called also mild silver protein **b** : a more irritant preparation containing 7.5 to 8.5 percent of silver — called also strong silver protein

si·meth·i·cone \si-'me-thi-ˌkōn\ n : a liquid mixture of silicone polymers used as an antiflatulent — see MYLICON

Sim·monds' disease \'si-məndz-\ n : a disease that is characterized by extreme and progressive emaciation with atrophy of internal organs, loss of body hair, and evidences of premature aging resulting from atrophy or destruction of the anterior lobe of the pituitary gland

Simmonds, Morris (1855–1925), German physician.

¹sim·ple \'sim-pəl\ adj **sim·pler**; **simplest 1** : free from complexity or difficulty: as **a** : easily treated or cured **b** : controlled by a single gene ⟨∼ inherited characters⟩ **2** : of, relating to, or being an epithelium in which the cells are arranged in a single layer

²simple n **1** : a medicinal plant **2** : a vegetable drug having only one ingredient

simple fracture n : a bone fracture that does not form an open wound in the skin — compare COMPOUND FRACTURE

simple ointment n : WHITE OINTMENT

simple sugar n : MONOSACCHARIDE

simplex — see GENITAL HERPES SIMPLEX, HERPES SIMPLEX, PERIODONTITIS SIMPLEX

sim·u·late \'sim-yə-ˌlāt\ vb **-lat·ed**; **-lat·ing** : to have or produce a symptomatic resemblance to ⟨lesions simulating leprosy⟩ — **sim·u·la·tion** \ˌsim-yə-'lā-shən\ n

Si·mu·li·um \si-'myü-lē-əm\ n : a genus of dark-colored bloodsucking dipteran flies (family Simuliidae) of which some are vectors of onchocerciasis or of protozoan diseases of birds — see BLACKFLY

si·nal \'sin-əl\ adj : of, relating to, or coming from a sinus ⟨a ∼ discharge⟩

Sind·bis virus \'sind-bis-\ n : an RNA-containing spherical arbovirus that is transmitted by mosquitoes and is related to the virus causing western equine encephalomyelitis

Sin·e·quan \'si-nə-ˌkwan\ trademark — used for a preparation of doxepin

sin·ew \'sin-yü\ n : TENDON

single-blind adj : of, relating to, or being an experimental procedure in which while the experiment is actually in progress either the subjects or the experimenters but not both know which individuals are assigned to the test group and which to the control group — compare DOUBLE-BLIND

single bond n : a chemical bond consisting of one covalent bond between two atoms in a molecule esp. when the atoms can have more than one bond

single photon emission computed tomography n : a medical imaging technique that is used esp. for mapping brain function and that is similar to positron-emission tomography in using the photons emitted by the agency of a radioactive tracer to create an image but that differs in being able to detect only a single photon for each nuclear disintegration and in generating a lower-quality image — abbr. SPECT

sin·gle·ton \'siŋ-gəl-tən\ n : an offspring born singly 〈~s are more common than twins〉

¹si·nis·tral \'si-nəs-trəl, sə-'nis-\ adj : relating to, or inclined to the left; esp : LEFT-HANDED

²sinistral n : a person exhibiting dominance of the left hand and eye : a left-handed person

sin·is·tral·i·ty \si-nə-'stra-lə-tē\ n, pl **-ties** : the quality or state of having the left side or one or more of its parts (as the hand or eye) different from and usu. more efficient than the right or its corresponding parts; also : LEFT-HANDEDNESS

sino- also **sinu-** comb form : relating to a sinus or sinuses and 〈sinoatrial node〉

si·no·atri·al \si-nō-'ā-trē-əl\ adj : of, involving, or being the sinoatrial node

sinoatrial node n : a small mass of tissue that is made up of Purkinje fibers, ganglion cells, and nerve fibers, that is embedded in the musculature of the right atrium, and that originates the impulses stimulating the heartbeat — called also S-A node, sinus node

si·no·au·ric·u·lar \-ȯ-'ri-kyə-lər\ adj : SINOATRIAL

sin·se·mil·la \sin-sə-'mē-lə, -'mi-, -yə, -lyə\ n : highly potent marijuana from female plants that are specially tended and kept seedless by preventing pollination in order to induce a high resin content; also : a female hemp plant grown to produce sinsemilla

si·nu·atri·al \si-nyü-\ or \-nü-\ var of SINOATRIAL

si·nus \'sī-nəs\ n : a cavity or hollow in the body: as **a** : a narrow elongated tract extending from a focus of suppuration and serving for the discharge of pus 〈a tuberculous ~〉 **b** (1) : a cavity in the substance of a bone of the skull that usu. communicates with the nostrils and contains air (2) : a channel for venous blood (3) : a dilatation in a bodily canal or vessel

sinus bradycardia n : abnormally slow sinus rhythm; specif : sinus rhythm at a rate lower than 60 beats per minute

si·nus·itis \si-nə-'sī-təs, -nyə-\ n : inflammation of a sinus of the skull

sinus node n : SINOATRIAL NODE

sinus of the dura mater n : any of numerous venous channels (as the sagittal sinuses) that are situated between the two layers of the dura mater and drain blood from the brain and the bones forming the cranium and empty it into the internal jugular vein — called also dural sinus

sinus of Val·sal·va \-väl-'säl-və\ n : any one of the pouches of the aorta and pulmonary artery which are located behind the flaps of the semilunar valves and into which the blood in its regurgitation toward the heart enters and thereby closes the valves — called also aortic sinus

Valsalva, Antonio Maria (1666–1723), Italian anatomist.

si·nu·soid \'sī-nə-ˌsȯid, -nyə-\ n : a minute endothelium-lined space or passage for blood in the tissues of an organ (as the liver) — **si·nu·soi·dal** \ˌsī-nə-'sȯid-əl, -nyə-\ adj — **si·nu·soi·dal·ly** adv

si·nus·ot·o·my \ˌsī-nə-'sä-tə-mē, -nyə-\ n, pl **-mies** : surgical incision into a sinus of the skull

sinus rhythm n : the rhythm of the heart produced by impulses from the sinoatrial node

sinus tachycardia n : abnormally rapid sinus rhythm; specif : sinus rhythm at a rate greater than 100 beats per minute

si·nus ve·no·sus \ˌsī-nəs-vi-'nō-səs\ n : an enlarged pouch that adjoins the heart, is formed by the union of the large systemic veins, and is the passage through which venous blood enters the embryonic heart

sinus venosus scle·rae \-'sklē-rē\ n : CANAL OF SCHLEMM

si·pho·no·phore \sī-'fä-nə-ˌfȯr, 'sī-fə-nə-\ n : any of an order (Siphonophora) of compound free-swimming or floating oceanic coelenterates — see PORTUGUESE MAN-OF-WAR

si·re·no·me·lia \ˌsī-rə-nō-'mē-lē-ə\ n : a congenital malformation in which the lower limbs are fused

sir·up var of SYRUP

sis·ter \'sis-tər\ n, chiefly Brit : a head nurse in a hospital ward or clinic; broadly : NURSE

sister chromatid n : any of the chromatids formed by replication of one chromosome during interphase of the cell cycle esp. while they are still joined by a centromere

Sis·tru·rus \si-'strür-əs\ n : a genus of small rattlesnakes having the top of the head covered with scales

site \'sīt\ n : the place, scene, or point of something 〈~ of inflammation〉

si·tos·ter·ol \sī-'täs-tə-ˌrȯl, sə-, -ˌrōl\ n : any of several sterols that are widespread esp. in plant products (as wheat germ) and are used in the synthesis of steroid hormones

situ — see IN SITU

sit·u·a·tion·al \ˌsi-chə-'wā-shə-nəl\ adj : of, relating to, or occurring in a particular set of circumstances 〈~ impotence〉 〈~ hypertension〉

si·tus \'sī-təs\ n : the place where something exists or originates : SITE

situs in·ver·sus \-in-'vər-səs\ n : a congenital abnormality characterized by lateral transposition of the viscera (as of the heart or the liver)

sitz bath \'sits-\ n **1** : a tub in which one

bathes in a sitting posture **2** : a bath in which the hips and buttocks are immersed in hot water for the therapeutic effect of moist heat in the perineal and anal regions

six–o–six or **606** \ˌsiks-ˌō-ˈsiks\ n : ARSPHENAMINE

sixth cranial nerve n : ABDUCENS NERVE

six–year molar n : one of the first permanent molar teeth of which there are four including one on each side of the upper and lower jaws and which erupt at about six years of age — called also *sixth-year molar*; compare TWELVE-YEAR MOLAR

Sjö·gren's syndrome \ˈshœ̄-ˌgrenz-\ also **Sjögren syndrome** \-ˌgren-\ n : a chronic inflammatory autoimmune disease that affects esp. older women, that is characterized by dryness of mucous membranes esp. of the eyes and mouth and by infiltration of the affected tissues by lymphocytes, and that is often associated with rheumatoid arthritis — called also *sicca syndrome, Sjögren's disease*

Sjögren, Henrik Samuel Conrad (1899–1986), Swedish ophthalmologist.

skelet- or **skeleto-** comb form **1** : skeleton ⟨*skeletal*⟩ **2** : skeletal and ⟨*skeletomuscular*⟩

skel·e·tal \ˈske-lət-ᵊl\ adj : of, relating to, forming, attached to, or resembling a skeleton ⟨∼ structures⟩

skeletal muscle n : striated muscle that is usu. attached to the skeleton and is usu. under voluntary control

skel·e·to·mus·cu·lar \ˌske-lə-tō-ˈməs-kyə-lər\ adj : constituting, belonging to, or dependent upon the skeleton and the muscles that move it

skel·e·ton \ˈske-lət-ᵊn\ n : a usu. rigid supportive or protective structure or framework of an organism; esp : the bony or more or less cartilaginous framework supporting the soft tissues and protecting the internal organs of a vertebrate

Skene's gland \ˈskēns-\ n : PARAURETHRAL GLAND

Skene, Alexander Johnston Chalmers (1838–1900), American gynecologist.

skia·gram \ˈskī-ə-ˌgram\ n : RADIOGRAPH

skia·graph \-ˌgraf\ n : RADIOGRAPH

skilled nursing facility n : a health-care institution that meets federal criteria for Medicaid and Medicare reimbursement for nursing care including esp. the supervision of the care of every patient by a physician, the employment full-time of at least one registered nurse, the maintenance of records concerning the care and condition of every patient, the availability of nursing care 24 hours a day, the presence of facilities for storing and dispensing drugs, the implementation

of a utilization review plan, and overall financial planning including an annual operating budget and a three-year capital expenditures program

skim milk n : milk from which the cream has been taken — called also *skimmed milk*

¹**skin** \ˈskin\ n : the 2-layered covering of the body consisting of an outer ectodermal epidermis that is more or less cornified and penetrated by the openings of sweat and sebaceous glands and an inner mesodermal dermis that is composed largely of connective tissue and is richly supplied with blood vessels and nerves

²**skin** vb **skinned; skin·ning** : to cut or scrape the skin of ⟨*skinned* his knee⟩

skin graft n : a piece of skin that is taken from a donor area to replace skin in a defective or denuded area (as one that has been burned)

skinned \ˈskind\ adj : having skin esp. of a specified kind — usu. used in combination ⟨dark-*skinned*⟩

Skin·ner box \ˈski-nər-ˌbäks\ n : a laboratory apparatus in which an animal is caged for experiments in operant conditioning and which typically contains a lever that must be pressed by the animal to gain reward or avoid punishment

Skinner, Burrhus Frederic (b 1904), American psychologist.

Skin·ner·ian \ski-ˈnir-ē-ən, -ˈner-\ adj : of, relating to, or suggestive of the behavioristic theories of B. F. Skinner ⟨∼ behaviorism⟩

skin tag \-ˌtag\ n : a small soft pendulous growth on the skin esp. around the eyes or on the neck, armpits, or groin — called also *acrochordon*

skin test n : a test (as a scratch test) performed on the skin and used in detecting allergic hypersensitivity

skull \ˈskəl\ n : the skeleton of the head forming a bony case that encloses and protects the brain and chief sense organs and supports the jaws

skull·cap \ˈskəl-ˌkap\ n : the upper portion of the skull : CALVARIUM

SLE abbr systemic lupus erythematosus

sleep \ˈslēp\ n **1** : the natural periodic suspension of consciousness during which the powers of the body are restored **2** : a state resembling sleep: as **a** : DEATH 1 ⟨put a pet cat to ∼⟩ **b** : a state marked by a diminution of feeling followed by tingling ⟨his foot went to ∼⟩ — **sleep** vb — **sleep·i·ness** \ˈslē-pē-nəs\ n — **sleepy** adj

sleep apnea n : intermittent apnea occurring as a sleep disorder

sleeping pill n : a drug and esp. a barbiturate that is taken as a tablet or capsule to induce sleep — called also *sleeping tablet*

sleeping sickness n **1** : a serious disease that is prevalent in much of tropical Africa, is marked by fever, protracted lethargy, tremors, and loss of weight, is caused by either of two trypanosomes (*Trypanosoma brucei gambiense* and *T. b. rhodesiense*), and is transmitted by tsetse flies — called also *African sleeping sickness* **2** : any of various viral encephalitides or encephalomyelitides of which lethargy or somnolence is a prominent feature; *esp* : EQUINE ENCEPHALOMYELITIS

sleeping tablet *n* : SLEEPING PILL

sleep·less \'slē-pləs\ *adj* : not able to sleep : INSOMNIAC — **sleep·less·ness** *n*

sleep spindle *n* : a burst of synchronous alpha waves that occurs during light sleep

sleep·walk·er \'slēp-ˌwȯ-kər\ *n* : one who is subject to somnambulism : one who walks while sleeping — called also *somnambulist* — **sleepwalk** \-ˌwȯk\ *vb*

sleepy sickness *n*, *Brit* : ENCEPHALITIS LETHARGICA

slide \'slīd\ *n* : a flat piece of glass on which an object is mounted for microscopic examination

sliding filament hypothesis *n* : a theory in physiology holding that muscle contraction occurs when the actin filaments next to the Z line at each end of a sarcomere are drawn toward each other between the thicker myosin filaments more centrally located in the sarcomere by the projecting globular heads of myosin molecules that form temporary attachments to the actin filaments — called also *sliding filament theory;* see CROSSBRIDGE

slim disease \'slim-\ *n* : AIDS; *also* : severe wasting of the body in the later stages of AIDS

sling \'slin\ *n* : a hanging bandage suspended from the neck to support an arm or hand

slipped disk *n* : a protrusion of an intervertebral disk and its nucleus pulposus that produces pressure upon spinal nerves resulting in low-back pain and often sciatic pain

slipped tendon *n* : PEROSIS

slit lamp \'slit-ˌlamp\ *n* : a lamp for projecting a narrow beam of intense light into an eye to facilitate microscopic study (as of the conjunctiva or cornea)

¹**slough** \'sləf\ *n* : dead tissue separating from living tissue; *esp* : a mass of dead tissue separating from an ulcer

²**slough** \'sləf\ *vb* : to separate in the form of dead tissue from living tissue (dermal ~*ing*)

slow infection *n* : a degenerative disease caused by a slow virus

slow–reacting substance of anaphylaxis *n* : a mixture of three leukotrienes produced in anaphylaxis that causes contraction of smooth muscle after minutes in contrast to histamine which acts in seconds and that is prob. responsible for the bronchoconstriction occurring in anaphylaxis —

abbr. *SRS-A;* called also *slow-reacting substance*

slow–twitch \'slō-ˌtwich\ *adj* : of, relating to, or being muscle fiber that contracts slowly esp. during sustained physical activity requiring endurance — compare FAST-TWITCH

slow virus *n* : any of various viruses with a long incubation period between infection and development of the degenerative disease (as kuru or Creutzfeldt-Jakob disease) associated with it

slow wave *n* : DELTA WAVE

slow–wave sleep *n* : a state of deep dreamless sleep that occurs regularly during a normal period of sleep with intervening periods of REM sleep and that is characterized by delta waves and a low level of autonomic physiological activity — called also *NREM sleep, orthodox sleep, S sleep, synchronized sleep*

slug·gish \'slə-gish\ *adj* : markedly slow in movement, progression, or response (~ healing) — **slug·gish·ly** *adv* — **slug·gish·ness** *n*

Sm *symbol* samarium

small bowel *n* : SMALL INTESTINE

small calorie *n* : CALORIE 1a

small–cell *adj* : OAT-CELL

small intestine *n* : the part of the intestine that lies between the stomach and colon, consists of duodenum, jejunum, and ileum, secretes digestive enzymes, and is the chief site of the absorption of digested nutrients — called also *small bowel*

small·pox \'smȯl-ˌpäks\ *n* : an acute contagious febrile disease caused by a poxvirus and characterized by skin eruption with pustules, sloughing, and scar formation

small saphenous vein *n* : SAPHENOUS VEIN b

smart \'smärt\ *vb* : to cause or be the cause or seat of a sharp poignant pain; *also* : to feel or have such a pain

smear \'smir\ *n* : material spread on a surface (as of a microscopic slide); *also* : a preparation made by spreading material on a surface (a vaginal ~) — see PAP SMEAR — **smear** *vb*

smeg·ma \'smeg-mə\ *n* : the secretion of a sebaceous gland; *specif* : the cheesy sebaceous matter that collects between the glans penis and the foreskin or around the clitoris and labia minora

¹**smell** \'smel\ *vb* **smelled** \'smeld\ *or* **smelt** \'smelt\; **smell·ing** : to perceive the odor or scent of through stimuli affecting the olfactory nerves : get the odor or scent of with the nose

²**smell** *n* **1** : the property of a thing that affects the olfactory organs : ODOR **2** : the special sense concerned with the perception of odor

smell brain *n* : RHINENCEPHALON

smelling salts *n pl* : a usu. scented aromatic preparation of ammonium carbonate and ammonia water used as a stimulant and restorative

Smith fracture \'smith-\ *or* **Smith's fracture** \'smiths-\ *n* : a fracture of the lower portion of the radius with forward displacement of the lower fragment — compare COLLES' FRACTURE

   Smith, Robert William (1807–1873), British surgeon.

Smith-Pe·ter·sen nail \'smith-'pē-tər-sən-\ *n* : a metal nail used to fix the femoral head in fractures of the neck of the femur

   Smith–Petersen, Marius Nygaard (1886–1953), American orthopedic surgeon.

smog \'smäg, 'smóg\ *n* : a fog made heavier and darker by smoke and chemical fumes; *also* : a photochemical haze caused by the action of solar ultraviolet radiation on atmosphere polluted with hydrocarbons and oxides of nitrogen from automobile exhaust

smoke \'smōk\ *vb* **smoked; smok·ing** : to inhale and exhale the fumes of burning plant material and esp. tobacco; *esp* : to smoke tobacco habitually

smok·er \'smō-kər\ *n* : a person who smokes habitually

smooth \'smüth\ *adj* : forming or being a colony with a flat shiny surface usu. made up of organisms that form no chains or filaments, show characteristic internal changes, and tend toward marked increase in capsule formation and virulence — used of dissociated strains of bacteria; compare ROUGH

smooth muscle *n* : muscle tissue that lacks cross striations, that is made up of elongated spindle-shaped cells having a central nucleus, and that is found in vertebrate visceral structures (as the stomach and bladder) as thin sheets performing functions not subject to conscious control by the mind and in all or most of the musculature of invertebrates other than arthropods — called also *nonstriated muscle, unstriated muscle;* compare CARDIAC MUSCLE, STRIATED MUSCLE

Sn *symbol* tin

snail \'snāl\ *n* : any of various gastropod mollusks and esp. those having an external enclosing spiral shell including some which are important in medicine as intermediate hosts of trematodes

snail fever *n* : SCHISTOSOMIASIS

snake \'snāk\ *n* : any of numerous limbless scaled reptiles (suborder Serpentes syn. Ophidia) with a long tapering body and with salivary glands often modified to produce venom which is injected through grooved or tubular fangs

snake·bite \-ˌbīt\ *n* : the bite of a snake; *also* : the condition of having been

bitten by a venomous snake characterized by stinging pain in the puncture wound, constitutional symptoms, and injury to blood or nerve tissue

snare \'snar\ *n* : a surgical instrument consisting usu. of a wire loop constricted by a mechanism in the handle and used for removing tissue masses (as tonsils or polyps)

sneeze \'snēz\ *vb* **sneezed; sneez·ing** : to make a sudden violent spasmodic audible expiration of breath through the nose and mouth esp. as a reflex act following irritation of the nasal mucous membrane — **sneeze** *n*

Snel·len chart \'sne-lən-\ *n* : the chart used in the Snellen test with black letters of various sizes against a white background

   Snellen, Hermann (1834–1908), Dutch ophthalmologist.

Snellen test *n* : a test for visual acuity presenting letters of graduated sizes to determine the smallest size that can be read at a standard distance

SNF *abbr* skilled nursing facility

snif·fles \'sni-fəlz\ *n pl* 1 : a head cold marked by nasal discharge (a case of the ~) 2 : BULLNOSE — usu. used with a sing. verb

snore \'snȯr\ *vb* **snored; snor·ing** : to breathe during sleep with a rough hoarse noise due to vibration of the soft palate — **snore** *n* — **snor·er** *n*

snort \'snȯrt\ *vb* : to inhale (a narcotic drug in powdered form) through the nostrils (~ cocaine)

snow \'snō\ *n, slang* 1 : COCAINE 2 : HEROIN

snow blindness *n* : inflammation and photophobia caused by exposure of the eyes to ultraviolet rays reflected from snow or ice — **snow–blind** \-ˌblīnd\ *or* **snow–blind·ed** \-ˌblīn-dəd\ *adj*

snuff \'snəf\ *n* : a preparation of pulverized tobacco to be inhaled through the nostrils, chewed, or placed against the gums; *also* : a preparation of a powdered drug to be inhaled through the nostrils

snuf·fles \'snə-fəlz\ *n pl* 1 : SNIFFLES 1 2 : a respiratory disorder (as bullnose) in animals marked esp. by catarrhal inflammation and sniffling — usu. used with a sing. verb

soak \'sōk\ *n* : an often hot medicated solution with which a body part is soaked usu. long or repeatedly esp. to promote healing, relieve pain, or stimulate local circulation

soap \'sōp\ *n* 1 : a cleansing and emulsifying agent made usu. by action of alkali on fat or fatty acids and consisting essentially of sodium or potassium salts of such acids 2 : a salt of a fatty acid and a metal

SOB *abbr* short of breath

so·cial \'sō-shəl\ *adj* 1 : tending to form cooperative and interdependent relationships with others of one's kind **2** : of or relating to human society, the interaction of the individual and the group, or the welfare of human beings as members of society ⟨immature ~ behavior⟩ — **so·cial·ly** *adv*

social disease *n* **1** : VENEREAL DISEASE **2** : a disease (as tuberculosis) whose incidence is directly related to social and economic factors

so·cial·i·za·tion \ˌsō-shə-lə-ˈzā-shən\ *n* : the process by which a human being beginning at infancy acquires the habits, beliefs, and accumulated knowledge of society through education and training for adult status — **so·cial·ize** \ˈsō-shə-ˌlīz\ *vb*

socialized medicine *n* : medical and hospital services for the members of a class or population administered by an organized group (as a state agency) and paid for from funds obtained usu. by assessments, philanthropy, or taxation

social psychiatry *n* **1** : a branch of psychiatry that deals in collaboration with related specialties (as sociology and anthropology) with the influence of social and cultural factors on the causation, course, and outcome of mental illness **2** : the application of psychodynamic principles to the solution of social problems

social psychology *n* : the study of the manner in which the personality, attitudes, motivations, and behavior of the individual is influenced by social groups — **social psychologist** *n*

social recovery *n* : an improvement in a psychiatric patient's clinical status that is not a total recovery but is sufficient to permit the patient's return to his or her former social milieu

social work *n* : any of various professional services, activities, or methods concretely concerned with the investigation, treatment, and material aid of the economically underprivileged and socially maladjusted — **social worker** *n*

socio- *comb form* **1** : society : social ⟨*sociopath*⟩ **2** : social and ⟨*sociopsychological*⟩

so·cio·cul·tur·al \ˌsō-sē-ō-ˈkəl-chə-rəl, ˌsō-shē-\ *adj* : of, relating to, or involving a combination of social and cultural factors — **so·cio·cul·tur·al·ly** *adv*

so·ci·ol·o·gy \ˌsō-sē-ˈä-lə-jē, ˌsō-shē-\ *n, pl* **-gies** : the science of society, social institutions, and social relationships; *specif* : the systematic study of the development, structure, interaction, and collective behavior of organized groups of human beings — **so·cio·log·i·cal** \ˌsō-sē-ə-ˈlä-ji-kəl, ˌsō-shē-ə-\ *also* **so·cio·log·ic** \-jik\ *adj* — **so·cio·log·i·cal·ly** *adv* — **so·ci·ol·o·gist** \ˌsō-sē-ˈä-lə-jist, ˌsō-shē-\ *n*

so·cio·med·i·cal \ˌsō-sē-ō-ˈme-di-kəl, ˌsō-shē-\ *adj* : of or relating to the interrelations of medicine and social welfare

so·cio·path \ˈsō-sē-ə-ˌpath, ˈsō-shē-ə-\ *n* : a sociopathic person : PSYCHOPATH

so·cio·path·ic \ˌsō-sē-ə-ˈpa-thik, ˌsō-shē-ə-\ *adj* : of, relating to, or characterized by antisocial behavior or a psychopathic personality — **so·ci·op·a·thy** \ˌsō-sē-ˈä-pə-thē, ˌsō-shē-\ *n*

so·cio·psy·cho·log·i·cal \ˌsō-sē-ō-ˌsī-kə-ˈlä-ji-kəl, ˌsō-shē-\ *adj* **1** : of, relating to, or involving a combination of social and psychological factors **2** : of or relating to social psychology

so·cio·sex·u·al \-ˈsek-shə-wəl\ *adj* : of or relating to the interpersonal aspects of sexuality

sock·et \ˈsä-kət\ *n* : an opening or hollow that forms a holder for something: as **a** : any of various hollows in body structures in which some other part normally lodges ⟨the bony ~ of the eye⟩ ⟨an inflamed tooth ~⟩; *esp* : the depression in a bone with which the rounded head of another bone fits in a ball-and-socket joint **b** : a cavity terminating an artificial limb into which the bodily stump fits

so·da \ˈsō-də\ *n* **1** : any of several compounds containing sodium; *esp* : SODIUM BICARBONATE **2** : SODIUM ⟨~ alum⟩

soda lime *n* : a granular mixture of calcium hydroxide with sodium hydroxide or potassium hydroxide or both that is used to absorb moisture and acid gases and esp. carbon dioxide (as in gas masks and in oxygen therapy)

sod disease \ˈsäd-\ *n* : VESICULAR DERMATITIS

so·di·um \ˈsō-dē-əm\ *n* : a silver white soft waxy ductile element — symbol *Na*; see ELEMENT table

sodium ascorbate *n* : the sodium salt $C_6H_7NaO_6$ of vitamin C

sodium benzoate *n* : a crystalline or granular salt $C_7H_5O_2Na$ used chiefly as a food preservative

sodium bicarbonate *n* : a white crystalline weakly alkaline salt $NaHCO_3$ used in medicine esp. as an antacid — called also *baking soda, bicarb, bicarbonate of soda*

sodium bromide *n* : a crystalline salt $NaBr$ having a biting saline taste that is used in medicine as a sedative, hypnotic, and anticonvulsant

sodium caprylate *n* : the sodium salt $C_8H_{15}O_2Na$ of caprylic acid used esp. in the topical treatment of fungal infections

sodium carbonate *n* : any of several salts (as Na_2CO_3) of carbonic acid

sodium chloride *n* : SALT 1a

sodium citrate *n* : a crystalline salt $C_6H_5Na_3O_7$ used chiefly as an expectorant, a systemic and urinary alkalizer, a chelating agent to increase urinary excretion of calcium in hypercalcemia and lead in lead poisoning, and in combination as an anticoagulant (as in stored blood)

sodium cro·mo·gly·cate \-ˌkrō-mō-ˈglī-ˌkāt\ *n* : CROMOLYN SODIUM

sodium di·hy·dro·gen phosphate \-ˌdī-ˈhī-drə-jən-\ *n* : SODIUM PHOSPHATE 1

sodium fluoride *n* : a poisonous crystalline salt NaF that is used in trace amounts in the fluoridation of water, as an antiseptic, and as a pesticide — see LURIDE

sodium glutamate *n* : MONOSODIUM GLUTAMATE

sodium hydroxide *n* : a white brittle solid NaOH that dissolves readily in water to form a strongly alkaline and caustic solution and that is used in pharmacy as an alkalizing agent

sodium hypochlorite *n* : an unstable salt NaOCl produced usu. in aqueous solution and used as a bleaching and disinfecting agent

sodium iodide *n* : a crystalline salt NaI used as an iodine supplement and expectorant

sodium io·do·hip·pu·rate \-ˌī-ˌō-dō-ˈhi-pyə-ˌrāt\ *n* : HIPPURAN

sodium lactate *n* : a hygroscopic syrupy salt $C_3H_5NaO_3$ used chiefly as an antacid in medicine and as a substitute for glycerol

sodium lau·ryl sulfate \-ˌlȯ-ril-\ *n* : a crystalline sodium salt $C_{12}H_{25}$NaO₄S; *also* : a mixture of sulfates of sodium consisting principally of this salt and used as a detergent, wetting, and emulsifying agent (as in toothpastes, ointments, and shampoos)

sodium mor·rhu·ate \-ˈmȯr-ü-ˌāt\ *n* : a pale yellow granular salt administered in solution intravenously as a sclerosing agent esp. in the treatment of varicose veins

sodium nitrate *n* : a crystalline salt NaNO₃ used in curing meat — called also *saltpeter*

sodium nitrite *n* : a colorless or yellowish salt NaNO₂ that is used as a meat preservative and in medicine as a vasodilator and an antidote for cyanide poisoning

sodium ni·tro·prus·side \-ˌnī-trō-ˈprə-ˌsid\ *n* : a red crystalline salt C_5Fe-N_6Na_2O administered intravenously as a vasodilator esp. in hypertensive emergencies — see NIPRIDE

sodium pentobarbital *n* : the sodium salt of pentobarbital

sodium pentobarbitone *n, Brit* : SODIUM PENTOBARBITAL

sodium per·bor·ate \-pər-ˈbȯr-ˌāt\ *n* : a white crystalline powder NaBO₃·4H₂O used as an oral antiseptic

sodium phosphate *n* 1 : a phosphate NaH₂PO₄ of sodium containing one sodium atom per molecule that with the phosphate containing two sodium atoms per molecule constitutes the principal buffer system of the urine — called also *sodium dihydrogen phosphate* 2 : a phosphate Na₂HPO₄ of sodium containing two sodium atoms per molecule that is used in medicine as a laxative and antacid

sodium potassium tartrate *n* : RO-CHELLE SALT

sodium pump *n* : a molecular mechanism by which sodium ions are actively transported across a cell membrane; *esp* : the one by which the appropriate internal and external concentrations of sodium and potassium ions are maintained in a nerve fiber and which involves the active transport of sodium ions outward with movement of potassium ions to the interior

sodium salicylate *n* : a crystalline salt $NaC_7H_5O_3$ that has a sweetish saline taste and is used chiefly as an analgesic, antipyretic, and antirheumatic

sodium secobarbital *n* : the sodium salt $C_{12}H_{17}N_2NaO_3$ of secobarbital

sodium stearate *n* : a white powdery water-soluble salt $C_{18}H_{35}NaO_2$ used esp. in glycerin suppositories, cosmetics, and some toothpastes

sodium sulfate *n* : a bitter salt Na₂SO₄ used in its hydrated form as a cathartic — see GLAUBER'S SALT

sodium thiosulfate *n* : a hygroscopic crystalline salt $Na_2O_3S_2$ used in medicine as an antidote in poisoning by cyanides or iodine, in the treatment of tinea versicolor, and to prevent ringworm (as in a football)

sodium valproate *n* : the sodium salt $C_8H_{15}NaO_2$ of valproic acid used as an anticonvulsant

so·do·ku \ˈsō-də-ˌkü\ *n* : RAT-BITE FEVER b

sod·om·ist \ˈsä-də-mist\ *n* : SODOMITE

sod·om·ite \-ˌmit\ *n* : one who practices sodomy

sod·omy \ˈsä-də-mē\ *n, pl* **-om·ies** 1 : copulation with a member of the same sex or with an animal 2 : noncoital and esp. anal or oral copulation with a member of the opposite sex — **sod·om·it·ic** \ˌsä-də-ˈmi-tik\ *or* **sod·om·it·i·cal** \-ti-kəl\ *adj* — **sod·om·ize** \ˈsä-də-ˌmīz\ *vb*

soft \ˈsȯft\ *adj* 1 : yielding to physical pressure 2 : deficient in or free from substances (as calcium and magnesium salts) that prevent lathering of soap (~ water) 3 : having relatively low energy (~ X rays) 4 : BIODEGRADABLE 5 *of a drug* : considered less detrimental than a hard narcotic (marijuana is usually regarded as a ~ drug) 6 : being or based on interpretive or speculative data (~ evidence)

soft chancre *n* : CHANCROID

soft contact lens *n* : a contact lens made of soft water-absorbing plastic that adheres closely and with minimal discomfort to the eye

soft lens *n* : SOFT CONTACT LENS

soft palate *n* : the membranous and

muscular fold suspended from the posterior margin of the hard palate and partially separating the mouth cavity from the pharynx

soft spot n : a fontanel of a fetal or young skull

sol \'säl, 'sól\ n : a fluid colloidal system; *esp* : one in which the dispersion medium is a liquid

so·la·nine *or* **so·la·nin** \'sō-lə-ˌnēn, -nən\ n : a bitter poisonous crystalline alkaloid $C_{45}H_{72}NO_{15}$ from several plants (as some potatoes or tomatoes) of the nightshade family (Solanaceae)

so·la·num \sə-'lā-nəm, -'lä-, -'la-\ n 1 *cap* : a genus of chiefly herbs and shrubs of the nightshade family (Solanaceae) that have often prickly-veined leaves, white, purple, or yellow flowers, and a fruit that is a berry 2 : any plant of the genus *Solanum*

so·lar·i·um \sō-'lar-ē-əm, sə-\ n, pl **-ia** \-ē-ə\ *also* **-ums** : a room (as in a hospital) used esp. for sunbathing or therapeutic exposure to light

solar plex·us \-'sō-lər-'plek-səs\ n 1 : CELIAC PLEXUS 2 : the part of the abdomen including the stomach and celiac plexus that is particularly vulnerable to the effects of a blow to the body wall in front of it — not used technically

soldier's heart n : NEUROCIRCULATORY ASTHENIA

sole \'sōl\ n : the undersurface of a foot

So·le·nop·sis \ˌsō-lə-'näp-səs\ n : a genus of small stinging ants including several tropical and subtropical forms (as the imported fire ants)

so·le·us \'sō-lē-əs\ n, pl **so·lei** \-lē-ˌī\ *also* **soleuses** : a broad flat muscle of the calf of the leg that lies deep to the gastrocnemius, arises from the back and upper part of the tibia and fibula and from a tendinous arch between them, inserts by a tendon that unites with that of the gastrocnemius to form the Achilles tendon, and acts to flex the foot

¹**sol·id** \'sä-ləd\ adj 1 : not hollow : being without an internal cavity ⟨~ tumors⟩ 2 : neither gaseous nor liquid

²**solid** n 1 : a substance that does not flow perceptibly under moderate stress 2 : the part of a solution or suspension that when freed from solvent or suspending medium has the qualities of a solid — usu. used in pl. ⟨milk ~s⟩

solitarius — see TRACTUS SOLITARIUS

sol·i·tary \'sä-lə-ˌter-ē\ adj : occurring singly and not as part of a group ⟨a ~ lesion⟩

sol·u·bil·i·ty \ˌsäl-yə-'bi-lə-tē\ n, pl **-ties** 1 : the quality or state of being soluble 2 : the amount of a substance that will dissolve in a given amount of another substance

sol·u·ble \'säl-yə-bəl\ adj 1 : susceptible of being dissolved in or as if in a fluid 2 : capable of being emulsified

soluble RNA n : TRANSFER RNA

sol·ute \'säl-ˌyüt\ n : a dissolved substance; *esp* : a component of a solution present in smaller amount than the solvent

so·lu·tion \sə-'lü-shən\ n 1 **a** : an act or the process by which a solid, liquid, or gaseous substance is homogeneously mixed with a liquid or sometimes a gas or solid **b** : a homogeneous mixture formed by this process 2 **a** : a liquid containing a dissolved substance ⟨an aqueous ~⟩ **b** : a liquid and usu. aqueous medicinal preparation with the solid ingredients soluble **c** : the condition of being dissolved ⟨a substance in ~⟩

¹**sol·vent** \'säl-vənt, 'sòl-\ adj : that dissolves or can dissolve ⟨~ fluids⟩ ⟨~ action of water⟩

²**solvent** n : a substance capable of or used in dissolving or dispersing one or more other substances; *esp* : a liquid component of a solution present in greater amount than the solute

so·ma \'sō-mə\ n, pl **so·ma·ta** \'sō-mə-tə\ *or* **somas** 1 : the body of an organism 2 : all of an organism except the germ cells 3 : CELL BODY

som·aes·thet·ic *chiefly Brit var of* SOMESTHETIC

somat- *or* **somato-** *comb form* 1 : body ⟨*somato*sensory⟩ 2 : somatic and ⟨*somato*psychic⟩

so·mat·ic \sō-'ma-tik, sə-\ adj 1 **a** : of, relating to, or affecting the body esp. as distinguished from the germ plasm or psyche : PHYSICAL **b** : of, relating to, supplying, or involving skeletal muscles ⟨~ nervous system⟩ **c** : of or relating to the wall of the body as distinguished from the viscera : PARIETAL — **so·mat·i·cal·ly** adv

somatic cell n : any of the cells of the body that compose the tissues, organs, and parts of that individual other than the germ cells

somatic mutation n : a mutation occurring in a somatic cell

so·ma·ti·za·tion disorder \ˌsō-mə-tə-'zā-shən-\ n : a somatoform disorder characterized by multiple and recurring physical complaints for which the patient has sought medical treatment over several years without any organic or physiological basis for the symptoms being found

so·ma·to·form \'sō-mə-tə-ˌfòrm, sə-'ma-tə-\ adj : relating to or being any of a group of psychological disorders or symptoms involving physical complaints for which no organic or physiological explanation is found and for which there is a strong likelihood that psychological factors are involved ⟨~ pain disorder⟩

so·ma·to·me·din \ˌsō-ˌma-tə-'mēd-ᵊn, ˌsō-mə-tə-\ n : any of several endogenous peptides produced esp. in the liver that are dependent on and prob. mediate growth hormone activity (as

in sulfate uptake by epiphyseal cartilage)

so·ma·to·plasm \sō-'ma-tə-ˌpla-zəm,
'sō-mət-ə-\ n 1 : protoplasm of somatic cells as distinguished from that of
germ cells 2 : somatic cells as distinguished from germ cells

so·ma·to·pleure \sō-'ma-tə-ˌplúr, 'sō-
mə-tə-\ n : a complex fold of tissue in
the embryo consisting of an outer layer of mesoderm together with the ectoderm that sheathes it and giving
rise to the amnion and chorion —
compare SPLANCHNOPLEURE

so·ma·to·psy·chic \ˌsō-ˌma-tə-'sī-kik,
ˌsō-mə-tə-\ adj : of or relating to the
body and the mind

so·ma·to·sen·so·ry \ˌsō-ˌma-tə-'sens-ə-
rē, ˌsō-mə-tə-\ adj : of, relating to, or
being sensory activity having its origin elsewhere than in the special
sense organs (as eyes and ears) and
conveying information about the
state of the body proper and its immediate environment (~ pathways)

so·ma·to·stat·in \ˌsō-mə-tə-'stat-ən\ n
: a polypeptide neurohormone that is
found esp. in the hypothalamus, is
composed of a chain of 14 amino-acid
residues, and inhibits the secretion of
several other hormones (as growth
hormone, insulin, and gastrin)

so·ma·to·ther·a·py \ˌsō-mə-tə-'ther-ə-
pē, sō-ˌma-tə-\ n, pl -pies : therapy for
psychological problems that uses
physiological intervention (as by
drugs or surgery) to modify behavior
— **so·ma·to·ther·a·peu·tic** \-ˌther-ə-
'pyü-tik\ adj

so·ma·to·top·ic \-'tä-pik\ adj : of, relating to, or mediating the orderly and
specific relation between particular
body regions (as a hand or the tongue)
and corresponding motor areas of the
brain — **so·ma·to·top·i·cal·ly** adv

so·ma·to·troph·ic \-'trō-fik\, **so·ma·to·
troph·in** \-'trō-fən\ var of SOMATO-
TROPIC, SOMATOTROPIN

so·ma·to·trop·ic \-'trō-pik, -'trä-\ adj
: promoting growth (~ activity)

somatotropic hormone n : GROWTH HOR-
MONE

so·ma·to·tro·pin \-'trō-pən\ n : GROWTH
HORMONE

so·ma·to·type \'sō-mə-tə-ˌtīp, sō-'ma-
tə-\ n : a body type or physique esp.
in a system of classification based on
the relative development of ectomorphic, endomorphic, and mesomorphic components — **somatotype** vb

-some \ˌsōm\ n comb form 1 : body
(chromosome) 2 : chromosome
(monosome)

som·es·thet·ic \ˌsō-mes-'the-tik\ adj
: of, relating to, or concerned with
bodily sensations (a ~ area of the
brain)

-so·mia \'sō-mē-ə\ n comb form : condition of having (such) a body (mi-
crosomia)

-som·ic \ˌsō-mik\ adj comb form : hav-

ing or being a chromosome complement of which one or more but not all
chromosomes or genomes exhibit
(such) a degree of reduplication
(monosomic)

so·mite \'sō-ˌmīt\ n : one of the longitudinal series of segments into which
the body of many animals is divided
: METAMERE

somnambul- comb form : somnambulism : somnambulist (somnambulant)

som·nam·bu·lant \säm-'nam-byə-lənt\
adj : walking or addicted to walking
while asleep

som·nam·bu·late \-ˌlāt\ vb -lat·ed; -lat-
ing : to walk while asleep — **som·
nam·bu·la·tion** \-ˌnam-byə-'lā-shən\ n

som·nam·bu·lism \säm-'nam-byə-ˌli-
zəm\ n 1 : an abnormal condition of
sleep in which motor acts (as walking) are performed 2 : actions characteristic of somnambulism — **som·
nam·bu·lis·tic** \-ˌnam-byə-'lis-tik\ adj

som·nam·bu·list \säm-'nam-byə-list\ n
: SLEEPWALKER

somni- comb form : sleep (somnifacient)

som·ni·fa·cient \ˌsäm-nə-'fā-shənt\ adj
: inducing sleep : HYPNOTIC (a ~
drug)

²somnifacient n : a somnifacient agent
(as a drug) : HYPNOTIC 1

som·nif·er·ous \säm-'ni-fə-rəs\ adj
: SOPORIFIC

som·no·lence \säm-nə-ləns\ n : the
quality or state of being drowsy —
som·no·lent \-lənt\ adj

son- or **sono-** comb form : sound
(sonogram)

sono·gram \'sä-nə-ˌgram\ n : an image
produced by ultrasound

so·nog·ra·pher \sō-'nä-grə-fər\ n : a
person trained in the use of ultrasound

so·nog·ra·phy \sō-'nä-grə-fē\ n, pl
-phies : ULTRASOUND 2 — **sono·graph·
ic** \ˌsä-nə-'gra-fik\ adj

so·po·rif·er·ous \ˌsä-pə-'ri-fə-rəs, ˌsō-\
adj : SOPORIFIC

¹so·po·rif·ic \-'ri-fik\ adj : causing or
tending to cause sleep

²soporific n : a soporific agent (as a
drug)

sorb \'sórb\ vb : to take up and hold by
either adsorption or absorption

sor·bic acid \'sór-bik-\ n : a crystalline
acid $C_6H_8O_2$ obtained from the un-
ripe fruits of the mountain ash (genus
Sorbus) or synthesized and used esp.
as a fungicide and food preservative

sor·bi·tol \'sór-bə-ˌtól, -ˌtōl\ n : a faintly sweet alcohol $C_6H_{14}O_6$ that occurs
esp. in fruits of the mountain ash (genus Sorbus), is made synthetically,
and is used esp. as a humectant, a
softener, and a sweetener and in making ascorbic acid

sor·des \'sór-(ˌ)dēz\ n, pl **sordes** : the
crusts that collect on the teeth and
lips in debilitating diseases with protracted low fever

¹sore \'sōr\ adj sor·er; sor·est : causing, characterized by, or affected with pain : PAINFUL (~ muscles) (a ~ wound) — sore·ly adv — sore·ness n

²sore n : a localized sore spot on the body; esp : one (as an ulcer) with the tissues ruptured or abraded and usu. with infection

sore mouth n 1 : a highly contagious disease of sheep and goats that is caused by a poxvirus, occurs esp. in young animals, and is characterized by extensive vesiculation and subsequent ulceration about the lips, gums, and tongue — called also scabby mouth 2 : necrobacillosis affecting the mouth: esp : CALF DIPHTHERIA

sore·muz·zle \-ˌməz-ᵊl\ n : BLUETONGUE

sore throat n : painful throat due to inflammation of the fauces and pharynx

SOS abbr [Latin si opus sit] if occasion require; if necessary — used in writing prescriptions

so·ta·lol \'sō-tə-ˌlȯl, -ˌlōl\ n : a beta=adrenergic blocking agent $C_{12}H_{20}$ N_2O_3S administered in the form of its hydrochloride to treat ventricular arrhythmias

souf·fle \'sü-fəl\ n : a blowing sound heard on auscultation (the uterine ~ heard in pregnancy)

¹sound \'saúnd\ adj 1 : free from injury or disease : exhibiting normal health 2 : deep and undisturbed (a ~ sleep) — sound·ness n

²sound n 1 : a particular auditory impression (heart ~s heard by auscultation) 2 : the sensation perceived by the sense of hearing 3 : mechanical radiant energy that is transmitted by waves of pressure in a material medium (as air) and is the objective cause of hearing

³sound vb : to explore or examine (a body cavity) with a sound

⁴sound n : an elongated instrument for exploring or examining body cavities (a uterine ~)

sound pollution n : NOISE POLLUTION

sound wave n 1 : SOUND 1 2 pl : waves of pressure esp. when transmitting audible sound

sour \'saúr\ adj : causing, characterized by, or being the one of the four basic taste sensations that is produced chiefly by acids — compare BITTER, SALT, SWEET — sour·ness n

South American blastomycosis n : blastomycosis caused by a fungus of the genus Paracoccidioides (P. brasiliensis syn. Blastomyces brasiliensis) and characterized by formation of ulcers on the mucosal surfaces of the mouth that spread to lips, nose, and cheeks, by great enlargement of lymph nodes esp. of the throat and chest, and by involvement of the gastrointestinal tract — called also paracoccidioidomycosis

South·ern blot \'sə-thərn-\ n : a blot consisting of a sheet of a cellulose derivative that contains spots of DNA for identification by a suitable molecular probe — compare NORTHERN BLOT, WESTERN BLOT — Southern blotting n

Southern, Edwin M. (fl 20th century), British biologist.

spa \'spä, 'spȯ\ n 1 a : a mineral spring b : a resort with mineral springs 2 : a commercial establishment with facilities for exercising and bathing: esp : HEALTH SPA

space maintainer n : a temporary orthodontic appliance used following the loss or extraction of a tooth (as a milk tooth) to prevent the shifting of adjacent teeth into the resulting space — called also space retainer

space medicine n : a branch of medicine concerned with the physiological and biological effects on the human body of spaceflight

space perception n : the perception of the properties and relationships of objects in space esp. with respect to direction, size, distance, and orientation

spac·er \'spä-sər\ n : a region of chromosomal DNA between genes that is not transcribed into messenger RNA and is of uncertain function

space retainer n : SPACE MAINTAINER

space sickness n : sickness and esp. nausea and dizziness that occurs under the conditions of sustained spaceflight — space·sick \'späs-ˌsik\ adj

Spanish fly n : a green beetle (Lytta vesicatoria of the family Meloidae) of southern Europe that is the source of cantharides 2 : CANTHARIS 2

Spanish influenza n : pandemic influenza; specif : an outbreak of pandemic influenza which occurred in 1918

spar·ga·no·sis \ˌspär-gə-'nō-səs\ n, pl -no·ses \-ˌsēz\ : the condition of being infected with spargana

spar·ga·num \'spär-gə-nəm\ n, pl -na \-nä\ also -nums : an intramuscular or subcutaneous vermiform parasite that is the larva of the fish tapeworm (Diphyllobothrium latum) or of a related tapeworm

Spar·ine \'spär-ˌēn\ trademark — used for a preparation of promazine

spar·te·ine \'spär-tē-ən, 'spär-ˌtēn\ n : a liquid alkaloid $C_{15}H_{26}N_2$ used in medicine in the form of its sulfate esp. as an oxytocic drug

spasm \'spa-zəm\ n 1 : an involuntary and abnormal contraction of muscle or muscle fibers or of a hollow organ (as the esophagus) that consists largely of involuntary muscle fibers 2 : the state or condition of a muscle or organ affected with spasms — spas·mod·ic \spaz-'mä-dik\ adj — spas·mod·i·cal·ly adv

spasmodic dysmenorrhea n : dysmenorrhea associated with painful contractions of the uterus

spas·mo·gen·ic \ˌspaz-mə-ˈje-nik\ *adj* : inducing spasm ⟨a ~ drug⟩

¹**spas·mo·lyt·ic** \ˌspaz-mə-ˈli-tik\ *adj* : tending or having the power to relieve spasms or convulsions ⟨~ drugs⟩

²**spasmolytic** *n* : a spasmolytic agent

spas·mo·phil·ia \ˌspaz-mə-ˈfi-lē-ə\ *n* : an abnormal tendency to convulsions, tetany, or spasms from even slight mechanical or electrical stimulation ⟨~ associated with rickets⟩

¹**spas·tic** \ˈspas-tik\ *adj* : of, relating to, or affected with spasm ⟨a ~ colon⟩ ⟨a ~ patient⟩ — **spas·ti·cal·ly** *adv*

²**spastic** *n* : an individual affected with spastic paralysis

spastic colon *n* : IRRITABLE BOWEL SYNDROME

spas·tic·i·ty \spa-ˈsti-sə-tē\ *n, pl* **-ties** : a spastic state or condition; *esp* : muscular hypertonicity with increased tendon reflexes

spastic paralysis *n* : paralysis with tonic spasm of the affected muscles and with increased tendon reflexes

spat *past and past part of* SPIT

spatial summation *n* : sensory summation that involves stimulation of several spatially separated neurons at the same time

spat·u·la \ˈspa-chə-lə\ *n* : a flat thin instrument used for spreading or mixing soft substances, scooping, lifting, or scraping

spav·in \ˈspa-vən\ *n* : a bony enlargement of the hock of a horse associated with strain — **spav·ined** \-vənd\ *adj*

spay \ˈspā\ *vb* **spayed; spay·ing** : to remove the ovaries of a (female animal)

SPCA *abbr* Society for the Prevention of Cruelty to Animals

spe·cial·ist \ˈspe-shə-list\ *n* : a medical practitioner whose practice is limited to a particular class of patients (as children) or of diseases (as skin diseases) or of technique (as surgery); *esp* : a physician who is qualified by advanced training and certification by a specialty examining board to so limit his or her practice

special sense *n* : any of the senses of sight, hearing, equilibrium, smell, taste, or touch

spe·cial·ty \ˈspe-shəl-tē\ *n, pl* **-ties** : something (as a branch of medicine) in which one specializes

spe·cies \ˈspē-(ˌ)shēz, -(ˌ)sēz\ *n, pl* **species** 1 a : a category of biological classification ranking immediately below the genus or subgenus, comprising related organisms or populations potentially capable of interbreeding, and being designated by a binomial that consists of the name of the genus followed by an uncapitalized noun or adjective that is Latin or has a Latin form and agrees grammatically with the genus name b : an individual or kind belonging to a biological species 2 : a particular kind of atomic nucleus, atom, molecule, or ion ⟨a ~ of RNA⟩

¹**spe·cif·ic** \spi-ˈsi-fik\ *adj* 1 a : restricted by nature to a particular individual, situation, relation, or effect b : exerting a distinctive influence (as on a body part or a disease) ⟨~ antibodies⟩ 2 : of, relating to, or constituting a species and esp. a biological species

²**specific** *n* : a drug or remedy having a specific mitigating effect on a disease

specific epithet *n* : a noun or adjective that is Latin or has a Latin form and follows the genus name in a taxonomic binomial

specific gravity *n* : the ratio of the density of a substance to the density of some substance (as pure water or hydrogen) taken as a standard when both densities are obtained by weighing in air

spec·i·fic·i·ty \ˌspes-ə-ˈfi-sə-tē\ *n, pl* **-ties** : the quality or condition of being specific: as a : the condition of being peculiar to a particular individual or group of organisms ⟨host ~ of a parasite⟩ b : the condition of participating in or catalyzing only one or a few chemical reactions ⟨enzyme ~⟩

spec·i·men \ˈspe-sə-mən\ *n* 1 : an individual, item, or part typical of a group, class, or whole 2 : a portion or quantity of material for use in testing, examination, or study ⟨a urine ~⟩

SPECT *abbr* single photon emission computed tomography

spec·ta·cles \ˈspek-ti-kəlz\ *n pl* : GLASSES

spec·ti·no·my·cin \ˌspek-tə-nō-ˈmīs-ᵊn\ *n* : a white crystalline broad-spectrum antibiotic $C_{14}H_{24}N_2O_7$ extracted from a bacterium of the genus *Streptomyces* (*S. spectabilis*) and used clinically esp. in the form of its hydrochloride to treat gonorrhea — called also *actinospectacin*; see TROBICIN

spec·tral \ˈspek-trəl\ *adj* : of, relating to, or made by a spectrum

spec·trin \ˈspek-trən\ *n* : a large cytoskeletal protein that is found on the inner cell membrane of red blood cells and that functions esp. in maintaining cell shape

spec·trom·e·ter \spek-ˈträ-mə-tər\ *n* 1 : an instrument used in determining the index of refraction of a transparent solid in the form of a prism 2 : a spectroscope fitted for measurements of the spectra observed with it — **spec·tro·met·ric** \ˌspek-trə-ˈme-trik\ *adj* — **spec·trom·e·try** \spek-ˈträ-mə-trē\ *n*

spec·tro·pho·tom·e·ter \ˌspek-trō-fə-ˈtä-mə-tər\ *n* : a photometer for measuring the relative intensities of the light in different parts of a spectrum — **spec·tro·pho·to·met·ric** \-trə-ˌfō-tə-ˈme-trik\ *adj* — **spec·tro·pho·to·met·ri·cal·ly** *adv* — **spec·tro·pho·tom·e·try** \ˌspek-(ˌ)trō-fə-ˈtä-mə-trē\ *n*

spec·tro·scope \'spek-trə-ˌskōp\ *n* : an instrument for forming and examining optical spectra — **spec·tro·scop·ic** \ˌspek-trə-'skä-pik\ *adj* — **spec·tro·scop·i·cal·ly** *adv* — **spec·tros·co·pist** \spek-'träs-kə-pist\ *n* — **spec·tros·co·py** \spek-'träs-kə-pē\ *n*

spec·trum \'spek-trəm\ *n, pl* **spec·tra** \-trə\ *or* **spectrums 1** : an array of the components of an emission or wave separated and arranged in the order of some varying characteristic (as wavelength, mass, or energy) **2** : a continuous sequence or range; *specif* : a range of effectiveness against pathogenic organisms (an antibiotic with a broad ~)

spec·u·lum \'spe-kyə-ləm\ *n, pl* **-la** \-lə\ *also* **-lums** : any of various instruments for insertion into a body passage to facilitate visual inspection or medication (a vaginal ~) (a nasal ~) — **spec·u·lar** \-lər\ *adj*

speech \'spēch\ *n* : the communication or expression of thoughts in spoken words

speech center *n* : a brain center exerting control over speech : BROCA'S AREA

speech therapist *n* : a person specially trained in speech therapy

speech therapy *n* : therapeutic treatment of speech defects (as lisping and stuttering)

speed \'spēd\ *n* : METHAMPHETAMINE; *also* : a related stimulant drug and esp. an amphetamine

spell \'spel\ *n* : a period of bodily or mental distress or disorder (a ~ of coughing) (fainting ~s)

sperm \'spərm\ *n, pl* **sperm** *or* **sperms 1** : the male impregnating fluid : SEMEN **2** : a male gamete — **sper·mat·ic** \(ˌ)spər-'ma-tik\ *adj*

sperm- *or* **spermo-** *or* **sperma-** *or* **spermi-** *comb form* : seed : germ : sperm (*spermicidal*)

spermat- *or* **spermato-** *comb form* : seed : spermatozoon (*sperma*tid) (*spermato*cyte)

spermatic artery — see TESTICULAR ARTERY

spermatic cord *n* : a cord that suspends the testis within the scrotum, contains the vas deferens and vessels and nerves of the testis, and extends from the deep inguinal ring through the inguinal canal and superficial inguinal ring downward into the scrotum

spermatic duct *n* : VAS DEFERENS

spermatic plexus *n* : a nerve plexus that receives fibers from the renal plexus and a plexus associated with the aorta and that passes with the testicular artery to the testis

spermatic vein *n* : TESTICULAR VEIN

sper·ma·tid \'spər-mə-tid\ *n* : one of the haploid cells that are formed by division of the secondary spermatocytes and that differentiate into spermatozoa — compare OOTID

sper·mato·cele \(ˌ)spər-'ma-tə-ˌsēl\ *n*

: a cystic swelling of the ducts in the epididymis or in the rete testis usu. containing spermatozoa

sper·mato·cide \(ˌ)spər-'ma-tə-ˌsīd\ *n* : SPERMICIDE — **sper·mato·cid·al** \-ˌma-tə-'sīd-ᵊl\ *adj*

sper·mato·cyte \(ˌ)spər-'ma-tə-ˌsīt\ *n* : a cell giving rise to sperm cells: *esp* : a cell that is derived from a spermatogonium and ultimately gives rise to four haploid spermatids

sper·mato·gen·e·sis \(ˌ)spər-ˌma-tə-'je-nə-səs\ *n, pl* **-e·ses** \-ˌsēz\ : the process of male gamete formation including formation of a primary spermatocyte from a spermatogonium, meiotic division of the spermatocyte, and transformation of the four resulting spermatids into spermatozoa — **sper·mato·gen·ic** \-'je-nik\ *adj*

sper·mato·go·ni·um \-'gō-nē-əm\ *n, pl* **-nia** \-nē-ə\ : a primitive male germ cell — **sper·mato·go·ni·al** \-nē-əl\ *adj*

sper·ma·tor·rhea \ˌspər-mə-tə-'rē-ə, (ˌ)spər-ˌma-\ *n* : abnormally frequent or excessive emission of semen without orgasm

sper·ma·tor·rhoea *chiefly Brit var of* SPERMATORRHEA

spermatozoa *pl of* SPERMATOZOON

sper·ma·to·zo·al \ˌspər-mə-tə-'zō-əl, (ˌ)spər-ˌma-\ *adj* : of or relating to spermatozoa

sper·ma·to·zo·an \ˌspər-mə-tə-'zō-ən, ˌspər-mə-\ *n* : SPERMATOZOON — **spermatozoan** *adj*

sper·ma·to·zo·on \-'zō-ˌän, -'zō-ən\ *n, pl* **-zoa** \-'zō-ə\ : a motile male gamete of an animal usu. with rounded or elongate head and a long posterior flagellum

sperm cell *n* : a male gamete : a male germ cell

sperm duct *n* : VAS DEFERENS

spermi- *or* **spermo-** — see SPERM-

-sper·mia \'spər-mē-ə\ *n comb form* : condition of having or producing (such) sperm (aspermia)

-sper·mic \'spər-mik\ *adj comb form* : being the product of (such) a number of spermatozoa : resulting from (such) a multiple fertilization (poly*spermic*)

sper·mi·cide \'spər-mə-ˌsīd\ *n* : a preparation or substance (as nonoxynol-9) used to kill sperm — called also *spermatocide* — **sper·mi·cid·al** \ˌspər-mə-'sīd-ᵊl\ *adj* — **sper·mi·cid·al·ly** *adv*

sper·mio·gen·e·sis \ˌspər-mē-ō-'je-nə-səs\ *n, pl* **-e·ses** \-ˌsēz\ **1** : SPERMATOGENESIS **2** : transformation of a spermatid into a spermatozoon

-sper·my \'spər-mē\ *n comb form, pl* **-spermies** : state of exhibiting or resulting from (such) a fertilization (poly*spermy*)

SPF \ˌes-(ˌ)pē-'ef\ *abbr* sun protection factor — used for a number assigned to a sunscreen that is the factor by which the time required for unpro-

tected skin to become sunburned is increased when the sunscreen is used

S phase *n* : the period in the cell cycle during which DNA replication takes place — compare G₁ PHASE, G₂ PHASE, M PHASE

sphen- or **spheno-** *comb form* : sphenoidal and ⟨*spheno*palatine⟩

sphe·no·eth·moid recess \ˌsfē-nō-ˈeth-ˌmȯid-\ *n* : a small space between the sphenoid bone and the superior nasal concha into which the sphenoidal sinus opens

¹**sphe·noid** \ˈsfē-ˌnȯid\ or **sphe·noi·dal** \sfē-ˈnȯid-ᵊl\ *adj* : of, relating to, or being a compound bone of the base of the cranium formed by the fusion of several bony elements with the basisphenoid and in humans consisting of a median body from whose sides extend a pair of broad curved winglike expansions in front of which is another pair of much smaller triangular lateral processes while ventrally two large deeply cleft processes extend downward — see GREATER WING, LESSER WING

²**sphenoid** *n* : a sphenoid bone

sphenoid sinus or **sphenoidal sinus** *n* : either of two irregular cavities in the body of the sphenoid bone that communicate with the nasal cavities

sphe·no·man·dib·u·lar ligament \ˌsfē-nō-man-ˈdib-yə-lər-\ *n* : a flat thin band of fibrous tissue derived from Meckel's cartilage which extends downward from the sphenoid bone to the lingula of the mandibular foramen

sphe·no·max·il·lary fissure \ˌsfē-nō-ˈmak-sə-ˌler-ē-, -mak-ˈsi-lə-re-\ *n* : ORBITAL FISSURE b

¹**sphe·no·pal·a·tine** \ˌsfē-nō-ˈpal-ə-ˌtīn\ *adj* : of, relating to, lying in, or distributed to the vicinity of the sphenoid and palatine bones

²**sphenopalatine** *n* : a sphenopalatine part; *specif* : PTERYGOPALATINE GANGLION

sphenopalatine foramen *n* : a foramen between the sphenoidal and orbital parts of the vertical plate of the palatine bone; *also* : a deep notch between these parts that by articulation with the sphenoid bone is converted into a foramen

sphenopalatine ganglion *n* : PTERYGOPALATINE GANGLION

sphe·no·pa·ri·etal sinus \ˌsfē-nō-pə-ˈrī-ət-ᵊl-\ *n* : a venous sinus of the dura mater on each side of the cranium arising at a meningeal vein near the apex of the lesser wing of the sphenoid bone and draining into the anterior part of the cavernous sinus

spher- or **sphero-** *comb form* : spherical ⟨*sphero*cyte⟩

sphe·ro·cyte \ˈsfir-ə-ˌsīt, ˈsfer-\ *n* : a more or less globular red blood cell that is characteristic of some hemolytic anemias — **sphe·ro·cyt·ic** \ˌsfir-ə-ˈsi-tik, ˌsfer-\ *adj*

sphe·ro·cy·to·sis \ˌsfir-ō-sī-ˈtō-səs, ˌsfer-\ *n* : the presence of spherocytes in the blood; *esp* : HEREDITARY SPHEROCYTOSIS

sphinc·ter \ˈsfiŋk-tər\ *n* : an annular muscle surrounding and able to contract or close a bodily opening — see ANAL SPHINCTER — **sphinc·ter·al** \-tə-rəl\ *adj*

sphincter ani ex·ter·nus \-ˈā-ˌnī-ik-ˈstər-nəs\ *n* : ANAL SPHINCTER a

sphincter ani in·ter·nus \-in-ˈtər-nəs\ *n* : ANAL SPHINCTER b

sphinc·ter·ic \sfiŋk-ˈter-ik\ *adj* : of, relating to, or being a sphincter

sphincter of Od·di \-ˈä-dē\ *n* : a complex sphincter closing the duodenal orifice of the common bile duct

   Oddi, Ruggero (1864–1913), Italian physician.

sphinc·tero·plas·ty \ˈsfiŋk-tər-ə-ˌplas-tē\ *n, pl* **-ties** : plastic surgery of a sphincter ⟨anal ~⟩

sphinc·ter·ot·o·my \ˌsfiŋk-tər-ˈä-tə-mē\ *n, pl* **-mies** : surgical incision of a sphincter

sphincter pu·pil·lae \-pyü-ˈpi-lē\ *n* : a broad flat band of smooth muscle in the iris that surrounds the pupil of the eye

sphincter ure·thrae \-yů-ˈrē-thrē\ *n* : a muscle composed of fibers that arise from the inferior ramus of the ischium and that interdigitate with those from the opposite side of the body to form in the male a narrow ring of muscle around the urethra — called also *urethral sphincter*

sphincter va·gi·nae \-və-ˈjī-nē\ *n* : the bulbocavernosus of the female

sphingo- *comb form* : sphingomyelin ⟨*sphingo*sine⟩

sphin·go·lip·id \ˌsfiŋ-gō-ˈli-pəd\ *n* : any of a group of lipids (as sphingomyelins and cerebrosides) that yield sphingosine or one of its derivatives as one product of hydrolysis

sphin·go·lip·i·do·sis \-ˌli-pə-ˈdō-səs\ *n, pl* **-do·ses** \-ˌsēz\ : any of various usu. hereditary disorders (as Gaucher's disease and Tay-Sachs disease) characterized by abnormal metabolism and storage of sphingolipids

sphin·go·my·elin \ˌsfiŋ-gō-ˈmī-ə-lən\ *n* : any of a group of crystalline phosphatides that are obtained esp. from nerve tissue and that on hydrolysis yield a fatty acid, sphingosine, choline, and phosphoric acid

sphin·go·my·elin·ase \-ˈmī-ə-lə-ˌnās, -ˌnāz\ *n* : any of several enzymes that catalyze the hydrolysis of sphingomyelin and are lacking in some metabolic deficiency diseases (as Niemann-Pick disease)

sphin·go·sine \ˈsfiŋ-gə-ˌsēn, -sən\ *n* : an unsaturated amino compound C₁₈H₃₇NO₂ containing two hydroxyl groups and obtained by hydrolysis of various sphingomyelins, cerebrosides, and gangliosides

sphygmo- *comb form* : pulse (*sphygmo-gram*)

sphyg·mo·gram \'sfig-mə-₁gram\ *n* : a tracing made by a sphygmograph and consisting of a series of curves that correspond to the beats of the heart

sphyg·mo·graph \'sfig-mə-₁graf\ *n* : an instrument that records graphically the movements or character of the pulse — **sphyg·mo·graph·ic** \₁sfig-mə-'gra-fik\ *adj*

sphyg·mo·ma·nom·e·ter \₁sfig-mō-mə-'nä-mə-tər\ *n* : an instrument for measuring blood pressure and esp. arterial blood pressure — **sphyg·mo·ma·nom·e·try** \-mə-trē\ *n*

spi·ca \'spī-kə\ *n, pl* **spi·cae** \-₁kē\ *or* **spicas** : a bandage that is applied in successive V-shaped crossings and is used to immobilize a limb esp. at a joint; *also* : such a bandage impregnated with plaster of paris

spic·ule \'spi-(₁)kyül\ *n* : a minute slender pointed usu. hard body (as of bone)

spi·der \'spī-dər\ *n* **1** : any of an order (Araneae syn. Araneida) of arachnids having a body with two main divisions, four pairs of walking legs, and two or more pairs of abdominal organs for spinning threads of silk used esp. in making webs for catching prey **2** : SPIDER NEVUS (an arterial ~)

spider nevus *n* : a pigmented area on the skin formed of dilated capillaries or arterioles radiating from a central point like the legs of a spider — called also *spider angioma*, *spider vein*

Spiel·mey·er–Vogt disease \'shpēl-₁mī-ər-'fōkt-\ *n* : an inherited progressive fatal disorder of lipid metabolism having an onset at about five years of age and characterized by blindness, paralysis, and dementia — called also *juvenile amaurotic idiocy*

    Spielmeyer, Walter (1879–1935), German neurologist.

    Vogt, Oskar (1870–1959), German neurologist.

spi·ge·lian hernia \spī-'jē-lē-ən-\ *n, often cap S* : a hernia occurring along the linea semilunaris

    Spie·ghel \'spē-gəl\, **Adriaan van den (1578–1625),** Flemish anatomist.

spigelian lobe *n, often cap S* : CAUDATE LOBE

¹spike \'spīk\ *n* **1** : the pointed element in the wave tracing in an electroencephalogram **2** : a sharp increase in body temperature followed by a rapid fall (a fever with ~s to 103°) **3** : a momentary sharp increase and fall in the record of an action potential; *also* : ACTION POTENTIAL

²spike *vb* **spiked; spik·ing** : to undergo a sudden sharp increase in (temperature or fever) usu. up to an indicated level

spike potential *n* **1** : SPIKE **3 2** : ACTION POTENTIAL

spik·ing *adj* : characterized by recurrent sharp rises in body temperature (a ~ fever); *also* : resulting from a sharp rise in body temperature (a ~ temperature of 105°)

spin- *or* **spini-** *or* **spino-** *comb form* **1** : spinal column : spinal cord (*spino-tectal tract*) **2** : of, relating to, or involving the spinal cord and (*spino-thalamic*)

spi·na \'spī-nə\ *n, pl* **spi·nae** \-₁nē\ : an anatomical spine or spinelike process

spina bi·fi·da \-'bī-fə-də, -'bī-\ *n* : a congenital cleft of the spinal column with hernial protrusion of the meninges and sometimes the spinal cord

spina bifida oc·cul·ta \-ə-'kəl-tə\ *n* : a congenital cleft of the spinal column without hernial protrusion of the meninges

spinae — see ERECTOR SPINAE

¹spi·nal \'spīn-əl\ *adj* **1** : of, relating to, or situated near the spinal column **2 a** : of, relating to, or affecting the spinal cord (~ reflexes) **b** : having the spinal cord functionally isolated (as by surgical section) from the brain (experiments on ~ animals) **c** : used for spinal anesthesia (a ~ anesthetic) **3** : made for or fitted to the spinal column (a ~ brace) — **spi·nal·ly** *adv*

²spinal *n* : a spinal anesthetic

spinal accessory nerve *n* : ACCESSORY NERVE

spinal anesthesia *n* : anesthesia produced by injection of an anesthetic into the subarachnoid space of the spine

spinal artery *n* : any of three arteries that supply the spinal cord and its membranes and adjacent structures: **a** : a single unpaired artery that is formed by the anastomosis of a branch of the vertebral artery on each side — called also *anterior spinal artery* **b** : either of two arteries of which one arises from a vertebral artery on each side below the level at which the corresponding branch of the anterior spinal artery arises — called also *posterior spinal artery*

spinal canal *n* : VERTEBRAL CANAL

spinal column *n* : the articulated series of vertebrae connected by ligaments and separated by more or less elastic intervertebral fibrocartilages that forms the supporting axis of the body and a protection for the spinal cord and that extends from the hind end of the skull through the median dorsal part of the body to the coccyx — called also *backbone*, *spine*, *vertebral column*

spinal cord *n* : the thick longitudinal cord of nervous tissue that in vertebrates extends along the back dorsal to the bodies of the vertebrae and is enclosed in the vertebral canal formed by their neural arches, is continued anteriorly with the medulla oblongata, gives off at intervals pairs of spinal nerves to the various parts of the trunk and limbs, serves not only as a pathway for nervous impulses to and from the brain but as a center for carrying out and coordinating many reflex actions independently of the brain, and is composed largely of white matter arranged in columns and tracts of longitudinal fibers about a large central core of gray matter — called also *medulla spinalis*

spinales *pl of* SPINALIS

spinal fluid *n* : CEREBROSPINAL FLUID

spinal fusion *n* : surgical fusion of two or more vertebrae for remedial immobilization of the spine

spinal ganglion *n* : a ganglion on the dorsal root of each spinal nerve that is one of a series of ganglia containing cell bodies of sensory neurons — called also *dorsal root ganglion*

spi·na·lis \spī-ˈnā-ləs, spi-ˈna-lis\ *n, pl* **spi·na·les** \-(ˌ)lēz\ : the most medial division of the sacrospinalis situated next to the spinal column and acting to extend it or any of the three muscles making up this division: a : SPINALIS THORACIS b : SPINALIS CERVICIS c : SPINALIS CAPITIS

spinalis ca·pi·tis \-ˈka-pə-təs\ *n* : a muscle that arises with, inserts with, and is intimately associated with the semispinalis capitis

spinalis cer·vi·cis \-ˈsər-və-səs\ *n* : an inconstant muscle that arises esp. from the spinous processes of the lower cervical and upper thoracic vertebrae and inserts esp. into the spinous process of the axis

spinalis tho·ra·cis \-ˈthō-ˈrā-səs\ *n* : an upward continuation of the sacrospinalis that is situated medially to and blends with the longissimus thoracis, arises from the spinous processes of the first two lumbar and last two thoracic vertebrae, and inserts into the spinous processes of the upper thoracic vertebrae

spinal meningitis *n* : inflammation of the meninges of the spinal cord; *also* : CEREBROSPINAL MENINGITIS

spinal nerve *n* : any of the paired nerves which leave the spinal cord, supply muscles of the trunk and limbs, and connect with the nerves of the sympathetic nervous system, which arise by a short motor ventral root and a short sensory dorsal root, and of which there are 31 pairs in humans classified according to the part of the spinal cord from which they arise into 8 pairs of cervical nerves, 12 pairs of thoracic nerves, 5 pairs of lumbar nerves, 5 pairs of sacral nerves, and one pair of coccygeal nerves

spinal puncture *n* : LUMBAR PUNCTURE

spinal shock *n* : a temporary condition following transection of the spinal cord that is characterized by muscular flaccidity and loss of motor reflex-

es in all parts of the body below the point of transection

spinal tap *n* : LUMBAR PUNCTURE

spin·dle \ˈspind-ᵊl\ *n* 1 : something shaped like a round stick or pin with tapered ends: as a : a network of chiefly microtubular fibers along which the chromosomes are distributed during mitosis and meiosis b : MUSCLE SPINDLE 2 : SLEEP SPINDLE

spindle cell *n* : a spindle-shaped cell (as in some tumors)

spindle–cell sarcoma *n* : a sarcoma (as a fibrosarcoma) composed chiefly or entirely of spindle cells

spindle fiber *n* : any of the apparent filaments constituting a mitotic spindle

spine \ˈspīn\ *n* 1 : SPINAL COLUMN 2 : a pointed prominence or process (as on a bone)

spine of the scapula *n* : a projecting triangular bony process on the dorsal surface of the scapula that divides it obliquely into the area of origin of parts of the supraspinatus and infraspinatus muscles and that terminates in the acromion

spini- *or* **spino-** — *see* SPIN-

spinn·bar·keit \ˈspin-ˌbär-ˌkīt, ˈshpin-\ *n* : the elastic quality that is characteristic of mucus of the uterine cervix esp. shortly before ovulation

spi·no·cer·e·bel·lar \ˌspī-nō-ˌser-ə-ˈbe-lər\ *adj* : of or relating to the spinal cord and cerebellum (~ pathways)

spinocerebellar tract *n* : any of four nerve tracts which pass from the spinal cord to the cerebellum and of which two are situated on each side external to the crossed corticospinal tracts: a : a posterior tract on each side that begins at the level of the attachments of the second or third lumbar spinal nerves and ascends to the inferior cerebellar peduncle and vermis of the cerebellum — called also *dorsal spinocerebellar tract, posterior spinocerebellar tract* b : an anterior tract on each side that arises from cells mostly in the dorsal column of gray matter on the same or opposite side and passes through the medulla oblongata and pons to the superior cerebellar peduncle and vermis — called also *ventral spinocerebellar tract*

spi·no·ol·i·vary \-ˈä-lə-ˌver-ē\ *adj* : connecting the spinal cord with the olivary nuclei (~ fibers) (the ~ tract)

spi·nose ear tick \ˈspī-ˌnōs-\ *n* : an ear tick of the genus *Otobius* (*O. megnini*) of the southwestern U.S. and Mexico that is a serious pest of cattle, horses, sheep, and goats

spinosum — *see* FORAMEN SPINOSUM, STRATUM SPINOSUM

spi·no·tec·tal tract \ˌspī-nō-ˈtekt-ᵊl-\ *n* : an ascending tract of nerve fibers in each lateral funiculus of white matter of the spinal cord that passes upward and terminates in the superior colliculus of the opposite side

spi·no·tha·lam·ic \ˌspī-nō-thə-ˈla-mik\ *adj* : of, relating to, comprising, or associated with the spinothalamic tracts (the ~ system)

spinothalamic tract *n* : any of four tracts of nerve fibers of the spinal cord that are arranged in pairs with one member of a pair on each side and that ascend to the thalamus by way of the brain stem: **a** : one on each side of the anterior median fissure that carries nerve impulses relating to the sense of touch — called also *anterior spinothalamic tract, ventral spinothalamic tract* **b** : one on each lateral part of the spinal cord that carries nerve impulses relating to the senses of touch, pain, and temperature — called also *lateral spinothalamic tract*

spi·nous \ˈspī-nəs\ *adj* : slender and pointed like a spine

spinous process *n* : SPINE 2; *specif* : the median spinelike or platelike dorsal process of the neural arch of a vertebra

spiny–headed worm *n* : ACANTHOCEPHALAN

spi·ral \ˈspī-rəl\ *adj* **1 a** : winding around a center or pole and gradually receding from or approaching it **b** : HELICAL (the ~ structure of DNA) **2** : being a fracture in which the break is produced by twisting apart the bone (a double ~ break) — **spiral** *n* — **spi·ral·ly** *adv*

spiral ganglion *n* : a mass of bipolar cell bodies occurring in the modiolus of the organ of Corti and giving off axons which comprise the cochlear nerve

spiralis — see LAMINA SPIRALIS

spiral lamina *n* : a twisting shelf of bone which projects from the modiolus into the canal of the cochlea — called also *lamina spiralis*

spiral ligament *n* : the thick periosteum that forms the outer wall of the scala media

spiral organ *n* : ORGAN OF CORTI

spiral valve *n* : a series of crescentic folds of mucous membrane somewhat spirally arranged on the interior of the gallbladder and continuing into the cystic duct

spi·ra·my·cin \ˌspī-rə-ˈmīs-ᵊn\ *n* : a mixture of macrolide antibiotics produced by a soil bacterium of the genus *Streptomyces* (*S. ambofaciens*) and having antibacterial activity

spi·ril·lum \spī-ˈri-ləm\ *n* **1** *cap* : a genus of gram-negative bacteria having tufts of flagella at both poles and usu. living in stagnant water rich in organic matter — see RAT-BITE FEVER b **2** *pl* **-ril·la** \-ˈri-lə\ : any bacterium of the genus *Spirillum*

spir·it \ˈspir-ət\ *n* **1 a** (1) : the liquid containing ethyl alcohol and water that is distilled from an alcoholic liquid or mash — often used in pl. (2) : ALCOHOL 1a **b** : a usu. volatile organic solvent (as an alcohol, ester, or hydrocarbon) **2** : an alcoholic solution of a volatile substance (~ of camphor)

spirit of hartshorn *or* **spirits of hartshorn** \-ˈhärts-ˌhȯrn\ *n* : AMMONIA WATER

spiro- *comb form* : respiration (*spirometer*)

Spi·ro·cer·ca \ˌspī-rō-ˈsər-kə\ *n* : a genus of red filarial worms (family Thelaziidae) forming nodules in the walls of the digestive tract and sometimes the aorta of canines esp. in warm regions

spi·ro·chaet·ae·mia, spi·ro·chaete, spi·ro·chae·ti·ci·dal, spi·ro·chaet·osis *chiefly Brit var of* SPIROCHETEMIA, SPIROCHETE, SPIROCHETICIDAL, SPIROCHETOSIS

spi·ro·chete \ˈspī-rə-ˌkēt\ *n* : any of an order (Spirochaetales) of slender spirally undulating bacteria including those causing syphilis and relapsing fever — **spi·ro·chet·al** \ˌspī-rə-ˈkēt-ᵊl\ *adj*

spi·ro·chet·emia \ˌspī-rə-ˌkē-ˈtē-mē-ə\ *n* : the abnormal presence of spirochetes in the circulating blood

spi·ro·che·ti·ci·dal \ˌspī-rə-ˌkē-tə-ˈsīd-ᵊl\ *adj* : destructive to spirochetes esp. within the body of an animal host (a ~ drug) — **spi·ro·che·ti·cide** \ˌspī-rə-ˈkē-tə-ˌsīd\ *n*

spi·ro·chet·osis \ˌspī-rə-ˌkē-ˈtō-səs\ *n*, *pl* **-oses** \-ˌsēz\ : infection with or a disease caused by spirochetes

spi·ro·gram \ˈspī-rə-ˌgram\ *n* : a graphic record of respiratory movements traced on a revolving drum

spi·ro·graph \ˈspī-rə-ˌgraf\ *n* : an instrument for recording respiratory movements — **spi·ro·graph·ic** \ˌspī-rə-ˈgra-fik\ *adj* — **spi·rog·ra·phy** \spī-ˈrä-grə-fē\ *n*

spi·rom·e·ter \spī-ˈrä-mə-tər\ *n* : an instrument for measuring the air entering and leaving the lungs — **spi·ro·met·ric** \ˌspī-rə-ˈme-trik\ *adj* — **spi·rom·e·try** \-ˈrä-mə-trē\ *n*

spi·ro·no·lac·tone \ˌspī-rə-nō-ˈlak-ˌtōn, spī-ˌrō-nə-\ *n* : an aldosterone antagonist $C_{24}H_{32}O_4S$ that promotes diuresis and sodium excretion and is used to treat essential hypertension, edema with congestive heart failure, hepatic cirrhosis with ascites, nephrotic syndrome, and idiopathic edema

¹spit \ˈspit\ *vb* **spit** *or* **spat** \ˈspat\; **spit·ting** : to eject (as saliva) from the mouth

²spit *n* : SALIVA

spitting cobra *n* : either of two African cobras (*Naja nigricollis* and *Hemachatus hemachatus*) that in defense typically eject their venom toward the victim without striking

spit·tle \ˈspit-ᵊl\ *n* : SALIVA

splanch·nic \'splaŋk-nik\ *adj* : of or relating to the viscera : VISCERAL

splanch·ni·cec·to·my \,splaŋk-nə-'sek-tə-mē\ *n, pl* **-mies** : surgical excision of a segment of one or more splanchnic nerves to relieve hypertension

splanchnic ganglion *n* : a small ganglion on the greater splanchnic nerve that is usually located near the eleventh or twelfth thoracic vertebra

splanchnic nerve *n* : any of three nerves situated on each side of the body and formed by the union of branches from the six or seven lower thoracic and first lumbar ganglia of the sympathetic system: **a** : a superior one ending in the celiac ganglion — called also *greater splanchnic nerve* **b** : a middle one ending in a detached ganglionic mass of the celiac ganglion — called also *lesser splanchnic nerve* **c** : an inferior one ending in the renal plexus — called also *least splanchnic nerve, lowest splanchnic nerve*

splanchno- *comb form* : viscera (*splanchnology*)

splanch·nol·o·gy \splaŋk-'näl-ə-jē\ *n, pl* **-gies** : a branch of anatomy concerned with the viscera

splanch·no·pleure \'splaŋk-nə-,plu̇r\ *n* : a layer of tissue that consists of the inner of the two layers into which the unsegmented sheet of mesoderm splits in the embryo together with the endoderm internal to it and that forms most of the walls and substance of the visceral organs — compare SOMATOPLEURE

splay·foot \'splā-,fu̇t, -'fu̇t\ *n* : a foot abnormally flattened and spread out: *specif* : FLATFOOT — **splay·foot·ed** \-'fu̇-təd\ *adj*

spleen \'splēn\ *n* : a highly vascular ductless organ that is concerned with final destruction of red blood cells, filtration and storage of blood, and production of lymphocytes, and that in humans is a dark purplish flattened oblong object of a soft fragile consistency lying in the upper left part of the abdominal cavity near the cardiac end of the stomach and which is divisible into a loose friable red pulp in intimate connection with the blood supply and with red blood cells free in its interstices and a denser white pulp chiefly of lymphoid tissue condensed in masses about the small arteries

splen- *or* **spleno-** *comb form* : spleen (*splenectomy*) (*spleno*megaly)

sple·nec·to·my \spli-'nek-tə-mē\ *n, pl* **-mies** : surgical excision of the spleen — **sple·nec·to·mize** \spli-'nek-tə-,mīz\ *vb*

splen·ic \'sple-nik\ *adj* : of, relating to, or located in the spleen

splenic artery *n* : the branch of the celiac artery that carries blood to the spleen and sends branches also to the pancreas and the cardiac end of the stomach

splenic fever *n* : ANTHRAX

splenic flexure *n* : the sharp bend of the colon under the spleen where the transverse colon joins the descending colon — called also *left colic flexure*

splenic flexure syndrome *n* : pain in the upper left quadrant of the abdomen that may radiate upward to the left shoulder and inner aspect of the left arm and that sometimes mimics angina pectoris but is caused by bloating and gas in the colon

splenic pulp *n* : the characteristic tissue of the spleen

splenic vein *n* : the vein that carries blood away from the spleen and that joins the superior mesenteric vein to form the portal vein — called also *lienal vein*

sple·ni·um \'splē-nē-əm\ *n, pl* **-nia** \-nē-ə\ : the thick rounded fold that forms the posterior border of the corpus callosum and is continuous by its undersurface with the fornix

sple·ni·us \-nē-əs\ *n, pl* **-nii** \-nē-,ī\ : either of two flat oblique muscles on each side of the back of the neck and upper thoracic region: **a** : SPLENIUS CAPITIS **b** : SPLENIUS CERVICIS

splenius cap·i·tis \-'ka-pi-təs\ *n* : a flat muscle on each side of the back of the neck and the upper thoracic region that arises from the caudal half of the ligamentum nuchae and the spinous processes of the seventh cervical and the first three or four thoracic vertebrae, that is inserted into the occipital bone and the mastoid process of the temporal bone, and that rotates the head to the side on which it is located and with the help of the muscle on the opposite side extends it

splenius cer·vi·cis \-'sər-vi-kəs\ *n* : a flat narrow muscle on each side of the back of the neck and the upper thoracic region that arises from the spinous processes of the third to sixth thoracic vertebrae, is inserted into the transverse processes of the first two or three cervical vertebrae, and acts to rotate the head to the side on which it is located and with the help of the muscle on the opposite side to extend and arch the neck

spleno- — see SPLEN-

sple·no·cyte \'splē-nə-,sīt, 'sple-\ *n* : a macrophage of the spleen

spleno·meg·a·ly \,sple-nō-'me-gə-lē\ *n, pl* **-lies** : abnormal enlargement of the spleen

spleno·re·nal \,sple-nō-'rēn-əl\ *adj* : of, relating to, or joining the splenic and renal veins or arteries

sple·no·sis \splē-'nō-səs\ *n, pl* **-no·ses** \-,sēs\ *or* **-no·sis·es** : a rare condition in which fragments of tissue from a ruptured spleen become implanted throughout the peritoneal cavity and often undergo regeneration and vascularization

splice \'splīs\ *vb* **spliced; splic·ing** : to

combine (genetic information) from either the same organism or different organisms — see GENE-SPLICING

¹splint \'splint\ n **1** : material or a device used to protect and immobilize a body part **2** : a bony enlargement on the upper part of the cannon bone of a horse usu. on the inside of the leg

²splint vb **1** : to support and immobilize (as a broken bone) with a splint **2** : to protect against pain by reducing the motion of

splin·ter \'splin-tər\ n : a thin piece (as of wood) split or rent off lengthwise; esp : such a piece embedded in the skin ⟨used tweezers to remove a ∼⟩ — **splinter** vb

split \'split\ vb **split; split·ting** : to divide or break down (a chemical compound) into constituents; also : to remove by such separation

split–brain \'split-'brān\ adj : of, relating to, concerned with, or having undergone separation of the two cerebral hemispheres by surgical division of the optic chiasma and corpus callosum ⟨∼ patients⟩

split personality n : SCHIZOPHRENIA; also : MULTIPLE PERSONALITY

spondyl- or **spondylo-** comb form : vertebra : vertebrae ⟨spondylarthritis⟩ ⟨spondylopathy⟩

spon·dyl·ar·thri·tis \spän-di-lär-'thrī-təs\ n, pl **-thrit·i·des** \-'thri-tə-dēz\ : arthritis of the spine

spon·dy·li·tis \spän-də-'lī-təs\ n : inflammation of the vertebrae ⟨tuberculous ∼⟩ — see ANKYLOSING SPONDYLITIS — **spon·dy·lit·ic** \-'li-tik\ adj

spon·dy·lar·throp·a·thy \spän-də-lö-är-'thrä-pə-thē\ also **spon·dyl·ar·throp·a·thy** \spän-də-lär-'thrä-\ n, pl **-thies** : any of several diseases (as ankylosing spondylitis) affecting the joints of the spine

spon·dy·lo·lis·the·sis \spän-də-lō-lis-'thē-səs\ n : forward displacement of a lumbar vertebra on the one below it and esp. of the fifth lumbar vertebra on the sacrum producing pain by compression of nerve roots

spon·dy·lol·y·sis \spän-də-'lä-lə-səs\ n, pl **-y·ses** \-sēz\ : disintegration or dissolution of a vertebra

spon·dy·lop·a·thy \spän-də-'lä-pə-thē\ n, pl **-thies** : any disease or disorder of the vertebrae

spon·dy·lo·sis \spän-də-'lō-səs\ n, pl **-lo·ses** \-sēz\ or **-lo·sis·es** : any of various degenerative diseases of the spine

sponge \'spənj\ n **1 a** : a small pad made of multiple folds of gauze or of cotton and gauze used to mop blood from a surgical incision, to carry inhalant medicaments to the nose, or to cover a superficial wound as a dressing **b** : a porous dressing (as of fibrin or gelatin) applied to promote wound healing **c** : a plastic prosthesis used in chest cavities following lung surgery

2 : an absorbent contraceptive device impregnated with spermicide that is inserted into the vagina before sexual intercourse to cover the cervix and act as a barrier to sperm — **sponge** vb

sponge bath n : a bath in which water is applied to the body without actual immersion

sponge biopsy n : biopsy performed on matter collected with a sponge from a lesion

spongi- or **spongio-** comb form : spongy ⟨spongioblast⟩

spon·gi·form \'spən-ji-form\ adj : of, relating to, or being a degenerative disease which causes the brain tissue to have a porous structure like that of a sponge ⟨acute ∼ encephalopathies⟩

spon·gi·o·blast \'spən-jē-ō-blast, 'spän-\ n : any of the ectodermal cells of the embryonic spinal cord or other nerve center that are at first columnar but become branched at one end and that give rise to the neuroglia cells

spon·gi·o·blas·to·ma \spän-jē-ō-(₍)bla-'stō-mə, spän-\ n, pl **-mas** or **-ma·ta** \-mə-tə\ : GLIOBLASTOMA

spon·gi·o·cyte \'spən-jē-ō-sīt, 'spän-\ n : any of the cells of the adrenal cortex that have a spongy appearance due to lipid vacuoles the contents of which have been dissolved out

spon·gi·o·sa \spən-jē-'ō-sə, spän-\ n : the part of a bone (as much of the epiphyseal area of long bones) made up of spongy cancellous bone

spon·gi·o·sis \spən-jē-'ō-səs, spän-\ n : swelling localized in the epidermis and often occurring in eczema

spongiosum — see CORPUS SPONGIOSUM, STRATUM SPONGIOSUM

spongy \'spən-jē\ adj **spong·i·er; -est** : resembling a sponge; esp : full of cavities : CANCELLOUS ⟨∼ bone⟩

spon·ta·ne·ous \spän-'tā-nē-əs\ adj **1** : proceeding from natural feeling or native tendency without external constraint **2** : developing without apparent external influence, force, cause, or treatment ⟨∼ nosebleed⟩ — **spon·ta·ne·ous·ly** adv

spontaneous abortion n : naturally occurring expulsion of a nonviable fetus

spontaneous recovery n : reappearance of an extinguished conditioned response without positive reinforcement

spoon nails \'spün-\ n : KOILONYCHIA

spor- or **spori-** or **sporo-** comb form : seed : spore ⟨sporocyst⟩

spo·rad·ic \spə-'ra-dik\ adj : occurring occasionally, singly, or in scattered instances ⟨∼ diseases⟩ — compare ENDEMIC, EPIDEMIC 1 — **spo·rad·i·cal·ly** adv

spore \'spōr\ n : a primitive usu. unicellular often environmentally resistant dormant or reproductive body produced by plants and some microorganisms and capable of development into a new individual either directly or after fusion with another spore — **spore** *vb*

spo·ro·blast \'spō-rə-ˌblast\ *n* : a cell of a sporozoan resulting from sexual reproduction and producing spores and sporozoites

spo·ro·cyst \-ˌsist\ *n* 1 : a case or cyst secreted by some sporozoans preliminary to sporogony; *also* : a sporozoan encysted in such a case 2 : a saccular body that is the first asexual reproductive form of a digenetic trematode, develops from a miracidium, and buds off cells from its inner surface which develop into rediae

spo·ro·gen·e·sis \ˌspōr-ə-'je-nə-səs\ *n, pl* **-e·ses** \-ˌsēz\ 1 : reproduction by spores 2 : spore formation — **spo·rog·e·nous** \spə-'rä-jə-nəs, spō-\ *also* **spo·ro·gen·ic** \ˌspōr-ə-'je-nik\ *adj*

spo·rog·o·ny \spə-'rä-gə-nē\ *n, pl* **-nies** : reproduction by spores; *specif* : formation of spores containing sporozoites that is characteristic of some sporozoans and that results from the encystment and subsequent division of a zygote — **spo·ro·gon·ic** \ˌspōr-ə-'gä-nik\ *adj*

spo·ront \'spōr-ˌänt\ *n* : a sporozoan that engages in sporogony

spo·ro·phore \'spōr-ə-ˌfōr\ *n* : the spore-producing organ esp. of a fungus

spo·ro·thrix \-ˌthriks\ *n* 1 *cap* : a genus of imperfect fungi (family Moniliaceae) that includes the causative agent (*S. schenckii*) of sporotrichosis 2 : any fungus of the genus *Sporothrix*

spo·ro·tri·cho·sis \spə-ˌrä-tri-'kō-səs, ˌspōr-ə-tri-\ *n, pl* **-cho·ses** \-ˌsēz\ : infection with or disease caused by a fungus of the genus *Sporothrix* (*S. schenckii* syn. *Sporotrichum schenckii*) that is characterized by nodules and abscesses in the superficial lymph nodes, skin, and subcutaneous tissues and that is usu. transmitted by entry of the fungus through a skin abrasion or wound

spo·ro·zo·an \ˌspōr-ə-'zō-ən\ *n* : any of a large class (Sporozoa) of strictly parasitic protozoans that have a complicated life cycle usu. involving both asexual and sexual generations often in different hosts and that include many serious pathogens (as malaria parasites and babesias) — **sporozoan** *adj*

spo·ro·zo·ite \-'zō-ˌīt\ *n* : a usu. motile infective form of some sporozoans (as the malaria parasite) that is a product of sporogony and initiates an asexual cycle in the new host

sport \'spōrt\ *n* : an individual exhibiting a sudden deviation from type beyond the normal limits of individual variation usu. as a result of mutation esp. of somatic tissue

sports medicine *n* : a medical specialty concerned with the prevention and treatment of injuries and diseases that are related to participation in sports

spor·u·la·tion \ˌspōr-ə-'lā-shən, ˌspōr-yə-\ *n* : the formation of spores; *esp* : division into many small spores (as after encystment) — **spor·u·late** \'spōr-ə-ˌlāt, 'spōr-yə-\ *vb*

¹spot \'spät\ *n* : a circumscribed mark or area: as **a** : a circumscribed surface lesion of disease (as measles) **b** : a circumscribed abnormality in an organ seen by means of X rays or an instrument (a ~ on the lung)

²spot *vb* **spot·ted; spot·ting** : to experience abnormal and sporadic bleeding in small amounts from the uterus

spot film *n* : a roentgenogram of a restricted area in the body

spotted cow·bane \-'kau̇-ˌbān\ *n* : a tall biennial No. American herb (*Cicuta maculata*) of the carrot family (Umbelliferae) with clusters of tuberous roots that resemble small sweet potatoes and are extremely poisonous — called also *spotted hemlock*

spotted fever *n* : any of various eruptive fevers; *esp* : ROCKY MOUNTAIN SPOTTED FEVER

sprain \'sprān\ *n* : a sudden or violent twist or wrench of a joint causing the stretching or tearing of ligaments and often rupture of blood vessels with hemorrhage into the tissues; *also* : the condition resulting from a sprain that is usu. marked by swelling, inflammation, hemorrhage, and discoloration — compare ³STRAIN b — **sprain** *vb*

sprain fracture *n* : the rupture of a tendon or ligament from its point of insertion at a joint with detachment of a splinter of bone

¹spray \'sprā\ *n* : a jet of vapor or finely divided liquid; *specif* : a jet of fine medicated vapor used as an application to a diseased part or to charge the air of a room with a disinfectant or deodorant

²spray *vb* : to emit a stream or spray of urine (a cat may ~ to mark its territory)

spreading factor *n* : HYALURONIDASE

Spreng·el's deformity \'shpreŋ-əlz-, -gəlz-\ *n* : a congenital elevation of the scapula

Sprengel, Otto Gerhard Karl (1852–1915), German surgeon.

spring \'spriŋ\ *n* : any of various elastic orthodontic devices used esp. to apply constant pressure to misaligned teeth

spring ligament *n* : PLANTAR CALCANEONAVICULAR LIGAMENT

¹sprout \'spraut\ *vb* : to send out new growth : produce sprouts

²sprout *n* : a new outgrowth (as of nerve tissue)

sprue \'sprü\ *n* 1 : CELIAC DISEASE 2 : a disease of tropical regions that is of unknown cause and is characterized by fatty diarrhea and malabsorption of nutrients — called also *tropical sprue*

spud \\'spəd\ n : any of various small surgical instruments with a shape resembling that of a spade

spur \\'spər\ n : a sharp and esp. bony outgrowth (as on the heel of the foot) — **spurred** \\'spərd\ adj

spu·ri·ous \\'spyur-ē-əs\ adj : simulating a symptom or condition without being pathologically or morphologically genuine ⟨∼ labor pains⟩

spu·tum \\'spü-təm, 'spyü-\ n, pl **spu·ta** \-tə\ : expectorated matter made up of saliva and often discharges from the respiratory passages

squa·ma \\'skwā-mə, 'skwä-\ n, pl **squa·mae** \\'skwā-ˌmē, 'skwä-ˌmī\ : a structure resembling a scale or plate: as a : the curved platelike posterior portion of the occipital bone b : the vertical portion of the frontal bone that forms the forehead c : the thin anterior upper portion of the temporal bone

squame \\'skwām\ n : a scale or flake (as of skin)

squa·mous \\'skwä-məs\ adj 1 a : covered with or consisting of scales b : of, relating to, or being a stratified epithelium that consists at least in its outer layers of small scalelike cells 2 : resembling a scale or plate; esp : of, relating to, or being the thin anterior upper portion of the temporal bone

squamous carcinoma n : SQUAMOUS CELL CARCINOMA

squamous cell n : a cell of or derived from squamous epithelium

squamous cell carcinoma n : a carcinoma made up of or arising from squamous cells

squash bite \\'skwäsh-, 'skwósh-\ n : an impression of the teeth and mouth made by closing the teeth on modeling composition or wax

squill \\'skwil\ n 1 : a Mediterranean bulbous herb of the genus *Urginea* (esp. *U. maritima*) 2 : the dried sliced bulb scales of a white-bulbed form of the squill (*Urginea maritima*) of the Mediterranean region used as an expectorant, cardiac stimulant, and diuretic — called also *white squill*

¹**squint** \\'skwint\ vb 1 : to be cross-eyed 2 : to look or peer with eyes partly closed

²**squint** n 1 : STRABISMUS 2 : an instance or habit of squinting

squir·rel corn \\'skwər-əl-\ n : a poisonous No. American herb (*Dicentra canadensis* of the family Fumariaceae)

Sr symbol strontium

sRNA \\'es-ˌär-(ˌ)en-'ā\ n : TRANSFER RNA

SRS–A abbr slow-reacting substance of anaphylaxis

ss abbr [Latin *semis*] one half — used in writing prescriptions

S sleep n : SLOW-WAVE SLEEP

SSPE abbr subacute sclerosing panencephalitis

SSSS abbr staphylococcal scalded skin syndrome

ST \\'es-ˌtē\ n : ST SEGMENT

stab \\'stab\ n : a wound produced by a pointed weapon — **stab** vb

stab·bing adj : having a sharp piercing quality ⟨∼ pain⟩

stab cell n : BAND FORM

sta·bil·i·ty \stə-'bil-ə-tē\ n, pl **-ties** : the quality, state, or degree of being stable ⟨emotional ∼⟩

sta·bi·lize \\'stā-bə-ˌlīz\ vb **-lized; -lizing** : to make or become stable ⟨∼ a patient's condition⟩ — **sta·bi·li·za·tion** \ˌstā-bə-lə-'zā-shən\ n — **sta·bi·liz·er** \\'stā-bə-ˌlī-zər\ n

sta·ble \\'stā-bəl\ adj **sta·bler; sta·blest** 1 : not changing or fluctuating ⟨the patient's condition was listed as ∼⟩ 2 : not subject to insecurity or emotional illness ⟨a ∼ personality⟩ 3 a : not readily altering in chemical makeup or physical state b : not spontaneously radioactive

stable factor n : FACTOR VII

stable fly n : a biting dipteran fly of the genus *Stomoxys* (*S. calcitrans*) that is abundant about stables and often enters dwellings esp. in autumn

stachy·bot·ryo·tox·i·co·sis \ˌsta-ki-ˌbä-trē-ō-ˌtäk-sə-'kō-səs\ n, pl **-co·ses** \-ˌsēz\ : a serious and sometimes fatal intoxication chiefly affecting domestic animals (as horses) that is due to ingestion of a toxic substance elaborated by a mold (*Stachybotrys alternans*)

staff \\'staf\ n : the doctors and surgeons regularly attached to a hospital and helping to determine its policies and guide its activities

staff nurse n : a registered nurse employed by a medical facility who does not assist in surgery

staff of Aes·cu·la·pi·us \-ˌes-kyə-'lā-pē-əs\ n : a conventionalized representation of a staff branched at the top with a single snake twined around it that is used as a symbol of medicine and as the official insignia of the American Medical Association — called also *Aesculapian staff*

stage \\'stāj\ n 1 : the small platform of a microscope on which an object is placed for examination 2 : a period or step in a progress, activity, or development: as a : one of the distinguishable periods of growth and development of a plant or animal b : a period or phase in the course of a disease ⟨the sweating ∼ of malaria⟩ c : one of two or more operations performed at different times but constituting a single procedure ⟨a two-*stage* thoracoplasty⟩ d : any of the four degrees indicating depth of general anesthesia

stag·gers \\'sta-gərz\ n pl 1 : any of various abnormal conditions of domestic animals associated with damage to the central nervous system and marked by incoordination and a reeling unsteady gait — used with a sing. or pl. verb; see BLIND STAGGERS; compare GRASS TETANY 2 : vertigo occurring as a symptom of decompression sickness

stag·horn calculus \'stag-ˌhȯrn-\ *n* : a large renal calculus with multiple irregular branches

stag·ing \'stā-jiṅ\ *n* : the classification of the severity of a disease in distinct stages on the basis of established symptomatic criteria

¹**stain** \'stān\ *vb* **1 a** : to cause discoloration of **b** : to color by processes affecting chemically or otherwise the material itself ⟨∼ bacteria with a fluorescent dye⟩ **2** : to receive a stain

²**stain** *n* **1** : a discolored spot or area (as on the skin or teeth) — see PORT-WINE STAIN **2** : a dye or mixture of dyes used in microscopy to make visible minute and transparent structures, to differentiate tissue elements, or to produce specific chemical reactions

stair·case effect \'star-ˌkās-\ *n* : TREPPE

stalk \'stȯk\ *n* : a slender supporting or connecting part : PEDUNCLE (the pituitary ∼) — **stalked** \'stȯkt\ *adj* — **stalk·less** *adj*

stam·i·na \'sta-mi-nə\ *n* : the strength or vigor of bodily constitution : capacity for standing fatigue or resisting disease

stam·mer \'sta-mər\ *vb* **stam·mered; stam·mer·ing** : to make involuntary stops and repetitions in speaking — **stammer** *n* — **stam·mer·er** \'sta-mər-ər\ *n*

stammering *n* **1** : the act of one who stammers **2** : a defective condition of speech characterized by involuntary stops and repetitions or blocking of utterance — compare STUTTERING 2

stanch \'stȯnch, 'stänch\ *vb* : to check or stop the flowing of ⟨∼ bleeding⟩; *also* : to stop the flow of blood from ⟨∼ a wound⟩

stand·still \'stand-ˌstil\ *n* : a state characterized by absence of motion or of progress : ARREST ⟨cardiac ∼⟩

Stan·ford-Bi·net test \'stan-fərd-bi-'nā-\ *n* : an intelligence test prepared at Stanford University as a revision of the Binet-Simon scale and commonly employed with children — called also *Stanford-Binet*

A. Binet — see BINET AGE

stan·nous fluoride \'sta-nəs-\ *n* : a white compound SnF₂ of tin and fluorine used in toothpaste to combat tooth decay

stan·o·lone \'sta-nə-ˌlōn\ *n* : an androgen C₁₉H₃₀O₂ used esp. in the treatment of breast cancer

stan·o·zol·ol \'sta-nə-zō-ˌlȯl\ *n* : an anabolic steroid C₂₁H₃₂N₂O

sta·pe·dec·to·my \ˌstā-pi-'dek-tə-mē\ *n*, *pl* **-mies** : surgical removal and prosthetic replacement of part or all of the stapes to relieve deafness

sta·pe·di·al \stā-'pē-dē-əl, stə-\ *adj* : of, relating to, or located near the stapes

sta·pe·di·us \stə-'pē-dē-əs\ *n*, *pl* **-dii** \-dē-ˌī\ : a small muscle of the middle ear that arises from the wall of the tympanum, is inserted into the neck of the stapes by a tendon that sometimes contains a slender spine of bone, and serves to check and dampen vibration of the stapes — called also *stapedius muscle*

sta·pes \'stā-(ˌ)pēz\ *n*, *pl* **stapes** or **sta·pe·des** \stə-'pē-ˌdēz\ : the innermost of the chain of ossicles of the ear which has the form of a stirrup, a base that occupies the oval window of the tympanum, and a head that is connected with the incus — called also *stirrup*

staph \'staf\ *n* : STAPHYLOCOCCUS 2; *also* : an infection with staphylococci

staphyl- *or* **staphylo-** *comb form* : staphylococcal ⟨*staphylotoxin*⟩

staph·y·lo·coc·cal \ˌsta-fə-lō-'kä-kəl\ *also* **staph·y·lo·coc·cic** \-'kä-kik, -'käk-sik\ *adj* : of, relating to, caused by, or being a staphylococcus ⟨∼ infection⟩

staphylococcal scalded skin syndrome *n* : an acute skin disorder esp. of infants and immunocompromised individuals that is characterized by widespread erythema, peeling, and necrosis of the skin, that is caused by a toxin produced by a bacterium of the genus *Staphyloccus* (*S. aureus*), and that exposes the affected individual to serious infections but is rarely fatal if diagnosed and treated promptly — abbr. *SSSS*; compare TOXIC EPIDERMAL NECROLYSIS

staph·y·lo·coc·co·sis \ˌsta-fə-lō-kä-'kō-səs\ *n* : infection with or disease caused by staphylococci

staph·y·lo·coc·cus \ˌsta-fə-lō-'kä-kəs\ *n* **1** *cap* : a genus of nonmotile grampositive spherical bacteria (family Micrococcaceae) that occur singly, in pairs of tetrads, or in irregular clusters and include pathogens (as *S. aureus*) which infect the skin and mucous membranes **2** *pl* **-coc·ci** \-'käk-ˌsī\ : any bacterium of the genus *Staphylococcus*; *broadly* : MICROCOCCUS 2

staph·y·lo·ki·nase \-'kī-ˌnās, -ˌnāz\ *n* : a proteinase from some pathogenic staphylococci that converts plasminogen to plasmin

staph·y·lo·ma \ˌsta-fə-'lō-mə\ *n* : a protrusion of the cornea or sclera of the eye

staph·y·lo·tox·in \ˌsta-fə-lō-'täk-sən\ *n* : a toxin produced by staphylococci

sta·ple \'stā-pəl\ *n* : a usu. U-shaped and typically metal surgical fastener used to hold layers of tissue together (as in the closure of an incision) — **staple** *vb* — **sta·pler** \-plər\ *n*

starch \'stärch\ n : a white odorless tasteless granular or powdery complex carbohydrate $(C_6H_{10}O_5)_x$ that is the chief storage form of carbohydrate in plants, is an important foodstuff, has demulcent and absorbent properties, and is used in pharmacy esp. as a dusting powder and as a constituent of ointments and pastes — **starchy** \'stär-chē\ adj

Star·ling hypothesis \'stär-liŋ-\ n : a hypothesis in physiology: the flow of fluids across capillary walls depends on the balance between the force of blood pressure on the walls and the osmotic pressure across the walls so that the declining gradient in blood pressure from the arterial to the venous end of the capillary results in an outflow of fluids at its arterial end with an increasing inflow toward its venous end

E. H. Starling — see FRANK-STARLING LAW

Starling's law of the heart n : a statement in physiology: the strength of the heart's systolic contraction is directly proportional to its diastolic expansion with the result that under normal physiological conditions the heart pumps out of the right atrium all the blood returned to it without letting any back up in the veins — called also *Frank-Starling law*, *Frank-Starling law of the heart*, *Starling's law*

starve \'stärv\ vb **starved; starv·ing 1 a** : to perish from lack of food **b** : to suffer extreme hunger **2** : to deprive of nourishment — **star·va·tion** \stär-'vā-shən\ n

sta·sis \'stā-səs, 'sta-\ n, pl **sta·ses** \'stā-ˌsēz, 'sta-\ : a slowing or stoppage of the normal flow of the bodily fluid or semifluid (biliary ~): as **a** : slowing of the current of circulating blood **b** : reduced motility of the intestines with retention of feces

stasis ulcer n : an ulcer (as on the lower leg) caused by localized slowing or stoppage of blood flow

stat \'stat\ adv : STATIM

-stat \ˌstat\ n comb form : agent causing inhibition of growth without destruction ⟨bacterio*stat*⟩

state \'stāt\ n : mode or condition of being: as **a** : condition of mind or temperament ⟨a manic ~⟩ **b** : a condition or stage in the physical being of something ⟨the gaseous ~ of water⟩

state hospital n : a hospital for the mentally ill that is run by a state

stat·im \'sta-tim\ adv : without delay or immediately

sta·tion \'stā-shən\ n **1** : the place at which someone is positioned or is assigned to remain (the nurse's ~ on a hospital ward) **2** : the act or manner of standing : POSTURE

sta·tion·ary \'stā-shə-ˌner-ē\ adj **1** : fixed in position : not moving **2**

: characterized by a lack of change

stato- comb form : balance : equilibrium ⟨*stato*lith⟩

sta·to·co·nia \ˌsta-tə-'kō-nē-ə\ n, pl : OTOCONIA

stato·lith \'stat-ᵊl-ˌith\ n : OTOLITH

sta·tus \'stā-təs, 'sta-\ n, pl **sta·tus·es** : a particular state or condition

status asth·mat·i·cus \-az-'ma-ti-kəs\ n : an attack of asthma of long duration characterized by dyspnea, cyanosis, exhaustion, and sometimes collapse

status ep·i·lep·ti·cus \-ˌe-pə-'lep-ti-kəs\ n : a state in epilepsy in which the attacks occur in rapid succession without recovery of consciousness

stat·u·to·ry rape \'sta-chə-ˌtōr-ē-\ n : sexual intercourse with a person who is below the age of consent as defined by law

staunch var of STANCH

STD \ˌes-(ˌ)tē-'dē\ n : SEXUALLY TRANSMITTED DISEASE

steady state n : a state of physiological equilibrium esp. in connection with a specified metabolic relation or activity

steal \'stēl\ n : abnormal circulation characterized by deviation (as through collateral vessels or by backward flow) of blood to tissues where the normal flow of blood has been cut off by occlusion of an artery (coronary ~)

ste·ap·sin \stē-'ap-sən\ n : the lipase in pancreatic juice

stea·rate \'stē-ə-ˌrāt, 'stir-ˌāt\ n : a salt or ester of stearic acid

stea·ric acid \stē-'ar-ik-, 'stir-ik-\ n : a white crystalline fatty acid $C_{18}H_{36}O_2$ obtained from tallow and some other hard fats; also : a commercial mixture of stearic and palmitic acids

stea·rin \'stē-ə-rən, 'stir-ən\ n : an ester of glycerol and stearic acid $C_3H_5(C_{18}H_{35}O_2)_3$ that is a predominant constituent of many hard fats

steat- or **steato-** comb form : fat ⟨*steato*ma⟩

ste·a·ti·tis \ˌstē-ə-'tī-təs\ n : inflammation of fatty tissue; esp : YELLOW FAT DISEASE

ste·a·to·ma \ˌstē-ə-'tō-mə\ n, pl **-mas** or **-ma·ta** \-mə-tə\ : SEBACEOUS CYST

ste·a·to·py·gia \ˌstē-ə-tə-'pi-jē-ə, ˌstē-ˌa-tō-, -'pī-\ n : an accumulation of a large amount of fat on the buttocks that occurs esp. among women of some peoples of African descent — **ste·a·to·py·gous** \-'pī-gəs\ or **ste·a·to·py·gic** \-'pi-jik, -'pī-\ adj

ste·at·or·rhea \ˌstē-ˌa-tə-'rē-ə\ n : an excess of fat in the stools (idiopathic ~)

ste·at·or·rhoea chiefly Brit var of STEATORRHEA

ste·a·to·sis \ˌstē-ə-'tō-səs\ n, pl **-to·ses** \-ˌsēz\ : FATTY DEGENERATION

Stein–Lev·en·thal syndrome \'stin-'lev-ᵊn-ˌthäl-\ n : POLYCYSTIC OVARY SYNDROME

Stein, Irving Freiler (1887–1976), and **Leventhal, Michael Leo** (1901–1971), American gynecologists.

Stein·mann pin \'stīn-mən-\ *n* : a stainless steel spike used for the internal fixation of fractures of long bones

Steinmann, Fritz (1872–1932), Swiss surgeon.

Stel·a·zine \'ste-lə-ˌzēn\ *trademark* — used for a preparation of trifluoperazine

stel·late \'ste-ˌlāt\ *adj* : shaped like a star ⟨a ~ ulcer⟩

stellate cell *n* : a cell (as a Kupffer cell) with radiating cytoplasmic processes

stellate ganglion *n* : a composite ganglion formed by fusion of the most inferior of the three cervical ganglia with the first thoracic ganglion of the sympathetic chain

stellate ligament *n* : RADIATE LIGAMENT

stellate reticulum *n* : a loosely-connected mass of stellate epithelial cells that in early developmental stages makes up a large portion of the enamel organ

stem cell *n* : an unspecialized cell that gives rise to differentiated cells ⟨hematopoietic *stem cells* in bone marrow⟩

ste·nosed \ste-'nōst, -'nōzd\ *adj* : affected with stenosis : abnormally constricted ⟨a ~ eustachian tube⟩

ste·nos·ing \ste-'nō-siŋ, -ziŋ\ *adj* : causing or characterized by stenosis (as of a tendon sheath)

ste·no·sis \stə-'nō-səs\ *n, pl* **-no·ses** \-ˌsēz\ : a narrowing or constriction of the diameter of a bodily passage or orifice ⟨esophageal ~⟩

ste·not·ic \stə-'nä-tik\ *adj* : of, relating to, characterized by, or causing stenosis ⟨~ lesions⟩

Sten·sen's duct *also* **Sten·son's duct** \'sten-sənz-\ *n* : PAROTID DUCT

Sten·sen *or* **Steen·sen** \'stän-sən\. **Niels** (*Latin* **Nicolaus Steno**) (1638–1686), Danish anatomist and geologist.

stent \'stent\ *n* : a mold formed from a resinous compound and used for holding a surgical graft in place; *also* : something (as a pad of gauze immobilized by sutures) used like a stent

Stent, Charles R. (1845–1901), British dentist.

Steph·a·no·fi·lar·ia \ˌste-fə-ˌnō-fi-'lar-ē-ə\ *n* : a genus of filarial worms parasitic in the skin and subcutaneous tissues of ruminants and horses where they may cause dermatitis and extensive degenerative lesions

Steph·a·nu·rus \ˌste-fə-'nur-əs, -'nyur-\ *n* : a genus of strongylid nematode worms that includes the kidney worm (*S. dentatus*) of swine

ster·co·ra·ceous \ˌstər-kə-'rā-shəs\ *adj* : of, relating to, containing, produced by, or being feces : FECAL

ster·cu·lia gum \stər-'kül-yə-, -'kyül-\ *n* : KARAYA GUM

stere- *or* **stereo-** *comb form* **1** : stereoscopic ⟨*stereo*psis⟩ **2** : having or dealing with three dimensions of space ⟨*stereo*taxic⟩

ste·reo·cil·i·um \ˌster-ē-ō-'si-lē-əm. ˌstir-\ *n, pl* **-ia** \-lē-ə\ : any of the immobile processes that resemble cilia and occur on the free border of various epithelia — see KINOCILIUM

ste·re·og·no·sis \ˌster-ē-äg-'nō-səs. ˌstir-\ *n* : ability to perceive or the perception of material qualities (as form and weight) of an object by handling or lifting it : tactile recognition

ste·reo·iso·mer \ˌster-ē-ō-'ī-sə-mər. ˌstir-\ *n* : any of a group of isomers in which atoms are linked in the same order but differ in their spatial arrangement — **ste·reo·iso·mer·ic** \-ˌī-sə-'mer-ik\ *adj* — **ste·reo·isom·er·ism** \-ī-'sä-mə-ˌri-zəm\ *n*

ste·re·op·sis \ˌster-ē-'äp-səs, ˌstir-\ *n* : stereoscopic vision

ste·reo·scope \'ster-ē-ə-ˌskōp, 'stir-\ *n* : an optical instrument with two eyepieces for helping the observer to combine the images of two pictures taken from points of view a little way apart and thus to get the effect of solidity or depth

ste·reo·scop·ic \ˌster-ē-ə-'skä-pik, ˌstir-\ *adj* **1** : of or relating to the stereoscope or the production of three-dimensional images **2** : characterized by the seeing of objects in three dimensions ⟨~ vision⟩ — **ste·reo·scop·i·cal·ly** *adv* — **ste·reos·co·py** \ster-ē-'äs-kə-pē, ˌstir-; 'ster-ē-ə-ˌskō-pē, 'stir-\ *n*

ste·reo·tac·tic \ˌster-ē-ə-'tak-tik, ˌstir-\ *adj* : STEREOTAXIC — **ste·reo·tac·ti·cal·ly** *adv*

ste·reo·tax·ic \ˌster-ē-ə-'tak-sik, ˌstir-\ *adj* : of, relating to, or being a technique or apparatus used in neurological research or surgery for directing the tip of a delicate instrument (as a needle or an electrode) in three planes in attempting to reach a specific locus in the brain — **ste·reo·tax·i·cal·ly** *adv*

ste·reo·tax·is \-'tak-səs\ *n, pl* **-tax·es** \-ˌsēz\ : a stereotaxic technique or procedure

¹ste·reo·type \'ster-ē-ə-ˌtīp, 'stir-\ *vb* **-typed; -typ·ing** **1** : to repeat without variation ⟨*stereotyped* behavior⟩ **2** : to develop a mental stereotype about

²stereotype *n* : something conforming to a fixed or general pattern; *esp* : an often oversimplified or biased mental picture held to characterize the typical individual of a group — **ste·reo·typ·i·cal** \ˌster-ē-ə-'ti-pi-kəl\ *also* **ste·reo·typ·ic** \-pik\ *adj*

ste·reo·ty·py \'ster-ē-ə-ˌtī-pē, 'stir-\ *n, pl* **-pies** : frequent almost mechanical repetition of the same posture, movement, or form of speech (as in schizophrenia)

ster·il·ant \'ster-ə-lənt\ *n* : a sterilizing agent

ster·ile \'ster-əl\ *adj* **1** : failing to produce or incapable of producing offspring ⟨a ~ hybrid⟩ **2** : free from living organisms and esp. microorganisms ⟨a ~ cyst⟩ — **ster·ile·ly** *adv* — **ste·ril·i·ty** \stə-'ri-lə-tē\ *n*

ster·il·ize \'ster-ə-ˌlīz\ *vb* **-ized; -iz·ing** : to make sterile: **a** : to deprive of the power of reproducing **b** : to free from living microorganisms usu. by the use of physical or chemical agents — **ster·il·i·za·tion** \ˌster-ə-lə-'zā-shən\ *n* — **ster·il·iz·er** \'ster-ə-ˌlī-zər\ *n*

stern- or **sterno-** *comb form* **1** : breast : sternum : breastbone ⟨*sterno*tomy⟩ **2** : sternal and ⟨*sterno*costal⟩

ster·nal \'stərn-ᵊl\ *adj* : of or relating to the sternum

ster·ne·bra \'stər-nə-brə\ *n, pl* **-brae** \-ˌbrē, -ˌbrī\ : any of the four segments into which the body of the sternum is divided in childhood and which fuse to form the gladiolus

ster·no·cla·vic·u·lar \ˌstər-nō-kla-'vi-kyə-lər\ *adj* : of, relating to, or being articulation of the sternum and the clavicle ⟨the ~ joint⟩ ⟨~ dislocation⟩

ster·no·clei·do·mas·toid \ˌstər-nō-ˌklī-də-'mas-ˌtòid\ *n* : a thick superficial muscle on each side that arises by one head from the first segment of the sternum and by a second from the inner part of the clavicle, that inserts into the mastoid process and occipital bone, and that acts esp. to bend, rotate, flex, and extend the head — **sternocleidomastoid** *adj*

ster·no·clei·do·mas·toi·de·us \-ˌmas-'tòi-dē-əs\ *n, pl* **-dei** \-dē-ˌī\ : STERNOCLEIDOMASTOID

ster·no·cos·tal \ˌstər-nō-'käst-ᵊl\ *adj* : of, relating to, or situated between the sternum and the ribs

ster·no·hy·oid \ˌstər-nō-'hī-ˌòid\ *n* : an infrahyoid muscle on each side of the midline that arises from the medial end of the clavicle and the first segment of the sternum, inserts into the body of the hyoid bone, and acts to depress the hyoid bone and the larynx — **sternohyoid** *adj*

ster·no·hy·oi·de·us \-hī-'òi-dē-əs\ *n, pl* **-dei** \-dē-ˌī\ : STERNOHYOID

ster·no·mas·toid muscle \-'mas-ˌtòid-\ *n* : STERNOCLEIDOMASTOID

ster·no·thy·roid \ˌstər-nō-'thī-ˌròid\ *n* : an infrahyoid muscle on each side of the body below the sternohyoid that arises from the sternum and from the cartilage of the first and sometimes of the second ribs, inserts into the thyroid cartilage, and acts to draw the larynx downward by depressing the thyroid cartilage — **sternothyroid** *adj*

ster·no·thy·roi·de·us \-thī-'ròi-dē-əs\ *n, pl* **-dei** \-dē-ˌī\ : STERNOTHYROID

ster·not·o·my \stər-'nä-tə-mē\ *n, pl* **-mies** : surgical incision through the sternum

ster·num \'stər-nəm\ *n, pl* **-nums** or **-na** \-nə\ : a compound ventral bone or cartilage that lies in the median central part of the body of most vertebrates other than fishes and that in humans is about seven inches (18 centimeters) long, consists in the adult of three parts, and connects with the clavicles and the cartilages of the upper seven pairs of ribs — called also *breastbone*

ster·nu·ta·tion \ˌstər-nyə-'tā-shən\ *n* : the act, fact, or noise of sneezing

ster·nu·ta·tor \'stər-nyə-ˌtā-tər\ *n* : an agent that induces sneezing and often lacrimation and vomiting

ste·roid \'ster-ˌòid, 'stir-\ *n* : any of numerous compounds containing a 17-carbon 4-ring system and including the sterols and various hormones and glycosides — **steroid** or **ste·roi·dal** \stə-'ròid-ᵊl\ *adj*

steroid hormone *n* : any of numerous hormones (as estrogen, testosterone, cortisone, and aldosterone) having the characteristic ring structure of steroids and formed in the body from cholesterol

ste·roi·do·gen·e·sis \stə-ˌròi-də-'je-nə-səs; ˌstir-ˌòi-, ˌster-\ *n, pl* **-e·ses** \-ˌsēz\ : synthesis of steroids (adrenal ~) — **ste·roi·do·gen·ic** \-'je-nik\ *adj*

ste·rol \'stir-ˌòl, 'ster-, -ˌòl\ *n* : any of various solid steroid alcohols (as cholesterol) widely distributed in animal and plant lipids

ster·to·rous \'stər-tə-rəs\ *adj* : characterized by a harsh snoring or gasping sound — **ster·to·rous·ly** *adv*

stetho·scope \'ste-thə-ˌskōp\ *n* : an instrument used to detect and study sounds produced in the body that are conveyed to the ears of the listener through rubber tubing connected with a usu. cup-shaped piece placed upon the area to be examined — **stetho·scop·ic** \ˌste-thə-'skä-pik\ *adj* — **stetho·scop·i·cal·ly** *adv*

Ste·vens–John·son syndrome \'stē-vənz-'jän-sən-\ *n* : a severe and sometimes fatal form of erythema multiforme that is characterized esp. by purulent conjunctivitis, Vincent's angina, and ulceration of the genitals and anus and that often results in blindness

Stevens, Albert Mason (1884–1945), and **Johnson, Frank Chambliss (1894–1934)**, American pediatricians.

STH *abbr* somatotropic hormone

sthen·ic \'sthe-nik\ *adj* **1** : notably or excessively vigorous or active ⟨~ fever⟩ ⟨~ emotions⟩ **2** : PYKNIC

stib·o·phen \'sti-bə-ˌfen\ *n* : a crystalline antimony compound $C_{12}H_4Na_5-O_{16}S_4Sb \cdot 7H_2O$ used in the treatment of various tropical diseases

stick·tight flea \'stik-ˌtīt-\ *n* : a flea of the genus *Echidnophaga* (*E. gallin-*

acea) that is parasitic esp. on the heads of chickens

sties *pl of* STY

stiff \'stif\ *adj* : lacking in suppleness (~ muscles) — **stiff·ness** *n*

stiff–lamb disease \'stif-,lam-\ *n* : white muscle disease occurring in lambs

stiff–man syndrome *n* : a chronic progressive disorder of uncertain etiology that is characterized by painful spasms and increasing stiffness of the muscles

sti·fle \'stī-fəl\ *n* : the joint next above the hock in the hind leg of a quadruped (as a horse) corresponding to the knee in humans

stig·ma \'stig-mə\ *n, pl* **stig·ma·ta** \stig-'mä-tə, 'stig-mə-tə\ *or* **stigmas** 1 : an identifying mark or characteristic; *specif* : a specific diagnostic sign of a disease (the *stigmata* of syphilis) 2 : PETECHIA 3 : a small spot, scar, or opening on a plant or animal

stilb·am·i·dine \stil-'ba-mə-,dēn\ *n* : a drug $C_{16}H_{16}N_4$ used chiefly in the form of one of its salts in treating various fungal infections

stil·bes·trol \stil-'bes-,tról, -,tról\ *n* 1 : a crystalline compound $C_{14}H_{12}O_2$ that differs from the related diethylstilbestrol in lack of the ethyl groups and in possession of only slight estrogenic activity 2 : DIETHYLSTILBESTROL

sti·let \'stī-lət\ *or* **sti·lette** \sti-'let\ *n* : STYLET

still·birth \'stil-,bərth\ *n* : the birth of a dead fetus — compare LIVE BIRTH

still·born \-,bórn\ *adj* : dead at birth — compare LIVE-BORN, **stillborn** *n*

Still's disease \'stilz-\ *n* : rheumatoid arthritis esp. in children
    Still, Sir George Frederic (1868–1941), British pediatrician.

stim·u·lant \'stim-yə-lənt\ *n* 1 : an agent (as a drug) that produces a temporary increase of the functional activity or efficiency of an organism or any of its parts 2 : STIMULUS 2

stim·u·late \-,lāt\ *vb* **-lat·ed; -lat·ing** 1 : to excite to activity or growth or to greater activity 2 a : to function as a physiological stimulus to (as a nerve or muscle) b : to arouse or affect by a stimulant (as a drug) — **stim·u·la·tion** \,stim-yə-'lā-shən\ *n* — **stim·u·la·tive** \'stim-yə-,lā-tiv\ *adj* — **stim·u·la·to·ry** \-lə-,tōr-ē\ *adj*

stim·u·la·tor \'stim-yə-,lā-tər\ *n* : one that stimulates; *specif* : an instrument used to provide a stimulus

stim·u·lus \'stim-yə-ləs\ *n, pl* **-li** \-,lī, -,lē\ 1 : STIMULANT 1 2 : an agent (as an environmental change) that directly influences the activity of living protoplasm (as by exciting a sensory organ or evoking muscular contraction or glandular secretion) (a visual ~)

stimulus–response *adj* : of, relating to, or being a reaction to a stimulus; *also*

: representing the activity of an organism as composed of such reactions (~ psychology)

sting \'stiŋ\ *vb* **stung** \'stəŋ\: **sting·ing** 1 : to prick painfully: as a : to pierce or wound with a poisonous or irritating process b : to affect with sharp quick pain 2 : to feel or cause a keen burning pain or smart (the injection *stung*) — **sting** *n*

sting·er \'stiŋ-ər\ *n* : a sharp organ (as of a bee or scorpion) that is usu. connected with a poison gland or otherwise adapted to wound by piercing and injecting a poison

sting·ray \'stiŋ-,rā\ *n* : any of numerous large flat cartilaginous fishes (order Rajiformes and esp. family Dasyatidae) with one or more large sharp barbed dorsal spines near the base of the whiplike tail capable of inflicting severe wounds

stint *var of* STENT

stip·pling \'stip-liŋ\ *n* : the appearance of spots : a spotted condition (as in basophilic red blood cells)

stir·rup \'stər-əp, 'stir-əp\ *n* 1 : STAPES 2 : an attachment to an examining or operating table designed to raise and spread the legs of a patient

stitch \'stich\ *n* 1 : a local sharp and sudden pain esp. in the side 2 a : one in-and-out movement of a threaded needle in suturing b : a portion of a suture left in the tissue after one stitch (removal of ~*es*) — **stitch** *vb*

stock·ing \'stäk-iŋ\ *n* — see ELASTIC STOCKING

Stokes–Ad·ams syndrome \'stōks-'a-dəmz-\ *n* : fainting and convulsions induced by complete heart block with a pulse rate of 40 beats per minute or less — called also *Adams-Stokes syndrome, Stokes-Adams attack, Stokes-Adams disease*
    W. Stokes — see CHEYNE-STOKES RESPIRATION
    Adams, Robert (1791–1875), British physician.

sto·ma \'stō-mə\ *n, pl* **-mas** : an artificial permanent opening esp. in the abdominal wall made in surgical procedures (a colostomy ~)

stom·ach \'stə-mik\ *n* 1 a : a dilatation of the alimentary canal communicating anteriorly with the esophagus and posteriorly with the duodenum and being typically a simple often curved sac with an outer serous coat, a strong complex muscular wall that contracts rhythmically, and a mucous lining membrane that contains gastric glands b : one of the compartments of a ruminant stomach 2 : the part of the body that contains the stomach : BELLY, ABDOMEN

stom·ach·ache \-,āk\ *n* : pain in or in the region of the stomach

sto·mach·ic \stə-'ma-kik\ *n* : a stimulant or tonic for the stomach

stomach pump *n* : a suction pump with

a flexible tube for removing liquid from the stomach

stomach tube *n* : a flexible rubber tube to be passed through the esophagus into the stomach for introduction of material or removal of gastric contents

stomach worm *n* : any of various nematode worms parasitic in the stomach of mammals or birds; *esp* : a worm of the genus *Haemonchus* (*H. contortus*) common in domestic ruminants

sto·mal \ˈstō-məl\ *adj* : of, relating to, or situated near a surgical stoma

stomat- *or* **stomato-** *comb form* : mouth ⟨*stoma*titis⟩ ⟨*stomato*logy⟩

sto·ma·ti·tis \ˌstō-mə-ˈtī-təs\ *n, pl* **-tit·i·des** \-ˈti-tə-ˌdēz\ *or* **-ti·tis·es** \ˈtī-tə-səz\ : any of numerous inflammatory diseases of the mouth having various causes (as mechanical trauma, irritants, allergy, vitamin deficiency, or infection) ⟨erosive ∼⟩

sto·ma·to·gnath·ic \ˌstō-mə-(ˌ)täg-ˈna-thik\ *adj* : of or relating to the jaws and the mouth

sto·ma·tol·o·gist \ˌstō-mə-ˈtä-lə-jist\ *n* : a specialist in stomatology

sto·ma·tol·o·gy \ˌstō-mə-ˈtä-lə-jē\ *n, pl* **-gies** : a branch of medical science dealing with the mouth and its disorders — **sto·ma·to·log·i·cal** \ˌstō-mət-ᵊl-ˈä-ji-kəl\ *also* **sto·ma·to·log·ic** \-ˈji-k\ *adj*

-stomia \ˈstō-mē-ə\ *n comb form* : mouth exhibiting (such) a condition ⟨xero*stomia*⟩

sto·mo·de·um *or* **sto·mo·dae·um** \ˌstō-mə-ˈdē-əm\ *n, pl* **-dea** *or* **-daea** \-ˈdē-ə\ *also* **-deums** *or* **-daeums** : the embryonic anterior ectodermal part of the alimentary canal or tract — **sto·mo·de·al** *or* **sto·mo·dae·al** \-ˈdē-əl\ *adj*

Sto·mox·ys \stə-ˈmäk-səs\ *n* : a genus of bloodsucking dipteran flies (family Muscidae) that includes the stable fly (*S. calcitrans*)

-s·to·my \s-tə-mē\ *n comb form, pl* **-s·to·mies** : surgical operation establishing a usu. permanent opening into (such) a part ⟨entero*stomy*⟩

stone \ˈstōn\ *n* : CALCULUS

stone-blind \ˈstōn-ˈblīnd\ *adj* : totally blind

stoned \ˈstōnd\ *adj* : being drunk or under the influence of a drug (as marijuana) taken esp. for pleasure

stone-deaf *adj* : totally deaf

stool \ˈstül\ *n* : a discharge of fecal matter

storage disease *n* : the abnormal accumulation in the body of one or more specific substances and esp. metabolic substances (as cerebrosides in Gaucher's disease)

sto·rax \ˈstōr-ˌaks\ *n* **1** : a fragrant balsam obtained from the bark of an Asian tree of the genus *Liquidambar* (*L. orientalis*) that is used as an expectorant — called also *Levant storax* **2** : a balsam similar to storax that is obtained from a No. American

tree of the genus *Liquidambar* (*L. styraciflua*) — called also *liquidambar*

storm \ˈstorm\ *n* : a crisis or sudden increase in the symptoms of a disease — see THYROID STORM

stormy \ˈstor-mē\ *adj* **storm·i·er; -est** : having alternating exacerbations and remissions of symptoms

STP \ˌes-(ˌ)tē-ˈpē\ *n* : a psychedelic drug chemically related to mescaline and amphetamine — called also *DOM*

stra·bis·mus \strə-ˈbiz-məs\ *n* : inability of one eye to attain binocular vision with the other because of imbalance of the muscles of the eyeball — called also *heterotropia*, *squint* — **stra·bis·mic** \strə-ˈbiz-mik\ *adj*

straight·jack·et *var of* STRAITJACKET

straight sinus *n* : a venous sinus of the brain that is located along the line of junction of the falx cerebri and tentorium cerebelli and passes posteriorly to terminate in the confluence of sinuses

¹**strain** \ˈstrān\ *n* : a group of presumed common ancestry with clear-cut physiological but usu. not morphological distinctions (a ∼ of bacteria)

²**strain** *vb* **1 a** : to exert (as oneself) to the utmost **b** : to injure by overuse, misuse, or excessive pressure ⟨∼ed his heart by overwork⟩ **2** : to contract the muscles forcefully in attempting to defecate — often used in the phrase *strain at stool*

³**strain** *n* : an act of straining or the condition of being strained; as **a** : excessive physical or mental tension; *also* : a force, influence, or factor causing such tension **b** : bodily injury from excessive tension, effort, or use ⟨heart ∼⟩; *esp* : one resulting from a wrench or twist and involving undue stretching of muscles or ligaments ⟨back ∼⟩ — compare SPRAIN

strait·jack·et \ˈstrāt-ˌja-kət\ *n* : a cover or garment of strong material (as canvas) used to bind the body and esp. the arms closely in restraining a violent prisoner or patient

stra·mo·ni·um \strə-ˈmō-nē-əm\ *n* **1** : the dried leaves of the jimsonweed (*Datura stramonium*) or of a related plant of the genus *Datura* that contain toxic alkaloids (as atropine) and are used in medicine similarly to belladonna **2** : JIMSONWEED

strand \ˈstrand\ *n* : something (as a molecular chain) resembling a thread

strand·ed \ˈstran-dəd\ *adj* : having a strand or strands esp. of a specified kind or number — usu. used in combination ⟨double-*stranded* DNA⟩ — **strand·ed·ness** *n*

stran·gle \ˈstraŋ-gəl\ *vb* **stran·gled; stran·gling 1** : to choke to death **2** : to obstruct seriously or fatally the normal breathing of

stran·gles \-gəlz\ *n sing or pl* : an infectious febrile disease of horses and other equines that is caused by a bacterium of the genus *Streptococcus* (*S. equi*)

stran·gu·lat·ed hernia \'straṅ-gyə-ˌlā-təd-\ *n* : a hernia in which the blood supply of the herniated viscus is so constricted by swelling and congestion as to arrest its circulation

stran·gu·la·tion \ˌstraṅ-gyə-'lā-shən\ *n* **1** : the action or process of strangling or of becoming constricted so as to stop circulation **2** : the state or condition resulting from strangulation; *esp* : excessive or pathological constriction or compression of a bodily tube (as a blood vessel or a loop of intestine) that interrupts its ability to act as a passage — **stran·gu·late** \'straṅ-gyə-ˌlāt\ *vb*

stran·gu·ry \'straṅ-gyə-rē, -ˌgyùr-ē\ *n, pl* **-ries** : a slow and painful discharge of urine drop by drop produced by spasmodic muscular contraction of the urethra and bladder

¹strap \'strap\ *n* : a flexible band or strip (as of adhesive plaster)

²strap *vb* **strapped; strap·ping 1** : to secure with or attach by means of a strap **2** : to support (as a sprained joint) with overlapping strips of adhesive plaster

strapping *n* : the application of adhesive plaster in overlapping strips upon or around a part (as a sprained ankle) to serve as a splint to reduce motion or to hold surgical dressings in place upon a surgical wound; *also* : material so used

strat·i·fied \'stra-tə-ˌfīd\ *adj* : arranged in layers; *esp* : of, relating to, or being an epithelium consisting of more than one layer of cells — **strat·i·fi·ca·tion** \ˌstra-tə-fə-'kā-shən\ *n*

stra·tum \'strā-təm, 'stra-\ *n, pl* **stra·ta** \'strā-tə, 'stra-\ : a layer of tissue

stratum ba·sa·le \-bā-'sā-lē\ *n, pl* **strata ba·sa·lia** \-lē-ə\ : the layer of stratum germinativum esp. in the endometrium that undergoes mitotic division

stratum com·pac·tum \-kəm-'pak-təm\ *n, pl* **strata com·pac·ta** \-'pak-tə\ : the relatively dense superficial layer of the endometrium

stratum corneum *n, pl* **strata cornea** : the outer more or less horny part of the epidermis

stratum ger·mi·na·ti·vum \-ˌjər-mə-nə-'tī-vəm\ *n, pl* **strata ger·mi·na·ti·va** \-və\ **1** : the innermost layer of the epidermis consisting of a single row of columnar or cuboidal epithelial cells that continually divide and replace the rest of the epidermis — see STRATUM BASALE **2** : MALPIGHIAN LAYER

stratum gran·u·lo·sum \-ˌgran-yə-'lō-səm\ *n, pl* **strata gran·u·lo·sa** \-sə\ : a layer of granular cells lying immediately above the stratum germinativum in most parts of the epidermis

stratum in·ter·me·di·um \-ˌin-tər-'mē-dē-əm\ *n, pl* **strata in·ter·me·dia** \-dē-ə\ : the cell layer of the enamel organ next to the layer of ameloblasts

stratum lu·ci·dum \-'lü-si-dəm\ *n, pl* **strata lu·ci·da** \-də\ : a thin somewhat translucent layer of cells lying under the stratum corneum esp. in thickened epidermis

stratum spi·no·sum \-spi-'nō-səm\ *n, pl* **strata spi·no·sa** \-sə\ : the layers of prickle cells over the layer of the stratum germinativum capable of undergoing mitosis — called also *prickle cell layer*

stratum spon·gi·o·sum \-ˌspən-jē-'ō-səm\ *n, pl* **strata spon·gi·o·sa** \-sə\ : the middle layer of the endometrium between the stratum basale and stratum compactum that contains dilated and tortuous portions of the uterine glands

strawberry gallbladder *n* : an abnormal condition characterized by the deposition of cholesterol in the lining of the gallbladder in a pattern resembling the surface of a strawberry

strawberry mark *n* : a tumor of the skin filled with small blood vessels and appearing usu. as a red and elevated birthmark

strawberry tongue *n* : a tongue that is red from swollen congested papillae and that occurs esp. in scarlet fever and Kawasaki disease

¹streak \'strēk\ *n* **1** : a usu. irregular line or stripe — see PRIMITIVE STREAK **2** : inoculum implanted in a line on a solid medium

²streak *vb* : to implant (inoculum) in a line on a solid medium

stream \'strēm\ *n* : an unbroken current or flow (as of a bodily fluid or a gas) — see BLOODSTREAM, MIDSTREAM

stream of consciousness *n* : the continuous unedited flow of conscious experience through the mind

street virus *n* : a naturally occurring rabies virus as distinguished from virus attenuated in the laboratory

strength \'streṅth, 'strenth\ *n, pl* **strengths 1** : the quality or state of being strong : capacity for exertion or endurance **2** : degree of potency of effect or of concentration **3** : degree of ionization of a solution — used of acids and bases

strep \'strep\ *n, often attrib* : STREPTOCOCCUS (a ~ infection)

strepho·sym·bo·lia \ˌstre-fō-sim-'bō-lē-ə\ *n* : a learning disorder in which symbols and esp. phrases, words, or letters appear to be reversed or transposed in reading

strep throat *n* : an inflammatory sore throat caused by hemolytic streptococci and marked by fever, prostration, and toxemia — called also *septic sore throat, strep sore throat*

strepto- *comb form* **1** : twisted : twisted

chain (*strepto*coccus) **2** : streptococ-cus (*strepto*kinase)

strep·to·ba·cil·lus \\strep-tō-bə-ˈsi-ləs\ *n 1 cap* : a genus of facultatively an-aerobic gram-negative rod bacteria that includes one (*S. moniliformis*) that is the causative agent of one form of rat-bite fever **2** *pl* **-li** \-ˌlī\ : any of various nonmotile gram-negative ba-cilli in which the individual cells are joined in a chain; *esp* : one of the ge-nus *Streptobacillus* — **strep·to·ba·cil·la·ry** \ˈba-sə-ˌler-ē, -bə-ˈsi-lə-rē\ *adj*

strep·to·coc·cal \\strep-tə-ˈkä-kəl\ *also* **strep·to·coc·cic** \-ˈkä-kik, -ˈkäk-sik\ *adj* : of, relating to, caused by, or be-ing streptococci (∼ gingivitis)

strep·to·coc·cus \-ˈkä-kəs\ *n 1 cap* : a genus of spherical or ovoid chiefly nonmotile and parasitic gram-pos-itive bacteria (family Streptococcace-ae) that divide only in one plane, oc-cur in pairs or chains, and include important pathogens of humans and domestic animals **2** *pl* **-coc·ci** \-ˈkä-ˌki, -ˈkäk-si\ : any bacterium of the genus *Streptococcus*; *broadly* : a coc-cus occurring in chains

strep·to·dor·nase \\strep-tō-ˈdȯr-ˌnās, -ˌnāz\ *n* : a deoxyribonuclease from hemolytic streptococci that dissolves pus and is usu. administered in a mix-ture with streptokinase — see VARI-DASE

strep·to·ki·nase \\strep-tō-ˈki-ˌnās, -ˌnāz\ *n* : a proteolytic enzyme from hemolytic streptococci active in pro-moting dissolution of blood clots — see VARIDASE

strep·to·ly·sin \\strep-tə-ˈlīs-ᵊn\ *n* : any of various antigenic hemolysins pro-duced by streptococci

strep·to·my·ces \-ˈmī-ˌsēz\ *n 1 cap* : a genus of mostly soil streptomycetes including some that form antibiotics as by-products of their metabolism **2** *pl* **streptomyces** : any bacterium of the genus *Streptomyces*

strep·to·my·cete \-ˈmī-ˌsēt, -ˌmī-ˈsēt\ *n* : any of a family (Streptomycetaceae) of actinomycetes (as a streptomyces) that are typically aerobic soil sapro-phytes but include a few parasites of plants and animals

strep·to·my·cin \-ˈmīs-ᵊn\ *n* : an antibi-otic $C_{21}H_{39}N_7O_{12}$ that is produced by a soil actinomycete of the genus *Streptomyces* (*S. griseus*), is active against bacteria, and is used esp. in the treatment of infections (as tuber-culosis) by gram-negative bacteria

strep·to·ni·grin \-ˈnī-grən\ *n* : a toxic antibiotic $C_{25}H_{22}N_4O_8$ from an acti-nomycete of the genus *Streptomyces* (*S. flocculus*) that is used as an anti-neoplastic agent

strep·to·zo·cin \\strep-tə-ˈzō-sən\ *n* : STREPTOZOTOCIN

strep·to·zot·o·cin \\strep-tə-ˈzä-tə-sən\ *n* : a broad-spectrum antibiotic $C_8H_{15}N_3O_7$ with antineoplastic and diabetogenic properties that has been isolated from a bacterium of the ge-nus *Streptomyces* (*S. achromogenes*)

stress \ˈstres\ *n 1* **a** : a force exerted when one body or body part presses on, pulls on, pushes against, or tends to compress or twist another body or body part **b** : the deformation caused in a body by such a force **2 a** : a phys-ical, chemical, or emotional factor that causes bodily or mental tension and may be a factor in disease causa-tion **b** : a state of bodily or mental ten-sion resulting from factors that tend to alter an existent equilibrium **3** : the force exerted between teeth of the upper and lower jaws during mastica-tion — **stress** *vb* — **stress·ful** \ˈstres-fəl\ *adj* — **stress·ful·ly** *adv*

stress breaker *n* : a flexible dental de-vice used to lessen the occlusal forces exerted on teeth to which a partial denture is attached

stress fracture *n* : a usu. hairline frac-ture of a bone that has been subjected to repeated stress

stress·or \ˈstre-sər, -ˌsȯr\ *n* : a stimulus that causes stress

stress test *n* : an electrocardiographic test of heart function before, during, and after a controlled period of in-creasingly strenuous exercise (as on a treadmill)

¹stretch \ˈstrech\ *vb 1* : to extend or be-come extended in length or breadth **2** : to enlarge or distend esp. by force

²stretch *n* : the act of stretching : the state of being stretched

stretch·er \ˈstre-chər\ *n* : a device for carrying a sick, injured, or dead per-son

stretch·er-bear·er \-ˌbar-ər\ *n* : one who carries one end of a stretcher

stretch marks *n pl* : striae on the skin (as of the hips, abdomen, and breasts) from excessive stretching and rupture of elastic fibers esp. due to pregnancy or obesity

stretch receptor *n* : MUSCLE SPINDLE

stretch reflex *n* : a spinal reflex involv-ing reflex contraction of a muscle in response to stretching — called also *myotatic reflex*

stria \ˈstrī-ə\ *n, pl* **stri·ae** \ˈstrī-ˌē\ **1** : STRIATION **2 2** : a narrow structural band esp. of nerve fibers **3** : a stripe or line (as in the skin) distinguished from surrounding tissue by color, tex-ture, or elevation — see STRETCH MARKS

striata *pl of* STRIATUM

stri·a·tal \strī-ˈāt-ᵊl\ *adj* : of or relating to the corpus striatum (∼ neurons)

stri·ate cortex \ˈstrī-ət-, -ˌāt-\ *n* : an area of the brain that receives visual impulses, contains a conspicuous band of myelinated fibers, and is lo-cated mostly in the walls and along the edges of the calcarine sulcus of the occipital lobe — called also *visual projection area*

stri·at·ed \'strī-ˌā-təd\ *adj* **1** : marked with striae **2** : of, relating to, or being striated muscle

striated muscle *n* : muscle tissue that is marked by transverse dark and light bands, that is made up of elongated multinuclear fibers, and that includes skeletal and cardiac muscle of vertebrates and most muscle of arthropods — compare SMOOTH MUSCLE, VOLUNTARY MUSCLE

stria ter·mi·na·lis \-ˌtər-mə-'nā-ləs\ *n* : a bundle of nerve fibers that passes from the amygdala mostly to the anterior part of the hypothalamus with a few fibers crossing the anterior commissure to the amygdala on the opposite side

stri·a·tion \strī-'ā-shən\ *n* **1** : the fact or state of being striated **2** : a minute groove, scratch, or channel esp. when one of a parallel series **3** : any of the alternate dark and light cross bands of a myofibril of striated muscle

stri·a·to·ni·gral \strī-ˌā-tə-'nī-grəl\ *adj* : connecting the corpus striatum and substantia nigra (~ axons)

stri·a·tum \strī-'ā-təm\ *n, pl* **stri·a·ta** \-'ā-tə\ **1** : CORPUS STRIATUM **2** : NEOSTRIATUM

stria vas·cu·la·ris \-ˌvas-kyə-'ler-əs\ *n* : the upper part of the spiral ligament of the scala media that contains numerous small blood vessels

stric·ture \'strik-chər\ *n* : an abnormal narrowing of a bodily passage (as from inflammation or the formation of scar tissue); *also* : the narrowed part

stri·dor \'strī-dər, -ˌdȯr\ *n* : a harsh vibrating sound heard during respiration in cases of obstruction of the air passages (laryngeal ~) — **strid·u·lous** \'stri-jə-ləs\ *adj*

stridulus — see LARYNGISMUS STRIDULUS

strike \'strīk\ *n* : cutaneous myiasis (as of sheep) (body ~) (blowfly ~)

string·halt \'striŋ-ˌhȯlt\ *n* : a condition of lameness in the hind legs of a horse caused by muscular spasms — **string·halt·ed** \-ˌhȯl-təd\ *adj*

strip \'strip\ *vb* **stripped** \'stript\ *also* **stript; strip·ping** : to remove (a vein) by means of a stripper

strip·per \'stri-pər\ *n* : a surgical instrument used for removal of a vein

stroke \'strōk\ *n* : sudden diminution or loss of consciousness, sensation, and voluntary motion caused by rupture or obstruction (as by a clot) of an artery of the brain — called also *apoplexy;* compare CEREBRAL ACCIDENT

stroke volume *n* : the volume of blood pumped from a ventricle of the heart in one beat

stro·ma \'strō-mə\ *n, pl* **stro·ma·ta** \-mə-tə\ **1** : the supporting framework of an animal organ typically consisting of connective tissue **2** : the spongy protoplasmic framework of some cells (as a red blood cell) — **stro·mal** \-məl\ *adj*

strong silver protein *n* : SILVER PROTEIN b

stron·gyle \'strän-ˌjīl\ *n* : STRONGYLID; *esp* : a worm of the genus *Strongylus* or closely related genera that is parasitic in the alimentary tract and tissues of the horse and may induce severe diarrhea and debility

stron·gy·lid \'strän-jə-lid\ *n* : any of a family (Strongylidae) of nematode worms that are parasites of vertebrates — **strongylid** *adj*

stron·gy·li·do·sis \ˌsträn-jə-lə-'dō-səs\ *n* : STRONGYLOSIS

stron·gy·loid \'strän-jə-ˌlȯid\ *n* : any of a superfamily (Strongyloidea) of nematode worms including the hookworms, strongyles, and related forms — **strongyloid** *adj*

Stron·gy·loi·des \ˌsträn-jə-'lȯi-ˌdēz\ *n* : a genus of nematode worms (family Strongyloididae) having both free-living males and females and parthenogenetic females parasitic in the intestine of various vertebrates and including some medically and economically important pests of humans

stron·gy·loi·di·a·sis \ˌsträn-jə-ˌlȯi-'dī-ə-səs\ *n, pl* **-a·ses** \-ˌsēz\ : infestation with or disease caused by nematodes of the genus *Strongyloides*

stron·gy·loi·do·sis \-'dō-səs\ *n* : STRONGYLOIDIASIS

stron·gy·lo·sis \ˌsträn-jə-'lō-səs\ *n* : infestation with or disease caused by strongyles — called also *strongylidosis*

Stron·gy·lus \'strän-jə-ləs\ *n* : a genus of strongylid nematode worms including gastrointestinal parasites of the horse

stron·ti·um \'strän-chəm, -chē-əm, -tē-əm\ *n* : a soft malleable ductile bivalent metallic element — symbol *Sr;* see ELEMENT table

strontium 90 *n* : a heavy radioactive isotope of strontium having the mass number 90 that is present in the fallout from nuclear explosions and is hazardous because like calcium it can be assimilated in biological processes and deposited in the bones — called also *radiostrontium*

stro·phan·thin \strō-'fan-thən\ *n* : a bitter toxic glycoside $C_{36}H_{54}O_{14}$ from a woody vine of the genus *Strophanthus* (*S. kombé*) used similarly to digitalis; *also* : a related glycoside (as ouabain)

stro·phan·thus \-thəs\ *n* **1** *cap* : a genus of Asian and African trees, shrubs, or woody vines of the dogbane family (Apocynaceae) including one (*S. kombé*) that furnishes strophanthin **2** : the dried cleaned ripe seeds of any of several plants of the genus *Strophanthus* (as *S. kombé* and *S. hispidus*) that are in moderate doses a cardiac stimulant like digitalis but in larger doses a violent poison and that have strophanthin as their most active constituent

struck \'strək\ *n* : enterotoxemia esp. of adult sheep

struc·tur·al \'strək-chə-rəl\ *adj* **1** : of or relating to the physical makeup of a plant or animal body (~ defects of the heart) — compare FUNCTIONAL 1a **2** : of, relating to, or affecting structure (~ stability) — **struc·tur·al·ly** *adv*

structural formula *n* : an expanded molecular formula (as HOCH₂(CHOH)₄CHO for glucose) showing the arrangement within the molecule of atoms and of bonds

structural gene *n* : a gene that codes for the amino acid sequence of a protein (as an enzyme) or for a ribosomal RNA or transfer RNA

struc·tur·al·ism \'strək-chə-rə-ˌli-zəm\ *n* : psychology concerned esp. with resolution of the mind into structural elements

struc·ture \'strək-chər\ *n* **1** : something (as an anatomical part) arranged in a definite pattern of organization **2 a** : the arrangement of particles or parts in a substance or body (molecular ~) **b** : organization of parts as dominated by the general character of the whole (personality ~) **3** : the aggregate of elements of an entity in their relationships to each other

stru·ma \'strü-mə\ *n, pl* **-mae** \-(ˌ)mē\ *or* **-mas** : GOITER

struma lym·pho·ma·to·sa \-ˌlim-ˌfō-mə-'tō-sə\ *n* : HASHIMOTO'S DISEASE

stru·vite \'strü-ˌvīt\ *n* : a hydrated magnesium-containing mineral Mg(NH₄)(PO₄)·6H₂O which is found in kidney stones associated with bacteria that cleave urea

strych·nine \'strik-ˌnīn, -nən, -ˌnēn\ *n* : a bitter poisonous alkaloid C₂₁H₂₂N₂O₂ that is obtained from nux vomica and related plants of the genus *Strychnos* and is used medicinally as a stimulant of the central nervous system

Strych·nos \'strik-nəs, -ˌnäs\ *n* : a large genus of tropical trees and woody vines (family Loganiaceae) — see CURARE, NUX VOMICA, STRYCHNINE

STS *abbr* serologic test for syphilis

ST segment *or* **S–T segment** \ˌes-'tē-\ *n* : the part of an electrocardiogram between the QRS complex and the T wave

Stu·art–Prow·er factor \'stü-ərt-'prau̇-ər-, -'styü-\ *n* : FACTOR X

Stuart and Prower, 20th century hospital patients.

stuff \'stəf\ *vb* : to choke or block up (as nasal passages) (a ~*ed* up nose) — **stuff·i·ness** \'stə-fē-nəs\ *n* — **stuffy** \'stəf-ē\ *adj*

stump \'stəmp\ *n* **1** : the basal portion of a bodily part (as a limb) remaining

after the rest is removed **2** : a rudimentary or vestigial bodily part

stung *past and past part of* STING

stunt \'stənt\ *vb* : to hinder the normal growth, development, or progress of

stupe \'stüp, 'styüp\ *n* : a hot wet often medicated cloth applied externally (as to stimulate circulation)

stu·pe·fy \'stü-pə-ˌfī, 'styü-\ *vb* **-fied; -fy·ing** : to make stupid, groggy, or insensible — **stu·pe·fac·tion** \ˌstü-pə-'fak-shən, ˌstyü-\ *n*

stu·por \'stü-pər, 'styü-\ *n* : a condition of greatly dulled or completely suspended sense or sensibility (a drunken ~); *specif* : a chiefly mental condition marked by absence of spontaneous movement, greatly diminished responsiveness to stimulation, and usu. impaired consciousness — **stu·por·ous** \'stü-pə-rəs, 'styü-\ *adj*

stur·dy \'stər-dē\ *n, pl* **stur·dies** : GID

Sturge–Web·er syndrome \'stərj-'web-ər-\ *n* : a rare congenital condition that is characterized by a port-wine stain affecting the facial skin on one side in the area innervated by the first branch of the trigeminal nerve and by malformed blood vessels in the brain that may cause progressive mental retardation, epilepsy, and glaucoma in the eye on the affected side — called also *Sturge–Weber disease*

Sturge, William Allen (1850–1919), and Weber, Frederick Parkes (1863–1962), British physicians.

¹stut·ter \'stə-tər\ *vb* : to speak with involuntary disruption or blocking of speech (as by spasmodic repetition or prolongation of vocal sounds) — **stut·ter·er** \'stə-tər-ər-\ *n*

²stutter *n* **1** : an act or instance of stuttering **2** : a speech disorder involving stuttering

stuttering *n* **1** : the act of one who stutters **2** : a disorder of vocal communication marked by involuntary disruption or blocking of speech (as by spasmodic repetition or prolongation of vocal sounds), by fear and anxiety, and by a struggle to avoid speech errors — compare STAMMERING 2

sty *or* **stye** \'stī\ *n, pl* **sties** *or* **styes** : an inflamed swelling of a sebaceous gland at the margin of an eyelid — called also *hordeolum*

styl- *or* **stylo-** *comb form* : styloid process (*stylo*glossus)

sty·let \ˌstī-'let, 'stī-lət\ *also* **sty·lette** \stī-'let\ *n* **1** : a slender surgical probe **2** : a thin wire inserted into a catheter to maintain rigidity or into a hollow needle to maintain patency

sty·lo·glos·sus \ˌstī-lō-'glä-səs, -'glȯ-\ *n, pl* **-glos·si** \-'glä-ˌsī, -'glȯ-\ : a muscle that arises from the styloid process of the temporal bone, inserts along the side and underpart of the tongue, and functions to draw the tongue upwards

sty·lo·hy·oid \ˌstī-lō-ˈhī-ˌóid\ *n* : STYLO-HYOID MUSCLE

sty·lo·hy·oi·de·us \-hī-ˈói-dē-əs\ *n, pl* **-dei** \-dē-ˌī\ : STYLOHYOID MUSCLE

stylohyoid ligament *n* : a band of fibrous tissue connecting the tip of the styloid process of the temporal bone to the ceratohyal of the hyoid bone

stylohyoid muscle *n* : a slender muscle that arises from the posterior surface of the styloid process of the temporal bone, inserts into the body of the hyoid bone, and acts to elevate and retract the hyoid bone resulting in elongation of the floor of the mouth — called also *stylohyoid, stylohyoideus*

sty·loid \ˈstī-ˌlóid\ *adj* : having a slender pointed shape

styloid process *n* : any of several long slender pointed bony processes: as **a** : a sharp spine that projects downward and forward from the inferior surface of the temporal bone just in front of the stylomastoid foramen **b** : an eminence on the distal extremity of the ulna giving attachment to a ligament of the wrist joint **c** : a conical prolongation of the lateral surface of the distal extremity of the radius that gives attachment to several tendons and ligaments

sty·lo·man·dib·u·lar ligament \ˌstī-lō-man-ˈdi-byə-lər\ *n* : a band of deep fascia that connects the styloid process of the temporal bone to the gonial angle

sty·lo·mas·toid foramen \-ˈmas-ˌtóid-\ *n* : a foramen that occurs on the lower surface of the temporal bone between the styloid and mastoid processes

sty·lo·pha·ryn·ge·us \ˌstī-lō-fə-ˈrin-jē-əs, -ˌfar-ən-ˈjē-əs\ *n, pl* **-gei** \-jē-ˌī\ : a slender muscle that arises from the base of the styloid process of the temporal bone, inserts into the side of the pharynx, and acts with the contralateral muscle in swallowing to increase the transverse diameter of the pharynx by drawing its sides upward and laterally

¹styp·tic \ˈstip-tik\ *adj* : tending to check bleeding; *esp* : having the property of arresting oozing of blood (as from a shallow surface injury) when applied to a bleeding part ⟨~ agent⟩

²styptic *n* : an agent (as a drug) having a styptic effect

styptic pencil *n* : a cylindrical stick of a medicated styptic substance used esp. in shaving to stop the bleeding from small cuts

sub- *prefix* **1** : under : beneath : below ⟨*sub*coastal⟩ **2** : subordinate portion of : subdivision of ⟨*sub*species⟩ **3** : less than completely or perfectly ⟨*sub*normal⟩

sub·acro·mi·al \ˌsəb-ə-ˈkrō-mē-əl\ *adj* : of, relating to, or affecting the subacromial bursa ⟨~ bursitis⟩

subacromial bursa *n* : a bursa lying between the acromion and the capsule of the shoulder joint

sub·acute \ˌsəb-ə-ˈkyüt\ *adj* **1** : falling between acute and chronic in character esp. when closer to acute ⟨~ endocarditis⟩ **2** : less marked in severity or duration than a corresponding acute state ⟨~ pain⟩ — **sub·acute·ly** *adv*

subacute sclerosing panencephalitis *n* : a central nervous system disease of children and young adults caused by infection of the brain by the measles virus or a closely related virus and marked by intellectual deterioration, convulsions, and paralysis — abbr. *SSPE*

sub·aor·tic stenosis \ˌsəb-ā-ˈór-tik-\ *n* : aortic stenosis produced by an obstruction in the left ventricle below the aortic valve

sub·arach·noid \ˌsəb-ə-ˈrak-ˌnóid\ *also* **sub·arach·noid·al** \-rak-ˈnóid-ᵊl\ *adj* **1** : situated or occurring under the arachnoid membrane ⟨~ hemorrhage⟩ **2** : of, relating to, or involving the subarachnoid space and the fluid within it ⟨~ meningitis⟩

subarachnoid space *n* : the space between the arachnoid and the pia mater through which the cerebrospinal fluid circulates

sub·cal·lo·sal \ˌsəb-ka-ˈlō-səl\ *adj* : situated below the corpus callosum

subcallosal area *n* : a small area of cortex in each cerebral hemisphere below the genu of the corpus callosum

sub·cap·su·lar \ˌsəb-ˈkap-sə-lər\ *adj* : situated or occurring beneath or within a capsule ⟨~ cataracts⟩

subcarbonate — see BISMUTH SUBCARBONATE

sub·cel·lu·lar \ˌsəb-ˈsel-yə-lər\ *adj* : INTRACELLULAR

sub·chon·dral \-ˈkän-drəl\ *adj* : situated beneath cartilage ⟨~ bone⟩

sub·cho·roi·dal \ˌsəb-kə-ˈróid-ᵊl\ *adj* : situated or occurring between the choroid and the retina ⟨~ fluid⟩

sub·class \ˈsəb-ˌklas\ *n* : a category in biological classification ranking below a class and above an order

subclavia — see ANSA SUBCLAVIA

¹sub·cla·vi·an \ˌsəb-ˈklā-vē-ən\ *adj* : of, relating to, being, or performed on a part (as an artery or vein) located under the clavicle ⟨~ angioplasty⟩

²subclavian *n* : a subclavian part

subclavian artery *n* : the proximal part of the main artery of the arm that arises on the right side from the innominate artery and on the left side from the arch of the aorta and that supplies or gives off branches supplying the brain, neck, anterior wall of the thorax, and shoulder

subclavian trunk *n* : a large lymphatic vessel on each side of the body that receives lymph from the axilla and arms and that on the right side empties into the right lymphatic duct and on the left side into the thoracic duct

subclavian vein *n* : the proximal part of the main vein of the arm that is a continuation of the axillary vein and extends from the level of the first rib to the sternal end of the clavicle where it unites with the internal jugular vein to form the innominate vein

sub·cla·vi·us \ˌsəb-ˈklā-vē-əs\ *n, pl* -vii \-vē-ˌī\ : a small muscle on each side of the body that arises from the junction of the first rib and its cartilage, inserts into the inferior surface of the clavicle, and acts to stabilize the clavicle by depressing and drawing forward its lateral end during movements of the shoulder joint

sub·clin·i·cal \-ˈkli-ni-kəl\ *adj* : not detectable or producing effects that are not detectable by the usual clinical tests (a ~ infection) (~ cancer) — **sub·clin·i·cal·ly** *adv*

sub·con·junc·ti·val \ˌsəb-kän-ˌjəŋk-ˈtī-vəl\ *adj* : situated or occurring beneath the conjunctiva — **sub·con·junc·ti·val·ly** *adv*

¹sub·con·scious \ˌsəb-ˈkän-chəs\ *adj* 1 : existing in the mind but not immediately available to consciousness : affecting thought, feeling, and behavior without entering awareness 2 : imperfectly conscious : partially but not fully aware — **sub·con·scious·ly** *adv* — **sub·con·scious·ness** *n*

²subconscious *n* : the mental activities just below the threshold of consciousness; *also* : the aspect of the mind concerned with such activities — compare UNCONSCIOUS

sub·cor·a·coid \-ˈkȯr-ə-ˌkȯid\ *adj* : situated or occurring under the coracoid process of the scapula (a ~ dislocation of the humerus)

sub·cor·ti·cal \-ˈkȯr-ti-kəl\ *adj* : of, relating to, involving, or being nerve centers below the cerebral cortex — **sub·cor·ti·cal·ly** *adv*

sub·cos·tal \-ˈkäs-təl, -ˈkȯs-\ *adj* : situated or performed below a rib

subcostal artery *n* : either of a pair of arteries that are the most posterior branches of the thoracic aorta and follow a course beneath the last pair of ribs

sub·cos·ta·lis \-käs-ˈtā-ləs, -ˌkȯs-\ *n, pl* -ta·les \-ˌlēz\ : any of a variable number of small muscles that arise on the inner surface of a rib, are inserted into the inner surface of the second or third rib below, and prob. function to draw adjacent ribs together

subcostal vein *n* : either of two veins: **a** : one that arises on the right side of the anterior abdominal wall and joins in the formation of the azygos vein — called also *right subcostal vein* **b** : one on the left side of the body that usually empties into the hemiazygos vein — called also *left subcostal vein*

sub·cul·ture \ˈsəb-ˌkəl-chər\ *n* 1 : a culture (as of bacteria) derived from an-

other culture 2 : an act or instance of producing a subculture — **subculture** *vb*

subcutanea — see TELA SUBCUTANEA

sub·cu·ta·ne·ous \ˌsəb-kyù-ˈtā-nē-əs\ *adj* : being, living, used, or made under the skin (~ parasites) — **sub·cu·ta·ne·ous·ly** *adv*

subcutaneous bursa *n* : a bursa lying between the skin and a bony process or a ligament

subcutaneous emphysema *n* : the presence of a gas and esp. air in the subcutaneous tissue

sub·cu·tic·u·lar \-kyù-ˈti-kyə-lər\ *adj* : situated or occurring beneath a cuticle (~ sutures) (~ tissues)

sub·cu·tis \ˌsəb-ˈkyü-təs\ *n* : the deeper part of the dermis

sub·del·toid \ˌsəb-ˈdel-ˌtȯid\ *adj* : situated underneath or inferior to the deltoid muscle (~ calcareous deposits)

subdeltoid bursa *n* : the bursa that lies beneath the deltoid muscle

sub·der·mal \-ˈdər-məl\ *adj* : SUBCUTANEOUS — **sub·der·mal·ly** *adv*

sub·di·a·phrag·mat·ic \ˌsəb-ˌdī-ə-frə-ˈma-tik, -ˌfrag-\ *adj* : situated, occurring, or performed below the diaphragm (a ~ abscess)

subdivision *n* : a category in botanical classification ranking below a division and above a class

sub·du·ral \ˌsəb-ˈdür-əl, -ˈdyür-\ *adj* : situated, occurring, or performed under the dura mater or between the dura mater and the arachnoid (~ hematoma) — **sub·du·ral·ly** *adv*

subdural space *n* : a fluid-filled space or potential space between the dura mater and the arachnoid

sub·en·do·car·di·al \ˌsəb-ˌen-dō-ˈkär-dē-əl\ *adj* : situated or occurring beneath the endocardium or between the endocardium and myocardium

sub·en·do·the·li·al \-ˌen-dō-ˈthē-lē-əl\ *adj* : situated under an endothelium

sub·ep·en·dy·mal \-e-ˈpen-də-məl\ *adj* : situated under the ependyma

sub·epi·der·mal \ˌsəb-ˌe-pə-ˈdər-məl\ *adj* : lying beneath or constituting the innermost part of the epidermis

sub·epi·the·li·al \-ˌe-pə-ˈthē-lē-əl\ *adj* : situated or occurring beneath an epithelial layer; *also* : SUBCUTANEOUS

sub·fam·i·ly \ˈsəb-ˌfam-lē\ *n* : a category in biological classification ranking below a family and above a genus

sub·fas·cial \ˈfa-shəl, -shē-əl\ *adj* : situated, occurring, or performed below a fascia (a ~ tumor) (~ suturing)

sub·fe·brile \-ˈfe-ˌbrīl, -ˈfē-\ *adj* : of, relating to, or constituting a body temperature very slightly above normal but not febrile

sub·fer·til·i·ty \-fər-ˈti-lə-tē\ *n, pl* -ties : the condition of being less than normally fertile though still capable of effecting fertilization — **sub·fer·tile** \-ˈfərt-əl\ *adj*

sub·ge·nus \ˈsəb-ˌjē-nəs\ *n, pl* -gene•ra \-.je-nər-ə\ : a category in biological taxonomy ranking below a genus and above a species

sub•gin•gi•val \.səb-ˈjin-jə-vəl\ adj : situated, performed, or occurring beneath the gums and esp. between the gums and the basal part of the crowns of the teeth (~ calculus) (~ curettage) — sub•gin•gi•val•ly adv

sub•glot•tic \-ˈglä-tik\ adj : situated or occurring below the glottis

su•bic•u•lum \sə-ˈbi-kyə-ləm\ n, pl -la \-lə\ : a part of the hippocampal gyrus that is a ventral continuation of the hippocampus and is situated ventrally and medially to the dentate gyrus; also : a section of that that borders the hippocampal sulcus — su•bic•u•lar \-lər\ adj

sub•in•tern \-ˈin-.tərn\ n : a medical student in the last year of medical school who performs work supervised by interns and residents in a hospital

sub•in•ti•mal \-ˈin-tə-məl\ adj : situated beneath an intima and esp. between the intima and media of an artery

sub•in•vo•lu•tion \-.in-və-ˈlü-shən\ n : partial or incomplete involution

sub•ja•cent \.səb-ˈjās-ᵊnt\ adj : lying immediately under or below (~ tissue)

sub•ject \ˈsəb-jikt\ n 1 : an individual whose reactions or responses are studied 2 : a dead body for anatomical study and dissection

sub•jec•tive \(.)səb-ˈjek-tiv\ adj 1 a : relating to or determined by the mind as the subject of experience (~ reality) b : characteristic of or belonging to reality as perceived rather than as independent of mind c : relating to or being experience or knowledge as conditioned by personal mental characteristics or states 2 a : arising from conditions within the brain or sense organs and not directly caused by external stimuli (~ sensations) b : arising out of or identified by means of one's perception of one's own states and processes and not observable by an examiner (a ~ symptom of disease) — compare OBJECTIVE 2 — sub•jec•tive•ly adv

subjective vertigo n : vertigo characterized by a sensation that one's body is revolving in space

sub•le•thal \.səb-ˈlē-thəl\ adj : less than but usu. only slightly less than lethal (a ~ dose)

sub•li•ma•tion \.sə-blə-ˈmā-shən\ n : the process of converting and expressing a primitive instinctual desire or impulse to a form that is socially and culturally acceptable — sub•li•mate \ˈsə-blə-.māt\ vb

sub•lim•i•nal \(.)səb-ˈli-mə-nəl\ adj 1 : inadequate to produce a sensation or a perception 2 : existing or functioning below the threshold of consciousness (the ~ mind) (~ advertising) — sub•lim•i•nal•ly adv

sub•lin•gual \.səb-ˈliŋ-gwəl, -gyə-wəl\ adj 1 : situated or administered under the tongue (~ tablets) (~ glands) 2 : of or relating to the sublingual glands — sub•lin•gual•ly adv

²sublingual n : SUBLINGUAL GLAND

sublingual gland n : a small salivary gland on each side of the mouth lying beneath the mucous membrane in a fossa in the mandible near the symphysis — called also sublingual salivary gland

sub•lob•u•lar vein \.səb-ˈlä-byə-lər-\ : one of several veins in the liver into which the central veins empty and which in turn empty into the hepatic veins

sub•lux•a•tion \.səb-.lək-ˈsā-shən\ n : partial dislocation (as of one of the bones in a joint) — sub•lux•at•ed \ˈsəb-.lək-.sā-təd\ adj

¹sub•man•dib•u•lar \.səb-man-ˈdi-byə-lər\ adj 1 : of, relating to, situated, or performed in the region below the lower jaw 2 : of, relating to, or associated with the submandibular glands

²submandibular n : a submandibular part (as an artery or bone)

submandibular ganglion n : an autonomic ganglion that is situated on the hyoglossus muscle above the deep part of the submandibular gland, receives preganglionic fibers from the facial nerve, and sends postganglionic fibers to the submandibular and sublingual glands — called also submaxillary ganglion

submandibular gland n : a salivary gland inside of and near the lower edge of the mandible on each side and discharging by Wharton's duct into the mouth under the tongue — called also submandibular salivary gland, submaxillary gland, submaxillary salivary gland

sub•max•il•lary \.səb-ˈmak-sə-.ler-ē\ adj or n : SUBMANDIBULAR

submaxillary ganglion n : SUBMANDIBULAR GANGLION

submaxillary gland n : SUBMANDIBULAR GLAND

submaxillary salivary gland n : SUBMANDIBULAR GLAND

sub•max•i•mal \.səb-ˈmak-sə-məl\ adj : being less than the maximum of which an individual is capable

sub•men•tal \-ˈment-ᵊl\ adj : located in, affecting, or performed on the area under the chin

submental artery n : a branch of the facial artery that branches off near the submandibular gland and is distributed to the muscles of the jaw

sub•meta•cen•tric \.səb-.me-tə-ˈsen-trik\ adj : having the centromere situated so that one chromosome arm is somewhat shorter than the other — submetacentric n

sub•mi•cro•scop•ic \.səb-.mī-krə-ˈskä-pik\ adj : too small to be seen in an ordinary light microscope (~ particles\ — compare MACROSCOPIC, MI-CROSCOPIC 2, ULTRAMICROSCOPIC 1 — **sub·mi·cro·scop·i·cal·ly** *adv*

sub·mis·sion \səb-ˈmi-shən\ *n* : the condition of being submissive

sub·mis·sive \-ˈmi-səv\ *adj* : characterized by tendencies to yield to the will or authority of others ⟨a ~ personality⟩ — **sub·mis·sive·ness** *n*

sub·mu·co·sa \ˌsəb-myü-ˈkō-sə\ *n* : a supporting layer of loose connective tissue directly under a mucous membrane — **sub·mu·co·sal** \-zəl\ *adj*

sub·mu·cous \ˌsəb-ˈmyü-kəs\ *adj* : lying under or involving the tissues under a mucous membrane

subnitrate — see BISMUTH SUBNITRATE

sub·nor·mal \ˌsəb-ˈnȯr-məl\ *adj* **1** : lower or smaller than normal ⟨a ~ temperature⟩ **2** : having less of something and esp. of intelligence than is normal — **sub·nor·mal·i·ty** \ˌsəb-nȯr-ˈma-lə-tē\ *n*

sub·oc·cip·i·tal \-äk-ˈsi-pət-ᵊl\ *adj* **1** : situated or performed below the occipital bone **2** : situated or performed below the occipital lobe of the brain

suboccipital nerve *n* : the first cervical nerve that supplies muscles around the suboccipital triangle and that sends branches to the rectus capitis posterior minor and semispinalis capitis

suboccipital triangle *n* : a space of the suboccipital region on each side of the dorsal cervical region that is bounded superiorly and medially by a muscle arising by a tendon from a spinous process of the axis and inserting into the inferior nuchal line and the adjacent inferior region of the occipital bone, that is bounded superiorly and laterally by the obliquus capitis superior, and that is bounded inferiorly and laterally by the obliquus capitis inferior

sub·op·ti·mal \ˌsəb-ˈäp-tə-məl\ *adj* : less than optimal ⟨a ~ diet⟩ ⟨a ~ dose of a drug⟩

sub·or·der \ˈsəb-ˌȯr-dər\ *n* : a category in biological classification ranking below an order and above a family

sub·peri·os·te·al \-ˌper-ē-ˈäs-tē-əl\ *adj* : situated or occurring beneath the periosteum ⟨~ bone deposition⟩ ⟨a ~ fibroma⟩ — **sub·peri·os·te·al·ly** *adv*

sub·phren·ic \ˌsəb-ˈfre-nik\ *adj* : situated or occurring below the diaphragm

subphrenic space *n* : a space on each side of the falciform ligament between the underside of the diaphragm and the upper side of the liver

sub·phy·lum \ˈsəb-ˌfī-ləm\ *n*, *pl* **-la** \-lə\ : a category in biological classification ranking below a phylum and above a class

sub·pleu·ral \-ˈplu̇r-əl\ *adj* : situated or occurring between the pleura and the body wall — **sub·pleu·ral·ly** *adv*

sub·pop·u·la·tion \ˌsəb-ˌpä-pyə-ˈlā-

shən\ *n* : an identifiable fraction or subdivision of a population

sub·po·tent \ˌsəb-ˈpōt-ᵊnt\ *adj* : less potent than normal ⟨~ drugs⟩ — **sub·po·ten·cy** \-ˈpōt-ᵊn-sē\ *n*

sub·pu·bic angle \ˌsəb-ˈpyü-bik-\ *n* : the angle that is formed just below the pubic symphysis by the meeting of the inferior ramus of the pubis on one side with the corresponding part on the other side

sub·ret·i·nal \-ˈret-ᵊn-əl\ *adj* : situated or occurring beneath the retina

sub·scap·u·lar \ˌsəb-ˈska-pyə-lər\ *adj* : situated under the scapula

subscapular artery *n* : an artery that is usu. the largest branch of the axillary artery, that arises opposite the lower border of the subscapularis muscle, and that passes down and back to the lower part of the scapula where it forms branches and anastomoses with arteries in that region

subscapular fossa *n* : the concave depression of the anterior surface of the scapula

sub·scap·u·lar·is \ˌsəb-ˌska-pyə-ˈlar-əs\ *n* : a large triangular muscle that fills up the subscapular fossa, that arises from the surface of the scapula, that is inserted into the lesser tubercle of the humerus, and that stabilizes the shoulder joint as part of the rotator cuff and rotates the humerus medially when the arm is held by the side of the body

sub·scrip·tion \səb-ˈskrip-shən\ *n* : a part of a prescription that contains directions to the pharmacist

sub·se·rous \ˌsəb-ˈsir-əs\ *or* **sub·se·ro·sal** \-sə-ˈrō-zəl\ *adj* : situated or occurring under a serous membrane ⟨a ~ uterine fibroid⟩ ⟨~ fat⟩

sub·side \səb-ˈsīd\ *vb* **sub·sid·ed**; **sub·sid·ing** : to lessen in severity : become diminished ⟨the fever subsided⟩ — **sub·si·dence** \səb-ˈsīd-ᵊns, ˈsəb-səd-ᵊns\ *n*

sub·spe·cial·ty \ˌsəb-ˈspe-shəl-tē\ *n*, *pl* **-ties** : a subordinate field of specialization

sub·spe·cies \ˈsəb-ˌspē-shēz, -sēz\ *n* : a subdivision of a species: as **a** : a category in biological classification that ranks immediately below a species and designates a population of a particular geographical region genetically distinguishable from other such populations of the same species and capable of interbreeding successfully with them where its range overlaps theirs **b** : a named subdivision (as a race or variety) of a species — **sub·spe·cif·ic** \ˌsəb-spi-ˈsi-fik\ *adj*

sub·stage \ˈsəb-ˌstāj\ *n* : an attachment to a microscope by means of which accessories (as mirrors, diaphragms, or condensers) are held in place beneath the stage of the instrument

sub·stance \ˈsəb-stəns\ *n* : something (as drugs or alcoholic beverages) deemed harmful and usu. subject to legal restrictions (possession of a controlled ∼)

substance abuse n : excessive use of a drug (as alcohol, narcotics, or cocaine) : use of a drug without medical justification — **substance abuser** n

substance P n : a neuropeptide that consists of 11 amino-acid residues, that is widely distributed in the brain, spinal cord, and peripheral nervous system, and that acts across nerve synapses to produce prolonged postsynaptic excitation

sub·stan·tia ge·la·ti·no·sa \səb-'stan-chə-ˌje-lə-tə-'nō-sə\ n : a mass of gelatinous gray matter that lies on the dorsal surface of the dorsal column and extends the entire length of the spinal cord into the medulla oblongata and that functions in the transmission of painful sensory information

substantia in·nom·i·na·ta \-i-ˌnä-mə-'nä-tə\ n : a band of large cells of indeterminate function that lie just under the surface of the globus pallidus

sub·stan·tia ni·gra \səb-'stan-chə-'nī-grə, -'ni-\ n, pl **sub·stan·ti·ae ni·grae** \-chē-ˌē-'nī-ˌgrē, -'ni-\ : a layer of deeply pigmented gray matter situated in the midbrain and containing the cell bodies of a tract of dopamine-producing nerve cells whose secretion tends to be deficient in Parkinson's disease

substantia pro·pria \-'prō-prē-ə\ n, pl **substantiae pro·pri·ae** \-prē-ˌē\ : the layer of lamellated transparent fibrous connective tissue that makes up the bulk of the cornea of the eye

sub·ster·nal \ˌsəb-'stər-nəl\ adj : situated or perceived behind or below the sternum (∼ pain)

sub·stit·u·ent \səb-'sti-chə-wənt\ n : an atom or group that replaces another atom or group in a molecule — **substituent** adj

sub·sti·tute \'səb-stə-ˌtüt, -ˌtyüt\ n : a person or thing that takes the place or function of another (father and mother ∼s) — **substitute** adj

sub·sti·tu·tion \ˌsəb-stə-'tü-shən, -'tyü-\ n 1 : the turning from an obstructed desire to another desire whose gratification is socially acceptable 2 : the turning from an obstructed form of behavior to a different and often more primitive expression of the same tendency (a ∼ neurosis)

sub·strate \'səb-ˌstrāt\ n 1 : the base on which an organism lives 2 : a substance acted upon (as by an enzyme)

sub·stra·tum \'səb-ˌstrā-təm, -ˌstra-\ n, pl **-stra·ta** \-tə\ : SUBSTRATE 1

sub·struc·ture \'səb-ˌstrək-chər\ n : an underlying or supporting structure — **sub·struc·tur·al** \-chə-rəl\ adj

sub·ta·lar \ˌsəb-'tā-lər\ adj : situated or occurring beneath the talus; specif : of, relating to, or being the articula-

tion formed between the posterior facet of the inferior surface of the talus and the posterior facet of the superior surface of the calcaneus

sub·tem·po·ral decompression \-'tem-pə-rəl-\ n : relief of intracranial pressure by excision of a portion of the temporal bone

sub·tha·lam·ic \ˌsəb-thə-'la-mik\ adj : of or relating to the subthalamus

subthalamic nucleus n : an oval mass of gray matter that is located in the caudal part of the subthalamus and when affected with lesions is associated with hemiballismus of the contralateral side of the body

sub·thal·a·mus \ˌsəb-'tha-lə-məs\ n, pl **-mi** \-ˌmī\ : the ventral part of the thalamus

sub·ther·a·peu·tic \-ˌther-ə-'pyü-tik\ adj : not producing a therapeutic effect (∼ doses of penicillin)

sub·thresh·old \ˌsəb-'thresh-ˌhōld\ adj : inadequate to produce a response (∼ dosage) (a ∼ stimulus)

sub·to·tal \ˌsəb-'tōt-ᵊl\ adj : somewhat less than complete : nearly total (∼ thyroidectomy)

sub·tro·chan·ter·ic \ˌsəb-strō-kən-'ter-ik, -ˌkan-\ adj : situated or occurring below a trochanter

sub·un·gual \ˌsəb-'əŋ-gwəl, -'ən-\ adj : situated or occurring under a fingernail or toenail (a ∼ abscess)

sub·val·vu·lar \ˌsəb-'val-vyə-lər\ adj : situated or occurring below a valve (as a semilunar valve) (∼ stenosis)

sub·vi·ral \ˌsəb-'vī-rəl\ adj : relating to, being, or caused by a piece or a structural part (as a protein) of a virus

succedaneum — see CAPUT SUCCEDANEUM

suc·ci·nate \'sək-sə-ˌnāt\ n : a salt or ester of succinic acid

succinate dehydrogenase n : an iron-containing flavoprotein enzyme that catalyzes often reversibly the dehydrogenation of succinic acid to fumaric acid — called also *succinic dehydrogenase*

suc·cin·ic acid \(ˌ)sək-'si-nik-\ n : a crystalline acid $C_4H_6O_4$ containing two carboxyl groups that is formed in the Krebs cycle and in various fermentation processes

suc·ci·nyl·cho·line \ˌsək-sə-nəl-'kō-ˌlēn, -ˌnil-\ n : a basic compound that acts similarly to curare and is used intravenously chiefly in the form of a hydrated chloride $C_{14}H_{30}Cl_2N_2O_4 \cdot 2H_2O$ as a muscle relaxant in surgery — called also *suxamethonium*; see ANECTINE

suc·ci·nyl·sul·fa·thi·a·zole \ˌsək-sə-nəl-ˌsəl-fə-'thī-ə-ˌzōl, -ˌnil-\ n : a crystalline sulfa drug $C_{13}H_{13}N_3O_5S_2$ used esp. for treating gastrointestinal infections

suc·cus en·ter·i·cus \ˌsə-kəs-en-'ter-i-kəs\ n : INTESTINAL JUICE

suc·cus·sion \sə-'kə-shən\ n : the action

or process of shaking or the condition of being shaken esp. with violence: **a** : a shaking of the body to ascertain if fluid is present in a cavity and esp. in the thorax **b** : the splashing sound made by succussion

suck \'sək\ *vb* **1** : to draw (as liquid) into the mouth through a suction force produced by movements of the lips and tongue **2** : to draw out by suction

suck·er \'sə-kər\ *n* **1** : an organ in various animals (as a trematode or tapeworm) used for adhering or holding **2** : a mouth (as of a leech) adapted for sucking or adhering

sucking louse *n* : any of an order (Anoplura) of wingless insects comprising the true lice with mouthparts adapted for sucking body fluids

suck·le \'sə-kəl\ *vb* **suck·led; suck·ling 1** : to give milk to from the breast or udder **2** : to draw milk from the breast or udder of

su·cral·fate \sü-'kral-ˌfāt\ *n* : an aluminum complex $C_{12}H_mAl_{16}O_nS_8$ where *m* and *n* are approximately 54 and 75 that is used in the treatment of duodenal ulcers

su·crase \'sü-ˌkrās, -ˌkrāz\ *n* : INVERTASE

su·crose \'sü-ˌkrōs, -ˌkrōz\ *n* : a sweet crystalline dextrorotatory disaccharide sugar $C_{12}H_{22}O_{11}$ that occurs naturally in most land plants and is the sugar obtained from sugarcane or sugar beets

¹suc·tion \'sək-shən\ *n* **1** : the act or process of sucking **2 a** : the act or process of exerting a force upon a solid, liquid, or gaseous body by reason of reduced air pressure over part of its surface **b** : force so exerted **3** : the act or process of removing secretions or fluids from hollow or tubular organs or cavities by means of a tube and a device (as a suction pump) that operates on negative pressure

²suction *vb* : to remove (as from a body cavity or passage) by suction

suction pump *n* : a common pump in which the liquid to be raised is pushed by atmospheric pressure into the partial vacuum under a retreating valved piston on the upstroke and reflux is prevented by a valve in the pipe that permits flow in only one direction — see STOMACH PUMP

su·dam·i·na \sü-'da-mə-nə\ *n pl* : a transient eruption of minute translucent vesicles caused by retention of sweat in the sweat glands and in the corneous layer of the skin and occurring after profuse perspiration — called also *miliaria crystallina* — **su·dam·i·nal** \-nəl\ *adj*

Su·dan \sü-'dan\ *n* : any of several azo solvent dyes including some which have a specific affinity for fatty substances

Sudan IV \-'fōr\ *n* : a red dye used

chiefly as a biological stain and in ointments for promoting (as in the treatment of burns, wounds, or ulcers) the growth of epithelium — called also *scarlet red*

su·dan·o·phil·ia \sü-ˌda-nə-'fi-lē-ə\ *n* : the quality or state of being sudanophilic

su·dan·o·phil·ic \sü-ˌda-nə-'fi-lik\ *also* **su·dan·o·phil** \sü-'da-nə-ˌfil\ *adj* : staining selectively with Sudan dyes; *also* : containing lipids

sudden death *n* : unexpected death that is instantaneous or occurs within minutes from any cause other than violence (*sudden death* following coronary occlusion)

sudden infant death syndrome *n* : death of an apparently healthy infant usu. before one year of age that is of unknown cause and occurs esp. during sleep — abbr. *SIDS*; called also *cot death, crib death*

su·do·mo·tor \'sü-də-ˌmō-tər\ *adj* : of, relating to, or being nerve fibers controlling the activity of sweat glands

su·do·rif·er·ous gland \ˌsü-də-'ri-fə-rəs-\ *n* : SWEAT GLAND

¹su·do·rif·ic \-'ri-fik\ *adj* : causing or inducing sweat : DIAPHORETIC

²sudorific *n* : a sudorific agent or medicine

su·fen·ta·nil \sü-'fen-tə-ˌnil\ *n* : an opioid analgesic $C_{22}H_{30}N_2O_2S$ that is administered intravenously in the form of its citrate as an anesthetic or an anesthetic adjunct

suf·fo·cate \'sə-fə-ˌkāt\ *vb* **-cat·ed; -cat·ing 1** : to stop the respiration of (as by strangling or asphyxiation) **2** : to deprive of oxygen **3** : to die from being unable to breathe — **suf·fo·ca·tion** \ˌsə-fə-'kā-shən\ *n* — **suf·fo·ca·tive** \'sə-fə-ˌkā-tiv\ *adj*

suf·fuse \sə-'fyüz\ *vb* **suf·fused; suf·fus·ing** : to flush or spread over or through in the manner of a fluid and esp. blood — **suf·fu·sion** \sə-'fyü-zhən\ *n*

sug·ar \'shu̇-gər\ *n* **1** : a sweet substance that is colorless or white when pure, consists chiefly of sucrose, and is obtained esp. from sugarcane or sugar beets **2** : any of various water-soluble compounds that vary widely in sweetness and comprise the saccharides of smaller molecular size including sucrose

sugar diabetes *n* : DIABETES MELLITUS

sui·cide \'sü-ə-ˌsīd\ *n* **1** : the act or an instance of taking one's own life voluntarily and intentionally **2** : a person who commits or attempts suicide — **sui·cid·al** \ˌsü-ə-'sīd-ᵊl\ *adj* — **sui·cid·al·ly** \-ᵊl-ē\ *adv* — **suicide** *vb*

sui·cid·ol·o·gy \ˌsü-ə-ˌsī-'dä-lə-jē\ *n, pl* **-gies** : the study of suicide and suicide prevention — **sui·cid·ol·o·gist** \-jist\ *n*

suit — see G SUIT, PRESSURE SUIT

suite \'swēt\ *n* : a group of rooms in a medical facility dedicated to a specified function or specialty ⟨surgical ∼⟩

sul·bac·tam \səl-ˈbak-ˌtam, -təm\ *n* : a penicillinase inhibitor $C_8H_{11}NO_5S$ that is usu. administered in the form of its sodium salt in combination with a beta-lactam antibiotic (as ampicillin)

sul·cus \ˈsəl-kəs\ *n, pl* **sul·ci** \-ˌkī, -ˌsī\ : FURROW, GROOVE; *esp* : a shallow furrow on the surface of the brain separating adjacent convolutions — compare FISSURE 1c — **sul·cal** \ˈsəl-kəl\ *adj*

sulcus ter·mi·na·lis \-ˌtər-mə-ˈnā-ləs\, *pl* **sulci ter·mi·na·les** \-ˌlēz\ 1 : a V-shaped groove separating the anterior two thirds of the tongue from the posterior third and containing the circumvallate papillae 2 : a shallow groove on the outside of the right atrium of the heart

sulf- *or* **sulfo-** *comb form* : sulfur : containing sulfur ⟨*sulf*arsphenamine⟩

¹**sul·fa** \ˈsəl-fə\ *adj* 1 : related chemically to sulfanilamide 2 : of, relating to, employing, or containing sulfa drugs ⟨∼ therapy⟩

²**sulfa** *n* : SULFA DRUG

sul·fa·cet·a·mide *also* **sul·fa·cet·i·mide** \ˌsəl-fə-ˈse-tə-ˌmīd, -məd\ *n* : a sulfa drug $C_8H_{10}N_2O_3S$ that is used chiefly for treating infections of the urinary tract and in the form of its sodium derivative for infections of the eye

sul·fa·di·a·zine \ˌsəl-fə-ˈdī-ə-ˌzēn\ *n* : a sulfa drug $C_{10}H_{10}N_4O_2S$ that is used esp. in the treatment of meningitis, pneumonia, and intestinal infections

sulfa drug *n* : any of various synthetic organic bacteria-inhibiting drugs that are sulfonamides closely related chemically to sulfanilamide — called also *sulfa*

sul·fa·gua·ni·dine \ˌsəl-fə-ˈgwä-nə-ˌdēn\ *n* : a sulfa drug $C_7H_{10}N_4O_2S$ used esp. in veterinary medicine — called also *sulfanilylguanidine*

sul·fa·mer·a·zine \ˌsəl-fə-ˈmer-ə-ˌzēn\ *n* : a sulfa drug $C_{11}H_{12}N_4O_2S$ that is a derivative of sulfadiazine and is used similarly

sul·fa·meth·a·zine \-ˈme-thə-ˌzēn\ *n* : a sulfa drug $C_{12}H_{14}N_4O_2S$ that is a derivative of sulfadiazine and is used similarly

sul·fa·meth·ox·a·zole \-ˌme-ˈthäk-sə-ˌzōl\ *n* : a sulfonamide $C_{10}H_{11}N_3O_3S$ often combined with trimethoprim and used as an antibacterial esp. in the treatment of urinary tract infections — see BACTRIM

sul·fa·mez·a·thine \-ˈme-zə-ˌthēn\ *n* : SULFAMETHAZINE

Sul·fa·my·lon \ˌsəl-fə-ˈmī-ˌlän\ *trademark* — used for a preparation of mafenide

sul·fa·nil·amide \ˌsəl-fə-ˈni-lə-ˌmīd, -məd\ *n* : a crystalline sulfonamide $C_6H_8N_2O_3S$ that is the amide of sulfanilic acid and the parent compound of most of the sulfa drugs

sul·fan·i·lyl·gua·ni·dine \səl-ˌfa-ni-lil-ˈgwä-nə-ˌdēn\ *n* : SULFAGUANIDINE

sul·fa·pyr·i·dine \ˌsəl-fə-ˈpir-ə-ˌdēn\ *n* : a sulfa drug $C_{11}H_{11}N_3O_2S$ that is derived from pyridine and sulfanilamide and is used in small doses in the treatment of one type of dermatitis and esp. formerly against pneumococcal and gonococcal infections

sul·fa·qui·nox·a·line \-kwi-ˈnäk-sə-ˌlēn\ *n* : a sulfa drug $C_{14}H_{12}N_4O_2S$ used esp. in veterinary medicine

sulf·ars·phen·a·mine \ˌsəl-ˌfärs-ˈfe-nə-ˌmēn, -mən\ *n* : an orange-yellow powder essentially $C_{12}H_{10}As_2N_2O_2$-$(CH_2SO_3Na)_2$ that is similar to neoarsphenamine and arsphenamine in structure and uses

sul·fa·sal·a·zine \ˌsəl-fə-ˈsa-lə-ˌzēn\ *n* : SALICYLAZOSULFAPYRIDINE

¹**sul·fate** \ˈsəl-ˌfāt\ *n* 1 : a salt or ester of sulfuric acid 2 : a bivalent group or anion SO_4 characteristic of sulfuric acid and the sulfates

²**sulfate** *vb* **sul·fat·ed; sul·fat·ing** 1 : to treat or combine with sulfuric acid or a sulfate 2 : to convert into a sulfate

sul·fa·thi·a·zole \ˌsəl-fə-ˈthī-ə-ˌzōl\ *n* : a sulfa drug $C_9H_9N_3O_2S_2$ derived from thiazole and sulfanilamide but seldom prescribed because of its toxicity

sul·fa·tide \ˈsəl-fə-ˌtīd\ *n* : any of the sulfates of cerebrosides that often accumulate in the central nervous systems of individuals affected with one form of leukodystrophy

sulf·he·mo·glo·bin \ˌsəlf-ˈhē-mə-ˌglō-bən\ *n* : a green pigment formed from hemoglobin and found in putrefied organs and cadavers

sulf·he·mo·glo·bi·ne·mia \ˌsəlf-ˌhē-mə-ˌglō-bə-ˈnē-mē-ə\ *n* : the presence of sulfhemoglobin in the blood

sulf·hy·dryl \ˌsəlf-ˈhī-drəl\ *n* : THIOL 2 — used chiefly in molecular biology

sul·fide \ˈsəl-ˌfīd\ *n* 1 : any of various organic compounds characterized by a sulfur atom attached to two carbon atoms 2 : a binary compound (as CuS) of sulfur usu. with a more electrically positive element or group

sul·fin·py·ra·zone \ˌsəl-fən-ˈpī-rə-ˌzōn\ *n* : a uricosuric drug $C_{23}H_{20}N_2O_3S$ used in long-term treatment of chronic gout

sul·fi·sox·a·zole \ˌsəl-fə-ˈsäk-sə-ˌzōl\ *n* : a sulfa drug $C_{11}H_{13}N_3O_3S$ derived from sulfanilamide that is used similarly to other sulfanilamide derivatives but is less likely to produce renal damage because of its greater solubility

sulfo- — see SULF-

sul·fo·bro·mo·phtha·lein \ˌsəl-fə-ˌbrō-mō-ˈtha-lē-ən, -ˈthā-ˌlēn\ *n* : a diagnostic material used in the form of its sodium salt $C_{20}H_8Br_4Na_2O_{10}S_2$ in a liver function test

sul·fon·amide \ˌsəl-ˈfä-nə-ˌmīd, -məd; -ˈfō-nə-ˌmid\ *n* : any of various amides (as sulfanilamide) of a sulfonic acid; *also* : SULFA DRUG

sul·fon·eth·yl·meth·ane \ˌsəl-ˌfō-ˌne-thəl-ˈme-ˌthān\ *n* : a crystalline hypnotic $C_8H_{18}O_4S_2$ that is an ethyl analog of sulfonmethane

sul·fon·ic acid \ˌsəl-ˈfä-nik-, -ˈfō-\ *n* : any of numerous acids that contain the SO_3H group

sul·fon·meth·ane \ˌsəl-ˈfōn-ˈme-ˌthān\ *n* : a crystalline hypnotic $C_5H_{10}O_4S_2$

sul·fo·nyl·urea \ˌsəl-fə-ˌnil-ˈyur-ē-ə, -ˌni-ˈlur-\ *n* : any of several hypoglycemic compounds related to the sulfonamides and used in the oral treatment of diabetes

sul·fo·sal·i·cyl·ic acid \ˌsəl-fō-ˌsa-lə-ˈsi-lik-\ *n* : a sulfonic acid derivative $C_7H_6O_6S_3$ used esp. to detect and precipitate proteins (as albumin) from urine

sulf·ox·one sodium \ˌsəl-ˈfäk-ˌsōn-\ *n* : a crystalline salt $C_{14}H_{14}N_2Na_2O_6S_3$ used in the treatment of leprosy

sul·fur \ˈsəl-fər\ *n* : a nonmetallic element that occurs either free or combined esp. in sulfides and sulfates — symbol *S*; see ELEMENT table — **sul·fur** *adj*

sul·fu·rat·ed lime solution \ˈsəl-fyə-ˌrā-təd-\ *n* : an orange-colored solution containing sulfides of calcium and used as a topical antiseptic and scabicide

sulfurated potash *n* : a mixture composed principally of sulfurated potassium compounds that is used in treating skin diseases

sulfur dioxide *n* : a heavy pungent toxic gas SO_2 that is a major air pollutant esp. in industrial areas

sul·fu·ric \ˌsəl-ˈfyur-ik\ *adj* : of, relating to, or containing sulfur esp. with a higher valence than sulfurous compounds

sulfuric acid *n* : a heavy corrosive oily strong acid H_2SO_4 having two replaceable hydrogen atoms

sul·fu·rous \ˈsəl-fə-rəs, -fyə-; ˌsəl-ˈfyur-əs\ *adj* **1** : of, relating to, or containing sulfur esp. with a lower valence than sulfuric compounds **2** : resembling or emanating from sulfur and esp. burning sulfur

sulfurous acid *n* : a weak unstable acid H_2SO_3 known in solution and through its salts and used in medicine as an antiseptic

su·lin·dac \sə-ˈlin-ˌdak\ *n* : an anti-inflammatory drug $C_{20}H_{17}FO_3S$ used esp. in the treatment of rheumatoid arthritis

sul·i·so·ben·zone \ˌsə-li-sō-ˈben-ˌzōn\ *n* : a sunscreening agent $C_{14}H_{12}O_6S$

sulph- *or* **sulpho-** *chiefly Brit var of* SULF-

sul·pha, sul·phate, sul·phide, sul·phur, sul·phu·ric *chiefly Brit var of* SULFA, SULFATE, SULFIDE, SULFUR, SULFURIC

su·mac *also* **su·mach** \ˈsü-ˌmak, ˈshü-\

n : any of various plants of the genus *Rhus* including several (as poison sumac, *R. vernix*) having foliage poisonous to the touch

su·ma·trip·tan \ˌsü-mə-ˈtrip-ˌtan, -tən\ *n* : a serotonin agonist $C_{14}H_{21}N_3O_2S$ administered by injection in the form of its succinate in the treatment of migraine headaches

sum·ma·tion \(ˌ)sə-ˈmā-shən\ *n* : cumulative action or effect; *esp* : the process by which a sequence of stimuli that are individually inadequate to produce a response are cumulatively able to induce a nerve impulse — see SPATIAL SUMMATION, TEMPORAL SUMMATION

summer complaint *n* : SUMMER DIARRHEA

summer diarrhea *n* : diarrhea esp. of children that is prevalent in hot weather and is usu. caused by ingestion of food contaminated by various microorganisms

summer sores *n sing or pl* : a skin disease of the horse caused by larval roundworms of the genus *Habronema*

sun block *n* : a chemical agent (as zinc oxide or para-aminobenzoic acid) or a preparation of this that is applied to the skin to prevent sunburn by blocking out all or most of the sun's rays — compare SUNSCREEN

sun·burn \ˈsən-ˌbərn\ *n* : inflammation of the skin caused by overexposure to ultraviolet radiation esp. from sunlight — **sunburn** *vb*

sun·glass·es \-ˌgla-səs\ *n pl* : glasses used to protect the eyes from the sun

sun·lamp \ˈsən-ˌlamp\ *n* : an electric lamp designed to emit radiation of wavelengths from ultraviolet to infrared and used esp. for therapeutic purposes or for producing tan artificially

sun·screen \-ˌskrēn\ *n* : a substance (as para-aminobenzoic acid) used in suntan preparations to protect the skin from excessive ultraviolet radiation — **sun·screen·ing** *adj*

sunshine vitamin *n* : VITAMIN D

sun·stroke \-ˌstrōk\ *n* : heatstroke caused by direct exposure to the sun

sun·tan \-ˌtan\ *n* : a browning of the skin from exposure to the rays of the sun — **sun·tanned** \-ˌtand\ *adj*

super- *prefix* **1** : greater than normal : excessive ⟨*super*ovulation⟩ **2** : situated or placed above, on, or at the top of ⟨*super*ciliary⟩; *specif* : situated on the dorsal side of

su·per·cil·i·ary \ˌsü-pər-ˈsi-lē-ˌer-ē\ *adj* : of, relating to, or adjoining the eyebrow : SUPRAORBITAL

superciliary arch *n* : SUPERCILIARY RIDGE

superciliary ridge *n* : a prominence of the frontal bone above the eye caused by the projection of the frontal sinuses — called also *browridge, superciliary arch, supraorbital ridge*

su·per·coil \'sü-pər-ˌkȯil\ n : SUPERHE-
LIX — **supercoil** vb

su·per·ego \ˌsü-pər-ˈē-(ˌ)gō, ˈsü-pər-ˌ,
-ˈe-(ˌ)gō\ n : the one of the three divisions of the psyche in psychoanalytic theory that is only partly
conscious, represents internalization
of parental conscience and the rules
of society, and functions to reward
and punish through a system of moral
attitudes, conscience, and a sense of
guilt — compare EGO, ¹ID

su·per·fam·i·ly \'sü-pər-ˌfam-lē\ n, pl
-lies : a category of taxonomic classification ranking next above a family

su·per·fat·ted \'sü-pər-ˌfa-təd\ adj
: containing extra oil or fat (~ soap)

su·per·fe·cun·da·tion \ˌsü-pər-ˌfe-kən-
ˈdā-shən, -ˌfē-\ n : successive fertilization of two or more ova from the
same ovulation esp. by different
mates

su·per·fe·ta·tion \ˌsü-pər-fē-ˈtā-shən\ n
: successive fertilization of two or
more ova of different ovulations resulting in the presence of embryos of
unlike ages in the same uterus

su·per·fi·cial \ˌsü-pər-ˈfi-shəl\ adj 1
: of, relating to, or located near the
surface (~ blood vessels) 2 : penetrating below or affecting only the
surface (~ wounds) — **su·per·fi·cial-
ly** adv

superficial external pudendal artery n
: EXTERNAL PUDENDAL ARTERY a

superficial fascia n : the thin layer of
loose fatty connective tissue underlying the skin and binding it to the parts
beneath — called also hypodermis,
tela subcutanea; compare DEEP FAS-
CIA

superficial inguinal ring n : the inguinal
ring that is the external opening of the
inguinal canal — called also external
inguinal ring; compare DEEP INGUI-
NAL RING

superficialis — see FLEXOR DIGITORUM
SUPERFICIALIS

superficial palmar arch n : PALMAR
ARCH b

superficial peroneal nerve n : a nerve
that arises as a branch of the common
peroneal nerve and that innervates or
supplies branches innervating the
muscles of the anterior part of the leg
and the skin on the lower anterior
part of the leg, on the dorsum of the
foot, on the lateral and medial sides
of the foot, and between the toes —
called also musculocutaneous nerve;
compare DEEP PERONEAL NERVE

superficial temporal artery n : the one
of the two terminal branches of each
external carotid artery that arises in
the substance of the parotid gland,
passes upward over the zygomatic
process of the temporal bone, and is
distributed by way of branches esp.
to the more superficial parts of the
side of the face and head

superficial temporal vein n : TEMPORAL
VEIN a(1)

**superficial transverse metacarpal liga-
ment** n : a transverse ligamentous
band across the palm of the hand in
the superficial fascia at the base of
the fingers — called also superficial
transverse ligament

superficial transverse perineal muscle n
: TRANSVERSUS PERINEI SUPERFICIA-
LIS

su·per·fuse \ˌsü-pər-ˈfyüz\ vb -fused;
-fus·ing : to maintain the metabolic or
physiological activity of (as an isolated organ) by submitting to a continuous flow of a sustaining medium over
the outside — **su·per·fu·sion** \-ˈfyü-
zhən\ n

su·per·gene \'sü-pər-ˌjēn\ n : a group of
linked genes acting as an allelic unit
esp. when due to the suppression of
crossing-over

su·per·he·lix \'sü-pər-ˌhē-liks\ n : a helix (as of DNA) which has its axis arranged in a helical coil — called also
supercoil — **su·per·he·li·cal** \ˌsü-pər-
ˈhe-li-kəl, -ˈhē-\ adj

su·per·in·fec·tion \ˌsü-pər-in-ˈfek-shən\
n : a second infection superimposed
on an earlier one esp. by a different
microbial agent of exogenous or endogenous origin that is resistant to
the treatment used against the first infection — **su·per·in·fect** \-in-ˈfekt\ vb

su·pe·ri·or \sù-ˈpir-ē-ər\ adj 1 : situated
toward the head and further away
from the feet than another and esp.
another similar part — compare INFE-
RIOR 1 2 : situated in a more anterior
or dorsal position in the body of a
quadruped — compare INFERIOR 2

superior alveolar nerve n : any of the
branches of the maxillary nerve or of
the infraorbital nerve that supply the
teeth and gums of the upper jaw

superior articular process n : ARTICU-
LAR PROCESS a

superior carotid triangle n : a space in
each lateral half of the neck that is
bounded in back by the sternocleidomastoid muscle, below by the omohyoid muscle, and above by the
stylohyoid and digastric muscles

superior cerebellar artery n : an artery
that arises from the basilar artery just
before it divides to form the posterior
cerebral arteries and supplies or
gives off branches supplying the superior part of the cerebellum, midbrain, pineal gland, and choroid
plexus of the third ventricle

superior cerebellar peduncle n : CERE-
BELLAR PEDUNCLE a

superior colliculus n : either member of
the anterior and higher pair of corpora quadrigemina that together constitute a primitive center for vision —
called also optic lobe, optic tectum;
compare INFERIOR COLLICULUS

superior concha n : NASAL CONCHA c

superior constrictor n : a 4-sided muscle of the pharynx that acts to constrict part of the pharynx in swallowing — called also *constrictor pharyngis superior, superior pharyngeal constrictor muscle;* compare INFERIOR CONSTRICTOR, MIDDLE CONSTRICTOR

superior extensor retinaculum *n* : EXTENSOR RETINACULUM 1b

superior ganglion *n* 1 : the upper and smaller of the two sensory ganglia of the glossopharyngeal nerve that may be absent but when present is situated in a groove in which the nerve passes through the jugular foramen — called also *jugular ganglion;* compare INFERIOR GANGLION 1 2 : the upper of the two ganglia of the vagus nerve that is situated at the point where it exits through the jugular foramen — called also *jugular ganglion, superior vagal ganglion;* compare INFERIOR GANGLION 2

superior gluteal artery *n* : GLUTEAL ARTERY a

superior gluteal nerve *n* : GLUTEAL NERVE a

superior gluteal vein *n* : any of several veins that accompany the superior gluteal artery and empty into the internal iliac vein

superior hemorrhoidal artery *n* : RECTAL ARTERY c

superior hemorrhoidal vein *n* : RECTAL VEIN c

superior intercostal vein *n* : a vein on each side formed by the union of the veins draining the first two or three intercostal spaces of which the one on the right usu. empties into the azygos vein but sometimes into the right innominate vein and the one on the left empties into the left innominate vein after crossing the arch of the aorta

superioris — see LEVATOR LABII SUPERIORIS, LEVATOR LABII SUPERIORIS ALAEQUE NASI, LEVATOR PALPEBRAE SUPERIORIS, QUADRATUS LABII SUPERIORIS

superiority complex *n* : an excessive striving for or pretense of superiority to compensate for supposed inferiority

superior laryngeal artery *n* : LARYNGEAL ARTERY b

superior laryngeal nerve *n* : LARYNGEAL NERVE a — called also *superior laryngeal*

superior longitudinal fasciculus *n* : a large bundle of association fibers in the white matter of each cerebral hemisphere that extends above the insula from the frontal lobe to the occipital lobe where it curves downward and forward into the temporal lobe

su·pe·ri·or·ly *adv* : in or to a more superior position or direction

superior meatus *n* : a curved relatively short anteroposterior passage on

each side of the nose that occupies the middle third of the lateral wall of a nasal cavity between the superior and middle nasal conchae — compare INFERIOR MEATUS, MIDDLE MEATUS

superior mesenteric artery *n* : MESENTERIC ARTERY b

superior mesenteric ganglion *n* : MESENTERIC GANGLION b

superior mesenteric plexus *n* : MESENTERIC PLEXUS b

superior mesenteric vein *n* : MESENTERIC VEIN b

superior nasal concha *n* : NASAL CONCHA c

superior nuchal line *n* : NUCHAL LINE a

superior oblique *n* : OBLIQUE b(1)

superior olive *n* : a small gray nucleus situated on the dorsolateral aspect of the trapezoid body — called also *superior olivary nucleus;* compare INFERIOR OLIVE

superior ophthalmic vein *n* : OPHTHALMIC VEIN a

superior orbital fissure *n* : ORBITAL FISSURE a

superior pancreaticoduodenal artery *n* : PANCREATICODUODENAL ARTERY b

superior pectoral nerve *n* : PECTORAL NERVE a

superior peroneal retinaculum *n* : PERONEAL RETINACULUM a

superior petrosal sinus *n* : PETROSAL SINUS a

superior pharyngeal constrictor muscle *n* : SUPERIOR CONSTRICTOR

superior phrenic artery *n* : PHRENIC ARTERY a

superior phrenic vein *n* : PHRENIC VEIN a

superior ramus *n* : RAMUS b(1)

superior rectal artery *n* : RECTAL ARTERY c

superior rectal vein *n* : RECTAL VEIN c

superior rectus *n* : RECTUS 2a

superior sagittal sinus *n* : SAGITTAL SINUS a

superior temporal gyrus *n* : TEMPORAL GYRUS a

superior thyroid artery *n* : THYROID ARTERY a

superior turbinate *n* : NASAL CONCHA c

superior turbinate bone *n* : NASAL CONCHA c

superior ulnar collateral artery *n* : a long slender artery that arises from the brachial artery or one of its branches just below the middle of the upper arm, descends to the elbow following the course of the ulnar nerve, and terminates under the flexor carpi ulnaris — compare INFERIOR ULNAR COLLATERAL ARTERY

superior vagal ganglion *n* : SUPERIOR GANGLION 2

superior vena cava *n* : a vein that is the second largest vein in the human body, is formed by the union of the two innominate veins at the level of the space between the first two ribs, and returns blood to the right atrium of the heart from the upper half of the body

superior vena cava syndrome *n* : a condition characterized by elevated venous pressure of the upper extremities with accompanying distension of the affected veins and swelling of the face and neck and caused by blockage (as by a thrombus) or compression (as by a neoplasm) of the superior vena cava

superior vermis *n* : VERMIS 1a

superior vesical *n* : VESICAL ARTERY a

superior vesical artery *n* : VESICAL ARTERY a

superior vestibular nucleus *n* : the one of the four vestibular nuclei on each side of the medulla oblongata that sends ascending fibers to the oculomotor and trochlear nuclei in the cerebrum on the same side of the brain

superior vocal cords *n pl* : FALSE VOCAL CORDS

su·per·na·tant \ˌsü-pər-ˈnāt-ᵊnt\ *n* : the usu. clear liquid overlying material deposited by settling, precipitation, or centrifugation — **supernatant** *adj*

su·per·nu·mer·ary \ˌsü-pər-ˈnü-mə-ˌrer-ē, -ˈnyü-\ *adj* : exceeding the usual or normal number (∼ teeth)

supero- *comb form* : situated above ⟨*supero*lateral⟩

su·pero·lat·er·al \ˌsü-pə-rō-ˈla-tə-rəl\ *adj* : situated above and toward the side

su·per·ovu·la·tion \-ˌä-vyə-ˈlā-shən\ *n* : production of exceptional numbers of ova at one time — **su·per·ovu·late** \-ˈä-vyə-ˌlāt\ *vb*

su·per·ox·ide \-ˈäk-ˌsīd\ *n* : the monovalent anion O⁻₂ or a compound containing it (potassium ∼ KO₂)

superoxide dis·mu·tase \-dis-ˈmyü-ˌtās, -ˌtāz\ *n* : a metal-containing enzyme that reduces potentially harmful free radicals of oxygen formed during normal metabolic cell processes to oxygen and hydrogen peroxide

su·per·po·tent \ˌsü-pər-ˈpōt-ᵊnt\ *adj* : of greater than normal or acceptable potency — **su·per·po·ten·cy** \-ᵊn-sē\ *n*

su·per·scrip·tion \ˌsü-pər-ˈskrip-shən\ *n* : the part of a pharmaceutical prescription which contains or consists of the Latin word *recipe* or the sign ℞

su·per·son·ic \-ˈsä-nik\ *adj* 1 : having a frequency above the human ear's audibility limit of about 20,000 cycles per second (∼ vibrations) 2 : utilizing, produced by, or relating to supersonic waves or vibrations — **su·per·son·i·cal·ly** *adv*

su·per·vene \ˌsü-pər-ˈvēn\ *vb* -**vened**; -**ven·ing** : to follow or result as an additional, adventitious, or unlooked-for development (as in the course of a disease)

su·pi·na·tion \ˌsü-pə-ˈnā-shən\ *n* 1 : rotation of the forearm and hand so that the palm faces forward or upward and the radius lies parallel to the

ulna; *also* : aᵉ corresponding movement of the foot and leg 2 : the position resulting from supination — **su·pi·nate** \ˈsü-pə-ˌnāt\ *vb*

su·pi·na·tor \ˈsü-pə-ˌnāt-ər\ *n* : a muscle that produces the motion of supination: *specif* : a deeply situated muscle of the forearm that arises in two layers from the lateral epicondyle of the humerus and adjacent parts of the ligaments and bones of the elbow and that passes over the head of the radius to insert into its neck and the lateral surface of its shaft

supinator crest *n* : a bony ridge on the upper lateral surface of the shaft of the ulna that is the origin for part of the supinator muscle

su·pine \sü-ˈpīn, ˈsü-ˌpīn\ *adj* 1 : lying on the back or with the face upward 2 : marked by supination

¹**sup·ple·ment** \ˈsə-plə-mənt\ *n* : something that completes or makes an addition (dietary ∼s)

²**sup·ple·ment** \-ˌment\ *vb* : to add a supplement to : serve as a supplement for — **sup·ple·men·ta·tion** \ˌsə-plə-ˌmen-ˈtā-shən, -mən-\ *n*

sup·ple·men·tal \ˌsə-plə-ˈment-ᵊl\ *adj* : serving to supplement : SUPPLEMENTARY

supplemental air *n* : the air that can still be expelled from the lungs after an ordinary expiration — compare RESIDUAL AIR

sup·ple·men·ta·ry \ˌsə-plə-ˈmen-tə-rē\ *adj* : added or serving as a supplement (∼ vitamins)

sup·ply \sə-ˈplī\ *vb* **sup·plied**; **sup·ply·ing** : to furnish (organs, tissues, or cells) with a vital element (as blood or nerve fibers) — used of nerves and blood vessels

¹**sup·port** \sə-ˈpōrt\ *vb* 1 : to hold up or serve as a foundation or prop for 2 : to maintain in condition, action, or existence (∼ life) — **sup·por·tive** \-ˈpōr-tiv\ *adj*

²**support** *n* 1 : the act or process of supporting : the condition of being supported (respiratory ∼) 2 : SUPPORTER

sup·port·er *n* : a woven or knitted band or elastic device supporting a part; *esp* : ATHLETIC SUPPORTER

support group *n* : a group of people with common experiences and concerns who provide emotional and moral support for one another

support hose *n* : stockings (as elastic stockings) worn to supply mild compression to assist the veins of the legs — usu. used with a pl. verb: called also *support hosiery*

sup·pos·i·to·ry \sə-ˈpä-zə-ˌtōr-ē\ *n, pl* -**ries** : a solid but readily melting cone or cylinder of usu. medicated material for insertion into a bodily passage or cavity (as the rectum)

sup·press \sə-ˈpres\ *vb* 1 : to exclude from consciousness (∼ed anxiety) 2 : to restrain from a usual course or action (~ a cough) **3** : to inhibit the genetic expression of (~ a mutation) — **sup·press·ible** \-'pre-sə-bəl\ adj

¹**sup·press·ant** \sə-'pres-ənt\ adj : SUPPRESSIVE

²**suppressant** n : an agent (as a drug) that tends to suppress or reduce in intensity rather than eliminate something

sup·pres·sion \sə-'pre-shən\ n : an act or instance of suppressing: as **a** : stoppage of a bodily function or a symptom **b** : the failure of development of a bodily part or organ **c** : the conscious intentional exclusion from consciousness of a thought or feeling — compare REPRESSION 2a

sup·pres·sive \sə-'pre-siv\ adj : tending or serving to suppress something (as the symptoms of a disease) (~ drugs)

sup·pres·sor \sə-'pre-sər\ n : one that suppresses: esp : a mutant gene that suppresses the expression of another nonallelic mutant gene when both are present

suppressor T cell n : a T cell that suppresses the immune response of B cells and other T cells to an antigen — called also *suppressor lymphocyte*, *suppressor cell*, *suppressor T lymphocyte*

sup·pu·ra·tion \ˌsə-pyə-'rā-shən\ n : the formation of, conversion into, or process of discharging pus (~ in a wound) — **sup·pu·rate** \'sə-pyə-ˌrāt\ vb — **sup·pu·ra·tive** \'sə-pyə-ˌrā-tiv\ adj

suppurativa — see HIDRADENITIS SUPPURATIVA

supra- prefix **1** : SUPER- 2 (supraorbital) **2** : transcending (supramolecular)

su·pra·cer·vi·cal hysterectomy \ˌsü-prə-'sər-vi-kəl-\ n : a hysterectomy in which the uterine cervix is not removed

su·pra·chi·as·mat·ic \-ˌkī-əz-'ma-tik\ adj : SUPRAOPTIC

suprachiasmatic nucleus n : a small group of neurons situated immediately dorsal to the optic chiasma

su·pra·cla·vic·u·lar \ˌkla-'vi-kyə-lər, -klə-\ adj : situated or occurring above the clavicle (~ lymph nodes)

supraclavicular nerve n : any of three nerves that are descending branches of the cervical plexus arising from the third and fourth cervical nerves and that supply the skin over the upper chest and shoulder

su·pra·clu·sion \ˌsü-prə-'klü-zhən\ n : SUPRAOCCLUSION

su·pra·con·dy·lar \ˌsü-prə-'kän-də-lər, -ˌprä-\ adj : of, relating to, affecting, or being the part of a bone situated above a condyle (a ~ fracture)

supracondylar ridge n : either of two ridges above the condyle of the humerus of which one is situated laterally and the other medially and which give attachment to muscles

su·pra·gin·gi·val \-'jin-jə-vəl\ adj : located on the surface of a tooth not surrounded by gingiva (~ calculus)

su·pra·gle·noid \-'gle-ˌnoid, -'glē-\ adj : situated or occurring superior to the glenoid cavity

su·pra·glot·tic \-'glä-tik\ adj : situated or occurring above the glottis

su·pra·hy·oid \-'hi-ˌoid\ adj : situated or occurring superior to the hyoid bone (~ lymphadenectomy)

suprahyoid muscle n : any of several muscles (as the mylohyoid and geniohyoid) passing upward to the jaw and face from the hyoid bone

su·pra·mar·gi·nal gyrus \-ˌmär-jən-ᵊl-\ n : a gyrus of the inferior part of the parietal lobe that is continuous in front with the postcentral gyrus and posteriorly and inferiorly with the superior temporal gyrus

su·pra·mo·lec·u·lar \-mə-'le-kyə-lər\ adj : more complex than a molecule: also : composed of many molecules

su·pra·nu·cle·ar \-'nü-klē-ər, -'nyü-\ adj : situated, occurring, or produced by a lesion superior or cortical to a nucleus esp. of the brain

su·pra·oc·clu·sion \-ə-'klü-zhən\ n : the projection of a tooth beyond the plane of occlusion

su·pra·op·tic \-'äp-tik\ adj : situated or occurring above the optic chiasma

supraoptic nucleus n : a small nucleus of closely packed neurons that overlies the optic chiasma and is intimately connected with the neurohypophysis

su·pra·or·bit·al \-'ȯr-bət-ᵊl\ adj : situated or occurring above the orbit of the eye

supraorbital artery n : a branch of the ophthalmic artery supplying the orbit and parts of the forehead

supraorbital fissure n : ORBITAL FISSURE a

supraorbital foramen n : SUPRAORBITAL NOTCH

supraorbital nerve n : a branch of the frontal nerve supplying the forehead, scalp, cranial periosteum, and adjacent parts

supraorbital notch n : a notch or foramen in the bony border of the upper inner part of the orbit serving for the passage of the supraorbital nerve, artery, and vein

supraorbital ridge n : SUPERCILIARY RIDGE

supraorbital vein n : a vein that drains the supraorbital region and unites with the frontal vein to form the angular vein

su·pra·pu·bic \-'pyü-bik\ adj : situated, occurring, or performed from above the pubis (~ prostatectomy) — **su·pra·pu·bi·cal·ly** adv

¹**su·pra·re·nal** \-'rēn-ᵊl\ adj : situated above or anterior to the kidneys; specif : ADRENAL

²**suprarenal** n : a suprarenal part; esp : ADRENAL GLAND

suprarenal artery n : any of three arteries on each side of the body that supply the adrenal gland located on the same side and that arise from the inferior phrenic artery, the abdominal aorta, or the renal artery

suprarenal gland n : ADRENAL GLAND

suprarenal vein n : either of two veins of which one arises from the right adrenal gland and empties directly into the inferior vena cava while the other arises from the left adrenal gland, passes behind the pancreas, and empties into the renal vein on the left side

su·pra·scap·u·lar \ˌsü-prə-ˈska-pyə-lər, -ˌprä-\ adj : situated or occurring superior to the scapula

suprascapular artery n : a branch of the thyrocervical trunk that passes over the suprascapular ligament to the back of the scapula

suprascapular ligament n : a thin flat ligament that is attached at one end to the coracoid process and at the other end to the upper margin of the scapula on its dorsal surface

suprascapular nerve n : a branch of the brachial plexus that supplies the supraspinatus and infraspinatus muscles

suprascapular notch n : a deep notch in the upper border of the scapula at the base of the coracoid process giving passage to the suprascapular nerve

su·pra·sel·lar \-ˈse-lər\ adj : situated or rising above the sella turcica — used chiefly of tumors of the hypophysis

su·pra·spi·nal \-ˈspī-nəl\ adj : situated or occurring above a spine

supraspinal ligament n : a fibrous cord that joins the tips of the spinous processes of the vertebrae from the seventh cervical vertebra to the sacrum and that continues forward to the skull as the ligamentum nuchae — called also supraspinous ligament

su·pra·spi·na·tus \-ˌspī-ˈnā-təs\ n : a muscle of the back of the shoulder that arises from the supraspinous fossa of the scapula, that inserts into the top of the greater tubercle of the humerus, that is one of the muscles making up the rotator cuff of the shoulder, and that rotates the humerus laterally and helps to abduct the arm

su·pra·spi·nous fossa \ˌsü-prə-ˈspī-nəs-\ n : a smooth concavity above the spine on the dorsal surface of the scapula that gives origin to the supraspinatus muscle

supraspinous ligament n : SUPRASPINAL LIGAMENT

su·pra·ster·nal \-ˈstərn-əl\ adj : situated above or measured from the top of the sternum (~ height)

suprasternal notch n : the depression in the top of the sternum between its articulations with the two clavicles

suprasternal space n : a long narrow space in the lower part of the deep fascia of the cervical region contain-

ing areolar tissue, the sternal part of the sternocleidomastoid muscles, and the lower part of the anterior jugular veins

su·pra·ten·to·ri·al \-ten-ˈtōr-ē-əl\ adj : relating to, occurring in, affecting, or being the tissues overlying the tentorium cerebelli (a ~ glioma)

su·pra·thresh·old \-ˈthresh-ˌhōld\ adj : of sufficient strength or quantity to produce a perceptible physiological effect

su·pra·troch·le·ar artery \-ˈträ-klē-ər-\ n : one of the terminal branches of the ophthalmic artery that ascends upon the forehead from the inner angle of the orbit

supratrochlear nerve n : a branch of the frontal nerve supplying the skin of the forehead and the upper eyelid

su·pra·val·vu·lar \-ˈval-vyə-lər\ adj : situated or occurring above a valve (~ aortic stenosis)

su·pra·ven·tric·u·lar \-ven-ˈtri-kyə-lər\ adj : relating to or being a rhythmic abnormality of the heart caused by impulses originating above the ventricles (as in the atrioventricular node) (~ tachycardia)

su·pra·vi·tal \-ˈvīt-əl\ adj : constituting or relating to the staining of living tissues or cells surviving after removal from a living body by dyes that penetrate living substance but induce more or less rapid degenerative changes — compare INTRAVITAL 2 — **su·pra·vi·tal·ly** adv

supreme thoracic artery n : THORACIC ARTERY 1a

su·ral nerve \ˈsür-əl-\ n : any of several nerves in the region of the calf of the leg; esp : one formed by the union of a branch of the tibial nerve with a branch of the common peroneal nerve that supplies branches to the skin of the back of the leg and sends a continuation to the little toe by way of the lateral side of the foot

sur·a·min \ˈsür-ə-mən\ n : a trypanocidal drug $C_{51}H_{34}N_6Na_6O_{23}S_6$ obtained as a white powder and administered intravenously in the early stages of African sleeping sickness — called also germanin, suramin sodium; see NAPHURIDE

surface–active adj : altering the properties and esp. lowering the tension at the surface of contact between phases (soaps are typical ~ substances)

surface tension n : a condition that exists at the free surface of a body (as a liquid) by reason of molecular forces about the individual surface molecules and is manifested by properties resembling those of an elastic skin under tension

sur·fac·tant \(ˌ)sər-ˈfak-tənt, ˈsər-ˌ\ n : a surface-active substance: specif : a surface-active lipoprotein mixture which coats the alveoli and which prevents collapse of the lungs by reducing the surface tension of pulmonary fluids — **surfactant** *adj*

surfer's knot *n* : a knobby lump just below a surfer's knee or on the upper surface of the foot caused by friction and pressure between surfboard and skin — called also *surfer's knob, surfer's lump, surfer's nodule*

surg *abbr* 1 surgeon 2 surgery 3 surgical

sur·geon \ˈsər-jən\ *n* 1 : a medical specialist who performs surgery : a physician qualified to treat those diseases that are amenable to or require surgery — compare INTERNIST 2 : the senior medical officer of a military unit

surgeon general *n, pl* **surgeons general** : the chief medical officer of a branch of the armed services or of a public health service

sur·gery \ˈsər-jə-rē\ *n, pl* **-ger·ies** 1 : a branch of medicine concerned with diseases and conditions requiring or amenable to operative or manual procedures 2 a *Brit* : a physician's or dentist's office b : a room or area where surgery is performed 3 a : the work done by a surgeon b : OPERATION

sur·gi·cal \ˈsər-ji-kəl\ *adj* 1 : of, relating to, or concerned with surgeons or surgery 2 : requiring surgical treatment ⟨a ~ appendix⟩ 3 : resulting from surgery ⟨~ fever⟩ 4 : done by or used in surgery or surgical conditions

sur·gi·cal·ly \ˈsər-ji-klē, -kə-lē\ *adv* : by means of surgery

surgical neck *n* : a slightly narrowed part of the humerus below the greater and lesser tubercles that is frequently the site of fractures

sur·gi·cen·ter \ˈsər-jə-ˌsen-tər\ *n* : a medical facility that performs minor surgery on an outpatient basis

sur·ra \ˈsur-ə\ *n* : a severe febrile and hemorrhagic disease of domestic animals that is caused by a protozoan of the genus *Trypanosoma* (*T. evansi*)

sur·ro·ga·cy \ˈsər-ə-gə-sē\ *n, pl* **-cies** : the practice of serving as a surrogate mother

sur·ro·gate \-gət\ *n* : one that serves as a substitute: as a : a representation of a person substituted through symbolizing (as in a dream) for conscious recognition of the person b : a drug substituted for another drug c : SURROGATE MOTHER

surrogate mother *n* : a woman who becomes pregnant usu. by artificial insemination or surgical implantation of a fertilized egg for the purpose of carrying the fetus to term for another woman — **surrogate motherhood** *n*

sur·veil·lance \sər-ˈvā-ləns, -ˈlyəns\ *n* : close and continuous observation or testing ⟨serological ~⟩ — see IMMUNOLOGICAL SURVEILLANCE

¹**sus·cep·ti·ble** \sə-ˈsep-tə-bəl\ *adj* 1 : having little resistance to a specific infectious disease : capable of being infected 2 : predisposed to develop a noninfectious disease ⟨~ to diabetes⟩ 3 : abnormally reactive to various drugs — **sus·cep·ti·bil·i·ty** \sə-ˌsep-tə-ˈbi-lə-tē\ *n*

²**susceptible** *n* : one that is susceptible (as to a disease)

suspended animation *n* : temporary suspension of the vital functions

sus·pen·sion \sə-ˈspen-chən\ *n* 1 a : the state of a substance when its particles are mixed with but undissolved in a fluid or solid b : a substance in this state 2 : a system consisting of a solid dispersed in a solid, liquid, or gas usu. in particles of larger than colloidal size

¹**sus·pen·so·ry** \sə-ˈspen-sə-rē\ *adj* : serving to suspend : providing support

²**suspensory** *n, pl* **-ries** : something that suspends or holds up : *esp* : a fabric supporter for the scrotum

suspensory ligament *n* : a ligament or fibrous membrane suspending an organ or part: as a : a ringlike fibrous membrane connecting the ciliary body and the lens of the eye and holding the lens in place b : FALCIFORM LIGAMENT

suspensory ligament of the ovary *n* : a fold of peritoneum that consists of a part of the broad ligament that is attached to the ovary near the end joining the fallopian tube and that contains blood and lymph vessels passing to and from the ovary — called also *infundibulopelvic ligament*; compare LIGAMENT OF THE OVARY

sus·ten·tac·u·lar cell \ˌsəs-tən-ˈta-kyə-lər-\ *n* : a supporting epithelial cell (as of the olfactory epithelium) that lacks a specialized function

sustentacular fiber of Müller *n* : FIBER OF MÜLLER

sus·ten·tac·u·lum ta·li \ˌsəs-tən-ˈta-kyə-ləm-ˈtā-ˌlī\ *n* : a medial process of the calcaneus supporting part of the talus

su·ture \ˈsü-chər\ *n* 1 a : a stitch made with a suture b : a strand or fiber used to sew parts of the living body c : the act or process of sewing with sutures 2 a : the line of union in an immovable articulation (as between the bones of the skull); *also* : such an articulation b : a furrow at the junction of adjacent bodily parts — **su·tur·al** \ˈsü-chə-rəl\ *adj* — **suture** *vb*

suxa·me·tho·ni·um \ˌsük-sə-mə-ˈthō-nē-əm\ *n, chiefly Brit* : SUCCINYLCHOLINE

sved·berg \ˈsfed-ˌbərg, -ˌber-ē\ *n* : a unit of time amounting to 10^{-13} second that is used to measure the sedimentation velocity of a colloidal solution (as of a protein) in an ultracentrifuge and to determine molecular weight by substitution in an equation — called also *svedberg unit*
    Svedberg, Theodor (1884–1971), Swedish chemist.

¹swab \'swäb\ *n* **1** : a wad of absorbent material usu. wound around one end of a small stick and used for applying medication or for removing material from an area **2** : a specimen taken with a swab (a throat ∼)

²swab *vb* **swabbed; swab·bing** : to apply medication to with a swab

swamp fever *n* : EQUINE INFECTIOUS ANEMIA

Swan–Ganz catheter \'swän-'ganz-\ *n* : a soft catheter with a balloon tip that is used for measuring blood pressure in the pulmonary artery

Swan, Harold James Charles (*b* 1922), and **Ganz, William** (*b* 1919), American cardiologists.

S wave \'es-₊\ *n* : the negative downward deflection in the QRS complex of an electrocardiogram that follows the R wave

sway·back \'swā-₊bak\ *n* **1** : an abnormally hollow condition or sagging of the back found esp. in horses; *also* : a back so shaped **2** : LORDOSIS **3** : a copper-deficiency disease of young or newborn lambs that is marked by demyelination of the brain resulting in weakness, staggering gait, and collapse and is almost universally fatal but is readily preventable by copper supplementation of the diet of the pregnant ewe — **sway·backed** \-₊bakt\ *adj*

¹sweat \'swet\ *vb* **sweat** *or* **sweat·ed; sweat·ing** : to excrete moisture in visible quantities through the opening of the sweat glands : PERSPIRE

²sweat *n* **1** : the fluid excreted from the sweat glands of the skin : PERSPIRATION **2** : abnormally profuse sweating — often used in pl. (soaking ∼s)

sweat duct *n* : the part of a sweat gland which extends through the dermis to the surface of the skin

sweat gland *n* : a simple tubular gland of the skin that secretes perspiration and in humans is widely distributed in nearly all parts of the skin — called also *sudoriferous gland*

sweat test *n* : a test for cystic fibrosis that involves measuring the subject's sweat for abnormally high sodium chloride content

swee·ny \'swē-nē\ *n, pl* **sweenies** : an atrophy of the shoulder muscles of a horse; *broadly* : any muscular atrophy of a horse

sweet \'swēt\ *adj* : being or inducing the one of the four basic taste sensations that is typically induced by disaccharides and is mediated esp. by receptors in taste buds at the front of the tongue — compare BITTER, SALT 2, SOUR — **sweet·ness** *n*

sweet clover disease *n* : a hemorrhagic diathesis of sheep and cattle feeding on sweet clover (genus *Melilotus* of the family Leguminosae) containing excess quantities of dicumarol

Sweet's syndrome \'swēts-\ *n* : a disease that occurs esp. in middle-aged women, that is characterized by red raised often painful patches on the skin, fever, and neutrophilia in the peripheral blood, that responds to treatment with corticosteroids but not antibiotics, and that is of unknown cause but is sometimes associated with an underlying malignant disorder — called also *acute febrile neutrophilic dermatosis*

Sweet, Robert (*fl* 1942–64), British dermatologist.

swell \'swel\ *vb* **swelled; swelled** *or* **swol·len** \'swō-lən\; **swell·ing** : to become distended or puffed up

swell·ing \'swel-iŋ\ *n* : an abnormal bodily protuberance or localized enlargement (an inflammatory ∼)

Swift's disease \'swifts-\ *n* : ACRODYNIA

Swift, H. (*fl* 1918), Australian physician.

swimmer's itch *n* : an itching inflammation that is a reaction to the invasion of the skin by schistosomes that are not normally parasites of humans — called also *schistosome dermatitis*

swine \'swīn\ *n* : any of various stout-bodied short-legged mammals (family Suidae) with a thick bristly skin and a long mobile snout; *esp* : a domesticated member of a species (*Sus scrofa*) that occurs wild in the Old World

swine dysentery *n* : an acute infectious hemorrhagic dysentery of swine

swine erysipelas *n* : a destructive contagious disease of various mammals and birds that is caused by a bacterium of the genus *Erysipelothrix* (*E. rhusiopathiae*) — called also *erysipelas*

swine fever *n* : HOG CHOLERA

swineherd's disease *n* : a form of leptospirosis contracted from swine

swine influenza *n* : an acute contagious febrile disease of swine caused by interaction of a specific virus introduced by the lungworm (*Metastrongylus elongatus*) of swine and a bacterium of the genus *Haemophilus* (*H. suis*) related to that causing human influenza — called also *swine flu*

swine pox *n* : a mild virus disease of young pigs marked by fever, loss of appetite, dullness, and production of skin lesions

swol·len *adj* : protuberant or abnormally distended (as by injury or disease)

sy·co·sis \sī-'kō-səs\ *n, pl* **sy·co·ses** \-₊sēz\ : a chronic inflammatory disease involving the hair follicles esp. of the bearded part of the face and marked by papules, pustules, and tubercles perforated by hairs with crusting

sycosis bar·bae \-'bär-bē\ *n* : sycosis of the bearded part of the face

Syd·en·ham's chorea \'sid-ᵊn-əmz-\ *n* : chorea following infection (as rheumatic fever) and occurring usu. in children and adolescents

Sydenham, Thomas (1624–1689), British physician.

syl·vat·ic \sil-'va-tik\ adj : occurring in, affecting, or transmitted by wild animals ⟨~ diseases⟩

sylvatic plague n : a form of plague of which wild rodents and their fleas are the reservoirs and vectors and which is widely distributed in western No. and So. America though rarely affecting humans

Syl·vi·an \'sil-vē-ən\ adj : of or relating to the fissure of Sylvius

F. Dubois or **De Le Boë** — see FISSURE OF SYLVIUS

Sylvian fissure n : FISSURE OF SYLVIUS

sym- — see SYN-

sym·bi·ont \'sim-bī-änt, -bē-\ n : an organism living in symbiosis; esp : the smaller member of a symbiotic pair

sym·bi·o·sis \sim-bī-'ō-səs, -bē-\ n, pl **-bi·o·ses** \-sēz\ 1 : the living together in more or less intimate association or close union of two dissimilar organisms 2 : the intimate living together of two dissimilar organisms in a mutually beneficial relationship — **sym·bi·ot·ic** \sim-bī-'ä-tik, -bē-\ adj — **sym·bi·ot·i·cal·ly** adv

sym·bi·ote \'sim-bī-ōt, -bē-\ n : SYMBIONT

sym·bleph·a·ron \sim-'ble-fə-rän\ n : adhesion between an eyelid and the eyeball

sym·bol \'sim-bəl\ n : something that stands for or suggests something else; esp : an object or act representing something in the unconscious mind that has been repressed ⟨phallic ~s⟩ — **sym·bol·ic** \sim-'bä-lik\ adj — **sym·bol·i·cal·ly** adv

Syme's amputation \'sīmz-\ or **Syme amputation** \'sīm-\ n : amputation of the foot through the articulation of the ankle with removal of the malleoli of the tibia and fibula — compare PIROGOFF'S AMPUTATION

Syme, James (1799–1870), British surgeon.

Sym·me·trel \'si-mə-ˌtrel\ trademark — used for a preparation of amantadine

sym·me·try \'si-mə-trē\ n, pl **-tries** : correspondence in size, shape, and relative position of parts on opposite sides of a dividing line or median plane or about a center or axis — see BILATERAL SYMMETRY — **sym·met·ri·cal** \sə-'me-tri-kəl\ or **sym·met·ric** \-trik\ adj — **sym·met·ri·cal·ly** adv

sympath- or **sympatho-** comb form : sympathetic nerve : sympathetic nervous system ⟨sympatholytic⟩

sym·pa·thec·to·my \sim-pə-'thek-tə-mē\ n, pl **-mies** : surgical interruption of sympathetic nerve pathways — **sym·pa·thec·to·mized** \-ˌmīzd\ adj

¹sym·pa·thet·ic \sim-pə-'the-tik\ adj 1 : of or relating to the sympathetic nervous system 2 : mediated by or

acting on the sympathetic nerves — **sym·pa·thet·i·cal·ly** adv

²sympathetic n : a sympathetic structure; esp : SYMPATHETIC NERVOUS SYSTEM

sympathetic chain n : either of the pair of ganglionated longitudinal cords of the sympathetic nervous system of which one is situated on each side of the spinal column — called also sympathetic trunk; compare VERTEBRAL GANGLION

sympathetic nerve n : a nerve of the sympathetic nervous system

sympathetic nervous system n : the part of the autonomic nervous system that contains chiefly adrenergic fibers and tends to depress secretion, decrease the tone and contractility of smooth muscle, and increase heart rate and that consists essentially of preganglionic fibers arising in the thoracic and upper lumbar parts of the spinal cord and passing through delicate white rami communicantes to ganglia located in a pair of sympathetic chains situated one on each side of the spinal column or to more peripheral ganglia or ganglionated plexuses and postganglionic fibers passing typically through gray rami communicantes to spinal nerves with which they are distributed to various end organs — called also sympathetic system; compare PARASYMPATHETIC NERVOUS SYSTEM

sympathetico- comb form : SYMPATH- ⟨sympatheticomimetic⟩

sym·pa·thet·i·co·mi·met·ic \sim-pə-ˌthe-ti-kō-mə-'me-tik\ adj or n : SYMPATHOMIMETIC

sympathetic ophthalmia n : inflammation in an uninjured eye as a result of injury and inflammation of the other

sym·pa·thet·i·co·to·nia \sim-pə-ˌthe-ti-kə-'tō-nē-ə\ n : SYMPATHICOTONIA

sympathetic system n : SYMPATHETIC NERVOUS SYSTEM

sympathetic trunk n : SYMPATHETIC CHAIN

sympathico- comb form : SYMPATH- ⟨sympathicotonia⟩

sym·path·i·co·lyt·ic \sim-ˌpa-thi-kō-'li-tik\ adj or n : SYMPATHOLYTIC

sym·path·i·co·mi·met·ic \-mə-'me-tik, -mī-\ adj or n : SYMPATHOMIMETIC

sym·path·i·co·to·nia \sim-ˌpa-thi-kō-'tō-nē-ə\ n : a condition produced by relatively great activity or stimulation of the sympathetic nervous system and characterized by goose bumps, vascular spasm, and abnormally high blood pressure — called also sympatheticotonia; compare VAGOTONIA — **sym·path·i·co·ton·ic** \-'tä-nik\ adj

sym·pa·thin \'sim-pə-thən\ n : a substance (as norepinephrine) that is secreted by sympathetic nerve endings and acts as a chemical mediator

sym·pa·tho·ad·re·nal \sim-pə-thō-ə-'drē-nəl\ adj : relating to or involving the sympathetic nervous system and the adrenal medulla

sym·pa·tho·go·nia \sim-pə-thō-ˈgō-nē-ə\ n : precursor cells of the sympathetic nervous system

sym·pa·tho·go·ni·o·ma \-ˌgō-nē-ˈō-mə\ n, pl -ma·ta \-mə-tə\ or -mas : a tumor derived from sympathogonia; also : NEUROBLASTOMA

¹**sym·pa·tho·lyt·ic** \ˌsim-pə-thō-ˈli-tik\ adj : tending to oppose the physiological results of sympathetic nervous activity or of sympathomimetic drugs — compare PARASYMPATHOLYTIC

²**sympatholytic** n : a sympatholytic agent

¹**sym·pa·tho·mi·met·ic** \-mə-ˈme-tik, -(ˌ)mī-\ adj : simulating sympathetic nervous action in physiological effect — compare PARASYMPATHOMIMETIC

²**sympathomimetic** n : a sympathomimetic agent

sym·phal·an·gism \(ˌ)sim-ˈfa-lən-ˌji-zəm\ n : ankylosis of the joints of one or more digits

sym·phy·se·al \ˌsim-fə-ˈsē-əl\ adj : of, relating to, or constituting a symphysis

sym·phy·si·ot·o·my \ˌsim-fə-zē-ˈä-tə-mē, sim-ˌfi-zē-\ n, pl -mies : the operation of dividing the pubic symphysis

sym·phy·sis \ˈsim-fə-səs\ n, pl -phy·ses \-ˌsēz\ 1 : an immovable or more or less movable articulation of various bones in the median plane of the body 2 : an articulation (as between the bodies of vertebrae) in which the bony surfaces are connected by pads of fibrous cartilage without a synovial membrane

symphysis pubis n : PUBIC SYMPHYSIS

symp·tom \ˈsimp-təm\ n : subjective evidence of disease or physical disturbance observed by the patient (headache is a ~ of many diseases); broadly : something that indicates the presence of a physical disorder — compare SIGN 2

symp·tom·at·ic \ˌsimp-tə-ˈma-tik\ adj 1 a : being a symptom of a disease b : having the characteristics of a particular disease but arising from another cause (~ epilepsy resulting from brain damage) 2 : concerned with or affecting symptoms (~ treatment) 3 : having symptoms (a ~ patient) — **symp·tom·at·i·cal·ly** adv

symp·tom·atol·o·gy \ˌsimp-tə-mə-ˈtä-lə-jē\ n, pl -gies 1 : SYMPTOM COMPLEX 2 : a branch of medical science concerned with symptoms of diseases — **symp·tom·at·o·log·i·cal** \-ˌmat-ᵊl-ˈä-ji-kəl\ or **symp·tom·at·o·log·ic** \-ˈä-jik\ adj — **symp·tom·at·o·log·i·cal·ly** adv

symptom complex n : a group of symptoms occurring together and characterizing a particular disease

symp·tom·less \ˈsimp-təm-ləs\ adj : exhibiting no symptoms

syn- or **sym-** prefix 1 : with : along with

: together (symbiosis) 2 : at the same time (synesthesia)

syn·aes·the·sia chiefly Brit var of SYNESTHESIA

syn·an·throp·ic \ˌsi-nan-ˈthrä-pik\ adj : ecologically associated with humans (~ flies) — **syn·an·thro·py** \sin-ˈan-thrə-pē\ n

¹**syn·apse** \ˈsi-ˌnaps, sə-ˈnaps\ n 1 : the place at which a nervous impulse passes from one neuron to another 2 : SYNAPSIS

²**synapse** vb **syn·apsed; syn·aps·ing** : to form a synapse or come together in synapsis

syn·ap·sis \sə-ˈnap-səs\ n, pl -ap·ses \-ˌsēz\ : the association of homologous chromosomes with chiasma formation that is characteristic of the first meiotic prophase and is held to be the mechanism for genetic crossing-over

syn·ap·tic \si-ˈnap-tik\ adj : of or relating to a synapse or to synapsis (~ transmission) — **syn·ap·ti·cal·ly** adv

synaptic cleft n : the space between neurons at a nerve synapse across which a nerve impulse is transmitted by a neurotransmitter — called also synaptic gap

synaptic vesicle n : a small secretory vesicle that contains a neurotransmitter, is found inside an axon near the presynaptic membrane, and releases its contents into the synaptic cleft after fusing with the membrane

syn·ap·to·gen·e·sis \sə-ˌnap-tə-ˈje-nə-səs\ n, pl -e·ses \-ˌsēz\ : the formation of nerve synapses

syn·ap·tol·o·gy \ˌsi-nap-ˈtä-lə-jē\ n, pl -gies : the scientific study of nerve synapses

syn·ap·to·some \sə-ˈnap-tə-ˌsōm\ n : a nerve ending that is isolated from homogenized nerve tissue — **syn·ap·to·som·al** \-ˌnap-tə-ˈsō-məl\ adj

syn·ar·thro·sis \ˌsi-när-ˈthrō-səs\ n, pl -thro·ses \-ˌsēz\ : an immovable articulation in which the bones are united by intervening fibrous connective tissues

syn·chon·dro·sis \ˌsin-kän-ˈdrō-səs\ n, pl -dro·ses \-ˌsēz\ : an immovable skeletal articulation in which the union is cartilaginous

syn·cho·ri·al \sin-ˈkōr-ē-əl, siŋ-\ adj : having a common placenta — used of multiple fetuses

syn·chro·nized sleep \ˈsiŋ-krə-ˌnīzd-, ˈsin-\ n : SLOW-WAVE SLEEP

syn·co·pe \ˈsiŋ-kə-pē, ˈsin-\ n : loss of consciousness resulting from insufficient blood flow to the brain : FAINT — **syn·co·pal** \ˈsiŋ-kə-pəl, ˈsin-\ adj

syn·cy·tial \sin-ˈsi-shəl, -shē-əl\ adj : of, relating to, or constituting syncytium

syn·cy·tio·tro·pho·blast \sin-ˌsi-shē-ō-ˈtrō-fə-ˌblast\ n : the outer syncytial layer of the trophoblast that actively invades the uterine wall forming the outermost fetal component of the placenta — called also *syntrophoblast*; compare CYTOTROPHOBLAST

syn·cy·tium \sin-ˈsi-shəm, -shē-əm\ *n*, *pl* **-tia** \-shə-, -shē-ə\ : a multinucleate mass of protoplasm resulting from fusion of cells

syn·dac·tyl \sin-ˈdakt-ᵊl\ *adj* : having two or more digits wholly or partly united

syn·dac·ty·lism \sin-ˈdak-tə-li-zəm\ *n* : SYNDACTYLY

syn·dac·ty·lous \sin-ˈdak-tə-ləs\ *adj* : SYNDACTYL

syn·dac·ty·ly \-lē\ *n*, *pl* **-lies** : a union of two or more digits that occurs as a human hereditary disorder marked by webbing of two or more fingers or toes

syndesm- or **syndesmo-** *comb form* : ligament ⟨*syndesm*osis⟩

syn·des·mo·sis \sin-dez-ˈmō-səs, -des-\ *n*, *pl* **-mo·ses** \-ˈsēz\ : an articulation in which the contiguous surfaces of the bones are rough and are bound together by a ligament

syn·drome \ˈsin-drōm\ *n* : a group of signs and symptoms that occur together and characterize a particular abnormality

syn·echia \si-ˈne-kē-ə, -ˈnē-\ *n*, *pl* **-chiae** \-kē-ē, -iˈ\ : an adhesion of parts and esp. one involving the iris of the eye: as **a** : adhesion of the iris to the cornea — called also *anterior synechia* **b** : adhesion of the iris to the crystalline lens — called also *posterior synechia*

syn·eph·rine \sə-ˈne-frən\ *n* : a crystalline sympathomimetic amine $C_9H_{13}NO_2$ isomeric with phenylephrine

syn·er·gic \si-ˈnər-jik\ *adj* : working together ⟨~ muscle contraction⟩ — **syn·er·gi·cal·ly** *adv*

syn·er·gism \ˈsi-nər-ji-zəm\ *n* : interaction of discrete agents (as drugs) such that the total effect is greater than the sum of the individual effects — called also *synergy*; compare ANTAGONISM b — **syn·er·gis·tic** \si-nər-ˈjis-tik\ *adj* — **syn·er·gis·ti·cal·ly** *adv*

syn·er·gist \-jist\ *n* **1** : an agent that increases the effectiveness of another agent when combined with it; *esp* : a drug that acts in synergism with another **2** : an organ (as a muscle) that acts in concert with another to enhance its effect — compare AGONIST 1, ANTAGONIST 1

syn·er·gize \ˈsi-nər-jīz\ *vb* **-gized; -giz·ing 1** : to act as synergists : exhibit synergism **2** : to increase the activity of (a substance)

syn·er·gy \-jē\ *n*, *pl* **-gies** : SYNERGISM

syn·es·the·sia \si-nəs-ˈthē-zhə, -zhē-ə\ *n* : a subjective sensation or image of a sense (as of color) other than the one (as of sound) being stimulated — **syn·es·thet·ic** \-ˈthe-tik\ *adj*

Syn·ga·mus \ˈsiŋ-gə-məs\ *n* : a genus (family Syngamidae) of nematode

worms that are parasitic in the trachea or esophagus of various birds and mammals and include the gapeworm (*S. trachea*)

syn·ga·my \ˈsiŋ-gə-mē\ *n*, *pl* **-mies** : sexual reproduction by union of gametes

syn·ge·ne·ic \sin-jə-ˈnē-ik\ *adj* : genetically identical esp. with respect to antigens or immunological reactions ⟨~ tumor cells⟩ — compare ALLOGENEIC, XENOGENEIC

syn·kary·on \sin-ˈkar-ē-än, -ē-ən\ *n* : a cell nucleus formed by the fusion of two preexisting nuclei

syn·ki·ne·sia \sin-kə-ˈnē-zhə, -kī-, -zhē-ə\ *n* : SYNKINESIS

syn·ki·ne·sis \-ˈnē-səs\ *n*, *pl* **-ne·ses** \-sēz\ : involuntary movement in one part when another part is moved : an associated movement — **syn·ki·net·ic** \-ˈne-tik\ *adj*

syn·os·to·sis \si-näs-ˈtō-səs\ *n*, *pl* **-to·ses** \-sēz\ : union of two or more separate bones to form a single bone; *also* : the union so formed (as at an epiphyseal line) — **syn·os·tot·ic** \-ˈtä-tik\ *adj*

syn·o·vec·to·my \si-nə-ˈvek-tə-mē\ *n*, *pl* **-mies** : surgical removal of a synovial membrane

sy·no·via \sə-ˈnō-vē-ə, sī-\ *n* : a transparent viscid lubricating fluid secreted by a membrane of an articulation, bursa, or tendon sheath — called also *synovial fluid*

sy·no·vi·al \-vē-əl\ *adj* : of, relating to, or secreting synovia ⟨~ effusion⟩; *also* : lined with synovial membrane ⟨a ~ bursa⟩ ⟨~ tendon sheaths⟩

synovial fluid *n* : SYNOVIA

synovial joint *n* : DIARTHROSIS

synovial membrane *n* : the dense connective-tissue membrane that secretes synovia and that lines the ligamentous surfaces of articular capsules, tendon sheaths where free movement is necessary, and bursae

sy·no·vi·tis \si-nə-ˈvī-təs\ *n* : inflammation of a synovial membrane usu. with pain and swelling of the joint

sy·no·vi·um \sə-ˈnō-vē-əm, sī-\ *n* : SYNOVIAL MEMBRANE

syn·the·sis \sin-thə-səs\ *n*, *pl* **-the·ses** \-sēz\ **1** : the composition or combination of parts or elements so as to form a whole **2** : the production of a substance by the union of chemical elements, groups, or simpler compounds or by the degradation of a complex compound ⟨protein ~⟩ — **syn·the·size** \-siz\ *vb*

syn·the·tase \ˈsin-thə-tās, -tāz\ *n* : an enzyme that catalyzes the linking together of two molecules esp. by using the energy derived from the concurrent splitting off of a group from a triphosphate (as ATP) — called also *ligase*

¹**syn·thet·ic** \sin-ˈthe-tik\ *adj* : of, relating to, or produced by chemical or biochemical synthesis; *esp* : pro-

duced artificially (∼ drugs) — **syn·thet·i·cal·ly** *adv*

²synthetic *n* : a product (as a drug) of chemical synthesis

syn·tro·pho·blast \sin-'trō-fə-ˌblast\ *n* : SYNCYTIOTROPHOBLAST

syphil- *or* **syphilo-** *comb form* : syphilis (*syphiloma*)

syph·i·lid \'si-fə-lid\ *n* : a skin eruption caused by syphilis

syph·i·lis \'si-fə-ləs\ *n* : a chronic contagious usu. venereal and often congenital disease that is caused by a spirochete of the genus *Treponema* (*T. pallidum*) and if left untreated produces chancres, rashes, and systemic lesions in a clinical course with three stages continued over many years — called also *lues;* see PRIMARY SYPHILIS, SECONDARY SYPHILIS, TERTIARY SYPHILIS

¹syph·i·lit·ic \ˌsi-fə-'li-tik\ *adj* : of, relating to, or infected with syphilis — **syph·i·lit·i·cal·ly** *adv*

²syphilitic *n* : a person infected with syphilis

syph·i·lo·ma \ˌsi-fə-'lō-mə\ *n, pl* **-mas** *or* **-ma·ta** \-mə-tə\ : a syphilitic tumor : GUMMA (a testicular ∼)

syph·i·lo·ther·a·py \ˌsi-fə-lō-'ther-ə-pē\ *n, pl* **-pies** : the treatment of syphilis

Sy·rette \sə-'ret\ *trademark* — used for a small collapsible tube fitted with a hypodermic needle for injecting a single dose of a medicinal agent

syring- *or* **syringo-** *comb form* : tube : fistula (*syringo*bulbia)

sy·ringe \sə-'rinj, 'sir-inj\ *n* : a device used to inject fluids into or withdraw them from something (as the body or its cavities): as **a** : a device that consists of a nozzle of varying length and a compressible rubber bulb and is used for injection or irrigation (an ear ∼) **b** : an instrument (as for the injection of medicine or the withdrawal of bodily fluids) that consists of a hollow barrel fitted with a plunger and a hollow needle **c** : a gravity device consisting of a reservoir fitted with a long rubber tube ending with an exchangeable nozzle that is used for irrigation of the vagina or bowel — **syringe** *vb*

sy·rin·go·bul·bia \sə-ˌriŋ-gō-'bəl-bē-ə\ *n* : the presence of abnormal cavities in the medulla oblongata

sy·rin·go·my·elia \sə-ˌriŋ-gō-mī-'ē-lē-ə\ *n* : a chronic progressive disease of the spinal cord associated with sensory disturbances, muscle atrophy, and spasticity

syr·o·sin·go·pine \ˌsir-ō-'siŋ-gə-ˌpēn, -ˌpin\ *n* : a white crystalline powder $C_{35}H_{42}N_2O_{11}$ that is closely related to reserpine and is used as an antihypertensive drug

syr·up \'sər-əp, 'sir-əp\ *n* : a thick sticky liquid consisting of a concentrated solution of sugar and water with or without the addition of a flavoring agent or medicinal substance (∼ of ipecac) — **syr·upy** \-ə-pē\ *adj*

sys·tem \'sis-təm\ *n* **1** : a group of body organs that together perform one or more vital functions — see CIRCULATORY SYSTEM, NERVOUS SYSTEM, REPRODUCTIVE SYSTEM, RESPIRATORY SYSTEM **2** : the body considered as a functional unit

¹sys·tem·ic \sis-'te-mik\ *adj* : of, relating to, or common to a system: as **a** : affecting the body generally — compare LOCAL **b** : supplying those parts of the body that receive blood through the aorta rather than through the pulmonary artery **c** : being a pesticide that as used is harmless to a higher animal or a plant but when absorbed into the bloodstream or the sap makes the whole organism toxic to pests (as cattle grubs) — **sys·tem·i·cal·ly** *adv*

²systemic *n* : a systemic pesticide

systemic circulation *n* : the passage of arterial blood from the left atrium of the heart through the left ventricle, the systemic arteries, and the capillaries to the organs and tissues that receive much of its oxygen in exchange for carbon dioxide and the return of the carbon-dioxide carrying blood via the systemic veins to enter the right atrium of the heart and to participate in the pulmonary circulation

systemic lupus erythematosus *n* : an inflammatory connective tissue disease of unknown cause that occurs chiefly in women and is characterized esp. by fever, skin rash, and arthritis, often by acute hemolytic anemia, by small hemorrhages in the skin and mucous membranes, by inflammation of the pericardium, and in serious cases by involvement of the kidneys and central nervous system

sys·to·le \'sis-tə-(ˌ)lē\ *n* : the contraction of the heart by which the blood is forced onward and the circulation kept up — compare DIASTOLE — **sys·tol·ic** \sis-'tä-lik\ *adj*

systolic pressure *n* : the highest arterial blood pressure of a cardiac cycle occurring immediately after systole of the left ventricle of the heart — compare DIASTOLIC PRESSURE

T

¹**T** abbr 1 thoracic — used with a number from 1 to 12 to indicate a vertebra or segment of the spinal cord ⟨multiple injuries with a fracture of *T-12*⟩ 2 thymine

²**T** symbol tritium

2,4,5-T — see entry alphabetized as TWO,FOUR,FIVE-T

Ta symbol tantalum

TA abbr transactional analysis

tab \ˈtab\ n : TABLET

ta·bar·dil·lo \ˌtä-bär-ˈdē-yō\ n : murine typhus occurring esp. in Mexico

ta·bel·la \tə-ˈbe-lə\ n, pl **-lae** \-ˌlē\ a : a medicated lozenge or tablet

ta·bes \ˈtā-(ˌ)bēz\ n, pl **tabes** 1 : wasting accompanying a chronic disease 2 : TABES DORSALIS

tabes dor·sa·lis \-ˌdor-ˈsā-ləs, -ˈsa-\ n : a syphilitic disorder that involves the dorsal horns of the spinal cord and the sensory nerve trunks and that is marked by wasting, pain, lack of coordination of voluntary movements and reflexes, and disorders of sensation, nutrition, and vision — called also *locomotor ataxia*

ta·bet·ic \tə-ˈbe-tik\ adj : of, relating to, or affected with tabes and esp. tabes dorsalis ⟨~ pains⟩ ⟨a ~ joint⟩

ta·ble·spoon \ˈtā-bəl-ˌspün\ n : a unit of measure equal to 4 fluid drams or ½ fluid ounce or 15 milliliters

ta·ble·spoon·ful \ˌtā-bəl-ˈspün-ˌfül, ˈtā-bəl-ˌ\ n, pl **tablespoonfuls** \-ˌfülz\ also **ta·ble·spoons·ful** \-ˈspünz-ˌfül, -ˌspünz-\ : TABLESPOON

tab·let \ˈta-blət\ n : a small mass of medicated material (as in the shape of a disk) ⟨an aspirin ~⟩

tabo- comb form : progressive wasting : tabes ⟨*taboparesis*⟩

ta·bo·pa·re·sis \ˌtä-bō-pə-ˈrē-səs, -ˈpar-ə-səs\ n, pl **-reses** \-ˌsēz\ : paresis occurring with tabes and esp. with tabes dorsalis

tache noire \ˈtäsh-ˈnwär\ n, pl **taches noires** \same or -ˈnwärz\ : a small dark-centered ulcer that appears at the site of a tick bite and that is the primary lesion of boutonneuse fever

ta·chis·to·scope \tə-ˈkis-tə-ˌskōp-, tä-\ n : an apparatus for the brief exposure of visual stimuli that is used in the study of learning, attention, and perception — **ta·chis·to·scop·ic** \-ˌkis-tə-ˈskä-pik\ adj — **ta·chis·to·scop·i·cal·ly** adv

tachy- comb form : rapid : accelerated ⟨*tachycardia*⟩

tachy·ar·rhyth·mia \ˌta-kē-ā-ˈrith-mē-ə\ n : arrhythmia characterized by a rapid irregular heartbeat

tachy·car·dia \ˌta-ki-ˈkär-dē-ə\ n : relatively rapid heart action whether physiological (as after exercise) or pathological — see PAROXYSMAL TACHYCARDIA; compare BRADYCARDIA — **tachy·car·di·ac** \-dē-ˌak\ adj

tachy·phy·lax·is \ˌta-ki-fi-ˈlak-səs\ n, pl **-lax·es** \-ˌsēz\ : diminished response to later increments in a sequence of applications of a physiologically active substance — **tachy·phy·lac·tic** \-fi-ˈlak-tik\ adj

tachy·pnea \ˌta-kip-ˈnē-ə\ n : increased rate of respiration — **tachy·pne·ic** \-ˈnē-ik\ adj

tachy·pnoea chiefly Brit var of TACHYPNEA

tac·rine \ˈta-ˌkrēn, -ˌkrīn\ n : an anticholinesterase $C_{13}H_{14}N_2$ that crosses the blood-brain barrier and is used esp. in the palliative treatment of cognitive deficits in learning, memory, and mood occurring early in Alzheimer's disease

¹**tac·tile** \ˈtak-təl, -ˌtīl\ adj 1 : of, relating to, mediated by, or affecting the sense of touch 2 : having or being organs or receptors for the sense of touch — **tac·tile·ly** adv

²**tactile** n : a person whose prevailing mental imagery is tactile rather than visual, auditory, or motor — compare AUDILE, VISUALIZER

tactile corpuscle n : one of the numerous minute bodies (as a Meissner's corpuscle) in the skin and some mucous membranes that usu. consist of a group of cells enclosed in a capsule, contain nerve terminations, and are held to be end organs of touch

tactile receptor n : an end organ (as a Meissner's corpuscle or a Pacinian corpuscle) that responds to light touch

tac·toid \ˈtak-ˌtȯid\ n : an elongated particle (as in a sickle cell) that appears as a spindle-shaped body under a polarizing microscope

tac·tual \ˈtak-chə-wəl\ adj : of or relating to the sense or the organs of touch : derived from or producing the sensation of touch : TACTILE ⟨a ~ sense⟩

taen- or **taeni-** also **ten-** or **teni-** comb form : tapeworm ⟨*taeniasis*⟩

tae·nia \ˈtē-nē-ə\ n 1 a \ˈtē-nē-ə\ pl **tae·nias** : TAPEWORM b cap : a genus of taeniid tapeworms that comprises forms usu. occurring as adults in the intestines of carnivores and as larvae in various ruminants, and that includes the beef tapeworm (*T. saginata*) and the pork tapeworm (*T. solium*) of humans 2 pl **tae·ni·ae** \-nē-ˌē, -ˌī\ or **taenias** : a band of nervous tissue or of muscle

taenia co·li \-ˈkō-ˌlī\ n, pl **taeniae coli** : any of three external longitudinal muscle bands of the large intestine

tae·ni·a·sis \tē-ˈnī-ə-səs\ n : infestation with or disease caused by tapeworms

tae·ni·id \ˈtē-nē-əd\ n : any of a family

(Taeniidae) of tapeworms that includes numerous forms of medical or veterinary importance — **taeniid** *adj*

tae·ni·oid \'tē-nē-ˌȯid\ *adj* : resembling or related to the taeniid tapeworms

¹**tag** \'tag\ *n* **1 a** : a shred of flesh or muscle **b** : a small abnormal projecting piece of tissue esp. when potentially or actually neoplastic in character **2** : LABEL

²**tag** *vb* **tagged; tag·ging** : LABEL

Tag·a·met \'ta-gə-ˌmet\ *trademark* — used for a preparation of cimetidine

tail \'tāl\ *n, often attrib* **1** : the rear end or a process or prolongation of the rear end of the body of an animal **2** : any of various parts of bodily structures that are terminal: as **a** : the distal tendon of a muscle **b** : the slender left end of the human pancreas **c** : the common convoluted tube that forms the lower part of the epididymis **3** : the part of a sperm consisting of the middle portion and the terminal flagellum

tail·bone \-ˌbōn\ *n* **1** : a caudal vertebra **2** : COCCYX

tail bud *n* : a knob of embryonic tissue that contributes to the formation of the posterior part of the vertebrate body — called also *end bud*

Ta·ka·ya·su's disease \ˌtä-kə-ˈyä-süz-\ *n* : progressive obliteration of the arteries branching from the arch of the aorta and comprising the innominate artery, left common carotid artery, and left subclavian artery that is marked by diminution or loss of the pulse in and symptoms of ischemia in the head, neck, and arms

Takayasu, Michishige (1872–1938), Japanese physician.

¹**take** \'tāk\ *vb* **took** \'tuk\; **tak·en** \'tā-kən\; **tak·ing 1** : to establish a take esp. by uniting or growing **2** *of a vaccine or vaccination* : to produce a take

²**take** *n* **1** : a local or systemic reaction indicative of successful vaccination **2** : a successful union (as of a graft)

take up *vb* : to absorb or incorporate into itself — **take–up** *n*

tali *pl of* TALUS

tal·i·pes \'ta-lə-ˌpēz\ *n* : CLUBFOOT I

talipes equi·no·var·us \-ˌe-kwi-nō-'var-əs\ *n* : a congenital deformity of the foot in which both talipes equinus and talipes varus occur so that walking is done on the toes and outer side of the sole

talipes equi·nus \-'e-kwi-nəs\ *n* : a congenital deformity of the foot in which the sole is permanently flexed so that walking is done on the toes without touching the heel to the ground

talipes valgus *n* : a congenital deformity of the foot in which it is rotated inward so that walking is done on the inner side of the sole

talipes varus *n* : a congenital deformity of the foot in which it is rotated out-

ward so that walking is done on the outer side of the sole

talo- *comb form* : astragalar and ⟨*talo*tibial⟩

ta·lo·cru·ral \ˌtā-lō-ˈkrür-əl\ *adj* : relating to or being the ankle joint

ta·lo·na·vic·u·lar \ˌtā-lō-nə-ˈvi-kyə-lər\ *adj* : of or relating to the talus and the navicular of the tarsus

ta·lo·tib·i·al \ˌtā-lō-ˈti-bē-əl\ *adj* : of or relating to the talus and the tibia

ta·lus \'tā-ləs\ *n, pl* **ta·li** \'tā-ˌlī\ **1** : the human astragalus that bears the weight of the body and together with the tibia and fibula forms the ankle joint — called also *anklebone* **2** : the entire ankle

Tal·win \'tal-ˌwin\ *trademark* — used for a preparation of pentazocine

ta·mox·i·fen \ta-ˈmäk-si-ˌfen\ *n* : an estrogen antagonist $C_{26}H_{29}NO$ used esp. to treat postmenopausal breast cancer

¹**tam·pon** \'tam-ˌpän\ *n* : a plug (as of cotton) introduced into a cavity usu. to absorb secretions (as from menstruation) or to arrest hemorrhaging

²**tampon** *vb* : to plug with a tampon

tam·pon·ade \ˌtam-pə-ˈnād\ *n* **1** : the closure or blockage (as of a wound or body cavity) by or as if by a tampon esp. to stop bleeding **2** : CARDIAC TAMPONADE

tan \'tan\ *n* : a brown color imparted to the skin by exposure to the sun or wind — **tan** *vb*

T and A *abbr* tonsillectomy and adenoidectomy

tan·gle \'taŋ-gəl\ *n* : NEUROFIBRILLARY TANGLE

tan·ta·lum \'tant-ᵊl-əm\ *n* : a hard ductile gray-white acid-resisting metallic element sometimes used in surgical implants and sutures — symbol *Ta*; see ELEMENT table

T antigen \'tē-\ *n* : an antigen occurring in the nuclei of cells transformed into tumor cells or tumorigenic cells by adenoviruses

tap \'tap\ *n* : the procedure of removing fluid (as from a body cavity) — see LUMBAR PUNCTURE — **tap** *vb*

¹**tape** \'tāp\ *n* : a narrow band of woven fabric; *esp* : ADHESIVE TAPE

²**tape** *vb* **taped; tap·ing** : to fasten, tie, bind, cover, or support with tape and esp. adhesive tape

ta·pe·tum \tə-ˈpē-təm\ *n, pl* **ta·pe·ta** \-ˈpē-tə\ **1** : any of various membranous layers or areas esp. of the choroid and retina of the eye **2** : a layer of nerve fibers derived from the corpus callosum and forming part of the roof of each lateral ventricle of the brain — **ta·pe·tal** \-ˈtāl\ *adj*

tape·worm \'tāp-ˌwərm\ *n* : any of a class (Cestoda) of platyhelminthic worms that are parasitic as adults in the alimentary tract of vertebrates including humans and as larvae in a great variety of vertebrates and invertebrates and that typically consist of an attachment organ usu. with suckers, grooves, hooks, or other devices for adhering to the host's intestine followed by an undifferentiated growth region from which buds off a chain of segments of which the anterior members are little more than blocks of tissue, the median members have fully developed organs of both sexes, and the posterior members are egg-filled sacs — called also *cestode*; see BEEF TAPEWORM, CAT TAPEWORM, FISH TAPEWORM, PORK TAPEWORM, ECHINOCOCCUS

ta·pote·ment \tə-ˈpōt-mənt\ *n* : PERCUSSION 2

tar \ˈtär\ *n* 1 : any of various dark brown or black viscous liquids obtained by distillation of organic material (as wood or coal); *esp* : one used medicinally — see JUNIPER TAR 2 : a substance in some respects resembling tar; *esp* : a residue present in smoke from burning tobacco that contains combustion by-products (as resins and phenols)

ta·ran·tu·la \tə-ˈran-chə-lə, -tə-lə\ *n, pl* **ta·ran·tu·las** *also* **ta·ran·tu·lae** \-ˌlē\ : any of a family (Theraphosidae) of large hairy American spiders that are typically rather sluggish and capable of biting sharply though most forms are not significantly poisonous to humans

tarda — see OSTEOGENESIS IMPERFECTA TARDA

tar·dive \ˈtär-div\ *adj* : tending to or characterized by lateness esp. in development or maturity

tardive dyskinesia *n* : a central nervous system disorder characterized by twitching of the face and tongue and involuntary motor movements of the trunk and limbs and occurring esp. as a side effect of prolonged use of antipsychotic drugs (as phenothiazine) — abbr. *TD*

tar·get \ˈtär-gət\ *n* 1 : something to be affected by an action or development; *specif* : an organ, part, or tissue that is affected by the action of a hormone 2 : a body, surface, or material bombarded with nuclear particles or electrons 3 : the thought or object that is to be recognized (as by telepathy) or affected (as by psychokinesis) in a parapsychological experiment

target cell *n* : a cell that is acted on preferentially by a specific agent (as a virus, drug, or hormone)

tar·ry stool \ˈtär-ē-\ *n* : an evacuation from the bowels having the color of tar caused esp. by hemorrhage in the stomach or upper intestines

¹tar·sal \ˈtär-səl\ *adj* 1 : of or relating to the tarsus 2 : being or relating to plates of dense connective tissue that serve to stiffen the eyelids

²tarsal *n* : a tarsal part (as a bone)

tarsal gland *n* : MEIBOMIAN GLAND

tarsal plate *n* : the plate of strong dense fibrous connective tissue that forms the supporting structure of the eyelid

tarso- *comb form* 1 : tarsus (*tarsometatarsal*) 2 : tarsal plate (*tarsorrhaphy*)

tar·so·meta·tar·sal \ˌtär-sō-ˌme-tə-ˈtär-səl\ *adj* : of or relating to the tarsus and metatarsus (~ articulations)

tar·sor·rha·phy \tär-ˈsȯr-ə-fē\ *n, pl* **-phies** : the operation of suturing the eyelids together entirely or in part

tar·sus \ˈtär-səs\ *n, pl* **tar·si** \-ˌsī, -ˌsē\ 1 : the part of the foot between the metatarsus and the leg; *also* : the small bones that support this part of the limb 2 : TARSAL PLATE

tar·tar \ˈtär-tər\ *n* : an incrustation on the teeth consisting of salivary secretion, food residue, and various salts (as calcium carbonate)

tartar emetic *n* : a poisonous crystalline salt $KSbOC_4H_4O_6 \cdot \frac{1}{2}H_2O$ of sweetish metallic taste that is used in medicine as an expectorant, in the treatment of amebiasis, and formerly as an emetic — called also *antimony potassium tartrate*, *potassium antimonyltartrate*

tar·tar·ic acid \(ˌ)tär-ˈtar-ik-\ *n* : a strong acid $C_4H_6O_6$ of plant origin that contains two carboxyl groups and occurs in three isomeric crystalline forms of which two are optically active

tar·trate \ˈtär-ˌtrāt\ *n* : a salt or ester of tartaric acid

tar·tra·zine \ˈtär-trə-ˌzēn, -zən\ *n* : a yellow azo dye used in coloring foods and drugs that sometimes causes bronchoconstriction in individuals with asthma

¹taste \ˈtāst\ *vb* **tast·ed; tast·ing** 1 : to ascertain the flavor of by taking a little into the mouth 2 : to have a specific flavor

²taste *n* 1 : the special sense that is concerned with distinguishing the sweet, sour, bitter, or salty quality of a dissolved substance and is mediated by taste buds on the tongue 2 : the objective sweet, sour, bitter, or salty quality of a dissolved substance as perceived by the sense of taste 3 : a sensation obtained from a substance in the mouth that is typically produced by the stimulation of the sense of taste combined with those of touch and smell

taste bud *n* : an end organ mediating the sensation of taste and lying chiefly in the epithelium of the tongue and esp. in the walls of the circumvallate papillae

taste cell *n* : a neuroepithelial cell that is located in a taste bud and is the actual receptor of the sensation of taste

taste hair *n* : the hairlike free end of a taste cell

tast·er \ˈtās-tər\ *n* : a person able to

taste the chemical phenylthiocarba-mide

TAT *abbr* thematic apperception test

tat·too \ta-ˈtü\ *n, pl* **tattoos** : an indelible mark or figure fixed upon the body by insertion of pigment under the skin or by production of scars — **tattoo** *vb*

tau·rine \ˈtò-ˌrēn\ *n* : a colorless crystalline cysteine derivative $C_2H_7NO_3S$ found in nerve tissue, in bile, and in the juices of muscle esp. in invertebrates

tau·ro·cho·lic acid \ˌtòr-ə-ˈkō-lik-, -ˈkä-\ *n* : a deliquescent acid C_{26}-$H_{45}NO_7S$ occurring as the sodium salt in bile

tau·tom·er·ism \ˈtò-ˈtä-mə-ˌri-zəm\ *n* : isomerism in which the isomers change into one another with great ease so that they ordinarily exist together in equilibrium — **tau·to·mer·ic** \ˌtò-tə-ˈmer-ik\ *adj*

tax·is \ˈtak-səs\ *n, pl* **tax·es** \-ˌsēz\ **1** : the manual restoration of a displaced body part; *specif* : the reduction of a hernia manually **2 a** : reflex movement in relation to a source of stimulation (as a light) **b** : a reflex reaction involving a taxis

tax·ol \ˈtak-ˌsòl\ *n* : an antineoplastic agent $C_{47}H_{51}NO_{14}$ derived esp. from the bark of a yew tree (*Taxus brevifolia* of the family Taxaceae) of the western U.S. and British Columbia and administered intravenously in the treatment of ovarian cancer which has not responded to conventional chemotherapy

tax·on \ˈtak-ˌsän\ *n, pl* **taxa** \-sə\ *also* **tax·ons 1** : a taxonomic group or entity **2** : the name applied to a taxonomic group in a formal system of nomenclature

tax·on·o·my \tak-ˈsä-nə-mē\ *n, pl* **-mies 1** : the study of the general principles of scientific classification **2** : orderly classification of plants and animals according to their presumed natural relationships — **tax·o·nom·ic** \ˌtak-sə-ˈnä-mik\ *adj* — **tax·o·nom·i·cal·ly** *adv* — **tax·on·o·mist** \-mist\ *n*

Tay–Sachs disease \ˈtā-ˈsaks-\ *n* : a hereditary disorder of lipid metabolism typically affecting individuals of eastern European Jewish ancestry that is characterized by the accumulation of lipids esp. in nervous tissue due to a deficiency of hexosaminidase and causes death in early childhood — called also *Tay-Sachs*; see SANDHOFF'S DISEASE

Tay, Warren (1843–1927), British physician.

Sachs, Bernard (1858–1944), American neurologist.

Tb *symbol* terbium

TB \ˌtē-ˈbē\ *n* : TUBERCULOSIS

TB *abbr* tubercle bacillus

TBG *abbr* thyroid-binding globulin; thyroxine-binding globulin

Tc *symbol* technetium

TCA *abbr* tricyclic antidepressant

TCDD \ˌtē-(ˌ)sē-(ˌ)dē-ˈdē\ *n* : a carcinogenic dioxin $C_{12}H_4O_2Cl_4$ found esp. as a contaminant in 2,4,5-T

TCE \ˌtē-(ˌ)sē-ˈē\ *n* : TRICHLOROETH-YLENE

T cell *n* : any of several lymphocytes (as a helper T cell) that differentiate in the thymus, possess highly specific cell-surface antigen receptors, and include some that control the initiation or suppression of cell-mediated and humoral immunity (as by the regulation of T and B cell maturation and proliferation) and others that lyse antigen-bearing cells — called also *T lymphocyte*; see HELPER T CELL, KILLER CELL, SUPPRESSOR T CELL

TD *abbr* tardive dyskinesia

tds *abbr* [Latin *ter die sumendum*] to be taken three times a day — used in writing prescriptions

Te *symbol* tellurium

TEA *abbr* tetraethylammonium

teaching hospital *n* : a hospital that is affiliated with a medical school and provides the means for medical education to students, interns, residents, and sometimes postgraduates

¹tear \ˈtir\ *n* **1** : a drop of clear saline fluid secreted by the lacrimal gland and diffused between the eye and eyelids to moisten the parts and facilitate their motion **2** *pl* : a secretion of profuse tears that overflow the eyelids and dampen the face

²tear *vb* : to fill with tears : shed tears

³tear \ˈtar\ *vb* **tore** \ˈtōr\; **torn** \ˈtōrn\; **tear·ing** : to wound by or as if by pulling apart by force

⁴tear *n* : a wound made by tearing a bodily part ⟨a muscle ~⟩

tear duct *n* : LACRIMAL DUCT

tear gas *n* : a solid, liquid, or gaseous substance that on dispersion in the atmosphere blinds the eyes with tears

tear gland *n* : LACRIMAL GLAND

tease \ˈtēz\ *vb* **teased**; **teas·ing** : to tear in pieces; *esp* : to shred (a tissue or specimen) for microscopic examination

tea·spoon \ˈtē-ˌspün\ *n* : a unit of measure equal to ⅙ fluid ounce or ⅓ tablespoon or 5 milliliters

tea·spoon·ful \-ˌfül\ *n, pl* **teaspoonfuls** \-ˌfülz\ *also* **tea·spoons·ful** \-ˌspünz-ˌfül\ : TEASPOON

teat \ˈtit, ˈtēt\ *n* : the protuberance through which milk is drawn from an udder or breast : NIPPLE

tech *abbr* technician

tech·ne·tium \tek-ˈnē-shəm, -shē-əm\ *n* : a metallic element that is obtained by bombarding molybdenum with deuterons or neutrons and in the fission of uranium and that is used in medicine in the preparation of radiopharmaceuticals — symbol *Tc;* see ELEMENT table

tech·nic \'tek-nik\ *n* : TECHNIQUE

tech·ni·cian \tek-'ni-shən\ *n* : a specialist in the technical details of a subject or occupation ⟨a medical ∼⟩

tech·nique \tek-'nēk\ *n* : a method or body of methods for accomplishing a desired end ⟨new surgical ∼s⟩

tecta *pl of* TECTUM

tec·tal \'tek-təl\ *adj* : of or relating to a tectum

tec·to·ri·al membrane \tek-'tōr-ē-əl-\ *n* : a membrane having the consistency of jelly that covers the surface of the organ of Corti

tec·to·spi·nal \tek-tō-'spīn-əl\ *adj* : of, relating to, or being a tract of myelinated nerve fibers that mediate various visual and auditory reflexes and that originate in the superior colliculus, cross to the opposite side, and terminate in the ventral horn of gray matter in the cervical region of the spinal cord

tec·tum \'tek-təm\ *n, pl* **tec·ta** \-tə\ **1** : a bodily structure resembling or serving as a roof **2** : the dorsal part of the midbrain including the corpora quadrigemina

teeth *pl of* TOOTH

teethe \'tēth\ *vb* **teethed; teeth·ing** : to cut one's teeth : grow teeth

teeth·ing \'tē-thiŋ\ *n* **1** : the first growth of teeth **2** : the phenomena accompanying the growth of teeth through the gums

Tef·lon \'te-ˌflän\ *trademark* — used for synthetic fluorine-containing resins used esp. for molding articles and for coatings to prevent sticking

teg·men \'teg-mən\ *n, pl* **teg·mi·na** \-mə-nə\ : an anatomical layer or cover; *specif* : TEGMEN TYMPANI

teg·men·tum \teg-'men-təm\ *n, pl* **-men·ta** \-tə\ : an anatomical covering : TEGMEN; *esp* : the part of the ventral midbrain above the substantia nigra — **teg·men·tal** \-təl\ *adj*

tegmen tym·pa·ni \-'tim-pə-ˌnī\ *n* : a thin plate of bone that covers the middle ear

tegmina *pl of* TEGMEN

Teg·o·pen \'te-gə-ˌpen\ *trademark* — used for a preparation of cloxacillin

Teg·re·tol \'te-grə-ˌtōl\ *trademark* — used for a preparation of carbamazepine

tel- *or* **telo-** *also* **tele-** *comb form* : end ⟨*tel*angiectasia⟩

te·la \'tē-lə\ *n, pl* **te·lae** \-ˌlē\ : an anatomical tissue or layer of tissue

tela cho·roi·dea \-kō-'rói-dē-ə\ *n* : a fold of pia mater roofing a ventricle of the brain

tel·an·gi·ec·ta·sia \te-ˌlan-jē-ˌek-'tā-zhə, ˌtē-, tə-, -zhē-ə\ *or* **tel·an·gi·ec·ta·sis** \-'ek-tə-səs\ *n, pl* **-ta·sias** *or* **-ta·ses** \-tə-ˌsēz\ **1** : an abnormal dilatation of capillary vessels and arterioles that often forms an angioma **2**

: HEREDITARY HEMORRHAGIC TELANGIECTASIA — **tel·an·gi·ec·tat·ic** \-ˌek-'ta-tik\ *adj*

te·la sub·cu·ta·nea \'tē-lə-ˌsəb-kyü-'tā-nē-ə\ *n* : SUPERFICIAL FASCIA

tele·di·ag·no·sis \ˌte-lə-ˌdī-əg-'nō-səs\ *n, pl* **-no·ses** \-ˌsēz\ : the diagnosis of physical or mental ailments based on data received from a patient by means of telemetry and closed-circuit television

tele·ki·ne·sis \ˌte-lə-kə-'nē-səs, -kī-\ *n, pl* **-ne·ses** \-ˌsēz\ : the apparent production of motion in objects (as by a spiritualistic medium) without contact or other physical means — compare PRECOGNITION, PSYCHOKINESIS — **tele·ki·net·ic** \-'ne-tik\ *adj* — **tele·ki·net·i·cal·ly** *adv*

tele·med·i·cine \-'me-də-sən\ *n* : the practice of medicine when the doctor and patient are widely separated using two-way voice and visual communication esp. by satellite, telemetry, or closed-circuit television

¹te·le·me·ter \te-lə-'mē-tər\ *n* : an electrical apparatus for measuring a quantity (as pressure, speed, or temperature), transmitting the result esp. by radio to a distant station, and there indicating or recording the quantity measured

²telemeter *vb* : to transmit (as the measurement of a quantity) by telemeter

te·lem·e·try \tə-'le-mə-trē\ *n, pl* **-tries 1** : the science or process of telemetering data **2** : data transmitted by telemetry **3** : BIOTELEMETRY — **tele·met·ric** \ˌte-lə-'me-trik\ *adj*

tel·en·ceph·a·lon \ˌte-len-'se-fə-ˌlän, -lən\ *n* : the anterior subdivision of the embryonic forebrain or the corresponding part of the adult forebrain that includes the cerebral hemispheres and associated structures — **tel·en·ce·phal·ic** \-ˌen-sə-'fa-lik\ *adj*

te·lep·a·thy \tə-'le-pə-thē\ *n, pl* **-thies** : apparent communication from one mind to another by extrasensory means — **tele·path·ic** \ˌte-lə-'pa-thik\ *adj* — **tele·path·i·cal·ly** *adv*

tele·ther·a·py \ˌte-lə-'ther-ə-pē\ *n, pl* **-pies** : the treatment of diseased tissue with high-intensity radiation (as gamma rays from radioactive cobalt)

tel·lu·ri·um \tə-'lur-ē-əm, te-\ *n* : a semimetallic element related to selenium and sulfur — symbol *Te;* see ELEMENT table

telo- — see TEL-

te·lo·cen·tric \ˌte-lə-'sen-trik, ˌtē-\ *adj* : having the centromere terminally situated so that there is only one chromosomal arm — compare ACROCENTRIC, METACENTRIC — **telocentric** *n*

te·lo·gen \'tē-lə-ˌjen\ *n* : the resting phase of the hair growth cycle following anagen and preceding shedding

telo·mere \'te-lə-ˌmir, 'tē-\ *n* : the natural end of a chromosome

telo·phase \'te-lə-ˌfāz, 'tē-\ n 1 : the final stage of mitosis and of the second division of meiosis in which the spindle disappears and the nuclear envelope reforms around each set of chromosomes 2 : the final stage in the first division of meiosis that may be missing in some organisms and that is characterized by the gathering at opposite poles of the cell of half the original number of chromosomes including one from each homologous pair

TEM \ˌtē-(ˌ)ē-'em\ n : TRIETHYLENE-MELAMINE

Tem·a·ril \'te-mə-ˌril\ trademark — used for a preparation of trimeprazine

te·maz·e·pam \tə-'ma-zə-ˌpam\ n : a benzodiazepine used for its sedative and tranquilizing effects in the treatment of insomnia — see RESTORIL

temp \'temp\ n : TEMPERATURE

tem·per·ate \'tem-pə-rət\ adj : existing as a prophage in infected cells and rarely causing lysis (∼ bacteriophages)

tem·per·a·ture \'tem-pər-ˌchùr, -pə-rə-, -chər, -ˌtyùr\ n 1 : degree of hotness or coldness measured on a definite scale — see THERMOMETER 2 a : the degree of heat that is natural to a living body b : a condition of abnormally high body heat

tem·plate \'tem-plət\ n : a molecule (as of DNA) that serves as a pattern for the generation of another macromolecule (as messenger RNA)

tem·ple \'tem-pəl\ n 1 : the flattened space on each side of the forehead 2 : one of the side supports of a pair of glasses jointed to the bows and passing on each side of the head

¹**tem·po·ral** \'tem-pə-rəl\ n : a temporal part (as a bone or muscle)

²**temporal** adj : of or relating to the temples or the sides of the skull behind the orbits

temporal arteritis n : GIANT CELL ARTERITIS

temporal artery n 1 : either of two branches of the maxillary artery that supply the temporalis and anastomose with the middle temporal artery — called also deep temporal artery 2 a : SUPERFICIAL TEMPORAL ARTERY b : a branch of the superficial temporal artery that arises just above the zygomatic arch and sends branches to the temporalis — called also middle temporal artery 3 : any of three branches of the middle cerebral artery: a : one that supplies the anterior parts of the superior, middle, and inferior temporal gyri — called also anterior temporal artery b : one that supplies the middle parts of the superior and middle temporal gyri — called also intermediate temporal artery c : one that supplies the middle and posterior parts of the superior temporal gyrus and the posterior parts of the middle

and inferior temporal gyri — called also posterior temporal artery

temporal bone n : a compound bone of the side of the skull that has four principal parts including the squamous, petrous, and tympanic portions and the mastoid process

temporal fossa n : a broad fossa on the side of the skull behind the orbit that contains muscles for raising the lower jaw and that in humans is occupied by the temporalis muscle

temporal gyrus n : any of three major convolutions of the external surface of the temporal lobe: a : the one that is uppermost and borders the fissure of Sylvius — called also superior temporal gyrus b : one lying in the middle between the other two — called also middle temporal gyrus c : the lowest of the three — called also inferior temporal gyrus

tem·po·ral·is \ˌtem-pə-'rā-ˌləs\ n : a large muscle in the temporal fossa that serves to raise the lower jaw — called also temporalis muscle, temporal muscle

temporal line n : either of two nearly parallel ridges or lines on each side of the skull

temporal lobe n : a large lobe of each cerebral hemisphere that is situated in front of the occipital lobe and contains a sensory area associated with the organ of hearing

temporal lobe epilepsy n : PSYCHOMOTOR EPILEPSY

temporal muscle n : TEMPORALIS

temporal nerve — see DEEP TEMPORAL NERVE

temporal process n : a process of the zygomatic bone that forms part of the zygomatic arch

temporal summation n : sensory summation that involves the addition of single stimuli over a short period of time

temporal vein n : any of several veins draining the temporal region: as a (1) : a large vein on each side of the head that unites with the maxillary vein to form a vein that contributes to the formation of the external jugular vein (2) : a vein that drains the lateral orbital region and empties into the superficial temporal vein just above the zygomatic arch — called also middle temporal vein b : any of several veins arising from behind the temporalis and emptying into the pterygoid plexus — called also deep temporal vein

temporo- comb form : temporal and ⟨temporomandibular⟩

tem·po·ro·man·dib·u·lar \ˌtem-pə-rō-man-'di-byə-lər\ adj : of, relating to, or affecting the temporomandibular joint (∼ dysfunction)

temporomandibular joint n : the synovial joint between the temporal bone and mandible that includes the condyloid process below separated by an articular disk from the glenoid fossa above and that allows for the opening, closing, protrusion, retraction, and lateral movement of the mandible — abbr. *TMJ*

tem·po·ro·pa·ri·etal \-pə-ˈrī-ət-ᵊl\ *adj* : of or relating to the temporal and parietal bones or lobes (the ∼ region)

ten- — see TAEN-

te·na·cious \tə-ˈnā-shəs\ *adj* : tending to adhere or cling esp. to another substance : VISCOUS (∼ sputum)

te·nac·u·lum \tə-ˈna-kyə-ləm\ *n, pl* **-la** \-lə\ *or* **-lums** : a slender sharp-pointed hook attached to a handle and used mainly in surgery for seizing and holding parts (as arteries)

ten·der \ˈten-dər\ *adj* : sensitive to touch or palpation (a ∼ spleen) — **ten·der·ness** *n*

ten·di·ni·tis \ten-də-ˈnī-təs\ *n* : inflammation of a tendon

ten·di·nous \ˈten-də-nəs\ *adj* **1** : consisting of tendons (∼ tissue) **2** : of, relating to, or resembling a tendon

tendinous arch *n* : a thickened arch of fascia which gives origin to muscles or ligaments or through which pass vessels or nerves; *esp* : a thickening in the pelvic fascia that gives attachment to supporting ligaments

ten·do cal·ca·ne·us \ˈten-dō-kal-ˈkā-nē-əs\ *n* : ACHILLES TENDON

ten·don \ˈten-dən\ *n* : a tough cord or band of dense white fibrous connective tissue that unites a muscle with some other part, transmits the force which the muscle exerts, and is continuous with the connective-tissue epimysium and perimysium of the muscle and when inserted into a bone is continuous with the periosteum of the bone — see APONEUROSIS

ten·do·ni·tis *var of* TENDINITIS

tendon of Achil·les \-ə-ˈki-lēz\ *n* : ACHILLES TENDON

tendon of Zinn \-ˈtsin\ *n* : LIGAMENT OF ZINN

tendon organ *n* : GOLGI TENDON ORGAN

ten·do·nous *var of* TENDINOUS

tendon reflex *n* : a reflex act (as a knee jerk) in which a muscle is made to contract by a blow upon its tendon

tendon sheath *n* : a synovial sheath covering a tendon (as in the hand)

¹-tene \ˌtēn\ *adj comb form* : having (such or so many) chromosomal filaments (poly*tene*) (pachy*tene*)

²-tene *n comb form* : stage of meiotic prophase characterized by (such) chromosomal filaments (diplo*tene*) (pachy*tene*)

tenens, tenentes — see LOCUM TENENS

te·nes·mus \tə-ˈnez-məs\ *n* : a distressing but ineffectual urge to evacuate the rectum or urinary bladder

teni- — see TAEN-

te·nia, tenia coli, te·ni·a·sis *var of* TAENIA, TAENIA COLI, TAENIASIS

tennis elbow *n* : inflammation and pain over the outer side of the elbow involving the lateral epicondyle of the humerus and usu. resulting from excessive strain on and twisting of the forearm

teno- *comb form* : tendon (*teno*synovitis)

te·no·de·sis \ˌte-nə-ˈdē-səs\ *n, pl* **-de·ses** \-ˌsēz\ : the operation of suturing the end of a tendon to a bone

te·nol·y·sis \te-ˈnä-lə-səs\ *n, pl* **-y·ses** \-ˌsēz\ : a surgical procedure to free a tendon from surrounding adhesions

teno·my·ot·o·my \ˌte-nō-mī-ˈä-tə-mē\ *n, pl* **-mies** : surgical excision of a portion of a tendon and muscle

Te·non's capsule \tə-ˈnōnz-, ˈte-nənz-\ *n* : a thin connective-tissue membrane ensheathing the eyeball behind the conjunctiva

Te·non \tə-ˈnōⁿ, Jacques René (1724–1816), French surgeon.

teno·syn·o·vi·tis \ˌte-nō-ˌsi-nə-ˈvī-təs\ *n* : inflammation of a tendon sheath

te·not·o·my \te-ˈnä-tə-mē\ *n, pl* **-mies** : surgical division of a tendon

tense \ˈtens\ *adj* **tens·er; tens·est** **1** : stretched tight : made taut or rigid **2** : feeling or showing nervous tension — **tense** *vb* — **tense·ness** *n*

Ten·si·lon \ˈten-si-ˌlän\ *trademark* — used for a preparation of edrophonium

ten·sion \ˈten-chən\ *n* **1 a** : the act or action of stretching or the condition or degree of being stretched to stiffness (muscular ∼) **b** : STRESS 1b **2 a** : either of two balancing forces causing or tending to cause extension **b** : the stress resulting from the elongation of an elastic body **3** : inner striving, unrest, or imbalance often with physiological indication of emotion **4** : PARTIAL PRESSURE (arterial carbon dioxide ∼) — **ten·sion·al** \ˈten-chə-nəl\ *adj* — **ten·sion·less** *adj*

tension headache *n* : headache due primarily to contraction of the muscles of the neck and scalp

tension pneumothorax *n* : pneumothorax resulting from a wound in the chest wall which acts as a valve that permits air to enter the pleural cavity but prevents its escape

tension–time index *n* : a measure of ventricular work and oxygen demand that is found by multiplying the average pressure in the ventricle during the period in which it ejects blood by the time it takes to do this

ten·sor \ˈten(t)-sər, ˈten-ˌsȯ(ə)r\ *n* : a muscle that stretches a part or makes it tense — called also *tensor muscle*

tensor fas·ci·ae la·tae \-ˈfa-shē-ē-ˈlā-tē\ *or* **tensor fas·cia la·ta** \-ˈfa-shē-ə-ˈlā-tə\ *n* : a muscle that arises esp. from the anterior part of the iliac crest and from the anterior superior iliac spine, is inserted into the iliotibial band of the fascia lata, and acts to flex and abduct the thigh

tensor pa·la·ti \-ˈpa-lə-ˌtī\ *n* : TENSOR VELI PALATINI

tensor tym·pa·ni \-ˈtim-pə-ˌnī\ *n* : a small muscle of the middle ear that is located in the bony canal just above the bony part of the eustachian tube and that serves to adjust the tension of the tympanic membrane — called also *tensor tympani muscle*

tensor ve·li pa·la·ti·ni \-ˈvē-ˌlī-ˌpa-lə-ˈtī-ˌnī\ *n* : a ribbonlike muscle of the palate that acts esp. to tense the soft palate

tent \ˈtent\ *n* : a canopy or enclosure placed over the head and shoulders to retain vapors or oxygen during medical administration

tenth cranial nerve *n* : VAGUS NERVE

ten·to·ri·al \ten-ˈtōr-ē-əl\ *adj* : of, relating to, or involving the tentorium cerebelli

tentorial notch *n* : an oval opening that is bounded by the anterior border of the tentorium cerebelli, that surrounds the midbrain, and that gives passage to the posterior cerebral arteries — called also *tentorial incisure*

ten·to·ri·um \-ē-əm\ *n, pl* **-ria** \-ē-ə\ : TENTORIUM CEREBELLI

tentorium ce·re·bel·li \-ˌser-ə-ˈbe-ˌlī\ *n* : an arched fold of dura mater that covers the upper surface of the cerebellum and supports the occipital lobes of the cerebrum

Ten·u·ate \ˈten-yə-ˌwāt\ *trademark* — used for a preparation of diethylpropion

te·pa \ˈtē-pə\ *n* : a soluble crystalline compound $C_6H_{12}N_3OP$ used esp. as a chemical sterilizing agent of insects and in medicine as a palliative in some kinds of cancer — see THIOTEPA

terat- *or* **terato-** *comb form* : developmental malformation ⟨*teratogenic*⟩

te·ra·to·car·ci·no·ma \ˌter-ə-tō-ˌkärs-ᵊn-ˈō-mə\ *n, pl* **-mas** *or* **-ma·ta** \-mə-tə\ : a malignant teratoma; *esp* : one involving germinal cells of the testis or ovary

te·ra·to·gen \tə-ˈra-tə-jən\ *n* : a teratogenic agent (as a drug or virus)

te·ra·to·gen·e·sis \ˌter-ə-tə-ˈje-nə-səs\ *n, pl* **-e·ses** \-ˌsēz\ : production of developmental malformations

te·ra·to·gen·ic \-ˈje-nik\ *adj* : of, relating to, or causing developmental malformations ⟨~ substances⟩ ⟨~ effects⟩ — **te·ra·to·ge·nic·i·ty** \-jə-ˈni-sə-tē\ *n*

te·ra·to·log·i·cal \ˌter-ət-ᵊl-ˈä-ji-kəl\ *or* **te·ra·to·log·ic** \-jik\ *adj* **1** : abnormal in growth or structure **2** : of or relating to teratology

te·ra·tol·o·gy \ˌter-ə-ˈtä-lə-jē\ *n, pl* **-gies** : the study of malformations or serious deviations from the normal type in organisms — **te·ra·tol·o·gist** \-jist\ *n*

te·ra·to·ma \ˌter-ə-ˈtō-mə\ *n, pl* **-mas** *or* **-ma·ta** \-mə-tə\ : a tumor derived from

more than one embryonic layer and made up of a heterogeneous mixture of tissues (as epithelium, bone, cartilage, or muscle)

ter·bi·um \ˈtər-bē-əm\ *n* : a usu. trivalent metallic element — symbol *Tb*; see ELEMENT table

ter·bu·ta·line \tər-ˈbyü-tə-ˌlēn\ *n* : a bronchodilator $C_{12}H_{19}NO_3$ used esp. in the form of its sulfate

ter·e·bene \ˈter-ə-ˌbēn\ *n* : a mixture of terpenes that has been used as an expectorant

teres — see LIGAMENTUM TERES, PRONATOR TERES

te·res major \ˈter-ēz-, ˈtir-\ *n* : a thick somewhat flattened muscle that arises from the lower axillary border of the scapula, inserts on the medial border of the bicipital groove of the humerus, and functions in opposition to the muscles comprising the rotator cuff by extending the arm when it is in the flexed position and by rotating it medially

teres minor *n* : a long cylindrical muscle that arises from the upper axillary border of the scapula, inserts chiefly on the greater tubercle of the humerus, contributes to the formation of the rotator cuff of the shoulder, and acts to rotate the arm laterally and draw the humerus toward the glenoid fossa

ter·fen·a·dine \(ˌ)tər-ˈfe-nə-ˌdēn\ *n* : an antihistamine $C_{32}H_{41}NO_2$ that does not produce the drowsiness associated with many antihistamines — see SELDANE

¹**term** \ˈtərm\ *n* : the time at which a pregnancy of normal length terminates ⟨had her baby at full ~⟩

²**term** *adj* : carried to, occurring at, or associated with full term

¹**ter·mi·nal** \ˈtər-mə-nəl\ *adj* **1** : of, relating to, or being at an end, extremity, boundary, or terminus ⟨the ~ phalanx of a finger⟩ **2 a** : leading ultimately to death : FATAL ⟨~ cancer⟩ **b** : approaching or close to death : being in the final stages of a fatal disease ⟨a ~ patient⟩ **3** : being at or near the end of a chain of atoms making up a molecule — **ter·mi·nal·ly** *adv*

²**terminal** *n* : a part that forms an end; *esp* : NERVE ENDING

terminal ganglion *n* : a usu. parasympathetic ganglion situated on or close to an innervated organ and being the site where preganglionic nerve fibers terminate

terminalis — see LAMINA TERMINALIS, STRIA TERMINALIS, SULCUS TERMINALIS

terminal nerve *n* : NERVUS TERMINALIS

ter·mi·na·tor \ˈtər-mə-ˌnā-tər\ *n* : a codon that stops protein synthesis since it does not code for a transfer RNA — called also *termination codon, terminator codon*; compare INITIATION CODON

ter·pene \ˈtər-ˌpēn\ *n* : any of various

isomeric hydrocarbons $C_{10}H_{16}$ found in essential oils: *broadly* : any of numerous hydrocarbons $(C_5H_8)_n$ found esp. in essential oils, resins, and balsams

ter·pin hydrate \'tər-pin-\ *n* : a crystalline or powdery compound $C_{10}H_{18}$-$(OH)_2$·H_2O used as an expectorant for coughs

Ter·ra·my·cin \ˌter-ə-'mīs-ᵊn\ *trademark* — used for a preparation of oxytetracycline

¹**ter·tian** \'tər-shən\ *adj* : recurring at approximately 48-hour intervals — used chiefly of vivax malaria: compare QUARTAN

²**tertian** *n* : a tertian fever; *specif* : VIVAX MALARIA

ter·tia·ry \'tər-shē-ˌer-ē, -shə-rē\ *adj* 1 : of third rank, importance, or value 2 : of, relating to, or being the normal folded structure of the coiled chain of a protein or of a DNA or RNA — compare PRIMARY 3, SECONDARY 3 3 : occurring in or being a third stage ($\sim$ lesions of syphilis)

tertiary care *n* : highly specialized health care usu. over an extended period of time that involves advanced and complex procedures and treatments performed by medical specialists in state-of-the-art facilities

tertiary syphilis *n* : the third stage of syphilis that develops after the disappearance of the secondary symptoms and is marked by ulcers in and gummas under the skin and commonly by involvement of the skeletal, cardiovascular, and nervous systems

tertius — see PERONEUS TERTIUS

Tesch·en disease \'te-shən-\ *n* : a severe virus encephalomyelitis of swine

test \'test\ *n* 1 : a critical examination, observation, evaluation, or trial 2 : a means of testing: as a (1) : a procedure or reaction used to identify or characterize a substance or constituent (2) : a reagent used in such a test b : a diagnostic procedure for determining the nature of a condition or disease or for revealing a change in function — see BLOOD TEST, DICK TEST, PATCH TEST, TUBERCULIN TEST, WASSERMANN TEST c : something (as a series of questions) for measuring the skill, knowledge, intelligence, capacities, or aptitudes of an individual or group — see INTELLIGENCE TEST, PERSONALITY INVENTORY 3 : a result or value determined by testing — test *adj or vb*

test·cross \'test-ˌkrós\ *n* : a genetic cross between a homozygous recessive individual and a corresponding suspected heterozygote to determine the genotype of the latter — **testcross** *vb*

testes *pl of* TESTIS

tes·ti·cle \'tes-ti-kəl\ *n* : TESTIS; *esp* : one usu. with its enclosing structures

tes·tic·u·lar \tes-'ti-kyə-lər\ *adj* : of, relating to, or derived from the testes

testicular artery *n* : either of a pair of arteries which supply blood to the testes and of which one arises on each side from the front of the aorta a little below the corresponding renal artery and passes downward to the spermatic cord of the same side and along it to the testis — called also *internal spermatic artery*

testicular feminization *n* : a genetic defect characterized by the presence in a phenotypically female individual of the normal X and Y chromosomes of a male, undeveloped and undescended testes, and functional sterility — called also *testicular feminization syndrome*

testicular vein *n* : any of the veins leading from the testes, forming with tributaries from the epididymis the pampiniform plexus in the spermatic cord, and thence accompanying the testicular artery and eventually uniting to form a single trunk which on the right side opens into the vena cava and on the left into the renal vein — called also *spermatic vein*

tes·tis \'tes-təs\ *n, pl* **tes·tes** \'tes-ˌtēz\ : a typically paired male reproductive gland that usu. consists largely of seminiferous tubules from the epithelium of which spermatozoa develop and that descends into the scrotum before the attainment of sexual maturity and in many cases before birth

tes·tos·ter·one \te-'stäs-tə-ˌrōn\ *n* : a hormone that is a hydroxy steroid ketone $C_{19}H_{28}O_2$ produced by the testes or made synthetically and that is responsible for inducing and maintaining male secondary sex characters

testosterone enan·thate \-ē-'nan-ˌthāt\ *n* : a white or whitish crystalline ester $C_{26}H_{40}O_3$ of testosterone that is used esp. in the treatment of eunuchism, eunuchoidism, androgen deficiency after castration, symptoms of the male climacteric, and oligospermia

testosterone propionate *n* : a white or whitish crystalline ester $C_{22}H_{32}O_3$ of testosterone that is used esp. in the treatment of postpubertal cryptorchidism, symptoms of the male climacteric, palliation of inoperable breast cancer, and the prevention of postpartum pain and breast engorgement

test-tube *adj* : produced by fertilization in laboratory apparatus and implantation in the uterus, by fertilization and growth in laboratory apparatus, or sometimes by artificial insemination ($\sim$ babies)

test tube *n* : a plain or lipped tube usu. of thin glass closed at one end

te·tan·ic \te-'ta-nik\ *adj* : of, relating to, being, or tending to produce tetany or tetanus (a $\sim$ condition)

tet·a·nize \'tet-ᵊn-ˌīz\ *vb* **-nized; -niz-**

ing : to induce tetanus in ⟨∼ a muscle⟩

tet·a·nus \'tet-ᵊn-əs, 'tet-nəs\ n **1 a** : an acute infectious disease characterized by tonic spasm of voluntary muscles and esp. of the muscles of the jaw and caused by the specific toxin produced by the tetanus bacterium which is usu. introduced through a wound — compare LOCK-JAW **b** : TETANUS BACILLUS **2** : prolonged contraction of a muscle resulting from a series of motor impulses following one another too rapidly to permit intervening relaxation of the muscle

tetanus bacillus n : a bacterium of the genus *Clostridium* (*C. tetani*) that causes tetanus

tet·a·ny \'tet-ᵊn-ē, 'tet-nē\ n, pl **-nies** : a condition of physiological calcium imbalance that is marked by intermittent tonic spasm of the voluntary muscles and is associated with deficiencies of parathyroid secretion or other disturbances (as vitamin D deficiency)

tet·ra·ben·a·zine \₁te-trə-'be-nə-₁zēn\ n : a serotonin antagonist $C_{19}H_{27}NO_3$ that is used esp. in the treatment of psychosis and anxiety

tet·ra·caine \'te-trə-₁kān\ n : a crystalline basic ester $C_{15}H_{24}N_2O_2$ that is closely related chemically to procaine and is used chiefly in the form of its hydrochloride as a local anesthetic — called also *amethocaine, pantocaine*; see PONTOCAINE

tet·ra·chlo·ride \₁te-trə-'klōr-₁īd\ n : a chloride containing four atoms of chlorine

tet·ra·cy·cline \₁te-trə-'sī-₁klēn\ n : a yellow crystalline broad-spectrum antibiotic $C_{22}H_{24}N_2O_8$ produced by a soil actinomycete of the genus *Streptomyces* (*S. virdifaciens*) or synthetically; *also* : any of various derivatives of tetracycline

tet·rad \'te-₁trad\ n : a group or arrangement of four: as **a** : a group of four cells produced by the successive divisions of a mother cell (a ∼ of spores) **b** : a group of four synapsed chromatids that become visibly evident in the pachytene stage of meiotic prophase

tet·ra·eth·yl·am·mo·ni·um \₁te-trə-₁e-thə-lə-'mō-nē-əm\ n : the quaternary ammonium ion ($C_2H_5)_4N^+$ containing four ethyl groups; *also* : a salt of this ion (as the crystalline chloride used as a ganglionic blocking agent) — abbr. TEA

tet·ra·eth·yl·thi·u·ram di·sul·fide \₁te-trə-₁e-thəl-'thī-yü-₁ram-₁dī-'səl-₁fīd\ n : DISULFIRAM

tet·ra·hy·dro·can·nab·i·nol \-₁hī-drə-kə-'na-bə-₁nȯl, -₁nōl\ n : THC

te·tral·o·gy of Fal·lot \te-'tra-lə-jē-əv-fā-'lō\ n : a congenital abnormality of the heart characterized by pulmonary

stenosis, an opening in the interventricular septum, malposition of the aorta over both ventricles, and hypertrophy of the right ventricle

Fallot, Etienne–Louis–Arthur (1850–1911), French physician.

tetranitrate — see ERYTHRITYL TETRANITRATE, PENTAERYTHRITOL TETRANITRATE

tet·ra·ple·gia \₁te-trə-'plē-jə, -jē-ə\ n : QUADRIPLEGIA

tet·ra·ploid \'te-trə-₁plȯid\ adj : having or being a chromosome number four times the monoploid number — **tet·ra·ploi·dy** \-₁plȯi-dē\ n

tet·ra·zo·li·um \₁te-trə-'zō-lē-əm\ n : a cation or group CH_3N_4 that is analogous to ammonium; *also* : any of several derivatives used esp. as electron acceptors to test for metabolic activity in living cells

te·tro·do·tox·in \₁te-₁trō-də-'täk-sən\ n : a neurotoxin $C_{11}H_{17}N_3O_8$ that is found esp. in puffer fish and that blocks nerve conduction by suppressing permeability of the nerve fiber to sodium ions

te·trox·ide \te-'träk-₁sīd\ n : a compound of an element or group with four atoms of oxygen — see OSMIUM TETROXIDE

Texas fever n : an infectious disease of cattle transmitted by the cattle tick and caused by a sporozoan of the genus *Babesia* (*B. bigemina*) that destroys red blood cells — called also *Texas cattle fever*

T–4 \'tē-'fȯr\ n : THYROXINE

T4 cell n : any of the T cells (as a helper T cell) that bear the CD4 molecular marker and become severely depleted in AIDS — called also *T4 lymphocyte*

TGF abbr transforming growth factor

T–group \'tē-₁grüp\ n : a group of people under the leadership of a trainer who seek to develop self-awareness and sensitivity to others by verbalizing feelings uninhibitedly at group sessions — compare ENCOUNTER GROUP

Th symbol thorium

thalam- or **thalamo-** comb form **1** : thalamus (*thalamo*tomy) **2** : thalamic and (*thalamo*cortical)

tha·lam·ic \thə-'la-mik\ adj : of, relating to, or involving the thalamus

thal·a·mo·cor·ti·cal \₁tha-lə-mō-'kȯr-ti-kəl\ adj : of, relating to, or connecting the thalamus and the cerebral cortex

thal·a·mot·o·my \₁tha-lə-'mä-tə-mē\ n, pl **-mies** : a surgical operation involving electrocoagulation of areas of the thalamus to interrupt pathways of nervous transmission through the thalamus for relief of certain mental and psychomotor disorders

thal·a·mus \'tha-lə-məs\ n, pl **-mi** \-₁mī, -₁mē\ : the largest subdivision of the diencephalon that consists chiefly of an ovoid mass of nuclei in each lateral wall of the third ventricle and serves to relay impulses and esp. sensory impulses to and from the cerebral cortex

thal·as·sae·mia, thal·as·sae·mic *chiefly Brit* var of THALASSEMIA, THALASSEMIC

thal·as·se·mia \ˌtha-lə-ˈsē-mē-ə\ *n* : any of a group of inherited hypochromic anemias and esp. Cooley's anemia controlled by a series of allelic genes that cause reduction in or failure of synthesis of one of the globin chains making up hemoglobin and that tend to occur esp. in individuals of Mediterranean, African, or southeastern Asian ancestry — called also *Mediterranean anemia;* sometimes used with a prefix (as alpha-, beta-, or delta-) to indicate the hemoglobin chain affected; see BETA-THALASSEMIA

thalassemia major *n* : COOLEY'S ANEMIA

thalassemia minor *n* : a mild form of thalassemia associated with the heterozygous condition for the gene involved

¹**thal·as·se·mic** \ˌtha-lə-ˈsē-mik\ *adj* : of, relating to, or affected with thalassemia

²**thalassemic** *n* : a person affected with thalassemia

tha·las·so·ther·a·py \thə-ˌla-sō-ˈther-ə-pē\ *n, pl* **-pies** : the treatment of disease by bathing in sea water, by exposure to sea air, or by taking a sea voyage

tha·lid·o·mide \thə-ˈli-də-ˌmīd, -məd\ *n* : a sedative and hypnotic drug $C_{13}H_{10}N_2O_4$ that has been the cause of malformation in infants born to mothers using it during pregnancy

thal·li·um \ˈtha-lē-əm\ *n* : a sparsely but widely distributed poisonous metallic element — symbol *Tl;* see ELEMENT table

thanat- *or* **thanato-** *comb form* : death (*thanatology*)

than·a·tol·o·gy \ˌtha-nə-ˈtä-lə-jē\ *n, pl* **-gies** : the description or study of the phenomena of death and of psychological mechanisms for coping with them — **than·a·to·log·i·cal** \ˌtha-nə-tə-ˈlä-ji-kəl\ *adj* — **than·a·tol·o·gist** \ˌtha-nə-ˈtä-lə-jist\ *n*

than·a·to·pho·ric \ˌtha-nə-tə-ˈför-ik\ *adj* : relating to, affected with, or being a severe form of congenital dwarfism which results in early death

Than·a·tos \ˈtha-nə-ˌtäs\ *n* : DEATH INSTINCT

THC \ˌtē-(ˌ)āch-ˈsē\ *n* : a physiologically active chemical $C_{21}H_{30}O_2$ from hemp plant resin that is the chief intoxicant in marijuana — called also *tetrahydrocannabinol*

the·ater *or* **the·atre** \ˈthē-ə-tər\ *n* 1 : a room often with rising tiers of seats for assemblies (as for lectures or sur-

gical demonstrations) 2 *usu* theatre, *Brit* : a hospital operating room

the·ba·ine \thə-ˈbā-ˌēn\ *n* : a poisonous crystalline alkaloid $C_{19}H_{21}NO_3$ found in opium in small quantities

The·be·sian vein \thə-ˈbē-zhən-\ *n* : any of the minute veins of the heart wall that drain directly into the cavity of the heart — called also *Thebesian vessel*

    The·be·si·us \te-ˈbā-zē-əs\, **Adam Christian (1686–1732),** German anatomist.

the·ca \ˈthē-kə\ *n, pl* **the·cae** \ˈthē-ˌsē, -ˌkē\ : an enveloping case or sheath of an anatomical part — **the·cal** \-kəl\ *adj*

theca cell *n* 1 : an epithelioid cell of the corpus luteum derived from the theca interna — called also *theca lutein cell* 2 : a cell of the columnar epithelium lining the gastric pits of the stomach

theca ex·ter·na \-ek-ˈstər-nə\ *n* : the outer layer of the theca folliculi that is composed of fibrous and muscular tissue

theca fol·lic·u·li \-fə-ˈli-kyə-ˌlī\ *n* : the outer covering of a graafian follicle that is made up of the theca externa and theca interna

theca in·ter·na \-in-ˈtər-nə\ *n* : the inner layer of the theca folliculi that is highly vascular and that contributes theca cells to the formation of the corpus luteum

theca lutein cell *n* : THECA CELL 1

Thee·lin \ˈthē-lən, ˈthē-ə-\ *trademark* — used for a preparation of estrone

thei·le·ria \thī-ˈlir-ē-ə\ *n* 1 *cap* : a genus of parasitic protozoans that includes one (*T. parva*) causing east coast fever of cattle 2 *pl* **-ri·ae** \-ē-ˌē\ *also* **-rias** : any organism of the genus *Theileria* — **thei·le·ri·al** \-ē-əl\ *adj*

    Thei·ler \ˈtī-lər\, **Sir Arnold (1867–1936),** South African veterinary bacteriologist.

thei·le·ri·a·sis \thī-lə-ˈrī-ə-səs\ *n, pl* **-a·ses** \-ˌsēz\ : THEILERIOSIS

thei·le·ri·o·sis \thī-ˌlir-ē-ˈō-səs\ *n, pl* **-o·ses** \-ˌsēz\ *or* **-osises** : infection with or disease caused by a protozoan of the genus *Theileria; esp* : EAST COAST FEVER

the·lar·che \thē-ˈlär-kē\ *n* : the beginning of breast development at the onset of puberty (premature ~)

The·la·zia \thə-ˈlā-zē-ə\ *n* : a genus of nematode worms (family Thelaziidae) that includes various eye worms

T–help·er cell \ˌtē-ˈhel-pər-\ *n* : HELPER T CELL

thematic apperception test *n* : a projective technique that is widely used in clinical psychology to make personality, psychodynamic, and diagnostic assessments based on the subject's verbal responses to a series of black and white pictures — abbr. *TAT*

the·nar \ˈthē-ˌnär, -nər\ *adj* : of, relating to, involving, or constituting the thenar eminence or the thenar muscles

thenar eminence *n* : the ball of the thumb

thenar muscle *n* : any of the muscles that comprise the intrinsic musculature of the thumb and include the abductor pollicis brevis, adductor pollicis, flexor pollicis brevis, and opponens pollicis

the·o·bro·ma oil \thē-ə-'brō-mə-\ *n* : COCOA BUTTER — used esp. in pharmacy

theo·bro·mine \thē-ə-'brō-ˌmēn, -mən\ *n* : a bitter alkaloid $C_7H_8N_4O_2$ closely related to caffeine that is used as a diuretic, myocardial stimulant, and vasodilator

the·oph·yl·line \thē-'ä-fə-lən\ *n* : a feebly basic bitter crystalline compound $C_7H_8N_4O_2$ that is present in small amounts in tea, is isomeric with theobromine, and is used in medicine esp. as a bronchodilator

theophylline ethylenediamine *n* : AMINOPHYLLINE

the·o·ry \'thir-ē\ *n, pl* **-ries** 1 : the general or abstract principles of a body of fact, a science, or an art 2 : a plausible or scientifically acceptable general principle or body of principles offered to explain natural phenomena — see CELL THEORY, GERM THEORY 3 : a working hypothesis that is considered probable based on experimental evidence of factual or conceptual analysis and is accepted as a basis for experimentation — **the·o·ret·i·cal** \thē-ə-'re-ti-kəl\ *also* **the·o·ret·ic** \-tik\ *adj* — **the·o·ret·i·cal·ly** *adv*

ther·a·peu·sis \ther-ə-'pyü-səs\ *n, pl* **-peu·ses** \-ˌsēz\ : THERAPEUTICS

ther·a·peu·tic \-'pyü-tik\ *adj* 1 : of or relating to the treatment of disease or disorders by remedial agents or methods 2 : CURATIVE, MEDICINAL — **ther·a·peu·ti·cal·ly** *adv*

therapeutic abortion *n* : abortion induced when pregnancy constitutes a threat to the physical or mental health of the mother

therapeutic index *n* : a measure of the relative desirability of a drug for the attaining of a particular medical end that is usu. expressed as the ratio of the largest dose producing no toxic symptoms to the smallest dose routinely producing cures

ther·a·peu·tics \ther-ə-'pyü-tiks\ *n sing or pl* : a branch of medical science dealing with the application of remedies to diseases ⟨cancer ∼⟩ — called also *therapeusis*

ther·a·peu·tist \-'pyü-tist\ *n* : a person skilled in therapeutics

ther·a·py \'ther-ə-pē\ *n, pl* **-pies** : therapeutic treatment esp. of bodily, mental, or behavioral disorder — see ELECTROSHOCK THERAPY, OCCUPATIONAL THERAPY, PHYSICAL THERAPY, PSYCHOTHERAPY, RESPIRATORY THER-APY, SPEECH THERAPY — **ther·a·pist** \'ther-ə-pist\ *n*

the·rio·ge·nol·o·gy \thir-ē-ō-jə-'nä-lə-jē\ *n, pl* **-gies** : a branch of veterinary medicine concerned with veterinary obstetrics and with the diseases and physiology of animal reproductive systems — **the·rio·gen·o·log·i·cal** \thir-ē-ō-ˌje-nə-'lä-ji-kəl\ *adj* — **the·rio·ge·nol·o·gist** \thir-ē-ō-jə-'nä-lə-jist\ *n*

therm- *or* **thermo-** *comb form* : heat ⟨*thermo*receptor⟩

ther·mal \'thər-məl\ *adj* 1 : of, relating to, or caused by heat 2 : being or involving a state of matter dependent upon temperature ⟨∼ agitation of molecular structure⟩ — **ther·mal·ly** *adv*

-ther·mia \'thər-mē-ə\ *or* **-ther·my** \ˌthər-mē\ *n comb form, pl* **-thermias** *or* **-thermies** : state of heat : generation of heat ⟨dia*thermy*⟩ ⟨hypo*thermia*⟩

ther·mo·co·ag·u·la·tion \ˌthər-mō-kō-ˌag-yə-'lā-shən\ *n* : surgical coagulation of tissue by the application of heat

ther·mo·di·lu·tion \ˌthər-mō-dī-'lü-shən\ *adj* : relating to or being a method of determining cardiac output by measurement of the change in temperature in the bloodstream after injecting a measured amount of cool fluid (as saline)

ther·mo·gen·e·sis \ˌthər-mō-'je-nə-səs\ *n, pl* **-e·ses** \-ˌsēz\ : the production of heat esp. in the body — **ther·mo·gen·ic** \-'je-nik\ *adj*

ther·mo·gram \'thər-mə-ˌgram\ *n* 1 : the record made by a thermograph 2 : a photographic record made by thermography

ther·mo·graph \-ˌgraf\ *n* 1 : THERMOGRAM 2 : the apparatus used in thermography 3 : a thermometer that produces an automatic record

ther·mog·ra·phy \ˌthər-'mä-grə-fē\ *n, pl* **-phies** : a technique for detecting and measuring variations in the heat emitted by various regions of the body and transforming them into visible signals that can be recorded photographically — **ther·mo·graph·ic** \ˌthər-mə-'gra-fik\ *adj* — **ther·mo·graph·i·cal·ly** *adv*

ther·mo·la·bile \ˌthər-mō-'lā-ˌbīl, -bəl\ *adj* : unstable when heated — **ther·mo·la·bil·i·ty** \-lā-'bi-lə-tē\ *n*

ther·mol·y·sis \(ˌ)thər-'mä-lə-səs\ *n, pl* **-y·ses** \-ˌsēz\ 1 : the dissipation of heat from the living body 2 : decomposition by heat

ther·mom·e·ter \thər-'mä-mə-tər\ *n* : an instrument for determining temperature

ther·mo·met·ric \ˌthər-mə-'me-trik\ *adj* : of or relating to a thermometer or to thermometry

ther·mom·e·try \thər-'mä-mə-trē\ *n, pl* **-tries** : the measurement of temperature

ther·mo·plas·tic \ˌthər-mə-'plas-tik\ *adj*

: capable of softening or fusing when heated and of hardening again when cooled ⟨∼ synthetic resins⟩ — **ther-moplastic** n

ther-mo-re-cep-tor \thər-mō-ri-ˈsep-tər\ n : a sensory end organ that is stimulated by heat or cold

ther-mo-reg-u-la-tion \-ˌre-gyə-ˈlā-shən\ n : the maintenance or regulation of temperature: *specif* : the maintenance of a particular temperature of the living body — **ther-mo-reg-u-late** \-ˈre-gyə-ˌlāt\ vb — **ther-mo-reg-u-la-to-ry** \-ˈre-gyə-lə-ˌtōr-ē\ adj

ther-mo-sta-ble \thər-mō-ˈstā-bəl\ adj : stable when heated — **ther-mo-sta-bil-i-ty** \-stə-ˈbi-lə-tē\ n

ther-mo-ther-a-py \ˌthər-mō-ˈther-ə-pē\ n, pl -**pies** : treatment of disease by heat (as by hot air or hot baths)

-thermy — see -THERMIA

the-ta rhythm \ˈthā-tə-ˌrith-əm\ n : a relatively high amplitude brain wave pattern between approximately 4 and 9 hertz that is characteristic esp. of the hippocampus but occurs in many regions of the brain including the cortex — called also *theta, theta wave*

thi- or **thio-** *comb form* : containing sulfur (*thiamine*) (*thiopental*)

thia-ben-da-zole \ˌthī-ə-ˈben-də-ˌzōl\ n : a drug $C_{10}H_7N_3S$ used in the control of parasitic nematodes and in the treatment of fungus infections

thi-acet-azone \ˌthī-ə-ˈse-tə-ˌzōn\ n : a bitter pale yellow crystalline tuberculostatic drug $C_{10}H_{12}N_4OS$

thi-ami-nase \thī-ˈa-mə-ˌnās, ˈthī-ə-mə-, -ˌnāz\ n : an enzyme that catalyzes the breakdown of thiamine

thi-a-mine \ˈthī-ə-mən, -ˌmēn\ *also* **thi-a-min** \-mən\ n : a vitamin $(C_{12}H_{17}N_4OS)Cl$ of the B complex that is a water-soluble salt occurring widely both in plants and animals and that is essential for conversion of carbohydrate to fat and for normal nerve function — called also *vitamin B₁*

Thi-ara \thī-ˈar-ə\ n : a genus of freshwater snails (family Thiaridae) that includes several forms (as *T. granifera* of eastern Asia and the western Pacific islands) which are intermediate hosts of medically important trematodes

thi-a-zide \ˈthī-ə-ˌzīd, -zəd\ n : any of a group of drugs used as oral diuretics esp. in the control of high blood pressure

thi-a-zine \ˈthī-ə-ˌzēn\ n : any of various compounds that are characterized by a ring composed of four carbon atoms, one sulfur atom, and one nitrogen atom — see PHENOTHIAZINE

thi-a-zole \ˈthī-ə-ˌzōl\ n 1 : a colorless basic liquid C_3H_3NS; *also* : any of various thiazole derivatives including some used in medicine

thick filament n : a myofilament of one

of the two types making up myofibrils that is 100 to 120 angstroms in width and is composed of the protein myosin — compare THIN FILAMENT

Thiersch graft \ˈtirsh-\ n : a skin graft that consists of thin strips or sheets of epithelium with the tops of the dermal papillae and that is split off with a sharp knife

Thiersch, Carl (1822–1895), German surgeon.

thigh \ˈthī\ n : the proximal segment of the leg extending from the hip to the knee and supported by a single large bone — compare FEMUR

thigh-bone \ˈthī-ˌbōn\ n : FEMUR

thi-mer-o-sal \thī-ˈmer-ə-ˌsal\ n : a crystalline mercurial antiseptic $C_9H_9HgNaO_2S$ used esp. for its antifungal and bacteriostatic properties — see MERTHIOLATE

thin filament n : a myofilament of the one of the two types making up myofibrils that is about 50 angstroms in width and is composed chiefly of the protein actin — compare THICK FILAMENT

thin-layer chromatography n : chromatography in which the stationary phase is an absorbent medium (as silica gel or alumina) arranged as a thin layer on a rigid support (as a glass plate) — compare COLUMN CHROMATOGRAPHY, PAPER CHROMATOGRAPHY — **thin-layer chromatogram** n — **thin-layer chromatographic** adj

thio \ˈthī-ō\ adj : relating to or containing sulfur esp. in place of oxygen

thio- — see THI-

thio acid n : an acid in which oxygen is partly or wholly replaced by sulfur

thio-amide \ˌthī-ō-ˈa-ˌmid, -məd\ n : an amide of a thio acid

thio-car-ba-mide \ˌthī-ō-ˈkär-bə-ˌmid, -ˌkär-ˈba-mid\ n : THIOUREA

thi-oc-tic acid *also* **6,8-thi-oc-tic acid** \(ˌsiks-ˌāt-)thī-ˈäk-tik-\ n : the lipoic acid $C_8H_{14}O_2S_2$ that is held by some to ameliorate the effects of poisoning by mushrooms (as the death cap) of the genus *Amanita*

thio-cy-a-nate \ˌthī-ō-ˈsī-ə-ˌnāt, -nət\ n : a compound that consists of the chemical group SCN bonded by the sulfur atom to a group or an atom other than a hydrogen atom

thiocyanoacetate — see ISOBORNYL THIOCYANOACETATE

thio-es-ter \ˌthī-ō-ˈes-tər\ n : an ester formed by uniting a carboxyl group of one compound (as acetic acid) with a sulfhydryl group of another (as coenzyme A)

thio-gua-nine \-ˈgwä-ˌnēn\ n : a crystalline compound $C_5H_5N_5S$ that is an antimetabolite and has been used in the treatment of leukemia

thi-ol \ˈthī-ˌól, -ōl\ n 1 : any of various compounds having the general formula RSH which are analogous to alcohols but in which sulfur replaces the oxygen of the hydroxyl group and which have disagreeable odors 2 : the functional group –SH characteristic of thiols — **thi·o·lic** \thī-'ō-lik\ *adj*

thio·pen·tal \ˌthī-ō-'pen-ˌtal, -ˌtól\ *n* : a barbiturate $C_{11}H_{18}N_2O_2S$ used in the form of its sodium salt esp. as an intravenous anesthetic — see PENTOTHAL

thio·pen·tone \-ˌtōn\ *n*, *Brit* : THIOPENTAL

thio·rid·a·zine \ˌthī-ə-'ri-də-ˌzēn, -zən\ *n* : a phenothiazine tranquilizer used in the form of its hydrochloride $C_{21}H_{26}N_2S_2·HCl$ for relief of anxiety states and in the treatment of schizophrenia — see MELLARIL

thio·te·pa \ˌthī-ə-'tē-pə\ *n* : a sulfur analog of tepa $C_6H_{12}N_3PS$ that is used esp. as an antineoplastic agent and is less toxic than tepa

thio·thix·ene \ˌthī-ō-'thik-ˌsēn\ *n* : an antipsychotic drug $C_{23}H_{29}N_3O_2S_2$ used esp. in the treatment of schizophrenia — see NAVANE

thio·ura·cil \ˌthī-ō-'yur-ə-ˌsil\ *n* : a bitter crystalline compound $C_4H_4N_2OS$ that depresses the function of the thyroid gland

thio·urea \-yù-'rē-ə\ *n* : a colorless bitter crystalline compound $CS(NH_2)_2$ analogous to and resembling urea that is used esp. in medicine as an antithyroid drug — called also *thiocarbamide*

thio·xan·thene \ˌthī-ō-'zan-ˌthēn\ *n* : a compound $C_{13}H_{10}S$ that is the parent compound of various antipsychotic drugs (as thiothixene); *also* : a derivative of thioxanthene

third cranial nerve *n* : OCULOMOTOR NERVE

third-degree burn *n* : a severe burn characterized by destruction of the skin through the depth of the dermis and possibly into underlying tissues, loss of fluid, and sometimes shock

third eyelid *n* : NICTITATING MEMBRANE

third ventricle *n* : the median unpaired ventricle of the brain bounded by parts of the telencephalon and diencephalon

thirst \'thərst\ *n* : a sensation of dryness in the mouth and throat associated with a desire for liquids; *also* : the bodily condition (as of dehydration) that induces this sensation — **thirsty** \'thər-stē\ *adj*

Thom·as splint \'tä-məs-\ *n* : a metal splint for fractures of the arm or leg that consists of a ring at one end to fit around the upper arm or leg and two metal shafts extending down the sides of the limb in a long U with a crosspiece at the bottom where traction is applied

Thomas, Hugh Owen (1834–1891), British orthopedic surgeon.

Thom·sen's disease \'tóm-sənz-, 'täm-\ *n* : MYOTONIA CONGENITA

Thomsen, Asmus Julius Thomas (1815–1896), Danish physician.

thon·zyl·a·mine \thän-'zi-lə-ˌmēn, -mən\ *n* : an antihistaminic drug $C_{16}H_{22}N_4O$ derived from pyrimidine and used in the form of its crystalline hydrochloride — see NEOHETRAMINE

thorac- *or* **thoraci-** *or* **thoraco-** *comb form* 1 : chest : thorax ⟨*thoracoplasty*⟩ 2 : thoracic and ⟨*thoracolumbar*⟩

tho·ra·cen·te·sis \ˌthō-rə-sen-'tē-səs\ *n*, *pl* **-te·ses** \-ˌsēz\ : aspiration of fluid from the chest (as in empyema) — called also *thoracocentesis*

thoraces *pl of* THORAX

tho·rac·ic \thə-'ra-sik\ *adj* : of, relating to, located within, or involving the thorax ⟨~ trauma⟩ ⟨~ surgery⟩ — **tho·rac·i·cal·ly** *adv*

thoracic aorta *n* : the part of the aorta that lies in the thorax and extends from the arch to the diaphragm

thoracic artery *n* 1 : either of two arteries that branch from the axillary artery or from one of its branches: **a** : a small artery that supplies or sends branches to the two pectoralis muscles and the walls of the chest — called also *supreme thoracic artery* **b** : an artery that supplies both pectoralis muscles and the serratus anterior and sends branches to the lymph nodes of the axilla and to the subscapularis muscle — called also *lateral thoracic artery* 2 — see INTERNAL THORACIC ARTERY

thoracic cage *n* : RIB CAGE

thoracic cavity *n* : the division of the body cavity that lies above the diaphragm, is bounded peripherally by the wall of the chest, and contains the heart and lungs

thoracic duct *n* : the main trunk of the system of lymphatic vessels that lies along the front of the spinal column and receives chyle from the intestine and lymph from the abdomen, the lower limbs, and the entire left side of the body — called also *left lymphatic duct*

thoracic ganglion *n* : any of the ganglia of the sympathetic chain in the thoracic region that occur in 12 or fewer pairs

thoracic nerve *n* : any of the spinal nerves of the thoracic region that consist of 12 pairs of which one pair emerges just below each thoracic vertebra

thoracic vertebra *n* : any of the 12 vertebrae dorsal to the thoracic region and characterized by articulation with the ribs

thoracis — see ILIOCOSTALIS THORACIS, LONGISSIMUS THORACIS, SEMISPINALIS THORACIS, SPINALIS THORACIS, TRANSVERSUS THORACIS

thoraco- — see THORAC-

tho·ra·co·ab·dom·i·nal \ˌthō-rə-ˌkō-ab-'dä-mə-nəl\ *also* **tho·rac·i·co·ab·dom·i·nal** \thə-ˌra-si-ˌkō-\ *adj* : of, relating to, involving, or affecting the thorax and the abdomen (a ~ incision)

tho·ra·co·acro·mi·al artery \ˌthō-rə-ˌkō-ə-'krō-mē-əl-\ n : a short branch of the axillary artery that divides into four branches supplying the region of the pectoralis muscles, deltoid, subclavius, and sternoclavicular joint

tho·ra·co·cen·te·sis \-sen-'tē-səs\ n, pl **-te·ses** \-ˌsēz\ : THORACENTESIS

tho·ra·co·dor·sal artery \ˌthō-rə-kō-'dór-səl-\ n : an artery that is continuous with the axillary artery and supplies or gives off branches supplying the subscapularis muscle, latissimus dorsi, serratus anterior, and the intercostal muscles

thoracodorsal nerve n : a branch of the posterior cord of the brachial plexus that supplies the latissimus dorsi

tho·ra·co·lum·bar \-'ləm-bər, -ˌbär\ adj **1** : of, relating to, arising in, or involving the thoracic and lumbar regions **2** : SYMPATHETIC 1 (~ nerve fibers)

tho·ra·co·plas·ty \'thôr-ə-kō-ˌplas-tē\ n, pl **-ties** : the surgical operation of removing or resecting one or more ribs so as to obliterate the pleural cavity and collapse a diseased lung

tho·ra·co·scope \thə-'rā-kə-ˌskōp, -'ra-\ n : an instrument that is designed to permit visual inspection within the chest cavity and is inserted through a puncture in the chest wall in an intercostal space

tho·ra·cos·co·py \ˌthôr-ə-'käs-kə-pē\ n, pl **-pies** : examination of the chest and esp. the pleural cavity by means of a thoracoscope

tho·ra·cos·to·my \ˌthôr-ə-'käs-tə-mē\ n, pl **-mies** : surgical opening of the chest (as for drainage)

tho·ra·cot·o·my \ˌthôr-ə-'kä-tə-mē\ n, pl **-mies** : surgical incision of the chest wall

tho·rax \'thôr-ˌaks\ n, pl **tho·rax·es** or **tho·ra·ces** \'thôr-ə-ˌsēz\ **1** : the part of the body that is situated between the neck and the abdomen and is supported by the ribs, costal cartilages, and sternum; also : THORACIC CAVITY **2** : the middle of the three chief divisions of the body of an insect; also : the corresponding part of a crustacean or an arachnid

Tho·ra·zine \'thôr-ə-ˌzēn\ trademark — used for a preparation of chlorpromazine

tho·ri·um \'thôr-ē-əm\ n : a radioactive metallic element — symbol Th; see ELEMENT table

thorn-headed worm or **thorny-headed worm** n : ACANTHOCEPHALAN

thor·ough·pin \'thər-ō-ˌpin\ n : a synovial swelling just above the hock of a horse that is often associated with lameness

thread lungworm n : a slender nematode worm of the genus Dictyocaulus (D. filaria) that parasitizes the air passages of the lungs of sheep

thread·worm \'thred-ˌwərm\ n : any long slender nematode worm

thready pulse \'thre-dē-\ n : a scarcely perceptible and commonly rapid pulse that feels like a fine mobile thread under a palpating finger

three-day fever n : a fever or febrile state lasting three days; esp : SANDFLY FEVER

three-o-nine \'thrē-ə-ˌnēn\ n : a colorless crystalline essential amino acid $C_4H_9NO_3$

thresh·old \'thresh-ˌhōld\ n : the point at which a physiological or psychological effect begins to be produced (as the degree of stimulation of a nerve which just produces a response) — called also limen

thrill \'thril\ n : an abnormal fine tremor or vibration in the respiratory or circulatory systems felt on palpation

throat \'thrōt\ n **1** : the part of the neck in front of the spinal column **2** : the passage through the throat to the stomach and lungs containing the pharynx and upper part of the esophagus, the larynx, and the trachea

throat botfly n : a botfly of the genus Gasterophilus (G. nasalis) that lays its eggs on the hairs about the mouth of the horse from where the larvae migrate on hatching and attach themselves to the walls of the stomach and intestine — called also throat fly

¹throb \'thräb\ vb **throbbed; throb·bing** : to pulsate or pound esp. with abnormal force or rapidity

²throb n : a single pulse of a pulsating movement or sensation

throe \'thrō\ n : PANG, SPASM — usu. used in pl. (death ~s)

thromb- or **thrombo-** comb form **1** : blood clot : clotting of blood (thrombin) (thromboplastic) **2** : marked by or associated with thrombosis (thromboangiitis)

throm·base \'thräm-ˌbās\ n : THROMBIN

throm·bas·the·nia \ˌthräm-bəs-'thē-nē-ə\ n : an inherited abnormality of the blood platelets characterized esp. by defective clot retraction and often prolonged bleeding time

throm·bec·to·my \thräm-'bek-tə-mē\ n, pl **-mies** : surgical excision of a thrombus

thrombi pl of THROMBUS

throm·bin \'thräm-bən\ n : a proteolytic enzyme formed from prothrombin that facilitates the clotting of blood by catalyzing conversion of fibrinogen to fibrin

throm·bo·an·gi·itis \ˌthräm-bō-ˌan-jē-'ī-təs\ n, pl **-it·i·des** \-'ī-tə-ˌdēz\ : inflammation of the lining of a blood vessel with thrombus formation

thromboangiitis ob·lit·er·ans \-ə-'bli-tə-ˌranz\ n : thromboangiitis of the small arteries and veins of the extremities and esp. the feet resulting in occlusion, ischemia, and gangrene — called also Buerger's disease

throm·bo·cyte \\'thräm-bə-₁sīt\ n : BLOOD PLATELET — **throm·bo·cyt·ic** \₁thräm-bə-'si-tik\ adj

throm·bo·cy·to·pa·thy \₁thräm-bə-₁sī-'tä-pə-thē\ n, pl **-thies** : any of various functional disorders of the blood platelets

throm·bo·cy·to·pe·nia \₁thräm-bə-₁sī-tə-'pē-nē-ə, -nyə\ n : persistent decrease in the number of blood platelets that is often associated with hemorrhagic conditions — called also *thrombopenia* — **throm·bo·cy·to·pe·nic** \-nik\ adj

thrombocytopenic purpura n : a condition that is characterized by bleeding into the skin with the production of petechiae or ecchymoses and by hemorrhages into mucous membranes and that is associated with a reduction in circulating blood platelets and prolonged bleeding time (idiopathic *thrombocytopenic purpura*) — called also *purpura hemorrhagica*, *Werlhof's disease*

throm·bo·cy·to·sis \₁thräm-bə-₁sī-'tō-səs\ n, pl **-to·ses** \-'tō-₁sēz\ : increase and esp. abnormal increase in the number of blood platelets

throm·bo·em·bo·lism \₁thräm-bō-'em-bə-₁li-zəm\ n : the blocking of a blood vessel by a particle that has broken away from a blood clot at its site of formation — **throm·bo·em·bol·ic** \-em-'bä-lik\ adj

throm·bo·end·ar·te·rec·to·my \₁thräm-bō-₁en-₁där-tə-'rek-tə-mē\ n, pl **-mies** : surgical excision of a thrombus and the adjacent arterial lining

throm·bo·gen·ic \₁thräm-bə-'je-nik\ adj : tending to produce a thrombus — **throm·bo·ge·nic·i·ty** \-jə-'ni-sə-tē\ n

throm·bo·ki·nase \₁thräm-bō-'kī-₁nās, -₁nāz\ n : THROMBOPLASTIN

throm·bo·lyt·ic \₁thräm-bə-'li-tik\ adj : destroying or breaking up a thrombus ⟨a ~ agent⟩ ⟨~ therapy⟩ — **throm·bol·y·sis** \₁thräm-'bä-lə-səs\ n

throm·bo·pe·nia \₁thräm-bō-'pē-nē-ə\ n : THROMBOCYTOPENIA — **throm·bo·pe·nic** \-'pē-nik\ adj

throm·bo·phle·bi·tis \-fli-'bī-təs\ n, pl **-bit·i·des** \-'bī-tə-₁dēz\ : inflammation of a vein with formation of a thrombus — compare PHLEBOTHROMBOSIS

throm·bo·plas·tic \₁thräm-bō-'plas-tik\ adj : initiating or accelerating the clotting of blood ⟨a ~ substance⟩

throm·bo·plas·tin \₁thräm-bō-'plas-tən\ n : a complex enzyme that is found esp. in blood platelets and functions in the conversion of prothrombin to thrombin in the clotting of blood — called also *thrombokinase*

throm·bo·plas·tin·o·gen \-plas-'ti-nə-jən\ n : FACTOR VIII

throm·bo·sis \thräm-'bō-səs, thrəm-\ n, pl **-bo·ses** \-₁sēz\ : the formation or presence of a blood clot within a blood vessel during life — **throm·bose** \'thräm-₁bōs, -₁bōz\ vb — **throm·bot·ic** \thräm-'bä-tik\ adj

throm·box·ane \thräm-'bäk-₁sān\ n : any of several substances that are formed from endoperoxides, cause constriction of vascular and bronchial smooth muscle, and promote blood coagulation

throm·bus \'thräm-bəs\ n, pl **throm·bi** \-₁bī, -₁bē\ : a clot of blood formed within a blood vessel and remaining attached to its place of origin — compare EMBOLUS

throw·back \'thrō-₁bak\ n **1** : reversion to an earlier type or phase : ATAVISM **2** : an instance or product of atavistic reversion

throw up vb : VOMIT

thrush \'thrəsh\ n **1** : a disease that is caused by a fungus of the genus *Candida* (C. albicans), occurs esp. in infants and children, and is marked by white patches in the oral cavity; broadly : CANDIDIASIS ⟨vaginal ~⟩ **2** : a suppurative disorder of the feet in various animals (as the horse)

thu·li·um \'thü-lē-əm, 'thyü-\ n : a metallic element — symbol *Tm*; see ELEMENT table

thumb \'thəm\ n : the short and thick first or most preaxial digit of the human hand that differs from the other fingers in having only two phalanges, in having greater freedom of movement, and in being opposable to the other fingers

thumb-suck·ing \-₁sə-kiŋ\ n : the habit of sucking a thumb beyond the period of physiological need — **thumb-suck·er** n

thym- or **thymo-** comb form : thymus ⟨thymic⟩ ⟨thymocyte⟩

thy·mec·to·my \thī-'mek-tə-mē\ n, pl **-mies** : surgical excision of the thymus — **thy·mec·to·mize** \-₁mīz\ vb

thyme oil \'tīm-, 'thīm-\ n : a fragrant essential oil that is obtained from various thymes (genus *Thymus* of the mint family, Labiatae) and is used chiefly as an antiseptic in pharmaceutical and dental preparations

-thy·mia \'thī-mē-ə\ n comb form : condition of mind and will ⟨cyclothymia⟩ ⟨dysthymia⟩

thy·mic \'thī-mik\ adj : of or relating to the thymus ⟨a ~ tumor⟩

thymic corpuscle n : HASSALL'S CORPUSCLE

thy·mi·co·lym·phat·ic \₁thī-mi-(₁)kō-lim-'fa-tik\ adj : of, relating to, or affecting both the thymus and the lymphatic system ⟨~ involution⟩

thy·mi·dine \'thī-mə-₁dēn\ n : a nucleoside $C_{10}H_{14}N_2O_5$ that is composed of thymine and deoxyribose and occurs as a structural part of DNA

thymidine kinase n : an enzyme that is involved in DNA replication and that increases greatly during infection with some viruses (as the herpesvirus causing herpes simplex) and during periods of increased growth rate (as in liver regeneration)

thy·mine \'thī-ˌmēn\ *n* : a pyrimidine base $C_5H_6N_2O_2$ that is one of the four bases coding genetic information in the polynucleotide chain of DNA — compare ADENINE, CYTOSINE, GUANINE, URACIL

thy·mo·cyte \'thī-mə-ˌsīt\ *n* : a cell of the thymus; *esp* : a thymic lymphocyte

thy·mol \'thī-ˌmȯl, -ˌmōl\ *n* : a crystalline phenol $C_{10}H_{14}O$ of aromatic odor and antiseptic properties found esp. in thyme oil or made synthetically and used chiefly as a fungicide and preservative

thy·mo·ma \thī-'mō-mə\ *n, pl* **-mas** *or* **-ma·ta** \-mə-tə\ : a tumor that arises from the tissue elements of the thymus

thy·mo·sin \'thī-mə-sən\ *n* : a mixture of polypeptides isolated from the thymus; *also* : any of these

thy·mus \'thī-məs\ *n* : a glandular structure of largely lymphoid tissue that functions in cell-mediated immunity by being the site where T cells develop, that is present in the young of most vertebrates typically in the upper anterior chest or at the base of the neck, and that tends to disappear or become rudimentary in the adult — called also *thymus gland*

thyr- *or* **thyro-** *comb form* 1 : thyroid ⟨*thyro*globulin⟩ 2 : thyroid and ⟨*thyro*arytenoid⟩

thy·ro·ac·tive \ˌthī-rō-'ak-tiv\ *adj* 1 : capable of entering into the thyroid metabolism and of being incorporated into the thyroid hormone ⟨~ iodine⟩ 2 : simulating the action of the thyroid hormone ⟨~ iodinated casein⟩

thy·ro·ar·y·te·noid \-ˌar-ə-'tē-ˌnȯid, -ə-'rit-ᵊn-ˌȯid\ *n* : a broad thin muscle that arises esp. from the thyroid cartilage, inserts into the arytenoid cartilage, and that functions to relax and shorten the vocal cords — called also *thyroarytenoid muscle*; see INFERIOR THYROARYTENOID LIGAMENT

thy·ro·ar·y·te·noi·de·us \-ˌar-ə-tə-'nȯi-dē-əs\ *n* : THYROARYTENOID

thy·ro·cal·ci·to·nin \ˌthī-rō-ˌkal-sə-'tō-nən\ *n* : CALCITONIN

thy·ro·cer·vi·cal \-'sər-vi-kəl\ *adj* : of, relating to, or being the thyrocervical trunk ⟨the ~ artery⟩

thyrocervical trunk *n* : a short thick branch of the subclavian artery that divides into the inferior thyroid, suprascapular, and transverse cervical arteries

thy·ro·epi·glot·tic ligament \ˌthī-rō-ˌe-pə-'glä-tik-\ *n* : a long narrow ligamentous cord connecting the thyroid cartilage and epiglottis

thy·ro·glob·u·lin \ˌthī-rō-'glä-byə-lən\ *n* : an iodine-containing protein of the thyroid gland that on proteolysis yields thyroxine and triiodothyronine

thy·ro·glos·sal \ˌthī-rō-'glä-səl\ *adj* : of,

relating to, or originating in the thyroglossal duct ⟨~ cysts⟩

thyroglossal duct *n* : a temporary duct connecting the embryonic thyroid gland and the tongue

thy·ro·hy·al \ˌthī-rō-'hī-əl\ *n* : the larger and more lateral of the two lateral projections on each side of the human hyoid bone — called also *greater cornu*; compare CERATOHYAL

¹**thy·ro·hy·oid** \-'hī-ˌȯid\ *adj* : of, relating to, or supplying the thyrohyoid muscle

²**thyrohyoid** *n* : a thyrohyoid part; *esp* : THYROHYOID MUSCLE

thyrohyoid membrane *n* : a broad fibroelastic sheet that connects the upper margin of the thyroid cartilage and the upper margin of the back of the hyoid bone

thyrohyoid muscle *n* : a small quadrilateral muscle that arises from the thyroid cartilage, inserts into the thyrohyal of the hyoid bone, and functions to depress the hyoid bone and to elevate the thyroid cartilage — called also *thyrohyoid*

¹**thy·roid** \'thī-ˌrȯid\ *also* **thy·roi·dal** \thī-'rȯid-ᵊl\ *adj* 1 : of, relating to, or being the thyroid gland ⟨~ cancer⟩ 2 : of, relating to, or being the thyroid cartilage

²**thyroid** *n* 1 : a large bilobed endocrine gland that arises as a median ventral outgrowth of the pharynx, lies in the anterior base of the neck, and produces esp. the hormones thyroxine and triiodothyronine — called also *thyroid gland* 2 : a preparation of the thyroid gland containing approximately 1/10 percent of iodine combined in thyroxine and used in treating thyroid disorders — called also *thyroid extract*

thyroid artery *n* : either of two arteries supplying the thyroid gland and nearby structures at the front of the neck: **a** : one that branches from the external carotid artery or sometimes from the common carotid artery — called also *superior thyroid artery* **b** : one that branches from the thyrocervical trunk — called also *inferior thyroid artery*

thyroid–binding globulin *n* : THYROXINE-BINDING GLOBULIN

thyroid cartilage *n* : the chief cartilage of the larynx that consists of two broad lamellae joined at an angle and that forms the Adam's apple

thy·roid·ec·to·my \ˌthī-ˌrȯi-'dek-tə-mē\ *n, pl* **-mies** : surgical excision of thyroid gland tissue — **thy·roid·ec·to·mize** \-ˌmīz\ *vb*

thyroid extract *n* : THYROID 2

thyroid gland *n* : THYROID 1

thyroid hormone *n* : any of several closely related metabolically active compounds (as triiodothyronine) that are stored in the thyroid gland in the form of thyroglobulin or circulate in the blood apparently bound to plasma protein; *esp* : THYROXINE

thy·roid·itis \ˌthī-ˌròi-ˈdī-təs\ *n* : inflammation of the thyroid gland

thyroid–stimulating hormone *n* : THYROTROPIN

thyroid storm *n* : a sudden life-threatening exacerbation of the symptoms (as high fever, tachycardia, weakness, or extreme restlessness) of hyperthyroidism that is brought on by various causes (as infection, surgery, or stress)

thyroid vein *n* : any of several small veins draining blood from the thyroid gland and nearby structures in the front of the neck

thy·ro·nine \ˈthī-rə-ˌnēn, -nən\ *n* : a phenolic amino acid $C_{15}H_{15}NO_4$ of which thyroxine is a derivative; *also* : any of various derivatives and esp. iodine-containing derivatives of this

thy·rot·o·my \thī-ˈrä-tə-mē\ *n, pl* **-mies** : surgical incision or division of the thyroid cartilage

thy·ro·tox·ic \ˌthī-rō-ˈtäk-sik\ *adj* : of, relating to, induced by, or affected with hyperthyroidism

thy·ro·tox·i·co·sis \ˈthī-rō-ˌtäk-sə-ˈkō-səs\ *n, pl* **-co·ses** \-ˌsēz\ : HYPERTHYROIDISM

thy·ro·tro·pic \ˌthī-rə-ˈtrō-pik, -ˈträ-\ *also* **thy·ro·tro·phic** \-ˈtrō-fik\ *adj* : exerting or characterized by a direct influence on the secretory activity of the thyroid gland (~ functions)

thyrotropic hormone *n* : THYROTROPIN

thy·ro·tro·pin \ˌthī-rə-ˈtrō-pən\ *also* **thy·ro·tro·phin** \-fən\ *n* : a hormone secreted by the adenohypophysis of the pituitary gland that stimulates the thyroid — called also *thyroid= stimulating hormone, TSH*

thyrotropin–releasing hormone *n* : a tripeptide hormone synthesized in the hypothalamus that stimulates secretion of thyrotropin by the anterior lobe of the pituitary gland — abbr. *TRH;* called also *protirelin, thyrotropin-releasing factor*

thy·rox·ine *or* **thy·rox·in** \thī-ˈräk-ˌsēn, -sən\ *n* : an iodine-containing hormone $C_{15}H_{11}I_4NO_4$ that is an amino acid produced by the thyroid gland as a product of the cleavage of thyroglobulin, increases metabolic rate, and is used to treat thyroid disorders — called also *T-4*

thyroxine–binding globulin *n* : a blood serum glycoprotein that is synthesized in the liver and that binds tightly to thyroxine and less firmly to triiodothyronine preventing their removal from the blood by the kidneys and releasing them as needed at sites of activity — abbr. *TBG;* called also *thyroid-binding globulin*

Thysa·no·so·ma \ˌthī-sə-nō-ˈsō-mə\ *n* : a genus of tapeworms (family Anoplocephalidae) including the common fringed tapeworm of ruminants

Ti *symbol* titanium

TIA *abbr* transient ischemic attack

tib·ia \ˈti-bē-ə\ *n, pl* **-i·ae** \-bē-ˌē, -bē-ˌī\ *also* **-i·as** : the inner and usu. larger of the two bones of the leg between the knee and ankle that articulates above with the femur and below with the talus — called also *shinbone* — **tib·i·al** \-bē-əl\ *adj*

tibial artery *n* : either of the two arteries of the lower leg formed by the bifurcation of the popliteal artery: **a** : a larger posterior artery that divides into the lateral and medial plantar arteries — called also *posterior tibial artery* **b** : a smaller anterior artery that continues beyond the ankle joint into the foot as the dorsalis pedis artery — called also *anterior tibial artery*

tibial collateral ligament *n* : MEDIAL COLLATERAL LIGAMENT

tib·i·a·lis \ˌti-bē-ˈä-ləs\ *n, pl* **tib·i·a·les** \-(ˌ)lēz\ : either of two muscles of the calf of the leg: **a** : a muscle arising chiefly from the lateral condyle and part of the shaft of the tibia, inserting by a long tendon into the first cuneiform and first metatarsal bones, and acting to flex the foot dorsally and to invert it — called also *tibialis anterior, tibialis anticus* **b** : a deeply situated muscle that arises from the tibia and fibula, interosseous membrane, and intermuscular septa, that is inserted by a tendon passing under the medial malleolus into the navicular and first cuneiform bones, and that flexes the foot in the direction of the sole and tends to invert it — called also *tibialis posterior, tibialis posticus*

tibialis anterior *n* : TIBIALIS a

tibialis an·ti·cus \-an-ˈti-kəs\ *n* : TIBIALIS a

tibialis pos·ti·cus \-pōs-ˈti-kəs\ *n* : TIBIALIS b

tibial nerve *n* : the large nerve in the back of the leg that is a continuation of the sciatic nerve and terminates at the medial malleolus in the lateral and medial plantar nerves — called also *medial popliteal nerve*

tibial vein *n* : any of several veins that accompany the corresponding tibial arteries and that unite to form the popliteal vein: **a** : one accompanying the posterior tibial artery — called also *posterior tibial vein* **b** : one accompanying the anterior tibial artery — called also *anterior tibial vein*

tibio- *comb form* : tibial and (*tibio*femoral)

tib·io·fem·o·ral \ˌti-bē-ō-ˈfe-mə-rəl\ *adj* : relating to or being the articulation occurring between the tibia and the femur (the ~ joint)

tib·io·fib·u·lar \-ˈfi-byə-lər\ *adj* : of, relating to, or connecting the tibia and fibula (the proximal ~ joint)

tib·io·tar·sal \-ˈtar-səl\ *adj* : of, relating

to, or affecting the tibia and the tarsus (~ abnormalities)

ti·bric acid \'tī-brik-\ n : an antihyperlipidemic drug $C_{14}H_{18}ClNO_4S$

tic \'tik\ n : local and habitual spasmodic motion of particular muscles esp. of the face : TWITCHING

ti·car·cil·lin \ˌtī-kär-'si-lən\ n : a semisynthetic antibiotic $C_{15}H_{16}N_2O_6S_2$ used esp. as the disodium salt

tic dou·lou·reux \'tik-ˌdü-lə-'rü, -'rœ\ n : TRIGEMINAL NEURALGIA

tick \'tik\ n 1 : any of a superfamily (Ixodoidea of the order Acarina) of bloodsucking arachnids that are larger than the closely related mites, attach themselves to warm-blooded vertebrates to feed, and include important vectors of various infectious diseases 2 : any of various usu. wingless parasitic dipteran flies (as the sheep ked)

tick–borne adj : capable of being transmitted by the bites of ticks (~ encephalitis)

tick–borne fever n : a mild rickettsial disease of sheep esp. in Great Britain that is transmitted by a tick of the genus *Ixodes; also* : a related disease of cattle

tick fever n 1 : TEXAS FEVER 2 : a febrile disease (as Rocky Mountain spotted fever or relapsing fever) transmitted by the bites of ticks

tick paralysis n : a progressive spinal paralysis that moves upward toward the brain and is caused by a neurotoxin secreted by some ticks (as *Dermacentor andersoni*)

tick typhus n : any of various tick–borne rickettsial spotted fevers (as Rocky Mountain spotted fever or boutonneuse fever)

ti·cryn·a·fen \ˌtī-'kri-nə-ˌfen\ n : a diuretic, uricosuric, and antihypertensive agent $C_{13}H_8Cl_2O_4S$ recalled from the drug market because of a high incidence of hepatic disorders associated with its use

tid abbr [Latin *ter in die*] three times a day — used in writing prescriptions

tid·al \'tīd-əl\ adj : of, relating to, or constituting tidal air

tidal air n : the air that passes in and out of the lungs in an ordinary breath

tidal volume n : the volume of the tidal air

tide \'tīd\ n : a temporary increase or decrease in a specified substance or quality in the body or one of its systems (an acid ~ during fasting)

tie off vb **tied off; ty·ing off** or **tie·ing off** : to close by means of an encircling or enveloping ligature (*tie off* a bleeding vessel)

Tiet·ze's syndrome \'tēt-səz-\ n : a condition of unknown origin that is characterized by inflammation of costochondral cartilage — called also *costochondritis, Tietze's disease*

tiger mosquito n : YELLOW-FEVER MOSQUITO

tiger rattlesnake n : a rather small rattlesnake of the genus *Crotalus* (*C. tigris*) that occurs in mountainous deserts of western No. America

ti·groid substance \'tī-ˌgroid-\ n : NISSL BODIES

TIL \ˌtē-(ˌ)ī-'el\ n : TUMOR-INFILTRATING LYMPHOCYTE

timber rattlesnake n : a moderate-sized rattlesnake of the genus *Crotalus* (*C. horridus horridus*) that is widely distributed through the eastern half of the U.S.

time \'tīm\ n : the measured or measurable period during which an action, process, or condition exists or continues — see COAGULATION TIME, PROTHROMBIN TIME, REACTION TIME

timed–release or **time–release** adj : consisting of or containing a drug that is released in small amounts over time (as by dissolution of a coating) usu. in the gastrointestinal tract (*timed=release* capsules)

ti·mo·lol \'tī-mə-ˌlȯl\ n : a beta-blocker $C_{13}H_{24}N_4O_3S$ used in the form of its maleate salt to treat glaucoma and to reduce the risk of second heart attacks

tin \'tin\ n : a soft white metallic metallic element malleable at ordinary temperatures — symbol *Sn*; see ELEMENT table

tinc·to·ri·al \tiŋk-'tōr-ē-əl\ adj : of or relating to dyeing or staining

tinc·tu·ra \tiŋk-'tür-ə, -'tyür-\ n, pl **-rae** \-rē\ : TINCTURE

tinc·ture \'tiŋk-chər\ n : a solution of a medicinal substance in an alcoholic menstruum — compare LIQUOR

tin·ea \'ti-nē-ə\ n : any of several fungal diseases of the skin; *esp* : RINGWORM

tinea ca·pi·tis \-'ka-pə-təs\ n : an infection of the scalp caused by fungi of the genera *Trichophyton* and *Microsporum* and characterized by scaly patches penetrated by a few dry brittle hairs

tinea cor·po·ris \-'kȯr-pə-rəs\ n : a fungal infection involving parts of the body not covered with hair

tinea cru·ris \-'krür-əs\ n : a fungal infection involving esp. the groin and perineum

tinea pe·dis \-'pe-dəs\ n : ATHLETE'S FOOT

tinea ver·si·col·or \-'vər-si-ˌkə-lər\ n : a chronic noninflammatory infection of the skin esp. of the trunk that is caused by a lipophilic fungus (*Pityrosporum orbiculare* syn. *Melassezia furfur*) and is marked by the formation of irregular macular patches — called also *pityriasis versicolor*

Ti·nel's sign \ti-'nelz-\ n : a tingling sensation felt in the distal portion of a limb upon percussion of the skin over a regenerating nerve in the limb

Tinel, Jules (1879-1952), French neurologist.

tine test \'tīn-\ n : a tuberculin test in which the tuberculin is introduced subcutaneously by means of four tines on a stainless steel disk

tin·ni·tus \'ti-nə-təs, ti-'nī-təs\ n : a sensation of noise (as a ringing or roaring) that is caused by a bodily condition (as a disturbance of the auditory nerve or wax in the ear) and can usu. be heard only by the one affected

tis·sue \'ti-(ˌ)shü\ n : an aggregate of cells usu. of a particular kind together with their intercellular substance that form one of the structural materials of a plant or an animal and that in animals include connective tissue, epithelium, muscle tissue, and nerve tissue

tissue culture n : the process or technique of making body tissue grow in a culture medium outside the organism; also : a culture of tissue (as epithelium)

tissue fluid n : a fluid that permeates the spaces between individual cells, that is in osmotic contact with the blood and lymph, and that serves in interstitial transport of nutrients and waste

tissue plasminogen activator n : a clot-dissolving enzyme with an affinity for fibrin that is produced naturally in blood vessel linings and is used in a genetically engineered form to prevent damage to heart muscle following a heart attack — abbr. TPA

tissue typing n : the determination of the degree of compatibility of tissues or organs from different individuals based on the similarity of histocompatibility antigens esp. on lymphocytes and used esp. as a measure of potential rejection in an organ transplant procedure

tis·su·lar \'ti-shyə-lər\ adj : of, relating to, or affecting organismic tissue

ti·ta·ni·um \ti-'tā-nē-əm, -'ta-\ n : a silvery gray metallic element — symbol Ti; see ELEMENT table

titanium dioxide n : an oxide TiO_2 of titanium that is used in sunscreens

ti·ter \'tī-tər\ n 1 : the strength of a solution or the concentration of a substance in solution as determined by titration 2 : the dilution of a serum containing a specific antibody at which the solution just retains a specific activity (as neutralizing or precipitating an antigen) which it loses at any greater dilution — **ti·tered** \-tərd\ adj

ti·tra·tion \tī-'trā-shən\ n : a method or the process of determining the concentration of a dissolved substance in terms of the smallest amount of a reagent of known concentration required to bring about a given effect in reaction with a known volume of the test solution — **ti·trate** \'tī-ˌtrāt\ vb

ti·tre chiefly Brit var of TITER

tit·u·ba·tion \ˌti-chə-'bā-shən\ n : a staggering gait observed in some nervous disturbances

Tl symbol thallium

TLC abbr 1 tender loving care 2 thin-layer chromatography

T lym·pho·cyte \'tē-'lim-fə-ˌsīt\ n : T CELL

Tm symbol thulium

TMJ abbr temporomandibular joint

TNF abbr tumor necrosis factor

toad·stool \'tōd-ˌstül\ n : a fungus having an umbrella-shaped spore-bearing structure : MUSHROOM; esp : a poisonous or inedible one as distinguished from an edible mushroom

to·bac·co \tə-'ba-(ˌ)kō\ n, pl -cos 1 : any of a genus (Nicotiana) of plants of the nightshade family (Solanaceae); esp : an annual So. American herb (N. tabacum) cultivated for its leaves 2 : the leaves of cultivated tobacco prepared for use in smoking or chewing or as snuff 3 : manufactured products of tobacco; also : the use of tobacco as a practice

to·bra·my·cin \ˌtō-brə-'mī-sᵊn\ n : a colorless water-soluble antibiotic $C_{18}H_{37}N_5O_9$ isolated from a soil bacterium of the genus Streptomyces (S. tenebrarius) and effective esp. against gram-negative bacteria

to·co·dy·na·mom·e·ter var of TOKODYNAMOMETER

to·coph·er·ol \tō-'kä-fə-ˌrȯl, -ˌrōl\ n : any of several fat-soluble oily phenolic compounds with varying degrees of antioxidant vitamin E activity; esp : ALPHA-TOCOPHEROL

toe \'tō\ n : one of the terminal members of a foot

toed \'tōd\ adj : having a toe or toes esp. of a specified kind or number — usu. used in combination (five-toed)

toe·nail \'tō-ˌnāl\ n : a nail of a toe

To·fra·nil \tō-'frā-nil\ trademark — used for a preparation of imipramine

to·ga·vi·rus \'tō-gə-ˌvī-rəs\ n : any of a group of medium-sized viruses 50 to 70 nanometers in diameter that are sometimes included in the arboviruses, contain single-stranded RNA, and include the causative agents of encephalitis and rubella

toi·let \'tȯi-lət\ n : cleansing in preparation for or in association with a medical or surgical procedure (a pharyngeal ~)

toilet training n : the process of training a child to control bladder and bowel movements and to use the toilet — **toilet train** \-ˌtrān\ vb

to·ko·dy·na·mom·e·ter \ˌtō-kō-ˌdī-nə-'mä-mə-tər\ n : an instrument by means of which the force of uterine puerperal contractions can be measured

tol·az·amide \tō-'la-zə-ˌmīd\ n : a hypoglycemic sulfonamide $C_{14}H_{21}N_3$-

O_3S used in the treatment of diabetes mellitus — see TOLINASE

to·laz·o·line \tō-ᵈla-zə-ˌlēn\ *n* : a weak alpha-adrenergic blocking agent $C_{10}H_{12}N_2$ used in the form of its hydrochloride to produce peripheral vasodilation

tol·bu·ta·mide \tǎl-ᵇbyü-tə-ˌmīd\ *n* : a sulfonylurea $C_{12}H_{18}N_2O_3S$ that lowers blood sugar level and is used in the treatment of diabetes mellitus

Tol·ec·tin \ᵈtǎ-lek-tin\ *trademark* — used for a preparation of tolmetin

tol·er·ance \ᵈtä-lə-rəns\ *n* : the capacity of the body to endure or become less responsive to a substance (as a drug) or a physiological insult with repeated use or exposure (immunological ∼ to a virus) (an addict's increasing ∼ for a drug) — **tol·er·ant** \-rənt\ *adj*

tol·er·ate \-ˌrāt\ *vb*

tol·er·a·tion \ˌtä-lə-ᵈrä-shən\ *n* : TOLERANCE

tol·er·o·gen \ᵈtä-lə-rə-jən\ *n* : a tolerogenic antigen

tol·er·o·gen·ic \ˌtä-lə-rə-ᵇje-nik\ *adj* : capable of producing immunological tolerance (∼ antigens)

To·li·nase \ᵈtō-lə-ˌnās, ᵇtä-lə-ˌnāz\ *trademark* — used for a preparation of tolazamide

tol·met·in \ᵇtäl-mə-tən\ *n* : an antiinflammatory drug $C_{15}H_{15}NO_3$ often administered in the form of its sodium salt — see TOLECTIN

tol·naf·tate \ᵇtäl-ᵇnaf-ˌtāt\ *n* : a topical antifungal drug $C_{19}H_{17}NOS$

to·lu \tə-ᵇlü, tō-\ *n* : BALSAM OF TOLU

tolu balsam *n* : BALSAM OF TOLU

tol·u·ene·sul·fon·ic acid \ˌtäl-yə-ˌwēn-səl-ᵇfä-nik-\ *n* : any of three isomeric crystalline oily liquid strong acids $CH_3C_6H_4SO_3H$

-tome \ˌtōm\ *n comb form* 1 : part : segment (myoᵗtome) 2 : cutting instrument (microᵗtome)

Tomes' fiber \ᵇtōmz-\ *n* : any of the fibers extending from the odontoblasts into the alveolar canals : a dentinal fiber — called also *Tomes' process*

Tomes, Sir John (1815–1895), British dental surgeon.

to·mo·gram \ᵇtō-mə-ˌgram\ *n* : a roentgenogram made by tomography

to·mo·graph \-ˌgraf\ *n* : an X-ray machine used for tomography

to·mog·ra·phy \tō-ᵇmä-grə-fē\ *n, pl* **-phies** : a method of producing a three-dimensional image of the internal structures of a solid object (as the human body) by the observation and recording of the differences in the effects on the passage of waves of energy impinging on those structures; see COMPUTED TOMOGRAPHY, POSITRON EMISSION TOMOGRAPHY — **to·mo·graph·ic** \ˌtō-mə-ᵇgra-fik\ *adj*

-to·my \t-ə-mē\ *n comb form, pl* **-t-o·mies** : incision : section (laparotoᵗmy)

¹**tone** \ᵇtōn\ *n* 1 : a sound of definite pitch and vibration 2 a : the state of a living body or of any of its organs or parts in which the functions are healthy and performed with due vigor b : normal tension or responsiveness to stimuli; *specif* : TONUS 2

²**tone** *vb* **toned; ton·ing** : to impart tone to

tone–deaf \ᵇtōn-ˌdef\ *adj* : relatively insensitive to differences in musical pitch — **tone deafness** *n*

tongue \ᵇtəŋ\ *n* : a process of the floor of the mouth that is attached basally to the hyoid bone, that consists essentially of a mass of extrinsic muscle attaching its base to other parts, intrinsic muscle by which parts of the structure move in relation to each other, and an epithelial covering rich in sensory end organs and small glands, and that functions esp. in taking and swallowing food and as a speech organ

tongue depressor *n* : a thin wooden blade rounded at both ends that is used to depress the tongue to allow for inspection of the mouth and throat — called also *tongue blade*

tongue roll·er \-ˌrō-lər\ *n* : a person who carries a dominant gene which confers the capacity to roll the tongue into the shape of a U

tongue thrust \-ˌthrəst\ *n* : the thrusting of the tongue against or between the incisors during the act of swallowing which if persistent in early childhood can lead to various dental abnormalities

tongue–tie *n* : a congenital defect characterized by limited mobility of the tongue due to shortness of its frenulum — **tongue–tied** *adj*

tongue worm *n* : any of a phylum or arthropod class (Pentastomida) of parasitic invertebrates that live as adults in the respiratory passages of reptiles, birds, or mammals — see HALZOUN

-to·nia \ᵇtō-nē-ə\ *n comb form* : condition or degree of tonus (myoᵗtonia)

¹**ton·ic** \ᵇtä-nik\ *adj* 1 a : characterized by tonus (∼ contraction of muscle); *also* : marked by or being prolonged muscular contraction (∼ convulsions) b : producing or adapted to produce healthy muscular condition and reaction of organs (as muscles) 2 a : increasing or restoring physical or mental tone b : yielding a tonic substance — **ton·i·cal·ly** *adv*

²**tonic** *n* : an agent (as a drug) that increases body tone

to·nic·i·ty \tō-ᵇni-sə-tē\ *n, pl* **-ties** 1 : the property of possessing tone; *esp* : healthy vigor of body or mind 2 : TONUS 2

ton·i·co·clon·ic \ˌtä-ni-kō-ᵇklä-nik\ *adj* : both tonic and clonic (∼ seizures)

tono- *comb form* 1 : tone (tonoᵗtopic) 2 : pressure (tonoᵗmeter)

tonoclonic • torpor

tono·clon·ic \ˌtä-nō-ˈklä-nik\ *adj* : TONI-COCLONIC

tono·fi·bril \-ˈfī-brəl, -ˈfi-\ *n* : a thin fibril made up of tonofilaments

tono·fil·a·ment \-ˈfi-lə-mənt\ *n* : a slender cytoplasmic organelle found esp. in some epithelial cells

to·nog·ra·phy \tō-ˈnä-grə-fē\ *n, pl* **-phies** : the procedure of recording measurements (as of intraocular pressure) with a tonometer — **to·no·graph·ic** \ˌtō-nə-ˈgra-fik, ˌtä-\ *adj*

to·nom·e·ter \tō-ˈnä-mə-tər\ *n* : an instrument for measuring tension or pressure and esp. intraocular pressure — **to·no·met·ric** \ˌtō-nə-ˈme-trik, ˌtä-\ *adj* — **to·nom·e·try** \tō-ˈnä-mə-trē\ *n*

to·no·top·ic \ˌtō-nə-ˈtä-pik\ *adj* : relating to or being the anatomic organization by which specific sound frequencies are received by specific receptors in the inner ear with nerve impulses traveling along selected pathways to specific sites in the brain

ton·sil \ˈtän-səl\ *n* **1 a** : either of a pair of prominent masses of lymphoid tissue that lie one on each side of the throat between the anterior and posterior pillars of the fauces and are composed of lymph follicles grouped around one or more deep crypts — called also *palatine tonsil* **b** : PHARYNGEAL TONSIL **c** : LINGUAL TONSIL **2** : a rounded prominence situated medially on the lower surface of each lateral hemisphere of the cerebellum (the cerebellar ~s) — **ton·sil·lar** \ˈtän-sə-lər\ *adj*

tonsill- *or* **tonsillo-** *comb form* : tonsil ⟨*tonsill*ectomy⟩

tonsillar crypt *n* : any of the deep invaginations occurring on the surface of the palatine and pharyngeal tonsils

ton·sil·lec·to·my \ˌtän-sə-ˈlek-tə-mē\ *n, pl* **-mies** : surgical excision of the tonsils

ton·sil·li·tis \ˌtän-sə-ˈlī-təs\ *n* : inflammation of the tonsils of varying degrees of severity and involving simple inflammation associated with acute pharyngitis, streptococcus infection, or formation of an abscess

ton·sil·lo·pha·ryn·ge·al \ˌtän-sə-lō-ˌfar-ən-ˈjē-əl, -fə-ˈrin-jəl, -jē-əl\ *adj* : of, relating to, or involving the tonsils and pharynx (the ~ area)

ton·sil·lo·phar·yn·gi·tis \-ˌfar-ən-ˈjī-təs\ *n, pl* **-git·i·des** \-ˈji-tə-ˌdēz\ : inflammation of the tonsils and pharynx

to·nus \ˈtō-nəs\ *n* **1** : TONE **2 a** : a state of partial contraction that is characteristic of normal muscle, is maintained at least in part by a continuous bombardment of motor impulses originating reflexly, and serves to maintain body posture — called also *muscle tone*; compare CLONUS

-to·ny \ˌtō-nē, tⁿ-ē\ *n comb form, pl* **-to·nies** : -TONIA ⟨hypo*tony*⟩

tooth \ˈtüth\ *n, pl* **teeth** \ˈtēth\ : any of the hard bony appendages that are borne on the jaws and serve esp. for the prehension and mastication of food — see MILK TOOTH, PERMANENT TOOTH

tooth·ache \ˈtüth-ˌāk\ *n* : pain in or about a tooth — called also *odontalgia*

tooth·brush \-ˌbrəsh\ *n* : a brush for cleaning the teeth — **tooth·brush·ing** *n*

tooth bud *n* : a mass of tissue having the potentiality of differentiating into a tooth

tooth germ *n* : TOOTH BUD

tooth·less \ˈtüth-ləs\ *adj* : having no teeth

tooth·paste \ˈtüth-ˌpāst\ *n* : a paste for cleaning the teeth

tooth·pick \-ˌpik\ *n* : a pointed instrument (as a slender tapering piece of wood) used for removing food particles lodged between the teeth

top- *or* **topo-** *comb form* : local ⟨*top*ectomy⟩ ⟨*topo*gnosia⟩

to·pec·to·my \tə-ˈpek-tə-mē\ *n, pl* **-mies** : surgical excision of selected portions of the frontal cortex of the brain for the relief of mental disorders

to·pha·ceous \tə-ˈfā-shəs\ *adj* : relating to, being, or characterized by the occurrence of tophi (~ gout)

to·phus \ˈtō-fəs\ *n, pl* **to·phi** \ˈtō-ˌfī, -ˌfē\ : a deposit of urates in tissues (as cartilage) characteristic of gout

top·i·cal \ˈtä-pi-kəl\ *adj* : designed for or involving local application to or action on a bodily part (a ~ remedy) (a ~ anesthetic) — **top·i·cal·ly** *adv*

top·og·no·sia \ˌtä-ˌpäg-ˈnō-zhə, ˌtō-, -zhē-ə\ *n* : recognition of the location of a stimulus on the skin or elsewhere in the body

topo·graph·i·cal \ˌtä-pə-ˈgra-fi-kəl\ *or* **topo·graph·ic** \-fik\ *adj* **1** : of, relating to, or concerned with topography **2** : of or relating to a mind made up of different strata and esp. of the conscious, preconscious, and unconscious — **topo·graph·i·cal·ly** *adv*

topographic anatomy *n* : REGIONAL ANATOMY

to·pog·ra·phy \tə-ˈpä-grə-fē\ *n, pl* **-phies 1** : the physical or natural features of an object or entity and their structural relationships (the ~ of the abdomen) **2** : REGIONAL ANATOMY

tori *pl of* TORUS

to·ric \ˈtōr-ik\ *adj* : of, relating to, or shaped like a torus or segment of a torus; *specif* : being a simple lens having for one of its surfaces a segment of an equilateral zone of a torus and consequently having different refracting power in different meridians

tor·pid \ˈtȯr-pəd\ *adj* : sluggish in functioning or acting : characterized by torpor — **tor·pid·i·ty** \tȯr-ˈpi-də-tē\ *n*

tor·por \ˈtȯr-pər\ *n* : a state of mental and motor inactivity with partial or total insensibility : extreme sluggishness or stagnation of function

torque \'tȯrk\ *n* : a force that produces or tends to produce rotation or torsion; *also* : a measure of the effectiveness of such a force

²**torque** *vb* **torqued; torqu·ing** : to impart torque to : cause to twist (as a tooth about its long axis)

tor·sion \'tȯr-shən\ *n* 1 : the twisting of a bodily organ or part on its own axis (intestinal ~) 2 : the twisting or wrenching of a body by the exertion of forces tending to turn one end or part about a longitudinal axis while the other is held fast or turned in the opposite direction; *also* : the state of being twisted — **tor·sion·al** \'tȯr-shə-nəl\ *adj*

torsion dystonia *n* : DYSTONIA MUSCULORUM DEFORMANS

tor·so \'tȯr-(ˌ)sō\ *n, pl* **torsos** *or* **tor·si** \'tȯr-ˌsē\ : the human trunk

tor·ti·col·lis \ˌtȯr-tə-'kä-ləs\ *n* : a twisting of the head and neck to one side that results in abnormal carriage of the head and is usu. caused by muscle spasms — called also **wryneck**

tor·tu·ous \'tȯr-chə-wəs\ *adj* : marked by repeated twists, bends, or turns (a ~ blood vessel) — **tor·tu·os·i·ty** \ˌtȯr-chə-'wä-sə-tē\ *n*

tor·u·la \'tȯr-yə-lə, 'tär-\ *n* 1 *pl* **-lae** \-ˌlē, -ˌlī\ *also* **-las** : CRYPTOCOCCOSIS 2 *cap, in some classifications* : a genus of yeasts including pathogens (as *T. histolytica* syn. *Cryptococcus neoformans* that causes cryptococcosis) usu. placed in the genus *Cryptococcus*

Tor·u·lop·sis \ˌtȯr-yə-'läp-səs, ˌtär-\ *n* : a genus of round, oval, or cylindrical yeasts that form no spores and no pellicle when growing in a liquid culture medium and that include forms which in other classifications are placed in *Torula* or *Cryptococcus*

tor·u·lo·sis \ˌtȯr-yə-'lō-səs, ˌtär-\ *n* : CRYPTOCOCCOSIS

to·rus \'tȯr-əs\ *n, pl* **to·ri** \'tȯr-ˌī, -ē\ : a smooth rounded anatomical protuberance (as a bony ridge on the skull)

torus tu·ba·ri·us \-tü-'ber-ē-əs, -tyü-\ *n* : a protrusion on the lateral wall of the nasopharynx marking the pharyngeal end of the cartilaginous part of the eustachian tube

torus ure·ter·i·cus \-ˌyür-ə-'ter-i-kəs\ *n* : a band of smooth muscle joining the orifices of the ureter and forming the base of the trigone of the bladder

tos·yl·ate \'tä-sə-ˌlāt\ *n* : an ester of the para isomer of toluenesulfonic acid

to·ti·po·ten·cy \ˌtō-tə-'pōt-ᵊn-sē\ *n, pl* **-cies** : ability of a cell or bodily part to generate or regenerate the whole organism

to·ti·po·tent \tō-'ti-pə-tənt\ *adj* : capable of developing into a complete organism or differentiating into any of its cells or tissues (~ blastomeres)

touch \'təch\ *n* 1 : the special sense by which pressure or traction exerted on

the skin or mucous membrane is perceived 2 : a light attack (a ~ of fever)

Tou·rette's syndrome \tur-'ets-\ *also* **Tou·rette syndrome** \-'et-\ *n* : a rare disease characterized by involuntary tics and by uncontrollable verbalizations involving esp. echolalia and coprolalia — called also *Gilles de la Tourette syndrome, Tourette's disease, Tourette's disorder*

Gilles de la Tourette \'zhēl-də-lä-'tür-et'\, **Georges** (1857–1904), French physician.

tour·ni·quet \'tür-ni-kət, 'tər-\ *n* : a device (as a bandage twisted tight with a stick) to check bleeding or blood flow

tower head *n* : OXYCEPHALY

tower skull *n* : OXYCEPHALY

tox- *or* **toxi-** *or* **toxo-** *comb form* 1 : toxic : poisonous (*toxin*) 2 : toxin : poison (*toxigenic*)

tox·ae·mia *chiefly Brit var of* TOXEMIA

Tox·as·ca·ris \täk-'sas-kə-rəs\ *n* : a genus of ascarid roundworms that infest the small intestine of the dog and cat and related wild animals

tox·e·mia \täk-'sē-mē-ə\ *n* : an abnormal condition associated with the presence of toxic substances in the blood: as **a** : a generalized intoxication due to absorption and systemic dissemination of bacterial toxins from a focus of infection **b** : intoxication due to dissemination of toxic substances (as some by-products of protein metabolism) that cause functional or organic disturbances (as in the kidneys) — **tox·e·mic** \-mik\ *adj*

toxemia of pregnancy *n* : a disorder of unknown cause that is peculiar to pregnancy, is usu. of sudden onset, is marked by hypertension, albuminuria, edema, headache, and visual disturbances, and may or may not be accompanied by convulsions — compare ECLAMPSIA a, PREECLAMPSIA

toxi- — see TOX-

¹**tox·ic** \'täk-sik\ *adj* 1 : of, relating to, or caused by a poison or toxin 2 **a** : affected by a poison or toxin **b** : affected with toxemia of pregnancy 3 : POISONOUS (~ drugs) — **tox·ic·i·ty** \täk-'si-sə-tē\ *n*

²**toxic** *n* : a toxic substance

toxic- *or* **toxico-** *comb form* : poison (*toxicology*) (*toxicosis*)

toxic epidermal necrolysis *n* : a skin disorder characterized by widespread erythema and the formation of flaccid bullae and later by skin that is scalded in appearance and separates from the body in large sheets — called also *epidermal necrolysis, Lyell's syndrome, scalded-skin syndrome;* compare STAPHYLOCOCCAL SCALDED SKIN SYNDROME

Tox·i·co·den·dron \ˌtäk-si-kō-'den-ˌdrän\ *n* : a genus of shrubs and trees (family Anacardiaceae) that includes poison ivy and related plants when they are split off from the genus *Rhus*

tox·i·co·gen·ic \ˌtäk-si-kō-ˈje-nik\ *adj* : producing toxins or poisons

tox·i·co·log·i·cal \ˌtäk-si-kə-ˈlä-ji-kəl\ *or* **tox·i·co·log·ic** \-jik\ *adj* : of or relating to toxicology or toxins — **tox·i·co·log·i·cal·ly** *adv*

tox·i·col·o·gy \ˌtäk-si-ˈkä-lə-jē\ *n, pl* **-gies** : a science that deals with poisons and their effect and with the problems involved (as clinical, industrial, or legal) — **tox·i·col·o·gist** *n*

tox·i·co·sis \ˌtäk-sə-ˈkō-səs\ *n, pl* **-co·ses** \-ˌsēz\ : a pathological condition caused by the action of a poison or toxin

toxic shock *n* : TOXIC SHOCK SYNDROME

toxic shock syndrome *n* : an acute and sometimes fatal disease that is characterized by fever, nausea, diarrhea, diffuse erythema, and shock, that is associated esp. with the presence of a bacterium of the genus *Staphylococcus* (*S. aureus*), and that occurs esp. in menstruating females using tampons — called also *toxic shock*

toxi·gen·ic \ˌtäk-sə-ˈje-nik\ *adj* : producing toxin ⟨∼ bacteria⟩ — **toxi·ge·nic·i·ty** \ˌtäk-si-jə-ˈni-sə-tē\ *n*

tox·in \ˈtäk-sən\ *n* : a poisonous substance that is a specific product of the metabolic activities of a living organism and is usu. very unstable, notably toxic when introduced into the tissues, and typically capable of inducing antibody formation — see ANTITOXIN, ENDOTOXIN, EXOTOXIN

toxin–antitoxin *n* : a mixture of toxin and antitoxin used esp. formerly in immunizing against a disease (as diphtheria) for which they are specific

toxo- — see TOX-

Tox·o·cara \ˌtäk-sə-ˈkar-ə\ *n* : a genus of nematode worms including the common ascarids (*T. canis* and *T. cati*) of the dog and cat

tox·o·ca·ri·a·sis \ˌtäk-sə-kə-ˈrī-ə-səs\ *n, pl* **-a·ses** \-ˌsēz\ : infection with or disease caused by nematode worms of the genus *Toxocara*

tox·oid \ˈtäk-ˌsöid\ *n* : a toxin of a pathogenic organism treated so as to destroy its toxicity but leave it capable of inducing the formation of antibodies on injection (diphtheria ∼) — called also *anatoxin*

toxo·plas·ma \ˌtäk-sə-ˈplaz-mə\ *n* **1** *cap* : a genus of sporozoans that are typically serious pathogens of vertebrates **2** *pl* **-mas** *or* **-ma·ta** \-mə-tə\ *also* **-ma** : any sporozoan of the genus *Toxoplasma* — **toxo·plas·mic** \-mik\ *adj*

toxo·plas·mo·sis \-ˌplaz-ˈmō-səs\ *n, pl* **-mo·ses** \-ˌsēz\ : infection with or disease caused by a sporozoan of the genus *Toxoplasma* (*T. gondii*) that invades the tissues and may seriously damage the central nervous system esp. of infants

TPA *abbr* tissue plasminogen activator

TPI *abbr* Treponema pallidum immobilization (test)

TPN \ˌtē-(ˌ)pē-ˈen\ *n* : NADP

TPR *abbr* temperature, pulse, respiration

tra·bec·u·la \trə-ˈbe-kyə-lə\ *n, pl* **-lae** \-ˌlē\ *also* **-las 1** : a small bar, rod, bundle of fibers, or septal membrane in the framework of a bodily organ or part (as the spleen) **2** : any of the intersecting osseous bars occurring in cancellous bone — **tra·bec·u·lar** \-lər\ *adj* — **tra·bec·u·la·tion** \trə-ˌbe-kyə-ˈlā-shən\ *n*

tra·bec·u·lec·to·my \trə-ˌbe-kyə-ˈlek-tə-mē\ *n, pl* **-mies** : surgical excision of a small portion of the trabecular tissue lying between the anterior chamber of the eye and the canal of Schlemm in order to facilitate drainage of aqueous humor for the relief of glaucoma

trace \ˈtrās\ *n* **1** : the marking made by a recording instrument (as a kymograph) **2** : an amount of a chemical constituent not always quantitatively determinable because of minuteness **3** : ENGRAM — **trace** *vb* — **trace·able** \ˈtrā-sə-bəl\ *adj*

trace element *n* : a chemical element present in minute quantities; *esp* : one used by organisms and held essential to their physiology — compare MICRONUTRIENT

trac·er \ˈtrā-sər\ *n* : a substance used to trace the course of a process; *specif* : a labeled element or atom that can be traced throughout chemical or biological processes by its radioactivity or its unusual isotopic mass

trache- *or* **tracheo-** *comb form* **1** : trachea (*trache*oscopy) **2** : tracheal and (*tracheo*bronchial)

tra·chea \ˈtrā-kē-ə\ *n, pl* **tra·che·ae** \-kē-ˌē\ *also* **tra·che·as** : the main trunk of the system of tubes by which air passes to and from the lungs that is about four inches (10 centimeters) long and somewhat less than an inch (2.5 centimeters) in diameter, extends down the front of the neck from the larynx, divides in two to form the bronchi, has walls of fibrous and muscular tissue stiffened by incomplete cartilaginous rings which keep it from collapsing, and is lined with mucous membrane whose epithelium is composed of columnar ciliated mucus-secreting cells — called also *windpipe* — **tra·che·al** \-əl\ *adj*

tracheal node *n* : any of a group of lymph nodes arranged along each side of the thoracic part of the trachea

tracheal ring *n* : any of the 16 to 20 C-shaped bands of highly elastic cartilage which are found as incomplete rings in the anterior two thirds of the tracheal wall and of which there are usu. 6 to 8 in the right bronchus and 9 to 12 in the left

tra·che·itis \ˌtrā-kē-ˈī-təs\ *n* : inflammation of the trachea

trachel- or **trachelo-** *comb form* 1 : neck ⟨*trachelo*mastoid muscle⟩ 2 : uterine cervix ⟨*trachelo*plasty⟩

trach·e·lec·to·my \ˌtrak-ə-ˈlek-tə-mē\ *n*, *pl* **-mies** : CERVICECTOMY

trach·e·lo·mas·toid muscle \ˌtra-kə-lō-ˈmas-ˌtȯid-\ *n* : LONGISSIMUS CAPITIS

trach·e·lo·plas·ty \ˈtra-kə-lō-ˌplas-tē\ *n*, *pl* **-ties** : a plastic operation on the neck of the uterus

trach·e·lor·rha·phy \ˌtra-kə-ˈlȯr-ə-fē\ *n*, *pl* **-phies** : the operation of sewing up a laceration of the uterine cervix

tra·cheo·bron·chi·al \ˌtrā-kē-ō-ˈbräŋ-kē-əl\ *adj* : of, relating to, affecting, or produced in the trachea and bronchi ⟨∼ secretion⟩ ⟨∼ lesions⟩

tracheobronchial node *n* : any of the lymph nodes arranged in four or five groups along the trachea and bronchi — called also *tracheobronchial lymph node*

tracheobronchial tree *n* : the trachea and bronchial tree considered together

tra·cheo·bron·chi·tis \ˌtrā-kē-ō-bräŋ-ˈkī-təs\ *n*, *pl* **-chit·i·des** \-ˈki-tə-ˌdēz\ : inflammation of the trachea and bronchi

tra·cheo·esoph·a·ge·al \-i-ˌsä-fə-ˈjē-əl\ *adj* : relating to or connecting the trachea and the esophagus ⟨a ∼ fistula⟩

tra·cheo·plas·ty \ˈtrā-kē-ə-ˌplas-tē\ *n*, *pl* **-ties** : a plastic operation on the trachea

tra·che·os·co·py \ˌtrā-kē-ˈäs-kə-pē\ *n*, *pl* **-pies** : inspection of the interior of the trachea (as by a bronchoscope)

tra·che·os·to·my \ˌtrā-kē-ˈäs-tə-mē\ *n*, *pl* **-mies** : the surgical formation of an opening into the trachea through the neck esp. to allow the passage of air; *also* : the opening itself

tra·che·ot·o·my \ˌtrā-kē-ˈä-tə-mē\ *n*, *pl* **-mies** 1 : the surgical operation of cutting into the trachea esp. through the skin 2 : the opening created by a tracheotomy

tra·cho·ma \trə-ˈkō-mə\ *n* : a chronic contagious conjunctivitis marked by inflammatory granulations on the conjunctival surfaces, caused by a bacterium of the genus *Chlamydia* (*C. trachomatis*), and commonly resulting in blindness if left untreated — **tra·cho·ma·tous** \trə-ˈkō-mə-təs, -ˈkä-\ *adj*

trac·ing \ˈtrā-siŋ\ *n* : a graphic record made by an instrument (as an electrocardiograph) that registers some movement

tract \ˈtrakt\ *n* 1 : a system of body parts or organs that act together to perform some function (the digestive ∼) — see GASTROINTESTINAL TRACT, LOWER RESPIRATORY TRACT, UPPER RESPIRATORY TRACT 2 : a bundle of

nerve fibers having a common origin, termination, and function and esp. one within the spinal cord or brain — called also *fiber tract*; compare FASCICULUS b: see CORTICOSPINAL TRACT, OLFACTORY TRACT, OPTIC TRACT, SPINOTHALAMIC TRACT

trac·tion \ˈtrak-shən\ *n* 1 : the pulling of or tension established in one body part by another 2 : a pulling force exerted on a skeletal structure (as in a fracture) by means of a special device or apparatus (a ∼ splint); *also* : a state of tension created by such a pulling force (a leg in ∼)

tract of Burdach *n* : FASCICULUS CUNEATUS

   K. F. Burdach — see COLUMN OF BURDACH

tract of Lissauer *n* : DORSOLATERAL TRACT

   Lissauer, Heinrich (1861–1891), German neurologist.

trac·tot·o·my \ˌtrak-ˈtä-tə-mē\ *n*, *pl* **-mies** : surgical division of a nerve tract

trac·tus \ˈtrak-təs\ *n*, *pl* **tractus** : TRACT 2

tractus sol·i·ta·ri·us \-ˌsä-li-ˈtar-ē-əs\ *n* : a descending tract of nerve fibers that is situated near the dorsal surface of the medulla oblongata, mediates esp. the sense of taste, and includes fibers from the facial, glossopharyngeal, and vagus nerves

trade·mark \ˈtrād-ˌmärk\ *n* : a device (as a word or mark) that points distinctly to the origin or ownership of merchandise to which it is applied and that is legally reserved for the exclusive use of the owner — compare SERVICE MARK

trag·a·canth \ˈtra-jə-ˌkanth, -gə-, -kanth; ˈtra-gə-ˌsanth\ *n* : a gum obtained from various Asian or East European plants (genus *Astragalus* and esp. *A. gummifer*) of the legume family (Leguminosae) and is used as an emulsifying, suspending, and thickening agent and as a demulcent — called also *gum tragacanth*

tra·gus \ˈtrā-gəs\ *n*, *pl* **tra·gi** \-ˌgī, -ˌjī\ : a small projection in front of the external opening of the ear

train·able \ˈtrā-nə-bəl\ *adj* : affected with moderate mental retardation and capable of being trained in self-care and in simple social and work skills in a sheltered environment — compare EDUCABLE

trained nurse *n* : GRADUATE NURSE

trait \ˈtrāt\ *n* : an inherited characteristic

Tral \ˈtral\ *trademark* — used for a preparation of hexocyclium methylsulfate

trance \ˈtrans\ *n* 1 : a state of partly suspended animation or inability to function 2 : a somnolent state (as of deep hypnosis) characterized by limited sensory and motor contact with one's surroundings and subsequent lack of recall — **trance·like** \-₁līk\ *adj*

tran·ex·am·ic acid \₁tra-nek-¹sa-mik-\ *n* : an antifibrinolytic drug $C_8H_{15}NO_2$

tran·quil·ize *also* **tran·quil·lize** \¹traŋ-kwə-₁līz, ¹tran-\ *vb* **-ized** *also* **-lized; -iz·ing** *also* **-liz·ing** : to make tranquil or calm; *esp* : to relieve of mental tension and anxiety by means of drugs — **tran·quil·i·za·tion** \₁traŋ-kwə-lə-¹zā-shən, ₁tran-\ *n*

tran·quil·iz·er *also* **tran·quil·liz·er** \-₁lī-zər\ *n* : a drug used to reduce mental disturbance (as anxiety and tension)

trans·ab·dom·i·nal \₁trans-ab-¹dä-mə-nəl, ₁tranz-\ *adj* : passing through or performed by passing through the abdomen or the abdominal wall 〈~ amniocentesis〉

trans·ac·tion·al analysis \-₁ak-shə-nəl-\ *n* : a system of psychotherapy involving analysis of individual episodes of social interaction for insight that will aid communication — abbr. *TA*

trans·am·i·nase \-¹a-mə-₁nās, -₁nāz\ *n* : an enzyme promoting transamination

trans·am·i·na·tion \-₁a-mə-¹nā-shən\ *n* : a reversible oxidation-reduction reaction in which an amino group is transferred typically from an alpha-amino acid to an alpha-keto acid

trans·cap·il·lary \-¹ka-pə-₁ler-ē\ *adj* : existing or taking place across the capillary walls

trans·cath·e·ter \-¹ka-thə-tər\ *adj* : performed through the lumen of a catheter 〈~ embolization〉

trans·con·dy·lar \-¹kän-də-lər\ *adj* : passing through a pair of condyles (a ~ fracture of the humerus)

trans·cor·ti·cal \-¹kör-ti-kəl\ *adj* : crossing the cortex of the brain; *esp* : passing from the cortex of one hemisphere to that of the other

trans·cor·tin \-¹kört-²n\ *n* : an alpha globulin produced in the liver that binds with and transports hydrocortisone in the blood

tran·scribe \trans-¹krīb\ *vb* **transcribed; tran·scrib·ing** : to cause (as DNA) to undergo genetic transcription

tran·script \¹trans-₁kript\ *n* : a sequence of RNA produced by transcription from a DNA template

tran·scrip·tase \tran-¹skrip-₁tās, -₁tāz\ *n* : RNA POLYMERASE; *also* : REVERSE TRANSCRIPTASE

tran·scrip·tion \trans-¹krip-shən\ *n* : the process of constructing a messenger RNA molecule using a DNA molecule as a template with resulting transfer of genetic information to the messenger RNA — compare REVERSE TRANSCRIPTION, TRANSLATION — **tran·scrip·tion·al** \-shə-nəl\ *adj* — **tran·scrip·tion·al·ly** *adv*

tran·scrip·tion·ist \-shə-nist\ *n* : one that transcribes; *esp* : MEDICAL TRANSCRIPTIONIST

trans·cu·ta·ne·ous \₁trans-kyü-¹tā-nē-əs\ *adj* : passing, entering, or made by penetration through the skin

trans·der·mal \₁trans-¹dər-məl, ₁tranz-\ *adj* : relating to, being, or supplying a medication in a form for absorption through the skin into the bloodstream 〈~ drug delivery〉 〈~ nitroglycerin〉 〈~ nicotine patch〉

trans·dia·phrag·mat·ic \-₁dī-ə-frəg-¹ma-tik, -₁frag-\ *adj* : occurring, passing, or performed through the diaphragm 〈~ hernia〉

trans·duce \-¹düs, -¹dyüs\ *vb* **transduced; trans·duc·ing 1** : to convert (as energy) into another form **2** : to bring about the transfer of (as a gene) from one microorganism to another by means of a viral agent

trans·duc·tion \-¹dek-shən\ *n* : the action or process of transducing; *esp* : the transfer of genetic material from one microorganism to another by a viral agent (as a bacteriophage) — compare TRANSFORMATION 2 — **trans·duc·tion·al** \-shə-nəl\ *adj*

trans·duo·de·nal \-₁dü-ə-¹dē-nəl, -₁dyü-; -₁dü-¹äd-²n-əl, -dyü-\ *adj* : performed by cutting across or through the duodenum

tran·sect \tran-¹sekt\ *vb* : to cut transversely — **tran·sec·tion** \-¹sek-shən\ *n*

trans·epi·the·li·al \₁trans-₁e-pə-¹thē-lē-əl, ₁tranz-\ *adj* : existing or taking place across an epithelium 〈~ sodium transport〉

trans·sep·tal \tran-¹sep-təl\ *adj* **1** : passing across a septum **2** : passing or performed through a septum 〈~ cardiac catheterization〉

trans·esoph·a·ge·al \-i-₁sä-fə-¹jē-əl\ *adj* : passing through or performed by way of the esophagus 〈~ echocardiography〉

trans·fec·tion \trans-¹fek-shən\ *n* : infection of a cell with isolated viral nucleic acid followed by production of the complete virus in the cell; *also* : the incorporation of exogenous DNA into a cell — **trans·fect** \-¹fekt\ *vb*

trans·fer \¹trans-₁fər\ *n* **1** : TRANSFERENCE **2** : the carryover or generalization of learned responses from one type of situation to another — see NEGATIVE TRANSFER

trans·fer·ase \¹trans-(₁)fər-₁ās, -₁āz\ *n* : an enzyme that promotes transfer of a group from one molecule to another

trans·fer·ence \trans-¹fər-əns, ¹trans-(₁)\ *n* : the redirection of feelings and desires and esp. of those unconsciously retained from childhood toward a new object (as a psychoanalyst conducting therapy)

transference neurosis *n* : a neurosis developed in the course of psychoanalytic treatment and manifested by the reliving of infantile experiences in the presence of the analyst

transfer factor *n* : a substance that is

produced and secreted by a lymphocyte functioning in cell-mediated immunity and that upon incorporation into a lymphocyte which has not been sensitized confers on it the same immunological specificity as the sensitized cell

trans·fer·rin \trans-ˈfer-ən\ *n* : a beta globulin in blood plasma capable of combining with ferric ions and transporting iron in the body

transfer RNA *n* : a relatively small RNA that transfers a particular amino acid to a growing polypeptide chain at the ribosomal site of protein synthesis during translation — called also *soluble RNA, tRNA;* compare MESSENGER RNA

trans·fix·ion \trans-ˈfik-shən\ *n* : a piercing of a part of the body (as by a suture or pin) in order to fix it in position — **trans·fix** \-ˈfiks\ *vb*

trans·form \trans-ˈfòrm\ *vb* **1** : to change or become changed in structure, appearance, or character **2** : to cause (a cell) to undergo genetic transformation

trans·for·ma·tion \ˌtrans-fər-ˈmā-shən, -fòr-\ *n* **1** : an act, process, or instance of transforming or being transformed ⟨~ of a normal into a malignant cell⟩ **2 a** : genetic modification of a bacterium by incorporation of free DNA from another ruptured bacterial cell — compare TRANSDUCTION **b** : genetic modification of a cell by the uptake and incorporation of exogenous DNA

transforming growth factor *n* : any of a group of polypeptides that are secreted by a variety of cells (as monocytes, T cells, or blood platelets) and have diverse effects (as inducing angiogenesis, stimulating fibroblast proliferation, or inhibiting T cell proliferation) on the division and activity of cells — abbr. *TGF*

trans·fuse \trans-ˈfyüz\ *vb* **trans·fused**; **trans·fus·ing 1** : to transfer (as blood) into a vein or artery of a human being or an animal **2** : to subject (a patient) to transfusion — **trans·fus·ible** *or* **trans·fus·able** \trans-ˈfyü-zə-bəl\ *adj*

trans·fu·sion \trans-ˈfyü-zhən\ *n* **1** : the process of transfusing fluid into a vein or artery **2** : something transfused — **trans·fu·sion·al** \-zhə-nəl\ *adj*

trans·fu·sion·ist \-zhə-nist\ *n* : one skilled in performing transfusions

trans·gen·ic \ˌtrans-ˈje-nik, ˌtranz-\ *adj* : having chromosomes into which one or more heterologous genes have been incorporated either artificially or naturally ⟨~ mice⟩

trans·glu·ta·min·ase \-ˈglü-tə-mə-ˌnās, -glü-ˈta-mə-ˌnāz\ *n* : a clotting factor that is a variant of factor XIII and that promotes the formation of links between strands of fibrin

trans·he·pat·ic \-hi-ˈpa-tik\ *adj* : involving direct injection (as of a radi-

opaque medium) into the biliary ducts

tran·sient \ˈtran-zē-ənt, -shənt, -chənt\ *adj* : passing away in time : existing temporarily ⟨~ symptoms⟩

transient ischemic attack *n* : a brief episode of cerebral ischemia that is usu. characterized by blurring of vision, slurring of speech, numbness, paralysis, or syncope and that is sometimes a forerunner of more serious cerebral accidents — abbr. *TIA*

trans·il·lu·mi·nate \ˌtrans-ə-ˈlü-mə-ˌnāt, ˌtranz-\ *vb* **-nat·ed; -nat·ing** : to pass light through (a body part) for medical examination ⟨~ the sinuses⟩ — **trans·il·lu·mi·na·tion** \-ə-ˌlü-mə-ˈnā-shən\ *n*

tran·si·tion·al \tran-ˈsi-shə-nəl, -ˈzi-\ *adj* : of, relating to, or being an epithelium (as in the urinary bladder) that consists of several layers of soft cuboidal cells which become flattened when stretched

trans·la·tion \trans-ˈlā-shən, tranz-\ *n* : the process of forming a protein molecule at a ribosomal site of protein synthesis from information contained in messenger RNA — compare TRANSCRIPTION — **trans·late** \-ˈlāt\ *vb* — **trans·la·tion·al** \-ˈlā-shə-nəl\ *adj*

trans·lo·ca·tion \ˌtrans-lō-ˈkā-shən, ˌtranz-\ *n* **1** : transfer of part of a chromosome to a different position esp. on a nonhomologous chromosome; *esp* : the exchange of parts between nonhomologous chromosomes **2** : a chromosome or part of a chromosome that has undergone translocation — **trans·lo·cate** \-ˈlō-ˌkāt\ *vb*

trans·lum·bar \ˌtrans-ˈləm-bər, ˌtranz-, -ˈbär\ *adj* : passing through or performed by way of the lumbar region; *specif* : involving the injection of a radiopaque medium through the lumbar region

trans·lu·mi·nal \-ˈlü-mə-nəl\ *adj* : passing across or performed by way of a lumen; *specif* : involving the passage of an inflatable catheter along the lumen of a blood vessel ⟨~ angioplasty⟩

trans·mem·brane \-ˈmem-ˌbrān\ *adj* : taking place, existing, or arranged from one side to the other of a membrane

trans·mis·si·ble \trans-ˈmi-sə-bəl, tranz-\ *adj* : capable of being transmitted ⟨~ diseases⟩ — **trans·mis·si·bil·i·ty** \-ˌmi-sə-ˈbi-lə-tē\ *n*

trans·mis·sion \trans-ˈmi-shən, tranz-\ *n* : an act, process, or instance of transmitting ⟨~ of rabies⟩ ⟨~ of a nerve impulse across a synapse⟩

transmission deafness *n* : CONDUCTION DEAFNESS

transmission electron microscope *n* : a conventional electron microscope which produces an image of a cross-sectional slice of a specimen all points of which are illuminated by the electron beam at the same time —

compare SCANNING ELECTRON MICROSCOPE — **transmission electron microscopy** n

trans·mit \trans-'mit, tranz-\ vb **transmit·ted; trans·mit·ting** : to pass, transfer, or convey from one person or place to another: as a : to pass or convey by heredity 〈~ a genetic abnormality〉 b : to convey (infection) abroad or to another 〈mosquitoes ~ malaria〉 c : to cause (energy) to be conveyed through space or a medium 〈substances that ~ nerve impulses〉

trans·mit·ta·ble \-'mi-tə-bəl\ adj : TRANSMISSIBLE

trans·mit·ter \-'mi-tər\ n : one that transmits; specif : NEUROTRANSMITTER

trans·mu·ral \trans-'myùr-əl, ,tranz-\ adj : passing or administered through an anatomical wall 〈~ stimulation of the ileum〉; also : involving the whole thickness of a wall 〈~ myocardial infarction〉 — **trans·mu·ral·ly** adv

trans·neu·ro·nal \-nü-'rōn-ᵊl, -nyü-: -ᵊnür-ən-ᵊl, -'nyùr-\ adj : TRANSSYNAPTIC 〈~ cell atrophy〉

trans·or·bit·al \-'ör-bət-ᵊl\ adj : passing through or performed by way of the eye socket

trans·ovar·i·al \-ō-'var-ē-əl\ adj : relating to or being transmission of a pathogen from an organism (as a tick) to its offspring by infection of eggs in its ovary — **trans·ovar·i·al·ly** adv

trans·ovar·i·an \-ē-ən\ adj : TRANSOVARIAL

trans·par·ent \trans-'par-ənt\ adj 1 : having the property of transmitting light so that bodies lying beyond are entirely visible 2 : pervious to a specified form of radiation (as X rays)

trans·pep·ti·dase \trans-'pep-tə-ˌdās, tranz-, -ˌdāz\ n : an enzyme that catalyzes the transfer of an amino acid residue or a peptide residue from one amino compound to another

trans·peri·to·ne·al \-ˌper-ə-tə-'nē-əl\ adj : passing or performed through the peritoneum

trans·pla·cen·tal \ˌtrans-plə-'sent-ᵊl\ adj : relating to, involving, or being passage (as of an antibody) between mother and fetus through the placenta — **trans·pla·cen·tal·ly** adv

¹**trans·plant** \trans-'plant\ vb : to transfer from one place to another; esp : to transfer (an organ or tissue) from one part or individual to another — **transplant·abil·i·ty** \-ˌplan-tə-'bi-lə-tē\ n — **trans·plant·able** \-'plan-tə-bəl\ adj — **trans·plan·ta·tion** \ˌtrans-ˌplan-'tā-shən\ n

²**trans·plant** \'trans-ˌplant\ n 1 : something (as an organ or part) that is transplanted 2 : the act or process of transplanting 〈a liver ~〉

trans·pleu·ral \-'plùr-əl\ adj : passing through or requiring passage through the pleura 〈a ~ surgical procedure〉

¹**trans·port** \trans-'pört, 'trans-ˌ\ vb : to transfer or convey from one place to another

²**trans·port** \'trans-ˌpört\ n : an act or process of transporting; specif : ACTIVE TRANSPORT

transposable element n : a segment of genetic material that is capable of changing its location in the genome or in some bacteria of undergoing transfer between an extrachromosomal plasmid and a chromosome — called also **transposable genetic element**

trans·pose \trans-'pōz\ vb **transposed; trans·pos·ing** : to transfer from one place or period to another; specif : to subject to or undergo genetic transposition — **trans·pos·able** \-'pō-zə-bəl\ adj

trans·po·si·tion \ˌtrans-pə-'zi-shən\ n : an act, process, or instance of transposing or being transposed: as a : the displacement of a viscus to a side opposite from that which it normally occupies 〈~ of the heart〉 b : the transfer of a segment of DNA from one site to another in the genome either between chromosomal sites or between an extrachromosomal site (as on a plasmid) and a chromosome — **trans·po·si·tion·al** \-'zi-shə-nəl\ adj

trans·po·son \trans-'pō-ˌzän\ n : a transposable element esp. when it contains genetic material controlling functions other than those related to its relocation

trans·py·lor·ic \-pī-'lör-ik\ adj : relating to or being the transverse plane or the line marking its intersection with the surface of the abdomen that passes below the rib cage cutting the pylorus of the stomach and the first lumbar vertebra and that is one of the four planes marking off the nine abdominal regions

trans·rec·tal \-'rekt-ᵊl\ adj : passing through or performed by way of the rectum 〈~ prostatic biopsy〉

trans·sep·tal \-'sept-ᵊl\ adj : passing through a septum

trans·sex·u·al \-'sek-shə-wəl\ n : a person with a psychological urge to belong to the opposite sex that may be carried to the point of undergoing surgery to modify the sex organs to mimic the opposite sex — **transsexual** adj — **trans·sex·u·al·ism** \-wə-ˌli-zəm\ n — **trans·sex·u·al·i·ty** \-ˌsek-shə-'wa-lə-tē\ n

trans·sphe·noi·dal \-sfi-'nöid-ᵊl\ adj : performed by entry through the sphenoid bone 〈~ hypophysectomy〉

trans·syn·ap·tic \-sə-'nap-tik\ adj : occurring or taking place across nerve synapses 〈~ degeneration〉

trans·tho·rac·ic \-thə-'ra-sik\ adj 1 : performed or made by way of the thoracic cavity 2 : crossing or having connections that cross the thoracic cavity 〈a ~ pacemaker〉 — **trans·tho·rac·i·cal·ly** adv

trans·thy·re·tin \-'thī-rə-tin\ n : a pro-

713

transtracheal • transvestite

tein component of blood serum that functions esp. in the transport of thyroxine — called also *prealbumin*

trans·tra·che·al \-'trā-kē-əl\ *adj* : passing through or administered by way of the trachea (~ anesthesia)

tran·su·date \'tran-'sü-dət, -'syü-, -'zü-, -'zyü-, -dāt\ *n* : a transuded substance

tran·su·da·tion \tran-sü-'dā-shən, -syü-, -zü-, -zyü-\ *n* 1 : the act or process of transuding or being transuded 2 : TRANSUDATE

tran·sude \tran-'süd, -'syüd, -'züd, -'zyüd\ *vb* **tran·sud·ed; tran·sud·ing** : to pass or permit passage of through a membrane or permeable substance

trans·ure·tero·ure·ter·os·to·my \trans-yü-'rē-tə-ō-yü-'rē-tə-'räs-tə-mē\ *n, pl* **-mies** : anastomosis of a ureter to the contralateral ureter

trans·ure·thral \-yü-'rē-thrəl\ *adj* : passing through or performed by way of the urethra (~ prostatectomy)

trans·vag·i·nal \-'va·jən-əl\ *adj* : passing through or performed by way of the vagina (~ laparoscopy)

trans·ve·nous \-'vē-nəs\ *adj* : relating to or involving the use of an intravenous catheter containing an electrode carrying electrical impulses from an extracorporeal source to the heart

trans·ven·tric·u·lar \-ven-'tri·kyə-lər, -vən-\ *adj* : passing through or performed by way of a ventricle

transversa, transversum — see SEPTUM TRANSVERSUM

trans·ver·sa·lis cer·vi·cis \trans-vər-'sā-ləs-'sər-vi-səs\ *n* : LONGISSIMUS CERVICIS

transversalis fascia *n* : the whole deep layer of fascia lining the abdominal wall; *also* : the part of this covering the inner surface of the transversus abdominis and separating it from the peritoneum

trans·verse \trans-'vərs, tranz-, 'trans-, 'tranz-\ *adj* 1 : acting, lying, or being across : set crosswise 2 : made at right angles to the anterior-posterior axis of the body (a ~ section) — **trans·verse·ly** *adv*

transverse carpal ligament *n* : FLEXOR RETINACULUM 2

transverse cervical artery *n* : an inconstant branch of the thyrocervical trunk or of the subclavian artery that supplies the region at the base of the neck and the muscles of the scapula

transverse colon *n* : the part of the large intestine that extends across the abdominal cavity joining the ascending colon to the descending colon

transverse crural ligament *n* : EXTENSOR RETINACULUM 1b

transverse facial artery *n* : a large branch of the superficial temporal artery that arises in the parotid gland and supplies the parotid gland, masseter muscle, and adjacent parts

transverse fissure *n* : PORTA HEPATIS

transverse foramen *n* : a foramen in each transverse process of a cervical vertebra through which the cervical artery and vertebral vein pass in each cervical vertebra except the seventh

transverse ligament *n* : any of various ligaments situated transversely with respect to a bodily axis or part: as a : the transverse part of the cruciate ligament of the atlas b : one in the anterior part of the knee connecting the anterior margins of the lateral and medial menisci

transverse process *n* : a process that projects on the dorsolateral aspect of each side of the neural arch of a vertebra

transverse sinus *n* : either of two large venous sinuses of the cranium that begin at the bony protuberance on the middle of the inner surface of the occipital bone at the intersection of its bony ridges and that terminate at the jugular foramen on either side to become the internal jugular vein

transverse thoracic muscle *n* : TRANSVERSUS THORACIS

transverse tubule *n* : T TUBULE

trans·ver·sion \trans-'vər-zhən, tranz-\ *n* : the eruption of a tooth in an abnormal position on the jaw

trans·ver·sus ab·dom·i·nis \trans-'vər-səs-əb-'dä-mə-nəs\ *n* : a flat muscle with transverse fibers that forms the innermost layer of the anterolateral wall of the abdomen and that acts to constrict the abdominal viscera and assist in expulsion of the contents of various abdominal organs (as in urination, defecation, vomiting, and parturition)

transversus pe·rin·ei su·per·fi·ci·a·lis \-pe-'ri-nē-ı-ı-sü-pər-ıfi-shē-'ā-ləs\ *n* : a small band of muscle of the urogenital region of the perineum that arises from the ischial tuberosity and that with the contralateral muscle inserts into and acts to stabilize the mass of tissue in the midline between the anus and the penis or vagina — called also *superficial transverse perineal muscle*

transversus tho·ra·cis \-thō-'rā-səs\ *n* : a thin flat sheet of muscle and tendon fibers of the anterior wall of the chest that arises esp. from the xiphoid process and lower third of the sternum, inserts into the costal cartilages of the second to sixth ribs, and acts to draw the ribs downward — called also *transverse thoracic muscle*

trans·ves·i·cal \trans-'ve-si-kəl, tranz-\ *adj* : passing through or performed by way of the urinary bladder

trans·ves·tism \trans-'ves-ıti-zəm, tranz-\ *n* : adoption of the dress and often the behavior of the opposite sex — called also *eonism*

trans·ves·tite \trans-'ves-ıtīt, tranz-\ *n* : a person and esp. a male who adopts the dress and often the behavior typical of the opposite sex esp. for purposes of emotional or sexual gratification — **transvestite** *adj*

tran·yl·cy·pro·mine \ˌtran-əl-ˈsī-prə-ˌmēn\ *n* : an antidepressant drug C₉H₁₁N that is an inhibitor of monoamine oxidase and is administered in the form of its sulfate

tra·pe·zi·um \trə-ˈpē-zē-əm, tra-\ *n, pl* **-zi·ums** *or* **-zia** \-zē-ə\ : a bone in the distal row of the carpus at the base of the thumb — called also *greater multangular*

tra·pe·zi·us \trə-ˈpē-zē-əs, tra-\ *n* : a large flat triangular superficial muscle of each side of the upper back that arises from the occipital bone, the ligamentum nuchae, and the spinous processes of the last cervical and all the thoracic vertebrae, is inserted into the outer part of the clavicle, the acromion, and the spine of the scapula, and serves chiefly to rotate the scapula so as to present the glenoid cavity upward

trap·e·zoid \ˈtra-pə-ˌzȯid\ *n* : a bone in the distal row of the carpus at the base of the forefinger — called also *lesser multangular, trapezoid bone, trapezoideum*

trapezoid body *n* : a bundle of transverse fibers in the dorsal part of the pons

trap·e·zoi·de·um \ˌtra-pə-ˈzȯi-dē-əm\ *n* : TRAPEZOID

Tras·en·tine \ˈtra-sən-ˌtīn\ *trademark* — used for a preparation of adiphenine

Tras·y·lol \ˈtra-sə-ˌlȯl\ *trademark* — used for a preparation of aprotinin

trau·ma \ˈtrau̇-mə, ˈtrȯ-\ *n, pl* **traumas** *also* **trau·ma·ta** \-mə-tə\ **1 a** : an injury (as a wound) to living tissue caused by an extrinsic agent (surgical ∼) **b** : a disordered psychic or behavioral state resulting from mental or emotional stress or physical injury **2** : an agent, force, or mechanism that causes trauma — **trau·mat·ic** \trə-ˈma-tik, trȯ-, trau̇-\ *adj* — **trau·mat·i·cal·ly** *adv*

traumat- *or* **traumato-** *comb form* : wound : trauma (*traumatism*)

trau·ma·tism \ˈtrau̇-mə-ˌti-zəm, ˈtrȯ-\ *n* : the development or occurrence of trauma; *also* : TRAUMA

trau·ma·tize \-ˌtīz\ *vb* **-tized; -tiz·ing** : to inflict a trauma upon — **trau·ma·ti·za·tion** \ˌtrau̇-mə-tə-ˈzā-shən, ˌtrȯ-\ *n*

trau·ma·tol·o·gy \ˌtrau̇-mə-ˈtä-lə-jē, ˌtrȯ-\ *n, pl* **-gies** : the surgical treatment of wounds (pediatric ∼) — **trau·ma·tol·o·gist** \-ˈtä-lə-jist\ *n*

tra·vail \trə-ˈvāl, ˈtra-ˌvāl\ *n* : LABOR, PARTURITION

traveler's diarrhea *n* : TURISTA

travel sickness *n* : MOTION SICKNESS

tray \ˈtrā\ *n* : an appliance consisting of a rimmed body and a handle for use in holding plastic material against the gums or teeth in making negative impressions for dentures

traz·o·done \ˈtra-zə-ˌdōn\ *n* : an antidepressant drug C₁₉H₂₂ClN₅O that is administered in the form of its hydrochloride and inhibits the uptake of serotonin by the brain

Trea·cher Col·lins syndrome \ˈtrē-chər-ˈkä-lənz-\ *n* : MANDIBULOFACIAL DYSOSTOSIS

Collins, Edward Treacher (1862–1932), British ophthalmologist.

tread·mill \ˈtred-ˌmil\ *n* : a device having an endless belt on which an individual walks or runs in place that is used for exercise and in tests of physiological functions — see STRESS TEST

treat \ˈtrēt\ *vb* : to care for or deal with medically or surgically : deal with by medical or surgical means (∼*ed* their diseases) (∼*s* a patient) — **treat·abil·i·ty** \ˌtrē-tə-ˈbi-lə-tē\ *n* — **treat·able** \ˈtrē-tə-bəl\ *adj* — **treat·ment** \ˈtrēt-mənt\ *n*

tree \ˈtrē\ *n* : an anatomical system or structure having many branches — see BILIARY TREE, BRONCHIAL TREE, TRACHEOBRONCHIAL TREE

-tre·ma \ˈtrē-mə\ *n comb form, pl* **-tremas** *or* **-tre·ma·ta** \ˈtrē-mə-tə\ : hole : orifice : opening (helicotrema)

trem·a·tode \ˈtre-mə-ˌtōd\ *n* : any of a class (Trematoda) of parasitic platyhelminthic flatworms including the flukes — **trematode** *adj*

trem·bles \ˈtrem-bəlz\ *n* : severe poisoning of livestock and esp. cattle by a toxic alcohol present in several plants (as white snakeroot and rayless goldenrod) of the daisy family (Compositae)

tremens — see DELIRIUM TREMENS

trem·or \ˈtre-mər\ *n* : a trembling or shaking usu. from physical weakness, emotional stress, or disease

trem·u·lous \ˈtrem-yə-ləs\ *adj* : characterized by or affected with trembling or tremors — **trem·u·lous·ness** *n*

trench fever *n* : a disease that is marked by fever and pain in muscles, bones, and joints and that is caused by a bacterium (*Rochalimaea quintana*) transmitted by the human body louse (*Pediculus humanus*)

trench foot *n* : a painful foot disorder resembling frostbite and resulting from exposure to cold and wet

trench mouth *n* **1** : VINCENT'S ANGINA 2 : VINCENT'S INFECTION

Tren·de·len·burg position \ˈtrend-əl-ən-ˌbərg-\ *n* : a position of the body for medical examination or operation in which the patient is placed head down on a table inclined at about 45 degrees from the floor with the knees uppermost and the legs hanging over the end of the table

Trendelenburg, Friedrich (1844–1924), German surgeon.

Tren·tal \ˈtren-ˌtal\ *trademark* — used for a preparation of pentoxifylline

treph·i·na·tion \ˌtre-fə-ˈnā-shən\ *n* : an

act or instance of using a trephine (as to perforate the skull)

tre·phine \'trē-₁fīn\ *n* : a surgical instrument for cutting out circular sections (as of bone or corneal tissue) — **trephine** \'trē-₁fīn, tri-'\ *vb*

trep·o·ne·ma \₁tre-pə-'nē-mə\ *n* **1** *cap* : a genus of anaerobic spirochetes (family Spirochaetaceae) that are pathogenic in humans and other warm-blooded animals and include one (*T. pallidum*) causing syphilis and another (*T. pertenue*) causing yaws **2** *pl* **-ma·ta** \-mə-tə\ *or* **-mas** : any spirochete of the genus *Treponema* — **trep·o·ne·mal** \-'nē-məl\ *adj*

Treponema pal·li·dum immobilization test \-'pa-lə-dəm-\ *n* : a serological test for syphilis — abbr. *TPI*

trep·o·ne·ma·to·sis \₁tre-pə-₁nē-mə-'tō-səs, -₁ne-\ *n, pl* **-to·ses** \-₁sēz\ : infection with or disease caused by spirochetes of the genus *Treponema*

trep·o·neme \'tre-pə-₁nēm\ *n* : TREPONEMA 2

trep·pe \'tre-pə\ *n* : the graduated series of increasingly vigorous contractions that results when a corresponding series of identical stimuli is applied to a rested muscle — called also *staircase effect*

Trest \'trest\ *trademark* — used for a preparation of methixene

tre·tin·o·in \tre-'ti-nō-ən\ *n* : RETINOIC ACID

TRF *abbr* thyrotropin-releasing factor

TRH *abbr* thyrotropin-releasing hormone

tri·ac·e·tyl·ole·an·do·my·cin \(₁)trī-₁a-sət-ᵊl-₁ō-lē-₁an-dō-'mīs-ᵊn\ *n* : TROLEANDOMYCIN

tri·ad \'trī-₁ad\ *n* : a union or group of three (a ~ of symptoms)

tri·age \trē-'äzh, 'trē-₁\ *n* **1** : the sorting of and allocation of treatment to patients and esp. battle and disaster victims according to a system of priorities designed to maximize the number of survivors **2** : the sorting of patients (as in an emergency room or an HMO) according to the urgency of their need for care — **triage** *vb*

tri·al \'trī-əl\ *n* **1** : a tryout or experiment to test quality, value, or usefulness (a clinical ~ of a drug) **2** : one of a number of repetitions of an experiment

tri·am·cin·o·lone \₁trī-am-'sin-ᵊl-₁ōn\ *n* : a glucocorticoid drug C₂₁H₂₇FO₆ used esp. in treating psoriasis and allergic skin and respiratory disorders — see KENACORT

tri·am·ter·ene \trī-'am-tər-₁ēn\ *n* : a diuretic drug C₁₂H₁₁N₇ that promotes potassium retention

tri·an·gle \'trī-₁aŋ-gəl\ *n* : a three-sided region or space and esp. an anatomical one — see ANTERIOR TRIANGLE, POSTERIOR TRIANGLE, SCARPA'S TRIANGLE, SUBOCCIPITAL TRIANGLE, SUPERIOR CAROTID TRIANGLE

tri·an·gu·lar \trī-'aŋ-gyə-lər\ *n* : TRIQUETRAL BONE

triangular bone *n* : TRIQUETRAL BONE

triangular fossa *n* : a shallow depression in the anterior part of the top of the ear's auricle between the two crura into which the antihelix divides

tri·an·gu·la·ris \trī-₁aŋ-gyə-'lar-əs\ *n, pl* **-la·res** \-'lar-₁ēz\ **1** : a flat triangular muscle that extends from the base of the mandible to the angle formed by the joining of the upper and lower lips and that acts to depress this angle **2** : TRIQUETRAL BONE

triangular ridge *n* : a triangular surface that slopes downward from the tip of a cusp of a molar or premolar toward the center of its occlusal surface

tri·at·o·ma \trī-'a-tə-mə\ *n* **1** *cap* : a genus of large blood-sucking bugs (family Reduviidae) that feed on mammals and sometimes transmit Chagas' disease to their hosts — see CONENOSE **2** : any bug of the genus *Triatoma*

¹**tri·at·o·mid** \trī-'a-tə-mid\ *adj* : belonging to the genus *Triatoma*

²**triatomid** *n* : TRIATOMA 2

tri·az·i·quone \trī-'a-zə-₁kwōn\ *n* : an antineoplastic drug C₁₂H₁₃N₃O₂

tri·az·o·lam \trī-'a-zə-₁lam\ *n* : a benzodiazepine C₁₇H₁₂Cl₂N₄ used as a sedative in the short-term treatment of insomnia

trib·a·dism \'tri-bə-₁di-zəm\ *n* : a homosexual practice among women which attempts to simulate heterosexual intercourse

tri·bro·mo·eth·a·nol \₁trī-₁brō-mō-'e-thə-₁nȯl, -₁nōl\ *n* : a crystalline bromine derivative C₂H₃Br₃O of ethyl alcohol used as a basal anesthetic

trib·u·tary \'tri-byə-₁ter-ē\ *n, pl* **-tar·ies** : a vein that empties into a larger vein

tri·car·box·yl·ic acid cycle \₁trī-₁kär-₁bäk-'si-lik-\ *n* : KREBS CYCLE

tri·ceps \'trī-₁seps\ *n, pl* **triceps** : a muscle that arises from three heads: **a** : the large extensor muscle that is situated along the back of the upper arm, arises by the long head from the infraglenoid tubercle of the scapula and by two heads from the shaft of the humerus, is inserted into the olecranon at the elbow, and extends the forearm at the elbow joint — called also *triceps brachii* **b** : the gastrocnemius and soleus muscles viewed as constituting together one muscle

triceps bra·chii \-'brā-kē-₁ī\ *n* : TRICEPS a

trich- *or* **tricho-** *comb form* : hair : filament (*trichobezoar*)

-trich·ia \'tri-kē-ə\ *n comb form* : condition of having (such) hair (*atrichia*)

tri·chi·a·sis \tri-'kī-ə-səs\ *n* : a turning inward of the eyelashes often causing irritation of the eyeball

tri·chi·na \tri-'kī-nə\ *n, pl* **-nae** \-(₁)nē\ *also* **-nas** : a small slender nematode worm of the genus *Trichinella* (*T. spi-*

ralis) that as an adult is a short-lived parasite of the intestines of a flesh-eating mammal where it produces immense numbers of larvae which migrate to the muscles, become encysted, may persist for years, and if consumed by a new host in raw or insufficiently cooked meat are liberated by the digestive processes and rapidly become adult to initiate a new parasitic cycle — see TRICHINOSIS

Trichina *n, syn of* TRICHINELLA

trich·i·nel·la \ˌtri-kə-ˈne-lə\ *n* 1 *cap* : a genus of nematode worms (family Trichinellidae) comprising the trichinae 2 *pl* -lae \-ˌlē\ : TRICHINA

trich·i·ni·a·sis \ˌtri-kə-ˈnī-ə-səs\ *n, pl* -ases \-ˌsēz\ : TRICHINOSIS

trich·i·no·sis \ˌtri-kə-ˈnō-səs\ *n, pl* -noses \-ˌsēz\ : infestation with or disease caused by trichinae contracted by eating raw or insufficiently cooked infested food and esp. pork and marked initially by colicky pains, nausea, and diarrhea and later by muscular pain, dyspnea, fever, and edema — called also *trichiniasis*

tri·chlor·ace·tic acid \ˌtrī-ˌklōr-ə-ˈsē-tik\ *var of* TRICHLOROACETIC ACID

tri·chlor·eth·y·lene \-ˈe-thə-ˌlēn\ *var of* TRICHLOROETHYLENE

tri·chlor·fon \(ˌ)trī-ˈklōr-ˌfän\ *n* : an organophosphate $C_4H_8Cl_3O_4P$ used as a parasiticide in veterinary medicine

tri·chlor·me·thi·a·zide \ˌtrī-ˌklōr-me-ˈthī-ə-ˌzīd\ *n* : a diuretic and antihypertensive drug $C_8H_8Cl_3N_3O_4S_2$ — see METAHYDRIN, NAQUA

tri·chlo·ro·ace·tic acid \ˌtrī-ˌklōr-ō-ə-ˈsē-tik\ *n* : a strong acid $C_2Cl_3HO_2$ used in medicine as a caustic and astringent

tri·chlo·ro·eth·y·lene \-ˈe-thə-ˌlēn\ *n* : a nonflammable liquid C_2HCl_3 used in medicine as an anesthetic and analgesic

tri·chlo·ro·meth·ane \-ˈme-ˌthān\ *n* : CHLOROFORM

tri·chlo·ro·phe·nol \-ˈfē-ˌnōl, -ˌnōl, -fi-ˈ\ *n* : a bactericide and fungicide $C_6H_3Cl_3O$ that is a major constituent of hexachlorophene

tri·chlo·ro·phen·oxy·ace·tic acid \(ˌ)trī-ˌklōr-ō-fə-ˌnäk-sē-ə-ˈsē-tik\ *n* : 2,4,-5-T

tri·chlor·phon *var of* TRICHLORFON

tricho·be·zoar \ˌtri-kō-ˈbē-ˌzōr\ *n* : HAIR BALL

Tricho·bil·har·zia \ˌtri-kō-bil-ˈhär-zē-ə, -ˈhärt-sē-ə\ *n* : a genus of digenetic trematode worms (family Schistosomatidae) including forms that normally parasitize aquatic birds and are leading causes of swimmer's itch in humans

Tricho·dec·tes \ˌtri-kə-ˈdek-ˌtēz\ *n* : a genus of bird lice (family Trichodectidae) of domesticated mammals

tricho·epi·the·li·o·ma \ˌtri-kō-ˌe-pə-ˌthē-lē-ˈō-ma\ *n, pl* -mas *or* -ma·ta \-mə-tə\ : a benign epithelial tumor developing from the hair follicles esp. on the face

tri·chol·o·gy \tri-ˈkä-lə-jē\ *n, pl* -gies : scientific study of hair and its diseases

tricho·mo·na·cide \ˌtri-kə-ˈmō-nə-ˌsīd\ *n* : an agent used to destroy trichomonads — **tricho·mo·na·cid·al** \-ˌmō-nə-ˈsīd-əl\ *adj*

¹tricho·mo·nad \ˌtri-kə-ˈmō-ˌnad, -nəd\ *n* : any protozoan of the genus *Trichomonas*

²trichomonad *adj* : TRICHOMONAL

tricho·mo·nal \ˌtri-kə-ˈmō-nəl\ *adj* : of, relating to, or caused by flagellated protozoans of the genus *Trichomonas*

Trich·o·mo·nas \ˌtri-kə-ˈmō-nəs\ *n* : a genus of flagellated protozoans (family Trichomonadidae) that are parasites of the alimentary or genitourinary tracts of numerous vertebrate and invertebrate hosts including one (*T. vaginalis*) causing human vaginitis

tricho·mo·ni·a·sis \ˌtri-kə-mə-ˈnī-ə-səs\ *n, pl* -ases \-ˌsēz\ : infection with or disease caused by trichomonads: as **a** : a human sexually transmitted disease occurring esp. as vaginitis with a persistent discharge and caused by a trichomonad (*Trichomonas vaginalis*) that may also invade the male urethra and bladder **b** : a venereal disease of domestic cattle caused by a trichomonad (*T. foetus*) and marked by abortion and sterility **c** : one or more diseases of various birds apparently caused by trichomonads (as *T. diversa* or *T. gallinorum*) and resembling blackhead — called also *roup*

tricho·phy·ton \ˌtri-kə-ˈfī-ˌtän, tri-fə-ˈtän\ *n* 1 *cap* : a genus of ringworm fungi (family Moniliaceae) that are parasitic in the skin and hair follicles — see EPIDERMOPHYTON 2 : any fungus of the genus *Trichophyton*

Tricho·spo·ron \ˌtri-kə-ˈspōr-ˌän, tri-ˈkäs-pə-ˌrän\ *n* : a genus of parasitic imperfect fungi (order Moniliales) of which some are reputed skin or hair parasites of humans

tricho·stron·gyle \ˌtri-kə-ˈsträn-ˌjil\ *n* : any worm of the genus *Trichostrongylus*

tricho·stron·gy·lo·sis \ˌtri-kō-ˌsträn-jə-ˈlō-səs\ *n* : infestation with or disease caused by roundworms of the genus *Trichostrongylus* chiefly in young sheep and cattle

Tricho·stron·gy·lus \ˌtri-kō-ˈsträn-jə-ləs\ *n* : a genus of nematode worms (family Trichostrongylidae) parasitic in birds and mammals including humans that comprises forms formerly placed in the genus *Strongylus*

tricho·til·lo·ma·nia \-ti-lə-ˈmā-nē-ə\ *n* : abnormal desire to pull out one's hair — **tricho·til·lo·man·ic** \-ˈma-nik\ *adj*

tri·chro·mat \ˈtrī-krō-ˌmat, (ˌ)trī-ˈ\ *n* : a person with trichromatism

tri·chro·mat·ic \ˌtrī-krō-ˈma-tik\ *adj* 1

: of, relating to, or consisting of three colors (~ light) **2 a** : relating to or being the theory that human color vision involves three types of retinal sensory receptors **b** : characterized by trichromatism (~ vision)

tri·chro·ma·tism \(₊)trī-ˈkrō-mə-₊ti-zəm\ n : color vision based on the perception of three primary colors and esp. red, green, and blue — compare DEUTERANOMALY, PROTANOMALY

trich·u·ri·a·sis \₊tri-kyə-ˈri-ə-səs\ n, pl **-a·ses** \-₊sēz\ : infestation with or disease caused by nematode worms of the genus *Trichuris*

Trich·u·ris \tri-ˈkyùr-əs\ n : a genus of nematode worms (family Trichuridae) comprising the whipworms

tri·clo·car·ban \₊trī-ˈklō-ˈkär-₊ban\ : an antiseptic $C_{13}H_9Cl_3N_2O$ used esp. in soaps

tri·cus·pid \(₊)trī-ˈkəs-pəd\ adj **1** : having three cusps (~ molars) **2** : of, relating to, or involving the tricuspid valve of the heart (~ disease)

tricuspid valve n : a valve that is situated at the opening of the right atrium of the heart into the right ventricle and that resembles in structure the bicuspid valve but consists of three triangular membranous flaps — called also *right atrioventricular valve*

¹tri·cy·clic \(₊)trī-ˈsī-klik, -ˈsi-\ adj : being a chemical with three usu. fused rings in the molecular structure and esp. a tricyclic antidepressant

²tricyclic n : TRICYCLIC ANTIDEPRESSANT

tricyclic antidepressant n : any of a group of antidepressant drugs (as imipramine, amitriptyline, desipramine, and nortriptyline) that contain three fused benzene rings, potentiate the action of catecholamines, and do not inhibit the action of monoamine oxidase

tri·di·hex·eth·yl chloride \₊trī-₊dī-₊heks-ˈeth-əl-\ n : a quaternary ammonium compound $C_{21}H_{36}ClNO$ used as an anticholinergic drug — see PATHILON

Tri·di·one \trī-ˈdī-₊ōn\ trademark — used for a preparation of trimethadione

triethiodide — see GALLAMINE TRIETHIODIDE

tri·eth·yl·ene gly·col \(₊)trī-ˌe-thə-₊len-ˈglī-₊kòl, -₊kōl\ n : a hygroscopic liquid alcohol $C_6H_{14}O_4$ that is used in medicine as an air disinfectant

tri·eth·yl·ene·mel·amine \-₊e-thə-₊len-ˈmel-ə-₊mēn, -mən\ n : a cytotoxic crystalline compound $C_9H_{12}N_6$ used as an antineoplastic drug — called also *TEM*

tri·fa·cial nerve \₊trī-ˈfā-shəl-\ n : TRIGEMINAL NERVE

trifacial neuralgia n : TRIGEMINAL NEURALGIA

tri·fluo·per·a·zine \₊trī-₊flü-ō-ˈper-ə-₊zēn, -zən\ n : a phenothiazine tranquilizer $C_{21}H_{24}F_3N_3S$ used to treat

psychotic conditions and esp. schizophrenia — see STELAZINE

tri·flu·pro·ma·zine \₊trī-₊flü-ˈprō-mə-₊zēn, -zən\ n : a phenothiazine tranquilizer $C_{18}H_{19}F_3N_2S$ used esp. in the treatment of psychoses and as an antiemetic — see VESPRIN

¹tri·fo·cal \(₊)trī-ˈfō-kəl\ adj, of an eyeglass lens : having one part that corrects for near vision, one for intermediate vision (as at arm's length), and one for distant vision

²tri·fo·cal \ˈtrī-₊fō-kəl\ n **1** : a trifocal glass or lens **2** pl : eyeglasses with trifocal lenses

¹tri·gem·i·nal \trī-ˈje-mə-nəl\ adj : of or relating to the trigeminal nerve

²trigeminal n : TRIGEMINAL NERVE

trigeminal ganglion n : the large flattened sensory root ganglion of the trigeminal nerve that lies within the skull and behind the orbit — called also *gasserian ganglion, semilunar ganglion*

trigeminal nerve n : either of the fifth pair of cranial nerves that are mixed nerves and in humans are the largest of the cranial nerves and that arise by a small motor and a larger sensory root which both emerge from the side of the pons with the sensory root bearing the trigeminal ganglion and dividing into ophthalmic, maxillary, and mandibular nerves and the motor root supplying fibers to the mandibular nerve and through this to the muscles of mastication — called also *fifth cranial nerve, trifacial nerve, trigeminus*

trigeminal neuralgia n : an intense paroxysmal neuralgia involving one or more branches of the trigeminal nerve — called also *tic douloureux*

trigger finger n : an abnormal condition in which flexion or extension of a finger may be momentarily obstructed by spasm followed by a snapping into place

trigger point n : a sensitive area of the body which when stimulated gives rise to reaction elsewhere in the body; esp : a hypersensitive area that evokes referred pain elsewhere when stimulated — called also *trigger zone*

tri·glyc·er·ide \(₊)trī-ˈgli-sə-₊rīd\ n : any of a group of lipids that are esters composed of one molecule of glycerol and three molecules of one or more fatty acids, are widespread in adipose tissue, and commonly circulate in the blood in the form of lipoproteins — called also *neutral fat*

tri·gone \ˈtrī-₊gōn\ also **tri·gon** \-₊gän\ : a triangular body part; specif : a smooth triangular area on the inner surface of the bladder limited by the apertures of the ureters and urethra

tri·go·ni·tis \₊trī-gə-ˈnī-təs\ n : inflammation of the trigone of the bladder

tri·go·no·ceph·a·ly \₊trī-gə-nə-ˈse-fə-lē, ₊trī-₊gō-nō-\ n, pl **-lies** : a congenital deformity in which the head is somewhat triangular and flat

tri-go-num \trī-'gō-nəm\ n, pl **-nums** or **-na** \-nə\ : a triangular anatomical part : TRIGONE

trigonum ha-ben-u-lae \-hə-'ben-yə-ˌlē\ n : a triangular area on the dorsomedial surface of the lateral geniculate body rostral to the pineal gland

trigonum ves-i-cae \-'ve-si-ˌkē\ n : the trigone of the urinary bladder

tri-io-do-thy-ro-nine \trī-ˌi-ə-dō-'thī-rə-ˌnēn\ n : a crystalline iodine-containing hormone $C_{15}H_{12}I_3NO_4$ that is an amino acid derived from thyroxine, and is used esp. in the form of its soluble sodium salt in the treatment of hypothyroidism and metabolic insufficiency — called also *liothyronine*, T_3

tri-mep-ra-zine \trī-'me-prə-ˌzēn\ n : a phenothiazine $C_{18}H_{22}N_2S$ used esp. in the form of its tartrate salt as an antipruritic — see TEMARIL

tri-mes-ter \(ˌ)trī-'mes-tər, 'trī-ˌ\ n : a period of three or about three months; *esp* : any of three periods of approximately three months each into which a human pregnancy is divided

tri-metha-di-one \ˌtrī-ˌme-thə-'dī-ˌōn\ n : a crystalline anticonvulsant $C_6H_9NO_3$ used chiefly in the treatment of petit mal epilepsy — see TRIDIONE

tri-meth-a-phan \trī-'me-thə-ˌfan\ n : a ganglionic blocking agent used as a salt $C_{32}H_{40}N_2O_5S_2$ to lower blood pressure esp. in hypertensive emergencies

tri-metho-ben-za-mide \ˌtrī-ˌme-thə-'ben-zə-ˌmid\ n : an antiemetic drug $C_{21}H_{28}N_2O_5$ used esp. in the form of its hydrochloride salt

tri-meth-o-prim \trī-'me-thə-ˌprim\ : a synthetic antibacterial and antimalarial drug $C_{14}H_{18}N_4O_3$ — see BACTRIM

tri-ni-tro-phe-nol \(ˌ)trī-ˌnī-trō-'fē-ˌnōl, -ˌnōl, -fi-'nōl\ or 2,4,6-**trinitrophenol** \ˌtü-ˌfōr-ˌsiks-\ n : PICRIC ACID

tri-nu-cle-o-tide \(ˌ)trī-'nü-klē-ə-ˌtīd, -'nyü-\ n : a nucleotide consisting of three mononucleotides in combination : CODON

tri-or-tho-cre-syl phosphate \ˌtrī-ˌôr-thō-ˌkre-səl-, -ˌkrē-\ n : a usu. colorless, odorless, tasteless neurotoxin $C_{21}H_{21}O_2P$

tri-ox-sa-len \ˌtrī-'äk-sə-lən\ n : a synthetic psoralen $C_{14}H_{12}O_3$ that promotes tanning of the skin

tri-pal-mi-tin \(ˌ)trī-'pal-mə-tən, -'päl-, -'pä-\ n : PALMITIN

tri-par-a-nol \trī-'par-ə-ˌnol, -ˌnōl\ n : a drug $C_{27}H_{32}ClNO_2$ that inhibits the formation of cholesterol but that has numerous toxic side effects

tri-pel-en-na-mine \ˌtrī-pe-'le-nə-ˌmēn, -mən\ n : an antihistamine drug $C_{16}H_{21}N_3$ used in the form of its crystalline citrate or hydrochloride — see PYRIBENZAMINE

tri-pep-tide \(ˌ)trī-'pep-ˌtīd\ n : a peptide that yields three amino acid residues on hydrolysis

tri-phe-nyl-meth-ane \ˌtrī-ˌfen-ə¹-l-'me-ˌthān, -ˌfēn-\ n : a crystalline hydrocarbon $CH(C_6H_5)_3$

triphenylmethane dye n : any of a group of dyes (as pararosaniline) derived from triphenylmethane

tri-phos-pha-tase \(ˌ)trī-'fäs-fə-ˌtās, -ˌtāz\ n : an enzyme that catalyzes hydrolysis of a triphosphate — see ATPASE

tri-phos-phate \(ˌ)trī-'fäs-ˌfāt\ n : a salt or acid that contains three phosphate groups — see ATP, GTP

tri-phos-pho-pyr-i-dine nucleotide \ˌtrī-ˌfäs-fō-'pir-ə-ˌdēn-\ n : NADP

triple bond n : a chemical bond consisting of three covalent bonds between two atoms in a molecule and usu. represented in structural formulas by three lines, three dots, or six dots that denote three pairs of electrons — compare DOUBLE BOND, UNSATURATED b

tri-ple-gia \(ˌ)trī-'plē-jə, -jē-ə\ n : hemiplegia plus paralysis of a limb on the opposite side

triple point n : the condition of temperature and pressure under which the gaseous, liquid, and solid phases of a substance can exist in equilibrium

trip-let \'tri-plət\ n **1 a** : a combination, set, or group of three **b** : CODON 2 : one of three children or offspring born at one birth

¹**trip-loid** \'tri-ˌploid\ adj : having or being a chromosome number three times the monoploid number — **trip-loi-dy** \-ˌploi-dē\ n

²**triploid** n : a triploid individual

tri-que-tral bone \trī-'kwē-trel-\ n : the bone in the proximal row of the carpus that is third counting from the thumb side of the wrist, has a pyramidal shape, and is situated between the lunate and pisiform bones — called also *triangular, triangular bone, triangularis, triquetral*

tri-que-trum \trī-'kwē-trəm\ n, pl **tri-que-tra** \-trə\ : TRIQUETRAL BONE

tris \'tris\ n, often cap : a white crystalline powder $C_4H_{11}NO_3$ used as a buffer (as in the treatment of acidosis) — called also *tris buffer*, *tromethamine*

tri-sac-cha-ride \(ˌ)trī-'sa-kə-ˌrīd\ n : a sugar that yields on complete hydrolysis three monosaccharide molecules

tris buffer n : TRIS

tris-kai-deka-pho-bia \ˌtris-ˌki-ˌde-kə-'fō-bē-ə, ˌtris-kə-\ n : fear of the number 13

tris-mus \'triz-məs\ n : spasm of the muscles of mastication resulting from any of various abnormal conditions or diseases (as tetanus)

¹**tri-so-mic** \(ˌ)trī-'sō-mik\ adj : relating

to, caused by, or characterized by trisomy (~ cells)

²trisomic n : a trisomic individual

tri·so·my \'trī-,sō-mē\ n, pl **-mies** : the condition (as in Down's syndrome) of having one or a few chromosomes triploid in an otherwise diploid set

trisomy 21 \-,twen-tē-'wən\ n : DOWN'S SYNDROME

trit·an·ope \'trit-³n-,ōp, 'trīt-\ n : a person affected with tritanopia

trit·an·opia \,trit-³n-'ō-pē-ə, ,trīt-\ n : dichromatism in which the spectrum is seen in tones of red and green — **trit·an·op·ic** \,trit-³n-'ō-pik, ,trīt-³n-'ä-\ adj

tri·ti·um \'tri-tē-əm, -shəm, -shē-əm\ n : a radioactive isotope of hydrogen with atoms of three times the mass of ordinary light hydrogen atoms — symbol T

¹trit·u·rate \'tri-chə-,rāt\ vb **-rat·ed; -rat·ing** : to pulverize thoroughly by rubbing or grinding — **trit·u·ra·tion** \,tri-chə-'rā-shən\ n

²trit·u·rate \-rət\ n : a triturated substance

tri·va·lent \(,)trī-'vā-lənt\ adj : reacting immunologically with three different combining sites (as of antigens or antibodies)

tRNA \,tē-,är-,en-'ā\ n : TRANSFER RNA

Tro·bi·cin \trō-'bīs-³n\ trademark — used for a preparation of spectinomycin

tro·car \'trō-,kär\ n : a sharp-pointed surgical instrument fitted with a cannula and used esp. to insert the cannula into a body cavity as a drainage outlet

tro·chan·ter \trō-'kan-tər\ n : a rough prominence or process at the upper part of the femur serving usu. for the attachment of muscles and being usu. two on each femur: **a** : a larger one situated on the outer part of the upper end of the shaft at its junction with the neck — called also *greater trochanter* **b** : a smaller one situated at the lower back part of the junction of the shaft and neck — called also *lesser trochanter* — **tro·chan·ter·ic** \,trō-kən-'ter-ik, -kan-\ adj

trochanteric fossa n : a depression at the base of the internal surface of the greater trochanter of the femur for the attachment of the tendon of the obturator externus

tro·char var of TROCAR

tro·che \'trō-kē\ n : LOZENGE

troch·lea \'trä-klē-ə\ n : an anatomical structure held to resemble a pulley: as **a** : the articular surface on the medial condyle of the humerus that articulates with the ulna **b** : the fibrous ring in the inner upper part of the orbit through which the tendon of the superior oblique muscle of the eye passes

troch·le·ar \-ər\ adj **1** : of, relating to, or

being a trochlea **2** : of, relating to, or being a trochlear nerve (~ fibers)

trochlear fovea n : a depression that is located in the orbital surface of each bony plate of the frontal bone and that forms a point of attachment for the superior oblique muscle of the eye

trochlear nerve n : either of the 4th pair of cranial nerves that arise from the dorsal aspect of the brainstem just below the inferior colliculus and supply the superior oblique muscle of the eye with motor fibers

trochlear nucleus n : a nucleus that is situated behind the oculomotor nucleus and is the source of the motor fibers of the trochlear nerve

tro·choid \'trō-,kȯid\ n : PIVOT JOINT

tro·land \'trō-lənd\ n : PHOTON 2

Troland, Leonard Thompson (1889–1932), American psychologist and physicist.

tro·le·an·do·my·cin \,trō-lē-,an-də-'mis-³n\ n : an orally administered antibacterial drug $C_{41}H_{67}NO_{15}$ — called also *triacetyloleandomycin*

trol·ley also **trol·ly** \'trä-lē\ n, pl **trolleys** also **trollies** Brit : a stretcher with four wheels used to transport patients in a hospital

trol·ni·trate \,träl-'nī-,trāt\ n : an organic nitrate with vasodilator activity that is used in the form of its diphosphate salt $C_6H_{12}N_4O_9 \cdot 2H_3PO_4$ to prevent or ameliorate attacks of angina pectoris — see METAMINE

Trom·bic·u·la \träm-'bi-kyə-lə\ n : a genus of mites (family Trombiculidae) including some forms that in Asia transmit tsutsugamushi disease

tro·meth·a·mine \trō-'me-thə-,mēn\ n : TRIS

troph- or **tropho-** comb form : nutritive (*troph*oblast)

troph·ec·to·derm \,trō-'fek-tə-,dərm\ n : TROPHOBLAST; esp : the outer layer of the blastocyst after differentiation of the ectoderm, mesoderm, and endoderm when the outer layer is continuous with the embryonic ectoderm

tro·phic \'trō-fik\ adj **1** : of or relating to nutrition : NUTRITIONAL (~ disorders) **2** : TROPIC — **tro·phi·cal·ly** adv

-tro·phic \'trō-fik\ adj comb form **1** : of, relating to, or characterized by (such) nutrition or growth (hyper*trophic*) **2** : -TROPIC (gonado*trophic*)

trophic ulcer n : an ulcer (as a bedsore) caused by faulty nutrition in the affected part

tro·pho·blast \'trō-fə-,blast\ n : the outer layer of the blastocyst that supplies nutrition to the embryo, facilitates implantation by eroding away the tissues of the uterus with which it comes in contact, and differentiates into the extraembryonic membranes surrounding the embryo — **tro·pho·blas·tic** \,trō-fə-'blas-tik\ adj

troph·o·derm \'trō-fə-ˌdərm\ n : TRO-PHOBLAST

tro·pho·zo·ite \ˌtrō-fə-'zō-ˌīt\ n : a protozoan of a vegetative form as distinguished from one of a reproductive or resting form

-tro·phy \trə-fē\ n comb form, pl **-trophies** : nutrition : nurture : growth (hypo*trophy*)

tro·pia \'trō-pē-ə\ n : deviation of an eye from the normal position with respect to the line of vision when the eyes are open : STRABISMUS — see ESOTROPIA, HYPERTROPIA

tro·pic \'trō-pik\ adj 1 : of, relating to, or characteristic of tropism or of a tropism 2 *of a hormone* : influencing the activity of a specified gland

-tro·pic \'trō-pik\ adj comb form : attracted to or acting upon (something specified) (neuro*tropic*)

tropical medicine n : a branch of medicine dealing with tropical diseases and other special medical problems of tropical regions

tropical oil n : any of several oils (as coconut oil and palm oil) that are high in saturated fatty acids

tropical sprue n : SPRUE 2

tropical ulcer n : a chronic sloughing sore of unknown cause occurring usu. on the legs and prevalent in wet tropical regions

tro·pic·amide \trə-'pi-kə-ˌmīd\ n : a synthetic anticholinergic $C_{17}H_{20}N_2O_2$ used esp. to dilate pupils in ophthalmological examinations — see MYDRIACYL

-tro·pin \'trō-pən\ or **-tro·phin** \-fən\ n comb form : hormone (gonado*tropin*) (somato*tropin*)

tro·pism \'trō-ˌpi-zəm\ n : an automatic movement by an organism in response to a source of stimulation; *also* : a reflex reaction involving a tropism

tro·po·col·la·gen \ˌträ-pə-'kä-lə-jən, ˌtrō-\ n : a subunit of collagen fibrils consisting of three polypeptide strands arranged in a helix

tro·po·my·o·sin \ˌträ-pə-'mī-ə-sən, ˌtrō-\ n : a protein of muscle that forms a complex with troponin regulating the interaction of actin and myosin in muscular contraction

tro·po·nin \'trō-pə-nən, 'trä-, -ˌnin\ n : a protein of muscle that together with tropomyosin forms a regulatory protein complex controlling the interaction of actin and myosin and that when combined with calcium ions permits muscular contraction

trough \'tróf\ n — see GINGIVAL CREVICE

troy \'tròi\ adj : expressed in troy weight (a ~ ounce)

troy pound n : POUND a

troy weight n : a series of units of weight based on a pound of 12 ounces and an ounce of 480 grains or 31.103 grams

true bug \'trü-\ n : BUG 1c

true conjugate n : CONJUGATE DIAMETER

true pelvis n : the lower more contracted part of the pelvic cavity — called also *true pelvic cavity;* compare FALSE PELVIS

true rib n : any of the ribs having costal cartilages connected directly with the sternum and in humans constituting the first seven pairs — called also *vertebrosternal rib*

true vocal cords n pl : the lower pair of vocal cords each of which encloses a vocal ligament, extends from the inner surface of one side of the thyroid cartilage near the median line to a process of the corresponding arytenoid cartilage on the same side of the larynx, and when drawn taut, approximated to the contralateral member of the pair, and subjected to a flow of breath produces the voice — called also *inferior vocal cords, vocal folds*

trun·cal \'trəŋ-kəl\ adj : of or relating to the trunk of the body or of a bodily part (as a nerve) (~ obesity)

trun·cus \'trəŋ-kəs\ n : TRUNK 2

truncus bra·chio·ce·phal·i·cus \-ˌbrā-kē-(ˌ)ō-se-'fa-li-kəs\ n : BRACHIOCEPHALIC ARTERY

truncus ce·li·a·cus \-se-'lī-ə-kəs\ n : CELIAC ARTERY

trunk \'trəŋk\ n 1 : the human body apart from the head and appendages : TORSO 2 : the main body of an anatomical part (as a nerve or blood vessel) that divides into branches

truss \'trəs\ n : a device worn to reduce a hernia by pressure

truth serum n : a hypnotic or anesthetic (as thiopental) held to induce a subject under questioning to talk freely

trypan- or **trypano-** comb form : trypanosome (*trypanocidal*)

try·pano·ci·dal \tri-ˌpa-nə-'sīd-ᵊl\ adj : destroying trypanosomes (a ~ drug) — **try·pano·cide** \tri-'pa-nə-ˌsīd\ n

try·pano·so·ma \tri-ˌpa-nə-'sō-mə\ n 1 cap : a genus of parasitic flagellate protozoans (family Trypanosomatidae) that infest the blood of various vertebrates including humans, are usu. transmitted by the bite of an insect, and include some that cause serious diseases (as Chagas' disease, sleeping sickness, and surra) 2 pl **-mas** or **-ma·ta** \-mə-tə\ : TRYPANOSOME

try·pano·some \tri-'pa-nə-ˌsōm\ n : any flagellate of the genus *Trypanosoma* — **try·pano·so·mal** \-ˌpa-nə-'sō-məl\ adj

try·pano·so·mi·a·sis \tri-ˌpa-nə-sə-'mī-ə-səs\ n, pl **-a·ses** \-ˌsēz\ : infection with or disease caused by flagellates of the genus *Trypanosoma*

tryp·ars·amide \tri-'pär-sə-ˌmīd\ n : an organic arsenical $C_8H_{10}AsN_2O_4Na·½H_2O$ used in the treatment of African sleeping sickness and syphilis

tryp·sin \'trip-sən\ *n* 1 : a crystallizable proteolytic enzyme that is produced and secreted in the pancreatic juice in the form of inactive trypsinogen and activated in the intestine — compare CHYMOTRYPSIN 2 : a preparation from the pancreatic juice containing principally proteolytic enzymes and used chiefly as a digestive and lytic agent

tryp·sin·ize \'trip-sə-ˌnīz\ *vb* **-ized; -izing** : to subject to the action of trypsin ⟨*trypsinized* tissue cells⟩ — **tryp·sin·i·za·tion** \ˌtrip-sə-nə-'zā-shən\ *n*

tryp·sin·o·gen \trip-'si-nə-jən\ *n* : the inactive substance released by the pancreas into the duodenum to form trypsin

tryp·tic \'trip-tik\ *adj* : of, relating to, or produced by trypsin or its action

tryp·to·phan \'trip-tə-ˌfan\ *also* **tryp·to·phane** \-ˌfān\ *n* : a crystalline essential amino acid $C_{11}H_{12}N_2O_2$ that is widely distributed in proteins

tset·se \'tset-sē, 'tsēt-, 'tet-, 'tēt-\ *n*, *pl* **tsetse** *or* **tsetses** : TSETSE FLY

tsetse fly *n* : any of several dipteran flies of the genus *Glossina* that occur in sub-Saharan Africa and include vectors of human and animal trypanosomes (as those causing sleeping sickness) — called also *tsetse*

TSH \ˌtē-(ˌ)es-'āch\ *n* : THYROTROPIN

TSS *abbr* toxic shock syndrome

tsu·tsu·ga·mu·shi disease \tsüt-sə-gə-'mü-shē-, ˌtüt-, ˌsüt-, -'gä-mü-shē-\ *n* : an acute febrile bacterial disease that is caused by a rickettsial bacterium (*Rickettsia tsutsugamushi*) transmitted by mite larvae, resembles louse-borne typhus, and is widespread in the western Pacific area — called also *scrub typhus, tsutsugamushi*

T system *n* : the system of T tubules in striated muscle

T₃ *or* **T-3** \ˌtē-'thrē\ *n* : TRIIODOTHYRONINE

T-tube *n* : a narrow flexible tube in the form of a T that is used for drainage esp. of the common bile duct

T tubule *n* : any of the small tubules which run transversely through a striated muscle fiber and through which electrical impulses are transmitted from the sarcoplasm to the fiber's interior

tub·al \'tü-bəl, 'tyü-\ *adj* : of, relating to, or involving a tube and esp. a fallopian tube ⟨∼ lumens⟩ ⟨a ∼ infection⟩

tubal abortion *n* : an aborted tubal pregnancy

tubal ligation *n* : ligation of the fallopian tubes to prevent passage of ova from the ovaries to the uterus used as a method of female sterilization

tubal pregnancy *n* : ectopic pregnancy in a fallopian tube

tubarius — see TORUS TUBARIUS

¹tube \'tüb, 'tyüb\ *n* 1 : a slender channel within a plant or animal body : DUCT — see BRONCHIAL TUBE, EUSTACHIAN TUBE, FALLOPIAN TUBE 2 a : a piece of laboratory or technical apparatus commonly serving to isolate or convey a product of reaction ⟨a distillation ∼⟩ b : TEST TUBE 3 : a hollow cylindrical device (as a cannula) used for insertion into bodily passages or hollow organs for removal or injection of materials

²tube *vb* **tubed; tub·ing** : to furnish with, enclose in, or pass through a tube

tube curare *n* : CURARE

tubed *adj* : having the sides sewn together so as to form a tube

tuberalis — see PARS TUBERALIS

tu·ber ci·ne·re·um \'tü-bər-si-'nir-ē-əm, 'tyü-\ *n* : an eminence of gray matter which lies on the lower surface of the brain and of which the upper surface forms part of the floor of the third ventricle and the lower surface bears the infundibulum to which the pituitary gland is attached

tu·ber·cle \'tü-bər-kəl, 'tyü-\ *n* 1 a : a small knobby prominence or excrescence: as **a** : a prominence on the crown of a molar tooth **b** : a small rough prominence on a bone usu. being smaller than a tuberosity and serving for the attachment of one or more muscles or ligaments — see GREATER TUBERCLE, LESSER TUBERCLE **c** : an eminence near the head of a rib that articulates with the transverse process of a vertebra **d** : any of several prominences in the central nervous system that mark the nuclei of various nerves 2 : a small discrete lump in the substance of an organ or in the skin; *esp* : the specific lesion of tuberculosis consisting of a packed mass of epithelioid cells, giant cells, disintegration products of leukocytes and bacilli, and usu. a necrotic center

tubercle bacillus *n* : a bacterium of the genus *Mycobacterium* (*M. tuberculosis*) that is a causative agent of tuberculosis

tubercul- *or* **tuberculo-** *comb form* 1 : tubercle ⟨*tubercular*⟩ 2 : tubercle bacillus ⟨*tuberculin*⟩ 3 : tuberculosis ⟨*tuberculoid*⟩

¹tu·ber·cu·lar \tü-'bər-kyə-lər, tyü-\ *adj* 1 a : of, relating to, or affected with tuberculosis : TUBERCULOUS **b** : caused by the tubercle bacillus ⟨∼ meningitis⟩ 2 : characterized by lesions that are or resemble tubercles ⟨∼ leprosy⟩ 3 : relating to, resembling, or constituting a tubercle

²tubercular *n* : an individual with tuberculosis

tu·ber·cu·lid \tü-'bər-kyə-lid, tyü-\ *n* : a tuberculous lesion of the skin; *esp* : one that is an id

tu·ber·cu·lin \tü-'bər-kyə-lən, tyü-\ *n* : a sterile liquid containing the growth products of or specific substances extracted from the tubercle bacillus and used in the diagnosis of tuberculosis

tu·ber·cu·lin reaction *n* : TUBERCULIN TEST

tuberculin test *n* : a test for hypersensitivity to tuberculin in which tuberculin is injected usu. into the skin of the individual tested and the appearance of inflammation at the site of injection is construed as indicating past or present tubercular infection — compare MANTOUX TEST

tu·ber·cu·loid \tü-'bər-kyə-ˌlöid, tyü-\ *adj* 1 : resembling tuberculosis and esp. the tubercles characteristic of it 2 : of, relating to, characterized by, or affected with tuberculoid leprosy

tuberculoid leprosy *n* : the one of the two major forms of leprosy that is characterized by the presence of few or no Hansen's bacilli in the lesions and by the loss of sensation in affected areas of the skin — compare LEPROMATOUS LEPROSY

tu·ber·cu·lo·ma \tü-ˌbər-kyə-'lö-mə, tyü-\ *n, pl* **-mas** \-məz\ *also* **-ma·ta** \-mə-tə\ : a large solitary caseous tubercle of tuberculous character occurring esp. in the brain

tu·ber·cu·lo·sis \tü-ˌbər-kyə-'lö-səs, tyü-\ *n, pl* **-lo·ses** \-ˌsēz\ : a usu. chronic highly variable disease that is caused by the tubercle bacillus and rarely in the U.S. by a related mycobacterium (*Mycobacterium bovis*), is usu. communicated by inhalation of the airborne causative agent, affects esp. the lungs but may spread to other areas (as the kidney or spinal column) from local lesions or by way of the lymph or blood vessels, and is characterized by fever, cough, difficulty in breathing, inflammatory infiltrations, formation of tubercles, caseation, pleural effusion, and fibrosis — called also *TB*

¹**tu·ber·cu·lo·stat·ic** \tü-ˌbər-kyə-lö-'statik, tyü-\ *adj* : inhibiting the growth of the tubercle bacillus (a ~ drug)

²**tuberculostatic** *n* : a tuberculostatic agent

tu·ber·cu·lous \tü-'bər-kyə-ləs, tyü-\ *adj* 1 : constituting or affected with tuberculosis 2 : caused by or resulting from the presence or products of the tubercle bacillus (~ peritonitis)

tu·ber·os·i·ty \tü-bə-'rä-sə-tē, tyü-\ *n, pl* **-ties** : a rounded prominence; *esp* : a large prominence on a bone usu. serving for the attachment of muscles or ligaments

tuberous sclerosis *n* : EPILOIA

tu·bo·cu·ra·rine \tü-bō-kyü-'rär-ən, -ˌēn, tyü-\ *n* : a toxic alkaloid or its crystalline hydrated hydrochloride salt $C_{37}H_{41}ClN_2O_6 \cdot HCl \cdot 5H_2O$ that is obtained chiefly from the bark and stems of a So. American vine (*Chondrodendron tomentosum* of the family Menispermaceae) and in its dextrorotatory form constitutes the chief active constituent of curare and is

used esp. as a skeletal muscle relaxant

tu·bo-ovar·i·an \tü-bō-ō-'var-ē-ən, ˌtyü-\ *adj* : of, relating to, or affecting a fallopian tube and ovary (a ~ abscess)

tu·bu·lar \'tü-byə-lər, 'tyü-\ *adj* 1 : having the form of or consisting of a tube 2 : of, relating to, or sounding as if produced through a tube or tubule (~ rales)

tu·bule \'tü-(ˌ)byül, 'tyü-\ *n* : a small tube; *esp* : a slender elongated anatomical channel

tu·bu·lin \'tü-byə-lən, 'tyü-\ *n* : a globular protein that polymerizes to form microtubules

tu·bu·lo·aci·nar \tü-byə-lō-'a-sə-nər, ˌtyü-\ *or* **tu·bu·lo·aci·nous** \-nəs\ *adj* : TUBULOALVEOLAR

tu·bu·lo·al·ve·o·lar \tü-byə-lō-al-'vē-ə-lər, ˌtyü-\ *adj* : of, relating to, or being a gland having branching tubules which end in secretory alveoli

tu·bu·lo·in·ter·sti·tial \tü-byə-lō-ˌin-tər-'sti-shəl, ˌtyü-\ *adj* : affecting or involving the tubules and interstitial tissue of the kidney (~ disease)

tu·bu·lus \'tü-byə-ləs, 'tyü-\ *n, pl* **tu·bu·li** \-ˌlī\ : TUBULE

tuck \'tək\ *n* : a cosmetic surgical operation for the removal of excess skin or fat from a body part — see TUMMY TUCK

Tu·i·nal \'tü-i-ˌnäl\ *trademark* — used for a preparation of amobarbital and secobarbital

tu·lar·ae·mia *chiefly Brit var of* TULAREMIA

tu·la·re·mia \ˌtü-lə-'rē-mē-ə, ˌtyü-\ *n* : an infectious disease esp. of wild rabbits, rodents, humans, and some domestic animals that is caused by a bacterium (*Francisella tularensis*), is transmitted esp. by the bites of insects, and in humans is marked by symptoms (as fever) of toxemia — called also *rabbit fever* — **tu·la·re·mic** \-mik\ *adj*

tulle gras \ˌtül-'grä\ *n* : fine-meshed gauze impregnated with a fatty substance (as soft paraffin)

tu·me·fa·cient \ˌtü-mə-'fā-shənt, ˌtyü-\ *adj* : producing swelling

tu·me·fac·tion \-'fak-shən\ *n* 1 : an action or process of swelling or becoming tumorous 2 : SWELLING

tu·me·fac·tive \-'fak-tiv\ *adj* : producing swelling (~ lesions)

tu·mes·cence \tü-'mes-ᵊns, tyü-\ *n* : the quality or state of being tumescent; *esp* : readiness for sexual activity marked esp. by vascular congestion of the sex organs

tu·mes·cent \-'mes-ᵊnt\ *adj* : somewhat swollen (~ tissue)

tummy tuck *n* : a surgical operation for removal of excess skin and fat in the abdominal area

tu·mor \'tü-mər, 'tyü-\ *n* : an abnormal benign or malignant mass of tissue that is not inflammatory, arises without obvious cause from cells of preexistent tissue, and possesses no physiological function — compare CANCER 1, CARCINOMA, SARCOMA — **tu·mor·al** \'t(y)ü-mə-rəl\ *adj* — **tu·mor·like** \-,lïk\ *adj*

tu·mor·i·cid·al \,tü-mə-rə-'sïd-°l, ,tyü-\ *adj* : destroying tumor cells ⟨∼ activity⟩

tu·mor·i·gen·ic \-'je-nik\ *adj* : producing or tending to produce tumors; *also* : CARCINOGENIC — **tu·mor·i·gen·e·sis** \-'je-nə-səs\ *n* — **tu·mor·i·ge·nic·i·ty** \-jə-'ni-sə-tē\ *n*

tumor–infiltrating lymphocyte *n* : a T cell that is isolated from a malignant tumor, cultured with interleukin-2, and injected back into the patient as a tumor-killing cell and that has greater cytotoxicity than lymphokine-activated killer cells — called also *TIL*

tumor necrosis factor *n* : a protein that is produced by monocytes and macrophages in response esp. to endotoxins and that activates leukocytes and has antitumor activity — abbr. *TNF*

tu·mor·ous \'tü-mə-rəs, 'tyü-\ *adj* : of, relating to, or resembling a tumor

tumor virus *n* : a virus (as Rous sarcoma virus) that causes neoplastic or cancerous growth

tu·mour *chiefly Brit var of* TUMOR

Tun·ga \'təŋ-gə\ *n* : a genus of fleas (family Tungidae) that include the chigoe (*T. penetrans*)

tung·sten \'təŋ-stən\ *n* : a gray-white high-melting ductile metallic element — called also *wolfram*; symbol *W*; see ELEMENT table

tu·nic \'tü-nik, 'tyü-\ *n* : an enclosing or covering membrane or tissue : TUNICA (the ∼*s* of the eye)

tu·ni·ca \'tü-ni-kə, 'tyü-\ *n, pl* **tu·ni·cae** \-nə-,kē, -,kï, -,sē\ : an enveloping membrane or layer of body tissue

tunica adventitia *n* : ADVENTITIA

tunica al·bu·gin·ea \-,al-bu-'ji-nē-ə, -byü-\ *n, pl* **tunicae al·bu·gin·e·ae** \-'ji-nē-,ē, -,ï\ : a white fibrous capsule esp. of the testis

tunica intima *n* : INTIMA

tunica media *n* : MEDIA

tunica mucosa *n* : mucous membrane and esp. that lining the digestive tract

tunica muscularis *n* : MUSCULAR COAT

tunica pro·pria \-'prō-prē-ə\ *n* : LAMINA PROPRIA

tunica va·gi·na·lis \-,va-jə-'nā-ləs, -,na-\ *n, pl* **tunicae va·gi·na·les** \-(,)lez\ : a pouch of serous membrane covering the testis and derived from the peritoneum

tuning fork *n* : a 2-pronged metal implement that gives a fixed tone when struck

tun·nel \'tən-°l\ *n* : a bodily channel — see CARPAL TUNNEL

tunnel of Cor·ti \-'kȯr-tē\ *n* : a spiral passage in the organ of Corti

tunnel vision *n* : constriction of the visual field resulting in loss of peripheral vision

tur·bel·lar·i·an \,tər-bə-'lar-ē-ən\ *n* : any of a class (Turbellaria) of mostly aquatic and free-living flatworms — **turbellarian** *adj*

tur·bid \'tər-bəd\ *adj* : thick or opaque with matter in suspension : cloudy or muddy in appearance ⟨∼ urine⟩ — **tur·bid·i·ty** \tər-'bi-də-tē\ *n*

tur·bi·dim·e·ter \,tər-bə-'di-mə-tər\ *n* 1 : an instrument for measuring and comparing the turbidity of liquids by viewing light through them and determining how much light is cut off 2 : NEPHELOMETER — **tur·bi·di·met·ric** \,tər-bə-də-'me-trik, ,tər-,bi-\ *adj* — **tur·bi·dim·e·try** \,tər-bə-'di-mə-trē\ *n*

¹**tur·bi·nate** \'tər-bə-nət, -,nāt\ *adj* : of, relating to, or being a nasal concha

²**turbinate** *n* : NASAL CONCHA

turbinate bone *also* **tur·bi·nat·ed bone** \'tər-bə-,nā-təd-\ *n* : NASAL CONCHA

turcica — see SELLA TURCICA

turf toe *n* : a minor but painful usu. sports-related injury involving hyperextension of the big toe resulting in sprain of the ligament of the metatarsophalangeal joint

tur·ges·cent \,tər-'jes-°nt\ *adj* : becoming turgid, distended, or swollen — **tur·ges·cence** \-'jes-°ns\ *n*

tur·gid \'tər-jəd\ *adj* : being in a normal or abnormal state of distension : SWOLLEN ⟨∼ limbs⟩ — **tur·gid·i·ty** \,tər-'ji-də-tē\ *n*

tur·gor \'tər-gər, -,gȯr\ *n* : the normal state of turgidity and tension in living cells

tu·ris·ta \tü-'rē-stə\ *n* : intestinal sickness and diarrhea commonly affecting a tourist in a foreign country; *esp* : MONTEZUMA'S REVENGE

turn \'tərn\ *vb* : to injure by twisting or wrenching ⟨∼*ed* his ankle⟩

Tur·ner's syndrome \'tər-nərz-\ *n* : a genetically determined condition that is associated with the presence of only one complete X chromosome and no Y chromosome and that is characterized by a female phenotype with underdeveloped and infertile ovaries

  Turner, Henry Hubert (1892–1970), American endocrinologist.

tur·ri·ceph·a·ly \,tər-ə-'se-fə-lē\ *n, pl* **-lies** : OXYCEPHALY

tus·sive \'tə-siv\ *adj* : of, relating to, or involved in coughing ⟨∼ force⟩

T wave \'tē-,wāv\ *n* : the deflection in an electrocardiogram that represents the electrical activity produced by ventricular repolarization — compare P WAVE, QRS COMPLEX

Tween \'twēn\ *trademark* — used for any of several preparations of polysorbates

tween–brain \'twēn-,brān\ *n* : DIENCEPHALON

tweez·ers \'twē-zərz\ *n sing or pl* : any of various small metal instruments that are usu. held between the thumb and forefinger, are used for plucking, holding, or manipulating, and consist of two legs joined at one end

twelfth cranial nerve *n* : HYPOGLOSSAL NERVE

twelve–year molar *n* : any of the second permanent molar teeth which erupt at about 12 years of age and include four of which one is located on each side of the upper and lower jaws — compare SIX-YEAR MOLAR

twen·ty–twen·ty *or* **20/20** *adj* : having the normal visual acuity of the human eye that according to one common scale can distinguish at a distance of 20 feet characters one-third inch in diameter

twig \'twig\ *n* : a minute branch of a nerve or artery

twi·light sleep \'twī-ˌlīt-\ *n* : a state in which awareness of pain is dulled and memory of pain is dimmed or effaced and which is produced by hypodermic injection of morphine and scopolamine and used esp. formerly chiefly in childbirth

twilight state *n* : a dreamy state lacking touch with present reality, occurring in epilepsy, hysteria, and schizophrenia, and sometimes induced with narcotics

¹twin \'twin\ *adj* : born with one other or as a pair at one birth ⟨∼ girls⟩

²twin *n* : either of two offspring produced at a birth — **twin·ship** \-ˌship\ *n*

twinge \'twinj\ *n* : a sudden sharp stab of pain

twin·ning \'twi-niŋ\ *n* : the bearing of twins

twitch \'twich\ *n* : a short spastic contraction of muscle fibers; *also* : a slight jerk of a body part caused by such a contraction — **twitch** *vb*

two–egg *adj* : DIZYGOTIC ⟨∼ twins⟩

2,4–D \ˌtü-ˌfȯr-'dē\ *n* : a white crystalline irritant compound $C_8H_6Cl_2O_3$ used as a weed killer — called also *2,4-dichlorophenoxyacetic acid*; see AGENT ORANGE

2,4,5–T \-ˌfīv-'tē\ *n* : an irritant compound $C_8H_5Cl_3O_3$ used esp. as an herbicide and defoliant — called also *trichlorophenoxyacetic acid*; see AGENT ORANGE

two–winged fly *n* : FLY 2

ty·ba·mate \'tī-bə-ˌmāt\ *n* : a tranquilizing drug $C_{13}H_{26}N_2O_4$

ty·lec·to·my \tī-'lek-tə-mē\ *n*, *pl* **-mies** : LUMPECTOMY

Ty·le·nol \'tī-lə-ˌnȯl\ *trademark* — used for a preparation of acetaminophen

ty·lo·sin \'tī-lə-sən\ *n* : an antibacterial antibiotic $C_{45}H_{77}NO_{17}$ from an actinomycete of the genus *Streptomyces* (*S. fradiae*) used in veterinary medicine and as a feed additive

ty·lo·sis \tī-'lō-səs\ *n*, *pl* **ty·lo·ses** \-'lō-sēz\ : a thickening and hardening of the skin : CALLOSITY

tympani — see CHORDA TYMPANI, SCALA TYMPANI, TEGMEN TYMPANI, TENSOR TYMPANI

tym·pan·ic \tim-'pa-nik\ *adj* : of, relating to, or being a tympanum

tympanic antrum *n* : a large air-containing cavity in the mastoid process communicating with the tympanum and often being the location of dangerous inflammation — called also *mastoid antrum*

tympanic canal *n* : SCALA TYMPANI

tympanic cavity *n* : MIDDLE EAR

tympanic membrane *n* : a thin membrane that separates the middle ear from the inner part of the external auditory meatus and functions in the mechanical reception of sound waves and in their transmission to the site of sensory reception — called also *eardrum, tympanum*

tympanic nerve *n* : a branch of the glossopharyngeal nerve arising from the petrosal ganglion and entering the middle ear where it takes part in forming the tympanic plexus — called also *Jacobson's nerve*

tympanic plate *n* : a curved platelike bone that is part of the temporal bone and forms the floor and anterior wall of the external auditory meatus

tympanic plexus *n* : a nerve plexus of the middle ear that is formed by the tympanic nerve and two or three filaments from the carotid plexus, sends fibers to the mucous membranes of the middle ear, the eustachian tube, and the mastoid cells, and gives off the lesser petrosal nerve to the otic ganglion

tym·pa·ni·tes \ˌtim-pə-'nī-tēz\ *n* : a distension of the abdomen caused by accumulation of gas in the intestinal tract or peritoneal cavity

tym·pa·nit·ic \ˌtim-pə-'ni-tik\ *adj* **1** : of, relating to, or affected with tympanites ⟨a ∼ abdomen⟩ **2** : resonant on percussion : hollow-sounding

tym·pa·no·plas·ty \'tim-pə-nō-ˌplas-tē\ *n*, *pl* **-ties** : a reparative surgical operation performed on the middle ear

tym·pa·nos·to·my \ˌtim-pa-'näs-tə-mē\ *n*, *pl* **-mies** : MYRINGOTOMY

tym·pa·not·o·my \ˌtim-pə-'nä-tə-mē\ *n*, *pl* **-mies** : MYRINGOTOMY

tym·pa·num \'tim-pə-nəm\ *n*, *pl* **-na** \-nə\ *also* **-nums 1** : TYMPANIC MEMBRANE **2** : MIDDLE EAR

tym·pa·ny \-nē\ *n*, *pl* **-nies 1** : TYMPANITES **2** : a resonant sound heard in percussion (as of the abdomen)

¹type \'tīp\ *n* : a particular kind, class, or group ⟨personality ∼s⟩; *specif* : a group distinguishable on physiological or serological bases ⟨salmonella ∼s⟩

²type *vb* **typed; typ·ing** : to determine the type of (as a sample of blood or a culture of bacteria)

type A *adj* : relating to, characteristic of, having, or being a personality that is marked by impatience, aggressiveness, and competitiveness and that is held to be associated with increased risk of cardiovascular disease

type B *adj* : relating to, characteristic of, having, or being a personality that is marked by a lack of excessive aggressiveness and tension and that is held to be associated with reduced risk of cardiovascular disease

type C *adj* : relating to or being any of the oncornaviruses in which the structure containing the nucleic acid is spherical and centrally located

type I diabetes *n* : INSULIN-DEPENDENT DIABETES MELLITUS — called also *type I diabetes mellitus*

type II diabetes *n* : NON-INSULIN-DEPENDENT DIABETES MELLITUS — called also *type II diabetes mellitus*

¹**ty•phoid** \'tī-,fóid, (,)tī-'\ *adj* 1 : of, relating to, or suggestive of typhus 2 : of, relating to, affected with, or constituting typhoid fever

²**typhoid** *n* 1 : TYPHOID FEVER 2 : any of several diseases of domestic animals resembling human typhus or typhoid fever

ty•phoi•dal \tī-'fóid-³l\ *adj* : of, relating to, or resembling typhoid fever

typhoid fever *n* : a communicable disease marked by fever, diarrhea, prostration, headache, splenomegaly, eruption of rose-colored spots, leukopenia, and intestinal inflammation and caused by a bacterium of the genus *Salmonella* (*S. typhi*)

ty•phus \'tī-fəs\ *n* : any of various bacterial diseases caused by rickettsial bacteria: as **a** : a severe human febrile disease that is caused by one (*Rickettsia prowazekii*) transmitted esp. by body lice and is marked by high fever, stupor alternating with delirium, intense headache, and a dark red rash — called also *louse-borne typhus* **b** : MURINE TYPHUS **c** : TSUTSUGAMUSHI DISEASE

typhus fever *n* : TYPHUS

ty•ra•mine \'tī-rə-,mēn\ *n* : a phenolic amine C₈H₁₁NO that is found in various foods and beverages (as cheese and red wine), has a sympathomimetic action, and is derived from tyrosine

ty•ro•ci•dine *also* **ty•ro•ci•din** \,tī-rə-'sīd-³n\ *n* : a basic polypeptide antibiotic produced by a soil bacterium of the genus *Bacillus* (*B. brevis*) and constituting the major component of tyrothricin

Ty•rode solution \'tī-,rōd-\ *or* **Ty•rode's solution** \-,rōdz-\ *n* : physiological saline containing sodium chloride 0.8, potassium chloride 0.02, calcium chloride 0.02, magnesium chloride 0.01, sodium bicarbonate 0.1, and sodium dihydrogen phosphate 0.005 percent

> **Tyrode, Maurice Vejux (1878–1930),** American pharmacologist.

ty•ro•sin•ae•mia *chiefly Brit var of* TYROSINEMIA

ty•ro•sine \'tī-rə-,sēn\ *n* : a phenolic amino acid C₉H₁₁NO₃ that is a precursor of several important substances (as epinephrine and melanin)

tyrosine hydroxylase *n* : an enzyme that catalyzes the first step in the biosynthesis of catecholamines (as dopamine and norepinephrine)

ty•ro•sin•emia \,tī-rō-si-'nē-mē-ə\ *n* : a rare inherited disorder of tyrosine metabolism that is characterized by abnormally high concentrations of tyrosine in the blood and urine with associated abnormalities esp. of the liver and kidneys

ty•ro•sin•osis \,tī-rō-si-'nō-səs\ *n* : a condition of faulty metabolism of tyrosine marked by the excretion of unusual amounts of tyrosine in the urine

ty•ro•sin•uria \,tī-rō-si-'nŭr-ē-ə, -'nyur-\ *n* : the excretion of tyrosine in the urine

ty•ro•thri•cin \,tī-rə-'thrīs-³n\ *n* : an antibiotic mixture that consists chiefly of tyrocidine and gramicidin, is usu. extracted from a soil bacterium of the genus *Bacillus* (*B. brevis*), and is used for local applications esp. for infection caused by gram-positive bacteria

U

¹**U** *abbr* uracil

²**U** *symbol* uranium

ubi•qui•none \yū-'bi-kwə-,nōn, ,yü-bi-kwi-'nōn\ *n* : any of a group of lipid-soluble quinones that function in the part of cellular respiration comprising oxidative phosphorylation

ud•der \'ə-dər\ *n* : a large pendulous organ (as of a cow) consisting of two or more mammary glands enclosed in a common envelope and each provided with a single nipple

¹**ul•cer** \'əl-sər\ *n* : a break in skin or mucous membrane with loss of surface tissue, disintegration and necrosis of epithelial tissue, and often pus (a stomach ∼)

²**ulcer** *vb* **ul•cered; ul•cer•ing** : ULCERATE

ul•cer•ate \'əl-sə-,rāt\ *vb* **-at•ed; -at•ing** : to become affected with or as if with an ulcer — **ul•cer•a•tion** \,əl-sə-'rā-shən\ *n*

ul•cer•a•tive \'əl-sə-,rā-tiv, -rə-\ *adj* : of, relating to, or characterized by an ulcer or by ulceration

ulcerative colitis *n* : a nonspecific inflammatory disease of the colon of unknown cause characterized by diarrhea with discharge of mucus and blood, cramping abdominal pain, and inflammation and edema of the mucous membrane with patches of ulceration

ulcero- *comb form* **1** : ulcer (*ulcero*genic) **2** : ulcerous and (*ulcero*glandular)

ul·cero·gen·ic \əl-sə-rō-'je-nik\ *adj* : tending to produce or develop into ulcers or ulceration (an ~ drug)

ul·cero·glan·du·lar \əl-sə-rō-'glan-jə-lər\ *adj* : being a type of tularemia in which the place of infection is the skin where a papule and then an ulcer develops with enlargement of the lymph nodes in the associated region

ul·cero·mem·bra·nous gingivitis \əl-sə-rō-'mem-brə-nəs-\ *n* : VINCENT'S ANGINA

ul·cer·ous \'əl-sə-rəs\ *adj* **1** : characterized or caused by ulceration **2** : affected with an ulcer

ul·cus \'əl-kəs\ *n, pl* **ul·cera** \'əl-sə-rə\ : ULCER

ul·na \'əl-nə\ *n, pl* **ul·nae** \-nē\ *or* **ul·nas** : the bone on the little-finger side of the forearm that forms with the humerus the elbow joint and serves as a pivot in rotation of the hand

¹ul·nar \'əl-nər\ *adj* **1** : of or relating to the ulna **2** : located on the same side of the forearm as the ulna

²ulnar *n* : an ulnar anatomical part (as the ulnar nerve or the ulnar artery)

ulnar artery *n* : an artery that is the larger of the two terminal branches of the brachial artery, runs along the ulnar side of the forearm, and gives off near its origin the anterior and posterior ulnar recurrent arteries

ulnar collateral artery — see INFERIOR ULNAR COLLATERAL ARTERY, SUPERIOR ULNAR COLLATERAL ARTERY

ulnaris — see EXTENSOR CARPI ULNARIS, FLEXOR CARPI ULNARIS

ulnar nerve *n* : a large superficial nerve of the arm that is a continuation of the medial cord of the brachial plexus, passes around the elbow superficially in a groove between the olecranon and the medial epicondyle of the humerus, and continues down the inner side of the forearm to supply the skin and muscles of the little-finger side of the forearm and hand — see FUNNY BONE

ulnar notch *n* : the narrow medial concave surface on the lower end of the radius that articulates with the ulna

ulnar recurrent artery *n* : either of the two small branches of the ulnar artery arising from its medial side: **a** : one that arises just below the elbow and supplies the brachialis muscle and the pronator teres — called also *anterior ulnar recurrent artery* **b** : one that is larger, arises lower on the arm, and supplies the elbow and associated muscles — called also *posterior ulnar recurrent artery*

ulnar vein *n* : any of several deep veins of the forearm that accompany the ulnar artery and unite at the elbow with the radial veins to form the brachial veins

ul·tra·cen·tri·fuge \əl-trə-'sen-tri-fyüj\ *n* : a high-speed centrifuge able to sediment colloidal and other small particles and used esp. in determining sizes of such particles and molecular weights of large molecules — **ul·tra·cen·trif·u·gal** \-sen-'tri-fyə-gəl, -fi-\ *adj* — **ul·tra·cen·tri·fu·ga·tion** \-sen-trə-fyü-'gā-shən\ *n* — **ultracentrifuge** *vb*

ul·tra·fil·tra·tion \əl-trə-fil-'trā-shən\ *n* : filtration through a medium (as a semipermeable capillary wall) which allows small molecules (as of water) to pass but holds back larger ones (as of protein) — **ul·tra·fil·tra·ble** \-'fil-trə-bəl\ *adj* — **ul·tra·fil·trate** \-'fil-trāt\ *n*

ul·tra·mi·cro·scope \əl-trə-'mī-krə-skōp\ *n* : an apparatus for making visible by scattered light particles too small to be perceived by the ordinary microscope — called also *dark-field microscope* — **ul·tra·mi·cros·co·py** \-mī-'kräs-kə-pē\ *n*

ul·tra·mi·cro·scop·ic \-mī-krə-'skä-pik\ *also* **ul·tra·mi·cro·scop·i·cal** \-pi-kəl\ *adj* **1** : too small to be seen with an ordinary microscope — compare MACROSCOPIC, MICROSCOPIC 2, SUBMICROSCOPIC **2** : of or relating to an ultramicroscope — **ul·tra·mi·cro·scop·i·cal·ly** *adv*

ul·tra·mi·cro·tome \-'mī-krə-tōm\ *n* : a microtome for cutting extremely thin sections for electron microscopy — **ul·tra·mi·crot·o·my** \-mī-'krä-tə-mē\ *n*

ul·tra·son·ic \-'sä-nik\ *adj* **1** : SUPERSONIC: **a** : having a frequency above the human ear's audibility limit of about 20,000 cycles per second — used of waves and vibrations **b** : utilizing, produced by, or relating to ultrasonic waves or vibrations (removal of tartar with an ~ scaler) **2** : ULTRASOUND — **ul·tra·son·i·cal·ly** *adv*

ul·tra·sono·gram \-'sä-nə-gram\ *n* : ECHOGRAM

ul·tra·so·nog·ra·pher \əl-trə-sə-'nä-grə-fər\ *n* : a specialist in the use of ultrasound

ul·tra·so·nog·ra·phy \-fē\ *n, pl* **-phies** : ULTRASOUND 2 — **ul·tra·so·no·graph·ic** \-sä-nə-'gra-fik, -sō-\ *adj*

¹ul·tra·sound \'əl-trə-saund\ *n* **1** : vibrations of the same physical nature as sound but with frequencies above the range of human hearing **2** : the diagnostic or therapeutic use of ultrasound and esp. a technique involving the formation of a two-dimensional image used for the examination and measurement of internal body structures and the detection of bodily abnormalities — called also *echography, sonography, ultrasonography* **3** : a diagnostic examination using ultrasound

²ultrasound *adj* : of, relating to, performed by, using, or expert in ultrasound ⟨an ∼ technician⟩ ⟨∼ imaging⟩

ul·tra·vi·o·let \\ˌəl-trə-ˈvī-ə-lət\\ *adj* 1 : situated beyond the visible spectrum at its violet end — used of radiation having a wavelength shorter than wavelengths of visible light and longer than those of X rays 2 : relating to, producing, or employing ultraviolet radiation — **ultraviolet** *n*

ultraviolet microscope *n* : a microscope equipped to irradiate material under examination with ultraviolet radiation in order to detect or study fluorescent components — called also *fluorescence microscope*

um·bi·lec·to·my \\ˌəm-bi-ˈlek-tə-mē\\ *n*, *pl* **-mies** : OMPHALECTOMY

um·bil·i·cal \\ˌəm-ˈbi-li-kəl\\ *adj* 1 : of, relating to, or used at the umbilicus ⟨∼ infection⟩ 2 : of or relating to the central abdominal region that is situated between the right and left lumbar regions and between the epigastric region above and the hypogastric region below

umbilical artery *n* : either of a pair of arteries that arise from the fetal hypogastric arteries and pass through the umbilical cord to the placenta to which they carry the deoxygenated blood from the fetus

umbilical cord *n* : a cord arising from the navel that connects the fetus with the placenta and contains the two umbilical arteries and the umbilical vein

umbilical hernia *n* : a hernia of abdominal viscera at the umbilicus

umbilical ligament — see MEDIAL UMBILICAL LIGAMENT, MEDIAN UMBILICAL LIGAMENT

umbilical vein *n* : a vein that passes through the umbilical cord to the fetus and returns the oxygenated and nutrient blood from the placenta to the fetus

umbilical vesicle *n* : the yolk sac of a mammalian embryo having a transitory connection with the alimentary canal by way of the omphalomesenteric duct

um·bil·i·cat·ed \\ˌəm-ˈbi-lə-ˌkā-təd\\ *adj* : having a small depression that resembles an umbilicus ⟨∼ vesicles⟩ — **um·bil·i·cate** \\-ˌkāt\\ *vb*

um·bi·li·cus \\ˌəm-bə-ˈlī-kəs, ˌəm-ˈbi-li-\\ *n*, *pl* **um·bi·li·ci** \\ˌəm-bə-ˈlī-ˌsī, -ˌkī; ˌəm-ˈbi-lə-ˌkī, -ˌkē\\ *or* **um·bi·li·cus·es** : NAVEL

um·bo \\ˈəm-(ˌ)bō\\ *n*, *pl* **um·bo·nes** \\ˌəm-ˈbō-(ˌ)nēz\\ *or* **um·bos** : an elevation in the tympanic membrane of the ear

un·anes·the·tized \\ˌən-ə-ˈnes-thə-ˌtīzd\\ *adj* : not having been subjected to an anesthetic

un·bal·anced \\ˌən-ˈba-lənst\\ *adj* : mentally disordered or deranged

un·blind·ed \\-ˈblīn-dəd\\ *adj* : made or done with knowledge of significant facts by the participants : not blind

⟨an ∼ study of a drug's effectiveness⟩

un·born \\-ˈborn\\ *adj* : not yet born : existing in utero ⟨∼ children⟩

un·bro·ken \\-ˈbrō-kən\\ *adj* : not broken ⟨∼ skin⟩ ⟨an ∼ blister⟩

un·cal \\ˈeŋ-kəl\\ *adj* : of or relating to the uncus ⟨the ∼ region⟩

un·cal·ci·fied \\ˌən-ˈkal-sə-ˌfīd\\ *adj* : not calcified ⟨∼ osteoid tissue⟩

uncal herniation *n* : downward displacement of the uncus and adjacent structures into the tentorial notch

unci *pl of* UNCUS

un·ci·form \\ˈən-sə-ˌform\\ *n* : HAMATE

unciform bone *n* : HAMATE

Un·ci·nar·ia \\ˌən-sə-ˈnar-ē-ə\\ *n* : a genus of hookworms (family Ancylostomatidae) now usu. restricted to a few parasites of carnivorous mammals but formerly often including most of the common hookworms

un·ci·nate fasciculus \\ˈən-sə-ˌnāt-\\ *n* : a hook-shaped bundle of long association fibers connecting the frontal lobe with the anterior portion of the temporal lobe

uncinate fit *n* : a psychomotor epileptic seizure that is characterized by hallucinations of taste and odor and disturbances of consciousness and that originates in the region of the uncus

un·cir·cum·cised \\ˌən-ˈsər-kəm-ˌsīzd\\ *adj* : not circumcised

un·com·pen·sat·ed \\-ˈkäm-pən-ˌsā-təd, -ˌpen-\\ *adj* 1 : accompanied by a change in the pH of the blood ⟨∼ acidosis⟩ ⟨∼ alkalosis⟩ — compare COMPENSATED 2 : not corrected or affected by physiological compensation ⟨∼ congestive heart failure⟩

un·com·pli·cat·ed \\ˌən-ˈkäm-plə-ˌkā-təd\\ *adj* : not involving or marked by complications ⟨∼ peptic ulcer⟩

un·con·di·tion·al \\ˌən-kən-ˈdi-shə-nəl\\ *adj* : UNCONDITIONED 2

un·con·di·tioned \\-ˈdi-shənd\\ *adj* 1 : not dependent on or subjected to conditioning or learning 2 : producing an unconditioned response

¹un·con·scious \\ˌən-ˈkän-chəs\\ *adj* 1 : not marked by conscious thought, sensation, or feeling ⟨∼ motivation⟩ 2 : of or relating to the unconscious 3 : having lost consciousness ⟨was ∼ for three days⟩ — **un·con·scious·ly** *adv* — **un·con·scious·ness** *n*

²unconscious *n* : the greater part of the psychic apparatus accumulated through life experience that is not ordinarily integrated or available to consciousness yet is manifested as a powerful motive force in overt behavior esp. in neurosis and is often revealed (as through dreams, slips of the tongue, or dissociated acts) — compare SUBCONSCIOUS

un·con·trolled \\ˌən-kən-ˈtrōld\\ *adj* : not being under control ⟨∼ diabetes⟩

un·co·or·di·nat·ed \\-kō-ˈord-ᵊn-ˌā-təd\\ *adj* : not coordinated : lacking proper or effective coordination ⟨∼ muscles⟩

un·crossed \-ˈkröst\ adj : not forming a decussation ⟨an ~ tract of nerve fibers⟩

unc·tu·ous \ˈəŋk-chə-wəs, -shə-\ adj : rich in oil or fat : FATTY

un·cur·able \ˌən-ˈkyür-ə-bəl\ adj : INCURABLE

un·cus \ˈəŋ-kəs\ n, pl **un·ci** \ˈən-ˌsī\ : a hooked anatomical part or process; specif : the anterior curved end of the hippocampal gyrus

un·de·cy·le·nic acid \ˌən-ˌde-sə-ˈle-nik-, -ˌlē-\ n : an acid $C_{11}H_{20}O_2$ used in the treatment of fungal infections (as ringworm) of the skin

¹**un·der** \ˈən-dər\ adv : in or into a condition of unconsciousness ⟨put the patient ~ prior to surgery⟩

²**under** prep : receiving or using the action or application of ⟨an operation performed ~ local anesthesia⟩

³**under** adj : being in an induced state of unconsciousness

un·der·achiev·er \ˌən-dər-ə-ˈchē-vər\ : a person and esp. a student who fails to achieve his or her potential or does not do as well as expected — **un·der·achieve** \-ˈchēv\ vb — **un·der·achieve·ment** \-mənt\ n

un·der·ac·tive \-ˈak-tiv\ adj : characterized by an abnormally low level of activity ⟨an ~ thyroid gland⟩ — **un·der·ac·tiv·i·ty** \-ˌak-ˈti-və-tē\ n

un·der·arm \ˈən-dər-ˌärm\ n : ARMPIT

un·der·cut \ˈən-dər-ˌkət\ n : the part of a tooth lying between the gum and the points of maximum outward bulge on the tooth's surfaces

un·der·de·vel·oped \ˌən-dər-di-ˈve-ləpt\ adj : not normally or adequately developed ⟨~ muscles⟩ — **un·der·de·vel·op·ment** \-əp-mənt\ n

un·der·dos·age \-ˈdō-sij\ n : the administration or taking of an insufficient dose ⟨~ of a drug⟩

un·der·feed \ˌən-dər-ˈfēd\ vb **-fed** \-ˈfed\ ; **-feed·ing** : to feed with too little food

un·der·nour·ished \ˌən-dər-ˈnər-isht\ adj : supplied with less than the minimum amount of the foods essential for sound health and growth — **un·der·nour·ish·ment** \-ˈnər-ish-mənt\ n

un·der·nu·tri·tion \-nü-ˈtri-shən, -nyü-\ n : deficient bodily nutrition due to inadequate food intake or faulty assimilation — **un·der·nu·tri·tion·al** \-shə-nəl\ adj

un·der·sexed \-ˈsekst\ adj : deficient in sexual desire

un·der·shot \ˈən-dər-ˌshät\ adj : having the lower incisor teeth or lower jaw projecting beyond the upper when the mouth is closed — used chiefly of animals

un·der·tak·er \ˈən-dər-ˌtā-kər\ n : one whose business is to prepare the dead for burial and to arrange and manage funerals — called also *mortician*

un·der·ven·ti·la·tion \ˌən-dər-ˌven-ti-ˈlā-shən\ n : HYPOVENTILATION

un·der·weight \-ˈwāt\ adj : weighing less than the normal amount

un·de·scend·ed \ˌən-di-ˈsen-dəd\ : retained within the inguinal region rather than descending into the scrotum ⟨an ~ testis⟩

un·de·vel·oped \ˌən-di-ˈve-ləpt\ adj : lacking in development : not developed ⟨physiologically ~⟩

un·di·ag·nos·able \-ˌdī-ig-ˈnō-sə-bəl\ adj : not capable of being diagnosed

un·di·ag·nosed \-ˈnōst\ adj : not diagnosed : eluding diagnosis ⟨~ disease⟩

un·dif·fer·en·ti·at·ed \-ˌdi-fə-ˈren-chē-ˌā-təd\ adj : not differentiated ⟨an ~ sarcoma⟩

un·di·gest·ed \ˌən-dī-ˈjes-təd\ adj : not digested ⟨~ food⟩

un·di·gest·ible \-dī-ˈjes-tə-bəl\ adj : not capable of being digested

un·du·lant fever \ˈən-jə-lənt-, -dyə-\ : BRUCELLOSIS a

un·erupt·ed \ˌən-i-ˈrəp-təd\ adj, of a tooth : not yet having emerged through the gum

un·fer·til·ized \-ˈfərt-ᵊl-ˌīzd\ adj : not fertilized ⟨an ~ egg⟩

ung abbr [Latin *unguentum*] ointment — used in writing prescriptions

un·gual \ˈəŋ-gwəl, ˈən-\ adj : of or relating to a fingernail or toenail

un·guent \ˈəŋ-gwənt, ˈən-jənt\ n : a soothing or healing salve : OINTMENT

un·guis \ˈəŋ-gwəs, ˈən-\ n, pl **un·gues** \-ˌgwēz\ : a fingernail or toenail

un·gu·late \ˈəŋ-gyə-lət, ˈən-, -ˌlāt\ n : a hoofed typically herbivorous quadruped mammal (as a ruminant, swine, camel, or horse) of an evolutionarily diverse group formerly considered a major mammalian taxon (Ungulata) — **ungulate** adj

Unh symbol unnilhexium

un·healed \-ˈhēld\ adj : not healed

un·health·ful \-ˈhelth-fəl\ adj : detrimental to good health ⟨~ working conditions⟩ — **un·health·ful·ness** n

un·healthy \-ˈhel-thē\ adj **un·health·i·er; -est** 1 : not conducive to health ⟨an ~ climate⟩ 2 : not in good health : SICKLY — **un·health·i·ness** n

un·hy·gien·ic \ˌən-ˌhi-ˈje-nik, -ˈjē-, -jē-ˈe-\ adj : not healthful or sanitary — **un·hy·gien·i·cal·ly** \-ni-k(ə-)lē\ adv

uni·cel·lu·lar \ˌyü-ni-ˈsel-yə-lər\ adj : having or consisting of a single cell ⟨~ organisms⟩ — **uni·cel·lu·lar·i·ty** \-ˌsel-yə-ˈlar-ə-tē\ n

uni·fo·cal \ˌyü-ni-ˈfō-kəl\ adj : arising from or occurring in a single focus or location ⟨~ infection⟩

uni·la·mel·lar \ˌyü-ni-lə-ˈme-lər\ adj : having only one lamella or layer

uni·lat·er·al \ˌyü-ni-ˈla-tə-rəl\ adj : occurring on, performed on, or affecting one side of the body or one of its parts ⟨~ exophthalmos⟩ — **uni·lat·er·al·ly** adv

uni·loc·u·lar \ˌyü-ni-ˈlä-kyə-lər\ adj : containing a single cavity

un·im·mu·nized \(ˌ)ən-'i-myə-ˌnīzd\ *adj* : not immunized

un·in·fect·ed \ˌən-in-'fek-təd\ *adj* : free from infection (an ∼ fracture)

uni·nu·cle·ate \ˌyü-ni-'nü-klē-ət, -'nyü-\ *also* **uni·nu·cle·at·ed** \-ˌā-təd\ *adj* : having a single nucleus : MONONUCLEAR

union \'yü-nyən\ *n* : an act or instance of uniting or joining two or more things into one: as **a** : the growing together of severed parts (∼ of a fractured bone) **b** : the joining of two germ cells in the process of fertilization

uni·ovu·lar \ˌyü-nē-'ä-vyə-lər\ *adj* : MONOZYGOTIC (∼ twins)

unip·a·ra \yü-'ni-pə-rə\ *n, pl* **-ras** *or* **-rae** : a woman who has borne one child

uni·pen·nate \ˌyü-ni-'pe-ˌnāt\ *adj* : having the fibers arranged obliquely and inserting into a tendon on one side only in the manner of a feather barbed on one side (a ∼ muscle)

uni·po·lar \ˌyü-ni-'pō-lər\ *adj* 1 : having, produced by, or acting by a single magnetic or electrical pole (a ∼ ECG lead) 2 : having but one process (a ∼ neuron) 3 : relating to or being a manic-depressive disorder in which there is a depressive phase only (∼ depressive illness)

un·ir·ra·di·at·ed \ˌun-ir-'ā-dē-ˌā-təd\ *adj* : not having been exposed to radiation (∼ lymphocytes)

unit \'yü-nət\ *n* 1 : an amount of a biologically active agent (as a drug or antigen) required to produce a specific result under strictly controlled conditions (a ∼ of penicillin) 2 : a molecule or portion of a molecule esp. as combined in a larger molecule

unit·age \'yü-nə-tij\ *n* 1 : specification of the amount constituting a unit (as of a vitamin) 2 : amount in units (a ∼ of 50,000 per capsule)

unit membrane *n* : a 3-layered membrane that consists of an inner lipid layer surrounded by a protein layer on each side

¹**uni·va·lent** \ˌyü-ni-'vā-lənt\ *n* : a chromosome that lacks a synaptic mate

²**univalent** *adj* 1 : MONOVALENT 1 2 : being a chromosomal univalent 3 *of an antibody* : capable of agglutinating or precipitating but not both : having only one combining group

universal antidote *n* : an antidote for ingested poisons having activated charcoal as its principal ingredient

universal donor *n* 1 : the blood group O characterized by a serum that does not agglutinate the cells of any other ABO blood group 2 **a** : a person with blood group O blood **b** : the blood of such a person

universal recipient *n* 1 : the blood group AB characterized by a serum that is not agglutinated by any other ABO blood group 2 **a** : a person with blood

group AB blood **b** : the blood of such a person

un·la·beled *or* **un·la·belled** \ˌən-'lā-bəld\ *adj* : not labeled esp. with an isotopic label

un·la·bored \ˌən-'lā-bərd\ *adj* : produced without exertion, pain, or undue effort (∼ breathing)

un·my·elin·at·ed \-'mī-ə-lə-ˌnā-təd\ *adj* : lacking a myelin sheath (∼ axons)

Un·na's boot \'ü-nəz-\ *or* **Un·na boot** \-nə-\ *n* : a compression dressing for varicose veins or ulcers consisting of a paste made of zinc oxide, gelatin, glycerin, and water

Unna, Paul Gerson (1850–1929), German dermatologist.

Unna's paste boot *n* : UNNA'S BOOT

un·nil·hex·i·um \ˌyün-əl-'hek-sē-əm\ *n* : the chemical element of atomic number 106 — symbol *Unh;* see ELEMENT table

un·nil·pen·ti·um \ˌyün-əl-'pen-tē-əm\ *n* : the chemical element of atomic number 105 — symbol *Unp;* see ELEMENT table

un·nil·qua·di·um \ˌyün-əl-'kwä-dē-əm\ *n* : the chemical element of atomic number 104 — symbol *Unq;* see ELEMENT table

un·of·fi·cial \ˌən-ə-'fi-shəl\ *adj* : not official; *specif* : of, relating to, or being a drug not described in the *U.S. Pharmacopeia* and *National Formulary* — compare NONOFFICIAL, OFFICIAL

un·os·si·fied \-'ä-sə-ˌfīd\ *adj* : not ossified

un·ox·y·gen·at·ed \-'äk-si-jə-ˌnā-təd, -ˌäk-'si-jə-\ *adj* : not oxygenated (∼ blood)

Unp *symbol* unnilpentium

un·paired \-'pard\ *adj* 1 **a** : not paired; *esp* : not matched or mated **b** : characterized by the absence of pairing (electrons in the ∼ state) 2 : situated in the median plane of the body (an ∼ anatomical part); *also* : not matched by a corresponding part on the opposite side

un·pig·ment·ed \-'pig-mən-təd\ *adj* : not pigmented : having no pigment

Unq *symbol* unnilquadium

un·re·ac·tive \-rē-'ak-tiv\ *adj* : not reactive (pupils ∼ to light)

un·re·solved \-ri-'zäld, -'zólvd\ *adj* : not resolved : not having undergone resolution (∼ pneumonia)

un·re·spon·sive \ˌən-ri-'spän-siv\ *adj* : not responsive (as to a stimulus or treatment) — **un·re·spon·sive·ness** *n*

un·san·i·tary \-'sa-nə-ˌter-ē\ *adj* : not sanitary : INSANITARY (∼ conditions)

un·sat·u·rate \-'sa-chə-rət\ *n* : an unsaturated chemical compound

un·sat·u·rat·ed \-'sa-chə-ˌrā-təd\ *adj* : not saturated: as **a** : capable of absorbing or dissolving more of something (an ∼ solution) **b** : able to form products by chemical addition; *esp* : containing double or triple bonds between carbon atoms ⟨∼ oils⟩ — **un-sat-u-ra-tion** \-₁sa-chə-'rā-shən\ n

un-seg-ment-ed \-'seg-₁men-təd\ adj : not divided into or made up of segments

un-sound \-'saůnd\ adj : not sound: as **a** : not healthy or whole ⟨an ∼ limb⟩ **b** : not mentally normal : not wholly sane ⟨of ∼ mind⟩ **c** : not fit to be eaten ⟨∼ food⟩ — **un-sound-ness** n

un-sta-ble \-'stā-bəl\ adj : not stable: as **a** : characterized by frequent or unpredictable changes ⟨a patient in ∼ condition⟩ **b** : readily changing in chemical composition or biological activity **c** : characterized by inability to control the emotions

unstable angina n : angina pectoris characterized by sudden changes ⟨as an increase in the severity or length of anginal attacks or a decrease in the exertion required to precipitate an attack⟩ esp. when symptoms were previously stable

un-stri-at-ed muscle \₁ən-'strī-₁ā-təd-\ n : SMOOTH MUSCLE

un-struc-tured \-'strək-chərd\ adj : lacking structure : not formally organized ⟨∼ psychological tests⟩

un-trau-ma-tized \-'traů-mə-₁tīzd, -'trỏ-\ adj : not subjected to trauma ⟨∼ skin⟩

un-treat-ed \-'trē-təd\ adj : not subjected to treatment ⟨an ∼ disease⟩ — **un-treat-able** \-'trē-tə-bəl\ adj

un-vac-ci-nat-ed \-'vak-sə-₁nā-təd\ adj : not vaccinated ⟨∼ children⟩

un-well \-'wel\ adj **1** : being in poor health : SICK **2** : undergoing menstruation

¹up-per \'ə-pər\ n : an upper tooth or denture

²upper n : a stimulant drug; esp : AMPHETAMINE

upper jaw n : JAW 1a

upper respiratory adj : of, relating to, or affecting the upper respiratory tract ⟨upper respiratory infection⟩

upper respiratory tract n : the part of the respiratory system including the nose, nasal passages, and nasopharynx — compare LOWER RESPIRATORY TRACT

up-set \'əp-₁set\ n **1** : a minor physical disorder ⟨a stomach ∼⟩ **2** : an emotional disturbance — **upset** \(₁)əp-'set\ vb — **upset** \'əp-₁set\ adj

up-stream \₁əp-'strēm\ adv or adj : in a direction along a molecule of DNA or RNA opposite to that in which transcription and translation take place and toward the end having a hydroxyl group attached to the position labeled 5' in the terminal nucleotide — compare DOWNSTREAM

up-take \'əp-₁tāk\ n : an act or instance of absorbing and incorporating something esp. into a living organism

ur- or **uro-** comb form **1** : urine ⟨uric⟩ **2** : urinary tract ⟨urology⟩ **3** : urinary and ⟨urogenital⟩ **4** : urea ⟨uracil⟩

ura-chal \'yůr-ə-kəl\ adj : of or relating to the urachus ⟨a ∼ cyst⟩

ura-chus \-kəs\ n : a cord of fibrous tissue extending from the bladder to the umbilicus and constituting the functionless remnant of a part of the duct of the allantois of the embryo

ura-cil \'yůr-ə-₁sil, -səl\ n : a pyrimidine base $C_4H_4N_2O_2$ that is one of the four bases coding genetic information in the polynucleotide chain of RNA — compare ADENINE, CYTOSINE, GUANINE, THYMINE

ur-ae-mia chiefly Brit var of UREMIA

ura-ni-um \yů-'rā-nē-əm\ n : a silvery heavy radioactive metallic element that exists naturally as a mixture of three isotopes of mass number 234, 235, and 238 — symbol U; see ELEMENT table

uranium 235 n : a light isotope of uranium of mass number 235 that is physically separable from natural uranium and that when bombarded with slow neutrons undergoes rapid fission into smaller atoms with the release of neutrons and atomic energy

urate \'yůr-₁āt\ n : a salt of uric acid

ure- or **ureo-** comb form : urea ⟨urease⟩

urea \yů-'rē-ə\ n : a soluble weakly basic nitrogenous compound CH_4N_2O that is the chief solid component of mammalian urine and an end product of protein decomposition and that is administered intravenously as a diuretic drug

urea-plas-ma \yů-'rē-ə-₁plaz-mə\ n **1** cap : a genus of mycoplasmas (family Mycoplasmataceae) that are able to hydrolyze urea with the formation of ammonia and that include one ⟨U. urealyticum⟩ found in the human genitourinary tract, oropharynx, and anal canal **2** : a mycoplasma of the genus Ureaplasma

ure-ase \'yůr-ē-₁ās, -₁āz\ n : an enzyme that catalyzes the hydrolysis of urea into ammonia and carbon dioxide

Ure-cho-line \₁yůr-ə-'kō-₁lēn\ trademark — used for a preparation of bethanechol

ure-mia \yů-'rē-mē-ə\ n **1** : accumulation in the blood of constituents normally eliminated in the urine that produces a severe toxic condition and usu. occurs in severe kidney disease **2** : the toxic bodily condition associated with uremia — **ure-mic** \-mik\ adj

ure-ter \'yůr-ə-tər, yů-'rē-tər\ n : either of the paired ducts that carry away urine from a kidney to the bladder or cloaca and that in humans are slender membranous epithelium-lined flat tubes about sixteen inches (41 centimeters) long which open above into the pelvis of a kidney and below into the back part of the same side of the bladder — **ure-ter-al** \yů-'rē-tə-rəl\ or **ure-ter-ic** \₁yůr-ə-'ter-ik\ adj

ure-ter-ec-ta-sis \₁yůr-ə-tər-'ek-tə-səs,

yù-₁rē-tər-\ *n, pl* -ta·ses \-₁sēz\ : dilation of a ureter

ure·ter·ec·to·my \₁yúr-ə-tər-ˈek-tə-mē, yù-ˈrē-tər-\ *n, pl* -mies : surgical excision of all or part of a ureter

ure·ter·itis \₁yùr-ə-tər-ˈī-təs, yù-ˈrē-tər-\ *n* : inflammation of a ureter

uretero- *comb form* 1 : ureter ⟨*ureter*ography⟩ 2 : ureteral and ⟨*ureter*oileal⟩

ure·tero·cele \yù-ˈrē-tə-rə-₁sēl\ *n* : cystic dilation of the lower part of a ureter into the bladder

ure·tero·en·ter·os·to·my \yù-₁rē-tə-rō-₁en-tə-ˈräs-tə-mē\ *n, pl* -mies : surgical formation of an artificial opening between a ureter and the intestine

ure·tero·gram \yù-ˈrē-tə-rə-₁gram\ *n* : an X-ray photograph of the ureters after injection of a radiopaque substance — ure·ter·og·ra·phy \yù-ˌrē-tə-ˈrä-grə-fē, ₁yúr-ə-tə-\ *n*

ure·tero·il·e·al \yù-₁rē-tə-rō-ˈi-lē-əl\ *adj* : relating to or connecting a ureter and the ileum

ure·tero·li·thot·o·my \yù-₁rē-tə-rō-li-ˈthä-tə-mē\ *n, pl* -mies : removal of a calculus by incision of a ureter

ure·ter·ol·y·sis \₁yùr-ə-tər-ˈä-lə-səs, yù-₁rē-tər-\ *n, pl* -y·ses \-₁sēz\ : a surgical procedure to free a ureter from abnormal adhesions or surrounding tissue (as in retroperitoneal fibrosis)

ure·tero·neo·cys·tos·to·my \yù-₁rē-tər-ō-₁nē-ō-sis-ˈtäs-tə-mē\ *n, pl* -mies : surgical reimplantation of a ureter into the bladder

ure·tero·pel·vic \yù-₁rē-tə-rō-ˈpel-vik\ *adj* : of, relating to, or involving a ureter and the adjoining renal pelvis ⟨∼ obstruction⟩

ure·tero·plas·ty \yù-ˈrē-tə-rə-₁plas-tē\ *n, pl* -ties : a plastic operation performed on a ureter

ure·tero·py·elog·ra·phy \yù-₁rē-tə-rō-₁pī-ə-ˈlä-grə-fē\ *n, pl* -phies : X-ray photography of a renal pelvis and a ureter following the injection of a radiopaque medium

ure·tero·py·elo·ne·os·to·my \yù-₁rē-tə-rō-₁pī-ə-lō-nē-ˈäs-tə-mē\ *n, pl* -mies : surgical creation of a new channel joining a renal pelvis to a ureter

ure·tero·py·e·los·to·my \-₁pī-ə-ˈläs-tə-mē\ *n, pl* -mies : URETEROPYELONEOSTOMY

ure·ter·or·rha·phy \yù-₁rē-tə-ˈrór-ə-fē, ₁yúr-ə-tə-\ *n, pl* -phies : the surgical operation of suturing a ureter

ure·tero·sco·py \yù-₁rē-tə-ˈräs-kə-pē, ₁yúr-ə-tə-\ *n, pl* -pies : visual examination of the interior of a ureter

ure·tero·sig·moid·os·to·my \yù-₁rē-tə-rō-₁sig-₁moi-ˈdäs-tə-mē\ *n, pl* -mies : surgical implantation of a ureter in the sigmoid flexure

ure·ter·os·to·my \₁yùr-ə-tər-ˈäs-tə-mē, yù-₁rē-tər-\ *n, pl* -mies : surgical creation of an opening on the surface of the body for the ureters

ure·ter·ot·o·my \₁yùr-ə-tər-ˈä-tə-mē,

yù-₁rē-tər-\ *n, pl* -mies : the operation of cutting into a ureter

ure·tero·ure·ter·os·to·my \yù-₁rē-tə-rō-yù-₁rē-tər-ˈäs-tə-mē\ *n, pl* -mies : surgical establishment of an artificial communication between two ureters or between different parts of the same ureter

ure·tero·ves·i·cal \yù-₁rē-tə-rō-ˈve-si-kəl\ *adj* : of or relating to the ureters and the urinary bladder

ure·thane \ˈyùr-ə-₁thān\ *or* ure·than \-₁than\ *n* : a crystalline compound $C_3H_7NO_2$ that is used esp. as a solvent and medicinally as an antineoplastic agent — called also *ethyl carbamate*

urethr- *or* urethro- *comb form* : urethra ⟨*urethr*itis⟩ ⟨*urethro*scope⟩

ure·thra \yù-ˈrē-thrə\ *n, pl* -thras *or* -thrae \-(₁)thrē\ : the canal that carries off the urine from the bladder and in the male serves also as a genital duct — ure·thral \-thrəl\ *adj*

urethral crest *n* : a narrow longitudinal fold or ridge along the posterior wall or floor of the female urethra or the prostatic portion of the male urethra

urethral gland *n* : any of the small mucous glands in the wall of the urethra — see GLAND OF LITTRÉ

urethral intercourse *n* : sexual intercourse in which the penis is inserted into the female urethra

urethral sphincter *n* : SPHINCTER URETHRAE

ure·threc·to·my \₁yùr-i-ˈthrek-tə-mē\ *n, pl* -mies : total or partial surgical excision of the urethra

ure·thri·tis \₁yùr-i-ˈthrī-təs\ *n* : inflammation of the urethra

ure·thro·cele \yə-ˈrē-thrə-₁sēl\ *n* : a pouched protrusion of urethral mucous membrane in the female

ure·thro·cu·ta·ne·ous \yù-₁rē-thrō-kyù-ˈtā-nē-əs\ *adj* : of, relating to, or joining the urethra and the skin

ure·thro·cys·tog·ra·phy \yù-₁rē-thrō-sis-ˈtä-grə-fē\ *n, pl* -phies : roentgenography of the urethra and bladder that utilizes a radiopaque substance

ure·throg·ra·phy \₁yùr-i-ˈthrä-grə-fē\ *n, pl* -phies : roentgenography of the urethra after injection of a radiopaque substance

ure·thro·pexy \yù-ˈrē-thrə-₁pek-sē\ *n, pl* -pex·ies : surgical fixation to nearby tissue of a displaced urethra that is causing incontinence by placing stress on the opening from the bladder

ure·thro·plas·ty \yù-ˈrē-thrə-₁plas-tē\ *n, pl* -ties : plastic surgery of the urethra

ure·thro·rec·tal \yù-₁rē-thrō-ˈrekt-əl\ *adj* : of, relating to, or joining the urethra and the rectum ⟨a ∼ fistula⟩

ure·thror·rha·phy \₁yùr-ə-ˈthrór-ə-fē\ *n, pl* -phies : suture of the urethra for an injury or fistula

ure·thro·scope \yù-ˈrē-thrə-₁skōp\ *n*

: an instrument for viewing the interior of the urethra — **ure·thro·scop·ic** \ yů-ˌrē-thrə-ˈskä-pik\ *adj* — **ure·thros·co·py** \ˌyůr-ə-ˈthräs-kə-pē\ *n*

ure·thros·to·my \ˌyůr-ə-ˈthräs-tə-mē\ *n, pl* **-mies** : the creation of a surgical opening between the perineum and the urethra

ure·throt·o·my \ˌyůr-ə-ˈthrä-tə-mē\ *n, pl* **-mies** : surgical incision into the urethra esp. for the relief of stricture

ure·thro·vag·i·nal \ yů-ˌrē-thrō-ˈva-jən-ᵊl\ *adj* : of, relating to, or joining the urethra and the vagina (a ∼ fistula)

ur·gen·cy \ˈər-jən-sē\ *n, pl* **-cies** : a compelling desire to urinate or defecate due to some abnormal stress

ur·gin·ea \ər-ˈji-nē-ə\ *n* **1** *cap* : a genus of bulbous herbs native to the Old World and esp. to the Mediterranean region — see SQUILL 2 *often cap* : squill for medicinal use composed of the sliced young bulbs of the squill (*Urginea indica*) of the Orient — used in the British Pharmacopoeia

URI *abbr* upper respiratory infection

-uria \ˈyůr-ē-ə, ˈyůr-\ *n comb form* **1** : presence of (a specified substance) in urine (albumin*uria*) **2** : condition of having (such) urine (poly*uria*); *esp* : abnormal or diseased condition marked by the presence of (a specified substance) (py*uria*)

uric \ˈyůr-ik\ *adj* : of, relating to, or found in urine

uric- or **urico-** *comb form* : uric acid (*urico*suric)

uric acid *n* : a white odorless and tasteless nearly insoluble acid $C_5H_4N_4O_3$ that is present in small quantity in human urine and occurs pathologically in renal calculi and the tophi of gout

uric·ac·id·uria \ˌyůr-ik-ˌa-sə-ˈdůr-ē-ə, -ˈdyůr-\ *n* : the presence of excess uric acid in the urine

uri·cae·mia *chiefly Brit var of* URICEMIA

uri·ce·mia \ˌyůr-ə-ˈsē-mē-ə\ *n* : HYPERURICEMIA — **uri·ce·mic** \-mik\ *adj*

uri·co·su·ric \ˌyůr-i-kə-ˈsůr-ik, -ˈsyůr-\ *adj* : relating to or promoting the excretion of uric acid in the urine

uri·dine \ˈyůr-ə-ˌdēn\ *n* : a pyrimidine nucleoside $C_9H_{12}N_2O_6$ that is composed of uracil attached to ribose and plays an important role in carbohydrate metabolism

urin- or **urino-** *comb form* — see UR- (*urinary*)

urinae — see DETRUSOR URINAE

uri·nal \ˈyůr-ən-ᵊl\ *n* **1** : a vessel so constructed that it can be used for urination by a bedridden patient **2** : a container worn by a person with urinary incontinence

uri·nal·y·sis \ˌyůr-ə-ˈna-lə-səs\ *n, pl* **-yses** \-ˌsēz\ : chemical analysis of urine

uri·nary \ˈyůr-ə-ˌner-ē\ *adj* **1** : relating to, occurring in, or constituting the organs concerned with the formation and discharge of urine **2** : of, relating

to, or for urine **3** : excreted as or in urine

urinary bladder *n* : a distensible membranous sac that serves for the temporary retention of the urine, is situated in the pelvis in front of the rectum, receives the urine from the two ureters, and discharges it at intervals into the urethra through an orifice closed by a sphincter

urinary calculus *n* : a calculus occurring in any portion of the urinary tract and esp. in the pelvis of the kidney — called also *urinary stone, urolith*

urinary system *n* : the organs of the urinary tract comprising the kidneys, ureters, urinary bladder, and urethra

urinary tract *n* : the tract through which urine passes and which consists of the renal tubules and renal pelvis, the ureters, the bladder, and the urethra

uri·nate \ˈyůr-ə-ˌnāt\ *vb* **-nat·ed; -nat·ing** : to discharge urine

uri·na·tion \ˌyůr-ə-ˈnā-shən\ *n* : the act of urinating — called also *micturition*

urine \ˈyůr-ən\ *n* : waste material that is secreted by the kidney, is rich in end products (as urea, uric acid, and creatinine) of protein metabolism together with salts and pigments, and forms a clear amber and usu. slightly acid fluid

uri·nif·er·ous tubule \ˌyůr-ə-ˈni-fə-rəs\ *n* : a tubule of the kidney that collects or conducts urine

uri·no·ma \ˌyůr-ə-ˈnō-mə\ *n, pl* **-mas** or **-ma·ta** \-mə-tə\ : a cyst that contains urine

uri·nom·e·ter \ˌyůr-ə-ˈnä-mə-tər\ *n* : a small hydrometer for determining the specific gravity of urine

uro- — see UR-

uro·bi·lin \ˌyůr-ə-ˈbī-lən\ *n* : any of several brown bile pigments formed from urobilinogens and found in normal feces, in normal urine in small amounts, and in pathological urines in larger amounts

uro·bi·lin·o·gen \ˌyůr-ə-bī-ˈli-nə-jən, -ˌjen\ *n* : any of several chromogens that are reduction products of bilirubin

uro·ca·nic acid \ˌyůr-ə-ˈkä-nik-, -ˈka-\ *n* : a crystalline acid $C_6H_6N_2O_2$ normally present in human skin that is held to act as a screening agent for ultraviolet radiation

uro·dy·nam·ics \ˌyůr-ə-dī-ˈna-miks\ *n* : the hydrodynamics of the urinary tract — **uro·dy·nam·ic** \-mik\ *adj*

uro·ery·thrin \ˌyůr-ō-ˈer-ə-thrən\ *n* : a pink or reddish pigment found in many pathological urines and also frequently in normal urine in very small quantity

uro·gas·trone \ˌyůr-ə-ˈgas-ˌtrōn\ *n* : a polypeptide that has been isolated from urine and inhibits gastric secretion — compare ENTEROGASTRONE

uro·gen·i·tal \ˌyùr-ō-ᵊje-nə-tᵊl\ *adj* : of, relating to, affecting, treating, or being the organs or functions of excretion and reproduction

urogenital diaphragm *n* : a double layer of pelvic fascia with its included muscle that is situated between the ischial and pubic rami, supports the prostate in the male, is traversed by the vagina in the female, gives passage to the membranous part of the urethra, and encloses the sphincter urethrae

urogenital sinus *n* : the ventral part of the embryonic mammalian cloaca that eventually forms the neck of the bladder and some of the more distal portions of the genitourinary tract

urogenital system *n* : GENITOURINARY TRACT

urogenital tract *n* : GENITOURINARY TRACT

uro·gram \ˈyùr-ə-ˌgram\ *n* : a roentgenogram made by urography

urog·ra·phy \yù-ˈrä-grə-fē\ *n, pl* **-phies** : roentgenography of a part of the urinary tract (as a kidney or ureter) after injection of a radiopaque substance — **uro·graph·ic** \ˌyùr-ə-ˈgra-fik\ *adj*

uro·ki·nase \ˌyùr-ō-ˈkī-ˌnās, -ˌnāz\ *n* : an enzyme that is produced by the kidney and is found in urine, that activates plasminogen, and that is used therapeutically to dissolve blood clots (as in the heart)

uro·lag·nia \ˌyùr-ō-ˈlag-nē-ə\ *n* : sexual excitement associated with urine or with urination

uro·lith \ˈyùr-ə-ˌlith\ *n* : URINARY CALCULUS

uro·lith·i·a·sis \ˌyùr-ə-li-ˈthī-ə-səs\ *n, pl* **-a·ses** \-ˌsēz\ : a condition that is characterized by the formation or presence of calculi in the urinary tract

urol·o·gist \yù-ˈrä-lə-jist\ *n* : a physician who specializes in urology

urol·o·gy \-jē\ *n, pl* **-gies** : a branch of medicine dealing with the urinary or urogenital organs — **uro·log·ic** \ˌyùr-ə-ˈlä-jik\ *also* **uro·log·i·cal** \-ji-kəl\ *adj*

urop·a·thy \yù-ˈrä-pə-thē\ *n, pl* **-thies** : a disease of the urinary or urogenital organs — **uro·path·ic** \ˌyùr-ə-ˈpa-thik\ *adj*

uro·pep·sin \ˌyùr-ō-ˈpep-sən\ *n* : a proteolytic hormone found in urine esp. in cases of peptic ulcers and other disorders of the digestive tract

uro·por·phy·rin \ˌyùr-ō-ˈpòr-fə-rən\ *n* : any of four isomeric porphyrins C₄₀H₃₈N₄O₁₆ closely related to the coproporphyrins

uro·ra·di·ol·o·gy \ˌyùr-ō-ˌrā-dē-ˈä-lə-jē\ *n, pl* **-gies** : radiology of the urinary tract — **uro·ra·dio·log·ic** \-ˌrā-dē-ə-ˈlä-jik\ *adj*

uros·co·py \yùr-ˈäs-kə-pē\ *n, pl* **-pies** : examination or analysis of the urine

uro·sep·sis \ˌyùr-ō-ˈsep-səs\ *n, pl* **-sep·ses** \-ˌsēz\ : a toxic condition caused

by the extravasation of urine into bodily tissues

uros·to·my \yù-ˈräs-tə-mē\ *n, pl* **-mies** : an ostomy for the elimination of urine from the body

Urot·ro·pin \yùr-ˈä-trə-pən\ *trademark* — used for a preparation of methenamine

ur·so·de·oxy·cho·lic acid \ˌər-sō-dē-ˌäk-sē-ˈkō-lik-\ *n* : URSODIOL

ur·so·di·ol \ˌər-sō-ˈdī-ˌol, -ˌōl\ *n* : a bile acid C₂₄H₄₀O₄ stereoisomeric with chenodeoxycholic acid that is used to dissolve uncalcified radiolucent gallstones — called also *ursodeoxycholic acid*

ur·ti·ca \ˈ ər-ti-kə\ *n* **1** *cap* : a genus of widely distributed plants of the nettle family (family Urticaceae) comprising the nettles with leaves having stinging hairs **2** : NETTLE 1

ur·ti·car·ia \ˌər-tə-ˈkar-ē-ə\ *n* : HIVES — **ur·ti·car·i·al** \-ē-əl\ *adj*

urticata — see ACNE URTICATA

uru·shi·ol \yù-ˈrü-shē-ˌol, -ˌōl\ *n* : an oily toxic irritant mixture present in poison ivy and some related plants of the genus *Rhus*

USAN *abbr* United States Adopted Names — used to designate officially recognized nonproprietary names of drugs as established by a joint committee of medical and pharmaceutical professionals

us·nic acid \ˈ əs-nik-\ *n* : a yellow crystalline antibiotic C₁₈H₁₆O₇ that is obtained from various lichens (as *Usnea barbata*)

USP *abbr* United States Pharmacopeia

uta \ˈü-tə\ *n* : a leishmaniasis of the skin occurring in Peru : ESPUNDIA

ut dict *abbr* [Latin *ut dictum*] as directed — used in writing prescriptions

uter- *or* **utero-** \ *for 2,* ˌyù-tə-rō\ *comb form* **1** : uterus ⟨*uterosalpingography*⟩ **2** : uterine and ⟨*utero*placental⟩

uteri *pl of* UTERUS

uter·ine \ˈyü-tə-rən, -ˌrīn\ *adj* : of, relating to, occurring in, or affecting the uterus ⟨∼ tissue⟩ ⟨∼ cancer⟩

uterine artery *n* : an artery that arises from the internal iliac artery and supplies the uterus and adjacent parts and during pregnancy the placenta

uterine gland *n* : any of the branched tubular glands in the mucous membrane of the uterus

uterine plexus *n* : a plexus of veins tributary to the internal iliac vein by which blood is returned from the uterus

uterine tube *n* : FALLOPIAN TUBE

uterine vein *n* : any of the veins that make up the uterine plexus

utero-ovar·ian \ˌyù-tə-(ˌ)rō-ō-ˈvar-ē-ən\ *adj* : of or relating to the uterus and the ovary ⟨∼ blood flow⟩

utero·pla·cen·tal \-plə-ˈsent-ᵊl\ *adj* : of or relating to the uterus and the placenta ⟨∼ circulation⟩

utero·sa·cral ligament \ˌyü-tə-rō-ˈsa-krəl-, -ˈsä-\ *n* : a fibrous fascial band on each side of the uterus that passes along the lateral wall of the pelvis from the uterine cervix to the sacrum and that serves to support the uterus and hold it in place — called also *sacrouterine ligament*

utero·sal·pin·gog·ra·phy \-ˌsal-ˌpiŋ-ˈgä-grə-fē\ *n, pl* **-phies** : HYSTEROSALPINGOGRAPHY

utero·ton·ic \ˌyü-tə-rō-ˈtä-nik\ *adj* : stimulating muscular tone in the uterus (a ~ substance)

utero·tub·al \-ˈtü-bəl, -ˈtyü-\ *adj* : of or relating to the uterus and fallopian tubes

utero·vag·i·nal \-ˈva-jən-əl\ *adj* : of or relating to the uterus and the vagina

utero·ves·i·cal pouch \-ˈve-si-kəl\ *n* : a pouch formed by the peritoneum between the uterus and the bladder

uter·us \ˈyü-tə-rəs\ *n, pl* **uteri** \-ˌrī\ *also* **uter·us·es** : an organ in female mammals for containing and usu. for nourishing the young during development previous to birth that has thick walls consisting of an external serous coat, a very thick muscular coat of smooth muscle, and a mucous coat containing numerous glands — called also *womb*; see CERVIX 2a, CORPUS UTERI

UTI *abbr* urinary tract infection

utilization review *n* : the critical examination of health-care services esp. to detect wasteful practices and unnecessary care

utri·cle \ˈyü-tri-kəl\ *n* : a small anatomical pouch: as a : the part of the membranous labyrinth of the ear into which the semicircular canals open — called also *utriculus* b : PROSTATIC UTRICLE — **utric·u·lar** \yü-ˈtri-kyə-lər\ *adj*

utric·u·lo·sac·cu·lar duct \yü-ˌtri-kyə-lō-ˈsa-kyə-lər-\ *n* : a narrow tube connecting the utricle to the saccule in the membranous labyrinth of the ear

utric·u·lus \yü-ˈtri-kyə-ləs\ *n, pl* **-li** \-ˌlī\ : UTRICLE a

UV *abbr* ultraviolet

UV–A \ˌyü-ˌvē-ˈā\ *n* : the region of the ultraviolet spectrum which is nearest to visible light and extends from 320 to 400 nm in wavelength and from which comes the radiation that causes tanning and contributes to aging of the skin

UV–B \ˌyü-ˌvē-ˈbē\ *n* : the region of the ultraviolet spectrum which extends from 280 to 320 nm in wavelength and from which comes the radiation primarily responsible for sunburn, aging of the skin, and the development of skin cancer

uvea \ˈyü-vē-ə\ *n* : the middle layer of the eye consisting of the iris and ciliary body together with the choroid coat — called also *vascular tunic* — **uve·al** \ˈyü-vē-əl\ *adj*

uve·itis \ˌyü-vē-ˈī-təs\ *n, pl* **uve·it·i·des** \-ˈi-tə-ˌdēz\ : inflammation of the uvea

uveo·pa·rot·id fever \ˌyü-vē-ō-pə-ˈrä-təd-\ *n* : chronic inflammation of the parotid gland and uvea marked by low-grade fever, lassitude, and bilateral iridocyclitis and sometimes associated with sarcoidosis — called also *Heerfordt's syndrome*

uvu·la \ˈyü-vyə-lə\ *n, pl* **-las** \-ləz\ *or* **-lae** \-ˌlē\ 1 : the pendent fleshy lobe in the middle of the posterior border of the soft palate 2 : a lobe of the inferior vermis of the cerebellum located in front of the pyramid — **uvu·lar** \-lər\ *adj*

uvu·lec·to·my \ˌyü-vyə-ˈlek-tə-mē\ *n, pl* **-mies** : surgical excision of the uvula

U wave \ˈyü-ˌ\ *n* : a positive wave following the T wave on an electrocardiogram

V

V *symbol* vanadium

vac·ci·nal \ˈvak-sən-əl, vak-ˈsēn-\ *adj* : of or relating to vaccine or vaccination (~ control of a disease)

vac·ci·nate \ˈvak-sə-ˌnāt\ *vb* **-nat·ed; -nat·ing** 1 : to inoculate (a person) with cowpox virus in order to produce immunity to smallpox 2 : to administer a vaccine to usu. by injection — **vac·ci·na·tor** \-ˌnā-tər\ *n*

vac·ci·na·tion \ˌvak-sə-ˈnā-shən\ *n* 1 : the act of vaccinating 2 : the scar left by vaccinating

vac·cine \vak-ˈsēn, ˈvak-ˌ\ *n* 1 : matter or a preparation containing the virus of cowpox in a form used for vaccination 2 : a preparation of killed microorganisms, living attenuated organisms, or living fully virulent organisms that is administered to produce or artificially increase immunity to a particular disease; *also* : a mixture of several such vaccines

vac·ci·nee \ˌvak-sə-ˈnē\ *n* : a vaccinated individual

vac·cin·ia \vak-ˈsi-nē-ə\ *n* 1 a : COWPOX b : the usu. mild systemic reaction of an individual following vaccination against smallpox 2 : the poxvirus that is the causative agent of cowpox and is used for vaccination against smallpox — **vac·cin·i·al** \-nē-əl\ *adj*

vac·u·o·late \ˈva-kyü-ō-ˌlāt\ *or* **vac·u·o·lat·ed** \-ˌlā-təd\ *adj* : containing one or more vacuoles

vac·u·o·la·tion \ˌva-kyü-ō-ˈlā-shən\ *n* : the development or formation of vacuoles (neuronal ~)

vac·u·ole \'va-kyü-ˌōl\ *n* 1 : a small cavity or space in the tissues of an organism containing air or fluid 2 : a cavity or vesicle in the cytoplasm of a cell usu. containing fluid — **vac·u·o·lar** \ˌva-kyü-ˈō-lər, -ˌlär\ *adj*

vac·u·ol·i·za·tion \ˌva-kyü-ˌō-lə-ˈzā-shən\ *n* : VACUOLATION ⟨∼ of erythroid cells⟩

vac·u·um aspiration \'va-(ˌ)kyüm-, -kyəm-\ *n* : abortion in the early stages of pregnancy by aspiration of the contents of the uterus through a narrow tube — **vacuum aspirator** *n*

VAD \ˌvē-(ˌ)ā-ˈdē\ *n* : an artificial device that is implanted in the chest to assist a damaged or weakened heart in pumping blood — called also *ventricular assist device*

vag- *or* **vago-** *comb form* : vagus nerve ⟨*vagotomy*⟩ ⟨*vagotonia*⟩

va·gal \'vā-gəl\ *adj* : of, relating to, mediated by, or being the vagus nerve — **va·gal·ly** *adv*

vagal escape *n* : resumption of the heartbeat that takes place after stimulation of the vagus nerve has caused it to stop and that occurs despite the continuing of such stimulation

vagal tone *n* : impulses from the vagus nerve producing inhibition of the heartbeat

vagi *pl of* VAGUS

vagin- *also* **vagini-** *comb form* : vagina ⟨*vaginectomy*⟩

va·gi·na \və-ˈji-nə\ *n, pl* **-nae** \-(ˌ)nē\ *or* **-nas** : a canal in a female mammal that leads from the uterus to the external orifice opening into the vestibule between the labia minora

vaginae — see SPHINCTER VAGINAE

vag·i·nal \'va-jən-ᵊl, və-ˈji-nᵊl\ *adj* 1 : of, relating to, or resembling a vagina : THECAL 2 : of, relating to, or affecting the genital vagina — **va·gi·nal·ly** *adv*

vaginal artery *n* : any of the several arteries that supply the vagina and that usu. arise from the internal iliac artery or the uterine artery

vaginal hysterectomy *n* : a hysterectomy performed through the vagina

vaginal process *n* 1 : a projecting lamina of bone on the inferior surface of the petrous portion of the temporal bone that is continuous with the tympanic plate and surrounds the root of the styloid process 2 : either of a pair of projecting laminae on the inferior surface of the sphenoid that articulate with the alae of the vomer

vaginal smear *n* : a smear taken from the vaginal mucosa for cytological diagnosis

vaginal thrush *n* : candidiasis of the vagina or vulva

vag·i·nec·to·my \ˌva-jə-ˈnek-tə-mē\ *n, pl* **-mies** : COLPECTOMY

vag·i·nis·mus \ˌva-jə-ˈniz-məs\ *n* : a painful spasmodic contraction of the vagina

vag·i·ni·tis \ˌva-jə-ˈnī-təs\ *n, pl* **-nit·i·des** \-ˈni-tə-ˌdēz\ : inflammation of the vagina or of a sheath (as a tendon sheath)

vag·i·no·plas·ty \'va-jə-nə-ˌplas-tē\ *n, pl* **-ties** : plastic surgery of the vagina

vago- — see VAG-

va·go·lyt·ic \ˌvā-gə-ˈli-tik\ *adj* : PARASYMPATHOLYTIC ⟨∼ effects⟩ ⟨∼ drugs⟩

va·got·o·my \vā-ˈgä-tə-mē\ *n, pl* **-mies** : surgical division of the vagus nerve — **va·got·o·mize** \-ˌmīz\ *vb*

va·go·to·nia \ˌvā-gə-ˈtō-nē-ə\ *n* : excessive excitability of the vagus nerve resulting typically in vasomotor instability, constipation, and sweating — compare SYMPATHICOTONIA — **va·go·ton·ic** \-ˈtä-nik\ *adj*

va·go·va·gal \ˌvā-gō-ˈvā-gəl\ *adj* : relating to or arising from both afferent and efferent impulses of the vagus nerve ⟨a ∼ reflex⟩

va·gus \'vā-gəs\ *n, pl* **va·gi** \'vā-ˌgī, -ˌjī\ : VAGUS NERVE

vagus nerve *n* : either of the tenth pair of cranial nerves that arise from the medulla and supply chiefly the viscera esp. with autonomic sensory and motor fibers — called also *pneumogastric nerve, tenth cranial nerve, vagus*

va·lence \'vā-ləns\ *n* 1 : the degree of combining power of an element or radical as shown by the number of atomic weights of a monovalent element (as hydrogen) with which the atomic weight of the element or the partial molecular weight of the radical will combine or for which it can be substituted or with which it can be compared 2 : relative capacity to unite, react, or interact (as with antigens or a biological substrate)

-va·lent \'vā-lənt\ *adj comb form* : having (so many) chromosomal strands or homologous chromosomes ⟨*bivalent*⟩

valgum — see GENU VALGUM

val·gus \'val-gəs\ *adj* : turned outward; *esp* : of, relating to, or being a deformity in which an anatomical part is turned outward away from the midline of the body to an abnormal degree ⟨∼ deformity of the ankle⟩ — see CUBITUS VALGUS, HALLUX VALGUS, TALIPES VALGUS; compare GENU VALGUM, GENU VARUM, VARUS — **valgus** *n*

va·line \'vā-ˌlēn, 'va-\ *n* : a crystalline essential amino acid $C_5H_{11}NO_2$

val·in·o·my·cin \ˌva-lə-nō-ˈmīs-ᵊn\ *n* : an antibiotic $C_{54}H_{90}N_6O_{18}$ produced by a bacterium of the genus *Streptomyces* (*S. fulvissimus*)

Val·ium \'va-lē-əm, 'val-yəm\ *trademark* — used for a preparation of diazepam

val·late \'va-ˌlāt\ *adj* : having a raised edge surrounding a depression

vallate papilla *n* : CIRCUMVALLATE PAPILLA

val·lec·u·la \va-ˈle-kyə-lə\ *n, pl* **-lae**

\-ₐlē\ : an anatomical groove, channel, or depression: as a : a groove between the base of the tongue and the epiglottis b : a fossa on the underside of the cerebellum separating the hemispheres and including the inferior vermis — **val·lec·u·lar** \-lər\ *adj*

valley fever *n* : COCCIDIOIDOMYCOSIS

val·pro·ate \val-ˈprō-ₐāt\ *n* : a salt or ester of valproic acid

val·pro·ic acid \val-ˈprō-ik-\ *n* : a valeric-acid derivative $C_8H_{16}O_2$ used as an anticonvulsant esp. in the form of its sodium salt — see SODIUM VALPROATE

Val·sal·va maneuver \val-ˈsal-və-\ *also* **Val·sal·va's maneuver** \-vəz-\ *n* : a forceful attempt at expiration when the airway is closed at some point; *esp* : a conscious effort made while holding the nostrils closed and keeping the mouth shut for the purpose of testing the patency of the eustachian tubes or of adjusting middle ear pressure — called also *Valsalva*

A. M. Valsalva — see SINUS OF VALSALVA

val·va \ˈval-və\ *n, pl* **val·vae** \-ₐvē\ : VALVE

valve \ˈvalv\ *n* 1 : a structure esp. in a vein or lymphatic that closes temporarily a passage or orifice or permits movement of fluid in one direction only 2 : any of various mechanical devices by which the flow of liquid (as blood) may be started, stopped, or regulated by a movable part that opens, shuts, or partially obstructs one or more ports or passageways; *also* : the movable part of such a device

valve of Kerck·ring *or* **valve of Kerkring** \-ˈker-kriŋ\ *n* : PLICAE CIRCULARES

Kerck·ring \ˈker-kriŋ\. **Theodor** (1640-1693), Dutch anatomist.

val·vot·o·my \val-ˈvä-tə-mē\ *n, pl* **-mies** : VALVULOTOMY

valvul- *or* **valvulo-** *comb form* : small valve : fold (*valvulitis*) (*valvulo*tome)

val·vu·la \ˈval-vyə-lə\ *n, pl* **-lae** \-ₐlē, -ₐlī\ : a small valve or fold

val·vu·lae con·ni·ven·tes \-ₐkä-nə-ˈven-ₐtēz\ *n pl* : PLICAE CIRCULARES

val·vu·lar \ˈval-vyə-lər\ *adj* 1 : resembling or functioning as a valve 2 : of, relating to, or affecting a valve esp. of the heart (~ heart disease)

val·vu·li·tis \ₐval-vyə-ˈlī-təs\ *n* : inflammation of a valve esp. of the heart

val·vu·lo·plas·ty \ˈval-vyə-lō-ₐplas-tē\ *n, pl* **-ties** : a plastic operation performed on a heart valve

val·vu·lo·tome \ˈval-vyə-lō-ₐtōm\ *n* : a surgical blade designed for valvulotomy or commissurotomy

val·vu·lot·o·my \ₐval-vyə-ˈlä-tə-mē\ *n, pl* **-mies** : surgical incision of a valve; *specif* : the operation of enlarging a narrowed heart valve by cutting through the mitral commissures with a knife or by a finger thrust to relieve the symptoms of mitral stenosis

vampire bat *n* : any of several Central and So. American bats (*Desmodus rotundus*, *Diaemus youngi*, and *Diphylla ecaudata*) that feed on the blood of birds and mammals and esp. domestic animals and that are sometimes vectors of equine trypanosomiasis and of rabies; *also* : any of several other bats that do not feed on blood but are sometimes reputed to do so

va·na·di·um \və-ˈnā-dē-əm\ *n* : a grayish malleable ductile metallic element — symbol *V*; see ELEMENT table

Van·co·cin \ˈvan-kə-ₐsin\ *trademark* — used for a preparation of vancomycin

van·co·my·cin \ₐvaŋ-kə-ˈmīs-ᵊn\ *n* : an antimicrobial agent from an actinomycete of the genus *Streptomyces* (*S. orientalis*) that is used esp. in the form of its hydrochloride salt against staphylococci resistant to other antibiotics — see VANCOCIN

van den Bergh test \ˈvan-dən-ₐbərg-\ *also* **van den Bergh's test** \-ₐbərgz-\ *n* : a test indicating presence of bilirubin in the blood (as in jaundice)

Van den Bergh, Albert Abraham Hijmans (1869-1943), Dutch physician.

van·il·lyl·man·de·lic acid \ₐva-nə-ₐlil-man-ˈdē-lik-\ *n* : a principal catecholamine metabolite $C_9H_{10}O_5$ whose presence in excess in the urine is used as a test for pheochromocytoma — abbr. *VMA*

van·il·man·de·lic acid \ₐvan-ᵊl-man-ˈdē-lik-\ *n* : VANILLYLMANDELIC ACID

va·por \ˈvā-pər\ *n* : a substance in the gaseous state as distinguished from the liquid or solid state — **va·por·ize** \ˈvā-pə-ₐrīz\ *vb* — **va·por·iz·able** \ˈvā-pə-ˈrī-zə-bəl\ *adj*

va·por·iz·er \ˈvā-pə-ₐrī-zər\ *n* : one that vaporizes: as a : ATOMIZER b : a device for converting water or a medicated liquid into a vapor for inhalation

va·pour *chiefly Brit var of* VAPOR

Va·quez's disease \vä-ˈke-zəz-\ *n* : POLYCYTHEMIA VERA

Vaquez, Louis Henri (1860-1936), French physician.

variable region *n* : the part of the polypeptide chain of a light or heavy chain of an antibody that ends in a free amino group $-NH_2$, that varies greatly in its sequence of amino-acid residues from one immunoglobulin to another, and that prob. determines the conformation of the combining site which confers the specificity of the antibody for a particular antigen — called also *variable domain;* compare CONSTANT REGION

varic- *or* **varico-** *comb form* : varix (*varicosis*) (*varicocele*)

var·i·ce·al \ₐvar-ə-ˈsē-əl, və-ˈri-sē-əl\

adj : of, relating to, or caused by varices 〈∼ hemorrhage〉

var·i·cel·la \ˌvar-ə-ˈse-lə\ *n* : CHICKEN POX

varicella zoster *n* : a herpesvirus that causes chicken pox and shingles — called also *varicella-zoster virus*

var·i·cel·li·form \ˌvar-ə-ˈse-lə-ˌförm\ *adj* : resembling chicken pox 〈a ∼ eruption〉

varices *pl of* VARIX

var·i·co·cele \ˈvar-i-kō-ˌsēl\ *n* : a varicose enlargement of the veins of the spermatic cord producing a soft compressible tumor mass in the scrotum

var·i·co·cel·ec·to·my \ˌvar-i-kō-sē-ˈlek-tə-mē\ *n*, *pl* **-mies** : surgical treatment of varicocele by excision of the affected veins often with removal of part of the scrotum

var·i·cose \ˈvar-ə-ˌkōs\ *also* **var·i·cosed** \-ˌkōst\ *adj* 1 : abnormally swollen or dilated 〈∼ lymph vessels〉 2 : affected with varicose veins 〈∼ legs〉

varicose vein *n* : an abnormal swelling and tortuosity esp. of a superficial vein of the legs — usu. used in pl.

var·i·co·sis \ˌvar-ə-ˈkō-səs\ *n*, *pl* **-co·ses** \-ˌsēz\ : the condition of being varicose or of having varicose vessels

var·i·cos·i·ty \ˌvar-ə-ˈkä-sə-tē\ *n*, *pl* **-ties** 1 : the quality or state of being abnormally or markedly swollen or dilated 2 : VARIX

Var·i·dase \ˈvar-ə-ˌdās\ *trademark* — used for a preparation containing a mixture of streptodornase and streptokinase

va·ri·ety \və-ˈrī-ə-tē\ *n*, *pl* **-et·ies** : any of various groups of plants or animals ranking below a species : SUBSPECIES

va·ri·o·la \və-ˈrī-ə-lə\ *n* : SMALLPOX

variola major *n* : a severe form of smallpox characterized historically by a death rate up to 40% or more

variola minor *n* : a mild form of smallpox of low mortality — called also *alastrim*

var·i·o·la·tion \ˌvar-ē-ə-ˈlā-shən\ *n* : the deliberate inoculation of an uninfected person with the smallpox virus (as by contact with pustular matter) that was widely practiced before the era of vaccination as prophylaxis against the severe form of smallpox

variola vac·cin·ia \-vak-ˈsi-nē-ə\ *n* : COWPOX

var·i·ol·i·form \ˌvar-ē-ˈō-lə-ˌförm\ *adj* : resembling smallpox

varioliformis — see PITYRIASIS LICHENOIDES ET VARIOLIFORMIS ACUTA

va·ri·o·loid \ˈvar-ē-ə-ˌloid, və-ˈrī-ə-ˌloid\ *n* : a modified mild form of smallpox occurring in persons who have been vaccinated or who have had smallpox

var·ix \ˈvar-iks\ *n*, *pl* **var·i·ces** \ˈvar-ə-ˌsēz\ : an abnormally dilated and lengthened vein, artery, or lymph vessel; *esp* : VARICOSE VEIN

Varolii — see PONS VAROLII

varum — see GENU VARUM

var·us \ˈvar-əs\ *adj* : of, relating to, or being a deformity of a bodily part characterized by bending or turning inward toward the midline of the body to an abnormal degree — see CUBITUS VARUS, TALIPES VARUS; compare GENU VALGUM, GENU VARUM, VALGUS — **varus** *n*

vas \ˈvas\ *n*, *pl* **va·sa** \ˈvā-zə\ : an anatomical vessel : DUCT

vas- *or* **vaso-** *comb form* 1 : vessel: as **a** : blood vessel 〈*vaso*motor〉 **b** : vas deferens 〈*vas*ectomy〉 2 : vascular and 〈*vaso*vagal〉

vasa ab·er·ran·tia \-ˌa-bə-ˈran-chə, -chē-ə\ *n pl* : slender arteries that are only occas. present and that connect the axillary or brachial artery with an artery (as the radial artery) of the forearm or with its branches

vas ab·er·rans of Hal·ler \-ˈa-bə-ˌranz . . . -ˈhä-lər\ *n*, *pl* **vasa ab·er·ran·tia of Haller** \ˌa-bə-ˈran-chə-, -chē-ə-\ : a blind tube that is occas. present parallel to the first part of the vas deferens

Haller, Albrecht von (1708–1777), Swiss biologist.

vasa deferentia *pl of* VAS DEFERENS

vasa ef·fer·en·tia \-ˌe-fə-ˈren-chə, -chē-ə\ *n pl* : the 12 to 20 ductules that lead from the rete testis to the vas deferens and except near their commencement are greatly convoluted and form the compact head of the epididymis

va·sal \ˈvā-zəl\ *adj* : of, relating to, or constituting an anatomical vessel

vasa rec·ta \-ˈrek-tə\ *n pl* 1 : numerous small vessels that arise from the terminal branches of arteries supplying the intestine, encircle the intestine, and divide into more branches between its layers 2 : hairpin-shaped vessels that arise from the arteriole leading away from a renal glomerulus, descend into the renal pyramids, reunite as they ascend, and play a role in the concentration of urine

vasa va·so·rum \-vā-ˈsōr-əm\ *n pl* : small blood vessels that supply or drain the walls of the larger arteries and veins and connect with a branch of the same vessel or a neighboring vessel

vascul- *or* **vasculo-** *comb form* : vessel; *esp* : blood vessel 〈*vasculo*toxic〉

vas·cu·lar \ˈvas-kyə-lər\ *adj* 1 : of, relating to, constituting, or affecting a tube or a system of tubes for the conveyance of a body fluid (as blood or lymph) 2 : supplied with or containing ducts and esp. blood vessels — **vas·cu·lar·i·ty** \ˌvas-kyə-ˈlar-ə-tē\ *n*

vascular bed *n* : an intricate network of minute blood vessels that ramifies through the tissues of the body or of one of its parts

vascularis — see STRIA VASCULARIS

vas·cu·lar·iza·tion \ˌvas-kyə-lə-rə-ˈzā-shən\ *n* : the process of becoming

vascular; *also* : abnormal or excessive formation of blood vessels (as in the retina or on the cornea) — **vas-cu-lar-ize** \'vas-kyə-lə-ˌrīz\ *vb*

vascular tunic *n* : UVEA

vas-cu-la-ture \'vas-kyə-lə-ˌchùr, -ˌtyùr, -ˌtùr\ *n* : the arrangement of blood vessels in an organ or part

vas-cu-li-tis \ˌvas-kyə-'lī-təs\ *n, pl* -lit-i-des \-'li-tə-ˌdēz\ : inflammation of a blood or lymph vessel — **vas-cu-lit-ic** \ˌvas-kyə-'li-tik\ *adj*

vas-cu-lo-gen-ic \ˌvas-kyə-lō-'je-nik\ *adj* : caused by disorder or dysfunction of the blood vessels (~ impotence) (~ migraine)

vas-cu-lo-tox-ic \ˌvas-kyə-lō-'täk-sik\ *adj* : destructive to blood vessels or the vascular system (~ effects)

vas def-er-ens \'de-fə-rənz, -ˌrenz\ *n, pl* **vasa def-er-en-tia** \-ˌde-fə-'ren-chə, -chē-ə\ : a spermatic duct that is a small but thick-walled tube about two feet (0.61 meter) long that begins at and is continuous with the tail of the epididymis, runs in the spermatic cord through the inguinal canal, and descends into the pelvis where it joins the duct of the seminal vesicle to form the ejaculatory duct — called also *ductus deferens, spermatic duct*

va-sec-to-my \va-'sek-tə-mē, vā-'zek-\ *n, pl* -mies : surgical division or resection of all or part of the vas deferens usu. to induce sterility — **va-sec-to-mize** \-ˌmīz\ *vb*

Vas-e-line \ˌva-sə-'lēn\ *trademark* — used for a preparation of petroleum jelly

vaso- — see VAS

va-so-ac-tive \ˌvā-zō-'ak-tiv\ *adj* : affecting the blood vessels esp. in respect to the degree of their relaxation or contraction — **va-so-ac-tiv-i-ty** \-ak-'ti-və-tē\ *n*

vasoactive intestinal polypeptide *n* : a protein hormone that consists of a chain of 28 amino-acid residues, has been implicated as a neurotransmitter, and has a wide range of physiological activities (as stimulation of secretion by the pancreas and small intestine, vasodilation, and inhibition of gastric juice production) — abbr. *VIP*; called also *vasoactive intestinal peptide*

va-so-con-stric-tion \ˌvā-zō-kən-'strik-shən\ *n* : narrowing of the lumen of blood vessels esp. as a result of vasomotor action — **va-so-con-stric-tive** \-'strik-tiv\ *adj*

va-so-con-stric-tor \ˌvā-zō-kən-'strik-tər\ *n* : an agent (as a sympathetic nerve fiber or a drug) that induces or initiates vasoconstriction — **vasoconstrictor** *adj*

va-so-de-pres-sor \ˌvā-zō-di-'pre-sər\ *adj* : causing or characterized by a vasomotor depression resulting in lowering of the blood pressure

va-so-di-la-tion \ˌvā-zo-dī-'lā-shən\ *or*

va-so-di-la-ta-tion \-ˌdi-lə-'tā-shən, -ˌdī-\ *n* : widening of the lumen of blood vessels

va-so-di-la-tor \ˌvā-zō-'dī-ˌlā-tər\ *n* : an agent (as a parasympathetic nerve fiber or a drug) that induces or initiates vasodilation — **vasodilator** *also* **va-so-di-la-to-ry** \-'dī-lə-ˌtōr-ē, -'dil-\ *adj*

va-so-for-ma-tive \ˌvā-zō-'fòr-mə-tiv\ *adj* : functioning in the development and formation of vessels and esp. blood vessels (~ cells)

va-sog-ra-phy \vā-'zä-grə-fē\ *n, pl* -phies : roentgenography of blood vessels

va-so-li-ga-tion \ˌvā-zō-lī-'gā-shən\ *n* : surgical ligation of a vessel and esp. of the vas deferens

va-so-mo-tion \ˌvā-zō-'mō-shən\ *n* : alteration in the caliber of blood vessels

va-so-mo-tor \ˌvā-zō-'mō-tər\ *adj* : of, relating to, affecting, or being those nerves or the centers (as in the medulla and spinal cord) from which they arise that supply the muscle fibers of the walls of blood vessels, include sympathetic vasoconstrictors and parasympathetic vasodilators, and by their effect on vascular diameter regulate the amount of blood passing to a particular body part or organ

vasomotor rhinitis *n* : rhinitis caused by an allergen : allergic rhinitis

va-so-pres-sin \ˌvā-zō-'pres-²n\ *n* : a polypeptide hormone that is secreted together with oxytocin by the posterior lobe of the pituitary gland, that is also obtained synthetically, and that increases blood pressure and exerts an antidiuretic effect — called also *antidiuretic hormone*; see PITRESSIN

¹**va-so-pres-sor** \-'pre-sər\ *adj* : causing a rise in blood pressure by exerting a vasoconstrictor effect

²**vasopressor** *n* : a vasopressor agent

vasorum — see VASA VASORUM

va-so-spasm \'vā-zō-ˌspa-zəm\ *n* : sharp and often persistent contraction of a blood vessel reducing its caliber and blood flow — **va-so-spas-tic** \ˌvā-zō-'spas-tik\ *adj*

Va-so-tec \'vā-zō-ˌtek\ *trademark* — used for a preparation of enalapril

va-sot-o-my \vā-'zä-tə-mē\ *n, pl* -mies : surgical incision of the vas deferens

va-so-va-gal \ˌvā-zō-'vā-gəl\ *adj* : of, relating to, or involving both vascular and vagal factors

vasovagal syncope *n* : a usu. transitory condition that is marked by anxiety, nausea, respiratory distress, and fainting and that is believed to be due to joint vasomotor and vagal disturbances

va-so-va-sos-to-my \ˌvā-zō-vā-'zäs-tə-mē\ *n, pl* -mies : surgical anastomosis of a divided vas deferens to reverse a previous vasectomy

Va-sox-yl \vā-'zäk-səl\ *trademark* —

used for a preparation of methoxamine

vas·tus in·ter·me·di·us \'vas-təs-₁in-tər-'mē-dē-əs\ *n* : the division of the quadriceps muscle that arises from and covers the front of the shaft of the femur

vastus in·ter·nus \-in-'tər-nəs\ *n* : VASTUS MEDIALIS

vastus lat·er·a·lis \-₁la-tər-'ā-ləs, -'a-\ *n* : the division of the quadriceps muscle that covers the outer anterior aspect of the femur, arises chiefly from the femur, and inserts into the outer border of the patella by a flat tendon — called also *vastus externus*

vastus me·di·a·lis \-₁mē-dē-'ā-ləs, -'a-\ *n* : the division of the quadriceps muscle that covers the inner anterior aspect of the femur, arises chiefly from the femur and the adjacent intermuscular septum, inserts into the inner border of the patella and into the tendon of the other divisions of the muscle, sends also a tendinous expansion to the capsule of the knee joint, and is closely united in the upper part often inseparably united with the vastus intermedius — called also *vastus internus*

vault \'vȯlt\ *n* : an arched or domeshaped anatomical structure: as **a** : SKULLCAP, CALVARIUM (the cranial ~) **b** : FORNIX d

VCG *abbr* vectorcardiogram

VD *abbr* venereal disease

VDRL \₁vē-(₁)dē-(₁)är-'el\ *n* : VDRL TEST

VDRL *abbr* venereal disease research laboratory

VDRL slide test *n* : VDRL TEST

VDRL test *n* : a flocculation test for syphilis employing cardiolipin in combination with lecithin and cholesterol

¹**vec·tor** \'vek-tər\ *n* **1** : a quantity that has magnitude and direction and that is usu. represented by part of a straight line with the given direction and with a length representing the magnitude **2** : an organism (as an insect) that transmits a pathogen from one organism to another (fleas are ~s of plague) — compare CARRIER 1a **3** : a sequence of genetic material (as a transposon or the genome of a bacteriophage) that can be used to introduce specific genes into the genome of an organism — **vec·to·ri·al** \vek-'tōr-ē-əl\ *adj*

²**vector** *vb* **vec·tored; vec·tor·ing** : to transmit (a pathogen or disease) from one organism to another : act as a vector for (a disease ~*ed* by flies)

vec·tor·car·dio·gram \₁vek-tər-'kär-dē-ə-₁gram\ *n* : a graphic record made by vectorcardiography

vec·tor·car·di·og·ra·phy \-₁kär-dē-'ä-grə-fē\ *n, pl* **-phies** : a method of recording the direction and magnitude of the electrical forces of the heart by

means of a continuous series of vectors that form a curving line around a center — **vec·tor·car·dio·graph·ic** \-dē-ə-'gra-fik\ *adj*

veg·an \'vē-jən, -₁jan; 'vē-gən\ *n* : a strict vegetarian : one that consumes no animal food or dairy products — **veg·an·ism** \'vē-jə-₁ni-zəm, 'vē-gə-\ *n*

veg·e·tar·i·an·ism \₁ve-jə-'ter-ē-ə-₁ni-zəm\ *n* : the theory or practice of living on a diet made up of vegetables, fruits, grains, nuts, and sometimes animal products (as milk and cheese) — **veg·e·tar·i·an** \-'ter-ē-ən\ *n or adj*

veg·e·ta·tion \₁ve-jə-'tā-shən\ *n* : an abnormal outgrowth upon a body part; *specif* : any of the warty excrescences on the valves of the heart that are composed of various tissue elements including fibrin and collagen and that are typical of endocarditis

veg·e·ta·tive \'ve-jə-₁tā-tiv\ *adj* **1 a (1)** : growing or having the power of growing **(2)** : of, relating to, or engaged in nutritive and growth functions as contrasted with reproductive functions (a ~ nucleus) **b** : of, relating to, or involving propagation by nonsexual processes or methods **2** : affecting, arising from, or relating to involuntary bodily functions **3** : characterized by, resulting from, or being a state of severe mental impairment in which only involuntary bodily functions are sustained (a ~ existence) — **veg·e·ta·tive·ly** *adv*

ve·hi·cle \'vē-i-kəl, -₁hi-\ *n* **1** : an inert medium in which a medicinally active agent is administered **2** : an agent of transmission

vein \'vān\ *n* : any of the tubular branching vessels that carry blood from the capillaries toward the heart and have thinner walls than the arteries and often valves at intervals to prevent reflux of the blood which flows in a steady stream and is in most cases dark-colored due to the presence of reduced hemoglobin — **veiny** \'vā-nē\ *adj*

vein·ous \'vā-nəs\ *adj* **1** : having veins that are esp. prominent (~ hands) **2** : VENOUS

vela *pl of* VELUM

veli — see LEVATOR VELI PALATINI, TENSOR VELI PALATINI

ve·lo·pha·ryn·geal \₁vē-lō-₁far-ən-'jē-əl, -fə-'rin-jəl, -jē-əl\ *adj* : of or relating to the soft palate and the pharynx

Vel·peau bandage \vel-'pō\ or **Vel·peau's bandage** \-'pōz\ *n* : a bandage used to support and immobilize the arm when the clavicle is fractured

Velpeau, Alfred–Armand–Louis-Marie (1795–1867), French surgeon.

ve·lum \'vē-ləm\ *n, pl* **ve·la** \-lə\ : a membrane or membranous part resembling a veil or curtain: as **a** : SOFT PALATE **b** : SEMILUNAR CUSP

ven- *or* **veni-** *or* **veno-** *comb form* : vein (*veni*puncture)

ve·na ca·va \və-nə-ˈkā-və\ *n, pl* **ve·nae ca·vae** \ˌvē-nē-ˈkā-(ˌ)vē\ : either of two large veins by which the blood is returned to the right atrium of the heart: **a** : INFERIOR VENA CAVA **b** : SUPERIOR VENA CAVA — **vena ca·val** \-vəl\ *adj*

vena co·mi·tans \-ˈkō-mə-ˌtanz\ *n, pl* **venae co·mi·tan·tes** \-ˌkō-mə-ˈtan-ˌtēz\ : a vein accompanying an artery

venae cor·dis min·i·mae \-ˈkor-dəs-ˈmi-nə-ˌmē\ *n pl* : minute veins in the wall of the heart that empty into the atria or ventricles

vena vor·ti·co·sa \-ˌvor-tə-ˈkō-sə\ *n, pl* **venae vor·ti·co·sae** \-(ˌ)sē\ : any of the veins of the outer layer of the choroid of the eye — called also *vorticose vein*

ve·neer \və-ˈnir\ *n* : a plastic or porcelain coating bonded to the surface of a cosmetically imperfect tooth

ve·ne·re·al \və-ˈnir-ē-əl\ *adj* **1** : resulting from or contracted during sexual intercourse (~ infections) **2** : of, relating to, or affected with venereal disease (a high ~ rate) **3** : involving the genital organs (~ sarcoma) — **ve·ne·re·al·ly** *adv*

venereal disease *n* : a contagious disease (as gonorrhea or syphilis) that is typically acquired in sexual intercourse — abbr. *VD*; compare SEXUALLY TRANSMITTED DISEASE

venereal wart *n* : CONDYLOMA ACUMINATUM

ve·ne·re·ol·o·gy \və-ˌnir-ē-ˈä-lə-jē\ *also* **ven·er·ol·o·gy** \ˌve-nə-ˈrä-lə-jē\ *n, pl* **-gies** : a branch of medical science concerned with venereal diseases — **ve·ne·re·o·log·i·cal** \və-ˌnir-ē-ə-ˈlä-ji-kəl\ *adj* — **ve·ne·re·ol·o·gist** \və-ˌnir-ē-ˈä-lə-jist\ *n*

venereum — see LYMPHOGRANULOMA VENEREUM, LYMPHOPATHIA VENEREUM

veneris — see MONS VENERIS

vene·sec·tion \ˈve-nə-ˌsek-shən, ˈvē-\ *n* : PHLEBOTOMY

Venezuelan equine encephalitis *n* : EQUINE ENCEPHALOMYELITIS c

Venezuelan equine encephalomyelitis *n* : EQUINE ENCEPHALOMYELITIS c

veni- — see VEN-

ve·ni·punc·ture \ˈvē-nə-ˌpəŋk-chər, ˈve-\ *n* : surgical puncture of a vein esp. for the withdrawal of blood or for intravenous medication

veni·sec·tion *var of* VENESECTION

veno- — see VEN-

ve·no·ar·te·ri·al \ˌvē-nō-är-ˈtir-ē-əl\ *adj* : relating to or involving an artery and vein

ve·noc·ly·sis \vē-ˈnä-klə-səs\ *n, pl* **-ly·ses** \-ˌsēz\ : clysis into a vein

ve·no·con·stric·tion \ˌvē-nō-kən-ˈstrik-shən\ *n* : constriction of a vein

ve·no·gram \ˈvē-nə-ˌgram\ *n* : a roentgenogram after the injection of an opaque substance into a vein

ve·nog·ra·phy \vi-ˈnä-grə-fē, vā-\ *n, pl* **-phies** : roentgenography of a vein after injection of an opaque substance — **ve·no·graph·ic** \ˌvē-nə-ˈgra-fik\ *adj*

ven·om \ˈve-nəm\ *n* : poisonous matter normally secreted by some animals (as snakes, scorpions, or bees) and transmitted to prey or an enemy chiefly by biting or stinging

ven·om·ous \ˈve-nə-məs\ *adj* **1** : POISONOUS **2** : having a venom-producing gland and able to inflict a poisoned wound (~ snakes)

venosum — see LIGAMENTUM VENOSUM

venosus — see DUCTUS VENOSUS, SINUS VENOSUS, SINUS VENOSUS SCLERAE

ve·not·o·my \vi-ˈnä-tə-mē\ *n, pl* **-mies** : PHLEBOTOMY

ve·nous \ˈvē-nəs\ *adj* **1 a** : full of or characterized by veins **b** : made up of or carried on by veins (the ~ circulation) **2** : of, relating to, or performing the functions of a vein (a ~ inflammation) **3** *of blood* : having passed through the capillaries and given up oxygen for the tissues and become charged with carbon dioxide and ready to pass through the respiratory organs to release its carbon dioxide and renew its oxygen supply : dark red from reduced hemoglobin — compare ARTERIAL 2

venous hum *n* : a humming sound sometimes heard during auscultation of the veins of the neck esp. in anemia

venous return *n* : the flow of blood from the venous system into the right atrium of the heart

venous sinus *n* **1** : a large vein or passage (as the canal of Schlemm) for venous blood **2** : SINUS VENOSUS

vent \ˈvent\ *n* : the external opening of the rectum or cloaca : ANUS

vent gleet *n* : CLOACITIS

ven·ti·late \ˈvent-ᵊl-ˌāt\ *vb* **-lat·ed; -lat·ing 1** : to expose to air and esp. to a current of fresh air for purifying or refreshing **2 a** : OXYGENATE, AERATE (~ blood in the lungs) **b** : to subject the lungs of (an individual) to ventilation **3** : to give verbal expression to (as mental or emotional conflicts)

ven·ti·la·tion \ˌvent-ᵊl-ˈā-shən\ *n* **1** : the act or process of ventilating **2** : the circulation and exchange of gases in the lungs or gills that is basic to respiration — **ven·ti·la·to·ry** \ˈvent-ᵊl-ə-ˌtōr-ē\ *adj*

ven·ti·la·tor \ˈvent-ᵊl-ˌā-tər\ *n* : RESPIRATOR 2

ventr- *or* **ventri-** *or* **ventro-** *comb form* **1** : abdomen (*ventral*) **2** : ventral and (*ventromedial*)

ven·tral \ˈven-trəl\ *adj* **1** : of or relating to the belly : ABDOMINAL **2 a** : being or located near, on, or toward the lower surface of an animal (as a quadruped) opposite the back or dorsal surface **b** : being or located near, on, or toward the front or anterior part of the human body — **ven·tral·ly** *adv*

ventral column *n* : VENTRAL HORN

ventral corticospinal tract *n* : a band of nerve fibers that descends in the ventrolateral part of the spinal cord and consists of fibers arising from the motor cortex of the brain on the same side of the body — called also *anterior corticospinal tract, direct pyramidal tract*

ventral funiculus *n* : ANTERIOR FUNICULUS

ventral gray column *n* : VENTRAL HORN

ventral horn *n* : a longitudinal subdivision of gray matter in the anterior part of each lateral half of the spinal cord that contains neurons giving rise to motor fibers of the ventral roots of the spinal nerves — called also *anterior column, anterior gray column, anterior horn, ventral column, ventral gray column*; compare DORSAL HORN, LATERAL COLUMN 1

ventralis — see SACROCOCCYGEUS VENTRALIS

ventral median fissure *n* : ANTERIOR MEDIAN FISSURE

ventral mesogastrium *n* : MESOGASTRIUM 1

ventral root *n* : the one of the two roots of a spinal nerve that passes anteriorly from the spinal cord separating the anterior and lateral funiculi and that consists of motor fibers — called also *anterior root*; compare DORSAL ROOT

ventral spinocerebellar tract *n* : SPINOCEREBELLAR TRACT b

ventral spinothalamic tract *n* : SPINOTHALAMIC TRACT a

ventri- — see VENTR-

ven·tri·cle \'ven-tri-kəl\ *n* : a cavity of a bodily part or organ: as **a** : a chamber of the heart which receives blood from a corresponding atrium and from which blood is forced into the arteries **b** : one of the communicating cavities in the brain that form a system and are continuous with the central canal of the spinal cord — see LATERAL VENTRICLE, THIRD VENTRICLE, FOURTH VENTRICLE **c** : a fossa or pouch on each side of the larynx between the false vocal cords above and the true vocal cords below

ven·tric·u·lar \ven-'tri-kyə-lər, vən-\ *adj* : of, relating to, or being a ventricle esp. of the heart or brain (∼ tachycardia)

ventricular assist device *n* : VAD

ventricular fibrillation *n* : very rapid uncoordinated fluttering contractions of the ventricles of the heart resulting in loss of synchronization between heartbeat and pulse beat

ventricular folds *n pl* : FALSE VOCAL CORDS

ventricular septal defect *n* : a congenital defect in the interventricular septum — abbr. *VSD*

ven·tric·u·li·tis \ven-ˌtri-kyə-'lī-təs\ *n* : inflammation of the ventricles of the brain

ven·tric·u·lo·atri·al \ven-ˌtri-kyə-lō-'ā-trē-əl\ *adj* **1** : of, relating to, or being an artificial shunt between a ventricle of the brain and an atrium of the heart esp. to drain cerebrospinal fluid (as in hydrocephalus) **2** : of, relating to, or being conduction from the ventricle to the atrium of the heart

ven·tric·u·lo·atri·os·to·my \-ˌā-trē-'äs-tə-mē\ *n, pl* **-mies** : surgical establishment of a shunt to drain cerebrospinal fluid (as in hydrocephalus) from a ventricle of the brain to the right atrium

ven·tric·u·lo·cis·ter·nos·to·my \-ˌsis-tər-'näs-tə-mē\ *n, pl* **-mies** : the surgical establishment of a communication between a ventricle of the brain and the subarachnoid space and esp. the cisterna magna to drain cerebrospinal fluid esp. in hydrocephalus

ven·tric·u·lo·gram \ven-'tri-kyə-lə-ˌgram\ *n* : an X-ray photograph made by ventriculography

ven·tric·u·log·ra·phy \ven-ˌtri-kyə-'lä-grə-fē\ *n, pl* **-phies 1** : the act or process of making an X-ray photograph of the ventricles of the brain after withdrawing fluid from the ventricles and replacing it with air or a radiopaque substance **2** : the act or process of making an X-ray photograph of a ventricle of the heart after injecting a radiopaque substance — **ven·tric·u·lo·graph·ic** \-kyə-lō-'gra-fik\ *adj*

ven·tric·u·lo·peri·to·ne·al \ven-ˌtri-kyə-lō-ˌper-ə-tə-'nē-əl\ *adj* : relating to or serving to communicate between a ventricle of the brain and the peritoneal cavity (a plastic ∼ shunt)

ven·tric·u·los·to·my \ven-ˌtri-kyə-'läs-tə-mē\ *n, pl* **-mies** : the surgical establishment of an opening in a ventricle of the brain to drain cerebrospinal fluid esp. in hydrocephalus

ven·tric·u·lot·o·my \ven-ˌtri-kyə-'lä-tə-mē\ *n, pl* **-mies** : surgical incision of a ventricle (as of the heart)

ventro- — see VENTR-

ven·tro·lat·er·al \ven-ˌtrō-'la-tə-rəl\ *adj* : ventral and lateral — **ven·tro·lat·er·al·ly** *adv*

ven·tro·me·di·al \-'mē-dē-əl\ *adj* : ventral and medial — **ven·tro·me·di·al·ly** *adv*

ventromedial nucleus *n* : a medially located nucleus of the hypothalamus that is situated between the lateral wall of the third ventricle and the fornix

ven·ule \'vēn-(ˌ)yül, 'ven-\ *n* : a small vein; *esp* : any of the minute veins connecting the capillaries with the larger systemic veins — **ven·u·lar** \'ven-yə-lər\ *adj*

vera — see DECIDUA VERA, POLYCYTHEMIA VERA

ver·ap·am·il \və-'ra-pə-ˌmil\ *n* : a calcium channel blocker $C_{27}H_{38}N_2O_4$ with vasodilating properties that is used esp. in the form of its hydrochloride

ver·a·trine \'ver-ə-ˌtrēn\ n : a mixture of alkaloids that is obtained from the seeds of a Mexican plant (*Schoeno-caulon officinalis*) of the lily family (Liliaceae) that is an intense local irritant and a powerful muscle and nerve poison, and that has been used as a counterirritant in neuralgia and arthritis

ve·ra·trum \və-'rā-trəm\ n 1 a cap : a genus of herbs having short poisonous rootstocks b : any hellebore of the genus Veratrum 2 : HELLEBORE 2b

ver·big·er·a·tion \(ˌ)vər-ˌbi-jə-'rā-shən\ n : continual repetition of stereotyped phrases (as in some forms of mental illness)

verge — see ANAL VERGE

ver·gence \'vər-jəns\ n : a movement of one eye in relation to the other

vermes pl of VERMIS

vermi- comb form : worm ⟨vermicide⟩ ⟨vermiform⟩

ver·mi·cide \'vər-mə-ˌsīd\ n : an agent that destroys worms; esp : ANTHELMINTIC

ver·mi·form \'vər-mə-ˌfȯrm\ adj : resembling a worm in shape

vermiform appendix n : a narrow blind tube usu. about three or four inches (7.6 to 10.2 centimeters) long that extends from the cecum in the lower right-hand part of the abdomen and represents an atrophied terminal part of the cecum

ver·mi·fuge \'vər-mə-ˌfyüj\ n : an agent that serves to destroy or expel parasitic worms : ANTHELMINTIC — **ver·mif·u·gal** \vər-'mi-fyə-gəl, ˌvər-mə-'fyü-gəl\ adj

ver·mil·ion border \vər-'mil-yən-\ n : the exposed pink or reddish margin of a lip

ver·mil·ion·ec·to·my \vər-ˌmil-yə-'nek-tə-mē\ n, pl **-mies** : surgical excision of the vermilion border

ver·min \'vər-mən\ n, pl **vermin** : small common harmful or objectionable animals (as lice or fleas) that are difficult to control

ver·min·ous \'vər-mə-nəs\ adj 1 : consisting of, infested with, or being vermin 2 : caused by parasitic worms

ver·mis \'vər-mis\ n, pl **ver·mes** \-ˌmēz\ 1 : either of two parts of the median lobe of the cerebellum: a : one slightly prominent on the upper surface — called also superior vermis b : one on the lower surface sunk in the vallecula — called also inferior vermis 2 : the median lobe or part of the cerebellum

vernal conjunctivitis n : conjunctivitis occurring in warm seasons as a result of exposure to allergens

Ver·ner–Mor·ri·son syndrome \'vər-nər-'mȯr-ə-sən-, -'mär-\ n : a syndrome characterized esp. by severe watery diarrhea and hypokalemia that is often due to an excessive secretion of vasoactive intestinal peptide from a vipoma esp. of the pancreas — called also pancreatic cholera

Verner, John Victor (b 1927), American physician. and **Morrison, Ashton Byrom** (b 1922), American pathologist.

ver·nix \'vər-niks\ n : VERNIX CASEOSA

vernix ca·se·o·sa \-ˌka-sē-'ō-sə\ n : a pasty covering chiefly of dead cells and sebaceous secretions that protects the skin of the fetus

Ver·o·nal \'ver-ə-ˌnȯl, -nəl\ trademark — used for a preparation of barbital

ver·ru·ca \və-'rü-kə\ n, pl **-cae** \-(ˌ)kē\ : a wart or warty skin lesion

verruca acu·mi·na·ta \-ə-ˌkyü-mə-'nā-tə\ n : CONDYLOMA ACUMINATUM

verruca plan·ta·ris \-ˌplan-'tar-əs\ n : PLANTAR WART

verruca vul·ga·ris \-ˌvəl-'gar-əs\ n : WART 1

ver·ru·cose \və-'rü-ˌkōs\ adj 1 : covered with warty elevations 2 : having the form of a wart ⟨a ∼ nevus⟩

ver·ru·cous \və-'rü-kəs\ adj 1 : VERRUCOSE 2 : characterized by the formation of warty lesions ⟨∼ dermatitis⟩

verrucous endocarditis n : endocarditis marked by the formation or presence of warty nodules of fibrin on the lips of the heart valves

ver·ru·ga \və-'rü-gə\ n 1 : VERRUCA 2 : VERRUGA PERUANA

verruga per·u·a·na \-ˌper-ə-'wä-nə\ also **verruga pe·ru·vi·ana** \-pə-ˌrü-vē-'a-nə\ n : the second stage of bartonellosis characterized by warty nodules tending to ulcerate and bleed

versicolor — see TINEA VERSICOLOR

ver·sion \'vər-zhən, -shən\ n 1 : a condition in which an organ and esp. the uterus is turned from its normal position 2 : manual turning of a fetus in the uterus to aid delivery

ver·te·bra \'vər-tə-brə\ n, pl **-brae** \-ˌbrā, -(ˌ)brē\ or **-bras** : any of the bony or cartilaginous segments that make up the spinal column and that have a short more or less cylindrical body whose ends articulate by pads of elastic or cartilaginous tissue with those of adjacent vertebrae and a bony arch that encloses the spinal cord

¹**ver·te·bral** \(ˌ)vər-'tē-brəl, 'vər-tə-\ adj 1 : of, relating to, or being vertebrae or the spinal column : SPINAL 2 : composed of or having vertebrae

²**vertebral** n : a vertebral part or element (as an artery)

vertebral arch n : NEURAL ARCH

vertebral artery n : a large branch of the subclavian artery that ascends through the foramina in the transverse processes of each of the cervical vertebrae except the last one or two, enters the cranium through the foramen magnum, and unites with the corresponding artery of the opposite side to form the basilar artery

vertebral canal n : a canal that contains the spinal cord and is delimited by the neural arches on the dorsal side of the vertebrae — called also *spinal canal*

vertebral column n : SPINAL COLUMN

vertebral foramen n : the opening formed by a neural arch through which the spinal cord passes

vertebral ganglion n : any of a group of sympathetic ganglia which form two chains extending from the base of the skull to the coccyx along the sides of the spinal column — compare SYMPA-THETIC CHAIN

vertebral notch n : either of two concave constrictions of which one occurs on the inferior surface and one on the superior surface of the pedicle on each side of a vertebra and which are arranged so that the superior notches of one vertebra and the corresponding inferior notches of a contiguous vertebra combine to form an intervertebral foramen on each side

vertebral plexus n : a plexus of veins associated with the spinal column

vertebral vein n : a tributary of the brachiocephalic vein that is formed by the union of branches originating in the occipital region and forming a plexus about the vertebral artery in its passage through the foramina of the cervical vertebrae

vertebra pro·mi·nens \-ˈprä-mi-ˌnenz\ n : the seventh cervical vertebra characterized by a prominent spinous process which can be felt at the base of the neck

ver·te·brate \ˈvər-tə-brət, -ˌbrāt\ n : any of a subphylum (Vertebrata) of animals with a spinal column including the mammals, birds, reptiles, amphibians, and fishes — **vertebrate** adj

ver·te·bro·ba·si·lar \ˌvər-tə-brō-ˈbā-sə-lər\ adj : of, relating to, or being the vertebral and basilar arteries

ver·te·bro·chon·dral rib \ˌvər-tə-brō-ˈkän-drəl-\ n : any of the three false ribs that are located above the floating ribs and that are attached to each other by costal cartilages

ver·te·bro·ster·nal rib \-ˈstər-nəl-\ n : TRUE RIB

ver·tex \ˈvər-ˌteks\ n, pl **ver·ti·ces** \ˈvər-tə-ˌsēz\ also **ver·tex·es** 1 : the top of the head 2 : the highest point of the skull

vertex presentation n : normal obstetric presentation in which the fetal occiput lies at the mouth of the uterus

ver·ti·cal \ˈvər-ti-kəl\ adj : relating to or being transmission (as of a disease) by inheritance in contrast to physical contact or proximity — compare HOR-IZONTAL 2 — **ver·ti·cal·ly** adv

vertical dimension n : the distance between two arbitrarily chosen points on the face above and below the

mouth when the teeth are in occlusion

vertical nystagmus n : nystagmus characterized by up-and-down movement of the eyes

ver·tig·i·nous \(ˌ)vər-ˈti-jə-nəs\ adj : of, relating to, characterized by, or affected with vertigo or dizziness

ver·ti·go \ˈvər-ti-ˌgō\ n, pl **-goes** or **-gos** 1 : a disordered state which is associated with various disorders (as of the inner ear) and in which the individual or the individual's surroundings seem to whirl dizzily — see SUBJECTIVE VERTIGO; compare DIZZINESS 2 : disordered vertiginous movement as a symptom of disease in lower animals; also : a disease (as gid) causing this

very low–density lipoprotein n : VLDL

vesicae — see TRIGONUM VESICAE, UVULA VESICAE

ves·i·ca fel·lea \ˈve-si-kə-ˈfe-lē-ə\ n : GALLBLADDER

¹**ves·i·cal** \ˈve-si-kəl\ adj : of or relating to a bladder and esp. to the urinary bladder (~ burning)

²**vesical** n : VESICAL ARTERY

vesical artery n : any of several arteries that arise from the internal iliac artery or one of its branches and that supply the urinary bladder and adjacent parts: as **a** : any of several arteries that arise from the umbilical artery and supply the upper part of the bladder — called also *superior vesical, superior vesical artery* **b** : one that arises from the internal iliac artery or the internal pudendal artery and that supplies the bladder, prostate, and seminal vesicles — called also *inferior vesical, inferior vesical artery*

vesical plexus n : a plexus of nerves that comprises preganglionic fibers derived chiefly from the hypogastric plexus and postganglionic neurons whose fibers are distributed to the bladder and adjacent parts

vesical venous plexus n : a plexus of veins surrounding the neck of the bladder and the base of the prostate gland

ves·i·cant \ˈve-si-kənt\ adj : producing or tending to produce blisters (a ~ substance) — **vesicant** n

vesica uri·nar·ia \-ˌyùr-i-ˈnar-ē-ə\ n : URINARY BLADDER

ves·i·cle \ˈve-si-kəl\ n 1 **a** : a membranous and usu. fluid-filled pouch (as a cyst or cell) in a plant or animal **b** : SYNAPTIC VESICLE 2 : a small abnormal elevation of the outer layer of skin enclosing a watery liquid : BLISTER 3 : a pocket of embryonic tissue that is the beginning of an organ — see BRAIN VESICLE, OPTIC VESICLE

vesico- comb form : of or relating to the urinary bladder and (vesicouterine)

ves·i·co·en·ter·ic \ˌve-si-kō-en-ˈter-ik\ adj : of, relating to, or connecting the urinary bladder and the intestinal tract (a ~ fistula)

ves·i·cos·to·my \ve-si-ˈkäs-tə-mē\ *n, pl* **-mies** : CYSTOSTOMY

ves·i·co·ure·ter·al reflux \ˌve-si-kō-yü-ˈrē-tə-rəl-\ *n* : reflux of urine from the bladder into a ureter

ves·i·co·ure·ter·ic reflux \-tə-rik-\ *n* : VESICOURETERAL REFLUX

ves·i·co·uter·ine \ˌve-si-kō-ˈyü-tə-ˌrīn, -rən\ *adj* : of, relating to, or connecting the urinary bladder and the uterus

ves·i·co·vag·i·nal \ˌve-si-kō-ˈva-jən-ᵊl\ *adj* : of, relating to, or connecting the urinary bladder and vagina

vesicul- *or* **vesiculo-** *comb form* 1 : vesicle (*vesiculectomy*) 2 : vesicular and (*vesiculobullous*)

ve·sic·u·lar \və-ˈsi-kyə-lər, ve-\ *adj* 1 : characterized by the presence or formation of vesicles (a ~ rash) 2 : having the form of a vesicle

vesicular breathing *n* : normal breathing that is soft and low-pitched when heard in auscultation

vesicular dermatitis *n* : a severe dermatitis esp. of young chickens and turkeys — called also *sod disease*

vesicular exanthema *n* : an acute virus disease of swine that closely resembles foot-and-mouth disease

vesicular ovarian follicle *n* : GRAAFIAN FOLLICLE

vesicular stomatitis *n* : an acute virus disease esp. of horses and mules that is marked by erosive blisters in and about the mouth

ve·sic·u·la·tion \və-ˌsi-kyə-ˈlā-shən\ *n* 1 : the presence or formation of vesicles 2 : the process of becoming vesicular (~ of a papule)

ve·sic·u·lec·to·my \və-ˌsi-kyə-ˈlek-tə-mē\ *n, pl* **-mies** : surgical excision of a seminal vesicle

ve·sic·u·li·tis \və-ˌsi-kyə-ˈlī-təs\ *n* : inflammation of a vesicle and esp. a seminal vesicle

ve·sic·u·lo·bul·lous \və-ˌsi-kyə-lō-ˈbu-ləs\ *adj* : of, relating to, or being both vesicles and bullae (a ~ rash)

ve·sic·u·lo·gram \və-ˈsi-kyə-lə-ˌgram\ *n* : a radiograph produced by vesiculography

ve·sic·u·log·ra·phy \və-ˌsi-kyə-ˈlä-grə-fē\ *n, pl* **-phies** : radiography of the seminal vesicles following the injection of a radiopaque medium

ve·sic·u·lo·pus·tu·lar \və-ˌsi-kyə-lō-ˈpəs-chə-lär\ *adj* : of, relating to, or marked by both vesicles and pustules

ve·sic·u·lot·o·my \və-ˌsi-kyə-ˈlä-tə-mē\ *n, pl* **-mies** : surgical incision of a seminal vesicle

Ves·prin \ˈves-prən\ *trademark* — used for a preparation of triflupromazine

ves·sel \ˈve-səl\ *n* : a tube or canal (as an artery, vein, or lymphatic) in which a body fluid (as blood or lymph) is contained and conveyed or circulated

ves·tib·u·lar \ve-ˈsti-byə-lər\ *adj* 1 : of

or relating to the vestibule of the inner ear, the vestibular apparatus, the vestibular nerve, or the labyrinthine sense 2 : lying within or facing the vestibule of the mouth (the ~ surface of a tooth) — **ves·tib·u·lar·ly** *adv*

vestibular apparatus *n* : the vestibule of the inner ear together with the end organs and nerve fibers that function in mediating the labyrinthine sense

vestibular folds *n pl* : FALSE VOCAL CORDS

vestibular ganglion *n* : a sensory ganglion in the trunk of the vestibular nerve in the internal auditory meatus that contains cell bodies supplying nerve fibers comprising the vestibular nerve

vestibular gland *n* : any of the glands (as Bartholin's glands) that open into the vestibule of the vagina

vestibular ligament *n* : the narrow band of fibrous tissue contained in each of the false vocal cords and stretching between the thyroid and arytenoid cartilages

vestibular membrane *n* : a thin cellular membrane separating the scala media and scala vestibuli — called also *Reissner's membrane*

vestibular nerve *n* : a branch of the auditory nerve that consists of bipolar neurons with cell bodies collected in the vestibular ganglion, with peripheral processes passing to the semicircular canals, utricle, and saccule, and with central processes passing to the vestibular nuclei of the medulla oblongata

vestibular neuronitis *n* : a disorder of uncertain etiology that is characterized by transitory attacks of severe vertigo

vestibular nucleus *n* : any of four nuclei in the medulla oblongata on each side of the floor of the fourth ventricle of the brain in which fibers of the vestibular nerve terminate — see INFERIOR VESTIBULAR NUCLEUS, LATERAL VESTIBULAR NUCLEUS, MEDIAL VESTIBULAR NUCLEUS, SUPERIOR VESTIBULAR NUCLEUS

vestibular system *n* : VESTIBULAR APPARATUS

ves·ti·bule \ˈves-tə-ˌbyül\ *n* : any of various bodily cavities esp. when serving as or resembling an entrance to some other cavity or space: as **a** (1) : the central cavity of the bony labyrinth of the ear (2) : the parts of the membranous labyrinth comprising the utricle and the saccule and contained in the cavity of the bony labyrinth **b** : the space between the labia minora containing the orifice of the urethra **c** : the part of the left ventricle of the heart immediately below the aortic orifice **d** : the part of the mouth cavity outside the teeth and gums

vestibuli — see FENESTRA VESTIBULI, SCALA VESTIBULI

ves·tib·u·lo·co·chle·ar nerve \ve-ˌsti-byə-lō-ˈkŏ-klē-ər-, -ˈkä-\ n : AUDITORY NERVE

ves·tib·u·lo·plas·ty \ve-ˈsti-byə-lō-ˌplas-tē\ n, pl **-ties** : plastic surgery of the vestibular region of the mouth

vestibulorum — see SCALA VESTIBULI

ves·tib·u·lo·spi·nal tract \ve-ˌsti-byə-lō-ˈspī-nəl-\ n : a nerve tract on each side of the central nervous system containing nerve fibers that arise from cell bodies in the lateral vestibular nucleus on one side of the medulla oblongata and that descend on the same side in the lateral and anterior funiculi of the spinal cord to synapse with motoneurons in the ventral roots

ves·tige \ˈves-tij\ n : a bodily part or organ that is small and degenerate or imperfectly developed in comparison to one more fully developed in an earlier stage of the individual, in a past generation, or in closely related forms — **ves·tig·ial** \ve-ˈsti-jəl, -jē-əl\ adj

vestigial fold of Mar·shall \-ˈmär-shəl\ n : a fold of endocardium that extends from the left pulmonary artery to the more superior of the two left pulmonary veins

J. Marshall — see OBLIQUE VEIN OF MARSHALL

vet \ˈvet\ n : VETERINARIAN

vet·er·i·nar·i·an \ˌve-tə-rə-ˈner-ē-ən, ˌve-trə-\ n : a person qualified and authorized to practice veterinary medicine

¹**vet·er·i·nary** \ˈve-tə-rə-ˌner-ē, ˈve-trə-\ adj : of, relating to, or being the science and art of prevention, cure, or alleviation of disease and injury in animals and esp. domestic animals (~ medicine)

²**veterinary** n, pl **-nar·ies** : VETERINARIAN

veterinary surgeon n, Brit : VETERINARIAN

vi·a·ble \ˈvī-ə-bəl\ adj **1** : capable of living (~ cancer cells); esp : having attained such form and development of organs as to be normally capable of living outside the uterus — often used of a human fetus at seven months but may be interpreted according to the state of the art of medicine (a ~ fetus) **2** : capable of growing or developing (~ eggs) — **vi·a·bil·i·ty** \ˌvī-ə-ˈbi-lə-tē\ n

vi·al \ˈvī-əl, ˈvīl\ n : a small closed or closable vessel esp. for liquids — called also phial

Vi antigen \ˈvē-ˈī-\ n : a heat-labile somatic antigen associated with virulence in some bacteria (as of the genus Salmonella) and esp. in the typhoid fever bacterium

Vi·bra·my·cin \ˌvī-brə-ˈmīs-ᵊn\ trademark — used for a preparation of doxycycline

vi·bra·tor \ˈvī-ˌbrā-tər\ n : a vibrating electrical apparatus used in massage or for sexual stimulation

vib·rio \ˈvi-brē-ō\ n **1** cap : a genus of motile gram-negative bacteria (family Vibrionaceae) that are curved rods and include various saprophytes and a few pathogens (as V. cholerae, the cause of cholera in humans) **2** : any bacterium of the genus Vibrio; broadly : a curved rod-shaped bacterium

vib·ri·on·ic abortion \ˌvi-brē-ˈä-nik-\ n : abortion in sheep and cattle caused by a bacterium of the genus Campylobacter (C. fetus syn. Vibrio fetus)

vib·ri·o·sis \ˌvi-brē-ˈō-səs\ n, pl **-o·ses** \-ˌsēz\ : infestation with or disease caused by bacteria of the genus Vibrio or Campylobacter; specif : VIBRIONIC ABORTION

vi·bris·sa \vī-ˈbri-sə, və-\ n, pl **vi·bris·sae** \vī-ˈbri-(ˌ)sē; və-ˈbri-(ˌ)sē, -ˌsī\ : any of the stiff hairs growing within the nostrils that serve to impede the inhalation of foreign substances

vi·car·i·ous \vī-ˈkar-ē-əs, və-\ adj : occurring in an unexpected or abnormal part of the body instead of the usual one (bleeding from the gums sometimes occurs in the absence of the normal discharge from the uterus in ~ menstruation)

vice \ˈvīs\ n : an abnormal behavior pattern in a domestic animal detrimental to its health or usefulness

vid·ar·a·bine \vi-ˈdär-ə-ˌbēn\ n : an antiviral agent $C_{10}H_{13}N_5O_4 \cdot H_2O$ derived from adenine and arabinoside and used esp. to treat keratitis and encephalitis caused by the herpes simplex virus — called also ara-A, adenine arabinoside

Vi·dex \ˈvī-ˌdeks\ trademark — used for a preparation of DDI

Vid·i·an artery \ˈvi-dē-ən-\ n : a branch of the maxillary artery passing through the pterygoid canal of the sphenoid bone

Gui·di \ˈgwē-dē\, **Guido** (Latin **Vidus Vidius**) (1508–1569), Italian anatomist and surgeon.

Vidian canal n : PTERYGOID CANAL

Vidian nerve n : a nerve formed by the union of the greater petrosal and the deep petrosal nerves that passes forward through the pterygoid canal in the sphenoid bone and joins the pterygopalatine ganglion

vil·li·ki·nin \ˌvi-lə-ˈki-nən\ n : a hormone postulated to exist in order to explain the activity of intestinal extracts in stimulating the intestinal villi

vil·lo·nod·u·lar \ˌvi-lō-ˈnä-jə-lər\ adj : characterized by villous and nodular thickening (as of a synovial membrane) (~ synovitis)

vil·lus \ˈvi-ləs\ n, pl **vil·li** \-ˌlī\ : a small slender vascular process: as **a** : one of the minute fingerlike processes of the mucous membrane of the small intestine that serve in the absorption of nutriment **b** : one of the branching processes of the surface of the chorion of the developing embryo of most mammals that help to form the placenta — **vil·lous** \'vi-ləs\ *adj*

vin·blas·tine \(ˌ)vin-'blas-ˌtēn\ *n* : an alkaloid $C_{46}H_{58}N_4O_9$ that is obtained from a periwinkle (*Catharanthus roseus*) and that is used esp. in the form of its sulfate to treat human neoplastic diseases (as leukemias and testicular carcinoma) — called also *vincaleukoblastine*

vin·ca \'viŋ-kə\ *n* : PERIWINKLE

vin·ca·leu·ko·blas·tine \ˌviŋ-kə-ˌlü-kə-'blas-ˌtēn\ *n* : VINBLASTINE

Vin·cent's angina \'vin-sənts-, (ˌ)van-'sän²z-\ *n* : Vincent's infection in which the ulceration has spread to surrounding tissues (as of the pharynx and tonsils) — called also *trench mouth*, *ulceromembranous gingivitis*

Vincent, Jean Hyacinthe (1862–1950), French bacteriologist.

Vincent's disease *n* : a disease marked by infection with Vincent's organisms; *esp* : VINCENT'S ANGINA

Vincent's infection *n* : a progressive painful disease of the mouth that is marked esp. by dirty gray ulceration of the mucous membranes, spontaneous hemorrhaging of the gums, and a foul odor to the breath and that is associated with the presence of large numbers of Vincent's organisms — called also *trench mouth*

Vincent's organisms *n pl* : a bacterium of the genus *Fusobacterium* (*F. nucleatum* syn. *F. fusiforme*) and a spirochete of the genus *Treponema* (*T. vincentii* syn. *Borrelia vincentii*) that are part of the normal oral flora and undergo a great increase in numbers in the mucous membrane of the mouth and adjacent parts in Vincent's infection and Vincent's angina

Vincent's stomatitis *n* : VINCENT'S ANGINA

Vincent's ulcer *n* **1** : TROPICAL ULCER **2** : an ulcer of the mucous membranes symptomatic of Vincent's infection or Vincent's angina

vin·cris·tine \(ˌ)vin-'kris-ˌtēn\ *n* : an alkaloid $C_{46}H_{56}N_4O_{10}$ that is obtained from a periwinkle (*Catharanthus roseus*) and that is used esp. in the form of its sulfate to treat human neoplastic diseases (as leukemias and Wilms' tumor) — called also *leurocristine*; see ONCOVIN

Vine·berg procedure \'vīn-ˌbərg-\ *n* : surgical implantation of an internal thoracic artery into the myocardium

Vineberg, Arthur Martin (1903–1988), Canadian surgeon.

vi·nyl chloride \'vīn-ᵊl-\ *n* : a flammable gaseous carcinogenic compound C_2H_3Cl

vinyl ether *n* : a volatile flammable liquid unsaturated ether C_4H_6O that is used as an inhalation anesthetic for short operative procedures

vio·my·cin \ˌvī-ə-'mīs-ᵊn\ *n* : a polypeptide antibiotic $C_{25}H_{43}N_{13}O_{10}$ that is produced by several soil actinomycetes of the genus *Streptomyces* and is administered intramuscularly in the form of its sulfate in the treatment of tuberculosis esp. in combination with other antituberculous drugs

vi·os·ter·ol \vī-'äs-tə-ˌrȯl, -ˌrōl\ *n* : CALCIFEROL

VIP *abbr* vasoactive intestinal peptide

vi·per \'vī-pər\ *n* : a common Eurasian venomous snake of the genus *Vipera* (*V. berus*) whose bite is usu. not fatal to humans; *broadly* : any of a family (Viperidae) of venomous snakes that includes Old World snakes (subfamily Viperinae) and the pit vipers

Vi·pera \'vī-pə-rə\ *n* : a genus of Old World venomous snakes (family Viperidae)

vi·po·ma \vī-'pō-mə, vi-\ *n* : a tumor of endocrine tissue esp. in the pancreas that secretes vasoactive intestinal polypeptide

vi·rae·mia *chiefly Brit var of* VIREMIA

vi·ral \'vī-rəl\ *adj* : of, relating to, or caused by a virus — **vi·ral·ly** *adv*

Vir·chow–Ro·bin space \'fir-ˌkō-rō-'ban-\ *n* : any of the spaces that surround blood vessels as they enter the brain and that communicate with the subarachnoid space

Virchow, Rudolf Ludwig Karl (1821–1902), German pathologist, anthropologist, and statesman.

Robin, Charles–Philippe (1821–1885), French anatomist and histologist.

Virchow's node *n* : SIGNAL NODE

vi·re·mia \vī-'rē-mē-ə\ *n* : the presence of virus in the blood of a host — **vi·re·mic** \-mik\ *adj*

vir·gin \'vər-jən\ *n* : a person who has not had sexual intercourse — **vir·gin·i·ty** \(ˌ)vər-'jin-ə-tē\ *n*

vi·ri·ci·dal \ˌvī-rə-'sīd-ᵊl\ *adj* : VIRUCIDAL

vi·ri·cide \'vī-rə-ˌsīd\ *n* : VIRUCIDE

vir·ile \'vir-əl, -ˌīl\ *adj* **1** : having the nature, properties, or qualities of an adult male; *specif* : capable of functioning as a male in copulation **2** : characteristic of or associated with men : MASCULINE — **vi·ril·i·ty** \və-'ri-lə-tē\ *n*

vir·il·ism \'vir-ə-ˌli-zəm\ *n* **1** : precocious development of secondary sex characteristics in the male **2** : the appearance of secondary sex characteristics of the male in a female

vir·il·ize \'vir-ə-ˌlīz\ *vb* -**ized**; -**iz·ing** : to make virile; *esp* : to cause or produce virilism in — **vir·il·iza·tion** \ˌvir-ə-lə-'zā-shən\ *n*

vi·ri·on \'vī-rē-ˌän, 'vir-ē-\ *n* : a complete virus particle that consists of an RNA or DNA core with a protein coat sometimes with external envelopes and that is the extracellular infective form of a virus

vi·rol·o·gy \vī-'rä-lə-jē\ n, pl **-gies** : a branch of science that deals with viruses — **vi·ro·log·i·cal** \ˌvī-rə-'lä-ji-kəl\ or **vi·ro·log·ic** \-jik\ adj — **vi·ro·log·i·cal·ly** adv — **vi·rol·o·gist** \vī-'rä-lə-jist\ n

virtual dead space n : PHYSIOLOGICAL DEAD SPACE

vi·ru·cid·al \ˌvī-rə-'sīd-əl\ adj : having the capacity to or tending to destroy or inactivate viruses (~ activity)

vi·ru·cide \'vī-rə-ˌsīd\ n : an agent having the capacity to destroy or inactivate viruses — called also *viricide*

vir·u·lence \'vir-yə-ləns, 'vir-ə-\ n : the quality or state of being virulent: as a : relative severity and malignancy b : the relative capacity of a pathogen to overcome body defenses — compare INFECTIVITY

vir·u·len·cy \-lən-sē\ n, pl **-cies** : VIRULENCE

vir·u·lent \-lənt\ adj **1 a** : marked by a rapid, severe, and malignant course (a ~ infection) **b** : able to overcome bodily defense mechanisms (a ~ pathogen) **2** : extremely poisonous or venomous : NOXIOUS

vi·rus \'vī-rəs\ n **1** : the causative agent of an infectious disease **2** : any of a large group of submicroscopic infective agents that are regarded either as extremely simple microorganisms or as extremely complex molecules, that typically contain a protein coat surrounding an RNA or DNA core of genetic material but no semipermeable membrane, that are capable of growth and multiplication only in living cells, and that cause various important diseases — see FILTERABLE VIRUS **3** : a disease caused by a virus

virus pneumonia n : pneumonia caused or thought to be caused by a virus; *esp* : PRIMARY ATYPICAL PNEUMONIA

viscer- or **visceri-** or **viscero-** comb form : visceral : viscera (*viscero*tropic)

viscera pl of VISCUS

vis·cer·al \'vi-sə-rəl\ adj : of, relating to, or located on or among the viscera — compare PARIETAL 1 — **vis·cer·al·ly** adv

visceral arch n : BRANCHIAL ARCH

visceral leishmaniasis n : KALA-AZAR

visceral muscle n : smooth muscle esp. in visceral structures

visceral pericardium n : EPICARDIUM

visceral peritoneum n : the part of the peritoneum that lines the abdominal viscera — compare PARIETAL PERITONEUM

visceral reflex n : a reflex mediated by autonomic nerves and initiated in the viscera

vis·cero·mo·tor \ˌvi-sə-rō-'mō-tər\ adj : causing or concerned in the functional activity of the viscera (~ nerves)

vis·cer·op·to·sis \ˌvi-sə- räp-'tō-səs\ n, pl **-to·ses** \-ˌsēz\ : downward displacement of the abdominal viscera

vis·cer·o·trop·ic \ˌvi-sə-rə-'trä-pik\ adj : tending to affect or having an affinity for the viscera — used esp. of a virus — **vis·cer·ot·ro·pism** \ˌvi-sə-'rä-trə-ˌpi-zəm\ n

vis·cid \'vi-səd\ adj **1** : having an adhesive quality **2** : having a glutinous consistency

vis·com·e·ter \vis-'kä-mə-tər\ n : an instrument used to measure viscosity (a blood ~) — called also *viscosimeter* — **vis·co·met·ric** \ˌvis-kə-'me-trik\ adj

vis·cos·i·ty \vis-'kä-sə-tē\ n, pl **-ties** : the quality of being viscous; *esp* : the property of resistance to flow in a fluid

vis·cous \'vis-kəs\ adj **1** : having a glutinous consistency and the quality of sticking or adhering : VISCID **2** : having or characterized by viscosity

vis·cus \'vis-kəs\ n, pl **vis·cera** \'vi-sə-rə\ : an internal organ of the body: *esp* : one (as the heart, liver, or intestine) located in the large cavity of the trunk

vis·i·ble \'vi-zə-bəl\ adj **1** : capable of being seen : perceptible to vision **2** : situated in the region of the visible spectrum

visible spectrum n : the part of the electromagnetic spectrum to which the human eye is sensitive extending from a wavelength of about 400 nm (3800 angstroms) for violet light to about 700 nm (7600 angstroms) for red light

vi·sion \'vi-zhən\ n **1** : the act or power of seeing **2** : the special sense by which the qualities of an object (as color, shape, and size) constituting its appearance are perceived and which is mediated by the eye

vis·it \'vi-zət\ n **1** : a professional call (as by a physician to treat a patient) **2** : a call upon a professional person (as a physician or dentist) for consultation or treatment — **visit** vb

visiting nurse n : a nurse employed (as by a hospital or social-service agency) to perform public health services and esp. to visit sick persons in a community — called also *public health nurse*

vis·na \'vis-nə\ n : a chronic retroviral encephalomyelitis of sheep

Vis·ta·ril \'vis-tə-ˌril\ trademark — used for a preparation of hydroxyzine

vi·su·al \'vi-zhə-wəl\ adj **1** : of, relating to, or used in vision (~ organs) **2** : attained or maintained by sight (~ impressions) — **vi·su·al·ly** adv

visual acuity n : the relative ability of the visual organ to resolve detail

visual area n : a sensory area of the occipital lobe of the cerebral cortex receiving afferent projection fibers concerned with the sense of sight — called also *visual cortex*

visual cortex n : VISUAL AREA

visual field n : the entire expanse of space visible at a given instant without moving the eyes — called also *field of vision*

vi·su·al·i·za·tion \ˌvi-zhə-wə-lə-ˈzā-shən\ *n* **1** : formation of mental visual images **2** : the process of making an internal organ visible by the introduction (as by swallowing, by an injection, or by an enema) of a radiopaque substance followed by roentgenography — **vi·su·al·ize** \ˈvi-zhə-wə-ˌlīz\ *vb*

vi·su·al·iz·er \-ˌlī-zər\ *n* : one that visualizes; *esp* : one whose mental imagery is prevailingly visual — compare AUDILE, TACTILE

visual projection area *n* : STRIATE CORTEX

visual purple *n* : RHODOPSIN

vi·suo·mo·tor \ˌvi-zhə-wō-ˈmō-tər\ *adj* : of or relating to vision and muscular movement 〈~ coordination〉

vi·suo·spa·tial \-ˈspā-shəl\ *adj* : of or relating to thought processes that involve visual and spatial awareness

vi·tal \ˈvīt-ᵊl\ *adj* **1 a** : existing as a manifestation of life **b** : concerned with or necessary to the maintenance of life 〈~ organs〉 **2** : characteristic of life or living beings **3** : recording data relating to lives **4** : of, relating to, or constituting the staining of living tissues — **vi·tal·ly** *adv*

vital capacity *n* : the breathing capacity of the lungs expressed as the number of cubic inches or cubic centimeters of air that can be forcibly exhaled after a full inspiration

vital function *n* : a function of the body (as respiration) on which life is directly dependent

vi·tal·i·ty \vī-ˈta-lə-tē\ *n, pl* **-ties** : capacity to live and develop; *also* : physical or mental vigor esp. when highly developed

Vi·tal·li·um \vī-ˈta-lē-əm\ *trademark* — used for a cobalt-chromium alloy of platinum-white color used esp. for cast dentures and prostheses

vi·tals \ˈvīt-ᵊlz\ *n pl* : vital organs (as the heart, liver, lungs, and brain)

vital signs *n pl* : signs of life: *specif* : the pulse rate, respiratory rate, body temperature, and often blood pressure of a person

vital statistics *n pl* : statistics relating to births, deaths, marriages, health, and disease

vi·ta·min \ˈvī-tə-mən\ *n* : any of various organic substances that are essential in minute quantities to the nutrition of most animals and some plants, act esp. as coenzymes and precursors of coenzymes in the regulation of metabolic processes but do not provide energy or serve as building units, and are present in natural foodstuffs or sometimes produced within the body

vitamin A *n* : any of several fat-soluble vitamins or a mixture of two or more of them whose lack in the animal body causes keratinization of epithelial tissues (as in the eye with result-

ing night blindness and xerophthalmia): as **a** : a pale yellow crystalline alcohol $C_{20}H_{29}OH$ that is found in animal products (as egg yolk, milk, and butter) and esp. in marine fish-liver oils (as of cod, halibut, and shark) — called also *retinol, vitamin A₁* **b** : a yellow viscous liquid alcohol $C_{20}H_{27}OH$ that contains one more double bond in a molecule than vitamin A₁ and is less active biologically in mammals and that occurs esp. in the liver oil of freshwater fish — called also *vitamin A₂*

vitamin A aldehyde *n* : RETINAL

vitamin A₁ \-ˌā-ˈwən\ *n* : VITAMIN A a

vitamin A₂ \-ˌā-ˈtü\ *n* : VITAMIN A b

vitamin B *n* **1** : VITAMIN B COMPLEX **2** : any of numerous members of the vitamin B complex; *esp* : THIAMINE

vitamin B_c \-ˌbē-ˈsē\ *n* : FOLIC ACID

vitamin B complex *n* : a group of water-soluble vitamins found esp. in yeast, seed germs, eggs, liver and flesh, and vegetables that have varied metabolic functions and include coenzymes and growth factors — called also *B complex;* see BIOTIN, CHOLINE, NIACIN, PANTOTHENIC ACID

vitamin B₁ \-ˌbē-ˈwən\ *n* : THIAMINE

vitamin B₁₇ \-ˌbē-ˌse-vən-ˈtēn\ *n* : LAETRILE

vitamin B₆ \-ˌbē-ˈsiks\ *n* : pyridoxine or a closely related compound found widely in combined form and considered essential to vertebrate nutrition

vitamin B_T \-ˌbē-ˈtē\ *n* : CARNITINE

vitamin B₃ \-ˌbē-ˈthrē\ *n* : NIACIN

vitamin B₁₂ \-ˌbē-ˈtwelv\ *n* **1** : a complex cobalt-containing compound $C_{63}H_{88}CoN_{14}O_{14}P$ that occurs esp. in liver, is essential to normal blood formation, neural function, and growth, and is used esp. in treating pernicious and related anemias and in animal feed as a growth factor — called also *cyanocobalamin* **2** : any of several compounds similar to vitamin B₁₂ in action but having different chemistry

vitamin B₂ \-ˌbē-ˈtü\ *n* : RIBOFLAVIN

vitamin C *n* : a water-soluble vitamin $C_6H_8O_6$ found in plants and esp. in fruits and leafy vegetables or made synthetically and used in the prevention and treatment of scurvy and as an antioxidant for foods — called also *ascorbic acid*

vitamin D *n* : any or all of several fat-soluble vitamins chemically related to steroids, essential for normal bone and tooth structure, and found esp. in fish-liver oils, egg yolk, and milk or produced by activation (as by ultraviolet irradiation) of sterols: as **a** : CALCIFEROL **b** : CHOLECALCIFEROL — called also *sunshine vitamin*

vitamin D₃ \-ˌdē-ˈthrē\ *n* : CHOLECALCIFEROL

vitamin D₂ \-ˌdē-ˈtü\ *n* : CALCIFEROL

vitamin E *n* : any of several fat-soluble vitamins that are chemically tocopherols, are essential in the nutrition of various vertebrates in which their absence is associated with infertility, degenerative changes in muscle, or vascular abnormalities, are found esp. in leaves and in seed germ oils, and are used chiefly in animal feeds and as antioxidants; *esp* : ALPHA-TOCOPHEROL

vitamin G *n* : RIBOFLAVIN

vitamin H *n* : BIOTIN

vitamin K *n* **1** : either of two naturally occurring fat-soluble vitamins that are essential for the clotting of blood because of their role in the production of prothrombin in the liver and that are used in preventing and treating hypoprothrombinemia and hemorrhage: **a** : an oily naphthoquinone $C_{31}H_{46}O_2$ that is obtained esp. from alfalfa or made synthetically and that has a fast, potent, and prolonged biological effect — called also *phylloquinone, phytonadione, vitamin K_1;* see MEPHYTON **b** : a crystalline naphthoquinone $C_{41}H_{56}O_2$ that is obtained esp. from putrefied fish meal and is synthesized by various bacteria (as in the intestines) and that is slightly less active biologically than vitamin K_1 — called also *menaquinone, vitamin K_2* **2** : any of several synthetic compounds that are closely related chemically to vitamins K_1 and K_2 but are simpler in structure; *esp* : MENADIONE

vitamin K₁ \-ₐkā-¹wən\ *n* : VITAMIN K 1a

vitamin K₃ \-ₐkā-¹thrē\ *n* : MENADIONE

vitamin K₂ \-ₐkā-¹tü\ *n* : VITAMIN K 1b

vitamin M *n* : FOLIC ACID

vi•ta•min•ol•o•gy \ₐvī-tə-mə-¹nä-lə-jē\ *n, pl* **-gies** : a branch of knowledge dealing with vitamins, their nature, action, and use

vitamin PP \-ₐpē-¹pē\ *n* : NIACIN

vitell- *or* **vitello-** *comb form* : yolk : vitellus ⟨*vitellogenesis*⟩

vi•tel•lin \vī-¹te-lən, və-\ *n* : a phosphoprotein in egg yolk — called also *ovovitellin*

vi•tel•line \-¹te-lən, -ₐlēn, -ₐlīn\ *adj* : of, relating to, or producing yolk

vitelline duct *n* : OMPHALOMESENTERIC DUCT

vitelline membrane *n* : a membrane enclosing the egg proper and corresponding to the plasma membrane of an ordinary cell

vi•tel•lo•gen•e•sis \vī-ₐte-lō-¹je-nə-səs, və-\ *n, pl* **-e•ses** \-ₐsēz\ : yolk formation — **vi•tel•lo•gen•ic** \-¹je-nik\ *adj*

vi•tel•lus \vī-¹te-ləs, və-\ *n* : the egg cell proper including the yolk but excluding any albuminous or membranous envelopes; *also* : YOLK

vit•il•i•go \ₐvi-tə-¹lī-gō, -¹lē-\ *n* : a skin disorder manifested by smooth white spots on various parts of the body — compare LEUKODERMA

vit•rec•to•my \və-¹trek-tə-mē\ *n, pl*

-mies : surgical removal of all or part of the vitreous humor

¹vit•re•ous \¹vi-trē-əs\ *adj* : of, relating to, constituting, or affecting the vitreous humor ⟨∼ hemorrhages⟩

²vitreous *n* : VITREOUS HUMOR

vitreous body *n* : VITREOUS HUMOR

vitreous humor *n* : the clear colorless transparent jelly that fills the eyeball posterior to the lens and is enclosed by a delicate hyaloid membrane

vitro — see IN VITRO

Vi•vac•til \vī-¹vak-til\ *trademark* — used for a preparation of protriptyline

vivax malaria \¹vī-ₐvaks-\ *n* : malaria caused by a plasmodium (*Plasmodium vivax*) that induces paroxysms at 48-hour intervals — compare FALCIPARUM MALARIA

vivi- *comb form* : alive : living ⟨*vivisection*⟩

vi•vip•a•rous \vī-¹vi-pə-rəs, və-\ *adj* : producing living young instead of eggs from within the body in the manner of nearly all mammals, many reptiles, and a few fishes — compare OVIPAROUS, OVOVIVIPAROUS — **vi•vi•par•i•ty** \ₐvī-və-¹par-ə-tē, ₐvi-\ *n*

vivi•sec•tion \ₐvi-və-¹sek-shən, ¹vi-və-\ *n* : the cutting of or operation on a living animal usu. for physiological or pathological investigation — **vivi•sect** \-¹sekt\ *vb* — **vivi•sec•tion•ist** \ₐvi-və-¹sek-sh(ə-)nəst\ *n*

vivo — see IN VIVO

VLDL \ₐvē-(ₐ)el-(ₐ)dē-¹el\ *n* : a plasma lipoprotein that is produced primarily by the liver with lesser amounts contributed by the intestine, that contains relatively large amounts of triglycerides compared to protein, and that leaves a residue of cholesterol in the tissues during the process of conversion to LDL — called also *very low-density lipoprotein;* compare HDL, LDL

VMA *abbr* vanillylmandelic acid

VMD *abbr* doctor of veterinary medicine

VNA *abbr* Visiting Nurse Association

vo•cal \¹vō-kəl\ *adj* **1** : uttered by the voice : ORAL **2** : having or exercising the power of producing voice, speech, or sound **3** : of, relating to, or resembling the voice — **vo•cal•ly** *adv*

vocal cord *n* **1** *pl* : either of two pairs of folds of mucous membrane of which each member of each pair stretches from the thyroid cartilage in front to the arytenoid cartilage in back, contains a band of fibrous or elastic tissue, and has a free edge projecting into the cavity of the larynx toward the contralateral member of the same pair forming a cleft which can be opened or closed: **a** : FALSE VOCAL CORDS **b** : TRUE VOCAL CORDS **2** : VOCAL LIGAMENT

vocal folds *n pl* : TRUE VOCAL CORDS

vo•ca•lis \vō-¹kä-ləs\ *n* : a small muscle that is the medial part of the thyroarytenoid, originates in the lamina of the thyroid cartilage, inserts in the vocal process of the arytenoid cartilage, and modulates the tension of the true vocal cords

vo·cal·i·za·tion \ˌvō-kə-lə-ˈzā-shən\ n : the act or process of producing sounds with the voice; also : a sound thus produced — **vo·cal·ize** vb

vocal ligament n : the band of yellow elastic tissue contained in each true vocal cord and stretching between the thyroid and arytenoid cartilages — called also *inferior thyroarytenoid ligament*

vocal process n : the anterior angle of the arytenoid cartilage on each side of the larynx to which the vocal ligament of the corresponding side is attached

voice \ˈvȯis\ n 1 : sound produced esp. by means of lungs or larynx; esp : sound so produced by human beings 2 : the faculty of utterance : SPEECH

voice box n : LARYNX

void \ˈvȯid\ vb : to discharge or emit (as excrement)

vol abbr volume

vo·lar \ˈvō-lər, -ˌlär\ adj : relating to the palm of the hand or the sole of the foot; specif : located on the same side as the palm of the hand

vol·a·tile \ˈvä-lə-təl, -ˌtīl\ adj : readily vaporizable at a relatively low temperature — **vol·a·til·i·ty** \ˌvä-lə-ˈti-lə-tē\ n

volatile oil n : an oil that vaporizes readily; esp : ESSENTIAL OIL

volitantes — see MUSCAE VOLITANTES

vo·li·tion \vō-ˈli-shən, və-\ n 1 : an act of making a choice or decision; also : a choice or decision made 2 : the power of choosing or determining — **vo·li·tion·al** \-ˈli-shə-nəl\ adj

Volk·mann's canal \ˈfōlk-mənz-\ n : any of the small channels in bone that transmit blood vessels from the periosteum into the bone and that lie perpendicular to and communicate with the Haversian canals

> Volkmann, Alfred Wilhelm (1800–1877), German physiologist.

Volkmann's contracture or **Volkmann contracture** n : ischemic contracture of an extremity and esp. of a hand

volt \ˈvōlt\ n : the practical mks unit of electrical potential difference and electromotive force equal to the difference of potential between two points in a conducting wire carrying a constant current of one ampere when the power dissipated between these two points is equal to one watt

> Vol·ta \ˈvōl-tä\, Alessandro Giuseppe Antonio Anastasio (1745–1827), Italian physicist.

volt·age \ˈvōl-tij\ n : electrical potential or potential difference expressed in volts

voltage clamp n, often attrib : stabilization of a membrane potential by de-

polarization and maintenance at a given potential by means of a current from a source outside the living system — **voltage clamp** vb

vol·un·tary \ˈvä-lən-ˌter-ē\ adj 1 : proceeding from the will or from one's own choice or consent 2 : of, relating to, subject to, or regulated by the will (~ behavior) — **vol·un·tari·ly** adv

voluntary hospital n : a hospital that is operated under individual, partnership, or corporation control usu. for little or no profit and provides mainly semiprivate and private care

voluntary muscle n : muscle (as most striated muscle) under voluntary control

vol·vu·lus \ˈväl-vyə-ləs\ n : a twisting of the intestine upon itself that causes obstruction — compare ILEUS

vo·mer \ˈvō-mər\ n : a bone of the skull that in humans forms the posterior and inferior part of the nasal septum comprising a vertical plate pointed in front and expanding at the upper back part into lateral wings

vom·ero·na·sal \ˌvä-mə-rō-ˈnā-zəl, ˌvō-\ adj : of or relating to the vomer and the nasal region and esp. to Jacobson's organ or the vomeronasal cartilage

vomeronasal cartilage n : a narrow process of cartilage between the vomer and the cartilage of the nasal septum

vomeronasal organ n : JACOBSON'S ORGAN

vomica — see NUX VOMICA

¹**vom·it** \ˈvä-mət\ n 1 : VOMITING 2 : stomach contents disgorged through the mouth — called also *vomitus*

²**vomit** vb : to disgorge the contents of the stomach through the mouth

vomiting n : an act or instance of disgorging the contents of the stomach through the mouth — called also *emesis*

vomiting center n : a nerve center in the medulla oblongata concerned in the act of vomiting

vom·i·tus \ˈvä-mə-təs\ n : VOMIT 2

von Grae·fe's sign \vän-ˈgrā-fəz-\ n : the failure of the upper eyelid to follow promptly and smoothly the downward movement of the eyeball that is seen in exophthalmic goiter

> von Grae·fe \fȯn-ˈgre-fə\, Albrecht Friedrich Wilhelm Ernst (1828–1870), German ophthalmologist.

von Hip·pel–Lin·dau disease \vän-ˈhipal-ˈlin-ˌdau-\ n : a rare genetically determined disease that is characterized by angiomatosis of the retina and cerebellum and often by cysts or neoplasms of the liver, pancreas, and kidneys — called also *Lindau's disease*

> von Hippel, Eugen (1867–1939), German ophthalmologist.
> Lindau, Arvid Vilhelm (1892–1958), Swedish pathologist.

von Reck·ling·hau·sen's disease \-ˈreklin-ˌhaù-zənz-\ *n* : NEUROFIBROMA-TOSIS

F. D. Recklinghausen — see RECK-LINGHAUSEN'S DISEASE

on Wil·le·brand's disease \vän-ˈvi-lə-ˌbränts-\ *n* : a genetic disorder that is inherited as an autosomal recessive trait and is characterized by deficiency of a plasma clotting factor and by mucosal and petechial bleeding due to abnormal blood vessels

Willebrand, Erik Adolf von (1870–1949), Finnish physician.

orticosa — see VENA VORTICOSA

or·ti·cose vein \ˈvòr-tə-ˌkōs-\ *n* : VENA VORTICOSA

oy·eur \vòi-ˈyər, vwä-\ *n* : one obtaining sexual gratification from seeing sex organs and sexual acts; *broadly* : one who habitually seeks sexual stimulation by visual means — **voy·eur·ism** \-ˌi-zəm\ *n* — **voy·eur·is·tic** \ˌvwä-(ˌ)yər-ˈis-tik, ˌvòi-ər-\ *adj*

'S *abbr* vesicular stomatitis

SD *abbr* ventricular septal defect

ulgaris — see ACNE VULGARIS, ICH-THYOSIS VULGARIS, LUPUS VULGARIS, PEMPHIGUS VULGARIS, VERRUCA VULGARIS

ul·ner·a·ble \ˈvəl-nə-rə-bəl\ *adj* : capable of being hurt : susceptible to injury or disease — **vul·ner·a·bil·i·ty** \ˌvəl-nə-rə-ˈbi-lə-tē\ *n*

vul·sel·lum \vəl-ˈse-ləm\ *n, pl* **-sel·la** \-ˈse-lə\ : a surgical forceps with serrated, clawed, or hooked blades

vulv- *or* **vulvo-** *comb form* 1 : vulva (*vulvitis*) 2 : vulvar and (*vulvovaginal*)

vul·va \ˈvəl-və\ *n, pl* **vul·vae** \-ˌvē, -ˌvī\ : the external parts of the female genital organs comprising the mons pubis, labia majora, labia minora, clitoris, vestibule of the vagina, bulb of the vestibule, and Bartholin's glands — **vul·val** \ˈvəl-vəl\ *or* **vul·var** \-vər\ *adj*

vulvae — see KRAUROSIS VULVAE, PRURITUS VULVAE

vul·vec·to·my \ˌvəl-ˈvek-tə-mē\ *n, pl* **-mies** : surgical excision of the vulva

vul·vi·tis \ˌvəl-ˈvī-təs\ *n* : inflammation of the vulva

vul·vo·vag·i·nal \ˌvəl-vō-ˈva-jən-ᵊl\ *adj* : of or relating to the vulva and the vagina (∼ hematoma)

vul·vo·vag·i·ni·tis \ˌvəl-vō-ˌva-jə-ˈnī-təs\ *n, pl* **-nit·i·des** \-ˈni-tə-ˌdēz\ : coincident inflammation of the vulva and vagina

W

V *symbol* [German *wolfram*] tungsten

Vaar·den·burg's syndrome \ˈvar-dən-ˌbergz-\ *n* : a highly variable genetic disorder inherited as an autosomal dominant trait and accompanied by all, any, or none of deafness, a white forelock, widely spaced eyes, and heterochromia of the irises

Waardenburg, Petrus Johannes (*b* 1886), Dutch ophthalmologist.

vad·ding \ˈwä-diŋ\ *n* : a soft absorbent sheet of cotton, wool, or cellulose used esp. in hospitals for surgical dressings

WAIS *abbr* Wechsler Adult Intelligence Scale

vaist \ˈwāst\ *n* : the narrowed part of the body between the thorax and hips

vaist·line \ˈwāst-ˌlīn\ *n* : body circumference at the waist

'ake·ful \ˈwāk-fəl\ *adj* : not sleeping or able to sleep : SLEEPLESS — **wake·ful·ness** *n*

Val·den·ström's macroglobulinemia \ˈväl-dən-ˌstremz-\ *n* : a rare progressive syndrome associated with a high serum concentration of a monoclonal antibody of the class IgM and characterized by adenopathy, hepatomegaly, splenomegaly, anemia, and lymphocytosis and plasmacytosis of the bone marrow

Waldenström, Jan Gosta (*b* 1906), Swedish physician.

Val·dey·er's ring \ˈväl-ˌdī-ərz-\ *n* : a ring of lymphatic tissue formed by the two palatine tonsils, the pharyngeal tonsil, the lingual tonsil, and intervening lymphoid tissue

Wal·dey·er-Hartz \ˈväl-ˌdī-ər-ˈhärts\, **Heinrich Wilhelm Gottfried von** (1836–1921), German anatomist.

walk·er \ˈwò-kər\ *n* : a framework designed to support a baby learning to walk or an infirm or handicapped person

'walk–in \ˈwòk-ˌin\ *adj* : providing medical services to ambulatory patients without an appointment (a ∼ clinic); *also* : being an individual who uses such services

²walk–in *n* : a walk-in patient

walk·ing \ˈwò-kiŋ\ *adj* : able to walk : AMBULATORY (the ∼ wounded)

walking cast *n* : a cast that is worn on a patient's leg and has a stirrup with a heel or other supporting device embedded in the plaster to facilitate walking

walking pneumonia *n* : a usu. mild pneumonia caused by a microorganism of the genus *Mycoplasma* (*M. pneumoniae*) and characterized by malaise, cough, and often fever

wall \ˈwòl\ *n* : a structural layer surrounding a cavity, hollow organ, or mass of material (the intestinal ∼s) — **walled** \ˈwòld\ *adj*

Wal·le·ri·an degeneration \wä-ˈlir-ē-ən-\ *n* : degeneration of nerve fibers that occurs following injury or disease and that progresses from the place of injury along the axon away from the cell body while the part between the place of injury and the cell body remains intact

Wal·ler \'wä-lər\, **Augustus Volney** (1816–1870), British physiologist.

wall·eye \'wo-ˌlī\ n **1a** : an eye with a whitish or bluish white iris **b** : an eye with an opaque white cornea **2a** : strabismus in which the eye turns outward away from the nose — called also *exotropia*; compare CROSS-EYE 1 **b** *pl* : eyes affected with divergent strabismus — **wall·eyed** \-ˈlīd\ *adj*

¹**wan·der·ing** \'wän-də-riŋ\ *adj* : FLOATING ⟨a ~ spleen⟩

²**wandering** n : movement of a tooth out of its normal position esp. as a result of periodontal disease

wandering cell n : any of various ameboid phagocytic tissue cells

wandering pacemaker n : a back and forth shift in the location of cardiac pacemaking esp. from the sinoatrial node to or near the atrioventricular node

Wan·gen·steen apparatus \'waŋ-ən-ˌstēn-, -gən-\ n : the apparatus used in Wangensteen suction — called also *Wangensteen appliance*

Wangensteen, Owen Harding (1898–1981), American surgeon.

Wangensteen suction n : a method of draining fluid or secretions from body cavities (as the stomach) by means of an apparatus that operates on negative pressure

war·ble \'wor-bəl\ n **1** : a swelling under the hide esp. of the back of cattle, horses, and wild mammals caused by the maggot of a botfly or warble fly **2** : the maggot of a warble fly — **war·bled** \-bəld\ *adj*

warble fly n : any of various dipteran flies (family Oestridae) whose larvae live under the skin of various mammals and cause warbles

ward \'word\ n : a division in a hospital; *esp* : a large room in a hospital where a number of patients often requiring similar treatment are accommodated ⟨a diabetic ~⟩

war·fa·rin \'wor-fə-rən\ n : an anticoagulant coumarin-derivative $C_{19}H_{16}O_4$ related to dicumarol that inhibits the production of prothrombin by vitamin K and is used as a rodent poison and in medicine; *also* : its sodium salt $C_{19}H_{15}N_4O_4$ used esp. in the prevention or treatment of thromboembolic disease — see COUMADIN

war gas n : a gas for use in warfare — compare LACRIMATOR, NERVE GAS, STERNUTATOR

warm-blood·ed \'worm-ˈblə-dəd\ *adj* : having a relatively high and constant body temperature relatively independent of the surroundings — **warm-blood·ed·ness** n

warm up *vb* : to engage in preliminary

exercise (as to stretch the muscles) — **warm-up** \'wor-ˌməp\ n

war neurosis n : a neurosis (as hysteri[a] or anxiety) occurring in soldiers du[r]ing war and attributed to their war ex[-] periences

wart \'wort\ n **1** : a horny projection o[n] the skin usu. of the extremities pr[o]duced by proliferation of the skin pa[-] pillae and caused by a virus — calle[d] also *verruca vulgaris* **2** : any of n[u]merous verrucous skin lesions — **warty** \'wär-tē\ *adj*

War·thin–Star·ry stain \'wor-thən-ˈstär-ē-\ n : a silver nitrate stain use[d] to show the presence of bacilli

Warthin, Aldred Scott (1866–1931[)] and **Starry, Allen Chronister** ([b.] 1890), American pathologists.

¹**wash** \'wosh, 'wäsh\ *vb* **1** : to cleans[e] by or as if by the action of liquid (a[s] water) **2** : to flush or moisten (a bodil[y] part or injury) with a liquid **3** : to pas[s] through a liquid to carry off impur[i]ties or soluble components

²**wash** n : a liquid medicinal preparatio[n] used esp. for cleansing or antisepsi[s] — see EYEWASH, MOUTHWASH

wash·able \'wo-shə-bəl, 'wä-\ *adj* : so[l]uble in water ⟨~ ointment bases⟩

washings n pl : material collected b[y] the washing of a bodily cavity

wash·out \'wosh-ˌaut, 'wäsh-\ n : th[e] action or process of progressively re[-] ducing the concentration of a sub[-] stance (as a dye injected into the le[ft] ventricle of the heart)

wasp \'wäsp, 'wosp\ n : any of numer[-] ous social or solitary winged hyme[n]nopteran insects (esp. familie[s] Sphecidae and Vespidae) that usu[.] have a slender smooth body with th[e] abdomen attached by a narrow stalk[,] biting mouthparts, and in the female[s] and workers an often formidabl[e] sting

Was·ser·mann \'wä-sər-mən, 'vä-\ : WASSERMANN TEST

Wassermann reaction n : the comple[-] ment-fixing reaction that occurs in [a] positive complement-fixation test fo[r] syphilis using the serum of an infect[-] ed individual

Wassermann, August Paul von (1866[–] 1925), German bacteriologist.

Wassermann test n : a test for the de[-] tection of syphilitic infection usin[g] the Wassermann reaction — calle[d] also *Wasserman*

¹**waste** \'wāst\ n **1** : loss through break[-] ing down of bodily tissue **2** pl : bodil[y] waste materials : EXCREMENT

²**waste** *vb* **wast·ed; wast·ing** : to lose o[r] cause to lose weight, strength, or vi[-] tality : EMACIATE — often used wit[h] *away*

³**waste** *adj* : excreted from or stored i[n] inert form in a living body as a by[-] product of vital activity ⟨~ materials⟩

wast·ing \'wās-tiŋ\ *adj* : undergoing o[r] causing decay or loss of strength

wasting *n* : the process or condition of wasting away : gradual loss of strength or substance : ATROPHY

wa·ter \'wȯ-tər, 'wä-\ *n* **1** : the liquid that descends from the clouds as rain, is a major constituent of all living matter, is an odorless, tasteless, very slightly compressible liquid oxide of hydrogen H_2O, and freezes at 0° C (32° F) and boils at 100° C (212° F) **2** : liquid containing or resembling water: as **a** (1) : a pharmaceutical or cosmetic preparation made with water (2) : a watery solution of a gaseous or readily volatile substance — see AMMONIA WATER **b** : a watery fluid (as tears or urine) formed or circulating in a living body **c** : AMNIOTIC FLUID — often used in pl.; *also* : BAG OF WATERS

water balance *n* : the ratio between the water assimilated into the body and that lost from the body; *also* : the condition of the body when this ratio approximates unity

water blister *n* : a blister with a clear watery content that is not purulent or sanguineous

wa·ter·borne \'wȯ-tər-ˌbōrn, 'wä-\ *adj* : carried or transmitted by water and esp. by drinking water

water brash *n* : regurgitation of an excessive accumulation of saliva from the lower part of the esophagus often with some acid material from the stomach — compare HEARTBURN

water–hammer pulse *n* : CORRIGAN'S PULSE

water hemlock *n* : a Eurasian perennial herb (*Cicuta virosa*) of the carrot family (Umbelliferae) that is highly poisonous; *also* : any of several related plants

Wa·ter·house–Frid·er·ich·sen syndrome \'wȯ-tər-ˌhaus-'fri-də-rik-sən-\ *n* : acute and severe meningococcemia with hemorrhage into the adrenal glands

    Waterhouse, Rupert (1873–1958), British physician, and **Friderichsen, Carl** (*b* 1886), Danish physician.

wa·ter·logged \-ˌlägd\ *adj* : EDEMATOUS

water moc·ca·sin \-'mä-kə-sən\ *n* : a venomous pit viper (*Agkistrodon piscivorus*) of the southern U.S. closely related to the copperhead — called also *cottonmouth, cottonmouth moccasin*

water on the brain *n* : HYDROCEPHALUS

water on the knee *n* : an accumulation of inflammatory exudate in the knee joint often following an injury

water pick \-ˌpik\ *n* : a tooth-cleaning device that cleans by directing a stream of water over and between teeth

water pill *n* : a diuretic pill

water–soluble *adj* : soluble in water (∼ vitamin B)

wa·tery \'wȯ-tə-rē, 'wä-\ *adj* **1** : consisting of or filled with water **2** : containing, sodden with, or yielding water or a thin liquid (∼ stools)

Wat·son–Crick \'wät-sən-'krik\ *adj* : of or relating to the Watson-Crick model (*Watson-Crick* helix)

    Watson, James Dewey (*b* 1928), American molecular biologist.
    Crick, Francis Harry Compton (*b* 1916), British molecular biologist.

Watson–Crick model *n* : a model of DNA structure in which the molecule is a double-stranded helix, each strand is composed of alternating links of phosphate and deoxyribose, and the strands are linked by pairs of purine and pyrimidine bases projecting inward from the deoxyribose sugars and joined by hydrogen bonds with adenine paired with thymine and with cytosine paired with guanine — compare DOUBLE HELIX

watt \'wät\ *n* : the mks unit of power equal to the work done at the rate of one joule per second or to the power produced by a current of one ampere across a potential difference of one volt

    Watt, James (1736–1819), British engineer and inventor.

wave \'wāv\ *n* **1a** : a disturbance or variation that transfers energy progressively from point to point in a medium and that may take the form of an elastic deformation or of a variation of pressure, electric or magnetic intensity, electric potential, or temperature **b** : one complete cycle of such a disturbance **2** : an undulating or jagged line constituting a graphic representation of an action (an electroencephalographic ∼)

wave·form \'wāv-ˌfȯrm\ *n* : a usu. graphic representation of a wave that indicates its characteristics (as frequency and amplitude) — called also *waveshape*

wave·length \-ˌleŋkth\ *n* : the distance in the line of advance of a wave from any one point to the next point of corresponding phase — symbol λ

wax \'waks\ *n* **1** : a substance secreted by bees that is a dull yellow solid plastic when warm — called also *beeswax* **2** : any of various substances resembling beeswax: as **a** : any of numerous substances of plant or animal origin that differ from fats in being less greasy, harder, and more brittle and in containing principally compounds of high molecular weight **b** : a pliable or liquid composition used esp. in uniting surfaces, making patterns or impressions, or producing a polished surface (dental ∼es) **3** : a waxy secretion; *esp* : EARWAX

wax·ing *n* : the process of removing body hair with a depilatory wax

waxy \'wak-sē\ *adj* **wax·i·er; -est 1** : made of, abounding in, or covered with wax **2** : resembling wax (∼ secretions)

waxy flexibility *n* : a condition in which a patient's limbs retain any position into which they are manipulated by another person and which occurs esp. in catatonic schizophrenia

WBC *abbr* white blood cell

weal \'wēl\ *n* : WELT

wean \'wēn\ *vb* **1** : to accustom (as a child) to take food otherwise than by nursing **2** : to detach usu. gradually from a cause of dependence or form of treatment

web \'web\ *n* : a tissue or membrane of an animal or plant; *esp* : that uniting fingers or toes at their bases — **webbed** \'webd\ *adj*

Web·er–Chris·tian disease \'we-bər-'kris-chən-\ *also* **Web·er–Chris·tian's disease** \-chənz-\ *n* : PANNICULITIS 2
Weber, Frederick Parkes (1863–1962), British physician.
H. A. Christian — see HAND-SCHÜLLER-CHRISTIAN DISEASE

We·ber–Fech·ner law \'we-bər-'fek-nər-, 'vā-bər-'fek-nər-\ *n* : an approximately accurate generalization in psychology: the intensity of a sensation is proportional to the logarithm of the intensity of the stimulus causing it — called also *Fechner's law*
Weber, Ernst Heinrich (1795–1878), German anatomist and physiologist.
Fechner, Gustav Theodor (1801–1887), German physicist and psychologist.

We·ber's law \'we-bərz-, 'vā-bərz-\ *n* : an approximately accurate generalization in psychology: the smallest change in the intensity of a stimulus capable of being perceived is proportional to the intensity of the original stimulus
E. H. Weber — see WEBER-FECHNER LAW

We·ber test \'we-bər-, 'vā-\ *or* **We·ber's test** \-bərz-\ *n* : a test to determine the nature of unilateral hearing loss in which a vibrating tuning fork is held against the forehead at the midline and conduction deafness is indicated if the sound is heard more loudly in the affected ear and nerve deafness is indicated if it is heard more loudly in the normal ear
We·ber–Liel \'vā-bər-'lēl\, Friedrich Eugen (1832–1891), German otologist.

Wechs·ler Adult Intelligence Scale \'weks-lər-\ *n* : an updated version of the Wechsler-Bellevue test having the same structure but standardized against a different population to more accurately reflect the general population — abbr. WAIS
Wechsler, David (1896–1981), American psychologist.

Wechs·ler–Belle·vue test \-'bel-ˌvyü-\ *n* : a test of general intelligence and coordination in adults that involves both verbal and performance tests and is now superseded by the Wechsler Adult Intelligence Scale — called also *Wechsler-Bellevue scale*

wedge pressure \'wej-\ *n* : intravascular pressure that is measured by means of a catheter wedged into the pulmonary artery so as to block the flow of blood and that is equivalent to the pressure in the left atrium — called also *pulmonary capillary wedge pressure, pulmonary wedge pressure*

wedge resection *n* : any of several surgical procedures for removal of a wedge-shaped mass of tissue (as from the ovary or a lung)

WEE *abbr* western equine encephalomyelitis

weep \'wēp\ *vb* **wept** \'wept\; **weeping 1** : to pour forth (tears) from the eyes **2** : to exude (a fluid) slowly

Weg·e·ner's granulomatosis \'ve-gə-nərz-\ *n* : an uncommon disease of unknown cause that is characterized esp. by granuloma formation in the respiratory tract, glomerulonephritis, and necrotizing granulomatous vasculitis
Wegener, F. (*fl* 1936–39), German pathologist.

weigh \'wā\ *vb* **1** : to find the heaviness of **2** : to measure or apportion (a definite quantity) on or as if on a scale **3** : to have weight or a specified weight

weight \'wāt\ *n* **1** : the amount that a thing weighs **2** : a unit of weight or mass

weight·less·ness \'wāt-ləs-nəs\ *n* : the state or condition of having little or no weight due to lack of apparent gravitational pull — **weight·less** *adj*

Weil–Fe·lix reaction \'vīl-'fā-liks-\ *n* : an agglutination test for various rickettsial infections (as typhus and tsutsugamushi disease) using particular strains of bacteria of the genus *Proteus* that have antigens in common with the rickettsias to be identified — called also *Weil-Felix test*
Weil, Edmund (1880–1922), and Felix, Arthur (1887–1956), Austrian bacteriologists.

Weil's disease \'vīlz-, 'wīlz-\ *n* : a leptospirosis that is characterized by chills, fever, muscle pain, and hepatitis manifested by more or less severe jaundice and that is caused by a spirochete of the genus *Leptospira* (*L. interrogans* serotype *icterohaemorrhagiae*)
Weil, Adolf (1848–1916), German physician.

well \'wel\ *adj* **1** : free or recovered from infirmity or disease : HEALTHY **2** : completely cured or healed

well–adjusted *adj* : WELL-BALANCED 2

well–balanced *adj* **1** : nicely or evenly balanced, arranged, or regulated (a ∼ diet) **2** : emotionally or psychologically untroubled

well·ness *n* : the quality or state of being in good health esp. as an actively sought goal

welt \'welt\ *n* : a ridge or lump raised on the body usu. by a blow

wen \'wen\ *n* : SEBACEOUS CYST; *broadly* : an abnormal growth or a cyst protruding from a surface esp. of the skin

Wencke·bach period \'weŋ-kə-ˌbäk-\ *n* : WENCKEBACH PHENOMENON

Wenckebach, Karel Frederik (1864–1940), Dutch internist.

Wenckebach phenomenon *n* : heart block in which a pulse from the atrium periodically does not reach the ventricle and which is characterized by progressive prolongation of the P-R interval until a pulse is skipped

Werd·nig–Hoff·mann disease \'vert-nik-'hóf-ˌmän-\ *n* : muscular atrophy that is caused by degeneration of the ventral horn cells of the spinal cord, is inherited as an autosomal recessive trait, becomes symptomatic during early infancy, is characterized by hypotonia and flaccid paralysis, and is often fatal during childhood — called also *Werdnig-Hoffmann syndrome*

Werdnig, Guido (1844–1919), Austrian neurologist, and **Hoffmann, Johann** (1857–1919), German neurologist.

Werl·hof's disease \'verl-ˌhófs-\ *n* : THROMBOCYTOPENIC PURPURA

Werlhof, Paul Gottlieb (1699–1767), German physician.

Wer·ner's syndrome \'ver-nərz-\ *n* : a rare hereditary disorder characterized by premature aging with associated abnormalities (as dwarfism, cataracts, osteoporosis, and hypogonadism)

Werner, Otto (*b* 1879), German physician.

Wer·nick·e's area \'ver-nə-kəs-\ *n* : an area located in the posterior part of the superior temporal gyrus that plays an important role in the comprehension of language

Wernicke, Carl (1848–1905), German neurologist.

Wernicke's encephalopathy *n* : an inflammatory hemorrhagic encephalopathy that is caused by thiamine deficiency, affects esp. chronic alcoholics, and is characterized by nystagmus, diplopia, ataxia, and degenerative mental disorders (as Korsakoff's psychosis)

Wert·heim operation \'vert-ˌhīm-\ *or* **Wert·heim's operation** \-ˌhīmz-\ *n* : radical hysterectomy for cancer of the uterine cervix

Wertheim, Ernst (1864–1920), Austrian gynecologist.

Wes·ter·gren erythrocyte sedimentation rate \'ves-tər-grən-\ *n* : sedimentation rate of red blood cells determined by the Westergren method — called also *Westergren sedimentation rate*

Westergren, Alf Vilhelm (*b* 1891), Swedish physician.

Westergren method *n* : a method for estimating the sedimentation rate of red blood cells in fluid blood

Western blot *n* : a blot consisting of a sheet of a cellulose derivative that contains spots of protein for identification by a suitable molecular probe and is used esp. for the detection of antibodies — compare NORTHERN BLOT, SOUTHERN BLOT — **Western blotting** *n*

western equine encephalomyelitis *n* : EQUINE ENCEPHALOMYELITIS b

wet dream *n* : an erotic dream culminating in orgasm and in the male accompanied by seminal emission

wet mount *n* : a glass slide holding a specimen suspended in a drop of liquid (as water) for microscopic examination; *also* : a specimen mounted in this way — **wet–mount** *adj*

wet nurse *n* : a woman who cares for and suckles young not her own

wetting agent *n* : any of numerous water-soluble or liquid organic substances that promote spreading of a liquid on a surface or penetration into a material esp. by their oriented adsorption on the surfaces in such a way that the wetting liquid is no longer repelled

Whar·ton's duct \'hwórt-ᵊnz-, 'wórt-\ *n* : the duct of the submandibular gland that opens into the mouth on a papilla at the side of the frenulum of the tongue

Wharton, Thomas (1614–1673), British anatomist.

Wharton's jelly *n* : a soft connective tissue that occurs in the umbilical cord and consists of large stellate fibroblasts and a few wandering cells and macrophages embedded in a homogeneous jellylike intercellular substance

wheal \'hwēl, 'wēl\ *n* : a suddenly formed elevation of the skin surface: as a : WELT b : the transient lump occurring at the site of injection of a solution before the solution is normally dispersed c : a flat burning or itching eminence on the skin (urticarial ∼s)

whealing *n* : the presence or development of wheals

wheat germ *n* : the embryo of the wheat kernel separated in milling and used esp. as a source of vitamins and protein

wheel·chair \'hwēl-ˌchar, 'wēl-\ *n* : a chair mounted on wheels esp. for the use of disabled persons

¹**wheeze** \'hwēz, 'wēz\ *vb* **wheezed; wheez·ing** : to breathe with difficulty usu. with a whistling sound

²**wheeze** *n* : a sibilant whistling sound caused by difficult or obstructed respiration

whey \'hwā, 'wā\ *n* : the serum or watery part of milk that is separated from the coagulable part or curd, is rich in lactose, minerals, and ˌvitamins, and contains lactalbumin and traces of fat

whip-lash *hwip-₊lash, *wip-\ *n* : WHIP-LASH INJURY

whiplash injury *n* : injury resulting from a sudden sharp whipping movement of the neck and head (as of a person in a vehicle that is struck head-on or from the rear by another vehicle)

Whip-ple's disease *hwi-pəlz-, *wi-\ *n* ; a rare malabsorption syndrome that is often associated with the presence of an actinomycetous fungus (*Tropheryma whippelli*) in the mucous membrane of the intestine, that affects primarily the small intestine but becomes more generalized affecting esp. the joints, brain, liver, and heart, that is marked by the accumulation of lipid deposits in the intestinal lymphatic tissues, weight loss, joint pain, mental confusion, and generalized lymphadenopathy, and that is diagnosed by the presence of macrophages in the lamina propria of the small intestine which give a positive reaction to a periodic acid-Schiff test — called also *intestinal lipodystrophy*

Whipple, George Hoyt (1878–1976), American pathologist.

whip-worm *hwip-₊wərm, *wip-\ *n* : a parasitic nematode worm of the genus *Trichuris* having a body that is thickened posteriorly and is very long and slender anteriorly: *esp* : one (*T. trichiura*) that parasitizes the human intestine

whirl-pool bath *hwərl-₊pūl-, *wərl-\ *n* : a therapeutic bath in which all or part of the body is exposed to forceful whirling currents of hot water — called also *whirlpool*

white blood cell *n* : any of the blood cells that are colorless, lack hemoglobin, contain a nucleus, and include the lymphocytes, monocytes, neutrophils, eosinophils, and basophils — called also *white blood corpuscle, white cell, white corpuscle;* compare RED BLOOD CELL

white count *n* : the count or the total number of white blood cells in blood usu. stated as the number in one cubic millimeter — compare DIFFERENTIAL BLOOD COUNT

white fat *n* : normal fat tissue that replaces brown fat in infants during the first year of life

white-head *hwīt-₊hed, *wīt-\ *n* : MILIUM

white lotion *n* : a preparation made of sulfurated potash and zinc sulfate that is applied topically in the treatment of various skin disorders

white matter *n* : neural tissue that consists largely of myelinated nerve fibers, has a whitish color, and underlies the gray matter of the brain and spinal cord or is gathered into nerves

white muscle disease *n* : a disease of young domestic animals (as lambs and calves) that is characterized by muscular degeneration — see STIFF= LAMB DISEASE

white noise *n* : a heterogeneous mixture of sound waves extending over a wide frequency range that has been used to mask out unwanted noise interfering with sleep — called also *white sound*

white ointment *n* : an ointment consisting of 5 percent white wax and 95 percent white petrolatum — called also *simple ointment*

white petrolatum *n* : decolorized petroleum jelly — called also *white petroleum jelly*

white piedra *n* : a form of piedra that affects esp. the facial hairs and is caused by a fungus of the genus *Trichosporan* (*T. beigelii*)

white pulp *n* : a parenchymatous tissue of the spleen that consists of compact masses of lymphatic cells and that forms the Malpighian corpuscles — compare RED PULP

white ramus *n* : RAMUS COMMUNICANS a

white ramus communicans *n* : RAMUS COMMUNICANS a

whites *n pl* : LEUKORRHEA

white shark *n* : GREAT WHITE SHARK

white snake-root \-*snāk-₊rūt, -₊rüt\ *n* : a poisonous No. American herb (*Eupatorium rugosum*) of the daisy family (Compositae) that is a cause of trembles and milk sickness

white sound *n* : WHITE NOISE

white squill *n* : SQUILL 2

Whit-field's ointment *hwit-₊fēldz-, *wit-\ *also* **Whit-field ointment** \-₊fēld-\ *n* : an ointment that contains benzoic acid and salicylic acid and is used for its keratolytic effect in treating fungus skin diseases (as ringworm)

Whitfield, Arthur (1868–1947), British dermatologist.

whit-low *hwit-(₊)lō, *wit-\ *n* : a deep usu. suppurative inflammation of the finger or toe esp. near the end or around the nail — called also *felon;* compare PARONYCHIA

WHO *abbr* World Health Organization

whole *hōl\ *adj* : containing all its natural constituents, components, or elements (~ blood)

whole–body *adj* : of, relating to, or affecting the entire body (~ radiation) (~ hyperthermia)

whoop *hüp, *hup, *hwüp\ *n* : the crowing intake of breath following a paroxysm in whooping cough — **whoop** *vb*

whooping cough *n* : an infectious disease esp. of children caused by a bacterium of the genus *Bordetella* (*B. pertussis*) and marked by a convulsive spasmodic cough sometimes followed by a crowing intake of breath — called also *pertussis*

whorl *hwórl, *wórl, *hwərl, *wərl\ *n*

: a fingerprint in which the central papillary ridges turn through at least one complete turn

Wi-dal reaction \vē-ˈdäl- *also* **Wi-dal's reaction** \-ˈdälz-\ *n* : a specific reaction consisting in agglutination of typhoid bacilli or other salmonellas when mixed with serum from a patient having typhoid fever or other salmonella infection and constituting a test for the disease

    Widal, Georges–Fernand–Isidore (1862–1929), French physician and bacteriologist.

Widal test *also* **Widal's test** *n* : a test for detecting typhoid fever and other salmonella infections using the Widal reaction

wide–spectrum *adj* : BROAD-SPECTRUM

wild type *n* : a phenotype, genotype, or gene that predominates in a natural population of organisms or strain of organisms in contrast to that of natural or laboratory mutant forms; *also* : an organism or strain displaying the wild type — **wild–type** *adj*

Wilms' tumor \ˈvilmz-\ *also* **Wilms's tumor** \ˈvilm-zəz-\ *n* : a malignant tumor of the kidney that primarily affects children and is made up of embryonic elements — called also *nephroblastoma*

    Wilms, Max (1867–1918), German surgeon.

Wil-son's disease \ˈwil-sənz-\ *n* : a hereditary disease that is determined by an autosomal recessive gene and is marked esp. by cirrhotic changes in the liver and severe mental disorder due to a ceruloplasmin deficiency and resulting inability to metabolize copper — called also *hepatolenticular degeneration;* see KAYSER-FLEISCHER RING

    Wilson, Samuel Alexander Kinnier (1877–1937), British neurologist.

wind–broken \ˈwind-ˌbrō-kən\ *adj, of a horse* : affected with pulmonary emphysema or with heaves

wind–burn \ˈwind-ˌbərn\ *n* : irritation of the skin caused by wind — **wind-burned** \-ˌbərnd\ *adj*

wind–chill \-ˌchil\ *n* : a still-air temperature that would have the same cooling effect on exposed human flesh as a given combination of temperature and wind speed — called also *chill factor, windchill factor, windchill index*

wind–gall \-ˌgȯl\ *n* : a soft tumor or synovial swelling on a horse's leg in the region of the fetlock joint

win-dow \ˈwin-(ˌ)dō\ *n* 1 : FENESTRA 1 2 : a small surgically created opening : FENESTRA 2a

wind–pipe \ˈwind-ˌpīp\ *n* : TRACHEA

wind puff \-ˌpəf\ *n* : WINDGALL

wing \ˈwiŋ\ *n* 1 : one of the movable feathered or membranous paired appendages by means of which a bird, bat, or insect is able to fly 2 : a wing-

like anatomical part or process : ALA; *esp* : any of the four winglike processes of the sphenoid bone — see GREATER WING, LESSER WING — **winged** \ˈwiŋd, ˈwiŋ-əd\ *adj*

win-ter-green \ˈwin-tər-ˌgrēn\ *n* 1 : any plant of the genus *Gaultheria; esp* : a low evergreen plant (*G. procumbens*) with white flowers and spicy red berries 2 : OIL OF WINTERGREEN

wintergreen oil *n* : OIL OF WINTERGREEN

winter itch *n* : an itching disorder caused by prolonged exposure to cold dry air

winter tick *n* : an ixodid tick of the genus *Dermacentor* (*D. albipictus*) that is actively parasitic during the winter months on domestic and big-game animals in parts of Canada and northern and western U.S.

wire \ˈwir\ *n* : metal thread or a rod used in surgery to suture soft tissue or transfix fractured bone and in orthodontic dentistry to position teeth — **wire** *vb*

Wir-sung's duct \ˈvir-ˌsu̇ŋz-\ *n* : PANCREATIC DUCT a

    J. G. Wirsung — see DUCT OF WIRSUNG

wisdom tooth *n* : the third molar that is the last tooth to erupt on each side of the upper and lower jaws

wish–fulfillment *n* : the gratification of a desire esp. symbolically (as in dreams or neurotic symptoms)

Wis-kott–Al-drich syndrome \ˈvis-ˌkät-ˈȯl-ˌdrich-\ *n* : an inherited usu. fatal childhood immunodeficiency disease characterized esp. by thrombocytopenia, leukopenia, recurrent infections, eczema, and abnormal bleeding

    Wiskott, Alfred (*b* 1898), German pediatrician.

    Aldrich, Robert Anderson (*b* 1917), American pediatrician.

witch ha-zel \ˈwich-ˌhā-zəl\ *n* 1 : a small tree or shrub (*Hamamelis virginiana* of the family Hamamelidaceae) of eastern No. America that blooms in the fall 2 : an alcoholic solution of a distillate of the bark of the witch hazel used as a soothing and mildly astringent lotion

with-draw-al \with-ˈdrȯ-əl, with-\ *n* 1 a : a pathological retreat from objective reality (as in some schizophrenic states) b : social or emotional detachment 2 a : the discontinuance of administration or use of a drug b : the syndrome of often painful physical and psychological symptoms that follows discontinuance of an addicting drug 3 : COITUS INTERRUPTUS — **withdraw** \-ˈdrȯ\ *vb*

withdrawal symptom *n* : one of a group of symptoms (as nausea, sweating, or depression) produced by deprivation of an addicting drug

with-drawn \with-ˈdrȯn\ *adj* : socially

detached and unresponsive : exhibiting withdrawal : INTROVERTED

with·ers \'wi-thərz\ *n pl* 1 : the ridge between the shoulder bones of a horse 2 : a part corresponding to the withers in a quadruped other than a horse

Wit·zel·sucht \'vit-səl-ˌzükt\ *n* : excessive facetiousness and inappropriate or pointless humor esp. when considered as part of an abnormal condition

wohl·fahr·tia \ˌvōl-'fär-tē-ə\ *n* 1 *cap* : a genus of dipteran flies (family Sarcophagidae) that commonly deposit their larvae in wounds or on the intact skin of humans and domestic animals causing severe cutaneous myiasis 2 : any fly of the genus *Wohlfahrtia*
  Wol·fart \'vōl-ˌfärt\, **Peter** (1675–1726), German physician.

Wolff·ian body \'wol-fē-ən-\ *n* : MESONEPHROS
  Wolff \'volf\, **Caspar Friedrich** (1734–1794), German anatomist and embryologist.

Wolffian duct *n* : the duct of the mesonephros that persists in the female chiefly as part of the epoophoron and in the male as the duct system leaving the testis and including the epididymis, vas deferens, and ejaculatory duct — called also *mesonephric duct*

Wolff–Par·kin·son–White syndrome \'wulf-'pär-kən-sən-'hwīt-, -'wit-\ *n* : an abnormal heart condition characterized by premature activation of the ventricle by atrial impulses and an electrocardiographic tracing with a shortened P-R interval and a widened QRS complex
  Wolff, Louis (*b* 1898), American cardiologist.
  Parkinson, Sir John (*b* 1885), British cardiologist.
  White, Paul Dudley (1886–1973), American cardiologist.

wol·fram \'wul-frəm\ *n* : TUNGSTEN

womb \'wüm\ *n* : UTERUS

wonder drug *n* : MIRACLE DRUG

wood alcohol *n* : METHANOL

wooden tongue *n* : actinobacillosis or actinomycosis of cattle esp. when chiefly affecting the tongue

wood tick *n* : any of several ixodid ticks: as **a** : ROCKY MOUNTAIN WOOD TICK **b** : AMERICAN DOG TICK

wool fat \'wul-\ *n* : wool grease esp. after refining : LANOLIN

wool grease *n* : a fatty slightly sticky wax coating the surface of the fibers of sheep's wool that is used as a source of lanolin

wool·sort·er's disease \'wul-ˌsor-tərz-\ *n* : pulmonary anthrax resulting esp. from inhalation of bacterial spores (*Bacillus anthracis*) from contaminated wool or hair

word–association test *n* : a test of personality and mental function in which the subject is required to respond to each of a series of words with the first

one that comes to mind or with one of a specified class of words

word blindness *n* : ALEXIA

word salad *n* : a jumble of extremely incoherent speech as sometimes observed in schizophrenia

work·up \'wər-ˌkəp\ *n* : an intensive diagnostic study (a gastrointestinal ∼)

work up \ˌwər-'kəp, 'wər-\ *vb* : to perform a diagnostic workup upon ⟨*work up* a patient⟩

¹**worm** \'wərm\ *n* 1 : any of various relatively small elongated usu. naked and soft-bodied parasitic animals (as a platyhelminth) 2 : HELMINTHIASIS — usu. used in pl. ⟨a dog with ∼s⟩
  worm·like *adj*

²**worm** *vb* : to treat (an animal) with a drug to destroy or expel parasitic worms

worm·er \'wər-mər\ *n* : a worming agent used in veterinary medicine

Wor·mi·an bone \'wòr-mē-ən-\ *n* : a small irregular inconstant plate of bone interposed in a suture between large cranial bones
  Worm \'vòrm\, **Ole** (1588–1654), Danish physician.

worm·seed \'wərm-ˌsēd\ *n* 1 : any of various plants (as of the genera *Artemisia* or *Chenopodium*) whose seeds possess anthelmintic properties

worm·wood \'wərm-ˌwud\ *n* : any of various aromatic shrubs and herbs (genus *Artemisia* and esp. *A. absinthium*) of the daisy family (Compositae)

wound \'wünd\ *n* **1a** : an injury to the body consisting of a laceration or breaking of the skin or mucous membrane usu. by a hard or sharp instrument forcefully driven or applied **b** : an opening made in the skin or a membrane of the body incidental to a surgical operation or procedure 2 : a mental or emotional hurt or blow — **wound** *vb*

wrench \'rench\ *n* : a sharp twist or sudden jerk straining muscles or ligaments; *also* : the resultant injury (as of a joint) — **wrench** *vb*

Wright's stain \'rits-\ *n* : a stain used in staining blood and parasites living in blood
  Wright, James Homer (1869–1928), American pathologist.

wrin·kle \'riŋ-kəl\ *n* : a small ridge or furrow in the skin esp. when due to age, care, or fatigue — **wrinkle** *vb*

wrist \'rist\ *n* : the joint or the region of the joint between the human hand and the arm

wrist·bone \-ˌbōn\ *n* 1 : a carpal bone 2 : the styloid process of the human radius that forms a prominence on the outer side of the wrist above the thumb

wrist–drop \-ˌdräp\ *n* : paralysis of the extensor muscles of the hand causing the hand to hang down at the wrist

wrist joint n : the articulation at the wrist

writer's cramp n : a painful spasmodic cramp of muscles of the hand or fingers brought on by excessive writing — called also *graphospasm*

wry·neck \'rī-ˌnek\ n : TORTICOLLIS

wt abbr weight

Wuch·er·e·ria \ˌwü-kə-'rir-ē-ə\ n : a genus of filarial worms (family Dipetalonematidae) including a parasite (*W. bancrofti*) that causes elephantiasis

Wu·cher·er \'vü-kər-ər\. **Otto Eduard Heinrich** (1820–1873), German physician.

X

x \'eks\ n, pl **x's** or **xs** \'ek-səz\ : the basic or haploid number of chromosomes of a polyploid series : the number contained in a single genome — compare N 1

x symbol power of magnification

Xan·ax \'za-ˌnaks\ trademark — used for a preparation of alprazolam

xanth- or **xantho-** comb form : yellow (*xanthoma*)

xan·than gum \'zan-thən-\ n : a polysaccharide that is produced by fermentation of carbohydrates by a bacterium (*Xanthomonas campestris*) and is a thickening and suspending agent used esp. in pharmaceuticals and prepared foods — called also *xanthan*

xan·the·las·ma \ˌzan-thə-'laz-mə\ n : xanthoma of the eyelid

xanthelasma pal·pe·bra·rum \-ˌpal-pē-'brar-əm\ n : XANTHELASMA

xan·thene dye \'zan-ˌthēn-\ n : any of various brilliant fluorescent yellow to pink to bluish red dyes

xan·thine \'zan-ˌthēn\ n : a feebly basic compound $C_5H_4N_4O_2$ that occurs esp. in animal or plant tissue, is derived from guanine and hypoxanthine, and yields uric acid on oxidation; also : any of various derivatives of this

xan·tho·chro·mia \ˌzan-thə-'krō-mē-ə\ n : xanthochromic discoloration

xan·tho·chro·mic \-'krō-mik\ adj : having a yellowish discoloration (~ cerebrospinal fluid)

xan·tho·ma \zan-'thō-mə\ n, pl **-mas** or **-ma·ta** \-mə-tə\ : a fatty irregular yellow patch or nodule on the skin (as of the eyelids, neck, or back) that is associated esp. with disturbances of cholesterol metabolism

xan·tho·ma·to·sis \ˌzan-ˌthō-mə-'tō-səs\ n, pl **-to·ses** \-ˌsēz\ : any of several metabolic disorders characterized by the accumulation of yellow fatty deposits in the skin and in internal tissues

xan·tho·ma·tous \zan-'thō-mə-təs\ adj : of, relating to, marked by, or characteristic of a xanthoma or xanthomatosis

xan·tho·phyll \'zan-thə-ˌfil\ n : any of several neutral yellow to orange carotenoid pigments that are oxygen derivatives of carotenes; esp : LUTEIN

xan·thop·sia \zan-'thäp-sē-ə\ n : a visual disturbance in which objects appear yellow

xan·tho·tox·in \'zan-thə-ˌtäk-sən\ n : METHOXSALEN

xanth·uren·ic acid \ˌzanth-yə-'re-nik-\ n : a yellow crystalline phenolic acid $C_{10}H_7NO_4$ excreted in the urine when tryptophan is added to the diet of experimental animals deficient in pyridoxine

X chromosome n : a sex chromosome that usu. occurs paired in each female cell and single in each male cell in species in which the male typically has two unlike sex chromosomes — compare Y CHROMOSOME

X–disease n : any of various usu. virus diseases of obscure etiology and relationships; esp : a viral encephalitis of humans first detected in Australia

Xe symbol xenon

xen- or **xeno-** comb form 1 : strange : foreign (*xenobiotic*) 2 : HETER- (*xenograft*)

xe·no·bi·ot·ic \ˌzē-nō-bī-'ä-tik, ˌzē-, -bē-\ n : a chemical compound (as a drug, pesticide, or carcinogen) that is foreign to a living organism — **xenobiotic** adj

xe·no·di·ag·no·sis \ˌzē-nō-ˌdī-ig-'nō-səs, ˌzē-\ n, pl **-no·ses** \-ˌsēz\ : the detection of a parasite by feeding test material (as blood) from a suspected host (as a human) to a suitable intermediate host (as an insect) and later examining the intermediate host for the parasite — **xe·no·di·ag·nos·tic** \-'näs-tik\ adj

xe·no·ge·ne·ic \ˌzē-nō-jə-'nē-ik, ˌzē-\ also **xe·no·gen·ic** \-'je-nik\ adj : derived from, originating in, or being a member of another species — compare ALLOGENEIC, SYNGENEIC

xe·no·graft \'ze-nə-ˌgraft, 'zē-\ n : a graft of tissue taken from a donor of one species and grafted into a recipient of another species — called also *heterograft, heterotransplant;* compare HOMOGRAFT

xe·non \'zē-ˌnän, 'ze-\ n : a heavy, colorless, and relatively inert gaseous element — symbol *Xe;* see ELEMENT table

xe·no·phobe \'ze-nə-ˌfōb, 'zē-\ n : one unduly fearful of what is foreign and esp. of people of foreign origin — **xe·no·pho·bic** \ˌze-nə-'fō-bik, ˌzē-\ adj

xe·no·pho·bia \ˌze-nə-'fō-bē-ə, ˌzē-\

: fear and hatred of strangers or foreigners or of anything that is strange or foreign

Xen·op·syl·la \ze-näp-'si-lə\ n : a genus of fleas (family Pulicidae) including several (as the oriental rat flea) that are important as vectors of plague

xe·no·tro·pic \ze-nə-'trä-pik, zē-nə-'trō-pik\ adj : replicating or reproducing only in cells other than those of the host species (∼ viruses)

xer- or **xero-** comb form : dry : arid ⟨xeroderma⟩

xe·ro·der·ma \zir-ə-'dər-mə\ n : a disease of the skin characterized by dryness and roughness and a fine scaly desquamation

xeroderma pig·men·to·sum \-pig-mən-'tō-səm, -men-\ n : a genetic condition inherited as a recessive autosomal trait that is caused by a defect in mechanisms that repair DNA mutations and is characterized by the development of pigment abnormalities and multiple skin cancers in body areas exposed to the sun — abbr. XP

xe·rog·ra·phy \zə-'räg-rə-fē, zir-'ä-\ n, pl **-phies** 1 : a process for copying graphic matter by the action of light on an electrically charged surface in which the latent image is developed with a resinous powder 2 : XERORADIOGRAPHY — **xe·ro·graph·ic** \zir-ə-'gra-fik\ adj — **xe·ro·graph·i·cal·ly** adv

xe·ro·mam·mog·ra·phy \zir-ō-ma-'mäg-rə-fē\ n, pl **-phies** : xeroradiography of the breast — **xe·ro·mam·mo·gram** \-'ma-mə-gram\ n

xe·roph·thal·mia \zir-äf-'thal-mē-ə, -äp-'thal-\ n : a dry thickened lusterless condition of the eyeball resulting esp. from a severe systemic deficiency of vitamin A — compare KERATOMALACIA — **xe·roph·thal·mic** \-mik\ adj

xe·ro·ra·di·og·ra·phy \zir-ō-rā-dē-'ä-grə-fē\ n, pl **-phies** : radiography used esp. in mammography for breast cancer that produces an image using X rays in a manner similar to the way an image is produced by light in xerography — **xe·ro·ra·dio·graph·ic** \-rā-dē-ō-'gra-fik\ adj

xe·ro·sis \zi-'rō-səs\ n, pl **xe·ro·ses** \-sēz\ : abnormal dryness of a body part or tissue (as the skin)

xe·ro·sto·mia \zir-ə-'stō-mē-ə\ n : abnormal dryness of the mouth due to insufficient secretions — called also dry mouth

xiph- or **xiphi-** or **xipho-** comb form : sword-shaped ⟨xiphisternum⟩

xi·phi·ster·num \zi-fə-'stər-nəm, zi-\ n, pl **-na** \-nə\ : XIPHOID PROCESS

xi·phoid \'zī-föid, 'zi-\ n : XIPHOID PROCESS — **xiphoid** adj

xiphoid process n : the smallest and lowest division of the human sternum that is cartilaginous early in life but becomes more or less ossified during adulthood — called also ensiform cartilage, ensiform process

x-ir·ra·di·a·tion \eks-\ n, often cap X : X-RADIATION 1 — **x-ir·ra·di·ate** vb, often cap X

X-linked adj : located in an X chromosome (an ∼ gene); also : transmitted by an X-linked gene ⟨an ∼ mutation⟩

XP abbr xeroderma pigmentosum

x-ra·di·a·tion n, often cap X 1 : exposure to X rays 2 : radiation composed of X rays

x-ra·di·og·ra·phy n, often cap X, pl **-phies** : radiography by means of X rays : ROENTGENOGRAPHY

x-ray \'eks-rā\ vb, often cap X : to examine, treat, or photograph with X rays

X ray n 1 : any of the electromagnetic radiations of the same nature as visible radiation but of an extremely short wavelength that has the properties of ionizing a gas upon passage through it, of penetrating various thicknesses of all solids, of producing secondary radiations by impinging on material bodies, of acting on photographic films and plates as light does, and of causing fluorescent screens to emit light — called also roentgen ray 2 : a photograph obtained by use of X rays ⟨a chest X ray⟩ — **X-ray** adj

X-ray therapy n : medical treatment (as of cancer) by controlled application of X rays

xy·lene \'zī-lēn\ n : any of three toxic flammable oily isomeric aromatic hydrocarbons C_8H_{10}

xy·li·tol \'zī-lə-töl, -tōl\ n : a crystalline alcohol $C_5H_{12}O_5$ that is a derivative of xylose and is used as a sweetener

Xy·lo·caine \'zī-lə-kān\ trademark — used for a preparation of lidocaine

xy·lose \'zī-lōs, -lōz\ n : a crystalline aldose sugar $C_5H_{10}O_5$

xy·lu·lose \'zīl-yü-lōs, 'zī-lü-, -lōz\ n : a ketose sugar $C_5H_{10}O_5$ of the pentose class that plays a role in carbohydrate metabolism and is found in the urine in cases of pentosuria

Y

Y *symbol* yttrium

yaw \'yo\ *n* : one of the lesions characteristic of yaws

yawn \'yon, 'yän\ *n* : a deep usu. involuntary intake of breath through the wide open mouth often as an involuntary reaction to fatigue or boredom — **yawn** *vb*

yaws \'yoz\ *n sing or pl* : an infectious contagious tropical disease that is caused by a spirochete of the genus *Treponema* (*T. pertenue*) and that is characterized by a primary ulcerating lesion on the skin followed by a secondary stage in which ulcers develop all over the body and by a third stage in which the bones are involved — called also *frambesia, pian*

Yb *symbol* ytterbium

Y chromosome \'wī-\ *n* : a sex chromosome that is characteristic of male cells in species in which the male typically has two unlike sex chromosomes — compare X CHROMOSOME

yeast \'yēst\ *n* **1 a** : a yellowish surface froth or sediment that occurs esp. in saccharine liquids (as fruit juices) in which it promotes alcoholic fermentation, consists largely of cells of a fungus (family Saccharomycetaceae), and is used esp. in the making of alcoholic liquors and as a leaven in baking **b** : a commercial product containing yeast plants in a moist or dry medium **2 a** : a minute fungus (esp. *Saccharomyces cerevisiae*) that is present and functionally active in yeast, usu. has little or no mycelium, and reproduces by budding **b** : any of various similar fungi (esp. orders Endomycetales and Moniliales) — **yeastlike** \-ˌlīk\ *adj*

yeast infection *n* : an infection of the female genital tract by a yeast of the genus *Candida* (*C. albicans*) and characterized by vaginal discharge and vulvovaginitis; *broadly* : an infection (as thrush or tinea versicolor) caused by a yeast fungus

yellow body *n* : CORPUS LUTEUM

yellow fat disease *n* : a disease esp. of swine, cats, and ranch-raised mink that is associated with a deficiency of vitamin E and is marked by inflammation of the fatty tissue, subcutaneous edema, and varied visceral lesions — called also *steatitis, yellow fat*

yellow fever *n* : an acute destructive disease of warm regions marked by sudden onset, prostration, fever, albuminuria, jaundice, and often hemorrhage and caused by a flavivirus transmitted esp. by a mosquito of the genus *Aedes* (*A. aegypti*)

yellow-fever mosquito *n* : a small darkcolored mosquito of the genus *Aedes* (*A. aegypti*) that is the usual vector of yellow fever — called also *tiger mosquito*

yellow jacket *n* **1** : any of various yellow-marked social wasps (esp. genus *Vespula* of the family Vespidae) that usu. nest in the ground and can sting repeatedly and painfully **2** : a yellow capsule containing a preparation of pentobarbital — usu. used in pl.

yellow marrow *n* : MARROW 1a

yellow petrolatum *n* : petrolatum that has not been wholly or mostly decolorized

yellows \'ye-(ˌ)lōz\ *n sing or pl* : any of several diseases of domestic animals (as sheep) that are characterized by jaundice

yellow wax *n* : a wax obtained as a yellow to brown solid by melting a honeycomb with boiling water, straining, and cooling — called also *beeswax*

yerba santa \'yer-bə-'sän-tə, 'yər-, -'san-\ *n* **1** : an evergreen shrub (*Eriodictyon californicum* of the family Hydrophyllaceae) of California with aromatic leaves **2** : ERIODICTYON

Yersinia \yər-'si-nē-ə\ *n* : a genus of enterobacteria that includes several important pathogens (as the plague bacterium, *Y. pestis*) formerly included in the genus *Pasteurella* — see PLAGUE 2

Yersin \yer-'seⁿ\, **Alexandre-Émile-John** (1863–1943), French bacteriologist.

Y ligament *n* : ILIOFEMORAL LIGAMENT

yogurt *also* **yoghurt** \'yō-gərt\ *n* : a fermented slightly acid often flavored semisolid food made of whole or skimmed cow's milk and milk solids to which cultures of bacteria of the genus *Lactobacillus* (*L. bulgarius*) and *Streptococcus* (*S. thermophilus*) have been added

yohimbine \yō-'him-ˌbēn, -bən\ *n* : an alkaloid $C_{21}H_{26}N_2O_3$ that is a weak blocker of alpha-adrenergic receptors and has been used as an aphrodisiac

yolk \'yōk\ *n* : material stored in an ovum that supplies food to the developing embryo and consists chiefly of proteins, lecithin, and cholesterol

yolk sac *n* : a membranous sac that is attached to an embryo and encloses food yolk, that is continuous in most forms through the omphalomesenteric duct with the intestinal cavity of the embryo, that being abundantly supplied with blood vessels is throughout embryonic life and in some forms later the chief organ of nutrition, and that in the mammals having a placenta is nearly vestigial and functions chiefly prior to the formation of the placenta

yolk stalk *n* : OMPHALOMESENTERIC DUCT

Young–Helm·holtz theory \\'yəŋ-'helm-ˌhōlts-\ *n* : a theory in color vision: the eye has three separate elements each of which is stimulated by a different primary color

Young, Thomas (1773–1829), British physician, physicist, and archeologist.

Helmholtz, Hermann Ludwig Ferdinand von (1821–1894), German physicist and physiologist.

yt·ter·bi·um \i-'tər-bē-əm\ *n* : a bivalent or trivalent metallic element — symbol *Yb;* see ELEMENT table

yt·tri·um \'i-trē-əm\ *n* : a trivalent metallic element — symbol *Y;* see ELEMENT table

yup·pie flu \'yə-pē-\ *n* : CHRONIC FATIGUE SYNDROME

Z

zal·cit·a·bine \zal-'si-tə-ˌbēn, -ˌbin\ *n* : DDC

Zan·tac \'zan-ˌtak\ *trademark* — used for a preparation of the hydrochloride of ranitidine

Z–DNA \'zē-\ *n* : a section of DNA that spirals to the left rather than to the right and that may exert some control over the activity of adjacent genes

Zei·gar·nik effect \zī-'gär-nik-\ *n* : the psychological tendency to remember an uncompleted task rather than a completed one

Zeigarnik, Bluma (*b* 1900), Russian psychologist.

Zen·ker's diverticulum \'zeŋ-kərz-, 'tseŋ-\ *n* : an abnormal pouch in the upper part of the esophagus in which food may become trapped causing bad breath, irritation, difficulty in swallowing, and regurgitation — called also *pharyngoesophageal diverticulum*

Zenker, Friedrich Albert von (1825–1898), German pathologist and anatomist.

Zeph·i·ran \'ze-fə-ˌran\ *trademark* — used for a preparation of benzalkonium chloride

Zes·tril \'zes-tril\ *trademark* — used for a preparation of lisinopril

zi·do·vu·dine \zī-'dō-vü-ˌdēn, -vyü-\ *n* : AZIDOTHYMIDINE

Ziehl–Neel·sen stain \'tsēl-'nāl-sən-\ *n* : a stain used esp. for detecting the tubercle bacillus

Ziehl, Franz (1857–1926), German bacteriologist.

Neelsen, Friedrich Carl Adolf (1854–1894), German pathologist.

zi·mel·i·dine \zi-'me-lə-ˌdēn\ *n* : a bicyclic antidepressant drug $C_{16}H_{17}BrN_2$

zinc \'ziŋk\ *n* : a bluish white crystalline bivalent metallic element that is an essential micronutrient for both plants and animals — symbol *Zn;* see ELEMENT table

zinc carbonate *n* : a crystalline salt $ZnCO_3$ having astringent and antiseptic properties

zinc chloride *n* : a poisonous caustic salt $ZnCl_2$ that is used as a disinfectant and astringent

zinc ointment *n* : ZINC OXIDE OINTMENT

zinc oxide *n* : a white solid ZnO used in pharmaceutical and cosmetic preparations (as ointments and powders)

zinc oxide ointment *n* : an ointment that contains about 20 percent of zinc oxide and is used in treating skin disorders

zinc peroxide *n* : any of various white to yellowish white powders that have the peroxide ZnO_2 of zinc as their chief ingredient and are used chiefly as disinfectants, astringents, and deodorants

zinc pyr·i·thi·one \-ˌpir-i-'thī-ˌōn\ *n* : a powder $C_{10}H_8N_2O_2S_2Zn$ that is nearly insoluble in water, possesses cytostatic activity against epidermal cells, and is the active ingredient in various shampoos used to control dandruff and seborrheic dermatitis — called also *pyrithione zinc*

zinc stearate *n* : an insoluble salt usu. of commercial stearic acid and usu. containing some zinc oxide that has astringent and antiseptic properties and is used as a constituent of ointments and powders

zinc sulfate *n* : a crystalline salt $ZnSO_4$ used in medicine as an astringent, emetic, and weak antiseptic

zinc un·dec·y·len·ate \-ˌən-ˌde-si-'le-ˌnāt\ *n* : a fine white powder $C_{22}H_{38}O_4Zn$ that is used as a fungistatic agent

zinc white *n* : ZINC OXIDE

zir·co·ni·um \ˌzər-'kō-nē-əm\ *n* : a strong ductile metallic element — symbol *Zr;* see ELEMENT table

zit \'zit\ *n* : PIMPLE 1

Z line *n* : any of the dark thin lines across a striated muscle fiber that mark the boundaries between adjacent sarcomeres

Zn *symbol* zinc

zo- *or* **zoo-** *comb form* : animal (*zoonosis*)

-zo·ic \'zō-ik\ *adj comb form* : having a (specified) animal mode of existence (*saprozoic*)

Zol·ling·er–El·li·son syndrome \'zä-liŋ-ər-'e-li-sən-\ *n* : a syndrome consisting of fulminating intractable peptic ulcers, gastric hypersecretion and hyperacidity, and the occurrence of gastrinomas of the pancreatic cells of the islets of Langerhans

Zollinger, Robert Milton (1903–1992), American surgeon.

Ellison, Edwin Homer (1918–1970), American surgeon.

Zo·max \'zō-₁maks\ *trademark* — used for a preparation of zomepirac

zo·me·pir·ac \₁zō-mə-'pir-₁ak\ *n* : an anti-inflammatory and analgesic drug administered in the form of the sodium salt $C_{15}H_{13}ClNNaO_3 \cdot 2H_2O$ — see ZOMAX

zo·na \'zō-nə\ *n, pl* **zo·nae** \-₁nē, -₁nī\ *or* **zonas** 1 : an anatomical zone or layer; *esp* : ZONA PELLUCIDA 2 : SHINGLES

zona fas·ci·cu·la·ta \-fa-₁si-kyə-'lä-tə\ *n* : the middle of the three layers of the adrenal cortex that consists of radially arranged columnar epithelial cells

zona glo·mer·u·lo·sa \-glō-₁mer-yə-'lō-sə\ *n* : the outermost of the three layers of the adrenal cortex that consists of round masses of granular epithelial cells that stain deeply — called also *glomerulosa*

zona pel·lu·ci·da \-pə-'lü-sə-də\ *n* : the transparent more or less elastic outer layer or envelope of a mammalian ovum often traversed by numerous radiating striae

zona re·tic·u·lar·is \-re-₁ti-kyə-'lar-əs\ *n* : the innermost of the three layers of the adrenal cortex that consists of irregularly arranged cylindrical masses of epithelial cells

zone \'zōn\ *n* 1 : an encircling anatomical structure 2 : a region or area set off as distinct

zo·nu·la \'zōn-yə-lə\ *n, pl* **-lae** \-₁lē\ *or* **-las** : ZONULE OF ZINN

zonula cil·i·ar·is \-₁si-lē-'ar-əs\ *n* : ZONULE OF ZINN

zo·nu·lar \'zōn-yə-lər\ *adj* : of or relating to the zonule of Zinn ⟨~ attachments⟩

zon·ule \'zōn-₁yül\ *n* : ZONULE OF ZINN

zonule of Zinn \-'tsin\ *n* : the suspensory ligament of the crystalline lens of the eye — called also *zonula, zonula ciliaris*

J. G. Zinn — see LIGAMENT OF ZINN

zoo- — see ZO-

zo·ol·o·gy \zō-'äl-ə-jē\ *n, pl* **-gies** 1 : a branch of biology that deals with the classification and the properties and vital phenomena of animals 2 : the properties and vital phenomena exhibited by an animal, animal type, or group — **zoo·log·i·cal** \₁zō-ə-'läj-i-kəl\ *also* **zoo·log·ic** \-ik\ *adj* — **zo·ol·o·gist** \zō-'äl-ə-jəst\ *n*

-zo·on \'zō-₁än, -ən\ *n comb form* : animal ⟨spermatozoon⟩

zoo·no·sis \₁zō-ə-'nō-səs, zō-'ä-nə-səs\ *n, pl* **-no·ses** \-₁sēz\ : a disease communicable from animals to humans under natural conditions — **zoo·not·ic** \₁zō-ə-'nät-ik\ *adj*

zoo·par·a·site \₁zō-ə-'par-ə-₁sīt\ *n* : a parasitic animal

zoo·phil·ia \₁zō-ə-'fil-ē-ə\ *n* : an erotic fixation on animals that may result in sexual excitement through real or fancied contact

zoo·pho·bia \₁zō-ə-'fō-bē-ə\ *n* : abnormal fear of animals

zos·ter \'zäs-tər\ *n* : SHINGLES

Zo·vi·rax \'zō-'vī-₁raks\ *trademark* — used for a preparation of acyclovir

zox·a·zol·amine \₁zäk-sə-'zäl-ə-₁mēn\ *n* : a drug $C_7H_5ClN_2O$ used esp. formerly as a skeletal muscle relaxant and uricosuric agent

ZPG *abbr* zero population growth

Z-plas·ty \'zē-₁plas-tē\ *n, pl* **-ties** : a surgical procedure for the repair of constricted scar tissue in which a Z-shaped incision is made in the skin and the two resulting flaps are interposed

Zr *symbol* zirconium

zyg- *or* **zygo-** *comb form* 1 : pair ⟨zygapophysis⟩ 2 : union : fusion ⟨zygogenesis⟩

zyg·apoph·y·sis \₁zī-gə-'pä-fə-səs\ *n, pl* **-y·ses** \-₁sēz\ : any of the articular processes of the neural arch of a vertebra of which there are usu. two anterior and two posterior

zy·go·gen·e·sis \₁zī-gō-'je-nə-səs\ *n, pl* **-e·ses** \-₁sēz\ : reproduction by means of specialized germ cells or gametes : sexual reproduction

zy·go·ma \zī-'gō-mə\ *n, pl* **-ma·ta** \-mə-tə\ *also* **-mas** 1 : ZYGOMATIC ARCH 2 : ZYGOMATIC BONE

¹**zy·go·mat·ic** \₁zī-gə-'ma-tik\ *adj* : of, relating to, constituting, or situated in the region of the zygomatic bone and the zygomatic arch

²**zygomatic** *n* : ZYGOMATIC BONE

zygomatic arch *n* : the arch of bone that extends along the front or side of the skull beneath the orbit and that is formed by the union of the temporal process of the zygomatic bone in front with the zygomatic process of the temporal bone behind

zygomatic bone *n* : a bone of the side of the face below the eye that forms part of the zygomatic arch and part of the orbit and articulates with the temporal, sphenoid, and frontal bones and with the maxilla of the upper jaw — called also *cheekbone, jugal, malar bone, zygoma*

zygomatic nerve *n* : a branch of the maxillary nerve that divides into a facial branch supplying the skin of the prominent part of the cheek and a temporal branch supplying the skin of the anterior temporal region

zygomatico- *comb form* : zygomatic and ⟨zygomaticofacial⟩

zy·go·mat·i·co·fa·cial \₁zī-gə-₁ma-ti-kō-'fā-shəl\ *adj* 1 : of, relating to, or being the branch of the zygomatic nerve that supplies the skin of the prominent part of the cheek 2 : of, relating to, or being a foramen in the zygomatic bone that gives passage to the zygomaticofacial branch of the zygomatic nerve

zy·go·mat·i·co·max·il·lary \-'mak-sə-‖ler-ē\ *adj* : of, relating to, or uniting the zygomatic bone and the maxilla of the upper jaw ⟨the ~ suture⟩

zy·go·mat·i·co·tem·po·ral \-'tem-pə-rəl\ *adj* **1** : of, relating to, or uniting the zygomatic arch and the temporal bone ⟨the ~ suture⟩ **2 a** : of, relating to, or being the branch of the zygomatic nerve that supplies the skin of the anterior temporal region **b** : of, relating to, or being a foramen in the zygomatic bone that gives passage to the zygomaticotemporal branch of the zygomatic nerve

zygomatic process *n* : any of several bony processes that articulate with the zygomatic bone: as **a** : a long slender process of the temporal bone helping to form the zygomatic arch **b** : a narrow process of the frontal bone articulating with the zygomatic bone **c** : a rough triangular eminence of the maxilla of the upper jaw articulating with the zygomatic bone

zy·go·mat·i·cus \‖zī-gə-'ma-ti-kəs\ *n* **1** : ZYGOMATICUS MAJOR **2** : ZYGOMATICUS MINOR

zygomaticus major *n* : a slender band of muscle on each side of the face that arises from the zygomatic bone, inserts into the orbicularis oris and skin at the corner of the mouth, and acts to pull the corner of the mouth upward and backward when smiling or laughing

zygomaticus minor *n* : a slender band of muscle on each side of the face that arises from the zygomatic bone, inserts into the upper lip between the zygomaticus major and the levator labii superioris, and acts to raise the upper lip upward and laterally

zy·gos·i·ty \zī-'gä-sə-tē\ *n, pl* **-ties** : the makeup or characteristics of a particular zygote

zy·gote \'zī-‖gōt\ *n* : a cell formed by the union of two gametes; *broadly* : the developing individual produced from such a cell — **zy·got·ic** \zī-'gä-tik\ *adj* — **zy·got·i·cal·ly** *adv*

zy·go·tene \'zī-gə-‖tēn\ *n* : the stage of meiotic prophase which immediately follows the leptotene and during which synapsis of homologous chromosomes occurs — **zygotene** *adj*

-zy·gous \'zī-gəs\ *adj comb form* : having (such) a zygotic constitution ⟨heterozygous⟩

zym- *or* **zymo-** *comb form* : enzyme ⟨zymogen⟩

-zyme \‖zīm\ *n comb form* : enzyme ⟨lysozyme⟩

zy·mo·gen \'zī-mə-jən\ *n* : a protein that is an inactive precursor of an enzyme, is secreted by living cells, and is activated by catalysis (as by a kinase or an acid) — called also *proenzyme*

zy·mo·gram \'zī-mə-‖gram\ *n* : an electrophoretic strip (as of starch gel) or a representation of it exhibiting the pattern of separated enzymes and esp. isoenzymes after electrophoresis

zy·mo·san \'zī-mə-‖san\ *n* : an insoluble largely polysaccharide fraction of yeast cell walls

Signs and Symbols

Biology

○	an individual, specif., a female—used chiefly in inheritance charts
□	an individual, specif., a male—used chiefly in inheritance charts
♀	female
♂ or ♂	male
×	crossed with; hybrid
+	wild type
F_1	offspring of the first generation
F_2	offspring of the second generation
F_3, F_4, F_5, etc.	offspring of the third, fourth, fifth, etc. generation

Chemistry and Physics

(for element symbols see ELEMENT table)

α	alpha particle
β	beta particle, beta ray
λ	wavelength
+	signifies "plus", "and", "together with" and is used between the symbols of substances brought together for, or produced by, a reaction;
	signifies a unit charge of positive electricity when placed to the right of a symbol as a superscript: Ca^{++} denotes the ion of calcium, which carries two positive charges;
	signifies a dextrorotatory compound when preceding in parentheses a compound name, as in (+) tartaric acid

    —   signifies a unit charge of negative electricity when placed to the right of a symbol as a superscript: Cl^- denotes a chlorine ion carrying a negative charge;

        signifies a levorotatory compound when preceding in parentheses a compound name, as in (−) quinine;

        signifies removal or loss of a part from a compound during a reaction (as $-CO_2$)

    —   signifies a single bond and is used between the symbols of elements or groups which unite to form a compound: H—Cl for HCl, H—O—H for H_2O

    >   signifies separate single bonds from an atom to two other atoms or groups (as in the grouping >C=NNHR characteristic of hydrazone)

    ·   used to separate parts of a substance regarded as loosely joined (as $CuSO_4 \cdot 5H_2O$);

        also used to denote the presence of a single unpaired electron (as H·)

    =   indicates a double bond;

        signifies two unit charges of negative electricity when placed to the right of a symbol as a superscript (as $SO_4^=$, the negative ion of sulfuric acid)

    ≡   signifies a triple bond or a triple negative charge

    :   signifies a pair of electrons belonging to an atom that is not shared with another atom (as in : NH_3);

        sometimes signifies a double bond (as in $CH_2 : CH_2$)

    ( )   marks groups within a compound, as in $C_6H_4(CH_3)_2$, the formula for xylene which contains two methyl groups (CH_3)

  — or —   joins attached atoms or groups in structural formulas for cyclic compounds, as that for glucose

$$\overbrace{\qquad}^{O}$$

$$CH_2OHCH(CHOH)_3CHOH$$

  1-, 2-, etc.   used initially in names, referring to the positions of substituting groups, attached to the first, second, etc., of the numbered atoms of the parent compound

  x, m, n used as subscripts following an atom or group in a chemical formula to indicate that the number of times the atom or group occurs is indefinite, as in $(C_6H_{10}O_5)_x$ for glycogen, or approximate, as in

$C_{12}H_mAl_{16}O_nS_8$ for sucralfate where m and n are approximately 54 and 75

R   group—used esp. of an organic group

$'$ used to distinguish between different substituents of the same kind (as R$'$, R$''$, R$'''$ to indicate different organic groups)

Medicine

℞   take—used on prescriptions; prescription; treatment

☠   poison

APOTHECARIES' MEASURES

℥   ounce

f℥   fluid ounce

f℈   fluid dram

min *or* ℳ   minim

APOTHECARIES' WEIGHTS

℔   pound

℥   ounce: as

       ℥ i or ℥ j, one ounce;

       ℥ ss, half an ounce;

       ℥ iss or ℥ jss, one ounce and a half;

       ℥ ij, two ounces

℈   dram

℈   scruple

768

create a complete medical reference library

Merriam-Webster's Medical Speller, Second Edition

"...the usefulness of this book is unquestionable..."
— THE NEW YORK STATE JOURNAL OF MEDICINE

Is the old adage "i" before "e" except after "c" enough to ensure that you are spelling medical terms correctly? If you think it is, check out *meiosis* in *Webster's Medical Speller.* While you're at the entry, be sure to note how you would hyphenate the word at the end of a line (in case you don't have a copy yet, you should break it up like so: **mei•o•sis**).

Correct spelling is vital in medicine and health care.

Webster's Medical Speller is a handy, quick-reference guide that helps you ensure that the medical terms you use in your writing are correctly spelled and hyphenated. This pocket-size resource contains spellings and end-of-line divisions for 35,000 of today's most frequently used medical terms, plus special sections including:

• 1,000 medical abbreviations, including those used in prescriptions

• Medical weights and measures

• Medical signs and symbols

Before you write another letter or report containing medical terms, make sure you have *Webster's Medical Speller* to give you fast, reliable answers to your spelling questions.

Compact hardcover volume for durability (See order form on page 772)

Merriam-Webster's Vocabulary Builder

Informative and entertaining discussions of English words derived from 200 Greek and Latin roots form the framework for gaining a greater command of the language right now—and for continuing lifelong vocabulary acquisition.

For adult readers and learners as well as high-school and college students, especially those preparing for standardized tests.

Following is an example from *Merriam-Webster's Vocabulary Builder* including one of the quizzes used throughout the book:

PUNG/PUNC comes from the Latin verb *pungere,* meaning "to prick or stab," and the noun *punctum,* meaning "point." A period is a form of *punctuation* that is literally a point. A *punctured* tire, pricked by a sharp point, can make it hard to be *punctual*—that is, to arrive "on the dot" or at a precise point in time.

---

compunction \kəm-'pəŋk-shən\ (1) Anxiety caused by guilt. (2) A slight misgiving or scruple.

• Speeding is something many people seem to do without compunction.

To feel compunction is to feel the sharp sting or prick of conscience. The word *compunction* is most often used in describing people who don't feel it. Hardened criminals have no compunctions about committing their crimes. Ruthless businessmen steal clients and contracts from other ruthless businessmen without compunction.

expunge \ik-'spənj\ To remove, erase, or destroy.

• After years of good behavior, all mention of his juvenile criminal career was expunged from his record.

Expunge comes directly from the Latin *expungere,* which means "to

770

mark for deletion with dots." In English, the material expunged is no longer marked with dots but is erased or removed completely. It is easier to expunge something written down than it is to expunge a memory.

punctilious \ ,pəŋk-'ti-lē-əs\ Marked by exact agreement or conformity to the details of codes or conventions.

• A good proofreader has to be punctilious about matters of spelling and punctuation.

A *punctilio* is a small point—a minor detail of conduct in a ceremony or in the observance of a code. A person who pays close attention to such minor details is punctilious. *Punctiliousness* can be valuable in the right circumstances, but you don't want to become so concerned about small points that you fail to pay attention to the large ones.

pungent \pən-jənt\ (1) Having a sharp, cutting quality. (2) Sharp or harsh to the sense of taste or smell.

• We could smell the pungent aroma of the spicy Indian food before we even entered the restaurant.

Someone with a pungent wit has a sharp sense of humor. Many people enjoy the aroma and flavor of pungent food, even if it does make their eyes water. The *pungency* of a cheap cigar can have the same effect, but it's more likely to clear a room than to draw a crowd.

Quizzes

A. Choose the closest definition:

1. expunge   a. mop up b. partially restore c. remove completely d. hesitate slightly
2. pungent   a. sharp b. rotten c. round d. funny
3. punctilious   a. pointed b. careful c. prompt d. unusual
4. compunction   a. desire b. bravery c. scruple d. conviction

B. Indicate whether the following pairs of words have the same or different meanings:

1. pungent / smoky   same___ / different___
2. expunge / erase   same___ / different___
3. compunction / threat   same___ / different___
4. punctilious / absurd   same___ / different___

Answers: A. 1. c.; 2. a.; 3. b.; 4. c.   **B.** 1. different; 2. same; 3. different; 4. different

America's Finest Language Reference Products
available from your local bookseller
or order directly from Merriam-Webster